THE NEW CAMBRIDGE EDITION

GEOFFREY CHAUCER

From an early painting on wood
now in the possession of Harvard University

THE WORKS OF

GEOFFREY

CHAUCER

Second Edition

Edited by F. N. ROBINSON

Houghton Mifflin Company : Boston

Printed in the U.S.A.

ॐ

Printed in the U.S.A.

To My Beloved Wife

TWENTY-FOUR years have passed since the first edition of the present work, and in that period the scholarly investigation of Chaucer has moved on at an unslackened pace. There have perhaps been fewer significant discoveries about the poet's life and the sources and chronology of his works than in the decades between 1890 and 1930, but there has been a great body of publications of which it is now time to take account. I am therefore offering my fellow-Chaucerians this new edition, and since it is the first real revision, as distinguished from reprints with minor corrections, I ought briefly to explain what has been my procedure.

Two of the works published during the period may be singled out as of outstanding importance: the new compilation of *Sources and Analogues to Chaucer's Canterbury Tales* (Chicago University Press, 1941), and the great Chicago critical edition of the *Tales*. Both these works are the result of the collaboration of many scholars, and the second is a supreme example of collaboration on a vast scale brought into a consistent whole by the wise control of a general editor. In the *Sources and Analogues* is collected, up to the date of publication, the widely scattered information on the sources of the *Tales*, and I have tried to incorporate this material in my revised notes. Of the Manly-Rickert edition I have of course made still more extensive use. As was predicted in my first edition, the investigations of the Chicago scholars, based upon collations of all known manuscripts of the *Canterbury Tales*, provided extensive, indeed exhaustive, materials not only for the determination of textual readings, but also for constructing the history of the different stages in the composition of the *Tales*. I have made no attempt to present here the voluminous information there assembled concerning manuscript relations. Any summary of Manly's highly complicated classification, if it had seemed proper to make one, would have been either too extensive for the

scope of this book or too inadequate really to serve the purposes of textual investigation. I have accordingly assumed that scholars will resort to Manly's complete presentation of the material, and have simply reprinted, with minor corrections, the textual variants recorded in my first edition as exhibiting the basis of my readings. Similarly, since I have seen no reason for changing my general method of dealing with orthography, grammatical rectification, and such matters, often not to be settled simply by comparison of manuscripts, I am republishing, practically without change, the introductory chapter on the text. Fortunately, although I had only some dozen more or less complete authorities to work with, the manuscripts provided by the Chaucer Society had been so well selected from different groups that they made possible, when supplemented by textual studies then available, the application of critical method. Manly's rigorous procedure of printing his reconstructed archetype even when he rejects a reading as unlikely to have been Chaucer's — a method wholly correct for his edition — would have been unsuited to my purpose. As was to be expected, however, there are many cases of doubtful readings in which the new evidence assembled by Manly supports decisions different from those I originally made. I have therefore, in the light of such evidence or sometimes under the influence of Manly's discussion, changed some two hundred readings significant for sense, style, or metre, and a list of the altered passages will be found at the beginning of my Textual Notes. A good many of these changes are due to Manly's argument, if not demonstration, that readings peculiar to the Ellesmere group of manuscripts are often due to emendation. But he also recognized that in some cases the Ellesmere scribes may have had access to Chaucer's own revision, and an editor cannot evade the responsibility of exercising his own judgment. I have substituted a considerable number of "critical" readings for readings taken from the Ellesmere manuscript in my first edition, especially in the case of headless lines which are not so lame as to seem un-Chaucerian. In so doing I may have sacrificed some superior readings due to the poet's own revision. But the critical text of Manly's reconstructed archetype, except in cases of manifest corruption, is likely to represent what Chaucer at some stage wrote.

As already remarked, the Manly-Rickert edition has provided abundant material for the study of the different stages in the composition of the *Tales*. Manly's opinions on this subject are more or less systematically set forth in his edition, and no attempt has been made to summarize them here. But they are cited at relevant places in the Explanatory and Textual Notes, together with references to later discussions by other scholars. Special mention should be made of the articles of Mrs. A. J. Dempster (cited frequently in the Notes), who was one of Manly's principal collaborators.

One problem concerning the order of the *Tales*, that of the adoption of the so-called "Bradshaw shift," has been discussed afresh by many scholars since the publication of the Manly-Rickert edition, and many Chaucerians will be disappointed by my decision to retain the manuscript order which was followed in my first edition. The question at issue and the main considerations involved are explained in the introduction to the Notes on the *Canterbury Tales*. I freely grant that the scholars who have urged the adoption of the Bradshaw order — especially Professor Pratt, whose statement of the case is very reasonable — have made it seem probable that Chaucer was on his way to the rectification of the inconsistencies in the traditional order. But after considerable deliberation I decided to leave the text in the form, manifestly uncompleted, in which it has come down in the manuscripts.

In the case of works other than the *Canterbury Tales* very few changes have been made in my text. The Textual Notes to these works have accordingly been reprinted practically without revision except in the case of a few of the Short Poems of which textual studies have recently been published.

Unlike the Textual Notes, the Explanatory Notes throughout the book have been very much expanded in my revision. It is in them chiefly that I have taken account of recent contributions to Chaucer scholarship. My headnotes to the various works, since they dealt in a general way with chronology, sources, literary types, and critical comments, have not required extensive revision and are reprinted with only minor additions and corrections, mainly factual. This is true also of the general Introduction at the beginning of the book. But I have tried to expand the Explanatory Notes so as to cover the more significant contributions of recent years to the historical and literary background and critical study of the works and to the detailed interpretation of the texts. But I ought to point out with emphasis, as I did in the first edition, that my notes, like my bibliographies, are selective and not exhaustive. This is not a "variorum" Chaucer. I have often tried to save space by selecting references which will supply further bibliographical information, and I hope my notes will serve the practical needs of readers and scholars. My classified book lists at the beginning of the Notes are also selective, and for a complete survey of recent scholarly work on Chaucer, students must resort to the annual bibliographies and to Professor Griffith's recent comprehensive volume.

In one other respect the scope of my Notes has been restricted by limitations of space. There has been little or no room for purely illustrative material such as many of us recall with pleasure in Skeat's edition of over sixty years ago. I have had to confine myself to essential matters of interpretation or historical background. If I have sometimes overstepped these limits, it has usually been to give some indication of the history and diffusion of ideas or of literary conventions.

When I had nearly finished my work of revision a new practical problem was presented to the publishers and myself by the discovery of the Peterhouse manuscript of the *Equatorie of the Planetis*. This work was precisely dated in 1392, and was thus closely contemporary with Chaucer's *Astrolabe*. The newly discovered treatise, like the *Astrolabe,* describes the construction and use of an astronomical instrument. It contains also extensive astronomical tables, in one of which appears the term "Radix Chaucer," and the word "Chaucer" is in a handwriting closely similar to that of the same name in a document of 1378 held to have been possibly in Chaucer's hand. In view of these facts the manuscript was hailed as an author's holograph copy of a treatise by Chaucer himself. Later investigation, while by no means disproving, has not conclusively substantiated this claim. The entry "Radix Chaucer" hardly constitutes an ascription of the treatise to the poet, and might even seem more natural if written by a person other than the author. The argument from handwriting, which is based on the comparison of the Peterhouse entry with a Record Office note made fourteen years earlier and not proved to be in Chaucer's hand, also rests upon slender evidence. The language of the *Equatorie* — its phonology, inflections, and syntax — seems consistent with Chaucer's usage. But it is difficult to compare the two treatises stylistically while the source of the *Equatorie* is unknown. Since for these reasons the authorship must be regarded as uncertain, and since the *Equatorie* is of exclusively scientific interest, I decided, after consultation with the publishers, not to include it here. Happily it has now been made available to Chaucer scholars in a masterly edition, with photographic reproductions of the manuscript, transcription, translation and commentary, and ample illustrative scientific material, by Dr. Derek J. Price (Cambridge University Press, 1955). The problem of authorship is discussed by Mr. Price with admirable fair-mindedness. An analysis of the language, in a separate chapter, is contributed by Mr. R. M. Wilson.

A German scholar of the last century, in an edition of Middle English texts which I used in my early years of teaching, described the inevitable indebtedness of one scholar to others in the words: "Das beste was er ist verdankt er anderen," — a sentence which James Russell Lowell observed made "an accidental pentam-

eter that might seem to have dropped out of *Nathan der Weise*." Certainly throughout the preparation of this revision, which has involved so much compilation of the results of other men's labors, I have had a keen sense of such obligations. I welcome the opportunity to acknowledge my debt, not only to such published works as I have already mentioned, but also to many colleagues and friends who have come personally to my aid.

I should like to begin with a general expression of gratitude to the numerous fellow-Chaucerians who have sent me copies of their books and articles, sometimes in advance of publication, thus often bringing to my attention information I might otherwise have missed, and placing the material conveniently within reach. Most of these contributions are recorded in my notes in appropriate places. Some of course could not be taken into account because of limitations of space, and a number of recent communications came to hand too late to be utilized. But I hope the authors will accept this general expression of thanks for a courtesy which has been of the greatest help to me in my work.

A number of scholars may be singled out for the personal assistance they have given me, often in reply to appeals for help. My friend Professor Tatlock, up to the end of his life, called my attention to items of information, usually growing out of his own researches. I also had the advantage, during the earlier years of my work of revision, of correspondence and occasional conference with my friend Dr. G. G. Coulton of Cambridge University, by whose learning I have profited. My late colleague at Harvard, Professor George Sarton, was thoughtful and generous with assistance on matters relating to mediæval science, and Professor E. H. Warren of the Harvard Law School, also deceased, gave me help in the field of legal antiquities. Professor William Thomson, now retired from the Harvard chair of Arabic, and Dr. A. R. Nykl, also formerly at Harvard, have occasionally assisted me in finding or interpreting Arabic material used in my notes, and Professor Cleaves, of the Far Eastern Department at Harvard, has with similar kindness answered inquiries about Mongolian place-names. The Reverend Dr. Gerald Ellard, S.J., of St. Louis University, has courteously replied to my appeal for information about liturgical matters. Among other scholars to whom I am indebted in various ways for information or counsel are Professor Ernest H. Wilkins, Professor George C. Homans, and Dr. Walter M. Whitehill, all colleagues at Harvard. The officers and staff of the Harvard Library, of which in my retirement I still enjoy the hospitality, have continued to do everything possible to aid and expedite my labors.

Thanks to the great kindness of my friend Mr. Boies Penrose of Philadelphia, it has been possible to enrich the textual material of this revised edition by adding a collation of his manuscript of the *Astrolabe*, which he placed for a long time at my disposal in the Harvard Library. Fortunately, too, another manuscript of the same work, presented to the Library by Mr. David Wheatland, came in at about the same time, and variant readings from it have also been added.

Among scholars actively engaged in Chaucerian research I am under special obligation to Professor J. Burke Severs, who has kept me continually informed about the plans and progress of the "Chaucer Library" of the Modern Language Association, and to Professor Robert A. Pratt, who, besides helping me frequently with information and advice, has supplied me with advance reports of his own investigations. Professors Magoun and Whiting of Harvard, by virtue of our long and intimate association and of their own active occupation with Chaucer studies, have both been exceptionally exposed to my appeals for help, and have given me information and counsel at every turn. Professor Whiting also made it possible for me to consult a bibliography of recent Chaucerian publications prepared in his seminar and a second catalogue which was lent me by the compiler, Mr. Alfred David of the Harvard Graduate School. Professor Griffith's published bibliography did not come to hand until my book was in the process of printing, but it was helpful in the late correction of copy and proofs.

I most gladly acknowledge the unfailing courtesy and considerateness of the Houghton Mifflin Company, my publishers, who have had to deal with an author no longer able to work at the speed of middle life. It has always been a pleasure to work with my friend Mr. Henry F. Thoma, who has had the immediate supervision of the book, and with the manuscript editor, Miss Eleanor Wiles.

It remains for me to record with gratitude the indispensable help I have received from my secretary, Mr. George F. Reinecke, formerly an assistant at Harvard and now teaching at Loyola University in New Orleans. For the past year or two my eyes have been unequal to the strain of continuous collation or proofreading, and I have been more dependent than ever before on secretarial aid. The actual work of revision of the text and notes I completed by myself. But Mr. Reinecke prepared the typescript for the press, attended to the verification of new references, and read all the proofs, submitting changes to me, of course, for final decision. At considerable sacrifice to himself he has continued the work to the end, and in general his secretarial service has been "above and beyond the call of duty." I am well aware of the ease with which, by reason of oversight or misunderstanding, errors can slip through between a secretary and an author, and I hope the number in this book will not have increased because of our procedure. At all events there would have been many more if I had tried to work without such help as Mr. Reinecke has given me.

After this long recital of explanations and acknowledgments I would express the hope that the book in its revised form may better serve the convenience of readers of Chaucer and the research of scholars. The number of books and articles that have come to hand too late to be noted in these pages is at least an encouraging sign that Chaucer studies are not likely soon to fall into neglect. To conclude with the words of the poet himself, than whom few men ever did less to incur unfriendly criticism, "With this swerd shal I sleen envie."

F. N. R.

PREFACE TO THE FIRST EDITION

IN OFFERING to the readers of Chaucer this edition, which has been the interrupted occupation of many years, I wish to make a few explanations and acknowledgments.

It was my original plan, and my understanding with the publishers, that the text should be based on such manuscript materials only as were accessible in print. In previous editions, even those of Skeat (1894) and the Globe editors (1898), very incomplete account had been taken of modern investigations of Chaucer's grammar, and I felt that one of the chief services an editor could render would be in the grammatical purification of the text. Having that, perhaps, primarily in view at the outset, I proceeded to make my text afresh from the Chaucer Society's reprints of the various pieces, endeavoring, of course, at the same time to follow sound critical principles in the determination of readings. For certain works I found it necessary to supplement the printed materials by photographs or copies of unpublished manuscripts, or even to base my text (as in the case of the *Boece* and the *Astrolabe*) upon such reproductions of unprinted sources. But for most of the poems the accessible reprints and collations were either complete or extensive enough to serve as a satisfactory basis for a text.

During the progress of my work there appeared a number of important investigations of Chaucer manuscripts, of which I have made full use. Miss Hammond's study of the manuscripts of the *Parliament of Fowls*, for example, and the exhaustive analysis of the manuscripts of the *Troilus* by Professor Root and the late Sir William McCormick were both published after I had first constituted my text of those poems, and I revised my work in the light of them. More recently, the Chaucer Tradition of the late Professor Brusendorff has led to the further reconsideration of many matters. I am greatly indebted to all these

studies, and to others that are cited in the textual notes.

For my text of the *Canterbury Tales* I used primarily the eight printed manuscripts and Thynne's edition. I collated also the Cardigan and Morgan copies, and took account of the various textual studies of Zupitza and Koch, McCormick, Tatlock, and Brusendorff. Although I knew I might have access to the photographic reproductions of manuscripts assembled by my friend Professor Manly at the University of Chicago, it did not seem to me either proper or profitable to make a partial and piecemeal use of the material which he and his associates are to publish in full. I felt, too, that the printed manuscripts represent so well the different classes of authorities that their readings, supplemented by my collations and the published reports of other copies, gave me in most cases the necessary evidence for the determination of the text. But, of course, in common with all other Chaucerians, I am eagerly awaiting the light that the Chicago edition will throw upon doubtful passages and upon the history of the composition of the tales.

I at first intended to publish a very full *apparatus criticus*, and collected at least four times as many variant readings of all the poems as are actually printed in the present volume. A number of considerations — chiefly limitations of space, the publication of Professor Root's *Troilus* with copious variants, and the announcement of Professor Manly's forthcoming edition of the *Canterbury Tales* — led me to change my plan and restrict my textual notes to selected variants of especial interest. I hope they will be found to include such readings as concern the student of Chaucer's poetic vocabulary or of his methods in revision. I may add that a good many readings not printed in my notes were reported to Professor Tatlock when he was preparing his

Concordance, and were registered in that work.

The explanatory notes, though much more extensive than those on the text, have also been limited by considerations of space. I had very little room for purely illustrative material, for which the reader may profitably consult the previous commentaries, especially those in Skeat's Oxford Chaucer and Professor Manly's selections from the *Canterbury Tales.* I have also not undertaken to give the history of interpretations or to list in full the opinions of commentators, as would be done in a variorum edition. But I have meant to supply the reader, either in the notes or in the glossary, with all necessary help for the understanding of the text; and I have tried to register fully, though in brief form, such literary sources of Chaucer's writings as have been discovered. Matters of common knowledge are stated without citation of authority, or with a general acknowledgment of indebtedness to previous editors. But where special credit seems due, or further information may be desired, references are added; and doubtful interpretations or new suggestions are occasionally discussed at some length.

Both in the notes and in the introductions to the various works, besides citing Chaucer's specific sources, I have given some account of the history of his ideas and the development of the literary forms and fashions exemplified in his writings. Such indications have had to be extremely brief, and I have undoubtedly overlooked both sources and parallels for which I might well have found room, even in my limited space. But I hope that my notes may help the reader who is unfamiliar with Chaucer and his period to understand the place of his works in the history of literature. Perhaps some of the discussions will point the way to profitable investigation. And it may be convenient even for the seasoned Chaucerian and the expert in other fields of literature to have in a continuous commentary a brief digest of the results obtained in the numerous source-studies of the past forty years.

Throughout the course of my work I have been indebted to Chaucer scholars, both friends and strangers, for innumerable courtesies, and I have tried to acknowledge such obligations in the proper places. But I should like to repeat here the expression of my thanks to the authorities of the Bodleian Library for allowing me to have a photograph of a manuscript of the *Astrolabe;* to the late librarian of the Cambridge University Library, Mr. Francis J. H. Jenkinson, for a photograph of the manuscript of the *Boece;* to Miss Belle da Costa Greene, for generously placing at my disposal the Morgan manuscript of the *Canterbury Tales;* to President MacCracken of Vassar College, for permitting me to collate the Cardigan manuscript of the *Canterbury Tales* while it was in his possession; and to Mr. G. A. Plimpton, for giving me access to his manuscripts of the *Canterbury Tales* and the *Astrolabe.* And I see no reason why, as a member of Harvard University, I should take for granted the inestimable privileges of the Harvard Library and refrain from thanking the authorities of that institution for their constant liberality and helpfulness. I wish to thank my friends Dr. Grace W. Landrum, Dr. J. P. Bethel, Dr. B. J. Whiting, and Mr. Joseph Butterworth for communicating to me the results of their unpublished investigations. In the typewriting of my manuscript and the verification of references and readings I had the assistance, in the early stages of the work, of Professor Paull F. Baum, and more recently, of Dr. Whiting, Dr. Harold O. White, Dr. Mark Eccles, and Miss Laura Gustafson, from all of whom I have received information and helpful suggestions beyond the ordinary range of secretarial aid. I am particularly indebted to Dr. White for his untiring assistance in the task of seeing the book through the press.

My obligations to a number of friends are so general that they could not be adequately acknowledged in special notes. In the beginning of the work I had the advantage of the advice of President W. A. Neilson, and I have received information and counsel, at various times, from Professors J. M. Manly, J. S. P. Tatlock, and Karl Young, and Mr. Henry B. Hinckley; and my friends and colleagues at Harvard,

Professors Lowes, Rand, Ford, and Magoun, have been constantly exposed, by near access and intimate association, to my appeals for help. In this work as in everything I have undertaken, I have owed most to Professor Kittredge, under whom I began the study of Chaucer very long ago. He has been my master since my student days, and I have drawn freely upon his learning and wisdom during a friendship of more than forty years.

Other obligations, which I shall not attempt to describe, are acknowledged in the dedication of the book to one who did not live to see it published, but who has shared and sustained all my labors.

F. N. R.

CONTENTS

INTRODUCTION

The Life of Chaucer

An eminent French critic of the last generation, complaining that the biographers of men of letters had given more attention to their correspondence, diaries, and other intimate records than to their literary productions, expressed the fear that his period in criticism might be remembered as "l'âge des petits papiers." The writer of the life of Chaucer is at least in no danger of going to the extreme described. He may resort too freely to conjecture, as scholars have occasionally done in the attempt to use every scrap of evidence for the reconstruction of Chaucer's life and times. But he will have no private papers to draw upon, and the public records at his disposal deal almost entirely with official appointments and business transactions — the external facts of the poet's career. In the end, for the most part, the biographer will have to let Chaucer's works speak for themselves, rather interpreting him by them than interpeting the writings by the personal experiences of the author.

Within their limited range, however, the recorded facts about Chaucer and his family are rather numerous. Hundreds of entries have been discovered, besides many relating to Thomas Chaucer, and more are constantly coming to light. But the story that they yield can be briefly recapitulated.

The year of Chaucer's birth is unknown. His own testimony, at the Scrope-Grosvenor trial in 1386, that he was then "forty years old and more" makes probable a date somewhat later than 1340. The fact that he was in military service in France in 1359 is also consistent with the assumption that he was born about 1343–44.

His father was John Chaucer and his mother probably Agnes, mentioned as John Chaucer's wife in 1349. She is described in the same document as a relative and heir of Hamo de Copton, and is to be identified, on the evidence of a cartulary of Holy Trinity, Aldgate, with his niece Agnes, daughter of John de Copton. She cannot have been married to John Chaucer before 1328, when, according to documentary evidence, he was still single, and a date considerably later seems likely in view of the fact that she had been married earlier to a man named Northwell, kinsman of William de Northwell, keeper of the King's wardrobe, and that after John Chaucer's death, in 1366 or 1367, she became the wife of Bartholomew atte Chapel. John Chaucer, born between 1310 and 1312, was the son of Robert Chaucer, who in 1307 had married a widow, Mary Heyroun (perhaps born Stace). Robert Chaucer died before 1316, and in 1323 Mary married Richard Chaucer, perhaps a kinsman of Robert. She died before April 12, 1349, as appears from Richard's will, which was proved in July of the same year.

According to John Philipot's Visitation of Kent, Geoffrey Chaucer had a sister Catherine, who was married to Simon Manning of Codham, and through her many New England families trace a connection with the poet's line. Of other children of John Chaucer nothing is known. Elizabeth Chaucy, for whose admission to Barking Abbey John of Gaunt gave £51–8–2 in 1381, is held by some to have been a sister of Geoffrey, and by others to have been his daughter. She is probably to be identified with the Elizabeth Chausier who took the oath of obedience to a new abbess in 1399.

The name of Chaucer or Chaucier (Fr. "Chaussier") would indicate that the family was once occupied with shoe-making, and their earliest known residence in London was in Cordwainers' Street. But Chaucer's immediate ancestors — his father, grandfather, and step-grandfather — were vintners or wine-merchants. They appear to have been prosperous people, with rising fortunes and some standing at court. In 1310 Robert Chaucer was collector of customs on wines from Aquitaine. John Chaucer attended Edward III in Flanders in 1338, and in 1348 he was appointed to collect the custom on cloths in certain ports. He was also deputy to the King's Butler in Southampton. Thus the family had made a modest beginning in the career of public service which Geoffrey Chaucer successfully continued.

The earliest known records of Geoffrey Chaucer himself are in the household accounts of Elizabeth, Countess of Ulster and wife of Prince Lionel. They state that in May, 1357, he received clothing from her wardrobe in London, and that in December of that year, at Hatfield in Yorkshire, he was allowed twenty shillings "for necessaries at Christmas." The same account-book records the journeys of Elizabeth to Reading, Stratford-atte-Bowe, and other places, and her attendance at several great entertainments, such as the Feast of St. George, given by Edward III in 1358 to the King of France, the Queen of Scotland, the King of Cyprus, and other notables. It is probable that Chaucer, as a page in the household, would have been present on many such occasions, and his acquaintance with John of Gaunt may date from Christmas, 1357, when that nobleman, then Earl of Richmond, was a guest at Hatfield.

It is not known how long Chaucer was in the service of Lionel and Elizabeth. In 1359–60 he was in the English army in France, and was taken prisoner near Reims. On March 1, 1360, he was released for a ransom, to which the King contributed £16, and in May he returned to England. Later in the year, during the peace negotiations, he was back in France and carried letters from Calais to England. That he was still in Lionel's service is shown by the fact that his payment is recorded in the Prince's expense book. But for the following seven years information about him is lacking, and at the end of that period he seems to have been in the service of the King. On June 20, 1367, he received from Edward a pension of twenty marks for life, and was described

as "dilectus vallectus noster." If he had been attached particularly to the train of Elizabeth, he may have left Lionel's household after her death in 1363; or he may have continued in the Prince's service till 1367. In any case he can hardly have been with Lionel on the occasion of the Prince's second marriage, May 28, 1368, to Violante, the niece of Bernabò Visconti of Milan. For there has recently been discovered a bill of privy seal, dated July 17, 1368, granting Chaucer a passport from Dover and an allowance of £10 for traveling expenses. The purpose of his journey is entirely unknown. He may have gone to join Lionel in Italy, but it seems more probable that he was traveling in the service of the King. In fact this may be the first of the series of diplomatic missions that took him repeatedly to the Continent during a period of ten years. If Chaucer continued to be attached to Lionel till 1366 or 1367, one other possibility must be considered. It has been suggested that he spent some time with the Prince in Ireland; and it is rather striking that the gap in our records of Chaucer very nearly coincides with the period (1361–66) of Lionel's service in Ireland as the King's Lieutenant.

Chaucer was married, probably as early as 1366, to Philippa, daughter of Sir Payne Roet, and sister of Katherine Swynford, afterwards the third wife of John of Gaunt. In that year Philippa Chaucer, in the service of the Queen, was granted an annual stipend of ten marks. In 1369 both Geoffrey and Philippa received cloth for mourning after the death of Queen Philippa. But Philippa Chaucer is not actually described as Geoffrey's wife until 1374, when Chaucer received a pension of ten pounds from John of Gaunt. Two years earlier the Duke had granted a similar stipend to Philippa for her services to Constance, his wife. In 1374 Chaucer received from the King an award of a daily pitcher of wine, which was commuted, in 1378, to an additional pension of twenty marks. The payments of the royal pensions are recorded year by year, though with some irregularity, in Philippa's case until 1387, when she apparently died, and in Chaucer's case until May 1, 1388, when he assigned his claim to John Scalby. The nature of this transaction is not quite clear. Perhaps Chaucer made over the annuity to secure ready money. On the face of the royal grant it appears simply that at Chaucer's request the pension was transferred to Scalby, who is also described as a deserving subject. It is unknown how long Chaucer received the annuity from John of Gaunt. When it was granted it was said to be for life, but very few records of payments have been published, and the accounts in which they would have been entered appear to be lost. The Lancaster Register shows several payments by the Duke for New Year's gifts for Philippa — in 1373 for a silver-gilt buttoner with six buttons, and in 1380, 1381, and 1382 for silver-gilt cups.

To return to Chaucer's offices at court and in the civil service, he is enrolled, in a list apparently dating from 1368, among the Esquires of the Royal Household, and he is still called "scutifer regis" in Beverlee's accounts in 1377. In 1368, as already noted, he was abroad on unknown business. In 1369 he saw military service for the second time in France, doubtless in the campaign in Picardy conducted by John of Gaunt. In 1370 he received letters of protection from June till Michaelmas because of his absence abroad in the King's service. The business on which he was engaged is again unknown. From December 1, 1372, till May 23, 1373, he was once more on the Continent, on what is usually regarded as his first Italian journey. He was commissioned to negotiate with the Genoese about the choice of an English port for their commerce, but the records show that he visited Florence as well as Genoa. From this famous journey, which has a place in Chaucer's intellectual development comparable to that of the "Italienische Reise" in Goethe's, has usually been dated his first acquaintance with the Italian language and literature. But he may have been chosen for the mission because he already had some knowledge of Italian. It is possible, too, though not very probable, that he had been in Italy with Lionel four years before. Shortly after his return to England in 1373, according to a writ recently discovered, Chaucer was directed to investigate an affair relative to a Genoese tarit at Dartmouth. This assignment has been reasonably taken as evidence of his knowledge of Italian, but does not indicate how early he acquired it.

On May 10, 1374, Chaucer obtained rent-free from the municipality the house above Aldgate which he did not give up till 1388. This seems to fix his settlement in the City, after having lived seventeen years or more (with one interval of which we have no record) in the households of Lionel and Edward. It also marks the beginning of a long series of official and professional appointments. On June 2, 1374, he was made Controller of Customs and Subsidy of Wools, Skins, and Hides in the port of London, on condition that he should write his rolls with his own hand. The regular stipend of this office was ten pounds a year, in addition to which Chaucer seems to have received annually, as a reward for diligent service, a gift of ten marks. Such payments to the controller are recorded as early as 1373 (before Chaucer held the office), and the entries continue with some irregularity during his term of service.

In November, 1375, Chaucer was granted the wardship of the lands and heir of Edward Staplegate, in Kent, an appointment which brought him emoluments of £104; and in December of the same year he received the wardship of another Kentish minor, William de Solys, in the parish of Nonington. In July, 1376, he was granted the substantial sum of £71–4–6, the fine of John Kent for exporting wool without license or the payment of custom. Chaucer's receipts from these grants, it has been estimated, must have been equal to approximately five thousand pounds in modern currency. A writ of July, 1375, recently reported, which shows Chaucer to have been manucaptor for John de Romesey, treasurer of Calais, in an action connected with the seizure of goods of Thomas Langton on a charge of felony, brings further evidence of Chaucer's standing at the time as a substantial man of affairs.

Between 1376 and 1381 Chaucer was again employed on several missions or embassies, of some of which the exact nature is unknown. In December, 1376, he received, with Sir John de Burley, a sum of money for secret service to the King. But no record of this journey appears to be preserved. In February, 1377, according to the Exchequer Rolls, Chaucer was sent to Flanders with Sir Thomas Percy, again "on the King's secret affairs." Froissart says that he and Sir Guichard d'Angle and Sir Richard Stury were commissioners to treat of peace. But none of the three is mentioned in the royal commission of February 20. Chaucer's accounts show that he was away from London from February 17, to March 25, and that he actually went to Paris and Montreuil. He was in France again, between April 30 and June 26, for fourteen days, and received £26–13–4 for this service, which seems to have been connected with the second negotiations for peace. Though Chaucer is again not named in the commission directed to the Bishops of St. Davids, Hereford, and others, Stow asserts, in his Annals, that he was sent with the bishops. Because of his frequent absences in the King's service Chaucer was given permission, during that same year, to employ Thomas de Evesham, a substantial London merchant, as deputy for the controllership of wools and hides.

On June 22, 1377, Richard II became King, and he at once confirmed Chaucer in his office of controller. The following March he confirmed the annuities awarded by Edward III to both Chaucer and Philippa.

According to a record of March 6, 1381, Chaucer took part, after Richard's accession, on a commission to negotiate a marriage between the King and a daughter of the King of France. He may have accompanied the Earl of Salisbury and Sir Guichard d'Angle, who were sent to France on this business in the summer of 1377. Another commission was appointed for the same purpose in January, 1378, but Chaucer is not mentioned as a member. If he did go to France at that time, he apparently returned to England before March 9, when he became a surety for William de Beauchamp on matters pertaining to Pembroke Castle. But again in May he was sent abroad on

the King's service. He went in the retinue of Sir Edward de Berkeley to Lombardy to negotiate with Bernabò Visconti, Lord of Milan, and Sir John Hawkwood "for certain affairs touching the expedition of the King's war." Chaucer was absent from May 28 to September 19. He received at the time, through Walworth and Philipot, the sum of £66–13–4 for wages and expenses. But his actual expenses exceeded his allowance by fourteen pounds, and the balance was apparently not paid him until February, 1380. During his absence on this second (or possibly third) Italian journey he left powers of attorney with John Gower, the poet, and Richard Forester.

After the year 1378 there is only one record known of Chaucer's service on a mission abroad. In July, 1387, according to an entry recently discovered, he was granted protection for a year, to go to Calais in the retinue of Sir William Beauchamp. This time again his duties are unknown, and there is no mention of him in the account of William de la Pole, Beauchamp's controller. If Chaucer was away from England for any length of time during that year, the question naturally arises (as raised by Miss Rickert, who called attention to the record) whether the date usually assumed for the beginning of the *Canterbury Tales* should be put somewhat later.

Except for this single mission, Chaucer's public services after 1378, so far as is known, were performed in England. In 1374, the year of his appointment as Controller of the Customs, as already noted, he had leased the house over Aldgate which he occupied for the twelve years of his service at the Custom House. His residence was of course interrupted by the foreign journeys that have been mentioned, and also, it seems, by absences on private business in 1383, when he obtained leave to appoint a deputy for four months, and in 1384, when he was granted the same privilege for a month. In 1382 he was appointed Controller of the Petty Custom on wines and other merchandise, with permission to have a permanent deputy. In February, 1385, he obtained leave to have a permanent deputy in the wool custom. But the following year his employment at the Custom House came to an end — whether through voluntary resignation, or through the hostile action of Gloucester's commission, is unknown. He gave up his house over Aldgate, which was leased in October, 1386, to Richard Forster, or Forester. He must have already retired to live in Kent, for which county he had been appointed justice of the peace in 1385, and was elected Knight of the Shire in the summer of 1386.

At this point may be mentioned an incident of the period of Chaucer's controllership which has occasioned considerable discussion. On May 1, 1380, a certain Cecily Chaumpaigne released Chaucer of every sort of action "tam de raptu meo, tam de alia re vel causa." It has sometimes been supposed that this referred to an act of physical rape, and Skeat even suggested that "Little Lewis," for whom Chaucer composed the *Astrolabe*, was Cecily's son. But it is more generally believed that the case was one of civil "raptus," or abduction. Chaucer's own father had been abducted as a child in an attempt to force him to marry Joan de Westhale; and in 1387, Chaucer himself served on a commission to inquire into the "raptus," or abduction, of a Kentish heiress, Isabella atte Halle. It has been recently argued that in 1380, after the passage of the Statute of Westminster, "raptus" would have meant "rape," as it is there defined. But the circumstances of the Chaumpaigne case, and Chaucer's connection with them, still remain unknown.

On February 19, 1386, Philippa Chaucer, whose close relation to the family of John of Gaunt and Constance of Castile has already been mentioned, was admitted to the fraternity of Lincoln Cathedral, along with Henry, Earl of Derby, John Beaufort, Sir Thomas Swynford, and several members of the Duke's household. In the following year she apparently died, for there is no record of the payment of her annuity after June 18, 1387.

It is uncertain, as has already been remarked, whether Chaucer's retirement from the Custom House was voluntary, or was due to the hostility of Gloucester and his faction toward the King's appointees. Possibly Gloucester's influence may be responsible, too, for Chaucer's failure to be reëlected to Parliament, in which he sat only for the session of 1386. At any rate it was not until 1389, when Richard became of age and assumed control of affairs, that Chaucer began to receive new preferments. Nothing definite is known about his financial condition in the interval. But a series of writs have been discovered, issued between April and June, 1388, enjoining his attachment for debt.

In 1389 Chaucer was appointed to the important and responsible office of Clerk of the King's Works, which he held for twenty-three months. He had charge of buildings and repairs in the Tower, Westminster Palace, and eight other royal residences, together with lodges, mews, parks, and other belongings. In 1390 he was given a special commission to attend to repairs in St. George's Chapel, Windsor. It was part of his business, in the same year, to construct scaffolds for two tournaments at Smithfield; and, in addition to the regular duties of his office as Clerk, he was appointed in March to a commission, headed by Sir Richard Stury, to look after the walls, bridges, sewers, and ditches along the Thames from Greenwich to Woolwich. Thus during his clerkship Chaucer must have been a very active man of affairs. He had the management of large numbers of workmen and very considerable sums of money. He must have been obliged to travel constantly from place to place in supervising his various pieces of construction. The records show that in September, 1390, he was robbed either twice or three times within four days, and on one of these occasions he was assaulted and beaten. Perhaps as a result of this experience, or because he found his office routine burdensome, or wished to have leisure for writing, he gave up the clerkship in the following year. The reasons for his withdrawal are a matter of conjecture. Some scholars have inferred from the recorded writs requiring him to settle his accounts and turn his offices over to John Gedney, his successor, that he was forced to resign because of dilatoriness or other kind of delinquency. It is even suggested that he was blamed for allowing himself to be robbed. But the assault and robbery is at least equally likely to have been a reason for his voluntary resignation. His accounts, moreover, when finally rendered, showed the government to be in his debt for the sum of £21, the equivalent of approximately six hundred pounds today. On this score, then, also, Chaucer might have had reason for voluntarily relinquishing the office.

At some date before June 22, 1391 — and perhaps before June 17, when he gave up the Clerkship of the Works — he was appointed deputy forester of the royal forest of North Petherton in Somerset. The appointment was renewed in 1398. The manor of Newton Plecy and the forestership, which was an appurtenance thereof, belonged to the Mortimers, earls of March, from 1359 until, by the failure of the Mortimer line, they passed into the hands of the Duke of York. It has been supposed that Chaucer received his first appointment from Edward Mortimer, the third earl, and his second from Eleanor, the dowager countess. But it has been recently shown that Sir Peter Courtenay had the administration of the forestership continuously from 1382 till 1405, first as custodian during the minority of the third earl, and after 1393 as lessee. So Chaucer appears to have owed his appointments to Courtenay. Since Courtenay was Constable of Windsor Castle during the time when Chaucer was in charge of the repairs of St. George's Chapel, this Petherton appointment may have some bearing on the theory that Chaucer's services as Clerk of the Works were terminated for inefficiency. It is not known how long Chaucer continued his work as forester after the renewal of his appointment in 1398.

The Petherton forestership is the last regular office that Chaucer is known to have held. In the discharge of its duties he may have spent a good deal of time in Somerset during the last decade of his life. But his designation, in April, 1396, as a member of a board of Greenwich freeholders to represent Gregory Ballard in an action concerning real estate would indicate that he retained his residence in Kent. Occasional entries in the records give evidence of his presence in London, and show that he continued to enjoy the royal favor. In January, 1393, he received a gift of ten pounds for "good service rendered to the King during the year now present." In February, 1394, after he had received all the arrears due him as Clerk of the Works, the King granted him a new annuity of twenty pounds, equal in value to about two-thirds of the annuity of forty marks he had assigned to Scalby in 1388. It is possible that during the year 1395–96 Chaucer was in attendance upon Henry, Earl of Derby (afterwards Henry IV). For at Christmas, 1395, and again in the following February, he appears to have delivered £10 to Henry from the clerk of the wardrobe. He also received from Henry a gift of a scarlet robe trimmed with fur, valued at over eight pounds. In December, 1397, Chaucer received a further mark of the King's favor in the grant of a butt of wine yearly. The informal promise apparently made at that time was confirmed by letters patent in the following October. Henry IV, immediately after his coronation in October, 1399, renewed Richard's grants of the annuity of £20 and the hogshead of wine, and gave Chaucer an additional annuity of forty marks.

The payments of these stipends in Chaucer's last years appear from the records to have been very irregular. From the fact that he obtained a number of advances or loans from the Exchequer it has been inferred that he was in financial need. His begging poems, the *Envoy to Scogan* and the *Complaint to his Purse,* have also been cited in support of the opinion. But the poems are not to be taken too seriously, and the records give very little evidence of poverty, though Chaucer may have been in temporary embarrassment as the result of a suit for over £14 brought against him by Isabella Bukholt. He was given letters of protection for two years, "that certain jealous persons might not interfere with his performance of the king's business." The grounds of the Bukholt claim are unknown, but since the claimant's husband had been keeper of the royal park at Clarendon and the mews at Charing Cross, and thus a subordinate of Chaucer as Clerk of the Works, it has been reasonably inferred that the suit had to do with the conduct of that office or the distribution of its perquisites.

On December 4, 1399, Chaucer took a long lease, for fifty-three years, of a house in the garden of Westminster Abbey. But his actual occupation of it was brief. The last recorded payment of his pension was on June 5, 1400, and according to the generally accepted date inscribed on his tomb in Westminster Abbey, he died on October 25, 1400.

The foregoing summary, which has been of necessity in large part a recital of dates and figures, includes all the more significant of the recorded facts of Chaucer's life that have thus far come to light. The account has been condensed by the omission of many entries relating to gifts, loans, and payments, and other transactions of minor importance. But the substance of the story, as it is now understood, has been here related. As shown by the comments made in the course of the narrative, the records are often of uncertain interpretation. They also leave us without positive information on such important matters as the dates of the poet's birth and marriage, the circumstances of his education, or the names and history of his children. They tell us little, except by implication, about his more intimate personal life or his intellectual interests. And, far from giving any information about his literary work, the contemporary documents cited do not once betray the fact that he was a man of letters.

On some of these points, however, information is supplied by other sources, and the story has been pieced out with tradition and conjecture, especially by the earlier biographers. In fact the more critical modern historians have rejected a whole series of traditions, which make up what Lounsbury called "the Chaucer legend."

It has not been easy to separate fact from legend in the case of assertions made on entirely unknown authority. With respect to Chaucer's education, for example, the older biographers reported a tradition that he studied at one or both of the universities. But

no support has been found for the statement, and it is now generally rejected. Unpublished records, cited recently by Professor Crow, make it probable that Chaucer received part at least of his early education at St. Paul's Cathedral School, London. Another tradition, that Chaucer was a member of one of the Inns of Court, which was rejected as legendary by Lounsbury, has lately been shown to be very probably true. It rests upon the declaration of Speght that Master Buckley had seen a record of the Inner Temple to the effect that Chaucer was fined two shillings for beating a Franciscan friar in Fleet Street. The records of the Inner Temple for the period have perished or disappeared, but since Master Buckley was their keeper in the sixteenth century his testimony is entitled to respect. The story in itself is perfectly credible, even the two-shilling fine being the kind of penalty commonly exacted for such an offense as is described. Legal training, moreover, would have been a natural preparation for Chaucer's career in business and public affairs, and in his writings — though this point should not be unduly pressed as evidence — he shows considerable acquaintance with the law. His study at the Temple may have fallen between 1361 and 1367 — a period, it will be remembered, during which we have no records of his doings.

With reference to Chaucer's family very little information has been found outside the records. Mention has already been made of Catherine Chaucer, his sister, and of Elizabeth Chaucy, who may have been his daughter. The "little Lewis" for whom he composed the *Astrolabe* was probably his son. Reasons have been given for identifying him with the younger Lewis Clifford, who was perhaps Chaucer's godson, and could therefore have been addressed as "son" in the treatise. But the recent discovery of the name of Lewis Chaucer in a record supports the usual belief that the boy was Chaucer's own child. He may have been a namesake and godson of Sir Lewis Clifford.

It is commonly held, and is highly probable, that Thomas Chaucer, who rose to wealth and influence in the beginning of the fifteenth century, was also the poet's son. In the numerous records that have been preserved of both men there is very little direct evidence of this relationship. But Manly, in 1933, cited a lawsuit of The London Skinners against "Thomam Chaucerum Armigerum filium Galfridi Chauceri Armigeri," and the relationship is positively asserted by Thomas Gascoigne in his Dictionarium Theologicum. Thomas Chaucer is known to have used the poet's seal, and the arms on his tomb clearly prove his connection with the Roets, the family of Chaucer's wife. In fact it is now generally agreed that Thomas was the son of Philippa, and passed as the poet's son. But it has been suspected by a few investigators, and has recently been argued by Dr. Russell Krauss, that Thomas's father was John of Gaunt. Documentary evidence would not be likely to prove or to disprove such a secret liaison. But when all allowance is made for the laxity of standards in the English court in the fourteenth century, and for the rather helpless position of retainers or subordinates in the households of the great, and even for the notoriously loose life of John of Gaunt, it still seems improbable that he injured and humiliated Chaucer, and entered into a relation with two sisters which would have been regarded as incestuous. For it is well known that Katherine, Philippa's sister, was first his mistress and afterwards his wife. The antecedent improbability of such action the evidence well presented by Dr. Krauss is not strong enough to overcome. Neither the Lancastrian arms on Thomas's tomb, nor John of Gaunt's gifts and favors to Philippa and her husband, and to Thomas Chaucer himself, demand the explanation assumed. Moreover, the silence of the poet's contemporaries with regard to his relationship to Thomas really proves nothing. For, by hypothesis, Thomas was the son of Geoffrey's wife. Since he bore Chaucer's name he must have passed as his son, and this apparent relationship between the two men must have been a matter of common knowledge. If it was also an open secret that Thomas was a bastard, and for that reason contemporary writers never refer to him as Geoffrey's son, it is a little strange that the fact was not disclosed by some

of the scribes or chroniclers who have preserved reports of other court scandals. Moreover, Gascoigne's testimony deserves respect as coming from a man of standing and an Oxfordshire neighbor of Thomas Chaucer.

The life of Thomas Chaucer is not strictly a part of the present story. But it may be of interest to note that he was in the service of John of Gaunt and Henry IV, and received annuities, like Geoffrey Chaucer, from both Richard and Henry. About 1394–95 he married Maud Burgersh. Their daughter, Alice, was married successively to the Earl of Salisbury and William de la Pole, later Duke of Suffolk. After 1411 Thomas paid the rent on the house at Westminster which Geoffrey had occupied at the end of his life. In 1413 he became forester of North Petherton, and is often referred to as Geoffrey's successor in that office. But it is more accurate to say that he followed Courtenay in the lease of the bailiwick of the forests of Somerset. Neither his occupation of the Westminster house nor his Petherton forestership proves anything with regard to his relationship to Geoffrey. His public career was distinguished. He was chief butler to Richard II and his three successors, envoy to France, member of the King's Council, and several times Speaker of the House of Commons.

To return to Geoffrey Chaucer, the life-records, of which a chronological outline has here been presented, tell a very incomplete story, but they show at least the range of his experience and acquaintance. From boyhood he had personal knowledge of the court, living in close association successively with the households of Lionel, Edward III, and John of Gaunt. His biographers disagree as to the extent of patronage and protection accorded to him by Lancaster. But the *Book of the Duchess* suggests that the poet stood in some dependent relation to the Duke, to whom he was certainly indebted for important favors in the early seventies. How long they were continued is not a matter of record, and it is uncertain how far Lancaster concerned himself with Chaucer's official appointments. Chaucer's association with Henry of Derby in the nineties may have no connection with his earlier relations to Gaunt, though it indicates a continued adherence to the Lancastrian house. For a part, at least, of the favors that the young poet received during the reign of Edward III it has been plausibly suggested, though documentary evidence seems to be lacking, that he was indebted to the influence of the King's mistress, Dame Alice Perrers.

It is uncertain to what degree Chaucer enjoyed the special favor of Richard and Anne. Complimentary references to the Queen have been recognized in the *Knight's Tale* and the *Troilus,* and the *Legend* was apparently to be presented to her, — perhaps was written at the royal command. But the evidence is not sufficient to show, what has sometimes been conjectured, that Anne intervened personally in the appointment of a deputy to relieve Chaucer in 1385. In one case the King's favor may have worked to Chaucer's disadvantage. The loss of his controllership in 1386 he may have owed to the fact that he was regarded by Gloucester's party, in Professor Tout's phrase, as "one of the King's gang."

Throughout his long public career Chaucer came into contact with most of the men of importance in London, as well as with continental diplomats and rulers. The list of those with whom he appears to have had frequent dealings includes the great merchants Sir William Walworth, Sir Nicholas Brembre, and Sir John Philipot, and a number of ambassadors and officials of various sorts — Sir William de Beauchamp, Sir Guichard d'Angle, Sir John Burley, Sir Peter Courtenay, Walter Skirley, Bishop of Durham, and the so-called Lollard Knights — at one time followers of Wyclif — Sir Lewis Clifford, Sir William Neville, Sir John Clanvowe, and Sir Richard Stury. To these men, whom the records show to have been in one way or another associated with Chaucer, may be added, on the evidence of his own writings, Sir Philip de Vache, Clifford's son-in-law, and one of the Buktons, Sir Peter or Sir Robert.

This is a brilliant circle of courtiers and men of affairs. With regard to Chaucer's literary friendships the records give little information, but it is fair to assume without documentary evidence that he would have been acquainted with all the writers of importance in London. It is known that when he went to Italy in 1378 he named John Gower as his attorney. From the dedication of the *Troilus* to Gower, and the complimentary lines on Chaucer in the *Confessio Amantis,* it has been inferred that the two poets were in friendly, if not intimate, relations. Ralph Strode — *philosophical Strode,* who shares with Gower the dedication of the *Troilus* — is also brought by at least one record into connection with Chaucer in a business transaction. Other literary friends or acquaintances were Scogan, to whom he addressed his *Envoy* — doubtless Henry Scogan, a younger poet and disciple, afterwards tutor to the sons of Henry IV and author of a Moral Balade; probably Otes de Granson, a French poet who lived for a time in England and to whom he makes complimentary reference in the *Complaint of Venus;* and certainly Eustache Deschamps, who sent Chaucer by the hand of Clifford one of his productions with a request for a critical judgment upon it. Chaucer may have seen both Deschamps and Guillaume Machaut in France, though there appears to be no record of such a meeting. In his youth he would naturally have seen Froissart, who was attached to the household of Queen Philippa. During his London life he must have come into contact with Thomas Usk, the political associate of Brembre, whose execution shortly followed Brembre's in 1388. Usk's Testament of Love, it will be remembered, is full of borrowings from Chaucer's writings. Chaucer can hardly have failed also to know Wyclif, who preached for a time at the royal court, enjoyed the protection of John of Gaunt, and numbered among his followers, as already indicated, several of Chaucer's friends.

Chaucer's literary acquaintance may well have extended beyond England and France to Italy. For it would have been possible for him, at least, on his visits to that country to see Sercambi, whose Novelle, like the *Canterbury Tales,* describe a pilgrimage; Giovanni da Legnano, the great jurist whom he praises in the *Clerk's Prologue;* and Boccaccio and

Petrarch, to both of whom he is indebted for important material. But no record has been found of his meeting any of these Italians, and the passage in the *Clerk's Prologue,* which is often cited to prove his personal acquaintance with Petrarch, is not really valid evidence.

This survey of Chaucer's friends and associates, though it discloses little of his more intimate personal life, helps us to reconstruct the world he lived in, and makes it easier to understand how he was able to give as complete a description as he did of the England of his day. In a measure, too, it reveals the kind of man he was, and for that reason is not without bearing on the literary judgment of his works. For example, anyone who contemplates his career will be slow to follow those critics who find in his writings the quality of simple-minded naïveté. It would seem unnecessary to labor this point did not the conception of a *naïf* Chaucer keep reappearing in critical comment. If the term were used in the sense made familiar by Schiller in his essay Ueber Naïve und Sentimentalische Dichtung, there would be no reason to object. For Chaucer may well be classified with the naïve rather than the sentimental poets. But the critics here referred to appear to have in mind not the higher naïveté of genius, but rather the lower naïveté of children and simple people. It is easy, moreover, to see some of the reasons for the persistent attribution of this quality to Chaucer. There is a real simplicity in the English language of Chaucer's period, as contrasted with modern English, and simple directness is a marked characteristic of Chaucer's individual style. He is fond, too, of using the proverbs and other formulas of common speech. The society he describes was doubtless less mature and sophisticated than that of today, though not so childlike as the condescending modern likes to suppose. Perhaps some of the ideas Chaucer expresses about science and religion make him now seem credulous and uncritical. But it is not necessarily a mark of naïveté to accept the beliefs of one's age, and as a matter of fact Chaucer often shows independence and discrimination in his comments on received opinions. In actual life

he proved himself able to deal with the shrewdest and most sophisticated men of affairs, and in his writings he displays an understanding of human nature that is altogether extraordinary.

Canon and Chronology of Chaucer's Writings

The life-records, as already explained, give no direct information about Chaucer's works. For evidence about the date and authenticity of these it is necessary to go to the writings themselves, to the statements of the copyists who have preserved them, and to such testimony as can be found in the literature of the period. Chaucer's own lists in the *Introduction to the Man of Law's Tale,* the *Prologue to the Legend,* and the *Retractation* (if it is genuine) are of course of primary importance. The information derived from these various sources is treated with some fullness later, in the discussion of the separate works, and a brief summary statement is all that is necessary here.

In the early editions of Chaucer, even down to the middle of the last century, many writings were included, his authorship of which is either unsupported by evidence or demonstrably impossible. Some of them were not attributed to Chaucer by the first editors, but came gradually to be associated with him. They finally swelled the volume of the works which passed for his in the seventeenth and eighteenth centuries, and they must be taken into account in any study of the opinion of Chaucer held by English poets and critics of those periods.

Skeat's Oxford Chaucer (six volumes, 1894) and the Globe Chaucer (1898) were the first modern collected editions from which such spurious works were rigorously excluded. Skeat published an additional seventh volume of Chaucerian Pieces (1897), in which a number of the most important writings of the Chaucer Apocrypha were made easily accessible. Of the pieces included in the present edition, there is no serious question of the authorship of any except the few short poems listed as doubtful (printed on pages 540–543) and the *Romaunt of the Rose*.

With regard to the chronological order of the works there is more uncertainty. It is perhaps surprising that hardly any of them can be dated from a connection with a definite event. Among the longer poems the *Book of the Duchess* is the only exception, and even in that case the traditional opinion has been called in question. But there is no strong reason for doubting that the work was composed to commemorate the death of Blanche, Duchess of Lancaster, which took place in 1369. A very few of the short pieces — the *Complaint to his Purse,* less positively the envoys to *Bukton* and *Scogan,* and possibly the *Fortune* — can be brought into association with particular occurrences. The *Astrolabe,* on the evidence of one of its calculations, may be safely assigned to 1391 or 1392. A few other works, like the *Knight's Tale,* the *Troilus,* the *Man of Law's Tale,* can be approximately dated by more or less doubtful allusions. But the greater number of Chaucer's writings can be only arranged in a probable order, based partly upon their relations to one another, and partly upon the consideration of their sources. Of course Chaucer's own lists are helpful in determining their dates as well as their authenticity. The allegorical interpretations that have been proposed for several pieces — the *House of Fame,* the *Anelida,* the *Parliament of Fowls,* and a number of the *Canterbury Tales* — are too dubious to be used as evidence.

To illustrate some of the more positive data in the solution of the problem, the *Palamon* (the original form of the *Knight's Tale*) and the *Troilus* must both precede the *Prologue to the Legend,* in which they are mentioned; and the *Legend* must have been at least partly written before the *Introduction to the Man of Law's Tale,* which refers to it. It has not been conclusively proved whether the *Knight's Tale* or the *Troilus* was written first. But there is reason (in an astronomical allusion) for dating the completion of the *Troilus* not earlier than 1385. The *Troilus* appears, also, to have been followed at no long interval by the *Prologue to the Legend,* and the first form of that

has been reasonably assigned, on the evidence of Chaucer's use of Deschamps, to the year 1386. The *Palamon,* therefore, should probably be put before the *Troilus,* and there is nothing in the two poems themselves to make this order unlikely. Some of the individual legends of *Good Women* look like rather early work, and may have preceded the *Prologue.* If the dates suggested for these various writings are accepted, the years from 1387 onward remain fairly free for Chaucer's consecutive work on the *Canterbury Tales.*

By the use of such evidence as has been described, supplemented by literary considerations, the following chronological table may be tentatively constructed:

Before 1372: The *ABC* (if composed for the Duchess Blanche); *The Book of the Duchess* (1369–70); and probably some of the early lyrics and complaints of the French type.

1372–80: Transitional works, partly of the French tradition, but showing the beginnings of Italian influence; *The House of Fame; Saint Cecilia* (the *Second Nun's Tale*); the tragedies afterward used for the *Monk's Tale; Anelida;* some of the lyrics.

1380–86: Works in which the Italian influence is fully assimilated; the *Parliament of Fowls* (possibly a little earlier); *Palamon; Troilus,* probably preceded shortly by the *Boece;* some of the short poems, probably including the Boethian group of ballades; the *Legend of Good Women.*

1387–92: The *General Prologue* and the earlier *Canterbury Tales;* the *Astrolabe* (1391–92).

1393–1400: The later *Canterbury Tales* (including the "Marriage Group"); the latest short poems, including *Scogan, Bukton,* and the *Complaint to his Purse.*

Some of the minor poems of uncertain date have been omitted from the table, as has also the *Romaunt of the Rose,* of which Chaucer's authorship is altogether doubtful. If Fragment A is his, the style and verse-form would point to its classification with the *Book of the Duchess* in the French period. But Chaucer's version may have been in a different form, and the association of it with the *Troilus* in the

Prologue to the Legend has led some scholars to put it in the decade of the eighties.

Language and Meter

Professor Scherillo, in his history of the origins of Italian literature, commenting upon the statement frequently made that Dante created the Italian language, reminds his readers that this is claiming for the Italian poet a function like that of Adam in Eden, when he gave names to all the beasts of the field and the fowls of the air! A similar reminder might appropriately have been addressed to those writers who have called Chaucer the creator of English. Such a statement of course totally misrepresents the development of the language. Chaucer employed the London speech of his time, and a minute comparison of his usage with that of the contemporary London archives shows the two to correspond in all essentials. He not only did not invent or alter the grammatical inflections, but he also appears to have added few words to the English vocabulary. At least Mr. Henry Bradley, in the light of his experience in editing the New English Dictionary, was very cautious about attributing such contributions to the poet. It is even doubtful if Chaucer had any important part in making the East Midland the dominant dialect. The speech of the capital would have become standard English if he had never written a line. But he did add greatly to its prestige and distinction. The very fact that he wrote in English instead of French was significant. He developed the resources of the language for literary use, and set an example which was followed by a long line of poets.

Chaucer's language, then, is late Middle English of the South East Midland type. As compared with Anglo-Saxon or some of the other dialects of Middle English, its inflections are simple and offer little difficulty to the reader of today. But many words retained a syllabic -*e*, either final or in the ending -*es* or -*en*, which afterwards ceased to be pronounced, and the vowels had in general their present continental rather than their English sound. For metrical purposes, consequently, Chau-

cer's language was very different from ours, and it is impossible to read his verse properly — to say nothing of appreciating it — without having some knowledge of the older pronunciation and grammatical forms. It is because this knowledge was lost from the fifteenth century down to the middle of the nineteenth that many of Chaucer's most enthusiastic admirers among English poets and critics have regarded his meter as irregular and rough.

The brief grammatical outline that follows is intended to supply the reader or student with such knowledge of Chaucer's sounds and inflections as is necessary for the intelligent reading of the verse. To save space, certain inflectional forms, such as the principal parts of strong verbs, which are registered in the Glossary, are not repeated here. The Glossary also records exceptional forms, like the contracted third singular present indicative of verbs or "petrified" datives of nouns, and it shows the nominative forms of nouns and adjectives when they are likely to give any trouble because of their unlikeness to modern English. In general, final *e*'s that appear in the present text may be assumed to represent correct Chaucerian usage. For it has been the editor's intention to remove all the incorrect scribal *e*'s, which abound in the manuscripts.

PRONUNCIATION

VOWELS AND DIPHTHONGS. There is considerable inconsistency in the spelling of the vowels and diphthongs. Vowels are commonly, but not regularly, doubled to indicate length — not only *e*, as in modern English e.g. "deed," but also *a* and *o*, and rarely *i*.

Some of the pronunciations indicated in the accompanying table are only approximate, and others are doubtful. Chaucer's close $\bar{e}$ and $\bar{o}$ did not quite correspond to the vowels now heard in "name" and "note," which are really diphthongal ($\bar{e}$ + a transitional *i*, $\bar{o}$ + *u*). It is hard to judge in how many cases Chaucer's $\breve{a}$ preserved the sound of *a* in German "Mann," and when it had the sound of *æ*, as in modern English "that" (and AS. "þæt"). The combinations *eu*, *ew*, represented not only the descending diphthong $\bar{e}u$, $\breve{e}u$ (as in *knew*, from AS.

Sound	Pronunciation	Spelling	Examples
ā	like *a* in "father"	a, aa	*name, caas.*
ă	like *a* in Ger. "Mann"	a	*can, that.*
ē (close)	like *a* in "fate"	e, ee	*sweete.*
ę̄ (open)	like *e* in "there"	e, ee	*heeth.*
ĕ	like *e* in "set"	e	*tendre.*
e (the neutral vowel)	like *a* in "about"	e	*yonge, sonne.*
ī	like *i* in "machine"	i, y	*ryden, shires.*
ĭ	like *i* in "sit"	i, y	*this, thyng.*
ō (close)	like *o* in "note"	o, oo	*good, bote.*
ǭ (open)	like *oa* in "broad"	o, oo	*holy, rood (vb.).*
ŏ	like *o* in "hot"	o	*oft, lot.*
ū	like *oo* in "boot"	ou, ow, ogh	*fowles, droghte.*
ŭ	like *u* in "full"	u, o	*but, yong, songen (pt. pl.).*
iū	like *u* in "mute"	u, eu, ew	*Pruce, vertu, salewe.*
ę̄i	like *ę̄ + i*	ai, ay, ei, ey	*sayle, day, wey.*
au	like *ou* in "house"	au, aw	*cause, draughte.*
ēu	like *ē + u*	eu, ew	*knew.*
ę̄u	like *ę̄ + u*	eu, ew	*lewed.*
oi	like *oy* in "boy"	oi, oy	*coy, joye.*
ōu	like *ō + u*	ou, ow	*growen.*
ǭu	like *ǭ + u*	ou, ow	*knowen, sowle.*
ou	like *ŏ + u*	o(u), before gh	*fo(u)ghte, tho(u)ght.*

cnéow; lewed, AS. *læwed*), but also the ascending diphthong *iu* (as probably in *salewen*, Fr. "saluer"). The first sound ultimately developed into the second (as in modern English "knew," "lewd"), and it is uncertain just what Chaucer's pronunciation was in individual cases. Similarly, in the combinations *ou, ow*, the original distinction between *ōu* (with close *ō*) and *ǭu* (with open *ǭ*) was apparently breaking down, and the two classes of words are not kept apart in rime. But the diphthong *ou* (of various origins) before *gh* had a different sound, which developed into the modern long vowel in "thought" and "fought." The pronunciation of the diphthongs variously spelled *ai, ay, ei, ey* is a matter of disagreement. The sounds concerned are of different origins, some coming from *e + i* or *e + g* (as in *seylen, wey, counseil*), others from *æ + g* (as in *day, fayn*), and others from *a + i* (as in *batayle, fayle*). They had all fallen together so as to rime acceptably one with another. It is doubtful whether the pronunciation was *āi* (as in "aisle") or *æi* (approaching the modern pronunciation of "way," "day"). But a sound intermediate between the two seems probable.

The distinction between open and close *ē* and *ō* does not appear in Chaucer's spelling, and no simple rule can be given which will guide the reader in all cases. The modern spellings *ea* and *oa* ("heath," "boat") usually point to the broad pronunciation in Middle English, but there are many exceptions. The modern pronunciation — *ō* for Chaucer's *ǭ* (as in "rode") and *oo* (i.e., long *u*) for his *ō* (as in "noon") — is a better test in the case of *ō*, but it fails with *ē*, where the two classes of sounds have fallen together (as in "seek" and "heath"). Even the evidence of etymology is not always decisive, for special conditions sometimes affected the development of words. But as a general rule *ē* (close) corresponds to AS. (or Old Mercian) *ē, ēo,* ON. *ē* and *ø,* OF. (and Anglo-Norman) *ẹ̄* (close); *ę̄* (open), to AS. *ǣ, ēa,* and *ĕ* (when lengthened in Middle English), ON. *æ,* and OF. (or Anglo-Norman) *ę̄; ō* (close), to AS. *ō* or *ŏ* lengthened before consonantal combinations, ON. *ō,* and OF. (or Anglo-Norman) *ọ̄* (close); *ǭ* (open), to AS. or ON. *ā* and *ŏ* (when lengthened before a nasal or in open syllables) and OF. *ŏ* (when lengthened in open syllables). For the assistance of readers who find it difficult to apply these tests, cases of open *ē* and *ō* have been marked (*ę̄* and *ǭ*) in the Glossary of the present edition. Full treatment of the history of the sounds will of course be found in the Middle English grammars listed in the Bibliography, especially those of Luick and Jordan.

CONSONANTS. Chaucer's consonants are pronounced for the most part as in Modern English. But there were no silent consonants, except *h* in French words like *honour* and *g* in French *gn,* which had the sound of single *n* (as in *resigne,* riming with *medicyne*). Ordinarily in the combinations *gn* (in native English words), *kn* (or *cn*), and *wr, g, k,* and *w* were pronounced, and *l* was pronounced before *f, k,* and *m* (as in *half, folk, palmer*). The sound of *ng* is held to have been regularly that of *ng* in "finger." Double *g* had sometimes the sound of *dg* (as in *juggen*), sometimes that of *gg* in "bigger" (as in *frogges*). The modern pronunciation is a safe guide. *ch* had the English sound (as in "church"), not the French (as in "machine"). The spirant *gh,* which became silent in later English, had the sound of the German *ch* in "ich" and "doch" (palatal after a front vowel, and guttural after a back vowel). *r* was trilled. *s* and *th* ought regularly to have been unvoiced (i.e., with the sound of *s* in "sit" and *th* in "thin"), except when between vowels. Between vowels they were voiced (sounded as in Mod. Eng. "those"). But the distinction may not have been observed consistently, and the later voicing in many words (*th* in "these," "those," and *s* in "is," "was") may have begun in Chaucer's period. The suffix *-cion* (Mod. Eng. *-tion*) had two syllables, and could rime with words in *-on* or in *-oun.* The spellings of the ending

in the MSS. are very inconsistent. For their treatment in the present edition see the introductory account of the textual method, p. xliii, below.

INFLECTIONS

The inflectional endings in Chaucer's language which differ from those in modern English can be briefly indicated for the various parts of speech. In many cases they consist simply of a final *-e* which in later English ceased to be pronounced.

NOUNS. Many nouns have in the nominative case a final *-e* which is lost in modern English. It is not strictly an inflectional ending, but usually represents a final vowel in the language from which the word descends or is derived. Examples: *ende,* from AS. "ende"; *name,* from AS. "nama"; *sone,* from AS. "sunu"; *entente,* from OF. "entente." When the *-e* does not have a corresponding vowel in the source (as in *carte,* from AS. "cræt"), it is called unhistoric or inorganic. In a number of nouns Chaucer had two forms, one with and one without final *-e.* Such words are entered in the Glossary with an *-e* in parenthesis — as, for example, *bliss(e)*.

The regular inflectional endings in the great majority of Chaucerian nouns are the same as in Modern English — *s* or *es* in the genitive (or possessive) singular and in the plural. But there are a few exceptional forms to be noted, all of them obvious survivals of older inflections. Of course some of them, like the umlauting plurals, are familiar in modern English.

Gen. sg. without ending: *a*) in nouns of the AS. *n*-declension (*chirche, lady, herte*); *b*) in nouns of the AS. *r*-declension (*fader, brother*); *c*) in nouns with final *s* (*Venus sone*).

Dat. sg. This is normally without ending in Chaucer (*in the hous, in my lyf*). But in certain stereotyped phrases the old dative ending survived. Examples: *on lyve, a-lyve,* Mod. Eng. "alive"; *on fyre,* "afire"; *to bedde, to shippe, with childe.* Many of the phrases in which this so-called "petrified" dative survives are recorded in the Glossary.

Plural without ending: *a*) in AS. neuter

nouns, and others, which had no ending in the nom. acc. pl. (*yeer,* but also *yeres, deer, sheep, freend*); *b*) nouns in *-s* (*caas, paas*); *c*) in umlauting nouns, which still form their plural by a change of vowel (*men, gees, feet*).

Plural in *-en:* now rare, but common in AS. and represented by a number of cases in Chaucer (*asshen, eyen* or *yën, hosen, fon, pesen, been*). Parallel forms in *-es* usually also occurred.

ADJECTIVES. The adjective, like the noun, sometimes has a final *-e* in the nominative case (*swete, grene, drye*). Such forms are recorded in the Glossary.

The English of Chaucer's period still preserved the old Germanic distinction, since lost, between the strong and the weak declensions. The latter occurs: *a*) when the adjective follows the article, a demonstrative or possessive pronoun, or a noun in the genitive (*the yonge sonne, his halve cours, Epicurus owne sone*); *b*) when it is used with a noun in the vocative (*O stronge God*); *c*) often when it is used with proper names (*faire Venus*); *d*) perhaps in a few other cases when the adjective is used substantively, though other explanations of the ending can usually be found (*the beste,* where the article precedes; *by weste,* perhaps a dative). The ending of the weak adjective is *-e,* which is also the regular ending of the strong plural. The following paradigm represents Chaucer's regular usage:

	Strong	Weak	Strong	Weak
Singular	*yong*	*yonge*	*swete*	*swete*
Plural	*yonge*	*yonge*	*swete*	*swete*

The inflectional *-e,* whether of the weak form or the plural, is usually not found in predicate adjectives, which are undeclined. It is also rarely pronounced, though often written, in adjectives of two syllables, where it does not fall in with the rhythm of the verse (or, probably, of prose speech). In trisyllabic adjectives, however, where it makes a fourth syllable, it is often preserved. Compare *the holy blisful martir* with *the semelieste man, O wommanliche wyf.*

In addition to the regular weak and plural endings, Chaucer's adjectives show some exceptional forms. The old strong ending of the genitive singular in *-es* is preserved in *alleskinnes,* "of every kind," *noskinnes,* "of no kind." There appear to be a very few datives in *-e,* survivals of the old strong dative inflection, though in most of the cases concerned other explanations of the ending are possible. Examples: *of olde tyme, with harde grace, of purpos grete, in salte see, by weste* — some of which may be explained as extensions of the use of the weak inflection. An old accusative ending is preserved in the combination *halvendel* (AS. "halfne dǽl"). The AS. strong genitive plural survives in one word *aller* (also *aller-, alder-,* in composition), from "ealra." There are a few examples of plural adjectives with the French ending *-es* (*places delitables, houres inequales*). These occur chiefly in the works translated from the French.

The regular suffixes for the comparison of adjectives are the same as in modern English, *-er* and *-est.* In Anglo-Saxon both the comparative and the superlative took the weak inflection, and the corresponding forms are often spelled with a final *-e* (*-ere, -este*) in Chaucer. But the ending is seldom pronounced in the verse except where it constitutes a second or a fourth syllable (*the semelieste man*). A few forms show the umlaut of the root vowel, as in Anglo-Saxon (*lenger, strenger, elder,* etc.), or the doubling of a final consonant (*gretter, sonner*). A number of adjectives are irregularly compared: *good, bettre, beste; bad, badder,* or *werse* (*worse*), *werste* (*worste*); *muche*(*l*), *more* or *mo, moste* (*mẹste*); *lytel, lasse* (*lesse*), *leeste;* etc. Such exceptional forms are registered in the Glossary.

ADVERBS. The regular endings of Chaucer's adverbs are *-e* and *-ly* or *-liche* (the last two coming from the adjectival ending *-lich* with the adverbial ending). Examples: *brighte, smerte, royalliche* or *royally.* There are a few adverbs in *-es* or *-en,* which correspond to AS. ending in *-es* or *-an.* Examples: *ones, twyes, hennes, aboven, abuten.* With the forms in *-es,* properly genitives in origin, may be compared the adverbial phrase *his thankes,* "willingly." The exceptional form *whilom* appears to correspond to the AS. dat. pl. *hwílum*, but is probably to be explained as a late modification of Middle English *whilen*, into which the AS. form normally developed.

PRONOUNS. The pronouns are mostly like those in modern English. Exceptional forms, which might give the reader trouble, are registered in the Glossary. The following special cases may be noted here.

In the first person, *ich* (Northern *ik*) occurs beside *I*. The possessive adjectives *myn* and *thyn* take the regular *-e* in the plural. In the third person singular, the neuter genitive is the same as the masculine — *his* (not "its"). The spelling *hise* ("his," "its") is often found, in the manuscripts, with plural nouns, but the *-e* appears not to have been pronounced and has been struck off in the present text. The plural forms of the personal pronoun in the third person were: nom. *they*, gen. *hire*, *here*, dat., acc. *hem*, (the forms "their" and "them" not having yet come into London English). In the plural possessives *oure*, *youre*, *hire*, the *-e* seems to have been regularly unpronounced.

In the demonstrative *thise* (*these*) the final *-e* was almost invariably silent, and usually in the plural forms *some*, *swiche*, and *whiche*, when used pronominally. When used adjectivally these words are more likely to show an inflectional *-e*.

VERBS. Chaucer's verbs show the characteristic Germanic distinction between the weak and the strong conjugations. Strong verbs, often called irregular, make their preterite tense by the change of the root vowel (ablaut), and weak verbs, by the addition of an ending (*-de* or *-te*). The principal parts of the strong verbs, which for the most part resemble those in modern English so closely as to be easily recognizable, are fully registered in the Glossary, as are also the forms of weak verbs that present any peculiarities. The inflectional endings are shown in the following tables. Parentheses are used to indicate alternative forms. Thus *n* may always be dropped in the verbal ending *-en*, and the prefix *y-* may or may not be used with participles.

Present tense (strong and weak alike)

Indicative		Subjunctive	
Singular 1.	*singe*	Singular	*singe*
2.	*singest*	Plural	*singe(n)*
3.	*singeth*		
Plural	*singe(n)*		

A number of verbs have contracted forms in the second and third singular: *lixt* (liest), *bit* (biddeth), *fint* (findeth), *set* (setteth), *stont* (stondeth), *worth* (wortheth). Such forms, when not easily recognizable, are recorded in the Glossary.

Preterite Indicative

Strong

Singular 1.	*song, sang*
2.	*song(e)*
3.	*song, sang*
Plural	*songe(n)*

Weak

Singular 1.	*wende*	*lovede*
2.	*wendest*	*lovedest*
3.	*wende*	*lovede*
Plural	*wende(n)*	*lovede(n)*

The preterite subjunctive, like the present, has *-e* in the singular and *-e(n)* in the plural.

Imperative

Strong

Singular 2.	*sing*
Plural 2.	*singeth, -e*

Weak

Singular 2.	*loke*	*her*
Plural 2.	*loketh, -e*	*hereth, -e*

Strong verbs and long-stemmed weak verbs of the first class in Anglo-Saxon have regularly no *-e* in the second singular; other weak verbs have *-e*. But *-e* is often written in the manuscripts, and sometimes pronounced in the verse, in forms not historically entitled to it. Example: *As sende love and pees bitwixe hem two*. Such forms, which appear in long-stemmed weak verbs in late Anglo-Saxon, are perhaps sometimes to be regarded as jussive subjunctives.

Infinitive: — The ending is *-en* or *-e* in strong and weak verbs alike: *singe(n)*, *wene(n)*.

In a very few verbs there is preserved an old gerundive or inflected infinitive with a dative *-e: to done, to sene, to seyne.*

Participles: — The present active participle of all verbs, weak and strong, ends in *-ing* or *-inge: singing(e), loving(e).* The preterite passive participle of strong verbs ends in *-e(n),* of weak verbs, in *-d* or *-t.* Examples: *(y-)sunge(n), (y-)loved, (y-)taught.* The prefix *y-* (from AS. *ge-*) is frequent with both strong and weak verbs. The preterite participle is ordinarily uninflected, but in a few cases has the adjectival plural ending in *-e.* Examples: *Sin they ben tolde; with eres spradde.*

Preterite-present (or strong-weak) verbs. — There is a small class of verbs in the Germanic languages in which an old strong preterite came to be used as a present tense, and a new weak preterite was formed to express past time. For example:

Present		Preterite	
Singular 1.	*shal*	Singular 1.	*sholde*
2.	*shalt*	2.	*sholdest*
3.	*shal*	3.	*sholde*
Plural	*shull(en), shal*	Plural	*sholde(n).*

The other preterite-present verbs are *can* (pret. *kouthe, koude*); *dar* (pret. *dorste*); *may* (pret. *mighte*); *most* (pret. *moste*); *owe* (pret. *oughte*); *thar* (pret. *thurfte,* but confused with *dorste*); and *woot* (pret. *wiste*). The peculiar forms of all these verbs are entered in the Glossary.

Anomalous verbs. — The following four verbs show exceptional irregularities.

Goon, pret. *yede* and *wente.*

Doon, pret. *dide.*

Wil(e), wol(e), 2 sg. *wilt, wolt,* 3 sg. *wil(e), wol(e),* pl., *willen, wil, wollen, wol;* pret. *wolde.* The *-e* of the 1 and 3 sg. present indicative, though apparently always silent, is often found in the manuscripts, and is historically justified (AS. *wile,* originally subjunctive).

Been. Pres. ind. sg. *am, art, is;* pl. *been, be,* rarely *are(n).* Pres. sbj. sg. *be;* pl. *been, be.* Pret. ind. sg. *was, were, was;* pl. *were(n).* Pret. sbj. sg. *were;* pl. *were(n).* Imperative sg. *be;* pl. *beeth.*

VERSIFICATION

The various verse-forms used by Chaucer are discussed in the introductions and notes to the separate works. But a few general directions may be given here for the reading of his lines.

The most important difference between Chaucer's English and modern English, for the purpose of versification, lies in the numerous final *-e*'s and other light inflectional endings described in the preceding pages. These endings are ordinarily pronounced in the verse, and indeed are essential to the rhythm. They are also pronounced in rime, and Chaucer with almost complete consistency avoided riming words in *-e* with words not etymologically or grammatically entitled to that ending. But within the verse final *-e* is regularly elided before an initial vowel or before an *h* which is either silent (as in *honour*) or slightly pronounced (as in *he, his, her, him, hem, hadde,* and a few other words). Before initial consonants *-e* is ordinarily sounded, though there are cases on almost every page where it must have been either slurred or entirely apocopated. These statements apply, of course, only to the light, unstressed final *-e,* and not to the long *ē* (often spelled *ee*) in words like *majestee* or *charitee.*

Most of Chaucer's lines, if read naturally and with a proper regard to grammatical endings, have an obvious rhythm. But there are many cases, apart from doubtful textual readings, where there is uncertainty as to elision or apocopation, or even a reasonable choice between two ways of rendering a line. Probably no rules can ever be laid down to settle all such questions. Certain characteristics of Chaucer's versification may, however, be borne in mind. His lines — as contrasted, for example, with those of Gower — have great freedom and variety of movement. He constantly shifts the position of the caesural pause. He often reverses the rhythm of a foot, substituting a trochaic for an iambic movement. Like most English poets, he not infrequently has an extra light syllable in a line (a trisyllabic foot in place of the regular iambus), though in such cases it is often impossible to determine whether to resort to apocopation. The extra syllable seems to have been most frequent in the caesural pause. One other irregularity, which some critics have condemned and the scribes themselves sometimes tried to correct by emendation, Chaucer certainly allowed himself. He not infrequently omitted the unaccented syllable at the beginning of a line. These headless, or nine-syllable, lines — seven-syllable in the case of the octosyllabic meter — are by no means objectionable when the initial stress falls upon an important word. When a preposition or conjunction gets this initial accent, there is perhaps more reason for the objections of the critics, but the evidence of the manuscripts makes it necessary to admit many such lines to the text.

In the following short passage from the *General Prologue*, which will serve as a specimen of scansion, the metrical stresses are marked with an accent ('), syllabic light *e*'s have a diaeresis (¨), and elided or apocopated *e*'s are underdotted. It will be understood, of course, that the metrical accents varied in strength, unimportant words receiving only a secondary stress.

A Clérk ther wás of Óxenfórd alsó,
That únto lógyk háddë lónge ygó.
As léenë wás his hórs as ís a rákë,
And hé nas nát right fát, I úndertákë,
But lóoked hólwë, and thérto sóbrelý.
Ful thrédbarẹ wás his óverestẹ coúrtepý;
For hé haddẹ géten hym yét no bénefícë,
Ne wás so wórldly fór to hávẹ officé.
For hým was lévere hávẹ at his béddes héed
Twénty bóokës, clád in blák or réed,
Of Áristótle and hís philósophië,
Than róbes ríchẹ, or fíthele, or gáy sautríë.
But ál be thát he wás a phílosóphrë,
Yet háddë hé but lítel góld in cófrë;
But ál that hé mýght of his fréendës héntë,
On bóokës ánd on lérnynge hé it spéntë,
And bísilý gán for the sóulës préyë
Of hém that yáf hym whérwith tó scoléyë.
Of stúdie tóok he móost curẹ and móost héedë.
Noght ó word spák he móorë thán was néedë,
And thát was séyd in fórme and réveréncë,
And shórt and quýk and fúl of hý senténcë;
Sównynge in móral vértu wás his spéchë,
And gládlý wóldẹ he lérnẹ and gládly téchë.

The Text

As already explained in the Preface to the present revised edition, and for the reasons there given, the following general introduction on the text has been reprinted here in substantially its original form. It sets forth the principles followed by the editor in the construction of his text, and the same principles hold for the second edition. In most of the works, too, very few textual changes have been made in revision. But in the case of the *Canterbury Tales* the Manly-Rickert edition, referred to expectantly in the original Preface and in the following pages, appeared in 1940. Since it was based upon all known manuscripts, over eighty in number, the classification of authorities there given completely supersedes the tentative one in this work, which is here reprinted simply to show the basis of the editor's decisions. The variants recorded in the Textual Notes are reprinted for the same reason, and for fuller information on both matters the reader should consult the Manly-Rickert edition. But a considerable number of readings have been altered in the text in the light of the new evidence in Manly's apparatus, and a list of these will be found on pages 883–885 at the beginning of the Textual Notes.

In the Textual Notes on the separate works will be found lists of the manuscripts and other authorities for the text, together with references to previous studies in their classification. Special problems, also, are discussed in the notes on the works in connection with which they arise. But here, in the introduction, may properly be given some account of the general method of the present edition.

The entire text has been made afresh by the editor. It is based upon his examination of all the published manuscript materials and photographs or collations of some of the more important unpublished sources. Account has been taken of the numerous studies that have been made of the character and relations of the manuscripts, and it has been the editor's intention to pay due regard to critical principles. In fact the text may be called a critical edition, with one reservation. In the case of some of the more important works, including the *Canterbury Tales,* the manuscript materials accessible to the editor have not been exhaustive. But the best copies of all the works have been available for use as the basis of the edition, and enough others have been compared to make possible, in the editor's belief, the establishment of trustworthy texts.

The *Canterbury Tales,* for example, are preserved in some ninety manuscripts and early prints, complete or fragmentary. Photographs of all these copies have recently been brought together at the University of Chicago by Professor Manly and his associates, who are preparing a great critical edition. Their work, which is eagerly awaited by all Chaucerians, will shed new light on doubtful readings, and will probably make it possible for the first time to reconstruct the successive stages in the composition of the *Canterbury Tales.* But it does not appear likely that a text based upon the complete collation would be materially different from one that can be constructed from the eight published manuscripts, which include the best copy, the Ellesmere MS., and are so distributed as to represent all the important groups of authorities. For the *Pardoner's Prologue* and *Tale,* of course, the editor has used the specimens published by the Chaucer Society, representing in all over fifty copies, upon which Zupitza and Koch based their classification of the authorities; and for the *Clerk's Tale* he has had the published specimens from eight additional manuscripts. He has been further aided by the numerous citations of the readings of special passages printed in such textual studies as Professor Tatlock's paper on the Harleian Manuscript and the late Professor Brusendorff's Chaucer Tradition. In addition to all this printed material, the editor has collated the Cardigan MS., a superior copy which was not represented among the specimens printed by the Chaucer Society, and the Morgan MS., which is classified with those of less authority.

In textual method the present editor does not belong to the severest critical school. When the readings of the "critical text" or of a superior archetype appeared unsatisfactory or manifestly inferior, he has accepted help from other authorities more often than the strict constructionists might approve. He has seen no way of avoiding the exercise of personal judgment. But he has not practiced mere eclecticism, and in making his decisions he has endeavored to give constant attention to the relation of the manuscripts and to all relevant consideration of language, meter, and usage. Some of the problems that have arisen — and they vary considerably in the different works of Chaucer — may be briefly described.

In the *Canterbury Tales,* for example, as is fully set forth in the Textual Notes below, the A type of manuscripts, represented by Ellesmere, Hengwrt, Cambridge Dd, and Cambridge Gg — whether or not they all go back to a single archetype below the original — is generally accepted as of superior authority to the B type, which includes Harleian 7334, Corpus, Petworth, and Lansdowne. They are the basis of the present text, as of all recent editions. In the *Pardoner's Tale,* for which nearly all the authorities have been printed and compared, there seems to be no case where the reading of the more numerous manuscripts of type B is preferable. But elsewhere in the tales there are a few passages where the B readings seem to the editor superior to the A readings, and he has not hesitated to adopt them. Thus in the *General Prologue,* I, 510 (where, of course, only the eight published manuscripts and the Cardigan and Morgan copies were considered) *chaunterie* (B) clearly affords a better and more Chaucerian rhythm than *chauntrye* (A), which Professor Liddell, in his critical edition, retained in strict adherence to his archetype. Other examples of B readings accepted in the present text are *ben* (A *leyn*), *PrT*, VII, 676; *Odenake* (A *Onedake*), *MkT*, VII, 2072; *out of the yerd* (A *into this yerd*), *NPT*, VII, 3422; *giltelees* (A *giltlees*), *FranklT*, V, 1318; *fayerye* (A *fairye*), *MerchT*, IV, 1743.

Although some editors would follow their archetype more strictly, the readings mentioned are of course entirely defensible from the point of view of critical method, since the original of the A manuscripts need not have been at all points superior to that of type B. More serious difficulties in adhering to critical procedure arise in connection with the baffling MS. Harl. 7334, the peculiar relations of which are said to have deterred Mr. Henry Bradshaw from editing the *Canterbury Tales.* Classified somewhat doubtfully by the textual critics among the manuscripts of type B, the Harleian copy shows evidence of contamination with the superior type A, and has many unique readings of great interest. Some editors, among them Professor Skeat and Mr. Pollard, have held it to contain Chaucerian revisions, and they have consequently felt free to draw upon any of its readings that seem intrinsically attractive. Other scholars have doubted the special authority of the manuscript, and, in the opinion of the present editor, it has been virtually disproved by Professor Tatlock in his study on the subject. Taking the more important passages where the Harleian readings are unique among the eight published manuscripts, Mr. Tatlock collated them with some thirty-five other copies to discover how much support they might have, and then examined the readings themselves to determine their character and value. He showed that many which have been adopted by the editors were clearly scribal emendations, and in some cases very poor ones. The officious and entirely unnecessary substitution of *cloysterlees* for *recchelees* in the familiar passage of the *General Prologue* (I, 179) is typical of the procedure of this anonymous editor. Again, in *KnT*, I, 1906, the Harleian reading *And westward in the mynde and in memorye* may safely be regarded as the scribe's emendation of the defective reading of most manuscripts, *And on* (or *in*) *the westward in memorye.* Professor Tatlock in the study in which he discredited the Harleian text as a whole was inclined to accept its authority in this passage. But the reading, *And on the gate westward in memorye,* which has been found in a few scattered manuscripts, is more likely to have been what Chaucer wrote, and would explain easily the corrupted forms in which the line is preserved. Similarly the greater number of unique Harleian readings appear on examination to be emendations, and many of them can be traced to the scribe's dis-

like of headless, or nine-syllable, lines. There remain, however, a few passages in which it is hard not to follow the Harleian text. In *KnT*, I, 2037, where all the printed manuscripts have the obvious blunder *sertres, certres* (or a variant thereof), the Harleian reads correctly *sterres,* which all editors adopt (except Koch, who emends to *cercles*). Again in *Gen Prol,* I, 485, *And swich he was ypreved ofte sithes,* all the manuscripts except the Harleian read *preved,* to the decided impairment of the rhythm. In this case Professor Liddell, whose definitely announced policy was to "boycott the Harleian," adopted its reading, as he did also in *KnT*, I, 3104, *And he hire serveth also gentilly* (where all the other printed manuscripts read *so*). On the other hand in *KnT*, I, 2892, Mr. Liddell read *Upon thise stedes grete and white,* rejecting the relief afforded by the Harleian text (*that weren grete and white*), though the other reading compels us to accent *upon* unnaturally on the first syllable and to pronounce the final *-e* of *thise,* which is usually silent. Possibly the correct reading of this line is *Upon thise steedes grete and lilye whyte,* which is found in MS. Cardigan. Again in *KnT*, I, 3071, Mr. Liddell reads *I rede we makë of sorwes two,* with objectionable rhythm and questionable hiatus, and refuses to insert *that* on the sole authority of the Harleian. It is difficult for any editor to proceed consistently, and improbable that any two editors would always agree, in dealing with these readings. In the present edition they are accepted sparingly, and only when the alternative readings are so unsatisfactory, or those of the Harleian manuscript so intrinsically superior, as to justify the risk. In its wholesale correction of headless lines the editor has not followed the Harleian scribe, for there is abundant evidence that Chaucer wrote them in both his decasyllabic and his octosyllabic verse. But in lines where the rhythm is otherwise objectionable or open to question the help of the Harleian manuscript has sometimes been accepted, and special considerations have sometimes entered into the editor's decision. Thus in *Gen Prol,* I, 752, the Harleian reading, *For to have been a marchal in an halle,* has been adopted in place of the shorter *For to been* of the other manuscripts, not simply because of the headless line, but because of the possibility that the Harleian reading preserves, or restores, the good old use of the perfect infinitive to express action contrary to fact. In the case of all doubtful readings the editor has tried to give special consideration to old grammatical forms or idioms which might have been lost or corrupted by the scribes.

The presence of correct unique readings in the Harleian copy may be explained either on the theory of emendation, or on that of contamination with some good lost manuscript, and there is other evidence that the Harleian text is derived in part from a source which belonged to type A. It is perhaps even possible that the Harleian preserved some good readings which were coincidently corrupted in the A manuscripts and in the remaining manuscripts of type B. But of course the chances of this are slight.

The problem of unique readings arises sometimes with superior manuscripts, like the Ellesmere copy of the *Canterbury Tales* or the Cambridge Gg copy of the *Parliament of Fowls*. In the case of Ellesmere the editor has had no such means of testing them as was afforded for the Harleian manuscript by Professor Tatlock's study. The Chicago collations, when published, will show just how much scattered support such readings may have. But from the evidence furnished by printed texts and the editor's collation of the Cardigan and Morgan manuscripts it does not appear that they are to be accepted without scrutiny on the bare authority of Ellesmere. That manuscript, though superior to all others, has its proportion of errors, some of which it shares with other manuscripts of the *a* group. It therefore cannot be regarded as an independent witness to the original text; nor do its peculiar readings look like revisions by the author. It does, however, preserve some lines, apparently genuine, and marginal glosses, very likely due to Chaucer, which are not found in any of the other published texts. These passages, at least, it seems to have derived from a good copy outside its immediate source and now unknown. There is conse-

quently justification for considering its unique readings, and the editor has accepted them in a very few cases, especially where they preserve good old forms or idioms that might have been lost through scribal corruption. Examples of the cases where this consideration has affected the decision are *KnT*, I, 1176, *wistest; KnT*, I, 1573, *after he* (rest, *afterward he,* with variants); *KnT*, I, 1260, *witen* (rest, *woot, wote,* etc.); *MLT*, II, 336, *hastifliche* (rest, *hastiliche, hastily*). In mere matters of orthography, when verbal variants are not involved, the Ellesmere copy has been followed, as representing a good scribal tradition. But throughout all Chaucer's works, as explained below, the spellings of the manuscripts have been corrected for grammatical accuracy and for the adjustment of rimes.

The question of the authority of a superior manuscript arises again in connection with the *Parliament of Fowls*. The Cambridge MS. Gg. 1. 27, like the Ellesmere copy of the *Canterbury Tales*, belongs to the best group of authorities, and is commonly adopted as the basis of the text. But there are two opinions as to the value of its testimony when it stands alone or has very slight support from other manuscripts. Miss Hammond, in an admirably sound and thorough study of the manuscripts of the *Parliament,* granted that some of the unique Gg readings are almost certainly right, but argued that they are the result of scribal emendation, and are therefore not to be adopted by an editor without special justification in every case. Professor Koch, on the other hand, has defended the opinion that Gg goes back in some fashion to an original above the archetype of the other manuscripts, and that its variants may therefore be accepted freely in preference to readings determined by the "critical" method. It is not easy to decide this question. The present editor finds about twenty readings, either peculiar to Gg or having slight support in other manuscripts, which are clearly right or so strongly preferable to the critical text as practically to demand adoption. Some thirty-five more appear to deserve serious consideration, and a few of them have been hesitatingly adopted. Still other Gg readings would have a strong claim for adoption if the manuscript were known to be derived in any fashion from a source independent of all the rest. But the evidence of this is insufficient, and it has seemed safest to give the preference in general to a critical text, resorting to Gg only where there is special need or justification. A few of its readings have been adopted for reasons connected with grammar or meter. Gg variants in mere phraseology have been in nearly every case rejected, though some of them are tempting. The fact that the manuscript preserves the unique copy of the revised *Prologue to the Legend of Good Women* makes easier the assumption that it contains the author's corrections of the text of the *Parliament*. But the variants themselves do not seem to bear out this theory.

A textual problem fundamentally different from that offered by the *Canterbury Tales* or the *Parliament* is presented by the *Troilus*. In the *Canterbury Tales,* although there are numerous cases of correction, cancellation, or rearrangement, there is no thoroughgoing and systematic revision. In fact, far from having prepared a second edition, Chaucer never completed a first. But in the *Troilus* it is agreed that the manuscripts show either two or three distinct stages of composition. Details about the classification of the authorities are given below in the Textual Notes and need not be repeated here. The essential facts are that all scholars recognize a first version, *a*, which stands in many respects closest to the Italian original, and a second (or third) version, γ, which is preserved in the most correct and best authenticated manuscripts. A third form of the text, preserved in manuscripts not wholly distinct from those which contain *a* and γ, is held by Professor Root, as by his predecessor in the study of the problem, the late Sir William McCormick, to represent a separate version β, which those two scholars have conceived in different ways. McCormick, in the Globe edition, took version β (as his lettering would indicate) to be intermediate between *a* and γ, though the excellence of one of the β manuscripts (St. John's College L. 1) led him to make considerable use of its readings. He held the γ text

to have been "either carelessly corrected by the author, or collated by some hand after Chaucer's death." More recently Professor Root, who continued and completed McCormick's thorough and elaborate study of all the manuscripts, has arrived at the opinion that β represents Chaucer's final revision — that is, the third stage of his text. While he recognizes the superiority of the best γ manuscripts, he holds that to arrive at Chaucer's authoritative version an editor should correct the γ text by β readings wherever these are susceptible of sure determination. The description and classification of manuscripts by McCormick and Root the present editor has found to be thorough and trustworthy. It is, in fact, one of the most substantial achievements of Chaucerian scholarship. Professor Root's selection of the Corpus manuscript as the best basis for the text confirms the editor's choice of nearly twenty years ago. But with the preference accorded by Mr. Root to the peculiar readings of the β version he has not been able to agree. Those readings appear to him to be rather scribal than authoritative — to stand, in short, somewhat in the position of the unique readings of MS. Harleian 7334 in the *Canterbury Tales*. It is doubtful, as Professor Tatlock long ago argued, whether more than a single revision of the *Troilus* can be made out. But even if two stages are recognized, that represented by the γ manuscripts has, in the opinion of the present editor, the best authority. The β readings have consequently not been accepted in this text, which is based consistently on the γ version. The reconstruction of γ has of course not been in itself always easy, since the γ manuscripts contain errors and omissions. Exclusive γ readings have been examined with especial care because of the uncertainty whether they are due to Chaucer or a scribe. But the authority of the γ group, even when it stands alone, seems better to the present editor than it does to Mr. Root. It should be added, however, that the differences between the γ text and Mr. Root's β version are few and unimportant.

The question of revision arises in relation to several other works of Chaucer besides the *Troilus,* but it nowhere else presents so serious a practical problem to the editor. In the case of several of the *Canterbury Tales,* it has been argued that Chaucer made over early poems for use in the collection. There is no question in editing, however, of a choice between versions. Similarly in the case of passages possibly unauthentic or canceled by the author, the editor has simply to decide whether and where to admit them to his text. In the *Prologue to the Legend* alone is there another instance of thoroughgoing revision, resulting in parallel versions, and in this case it is clear that both texts should be printed side by side, as has been done in most recent editions.

An editorial problem somewhat different from those thus far discussed is raised by the *Book of the Duchess* and, in less degree, by the *House of Fame.* It may be illustrated by some account of the character of the text in the former of these works. There are only four authorities — the Fairfax, Bodley, and Tanner manuscripts, and Thynne's edition. Fairfax and Bodley are, as usual, closely related, and in this poem they offer the best text. Thynne furnishes a number of good corrections of their readings. The critical text is easy to construct, and there are very few cases where a choice of readings is difficult. But there are many cases where the authorities agree in readings unsatisfactory in sense or in meter, and it is hard to decide how far an editor should go in mending such passages. Skeat transposed or supplied words freely, with the result that he secured a fairly smooth Chaucerian movement for the lines. Mr. Heath, the Globe editor, was much more conservative, retaining many words that clog the movement of the verse, and leaving many lines deficient in a syllable. This procedure seems to the present editor the safer, though no two men might agree as to the exact application of it. It may be freely admitted that the manuscripts are late and none too trustworthy. At the same time it should be remembered that some roughness of workmanship might be expected in so early a work as the *Book of the Duchess* and in a meter of such free traditions as the English octosyllabic couplet. Headless lines were quite as natural there as in the decasyllabic verse, and extra syllables within the line are not hard to accept, though some of them may be due to scribes who supplied words to take the place of final -*e*'s they had wrongfully suppressed. Lines which lack an unaccented syllable in the middle are very unlikely to be right. For verses so constructed, with two abutting stresses — a metrical type sometimes called Lydgatian because of its frequent occurrence in Lydgate's poems — are almost unknown in those works of Chaucer of which a good text is preserved. All these irregularities, which occur commonly in the *Book of the Duchess,* are easy to remove if an editor feels at liberty to emend his manuscripts at will. The present text is less freely corrected than Skeat's, and for that reason less smooth in many places, as the editor is well aware. But one kind of emendation, the restoration of full grammatical forms apocopated in the manuscript to the detriment of the meter, is certainly justifiable and has been freely employed.

The editor of Chaucer, after he has settled the matter of authorities and readings and made his critical texts, still has to consider the question of grammatical rectification. For the best manuscripts contain many forms that are demonstrably incorrect — nouns and adjectives with meaningless final -*e*'s, or strong preterites with the same ending incorrectly added in the singular number. These errors cannot be removed by a critical comparison of the manuscripts; they must be treated, if regulated at all, in the light of Middle English grammar. Fortunately the materials are abundant for constructing a grammar of Chaucer's dialect, and the inflections he employed are very fully and precisely known. It is therefore possible to correct with confidence most of the grammatical errors of the scribes. But the practice of editors in making such corrections has varied considerably. Skeat's general policy was to normalize both the spelling and the grammar of his texts, though he was not quite thorough or consistent in removing erroneous forms. The Globe editors differed one from another in their practice, but many incorrect endings were allowed to stand in their text. Professor Root, in his edition of the *Troilus,* though recognizing that numerous final -*e*'s in his text did not represent a syllable, thought it most consistent with his purpose to follow the actual usage of his scribes. His method and that of the Globe edition is of course defensible, and it has its advantage, especially for an investigator of the history of English orthography. For many of the forms under discussion are not, strictly speaking, incorrect, but are rather specimens of a system of spelling divergent from the ordinary practice in Middle English. According to that system final -e may denote not only a pronounced final syllable but also, as in modern English, the long quantity of a preceding vowel (as in "*hate*," over against "*hat*"). This principle is doubtless to be recognized in some of the spellings of the Chaucerian scribes. But in a library edition, like the present one, there seems to be no purpose in preserving two inconsistent systems of orthography, or in printing final -*e*'s which would appear to indicate incorrect endings, and so would confuse the reader or student. The editor has consequently gone farther than any of his predecessors in removing such scribal, or ungrammatical, -*e*'s. In the great majority of cases the Chaucerian form or inflection is well known, and the correction of the text is easy. But there are a few words, or classes of words, in which the application of the method is not so clear. In a small number of nouns and adjectives it is not certain whether Chaucer's nominative form had a final -*e;* and in others he clearly used two forms, one with -*e* and one without. Words of the latter sort are entered in the Glossary of this edition with a bracketed -*e* (e.g., *bliss(e)*, *cler(e)*), and in the text the form which occurs in manuscript is usually preserved. But the editor's practice has probably not been perfectly consistent in this matter, and the final -*e* may sometimes have been struck off when unpronounced in the verse. In the case of nouns in the dative construction it is sometimes difficult to decide whether to allow the inflectional -*e* outside of the stereotyped or "petrified" phrases to which it is mainly restricted. Its use undoubtedly spread somewhat, even to cases other than the dative, but Chaucer's dative was usually without ending, and the dative -*e*'s have been struck off in this text unless there was special reason for supposing

them to have been preserved. Perhaps the inflectional form that makes most trouble with regard to this matter of final -*e* is the second person singular of the imperative of strong verbs and of long-stemmed weak verbs of the first Anglo-Saxon conjugation. Strictly speaking these forms should have no ending (*sing*, *send*, *heer*, etc.). But they are commonly spelled with a final -*e*, and the ending is occasionally demanded by the rime or verse-rhythm. It can be accounted for as a subjunctive form used in a jussive sense, or as an ending which was developed in the imperative of the verbs mentioned above because of the analogy of the subjunctive and the other weak classes in the imperative. It would be defensible to keep such forms in the text when they occur in the manuscript. In this edition the practice is again not wholly consistent, but in most cases the -*e*'s have been struck off and the correct historical forms restored. One other form, of frequent occurrence, may be cited to illustrate this editorial problem. The possessive pronoun *his,* when used with a plural noun, frequently takes a final -*e* (*hise*) in the best manuscripts. This is very common, almost regular, with the Ellesmere scribe. But the -*e* is not justified by the Anglo-Saxon form (*his*) and appears never, or almost never, to be pronounced in Chaucer's verse. It has been struck off in the present edition. But since the form with -*e* clearly occurs in Middle English, an editor might with equal propriety allow it to stand where his manuscript has it.

The examples cited will show the method of the present edition in the grammatical rectification of the text. Errors and omissions excepted, incorrect final -*e*'s (in the sense explained above) have been removed. In the treatment of final -*e*'s that are in some respect irregular but not inadmissible there has been some inconsistency during the long period of the preparation of the edition. But the text throughout, it is hoped, will be found to give a true representation of Chaucer's language.

In matters of spelling, apart from questions of inflections or dialect, the procedure of the editor has been conservative. The lack of any autograph manuscripts leaves us without an authoritative Chaucerian standard, and any attempt to construct such a standard (like that of Professor Koch in his early edition of the Minor Poems) is sure to encounter many uncertainties. The ordinary critical method fails entirely at this point, since the scribes modified spelling rather freely in copying. A variety of practices is consequently open to the editor, ranging from the "diplomatic" reproduction of a given manuscript to the introduction of a new phonetic spelling of his own. For the purpose of teaching pronunciation and meter this last method would have its advantages, and it has been adopted with selected specimens of the verse (as, for example, with the whole *Manciple's Tale* in Dr. Plessow's edition). But there are obvious objections to its use in a library edition of the entire works of the poet; and half-way normalization, like that of Skeat's edition, though in some respects convenient, is hardly worth while. The present text, therefore, in the case of those works that are preserved in the best manuscripts, follows the spelling of the scribe where it is not absolutely or probably incorrect. Final -*e*'s omitted in the manuscripts have not been supplied if they were elided or apocopated in the verse, but they have been restored when necessary to the meter. Grammatical errors, as already explained, and dialectal spellings, where not appropriate and presumably intentional, have been mended with care. But no effort has been made to introduce uniformity in less important matters, such as the use of *u* and *w* or of *i* and *y*, or the doubling of long *o* and long *e*. Such slight modernization as has been adopted in printing will be explained below.

In the case of nearly all Chaucer's works it has been possible to follow this method of close adherence to the spelling of the manuscripts. Indeed such is the excellence and general agreement in these matters, of the Ellesmere copy of the *Canterbury Tales* and the Corpus and Campsall copies of the *Troilus*, that those manuscripts may be reasonably supposed to represent practices closely similar to Chaucer's own. But there are a few poems in which the manuscript of best verbal authority presents a dialectal or otherwise vagarious orthography. This is notably true of the *Legend of Good Women*, where the Cambridge Gg manuscript is the only source of the revised text of the *Prologue;* and the case is similar with the *Parliament of Fowls* and some of the short poems. Under such circumstances an editor has to choose between printing a text of strange and un-Chaucerian appearance and making the spelling conform to Ellesmere and Corpus standards. The latter method seems decidedly preferable, and the orthography of the *Legend* and of a number of the minor poems has accordingly been freely normalized.

In minor matters of printing — spacing, capitalization, punctuation, and the like — modern usage has been followed as far as circumstances permit. Capitals have been used at the beginning of lines of verse. Capital *F* has been substituted for *ff*, which often takes the place of a majuscular sign in the manuscripts; *th* for the archaic "thorn" (þ); and *j* for the capital *I* which sometimes represents it. The letters *u* and *v* have been adjusted to modern practice (*use, vertu, love,* for the manuscript spellings *vse, uertu, loue*). The apostrophe has been employed with *n', t',* and *th',* when the vowel of *ne, to,* and *the* (or *thee*) is elided before a following initial. Contractions, like the stroke which designates a final nasal, have been silently expanded unless there was real doubt about their meaning. In the case of words in -*on,* -*oun* (*nacioun, condicioun,* etc.), which are spelled very inconsistently and may be pronounced with the sound of either *o* or *ou*, it has been necessary to adopt an arbitrary practice. The ending is commonly abbreviated in the manuscript, sometimes with *w* (*n* with an upper return stroke), sometimes with *n̄* or *ū*. These signs are used inconsistently by the scribes. In the present text, when words of this class have their pronunciation determined by rime (as by such unambiguous rime-words as *toun* or *oon*), they are spelled accordingly. When two words of the *nacioun* (*nacion*) type rime with each other, *n* with the return stroke is expanded as *n*, and *n* or *u* with the makron as *un*. When the scribes use both abbreviations in a single pair of rime-words (*nacion : condicioū*), as occasionally happens, both are normalized with the spelling *-oun*.

In spacing (which varies greatly in the manuscripts) modern usage has been followed except when Middle English appears to have had a different sense of unity. Thus *upon, unto, into, therto, theron, withoute, also, whoso, nowher,* and the participial compound with *y-* and *for-* are regularly printed without spacing or hyphen. But combinations which were less clearly recognized as units (such as *for sothe, but if, by cause, over al,* in the sense of the German *überall*) are either hyphenated or separated entirely. In this second class of words consistency of practice has been hard to attain, just as in modern spelling there is considerable variation in the use of the hyphen.

To the foregoing explanations of editorial method may be added a word about the Textual Notes in the present edition. They contain accounts of the manuscripts and other authorities for the text of each work, with information about their relations, and lists of the more important variant readings. It was the editor's original plan to register variants much more fully than he has finally done in print. But various considerations — lack of space, the appearance of Professor Root's edition of the *Troilus* with full textual apparatus, and the announcement of Professor Manly's projected work on the *Canterbury Tales* — led him to reduce his citations to about one quarter of those originally collected. The selected list now printed is not intended to exhibit the characteristics of manuscripts or to supply adequate materials for textual investigation. Scholars having these interests in mind will naturally resort directly to the manuscripts or to complete reprints and reproductions. But it is hoped that the variants here given will be found to include such alternative readings as have any literary interest. The different versions of the *Troilus* have been recorded with some fullness; also rejected passages (including some that are spurious) from the *Canterbury Tales*. Some variants in phraseology have been registered because they have a bearing on the poet's vocabulary. Finally, in a good many cases where the readings are doubtful the editor has supplied his readers with the material for testing his decisions.

THE CANTERBURY TALES

CHAUCER's most comprehensive work, *The Canterbury Tales,* was without doubt largely the production of his later years. But it includes writings of his early and middle life, and cannot be given a definite place in the chronological sequence of his poems. Since it is the one of his works first approached by most readers, it may fitly stand at the beginning of an edition.

The plan of the tales was probably adopted soon after 1386, in which year, according to generally received opinion, Chaucer composed the *Prologue to the Legend of Good Women.* But that date has been recently challenged, and in any case it is not definitely known how long he was occupied with the *Legend.* A passage in The Man of Law's headlink, written when *The Canterbury Tales* must have been well under way, implies that Chaucer still meant to compose additional accounts of "Good Women," and he appears to have made his revision of the *Prologue to the Legend* as late as 1394. For several years, then, he had both collections of tales in hand, or at least in mind. But it is clear that the rather conventional scheme of the *Legend* was rapidly superseded in his interest by the far more absorbing drama of the Canterbury pilgrimage.

The composition of the *General Prologue* to the tales is commonly associated with 1387. It has even been assumed that Chaucer himself took part in a pilgrimage in April of that year, perhaps because of the illness of his wife Philippa, who probably died a few months later. The calendar of the year, it has been shown, would provide very well for the dates mentioned in the tales. But these indications prove nothing, and, in general, it is altogether uncertain how much there is of fact, and how much of fiction, in the account of the pilgrimage. On the whole, 1387 seems a reasonable date for the *General Prologue,* unless Chaucer's absence in Calais (of which evidence has recently come to light) makes it necessary to assume a longer interval between

the *Prologue to the Legend* and the *Canterbury Tales.*

There is also no sure indication of how long Chaucer worked on the Canterbury collection. Reasons have been found for dating certain tales in 1393 or 1394, and no tale has been definitely proved to be later. The unfinished state of the work as a whole might be taken as evidence that Chaucer was occupied with it till the very end of his life. But such an inference would not be safe in the case of the man who left successively incomplete the *House of Fame,* the *Anelida,* the *Legend of Good Women,* and the *Astrolabe.* In fact very little is positively known about the productions of Chaucer's last years.

There has been much speculation as to what suggested to Chaucer the idea of a pilgrimage. He may, of course, have been describing an actual experience, or more than one. At all events he had no occasion to resort to books for knowledge of the pilgrimage as an institution. In the general device of a frame-story, or series of tales within an enclosing narrative, it has often been thought that he imitated the Decameron. But it now appears improbable that Chaucer knew Boccaccio's great collection of *novelle,* and the idea of tales within a tale was so familiar that no particular model need be sought. Popular from antiquity in the orient (from which Europe derived in modern times one of the most famous examples, The Thousand and One Nights), the type was well known in classical and mediæval literature. Ovid's Metamorphoses, The Disciplina Clericalis of Peter Alphonsus, the romance of the Seven Sages, Gower's Confessio Amantis, and Chaucer's own *Legend of Good Women* all occur to the mind at once as illustrations, very different one from another. But the *Canterbury Tales* are unlike most collections of the sort in the fact that the enclosing narrative is not formal or mechanical or merely introductory, but provides, and keeps in action, a social group engaged naturally in mutual enter-

1

tainment. In this respect it resembles the Decameron, which, as already remarked, Chaucer is believed not to have known. A little group, similarly engaged in story-telling, is represented in Ovid's account of the daughters of Minyas, in the fourth book of the Metamorphoses, and another appears in Boccaccio's prose romance, the Ameto. But it may be doubted whether Chaucer owed a suggestion to either of these mere episodes. A more significant parallel is afforded by the Novelle of Giovanni Sercambi, a work which actually employs the setting of a pilgrimage. It was probably written about 1374, and both the collection and the author may have been known to Chaucer. If so, Sercambi may have given him the hint upon which he wrote. But Chaucer's debt to the Novelle, if he owed one, was for little more than the bare suggestion of the pilgrimage. Sercambi's plan is very different from that of the *Canterbury Tales*. His *brigata* of pilgrims is large, and wanders all over Italy. The stories are told, not by the various fellow-travelers, but by the author, who, like Chaucer, represents himself as a member of the company. Of the individual tales only two are analogues of those in the Canterbury collection, and neither of these appears to have been the version used by Chaucer. And although in the conduct of Sercambi's pilgrims and of the Proposto, who corresponds in a way to Chaucer's Host, there are incidents which remind one of the Canterbury pilgrimage, no clear evidence has been found that Chaucer borrowed from Sercambi in matters of detail.

Whatever the reason for its adoption, the device of the pilgrimage is one of the happiest ever employed in a collection of stories. It afforded Chaucer an opportunity to bring together a representative group of various classes of society, united by a common religious purpose, yet not so dominated by that purpose as to be unable to give themselves over to enjoyment. Whether such a company would ever have mingled as Chaucer's pilgrims do, or would have entered upon such a round of story-telling, it is idle to discuss, as idle as to question whether the speakers could have been heard from horseback on the road. Literal truth of fact the *Canterbury Tales* obviously

do not represent. In their very metrical form there is, if one chooses to be literal-minded, a convention of unreality. But there is essential, poetic truth in the portrayal of the characters, in their sentiments and personal relations, and, no less, in the representation of the pilgrimage as a social assemblage.

The plan of the *Canterbury Tales* was never brought anywhere near to completion. It is provided in the *Prologue* that each pilgrim shall tell four tales, two on the outward and two on the homeward journey. But the company never reaches Canterbury, and only twenty-three of the thirty pilgrims get their turn. Some tales are left unfinished; others are manifestly unadapted to the tellers. The Second Nun, for example, refers to herself as an "unworthy son of Eve," and the Shipman several times classes himself among women. These and many other trifling oversights and discrepancies show that Chaucer never really prepared his text for publication. Nor, apparently, did he get to the point of arranging the tales he had written. They have come down in a series of fragments (usually lettered A to I), and in the best group of manuscripts some of the tales told near Canterbury precede those which are put at an earlier stage of the journey. In most recent editions this inconsistency is removed, but the order they adopt is a modern arrangement suggested by Bradshaw and followed in the Six-Text reprint, and has no real authority. In the present edition the inconsistent arrangement of the best manuscripts is followed, and no attempt is made to correct discrepancies left standing by the author, or to reconstruct the stages of a pilgrimage which he seems never to have completely planned.

Fragment I (Group A)

The General Prologue. For the *Prologue*, as for the general device of the Canterbury pilgrimage, no real model has been found. Individual sketches of knights or priests or peasants are common enough in the mediæval literature of France and England, and some of them — like the lazy priest in Piers Plowman, who knew his Robin Hood better than his paternoster — have often been adduced to illustrate one or another of Chaucer's characters. The allegorical writings of the age, both sacred and secular, abound in personified types — Courtesy, Gentleness, Envy, Slander, Hypocrisy — some of which Chaucer clearly imitates. Whole works, too, were devoted to the description of the various orders of society, and others to the classification of men and women by physical and temperamental characteristics. With this lore of the physiognomists and social philosophers Chaucer was doubtless familiar. But in none of his predecessors has there been found a gallery of portraits like that in the *Prologue,* and there is very little that is comparable in later English poetry except in Chaucer's avowed imitators. As representative figures Chaucer's portraits suggest in a way the formal "characters" of the type brought to perfection by La Bruyère. But Chaucer can hardly have known the Theophrastan tradition, and character-writing in French and English did not come into vogue until the sixteenth century.

Chaucer's pilgrims are far more vivid and personal than either the Theophrastan characters or the mediæval figures with which they have been compared. This is perhaps sufficiently accounted for by Chaucer's creative imagination. But it is hard to believe that his men and women were not in some measure drawn from life, and a number of facts confirm this suspicion. Harry Bailly, the Host, has the same name as Henricus Bailly or Baillif, known to have been an innkeeper in Southwark and a member of Parliament from that borough. The other pilgrims are not mentioned by surname, and it would be hard to identify in records Roger, the Cook, Hubert, the Friar, or Dame Alice, the Wife of Bath. But in these and several other instances details of locality, occupation, and character are given with so much particularity that the temptation has proved irresistible to look for historical counterparts. A certain Peter Risshenden, known to have sailed a ship "The Maudelayne," was long ago pointed out as a possible model for the Shipman. The Knight's career has been shown to correspond in part to that of a number of Chaucer's contemporaries. And Professor Manly brought together a large body of interesting biographical data about men whose personal history or circumstances in life resemble those of various pilgrims. For one, at least, the Man of Law, he found a very likely original. For the names are recorded of the small group of barristers who held the high rank of Sergeant-at-Law, and Thomas Pinchbek alone appears to fit the description. The case for the identification of other pilgrims is usually not so strong because the field of search is less precisely limited. But even where he had no individual prototypes to suggest, Manly was sometimes able to show that the localities mentioned are significant. In such identifications demonstration is not to be looked for. It is hard enough to establish them in the work of living novelists, or to induce an author to admit them. But the probability is strong that Chaucer had contemporary models for his characters. And curiosity on this subject, it is proper to add, is not merely trivial. Such inquiries and conjectures, like the search for literary sources, help toward an understanding of the poet's imagination and of the material on which it worked.

Individual as the pilgrims are, they are also representative. Many of them exhibit types of character or of professional conduct — the gentle Knight, the venal Friar, the hypocrite in the person of the Pardoner — such as were familiar in the literature of the age. And taken together, they cover nearly the whole range of life in Chaucer's England. The circle of the royalty and the higher nobility, to be sure, is not directly represented. Men of such rank and station could hardly have been included in the company. But the mind and manners of courtly society are well expressed by the Knight, who had seen honorable service at home and abroad; by his son, the Squire, the typical courtly lover; again, from a different angle, by the Prioress, who "peyned hire to countrefete chere of court"; and, best of all, by Chaucer himself, the accomplished courtier and man of the world, who as author creates the atmosphere and medium of the whole narrative. The clergy, regular and secular, are included in liberal number, and there are also represented the learned professions of law and medicine, the merchants and the craftsmen of the guild, officials of the manor, the sailor, and the common peasant farmer. Possibly Chaucer did not set out deliberately to make the group so inclusive and well-distributed. But whatever chance or purpose governed his choice, it would be hard to find such a description of English society between the Beowulf, with its picture of the heroic age, and the broader canvas of the Elizabethan drama.

In keeping with the miscellaneous character of the company is the wide range of tastes and interests represented by the stories they relate. The romance of chivalry, the courtly lay, the coarse realistic *fabliau*, the beast-epic, the legend or saint's life, the mock sermon with its illustrative *exemplum* — all are included, along with the moral allegory and the ethical treatise, which only by a stretch of terminology can be called a tale at all. Nearly every type of mediæval fiction appears, and appears at its best. Just as Milton, in the seventeenth century, took up one literary form after another — the masque, the pastoral elegy, the epic, the Greek drama — and gave us a supreme example of each, so Chaucer used every important narrative type of his age, and in each was unsurpassed.

In almost every case Chaucer assigned to a pilgrim a tale suited to his character and vocation. He represents the party as engaged in free and natural social intercourse, and oftener than not the tales are evoked by the talks along the way. Sometimes they are told to illustrate a point or enforce an argument; sometimes they grow out of an altercation, as when the Friar and the Summoner abuse each other's callings. Sometimes they are given simply in response to the request of the Host, who is chosen at the outset to be toastmaster, or "lord and governour." But Chaucer found ways of relieving the monotony of this procedure, and from the time when the drunken Miller insists on being heard after the Knight the company shows frequent inclination to take things into its own hands. In fact, from one point of view, the pilgrimage is a continuous and lively drama, in which the stories themselves contribute to the action. Because of this sustained dramatic interest and the vivid reality of the characters, as well as for the inclusive representation of English society, the *Canterbury Tales* has been called a Human Comedy. The implied comparison with Balzac's great series of stories of the life of modern France is not inappropriate. Chaucer might have used without exaggeration the words of the Frenchman, "J'aurai porté une société entière dans ma tête." Like Balzac he achieved "l'évocation vivante de tout un monde."

The Knight's Tale. The Knight very properly begins the story-telling with a specimen of chivalric romance. To speak more strictly, his tale of Palamon and Arcite combines the traditions of mediæval romance and classical epic, though the ancient type is more apparent in the title and structure of the Italian original, Boccaccio's Teseida, or epic of Theseus. The classical forerunner of both poets was Statius, the author of the Thebaid, whom Chaucer, somewhat misleadingly, cites as a source. In the *Knight's Tale*, as in the *Anelida* and the *Troilus*, he chooses to claim ancient authority for his mediæval fiction, but in all the essentials of the story he actually follows the Teseida. Even in characterization, in which he usually showed independence, he here departs very little from Boccaccio. Yet the *Knight's Tale* is a very different poem from its Italian source. In the first place it is only about a quarter as long as the original. At the outset Chaucer strikes his pace and passes over in a dozen swift lines the campaign of Theseus against the Amazons, to which Boccaccio devotes his whole first book. And he continues to hasten the development of Boccaccio's very leisurely narrative. Nevertheless he finds room for significant additions of his own. Only about a third of the English poem is actually translated from the Italian, and some of its most memorable features — the descriptions of the temples, the account of the tournament, the passages of philosophical reflection — are in large part independent of the Teseida. By adapting both action and setting to the life of his time Chaucer made the tale more real and vivid. Its pervading humor, too, he greatly heightened, so that some critics have been led, unjustifiably, to pronounce the *Knight's Tale* a satire on chivalry or courtly love. Of course in the drastic reduction of the scale of the Italian narrative some charming descriptions and much delightful poetry had to be sacrificed. But on the whole,

Chaucer improved on his original. Yet his debt to Boccaccio, both here and in the *Troilus,* can hardly be overstated. Professor Manly has justly observed that Chaucer did not borrow the Italian technique. But he found in the Teseida and the Filostrato examples of narrative structure far superior to most of the French and English romances and allegories that he knew in his youth. And though he always told a story in his own way, there is a vast difference between his early tales and those that he wrote after he came into contact with Italian poetry.

The *Knight's Tale,* at least in its original form, was not written for the Canterbury series. For the story of Palamon and Arcite is included among the works of Chaucer mentioned in the *Prologue* to the *Legend of Good Women,* and this first version of his translation or redaction of the Teseida is now generally assigned to the early eighties. Its precise relation to the version preserved as the *Knight's Tale* is unknown. But there is little support for the theory held by some eminent Chaucerians, that the original *Palamon* was in seven-line stanzas, some of which Chaucer used in the *Anelida* and the *Troilus* before he transposed the poem into decasyllabic couplets. The *Knight's Tale* bears obvious marks of adaptation to the teller. But there is no evidence that the *Palamon* was seriously altered in form or substance.

The Tales of the Miller, Reeve, and Cook. In determining the order of the earlier tales in the series Chaucer was evidently governed by the principle of contrast. For the stories that follow the Knight's and complete Group A are of an utterly different character. They are introduced by a simple dramatic device. When the Knight has finished speaking, the Host turns to the Monk as a suitable personage to follow him. But the Miller insists on being heard, and the Host, seeing that he is "dronke of ale," lets him have his way. The Miller's story is at the expense of a carpenter, and the Reeve, who has followed that craft, takes offense and makes an immediate rejoinder with a story of a dishonest miller. And now that the churls have got under way, the Host makes no attempt to check the Cook, when he claims

the next turn. Of the Cook's tale only a fragment was written, but enough to show that it was of the same scurrilous character as the stories of the Miller and the Reeve. All three belong to the narrative type most extensively cultivated in mediæval France, and known as the *fabliau.* The term *fabliau* means by its derivation simply "short story," and cannot be safely given a much more precise definition. For stories of many varieties were designated by the name. But the majority were tales of the bourgeois or lower social orders; they were realistic in character, generally humorous, and often indecent; and they turned more upon plot and intrigue than upon description or sentiment. In Chaucer's hands they retain their essential character. They remain short, though the setting is somewhat elaborated, and Chaucer finds an opportunity for descriptions which might be compared to the *genre* painting of the Dutch artists. They remain plain-spoken and even indecent. But the emphasis in them is perhaps less on pure animalism than in the usual French *fabliau,* and a kind of moral quality has been observed in their tendency to emphasize poetic justice. No definite source is known for any of the three here grouped together, and the Cook's fragment is hardly long enough to disclose what the plot was to be. But for the *Miller's Tale* and *Reeve's Tale* numerous analogues have been found in various languages.

Fragment II (Group B¹)

Man of Law's Prologue and Tale. The first group of tales (A) ends with the Cook's fragment, which, because of its incompleteness, gives no indication of what was to follow. But in the regular arrangement of the rest, the next tale is that of the Man of Law, preceded by an interesting and somewhat puzzling introduction or headlink. At ten o'clock in the morning of April eighteenth (the mention of this precise date lends some color to the belief that Chaucer had in mind a real pilgrimage), the Host reminds the pilgrims that time is passing and exhorts them to go on with their storytelling. He appeals in particular to the Man of Law to keep his contract and entertain the company. The lawyer, with some parade of technical terms which are not without bearing on the theory that Chaucer himself had a legal education, promises to fulfill his obligation. But he protests that Chaucer, "in such English as he can," has spoiled all the good stories. He mentions by name the tales of lovers in the *Book of the Duchess* and the *Legend of Good Women* (including some that are not there), gets in what appears to be a humorous fling at Gower for telling such tales as he and Chaucer do not approve, and ends by declaring that he will not court comparison with the Muses but will tell his tale in prose. Then he proceeds to relate the story of Constance in seven-line stanzas! Doubtless when Chaucer wrote the headlink, he meant to assign a prose tale to the Man of Law. But the Constance story, though not so conspicuously adapted to the teller as the tales of many of the other pilgrims, is sufficiently appropriate.

It purports to be an account of the adventures of a daughter of the Roman Emperor Tiberius Constantinus. In reality, though attached to historical characters, it is a *märchen* found in many forms the world over and known to students of folk-lore as the story of the Calumniated Wife. Of the special type to which Chaucer's tale belongs some sixty versions, popular and literary, have been collected. The best known Middle-English analogues are the Lay of Emare and Gower's account of Constance in the Confessio Amantis. The latter was pretty surely known to Chaucer. In fact he appears to refer to it in his version, and he and Gower used the same immediate source, Nicholas Trivet's Anglo-Norman Chronicle. But Chaucer handled the material with considerable freedom, punctuating the narrative, so to speak, with moral and philosophical reflections like those of a Greek chorus. He tells the whole story in the manner and spirit of a legend. The interest centers in the sufferings and miraculous deliverances of Constance, which are compared with those of biblical heroes or of the Christian saints. Husband, kindred, and the child Maurice are mere incidents in this spiritual life-history. And the character of Constance, in contrast to the highly realistic figures which fill most of the works of Chaucer's maturity, is drawn in the mediæval manner. She is almost an allegorical symbol, and as Griselda in the *Clerk's Tale* represents Patience, so Constance is an incarnation of Fortitude.

In the best manuscripts the *Man of Law's Tale* constitutes a fragment by itself, and is not attached to the following story. But in a considerable number of copies it is followed by a very lively *Epilogue*. The Host, enthusiastic about the Man of Law's performance, calls upon the Parson, another "learned man in lore," to follow him. "Sir Parish Preest, quod he, for Goddes bones, tel us a tale!" But the Parson takes occasion to rebuke him for his profanity, and the Host ironically calls upon the company to listen to a sermon. Thereupon another pilgrim, variously referred to in the manuscripts as the Squire, the Summoner, or the Shipman — obviously, in any case, not the Squire, but one of the ruder members of the company — springs up as a defender of the faith and protests that the Lollard Parson would corrupt their religion. So he, a plain man, with "little Latin in his maw," will tell a tale which, he implies, will keep them awake better than that of his predecessor. The name of the speaker is uncertain, as is also the story which the dialogue was meant to introduce. In most modern editions the speech is ascribed to the Shipman and prefixed to his tale. But the authority for this arrangement is very slight. From the fact that the *Epilogue* is missing in the best manuscripts it is a reasonable inference that Chaucer himself meant to cancel it. But there can be no doubt of its genuineness. It is one of the most spirited of the talks by the way and gives a picture of the Parson in his "snibbing" mood, which we should not willingly spare.

Fragment III (Group D)

Wife of Bath's Prologue and Tale. With the third fragment (Group D in the Six-Text arrangement) begins a series of seven tales which, though not completely welded together, seem to have received something like their final arrangement at Chaucer's hands. They have been commonly known as the Marriage Group, since they were so designated by Professor Kittredge in an essay in which he pointed out the continuity which sets them apart from the rest of the *Canterbury Tales*. They deal — though, to be sure, with skillfully managed dramatic interruptions — with a single subject or topic, the seat and conduct of authority in married life. The wife argues for the supreme authority — the *souverainetee* — of a woman over her husband. The Friar and Summoner then break in with an altercation and tell their stories at each other's expense. After they have had their quarrel out, the Clerk follows with his tale of the complete subjugation of the Wife in the person of the incredibly patient Griselda. In the *Merchant's Tale* the tables are turned again, and the poor old dotard, January, is deceived by his young wife. Though her conduct is more than half excused by his folly, the whole picture of matrimony is bitterly satirical. The romantic story of the Squire, though it deals also with unfaithfulness in love, does not continue the treatment of the domestic issue and may be regarded as a second interruption in the discussion. Then follows the *Franklin's Tale,* which, at least incidentally, provides a solution of the problem. The two morals explicitly taught in the story are the duties of "keeping truth" and practicing courtesy. But while exemplifying these virtues Arviragus and Dorigen also live in ideally harmonious relations as man and wife. Whether Chaucer wrote the tale with this fact in view has been disputed, and reasons have even been adduced for dating it, before the Canterbury series, in the period of the *Knight's Tale.* But there is a clear connection of thought running from the *Wife's Prologue* to the *Franklin's Tale.* The Clerk and the Merchant both refer explicitly to the Wife, and the Franklin's discussion of sovereignty, once mentioned by name, has a relevance that can hardly have been unintentional. If Chaucer did use an early composition for the *Franklin's Tale,* he must have adapted it to its position. It is happily placed at the end of the series, if only for the contrast it affords with the various kinds of domestic infelicity that precede. Not only are the tales of the Marriage Group bound together in subject, in the way that has been indicated, but there are also reasons for believing, at least in the case of the *Wife's Prologue and Tale* and the *Merchant's Tale,* which give the tone for the series, that they were composed at about the same time, and rather late in the Canterbury period.

The *Wife of Bath's Prologue* is one of the most remarkable of Chaucer's productions. It is at once a confession, an *apologia*, and a program of matrimonial reform. Out of a rich experience, as she herself declares, but with no lack of knowledge of the *auctoritees*, the "literature of her subject," she expounds and defends two theses: first, that the married state is not to be held inferior to virginity; and second, that in marriage the sovereignty should rest with the wife. She relates at length — the Friar complained that it was *a long preamble of a tale* — the life she has lived with her five husbands, and shows triumphantly how all went for the best when she exercised control. The character revealed in the *Prologue* became a type for later English literature, but in itself it is far more than a type and possesses individualizing traits which make it one of the most real and complex of all the personalities drawn by Chaucer. From another point of view the *Prologue* is a most brilliant discussion of the "woman question" as it was understood in Chaucer's epoch. Nothing could be more skillful than the way in which Chaucer has put into the mouth of this "arch-wife" the confession, boastful and cynical, but none the less engaging, of all the deceits and vices charged against women in satire from antiquity down. And the author enters so dramatically into the spirit of the speaker that it might well be debated whether the *Prologue* is a document on the feminist or the anti-feminist side of the controversy.

The *Wife's Tale* is a brilliant continuation of her argument. It illustrates and confirms her doctrine, serving, as has often been noted, as a kind of *exemplum* in a lay sermon. She uses the familiar and widely disseminated popular tale of the Loathly Lady, skillfully adapted to the purpose in hand. In its more typical and original form a hag, the victim of enchantment, is released from her spell by the embrace of a hero, to whom she first offers the choice of having her "fair by day and foul (that is, ugly) by night" or "fair by night and foul by day." Chaucer substitutes the alternative of having her foul and faithful, or fair and free to bestow her favors where she will. The Knight, courteously — and, as it turns out, wisely — leaves the decision to her. When she is assured that she has the sovereignty securely in her hands she promises to be to him both fair and true. The moral is obvious. The story itself is one of the best of the fairy tales that have received literary treatment. In an early Irish version, with which Chaucer's has been held to be indirectly related, the hag is made to stand allegorically for Royal Rule, at first hard to obtain, but afterwards pleasant and honorable. In Gower's Confessio Amantis the same tale is told as an illustration of the virtue of Obedience. In the ballad of the Marriage of Gawain and in the romance of the Wedding of Gawain and Dame Ragnell, as in Chaucer's version, the adventure is attached to a Knight of Arthur's court. These analogues are interesting in themselves and as showing the kind of material with which Chaucer was working. But in its delightful combination of romantic adventure and fairy mythology with shrewd humor the *Wife of Bath's Tale* far surpasses them all.

The Friar's Tale and the Summoner's Tale. The *Friar's Tale* and the *Summoner's Tale* are both *fabliaux*, for which various parallels have been found. In neither case is Chaucer's source known, and its discovery would probably be unimportant. For the slight anecdotes are richly overlaid by description, characterization, and witty dialogue obviously original with the poet. The satirical account of the ecclesiastical court, the highly comical encounter of the Summoner with the diabolical "bailly," the description of the Friar's visit to the house of Thomas, the villager — all these are specimens of Chaucer's most accomplished workmanship. Though the tales contain no definite indication of date, the free handling of the material places them unquestionably at the period of the full development of Chaucer's art.

Fragment IV (Group E)

The Clerk's Tale. In the *Clerk's Tale* of Patient Griselda Chaucer is once again dealing with what was originally a story from folklore. But it had been given literary form by two of the greatest men of letters on the continent. Boccaccio, who, whatever material he had to work with, must be regarded as the creator of the character of Griselda as it is actually known to literature, included the story in his Decameron as the tenth tale of the tenth day. Then Petrarch made a Latin rendering of it; and this was Chaucer's source, as he acknowledges gracefully, and by the use of a recognized convention, when he makes the Clerk declare that he learned the story from Petrarch in Padua. In all the essentials of the narrative Chaucer's version follows its original. It is a close rendering, as poetical translations go. Though some details have been pointed out in which it resembles Boccaccio's Italian rather than Petrarch's Latin, Chaucer's knowledge and use of the Decameron remain uncertain, if not unlikely. Other variations from Petrarch's Latin have been shown to agree with a contemporary French translation of which Chaucer made extensive use. In its ultimate origin the tale is related to the ancient legend of Cupid and Psyche which was somewhere combined in popular tradition with another *märchen* of the type represented in the ballad of Fair Annie. As narrated by Boccaccio, Petrarch, and Chaucer, it is a beautiful and sympathetic narrative of the sufferings inflicted on Griselda by her misguided husband. It is not only sympathetic but moving if we accept, as we must, the convention in conformity to which it was written. Judged by the standards of realistic fiction, the action is preposterous and the character of Griselda, in its imperturbable meekness, neither real nor admirable. Petrarch recognized this and explained, in pointing a moral which the Clerk repeats, that her behavior is meant to teach how human beings should submit to the Providence of God. Chaucer saw the absurdities of the tale just as clearly, and his humorous comment finds expression in the Clerk's rollicking *envoy*, in which he declares that it would be intolerable if women were like Griselda, and bids wives to stand at defense and be as "egre as is a tygre yond in Ynde." Yet Petrarch also testifies that he found an Italian, after the reading of the tale, dissolved in tears, and the primary effect of Chaucer's poem is, and was unquestionably meant to be, pathetic. To accept the action calls for no more suspense of critical judgment than is required by many a myth or drama or tale of adventure. And to understand Griselda it is necessary to bear in mind that she was not drawn as a complex human creature like the Pardoner or the Prioress or the Wife of Bath. She belongs rather, like Constance in the *Man of Law's Tale*, with the simple, almost allegorical, types which the Middle Ages loved to contemplate. From the mediæval character of the *Clerk's Tale* and *Man of Law's Tale* critics have inferred that both were written rather early. But such uncertain indications of date as have been noted point rather to their composition during the Canterbury period.

The Merchant's Tale. In the *Merchant's Tale* of January and May, once again the kernel of the story is a popular *märchen*. It is known to folk-lorists as the "Pear-Tree Episode," and is widely disseminated in Europe and Asia. It serves the Merchant as an example of the wicked wiles of women. But the pear-tree story, which supplies the final incident of the deception of the husband, is only a small part of the Merchant's discourse. Here, as in the case of most of Chaucer's latest writings, the simple plot is richly elaborated by description, comment, and characterization. In the story itself there is introduced, with serio-comic effect, a bit of "machinery" from fairy mythology about Pluto and Proserpina. The figure of January affords one of the most vivid portrayals in literature of the type, at once amusing and repulsive, of the superannuated lover, *senex amans*. And the whole story is handled with great dramatic effect by the Merchant, himself unhappily mated, to give point to his bitter condemnation of matrimony and of the women to whose evil devices it exposes men.

Fragment V (Group F)

The Squire's Tale. With the *Squire's Tale*, as has been already remarked, Chaucer drops the theme of the marriage problem and turns to an interlude of pure romance. The Squire tells a story of adventure and enchantment,

laid in the distant land of Cambyuskan. It contains, to be sure, the sad history of a deserted lady, but even this is made less real by the metamorphosis of the actors into birds. The tale is a perfect expression of the joy and wonder and simple human feeling which gives enduring charm to the numerous metrical romances, many of them defective in literary form, of mediæval Europe. It is clear that Chaucer, with all the skepticism and sophistication that have been attributed to him, could enter heartily into the spirit of this literature. He "left half-told the story of Cambuscan bold," probably because he had in mind no plan for continuing it. No definite source has been discovered for the tale, and Chaucer was not much given to inventing plots. For what he did write he very likely found suggestions in the romance of Cleomades and in accounts then current of travels in the East. He may have picked up some of his lore from the oral reports of the traders and sailors with whom he was in frequent contact in the port of London. For it is not to be assumed that everything he used came out of books. And though it is seldom possible to trace non-literary channels of information, it is interesting to speculate about them and important to recognize their existence.

The *Franklin's Tale* is of a *genre* not elsewhere represented among Chaucer's writings. It purports to be a "Breton lay," that is, a short romance or tale of adventure such as the "ancient gentle Britons" were believed to have composed in their Celtic tongue. No poems of the exact type appear to have been preserved in early Welsh or Breton, but a number have come down in French and English. The finest specimens are the lays of Marie de France, the truly British character of which — whatever exact sources lay behind them — appears in their setting, in incidents and other features paralleled in Welsh and Irish saga, in occasional traces of the Breton language, and in the delicate fancy commonly recognized as characteristic of Celtic literature. Among the English lays that of Le Fraisne, translated from Marie, and that of Sir Orfeo perhaps best illustrate the same Celtic qualities. Whether Chaucer actually had a Breton lay (he would doubtless have known it in French or English) from which he derived the *Franklin's Tale*, is a matter of disagreement. At first sight the names of Arviragus and Dorigen and the localization in Brittany seem to favor the supposition. But the substance of the story is sufficiently accounted for by Boccaccio's version in the Filocolo, which was probably known to Chaucer, and it is now the prevalent opinion that he had no other source. He could easily have supplied the Celtic names of persons and places, though the description of Brittany, if due to him, affords an instance of unusual care in providing an appropriate setting for a tale. If he did not have a Breton lay as his source and model, he at all events knew very well what a lay ought to be. The romantic theme, the resort to magic or other incidents of supernatural character, the spirit of chivalry and courtesy — all these features of the *Franklin's Tale* are characteristic of the poems of Marie and her successors. Beyond this, in its urbanity and humor, the *Franklin's Tale* is both appropriate to the fictitious teller and delightfully expressive of the author. It is happily placed, as has already been observed, in the sequence of the tales of the Marriage Group. Thus considered in its relation to the Canterbury series, it fulfills a dramatic purpose, and considered by itself, it is an example of an interesting literary type, which it at once reproduces and transcends.

Fragment VI (Group C)

The Physician's Tale. With the end of Fragment V (Group F) the continuity of the *Canterbury Tales* is once more broken. In the best manuscripts the *Franklin's Tale* is followed by those of the Doctor and the Pardoner, but this pair (Group C) are not connected by genuine links with any of the other tales.

The *Physician's Tale* is the old Roman story of Appius and Virginia. It is told on the authority of Livy, but Chaucer's actual source seems clearly to have been the Roman de la Rose, from which he took even the citation of the Latin historian. In the simplicity of its structure and the directness with which it follows its source the *Physician's Tale* differs

strikingly from the tales of the Marriage Group which we have been considering, and ranges itself rather with the narratives that make up the *Legend of Good Women*. It has even been conjectured that Chaucer originally meant the story of Virginia for that collection. Like the legends, the *Physician's Tale* is by no means without art, but it is certainly not in what we have come to recognize as Chaucer's latest manner. The composition should perhaps be assigned to the late eighties, a date which is supported by personal allusions conjecturally recognized in the tale. The narrative, in general simple and straightforward, is interrupted by a long digression on the character and education of young girls. This discussion may have been prompted by a scandalous occurrence in the family of John of Gaunt. The remarks are also not inappropriate to the Doctor, and were perhaps introduced by way of adapting the tale to the teller.

The Pardoner's Prologue and Tale. Joined to the *Physician's Tale* are the prologue and tale of the Pardoner, which constitute one of Chaucer's most remarkable productions. They contain no definite indication of date, but clearly belong to a time when the plan of the *Canterbury Tales* was fully developed. The rascally Pardoner, suitably described by Professor Kittredge as "perhaps the one lost soul on the pilgrimage," begins with a confession, or rather a boastful relation, of all his vices and fraudulent acts. Then he preaches a sample sermon, such as he is in the habit of using to extract money from his congregations. Feeling, no doubt, that in such a company of "good felawes," whatever he tells will be privileged information, he keeps nothing back, but confesses all his dishonest motives and evil practices. At last, reaching the height of insolent jocularity, he recommends his false relics to his fellow-pilgrims and invites the Host, as most "envoluped in synne," to make the first offering. Thereupon ensues a bitter quarrel which it takes the best offices of the Knight to compose.

In spite of his contemptible nature, physical and moral, the Pardoner is one of the most intellectual figures among the pilgrims and his performance is worthy of his powers. His tale has sometimes been called the best short story in existence. Embodied in the sermon as an *exemplum,* or illustrative example, it is the old anecdote of the three revelers who found death in a heap of gold. It has been current in Asia as a moral fable from the time of the birth-tales of the Buddha, and Kipling included a modern version in his Jungle Book. Numerous European analogues have been collected, some of which are similar to Chaucer's version, but no one of them appears to have been his source. Certainly the tale was never better told than by the Pardoner. In the management of the intrigue and the swift *dénouement* it is a model of short-story method. In atmosphere and characterization it is vividly conceived, and in the dialogue not a word is wasted. And the Old Man, the Messenger of Death, in his mystery and moral sublimity is one of the most impressive apparitions in poetry.

Fragment VII (Group B²)

The *Pardoner's Tale* ends another fragment. It is followed in the best manuscripts by the series of tales (Group B²) which in most recent editions come after that of the Man of Law. Chaucer may well have been working toward the arrangement adopted by these editors, but the present edition, as explained above (page 2), adheres to the manuscript tradition. Within the group there seems to be no principle of arrangement save that of contrast or variety.

The *Shipman's Tale* is a *fabliau* and relates how a merchant was doubly cheated by a monk, first of his wife's favors, and second of his money. The anecdote is widely dispersed in popular tradition and is still current in America, where it is told at the expense of nationalities reputed to be parsimonious. The best known literary version except Chaucer's is in Boccaccio's Decameron.

The Prioress's Tale. In complete contrast with the scandalous anecdote of the Shipman is the Tale of the Prioress which follows. Requested by the Host, in what may be called without exaggeration the politest speech in English literature, to tell her story, the Prioress first recites an Invocation to the Blessed Virgin,

and then relates a legend of a little "clergeoun," or school-boy, murdered by the Jews. A vast cycle of such stories have been current since the early Christian centuries, and they still spring up when hostile feelings develop between Jews and Christians. In the special form which the legend takes in the *Prioress's Tale* and related versions, it is a "miracle of Our Lady," and the murdered child, by the intervention of the Virgin, is made to speak and declare the manner of his death. In most accounts of the miracle, and probably in its original form, the story ends happily with the restoration of the child to life. But Chaucer's version, and without doubt his source, have a tragic ending, probably taken over from current stories of children murdered by the Jews. The *Prioress's Tale,* though in the stanzaic form characteristic of Chaucer's middle period, is generally assigned, by reason of its flawless workmanship and its perfect adaptation to the teller, to the time of the fully developed plan of the Canterbury Tales. By a comparison of the numerous extant versions of the miracle it is possible to discover almost exactly what Chaucer had before him in his source. And we find that working here on a small scale and with almost fragile delicacy of materials he contributed the same new elements of descriptive setting and dramatic characterization which he brought to his larger works. But here, in the interest of dramatic propriety, his humor was held completely in abeyance and the story is told in a spirit of consistent pathos. Surely that criticism is perverse which maintains that Chaucer wrote the *Prioress's Tale* as a satire on childish legends. He is as far from showing disrespect for the story as for the devout lady who tells it. And when the miracle was related even the ruder and more boisterous members of the company were reduced to silence.

The adaptation of the story to the Prioress is almost too obvious to mention. Everywhere in it are apparent her religious devotion, her elegance and refinement, her "conscience and tendre herte" — unhappily not incompatible with a bigoted hatred for the "cursed Jewes." The story and, hardly less, the revealing introductory dialogue with the Host, serve admirably to complete the portrait of the Prioress in the *Prologue*.

The Rime of Sir Thopas. To recall the company from the solemn mood induced by the Prioress's legend, the Host calls upon Chaucer, who looks as if he could contribute something good, for the next story. The creator of all the pilgrims modestly protests that he has nothing to offer but an old rime he learned long ago, and then launches out into the doggerel jog-trot of the stanzas of *Sir Thopas*. He is allowed to finish only one canto, or "fit," and begin a second, when the Host declares he can stand no more of it. Chaucer asks, with injured sensibility, why he should be stopped in his tale more than any other man, but the Host is obdurate and tells him he shall no longer rime. Chaucer obediently accepts the ruling of the "lord and governour," and tells the prose tale of *Melibee*.

The rime of *Sir Thopas* is hardly a tale at all. It starts out, in the language and measure of the more popular minstrel romances, to recount the adventures of the paragon of knighthood whose name it bears, and before it is cut short it relates his enamourment with a fairy queen and one inglorious exploit against a giant "with hevedes three." The whole piece is preposterous in the extreme and obviously satirical in purpose. But there is some difference of opinion as to the object of the satire. It has long been recognized that the rime reproduces many of the absurd features of the poorer romances — their padded style and doggerel movement; their catalogue method of description, with endless lists of food and clothing, birds and trees, or the physical features of men and women; their stock adventures of heroes in love or war; their commonplaces of sentiment or of moral teaching. To the reader familiar with the metrical romances nearly every line of *Sir Thopas* recalls some figure or incident or trick of style, not necessarily absurd in itself, and makes it ridiculous. It has been commonly held that Chaucer's main purpose in the parody was to show up these defects of the romances, and some readers have drawn the unwarrantable inference that he meant to disparage the whole body of such compositions. But recent critics have seen in

Sir Thopas, in addition to the literary satire, or even in place of it, social satire at the expense of the Flemish knighthood. It is clear, especially from accounts cited by Miss Winstanley and Professor Manly, that the knights of Flanders were the subject of ridicule at the French and English courts, and *Sir Thopas*, born at "Poperyng, in the place," was very likely intended as a representative of the type. The descriptions of his food and clothing, appearance, and behavior all seem to convey such jokes as were made by the older aristocracy in contempt for the Flemish *nouveaux riches*, bourgeois intruders into the circle of chivalry. This application of the satire in *Sir Thopas*, when once pointed out, appears altogether reasonable. But it does not exclude the older interpretation, and it is probable that we should recognize in the poem a twofold satire, literary and social. And after all, the Host's comments, which, here and elsewhere, afford some indication of Chaucer's purposes, point rather to the former. He makes no reference to Flemish or other upstart knights, but condemns *Sir Thopas* as a wretched rime.

The Tale of Melibee. "Cut off in the midst of *Sir Thopas*," one American critic observes, "Chaucer revenges himself by telling the dull tale of *Melibee*." Most modern readers will doubtless agree in this appraisal of the "moral tale and virtuous" of Melibeus and Dame Prudence. Chaucer's prose, at its best, is heavy in comparison with his verse. Allegory is now out of fashion, and the moral instruction in *Melibee* is commonplace and tiresomely schematic. Except for the collector of proverbs and apophthegms it has now small literary interest. Yet some allowance must undoubtedly be made for change of taste. The Host — who, to be sure, has in mind practical rather than artistic considerations — receives the tale enthusiastically. This is the more significant since he has just cut short *Sir Thopas*, and since the *Monk's Tale*, which immediately follows, is interrupted by the Knight when he can no longer endure the dismal tragedies. In so far as the pilgrims' comments are intended to represent the taste and fashion of the time, the *Melibee* at least escapes condemnation. Lydgate, writing in the next generation, speaks of it with respect. Chaucer himself, too, had enough interest in the plot, slight as it is, to utilize it in the *Merchant's Tale*. On the whole, there is no reason to suppose that he or his age thought ill of *Melibee*. And the *Parson's Tale*, on the Seven Deadly Sins, and the lost translation of Pope Innocent's De Contemptu Mundi testify to his interest in much more uninviting specimens of what Lord Bacon would call "friar's books of edification and mortification."

The *Melibee* is a close translation of the French Livre de Melibé et de Dame Prudence, ascribed to Renaud de Louens, and this in turn is a free rendering of the Liber Consolationis et Consilii of Albertanus of Brescia. The date of Chaucer's version is unknown, but it probably belongs among the earlier productions of the Canterbury period.

The Monk's Tale. After an extremely personal outburst, in which the Host laments that Godelief, his wife, is not more like Dame Prudence, and shows that she uses all the arguments of a Lady Macbeth to make him resort to violence against the men who have given her offense, he turns for the second time to the Monk and asks him for a tale. Presuming, it would seem, upon the jovial character of the hunting cleric, he begins in a familiar tone to ask him his name, becomes more and more personal, and ends by declaring that if he were pope such a vigorous man would not be restrained from begetting offspring. This eugenic argument, which is repeated in the canceled Epilogue to the *Nun's Priest's Tale*, is rather unusual in the contemporary discussions of sacerdotal celibacy. Pursuing his attack, and confident of provoking a lively response, the Host asks for an entertaining story, and in particular, for something about hunting. The Monk, unexpectedly — but, in view of the Host's rather impudent onslaught, not unnaturally — preserves the dignity of the cloth. Without taking direct offense he ignores the Host's challenging remarks and offers to relate, for the edification of the company, either a life of St. Edward or a series of "tragedies," of which he has a hundred in his cell. Then after giving, with pedantic solemnity, a dictionary definition of a tragedy, he tells a string of dismal tales of the fall of men from high estate. When

he has finished some fifteen of his inexhaustible supply the Knight stops him, declaring that he cannot endure to hear any more about "wo and hevinesse." The Host gives the Monk one more chance to tell a tale which would be in character. But he refuses to play the expected part, and the Host turns to the Nun's Priest, who proves more tractable.

For the scheme of the *Monk's Tale*, Chaucer was indebted principally to two sources: the Roman de la Rose, which supplied him with the moral concerning Fortune and with some of the individual instances, and Boccaccio's De Casibus Virorum et Feminarum Illustrium, which gave him his sub-title and also several of the tragedies. The other examples he gathered from Boccaccio's De Mulieribus Claris, the Bible, Boethius and Dante, and in three instances — Peter of Spain, Peter of Cyprus, and Bernabò Visconti — from contemporary life. In the case of a few, which contain familiar historical information, the exact source has not been determined. The date of the collection, except for the account of Bernabò, was almost certainly early. The death of Bernabò — one of the very few contemporary events specifically mentioned by Chaucer — did not take place until December, 1385, and Chaucer's lines about it could hardly have been written before the early weeks of 1386. But the single stanza bears every indication of having been interpolated, and the rest of the work belongs to the period of transition from French to Italian influence. The early seventies seem the most reasonable date. The literary interest of the compilation is small, as was inevitable with a series of encyclopedic sketches of the "falls of princes." The Bernabò stanza has vigor and warmth of feeling, and the tragedy of Ugolino, alone perhaps, has moving power. For this deals, not with the summary of a career, but with a tragic moment which could be presented in the small compass of the poem; and Chaucer had a supremely excellent model in Dante's Inferno.

The Nun's Priest's Tale. The tale of the Nun's Priest, in contrast to the apprentice work of the Monk's tragedies, shows Chaucer again at the height of his powers. It was not merely written with the Nun's Priest in mind, but was adapted with more than usual care to the character and calling of the teller. His habit of life as a preacher appears in pulpit mannerisms and in the frequent use of homiletic material. His relation to the Prioress as father confessor and spiritual adviser, and at the same time social dependent or beneficiary, seems to be reflected in the cautious protest, "I kan noon harm of no woman divyne." His own character, in its combination of modesty and good humor with quick wit and high intelligence, is one of the most vivid among the pilgrims. Yet it is revealed only as it appears dramatically in his tale, for there is no sketch of him in the *General Prologue*. The story itself is the familiar incident of the cock who was seized by a fox and made his escape by inducing his captor to open his mouth in speech. It is preserved both in fables and in an episode of the beast-epic known in various languages as the romance of Renard. It used to be held that Chaucer's version was derived from the fable, Dou Coc et Dou Werpil, of Marie de France. But a careful comparison of numerous forms of the story has shown that the *Nun's Priest's Tale* belongs rather with the epic than with the fables. The type of literature with which Chaucer was working can be best observed in the old French Roman de Renart or the Netherlandish Reinaert Vos, and it received its classic treatment in modern times in Goethe's Reinecke Fuchs. But Chaucer's source, or, for that matter, the simple incident itself which constitutes the action, counts for little in the poem compared with the brilliant presentation. In none of Chaucer's tales — perhaps in no story that could be cited — is the narrative more enlivened by variety of method, by apt description, witty dialogue, or wealth of literary allusion and philosophical comment. The cock's tragic adventure is presented, almost from the outset, against a background of universal history and divine providence. In the discussion of dreams and destiny the Priest draws upon the sermon-books, which are great treasure-houses of mediæval fiction. The catastrophe, thus prepared for, is related in the grand style, making the poem the first notable English example of mock-heroic. And this method is extended with amazing subtlety of humor, to the presentation of the characters of Chauntecleer and Pertelote. The balance is most delicately maintained between the barnyard and the boudoir — or, in contemporary language, the bower. At one moment the characters are in most physical literalness the cock and hen, and in the next Chauntecleer is an educated gentleman, quoting *auctoritees* and translating Latin for the ladies, and Pertelote, the object of his courtly attentions, is a practical and rather disillusioned woman of the world. In her skeptical habit of mind, as Professor Kittredge long ago pointed out, she is an amusing counterpart of the tragic heroine, Criseyde.

The *Nun's Priest's Tale* is followed by an *Epilogue* which repeats in a measure the argument of the earlier words of the Host to the Monk, and which, probably for that reason, appears to have been canceled by Chaucer. Even if retained it does not furnish a definite introduction to any following tale. It therefore marks the end of the seventh fragment.

Fragment VIII (Group G)

The Second Nun's Tale. The "nonne chapeleyne," like her superior, the Prioress, relates a Christian legend. It is the life of the famous Roman martyr, St. Cecilia, and was taken by Chaucer from the Legenda Aurea, or a version almost identical with that of Jacobus Januensis. Chaucer's text closely follows the Latin original, and is regarded by common consent as the work of his early years. The *Prologue*, which some scholars hold to have been composed later than the legend, is partly based upon the noble prayer of St. Bernard to the Virgin in the thirty-third canto of Dante's Paradiso. So at least that passage may be assigned to the period after Chaucer's first Italian journey, and the whole composition, along with the *Monk's Tale*, which also shows the beginning of Italian influence, probably belongs to the early seventies. The legend, by reason alike of subject-matter and of treatment, lacks the vivid and varied human interest of Chaucer's later writings. But with all its simplicity, it is by no means devoid of poetic beauty, and the truly reverent spirit of the narrative — which was not dramatically composed for the Nun —

should be taken into account by those critics who think of Chaucer as out of sympathy with the religion of his age. To the student of literary history it is an excellent specimen of the saints' lives, which constituted a very large part of the narrative writings of the Middle Ages. It also gives, as Professor Tatlock has remarked, an expression, rarely to be matched in literature, of the triumphant spirit of early Christianity.

The Canon's Yeoman's Tale. The Nun's account of the remote martyrdom of St. Cecilia is followed immediately by what is perhaps the most closely personal and contemporaneous story in the collection, the Canon's Yeoman's anecdote of a swindling alchemist. It has even been conjectured that Chaucer wrote the tale in indignation at his own treatment by a follower of the "sliding craft," and a particular canon of Windsor, William Shuchirch, known to have practiced the art, has been identified as a possible subject of the satire. Be that as it may, the tale reveals keen interest if not strong feeling, and the exposure and denunciation of the alchemist's trickery is thoroughgoing. It does not follow, of course, that Chaucer regarded alchemy as wholly an imposture. The tale shows that he had a considerable acquaintance with alchemical writings, which did have scientific standing in his age; and it would be strange if he did not recognize that there was a legitimate practice of the art.

The Yeoman is represented as overtaking the pilgrims after a mad gallop with his master, who takes abrupt leave upon discovering that his rascality is to be revealed. Whether the pair were really an afterthought with Chaucer we do not know. The device by which they are brought in may have been in his mind from the beginning. In any case it gives variety to the narrative, and provides a natural and dramatic introduction for the Yeoman's story. He begins, like the Wife of Bath and the Pardoner, with a personal confession, though in this case the speaker is not the principal culprit. He is himself the victim of his dishonest lord, from whom he set out to learn the art of "multiplying." He describes at considerable length the processes of alchemy, and then tells of a double swindling trick played by a canon upon a priest.

No literary source need be sought for the anecdote, though records have been found of very similar incidents. Probably they were a matter of too common experience. They make a good story, and the Canon and his Yeoman, whether or not drawn from life, are among the most lifelike of Chaucer's characters.

Fragment IX (Group H)

The Manciple's Prologue and Tale. When overtaken by the Canon's Yeoman, the pilgrims are said to have been at "Boughton-under-Blee." In the *Manciple's Prologue*, which begins the next fragment, they are at Bob-up-and-Down, identified conjecturally as Harbledown, or a field in the vicinity between Boughton under Blean and Canterbury. It is usually understood that the company was now approaching Canterbury, and that the tales of the Manciple and the Parson were intended to close the outward journey. But it is entirely possible, as has been recently suggested, that Chaucer meant the *Manciple's Tale* to be told early on the way back to London, and that he was holding the *Parson's Tale* in reserve for the very end.

The subject of the Manciple's story is the Tell-tale Bird, famous in popular tradition in both orient and occident. The tale obtained wide diffusion in the Middle Ages as one of the stories in the romance of the Seven Sages, and in this form was very probably known to Chaucer. But his own version is derived rather from the Metamorphoses of Ovid, considerably elaborated by description, illustrative *exempla,* and other digressions. The treatment is rhetorically formal, even somewhat pedantic, and seems to indicate early composition. This supposition is supported, positively, by the extensive use of the Roman de la Rose and, negatively, by the fact that the tale bears no indication of having been written for one of the Canterbury pilgrims.

Fragment X (Group I)

The Parson's Prologue and Tale. The Parson, when called upon by the Host to play his part in the game, refuses to tell a "fable," or "idle story," but declares himself willing to speak of "moralitee and vertuous matere." Being a Southern man, however, he cannot compose alliterative verse (which in Chaucer's century was especially cultivated in the dialects of the north and northwest), and he "holds rime but little better"; so he offers to tell what he calls a "merry tale in prose." This description is so ludicrously inappropriate to the discourse that follows — a treatise on the Seven Deadly Sins — that some critics have thought that Chaucer must have meant it to introduce a different tale. They have even questioned whether he intended what is known as the *Parson's Tale* to be included at all in the Canterbury collection. But, after all, the treatise is exactly the kind of entertainment the Parson said he was willing to provide, and in calling it a "merry tale" he was only having his little joke — very much as Chaucer did in introducing his *Melibee.* In spite of the Host's exhortation, "Beth fructuous, and that in litel space," the *Parson's Tale* is by far the longest in the series. Whatever claim it had to consideration in the competition of the pilgrims certainly rests rather upon "sentence" than upon "solas." It deals with the Deadly Sins according to the usual classification and by the regular method of a manual of confession. The greater part has been shown to correspond closely to a portion of the third book of the De Poenitentia of Raymond de Pennaforte. Into this has been inserted a section derived from the Summa de Vitiis of Guilielmus Peraldus. The exact form in which Chaucer had these treatises is not yet known, and it is not even possible to say whether he first made the combination. But it seems probable that he found it ready to hand in the work of a predecessor.

Chaucer's Retracciouns. The *Parson's Tale* is followed by the much discussed *Retracciouns,* or Retractations, of the author. In them Chaucer revokes all his "translacions and enditynges of worldly vanitees," mentioning by name not only those Canterbury tales "that sownen into synne" but also some works which seem quite inoffensive. Partly because of the inclusion, among disavowed writings, of the

Book of the Duchess, the *House of Fame,* the *Parliament of Fowls,* and the *Legend of Good Women,* some critics have denied the authenticity of the *Retracciouns.* But it is to be observed that the author is repudiating not merely downright sin, but all worldly vanities, and the poems in question celebrate, in one aspect or other, romantic love. To Chaucer, in the mood in which he wrote the *Retracciouns,* nothing seemed worthy except works on philosophy and religion, and he specifically excepts from his condemnation only the translation of Boethius "and other bookes of legendes of seintes, and omelies, and moralitee, and devocion." Such a repudiation of most of his life work may be deplored as weakness of mind or explained as a sign of broken health in old age. But it can hardly be regarded as impossible, or even improbable. Literary history affords many examples, from St. Augustine down to modern times, of similar changes of heart. In Chaucer's own century Boccaccio, who is so much like him in temperament, is reported, while still in middle life, to have undergone a religious experience which led him to renounce his frivolous and licentious writings in the vernacular and devote himself to learned treatises in Latin. And it was not only men of letters who were moved in old age to make amends for what they regarded as sinful lives. Chaucer's own friend, Sir Lewis Clifford, the Lollard Knight, was another conspicuous example. It is not to be supposed that Chaucer was necessarily immune from such revulsion of feeling. Moreover, many of his writings contain passages which, by the standards of any age, would be pronounced vulgar and indecent. If we are more lenient toward them than was the aged author himself, it is partly because some of the "cherles tales" are examples of his most masterly narrative art, and partly because in the work of a great realist vice and depravity cannot be excluded. And it may at least be said for Chaucer, in contrast to many of the modern practitioners of realism, that he is never morbid or unhealthy, and that he sees life in a true perspective.

THE CANTERBURY TALES

Fragment I (Group A)

General Prologue

Here bygynneth the Book of the Tales of Caunterbury.

Whan that Aprill with his shoures soote
The droghte of March hath perced to the
    roote,
And bathed every veyne in swich licour
Of which vertu engendred is the flour;
Whan Zephirus eek with his sweete breeth   5
Inspired hath in every holt and heeth
The tendre croppes, and the yonge sonne
Hath in the Ram his halve cours yronne,
And smale foweles maken melodye,
That slepen al the nyght with open ye   10
(So priketh hem nature in hir corages);
Thanne longen folk to goon on pilgrimages,
And palmeres for to seken straunge strondes,
To ferne halwes, kowthe in sondry londes;
And specially from every shires ende   15
Of Engelond to Caunterbury they wende,
The hooly blisful martir for to seke,
That hem hath holpen whan that they were
    seeke.
  Bifil that in that seson on a day,
In Southwerk at the Tabard as I lay   20
Redy to wenden on my pilgrymage
To Caunterbury with ful devout corage,
At nyght was come into that hostelrye
Wel nyne and twenty in a compaignye,
Of sondry folk, by aventure yfalle   25
In felaweshipe, and pilgrimes were they alle,
That toward Caunterbury wolden ryde.
The chambres and the stables weren wyde,
And wel we weren esed atte beste.
And shortly, whan the sonne was to reste,   30
So hadde I spoken with hem everichon
That I was of hir felaweshipe anon,
And made forward erly for to ryse,

To take oure wey ther as I yow devyse.
  But nathelees, whil I have tyme and
    space,   35
Er that I ferther in this tale pace,
Me thynketh it acordaunt to resoun
To telle yow al the condicioun
Of ech of hem, so as it semed me,
And whiche they weren, and of what de-
    gree,   40
And eek in what array that they were inne;
And at a knyght than wol I first bigynne.
  A KNYGHT ther was, and that a worthy man,
That fro the tyme that he first bigan
To riden out, he loved chivalrie,   45
Trouthe and honour, fredom and curteisie.
Ful worthy was he in his lordes werre,
And therto hadde he riden, no man ferre,
As wel in cristendom as in hethenesse,
And evere honoured for his worthynesse.   50
At Alisaundre he was whan it was wonne.
Ful ofte tyme he hadde the bord bigonne
Aboven alle nacions in Pruce;
In Lettow hadde he reysed and in Ruce,
No Cristen man so ofte of his degree.   55
In Gernade at the seege eek hadde he be
Of Algezir, and riden in Belmarye.
At Lyeys was he and at Satalye,
Whan they were wonne; and in the Grete See
At many a noble armee hadde he be.   60
At mortal batailles hadde he been fiftene,
And foughten for oure feith at Tramyssene
In lystes thries, and ay slayn his foo.
This ilke worthy knyght hadde been also
Somtyme with the lord of Palatye   65
Agayn another hethen in Turkye.

17

And everemoore he hadde a sovereyn prys;
And though that he were worthy, he was wys,
And of his port as meeke as is a mayde.
He nevere yet no vileynye ne sayde   70
In al his lyf unto no maner wight.
He was a verray, parfit gentil knyght.
But, for to tellen yow of his array,
His hors were goode, but he was nat gay.
Of fustian he wered a gypon   75
Al bismotered with his habergeon,
For he was late ycome from his viage,
And wente for to doon his pilgrymage.
    With hym ther was his sone, a yong SQUIER,
A lovyere and a lusty bacheler,   80
With lokkes crulle as they were leyd in presse.
Of twenty yeer of age he was, I gesse.
Of his stature he was of evene lengthe,
And wonderly delyvere, and of greet strengthe.
And he hadde been somtyme in chyvachie   85
In Flaundres, in Artoys, and Pycardie,
And born hym weel, as of so litel space,
In hope to stonden in his lady grace.
Embrouded was he, as it were a meede
Al ful of fresshe floures, whyte and reede.   90
Syngynge he was, or floytynge, al the day;
He was as fressh as is the month of May.
Short was his gowne, with sleves longe and
        wyde.
Wel koude he sitte on hors and faire ryde.
He koude songes make and wel endite,   95
Juste and eek daunce, and weel purtreye and
        write.
So hoote he lovede that by nyghtertale
He sleep namoore than dooth a nyghtyngale.
Curteis he was, lowely, and servysable,
And carf biforn his fader at the table.   100
    A YEMAN hadde he and servantz namo
At that tyme, for hym liste ride so,
And he was clad in cote and hood of grene.
A sheef of pecok arwes, bright and kene,
Under his belt he bar ful thriftily,   105
(Wel koude he dresse his takel yemanly:
His arwes drouped noght with fetheres lowe)
And in his hand he baar a myghty bowe.
A not heed hadde he, with a broun visage.
Of wodecraft wel koude he al the usage.   110
Upon his arm he baar a gay bracer,
And by his syde a swerd and a bokeler,
And on that oother syde a gay daggere
Harneised wel and sharp as point of spere;
A Cristopher on his brest of silver sheene. 115
An horn he bar, the bawdryk was of grene;
A forster was he, soothly, as I gesse.
    Ther was also a Nonne, a PRIORESSE,

That of hir smylyng was ful symple and coy;
Hire gretteste ooth was but by Seinte Loy;   120
And she was cleped madame Eglentyne.
Ful weel she soong the service dyvyne,
Entuned in hir nose ful semely,
And Frenssh she spak ful faire and fetisly,
After the scole of Stratford atte Bowe,   125
For Frenssh of Parys was to hire unknowe.
At mete wel ytaught was she with alle:
She leet no morsel from hir lippes falle,
Ne wette hir fyngres in hir sauce depe;
Wel koude she carie a morsel and wel kepe   130
That no drope ne fille upon hire brest.
In curteisie was set ful muchel hir lest.
Hir over-lippe wyped she so clene
That in hir coppe ther was no ferthyng sene
Of grece, whan she dronken hadde hir draughte.
Ful semely after hir mete she raughte.   136
And sikerly she was of greet desport,
And ful plesaunt, and amyable of port,
And peyned hire to countrefete cheere
Of court, and to been estatlich of manere,   140
And to ben holden digne of reverence.
But, for to speken of hire conscience,
She was so charitable and so pitous
She wolde wepe, if that she saugh a mous   144
Kaught in a trappe, if it were deed or bledde.
Of smale houndes hadde she that she fedde
With rosted flessh, or milk and wastel-breed.
But soore wepte she if oon of hem were deed,
Or if men smoot it with a yerde smerte;
And al was conscience and tendre herte.   150
Ful semyly hir wympul pynched was,
Hir nose tretys, hir eyen greye as glas,
Hir mouth ful smal, and therto softe and reed;
But sikerly she hadde a fair forheed;
It was almoost a spanne brood, I trowe;   155
For, hardily, she was nat undergrowe.
Ful fetys was hir cloke, as I was war.
Of smal coral aboute hire arm she bar
A peire of bedes, gauded al with grene,   159
And theron heng a brooch of gold ful sheene,
On which ther was first write a crowned A,
And after *Amor vincit omnia.*
    Another NONNE with hire hadde she,
That was hir chapeleyne, and preestes thre.
    A MONK ther was, a fair for the maistrie, 165
An outridere, that lovede venerie,
A manly man, to been an abbot able.
Ful many a deyntee hors hadde he in stable,
And whan he rood, men myghte his brydel
        heere
Cynglen in a whistlynge wynd als cleere   170
And eek as loude as dooth the chapel belle.

Ther as this lord was kepere of the celle,
The reule of seint Maure or of seint Beneit,
By cause that it was old and somdel streit
This ilke Monk leet olde thynges pace,   175
And heeld after the newe world the space.
He yaf nat of that text a pulled hen,
That seith that hunters ben nat hooly men,
Ne that a monk, whan he is recchelees,
Is likned til a fissh that is waterlees, —   180
This is to seyn, a monk out of his cloystre.
But thilke text heeld he nat worth an oystre;
And I seyde his opinion was good.
What sholde he studie and make hymselven
        wood,
Upon a book in cloystre alwey to poure,   185
Or swynken with his handes, and laboure,
As Austyn bit? How shal the world be served?
Lat Austyn have his swynk to hym reserved!
Therfore he was a prikasour aright:
Grehoundes he hadde as swift as fowel in flight;
Of prikyng and of huntyng for the hare   191
Was al his lust, for no cost wolde he spare.
I seigh his sleves purfiled at the hond
With grys, and that the fyneste of a lond;
And, for to festne his hood under his chyn,   195
He hadde of gold ywroght a ful curious pyn;
A love-knotte in the gretter ende ther was.
His heed was balled, that shoon as any glas,
And eek his face, as he hadde been enoynt.
He was a lord ful fat and in good poynt;   200
His eyen stepe, and rollynge in his heed,
That stemed as a forneys of a leed;
His bootes souple, his hors in greet estaat.
Now certeinly he was a fair prelaat;
He was nat pale as a forpyned goost.   205
A fat swan loved he best of any roost.
His palfrey was as broun as is a berye.
    A FRERE ther was, a wantowne and a merye,
A lymytour, a ful solempne man.
In alle the ordres foure is noon that kan   210
So muchel of daliaunce and fair langage.
He hadde maad ful many a mariage
Of yonge wommen at his owene cost.
Unto his ordre he was a noble post.
Ful wel biloved and famulier was he   215
With frankeleyns over al in his contree,
And eek with worthy wommen of the toun;
For he hadde power of confessioun,
As seyde hymself, moore than a curat,
For of his ordre he was licenciat.   220
Ful swetely herde he confessioun,
And plesaunt was his absolucioun:
He was an esy man to yeve penaunce,
Ther as he wiste to have a good pitaunce.

For unto a povre ordre for to yive   225
Is signe that a man is wel yshryve;
For if he yaf, he dorste make avaunt,
He wiste that a man was repentaunt;
For many a man so hard is of his herte,   229
He may nat wepe, althogh hym soore smerte.
Therfore in stede of wepynge and preyeres
Men moote yeve silver to the povre freres.
His typet was ay farsed ful of knyves
And pynnes, for to yeven faire wyves.
And certeinly he hadde a murye note: 235
Wel koude he synge and pleyen on a rote;
Of yeddynges he baar outrely the pris.
His nekke whit was as the flour-de-lys;
Therto he strong was as a champioun.
He knew the tavernes wel in every toun   240
And everich hostiler and tappestere
Bet than a lazar or a beggestere;
For unto swich a worthy man as he
Acorded nat, as by his facultee,
To have with sike lazars aqueyntaunce.   245
It is nat honest, it may nat avaunce,
For to deelen with no swich poraille,
But al with riche and selleres of vitaille.
And over al, ther as profit sholde arise,
Curteis he was and lowely of servyse.   250
Ther nas no man nowher so vertuous.
He was the beste beggere in his hous;
[And yaf a certeyn ferme for the graunt;   252a
Noon of his bretheren cam ther in his
        haunt;]   252b
For thogh a wydwe hadde noght a sho,
So plesaunt was his *In principio,*
Yet wolde he have a ferthyng, er he wente.   255
His purchas was wel bettre than his rente.
And rage he koude, as it were right a whelp.
In love-dayes ther koude he muchel help,
For ther he was nat lyk a cloysterer
With a thredbare cope, as is a povre scoler,   260
But he was lyk a maister or a pope.
Of double worstede was his semycope,
That rounded as a belle out of the presse.
Somwhat he lipsed, for his wantownesse,   264
To make his Englissh sweete upon his tonge;
And in his harpyng, whan that he hadde songe,
His eyen twynkled in his heed aryght,
As doon the sterres in the frosty nyght.
This worthy lymytour was cleped Huberd.
    A MARCHANT was ther with a forked berd,
In mottelee, and hye on horse he sat;   271
Upon his heed a Flaundryssh bever hat,
His bootes clasped faire and fetisly.
His resons he spak ful solempnely,
Sownynge alwey th'encrees of his wynnyng.

He wolde the see were kept for any thyng 276
Bitwixe Middelburgh and Orewelle.
Wel koude he in eschaunge sheeldes selle.
This worthy man ful wel his wit bisette:
Ther wiste no wight that he was in dette, 280
So estatly was he of his governaunce
With his bargaynes and with his chevyssaunce.
For sothe he was a worthy man with alle,
But, sooth to seyn, I noot how men hym calle.
    A Clerk ther was of Oxenford also, 285
That unto logyk hadde longe ygo.
As leene was his hors as is a rake,
And he nas nat right fat, I undertake,
But looked holwe, and therto sobrely.
Ful thredbare was his overeste courtepy; 290
For he hadde geten hym yet no benefice,
Ne was so worldly for to have office.
For hym was levere have at his beddes heed
Twenty bookes, clad in blak or reed,
Of Aristotle and his philosophie, 295
Than robes riche, or fithele, or gay sautrie.
But al be that he was a philosophre,
Yet hadde he but litel gold in cofre;
But al that he myghte of his freendes hente,
On bookes and on lernynge he it spente, 300
And bisily gan for the soules preye
Of hem that yaf hym wherwith to scoleye.
Of studie took he moost cure and moost heede.
Noght o word spak he moore than was neede,
And that was seyd in forme and reverence, 305
And short and quyk and ful of hy sentence;
Sownynge in moral vertu was his speche,
And gladly wolde he lerne and gladly teche.
    A Sergeant of the Lawe, war and wys,
That often hadde been at the Parvys, 310
Ther was also, ful riche of excellence.
Discreet he was and of greet reverence —
He semed swich, his wordes weren so wise.
Justice he was ful often in assise,
By patente and by pleyn commissioun. 315
For his science and for his heigh renoun,
Of fees and robes hadde he many oon.
So greet a purchasour was nowher noon:
Al was fee symple to hym in effect;
His purchasyng myghte nat been infect. 320
Nowher so bisy a man as he ther nas,
And yet he semed bisier than he was.
In termes hadde he caas and doomes alle
That from the tyme of kyng William were
        falle. 324
Therto he koude endite, and make a thyng,
Ther koude no wight pynche at his writyng;
And every statut koude he pleyn by rote.
He rood but hoomly in a medlee cote.

Girt with a ceint of silk, with barres smale;
Of his array telle I no lenger tale. 330
    A Frankeleyn was in his compaignye.
Whit was his berd as is the dayesye;
Of his complexioun he was sangwyn.
Wel loved he by the morwe a sop in wyn;
To lyven in delit was evere his wone, 335
For he was Epicurus owene sone,
That heeld opinioun that pleyn delit
Was verray felicitee parfit.
An housholdere, and that a greet, was he;
Seint Julian he was in his contree. 340
His breed, his ale, was alweys after oon;
A bettre envyned man was nowher noon.
Withoute bake mete was nevere his hous
Of fissh and flessh, and that so plentevous,
It snewed in his hous of mete and drynke, 345
Of alle deyntees that men koude thynke.
After the sondry sesons of the yeer,
So chaunged he his mete and his soper.
Ful many a fat partrich hadde he in muwe,
And many a breem and many a luce in stuwe.
Wo was his cook but if his sauce were 351
Poynaunt and sharp, and redy al his geere.
His table dormant in his halle alway
Stood redy covered al the longe day.
At sessiouns ther was he lord and sire; 355
Ful ofte tyme he was knyght of the shire.
An anlaas and a gipser al of silk
Heeng at his girdel, whit as morne milk.
A shirreve hadde he been, and a contour.
Was nowher swich a worthy vavasour. 360
    An Haberdasshere and a Carpenter,
A Webbe, a Dyere, and a Tapycer, —
And they were clothed alle in o lyveree
Of a solempne and a greet fraternitee.
Ful fressh and newe hir geere apiked was; 365
Hir knyves were chaped noght with bras
But al with silver; wroght ful clene and weel
Hire girdles and hir pouches everydeel.
Wel semed ech of hem a fair burgeys
To sitten in a yeldehalle on a deys. 370
Everich, for the wisdom that he kan,
Was shaply for to been an alderman.
For catel hadde they ynogh and rente,
And eek hir wyves wolde it wel assente;
And elles certeyn were they to blame. 375
It is ful fair to been ycleped "madame,"
And goon to vigilies al bifore,
And have a mantel roialliche ybore.
    A Cook they hadde with hem for the nones
To boille the chiknes with the marybones, 380
And poudre-marchant tart and galyngale.
Wel koude he knowe a draughte of Londoun ale.

He koude rooste, and sethe, and broille, and
    frye,
Maken mortreux, and wel bake a pye.
But greet harm was it, as it thoughte me,   385
That on his shyne a mormal hadde he.
For blankmanger, that made he with the beste.

    A SHIPMAN was ther, wonynge fer by weste;
For aught I woot, he was of Dertemouthe.
He rood upon a rouncy, as he kouthe,   390
In a gowne of faldyng to the knee.
A daggere hangynge on a laas hadde he
Aboute his nekke, under his arm adoun.
The hoote somer hadde maad his hewe al
    broun;
And certeinly he was a good felawe.   395
Ful many a draughte of wyn had he ydrawe
Fro Burdeux-ward, whil that the chapman
    sleep.
Of nyce conscience took he no keep.
If that he faught, and hadde the hyer hond,
By water he sente hem hoom to every lond.
But of his craft to rekene wel his tydes,   401
His stremes, and his daungers hym bisides,
His herberwe, and his moone, his lodemenage,
Ther nas noon swich from Hulle to Cartage.
Hardy he was and wys to undertake;   405
With many a tempest hadde his berd been
    shake.
He knew alle the havenes, as they were,
Fro Gootlond to the cape of Fynystere,
And every cryke in Britaigne and in Spayne.
His barge ycleped was the Maudelayne.   410

    With us ther was a DOCTOUR OF PHISIK;
In al this world ne was ther noon hym lik,
To speke of phisik and of surgerye,
For he was grounded in astronomye.
He kepte his pacient a ful greet deel   415
In houres by his magyk natureel.
Wel koude he fortunen the ascendent
Of his ymages for his pacient.
He knew the cause of everich maladye,   419
Were it of hoot, or coold, or moyste, or drye,
And where they engendred, and of what hu-
    mour.
He was a verray, parfit praktisour:
The cause yknowe, and of his harm the roote,
Anon he yaf the sike man his boote.
Ful redy hadde he his apothecaries   425
To sende hym drogges and his letuaries,
For ech of hem made oother for to wynne —
Hir frendshipe nas nat newe to bigynne.
Wel knew he the olde Esculapius,
And Deyscorides, and eek Rufus,   430
Olde Ypocras, Haly, and Galyen,

Serapion, Razis, and Avycen,
Averrois, Damascien, and Constantyn,
Bernard, and Gatesden, and Gilbertyn.
Of his diete mesurable was he,   435
For it was of no superfluitee,
But of greet norissyng and digestible.
His studie was but litel on the Bible.
In sangwyn and in pers he clad was al,
Lyned with taffata and with sendal;   440
And yet he was but esy of dispence;
He kepte that he wan in pestilence.
For gold in phisik is a cordial,
Therefore he lovede gold in special.

    A good WIF was ther OF biside BATHE,   445
But she was somdel deef, and that was scathe.
Of clooth-makyng she hadde swich an haunt,
She passed hem of Ypres and of Gaunt.
In al the parisshe wif ne was ther noon   449
That to the offrynge bifore hire sholde goon;
And if ther dide, certeyn so wrooth was she,
That she was out of alle charitee.
Hir coverchiefs ful fyne weren of ground;
I dorste swere they weyeden ten pound
That on a Sonday weren upon hir heed.   455
Hir hosen weren of fyn scarlet reed,
Ful streite yteyd, and shoes ful moyste and
    newe.
Boold was hir face, and fair, and reed of hewe.
She was a worthy womman al hir lyve: 459
Housbondes at chirche dore she hadde fyve,
Withouten oother compaignye in youthe, —
But therof nedeth nat to speke as nowthe.
And thries hadde she been at Jerusalem;
She hadde passed many a straunge strem;
At Rome she hadde been, and at Boloigne,   465
In Galice at Seint-Jame, and at Coloigne.
She koude muchel of wandrynge by the weye.
Gat-tothed was she, soothly for to seye.
Upon an amblere esily she sat,
Ywympled wel, and on hir heed an hat   470
As brood as is a bokeler or a targe;
A foot-mantel aboute hir hipes large,
And on hir feet a paire of spores sharpe.
In felaweshipe wel koude she laughe and carpe.
Of remedies of love she knew per chaunce,
For she koude of that art the olde daunce.   476

    A good man was ther of religioun,
And was a povre PERSOUN OF A TOUN,
But riche he was of hooly thoght and werk.
He was also a lerned man, a clerk,   480
That Cristes gospel trewely wolde preche;
His parisshens devoutly wolde he teche.
Benygne he was, and wonder diligent,
And in adversitee ful pacient,

And swich he was ypreved ofte sithes.   485
Ful looth were hym to cursen for his tithes,
But rather wolde he yeven, out of doute,
Unto his povre parisshens aboute
Of his offryng and eek of his substaunce.
He koude in litel thyng have suffisaunce.   490
Wyd was his parisshe, and houses fer asonder,
But he ne lefte nat, for reyn ne thonder,
In siknesse nor in meschief to visite
The ferreste in his parisshe, muche and lite,
Upon his feet, and in his hand a staf.   495
This noble ensample to his sheep he yaf,
That first he wroghte, and afterward he
        taughte.
Out of the gospel he tho wordes caughte,
And this figure he added eek therto,
That if gold ruste, what shal iren do?   500
For if a preest be foul, on whom we truste,
No wonder is a lewed man to ruste;
And shame it is, if a prest take keep,
A shiten shepherde and a clene sheep.
Wel oghte a preest ensample for to yive,   505
By his clennesse, how that his sheep sholde
        lyve.
He sette nat his benefice to hyre
And leet his sheep encombred in the myre
And ran to Londoun unto Seinte Poules
To seken hym a chaunterie for soules,   510
Or with a bretherhed to been withholde;
But dwelte at hoom, and kepte wel his folde,
So that the wolf ne made it nat myscarie;
He was a shepherde and noght a mercenarie.
And though he hooly were and vertuous,   515
He was to synful men nat despitous,
Ne of his speche daungerous ne digne,
But in his techyng discreet and benygne,
To drawen folk to hevene by fairnesse,
By good ensample, this was his bisynesse.   520
But it were any persone obstinat,
What so he were, of heigh or lough estat,
Hym wolde he snybben sharply for the nonys.
A bettre preest I trowe that nowher noon ys.
He waited after no pompe and reverence,   525
Ne maked him a spiced conscience,
But Cristes loore and his apostles twelve
He taughte, but first he folwed it hymselve.
    With hym ther was a PLOWMAN, was his
        brother,
That hadde ylad of dong ful many a fother;
A trewe swynkere and a good was he,   531
Lyvynge in pees and parfit charitee.
God loved he best with al his hoole herte
At alle tymes, thogh him gamed or smerte,
And thanne his neighebor right as hymselve.

He wolde thresshe, and therto dyke and delve,
For Cristes sake, for every povre wight,   537
Withouten hire, if it lay in his myght.
His tithes payde he ful faire and wel,
Bothe of his propre swynk and his catel.   540
In a tabard he rood upon a mere.
    Ther was also a REVE, and a MILLERE,
A SOMNOUR, and a PARDONER also,
A MAUNCIPLE, and myself — ther were namo.
    The MILLERE was a stout carl for the nones;
Ful byg he was of brawn, and eek of bones.   546
That proved wel, for over al ther he cam,
At wrastlynge he wolde have alwey the ram.
He was short-sholdred, brood, a thikke knarre;
Ther was no dore that he nolde heve of harre,
Or breke it at a rennyng with his heed.   551
His berd as any sowe or fox was reed,
And therto brood, as though it were a spade.
Upon the cop right of his nose he hade
A werte, and theron stood a toft of herys,   555
Reed as the brustles of a sowes erys;
His nosethirles blake were and wyde.
A swerd and bokeler bar he by his syde.
His mouth as greet was as a greet forneys.
He was a janglere and a goliardeys,   560
And that was moost of synne and harlotries.
Wel koude he stelen corn and tollen thries;
And yet he hadde a thombe of gold, pardee.
A whit cote and a blew hood wered he.   564
A baggepipe wel koude he blowe and sowne,
And therwithal he broghte us out of towne.
    A gentil MAUNCIPLE was ther of a temple,
Of which achatours myghte take exemple
For to be wise in byynge of vitaille;
For wheither that he payde or took by taille,
Algate he wayted so in his achaat   571
That he was ay biforn and in good staat.
Now is nat that of God a ful fair grace
That swich a lewed mannes wit shal pace
The wisdom of an heep of lerned men?   575
Of maistres hadde he mo than thries ten,
That weren of lawe expert and curious,
Of which ther were a duszeyne in that hous
Worthy to been stywardes of rente and lond
Of any lord that is in Engelond,   580
To make hym lyve by his propre good
In honour dettelees (but if he were wood),
Or lyve as scarsly as hym list desire;
And able for to helpen al a shire
In any caas that myghte falle or happe;   585
And yet this Manciple sette hir aller cappe.
    The REVE was a sclendre colerik man.
His berd was shave as ny as ever he kan;
His heer was by his erys ful round yshorn;

His top was dokked lyk a preest biforn   590
Ful longe were his legges and ful lene,
Ylyk a staf, ther was no calf ysene.
Wel koude he kepe a gerner and a bynne;
Ther was noon auditour koude on him wynne.
Wel wiste he by the droghte and by the reyn
The yeldynge of his seed and of his greyn.   596
His lordes sheep, his neet, his dayerye,
His swyn, his hors, his stoor, and his pultrye
Was hoolly in this Reves governynge,
And by his covenant yaf the rekenynge,   600
Syn that his lord was twenty yeer of age.
Ther koude no man brynge hym in arrerage.
Ther nas baillif, ne hierde, nor oother hyne,
That he ne knew his sleighte and his covyne;
They were adrad of hym as of the deeth.   605
His wonyng was ful faire upon an heeth;
With grene trees yshadwed was his place.
He koude bettre than his lord purchace.
Ful riche he was astored pryvely:
His lord wel koude he plesen subtilly,   610
To yeve and lene hym of his owene good,
And have a thank, and yet a cote and hood.
In youthe he hadde lerned a good myster;
He was a wel good wrighte, a carpenter.
This Reve sat upon a ful good stot,   615
That was al pomely grey and highte Scot.
A long surcote of pers upon he hade,
And by his syde he baar a rusty blade.
Of Northfolk was this Reve of which I telle,
Biside a toun men clepen Baldeswelle.   620
Tukked he was as is a frere aboute,
And evere he rood the hyndreste of oure route.
    A SOMONOUR was ther with us in that place,
That hadde a fyr-reed cherubynnes face,
For saucefleem he was, with eyen narwe.   625
As hoot he was and lecherous as a sparwe,
With scalled browes blake and piled berd.
Of his visage children were aferd.
Ther nas quyk-silver, lytarge, ne brymstoon,
Boras, ceruce, ne oille of tartre noon;   630
Ne oynement that wolde clense and byte,
That hym myghte helpen of his whelkes white,
Nor of the knobbes sittynge on his chekes.
Wel loved he garleek, oynons, and eek lekes,
And for to drynken strong wyn, reed as
        blood;   635
Thanne wolde he speke and crie as he were
        wood.
And whan that he wel dronken hadde the wyn,
Thanne wolde he speke no word but Latyn.
A fewe termes hadde he, two or thre,
That he had lerned out of som decree —   640
No wonder is, he herde it al the day;

And eek ye knowen wel how that a jay
Kan clepen "Watte" as wel as kan the pope.
But whoso koude in oother thyng hym grope,
Thanne hadde he spent al his philosophie;   645
Ay "*Questio quid iuris*" wolde he crie.
He was a gentil harlot and a kynde;
A bettre felawe sholde men noght fynde.
He wolde suffre for a quart of wyn
A good felawe to have his concubyn   650
A twelf month, and excuse hym atte fulle;
Ful prively a fynch eek koude he pulle.
And if he foond owher a good felawe,
He wolde techen him to have noon awe
In swich caas of the ercedekenes curs,   655
But if a mannes soule were in his purs;
For in his purs he sholde ypunysshed be.
"Purs is the ercedekenes helle," seyde he.
But wel I woot he lyed right in dede;   659
Of cursyng oghte ech gilty man him drede,
For curs wol slee right as assoillyng savith,
And also war hym of a *Significavit*.
In daunger hadde he at his owene gise
The yonge girles of the diocise,
And knew hir conseil, and was al hir reed.   665
A gerland hadde he set upon his heed
As greet as it were for an ale-stake.
A bokeleer hadde he maad hym of a cake.
    With hym ther rood a gentil PARDONER
Of Rouncivale, his freend and his compeer,   670
That streight was comen fro the court of Rome.
Ful loude he soong "Com hider, love, to me!"
This Somonour bar to hym a stif burdoun;
Was nevere trompe of half so greet a soun.
This Pardoner hadde heer as yelow as wex,   675
But smothe it heeng as dooth a strike of flex;
By ounces henge his lokkes that he hadde,
And therwith he his shuldres overspradde;
But thynne it lay, by colpons oon and oon.
But hood, for jolitee, wered he noon,   680
For it was trussed up in his walet.
Hym thoughte he rood al of the newe jet;
Dischevelee, save his cappe, he rood al bare.
Swiche glarynge eyen hadde he as an hare.
A vernycle hadde he sowed upon his cappe.
His walet lay biforn hym in his lappe,   686
Bretful of pardoun, comen from Rome al hoot.
A voys he hadde as smal as hath a goot.
No berd hadde he, ne nevere sholde have;
As smothe it was as it were late shave.   690
I trowe he were a geldyng or a mare.
But of his craft, fro Berwyk into Ware,
Ne was ther swich another pardoner.
For in his male he hadde a pilwe-beer,
Which that he seyde was Oure Lady veyl: 695

He seyde he hadde a gobet of the seyl
That Seint Peter hadde, whan that he wente
Upon the see, til Jhesu Crist hym hente.
He hadde a croys of latoun ful of stones,
And in a glas he hadde pigges bones.   700
But with thise relikes, whan that he fond
A povre person dwellynge upon lond,
Upon a day he gat hym moore moneye
Than that the person gat in monthes tweye;
And thus, with feyned flaterye and japes,   705
He made the person and the peple his apes.
But trewely to tellen atte laste,
He was in chirche a noble ecclesiaste.
Wel koude he rede a lessoun or a storie,
But alderbest he song an offertorie;   710
For wel he wiste, whan that song was songe,
He moste preche and wel affile his tonge
To wynne silver, as he ful wel koude;
Therefore he song the murierly and loude.   714
    Now have I toold you soothly, in a clause,
Th'estaat, th'array, the nombre, and eek the
        cause
Why that assembled was this compaignye
In Southwerk at this gentil hostelrye
That highte the Tabard, faste by the Belle.
But now is tyme to yow for to telle   720
How that we baren us that ilke nyght,
Whan we were in that hostelrie alyght;
And after wol I telle of our viage
And al the remenaunt of oure pilgrimage.
But first I pray yow, of youre curteisye,   725
That ye n'arette it nat my vileynye,
Thogh that I pleynly speke in this mateere,
To telle yow hir wordes and hir cheere,
Ne thogh I speke hir wordes proprely.
For this ye knowen al so wel as I,   730
Whoso shal telle a tale after a man,
He moot reherce as ny as evere he kan
Everich a word, if it be in his charge,
Al speke he never so rudeliche and large,
Or ellis he moot telle his tale untrewe,   735
Or feyne thyng, or fynde wordes newe.
He may nat spare, althogh he were his brother;
He moot as wel seye o word as another.
Crist spak hymself ful brode in hooly writ,
And wel ye woot no vileynye is it.   740
Eek Plato seith, whoso that kan hym rede,
The wordes moote be cosyn to the dede.
Also I prey yow to foryeve it me,
Al have I nat set folk in hir degree   744
Heere in this tale, as that they sholde stonde.
My wit is short, ye may wel understonde.
    Greet chiere made oure Hoost us everichon,
And to the soper sette he us anon.

He served us with vitaille at the beste;   749
Strong was the wyn, and wel to drynke us leste.
A semely man OURE HOOSTE was withalle
For to han been a marchal in an halle.
A large man he was with eyen stepe —
A fairer burgeys is ther noon in Chepe —   754
Boold of his speche, and wys, and wel ytaught,
And of manhod hym lakkede right naught.
Eek therto he was right a myrie man,
And after soper pleyen he bigan,
And spak of myrthe amonges othere thynges,
Whan that we hadde maad oure rekenynges,   760
And seyde thus: "Now, lordynges, trewely,
Ye been to me right welcome, hertely;
For by my trouthe, if that I shal nat lye,
I saugh nat this yeer so myrie a compaignye
Atones in this herberwe as is now.   765
Fayn wolde I doon yow myrthe, wiste I how.
And of a myrthe I am right now bythoght,
To doon yow ese, and it shal coste noght.
    Ye goon to Caunterbury — God yow speede,
The blisful martir quite yow youre meede!   770
And wel I woot, as ye goon by the weye,
Ye shapen yow to talen and to pleye;
For trewely, confort ne myrthe is noon
To ride by the weye doumb as a stoon;
And therfore wol I maken yow disport,   775
As I seyde erst, and doon yow som confort.
And if yow liketh alle by oon assent
For to stonden at my juggement,
And for to werken as I shal yow seye,
To-morwe, whan ye riden by the weye,   780
Now, by my fader soule that is deed,
But ye be myrie, I wol yeve yow myn heed!
Hoold up youre hondes, withouten moore
        speche."
    Oure conseil was nat longe for to seche.   784
Us thoughte it was noght worth to make it wys,
And graunted hym withouten moore avys,
And bad him seye his voirdit as hym leste.
"Lordynges," quod he, "now herkneth for the
        beste;
But taak it nought, I prey yow, in desdeyn.   789
This is the poynt, to speken short and pleyn,
That ech of yow, to shorte with oure weye,
In this viage shal telle tales tweye
To Caunterbury-ward, I mene it so,
And homward he shal tellen othere two,
Of aventures that whilom han bifalle.   795
And which of yow that bereth hym best of alle,
That is to seyn, that telleth in this caas
Tales of best sentence and moost solaas,
Shal have a soper at oure aller cost
Heere in this place, sittynge by this post,   800

Whan that we come agayn fro Caunterbury.
And for to make yow the moore mury,
I wol myselven goodly with yow ryde,
Right at myn owene cost, and be youre gyde;
And whoso wole my juggement withseye   805
Shal paye al that we spenden by the weye.
And if ye vouche sauf that it be so,
Tel me anon, withouten wordes mo,
And I wol erly shape me therfore."

   This thyng was graunted, and oure othes
      swore   810
With ful glad herte, and preyden hym also
That he wolde vouche sauf for to do so,
And that he wolde been oure governour,
And of oure tales juge and reportour,
And sette a soper at a certeyn pris,   815
And we wol reuled been at his devys
In heigh and lough; and thus by oon assent
We been acorded to his juggement.
And therupon the wyn was fet anon;
We dronken, and to reste wente echon,   820
Withouten any lenger taryynge.

   Amorwe, whan that day bigan to sprynge,
Up roos oure Hoost, and was oure aller cok,
And gadrede us togidre alle in a flok,
And forth we riden a litel moore than paas   825
Unto the wateryng of Seint Thomas;
And there oure Hoost bigan his hors areste
And seyde, "Lordynges, herkneth, if yow leste.
Ye woot youre foreward, and I it yow recorde.

If even-song and morwe-song accorde,   830
Lat se now who shal telle the firste tale.
As evere mote I drynke wyn or ale,
Whoso be rebel to my juggement
Shal paye for al that by the wey is spent.   834
Now draweth cut, er that we ferrer twynne;
He which that hath the shorteste shal bigynne.
Sire Knyght," quod he, "my mayster and my
      lord,
Now draweth cut, for that is myn accord.
Cometh neer," quod he, "my lady Prioresse.
And ye, sire Clerk, lat be youre shamefastnesse,
Ne studieth noght; ley hond to, every man!"
Anon to drawen every wight bigan,   842
And shortly for to tellen as it was,
Were it by aventure, or sort, or cas,
The sothe is this, the cut fil to the Knyght,   845
Of which ful blithe and glad was every wyght,
And telle he moste his tale, as was resoun,
By foreward and by composicioun,
As ye han herd; what nedeth wordes mo?
And whan this goode man saugh that it was so,
As he that wys was and obedient   851
To kepe his foreward by his free assent,
He seyde, "Syn I shal bigynne the game,
What, welcome be the cut, a Goddes name!
Now lat us ryde, and herkneth what I seye."   855
And with that word we ryden forth oure weye,
And he bigan with right a myrie cheere
His tale anon, and seyde as ye may heere.

The Knight's Tale

Heere bigynneth the Knyghtes Tale.

*Iamque domos patrias, Scithice post aspera gentis
Prelia, laurigero, &c.*

Whilom, as olde stories tellen us,
Ther was a duc that highte Theseus;   860
Of Atthenes he was lord and governour,
And in his tyme swich a conquerour,
That gretter was ther noon under the sonne.
Ful many a riche contree hadde he wonne;
What with his wysdom and his chivalrie,   865
He conquered al the regne of Femenye,
That whilom was ycleped Scithia,
And weddede the queene Ypolita,
And broghte hire hoom with hym in his contree

With muchel glorie and greet solempnytee,
And eek hir yonge suster Emelye.   87..
And thus with victorie and with melodye
Lete I this noble duc to Atthenes ryde,
And al his hoost in armes hym bisyde.

   And certes, if it nere to long to heere,   875
I wolde have toold yow fully the manere
How wonnen was the regne of Femenye
By Theseus and by his chivalrye;
And of the grete bataille for the nones
Bitwixen Atthenes and Amazones;   880

And how asseged was Ypolita,
The faire, hardy queene of Scithia;
And of the feste that was at hir weddynge,
And of the tempest at hir hoom-comynge;
But al that thyng I moot as now forbere.   885
I have, God woot, a large feeld to ere,
And wayke been the oxen in my plough.
The remenant of the tale is long ynough.
I wol nat letten eek noon of this route;
Lat every felawe telle his tale aboute,   890
And lat se now who shal the soper wynne;
And ther I lefte, I wol ayeyn bigynne.

    This duc, of whom I make mencioun,
Whan he was come almoost unto the toun,
In al his wele and in his mooste pride,   895
He was war, as he caste his eye aside,
Where that ther kneled in the heighe weye
A compaignye of ladyes, tweye and tweye,
Ech after oother, clad in clothes blake;
But swich a cry and swich a wo they make   900
That in this world nys creature lyvynge
That herde swich another waymentynge;
And of this cry they nolde nevere stenten
Til they the reynes of his brydel henten.
    "What folk been ye, that at myn hom-   905
        comynge
Perturben so my feste with criynge?"
Quod Theseus. "Have ye so greet envye
Of myn honour, that thus compleyne and crye?
Or who hath yow mysboden or offended?
And telleth me if it may been amended,   910
And why that ye been clothed thus in blak."
    The eldeste lady of hem alle spak,
Whan she hadde swowned with a deedly cheere,
That it was routhe for to seen and heere.
She seyde: "Lord, to whom Fortune hath yiven
Victorie, and as a conqueror to lyven,   916
Nat greveth us youre glorie and youre honour,
But we biseken mercy and socour.
Have mercy on oure wo and oure distresse!
Som drope of pitee, thurgh thy gentillesse,
Upon us wrecched wommen lat thou falle.   921
For, certes, lord, ther is noon of us alle,
That she ne hath been a duchesse or a queene.
Now be we caytyves, as it is wel seene,
Thanked be Fortune and hire false wheel,   925
That noon estaat assureth to be weel.
And certes, lord, to abyden youre presence,
Heere in this temple of the goddesse Clemence
We han ben waitynge al this fourtenyght.
Now help us, lord, sith it is in thy myght.   930
    I, wrecche, which that wepe and wayle thus,
Was whilom wyf to kyng Cappaneus,
That starf at Thebes—cursed be that day! —

And alle we that been in this array
And maken al this lamentacioun,   935
We losten alle oure housbondes at that toun,
Whil that the seege theraboute lay.
And yet now the olde Creon, weylaway!
That lord is now of Thebes the citee,
Fulfild of ire and of iniquitee,   940
He, for despit and for his tirannye,
To do the dede bodyes vileynye
Of alle oure lordes whiche that been yslawe,
Hath alle the bodyes on an heep ydrawe,
And wol nat suffren hem, by noon assent,   945
Neither to been yburyed nor ybrent,
But maketh houndes ete hem in despit."
    And with that word, withouten moore respit,
They fillen gruf and criden pitously,   949
"Have on us wrecched wommen som mercy,
And lat oure sorwe synken in thyn herte."
    This gentil duc doun from his courser sterte
With herte pitous, whan he herde hem speke.
Hym thoughte that his herte wolde breke,   954
Whan he saugh hem so pitous and so maat,
That whilom weren of so greet estaat;
And in his armes he hem alle up hente,
And hem conforteth in ful good entente,
And swoor his ooth, as he was trewe knyght,
He wolde doon so ferforthly his myght   960
Upon the tiraunt Creon hem to wreke,
That al the peple of Grece sholde speke
How Creon was of Theseus yserved
As he that hadde his deeth ful wel deserved.
And right anoon, withouten moore abood,   965
His baner he desplayeth, and forth rood
To Thebes-ward, and al his hoost biside.
No neer Atthenes wolde he go ne ride,
Ne take his ese fully half a day,
But onward on his wey that nyght he lay,   970
And sente anon Ypolita the queene,
And Emelye, hir yonge suster sheene,
Unto the toun of Atthenes to dwelle,
And forth he rit; ther is namoore to telle.
    The rede statue of Mars, with spere and   975
        targe,
So shyneth in his white baner large,
That alle the feeldes glyteren up and doun;
And by his baner born is his penoun
Of gold ful riche, in which ther was ybete   979
The Mynotaur, which that he slough in Crete.
Thus rit this duc, thus rit this conquerour,
And in his hoost of chivalrie the flour,
Til that he cam to Thebes and alighte
Faire in a feeld, ther as he thoughte to fighte.
But shortly for to speken of this thyng,   985
With Creon, which that was of Thebes kyng,

He faught, and slough hym manly as a knyght
In pleyn bataille, and putte the folk to flyght;
And by assaut he wan the citee after,
And rente adoun bothe wall and sparre and
    rafter;
And to the ladyes he restored agayn   991
The bones of hir housbondes that were slayn,
To doon obsequies, as was tho the gyse.
But it were al to longe for to devyse
The grete clamour and the waymentynge   995
That the ladyes made at the brennynge
Of the bodies, and the grete honour
That Theseus, the noble conquerour,
Dooth to the ladyes, whan they from hym
    wente;
But shortly for to telle is myn entente.   1000

    Whan that this worthy duc, this Theseus,
Hath Creon slayn, and wonne Thebes thus,
Stille in that feeld he took al nyght his reste,
And dide with al the contree as hym leste.

    To ransake in the taas of bodyes dede,   1005
Hem for to strepe of harneys and of wede,
The pilours diden bisynesse and cure
After the bataille and disconfiture.
And so bifel that in the taas they founde,   1009
Thurgh-girt with many a grevous blody
    wounde,
Two yonge knyghtes liggynge by and by,
Bothe in oon armes, wroght ful richely,
Of whiche two Arcita highte that oon,
And that oother knyght highte Palamon.
Nat fully quyke, ne fully dede they were,   1015
But by hir cote-armures and by hir gere
The heraudes knewe hem best in special
As they that weren of the blood roial
Of Thebes, and of sustren two yborn.
Out of the taas the pilours han hem torn,   1020
And han hem caried softe unto the tente
Of Theseus; and he ful soone hem sente
To Atthenes, to dwellen in prisoun
Perpetuelly, — he nolde no raunsoun.   1024
And whan this worthy duc hath thus ydon,
He took his hoost, and hoom he rit anon
With laurer crowned as a conquerour;
And ther he lyveth in joye and in honour
Terme of his lyf; what nedeth wordes mo?
And in a tour, in angwissh and in wo,   1030
This Palamon and his felawe Arcite
For everemoore; ther may no gold hem quite.

    This passeth yeer by yeer and day by day,
Till it fil ones, in a morwe of May,
That Emelye, that fairer was to sene   1035
Than is the lylie upon his stalke grene,
And fressher than the May with floures newe —

For with the rose colour stroof hire hewe,
I noot which was the fyner of hem two —
Er it were day, as was hir wone to do,   1040
She was arisen and al redy dight;
For May wole have no slogardie a-nyght.
The sesoun priketh every gentil herte,
And maketh hym out of his slep to sterte,
And seith "Arys, and do thyn observaunce."
This maked Emelye have remembraunce   1046
To doon honour to May, and for to ryse.
Yclothed was she fressh, for to devyse:
Hir yelow heer was broyded in a tresse
Bihynde hir bak, a yerde long, I gesse.   1050
And in the gardyn, at the sonne upriste,
She walketh up and doun, and as hire liste
She gadereth floures, party white and rede,
To make a subtil gerland for hire hede;
And as an aungel hevenysshly she soong.   1055
The grete tour, that was so thikke and stroong,
Which of the castel was the chief dongeoun,
(Ther as the knyghtes weren in prisoun
Of which I tolde yow and tellen shal)
Was evene joynant to the gardyn wal   1060
Ther as this Emelye hadde hir pleyynge.

    Bright was the sonne and cleer that morwen-
      ynge,
And Palamoun, this woful prisoner,
As was his wone, by leve of his gayler,
Was risen and romed in a chambre an heigh,
In which he al the noble citee seigh,   1066
And eek the gardyn, ful of braunches grene,
Ther as this fresshe Emelye the shene
Was in hire walk, and romed up and doun.
This sorweful prisoner, this Palamoun,   1070
Goth in the chambre romynge to and fro,
And to hymself compleynynge of his wo.
That he was born, ful ofte he seyde, "allas!"
And so bifel, by aventure or cas,   1074
That thurgh a wyndow, thikke of many a barre
Of iren greet and square as any sparre,
He cast his eye upon Emelya,
And therwithal he bleynte and cride, "A!"
As though he stongen were unto the herte.
And with that cry Arcite anon up sterte,   1080
And seyde, "Cosyn myn, what eyleth thee,
That art so pale and deedly on to see?
Why cridestow? Who hath thee doon offence?
For Goddes love, taak al in pacience
Oure prisoun, for it may noon oother be.   1085
Fortune hath yeven us this adversitee.
Som wikke aspect or disposicioun
Of Saturne, by som constellacioun,
Hath yeven us this, although we hadde it
    sworn;

So stood the hevene whan that we were
    born.   1090
We moste endure it; this is the short and
    playn."
    This Palamon answerde and seyde agayn:
"Cosyn, for sothe, of this opinioun
Thow hast a veyn ymaginacioun.
This prison caused me nat for to crye,   1095
But I was hurt right now thurghout myn ye
Into myn herte, that wol my bane be.
The fairnesse of that lady that I see
Yond in the gardyn romen to and fro
Is cause of al my criyng and my wo.   1100
I noot wher she be womman or goddesse,
But Venus is it soothly, as I gesse."
And therwithal on knees doun he fil,
And seyde: "Venus, if it be thy wil
Yow in this gardyn thus to transfigure   1105
Bifore me, sorweful, wrecched creature,
Out of this prisoun help that we may scapen.
And if so be my destynee be shapen
By eterne word to dyen in prisoun,
Of oure lynage have som compassioun,   1110
That is so lowe ybroght by tirannye."
And with that word Arcite gan espye
Wher as this lady romed to and fro,
And with that sighte hir beautee hurte hym so,
That, if that Palamon was wounded sore,   1115
Arcite is hurt as muche as he, or moore.
And with a sigh he seyde pitously:
"The fresshe beautee sleeth me sodeynly
Of hire that rometh in the yonder place,
And but I have hir mercy and hir grace,   1120
That I may seen hire atte leeste weye,
I nam but deed; ther nis namoore to seye."
    This Palamon, whan he tho wordes herde,
Dispitously he looked and answerde,   1124
"Wheither seistow this in ernest or in pley?"
    "Nay," quod Arcite, "in ernest, by my fey!
God helpe me so, me list ful yvele pleye."
    This Palamon gan knytte his browes tweye.
"It nere," quod he, "to thee no greet honour
For to be fals, ne for to be traitour   1130
To me, that am thy cosyn and thy brother
Ysworn ful depe, and ech of us til oother,
That nevere, for to dyen in the peyne,
Til that the deeth departe shal us tweyne,
Neither of us in love to hyndre oother,   1135
Ne in noon oother cas, my leeve brother;
But that thou sholdest trewely forthren me
In every cas, as I shal forthren thee, —
This was thyn ooth, and myn also, certeyn;
I woot right wel, thou darst it nat withseyn.
Thus artow of my conseil, out of doute,   1141

And now thow woldest falsly been aboute
To love my lady, whom I love and serve,
And evere shal til that myn herte sterve.
Nay, certes, false Arcite, thow shalt nat so.
I loved hire first, and tolde thee my wo   1146
As to my conseil and my brother sworn
To forthre me, as I have toold biforn.
For which thou art ybounden as a knyght
To helpen me, if it lay in thy myght,   1150
Or elles artow fals, I dar wel seyn."
    This Arcite ful proudly spak ageyn:
"Thow shalt," quod he, "be rather fals than I;
And thou art fals, I telle thee outrely,
For paramour I loved hire first er thow.   1155
What wiltow seyen? Thou woost nat yet now
Wheither she be a womman or goddesse!
Thyn is affeccioun of hoolynesse,
And myn is love, as to a creature;
For which I tolde thee myn aventure   1160
As to my cosyn and my brother sworn.
I pose that thow lovedest hire biforn;
Wostow nat wel the olde clerkes sawe,
That 'who shal yeve a lovere any lawe?'
Love is a gretter lawe, by my pan,   1165
Than may be yeve to any erthely man;
And therfore positif lawe and swich decree
Is broken al day for love in ech degree.
A man moot nedes love, maugree his heed.
He may nat fleen it, thogh he sholde be deed,
Al be she mayde, or wydwe, or elles wyf.   1171
And eek it is nat likly al thy lyf
To stonden in hir grace; namoore shal I;
For wel thou woost thyselven, verraily,
That thou and I be dampned to prisoun   1175
Perpetuelly; us gayneth no raunsoun.
We stryve as dide the houndes for the boon;
They foughte al day, and yet hir part was noon.
Ther cam a kyte, whil that they were so
    wrothe,
And baar awey the boon bitwixe hem bothe.
And therfore, at the kynges court, my brother,
Ech man for hymself, ther is noon oother. 1182
Love, if thee list, for I love and ay shal;
And soothly, leeve brother, this is al.
Heere in this prisoun moote we endure,   1185
And everich of us take his aventure."
    Greet was the strif and long bitwix hem
    tweye,
If that I hadde leyser for to seye,
But to th'effect. It happed on a day,
To telle it yow as shortly as I may,   1190
A worthy duc that highte Perotheus,
That felawe was unto duc Theseus
Syn thilke day that they were children lite,

Was come to Atthenes his felawe to visite,
And for to pleye as he was wont to do; 1195
For in this world he loved no man so,
And he loved hym als tendrely agayn.
So wel they lovede, as olde bookes sayn,
That whan that oon was deed, soothly to telle,
His felawe wente and soughte hym doun in
    helle, —
But of that storie list me nat to write. 1201
Duc Perotheus loved wel Arcite,
And hadde hym knowe at Thebes yeer by yere,
And finally at requeste and preyere
Of Perotheus, withouten any raunsoun, 1205
Duc Theseus hym leet out of prisoun
Frely to goon wher that hym liste over al,
In swich a gyse as I you tellen shal.
    This was the forward, pleynly for t'endite,
Bitwixen Theseus and hym Arcite 1210
That if so were that Arcite were yfounde
Evere in his lif, by day or nyght, oo stounde
In any contree of this Theseus,
And he were caught, it was acorded thus,
That with a swerd he sholde lese his heed.
Ther nas noon oother remedie ne reed; 1216
But taketh his leve, and homward he him
    spedde.
Lat hym be war! his nekke lith to wedde.
    How greet a sorwe suffreth now Arcite!
The deeth he feeleth thurgh his herte smyte;
He wepeth, wayleth, crieth pitously; 1221
To sleen hymself he waiteth prively.
He seyde, "Allas that day that I was born!
Now is my prisoun worse than biforn;
Now is me shape eternally to dwelle. 1225
Noght in purgatorie, but in helle.
Allas, that evere knew I Perotheus!
For elles hadde I dwelled with Theseus,
Yfetered in his prisoun everemo. 1229
Thanne hadde I been in blisse, and nat in wo.
Oonly the sighte of hire whom that I serve,
Though that I nevere hir grace may deserve,
Wolde han suffised right ynough for me.
O deere cosyn Palamon," quod he,
"Thyn is the victorie of this aventure. 1235
Ful blisfully in prison maistow dure, —
In prison? certes nay, but in paradys!
Wel hath Fortune yturned thee the dys,
That hast the sighte of hire, and I th'absence.
For possible is, syn thou hast hire presence,
And art a knyght, a worthy and an able, 1241
That by som cas, syn Fortune is chaungeable,
Thow maist to thy desir somtyme atteyne.
But I, that am exiled and bareyne
Of alle grace, and in so greet dispeir, 1245

That ther nys erthe, water, fir, ne eir,
Ne creature that of hem maked is,
That may me helpe or doon confort in this,
Wel oughte I sterve in wanhope and distresse.
Farwel my lif, my lust, and my gladnesse! 1250
    Allas, why pleynen folk so in commune
On purveiaunce of God, or of Fortune,
That yeveth hem ful ofte in many a gyse
Wel bettre than they kan hemself devyse?
Som man desireth for to han richesse, 1255
That cause is of his mordre or greet siknesse;
And som man wolde out of his prisoun fayn,
That in his hous is of his meynee slayn.
Infinite harmes been in this mateere. 1259
We witen nat what thing we preyen heere:
We faren as he that dronke is as a mous.
A dronke man woot wel he hath an hous,
But he noot which the righte wey is thider,
And to a dronke man the wey is slider.
And certes, in this world so faren we; 1265
We seken faste after felicitee,
But we goon wrong ful often, trewely.
Thus may we seyen alle, and namely I,
That wende and hadde a greet opinioun
That if I myghte escapen from prisoun, 1270
Thanne hadde I been in joye and perfit heele,
Ther now I am exiled fro my wele.
Syn that I may nat seen you, Emelye,
I nam but deed; ther nys no remedye."
    Upon that oother syde Palamon, 1275
Whan that he wiste Arcite was agon,
Swich sorwe he maketh that the grete tour
Resouneth of his youlyng and clamour.
The pure fettres on his shynes grete
Weren of his bittre, salte teeres wete. 1280
"Allas," quod he, "Arcita, cosyn myn,
Of al oure strif, God woot, the fruyt is thyn.
Thow walkest now in Thebes at thy large,
And of my wo thow yevest litel charge. 1284
Thou mayst, syn thou hast wisdom and man-
    hede,
Assemblen alle the folk of oure kynrede,
And make a werre so sharp on this citee,
That by som aventure or some tretee
Thow mayst have hire to lady and to wyf
For whom that I moste nedes lese my lyf. 1290
For, as by wey of possibilitee,
Sith thou art at thy large, of prisoun free,
And art a lord, greet is thyn avauntage
Moore than is myn, that sterve here in a cage.
For I moot wepe and wayle, whil I lyve, 1295
With al the wo that prison may me yive,
And eek with peyne that love me yeveth also,
That doubleth al my torment and my wo."

Therwith the fyr of jalousie up sterte   1299
Withinne his brest, and hente him by the herte
So woodly that he lyk was to biholde
The boxtree or the asshen dede and colde.

    Thanne seyde he, "O crueel goddes that
       governe
This world with byndyng of youre word eterne,
And writen in the table of atthamaunt   1305
Youre parlement and youre eterne graunt,
What is mankynde moore unto you holde
Than is the sheep that rouketh in the folde?
For slayn is man right as another beest,
And dwelleth eek in prison and arreest,   1310
And hath siknesse and greet adversitee,
And ofte tymes giltelees, pardee.
    What governance is in this prescience,
That giltelees tormenteth innocence?   1314
And yet encresseth this al my penaunce,
That man is bounden to his observaunce,
For Goddes sake, to letten of his wille,
Ther as a beest may al his lust fulfille.
And whan a beest is deed he hath no peyne;
But man after his deeth moot wepe and
      pleyne,   1320
Though in this world he have care and wo.
Withouten doute it may stonden so.
The answere of this lete I to dyvynys,
But wel I woot that in this world greet pyne ys.
Allas, I se a serpent or a theef,   1325
That many a trewe man hath doon mescheef,
Goon at his large, and where hym list may
      turne.
But I moot been in prisoun thurgh Saturne,
And eek thurgh Juno, jalous and eek wood,
That hath destroyed wel ny al the blood   1330
Of Thebes with his waste walles wyde;
And Venus sleeth me on that oother syde
For jalousie and fere of hym Arcite."
    Now wol I stynte of Palamon a lite,
And lete hym in his prisoun stille dwelle,   1335
And of Arcita forth I wol yow telle.
    The somer passeth, and the nyghtes longe
Encressen double wise the peynes stronge
Bothe of the lovere and the prisoner.
I noot which hath the wofuller mester.   1340
For, shortly for to seyn, this Palamoun
Perpetuelly is dampned to prisoun,
In cheynes and in fettres to been deed;
And Arcite is exiled upon his heed
For everemo, as out of that contree,   1345
Ne nevere mo he shal his lady see.
    Yow loveres axe I now this questioun:
Who hath the worse, Arcite or Palamoun?
That oon may seen his lady day by day,

But in prison he moot dwelle alway;   1350
That oother wher hym list may ride or go,
But seen his lady shal he nevere mo.
Now demeth as yow liste, ye that kan,
For I wol telle forth as I bigan.   1354

Explicit prima pars

Sequitur pars secunda

    Whan that Arcite to Thebes comen was,
Ful ofte a day he swelte and seyde "Allas!"
For seen his lady shal he nevere mo.
And shortly to concluden al his wo,
So muche sorwe hadde nevere creature   1359
That is, or shal, whil that the world may dure.
His slep, his mete, his drynke, is hym biraft,
That lene he wex and drye as is a shaft;
His eyen holwe, and grisly to biholde,
His hewe falow and pale as asshen colde,
And solitarie he was and evere allone,   1365
And waillynge al the nyght, makynge his mone;
And if he herde song or instrument,
Thanne wolde he wepe, he myghte nat be stent.
So feble eek were his spiritz, and so lowe,   1369
And chaunged so, that no man koude knowe
His speche nor his voys, though men it herde.
And in his geere for al the world he ferde,
Nat oonly lik the loveris maladye
Of Hereos, but rather lyk manye,
Engendred of humour malencolik,   1375
Biforen, in his celle fantastik.
And shortly, turned was al up so doun
Bothe habit and eek disposicioun
Of hym, this woful lovere daun Arcite.
    What sholde I al day of his wo endite?   1380
Whan he endured hadde a yeer or two
This crueel torment and this peyne and wo,
At Thebes, in his contree, as I seyde,
Upon a nyght in sleep as he hym leyde,   1384
Hym thoughte how that the wynged god Mer-
      curie
Biforn hym stood and bad hym to be murie.
His slepy yerde in hond he bar uprighte;
An hat he werede upon his heris brighte.
Arrayed was this god, as he took keep,
As he was whan that Argus took his sleep;   1390
And seyde hym thus: "To Atthenes shaltou
      wende,
Ther is thee shapen of thy wo an ende."
And with that word Arcite wook and sterte.
"Now trewely, hou soore that me smerte,"   1394
Quod he, "to Atthenes right now wol I fare,
Ne for the drede of deeth shal I nat spare
To se my lady, that I love and serve.

In hire presence I recche nat to sterve."
  And with that word he caughte a greet
          mirour,   1399
And saugh that chaunged was al his colour,
And saugh his visage al in another kynde.
And right anon it ran hym in his mynde,
That, sith his face was so disfigured
Of maladye the which he hadde endured,
He myghte wel, if that he bar hym lowe,   1405
Lyve in Atthenes everemoore unknowe.
And seen his lady wel ny day by day.
And right anon he chaunged his array,
And cladde hym as a povre laborer,
And al allone, save oonly a squier   1410
That knew his privetee and al his cas,
Which was disguised povrely as he was,
To Atthenes is he goon the nexte way.
And to the court he wente upon a day,
And at the gate he profreth his servyse   1415
To drugge and drawe, what so men wol devyse.
And shortly of this matere for to seyn,
He fil in office with a chamberleyn
The which that dwellynge was with Emelye;
For he was wys and koude soone espye   1420
Of every servaunt which that serveth here.
Wel koude he hewen wode, and water bere,
For he was yong and myghty for the nones,
And therto he was long and big of bones
To doon that any wight kan hym devyse.   1425
A yeer or two he was in this servyse,
Page of the chambre of Emelye the brighte;
And Philostrate he seyde that he highte.
But half so wel biloved a man as he
Ne was ther nevere in court of his degree;
He was so gentil of condicioun   1431
That thurghout al the court was his renoun.
They seyden that it were a charitee
That Theseus wolde enhauncen his degree,
And putten hym in worshipful servyse,   1435
Ther as he myghte his vertu excercise.
And thus withinne a while his name is spronge,
Bothe of his dedes and his goode tonge,
That Theseus hath taken hym so neer,   1439
That of his chambre he made hym a squier,
And gaf hym gold to mayntene his degree.
And eek men broghte hym out of his contree,
From yeer to yeer, ful pryvely his rente;
But honestly and slyly he it spente,   1444
That no man wondred how that he it hadde.
And thre yeer in this wise his lif he ladde,
And bar hym so, in pees and eek in werre,
Ther was no man that Theseus hath derre.
And in this blisse lete I now Arcite,
And speke I wole of Palamon a lite.   1450

In derknesse and horrible and strong prisoun
Thise seven yeer hath seten Palamoun
Forpyned, what for wo and for distresse.
Who feeleth double soor and hevynesse
But Palamon, that love destreyneth so   1455
That wood out of his wit he goth for wo?
And eek therto he is a prisoner
Perpetuelly, noght oonly for a yer.
  Who koude ryme in Englyssh proprely
His martirdom? for sothe it am nat I;   1460
Therfore I passe as lightly as I may.
  It fel that in the seventhe yer, of May
The thridde nyght, (as olde bookes seyn,
That al this storie tellen moore pleyn)
Were it by aventure or destynee —   1465
As, whan a thyng is shapen, it shal be —
That soone after the mydnyght Palamoun,
By helpyng of a freend, brak his prisoun
And fleeth the citee faste as he may go.
For he hadde yeve his gayler drynke so   1470
Of a clarree maad of a certeyn wyn,
With nercotikes and opie of Thebes fyn,
That al that nyght, thogh that men wolde him
          shake,
The gayler sleep, he myghte nat awake;   1474
And thus he fleeth as faste as evere he may.
The nyght was short and faste by the day,
That nedes cost he moot hymselven hyde;
And til a grove faste ther bisyde
With dredeful foot thanne stalketh Palamon.
For, shortly, this was his opinion,   1480
That in that grove he wolde hym hyde al day,
And in the nyght thanne wolde he take his way
To Thebes-ward, his freendes for to preye
On Theseus to helpe him to werreye;
And shortly, outher he wolde lese his lif,   1485
Or wynnen Emelye unto his wyf.
This is th'effect and his entente pleyn.
  Now wol I turne to Arcite ageyn,
That litel wiste how ny that was his care,   1489
Til that Fortune had broght him in the snare.
  The bisy larke, messager of day,
Salueth in hir song the morwe gray,
And firy Phebus riseth up so bright
That al the orient laugheth of the light,
And with his stremes dryeth in the greves   1495
The silver dropes hangynge on the leves.
And Arcita, that in the court roial
With Theseus is squier principal,
Is risen and looketh on the myrie day.
And for to doon his observaunce to May,   1500
Remembrynge on the poynt of his desir,
He on a courser, startlynge as the fir,
Is riden into the feeldes hym to pleye,

Out of the court, were it a myle or tweye.
And to the grove of which that I yow tolde
By aventure his wey he gan to holde,   1506
To maken hym a gerland of the greves
Were it of wodebynde or hawethorn leves,
And loude he song ayeyn the sonne shene:
"May, with alle thy floures and thy grene,
Welcome be thou, faire, fresshe May,   1511
In hope that I som grene gete may."
And from his courser, with a lusty herte,
Into the grove ful hastily he sterte,
And in a path he rometh up and doun,   1515
Ther as by aventure this Palamoun
Was in a bussh, that no man myghte hym se,
For soore afered of his deeth was he.
No thyng ne knew he that it was Arcite;
God woot he wolde have trowed it ful lite.
But sooth is seyd, go sithen many yeres,   1521
That "feeld hath eyen and the wode hath eres."
It is ful fair a man to bere hym evene,
For al day meeteth men at unset stevene.
Ful litel woot Arcite of his felawe,   1525
That was so ny to herknen al his sawe,
For in the bussh he sitteth now ful stille.
    Whan that Arcite hadde romed al his fille,
And songen al the roundel lustily,
Into a studie he fil sodeynly,   1530
As doon thise loveres in hir queynte geres,
Now in the crope, now doun in the breres,
Now up, now doun, as boket in a welle.
Right as the Friday, soothly for to telle,
Now it shyneth, now it reyneth faste,   1535
Right so kan geery Venus overcaste
The hertes of hir folk; right as hir day
Is gereful, right so chaungeth she array.
Selde is the Friday al the wowke ylike.   1539
    Whan that Arcite had songe, he gan to sike,
And sette hym doun withouten any moore.
"Allas," quod he, "that day that I was bore!
How longe, Juno, thurgh thy crueltee,
Woltow werreyen Thebes the citee?
Allas, ybroght is to confusioun   1545
The blood roial of Cadme and Amphioun, —
Of Cadmus, which that was the firste man
That Thebes bulte, or first the toun bigan,
And of the citee first was crouned kyng.
Of his lynage am I and his ofspryng   1550
By verray ligne, as of the stok roial,
And now I am so caytyf and so thral,
That he that is my mortal enemy,
I serve hym as his squier povrely.
And yet dooth Juno me wel moore shame,   1555
For I dar noght biknowe myn owene name;
But ther as I was wont to highte Arcite,

Now highte I Philostrate, noght worth a myte.
Allas, thou felle Mars! allas, Juno!
Thus hath youre ire oure lynage al fordo,   1560
Save oonly me and wrecched Palamoun,
That Theseus martireth in prisoun.
And over al this, to sleen me outrely,
Love hath his firy dart so brennyngly
Ystiked thurgh my trewe, careful herte,   1565
That shapen was my deeth erst than my sherte.
Ye sleen me with youre eyen, Emelye!
Ye been the cause wherfore that I dye.
Of al the remenant of myn oother care
Ne sette I nat the montance of a tare,   1570
So that I koude doon aught to youre ples-
        aunce."
And with that word he fil doun in a traunce
A longe tyme, and after he up sterte.
    This Palamoun, that thoughte that thurgh his
        herte
He felte a coold swerd sodeynliche glyde,   1575
For ire he quook, no lenger wolde he byde.
And whan that he had herd Arcites tale,
As he were wood, with face deed and pale,
He stirte hym up out of the buskes thikke,
And seide: "Arcite, false traytour wikke,   1580
Now artow hent, that lovest my lady so,
For whom that I have al this peyne and wo,
And art my blood, and to my conseil sworn,
As I ful ofte have told thee heerbiforn,
And hast byjaped heere duc Theseus,   1585
And falsly chaunged hast thy name thus!
I wol be deed, or elles thou shalt dye.
Thou shalt nat love my lady Emelye,
But I wol love hire oonly and namo;
For I am Palamon, thy mortal foo.   1590
And though that I no wepene have in this
        place,
But out of prison am astert by grace,
I drede noght that outher thow shalt dye,
Or thow ne shalt nat loven Emelye.
Chees which thou wolt, for thou shalt nat
        asterte!"   1595
    This Arcite, with ful despitous herte,
Whan he hym knew, and hadde his tale herd,
As fiers as leon pulled out his swerd,
And seyde thus: "By God that sit above,
Nere it that thou art sik and wood for love, 1600
And eek that thow no wepne hast in this place,
Thou sholdest nevere out of this grove pace,
That thou ne sholdest dyen of myn hond.
For I defye the seurete and the bond   1604
Which that thou seist that I have maad to thee.
What, verray fool, thynk wel that love is free,
And I wol love hire maugree al thy myght!

But for as muche thou art a worthy knyght;
And wilnest to darreyne hire by bataille,
Have heer my trouthe, tomorwe I wol nat faille,
Withoute wityng of any oother wight, 1611
That heere I wol be founden as a knyght,
And bryngen harneys right ynough for thee;
And ches the beste, and leef the worste for me.
And mete and drynke this nyght wol I
    brynge 1615
Ynough for thee, and clothes for thy beddynge.
And if so be that thou my lady wynne,
And sle me in this wode ther I am inne,
Thow mayst wel have thy lady as for me."
    This Palamon answerde, "I graunte it thee."
And thus they been departed til amorwe, 1621
Whan ech of hem had leyd his feith to borwe.
    O Cupide, out of alle charitee!
O regne, that wolt no felawe have with thee!
Ful sooth is seyd that love ne lordshipe 1625
Wol noght, his thankes, have no felaweshipe.
Wel fynden that Arcite and Palamoun.
Arcite is riden anon unto the toun,
And on the morwe, er it were dayes light,
Ful prively two harneys hath he dight, 1630
Bothe suffisaunt and mete to darreyne
The bataille in the feeld bitwix hem tweyne;
And on his hors, allone as he was born,
He carieth al the harneys hym biforn.
And in the grove, at tyme and place yset, 1635
This Arcite and this Palamon ben met.
Tho chaungen gan the colour in hir face,
Right as the hunters in the regne of Trace,
That stondeth at the gappe with a spere,
Whan hunted is the leon or the bere, 1640
And hereth hym come russhyng in the greves,
And breketh bothe bowes and the leves,
And thynketh, "Heere cometh my mortal en-
    emy!
Withoute faille, he moot be deed, or I; 1644
For outher I moot sleen hym at the gappe,
Or he moot sleen me, if that me myshappe," —
So ferden they in chaungyng of hir hewe,
As fer as everich of hem oother knewe.
    Ther nas no good day, ne no saluyng, 1649
But streight, withouten word or rehersyng,
Everich of hem heelp for to armen oother
As freendly as he were his owene brother;
And after that, with sharpe speres stronge
They foynen ech at oother wonder longe.
Thou myghtest wene that this Palamon 1655
In his fightyng were a wood leon,
And as a crueel tigre was Arcite;
As wilde bores gonne they to smyte,
That frothen whit as foom for ire wood.

Up to the ancle foghte they in hir blood. 1660
And in this wise I lete hem fightyng dwelle,
And forth I wole of Theseus yow telle.
    The destinee, ministre general,
That executeth in the world over al 1664
The purveiaunce that God hath seyn biforn,
So strong it is that, though the world had sworn
The contrarie of a thyng by ye or nay,
Yet somtyme it shal fallen on a day
That falleth nat eft withinne a thousand yeer.
For certeinly, oure appetites heer, 1670
Be it of werre, or pees, or hate, or love,
Al is this reuled by the sighte above.
    This mene I now by myghty Theseus,
That for to hunten is so desirus,
And namely at the grete hert in May, 1675
That in his bed ther daweth hym no day
That he nys clad, and redy for to ryde
With hunte and horn and houndes hym bisyde.
For in his huntyng hath he swich delit
That it is al his joye and appetit 1680
To been hymself the grete hertes bane,
For after Mars he serveth now Dyane.
    Cleer was the day, as I have toold er this,
And Theseus with alle joye and blis,
With his Ypolita, the faire queene, 1685
And Emelye, clothed al in grene,
On huntyng be they riden roially.
And to the grove that stood ful faste by,
In which ther was an hert, as men hym tolde,
Duc Theseus the streighte wey hath holde.
And to the launde he rideth hym ful right, 1691
For thider was the hert wont have his flight,
And over a brook, and so forth on his weye.
This duc wol han a cours at hym or tweye
With houndes swiche as that hym list com-
    aunde. 1695
    And whan this duc was come unto the
    launde,
Under the sonne he looketh, and anon
He was war of Arcite and Palamon,
That foughten breme, as it were bores two.
The brighte swerdes wenten to and fro 1700
So hidously that with the leeste strook
It semed as it wolde felle an ook.
But what they were, no thyng he ne woot.
This duc his courser with his spores smoot,
And at a stert he was bitwix hem two, 1705
And pulled out a swerd, and cride, "Hoo!
Namoore, up peyne of lesynge of youre heed!
By myghty Mars, he shal anon be deed
That smyteth any strook that I may seen.
But telleth me what myster men ye been, 1710
That been so hardy for to fighten heere

Withouten juge or oother officere,
As it were in a lystes roially."
    This Palamon answerde hastily,   1714
And seyde, "Sire, what nedeth wordes mo?
We have the deeth disserved bothe two.
Two woful wrecches been we, two caytyves,
That been encombred of oure owene lyves;
And as thou art a rightful lord and juge,
Ne yif us neither mercy ne refuge,   1720
But sle me first, for seinte charitee!
But sle my felawe eek as wel as me;
Or sle hym first, for though thow knowest it
    lite,
This is thy mortal foo, this is Arcite,   1724
That fro thy lond is banysshed on his heed,
For which he hath deserved to be deed.
For this is he that cam unto thy gate
And seyde that he highte Philostrate.
Thus hath he japed thee ful many a yer,
And thou hast maked hym thy chief squier;
And this is he that loveth Emelye.   1731
For sith the day is come that I shal dye,
I make pleynly my confessioun
That I am thilke woful Palamoun
That hath thy prisoun broken wikkedly.   1735
I am thy mortal foo, and it am I
That loveth so hoote Emelye the brighte
That I wol dye present in hir sighte.
Wherfore I axe deeth and my juwise;
But sle my felawe in the same wise,   1740
For bothe han we deserved to be slayn."
    This worthy duc answerde anon agayn,
And seyde, "This is a short conclusioun.
Youre owene mouth, by youre confessioun,
Hath dampned yow, and I wol it recorde;   1745
It nedeth noght to pyne yow with the corde.
Ye shal be deed, by myghty Mars the rede!"
    The queene anon, for verray wommanhede,
Gan for to wepe, and so dide Emelye,
And alle the ladyes in the compaignye.   1750
Greet pitee was it, as it thoughte hem alle,
That evere swich a chaunce sholde falle;
For gentil men they were of greet estaat,
And no thyng but for love was this debaat;
And saugh hir blody woundes wyde and soore,
And alle crieden, bothe lasse and moore,   1756
"Have mercy, Lord, upon us wommen alle!"
And on hir bare knees adoun they falle,
And wolde have kist his feet ther as he stood;
Til at the laste aslaked was his mood,   1760
For pitee renneth soone in gentil herte.
And though he first for ire quook and sterte,
He hath considered shortly, in a clause,
The trespas of hem bothe, and eek the cause,

And although that his ire hir gilt accused,   1765
Yet in his resoun he hem bothe excused,
As thus: he thoghte wel that every man
Wol helpe hymself in love, if that he kan,
And eek delivere hymself out of prisoun.
And eek his herte hadde compassioun   1770
Of wommen, for they wepen evere in oon;
And in his gentil herte he thoughte anon,
And softe unto hymself he seyde, "Fy
Upon a lord that wol have no mercy,
But been a leon, bothe in word and dede,   1775
To hem that been in repentaunce and drede,
As wel as to a proud despitous man
That wol mayntene that he first bigan.
That lord hath litel of discrecioun,
That in swich cas kan no divisioun,   1780
But weyeth pride and humblesse after oon."
And shortly, whan his ire is thus agoon,
He gan to looken up with eyen lighte,
And spak thise same wordes al on highte:
    "The god of love, a, *benedicite!*   1785
How myghty and how greet a lord is he!
Ayeyns his myght ther gayneth none obstacles.
He may be cleped a god for his myracles;
For he kan maken, at his owene gyse,
Of everich herte as that hym list divyse.   1790
Lo heere this Arcite and this Palamoun,
That quitly weren out of my prisoun,
And myghte han lyved in Thebes roially,
And witen I am hir mortal enemy,
And that hir deth lith in my myght also;   1795
And yet hath love, maugree hir eyen two,
Broght hem hyder bothe for to dye.
Now looketh, is nat that an heigh folye?
Who may been a fool, but if he love?
Bihoold, for Goddes sake that sit above,   1800
Se how they blede! be they noght wel arrayed?
Thus hath hir lord, the god of love, ypayed
Hir wages and hir fees for hir servyse!
And yet they wenen for to been ful wyse
That serven love, for aught that may bifalle.
But this is yet the beste game of alle,   1806
That she for whom they han this jolitee
Kan hem therfore as muche thank as me.
She woot namoore of al this hoote fare,
By God, than woot a cokkow or an hare!   1810
But all moot ben assayed, hoot and coold;
A man moot ben a fool, or yong or oold, —
I woot it by myself ful yore agon,
For in my tyme a servant was I oon.
And therfore, syn I knowe of loves peyne,   1815
And woot hou soore it kan a man distreyne,
As he that hath ben caught ofte in his laas,
I yow foryeve al hoolly this trespaas,

At requeste of the queene, that kneleth heere,
And eek of Emelye, my suster deere. 1820
And ye shul bothe anon unto me swere
That nevere mo ye shal my contree dere,
Ne make werre upon me nyght ne day,
But been my freendes in all that ye may.
I yow foryeve this trespas every deel." 1825
And they hym sworen his axyng faire and weel,
And hym of lordshipe and of mercy preyde,
And he hem graunteth grace, and thus he
    seyde:
"To speke of roial lynage and richesse,
Though that she were a queene or a princesse,
Ech of you bothe is worthy, doutelees, 1831
To wedden whan tyme is, but nathelees
I speke as for my suster Emelye,
For whom ye have this strif and jalousye.
Ye woot yourself she may nat wedden two 1835
Atones, though ye fighten everemo.
That oon of you, al be hym looth or lief,
He moot go pipen in an yvy leef;
This is to seyn, she may nat now han bothe,
Al be ye nevere so jalouse ne so wrothe. 1840
And forthy I yow putte in this degree,
That ech of yow shal have his destynee
As hym is shape, and herkneth in what wyse;
Lo heere youre ende of that I shal devyse.
    My wyl is this, for plat conclusioun, 1845
Withouten any repplicacioun, —
If that you liketh, take it for the beste:
That everich of you shal goon where hym leste
Frely, withouten raunson or daunger;
And this day fifty wykes, fer ne ner, 1850
Everich of you shal brynge an hundred
    knyghtes
Armed for lystes up at alle rightes,
Al redy to darreyne hire by bataille.
And this bihote I yow withouten faille,
Upon my trouthe, and as I am a knyght, 1855
That wheither of yow bothe that hath
    myght, —
This is to seyn, that wheither he or thow
May with his hundred, as I spak of now,
Sleen his contrarie, or out of lystes dryve,
Thanne shal I yeve Emelya to wyve 1860
To whom that Fortune yeveth so fair a grace.
The lystes shal I maken in this place,
And God so wisly on my soule rewe,
As I shal evene juge been and trewe. 1864
Ye shul noon oother ende with me maken,
That oon of yow ne shal be deed or taken.
And if yow thynketh this is weel ysayd,
Seyeth youre avys, and holdeth you apayd.
This is youre ende and youre conclusioun."

Who looketh lightly now but Palamoun?
Who spryngeth up for joye but Arcite? 1871
Who kouthe telle, or who kouthe it endite,
The joye that is maked in the place
Whan Theseus hath doon so fair a grace? 1874
But doun on knees wente every maner wight,
And thonked hym with al hir herte and myght,
And namely the Thebans often sithe.
And thus with good hope and with herte blithe
They taken hir leve, and homward gonne they
    ride
To Thebes, with his olde walles wyde. 1880

Explicit secunda pars

Sequitur pars tercia

I trowe men wolde deme it necligence
If I foryete to tellen the dispence
Of Theseus, that gooth so bisily
To maken up the lystes roially,
That swich a noble theatre as it was, 1885
I dar wel seyen in this world ther nas.
The circuit a myle was aboute,
Walled of stoon, and dyched al withoute.
Round was the shap, in manere of compas,
Ful of degrees, the heighte of sixty pas, 1890
That whan a man was set on o degree,
He letted nat his felawe for to see.
    Estward ther stood a gate of marbul whit,
Westward right swich another in the opposit.
And shortly to concluden, swich a place 1895
Was noon in erthe, as in so litel space;
For in the lond ther was no crafty man
That geometrie or ars-metrike kan,
Ne portreyour, ne kervere of ymages,
That Theseus ne yaf him mete and wages,
The theatre for to maken and devyse. 1901
And for to doon his ryte and sacrifise,
He estward hath, upon the gate above,
In worshipe of Venus, goddesse of love,
Doon make an auter and an oratorie; 1905
And on the gate westward, in memorie
Of Mars, he maked hath right swich another,
That coste largely of gold a fother.
And northward, in a touret on the wal,
Of alabastre whit and reed coral, 1910
An oratorie, riche for to see,
In worshipe of Dyane of chastitee,
Hath Theseus doon wroght in noble wyse.
    But yet hadde I foryeten to devyse
The noble kervyng and the portreitures, 1915
The shap, the contenaunce, and the figures,
That weren in thise oratories thre.

First in the temple of Venus maystow se
Wroght on the wal, ful pitous to biholde,
The broken slepes, and the sikes colde,   1920
The sacred teeris, and the waymentynge,
The firy strokes of the desirynge
That loves servantz in this lyf enduren;
The othes that hir covenantz assuren;   1924
Plesaunce and Hope, Desir, Foolhardynesse,
Beautee and Youthe, Bauderie, Richesse,
Charmes and Force, Lesynges, Flaterye,
Despense, Bisynesse, and Jalousye,
That wered of yelewe gooldes a gerland,
And a cokkow sittynge on hir hand;   1930
Festes, instrumentz, caroles, daunces,
Lust and array, and alle the circumstaunces
Of love, which that I rekned and rekne shal,
By ordre weren peynted on the wal,
And mo than I kan make of mencioun.   1935
For soothly al the mount of Citheroun,
Ther Venus hath hir principal dwellynge,
Was shewed on the wal in portreyynge,
With al the gardyn and the lustynesse.
Nat was foryeten the porter, Ydelnesse,   1940
Ne Narcisus the faire of yore agon,
Ne yet the folye of kyng Salomon,
Ne yet the grete strengthe of Ercules —
Th'enchauntementz of Medea and Circes —
Ne of Turnus, with the hardy fiers corage,
The riche Cresus, kaytyf in servage.   1946
Thus may ye seen that wysdom ne richesse,
Beautee ne sleighte, strengthe ne hardynesse,
Ne may with Venus holde champartie,   1949
For as hir list the world than may she gye.
Lo, alle thise folk so caught were in hir las,
Til they for wo ful ofte seyde "allas!"
Suffiseth heere ensamples oon or two,
And though I koude rekene a thousand mo.
     The statue of Venus, glorious for to se,   1955
Was naked, fletynge in the large see,
And fro the navele doun al covered was
With wawes grene, and brighte as any glas.
A citole in hir right hand hadde she,
And on hir heed, ful semely for to se,   1960
A rose gerland, fressh and wel smellynge;
Above hir heed hir dowves flikerynge.
Biforn hire stood hir sone Cupido;
Upon his shuldres wynges hadde he two,
And blynd he was, as it is often seene;   1965
A bowe he bar and arwes brighte and kene.
     Why sholde I noght as wel eek telle yow al
The portreiture that was upon the wal
Withinne the temple of myghty Mars the rede?
Al peynted was the wal, in lengthe and brede,
Lyk to the estres of the grisly place   1971

That highte the grete temple of Mars in Trace,
In thilke colde, frosty regioun
Ther as Mars hath his sovereyn mansioun.
     First on the wal was peynted a forest,   1975
In which ther dwelleth neither man ne best,
With knotty, knarry, bareyne trees olde,
Of stubbes sharpe and hidouse to biholde,
In which ther ran a rumbel in a swough,   1979
As though a storm sholde bresten every bough.
And dounward from an hille, under a bente,
Ther stood the temple of Mars armypotente,
Wroght al of burned steel, of which the entree
Was long and streit, and gastly for to see.
And therout came a rage and swich a veze
That it made al the gate for to rese.   1986
The northren lyght in at the dores shoon,
For wyndowe on the wal ne was ther noon,
Thurgh which men myghten any light discerne.
The dore was al of adamant eterne,   1990
Yclenched overthwart and endelong
With iren tough; and for to make it strong,
Every pyler, the temple to sustene,
Was tonne-greet, of iren bright and shene.
     Ther saugh I first the derke ymaginyng
Of Felonye, and al the compassyng;   1996
The crueel Ire, reed as any gleede;
The pykepurs, and eek the pale Drede;
The smylere with the knyf under the cloke;
The shepne brennynge with the blake
       smoke;   2000
The tresoun of the mordrynge in the bedde;
The open werre, with woundes al bibledde;
Contek, with blody knyf and sharp manace.
Al ful of chirkyng was that sory place.   2004
The sleere of hymself yet saugh I ther, —
His herte-blood hath bathed al his heer;
The nayl ydryven in the shode a-nyght;
The colde deeth, with mouth gapyng upright.
Amyddes of the temple sat Meschaunce,
With disconfort and sory contenaunce.   2010
Yet saugh I Woodnesse, laughynge in his rage,
Armed Compleint, Outhees, and fiers Outrage;
The careyne in the busk, with throte ycorve;
A thousand slayn, and nat of qualm ystorve;
The tiraunt, with the pray by force yraft;   2015
The toun destroyed, ther was no thyng laft.
Yet saugh I brent the shippes hoppesteres;
The hunte strangled with the wilde beres;
The sowe freten the child right in the cradel;
The cook yscalded, for al his longe ladel.   2020
Noght was foryeten by the infortune of Marte
The cartere overryden with his carte:
Under the wheel ful lowe he lay adoun.
Ther were also, of Martes divisioun,   2024

The barbour, and the bocher, and the smyth,
That forgeth sharpe swerdes on his styth.
And al above, depeynted in a tour,
Saugh I Conquest, sittynge in greet honour,
With the sharpe swerd over his heed
Hangynge by a soutil twynes threed.   2030
Depeynted was the slaughtre of Julius,
Of grete Nero, and of Antonius;
Al be that thilke tyme they were unborn,
Yet was hir deth depeynted ther-biforn
By manasynge of Mars, right by figure.   2035
So was it shewed in that portreiture,
As is depeynted in the sterres above
Who shal be slayn or elles deed for love.
Suffiseth oon ensample in stories olde;   2039
I may nat rekene hem alle though I wolde.
    The statue of Mars upon a carte stood
Armed, and looked grym as he were wood;
And over his heed ther shynen two figures
Of sterres, that been cleped in scriptures,
That oon Puella, that oother Rubeus —   2045
This god of armes was arrayed thus.
A wolf ther stood biforn hym at his feet
With eyen rede, and of a man he eet;
With soutil pencel depeynted was this storie
In redoutynge of Mars and of his glorie.   2050
    Now to the temple of Dyane the chaste,
As shortly as I kan, I wol me haste,
To telle yow al the descripsioun.
Depeynted been the walles up and doun
Of huntyng and of shamefast chastitee.   2055
Ther saugh I how woful Calistopee,
Whan that Diane agreved was with here,
Was turned from a womman til a bere,
And after was she maad the loode-sterre;   2059
Thus was it peynted, I kan sey yow no ferre.
Hir sone is eek a sterre, as men may see.
Ther saugh I Dane, yturned til a tree, —
I mene nat the goddesse Diane,
But Penneus doghter, which that highte Dane.
Ther saugh I Attheon an hert ymaked,   2065
For vengeaunce that he saugh Diane al naked;
I saugh how that his houndes have hym caught
And freeten hym, for that they knewe hym
    naught.
Yet peynted was a litel forther moor
How Atthalante hunted the wilde boor,   2070
And Meleagre, and many another mo,
For which Dyane wroghte hym care and wo.
Ther saugh I many another wonder storie,
The which me list nat drawen to memorie.
    This goddesse on an hert ful hye seet,   2075
With smale houndes al aboute hir feet;
And undernethe hir feet she hadde a moone, —

Wexynge it was and sholde wanye soone.
In gaude grene hir statue clothed was,
With bowe in honde, and arwes in a cas.   2080
Hir eyen caste she ful lowe adoun,
Ther Pluto hath his derke regioun.
A womman travaillynge was hire biforn;
But for hir child so longe was unborn,
Ful pitously Lucyna gan she calle,   2085
And seyde, "Help, for thou mayst best of alle!"
Wel koude he peynten lifly that it wroghte;
With many a floryn he the hewes boghte.
    Now been thise lystes maad, and Theseus,
That at his grete cost arrayed thus   2090
The temples and the theatre every deel,
Whan it was doon, hym lyked wonder weel.
But stynte I wole of Theseus a lite,
And speke of Palamon and of Arcite.
    The day approcheth of hir retournynge,   2095
That everich sholde an hundred knyghtes
    brynge
The bataille to darreyne, as I yow tolde.
And til Atthenes, hir covenant for to holde,
Hath everich of hem broght an hundred
    knyghtes,
Wel armed for the werre at alle rightes.   2100
And sikerly ther trowed many a man
That nevere, sithen that the world bigan,
As for to speke of knyghthod of hir hond,
As fer as God hath maked see or lond,
Nas of so fewe so noble a compaignye.   2105
For every wight that lovede chivalrye,
And wolde, his thankes, han a passant name,
Hath preyed that he myghte been of that game;
And wel was hym that therto chosen was.
For if ther fille tomorwe swich a cas,   2110
Ye knowen wel that every lusty knyght
That loveth paramours and hath his myght,
Were it in Engelond or elleswhere,
They wolde, hir thankes, wilnen to be there, —
To fighte for a lady, *benedicitee!*   2115
It were a lusty sighte for to see.
    And right so ferden they with Palamon.
With hym ther wenten knyghtes many on;
Som wol ben armed in an haubergeoun,
And in a brestplate and a light gypoun;   2120
And som wol have a paire plates large;
And som wol have a Pruce sheeld or a targe;
Som wol ben armed on his legges weel,
And have an ax, and som a mace of steel —
Ther is no newe gyse that it nas old.   2125
Armed were they, as I have yow told,
Everych after his opinioun.
    Ther maistow seen, comynge with Palamoun,
Lygurge hymself, the grete kyng of Trace.

Blak was his berd, and manly was his face;
The cercles of his eyen in his heed,   2131
They gloweden bitwixen yelow and reed,
And lik a grifphon looked he aboute,
With kempe heeris on his browes stoute;   2134
His lymes grete, his brawnes harde and stronge,
His shuldres brode, his armes rounde and longe;
And as the gyse was in his contree,
Ful hye upon a chaar of gold stood he,
With foure white boles in the trays.
In stede of cote-armure over his harnays,   2140
With nayles yelewe and brighte as any gold,
He hadde a beres skyn, col-blak for old.
His longe heer was kembd bihynde his bak;
As any ravenes fethere it shoon for blak;   2144
A wrethe of gold, arm-greet, of huge wighte,
Upon his heed, set ful of stones brighte,
Of fyne rubyes and of dyamauntz.
Aboute his chaar ther wenten white alauntz,
Twenty and mo, as grete as any steer,
To hunten at the leoun or the deer,   2150
And folwed hym with mosel faste ybounde,
Colered of gold, and tourettes fyled rounde.
An hundred lordes hadde he in his route,
Armed ful wel, with hertes stierne and stoute.

   With Arcita, in stories as men fynde,   2155
The grete Emetreus, the kyng of Inde,
Upon a steede bay trapped in steel,
Covered in clooth of gold, dyapred weel,
Cam ridynge lyk the god of armes, Mars.
His cote-armure was of clooth of Tars   2160
Couched with perles white and rounde and grete;
His sadel was of brend gold newe ybete;
A mantelet upon his shulder hangynge,
Bret-ful of rubyes rede as fyr sparklynge;
His crispe heer lyk rynges was yronne,   2165
And that was yelow, and glytered as the sonne.
His nose was heigh, his eyen bright citryn,
His lippes rounde, his colour was sangwyn;
A fewe frakenes in his face yspreynd,
Bitwixen yelow and somdel blak ymeynd;   2170
And as a leon he his lookyng caste.
Of fyve and twenty yeer his age I caste.
His berd was wel bigonne for to sprynge;
His voys was as a trompe thonderynge.
Upon his heed he wered of laurer grene   2175
A gerland, fressh and lusty for to sene.
Upon his hand he bar for his deduyt
An egle tame, as any lilye whyt.
An hundred lordes hadde he with hym there,
Al armed, save hir heddes, in al hir gere,   2180
Ful richely in alle maner thynges.
For trusteth wel that dukes, erles, kynges

Were gadered in this noble compaignye,
For love and for encrees of chivalrye.
Aboute this kyng ther ran on every part   2185
Ful many a tame leon and leopart.
And in this wise thise lordes, alle and some,
Been on the Sonday to the citee come
Aboute pryme, and in the toun alight.   2189

   This Theseus, this duc, this worthy knyght,
Whan he had broght hem into his citee,
And inned hem, everich at his degree,
He festeth hem, and dooth so greet labour
To esen hem and doon hem al honour,
That yet men wenen that no mannes wit   2195
Of noon estaat ne koude amenden it.
   The mynstralcye, the service at the feeste,
The grete yiftes to the meeste and leeste,
The riche array of Theseus paleys,
Ne who sat first ne last upon the deys,   2200
What ladyes fairest been or best daunsynge,
Or which of hem kan dauncen best and synge,
Ne who moost felyngly speketh of love;
What haukes sitten on the perche above,
What houndes liggen on the floor adoun, —
Of al this make I now no mencioun,   2206
But al th'effect, that thynketh me the beste.
Now cometh the point, and herkneth if yow leste.

   The Sonday nyght, er day bigan to sprynge,
Whan Palamon the larke herde synge,   2210
(Although it nere nat day by houres two,
Yet song the larke) and Palamon right tho
With hooly herte and with an heigh corage,
He roos to wenden on his pilgrymage
Unto the blisful Citherea benigne, —   2215
I mene Venus, honurable and digne.
And in hir houre he walketh forth a pas
Unto the lystes ther hire temple was,
And doun he kneleth, and with humble cheere
And herte soor, he seyde as ye shal heere: 2220
   "Faireste of faire, O lady myn, Venus,
Doughter to Jove, and spouse of Vulcanus,
Thow gladere of the mount of Citheron,
For thilke love thow haddest to Adoon,
Have pitee of my bittre teeris smerte,   2225
And taak myn humble preyere at thyn herte.
Allas! I ne have no langage to telle
Th'effectes ne the tormentz of myn helle;
Myn herte may myne harmes nat biwreye;
I am so confus that I kan noght seye   2230
But, 'Mercy, lady bright, that knowest weele
My thought, and seest what harmes that I feele!'
Considere al this and rewe upon my soore,
As wisly as I shal for everemoore,   2234

Emforth my myght, thy trewe servant be,
And holden werre alwey with chastitee.
That make I myn avow, so ye me helpe!
I kepe noght of armes for to yelpe,
Ne I ne axe nat tomorwe to have victorie,
Ne renoun in this cas, ne veyne glorie   2240
Of pris of armes blowen up and doun;
But I wolde have fully possessioun
Of Emelye, and dye in thy servyse.
Fynd thow the manere hou, and in what wyse:
I recche nat but it may bettre be   2245
To have victorie of hem, or they of me,
So that I have my lady in myne armes.
For though so be that Mars is god of armes,
Youre vertu is so greet in hevene above
That if yow list, I shal wel have my love.   2250
Thy temple wol I worshipe everemo,
And on thyn auter, where I ride or go,
I wol doon sacrifice and fires beete.
And if ye wol nat so, my lady sweete,
Thanne preye I thee, tomorwe with a spere
That Arcita me thurgh the herte bere.   2256
Thanne rekke I noght, whan I have lost my lyf,
Though that Arcita wynne hire to his wyf.
This is th'effect and ende of my preyere:
Yif me my love, thow blisful lady deere."   2260
    Whan the orison was doon of Palamon,
His sacrifice he dide, and that anon,
Ful pitously, with alle circumstaunces,
Al telle I noght as now his observaunces;
But atte laste the statue of Venus shook,   2265
And made a signe, wherby that he took
That his preyere accepted was that day.
For thogh the signe shewed a delay,
Yet wiste he wel that graunted was his boone;
And with glad herte he wente hym hoom ful
          soone.   2270
    The thridde houre inequal that Palamon
Bigan to Venus temple for to gon,
Up roos the sonne, and up roos Emelye,
And to the temple of Dyane gan hye.
Hir maydens, that she thider with hire ladde,
Ful redily with hem the fyr they hadde,   2276
Th'encens, the clothes, and the remenant al
That to the sacrifice longen shal;
The hornes fulle of meeth, as was the gyse:
Ther lakked noght to doon hir sacrifise.   2280
Smokynge the temple, ful of clothes faire,
This Emelye, with herte debonaire,
Hir body wessh with water of a welle.
But hou she dide hir ryte I dar nat telle,
But it be any thing in general;   2285
And yet it were a game to heeren al.
To hym that meneth wel it were no charge;

But it is good a man been at his large.
Hir brighte heer was kembd, untressed al;
A coroune of a grene ook cerial   2290
Upon hir heed was set ful fair and meete.
Two fyres on the auter gan she beete,
And dide hir thynges, as men may biholde
In Stace of Thebes and thise bookes olde.
Whan kyndled was the fyr, with pitous cheere
Unto Dyane she spak as ye may heere: 2296
    "O chaste goddesse of the wodes grene,
To whom bothe hevene and erthe and see is
          sene,
Queene of the regne of Pluto derk and lowe,
Goddesse of maydens, that myn herte hast
          knowe   2300
Ful many a yeer, and woost what I desire,
As keepe me fro thy vengeaunce and thyn ire,
That Attheon aboughte cruelly.
Chaste goddesse, wel wostow that I
Desire to ben a mayden al my lyf,   2305
Ne nevere wol I be no love ne wyf.
I am, thow woost, yet of thy compaignye,
A mayde, and love huntynge and venerye,
And for to walken in the wodes wilde,   2309
And noght to ben a wyf and be with childe.
Noght wol I knowe compaignye of man.
Now help me, lady, sith ye may and kan,
For tho thre formes that thou hast in thee.
And Palamon, that hath swich love to me,
And eek Arcite, that loveth me so soore,   2315
(This grace I preye thee withoute moore)
As sende love and pees bitwixe hem two,
And fro me turne awey hir hertes so
That al hire hoote love and hir desir,
And al hir bisy torment, and hir fir   2320
Be queynt, or turned in another place.
And if so be thou wolt nat do me grace,
Or if my destynee be shapen so
That I shal nedes have oon of hem two,
As sende me hym that moost desireth me.   2325
Bihoold, goddesse of clene chastitee,
The bittre teeris that on my chekes falle.
Syn thou art mayde and kepere of us alle,
My maydenhede thou kepe and wel conserve,
And whil I lyve, a mayde I wol thee serve."
    The fires brenne upon the auter cleere,   2331
Whil Emelye was thus in hir preyere.
But sodeynly she saugh a sighte queynte,
For right anon oon of the fyres queynte,
And quyked agayn, and after that anon   2335
That oother fyr was queynt and al agon;
And as it queynte it made a whistelynge,
As doon thise wete brondes in hir brennynge,
And at the brondes ende out ran anon

As it were blody dropes many oon; 2340
For which so soore agast was Emelye
That she was wel ny mad, and gan to crye,
For she ne wiste what it signyfied;
But oonly for the feere thus hath she cried,
And weep that it was pitee for to heere. 2345
And therwithal Dyane gan appeere,
With bowe in honde, right as an hunteresse,
And seyde, "Doghter, stynt thyn hevynesse.
Among the goddes hye it is affermed, 2349
And by eterne word writen and confermed,
Thou shalt ben wedded unto oon of tho
That han for thee so muchel care and wo;
But unto which of hem I may nat telle.
Farwel, for I ne may no lenger dwelle.
The fires which that on myn auter brenne 2355
Shulle thee declaren, er that thou go henne,
Thyn aventure of love, as in this cas."
And with that word, the arwes in the caas
Of the goddesse clateren faste and rynge,
And forth she wente, and made a vanysshynge;
For which this Emelye astoned was, 2361
And seyde, "What amounteth this, allas?
I putte me in thy proteccioun,
Dyane, and in thy disposicioun."
And hoom she goth anon the nexte weye. 2365
This is th'effect; ther is namoore to seye.
　　The nexte houre of Mars folwynge this,
Arcite unto the temple walked is
Of fierse Mars, to doon his sacrifise,
With alle the rytes of his payen wyse. 2370
With pitous herte and heigh devocioun,
Right thus to Mars he seyde his orisoun:
"O stronge god, that in the regnes colde
Of Trace honoured art and lord yholde,
And hast in every regne and every lond 2375
Of armes al the brydel in thyn hond,
And hem fortunest as thee lyst devyse,
Accepte of me my pitous sacrifise.
If so be that my youthe may deserve, 2379
And that my myght be worthy for to serve
Thy godhede, that I may been oon of thyne,
Thanne preye I thee to rewe upon my pyne.
For thilke peyne, and thilke hoote fir
In which thow whilom brendest for desir,
Whan that thow usedest the beautee 2385
Of faire, yonge, fresshe Venus free,
And haddest hire in armes at thy wille —
Although thee ones on a tyme mysfille,
Whan Vulcanus hadde caught thee in his las,
And foond thee liggynge by his wyf, allas!—
For thilke sorwe that was in thyn herte, 2391
Have routhe as wel upon my peynes smerte.
I am yong and unkonnynge, as thow woost,

And, as I trowe, with love offended moost
That evere was any lyves creature; 2395
For she that dooth me al this wo endure
Ne reccheth nevere wher I synke or fleete.
And wel I woot, er she me mercy heete,
I moot with strengthe wynne hire in the place,
And, wel I woot, withouten help or grace 2400
Of thee, ne may my strengthe noght availle.
Thanne help me, lord, tomorwe in my bataille,
For thilke fyr that whilom brente thee,
As wel as thilke fyr now brenneth me,
And do that I tomorwe have victorie. 2405
Myn be the travaille, and thyn be the glorie!
Thy sovereyn temple wol I moost honouren
Of any place, and alwey moost labouren
In thy plesaunce and in thy craftes stronge,
And in thy temple I wol my baner honge 2410
And alle the armes of my compaignye;
And everemo, unto that day I dye,
Eterne fir I wol bifore thee fynde.
And eek to this avow I wol me bynde:
My beerd, myn heer, that hongeth long adoun,
That nevere yet ne felte offensioun 2416
Of rasour nor of shere, I wol thee yive,
And ben thy trewe servant whil I lyve.
Now, lord, have routhe upon my sorwes soore;
Yif me victorie, I aske thee namoore." 2420
　　The preyere stynt of Arcita the stronge,
The rynges on the temple dore that honge,
And eek the dores, clatereden ful faste,
Of which Arcita somwhat hym agaste. 2424
The fyres brenden upon the auter brighte,
That it gan al the temple for to lighte;
A sweete smel the ground anon up yaf,
And Arcita anon his hand up haf,
And moore encens into the fyr he caste,
With othere rytes mo; and atte laste 2430
The statue of Mars bigan his hauberk rynge;
And with that soun he herde a murmurynge
Ful lowe and dym, and seyde thus, "Victorie!"
For which he yaf to Mars honour and glorie.
And thus with joye and hope wel to fare 2435
Arcite anon unto his in is fare,
As fayn as fowel is of the brighte sonne.
　　And right anon swich strif ther is bigonne,
For thilke grauntyng, in the hevene above,
Bitwixe Venus, the goddesse of love, 2440
And Mars, the stierne god armypotente,
That Juppiter was bisy it to stente;
Til that the pale Saturnus the colde,
That knew so manye of aventures olde,
Foond in his olde experience an art 2445
That he ful soone hath plesed every part.
As sooth is seyd, elde hath greet avantage;

In elde is bothe wysdom and usage;
Men may the olde atrenne, and noght atrede.
Saturne anon, to stynten strif and drede,   2450
Al be it that it is agayn his kynde,
Of al this strif he gan remedie fynde.
"My deere doghter Venus," quod Saturne,
"My cours, that hath so wyde for to turne,
Hath moore power than woot any man.   2455
Myn is the drenchyng in the see so wan;
Myn is the prison in the derke cote;
Myn is the stranglyng and hangyng by the
  throte,
The murmure and the cherles rebellyng,
The groynynge, and the pryvee empoysonyng;
I do vengeance and pleyn correccioun,   2461
Whil I dwelle in the signe of the leoun.
Myn is the ruyne of the hye halles,
The fallynge of the toures and of the walles
Upon the mynour or the carpenter.   2465
I slow Sampsoun, shakynge the piler;
And myne be the maladyes colde,
The derke tresons, and the castes olde;
My lookyng is the fader of pestilence.
Now weep namoore, I shal doon diligence   2470
That Palamon, that is thyn owene knyght,
Shal have his lady, as thou hast him hight.
Though Mars shal helpe his knyght, yet nathe-
  lees
Bitwixe yow ther moot be som tyme pees,
Al be ye noght of o compleccioun,   2475
That causeth al day swich divisioun.
I am thyn aiel, redy at thy wille;
Weep now namoore, I wol thy lust fulfille."
  Now wol I stynten of the goddes above,
Of Mars, and of Venus, goddesse of love,   2480
And telle yow as pleynly as I kan
The grete effect, for which that I bygan.

Explicit tercia pars

Sequitur pars quarta

  Greet was the feeste in Atthenes that day,
And eek the lusty seson of that May   2484
Made every wight to been in swich plesaunce
That al that Monday justen they and daunce,
And spenden it in Venus heigh servyse.
But by the cause that they sholde ryse
Eerly, for to seen the grete fight,
Unto hir reste wenten they at nyght.   2490
And on the morwe, whan that day gan sprynge,
Of hors and harneys noyse and claterynge
Ther was in hostelryes al aboute;
And to the paleys rood ther many a route

Of lordes upon steedes and palfreys.   2495
Ther maystow seen devisynge of harneys
So unkouth and so riche, and wroght so weel
Of goldsmythrye, of browdynge, and of steel;
The sheeldes brighte, testeres, and trappures,
Gold-hewen helmes, hauberkes, cote-armures;
Lordes in paramentz on hir courseres,   2501
Knyghtes of retenue, and eek squieres
Nailynge the speres, and helmes bokelynge;
Giggynge of sheeldes, with layneres lacynge
(There as nede is they weren no thyng ydel);
The fomy steedes on the golden brydel   2506
Gnawynge, and faste the armurers also
With fyle and hamer prikynge to and fro;
Yemen on foote, and communes many oon
With shorte staves, thikke as they may goon;
Pypes, trompes, nakers, clariounes,   2511
That in the bataille blowen blody sounes;
The paleys ful of peple up and doun,
Heere thre, ther ten, holdynge hir questioun,
Dyvynynge of thise Thebane knyghtes
  two.   2515
Somme seyden thus, somme seyde "it shal be
  so";
Somme helden with hym with the blake berd,
Somme with the balled, somme with the thikke
  herd;
Somme seyde he looked grymme, and he wolde
  fighte;
"He hath a sparth of twenty pound of wighte."
Thus was the halle ful of divynynge,   2521
Longe after that the sonne gan to sprynge.
  The grete Theseus, that of his sleep awaked
With mynstralcie and noyse that was maked,
Heeld yet the chambre of his paleys riche,
Til that the Thebane knyghtes, bothe yliche
Honured, were into the paleys fet.   2527
Duc Theseus was at a wyndow set,
Arrayed right as he were a god in trone.
The peple preesseth thiderward ful soone   2530
Hym for to seen, and doon heigh reverence,
And eek to herkne his heste and his sentence.
An heraud on a scaffold made an "Oo!"
Til al the noyse of peple was ydo,   2534
And whan he saugh the peple of noyse al stille,
Tho shewed he the myghty dukes wille.
  "The lord hath of his heigh discrecioun
Considered that it were destruccioun
To gentil blood to fighten in the gyse
Of mortal bataille now in this emprise.   2540
Wherfore, to shapen that they shal nat dye,
He wol his firste purpos modifye.
No man therfore, up peyne of los of lyf,
No maner shot, ne polax, ne short knyf

Into the lystes sende, or thider brynge;   2545
Ne short swerd, for to stoke with poynt
    bitynge,
No man ne drawe, ne bere it by his syde.
Ne no man shal unto his felawe ryde
But o cours, with a sharpe ygrounde spere;
Foyne, if hym list, on foote, hymself to were.
And he that is at meschief shal be take   2551
And noght slayn, but be broght unto the stake
That shal ben ordeyned on either syde;
But thider he shal by force, and there abyde.
And if so falle the chieftayn be take   2555
On outher syde, or elles sleen his make,
No lenger shal the turneiynge laste.
God spede you! gooth forth, and ley on faste!
With long swerd and with maces fighteth youre
    fille.
Gooth now youre wey, this is the lordes
    wille."   2560
    The voys of peple touchede the hevene,
So loude cride they with murie stevene,
"God save swich a lord, that is so good,
He wilneth no destruccion of blood!"
Up goon the trompes and the melodye,   2565
And to the lystes rit the compaignye,
By ordinance, thurghout the citee large,
Hanged with clooth of gold, and nat with sarge.
    Ful lik a lord this noble duc gan ryde,
Thise two Thebans upon either syde;   2570
And after rood the queene, and Emelye,
And after that another compaignye
Of oon and oother, after hir degree.
And thus they passen thurghout the citee,
And to the lystes come they by tyme.   2575
It nas nat of the day yet fully pryme
Whan set was Theseus ful riche and hye,
Ypolita the queene, and Emelye,
And othere ladys in degrees aboute.
Unto the seetes preesseth al the route.   2580
And westward, thurgh the gates under Marte,
Arcite, and eek the hondred of his parte,
With baner reed is entred right anon;
And in that selve moment Palamon
Is under Venus, estward in the place,   2585
With baner whyt, and hardy chiere and face.
In al the world, to seken up and doun,
So evene, withouten variacioun,
Ther nere swiche compaignyes tweye;
For ther was noon so wys that koude seye   2590
That any hadde of oother avauntage
Of worthynesse, ne of estaat, ne age,
So evene were they chosen, for to gesse.
And in two renges faire they hem dresse.
Whan that hir names rad were everichon,

That in hir nombre gyle were ther noon,   2596
Tho were the gates shet, and cried was loude:
"Do now youre devoir, yonge knyghtes
    proude!"
    The heraudes lefte hir prikyng up and doun;
Now ryngen trompes loude and clarioun.   2600
Ther is namoore to seyn, but west and est
In goon the speres ful sadly in arrest;
In gooth the sharpe spore into the syde.
Ther seen men who kan juste and who kan
    ryde;   2604
Ther shyveren shaftes upon sheeldes thikke;
He feeleth thurgh the herte-spoon the prikke.
Up spryngen speres twenty foot on highte;
Out goon the swerdes as the silver brighte;
The helmes they tohewen and toshrede;   2609
Out brest the blood with stierne stremes rede;
With myghty maces the bones they tobreste.
He thurgh the thikkeste of the throng gan
    threste;
Ther stomblen steedes stronge, and doun
    gooth al;
He rolleth under foot as dooth a bal;   2614
He foyneth on his feet with his tronchoun,
And he hym hurtleth with his hors adoun;
He thurgh the body is hurt and sithen take,
Maugree his heed, and broght unto the stake:
As forward was, right there he moste abyde.
Another lad is on that oother syde.   2620
And some tyme dooth hem Theseus to reste,
Hem to refresshe and drynken, if hem leste.
Ful ofte a day han thise Thebanes two
Togydre ymet, and wroght his felawe wo;
Unhorsed hath ech oother of hem tweye.   2625
Ther nas no tygre in the vale of Galgopheye,
Whan that hir whelp is stole whan it is lite,
So crueel on the hunte as is Arcite
For jelous herte upon this Palamon.
Ne in Belmarye ther nys so fel leon,   2630
That hunted is, or for his hunger wood,
Ne of his praye desireth so the blood,
As Palamon to sleen his foo Arcite.
The jelous strokes on hir helmes byte;   2634
Out renneth blood on bothe hir sydes rede.
    Som tyme an ende ther is of every dede.
For er the sonne unto the reste wente,
The stronge kyng Emetreus gan hente
This Palamon, as he faught with Arcite,
And made his swerd depe in his flessh to byte;
And by the force of twenty is he take   2641
Unyolden, and ydrawe unto the stake.
And in the rescus of this Palamoun
The stronge kyng Lygurge is born adoun,
And kyng Emetreus, for al his strengthe,   2645

Is born out of his sadel a swerdes lengthe,
So hitte him Palamoun er he were take;
But al for noght, he was broght to the stake.
His hardy herte myghte hym helpe naught:
He moste abyde, whan that he was caught,
By force and eek by composicioun.   2651

Who sorweth now but woful Palamoun,
That moot namoore goon agayn to fighte?
And whan that Theseus hadde seyn this sighte,
Unto the folk that foghten thus echon   2655
He cryde, "Hoo! namoore, for it is doon!
I wol be trewe juge, and no partie.
Arcite of Thebes shal have Emelie,
That by his fortune hath hire faire ywonne."
Anon ther is a noyse of peple bigonne   2660
For joye of this, so loude and heighe withalle,
It semed that the lystes sholde falle.

What kan now faire Venus doon above?
What seith she now? What dooth this queene
        of love,
But wepeth so, for wantynge of hir wille,   2665
Til that hir teeres in the lystes fille?
She seyde, "I am ashamed, doutelees."

Saturnus seyde, "Doghter, hoold thy pees!
Mars hath his wille, his knyght hath al his
        boone,   2669
And, by myn heed, thow shalt been esed soone."
The trompours, with the loude mynstralcie,
The heraudes, that ful loude yelle and crie,
Been in hire wele for joye of daun Arcite.
But herkneth me, and stynteth noyse a lite,
Which a myracle ther bifel anon.   2675

This fierse Arcite hath of his helm ydon,
And on a courser, for to shewe his face,
He priketh endelong the large place
Lokynge upward upon this Emelye;
And she agayn hym caste a freendlich ye   2680
(For wommen, as to speken in comune,
Thei folwen alle the favour of Fortune)
And was al his chiere, as in his herte.

Out of the ground a furie infernal sterte,
From Pluto sent at requeste of Saturne,   2685
For which his hors for fere gan to turne,
And leep aside, and foundred as he leep;
And er that Arcite may taken keep,
He pighte hym on the pomel of his heed,
That in the place he lay as he were deed,   2690
His brest tobrosten with his sadel-bowe.
As blak he lay as any cole or crowe,
So was the blood yronnen in his face.
Anon he was yborn out of the place,
With herte soor, to Theseus paleys.   2695
Tho was he korven out of his harneys,
And in a bed ybrought ful faire and blyve;

For he was yet in memorie and alyve,
And alwey criynge after Emelye.

Duc Theseus, with al his compaignye,   2700
Is comen hoom to Atthenes his citee,
With alle blisse and greet solempnitee.
Al be it that this aventure was falle,
He nolde noght disconforten hem alle.
Men seyde eek that Arcite shal nat dye;   2705
He shal been heeled of his maladye.
And of another thyng they weren as fayn,
That of hem alle was ther noon yslayn,
Al were they soore yhurt, and namely oon,
That with a spere was thirled his brest boon.
To othere woundes and to broken armes   2711
Somme hadden salves, and somme hadden
        charmes;
Fermacies of herbes, and eek save
They dronken, for they wolde hir lymes have.
For which this noble duc, as he wel kan,   2715
Conforteth and honoureth every man,
And made revel al the longe nyght
Unto the straunge lordes, as was right.
Ne ther was holden no disconfitynge
But as a justes, or a tourneiynge;   2720
For soothly ther was no disconfiture.
For fallyng nys nat but an aventure,
Ne to be lad by force unto the stake
Unyolden, and with twenty knyghtes take,
O persone allone, withouten mo,   2725
And haryed forth by arme, foot, and too,
And eke his steede dryven forth with staves
With footmen, bothe yemen and eek knaves,—
It nas arretted hym no vileynye;
Ther may no man clepen it cowardye.   2730
For which anon duc Theseus leet crye,
To stynten alle rancour and envye,
The gree as wel of o syde as of oother,
And eyther syde ylik as ootheres brother;
And yaf hem yiftes after hir degree,   2735
And fully heeld a feeste dayes three,
And conveyed the kynges worthily
Out of his toun a journee largely.
And hoom wente every man the righte way.
Ther was namoore but "Fare wel, have good
        day!"
Of this bataille I wol namoore endite,   2741
But speke of Palamon and of Arcite.

Swelleth the brest of Arcite, and the soore
Encreesseth at his herte moore and moore.
The clothered blood, for any lechecraft,   2745
Corrupteth, and is in his bouk ylaft,
That neither veyne-blood, ne ventusynge,
Ne drynke of herbes may ben his helpynge.
The vertu expulsif, or animal,

Fro thilke vertu cleped natural   2750
Ne may the venym voyden ne expelle.
The pipes of his longes gonne to swelle,
And every lacerte in his brest adoun
Is shent with venym and corrupcioun.
Hym gayneth neither, for to gete his lif,   2755
Vomyt upward, ne dounward laxatif.
Al is tobrosten thilke regioun;
Nature hath now no dominacioun.
And certeinly, ther Nature wol nat wirche,
Fare wel phisik! go ber the man to chirche!
This al and som, that Arcita moot dye;   2761
For which he sendeth after Emelye,
And Palamon, that was his cosyn deere.
Thanne seyde he thus, as ye shal after heere:
"Naught may the woful spirit in myn herte
Declare o point of alle my sorwes smerte   2766
To yow, my lady, that I love moost;
But I biquethe the servyce of my goost
To yow aboven every creature,
Syn that my lyf may no lenger dure.   2770
Allas, the wo! allas, the peynes stronge,
That I for yow have suffred, and so longe!
Allas, the deeth! allas, myn Emelye!
Allas, departynge of oure compaignye!
Allas, myn hertes queene! allas, my wyf!   2775
Myn hertes lady, endere of my lyf!
What is this world? what asketh men to have?
Now with his love, now in his colde grave
Allone, withouten any compaignye.
Fare wel, my sweete foo, myn Emelye!   2780
And softe taak me in youre armes tweye,
For love of God, and herkneth what I seye.
   I have heer with my cosyn Palamon
Had strif and rancour many a day agon
For love of yow, and for my jalousye.   2785
And Juppiter so wys my soule gye,
To speken of a servaunt proprely,
With alle circumstances trewely —
That is to seyen, trouthe, honour, knyghthede,
Wysdom, humblesse, estaat, and heigh kyn-
      rede,
Fredom, and al that longeth to that art —   2791
So Juppiter have of my soule part,
As in this world right now ne knowe I non
So worthy to ben loved as Palamon,
That serveth yow, and wol doon al his lyf.
And if that evere ye shul ben a wyf,   2796
Foryet nat Palamon, the gentil man."
And with that word his speche faille gan,
For from his feet up to his brest was come
The coold of deeth, that hadde hym overcome,
And yet moreover, for in his armes two   2801
The vital strengthe is lost and al ago.

Oonly the intellect, withouten moore,
That dwelled in his herte syk and soore,
Gan faillen whan the herte felte deeth.   2805
Dusked his eyen two, and failled breeth,
But on his lady yet caste he his ye;
His laste word was, "Mercy, Emelye!"
His spirit chaunged hous and wente ther,
As I cam nevere, I kan nat tellen wher.   2810
Therfore I stynte, I nam no divinistre;
Of soules fynde I nat in this registre,
Ne me ne list thilke opinions to telle
Of hem, though that they writen wher they
      dwelle.
Arcite is coold, ther Mars his soule gye!   2815
Now wol I speken forth of Emelye.
   Shrighte Emelye, and howleth Palamon,
And Theseus his suster took anon
Swownynge, and baar hire fro the corps away.
What helpeth it to tarien forth the day   2820
To tellen how she weep bothe eve and morwe?
For in swich cas wommen have swich sorwe,
Whan that hir housbondes ben from hem ago,
That for the moore part they sorwen so,
Or ellis fallen in swich maladye,   2825
That at the laste certeinly they dye.
   Infinite been the sorwes and the teeres
Of olde folk, and folk of tendre yeeres,
In al the toun for deeth of this Theban.   2829
For hym ther wepeth bothe child and man;
So greet wepyng was ther noon, certayn,
Whan Ector was ybroght, al fressh yslayn,
To Troye. Allas, the pitee that was ther,
Cracchynge of chekes, rentynge eek of heer.
"Why woldestow be deed," thise wommen
      crye,   2835
"And haddest gold ynough, and Emelye?"
   No man myghte gladen Theseus,
Savynge his olde fader Egeus,
That knew this worldes transmutacioun,
As he hadde seyn it chaunge bothe up and
      doun,
Joye after wo, and wo after gladnesse,   2841
And shewed hem ensamples and liknesse.
   "Right as ther dyed nevere man," quod he,
"That he ne lyvede in erthe in some degree,
Right so ther lyvede never man," he seyde,   2845
"In al this world, that som tyme he ne deyde.
This world nys but a thurghfare ful of wo,
And we been pilgrymes, passynge to and fro.
Deeth is an ende of every worldly soore."
And over al this yet seyde he muchel moore
To this effect, ful wisely to enhorte   2851
The peple that they sholde hem reconforte.
   Duc Theseus, with al his bisy cure,

Caste now wher that the sepulture
Of goode Arcite may best ymaked be,   2855
And eek moost honurable in his degree.
And at the laste he took conclusioun
That ther as first Arcite and Palamoun
Hadden for love the bataille hem bitwene,
That in that selve grove, swoote and grene,
Ther as he hadde his amorouse desires,   2861
His compleynte, and for love his hoote fires,
He wolde make a fyr in which the office
Funeral he myghte al accomplice.   2864
And leet comande anon to hakke and hewe
The okes olde, and leye hem on a rewe
In colpons wel arrayed for to brenne.
His officers with swifte feet they renne
And ryde anon at his comandement.
And after this, Theseus hath ysent   2870
After a beere, and it al over spradde
With clooth of gold, the richeste that he hadde.
And of the same suyte he cladde Arcite;
Upon his hondes hadde he gloves white,   2874
Eek on his heed a coroune of laurer grene,
And in his hond a swerd ful bright and kene.
He leyde hym, bare the visage, on the beere;
Therwith he weep that pitee was to heere.
And for the peple sholde seen hym alle,
Whan it was day, he broghte hym to the halle,
That roreth of the criyng and the soun.   2881
     Tho cam this woful Theban Palamoun,
With flotery berd and ruggy, asshy heeres,
In clothes blake, ydropped al with teeres;
And, passynge othere of wepynge, Emelye,
The rewefulleste of al the compaignye.   2886
In as muche as the servyce sholde be
The moore noble and riche in his degree,
Duc Theseus leet forth thre steedes brynge,
That trapped were in steel al gliterynge,   2890
And covered with the armes of daun Arcite.
Upon thise steedes, that weren grete and white,
Ther seten folk, of whiche oon baar his sheeld,
Another his spere up on his hondes heeld,
The thridde baar with hym his bowe Tur-
     keys   2895
(Of brend gold was the caas and eek the
     harneys);
And riden forth a paas with sorweful cheere
Toward the grove, as ye shul after heere.
The nobleste of the Grekes that ther were
Upon hir shuldres caryeden the beere,   2900
With slakke paas, and eyen rede and wete,
Thurghout the citee by the maister strete,
That sprad was al with blak, and wonder hye
Right of the same is the strete ywrye.
Upon the right hond wente olde Egeus,   2905

And on that oother syde duc Theseus,
With vessels in hir hand of gold ful fyn,
Al ful of hony, milk, and blood, and wyn;
Eek Palamon, with ful greet compaignye;
And after that cam woful Emelye,   2910
With fyr in honde, as was that tyme the gyse,
To do the office of funeral servyse.
     Heigh labour and ful greet apparaillynge
Was at the service and the fyr-makynge,   2914
That with his grene top the hevene raughte;
And twenty fadme of brede the armes
     straughte—
This is to seyn, the bowes weren so brode.
Of stree first ther was leyd ful many a lode.
But how the fyr was maked upon highte,
Ne eek the names that the trees highte,   2920
As ook, firre, birch, aspe, alder, holm, popler,
Wylugh, elm, plane, assh, box, chasteyn, lynde,
     laurer,
Mapul, thorn, bech, hasel, ew, whippeltree, --
How they weren feld, shal nat be toold for me;
Ne hou the goddes ronnen up and doun,   2925
Disherited of hire habitacioun,
In which they woneden in reste and pees,
Nymphes, fawnes and amadrides;
Ne hou the beestes and the briddes alle   2929
Fledden for fere, whan the wode was falle;
Ne how the ground agast was of the light,
That was nat wont to seen the sonne bright;
Ne how the fyr was couched first with stree,
And thanne with drye stikkes cloven a thre,
And thanne with grene wode and spicerye,
And thanne with clooth of gold and with
     perrye,   2936
And gerlandes, hangynge with ful many a flour;
The mirre, th'encens, with al so greet odour;
Ne how Arcite lay among al this,
Ne what richesse aboute his body is;   2940
Ne how that Emelye, as was the gyse,
Putte in the fyr of funeral servyse;
Ne how she swowned whan men made the fyr,
Ne what she spak, ne what was hir desir;
Ne what jeweles men in the fyre caste,   2945
Whan that the fyr was greet and brente faste;
Ne how somme caste hir sheeld, and somme hir
     spere,
And of hire vestimentz, whiche that they were,
And coppes fulle of wyn, and milk, and blood,
Into the fyr, that brente as it were wood;   2950
Ne how the Grekes, with an huge route,
Thries riden al the fyr aboute
Upon the left hand, with a loud shoutynge,
And thries with hir speres claterynge;
And thries how the ladyes gonne crye;   2955

Ne how that lad was homward Emelye;
Ne how Arcite is brent to asshen colde;
Ne how that lyche-wake was yholde
Al thilke nyght; ne how the Grekes pleye
The wake-pleyes, ne kepe I nat to seye;   2960
Who wrastleth best naked with oille enoynt,
Ne who that baar hym best, in no disjoynt.
I wol nat tellen eek how that they goon
Hoom til Atthenes, whan the pley is doon;
But shortly to the point thanne wol I wende,
And maken of my longe tale an ende.   2966

By processe and by lengthe of certeyn yeres,
Al stynted is the moornynge and the teres
Of Grekes, by oon general assent.
Thanne semed me ther was a parlement   2970
At Atthenes, upon certein pointz and caas;
Among the whiche pointz yspoken was,
To have with certein contrees alliaunce,
And have fully of Thebans obeisaunce.
For which this noble Theseus anon   2975
Leet senden after gentil Palamon,
Unwist of hym what was the cause and why;
But in his blake clothes sorwefully
He cam at his comandement in hye.
Tho sente Theseus for Emelye.   2980
Whan they were set, and hust was al the place,
And Theseus abiden hadde a space
Er any word cam fram his wise brest,
His eyen sette he ther as was his lest.
And with a sad visage he siked stille,   2985
And after that right thus he seyde his wille:
"The Firste Moevere of the cause above,
Whan he first made the faire cheyne of love,
Greet was th'effect, and heigh was his entente.
Wel wiste he why, and what thereof he mente;
For with that faire cheyne of love he bond   2991
The fyr, the eyr, the water, and the lond
In certeyn boundes, that they may nat flee.
That same Prince and that Moevere," quod he,
"Hath stablissed in this wrecched world adoun
Certeyne dayes and duracioun   2996
To al that is engendred in this place,
Over the whiche day they may nat pace,
Al mowe they yet tho dayes wel abregge.   2999
Ther nedeth noght noon auctoritee t'allegge,
For it is preeved by experience,
But that me list declaren my sentence.
Thanne may men by this ordre wel discerne
That thilke Moevere stable is and eterne.
Wel may men knowe, but it be a fool,   3005
That every part dirryveth from his hool;
For nature hath nat taken his bigynnyng
Of no partie or cantel of a thyng,
But of a thyng that parfit is and stable,

Descendynge so til it be corrumpable.   3010
And therfore, of his wise purveiaunce,
He hath so wel biset his ordinaunce,
That speces of thynges and progressiouns
Shullen enduren by successiouns,
And nat eterne, withouten any lye.   3015
This maystow understonde and seen at ye.
   Loo the ook, that hath so long a norisshynge
From tyme that it first bigynneth to sprynge,
And hath so long a lif, as we may see,
Yet at the laste wasted is the tree.   3020
   Considereth eek how that the harde stoon
Under oure feet, on which we trede and goon,
Yet wasteth it as it lyth by the weye.
The brode ryver somtyme wexeth dreye;   3024
The grete tounes se we wane and wende.
Thanne may ye se that al this thyng hath ende.
   Of man and womman seen we wel also
That nedes, in oon of thise termes two,
This is to seyn, in youthe or elles age,
He moot be deed, the kyng as shal a page;
Som in his bed, som in the depe see,   3031
Som in the large feeld, as men may see;
Ther helpeth noght, al goth that ilke weye.
Thanne may I seyn that al this thyng moot
     deye.
   What maketh this but Juppiter, the kyng,
That is prince and cause of alle thyng,   3036
Convertynge al unto his propre welle
From which it is dirryved, sooth to telle?
And heer-agayns no creature on lyve,
Of no degree, availleth for to stryve.   3040
   Thanne is it wysdom, as it thynketh me,
To maken vertu of necessitee,
And take it weel that we may nat eschue,
And namely that to us alle is due.
And whoso grucccheth ought, he dooth folye,
And rebel is to hym that al may gye.   3046
And certeinly a man hath moost honour
To dyen in his excellence and flour,
Whan he is siker of his goode name;   3049
Thanne hath he doon his freend, ne hym, no
     shame.
And gladder oghte his freend been of his deeth,
Whan with honour up yolden is his breeth,
Than whan his name apalled is for age,
For al forgeten is his vassellage.
Thanne is it best, as for a worthy fame,   3055
To dyen whan that he is best of name.
   The contrarie of al this is wilfulnesse.
Why grucchen we, why have we hevynesse,
That goode Arcite, of chivalrie the flour,
Departed is with duetee and honour   3060
Out of this foule prisoun of this lyf?

Why grucchen heere his cosyn and his wyf
Of his welfare, that loved hem so weel?
Kan he hem thank? Nay, God woot, never a
    deel,
That both his soule and eek hemself offende,
And yet they mowe hir lustes nat amende.   3066

    What may I conclude of this longe serye,
But after wo I rede us to be merye,
And thanken Juppiter of al his grace?
And er that we departen from this place   3070
I rede that we make of sorwes two
O parfit joye, lastynge everemo.
And looketh now, wher moost sorwe is herinne,
Ther wol we first amenden and bigynne.

    "Suster," quod he, "this is my fulle assent,
With al th'avys heere of my parlement,   3076
That gentil Palamon, youre owene knyght,
That serveth yow with wille herte, and myght,
And ever hath doon syn ye first hym knewe,
That ye shul of youre grace upon hym rewe,
And taken hym for housbonde and for lord.   3081
Lene me youre hond, for this is oure accord.
Lat se now of youre wommanly pitee.
He is a kynges brother sone, pardee;

And though he were a povre bacheler,   3085
Syn he hath served yow so many a yeer,
And had for yow so greet adversitee,
It moste been considered, leeveth me;
For gentil mercy oghte to passen right."   3089
    Thanne seyde he thus to Palamon the knight:
"I trowe ther nedeth litel sermonyng
To make yow assente to this thyng.
    Com neer, and taak youre lady by the hond."
Bitwixen hem was maad anon the bond
That highte matrimoigne or mariage,   3095
By al the conseil and the baronage.
And thus with alle blisse and melodye
Hath Palamon ywedded Emelye.
And God, that al this wyde world hath wroght,
Sende hym his love that hath it deere aboght;
For now is Palamon in alle wele,   3101
Lyvynge in blisse, in richesse, and in heele,
And Emelye hym loveth so tendrely,
And he hire serveth al so gentilly,
That nevere was ther no word hem bitwene
Of jalousie or any oother teene.   3106
Thus endeth Palamon and Emelye;
And God save al this faire compaignye! Amen.

Heere is ended the Knyghtes Tale.

The Miller's Prologue

Heere folwen the wordes bitwene the Hoost and the Millere.

    Whan that the Knyght had thus his tale
    ytoold,
In al the route nas ther yong ne oold   3110
That he ne seyde it was a noble storie,
And worthy for to drawen to memorie;
And namely the gentils everichon.
Oure Hooste lough and swoor, "So moot I gon,
This gooth aright; unbokeled is the male.   3115
Lat se now who shal telle another tale;
For trewely the game is wel bigonne.
Now telleth ye, sir Monk, if that ye konne
Somwhat to quite with the Knyghtes tale."
The Millere, that for dronken was al pale,
So that unnethe upon his hors he sat,   3121
He nolde avalen neither hood ne hat,
Ne abyde no man for his curteisie,
But in Pilates voys he gan to crie,

And swoor, "By armes, and by blood and bones,
I kan a noble tale for the nones,   3126
With which I wol now quite the Knyghtes
    tale."
Oure Hooste saugh that he was dronke of ale,
And seyde, "Abyd, Robyn, my leeve brother;
Som bettre man shal telle us first another.
Abyd, and lat us werken thriftily."   3131
    "By Goddes soule," quod he, "that wol nat I;
For I wol speke, or elles go my wey."
Oure Hoost answerde, "Tel on, a devel wey!
Thou art a fool; thy wit is overcome."   3135
    "Now herkneth," quod the Millere, "alle and
    some!
But first I make a protestacioun
That I am dronke, I knowe it by my soun;
And therfore if that I mysspeke or seye,

Wyte it the ale of Southwerk, I you preye.
For I wol telle a legende and a lyf   3141
Bothe of a carpenter and of his wyf,
How that a clerk hath set the wrightes cappe."
  The Reve answerde and seyde, "Stynt thy clappe!
Lat be thy lewed dronken harlotrye. 3145
It is a synne and eek a greet folye
To apeyren any man, or hym defame,
And eek to bryngen wyves in swich fame.
Thou mayst ynogh of othere thynges seyn."
  This dronke Millere spak ful soone ageyn
And seyde, "Leve brother Osewold, 3151
Who hath no wyf, he is no cokewold.
But I sey nat therfore that thou art oon;
Ther been ful goode wyves many oon, 3154
And evere a thousand goode ayeyns oon badde.
That knowestow wel thyself, but if thou madde.
Why artow angry with my tale now?
I have a wyf, pardee, as wel as thow;
Yet nolde I, for the oxen in my plogh,
Take upon me moore than ynogh, 3160
As demen of myself that I were oon;
I wol bileve wel that I am noon.

An housbonde shal nat been inquisityf
Of Goddes pryvetee, nor of his wyf.
So he may fynde Goddes foyson there, 3165
Of the remenant nedeth nat enquere."
  What sholde I moore seyn, but this Millere
He nolde his wordes for no man forbere,
But tolde his cherles tale in his manere.
M'athynketh that I shal reherce it heere. 3170
And therfore every gentil wight I preye,
For Goddes love, demeth nat that I seye
Of yvel entente, but for I moot reherce
Hir tales alle, be they bettre or werse,
Or elles falsen som of my mateere. 3175
And therfore, whoso list it nat yheere,
Turne over the leef and chese another tale;
For he shal fynde ynowe, grete and smale,
Of storial thyng that toucheth gentillesse,
And eek moralitee and hoolynesse. 3180
Blameth nat me if that ye chese amys.
The Millere is a cherl, ye knowe wel this;
So was the Reve eek and othere mo,
And harlotrie they tolden bothe two.
Avyseth yow, and put me out of blame; 3185
And eek men shal nat maken ernest of game.

The Miller's Tale

Heere bigynneth the Millere his tale.

Whilom ther was dwellynge at Oxenford
A riche gnof, that gestes heeld to bord,
And of his craft he was a carpenter. 3189
With hym ther was dwellynge a poure scoler,
Hadde lerned art, but al his fantasye
Was turned for to lerne astrologye,
And koude a certeyn of conclusiouns,
To demen by interrogaciouns,
If that men asked hym in certein houres 3195
Whan that men sholde have droghte or elles shoures,
Or if men asked hym what sholde bifalle
Of every thyng; I may nat rekene hem alle.
  This clerk was cleped hende Nicholas.
Of deerne love he koude and of solas; 3200
And therto he was sleigh and ful privee,
And lyk a mayden meke for to see.
A chambre hadde he in that hostelrye
Allone, withouten any compaignye,
Ful fetisly ydight with herbes swoote; 3205

And he hymself as sweete as is the roote
Of lycorys, or any cetewale.
His Almageste, and bookes grete and smale,
His astrelabie, longynge for his art,
His augrym stones layen faire apart, 3210
On shelves couched at his beddes heed;
His presse ycovered with a faldyng reed;
And al above ther lay a gay sautrie,
On which he made a-nyghtes melodie
So swetely that all the chambre rong; 3215
And *Angelus ad virginem* he song;
And after that he song the Kynges Noote.
Ful often blessed was his myrie throte.
And thus this sweete clerk his tyme spente
After his freendes fyndyng and his rente. 3220
  This carpenter hadde wedded newe a wyf,
Which that he lovede moore than his lyf;
Of eighteteene yeer she was of age.
Jalous he was, and heeld hire narwe in cage,
For she was wylde and yong, and he was old,

And demed hymself been lik a cokewold.   3226
He knew nat Catoun, for his wit was rude,
That bad man sholde wedde his simylitude.
Men sholde wedden after hire estaat,
For youthe and elde is often at debaat.   3230
But sith that he was fallen in the snare,
He moste endure, as oother folk, his care.

    Fair was this yonge wyf, and therwithal
As any wezele hir body gent and smal.
A ceynt she werede, barred al of silk,   3235
A barmclooth eek as whit as morne milk
Upon hir lendes, ful of many a goore.
Whit was hir smok, and broyden al bifoore
And eek bihynde, on hir coler aboute,
Of col-blak silk, withinne and eek withoute.
The tapes of hir white voluper   3241
Were of the same suyte of hir coler;
Hir filet brood of silk, and set ful hye.
And sikerly she hadde a likerous ye;
Ful smale ypulled were hire browes two,   3245
And tho were bent and blake as any sloo.
She was ful moore blisful on to see
Than is the newe pere-jonette tree,
And softer than the wolle is of a wether.
And by hir girdel heeng a purs of lether,   3250
Tasseled with silk, and perled with latoun.
In al this world, to seken up and doun,
There nys no man so wys that koude thenche
So gay a popelote or swich a wenche.   3254
Ful brighter was the shynyng of hir hewe
Than in the Tour the noble yforged newe.
But of hir song, it was as loude and yerne
As any swalwe sittynge on a berne.
Therto she koude skippe and make game,
As any kyde or calf folwynge his dame.   3260
Hir mouth was sweete as bragot or the meeth,
Or hoord of apples leyd in hey or heeth.
Wynsynge she was, as is a joly colt,
Long as a mast, and upright as a bolt.
A brooch she baar upon hir lowe coler,   3265
As brood as is the boos of a bokeler.
Hir shoes were laced on hir legges hye.
She was a prymerole, a piggesnye,
For any lord to leggen in his bedde,
Or yet for any good yeman to wedde.   3270

    Now, sire, and eft, sire, so bifel the cas,
That on a day this hende Nicholas
Fil with this yonge wyf to rage and pleye,
Whil that hir housbonde was at Oseneye,   3274
As clerkes ben ful subtile and ful queynte;
And prively he caughte hire by the queynte,
And seyde, "Ywis, but if ich have my wille,
For deerne love of thee, lemman, I spille."
And heeld hire harde by the haunchebones,

And seyde, "Lemman, love me al atones,   3280
Or I wol dyen, also God me save!"
And she sproong as a colt dooth in the trave,
And with hir heed she wryed faste awey,
And seyde, "I wol nat kisse thee, by my fey!
Why, lat be," quod she, "lat be, Nicholas,
Or I wol crie 'out, harrow' and 'allas'!   3286
Do wey youre handes, for youre curteisye!"

    This Nicholas gan mercy for to crye,
And spak so faire, and profred him so faste,
That she hir love hym graunted atte laste,
And swoor hir ooth, by seint Thomas of Kent,
That she wol been at his comandement,   3292
Whan that she may hir leyser wel espie.
"Myn housbonde is so ful of jalousie
That but ye wayte wel and been privee,   3295
I woot right wel I nam but deed," quod she.
"Ye moste been ful deerne, as in this cas."

    "Nay, therof care thee noght," quod Nicholas.
"A clerk hadde litherly biset his whyle,
But if he koude a carpenter bigyle."   3300
And thus they been accorded and ysworn
To wayte a tyme, as I have told biforn.
Whan Nicholas had doon thus everideel,
And thakked hire aboute the lendes weel,
He kiste hire sweete and taketh his sawtrie,
And pleyeth faste, and maketh melodie.   3306

    Thanne fil it thus, that to the paryssh chirche,
Cristes owene werkes for to wirche,
This goode wyf went on an haliday.
Hir forheed shoon as bright as any day,   3310
So was it wasshen whan she leet hir werk.
Now was ther of that chirche a parissh clerk,
The which that was ycleped Absolon.
Crul was his heer, and as the gold it shoon,
And strouted as a fanne large and brode;
Ful streight and evene lay his joly shode.   3316
His rode was reed, his eyen greye as goos.
With Poules wyndow corven on his shoos,
In hoses rede he wente fetisly.
Yclad he was ful smal and proprely   3320
Al in a kirtel of a lyght waget;
Ful faire and thikke been the poyntes set.
And therupon he hadde a gay surplys
As whit as is the blosme upon the rys.
A myrie child he was, so God me save.   3325
Wel koude he laten blood and clippe and
                                        shave,
And maken a chartre of lond or acquitaunce.
In twenty manere koude he trippe and daunce
After the scole of Oxenforde tho,
And with his legges casten to and fro,   3330
And pleyen songes on a smal rubible;
Therto he song som tyme a loud quynyble;

And as wel koude he pleye on a giterne.
In al the toun nas brewhous ne taverne
That he ne visited with his solas,   3335
Ther any gaylard tappestere was.
But sooth to seyn, he was somdeel squaymous
Of fartyng, and of speche daungerous.
   This Absolon, that jolif was and gay,
Gooth with a sencer on the haliday,   3340
Sensynge the wyves of the parisshe faste;
And many a lovely look on hem he caste,
And namely on this carpenteris wyf.
To looke on hire hym thoughte a myrie lyf,
She was so propre and sweete and likerous.
I dar wel seyn, if she hadde been a mous,   3346
And he a cat, he wolde hire hente anon.
This parissh clerk, this joly Absolon,
Hath in his herte swich a love-longynge
That of no wyf took he noon offrynge;   3350
For curteisie, he seyde, he wolde noon.
   The moone, whan it was nyght, ful brighte
     shoon,
And Absolon his gyterne hath ytake,
For paramours he thoghte for to wake.
And forth he gooth, jolif and amorous,   3355
Til he cam to the carpenteres hous
A litel after cokkes hadde ycrowe,
And dressed hym up by a shot-wyndowe
That was upon the carpenteris wal.
He syngeth in his voys gentil and smal,   3360
"Now, deere lady, if thy wille be,
I praye yow that ye wole rewe on me,"
Ful wel acordaunt to his gyternynge.
This carpenter awook, and herde him synge,
And spak unto his wyf, and seyde anon,   3365
"What! Alison! herestow nat Absolon,
That chaunteth thus under oure boures wal?"
And she answerde hir housbonde therwithal,
"Yis, God woot, John, I heere it every deel."
   This passeth forth; what wol ye bet than
     weel?
Fro day to day this joly Absolon   3371
So woweth hire that hym is wo bigon.
He waketh al the nyght and al the day;
He kembeth his lokkes brode, and made hym
     gay;
He woweth hire by meenes and brocage,   3375
And swoor he wolde been hir owene page;
He syngeth, brokkynge as a nyghtyngale;
He sente hire pyment, meeth, and spiced ale,
And wafres, pipyng hoot out of the gleede;
And, for she was of town, he profred meede.
For som folk wol ben wonnen for richesse,   3381
And somme for strokes, and somme for gen-
     tillesse.

Somtyme, to shewe his lightnesse and
     maistrye,
He pleyeth Herodes upon a scaffold hye.
But what availleth hym as in this cas?   3385
She loveth so this hende Nicholas
That Absolon may blowe the bukkes horn;
He ne hadde for his labour but a scorn.
And thus she maketh Absolon hire ape,
And al his ernest turneth til a jape.   3390
Ful sooth is this proverbe, it is no lye,
Men seyn right thus, "Alwey the nye slye
Maketh the ferre leeve to be looth."
For though that Absolon be wood or wrooth,
By cause that he fer was from hire sight,   3395
This nye Nicholas stood in his light.
   Now ber thee wel, thou hende Nicholas,
For Absolon may waille and synge "allas."
And so bifel it on a Saterday,
This carpenter was goon til Osenay;   3400
And hende Nicholas and Alisoun
Acorded been to this conclusioun,
That Nicholas shal shapen hym a wyle
This sely jalous housbonde to bigyle;
And if so be the game wente aright,   3405
She sholde slepen in his arm al nyght,
For this was his desir and hire also.
And right anon, withouten wordes mo,
This Nicholas no lenger wolde tarie,   3409
But dooth ful softe unto his chambre carie
Bothe mete and drynke for a day or tweye,
And to hire housbonde bad hire for to seye,
If that he axed after Nicholas,
She sholde seye she nyste where he was,
Of al that day she saugh hym nat with ye;
She trowed that he was in maladye,   3416
For for no cry hir mayde koude hym calle,
He nolde answere for thyng that myghte falle.
   This passeth forth al thilke Saterday,
That Nicholas stille in his chambre lay,   3420
And eet and sleep, or dide what hym leste,
Til Sonday, that the sonne gooth to reste.
This sely carpenter hath greet merveyle
Of Nicholas, or what thyng myghte hym eyle,
And seyde, "I am adrad, by Seint Thomas,
It stondeth nat aright with Nicholas.   3426
God shilde that he deyde sodeynly!
This world is now ful tikel, sikerly.
I saugh to-day a cors yborn to chirche   3429
That now, on Monday last, I saugh hym
     wirche.
   "Go up," quod he unto his knave anoon,
"Clepe at his dore, or knokke with a stoon.
Looke how it is, and tel me boldely."
   This knave gooth hym up ful sturdily,   3434

And at the chambre dore whil that he stood,
He cride and knokked as that he were wood,
"What! how! what do ye, maister Nicholay?
How may ye slepen al the longe day?"

But al for noght, he herde nat a word.
An hole he foond, ful lowe upon a bord, 3440
Ther as the cat was wont in for to crepe,
And at that hole he looked in ful depe,
And at the laste he hadde of hym a sight.
This Nicholas sat evere capyng upright,
As he had kiked on the newe moone. 3445
Adoun he gooth, and tolde his maister soone
In what array he saugh this ilke man.

This carpenter to blessen hym bigan,
And seyde, "Help us, seinte Frydeswyde!
A man woot litel what hym shal bityde. 3450
This man is falle, with his astromye,
In some woodnesse or in som agonye.
I thoghte ay wel how that it sholde be!
Men sholde nat knowe of Goddes pryvetee.
Ye, blessed be alwey a lewed man 3455
That noght but oonly his bileve kan!
So ferde another clerk with astromye;
He walked in the feeldes, for to prye
Upon the sterres, what ther sholde bifalle,
Til he was in a marle-pit yfalle; 3460
He saugh nat that. But yet, by seint Thomas,
Me reweth soore of hende Nicholas.
He shal be rated of his studiyng,
If that I may, by Jhesus, hevene kyng!
Get me a staf, that I may underspore, 3465
Whil that thou, Robyn, hevest up the dore.
He shal out of his studiyng, as I gesse" —
And to the chambre dore he gan hym dresse.
His knave was a strong carl for the nones,
And by the haspe he haaf it of atones; 3470
Into the floor the dore fil anon.
This Nicholas sat ay as stille as stoon,
And evere caped upward into the eir.
This carpenter wende he were in despeir,
And hente hym by the sholdres myghtily, 3475
And shook hym harde, and cride spitously,
"What! Nicholay! what, how! what, looke
    adoun!
Awak, and thenk on Cristes passioun!
I crouche thee from elves and fro wightes.
Therwith the nyght-spel seyde he anon-rightes
On foure halves of the hous aboute, 3481
And on the threshfold of the dore withoute:
"Jhesu Crist and seinte Benedight,
Blesse this hous from every wikked wight,
For nyghtes verye, the white *pater-noster*! 3485
Where wentestow, seinte Petres soster?"

And atte laste this hende Nicholas

Gan for to sik soore, and seyde, "Allas!
Shal al the world be lost eftsoones now?" 3489

This carpenter answerde, "What seystow?
What! thynk on God, as we doon, men that
    swynke."

This Nicholas answerde, "Fecche me drynke,
And after wol I speke in pryvetee
Of certeyn thyng that toucheth me and thee.
I wol telle it noon oother man, certeyn." 3495

This carpenter goth doun, and comth ageyn,
And broghte of myghty ale a large quart;
And whan that ech of hem had dronke his part,
This Nicholas his dore faste shette,
And doun the carpenter by hym he sette. 3500

He seyde "John, myn hooste, lief and deere,
Thou shalt upon thy trouthe swere me heere
That to no wight thou shalt this conseil wreye;
For it is Cristes conseil that I seye,
And if thou telle it man, thou art forlore; 3505
For this vengeaunce thou shalt han therfore,
That if thou wreye me, thou shalt be wood."
"Nay, Crist forbede it, for his hooly blood!"
Quod tho this sely man, "I nam no labbe; 3509
Ne, though I seye, I nam nat lief to gabbe.
Sey what thou wolt, I shal it nevere telle
To child ne wyf, by hym that harwed helle!"

"Now John," quod Nicholas, "I wol nat lye;
I have yfounde in myn astrologye,
As I have looked in the moone bright, 3515
That now a Monday next, at quarter nyght,
Shal falle a reyn, and that so wilde and wood,
That half so greet was nevere Noes flood.
This world," he seyde, "in lasse than an hour
Shal al be dreynt, so hidous is the shour. 3520
Thus shal mankynde drenche, and lese hir lyf."

This carpenter answerde, "Allas, my wyf!
And shal she drenche? allas, myn Alisoun!"
For sorwe of this he fil almoost adoun, 3524
And seyde, "Is ther no remedie in this cas?"

"Why, yis, for Gode," quod hende Nicholas,
"If thou wolt werken after loore and reed.
Thou mayst nat werken after thyn owene heed;
For thus seith Salomon, that was ful trewe,
'Werk al by conseil, and thou shalt nat rewe.'
And if thou werken wolt by good conseil, 3531
I undertake, withouten mast and seyl,
Yet shal I saven hire and thee and me.
Hastow nat herd hou saved was Noe, 3534
Whan that oure Lord hadde warned hym
    biforn
That al the world with water sholde be lorn?"

"Yis," quod this Carpenter, "ful yoore ago."
"Hastou nat herd," quod Nicholas, "also
The sorwe of Noe with his felaweshipe,

Er that he myghte gete his wyf to shipe? 3540
Hym hadde be levere, I dar wel undertake
At thilke tyme, than alle his wetheres blake
That she hadde had a ship hirself allone.
And therfore, woostou what is best to doone?
This asketh haste, and of an hastif thyng 3545
Men may nat preche or maken tariyng.

Anon go gete us faste into this in
A knedyng trogh, or ellis a kymelyn,
For ech of us, but looke that they be large,
In which we mowe swymme as in a barge,
And han therinne vitaille suffisant 3551
But for a day, — fy on the remenant!
The water shal aslake and goon away
Aboute pryme upon the nexte day. 3554
But Robyn may nat wite of this, thy knave,
Ne eek thy mayde Gille I may nat save;
Axe nat why, for though thou aske me,
I wol nat tellen Goddes pryvetee.
Suffiseth thee, but if thy wittes madde,
To han as greet a grace as Noe hadde. 3560
Thy wyf shal I wel saven, out of doute.
Go now thy wey, and speed thee heer-aboute.

But whan thou hast, for hire and thee and
    me,
Ygeten us thise knedyng tubbes thre, 3564
Thanne shaltow hange hem in the roof ful hye,
That no man of oure purveiaunce spye.
And whan thou thus hast doon, as I have seyd,
And hast oure vitaille faire in hem yleyd,
And eek an ax, to smyte the corde atwo, 3569
Whan that the water comth, that we may go,
And breke an hole an heigh, upon the gable,
Unto the gardyn-ward, over the stable,
That we may frely passen forth oure way,
Whan that the grete shour is goon away,
Thanne shaltou swymme as myrie, I undertake,
As dooth the white doke after hire drake. 3576
Thanne wol I clepe, 'How, Alison! how, John!
Be myrie, for the flood wol passe anon.'
And thou wolt seyn, 'Hayl, maister Nicholay!
Good morwe, I se thee wel, for it is day.' 3580
And thanne shul we be lordes al oure lyf
Of al the world, as Noe and his wyf.

But of o thyng I warne thee ful right:
Be wel avysed on that ilke nyght
That we ben entred into shippes bord, 3585
That noon of us ne speke nat a word,
Ne clepe, ne crie, but be in his preyere;
For it is Goddes owene heeste deere.

Thy wyf and thou moote hange fer atwynne;
For that bitwixe yow shal be no synne, 3590
Namoore in lookyng than ther shal in deede,
This ordinance is seyd. Go, God thee speede!

Tomorwe at nyght, whan men ben alle aslepe,
Into oure knedyng-tubbes wol we crepe,
And sitten there, abidyng Goddes grace. 3595
Go now thy wey, I have no lenger space
To make of this no lenger sermonyng.
Men seyn thus, 'sende the wise, and sey no
    thyng:'
Thou art so wys, it needeth thee nat teche.
Go, save oure lyf, and that I the biseche." 3600

This sely carpenter goth forth his wey.
Ful ofte he seide "allas" and "weylawey,"
And to his wyf he tolde his pryvetee, 3603
And she was war, and knew it bet than he,
What al this queynte cast was for to seye.
But nathelees she ferde as she wolde deye,
And seyde, "Allas! go forth thy wey anon,
Help us to scape, or we been dede echon!
I am thy trewe, verray wedded wyf; 3609
Go, deere spouse, and help to save oure lyf."

Lo, which a greet thyng is affeccioun!
Men may dyen of ymaginacioun,
So depe may impressioun be take.
This sely carpenter bigynneth quake;
Hym thynketh verraily that he may see 3615
Noees flood come walwynge as the see
To drenchen Alisoun, his hony deere.
He wepeth, weyleth, maketh sory cheere;
He siketh with ful many a sory swogh; 3619
He gooth and geteth hym a knedyng trogh,
And after that a tubbe and a kymelyn,
And pryvely he sente hem to his in,
And heng hem in the roof in pryvetee.
His owene hand he made laddres thre, 3624
To clymben by the ronges and the stalkes
Unto the tubbes hangynge in the balkes,
And hem vitailled, bothe trogh and tubbe,
With breed and chese, and good ale in a jubbe,
Suffisynge right ynogh as for a day.
But er that he hadde maad al this array, 3630
He sente his knave, and eek his wenche also,
Upon his nede to London for to go.
And on the Monday, whan it drow to nyght,
He shette his dore withoute candel-lyght,
And dressed alle thyng as it sholde be. 3635
And shortly, up they clomben alle thre;
They seten stille wel a furlong way.
"Now, *Pater-noster*, clom!" seyde Nicholay,
And "clom," quod John, and "clom," seyde Ali-
    soun.
This carpenter seyde his devocioun, 3640
And stille he sit, and biddeth his preyere,
Awaitynge on the reyn, if he it heere.

The dede sleep, for wery bisynesse,
Fil on this carpenter right, as I gesse,

Aboute corfew-tyme, or litel moore;   3645
For travaille of his goost he groneth soore,
And eft he routeth, for his heed myslay.
Doun of the laddre stalketh Nicholay,
And Alisoun ful softe adoun she spedde;
Withouten wordes mo they goon to bedde,
Ther as the carpenter is wont to lye.   3651
Ther was the revel and the melodye;
And thus lith Alison and Nicholas,
In bisynesse of myrthe and of solas,
Til that the belle of laudes gan to rynge,   3655
And freres in the chauncel gonne synge.

This parissh clerk, this amorous Absolon,
That is for love alwey so wo bigon,
Upon the Monday was at Oseneye   3659
With compaignye, hym to disporte and pleye,
And axed upon cas a cloisterer
Ful prively after John the carpenter;
And he drough hym apart out of the chirche,
And seyde, "I noot, I saugh hym heere nat
     wirche
Syn Saterday; I trowe that he be went   3665
For tymber, ther oure abbot hath hym sent;
For he is wont for tymber for to go,
And dwellen at the grange a day or two;
Or elles he is at his hous, certeyn.
Where that he be, I kan nat soothly seyn."   3670

This Absolon ful joly was and light,
And thoghte, "Now is tyme to wake al nyght;
For sikirly I saugh hym nat stirynge
Aboute his dore, syn day bigan to sprynge.

So moot I thryve, I shal, at cokkes crowe,
Ful pryvely knokken at his wyndowe   3676
That stant ful lowe upon his boures wal.
To Alison now wol I tellen al
My love-longynge, for yet I shal nat mysse
That at the leeste wey I shal hire kisse.   3680
Som maner confort shal I have, parfay.
My mouth hath icched al this longe day;
That is a signe of kissyng atte leeste.
Al nyght me mette eek I was at a feeste.   3684
Therfore I wol go slepe an houre or tweye,
And al the nyght thanne wol I wake and
     pleye."

Whan that the firste cok hath crowe, anon
Up rist this joly lovere Absolon,
And hym arraieth gay, at poynt-devys.
But first he cheweth greyn and lycorys,   3690
To smellen sweete, er he hadde kembd his heer.
Under his tonge a trewe-love he beer,
For therby wende he to ben gracious.
He rometh to the carpenteres hous,   3694
And stille he stant under the shot-wyndowe –
Unto his brest it raughte, it was so lowe –

And softe he cougheth with a semy soun:
"What do ye, hony-comb, sweete Alisoun,
My faire bryd, my sweete cynamome?   3699
Awaketh, lemman myn, and speketh to me!
Wel litel thynken ye upon my wo,
That for youre love I swete ther I go.
No wonder is thogh that I swelte and swete;
I moorne as dooth a lamb after the tete.   3704
Ywis, lemman, I have swich love-longynge,
That lik a turtel trewe is my moornynge.
I may nat ete na moore than a mayde."

"Go fro the wyndow, Jakke fool," she sayde;
"As help me God, it wol nat be 'com pa me.'
I love another – and elles I were to blame –
Wel bet than thee, by Jhesu, Absolon.   3711
Go forth thy wey, or I wol caste a ston,
And lat me slepe, a twenty devel wey!"

"Allas," quod Absolon, "and weylawey,
That trewe love was evere so yvel biset!   3715
Thanne kysse me, syn it may be no bet,
For Jhesus love, and for the love of me."

"Wiltow thanne go thy wey therwith?" quod
     she.

"Ye, certes, lemman," quod this Absolon.

"Thanne make thee redy," quod she, "I come
     anon."
And unto Nicholas she seyde stille,   3721
"Now hust, and thou shalt laughen al thy fille."

This Absolon doun sette hym on his knees
And seyde, "I am a lord at alle degrees;
For after this I hope ther cometh moore.   3725
Lemman, thy grace, and sweete bryd, thyn
     oore!"

The wyndow she undoth, and that in haste.
"Have do," quod she, "com of, and speed the
     faste,
Lest that oure neighebores thee espie."   3729

This Absolon gan wype his mouth ful drie.
Derk was the nyght as pich, or as the cole,
And at the wyndow out she putte hir hole,
And Absolon, hym fil no bet ne wers,
But with his mouth he kiste hir naked ers
Ful savourly, er he were war of this.   3735
Abak he stirte, and thoughte it was amys,
For wel he wiste a womman hath no berd.
He felte a thyng al rough and long yherd,
And seyde, "Fy! allas! what have I do?"

"Tehee!" quod she, and clapte the wyndow
     to,
And Absolon gooth forth a sory pas.   3741

"A berd! a berd!" quod hende Nicholas,
"By Goddes corpus, this goth faire and weel."
This sely Absolon herde every deel,
And on his lippe he gan for anger byte,   3745

And to hymself he seyde, "I shal thee quyte."
 Who rubbeth now, who froteth now his
  lippes
With dust, with sond, with straw, with clooth,
  with chippes,
But Absolon, that seith ful ofte, "Allas!"
"My soule bitake I unto Sathanas,   3750
But me were levere than al this toun," quod he,
"Of this despit awroken for to be.
Allas," quod he, "allas, I ne hadde ybleynt!"
His hoote love was coold and al yqueynt;
For fro that tyme that he hadde kist hir ers,
Of paramours he sette nat a kers;   3756
For he was heeled of his maladie.
Ful ofte paramours he gan deffie,
And weep as dooth a child that is ybete.
A softe paas he wente over the strete 3760
Until a smyth men cleped daun Gerveys,
That in his forge smythed plough harneys;
He sharpeth shaar and kultour bisily.
This Absolon knokketh al esily,   3764
And seyde, "Undo, Gerveys, and that anon."
 "What, who artow?" "It am I, Absolon."
"What, Absolon! for Cristes sweete tree,
Why rise ye so rathe? ey, *benedicitee!*
What eyleth yow? Som gay gerl, God it woot,
Hath broght yow thus upon the viritoot. 3770
By seinte Note, ye woot wel what I mene."
 This Absolon ne roghte nat a bene
Of al his pley; no word agayn he yaf;
He hadde moore tow on his distaf   3774
Than Gerveys knew, and seyde, "Freend so
  deere,
That hoote kultour in the chymenee heere,
As lene it me, I have therwith to doone,
And I wol brynge it thee agayn ful soone."
 Gerveys answerde, "Certes, were it gold,
Or in a poke nobles alle untold,   3780
Thou sholdest have, as I am trewe smyth.
Ey, Cristes foo! what wol ye do therwith?"
 "Therof," quod Absolon, "be as be may.
I shal wel telle it thee to-morwe day"—
And caughte the kultour by the colde stele.
Ful softe out at the dore he gan to stele, 3786
And wente unto the carpenteris wal.
He cogheth first, and knokketh therwithal
Upon the wyndowe, right as he dide er.
 This Alison answerde, "Who is ther 3790
That knokketh so? I warante it a theef."
 "Why, nay," quod he, "God woot, my sweete
  leef,
I am thyn Absolon, my deerelyng.
Of gold," quod he, "I have thee broght a ryng.
My mooder yaf it me, so God me save; 3795

Ful fyn it is, and therto wel ygrave.
This wol I yeve thee, if thou me kisse."
 This Nicholas was risen for to pisse,
And thoughte he wolde amenden al the jape;
He sholde kisse his ers er that he scape. 3800
And up the wyndowe dide he hastily,
And out his ers he putteth pryvely
Over the buttok, to the haunche-bon;
And therwith spak this clerk, this Absolon,
"Spek, sweete bryd, I noot nat where thou
  art."
 This Nicholas anon leet fle a fart, 3806
As greet as it had been a thonder-dent,
That with the strook he was almoost yblent;
And he was redy with his iren hoot,
And Nicholas amydde the ers he smoot. 3810
 Of gooth the skyn an hande-brede aboute,
The hoote kultour brende so his toute,
And for the smert he wende for to dye.
As he were wood, for wo he gan to crye, 3814
"Help! water! water! help, for Goddes herte!"
 This carpenter out of his slomber sterte,
And herde oon crien "water" as he were wood,
And thoughte, "Allas, now comth Nowelis
  flood!"
He sit hym up withouten wordes mo, 3819
And with his ax he smoot the corde atwo,
And doun gooth al; he foond neither to selle,
Ne breed ne ale, til he cam to the celle
Upon the floor, and ther aswowne he lay.
 Up stirte hire Alison and Nicholay, 3824
And criden "out" and "harrow" in the strete.
The neighebores, bothe smale and grete,
In ronnen for to gauren on this man,
That yet aswowne lay, bothe pale and wan,
For with the fal he brosten hadde his arm.
But stonde he moste unto his owene harm;
For whan he spak, he was anon bore doun 3831
With hende Nicholas and Alisoun.
They tolden every man that he was wood,
He was agast so of Nowelis flood
Thurgh fantasie, that of his vanytee 3835
He hadde yboght hym knedyng tubbes thre,
And hadde hem hanged in the roof above;
And that he preyed hem, for Goddes love,
To sitten in the roof, *par compaignye.*
 The folk gan laughen at his fantasye; 3840
Into the roof they kiken and they cape,
And turned al his harm unto a jape.
For what so that this carpenter answerde,
It was for noght, no man his reson herde.
With othes grete he was so sworn adoun 3845
That he was holde wood in al the toun;
For every clerk anonright heeld with oother.

They seyde, "The man is wood, my leeve
    brother";
And every wight gan laughen at this stryf.
Thus swyved was this carpenteris wyf,   3850

For al his kepyng and his jalousye;
And Absolon hath kist hir nether ye;
And Nicholas is scalded in the towte.
This tale is doon, and God save al the rowte!

Heere endeth the Millere his tale.

The Reeve's Prologue

The prologe of the Reves Tale.

Whan folk hadde laughen at this nyce cas
Of Absolon and hende Nicholas,   3856
Diverse folk diversely they seyde,
But for the moore part they loughe and pleyde.
Ne at this tale I saugh no man hym greve,
But it were oonly Osewold the Reve.   3860
By cause he was of carpenteris craft,
A litel ire is in his herte ylaft;
He gan to grucche, and blamed it a lite.
    "So theek," quod he, "ful wel koude I thee
    quite
With bleryng of a proud milleres ye,   3865
If that me liste speke of ribaudye.
But ik am oold, me list not pley for age;
Gras tyme is doon, my fodder is now forage;
This white top writeth myne olde yeris;
Myn herte is also mowled as myne heris,   3870
But if I fare as dooth an open-ers, —
That ilke fruyt is ever lenger the wers,
Til it be roten in mullok or in stree.
We olde men, I drede, so fare we:
Til we be roten, kan we nat be rype;   3875
We hoppen alwey whil the world wol pype.
For in oure wyl ther stiketh evere a nayl,
To have an hoor heed and a grene tayl,
As hath a leek; for thogh oure myght be goon,
Oure wyl desireth folie evere in oon.   3880
For whan we may nat doon, than wol we speke;
Yet in oure asshen olde is fyr yreke.
    Foure gleedes han we, which I shal de-
    vyse, —
Avauntyng, liyng, anger, coveitise;
Thise foure sparkles longen unto eelde.   3885
Oure olde lemes mowe wel been unweelde,
But wyl ne shal nat faillen, that is sooth.

And yet ik have alwey a coltes tooth,
As many a yeer as it is passed henne
Syn that my tappe of lif bigan to renne.   3890
For sikerly, whan I was bore, anon
Deeth drough the tappe of lyf and leet it
    gon;
And ever sithe hath so the tappe yronne
Til that almoost al empty is the tonne.   3894
The streem of lyf now droppeth on the chymbe.
The sely tonge may wel rynge and chymbe
Of wrecchednesse that passed is ful yoore;
With olde folk, save dotage, is namoore!"
    Whan that oure Hoost hadde herd this ser-
    monyng,
He gan to speke as lordly as a kyng.   3900
He seide, "What amounteth al this wit?
What shul we speke alday of hooly writ?
The devel made a reve for to preche,
Or of a soutere a shipman or a leche.
Sey forth thy tale, and tarie nat the tyme   3905
Lo Depeford! and it is half-wey pryme.
Lo Grenewych, ther many a shrewe is inne!
It were al tyme thy tale to bigynne."
    "Now, sires," quod this Osewold the Reve,
"I pray yow alle that ye nat yow greve,   3910
Thogh I answere, and somdeel sette his howve;
For leveful is with force force of-showve.
    This dronke Millere hath ytoold us heer
How that bigyled was a carpenteer,
Peraventure in scorn, for I am oon.   3915
And, by youre leve, I shal hym quite anoon;
Right in his cherles termes wol I speke.
I pray to God his nekke mote to-breke;
He kan wel in myn eye seen a stalke,
But in his owene he kan nat seen a balke.   3920

The Reeve's Tale

Heere bigynneth the Reves Tale.

At Trumpyngtoun, nat fer fro Cantebrigge,
Ther gooth a brook, and over that a brigge,
Upon the whiche brook ther stant a melle;
And this is verray sooth that I yow telle:
A millere was ther dwellynge many a day.   3925
As any pecok he was proud and gay.
Pipen he koude and fisshe, and nettes beete,
And turne coppes, and wel wrastle and sheete;
Ay by his belt he baar a long panade,
And of a swerd ful trenchant was the blade.
A joly poppere baar he is in his pouche;   3931
Ther was no man, for peril, dorste hym touche.
A Sheffeld thwitel baar he in his hose.
Round was his face, and camus was his nose;
As piled as an ape was his skulle.   3935
He was a market-betere atte fulle.
Ther dorste no wight hand upon hym legge,
That he ne swoor he sholde anon abegge.
A theef he was for sothe of corn and mele,
And that a sly, and usaunt for to stele.   3940
His name was hoote deynous Symkyn.
A wyf he hadde, ycomen of noble kyn;
The person of the toun hir fader was.
With hire he yaf ful many a panne of bras,
For that Symkyn sholde in his blood allye.
She was yfostred in a nonnerye;   3946
For Symkyn wolde no wyf, as he sayde,
But she were wel ynorissed and a mayde,
To saven his estaat of yomanrye.
And she was proud, and peert as is a pye.   3950
A ful fair sighte was it upon hem two;
On halydayes biforn hire wolde he go
With his typet bounden aboute his heed,
And she cam after in a gyte of reed;
And Symkyn hadde hosen of the same.   3955
Ther dorste no wight clepen hire but "dame";
Was noon so hardy that wente by the weye
That with hire dorste rage or ones pleye,
But if he wolde be slayn of Symkyn
With panade, or with knyf, or boidekyn.   3960
For jalous folk ben perilous everemo;
Algate they wolde hire wyves wenden so.
And eek, for she was somdel smoterlich,
She was as digne as water in a dich,
And ful of hoker and of bisemare.   3965
Hir thoughte that a lady sholde hire spare,
What for hire kynrede and hir nortelrie
That she hadde lerned in the nonnerie.

A doghter hadde they bitwixe hem two
Of twenty yeer, withouten any mo,   3970
Savynge a child that was of half yeer age;
In cradel it lay and was a propre page.
This wenche thikke and wel ygrowen was,
With kamus nose, and eyen greye as glas,
With buttokes brode, and brestes rounde and
     hye;
But right fair was hire heer, I wol nat lye.   3976
This person of the toun, for she was feir,
In purpos was to maken hire his heir,
Bothe of his catel and his mesuage,
And straunge he made it of hir mariage.   3980
His purpos was for to bistowe hire hye
Into som worthy blood of auncetrye;
For hooly chirches good moot been despended
On hooly chirches blood, that is descended.
Therfore he wolde his hooly blood hon-
     oure,   3985
Though that he hooly chirche sholde devoure.
Greet sokene hath this millere, out of doute,
With whete and malt of al the land aboute;
And nameliche ther was a greet collegge   3989
Men clepen the Soler Halle at Cantebregge;
Ther was hir whete and eek hir malt ygrounde.
And on a day it happed, in a stounde,
Sik lay the maunciple on a maladye;
Men wenden wisly that he sholde dye.   3994
For which this millere stal bothe mele and corn
An hundred tyme moore than biforn;
For therbiforn he stal but curteisly,
But now he was a theef outrageously,
For which the wardeyn chidde and made fare.
But therof sette the millere nat a tare;   4000
He craketh boost, and swoor it was nat so.
Thanne were ther yonge povre scolers two,
That dwelten in this halle, of which I seye.
Testif they were, and lusty for to pleye,
And, oonly for hire myrthe and revelrye,   4005
Upon the wardeyn bisily they crye
To yeve hem leve, but a litel stounde,
To goon to mille and seen hir corn ygrounde;
And hardily they dorste leye hir nekke   4009
The millere sholde not stele hem half a pekke
Of corn by sleighte, ne by force hem reve;
And at the laste the wardeyn yaf hem leve.
John highte that oon, and Aleyn highte that
     oother;

Of o toun were they born, that highte Strother,
Fer in the north, I kan nat telle where. 4015
  This Aleyn maketh redy al his gere,
And on an hors the sak he caste anon.
Forth goth Aleyn the clerk, and also John,
With good swerd and with bokeler by hir syde.
John knew the wey, — hem nedede no gyde, —
And at the mille the sak adoun he layth. 4021
Aleyn spak first, "Al hayl, Symond, y-fayth!
Hou fares thy faire doghter and thy wyf?"
  "Aleyn, welcome," quod Symkyn, "by my
      lyf!
And John also, how now, what do ye
      heer?" 4025
  "Symond," quod John, "by God, nede has na
      peer.
Hym boes serve hymself that has na swayn,
Or elles he is a fool, as clerkes sayn.
Oure manciple, I hope he wil be deed,
Swa werkes ay the wanges in his heed; 4030
And forthy is I come, and eek Alayn,
To grynde oure corn and carie it ham agayn;
I pray yow spede us heythen that ye may."
  "It shal be doon," quod Symkyn, "by my
      fay! 4034
What wol ye doon whil that it is in hande?"
  "By God, right by the hopur wil I stande,"
Quod John, "and se howgates the corn gas in.
Yet saugh I nevere, by my fader kyn,
How that the hopur wagges til and fra."
  Aleyn answerde, "John, and wiltow swa?
Thanne wil I be bynethe, by my croun, 4041
And se how that the mele falles doun
Into the trough; that sal be my disport.
For John, y-faith, I may been of youre sort;
I is as ille a millere as ar ye." 4045
  This millere smyled of hir nycetee,
And thoghte, "Al this nys doon but for a wyle.
They wene that no man may hem bigyle,
But by my thrift, yet shal I blere hir ye,
For al the sleighte in hir philosophye. 4050
The moore queynte crekes that they make,
The moore wol I stele whan I take.
In stide of flour yet wol I yeve hem bren.
'The gretteste clerkes been noght wisest men,'
As whilom to the wolf thus spak the mare.
Of al hir art ne counte I noght a tare." 4056
  Out at the dore he gooth ful pryvely,
Whan that he saugh his tyme, softely.
He looketh up and doun til he hath founde
The clerkes hors, ther as it stood ybounde 4060
Bihynde the mille, under a levesel;
And to the hors he gooth hym faire and wel;
He strepeth of the brydel right anon.

And whan the hors was laus, he gynneth gon
Toward the fen, ther wilde mares renne, 4065
And forth with "wehee," thurgh thikke and
      thurgh thenne.
  This millere gooth agayn, no word he seyde,
But dooth his note, and with the clerkes
      pleyde,
Til that hir corn was faire and weel ygrounde.
And whan the mele is sakked and ybounde,
This John goth out and fynt his hors away, 4071
And gan to crie "Harrow!" and "Weylaway!
Oure hors is lorn, Alayn, for Goddes banes,
Step on thy feet! Com of, man, al atanes!
Allas, our wardeyn has his palfrey lorn." 4075
This Aleyn al forgat, bothe mele and corn;
Al was out of his mynde his housbondrie.
"What, whilk way is he geen?" he gan to crie.
  The wyf cam lepynge inward with a ren.
She seyde, "Allas! youre hors goth to the fen
With wilde mares, as faste as he may go. 4081
Unthank come on his hand that boond hym so,
And he that bettre sholde han knyt the reyne!"
  "Allas," quod John, "Aleyn, for Cristes peyne
Lay doun thy swerd, and I wil myn alswa.
I is ful wight, God waat, as is a raa; 4086
By Goddes herte, he sal nat scape us bathe!
Why ne had thow pit the capul in the lathe?
Ilhayl! by God, Alayn, thou is a fonne!"
  Thise sely clerkes han ful faste yronne 4090
Toward the fen, bothe Aleyn and eek John.
  And whan the millere saugh that they were
      gon,
He half a busshel of hir flour hath take,
And bad his wyf go knede it in a cake.
He seyde, "I trowe the clerkes were aferd.
Yet kan a millere make a clerkes berd, 4096
For al his art; now lat hem goon hir weye!
Lo, wher he gooth! ye, lat the children pleye.
They gete hym nat so lightly, by my croun."
  Thise sely clerkes rennen up and doun 4100
With "Keep! keep! stand! stand! jossa, war-
      derere,
Ga whistle thou, and I shal kepe hym heere!"
But shortly, til that it was verray nyght,
They koude nat, though they dide al hir myght,
Hir capul cacche, he ran alwey so faste, 4105
Til in a dych they caughte hym atte laste.
  Wery and weet, as beest is in the reyn,
Comth sely John, and with him comth Aleyn.
"Allas," quod John, "the day that I was born!
Now are we dryve til hethyng and til scorn.
Oure corn is stoln, men wil us fooles calle, 4111
Bathe the wardeyn and oure felawes alle,
And namely the millere, weylaway!"

Thus pleyneth John as he gooth by the way
Toward the mille, and Bayard in his hond.
The millere sittynge by the fyr he fond,   4116
For it was nyght, and forther myghte they
    noght;
But for the love of God they hym bisoght
Of herberwe and of ese, as for hir peny.   4119
    The millere seyde agayn, "If ther be eny,
Swich as it is, yet shal ye have youre part.
Myn hous is streit, but ye han lerned art;
Ye konne by argumentes make a place
A myle brood of twenty foot of space.
Lat se now if this place may suffise,   4125
Or make it rowm with speche, as is youre gise."
    "Now, Symond," seyde John, "by seint Cut-
    berd,
Ay is thou myrie, and this is faire answerd.
I have herd seyd, 'man sal taa of twa thynges
Slyk as he fyndes, or taa slyk as he brynges.'
But specially I pray thee, hooste deere,   4131
Get us som mete and drynke, and make us
    cheere,
And we wil payen trewely atte fulle.
With empty hand men may na haukes tulle;
Loo, heere oure silver, redy for to spende."
    This millere into toun his doghter sende   4136
For ale and breed, and rosted hem a goos,
And boond hire hors, it sholde namoore go loos;
And in his owene chambre hem made a bed,
With sheetes and with chalons faire yspred   4140
Noght from his owene bed ten foot or twelve.
His doghter hadde a bed, al by hirselve,
Right in the same chambre by and by.
It myghte be no bet, and cause why?   4144
Ther was no roumer herberwe in the place.
They soupen and they speke, hem to solace,
And drynken evere strong ale atte beste.
Aboute mydnyght wente they to reste.
    Wel hath this millere vernysshed his heed;
Ful pale he was for dronken, and nat reed.   4150
He yexeth, and he speketh thurgh the nose
As he were on the quakke, or on the pose.
To bedde he goth, and with hym goth his wyf.
As any jay she light was and jolyf,
So was hir joly whistle wel ywet.   4155
The cradel at hir beddes feet is set,
To rokken, and to yeve the child to sowke.
And whan that dronken al was in the crowke,
To bedde wente the doghter right anon;
To bedde goth Aleyn and also John;   4160
Ther nas na moore, – hem nedede no dwale.
This millere hath so wisely bibbed ale
That as an hors he fnorteth in his sleep,
Ne of his tayl bihynde he took no keep.

His wyf bar hym a burdon, a ful strong;   4165
Men myghte hir rowtyng heere two furlong;
The wenche rowteth eek, *par compaignye*.
    Aleyn the clerk, that herde this melodye,
He poked John, and seyde, "Slepestow?
Herdestow evere slyk a sang er now?   4170
Lo, swilk a complyn is ymel hem alle,
A wilde fyr upon thair bodyes falle!
Wha herkned evere slyk a ferly thyng?
Ye, they sal have the flour of il endyng.
This lange nyght ther tydes me na reste;   4175
But yet, nafors, al sal be for the beste.
For, John," seyde he, "als evere moot I thryve,
If that I may, yon wenche wil I swyve.
Som esement has lawe yshapen us;
For, John, ther is a lawe that says thus,   4180
That gif a man in a point be agreved,
That in another he sal be releved.
Oure corn is stoln, sothly, it is na nay,
And we han had an il fit al this day;
And syn I sal have neen amendement   4185
Agayn my los, I will have esement.
By Goddes sale, it sal neen other bee!"
    This John answerde, "Alayn, avyse thee!
The millere is a perilous man," he seyde,
"And gif that he out of his sleep abreyde,   4190
He myghte doon us bathe a vileynye."
    Aleyn answerde, "I counte hym nat a flye."
And up he rist, and by the wenche he crepte.
This wenche lay uprighte, and faste slepte,
Til he so ny was, er she myghte espie,   4195
That it had been to late for to crie,
And shortly for to seyn, they were aton.
Now pley, Aleyn, for I wol speke of John.
    This John lith stille a furlong wey or two,
And to hymself he maketh routhe and wo.   4200
"Allas!" quod he, "this is a wikked jape;
Now may I seyn that I is but an ape.
Yet has my felawe somwhat for his harm;
He has the milleris doghter in his arm.
He auntred hym, and has his nedes sped,   4205
And I lye as a draf-sak in my bed;
And when this jape is tald another day,
I sal been halde a daf, a cokenay!
I wil arise and auntre it, by my fayth!
'Unhardy is unseely,' thus men sayth."   4210
And up he roos, and softely he wente
Unto the cradel, and in his hand it hente,
And baar it softe unto his beddes feet.
    Soone after this the wyf hir rowtyng leet,
And gan awake, and wente hire out to
    pisse,   4215
And cam agayn, and gan hir cradel mysse,
And groped heer and ther, but she foond noon.

"Allas!" quod she, "I hadde almoost mysgoon;
I hadde almoost goon to the clerkes bed.
Ey, benedicite! thanne hadde I foule ysped."
And forth she gooth til she the cradel fond.
She gropeth alwey forther with hir hond,   4222
And foond the bed, and thoghte noght but good,
By cause that the cradel by it stood,
And nyste wher she was, for it was derk;   4225
But faire and wel she creep in to the clerk,
And lith ful stille, and wolde han caught a sleep.
Withinne a while this John the clerk up leep,
And on this goode wyf he leith on soore.
So myrie a fit ne hadde she nat ful yoore;   4230
He priketh harde and depe as he were mad.
This joly lyf han thise two clerkes lad
Til that the thridde cok bigan to synge.
   Aleyn wax wery in the dawenynge,
For he had swonken al the longe nyght,   4235
And seyde, "Fare weel, Malyne, sweete wight!
The day is come, I may no lenger byde;
But everemo, wher so I go or ryde,
I is thyn awen clerk, swa have I seel!"   4239
   "Now, deere lemman," quod she, "go, far weel!
But er thow go, o thyng I wol thee telle:
Whan that thou wendest homward by the melle,
Right at the entree of the dore bihynde
Thou shalt a cake of half a busshel fynde
That was ymaked of thyn owene mele,   4245
Which that I heelp my sire for to stele.
And, goode lemman, God thee save and kepe!"
And with that word almoost she gan to wepe.
   Aleyn up rist, and thoughte, "Er that it dawe,
I wol go crepen in by my felawe";   4250
And fond the cradel with his hand anon.
"By God," thoughte he, "al wrang I have mysgon.
Myn heed is toty of my swynk to-nyght,
That makes me that I ga nat aright.
I woot wel by the cradel I have mysgo;   4255
Heere lith the millere and his wyf also."
And forth he goth, a twenty devel way,
Unto the bed ther as the millere lay.
He wende have cropen by his felawe John,
And by the millere in he creep anon,   4260
And caughte hym by the nekke, and softe he spak.
He seyde, "Thou John, thou swynes-heed, awak,
For Cristes saule, and heer a noble game.
For by that lord that called is seint Jame,

As I have thries in this shorte nyght   4265
Swyved the milleres doghter bolt upright,
Whil thow hast, as a coward, been agast."
   "Ye, false harlot," quod the millere, "hast?
A, false traitour! false clerk!" quod he,
Thow shalt be deed, by Goddes dignitee!   4270
Who dorste be so boold to disparage
My doghter, that is come of swich lynage?"
And by the throte-bolle he caughte Alayn,
And he hente hym despitously agayn,   4274
And on the nose he smoot hym with his fest.
Doun ran the blody streem upon his brest;
And in the floor, with nose and mouth tobroke,
They walwe as doon two pigges in a poke;
And up they goon, and doun agayn anon,
Til that the millere sporned at a stoon,   4280
And doun he fil bakward upon his wyf,
That wiste no thyng of this nyce stryf;
For she was falle aslepe a lite wight
With John the clerk, that waked hadde al nyght.
And with the fal out of hir sleep she breyde.   4285
"Help! hooly croys of Bromeholm," she seyde,
In manus tuas! Lord, to thee I calle!
Awak, Symond! the feend is on me falle.
Myn herte is broken; help! I nam but deed!
Ther lyth oon upon my wombe and on myn heed.   4290
Help, Symkyn, for the false clerkes fighte!"
   This John stirte up as faste as ever he myghte,
And graspeth by the walles to and fro,
To fynde a staf; and she stirte up also,
And knew the estres bet than dide this John,
And by the wal a staf she foond anon,   4296
And saugh a litel shymeryng of a light,
For at an hole in shoon the moone bright;
And by that light she saugh hem bothe two,
But sikerly she nyste who was who,   4300
But as she saugh a whit thyng in hir ye.
And whan she gan this white thyng espye,
She wende the clerk hadde wered a volupeer,
And with the staf she drow ay neer and neer,
And wende han hit this Aleyn at the fulle,   4305
And smoot the millere on the pyled skulle,
That doun he gooth, and cride, "Harrow! I dye!"
Thise clerkes beete hym weel and lete hym lye;
And greythen hem, and tooke hir hors anon,
And eek hire mele, and on hir wey they gon.
And at the mille yet they tooke hir cake   4311
Of half a busshel flour, ful wel ybake.

Thus is the proude millere wel ybete,
And hath ylost the gryndynge of the whete,
And payed for the soper everideel   4315
Of Aleyn and of John, that bette hym weel.
His wyf is swyved, and his doghter als.
Lo, swich it is a millere to be fals!

And therfore this proverbe is seyd ful sooth,
"Hym thar nat wene wel that yvele dooth";
A gylour shal hymself bigyled be.   4321
And God, that sitteth heighe in magestee,
Save al this compaignye, grete and smale!
Thus have I quyt the Millere in my tale.   4324

Heere is ended the Reves tale.

The Cook's Prologue

The prologe of the Cokes Tale.

The Cook of Londoun, whil the Reve spak,
For joye him thoughte he clawed him on the
     bak.
"Ha! ha!" quod he, "for Cristes passion,
This millere hadde a sharp conclusion
Upon his argument of herbergage!
Wel seyde Salomon in his langage,   4330
'Ne bryng nat every man into thyn hous';
For herberwynge by nyghte is perilous.
Wel oghte a man avysed for to be
Whom that he broghte into his pryvetee.
I pray to God, so yeve me sorwe and care   4335
If evere, sitthe I highte Hogge of Ware,
Herde I a millere bettre yset a-werk.
He hadde a jape of malice in the derk.
But God forbede that we stynte heere;
And therfore, if ye vouche-sauf to heere   4340
A tale of me, that am a povre man,
I wol yow telle, as wel as evere I kan,
A litel jape that fil in oure citee."
     Oure Hoost answerde and seide, "I graunte
          it thee.

Now telle on, Roger, looke that it be good;
For many a pastee hastow laten blood,   4346
And many a Jakke of Dovere hastow soold
That hath been twies hoot and twies coold.
Of many a pilgrym hastow Cristes curs,
For of thy percely yet they fare the wors,   4350
That they han eten with thy stubbel goos;
For in thy shoppe is many a flye loos.
Now telle on, gentil Roger by thy name.
But yet I pray thee, be nat wroth for game;
A man may seye ful sooth in game and pley."
     "Thou seist ful sooth," quod Roger, "by my
          fey!   4356
But 'sooth pley, quaad pley,' as the Flemyng
          seith.
And therfore, Herry Bailly, by thy feith,
Be thou nat wrooth, er we departen heer,
Though that my tale be of an hostileer.   4360
But nathelees I wol nat telle it yit;
But er we parte, ywis, thou shalt be quit."
And therwithal he lough and made cheere,
And seyde his tale, as ye shul after heere.

The Cook's Tale

Heere bigynneth the Cookes Tale.

A prentys whilom dwelled in oure citee,
And of a craft of vitailliers was hee.   4366
Gaillard he was as goldfynch in the shawe,
Broun as a berye, a propre short felawe,
With lokkes blake, ykembd ful fetisly.

Dauncen he koude so wel and jolily   4370
That he was cleped Perkyn Revelour.
He was as ful of love and paramour
As is the hyve ful of hony sweete:
Wel was the wenche with hym myghte meete.

At every bridale wolde he synge and
    hoppe;   4375
He loved bet the taverne than the shoppe.
For whan ther any ridyng was in Chepe,
Out of the shoppe thider wolde he lepe —
Til that he hadde al the sighte yseyn,
And daunced wel, he wolde nat come ayeyn —
And gadered hym a meynee of his sort   4381
To hoppe and synge and maken swich disport;
And ther they setten stevene for to meete,
To pleyen at the dys in swich a streete.
For in the toune nas ther no prentys   4385
That fairer koude caste a paire of dys
Than Perkyn koude, and therto he was free
Of his dispense, in place of pryvetee.
That fond his maister wel in his chaffare;
For often tyme he foond his box ful bare.
For sikerly a prentys revelour   4391
That haunteth dys, riot, or paramour,
His maister shal it in his shoppe abye,
Al have he no part of the mynstralcye.
For thefte and riot, they been convertible,
Al konne he pleye on gyterne or ribible.   4396
Revel and trouthe, as in a lowe degree,
They been ful wrothe al day, as men may see.

This joly prentys with his maister bood,
Til he were ny out of his prentishood,   4400
Al were he snybbed bothe erly and late,
And somtyme lad with revel to Newegate.
But atte laste his maister hym bithoghte,
Upon a day, whan he his papir soghte,
Of a proverbe that seith this same word,   4405
"Wel bet is roten appul out of hoord
Than that it rotie al the remenaunt."
So fareth it by a riotous servaunt;
It is ful lasse harm to lete hym pace,   4409
Than he shende alle the servantz in the place.
Therfore his maister yaf hym acquitance,
And bad hym go, with sorwe and with mes-
    chance!
And thus this joly prentys hadde his leve.
Now lat hym riote al the nyght or leve.   4414
And for ther is no theef withoute a lowke,
That helpeth hym to wasten and to sowke
Of that he brybe kan or borwe may,
Anon he sente his bed and his array
Unto a compeer of his owene sort,
That lovede dys, and revel, and disport,   4420
And hadde a wyf that heeld for contenance
A shoppe, and swyved for hir sustenance.

Introduction to The Man of Law's Tale

The wordes of the Hoost to the compaignye.

OURE HOOSTE saugh wel that the brighte
    sonne
The ark of his artificial day hath ronne
The ferthe part, and half an houre and moore,
And though he were nat depe ystert in loore,
He wiste it was the eightetethe day   5
Of Aprill, that is messager to May;
And saugh wel that the shadwe of every tree
Was as in lengthe the same quantitee
That was the body erect that caused it.
And therfore by the shadwe he took his wit   10
That Phebus, which that shoon so clere and
    brighte,
Degrees was fyve and fourty clombe on highte;
And for that day, as in that latitude,
It was ten of the clokke, he gan conclude,
And sodeynly he plighte his hors aboute.   15
   "Lordynges," quod he, "I warne yow, al this
    route,
The fourthe party of this day is gon.
Now, for the love of God and of Seint John,
Leseth no tyme, as ferforth as ye may.   19
Lordynges, the tyme wasteth nyght and day,
And steleth from us, what pryvely slepynge,
And what thurgh necligence in oure wakynge,
As dooth the streem that turneth nevere agayn,
Descendynge fro the montaigne into playn.
Wel kan Senec and many a philosophre   25
Biwaillen tyme moore than gold in cofre;
For 'los of catel may recovered be,
But los of tyme shendeth us,' quod he.
It wol nat come agayn, withouten drede,   29
Namoore than wole Malkynes maydenhede,
Whan she hath lost it in hir wantownesse.
Lat us nat mowlen thus in ydelnesse.
   "Sire Man of Lawe," quod he, "so have ye
    blis,
Telle us a tale anon, as forward is.   34
Ye been submytted, thurgh youre free assent,
To stonden in this cas at my juggement.
Acquiteth yow now of youre biheeste;
Thanne have ye do youre devoir atte leeste."
   "Hooste," quod he, "*depardieux*, ich assente;
To breke forward is nat myn entente.   40
Biheste is dette, and I wole holde fayn

Al my biheste, I kan no bettre sayn.
For swich lawe as a man yeveth another wight,
He sholde hymselven usen it, by right;
Thus wole oure text. But nathelees, certeyn,
I kan right now no thrifty tale seyn   46
That Chaucer, thogh he kan but lewedly
On metres and on rymyng craftily,
Hath seyd hem in swich Englissh as he kan
Of olde tyme, as knoweth many a man;   50
And if he have noght seyd hem, leve brother,
In o book, he hath seyd hem in another.
For he hath toold of loveris up and doun
Mo than Ovide made of mencioun
In his Episteles, that been ful olde.   55
What sholde I tellen hem, syn they been tolde?
   In youthe he made of Ceys and Alcione,
And sitthen hath he spoken of everichone,
Thise noble wyves and thise loveris eke.
Whoso that wole his large volume seke,   60
Cleped the Seintes Legende of Cupide,
Ther may he seen the large woundes wyde
Of Lucresse, and of Babilan Tesbee;
The swerd of Dido for the false Enee;
The tree of Phillis for hire Demophon;   65
The pleinte of Dianire and of Hermyon,
Of Adriane, and of Isiphilee;
The bareyne yle stondynge in the see;
The dreynte Leandre for his Erro;
The teeris of Eleyne, and eek the wo   70
Of Brixseyde, and of the, Ladomya;
The crueltee of the, queene Medea,
Thy litel children hangynge by the hals,
For thy Jason, that was of love so fals!
O Ypermystra, Penelopee, Alceste,   75
Youre wifhod he comendeth with the beste!
   But certeinly no word ne writeth he
Of thilke wikke ensample of Canacee,
That loved hir owene brother synfully;
(Of swiche cursed stories I sey fy!)   80
Or ellis of Tyro Appollonius,
How that the cursed kyng Antiochus
Birafte his doghter of hir maydenhede,
That is so horrible a tale for to rede,
Whan he hir threw upon the pavement.   85
And therfore he, of ful avysement,

Nolde nevere write in none of his sermons
Of swiche unkynde abhomynacions,
Ne I wol noon reherce, if that I may.

But of my tale how shal I doon this day?   90
Me were looth be likned, doutelees,
To Muses that men clepe Pierides —
Methamorphosios woot what I mene;
But nathelees, I recche noght a bene
Though I come after hym with hawebake.   95
I speke in prose, and lat him rymes make."
And with that word he, with a sobre cheere,
Bigan his tale, as ye shal after heere.

The prologe of the Mannes Tale of Lawe.

O hateful harm, condicion of poverte!   99
With thurst, with coold, with hunger so con-
      foundid!
To asken help thee shameth in thyn herte;
If thou noon aske, with nede artow so woundid
That verray nede unwrappeth al thy wounde
      hid!
Maugree thyn heed, thou most for indigence
Or stele, or begge, or borwe thy despence!   105

Thow blamest Crist, and seist ful bitterly,
He mysdeparteth richesse temporal;
Thy neighebor thou wytest synfully,

And seist thou hast to lite, and he hath al.   109
"Parfay," seistow, "somtyme he rekene shal,
Whan that his tayl shal brennen in the gleede,
For he noght helpeth needfulle in hir neede."

Herkne what is the sentence of the wise:
"Bet is to dyen than have indigence";
"Thy selve neighebor wol thee despise."   115
If thou be povre, farwel thy reverence!
Yet of the wise man take this sentence:
"Alle the dayes of povre men been wikke."
Be war, therfore, er thou come to that prikke!

If thou be povre, thy brother hateth thee,   120
And alle thy freendes fleen from thee, allas!
O riche marchauntz, ful of wele been yee,
O noble, o prudent folk, as in this cas!
Youre bagges been nat fild with ambes as,
But with sys cynk, that renneth for youre
      chaunce;
At Cristemasse myrie may ye daunce!   126

Ye seken lond and see for yowre wynnynges;
As wise folk ye knowen al th'estaat
Of regnes; ye been fadres of tidynges
And tales, bothe of pees and of debaat.   130
I were right now of tales desolaat,
Nere that a marchant, goon is many a yeere,
Me taughte a tale, which that ye shal heere.

The Man of Law's Tale

Heere begynneth the Man of Lawe his tale.

In Surrye whilom dwelte a compaignye
Of chapmen riche, and therto sadde and trewe,
That wyde-where senten hir spicerye,   136
Clothes of gold, and satyns riche of hewe.
Hir chaffare was so thrifty and so newe
That every wight hath deyntee to chaffare
With hem, and eek to sellen hem hire ware.

Now fil it that the maistres of that sort   141
Han shapen hem to Rome for to wende;
Were it for chapmanhod or for disport,
Noon oother message wolde they thider sende,
But comen hemself to Rome, this is the ende;
And in swich place as thoughte hem avantage
For hire entente, they take hir herbergage.   147

Sojourned han thise merchantz in that toun
A certein tyme, as fil to hire plesance.
And so bifel that th'excellent renoun   150
Of the Emperoures doghter, dame Custance,
Reported was, with every circumstance,
Unto thise Surryen marchantz in swich wyse.
Fro day to day, as I shal yow devyse.   154

This was the commune voys of every man:
"Oure Emperour of Rome — God hym see! —
A doghter hath that, syn the world bigan,
To rekene as wel hir goodnesse as beautee,
Nas nevere swich another as is shee.
I prey to God in honour hire susteene,   160
And wolde she were of al Europe the queene.

"In hire is heigh beautee, withoute pride,
Yowthe, withoute grenehede or folye;
To alle hire werkes vertu is hir gyde;
Humblesse hath slayn in hire al tirannye.   165
She is mirour of alle curteisye;
Hir herte is verray chambre of hoolynesse,
Hir hand, ministre of fredam for almesse."

And al this voys was sooth, as God is trewe.
But now to purpos lat us turne agayn.   170
Thise marchantz han doon fraught hir shippes
              newe,
And whan they han this blisful mayden sayn,
Hoom to Surrye been they went ful fayn,
And doon hir nedes as they han doon yoore,
And lyven in wele; I kan sey yow namoore.   175

    Now fil it that thise marchantz stode in grace
Of hym that was the Sowdan of Surrye;
For whan they cam from any strange place,
He wolde, of his benigne curteisye,
Make hem good chiere, and bisily espye   180
Tidynges of sondry regnes, for to leere
The wondres that they myghte seen or heere.

Amonges othere thynges, specially,
Thise marchantz han hym toold of dame Cus-
              tance
So greet noblesse in ernest, ceriously,   185
That this Sowdan hath caught so greet plesance
To han hir figure in his remembrance,
That al his lust and al his bisy cure
Was for to love hire while his lyf may dure.

Paraventure in thilke large book   190
Which that men clepe the hevene ywriten was
With sterres, whan that he his birthe took,
That he for love sholde han his deeth, allas!
For in the sterres, clerer than is glas,
Is writen, God woot, whoso koude it rede,   195
The deeth of every man, withouten drede.

In sterres, many a wynter therbiforn,
Was writen the deeth of Ector, Achilles,
Of Pompei, Julius, er they were born;
The strif of Thebes; and of Ercules,   200
Of Sampson, Turnus, and of Socrates
The deeth; but mennes wittes ben so dulle
That no wight kan wel rede it atte fulle.

    This Sowdan for his privee conseil sente,
And, shortly of this matiere for to pace,   205
He hath to hem declared his entente,
And seyde hem, certein, but he myghte have
              grace

To han Custance withinne a litel space,
He nas but deed; and charged hem in hye
To shapen for his lyf som remedye.   210

    Diverse men diverse thynges seyden;
They argumenten, casten up and doun;
Many a subtil resoun forth they leyden;
They speken of magyk and abusioun.
But finally, as in conclusioun,   215
They kan nat seen in that noon avantage,
Ne in noon oother wey, save mariage.

Thanne sawe they therinne swich difficultee
By wey of reson, for to speke al playn,
By cause that ther was swich diversitee   220
Bitwene hir bothe lawes, that they sayn
They trowe, "that no Cristen prince wolde fayn
Wedden his child under oure lawe sweete
That us was taught by Mahoun, oure prophete."

    And he answerde, "Rather than I lese   225
Custance, I wol be cristned, doutelees.
I moot been hires, I may noon oother chese.
I prey yow hoold youre argumentz in pees;
Saveth my lyf, and beth noght recchelees
To geten hire that hath my lyf in cure;   230
For in this wo I may nat longe endure."

    What nedeth gretter dilatacioun?
I seye, by tretys and embassadrie,
And by the popes mediacioun,
And al the chirche, and al the chivalrie,   235
That in destruccioun of mawmettrie,
And in encrees of Cristes lawe deere,
They been acorded, so as ye shal heere:

How that the Sowdan and his baronage
And alle his liges sholde ycristned be,   240
And he shal han Custance in mariage,
And certein gold, I noot what quantitee;
And heer-to founden sufficient suretee.
This same accord was sworn on eyther syde;
Now, faire Custance, almyghty God thee gyde!

    Now wolde som men waiten, as I gesse,   246
That I sholde tellen al the purveiance
That th'Emperour, of his grete noblesse,
Hath shapen for his doghter, dame Custance.
Wel may men knowen that so greet ordinance
May no man tellen in a litel clause   251
As was arrayed for so heigh a cause.

Bisshopes been shapen with hire for to wende,
Lordes, ladies, knyghtes of renoun,

And oother folk ynowe, this is th'ende;   255
And notified is thurghout the toun
That every wight, with greet devocioun,
Sholde preyen Crist that he this mariage
Receyve in gree, and spede this viage.

The day is comen of hir departynge;   260
I seye, the woful day fatal is come,
That ther may be no lenger tariynge,
But forthward they hem dressen, alle and some.
Custance, that was with sorwe al overcome,
Ful pale arist, and dresseth hire to wende;   265
For wel she seeth ther is noon oother ende.

Allas! what wonder is it thogh she wepte,
That shal be sent to strange nacioun
Fro freendes that so tendrely hire kepte,
And to be bounden under subjeccioun   270
Of oon, she knoweth nat his condicioun?
Housbondes been alle goode, and han ben
          yoore;
That knowen wyves; I dar sey yow na moore.

"Fader," she seyde, "thy wrecched child
          Custance,
Thy yonge doghter fostred up so softe,   275
And ye, my mooder, my soverayn plesance
Over alle thyng, out-taken Crist on-lofte,
Custance youre child hire recomandeth ofte
Unto youre grace, for I shal to Surrye,
Ne shal I nevere seen yow moore with ye.   280

"Allas! unto the Barbre nacioun
I moste anoon, syn that it is youre wille;
But Crist, that starf for our redempcioun
So yeve me grace his heestes to fulfille!   284
I, wrecche womman, no fors though I spille!
Wommen are born to thraldom and penance,
And to been under mannes governance."

I trowe at Troye, whan Pirrus brak the wal,
Or Ilion brende, at Thebes the citee,
N'at Rome, for the harm thurgh Hanybal   290
That Romayns hath venquysshed tymes thre,
Nas herd swich tendre wepyng for pitee
As in the chambre was for hire departynge;
But forth she moot, wher-so she wepe or synge.

O firste moevyng! crueel firmament,   295
With thy diurnal sweigh that crowdest ay
And hurlest al from est til occident
That naturelly wolde holde another way,
Thy crowdyng set the hevene in swich array
At the bigynnyng of this fiers viage,   300
That crueel Mars hath slayn this mariage.

Infortunat ascendent tortuous,
Of which the lord is helplees falle, allas,
Out of his angle into the derkeste hous!
O Mars, o atazir, as in this cas!   305
O fieble moone, unhappy been thy paas!
Thou knyttest thee ther thou art nat receyved;
Ther thou were weel, fro thennes artow
          weyved.

Imprudent Emperour of Rome, allas!
Was ther no philosophre in al thy toun?   310
Is no tyme bet than oother in swich cas?
Of viage is ther noon eleccioun,
Namely to folk of heigh condicioun?
Noght whan a roote is of a burthe yknowe?
Allas, we been to lewed or to slowe!   315

To shippe is brought this woful faire mayde
Solempnely, with every circumstance.
"Now Jhesu Crist be with yow alle!" she sayde;
Ther nys namoore, but "Farewel, faire Cus-
          tance!"
She peyneth hire to make good contenance;
And forth I lete hire saille in this manere,   321
And turne I wole agayn to my matere.

The mooder of the Sowdan, welle of vices,
Espied hath hir sones pleyn entente,
How he wol lete his olde sacrifices;   325
And right anon she for hir conseil sente,
And they been come to knowe what she mente.
And whan assembled was this folk in-feere,
She sette hire doun, and seyde as ye shal heere.

"Lordes," quod she, "ye knowen everichon,
How that my sone in point is for to lete   331
The hooly lawes of our Alkaron,
Yeven by Goddes message Makomete.
But oon avow to grete God I heete,
The lyf shal rather out of my body sterte   335
Or Makometes lawe out of myn herte!

"What sholde us tyden of this newe lawe
But thraldom to oure bodies and penance,
And afterward in helle to be drawe,
For we reneyed Mahoun oure creance?   340
But, lordes, wol ye maken assurance,
As I shal seyn, assentynge to my loore,
And I shal make us sauf for everemoore?"

They sworen and assenten, every man,
To lyve with hire and dye, and by hire stonde,
And everich, in the beste wise he kan,   346
To strengthen hire shal alle his frendes fonde;

And she hath this emprise ytake on honde,
Which ye shal heren that I shal devyse,   349
And to hem alle she spak right in this wyse:

"We shul first feyne us cristendom to take, —
Coold water shal nat greve us but a lite!
And I shal swich a feeste and revel make
That, as I trowe, I shal the Sowdan quite.   354
For thogh his wyf be cristned never so white,
She shal have nede to wasshe awey the rede,
Thogh she a font-ful water with hire lede."

O Sowdanesse, roote of iniquitee!
Virago, thou Semyrame the secounde!
O serpent under femynynytee,   360
Lik to the serpent depe in helle ybounde!
O feyned womman, al that may confounde
Vertu and innocence, thurgh thy malice,
Is bred in thee, as nest of every vice!

O Sathan, envious syn thilke day   365
That thou were chaced from oure heritage,
Wel knowestow to wommen the olde way!
Thou madest Eva brynge us in servage;
Thou wolt fordoon this Cristen mariage.
Thyn instrument so, weylawey the while!   370
Makestow of wommen, whan thou wolt bigile.

This Sowdanesse, whom I thus blame and
      warye,
Leet prively hire conseil goon hire way.
What sholde I in this tale lenger tarye?
She rydeth to the Sowdan on a day,   375
And seyde hym that she wolde reneye hir lay,
And cristendom of preestes handes fonge,
Repentynge hire she hethen was so longe;

Bisechynge hym to doon hire that honour,
That she moste han the Cristen folk to
      feeste,—   380
"To plesen hem I wol do my labour."
The Sowdan seith, "I wol doon at youre heeste";
And knelynge thanketh hire of that requeste.
So glad he was, he nyste what to seye.
She kiste hir sone, and hoom she gooth hir
      weye.   385

Explicit prima pars.

Sequitur pars secunda.

Arryved been this Cristen folk to londe
In Surrye, with a greet solempne route,
And hastifliche this Sowdan sente his sonde,
First to his mooder, and al the regne aboute,

And seyde his wyf was comen, out of doute,
And preyde hire for to ryde agayn the queene,
The honour of his regne to susteene.   392

Greet was the prees, and riche was th'array
Of Surryens and Romayns met yfeere;
The mooder of the Sowdan, riche and gay,   395
Receyveth hire with also glad a cheere
As any mooder myghte hir doghter deere,
And to the nexte citee ther bisyde
A softe paas solempnely they ryde.

Noght trowe I the triumphe of Julius,   400
Of which that Lucan maketh swich a boost,
Was roialler ne moore curius
Than was th'assemblee of this blisful hoost.
But this scorpioun, this wikked goost,
The Sowdanesse, for al hire flaterynge,   405
Caste under this ful mortally to stynge.

The Sowdan comth hymself soone after this
So roially, that wonder is to telle,
And welcometh hire with alle joye and blis.
And thus in murthe and joye I lete hem dwelle;
The fruyt of this matiere is that I telle.   411
Whan tyme cam, men thoughte it for the beste
That revel stynte, and men goon to hir reste.

The tyme cam, this olde Sowdanesse   414
Ordeyned hath this feeste of which I tolde,
And to the feeste Cristen folk hem dresse
In general, ye, bothe yonge and olde.
Heere may men feeste and roialtee biholde,
And deyntees mo than I kan yow devyse;
But al to deere they boghte it er they ryse.   420

O sodeyn wo, that evere art successour
To worldly blisse, spreynd with bitternesse!
The ende of the joye of oure worldly labour!
Wo occupieth the fyn of oure gladnesse.
Herke this conseil for thy sikernesse: 425
Upon thy glade day have in thy mynde
The unwar wo or harm that comth bihynde.

For shortly for to tellen, at o word,
The Sowdan and the Cristen everichone
Been al tohewe and stiked at the bord,   430
But it were oonly dame Custance allone.
This olde Sowdanesse, cursed krone,
Hath with hir freendes doon this cursed dede,
For she hirself wolde al the contree lede.

Ne ther was Surryen noon that was converted,
That of the conseil of the Sowdan woot,   436

That he nas al tohewe er he asterted.
And Custance han they take anon, foot-hoot,
And in a ship al steerelees, God woot,
They han hir set, and bidde hire lerne saille
Out of Surrye agaynward to Ytaille.   441

A certein tresor that she thider ladde,
And, sooth to seyn, vitaille greet plentee
They han hire yeven, and clothes eek she
    hadde,
And forth she sailleth in the salte see.   445
O my Custance, ful of benignytee,
O Emperoures yonge doghter deere,
He that is lord of Fortune be thy steere!

She blesseth hire, and with ful pitous voys
Unto the croys of Crist thus seyde she: 450
"O cleere, o welful auter, hooly croys,
Reed of the Lambes blood ful of pitee,
That wessh the world fro the olde iniquitee,
Me fro the feend and fro his clawes kepe,
That day that I shal drenchen in the depe.

Victorious tree, proteccioun of trewe,   456
That oonly worthy were for to bere
The Kyng of Hevene with his woundes newe,
The white Lamb, that hurt was with a spere,
Flemere of feendes out of hym and here   460
On which thy lymes feithfully extenden,
Me kepe, and yif me mygth my lyf t'amenden."

   Yeres and dayes fleet this creature
Thurghout the See of Grece unto the Strayte
Of Marrok, as it was hire aventure.   465
On many a sory meel now may she bayte;
After hir deeth ful often may she wayte,
Er that the wilde wawes wol hire dryve
Unto the place ther she shal arryve.   469

   Men myghten asken why she was nat slayn
Eek at the feeste? who myghte hir body save?
And I answere to that demande agayn,
Who saved Danyel in the horrible cave
Ther every wight save he, maister and knave,
Was with the leon frete er he asterte?   475
No wight but God, that he bar in his herte.

God liste to shewe his wonderful myracle
In hire, for we sholde seen his myghty werkis;
Crist, which that is to every harm triacle,   479
By certeine meenes ofte, as knowen clerkis,
Dooth thyng for certein ende that ful derk is
To mannes wit, that for oure ignorance
Ne konne noght knowe his prudent purveiance.

Now sith she was nat at the feeste yslawe,
Who kepte hire fro the drenchyng in the see?
Who kepte Jonas in the fisshes mawe   486
Til he was spouted up at Nynyvee?
Wel may men knowe it was no wight but he
That kepte peple Ebrayk from hir drenchynge,
With drye feet thurghout the see passynge.

Who bad the foure spirites of tempest   491
That power han t'anoyen lond and see,
Bothe north and south, and also west and est,
"Anoyeth, neither see, ne land, ne tree"?
Soothly, the comandour of that was he   495
That fro the tempest ay this womman kepte
As wel whan she wook as whan she slepte.

Where myghte this womman mete and
    drynke have
Thre yeer and moore? how lasteth hire vitaille?
Who fedde the Egipcien Marie in the
    cave,   500
Or in desert? No wight but Crist, sanz faille.
Fyve thousand folk it was as greet mervaille
With loves fyve and fisshes two to feede.
God sente his foyson at hir grete neede.

She dryveth forth into oure occian   505
Thurghout oure wilde see, til atte laste
Under an hoold that nempnen I ne kan,
Fer in Northhumberlond the wawe hire caste,
And in the sond hir ship stiked so faste
That thennes wolde it noght of al a tyde;   510
The wyl of Crist was that she sholde abyde.

   The constable of the castel doun is fare
To seen this wrak, and al the ship he soghte,
And foond this wery womman ful of care;
He foond also the tresor that she broghte.   515
In hir langage mercy she bisoghte,
The lyf out of hir body for to twynne,
Hire to delivere of wo that she was inne.

A maner Latyn corrupt was hir speche,
But algates therby was she understonde.   520
The constable, whan hym lyst no longer seche,
This woful womman broghte he to the londe.
She kneleth doun and thanketh Goddes sonde;
But what she was she wolde no man seye,
For foul ne fair, thogh that she sholde deye.

She seyde she was so mazed in the see   526
That she forgat hir mynde, by hir trouthe.
The constable hath of hire so greet pitee,
And eek his wyf, that they wepen for routhe.

She was so diligent, withouten slouthe,   530
To serve and plesen everich in that place,
That alle hir loven that looken in hir face.

    This constable and dame Hermengyld, his
      wyf,
Were payens, and that contree everywhere;
But Hermengyld loved hire right as hir lyf,
And Custance hath so longe sojourned there,
In orisons, with many a bitter teere,   537
Til Jhesu hath converted thurgh his grace
Dame Hermengyld, constablesse of that place.

In al that lond no Cristen dorste route;   540
Alle Cristen folk been fled fro that contree
Thurgh payens, that conquereden al aboute
The plages of the north, by land and see.
To Walys fledde the Cristyanytee
Of olde Britons dwellynge in this ile;   545
Ther was hir refut for the meene while.

But yet nere Cristene Britons so exiled
That ther nere somme that in hir privetee
Honoured Crist and hethen folk bigiled,   549
And ny the castel swiche ther dwelten three.
That oon of hem was blynd and myghte nat see,
But it were with thilke eyen of his mynde
With whiche men seen, after that they ben
    blynde.

    Bright was the sonne as in that someres day,
For which the constable and his wyf also   555
And Custance han ytake the righte way
Toward the see a furlong wey or two,
To pleyen and to romen to and fro;
And in hir walk this blynde man they mette,
Croked and oold, with eyen faste yshette.   560

"In name of Crist," cride this blinde Britoun,
"Dame Hermengyld, yif me my sighte agayn!"
This lady weex affrayed of the soun,
Lest that hir housbonde, shortly for to sayn,
Wolde hire for Jhesu Cristes love han
    slayn,   565
Til Custance made hire boold, and bad hire
    wirche
The wyl of Crist, as doghter of his chirche.

    The constable weex abasshed of that sight,
And seyde, "What amounteth al this fare?"
Custance answerde, "Sire, it is Cristes myght,
That helpeth folk out of the feendes snare."
And so ferforth she gan oure lay declare   572
That she the constable, er that it was eve
Converted, and on Crist made hym bileve.

This constable was nothyng lord of this place
Of which I speke, ther he Custance fond,   576
But kepte it strongly many a wyntres space
Under Alla, kyng of al Northhumbrelond,
That was ful wys, and worthy of his hond
Agayn the Scottes, as men may wel heere;   580
But turne I wole agayn to my mateere.

    Sathan, that evere us waiteth to bigile,
Saugh of Custance al hire perfeccioun,
And caste anon how he myghte quite hir while,
And made a yong knyght that dwelte in that
    toun
Love hire so hoote, of foul affeccioun,   586
That verraily hym thoughte he sholde spille,
But he of hire myghte ones have his wille.

He woweth hire, but it availleth noght;
She wolde do no synne, by no weye;   590
And for despit he compassed in his thoght
To maken hire on shameful deeth to deye.
He wayteth whan the constable was aweye,
And pryvely upon a nyght he crepte
In Hermengyldes chambre, whil she slepte.

    Wery, forwaked in hire orisouns,   596
Slepeth Custance, and Hermengyld also.
This knyght, thurgh Sathanas temptaciouns,
Al softely is to the bed ygo,
And kitte the throte of Hermengyld atwo,   600
And leyde the blody knyf by dame Custance,
And wente his wey, ther God yeve hym mes-
    chance!

    Soone after cometh this constable hoom
    agayn,
And eek Alla, that kyng was of that lond,
And saugh his wyf despitously yslayn,   605
For which ful ofte he weep and wroong his
    hond,
And in the bed the blody knyf he fond
By Dame Custance. Allas! what myghte she
    seye?
For verray wo hir wit was al aweye.   609

    To kyng Alla was toold al this meschance,
And eek the tyme, and where, and in what wise
That in a ship was founden this Custance,
As heer-biforn that ye han herd devyse.
The kynges herte of pitee gan agryse,
Whan he saugh so benigne a creature   615
Falle in disese and in mysaventure.

For as the lomb toward his deeth is broght,
So stant this innocent bifore the kyng.

This false knyght, that hath this tresoun wroght,
Berth hire on hond that she hath doon thys thyng. 620
But nathelees, ther was greet moornyng
Among the peple, and seyn they kan nat gesse
That she had doon so greet a wikkednesse;

For they han seyn hire evere so vertuous,
And lovynge Hermengyld right as hir lyf. 625
Of this baar witnesse everich in that hous,
Save he that Hermengyld slow with his knyf.
This gentil kyng hath caught a greet motyf
Of this witnesse, and thoghte he wolde enquere
Depper in this, a trouthe for to lere. 630

Allas! Custance, thou hast no champioun,
Ne fighte kanstow noght, so weylaway!
But he that starf for our redempcioun,
And boond Sathan (and yet lith ther he lay),
So be thy stronge champion this day! 635
For, but if Crist open myracle kithe,
Withouten gilt thou shalt be slayn as swithe.

She sette hire doun on knees, and thus she sayde:
"Immortal God, that savedest Susanne
Fro false blame, and thou, merciful mayde, 640
Marie I meene, doghter to Seint Anne, 641
Bifore whos child angeles synge Osanne,
If I be giltlees of this felonye,
My socour be, for ellis shal I dye!"

Have ye nat seyn somtyme a pale face, 645
Among a prees, of hym that hath be lad
Toward his deeth, wher as hym gat no grace,
And swich a colour in his face hath had,
Men myghte knowe his face that was bistad,
Amonges alle the faces in that route? 650
So stant Custance, and looketh hire aboute.

O queenes, lyvynge in prosperitee,
Duchesses, and ye ladyes everichone,
Haveth som routhe on hire adversitee!
An Emperoures doghter stant allone; 655
She hath no wight to whom to make hir mone.
O blood roial, that stondest in this drede,
Fer been thy freendes at thy grete nede!

This Alla kyng hath swich compassioun,
As gentil herte is fulfild of pitee, 660
That from his eyen ran the water doun.
"Now hastily do fecche a book," quod he,
"And if this knyght wol sweren how that she

This womman slow, yet wol we us avyse 664
Whom that we wole that shal been oure justise."

A Britoun book, written with Evaungiles,
Was fet, and on this book he swoor anoon
She gilty was, and in the meene whiles
An hand hym smoot upon the nekke-boon,
That doun he fil atones as a stoon, 670
And bothe his eyen broste out of his face
In sighte of every body in that place.

A voys was herd in general audience,
And seyde, "Thou hast desclaundred, giltelees,
The doghter of hooly chirche in heigh pres-
ence; 675
Thus hastou doon, and yet holde I my pees!"
Of this mervaille agast was al the prees;
As mazed folk they stoden everichone,
For drede of wreche, save Custance allone.

Greet was the drede and eek the repentance
Of hem that hadden wrong suspecioun 681
Upon this sely innocent, Custance;
And for this miracle, in conclusioun,
And by Custances mediacioun, 684
The kyng — and many another in that place —
Converted was, thanked be Cristes grace!

This false knyght was slayn for his untrouthe
By juggement of Alla hastifly;
And yet Custance hadde of his deeth greet routhe.
And after this Jhesus, of his mercy, 690
Made Alla wedden ful solempnely
This hooly mayden, that is so bright and sheene;
And thus hath Crist ymaad Custance a queene.

But who was woful, if I shal nat lye,
Of this weddyng but Donegild, and namo, 695
The kynges mooder, ful of tirannye?
Hir thoughte hir cursed herte brast atwo.
She wolde noght hir sone had do so;
Hir thoughte a despit that he sholde take
So strange a creature unto his make. 700

Me list nat of the chaf, ne of the stree,
Maken so long a tale as of the corn.
What sholde I tellen of the roialtee
At mariage, or which cours goth biforn;
Who bloweth in a trumpe or in an horn? 705
The fruyt of every tale is for to seye:
They ete, and drynke, and daunce, and synge, and pleye.

They goon to bedde, as it was skile and right;
For thogh that wyves be ful hooly thynges,
They moste take in pacience at nyght   710
Swiche manere necessaries as been plesynges
To folk that han ywedded hem with rynges,
And leye a lite hir hoolynesse aside,
As for the tyme, — it may no bet bitide.

On hire he gat a knave child anon,   715
And to a bisshop, and his constable eke,
He took his wyf to kepe, whan he is gon
To Scotlond-ward, his foomen for to seke.
Now faire Custance, that is so humble and
          meke,
So longe is goon with childe, til that stille 720
She halt hire chambre, abidyng Cristes wille.

The tyme is come a knave child she beer;
Mauricius at the fontstoon they hym calle.
This constable dooth forth come a messageer,
And wroot unto his kyng, that cleped was Alle,
How that this blisful tidyng is bifalle,   726
And othere tidynges spedeful for to seye.
He taketh the lettre, and forth he gooth his
          weye.

   This messager, to doon his avantage,
Unto the kynges mooder rideth swithe,   730
And salueth hire ful faire in his langage:
"Madame," quod he, "ye may be glad and
          blithe,
And thanketh God an hundred thousand sithe!
My lady queene hath child, withouten doute,
To joye and blisse to al this regne aboute.   735

Lo, heere the lettres seled of this thyng,
That I moot bere with al the haste I may.
If ye wol aught unto youre sone the kyng,
I am youre servant, bothe nyght and day."
Donegild answerde, "As now at this tyme,
          nay;   740
But heere al nyght I wol thou take thy reste.
To-morwe wol I seye thee what me leste."

   This messager drank sadly ale and wyn,
And stolen were his lettres pryvely
Out of his box, whil he sleep as a swyn;   745
And countrefeted was ful subtilly
Another lettre, wroght ful synfully,
Unto the kyng direct of this mateere
Fro his constable, as ye shal after heere.

The lettre spak the queene delivered was   750
Of so horrible a feendly creature

That in the castel noon so hardy was
That any while dorste ther endure.
The mooder was an elf, by aventure
Ycomen, by charmes or by sorcerie,   755
And every wight hateth hir compaignye.

   Wo was this kyng whan he this lettre had
          sayn,
But to no wight he tolde his sorwes soore,
But of his owene hand he wroot agayn,
"Welcome the sonde of Crist for everemoore
To me that am now lerned in his loore!   761
Lord, welcome be thy lust and thy plesaunce;
My lust I putte al in thyn ordinaunce.

Kepeth this child, al be it foul or feir,
And eek my wyf, unto myn hoom-comynge.
Crist, whan hym list, may sende me an heir   766
Moore agreable than this to my likynge."
This lettre he seleth, pryvely wepynge,
Which to the messager was take soone,
And forth he gooth; ther is na moore to doone.

   O messager, fulfild of dronkenesse,   771
Strong is thy breeth, thy lymes faltren ay,
And thou biwreyest alle secreenesse.
Thy mynde is lorn, thou janglest as a jay,
Thy face is turned in a newe array.   775
Ther dronkenesse regneth in any route,
Ther is no conseil hyd, withouten doute.

   O Donegild, I ne have noon Englissh digne
Unto thy malice and thy tirannye!
And therfore to the feend I thee resigne;   780
Lat hym enditen of thy traitorie!
Fy, mannysh, fy! — o nay, by God, I lye —
Fy, feendlych spirit, for I dar wel telle,
Thogh thou heere walke, thy spirit is in helle!

   This messager comth fro the kyng agayn,
And at the kynges moodres court he lighte,   786
And she was of this messager ful fayn,
And plesed hym in al that ever she myghte.
He drank, and wel his girdel underpighte;
He slepeth, and he fnorteth in his gyse   790
Al nyght, til the sonne gan aryse.

   Eft were his lettres stolen everychon,
And countrefeted lettres in this wyse:
"The king comandeth his constable anon,   794
Up peyne of hangyng, and on heigh juyse,
That he ne sholde suffren in no wyse
Custance in-with his reawme for t'abyde
Thre dayes and o quarter of a tyde;

"But in the same ship as he hire fond,
Hire, and hir yonge sone, and al hir geere, 800
He sholde putte, and croude hire fro the lond,
And charge hire that she never eft coome
      theere."
O my Custance, wel may thy goost have feere,
And, slepynge, in thy dreem been in penance,
Whan Donegild cast al this ordinance. 805

This messager on morwe, whan he wook,
Unto the castel halt the nexte way,
And to the constable he the lettre took;
And whan that he this pitous lettre say,
Ful ofte he seyde, "Allas! and weylaway!" 810
"Lord Crist," quod he, "how may this world
      endure,
So ful of synne is many a creature?

"O myghty God, if that it be thy wille,
Sith thou art rightful juge, how may it be
That thou wolt suffren innocentz to spille, 815
And wikked folk regne in prosperitee?
O goode Custance, allas! so wo is me
That I moot be thy tormentour, or deye
On shames deeth; ther is noon oother weye."

Wepen bothe yonge and olde in al that
      place 820
Whan that the kyng this cursed lettre sente,
And Custance, with a deedly pale face,
The ferthe day toward hir ship she wente.
But nathelees she taketh in good entente 824
The wyl of Crist, and knelynge on the stronde,
She seyde, "Lord, ay welcome be thy sonde!

"He that me kepte fro the false blame
While I was on the lond amonges yow,
He kan me kepe from harm and eek fro shame
In salte see, althogh I se noght how. 830
As strong as evere he was, he is yet now.
In hym triste I, and in his mooder deere,
That is to me my seyl and eek my steere."

Hir litel child lay wepyng in hir arm,
And knelynge, pitously to hym she seyde, 835
"Pees, litel sone, I wol do thee noon harm."
With that hir coverchief of hir heed she breyde,
And over his litel eyen she it leyde,
And in hir arm she lulleth it ful faste,
And into hevene hire eyen up she caste. 840

"Mooder," quod she, "and mayde bright,
      Marie,
Sooth is that thurgh wommanes eggement

Mankynde was lorn, and damned ay to dye,
For which thy child was on a croys yrent.
Thy blisful eyen sawe al his torment; 845
Thanne is ther no comparison bitwene
Thy wo and any wo man may sustene.

"Thow sawe thy child yslayn bifore thyne yen,
And yet now lyveth my litel child, parfay! 849
Now, lady bright, to whom alle woful cryen,
Thow glorie of wommanhede, thow faire may,
Thow haven of refut, brighte sterre of day,
Rewe on my child, that of thy gentillesse,
Rewest on every reweful in distresse.

"O litel child, allas! what is thy gilt, 855
That nevere wroghtest synne as yet, pardee?
Why wil thyn harde fader han thee spilt?
O mercy, deere constable," quod she,
"As lat my litel child dwelle heer with thee;
And if thou darst nat saven hym, for blame,
So kys hym ones in his fadres name!" 861

Therwith she looked bakward to the londe,
And seyde, "Farewel, housbonde routhelees!"
And up she rist, and walketh doun the stronde
Toward the ship, — hir folweth al the prees, —
And evere she preyeth hire child to holde his
      pees; 866
And taketh hir leve, and with an hooly entente
She blisseth hire, and into ship she wente.

Vitailled was the ship, it is no drede,
Habundantly for hire ful longe space, 870
And othere necessaries that sholde nede
She hadde ynogh, heryed be Goddes grace!
For wynd and weder almyghty God purchace,
And brynge hire hoom! I kan no bettre seye,
But in the see she dryveth forth hir weye. 875

Explicit secunda pars.

Sequitur pars tercia.

Alla the kyng comth hoom soone after this
Unto his castel, of the which I tolde,
And asketh where his wyf and his child is.
The constable gan aboute his herte colde,
And pleynly al the manere he hym tolde 880
As ye han herd — I kan telle it no bettre —
And sheweth the kyng his seel and eek his
      lettre,

And seyde, "Lord, as ye comanded me
Up peyne of deeth, so have I doon, certein."
This messager tormented was til he 885

Moste biknowe and tellen, plat and pleyn,
Fro nyght to nyght, in what place he had leyn;
And thus, by wit and sotil enquerynge,
Ymagined was by whom this harm gan sprynge.

The hand was knowe that the lettre wroot,
And al the venym of this cursed dede,   891
But in what wise, certeinly, I noot.
Th'effect is this, that Alla, out of drede,
His mooder slow — that may men pleynly rede —
For that she traitour was to hire ligeance.   895
Thus endeth olde Donegild, with meschance!

The sorwe that this Alla nyght and day
Maketh for his wyf, and for his child also,
Ther is no tonge that it telle may.
But now wol I unto Custance go,   900
That fleteth in the see, in peyne and wo,
Fyve yeer and moore, as liked Cristes sonde,
Er that hir ship approched unto londe.

Under an hethen castel, atte laste,   904
Of which the name in my text noght I fynde,
Custance, and eek hir child, the see up caste.
Almyghty God, that saveth al mankynde,
Have on Custance and on hir child som mynde,
That fallen is in hethen hand eft soone,
In point to spille, as I shal telle yow soone.   910

Doun fro the castel comth ther many a wight
To gauren on this ship and on Custance.
But shortly, from the castel, on a nyght,
The lordes styward — God yeve hym mes-
        chance! —
A theef, that hadde reneyed oure creance,   915
Cam into ship allone, and seyde he sholde
Hir lemman be, wher-so she wolde or nolde.

Wo was this wrecched womman tho bigon;
Hir child cride, and she cride pitously.
But blisful Marie heelp hire right anon;   920
For with hir struglyng wel and myghtily
The theef fil over bord al sodeynly,
And in the see he dreynte for vengeance;
And thus hath Crist unwemmed kept Custance.

O foule lust of luxurie, lo, thyn ende!   925
Nat oonly that thou feyntest mannes mynde,
But verraily thou wolt his body shende.
Th'ende of thy werk, or of thy lustes blynde,
Is compleynyng. Hou many oon may men fynde
That noght for werk somtyme, but for th'en-
        tente   930
To doon this synne, been outher slayn or shente!

How may this wayke womman han this
        strengthe
Hire to defende agayn this renegat?
O Golias, unmesurable of lengthe,
Hou myghte David make thee so maat,   935
So yong and of armure so desolaat?
Hou dorste he looke upon thy dredful face?
Wel may men seen, it nas but Goddes grace.

Who yaf Judith corage or hardynesse
To sleen hym Olofernus in his tente,   940
And to deliveren out of wrecchednesse
The peple of God? I seye, for this entente,
That right as God spirit of vigour sente
To hem, and saved hem out of meschance,
So sente he myght and vigour to Custance.   945

Forth gooth hir ship thurghout the narwe
        mouth
Of Jubaltare and Septe, dryvynge ay
Somtyme west, and somtyme north and south,
And somtyme est, ful many a wery day,
Til Cristes mooder — blessed be she ay! —   950
Hath shapen, thurgh hir endelees goodnesse,
To make an ende of al hir hevynesse.

Now lat us stynte of Custance but a throwe,
And speke we of the Romayn Emperour,
That out of Surrye hath by lettres knowe   955
The slaughtre of cristen folk, and dishonour
Doon to his doghter by a fals traytour,
I mene the cursed wikked Sowdanesse
That at the feeste leet sleen bothe moore and
        lesse.

For which this Emperour hath sent anon   960
His senatour, with roial ordinance,
And othere lordes, God woot, many oon,
On Surryens to taken heigh vengeance.
They brennen, sleen, and brynge hem to mes-
        chance
Ful many a day; but shortly, this is th'ende,
Homward to Rome they shapen hem to wende.

This senatour repaireth with victorie   967
To Rome-ward, saillynge ful roially,
And mette the ship dryvynge, as seith the
        storie,
In which Custance sit ful pitously.   970
Nothyng ne knew he what she was, ne why
She was in swich array, ne she nyl seye
Of hire estaat, althogh she sholde deye.

He bryngeth hire to Rome, and to his wyf
He yaf hire, and hir yonge sone also;   975

And with the senatour she ladde hir lyf.
Thus kan Oure Lady bryngen out of wo
Woful Custance, and many another mo.
And longe tyme dwelled she in that place,
In hooly werkes evere, as was hir grace.   980

The senatoures wyf hir aunte was,
But for al that she knew hire never the moore.
I wol no lenger tarien in this cas,
But to kyng Alla, which I spak of yoore,
That for his wyf wepeth and siketh soore,   985
I wol retourne, and lete I wol Custance
Under the senatoures governance.

Kyng Alla, which that hadde his mooder
    slayn,
Upon a day fil in swich repentance
That, if I shortly tellen shal and playn,   990
To Rome he comth to receyven his penance;
And putte hym in the Popes ordinance
In heigh and logh, and Jhesu Crist bisoghte
Foryeve his wikked werkes that he wroghte.

The fame anon thurgh Rome toun is born,
How Alla kyng shal comen in pilgrymage,   996
By herbergeours that wenten hym biforn;
For which the senatour, as was usage,
Rood hym agayns, and many of his lynage,
As wel to shewen his heighe magnificence
As to doon any kyng a reverence.   1001

Greet cheere dooth this noble senatour
To kyng Alla, and he to hym also;
Everich of hem dooth oother greet honour.
And so bifel that in a day or two   1005
This senatour is to kyng Alla go
To feste, and shortly, if I shal nat lye,
Custances sone wente in his compaignye.

Som men wolde seyn at requeste of Cus-
    tance
This senatour hath lad this child to feeste,
I may nat tellen every circumstance, —   1011
Be as be may, ther was he at the leeste.
But sooth is this, that at his moodres heeste
Biforn Alla, durynge the metes space,   1014
The child stood, lookynge in the kynges face.

This Alla kyng hath of this child greet won-
    der,
And to the senatour he seyde anon,
"Whos is that faire child that stondeth yon-
    der?"
"I noot," quod he, "by God, and by seint John!

A mooder he hath, but fader hath he noon   1020
That I of woot" — and shortly, in a stounde,
He tolde Alla how that this child was founde.

"But God woot," quod this senatour also,
"So vertuous a lyvere in my lyf
Ne saugh I nevere as she, ne herde of mo,   1025
Of worldly wommen, mayde, ne of wyf.
I dar wel seyn hir hadde levere a knyf
Thurghout hir brest, than ben a womman
    wikke,
There is no man koude brynge hire to that
    prikke."

Now was this child as lyk unto Custance
As possible is a creature to be.   1031
This Alla hath the face in remembrance
Of dame Custance, and ther on mused he
If that the childes mooder were aught she
That is his wyf, and pryvely he sighte,   1035
And spedde hym fro the table that he myghte.

"Parfay," thoghte he, "fantome is in myn heed!
I oghte deme, of skilful juggement,
That in the salte see my wyf is deed."
And afterward he made his argument: 1040
"What woot I if that Crist have hyder ysent
My wyf by see, as wel as he hire sente
To my contree fro thennes that she wente?"

And after noon, hoom with the senatour
Goth Alla, for to seen this wonder chaunce.
This senatour dooth Alla greet honour,   1046
And hastifly he sente after Custaunce.
But trusteth weel, hire liste nat to daunce,
Whan that she wiste wherfore was that sonde;
Unnethe upon hir feet she myghte stonde.   1050

Whan Alla saugh his wyf, faire he hire grette,
And weep, that it was routhe for to see;
For at the firste look he on hire sette,
He knew wel verraily that it was she.
And she, for sorwe, as doumb stant as a tree,
So was hir herte shet in hir distresse,   1056
Whan she remembred his unkyndenesse.

Twyes she swowned in his owene sighte;
He weep, and hym excuseth pitously.
"Now God," quod he, "and alle his halwes
    brighte
So wisly on my soule as have mercy,   1061
That of youre harm as giltelees am I
As is Maurice my sone, so lyk youre face;
Elles the feend me fecche out of this place!"

Long was the sobbyng and the bitter peyne,
Er that hir woful hertes myghte cesse;   1066
Greet was the pitee for to heere hem pleyne,
Thurgh whiche pleintes gan hir wo encresse.
I pray yow alle my labour to relesse;
I may nat telle hir wo until to-morwe,   1070
I am so wery for to speke of sorwe.

But finally, whan that the sothe is wist
That Alla giltelees was of hir wo,
I trowe an hundred tymes been they kist,
And swich a blisse is ther bitwix hem two   1075
That, save the joye that lasteth everemo,
Ther is noon lyk that any creature
Hath seyn or shal, whil that the world may
     dure.

Tho preyde she hir housbonde mekely,
In relief of hir longe, pitous pyne,   1080
That he wolde preye hir fader specially
That of his magestee he wolde enclyne
To vouche sauf som day with hym to dyne.
She preyde hym eek he sholde by no weye
Unto hir fader no word of hire seye.   1085

Som men wolde seyn how that the child
     Maurice
Dooth this message unto this Emperour;
But, as I gesse, Alla was nat so nyce
To hym that was of so sovereyn honour
As he that is of Cristen folk the flour,   1090
Sente any child, but it is bet to deeme
He wente hymself, and so it may wel seeme.

This Emperour hath graunted gentilly
To come to dyner, as he hym bisoughte;
And wel rede I he looked bisily   1095
Upon this child, and on his doghter thoghte.
Alla goth to his in, and as hym oghte,
Arrayed for this feste in every wise
As ferforth as his konnyng may suffise.   1099

The morwe cam, and Alla gan hym dresse,
And eek his wyf, this Emperour to meete;
And forth they ryde in joye and in gladnesse.
And whan she saugh hir fader in the strete,
She lighte doun, and falleth hym to feete.   1104
"Fader," quod she, "youre yonge child Cus-
     tance
Is now ful clene out of youre remembrance.

I am youre doghter Custance," quod she,
"That whilom ye han sent unto Surrye.
It am I, fader, that in the salte see

Was put allone and dampned for to dye.   1110
Now, goode fader, mercy I yow crye!
Sende me namoore unto noon hethenesse,
But thonketh my lord heere of his kyndenesse."

Who kan the pitous joye tellen al
Bitwixe hem thre, syn they been thus ymette?
But of my tale make an ende I shal;   1116
The day goth faste, I wol no lenger lette.
This glade folk to dyner they hem sette;
In joye and blisse at mete I lete hem dwelle
A thousand foold wel moore than I kan
     telle.   1120

This child Maurice with sithen Emperour
Maad by the Pope, and lyved cristenly;
To Cristes chirche he dide greet honour.
But I lete al his storie passen by;
Of Custance is my tale specially.   1125
In the olde Romayn geestes may men fynde
Maurices lyf; I bere it noght in mynde.

This kyng Alla, whan he his tyme say,
With his Custance, his hooly wyf so sweete,
To Engelond been they come the righte way,
Wher as they lyve in joye and in quiete.   1131
But litel while it lasteth, I yow heete,
Joye of this world, for tyme wol nat abyde;
Fro day to nyght it changeth as the tyde.

Who lyved euere in swich delit o day   1135
That hym ne moeved outher conscience,
Or ire, or talent, or som kynnes affray,
Envye, or pride, or passion, or offence?
I ne seye but for this ende this sentence,
That litel while in joye or in plesance   1140
Lasteth the blisse of Alla with Custance.

For deeth, that taketh of heigh and logh his
     rente,
Whan passed was a yeer, evene as I gesse,
Out of this world this kyng Alla he hente,
For whom Custance hath ful greet hevynesse.
Now lat us prayen God his soule blesse!   1146
And dame Custance, finally to seye,
Toward the toun of Rome goth hir weye.

To Rome is come this hooly creature,
And fyndeth hire freendes hoole and sounde;
Now is she scaped al hire aventure.   1151
And whan that she hir fader hath yfounde,
Doun on hir knees falleth she to grounde;
Wepynge for tendrenesse in herte blithe,
She heryeth God an hundred thousand sithe.

In vertu and in hooly almus-dede   1156
They lyven alle, and nevere asonder wende;
Til deeth departeth hem, this lyf they lede.
And fareth now weel! my tale is at an ende.

Now Jhesu Crist, that of his myght may sende
Joye after wo, governe us in his grace,   1161
And kepe us alle that been in this place! Amen

Heere endeth the tale of the Man of Lawe.

The Epilogue of The Man of Law's Tale

[Owre Hoost upon his stiropes stood anon,
And seyde, "Goode men, herkeneth everych
on!
This was a thrifty tale for the nones!   1165
Sir Parisshe Prest," quod he, "for Goddes bones,
Telle us a tale, as was thi forward yore.
I se wel that ye lerned men in lore
Can moche good, by Goddes dignitee!"   1169
    The Parson hem answerde, "*Benedicite!*
What eyleth the man, so synfully to swere?"
Oure Host answerde, "O Jankin, be ye there?
I smelle a Lollere in the wynd," quod he.
"Now! goode men," quod oure Hoste, "herken-
eth me;
Abydeth, for Goddes digne passioun,   1175

For we schal han a predicacioun;
This Lollere heer wil prechen us somwhat."
    "Nay, by my fader soule, that schal he nat!"
Seyde the Shipman; "heer schal he nat preche;
He schal no gospel glosen here ne teche.   1180
We leven alle in the grete God," quod he;
"He wolde sowen som difficulte,
Or springen cokkel in our clene corn.
And therfore, Hoost, I warne thee biforn,
My joly body schal a tale telle,   1185
And I schal clynken you so mery a belle,
That I schal waken al this compaignie.
But it schal not ben of philosophie,
Ne phislyas, ne termes queinte of lawe,
Ther is but litel Latyn in my mawe!"]   1190

The Wife of Bath's Prologue

The Prologe of the Wyves Tale of Bathe.

"Experience, though noon auctoritee
Were in this world, is right ynogh for me
To speke of wo that is in mariage;
For, lordynges, sith I twelve yeer was of age,
Thonked be God that is eterne on lyve,   5
Housbondes at chirche dore I have had fyve, —
If I so ofte myghte have ywedded bee, —
And alle were worthy men in hir degree.
But me was toold, certeyn, nat longe agoon is,
That sith that Crist ne wente nevere but onis
To weddyng, in the Cane of Galilee,   11
That by the same ensample taughte he me
That I ne sholde wedded be but ones.
Herkne eek, lo, which a sharp word for the nones,
Biside a welle, Jhesus, God and man,   15
Spak in repreeve of the Samaritan:
"Thou hast yhad fyve housbondes,' quod he,
'And that ilke man that now hath thee
Is noght thyn housbonde,' thus seyde he cer-
   teyn.
What that he mente therby, I kan nat seyn;   20
But that I axe, why that the fifthe man
Was noon housbonde to the Samaritan?
How manye myghte she have in mariage?
Yet herde I nevere tellen in myn age
Upon this nombre diffinicioun.   25
Men may devyne and glosen, up and doun,
But wel I woot, expres, withoute lye,
God bad us for to wexe and multiplye;
That gentil text kan I wel understonde.
Eek wel I woot, he seyde myn housbonde   30
Sholde lete fader and mooder, and take to me.
But of no nombre mencion made he,
Of bigamye, or of octogamye,
Why sholde men thanne speke of it vileynye?
   Lo, heere the wise kyng, daun Salomon;   35
I trowe he hadde wyves mo than oon.
As wolde God it were leveful unto me
To be refresshed half so ofte as he!
Which yifte of God hadde he for alle his
   wyvys!
No man hath swich that in this world alyve is.
God woot, this noble kyng, as to my wit,   41
The firste nyght had many a myrie fit

With ech of hem, so wel was hym on lyve.
Yblessed be God that I have wedded fyve! [1]
Welcome the sixte, whan that evere he shal.
For sothe, I wol nat kepe me chaast in al.   46
Whan myn housbonde is fro the world ygon,
Som Cristen man shal wedde me anon,
For thanne, th'apostle seith that I am free
To wedde, a Goddes half, where it liketh me.
He seith that to be wedded is no synne;   51
Bet is to be wedded than to brynne
What rekketh me, thogh folk seye vileynye
Of shrewed Lameth and his bigamye?
I woot wel Abraham was an hooly man,   55
And Jacob eek, as ferforth as I kan;
And ech of hem hadde wyves mo than two,
And many another holy man also.
Wher can ye seye, in any manere age,
That hye God defended mariage   60
By expres word? I pray yow, telleth me.
Or where comanded he virginitee?
I woot as wel as ye, it is no drede,
Th'apostle, whan he speketh of maydenhede,
He seyde that precept therof hadde he noon.
Men may conseille a womman to been oon,   66
But conseillyng is no comandement.
He putte it in oure owene juggement;
For hadde God comanded maydenhede,
Thanne hadde he dampned weddyng with the
   dede.
And certes, if ther were no seed ysowe,   71
Virginitee, thanne wherof sholde it growe?
Poul dorste nat comanden, atte leeste,
A thyng of which his maister yaf noon heeste.
The dart is set up for virginitee: 75
Cacche whoso may, who renneth best lat see.
   But this word is nat taken of every wight,
But ther as God lust gyve it of his myght.
I woot wel that th'apostle was a mayde;   79

[1] ll. 44a–44f.
   Of whiche I have pyked out the beste,
   Bothe of here nether purs and of here cheste.
   Diverse scoles maken parfyt clerkes,
   And diverse practyk in many sondry werkes
   Maketh the werkman parfyt sekirly;
   Of fyve husbondes scoleiyng am I.

But nathelees, thogh that he wroot and sayde
He wolde that every wight were swich as he,
Al nys but conseil to virginitee.
And for to been a wyf he yaf me leve
Of indulgence; so nys it no repreve
To wedde me, if that my make dye,   85
Withouten excepcion of bigamye.
Al were it good no womman for to touche, —
He mente as in his bed or in his couche;
For peril is bothe fyr and tow t'assemble;
Ye knowe what this ensample may resemble.
This is al and som, he heeld virginitee   91
Moore parfit than weddyng in freletee.
Freletee clepe I, but if that he and she
Wolde leden al hir lyf in chastitee.
    I graunte it wel, I have noon envie,   95
Thogh maydenhede preferre bigamye.
It liketh hem to be clene, body and goost;
Of myn estaat I nyl nat make no boost.
For wel ye knowe, a lord in his houshold,
He nath nat every vessel al of gold;   100
Somme been of tree, and doon hir lord servyse.
God clepeth folk to hym in sondry wyse,
And everich hath of God a propre yifte,
Som this, som that, as hym liketh shifte.
    Virginitee is greet perfeccion,   105
And continence eek with devocion,
But Crist, that of perfeccion is welle,
Bad nat every wight he sholde go selle
Al that he hadde, and gyve it to the poore
And in swich wise folwe hym and his foore.
He spak to hem that wolde lyve parfitly;   111
And lordynges, by youre leve, that am nat I.
I wol bistowe the flour of al myn age
In the actes and in fruyt of mariage.
    Telle me also, to what conclusion   115
Were membres maad of generacion,
And of so parfit wys a wight ywroght?
Trusteth right wel, they were nat maad for
        noght.
Glose whoso wole, and seye bothe up and doun,
That they were maked for purgacioun   120
Of uryne, and oure bothe thynges smale
Were eek to knowe a femele from a male,
And for noon oother cause, — say ye no?
The experience woot wel it is noght so.
So that the clerkes be nat with me wrothe,   125
I sey this, that they maked ben for bothe,
This is to seye, for office, and for ese
Of engendrure, ther we nat God displese.
Why sholde men elles in hir bookes sette
That man shal yelde to his wyf hire dette?   130
Now wherwith sholde he make his paiement,
If he ne used his sely instrument?

Thanne were they maad upon a creature
To purge uryne, and eek for engendrure.   134
But I seye noght that every wight is holde,
That hath swich harneys as I to yow tolde,
To goon and usen hem in engendrure.
Thanne sholde men take of chastitee no cure.
Crist was a mayde, and shapen as a man,
And many a seint, sith that the world bigan;
Yet lyved they evere in parfit chastitee.   141
I nyl envye no virginitee.
Lat hem be breed of pured whete-seed,
And lat us wyves hoten barly-breed;
And yet with barly-breed, Mark telle kan,   145
Oure Lord Jhesu refresshed many a man.
In swich estaat as God hath cleped us
I wol persevere; I nam nat precius.
In wyfhod I wol use myn instrument
As frely as my Makere hath it sent.   150
If I be daungerous, God yeve me sorwe!
Myn housbonde shal it have bothe eve and
        morwe,
Whan that hym list come forth and paye his
        dette.
An housbonde I wol have, I wol nat lette,
Which shal be bothe my dettour and my thral,
And have his tribulacion withal   156
Upon his flessh, whil that I am his wyf.
I have the power durynge al my lyf
Upon his propre body, and noght he.
Right thus the Apostel tolde it unto me;   160
And bad oure housbondes for to love us weel.
Al this sentence me liketh every deel —
    Up stirte the Pardoner, and that anon:
"Now, dame," quod he, "by God and by seint
        John!
Ye been a noble prechour in this cas.   165
I was aboute to wedde a wyf; allas!
What sholde I bye it on my flessh so deere?
Yet hadde I levere wedde no wyf to-yeere!"
    "Abyde!" quod she, "my tale is nat bigonne.
Nay, thou shalt drynken of another tonne,   170
Er that I go, shal savoure wors than ale.
And whan that I have toold thee forth my tale
Of tribulacion in mariage,
Of which I am expert in al myn age,   174
This is to seyn, myself have been the whippe, —
Than maystow chese wheither thou wolt sippe
Of thilke tonne that I shal abroche.
Be war of it, er thou to ny approche;
For I shal telle ensamples mo than ten.
'Whoso that nyl be war by othere men,   180
By hym shul othere men corrected be.'
The same wordes writeth Ptholomee;
Rede in his Almageste, and take it there."

"Dame, I wolde praye yow, if youre wyl it
    were,"
Seyde this Pardoner, "as ye bigan, 185
Telle forth youre tale, spareth for no man,
And teche us yonge men of youre praktike."
    "Gladly," quod she, "sith it may yow like;
But that I praye to al this compaignye,
If that I speke after my fantasye, 190
As taketh not agrief of that I seye;
For myn entente is nat but for to pleye.
    Now, sire, now wol I telle forth my tale. —
As evere moote I drynken wyn or ale, 194
I shal seye sooth, tho housbondes that I hadde,
As thre of hem were goode, and two were
    badde.
The thre were goode men, and riche, and olde;
Unnethe myghte they the statut holde
In which that they were bounden unto me.
Ye woot wel what I meene of this, pardee! 200
As help me God, I laughe whan I thynke
How pitously a-nyght I made hem swynke!
And, by my fey, I tolde of it no stoor.
They had me yeven hir lond and hir tresoor;
Me neded nat do lenger diligence 205
To wynne hir love, or doon hem reverence.
They loved me so wel, by God above,
That I ne tolde no deyntee of hir love!
A wys womman wol bisye hire evere in oon
To gete hire love, ye, ther as she hath noon.
But sith I hadde hem hoolly in myn hond, 211
And sith they hadde me yeven al hir lond,
What sholde I taken keep hem for to plese,
But it were for my profit and myn ese?
I sette hem so a-werke, by my fey, 215
That many a nyght they songen 'weilawey!'
The bacon was nat fet for hem, I trowe,
That som men han in Essex at Dunmowe.
I governed hem so wel, after my lawe,
That ech of hem ful blisful was and fawe 220
To brynge me gaye thynges fro the fayre.
They were ful glad whan I spak to hem faire;
For, God it woot, I chidde hem spitously.
    Now herkneth hou I baar me proprely,
Ye wise wyves, that kan understonde. 225
Thus shulde ye speke and bere hem wrong
    on honde;
For half so boldely kan ther no man
Swere and lyen, as a womman kan.
I sey nat this by wyves that been wyse,
But if it be whan they hem mysavyse. 230
A wys wyf shal, if that she kan hir good,
Bere hym on honde that the cow is wood,
And take witnesse of hir owene mayde
Of hir assent; but herkneth how I sayde:

'Sire olde kaynard, is this thyn array? 235
Why is my neighebores wyf so gay?
She is honoured over al ther she gooth;
I sitte at hoom, I have no thrifty clooth.
What dostow at my neighebores hous?
Is she so fair? artow so amorous? 240
What rowne ye with oure mayde? *Benedicite!*
Sire olde lecchour, lat thy japes be!
And if I have a gossib or a freend,
Withouten gilt, thou chidest as a feend,
If that I walke or pleye unto his hous! 245
Thou comest hoom as dronken as a mous,
And prechest on thy bench, with yvel preef!
Thou seist to me it is a greet meschief
To wedde a povre womman, for costage;
And if that she be riche, of heigh parage, 250
Thanne seistow that it is a tormentrie
To soffre hire pride and hire malencolie.
And if that she be fair, thou verray knave,
Thou seyst that every holour wol hire have;
She may no while in chastitee abyde, 255
That is assailled upon ech a syde.
    Thou seyst som folk desiren us for richesse,
Somme for oure shap, and somme for oure fair-
    nesse,
And som for she kan outher synge or daunce,
And som for gentillesse and daliaunce; 260
Som for hir handes and hir armes smale:
Thus goth al to the devel, by thy tale.
Thou seyst men may nat kepe a castel wal,
It may so longe assailled been over al.
    And if that she be foul, thou seist that she
Coveiteth every man that she may se, 266
For as a spaynel she wol on hym lepe,
Til that she fynde som man hire to chepe.
Ne noon so grey goos gooth ther in the lake
As, sëistow, wol been withoute make. 270
And seyst it is an hard thyng for to welde
A thyng that no man wole, his thankes, helde.
Thus seistow, lorel, whan thow goost to bedde;
And that no wys man nedeth for to wedde,
Ne no man that entendeth unto hevene. 275
With wilde thonder-dynt and firy levene
Moote thy welked nekke be tobroke!
    Thow seyst that droppyng houses, and eek
    smoke,
And chidyng wyves maken men to flee
Out of hir owene hous; a! *benedicitee!* 280
What eyleth swich an old man for to chide?
    Thow seyst we wyves wol oure vices hide
Til we be fast, and thanne we wol hem
    shewe, —
Wel may that be a proverbe of a shrewe!
Thou seist that oxen, asses, hors, and houndes,

They been assayed at diverse stoundes;   286
Bacyns, lavours, er that men hem bye,
Spoones and stooles, and al swich housbondrye,
And so been pottes, clothes, and array;
But folk of wyves maken noon assay,   290
Til they be wedded; olde dotard shrewe!
And thanne, seistow, we wol oure vices shewe.

Thou seist also that it displeseth me
But if that thou wolt preyse my beautee,
And but thou poure alwey upon my face,   295
And clepe me "faire dame" in every place.
And but thou make a feeste on thilke day
That I was born, and make me fressh and gay;
And but thou do to my norice honour,
And to my chamberere withinne my bour,   300
And to my fadres folk and his allyes, —
Thus seistow, olde barel-ful of lyes!

And yet of oure apprentice Janekyn,
For his crispe heer, shynynge as gold so fyn,
And for he squiereth me bothe up and doun,
Yet hastow caught a fals suspecioun.   306
I wol hym noght, thogh thou were deed to-
        morwe!

But tel me this: why hydestow, with sorwe,
The keyes of thy cheste awey fro me?
It is my good as wel as thyn, pardee!   310
What, wenestow make an ydiot of oure dame?
Now by that lord that called is Seint Jame,
Thou shalt nat bothe, thogh that thou were
        wood,
Be maister of my body and of my good;   314
That oon thou shalt forgo, maugree thyne yen.
What helpith it of me to enquere or spyen?
I trowe thou woldest loke me in thy chiste!
Thou sholdest seye, "Wyf, go wher thee liste;
Taak youre disport, I wol nat leve no talys.
I knowe yow for a trewe wyf, dame Alys."
We love no man that taketh kep or charge   321
Wher that we goon; we wol ben at oure large.

Of alle men yblessed moot he be,
The wise astrologien, Daun Ptholome,
That seith this proverbe in his Almageste: 325
"Of alle men his wysdom is the hyeste
That rekketh nevere who hath the world in
        honde."
By this proverbe thou shalt understonde,
Have thou ynogh, what thar thee recche or
        care
How myrily that othere folkes fare?   330
For, certeyn, olde dotard, by youre leve,
Ye shul have queynte right ynogh at eve.
He is to greet a nygard that wolde werne
A man to lighte a candle at his lanterne;
He shal have never the lasse light, pardee.   335

Have thou ynogh, thee thar nat pleyne thee.
Thou seyst also, that if we make us gay
With clothyng, and with precious array,
That it is peril of oure chastitee;   339
And yet, with sorwe! thou most enforce thee,
And seye thise wordes in the Apostles name:
"In habit maad with chastitee and shame
Ye wommen shul apparaille yow," quod he,
"And noght in tressed heer and gay perree,
As perles, ne with gold, ne clothes riche."   345
After thy text, ne after thy rubriche,
I wol nat wirche as muchel as a gnat.

Thou seydest this, that I was lyk a cat;
For whoso wolde senge a cattes skyn,   349
Thanne wolde the cat wel dwellen in his in;
And if the cattes skyn be slyk and gay,
She wol nat dwelle in house half a day,
But forth she wole, er any day be dawed,
To shewe hir skyn, and goon a-caterwawed.
This is to seye, if I be gay, sire shrewe,   355
I wol renne out, my borel for to shewe.

Sire olde fool, what helpeth thee to spyen?
Thogh thou preye Argus with his hundred yen
To be my warde-cors, as he kan best,
In feith, he shal nat kepe me but me lest;   360
Yet koude I make his berd, so moot I thee!

Thou seydest eek that ther been thynges thre,
The whiche thynges troublen al this erthe,
And that no wight may endure the ferthe.
O leeve sire shrewe, Jhesu shorte thy lyf!   365
Yet prechestow and seyst an hateful wyf
Yrekened is for oon of thise meschances.
Been ther none othere maner resemblances
That ye may likne youre parables to,
But if a sely wyf be oon of tho?   370

Thou liknest eek wommenes love to helle,
To bareyne lond, ther water may nat dwelle.
Thou liknest it also to wilde fyr;
The moore it brenneth, the moore it hath desir
To consume every thyng that brent wole be.
Thou seyest, right as wormes shende a tree,   376
Right so a wyf destroyeth hire housbonde;
This knowe they that been to wyves bonde.'

Lordynges, right thus, as ye have under-
        stonde,
Baar I stifly myne olde housbondes on honde
That thus they seyden in hir dronkenesse;   381
And al was fals, but that I took witnesse
On Janekyn, and on my nece also.
O Lord! the peyne I dide hem and the wo,
Ful giltelees, by Goddes sweete pyne!   385
For as an hors I koude byte and whyne.
I koude pleyne, and yit was in the gilt,
Or elles often tyme hadde I been spilt.

Whoso that first to mille comth, first grynt;
I pleyned first, so was oure werre ystynt.   390
They were ful glade to excuse hem blyve
Of thyng of which they nevere agilte hir lyve.
Of wenches wolde I beren hem on honde,
Whan that for syk unnethes myghte they
    stonde.

Yet tikled I his herte, for that he   395
Wende that I hadde of hym so greet chiertee!
I swoor that al my walkynge out by nyghte
Was for t'espye wenches that he dighte;
Under that colour hadde I many a myrthe.   399
For al swich wit is yeven us in oure byrthe;
Deceite, wepyng, spynnyng God hath yive
To wommen kyndely, whil that they may lyve.
And thus of o thyng I avaunte me,
Atte ende I hadde the bettre in ech degree,
By sleighte, or force, or by som maner thyng,
As by continueel murmur or grucchyng.   406
Namely abedde hadden they meschaunce:
Ther wolde I chide, and do hem no plesaunce;
I wolde no lenger in the bed abyde,
If that I felte his arm over my syde,   410
Til he had maad his raunson unto me;
Thanne wolde I suffre hym do his nycetee.
And therfore every man this tale I telle,
Wynne whoso may, for al is for to selle;
With empty hand men may none haukes lure.
For wynnyng wolde I al his lust endure,   416
And make me a feyned appetit;
And yet in bacon hadde I nevere delit;
That made me that evere I wolde hem chide.
For thogh the pope hadde seten hem biside,
I wolde nat spare hem at hir owene bord;   421
For, by my trouthe, I quitte hem word for
    word.
As helpe me verray God omnipotent,
Though I right now sholde make my testament,
I ne owe hem nat a word that it nys quit.   425
I broghte it so aboute by my wit
That they moste yeve it up, as for the beste,
Or elles hadde we nevere been in reste.
For thogh he looked as a wood leon,
Yet sholde he faille of his conclusion.   430

Thanne wolde I seye, 'Goode lief, taak keep
How mekely looketh Wilkyn, oure sheep!
Com neer, my spouse, lat me ba thy cheke!
Ye sholde been al pacient and meke,
And han a sweete spiced conscience,   435
Sith ye so preche of Jobes pacience.
Suffreth alwey, syn ye so wel kan preche;
And but ye do, certein we shal yow teche
That it is fair to have a wyf in pees.
Oon of us two moste bowen, doutelees;   440

And sith a man is moore resonable
Than womman is, ye moste been suffrable.
What eyleth yow to grucche thus and grone?
Is it for ye wolde have my queynte allone?
Wy, taak it al! lo, have it every deel!   445
Peter! I shrewe yow, but ye love it weel;
For if I wolde selle my *bele chose,*
I koude walke as fressh as is a rose;
But I wol kepe it for youre owene tooth.
Ye be to blame, by God! I sey yow sooth.'   450

Swiche manere wordes hadde we on honde.
Now wol I speken of my fourthe housbonde.

My fourthe housbonde was a revelour;
This is to seyn, he hadde a paramour;
And I was yong and ful of ragerye,   455
Stibourn and strong, and joly as a pye.
How koude I daunce to an harpe smale,
And synge, ywis, as any nyghtyngale,
Whan I had dronke a draughte of sweete wyn!
Metellius, the foule cherl, the swyn,   460
That with a staf birafte his wyf hir lyf,
For she drank wyn, thogh I hadde been his wyf,
He sholde nat han daunted me fro drynke!
And after wyn on Venus moste I thynke,
For al so siker as cold engendreth hayl,   465
A likerous mouth moste han a likerous tayl.
In wommen vinolent is no defence, —
This knowen lecchours by experience.

But, Lord Crist! whan that it remembreth me
Upon my yowthe, and on my jolitee,   470
It tikleth me aboute myn herte roote.
Unto this day it dooth myn herte boote
That I have had my world as in my tyme.
But age, allas! that al wole envenyme,
Hath me biraft my beautee and my pith.   475
Lat go, farewel! the devel go therwith!
The flour is goon, ther is namoore to telle;
The bren, as I best kan, now moste I selle;
But yet to be right myrie wol I fonde.
Now wol I tellen of my fourthe housbonde.

I seye, I hadde in herte greet despit   481
That he of any oother had delit.
But he was quit, by God and by Seint Joce!
I made hym of the same wode a croce;
Nat of my body, in no foul manere,   485
But certeinly, I made folk swich cheere
That in his owene grece I made hym frye
For angre, and for verray jalousye.
By God! in erthe I was his purgatorie,
For which I hope his soule is in glorie.   490
For, God it woot, he sat ful ofte and song,
Whan that his shoo ful bitterly hym wrong.
Ther was no wight, save God and he, that
    wiste,

In many wise, how soore I hym twiste.
He deyde whan I cam fro Jerusalem,   495
And lith ygrave under the roode beem,
Al is his tombe noght so curyus
As was the sepulcre of hym Daryus,
Which that Appelles wroghte subtilly;
It nys but wast to burye hym preciously.   500
Lat hym fare wel, God yeve his soul reste!
He is now in his grave and in his cheste.
    Now of my fifthe housbonde wol I telle.
God lete his soule nevere come in helle!
And yet was he to me the mooste shrewe;   505
That feele I on my ribbes al by rewe,
And evere shal unto myn endyng day.
But in oure bed he was so fressh and gay,
And therwithal so wel koude he me glose,
Whan that he wolde han my *bele chose*,   510
That thogh he hadde me bete on every bon,
He koude wynne agayn my love anon.
I trowe I loved hym best, for that he
Was of his love daungerous to me.
We wommen han, if that I shal nat lye,   515
In this matere a queynte fantasye;
Wayte what thyng we may nat lightly have,
Therafter wol we crie al day and crave.
Forbede us thyng, and that desiren we;
Preesse on us faste, and thanne wol we fle.   520
With daunger oute we al oure chaffare;
Greet prees at market maketh deere ware,
And to greet cheep is holde at litel prys:
This knoweth every womman that is wys.   524
    My fifthe housbonde, God his soule blesse!
Which that I took for love, and no richesse,
He som tyme was a clerk of Oxenford,
And hadde left scole, and wente at hom to bord
With my gossib, dwellynge in oure toun;
God have hir soule! hir name was Alisoun.   530
She knew myn herte, and eek my privetee,
Bet than oure parisshe preest, so moot I thee!
To hire biwreyed I my conseil al.
For hadde myn housbonde pissed on a wal,
Or doon a thyng that sholde han cost his lyf,
To hire, and to another worthy wyf,   536
And to my nece, which that I loved weel,
I wolde han toold his conseil every deel.
And so I dide ful often, God it woot,
That made his face often reed and hoot   540
For verray shame, and blamed hymself for he
Had toold to me so greet a pryvetee.
    And so bifel that ones in a Lente —
So often tymes I to my gossyb wente,
For evere yet I loved to be gay,   545
And for to walke in March, Averill, and May,
Fro hous to hous, to heere sondry talys —

That Jankyn clerk, and my gossyb dame Alys,
And I myself, into the feeldes wente.
Myn housbonde was at Londoun al that Lente;
I hadde the bettre leyser for to pleye,   551
And for to se, and eek for to be seye
Of lusty folk. What wiste I wher my grace
Was shapen for to be, or in what place?
Therfore I made my visitaciouns   555
To vigilies and to processiouns,
To prechyng eek, and to thise pilgrimages,
To pleyes of myracles, and to mariages,
And wered upon my gaye scarlet gytes.   559
Thise wormes, ne thise motthes, ne thise mytes,
Upon my peril, frete hem never a deel;
And wostow why? for they were used weel.
    Now wol I tellen forth what happed me.
I seye that in the feeldes walked we,
Til trewely we hadde swich daliance,   565
This clerk and I, that of my purveiance
I spak to hym and seyde hym how that he,
If I were wydwe, sholde wedde me.
For certeinly, I sey for no bobance,
Yet was I nevere withouten purveiance   570
Of mariage, n'of othere thynges eek.
I holde a mouses herte nat worth a leek
That hath but oon hole for to sterte to,
And if that faille, thanne is al ydo.   574
    I bar hym on honde he hadde enchanted
        me, —
My dame taughte me that soutiltee.
And eek I seyde I mette of hym al nyght,
He wolde han slayn me as I lay upright,
And al my bed was ful of verray blood;
But yet I hope that he shal do me good,   580
For blood bitokeneth gold, as me was taught.
And al was fals; I dremed of it right naught,
But as I folwed ay my dames loore,
As wel of this as of othere thynges moore.
    But now, sire, lat me se, what I shal seyn?
A ha! by God, I have my tale ageyn.   586
    Whan that my fourthe housbonde was on
        beere,
I weep algate, and made sory cheere,
As wyves mooten, for it is usage,
And with my coverchief covered my visage,
But for that I was purveyed of a make,   591
I wepte but smal, and that I undertake.
    To chirche was myn housbonde born
        a-morwe
With neighebores, that for hym maden sorwe;
And Jankyn, oure clerk, was oon of tho.   595
As help me God! whan that I saugh hym go
After the beere, me thoughte he hadde a paire
Of legges and of feet so clene and faire

That al myn herte I yaf unto his hoold.
He was, I trowe, a twenty wynter oold,   600
And I was fourty, if I shal seye sooth;
But yet I hadde alwey a coltes tooth.
Gat-tothed I was, and that bicam me weel;
I hadde the prente of seinte Venus seel.
As help me God! I was a lusty oon,   605
And faire, and riche, and yong, and wel bigon;
And trewely, as myne housbondes tolde me,
I hadde the beste *quoniam* myghte be.
For certes, I am al Venerien
In feelynge, and myn herte is Marcien.   610
Venus me yaf my lust, my likerousnesse,
And Mars yaf me my sturdy hardynesse;
Myn ascendent was Taur, and Mars therinne.
Allas! allas! that evere love was synne!
I folwed ay myn inclinacioun   615
By vertu of my constellacioun;
That made me I koude noght withdrawe
My chambre of Venus from a good felawe.
Yet have I Martes mark upon my face,
And also in another privee place.   620
For God so wys be my savacioun,
I ne loved nevere by no discrecioun,
But evere folwede myn appetit,
Al were he short, or long, or blak, or whit;
I took no kep, so that he liked me,   625
How poore he was, ne eek of what degree.
    What sholde I seye? but, at the monthes ende,
This joly clerk, Jankyn, that was so hende,
Hath wedded me with greet solempnytee;
And to hym yaf I al the lond and fee   630
That evere was me yeven therbifoore.
But afterward repented me ful soore;
He nolde suffre nothyng of my list.
By God! he smoot me ones on the lyst,
For that I rente out of his book a leef,   635
That of the strook myn ere wax al deef.
Stibourn I was as is a leonesse,
And of my tonge a verray jangleresse,
And walke I wolde, as I had doon biforn,   639
From hous to hous, although he had it sworn;
For which he often tymes wolde preche,
And me of olde Romayn geestes teche,
How he Symplicius Gallus lefte his wyf,
And hire forsook for terme of al his lyf,
Noght but for open-heveded he hir say   645
Lookynge out at his dore upon a day.
    Another Romayn tolde he me by name,
That, for his wyf was at a someres game
Withouten his wityng, he forsook hire eke.
And thanne wolde he upon his Bible seke   650
That ilke proverbe of Ecclesiaste

Where he comandeth, and forbedeth faste,
Man shal nat suffre his wyf go roule aboute.
Thanne wolde he seye right thus, withouten
        doute:
'Whoso that buyldeth his hous al of salwes,
And priketh his blynde hors over the falwes,
And suffreth his wyf to go seken halwes,   657
Is worthy to been hanged on the galwes!'
But al for noght, I sette noght an hawe
Of his proverbes n'of his olde sawe,   660
Ne I wolde nat of hym corrected be.
I hate hym that my vices telleth me,
And so doo mo, God woot, of us than I.
This made hym with me wood al outrely;
I nolde noght forbere hym in no cas.   665
    Now wol I seye yow sooth, by seint Thomas,
Why that I rente out of his book a leef,
For which he smoot me so that I was deef.
    He hadde a book that gladly, nyght and day,
For his desport he wolde rede alway;   670
He cleped it Valerie and Theofraste,
At which book he lough alwey ful faste.
And eek ther was somtyme a clerk at Rome,
A cardinal, that highte Seint Jerome,
That made a book agayn Jovinian;   675
In which book eek ther was Tertulan,
Crisippus, Trotula, and Helowys,
That was abbesse nat fer fro Parys;
And eek the Parables of Salomon,
Ovides Art, and bookes many on,   680
And alle thise were bounden in o volume.
And every nyght and day was his custume,
Whan he hadde leyser and vacacioun
From oother worldly occupacioun,
To reden on this book of wikked wyves.   685
He knew of hem mo legendes and lyves
Than been of goode wyves in the Bible.
For trusteth wel, it is an impossible
That any clerk wol speke good of wyves,
But if it be of hooly seintes lyves,   690
Ne of noon oother womman never the mo.
Who peyntede the leon, tel me who?
By God! if wommen hadde writen stories,
As clerkes han withinne hire oratories,
They wolde han writen of men moore wikked-
        nesse
Than al the mark of Adam may redresse.   696
The children of Mercurie and of Venus
Been in hir wirkyng ful contrarius;
Mercurie loveth wysdam and science,
And Venus loveth ryot and dispence.   700
And, for hire diverse disposicioun,
Ech falleth in otheres exaltacioun.
And thus, God woot, Mercurie is desolat

In Pisces, wher Venus is exaltat;
And Venus falleth ther Mercurie is reysed.   705
Therfore no womman of no clerk is preysed.
The clerk, whan he is oold, and may noght do
Of Venus werkes worth his olde sho,
Thanne sit he doun, and writ in his dotage
That wommen kan nat kepe hir mariage!   710

But now to purpos, why I tolde thee
That I was beten for a book, pardee!
Upon a nyght Jankyn, that was oure sire,
Redde on his book, as he sat by the fire,
Of Eva first, that for hir wikkednesse   715
Was al mankynde broght to wrecchednesse,
For which that Jhesu Crist hymself was slayn,
That boghte us with his herte blood agayn.
Lo, heere expres of womman may ye fynde,
That womman was the los of al mankynde.   720

Tho redde he me how Sampson loste his
    heres:
Slepynge, his lemman kitte it with hir sheres;
Thurgh which treson loste he bothe his yen.

Tho redde he me, if that I shal nat lyen,
Of Hercules and of his Dianyre,   725
That caused hym to sette hymself afyre.

No thyng forgat he the care and the wo
That Socrates hadde with his wyves two;
How Xantippa caste pisse upon his heed.
This sely man sat stille as he were deed;   730
He wiped his heed, namoore dorste he seyn,
But 'Er that thonder stynte, comth a reyn!'

Of Phasipha, that was the queene of Crete,
For shrewednesse, hym thoughte the tale
    swete;
Fy! spek namoore — it is a grisly thyng —   735
Of hire horrible lust and hir likyng.

Of Clitermystra, for hire lecherye,
That falsly made hire housbonde for to dye,
He redde it with ful good devocioun.

He tolde me eek for what occasioun   740
Amphiorax at Thebes loste his lyf.
Myn housbonde hadde a legende of his wyf,
Eriphilem, that for an ouche of gold
Hath prively unto the Grekes told
Wher that hir housbonde hidde hym in a place,
For which he hadde at Thebes sory grace.   746

Of Lyvia tolde he me, and of Lucye:
They bothe made hir housbondes for to dye;
That oon for love, that oother was for hate.
Lyvia hir housbonde, on an even late,   750
Empoysoned hath, for that she was his fo;
Lucia, likerous, loved hire housbonde so
That, for he sholde alwey upon hire thynke,
She yaf hym swich a manere love-drynke
That he was deed er it were by the morwe;

And thus algates housbondes han sorwe.   756

Thanne tolde he me how oon Latumyus
Compleyned unto his felawe Arrius
That in his gardyn growed swich a tree
On which he seyde how that his wyves thre
Hanged hemself for herte despitus.   761
'O leeve brother,' quod this Arrius,
'Yif me a plante of thilke blissed tree,
And in my gardyn planted shal it bee.'

Of latter date, of wyves hath he red   765
That somme han slayn hir housbondes in hir
    bed,
And lete hir lecchour dighte hire al the nyght,
Whan that the corps lay in the floor upright.
And somme han dryve nayles in hir brayn,
Whil that they slepte, and thus they had hem
    slayn.   770
Somme han hem yeve poysoun in hire drynke.
He spak moore harm than herte may bithynke;
And therwithal he knew of mo proverbes
Than in this world ther growen gras or herbes.
'Bet is,' quod he, 'thyn habitacioun   775
Be with a leon or a foul dragoun,
Than with a womman usynge for to chyde.'
'Bet is,' quod he, 'hye in the roof abyde,
Than with an angry wyf doun in the hous;
They been so wikked and contrarious,   780
They haten that hir housbondes loven ay.'
He seyde, 'a womman cast hir shame away,
Whan she cast of hir smok;' and forthermo,
'A fair womman, but she be chaast also,
Is lyk a gold ryng in a sowes nose.'   785
Who wolde wene, or who wolde suppose,
The wo that in myn herte was, and pyne?

And whan I saugh he wolde nevere fyne
To reden on this cursed book al nyght,
Al sodeynly thre leves have I plyght   790
Out of his book, right as he radde, and eke
I with my fest so took hym on the cheke
That in oure fyr he fil bakward adoun.
And he up stirte as dooth a wood leoun,
And with his fest he smoot me on the heed,
That in the floor I lay as I were deed.   796
And whan he saugh how stille that I lay,
He was agast, and wolde han fled his way,
Til atte laste out of my swogh I breyde.
'O! hastow slayn me, false theef?' I seyde,   800
'And for my land thus hastow mordred me?
Er I be deed, yet wol I kisse thee.'

And neer he cam, and kneled faire adoun,
And seyde, 'Deere suster Alisoun,
As help me God! I shal thee nevere smyte.
That I have doon, it is thyself to wyte.   805
Foryeve it me, and that I thee biseke!'

And yet eftsoones I hitte hym on the cheke,
And seyde, 'Theef, thus muchel am I wreke;
Now wol I dye, I may no lenger speke.'   810
But atte laste, with muchel care and wo,
We fille acorded by us selven two.
He yaf me al the bridel in myn hond,
To han the governance of hous and lond,
And of his tonge, and of his hond also;   815
And made hym brenne his book anon right tho.
And whan that I hadde geten unto me,
By maistrie, al the soveraynetee,
And that he seyde, 'Myn owene trewe wyf,
Do as thee lust the terme of al thy lyf;   820
Keep thyn honour, and keep eek myn estaat' —
After that day we hadden never debaat.
God helpe me so, I was to hym as kynde
As any wyf from Denmark unto Ynde,
And also trewe, and so was he to me.   825
I prey to God, that sit in magestee,
So blesse his soule for his mercy deere.
Now wol I seye my tale, if ye wol heere."

Biholde the wordes bitwene the Somonour and the Frere.

The Frere lough, whan he hadde herd al this;
"Now dame," quod he, "so have I joye or blis,
This is a long preamble of a tale!"   831

And whan the Somonour herde the Frere gale,
"Lo," quod the Somonour, "Goddes armes two!
A frere wol entremette hym everemo.
Lo, goode men, a flye and eek a frere   835
Wol falle in every dyssh and eek mateere.
What spekestow of preambulacioun?
What! amble, or trotte, or pees, or go sit doun!
Thou lettest oure disport in this manere."
    "Ye, woltow so, sire Somonour?" quod the
        Frere;
"Now, by my feith, I shal, er that I go,   841
Telle of a somonour swich a tale or two,
That alle the folk shal laughen in this place."
    "Now elles, Frere, I bishrewe thy face,"
Quod this Somonour, "and I bishrewe me,   845
But if I telle tales two or thre
Of freres, er I come to Sidyngborne,
That I shal make thyn herte for to morne,
For wel I woot thy pacience is gon."   849
    Oure Hooste cride "Pees! and that anon!"
And seyde, "Lat the womman telle hire tale.
Ye fare as folk that dronken ben of ale.
Do, dame, telle forth youre tale, and that is
        best."
    "Al redy, sire," quod she, "right as yow lest,
If I have licence of this worthy Frere."   855
    "Yis, dame," quod he, "tel forth, and I wol
        heere."

Heere endeth the Wyf of Bathe hir Prologe.

The Wife of Bath's Tale

Heere bigynneth the Tale of the Wyf of Bathe.

In th'olde dayes of the Kyng Arthour,
Of which that Britons speken greet honour,
Al was this land fulfild of fayerye.
The elf-queene, with hir joly compaignye,   860
Daunced ful ofte in many a grene mede.
This was the olde opinion, as I rede;
I speke of manye hundred yeres ago.
But now kan no man se none elves mo,
For now the grete charitee and prayeres   865
Of lymytours and othere hooly freres,
That serchen every lond and every streem,
As thikke as motes in the sonne-beem,
Blessynge halles, chambres, kichenes, boures,
Citees, burghes, castels, hye toures,   870

Thropes, bernes, shipnes, dayeryes —
This maketh that ther ben no fayeryes.
For ther as wont to walken was an elf,
Ther walketh now the lymytour hymself
In undermeles and in morwenynges,   875
And seyth his matyns and his hooly thynges
As he gooth in his lymytacioun.
Wommen may go now saufly up and doun.
In every bussh or under every tree
Ther is noon oother incubus but he,   880
And he ne wol doon hem but dishonour.
    And so bifel it that this kyng Arthour
Hadde in his hous a lusty bacheler,
That on a day cam ridynge fro ryver;

And happed that, allone as he was born,   885
He saugh a mayde walkynge hym biforn,
Of which mayde anon, maugree hir heed,
By verray force, he rafte hire maydenhed;
For which oppressioun was swich clamour
And swich pursute unto the kyng Arthour,   890
That dampned was this knyght for to be deed,
By cours of lawe, and sholde han lost his
        heed —
Paraventure swich was the statut tho —
But that the queene and othere ladyes mo
So longe preyeden the kyng of grace,   895
Til he his lyf hym graunted in the place,
And yaf hym to the queene, al at hir wille,
To chese wheither she wolde hym save or
        spille.
    The queene thanketh the kyng with al hir
        myght,
And after this thus spak she to the knyght,   900
Whan that she saugh hir tyme, upon a day:
"Thou standest yet," quod she, "in swich array
That of thy lyf yet hastow no suretee.
I grante thee lyf, if thou kanst tellen me   904
What thyng is it that wommen moost desiren.
Be war, and keep thy nekke-boon from iren!
And if thou kanst nat tellen it anon,
Yet wol I yeve thee leve for to gon
A twelf-month and a day, to seche and leere
An answere suffisant in this mateere;   910
And suretee wol I han, er that thou pace,
Thy body for to yelden in this place."
    Wo was this knyght, and sorwefully he
        siketh;
But what! he may nat do al as hym liketh.
And at the laste he chees hym for to wende,
And come agayn, right at the yeres ende,   916
With swich answere as God wolde hym pur-
        veye;
And taketh his leve, and wendeth forth his
        weye.
    He seketh every hous and every place
Where as he hopeth for to fynde grace,   920
To lerne what thyng wommen loven moost;
But he ne koude arryven in no coost
Wher as he myghte fynde in this mateere
Two creatures accordynge in-feere.   924
Somme seyde wommen loven best richesse,
Somme seyde honour, somme seyde jolynesse,
Somme riche array, somme seyden lust abedde,
And oftetyme to be wydwe and wedde.
Somme seyde that oure hertes been moost esed
Whan that we been yflatered and yplesed.   930
He gooth ful ny the sothe, I wol nat lye.
A man shal wynne us best with flaterye;

And with attendance, and with bisynesse,
Been we ylymed, bothe moore and lesse.
    And somme seyen that we loven best   935
For to be free, and do right as us lest,
And that no man repreve us of oure vice,
But seye that we be wise, and no thyng nyce.
For trewely ther is noon of us alle,
If any wight wol clawe us on the galle,   940
That we nel kike, for he seith us sooth.
Assay, and he shal fynde it that so dooth;
For, be we never so vicious withinne,
We wol been holden wise and clene of synne.
    And somme seyn that greet delit han we   945
For to been holden stable, and eek secree,
And in o purpos stedefastly to dwelle,
And nat biwreye thyng that men us telle.
But that tale is nat worth a rake-stele.
Pardee, we wommen konne no thyng hele;   950
Witnesse on Myda, — wol ye heere the tale?
    Ovyde, amonges othere thynges smale,
Seyde Myda hadde, under his longe heres,
Growynge upon his heed two asses eres,   954
The whiche vice he hydde, as he best myghte,
Ful subtilly from every mannes sighte,
That, save his wyf, ther wiste of it namo.
He loved hire moost, and trusted hire also;
He preyede hire that to no creature
She sholde tellen of his disfigure.   960
    She swoor him, "Nay," for al this world to
        wynne,
She nolde do that vileynye or synne,
To make hir housbonde han so foul a name.
She nolde nat telle it for hir owene shame.
But nathelees, hir thoughte that she dyde,   965
That she so longe sholde a conseil hyde;
Hir thoughte it swal so soore aboute hir herte
That nedely som word hire moste asterte;
And sith she dorste telle it to no man,
Doun to a mareys faste by she ran —   970
Til she cam there, hir herte was a-fyre —
And as a bitore bombleth in the myre,
She leyde hir mouth unto the water doun:
"Biwreye me nat, thou water, with thy soun,"
Quod she; "to thee I telle it and namo;   975
Myn housbonde hath longe asses erys two!
Now is myn herte al hool, now is it oute.
I myghte no lenger kepe it, out of doute.
Heere may ye se, thogh we a tyme abyde,
Yet out it moot; we kan no conseil hyde.   980
The remenant of the tale if ye wol heere,
Redeth Ovyde, and ther ye may it leere.
    This knyght, of which my tale is specially,
Whan that he saugh he myghte nat come
        therby,

This is to seye, what wommen love moost,   985
Withinne his brest ful sorweful was the
    goost.
But hoom he gooth, he myghte nat sojourne;
The day was come that homward moste he
    tourne.
And in his wey it happed hym to ryde,
In al this care, under a forest syde,   990
Wher as he saugh upon a daunce go
Of ladyes foure and twenty, and yet mo;
Toward the whiche daunce he drow ful yerne,
In hope that som wysdom sholde he lerne.
But certeinly, er he cam fully there,   995
Vanysshed was this daunce, he nyste where.
No creature saugh he that bar lyf,
Save on the grene he saugh sittynge a wyf —
A fouler wight ther may no man devyse.
Agayn the knyght this olde wyf gan ryse,   1000
And seyde, "Sire knyght, heer forth ne lith no
    wey.
Tel me what that ye seken, by youre fey!
Paraventure it may the bettre be;
Thise olde folk kan muchel thyng," quod she.
   "My leeve mooder," quod this knyght, "cer-
    teyn
I nam but deed, but if that I kan seyn   1006
What thyng it is that wommen moost desire.
Koude ye me wisse, I wolde wel quite youre
    hire."
   "Plight me thy trouthe heere in myn hand,"
    quod she,
"The nexte thyng that I requere thee,   1010
Thou shalt it do, if it lye in thy myght,
And I wol telle it yow er it be nyght."
   "Have heer my trouthe," quod the knyght,
    "I grante."
   "Thanne," quod she, "I dar me wel avante
Thy lyf is sauf; for I wol stonde therby,   1015
Upon my lyf, the queene wol seye as I.
Lat se which is the proudeste of hem alle,
That wereth on a coverchief or a calle,
That dar seye nay of that I shal thee teche.
Lat us go forth, withouten lenger speche."
Tho rowned she a pistel in his ere,   1021
And bad hym to be glad, and have no fere.
   Whan they be comen to the court, this
    knyght
Seyde he had holde his day, as he hadde hight,
And redy was his answere, as he sayde.   1025
Ful many a noble wyf, and many a mayde,
And many a wydwe, for that they been wise,
The queene hirself sittynge as a justise,
Assembled been, his answere for to heere;
And afterward this knyght was bode appeere.

To every wight comanded was silence,   1031
And that the knyght sholde telle in audience
What thyng that worldly wommen loven best.
This knyght ne stood nat stille as doth a best,
But to his questioun anon answerde   1035
With manly voys, that al the court it herde:
   "My lige lady, generally," quod he,
"Wommen desiren to have sovereynetee
As wel over hir housbond as hir love,
And for to been in maistrie hym above.   1040
This is youre mooste desir, thogh ye me kille.
Dooth as yow list; I am heer at youre wille."
In al the court ne was ther wyf, ne mayde,
Ne wydwe, that contraried that he sayde,
But seyden he was worthy han his lyf.   1045
And with that word up stirte the olde wyf,
Which that the knyght saugh sittynge on the
    grene:
"Mercy," quod she, "my sovereyn lady queene!
Er that youre court departe, do me right.
I taughte this answere unto the knyght;   1050
For which he plighte me his trouthe there,
The firste thyng that I wolde hym requere,
He wolde it do, if it lay in his myghte.
Bifore the court thanne preye I thee, sir
    knyght,"
Quod she, "that thou me take unto thy wyf;
For wel thou woost that I have kept thy lyf.
If I seye fals, sey nay, upon thy fey!"   1057
   This knyght answerde, "Allas! and weyla-
    wey!
I woot right wel that swich was my biheste.
For Goddes love, as chees a newe requeste!
Taak al my good, and lat my body go."   1061
   "Nay, thanne," quod she, "I shrewe us bothe
    two!
For thogh that I be foul, and oold, and poore,
I nolde for al the metal, ne for oore,
That under erthe is grave, or lith above,   1065
But if thy wyf I were, and eek thy love."
   "My love?" quod he, "nay, my dampna-
    cioun!
Allas! that any of my nacioun
Sholde evere so foule disparaged be!"
But al for noght; the ende is this, that he   1070
Constreyned was, he nedes moste hire wedde;
And taketh his olde wyf, and gooth to bedde.
   Now wolden som men seye, paraventure,
That for my necligence I do no cure
To tellen yow the joye and al th'array   1075
That at the feeste was that ilke day.
To which thyng shortly answeren I shal:
I seye ther nas no joye ne feeste at al;
Ther nas but hevynesse and muche sorwe

For prively he wedded hire on the morwe,
And al day after hidde hym as an owle, 1081
So wo was hym, his wyf looked so foule.
　Greet was the wo the knyght hadde in his
　　thoght,
Whan he was with his wyf abedde ybroght;
He walweth and he turneth to and fro. 1085
His olde wyf lay smylynge everemo,
And seyde, "O deere housbonde, *benedicitee!*
Fareth every knyght thus with his wyf as ye?
Is this the lawe of kyng Arthures hous?
Is every knyght of his so dangerous? 1090
I am youre owene love and eek youre wyf;
I am she which that saved hath youre lyf,
And, certes, yet ne dide I yow nevere unright;
Why fare ye thus with me this firste nyght?
Ye faren lyk a man had lost his wit. 1095
What is my gilt? For Goddes love, tel me it,
And it shal been amended, if I may."
　"Amended?" quod this knyght, "allas! nay,
　　nay!
It wol nat been amended nevere mo.
Thou art so loothly, and so oold also, 1100
And therto comen of so lough a kynde,
That litel wonder is thogh I walwe and wynde.
So wolde God myn herte wolde breste!"
　"Is this," quod she, "the cause of youre un-
　　reste?"
　"Ye, certeinly," quod he, "no wonder is."
　"Now, sire," quod she, "I koude amende al
　　this,
If that me liste, er it were dayes thre, 1106
So wel ye myghte bere yow unto me.
　But, for ye speken of swich gentillesse
As is descended out of old richesse, 1110
That therfore sholden ye be gentil men,
Swich arrogance is nat worth an hen.
Looke who that is moost vertuous alway,
Pryvee and apert, and moost entendeth ay
To do the gentil dedes that he kan; 1115
Taak hym for the grettest gentil man.
Crist wole we clayme of hym oure gentillesse,
Nat of oure eldres for hire old richesse.
For thogh they yeve us al hir heritage, 1119
For which we clayme to been of heigh parage,
Yet may they nat biquethe, for no thyng,
To noon of us hir vertuous lyvyng,
That made hem gentil men ycalled be,
And bad us folwen hem in swich degree.
　Wel kan the wise poete of Florence, 1125
That highte Dant, speken in this sentence.
Lo, in swich maner rym is Dantes tale:
'Ful selde up riseth by his branches smale
Prowesse of man, for God, of his goodnesse,

Wole that of hym we clayme oure gentil-
　lesse'; 1130
For of oure eldres may we no thyng clayme
But temporel thyng, that man may hurte and
　mayme.
Eek every wight woot this as wel as I,
If gentillesse were planted natureelly
Unto a certeyn lynage doun the lyne, 1135
Pryvee and apert, thanne wolde they nevere
　fyne
To doon of gentillesse the faire office;
They myghte do no vileynye or vice.
　Taak fyr, and ber it in the derkeste hous
Bitwix this and the mount of Kaukasous, 1140
And lat men shette the dores and go thenne;
Yet wole the fyr as faire lye and brenne
As twenty thousand men myghte it biholde;
His office natureel ay wol it holde,
Up peril of my lyf, til that it dye. 1145
　Heere may ye se wel how that genterye
Is nat annexed to possessioun,
Sith folk ne doon hir operacioun
Alwey, as dooth the fyr, lo, in his kynde. 1149
For, God it woot, men may wel often fynde
A lordes sone do shame and vileynye;
And he that wole han pris of his gentrye,
For he was boren of a gentil hous,
And hadde his eldres noble and vertuous,
And nel hymselven do no gentil dedis, 1155
Ne folwen his gentil auncestre that deed is,
He nys nat gentil, be he duc or erl;
For vileyns synful dedes make a cherl.
For gentillesse nys but renomee 1159
Of thyne auncestres, for hire heigh bountee,
Which is a strange thyng to thy persone.
Thy gentillesse cometh fro God allone.
Thanne comth oure verray gentillesse of grace;
It was no thyng biquethe us with oure place.
　Thenketh hou noble, as seith Valerius, 1165
Was thilke Tullius Hostillius,
That out of poverte roos to heigh noblesse.
Reedeth Senek, and redeth eek Boece;
Ther shul ye seen expres that it no drede is
That he is gentil that dooth gentil dedis. 1170
And therfore, leeve housbonde, I thus con-
　clude:
Al were it that myne auncestres were rude,
Yet may the hye God, and so hope I,
Grante me grace to lyven vertuously.
Thanne am I gentil, whan that I bigynne 1175
To lyven vertuously and weyve synne.
　And ther as ye of poverte me repreeve,
The hye God, on whom that we bileeve,
In wilful poverte chees to lyve his lyf.

And certes every man, mayden, or wyf,   1180
May understonde that Jhesus, hevene kyng,
Ne wolde nat chese a vicious lyvyng.
Glad poverte is an honest thyng, certeyn;
This wole Senec and othere clerkes seyn.
Whoso that halt hym payd of his poverte,   1185
I holde hym riche, al hadde he nat a sherte.
He that coveiteth is a povre wight,
For he wolde han that is nat in his myght;
But he that noght hath, ne coveiteth have,
Is riche, although ye holde hym but a knave.
Verray poverte, it syngeth proprely;   1191
Juvenal seith of poverte myrily:
'The povre man, whan he goth by the weye,
Bifore the theves he may synge and pleye.'
Poverte is hateful good and, as I gesse,   1195
A ful greet bryngere out of bisynesse;
A greet amendere eek of sapience
To hym that taketh it in pacience.
Poverte is this, although it seme alenge,
Possessioun that no wight wol chalenge.   1200
Poverte ful ofte, whan a man is lowe,
Maketh his God and eek hymself to knowe.
Poverte a spectacle is, as thynketh me,
Thurgh which he may his verray freendes see.
And therfore, sire, syn that I noght yow greve,
Of my poverte namoore ye me repreve.   1206
   Now, sire, of elde ye repreve me;
And certes, sire, thogh noon auctoritee
Were in no book, ye gentils of honour
Seyn that men sholde an oold wight doon
      favour,   1210
And clepe hym fader, for youre gentillesse;
And auctours shal I fynden, as I gesse.
   Now ther ye seye that I am foul and old,
Than drede you noght to been a cokewold;
For filthe and eelde, also moot I thee,   1215
Been grete wardeyns upon chastitee.
But nathelees, syn I knowe youre delit,
I shal fulfille youre worldly appetit.
   Chese now," quod she, "oon of thise thynges
      tweye:
To han me foul and old til that I deye,   1220
And be to yow a trewe, humble wyf,
And nevere yow displese in al my lyf;

Or elles ye wol han me yong and fair,
And take youre aventure of the repair
That shal be to youre hous by cause of me,
Or in som oother place, may wel be.   1226
Now chese yourselven, wheither that yow
      liketh."
   This knyght avyseth hym and sore siketh,
But atte laste he seyde in this manere:
"My lady and my love, and wyf so deere,   1230
I put me in youre wise governance;
Cheseth youreself which may be moost ples-
      ance,
And moost honour to yow and me also.
I do no fors the wheither of the two;
For as yow liketh, it suffiseth me."   1235
   "Thanne have I gete of yow maistrie," quod
      she,
"Syn I may chese and governe as me lest?"
   "Ye, certes, wyf," quod he, "I holde it best."
   "Kys me," quod she, "we be no lenger wrothe;
For, by my trouthe, I wol be to yow bothe,
This is to seyn, ye, bothe fair and good.   1241
I prey to God that I moote sterven wood,
But I to yow be also good and trewe
As evere was wyf, syn that the world was newe.
And but I be to-morn as fair to seene   1245
As any lady, emperice, or queene,
That is bitwixe the est and eke the west,
Dooth with my lyf and deth right as yow lest.
Cast up the curtyn, looke how that it is."
   And whan the knyght saugh verraily al this,
That she so fair was, and so yong therto,   1251
For joye he hente hire in his armes two,
His herte bathed in a bath of blisse,
A thousand tyme a-rewe he gan hire kisse,
And she obeyed hym in every thyng   1255
That myghte doon hym plesance or likyng.
   And thus they lyve unto hir lyves ende
In parfit joye; and Jhesu Crist us sende
Housbondes meeke, yonge, and fressh abedde,
And grace t'overbyde hem that we wedde;
And eek I praye Jhesu shorte hir lyves   1261
That wol nat be governed by hir wyves;
And olde and angry nygardes of dispence,
God sende hem soone verray pestilence!

Heere endeth the Wyves Tale of Bathe.

The Friar's Prologue

The Prologe of the Freres Tale.

This worthy lymytour, this noble Frere, 1265
He made alwey a maner louryng chiere
Upon the Somonour, but for honestee
No vileyns word as yet to hym spak he.
But atte laste he seyde unto the wyf,
"Dame," quod he, "God yeve yow right good
　　lyf! 1270
Ye han heer touched, also moot I thee,
In scole-matere greet difficultee.
Ye han seyd muche thyng right wel, I seye;
But, dame, heere as we ryde by the weye,
Us nedeth nat to speken but of game, 1275
And lete auctoritees, on Goddes name,
To prechyng and to scole eek of clergye.
But if it lyke to this compaignye,
I wol yow of a somonour telle a game.
Pardee, ye may wel knowe by the name 1280
That of a somonour may no good be sayd;
I praye that noon of you be yvele apayd.
A somonour is a rennere up and doun

With mandementz for fornicacioun,
And is ybet at every townes ende." 1285
　　Oure Hoost tho spak, "A! sire, ye sholde be
　　hende
And curteys, as a man of youre estaat;
In compaignye we wol have no debaat.
Telleth youre tale, and lat the Somonour be."
　　"Nay," quod the Somonour, "lat hym seye to
　　me 1290
What so hym list; whan it comth to my lot,
By God! I shal hym quiten every grot.
I shal hym tellen which a greet honour
It is to be a flaterynge lymytour;
And eek of many another manere cryme 1295
Which nedeth nat rehercen at this tyme;
And his office I shal hym telle, ywis."
　　Oure Hoost answerde, "Pees, namoore of
　　this!"
And after this he seyde unto the Frere, 1299
"Tel youre tale, my leeve maister deere."

The Friar's Tale

Heere bigynneth the Freres Tale.

Whilom ther was dwellynge in my contree
An erchedeken, a man of heigh degree,
That boldely dide execucioun
In punysshynge of fornicacioun,
Of wicchecraft, and eek of bawderye, 1305
Of diffamacioun, and avowtrye,
Of chirche reves, and of testamentz,
Of contractes and of lakke of sacramentz,
Of usure, and of symonye also.
But certes, lecchours dide he grettest wo; 1310
They sholde syngen if that they were hent;
And smale tytheres weren foule yshent,
If any persoun wolde upon hem pleyne.
Ther myghte asterte hym no pecunyal peyne.
For smale tithes and for smal offrynge 1315
He made the peple pitously to synge.
For er the bisshop caughte hem with his hook,
They weren in the erchedeknes book.

Thanne hadde he, thurgh his jurisdiccioun,
Power to doon on hem correccioun. 1320
He hadde a somonour redy to his hond;
A slyer boye nas noon in Engelond;
For subtilly he hadde his espiaille,
That taughte hym wel wher that hym myghte
　　availle.
He koude spare of lecchours oon or two, 1325
To techen hym to foure and twenty mo.
For thogh this Somonour wood were as an hare,
To telle his harlotrye I wol nat spare;
For we been out of his correccioun.
They han of us no jurisdiccioun, 1330
Ne nevere shullen, terme of alle hir lyves. —
　　"Peter! so been the wommen of the styves,"
Quod the Somonour, "yput out of oure cure!"
　　"Pees! with myschance and with mysaven-
　　ture!"

Thus seyde oure Hoost, "and lat hym telle his
    tale.   1335
Now telleth forth, thogh that the Somonour gale;
Ne spareth nat, myn owene maister deere." —
    This false theef, this somonour, quod the
    Frere,
Hadde alwey bawdes redy to his hond,
As any hauk to lure in Engelond,   1340
That tolde hym al the secree that they knewe;
For hire acqueyntance was nat come of newe.
They weren his approwours prively.
He took hymself a greet profit therby;
His maister knew nat alwey what he wan.   1345
Withouten mandement a lewed man
He koude somne, on peyne of Cristes curs,
And they were glade for to fille his purs,
And make hym grete feestes atte nale.
And right as Judas hadde purses smale,   1350
And was a theef, right swich a theef was he;
His maister hadde but half his duetee.
He was, if I shal yeven hym his laude,
A theef, and eek a somnour, and a baude.
He hadde eek wenches at his retenue,   1355
That, wheither that sir Robert or sir Huwe,
Or Jakke, or Rauf, or whoso that it were
That lay by hem, they tolde it in his ere.
Thus was the wenche and he of oon assent;
And he wolde fecche a feyned mandement,
And somne hem to chapitre bothe two,   1361
And pile the man, and lete the wenche go.
Thanne wolde he seye, "Freend, I shal for thy
    sake
Do striken hire out of oure lettres blake;
Thee thar namoore as in this cas travaille.   1365
I am thy freend, ther I thee may availle."
Certeyn he knew of briberyes mo
Than possible is to telle in yeres two.
For in this world nys dogge for the bowe   1369
That kan an hurt deer from an hool yknowe
Bet than this somnour knew a sly lecchour,
Or an avowtier, or a paramour.
And for that was the fruyt of al his rente,
Therfore on it he sette al his entente.

    And so bifel that ones on a day   1375
This somonour, evere waityng on his pray,
Rood for to somne an old wydwe, a ribibe,
Feynynge a cause, for he wolde brybe.
And happed that he saugh bifore hym ryde
A gay yeman, under a forest syde.   1380
A bowe he bar, and arwes brighte and kene;
He hadde upon a courtepy of grene,
An hat upon his heed with frenges blake.
    "Sire," quod this somnour, "hayl, and wel
    atake!"   1384

"Welcome," quod he, "and every good felawe!
Wher rydestow, under this grene-wode shawe?"
Seyde this yeman, "wiltow fer to day?"
    This somnour hym answerde and seyde,
    "Nay;
Heere faste by," quod he, "is myn entente
To ryden, for to reysen up a rente   1390
That longeth to my lordes duetee."
    "Artow thanne a bailly?" "Ye," quod he.
He dorste nat, for verray filthe and shame
Seye that he was a somonour, for the name.
    "*Depardieux,*" quod this yeman, "deere
    broother,   1395
Thou art a bailly, and I am another.
I am unknowen as in this contree;
Of thyn aqueyntance I wolde praye thee,
And eek of bretherhede, if that yow leste.
I have gold and silver in my cheste;   1400
If that thee happe to comen in oure shire,
Al shal be thyn, right as thou wolt desire."
    "Grantmercy," quod this somonour, "by my
    feith!"
Everych in ootheres hand his trouthe leith,
For to be sworne bretheren til they deye.   1405
In daliance they ryden forth and pleye.
    This somonour, which that was as ful of
    jangles,
As ful of venym been thise waryangles,
And evere enqueryng upon every thyng,
"Brother," quod he, "where is now youre dwell-
    yng   1410
Another day if that I sholde yow seche?"
This yeman hym answerde in softe speche,
    "Brother," quod he, "fer in the north con-
    tree,
Where-as I hope som tyme I shal thee see.
Er we departe, I shal thee so wel wisse   1415
That of myn hous ne shaltow nevere mysse."
    "Now, brother," quod this somonour, "I yow
    preye,
Teche me, whil that we ryden by the weye,
Syn that ye been a baillif as am I,
Som subtiltee, and tel me feithfully   1420
In myn office how that I may moost wynne;
And spareth nat for conscience ne synne,
But as my brother tel me, how do ye."
    "Now, by my trouthe, brother deere," seyde
    he,
"As I shal tellen thee a feithful tale,   1425
My wages been ful streite and ful smale.
My lord is hard to me and daungerous,
And myn office is ful laborous,
And therfore by extorcions I lyve.
For sothe, I take al that men wol me yive.   1430

Algate, by sleyghte or by violence,
Fro yeer to yeer I wynne al my dispence.
I kan no bettre telle, feithfully."
   "Now certes," quod this Somonour, "so fare
     I.
I spare nat to taken, God it woot,   1435
But if it be to hevy or to hoot.
What I may gete in conseil prively,
No maner conscience of that have I.
Nere myn extorcioun, I myghte nat lyven,
Ne of swiche japes wol I nat be shryven.   1440
Stomak ne conscience ne knowe I noon;
I shrewe thise shrifte-fadres everychoon.
Wel be we met, by God and by Seint Jame!
But, leeve brother, tel me thanne thy name,"
Quod this somonour. In this meene while
This yeman gan a litel for to smyle.   1446
   "Brother," quod he, "wiltow that I thee telle?
I am a feend; my dwellyng is in helle,
And heere I ryde aboute my purchasyng,
To wite wher men wol yeve me any thyng.
My purchas is th'effect of al my rente.   1451
Looke how thou rydest for the same entente,
To wynne good, thou rekkest nevere how;
Right so fare I, for ryde wolde I now
Unto the worldes ende for a preye."   1455
   "A!" quod this somonour, "*benedicite!* what
     sey ye?
I wende ye were a yeman trewely.
Ye han a mannes shap as wel as I;
Han ye a figure thanne determinat
In helle, ther ye been in youre estat?"   1460
   "Nay, certeinly," quod he, "ther have we
     noon;
But whan us liketh, we kan take us oon,
Or elles make yow seme we been shape
Somtyme lyk a man, or lyk an ape,
Or lyk an angel kan I ryde or go.   1465
It is no wonder thyng thogh it be so;
A lowsy jogelour kan deceyve thee,
And pardee, yet kan I moore craft than he."
   "Why," quod this somonour, "ryde ye thanne
     or goon
In sondry shap, and nat alwey in oon?"   1470
   "For we," quod he, "wol us swiche formes
     make
As moost able is oure preyes for to take."
   "What maketh yow to han al this labour?"
   "Ful many a cause, leeve sire somonour,"
Seyde this feend, "but alle thyng hath tyme.
The day is short, and it is passed pryme,   1476
And yet ne wan I nothyng in this day.
I wol entende to wynnyng, if I may,
And nat entende oure wittes to declare.

For, brother myn, thy wit is al to bare   1480
To understonde, althogh I tolde hem thee.
But, for thou axest why labouren we —
For somtyme we been Goddes instrumentz,
And meenes to doon his comandementz,
Whan that hym list, upon his creatures,   1485
In divers art and in diverse figures.
Withouten hym we have no myght, certayn,
If that hym list to stonden ther-agayn.
And somtyme, at oure prayere, han we leve
Oonly the body and nat the soule greve;   1490
Witnesse on Job, whom that we diden wo.
And somtyme han we myght of bothe two,
This is to seyn, of soule and body eke.
And somtyme be we suffred for to seke
Upon a man, and doon his soule unreste,   1495
And nat his body, and al is for the beste.
Whan he withstandeth oure temptacioun,
It is a cause of his savacioun,
Al be it that it was nat oure entente
He sholde be sauf, but that we wolde hym
     hente.   1500
And somtyme be we servant unto man,
As to the erchebisshop Seint Dunstan,
And to the apostles servant eek was I."
   "Yet tel me," quod the somonour, "feithfully,
Make ye yow newe bodies thus alway   1505
Of elementz?" The feend answerde, "Nay.
Somtyme we feyne, and somtyme we aryse
With dede bodyes, in ful sondry wyse,
And speke as renably and faire and wel
As to the Phitonissa dide Samuel.   1510
(And yet wol som men seye it was nat he;
I do no fors of youre dyvynytee.)
But o thyng warne I thee, I wol nat jape, —
Thou wolt algates wite how we been shape;
Thou shalt herafterward, my brother deere,
Come there thee nedeth nat of me to
     leere.   1516
For thou shalt, by thyn owene experience,
Konne in a chayer rede of this sentence
Bet than Virgile, while he was on lyve,
Or Dant also. Now lat us ryde blyve,   1520
For I wole holde compaignye with thee
Til it be so that thou forsake me."
   "Nay," quod this somonour, "that shal nat
     bityde!
I am a yeman, knowen is ful wyde;
My trouthe wol I holde, as in this cas.   1525
For though thou were the devel Sathanas,
My trouthe wol I holde to my brother,
As I am sworn, and ech of us til oother,
For to be trewe brother in this cas;   1529
And bothe we goon abouten oure purchas.

Taak thou thy part, what that men wol thee
        yive,
And I shal myn; thus may we bothe lyve.
And if that any of us have moore than oother,
Lat hym be trewe, and parte it with his
        brother."
    "I graunte," quod the devel, "by my
        fey."   1535
And with that word they ryden forth hir wey.
And right at the entryng of the townes ende,
To which this somonour shoop hym for to
        wende,
They saugh a cart that charged was with hey,
Which that a cartere droof forth in his
        wey.   1540
Deep was the wey, for which the carte stood.
The cartere smoot, and cryde as he were wood,
"Hayt, Brok! hayt, Scot! what spare ye for the
        stones?
The feend," quod he, "yow fecche, body and
        bones,
As ferforthly as evere were ye foled,   1545
So muche wo as I have with yow tholed!
The devel have al, bothe hors and cart and
        hey!"
    This somonour seyde, "Heere shal we have a
        pley."
And neer the feend he drough, as noght ne
        were,
Ful prively, and rowned in his ere: 1550
"Herkne, my brother, herkne, by thy feith!
Herestow nat how that the cartere seith?
Hent it anon, for he hath yeve it thee,
Bothe hey and cart, and eek his caples thre."
    "Nay," quod the devel, "God woot, never a
        deel!   1555
It is nat his entente, trust me weel.
Axe hym thyself, if thou nat trowest me;
Or elles stynt a while, and thou shalt see."
    This cartere thakketh his hors upon the
        croupe,
And they bigonne to drawen and to stoupe.
"Heyt! now," quod he, "ther Jhesu Crist yow
        blesse,   1561
And al his handwerk, bothe moore and lesse!
That was wel twight, myn owene lyard boy.
I pray God save thee, and Seinte Loy!
Now is my cart out of the slow, pardee!"   1565
    "Lo, brother," quod the feend, "what tolde
        I thee?
Heere may ye se, myn owene deere brother,
The carl spak oo thing, but he thoghte another.
Lat us go forth abouten oure viage;
Heere wynne I nothyng upon cariage."   1570

Whan that they coomen somwhat out of
        towne,
This somonour to his brother gan to rowne:
"Brother," quod he, "heere woneth an old
        rebekke,
That hadde almoost as lief to lese hire nekke
As for to yeve a peny of hir good.   1575
I wole han twelf pens, though that she be wood,
Or I wol sompne hire unto oure office;
And yet, God woot, of hire knowe I no vice.
But for thou kanst nat, as in this contree,   1579
Wynne thy cost, taak heer ensample of me."
    This somonour clappeth at the wydwes gate.
"Com out," quod he, "thou olde virytrate!
I trowe thou hast som frere or preest with
        thee."
    "Who clappeth?" seyde this wyf, "*bene-
        dicitee!*
God save you, sire, what is youre sweete
        wille?"   1585
    "I have," quod he, "of somonce here a bille;
Up peyne of cursyng, looke that thou be
To-morn bifore the erchedeknes knee,
T'answere to the court of certeyn thynges."
    "Now, Lord," quod she, "Crist Jhesu, kyng
        of kynges,   1590
So wisly helpe me, as I ne may.
I have been syk, and that ful many a day.
I may nat go so fer," quod she, "ne ryde,
But I be deed, so priketh it in my syde.
May I nat axe a libel, sire somonour,   1595
And answere there by my procuratour
To swich thyng as men wole opposen me?"
    "Yis," quod this somonour, "pay anon, lat se,
Twelf pens to me, and I wol thee acquite.
I shal no profit han therby but lite;   1600
My maister hath the profit, and nat I.
Com of, and lat me ryden hastily;
Yif me twelf pens, I may no lenger tarye."
    "Twelf pens!" quod she, "now, lady Seinte
        Marie
So wisly help me out of care and synne,   1605
This wyde world thogh that I sholde wynne,
Ne have I nat twelf pens withinne myn hoold.
Ye knowen wel that I am povre and oold;
Kithe youre almesse on me povre wrecche."
    "Nay thanne," quod he, "the foule feend me
        fecche   1610
If I th'excuse, though thou shul be spilt!"
    "Allas!" quod she, "God woot, I have no gilt."
    "Pay me," quod he, "or by the sweete seinte
        Anne,
As I wol bere awey thy newe panne
For dette which thou owest me of old.   1615

Whan that thou madest thyn housbonde coke-
    wold,
I payde at hoom for thy correccioun."
    "Thou lixt!" quod she, "by my savacioun,
Ne was I nevere er now, wydwe ne wyf,
Somoned unto youre court in al my lyf;   1620
Ne nevere I nas but of my body trewe!
Unto the devel blak and rough of hewe
Yeve I thy body and my panne also!"
    And whan the devel herde hire cursen so
Upon hir knees, he seyde in this manere,   1625
"Now, Mabely, myn owene mooder deere,
Is this youre wyl in ernest that ye seye?"
    "The devel," quod she, "so fecche hym er he
    deye,
And panne and al, but he wol hym repente!"
    "Nay, olde stot, that is nat myn entente,"
Quod this somonour, "for to repente me   1631
For any thyng that I have had of thee.
I wolde I hadde thy smok and every clooth!"
    "Now, brother," quod the devel, "be nat
    wrooth;
Thy body and this panne been myne by right.
Thou shalt with me to helle yet to-nyght,   1636
Where thou shalt knowen of oure privetee
Moore than a maister of dyvynytee."
And with that word this foule feend hym hente;

Body and soule he with the devel wente   1640
Where as that somonours han hir heritage.
And God, that maked after his ymage
Mankynde, save and gyde us, alle and some,
And leve thise somonours goode men bicome!
    Lordynges, I koude han toold yow, quod this
    Frere,   1645
Hadde I had leyser for this Somnour heere,
After the text of Crist, Poul, and John,
And of oure othere doctours many oon,
Swiche peynes that youre hertes myghte agryse,
Al be it so no tonge may it devyse,   1650
Thogh that I myghte a thousand wynter telle
The peynes of thilke cursed hous of helle.
But for to kepe us fro that cursed place,
Waketh, and preyeth Jhesu for his grace
So kepe us fro the temptour Sathanas.   1655
Herketh this word! beth war, as in this cas:
"The leoun sit in his awayt alway
To sle the innocent, if that he may."
Disposeth ay youre hertes to withstonde
The feend, that yow wolde make thral and
    bonde.   1660
He may nat tempte yow over youre myght,
For Crist wol be youre champion and knyght.
And prayeth that thise somonours hem repente
Of hir mysdedes, er that the feend hem hente!

Heere endeth the Freres Tale.

The Summoner's Prologue

The Prologe of the Somonours Tale.

    This Somonour in his styropes hye stood;
Upon this Frere his herte was so wood   1666
That lyk an aspen leef he quook for ire.
    "Lordynges," quod he, "but o thyng I desire;
I yow biseke that, of youre curteisye,
Syn ye han herd this false Frere lye,   1670
As suffreth me I may my tale telle.
This Frere bosteth that he knoweth helle,
And God it woot, that it is litel wonder;
Freres and feendes been but lyte asonder.
For, pardee, ye han ofte tyme herd telle   1675
How that a frere ravysshed was to helle
In spirit ones by a visioun;
And as an angel ladde hym up and doun,
To shewen hym the peynes that ther were,

In al the place saugh he nat a frere;   1680
Of oother folk he saugh ynowe in wo.
Unto this angel spak the frere tho:
'Now, sire,' quod he, 'han freres swich a grace
That noon of hem shal come to this place?'
    'Yis,' quod this angel, 'many a millioun!'
And unto Sathanas he ladde hym doun.   1686
'And now hath Sathanas,' seith he, 'a tayl
Brodder than of a carryk is the sayl.
Hold up thy tayl, thou Sathanas!' quod he;
'Shewe forth thyn ers, and lat the frere se
Where is the nest of freres in this place!'   1691
And er that half a furlong wey of space,
Right so as bees out swarmen from an hyve,
Out of the develes ers ther gonne dryve

Twenty thousand freres on a route,   1695
And thurghout helle swarmed al aboute,
And comen agayn as faste as they may gon,
And in his ers they crepten everychon.
He clapte his tayl agayn and lay ful stille.
This frere, whan he looked hadde his fille   1700
Upon the tormentz of this sory place,

His spirit God restored, of his grace,
Unto his body agayn, and he awook.
But natheles, for fere yet he quook,
So was the develes ers ay in his mynde,   1705
That is his heritage of verray kynde.
God save yow alle, save this cursed Frere!
My prologe wol I ende in this manere."

The Summoner's Tale

Heere bigynneth the Somonour his Tale.

Lordynges, ther is in Yorkshire, as I gesse,
A mersshy contree called Holdernesse,   1710
In which ther wente a lymytour aboute,
To preche, and eek to begge, it is no doute.
And so bifel that on a day this frere
Hadde preched at a chirche in his manere,
And specially, aboven every thyng,   1715
Excited he the peple in his prechyng
To trentals, and to yeve, for Goddes sake,
Wherwith men myghte hooly houses make,
Ther as divine servyce is honoured,
Nat ther as it is wasted and devoured,   1720
Ne ther it nedeth nat for to be yive,
As to possessioners, that mowen lyve,
Thanked be God, in wele and habundaunce.
"Trentals," seyde he, "deliveren fro penaunce
Hir freendes soules, as wel olde as yonge, —
Ye, whan that they been hastily ysonge,   1726
Nat for to holde a preest joly and gay —
He syngeth nat but o masse in a day.
Delivereth out," quod he, "anon the soules!
Ful hard it is with flesshhook or with oules
To been yclawed, or to brenne or bake.   1731
Now spede yow hastily, for Cristes sake!"
And whan this frere had seyd al his entente,
With *qui cum patre* forth his wey he wente.
Whan folk in chirche had yeve him what
        hem leste,   1735
He wente his wey, no lenger wolde he reste.
With scrippe and tipped staf, ytukked hye,
In every hous he gan to poure and prye,
And beggeth mele and chese, or elles corn.
His felawe hadde a staf tipped with horn,   1740
A peyre of tables al of yvory,
And a poyntel polysshed fetisly,
And wroot the names alwey, as he stood,
Of alle folk that yaf hym any good,
Ascaunces that he wolde for hem preye.   1745

"Yif us a busshel whete, malt, or reye,
A Goddes kechyl, or a trype of chese,
Or elles what yow lyst, we may nat cheese;
A Goddes halfpeny, or a masse peny,
Or yif us of youre brawn, if ye have eny;   1750
A dagon of youre blanket, leeve dame,
Oure suster deere, — lo! heere I write youre
        name, —
Bacon or beef, or swich thyng as ye fynde."
A sturdy harlot wente ay hem bihynde,
That was hir hostes man, and bar a sak,   1755
And what men yaf hem, leyde it on his bak.
And whan that he was out at dore, anon
He planed awey the names everichon
That he biforn had writen in his tables;   1759
He served hem with nyfles and with fables.
"Nay, ther thou lixt, thou Somonour!" quod
        the Frere.
"Pees," quod oure Hoost, "for Cristes mooder
        deere!
Tel forth thy tale, and spare it nat at al."
"So thryve I," quod this Somonour, "so I
        shal!"
So longe he wente, hous by hous, til he   1765
Cam til an hous ther he was wont to be
Refresshed moore than in an hundred placis.
Syk lay the goode man whos that the place is;
Bedrede upon a couche lowe he lay.
"*Deus hic!*" quod he, "o Thomas, freend, good
        day!"   1770
Seyde this frere, curteisly and softe.
"Thomas," quod he, "God yelde yow! ful ofte
Have I upon this bench faren ful weel;
Heere have I eten many a myrie meel."
And fro the bench he droof awey the cat,   1775
And leyde adoun his potente and his hat,
And eek his scrippe, and sette hym softe adoun.
His felawe was go walked into toun

Forth with his knave, into that hostelrye
Where as he shoop hym thilke nyght to lye.
   "O deere maister," quod this sike man, 1781
"How han ye fare sith that March bigan?
I saugh yow noght this fourtenyght or moore."
"God woot," quod he, "laboured have I ful
     soore,
And specially, for thy savacion   1785
Have I seyd many a precious orison,
And for oure othere freendes, God hem blesse!
I have to day been at youre chirche at messe,
And seyd a sermon after my symple wit,
Nat al after the text of hooly writ;   1790
For it is hard to yow, as I suppose,
And therfore wol I teche yow al the glose.
Glosynge is a glorious thyng, certeyn,
For lettre sleeth, so as we clerkes seyn.
There have I taught hem to be charitable, 1795
And spende hir good ther it is resonable,
And there I saugh oure dame, — a! where is
     she?"
   "Yond in the yerd I trowe that she be,"
Seyde this man, "and she wol come anon."
   "Ey, maister, welcome be ye, by Seint John!"
Seyde this wyf, "how fare ye, hertely?"   1801
   The frere ariseth up ful curteisly,
And hire embraceth in his armes narwe,
And kiste hire sweete, and chirketh as a sparwe
With his lyppes: "Dame," quod he, "right weel,
As he that is youre servant every deel,   1806
Thanked be God, that yow yaf soule and lyf!
Yet saugh I nat this day so fair a wyf
In al the chirche, God so save me!"
   "Ye, God amende defautes, sire," quod she.
"Algates, welcome be ye, by my fey!"   1811
   "Graunt mercy, dame, this have I founde al-
     wey.
But of youre grete goodnesse, by youre leve,
I wolde prey yow that ye nat yow greve,
I wole with Thomas speke a litel throwe. 1815
Thise curatz been ful necligent and slowe
To grope tendrely a conscience
In shrift; in prechyng is my diligence,
And studie in Petres wordes and in Poules.
I walke, and fisshe Cristen mennes soules, 1820
To yelden Jhesu Crist his propre rente;
To sprede his word is set al myn entente."
   "Now, by youre leve, o deere sire," quod
     she,
"Chideth him weel, for seinte Trinitee!
He is as angry as a pissemyre,   1825
Though that he have al that he kan desire,
Though I hym wrye a-nyght and make hym
     warm,

And over hym leye my leg outher myn arm,
He groneth lyk oure boor, lith in oure sty.
Oother desport right noon of hym have I; 1830
I may nat plese hym in no maner cas."
   "O Thomas, *je vous dy*, Thomas! Thomas!
This maketh the feend; this moste ben
     amended.
Ire is a thyng that hye God defended,
And therof wol I speke a word or two."   1835
   "Now, maister," quod the wyf, "er that I go,
What wol ye dyne? I wol go theraboute."
   "Now, dame," quod he, "now *je vous dy sanz
     doute,*
Have I nat of a capon but the lyvere,
And of youre softe breed nat but a shyvere,
And after that a rosted pigges heed —   1841
But that I nolde no beest for me were deed —
Thanne hadde I with yow hoomly suffisaunce.
I am a man of litel sustenaunce;
My spirit hath his fostryng in the Bible. 1845
The body is ay so redy and penyble
To wake, that my stomak is destroyed.
I prey yow, dame, ye be nat anoyed,
Though I so freendly yow my conseil shewe.
By God! I wolde nat telle it but a fewe." 1850
   "Now, sire," quod she, "but o word er I go.
My child is deed withinne thise wykes two,
Soone after that ye wente out of this toun."
   "His deeth saugh I by revelacioun,"
Seide this frere, "at hoom in oure dortour. 1855
I dar wel seyn that, er that half an hour
After his deeth, I saugh hym born to blisse
In myn avision, so God me wisse!
So dide oure sexteyn and oure fermerer,
That han been trewe freres fifty yeer;   1860
They may now — God be thanked of his
     loone! —
Maken hir jubilee and walke allone.
And up I roos, and al oure covent eke,
With many a teere trillyng on my cheke,
Withouten noyse or claterynge of belles; 1865
Te Deum was oure song, and nothyng elles,
Save that to Crist I seyde an orison,
Thankynge hym of his revelacion.
For, sire and dame, trusteth me right weel,
Oure orisons been moore effectueel,   1870
And moore we seen of Cristes secree thynges,
Than burel folk, although they weren kynges.
We lyve in poverte and in abstinence,
And burell folk in richesse and despence
Of mete and drynke, and in hir foul delit.
We han this worldes lust al in despit.   1876
Lazar and Dives lyveden diversly,
And divers gerdon hadden they therby.

Whoso wol preye, he moot faste and be clene,
And fatte his soule, and make his body
          lene.   1880
We fare as seith th'apostle; clooth and foode
Suffisen us, though they be nat ful goode.
The clennesse and the fastynge of us freres
Maketh that Crist accepteth oure preyeres.

Lo, Moyses fourty dayes and fourty nyght
Fasted, er that the heighe God of myght   1886
Spak with hym in the mountayne of Synay.
With empty wombe, fastynge many a day,
Receyved he the lawe that was writen
With Goddes fynger; and Elye, wel ye witen,
In mount Oreb, er he hadde any speche   1891
With hye God, that is oure lyves leche,
He fasted longe, and was in contemplaunce.

Aaron, that hadde the temple in gover-
          naunce,
And eek the othere preestes everichon,   1895
Into the temple whan they sholde gon
To preye for the peple, and do servyse,
They nolden drynken in no maner wyse
No drynke which that myghte hem dronke
          make,
But there in abstinence preye and wake,   1900
Lest that they deyden. Taak heede what I
          seye!
But they be sobre that for the peple preye,
War that I seye — namoore, for it suffiseth.
Oure Lord Jhesu, as hooly writ devyseth,
Yaf us ensample of fastynge and preyeres.   1905
Therfore we mendynantz, we sely freres,
Been wedded to poverte and continence,
To charite, humblesse, and abstinence,
To persecucioun for rightwisnesse,
To wepynge, misericorde, and clennesse.   1910
And therfore may ye se that oure preyeres —
I speke of us, we mendynantz, we freres —
Been to the hye God moore acceptable
Than youres, with youre feestes at the table.
Fro Paradys first, if I shal nat lye,   1915
Was man out chaced for his glotonye;
And chaast was man in Paradys, certeyn.

But herkne now, Thomas, what I shal seyn.
I ne have no text of it, as I suppose,
But I shal fynde it in a maner glose,   1920
That specially oure sweete Lord Jhesus
Spak this by freres, whan he seyde thus:
'Blessed be they that povere in spirit been.'
And so forth al the gospel may ye seen,
Wher it be likker oure professioun,   1925
Or hirs that swymmen in possessioun.
Fy on hire pompe and on hire glotonye!
And for hir lewednesse I hem diffye.

Me thynketh they been lyk Jovinyan,
Fat as a whale, and walkynge as a swan,   1930
Al vinolent as botel in the spence.
Hir preyere is of ful greet reverence,
Whan they for soules seye the psalm of Davit;
Lo, 'buf!' they seye, *'cor meum eructavit!'*
Who folweth Cristes gospel and his foore,   1935
But we that humble been, and chaast, and
          poore,
Werkeris of Goddes word, nat auditours?
Therfore, right as an hauk up at a sours
Up springeth into th'eir, right so prayeres
Of charitable and chaste bisy freres   1940
Maken hir sours to Goddes eres two.
Thomas! Thomas! so moote I ryde or go,
And by that lord that clepid is Seint Yve,
Nere thou oure brother, sholdestou nat thryve.
In our chapitre praye we day and nyght   1945
To Crist, that he thee sende heele and myght
Thy body for to weelden hastily."

"God woot," quod he, "no thyng therof
          feele I!
As help me Crist, as I in fewe yeres,
Have spent upon diverse manere freres   1950
Ful many a pound; yet fare I never the bet.
Certeyn, my good have I almoost biset.
Farwel, my gold, for it is al ago!"

The frere answerde, "O Thomas, dostow so?
What nedeth yow diverse freres seche?   1955
What nedeth hym that hath a parfit leche
To sechen othere leches in the toun?
Youre inconstance is youre confusioun.
Holde ye thanne me, or elles oure covent,
To praye for yow been insufficient?   1960
Thomas, that jape nys nat worth a myte.
Youre maladye is for we han to lyte.
A! yif that covent half a quarter otes!
A! yif that covent foure and twenty grotes!
A! yif that frere a peny, and lat hym go!   1965
Nay, nay, Thomas, it may no thyng be so!
What is a ferthyng worth parted in twelve?
Lo, ech thyng that is oned in himselve
Is moore strong than whan it is toscatered.
Thomas, of me thou shalt nat been yflat-
          ered;   1970
Thou woldest han oure labour al for noght.
The hye God, that al this world hath wroght,
Seith that the werkman worthy is his hyre.
Thomas, noght of youre tresor I desire
As for myself, but that al oure covent   1975
To preye for yow is ay so diligent,
And for to buylden Cristes owene chirche.
Thomas, if ye wol lernen for to wirche,
Of buyldynge up of chirches may ye fynde,

If it be good, in Thomas lyf of Inde.   1980
Ye lye heere ful of anger and of ire,
With which the devel set youre herte afyre,
And chiden heere the sely innocent,
Youre wyf, that is so meke and pacient.   1984
And therfore, Thomas, trowe me if thee leste,
Ne stryve nat with thy wyf, as for thy beste;
And ber this word awey now, by thy feith,
Touchynge swich thyng, lo, what the wise seith:
'Withinne thyn hous ne be thou no leon;
To thy subgitz do noon oppression,   1990
Ne make thyne aqueyntances nat to flee.'
And, Thomas, yet eft-soones I charge thee,
Be war from hire that in thy bosom slepeth;
War fro the serpent that so slily crepeth
Under the gras, and styngeth subtilly.   1995
Be war, my sone, and herkne paciently,
That twenty thousand men han lost hir lyves
For stryvyng with hir lemmans and hir wyves.
Now sith ye han so hooly and meke a wyf,
What nedeth yow, Thomas, to maken stryf?
Ther nys, ywys, no serpent so cruel,   2001
Whan man tret on his tayl, ne half so fel,
As womman is, whan she hath caught an ire;
Vengeance is thanne al that they desire.
Ire is a synne, oon of the grete of sevene,   2005
Abhomynable unto the God of hevene;
And to hymself it is destruccion.
This every lewed viker or person
Kan seye, how ire engendreth homycide.
Ire is, in sooth, executour of pryde.   2010
I koude of ire seye so muche sorwe,
My tale sholde laste til to-morwe.
And therfore preye I God, bothe day and nyght,
An irous man, God sende hym litel myght!
It is greet harm and certes greet pitee   2015
To sette an irous man in heigh degree.
   Whilom ther was an irous potestat,
As seith Senek, that, durynge his estaat,
Upon a day out ryden knyghtes two,
And as Fortune wolde that it were so,   2020
That oon of hem cam hoom, that oother noght.
Anon the knyght bifore the juge is broght,
That seyde thus, 'Thou hast thy felawe slayn,
For which I deme thee to the deeth, certayn.'
And to another knyght comanded he,   2025
'Go lede hym to the deeth, I charge thee.'
And happed, as they wente by the weye
Toward the place ther he sholde deye,
The knyght cam which men wenden had be
   deed.
Thanne thoughte they it were the beste reed
To lede hem bothe to the juge agayn.   2031
They seiden, 'Lord, the knyght ne hath nat slayn

His felawe; heere he standeth hool alyve.'
'Ye shul be deed,' quod he, 'so moot I thryve!
That is to seyn, bothe oon, and two, and
   thre!'   2035
And to the firste knyght right thus spak he,
'I dampned thee; thou most algate be deed.
And thou also most nedes lese thyn heed,
For thou art cause why thy felawe deyth.'   2039
And to the thridde knyght right thus he seith,
'Thou hast nat doon that I comanded thee.'
And thus he dide doon sleen hem alle thre.
   Irous Cambises was eek dronkelewe,
And ay delited hym to been a shrewe.
And so bifel, a lord of his meynee,   2045
That loved vertuous moralitee,
Seyde on a day bitwix hem two right thus:
   'A lord is lost, if he be vicius;
And dronkenesse is eek a foul record
Of any man, and namely in a lord.   2050
Ther is ful many an eye and many an ere
Awaityng on a lord, and he noot where.
For Goddes love, drynk moore attemprely!
Wyn maketh man to lesen wrecchedly
His mynde and eek his lymes everichon.'   2055
   'The revers shaltou se,' quod he, 'anon,
And preve it by thyn owene experience,
That wyn ne dooth to folk no swich offence.
Ther is no wyn bireveth me my myght
Of hand ne foot, ne of myne eyen sight.'   2060
And for despit he drank ful muchel moore,
An hondred part, than he hadde don bifoore;
And right anon this irous, cursed wrecche
Leet this knyghtes sone bifore hym fecche,
Comandynge hym he sholde bifore hym stonde.
And sodeynly he took his bowe in honde,   2066
And up the streng he pulled to his ere,
And with an arwe he slow the child right there.
'Now wheither have I a siker hand or noon?'
Quod he; 'is al my myght and mynde agon?
Hath wyn bireved me myn eyen sight?'   2071
What sholde I telle th'answere of the knyght?
His sone was slayn, ther is namoore to seye.
Beth war, therfore, with lordes how ye pleye.
Syngeth *Placebo*, and 'I shal, if I kan,'   2075
But if it be unto a povre man.
To a povre man men sholde his vices telle,
But nat to a lord, thogh he sholde go to helle.
   Lo irous Cirus, thilke Percien,
How he destroyed the ryver of Gysen,   2080
For that an hors of his was dreynt therinne,
Whan that he wente Babiloigne to wynne.
He made that the ryver was so smal
That wommen myghte wade it over al.
Lo, what seyde he that so wel teche kan?   2085

'Ne be no felawe to an irous man,
Ne with no wood man walke by the weye,
Lest thee repente;' I wol no ferther seye.
　　Now, Thomas, leeve brother, lef thyn ire;
Thou shalt me fynde as just as is a squyre.　2090
Hoold nat the develes knyf ay at thyn herte —
Thyn angre dooth thee al to soore smerte —
But shewe to me al thy confessioun."
　　"Nay," quod the sike man, "by Seint Sy-
　　　moun!
I have be shryven this day at my curat.　2095
I have hym toold hoolly al myn estat;
Nedeth namoore to speken of it," seith he,
"But if me list, of myn humylitee."
　　"Yif me thanne of thy gold, to make oure
　　　cloystre,"
Quod he, "for many a muscle and many an
　　oystre,　2100
Whan othere men han ben ful wel at eyse,
Hath been oure foode, our cloystre for to reyse.
And yet, God woot, unnethe the fundement
Parfourned is, ne of our pavement
Nys nat a tyle yet withinne oure wones.　2105
By God! we owen fourty pound for stones.
　　Now help, Thomas, for hym that harwed
　　　helle!
For elles moste we oure bookes selle.
And if yow lakke oure predicacioun,　2109
Thanne goth the world al to destruccioun.
For whoso wolde us fro this world bireve,
So God me save, Thomas, by youre leve,
He wolde bireve out of this world the sonne.
For who kan teche and werchen as we konne?
And that is nat of litel tyme," quod he,　2115
"But syn Elye was, or Elise,
Han freres been, that fynde I of record,
In charitee, ythanked be oure Lord!
Now Thomas, help, for seinte charitee!"　2119
And doun anon he sette hym on his knee.
　　This sike man wax wel ny wood for ire;
He wolde that the frere had been on-fire,
With his false dissymulacioun.
"Swich thyng as is in my possessioun,"　2124
Quod he, "that may I yeve yow, and noon
　　oother.
Ye sey me thus, how that I am youre brother?"
　　"Ye, certes," quod the frere, "trusteth weel.
I took oure dame oure lettre with oure seel."
　　"Now wel," quod he, "and somwhat shal I
　　　yive
Unto youre hooly covent whil I lyve;　2130
And in thyn hand thou shalt it have anon,
On this condicion, and oother noon,
That thou departe it so, my deere brother,

That every frere have also muche as oother.
This shaltou swere on thy professioun,　2135
Withouten fraude or cavillacioun."
　　"I swere it," quod this frere, "by my feith!"
And therwithal his hand in his he leith,
"Lo, heer my feith; in me shal be no lak."　2139
　　"Now thanne, put in thyn hand doun by my
　　　bak,"
Seyde this man, "and grope wel bihynde.
Bynethe my buttok there shaltow fynde
A thyng that I have hyd in pryvetee."
　　"A!" thoghte this frere, "that shal go with
　　　me!"
And doun his hand he launcheth to the clifte,
In hope for to fynde there a yifte.　2146
And whan this sike man felte this frere
Aboute his tuwel grope there and heere,
Amydde his hand he leet the frere a fart,
Ther nys no capul, drawynge in a cart,　2150
That myghte have lete a fart of swich a soun.
　　The frere up stirte as dooth a wood leoun, —
"A! false cherl," quod he, "for Goddes bones!
This hastow for despit doon for the nones.
Thou shalt abye this fart, if that I may!"　2155
　　His meynee, whiche that herden this affray,
Cam lepynge in and chaced out the frere;
And forth he gooth, with a ful angry cheere,
And fette his felawe, ther as lay his stoor.
He looked as it were a wilde boor;　2160
He grynte with his teeth, so was he wrooth.
A sturdy paas doun to the court he gooth,
Wher as ther woned a man of greet honour,
To whom that he was alwey confessour.
This worthy man was lord of that village.　2165
This frere cam as he were in a rage,
Where as this lord sat etyng at his bord;
Unnethes myghte the frere speke a word,
Til atte laste he seyde, "God yow see!"　2169
　　This lord gan looke, and seide, "*Benedicitee!*
What, frere John, what maner world is this?
I se wel that som thyng ther is amys;
Ye looken as the wode were ful of thevys.
Sit doun anon, and tel me what youre grief is,
And it shal been amended, if I may."　2175
　　"I have," quod he, "had a despit this day,
God yelde yow, adoun in youre village,
That in this world is noon so povre a page
That he nolde have abhomynacioun
Of that I have receyved in youre toun.　2180
And yet ne greveth me nothyng so soore,
As that this olde cherl with lokkes hoore
Blasphemed hath oure hooly covent eke."
　　"Now, maister," quod this lord, "I yow
　　　biseke, —"

"No maister, sire," quod he, "but servitour,
Thogh I have had in scole that honour.   2186
God liketh nat that 'Raby' men us calle,
Neither in market ne in youre large halle."
    "No fors," quod he, "but tel me al youre
        grief."
    "Sire," quod this frere, "an odious meschief
This day bityd is to myn ordre and me,   2191
And so, *per consequens,* to ech degree
Of hooly chirche, God amende it soone!"
    "Sire," quod the lord, "ye woot what is to
        doone.
Distempre yow noght, ye be my confes-
        sour;   2195
Ye been the salt of the erthe and the savour.
For Goddes love, youre pacience ye holde!
Tel me youre grief"; and he anon hym tolde,
As ye han herd biforn, ye woot wel what.
    The lady of the hous ay stille sat   2200
Til she had herd what the frere sayde.
"Ey, Goddes mooder," quod she, "Blisful
        mayde!
Is ther oght elles? telle me feithfully."
    "Madame," quod he, "how thynke ye herby?"
    "How that me thynketh?" quod she, "so God
        me speede,   2205
I seye, a cherl hath doon a cherles dede.
What shold I seye? God lat hym nevere thee!
His sike heed is ful of vanytee;
I holde hym in a manere frenesye."
    "Madame," quod he, "by God, I shal nat lye,
But I on oother wyse may be wreke,   2211
I shal disclaundre hym over al ther I speke,
This false blasphemour, that charged me
To parte that wol nat departed be,
To every man yliche, with meschaunce!"   2215
    The lord sat stille as he were in a traunce,
And in his herte he rolled up and doun,
"How hadde this cherl ymaginacioun
To shewe swich a probleme to the frere?   2219
Nevere erst er now herde I of swich mateere.
I trowe the devel putte it in his mynde.
In ars-metrike shal ther no man fynde,
Biforn this day, of swich a question.
Who sholde make a demonstracion
That every man sholde have yliche his part
As of the soun or savour of a fart?   2226
O nyce, proude cherl, I shrewe his face!
Lo, sires," quod the lord, "with harde grace!
Who evere herde of swich a thyng er now?
To every man ylike, tel me how?   2230
It is an inpossible, it may nat be.
Ey, nyce cherl, God lete him nevere thee!
The rumblynge of a fart, and every soun,

Nis but of eir reverberacioun,
And evere it wasteth litel and litel awey. 2235
Ther is no man kan deemen, by my fey,
If that it were departed equally.
What, lo, my cherl, lo, yet how shrewedly
Unto my confessour to-day he spak!
I holde hym certeyn a demonyak!   2240
Now ete youre mete, and lat the cherl go
        pleye;
Lat hym go honge hymself a devel weye!"

The wordes of the lordes squier and his kervere for departynge of the fart on twelve.

    Now stood the lordes squier at the bord,
That karf his mete, and herde word by word
Of alle thynges whiche I have yow sayd.   2245
"My lord," quod he, "be ye nat yvele apayd,
I koude telle, for a gowne-clooth,
To yow, sire frere, so ye be nat wrooth,
How that this fart sholde evene deled be
Among youre covent, if it lyked me."   2250
    "Tel," quod the lord, "and thou shalt have
        anon
A gowne-clooth, by God and by Seint John!"
    "My lord," quod he, "whan that the weder
        is fair,
Withouten wynd or perturbynge of air,   2254
Lat brynge a cartwheel heere into this halle;
But looke that it have his spokes alle, —
Twelve spokes hath a cartwheel comunly.
And bryng me thanne twelve freres, woot ye
        why?
For thrittene is a covent, as I gesse.   2259
Youre confessour heere, for his worthynesse,
Shal parfourne up the nombre of his covent.
Thanne shal they knele doun, by oon assent,
And to every spokes ende, in this manere,
Ful sadly leye his nose shal a frere.   2264
Youre noble confessour — there God hym
        save! —
Shal holde his nose upright under the nave.
Thanne shal this cherl, with bely stif and toght
As any tabour, hyder been ybroght;
And sette hym on the wheel right of this cart,
Upon the nave, and make hym lete a fart.   2270
And ye shul seen, up peril of my lyf,
By preeve which that is demonstratif,
That equally the soun of it wol wende,
And eke the stynk, unto the spokes ende,
Save that this worthy man, youre confessour,
By cause he is a man of greet honour,   2276
Shal have the firste fruyt, as resoun is.

The noble usage of freres yet is this,
The worthy men of hem shul first be served;
And certeinly he hath it weel disserved.   2280
He hath to-day taught us so muche good
With prechyng in the pulpit ther he stood,
That I may vouche sauf, I sey for me,
He hadde the firste smel of fartes thre;
And so wolde al his covent hardily,   2285
He bereth hym so faire and hoolily."

The lord, the lady, and ech man, save the
    frere,
Seyde that Jankyn spak, in this matere,
As wel as Euclide dide or Ptholomee.   2289
Touchynge the cherl, they seyde, subtiltee
And heigh wit made hym speken as he spak;
He nys no fool, ne no demonyak.
And Jankyn hath ywonne a newe gowne. —
My tale is doon; we been almoost at towne.

Heere endeth the Somonours Tale.

The Clerk's Prologue

Heere folweth the Prologe of the Clerkes Tale of Oxenford.

"Sire Clerk of Oxenford," oure Hooste sayde,
"Ye ryde as coy and stille as dooth a mayde
Were newe spoused, sittynge at the bord;
This day ne herde I of youre tonge a word.
I trowe ye studie aboute som sophyme;   5
But Salomon seith 'every thyng hath tyme.'
  For Goddes sake, as beth of bettre cheere!
It is no tyme for to studien heere.
Telle us som myrie tale, by youre fey!
For what man that is entred in a pley,   10
He nedes moot unto the pley assente.
But precheth nat, as freres doon in Lente,
To make us for oure olde synnes wepe,
Ne that thy tale make us nat to slepe.
  Telle us som murie thyng of aventures.   15
Youre termes, youre colours, and youre figures,
Keepe hem in stoor til so be that ye endite
Heigh style, as whan that men to kynges write.
Speketh so pleyn at this tyme, we yow preye,
That we may understonde what ye seye."   20
  This worthy clerk benignely answerde:
"Hooste," quod he, "I am under youre yerde;
Ye han of us as now the governance,
And therfore wol I do yow obeisance,
As fer as resoun axeth, hardily.   25
I wol yow telle a tale which that I
Lerned at Padowe of a worthy clerk,
As preved by his wordes and his werk.

He is now deed and nayled in his cheste,
I prey to God so yeve his soule reste!   30
  Fraunceys Petrak, the lauriat poete,
Highte this clerk, whos rethorike sweete
Enlumyned al Ytaille of poetrie,
As Lynyan dide of philosophie,
Or lawe, or oother art particuler;   35
But deeth, that wol nat suffre us dwellen heer,
But as it were a twynklyng of an ye,
Hem bothe hath slayn, and alle shul we dye.
  But forth to tellen of this worthy man
That taughte me this tale, as I bigan,   40
I seye that first with heigh stile he enditeth,
Er he the body of his tale writeth,
A prohemye, in the which discryveth he
Pemond, and of Saluces the contree,
And speketh of Apennyn, the hilles hye,   45
That been the boundes of West Lumbardye,
And of Mount Vesulus in special,
Where as the Poo out of a welle smal
Taketh his firste spryngyng and his sours,
That estward ay encresseth in his cours   50
To Emele-ward, to Ferrare, and Venyse;
The which a long thyng were to devyse.
And trewely, as to my juggement,
Me thynketh it a thyng impertinent,
Save that he wole conveyen his mateere;   55
But this his tale, which that ye may heere."

The Clerk's Tale

Heere bigynneth the Tale of the Clerk of Oxenford.

Ther is, right at the west syde of Ytaille,
Doun at the roote of Vesulus the colde,
A lusty playn, habundant of vitaille,   59
Where many a tour and toun thou mayst biholde,
That founded were in tyme of fadres olde,
And many another delitable sighte,
And Saluces this noble contree highte.

  A markys whilom lord was of that lond,
As were his worthy eldres hym bifore;   65
And obeisant, ay redy to his hond,
Were alle his liges, bothe lasse and moore.
Thus in delit he lyveth, and hath doon yoore,
Biloved and drad, thurgh favour of Fortune,
Bothe of his lordes and of his commune.   70

Therwith he was, to speke as of lynage,
The gentilleste yborn of Lumbardye,
A fair persone, and strong, and yong of age,
And ful of honour and of curteisye;
Discreet ynogh his contree for to gye, 75
Save in somme thynges that he was to blame;
And Walter was this yonge lordes name.

I blame hym thus, that he considered noght
In tyme comynge what myghte hym bityde,
But on his lust present was al his thoght, 80
As for to hauke and hunte on every syde.
Wel ny alle othere cures leet he slyde,
And eek he nolde — and that was worst of alle —
Wedde no wyf, for noght that may bifalle.

Oonly that point his peple bar so soore 85
That flokmeele on a day they to hym wente,
And oon of hem, that wisest was of loore —
Or elles that the lord best wolde assente
That he sholde telle hym what his peple mente,
Or elles koude he shewe wel swich mateere —
He to the markys seyde as ye shul heere: 91

"O noble markys, youre humanitee
Asseureth us and yeveth us hardinesse,
As ofte as tyme is of necessitee, 94
That we to yow mowe telle oure hevynesse.
Accepteth, lord, now of youre gentillesse
That we with pitous herte unto yow pleyne,
And lat youre eres nat my voys desdeyne.

"Al have I noght to doone in this mateere
Moore than another man hath in this place,
Yet for as muche as ye, my lord so deere, 101
Han alwey shewed me favour and grace
I dar the bettre aske of yow a space
Of audience, to shewen oure requeste,
And ye, my lord, to doon right as yow leste.

"For certes, lord, so wel us liketh yow 106
And al youre werk, and evere han doon, that we
Ne koude nat us self devysen how
We myghte lyven in moore felicitee,
Save o thyng, lord, if it youre wille be, 110
That for to been a wedded man yow leste;
Thanne were youre peple in sovereyn hertes
 reste.

"Boweth youre nekke under that blisful yok
Of soveraynetee, noght of servyse, 114
Which that men clepe spousaille or wedlok;
And thenketh, lord, among youre thoghtes wyse
How that oure dayes passe in sondry wyse;

For thogh we slepe, or wake, or rome, or ryde,
Ay fleeth the tyme; it nyl no man abyde. 119

"And thogh youre grene youthe floure as yit,
In crepeth age alwey, as stille as stoon,
And deeth manaceth every age, and smyt
In ech estaat, for ther escapeth noon;
And al so certein as we knowe echoon
That we shul deye, as uncerteyn we alle 125
Been of that day whan deeth shal on us falle.

"Accepteth thanne of us the trewe entente,
That nevere yet refuseden thyn heeste,
And we wol, lord, if that ye wole assente,
Chese yow a wyf, in short tyme atte leeste,
Born of the gentilleste and of the meeste 131
Of al this land, so that it oghte seme
Honour to God and yow, as we kan deeme.

"Delivere us out of al this bisy drede,
And taak a wyf, for hye Goddes sake! 135
For if it so bifelle, as God forbede,
That thurgh youre deeth youre lynage sholde
 slake,
And that a straunge successour sholde take
Youre heritage, O, wo were us alyve!
Wherfore we pray you hastily to wyve." 140

Hir meeke preyere and hir pitous cheere
Made the markys herte han pitee.
"Ye wol," quod he, "myn owene peple deere,
To that I nevere erst thoughte streyne me.
I me rejoysed of my liberte, 145
That seelde tyme is founde in mariage;
Ther I was free, I moot been in servage.

"But nathelees I se youre trewe entente,
And truste upon youre wit, and have doon ay;
Wherfore of my free wyl I wole assente 150
To wedde me, as soone as evere I may.
But ther as ye han profred me to-day
To chese me a wyf, I yow relesse
That choys, and prey yow of that profre cesse.

"For God it woot, that children ofte been
Unlyk hir worthy eldres hem bifore; 156
Bountee comth al of God, nat of the streen
Of which they been engendred and ybore.
I truste in Goddes bountee, and therfore
My mariage and myn estaat and reste 160
I hym bitake; he may doon as hym leste.

"Lat me allone in chesynge of my wyf, —
That charge upon my bak I wole endure.

But I yow preye, and charge upon youre lyf,
That what wyf that I take, ye me assure   165
To worshipe hire, whil that hir lyf may dure,
In word and werk, bothe heere and every-
    wheere,
As she an emperoures doghter weere.

"And forthermoore, this shal ye swere, that ye
Agayn my choys shul neither grucche ne stryve;
For sith I shal forgoon my libertee   171
At youre requeste, as evere moot I thryve,
Ther as myn herte is set, ther wol I wyve;
And but ye wole assente in swich manere,   174
I prey yow, speketh namoore of this matere."

With hertely wyl they sworen and assenten
To al this thyng, ther seyde no wight nay;
Bisekynge hym of grace, er that they wenten,
That he wolde graunten hem a certein day
Of his spousaille, as soone as evere he may;
For yet alwey the peple somwhat dredde,   181
Lest that the markys no wyf wolde wedde.

He graunted hem a day, swich as hym leste,
On which he wolde be wedded sikerly,
And seyde he dide al this at hir requeste.   185
And they, with humble entente, buxomly,
Knelynge upon hir knees ful reverently,
Hym thonken alle; and thus they han an ende
Of hire entente, and hoom agayn they wende.

And heerupon he to his officeres   190
Comaundeth for the feste to purveye,
And to his privee knyghtes and squieres
Swich charge yaf as hym liste on hem leye;
And they to his comandement obeye,
And ech of hem dooth al his diligence   195
To doon unto the feeste reverence.

Explicit prima pars.

Incipit secunda pars.

Noght fer fro thilke paleys honurable,
Wher as this markys shoop his mariage,
There stood a throop, of site delitable,
In which that povre folk of that village   200
Hadden hir beestes and hir herbergage,
And of hire labour tooke hir sustenance,
After that the erthe yaf hem habundance.

Amonges thise povre folk ther dwelte a man
Which that was holden povrest of hem alle;
But hye God somtyme senden kan   206
His grace into a litel oxes stalle;

Janicula men of that throop hym calle.
A doghter hadde he, fair ynogh to sighte,
And Grisildis this yonge mayden highte.   210

But for to speke of vertuous beautee,
Thanne was she oon the faireste under sonne;
For povreliche yfostred up was she,
No likerous lust was thurgh hire herte yronne.
Wel ofter of the welle than of the tonne   215
She drank, and for she wolde vertu plese,
She knew wel labour, but noon ydel ese.

But thogh this mayde tendre were of age,
Yet in the brest of hire virginitee
Ther was enclosed rype and sad corage;   220
And in greet reverence and charitee
Hir olde povre fader fostred shee.
A fewe sheep, spynnynge, on feeld she kepte;
She wolde noght been ydel til she slepte.

And whan she homward cam, she wolde
    brynge   225
Wortes or othere herbes tymes ofte,
The whiche she shredde and seeth for hir lyv-
    ynge,
And made hir bed ful hard and nothyng softe;
And ay she kepte hir fadres lyf on-lofte
With everich obeisaunce and diligence   230
That child may doon to fadres reverence.

Upon Grisilde, this povre creature,
Ful ofte sithe this markys sette his ye
As he on huntyng rood paraventure;
And whan it fil that he myghte hire espye,   235
He noght with wantown lookyng of folye
His eyen caste on hire, but in sad wyse
Upon hir chiere he wolde hym ofte avyse,

Commendynge in his herte hir womman-
    hede,
And eek hir vertu, passynge any wight   240
Of so yong age, as wel in chiere as dede.
For thogh the peple have no greet insight
In vertu, he considered ful right
Hir bountee, and disposed that he wolde   244
Wedde hire oonly, if evere he wedde sholde.

The day of weddyng cam, but no wight kan
Telle what womman that it sholde be;
For which merveille wondred many a man,
And seyden, whan they were in privetee,
"Wol nat oure lord yet leve his vanytee?   250
Wol he nat wedde? allas; allas, the while!
Why wole he thus hymself and us bigile?"

But nathelees this markys hath doon make
Of gemmes, set in gold and in asure,
Brooches and rynges, for Grisildis sake;   255
And of hir clothyng took he the mesure
By a mayde lyk to hire stature,
And eek of othere aornementes alle
That unto swich a weddyng sholde falle.

The time of undren of the same day   260
Approcheth, that this weddyng sholde be;
And al the paleys put was in array,
Bothe halle and chambres, ech in his degree;
Houses of office stuffed with plentee
Ther maystow seen, of deyntevous vitaille
That may be founde as fer as last Ytaille.   266

This roial markys, richely arrayed,
Lordes and ladyes in his compaignye,
The whiche that to the feeste weren yprayed,
And of his retenue the bachelrye,   270
With many a soun of sondry melodye,
Unto the village of the which I tolde,
In this array the righte wey han holde.

Grisilde of this, God woot, ful innocent,
That for hire shapen was al this array,   275
To fecchen water at a welle is went,
And cometh hoom as soone as ever she may;
For wel she hadde herd seyd that thilke day
The markys sholde wedde, and if she myghte,
She wolde fayn han seyn som of that sighte. 280

She thoghte, "I wole with othere maydens
        stonde,
That been my felawes, in oure dore and se
The markysesse, and therfore wol I fonde
To doon at hoom, as soone as it may be,
The labour which that longeth unto me;   285
And thanne I may at leyser hire biholde,
If she this wey unto the castel holde."

And as she wolde over hir thresshfold gon,
The markys cam, and gan hire for to calle;
And she set doun hir water pot anon,   290
Biside the thresshfold, in an oxes stalle,
And doun upon hir knes she gan to falle,
And with sad contenance kneleth stille,
Til she had herd what was the lordes wille.

This thoghtful markys spak unto this mayde
Ful sobrely, and seyde in this manere: 296
"Where is youre fader, O Grisildis?" he sayde.
And she with reverence, in humble cheere,
Answerde, "Lord, he is al redy heere."

And in she gooth withouten lenger lette,   300
And to the markys she hir fader fette.

He by the hand thanne took this olde man,
And seyde thus, whan he hym hadde asyde:
"Janicula, I neither may ne kan
Lenger the plesance of myn herte hyde.   305
If that thou vouche sauf, what so bityde,
Thy doghter wol I take, er that I wende,
As for my wyf, unto hir lyves ende.

"Thou lovest me, I woot it wel certeyn,
And art my feithful lige man ybore;   310
And al that liketh me, I dar wel seyn
It liketh thee, and specially therfore
Tel me that poynt that I have seyd bifore,
If that thou wolt unto that purpos drawe,
To take me as for thy sone-in-lawe."   315

This sodeyn cas this man astonyed so
That reed he wax; abayst and al quakynge
He stood; unnethes seyde he wordes mo,
But oonly thus: "Lord," quod he, "my willynge
Is as ye wole, ne ayeynes youre likynge   320
I wol no thyng, ye be my lord so deere;
Right as yow lust, governeth this mateere."

"Yet wol I," quod this markys softely,
"That in thy chambre I and thou and she
Have a collacioun, and wostow why?   325
For I wol axe if it hire wille be
To be my wyf, and reule hire after me.
And al this shal be doon in thy presence;
I wol noght speke out of thyn audience."

And in the chambre, whil they were aboute
Hir tretys, which as ye shal after heere,   331
The peple cam unto the hous withoute,
And wondred hem in how honest manere
And tentifly she kepte hir fader deere.
But outrely Grisildis wondre myghte,   335
For nevere erst ne saugh she swich a sighte.

No wonder is thogh that she were astoned
To seen so greet a gest come in that place;
She nevere was to swiche gestes woned,
For which she looked with ful pale face.   340
But shortly forth this matere for to chace,
Thise arn the wordes that the markys sayde
To this benigne, verray, feithful mayde.

"Grisilde," he seyde, "ye shal wel under-
        stonde
It liketh to youre fader and to me   345

That I yow wedde, and eek it may so stonde,
As I suppose, ye wol that it so be.
But thise demandes axe I first," quod he,
"That, sith it shal be doon in hastif wyse,
Wol ye assente, or elles yow avyse?   350

"I seye this, be ye redy with good herte
To al my lust, and that I frely may,
As me best thynketh, do yow laughe or smerte,
And nevere ye to grucche it, nyght ne day?
And eek whan I sey 'ye,' ne sey nat 'nay,'   355
Neither by word ne frownyng contenance?
Swere this, and heere I swere oure alliance."

Wondrynge upon this word, quakynge for
    drede,
She seyde, "Lord, undigne and unworthy
Am I to thilke honour that ye me beede,   360
But as ye wole yourself, right so wol I.
And heere I swere that nevere willyngly,
In werk ne thoght, I nyl yow disobeye,
For to be deed, though me were looth to deye."

"This is ynogh, Grisilde myn," quod he.   365
And forth he gooth, with a ful sobre cheere,
Out at the dore, and after that cam she,
And to the peple he seyde in this manere:
"This is my wyf," quod he, "that standeth
    heere.
Honoureth hire and loveth hire, I preye,   370
Whoso me loveth; ther is namoore to seye."

And for that no thyng of hir olde geere
She sholde brynge into his hous, he bad
That wommen sholde dispoillen hire right
    theere;
Of which thise ladyes were nat right glad   375
To handle hir clothes, wherinne she was clad.
But nathelees, this mayde bright of hewe
Fro foot to heed they clothed han al newe.

Hir heris han they kembd, that lay untressed
Ful rudely, and with hir fyngres smale   380
A corone on hire heed they han ydressed,
And sette hire ful of nowches grete and smale.
Of hire array what sholde I make a tale?
Unnethe the peple hir knew for hire fairnesse,
Whan she translated was in swich richesse.   385

This markys hath hire spoused with a ryng
Broght for the same cause, and thanne hire sette
Upon an hors, snow-whit and wel amblyng,
And to his paleys, er he lenger lette,   389
With joyful peple that hire ladde and mette,

Conveyed hire, and thus the day they spende
In revel, til the sonne gan descende.

And shortly forth this tale for to chace,
I seye that to this newe markysesse
God hath swich favour sent hire of his grace,
That it ne semed nat by liklynesse   396
That she was born and fed in rudenesse,
As in a cote or in an oxe-stalle,
But norissed in an emperoures halle.

To every wight she woxen is so deere   400
And worshipful that folk ther she was bore,
And from hire birthe knewe hire yeer by yeere,
Unnethe trowed they, — but dorste han swore —
That to Janicle, of which I spak bifore,
She doghter were, for, as by conjecture,   405
Hem thoughte she was another creature.

For though that evere vertuous was she,
She was encressed in swich excellence
Of thewes goode, yset in heigh bountee,
And so discreet and fair of eloquence,   410
So benigne and so digne of reverence,
And koude so the peples herte embrace,
That ech hire lovede that looked in hir face.

Noght oonly of Saluces in the toun
Publiced was the bountee of hir name,   415
But eek biside in many a regioun,
If oon seide wel, another seyde the same;
So spradde of hire heighe bountee the fame
That men and wommen, as wel yonge as olde,
Goon to Saluce, upon hire to biholde.   420

Thus Walter lowely — nay, but roially —
Wedded with fortunat honestetee,
In Goddes pees lyveth ful esily
At hoom, and outward grace ynogh had he;
And for he saugh that under low degree   425
Was ofte vertu hid, the peple hym heelde
A prudent man, and that is seyn ful seelde.

Nat oonly this Grisildis thurgh hir wit
Koude al the feet of wyfly hoomlinesse,
But eek, whan that the cas required it,   430
The commune profit koude she redresse.
Ther nas discord, rancour, ne hevynesse
In al that land, that she ne koude apese,
And wisely brynge hem alle in reste and ese.

Though that hire housbonde absent were
    anon,   435
If gentil men or othere of hire contree

Were wrothe, she wolde bryngen hem aton;
So wise and rype wordes hadde she,
And juggementz of so greet equitee,
That she from hevene sent was, as men wende,
Peple to save and every wrong t'amende.   441

Nat longe tyme after that this Grisild
Was wedded, she a doghter hath ybore.
Al had hire levere have born a knave child,
Glad was this markys and the folk therfore;
For though a mayde child coome al bifore,   446
She may unto a knave child atteyne
By liklihede, syn she nys nat bareyne.

Explicit secunda pars.

Incipit tercia pars.

Ther fil, as it bifalleth tymes mo,
Whan that this child had souked but a throwe,
This markys in his herte longeth so   451
To tempte his wyf, hir sadnesse for to knowe,
That he ne myghte out of his herte throwe
This merveillous desir his wyf t'assaye;
Nedelees, God woot, he thoghte hire for
      t'affraye.   455

He hadde assayed hire ynogh bifore,
And foond hire evere good; what neded it
Hire for to tempte, and alwey moore and
      moore,
Though som men preise it for a subtil wit?
But as for me, I seye that yvele it sit   460
To assaye a wyf whan that it is no nede,
And putten hire in angwyssh and in drede.

For which this markys wroghte in this man-
      ere:
He cam allone a-nyght, ther as she lay,   464
With stierne face and with ful trouble cheere,
And seyde thus: "Grisilde," quod he, "that day
That I yow took out of youre povere array,
And putte yow in estaat of heigh noblesse, —
Ye have nat that forgeten, as I gesse?

"I seye, Grisilde, this present dignitee,   470
In which that I have put yow, as I trowe,
Maketh yow nat foryetful for to be
That I yow took in povre estaat ful lowe,
For any wele ye moot youreselven knowe.   474
Taak heede of every word that y yow seye;
Ther is no wight that hereth it but we tweye.

"Ye woot youreself wel how that ye cam heere
Into this hous, it is nat longe ago;

And though to me that ye be lief and deere,
Unto my gentils ye be no thyng so.   480
They seyn, to hem it is greet shame and wo
For to be subgetz and been in servage
To thee, that born art of a smal village.

"And namely sith thy doghter was ybore
Thise wordes han they spoken, doutelees.   485
But I desire, as I have doon bifore,
To lyve my lyf with hem in reste and pees.
I may nat in this caas be recchelees;
I moot doon with thy doghter for the beste,
Nat as I wolde, but as my peple leste.   490

"And yet, God woot, this is ful looth to me;
But nathelees withoute youre wityng
I wol nat doon; but this wol I," quod he,
"That ye to me assente as in this thyng.   494
Shewe now youre pacience in youre werkyng,
That ye me highte and swore in youre village
That day that maked was oure mariage."

Whan she had herd al this, she noght ameved
Neither in word, or chiere, or contenaunce;
For, as it semed, she was nat agreved.   500
She seyde, "Lord, al lyth in youre plesaunce.
My child and I, with hertely obeisaunce,
Been youres al, and ye mowe save or spille
Youre owene thyng; werketh after youre wille.

"Ther may no thyng, God so my soule save,
Liken to yow that may displese me;   506
Ne I desire no thyng for to have,
Ne drede for to leese, save oonly yee.
This wyl is in myn herte, and ay shal be;
No lengthe of tyme or deeth may this deface,
Ne chaunge my corage to another place."   511

Glad was this markys of hire answeryng,
But yet he feyned as he were nat so;
Al drery was his cheere and his lookyng,
Whan that he sholde out of the chambre go.
Soone after this, a furlong wey or two,   516
He prively hath toold al his entente
Unto a man, and to his wyf hym sente.

A maner sergeant was this privee man,   519
The which that feithful ofte he founden hadde
In thynges grete, and eek swich folk wel kan
Doon execucioun in thynges badde.
The lord knew wel that he hym loved and
      dradde;
And whan this sergeant wiste his lordes wille,
Into the chambre he stalked hym ful stille.   525

"Madame," he seyde, "ye moote foryeve it
    me,
Though I do thyng to which I am constreyned.
Ye been so wys that ful wel knowe ye
That lordes heestes mowe nat been yfeyned;
They mowe wel been biwailled or compleyned,
But men moote nede unto hire lust obeye, 531
And so wol I; ther is namoore to seye.

"This child I am comanded for to take," —
And spak namoore, but out the child he hente
Despitously, and gan a cheere make 535
As though he wolde han slayn it er he wente.
Grisildis moot al suffre and al consente;
And as a lamb she sitteth meke and stille,
And leet this crueel sergeant doon his wille.

Suspecious was the diffame of this man, 540
Suspect his face, suspect his word also;
Suspect the tyme in which he this bigan.
Allas! hir doghter that she loved so,
She wende he wolde han slawen it right tho.
But nathelees she neither weep ne syked, 545
Conformynge hire to that the markys lyked.

But atte laste to speken she bigan,
And mekely she to the sergeant preyde,
So as he was a worthy gentil man,
That she moste kisse hire child er that it deyde.
And in hir barm this litel child she leyde 551
With ful sad face, and gan the child to blisse,
And lulled it, and after gan it kisse.

And thus she seyde in hire benigne voys,
"Fareweel my child! I shal thee nevere see.
But sith I thee have marked with the croys 556
Of thilke Fader — blessed moote he be! —
That for us deyde upon a croys of tree,
Thy soule, litel child, I hym bitake,
For this nyght shaltow dyen for my sake." 560

I trowe that to a norice in this cas
It had been hard this reuthe for to se;
Wel myghte a mooder thanne han cryd "allas!"
But nathelees so sad stidefast was she
That she endured al adversitee, 565
And to the sergeant mekely she sayde,
"Have heer agayn youre litel yonge mayde.

"Gooth now," quod she, "and dooth my
    lordes heeste;
But o thyng wol I prey yow of youre grace,
That, but my lord forbad yow, atte leeste 570
Burieth this litel body in som place

That beestes ne no briddes it torace."
But he no word wol to that purpos seye,
But took the child and wente upon his weye.

This sergeant cam unto his lord ageyn, 575
And of Grisildis wordes and hire cheere
He tolde hym point for point, in short and
    pleyn,
And hym presenteth with his doghter deere.
Somwhat this lord hadde routhe in his manere,
But nathelees his purpos heeld he stille, 580
As lordes doon, whan they wol han hir wille;

And bad this sergeant that he pryvely
Sholde this child ful softe wynde and wrappe,
With alle circumstances tendrely,
And carie it in a cofre or in a lappe; 585
But, upon peyne his heed of for to swappe,
That no man sholde knowe of his entente,
Ne whenne he cam, ne whider that he wente;

But at Boloigne to his suster deere,
That thilke tyme of Panik was countesse, 590
He sholde it take, and shewe hire this mateere,
Bisekynge hire to doon hire bisynesse
This child to fostre in alle gentillesse;
And whos child that it was he bad hire hyde
From every wight, for oght that may bityde.

The sergeant gooth, and hath fulfild this
    thyng; 596
But to this markys now retourne we.
For now gooth he ful faste ymaginyng
If by his wyves cheere he myghte se,
Or by hire word aperceyve, that she 600
Were chaunged; but he nevere hire koude
    fynde
But evere in oon ylike sad and kynde.

As glad, as humble, as bisy in servyse,
And eek in love, as she was wont to be,
Was she to hym in every maner wyse; 605
Ne of hir doghter noght a word spak she.
Noon accident, for noon adversitee,
Was seyn in hire, ne nevere hir doghter name
Ne nempned she, in ernest nor in game. 609

Explicit tercia pars.

Sequitur pars quarta.

In this estaat ther passed been foure yeer
Er she with childe was, but, as God wolde,
A knave child she bar by this Walter,
Ful gracious and fair for to biholde.

And whan that folk it to his fader tolde,
Nat oonly he, but al his contree merye   615
Was for this child, and God they thanke and
      herye.

    Whan it was two yeer old, and fro the brest
Departed of his norice, on a day
This markys caughte yet another lest
To tempte his wyf yet ofter, if he may.   620
O nedelees was she tempted in assay!
But wedded men ne knowe no mesure,
Whan that they fynde a pacient creature.

    "Wyf," quod this markys, "ye han herd er
      this,
My peple sikly berth oure mariage;   625
And namely sith my sone yboren is,
Now is it worse than evere in al oure age.
The murmur sleeth myn herte and my corage,
For to myne eres comth the voys so smerte
That it wel ny destroyed hath myn herte.   630

    "Now sey they thus: 'Whan Walter is agon,
Thanne shal the blood of Janicle succede
And been oure lord, for oother have we noon.'
Swiche wordes seith my peple, out of drede.
Wel oughte I of swich murmur taken heede;
For certeinly I drede swich sentence,   636
Though they nat pleyn speke in myn audience.

    "I wolde lyve in pees, if that I myghte;
Wherfore I am disposed outrely,
As I his suster servede by nyghte,   640
Right so thenke I to serve hym pryvely.
This warne I yow, that ye nat sodeynly
Out of youreself for no wo sholde outreye;
Beth pacient, and therof I yow preye."

    "I have," quod she, "seyd thus, and evere
      shal: 645
I wol no thyng, ne nyl no thyng, certayn,
But as yow list. Naught greveth me at al,
Though that my doughter and my sone be
      slayn, —
At youre comandement, this is to sayn.   649
I have noght had no part of children tweyne
But first siknesse, and after, wo and peyne.

    "Ye been oure lord, dooth with youre owene
      thyng
Right as yow list; axeth no reed at me.
For as I lefte at hoom al my clothyng,
Whan I first cam to yow, right so," quod she,
"Lefte I my wyl and al my libertee,   656

And took youre clothyng; wherfore I yow
      preye,
Dooth youre plesaunce, I wol youre lust obeye.

    "And certes, if I hadde prescience   659
Youre wyl to knowe, er ye youre lust me tolde,
I wolde it doon withouten necligence;
But now I woot youre lust, and what ye wolde,
Al youre plesance ferme and stable I holde;
For wiste I that my deeth wolde do yow ese,
Right gladly wolde I dyen, yow to plese.   665

    "Deth may noght make no comparisoun
Unto youre love." And whan this markys say
The constance of his wyf, he caste adoun
His eyen two, and wondreth that she may
In pacience suffre al this array;   670
And forth he goth with drery contenance,
But to his herte it was ful greet plesance.

    This ugly sergeant, in the same wyse
That he hire doghter caughte, right so he,
Or worse, if men worse kan devyse,   675
Hath hent hire sone, that ful was of beautee.
And evere in oon so pacient was she
That she no chiere maade of hevynesse,
But kiste hir sone, and after gan it blesse;

    Save this, she preyede hym that, if he
      myghte,   680
Hir litel sone he wolde in erthe grave,
His tendre lymes, delicaat to sighte,
Fro foweles and fro beestes for to save.
But she noon answere of hym myghte have.
He wente his wey, as hym no thyng ne roghte;
But to Boloigne he tendrely it broghte.   686

    This markys wondred, evere lenger the
      moore,
Upon hir pacience, and if that he
Ne hadde soothly knowen therbifoore
That parfitly hir children loved she,   690
He wolde have wend that of som subtiltee,
And of malice, or for crueel corage,
That she hadde suffred this with sad visage.

    But wel he knew that next hymself, certayn,
She loved hir children best in every wyse.   695
But now of wommen wolde I axen fayn
If thise assayes myghte nat suffise?
What koude a sturdy housbonde moore devyse
To preeve hir wyfhod and hir stedefastnesse,
And he continuynge evere in sturdinesse?   700

But ther been folk of swich condicion
That whan they have a certein purpos take,
They kan nat stynte of hire entencion,
But, right as they were bounden to a stake,
They wol nat of that firste purpos slake.   705
Right so this markys fulliche hath purposed
To tempte his wyf as he was first disposed.

He waiteth if by word or contenance
That she to hym was changed of corage;
But nevere koude he fynde variance.   710
She was ay oon in herte and in visage;
And ay the forther that she was in age,
The moore trewe, if that it were possible,
She was to hym in love, and moore penyble.

For which it semed thus, that of hem two
Ther nas but o wyl; for, as Walter leste,   716
The same lust was hire plesance also.
And, God be thanked, al fil for the beste.
She shewed wel, for no worldly unreste
A wyf, as of hirself, nothing ne sholde   720
Wille in effect, but as hir housbonde wolde.

The sclaundre of Walter ofte and wyde
            spradde,
That of a crueel herte he wikkedly,
For he a povre womman wedded hadde,
Hath mordred bothe his children prively.   725
Swich murmur was among hem comunly.
No wonder is, for to the peples ere
Ther cam no word, but that they mordred were.

For which, where as his peple therbifore
Hadde loved hym wel, the sclaundre of his
            diffame   730
Made hem that they hym hatede therfore.
To been a mordrere is an hateful name;
But nathelees, for ernest ne for game,
He of his crueel purpos nolde stente;
To tempte his wyf was set al his entente.   735

Whan that his doghter twelve yeer was of
            age,
He to the court of Rome, in subtil wyse
Enformed of his wyl, sente his message,
Comaundynge hem swiche bulles to devyse
As to his crueel purpos may suffyse,   740
How that the pope, as for his peples reste,
Bad hym to wedde another, if hym leste.

I seye, he bad they sholde countrefete
The popes bulles, makynge mencion
That he hath leve his firste wyf to lete,   745

As by the popes dispensacion,
To stynte rancour and dissencion
Bitwixe his peple and hym; thus seyde the
            bulle,
The which they han publiced atte fulle.

The rude peple, as it no wonder is,   750
Wenden ful wel that it hadde be right so;
But whan thise tidynges came to Grisildis,
I deeme that hire herte was ful wo.
But she, ylike sad for everemo,
Disposed was, this humble creature,   755
The adversitee of Fortune al t'endure,

Abidynge evere his lust and his plesance,
To whom that she was yeven herte and al,
As to hire verray worldly suffisance.
But shortly if this storie I tellen shal,   760
This markys writen hath in special
A lettre, in which he sheweth his entente,
And secreely he to Boloigne it sente.

To the Erl of Panyk, which that hadde tho
Wedded his suster, preyde he specially   765
To bryngen hoom agayn his children two
In honurable estaat al openly.
But o thyng he hym preyede outrely,
That he to no wight, though men wolde en-
            quere,
Sholde nat telle whos children that they
            were,   770

But seye, the mayden sholde ywedded be
Unto the Markys of Saluce anon.
And as this erl was preyed, so dide he;
For at day set he on his wey is goon
Toward Saluce, and lordes many oon   775
In riche array, this mayden for to gyde,
Hir yonge brother ridynge hire bisyde.

Arrayed was toward hir mariage
This fresshe mayde, ful of gemmes cleere;
Hir brother, which that seven yeer was of age,
Arrayed eek ful fressh in his manere.   781
And thus in greet noblesse and with glad
            cheere,
Toward Saluces shapynge hir journey,
Fro day to day they ryden in hir wey.

Explicit quarta pars.

Sequitur pars quinta.

Among al this, after his wikke usage,   785
This markys, yet his wyf to tempte moore

To the outtreste preeve of hir corage,
Fully to han experience and loore
If that she were as stidefast as bifoore,
He on a day, in open audience,   790
Ful boistously hath seyd hire this sentence:

"Certes, Grisilde, I hadde ynogh plesance
To han yow to my wyf for youre goodnesse,
As for youre trouthe and for youre obeisance,
Noght for youre lynage, ne for youre richesse;
But now knowe I in verray soothfastnesse   796
That in greet lordshipe, if I wel avyse,
Ther is greet servitute in sondry wyse.

"I may nat doon as every plowman may.
My peple me constreyneth for to take   800
Another wyf, and crien day by day;
And eek the pope, rancour for to slake.
Consenteth it, that dar I undertake;
And trewely thus muche I wol yow seye,
My newe wyf is comynge by the weye.   805

"Be strong of herte, and voyde anon hir
    place,
And thilke dowere that ye broghten me,
Taak it agayn; I graunte it of my grace.
Retourneth to youre fadres hous," quod he;
"No man may alwey han prosperitee.   810
With evene herte I rede yow t'endure
The strook of Fortune or of aventure."

And she agayn answerde in pacience,
"My lord," quod she, "I woot, and wiste alway,
How that bitwixen youre magnificence   815
And my poverte no wight kan ne may
Maken comparison; it is no nay.
I ne heeld me nevere digne in no manere
To be youre wyf, no, ne youre chamberere.

"And in this hous, ther ye me lady maade —
The heighe God take I for my witnesse,   821
And also wysly he my soule glaade —
I nevere heeld me lady ne mistresse,
But humble servant to youre worthynesse,
And evere shal, whil that my lyf may dure,   825
Aboven every worldly creature.

"That ye so longe of youre benignitee
Han holden me in honour and nobleye,
Where as I was noght worthy for to bee,
That thonke I God and yow, to whom I preye
Foryelde it yow; ther is namoore to seye.   831
Unto my fader gladly wol I wende,
And with hym dwelle unto my lyves ende.

"Ther I was fostred of a child ful smal,
Til I be deed my lyf ther wol I lede,   835
A wydwe clene in body, herte, and al.
For sith I yaf to yow my maydenhede,
And am youre trewe wyf, it is no drede,
God shilde swich a lordes wyf to take
Another man to housbonde or to make!   840

"And of youre newe wyf God of his grace
So graunte yow wele and prosperitee!
For I wol gladly yelden hire my place,
In which that I was blisful wont to bee.
For sith it liketh yow, my lord," quod shee,   845
"That whilom weren al myn hertes reste,
That I shal goon, I wol goon whan yow leste.

"But ther as ye me profre swich dowaire
As I first broghte, it is wel in my mynde   849
It were my wrecched clothes, nothyng faire,
The whiche to me were hard now for to fynde.
O goode God! how gentil and how kynde
Ye semed by youre speche and youre visage
The day that maked was oure mariage!

"But sooth is seyd — algate I fynde it trewe,
For in effect it preeved is on me —   856
Love is noght oold as whan that it is newe.
But certes, lord, for noon adversitee,
To dyen in the cas, it shal nat bee
That evere in word or werk I shal repente   860
That I yow yaf myn herte in hool entente.

"My lord, ye woot that in my fadres place
Ye dide me streepe out of my povre weede,
And richely me cladden, of youre grace.
To yow broghte I noght elles, out of drede,   865
But feith, and nakednesse, and maydenhede;
And heere agayn your clothyng I restoore,
And eek your weddyng ryng, for everemore.

"The remenant of youre jueles redy be
Inwith youre chambre, dar I saufly sayn.   870
Naked out of my fadres hous," quod she,
"I cam, and naked moot I turne agayn.
Al youre plesance wol I folwen fayn;
But yet I hope it be nat youre entente   874
That I smoklees out of youre paleys wente.

"Ye koude nat doon so dishonest a thyng,
That thilke wombe in which youre children
    leye
Sholde biforn the peple, in my walkyng,
Be seyn al bare; wherfore I yow preye,
Lat me nat lyk a worm go by the weye.   880

Remembre yow, myn owene lord so deere,
I was youre wyf, though I unworthy weere.

"Wherfore, in gerdon of my maydenhede,
Which that I broghte, and noght agayn I bere,
As voucheth sauf to yeve me, to my meede,
But swich a smok as I was wont to were,   886
That I therwith may wrye the wombe of here
That was youre wyf. And heer take I my leeve
Of yow, myn owene lord, lest I yow greve."

"The smok," quod he, "that thou hast on thy
        bak,   890
Lat it be stille, and bere it forth with thee."
But wel unnethes thilke word he spak,
But wente his wey, for routhe and for pitee.
Biforn the folk hirselven strepeth she,
And in hir smok, with heed and foot al bare,
Toward hir fadre hous forth is she fare.   896

The folk hire folwe, wepynge in hir weye,
And Fortune ay they cursen as they goon;
But she fro wepyng kepte hire eyen dreye,
Ne in this tyme word ne spak she noon.   900
Hir fader, that this tidynge herde anoon,
Curseth the day and tyme that Nature
Shoop hym to been a lyves creature.

For out of doute this olde poure man
Was evere in suspect of hir mariage;   905
For evere he demed, sith that it bigan,
That whan the lord fulfild hadde his corage,
Hym wolde thynke it were a disparage
To his estaat so lowe for t'alighte,
And voyden hire as soone as ever he myghte.

Agayns his doghter hastily goth he,   911
For he by noyse of folk knew hire comynge,
And with hire olde coote, as it myghte be
He covered hire, ful sorwefully wepynge.
But on hire body myghte he it nat brynge,   915
For rude was the clooth, and moore of age
By dayes fele than at hire mariage.

Thus with hire fader, for a certeyn space,
Dwelleth this flour of wyfly pacience,
That neither by hire wordes ne hire face,   920
Biforn the folk, ne eek in hire absence,
Ne shewed she that hire was doon offence;
Ne of hire heighe estaat no remembraunce
Ne hadde she, as by hire contenaunce.

No wonder is, for in hire grete estaat   925
Hire goost was evere in pleyn humylitee;

No tendre mouth, noon herte delicaat,
No pompe, no semblant of roialtee,
But ful of pacient benyngnytee,
Discreet and pridelees, ay honurable,   930
And to hire housbonde evere meke and stable.

Men speke of Job, and moost for his hum-
        blesse,
As clerkes, whan hem list, konne wel endite,
Namely of men, but as in soothfastnesse,
Though clerkes preise wommen but a lite,   935
Ther kan no man in humblesse hym acquite
As womman kan, ne kan been half so trewe
As wommen been, but it be falle of newe.

[PART VI.]

Fro Boloigne is this Erl of Panyk come,
Of which the fame up sprang to moore and
        lesse,   940
And to the peples eres, alle and some,
Was kouth eek that a newe markysesse
He with hym broghte, in swich pompe and
        richesse
That nevere was ther seyn with mannes ye
So noble array in al West Lumbardye.   945

The markys, which that shoop and knew al
        this,
Er that this erl was come, sente his message
For thilke sely povre Grisildis;
And she with humble herte and glad visage,
Nat with no swollen thoght in hire corage,   950
Cam at his heste, and on hire knees hire sette,
And reverently and wisely she hym grette.

"Grisilde," quod he, "my wyl is outrely,
This mayden, that shal wedded been to me,
Received be to-morwe as roially   955
As it possible is in myn hous to be,
And eek that every wight in his degree
Have his estaat, in sittyng and servyse
And heigh plesaunce, as I kan best devyse.

"I have no wommen suffisaunt, certayn,   960
The chambres for t'arraye in ordinaunce
After my lust, and therfore wolde I fayn
That thyn were al swich manere governaunce.
Thou knowest eek of old al my plesaunce;
Thogh thyn array be badde and yvel biseye,
Do thou thy devoir at the leeste weye."   966

"Nat oonly, lord, that I am glad," quod she,
"To doon youre lust, but I desire also
Yow for to serve and plese in my degree

Withouten feyntyng, and shal everemo;   970
Ne nevere, for no wele ne no wo,
Ne shal the goost withinne myn herte stente
To love yow best with al my trewe entente."

And with that word she gan the hous to
     dighte,
And tables for to sette, and beddes make;   975
And peyned hire to doon al that she myghte,
Preyynge the chambereres, for Goddes sake,
To hasten hem, and faste swepe and shake;
And she, the mooste servysable of alle,
Hath every chambre arrayed and his halle.   980

Abouten undren gan this erl alighte,
That with hym broghte thise noble children
     tweye,
For which the peple ran to seen the sighte
Of hire array, so richely biseye;
And thanne at erst amonges hem they seye   985
That Walter was no fool, thogh that hym leste
To chaunge his wyf, for it was for the beste.

For she is fairer, as they deemen alle,
Than is Grisilde, and moore tendre of age,
And fairer fruyt bitwene hem sholde falle,   990
And moore plesant, for hire heigh lynage.
Hir brother eek so fair was of visage
That hem to seen the peple hath caught ples-
     aunce,
Commendynge now the markys governaunce. —

"O stormy peple! unsad and evere untrewe!
Ay undiscreet and chaungynge as a fane!   996
Delitynge evere in rumbul that is newe,
For lyk the moone ay wexe ye and wane!
Ay ful of clappyng, deere ynogh a jane!
Youre doom is fals, youre constance yvele   1000
     preeveth;
A ful greet fool is he that on yow leeveth."

Thus seyden sadde folk in that citee,
Whan that the peple gazed up and doun;
For they were glad, right for the noveltee,
To han a newe lady of hir toun.   1005
Namoore of this make I now mencioun,
But to Grisilde agayn wol I me dresse,
And telle hir constance and hir bisynesse. —

Ful bisy was Grisilde in every thyng
That to the feeste was apertinent.   1010
Right noght was she abayst of hire clothyng,
Thogh it were rude and somdeel eek torent;
But with glad cheere to the yate is went

With oother folk, to greete the markysesse,
And after that dooth forth hire bisynesse.   1015

With so glad chiere his gestes she receyveth,
And konnyngly, everich in his degree,
That no defaute no man aperceyveth,
But ay they wondren what she myghte bee
That in so povre array was for to see,   1020
And koude swich honour and reverence,
And worthily they preisen hire prudence.

In al this meene while she ne stente
This mayde and eek hir brother to commende
With al hir herte, in ful benyngne entente,   1025
So wel that no man koude hir pris amende.
But atte laste, whan that thise lordes wende
To sitten doun to mete, he gan to calle
Grisilde, as she was bisy in his halle.   1029

"Grisilde," quod he, as it were in his pley,
"How liketh thee my wyf and hire beautee?"
"Right wel," quod she, "my lord; for, in good
     fey,
A fairer saugh I nevere noon than she.
I prey to God yeve hire prosperitee;
And so hope I that he wol to yow sende   1035
Plesance ynogh unto youre lyves ende.

"O thyng biseke I yow, and warne also,
That ye ne prikke with no tormentynge
This tendre mayden, as ye han doon mo;
For she is fostred in hire norissynge   1040
Moore tendrely, and, to my supposynge,
She koude nat adversitee endure
As koude a povre fostred creature."

And whan this Walter saugh hire pacience,
Hir glade chiere, and no malice at al,   1045
And he so ofte had doon to hire offence,
And she ay sad and constant as a wal,
Continuynge evere hire innocence overal,
This sturdy markys gan his herte dresse
To rewen upon hire wyfly stedfastnesse.   1050

"This is ynogh, Grisilde myn," quod he;
"Be now namoore agast ne yvele apayed.
I have thy feith and thy benyngnytee,
As wel as evere womman was, assayed,
In greet estaat, and povreliche arrayed.   1055
Now knowe I, dere wyf, thy stedfastnesse," —
And hire in armes took and gan hire kesse.

And she for wonder took of it no keep;
She herde nat what thyng he to hire seyde;

She ferde as she had stert out of a sleep,   1060
Til she out of hire mazednesse abreyde.
"Grisilde," quod he, "by God, that for us deyde,
Thou art my wyf, ne noon oother I have,
Ne nevere hadde, as God my soule save!

"This is thy doghter, which thou hast sup-
            posed   1065
To be my wyf; that oother feithfully
Shal be myn heir, as I have ay disposed;
Thou bare hym in thy body trewely.
At Boloigne have I kept hem prively;   1069
Taak hem agayn, for now maystow nat seye
That thou hast lorn noon of thy children tweye.

"And folk that ootherweys han seyd of me,
I warne hem wel that I have doon this deede
For no malice, ne for no crueltee,   1074
But for t'assaye in thee thy wommanheede,
And nat to sleen my children — God for-
            beede! —
But for to kepe hem pryvely and stille,
Til I thy purpos knewe and al thy wille."

Whan she this herde, aswowne doun she
            falleth
For pitous joye, and after hire swownynge
She bothe hire yonge children to hire calleth,
And in hire armes, pitously wepynge,   1082
Embraceth hem, and tendrely kissynge
Ful lyk a mooder, with hire salte teeres
She bathed bothe hire visage and hire heeres.

O which a pitous thyng it was to se   1086
Hir swownyng, and hire humble voys to heere!
"Grauntmercy, lord, God thanke it yow," quod
            she,
"That ye han saved me my children deere!   1089
Now rekke I nevere to been deed right heere;
Sith I stonde in youre love and in youre grace,
No fors of deeth, ne whan my spirit pace!

"O tendre, o deere, o yonge children myne!
Youre woful mooder wende stedfastly
That cruel houndes or som foul vermyne   1095
Hadde eten yow; but God, of his mercy,
And youre benyngne fader tendrely
Hath doon yow kept," — and in that same
            stounde
Al sodeynly she swapte adoun to grounde.

And in hire swough so sadly holdeth she   1100
Hire children two, whan she gan hem t'em-
            brace,

That with greet sleighte and greet difficultee
The children from hire arm they gonne arace.
O many a teere on many a pitous face   1104
Doun ran of hem that stooden hire bisyde;
Unnethe abouten hire myghte they abyde.

Walter hire gladeth, and hire sorwe slaketh;
She riseth up, abaysed, from hire traunce,
And every wight hire joye and feeste maketh
Til she hath caught agayn hire contenaunce.
Walter hire dooth so feithfully plesaunce   1111
That it was deyntee for to seen the cheere
Bitwixe hem two, now they been met yfeere.

Thise ladyes, whan that they hir tyme say,
Han taken hire and into chambre gon,   1115
And strepen hire out of hire rude array,
And in a clooth of gold that brighte shoon,
With a coroune of many a riche stoon
Upon hire heed, they into halle hire broghte,
And ther she was honured as hire oghte.   1120

Thus hath this pitous day a blisful ende,
For every man and womman dooth his myght
This day in murthe and revel to dispende
Til on the welkne shoon the sterres lyght.   1124
For moore solempne in every mannes syght
This feste was, and gretter of costage,
Than was the revel of hire mariage.

Ful many a yeer in heigh prosperitee
Lyven thise two in concord and in reste,
And richely his doghter maryed he   1130
Unto a lord, oon of the worthieste
Of al Ytaille; and thanne in pees and reste
His wyves fader in his court he kepeth,
Til that the soule out of his body crepeth.

His sone succedeth in his heritage   1135
In reste and pees, after his fader day,
And fortunat was eek in mariage,
Al putte he nat his wyf in greet assay.
This world is nat so strong, it is no nay,
As it hath been in olde tymes yoore,   1140
And herkneth what this auctour seith therfoore.

This storie is seyd, nat for that wyves sholde
Folwen Grisilde as in humylitee,
For it were inportable, though they wolde;
But for that every wight, in his degree,   1145
Sholde be constant in adversitee
As was Grisilde; therfore Petrak writeth
This storie, which with heigh stile he enditeth.

For, sith a womman was so pacient
Unto a mortal man, wel moore us oghte 1150
Receyven al in gree that God us sent;
For greet skile is, he preeve that he wroghte.
But he ne tempteth no man that he boghte,
As seith Seint Jame, if ye his pistel rede;
He preeveth folk al day, it is no drede, 1155

And suffreth us, as for oure excercise,
With sharpe scourges of adversitee
Ful ofte to be bete in sondry wise;
Nat for to knowe oure wyl, for certes he,
Er we were born, knew al oure freletee; 1160
And for oure beste is al his governaunce.
Lat us thanne lyve in vertuous suffraunce.

But o word, lordynges, herkneth er I go:
It were ful hard to fynde now-a-dayes
In al a toun Grisildis thre or two; 1165
For if that they were put to swiche assayes,
The gold of hem hath now so badde alayes
With bras, that thogh the coyne be fair at ye,
It wolde rather breste a-two than plye.

For which heere, for the Wyves love of
  Bathe — 1170
Whos lyf and al hire secte God mayntene
In heigh maistrie, and elles were it scathe —
I wol with lusty herte, fressh and grene,
Seyn yow a song to glade yow, I wene;
And lat us stynte of ernestful matere. 1175
Herkneth my song that seith in this manere:

Lenvoy de Chaucer.

Grisilde is deed, and eek hire pacience,
And bothe atones buryed in Ytaille;
For which I crie in open audience,
No wedded man so hardy be t'assaille 1180
His wyves pacience in trust to fynde
Grisildis, for in certein he shal faille.

O noble wyves, ful of heigh prudence,
Lat noon humylitee youre tonge naille,
Ne lat no clerk have cause or diligence 1185
To write of yow a storie of swich mervaille
As of Grisildis pacient and kynde,
Lest Chichevache yow swelwe in hire entraille!

Folweth Ekko, that holdeth no silence,
But evere answereth at the countretaille. 1190
Beth nat bidaffed for youre innocence,
But sharply taak on yow the governaille.
Emprenteth wel this lessoun in youre mynde,
For commune profit sith it may availle.

Ye archewyves, stondeth at defense, 1195
Syn ye be strong as is a greet camaille;
Ne suffreth nat that men yow doon offense.
And sklendre wyves, fieble as in bataille,
Beth egre as is a tygre yond in Ynde;
Ay clappeth as a mille, I yow consaille. 1200

Ne dreed hem nat, doth hem no reverence,
For though thyn housbonde armed be in maille,
The arwes of thy crabbed eloquence
Shal perce his brest, and eek his aventaille.
In jalousie I rede eek thou hym bynde, 1205
And thou shalt make hym couche as doth a
  quaille.

If thou be fair, ther folk been in presence,
Shewe thou thy visage and thyn apparaille;
If thou be foul, be fre of thy dispence;
To gete thee freendes ay do thy travaille;
Be ay of chiere as light as leef on lynde, 1211
And lat hym care, and wepe, and wrynge, and
  waille!

[The following stanza, ll. 1212^(a-g), seems to have been the original ending of the tale. It stands after the Envoy in most of the manuscripts which preserve it, but it may have been meant to follow l. 1162 or l. 1169.]

Bihoold the murye words of the Hoost.

This worthy Clerk, whan ended was his
  tale, 1212^a
Oure Hooste seyde, and swoor, "By Goddes
  bones,
Me were levere than a barel ale
My wyf at hoom had herd this legende ones!
This is a gentil tale for the nones,
As to my purpos, wiste ye my wille;
But thyng that wol nat be, lat it be stille."]

Heere endeth the Tale of the Clerk of Oxenford.

The Merchant's Prologue

The Prologe of the Marchantes Tale.

"Wepyng and waylyng, care and oother sorwe
I knowe ynogh, on even and a-morwe,"   1214
Quod the Marchant, "and so doon other mo
That wedded been. I trowe that it be so,
For wel I woot it fareth so with me.
I have a wyf, the worste that may be;
For thogh the feend to hire ycoupled were,
She wolde hym overmacche, I dar wel swere.
What sholde I yow reherce in special   1221
Hir hye malice? She is a shrewe at al.
Ther is a long and large difference
Bitwix Grisildis grete pacience
And of my wyf the passyng crueltee.   1225
Were I unbounden, also moot I thee!
I wolde nevere eft comen in the snare.
We wedded men lyven in sorwe and care.
Assaye whoso wole, and he shal fynde

That I seye sooth, by Seint Thomas of Ynde,
As for the moore part, I sey nat alle.   1231
God shilde that it sholde so bifalle!
    A! goode sire Hoost, I have ywedded bee
Thise monthes two, and moore nat, pardee;
And yet, I trowe, he that al his lyve   1235
Wyflees hath been, though that men wolde him
        ryve
Unto the herte, ne koude in no manere
Tellen so muchel sorwe as I now heere
Koude tellen of my wyves cursednesse!"
    "Now," quod oure Hoost, "Marchaunt, so
        God yow blesse,   1240
Syn ye so muchel knowen of that art
Ful hertely I pray yow telle us part."
    "Gladly," quod he, "but of myn owene soore,
For soory herte, I telle may namoore."

The Merchant's Tale

Heere bigynneth the Marchantes Tale.

Whilom ther was dwellynge in Lumbardye
A worthy knyght, that born was of Pavye,   1246
In which he lyved in greet prosperitee;
And sixty yeer a wyflees man was hee,
And folwed ay his bodily delyt
On wommen, ther as was his appetyt,   1250
As doon thise fooles that been seculeer.
And whan that he was passed sixty yeer,
Were it for hoolynesse or for dotage,
I kan nat seye, but swich a greet corage   1254
Hadde this knyght to been a wedded man
That day and nyght he dooth al that he kan
T'espien where he myghte wedded be,
Preyinge oure Lord to graunten him that he
Mighte ones knowe of thilke blisful lyf
That is bitwixe an housbonde and his wyf,
And for to lyve under that hooly boond   1261
With which that first God man and womman
        bond.
"Noon oother lyf," seyde he, "is worth a bene;
For wedlok is so esy and so clene,
That in this world it is a paradys."   1265

Thus seyde this olde knyght, that was so wys.
    And certeinly, as sooth as God is kyng,
To take a wyf it is a glorious thyng,
And namely whan a man is oold and hoor;
Thanne is a wyf the fruyt of his tresor.   1270
Thanne sholde he take a yong wyf and a feir,
On which he myghte engendren hym an heir,
And lede his lyf in joye and in solas,
Where as thise bacheleris synge "allas,"
Whan that they fynden any adversitee   1275
In love, which nys but childyssh vanytee.
And trewely it sit wel to be so,
That bacheleris have often peyne and wo;
On brotel ground they buylde, and brotelnesse
They fynde, whan they wene sikernesse.   1280
They lyve but as a bryd or as a beest,
In libertee, and under noon arreest,
Ther as a wedded man in his estaat
Lyveth a lyf blisful and ordinaat,
Under this yok of mariage ybounde.   1285
Wel may his herte in joy and blisse habounde,
For who kan be so buxom as a wyf?

Who is so trewe, and eek so ententyf
To kepe hym, syk and hool, as is his make?
For wele or wo she wole hym nat forsake;   1290
She nys nat wery hym to love and serve,
Thogh that he lye bedrede, til he sterve.
And yet somme clerkes seyn it nys nat so,
Of whiche he Theofraste is oon of tho.
What force though Theofraste liste lye?   1295
"Ne take no wyf," quod he, "for housbondrye,
As for to spare in houshold thy dispence.
A trewe servant dooth moore diligence
Thy good to kepe, than thyn owene wyf,
For she wol clayme half part al hir lyf.   1300
And if that thou be syk, so God me save,
Thy verray freendes, or a trewe knave,
Wol kepe thee bet than she that waiteth ay
After thy good and hath doon many a day.
And if thou take a wyf unto thyn hoold,   1305
Ful lightly maystow been a cokewold."
This sentence, and an hundred thynges worse,
Writeth this man, ther God his bones corse!
But take no kep of al swich vanytee;
Deffie Theofraste, and herke me.   1310
     A wyf is Goddes yifte verraily;
Alle othere manere yiftes hardily,
As londes, rentes, pasture, or commune,
Or moebles, alle been yiftes of Fortune,
That passen as a shadwe upon a wal.   1315
But drede nat, if pleynly speke I shal,
A wyf wol laste, and in thyn hous endure,
Wel lenger than thee list, paraventure.
     Mariage is a ful greet sacrement.
He which that hath no wyf, I holde hym shent;
He lyveth helplees and al desolat, —   1321
I speke of folk in seculer estaat.
And herke why, I sey nat this for noght,
That womman is for mannes helpe ywroght.
The hye God, whan he hadde Adam maked,
And saugh him al allone, bely-naked,   1326
God of his grete goodnesse seyde than,
"Lat us now make an helpe unto this man
Lyk to hymself"; and thanne he made him Eve.
Heere may ye se, and heerby may ye preve,
That wyf is mannes helpe and his confort,   1331
His paradys terrestre, and his disport.
So buxom and so vertuous is she,
They moste nedes lyve in unitee.   1334
O flessh they been, and o fleesh, as I gesse,
Hath but oon herte, in wele and in distresse.
     A wyf! a, Seinte Marie, *benedicite!*
How myghte a man han any adversitee
That hath a wyf? Certes, I kan nat seye.
The blisse which that is bitwixe hem tweye
Ther may no tonge telle, or herte thynke.   1341

If he be povre, she helpeth hym to swynke;
She kepeth his good, and wasteth never a deel;
Al that hire housbonde lust, hire liketh weel;
She seith nat ones "nay," whan he seith
     "ye."   1345
"Do this," seith he; "Al redy, sire," seith she.
O blisful ordre of wedlok precious,
Thou art so murye, and eek so vertuous,
And so commended and approved eek
That every man that halt hym worth a leek,
Upon his bare knees oughte al his lyf   1351
Thanken his God that hym hath sent a wyf,
Or elles preye to God hym for to sende
A wyf, to laste unto his lyves ende.
For thanne his lyf is set in sikernesse;   1355
He may nat be deceyved, as I gesse,
So that he werke after his wyves reed.
Thanne may he boldely beren up his heed,
They been so trewe, and therwithal so wyse;
For which, if thou wolt werken as the wyse,
Do alwey so as wommen wol thee rede.   1361
     Lo, how that Jacob, as thise clerkes rede,
By good conseil of his mooder Rebekke,
Boond the kydes skyn aboute his nekke,
For which his fadres benyson he wan.   1365
     Lo Judith, as the storie eek telle kan,
By wys conseil she Goddes peple kepte,
And slow hym Olofernus, whil he slepte.
     Lo Abigayl, by good conseil, how she
Saved hir housbonde Nabal, whan that he   1370
Sholde han be slayn; and looke, Ester also
By good conseil delyvered out of wo
The peple of God, and made hym Mardochee
Of Assuere enhaunced for to be.
     Ther nys no thyng in gree superlatyf,   1375
As seith Senek, above an humble wyf.
     Suffre thy wyves tonge, as Catoun bit;
She shal comande, and thou shalt suffren it,
And yet she wole obeye of curteisye.
A wyf is kepere of thyn housbondrye;   1380
Wel may the sike man biwaille and wepe,
Ther as ther nys no wyf the hous to kepe.
I warne thee, if wisely thou wolt wirche,
Love wel thy wyf, as Crist loved his chirche.
If thou lovest thyself, thou lovest thy wyf;
No man hateth his flessh, but in his lyf   1386
He fostreth it, and therfore bidde I thee,
Cherisse thy wyf, or thou shalt nevere thee.
Housbonde and wyf, what so men jape or
     pleye,
Of worldly folk holden the siker weye;   1390
They been so knyt ther may noon harm bityde,
And namely upon the wyves syde.
For which this Januarie, of whom I tolde,

Considered hath, inwith his dayes olde,
The lusty lyf, the vertuous quyete,   1395
That is in mariage hony-sweete;
And for his freendes on a day he sente,
To tellen hem th'effect of his entente.
    With face sad his tale he hath hem toold.
He seyde, "Freendes, I am hoor and oold,   1400
And almoost, God woot, on my pittes brynke;
Upon my soule somwhat moste I thynke.
I have my body folily despended;
Blessed be God that it shal been amended!
For I wol be, certeyn, a wedded man,   1405
And that anoon in al the haste I kan.
Unto som mayde fair and tendre of age,
I prey yow, shapeth for my mariage
Al sodeynly, for I wol nat abyde;
And I wol fonde t'espien, on my syde,   1410
To whom I may be wedded hastily.
But forasmuche as ye been mo than I,
Ye shullen rather swich a thyng espyen
Than I, and where me best were to allyen.
    But o thyng warne I yow, my freendes deere,
I wol noon oold wyf han in no manere.   1416
She shal nat passe twenty yeer, certayn;
Oold fissh and yong flessh wolde I have ful
        fayn.
Bet is," quod he, "a pyk than a pykerel,
And bet than old boef is the tendre veel.   1420
I wol no womman thritty yeer of age;
It is but bene-straw and greet forage.
And eek thise olde wydwes, God it woot,
They konne so muchel craft on Wades boot,
So muchel broken harm, whan that hem
        leste,   1425
That with hem sholde I nevere lyve in reste.
For sondry scoles maken sotile clerkis;
Womman of manye scoles half a clerk is.
But certeynly, a yong thyng may men gye,
Right as men may warm wex with handes plye.
Wherfore I sey yow pleynly, in a clause,   1431
I wol noon oold wyf han right for this cause.
For if so were I hadde swich myschaunce,
That I in hire ne koude han no plesaunce,
Thanne sholde I lede my lyf in avoutrye,   1435
And go streight to the devel, whan I dye.
Ne children sholde I none upon hire geten;
Yet were me levere houndes had me eten,
Than that myn heritage sholde falle
In straunge hand, and this I telle yow alle.
I dote nat, I woot the cause why   1441
Men sholde wedde, and forthermoore woot I,
Ther speketh many a man of mariage
That woot namoore of it than woot my page,
For whiche causes man sholde take a wyf.   1445

If he ne may nat lyven chaast his lyf,
Take hym a wyf with greet devocioun,
By cause of leveful procreacioun
Of children, to th'onour of God above,
And nat oonly for paramour or love;   1450
And for they sholde leccherye eschue,
And yelde hir dette whan that it is due;
Or for that ech of hem sholde helpen oother
In meschief, as a suster shal the brother;
And lyve in chastitee ful holily.   1455
But sires, by youre leve, that am nat I.
For, God be thanked! I dar make avaunt,
I feele my lymes stark and suffisaunt
To do al that a man bilongeth to;
I woot myselven best what I may do.   1460
Though I be hoor, I fare as dooth a tree
That blosmeth er that fruyt ywoxen bee;
And blosmy tree nys neither drye ne deed.
I feele me nowhere hoor but on myn heed;
Myn herte and alle my lymes been as grene
As laurer thurgh the yeer is for to sene.   1466
And syn that ye han herd al myn entente,
I prey yow to my wyl ye wole assente."
    Diverse men diversely hym tolde
Of mariage manye ensamples olde.   1470
Somme blamed it, somme preysed it, certeyn;
But atte laste, shortly for to seyn,
As al day falleth altercacioun
Bitwixen freendes in disputisoun,
Ther fil a stryf bitwixe his bretheren two, 1475
Of whiche that oon was cleped Placebo,
Justinus soothly called was that oother.
    Placebo seyde, "O Januarie, brother,
Ful litel nede hadde ye, my lord so deere,
Conseil to axe of any that is heere,   1480
But that ye been so ful of sapience
That yow ne liketh, for youre heighe prudence,
To weyven fro the word of Salomon.
This word seyde he unto us everychon:
'Wirk alle thyng by conseil,' thus seyde he,
'And thanne shaltow nat repente thee.'   1486
But though that Salomon spak swich a word,
Myn owene deere brother and my lord,
So wysly God my soule brynge at reste,
I holde youre owene conseil is the beste.   1490
For, brother myn, of me taak this motyf,
I have now been a court-man al my lyf,
And God it woot, though I unworthy be,
I have stonden in ful greet degree
Abouten lordes of ful heigh estaat;   1495
Yet hadde I nevere with noon of hem debaat.
I nevere hem contraried, trewely;
I woot wel that my lord kan moore than I.
With that he seith, I holde it ferme and stable;

I seye the same, or elles thyng semblable.   1500
A ful greet fool is any conseillour
That serveth any lord of heigh honour,
That dar presume, or elles thenken it,
That his conseil sholde passe his lordes wit.
Nay, lordes been no fooles, by my fay!   1505
Ye han youreselven shewed heer to-day
So heigh sentence, so holily and weel,
That I consente and conferme everydeel
Youre wordes alle and youre opinioun.
By God, ther nys no man in al this toun,   1510
Ne in Ytaille, that koude bet han sayd!
Crist halt hym of this conseil ful wel apayd.
And trewely, it is an heigh corage
Of any man that stapen is in age
To take a yong wyf; by my fader kyn,   1515
Youre herte hangeth on a joly pyn!
Dooth now in this matiere right as yow leste,
For finally I holde it for the beste."

   Justinus, that ay stille sat and herde,   1519
Right in this wise he to Placebo answerde:
"Now, brother myn, be pacient, I preye,
Syn ye han seyd, and herkneth what I seye.
Senek, amonges othere wordes wyse,
Seith that a man oghte hym right wel avyse
To whom he yeveth his lond or his catel.   1525
And syn I oghte avyse me right wel
To whom I yeve my good awey fro me,
Wel muchel moore I oghte avysed be
To whom I yeve my body for alwey.
I warne yow wel, it is no childes pley   1530
To take a wyf withouten avysement.
Men moste enquere, this is myn assent,
Wher she be wys, or sobre, or dronkelewe,
Or proud, or elles ootherweys a shrewe,
A chidestere, or wastour of thy good,   1535
Or riche, or poore, or elles mannyssh wood.
Al be it so that no man fynden shal
Noon in this world that trotteth hool in al,
Ne man, ne beest, swich as men koude devyse;
But nathelees it oghte ynough suffise   1540
With any wyf, if so were that she hadde
Mo goode thewes than hire vices badde;
And al this axeth leyser for t'enquere.
For, God it woot, I have wept many a teere
Ful pryvely, syn I have had a wyf.   1545
Preyse whoso wole a wedded mannes lyf,
Certein I fynde in it but cost and care
And observances, of alle blisses bare.
And yet, God woot, my neighebores aboute,
And namely of wommen many a route,   1550
Seyn that I have the mooste stedefast wyf,
And eek the mekeste oon that bereth lyf;
But I woot best where wryngeth me my sho.

Ye mowe, for me, right as yow liketh do;
Avyseth yow — ye been a man of age —   1555
How that ye entren into mariage,
And namely with a yong wyf and a fair.
By hym that made water, erthe, and air,
The yongeste man that is in al this route
Is bisy ynough to bryngen it aboute   1560
To han his wyf allone. Trusteth me,
Ye shul nat plesen hire fully yeres thre, —
This is to seyn, to doon hire ful plesaunce.
A wyf axeth ful many an observaunce.
I prey yow that ye be nat yvele apayd."   1565
   "Wel," quod this Januarie, "and hastow
       sayd?
Straw for thy Senek, and for thy proverbes!
I counte nat a panyer ful of herbes
Of scole-termes. Wyser men than thow,
As thou hast herd, assenteden right now   1570
To my purpos. Placebo, what sey ye?"
   "I seye it is a cursed man," quod he,
"That letteth matrimoigne, sikerly."
And with that word they rysen sodeynly,
And been assented fully that he sholde   1575
Be wedded whanne hym liste, and where he
       wolde.
   Heigh fantasye and curious bisynesse
Fro day to day gan in the soule impresse
Of Januarie aboute his mariage.
Many fair shap and many a fair visage   1580
Ther passeth thurgh his herte nyght by nyght,
As whoso tooke a mirour, polisshed bryght,
And sette it in a commune market-place,
Thanne sholde he se ful many a figure pace
By his mirour; and in the same wyse   1585
Gan Januarie inwith his thoght devyse
Of maydens whiche that dwelten hym bisyde.
He wiste nat wher that he myghte abyde.
For if that oon have beaute in hir face,
Another stant so in the peples grace   1590
For hire sadnesse and hire benyngnytee
That of the peple grettest voys hath she;
And somme were riche, and hadden badde
       name.
But nathelees, bitwixe ernest and game,
He atte laste apoynted hym on oon,   1595
And leet alle othere from his herte goon,
And chees hire of his owene auctoritee;
For love is blynd alday, and may nat see.
And whan that he was in his bed ybroght,
He purtreyed in his herte and in his thoght
Hir fresshe beautee and hir age tendre,   1601
Hir myddel smal, hire armes longe and sklen-
       dre,
Hir wise governaunce, hir gentillesse,

Hir wommanly berynge, and hire sadnesse.
And whan that he on hire was conde-
scended,   1605
Hym thoughte his choys myghte nat ben
amended.
For whan that he hymself concluded hadde,
Hym thoughte ech oother mannes wit so badde
That inpossible it were to repplye
Agayn his choys, this was his fantasye.   1610
His freendes sente he to, at his instaunce,
And preyed hem to doon hym that plesaunce,
That hastily they wolden to hym come;
He wolde abregge hir labour, alle and some.
Nedeth namoore for hym to go ne ryde;   1615
He was apoynted ther he wolde abyde.
  Placebo cam, and eek his freendes soone,
And alderfirst he bad hem alle a boone,
That noon of hem none argumentes make   1619
Agayn the purpos which that he hath take,
Which purpos was plesant to God, seyde he,
And verray ground of his prosperitee.
  He seyde ther was a mayden in the toun,
Which that of beautee hadde greet renoun,
Al were it so she were of smal degree;   1625
Suffiseth hym hir yowthe and hir beautee.
Which mayde, he seyde, he wolde han to his
wyf,
To lede in ese and hoolynesse his lyf;
And thanked God that he myghte han hire al,
That no wight his blisse parten shal.   1630
And preyed hem to laboure in this nede,
And shapen that he faille nat to spede;
For thanne, he seyde, his spirit was at ese.
"Thanne is," quod he, "no thyng may me dis-
plese,
Save o thyng priketh in my conscience,   1635
The which I wol reherce in youre presence.
  I have," quod he, "herd seyd, ful yoore ago,
Ther may no man han parfite blisses two, —
This is to seye, in erthe and eek in hevene.
For though he kepe hym fro the synnes sevene,
And eek from every branche of thilke tree, 1641
Yet is ther so parfit felicitee
And so greet ese and lust in mariage,
That evere I am agast now in myn age
That I shal lede now so myrie a lyf,   1645
So delicat, withouten wo and stryf,
That I shal have myn hevene in erthe heere.
For sith that verray hevene is boght so deere
With tribulacion and greet penaunce,
How sholde I thanne, that lyve in swich ples-
aunce   1650
As alle wedded men doon with hire wyvys,
Come to the blisse ther Crist eterne on lyve ys?

This is my drede, and ye, my bretheren tweye,
Assoilleth me this question, I preye."
  Justinus, which that hated his folye,   1655
Answerde anon right in his japerye;
And for he wolde his longe tale abregge,
He wolde noon auctoritee allegge,
But seyde, "Sire, so ther be noon obstacle
Oother than this, God of his hygh myracle
And of his mercy may so for yow wirche   1661
That, er ye have youre right of hooly chirche,
Ye may repente of wedded mannes lyf,
In which ye seyn ther is no wo ne stryf.
And elles, God forbede but he sente   1665
A wedded man hym grace to repente
Wel ofte rather than a sengle man!
And therfore, sire — the beste reed I kan —
Dispeire yow noght, but have in youre mem-
orie,
Paraunter she may be youre purgatorie!   1670
She may be Goddes meene and Goddes
whippe;
Thanne shal youre soule up to hevene skippe
Swifter than dooth an arwe out of a bowe.
I hope to God, herafter shul ye knowe
That ther nys no so greet felicitee   1675
In mariage, ne nevere mo shal bee,
That yow shal lette of youre savacion,
So that ye use, as skile is and reson,
The lustes of youre wyf attemprely,
And that ye plese hire nat to amorously,   1680
And that ye kepe yow eek from oother synne.
My tale is doon, for my wit is thynne.
Beth nat agast herof, my brother deere,
But lat us waden out of this mateere.
The Wyf of Bathe, if ye han understonde,   1685
Of mariage, which we have on honde,
Declared hath ful wel in litel space.
Fareth now wel, God have yow in his grace."
  And with this word this Justyn and his
brother
Han take hir leve, and ech of hem of
oother.   1690
For whan they saughe that it moste nedes be,
They wroghten so, by sly and wys tretee,
That she, this mayden, which that Mayus
highte,
As hastily as evere that she myghte,
Shal wedded be unto this Januarie.   1695
I trowe it were to longe yow to tarie,
If I yow tolde of every scrit and bond
By which that she was feffed in his lond,
Or for to herknen of hir riche array.
But finally ycomen is the day   1700
That to the chirche bothe be they went

For to receyve the hooly sacrement.
Forth comth the preest, with stole aboute his
    nekke,
And bad hire be lyk Sarra and Rebekke
In wysdom and in trouthe of mariage;   1705
And seyde his orisons, as is usage,
And croucheth hem, and bad God sholde hem
    blesse,
And made al siker ynogh with hoolynesse.
    Thus been they wedded with solempnitee,
And at the feeste sitteth he and she   1710
With othere worthy folk upon the deys.
Al ful of joye and blisse is the paleys,
And ful of instrumentz and of vitaille,
The mooste deyntevous of al Ytaille.
Biforn hem stoode instrumentz of swich soun
That Orpheus, ne of Thebes Amphioun,   1716
Ne maden nevere swich a melodye.
At every cours thanne cam loud mynstralcye,
That nevere tromped Joab for to heere,
Nor he Theodomas, yet half so cleere,   1720
At Thebes, whan the citee was in doute.
Bacus the wyn hem shynketh al aboute,
And Venus laugheth upon every wight,
For Januarie was bicome hir knyght,
And wolde bothe assayen his corage   1725
In libertee, and eek in mariage;
And with hire fyrbrond in hire hand aboute
Daunceth biforn the bryde and al the route.
And certeinly, I dar right wel seyn this,
Ymeneus, that god of weddyng is,   1730
Saugh nevere his lyf so myrie a wedded man.
Hoold thou thy pees, thou poete Marcian,
That writest us that ilke weddyng murie
Of hire Philologie and hym Mercurie,
And of the songes that the Muses songe!   1735
To smal is bothe thy penne, and eek thy tonge,
For to descryven of this mariage.
Whan tendre youthe hath wedded stoupyng
    age,
Ther is swich myrthe that it may nat be writen.
Assayeth it youreself, thanne may ye witen
If that I lye or noon in this matiere.   1741
    Mayus, that sit with so benyngne a chiere,
Hire to biholde it semed fayerye.
Queene Ester looked nevere with swich an ye
On Assuer, so meke a look hath she.   1745
I may yow nat devyse al hir beautee.
But thus muche of hire beautee telle I may,
That she was lyk the brighte morwe of May,
Fulfild of alle beautee and plesaunce.
    This Januarie is ravysshed in a traunce   1750
At every tyme he looked on hir face;
But in his herte he gan hire to manace

That he that nyght in armes wolde hire streyne
Harder than evere Parys dide Eleyne.
But nathelees yet hadde he greet pitee   1755
That thilke nyght offenden hire moste he,
And thoughte, "Allas! O tendre creature,
Now wolde God ye myghte wel endure
Al my corage, it is so sharp and keene!
I am agast ye shul it nat susteene.   1760
But God forbede that I dide al my myght!
Now wolde God that it were woxen nyght,
And that the nyght wolde lasten everemo.
I wolde that al this peple were ago."
And finally he dooth al his labour,   1765
As he best myghte, savynge his honour,
To haste hem fro the mete in subtil wyse.
    The tyme cam that resoun was to ryse;
And after that men daunce and drynken faste,
And spices al aboute the hous they caste,   1770
And ful of joye and blisse is every man, —
Al but a squyer, highte Damyan,
Which carf biforn the knyght ful many a day.
He was so ravysshed on his lady May   1774
That for the verray peyne he was ny wood.
Almoost he swelte and swowned ther he stood,
So soore hath Venus hurt hym with hire brond,
As that she bar it daunsynge in hire hond;
And to his bed he wente hym hastily.
Namoore of hym as at this tyme speke I,   1780
But there I lete hym wepe ynogh and pleyne,
Til fresshe May wol rewen on his peyne.
    O perilous fyr, that in the bedstraw bredeth!
O famulier foo, that his servyce bedeth!
O servant traytour, false hoomly hewe,   1785
Lyk to the naddre in bosom sly untrewe,
God shilde us alle from youre aqueyntaunce!
O Januarie, dronken in plesaunce
In mariage, se how thy Damyan,
Thyn owene squier and thy borne man,   1790
Entendeth for to do thee vileynye.
God graunte thee thyn hoomly fo t'espye!
For in this world nys worse pestilence
Than hoomly foo al day in thy presence.   1794
    Parfourned hath the sonne his ark diurne;
No lenger may the body of hym sojurne
On th'orisonte, as in that latitude.
Night with his mantel, that is derk and rude,
Gan oversprede the hemysperie aboute;
For which departed is this lusty route   1800
Fro Januarie, with thank on every syde.
Hoom to hir houses lustily they ryde,
Where as they doon hir thynges as hem leste,
And whan they sye hir tyme, goon to reste.
Soone after that, this hastif Januarie   1805
Wolde go to bedde, he wolde no lenger tarye.

He drynketh ypocras, clarree, and vernage
Of spices hoote, t'encreessen his corage;
And many a letuarie hath he ful fyn,
Swiche as the cursed monk, daun Constantyn,
Hath writen in his book *De Coitu;*   1811
To eten hem alle he nas no thyng eschu.
And to his privee freendes thus seyde he:
"For Goddes love, as soone as it may be,
Lat voyden al this hous in curteys wyse."   1815
And they han doon right as he wol devyse.
Men drynken, and the travers drawe anon.
The bryde was broght abedde as stille as stoon;
And whan the bed was with the preest yblessed,
Out of the chambre hath every wight hym
     dressed;   1820
And Januarie hath faste in armes take
His fresshe May, his paradys, his make.
He lulleth hire, he kisseth hire ful ofte;
With thikke brustles of his berd unsofte,
Lyk to the skyn of houndfyssh, sharp as brere —
For he was shave al newe in his manere —   1826
He rubbeth hire aboute hir tendre face,
And seyde thus, "Allas! I moot trespace
To yow, my spouse, and yow greetly offende,
Er tyme come that I wil doun descende.   1830
But nathelees, considereth this," quod he,
"Ther nys no werkman, whatsoevere he be,
That may bothe werke wel and hastily;
This wol be doon at leyser parfitly.
It is no fors how longe that we pleye;   1835
In trewe wedlok coupled be we tweye;
And blessed be the yok that we been inne,
For in oure actes we mowe do no synne.
A man may do no synne with his wyf,
Ne hurte hymselven with his owene knyf;   1840
For we han leve to pleye us by the lawe."
Thus laboureth he til that the day gan dawe;
And thanne he taketh a sop in fyn clarree,
And upright in his bed thanne sitteth he,   1844
And after that he sang ful loude and cleere,
And kiste his wyf, and made wantown cheere.
He was al coltissh, ful of ragerye,
And ful of jargon as a flekked pye.
The slakke skyn aboute his nekke shaketh,   1849
Whil that he sang, so chaunteth he and craketh.
But God woot what that May thoughte in hir
     herte,
Whan she hym saugh up sittynge in his sherte,
In his nyght-cappe, and with his nekke lene;
She preyseth nat his pleyyng worth a bene.
Thanne seide he thus, "My reste wol I take;
Now day is come, I may no lenger wake."   1856
And doun he leyde his heed, and sleep til
     pryme.

And afterward, whan that he saugh his tyme,
Up ryseth Januarie; but fresshe May   1859
Heeld hire chambre unto the fourthe day,
As usage is of wyves for the beste.
For every labour somtyme moot han reste,
Or elles longe may he nat endure;
This is to seyn, no lyves creature,
Be it of fyssh, or bryd, or beest, or man.   1865
    Now wol I speke of woful Damyan,
That langwissheth for love, as ye shul heere;
Therfore I speke to hym in this manere:
I seye, "O sely Damyan, allas!
Andswere to my demaunde, as in this cas.   1870
How shaltow to thy lady, fresshe May,
Telle thy wo? She wole alwey seye nay.
Eek if thou speke, she wol thy wo biwreye.
God be thyn helpe! I kan no bettre seye."
    This sike Damyan in Venus fyr   1875
So brenneth that he dyeth for desyr,
For which he putte his lyf in aventure.
No lenger myghte he in this wise endure,
But prively a penner gan he borwe,
And in a lettre wroot he al his sorwe,   1880
In manere of a compleynt or a lay,
Unto his faire, fresshe lady May;
And in a purs of sylk, heng on his sherte
He hath it put, and leyde it at his herte.   1884
    The moone, that at noon was thilke day
That Januarie hath wedded fresshe May
In two of Tawr, was into Cancre glyden;
So longe hath Mayus in hir chambre abyden,
As custume is unto thise nobles alle.
A bryde shal nat eten in the halle   1890
Til dayes foure, or thre dayes atte leeste,
Ypassed been; thanne lat hire go to feeste.
The fourthe day compleet fro noon to noon,
Whan that the heighe masse was ydoon,
In halle sit this Januarie and May,   1895
As fressh as is the brighte someres day.
And so bifel how that this goode man
Remembred hym upon this Damyan,
And seyde, "Seynte Marie! how may this be,
That Damyan entendeth nat to me?   1900
Is he ay syk, or how may this bityde?"
His squieres, whiche that stooden ther bisyde,
Excused hym by cause of his siknesse,
Which letted hym to doon his bisynesse;   1904
Noon oother cause myghte make hym tarye.
    "That me forthynketh," quod this Januarie,
"He is a gentil squier, by my trouthe!
If that he deyde, it were harm and routhe.
He is as wys, discreet, and as secree
As any man I woot of his degree,   1910
And therto manly, and eek servysable,

And for to been a thrifty man right able.
But after mete, as soone as evere I may,
I wol myself visite hym, and eek May,
To doon hym al the confort that I kan."   1915
And for that word hym blessed every man,
That of his bountee and his gentillesse
He wolde so conforten in siknesse
His squier, for it was a gentil dede.   1919
"Dame," quod this Januarie, "taak good hede,
At after-mete ye with youre wommen alle,
Whan ye han been in chambre out of this halle,
That alle ye go se this Damyan.
Dooth hym disport — he is a gentil man;
And telleth hym that I wol hym visite,   1925
Have I no thyng but rested me a lite;
And spede yow faste, for I wole abyde
Til that ye slepe faste by my syde."
And with that word he gan to hym to calle
A squier, that was marchal of his halle,   1930
And tolde hym certeyn thynges, what he wolde.
    This fresshe May hath streight hir wey
        yholde,
With alle hir wommen, unto Damyan.
Doun by his beddes syde sit she than,
Confortynge hym as goodly as she may.   1935
This Damyan, whan that his tyme he say,
In secree wise his purs and eek his bille,
In which that he ywriten hadde his wille,
Hath put into hire hand, withouten moore,
Save that he siketh wonder depe and soore,
And softely to hire right thus seyde he: 1941
"Mercy! and that ye nat discovere me,
For I am deed if that this thyng be kyd."
This purs hath she inwith hir bosom hyd,
And wente hire wey; ye gete namoore of me.
But unto Januarie ycomen is she,   1946
That on his beddes syde sit ful softe.
He taketh hire, and kisseth hire ful ofte,
And leyde hym doun to slepe, and that anon.
She feyned hire as that she moste gon   1950
Ther as ye woot that every wight moot neede;
And whan she of this bille hath taken heede,
She rente it al to cloutes atte laste,
And in the pryvee softely it caste.
    Who studieth now but faire fresshe May?
Adoun by olde Januarie she lay,   1956
That sleep til that the coughe hath hym
        awaked.
Anon he preyde hire strepen hire al naked;
He wolde of hire, he seyde, han som plesaunce,
And seyde hir clothes dide hym encombraunce,
And she obeyeth, be hire lief or looth.   1961
But lest that precious folk be with me wrooth,
How that he wroghte, I dar nat to yow telle;

Or wheither hire thoughte it paradys or helle.
But heere I lete hem werken in hir wyse   1965
Til evensong rong, and that they moste aryse.
    Were it by destynee or aventure,
Were it by influence or by nature,
Or constellacion, that in swich estaat
The hevene stood, that tyme fortunaat   1970
Was for to putte a bille of Venus werkes —
For alle thyng hath tyme, as seyn thise
        clerkes —
To any womman, for to gete hire love,
I kan nat seye; but grete God above,
That knoweth that noon act is causelees,   1975
He deme of al, for I wole holde my pees.
But sooth is this, how that this fresshe May
Hath take swich impression that day
Of pitee of this sike Damyan,
That from hire herte she ne dryve kan   1980
The remembrance for to doon hym ese.
"Certeyn," thoghte she, "whom that this thyng
        displese,
I rekke noght, for heere I hym assure
To love hym best of any creature,   1984
Though he namoore hadde than his sherte."
Lo, pitee renneth soone in gentil herte!
    Heere may ye se how excellent franchise
In wommen is, whan they hem narwe avyse.
Som tyrant is, as ther be many oon,
That hath an herte as hard as any stoon,   1990
Which wolde han lat hym sterven in the place
Wel rather than han graunted hym hire grace;
And hem rejoysen in hire crueel pryde,
And rekke nat to been an homycide.
    This gentil May, fulfilled of pitee,   1995
Right of hire hand a lettre made she,
In which she graunteth hym hire verray grace.
Ther lakketh noght, oonly but day and place,
Wher that she myghte unto his lust suffise;
For it shal be right as he wole devyse.   2000
And whan she saugh hir tyme, upon a day,
To visite this Damyan gooth May,
And sotilly this lettre doun she threste
Under his pilwe, rede it if hym leste.
She taketh hym by the hand, and harde hym
        twiste   2005
So secrely that no wight of it wiste,
And bad hym been al hool, and forth she wente
To Januarie, whan that he for hire sente.
    Up riseth Damyan the nexte morwe;
Al passed was his siknesse and his sorwe.   2010
He kembeth hym, he preyneth hym and pyketh,
He dooth al that his lady lust and lyketh;
And eek to Januarie he gooth as lowe
As evere dide a dogge for the bowe.

He is so plesant unto every man   2015
(For craft is al, whoso that do it kan)
That every wight is fayn to speke hym good;
And fully in his lady grace he stood.
Thus lete I Damyan aboute his nede,
And in my tale forth I wol procede.   2020
    Somme clerkes holden that felicitee
Stant in delit, and therfore certeyn he,
This noble Januarie, with al his myght,
In honest wyse, as longeth to a knyght,
Shoop hym to lyve ful deliciously.   2025
His housynge, his array, as honestly
To his degree was maked as a kynges.
Amonges othere of his honeste thynges,
He made a gardyn, walled al with stoon;
So fair a gardyn woot I nowher noon.   2030
For, out of doute, I verraily suppose
That he that wroot the Romance of the Rose
Ne koude of it the beautee wel devyse;
Ne Priapus ne myghte nat suffise,
Though he be god of gardyns, for to telle   2035
The beautee of the gardyn and the welle,
That stood under a laurer alwey grene.
Ful ofte tyme he Pluto and his queene,
Proserpina, and al hire fayerye,
Disporten hem and maken melodye   2040
Aboute that welle, and daunced, as men tolde.
    This noble knyght, this Januarie the olde,
Swich deyntee hath in it to walke and pleye,
That he wol no wight suffren bere the keye
Save he hymself; for of the smale wyket   2045
He baar alwey of silver a clyket,
With which, whan that hym leste, he it un-
    shette.
And whan he wolde paye his wyf hir dette
In somer seson, thider wolde he go,   2049
And May his wyf, and no wight but they two;
And thynges whiche that were nat doon
    abedde,
He in the gardyn parfourned hem and spedde.
And in this wyse, many a murye day,
Lyved this Januarie and fresshe May.
But worldly joye may nat alwey dure   2055
To Januarie, ne to no creature.
    O sodeyn hap! o thou Fortune unstable!
Lyk to the scorpion so deceyvable,
That flaterest with thyn heed whan thou wolt
    stynge;
Thy tayl is deeth, thurgh thyn envenymynge.
O brotil joye! o sweete venym queynte!   2061
O monstre, that so subtilly kanst peynte
Thy yiftes under hewe of stidefastnesse,
That thou deceyvest bothe moore and lesse!
Why hastow Januarie thus deceyved,   2065

That haddest hym for thy fulle freend re-
    ceyved?   2120
And now thou hast biraft hym bothe his yen,
For sorwe of which desireth he to dyen.
    Allas! this noble Januarie free,
Amydde his lust and his prosperitee,   2070
Is woxen blynd, and that al sodeynly.
He wepeth and he wayleth pitously;
And therwithal the fyr of jalousie,
Lest that his wyf sholde falle in som folye,
So brente his herte that he wolde fayn   2075
That som man bothe hire and hym had slayn.
For neither after his deeth, nor in his lyf,
Ne wolde he that she were love ne wyf,
But evere lyve as wydwe in clothes blake,
Soul as the turtle that lost hath hire make.   2080
But atte laste, after a month or tweye,
His sorwe gan aswage, sooth to seye;
For whan he wiste it may noon oother be,
He paciently took his adversitee,
Save, out of doute, he may nat forgoon   2085
That he nas jalous everemoore in oon;
Which jalousye it was so outrageous,
That neither in halle, n'yn noon oother hous,
Ne in noon oother place, neverthemo,
He nolde suffre hire for to ryde or go,   2090
But if that he had hond on hire alway;
For which ful ofte wepeth fresshe May,
That loveth Damyan so benyngnely
That she moot outher dyen sodeynly,
Or elles she moot han hym as hir leste.   2095
She wayteth whan hir herte wolde breste.
    Upon that oother syde Damyan
Bicomen is the sorwefulleste man
That evere was; for neither nyght ne day
Ne myghte he speke a word to fresshe May,
As to his purpos, of no swich mateere,   2101
But if that Januarie moste it heere,
That hadde an hand upon hire everemo.
But nathelees, by writyng to and fro,
And privee signes, wiste he what she mente,
And she knew eek the fyn of his entente.   2106
    O Januarie, what myghte it thee availle,
Thogh thou myghte se as fer as shippes saille?
For as good is blynd deceyved be
As to be deceyved whan a man may se.   2110
Lo, Argus, which that hadde an hondred yen,
For al that evere he koude poure or pryen,
Yet was he blent, and, God woot, so been mo,
That wenen wisly that it be nat so.
Passe over is an ese, I sey namoore.   2115
    This fresshe May, that I spak of so yoore,
In warm wex hath emprented the clyket
That Januarie bar of the smale wyket,

By which into his gardyn ofte he wente;
And Damyan, that knew al hire entente,   2120
The cliket countrefeted pryvely.
Ther nys namoore to seye, but hastily
Som wonder by this clyket shal bityde,
Which ye shul heeren, if ye wole abyde.   2124
 O noble Ovyde, ful sooth seystou, God woot,
What sleighte is it, thogh it be long and hoot,
That Love nyl fynde it out in som manere?
By Piramus and Tesbee may men leere;
Thogh they were kept ful longe streite overal,
They been accorded, rownynge thurgh a
 wal,   2130
Ther no wight koude han founde out swich a
 sleighte.
 But now to purpos: er that dayes eighte
Were passed, er the month of Juyn, bifil
That Januarie hath caught so greet a wil,   2134
Thurgh eggyng of his wyf, hym for to pleye
In his gardyn, and no wight but they tweye,
That in a morwe unto his May seith he:
"Rys up, my wyf, my love, my lady free!
The turtles voys is herd, my dowve sweete;
The wynter is goon with alle his reynes
 weete.   2140
Com forth now, with thyne eyen columbyn!
How fairer been thy brestes than is wyn!
The gardyn is enclosed al aboute;
Com forth, my white spouse! out of doute
Thou hast me wounded in myn herte, O wyf!
No spot of thee ne knew I al my lyf.   2146
Com forth, and lat us taken oure disport;
I chees thee for my wyf and my confort."
 Swiche olde lewed wordes used he.
On Damyan a signe made she,   2150
That he sholde go biforn with his cliket.
This Damyan thanne hath opened the wyket,
And in he stirte, and that in swich manere
That no wight myghte it se neither yheere,
And stille he sit under a bussh anon.   2155
 This Januarie, as blynd as is a stoon,
With Mayus in his hand, and no wight mo,
Into his fresshe gardyn is ago,
And clapte to the wyket sodeynly.
 "Now wyf," quod he, "heere nys but thou
 and I,   2160
That art the creature that I best love.
For by that Lord that sit in hevene above,
Levere ich hadde to dyen on a knyf,
Than thee offende, trewe deere wyf!
For Goddes sake, thenk how I thee chees,   2165
Noght for no coveitise, doutelees,
But oonly for the love I had to thee.
And though that I be oold, and may nat see,

Beth to me trewe, and I wol telle yow why.
Thre thynges, certes, shal ye wynne therby:
First, love of Crist, and to youreself honour,
And al myn heritage, toun and tour;   2172
I yeve it yow, maketh chartres as yow leste;
This shal be doon to-morwe er sonne reste,
So wisly God my soule brynge in blisse.   2175
I prey yow first, in covenant ye me kisse;
And though that I be jalous, wyte me noght.
Ye been so depe enprented in my thoght
That, whan that I considere youre beautee,
And therwithal the unlikly elde of me,   2180
I may nat, certes, though I sholde dye,
Forbere to been out of youre compaignye
For verray love; this is withouten doute.
Now kys me, wyf, and lat us rome aboute."
 This fresshe May, whan she thise wordes
 herde,   2185
Benyngnely to Januarie answerde,
But first and forward she bigan to wepe.
"I have," quod she, "a soule for to kepe
As wel as ye, and also myn honour,
And of my wyfhod thilke tendre flour,   2190
Which that I have assured in youre hond,
Whan that the preest to yow my body bond;
Wherfore I wole answere in this manere,
By the leve of yow, my lord so deere:
I prey to God that nevere dawe the day   2195
That I ne sterve, as foule as womman may,
If evere I do unto my kyn that shame,
Or elles I empeyre so my name,
That I be fals; and if I do that lak,
Do strepe me and put me in a sak,   2200
And in the nexte ryver do me drenche.
I am a gentil womman and no wenche.
Why speke ye thus? but men been evere un-
 trewe,
And wommen have repreve of yow ay newe.
Ye han noon oother contenance, I leeve,   2205
But speke to us of untrust and repreeve."
 And with that word she saugh wher Damyan
Sat in the bussh, and coughen she bigan,
And with hir fynger signes made she
That Damyan sholde clymbe upon a tree,   2210
That charged was with fruyt, and up he wente.
For verraily he knew al hire entente,
And every signe that she koude make,
Wel bet than Januarie, hir owene make;
For in a lettre she hadde toold hym al   2215
Of this matere, how he werchen shal.
And thus I lete hym sitte upon the pyrie,
And Januarie and May romynge ful myrie.
 Bright was the day, and blew the firmament;
Phebus hath of gold his stremes doun ysent,

To gladen every flour with his warmnesse.   2221
He was that tyme in Geminis, as I gesse,
But litel fro his declynacion
Of Cancer, Jovis exaltacion.
And so bifel, that brighte morwe-tyde,   2225
That in that gardyn, in the ferther syde,
Pluto, that is kyng of Fayerye,
And many a lady in his compaignye,
Folwynge his wyf, the queene Proserpyna,
Which that he ravysshed out of Ethna   2230
Whil that she gadered floures in the mede —
In Claudyan ye may the stories rede,
How in his grisely carte he hire fette —
This kyng of Fairye thanne adoun hym sette
Upon a bench of turves, fressh and grene,   2235
And right anon thus seyde he to his queene:
"My wyf," quod he, "ther may no wight seye
        nay;
Th'experience so preveth every day
The tresons whiche that wommen doon to man.
Ten hondred thousand [tales] tellen I kan
Notable of youre untrouthe and brotilnesse.
O Salomon, wys, and richest of richesse,   2242
Fulfild of sapience and of worldly glorie,
Ful worthy been thy wordes to memorie
To every wight that wit and reson kan.   2245
Thus preiseth he yet the bountee of man:
'Amonges a thousand men yet foond I oon,
But of wommen alle foond I noon.'
    Thus seith the kyng that knoweth youre
        wikkednesse.
And Jhesus, *filius Syrak*, as I gesse,   2250
Ne speketh of yow but seelde reverence.
A wylde fyr and corrupt pestilence
So falle upon youre bodyes yet to-nyght!
Ne se ye nat this honurable knyght,   2254
By cause, allas! that he is blynd and old,
His owene man shal make hym cokewold.
Lo, where he sit, the lechour, in the tree!
Now wol I graunten, of my magestee,
Unto this olde, blynde, worthy knyght
That he shal have ayen his eyen syght,   2260
Whan that his wyf wold doon hym vileynye.
Thanne shal he knowen al hire harlotrye,
Bothe in repreve of hire and othere mo."
    "Ye shal?" quod Proserpyne, "wol ye so?
Now by my moodres sires soule I swere   2265
That I shal yeven hire suffisant answere,
And alle wommen after, for hir sake;
That, though they be in any gilt ytake,
With face boold they shulle hemself excuse,
And bere hem doun that wolden hem accuse.
For lak of answere noon of hem shal dyen.   2271
Al hadde man seyn a thyng with bothe his yen,

Yit shul we wommen visage it hardily,
And wepe, and swere, and chyde subtilly,
So that ye men shul been as lewed as gees.   2275
    What rekketh me of youre auctoritees?
I woot wel that this Jew, this Salomon,
Foond of us wommen fooles many oon.
But though that he ne foond no good womman,
Yet hath ther founde many another man   2280
Wommen ful trewe, ful goode, and vertuous.
Witnesse on hem that dwelle in Cristes hous;
With martirdom they preved hire constance.
The Romayn geestes eek make remembrance
Of many a verray, trewe wyf also.   2285
But, sire, ne be nat wrooth, al be it so,
Though that he seyde he foond no good
        womman,
I prey yow take the sentence of the man;
He mente thus, that in sovereyn bontee
Nis noon but God, but neither he ne she.   2290
    Ey! for verray God, that nys but oon,
What make ye so muche of Salomon?
What though he made a temple, Goddes hous?
What though he were riche and glorious?
So made he eek a temple of false goddis.   2295
How myghte he do a thyng that moore for-
        bode is?
Pardee, as faire as ye his name emplastre,
He was a lecchour and an ydolastre,
And in his elde he verray God forsook;   2299
And if that God ne hadde, as seith the book,
Yspared him for his fadres sake, he sholde
Have lost his regne rather than he wolde.
I sette right noght, of al the vileynye
That ye of wommen write, a boterflye!
I am a womman, nedes moot I speke,   2305
Or elles swelle til myn herte breke.
For sithen he seyde that we been jangleresses,
As evere hool I moote brouke my tresses,
I shal nat spare, for no curteisye,   2309
To speke hym harm that wolde us vileynye."
    "Dame," quod this Pluto, "be no lenger
        wrooth;
I yeve it up! but sith I swoor myn ooth
That I wolde graunten hym his sighte ageyn,
My word shal stonde, I warne yow certeyn.
I am a kyng, it sit me noght to lye."   2315
    "And I," quod she, "a queene of Fayerye!
Hir answere shal she have, I undertake.
Lat us namoore wordes heerof make;
For sothe, I wol no lenger yow contrarie."
    Now lat us turne agayn to Januarie,   2320
That in the gardyn with his faire May
Syngeth ful murier than the papejay,
"Yow love I best, and shal, and oother noon."

So longe aboute the aleyes is he goon,
Til he was come agaynes thilke pyrie   2325
Where as this Damyan sitteth ful myrie
An heigh among the fresshe leves grene.
   This fresshe May, that is so bright and
     sheene,
Gan for to syke, and seyde, "Allas, my syde!
Now sire," quod she, "for aught that may
     bityde,   2330
I moste han of the peres that I see,
Or I moot dye, so soore longeth me
To eten of the smale peres grene.
Help, for hir love that is of hevene queene!
I telle yow wel, a womman in my plit   2335
May han to fruyt so greet an appetit
That she may dyen, but she of it have."
   "Allas!" quod he, "that I ne had heer a knave
That koude clymbe! Allas, allas," quod he,
"For I am blynd!" "Ye, sire, no fors," quod
     she;   2340
"But wolde ye vouche sauf, for Goddes sake,
The pyrie inwith youre armes for to take,
For wel I woot that ye mystruste me,
Thanne sholde I clymbe wel ynogh," quod she,
"So I my foot myghte sette upon youre
     bak."   2345
   "Certes," quod he, "theron shal be no lak,
Mighte I yow helpen with myn herte blood."
He stoupeth doun, and on his bak she stood,
And caughte hire by a twiste, and up she gooth —
Ladyes, I prey yow that ye be nat wrooth;
I kan nat glose, I am a rude man —   2351
And sodeynly anon this Damyan
Gan pullen up the smok, and in he throng.
   And whan that Pluto saugh this grete wrong,
To Januarie he gaf agayn his sighte,   2355
And made hym se as wel as evere he myghte.
And whan that he hadde caught his sighte
     agayn,
Ne was ther nevere man of thyng so fayn,
But on his wyf his thoght was everemo.
Up to the tree he caste his eyen two,   2360
And saugh that Damyan his wyf had dressed
In swich manere it may nat been expressed,
But if I wolde speke uncurteisly;
And up he yaf a roryng and a cry,   2364
As dooth the mooder whan the child shal dye:
"Out! help; allas! harrow!" he gan to crye,
"O stronge lady stoore, what dostow?"
   And she answerde, "Sire, what eyleth yow?
Have pacience and resoun in youre mynde!
I have yow holpe on bothe youre eyen blynde.

Up peril of my soule, I shal nat lyen,   2371
As me was taught, to heele with youre eyen,
Was no thyng bet, to make yow to see,
Than strugle with a man upon a tree.
God woot, I dide it in ful good entente."   2375
   "Strugle!" quod he, "ye algate in it wente!
God yeve yow bothe on shames deth to dyen!
He swyved thee, I saugh it with myne yen,
And elles be I hanged by the hals!"
   "Thanne is," quod she, "my medicyne fals;
For certeinly, if that ye myghte se,   2381
Ye wolde nat seyn thise wordes unto me.
Ye han som glymsyng, and no parfit sighte."
   "I se," quod he, "as wel as evere I myghte,
Thonked be God! with bothe myne eyen two,
And by my trouthe, me thoughte he dide thee
     so."   2386
   "Ye maze, maze, goode sire," quod she;
"This thank have I for I have maad yow see.
Allas," quod she, "that evere I was so kynde!"
   "Now, dame," quod he, "lat al passe out of
     mynde.   2390
Com doun, my lief, and if I have myssayd,
God helpe me so, as I am yvele apayd.
But, by my fader soule, I wende han seyn
How that this Damyan hadde by thee leyn,
And that thy smok hadde leyn upon his
     brest."   2395
   "Ye, sire," quod she, "ye may wene as yow
     lest.
But, sire, a man that waketh out of his sleep,
He may nat sodeynly wel taken keep
Upon a thyng, ne seen it parfitly,
Til that he be adawed verraily.   2400
Right so a man that longe hath blynd ybe,
Ne may nat sodeynly so wel yse,
First whan his sighte is newe come ageyn,
As he that hath a day or two yseyn.
Til that youre sighte ysatled be a while,   2405
Ther may ful many a sighte yow bigile.
Beth war, I prey yow; for, by hevene kyng,
Ful many a man weneth to seen a thyng,
And it is al another than it semeth.
He that mysconceyveth, he mysdemeth."   2410
And with that word she leep doun fro the tree.
   This Januarie, who is glad but he?
He kisseth hire, and clippeth hire ful ofte,
And on hire wombe he stroketh hire ful softe,
And to his palays hoom he hath hire lad.   2415
Now, goode men, I pray yow to be glad.
Thus endeth heere my tale of Januarie;
God blesse us, and his mooder Seinte Marie!

Heere is ended the Marchantes Tale of Januarie.

Epilogue to The Merchant's Tale

"Ey! Goddes mercy!" seyde oure Hooste tho,
"Now swich a wyf I pray God kepe me fro!
Lo, whiche sleightes and subtilitees   2421
In wommen been! for ay as bisy as bees
Been they, us sely men for to deceyve,
And from the soothe evere wol they weyve;
By this Marchauntes tale it preveth weel.   2425
But doutelees, as trewe as any steel
I have a wyf, though that she povre be,
But of hir tonge, a labbyng shrewe is she,
And yet she hath an heep of vices mo;

Therof no fors! lat alle swiche thynges go.   2430
But wyte ye what? In conseil be it seyd,
Me reweth soore I am unto hire teyd.
For, and I sholde rekenen every vice
Which that she hath, ywis I were to nyce;
And cause why, it sholde reported be   2435
And toold to hire of somme of this meynee, —
Of whom, it nedeth nat for to declare,
Syn wommen konnen outen swich chaffare;
And eek my wit suffiseth nat therto,
To tellen al, wherfore my tale is do."   2440

Fragment V (Group F)

Introduction to The Squire's Tale

"Squier, com neer, if it youre wille be,
And sey somwhat of love; for certes ye
Konnen theron as muche as any man."
　"Nay, sire," quod he, "but I wol seye as I kan
With hertly wyl; for I wol nat rebelle　　5
Agayn youre lust; a tale wol I telle.
Have me excused if I speke amys;
My wyl is good, and lo, my tale is this."

The Squire's Tale

Heere bigynneth the Squieres Tale.

At Sarray, in the land of Tartarye,
Ther dwelte a kyng that werreyed Russye,　10
Thurgh which ther dyde many a doughty man.
This noble kyng was cleped Cambyuskan,
Which in his tyme was of so greet renoun
That ther was nowher in no regioun
So excellent a lord in alle thyng.　　15
Hym lakked noght that longeth to a kyng.
As of the secte of which that he was born
He kepte his lay, to which that he was sworn;
And therto he was hardy, wys, and riche,
And pitous and just, alwey yliche;　　20
Sooth of his word, benigne, and honurable;
Of his corage as any centre stable;
Yong, fressh, and strong, in armes desirous
As any bacheler of al his hous.
A fair persone he was and fortunat,　　25
And kepte alwey so wel roial estat
That ther was nowher swich another man.
　This noble kyng, this Tartre Cambyuskan,
Hadde two sones on Elpheta his wyf,
Of whiche the eldeste highte Algarsyf,　　30
That oother sone was cleped Cambalo.
A doghter hadde this worthy kyng also,
That yongest was, and highte Canacee.
But for to telle yow al hir beautee,
It lyth nat in my tonge, n'yn my konnyng;
I dar nat undertake so heigh a thyng.　　36
Myn Englissh eek is insufficient.
It moste been a rethor excellent,
That koude his colours longynge for that art,
If he sholde hire discryven every part.　　40
I am noon swich, I moot speke as I kan.

And so bifel that whan this Cambyuskan
Hath twenty wynter born his diademe,
As he was wont fro yeer to yeer, I deme,
He leet the feeste of his nativitee　　45
Doon cryen thurghout Sarray his citee,
The laste Idus of March, after the yeer.
Phebus the sonne ful joly was and cleer;
For he was neigh his exaltacioun
In Martes face, and in his mansioun　　50
In Aries, the colerik hoote signe.
Ful lusty was the weder and benigne,
For which the foweles, agayn the sonne sheene,
What for the sesoun and the yonge grene,
Ful loude songen hire affecciouns.　　55
Hem semed han geten hem protecciouns
Agayn the swerd of wynter, keene and coold.
　This Cambyuskan, of which I have yow toold,
In roial vestiment sit on his deys,
With diademe, ful heighe in his paleys,　　60
And halt his feeste so solempne and so ryche
That in this world ne was ther noon it lyche;
Of which if I shal tellen al th'array,
Thanne wolde it occupie a someres day;
And eek it nedeth nat for to devyse　　65
At every cours the ordre of hire servyse.
I wol nat tellen of hir strange sewes,
Ne of hir swannes, ne of hire heronsewes.
Eek in that lond, as tellen knyghtes olde,
Ther is som mete that is ful deynte holde,　　70
That in this lond men recche of it but smal;
Ther nys no man that may reporten al.
I wol nat taryen yow, for it is pryme,

And for it is no fruyt, but los of tyme;
Unto my firste I wole have my recours. 75

    And so bifel that after the thridde cours,
Whil that this kyng sit thus in his nobleye,
Herknynge his mynstralles hir thynges pleye
Biforn hym at the bord deliciously,
In at the halle dore al sodeynly 80
Ther cam a knyght upon a steede of bras,
And in his hand a brood mirour of glas.
Upon his thombe he hadde of gold a ryng,
And by his syde a naked swerd hangyng;
And up he rideth to the heighe bord. 85
In al the halle ne was ther spoken a word
For merveille of this knyght; hym to biholde
Ful bisily they wayten, yonge and olde.

    This strange knyght, that cam thus sodeynly,
Al armed, save his heed, ful richely, 90
Saleweth kyng and queene and lordes alle,
By ordre, as they seten in the halle,
With so heigh reverence and obeisaunce,
As wel in speche as in his contenaunce,
That Gawayn, with his olde curteisye, 95
Though he were comen ayeyn out of Fairye,
Ne koude hym nat amende with a word.
And after this, biforn the heighe bord,
He with a manly voys seide his message,
After the forme used in his langage, 100
Withouten vice of silable or of lettre;
And, for his tale sholde seme the bettre,
Accordant to his wordes was his cheere,
As techeth art of speche hem that it leere.
Al be it that I kan nat sowne his stile, 105
Ne kan nat clymben over so heigh a style,
Yet seye I this, as to commune entente,
Thus muche amounteth al that evere he mente,
If it so be that I have it in mynde.

    He seyde, "The kyng of Arabe and of Inde,
My lige lord, on this solempne day 111
Saleweth yow, as he best kan and may,
And sendeth yow, in honour of youre feeste,
By me, that am al redy at youre heeste,
This steede of bras, that esily and weel 115
Kan in the space of o day natureel —
This is to seyn, in foure and twenty houres —
Wher-so yow lyst, in droghte or elles shoures,
Beren youre body into every place
To which youre herte wilneth for to pace;
Withouten wem of yow, thurgh foul or fair;
Or, if yow lyst to fleen as hye in the air 122
As dooth an egle whan hym list to soore,
This same steede shal bere yow evere moore,
Withouten harm, til ye be ther yow leste, 125
Though that ye slepen on his bak or reste,
And turne ayeyn with writhyng of a pyn.

He that it wroghte koude ful many a gyn.
He wayted many a constellacion
Er he had doon this operacion, 130
And knew ful many a seel and many a bond.

    This mirour eek, that I have in myn hond,
Hath swich a myght that men may in it see
Whan ther shal fallen any adversitee
Unto youre regne or to youreself also, 135
And openly who is youre freend or foo.

    And over al this, if any lady bright
Hath set hire herte on any maner wight,
If he be fals, she shal his tresoun see,
His newe love, and al his subtiltee, 140
So openly that ther shal no thyng hyde.
Wherfore, ageyn this lusty someres tyde,
This mirour and this ryng, that ye may see,
He hath sent to my lady Canacee,
Youre excellente doghter that is heere. 145

    The vertu of the ryng, if ye wol heere,
Is this, that if hire lust it for to were
Upon hir thombe, or in hir purs it bere,
Ther is no fowel that fleeth under the hevene
That she ne shal wel understonde his stevene,
And knowe his menyng openly and pleyn, 151
And answere hym in his langage ageyn;
And every gras that groweth upon roote
She shal eek knowe, and whom it wol do boote,
Al be his woundes never so depe and
    wyde. 155

    This naked swerd, that hangeth by my syde,
Swich vertu hath that, what man so ye smyte,
Thurgh out his armure it wole kerve and byte,
Were it as thikke as is a branched ook; 159
And what man that is wounded with the strook
Shal never be hool til that yow list, of grace,
To stroke hym with the plat in thilke place
Ther he is hurt; this is as muche to seyn,
Ye moote with the platte swerd ageyn 164
Stroke hym in the wounde, and it wol close.
This is a verray sooth, withouten glose;
It failleth nat whils it is in youre hoold."

    And whan this knyght hath thus his tale
    toold,
He rideth out of halle, and doun he lighte.
His steede, which that shoon as sonne brighte,
Stant in the court as stille as any stoon. 171
This knyght is to his chambre lad anoon,
And is unarmed, and to mete yset.

    The presentes been ful roially yfet, —
This is to seyn, the swerd and the mirour, 175
And born anon into the heighe tour
With certeine officers ordeyned therfore;
And unto Canacee this ryng is bore
Solempnely, ther she sit at the table.

But sikerly, withouten any fable,   180
The hors of bras, that may nat be remewed,
It stant as it were to the ground yglewed.
Ther may no man out of the place it dryve
For noon engyn of wyndas or polyve;
And cause why? for they kan nat the craft.   185
And therfore in the place they han it laft,
Til that the knyght hath taught hem the man-
        ere
To voyden hym, as ye shal after heere.
    Greet was the prees that swarmeth to and
        fro
To gauren on this hors that stondeth so;   190
For it so heigh was, and so brood and long,
So wel proporcioned for to been strong,
Right as it were a steede of Lumbardye,
Therwith so horsly, and so quyk of ye,
As it a gentil Poilleys courser were.   195
For certes, fro his tayl unto his ere,
Nature ne art ne koude hym nat amende
In no degree, as al the peple wende.
But everemoore hir mooste wonder was
How that it koude gon, and was of bras;   200
It was of Fairye, as the peple semed.
Diverse folk diversely they demed;
As many heddes, as manye wittes ther been.
They murmureden as dooth a swarm of been,
And maden skiles after hir fantasies,   205
Rehersynge of thise olde poetries,
And seyden it was lyk the Pegasee,
The hors that hadde wynges for to flee;
Or elles it was the Grekes hors Synon,
That broghte Troie to destruccion,   210
As men moun in thise olde geestes rede.
"Myn herte," quod oon, "is everemoore in
        drede;
I trowe som men of armes been therinne,
That shapen hem this citee for to wynne.
It were right good that al swich thyng were
        knowe."
Another rowned to his felawe lowe,   216
And seyde, "He lyeth, for it is rather lyk
An apparence ymaad by som magyk,
As jogelours pleyen at thise feestes grete."
Of sondry doutes thus they jangle and trete,
As lewed peple demeth comunly   221
Of thynges that been maad moore subtilly
Than they kan in hir lewednesse comprehende;
They demen gladly to the badder ende.
    And somme of hem wondred on the mirour,
That born was up into the maister-tour,   226
Hou men myghte in it swiche thynges se.
    Another answerde, and seyde it myghte wel
        be

Naturelly, by composiciouns
Of anglis and of slye reflexiouns,   230
And seyde that in Rome was swich oon
They speken of Alocen, and Vitulon,
And Aristotle, that writen in hir lyves
Of queynte mirours and of perspectives,
As knowen they that han hir bookes herd.   235
    And oother folk han wondred on the swerd
That wolde percen thurghout every thyng,
And fille in speche of Thelophus the kyng,
And of Achilles with his queynte spere,
For he koude with it bothe heele and dere.   240
Right in swich wise as men may with the swerd
Of which right now ye han youreselven herd.
They speken of sondry hardyng of metal,
And speke of medicynes therwithal,
And how and whanne it sholde yharded be,
Which is unknowe, algates unto me.   246
    Tho speeke they of Canacees ryng,
And seyden alle that swich a wonder thyng
Of craft of rynges herde they nevere noon,
Save that he Moyses and kyng Salomon   250
Hadde a name of konnyng in swich art.
Thus seyn the peple, and drawen hem apart.
But nathelees somme seiden that it was
Wonder to maken of fern-asshen glas,
And yet nys glas nat lyk asshen of fern;   255
But, for they han yknowen it so fern,
Therfore cesseth hir janglyng and hir wonder.
As soore wondren somme on cause of thonder,
On ebbe, on flood, on gossomer, and on myst,
And alle thyng, til that the cause is wyst.   260
Thus jangle they, and demen, and devyse,
Til that the kyng gan fro the bord aryse.
    Phebus hath laft the angle meridional,
And yet ascendynge was the beest roial,
The gentil Leon, with his Aldiran,   265
Whan that this Tartre kyng, this Cambyuskan,
Roos fro his bord, ther as he sat ful hye.
Toforn hym gooth the loude mynstralcye,
Til he cam to his chambre of paramentz,
Ther as they sownen diverse instrumentz,   270
That it is lyk an hevene for to heere.
Now dauncen lusty Venus children deere,
For in the Fyssh hir lady sat ful hye,
And looketh on hem with a freendly ye.
    This noble kyng is set upon his trone.   275
This strange knyght is fet to hym ful soone,
And on the daunce he gooth with Canacee.
Heere is the revel and the jolitee
That is nat able a dul man to devyse.   279
He moste han knowen love and his servyse,
And been a feestlych man as fressh as May,
That sholde yow devysen swich array.

Who koude telle yow the forme of daunces
So unkouthe, and swiche fresshe contenaunces.
Swich subtil lookyng and dissymulynges 285
For drede of jalouse mennes aperceyvynges?
No man but Launcelot, and he is deed.
Therfore I passe of al this lustiheed;
I sey namoore, but in this jolynesse
I lete hem, til men to the soper dresse. 290

The styward bit the spices for to hye,
And eek the wyn, in al this melodye.
The usshers and the squiers been ygoon,
The spices and the wyn is come anoon. 294
They ete and drynke; and whan this hadde an
    ende,
Unto the temple, as reson was, they wende.
The service doon, they soupen al by day.
What nedeth yow rehercen hire array?
Ech man woot wel that at a kynges feeste 299
Hath plentee to the meeste and to the leeste,
And deyntees mo than been in my knowyng.
At after-soper gooth this noble kyng
To seen this hors of bras, with al a route
Of lordes and of ladyes hym aboute. 304

Swich wondryng was ther on this hors of bras
That syn the grete sege of Troie was,
Theras men wondreden on an hors also,
Ne was ther swich a wondryng as was tho.
But fynally the kyng axeth this knyght
The vertu of this courser and the myght, 310
And preyde hym to telle his governaunce.

This hors anoon bigan to trippe and daunce,
Whan that this knyght leyde hand upon his
    reyne,
And seyde, "Sire, ther is namoore to seyne,
But, whan yow list to ryden anywhere, 315
Ye mooten trille a pyn, stant in his ere,
Which I shal telle yow bitwix us two.
Ye moote nempne hym to what place also,
Or to what contree, that yow list to ryde.
And whan ye come ther as yow list abyde, 320
Bidde hym descende, and trille another pyn,
For therin lith th'effect of al the gyn,
And he wol doun descende and doon youre
    wille,
And in that place he wol abyde stille.
Though al the world the contrarie hadde
    yswore, 325
He shal nat thennes been ydrawe ne ybore.
Or, if yow liste bidde hym thennes goon,
Trille this pyn, and he wol vanysshe anoon
Out of the sighte of every maner wight,
And come agayn, be it by day or nyght, 330
Whan that yow list to clepen hym ageyn
In swich a gyse as I shal to yow seyn

Bitwixe yow and me, and that ful soone.
Ride whan yow list, ther is namoore to doone."
Enformed whan the kyng was of that knyght,
And hath conceyved in his wit aright 336
The manere and the forme of al this thyng,
Ful glad and blithe, this noble doughty kyng
Repeireth to his revel as biforn.
The brydel is unto the tour yborn 340
And kept among his jueles leeve and deere,
The hors vanysshed, I noot in what manere,
Out of hir sighte; ye gete namoore of me.
But thus I lete in lust and jolitee
This Cambyuskan his lordes festeiynge, 345
Til wel ny the day bigan to sprynge.

Explicit prima pars.

Sequitur pars secunda.

The norice of digestioun, the sleep,
Gan on hem wynke and bad hem taken keep
That muchel drynke and labour wolde han
    reste;
And with a galpyng mouth hem alle he
    keste, 350
And seyde that it was tyme to lye adoun,
For blood was in his domynacioun.
"Cherisseth blood, natures freend," quod he.
They thanken hym galpynge, by two, by thre,
And every wight gan drawe hym to his
    reste, 355
As sleep hem bad; they tooke it for the beste.

Hire dremes shul nat now been toold for me;
Ful were hire heddes of fumositee,
That causeth dreem of which ther nys no
    charge.
They slepen til that it was pryme large, 360
The mooste part, but it were Canacee.
She was ful mesurable, as wommen be;
For of hir fader hadde she take leve
To goon to reste soone after it was eve.
Hir liste nat appalled for to be, 365
Ne on the morwe unfeestlich for to se,
And slepte hire firste sleep, and thanne awook.
For swich a joye she in hir herte took
Bothe of hir queynte ryng and hire mirour,
That twenty tyme she changed hir colour; 370
And in hire sleep, right for impressioun
Of hire mirour, she hadde a visioun.
Wherfore, er that the sonne gan up glyde,
She cleped on hir maistresse hire bisyde,
And seyde that hire liste for to ryse. 375

Thise olde wommen that been gladly wyse,
As is hire maistresse, answerde hire anon,
And seyde, "Madame, whider wil ye goon

Thus erly, for the folk been alle on reste?"
"I wol," quod she, "arise, for me leste   380
Ne lenger for to slepe, and walke aboute."
      Hire maistresse clepeth wommen a greet
            route,
And up they rysen, wel a ten or twelve;
Up riseth fresshe Canacee hireselve,   384
As rody and bright as dooth the yonge sonne,
That in the Ram is foure degrees up ronne —
Noon hyer was he whan she redy was —
And forth she walketh esily a pas,
Arrayed after the lusty seson soote
Lightly, for to pleye and walke on foote,   390
Nat but with fyve or sixe of hir meynee;
And in a trench forth in the park gooth she.
      The vapour which that fro the erthe glood
Made the sonne to seme rody and brood;
But nathelees it was so fair a sighte   395
That it made alle hire hertes for to lighte,
What for the seson and the morwenynge,
And for the foweles that she herde synge.
For right anon she wiste what they mente,
Right by hir song, and knew al hire entente.
      The knotte why that every tale is toold,   401
If it be taried til that lust be coold
Of hem that han it after herkned yoore,
The savour passeth ever lenger the moore,
For fulsomnesse of his prolixitee;   405
And by the same resoun, thynketh me,
I sholde to the knotte condescende,
And maken of hir walkyng soone an ende.
      Amydde a tree, for drye as whit as chalk,
As Canacee was pleyyng in hir walk,   410
Ther sat a faucon over hire heed ful hye,
That with a pitous voys so gan to crye
That all the wode resouned of hire cry.
Ybeten hadde she hirself so pitously
With bothe hir wynges, til the rede blood   415
Ran endelong the tree ther-as she stood.
And evere in oon she cryde alwey and shrighte,
And with hir beek hirselven so she prighte,
That ther nys tygre, ne noon so crueel beest,
That dwelleth outher in wode or in forest,   420
That nolde han wept, if that he wepe koude,
For sorwe of hire, she shrighte alwey so loude.
For ther nas nevere yet no man on lyve,
If that I koude a faucon wel discryve,
That herde of swich another of fairnesse,   425
As wel of plumage as of gentillesse
Of shap, of al that myghte yrekened be.
A faucon peregryn thanne semed she
Of fremde land; and everemoore, as she stood,
She swowneth now and now for lak of blood,
Til wel neigh is she fallen fro the tree.   431

This faire kynges doghter, Canacee,
That on hir fynger baar the queynte ryng,
Thurgh which she understood wel every thyng
That any fowel may in his leden seyn,   435
And koude answeren hym in his ledene ageyn,
Hath understonde what this faucon seyde,
And wel neigh for the routhe almoost she
            deyde.
And to the tree she gooth ful hastily,
And on this faukon looketh pitously,   440
And heeld hir lappe abrood, for wel she wiste
The faukon moste fallen fro the twiste,
Whan that it swowned next, for lak of blood.
A longe whil to wayten hire she stood,
Til atte laste she spak in this manere   445
Unto the hauk, as ye shal after heere:
      "What is the cause, if it be for to telle,
That ye be in this furial pyne of helle?"
Quod Canacee unto this hauk above.
"Is this for sorwe of deeth or los of love?   450
For, as I trowe, thise been causes two
That causen moost a gentil herte wo;
Of oother harm it nedeth nat to speke.
For ye youreself upon yourself yow wreke,
Which proveth wel that outher ire or drede   455
Moot been enchesoun of youre cruel dede,
Syn that I see noon oother wight yow chace.
For love of God, as dooth youreselven grace,
Or what may been youre help? for west nor est
Ne saugh I nevere er now no bryd ne beest
That ferde with hymself so pitously.   461
Ye sle me with youre sorwe verraily,
I have of yow so greet compassioun.
For Goddes love, com fro the tree adoun;
And as I am a kynges doghter trewe,   465
If that I verraily the cause knewe
Of youre disese, if it lay in my myght,
I wolde amenden it er that it were nyght,
As wisly helpe me grete God of kynde!
And herbes shal I right ynowe yfynde   470
To heel with youre hurtes hastily."
      Tho shrighte this faucon yet moore pitously
Than ever she dide, and fil to grounde anon,
And lith aswowne, deed and lyk a stoon,
Til Canacee hath in hire lappe hire take   475
Unto the tyme she gan of swough awake.
And after that she of hir swough gan breyde,
Right in hir haukes ledene thus she seyde:
"That pitee renneth soone in gentil herte,
Feelynge his similitude in peynes smerte,   480
Is preved alday, as men may it see,
As wel by werk as by auctoritee;
For gentil herte kitheth gentillesse.
I se wel that ye han of my distresse

Compassion, my faire Canacee,   485
Of verray wommanly benignytee
That Nature in youre principles hath set.
But for noon hope for to fare the bet,
But for to obeye unto youre herte free,
And for to maken othere be war by me,   490
As by the whelp chasted is the leon,
Right for that cause and that conclusion,
Whil that I have a leyser and a space,
Myn harm I wol confessen er I pace."
    And evere, whil that oon hir sorwe tolde,   495
That oother weep as she to water wolde,
Til that the faucon bad hire to be stille,
And, with a syk, right thus she seyde hir wille:
"Ther I was bred — allas, that ilke day! —
And fostred in a roche of marbul gray   500
So tendrely that no thyng eyled me,
I nyste nat what was adversitee,
Til I koude flee ful hye under the sky.
Tho dwelte a tercelet me faste by,
That semed welle of alle gentillesse;   505
Al were he ful of treson and falsnesse,
It was so wrapped under humble cheere,
And under hewe of trouthe in swich manere,
Under plesance, and under bisy peyne,
That no wight koude han wend he koude feyne,
So depe in greyn he dyed his coloures.   511
Right as a serpent hit hym under floures
Til he may seen his tyme for to byte,
Right so this god of loves ypocryte
Dooth so his cerymonyes and obeisaunces,   515
And kepeth in semblaunt alle his observaunces
That sownen into gentillesse of love.
As in a toumbe is al the faire above,
And under is the corps, swich as ye woot,
Swich was this ypocrite, bothe coold and hoot.
And in this wise he served his entente,   521
That, save the feend, noon wiste what he
          mente,
Til he so longe hadde wopen and compleyned,
And many a yeer his service to me feyned,
Til that myn herte, to pitous and to nyce,   525
Al innocent of his crouned malice,
Forfered of his deeth, as thoughte me,
Upon his othes and his seuretee,
Graunted hym love, on this condicioun,
That everemoore myn honour and renoun   530
Were saved, bothe privee and apert;
This is to seyn, that after his desert,
I yaf hym al myn herte and al my thoght —
God woot and he, that ootherwise noght —   534
And took his herte in chaunge of myn for ay.
But sooth is seyd, goon sithen many a day,
'A trewe wight and a theef thenken nat oon.'

And whan he saugh the thyng so fer ygoon
That I hadde graunted hym fully my love,
In swich a gyse as I have seyd above,   540
And yeven hym my trewe herte as free
As he swoor he yaf his herte to me;
Anon this tigre, ful of doublenesse,
Fil on his knees with so devout humblesse,
With so heigh reverence, and, as by his cheere,
So lyk a gentil lovere of manere,   546
So ravysshed, as it semed, for the joye,
That nevere Jason ne Parys of Troye —
Jason? certes, ne noon oother man
Syn Lameth was, that alderfirst bigan   550
To loven two, as writen folk biforn —
Ne nevere, syn the firste man was born,
Ne koude man, by twenty thousand part,
Countrefete the sophymes of his art,
Ne were worthy unbokelen his galoche,   555
Ther doublenesse or feynyng sholde approche,
Ne so koude thonke a wight as he dide me!
His manere was an hevene for to see
Til any womman, were she never so wys,
So peynted he and kembde at point-devys   560
As wel his wordes as his contenaunce.
And I so loved hym for his obeisaunce,
And for the trouthe I demed in his herte,
That if so were that any thyng hym smerte,
Al were it never so lite, and I it wiste,   565
Me thoughte I felte deeth myn herte twiste.
And shortly, so ferforth this thyng is went,
That my wyl was his willes instrument;
This is to seyn, my wyl obeyed his wyl
In alle thyng, as fer as reson fil,   570
Kepynge the boundes of my worshipe evere.
Ne nevere hadde I thyng so lief, ne levere,
As hym, God woot! ne nevere shal namo.
    This laste lenger than a yeer or two,
That I supposed of hym noght but good.   575
But finally, thus atte laste it stood,
That Fortune wolde that he moste twynne
Out of that place which that I was inne.
Wher me was wo, that is no questioun;
I kan nat make of it discripsioun;   580
For o thyng dar I tellen boldely,
I knowe what is the peyne of deeth therby;
Swich harm I felte for he ne myghte bileve.
So on a day of me he took his leve,
So sorwefully eek that I wende verraily   585
That he had felt as muche harm as I,
Whan that I herde hym speke, and saugh his
          hewe.
But nathelees, I thoughte he was so trewe,
And eek that he repaire sholde ageyn
Withinne a litel while, sooth to seyn;   59c

And resoun wolde eek that he moste go
For his honour, as ofte it happeth so,
That I made vertu of necessitee,
And took it wel, syn that it moste be.   594
As I best myghte, I hidde fro hym my sorwe,
And took hym by the hond, Seint John to
    borwe,
And seyde hym thus: 'Lo, I am youres al;
Beth swich as I to yow have been and shal.'
What he answerde, it nedeth noght reherce;
Who kan sey bet than he, who kan do
    werse?   600
Whan he hath al wel seyd, thanne hath he
    doon.
'Therfore bihoveth hire a ful long spoon
That shal ete with a feend,' thus herde I seye.
So atte laste he moste forth his weye,   604
And forth he fleeth til he cam ther hym leste.
Whan it cam hym to purpos for to reste,
I trowe he hadde thilke text in mynde,
That 'alle thyng, repeirynge to his kynde,
Gladeth hymself;' thus seyn men, as I gesse.
Men loven of propre kynde newefangelnesse,
As briddes doon that men in cages fede.   611
For though thou nyght and day take of hem
    hede,
And strawe hir cage faire and softe as silk,
And yeve hem sugre, hony, breed and milk,
Yet right anon as that his dore is uppe,   615
He with his feet wol spurne adoun his cuppe,
And to the wode he wole, and wormes ete;
So newefangel been they of hire mete,
And loven novelries of propre kynde;
No gentillesse of blood ne may hem bynde.
    So ferde this tercelet, allas the day!   621
Though he were gentil born, and fressh and
    gay,
And goodlich for to seen, and humble and free,
He saugh upon a tyme a kyte flee,
And sodeynly he loved this kyte so   625
That al his love is clene fro me ago;
And hath his trouthe falsed in this wyse.
Thus hath the kyte my love in hire servyse,
And I am lorn withouten remedie!"
And with that word this faucon gan to crie,
And swowned eft in Canacees barm.   631
    Greet was the sorwe for the haukes harm
That Canacee and alle hir wommen made;
They nyste hou they myghte the faucon glade.
But Canacee hom bereth hire in hir lappe,   635
And softely in plastres gan hire wrappe,
Ther as she with hire beek hadde hurt hirselve.
Now kan nat Canacee but herbes delve
Out of the ground, and make salves newe

Of herbes preciouse and fyne of hewe,   640
To heelen with this hauk. Fro day to nyght
She dooth hire bisynesse and al hire myght,
And by hire beddes heed she made a mewe,
And covered it with veluettes blewe,   644
In signe of trouthe that is in wommen sene.
And al withoute, the mewe is peynted grene,
In which were peynted alle thise false fowles,
As ben thise tidyves, tercelettes, and owles;
Right for despit were peynted hem bisyde,
Pyes, on hem for to crie and chyde.   650
    Thus lete I Canacee hir hauk kepyng;
I wol namoore as now speke of hir ryng,
Til it come eft to purpos for to seyn
How that this faucon gat hire love ageyn
Repentant, as the storie telleth us,   655
By mediacion of Cambalus,
The kynges sone, of which that I yow tolde.
But hennesforth I wol my proces holde
To speken of aventures and of batailles,
That nevere yet was herd so grete mervailles.
    First wol I telle yow of Cambyuskan,   661
That in his tyme many a citee wan;
And after wol I speke of Algarsif,
How that he wan Theodora to his wif,
For whom ful ofte in greet peril he was,   665
Ne hadde he ben holpen by the steede of bras;
And after wol I speke of Cambalo,
That faught in lystes with the bretheren two
For Canacee er that he myghte hire wynne.
And ther I lefte I wol ayeyn bigynne.   670

         Explicit secunda pars.

         Incipit pars tercia.

Appollo whirleth up his chaar so hye,
Til that the god Mercurius hous, the slye —
. . . .

Heere folwen the wordes of the
Frankeleyn to the Squier, and the
wordes of the Hoost to the Frankeleyn.

"In feith, Squier, thow hast thee wel yquit
And gentilly. I preise wel thy wit,"   674
Quod the Frankeleyn, "considerynge thy
    yowthe,
So feelyngly thou spekest, sire, I allow the!
As to my doom, ther is noon that is heere
Of eloquence that shal be thy peere,
If that thou lyve; God yeve thee good chaunce,
And in vertu sende thee continuaunce!   680
For of thy speche I have greet deyntee.

I have a sone, and by the Trinitee,
I hadde levere than twenty pound worth lond,
Though it right now were fallen in myn hond,
He were a man of swich discrecioun   685
As that ye been! Fy on possessioun,
But if a man be vertuous withal!
I have my sone snybbed, and yet shal,
For he to vertu listeth nat entende;
But for to pleye at dees, and to despende   690
And lese al that he hath, is his usage.
And he hath levere talken with a page
Than to comune with any gentil wight
Where he myghte lerne gentillesse aright."
   "Straw for youre gentillesse!" quod oure
   Hoost.   695

"What, Frankeleyn! pardee, sire, wel thou
   woost
That ech of yow moot tellen atte leste
A tale or two, or breken his biheste."
   "That knowe I wel, sire," quod the Frank-
   eleyn.
"I prey yow, haveth me nat in desdeyn,   700
Though to this man I speke a word or two."
   "Telle on thy tale withouten wordes mo."
   "Gladly, sire Hoost," quod he, "I wole obeye
Unto your wyl; now herkneth what I seye.
I wol yow nat contrarien in no wyse   705
As fer as that my wittes wol suffyse.
I prey to God that it may plesen yow;
Thanne woot I wel that it is good ynow."

The Franklin's Prologue

The Prologe of the Frankeleyns Tale.

Thise olde gentil Britouns in hir dayes
Of diverse aventures maden layes,   710
Rymeyed in hir firste Briton tonge;
Whiche layes with hir instrumentz they
   songe,
Or elles redden hem for hir plesaunce,
And oon of hem have I in remembraunce,
Which I shal seyn with good wyl as I kan.   715
   But, sires, by cause I am a burel man,
At my bigynnyng first I yow biseche,
Have me excused of my rude speche.

I lerned nevere rethorik, certeyn;
Thyng that I speke, it moot be bare and
   pleyn.   720
I sleep nevere on the Mount of Pernaso,
Ne lerned Marcus Tullius Scithero.
Colours ne knowe I none, withouten drede,
But swiche colours as growen in the mede,
Or elles swiche as men dye or peynte.   725
Colours of rethoryk been to me queynte;
My spirit feeleth noght of swich mateere.
But if yow list, my tale shul ye heere.

The Franklin's Tale

Here bigynneth the Frankeleyns Tale.

In Armorik, that called is Britayne,
Ther was a knyght that loved and dide his
   payne   730
To serve a lady in his beste wise;
And many a labour, many a greet emprise
He for his lady wroghte, er she were wonne.
For she was oon the faireste under sonne,
And eek therto comen of so heigh kynrede   735
That wel unnethes dorste this knyght, for
   drede,

Telle hire his wo, his peyne, and his distresse.
But atte laste she, for his worthynesse,
And namely for his meke obeysaunce,
Hath swich a pitee caught of his penaunce
That pryvely she fil of his accord   741
To take hym for hir housbonde and hir lord,
Of swich lordshipe as men han over hir wyves.
And for to lede the moore in blisse hir lyves,
Of his free wyl he swoor hire as a knyght   745
That nevere in al his lyf he, day ne nyght,

Ne sholde upon hym take no maistrie
Agayn hir wyl, ne kithe hire jalousie,
But hire obeye, and folwe hir wyl in al,
As any lovere to his lady shal,   750
Save that the name of soveraynetee,
That wolde he have for shame of his degree.
   She thanked hym, and with ful greet humblesse
She seyde, "Sire, sith of youre gentillesse
Ye profre me to have so large a reyne,   755
Ne wolde nevere God bitwixe us tweyne,
As in my gilt, were outher werre or stryf.
Sire, I wol be youre humble trewe wyf;
Have heer my trouthe, til that myn herte
    breste."
Thus been they bothe in quiete and in reste.
   For o thyng, sires, saufly dar I seye,   761
That freendes everych oother moot obeye,
If they wol longe holden compaignye.
Love wol nat been constreyned by maistrye.
Whan maistrie comth, the God of Love anon
Beteth his wynges, and farewel, he is gon!   766
Love is a thyng as any spirit free.
Wommen, of kynde, desiren libertee,
And nat to been constreyned as a thral;
And so doon men, if I sooth seyen shal.   770
Looke who that is moost pacient in love,
He is at his avantage al above.
Pacience is an heigh vertu, certeyn,
For it venquysseth, as thise clerkes seyn,
Thynges that rigour sholde nevere atteyne.   775
For every word men may nat chide or pleyne.
Lerneth to suffre, or elles, so moot I goon,
Ye shul it lerne, wher so ye wole or noon;
For in this world, certein, ther no wight is
That he ne dooth or seith somtyme amys.   780
Ire, siknesse, or constellacioun,
Wyn, wo, or chaungynge of complexioun
Causeth ful ofte to doon amys or speken.
On every wrong a man may nat be wreken.
After the tyme moste be temperaunce   785
To every wight that kan on governaunce.
And therfore hath this wise, worthy knyght,
To lyve in ese, suffrance hire bihight,
And she to hym ful wisly gan to swere   789
That nevere sholde ther be defaute in here.
   Heere may men seen an humble, wys accord;
Thus hath she take hir servant and hir lord, —
Servant in love, and lord in mariage.
Thanne was he bothe in lordshipe and servage.
Servage? nay, but in lordshipe above,   795
Sith he hath bothe his lady and his love;
His lady, certes, and his wyf also,
The which that lawe of love acordeth to.

And whan he was in this prosperitee,   799
Hoom with his wyf he gooth to his contree,
Nat fer fro Pedmark, ther his dwellyng was,
Where as he lyveth in blisse and in solas.
   Who koude telle, but he hadde wedded be,
The joye, the ese, and the prosperitee
That is bitwixe an housbonde and his wyf?
A yeer and moore lasted this blisful lyf,   806
Til that the knyght of which I speke of thus,
That of Kayrrud was cleped Arveragus,
Shoop hym to goon and dwelle a yeer or tweyne
In Engelond, that cleped was eek Briteyne,
To seke in armes worshipe and honour;   811
For al his lust he sette in swich labour;
And dwelled there two yeer, the book seith
    thus.
   Now wol I stynten of this Arveragus,
And speken I wole of Dorigen his wyf,   815
That loveth hire housbonde as hire hertes lyf.
For his absence wepeth she and siketh,
As doon thise noble wyves whan hem liketh.
She moorneth, waketh, wayleth, fasteth, pleyneth;
Desir of his presence hire so destreyneth   820
That al this wyde world she sette at noght.
Hire freendes, whiche that knewe hir hevy
    thoght,
Conforten hire in al that ever they may.
They prechen hire, they telle hire nyght and
    day
That causelees she sleeth hirself, allas!   825
And every confort possible in this cas
They doon to hire with al hire bisynesse,
Al for to make hire leve hire hevynesse.
   By proces, as ye knowen everichoon,
Men may so longe graven in a stoon   830
Til som figure therinne emprented be.
So longe han they conforted hire, til she
Receyved hath, by hope and by resoun,
The emprentyng of hire consolacioun,
Thurgh which hir grete sorwe gan aswage;   835
She may nat alwey duren in swich rage.
   And eek Arveragus, in al this care,
Hath sent hire lettres hoom of his welfare,
And that he wol come hastily agayn;
Or elles hadde this sorwe hir herte slayn.   840
   Hire freendes sawe hir sorwe gan to slake,
And preyde hire on knees, for Goddes sake,
To come and romen hire in compaignye,
Awey to dryve hire derke fantasye.
And finally she graunted that requeste,   845
For wel she saugh that it was for the beste.
   Now stood hire castel faste by the see,
And often with hire freendes walketh shee,

Hire to disporte, upon the bank an heigh,
Where as she many a ship and barge seigh
Seillynge hir cours, where as hem liste go. 851
But thanne was that a parcel of hire wo,
For to hirself ful ofte, "Allas!" seith she,
"Is ther no ship, of so manye as I se,
Wol bryngen hom my lord? Thanne were myn
      herte 855
Al warisshed of his bittre peynes smerte."
    Another tyme ther wolde she sitte and
      thynke,
And caste hir eyen dounward fro the brynke.
But whan she saugh the grisly rokkes blake,
For verray feere so wolde hir herte quake 860
That on hire feet she myghte hire noght sus-
      tene.
Thanne wolde she sitte adoun upon the grene,
And pitously into the see biholde,
And seyn right thus, with sorweful sikes colde:
    "Eterne God, that thurgh thy purveiaunce
Ledest the world by certein governaunce, 866
In ydel, as men seyn, ye no thyng make.
But, Lord, thise grisly feendly rokkes blake,
That semen rather a foul confusion
Of werk than any fair creacion 870
Of swich a parfit wys God and a stable,
Why han ye wroght this werk unresonable?
For by this werk, south, north, ne west, ne eest,
Ther nys yfostred man, ne bryd, ne beest;
It dooth no good, to my wit, but anoyeth. 875
Se ye nat, Lord, how mankynde it destroyeth?
An hundred thousand bodyes of mankynde
Han rokkes slayn, al be they nat in mynde,
Which mankynde is so fair part of thy werk
That thou it madest lyk to thyn owene merk.
Thanne semed it ye hadde a greet chiertee 881
Toward mankynde; but how thanne may it bee
That ye swiche meenes make it to destroyen,
Whiche meenes do no good, but evere anoyen?
I woot wel clerkes wol seyn as hem leste, 885
By argumentz, that al is for the beste,
Though I ne kan the causes nat yknowe.
But thilke God that made wynd to blowe
As kepe my lord! this my conclusion.
To clerkes lete I al disputison. 890
But wolde God that alle thise rokkes blake
Were sonken into helle for his sake!
Thise rokkes sleen myn herte for the feere."
Thus wolde she seyn, with many a pitous teere.
    Hire freendes sawe that it was no disport
To romen by the see, but disconfort, 896
And shopen for to pleyen somwher elles.
They leden hire by ryveres and by welles,
And eek in othere places delitables;

They dauncen, and they pleyen at ches and
      tables. 900
    So on a day, right in the morwe-tyde,
Unto a gardyn that was ther bisyde,
In which that they hadde maad hir ordinaunce
Of vitaille and of oother purveiaunce,
They goon and pleye hem al the longe day.
And this was on the sixte morwe of May, 906
Which May hadde peynted with his softe
      shoures
This gardyn ful of leves and of floures;
And craft of mannes hand so curiously
Arrayed hadde this gardyn, trewely, 910
That nevere was ther gardyn of swich prys,
But if it were the verray paradys.
The odour of floures and the fresshe sighte
Wolde han maked any herte lighte
That evere was born, but if to greet siknesse,
Or to greet sorwe, helde it in distresse; 916
So ful it was of beautee with plesaunce.
At after-dyner gonne they to daunce,
And synge also, save Dorigen allone,
Which made alwey hir compleint and hir
      moone, 920
For she ne saugh hym on the daunce go
That was hir housbonde and hir love also.
But nathelees she moste a tyme abyde,
And with good hope lete hir sorwe slyde.
    Upon this daunce, amonges othere men, 925
Daunced a squier biforn Dorigen,
That fressher was and jolyer of array,
As to my doom, than is the month of May.
He syngeth, daunceth, passynge any man
That is, or was, sith that the world bigan. 930
Therwith he was, if men sholde hym discryve,
Oon of the beste farynge man on lyve;
Yong, strong, right vertuous, and riche, and
      wys,
And wel biloved, and holden in greet prys.
And shortly, if the sothe I tellen shal, 935
Unwityng of this Dorigen at al,
This lusty squier, servant to Venus,
Which that ycleped was Aurelius,
Hadde loved hire best of any creature
Two yeer and moore, as was his aventure, 940
But nevere dorste he tellen hire his grevaunce.
Withouten coppe he drank al his penaunce.
He was despeyred; no thyng dorste he seye,
Save in his songes somwhat wolde he wreye
His wo, as in a general compleynyng; 945
He seyde he lovede, and was biloved no thyng.
Of swich matere made he manye layes,
Songes, compleintes, roundels, virelayes,
How that he dorste nat his sorwe telle, 949

But langwissheth as a furye dooth in helle;
And dye he moste, he seyde, as dide Ekko
For Narcisus, that dorste nat telle hir wo.
In oother manere than ye heere me seye,
Ne dorste he nat to hire his wo biwreye,   954
Save that, paraventure, somtyme at daunces,
Ther yonge folk kepen hir observaunces,
It may wel be he looked on hir face
In swich a wise as man that asketh grace;
But nothyng wiste she of his entente.
Nathelees it happed, er they thennes wente,
By cause that he was hire neighebour,   961
And was a man of worshipe and honour,
And hadde yknowen hym of tyme yoore,
They fille in speche; and forth, moore and
    moore,
Unto his purpos drough Aurelius,   965
And whan he saugh his tyme, he seyde thus:
    "Madame," quod he, "by God that this world
    made,
So that I wiste it myghte youre herte glade,
I wolde that day that youre Arveragus
Wente over the see, that I, Aurelius,   970
Hadde went ther nevere I sholde have come
    agayn.
For wel I woot my servyce is in vayn;
My gerdon is but brestyng of myn herte.
Madame, reweth upon my peynes smerte;
For with a word ye may me sleen or save.   975
Heere at youre feet God wolde that I were
    grave!
I ne have as now no leyser moore to seye;
Have mercy, sweete, or ye wol do me deye!"
    She gan to looke upon Aurelius: 979
"Is this youre wyl," quod she, "and sey ye thus?
Nevere erst," quod she, "ne wiste I what ye
    mente.
But now, Aurelie, I knowe youre entente,
By thilke God that yaf me soule and lyf,
Ne shal I nevere been untrewe wyf   985
In word ne werk, as fer as I have wit;
I wol been his to whom that I am knyt.
Taak this for fynal answere as of me."
But after that in pley thus seyde she:
    "Aurelie," quod she, "by heighe God above,
Yet wolde I graunte yow to been youre love,
Syn I yow se so pitously complayne.   991
Looke what day that endelong Britayne
Ye remoeve alle the rokkes, stoon by stoon,
That they ne lette ship ne boot to goon, —
I seye, whan ye han maad the coost so clene
Of rokkes that ther nys no stoon ysene,   996
Thanne wol I love yow best of any man,
Have heer my trouthe, in al that evere I kan."

"Is ther noon oother grace in yow?" quod he.
"No, by that Lord," quod she, "that maked
    me!   1000
For wel I woot that it shal never bityde.
Lat swiche folies out of youre herte slyde.
What deyntee sholde a man han in his lyf
For to go love another mannes wyf,
That hath hir body whan so that hym liketh?"
    Aurelius ful ofte soore siketh;   1006
Wo was Aurelie whan that he this herde,
And with a sorweful herte he thus answerde:
    "Madame," quod he, "this were an inpos-
    sible!
Thanne moot I dye of sodeyn deth horrible."
And with that word he turned hym anon.   1011
Tho coome hir othere freendes many oon,
And in the aleyes romeden up and doun,
And nothyng wiste of this conclusioun,
But sodeynly bigonne revel newe   1015
Til that the brighte sonne loste his hewe;
For th'orisonte hath reft the sonne his lyght, —
This is as muche to seye as it was nyght! —
And hoom they goon in joye and in solas,
Save oonly wrecche Aurelius, allas!   1020
He to his hous is goon with sorweful herte.
He seeth he may nat fro his deeth asterte;
Hym semed that he felte his herte colde.
Up to the hevene his handes he gan holde,
And on his knowes bare he sette hym doun,
And in his ravyng seyde his orisoun.   1026
For verray wo out of his wit he breyde.
He nyste what he spak, but thus he seyde;
With pitous herte his pleynt hath he bigonne
Unto the goddes, and first unto the sonne: 1030
    He seyde, "Appollo, god and governour
Of every plaunte, herbe, tree, and flour,
That yevest, after thy declinacion,
To ech of hem his tyme and his seson,
As thyn herberwe chaungeth lowe or heighe,
Lord Phebus, cast thy merciable eighe   1036
On wrecche Aurelie, which that am but lorn.
Lo, lord! my lady hath my deeth ysworn
Withoute gilt, but thy benignytee
Upon my dedly herte have som pitee.   1040
For wel I woot, lord Phebus, if yow lest,
Ye may me helpen, save my lady, best.
Now voucheth sauf that I may yow devyse
How that I may been holpen and in what wyse.
    Youre blisful suster, Lucina the sheene,   1045
That of the see is chief goddesse and queene
(Though Neptunus have deitee in the see,
Yet emperisse aboven hym is she),
Ye knowen wel, lord, that right as hir desir
Is to be quyked and lighted of youre fir,   1050

For which she folweth yow ful bisily,
Right so the see desireth naturelly
To folwen hire, as she that is goddesse
Bothe in the see and ryveres moore and lesse.
Wherfore, lord Phebus, this is my requeste —
Do this miracle, or do myn herte breste —   1056
That now next at this opposicion
Which in the signe shal be of the Leon,
As preieth hire so greet a flood to brynge   1059
That fyve fadme at the leeste it oversprynge
The hyeste rokke in Armorik Briteyne;
And lat this flood endure yeres tweyne.
Thanne certes to my lady may I seye,
'Holdeth youre heste, the rokkes been aweye.'
    Lord Phebus, dooth this miracle for me.   1065
Preye hire she go no faster cours than ye;
I seye, preyeth your suster that she go
No faster cours than ye thise yeres two.
Thanne shal she been evene atte fulle alway,
And spryng flood laste bothe nyght and day.
And but she vouche sauf in swich manere   1071
To graunte me my sovereyn lady deere,
Prey hire to synken every rok adoun
Into hir owene dirke regioun
Under the ground, ther Pluto dwelleth inne,
Or nevere mo shal I my lady wynne.   1076
Thy temple in Delphos wol I barefoot seke.
Lord Phebus, se the teeris on my cheke,
And of my peyne have som compassioun."
And with that word in swowne he fil adoun,
And longe tyme he lay forth in a traunce.   1081
    His brother, which that knew of his pen-
        aunce,
Up caughte hym, and to bedde he hath hym
        broght.
Dispeyred in this torment and this thoght
Lete I this woful creature lye;   1085
Chese he, for me, wheither he wol lyve or dye.
    Arveragus, with heele and greet honour,
As he that was of chivalrie the flour,
Is comen hoom, and othere worthy men.
O blisful artow now, thou Dorigen,   1090
That hast thy lusty housbonde in thyne armes,
The fresshe knyght, the worthy man of armes,
That loveth thee as his owene hertes lyf.
No thyng list hym to been ymaginatyf,
If any wight hadde spoke, whil he was oute,
To hire of love; he hadde of it no doute.   1096
He noght entendeth to no swich mateere,
But daunceth, justeth, maketh hire good
        cheere;
And thus in joye and blisse I lete hem dwelle,
And of the sike Aurelius wol I telle.   1100
    In langour and in torment furyus

Two yeer and moore lay wrecche Aurelyus,
Er any foot he myghte on erthe gon;
Ne confort in this tyme hadde he noon,
Save of his brother, which that was a clerk;
He knew of al this wo and al this werk;   1106
For to noon oother creature, certeyn,
Of this matere he dorste no word seyn.
Under his brest he baar it moore secree
Than evere dide Pamphilus for Galathee.   1110
His brest was hool, withoute for to sene,
But in his herte ay was the arwe kene.
And wel ye knowe that of a sursanure
In surgerye is perilous the cure,
But men myghte touche the arwe, or come
        therby.   1115
His brother weep and wayled pryvely,
Til atte laste hym fil in remembraunce,
That whiles he was at Orliens in Fraunce,
As yonge clerkes, that been lykerous
To reden artes that been curious,   1120
Seken in every halke and every herne
Particuler sciences for to lerne —
He hym remembred that, upon a day,
At Orliens in studie a book he say
Of magyk natureel, which his felawe,   1125
That was that tyme a bacheler of lawe,
Al were he ther to lerne another craft,
Hadde prively upon his desk ylaft;
Which book spak muchel of the operaciouns
Touchynge the eighte and twenty mansiouns
That longen to the moone, and swich folye
As in oure dayes is nat worth a flye, —   1132
For hooly chirches feith in oure bileve
Ne suffreth noon illusioun us to greve.
And whan this book was in his remembraunce,
Anon for joye his herte gan to daunce,   1136
And to hymself he seyde pryvely:
"My brother shal be warisshed hastily;
For I am siker that ther be sciences   1139
By whiche men make diverse apparences,
Swiche as thise subtile tregetoures pleye.
For ofte at feestes have I wel herd seye
That tregetours, withinne an halle large,
Have maad come in a water and a barge,
And in the halle rowen up and doun.   1145
Somtyme hath semed come a grym leoun;
And somtyme floures sprynge as in a mede;
Somtyme a vyne, and grapes white and rede;
Somtyme a castel, al of lym and stoon;
And whan hem lyked, voyded it anon.   1150
Thus semed it to every mannes sighte.
    Now thanne conclude I thus, that if I myghte
At Orliens som oold felawe yfynde
That hadde thise moones mansions in mynde,

Or oother magyk natureel above,   1155
He sholde wel make my brother han his love.
For with an apparence a clerk may make,
To mannes sighte, that alle the rokkes blake
Of Britaigne weren yvoyded everichon,   1159
And shippes by the brynke comen and gon,
And in swich forme enduren a wowke or two.
Thanne were my brother warisshed of his wo;
Thanne moste she nedes holden hire biheste,
Or elles he shal shame hire atte leeste."
    What sholde I make a lenger tale of this?
Unto his brotheres bed he comen is,   1166
And swich confort he yaf hym for to gon
To Orliens that he up stirte anon,
And on his wey forthward thanne is he fare
In hope for to been lissed of his care.   1170
    Whan they were come almoost to that citee,
But if it were a two furlong or thre,
A yong clerk romynge by hymself they mette,
Which that in Latyn thriftily hem grette,
And after that he seyde a wonder thyng: 1175
"I knowe," quod he, "the cause of youre com-
        yng."
And er they ferther any foote wente,
He tolde hem al that was in hire entente.
    This Briton clerk hym asked of felawes   1179
The whiche that he had knowe in olde dawes,
And he answerde hym that they dede were,
For which he weep ful ofte many a teere.
    Doun of his hors Aurelius lighte anon,
And with this magicien forth is he gon   1184
Hoom to his hous, and maden hem wel at ese.
Hem lakked no vitaille that myghte hem plese.
So wel arrayed hous as ther was oon
Aurelius in his lyf saugh nevere noon.
    He shewed hym, er he wente to sopeer,
Forestes, parkes ful of wilde deer;   1190
Ther saugh he hertes with hir hornes hye,
The gretteste that evere were seyn with ye.
He saugh of hem an hondred slayn with
        houndes,
And somme with arwes blede of bittre
        woundes.
He saugh, whan voyded were thise wilde deer,
Thise fauconers upon a fair ryver,   1196
That with hir haukes han the heron slayn.
    Tho saugh he knyghtes justyng in a playn;
And after this he dide hym swich plesaunce
That he hym shewed his lady on a daunce,
On which hymself he daunced, as hym
        thoughte.   1201
And whan this maister that this magyk
        wroughte
Saugh it was tyme, he clapte his handes two,

And farewel! al oure revel was ago.   1204
And yet remoeved they nevere out of the hous,
Whil they saugh al this sighte merveillous,
But in his studie, ther as his bookes be,
They seten stille, and no wight but they thre.
    To hym this maister called his squier,
And seyde hym thus: "Is redy oure soper?
Almoost an houre it is, I undertake,   1211
Sith I yow bad oure soper for to make,
Whan that thise worthy men wenten with me
Into my studie, ther as my bookes be."
    "Sire," quod this squier, "whan it liketh yow,
It is al redy, though ye wol right now."   1216
"Go we thanne soupe," quod he, "as for the
        beste.
Thise amorous folk somtyme moote han hir
        reste."
    At after-soper fille they in tretee
What somme sholde this maistres gerdon be,
To remoeven alle the rokkes of Britayne,   1221
And eek from Gerounde to the mouth of Sayne.
    He made it straunge, and swoor, so God hym
        save,
Lasse than a thousand pound he wolde nat
        have,
Ne gladly for that somme he wolde nat goon.
    Aurelius, with blisful herte anoon,   1226
Answerde thus: "Fy on a thousand pound!
This wyde world, which that men seye is
        round,
I wolde it yeve, if I were lord of it.
This bargayn is ful dryve, for we been knyt.
Ye shal be payed trewely, by my trouthe!   1231
But looketh now, for no necligence or slouthe
Ye tarie us heere no lenger than to-morwe."
    "Nay," quod this clerk, "have heer my feith
        to borwe."
    To bedde is goon Aurelius whan hym
        leste,   1235
And wel ny al that nyght he hadde his reste.
What for his labour and his hope of blisse,
His woful herte of penaunce hadde a lisse.
    Upon the morwe, whan that it was day,
To Britaigne tooke they the righte way,   1240
Aurelius and this magicien bisyde,
And been descended ther they wolde abyde.
And this was, as thise bookes me remembre,
The colde, frosty seson of Decembre.
    Phebus wax old, and hewed lyk laton,   1245
That in his hoote declynacion
Shoon as the burned gold with stremes brighte;
But now in Capricorn adoun he lighte,
Where as he shoon ful pale, I dar wel seyn.
The bittre frostes, with the sleet and reyn,   1250

Destroyed hath the grene in every yerd.
Janus sit by the fyr, with double berd,
And drynketh of his bugle horn the wyn;
Biforn hym stant brawen of the tusked swyn,
And "Nowel" crieth every lusty man.   1255
   Aurelius, in al that evere he kan,
Dooth to this maister chiere and reverence,
And preyeth hym to doon his diligence
To bryngen hym out of his peynes smerte,
Or with a swerd that he wolde slitte his
       herte.   1260
   This subtil clerk swich routhe had of this man
That nyght and day he spedde hym that he kan
To wayten a tyme of his conclusioun;
This is to seye, to maken illusioun,
By swich an apparence or jogelrye —   1265
I ne kan no termes of astrologye —
That she and every wight sholde wene and seye
That of Britaigne the rokkes were aweye,
Or ellis they were sonken under grounde.
So atte laste he hath his tyme yfounde   1270
To maken his japes and his wrecchednesse
Of swich a supersticious cursednesse.
His tables Tolletanes forth he brought,
Ful wel corrected, ne ther lakked nought,
Neither his collect ne his expans yeeris,   1275
Ne his rootes, ne his othere geeris,
As been his centris and his argumentz
And his proporcioneles convenientz
For his equacions in every thyng.
And by his eighte speere in his wirkyng   1280
He knew ful wel how fer Alnath was shove
Fro the heed of thilke fixe Aries above,
That in the ninthe speere considered is;
Ful subtilly he kalkuled al this.   1284
   Whan he hadde founde his firste mansioun,
He knew the remenaunt by proporcioun,
And knew the arisyng of his moone weel,
And in whos face, and terme, and everydeel;
And knew ful weel the moones mansioun
Acordaunt to his operacioun,   1290
And knew also his othere observaunces
For swiche illusiouns and swiche meschaunces
As hethen folk useden in thilke dayes.
For which no lenger maked he delayes,   1294
But thurgh his magik, for a wyke or tweye,
It semed that alle the rokkes were aweye.
   Aurelius, which that yet despeired is
Wher he shal han his love or fare amys,
Awaiteth nyght and day on this myracle;   1299
And whan he knew that ther was noon obstacle,
That voyded were thise rokkes everychon,
Doun to his maistres feet he fil anon,
And seyde, "I woful wrecche, Aurelius,

Thanke yow, lord, and lady myn Venus,
That me han holpen fro my cares colde."   1305
And to the temple his wey forth hath he holde,
Where as he knew he sholde his lady see.
And whan he saugh his tyme, anon-right hee,
With dredful herte and with ful humble cheere,
Salewed hath his sovereyn lady deere: 1310
   "My righte lady," quod this woful man,
"Whom I moost drede and love as I best kan,
And lothest were of al this world displese,
Nere it that I for yow have swich disese   1314
That I moste dyen heere at youre foot anon,
Noght wolde I telle how me is wo bigon.
But certes outher moste I dye or pleyne;
Ye sle me giltelees for verray peyne.
But of my deeth thogh that ye have no routhe,
Avyseth yow er that ye breke youre trouthe.
Repenteth yow, for thilke God above,   1321
Er ye me sleen by cause that I yow love.
For, madame, wel ye woot what ye han hight —
Nat that I chalange any thyng of right
Of yow, my sovereyn lady, but youre grace —
But in a gardyn yond, at swich a place,   1326
Ye woot right wel what ye bihighten me;
And in myn hand youre trouthe plighten ye
To love me best — God woot, ye seyde so,
Al be that I unworthy am therto.   1330
Madame, I speke it for the honour of yow
Moore than to save myn hertes lyf right now, —
I have do so as ye comanded me;
And if ye vouche sauf, ye may go see.   1334
Dooth as yow list; have youre biheste in mynde,
For, quyk or deed, right there ye shal me fynde.
In yow lith al to do me lyve or deye, —
But wel I woot the rokkes been aweye."
   He taketh his leve, and she astoned stood;
In al hir face nas a drope of blood.   1340
She wende nevere han come in swich a trappe.
"Allas," quod she, "that evere this sholde
      happe!
For wende I nevere by possibilitee
That swich a monstre or merveille myghte be!
It is agayns the proces of nature."   1345
And hoom she goth a sorweful creature;
For verray feere unnethe may she go.
She wepeth, wailleth, al a day or two,
And swowneth, that it routhe was to see.
But why it was to no wight tolde shee,   1350
For out of towne was goon Arveragus.
But to hirself she spak, and seyde thus,
With face pale and with ful sorweful cheere,
In hire compleynt, as ye shal after heere:
   "Allas," quod she, "on thee, Fortune, I
      pleyne,   1355

That unwar wrapped hast me in thy cheyne,
Fro which t'escape woot I no socour,
Save oonly deeth or elles dishonour;
Oon of thise two bihoveth me to chese.
But nathelees, yet have I levere to lese   1360
My lif than of my body to have a shame,
Or knowe myselven fals, or lese my name;
And with my deth I may be quyt, ywis.
Hath ther nat many a noble wyf er this,
And many a mayde, yslayn hirself, allas!   1365
Rather than with hir body doon trespas?
    Yis, certes, lo, thise stories beren witnesse:
Whan thritty tirauntz, ful of cursednesse,
Hadde slayn Phidon in Atthenes atte feste,
They comanded his doghtres for t'areste,   1370
And bryngen hem biforn hem in despit,
Al naked, to fulfille hir foul delit,
And in hir fadres blood they made hem daunce
Upon the pavement, God yeve hem mes-
          chaunce!
For which thise woful maydens, ful of drede,
Rather than they wolde lese hir maydenhede,
They prively been stirt into a welle,   1377
And dreynte hemselven, as the bookes telle.
    They of Mecene leete enquere and seke
Of Lacedomye fifty maydens eke,   1380
On whiche they wolden doon hir lecherye.
But was ther noon of al that compaignye
That she nas slayn, and with a good entente
Chees rather for to dye than assente
To been oppressed of hir maydenhede.   1385
Why sholde I thanne to dye been in drede?
Lo, eek, the tiraunt Aristoclides,
That loved a mayden, heet Stymphalides,
Whan that hir fader slayn was on a nyght,
Unto Dianes temple goth she right,   1390
And hente the ymage in hir handes two,
Fro which ymage wolde she nevere go.
No wight ne myghte hir handes of it arace
Til she was slayn, right in the selve place.
    Now sith that maydens hadden swich despit
To been defouled with mannes foul delit,   1396
Wel oghte a wyf rather hirselven slee
Than be defouled, as it thynketh me.
What shal I seyn of Hasdrubales wyf,
That at Cartage birafte hirself hir lyf?   1400
For whan she saugh that Romayns wan the
          toun,
She took hir children alle, and skipte adoun
Into the fyr, and chees rather to dye
Than any Romayn dide hire vileynye.
Hath nat Lucresse yslayn hirself, allas!   1405
At Rome, whan that she oppressed was
Of Tarquyn, for hire thoughte it was a shame

To lyven whan that she had lost hir name?
The sevene maydens of Milesie also   1409
Han slayn hemself, for verrey drede and wo,
Rather than folk of Gawle hem sholde oppresse.
Mo than a thousand stories, as I gesse,
Koude I now telle as touchynge this mateere.
Whan Habradate was slayn, his wyf so deere
Hirselven slow, and leet hir blood to glyde
In Habradates woundes depe and wyde,   1416
And seyde, 'My body, at the leeste way,
Ther shal no wight defoulen, if I may.'
    What sholde I mo ensamples heerof sayn,
Sith that so manye han hemselven slayn   1420
Wel rather than they wolde defouled be?
I wol conclude that it is bet for me
To sleen myself than been defouled thus.
I wol be trewe unto Arveragus,
Or rather sleen myself in som manere,   1425
As dide Demociones doghter deere
By cause that she wolde nat defouled be.
O Cedasus, it is ful greet pitee
To reden how thy doghtren deyde, allas!
That slowe hemself for swich a manere cas.   1431
As greet a pitee was it, or wel moore,
The Theban mayden that for Nichanore
Hirselven slow, right for swich manere wo.
Another Theban mayden dide right so;   1434
For oon of Macidonye hadde hire oppressed,
She with hire deeth hir maydenhede redressed.
What shal I seye of Nicerates wyf,
That for swich cas birafte hirself hir lyf?
How trewe eek was to Alcebiades
His love, that rather for to dyen chees   1440
Than for to suffre his body unburyed be.
Lo, which a wyf was Alceste," quod she.
"What seith Omer of goode Penalopee?
Al Grece knoweth of hire chastitee.
Pardee, of Laodomya is writen thus,   1445
That whan at Troie was slayn Protheselaus,
Ne lenger wolde she lyve after his day.
The same of noble Porcia telle I may;
Withoute Brutus koude she nat lyve,
To whom she hadde al hool hir herte yive.   1450
The parfit wyfhod of Arthemesie
Honured is thurgh al the Barbarie.
O Teuta, queene! thy wyfly chastitee
To alle wyves may a mirour bee.
The same thyng I seye of Bilyea,   1455
Of Rodogone, and eek Valeria."
    Thus pleyned Dorigen a day or tweye,
Purposynge evere that she wolde deye.
But nathelees, upon the thridde nyght,   1459
Hoom cam Arveragus, this worthy knyght,
And asked hire why that she weep so soore;

And she gan wepen ever lenger the moore.
"Allas," quod she, "that evere was I born!
Thus have I seyd," quod she, "thus have I
    sworn" —
And toold hym al as ye han herd bifore;   1465
It nedeth nat reherce it yow namoore.
This housbonde, with glad chiere, in freendly
    wyse
Answerde and seyde as I shal yow devyse:
"Is ther oght elles, Dorigen, but this?"
   "Nay, nay," quod she, "God helpe me so as
    wys!   1470
This is to muche, and it were Goddes wille."
   "Ye, wyf," quod he, "lat slepen that is stille.
It may be wel, paraventure, yet to day.
Ye shul youre trouthe holden, by my fay!
For God so wisly have mercy upon me,   1475
I hadde wel levere ystiked for to be
For verray love which that I to yow have,
But if ye sholde youre trouthe kepe and save.
Trouthe is the hyeste thyng that man may
    kepe" —
But with that word he brast anon to
    wepe,   1480
And seyde, "I yow forbede, up peyne of
    deeth,
That nevere, whil thee lasteth lyf ne breeth,
To no wight telle thou of this aventure, —
As I may best, I wol my wo endure, —
Ne make no contenance of hevynesse,   1485
That folk of yow may demen harm or gesse."
   And forth he cleped a squier and a mayde:
"Gooth forth anon with Dorigen," he sayde,
"And bryngeth hire to swich a place anon."
They take hir leve, and on hir wey they gon,
But they ne wiste why she thider wente.   1491
He nolde no wight tellen his entente.
   Paraventure an heep of yow, ywis,
Wol holden hym a lewed man in this
That he wol putte his wyf in jupartie.   1495
Herkneth the tale er ye upon hire crie.
She may have bettre fortune than yow semeth;
And whan that ye han herd the tale, demeth.
   This squier, which that highte Aurelius,
On Dorigen that was so amorus,   1500
Of aventure happed hire to meete
Amydde the toun, right in the quykkest strete,
As she was bown to goon the wey forth right
Toward the gardyn ther as she had hight.
And he was to the gardyn-ward also;   1505
For wel he spyed whan she wolde go
Out of hir hous to any maner place.
But thus they mette, of aventure or grace,
And he saleweth hire with glad entente,

And asked of hire whiderward she wente;   1510
And she answerde, half as she were mad,
"Unto the gardyn, as myn housbonde bad,
My trouthe for to holde, allas! allas!"
   Aurelius gan wondren on this cas,
And in his herte hadde greet compassioun   1515
Of hire and of hire lamentacioun,
And of Arveragus, the worthy knyght,
That bad hire holden al that she had hight,
So looth hym was his wyf sholde breke hir
    trouthe;
And in his herte he caughte of this greet routhe,
Considerynge the beste on every syde,   1521
That fro his lust yet were hym levere abyde
Than doon so heigh a cherlyssh wrecchednesse
Agayns franchise and alle gentillesse;
For which in fewe wordes seyde he thus: 1525
   "Madame, seyth to youre lord Arveragus,
That sith I se his grete gentillesse
To yow, and eek I se wel youre distresse,
That him were levere han shame (and that
    were routhe)
Than ye to me sholde breke thus youre trouthe,
I have wel levere evere to suffre wo   1531
Than I departe the love bitwix yow two.
I yow relesse, madame, into youre hond
Quyt every serement and every bond
That ye han maad to me as heerbiforn,   1535
Sith thilke tyme which that ye were born.
My trouthe I plighte, I shal yow never repreve
Of no biheste, and heere I take my leve,
As of the treweste and the beste wyf
That evere yet I knew in al my lyf."   1540
But every wyf be war of hire biheeste!
On Dorigen remembreth, atte leeste.
Thus kan a squier doon a gentil dede
As wel as kan a knyght, withouten drede.   1544
   She thonketh hym upon hir knees al bare,
And hoom unto hir housbonde is she fare,
And tolde hym al, as ye han herd me sayd;
And be ye siker, he was so weel apayd
That it were inpossible me to wryte.
What sholde I lenger of this cas endyte?   1550
   Arveragus and Dorigen his wyf
In sovereyn blisse leden forth hir lyf.
Nevere eft ne was ther angre hem bitwene.
He cherisseth hire as though she were a queene,
And she was to hym trewe for everemoore.
Of thise two folk ye gete of me namoore.   1556
   Aurelius, that his cost hath al forlorn,
Curseth the tyme that evere he was born:
"Allas," quod he, "allas, that I bihighte
Of pured gold a thousand pound of wighte
Unto this philosophre! How shal I do?   1561

I se namoore but that I am fordo.
Myn heritage moot I nedes selle,
And been a beggere; heere may I nat dwelle,
And shamen al my kynrede in this place,   1565
But I of hym may gete bettre grace.
But nathelees, I wole of hym assaye,
At certeyn dayes, yeer by yeer, to paye,
And thanke hym of his grete curteisye.
My trouthe wol I kepe, I wol nat lye."   1570

    With herte soor he gooth unto his cofre,
And broghte gold unto this philosophre,
The value of fyve hundred pound, I gesse,
And hym bisecheth, of his gentillesse,
To graunte hym dayes of the remenaunt;   1575
And seyde, "Maister, I dar wel make avaunt,
I failled nevere of my trouthe as yit.
For sikerly my dette shal be quyt
Towardes yow, howevere that I fare
To goon a-begged in my kirtle bare.   1580
But wolde ye vouche sauf, upon seuretee,
Two yeer or thre for to respiten me,
Thanne were I wel; for elles moot I selle
Myn heritage; ther is namoore to telle."

    This philosophre sobrely answerde,   1585
And seyde thus, whan he thise wordes herde:
"Have I nat holden covenant unto thee?"

    "Yes, certes, wel and trewely," quod he.

    "Hastow nat had thy lady as thee liketh?"

    "No, no," quod he, and sorwefully he siketh.

    "What was the cause? tel me if thou kan."
Aurelius his tale anon bigan,   1592
And tolde hym al, as ye han herd bifoore;
It nedeth nat to yow reherce it moore.

He seide, "Arveragus, of gentillesse,   1595
Hadde levere dye in sorwe and in distresse
Than that his wyf were of hir trouthe fals."
The sorwe of Dorigen he tolde hym als;
How looth hire was to been a wikked wyf,   1599
And that she levere had lost that day hir lyf,
And that hir trouthe she swoor thurgh inno-
          cence,
She nevere erst hadde herd speke of apparence.
"That made me han of hire so greet pitee;
And right as frely as he sente hire me,
As frely sente I hire to hym ageyn.   1605
This al and som; ther is namoore to seyn."

    This philosophre answerde, "Leeve brother,
Everich of yow dide gentilly til oother.
Thou art a squier, and he is a knyght;
But God forbede, for his blisful myght,   1610
But if a clerk koude doon a gentil dede
As wel as any of yow, it is no drede!

    Sire, I releesse thee thy thousand pound,
As thou right now were cropen out of the
          ground,
Ne nevere er now ne haddest knowen me.   1615
For, sire, I wol nat taken a peny of thee
For al my craft, ne noght for my travaille.
Thou hast ypayed wel for my vitaille.
It is ynogh, and farewel, have good day!"   1619
And took his hors, and forth he goth his way.
Lordynges, this question, thanne, wol I aske
          now,
Which was the mooste fre, as thynketh yow?
Now telleth me, er that ye ferther wende.
I kan namoore; my tale is at an ende.

Heere is ended the Frankeleyns Tale.

Fragment VI (Group C)

The Physician's Tale

Heere folweth the Phisiciens Tale.

Ther was, as telleth Titus Livius,
A knyght that called was Virginius,
Fulfild of honour and of worthynesse,
And strong of freendes, and of greet richesse.

This knyght a doghter hadde by his wyf; 5
No children hadde he mo in al his lyf.
Fair was this mayde in excellent beautee
Aboven every wight that man may see;
For Nature hath with sovereyn diligence
Yformed hire in so greet excellence, 10
As though she wolde seyn, "Lo! I, Nature,
Thus kan I forme and peynte a creature,
Whan that me list; who kan me countrefete?
Pigmalion noght, though he ay forge and bete,
Or grave, or peynte; for I dar wel seyn, 15
Apelles, Zanzis, sholde werche in veyn
Outher to grave, or peynte, or forge, or bete,
If they presumed me to countrefete.
For He that is the formere principal
Hath maked me his vicaire general, 20
To forme and peynten erthely creaturis
Right as me list, and ech thyng in my cure is
Under the moone, that may wane and waxe;
And for my werk right no thyng wol I axe;
My lord and I been ful of oon accord. 25
I made hire to the worshipe of my lord;
So do I alle myne othere creatures,
What colour that they han, or what figures."
Thus semeth me that Nature wolde seye.

This mayde of age twelve yeer was and
    tweye,
In which that Nature hadde swich delit. 31
For right as she kan peynte a lilie whit,
And reed a rose, right with swich peynture
She peynted hath this noble creature,
Er she were born, upon hir lymes fre, 35
Where as by right swiche colours sholde be;
And Phebus dyed hath hire tresses grete
Lyk to the stremes of his burned heete.
And if that excellent was hire beautee,
A thousand foold moore vertuous was she. 40
In hire ne lakked no condicioun
That is to preyse, as by discrecioun.
As wel in goost as body chast was she;
For which she floured in virginitee

With alle humylitee and abstinence, 45
With alle attemperaunce and pacience,
With mesure eek of beryng and array.
Discreet she was in answeryng alway;
Though she were wis as Pallas, dar I seyn,
Hir facound eek ful wommanly and pleyn, 50
No countrefeted termes hadde she
To seme wys; but after hir degree
She spak, and alle hire wordes, moore and
    lesse,
Sownynge in vertu and in gentillesse. 54
Shamefast she was in maydens shamefastnesse,
Constant in herte, and evere in bisynesse
To dryve hire out of ydel slogardye.
Bacus hadde of hir mouth right no maistrie;
For wyn and youthe dooth Venus encresse,
As men in fyr wol casten oille or greesse. 60
And of hir owene vertu, unconstreyned,
She hath ful ofte tyme syk hire feyned,
For that she wolde fleen the compaignye
Where likly was to treten of folye,
As is at feestes, revels, and at daunces, 65
That been occasions of daliaunces.
Swich thynges maken children for to be
To soone rype and boold, as men may se,
Which is ful perilous, and hath been yoore.
For al to soone may she lerne loore 70
Of booldnesse, whan she woxen is a wyf.

And ye maistresses, in youre olde lyf,
That lordes doghtres han in governaunce,
Ne taketh of my wordes no displesaunce.
Thenketh that ye been set in governynges 75
Of lordes doghtres, oonly for two thynges:
Outher for ye han kept youre honestee,
Or elles ye han falle in freletee,
And knowen wel ynough the olde daunce,
And han forsaken fully swich meschaunce 80
For everemo; therfore, for Cristes sake,
To teche hem vertu looke that ye ne slake.

A theef of venysoun, that hath forlaft
His likerousnesse and al his olde craft,
Kan kepe a forest best of any man. 85
Now kepeth wel, for if ye wole, ye kan.
Looke wel that ye unto no vice assente,
Lest ye be dampned for youre wikke entente;

145

For whoso dooth, a traitour is, certeyn.
And taketh kep of that that I shal seyn: 90
Of alle tresons sovereyn pestilence
Is whan a wight bitrayseth innocence.

Ye fadres and ye moodres eek also,
Though ye han children, be it oon or mo,
Youre is the charge of al hir surveiaunce,   95
Whil that they been under youre governaunce.
Beth war, that by ensample of youre lyvynge,
Or by youre necligence in chastisynge,
That they ne perisse; for I dar wel seye,
If that they doon, ye shul it deere abeye.   100
Under a shepherde softe and necligent
The wolf hath many a sheep and lamb torent.
Suffiseth oon ensample now as heere,
For I moot turne agayn to my matere.

This mayde, of which I wol this tale expresse,
So kepte hirself hir neded no maistresse;   106
For in hir lyvyng maydens myghten rede,
As in a book, every good word or dede
That longeth to a mayden vertuous,
She was so prudent and so bountevous.   110
For which the fame out sprong on every syde,
Bothe of hir beautee and hir bountee wyde,
That thurgh that land they preised hire echone
That loved vertu, save Envye allone,
That sory is of oother mennes wele,   115
And glad is of his sorwe and his unheele.
(The doctour maketh this descripcioun).

This mayde upon a day wente in the toun
Toward a temple, with hire mooder deere,
As is of yonge maydens the manere.   120
Now was ther thanne a justice in that toun,
That governour was of that regioun.
And so bifel this juge his eyen caste
Upon this mayde, avysynge hym ful faste,
As she cam forby ther as this juge stood.   125
Anon his herte chaunged and his mood,
So was he caught with beautee of this mayde,
And to hymself ful pryvely he sayde,
"This mayde shal be myn, for any man!"

Anon the feend into his herte ran,   130
And taughte hym sodeynly that he by slyghte
The mayden to his purpos wynne myghte.
For certes, by no force ne by no meede,
Hym thoughte, he was nat able for to speede;
For she was strong of freendes, and eek she   135
Confermed was in swich soverayn bountee,
That wel he wiste he myghte hire nevere wynne
As for to make hire with hir body synne.
For which, by greet deliberacioun,
He sente after a cherl, was in the toun,   140
Which that he knew for subtil and for boold.

This juge unto this cherl his tale hath toold
In secree wise, and made hym to ensure
He sholde telle it to no creature,
And if he dide, he sholde lese his heed.   145
Whan that assented was this cursed reed,
Glad was this juge, and maked him greet cheere,
And yaf hym yiftes preciouse and deere.

Whan shapen was al hire conspiracie
Fro point to point, how that his lecherie   150
Parfourned sholde been ful subtilly,
As ye shul heere it after openly,
Hoom gooth the cherl, that highte Claudius.
This false juge, that highte Apius,
(So was his name, for this is no fable,   155
But knowen for historial thyng notable;
The sentence of it sooth is, out of doute),
This false juge gooth now faste aboute
To hasten his delit al that he may.
And so bifel soone after, on a day,   160
This false juge, as telleth us the storie,
As he was wont, sat in his consistorie,
And yaf his doomes upon sondry cas.
This false cherl cam forth a ful greet pas,
And seyde, "Lord, if that it be youre wille,   165
As dooth me right upon this pitous bille,
In which I pleyne upon Virginius;
And if that he wol seyn it is nat thus,
I wol it preeve, and fynde good witnesse,
That sooth is that my bille wol expresse."   170

The juge answerde, "Of this, in his absence,
I may nat yeve diffynytyf sentence.
Lat do hym calle, and I wol gladly heere;
Thou shalt have al right, and no wrong heere."

Virginius cam to wite the juges wille,   175
And right anon was rad this cursed bille;
The sentence of it was as ye shul heere:
"To yow, my lord, sire Apius so deere,
Sheweth youre povre servant Claudius
How that a knyght, called Virginius,   180
Agayns the lawe, agayn al equitee,
Holdeth, expres agayn the wyl of me,
My servant, which that is my thral by right,
Which fro myn hous was stole upon a nyght,
Whil that she was ful yong; this wol I preeve   185
By witnesse, lord, so that it nat yow greeve.
She nys his doghter nat, what so he seye.
Wherfore to yow, my lord the juge, I preye,
Yeld me my thral, if that it be youre wille."
Lo, this was al the sentence of his bille.   190
Virginius gan upon the cherl biholde,
But hastily, er he his tale tolde,
And wolde have preeved it as sholde a knyght,
And eek by witnessyng of many a wight,

That al was fals that seyde his adversarie,   195
This cursed juge wolde no thyng tarie,
Ne heere a word moore of Virginius,
But yaf his juggement, and seyde thus:
    "I deeme anon this cherl his servant have;
Thou shalt no lenger in thyn hous hir save.   200
Go bryng hire forth, and put hire in oure
    warde.
The cherl shal have his thral, this I awarde."
    And whan this worthy knyght Virginius,
Thurgh sentence of this justice Apius,
Moste by force his deere doghter yiven   205
Unto the juge, in lecherie to lyven,
He gooth hym hoom, and sette him in his halle,
And leet anon his deere doghter calle,
And with a face deed as asshen colde
Upon hir humble face he gan biholde,   210
With fadres pitee stikynge thurgh his herte,
Al wolde he from his purpos nat converte.
    "Doghter," quod he, "Virginia, by thy name,
Ther been two weyes, outher deeth or shame,
That thou most suffre; allas, that I was bore!
For nevere thou deservedest wherfore   216
To dyen with a swerd or with a knyf.
O deere doghter, endere of my lyf,
Which I have fostred up with swich plesaunce
That thou were nevere out of my remem-
    braunce!   220
O doghter, which that art my laste wo,
And in my lyf my laste joye also,
O gemme of chastitee, in pacience
Take thou thy deeth, for this is my sentence.
For love, and nat for hate, thou most be
    deed;   225
My pitous hand moot smyten of thyn heed.
Allas, that evere Apius the say!
Thus hath he falsly jugged the to-day" —
And tolde hire al the cas, as ye bifore
Han herd; nat nedeth for to telle it moore.   230
    "O mercy, deere fader!" quod this mayde,
And with that word she bothe hir armes layde
Aboute his nekke, as she was wont to do.
The teeris bruste out of hir eyen two,
And seyde, "Goode fader, shal I dye?   235
Is ther no grace, is ther no remedye?"
    "No, certes, deere doghter myn," quod he.
"Thanne yif me leyser, fader myn," quod she,
"My deeth for to compleyne a litel space;
For, pardee, Jepte yaf his doghter grace   240

For to compleyne, er he hir slow, allas!
And, God it woot, no thyng was hir trespas,
But for she ran hir fader first to see,
To welcome hym with greet solempnitee."
And with that word she fil aswowne anon,   245
And after, whan hir swownyng is agon,
She riseth up, and to hir fader sayde,
"Blissed be God, that I shal dye a mayde!
Yif me my deeth, er that I have a shame;
Dooth with youre child youre wyl, a Goddes
    name!"   250
    And with that word she preyed hym ful ofte
That with his swerd he sholde smyte softe;
And with that word aswowne doun she fil.
Hir fader, with ful sorweful herte and wil,
Hir heed of smoot, and by the top it hente,   255
And to the juge he gan it to presente,
As he sat yet in doom in consistorie.
And whan the juge it saugh, as seith the storie,
He bad to take hym and anhange hym faste;
But right anon a thousand peple in thraste,   260
To save the knyght, for routhe and for pitee,
For knowen was the false iniquitee.
The peple anon had suspect in this thyng,
By manere of the cherles chalangyng,
That it was by the assent of Apius;   265
They wisten wel that he was lecherus.
For which unto this Apius they gon,
And caste hym in a prisoun right anon,
Ther as he slow hymself; and Claudius,
That servant was unto this Apius,   270
Was demed for to hange upon a tree,
But that Virginius, of his pitee,
So preyde for hym that he was exiled;
And elles, certes, he had been bigyled.   274
The remenant were anhanged, moore and lesse,
That were consentant of this cursednesse.
    Heere may men seen how synne hath his
        merite.
Beth war, for no man woot whom God wol
        smyte
In no degree, ne in which manere wyse
The worm of conscience may agryse   280
Of wikked lyf, though it so pryvee be
That no man woot therof but God and he.
For be he lewed man, or ellis lered,
He noot how soone that he shal been afered.
Therfore I rede yow this conseil take: 285
Forsaketh synne, er synne yow forsake.

Heere endeth the Phisiciens Tale.

The Introduction to The Pardoner's Tale

The wordes of the Hoost to the Phisicien and the Pardoner.

Oure Hooste gan to swere as he were wood;
"Harrow!" quod he, "by nayles and by blood!
This was a fals cherl and a fals justise.
As shameful deeth as herte may devyse   290
Come to thise juges and hire advocatz!
Algate this sely mayde is slayn, allas!
Allas, to deere boughte she beautee!
Wherfore I seye al day that men may see
That yiftes of Fortune and of Nature   295
Been cause of deeth to many a creature.
Hire beautee was hire deth, I dar wel sayn.
Allas, so pitously as she was slayn!
Of bothe yiftes that I speke of now
Men han ful ofte moore for harm than prow.
But trewely, myn owene maister deere,   301
This is a pitous tale for to heere.
But nathelees, passe over, is no fors.
I pray to God so save thy gentil cors,
And eek thyne urynals and thy jurdones,   305
Thyn ypocras, and eek thy galiones,
And every boyste ful of thy letuarie;
God blesse hem, and oure lady Seinte Marie!

So moot I theen, thou art a propre man,
And lyk a prelat, by Seint Ronyan!   310
Seyde I nat wel? I kan nat speke in terme;
But wel I woot thou doost myn herte to erme,
That I almoost have caught a cardynacle.
By corpus bones! but I have triacle,
Or elles a draughte of moyste and corny ale,
Or but I heere anon a myrie tale,   316
Myn herte is lost for pitee of this mayde.
Thou beel amy, thou Pardoner," he sayde,
"Telle us som myrthe or japes right anon."
"It shal be doon," quod he, "by Seint Ron-
          yon!   320
But first," quod he, "heere at this alestake
I wol bothe drynke, and eten of a cake."

But right anon thise gentils gonne to crye,
"Nay, lat hym telle us of no ribaudye!   324
Telle us som moral thyng, that we may leere
Som wit, and thanne wol we gladly heere."
"I graunte, ywis," quod he, "but I moot
          thynke
Upon som honest thyng while that I drynke."

The Pardoner's Prologue

Heere folweth the Prologe of the Pardoners Tale.

Radix malorum est Cupiditas. Ad Thimotheum, 6⁰.

"Lordynges," quod he, "in chirches whan I
      preche,
I peyne me to han an hauteyn speche,   330
And rynge it out as round as gooth a belle,
For I kan al by rote that I telle.
My theme is alwey oon, and evere was —
Radix malorum est Cupiditas.
First I pronounce whennes that I come,   335
And thanne my bulles shewe I, alle and some.
Oure lige lordes seel on my patente,
That shewe I first, my body to warente,
That no man be so boold, ne preest ne clerk,
Me to destourbe of Cristes hooly werk.   340
And after that thanne telle I forth my tales;
Bulles of popes and of cardynales,

Of patriarkes and bishopes I shewe,
And in Latyn I speke a wordes fewe,
To saffron with my predicacioun,   345
And for to stire hem to devocioun.
Thanne shewe I forth my longe cristal stones,
Ycrammed ful of cloutes and of bones, —
Relikes been they, as wenen they echoon.
Thanne have I in latoun a sholder-boon   350
Which that was of an hooly Jewes sheep.
'Goode men,' I seye, 'taak of my wordes keep;
If that this boon be wasshe in any welle,
If cow, or calf, or sheep, or oxe swelle
That any worm hath ete, or worm ystonge,   355
Taak water of that welle and wassh his tonge,
And it is hool anon; and forthermoore,

Of pokkes and of scabbe, and every soore
Shal every sheep be hool that of this welle   359
Drynketh a draughte. Taak kep eek what I telle:
If that the good-man that the beestes oweth
Wol every wyke, er that the cok hym croweth,
Fastynge, drynken of this welle a draughte,
As thilke hooly Jew oure eldres taughte,
His beestes and his stoor shal multiplie.   365
    And, sires, also it heeleth jalousie;
For though a man be falle in jalous rage,
Lat maken with this water his potage,
And nevere shal he moore his wyf mystriste,
Though he the soothe of hir defaute wiste,   370
Al had she taken prestes two or thre.
    Heere is a miteyn eek, that ye may se.
He that his hand wol putte in this mitayn,
He shal have multipliyng of his grayn,
Whan he hath sowen, be it whete or otes,   375
So that he offre pens, or elles grotes.
    Goode men and wommen, o thyng warne I
      yow:
If any wight be in this chirche now
That hath doon synne horrible, that he
Dar nat, for shame, of it yshryven be,   380
Or any womman, be she yong or old,
That hath ymaad hir housbonde cokewold,
Swich folk shal have no power ne no grace
To offren to my relikes in this place.   384
And whoso fyndeth hym out of swich blame,
He wol come up and offre in Goddes name,
And I assoille him by the auctoritee
Which that by bulle ygraunted was to me.'
    By this gaude have I wonne, yeer by yeer,
An hundred mark sith I was pardoner.   390
I stonde lyk a clerk in my pulpet,
And whan the lewed peple is doun yset,
I preche so as ye han herd bifoore,
And telle an hundred false japes moore.   394
Thanne peyne I me to strecche forth the nekke,
And est and west upon the peple I bekke,
As dooth a dowve sittynge on a berne.
Myne handes and my tonge goon so yerne
That it is joye to se my bisynesse.
Of avarice and of swich cursednesse   400
Is al my prechyng, for to make hem free
To yeven hir pens, and namely unto me.
For myn entente is nat but for to wynne,
And nothyng for correccioun of synne.   404
I rekke nevere, whan that they been beryed,
Though that hir soules goon a-blakeberyed!
For certes, many a predicacioun
Comth ofte tyme of yvel entencioun;
Som for plesance of folk and flaterye,

To been avaunced by ypocrisye,   410
And som for veyne glorie, and som for hate.
For whan I dar noon oother weyes debate,
Thanne wol I stynge hym with my tonge smerte
In prechyng, so that he shal nat asterte
To been defamed falsly, if that he   415
Hath trespased to my bretheren or to me.
For though I telle noght his propre name,
Men shal wel knowe that it is the same,
By signes, and by othere circumstances.   419
Thus quyte I folk that doon us displesances;
Thus spitte I out my venym under hewe
Of hoolynesse, to semen hooly and trewe.
    But shortly myn entente I wol devyse:
I preche of no thyng but for coveityse.
Therfore my theme is yet, and evere was,   425
Radix malorum est Cupiditas.
Thus kan I preche agayn that same vice
Which that I use, and that is avarice.
But though myself be gilty in that synne,
Yet kan I maken oother folk to twynne   430
From avarice, and soore to repente.
But that is nat my principal entente;
I preche nothyng but for coveitise.
Of this mateere it oghte ynogh suffise.
    Thanne telle I hem ensamples many oon   435
Of olde stories longe tyme agoon.
For lewed peple loven tales olde;
Swiche thynges kan they wel reporte and holde.
What, trowe ye, that whiles I may preche,
And wynne gold and silver for I teche,   440
That I wol lyve in poverte wilfully?
Nay, nay, I thoghte it nevere, trewely!
For I wol preche and begge in sondry landes;
I wol nat do no labour with myne handes,
Ne make baskettes, and lyve therby,   445
By cause I wol nat beggen ydelly.
I wol noon of the apostles countrefete;
I wol have moneie, wolle, chese, and whete,
Al were it yeven of the povereste page,
Or of the povereste wydwe in a village,   450
Al sholde hir children sterve for famyne.
Nay, I wol drynke licour of the vyne,
And have a joly wenche in every toun.
But herkneth, lordynges, in conclusioun:
Youre likyng is that I shal telle a tale.   455
Now have I dronke a draughte of corny ale,
By God, I hope I shal yow telle a thyng
That shal by reson been at youre likyng.
For though myself be a ful vicious man,
A moral tale yet I yow telle kan,   460
Which I am wont to preche for to wynne.
Now hoold youre pees! my tale I wol bigynne."

The Pardoner's Tale

Heere bigynneth the Pardoners Tale.

In Flaundres whilom was a compaignye
Of yonge folk that haunteden folye,
As riot, hasard, stywes, and tavernes,   465
Where as with harpes, lutes, and gyternes,
They daunce and pleyen at dees bothe day and
      nyght,
And eten also and drynken over hir myght,
Thurgh which they doon the devel sacrifise
Withinne that develes temple, in cursed wise,
By superfluytee abhomynable.   471
Hir othes been so grete and so dampnable
That it is grisly for to heere hem swere.
Oure blissed Lordes body they totere, —
Hem thoughte that Jewes rente hym noght
      ynough;   475
And ech of hem at otheres synne lough.
And right anon thanne comen tombesteres
Fetys and smale, and yonge frutesteres,
Syngeres with harpes, baudes, wafereres,
Whiche been the verray develes officeres   480
To kyndle and blowe the fyr of lecherye,
That is annexed unto glotonye.
The hooly writ take I to my witnesse
That luxurie is in wyn and dronkenesse.
   Lo, how that dronken Looth, unkyndely,   485
Lay by his doghtres two, unwityngly;
So dronke he was, he nyste what he wroghte.
   Herodes, whoso wel the stories soghte,
Whan he of wyn was repleet at his feeste,
Right at his owene table he yaf his heeste   490
To sleen the Baptist John, ful giltelees.
   Senec seith a good word doutelees;
He seith he kan no difference fynde
Bitwix a man that is out of his mynde
And a man which that is dronkelewe,   495
But that woodnesse, yfallen in a shrewe,
Persevereth lenger than doth dronkenesse.
O glotonye, ful of cursednesse!
O cause first of oure confusioun!
O original of oure dampnacioun,   500
Til Crist hadde boght us with his blood agayn!
Lo, how deere, shortly for to sayn,
Aboght was thilke cursed vileynye!
Corrupt was al this world for glotonye.
   Adam oure fader, and his wyf also,   505
Fro Paradys to labour and to wo
Were dryven for that vice, it is no drede.
For whil that Adam fasted, as I rede,

He was in Paradys; and whan that he
Eet of the fruyt deffended on the tree,   510
Anon he was out cast to wo and peyne.
O glotonye, on thee wel oghte us pleyne!
O, wiste a man how manye maladyes
Folwen of excesse and of glotonyes,
He wolde been the moore mesurable   515
Of his diete, sittynge at his table.
Allas! the shorte throte, the tendre mouth,
Maketh that est and west and north and south,
In erthe, in eir, in water, men to swynke   519
To gete a glotoun deyntee mete and drynke!
Of this matiere, o Paul, wel kanstow trete:
"Mete unto wombe, and wombe eek unto mete,
Shal God destroyen bothe," as Paulus seith.
Allas! a foul thyng is it, by my feith,
To seye this word, and fouler is the dede,   525
Whan man so drynketh of the white and rede
That of his throte he maketh his pryvee,
Thurgh thilke cursed superfluitee.
   The apostel wepyng seith ful pitously,
"Ther walken manye of whiche yow toold
      have I —   530
I seye it now wepyng, with pitous voys —
That they been enemys of Cristes croys,
Of whiche the ende is deeth, wombe is hir
      god!"
O wombe! O bely! O stynkyng cod,
Fulfilled of dong and of corrupcioun!   535
At either ende of thee foul is the soun.
How greet labour and cost is thee to fynde!
Thise cookes, how they stampe, and streyne,
      and grynde,
And turnen substaunce into accident,
To fulfille al thy likerous talent!   540
Out of the harde bones knokke they
The mary, for they caste noght awey
That may go thurgh the golet softe and swoote.
Of spicerie of leef, and bark, and roote
Shal been his sauce ymaked by delit,   545
To make hym yet a newer appetit.
But, certes, he that haunteth swiche delices
Is deed, whil that he lyveth in tho vices.
   A lecherous thyng is wyn, and dronkenesse
Is ful of stryvyng and of wrecchednesse.   550
O dronke man, disfigured is thy face,
Sour is thy breeth, foul artow to embrace,
And thurgh thy dronke nose semeth the soun

As though thou seydest ay "Sampsoun, Samp-
soun!"
And yet, God woot, Sampsoun drank nevere no
wyn.   555
Thou fallest as it were a styked swyn;
Thy tonge is lost, and al thyn honeste cure;
For dronkenesse is verray sepulture
Of mannes wit and his discrecioun.
In whom that drynke hath dominacioun   560
He kan no conseil kepe, it is no drede.
Now kepe yow fro the white and fro the rede,
And namely fro the white wyn of Lepe,
That is to selle in Fysshstrete or in Chepe.
This wyn of Spaigne crepeth subtilly   565
In othere wynes, growynge faste by,
Of which ther ryseth swich fumositee
That whan a man hath dronken draughtes thre,
And weneth that he be at hoom in Chepe,
He is in Spaigne, right at the toune of Lepe, —
Nat at the Rochele, ne at Burdeux toun;   571
And thanne wol he seye "Sampsoun, Samp-
soun!"

But herkneth, lordynges, o word, I yow
preye,
That alle the sovereyn actes, dar I seye,
Of victories in the Olde Testament,   575
Thurgh verray God, that is omnipotent,
Were doon in abstinence and in preyere.
Looketh the Bible, and ther ye may it leere.

Looke, Attilla, the grete conquerour,   579
Deyde in his sleep, with shame and dishonour,
Bledynge ay at his nose in dronkenesse.
A capitayn sholde lyve in sobrenesse.
And over al this, avyseth yow right wel
What was comaunded unto Lamuel —
Nat Samuel, but Lamuel, seye I;   585
Redeth the Bible, and fynde it expresly
Of wyn-yevyng to hem that han justise.
Namoore of this, for it may wel suffise.

And now that I have spoken of glotonye,
Now wol I yow deffenden hasardrye.   590
Hasard is verray mooder of lesynges,
And of deceite, and cursed forswerynges,
Blaspheme of Crist, manslaughtre, and wast
also
Of catel and of tyme; and forthermo,
It is repreeve and contrarie of honour   595
For to ben holde a commune hasardour.
And ever the hyer he is of estaat,
The moore is he yholden desolaat.
If that a prynce useth hasardrye,
In alle governaunce and policye   600
He is, as by commune opinioun,
Yholde the lasse in reputacioun.

Stilboun, that was a wys embassadour,
Was sent to Corynthe, in ful greet honour,
Fro Lacidomye, to make hire alliaunce.   605
And whan he cam, hym happede, par chaunce,
That alle the gretteste that were of that lond,
Pleyynge atte hasard he hem fond.
For which, as soone as it myghte be,
He stal hym hoom agayn to his contree,   610
And seyde, "Ther wol I nat lese my name,
Ne I wol nat take on me so greet defame,
Yow for to allie unto none hasardours.
Sendeth othere wise embassadours;
For, by my trouthe, me were levere dye   615
Than I yow sholde to hasardours allye.
For ye, that been so glorious in honours,
Shul nat allyen yow with hasardours
As by my wyl, ne as by my tretee."
This wise philosophre, thus seyde hee.   620

Looke eek that to the kyng Demetrius,
The kyng of Parthes, as the book seith us,
Sente him a paire of dees of gold in scorn,
For he hadde used hasard ther-biforn;
For which he heeld his glorie or his renoun   625
At no value or reputacioun.
Lordes may fynden oother maner pley
Honest ynough to dryve the day awey.

Now wol I speke of othes false and grete
A word or two, as olde bookes trete.   630
Gret sweryng is a thyng abhominable,
And fals sweryng is yet moore reprevable.
The heighe God forbad sweryng at al,
Witnesse on Mathew; but in special
Of sweryng seith the hooly Jeremye,   635
"Thou shalt swere sooth thyne othes, and nat
lye,
And swere in doom, and eek in rightwisnesse";
But ydel sweryng is a cursednesse.
Bihoold and se that in the firste table
Of heighe Goddes heestes honurable,   640
Hou that the seconde heeste of hym is this:
"Take nat my name in ydel or amys."
Lo, rather he forbedeth swich sweryng
Than homycide or many a cursed thyng;
I seye that, as by ordre, thus it stondeth;   645
This knoweth, that his heestes understondeth,
How that the seconde heeste of God is that.
And forther over, I wol thee telle al plat,
That vengeance shal nat parten from his hous
That of his othes is to outrageous.   650
"By Goddes precious herte," and "By his
nayles,"
And "By the blood of Crist that is in Hayles,
Sevene is my chaunce, and thyn is cynk and
treye!"

"By Goddes armes, if thou falsly pleye,   654
This daggere shal thurghout thyn herte go!" —
This fruyt cometh of the bicched bones two,
Forsweryng, ire, falsnesse, homycide.
Now, for the love of Crist, that for us dyde,
Lete youre othes, bothe grete and smale.
But, sires, now wol I telle forth my tale.   660
    Thise riotoures thre of whiche I telle,
Longe erst er prime rong of any belle,
Were set hem in a taverne for to drynke,
And as they sat, they herde a belle clynke
Biforn a cors, was caried to his grave.   665
That oon of hem gan callen to his knave:
"Go bet," quod he, "and axe redily
What cors is this that passeth heer forby;
And looke that thou reporte his name weel."
    "Sire," quod this boy, "it nedeth never-a-
      deel;   670
It was me toold er ye cam heer two houres.
He was, pardee, an old felawe of youres;
And sodeynly he was yslayn to-nyght,
Fordronke, as he sat on his bench upright.
Ther cam a privee theef men clepeth Deeth,
That in this contree al the peple sleeth,   676
And with his spere he smoot his herte atwo,
And wente his wey withouten wordes mo.
He hath a thousand slayn this pestilence.
And, maister, er ye come in his presence,   680
Me thynketh that it were necessarie
For to be war of swich an adversarie.
Beth redy for to meete hym everemoore;
Thus taughte me my dame; I sey namoore."
"By seinte Marie!" seyde this taverner,   685
"The child seith sooth, for he hath slayn this
      yeer,
Henne over a mile, withinne a greet village,
Bothe man and womman, child, and hyne, and
      page;
I trowe his habitacioun be there.
To been avysed greet wysdom it were,   690
Er that he dide a man a dishonour."
    "Ye, Goddes armes!" quod this riotour,
"Is it swich peril with hym for to meete?
I shal hym seke by wey and eek by strete,
I make avow to Goddes digne bones!   695
Herkneth, felawes, we thre been al ones;
Lat ech of us holde up his hand til oother,
And ech of us bicomen otheres brother,
And we wol sleen this false traytour Deeth.
He shal be slayn, he that so manye sleeth,   700
By Goddes dignitee, er it be nyght!"
    Togidres han thise thre hir trouthes plight
To lyve and dyen ech of hem for oother,
As though he were his owene ybore brother.

And up they stirte, al dronken in this rage,   705
And forth they goon towardes that village
Of which the taverner hadde spoke biforn.
And many a grisly ooth thanne han they sworn,
And Cristes blessed body al torente —   709
Deeth shal be deed, if that they may hym hente!
    Whan they han goon nat fully half a mile,
Right as they wolde han troden over a stile,
An oold man and a povre with hem mette.
This olde man ful mekely hem grette,
And seyde thus, "Now, lordes, God yow see!"
    The proudeste of thise riotoures three   716
Answerde agayn, "What, carl, with sory grace!
Why artow al forwrapped save thy face?
Why lyvestow so longe in so greet age?"
    This olde man gan looke in his visage,   720
And seyde thus: "For I ne kan nat fynde
A man, though that I walked into Ynde,
Neither in citee ne in no village,
That wolde chaunge his youthe for myn age;
And therfore moot I han myn age stille,   725
As longe tyme as it is Goddes wille.
Ne Deeth, allas! ne wol nat han my lyf
Thus walke I, lyk a restelees kaityf,
And on the ground, which is my moodres gate,
I knokke with my staf, bothe erly and late,   730
And seye 'Leeve mooder, leet me in!
Lo how I vanysshe, flessh, and blood, and skyn!
Allas! whan shul my bones been at reste?
Mooder, with yow wolde I chaunge my cheste
That in my chambre longe tyme hath be,   735
Ye, for an heyre clowt to wrappe in me!'
But yet to me she wol nat do that grace,
For which ful pale and welked is my face.
    But, sires, to yow it is no curteisye
To speken to an old man vileynye,   740
But he trespasse in word, or elles in dede.
In Hooly Writ ye may yourself wel rede:
'Agayns an oold man, hoor upon his heed,
Ye sholde arise;' wherfore I yeve yow reed,
Ne dooth unto an oold man noon harm
      now,   745
Namoore than that ye wolde men did to yow
In age, if that ye so longe abyde.
And God be with yow, where ye go or ryde!
I moot go thider as I have to go."
    "Nay, olde cherl, by God, thou shalt nat so,"
Seyde this oother hasardour anon;   751
"Thou partest nat so lightly, by Seint John!
Thou spak right now of thilke traytour Deeth,
That in this contree alle oure freendes sleeth.
Have heer my trouthe, as thou art his espye,
Telle where he is, or thou shalt it abye,   756
By God, and by the hooly sacrement!

For soothly thou art oon of his assent
To sleen us yonge folk, thou false theef!"   759
   "Now, sires," quod he, "if that yow be so leef
To fynde Deeth, turne up this croked wey,
For in that grove I lafte hym, by my fey,
Under a tree, and there he wole abyde;
Noght for youre boost he wole him no thyng
      hyde.
Se ye that ook? Right there ye shal hym
      fynde.   765
God save yow, that boghte agayn mankynde,
And yow amende!" Thus seyde this olde man;
And everich of thise riotoures ran
Til he cam to that tree, and ther they founde
Of floryns fyne of gold ycoyned rounde   770
Wel ny an eighte busshels, as hem thoughte.
No lenger thanne after Deeth they soughte,
But ech of hem so glad was of that sighte,
For that the floryns been so faire and brighte,
That doun they sette hem by this precious
      hoord.   775
The worste of hem, he spak the firste word.
   "Bretheren," quod he, "taak kep what that I
      seye;
My wit is greet, though that I bourde and
      pleye.
This tresor hath Fortune unto us yiven,
In myrthe and jolitee oure lyf to lyven,   780
And lightly as it comth, so wol we spende.
Ey! Goddes precious dignitee! who wende
To-day that we sholde han so fair a grace?
But myghte this gold be caried fro this place
Hoom to myn hous, or elles unto youres —   785
For wel ye woot that al this gold is oures —
Thanne were we in heigh felicitee.
But trewely, by daye it may nat bee.
Men wolde seyn that we were theves stronge,
And for oure owene tresor doon us honge.   790
This tresor moste ycaried be by nyghte
As wisely and as slyly as it myghte.
Wherfore I rede that cut among us alle
Be drawe, and lat se wher the cut wol falle;
And he that hath the cut with herte blithe   795
Shal renne to the town, and that ful swithe,
And brynge us breed and wyn ful prively.
And two of us shul kepen subtilly
This tresor wel; and if he wol nat tarie,
Whan it is nyght, we wol this tresor carie,   800
By oon assent, where as us thynketh best."
That oon of hem the cut broghte in his fest,
And bad hem drawe, and looke where it wol
      falle;
And it fil on the yongeste of hem alle,
And forth toward the toun he wente anon.   805

And also soone as that he was gon,
That oon of hem spak thus unto that oother:
"Thow knowest wel thou art my sworen
      brother;
Thy profit wol I telle thee anon.
Thou woost wel that oure felawe is agon.   810
And heere is gold, and that ful greet plentee,
That shal departed been among us thre.
But nathelees, if I kan shape it so
That it departed were among us two,
Hadde I nat doon a freendes torn to thee?"   815
   That oother answerde, "I noot hou that may
      be.
He woot wel that the gold is with us tweye;
What shal we doon? What shal we to hym
      seye?"
   "Shal it be conseil?" seyde the firste shrewe,
"And I shal tellen in a wordes fewe   820
What we shal doon, and brynge it wel aboute."
   "I graunte," quod that oother, "out of doute,
That, by my trouthe, I wol thee nat biwreye."
   "Now," quod the firste, "thou woost wel we
      be tweye,
And two of us shul strenger be than oon.   825
Looke whan that he is set, that right anoon
Arys as though thou woldest with hym pleye,
And I shal ryve hym thurgh the sydes tweye
Whil that thou strogelest with hym as in game,
And with thy daggere looke thou do the same;
And thanne shal al this gold departed be,   831
My deere freend, bitwixen me and thee.
Thanne may we bothe oure lustes all fulfille,
And pleye at dees right at oure owene wille."
And thus acorded been thise shrewes tweye
To sleen the thridde, as ye han herd me seye.   836
   This yongeste, which that wente to the toun,
Ful ofte in herte he rolleth up and doun
The beautee of thise floryns newe and brighte.
"O Lord!" quod he, "if so were that I myghte
Have al this tresor to myself allone,   841
Ther is no man that lyveth under the trone
Of God that sholde lyve so murye as I!"
And atte laste the feend, oure enemy,   844
Putte in his thought that he sholde poyson beye,
With which he myghte sleen his felawes tweye;
For-why the feend foond hym in swich lyvynge
That he hadde leve him to sorwe brynge.
For this was outrely his fulle entente,
To sleen hem bothe, and nevere to repente.   850
And forth he gooth, no lenger wolde he tarie,
Into the toun, unto a pothecarie,
And preyde hym that he hym wolde selle
Som poyson, that he myghte his rattes quelle;
And eek ther was a polcat in his hawe,   855

That, as he seyde, his capouns hadde yslawe,
And fayn he wolde wreke hym, if he myghte,
On vermyn that destroyed hym by nyghte.
   The pothecarie answerde, "And thou shalt
      have
A thyng that, also God my soule save,   860
In al this world ther is no creature,
That eten or dronken hath of this confiture
Noght but the montance of a corn of whete,
That he ne shal his lif anon forlete;
Ye, sterve he shal, and that in lasse while   865
Than thou wolt goon a paas nat but a mile,
This poysoun is so strong and violent."
   This cursed man hath in his hond yhent
This poysoun in a box, and sith he ran
Into the nexte strete unto a man,   870
And borwed of hym large botelles thre;
And in the two his poyson poured he;
The thridde he kepte clene for his drynke.
For al the nyght he shoop hym for to swynke
In cariynge of the gold out of that place.   875
And whan this riotour, with sory grace,
Hadde filled with wyn his grete botels thre,
To his felawes agayn repaireth he.
   What nedeth it to sermone of it moore?   879
For right as they hadde cast his deeth bifoore,
Right so they han hym slayn, and that anon.
And whan that this was doon, thus spak that
      oon:
"Now lat us sitte and drynke, and make us
      merie,
And afterward we wol his body berie."   884
And with that word it happed hym, par cas,
To take the botel ther the poyson was,
And drank, and yaf his felawe drynke also,
For which anon they storven bothe two.
   But certes, I suppose that Avycen
Wroot nevere in no canon, ne in no fen,   890
Mo wonder signes of empoisonyng
Than hadde thise wrecches two, er hir endyng.
Thus ended been thise homycides two,
And eek the false empoysonere also.
   O cursed synne of alle cursednesse!   895
O traytours homycide, O wikkednesse!
O glotonye, luxurie, and hasardrye!
Thou blasphemour of Crist with vileynye
And othes grete, of usage and of pride!
Allas! mankynde, how may it bitide   900
That to thy creatour, which that thee wroghte,
And with his precious herte-blood thee boghte,
Thou art so fals and so unkynde, allas?
   Now, goode men, God foryeve yow youre
      trespas,
And ware yow fro the synne of avarice!   905

Myn hooly pardoun may yow alle warice,
So that ye offre nobles or sterlynges,
Or elles silver broches, spoones, rynges.
Boweth youre heed under this hooly bulle!   909
Cometh up, ye wyves, offreth of youre wolle!
Youre names I entre heer in my rolle anon;
Into the blisse of hevene shul ye gon.
I yow assoille, by myn heigh power,
Yow that wol offre, as clene and eek as cleer
As ye were born. — And lo, sires, thus I preche.
And Jhesu Crist, that is oure soules leche,   916
So graunte yow his pardoun to receyve,
For that is best; I wol yow nat deceyve.
   But, sires, o word forgat I in my tale:
I have relikes and pardoun in my male,   920
As faire as any man in Engelond,
Whiche were me yeven by the popes hond.
If any of yow wole, of devocion,
Offren, and han myn absolucion,
Com forth anon, and kneleth heere adoun,   925
And mekely receyveth my pardoun;
Or elles taketh pardoun as ye wende,
Al newe and fressh at every miles ende,
So that ye offren, alwey newe and newe,
Nobles or pens, whiche that be goode and
      trewe.   930
It is an honour to everich that is heer
That ye mowe have a suffisant pardoneer
T'assoille yow, in contree as ye ryde,
For aventures whiche that may bityde.
Paraventure ther may fallen oon or two   935
Doun of his hors, and breke his nekke atwo.
Looke which a seuretee is it to yow alle
That I am in youre felaweshipe yfalle,
That may assoille yow, bothe moore and lasse,
Whan that the soule shal fro the body passe.
I rede that oure Hoost heere shal bigynne,   941
For he is moost envoluped in synne.
Com forth, sire Hoost, and offre first anon,
And thou shalt kisse the relikes everychon,
Ye, for a grote! Unbokele anon thy purs."   945
   "Nay, nay!" quod he, "thanne have I Cristes
      curs!
Lat be," quod he, "it shal nat be, so theech!
Thou woldest make me kisse thyn olde breech,
And swere it were a relyk of a seint,   949
Though it were with thy fundement depeint!
But, by the croys which that Seint Eleyne fond,
I wolde I hadde thy coillons in myn hond
In stide of relikes or of seintuarie.
Lat kutte hem of, I wol thee helpe hem carie;
They shul be shryned in an hogges toord!"   955
   This Pardoner answerde nat a word;
So wrooth he was, no word ne wolde he seye.

"Now," quod oure Hoost, "I wol no lenger pleye
With thee, ne with noon oother angry man."
But right anon the worthy Knyght bigan, 960
Whan that he saugh that al the peple lough,
"Namoore of this, for it is right ynough!

Sire Pardoner, be glad and myrie of cheere;
And ye, sire Hoost, that been to me so deere,
I prey yow that ye kisse the Pardoner. 965
And Pardoner, I prey thee, drawe thee neer,
And, as we diden, lat us laughe and pleye."
Anon they kiste, and ryden forth hir weye.

Heere is ended the Pardoners Tale.

"Now, quod oure Hoost, ... old and myrie of chere;
With thee, ne with noon oother angry man." . . . . I prey yow that ye kisse the Pardoner.   968
But right anon the worthy Knyght bigan, ... And Pardoner, I prey thee, drawe thee neer,
Whan that he saugh that al the peple lough, ... And, as we diden, lat us laughe and pleye."
"Namoore of this, for it is right ynough! . . . . Anon they kiste, and ryden forth hir weye.

Heere is ended the Pardoners Tale.

Fragment VII (Group B²)*

The Shipman's Tale

Heere bigynneth the Shipmannes Tale.

A marchant whilom dwelled at Seint-Denys,
That riche was, for which men helde hym wys.
A wyf he hadde of excellent beautee;
And compaignable and revelous was she,   4
Which is a thyng that causeth more dispence
Than worth is al the chiere and reverence
That men hem doon at festes and at daunces.
Swiche salutaciouns and contenaunces
Passen as dooth a shadwe upon the wal;
But wo is hym that payen moot for al!   *1200
The sely housbonde, algate he moot paye,
He moot us clothe, and he moot us arraye,
Al for his owene worshipe richely,
In which array we daunce jolily.
And if that he noght may, par aventure,   15
Or ellis list no swich dispence endure,
But thynketh it is wasted and ylost,
Thanne moot another payen for oure cost,
Or lene us gold, and that is perilous.
   This noble marchaunt heeld a worthy
      hous,   *1210
For which he hadde alday so greet repair
For his largesse, and for his wyf was fair,
That wonder is; but herkneth to my tale.
Amonges alle his gestes, grete and smale,
Ther was a monk, a fair man and a boold —   25
I trowe a thritty wynter he was oold —
That evere in oon was drawynge to that place.
This yonge monk, that was so fair of face,
Aqueynted was so with the goode man,
Sith that hir firste kneweliche bigan,   *1220
That in his hous as famulier was he
As it is possible any freend to be.
   And for as muchel as this goode man,
And eek this monk, of which that I bigan,
Were bothe two yborn in o village,   35
The monk hym claymeth as for cosynage;
And he agayn, he seith nat ones nay,
But was as glad therof as fowel of day;
For to his herte it was a greet plesaunce.
Thus been they knyt with eterne alli-
      aunce,   *1230

And ech of hem gan oother for t'assure
Of bretherhede, whil that hir lyf may dure.
   Free was daun John, and namely of dispence,
As in that hous, and ful of diligence
To doon plesaunce, and also greet costage.   45
He noght forgat to yeve the leeste page
In al that hous; but after hir degree,
He yaf the lord, and sitthe al his meynee,
Whan that he cam, som manere honest
      thyng;   *1239
For which they were as glad of his comyng
As fowel is fayn whan that the sonne up riseth.
Na moore of this as now, for it suffiseth.
   But so bifel, this marchant on a day
Shoop hym to make redy his array
Toward the toun of Brugges for to fare,   55
To byen there a porcioun of ware;
For which he hath to Parys sent anon
A messager, and preyed hath daun John
That he sholde come to Seint-Denys to pleye
With hym and with his wyf a day or
      tweye,   *1250
Er he to Brugges wente, in alle wise.
   This noble monk, of which I yow devyse,
Hath of his abbot, as hym list, licence,
By cause he was a man of heigh prudence,
And eek an officer, out for to ryde,   65
To seen hir graunges and hire bernes wyde,
And unto Seint-Denys he comth anon.
Who was so welcome as my lord daun John,
Oure deere cosyn, ful of curteisye?
With hym broghte he a jubbe of mal-
      vesye,   *1260
And eek another, ful of fyn vernage,
And volatyl, as ay was his usage.
And thus I lete hem ete and drynke and pleye,
This marchant and this monk, a day or tweye.
   The thridde day, this marchant up ariseth,
And on his nedes sadly hym avyseth,   76
And up into his countour-hous gooth he
To rekene with hymself, as wel may be,
Of thilke yeer how that it with hym stood,

*For the convenience of the reader in finding references, the traditional numbering of Group B², marked
with asterisks, is carried alternately with that of Fragment VII.

And how that he despended hadde his
    good,   *1270
And if that he encressed were or noon.
His bookes and his bagges many oon
He leith biforn hym on his countyng-bord.
Ful riche was his tresor and his hord,   84
For which ful faste his countour-dore he shette;
And eek he nolde that no man sholde hym lette
Of his acountes, for the meene tyme;
And thus he sit til it was passed pryme.

    Daun John was rysen in the morwe also,
And in the gardyn walketh to and fro,   *1280
And hath his thynges seyd ful curteisly.

    This goode wyf cam walkynge pryvely
Into the gardyn, there he walketh softe,
And hym saleweth, as she hath doon ofte.
A mayde child cam in hire compaignye,   95
Which as hir list she may governe and gye,
For yet under the yerde was the mayde.
"O deere cosyn myn, daun John," she sayde,
"What eyleth yow so rathe for to ryse?"
    "Nece," quod he, "it oghte ynough suf-
    fise   *1290
Fyve houres for to slepe upon a nyght,
But it were for an old appalled wight,
As been thise wedded men, that lye and dare
As in a fourme sit a wery hare,
Were al forstraught with houndes grete and
    smale.
But deere nece, why be ye so pale?   106
I trowe, certes, that oure goode man
Hath yow laboured sith the nyght bigan,
That yow were nede to resten hastily."
And with that word he lough ful murily,
And of his owene thought he wax al
    reed.   *1301

    This faire wyf gan for to shake hir heed
And seyde thus, "Ye, God woot al," quod she.
"Nay, cosyn myn, it stant nat so with me;
For, by that God that yaf me soule and lyf,
In al the reawme of France is ther no wyf   116
That lasse lust hath to that sory pley.
For I may synge 'allas and weylawey
That I was born,' but to no wight," quod she,
"Dar I nat telle how that it stant with
    me.   *1310
Wherfore I thynke out of this land to wende,
Or elles of myself to make an ende,
So ful am I of drede and eek of care."

    This monk bigan upon this wyf to stare,
And seyde, "Allas, my nece, God forbede   125
That ye, for any sorwe or any drede,
Fordo youreself; but telleth me youre grief.
Paraventure I may, in youre meschief,

Conseille or helpe; and therfore telleth me
Al youre anoy, for it shal been secree.   *1320
For on my porthors here I make an ooth
That nevere in my lyf, for lief ne looth,
Ne shal I of no conseil yow biwreye."
    "The same agayn to yow," quod she, "I seye.
By God and by this porthors I yow swere,   135
Though men me wolde al into pieces tere,
Ne shal I nevere, for to goon to helle,
Biwreye a word of thyng that ye me telle,
Nat for no cosynage ne alliance,
But verraily, for love and affiance."   *1330
Thus been they sworn, and heerupon they kiste,
And ech of hem tolde oother what hem liste.

    "Cosyn," quod she, "if that I hadde a space,
As I have noon, and namely in this place,
Thanne wolde I telle a legende of my lyf,   145
What I have suffred sith I was a wyf
With myn housbonde, al be he youre cosyn."
    "Nay," quod this monk, "by God and seint
    Martyn,
He is na moore cosyn unto me
Than is this leef that hangeth on the
    tree!   *1340
I clepe hym so, by Seint Denys of Fraunce,
To have the moore cause of aqueyntaunce
Of yow, which I have loved specially
Aboven alle wommen, sikerly.
This swere I yow on my professioun.   155
Telleth youre grief, lest that he come adoun;
And hasteth yow, and gooth youre wey anon."
    "My deere love," quod she, "O my daun
    John,
Ful lief were me this conseil for to hyde,
But out it moot, I may namoore abyde.
Myn housbonde is to me the worste man   *1351
That evere was sith that the world bigan.
But sith I am a wyf, it sit nat me
To tellen no wight of oure privetee,
Neither abedde, ne in noon oother place;   165
God shilde I sholde it tellen, for his grace!
A wyf ne shal nat seyn of hir housbonde
But al honour, as I kan understonde;
Save unto yow thus muche I tellen shal:
As helpe me God, he is noght worth at al   *1360
In no degree the value of a flye.
But yet me greveth moost his nygardye.
And wel ye woot that wommen naturelly
Desiren thynges sixe as wel as I:
They wolde that hir housbondes sholde be   175
Hardy, and wise, and riche, and therto free,
And buxom unto his wyf, and fressh abedde.
But by that ilke Lord that for us bledde,
For his honour, myself for to arraye,

A Sonday next I moste nedes paye   *1370
An hundred frankes, or ellis I am lorn.
Yet were me levere that I were unborn
Than me were doon a sclaundre or vileynye;
And if myn housbonde eek it myghte espye,
I nere but lost; and therfore I yow preye, 185
Lene me this somme, or ellis moot I deye.
Daun John, I seye, lene me thise hundred
    frankes.
Pardee, I wol nat faille yow my thankes,
If that yow list to doon that I yow praye.
For at a certeyn day I wol yow paye,   *1380
And doon to yow what plesance and service
That I may doon, right as yow list devise.
And but I do, God take on me vengeance
As foul as evere hadde Genylon of France."
    This gentil monk answerde in this manere:
"Now trewely, myn owene lady deere, 196
I have," quod he, "on yow so greet a routhe
That I yow swere, and plighte yow my trouthe,
That whan youre housbonde is to Flaundres
    fare,
I wol delyvere yow out of this care;   *1390
For I wol brynge yow an hundred frankes."
And with that word he caughte hire by the
    flankes,
And hire embraceth harde, and kiste hire ofte.
"Gooth now youre wey," quod he, "al stille and
    softe,
And lat us dyne as soone as that ye may; 205
For by my chilyndre it is pryme of day.
Gooth now, and beeth as trewe as I shal be."
    "Now elles God forbede, sire," quod she;
And forth she gooth as jolif as a pye,
And bad the cookes that they sholde hem
    hye,   *1400
So that men myghte dyne, and that anon.
Up to hir housbonde is this wyf ygon,
And knokketh at his countour boldely.
  "*Quy la?*" quod he. "Peter! it am I,"
Quod she; "what, sire, how longe wol ye faste?
How longe tyme wol ye rekene and caste 216
Youre sommes, and youre bookes, and youre
    thynges?
The devel have part on alle swiche rekenynges!
Ye have ynough, pardee, of Goddes sonde;
Com doun to-day, and lat youre bagges
    stonde.   *1410
Ne be ye nat ashamed that daun John
Shal fasting al this day alenge goon?
What! lat us heere a messe, and go we dyne."
  "Wyf," quod this man, "litel kanstow devyne
The curious bisynesse that we have. 225
For of us chapmen, also God me save,

And by that lord that clepid is Seint Yve,
Scarsly amonges twelve tweye shul thryve
Continuelly, lastynge unto oure age.
We may wel make chiere and good
    visage,   *1420
And dryve forth the world as it may be,
And kepen oure estaat in pryvetee,
Til we be deed, or elles that we pleye
A pilgrymage, or goon out of the weye.
And therfore have I greet necessitee 235
Upon this queynte world t'avyse me;
For everemoore we moote stonde in drede
Of hap and fortune in oure chapmanhede.
    To Flaundres wol I go to-morwe at day,
And come agayn, as soone as evere I
    may.   *1430
For which, my deere wyf, I thee biseke,
As be to every wight buxom and meke,
And for to kepe oure good be curious,
And honestly governe wel oure hous.
Thou hast ynough, in every maner wise, 245
That to a thrifty houshold may suffise.
Thee lakketh noon array ne no vitaille;
Of silver in thy purs shaltow nat faille."
And with that word his countour-dore he shette,
And doun he gooth, no lenger wolde he
    lette.   *1440
But hastily a messe was ther seyd,
And spedily the tables were yleyd,
And to the dyner faste they hem spedde,
And richely this monk the chapman fedde.
    At after-dyner daun John sobrely 255
This chapman took apart, and prively
He seyde hym thus: "Cosyn, it standeth so,
That wel I se to Brugges wol ye go.
God and seint Austyn spede yow and gyde!
I prey yow, cosyn, wisely that ye ryde.   *1450
Governeth yow also of youre diete
Atemprely, and namely in this hete.
Bitwix us two nedeth no strange fare;
Farewel, cosyn; God shilde yow fro care!
And if that any thyng by day or nyght, 265
If it lye in my power and my myght,
That ye me wol comande in any wyse,
It shal be doon, right as ye wol devyse.
    O thyng, er that ye goon, if it may be,
I wolde prey yow; for to lene me   *1460
An hundred frankes, for a wyke or tweye,
For certein beestes that I moste beye,
To stoore with a place that is oures.
God helpe me so, I wolde it were youres!
I shal nat faille surely of my day, 275
Nat for a thousand frankes, a mile way.
But lat this thyng be secree, I yow preye,

For yet to-nyght thise beestes moot I beye.
And fare now wel, myn owene cosyn deere;
Graunt mercy of youre cost and of youre
    cheere."   °1470
    This noble marchant gentilly anon
Answerde and seyde, "O cosyn myn, daun John,
Now sikerly this is a smal requeste.
My gold is youres, whan that it yow leste,
And nat oonly my gold, but my chaffare.   285
Take what yow list, God shilde that ye spare.
    But o thyng is, ye knowe it wel ynogh,
Of chapmen, that hir moneie is hir plogh.
We may creaunce whil we have a name;
But goldlees for to be, it is no game.   °1480
Paye it agayn whan it lith in youre ese;
After my myght ful fayn wolde I yow plese."
    Thise hundred frankes he fette forth anon,
And prively he took hem to daun John.   294
No wight in al this world wiste of this loone,
Savynge this marchant and daun John allone.
They drynke, and speke, and rome a while and
    pleye,
Til that daun John rideth to his abbeye.
    The morwe cam, and forth this marchant
    rideth
To Flaundres-ward; his prentys wel hym
    gydeth,   °1490
Til he came into Brugges murily.
Now gooth this marchant faste and bisily
Aboute his nede, and byeth and creaunceth.
He neither pleyeth at the dees ne daunceth,
But as a marchaunt, shortly for to telle,   305
He let him lyf, and there I lete hym dwelle.
    The Sonday next the marchant was agon,
To Seint-Denys ycomen is daun John,
With crowne and berd al fressh and newe
    yshave.   °1499
In al the hous ther nas so litel a knave,
Ne no wight elles, that he nas ful fayn
For that my lord daun John was come agayn.
And shortly to the point right for to gon,
This faire wyf acorded with daun John
That for thise hundred frankes he sholde al
    nyght   315
Have hire in his armes bolt upright;
And this acord parfourned was in dede.
In myrthe al nyght a bisy lyf they lede
Til it was day, that daun John wente his way,
And bad the meynee "farewel, have good
    day!"   °1510
For noon of hem, ne no wight in the toun,
Hath of daun John right no suspecioun.
And forth he rydeth hoom to his abbeye,
Or where hym list; namoore of hym I seye.

    This marchant, whan that ended was the
    faire,
To Seint-Denys he gan for to repaire,   326
And with his wyf he maketh feeste and cheere,
And telleth hire that chaffare is so deere
That nedes moste he make a chevyssaunce;
For he was bounden in a reconyssaunce   °1520
To paye twenty thousand sheeld anon.
For which this marchant is to Parys gon
To borwe of certeine freendes that he hadde
A certeyn frankes; and somme with him he
    ladde.
And whan that he was come into the toun,   335
For greet chiertee and greet affeccioun,
Unto daun John he gooth first, hym to pleye;
Nat for to axe or borwe of hym moneye,
But for to wite and seen of his welfare,
And for to tellen hym of his chaffare,
As freendes doon whan they been met
    yfeere.   °1531
Daun John hym maketh feeste and murye
    cheere,
And he hym tolde agayn, ful specially,
How he hadde wel yboght and graciously,
Thanked be God, al hool his marchandise;   345
Save that he moste, in alle maner wise,
Maken a chevyssaunce, as for his beste,
And thanne he sholde been in joye and reste.
    Daun John answerde, "Certes, I am
    fayn   °1539
That ye in heele ar comen hom agayn.
And if that I were riche, as have I blisse,
Of twenty thousand sheeld sholde ye nat mysse,
For ye so kyndely this oother day
Lente me gold; and as I kan and may,
I thanke yow, by God and by seint Jame!   355
But nathelees, I took unto oure dame,
Youre wyf, at hom, the same gold ageyn
Upon youre bench; she woot it wel, certeyn,
By certeyn tokenes that I kan hire telle.
Now, by youre leve, I may no lenger
    dwelle;   °1550
Oure abbot wole out of this toun anon,
And in his compaignye moot I goon.
Grete wel oure dame, myn owene nece sweete,
And fare wel, deere cosyn, til we meete!"
    This marchant, which that was ful war and
    wys,
Creanced hath, and payd eek in Parys   366
To certeyn Lumbardes, redy in hir hond,
The somme of gold, and gat of hem his bond;
And hoom he gooth, murie as a papejay,
For wel he knew he stood in swich array   °1560
That nedes moste he wynne in that viage

A thousand frankes aboven al his costage.
  His wyf ful redy mette hym atte gate,
As she was wont of oold usage algate,
And al that nyght in myrthe they bisette;   375
For he was riche and cleerly out of dette.
Whan it was day, this marchant gan embrace
His wyf al newe, and kiste hire on hir face,
And up he gooth and maketh it ful tough.
  "Namoore," quod she, "by God, ye have
    ynough!"   *1570
And wantownly agayn with hym she pleyde,
Til atte laste thus this marchant seyde:
"By God," quod he, "I am a litel wrooth
With yow, my wyf, although it be me looth.
And woot ye why? by God, as that I gesse   385
That ye han maad a manere straungenesse
Bitwixen me and my cosyn daun John.
Ye sholde han warned me, er I had gon,
That he yow hadde an hundred frankes payed
By redy token; and heeld hym yvele
    apayed,   *1580
For that I to hym spak of chevyssaunce;
Me semed so, as by his contenaunce.
But nathelees, by God, oure hevene kyng,
I thoughte nat to axen hym no thyng.
I prey thee, wyf, ne do namoore so;   395
Telle me alwey, er that I fro thee go,
If any dettour hath in myn absence
Ypayed thee, lest thurgh thy necligence
I myghte hym axe a thing that he hath payed."
  This wyf was nat afered nor affrayed,
But boldely she seyde, and that anon;   *1591
"Marie, I deffie the false monk, daun John!

I kepe nat of his tokenes never a deel;
He took me certeyn gold, that woot I weel, —
What! yvel thedam on his monkes snowte!   405
For, God it woot, I wende, withouten doute,
That he hadde yeve it me bycause of yow,
To doon therwith myn honour and my prow,
For cosynage, and eek for beele cheere
That he hath had ful ofte tymes heere.   *1600
But sith I se I stonde in this disjoynt,
I wol answere yow shortly to the poynt.
Ye han mo slakkere dettours than am I!
For I wol paye yow wel and redily
Fro day to day, and if so be I faille,   415
I am youre wyf; score it upon my taille,
And I shal paye as soone as ever I may.
For by my trouthe, I have on myn array,
And nat on wast, bistowed every deel;
And for I have bistowed it so weel   *1610
For youre honour, for Goddes sake, I seye,
As be nat wrooth, but lat us laughe and pleye.
Ye shal my joly body have to wedde;
By God, I wol nat paye yow but abedde!
Forgyve it me, myn owene spouse deere;   425
Turne hiderward, and maketh bettre cheere."
  This marchant saugh ther was no remedie,
And for to chide it nere but folie,
Sith that the thyng may nat amended be.
"Now wyf," he seyde, "and I foryeve it
    thee;   *1620
But, by thy lyf, ne be namoore so large.
Keep bet my good, this yeve I thee in charge."
Thus endeth now my tale, and God us sende
Taillynge ynough unto oure lyves ende. Amen

Heere endeth the Shipmannes Tale.

Bihoold the murie wordes of the Hoost to the Shipman
and to the lady Prioresse.

"Wel seyd, by *corpus dominus*," quod oure
    Hoost,
"Now longe moote thou saille by the cost,   436
Sire gentil maister, gentil maryneer!
God yeve the monk a thousand last quade yeer!
A ha! felawes! beth ware of swich a jape!
The monk putte in the mannes hood an ape,
And in his wyves eek, by Seint Austyn!   *1631
Draweth no monkes moore unto youre in.
  But now passe over, and lat us seke aboute,

Who shal now telle first of al this route
Another tale;" and with that word he sayde,
As curteisly as it had been a mayde,   445
"My lady Prioresse, by youre leve,
So that I wiste I sholde yow nat greve,
I wolde demen that ye tellen sholde
A tale next, if so were that ye wolde.   *1640
Now wol ye vouche sauf, my lady deere?"
  "Gladly," quod she, and seyde as ye shal
    heere.

Prologue of The Prioress's Tale

The Prologe of the Prioresses Tale.

Domine dominus noster.

"O Lord, oure Lord, thy name how merveil-
    lous
Is in this large world ysprad," quod she;
"For noght oonly thy laude precious   455
Parfourned is by men of dignitee,
But by the mouth of children thy bountee
Parfourned is, for on the brest soukynge
Somtyme shewen they thyn heriynge.

Wherfore in laude, as I best kan or may,   °1650
Of thee and of the white lylye flour
Which that the bar, and is a mayde alway,
To telle a storie I wol do my labour;
Nat that I may encressen hir honour,
For she hirself is honour and the roote   465
Of bountee, next hir Sone, and soules boote.

O mooder Mayde! o mayde Mooder free!
O bussh unbrent, brennynge in Moyses
    sighte,
That ravyshedest doun fro the Deitee,

Thurgh thyn humblesse, the Goost that in
    th'alighte,   °1660
Of whos vertu, whan he thyn herte lighte,
Conceyved was the Fadres sapience,
Help me to telle it in thy reverence!

Lady, thy bountee, thy magnificence,
Thy vertu, and thy grete humylitee,   475
Ther may no tonge expresse in no science;
For somtyme, Lady, er men praye to thee,
Thou goost biforn of thy benyngnytee,
And getest us the lyght, of thy preyere,
To gyden us unto thy Sone so deere.   °1670

My konnyng is so wayk, o blisful Queene,
For to declare thy grete worthynesse
That I ne may the weighte nat susteene;
But as a child of twelf month oold, or lesse,
That kan unnethes any word expresse,   485
Right so fare I, and therfore I yow preye,
Gydeth my song that I shal of yow seye."

Explicit.

The Prioress's Tale

Heere bigynneth the Prioresses Tale.

Ther was in Asye, in a greet citee,
Amonges Cristene folk, a Jewerye,
Sustened by a lord of that contree   °1680
For foule usure and lucre of vileynye,
Hateful to Crist and to his compaignye;
And thurgh the strete men myghte ride or
    wende,
For it was free and open at eyther ende.

A litel scole of Cristen folk ther stood   495
Doun at the ferther ende, in which ther were
Children an heep, ycomen of Cristen blood,
That lerned in that scole yeer by yere
Swich manere doctrine as men used there,

This is to seyn, to syngen and to rede,   °1690
As smale children doon in hire childhede.

Among thise children was a wydwes sone,
A litel clergeon, seven yeer of age,
That day by day to scole was his wone,
And eek also, where as he saugh th'ymage
Of Cristes mooder, hadde he in usage,   506
As hym was taught, to knele adoun and seye
His *Ave Marie*, as he goth by the weye.

Thus   hath   this   wydwe   hir   litel   sone
    ytaught   °1699
Oure blisful Lady, Cristes mooder deere,

To worshipe ay, and he forgat it naught,
For sely child wol alday soone leere.
But ay, whan I remembre on this mateere,
Seint Nicholas stant evere in my presence,
For he so yong to Crist dide reverence.   515

This litel child, his litel book lernynge,
As he sat in the scole at his prymer,
He *Alma redemptoris* herde synge,
As children lerned hire antiphoner;
And as he dorste, he drough hym ner and
          ner,   °1710
And herkned ay the wordes and the noote,
Til he the firste vers koude al by rote.

Noght wiste he what this Latyn was to seye,
For he so yong and tendre was of age.
But on a day his felawe gan he preye   525
T'expounden hym this song in his langage,
Or telle hym why this song was in usage;
This preyde he hym to construe and declare
Ful often tyme upon his knowes bare.

His felawe, which that elder was than
          he,   °1720
Answerde hym thus: "This song, I have herd
          seye,
Was maked of our blisful Lady free,
Hire to salue, and eek hire for to preye   533
To been oure help and socour whan we deye.
I kan namoore expounde in this mateere;
I lerne song, I kan but smal grammeere."

     "And is this song maked in reverence
Of Cristes mooder?" seyde this innocent.
"Now, certes, I wol do my diligence
To konne it al er Cristemasse be went.   °1730
Though that I for my prymer shal be shent,
And shal be beten thries in an houre,
I wol it konne Oure Lady for to honoure!"

His felawe taughte hym homward prively,
Fro day to day, til he koude it by rote,   545
And thanne he song it wel and boldely,
Fro word to word, acordynge with the note.
Twies a day it passed thurgh his throte,
To scoleward and homward whan he
          wente;   °1739
On Cristes mooder set was his entente.

     As I have seyd, thurghout the Juerie,
This litel child, as he cam to and fro,
Ful murily than wolde he synge and crie
O Alma redemptoris everemo.

The swetnesse hath his herte perced so   555
Of Cristes mooder that, to hire to preye,
He kan nat stynte of syngyng by the weye.

     Oure firste foo, the serpent Sathanas,
That hath in Jues herte his waspes nest,
Up swal, and seide, "O Hebrayk peple,
          allas!   °1750
Is this to yow a thyng that is honest,
That swich a boy shal walken as hym lest
In youre despit, and synge of swich sentence,
Which is agayn youre lawes reverence?"

Fro thennes forth the Jues han conspired   565
This innocent out of this world to chace.
An homycide therto han they hyred,
That in an aleye hadde a privee place;
And as the child gan forby for to pace,
This cursed Jew hym hente, and heeld hym
          faste,   °1760
And kitte his throte, and in a pit hym caste.

I seye that in a wardrobe they hym threwe
Where as thise Jewes purgen hire entraille.
O cursed folk of Herodes al newe,
What may youre yvel entente yow availle?   575
Mordre wol out, certeyn, it wol nat faille,
And namely ther th'onour of God shal sprede;
The blood out crieth on youre cursed dede.

     O martir, sowded to virginitee,
Now maystow syngen, folwynge evere in
          oon   °1770
The white Lamb celestial — quod she —
Of which the grete evaungelist, Seint John,
In Pathmos wroot, which seith that they that
          goon
Biforn this Lamb, and synge a song al newe,
That nevere, flesshly, wommen they ne
          knewe.   585

     This poure wydwe awaiteth al that nyght
After hir litel child, but he cam noght;
For which, as soone as it was dayes lyght,
With face pale of drede and bisy thoght,
She hath at scole and elleswhere hym
          soght,   °1780
Til finally she gan so fer espie
That he last seyn was in the Juerie.

With moodres pitee in hir brest enclosed,
She gooth, as she were half out of hir mynde,
To every place where she hath supposed   595
By liklihede hir litel child to fynde;

And evere on Cristes mooder meeke and kynde
She cride, and atte laste thus she wroghte:
Among the cursed Jues she hym soghte.

She frayneth and she preyeth pitously   *1790
To every Jew that dwelte in thilke place,
To telle hire if hir child wente oght forby.
They seyde "nay"; but Jhesu, of his grace,
Yaf in hir thoght, inwith a litel space,
That in that place after hir sone she cryde,   605
Where he was casten in a pit bisyde.

O grete God, that parfournest thy laude
By mouth of innocentz, lo, heere thy myght!
This gemme of chastite, this emeraude,
And eek of martirdom the ruby bright,
Ther he with throte ykorven lay upright,   *1801
He *Alma redemptoris* gan to synge
So loude that al the place gan to rynge.

The Cristene folk that thurgh the strete
    wente
In coomen for to wondre upon this thyng,   615
And hastily they for the provost sente;
He cam anon withouten tariyng,
And herieth Crist that is of hevene kyng,
And eek his mooder, honour of man-
    kynde,   *1809
And after that the Jewes leet he bynde.

This child with pitous lamentacioun
Up taken was, syngynge his song alway,
And with honour of greet processioun
They carien hym unto the nexte abbay.
His mooder swownynge by the beere lay;   625
Unnethe myghte the peple that was theere
This newe Rachel brynge fro his beere.

With torment and with shameful deeth echon
This provost dooth thise Jewes for to sterve
That of this mordre wiste, and that anon.   *1820
He nolde no swich cursednesse observe.
"Yvele shal have that yvele wol deserve";
Therfore with wilde hors he dide hem drawe,
And after that he heng hem by the lawe.

Upon this beere ay lith this innocent   635
Biforn the chief auter, whil masse laste;
And after that, the abbot with his covent
Han sped hem for to burien hym ful faste;
And whan they hooly water on hym caste,
Yet spak this child, whan spreynd was hooly
    water,   *1830
And song *O Alma redemptoris mater!*

This abbot, which that was an hooly man,
As monkes been—or elles oghte be—
This yonge child to conjure he bigan,
And seyde, "O deere child, I halse thee,   645
In vertu of the hooly Trinitee,
Tel me what is thy cause for to synge,
Sith that thy throte is kut to my semynge?"

"My throte is kut unto my nekke boon,"
Seyde this child, "and, as by wey of
    kynde,   *1840
I sholde have dyed, ye, longe tyme agon.
But Jesu Crist, as ye in bookes fynde,
Wil that his glorie laste and be in mynde,
And for the worship of his Mooder deere
Yet may I synge *O Alma* loude and cleere.   655

"This welle of mercy, Cristes mooder sweete,
I loved alwey, as after my konnynge;
And whan that I my lyf sholde forlete,
To me she cam, and bad me for to synge
This anthem verraily in my deyynge,
As ye han herd, and whan that I hadde
    songe,   *1851
Me thoughte she leyde a greyn upon my
    tonge.

"Wherfore I synge, and synge moot certeyn,
In honour of that blisful Mayden free,
Til fro my tonge of taken is the greyn;   665
And after that thus seyde she to me:
'My litel child, now wol I fecche thee,
Whan that the greyn is fro thy tonge ytake.
Be nat agast, I wol thee nat forsake.' "

This hooly monk, this abbot, hym meene
    I,   *1860
His tonge out caughte, and took awey the
    greyn,
And he yaf up the goost ful softely.
And whan this abbot hadde this wonder seyn,
His salte teeris trikled doun as reyn,
And gruf he fil al plat upon the grounde,   675
And stille he lay as he had ben ybounde.

The covent eek lay on the pavement
Wepynge, and herying Cristes mooder deere,
And after that they ryse, and forth been
    went,
And tooken awey this martir from his
    beere;   *1870
And in a tombe of marbul stones cleere
Enclosen they his litel body sweete.
Ther he is now, God leve us for to meete!

O yonge Hugh of Lyncoln, slayn also
With cursed Jewes, as it is notable,   685
For it is but a litel while ago,
Preye eek for us, we synful folk unstable,

That, of his mercy, God so merciable
On us his grete mercy multiplie,
For reverence of his mooder Marie.
         Amen   °1880

Heere is ended the Prioresses Tale.

Prologue to Sir Thopas

Bihoold the murye wordes of the Hoost to Chaucer.

Whan seyd was al this miracle, every man
As sobre was that wonder was to se,
Til that oure Hooste japen tho bigan,
And thanne at erst he looked upon me,
And seyde thus: "What man artow?" quod he;
"Thou lookest as thou woldest fynde an hare,
For evere upon the ground I se thee stare.

"Approche neer, and looke up murily.
Now war yow, sires, and lat this man have
     place!
He in the waast is shape as wel as I;   °1890
This were a popet in an arm t'enbrace

For any womman, smal and fair of face.
He semeth elvyssh by his contenaunce,
For unto no wight dooth he daliaunce.

"Sey now somwhat, syn oother folk han sayd;
Telle us a tale of myrthe, and that anon."   706
"Hooste," quod I, "ne beth nat yvele apayd,
For oother tale certes kan I noon,
But of a rym I lerned longe agoon."
"Ye, that is good," quod he; "now shul we
     heere   °1900
Som deyntee thyng, me thynketh by his
     cheere."

Sir Thopas

Heere bigynneth Chaucers Tale of Thopas.

The First Fit

Listeth, lordes, in good entent,
And I wol telle verrayment
     Of myrthe and of solas;
Al of a knyght was fair and gent   715
In bataille and in tourneyment,
     His name was sire Thopas.

Yborn he was in fer contree,
In Flaundres, al biyonde the see,
     At Poperyng, in the place.   °1910
His fader was a man ful free,
And lord he was of that contree,
     As it was Goddes grace.

Sire Thopas wax a doghty swayn;
Whit was his face as payndemayn,   725

His lippes rede as rose;
His rode is lyk scarlet in grayn,
And I yow telle in good certayn,
     He hadde a semely nose.

His heer, his berd was lyk saffroun,   °1920
That to his girdel raughte adoun;
     His shoon of cordewane.
Of Brugges were his hosen broun,
His robe was of syklatoun,
     That coste many a jane.   735

He koude hunte at wilde deer,
And ride an haukyng for river
     With grey goshauk on honde;
Therto he was a good archeer;
Of wrastlyng was ther noon his peer,   °1930
     Ther any ram shal stonde.

Ful many a mayde, bright in bour,
They moorne for hym paramour,
　　Whan hem were bet to slepe;
But he was chaast and no lechour,   745
And sweete as is the brembul flour
　　That bereth the rede hepe.

And so bifel upon a day,
For sothe, as I yow telle may,
　　Sire Thopas wolde out ride.   *1940
He worth upon his steede gray,
And in his hand a launcegay,
　　A long swerd by his side.

He priketh thurgh a fair forest,
Therinne is many a wilde best,   755
　　Ye, bothe bukke and hare;
And as he priketh north and est,
I telle it yow, hym hadde almest
　　Bitid a sory care.

Ther spryngen herbes grete and smale,
The lycorys and the cetewale,   *1951
　　And many a clowe-gylofre;
And notemuge to putte in ale,
Wheither it be moyste or stale,
　　Or for to leye in cofre.   765

The briddes synge, it is no nay,
The sparhauk and the papejay,
　　That joye it was to heere;
The thrustelcok made eek his lay,
The wodedowve upon the spray   *1960
　　She sang ful loude and cleere.

Sire Thopas fil in love-longynge,
Al whan he herde the thrustel synge,
　　And pryked as he were wood.
His faire steede in his prikynge   775
So swatte that men myghte him wrynge;
　　His sydes were al blood.

Sire Thopas eek so wery was
For prikyng on the softe gras,
　　So fiers was his corage,   *1970
That doun he leyde him in that plas
To make his steede som solas,
　　And yaf hym good forage.

"O seinte Marie, *benedicite!*
What eyleth this love at me   785
　　To bynde me so soore?
Me dremed al this nyght, pardee,
An elf-queene shal my lemman be
　　And slepe under my goore.

"An elf-queene wol I love, ywis,   *1980
For in this world no womman is
　　Worthy to be my make
　　　　In towne;
Alle othere wommen I forsake,
And to an elf-queene I me take   795
　　By dale and eek by downe!"

Into his sadel he clamb anon,
And priketh over stile and stoon
　　An elf-queene for t'espye,
Til he so longe hath riden and goon   *1990
That he foond, in a pryve woon,
　　The contree of Fairye
　　　　So wilde;
For in that contree was ther noon
That to him durste ride or goon,   805
　　Neither wyf ne childe;

Til that ther cam a greet geaunt,
His name was sire Olifaunt,
　　A perilous man of dede.
He seyde, "Child, by Termagaunt!   *2000
But if thou prike out of myn haunt,
　　Anon I sle thy steede
　　　　With mace.
Heere is the queene of Fayerye,
With harpe and pipe and symphonye,   815
　　Dwellynge in this place."

The child seyde, "Also moote I thee,
Tomorwe wol I meete with thee,
　　Whan I have myn armoure;
And yet I hope, *par ma fay,*   *2010
That thou shalt with this launcegay
　　Abyen it ful sowre.
　　　　Thy mawe
Shal I percen, if I may,
Er it be fully pryme of day,   825
　　For heere thow shalt be slawe."

Sire Thopas drow abak ful faste;
This geant at hym stones caste
　　Out of a fel staf-slynge.
But faire escapeth child Thopas,   *2020
And al it was thurgh Goddes gras,
　　And thurgh his fair berynge.

Yet listeth, lordes, to my tale
Murier than the nightyngale,
　　For now I wol yow rowne   835
How sir Thopas, with sydes smale,
Prikyng over hill and dale,
　　Is comen agayn to towne.

His myrie men comanded he
To make hym bothe game and glee,   *2030
    For nedes moste he fighte
With a geaunt with hevedes three,
For paramour and jolitee
    Of oon that shoon ful brighte.

"Do come," he seyde, "my mynstrales,   845
And geestours for to tellen tales,
    Anon in myn armynge,
Of romances that been roiales,
Of popes and of cardinales,
    And eek of love-likynge."   *2040

They fette hym first the sweete wyn,
And mede eek in a mazelyn,
    And roial spicerye
Of gyngebreed that was ful fyn,
And lycorys, and eek comyn,   855
    With sugre that is trye.

He dide next his white leere,
Of cloth of lake fyn and cleere,
    A breech and eek a sherte;
And next his sherte an aketoun,   *2050
And over that an haubergeoun
    For percynge of his herte;

And over that a fyn hawberk,
Was al ywroght of Jewes werk,
    Ful strong it was of plate;   865
And over that his cote-armour
As whit as is a lilye flour,
    In which he wol debate.

His sheeld was al of gold so reed,
And therinne was a bores heed,   *2060
    A charbocle bisyde;
And there he swoor on ale and breed
How that the geaunt shal be deed,
    Bityde what bityde!

His jambeux were of quyrboilly,   875
His swerdes shethe of yvory,
    His helm of latoun bright;
His sadel was of rewel boon,
His brydel as the sonne shoon,
    Or as the moone light.   *2070

His spere was of fyn ciprees,
That bodeth werre, and nothyng pees,
    The heed ful sharpe ygrounde;
His steede was al dappull gray,
It gooth an ambil in the way   885
    Ful softely and rounde
         In londe.

Loo, lordes myne, heere is a fit!
If ye wol any moore of it,
    To telle it wol I fonde.   *2080

The Second Fit

Now holde youre mouth, *par charitee*,
Bothe knyght and lady free,
    And herkneth to my spelle;
Of bataille and of chivalry,
And of ladyes love-drury   895
    Anon I wol yow telle.

Men speken of romances of prys,
Of Horn child and of Ypotys,
    Of Beves and sir Gy,
Of sir Lybeux and Pleyndamour, —   *2090
But sir Thopas, he bereth the flour
    Of roial chivalry!

His goode steede al he bistrood,
And forth upon his wey he glood
    As sparcle out of the bronde;   905
Upon his creest he bar a tour,
And therinne stiked a lilie flour,—
    God shilde his cors fro shonde!

And for he was a knyght auntrous,
He nolde slepen in noon hous,   *2100
    But liggen in his hoode;
His brighte helm was his wonger,
And by hym baiteth his dextrer
    Of herbes fyne and goode.

Hymself drank water of the well,   915
As dide the knyght sire Percyvell
    So worthy under wede,
Til on a day —

Heere the Hoost stynteth Chaucer of his Tale of Thopas.

"Namoore of this, for Goddes dignitee,"
Quod oure Hooste, "for thou makest me   *2110
So wery of thy verray lewednesse
That, also wisly God my soule blesse,
Myne eres aken of thy drasty speche.
Now swich a rym the devel I biteche!
This may wel be rym dogerel," quod he.   925
   "Why so?" quod I, "why wiltow lette me
Moore of my tale than another man,
Syn that it is the beste rym I kan?"
   "By God," quod he, "for pleynly, at a word,
Thy drasty rymyng is nat worth a toord!
Thou doost noght elles but despendest
      tyme.   *2121
Sire, at o word, thou shalt no lenger ryme.
Lat se wher thou kanst tellen aught in geeste,
Or telle in prose somwhat, at the leeste,
In which ther be som murthe or som doc-
      tryne."   935
   "Gladly," quod I, "by Goddes sweete pyne!
I wol yow telle a litel thyng in prose
That oghte liken yow, as I suppose,
Or elles, certes, ye been to daungerous.
It is a moral tale vertuous,   *2130
Al be it told somtyme in sondry wyse
Of sondry folk, as I shal yow devyse.

As thus: ye woot that every Evaungelist,
That telleth us the peyne of Jhesu Crist,
Ne seith nat alle thyng as his felawe dooth;
But nathelees hir sentence is al sooth,   946
And alle acorden as in hire sentence,
Al be ther in hir tellyng difference.
For somme of hem seyn moore, and somme
      seyn lesse,
Whan they his pitous passioun expresse —
I meene of Mark, Mathew, Luc, and
      John —   *2141
But doutelees hir sentence is al oon.
Therfore, lordynges alle, I yow biseche,
If that yow thynke I varie as in my speche,
As thus, though that I telle somwhat moore
Of proverbes than ye han herd bifoore   956
Comprehended in this litel tretys heere,
To enforce with th' effect of my mateere,
And though I nat the same wordes seye
As ye han herd, yet to yow alle I preye   *2150
Blameth me nat; for, as in my sentence,
Shul ye nowher fynden difference
Fro the sentence of this tretys lyte
After the which this murye tale I write.
And therfore herkneth what that I shal seye,
And lat me tellen al my tale, I preye."   966

The Tale of Melibee

Heere bigynneth Chaucers Tale of Melibee.

A yong man called Melibeus, myghty and
riche, bigat upon his wyf, that called was Prudence, a doghter which that called was Sophie./
   Upon a day bifel that he for his desport is
went into the feeldes hym to pleye./ His wyf
and eek his doghter hath he left inwith his hous,
of which the dores weren faste yshette./ Thre
of his olde foes han it espyed, and setten laddres
to the walles of his hous, and by wyndowes been entred,/   *2160
and betten his wyf,
and wounded his doghter with fyve mortal woundes in fyve sondry places, — / this is to
seyn, in hir feet, in hire handes, in hir erys, in
hir nose, and in hire mouth, — and leften hire
for deed, and wenten awey./

Whan Melibeus retourned was in to his hous,
and saugh al this meschief, he, lyk a mad man,
rentynge his clothes, gan to wepe and crie./
   Prudence, his wyf, as ferforth as she dorste,
bisoghte hym of his wepyng for to stynte;/ but
nat forthy he gan to crie and wepen
evere lenger the moore./   975
   This noble wyf Prudence remembred
hire upon the sentence of Ovide, in his book
that cleped is the Remedie of Love, where as
he seith/ "He is a fool that destourbeth the
mooder to wepen in the deeth of hire child,
til she have wept hir fille as for a certein tyme;/
and thanne shal man doon his diligence with
amyable wordes hire to reconforte, and preyen

hire of hir wepyng for to stynte."/ For which
resoun this noble wyf Prudence suffred hir
housbonde for to wepe and crie as for a certein
space;/ and whan she saugh hir tyme, she
seyde hym in this wise: "Allas, my lord," quod
she, "why make ye youreself for to be
lyk a fool?/ For sothe it aperteneth nat   *2170
to a wys man to maken swich a sorwe./
Youre doghter, with the grace of God, shal
warisshe and escape./ And, al were it so that
she right now were deed, ye ne oughte nat, as
for hir deeth, youreself to destroye./ Senek
seith: 'The wise man shal nat take to greet disconfort for the deeth of his children;/ but,
certes, he sholde suffren it in pacience as wel
as he abideth the deeth of his owene
propre persone.' "/   985
This Melibeus answerde anon, and
seyde, "What man," quod he, "sholde of his
wepyng stente that hath so greet a cause for
to wepe?/ Jhesu Crist, oure Lord, hymself
wepte for the deeth of Lazarus hys freend."/
Prudence answerde: "Certes, wel I woot attempree wepyng is no thyng deffended to hym
that sorweful is, amonges folk in sorwe, but it
is rather graunted hym to wepe./ The Apostle
Paul unto the Romayns writeth, 'Man shal rejoyse with hem that maken joye, and wepen
with swich folk as wepen.'/ But though attempree wepyng be ygraunted, outra-
geous wepyng certes is deffended./   *2180
Mesure of wepyng sholde be consid-
ered, after the loore that techeth us Senek:/
'Whan that thy frend is deed,' quod he, 'lat
nat thyne eyen to moyste been of teeris, ne
to muche drye; although the teeris come to
thyne eyen, lat hem nat falle;/ and whan thou
hast forgoon thy freend, do diligence to gete
another freend; and this is moore wysdom than
for to wepe for thy freend which that thou has
lorn, for therinne is no boote.'/ And therfore,
if ye governe yow by sapience, put awey sorwe
out of youre herte./ Remembre yow that
Jhesus Syrak seith, 'A man that is joyous and
glad in herte, it hym conserveth florissynge
in his age; but soothly sorweful herte
maketh his bones drye.'/ He seith eek   995
thus, that sorwe in herte sleeth ful many
a man./ Salomon seith that right as motthes
in the shepes flees anoyeth to the clothes, and
the smale wormes to the tree, right so anoyeth
sorwe to the herte./ Wherfore us oghte, as wel
in the deeth of oure children as in the los of
oure othere goodes temporels, have pacience./

Remembre yow upon the pacient Job. Whan
he hadde lost his children and his temporeel
substance, and in his body endured and receyved ful many a grevous tribulacion, yet
seyde he thus:/ 'Oure Lord hath yeve it me;
oure Lord hath biraft it me; right as oure Lord
hath wold, right so it is doon; blessed
be the name of oure Lord!' "/   *2190
To thise forseide thynges answerde
Melibeus unto his wyf Prudence: "Alle thy
wordes," quod he, "been sothe, and therto profitable; but trewely myn herte is troubled with
this sorwe so grevously that I noot what to
doone."/
"Lat calle," quod Prudence, "thy trewe
freendes alle, and thy lynage whiche that been
wise. Telleth youre cas, and herkneth what
they seye in conseillyng, and yow governe after
hire sentence./ Salomon seith, 'Werk alle thy
thynges by conseil, and thou shalt never repente.' "/
Thanne, by the conseil of his wyf Prudence,
this Melibeus leet callen a greet congregacion
of folk;/ as surgiens, phisiciens, olde folk and
yonge, and somme of his olde enemys reconsiled as by hir semblaunt to his love and
into his grace;/ and therwithal ther   1005
coomen somme of his neighebores that
diden hym reverence moore for drede than for
love, as it happeth ofte./ Ther coomen also
ful many subtille flatereres, and wise advocatz lerned in the lawe./
And whan this folk togidre assembled weren,
this Melibeus in sorweful wise shewed hem his
cas./ And by the manere of his speche it
semed that in herte he baar a crueel ire, redy
to doon vengeaunce upon his foes, and sodeynly desired that the werre sholde bigynne;/
but nathelees, yet axed he hire conseil
upon this matiere./ A surgien, by li-   *2200
cence and assent of swiche as weren
wise, up roos, and to Melibeus seyde as ye may
heere:/
"Sire," quod he, "as to us surgiens aperteneth that we do to every wight the beste that
we kan, where as we been withholde, and to
oure pacientz that we do no damage;/ wherfore it happeth many tyme and ofte that whan
twey men han everich wounded oother, oon
same surgien heeleth hem bothe;/ wherfore
unto oure art it is nat pertinent to norice werre
ne parties to supporte./ But certes, as to the
warisshynge of youre doghter, al be it so that
she perilously be wounded, we shullen do so

ententif bisynesse fro day to nyght that with
the grace of God she shal be hool and
sound as soone as is possible."/   1015

Almoost right in the same wise the
phisiciens answerden, save that they seyden a
fewe woordes moore:/ that right as maladies
been cured by hir contraries, right so shul men
warisshe werre by vengeaunce./

His neighebores ful of envye, his feyned
freendes that semeden reconsiled, and his flat-
ereres/ maden semblant of wepyng, and em-
peireden and agreggeden muchel of this matiere in preisynge greetly Melibee of myght, of
power, of richesse, and of freendes, despisynge
the power of his adversaries,/ and seiden outrely that he anon sholde wreken hym on
his foes, and bigynne werre./   °2210

Up roos thanne an advocat that was
wys, by leve and by conseil of othere that were
wise, and seide:/ "Lordynges, the nede for
which we been assembled in this place is a ful
hevy thyng and an heigh matiere,/ by cause
of the wrong and of the wikkednesse that hath
be doon, and eek by resoun of the grete damages that in tyme comynge been possible to
fallen for this same cause,/ and eek by resoun
of the grete richesse and power of the parties
bothe;/ for the whiche resouns it were a
ful greet peril to erren in this matiere./   1025
Wherfore, Melibeus, this is oure sen-
tence: we conseille yow aboven alle thyng
that right anon thou do thy diligence in
kepynge of thy propre persone in swich
a wise that thou ne wante noon espie ne
wacche, thy persone for to save./ And after
that, we conseille that in thyn hous thou sette
sufficeant garnisoun so that they may as wel
thy body as thyn hous defende./ But certes,
for to moeve werre, ne sodeynly for to doon
vengeaunce, we may nat demen in so litel
tyme that it were profitable./ Wherfore we
axen leyser and espace to have deliberacion in
this cas to deme./ For the commune proverbe
seith thus: 'He that soone deemeth,
soone shal repente.'/ And eek men seyn   °2220
that thilke juge is wys that soone understondeth a matiere and juggeth by leyser;/ for
al be it so that alle tariyng be anoyful, algates it
is nat to repreve in yevynge of juggement ne
in vengeance takyng, whan it is sufficeant
and resonable./ And that shewed oure Lord
Jhesu Crist by ensample; for whan that the
womman that was taken in avowtrie was broght
in his presence to knowen what sholde be doon

with hire persone, al be it so that he wiste wel
hymself what that he wolde answere, yet ne
wolde he nat answere sodeynly, but he wolde
have deliberacion, and in the ground he wroot
twies./ And by thise causes weaxen deliberacioun, and we shal thanne, by the grace of
God, conseille thee thyng that shal be profitable./

Up stirten thanne the yonge folk atones, and
the mooste partie of that compaignye han
scorned this olde wise man, and bigonnen to make noyse, and seyden that/   1035
right so as, whil that iren is hoot, men
sholden smyte, right so men sholde wreken hir
wronges whil that they been fresshe and newe;
and with loud voys they criden "Werre!
werre!"/

Up roos tho oon of thise olde wise, and with
his hand made contenaunce that men sholde
holden hem stille and yeven hym audience./
"Lordynges," quod he, "ther is ful many a man
that crieth 'Werre! werre!' that woot ful litel
what werre amounteth./ Werre at his bigynnyng hath so greet an entryng and so large, that
every wight may entre whan hym liketh, and
lightly fynde werre;/ but certes what ende
that shal therof bifalle, it is nat light to
knowe./ For soothly, whan that werre is   °2230
ones bigonne, ther is ful many a child
unborn of his mooder that shal sterve yong by
cause of thilke werre, or elles lyve in sorwe and
dye in wrecchednesse./ And therfore, er that
any werre bigynne, men moste have greet conseil and greet deliberacion."/ And whan this
olde man wende to enforcen his tale by resons,
wel ny alle atones bigonne they to rise for to
breken his tale, and beden hym ful ofte his
wordes for to abregge./ For soothly, he that
precheth to hem that listen nat heeren his
wordes, his sermon hem anoieth./ For Jhesus
Syrak seith that "musik in wepynge is a noyous
thyng"; this is to seyn: as muche availleth to
speken bifore folk to which his speche anoye-
eth, as it is to synge biforn hym that
wepeth./ And whan this wise man   1045
saugh that hym wanted audience, al
shamefast he sette hym doun agayn./ For
Salomon seith: "Ther as thou ne mayst have
noon audience, enforce thee nat to speke."/
"I see wel," quod this wise man, "that the commune proverbe is sooth, that 'good conseil
wanteth whan it is moost nede.'"/

Yet hadde this Melibeus in his conseil many
folk that prively in his eere conseilled hym

certeyn thyng, and conseilled hym the contrarie in general audience./

Whan Melibeus hadde herd that the gretteste partie of his conseil weren accorded that he sholde maken werre, anoon he consented to hir conseillyng, and fully affermed hire sentence./ Thanne dame Prudence, °2240 whan that she saugh how that hir housbonde shoop hym for to wreken hym on his foes, and to bigynne werre, she in ful humble wise, whan she saugh hir tyme, seide to hym thise wordes:/ "My lord," quod she, "I yow biseche as hertely as I dar and kan, ne haste yow nat to faste, and for alle gerdons, as yeveth me audience./ For Piers Alfonce seith, 'Whoso that dooth to thee oother good or harm, haste thee nat to quiten it; for in this wise thy freend wole abyde, and thyn enemy shal the lenger lyve in drede.'/ The proverbe seith, 'He hasteth wel that wisely kan abyde,' and in wikked haste is no profit."/

This Melibee answerde unto his wyf Prudence: "I purpose nat," quod he, "to werke by thy conseil, for many causes and resouns. For certes, every wight wolde holde me thanne a fool;/ this is to seyn, if I, for 1055 thy conseillyng, wolde chaungen thynges that been ordeyned and affermed by so manye wyse./ Secoundely, I seye that alle wommen been wikke, and noon good of hem alle. For 'of a thousand men,' seith Salomon, 'I foond o good man, but certes, of alle wommen, good womman foond I nevere.'/ And also, certes, if I governed me by thy conseil, it sholde seme that I hadde yeve to thee over me the maistrie; and God forbede that it so weere!/ For Jhesus Syrak seith that 'if the wyf have maistrie, she is contrarious to hir housbonde.'/ And Salomon seith: 'Nevere in thy lyf to thy wyf, ne to thy child, ne to thy freend, ne yeve no power over thyself; for bettre it were that thy children aske of thy persone thynges that hem nedeth, than thou see thyself in the handes of thy children.'/ And also if I wolde werke °2250 by thy conseillyng, certes, my conseil moste som tyme be secree, til it were tyme that it moste be knowe, and this ne may noght be./ [*Car il est escript, la genglerie des femmes ne puet riens celler fors ce qu'elle ne scet./ Apres, le philosophre dit, en mauvais conseil les femmes vainquent les hommes: et par ces raisons je ne dois point user de ton conseil.*]/

Whanne dame Prudence, ful debonairly and with greet pacience, hadde herd al that hir housbonde liked for to seye, thanne axed she of hym licence for to speke, and seyde in this wise:/ "My lord," quod she, "as to youre firste resoun, certes it may lightly been answered. For I seye that it is no folie to chaunge conseil whan the thyng is chaunged, or elles whan the thyng semeth ootherweyes than it was biforn./ And moreover, I seye 1065 that though ye han sworn and bihight to perfourne youre emprise, and nathelees ye weyve to perfourne thilke same emprise by juste cause, men sholde nat seyn therfore that ye were a liere ne forsworn./ For the book seith that 'the wise man maketh no lesyng whan he turneth his corage to the bettre.'/ And al be it so that youre emprise be establissed and ordeyned by greet multitude of folk, yet thar ye nat accomplice thilke ordinaunce, but yow like./ For the trouthe of thynges and the profit been rather founden in fewe folk that been wise and ful of resoun, than by greet multitude of folk ther every man crieth and clatereth what that hym liketh. Soothly swich multitude is nat honest./ And as to the seconde resoun, where as ye seyn that alle wommen been wikke; save youre grace, certes ye despisen alle wommen in this wyse, and 'he that al despiseth, al displeseth,' as seith the book./ And Senec seith that 'whoso °2260 wole have sapience shal no man dispreyse, but he shal gladly techen the science that he kan withouten presumpcion or pride;/ and swiche thynges as he noght ne kan, he shal nat been ashamed to lerne hem, and enquere of lasse folk than hymself.'/ And, sire, that ther hath been many a good womman, may lightly be preved./ For certes, sire, oure Lord Jhesu Crist wolde nevere have descended to be born of a womman, if alle wommen hadden been wikke./ And after that, for the grete bountee that is in wommen, oure Lord Jhesu Crist, whan he was risen fro deeth to lyve, appeered rather to a womman than to his Apostles./ And though that Salo- 1075 mon seith that he foond nevere womman good, it folweth nat therfore that alle wommen ben wikke./ For though that he ne foond no good womman, certes, many another man hath founden many a womman ful good and trewe./ Or elles, per aventure, the entente of Salomon was this, that, as in sovereyn bountee, he foond no womman;/ this is to seyn, that ther is no wight that hath sovereyn bountee save God allone, as he hymself recordeth in hys Evaungelie./ For ther nys no creature so good that hym ne wanteth somwhat of the perfeccioun of God, that is his makere./ *2270 Youre thridde reson is this: ye seyn that if ye governe yow by my conseil, it sholde seme that ye hadde yeve me the maistrie and the lordshipe over youre persone./ Sire, save youre grace, it is nat so. For if it so were that no man sholde be conseilled but oonly of hem that hadden lordshipe and maistrie of his persone, men wolden nat be conseilled so ofte./ For soothly thilke man that asketh conseil of a purpos, yet hath he free choys wheither he wole werke by that conseil or noon./ And as to youre fourthe resoun, ther ye seyn that the janglerie of wommen kan hyde thynges that they wot noght, as who seith that a womman kan nat hyde that she woot;/ sire, thise wordes been understonde of wommen that been jangleresses and wikked;/ of whiche 1085 wommen men seyn that thre thynges dryven a man out of his hous,—that is to seyn, smoke, droppyng of reyn, and wikked wyves;/ and of swiche wommen seith Salomon that 'it were bettre dwelle in desert than with a womman that is riotous.'/ And sire, by youre leve, that am nat I;/ for ye han ful ofte assayed my grete silence and my grete pacience, and eek how wel that I kan hyde and hele thynges that men oghte secreely to hyde./ And soothly, as to youre fifthe resoun, where as ye seyn that in wikked conseil wommen venquisshe men, God woot, thilke resoun stant heere in no stede./ For understoond now, ye *2280 asken conseil to do wikkednesse;/ and if ye wole werken wikkednesse, and youre wif restreyneth thilke wikked purpos, and overcometh yow by reson and by good conseil,/ certes youre wyf oghte rather to be preised than yblamed./ Thus sholde ye understonde the philosophre that seith, 'In wikked conseil wommen venquisshen hir housbondes.'/ And ther as ye blamen alle wommen and hir resouns, I shal shewe yow by manye ensamples that many a womman hath ben ful good, and yet been, and hir conseils ful hoolsome and profitable./ Eek som men han seyd 1095 that the conseillynge of wommen is outher to deere, or elles to litel of pris./ But al be it so that ful many a womman is badde, and hir conseil vile and noght worth, yet han men founde ful many a good womman, and ful dis-

cret and wis in conseillynge./ Loo, Jacob, by good conseil of his mooder Rebekka, wan the benysoun of Ysaak his fader, and the lordshipe over alle his bretheren./ Judith, by hire good conseil, delivered the citee of Bethulie, in which she dwelled, out of the handes of Olofernus, that hadde it biseged and wolde have al destroyed it./ Abygail delivered Nabal hir housbonde fro David the kyng, that wolde have slayn hym, and apaysed the ire of the kyng by hir wit and by hir good conseillyng./ Hester, by hir good conseil, *2290 enhaunced greetly the peple of God in the regne of Assuerus the kyng./ And the same bountee in good conseillyng of many a good womman may men telle./ And mooreover, whan oure Lord hadde creat Adam, oure forme fader, he seyde in this wise:/ 'It is nat good to been a man alloone; make we to hym an helpe semblable to hymself.'/ Heere may ye se that if that wommen were nat goode, and hir conseils goode and profitable,/ oure Lord God of hevene wolde 1105 nevere han wroght hem, ne called hem help of man, but rather confusioun of man./ And ther seyde oones a clerk in two vers, 'What is bettre than gold? Jaspre. What is bettre than jaspre? Wisedoom./ And what is better than wisedoom? Womman. And what is bettre than a good womman? Nothyng.'/ And, sire, by manye of othre resons may ye seen that manye wommen been goode, and hir conseils goode and profitable./ And therfore, sire, if ye wol triste to my conseil, I shal restoore yow youre doghter hool and sound./ And eek I wol do to yow so *2300 muche that ye shul have honour in this cause."/

Whan Melibee hadde herd the wordes of his wyf Prudence, he seyde thus:/ "I se wel that the word of Salomon is sooth. He seith that 'wordes that been spoken discreetly by ordinaunce been honycombes, for they yeven swetnesse to the soule and hoolsomnesse to the body.'/ And, wyf, by cause of thy sweete wordes, and eek for I have assayed and preved thy grete sapience and thy grete trouthe, I wol governe me by thy conseil in alle thyng."/

"Now, sire," quod dame Prudence, "and syn ye vouche sauf to been governed by my conseil, I wol enforme yow how ye shul governe yourself in chesynge of youre conseillours./ Ye shul first in alle youre werkes 1115 mekely biseken to the heighe God that

he wol be youre conseillour;/ and shapeth yow
to swich entente that he yeve yow conseil and
confort, as taughte Thobie his sone:/ 'At alle
tymes thou shalt blesse God, and praye hym
to dresse thy weyes, and looke that alle thy
conseils been in hym for everemoore.'/ Seint
Jame eek seith: 'If any of yow have nede of
sapience, axe it of God.'/ And afterward
thanne shul ye taken conseil in yourself, and
examyne wel youre thoghtes of swich thyng
as yow thynketh that is best for youre
profit./ And thanne shul ye dryve fro   *2310
youre herte thre thynges that been contrariouse to good conseil;/ that is to seyn, ire,
coveitise, and hastifnesse./

First, he that axeth conseil of hymself, certes
he moste been withouten ire, for manye
causes./ The firste is this: he that hath greet
ire and wratthe in hymself, he weneth alwey
that he may do thyng that he may nat do./
And secoundely, he that is irous and
wrooth, he ne may nat wel deme;/ and   1125
he that may nat wel deme, may nat wel
conseille./ The thridde is this, that he that is
irous and wrooth, as seith Senec, ne may nat
speke but blameful thynges,/ and with his
viciouse wordes he stireth oother folk to angre
and to ire./ And eek, sire, ye moste dryve
coveitise out of youre herte./ For the Apostle seith that coveitise is roote of alle
harmes./ And trust wel that a coveitous   *2320
man ne kan noght deme ne thynke, but
oonly to fulfille the ende of his coveitise;/ and
certes, that ne may nevere been accompliced;
for evere the moore habundaunce that he hath
of richesse, the moore he desireth./ And, sire,
ye moste also dryve out of youre herte hastifnesse; for certes,/ ye ne may nat deeme for
the beste by a sodeyn thought that falleth in
youre herte, but ye moste avyse yow on it
ful ofte./ For, as ye herde her biforn, the
commune proverbe is this, that 'he that
soone deemeth, soone repenteth.'/ Sire,   1135
ye ne be nat alwey in lyk disposicioun;/
for certes, somthyng that somtyme semeth to
yow that it is good for to do, another tyme it
semeth to yow the contrarie./

Whan ye han taken conseil in yourself, and
han deemed by good deliberacion swich thyng
as you semeth best,/ thanne rede I yow that
ye kepe it secree./ Biwrey nat youre conseil
to no persone, but if so be that ye wenen
sikerly that thurgh youre biwreyyng youre
condicioun shal be to yow the moore profit-

able./ For Jhesus Syrak seith, 'Neither   *2330
to thy foo, ne to thy frend, discovere nat
thy secree ne thy folie;/ for they wol yeve yow
audience and lookynge and supportacioun in
thy presence, and scorne thee in thyn absence.'/ Another clerk seith that 'scarsly
shaltou fynden any persone that may kepe conseil secrely.'/ The book seith, 'Whil that thou
kepest thy conseil in thyn herte, thou kepest
it in thy prisoun;/ and whan thou biwreyest
thy conseil to any wight, he holdeth
thee in his snare.'/ And therfore yow   1145
is bettre to hyde youre conseil in youre
herte than praye him to whom ye han biwreyed
youre conseil that he wole kepen it cloos and
stille./ For Seneca seith: 'If so be that thou
ne mayst nat thyn owene conseil hyde, how
darstou prayen any oother wight thy conseil
secrely to kepe?'/ But nathelees, if thou wene
sikerly that the biwreiyng of thy conseil to a
persone wol make thy condicion to stonden in
the bettre plyt, thanne shaltou tellen hym thy
conseil in this wise./ First thou shalt make no
semblant wheither thee were levere pees or
werre, or this or that, ne shewe hym nat thy
wille and thyn entente./ For trust wel that
comunli thise conseillours been flatereres,/ namely the conseillours of grete   *2340
lordes;/ for they enforcen hem alwey
rather to speken plesante wordes, enclynynge
to the lordes lust, than wordes that been trewe
or profitable./ And therfore men seyn that the
riche man hath seeld good conseil, but if he
have it of hymself./

And after that thou shalt considere thy
freendes and thyne enemys./ And as touchynge thy freendes, thou shalt considere which
of hem been moost feithful and moost wise
and eldest and most approved in conseillyng;/ and of hem shalt thou aske   1155
thy conseil, as the caas requireth./ I
seye that first ye shul clepe to youre conseil
youre freendes that been trewe./ For Salomon
seith that 'right as the herte of a man deliteth in
savour that is soote, right so the conseil of trewe
freendes yeveth swetnesse to the soule.'/ He
seith also, 'Ther may no thyng be likned to the
trewe freend;/ for certes gold ne silver ben nat
so muche worth as the goode wyl of a
trewe freend.'/ And eek he seith that   *2350
'a trewe freend is a strong deffense;
who so that it fyndeth, certes he fyndeth a
greet tresour.'/ Thanne shul ye eek considere
if that youre trewe freendes been discrete and

wise. For the book seith, 'Axe alwey thy conseil of hem that been wise.'/ And by this same
resoun shul ye clepen to youre conseil of youre
freendes that been of age, swiche as han seyn
and been expert in manye thynges and been
approved in conseillynges./ For the book seith
that 'in olde men is the sapience, and in longe
tyme the prudence.'/ And Tullius seith that
'grete thynges ne been nat ay accompliced by
strengthe, ne by delivernesse of body, but by
good conseil, by auctoritee of persones, and by
science; the whiche thre thynges ne been nat
fieble by age, but certes they enforcen
and encreescen day by day.'/ And   1165
thanne shul ye kepe this for a general
reule: First shul ye clepen to youre conseil a
fewe of youre freendes that been especiale;/
for Salomon seith, 'Manye freendes have thou,
but among a thousand chese thee oon to be
thy conseillour.'/ For al be it so that thou first
ne telle thy conseil but to a fewe, thou mayst
afterward telle it to mo folk if it be nede./ But
looke alwey that thy conseillours have thilke
thre condiciouns that I have seyd bifore, that
is to seyn, that they be trewe, wise, and of
oold experience./ And werke nat alwey in
every nede by oon counseillour allone; for somtyme bihooveth it to been conseilled by
manye./ For Salomon seith, 'Salvacion   *2360
of thynges is where as ther been manye
conseillours.'/

Now, sith that I have toold yow of which
folk ye sholde been counseilled, now wol I
teche yow which conseil ye oghte to eschewe./
First, ye shul eschue the conseillyng of fooles;
for Salomon seith, 'Taak no conseil of a fool,
for he ne kan noght conseille but after his
owene lust and his affeccioun.'/ The book
seith that 'the propretee of a fool is this: he
troweth lightly harm of every wight, and lightly
troweth alle bountee in hymself.'/ Thou shalt
eek eschue the conseillyng of alle flatereres,
swiche as enforcen hem rather to preise youre
persone by flaterye than for to telle yow
the soothfastnesse of thynges./ Wher-   1175
fore Tullius seith, 'Amonges alle the
pestilences that been in freendshipe the gretteste is flaterie.' And therfore is it moore nede
that thou eschue and drede flatereres than any
oother peple./ The book seith, 'Thou shalt
rather drede and flee fro the sweete wordes of
flaterynge preiseres than fro the egre wordes
of thy freend that seith thee thy sothes.'/ Salomon seith that 'the wordes of a flaterere is a
snare to cacche with innocentz.'/ He seith also
that 'he that speketh to his freend wordes of
swetnesse and of plesaunce, setteth a net biforn his feet to cacche hym.'/ And therfore
seith Tullius, 'Enclyne nat thyne eres to flatereres, ne taak no conseil of the wordes
of flaterye.'/ And Caton seith, 'Avyse   *2370
thee wel, and eschue the wordes of swetnesse and of plesaunce.'/ And eek thou shalt
eschue the conseillyng of thyne olde enemys
that been reconsiled./ The book seith that 'no
wight retourneth saufly into the grace of his
olde enemy.'/ And Isope seith, 'Ne trust nat
to hem to whiche thou hast had som tyme
werre or enemytee, ne telle hem nat thy
conseil.'/ And Seneca telleth the cause why:
'It may nat be,' seith he, 'that where greet
fyr hath longe tyme endured, that ther
ne dwelleth som vapour of warm-
nesse.'/ And therfore seith Salomon, 'In   1185
thyn olde foo trust nevere.'/ For sikerly,
though thyn enemy be reconsiled, and maketh thee chiere of humylitee, and lowteth to
thee with his heed, ne trust hym nevere./ For
certes he maketh thilke feyned humilitee moore
for his profit than for any love of thy persone,
by cause that he deemeth to have victorie over
thy persone by swich feyned contenance, the
which victorie he myghte nat have by strif or
werre./ And Peter Alfonce seith, 'Make no
felawshipe with thyne olde enemys; for if thou
do hem bountee, they wol perverten it into
wikkednesse.'/ And eek thou most eschue
the conseillyng of hem that been thy servantz and beren thee greet reverence, for
peraventure they seyn it moore for drede
than for love./ And therfore seith a phi-   *2380
losophre in this wise: 'Ther is no wight
parfitly trewe to hym that he to soore dredeth.'/ And Tullius seith, 'Ther nys no myght
so greet of any emperour that longe may endure, but if he have moore love of the peple
than drede.'/ Thou shalt also eschue the con-
seiling of folk that been dronkelewe, for they
ne kan no conseil hyde./ For Salomon seith,
'Ther is no privetee ther as regneth dronkenesse.'/ Ye shul also han in suspect the conseillyng of swich folk as conseille yow o thyng
prively, and conseille yow the contrarie
openly./ For Cassidorie seith that 'it   1195
is a manere sleighte to hyndre, whan he
sheweth to doon o thyng openly and werketh
prively the contrarie.'/ Thou shalt also have
in suspect the conseillyng of wikked folk. For

the book seith, 'The conseillyng of wikked folk
is alwey ful of fraude.'/ And David seith, 'Blisful is that man that hath nat folwed the con-
seilyng of shrewes.'/ Thou shalt also eschue
the conseillyng of yong folk, for hir conseil is
nat rype./

Now, sire, sith I have shewed yow of
which folk ye shul take youre conseil, and of
which folk ye shul folwe the con-
seil,/ now wol I teche yow how ye shal   *2390
examyne youre conseil, after the doctrine of Tullius./ In the examynynge thanne
of youre conseillour ye shul considere manye
thynges./ Alderfirst thou shalt considere that
in thilke thyng that thou purposest, and upon
what thyng thou wolt have conseil, that verray
trouthe be seyd and conserved; this is to seyn,
telle trewely thy tale./ For he that seith fals
may nat wel be conseilled in that cas of which
he lieth./ And after this thou shalt considere the
thynges that acorden to that thou purposest for
to do by thy conseillours, if resoun accorde therto;/ and eek if thy myght may   1205
atteine therto; and if the moore part and
the bettre part of thy conseillours acorde therto,
or noon./ Thanne shaltou considere what
thyng shal folwe of that conseillyng, as hate,
pees, werre, grace, profit, or damage, and
manye othere thynges./ And in alle thise
thynges thou shalt chese the beste, and weyve
alle othere thynges./ Thanne shaltow considere of what roote is engendred the matiere of
thy conseil, and what fruyt it may conceyve
and engendre./ Thou shalt eek considere
alle thise causes, fro whennes they been
sprongen./ And whan ye han exam-   *2400
yned youre conseil, as I have seyd, and
which partie is the bettre and moore profitable, and han approved it by manye wise folk
and olde,/ thanne shaltou considere if thou
mayst parfourne it and maken of it a good
ende./ For certes, resoun wol nat that any
man sholde bigynne a thyng, but if he myghte
parfourne it as hym oghte;/ ne no wight sholde
take upon hym so hevy a charge that he
myghte nat bere it./ For the proverbe seith,
'He that to muche embraceth, distrey-
neth litel.'/ And Catoun seith, 'Assay   1215
to do swich thyng as thou hast power to
doon, lest that the charge oppresse thee so
soore that thee bihoveth to weyve thyng that
thou hast bigonne.'/ And if so be that thou
be in doute wheither thou mayst parfourne a
thing or noon, chese rather to suffre than bi-

gynne./ And Piers Alphonce seith, 'If thou hast
myght to doon a thyng of which thou most
repente, it is bettre "nay" than "ye."'/ This is
to seyn, that thee is bettre holde thy tonge
stille than for to speke./ Thanne may ye understonde by strenger resons that if thou hast
power to parfourne a werk of which thou shalt
repente, thanne is it bettre that thou suffre than bigynne./ Wel seyn they that   *2410
defenden every wight to assaye a thyng
of which he is in doute wheither he may parfourne it or noon./ And after, whan ye han
examyned youre conseil, as I have seyd biforn,
and knowen wel that ye may parfourne youre
emprise, conferme it thanne sadly til it be at
an ende./

Now is it resoun and tyme that I shewe yow
whanne and wherfore that ye may chaunge
youre conseillours withouten youre repreve./
Soothly, a man may chaungen his purpos and
his conseil if the cause cesseth, or whan a newe
caas bitydeth./ For the lawe seith that 'upon
thynges that newely bityden bihoveth
newe conseil.'/ And Senec seith, 'If thy   1225
conseil is comen to the eeris of thyn enemy, chaunge thy conseil.'/ Thou mayst also
chaunge thy conseil if so be that thou fynde
that by errour, or by oother cause, harm or
damage may bityde./ Also if thy conseil be
dishonest, or ellis cometh of dishonest cause,
chaunge thy conseil./ For the lawes seyn that
'alle bihestes that been dishoneste been of no
value';/ and eek if so be that it be inpossible, or may nat goodly be parfourned
or kept./   *2420

And take this for a general reule, that
every conseil that is affermed so strongly that
it may nat be chaunged for no condicioun that
may bityde, I seye that thilke conseil is wikked."/

This Melibeus, whanne he hadde herd the
doctrine of his wyf dame Prudence, answerde
in this wyse:/ "Dame," quod he, "as yet into
this tyme ye han wel and covenably taught me
as in general, how I shal governe me in the
chesynge and in the withholdynge of my conseillours./ But now wolde I fayn that ye wolde
condescende in especial,/ and telle me how liketh yow, or what semeth yow, by oure conseillours that we han chosen in oure present nede."/   1235

"My lord," quod she, "I biseke yow in al
humblesse that ye wol nat wilfully replie agayn
my resouns, ne distempre youre herte, thogh I

speke thyng that yow displese./ For God woot
that, as in myn entente, I speke it for youre
beste, for youre honour, and for youre profite
eke./ And soothly, I hope that youre benyngnytee wol taken it in pacience./ Trusteth me
wel," quod she, "that youre conseil as in this
caas ne sholde nat, as to speke properly, be
called a conseillyng, but a mocioun or a moevyng of folye,/ in which conseil ye han
erred in many a sondry wise./

First and forward, ye han erred in
th'assemblynge of youre conseillours./ For ye
sholde first have cleped a fewe folk to youre
conseil, and after ye myghte han shewed it
to mo folk, if it hadde been nede./ But certes,
ye han sodeynly cleped to youre conseil a greet
multitude of peple, ful chargeant and ful anoyous for to heere./ Also ye han erred, for theras
ye sholden oonly have cleped to youre conseil
youre trewe frendes olde and wise,/ ye han
ycleped straunge folk, yonge folk, false flatereres,
and enemys reconsiled, and folk that
doon yow reverence withouten love./   1245
And eek also ye have erred, for ye han
broght with yow to youre conseil ire, coveitise,
and hastifnesse,/ the whiche thre thinges been
contrariouse to every conseil honest and profitable;/ the whiche thre thinges ye han nat
anientissed or destroyed hem, neither in youreself, ne in youre conseillours, as yow oghte./
Ye han erred also, for ye han shewed to youre
conseillours youre talent and youre affeccioun
to make werre anon, and for to do vengeance./
They han espied by youre wordes to
what thyng ye been enclyned;/ and   *2440
therfore han they rather conseilled
yow to youre talent that to youre profit./
Ye han erred also, for it semeth that yow
suffiseth to han been conseilled by thise
conseillours oonly, and with litel avys,/
whereas in so greet and so heigh a nede
it hadde been necessarie mo conseillours
and moore deliberacion to parfourne youre emprise./ Ye han erred also, for ye ne han nat
examyned youre conseil in the forseyde manere, ne in due manere, as the caas requireth./
Ye han erred also, for ye han maked no division bitwixe youre conseillours; this is to
seyn, bitwixen youre trewe freendes and
youre feyned conseillours;/ ne ye han   1255
nat knowe the wil of youre trewe
freendes olde and wise;/ but ye han cast alle
hire wordes in an hochepot, and enclyned
youre herte to the moore part and to the gretter

nombre, and there been ye condescended./
And sith ye woot wel that men shal alwey
fynde a gretter nombre of fooles than of wise
men,/ and therfore the conseils that been at
congregaciouns and multitudes of folk, there as
men take moore reward to the nombre than to
the sapience of persones,/ ye se wel that in
swiche conseillynges fooles han the maistrie."/   *2450
Melibeus answerde agayn, and seyde,
"I graunte wel that I have erred;/ but there
as thou hast toold me heerbiforn that he nys
nat to blame that chaungeth his conseillours in
certein caas and for certeine juste causes,/ I am
al redy to chaunge my conseillours right as thow
wolt devyse./ The proverbe seith that 'for
to do synne is mannyssh, but certes for to persevere longe in synne is werk of the devel.' "/
To this sentence answered anon dame
Prudence, and seyde:/ "Examineth,"   1265
quod she, "youre conseil, and lat us see
the whiche of hem han spoken most resonably,
and taught yow best conseil./ And for as
muche as that the examynacion is necessarie,
lat us bigynne at the surgiens and at the phisiciens, that first speeken in this matiere./ I sey
yow that the surgiens and phisiciens han
seyd yow in youre conseil discreetly, as hem
oughte;/ and in hir speche seyden ful wisely
that to the office of hem aperteneth to doon to
every wight honour and profit, and no wight
for to anoye;/ and after hir craft to doon greet
diligence unto the cure of hem which
that they han in hir governaunce./   *2460
And, sire, right as they han answered
wisely and discreetly,/ right so rede I that they
been heighly and sovereynly gerdoned for hir
noble speche;/ and eek for they sholde do the
moore ententif bisynesse in the curacion of
youre doghter deere./ For al be it so that they
been youre freendes, therfore shal ye nat suffren that they serve yow for noght,/ but ye
oghte the rather gerdone hem and shewe
hem youre largesse./ And as touchynge   1275
the proposicioun which that the phisiciens encreesceden in this caas, this is to seyn,/
that in maladies that oon contrarie is warisshed
by another contrarie,/ I wolde fayn knowe hou
ye understonde thilke text, and what is youre
sentence."/
"Certes," quod Melibeus, "I understonde
it in this wise:/ that right as they han
doon me a contrarie, right so sholde I
doon hem another./ For right as they   *2470

han venged hem on me and doon me wrong, right so shal I venge me upon hem and doon hem wrong;/ and thanne have I cured oon contrarie by another."/

"Lo, lo," quod dame Prudence, "how lightly is every man enclined to his owene desir and to his owene plesaunce!/ Certes," quod she, "the wordes of the phisiciens ne sholde nat han been understonden in thys wise./ For certes, wikkednesse is nat contrarie to wikkednesse, ne vengeance to vengeaunce, ne wrong to wrong, but they been semblable./ And therfore o vengeaunce is 1285 nat warisshed by another vengeaunce, ne o wroong by another wroong,/ but everich of hem encreesceth and aggreggeth oother./ But certes, the wordes of the phisiciens sholde been understonden in this wise:/ For good and wikkednesse been two contraries, and pees and werre, vengeaunce and suffraunce, discord and accord, and manye othere thynges./ But certes, wikkednesse shal be warisshed by goodnesse, discord by accord, werre by pees, and so forth of othere thynges./ And heerto °2480 accordeth Seint Paul the Apostle in manye places./ He seith: 'Ne yeldeth nat harm for harm, ne wikked speche for wikked speche;/ but do wel to hym that dooth thee harm, and blesse hym that seith to thee harm.'/ And in manye othere places he amonesteth pees and accord./ But now wol I speke to yow of the conseil which that was yeven to yow by the men of lawe and the wise folk,/ that seyden alle by oon accord, 1295 as ye han herd bifore,/ that over alle thynges ye shal doon youre diligence to kepen youre persone and to warnestoore youre hous;/ and seyden also that in this caas yow oghten for to werken ful avysely and with greet deliberacioun./ And, sire, as to the firste point, that toucheth to the kepyng of youre persone, ye shul understonde that he that hath werre shal everemoore mekely and devoutly preyen, biforn alle thynges,/ that Jhesus °2490 Crist of his mercy wol han hym in his proteccion and been his sovereyn helpyng at his nede./ For certes, in this world ther is no wight that may be conseilled ne kept sufficeantly withouten the kepyng of oure Lord Jhesu Crist./ To this sentence accordeth the prophete David, that seith,/ 'If God ne kepe the citee, in ydel waketh he that it kepeth.'/ Now, sire, thanne shul ye committe the kepyng of youre persone to youre trewe freendes,

that been approved and yknowe,/ and 1305 of hem shul ye axen help youre persone for to kepe. For Catoun seith: 'If thou hast nede of help, axe it of thy freendes;/ for ther nys noon so good a phisicien as thy trewe freend.'/ And after this thanne shul ye kepe yow fro alle straunge folk, and fro lyeres, and have alwey in suspect hire compaignye./ For Piers Alfonce seith, 'Ne taak no compaignye by the weye of a straunge man, but if so be that thou have knowe hym of a lenger tyme./ And if so be that he falle into thy compaignye paraventure, withouten thyn assent,/ en- °2500 quere thanne as subtilly as thou mayst of his conversacion, and of his lyf bifore, and feyne thy wey; seye that thou wolt thider as thou wolt nat go;/ and if he bereth a spere, hoold thee on the right syde, and if he bere a swerd, hoold thee on the lift syde.'/ And after this thanne shul ye kepe yow wisely from all swich manere peple as I have seyd bifore, and hem and hir conseil eschewe./ And after this thanne shul ye kepe yow in swich manere/ that, for any presumpcion of youre strengthe, that ye ne dispise nat, ne accompte nat the myght of youre adversarie so litel, that ye lete the kepyng of youre persone for youre presumpcioun;/ for every wys man 1315 dredeth his enemy./ And Salomon seith: 'Weleful is he that of alle hath drede;/ for certes, he that thurgh the hardynesse of his herte, and thurgh the hardynesse of hymself, hath to greet presumpcioun, hym shal yvel bityde.'/ Thanne shul ye everemoore contrewayte embusshementz and alle espiaille./ For Senec seith that 'the wise man that dredeth harmes, eschueth harmes,/ ne °2510 he ne falleth into perils that perils eschueth.'/ And al be it so that it seme that thou art in siker place, yet shaltow alwey do thy diligence in kepynge of thy persone;/ this is to seyn, ne be nat necligent to kepe thy persone, nat oonly fro thy gretteste enemys, but fro thy leeste enemy./ Senek seith: 'A man that is well avysed, he dredeth his leste enemy.'/ Ovyde seith that 'the litel wesele wol slee the grete bole and the wilde hert.'/ And the book seith, 'A litel 1325 thorn may prikke a kyng ful soore, and an hound wol holde the wilde boor.'/ But nathelees, I sey nat thou shalt be so coward that thou doute ther wher as is no drede./ The book seith that 'somme folk han greet lust to deceyve, but yet they dreden hem to be de-

ceyved.'/ Yet shaltou drede to been empoi-
soned, and kepe the from the compaignye of
scorneres./ For the book seith, 'With scorneres make no compaignye, but flee hire
wordes as venym.'/   *2520

Now, as to the seconde point, where
as youre wise conseillours conseilled yow to
warnestoore youre hous with gret diligence,/
I wolde fayn knowe how that ye understonde
thilke wordes and what is youre sentence."/

Melibeus answerde, and seyde, "Certes, I understande it in this wise: That I shal warnestoore myn hous with toures, swiche as han
castelles and othere manere edifices, and armure, and artelries;/ by whiche thynges I may
my persone and myn hous so kepen and deffenden that myne enemys shul been in drede
myn hous for to approche."/

To this sentence answerde anon Prudence:
"Warnestooryng," quod she, "of heighe toures
and of grete edifices apperteyneth somtyme to pryde./ And eek men make   1335
heighe toures, and grete edifices with
grete costages and with greet travaille; and
whan that they been accompliced, yet be they
nat worth a stree, but if they be defended by
trewe freendes that been olde and wise./ And
understoond wel that the gretteste and strong-
este garnysoun that a riche man may have, as
wel to kepen his persone as his goodes, is/
that he be biloved with hys subgetz and with
his neighebores./ For thus seith Tullius, that
'ther is a manere garnysoun that no man may
venquysse ne disconfite, and that is/ a lord to
be biloved of his citezeins and of his
peple.'/   *2530

Now, sire, as to the thridde point,
where as youre olde and wise conseillours
seyden that yow ne oghte nat sodeynly ne
hastily proceden in this nede,/ but that yow
oghte purveyen and apparaillen yow in this caas
with greet diligence and greet deliberacioun;/
trewely, I trowe that they seyden right wisely
and right sooth./ For Tullius seith: 'In every
nede, er thou bigynne it, apparaille thee with
greet diligence.'/ Thanne seye I that in ven-
geance-takyng, in werre, in bataille, and
in warnestooryng,/ er thow bigynne, I   1345
rede that thou apparaille thee therto,
and do it with greet deliberacion./ For Tullius seith that 'longe apparaillyng biforn the
bataille maketh short victorie.'/ And Cassidorus seith, 'The garnysoun is stronger, whan
it is longe tyme avysed.'/

But now lat us speken of the conseil that
was accorded by youre neighebores, swiche
as doon yow reverence withouten love,/
youre olde enemys reconsiled, youre flatereres,/ that conseilled yow certeyne   *2540
thynges prively, and openly conseilleden
yow the contrarie;/ the yonge folk also, that
conseilleden yow to venge yow, and make
werre anon./ And certes, sire, as I have seyd
biforn, ye han greetly erred to han cleped
swich manere folk to youre conseil,/ which
conseillours been ynogh repreved by the resouns aforeseyd./ But nathelees, lat us now
descende to the special. Ye shuln first
procede after the doctrine of Tullius./   1355
Certes, the trouthe of this matiere, or of
this conseil, nedeth nat diligently enquere;/
for it is wel wist whiche they been that han
doon to yow this trespas and vileynye,/ and
how manye trespassours, and in what manere
they han to yow doon al this wrong and al this
vileynye./ And after this, thanne shul ye examyne the seconde condicion which that the
same Tullius addeth in this matiere./ For Tullius put a thyng which that he clepeth
'consentynge'; this is to seyn,/ who been   *2550
they, and whiche been they and how
manye, that consenten to thy conseil in thy
wilfulnesse to doon hastif vengeance./ And
lat us considere also who been they, and how
manye been they, and whiche been they, that
consenteden to youre adversaries./ And certes,
as to the firste poynt, it is wel knowen whiche
folk been they that consenteden to youre hastif
wilfulnesse;/ for trewely, alle tho that conseilleden yow to maken sodeyn werre ne been nat
youre freendes./ Lat us now considere whiche
been they that ye holde so greetly youre
freendes as to youre persone./ For al   1365
be it so that ye be myghty and riche,
certes ye ne been but allone,/ for certes ye ne
han no child but a doghter,/ ne ye ne han
brotheren, ne cosyns germayns, ne noon oother
neigh kynrede,/ wherfore that youre enemys
for drede sholde stinte to plede with yow, or
to destroye youre persone./ Ye knowen also
that youre richesses mooten been dis-
pended in diverse parties,/ and whan   *2560
that every wight hath his part, they ne
wollen taken but litel reward to venge thy
deeth./ But thyne enemys been thre, and they
han manie children, bretheren, cosyns, and
oother ny kynrede./ And though so were that
thou haddest slayn of hem two or three, yet

dwellen ther ynowe to wreken hir deeth and
to sle thy persone./ And though so be that
youre kynrede be moore siker and stedefast
than the kyn of youre adversarie,/ yet nathelees youre kynrede nys but a fer kynrede; they been but litel syb to yow,/   1375
and the kyn of youre enemys been ny
syb to hem. And certes, as in that, hir condicioun is bet than youres./ Thanne lat us considere also if the conseillyng of hem that conseilleden yow to taken sodeyn vengeaunce,
wheither it accorde to resoun./ And certes, ye
knowe wel 'nay.'/ For, as by right and resoun,
ther may no man taken vengeance on no wight
but the juge that hath the jurisdiccioun of it,/
whan it is graunted hym to take thilke vengeance hastily or attemprely, as the lawe
requireth./ And yet mooreover of thilke   *2570
word that Tullius clepeth 'consent-
ynge,'/ thou shalt considere if thy myght and
thy power may consenten and suffise to thy
wilfulnesse and to thy conseillours./ And certes
thou mayst wel seyn that 'nay.'/ For sikerly, as for to speke proprely, we may do
no thyng, but oonly swich thyng as we may
doon rightfully./ And certes rightfully ne mowe
ye take no vengeance, as of youre
propre auctoritee./ Thanne mowe ye   1385
seen that youre power ne consenteth
nat, ne accordeth nat, with youre wilfulnesse./

Lat us now examyne the thridde point, that
Tullius clepeth 'consequent.'/ Thou shal understonde that the vengeance that thou purposest for to take is the consequent;/ and
therof folweth another vengeaunce, peril, and
werre, and othere damages withoute nombre,
of whiche we be nat war, as at this tyme./

And as touchynge the fourthe point,
that Tullius clepeth 'engendrynge,'/   *2580
thou shalt considere that this wrong
which that is doon to thee is engendred of the
hate of thyne enemys,/ and of the vengeance-
takynge upon that wolde engendre another
vengeance, and muchel sorwe and wastynge
of richesses, as I seyde./

Now, sire, as to the point that Tullius clepeth 'causes,' which that is the laste point,/ thou
shalt understonde that the wrong that thou hast
receyved hath certeine causes,/ whiche that
clerkes clepen *Oriens* and *Efficiens*, and *Causa
longinqua* and *Causa propinqua*, this is
to seyn, the fer cause and the ny cause./   1395
The fer cause is almyghty God, that is
cause of alle thynges./ The neer cause is thy

thre enemys./ The cause accidental was hate./
The cause material been the fyve woundes of
thy doghter./ The cause formal is the manere
of hir werkynge that broghten laddres
and cloumben in at thy wyndowes./   *2590
The cause final was for to sle thy doghter. It letted nat in as muche as in hem was./
But for to speken of the fer cause, as to what
ende they shul come, or what shal finally bityde
of hem in this caas, ne kan I nat deeme but
by conjectynge and by supposynge./ For we
shul suppose that they shul come to a wikked
ende,/ by cause that the Book of Decrees seith,
'Seelden, or with greet peyne, been causes
ybroght to good ende whanne they been baddely bigonne.'/

Now, sire, if men wolde axe me why that
God suffred men to do yow this vileynye, certes,
I kan nat wel answere, as for no soothfastnesse./ For th'apostle seith that 'the   1405
sciences and the juggementz of oure
Lord God almyghty been ful depe;/ ther may
no man comprehende ne serchen hem suffisantly.'/ Nathelees, by certeyne presump-
ciouns and conjectynges, I holde and bileeve/
that God, which that is ful of justice and of
rightwisnesse, hath suffred this bityde by juste
cause resonable./

Thy name is Melibee, this is to seyn,
'a man that drynketh hony.'/ Thou hast   *2600
ydronke so muchel hony of sweete temporeel richesses, and delices and honours of
this world,/ that thou art dronken, and hast
forgeten Jhesu Crist thy creatour./ Thou ne
hast nat doon to hym swich honour and reverence as thee oughte,/ ne thou ne hast nat
wel ytaken kep to the wordes of Ovide, that
seith,/ 'Under the hony of the goodes of
the body is hyd the venym that sleeth
the soule.'/ And Salomon seith, 'If thou   1415
hast founden hony, ete of it that suffiseth;/ for if thou ete of it out of mesure, thou
shalt spewe,' and be nedy and povre./ And
peraventure Crist hath thee in despit, and hath
turned awey fro thee his face and his eeris of
misericorde;/ and also he hath suffred that thou
hast been punysshed in the manere that thow
hast ytrespassed./ Thou hast doon
synne agayn oure Lord Crist;/ for certes,   *2610
the three enemys of mankynde, that is to
seyn, the flessh, the feend, and the world,/
thou hast suffred hem entre in to thyn herte
wilfully by the wyndowes of thy body,/ and
hast nat defended thyself suffisantly agayns

hire assautes and hire temptaciouns, so that they han wounded thy soule in fyve places;/ this is to seyn, the deedly synnes that been entred into thyn herte by thy fyve wittes./ And in the same manere oure Lord Crist hath woold and suffred that thy three enemys been entred into thyn house by the wyndowes,/ and han ywounded thy doghter in the forseyde manere."/

"Certes," quod Melibee, "I se wel that ye enforce yow muchel by wordes to overcome me in swich manere that I shal nat venge me of myne enemys,/ shewynge me the perils and the yveles that myghten falle of this vengeance./ But whoso wolde considere in alle vengeances the perils and yveles that myghte sewe of vengeance-takynge,/ a man wolde nevere take vengeance, and that were harm;/ for by the vengeance-takynge *2620 been the wikked men dissevered fro the goode men,/ and they that han wyl to do wikkednesse restreyne hir wikked purpos, whan they seen the punyssynge and chastisynge of the trespassours."/

[Et a ce respont dame Prudence, "Certes," dist elle, "je t'ottroye que de vengence vient molt de maulx et de biens;/ Mais vengence n'appartient pas a un chascun fors seulement aux juges et a ceulx qui ont la juridicion sur les malfaitteurs.]/ And yet seye I moore, that right as a singuler persone synneth in takynge vengeance of another man,/ 1435 right so synneth the juge if he do no vengeance of hem that it han disserved./ For Senec seith thus: 'That maister,' he seith, 'is good that proveth shrewes.'/ And as Cassidore seith, 'A man dredeth to do outrages whan he woot and knoweth that it displeseth to the juges and the sovereyns.'/ And another seith, 'The juge that dredeth to do right, maketh men shrewes.'/ And Seint Paul the Apostle seith in his Epistle, whan he writeth unto the Romayns, that 'the juges beren nat the spere withouten cause,/ but they *2630 beren it to punysse the shrewes and mysdoers, and for to defende the goode men./ If ye wol thanne take vengeance of youre enemys, ye shul retourne or have youre recours to the juge that hath the jurisdiccion upon hem,/ and he shal punysse hem as the lawe axeth and requireth."/

"A!" quod Melibee, "this vengeance liketh me no thyng./ I bithenke me now and take heede how Fortune hath norissed me fro my childhede, and hath holpen me to passe many a stroong paas./ Now wol I as- 1445 sayen hire, trowynge, with Goddes help, that she shal helpe me my shame for to venge."/

"Certes," quod Prudence, "if ye wol werke by my conseil, ye shul nat assaye Fortune by no wey,/ ne ye shul nat lene or bowe unto hire, after the word of Senec;/ for 'thynges that been folily doon, and that been in hope of Fortune, shullen nevere come to good ende.'/ And, as the same Senec seith, 'The moore cleer and the moore shynyng that Fortune is, the moore brotil and the sonner broken she is.'/ Trusteth nat in hire, for she nys *2640 nat stidefast ne stable;/ for whan thow trowest to be moost seur or siker of hire help, she wol faille thee and deceyve thee./ And where as ye seyn that Fortune hath norissed yow fro youre childhede,/ I seye that in so muchel shul ye the lasse truste in hire and in hir wit./ For Senec seith, 'What man that is norissed by Fortune, she maketh hym a greet fool.'/ Now thanne, syn ye de- 1455 sire and axe vengeance, and the vengeance that is doon after the lawe and bifore the juge ne liketh yow nat,/ and the vengeance that is doon in hope of Fortune is perilous and uncertein,/ thanne have ye noon oother remedie but for to have youre recours unto the sovereyn Juge that vengeth alle vileynyes and wronges./ And he shal venge yow after that hymself witnesseth, where as he seith,/ 'Leveth the vengeance to me, and I shal do it.'"/ *2650

Melibee answerde, "If I ne venge me nat of the vileynye that men han doon to me,/ I sompne or warne hem that han doon to me that vileynye, and alle othere, to do me another vileynye./ For it is writen, 'If thou take no vengeance of an oold vileynye, thou sompnest thyne adversaries to do thee a newe vileynye.'/ And also for my suffrance men wolden do me so muchel vileynye that I myghte neither bere it ne susteene,/ and so sholde I been put and holden overlowe./ For 1465 men seyn, 'In muchel suffrynge shul manye thynges falle unto thee whiche thou shalt nat mowe suffre.'"/

"Certes," quod Prudence, "I graunte yow that over-muchel suffraunce is nat good./ But yet ne folweth it nat therof that every persone to whom men doon vileynye take of it vengeance;/ for that aperteneth and longeth al oonly to the juges, for they shul venge the vileynyes and injuries./ And therfore tho two auctoritees that ye han seyd above been oonly understonden in the juges./ For   *2660 whan they suffren over-muchel the wronges and the vileynyes to be doon withouten punysshynge,/ they sompne nat a man al oonly for to do newe wronges, but they comanden it./ Also a wys man seith that 'the juge that correcteth nat the synnere comandeth and biddeth hym do synne.'/ And the juges and sovereyns myghten in hir land so muchel suffre of the shrewes and mysdoeres/ that they sholden, by swich suffrance, by proces of tyme wexen of swich power and myght that they sholden putte out the juges and the sovereyns from hir places,/ and atte laste   1475 maken hem lesen hire lordshipes./

But lat us now putte that ye have leve to venge yow./ I seye ye been nat of myght and power as now to venge yow;/ for if ye wole maken comparisoun unto the myght of youre adversaries, ye shul fynde in manye thynges that I have shewed yow er this that hire condicion is bettre than youres./ And therfore seye I that it is good as now that ye suffre and be pacient./   *2670

Forthermoore, ye knowen wel that after the comune sawe, 'it is a woodnesse a man to stryve with a strenger or a moore myghty man than he is hymself;/ and for to stryve with a man of evene strengthe, that is to seyn, with as strong a man as he is, it is peril;/ and for to stryve with a weyker man, it is folie.'/ And therfore sholde a man flee stryvynge as muchel as he myghte./ For Salomon seith, 'It is a greet worshipe to a man to kepen hym fro noyse and stryf.'/ And   1485 if it so bifalle or happe that a man of gretter myght and strengthe than thou art do thee grevaunce,/ studie and bisye thee rather to stille the same grevaunce than for to venge thee./ For Senec seith that 'he putteth hym in greet peril that stryveth with a gretter man than he is hymself.'/ And Catoun seith, 'If a man of hyer estaat or degree, or moore myghty than thou, do thee anoy or grevaunce, suffre hym;/ for he that oones hath greved thee, may another tyme releeve thee and helpe.'/ Yet sette I caas, ye have bothe   *2680 myght and licence for to venge yow,/ I seye that ther be ful manye thynges that shul restreyne yow of vengeance-takynge,/ and make yow for to enclyne to suffre, and for to

han pacience in the wronges that han been doon to yow./ First and foreward, if ye wole considere the defautes that been in youre owene persone,/ for whiche defautes God hath suffred yow have this tribulacioun, as I have seyd yow heer-biforn./ For the   1495 poete seith that 'we oghte paciently taken the tribulacions that comen to us, whan we thynken and consideren that we han disserved to have hem.'/ And Seint Gregorie seith that 'whan a man considereth wel the nombre of his defautes and of his synnes,/ the peynes and the tribulaciouns that he suffreth semen the lesse unto hym;/ and in as muche as hym thynketh his synnes moore hevy and grevous,/ in so muche semeth his peyne the lighter and the esier unto hym.'/   *2690 Also ye owen to enclyne and bowe youre herte to take the pacience of oure Lord Jhesu Crist, as seith seint Peter in his Epistles./ 'Jhesu Crist,' he seith, 'hath suffred for us and yeven ensample to every man to folwe and sewe hym;/ for he dide nevere synne, ne nevere cam ther a vileyns word out of his mouth./ Whan men cursed hym, he cursed hem noght; and whan men betten hym, he manaced hem noght.'/ Also the grete pacience which the seintes that been in Paradys han had in tribulaciouns that they han ysuffred, withouten hir desert or gilt,/ oghte muchel stiren   1505 yow to pacience./ Forthermoore ye sholde enforce yow to have pacience,/ considerynge that the tribulaciouns of this world but litel while endure, and soone passed been and goon,/ and the joye that a man seketh to have by pacience in tribulaciouns is perdurable, after that the Apostle seith in his epistle./ 'The joye of God,' he seith, 'is perdurable,' that is to seyn, everelastynge./ Also   *2700 troweth and bileveth stedefastly that he nys nat wel ynorissed, ne wel ytaught, that kan nat have pacience, or wol nat receyve pacience./ For Salomon seith that 'the doctrine and the wit of a man is knowen by pacience.'/ And in another place he seith that 'he that is pacient governeth hym by greet prudence.'/ And the same Salomon seith, 'The angry and wrathful man maketh noyses, and the pacient man atempreth hem and stilleth.'/ He seith also, 'It is moore worth to be pacient than for to be right strong;/ and he   1515 that may have the lordshipe of his owene herte is moore to preyse than he that by his force or strengthe taketh grete citees.'/

And therfore seith Seint Jame in his Epistle that 'pacience is a greet vertu of perfeccioun.' "/

"Certes," quod Melibee, "I graunte yow, dame Prudence, that pacience is a greet vertu of perfeccioun;/ but every man may nat have the perfeccioun that ye seken;/ ne I nam nat of the nombre of right parfite men,/ °2710 for myn herte may nevere been in pees unto the tyme it be venged./ And al be it so that it was greet peril to myne enemys to do me a vileynye in takynge vengeance upon me,/ yet tooken they noon heede of the peril, but fulfilleden hir wikked wyl and hir corage./ And therfore me thynketh men oghten nat repreve me, though I putte me in a litel peril for to venge me,/ and though I do a greet excesse, that is to seyn, that I venge oon outrage by another."/ 1525

"A," quod dame Prudence, "ye seyn youre wyl and as yow liketh,/ but in no caas of the world a man sholde nat doon outrage ne excesse for to vengen hym./ For Cassidore seith that 'as yvele dooth he that vengeth hym by outrage as he that dooth the outrage.'/ And therfore ye shul venge yow after the ordre of right, that is to seyn, by the lawe, and noght by excesse ne by outrage./ And also, if ye wol venge yow of the outrage of youre adversaries in oother manere than right comandeth, ye synnen./ And therfore seith Senec °2720 that 'a man shal nevere vengen shrewednesse by shrewednesse.'/ And if ye seye that right axeth a man to defenden violence by violence, and fightyng by fightyng,/ certes ye seye sooth, whan the defense is doon anon withouten intervalle or withouten tariyng or delay,/ for to deffenden hym and nat for to vengen hym./ And it bihoveth that a man putte swich attemperance in his deffense/ that men have no cause ne matiere to repreven hym that deffendeth 1535 hym of excesse and outrage, for ellis were it agayn resoun./ Pardee, ye knowen wel that ye maken no deffense as now for to deffende yow, but for to venge yow;/ and so seweth it that ye han no wyl to do youre dede attemprely./ And therfore me thynketh that pacience is good; for Salomon seith that 'he that is nat pacient shal have greet harm.' "/

"Certes," quod Melibee, "I graunte yow that whan a man is inpacient and wrooth, of that that toucheth hym noght and that aperteneth nat unto hym, though it harme hym, it is no wonder./ For the lawe seith that °2730

'he is coupable that entremetteth hym or medleth with swych thyng as aperteneth nat unto hym.'/ And Salomon seith that 'he that entremetteth hym of the noyse or strif of another man is lyk to hym that taketh an hound by the eris.'/ For right as he that taketh a straunge hound by the eris is outherwhile biten with the hound,/ right in the same wise is it resoun that he have harm that by his inpacience medleth hym of the noyse of another man, wheras it aperteneth nat unto hym./ But ye knowen wel that this dede, that is to seyn, my grief and my disese, toucheth me right ny./ And therfore, though I be 1545 wrooth and inpacient, it is no merveille./ And, savynge youre grace, I kan nat seen that it myghte greetly harme me though I tooke vengeaunce./ For I am richer and moore myghty than myne enemys been;/ and wel knowen ye that by moneye and by havynge grete possessions been alle the thynges of this world governed./ And Salomon seith that 'alle thynges obeyen to moneye.' "/ °2740

Whan Prudence hadde herd hir housbonde avanten hym of his richesse and of his moneye, dispreisynge the power of his adversaries, she spak, and seyde in this wise:/ "Certes, deere sire, I graunte yow that ye been riche and myghty,/ and that the richesses been goode to hem that han wel ygeten hem and wel konne usen hem./ For right as the body of a man may nat lyven withoute the soule, namoore may it lyve withouten temporeel goodes./ And by richesses may a man gete hym grete freendes./ And therfore seith Pam- 1555 philles: 'If a net-herdes doghter,' seith he, 'be riche, she may chesen of a thousand men which she wol take to hir housbonde;/ for, of a thousand men, oon wol nat forsaken hire ne refusen hire.'/ And this Pamphilles seith also: 'If thow be right happy — that is to seyn, if thou be right riche — thou shalt fynde a greet nombre of felawes and freendes./ And if thy fortune change that thou wexe povre, farewel freendshipe and felaweshipe;/ for thou shalt be alloone withouten any compaignye, but if it be the compaignye of povre folk.'/ And yet seith this Pamphilles °2750 moreover that 'they that been thralle and bonde of lynage shullen been maad worthy and noble by the richesses.'/ And right so as by richesses ther comen manye goodes, right so by poverte come ther manye harmes and yveles./ For greet poverte constreyneth a man

to do manye yveles./ And therfore clepeth
Cassidore poverte the mooder of ruyne,/ that
is to seyn, the mooder of overthrowynge
or fallynge doun./ And therfore seith   1565
Piers Alfonce: 'Oon of the gretteste ad-
versitees of this world is/ whan a free man by
kynde or of burthe is constreyned by poverte
to eten the almesse of his enemy,'/ and the
same seith Innocent in oon of his bookes. He
seith that 'sorweful and myshappy is the condicioun of a povre beggere;/ for if he axe nat
his mete, he dyeth for hunger;/ and if he axe,
he dyeth for shame; and algates necessitee constreyneth hym to axe.'/ And   *2760
seith Salomon that 'bet it is to dye than
for to have swich poverte.'/ And as the same
Salomon seith, 'Bettre it is to dye of bitter deeth
than for to lyven in swich wise.'/ By thise
resons that I have seid unto yow, and by manye
othere resons that I koude seye,/ I graunte yow
that richesses been goode to hem that geten
hem wel, and to hem that wel usen tho richesses./ And therfore wol I shewe yow hou ye
shul have yow and how ye shul bere yow in
gaderynge of richesses, and in what
manere ye shul usen hem./   1575
   First, ye shul geten hem withouten
greet desir, by good leyser, sokyngly and nat
over-hastily./ For a man that is to desirynge
to gete richesses abaundoneth hym first to
thefte, and to alle othere yveles;/ and therfore seith Salomon, 'He that hasteth hym to
bisily to wexe riche shal be noon innocent.'/
He seith also that 'the richesse that hastily cometh to a man, soone and lightly gooth and
passeth fro a man;/ but that richesse that
cometh litel and litel, wexeth alwey and
multiplieth.'/ And, sire, ye shul geten   *2770
richesses by youre wit and by youre
travaille unto youre profit;/ and that withouten
wrong or harm doynge to any oother persone./
For the lawe seith that 'ther maketh no man
himselven riche, if he do harm to another
wight.'/ This is to seyn, that nature deffendeth and forbedeth by right that no man make
hymself riche unto the harm of another persone./ And Tullius seith that 'no sorwe, ne no
drede of deeth, ne no thyng that may
falle unto a man,/ is so muchel agayns   1585
nature as a man to encressen his owene
profit to the harm of another man./ And
though the grete men and the myghty men
geten richesses moore lightly than thou,/ yet
shaltou nat been ydel ne slow to do thy profit,

for thou shalt in alle wise flee ydelnesse.'/ For
Salomon seith that 'ydelnesse techeth a man to
do manye yveles.'/ And the same Salomon
seith that 'he that travailleth and bisieth
hym to tilien his land, shal eten breed;/   *2780
but he that is ydel and casteth hym to
no bisynesse ne occupacioun, shal falle into
poverte, and dye for hunger.'/ And he that is
ydel and slow kan nevere fynde covenable
tyme for to doon his profit./ For ther is a
versifiour seith that 'the ydel man excuseth hym
in wynter by cause of the grete coold, and in
somer by enchesoun of the greete heete.'/ For
thise causes seith Caton, 'Waketh and enclyneth nat yow over-muchel for to slepe, for over-
muchel reste norisseth and causeth manye
vices.'/ And therfore seith Seint Jerome,
'Dooth somme goode dedes that the devel,
which is oure enemy, ne fynde yow nat
unocupied.'/ For the devel ne taketh   1595
nat lightly unto his werkynge swiche as
he fyndeth occupied in goode werkes./
   Thanne thus, in getynge richesses, ye mosten
flee ydelnesse./ And afterward, ye shul use
the richesses which ye have geten by youre wit
and by youre travaille,/ in swich a manere that
men holde yow nat to scars. ne to sparynge, ne
to fool-large, that is to seyen, over-large a
spendere./ For right as men blamen an avaricious man by cause of his scarsetee and
chyncherie,/ in the same wise is he to   *2790
blame that spendeth over-largely./ And
therfore seith Caton: 'Use,' he seith, 'thy richesses that thou hast geten/ in swich a manere
that men have no matiere ne cause to calle
thee neither wrecche ne chynche;/ for it is a
greet shame to a man to have a povere herte
and a riche purs.'/ He seith also: 'The goodes
that thou hast ygeten, use hem by mesure,'
that is to seyn, spende hem mesur-
ably;/ for they that folily wasten and   1605
despenden the goodes that they han,/
whan they han namoore propre of hir owene,
they shapen hem to take the goodes of another
man./ I seye thanne that ye shul fleen avarice;/ usynge youre richesses in swich manere
that men seye nat that youre richesses been
yburyed,/ but that ye have hem in
youre myght and in youre weeldynge./   *2800
For a wys man repreveth the avaricious
man, and seith thus in two vers:/ 'Wherto and
why burieth a man his goodes by his grete
avarice, and knoweth wel that nedes moste
he dye?/ For deeth is the ende of every man

as in this present lyf.'/ And for what cause or
enchesoun joyneth he hym or knytteth he hym
so faste unto his goodes/ that alle hise wittes
mowen nat disseveren hym or departen
hym from his goodes,/ and knoweth   1615
wel, or oghte knowe, that whan he is
deed he shal no thyng bere with hym out of
this world?/ And therfore seith Seint Austyn
that 'the avaricious man is likned unto helle,/
that the moore it swelweth. the moore desir it
hath to swelwe and devoure.'/ And as wel as
ye wolde eschewe to be called an avaricious
man or chynche,/ as wel sholde ye kepe yow
and governe yow in swich a wise that
men calle yow nat fool-large./   Ther-   *2810
fore seith Tullius: 'The goodes,' he seith,
'of thyn hous ne sholde nat been hyd ne kept
so cloos, but that they myghte been opened
by pitee and debonairetee;'/ that is to seyn, to
yeven part to hem that han greet nede;/ 'ne
thy goodes shullen nat been so opene to been
every mannes goodes.'/ Afterward, in getynge
of youre richesses and in usynge hem, ye shul
alwey have thre thynges in youre herte,/ that
is to seyn, oure Lord God, conscience,
and good name./ First, ye shul have   1625
God in youre herte,/ and for no richesse
ye shullen do no thyng which may in any
manere displese God, that is youre creatour
and makere./ For after the word of Salomon,
'It is bettre to have a litel good with the love
of God,/ than to have muchel good and tresour, and lese the love of his Lord God./ And
the prophete seith that 'bettre it is to been
a good man and have litel good and
tresour,/ than to been holden a shrewe   *2820
and have grete richesses.'/ And yet seye
I ferthermoore, that ye sholde alwey doon youre
bisynesse to gete yow richesses,/ so that ye
gete hem with good conscience./ And th'apostle seith that 'ther nys thyng in this world
of which we sholden have so greet joye as
whan oure conscience bereth us good witnesse.'/ And the wise man seith, 'The substance of a man is ful good, whan synne
is nat in mannes conscience.'/ After-   1635
ward, in getynge of youre richesses and
in usynge of hem,/ yow moste have greet bisynesse and greet diligence that youre goode
name be alwey kept and conserved./ For Salomon seith that 'bettre it is and moore it availleth a man to have a good name, than for
to have grete richesses.'/ And therfore he
seith in another place, 'Do greet diligence,'

seith Salomon, 'in kepyng of thy freend and
of thy goode name;/ for it shal lenger abide
with thee than any tresour, be it never
so precious.'/ And certes he sholde nat   *2830
be called a gentil man that after God
and good conscience, alle thynges left, ne
dooth his diligence and bisynesse to kepen his
goode name./ And Cassidore seith that 'it is
signe of a gentil herte, whan a man loveth and
desireth to han a good name.'/ And therfore
seith Seint Austyn that 'ther been two thynges
that arn necessarie and nedefulle,/ and that
is good conscience and good loos;/ that is to
seyn, good conscience to thyn owene persone
inward, and good loos for thy neighebor   1645
outward.'/ And he that trusteth hym so
muchel in his goode conscience/ that he
displeseth, and setteth at noght his goode
name or loos, and rekketh noght though he
kepe nat his goode name, nys but a crueel
cherl./
Sire, now have I shewed yow how ye shul
do in getynge richesses, and how ye shullen
usen hem,/ and I se wel that for the trust
that ye han in youre richesses ye wole moeve
werre and bataille./ I conseille yow that ye
bigynne no werre in trust of youre richesses,
for they ne suffisen noght werres to
mayntene./ And therfore seith a phi-   *2840
losophre, 'That man that desireth and
wole algates han werre, shal nevere have suffisaunce;/ for the richer that he is, the gretter
despenses moste he make, if he wole have worshipe and victorie.'/ And Salomon seith that
'the gretter richesses that a man hath, the mo
despendours he hath.'/ And, deere sire, al be
it so that for youre richesses ye mowe have
muchel folk,/ yet bihoveth it nat, ne it is nat
good, to bigynne werre, whereas ye mowe in
oother manere have pees unto youre
worshipe and profit./ For the victorie   1655
of batailles that been in this world lyth
nat in greet nombre or multitude of the peple,
ne in the vertu of man,/ but it lith in the wyl
and in the hand of oure Lord God Almyghty./
And therfore Judas Machabeus, which was
Goddes knyght,/ whan he sholde fighte agayn
his adversarie that hadde a gretter nombre and
a gretter multitude of folk and strenger than
was this peple of Machabee,/ yet he recon-
forted his litel compaignye, and seyde
right in this wise:/ 'Als lightly,' quod   *2850
he, 'may oure Lord God Almyghty yeve
victorie to a fewe folk as to many folk;/ for the

victorie of a bataile comth nat by the grete nombre of peple,/ but it cometh from oure Lord God of hevene.'/ And, deere sire, for as muchel as ther is no man certein if he be worthy that God yeve hym victorie, [*ne plus que il est certain se il est digne de l'amour de Dieu*], or naught, after that Salomon seith,/ therfore every man sholde greetly drede werres to bigynne./ And by cause that   1665 in batailles fallen manye perils,/ and happeth outher while that as soone is the grete man slayn as the litel man;/ and as it is writen in the seconde Book of Kynges, 'The dedes of batailles been aventurouse and nothyng certeyne,/ for as lightly is oon hurt with a spere as another';/ and for ther is gret peril in werre; therfore sholde a man flee and eschue werre, in as muchel as a man may goodly./ For Salomon seith, 'He that °2860 loveth peril shal falle in peril.' "/

After that Dame Prudence hadde spoken in this manere, Melibee answerde, and seyde:/ "I see wel, dame Prudence, that by youre faire wordes, and by youre resouns that ye han shewed me, that the werre liketh yow no thyng;/ but I have nat yet herd youre conseil, how I shal do in this nede."/

"Certes," quod she, "I conseille yow that ye accorde with youre adversaries and that ye have pees with hem./ For Seint Jame   1675 seith in his Epistles that 'by concord and pees the smale richesses wexen grete,/ and by debaat and discord the grete richesses fallen doun.'/ And ye knowen wel that oon of the gretteste and moost sovereyn thyng that is in this world is unytee and pees./ And therfore seyde oure Lord Jhesu Crist to his apostles in this wise:/ 'Wel happy and blessed been they that loven and purchacen pees, for they been called children of God.' "/   °2870

"A," quod Melibee, "now se I wel that ye loven nat myn honour ne my worshipe./ Ye knowen wel that myne adversaries han bigonnen this debaat and bryge by hire outrage,/ and ye se wel that they ne requeren ne preyen me nat of pees, ne they asken nat to be reconsiled./ Wol ye thanne that I go and meke me and obeye me to hem, and crie hem mercy?/ For sothe, that were nat my worshipe./ For right as men seyn that   1685 'over-greet hoomlynesse engendreth dispreisynge,' so fareth it by to greet humylitee or mekenesse."/

Thanne bigan dame Prudence to maken semblant of wratthe, and seyde:/ "Certes, sire, sauf youre grace, I love youre honour and youre profit as I do myn owene, and evere have doon;/ ne ye, ne noon oother, seyn nevere the contrarie./ And yit if I hadde seyd that ye sholde han purchaced the pees and the reconsiliacioun, I ne hadde nat muchel mystaken me, ne seyd amys./ For the °2880 wise man seith, 'The dissensioun bigynneth by another man, and the reconsilyng bygynneth by thyself.'/ And the prophete seith, 'Flee shrewednesse and do goodnesse;/ seke pees and folwe it, as muchel as in thee is.'/ Yet seye I nat that ye shul rather pursue to youre adversaries for pees than they shuln to yow./ For I knowe wel that ye been so hardherted that ye wol do no thyng for me./ And Salomon seith, 'He that hath   1695 over-hard an herte, atte laste he shal myshappe and mystyde.' "/

Whanne Melibee hadde herd dame Prudence maken semblant of wratthe, he seyde in this wise:/ "Dame, I prey yow that ye be nat displesed of thynges that I seye,/ for ye knowe wel that I am angry and wrooth, and that is no wonder;/ and they that been wrothe witen nat wel what they don, ne what they seyn./ Therfore the prophete seith that °2890 'troubled eyen han no cleer sighte.'/ But seyeth and conseileth me as yow liketh, for I am redy to do right as ye wol desire;/ and if ye repreve me of my folye, I am the moore holden to love yow and to preyse yow./ For Salomon seith that 'he that repreveth hym that dooth folye,/ he shal fynde gretter grace than he that deceyveth hym by sweete wordes.' "/   1705

Thanne seide dame Prudence, "I make no semblant of wratthe ne anger, but for youre grete profit./ For Salomon seith, 'He is moore worth that repreveth or chideth a fool for his folye, shewynge hym semblant of wratthe,/ than he that supporteth hym and preyseth hym in his mysdoynge, and laugheth at his folye.'/ And this same Salomon seith afterward that 'by the sorweful visage of a man,' that is to seyn by the sory and hevy contenaunce of a man,/ 'the fool correcteth and amendeth hymself.' "/   °2900

Thanne seyde Melibee, "I shal nat konne answere to so manye faire resouns as ye putten to me and shewen./ Seyeth shortly youre wyl and youre conseil, and I am al redy to fulfille and parfourne it."/

Thanne dame Prudence discovered al hir wyl to hym, and seyde,/ "I conseille yow," quod she, "aboven alle thynges, that ye make pees bitwene God and yow;/ and beth reconsiled unto hym and to his grace./ 1715 For, as I have seyd yow heer biforn, God hath suffred yow to have this tribulacioun and disese for youre synnes./ And if ye do as I sey yow, God wol sende youre adversaries unto yow,/ and maken hem fallen at youre feet, redy to do youre wyl and youre comandementz./ For Salomon seith, 'Whan the condicioun of man is plesaunt and likynge to God,/ he chaungeth the hertes of the mannes adversaries and constreyneth hem to biseken hym of pees and of grace.'/ And °2910 I prey yow lat me speke with youre adversaries in privee place;/ for they shul nat knowe that it be of youre wyl or of youre assent./ And thanne, whan I knowe hir wil and hire entente, I may conseille yow the moore seurely."/

"Dame," quod Melibee, "dooth youre wil and youre likynge;/ for I putte me hoolly in youre disposicioun and ordinaunce."/ 1725

Thanne dame Prudence, whan she saugh the goode wyl of hir housbonde, delibered and took avys in hirself,/ thinkinge how she myghte brynge this nede unto a good conclusioun and to a good ende./ And whan she saugh hir tyme, she sente for thise adversaries to come unto hire into a pryvee place,/ and shewed wisely unto hem the grete goodes that comen of pees,/ and the grete harmes and perils that been in werre;/ and °2920 seyde to hem in a goodly manere hou that hem oughten have greet repentaunce/ of the injurie and wrong that they hadden doon to Melibee hir lord, and unto hire, and to hire doghter./

And whan they herden the goodliche wordes of dame Prudence,/ they weren so supprised and ravysshed, and hadden so greet joye of hire that wonder was to telle./ "A, lady," quod they, "ye han shewed unto us the blessynge of swetnesse, after the sawe of David the prophete;/ for the reconsilynge which 1735 we been nat worthy to have in no manere,/ but we oghte requeren it with greet contricioun and humylitee,/ ye of youre grete goodnesse have presented unto us./ Now se we wel that the science and the konnynge of Salomon is ful trewe./ For he seith that 'sweete wordes multiplien and encreescen freendes, and maken shrewes to be debonaire and meeke.'/ °2930

"Certes," quod they, "we putten oure dede and al oure matere and cause al hoolly in youre goode wyl/ and been redy to obeye to the speche and comandement of my lord Melibee./ And therfore, deere and benygne lady, we preien yow and biseke yow as mekely as we konne and mowen,/ that it lyke unto youre grete goodnesse to fulfillen in dede youre goodliche wordes./ For we consideren and knowelichen that we han offended and greved my lord Melibee out of mesure,/ so fer- 1745 forth that we be nat of power to maken his amendes./ And therfore we oblige and bynden us and oure freendes for to doon al his wyl and his comandementz./ But peraventure he hath swich hevynesse and swich wratthe to us-ward, by cause of oure offense,/ that he wole enjoyne us swich a peyne as we mowe nat bere ne susteene./ And therfore, noble lady, we biseke to youre wommanly pitee/ to taken swich avysement in this °2940 nede that we, ne oure freendes, be nat desherited ne destroyed thurgh oure folye."/

"Certes," quod Prudence, "it is an hard thyng and right perilous/ that a man putte hym al outrely in the arbitracioun and juggement, and in the myght and power of his enemys./ For Salomon seith, 'Leeveth me, and yeveth credence to that I shal seyn: I seye,' quod he, 'ye peple, folk and governours of hooly chirche,/ to thy sone, to thy wyf, to thy freend, ne to thy broother,/ ne 1755 yeve thou nevere myght ne maistrie of thy body whil thou lyvest.'/ Now sithen he deffendeth that man sholde nat yeven to his broother ne to his freend the myght of his body,/ by a strenger resoun he deffendeth and forbedeth a man to yeven hymself to his enemy./ And nathelees I conseille you that ye mystruste nat my lord,/ for I woot wel and knowe verraily that he is debonaire and meeke, large, curteys,/ and nothyng de- °2950 sirous ne coveitous of good ne richesse./ For ther nys nothyng in this world that he desireth, save oonly worshipe and honour./ Forthermoore I knowe wel and am right seur that he shal nothyng doon in this nede withouten my conseil;/ and I shal so werken in this cause that, by the grace of oure Lord God, ye shul been reconsiled unto us."/

Thanne seyden they with o voys, "Worshipful lady, we putten us and oure goodes

al fully in youre wil and disposicioun,/   1765
and been redy to comen, what day that
it like unto youre noblesse to lymyte us or assigne us,/ for to maken oure obligacioun and
boond as strong as it liketh unto youre goodnesse,/ that we mowe fulfille the wille of yow
and of my lord Melibee."/

Whan dame Prudence hadde herd the answeres of thise men, she bad hem goon agayn
prively;/ and she retourned to hir lord Melibee, and tolde hym how she foond his
adversaries ful repentant,/ knowelech-   °2960
ynge ful lowely hir synnes and trespas,
and how they were redy to suffren all peyne,/
requirynge and preiynge hym of mercy and
pitee./

Thanne seyde Melibee: "He is wel worthy
to have pardoun and foryifnesse of his synne,
that excuseth nat his synne,/ but knowelecheth
it and repenteth hym, axinge indulgence./ For
Senec seith, 'Ther is the remissioun and
foryifnesse, where as the confessioun is';/   1775
for confessioun is neighebor to innocence./ And he seith in another place that 'he
that hath shame of his synne and knowlecheth
it, is worthy remissioun.' And therfore I assente and conferme me to have pees;/ but it
is good that we do it nat withouten the assent
and wyl of oure freendes."/

Thanne was Prudence right glad and joyeful, and seyde:/ "Certes, sire," quod
she, "ye han wel and goodly answered;/   °2970
for right as by the conseil, assent, and
help of youre freendes ye han been stired to
venge yow and maken werre,/ right so withouten hire conseil shul ye nat accorden yow
ne have pees with youre adversaries./ For the
lawe seith: 'Ther nys no thyng so good by wey
of kynde as a thyng to be unbounde by hym
that it was ybounde.' "/

And thanne dame Prudence, withouten delay or tariynge, sente anon hire messages for
hire kyn, and for hire olde freendes which
that were trewe and wyse,/ and tolde hem
by ordre in the presence of Melibee al this mateere as it is aboven expressed and declared,/ and preyden hem that they   1785
wolde yeven hire avys and conseil what
best were to doon in this nede./ And whan
Melibees freendes hadde taken hire avys and
deliberacioun of the forseide mateere,/ and
hadden examyned it by greet bisynesse and
greet diligence,/ they yave ful conseil for to
have pees and reste,/ and that Melibee sholde

receyve with good herte his adversaries
to foryifnesse and mercy./   °2980

And whan dame Prudence hadde herd
the assent of hir lord Melibee, and the conseil of his freendes/ accorde with hire wille
and hire entencioun,/ she was wonderly glad
in hire herte, and seyde:/ "Ther is an old
proverbe," quod she, "seith that 'the goodnesse that thou mayst do this day, do it,/
and abide nat ne delaye it nat til to-
morwe.' And therfore I conseille that   1795
ye sende youre messages, swiche as been
discrete and wise,/ unto youre adversaries,
tellynge hem on youre bihalve/ that if they
wole trete of pees and of accord,/ that they
shape hem withouten delay or tariyng to comen
unto us."/ Which thyng parfourned was
in dede./ And whanne thise trespas-   °2990
sours and repentynge folk of hire folies,
that is to seyn, the adversaries of Melibee,/
hadden herd what thise messagers seyden unto
hem,/ they weren right glad and joyeful, and
answereden ful mekely and benignely,/ yeldynge graces and thankynges to hir lord Melibee and to al his compaignye;/ and shopen
hem withouten delay to go with the messagers,
and obeye to the comandement of hir
lord Melibee./   1805

And right anon they tooken hire wey
to the court of Melibee,/ and tooken with hem
somme of hire trewe freendes to maken feith
for hem and for to been hire borwes./ And
whan they were comen to the presence of
Melibee, he seyde hem thise wordes:/ It standeth thus," quod Melibee, "and sooth it is, that
ye,/ causelees and withouten skile and
resoun,/ han doon grete injuries and   °3000
wronges to me and to my wyf Prudence,
and to my doghter also./ For ye han entred
into myn hous by violence,/ and have doon
swich outrage that alle men knowen wel that
ye have disserved the deeth./ And therfore
wol I knowe and wite of yow,/ wheither ye
wol putte the punyssement and the chastisynge
and the vengeance of this outrage in the wyl
of me and of my wyf Prudence, or ye
wol nat?"/   1815

Thanne the wiseste of hem thre answerde for hem alle, and seyde,/ "Sire," quod
he, "we knowen wel that we been unworthy
to comen unto the court of so greet a lord and
so worthy as ye been./ For we han so greetly
mystaken us, and han offended and agilt in
swich a wise agayn youre heigh lordshipe,/

that trewely we han disserved the deeth./ But yet, for the grete goodnesse and debonairetee that al the world witnesseth of youre persone,/ we submytten us to the excellence and benignitee of youre gracious lordshipe,/ and been redy to obeie to alle youre comandementz;/ bisekynge yow that of youre merciable pitee ye wol considere oure grete repentaunce and lowe submyssioun,/ and graunten us foryevenesse of oure outrageous trespas and offense./ For wel we knowe that youre liberal grace and mercy strecchen hem ferther into goodnesse than doon oure outrageouse giltes and trespas into wikkednesse,/ al be it that cursedly and   1825 dampnablely we han agilt agayn youre heigh lordshipe."/

Thanne Melibee took hem up fro the ground ful benignely,/ and receyved hire obligaciouns and hir boondes by hire othes upon hire plegges and borwes,/ and assigned hem a certeyn day to retourne unto his court,/ for to accepte and receyve the sentence and juggement that Melibee wolde comande to be doon on hem by the causes aforeseyd./ Whiche   *3020 thynges ordeyned, every man retourned to his hous./

And whan that dame Prudence saugh hir tyme, she freyned and axed hir lord Melibee/ what vengeance he thoughte to taken of his adversaries./

To which Melibee answerde, and seyde: "Certes," quod he, "I thynke and purpose me fully/ to desherite hem of al that evere they han, and for to putte hem in exil for evere."/   1835

"Certes," quod dame Prudence, "this were a crueel sentence and muchel agayn resoun./ For ye been riche ynough, and han no nede of oother mennes good;/ and ye myghte lightly in this wise gete yow a coveitous name,/ which is a vicious thyng, and oghte been eschued of every good man./ For after the sawe of the word of the Apostle, 'Coveitise is roote of alle harmes.'/   *3030 And therfore it were bettre for yow to lese so muchel good of youre owene, than for to taken of hir good in this manere;/ for bettre it is to lesen good with worshipe, than it is to wynne good with vileynye and shame./ And everi man oghte to doon his diligence and his bisynesse to geten hym a good name./ And yet shal he nat oonly bisie hym in kepynge of his good name,/ but he shal also en-

forcen hym alwey to do somthyng by which he may renovelle his good name./   1845 For it is writen that 'the olde good loos or good name of a man is soone goon and passed, whan it is nat newed ne renovelled.'/ And as touchynge that ye seyn ye wole exile youre adversaries,/ that thynketh me muchel agayn resoun and out of mesure,/ considered the power that they han yeve yow upon hemself./ And it is writen that 'he is worthy to lesen his privilege, that mysuseth the myght and the power that is yeven hym.'/ And I sette cas ye myghte en-   *3040 joyne hem that peyne by right and by lawe,/ which I trowe ye mowe nat do,/ I seye ye mighte nat putten it to execucioun peraventure,/ and thanne were it likly to retourne to the werre as it was biforn./ And therfore, if ye wole that men do yow obeisance, ye moste deemen moore curteisly;/ this   1855 is to seyn, ye moste yeven moore esy sentences and juggementz./ For it is writen that 'he that moost curteisly comandeth, to hym men moost obeyen.'/ And therfore I prey yow that in this necessitee and in this nede ye caste yow to overcome youre herte./ For Senec seith that 'he that overcometh his herte, overcometh twies.'/ And Tullius seith: 'Ther is no thyng so comendable in a greet lord/ as   *3050 whan he is debonaire and meeke, and appeseth him lightly.'/ And I prey yow that ye wole forbere now to do vengeance,/ in swich a manere that youre goode name may be kept and conserved,/ and that men mowe have cause and mateere to preyse yow of pitee and of mercy,/ and that ye have no cause to repente yow of thyng that ye doon./   1865 For Senec seith, 'He overcometh in an yvel manere that repenteth hym of his victorie.'/ Wherfore I pray yow, lat mercy been in youre herte,/ to th' effect and entente that God Almighty have mercy on yow in his laste juggement./ For Seint Jame seith in his Epistle: 'Juggement withouten mercy shal be doon to hym that hath no mercy of another wight.'/

Whanne Melibee hadde herd the grete skiles and resouns of dame Prudence, and hire wise informaciouns and techynges,/ his   *3060 herte gan enclyne to the wil of his wif, considerynge hir trewe entente,/ and conformed hym anon, and assented fully to werken after hir conseil;/ and thonked God, of whom procedeth al vertu and alle goodnesse, that hym sente a wyf of so greet discrecioun./ And whan the day cam that his adversaries sholde appieren in his presence,/ he spak unto hem ful goodly, and seyde in this wyse:/   1875 "Al be it so that of youre pride and heigh presumpcioun and folie, and of youre necligence and unkonnynge,/ ye have mysborn yow and trespassed unto me,/ yet for as muche as I see and biholde youre grete humylitee,/ and that ye been sory and repentant of youre giltes,/ it constreyneth me to doon yow grace and mercy./ Wherfore I receyve   *3070 yow to my grace,/ and foryeve yow out-rely alle the offenses, injuries, and wronges that ye have doon agayn me and myne,/ to this effect and to this ende that God of his endelees mercy/ wole at the tyme of oure diynge foryeven us oure giltes that we han trespassed to hym in this wrecched world./ For doutelees, if we be sory and repentant of the synnes and giltes which we han trespassed in the sighte of oure Lord God,/ he is so   1885 free and so merciable/ that he wole foryeven us oure giltes,/ and bryngen us to the blisse that nevere hath ende. Amen.

Heere is ended Chaucers Tale of Melibee and of Dame Prudence.

The Prologue of The Monk's Tale

The murye wordes of the Hoost to the Monk.

Whan ended was my tale of Melibee,
And of Prudence and hire benignytee,   *3080
Oure Hooste seyde, "As I am feithful man,
And by that precious corpus Madrian,
I hadde levere than a barel ale
That Goodelief, my wyf, hadde herd this tale!
For she nys no thyng of swich pacience   1895
As was this Melibeus wyf Prudence.
By Goddes bones! whan I bete my knaves,
She bryngeth me forth the grete clobbed staves,
And crieth, 'Slee the dogges everichoon,
And brek hem, bothe bak and every boon!'   *3090
And if that any neighebor of myne
Wol nat in chirche to my wyf enclyne,
Or be so hardy to hire to trespace,
Whan she comth hoom she rampeth in my face,
And crieth, 'False coward, wrek thy wyf!   1905
By corpus bones, I wol have thy knyf,
And thou shalt have my distaf and go spynne!'
Fro day to nyght right thus she wol bigynne.
'Allas!' she seith, 'that evere I was shape   *3099
To wedden a milksop, or a coward ape,
That wol been overlad with every wight!
Thou darst nat stonden by thy wyves right!'
This is my lif, but if that I wol fighte;
And out at dore anon I moot me dighte,
Or elles I am but lost, but if that I   1915
Be lik a wilde leoun, fool-hardy.

I woot wel she wol do me slee som day
Som neighebor, and thanne go my way;
For I am perilous with knyf in honde,
Al be it that I dar nat hire withstonde,
For she is byg in armes, by my feith: *3111
That shal he fynde that hire mysdooth or seith,—
But lat us passe awey fro this mateere.
My lord, the Monk," quod he, "be myrie of cheere,
For ye shul telle a tale trewely.   1925
Loo, Rouchestre stant heer faste by!
Ryde forth, myn owene lord, brek nat oure game.
But, by my trouthe, I knowe nat youre name.
Wher shal I calle yow my lord daun John,
Or daun Thomas, or elles daun Albon?   *3120
Of what hous be ye, by youre fader kyn?
I vowe to God, thou hast a ful fair skyn;
It is a gentil pasture ther thow goost.
Thou art nat lyk a penant or a goost:
Upon my feith, thou art som officer,   1935
Som worthy sexteyn, or som celerer,
For by my fader soule, as to my doom,
Thou art a maister whan thou art at hoom;
No povre cloysterer, ne no novys,
But a governour, wily and wys,   *3130
And therwithal of brawnes and of bones,
A wel farynge persone for the nones.
I pray to God, yeve hym confusioun
That first thee broghte unto religioun!
Thou woldest han been a tredefowel aright.

Haddestow as greet a leeve, as thou hast
    myght,   1946
To parfourne al thy lust in engendrure,
Thou haddest bigeten ful many a creature.
Allas, why werestow so wyd a cope?
God yeve me sorwe, but, and I were a
    pope,   *3140
Nat oonly thou, but every myghty man,
Though he were shorn ful hye upon his pan,
Sholde have a wyf; for al the world is lorn!
Religioun hath take up al the corn   1954
Of tredyng, and we borel men been shrympes.
Of fieble trees ther comen wrecched ympes.
This maketh that oure heires been so sklendre
And feble that they may nat wel engendre.
This maketh that oure wyves wole assaye
Religious folk, for ye mowe bettre paye
Of Venus paiementz than mowe we;   *3151
God woot, no lussheburghes payen ye!
But be nat wrooth, my lord, though that I
    pleye.
Ful ofte in game a sooth I have herd seye!"

    This worthy Monk took al in pacience,   1965
And seyde, "I wol doon al my diligence,

As fer as sowneth into honestee,
To telle yow a tale, or two, or three.
And if yow list to herkne hyderward,
I wol yow seyn the lyf of Seint Edward;
Or ellis, first, tragedies wol I telle,   *3167
Of whiche I have an hundred in my celle.
Tragedie is to seyn a certeyn storie,
As olde bookes maken us memorie,
Of hym that stood in greet prosperitee,   1975
And is yfallen out of heigh degree
Into myserie, and endeth wrecchedly.
And they ben versified communely
Of six feet, which men clepen *exametron*.
In prose eek been endited many oon,   *3170
And eek in meetre, in many a sondry wyse.
Lo, this declaryng oghte ynogh suffise.
    Now herkneth, if yow liketh for to heere.
But first I yow biseeke in this mateere,
Though I by ordre telle nat thise thynges,   1985
Be it of popes, emperours, or kynges,
After hir ages, as men writen fynde,
But tellen hem som bifore and som bihynde,
As it now comth unto my remembrarunce,
Have me excused of myn ignoraunce."   *3180

Explicit

The Monk's Tale

Heere bigynneth the Monkes Tale De Casibus Virorum Illustrium.

I wol biwaille, in manere of tragedie,
The harm of hem that stoode in heigh degree,
And fillen so that ther nas no remedie
To brynge hem out of hir adversitee.
For certein, whan that Fortune list to flee,
Ther may no man the cours of hire with-
    holde.   1996
Lat no man truste on blynd prosperitee;
Be war by thise ensamples trewe and olde.

Lucifer

    At Lucifer, though he an angel were,
And nat a man, at hym wol I bigynne.   *3190
For though Fortune may noon angel dere,
From heigh degree yet fel he for his synne
Doun into helle, where he yet is inne.
O Lucifer, brightest of angels alle,   2004
Now artow Sathanas, that mayst nat twynne
Out of miserie, in which that thou art falle.

Adam

    Loo Adam, in the feeld of Damyssene,
With Goddes owene fynger wroght was he,
And nat bigeten of mannes sperme unclene,
And welte al paradys savynge o tree.   *3200
Hadde nevere worldly man so heigh degree
As Adam, til he for mysgovernaunce
Was dryven out of hys hye prosperitee
To labour, and to helle, and to meschaunce.

Sampson

    Loo Sampsoun, which that was annunciat
By th' angel, longe er his nativitee,   2016
And was to God Almyghty consecrat,
And stood in noblesse whil he myghte see.
Was nevere swich another as was hee,
To speke of strengthe, and therwith hardy-
    nesse;   *3210

But to his wyves toolde he his secree,
Thurgh which he slow hymself for wrecched-
    nesse.

Sampsoun, this noble almyghty champioun,
Withouten wepen, save his handes tweye,
He slow and al torente the leoun, 2025
Toward his weddyng walkynge by the weye.
His false wyf koude hym so plese and preye
Til she his conseil knew; and she, untrewe,
Unto his foos his conseil gan biwreye,
And hym forsook, and took another newe.

Thre hundred foxes took Sampson for ire,
And alle hir tayles he togydre bond, *3222
And sette the foxes tayles alle on fire,
For he on every tayl had knyt a brond;
And they brende alle the cornes in that lond,
And alle hire olyveres, and vynes eke. 2036
A thousand men he slow eek with his hond,
And hadde no wepen but an asses cheke.

Whan they were slayn, so thursted hym that he
Was wel ny lorn, for which he gan to preye
That God wolde on his peyne han some
    pitee, *3231
And sende hym drynke, or elles moste he deye;
And of this asses cheke, that was dreye,
Out of a wang-tooth sprang anon a welle,
Of which he drank ynogh, shortly to seye;
Thus heelp hym God, as *Judicum* can
    telle. 2046

By verray force at Gazan, on a nyght,
Maugree Philistiens of that citee,
The gates of the toun he hath up plyght,
And on his bak ycaryed hem hath hee *3240
Hye on an hill whereas men myghte hem see.
O noble, almyghty Sampsoun, lief and deere,
Had thou nat toold to wommen thy secree,
In al this world ne hadde been thy peere!

This Sampson nevere ciser drank ne wyn, 2055
Ne on his heed cam rasour noon ne sheere,
By precept of the messager divyn,
For alle his strengthes in his heeres weere.
And fully twenty wynter, yeer by yeere,
He hadde of Israel the governaunce. *3250
But soone shal he wepe many a teere,
For wommen shal hym bryngen to meschaunce!

Unto his lemman Dalida he tolde
That in his heeris al his strengthe lay,
And falsly to his foomen she hym solde. 2065

And slepynge in hir barm, upon a day,
She made to clippe or shere his heres away,
And made his foomen al his craft espyen;
And whan that they hym foond in this array,
They bounde hym faste and putten out his
    yen. *3260

But er his heer were clipped or yshave,
Ther was no boond with which men myghte
    him bynde;
But now is he in prison in a cave,
Where-as they made hym at the queerne
    grynde. 2074
O noble Sampsoun, strongest of mankynde,
O whilom juge, in glorie and in richesse!
Now maystow wepen with thyne eyen blynde,
Sith thou fro wele art falle in wrecchednesse.

The ende of this caytyf was as I shal seye.
His foomen made a feeste upon a day, *3270
And made hym as hire fool biforn hem pleye;
And this was in a temple of greet array.
But atte laste he made a foul affray;
For he two pilers shook and made hem falle,
And doun fil temple and al, and ther it
    lay,— 2085
And slow hymself, and eek his foomen alle.

This is to seyn, the prynces everichoon,
And eek thre thousand bodyes, were ther slayn
With fallynge of the grete temple of stoon.
Of Sampson now wol I namoore sayn. *3280
Beth war by this ensample oold and playn
That no men telle hir conseil til hir wyves
Of swich thyng as they wolde han secree fayn,
If that it touche hir lymes or hir lyves.

Hercules

Of Hercules, the sovereyn conquerour, 2095
Syngen his werkes laude and heigh renoun;
For in his tyme of strengthe he was the flour.
He slow, and rafte the skyn of the leoun;
He of Centauros leyde the boost adoun;
He Arpies slow, the crueel bryddes felle;
He golden apples rafte of the dragoun; *3291
He drow out Cerberus, the hound of helle;

He slow the crueel tyrant Busirus,
And made his hors to frete hym, flessh and
    boon;
He slow the firy serpent venymus; 2105
Of Acheloys two hornes he brak oon;
And he slow Cacus in a cave of stoon;
He slow the geant Antheus the stronge;

He slow the grisly boor, and that anon;
And bar the hevene on his nekke longe.

Was nevere wight, sith that this world bi-
    gan,   *3301
That slow so manye monstres as dide he.
Thurghout this wyde world his name ran,
What for his strengthe and for his heigh
    bountee,
And every reawme wente he for to see.   2115
He was so stroong that no man myghte hym
    lette.
At bothe the worldes endes, seith Trophee,
In stide of boundes he a pileer sette.

A lemman hadde this noble champioun,
That highte Dianira, fressh as May;   *3310
And as thise clerkes maken mencioun,.
She hath hym sent a sherte, fressh and gay.
Allas! this sherte, allas and weylaway!
Envenymed was so subtilly withalle,
That er that he had wered it half a day,   2125
It made his flessh al from his bones falle.

But nathelees somme clerkes hire excusen
By oon that highte Nessus, that it maked.
Be as be may, I wol hire noght accusen;
But on his bak this sherte he wered al
    naked,   *3320
Til that his flessh was for the venym blaked.
And whan he saugh noon oother remedye,
In hoote coles he hath hymselven raked,
For with no venym deigned hym to dye.

Thus starf this worthy, myghty Hercules.   2135
Lo, who may truste on Fortune any throwe?
For hym that folweth al this world of prees,
Er he be war, is ofte yleyd ful lowe.
Ful wys is he that kan hymselven knowe!
Beth war, for whan that Fortune list to
    glose,   *3330
Thanne wayteth she her man to overthrowe
By swich a wey as he wolde leest suppose.

Nabugodonosor

The myghty trone, the precious tresor,
The glorious ceptre, and roial magestee
That hadde the kyng Nabugodonosor   2145
With tonge unnethe may discryved bee.
He twyes wan Jerusalem the citee;
The vessel of the temple he with hym ladde.
At Babiloigne was his sovereyn see,
In which his glorie and his delit he hadde.

The faireste children of the blood roial
Of Israel he leet do gelde anoon,   *3342
And maked ech of hem to been his thral.
Amonges othere Daniel was oon,
That was the wiseste child of everychon;   2155
For he the dremes of the kyng expowned,
Whereas in Chaldeye clerk ne was ther noon
That wiste to what fyn his dremes sowned.

This proude kyng leet maken a statue of gold,
Sixty cubites long and sevene in brede;   *3350
To which ymage bothe yong and oold
Comanded he to loute, and have in drede,
Or in a fourneys, ful of flambes rede,
He shal be brent that wolde noght obeye.
But nevere wolde assente to that dede   2165
Daniel, ne his yonge felawes tweye.

This kyng of kynges proud was and elaat;
He wende that God, that sit in magestee,
Ne myghte hym nat bireve of his estaat.
But sodeynly he loste his dignytee,   *3360
And lyk a beest hym semed for to bee,
And eet hey as an oxe, and lay theroute
In reyn; with wilde beestes walked hee,
Til certein tyme was ycome aboute.

And lik an egles fetheres wax his heres;   2175
His nayles lyk a briddes clawes weere;
Til God relessed hym a certeyn yeres,
And yaf hym wit, and thanne with many a teere
He thanked God, and evere his lyf in feere
Was he to doon amys or moore trespace;
And til that tyme he leyd was on his beere,
He knew that God was ful of myght and
    grace.   *3372

Balthasar

His sone, which that highte Balthasar,
That heeld the regne after his fader day,
He by his fader koude noght be war,   2185
For proud he was of herte and of array;
And eek an ydolastre was he ay.
His hye estaat assured hym in pryde;
But Fortune caste hym doun, and ther he lay,
And sodeynly his regne gan divide.   *3380

A feeste he made unto his lordes alle,
Upon a tyme, and bad hem blithe bee;
And thanne his officeres gan he calle:
"Gooth, bryngeth forth the vesseles," quod he,
"Whiche that my fader in his prosperitee
Out of the temple of Jerusalem birafte;   2196
And to oure hye goddes thanke we
Of honour that oure eldres with us lafte."

Hys wyf, his lordes, and his concubynes
Ay dronken, whil hire appetites laste,   °3390
Out of thise noble vessels sondry wynes.
And on a wal this kyng his eyen caste,
And saugh an hand, armlees, that wroot ful faste,
For feere of which he quook and siked soore.
This hand, that Balthasar so soore agaste,
Wroot *Mane*, *techel*, *phares*, and namoore.

In all that land magicien was noon   2207
That koude expoune what this lettre mente;
But Daniel expowned it anoon,
And seyde, "Kyng, God to thy fader lente
Glorie and honour, regne, tresour, rente;
And he was proud, and nothyng God ne dradde,   °3402
And therfore God greet wreche upon hym sente,
And hym birafte the regne that he hadde.

He was out cast of mannes compaignye;   2215
With asses was his habitacioun,
And eet hey as a beest in weet and drye,
Til that he knew, by grace and by resoun,
That God of hevene hath domynacioun
Over every regne and every creature;   °3410
And thanne hadde God of hym compassioun,
And hym restored his regne and his figure.

Eek thou, that art his sone, art proud also,
And knowest alle thise thynges verraily,
And art rebel to God, and art his foo.   2225
Thou drank eek of his vessels boldely;
Thy wyf eek, and thy wenches, synfully
Dronke of the same vessels sondry wynys;
And heryest false goddes cursedly;
Therfore to thee yshapen ful greet pyne ys.   °3420

This hand was sent from God that on the wal
Wroot *Mane*, *techel*, *phares*, truste me;
Thy regne is doon, thou weyest noght at al.
Dyvyded is thy regne, and it shal be
To Medes and to Perses yeven," quod he.   2235
And thilke same nyght this kyng was slawe,
And Darius occupieth his degree,
Thogh he therto hadde neither right ne lawe.

Lordynges, ensample heerby may ye take
How that in lordshipe is no sikernesse;   °3430
For whan Fortune wole a man forsake,
She bereth awey his regne and his richesse,
And eek his freendes, bothe moore and lesse.

For what man that hath freendes thurgh Fortune,
Mishap wol maken hem enemys, I gesse;   2245
This proverbe is ful sooth and ful commune.

Cenobia

Cenobia, of Palymerie queene,
As writen Persiens of hir noblesse,
So worthy was in armes and so keene,
That no wight passed hire in hardynesse,
Ne in lynage, ne in oother gentillesse.   °3441
Of kynges blood of Perce is she descended.
I seye nat that she hadde moost fairnesse,
But of hir shap she myghte nat been amended.

From hire childhede I fynde that she fledde   2255
Office of wommen, and to wode she wente,
And many a wilde hertes blood she shedde
With arwes brode that she to hem sente.
She was so swift that she anon hem hente;
And whan that she was elder, she wolde kille   °3450
Leouns, leopardes, and beres al torente,
And in hir armes weelde hem at hir wille.

She dorste wilde beestes dennes seke,
And rennen in the montaignes al the nyght,
And slepen under a bussh, and she koude eke   2265
Wrastlen, by verray force and verray myght,
With any yong man, were he never so wight.
Ther myghte no thyng in hir armes stonde.
She kepte hir maydenhod from every wight;   °3459
To no man deigned hire for to be bonde.

But atte laste hir freendes han hire maried
To Odenake, a prynce of that contree,
Al were it so that she hem longe taried.
And ye shul understonde how that he
Hadde swiche fantasies as hadde she.   2275
But natheless, whan they were knyt in-feere,
They lyved in joye and in felicitee;
For ech of hem hadde oother lief and deere.

Save o thyng, that she wolde nevere assente,
By no wey, that he sholde by hire lye   °3470
But ones, for it was hir pleyn entente
To have a child, the world to multiplye;
And also soone as that she myghte espye
That she was nat with childe with that dede,
Thanne wolde she suffre hym doon his fantasye   2285
Eft-soone, and nat but oones, out of drede.

And if she were with childe at thilke cast,
Namoore sholde he pleyen thilke game
Til fully fourty wikes weren past;
Thanne wolde she ones suffre hym do the
    same.   °3480
Al were this Odenake wilde or tame,
He gat namoore of hire, for thus she seyde,
It was to wyves lecherie and shame,
In oother caas, if that men with hem pleyde.

Two sones by this Odenake hadde she,   2295
The whiche she kepte in vertu and lettrure;
But now unto oure tale turne we.
I seye, so worshipful a creature,
And wys therwith, and large with mesure,
So penyble in the werre, and curteis eke,   °3490
Ne moore labour myghte in werre endure,
Was noon, though al this world men sholde
    seke.

Hir riche array ne myghte nat be told,
As wel in vessel as in hire clothyng.
She was al clad in perree and in gold,   2305
And eek she lafte noght, for noon huntyng,
To have of sondry tonges ful knowyng,
Whan that she leyser hadde; and for to en-
    tende
To lerne bookes was al hire likyng,   °3499
How she in vertu myghte hir lyf dispende.

And shortly of this storie for to trete,
So doghty was hir housbonde and eek she,
That they conquered manye regnes grete
In the orient, with many a fair citee
Apertenaunt unto the magestee   2315
Of Rome, and with strong hond held hem ful
    faste,
Ne nevere myghte hir foomen doon hem flee,
Ay whil that Odenakes dayes laste.

Hir batailles, whoso list hem for to rede,
Agayn Sapor the kyng and othere mo,   °3510
And how that al this proces fil in dede,
Why she conquered, and what title had therto,
And after, of hir meschief and hire wo,
How that she was biseged and ytake, —
Lat hym unto my maister Petrak go,   2325
That writ ynough of this, I undertake.

Whan Odenake was deed, she myghtily
The regnes heeld, and with hire propre hond
Agayn hir foos she faught so cruelly
That ther nas kyng ne prynce in al that
    lond   °3520

That he nas glad, if he that grace fond,
That she ne wolde upon his lond werreye.
With hire they maden alliance by bond
To been in pees, and lete hire ride and pleye.

The Emperour of Rome, Claudius   2335
Ne hym bifore, the Romayn Galien,
Ne dorste nevere been so corageus,
Ne noon Ermyn, ne noon Egipcien,
Ne Surrien, ne noon Arabyen,
Withinne the feeld that dorste with hire
    fighte,   °3530
Lest that she wolde hem with hir handes slen,
Or with hir meignee putten hem to flighte.

In kynges habit wente hir sones two,
As heires of hir fadres regnes alle,
And Hermanno and Thymalao   2345
Hir names were, as Persiens hem calle.
But ay Fortune hath in hire hony galle;
This myghty queene may no while endure.
Fortune out of hir regne made hire falle
To wrecchednesse and to mysaventure.   °3540

Aurelian, whan that the governaunce
Of Rome cam into his handes tweye,
He shoop upon this queene to doon ven-
    geaunce.
And with his legions he took his weye   2354
Toward Cenobie, and, shortly for to seye,
He made hire flee, and atte laste hire hente,
And fettred hire, and eek hire children tweye,
And wan the land, and hoom to Rome he
    wente.

Amonges othere thynges that he wan,
Hir chaar, that was with gold wroght and
    perree,   °3550
This grete Romayn, this Aurelian,
Hath with hym lad, for that men sholde it see.
Biforen his triumphe walketh shee,
With gilte cheynes on hire nekke hangynge.
Coroned was she, as after hir degree,   2365
And ful of perree charged hire clothynge.

Allas, Fortune! she that whilom was
Dredeful to kynges and to emperoures,
Now gaureth al the peple on hire, allas!
And she that helmed was in starke
    stoures,   °3560
And wan by force townes stronge and toures,
Shal on hir heed now were a vitremyte;
And she that bar the ceptre ful of floures
Shal bere a distaf, hire cost for to quyte.

De Petro Rege Ispannie

O noble, O worthy Petro, glorie of Spayne,
Whom Fortune heeld so hye in magestee,   2376
Wel oghten men thy pitous deeth complayne!
Out of thy land thy brother made thee flee,
And after, at a seege, by subtiltee,
Thou were bitraysed and lad unto his
    tente,   *3570
Where as he with his owene hand slow thee,
Succedynge in thy regne and in thy rente.

The feeld of snow, with th'egle of blak therinne,
Caught with the lymrod coloured as the gleede,
He brew this cursednesse and al this synne.
The wikked nest was werker of this nede.   2386
Noght Charles Olyver, that took ay heede
Of trouthe and honour, but of Armorike
Genylon-Olyver, corrupt for meede,
Broghte this worthy kyng in swich a
    brike.   *3580

De Petro Rege de Cipro

O worthy Petro, kyng of Cipre, also,
That Alisandre wan by heigh maistrie,
Ful many an hethen wroghtestow ful wo,
Of which thyne owene liges hadde envie,
And for no thyng but for thy chivalrie   2395
They in thy bed han slayn thee by the morwe.
Thus kan Fortune hir wheel governe and gye,
And out of joye brynge men to sorwe.

De Barnabo de Lumbardia

Off Melan grete Barnabo Viscounte,   *3589
God of delit, and scourge of Lumbardye,
Why sholde I nat thyn infortune acounte,
Sith in estaat thow cloumbe were so hye?
Thy brother sone, that was thy double allye,
For he thy nevew was, and sone-in-lawe,
Withinne his prisoun made thee to dye, —   2405
But why, ne how, noot I that thou were slawe.

De Hugelino Comite de Pize

Off the Erl Hugelyn of Pyze the langour
Ther may no tonge telle for pitee.
But litel out of Pize stant a tour,
In which tour in prisoun put was he,   *3600
And with hym been his litel children thre;
The eldest scarsly fyf yeer was of age.
Allas, Fortune! it was greet crueltee
Swiche briddes for to putte in swich a cage!

Dampned was he to dyen in that prisoun,   2415
For Roger, which that bisshop was of Pize,

Hadde on hym maad a fals suggestioun,
Thurgh which the peple gan upon hym rise,
And putten hym to prisoun, in swich wise
As ye han herd, and mete and drynke he
    hadde   *3610
So smal, that wel unnethe it may suffise,
And therwithal it was ful povre and badde.

And on a day bifil that in that hour
Whan that his mete wont was to be broght,
The gayler shette the dores of the tour.   2425
He herde it wel, but he spak right noght,
And in his herte anon ther fil a thoght
That they for hunger wolde doon hym dyen.
"Allas!" quod he, "allas, that I was wroght!"
Therwith the teeris fillen from his yen.   *3620

His yonge sone, that thre yeer was of age,
Unto hym seyde, "Fader, why do ye wepe?
Whanne wol the gayler bryngen oure potage?
Is ther no morsel breed that ye do kepe?
I am so hungry that I may nat slepe.   2435
Now wolde God that I myghte slepen evere!
Thanne sholde nat hunger in my wombe crepe;
Ther is no thyng, save breed, that me were
    levere."

Thus day by day this child bigan to crye,
Til in his fadres barm adoun it lay,   *3630
And seyde, "Farewel, fader, I moot dye!"
And kiste his fader, and dyde the same day.
And whan the woful fader deed it say,
For wo his armes two he gan to byte,   2444
And seyde, "Allas, Fortune, and weylaway!
Thy false wheel my wo al may I wyte."

His children wende that it for hunger was
That he his armes gnow, and nat for wo,
And seyde, "Fader, do nat so, allas!
But rather ete the flessh upon us two.   *3640
Oure flessh thou yaf us, take oure flessh us fro,
And ete ynogh," — right thus they to hym
    seyde,
And after that, withinne a day or two,
They leyde hem in his lappe adoun and deyde.

Hymself, despeired, eek for hunger starf;   2455
Thus ended is this myghty Erl of Pize.
From heigh estaat Fortune awey hym carf.
Of this tragedie it oghte ynough suffise;
Whoso wol here it in a lenger wise,
Redeth the grete poete of Ytaille   *3650
That highte Dant, for he kan al devyse
Fro point to point, nat o word wol he faille.

Nero

Although that Nero were as vicius
As any feend that lith ful lowe adoun,
Yet he, as telleth us Swetonius,   2465
This wyde world hadde in subjeccioun,
Bothe est and west, [south], and septemtrioun.
Of rubies, saphires, and of peerles white
Were alle his clothes brouded up and doun;
For he in gemmes greetly gan delite.   *3660

Moore delicaat, moore pompous of array,
Moore proud was nevere emperour than he;
That like clooth that he hadde wered o day,
After that tyme he nolde it nevere see.   2474
Nettes of gold threed hadde he greet plentee
To fisshe in Tybre, whan hym liste pleye.
His lustes were al lawe in his decree,
For Fortune as his freend hym wolde obeye.

He Rome brende for his delicasie;
The senatours he slow upon a day   *3670
To heere how that men wolde wepe and crie;
And slow his brother, and by his suster lay.
His mooder made he in pitous array,
For he hire wombe slitte to biholde
Where he conceyved was; so weilaway!   2485
That he so litel of his mooder tolde.

No teere out of his eyen for that sighte
Ne cam, but seyde, "A fair womman was she!"
Greet wonder is how that he koude or myghte
Be domesman of hire dede beautee.   *3680
The wyn to bryngen hym comanded he,
And drank anon, — noon oother wo he made.
Whan myght is joyned unto crueltee,
Allas, to depe wol the venym wade!

In yowthe a maister hadde this emperour   2495
To teche hym letterure and curteisye,
For of moralitee he was the flour,
As in his tyme, but if bookes lye;
And whil this maister hadde of hym mais-
      trye,   *3689
He maked hym so konnyng and so sowple
That longe tyme it was er tirannye
Or any vice dorste on hym uncowple.

This Seneca, of which that I devyse,
By cause Nero hadde of hym swich drede,
For he fro vices wolde hym ay chastise   2505
Discreetly, as by word and nat by dede, —
"Sire," wolde he seyn, "an emperour moot nede

Be vertuous and hate tirannye — "
For which he in a bath made hym to blede
On bothe his armes, til he moste dye.   *3700

This Nero hadde eek of acustumaunce
In youthe agayns his maister for to ryse,
Which afterward hym thoughte a greet grev-
      aunce;
Therefore he made hym dyen in this wise.
But natheless this Seneca the wise   2515
Chees in a bath to dye in this manere
Rather than han another tormentise;
And thus hath Nero slayn his maister deere.

Now fil it so that Fortune liste no lenger
The hye pryde of Nero to cherice,   *3710
For though that he were strong, yet was she
      strenger.
She thoughte thus, "By God! I am to nyce
To sette a man that is fulfild of vice
In heigh degree, and emperour hym calle.
By God! out of his sete I wol hym trice;   2525
Whan he leest weneth, sonnest shal he falle."

The peple roos upon hym on a nyght
For his defaute, and whan he it espied,
Out of his dores anon he hath hym dight
Allone, and ther he wende han been al-
      lied,   *3270
He knokked faste, and ay the moore he cried,
The fastere shette they the dores alle.
Tho wiste he wel, he hadde himself mysgyed,
And wente his wey; no lenger dorste he calle.

The   peple   cried   and   rombled   up   and
      doun,   2535
That with his erys herde he how they seyde,
"Where is this false tiraunt, this Neroun?"
For fere almoost out of his wit he breyde,
And to his goddes pitously he preyde
For socour, but it myghte nat bityde.   *3730
For drede of this, hym thoughte that he deyde,
And ran into a gardyn hym to hyde.

And in this gardyn foond he cherles tweye
That seten by a fyr ful greet and reed.
And to thise cherles two he gan to preye   2545
To sleen hym, and to girden of his heed,
That to his body, whan that he were deed,
Were no despit ydoon for his defame.
Hymself he slow, he koude no bettre reed,
Of   which   Fortune   lough,   and   hadde   a
      game.   *3740

De Oloferno

Was nevere capitayn under a kyng
That regnes mo putte in subjeccioun,
Ne strenger was in feeld of alle thyng,
As in his tyme, ne gretter of renoun,   2554
Ne moore pompous in heigh presumpcioun
Than Oloferne, which Fortune ay kiste
So likerously, and ladde hym up and doun,
Til that his heed was of, er that he wiste.

Nat oonly that this world hadde hym in awe
For lesynge of richesse or libertee,   *3750
But he made every man reneyen his lawe.
"Nabugodonosor was god," seyde hee;
"Noon oother god sholde adoured bee."
Agayns his heeste no wight dar trespace,
Save in Bethulia, a strong citee,   2565
Where Eliachim a preest was of that place.

But taak kep of the deth of Oloferne:
Amydde his hoost he dronke lay a-nyght,
Withinne his tente, large as is a berne,
And yet, for al his pompe and al his
     myght,   *3760
Judith, a womman, as he lay upright
Slepynge, his heed of smoot, and from his tente
Ful pryvely she stal from every wight,
And with his heed unto hir toun she wente.

De Rege Antiocho illustri

What nedeth it of kyng Anthiochus   2575
To telle his hye roial magestee,
His hye pride, his werkes venymus?
For swich another was ther noon as he.
Rede which that he was in Machabee,
And rede the proude wordes that he
     seyde,   *3770
And why he fil fro heigh prosperitee,
And in an hill how wrecchedly he deyde.

Fortune hym hadde enhaunced so in pride
That verraily he wende he myghte attayne
Unto the sterres upon every syde,   2585
And in balance weyen ech montayne,
And alle the floodes of the see restrayne.
And Goddes peple hadde he moost in hate;
Hem wolde he sleen in torment and in payne,
Wenynge that God ne myghte his pride
     abate.   *3780

And for that Nichanore and Thymothee
Of Jewes weren venquysshed myghtily,
Unto the Jewes swich an hate hadde he

That he bad greithen his chaar ful hastily,
And swoor, and seyde ful despitously   2595
Unto Jerusalem he wolde eftsoone,
To wreken his ire on it ful cruelly;
But of his purpos he was let ful soone.

God for his manace hym so soore smoot
With invisible wounde, ay incurable,   *3790
That in his guttes carf it so and boot
That his peynes weren importable.
And certeinly the wreche was resonable,
For many a mannes guttes dide he peyne.   2604
But from his purpos cursed and dampnable,
For al his smert, he wolde hym nat restreyne,

But bad anon apparaillen his hoost;
And sodeynly, er he was of it war,
God daunted al his pride and al his boost.
For he so soore fil out of his char   *3800
That it his limes and his skyn totar,
So that he neyther myghte go ne ryde,
But in a chayer men aboute hym bar,
Al forbrused, bothe bak and syde.

The wreche of God hym smoot so cruelly   2615
That thurgh his body wikked wormes crepte,
And therwithal he stank so horribly
That noon of al his meynee that hym kepte,
Wheither so he wook, or ellis slepte,
Ne myghte noght the stynk of hym en-
     dure.   *3810
In this meschief he wayled and eek wepte,
And knew God lord of every creature.

To al his hoost and to hymself also
Ful wlatsom was the stynk of his careyne;
No man ne myghte hym bere to ne fro.   2625
And in this stynk and this horrible peyne,
He starf ful wrecchedly in a monteyne.
Thus hath this robbour and this homycide,
That many a man made to wepe and
     pleyne,   *3819
Swich gerdoun as bilongeth unto pryde.

De Alexandro

The storie of Alisaundre is so commune
That every wight that hath discrecioun
Hath herd somwhat or al of his fortune.
This wyde world, as in conclusioun,   2634
He wan by strengthe, or for his hye renoun
They weren glad for pees unto hym sende.
The pride of man and beest he leyde adoun,
Wherso he cam, unto the worldes ende.

Comparisoun myghte nevere yet been
    maked   °3829
Bitwixe hym and another conquerour;
For al this world for drede of hym hath quaked.
He was of knyghthod and of fredom flour;
Fortune hym made the heir of hire honour.
Save wyn and wommen, no thing myghte
    aswage
His hye entente in armes and labour,   2645
So was he ful of leonyn corage.

What pris were it to hym, though I yow tolde
Of Darius, and an hundred thousand mo
Of kynges, princes, dukes, erles bolde
Whiche he conquered, and broghte hem into
    wo?   °3840
I seye, as fer as man may ryde or go,
The world was his, — what sholde I moore de-
    vyse?
For though I write or tolde yow everemo
Of his knyghthod, it myghte nat suffise.

Twelf yeer he regned, as seith Machabee.   2655
Philippes sone of Macidoyne he was,
That first was kyng in Grece the contree.
O worthy, gentil Alisandre, allas,
That evere sholde fallen swich a cas!
Empoysoned of thyn owene folk thou weere;
Thy sys Fortune hath turned into aas,   °3851
And yet for thee ne weep she never a teere.

Who shal me yeven teeris to compleyne
The deeth of gentillesse and of franchise,
That al the world weelded in his demeyne,
And yet hym thoughte it myghte nat suf-
    fise?   2666
So ful was his corage of heigh emprise.
Allas! who shal me helpe to endite
False Fortune, and poyson to despise,
The whiche two of al this wo I wyte?   °3860

De Julio Cesare

By wisedom, manhede, and by greet labour,
From humble bed to roial magestee
Up roos he Julius, the conquerour,
That wan al th'occident by land and see,
By strengthe of hand, or elles by tretee,
And unto Rome made hem tributarie;   2676
And sitthe of Rome the emperour was he,
Til that Fortune weex his adversarie.

O myghty Cesar, that in Thessalie
Agayn Pompeus, fader thyn in lawe,   °3870

That of the orient hadde al the chivalrie
As fer as that the day bigynneth dawe,
Thou thurgh thy knyghthod hast hem take and
    slawe,
Save fewe folk that with Pompeus fledde,
Thurgh which thou puttest al th'orient in awe.
Thanke Fortune, that so wel thee spedde!   2686

But now a litel while I wol biwaille
This Pompeus, this noble governour
Of Rome, which that fleigh at this bataille.
I seye, oon of his men, a fals traitour,   °3880
His heed of smoot, to wynnen hym favour
Of Julius, and hym the heed he broghte.
Allas, Pompeye, of th'orient conquerour,
That Fortune unto swich a fyn thee broghte!

To Rome agayn repaireth Julius   2695
With his triumphe, lauriat ful hye;
But on a tyme Brutus Cassius,
That evere hadde of his hye estaat envye,
Ful prively hath maad conspiracye
Agayns this Julius in subtil wise,   °3890
And caste the place in which he sholde dye
With boydekyns, as I shal yow devyse.

This Julius to the Capitolie wente
Upon a day, as he was wont to goon,
And in the Capitolie anon hym hente   2705
This false Brutus and his othere foon,
And stiked hym with boydekyns anoon
With many a wounde, and thus they lete hym
    lye;
But nevere gronte he at no strook but oon,
Or elles at two, but if his storie lye.   °3900

So manly was this Julius of herte,
And so wel lovede estaatly honestee,
That though his deedly woundes soore smerte,
His mantel over his hypes caste he,
For no man sholde seen his privetee;   2715
And as he lay of diyng in a traunce,
And wiste verraily that deed was hee,
Of honestee yet hadde he remembraunce.

Lucan, to thee this storie I recomende,
And to Swetoun, and to Valerie also,   °3910
That of this storie writen word and ende,
How that to thise grete conqueroures two
Fortune was first freend, and sitthe foo.
No man ne truste upon hire favour longe,
But have hire in awayt for everemoo;   2725
Witnesse on alle thise conqueroures stronge.

Cresus

This riche Cresus, whilom kyng of Lyde,
Of which Cresus Cirus soore hym dradde,
Yet was he caught amyddes al his pryde,
And to be brent men to the fyr hym
    ladde.   °3920
But swich a reyn doun fro the welkne shadde
That slow the fyr, and made hym to escape;
But to be war no grace yet he hadde,
Til Fortune on the galwes made hym gape.

Whanne he escaped was, he kan nat stente
For to bigynne a newe werre agayn.   2736
He wende wel, for that Fortune hym sente
Swich hap that he escaped thurgh the rayn,
That of his foos he myghte nat be slayn;
And eek a sweven upon a nyght he
    mette,   °3930
Of which he was so proud and eek so fayn
That in vengeance he al his herte sette.

Upon a tree he was, as that hym thoughte,
Ther Juppiter hym wessh, bothe bak and
    syde,
And Phebus eek a fair towaille hym
    broughte   2745

To dryen hym with; and therfore wax his pryde,
And to his doghter, that stood hym bisyde,
Which that he knew in heigh sentence ha-
    bounde,
He bad hire telle hym what it signyfyde,
And she his dreem bigan right thus ex-
    pounde: °3940

"The tree," quod she, "the galwes is to meene,
And Juppiter bitokneth snow and reyn,
And Phebus, with his towaille so clene,
Tho been the sonne stremes for to seyn.
Thou shalt anhanged be, fader, certeyn;   2755
Reyn shal thee wasshe, and sonne shal thee
    drye."
Thus warned hym ful plat and eek ful pleyn
His doghter, which that called was Phanye.

Anhanged was Cresus, the proude kyng;
His roial trone myghte hym nat availle.
Tragediës noon oother maner thyng   °3951
Ne kan in syngyng crie ne biwaille
But that Fortune alwey wole assaille
With unwar strook the regnes that been proude;
For whan men trusteth hire, thanne wol she
    faille,   2765
And covere hire brighte face with a clowde.

Explicit Tragedia.

Heere stynteth the Knyght the Monk of his tale.

The Prologue of The Nun's Priest's Tale

The prologe of the Nonnes Preestes Tale.

"Hoo!" quod the Knyght, "good sire, na-
    moore of this!
That ye han seyd is right ynough, ywis,
And muchel moore; for litel hevynesse
Is right ynough to muche folk, I gesse.   °3960
I seye for me, it is a greet disese,
Whereas men han been in greet welthe and ese,
To heeren of hire sodeyn fal, allas!
And the contrarie is joye and greet solas,
As whan a man hath been in povre estaat,   2775
And clymbeth up and wexeth fortunat,
And there abideth in prosperitee.
Swich thyng is gladsom, as it thynketh me,

And of swich thyng were goodly for to telle."
"Ye," quod oure Hooste, "by seint Poules
    belle!   °3970
Ye seye right sooth; this Monk he clappeth
    lowde.
He spak how Fortune covered with a clowde
I noot nevere what; and als of a tragedie
Right now ye herde, and, pardee, no remedie
It is for to biwaille ne compleyne   2785
That that is doon, and als it is a peyne,
As ye han seyd, to heere of hevynesse.
    Sire Monk, namoore of this, so God yow
    blesse!

Youre tale anoyeth al this compaignye.
Swich talkyng is nat worth a boterflye,   *3980
For therinne is ther no desport ne game.
Wherfore, sire Monk, or daun Piers by youre
　　　name,
I pray yow hertely telle us somwhat elles;
For sikerly, nere clynkyng of youre belles,
That on youre bridel hange on every syde,
By hevene kyng, that for us alle dyde,   2796
I sholde er this han fallen doun for sleep,
Althogh the slough had never been so deep;
Thanne hadde your tale al be toold in veyn.
For certeinly, as that thise clerkes seyn,
Whereas a man may have noon audi-
　　　ence,   *3991
Noght helpeth it to tellen his sentence.
　　And wel I woot the substance is in me,
If any thyng shal wel reported be.   2804
Sir, sey somwhat of huntyng, I yow preye."

"Nay," quod this Monk, "I have no lust to
　　　pleye.
Now lat another telle, as I have toold."
Thanne spak oure Hoost with rude speche and
　　　boold,
And seyde unto the Nonnes Preest anon,
"Com neer, thou preest, com hyder, thou sir
　　　John!   *4000
Telle us swich thyng as may oure hertes glade.
Be blithe, though thou ryde upon a jade.
What thogh thyn hors be bothe foul and lene?
If he wol serve thee, rekke nat a bene.
Looke that thyn herte be murie everemo."   2815
　　"Yis, sir," quod he, "yis, Hoost, so moot I go,
But I be myrie, ywis I wol be blamed."
And right anon his tale he hath attamed,
And thus he seyde unto us everichon,
This sweete preest, this goodly man sir
　　　John.   *4010

Explicit.

The Nun's Priest's Tale

Heere bigynneth the Nonnes Preestes Tale of the Cok and Hen, Chauntecleer and Pertelote.

A povre wydwe, somdeel stape in age
Was whilom dwellyng in a narwe cotage,
Biside a grove, stondynge in a dale.
This wydwe, of which I telle yow my tale,
Syn thilke day that she was last a wyf,   2825
In pacience ladde a ful symple lyf,
For litel was hir catel and hir rente.
By housbondrie of swich as God hire sente
She foond hirself and eek hir doghtren two.
Thre large sowes hadde she, and namo,   *4020
Three keen, and eek a sheep that highte Malle.
Ful sooty was hire bour and eek hir halle,
In which she eet ful many a sklendre meel.
Of poynaunt sauce hir neded never a deel.
No deyntee morsel passed thurgh hir throte;
Hir diete was accordant to hir cote.   2836
Repleccioun ne made hire nevere sik;
Attempree diete was al hir phisik,
And exercise, and hertes suffisaunce.
The goute lette hire nothyng for to
　　　daunce,   *4030
N'apoplexie shente nat hir heed.

No wyn ne drank she, neither whit ne reed;
Hir bord was served moost with whit and
　　　blak, —
Milk and broun breed, in which she foond no
　　　lak,
Seynd bacoun, and somtyme an ey or tweye;
For she was, as it were, a maner deye.   2846
　　A yeerd she hadde, enclosed al aboute
With stikkes, and a drye dych withoute,
In which she hadde a cok, hight Chaunte-
　　　cleer.   *4039
In al the land, of crowyng nas his peer.
His voys was murier than the murie orgon
On messe-dayes that in the chirche gon.
Wel sikerer was his crowyng in his logge
Than is a clokke or an abbey orlogge.
By nature he knew ech ascencioun   2855
Of the equynoxial in thilke toun;
For whan degrees fiftene weren ascended,
Thanne crew he, that it myghte nat been
　　　amended.
His coomb was redder than the fyn coral,

And batailled as it were a castel wal;   °4050
His byle was blak, and as the jeet it shoon;
Lyk asure were his legges and his toon;
His nayles whitter than the lylye flour,
And lyk the burned gold was his colour.
This gentil cok hadde in his governaunce   2865
Sevene hennes for to doon al his plesaunce,
Whiche were his sustres and his paramours,
And wonder lyk to hym, as of colours;
Of whiche the faireste hewed on hir throte
Was cleped faire damoysele Pertelote.   °4060
Curteys she was, discreet, and debonaire,
And compaignable, and bar hyrself so faire,
Syn thilke day that she was seven nyght oold,
That trewely she hath the herte in hoold
Of Chauntecleer, loken in every lith;   2875
He loved hire so that wel was hym therwith.
But swich a joye was it to here hem synge,
Whan that the brighte sonne gan to sprynge,
In sweete accord, "My lief is faren in londe!"
For thilke tyme, as I have understonde,
Beestes and briddes koude speke and
     synge.   °4071
    And so bifel that in a dawenynge,
As Chauntecleer among his wyves alle
Sat on his perche, that was in the halle,
And next hym sat this faire Pertelote,   2885
This Chauntecleer gan gronen in his throte,
As man that in his dreem is drecched soore.
And whan that Pertelote thus herde hym roore,
She was agast, and seyde, "Herte deere,
What eyleth yow, to grone in this man-
     ere?   °4080
Ye been a verray sleper; fy, for shame!"
    And he answerde, and seyde thus: "Madame,
I pray yow that ye take it nat agrief.
By God, me mette I was in swich meschief
Right now, that yet myn herte is soore
     afright.   2895
Now God," quod he, "my swevene recche
     aright,
And kepe my body out of foul prisoun!
Me mette how that I romed up and doun
Withinne our yeerd, wheer as I saugh a beest
Was lyk an hound, and wolde han maad
     areest °4090
Upon my body, and wolde han had me deed.
His colour was bitwixe yelow and reed,
And tipped was his tayl and bothe his eeris
With blak, unlyk the remenant of his heeris;
His snowte smal, with glowynge eyen tweye.
Yet of his look for feere almoost I deye;   2906
This caused me my gronyng, doutelees."
    "Avoy!" quod she, "fy on yow, hertelees!

Allas!" quod she, "for, by that God above,
Now han ye lost myn herte and al my love.
I kan nat love a coward, by my feith!   °4101
For certes, what so any womman seith,
We alle desiren, if it myghte bee,
To han housbondes hardy, wise, and free,
And secree, and no nygard, ne no fool,   2915
Ne hym that is agast of every tool,
Ne noon avauntour, by that God above!
How dorste ye seyn, for shame, unto youre love
That any thyng myghte make yow aferd?
Have ye no mannes herte, and han a
     berd?   °4110
Allas! and konne ye been agast of swevenys?
Nothyng, God woot, but vanitee in sweven is.
Swevenes engendren of replecciouns,
And ofte of fume and of complecciouns,   2924
Whan humours been to habundant in a wight.
Certes this dreem, which ye han met to-nyght,
Cometh of the greete superfluytee
Of youre rede colera, pardee,
Which causeth folk to dreden in hir dremes
Of arwes, and of fyr with rede lemes,   °4120
Of rede beestes, that they wol hem byte,
Of contek, and of whelpes, grete and lyte;
Right as the humour of malencolie
Causeth ful many a man in sleep to crie
For feere of blake beres, or boles blake,   2935
Or elles blake develes wole hem take.
Of othere humours koude I telle also
That werken many a man sleep ful wo;
But I wol passe as lightly as I kan.
    Lo Catoun, which that was so wys a
     man,   °4130
Seyde he nat thus, 'Ne do no fors of dremes?'
    Now sire," quod she, "whan we flee fro the
     bemes,
For Goddes love, as taak som laxatyf.
Up peril of my soule and of my lyf,
I conseille yow the beste, I wol nat lye,   2945
That bothe of colere and of malencolye
Ye purge yow; and for ye shal nat tarie,
Though in this toun is noon apothecarie,
I shal myself to herbes techen yow
That shul been for youre hele and for youre
     prow; °4140
And in oure yeerd tho herbes shal I fynde
The whiche han of hire propretee by kynde
To purge yow bynethe and eek above.
Foryet nat this, for Goddes owene love!
Ye been ful coleryk of compleccioun;   2955
Ware the sonne in his ascencioun
Ne fynde yow nat repleet of humours hoote.
And if it do, I dar wel leye a grote,

That ye shul have a fevere terciane,
Or an agu, that may be youre bane.   *4150
A day or two ye shul have digestyves
Of wormes, er ye take youre laxatyves
Of lawriol, centaure, and fumetere,
Or elles of ellebor, that groweth there,
Of katapuce, or of gaitrys beryis,   2965
Of herbe yve, growyng in oure yeerd, ther mery
          is;
Pekke hem up right as they growe and ete hem
          yn.
Be myrie, housbonde, for youre fader kyn!
Dredeth no dreem, I kan sey yow namoore."
     "Madame," quod he, "graunt mercy of youre
          loore.   *4160
But nathelees, as touchyng daun Catoun,
That hath of wysdom swich a greet renoun,
Though that he bad no dremes for to drede,
By God, men may in olde bookes rede
Of many a man moore of auctorite   2975
Than evere Caton was, so moot I thee,
That al the revers seyn of this sentence,
And han wel founden by experience
That dremes been significaciouns
As wel of joye as of tribulaciouns   *4170
That folk enduren in this lif present.
Ther nedeth make of this noon argument;
The verray preeve sheweth it in dede.
     Oon of the gretteste auctour that men rede
Seith thus: that whilom two felawes wente   2985
On pilgrimage, in a ful good entente;
And happed so, they coomen in a toun
Wher as ther was swich congregacioun
Of peple, and eek so streit of herbergage,
That they ne founde as muche as o   *4180
          cotage
In which they bothe myghte ylogged bee.
Wherfore they mosten of necessitee,
As for that nyght, departen compaignye;
And ech of hem gooth to his hostelrye,
And took his loggyng as it wolde falle.   2995
That oon of hem was logged in a stalle,
Fer in a yeerd, with oxen of the plough;
That oother man was logged wel ynough,
As was his aventure or his fortune,
That us governeth alle as in commune.   *4190
     And so bifel that, longe er it were day,
This man mette in his bed, ther as he lay,
How that his felawe gan upon hym calle,
And seyde, 'Allas! for in an oxes stalle
This nyght I shal be mordred ther I lye.   3005
Now help me, deere brother, or I dye.
In alle haste com to me!' he sayde.
This man out of his sleep for feere abrayde;

But whan that he was wakened of his sleep,
He turned hym, and took of this no
          keep.   *4200
Hym thoughte his dreem nas but a vanitee.
Thus twies in his slepyng dremed hee;
And atte thridde tyme yet his felawe
Cam, as hym thoughte, and seide, 'I am now
          slawe.
Bihoold my bloody woundes depe and wyde!
Arys up erly in the morwe tyde,   3016
And at the west gate of the toun,' quod he,
'A carte ful of dong ther shaltow se,
In which my body is hid ful prively;
Do thilke carte arresten boldely.   *4210
My gold caused my mordre, sooth to sayn.'
And tolde hym every point how he was slayn,
With a ful pitous face, pale of hewe.
And truste wel, his dreem he foond ful trewe,
For on the morwe, as soone as it was day,   3025
To his felawes in he took the way;
And whan that he cam to this oxes stalle,
After his felawe he bigan to calle.
     The hostiler answerede hym anon,
And seyde, 'Sire, your felawe is agon.   *4220
As soone as day he wente out of the toun.'
     This man gan fallen in suspecioun,
Remembrynge on his dremes that he mette,
And forth he gooth — no lenger wolde he
          lette —
Unto the west gate of the toun, and fond   3035
A dong-carte, wente as it were to donge lond,
That was arrayed in that same wise
As ye han herd the dede man devyse.
And with an hardy herte he gan to crye
Vengeance and justice of this felonye.   *4230
'My felawe mordred is this same nyght,
And in this carte he lith gapyng upright.
I crye out on the ministres,' quod he,
'That sholden kepe and reulen this citee.   3044
Harrow! allas! heere lith my felawe slayn!'
What sholde I moore unto this tale sayn?
The peple out sterte and caste the cart to
          grounde,
And in the myddel of the dong they founde
The dede man, that mordred was al newe.
     O blisful God, that art so just and
          trewe,   *4240
Lo, how that thou biwreyest mordre alway!
Mordre wol out, that se we day by day.
Mordre is so wlatsom and abhomynable
To God, that is so just and resonable,
That he ne wol nat suffre it heled be,   3055
Though it abyde a yeer, or two, or thre.
Mordre wol out, this my conclusioun.

And right anon, ministres of that toun
Han hent the carter and so soore hym pyned,
And eek the hostiler so soore engyned,   *4250
That they biknewe hire wikkednesse anon,
And were anhanged by the nekke-bon.
    Heere may men seen that dremes been to
        drede.
And certes in the same book I rede,
Right in the nexte chapitre after this —   3065
I gabbe nat, so have I joye or blis —
Two men that wolde han passed over see,
For certeyn cause, into a fer contree,
If that the wynd ne hadde been contrarie,
That made hem in a citee for to tarie   *4260
That stood ful myrie upon an haven-syde;
But on a day, agayn the even-tyde,
The wynd gan chaunge, and blew right as hem
        leste.
Jolif and glad they wente unto hir reste,
And casten hem ful erly for to saille.   3075
But to that o man fil a greet mervaille:
That oon of hem, in slepyng as he lay,
Hym mette a wonder dreem agayn the day.
Hym thoughte a man stood by his beddes syde,
And   hym   comanded   that   he   sholde
        abyde,   *4270
And seyde hym thus: 'If thou tomorwe wende,
Thow shalt be dreynt; my tale is at an ende.'
He wook, and tolde his felawe what he mette,
And preyde hym his viage for to lette;
As for that day, he preyde hym to byde.   3085
His felawe, that lay by his beddes syde,
Gan for to laughe, and scorned him ful faste.
'No dreem,' quod he, 'may so myn herte agaste
That I wol lette for to do my thynges.
I sette nat a straw by thy dremynges,   *4280
For swevenes been but vanytees and japes.
Men dreme alday of owles and of apes,
And eek of many a maze therwithal;
Men dreme of thyng that nevere was ne shal.
But sith I see that thou wolt heere abyde,   3095
And thus forslewthen wilfully thy tyde,
God woot, it reweth me; and have good day!'
And thus he took his leve, and wente his way.
But er that he hadde half his cours yseyled,
Noot I nat why, ne what myschaunce it
        eyled,   *4290
But casuelly the shippes botme rente,
And ship and man under the water wente
In sighte of othere shippes it bisyde,
That with hem seyled at the same tyde.
And therfore, faire Pertelote so deere,   3105
By swiche ensamples olde maistow leere
That no man sholde been to recchelees

Of dremes; for I seye thee, doutelees,
That many a dreem ful soore is for to drede.
    Lo, in the lyf of Seint Kenelm I rede,
That   was   Kenulphus   sone,   the   noble
        kyng   *4301
Of Mercenrike, how Kenelm mette a thyng.
A lite er he was mordred, on a day,
His mordre in his avysioun he say.
His norice hym expowned every deel   3115
His sweven, and bad hym for to kepe hym weel
For traisoun; but he nas but seven yeer oold,
And therfore litel tale hath he toold
Of any dreem, so hooly was his herte.
By God! I hadde levere than my sherte   *4310
That ye hadde rad his legende, as have I.
    Dame Pertelote, I sey yow trewely,
Macrobeus, that writ the avisioun
In Affrike of the worthy Cipioun,   3124
Affermeth dremes, and seith that they been
Warnynge of thynges that men after seen.
And forthermoore, I pray yow, looketh wel
In the olde testament, of Daniel,
If he heeld dremes any vanitee.
Reed eek of Joseph, and ther shul ye see   *4320
Wher dremes be somtyme — I sey nat alle —
Warnynge of thynges that shul after falle.
Looke of Egipte the kyng, daun Pharao,
His bakere and his butiller also,
Wher they ne felte noon effect in dremes.   3135
Whoso wol seken actes of sondry remes
May rede of dremes many a wonder thyng.
Lo Cresus, which that was of Lyde kyng,
Mette he nat that he sat upon a tree,
Which signified he sholde anhanged
        bee?   *4330
Lo heere Andromacha, Ectores wyf,
That day that Ector sholde lese his lyf,
She dremed on the same nyght biforn
How that the lyf of Ector sholde be lorn,
If thilke day he wente into bataille.   3145
She warned hym, but it myghte nat availle;
He wente for to fighte natheles,
But he was slayn anon of Achilles.
But thilke tale is al to longe to telle,
And eek it is ny day, I may nat dwelle.   *4340
Shortly I seye, as for conclusioun,
That I shal han of this avisioun
Adversitee; and I seye forthermoor,
That I ne telle of laxatyves no stoor,
For they been venymous, I woot it weel;   3155
I hem diffye, I love hem never a deel!
    Now let us speke of myrthe, and stynte al this.
Madame Pertelote, so have I blis,
Of o thyng God hath sent me large grace;

For whan I se the beautee of youre
    face,   *4350
Ye been so scarlet reed aboute youre yen,
It maketh al my drede for to dyen;
For al so siker as *In principio,*
Mulier est hominis confusio, —
Madame, the sentence of this Latyn is, 3165
'Womman is mannes joye and al his blis.'
For whan I feele a-nyght your softe syde,
Al be it that I may nat on yow ryde,
For that oure perche is maad so narwe, allas!
I am so ful of joye and of solas, *4360
That I diffye bothe sweven and dreem."
And with that word he fley doun fro the beem,
For it was day, and eke his hennes alle,
And with a chuk he gan hem for to calle,
For he hadde founde a corn, lay in the yerd.
Real he was, he was namoore aferd. 3176
He fethered Pertelote twenty tyme,
And trad hire eke as ofte, er it was pryme.
He looketh as it were a grym leoun,
And on his toos he rometh up and doun; *4370
Hym deigned nat to sette his foot to grounde.
He chukketh whan he hath a corn yfounde,
And to hym rennen thanne his wyves alle.
Thus roial, as a prince is in his halle,
Leve I this Chauntecleer in his pasture, 3185
And after wol I telle his aventure.

    Whan that the month in which the world
    bigan,
That highte March, whan God first maked man,
Was compleet, and passed were also,
Syn March bigan, thritty dayes and two, *4380
Bifel that Chauntecleer in al his pryde,
His sevene wyves walkynge by his syde,
Caste up his eyen to the brighte sonne,
That in the signe of Taurus hadde yronne 3194
Twenty degrees and oon, and somwhat moore,
And knew by kynde, and by noon oother loore,
That it was pryme, and crew with blisful
    stevene.
"The sonne," he seyde, "is clomben up on
    hevene
Fourty degrees and oon, and moore ywis.
Madame Pertelote, my worldes blis, *4390
Herkneth thise blisful briddes how they synge,
And se the fresshe floures how they sprynge;
Ful is myn herte of revel and solas!"
But sodeynly hym fil a sorweful cas,
For evere the latter ende of joye is wo. 3205
God woot that worldly joye is soone ago;
And if a rethor koude faire endite,
He in a cronycle saufly myghte it write
As for a sovereyn notabilitee.

Now every wys man, lat him herkne me; *4400
This storie is also trewe, I undertake,
As is the book of Launcelot de Lake,
That wommen holde in ful greet reverence.
Now wol I torne agayn to my sentence.

    A col-fox, ful of sly iniquitee, 3215
That in the grove hadde woned yeres three,
By heigh ymaginacioun forncast,
The same nyght thurghout the hegges brast
Into the yerd ther Chauntecleer the faire
Was wont, and eek his wyves, to re-
    paire; *4410
And in a bed of wortes stille he lay,
Til it was passed undren of the day,
Waitynge his tyme on Chauntecleer to falle,
As gladly doon thise homycides alle
That in await liggen to mordre men. 3225
O false mordrour, lurkynge in thy den!
O newe Scariot, newe Genylon,
False dissymulour, o Greek Synon,
That broghtest Troye al outrely to sorwe!
O Chauntecleer, acursed be that morwe
That thou into that yerd flaugh fro the
    bemes! *4421
Thou were ful wel ywarned by thy dremes
That thilke day was perilous to thee;
But what that God forwoot moot nedes bee,
After the opinioun of certein clerkis. 3235
Witnesse on hym that any parfit clerk is,
That in scole is greet altercacioun
In this mateere, and greet disputisoun,
And hath been of an hundred thousand men.
But I ne kan nat bulte it to the bren *4430
As kan the hooly doctour Augustyn,
Or Boece, or the Bisshop Bradwardyn,
Wheither that Goddes worthy forwityng
Streyneth me nedely for to doon a thyng, —
"Nedely" clepe I symple necessitee; 3245
Or elles, if free choys be graunted me
To do that same thyng, or do it noght,
Though God forwoot it er that was wroght;
Or if his wityng streyneth never a deel
But by necessitee condicioneel. *4440
I wol nat han to do of swich mateere;
My tale is of a cok, as ye may heere,
That tok his conseil of his wyf, with sorwe,
To walken in the yerd upon that morwe 3254
That he hadde met that dreem that I yow tolde.
Wommennes conseils been ful ofte colde;
Wommannes conseil broghte us first to wo,
And made Adam fro Paradys to go,
Ther as he was ful myrie and wel at ese.
But for I noot to whom it myght dis-
    plese, *4450

If I conseil of wommen wolde blame,
Passe over, for I seyde it in my game.
Rede auctours, where they trete of swich ma-
    teere,
And what they seyn of wommen ye may heere.
Thise been the cokkes wordes, and nat myne;
I kan noon harm of no womman divyne.   3266

    Faire in the soond, to bathe hire myrily,
Lith Pertelote, and alle hire sustres by,
Agayn the sonne, and Chauntecleer so free
Soong murier than the mermayde in the
    see;   *4460
For Phisiologus seith sikerly
How that they syngen wel and myrily.
And so bifel that, as he caste his ye
Among the wortes on a boterflye,
He was war of this fox, that lay ful lowe.   3275
Nothyng ne liste hym thanne for to crowe,
But cride anon, "Cok! cok!" and up he sterte
As man that was affrayed in his herte.
For natureelly a beest desireth flee
Fro his contrarie, if he may it see,   *4470
Though he never erst hadde seyn it with his ye.

    This Chauntecleer, whan he gan hym espye,
He wolde han fled, but that the fox anon
Seyde, "Gentil sire, allas! wher wol ye gon?
Be ye affrayed of me that am youre freend?
Now, certes, I were worse than a feend,   3286
If I to yow wolde harm or vileynye!
I am nat come youre conseil for t'espye,
But trewely, the cause of my comynge
Was oonly for to herkne how that ye
    synge.   *4480
For trewely, ye have as myrie a stevene
As any aungel hath that is in hevene.
Therwith ye han in musyk moore feelynge
Than hadde Boece, or any that kan synge.
My lord youre fader — God his soule blesse! —
And eek youre mooder, of hire gentillesse,   3296
Han in myn hous ybeen to my greet ese;
And certes, sire, ful fayn wolde I yow plese.
But, for men speke of syngyng, I wol seye,—
So moote I brouke wel myne eyen tweye,—
Save yow, I herde nevere man so synge   *4491
As dide youre fader in the morwenynge.
Certes, it was of herte, al that he song.
And for to make his voys the moore strong,
He wolde so peyne hym that with bothe his
    yen   3305
He moste wynke, so loude he wolde cryen,
And stonden on his tiptoon therwithal,
And strecche forth his nekke long and smal.
And eek he was of swich discrecioun
That ther nas no man in no regioun   *4500

That hym in song or wisedom myghte passe.
I have wel rad in 'Daun Burnel the Asse,'
Among his vers, how that ther was a cok,
For that a preestes sone yaf hym a knok
Upon his leg whil he was yong and nyce,   3315
He made hym for to lese his benefice.
But certeyn, ther nys no comparisoun
Bitwixe the wisedom and discrecioun
Of youre fader and of his subtiltee.
Now syngeth, sire, for seinte charitee;   *4510
Lat se, konne ye youre fader countrefete?"

    This Chauntecleer his wynges gan to bete,
As man that koude his traysoun nat espie,
So was he ravysshed with his flaterie.

    Allas! ye lordes, many a fals flatour   3325
Is in youre courtes, and many a losengeour,
That plesen yow wel moore, by my feith,
Than he that soothfastnesse unto yow seith.
Redeth Ecclesiaste of flaterye;
Beth war, ye lordes, of hir trecherye.   *4520

    This Chauntecleer stood hye upon his toos,
Strecchynge his nekke, and heeld his eyen cloos,
And gan to crowe loude for the nones.
And daun Russell the fox stirte up atones,
And by the gargat hente Chauntecleer,   3335
And on his bak toward the wode hym beer,
For yet ne was ther no man that hym sewed.

    O destinee, that mayst nat been eschewed!
Allas, that Chauntecleer fleigh fro the bemes!
Allas, his wyf ne roghte nat of dremes!   *4530
And on a Friday fil al this meschaunce.
O Venus, that art goddesse of plesaunce,
Syn that thy servant was this Chauntecleer,
And in thy servyce dide al his poweer,
Moore for delit than world to multiplye,   3345
Why woldestow suffre hym on thy day to dye?
    O Gaufred, deere maister soverayn,
That whan thy worthy kyng Richard was slayn
With shot, compleynedest his deeth so soore,
Why ne hadde I now thy sentence and thy
    loore,   *4540
The Friday for to chide, as diden ye?
For on a Friday, soothly, slayn was he.
Thanne wolde I shewe yow how that I koude
    pleyne
For Chauntecleres drede and for his peyne.

    Certes, swich cry ne lamentacion,   3355
Was nevere of ladyes maad whan Ylion
Was wonne, and Pirrus with his streite swerd,
Whan he hadde hent kyng Priam by the berd,
And slayn hym, as seith us *Eneydos*,
As maden alle the hennes in the clos,   *4550
Whan they had seyn of Chauntecleer the
    sighte.

But sovereynly dame Pertelote shrighte
Ful louder than dide Hasdrubales wyf,
Whan that hir housbonde hadde lost his lyf,
And that the Romayns hadde brend Cartage.
She was so ful of torment and of rage   3366
That wilfully into the fyr she sterte,
And brende hirselven with a stedefast herte.
 O woful hennes, right so criden ye,
As, whan that Nero brende the citee   °4560
Of Rome, cryden senatoures wyves
For that hir husbondes losten alle hir lyves, —
Withouten gilt this Nero hath hem slayn.
Now wole I turne to my tale agayn.   3374
 This sely wydwe and eek hir doghtres two
Herden thise hennes crie and maken wo,
And out at dores stirten they anon,
And syen the fox toward the grove gon,
And bar upon his bak the cok away,
And cryden, "Out! harrow! and weyl-
 away!   °4570
Ha! ha! the fox!" and after hym they ran,
And eek with staves many another man.
Ran Colle oure dogge, and Talbot and Gerland,
And Malkyn, with a dystaf in hir hand;
Ran cow and calf, and eek the verray hogges,
So fered for the berkyng of the dogges   3386
And shoutyng of the men and wommen eeke,
They ronne so hem thoughte hir herte breeke.
They yolleden as feendes doon in helle;
The dokes cryden as men wolde hem
 quelle;   °4580
The gees for feere flowen over the trees;
Out of the hyve cam the swarm of bees.
So hydous was the noyse, a, *benedicitee!*
Certes, he Jakke Straw and his meynee
Ne made nevere shoutes half so shrille   3395
Whan that they wolden any Flemyng kille,
As thilke day was maad upon the fox.
Of bras they broghten bemes, and of box,
Of horn, of boon, in whiche they blewe and
 powped,
And therwithal they skriked and they
 howped.   °4590
It semed as that hevene sholde falle.
 Now, goode men, I prey yow herkneth alle:
Lo, how Fortune turneth sodeynly
The hope and pryde eek of hir enemy!

This cok, that lay upon the foxes bak,   3405
In al his drede unto the fox he spak,
And seyde, "Sire, if that I were as ye,
Yet sholde I seyn, as wys God helpe me,
'Turneth agayn, ye proude cherles alle!
A verray pestilence upon yow falle!   °4600
Now am I come unto the wodes syde;
Maugree youre heed, the cok shal heere abyde.
I wol hym ete, in feith, and that anon!' "
 The fox answerde, "In feith, it shal be don."
And as he spak that word, al sodeynly   3415
This cok brak from his mouth delyverly,
And heighe upon a tree he fleigh anon.
And whan the fox saugh that the cok was gon,
 "Allas!" quod he, "O Chauntecleer, allas!
I have to yow," quod he, "ydoon tres-
 pas,   °4610
In as muche as I maked yow aferd
Whan I yow hente and broghte out of the yerd.
But, sire, I dide it in no wikke entente.
Com doun, and I shal telle yow what I mente;
I shal seye sooth to yow, God help me so!"   3425
 "Nay thanne," quod he, "I shrewe us bothe
 two.
And first I shrewe myself, bothe blood and
 bones,
If thou bigyle me ofter than ones.
Thou shalt namoore, thurgh thy flaterye,
Do me to synge and wynke with myn
 ye;   °4620
For he that wynketh, whan he sholde see,
Al wilfully, God lat him nevere thee!"
 "Nay," quod the fox, "but God yeve hym
 meschaunce,
That is so undiscreet of governaunce
That jangleth whan he sholde holde his pees."
 Lo, swich it is for to be recchelees   3436
And necligent, and truste on flaterye.
 But ye that holden this tale a folye,
As of a fox, or of a cok and hen,
Taketh the moralite, goode men.   °4630
For seint Paul seith that al that writen is,
To oure doctrine it is ywrite, ywis;
Taketh the fruyt, and lat the chaf be stille.
Now, goode God, if that it be thy wille,   3444
As seith my lord, so make us alle goode men,
And brynge us to his heighe blisse! Amen.

Heere is ended the Nonnes Preestes Tale.

[Epilogue to The Nun's Priest's Tale

"Sire Nonnes Preest," oure Hooste seide anoon,
"I-blessed be thy breche, and every stoon!
This was a murie tale of Chauntecleer.
But by my trouthe, if thou were seculer,
Thou woldest ben a trede-foul aright.   *4641
For if thou have corage as thou hast myght,
Thee were nede of hennes, as I wene,
Ya, moo than seven tymes seventene.   3454

See, whiche braunes hath this gentil preest,
So gret a nekke, and swich a large breest!
He loketh as a sperhauk with his yen;
Him nedeth nat his colour for to dyen
With brasile, ne with greyn of Portyngale.
Now, sire, faire falle yow for youre tale!"   *4650
    And after that he, with ful merie chere,
Seide unto another, as ye shuln heere.]

Fragment VIII (Group G)

The Second Nun's Prologue

The Prologe of the Seconde Nonnes Tale.

The ministre and the norice unto vices,
Which that men clepe in Englissh ydelnesse,
That porter of the gate is of delices,
To eschue, and by hire contrarie hire op-
    presse,
That is to seyn, by leveful bisynesse,   5
Wel oghten we to doon al oure entente,
Lest that the feend thurgh ydelnesse us hente.

For he that with his thousand cordes slye
Continuelly us waiteth to biclappe,
Whan he may man in ydelnesse espye,   10
He kan so lightly cache hym in his trappe,
Til that a man be hent right by the lappe,
He nys nat war the feend hath hym in honde.
Wel oghte us werche, and ydelnesse with-
    stonde.

And though men dradden nevere for to dye,
Yet seen men wel by resoun, douteles,   16
That ydelnesse is roten slogardye,
Of which ther nevere comth no good n'encrees,
And syn that slouthe hire holdeth in a lees
Oonly to slepe, and for to ete and drynke,   20
And to devouren al that othere swynke,

And for to putte us fro swich ydelnesse,
That cause is of so greet confusioun,
I have heer doon my feithful bisynesse
After the legende, in translacioun   25
Right of thy glorious lif and passioun,
Thou with thy gerland wroght with rose and
    lilie, —
Thee meene I, mayde and martyr, Seint Cecile.

Invocacio ad Mariam

And thow that flour of virgines art alle,
Of whom that Bernard list so wel to write,   30
To thee at my bigynnyng first I calle;
Thou confort of us wrecches, do me endite
Thy maydens deeth, that wan thurgh hire
    merite

The eterneel lyf, and of the feend victorie,
As man may after reden in hire storie.   35

Thow Mayde and Mooder, doghter of thy Sone,
Thow welle of mercy, synful soules cure,
In whom that God for bountee chees to wone,
Thow humble, and heigh over every creature,
Thow nobledest so ferforth oure nature,   40
That no desdeyn the Makere hadde of kynde
His Sone in blood and flessh to clothe and
    wynde.

Withinne the cloistre blisful of thy sydis
Took mannes shap the eterneel love and pees,
That of the tryne compas lord and gyde is,   45
Whom erthe and see and hevene, out of relees,
Ay heryen; and thou, Virgine wemmelees,
Baar of thy body — and dweltest mayden
    pure —
The Creatour of every creature.

Assembled is in thee magnificence   50
With mercy, goodnesse, and with swich pitee
That thou, that art the sonne of excellence
Nat oonly helpest hem that preyen thee,
But often tyme, of thy benygnytee,
Ful frely, er that men thyn help biseche,   55
Thou goost biforn, and art hir lyves leche.

Now help, thow meeke and blisful faire mayde,
Me, flemed wrecche, in this desert of galle;
Thynk on the womman Cananee, that sayde
That whelpes eten somme of the crommes alle
That from hir lordes table been yfalle;   61
And though that I, unworthy sone of Eve,
Be synful, yet accepte my bileve.

And, for that feith is deed withouten werkis,
So for to werken yif me wit and space,   65
That I be quit fro thennes that most derk is!
O thou, that art so fair and ful of grace,
Be myn advocat in that heighe place

Theras withouten ende is songe "Osanne,"
Thow Cristes mooder, doghter deere of Anne!

And of thy light my soule in prison lighte,   71
That troubled is by the contagioun
Of my body, and also by the wighte
Of erthely lust and fals affeccioun;
O havene of refut, o salvacioun   75
Of hem that been in sorwe and in distresse,
Now help, for to my werk I wol me dresse.

Yet preye I yow that reden that I write,
Foryeve me that I do no diligence
This ilke storie subtilly to endite,   80
For bothe have I the wordes and sentence
Of hym that at the seintes reverence
The storie wroot, and folwen hire legende,
And pray yow that ye wole my werk amende.

Interpretacio nominis Cecilie quam ponit
Frater Jacobus Januensis in Legenda

First wolde I yow the name of Seint Cecilie
Expowne, as men may in hir storie see.   86
It is to seye in Englissh "hevenes lilie,"
For pure chaastnesse of virginitee;
Or, for she whitnesse hadde of honestee,
And grene of conscience, and of good fame   90
The soote savour, "lilie" was hir name.

Or Cecilie is to seye "the wey to blynde,"
For she ensample was by good techynge;

Or elles Cecile, as I writen fynde,
Is joyned, by a manere conjoynynge   95
Of "hevene" and "Lia"; and heere, in figurynge,
The "hevene" is set for thoght of hoolynesse,
And "Lia" for hire lastynge bisynesse.

Cecile may eek be seyd in this manere,
"Wantynge of blyndnesse," for hir grete light
Of sapience, and for hire thewes cleere;   101
Or elles, loo, this maydens name bright
Of "hevene" and "leos" comth, for which by right
Men myghte hire wel "the hevene of peple" calle,
Ensample of goode and wise werkes alle.   105

For "leos" "peple" in Englissh is to seye,
And right as men may in the hevene see
The sonne and moone and sterres every weye,
Right so men goostly in this mayden free
Seyen of feith the magnanymytee,   110
And eek the cleernesse hool of sapience,
And sondry werkes, brighte of excellence.

And right so as thise philosophres write
That hevene is swift and round and eek brennynge,
Right so was faire Cecilie the white   115
Ful swift and bisy evere in good werkynge,
And round and hool in good perseverynge,
And brennynge evere in charite ful brighte.
Now have I yow declared what she highte.

Explicit

The Second Nun's Tale

Here bigynneth the Seconde Nonnes Tale of the lyf of Seinte Cecile.

This mayden bright Cecilie, as hir lif seith,   120
Was comen of Romayns, and of noble kynde,
And from hir cradel up fostred in the feith
Of Crist, and bar his gospel in hir mynde.
She nevere cessed, as I writen fynde,
Of hir preyere, and God to love and drede,   125
Bisekynge hym to kepe hir maydenhede.

And whan this mayden sholde unto a man
Ywedded be, that was ful yong of age,

Which that ycleped was Valerian,
And day was comen of hir marriage,   130
She, ful devout and humble in hir corage,
Under hir robe of gold, that sat ful faire,
Hadde next hire flessh yclad hire in an haire.

And whil the organs maden melodie,
To God allone in herte thus sang she: 135
"O Lord, my soule and eek my body gye
Unwemmed, lest that it confounded be."
And, for his love that dyde upon a tree,

Every seconde and thridde day she faste,
Ay biddynge in hire orisons ful faste.   140

The nyght cam, and to bedde moste she gon
With hire housbonde, as ofte is the manere,
And pryvely to hym she seyde anon,
"O sweete and wel biloved spouse deere,
Ther is a conseil, and ye wolde it heere,   145
Which that right fayn I wolde unto yow seye,
So that ye swere ye shul it nat biwreye."

Valerian gan faste unto hire swere
That for no cas, ne thyng that myghte be,
He sholde nevere mo biwreyen here;   150
And thanne at erst to hym thus seyde she:
"I have an aungel which that loveth me,
That with greet love, wher so I wake or sleepe,
Is redy ay my body for to kepe.

"And if that he may feelen, out of drede,   155
That ye me touche, or love in vileynye,
He right anon wol sle yow with the dede,
And in youre yowthe thus ye shullen dye;
And if that ye in clene love me gye,   159
He wol yow loven as me, for youre clennesse,
And shewen yow his joye and his brightnesse."

Valerian, corrected as God wolde,
Answerde agayn, "If I shal trusten thee,
Lat me that aungel se, and hym biholde;
And if that it a verray angel bee,   165
Thanne wol I doon as thou hast prayed me;
And if thou love another man, for sothe
Right with this swerd thanne wol I sle yow
            bothe."

Cecile answerde anon-right in this wise:
"If that yow list, the angel shul ye see,   170
So that ye trowe on Crist and yow baptize.
Gooth forth to Via Apia," quod shee,
"That fro this toun ne stant but miles three,
And to the povre folkes that ther dwelle,
Sey hem right thus, as that I shal yow telle.   175

"Telle hem that I, Cecile, yow to hem sente,
To shewen yow the goode Urban the olde,
For secree nedes and for good entente.
And whan that ye Seint Urban han biholde,
Telle hym the wordes whiche I to yow
            tolde;   180
And whan that he hath purged yow fro synne,
Thanne shul ye se that angel, er ye twynne."

Valerian is to the place ygon,
And right as hym was taught by his lernynge,
He foond this hooly olde Urban anon   185
Among the seintes buryeles lotynge.
And he anon, withouten tariynge,
Dide his message; and whan that he it tolde,
Urban for joye his handes gan up holde.

The teeris from his eyen leet he falle.   190
"Almyghty Lord, o Jhesu Crist," quod he,
"Sower of chaast conseil, hierde of us alle,
The fruyt of thilke seed of chastitee
That thou hast sowe in Cecile, taak to thee!
Lo, lyk a bisy bee, withouten gile,   195
Thee serveth ay thyn owene thral Cecile.

"For thilke spouse that she took but now
Ful lyk a fiers leoun, she sendeth heere,
As meke as evere was any lomb, to yow!"
And with that word anon ther gan appeere   200
An oold man, clad in white clothes cleere,
That hadde a book with lettre of gold in honde,
And gan bifore Valerian to stonde.

Valerian as deed fil doun for drede   204
Whan he hym saugh, and he up hente hym tho,
And on his book right thus he gan to rede:
"O Lord, o feith, o God, withouten mo,
O Cristendom, and Fader of alle also,
Aboven alle and over alle everywhere."
Thise wordes al with gold ywriten were.   210

Whan this was rad, thanne seyde this olde man,
"Leevestow this thyng or no? Sey ye or nay."
"I leeve al this thyng," quod Valerian,
"For sother thyng than this, I dar wel say,
Under the hevene no wight thynke may."   215
Tho vanysshed the olde man, he nyste where,
And Pope Urban hym cristned right there.

Valerian gooth hoom and fynt Cecilie
Withinne his chambre with an angel stonde.
This angel hadde of roses and of lilie   220
Corones two, the which he bar in honde;
And first to Cecile, as I understonde,
He yaf that oon, and after gan he take
That oother to Valerian, hir make.   224

"With body clene and with unwemmed thoght
Kepeth ay wel thise corones," quod he;
"Fro paradys to yow have I hem broght,
Ne nevere mo ne shal they roten bee,
Ne lese hir soote savour, trusteth me;

Ne nevere wight shal seen hem with his ye,   230
But he be chaast and hate vileynye.

"And thow, Valerian, for thow so soone
Assentedest to good conseil also,
Sey what thee list, and thou shalt han thy
    boone."
"I have a brother," quod Valerian tho,   235
"That in this world I love no man so.
I pray yow that my brother may han grace
To knowe the trouthe, as I do in this place."

The angel seyde, "God liketh thy requeste,
And bothe, with the palm of martirdom,   240
Ye shullen come unto his blisful feste."
And with that word Tiburce his brother coom.
And whan that he the savour undernoom,
Which that the roses and the lilies caste,
Withinne his herte he gan to wondre faste,   245

And seyde, "I wondre, this tyme of the yeer,
Whennes that soote savour cometh so
Of rose and lilies that I smelle heer.
For though I hadde hem in myne handes two,
The savour myghte in me no depper go.   250
The sweete smel that in myn herte I fynde
Hath chaunged me al in another kynde."

Valerian seyde: "Two corones han we,
Snow white and rose reed, that shynen cleere,
Whiche that thyne eyen han no myght to
    see;   255
And as thou smellest hem thurgh my preyere,
So shaltow seen hem, leeve brother deere,
If it so be thou wolt, withouten slouthe,
Bileve aright and knowen verray trouthe."

Tiburce answerde, "Seistow this to me   260
In soothnesse, or in dreem I herkne this?"
"In dremes," quod Valerian, "han we be
Unto this tyme, brother myn, ywis.
But now at erst in trouthe oure dwellyng is."
"How woostow this?" quod Tiburce, "and in
    what wyse?"   265
Quod Valerian, "That shal I thee devyse.

"The aungel of God hath me the trouthe
    ytaught
Which thou shalt seen, if that thou wolt reneye
The ydoles and be clene, and elles naught."
And of the myracle of thise corones tweye   270
Seint Ambrose in his preface list to seye;
Solempnely this noble doctour deere
Commendeth it, and seith in this manere:

"The palm of martirdom for to receyve,
Seinte Cecile, fulfild of Goddes yifte,   275
The world and eek hire chambre gan she
    weyve;
Witnesse Tyburces and Valerians shrifte,
To whiche God of his bountee wolde shifte
Corones two of floures wel smellynge,   279
And make his angel hem the corones brynge.

The mayde hath broght thise men to blisse
    above;
The world hath wist what it is worth, certeyn,
Devocioun of chastitee to love."
Tho shewed hym Cecile al open and pleyn
That alle ydoles nys but a thyng in veyn,   285
For they been dombe, and therto they been
    deve,
And charged hym his ydoles for to leve.

"Whoso that troweth nat this, a beest he is,"
Quod tho Tiburce, "if that I shal nat lye."
And she gan kisse his brest, that herde this,
And was ful glad he koude trouthe espye.   291
"This day I take thee for myn allye,"
Seyde this blisful faire mayde deere,
And after that, she seyde as ye may heere: 294

"Lo, right so as the love of Crist," quod she,
"Made me thy brotheres wyf, right in that wise
Anon for myn allye heer take I thee,
Syn that thou wolt thyne ydoles despise.
Go with thy brother now, and thee baptise,
And make thee clene, so that thou mowe bi-
    holde   300
The angels face of which thy brother tolde."

Tiburce answerde and seyde, "Brother deere,
First tel me whider I shal, and to what man?"
"To whom?" quod he, "com forth with right
    good cheere,
I wol thee lede unto the Pope Urban."   305
"Til Urban? brother myn Valerian,"
Quod tho Tiburce, "woltow me thider lede?
Me thynketh that it were a wonder dede.

"Ne menestow nat Urban," quod he tho,
"That is so ofte dampned to be deed,   310
And woneth in halkes alwey to and fro,
And dar nat ones putte forth his heed?
Men sholde hym brennen in a fyr so reed
If he were founde, or that men myghte hym
    spye,
And we also, to bere hym compaignye;   315

"And whil we seken thilke divinitee
That is yhid in hevene pryvely,
Algate ybrend in this world shul we be!"
To whom Cecile answerde boldely,
"Men myghten dreden wel and skilfully   320
This lyf to lese, myn owene deere brother,
If this were lyvynge oonly and noon oother.

"But ther is bettre lif in oother place,
That nevere shal be lost, ne drede thee noght,
Which Goddes Sone us tolde thurgh his
        grace.   325
That Fadres Sone hath alle thyng ywroght,
And al that wroght is with a skilful thoght,
The Goost, that fro the Fader gan procede,
Hath sowled hem, withouten any drede.   329

By word and by myracle heigh Goddes Sone,
Whan he was in this world, declared heere
That ther was oother lyf ther men may wone."
To whom answerde Tiburce, "O suster deere,
Ne seydestow right now in this manere,   334
Ther nys but o God, lord in soothfastnesse?
And now of three how maystow bere witnesse?"

    "That shal I telle," quod she, "er I go.
Right as a man hath sapiences three,
Memorie, engyn, and intellect also,
So in o beynge of divinitee,   340
Thre persones may ther right wel bee."
Tho gan she hym ful bisily to preche
Of Cristes come, and of his peynes teche,

And manye pointes of his passioun;
How Goddes Sone in this world was withholde
To doon mankynde pleyn remissioun,   346
That was ybounde in synne and cares colde;
Al this thyng she unto Tiburce tolde.
And after this, Tiburce in good entente
With Valerian to Pope Urban he wente,   350

That thanked God, and with glad herte and
        light
He cristned hym, and made hym in that place
Parfit in his lernynge, Goddes knyght.
And after this, Tiburce gat swich grace   354
That every day he saugh, in tyme and space,
The aungel of God; and every maner boone
That he God axed, it was sped ful soone.

    It were ful hard by ordre for to seyn
How manye wondres Jhesus for hem wroghte;
But atte laste, to tellen short and pleyn,   360
The sergeantz of the toun of Rome hem soghte,

And hem biforn Almache, the prefect, broghte,
Which hem apposed, and knew al hire entente,
And to the ymage of Juppiter hem sente,

And seyde, "Whoso wol nat sacrifise,   365
Swape of his heed; this my sentence heer."
Anon thise martirs that I yow devyse,
Oon Maximus, that was an officer
Of the prefectes, and his corniculer,
Hem hente, and whan he forth the seintes
        ladde,   370
Hymself he weep for pitee that he hadde.

Whan Maximus had herd the seintes loore,
He gat hym of the tormentoures leve,
And ladde hem to his hous withoute moore,
And with hir prechyng, er that it were eve,
They gonnen fro the tormentours to reve,   376
And fro Maxime, and fro his folk echone,
The false feith, to trowe in God allone.

    Cecile cam, whan it was woxen nyght,   379
With preestes that hem cristned alle yfeere;
And afterward, whan day was woxen light,
Cecile hem seyde with a ful stedefast cheere,
"Now, Cristes owene knyghtes leeve and deere,
Cast alle awey the werkes of derknesse,
And armeth yow in armure of brightnesse.   385

"Ye han for sothe ydoon a greet bataille,
Youre cours is doon, youre feith han ye con-
        served.
Gooth to the corone of lif that may nat faille;
The rightful Juge, which that ye han served,
Shal yeve it yow, as ye han it deserved."   390
And whan this thyng was seyd as I devyse,
Men ledde hem forth to doon the sacrefise.

But whan they weren to the place broght
To tellen shortly the conclusioun,
They nolde encense ne sacrifise right noght,
But on hir knees they setten hem adoun   396
With humble herte and sad devocioun,
And losten bothe hir hevedes in the place.
Hir soules wenten to the Kyng of grace.

This Maximus, that saugh this thyng bityde,
With pitous teeris tolde it anonright,   401
That he hir soules saugh to hevene glyde
With aungels ful of cleernesse and of light,
And with his word converted many a wight;
For which Almachius dide hym so tobete   405
With whippe of leed, til he his lif gan lete.

Cecile hym took and buryed hym anon
By Tiburce and Valerian softely
Withinne hire buriyng place, under the stoon;
And after this, Almachius hastily   410
Bad his ministres fecchen openly
Cecile, so that she myghte in his presence
Doon sacrifice, and Juppiter encense.

But they, converted at hir wise loore,
Wepten ful soore, and yaven ful credence   415
Unto hire word, and cryden moore and moore,
"Crist, Goddes Sone, withouten difference,
Is verray God — this is al oure sentence —
That hath so good a servant hym to serve.
This with o voys we trowen, thogh we sterve!"

Almachius, that herde of this doynge,   421
Bad fecchen Cecile, that he myghte hire see,
And alderfirst, lo! this was his axynge.
"What maner womman artow?" tho quod he.
"I am a gentil womman born," quod she.   425
"I axe thee," quod he, "though it thee greeve,
Of thy religioun and of thy bileeve."

"Ye han bigonne youre questioun folily,"
Quod she, "that wolden two answeres conclude
In o demande; ye axed lewedly."   430
Almache answerde unto that similitude,
"Of whennes comth thyn answeryng so rude?"
"Of whennes?" quod she, whan that she was
          freyned,
"Of conscience and of good feith unfeyned."

Almachius seyde, "Ne takestow noon heede
Of my power?" And she answerde hym
          this: 436
"Youre myght," quod she, "ful litel is to dreede,
For every mortal mannes power nys
But lyk a bladdre ful of wynd, ywys.
For with a nedles poynt, whan it is blowe,   440
May al the boost of it be leyd ful lowe."

"Ful wrongfully bigonne thow," quod he,
"And yet in wrong is thy perseveraunce.
Wostow nat how oure myghty princes free
Han thus comanded and maad ordinaunce,   445
That every Cristen wight shal han penaunce
But if that he his Cristendom withseye,
And goon al quit, if he wole it reneye?"

"Yowre princes erren, as youre nobleye dooth,"
Quod tho Cecile, "and with a wood sentence
Ye make us gilty, and it is nat sooth.   451
For ye, that knowen wel oure innocence,

For as muche as we doon a reverence
To Crist, and for we bere a Cristen name,
Ye putte on us a cryme, and eek a blame.   455

But we that knowen thilke name so
For vertuous, we may it nat withseye."
Almache answerde, "Chees oon of thise two:
Do sacrifice, or Cristendom reneye,   459
That thou mowe now escapen by that weye."
At which the hooly blisful faire mayde
Gan for to laughe, and to the juge sayde:

"O juge, confus in thy nycetee,
Woltow that I reneye innocence,
To make me a wikked wight?" quod shee.   465
"Lo, he dissymuleth heere in audience;
He stareth, and woodeth in his advertence!"
To whom Almachius, "Unsely wrecche,
Ne woostow nat how fer my myght may
          strecche?

Han noght oure myghty princes to me yiven,
Ye, bothe power and auctoritee   471
To maken folk to dyen or to lyven?
Why spekestow so proudly thanne to me?"
"I speke noght but stedfastly," quod she;
"Nat proudly, for I seye, as for my syde,   475
We haten deedly thilke vice of pryde.

And if thou drede nat a sooth to heere,
Thanne wol I shewe al openly, by right,
That thou hast maad a ful gret lesyng heere.
Thou seyst thy princes han thee yeven myght
Bothe for to sleen and for to quyken a wight;
Thou, that ne mayst but oonly lyf bireve,   482
Thou hast noon oother power ne no leve.

But thou mayst seyn thy princes han thee
          maked
Ministre of deeth; for if thou speke of mo,   485
Thou lyest, for thy power is ful naked."
"Do wey thy booldnesse," seyde Almachius tho,
"And sacrifice to oure goddes, er thou go!
I recche nat what wrong that thou me profre,
For I kan suffre it as a philosophre;   490

But thilke wronges may I nat endure
That thou spekest of oure goddes heere," quod
          he.
Cecile answerde, "O nyce creature!
Thou seydest no word syn thou spak to me
That I ne knew therwith thy nycetee;   495
And that thou were, in every maner wise,
A lewed officer and a veyn justise.

"Ther lakketh no thyng to thyne outter yën
That thou n'art blynd; for thyng that we seen alle
That it is stoon,—that men may wel espyen,— 500
That ilke stoon a god thow wolt it calle.
I rede thee, lat thyn hand upon it falle,
And taste it wel, and stoon thou shalt it fynde,
Syn that thou seest nat with thyne eyen blynde.

"It is a shame that the peple shal 505
So scorne thee, and laughe at thy folye;
For communly men woot it wel overal
That myghty God is in his hevenes hye;
And thise ymages, wel thou mayst espye,
To thee ne to hemself mowen noght profite,
For in effect they been nat worth a myte." 511

Thise wordes and swiche othere seyde she,
And he weex wroth, and bad men sholde hir lede
Hom til hir hous, and "In hire hous," quod he,
"Brenne hire right in a bath of flambes rede."
And as he bad, right so was doon the dede; 516
For in a bath they gonne hire faste shetten,
And nyght and day greet fyr they under betten.

The longe nyght, and eek a day also,
For al the fyr, and eek the bathes heete, 520
She sat al coold, and feelede no wo.
It made hire nat a drope for to sweete.
But in that bath hir lyf she moste lete,
For he Almachius, with ful wikke entente,
To sleen hire in the bath his sonde sente. 525

Thre strokes in the nekke he smoot hire tho,
The tormentour, but for no maner chaunce
He myghte noght smyte al hir nekke atwo;
And for ther was that tyme an ordinaunce
That no man sholde doon man swich penaunce
The ferthe strook to smyten, softe or soore, 531
This tormentour ne dorste do namoore,

But half deed, with hir nekke ycorven there,
He lefte hir lye, and on his wey is went.
The Cristen folk, which that aboute hire were,
With sheetes han the blood ful faire yhent. 536
Thre dayes lyved she in this torment,
And nevere cessed hem the feith to teche
That she hadde fostred; hem she gan to preche,

And hem she yaf hir moebles and hir thyng,
And to the Pope Urban bitook hem tho, 541
And seyde, "I axed this of hevene kyng,
To han respit thre dayes and namo,
To recomende to yow, er that I go,
Thise soules, lo! and that I myghte do werche
Heere of myn hous perpetuelly a cherche." 546

Seint Urban, with his deknes, prively
The body fette, and buryed it by nyghte
Among his othere seintes honestly. 549
Hir hous the chirche of Seint Cecilie highte;
Seint Urban halwed it, as he wel myghte;
In which, into this day, in noble wyse,
Men doon to Crist and to his seint servyse.

Heere is ended the Seconde Nonnes Tale.

The Canon's Yeoman's Prologue

The Prologe of the Chanouns Yemannes Tale.

Whan ended was the lyf of Seinte Cecile,
Er we hadde riden fully fyve mile, 555
At Boghtoun under Blee us gan atake
A man that clothed was in clothes blake,
And under-nethe he hadde a whyt surplys.
His hakeney, that was al pomely grys,
So swatte that it wonder was to see; 560
It semed as he had priked miles three.
The hors eek that his yeman rood upon
So swatte that unnethe myghte it gon.
Aboute the peytrel stood the foom ful hye;
He was of foom al flekked as a pye. 565

A male tweyfoold on his croper lay;
It semed that he caried lite array.
Al light for somer rood this worthy man,
And in myn herte wondren I bigan
What that he was, til that I understood 570
How that his cloke was sowed to his hood;
For which, whan I hadde longe avysed me,
I demed hym som chanoun for to be.
His hat heeng at his bak doun by a laas,
For he hadde riden moore than trot or paas;
He hadde ay priked lik as he were wood. 576
A clote-leef he hadde under his hood

For swoot, and for to keep his heed from heete.
But it was joye for to seen hym swete!
His forheed dropped as a stillatorie,   580
Were ful of plantayne and of paritorie.
And whan that he was come, he gan to crye,
"God save," quod he, "this joly compaignye!
Faste have I priked," quod he, "for youre sake,
By cause that I wolde yow atake,   585
To riden in this myrie compaignye."
His yeman eek was ful of curteisye,
And seyde, "Sires, now in the morwe-tyde
Out of youre hostelrie I saugh yow ryde,   589
And warned heer my lord and my soverayn,
Which that to ryden with yow is ful fayn
For his desport; he loveth daliaunce."
    "Freend, for thy warnyng God yeve thee
        good chaunce!"
Thanne seyde oure Hoost, "for certein it wolde
        seme
Thy lord were wys, and so I may wel deme.
He is ful jocunde also, dar I leye!   596
Can he oght telle a myrie tale or tweye,
With which he glade may this compaignye?"
    "Who, sire? my lord? ye, ye, withouten lye,
He kan of murthe and eek of jolitee   600
Nat but ynough; also, sire, trusteth me,
And ye hym knewe as wel as do I,
Ye wolde wondre how wel and craftily
He koude werke, and that in sondry wise.
He hath take on hym many a greet emprise,
Which were ful hard for any that is heere   606
To brynge aboute, but they of hym it leere.
As hoomly as he rit amonges yow,
If ye hym knewe, it wolde be for youre prow.
Ye wolde nat forgoon his aqueyntaunce   610
For muchel good, I dar leye in balaunce
Al that I have in my possessioun.
He is a man of heigh discrecioun;
I warne yow wel, he is a passyng man."
    "Wel," quod oure Hoost, "I pray thee, tel me
        than,   615
Is he a clerk, or noon? telle what he is."
    "Nay, he is gretter than a clerk, ywis,"
Seyde this Yeman, "and in wordes fewe,
Hoost, of his craft somwhat I wol yow shewe.
    I seye, my lord kan swich subtilitee —   620
But al his craft ye may nat wite at me,
And somwhat helpe I yet to his wirkyng —
That al this ground on which we been ridyng,
Til that we come to Caunterbury toun,
He koude al clene turne it up-so-doun,   625
And pave it al of silver and of gold."
    And whan this Yeman hadde this tale ytold
Unto oure Hoost, he seyde, "*Benedicitee!*

This thyng is wonder merveillous to me,
Syn that thy lord is of so heigh prudence,   630
By cause of which men sholde hym reverence,
That of his worshipe rekketh he so lite.
His overslope nys nat worth a myte,
As in effect, to hym, so moot I go!
It is al baudy and totore also.   635
Why is thy lord so sluttissh, I the preye,
And is of power bettre clooth to beye,
If that his dede accorde with thy speche?
Telle me that, and that I thee biseche."
    "Why?" quod this Yeman, "wherto axe ye
        me?   640
God help me so, for he shal nevere thee!
(But I wol nat avowe that I seye,
And therfore keepe it secree, I yow preye.)
He is to wys, in feith, as I bileeve.
That that is overdoon, it wol nat preeve   645
Aright, as clerkes seyn; it is a vice.
Wherfore in that I holde hym lewed and nyce.
For whan a man hath over-greet a wit,
Ful oft hym happeth to mysusen it.   649
So dooth my lord, and that me greveth soore;
God it amende! I kan sey yow namoore."
    "Ther-of no fors, good Yeman," quod oure
        Hoost;
"Syn of the konnyng of thy lord thow woost,
Telle how he dooth, I pray thee hertely,
Syn that he is so crafty and so sly.   655
Where dwelle ye, if it to telle be?"
    "In the suburbes of a toun," quod he,
"Lurkynge in hernes and in lanes blynde,
Whereas thise robbours and thise theves by
        kynde
Holden hir pryvee fereful residence,   660
As they that dar nat shewen hir presence;
So faren we, if I shal seye the sothe."
    "Now," quod oure Hoost, "yit lat me talke to
        the.
Why artow so discoloured of thy face?"
    "Peter!" quod he, "God yeve it harde grace,
I am so used in the fyr to blowe   666
That it hath chaunged my colour, I trowe.
I am nat wont in no mirour to prie,
But swynke soore and lerne multiplie.
We blondren evere and pouren in the fir,   670
And for al that we faille of oure desir,
For evere we lakken oure conclusioun.
To muchel folk we doon illusioun,
And borwe gold, be it a pound or two,
Or ten, or twelve, or manye sommes mo,   675
And make hem wenen, at the leeste weye,
That of a pound we koude make tweye.
Yet is it fals, but ay we han good hope

It for to doon, and after it we grope.
But that science is so fer us biforn,   680
We mowen nat, although we hadden it sworn,
It overtake, it slit awey so faste.
It wole us maken beggers atte laste."

    Whil this Yeman was thus in his talkyng,
This Chanoun drough hym neer, and herde al
    thyng   685
Which that this Yeman spak, for suspecioun
Of mennes speche evere hadde this Chanoun.
For Catoun seith that he that gilty is
Demeth alle thyng be spoke of hym, ywis.
That was the cause he gan so ny hym drawe
To his Yeman, to herknen al his sawe.   691
And thus he seyde unto his Yeman tho:
"Hoold thou thy pees, and spek no wordes mo,
For if thou do, thou shalt it deere abye.   694
Thou sclaundrest me heere in this compaignye,
And eek discoverest that thou sholdest hyde."

    "Ye," quod oure Hoost, "telle on, what so
    bityde.
Of al his thretyng rekke nat a myte!"

"In feith," quod he, "namoore I do but lyte."
And whan this Chanon saugh it wolde nat
    bee,   700
But his Yeman wolde telle his pryvetee,
He fledde awey for verray sorwe and shame.

    "A!" quod the Yeman, "heere shal arise game;
Al that I kan anon now wol I telle.
Syn he is goon, the foule feend hym quelle!   705
For nevere heerafter wol I with hym meete
For peny ne for pound, I yow biheete.
He that me broghte first unto that game,
Er that he dye, sorwe have he and shame!
For it is ernest to me, by my feith;   710
That feele I wel, what so any man seith.
And yet, for al my smert and al my grief,
For al my sorwe, labour, and meschief,
I koude nevere leve it in no wise.
Now wolde God my wit myghte suffise   715
To tellen al that longeth to that art!
But nathelees yow wol I tellen part.
Syn that my lord is goon, I wol nat spare;
Swich thyng as that I knowe, I wol declare.

Heere endeth the Prologe of the Chanouns Yemannes Tale.

The Canon's Yeoman's Tale

Heere bigynneth the Chanouns Yeman his Tale.

[Prima Pars]

    With this Chanoun I dwelt have seven yeer,
And of his science am I never the neer.   721
Al that I hadde I have lost therby,
And, God woot, so hath many mo than I.
Ther I was wont to be right fressh and gay
Of clothyng and of oother good array,   725
Now may I were an hose upon myn heed;
And wher my colour was bothe fressh and reed,
Now is it wan and of a leden hewe —
Whoso it useth, soore shal he rewe! —
And of my swynk yet blered is myn ye.   730
Lo! which avantage is to multiplie!
That slidynge science hath me maad so bare
That I have no good, wher that evere I fare;
And yet I am endetted so therby,
Of gold that I have borwed, trewely,   735
That whil I lyve I shal it quite nevere.
Lat every man be war by me for evere!
What maner man that casteth hym therto,

If he continue, I holde his thrift ydo.
For so helpe me God, therby shal he nat
    wynne,   740
But empte his purs, and make his wittes thynne.
And whan he, thurgh his madnesse and folye,
Hath lost his owene good thurgh jupartye,
Thanne he exciteth oother folk therto,
To lesen hir good, as he hymself hath do.   745
For unto shrewes joye it is and ese
To have hir felawes in peyne and disese.
Thus was I ones lerned of a clerk.
Of that no charge, I wol speke of oure werk.

    Whan we been there as we shul exercise   750
Oure elvysshe craft, we semen wonder wise,
Oure termes been so clergial and so queynte.
I blowe the fir til that myn herte feynte.
What sholde I tellen ech proporcion
Of thynges whiche that we werche upon —   755
As on fyve or sixe ounces, may wel be,
Of silver, or som oother quantitee —
And bisye me to telle yow the names

Of orpyment, brent bones, iren squames,
That into poudre grounden been ful smal;   760
And in an erthen pot how put is al,
And salt yput in, and also papeer,
Biforn thise poudres that I speke of heer;
And wel ycovered with a lampe of glas;
And of muche oother thyng which that ther
            was;   765
And of the pot and glasses enlutyng,
That of the eyr myghte passe out nothyng;
And of the esy fir, and smart also,
Which that was maad, and of the care and wo
That we hadde in oure matires sublymyng,   770
And in amalgamyng and calcenyng
Of quyksilver, yclept mercurie crude?
For alle oure sleightes we kan nat conclude.
Oure orpyment and sublymed mercurie,
Oure grounden litarge eek on the porfurie,   775
Of ech of thise of ounces a certeyn —
Noght helpeth us, oure labour is in veyn.
Ne eek oure spirites ascencioun,
Ne oure materes that lyen al fix adoun,
Mowe in oure werkyng no thyng us availle,   780
For lost is al oure labour and travaille;
And al the cost, a twenty devel waye,
Is lost also, which we upon it laye.
    Ther is also ful many another thyng
That is unto oure craft apertenyng.   785
Though I by ordre hem nat reherce kan,
By cause that I am a lewed man,
Yet wol I telle hem as they come to mynde,
Thogh I ne kan nat sette hem in hir kynde:
As boole armonyak, verdegrees, boras,   790
And sondry vessels maad of erthe and glas,
Oure urynales and oure descensories,
Violes, crosletz, and sublymatories,
Cucurbites and alambikes eek,
And othere swiche, deere ynough a leek.   795
Nat nedeth it for to reherce hem alle, —
Watres rubifiyng, and boles galle,
Arsenyk, sal armonyak, and brymstoon;
And herbes koude I telle eek many oon,
As egremoyne, valerian, and lunarie,   800
And othere swiche, if that me liste tarie;
Oure lampes brennyng bothe nyght and day,
To brynge aboute oure purpos, if we may;
Oure fourneys eek of calcinacioun,
And of watres albificacioun;   805
Unslekked lym, chalk, and gleyre of an ey,
Poudres diverse, asshes, donge, pisse, and cley,
Cered pokkets, sal peter, vitriole,
And diverse fires maad of wode and cole;
Sal tartre, alkaly, and sal preparat,   810
And combust materes and coagulat;

Cley maad with hors or mannes heer, and oille
Of tartre, alum glas, berme, wort, and argoille,
Resalgar, and oure materes enbibyng,
And eek of oure materes encorporyng,   815
And of oure silver citrinacioun,
Oure cementyng and fermentacioun,
Oure yngottes, testes, and many mo.
    I wol yow telle, as was me taught also,
The foure spirites and the bodies sevene,   820
By ordre, as ofte I herde my lord hem nevene.
    The firste spirit quyksilver called is,
The seconde orpyment, the thridde, ywis,
Sal armonyak, and the ferthe brymstoon.
The bodyes sevene eek, lo! hem heere anoon:
Sol gold is, and Luna silver we threpe,   826
Mars iren, Mercurie quyksilver we clepe,
Saturnus leed, and Juppiter is tyn,
And Venus coper, by my fader kyn!
    This cursed craft whoso wole excercise,   830
He shal no good han that hym may suffise;
For al the good he spendeth theraboute
He lese shal; therof have I no doute.
Whoso that listeth outen his folie,
Lat hym come forth and lerne multiplie;   835
And every man that oght hath in his cofre,
Lat hym appiere, and wexe a philosophre.
Ascaunce that craft is so light to leere?
Nay, nay, God woot, al be he monk or frere,
Preest or chanoun, or any oother wyght,   840
Though he sitte at his book bothe day and
            nyght
In lernyng of this elvysshe nyce loore,
Al is in veyn, and parde! muchel moore.
To lerne a lewed man this subtiltee —
Fy! spek nat therof, for it wol nat bee;   845
And konne he letterure, or konne he noon,
As in effect, he shal fynde it al oon.
For bothe two, by my savacioun,
Concluden in multiplicacioun
Ylike wel, whan they han al ydo;   850
This is to seyn, they faillen bothe two.
    Yet forgat I to maken rehersaille
Of watres corosif, and of lymaille,
And of bodies mollificacioun,
And also of hire induracioun;   855
Oilles, ablucions, and metal fusible, —
To tellen al wolde passen any bible
That owher is; wherfore, as for the beste,
Of alle thise names now wol I me reste.
For, as I trowe, I have yow toold ynowe   860
To reyse a feend, al looke he never so rowe.
    A! nay! lat be; the philosophres stoon,
Elixer clept, we sechen faste echoon;
For hadde we hym, thanne were we siker ynow.

But unto God of hevene I make avow,   865
For al oure craft, whan we han al ydo,
And al oure sleighte, he wol nat come us to.
He hath ymaad us spenden muchel good,
For sorwe of which almoost we wexen wood,
But that good hope crepeth in oure herte,   870
Supposynge evere, though we sore smerte,
To be releeved by hym afterward.
Swich supposyng and hope is sharp and hard;
I warne yow wel, it is to seken evere.   874
That futur temps hath maad men to dissevere,
In trust therof, from al that evere they hadde.
Yet of that art they kan nat wexen sadde,
For unto hem it is a bitter sweete, —
So semeth it, — for nadde they but a sheete,
Which that they myghte wrappe hem inne
          a-nyght,   880
And a brat to walken inne by daylyght,
They wolde hem selle and spenden on this craft.
They kan nat stynte til no thyng be laft.
And everemoore, where that evere they goon,
Men may hem knowe by smel of brymstoon.
For al the world they stynken as a goot;   886
Hir savour is so rammyssh and so hoot
That though a man from hem a mile be,
The savour wole infecte hym, trusteth me.
And thus by smel, and by threedbare array,
If that men liste, this folk they knowe may.   891
And if a man wole aske hem pryvely
Why they been clothed so unthriftily,
They right anon wol rownen in his ere,
And seyn that if that they espied were,   895
Men wolde hem slee by cause of hir science.
Lo, thus this folk bitrayen innocence!
    Passe over this; I go my tale unto.
Er that the pot be on the fir ydo,
Of metals with a certeyn quantitee,   900
My lord hem tempreth, and no man but he —
Now he is goon, I dar seyn boldely —
For, as men seyn, he kan doon craftily.
Algate I woot wel he hath swich a name,
And yet ful ofte he renneth in a blame.   905
And wite ye how? ful ofte it happeth so,
The pot tobreketh, and farewel, al is go!
Thise metals been of so greet violence,   908
Oure walles mowe nat make hem resistence,
But if they weren wroght of lym and stoon;
They percen so, and thurgh the wal they goon.
And somme of hem synken into the ground —
Thus han we lost by tymes many a pound —
And somme are scatered al the floor aboute;
Somme lepe into the roof. Withouten doute,
Though that the feend noght in oure sighte
          hym shewe,   916

I trowe he with us be, that ilke shrewe!
In helle, where that he lord is and sire,
Nis ther moore wo, ne moore rancour ne ire.
Whan that oure pot is broke, as I have
          sayd,   920
Every man chit, and halt hym yvele apayd.
    Somme seyde it was long on the fir makyng;
Somme seyde nay, it was on the blowyng, —
Thanne was I fered, for that was myn office.
"Straw!" quod the thridde, "ye been lewed and
          nyce.   925
It was nat tempred as it oghte be."
"Nay," quod the fourthe, "stynt and herkne me.
By cause oure fir ne was nat maad of beech,
That is the cause, and oother noon, so
          thee'ch!"
I kan nat telle wheron it was long,   930
But wel I woot greet strif is us among.
    "What," quod my lord, "ther is namoore to
          doone;
Of thise perils I wol be war eftsoone.
I am right siker that the pot was crased.
Be as be may, be ye no thyng amased;   935
As usage is, lat swepe the floor as swithe,
Plukke up youre hertes, and beeth glad and
          blithe."
    The mullok on an heep ysweped was,
And on the floor ycast a canevas,
And al this mullok in a syve ythrowe,   940
And sifted, and ypiked many a throwe.
    "Pardee," quod oon, "somwhat of oure metal
Yet is ther heere, though that we han nat al.
Although this thyng myshapped have as now,
Another tyme it may be well ynow.   945
Us moste putte oure good in aventure.
A marchant, pardee, may nat ay endure,
Trusteth me wel, in his prosperitee.
Somtyme his good is drowned in the see,   949
And somtyme comth it sauf unto the londe."
    "Pees!" quod my lord, "the nexte tyme I wol
          fonde
To bryngen oure craft al in another plite,
And but I do, sires, lat me han the wite.
Ther was defaute in somwhat, wel I woot."
    Another seyde the fir was over-hoot, —   955
But, be it hoot or coold, I dar seye this,
That we concluden everemoore amys.
We faille of that which that we wolden have,
And in oure madnesse everemoore we rave.
And whan we been togidres everichoon,   960
Every man semeth a Salomon.
But al thyng which that shineth as the gold
Nis nat gold, as that I have herd it told;
Ne every appul that is fair at eye

Ne is nat good, what so men clappe or crye.
Right so, lo, fareth it amonges us: 966
He that semeth the wiseste, by Jhesus!
Is moost fool, whan it cometh to the preef;
And he that semeth trewest is a theef.
That shul ye knowe, er that I fro yow wende,
By that I of my tale have maad an ende.   971

Explicit prima pars.

Et sequitur pars secunda.

Ther is a chanoun of religioun
Amonges us, wolde infecte al a toun,
Thogh it as greet were as was Nynyvee,
Rome, Alisaundre, Troye, and othere three.
His sleightes and his infinite falsnesse   976
Ther koude no man writen, as I gesse,
Though that he myghte lyve a thousand yeer.
In al this world of falshede nis his peer;
For in his termes he wol hym so wynde,   980
And speke his wordes in so sly a kynde,
Whanne he commune shal with any wight,
That he wol make hym doten anonright,
But it a feend be, as hymselven is.
Ful many a man hath he bigiled er this,   985
And wole, if that he lyve may a while;
And yet men ride and goon ful many a mile
Hym for to seke and have his aqueyntaunce,
Noght knowynge of his false governaunce.
And if yow list to yeve me audience,   990
I wol it tellen heere in youre presence.
But worshipful chanons religious,
Ne demeth nat that I sclaundre youre hous,
Although that my tale of a chanoun bee.
Of every ordre som shrewe is, pardee,   995
And God forbede that al a compaignye
Sholde rewe o singuleer mannes folye.
To sclaundre yow is no thyng myn entente,
But to correcten that is mys I mente.
This tale was nat oonly toold for yow,   1000
But eek for othere mo; ye woot wel how
That among Cristes apostelles twelve
Ther nas no traytour but Judas hymselve.
Thanne why sholde al the remenant have a
     blame
That giltlees were? By yow I seye the same,
Save oonly this, if ye wol herkne me: 1006
If any Judas in youre covent be,
Remoeveth hym bitymes, I yow rede,
If shame or los may causen any drede.
And beeth no thyng displesed, I yow preye,
But in this cas herkneth what I shal seye.   1011
In Londoun was a preest, an annueleer,

That therinne dwelled hadde many a yeer,
Which was so plesaunt and so servysable
Unto the wyf, where as he was at table,   1015
That she wolde suffre hym no thyng for to paye
For bord ne clothyng, wente he never so gaye;
And spendyng silver hadde he right ynow.
Therof no fors; I wol procede as now,
And telle forth my tale of the chanoun   1020
That broghte this preest to confusioun.
This false chanon cam upon a day
Unto this preestes chambre, wher he lay,
Bisechynge hym to lene hym a certeyn
Of gold, and he wolde quite it hym ageyn.   1025
"Leene me a marc," quod he, "but dayes three,
And at my day I wol it quiten thee.
And if so be that thow me fynde fals,
Another day do hange me by the hals!"
This preest hym took a marc, and that as
     swithe,   1030
And this chanoun hym thanked ofte sithe,
And took his leve, and wente forth his weye,
And at the thridde day broghte his moneye,
And to the preest he took his gold agayn,
Wherof this preest was wonder glad and
     fayn.   1035
"Certes," quod he, "no thyng anoyeth me
To lene a man a noble, or two, or thre,
Or what thyng were in my possessioun,
Whan he so trewe is of condicioun
That in no wise he breke wole his day;   1040
To swich a man I kan never seye nay."
"What!" quod this chanoun, "sholde I be
     untrewe?
Nay, that were thyng yfallen al of newe.
Trouthe is a thyng that I wol evere kepe
Unto that day in which that I shal crepe   1045
Into my grave, and ellis God forbede.
Bileveth this as siker as your Crede.
God thanke I, and in good tyme be it sayd,
That ther was nevere man yet yvele apayd
For gold ne silver that he to me lente,   1050
Ne nevere falshede in myn herte I mente.
And sire," quod he, "now of my pryvetee,
Syn ye so goodlich han been unto me,
And kithed to me so greet gentillesse,
Somwhat to quyte with youre kyndenesse   1055
I wol yow shewe, and if yow list to leere,
I wol yow teche pleynly the manere
How I kan werken in philosophie.
Taketh good heede, ye shul wel seen at yë
That I wol doon a maistrie er I go."   1060
"Ye," quod the preest, "ye, sire, and wol
     ye so?
Marie! therof I pray yow hertely."

"At youre comandement, sire, trewely,"
Quod the chanoun, "and ellis God forbeede!"
    Loo, how this theef koude his service beede!
Ful sooth it is that swich profred servyse   1066
Stynketh, as witnessen thise olde wyse,
And that, ful soone I wol it verifie
In this chanoun, roote of al trecherie,   1069
That everemoore delit hath and gladnesse —
Swiche feendly thoghtes in his herte impresse —
How Cristes peple he may to meschief brynge.
God kepe us from his false dissymulynge!
    Noght wiste this preest with whom that he
        delte,
Ne of his harm comynge he no thyng felte.
O sely preest! o sely innocent!   1076
With coveitise anon thou shalt be blent!
O gracelees, ful blynd is thy conceite,
No thyng ne artow war of the deceite
Which that this fox yshapen hath to thee!   1080
His wily wrenches thou ne mayst nat flee.
Wherfore, to go to the conclusion,
That refereth to thy confusion,
Unhappy man, anon I wol me hye
To tellen thyn unwit and thy folye,   1085
And eek the falsnesse of that oother wrecche,
As ferforth as that my konnyng wol strecche.
    This chanon was my lord, ye wolden weene?
Sire hoost, in feith, and by the hevenes queene,
It was another chanoun, and nat hee,   1090
That kan an hundred foold moore subtiltee.
He hath bitrayed folkes many tyme;
Of his falsnesse it dulleth me to ryme.
Evere whan that I speke of his falshede,
For shame of hym my chekes wexen rede.   1095
Algates they bigynnen for to glowe,
For reednesse have I noon, right wel I knowe,
In my visage; for fumes diverse
Of metals, whiche ye han herd me reherce,
Consumed and wasted han my reednesse.   1100
Now taak heede of this chanons cursednesse!
    "Sire," quod he to the preest, "lat youre man
        gon
For quyksilver, that we it hadde anon;
And lat hym bryngen ounces two or three;
And whan he comth, as faste shal ye see   1105
A wonder thyng, which ye saugh nevere er
        this."
    "Sire," quod the preest, "it shal be doon,
        ywis."
He bad his servant fecchen hym this thyng,
And he al redy was at his biddyng,
And wente hym forth, and cam anon agayn
With this quyksilver, shortly for to sayn,   1111
And took thise ounces thre to the chanoun;

And he hem leyde faire and wel adoun,
And bad the servant coles for to brynge,
That he anon myghte go to his werkynge.   1115
    The coles right anon weren yfet,
And this chanoun took out a crosselet
Of his bosom, and shewed it to the preest.
"This instrument," quod he, "which that thou
        seest,
Taak in thyn hand, and put thyself ther-
        inne   1120
Of this quyksilver an ounce, and heer bigynne,
In name of Crist, to wexe a philosofre.
Ther been ful fewe to whiche I wolde profre
To shewen hem thus muche of my science.
For ye shul seen heer, by experience,   1125
That this quyksilver I wol mortifye
Right in youre sighte anon, withouten lye,
And make it as good silver and as fyn
As ther is any in youre purs or myn,
Or elleswhere, and make it malliable;   1130
And elles holdeth me fals and unable
Amonges folk for evere to appeere.
I have a poudre heer, that coste me deere,
Shal make al good, for it is cause of al   1134
My konnyng, which that I yow shewen shal.
Voyde youre man, and lat hym be theroute,
And shette the dore, whils we been aboute
Oure pryvetee, that no man us espie,
Whils that we werke in this philosophie."
    Al as he bad fulfilled was in dede.   1140
This ilke servant anonright out yede
And his maister shette the dore anon,
And to hire labour spedily they gon.
    This preest, at this cursed chanons biddyng,
Upon the fir anon sette this thyng,   1145
And blew the fir, and bisyed hym ful faste.
And this chanoun into the crosselet caste
A poudre, noot I wherof that it was
Ymaad, outher of chalk, outher of glas,
Or somwhat elles, was nat worth a flye,   1150
To blynde with this preest; and bad hym hye
The coles for to couchen al above
The crosselet. "For in tokenyng I thee love,"
Quod this chanoun, "thyne owene handes two
Shul werche al thyng which that shal heer
        be do."   1155
    "Graunt mercy," quod the preest, and was
        ful glad,
And couched coles as that the chanoun bad.
And while he bisy was, this feendly wrecche,
This false chanoun — the foule feend hym
        fecche! —
Out of his bosom took a bechen cole,   1160
In which ful subtilly was maad an hole,

And therinne put was of silver lemaille
An ounce, and stopped was, withouten faille,
This hole with wex, to kepe the lemaille in.
And understondeth that this false gyn   1165
Was nat maad ther, but it was maad bifore;
And othere thynges I shal tellen moore
Herafterward, whiche that he with hym
    broghte.
Er he cam there, hym to bigile he thoghte,
And so he dide, er that they wente at wynne;
Til he had terved hym, koude he nat blynne.
It dulleth me whan that I of hym speke.   1172
On his falshede fayn wolde I me wreke,
If I wiste how, but he is heere and there;
He is so variaunt, he abit nowhere.   1175
    But taketh heede now, sires, for Goddes love!
He took his cole of which I spak above,
And in his hand he baar it pryvely.
And whiles the preest couched bisily
The coles, as I tolde yow er this,   1180
This chanoun seyde, "Freend, ye doon amys.
This is nat couched as it oghte be;
But soone I shal amenden it," quod he.
"Now lat me medle therwith but a while,
For of yow have I pitee, by Seint Gile!   1185
Ye been right hoot; I se wel how ye swete.
Have heere a clooth, and wipe awey the wete."
And whiles that the preest wiped his face,
This chanoun took his cole — with sory
    grace! —
And leyde it above upon the myddeward   1190
Of the crosselet, and blew wel afterward,
Til that the coles gonne faste brenne.
    "Now yeve us drynke," quod the chanoun
    thenne;
"As swithe al shal be wel, I undertake.
Sitte we doun, and lat us myrie make."   1195
And whan that this chanounes bechen cole
Was brent, al the lemaille out of the hole
Into the crosselet fil anon adoun;
And so it moste nedes, by resoun,
Syn it so evene aboven it couched was.   1200
But therof wiste the preest nothyng, alas!
He demed alle the coles yliche good;
For of that sleighte he nothyng understood.
And whan this alkamystre saugh his tyme,
"Ris up," quod he, "sire preest, and stondeth
    by me;   1205
And for I woot wel ingot have ye noon,
Gooth, walketh forth, and brynge us a chalk
    stoon;
For I wol make it of the same shap
That is an ingot, if I may han hap.
And bryngeth eek with yow a bolle or a panne

Ful of water, and ye shul se wel thanne   1211
How that oure bisynesse shal thryve and
    preeve.
And yet, for ye shul han no mysbileeve
Ne wrong conceite of me in youre absence,
I ne wol nat been out of youre presence,   1215
But go with yow, and come with yow ageyn."
The chambre dore, shortly for to seyn,
They opened and shette, and wente hir weye.
And forth with hem they carieden the keye,
And coome agayn withouten any delay.   1220
What sholde I tarien al the longe day?
He took the chalk, and shoop it in the wise
Of an ingot, as I shal yow devyse.
    I seye, he took out of his owene sleeve   1224
A teyne of silver — yvele moot he cheeve! —
Which that ne was nat but an ounce of weighte.
And taaketh heede now of his cursed sleighte!
    He shoop his ingot, in lengthe and in breede
Of this teyne, withouten any drede,
So slyly that the preest it nat espide,   1230
And in his sleve agayn he gan it hide,
And fro the fir he took up his mateere,
And in th'yngot putte it with myrie cheere,
And in the water-vessel he it caste,
Whan that hym luste, and bad the preest as
    faste,   1235
"Loke what ther is, put in thyn hand and grope.
Thow fynde shalt ther silver, as I hope.
What, devel of helle! sholde it elles be?
Shaving of silver silver is, pardee!"
He putte his hand in and took up a teyne   1240
Of silver fyn, and glad in every veyne
Was this preest, whan he saugh that it was so.
"Goddes blessyng, and his moodres also,
And alle halwes, have ye, sire chanoun,"
Seyde the preest, "and I hir malisoun,   1245
But, and ye vouche-sauf to techen me
This noble craft and this subtilitee,
I wol be youre in al that evere I may."
    Quod the chanoun, "Yet wol I make assay
The seconde tyme, that ye may taken heede
And been expert of this, and in youre neede
Another day assaye in myn absence   1252
This disciplyne and this crafty science.
Lat take another ounce," quod he tho,
"Of quyksilver, withouten wordes mo,   1255
And do therwith as ye han doon er this
With that oother, which that now silver is."
    This preest hym bisieth in al that he kan
To doon as this chanoun, this cursed man,
Comanded hym, and faste he blew the fir,   1260
For to come to th'effect of his desir.
And this chanon, right in the meene while,

Al redy was this preest eft to bigile,
And for a contenaunce in his hand he bar
An holwe stikke — taak kep and be war! —   1265
In the ende of which an ounce, and namoore,
Of silver lemaille put was, as bifore
Was in his cole, and stopped with wex weel
For to kepe in his lemaille every deel.
And whil this preest was in his bisynesse,   1270
This chanoun with his stikke gan hym dresse
To hym anon, and his poudre caste in
As he dide er — the devel out of his skyn
Hym terve, I pray to God, for his falshede!
For he was evere fals in thoght and dede —
And with this stikke, above the crosselet,   1276
That was ordeyned with that false jet
He stired the coles til relente gan
The wex agayn the fir, as every man,
But it a fool be, woot wel it moot nede,   1280
And al that in the stikke was out yede,
And in the crosselet hastily it fel.
   Now, good sires, what wol ye bet than wel?
Whan that this preest thus was bigiled ageyn,
Supposynge noght but treuthe, sooth to seyn,
He was so glad that I kan nat expresse   1286
In no manere his myrthe and his gladnesse;
And to the chanoun he profred eftsoone
Body and good. "Ye," quod the chanoun soone,
"Though poure I be, crafty thou shalt me fynde.
I warne thee, yet is ther moore bihynde.   1291
Is ther any coper herinne?" seyde he.
   "Ye," quod the preest, "sire, I trowe wel ther
      be."
   "Elles go bye us som, and that as swithe;
Now, goode sire, go forth thy wey and hy
      the."   1295
   He wente his wey, and with the coper cam,
And this chanon it in his handes nam,
And of that coper weyed out but an ounce.
Al to symple is my tonge to pronounce,
As ministre of my wit, the doublenesse   1300
Of this chanoun, roote of alle cursednesse!
He semed freendly to hem that knewe hym
      noght,
But he was feendly bothe in werk and thoght.
It weerieth me to telle of his falsnesse,
And nathelees yet wol I it expresse,   1305
To th'entente that men may be war therby,
And for noon oother cause, trewely.
   He putte this ounce of coper in the crosselet,
And on the fir as swithe he hath it set,
And caste in poudre, and made the preest to
      blowe,   1310
And in his werkyng for to stoupe lowe,
As he dide er, — and al nas but a jape;

Right as hym liste, the preest he made his ape!
And afterward in the ingot he it caste,
And in the panne putte it at the laste   1315
Of water, and in he putte his owene hand,
And in his sleve (as ye biforen-hand
Herde me telle) he hadde a silver teyne.
He slyly took it out, this cursed heyne,
Unwityng this preest of his false craft,   1320
And in the pannes botme he hath it laft;
And in the water rombled to and fro,
And wonder pryvely took up also
The coper teyne, noght knowynge this preest,
And hidde it, and hym hente by the breest,
And to hym spak, and thus seyde in his
      game: 1326
"Stoupeth adoun, by God, ye be to blame!
Helpeth me now, as I dide yow whileer;
Putte in youre hand, and looketh what is theer."
   This preest took up this silver teyne
      anon,   1330
And thanne seyde the chanoun, "Lat us gon
With thise thre teynes, whiche that we han
      wroght,
To som goldsmyth, and wite if they been oght.
For, by my feith, I nolde, for myn hood,
But if that they were silver fyn and good,   1335
And that as swithe preeved it shal bee."
   Unto the goldsmyth with thise teynes three
They wente, and putte thise teynes in assay
To fir and hamer; myghte no man seye nay,
But that they weren as hem oghte be.   1340
   This sotted preest, who was gladder than he?
Was nevere brid gladder agayn the day,
Ne nyghtyngale, in the sesoun of May,
Was nevere noon that luste bet to synge;
Ne lady lustier in carolynge,   1345
Or for to speke of love and wommanhede,
Ne knyght in armes to doon an hardy dede,
To stonden in grace of his lady deere,
Than hadde this preest this soory craft to leere.
And to the chanoun thus he spak and seyde:
"For love of God, that for us alle deyde,   1351
And as I may deserve it unto yow,
What shal this receite coste? telleth now!"
   "By oure Lady," quod this chanon, "it is
      deere,
I warne yow wel; for save I and a frere,   1355
In Engelond ther kan no man it make."
   "No fors," quod he, "now, sire, for Goddes
      sake,
What shal I paye? telleth me, I preye."
   "Ywis," quod he, "it is ful deere, I seye.
Sire, at o word, if that thee list it have,   1360
Ye shul paye fourty pound, so God me save!

And nere the freendshipe that ye dide er this
To me, ye sholde paye moore, ywis."
    This preest the somme of fourty pound anon
Of nobles fette, and took hem everichon   1365
To this chanoun, for this ilke receite.
Al his werkyng nas but fraude and deceite.
    "Sire preest," he seyde, "I kepe han no loos
Of my craft, for I wolde it kept were cloos;
And, as ye love me, kepeth it secree.   1370
For, and men knewen al my soutiltee,
By God, they wolden han so greet envye
To me, by cause of my philosophye,
I sholde be deed; ther were noon oother weye."
    "God it forbeede," quod the preest, "what
        sey ye?   1375
Yet hadde I levere spenden al the good
Which that I have, and elles wexe I wood,
Than that ye sholden falle in swich mescheef."
    "For youre good wyl, sire, have ye right good
        preef,"   1379
Quod the chanoun, "and farwel, grant mercy!"
He wente his wey, and never the preest hym sy
After that day; and whan that this preest
        shoolde
Maken assay, at swich tyme as he wolde,
Of this receit, farwel! it wolde nat be.
Lo, thus byjaped and bigiled was he!   1385
Thus maketh he his introduccioun,
To brynge folk to hir destruccioun.
    Considereth, sires, how that, in ech estaat,
Bitwixe men and gold ther is debaat
So ferforth that unnethes is ther noon.   1390
This multiplying blent so many oon
That in good feith I trowe that it bee
The cause grettest of swich scarsetee.
Philosophres speken so mystily   1394
In this craft that men kan nat come therby,
For any wit that men han now-a-dayes.
They mowe wel chiteren as doon thise jayes,
And in hir termes sette hir lust and peyne,
But to hir purpos shul they nevere atteyne.
A man may lightly lerne, if he have aught,   1400
To multiplie, and brynge his good to naught!
    Lo! swich a lucre is in this lusty game,
A mannes myrthe it wol turne unto grame,
And empten also grete and hevye purses,
And maken folk for to purchacen curses   1405
Of hem that han hir good therto ylent.
O! fy, for shame! they that han been brent,
Allas! kan they nat flee the fires heete?
Ye that it use, I rede ye it leete,
Lest ye lese al; for bet than nevere is late.   1410
Nevere to thryve were to long a date.
Though ye prolle ay, ye shul it nevere fynde.

Ye been as boold as is Bayard the blynde,
That blondreth forth, and peril casteth noon.
He is as boold to renne agayn a stoon   1415
As for to goon bisides in the weye.
So faren ye that multiplie, I seye.
If that youre eyen kan nat seen aright,
Looke that youre mynde lakke noght his sight.
For though ye looken never so brode and stare,
Ye shul nothyng wynne on that chaffare,   1421
But wasten al that ye may rape and renne.
Withdraweth the fir, lest it to faste brenne;
Medleth namoore with that art, I mene,   1424
For if ye doon, youre thrift is goon ful clene.
And right as swithe I wol yow tellen heere
What philosophres seyn in this mateere.
    Lo, thus seith Arnold of the Newe Toun,
As his Rosarie maketh mencioun;
He seith right thus, withouten any lye: 1430
"Ther may no man mercurie mortifie
But it be with his brother knowlechyng."
How be that he which that first seyde this thyng
Of philosophres fader was, Hermes —
He seith how that the dragon, doutelees,   1435
Ne dyeth nat, but if that he be slayn
With his brother; and that is for to sayn,
By the dragon, Mercurie, and noon oother
He understood, and brymstoon by his brother,
That out of Sol and Luna were ydrawe.   1440
    "And therfore," seyde he, — taak heede to my
        sawe —
"Lat no man bisye hym this art for to seche,
But if that he th'entencioun and speche
Of philosophres understonde kan;
And if he do, he is a lewed man.   1445
For this science and this konnyng," quod he,
"Is of the secree of secrees, pardee."
    Also ther was a disciple of Plato,
That on a tyme seyde his maister to,
As his book Senior wol bere witnesse,   1450
And this was his demande in soothfastnesse:
"Telle me the name of the privee stoon?"
    And Plato answerde unto hym anoon,
"Take the stoon that Titanos men name."
    "Which is that?" quod he. "Magnasia is the
        same,"   1455
Seyde Plato. "Ye, sire, and is it thus?
This is *ignotum per ignocius.*
What is Magnasia, good sire, I yow preye?"
    "It is a water that is maad, I seye,
Of elementes foure," quod Plato.   1460
    "Telle me the roote, good sire," quod he tho,
"Of that water, if it be youre wil."
    "Nay, nay," quod Plato, "certein, that I nyl.
The philosophres sworn were everychoon

That they sholden discovere it unto noon,   1465
Ne in no book it write in no manere.
For unto Crist it is so lief and deere
That he wol nat that it discovered bee,
But where it liketh to his deitee
Men for t'enspire, and eek for to deffende   1470
Whom that hym liketh; lo, this is the ende."
    Thanne conclude I thus, sith that God of
        hevene

Ne wil nat that the philosophres nevene
How that a man shal come unto this stoon,
I rede, as for the beste, lete it goon.   1475
For whoso maketh God his adversarie,
As for to werken any thyng in contrarie
Of his wil, certes, never shal he thryve,
Thogh that he multiplie terme of his lyve.
And there a poynt; for ended is my tale.   1480
God sende every trewe man boote of his bale!

Heere is ended the Chanouns Yemannes Tale.

Fragment IX (Group H)

The Manciple's Prologue

Heere folweth the Prologe of the Maunciples Tale.

Woot ye nat where ther stant a litel toun
Which that ycleped is Bobbe-up-and-doun,
Under the Blee, in Caunterbury Weye?
Ther gan oure Hooste for to jape and pleye,
And seyde, "Sires, what! Dun is in the myre!
Is ther no man, for preyere ne for hyre,   6
That wole awake oure felawe al bihynde?
A theef myghte hym ful lightly robbe and
      bynde.
See how he nappeth! see how, for cokkes bones,
That he wol falle fro his hors atones!   10
Is that a cook of Londoun, with meschaunce?
Do hym come forth, he knoweth his penaunce;
For he shal telle a tale, by my fey,
Although it be nat worth a botel hey.
Awake, thou Cook," quod he, "God yeve thee
      sorwe!   15
What eyleth thee to slepe by the morwe?
Hastow had fleen al nyght, or artow dronke?
Or hastow with som quene al nyght yswonke,
So that thow mayst nat holden up thyn heed?"
   This Cook, that was ful pale and no thyng
      reed,   20
Seyde to oure Hoost, "So God my soule blesse,
As ther is falle on me swich hevynesse,
Noot I nat why, that me were levere slepe
Than the beste galon wyn in Chepe."
   "Wel," quod the Maunciple, "if it may doon
      ese   25
To thee, sire Cook, and to no wight displese,
Which that heere rideth in this compaignye,
And that oure Hoost wole, of his curteisye,
I wol as now excuse thee of thy tale.
For, in good feith, thy visage is ful pale,   30
Thyne eyen daswen eek, as that me thynketh,
And, wel I woot, thy breeth ful soure stynketh:
That sheweth wel thou art nat wel disposed.
Of me, certeyn, thou shalt nat been yglosed.
See how he ganeth, lo! this dronken wight,   35
As though he wolde swolwe us anonright.
Hoold cloos thy mouth, man, by thy fader kyn!
The devel of helle sette his foot therin!
Thy cursed breeth infecte wole us alle.
Fy, stynkyng swyn! fy, foule moote thee falle!
A! taketh heede, sires, of this lusty man.   41

Now, sweete sire, wol ye justen atte fan?
Therto me thynketh ye been wel yshape!
I trowe that ye dronken han wyn ape,   44
And that is whan men pleyen with a straw."
And with this speche the Cook wax wrooth
      and wraw,
And on the Manciple he gan nodde faste
For lakke of speche, and doun the hors hym
      caste,
Where as he lay, til that men hym up took.
This was a fair chyvachee of a cook!   50
Allas! he nadde holde hym by his ladel!
And er that he agayn were in his sadel,
Ther was greet showvyng bothe to and fro
To lifte hym up, and muchel care and wo,
So unweeldy was this sory palled goost.   55
And to the Manciple thanne spak oure Hoost:
   "By cause drynke hath dominacioun
Upon this man, by my savacioun,
I trowe he lewedly wolde telle his tale.
For, were it wyn, or oold or moysty ale,   60
That he hath dronke, he speketh in his nose,
And fneseth faste, and eek he hath the pose.
   He hath also to do moore than ynough
To kepen hym and his capul out of the slough;
And if he falle from his capul eftsoone,   65
Thanne shal we alle have ynogh to doone
In liftyng up his hevy dronken cors.
Telle on thy tale; of hym make I no fors.
   But yet, Manciple, in feith thou art to nyce,
Thus openly repreve hym of his vice.   70
Another day he wole, peraventure,
Reclayme thee and brynge thee to lure;
I meene, he speke wole of smale thynges,
As for to pynchen at thy rekenynges,
That were nat honest, if it cam to preef."   75
   "No," quod the Manciple, "that were a greet
      mescheef!
So myghte he lightly brynge me in the snare.
Yet hadde I levere payen for the mare
Which he rit on, than he sholde with me stryve.
I wol nat wratthen hym, also moot I thryve!   80
That that I spak, I seyde it in my bourde.
And wite ye what? I have heer in a gourde
A draghte of wyn, ye, of a ripe grape,

224

And right anon ye shul seen a good jape.
This Cook shal drynke therof, if I may.   85
Up peyne of deeth, he wol nat seye me nay."
    And certeynly, to tellen as it was,
Of this vessel the Cook drank faste, allas!
What neded hym? he drank ynough biforn.
And whan he hadde pouped in this horn,   90
To the Manciple he took the gourde agayn;
And of that drynke the Cook was wonder fayn,
And thanked hym in swich wise as he koude.
    Thanne gan oure Hoost to laughen wonder
        loude,

And seyde, "I se wel it is necessarie,   95
Where that we goon, good drynke with us
        carie;
For that wol turne rancour and disese
T'acord and love, and many a wrong apese.
    O thou Bacus, yblessed be thy name,
That so kanst turnen ernest into game!   100
Worshipe and thank be to thy deitee!
Of that mateere ye gete namoore of me.
Telle on thy tale, Manciple, I thee preye."
    "Wel, sire," quod he, "now herkneth what I
        seye."

The Manciple's Tale

Heere bigynneth the Maunciples Tale of the Crowe.

Whan Phebus dwelled heere in this erthe
        adoun,   105
As olde bookes maken mencioun,
He was the mooste lusty bachiler
In al this world, and eek the beste archer.
He slow Phitoun, the serpent, as he lay
Slepynge agayn the soone upon a day;   110
And many another noble worthy dede
He with his bowe wroghte, as men may rede.
    Pleyen he koude on every mynstralcie,
And syngen, that it was a melodie
To heeren of his cleere voys the soun.   115
Certes the kyng of Thebes, Amphioun,
That with his syngyng walled that citee,
Koude nevere syngen half so wel as hee.
Therto he was the semelieste man
That is or was, sith that the world bigan.   120
What nedeth it his fetures to discryve?
For in this world was noon so faire on-lyve.
He was therwith fulfild of gentillesse,
Of honour, and of parfit worthynesse.
    This Phebus, that was flour of bachilrie, 125
As wel in fredom as in chivalrie,
For his desport, in signe eek of victorie
Of Phitoun, so as telleth us the storie,
Was wont to beren in his hand a bowe.   129
    Now hadde this Phebus in his hous a crowe
Which in a cage he fostred many a day,
And taughte it speken, as men teche a jay.
Whit was this crowe as is a snow-whit swan,
And countrefete the speche of every man
He koude, whan he sholde telle a tale.   135
Therwith in al this world no nyghtyngale

Ne koude, by an hondred thousand deel,
Syngen so wonder myrily and weel.
    Now hadde this Phebus in his hous a wyf
Which that he lovede moore than his lyf,   140
And nyght and day dide evere his diligence
Hir for to plese, and doon hire reverence,
Save oonly, if the sothe that I shal sayn,
Jalous he was, and wolde have kept hire fayn.
For hym were looth byjaped for to be,   145
And so is every wight in swich degree;
But al in ydel, for it availleth noght.
A good wyf, that is clene of werk and thoght,
Sholde nat been kept in noon awayt, certayn;
And trewely, the labour is in vayn   150
To kepe a shrewe, for it wol nat bee.
This holde I for a verray nycetee,
To spille labour for to kepe wyves:
Thus writen olde clerkes in hir lyves.
    But now to purpos, as I first bigan: 155
This worthy Phebus dooth al that he kan
To plesen hire, wenynge for swich plesaunce,
And for his manhede and his governaunce,
That no man sholde han put hym from hir
        grace.
But God it woot, ther may no man embrace
As to destreyne a thyng which that nature   161
Hath natureelly set in a creature.
    Taak any bryd, and put it in a cage,
And do al thyn entente and thy corage
To fostre it tendrely with mete and drynke   165
Of alle deyntees that thou kanst bithynke,
And keep it al so clenly as thou may,
Although his cage of gold be never so gay,

Yet hath this brid, by twenty thousand foold,
Levere in a forest, that is rude and coold, 170
Goon ete wormes and swich wrecchednesse.
For evere this brid wol doon his bisynesse
To escape out of his cage, yif he may.
His libertee this brid desireth ay. 174
    Lat take a cat, and fostre hym wel with milk
And tendre flessh, and make his couche of silk,
And lat hym seen a mous go by the wal,
Anon he weyveth milk and flessh and al,
And every deyntee that is in that hous,
Swich appetit hath he to ete a mous. 180
Lo, heere hath lust his dominacioun,
And appetit fleemeth discrecioun.
    A she-wolf hath also a vileyns kynde.
The lewedeste wolf that she may fynde,
Or leest of reputacioun, wol she take, 185
In tyme whan hir lust to han a make.
    Alle thise ensamples speke I by thise men
That been untrewe, and nothyng by wommen.
For men han evere a likerous appetit
On lower thyng to parfourne hire delit 190
Than on hire wyves, be they never so faire,
Ne never so trewe, ne so debonaire.
Flessh is so newefangel, with meschaunce,
That we ne konne in nothyng han plesaunce
That sowneth into vertu any while. 195
    This Phebus, which that thoghte upon no gile,
Deceyved was, for al his jolitee.
For under hym another hadde shee,
A man of litel reputacioun,
Nat worth to Phebus in comparisoun. 200
The moore harm is, it happeth ofte so,
Of which ther cometh muchel harm and wo.
    And so bifel, whan Phebus was absent,
His wyf anon hath for hir lemman sent. 204
Hir lemman? Certes, this is a knavyssh speche!
Foryeveth it me, and that I yow biseche.
    The wise Plato seith, as ye may rede,
The word moot nede accorde with the dede.
If men shal telle proprely a thyng,
The word moot cosyn be to the werkyng. 210
I am a boystous man, right thus seye I,
Ther nys no difference, trewely,
Bitwixe a wyf that is of heigh degree,
If of hir body dishonest she bee,
And a povre wenche, oother than this — 215
If it so be they werke bothe amys —
But that the gentile, in estaat above,
She shal be cleped his lady, as in love;
And for that oother is a povre womman, 219
She shal be cleped his wenche or his lemman.

And, God it woot, myn owene deere brother.
Men leyn that oon as lowe as lith that oother.
    Right so bitwixe a titlelees tiraunt
And an outlawe, or a theef erraunt,
The same I seye, ther is no difference. 225
To Alisaundre was toold this sentence,
That, for the tirant is of gretter myght,
By force of meynee, for to sleen dounright,
And brennen hous and hoom, and make al playn,
Lo, therfore is he cleped a capitayn; 230
And for the outlawe hath but smal meynee,
And may nat doon so greet an harm as he,
Ne brynge a contree to so greet mescheef,
Men clepen hym an outlawe or a theef.
But, for I am a man noght textueel, 235
I wol noght telle of textes never a deel;
I wol go to my tale, as I bigan.
Whan Phebus wyf had sent for hir lemman,
Anon they wroghten al hire lust volage. 239
    The white crowe, that heeng ay in the cage,
Biheeld hire werk, and seyde never a word.
And whan that hoom was come Phebus, the lord,
This crowe sang "Cokkow! cokkow! cokkow!"
    "What, bryd!" quod Phebus, "what song syngestow?
Ne were thow wont so myrily to synge 245
That to myn herte it was a rejoysynge
To heere thy voys? Allas! what song is this?"
    "By God!" quod he, "I synge nat amys.
Phebus," quod he, "for al thy worthynesse,
For al thy beautee and thy gentilesse, 250
For al thy song and al thy mynstralcye,
For al thy waityng, blered is thyn ye
With oon of litel reputacioun,
Noght worth to thee, as in comparisoun, 254
The montance of a gnat, so moote I thryve!
For on thy bed thy wyf I saugh hym swyve."
    What wol ye moore? The crowe anon hym tolde,
By sadde tokenes and by wordes bolde,
How that his wyf had doon hire lecherye,
Hym to greet shame and to greet vileynye; 260
And tolde hym ofte he saugh it with his yen.
    This Phebus gan aweyward for to wryen,
And thoughte his sorweful herte brast atwo.
His bowe he bente, and sette therinne a flo,
And in his ire his wyf thanne hath he slayn.
This is th'effect, ther is namoore to sayn; 266
For sorwe of which he brak his mynstralcie,
Bothe harpe, and lute, and gyterne, and sautrie;
And eek he brak his arwes and his bowe,
And after that thus spak he to the crowe: 270

"Traitour," quod he, "with tonge of scor-
    pioun,
Thou hast me broght to my confusioun;
Allas, that I was wroght! why nere I deed?
O deere wyf! o gemme of lustiheed!
That were to me so sad and eek so trewe,   275
Now listow deed, with face pale of hewe,
Ful giltelees, that dorste I swere, ywys!
O rakel hand, to doon so foule amys!
O trouble wit, o ire recchelees,
That unavysed smyteth gilteles!   280
O wantrust, ful of fals suspecion,
Where was thy wit and thy discrecion?
O every man, be war of rakelnesse!
Ne trowe no thyng withouten strong witnesse.
Smyt nat to soone, er that ye witen why,   285
And beeth avysed wel and sobrely
Er ye doon any execucion
Upon youre ire for suspecion.
Allas! a thousand folk hath rakel ire
Fully fordoon, and broght hem in the mire.
Allas! for sorwe I wol myselven slee!"   291
    And to the crowe, "O false theef!" seyde he,
"I wol thee quite anon thy false tale.
Thou songe whilom lyk a nyghtyngale;
Now shaltow, false theef, thy song forgon,   295
And eek thy white fetheres everichon,
Ne nevere in al thy lif ne shaltou speke.
Thus shal men on a traytour been awreke;
Thou and thyn ofspryng evere shul be blake,
Ne nevere sweete noyse shul ye make,   300
But evere crie agayn tempest and rayn,
In tokenynge that thurgh thee my wyf is slayn."
And to the crowe he stirte, and that anon,
And pulled his white fetheres everychon,   304
And made hym blak, and refte hym al his song,
And eek his speche, and out at dore hym slong
Unto the devel, which I hym bitake;
And for this caas been alle crowes blake.
    Lordynges, by this ensample I yow preye,
Beth war, and taketh kep what that ye seye:
Ne telleth nevere no man in youre lyf   311
How that another man hath dight his wyf;
He wol yow haten mortally, certeyn.
Daun Salomon, as wise clerkes seyn,
Techeth a man to kepen his tonge weel.   315
But, as I seyde, I am noght textueel.
But nathelees, thus taughte me my dame:
"My sone, thenk on the crowe, a Goddes name!

My sone, keep wel thy tonge, and keep thy
    freend.
A wikked tonge is worse than a feend;   320
My sone, from a feend men may hem blesse.
My sone, God of his endelees goodnesse
Walled a tonge with teeth and lippes eke,
For man sholde hym avyse what he speeke.
My sone, ful ofte, for to muche speche   325
Hath many a man been spilt, as clerkes teche;
But for litel speche avysely
Is no man shent, to speke generally.
My sone, thy tonge sholdestow restreyne   329
At alle tymes, but whan thou doost thy peyne
To speke of God, in honour and preyere.
The firste vertu, sone, if thou wolt leere,
Is to restreyne and kepe wel thy tonge;
Thus lerne children whan that they been yonge.
My sone, of muchel spekyng yvele avysed,   335
Ther lasse spekyng hadde ynough suffised,
Comth muchel harm; thus was me toold and
    taught.
In muchel speche synne wanteth naught.
Wostow wherof a rakel tonge serveth?
Right as a swerd forkutteth and forkerveth   340
An arm a-two, my deere sone, right so
A tonge kutteth freendshipe al a-two.
A jangler is to God abhomynable.
Reed Salomon, so wys and honurable;
Reed David in his psalmes, reed Senekke.   345
My sone, spek nat, but with thyn heed thou
    bekke.
Dissimule as thou were deef, if that thou heere
A janglere speke of perilous mateere.
The Flemyng seith, and lerne it if thee leste,
That litel janglyng causeth muchel reste.   350
My sone, if thou no wikked word hast seyd,
Thee thar nat drede for to be biwreyd;
But he that hath mysseyd, I dar wel sayn,
He may by no wey clepe his word agayn.   354
Thyng that is seyd is seyd, and forth it gooth,
Though hym repente, or be hym nevere so
    looth.
He is his thral to whom that he hath sayd
A tale of which he is now yvele apayd.
My sone, be war, and be noon auctour newe
Of tidynges, wheither they been false or trewe.
Whereso thou come, amonges hye or lowe,   361
Kepe wel thy tonge, and thenk upon the
    crowe."

Heere is ended the Maunciples Tale of the Crowe.

Fragment X (Group I)

The Parson's Prologue

Heere folweth the Prologe of the Persouns Tale.

By that the Maunciple hadde his tale al
    ended,
The sonne fro the south lyne was descended
So lowe that he nas nat, to my sighte,
Degreës nyne and twenty as in highte.
Foure of the clokke it was tho, as I gesse,   5
For ellevene foot, or litel moore or lesse,
My shadwe was at thilke tyme, as there,
Of swiche feet as my lengthe parted were
In sixe feet equal of proporcioun.
Therwith the moones exaltacioun,   10
I meene Libra, alwey gan ascende,
As we were entryng at a thropes ende;
For which oure Hoost, as he was wont to gye,
As in this caas, oure joly compaignye,
Seyde in this wise: "Lordynges everichoon,   15
Now lakketh us no tales mo than oon.
Fulfilled is my sentence and my decree;
I trowe that we han herd of ech degree;
Almoost fulfild is al myn ordinaunce.
I pray to God, so yeve hym right good chaunce,
That telleth this tale to us lustily.   21
    Sire preest," quod he, "artow a vicary?
Or arte a person? sey sooth, by thy fey!
Be what thou be, ne breke thou nat oure pley;
For every man, save thou, hath toold his
    tale.   25
Unbokele, and shewe us what is in thy male;
For, trewely, me thynketh by thy cheere
Thou sholdest knytte up wel a greet mateere.
Telle us a fable anon, for cokkes bones!"
    This Persoun answerde, al atones,   30
"Thou getest fable noon ytoold for me;
For Paul, that writeth unto Thymothee,
Repreveth hem that weyven soothfastnesse,
And tellen fables and swich wrecchednesse.
Why sholde I sowen draf out of my fest,   35
Whan I may sowen whete, if that me lest?

For which I seye, if that yow list to heere
Moralitee and vertuous mateere,
And thanne that ye wol yeve me audience,
I wol ful fayn, at Cristes reverence,   40
Do yow plesaunce leefful, as I kan.
But trusteth wel, I am a Southren man,
I kan nat geeste 'rum, ram, ruf,' by lettre,
Ne, God woot, rym holde I but litel bettre;
And therfore, if yow list — I wol nat glose —
I wol yow telle a myrie tale in prose   46
To knytte up al this feeste, and make an ende.
And Jhesu, for his grace, wit me sende
To shewe yow the wey, in this viage,
Of thilke parfit glorious pilgrymage   50
That highte Jerusalem celestial.
And if ye vouche sauf, anon I shal
Bigynne upon my tale, for which I preye
Telle youre avys, I kan no bettre seye.
    But nathelees, this meditacioun   55
I putte it ay under correccioun
Of clerkes, for I am nat textueel;
I take but the sentence, trusteth weel.
Therfore I make protestacioun
That I wol stonde to correccioun."   60
    Upon this word we han assented soone,
For, as it seemed, it was for to doone,
To enden in som vertuous sentence,
And for to yeve hym space and audience;
And bade oure Hoost he sholde to hym seye   65
That alle we to telle his tale hym preye.
    Oure Hoost hadde the wordes for us alle:
"Sire preest," quod he, "now faire yow bifalle!
Telleth," quod he, "youre meditacioun.
But hasteth yow, the sonne wole adoun;   70
Beth fructuous, and that in litel space,
And to do wel God sende yow his grace!
Sey what yow list, and we wol gladly heere."
And with that word he seyde in this manere.

Explicit prohemium.

The Parson's Tale

Heere bigynneth the Persouns Tale.

Jer. 6°. State super vias, et videte, et interrogate de viis antiquis que sit via bona, et ambulate in ea; et inuenietis refrigerium animabus vestris, etc.

Oure sweete Lord God of hevene, that no man wole perisse, but wole that we comen alle to the knoweleche of hym, and to the blisful lif that is perdurable,/ amonesteth us 75 by the prophete Jeremie, that seith in thys wyse:/ Stondeth upon the weyes, and seeth and axeth of olde pathes (that is to seyn, of olde sentences) which is the goode wey,/ and walketh in that wey, and ye shal fynde refresshynge for youre soules, etc./ Manye been the weyes espirituels that leden folk to oure Lord Jhesu Crist, and to the regne of glorie./ Of whiche weyes, ther is a ful noble wey and a ful covenable, which may nat fayle to man ne to womman that thurgh synne hath mysgoon fro the righte wey of Jerusalem celestial;/ and 80 this wey is cleped Penitence, of which man sholde gladly herknen and enquere with al his herte,/ to wyten what is Penitence, and whennes it is cleped Penitence, and in how manye maneres been the acciouns or werkynges of Penitence,/ and how manye speces ther been of Penitence, and whiche thynges apertenen and bihoven to Penitence, and whiche thynges destourben Penitence./

Seint Ambrose seith that Penitence is the pleynynge of man for the gilt that he hath doon, and namoore to do any thyng for which hym oghte to pleyne./ And som doctour seith, "Penitence is the waymentynge of man that sorweth for his synne, and pyneth hymself for he hath mysdoon."/ Penitence, 85 with certeyne circumstances, is verray repentance of a man that halt hymself in sorwe and oother peyne for his giltes./ And for he shal be verray penitent, he shal first biwaylen the synnes that he hath doon, and stidefastly purposen in his herte to have shrift of mouthe, and to doon satisfaccioun,/ and nevere to doon thyng for which hym oghte moore to biwayle or to compleyne, and to continue in goode werkes, or elles his repentance may nat availle./ For, as seith seint Ysidre, "he is a japere and a gabbere, and no verray repentant, that eft-soone dooth thyng for which hym oghte repente."/ Wepynge, and nat for to stynte to do synne, may nat avayle./ But nathelees, 90 men shal hope that every tyme that man falleth, be it never so ofte, that he may arise thurgh Penitence, if he have grace; but certeinly it is greet doute./ For, as seith Seint Gregorie, "unnethe ariseth he out of his synne, that is charged with the charge of yvel usage."/ And therfore repentant folk, that stynte for to synne, and forlete synne er that synne forlete hem, hooly chirche holdeth hem siker of hire savacioun./ And he that synneth and verraily repenteth hym in his laste, hooly chirche yet hopeth his savacioun, by the grete mercy of oure Lord Jhesu Crist, for his repentaunce; but taak the siker wey./

And now, sith I have declared yow what thyng is Penitence, now shul ye understonde that ther been three acciouns of Penitence./ The firste is that if a man be bap- 95 tized after that he hath synned,/ Seint Augustyn seith, "But he be penytent for his olde synful lyf, he may nat bigynne the newe clene lif."/ For, certes, if he be baptized withouten penitence of his olde gilt, he receyveth the mark of baptesme, but nat the grace ne the remission of his synnes, til he have repentance verray./ Another defaute is this, that men doon deedly synne after that they han receyved baptesme./ The thridde defaute is that men fallen in venial synnes after hir baptesme, fro day to day./ Therof seith Seint Augustyn that 100 penitence of goode and humble folk is the penitence of every day./

The speces of Penitence been three. That oon of hem is solempne, another is commune, and the thridde is privee./ Thilke penance that is solempne is in two maneres; as to be put out of hooly chirche in Lente, for slaughtre of children, and swich maner thyng./ Another is, whan a man hath synned openly, of which synne the fame is openly spoken in the contree, and thanne hooly chirche by juggement destreyneth hym for to do open penaunce./ Commune penaunce is that preestes enjoynen men communly in certeyn caas, as for to goon peraventure naked in pilgrimages, or bare-

foot./ Pryvee penaunce is thilke that men   105
doon alday for privee synnes, of whiche we
shryve us prively and receyve privee penaunce./

Now shaltow understande what is bihovely
and necessarie to verray perfit Penitence. And
this stant on three thynges:/ Contricioun of
herte, Confessioun of Mouth, and Satisfaccioun./ For which seith Seint John Crisostom:
"Penitence destreyneth a man to accepte benygnely every peyne that hym is enjoyned,
with contricioun of herte, and shrift of mouth,
with satisfaccioun; and in werkynge of alle
manere humylitee."/ And this is fruytful penitence agayn three thynges in which we
wratthe oure Lord Jhesu Crist:/ this is to   110
seyn, by delit in thynkynge, by reccheless-
nesse in spekynge, and by wikked synful werkynge./ And agayns thise wikkede giltes is Penitence, that may be likned unto a tree./

The roote of this tree is Contricioun, that
hideth hym in the herte of hym that is verray
repentaunt, right as the roote of a tree hydeth
hym in the erthe./ Of the roote of Contricioun
spryngeth a stalke that bereth braunches and
leves of Confessioun, and fruyt of Satisfaccioun./ For which Crist seith in his gospel:
"Dooth digne fruyt of Penitence"; for by this
fruyt may men knowe this tree, and nat by the
roote that is hyd in the herte of man, ne by the
braunches, ne by the leves of Confessioun./ And therfore oure Lord Jhesu   115
Crist seith thus: "By the fruyt of hem shul
ye knowen hem."/ Of this roote eek spryngeth
a seed of grace, the which seed is mooder of
sikernesse, and this seed is egre and hoot./ The
grace of this seed spryngeth of God thurgh remembrance of the day of doom and on the
peynes of helle./ Of this matere seith Salomon that in the drede of God man forleteth his
synne./ The heete of this seed is the love of
God, and the desiryng of the joye perdurable./ This heete draweth the herte   120
of a man to God, and dooth hym haten his
synne./ For soothly ther is nothyng that sa-
voureth so wel to a child as the milk of his
norice, ne nothyng is to hym moore abhomynable than thilke milk whan it is medled with
oother mete./ Right so the synful man that
loveth his synne, hym semeth that it is to him
moost sweete of any thyng;/ but fro that tyme
that he loveth sadly oure Lord Jhesu Crist, and
desireth the lif perdurable, ther nys to him no
thyng moore abhomynable./ For soothly the
lawe of God is the love of God; for which

David the prophete seith: "I have loved thy
lawe, and hated wikkednesse and hate"; he
that loveth God kepeth his lawe and his
word./ This tree saugh the prophete   125
Daniel in spirit, upon the avysioun of the
kyng Nabugodonosor, whan he conseiled hym
to do penitence./ Penaunce is the tree of lyf
to hem that it receyven, and he that holdeth
hym in verray penitence is blessed, after the
sentence of Salomon./

In this Penitence or Contricioun man shal
understonde foure thynges; that is to seyn, what
is Contricioun, and whiche been the causes that
moeven a man to Contricioun, and how he
sholde be contrit, and what Contricioun availleth to the soule./ Thanne is it thus: that Contricioun is the verray sorwe that a man receyveth in his herte for his synnes, with sad purpos
to shryve hym, and to do penaunce, and nev-
eremoore to do synne./ And this sorwe shal
been in this manere, as seith Seint Bernard: "It
shal been hevy and grevous, and ful sharp
and poynaunt in herte."/ First, for man   130
hath agilt his Lord and his Creatour; and
moore sharp and poynaunt, for he hath agilt hys
Fader celestial;/ and yet moore sharp and
poynaunt, for he hath wrathed and agilt hym
that boghte hym, that with his precious blood
hath delivered us fro the bondes of synne, and
fro the crueltee of the devel, and fro the peynes
of helle./

The causes that oghte moeve a man to Contricioun been sixe. First a man shal remembre
hym of his synnes;/ but looke he that thilke
remembraunce ne be to hym no delit by no
wey, but greet shame and sorwe for his gilt.
For Job seith, "Synful men doon werkes worthy
of confusioun."/ And therfore seith Ezechie,
"I wol remembre me alle the yeres of my
lyf in bitternesse of myn herte."/ And   135
God seith in the Apocalipse, "Remembreth
yow fro whennes that ye been falle"; for biforn
that tyme that ye synned, ye were the children
of God, and lymes of the regne of God;/ but for
youre synne ye been woxen thral, and foul, and
membres of the feend, hate of aungels, sclaundre of hooly chirche, and foode of the false
serpent; perpetueel matere of the fir of helle;/
and yet moore foul and abhomynable, for ye
trespassen so ofte tyme as dooth the hound that
retourneth to eten his spewyng./ And yet be
ye fouler for youre longe continuyng in synne
and youre synful usage, for which ye be roten
in youre synne, as a beest in his dong./ Swiche

manere of thoghtes maken a man to have shame
of his synne, and no delit, as God seith by
the prophete Ezechiel:/ "Ye shal remem-   140
bre yow of youre weyes, and they shuln
displese yow." Soothly synnes been the weyes
that leden folk to helle./

The seconde cause that oghte make a man
to have desdeyn of synne is this: that, as seith
Seint Peter, "whoso that dooth synne is thral
of synne"; and synne put a man in greet thraldom./ And therfore seith the prophete Ezechiel: "I wente sorweful in desdayn of myself."
Certes, wel oghte a man have desdayn of synne,
and withdrawe hym from that thraldom and
vileynye./ And lo, what seith Seneca in this
matere? He seith thus: "Though I wiste that
neither God ne man ne sholde nevere knowe
it, yet wolde I have desdayn for to do synne."/
And the same Seneca also seith: "I am born to
gretter thynges than to be thral to my body,
or than for to maken of my body a thral."/   145
Ne a fouler thral may no man ne womman
maken of his body than for to yeven his body
to synne./ Al were it the fouleste cherl or the
fouleste womman that lyveth, and leest of
value, yet is he thanne moore foul and moore
in servitute./ Evere fro the hyer degree that
man falleth, the moore is he thral, and moore
to God and to the world vile and abhomynable./ O goode God, wel oghte man have desdayn of synne, sith that thurgh synne, ther he
was free, now is he maked bonde./ And therfore seyth Seint Augustyn: "If thou hast desdayn of thy servant, if he agilte or synne, have
thou thanne desdayn that thou thyself
sholdest do synne."/ Tak reward of thy   150
value, that thou ne be to foul to thyself./
Allas! wel oghten they thanne have desdayn to
been servauntz and thralles to synne, and soore
been ashamed of hemself,/ that God of his
endelees goodnesse hath set hem in heigh estaat, or yeven hem wit, strengthe of body,
heele, beautee, prosperitee,/ and boghte hem
fro the deeth with his herte-blood, that they
so unkyndely, agayns his gentilesse, quiten hym
so vileynsly to slaughtre of hir owene soules./
O goode God, ye wommen that been of so greet
beautee, remembreth yow of the proverbe
of Salomon. He seith:/ "Likneth a fair   155
womman that is a fool of hire body lyk to
a ryng of gold that were in the groyn of a
soughe."/ For right as a soughe wroteth in
everich ordure, so wroteth she hire beautee in
the stynkynge ordure of synne./

The thridde cause that oghte moeve a man
to Contricioun is drede of the day of doom and
of the horrible peynes of helle./ For, as Seint
Jerome seith, "At every tyme that me remembreth of the day of doom I quake;/ for whan
I ete or drynke, or what so that I do, evere
semeth me that the trompe sowneth in
myn ere: 'Riseth up, ye that been dede,   160
and cometh to the juggement.' "/ O goode
God, muchel oghte a man to drede swich a
juggement, "ther as we shullen been alle," as
Seint Poul seith, "biforn the seete of oure Lord
Jhesu Crist;"/ whereas he shal make a general
congregacioun, whereas no man may been absent./ For certes there availleth noon essoyne
ne excusacioun./ And nat oonly that oure defautes shullen be jugged, but eek that alle
oure werkes shullen openly be knowe./   165
And, as seith Seint Bernard, "Ther ne shal
no pledynge availle, ne no sleighte; we shullen
yeven rekenynge of everich ydel word."/ Ther
shul we han a juge that may nat been deceyved ne corrupt. And why? For, certes, alle
oure thoghtes been discovered as to hym; ne
for preyere ne for meede he shal nat been corrupt./ And therfore seith Salomon, "The
wratthe of God ne wol nat spare no wight, for
preyere ne for yifte"; and therfore, at the day
of doom, ther nys noon hope to escape./ Wherfore, as seith Seint Anselm, "Ful greet angwyssh shul the synful folk have at that tyme;/
ther shal the stierne and wrothe juge sitte
above, and under hym the horrible pit of helle
open to destroyen hym that moot biknowen his
synnes, whiche synnes openly been shewed
biforn God and biforn every creature;/   170
and in the left syde mo develes than herte
may bithynke, for to harye and drawe the synful soules to the peyne of helle;/ and withinne
the hertes of folk shal be the bitynge conscience, and withoute forth shal be the world
al brennynge./ Whider shal thanne the
wrecched synful man flee to hiden hym?
Certes, he may nat hyden hym; he moste come
forth and shewen hym."/ For certes, as seith
Seint Jerome, "the erthe shal casten hym out
of hym, and the see also, and the eyr also, that
shal be ful of thonder-clappes and light-
nynges."/ Now soothly, whoso wel remembreth
hym of thise thynges, I gesse that his synne
shal nat turne hym into delit, but to greet
sorwe, for drede of the peyne of helle./   175
And therfore seith Job to God: "Suffre,
Lord, that I may a while biwaille and wepe,

er I go withoute returnyng to the derke lond, covered with the derknesse of deeth;/ to the lond of mysese and of derknesse, whereas is the shadwe of deeth; whereas ther is noon ordre or ordinaunce, but grisly drede that evere shal laste."/ Loo, heere may ye seen that Job preyde respit a while, to biwepe and waille his trespas; for soothly oo day of respit is bettre than al the tresor of this world./ And forasmuche as a man may acquiten hymself biforn God by penitence in this world, and nat by tresor, therfore sholde he preye to God to yeve hym respit a while to biwepe and biwaillen his trespas./ For certes, al the sorwe that a man myghte make fro the bigynnyng of the world nys but a litel thyng at regard of the sorwe of helle./ The cause why that Job 180 clepeth helle the lond of derknesse;/ understondeth that he clepeth it "lond" or erthe, for it is stable, and nevere shal faille; "derk," for he that is in helle hath defaute of light material./ For certes, the derke light that shal come out of the fyr that evere shal brenne, shal turne hym al to peyne that is in helle; for it sheweth him to the horrible develes that hym tormenten./ "Covered with the derknesse of deeth," that is to seyn, that he that is in helle shal have defaute of the sighte of God; for certes, the sighte of God is the lyf perdurable./ "The derknesse of deeth" been the synnes that the wrecched man hath doon, whiche that destourben hym to see the face of God, right as dooth a derk clowde bitwixe us and the sonne./ "Lond of misese," by cause that 185 ther been three maneres of defautes, agayn three thynges that folk of this world han in this present lyf, that is to seyn, honours, delices, and richesses./ Agayns honour, have they in helle shame and confusioun./ For wel ye woot that men clepen honour the reverence that man doth to man; but in helle is noon honour ne reverence. For certes, namoore reverence shal be doon there to a kyng than to a knave./ For which God seith by the prophete Jeremye, "Thilke folk that me despisen shul been in despit."/ Honour is eek cleped greet lordshipe; ther shal no wight serven other, but of harm and torment. Honour is eek cleped greet dignytee and heighnesse, but in helle shul they been al fortroden of develes./ And 190 God seith, "The horrible develes shulle goon and comen upon the hevedes of the dampned folk." And this is for as muche as the hyer that they were in this present lyf, the moore shulle they been abated and defouled in helle./ Agayns the richesse of this world shul they han mysese of poverte, and this poverte shal been in foure thynges:/ In defaute of tresor, of which that David seith, "The riche folk, that embraceden and oneden al hire herte to tresor of this world, shul slepe in the slepynge of deeth; and nothyng ne shal they fynden in hir handes of al hir tresor."/ And mooreover the myseyse of helle shal been in defaute of mete and drinke./ For God seith thus by Moyses: "They shul been wasted with hunger, and the briddes of helle shul devouren hem with bitter deeth, and the galle of the dragon shal been hire drynke, and the venym of the dragon hire morsels."/ And forther 195 over, hire myseyse shal been in defaute of clothyng; for they shulle be naked in body as of clothyng, save the fyr in which they brenne, and othere filthes;/ and naked shul they been of soule, as of alle manere vertues, which that is the clothyng of the soule. Where been thanne the gaye robes, and the softe shetes, and the smale shertes?/ Loo, what seith God of hem by the prophete Ysaye: that "under hem shul been strawed motthes, and hire covertures shulle been of wormes of helle."/ And forther over, hir myseyse shal been in defaute of freendes. For he nys nat povre that hath goode freendes; but there is no frend,/ for neither God ne no creature shal been freend to hem, and everich of hem shal haten oother with deedly hate./ "The sones and the 200 doghtren shullen rebellen agayns fader and mooder, and kynrede agayns kynrede, and chiden and despisen everich of hem oother bothe day and nyght," as God seith by the prophete Michias./ And the lovynge children, that whilom loveden so flesshly everich oother, wolden everich of hem eten oother if they myghte./ For how sholden they love hem togidre in the peyne of helle, whan they hated everich of hem oother in the prosperitee of this lyf?/ For truste wel, hir flesshly love was deedly hate, as seith the prophete David: "Whoso that loveth wikkednesse, he hateth his soule."/ And whoso hateth his owene soule, certes, he may love noon oother wight in no manere./ And therfore, in helle is no 205 solas ne no freendshipe, but evere the moore flesshly kynredes that been in helle, the moore cursynges, the more chidynges, and the moore deedly hate ther is among hem./ And forther over, they shul have defaute of alle manere delices. For certes, delices been after the appetites of the fyve wittes, as sighte, herynge, smellynge, savorynge, and touchynge./ But in helle hir sighte shal be ful of derknesse and of smoke, and therfore ful of teeres; and hir herynge ful of waymentynge and of gryntynge of teeth, as seith Jhesu Crist./ Hir nosethirles shullen be ful of stynkynge stynk; and, as seith Ysaye the prophete, "hir savoryng shal be ful of bitter galle";/ and touchynge of al hir body ycovered with "fir that nevere shal quenche, and with wormes that nevere shul dyen," as God seith by the mouth of Ysaye./ And for as muche as they shul 210 nat wene that they may dyen for peyne, and by hir deeth flee fro peyne, that may they understonden by the word of Job, that seith, "ther as is the shadwe of deeth."/ Certes, a shadwe hath the liknesse of the thyng of which it is shadwe, but shadwe is nat the same thyng of which it is shadwe./ Right so fareth the peyne of helle; it is lyk deeth for the horrible angwissh, and why? For it peyneth hem evere, as though they sholde dye anon; but certes, they shal nat dye./ For, as seith Seint Gregorie, "To wrecche caytyves shal be deeth withoute deeth, and ende withouten ende, and defaute withoute failynge./ For hir deeth shal alwey lyven, and hir ende shal everemo bigynne, and hir defaute shal nat faille."/ 215 And therfore seith Seint John the Evaungelist: "They shullen folwe deeth, and they shul nat fynde hym; and they shul desiren to dye, and deeth shal flee fro hem."/ And eek Job seith that in helle is noon ordre of rule./ And al be it so that God hath creat alle thynges in right ordre, and no thyng withouten ordre, but alle thynges been ordeyned and nombred; yet, nathelees, they that been dampned been nothyng in ordre, ne holden noon ordre./ For the erthe ne shal bere hem no fruyt./ For, as the prophete David seith, "God shal destroie the fruyt of the erthe as fro hem; ne water ne shal yeve hem no moisture, ne the eyr no refresshyng, ne fyr no light."/ For, as 220 seith Seint Basilie, "The brennynge of the fyr of this world shal God yeven in helle to hem that been dampned,/ but the light and the cleernesse shal be yeven in hevene to his children"; right as the goode man yeveth flessh to his children and bones to his houndes./ And for they shullen have noon hope to escape, seith Seint Job atte laste that "ther shal horrour and grisly drede dwellen withouten ende."/ Hor-

rour is alwey drede of harm that is to come, and this drede shal evere dwelle in the hertes of hem that been dampned. And therfore han they lorn al hire hope, for sevene causes./ First, for God, that is hir juge, shal be withouten mercy to hem; and they may nat plese hym ne noon of his halwes; ne they ne may yeve no thyng for hir raunsoun;/ ne 225 they have no voys to speke to hym; ne they may nat fle fro peyne; ne they have no goodnesse in hem, that they mowe shewe to delivere hem fro peyne./ And therfore seith Salomon: "The wikked man dyeth, and whan he is deed, he shal have noon hope to escape fro peyne."/ Whoso thanne wolde wel understande thise peynes, and bithynke hym weel that he hath deserved thilke peynes for his synnes, certes, he sholde have moore talent to siken and to wepe, than for to syngen and to pleye./ For, as that seith Salomon, "Whoso that hadde the science to knowe the peynes that been establissed and ordeyned for synne, he wolde make sorwe."/ "Thilke science," as seith Seint Augustyn, "maketh a man to waymenten in his herte."/ 230
The fourthe point that oghte maken a man to have contricion is the sorweful remembraunce of the good that he hath left to doon heere in erthe, and eek the good that he hath lorn./ Soothly, the goode werkes that he hath lost, outher they been the goode werkes that he wroghte er he fel into deedly synne, or elles the goode werkes that he wroghte while he lay in synne./ Soothly, the goode werkes that he dide biforn that he fil in synne been al mortefied and astoned and dulled by the ofte synnyng./ The othere goode werkes, that he wroghte whil he lay in deedly synne, thei been outrely dede, as to the lyf perdurable in hevene./ Thanne thilke goode werkes that been mortefied by ofte synnyng, whiche goode werkes he dide whil he was in charitee, ne mowe nevere quyken agayn withouten verray penitence./ And therof seith God by 235 the mouth of Ezechiel, that "if the rightful man returne agayn from his rightwisnesse and werke wikkednesse, shal he lyve?"/ Nay, for alle the goode werkes that he hath wroght ne shul nevere been in remembraunce, for he shal dyen in his synne./ And upon thilke chapitre seith Seint Gregorie thus: that "we shulle understonde this principally;/ that whan we doon deedly synne, it is for noght thanne to rehercen or drawen into memorie the goode werkes that

we han wroght biforn."/ For certes, in the werkynge of the deedly synne, ther is no trust to no good werk that we han doon biforn; that is to seyn, as for to have therby the lyf perdurable in hevene./ But nathelees, the 240 goode werkes quyken agayn, and comen agayn, and helpen, and availlen to have the lyf perdurable in hevene, whan we han con-tricioun./ But soothly, the goode werkes that men doon whil they been in deedly synne, for as muche as they were doon in deedly synne, they may nevere quyke agayn./ For certes, thyng that nevere hadde lyf may nevere quyk-ene; and nathelees, al be it that they ne availle noght to han the lyf perdurable, yet availlen they to abregge of the peyne of helle, or elles to geten temporal richesse,/ or elles that God wole the rather enlumyne and lightne the herte of the synful man to have repentaunce;/ and eek they availlen for to usen a man to doon goode werkes, that the feend have the 245 lasse power of his soule./ And thus the curteis Lord Jhesu Crist ne wole that no good werk be lost; for in somwhat it shal availle./ But, for as muche as the goode werkes that men doon whil they been in good lyf been al mortefied by synne folwynge, and eek sith that alle the goode werkes that men doon whil they been in deedly synne been outrely dede as for to have the lyf perdurable;/ wel may that man that no good werk ne dooth synge thilke newe Frenshe song, "*Jay tout perdu mon temps et mon labour.*"/ For certes, synne bireveth a man bothe goodnesse of nature and eek the goodnesse of grace./ For soothly, the grace of the Hooly Goost fareth lyk fyr, that may nat been ydel; for fyr fayleth anoon as it forleteth his wirkynge, and right so grace fayleth anoon as it forleteth his werkynge./ Then 250 leseth the synful man the goodnesse of glorie, that oonly is bihight to goode men that labouren and werken./ Wel may he be sory thanne, that oweth al his lif to God as longe as he hath lyved, and eek as longe as he shal lyve, that no goodnesse ne hath to paye with his dette to God to whom he oweth al his lyf./ For trust wel, "he shal yeven acountes," as seith Seint Bernard, "of alle the goodes that han be yeven hym in this present lyf, and how he hath hem despended;/ in so muche that ther shal nat perisse an heer of his heed, ne a moment of an houre ne shal nat perisse of his tyme, that he ne shal yeve of it a rekenyng."/ The fifthe thyng that oghte moeve a man to

contricioun is remembrance of the passioun that oure Lord Jhesu Crist suffred for oure synnes./ For, as seith Seint Bernard, 255 "Whil that I lyve I shal have remem-brance of the travailles that oure Lord Crist suffred in prechyng;/ his werynesse in travail-lyng, his temptaciouns whan he fasted, his longe wakynges whan he preyde, hise teeres whan that he weep for pitee of good peple;/ the wo and the shame and the filthe that men seyden to hym; of the foule spittyng that men spitte in his face, of the buffettes that men yaven hym, of the foule mowes, and of the re-preves that men to hym seyden;/ of the nayles with whiche he was nayled to the croys, and of al the remenant of his passioun that he suf-fred for my synnes, and no thyng for his gilt."/ And ye shul understonde that in mannes synne is every manere of ordre or ordinaunce turned up-so-doun./ For it is sooth that 260 God, and resoun, and sensualitee, and the body of man been so ordeyned that everich of thise foure thynges sholde have lordshipe over that oother;/ as thus: God sholde have lord-shipe over resoun, and resoun over sensualitee, and sensualitee over the body of man./ But soothly, whan man synneth, al this ordre or ordinaunce is turned up-so-doun./ And ther-fore, thanne, for as muche as the resoun of man ne wol nat be subget ne obeisant to God, that is his lord by right, therfore leseth it the lord-shipe that it sholde have over sensualitee, and eek over the body of man./ And why? For sensualitee rebelleth thanne agayns resoun, and by that way leseth resoun the lord-shipe over sensualitee and over the body./ 265 For right as resoun is rebel to God, right so is bothe sensualitee rebel to resoun and the body also./ And certes this disordinaunce and this rebellioun oure Lord Jhesu Crist aboghte upon his precious body ful deere, and herkneth in which wise./ For as muche thanne as re-soun is rebel to God, therfore is man worthy to have sorwe and to be deed./ This suffred oure Lord Jhesu Crist for man, after that he hadde be bitraysed of his disciple, and dis-treyned and bounde, so that his blood brast out at every nayl of his handes, as seith Seint Augustyn./ And forther over, for as muchel as resoun of man ne wol nat daunte sensuali-tee whan it may, therfore is man worthy to have shame; and this suffred oure Lord Jhesu Crist for man, whan they spetten in his visage./ And forther over, for as muchel 270

thanne as the caytyf body of man is rebel
bothe to resoun and to sensualitee, therfore is
it worthy the deeth./ And this suffred oure
Lord Jhesu Crist for man upon the croys,
where as ther was no part of his body free
withouten greet peyne and bitter passioun./
And al this suffred Jhesu Crist, that nevere
forfeted. And therfore resonably may be seyd
of Jhesu in this manere: "To muchel am I
peyned for the thynges that I nevere deserved,
and to muche defouled for shendshipe that
man is worthy to have."/ And therfore may
the synful man wel seye, as seith Seint Bernard,
"Acursed be the bitternesse of my synne, for
which ther moste be suffred so muchel bitternesse."/ For certes, after the diverse disordi-
naunces of oure wikkednesses was the passioun of Jhesu Crist ordeyned in diverse
thynges,/ as thus. Certes, synful mannes 275
soule is bitraysed of the devel by coveitise
of temporeel prosperitee, and scorned by deceite whan he cheseth flesshly delices; and yet
is it tormented by inpacience of adversitee,
and bispet by servage and subjeccioun of
synne; and atte laste it is slayn fynally./ For
this disordinaunce of synful man was Jhesu
Crist first bitraysed, and after that was he
bounde, that cam for to unbynden us of synne
and peyne./ Thanne was he byscorned, that
oonly sholde han been honoured in alle thynges
and of alle thynges./ Thanne was his visage,
that oghte be desired to be seyn of al mankynde, in which visage aungels desiren to looke,
vileynsly bispet./ Thanne was he scourged,
that no thyng hadde agilt; and finally,
thanne was he crucified and slayn./ 280
Thanne was acompliced the word of Ysaye,
"He was wounded for oure mysdedes and defouled for oure felonies."/ Now sith that Jhesu
Crist took upon hymself the peyne of alle oure
wikkednesses, muchel oghte synful man wepen
and biwayle, that for his synnes Goddes sone
of hevene sholde al this peyne endure./

The sixte thyng that oghte moeve a man to
contricioun is the hope of three thynges; that
is to seyn, foryifnesse of synne, and the yifte of
grace wel for to do, and the glorie of hevene,
with which God shal gerdone man for his
goode dedes./ And for as muche as Jhesu
Crist yeveth us thise yiftes of his largesse and
of his sovereyn bountee, therfore is he cleped
Jhesus Nazarenus rex Judeorum./ Jhesus is to
seyn "saveour" or "salvacioun," on whom men
shul hope to have foryifnesse of synnes,
which that is proprely salvacioun of
synnes./ And therfore seyde the aungel 285
to Joseph, "Thou shalt clepen his name
Jhesus, that shal saven his peple of hir synnes."/
And heerof seith Seint Peter: "Ther is noon
oother name under hevene that is yeve to any
man, by which a man may be saved, but oonly
Jhesus."/ *Nazarenus* is as muche for to seye as
"florisshynge," in which a man shal hope that
he that yeveth hym remissioun of synnes shal
yeve hym eek grace wel for to do. For in the
flour is hope of fruyt in tyme comynge, and in
foryifnesse of synnes hope of grace wel for to
do./ "I was atte dore of thyn herte," seith
Jhesus, "and cleped for to entre. He that openeth to me shal have foryifnesse of synne./ I
wol entre into hym by my grace, and soupe
with hym," by the goode werkes that he shal
doon, whiche werkes been the foode of God;
"and he shal soupe with me," by the grete
joye that I shal yeven hym./ Thus shal 290
man hope, for his werkes of penaunce,
that God shal yeven hym his regne, as he bi-
hooteth hym in the gospel./

Now shal a man understonde in which manere shal been his contricioun. I seye that it
shal been universal and total. This is to seyn,
a man shal be verray repentaunt for alle his
synnes that he hath doon in delit of his thoght;
for delit is ful perilous./ For ther been two
manere of consentynges: that oon of hem is
cleped consentynge of affeccioun, whan a man
is moeved to do synne, and deliteth hym longe
for to thynke on that synne;/ and his reson
aperceyveth it wel that it is synne agayns the
lawe of God, and yet his resoun refreyneth nat
his foul delit or talent, though he se wel apertly
that it is agayns the reverence of God. Although his resoun ne consente noght to doon
that synne in dede,/ yet seyn somme doctours
that swich delit that dwelleth longe, it is
ful perilous, al be it nevere so lite./ And 295
also a man sholde sorwe namely for al that
evere he hath desired agayn the lawe of God
with perfit consentynge of his resoun; for therof
is no doute, that it is deedly synne in consentynge./ For certes, ther is no deedly synne, that
it nas first in mannes thoght, and after that
in his delit, and so forth into consentynge and
into dede./ Wherfore I seye that many men
ne repenten hem nevere of swiche thoghtes and
delites, ne nevere shryven hem of it, but oonly
of the dede of grete synnes outward./ Wherfore I seye that swiche wikked delites and wik-

ked thoghtes been subtile bigileres of hem that shullen be dampned./ Mooreover man oghte to sorwe for his wikkede wordes as wel as for his wikkede dedes. For certes, the repentaunce of a synguler synne, and nat repente of alle his othere synnes, or elles repenten hym of alle his othere synnes, and nat of a synguler synne, may nat availle./ For certes, God al- 300 myghty is al good; and therfore he for- yeveth al, or elles right noght./ And heerof seith Seint Augustyn:/ "I wot certeynly that God is enemy to everich synnere"; and how thanne, he that observeth o synne, shal he have foryifnesse of the remenaunt of his othere synnes? Nay./ And forther over, contricioun sholde be wonder sorweful and angwissous; and therfore yeveth hym God pleynly his mercy; and therfore, whan my soule was an- gwissous withinne me, I hadde remembrance of God that my preyere myghte come to hym./ Forther over, contricioun moste be continueel, and that man have stedefast purpos to shriven hym, and for to amenden hym of his lyf./ For soothly, whil contricioun lasteth, 305 man may evere have hope of foryifnesse; and of this comth hate of synne, that destroy- eth synne, bothe in himself, and eek in oother folk, at his power./ For which seith David: "Ye that loven God, hateth wikkednesse." For trusteth wel, to love God is for to love that he loveth, and hate that he hateth./

The laste thyng that men shal understonde in contricioun is this: wherof avayleth contri- cioun. I seye that somtyme contricioun de- livereth a man fro synne;/ of which that David seith, "I seye," quod David (that is to seyn, I purposed fermely) "to shryve me, and thow, Lord, relessedest my synne."/ And right so as contricion availleth noght withouten sad pur- pos of shrifte, if man have oportunitee, right so litel worth is shrifte or satisfaccioun withouten contricioun./ And mooreover 310 contricion destroyeth the prisoun of helle, and maketh wayk and fieble alle the strengthes of the develes, and restoreth the yiftes of the Hooly Goost and of alle goode vertues;/ and it clenseth the soule of synne, and delivereth the soule fro the peyne of helle, and fro the compaignye of the devel, and fro the servage of synne, and restoreth it to alle goodes espir- ituels, and to the compaignye and communyoun of hooly chirche./ And forther over, it maketh hym that whilom was sone of ire to be sone of grace; and alle thise thynges been preved by hooly writ./ And therfore, he that wolde sette his entente to thise thynges, he were ful wys; for soothly he ne sholde nat thanne in al his lyf have corage to synne, but yeven his body and al his herte to the service of Jhesu Crist, and therof doon hym hommage./ For soothly oure sweete Lord Jhesu Crist hath spared us so debonairly in oure folies, that if he ne hadde pitee of mannes soule, a sory song we myghten alle synge./ 315

Explicit prima pars Penitentie; Et sequitur secunda pars eiusdem.

The seconde partie of Penitence is Confes- sioun, that is signe of contricioun./ Now shul ye understonde what is Confessioun, and wheither it oghte nedes be doon or noon, and whiche thynges been covenable to verray Con- fessioun./

First shaltow understonde that Confessioun is verray shewynge of synnes to the preest./ This is to seyn "verray," for he moste confessen hym of alle the condiciouns that bilongen to his synne, as ferforth as he kan./ Al moot be seyd, and no thyng excused ne hyd ne forwrapped, and noght avaunte thee of thy goode werkes./ And forther over, it is neces- 320 sarie to understonde whennes that synnes spryngen, and how they encreessen and whiche they been./

Of the spryngynge of synnes seith Seint Paul in this wise: that "right as by a man synne en- tred first into this world, and thurgh that synne deeth, right so thilke deeth entred into alle men that synneden."/ And this man was Adam, by whom synne entred into this world, whan he brak the comaundementz of God./ And therfore, he that first was so myghty that he sholde nat have dyed, bicam swich oon that he moste nedes dye, wheither he wolde or noon, and al his progenye in this world, that in thilke man synneden./ Looke that in th'estaat of in- nocence, whan Adam and Eve naked weren in Paradys, and nothyng ne hadden shame of hir nakednesse,/ how that the serpent, 325 that was moost wily of alle othere beestes that God hadde maked, seyde to the womman: "Why comaunded God to yow ye sholde nat eten of every tree in Paradys?"/ The womman answerde: "Of the fruyt," quod she, "of the trees in Paradys we feden us, but soothly, of the fruyt of the tree that is in the myddel of Paradys, God forbad us for to ete, ne nat touchen it, lest per aventure we sholde dyen."/ The serpent seyde to the womman: "Nay, nay, ye shul nat dyen of deeth; for sothe, God woot that what day that ye eten therof, youre eyen shul opene, and ye shul been as goddes, knowynge good and harm."/ The womman thanne saugh that the tree was good to feedyng, and fair to the eyen, and delitable to the sighte. She took of the fruyt of the tree, and eet it, and yaf to hire housbonde, and he eet, and anoon the eyen of hem bothe openeden./ And whan that they knewe that they were naked, they sowed of fige leves a maner of breches to hiden hire membres./ There may ye seen that deedly synne hath, first, suggestion of the feend, as sheweth heere by the naddre; and afterward, the delit of the flessh, as sheweth heere by Eve; and after that, the consentynge of resoun, as sheweth heere by Adam./ For trust wel, though so were that the feend tempted Eve, that is to seyn, the flessh, and the flessh hadde delit in the beautee of the fruyt defended, yet certes, til that resoun, that is to seyn, Adam, consented to the etynge of the fruyt, yet stood he in th' estaat of innocence./ Of thilke Adam tooke we thilke synne original; for of hym flesshly descended be we alle, and engendred of vile and corrupt mateere./ And whan the soule is put in oure body, right anon is contract original synne; and that that was erst but oonly peyne of concupiscence, is afterward bothe peyne and synne./ And therfore be we alle born sones of wratthe and of dampnacioun perdurable, if it nere baptesme that we receyven, which bynymeth us the culpe. But for sothe, the peyne dwelleth with us, as to temptacioun, which peyne highte concupiscence./ And this concupiscence, whan it is wrongfully disposed or ordeyned in man, it maketh hym coveite, by coveitise of flessh, flesshly synne, by sighte of his eyen as to erthely thynges, and eek coveitise of hynesse by pride of herte./

Now, as for to speken of the firste coveitise, that is concupiscence, after the lawe of oure membres, that weren lawefulliche ymaked and by rightful juggement of God;/ I seye, forasmuche as man is nat obeisaunt to God, that is his lord, therfore is the flessh to hym disobeisaunt thurgh concupiscence, which yet is

cleped norrissynge of synne and occasioun of synne./ Therfore, al the while that a man hath in hym the peyne of concupiscence, it is impossible but he be tempted somtime and moeved in his flessh to synne./ And this thyng may nat faille as longe as he lyveth; it may wel wexe fieble and faille by vertu of baptesme, and by the grace of God thurgh penitence;/ but fully ne shal it nevere quenche, that he ne shal som tyme be moeved in hymself, but if he were al refreyded by siknesse, or by malefice of sorcerie, or colde drynkes./ For lo, what seith Seint Paul: "The flessh coveiteth agayn the spirit, and the spirit agayn the flessh; they been so contrarie and so stryven that a man may nat alway doon as he wolde."/ The same Seint Paul, after his grete penaunce in water and in lond, — in water by nyght and by day in greet peril and in greet peyne; in lond, in famyne and thurst, in coold and cloothlees, and ones stoned almoost to the deeth,/ — yet seyde he, "Allas, I caytyf man! who shal delivere me fro the prisoun of my caytyf body?"/ And Seint Jerome, whan he longe tyme hadde woned in desert, where as he hadde no compaignye but of wilde beestes, where as he ne hadde no mete but herbes, and water to his drynke, ne no bed but the naked erthe, for which his flessh was blak as an Ethiopeen for heete, and ny destroyed for coold,/ yet seyde he that "the brennynge of lecherie boyled in al his body."/ Wherfore I woot wel sykerly that they been deceyved that seyn that they ne be nat tempted in hir body./ Witnesse on Seint Jame the Apostel, that seith that "every wight is tempted in his owene concupiscence"; that is to seyn, that everich of us hath matere and occasioun to be tempted of the norissynge of synne that is in his body./ And therfore seith Seint John the Evaungelist: "If that we seyn that we be withoute synne, we deceyve us selve, and trouthe is nat in us."/

Now shal ye understonde in what manere that synne wexeth or encreesseth in man. The firste thyng is thilke norissynge of synne of which I spak biforn, thilke flesshly concupiscence./ And after that comth the subjeccioun of the devel, this is to seyn, the develes bely, with which he bloweth in man the fir of flesshly concupiscence./ And after that, a man bithynketh hym wheither he wol doon, or no, thilke thing to which he is tempted./ And thanne, if that a man withstonde and weyve the firste entisynge of his flessh and of the feend, thanne is it no synne; and if it so be that he do nat so, thanne feeleth he anoon a flambe of delit./ And thanne is it good to be war, and kepen hym wel, or elles he wol falle anon into consentynge of synne; and thanne wol he do it, if he may have tyme and place./ And of this matere seith Moyses by the devel in this manere: "The feend seith, 'I wole chace and pursue the man by wikked suggestioun, and I wole hente hym by moevynge or stirynge of synne. And I wol departe my prise or my praye by deliberacioun, and my lust shal been acompliced in delit. I wol drawe my swerd in consentynge' —/ 355 for certes, right as a swerd departeth a thyng in two peces, right so consentynge departeth God fro man — 'and thanne wol I sleen hym with myn hand in dede of synne'; thus seith the feend."/ For certes, thanne is a man al deed in soule. And thus is synne acompliced by temptacioun, by delit, and by consentynge; and thanne is the synne cleped actueel./

For sothe, synne is in two maneres; outher it is venial, or deedly synne. Soothly, whan man loveth any creature moore than Jhesu Crist oure Creatour, thanne is it deedly synne. And venial synne is it, if man love Jhesu Crist lasse than hym oghte./ For sothe, the dede of this venial synne is ful perilous; for it amenuseth the love that men sholde han to God moore and moore./ And therfore, if a man charge hymself with manye swiche venial synnes, certes, but if so be that he somtyme descharge hym of hem by shrifte, they mowe ful lightly amenuse in hym al the love that he hath to Jhesu Crist;/ and in this wise 360 skippeth venial into deedly synne. For certes, the moore that a man chargeth his soule with venial synnes, the moore is he enclyned to fallen into deedly synne./ And therfore lat us nat be necligent to deschargen us of venial synnes. For the proverbe seith that "manye smale maken a greet."/ And herkne this ensample. A greet wawe of the see comth som tyme with so greet a violence that it drencheth the ship. And the same harm doon som tyme the smale dropes of water, that entren thurgh a litel crevace into the thurrok, and in the botme of the ship, if men be so necligent that they ne descharge hem nat by tyme./ And therfore, although ther be a difference bitwixe thise two causes of drenchynge,

algates the ship is dreynt./ Right so fareth it somtyme of deedly synne, and of anyouse veniale synnes, whan they multiplie in a man so greetly that the love of thilke worldly thynges that he loveth, thurgh whiche he synneth venyally, is as greet in his herte as the love of God, or moore./ And ther- 365 fore, the love of every thyng that is nat biset in God, ne doon principally for Goddes sake, although that a man love it lasse than God, yet is it venial synne;/ and deedly synne whan the love of any thyng weyeth in the herte of man as muchel as the love of God, or moore./ "Deedly synne," as seith Seint Augustyn, "is whan a man turneth his herte fro God, which that is verray sovereyn bountee, that may nat chaunge, and yeveth his herte to thyng that may chaunge and flitte."/ And certes, that is every thyng save God of hevene. For sooth is that if a man yeve his love, the which that he oweth al to God with al his herte, unto a creature, certes, as muche of his love as he yeveth to thilke creature, so muche he bireveth fro God;/ and therfore dooth he synne. For he that is dettour to God ne yeldeth nat to God al his dette, that is to seyn, al the love of his herte./ 370

Now sith man understondeth generally which is venial synne, thanne is it covenable to tellen specially of synnes whiche that many a man peraventure ne demeth hem nat synnes, and ne shryveth him nat of the same thynges, and yet natheless they been synnes;/ soothly, as thise clerkes writen, this is to seyn, that at every tyme that a man eteth or drynketh moore than suffiseth to the sustenaunce of his body, in certein he dooth synne./ And eek whan he speketh moore than it nedeth, it is synne. Eke whan he herkneth nat benignely the compleint of the povre;/ eke whan he is in heele of body, and wol nat faste whan other folk faste, withouten cause resonable; eke whan he slepeth moore than nedeth, or whan he comth by thilke enchesoun to late to chirche, or to othere werkes of charite;/ eke whan he useth his wyf, withouten sovereyn desir of engendrure to the honour of God, or for the entente to yelde to his wyf the dette of his body;/ eke whan 375 he wol nat visite the sike and the prisoner, if he may; eke if he love wyf or child, or oother worldly thyng, moore than resoun requireth; eke if he flatere or blandise moore than hym oghte for any necessitee;/ eke if he amenuse or withdrawe the almesse of the povre; eke if he apparailleth his mete moore deliciously than nede is, or ete it to hastily by likerousnesse;/ eke if he tale vanytees at chirche or at Goddes service, or that he be a talker of ydel wordes of folye or of vileynye, for he shal yelden acountes of it at the day of doom;/ eke whan he biheteth or assureth to do thynges that he may nat perfourne; eke whan that he by lightnesse or folie mysseyeth or scorneth his neighebor;/ eke whan he hath any wikked suspecioun of thyng ther he ne woot of it no soothfastnesse:/ thise thynges, and mo withoute nombre, been synnes, as seith Seint Augustyn./ 380

Now shal men understonde that, al be it so that noon erthely man may eschue alle venial synnes, yet may he refreyne hym by the brennynge love that he hath to oure Lord Jhesu Crist, and by preyeres and confessioun and othere goode werkes, so that it shal but litel greve./ For, as seith Seint Augustyn, "If a man love God in swich manere that al that evere he dooth is in the love of God, and for the love of God, verraily, for he brenneth in the love of God,/ looke, how muche that a drope of water that falleth in a fourneys ful of fyr anoyeth or greveth, so muche anoyeth a venial synne unto a man that is perfit in the love of Jhesu Crist."/ Men may also refreyne venial synne by receyvynge worthily of the precious body of Jhesu Crist;/ by receyvynge eek 385 of hooly water; by almesdede; by general confessioun of *Confiteor* at masse and at complyn; and by blessynge of bisshopes and of preestes, and by oothere goode werkes.

Explicit secunda pars Penitentie.

Sequitur de septem peccatis mortalibus et eorum dependenciis, circumstanciis, et speciebus.

Now is it bihovely thyng to telle whiche been the sevene deedly synnes, this is to seyn, chieftaynes of synnes. Alle they renne in o lees, but in diverse manneres. Now been they cleped chieftaynes, for as muche as they been chief and spryng of alle othere synnes./ Of the roote of thise sevene synnes, thanne, is Pride the general roote of alle harmes. For of this roote spryngen certein braunches, as Ire, Envye, Accidie or Slewthe, Avarice or Coveitise (to commune understondynge), Glotonye, and Lecherye./ And everich of thise chief synnes hath his braunches and his twigges, as shal be declared in hire chapitres folwynge./

De Superbia.

And thogh so be that no man kan outrely telle the nombre of the twigges and of the harmes that cometh of Pride, yet wol I shewe a partie of hem, as ye shul understonde./ Ther is Inobedience, Avaunt- 390 ynge, Ypocrisie, Despit, Arrogance, Inpudence, Swellynge of Herte, Insolence, Elacioun, Inpacience, Strif, Contumacie, Presumpcioun, Irreverence, Pertinacie, Veyne Glorie, and many another twig that I kan nat declare./ Inobedient is he that disobeyeth for despit to the comandementz of God, and to his sovereyns, and to his goostly fader./ Avauntour is he that bosteth of the harm or of the bountee that he hath doon./ Ypocrite is he that hideth to shewe hym swich as he is, and sheweth hym swich as he noght is./ Despitous is he that hath desdeyn of his neighebor, that is to seyn, of his evene-Cristene, or hath despit to doon that hym oghte to do./ Arrogant is he 395 that thynketh that he hath thilke bountees in hym that he hath noght, or weneth that he sholde have hem by his desertes, or elles he demeth that he be that he nys nat./ Inpudent is he that for his pride hath no shame of his synnes./ Swellynge of herte is whan a man rejoyseth hym of harm that he hath doon./ Insolent is he that despiseth in his juggement alle othere folk, as to regard of his value, and of his konnyng, and of his spekyng, and of his beryng./ Elacioun is whan he ne may neither suffre to have maister ne felawe./ Inpa- 400 cient is he that wol nat been ytaught ne undernome of his vice, and by strif werreieth trouthe wityngly, and deffendeth his folye./ *Contumax* is he that thurgh his indignacioun is agayns everich auctoritee or power of hem that been his sovereyns./ Presumpcioun is whan a man undertaketh an emprise that hym oghte nat do, or elles that he may nat do; and this is called Surquidrie. Irreverence is whan men do nat honour there as hem oghte to doon, and waiten to be reverenced./ Pertinacie is whan man deffendeth his folie, and trusteth to muchel to his owene wit./ Veyneglorie is for to have pompe and delit in his temporeel hynesse, and glorifie hym in this worldly estaat./ Janglynge is whan a man speketh   405 to muche biforn folk, and clappeth as a mille, and taketh no keep what he seith./

And yet is ther a privee spece of Pride, that waiteth first to be salewed er he wole salewe, al be he lasse worth than that oother is, per-aventure; and eek he waiteth or desireth to sitte, or elles to goon above hym in the wey, or kisse pax, or been encensed, or goon to offryng biforn his neighebor,/ and swiche sem-blable thynges, agayns his duetee, peraventure, but that he hath his herte and his entente in swich a proud desir to be magnified and hon-oured biforn the peple./

Now been ther two maneres of Pride: that oon of hem is withinne the herte of man, and that oother is withoute./ Of whiche, soothly, thise forseyde thynges, and mo than I have seyd, apertenen to Pride that is in the herte of man; and that othere speces of Pride been withoute./ But natheles that oon   410 of thise speces of Pride is signe of that oother, right as the gaye leefsel atte taverne is signe of the wyn that is in the celer./ And this is in manye thynges: as in speche and con-tenaunce, and in outrageous array of cloth-yng./ For certes, if ther ne hadde be no synne in clothyng, Crist wolde nat so soone have noted and spoken of the clothyng of thilke riche man in the gospel./ And, as seith Seint Gregorie, that "precious clothyng is cowpable for the derthe of it, and for his softenesse, and for his strangenesse and degisynesse, and for the superfluitee, or for the inordinat scantnesse of it."/ Allas! may man nat seen, as in oure dayes, the synful costlewe array of clothynge, and namely in to muche superfluite, or elles in to desordinat scantnesse?/   415

As to the first synne, that is in superflu-itee of clothynge, which that maketh it so deere, to harm of the peple;/ nat oonly the cost of embrowdynge, the degise endentynge or bar-rynge, owndynge, palynge, wyndynge or bend-ynge, and semblable wast of clooth in vanitee;/ but ther is also costlewe furrynge in hir gownes, so muche pownsonynge of chisels to maken holes, so muche daggynge of sheres;/ forth-with the superfluitee in lengthe of the forseide gownes, trailynge in the dong and in the mire, on horse and eek on foote, as wel of man as of womman, that al thilke trailyng is verraily as in effect wasted, consumed, thredbare, and roten with donge, rather than it is yeven to the povre, to greet damage of the forseyde povre folk./ And that in sondry wise; this is to seyn that the moore that clooth is wasted, the moore moot it coste to the peple for the scars-nesse./ And forther over, if so be that   420 they wolde yeven swich pownsoned and dagged clothyng to the povre folk, it is nat convenient to were for hire estaat, ne suf-fisant to beete hire necessitee, to kepe hem fro the distemperance of the firmament./ Upon that oother side, to speken of the horrible dis-ordinat scantnesse of clothyng, as been thise kutted sloppes, or haynselyns, that thurgh hire shortnesse ne covere nat the shameful mem-bres of man, to wikked entente./ Allas! somme of hem shewen the boce of hir shap, and the horrible swollen membres, that semeth lik the maladie of hirnia, in the wrappynge of hir hoses;/ and eek the buttokes of hem faren as it were the hyndre part of a she-ape in the fulle of the moone./ And mooreover, the wrecched swollen membres that they shewe thurgh dis-gisynge, in departynge of hire hoses in whit and reed, semeth that half hir shameful privee membres weren flayne./ And if so be that   425 they departen hire hoses in othere colours, as is whit and blak, or whit and blew, or blak and reed, and so forth,/ thanne semeth it, as by variaunce of colour, that half the partie of hire privee membres were corrupt by the fir of seint Antony, or by cancre, or by oother swich meschaunce./ Of the hyndre part of hir buttokes, it is ful horrible for to see. For certes, in that partie of hir body ther as they purgen hir stynkynge ordure,/ that foule partie shewe they to the peple prowdly in despit of hon-estitee, which honestitee that Jhesu Crist and his freendes observede to shewen in hir lyve./ Now, as of the outrageous array of wommen, God woot that though the visages of somme of hem seme ful chaast and debonaire, yet notifie they in hire array of atyr likerousnesse and pride./ I sey nat that honestitee in cloth-   430 ynge of man or womman is uncovenable, but certes the superfluitee or disordinat scanti-tee of clothynge is reprevable./ Also the synne of aornement or of apparaille is in thynges that apertenen to ridynge, as in to manye delicat horses that been hoolden for delit, that been so faire, fatte, and costlewe;/ and also in many a vicious knave that is sustened by cause of hem; and in to curious harneys, as in sadeles, in crouperes, peytrels, and bridles covered with precious clothyng, and riche barres and plates of gold and of silver./ For which God seith by Zakarie the prophete, "I wol confounde the rideres of swiche horses."/ This folk taken litel reward of the ridynge of Goddes sone of hevene, and of his harneys whan he rood upon the asse, and ne hadde noon oother harneys but the povre clothes of his disciples; ne we ne rede nat that evere he rood on oother beest./ I speke this for the synne of super- 435 fluitee, and nat for resonable honestitee, whan reson it requireth./ And forther over, certes, pride is greetly notified in holdynge of greet meynee, whan they be of litel profit or of right no profit;/ and namely whan that meynee is felonous and damageous to the peple by hardynesse of heigh lordshipe or by wey of offices./ For certes, swiche lordes sellen thanne hir lordshipe to the devel of helle, whanne they sustenen the wikkednesse of hir meynee./ Or elles, whan this folk of lowe degree, as thilke that holden hostelries, sustenen the thefte of hire hostilers, and that is in many manere of deceites./ Thilke manere of folk been 440 the flyes that folwen the hony, or elles the houndes that folwen the careyne. Swich forseyde folk stranglen spiritually hir lordshipes;/ for which thus seith David the prophete: "Wikked deeth moote come upon thilke lordshipes, and God yeve that they moote descenden into helle al doun; for in hire houses been iniquitees and shrewednesses, and nat God of hevene."/ And certes, but if they doon amendement, right as God yaf his benysoun to [Laban] by the service of Jacob, and to [Pharao] by the service of Joseph, right so God wol yeve his malisoun to swiche lordshipes as sustenen the wikkednesse of hir servauntz, but they come to amendement./ Pride of the table appeereth eek ful ofte; for certes, riche men been cleped to festes, and povre folk been put awey and rebuked./ Also in excesse of diverse metes and drynkes, and namely swich manere bake-metes and dissh-metes, brennynge of wilde fir and peynted and castelled with papir, and semblable wast, so that it is abusioun for to thynke./ And eek in to greet precious- 445 nesse of vessel and curiositee of mynstral-

cie, by whiche a man is stired the moore to delices of luxurie,/ if so be that he sette his herte the lasse upon oure Lord Jhesu Crist, certeyn it is a synne; and certeinly the delices myghte been so grete in this caas that man myghte lightly falle by hem into deedly synne./ The especes that sourden of Pride, soothly whan they sourden of malice ymagined, avised, and forncast, or elles of usage, been deedly synnes, it is no doute./ And whan they sourden by freletee unavysed, and sodeynly withdrawen ayeyn, al been they grevouse synnes, I gesse that they ne been nat deedly./ Now myghte men axe wherof that Pride sourdeth and spryngeth, and I seye, somtyme it spryngeth of the goodes of nature, and somtyme of the goodes of fortune, and somtyme of the goodes of grace./ Certes, the goodes of 450 nature stonden outher in goodes of body or in goodes of soule./ Certes, goodes of body been heele of body, strengthe, delivernesse, beautee, gentrice, franchise./ Goodes of nature of the soule been good wit, sharp understondynge, subtil engyn, vertu natureel, good memorie./ Goodes of fortune been richesse, hyghe degrees of lordshipes, preisynges of the peple./ Goodes of grace been science, power to suffre spiritueel travaille, benignitee, vertuous contemplacioun, withstondynge of temptacioun, and semblable thynges./ Of 455 whiche forseyde goodes, certes it is a ful greet folye a man to priden hym in any of hem alle./ Now as for to speken of goodes of nature, God woot that somtyme we han hem in nature as muche to oure damage as to oure profit./ As for to speken of heele of body, certes it passeth ful lightly, and eek it is ful ofte enchesoun of the siknesse of oure soule. For, God woot, the flessh is a ful greet enemy to the soule; and therfore, the moore that the body is hool, the moore be we in peril to falle./ Eke for to pride hym in his strengthe of body, it is an heigh folye. For certes, the flessh coveiteth agayn the spirit; and ay the moore strong that the flessh is, the sorier may the soule be./ And over al this, strengthe of body and worldly hardynesse causeth ful ofte many a man to peril and meschaunce./ Eek for to pride 460 hym of his gentrie is ful greet folie; for ofte tyme the gentrie of the body binymeth the gentrie of the soule; and eek we ben alle of o fader and of o mooder; and alle we been of o nature, roten and corrupt, bothe riche and povre./ For sothe, o manere gentrie is for to preise, that apparailleth mannes corage with vertues and moralitees, and maketh hym Cristes child./ For truste wel that over what man that synne hath maistrie, he is a verray cherl to synne./

Now been ther generale signes of gentillesse, as eschewynge of vice and ribaudye and servage of synne, in word, in werk, and contenaunce;/ and usynge vertu, curteisye, and clennesse, and to be liberal, that is to seyn, large by mesure; for thilke that passeth mesure is folie and synne./ Another is to remembre hym of   465 bountee, that he of oother folk hath receyved./ Another is to be benigne to his goode subgetis; wherfore seith Senek, "Ther is no thing moore covenable to a man of heigh estaat than debonairetee and pitee./ And therfore thise flyes that men clepen bees, whan they maken hir kyng, they chesen oon that hath no prikke wherwith he may stynge."/ Another is, a man to have a noble herte and a diligent, to attayne to heighe vertuouse thynges./ Now certes, a man to pride hym in the goodes of grace is eek an outrageous folie; for thilke yifte of grace that sholde have turned hym to goodnesse and to medicine, turneth hym to venym and to confusioun, as seith Seint Gregorie./ Certes also, whoso prid-   470 eth hym in the goodes of fortune, he is a ful greet fool; for somtyme is a man a greet lord by the morwe, that is a caytyf and a wrecche er it be nyght;/ and somtyme the richesse of a man is cause of his deth; somtyme the delices of a man ben cause of the grevous maladye thurgh which he dyeth./ Certes, the commendacioun of the peple is somtyme ful fals and ful brotel for to triste; this day they preyse, tomorwe they blame./ God woot, desir to have commendacioun eek of the peple hath caused deeth to many a bisy man./

*Remedium contra peccatum
Superbie.*

Now sith that so is that ye han understonde what is Pride, and whiche been the speces of it, and whennes Pride sourdeth and spryngeth,/ now shul ye understonde which is   475 the remedie agayns the synne of Pride; and that is humylitee, or mekenesse./ That is a vertu thurgh which a man hath verray knoweleche of hymself, and holdeth of hymself no pris ne deyntee, as in regard of his desertes, considerynge evere his freletee./ Now been ther three maneres of humylitee: as humylitee in herte; another humylitee is in his mouth; the thridde in his werkes./ The humilitee in herte is in foure maneres. That oon is whan a man holdeth hymself as noght worth biforn God of hevene. Another is whan he ne despiseth noon oother man./ The thridde is whan he rekketh nat, though men holde hym noght worth. The ferthe is whan he nys nat sory of his humiliacioun./ Also the   480 humilitee of mouth is in foure thynges: in attempree speche, and in humblesse of speche, and whan he biknoweth with his owene mouth that he is swich as hym thynketh that he is in his herte. Another is whan he preiseth the bountee of another man, and nothyng therof amenuseth./ Humilitee eek in werkes is in foure maneres. The firste is whan he putteth othere men biforn hym. The seconde is to chese the loweste place over al. The thridde is gladly to assente to good conseil./ The ferthe is to stonde gladly to the award of his sovereyns, or of hym that is in hyer degree. Certein, this is a greet werk of humylitee./

Sequitur de Invidia.

After Pride wol I speken of the foule synne of Envye, which that is, as by the word of the philosophre, "sorwe of oother mannes prosperitee"; and after the word of Seint Augustyn, it is "sorwe of oother mennes wele, and joye of othere mennes harm."/ This foule synne is platly agayns the Hooly Goost. Al be it so that every synne is agayns the Hooly Goost, yet nathelees, for as muche as bountee aperteneth proprely to the Hooly Goost, and Envye comth proprely of malice, therfore it is proprely agayn the bountee of the Hooly Goost./ Now hath   485 malice two speces; that is to seyn, hardnesse of herte in wikkednesse, or elles the flessh of man is so blynd that he considereth nat that he is in synne, or rekketh nat that he is in synne, which is the hardnesse of the devel./ That oother spece of malice is whan a man werreyeth trouthe, whan he woot that it is trouthe; and eek whan he werreyeth the grace that God hath yeve to his neighebor; and al this is by Envye./ Certes, thanne is Envye the worste synne that is. For soothly, alle othere synnes been somtyme oonly agayns o special vertu;/ but certes, Envye is agayns alle vertues and agayns alle goodnesses. For it is sory of alle

the bountees of his neighebor, and in this manere it is divers from alle othere synnes./ For
wel unnethe is ther any synne that it ne hath
som delit in itself, save oonly Envye, that
evere hath in itself angwissh and sorwe./ 490
The speces of Envye been thise. Ther is
first, sorwe of oother mannes goodnesse and
of his prosperitee; and prosperitee is kyndely
matere of joye; thanne is Envye a synne agayns
kynde./ The seconde spece of Envye is joye
of oother mannes harm; and that is proprely
lyk to the devel, that evere rejoyseth hym of
mannes harm./ Of thise two speces comth bakbityng; and this synne of bakbityng or detraccion hath certeine speces, as thus. Som man
preiseth his neighebor by a wikked entente;/
for he maketh alwey a wikked knotte atte laste
ende. Alwey he maketh a "but" atte laste ende,
that is digne of moore blame, than worth is al
the preisynge./ The seconde spece is that if a
man be good, and dooth or seith a thing to
good entente, the bakbitere wol turne al thilke
goodnesse up-so-doun to his shrewed entente./ The thridde is to amenuse the 495
bountee of his neighebor./ The fourthe
spece of bakbityng is this, that if men speke
goodnesse of a man, thanne wol the bakbitere
seyn, "parfey, swich a man is yet bet than he";
in dispreisynge of hym that men preise./ The
fifte spece is this, for to consente gladly and
herkne gladly to the harm that men speke of
oother folk. This synne is ful greet, and ay
encreesseth after the wikked entente of the
bakbitere./ After bakbityng cometh gruch-
chyng or murmuracioun; and somtyme it
spryngeth of inpacience agayns God, and somtyme agayns man./ Agayn God it is, whan
a man gruccheth agayn the peyne of helle, or
agayns poverte, or los of catel, or agayn reyn
or tempest; or elles gruccheth that shrewes
han prosperitee, or elles for that goode
men han adversitee./ And alle thise 500
thynges sholde man suffre paciently, for
they comen by the rightful juggement and
ordinaunce of God./ Somtyme comth gruch-
ing of avarice; as Judas grucched agayns the
Magdaleyne, whan she enoynted the heved of
oure Lord Jhesu Crist with hir precious oynement./ This manere murmure is swich as whan
man gruccheth of goodnesse that hymself
dooth, or that oother folk doon of hir owene
catel./ Somtyme comth murmure of Pride; as
whan Simon the Pharisee gruchched agayn the
Magdaleyne, whan she approched to Jhesu

Crist, and weep at his feet for hire synnes./
And somtyme grucchyng sourdeth of Envye;
whan men discovereth a mannes harm that
was pryvee, or bereth hym on hond
thyng that is fals./ Murmure eek is ofte 505
amonges servauntz that grucchen whan hir
sovereyns bidden hem doon leveful thynges;/
and forasmuche as they dar nat openly withseye the comaundementz of hir sovereyns, yet
wol they seyn harm, and grucche, and murmure prively for verray despit;/ whiche wordes
men clepen the develes *Pater noster*, though
so be that the devel ne hadde nevere *Pater
noster*, but that lewed folk yeven it swich a
name./ Somtyme it comth of Ire or prive hate,
that norisseth rancour in herte, as afterward I
shal declare./ Thanne cometh eek bitternesse
of herte, thurgh which bitternesse every good
dede of his neighebor semeth to hym bitter and unsavory./ Thanne cometh dis- 510
cord, that unbyndeth alle manere of
freendshipe. Thanne comth scornynge of his
neighebor, al do he never so weel./ Thanne
comth accusynge, as whan man seketh occasioun to anoyen his neighebor, which that is
lyk the craft of the devel, that waiteth bothe
nyght and day to accusen us alle./ Thanne
comth malignitee, thurgh which a man anoyeth his neighebor prively, if he may;/ and if
he noght may, algate his wikked wil ne shal
nat wante, as for to brennen his hous pryvely,
or empoysone or sleen his beestes, and semblable thynges./

Remedium contra peccatum Invidie

Now wol I speke of remedie agayns this
foule synne of Envye. First is the love of God
principal, and lovyng of his neighebor as hymself; for soothly, that oon ne may nat been
withoute that oother./ And truste wel that 515
in the name of thy neighebor thou shalt
understonde the name of thy brother; for certes
alle we have o fader flesshly, and o mooder,
that is to seyn, Adam and Eve; and eek o fader
espiritueel, and that is God of hevene./ Thy
neighebor artow holden for to love, and wilne
hym alle goodnesse; and therfore seith God,
"Love thy neighebor as thyselve," that is to
seyn, to salvacioun bothe of lyf and of soule./
And mooreover thou shalt love hym in word,
and in benigne amonestynge and chastisynge,
and conforten hym in his anoyes, and preye for
hym with al thyn herte./ And in dede thou

shalt love hym in swich wise that thou shalt doon to hym in charitee as thou woldest that it were doon to thyn owene persone./ And therfore thou ne shalt doon hym no damage in wikked word, ne harm in his body, ne in his catel, ne in his soule, by entissyng of wikked ensample./ Thou shalt nat desiren 520 his wyf, ne noon of his thynges. Understoond eek that in the name of neighebor is comprehended his enemy./ Certes, man shal loven his enemy, by the comandement of God; and soothly thy freend shaltow love in God./ I seye, thyn enemy shaltow love for Goddes sake, by his comandement. For if it were reson that man sholde haten his enemy, for sothe God nolde nat receyven us to his love that been his enemys./ Agayns three manere of wronges that his enemy dooth to hym, he shal doon three thynges, as thus./ Agayns hate and rancour of herte, he shal love hym in herte. Agayns chidyng and wikkede wordes, he shal preye for his enemy. Agayns the wikked dede of his enemy, he shal doon hym bountee./ For Crist seith: "Loveth youre ene- 525 mys, and preyeth for hem that speke yow harm, and eek for hem that yow chacen and pursewen, and dooth bountee to hem that yow haten." Loo, thus comaundeth us oure Lord Jhesu Crist to do to oure enemys./ For soothly, nature dryveth us to loven oure freendes, and parfey, oure enemys han moore nede to love than oure freendes; and they that moore nede have, certes to hem shal men doon goodnesse;/ and certes, in thilke dede have we remembraunce of the love of Jhesu Crist that deyde for his enemys./ And in as muche as thilke love is the moore grevous to perfourne, so muche is the moore gret the merite; and therfore the lovynge of oure enemy hath confounded the venym of the devel./ For right as the devel is disconfited by humylitee, right so is he wounded to the deeth by love of oure enemy./ Certes, thanne is love the 530 medicine that casteth out the venym of Envye fro mannes herte./ The speces of this paas shullen be moore largely declared in hir chapitres folwynge./

Sequitur de Ira

After Envye wol I discryven the synne of Ire. For soothly, whoso hath envye upon his neighebor, anon he wole comunly fynde hym a matere of wratthe, in word or in dede, agayns

hym to whom he hath envye./ And as wel comth Ire of Pride, as of Envye; for soothly, he that is proud or envyous is lightly wrooth./

This synne of Ire, after the discryvyng of Seint Augustyn, is wikked wil to been avenged by word or by dede./ Ire, after 535 the philosophre, is the fervent blood of man yquyked in his herte, thurgh which he wole harm to hym that he hateth./ For certes, the herte of man, by eschawfynge and moevynge of his blood, wexeth so trouble that he is out of alle juggement of resoun./ But ye shal understonde that Ire is in two maneres; that oon of hem is good, and that oother is wikked./ The goode Ire is by jalousie of goodnesse, thurgh which a man is wrooth with wikkednesse and agayns wikkednesse; and therfore seith a wys man that Ire is bet than pley./ This Ire is with debonairetee, and it is wrooth withouten bitternesse; nat wrooth agayns the man, but wrooth with the mysdede of the man, as seith the prophete David, "*Irascimini et nolite peccare.*" Now understondeth 540 that wikked Ire is in two maneres; that is to seyn, sodeyn Ire or hastif Ire, withouten avisement and consentynge of resoun./ The menyng and the sens of this is, that the resoun of a man ne consente nat to thilke sodeyn Ire; and thanne is it venial./ Another Ire is ful wikked, that comth of felonie of herte avysed and cast biforn, with wikked wil to do vengeance, and therto his resoun consenteth; and soothly this is deedly synne./ This Ire is so displesant to God that it troubleth his hous, and chaceth the Hooly Goost out of mannes soule, and wasteth and destroyeth the liknesse of God, that is to seyn, the vertu that is in mannes soule,/ and put in hym the liknesse of the devel, and bynymeth the man fro God, that is his rightful lord./ This Ire 545 is a ful greet plesaunce to the devel; for it is the develes fourneys, that is eschawfed with the fir of helle./ For certes, right so as fir is moore mighty to destroyen erthely thynges than any oother element, right so Ire is myghty to destroyen alle spiritueel thynges./ Looke how that fir of smale gleedes, that been almost dede under asshen, wollen quike agayn whan they been touched with brymstoon; right so Ire wol everemo quyken agayn, whan it is touched by the pride that is covered in mannes herte./ For certes, fir ne may nat comen out of no thyng, but if it were first in the same thyng natureelly, as fir is drawen out of flyntes with

steel./ And right so as pride is ofte tyme matere of Ire, right so is rancour norice and
kepere of Ire./ Ther is a maner tree, as   550
seith Seint Ysidre, that whan men maken
fir of thilke tree, and covere the coles of it
with asshen, soothly the fir of it wol lasten al
a yeer or moore./ And right so fareth it of
rancour; whan it is ones conceyved in the
hertes of som men, certein, it wol lasten peraventure from oon Estre day unto another
Estre day, and moore./ But certes, thilke man
is ful fer fro the mercy of God al thilke while./
In this forseyde develes fourneys ther forgen
three shrewes: Pride, that ay bloweth and encreesseth the fir by chidynge and wikked
wordes;/ thanne stant Envye, and holdeth the
hoote iren upon the herte of man with a
peire of longe toonges of long rancour;/   555
and thanne stant the synne of Contumelie,
or strif and cheeste, and batereth and forgeth
by vileyns reprevynges./ Certes, this cursed
synne anoyeth bothe to the man hymself and
eek to his neighebor. For soothly, almoost al
the harm that any man dooth to his neighebor
comth of wratthe./ For certes, outrageous
wratthe dooth al that evere the devel hym
comaundeth; for he ne spareth neither Crist ne
his sweete Mooder./ And in his outrageous anger and ire, allas! allas! ful many oon at that
tyme feeleth in his herte ful wikkedly, bothe
of Crist and eek of alle his halwes./ Is nat this
a cursed vice? Yis, certes. Allas! it bynymeth
from man his wit and his resoun, and al his debonaire lif espiritueel that sholde kepen his
soule./ Certes, it bynymeth eek Goddes   560
due lordshipe, and that is mannes soule,
and the love of his neighebores. It stryveth
eek alday agayn trouthe. It reveth hym the
quiete of his herte, and subverteth his soule./
Of Ire comen thise stynkynge engendrures:
First, hate, that is oold wratthe; discord, thurgh
which a man forsaketh his olde freend that he
hath loved ful longe;/ and thanne cometh
werre, and every manere of wrong that man
dooth to his neighebor, in body or in catel./
Of this cursed synne of Ire cometh eek manslaughtre. And understonde wel that homycide,
that is manslaughtre, is in diverse wise. Som
manere of homycide is spiritueel, and som is
bodily./ Spiritueel manslaughtre is in sixe
thynges. First by hate, as seith Seint John:
"He that hateth his brother is an homycide."/ Homycide is eek by bakbitynge,   565
of whiche bakbiteres seith Salomon that
"they han two swerdes with whiche they sleen
hire neighebores." For soothly, as wikke is to
bynyme his good name as his lyf./ Homycide is
eek in yevynge of wikked conseil by fraude;
as for to yeven conseil to areysen wrongful
custumes and taillages./ Of whiche seith Salomon: "Leon rorynge and bere hongry been like
to the crueel lordshipes in withholdynge or
abreggynge of the shepe (or the hyre), or of
the wages of servauntz, or elles in usure, or
in withdrawynge of the almesse of povre folk./
For which the wise man seith, "Fedeth hym that
almoost dyeth for honger"; for soothly, but if
thow feede hym, thou sleest hym; and alle thise
been deedly synnes./ Bodily manslaughtre is,
whan thow sleest him with thy tonge in oother
manere; as whan thou comandest to sleen a
man, or elles yevest hym conseil to sleen
a man./ Manslaughtre in dede is in foure   570
maneres. That oon is by lawe, right as a
justice dampneth hym that is coupable to the
deeth. But lat the justice be war that he do
it rightfully, and that he do it nat for delit to
spille blood, but for kepynge of rightwisnesse./
Another homycide is that is doon for necessitee,
as whan o man sleeth another in his defendaunt, and that he ne may noon oother wise escape from his owene deeth./ But certeinly if
he may escape withouten slaughtre of his adversarie, and sleeth hym, he dooth synne and
he shal bere penance as for deedly synne./
Eek if a man, by caas or aventure, shete an arwe,
or caste a stoon, with which he sleeth a man,
he is homycide./ Eek if a womman by necligence overlyeth hire child in hir slepyng,
it is homycide and deedly synne./ Eek   575
whan man destourbeth concepcioun of a
child, and maketh a womman outher bareyne
by drynkynge venenouse herbes thurgh which
she may nat conceyve, or sleeth a child by
drynkes wilfully, or elles putteth certeine material thynges in hire secree places to slee the
child,/ or elles dooth unkyndely synne, by
which man or womman shedeth hire nature
in manere or in place ther as a child may nat
be conceived, or elles if a woman have conceyved, and hurt hirself and sleeth the child,
yet is it homycide./ What seye we eek of
wommen that mordren hir children for drede
of worldly shame? Certes, an horrible homicide./ Homycide is eek if a man approcheth
to a womman by desir of lecherie, thurgh which
the child is perissed, or elles smyteth a womman
wityngly, thurgh which she leseth hir child.

Alle thise been homycides and horrible deedly synnes./ Yet comen ther of Ire manye mo synnes, as wel in word as in thoght and in dede; as he that arretteth upon God, or blameth God of thyng of which he is hymself gilty, or despiseth God and alle his halwes, as doon thise cursede hasardours in diverse contrees./ This cursed synne doon they, 580 whan they feelen in hir herte ful wikkedly of God and of his halwes./ Also whan they treten unreverently the sacrement of the auter, thilke synne is so greet that unnethe may it been releessed, but that the mercy of God passeth alle his werkes; it is so greet, and he so benigne./ Thanne comth of Ire attry angre. Whan a man is sharply amonested in his shrifte to forleten his synne,/ thanne wole he be angry, and answeren hokerly and angrily, and deffenden or excusen his synne by unstedefastnesse of his flessh; or elles he dide it for to holde compaignye with his felawes; or elles, he seith, the feend enticed hym;/ or elles he dide it for his youthe; or elles his compleccioun is so corageous that he may nat forbere; or elles it is his destinee, as he seith, unto a certein age; or elles, he seith, it cometh hym of gentillesse of his auncestres; and semblable thynges./ Alle thise manere of folk 585 so wrappen hem in hir synnes that they ne wol nat delivere hemself. For soothly, no wight that excuseth hym wilfully of his synne may nat been delivered of his synne, til that he mekely biknoweth his synne./ After this, thanne cometh sweryng, that is expres agayn the comandement of God; and this bifalleth ofte of anger and of Ire./ God seith: "Thow shalt nat take the name of thy Lord God in veyn or in ydel." Also oure Lord Jhesu Crist seith, by the word of Seint Mathew,/ "Ne wol ye nat swere in alle manere; neither by hevene, for it is Goddes trone; ne by erthe, for it is the bench of his feet; ne by Jerusalem, for it is the citee of a greet kyng; ne by thyn heed, for thou mayst nat make an heer whit ne blak./ But seyeth by youre word 'ye, ye,' and 'nay, nay'; and what that is moore, it is of yvel,"—thus seith Crist./ For Cristes 590 sake, ne swereth nat so synfully in dismembrynge of Crist by soule, herte, bones, and body. For certes, it semeth that ye thynke that the cursede Jewes ne dismembred nat ynough the precioure persone of Crist, but ye dismembre hym moore./ And if so be that the lawe compelle yow to swere, thanne rule yow after

the lawe of God in youre swerying, as seith Jeremye, *quarto capitulo*: "Thou shalt kepe three condicions: thou shalt swere in trouthe, in doom, and in rightwisnesse."/ This is to seyn, thou shalt swere sooth; for every lesynge is agayns Crist. For Crist is verray trouthe. And thynk wel this, that every greet swerere, nat compelled lawefully to swere, the wounde shal nat departe from his hous whil he useth swich unleveful swerying./ Thou shalt sweren eek in doom, whan thou art constreyned by thy domesman to witnessen the trouthe./ Eek thow shalt nat swere for envye, ne for favour, ne for meede, but for rightwisnesse, for declaracioun of it, to the worshipe of God and helpyng of thyne evene-Cristene./ And therfore 595 every man that taketh Goddes name in ydel, or falsly swereth with his mouth, or elles taketh on hym the name of Crist, to be called a Cristen man, and lyveth agayns Cristes lyvynge and his techynge, alle they taken Goddes name in ydel./ Looke eek what seint Peter seith, *Actuum, quarto, Non est aliud nomen sub celo, etc.*, "Ther nys noon oother name," seith Seint Peter, "under hevene yeven to men, in which they mowe be saved"; that is to seyn, but the name of Jhesu Crist./ Take kep eek how precious is the name of Crist, as seith Seint Paul, *ad Philipenses, secundo, In nomine Jhesu, etc.*, "that in the name of Jhesu every knee of hevenely creatures, or erthely, or of helle sholde bowe"; for it is so heigh and so worshipful that the cursede feend in helle sholde tremblen to heeren it ynempned./ Thanne semeth it that men that sweren so horribly by his blessed name, that they despise it moore booldely than dide the cursede Jewes, or elles the devel, that trembleth whan he heereth his name./

Now certes, sith that sweryng, but if it be lawefully doon, is so heighly deffended, muche worse is forsweryng falsly, and yet nedelees./ 600

What seye we eek of hem that deliten hem in sweryng, and holden it a gentrie or a manly dede to swere grete othes? And what of hem that of verray usage ne cesse nat to swere grete othes, al be the cause nat worth a straw? Certes, this is horrible synne./ Swerynge sodeynly withoute avysement is eek a synne./ But lat us go now to thilke horrible sweryng of adjuracioun and conjuracioun, as doon thise false enchauntours or nigromanciens in bacyns ful of water, or in a bright

swerd, in a cercle, or in a fir, or in a shulder-
boon of a sheep./ I kan nat seye but that they
doon cursedly and dampnably agayns Crist and
al the feith of hooly chirche./

What seye we of hem that bileeven on divynailes, as by flight or by noyse of briddes, or
of beestes, or by sort, by nigromancie, by dremes,
by chirkynge of dores, or crakkynge of houses,
by gnawynge of rattes, and swich manere
wrecchednesse?/ Certes, al this thyng is   605
deffended by God and by hooly chirche.
For which they been acursed, til they come
to amendement, that on swich filthe setten hire
bileeve./ Charmes for woundes or maladie of
men or of beestes, if they taken any effect, it
may be peraventure that God suffreth it, for
folk sholden yeve the moore feith and reverence to his name./

Now wol I speken of lesynges, which generally is fals signyficaunce of word, in entente to
deceyven his evene-Cristene./ Som lesynge is
of which ther comth noon avantage to no wight;
and som lesynge turneth to the ese and profit
of o man, and to disese and damage of another
man./ Another lesynge is for to saven his lyf
or his catel. Another lesynge comth of delit
for to lye, in which delit they wol forge a
long tale, and peynten it with alle circumstaunces, where al the ground of the tale
is fals./ Som lesynge comth, for he wole   610
sustene his word; and som lesynge comth
of reccheleesnesse withouten avisement; and
semblable thynges./

Lat us now touche the vice of flaterynge,
which ne comth nat gladly but for drede or
for coveitise./ Flaterye is generally wrongful
preisynge. Flatereres been the develes norices,
that norissen his children with milk of losengerie./ For sothe, Salomon seith that "flaterie
is wors than detraccioun." For somtyme detraccion maketh an hauteyn man be the moore
humble, for he dredeth detraccion; but certes
flaterye, that maketh a man to enhauncen his
herte and his contenaunce./ Flatereres been
the develes enchauntours; for they make a
man to wene of hymself be lyk that he nys
nat lyk./ They been lyk to Judas that bi-   615
traysen a man to sellen hym to his enemy,
that is to the devel./ Flatereres been the develes chapelleyns, that syngen evere *Placebo*./
I rekene flaterie in the vices of Ire; for ofte
tyme, if o man be wrooth with another, thanne
wole he flatere som wight to sustene hym in his
querele./

Speke we now of swich cursynge as comth
of irous herte. Malisoun generally may be
seyd every maner power of harm. Swich cursynge bireveth man fro the regne of God, as
seith Seint Paul./ And ofte tyme swich cursynge wrongfully retorneth agayn to hym that
curseth, as a bryd that retorneth agayn to
his owene nest./ And over alle thyng men   620
oghten eschewe to cursen hire children,
and yeven to the devel hire engendrure, as
ferforth as in hem is. Certes, it is greet peril
and greet synne./

Lat us thanne speken of chidynge and re-
proche, whiche been ful grete woundes in
mannes herte, for they unsowen the semes of
freendshipe in mannes herte./ For certes, unnethes may a man pleynly been accorded with
hym that hath hym openly revyled and repreved and disclaundred. This is a ful grisly
synne, as Crist seith in the gospel./ And taak
kep now, that he that repreveth his neighebor,
outher he repreveth hym by som harm of peyne
that he hath on his body, as "mesel," "croked
harlot," or by som synne that he dooth./ Now
if he repreve hym by harm of peyne, thanne
turneth the repreve to Jhesu Crist, for peyne
is sent by the rightwys sonde of God, and
by his suffrance, be it meselrie, or maheym, or maladie./ And if he repreve hym   625
uncharitably of synne, as "thou holour,"
"thou dronkelewe harlot," and so forth, thanne
aperteneth that to the rejoysynge of the devel,
that evere hath joye that men doon synne./
And certes, chidynge may nat come but out
of a vileyns herte. For after the habundance
of the herte speketh the mouth ful ofte./ And
ye shul understonde that looke, by any wey,
whan any man shal chastise another, that he
be war from chidynge or reprevynge. For
trewely, but he be war, he may ful lightly
quyken the fir of angre and of wratthe, which
that he sholde quenche, and peraventure sleeth
hym, which that he myghte chastise with benignitee./ For as seith Salomon, "The amyable
tonge is the tree of lyf," that is to seyn, of lyf
espiritueel; and soothly, a deslavee tonge sleeth
the spirites of hym that repreveth and eek of
hym that is repreved./ Loo, what seith Seint
Augustyn: "Ther is nothyng so lyk the develes
child as he that ofte chideth." Seint Paul seith
eek, "The servant of God bihoveth nat to
chide."/ And how that chidynge be a   630
vileyns thyng bitwixe alle manere folk,
yet is it certes moost uncovenable bitwixe **a**

man and his wyf; for there is nevere reste. And therfore seith Salomon, "An hous that is uncovered and droppynge, and a chidynge wyf, been lyke."/ A man that is in a droppynge hous in manye places, though he eschewe the droppynge in o place, it droppeth on hym in another place. So fareth it by a chydynge wyf; but she chide hym in o place, she wol chide hym in another./ And therfore, "bettre is a morsel of breed with joye than an hous ful of delices with chidynge," seith Salomon./ Seint Paul seith: "O ye wommen, be ye subgetes to youre housbondes as bihoveth in God, and ye men loveth youre wyves." *Ad Colossenses, tertio.*/

Afterward speke we of scornynge, which is a wikked synne, and namely whan he scorneth a man for his goode werkes./ 635 For certes, swiche scorneres faren lyk the foule tode, that may nat endure to smelle the soote savour of the vyne whanne it florisseth./ Thise scorneres been partyng felawes with the devel; for they han joye whan the devel wynneth, and sorwe whan he leseth./ They been adversaries of Jhesu Crist, for they haten that he loveth, that is to seyn, salvacioun of soule./

Speke we now of wikked conseil; for he that wikked conseil yeveth is a traytour. For he deceyveth hym that trusteth in hym, *ut Achitofel ad Absolonem.* But nathelees, yet is his wikked conseil first agayn hymself./ For, as seith the wise man, "Every fals lyvynge hath this propertee in hymself, that he that wole anoye another man, he anoyeth first hymself."/ 640 And men shul understonde that man shal nat taken his conseil of fals folk, ne of angry folk, or grevous folk, ne of folk that loven specially to muchel hir owene profit, ne to muche worldly folk, namely in conseilynge of soules./

Now comth the synne of hem that sowen and maken discord amonges folk, which is a synne that Crist hateth outrely. And no wonder is; for he deyde for to make concord./ And moore shame do they to Crist, than dide they that hym crucifiede; for God loveth bettre that freendshipe be amonges folk, than he dide his owene body, the which that he yaf for unitee. Therfore been they likned to the devel, that evere is aboute to maken discord./

Now comth the synne of double tonge; swiche as speken faire byforn folk, and wikkedly bihynde; or elles they maken semblant as though they speeke of good entencioun, or

elles in game and pley, and yet they speke of wikked entente./

Now comth biwreying of conseil, thurgh which a man is defamed; certes, unnethe may he restoore the damage./ 645

Now comth manace, that is an open folye; for he that ofte manaceth, he threteth moore than he may perfourne ful ofte tyme./

Now cometh ydel wordes, that is withouten profit of hym that speketh tho wordes, and eek of hym that herkneth tho wordes. Or elles ydel wordes been tho that been nedelees, or withouten entente of natureel profit./ And al be it that ydel wordes been somtyme venial synne, yet sholde men douten hem, for we shul yeve rekenynge of hem bifore God./

Now comth janglynge, that may nat been withoute synne. And, as seith Salomon, "It is a sygne of apert folye."/ And therfore a philosophre seyde, whan men axed hym how that men sholde plese the peple, and he answerde, "Do manye goode werkes, and spek fewe jangles."/ 650

After this comth the synne of japeres, that been the develes apes; for they maken folk to laughe at hire japerie as folk doon at the gawdes of an ape. Swiche japes deffendeth Seint Paul./ Looke how that vertuouse wordes and hooly conforten hem that travaillen in the service of Crist, right so conforten the vileyns wordes and knakkes of japeris hem that travaillen in the service of the devel./ Thise been the synnes that comen of the tonge, that comen of Ire and of othere synnes mo./

Sequitur remedium contra peccatum Ire

The remedie agayns Ire is a vertu that men clepen Mansuetude, that is Debonairetee; and eek another vertu, that men callen Pacience or Suffrance./

Debonairetee withdraweth and refreyneth the stirynges and the moevynges of mannes corage in his herte, in swich manere that they ne skippe nat out by angre ne by ire./ Suf- 655 france suffreth swetely alle the anoyaunces and the wronges that men doon to man outward./ Seint Jerome seith thus of debonairetee, that "it dooth noon harm to no wight ne seith; ne for noon harm that men doon or seyn, he ne eschawfeth nat agayns his resoun."/ This vertu somtyme comth of nature; for, as seith the philosophre, "A man is a quyk thyng, by

nature debonaire and tretable to goodnesse;
but whan debonairetee is enformed of grace,
thanne is it the moore worth."/

Pacience, that is another remedie agayns Ire,
is a vertu that suffreth swetely every mannes
goodnesse, and is nat wrooth for noon harm
that is doon to hym./ The philosophre seith
that pacience is thilke vertu that suffreth
debonairely alle the outrages of adversitee
and every wikked word./ This vertu mak-   660
eth a man lyk to God, and maketh hym
Goddes owene deere child, as seith Crist. This
vertu disconfiteth thyn enemy. And therfore
seith the wise man, "If thow wolt venquysse
thyn enemy, lerne to suffre."/ And thou shalt
understonde that man suffreth foure manere of
grevances in outward thynges, agayns the
whiche foure he moot have foure manere of
paciences./

The firste grevance is of wikkede wordes.
Thilke suffrede Jhesu Crist withouten grucchyng, ful paciently, whan the Jewes despised
and repreved hym ful ofte./ Suffre thou therfore paciently; for the wise man seith, "If thou
stryve with a fool, though the fool be wrooth
or though he laughe, algate thou shalt have no
reste."/ That oother grevance outward is to
have damage of thy catel. Theragayns suffred Crist ful paciently, whan he was despoyled
of al that he hadde in this lyf, and that nas
but his clothes./ The thridde grevance is a   665
man to have harm in his body. That suffred Crist ful paciently in al his passioun./ The
fourthe grevance is in outrageous labour in
werkes. Wherfore I seye that folk that maken
hir servantz to travaillen to grevously, or out
of tyme, as on haly dayes, soothly they do greet
synne./ Heer-agayns suffred Crist ful paciently
and taughte us pacience, whan he baar upon
his blissed shulder the croys upon which he
sholde suffren despitous deeth./ Heere may
men lerne to be pacient; for certes noght oonly
Cristen men been pacient, for love of Jhesu
Crist, and for gerdoun of the blisful lyf that
is perdurable, but certes, the olde payens that
nevere were Cristene, commendeden and useden the vertu of pacience./

A philosophre upon a tyme, that wolde have
beten his disciple for his grete trespas, for
which he was greetly amoeved, broghte
a yerde to scoure with the child;/ and   670
whan this child saugh the yerde, he seyde
to his maister, "What thenke ye do?" "I wol
bete thee," quod the maister, "for thy correc-

cioun."/ "For sothe," quod the child, "ye
oghten first correcte youreself, that han lost
al youre pacience for the gilt of a child."/
"For sothe," quod the maister al wepynge,
"thow seyst sooth. Have thow the yerde, my
deere sone, and correcte me for myn inpacience."/ Of pacience comth obedience, thurgh
which a man is obedient to Crist and to alle
hem to whiche he oghte to been obedient in
Crist./ And understond wel that obedience is
perfit, whan that a man dooth gladly and
hastily, with good herte entierly, al that
he sholde do./ Obedience generally is to   675
perfourne the doctrine of God and of his
sovereyns, to whiche hym oghte to ben obeisaunt in alle rightwisnesse./

Sequitur de Accidia

After the synne of Envye and of Ire, now
wol I speken of the synne of Accidie. For
Envye blyndeth the herte of a man, and Ire
troubleth a man, and Accidie maketh hym
hevy, thoghtful, and wraw./ Envye and Ire
maken bitternesse in herte, which bitternesse
is mooder of Accidie, and bynymeth hym the
love of alle goodnesse. Thanne is Accidie the
angwissh of troubled herte; and Seint Augustyn
seith, "It is anoy of goodnesse and Ioye of
harm."/ Certes, this is a dampnable synne;
for it dooth wrong to Jhesu Crist, in as muche
as it bynymeth the service that men oghte doon
to Crist with alle diligence, as seith Salomon./
But Accidie dooth no swich diligence. He
dooth alle thyng with anoy, and with wraw-
nesse, slaknesse, and excusacioun, and with
ydelnesse, and unlust; for which the book seith,
"Acursed be he that dooth the service of
God necligently."/ Thanne is Accidie en-   680
emy to everich estaat of man; for certes,
the estaat of man is in three maneres./ Outher
it is th'estaat of innocence, as was th'estaat of
Adam biforn that he fil into synne; in which
estaat he was holden to wirche as in heriynge
and adowrynge of God./ Another estaat is the
estaat of synful men, in which estaat men been
holden to laboure in preiynge to God for
amendement of hire synnes, and that he wole
graunte hem to arysen out of hir synnes./ Another estaat is th'estaat of grace; in which estaat
he is holden to werkes of penitence. And certes,
to alle thise thynges is Accidie enemy and contrarie, for he loveth no bisynesse at al./ Now
certes, this foule synne, Accidie, is eek a ful

greet enemy to the liflode of the body; for it
ne hath no purveaunce agayn temporeel necessitee; for it forsleweth and forsluggeth and destroyeth alle goodes temporeles by reccheleesnesse./   685

The fourthe thyng is that Accidie is lyk
hem that been in the peyne of helle, by cause
of hir slouthe and of hire hevynesse; for they
that been dampned been so bounde that they
ne may neither wel do ne wel thynke./ Of
Accidie comth first, that a man is anoyed and
encombred for to doon any goodnesse, and
maketh that God hath abhomynacion of swich
Accidie, as seith Seint John./

Now comth Slouthe, that wol nat suffre
noon hardnesse ne no penaunce. For soothly,
Slouthe is so tendre and so delicaat, as seith
Salomon, that he wol nat suffre noon hardnesse
ne penaunce, and therfore he shendeth al that
he dooth./ Agayns this roten-herted synne of
Accidie and Slouthe sholde men exercise hemself to doon goode werkes, and manly and vertuously cacchen corage wel to doon, thynkynge
that oure Lord Jhesu Crist quiteth every good
dede, be it never so lite./ Usage of labour is
a greet thyng, for it maketh, as seith Seint Bernard, the laborer to have stronge armes and
harde synwes; and slouthe maketh hem
feble and tendre./ Thanne comth drede   690
to bigynne to werke anye goode werkes.
For certes, he that is enclyned to synne, hym
thynketh it is so greet an emprise for to undertake to doon werkes of goodnesse,/ and
casteth in his herte that the circumstaunces of
goodnesse been so grevouse and so chargeaunt
for to suffre, that he dar nat undertake to do
werkes of goodnesse, as seith Seint Gregorie./

Now comth wanhope, that is despeir of the
mercy of God, that comth somtyme of to muche
outrageous sorwe, and somtyme of to muche
drede, ymaginynge that he hath doon so muche
synne that it wol nat availlen hym, though
he wolde repenten hym and forsake synne;/
thurgh which despeir or drede he abaundoneth al his herte to every maner synne, as seith
Seint Augustin./ Which dampnable synne, if
that it continue unto his ende, it is cleped
synnyng in the Hooly Goost./ This hor-   695
rible synne is so perilous that he that is
despeired, ther nys no felonye ne no synne that
he douteth for to do; as shewed wel by Judas./
Certes, aboven alle synnes thanne is this synne
moost displesant to Crist, and moost adversarie./ Soothly, he that despeireth hym is lyk

the coward champioun recreant, that seith
"creant" withoute nede, allas! allas! nedeles is
he recreant and nedelees despeired./ Certes,
the mercy of God is evere redy to the penitent,
and is aboven alle his werkes./ Allas! kan a
man nat bithynke hym on the gospel of Seint
Luc, 15, where as Crist seith that "as wel shal
ther be joye in hevene upon a synful man that
dooth penitence, as upon nynty and nyne
rightful men that neden no penitence."/   700
Looke forther, in the same gospel, the joye
and the feeste of the goode man that hadde
lost his sone, whan his sone with repentaunce
was retourned to his fader./ Kan they nat remembren hem eek that, as seith Seint Luc, 23,
how that the theef that was hanged bisyde
Jhesu Crist, seyde: "Lord, remembre of me,
whan thow comest into thy regne"?/ "For
sothe," seyde Crist, "I seye to thee, to-day
shaltow been with me in paradys."/ Certes,
ther is noon so horrible synne of man that it
ne may in his lyf be destroyed by penitence,
thurgh vertu of the passion and of the deeth
of Crist./ Allas! what nedeth man thanne to
been despeired, sith that his mercy so redy
is and large? Axe and have./ Thanne com-   705
eth sompnolence, that is, sloggy slombr-
ynge, which maketh a man be hevy and dul
in body and in soule; and this synne comth
of Slouthe./ And certes, the tyme that, by wey
of resoun, men sholde nat slepe, that is by the
morwe, but if ther were cause resonable./ For
soothly, the morwe tyde is moost covenable a
man to seye his preyeres, and for to thynken on
God, and for to honoure God, and to yeven
almesse to the povre that first cometh in the
name of Crist./ Lo, what seith Salomon:
"Whoso wolde by the morwe awaken and
seke me, he shal fynde."/ Thanne cometh necligence, or reccheleesnesse, that rekketh of
no thyng. And how that ignoraunce be
mooder of alle harm, certes, necligence
is the norice./ Necligence ne dooth no   710
fors, whan he shal doon a thyng, wheither
he do it weel or baddely./

Of the remedie of thise two synnes, as seith
the wise man, that "he that dredeth God, he
spareth nat to doon that him oghte doon."/
And he that loveth God, he wol doon diligence
to plese God by his werkes, and abaundone
hymself, with al his myght, wel for to doon./
Thanne comth ydelnesse, that is the yate of alle
harmes. An ydel man is lyk to a place that hath
no walles; the develes may entre on every syde,

or sheten at hym at discovert, by temptacion on every syde./ This ydelnesse is the thurrok of alle wikked and vileyns thoghtes, and of alle jangles, trufles, and of alle ordure./ 715 Certes, the hevene is yeven to hem that wol labourn, and nat to ydel folk. Eek David seith that "they ne been nat in the labour of men, ne they shul nat been whipped with men," that is to seyn, in purgatorie./ Certes, thanne semeth it, they shul be tormented with the devel in helle, but if they doon penitence./

Thanne comth the synne that men clepen *tarditas*, as whan a man is to laterede or tariynge, er he wole turne to God; and certes, that is a greet folie. He is lyk to hym that falleth in the dych, and wol nat arise./ And this vice comth of a fals hope, that he thynketh that he shal lyve longe; but that hope faileth ful ofte./ Thanne comth lachesse; that is he, that whan he biginneth any good werk, anon he shal forleten it and stynten; as doon they that han any wight to governe, and ne taken of hym namoore kep, anon as they fynden any contrarie or any anoy./ Thise been 720 the newe sheepherdes that leten hir sheep wityngly go renne to the wolf that is in the breres, or do no fors of hir owene governaunce./ Of this comth poverte and destruccioun, bothe of spiritueel and temporeel thynges. Thanne comth a manere cooldnesse, that freseth al the herte of a man./ Thanne comth undevocioun, thurgh which a man is so blent, as seith Seint Bernard, and hath swich langour in soule that he may neither rede ne singe in hooly chirche, ne heere ne thynke of no devocioun, ne travaille with his handes in no good werk, that it nys hym unsavory and al apalled./ Thanne wexeth he slough and slombry, and soone wol be wrooth, and soone is enclyned to hate and to envye./ Thanne comth the synne of worldly sorwe, swich as is cleped *tristicia*, that sleeth man, as seith Seint Paul./ For 725 certes, swich sorwe werketh to the deeth of the soule and of the body also; for therof comth that a man is anoyed of his owene lif./ Wherfore swich sorwe shorteth ful ofte the lif of man, er that his tyme be come by wey of kynde./

Remedium contra peccatum Accidie.

Agayns this horrible synne of Accidie, and the branches of the same, ther is a vertu that is called *fortitudo* or strengthe, that is an affeccioun thurgh which a man despiseth anoyouse thinges./ This vertu is so myghty and so vigerous that it dar withstonde myghtily and wisely kepen hymself fro perils that been wikked, and wrastle agayn the assautes of the devel./ For it enhaunceth and enforceth the soule, right as Accidie abateth it and maketh it fieble. For this *fortitudo* may endure by long suffraunce the travailles that been covenable./ 730

This vertu hath manye speces; and the firste is cleped magnanimitee, that is to seyn, greet corage. For certes, ther bihoveth greet corage agains Accidie, lest that it ne swolwe the soule by the synne of sorwe, or destroye it by wanhope./ This vertu maketh folk to undertake harde thynges and grevouse thynges, by hir owene wil, wisely and resonably./ And for as muchel as the devel fighteth agayns a man moore by queyntise and by sleighte than by strengthe, therfore men shal withstonden hym by wit and by resoun and by discrecioun./ Thanne arn ther the vertues of feith and hope in God and in his seintes, to acheve and acomplice the goode werkes in the whiche he purposeth fermely to continue./ Thanne comth seuretee or sikernesse; and that is whan a man ne douteth no travaille in tyme comynge of the goode werkes that a man hath bigonne./ Thanne comth magnificence, that 735 is to seyn, whan a man dooth and perfourneth grete werkes of goodnesse; and that is the ende why that men sholde do goode werkes, for in the acomplissynge of grete goode werkes lith the grete gerdoun./ Thanne is ther constaunce, that is, stablenesse of corage; and this sholde been in herte by stedefast feith, and in mouth, and in berynge, and in chiere, and in dede./ Eke ther been mo speciale remedies against Accidie in diverse werkes, and in consideracioun of the peynes of helle and of the joyes of hevene, and in the trust of the grace of the Holy Goost, that wole yeve hym myght to perfourne his goode entente./

Sequitur de Avaricia.

After Accidie wol I speke of Avarice and of Coveitise, of which synne seith Seint Paul that "the roote of alle harmes is Coveitise." *Ad Thimotheum Sexto.*/ For soothly, whan the herte of a man is confounded in itself and troubled, and that the soule hath lost the confort of God, thanne seketh he an ydel solas of worldly thynges./ 740

Avarice, after the descripcioun of Seint Augustyn, is a likerousnesse in herte to have erthely thynges./ Som oother folk seyn that Avarice is for to purchacen manye erthely thynges, and no thyng yeve to hem that han nede./ And understoond that Avarice ne stant nat oonly in lond ne catel, but somtyme in science and in glorie, and in every manere of outrageous thyng is Avarice and Coveitise./ And the difference bitwixe Avarice and Coveitise is this: Coveitise is for to coveite swiche thynges as thou hast nat; and Avarice is for to withholde and kepe swiche thynges as thou hast, withoute rightful nede./ Soothly, this Avarice is a synne that is ful dampnable; for al hooly writ curseth it, and speketh agayns that vice; for it dooth wrong to Jhesu Crist./ For it bireveth hym the love that   745 men to hym owen, and turneth it bakward agayns alle resoun,/ and maketh that the avaricious man hath moore hope in his catel than in Jhesu Crist, and dooth moore observance in kepynge of his tresor than he dooth to the service of Jhesu Crist./ And therfore seith Seint Paul *ad Ephesios, quinto,* that an avaricious man is in the thraldom of ydolatrie./

What difference is bitwixe an ydolastre and an avaricious man, but that an ydolastre, per aventure, ne hath but o mawmet or two, and the avaricious man hath manye? For certes, every floryn in his cofre is his mawmet./ And certes, the synne of mawmettrie is the firste thyng that God deffended in the ten comaundementz, as bereth witnesse in *Exodi capitulo vicesimo.*/ "Thou shalt have no false   750 goddes bifore me, ne thou shalt make to thee no grave thyng." Thus is an avaricious man, that loveth his tresor biforn God, an ydolastre,/ thurgh this cursed synne of avarice. Of Coveitise comen thise harde lordshipes, thurgh whiche men been distreyned by taylages, custumes, and cariages, moore than hire duetee or resoun is. And eek taken they of hire bonde-men amercimentz, whiche myghten moore resonably ben cleped extorcions than amercimentz./ Of whiche amercimentz and raunsonynge of boonde-men somme lordes stywardes seyn that it is rightful, for as muche as a cherl hath no temporeel thyng that it ne is his lordes, as they seyn./ But certes, thise lordshipes doon wrong that bireven hire bondefolk thynges that they nevere yave hem. *Augustinus, de Civitate, libro nono.*/ Sooth is that the condicioun of thraldom and the firste

cause of thraldom is for synne. *Genesis, nono.*/   755
Thus may ye seen that the gilt disserveth thraldom, but nat nature./ Wherfore thise lordes ne sholde nat muche glorifien hem in hir lordshipes, sith that by natureel condicion they been nat lordes over thralles, but that thraldom comth first by the desert of synne./ And forther over, ther as the lawe seith that temporeel goodes of boonde-folk been the goodes of hir lordshipes, ye, that is for to understonde, the goodes of the emperour, to deffenden hem in hir right, but nat for to robben hem ne reven hem./ And therfore seith Seneca, "Thy prudence sholde lyve benignely with thy thralles."/ Thilke that thou clepest thy thralles been Goddes peple; for humble folk been Cristes freendes; they been contubernyal with the Lord./   760
Thynk eek that of swich seed as cherles spryngen, of swich seed spryngen lordes. As wel may the cherl be saved as the lord./ The same deeth that taketh the cherl, swich deeth taketh the lord. Wherfore I rede, do right so with thy cherl, as thou woldest that thy lord dide with thee, if thou were in his plit./ Every synful man is a cherl to synne. I rede thee, certes, that thou, lord, werke in swich wise with thy cherles that they rather love thee than drede./ I woot wel ther is degree above degree, as reson is; and skile is that men do hir devoir ther as it is due; but certes, extorcions and despit of youre underlynges is dampnable./

And forther over, understoond wel that thise conquerours or tirauntz maken ful ofte thralles of hem that been born of as roial blood as been they that hem conqueren./ This   765 name of thraldom was nevere erst kowth, til that Noe seyde that his sone Canaan sholde be thral to his bretheren for his synne./ What seye we thanne of hem that pilen and doon extorcions to hooly chirche? Certes, the swerd that men yeven first to a knyght, whan he is newe dubbed, signifieth that he sholde deffenden hooly chirche, and nat robben it ne pilen it; and whoso dooth is traitour to Crist./ And, as seith Seint Augustyn, "they been the develes wolves that stranglen the sheep of Jhesu Crist"; and doon worse than wolves./ For soothly, whan the wolf hath ful his wombe, he stynteth to strangle sheep. But soothly, the pilours and destroyours of the godes of hooly chirche no do nat so, for they ne stynte nevere to pile./ Now as I have seyd, sith so is that synne was first cause of thraldom, thanne is it thus, that thilke tyme that al this world was in synne, thanne was al this world in thraldom and subjeccioun./ But certes, sith the 770 time of grace cam, God ordeyned that som folk sholde be moore heigh in estaat and in degree, and som folk moore lough, and that everich sholde be served in his estaat and in his degree./ And therfore in somme contrees, ther they byen thralles, whan they han turned hem to the feith, they maken hire thralles free out of thraldom. And therfore, certes, the lord oweth to his man that the man oweth to his lord./ The Pope calleth hymself servant of the servantz of God; but for as muche as the estaat of hooly chirche ne myghte nat han be, ne the commune profit myghte nat han be kept, ne pees and rest in erthe, but if God hadde ordeyned that som men hadde hyer degree and som men lower,/ therfore was sovereyntee ordeyned, to kepe and mayntene and deffenden hire underlynges or hire subgetz in resoun, as ferforth as it lith in hire power, and nat to destroyen hem ne confounde./ Wherfore I seye that thilke lordes that been lyk wolves, that devouren the possessiouns or the catel of povre folk wrongfully, withouten mercy or mesure,/ they shul receyven, by the same 775 mesure that they han mesured to povre folk, the mercy of Jhesu Crist, but if it be amended./ Now comth deceite bitwixe marchaunt and marchant. And thow shalt understonde that marchandise is in manye maneres; that oon is bodily, and that oother is goostly; that oon is honest and leveful, and that oother is deshonest and unleveful./ Of thilke bodily marchandise that is leveful and honest is this: that, there as God hath ordeyned that a regne or a contree is suffisaunt to hymself, thanne is it honest and leveful that of habundaunce of this contree, that men helpe another contree that is moore nedy./ And therfore ther moote been marchantz to bryngen fro that o contree to that oother hire marchandises./ That oother marchandise, that men haunten with fraude and trecherie and deceite, with lesynges and false othes, is cursed and dampnable./ Es- 780 pirituel marchandise is proprely symonye, that is, ententif desir to byen thyng espiritueel, that is, thyng that aperteneth to the seintuarie of God and to cure of the soule./ This desir, if so be that a man do his diligence to parfournen it, al be it that his desir ne take noon effect, yet is it to hym a deedly synne; and if

he be ordred, he is irreguleer./ Certes symonye is cleped of Simon Magus, that wolde han boght for temporeel catel the yifte that God hadde yeven, by the Hooly Goost, to Seint Peter and to the apostles./ And therfore understoond that bothe he that selleth and he that beyeth thynges espirituels been cleped symonyals, be it by catel, be it by procurynge, or by flesshly preyere of his freendes, flesshly freendes, or espiritueel freendes./ Flesshly in two maneres; as by kynrede, or othere freendes. Soothly, if they praye for hym that is nat worthy and able, it is symonye, if he take the benefice; and if he be worthy and able, ther nys noon./ That oother manere is 785 whan men or wommen preyen for folk to avauncen hem, oonly for wikked flesshly affeccioun that they han unto the persone; and that is foul symonye./ But certes, in service, for which men yeven thynges espirituels unto hir servantz, it moot been understonde that the service moot been honest, and elles nat; and eek that it be withouten bargaynynge, and that the persone be able./ For, as seith Seint Damasie, "Alle the synnes of the world, at regard of this synne, arn as thyng of noght." For it is the gretteste synne that may be, after the synne of Lucifer and Antecrist./ For by this synne God forleseth the chirche and the soule that he boghte with his precious blood, by hem that yeven chirches to hem that been nat digne./ For they putten in theves that stelen the soules of Jhesu Crist and destroyen his patrimoyne./ By swiche undigne preestes 790 and curates han lewed men the lasse reverence of the sacramentz of hooly chirche; and swiche yeveres of chirches putten out the children of Crist, and putten into the chirche the develes owene sone./ They sellen the soules that lambes sholde kepen to the wolf that strangleth hem. And therfore shul they nevere han part of the pasture of lambes, that is the blisse of hevene./ Now comth hasardrie with his apurtenaunces, as tables and rafles, of which comth deceite, false othes, chidynges, and alle ravynes, blasphemynge and reneiynge of God, and hate of his neighebores, wast of goodes, mysspendynge of tyme, and somtyme manslaughtre./ Certes, hasardours ne mowe nat been withouten greet synne whiles they haunte that craft./ Of Avarice comen eek lesynges, thefte, fals witnesse, and false othes. And ye shul understonde that thise been grete synnes, and expres agayn the comaundementz of

God, as I have seyd./ Fals witnesse is in 795
word and eek in dede. In word, as for to
bireve thy neighebores goode name by thy fals
witnessyng, or bireven hym his catel or his
heritage by thy fals witnessyng, whan thou for
ire, or for meede, or for envye, berest fals
witnesse, or accusest hym or excusest hym by
thy fals witnesse, or elles excusest thyself
falsly./ Ware yow, questemongeres and notaries! Certes, for fals witnessyng was Susanna
in ful gret sorwe and peyne, and many another
mo./ The synne of thefte is eek expres agayns
Goddes heeste, and that in two maneres, corporeel or spiritueel./ Corporeel, as for to take
thy neighebores catel agayn his wyl, be it by
force or by sleighte, be it by met or by mesure;/ by stelyng eek of false enditementz upon
hym, and in borwynge of thy neighebores catel,
in entente nevere to payen it agayn, and
semblable thynges./ Espiritueel thefte is 800
sacrilege, that is to seyn, hurtynge of hooly
thynges, or of thynges sacred to Crist, in two
maneres: by reson of the hooly place, as
chirches or chirche-hawes,/ for which every
vileyns synne that men doon in swiche places
may be cleped sacrilege, or every violence in
the semblable places; also, they that withdrawen falsly the rightes that longen to hooly
chirche./ And pleynly and generally, sacrilege
is to reven hooly thyng fro hooly place, or unhooly thyng out of hooly place, or hooly thing
out of unhooly place./

Relevacio contra peccatum Avaricie.

Now shul ye understonde that the releevynge
of Avarice is misericorde, and pitee largely
taken. And men myghten axe why that misericorde and pitee is releevynge of Avarice./
Certes, the avricious man sheweth no pitee ne
misericorde to the nedeful man, for he deliteth hym in the kepynge of his tresor, and nat
in the rescowynge ne releevynge of his evene-
Cristen. And therfore speke I first of misericorde./ Thanne is misericorde, as seith 805
the philosophre, a vertu by which the corage of a man is stired by the mysese of hym
that is mysesed./ Upon which misericorde
folweth pitee in parfournynge of charitable
werkes of misericorde./ And certes, thise
thynges moeven a man to the misericorde of
Jhesu Crist, that he yaf hymself for oure gilt,
and suffred deeth for misericorde, and forgaf
us oure originale synnes,/ and therby relessed

us fro the peynes of helle, and amenused the
peynes of purgatorie by penitence, and yeveth
grace wel to do, and atte laste the blisse of
hevene./ The speces of misericorde been, as
for to lene and for to yeve, and to foryeven
and relesse, and for to han pitee in herte
and compassioun of the meschief of his evene-
Cristene, and eek to chastise, there as nede
is./ Another manere of remedie agayns 810
avarice is resonable largesse; but soothly,
heere bihoveth the consideracioun of the grace
of Jhesu Crist, and of his temporeel goodes,
and eek of the goodes perdurables, that Crist
yaf to us;/ and to han remembrance of the
deeth that he shal receyve, he noot whanne,
where, ne how; and eek that he shal forgon al
that he hath, save oonly that he hath despended
in goode werkes./

But for as muche as som folk been unmesurable, men oghten eschue fool-largesse, that
men clepen wast./ Certes, he that is fool-large
ne yeveth nat his catel, but he leseth his catel.
Soothly, what thyng that he yeveth for veyne
glorie, as to mynstrals and to folk, for to beren
his renoun in the world, he hath synne therof,
and noon almesse./ Certes, he leseth foule his
good, that ne seketh with the yifte of his
good nothyng but synne./ He is lyk to an 815
hors that seketh rather to drynken drovy
or trouble water than for to drynken water of
the clere welle./ And for as muchel as they
yeven ther as they sholde nat yeven, to hem
aperteneth thilke malisoun that Crist shal
yeven at the day of doom to hem that shullen
been dampned./

Sequitur de Gulâ.

After Avarice comth Glotonye, which is expres eek agayn the comandement of God. Glotonye is unmesurable appetit to ete or to drynke,
or elles to doon ynogh to the unmesurable appetit and desordeynee coveitise to eten or to
drynke./ This synne corrumped al this world,
as is wel shewed in the synne of Adam and of
Eve. Looke eek what seith Seint Paul of Glotonye:/ "Manye," seith Saint Paul, "goon, of
whiche I have ofte seyd to yow, and now I
seye it wepynge, that been the enemys of the
croys of Crist; of whiche the ende is deeth, and
of whiche hire wombe is hire god, and hire
glorie in confusioun of hem that so sa-
vouren erthely thynges."/ He that is 820
usaunt to this synne of glotonye, he ne

may no synne withstonde. He moot been in servage of alle vices, for it is the develes hoord ther he hideth hym and resteth./ This synne hath manye speces. The firste is dronkenesse, that is the horrible sepulture of mannes resoun; and therfore, whan a man is dronken, he hath lost his resoun; and this is deedly synne./ But soothly, whan that a man is nat wont to strong drynke, and peraventure ne knoweth nat the strengthe of the drynke, or hath feblesse in his heed, or hath travailed, thurgh which he drynketh the moore, al be he sodeynly caught with drynke, it is no deedly synne, but venyal./ The seconde spece of glotonye is that the spirit of a man wexeth al trouble, for dronkenesse bireveth hym the discrecioun of his wit./ The thridde spece of glotonye is whan a man devoureth his mete, and hath no rightful manere of etynge./ The fourthe is whan, thurgh the grete habundaunce of his mete, the humours in his body been distempred./ The fifthe is foryetelnesse by to muchel drynkynge; for which somtyme a man foryeteth er the morwe what he dide at even, or on the nyght biforn./ 825

In oother manere been distinct the speces of Glotonye, after Seint Gregorie. The firste is for to ete biforn tyme to ete. The seconde is whan a man get hym to delicaat mete or drynke./ The thridde is whan men taken to muche over mesure. The fourthe is curiositee, with greet entente to maken and apparaillen his mete. The fifthe is for to eten to gredily./ Thise been the fyve fyngres of the develes hand, by whiche he draweth folk to synne./ 830

Remedium contra peccatum Gule.

Agayns Glotonye is the remedie abstinence, as seith Galien; but that holde I nat meritorie, if he do it oonly for the heele of his body. Seint Augustyn wole that abstinence be doon for vertu and with pacience./ "Abstinence," he seith, "is litel worth, but if a man have good wil therto, and but it be enforced by pacience and by charitee, and that men doon it for Godes sake, and in hope to have the blisse of hevene."/

The felawes of abstinence been attemperaunce, that holdeth the meene in alle thynges; eek shame, that eschueth alle deshonestee; suffisance, that seketh no riche metes ne drynkes, ne dooth no fors of to outrageous apparail-ynge of mete;/ mesure also, that restreyneth by resoun the deslavee appetit of etynge; sobrenesse also, that restreyneth the outrage of drynke;/ sparynge also, that restreyneth the delicaat ese to sitte longe at his mete and softely, wherfore some folk stonden of hir owene wyl to eten at the lasse leyser./ 835

Sequitur de Luxuria.

After Glotonye thanne comth Lecherie, for thise two synnes been so ny cosyns that ofte tyme they wol nat departe./ God woot, this synne is ful displesaunt thyng to God; for he seyde hymself, "Do no lecherie." And therfore he putte grete peynes agayns this synne in the olde lawe./ If womman thral were taken in this synne, she sholde be beten with staves to the deeth; and if she were a gentil womman, she sholde be slayn with stones; and if she were a bisshoppes doghter, she sholde been brent, by Goddes comandement./ Forther over, by the synne of lecherie God dreynte al the world at the diluge. And after that he brente fyve citees with thonder-leyt, and sank hem into helle./

Now lat us speke thanne of thilke stynkynge synne of Lecherie that men clepe avowtrie of wedded folk, that is to seyn, if that oon of hem be wedded, or elles bothe./ Seint John seith that avowtiers shullen been in helle, in a stank brennynge of fyr and of brymston; in fyr, for hire lecherye; in brymston, for the stynk of hire ordure./ Certes, the brekynge of this sacrement is an horrible thyng. It was maked of God hymself in paradys, and confermed by Jhesu Crist, as witnesseth Seint Mathew in the gospel: "A man shal lete fader and mooder, and taken hym to his wif, and they shullen be two in o flessh."/ This sacrement bitokneth the knyttynge togidre of Crist and of hooly chirche./ And nat oonly that God forbad avowtrie in dede, but eek he comanded that thou sholdest nat coveite thy neighebores wyf./ "In this heeste," seith Seint Augustyn, "is forboden alle manere coveitise to doon lecherie." Lo, what seith Seint Mathew in the gospel, that "whoso seeth a womman to coveitise of his lust, he hath doon lecherie with hire in his herte."/ Heere may ye seen that nat oonly the dede of this synne is forboden, but eek the desir to doon that synne./ This cursed synne anoyeth grevousliche hem that it haunten. And first to hire soule, for he 840 845

obligeth it to synne and to peyne of deeth that
is perdurable./ Unto the body anoyeth it grevously also, for it dreyeth hym, and wasteth him,
and shent hym, and of his blood he maketh sacrifice to the feend of helle. It wasteth eek his
catel and his substaunce./ And certes, if it be
a foul thyng a man to waste his catel on wommen, yet is it a fouler thyng whan that, for
swich ordure, wommen dispenden upon men
hir catel and substaunce./ This synne, as seith
the prophete, bireveth man and womman hir
goode fame and al hire honour; and it is ful
plesaunt to the devel, for therby wynneth
he the mooste partie of this world./ And   850
right as a marchant deliteth hym moost in
chaffare that he hath moost avantage of, right
so deliteth the fend in this ordure./

This is that oother hand of the devel with
fyve fyngres to cacche the peple to his vileynye./ The firste fynger is the fool lookynge
of the fool womman and of the fool man, that
sleeth, right as the basilicok sleeth folk by the
venym of his sighte; for the coveitise of eyen
folweth the coveitise of the herte./ The seconde fynger is the vileyns touchynge in wikkede manere. And therfore seith Salomon that
"whoso toucheth and handleth a womman, he
fareth lyk hym that handleth the scorpioun that
styngeth and sodeynly sleeth thurgh his envenymynge"; as whoso toucheth warm pych,
it shent his fyngres./ The thridde is foule
wordes, that fareth lyk fyr, that right anon
brenneth the herte./ The fourthe fynger   855
is the kissynge; and trewely he were a
greet fool that wolde kisse the mouth of a
brennynge oven or of a fourneys./ And moore
fooles been they that kissen in vileynye, for
that mouth is the mouth of helle; and namely
thise olde dotardes holours, yet wol they kisse,
though they may nat do, and smatre hem./
Certes, they been lyk to houndes; for an hound,
whan he comth by the roser or by othere
[bushes], though he may nat pisse, yet wole
he heve up his leg and make a contenaunce
to pisse./ And for that many man weneth that
he may nat synne, for no likerousnesse that
he dooth with his wyf, certes, that opinion is
fals. God woot, a man may sleen hymself with
his owene knyf, and make hymselve dronken
of his owene tonne./ Certes, be it wyf, be it
child, or any worldly thyng that he loveth biforn God, it is his mawmet, and he is an
ydolastre./ Man sholde loven hys wyf by   860
discrecioun, paciently and atemprely; and

thanne is she as though it were his suster./ The
fifthe fynger of the develes hand is the stynkynge dede of Leccherie./ Certes, the fyve fyngres of Glotonie the feend put in the wombe
of a man, and with his fyve fingres of Lecherie he gripeth hym by the reynes, for to
throwen hym into the fourneys of helle,/ ther
as they shul han the fyr and the wormes that
evere shul lasten, and wepynge and wailynge,
sharp hunger and thurst, and grymnesse of
develes, that shullen al totrede hem withouten
respit and withouten ende./ Of Leccherie, as
I seyde, sourden diverse speces, as fornicacioun,
that is bitwixe man and womman that been
nat maried; and this is deedly synne, and
agayns nature./ Al that is enemy and de-   865
struccioun to nature is agayns nature./
Parfay, the resoun of a man telleth eek hym
wel that it is deedly synne, for as muche as
God forbad leccherie. And Seint Paul yeveth
hem the regne that nys dewe to no wight but
to hem that doon deedly synne./ Another
synne of Leccherie is to bireve a mayden of
hir maydenhede; for he that so dooth, certes,
he casteth a mayden out of the hyeste degree
that is in this present lif,/ and bireveth hire
thilke precious fruyt that the book clepeth the
hundred fruyt. I ne kan seye it noon ootherweyes in Englissh, but in Latyn it highte *Centesimus fructus*./ Certes, he that so dooth is
cause of manye damages and vileynyes, mo
than any man kan rekene; right as he somtyme
is cause of alle damages that beestes don in
the feeld, that breketh the hegge or the closure,
thurgh which he destroyeth that may nat
been restoored./ For certes, namoore may   870
maydenhede be restoored than an arm that
is smyten fro the body may retourne agayn to
wexe./ She may have mercy, this woot I wel,
if she do penitence; but nevere shal it be that
she nas corrupt./ And al be it so that I have
spoken somwhat of avowtrie, it is good to
shewen mo perils that longen to avowtrie, for
to eschue that foule synne./ Avowtrie in Latyn
is for to seyn, approchynge of oother mannes
bed, thurgh which tho that whilom weren o
flessh abawndone hir bodyes to othere persones./ Of this synne, as seith the wise man,
folwen manye harmes. First, brekynge of feith;
and certes, in feith is the keye of Cristendom./ And whan that feith is broken   875
and lorn, soothly Cristendom stant veyn
and withouten fruyt./ This synne is eek a
thefte; for thefte generally is for to reve a

wight his thyng agayns his wille./ Certes, this is the foulest thefte that may be, whan a womman steleth hir body from hir housbonde, and yeveth it to hire holour to defoulen hire; and steleth hir soule fro Crist, and yeveth it to the devel./ This is a fouler thefte than for to breke a chirche and stele the chalice; for thise avowtiers breken the temple of God spiritually, and stelen the vessel of grace, that is the body and the soule, for which Crist shal destroyen hem, as seith Seint Paul./ Soothly, of this thefte douted gretly Joseph, whan that his lordes wyf preyed hym of vileynye, whan he seyde, "Lo, my lady, how my lord hath take to me under my warde al that he hath in this world, ne no thyng of his thynges is out of my power, but oonly ye, that been his wyf./ And how sholde I thanne do this 880 wikkednesse, and synne so horribly agayns God and agayns my lord? God it forbeede!" Allas! al to litel is swich trouthe now yfounde./ The thridde harm is the filthe thurgh which they breken the comandement of God, and defoulen the auctour of matrimoyne, that is Crist./ For certes, in so muche as the sacrement of mariage is so noble and so digne, so muche is it gretter synne for to breken it; for God made mariage in paradys, in the estaat of innocence, to multiplye mankynde to the service of God./ And therfore is the brekynge therof the moore grevous; of which brekynge comen false heires ofte tyme, that wrongfully ocupien folkes heritages. And therfore wol Crist putte hem out of the regne of hevene, that is heritage to goode folk./ Of this brekynge comth eek ofte tyme that folk unwar wedden or synnen with hire owene kynrede, and namely thilke harlotes that haunten bordels of thise fool wommen, that mowe be likned to a commune gong, where as men purgen hire ordure./ What seye we eek of pu- 885 tours that lyven by the horrible synne of putrie, and constreyne wommen to yelden hem a certeyn rente of hire bodily puterie, ye, somtyme of his owene wyf or his child, as doon thise bawdes? Certes, thise been cursede synnes./ Understoond eek that Avowtrie is set gladly in the ten comandementz bitwixe thefte and manslaughtre; for it is the gretteste thefte that may be, for it is thefte of body and of soule./ And it is lyk to homycide, for it kerveth atwo and breketh atwo hem that first were maked o flessh. And therfore, by the olde lawe of God, they sholde be slayn./ But nathelees, by the lawe of Jhesu Crist, that is lawe of pitee, whan he seyde to the womman that was founden in avowtrie, and sholde han been slayn with stones, after the wyl of the Jewes, as was hir lawe, "Go," quod Jhesu Crist, "and have namoore wyl to synne," or, "wille namoore to do synne."/ Soothly the vengeaunce of Avowtrie is awarded to the peynes of helle, but if so be that it be destourbed by penitence./ Yet been ther mo speces of this 890 cursed synne; as whan that oon of hem is religious, or elles bothe; or of folk that been entred into ordre, as subdekne, or dekne, or preest, or hospitaliers. And evere the hyer that he is in ordre, the gretter is the synne./ The thynges that gretly agreggen hire synne is the brekynge of hire avow of chastitee, whan they receyved the ordre./ And forther over, sooth is that hooly ordre is chief of al the tresorie of God, and his especial signe and mark of chastitee, to shewe that they been joyned to chastitee, which that is the moost precious lyf that is./ And thise ordred folk been specially titled to God, and of the special meignee of God, for which, whan they doon deedly synne, they been the special traytours of God and of his peple; for they lyven of the peple, to preye for the peple, and while they ben suche traitours, here preyer avayleth nat to the peple. Preestes been aungels, as by the dignitee of hir mysterye; but for sothe, Seint Paul seith that Sathanas transformeth hym in an aungel of light./ Soothly, the preest that haunt- 895 eth deedly synne, he may be likned to the aungel of derknesse transformed in the aungel of light. He semeth aungel of light, but for sothe he is aungel of derknesse./ Swiche preestes been the sones of Helie, as sheweth in the Book of Kynges, that they weren the sones of Belial, that is, the devel./ Belial is to seyn, "withouten juge"; and so faren they; hem thynketh they been free, and han no juge, namoore than hath a free bole that taketh which cow that hym liketh in the town./ So faren they by wommen. For right as a free bole is ynough for al a toun, right so is a wikked preest corrupcioun ynough for al a parisshe, or for al a contree./ Thise preestes, as seith the book, ne konne nat the mysterie of preesthod to the peple, ne God ne knowe they nat. They ne helde hem nat apayd, as seith the book, of soden flessh that was to hem offred, but they tooke by force the flessh that is rawe./ 900 Certes, so thise shrewes ne holden hem nat apayed of roosted flessh and sode flessh, with which the peple feden hem in greet reverence, but they wole have raw flessh of folkes wyves and hir doghtres./ And certes, thise wommen that consenten to hire harlotrie doon greet wrong to Crist, and to hooly chirche, and alle halwes, and to alle soules; for they bireven alle thise hym that sholde worshipe Crist and hooly chirche, and preye for Cristene soules./ And therfore han swiche preestes, and hire lemmanes eek that consenten to hir leccherie, the malisoun of al the court Cristien, til they come to amendement./ The thridde spece of avowtrie is somtyme bitwixe a man and his wyf, and that is whan they take no reward in hire assemblynge but oonly to hire flesshly delit, as seith Seint Jerome,/ and ne rekken of nothyng but that they been assembled; by cause that they been maried, al is good ynough, as thynketh to hem./ But in swich folk **905** hath the devel power, as seyde the aungel Raphael to Thobie, for in hire assemblynge they putten Jhesu Crist out of hire herte, and yeven hemself to alle ordure./ The fourthe spece is the assemblee of hem that been of hire kynrede, or of hem that been of oon affynytee, or elles with hem with whiche hir fadres or hir kynrede han deled in the synne of lecherie. This synne maketh hem lyk to houndes, that taken no kep to kynrede./ And certes, parentele is in two maneres, outher goostly or flesshly; goostly, as for to deelen with his godsibbes./ For right so as he that engendreth a child is his flesshly fader, right so is his godfader his fader espiritueel. For which a womman may in no lasse synne assemblen with hire godsib than with hire owene flesshly brother./ The fifthe spece is thilke abhomynable synne, of which that no man unnethe oghte speke ne write; nathelees it is openly reherced in holy writ./ This cur- **910** sednesse doon men and wommen in diverse entente and in diverse manere; but though that hooly writ speke of horrible synne, certes hooly writ may nat been defouled, namoore than the sonne that shyneth on the mixne./ Another synne aperteneth to leccherie, that comth in slepynge, and this synne cometh ofte to hem that been maydenes, and eek to hem that been corrupt; and this synne men clepen polucioun, that comth in foure maneres./ Somtyme of langwissynge of body, for the humours been to ranke and to habundaunt in the body of man; somtyme of infermetee, for the fieblesse

of the vertu retentif, as phisik maketh mencion; somtyme for surfeet of mete and drynke;/ and somtyme of vileyns thoghtes that been enclosed in mannes mynde whan he gooth to slepe, which may nat been withoute synne; for which men moste kepen hem wisely, or elles may men synnen ful grevously./

Remedium contra peccatum luxurie.

Now comth the remedie agayns Leccherie, and that is generally chastitee and continence, that restreyneth alle the desordeynee moevynges that comen of flesshly talentes./ And evere the gretter merite shal **915** he han, that moost restreyneth the wikkede eschawfynges of the ardour of this synne. And this is in two maneres, that is to seyn, chastitee in mariage, and chastitee of widwehod./ Now shaltow understonde that matrimoyne is leefful assemblynge of man and of womman that receyven by vertu of the sacrement the boond thurgh which they may nat be departed in al hir lyf, that is to seyn, whil that they lyven bothe./ This, as seith the book, is a ful greet sacrement. God maked it, as I have seyd, in paradys, and wolde hymself be born in mariage./ And for to halwen mariage he was at a weddynge, where as he turned water into wyn; which was the firste miracle that he wroghte in erthe biforn his disciples./ Trewe effect of mariage clenseth fornicacioun and replenysseth hooly chirche of good lynage; for that is the ende of mariage; and it chaungeth deedly synne into venial synne bitwixe hem that been ywedded, and maketh the hertes al oon of hem that been ywedded, as wel as the bodies./ This is verray mariage, that **920** was establissed by God, er that synne bigan, whan natureel lawe was in his right poynt in paradys; and it was ordeyned that o man sholde have but o womman, and o womman but o man, as seith Seint Augustyn, by manye resouns./ First, for mariage is figured bitwixe Crist and holy chirche. And that oother is for a man is heved of a womman; algate, by ordinaunce it sholde be so./ For if a womman hadde mo men than oon, thanne sholde she have moo hevedes than oon, and that were an horrible thyng biforn God; and eek a womman ne myghte nat plese to many folk at oones. And also ther ne sholde nevere be pees ne reste amonges hem; for everich wolde axen his owene thyng./ And forther over, no man ne sholde knowe his owene engendrure, ne who sholde have his heritage; and the womman sholde been the lasse biloved fro the tyme that she were conjoynt to many men./

Now comth how that a man sholde bere hym with his wif, and namely in two thynges, that is to seyn, in suffraunce and reverence, as shewed Crist whan he made first womman./ For he ne made hire nat 925 of the heved of Adam, for she sholde nat clayme to greet lordshipe./ For ther as the womman hath the maistrie, she maketh to muche desray. Ther neden none ensamples of this; the experience of day by day oghte suf- fise./ Also, certes, God ne made nat womman of the foot of Adam, for she ne sholde nat been holden to lowe; for she kan nat paciently suffre. But God made womman of the ryb of Adam, for womman sholde be felawe unto man./ Man sholde bere hym to his wyf in feith, in trouthe, and in love, as seith Seint Paul, that a man sholde loven his wyf as Crist loved hooly chirche, that loved it so wel that he deyde for it. So sholde a man for his wyf, if it were nede./

Now how that a womman sholde be sub- get to hire housbonde, that telleth Seint Peter. First, in obedience./ And eek, as 930 seith the decree, a womman that is wyf, as longe as she is a wyf, she hath noon auctori- tee to swere ne to bere witnesse withoute leve of hir housbonde, that is hire lord; algate, he sholde be so by resoun./ She sholde eek serven hym in alle honestee, and been attempree of hire array. I woot wel that they sholde setten hire entente to plesen hir housbondes, but nat by hire queyntise of array./ Seint Jerome seith that "wyves that been apparailled in silk and in precious purpre ne mowe nat clothen hem in Jhesu Crist." Loke what seith Seint John eek in thys matere?/ Seint Gregorie eek seith that "no wight seketh precious array but oonly for veyne glorie, to been honoured the moore biforn the peple."/ It is a greet folye, a womman to have a fair array outward and in hirself be foul inward./ A wyf 935 sholde eek be mesurable in lookynge and in berynge and in lawghynge, and discreet in alle hire wordes and hire dedes./ And aboven alle worldly thyng she sholde loven hire housbonde with al hire herte, and to hym be trewe of hir body./ So sholde an housbonde eek be to his wyf. For sith that al the body is the housbondes, so sholde hire herte been,

or elles ther is bitwixe hem two, as in that, no parfit mariage./ Thanne shal men under- stonde that for thre thynges a man and his wyf flesshly mowen assemble. The firste is in en- tente of engendrure of children to the service of God; for certes that is the cause final of matrimoyne./ Another cause is to yelden ev- erich of hem to oother the dette of hire bodies; for neither of hem hath power of his owene body. The thridde is for to eschewe lecch- erye and vileynye. The ferthe is for sothe deedly synne./ As to the firste, it is meri- 940 torie; the seconde also, for, as seith the decree, that she hath merite of chastitee that yeldeth to hire housbonde the dette of hir body, ye, though it be agayn hir likynge and the lust of hire herte./ The thridde manere is venyal synne; and, trewely, scarsly may ther any of thise be withoute venial synne, for the corrup- cion and for the delit./ The fourthe manere is for to understonde, as if they assemble oonly for amorous love and for noon of the foreseyde causes, but for to accomplice thilke brennynge delit, they rekke nevere how ofte. Soothly it is deedly synne; and yet, with sorwe, somme folk wol peynen hem moore to doon than to hire appetit suffiseth./

The seconde manere of chastitee is for to been a clene wydewe, and eschue the embrac- ynges of man, and desiren the embracynge of Jhesu Crist./ Thise been tho that han been wyves and han forgoon hire housbondes, and eek wommen that han doon leccherie and been releeved by penitence./ And certes, 945 if that a wyf koude kepen hire al chaast by licence of hir housbonde, so that she yeve nevere noon occasion that he agilte, it were to hire a greet merite./ Thise manere wom- men that observen chastitee moste be clene in herte as wel as in body and in thought, and mesurable in clothynge and in contenaunce; and been abstinent in etynge and drynkynge, in spekynge, and in dede. They been the ves- sel or the boyste of the blissed Magdelene, that fulfilleth hooly chirche of good odour./ The thridde manere of chastitee is virginitee, and it bihoveth that she be hooly in herte and clene of body. Thanne is she spouse to Jhesu Crist, and she is the lyf of angeles./ She is the preis- ynge of this world, and she is as thise martirs in egalitee; she hath in hire that tonge may nat telle ne herte thynke./ Virginitee baar oure Lord Jhesu Crist, and virgine was hymselve./ 956

Another remedie agayns Leccherie is specially to withdrawen swiche thynges as yeve
occasion to thilke vileynye, as ese, etynge, and
drynkynge. For certes, whan the pot boyleth
strongly, the beste remedie is to withdrawe the
fyr./ Slepynge longe in greet quiete is eek
a greet norice to Leccherie./

Another remedie agayns Leccherie is that a
man or a womman eschue the compaignye of
hem by whiche he douteth to be tempted; for
al be it so that the dede be withstonden, yet
is ther greet temptacioun./ Soothly, a whit
wal, although it ne brenne noght fully by
stikynge of a candele, yet is the wal blak of
the leyt./ Ful ofte tyme I rede that no man
truste in his owene perfeccioun, but he be
stronger than Sampson, and hoolier than
David, and wiser than Salomon./   955

Now after that I have declared yow, as
I kan, the sevene deedly synnes, and somme
of hire braunches and hire remedies, soothly,
if I koude, I wolde telle yow the ten comandementz./ But so heigh a doctrine I lete to divines. Nathelees, I hope to God, they been
touched in this tretice, everich of hem alle./

Sequitur secunda pars Penitencie.

Now for as muche as the seconde partie of
Penitence stant in Confessioun of mouth, as I
bigan in the firste chapitre, I seye, Seint Augustyn seith:/ "Synne is every word and every
dede, and al that men coveiten, agayn the lawe
of Jhesu Crist; and this is for to synne in herte,
in mouth, and in dede, by thy fyve wittes, that
been sighte, herynge, smellynge, tastynge or
savourynge, and feelynge."/ Now is it good
to understonde the circumstances that
agreggen muchel every synne./ Thou   960
shalt considere what thow art that doost
the synne, wheither thou be male or femele,
yong or oold, gentil or thral, free or servant,
hool or syk, wedded or sengle, ordred or unordred, wys or fool, clerk or seculeer;/ if she
be of thy kynrede, bodily or goostly, or noon;
if any of thy kynrede have synned with hire,
or noon; and manye mo thinges./

Another circumstaunce is this: wheither it
be doon in fornicacioun or in avowtrie or noon;
incest or noon; mayden or noon; in manere of
homicide or noon; horrible grete synnes or
smale; and how longe thou hast continued in
synne./ The thridde circumstaunce is the
place ther thou hast do synne; wheither in
oother mennes hous or in thyn owene; in feeld
or in chirche or in chirchehawe; in chirche
dedicaat or noon./ For if the chirche be
halwed, and man or womman spille his kynde
inwith that place, by wey of synne or by wikked temptacioun, the chirche is entredited
til it be reconsiled by the bysshop./ And   965
the preest sholde be enterdited that dide
swich a vileynye; to terme of al his lif he sholde
namoore synge masse, and if he dide, he sholde
doon deedly synne at every time that he so
songe masse./ The fourthe circumstaunce is
by whiche mediatours, or by whiche messagers, as for enticement, or for consentement to
bere compaignye with felaweshipe; for many
a wrecche, for to bere compaignye, wol go to
the devel of helle./ Wherfore they that eggen
or consenten to the synne been parteners of
the synne, and of the dampnacioun of the synnere./

The fifthe circumstaunce is how manye
tymes that he hath synned, if it be in his mynde,
and how ofte that he hath falle./ For he that
ofte falleth in synne, he despiseth the mercy
of God, and encreesseth hys synne, and is unkynde to Crist; and he wexeth the moore
fieble to withstonde synne, and synneth
the moore lightly,/ and the latter ariseth,   970
and is the moore eschew for to shryven
hym, and namely, to hym that is his confessour./
For which that folk, whan they falle agayn in
hir olde folies, outher they forleten hir olde
confessours al outrely, or elles they departen
hir shrift in diverse places; but soothly, swich
departed shrift deserveth no mercy of God of
his synnes./ The sixte circumstaunce is why
that a man synneth, as by which temptacioun;
and if hymself procure thilke temptacioun, or by
the excitynge of oother folk; or if he synne
with a womman by force, or by hire owene
assent;/ or if the womman, maugree hir hed,
hath been afforced, or noon. This shal she
telle: for coveitise, or for poverte, and if it was
hire procurynge, or noon; and swich manere
harneys./ The seventhe circumstaunce is in
what manere he hath doon his synne, or how
that she hath suffred that folk han doon
to hire./ And the same shal the man telle   975
pleynly with alle circumstaunces; and
wheither he hath synned with comune bordel
wommen, or noon;/ or doon his synne in hooly
tymes, or noon; in fastyng tymes, or noon; or
biforn his shrifte, or after his latter shrifte;/
and hath peraventure broken therfore his pen-

ance enjoyned; by whos help and whos conseil;
by sorcerie or craft; al moste be toold./ Alle
thise thynges, after that they been grete or
smale, engreggen the conscience of man. And
eek the preest, that is thy juge, may the bettre
been avysed of his juggement in yevynge of
thy penaunce, and that is after thy contricioun./ For understond wel that after tyme
that a man hath defouled his baptesme by
synne, if he wole come to salvacioun, ther is
noon other wey but by penitence and
shrifte and satisfaccioun;/ and namely by   980
the two, if ther be a confessour to which
he may shriven hym, and the thridde, if he
have lyf to parfournen it./

Thanne shal man looke and considere that
if he wole maken a trewe and a profitable confessioun, ther moste be foure condiciouns./
First, it moot been in sorweful bitternesse of
herte, as seyde the kyng Ezechias to God: "I
wol remembre me alle the yeres of my lif in
bitternesse of myn herte."/ This condicioun of
bitternesse hath fyve signes. The firste is that
confessioun moste be shamefast, nat for to covere ne hyden his synne, for he hath agilt his
God and defouled his soule./ And herof seith
Seint Augustyn: "The herte travailleth for
shame of his synne"; and for he hath greet
shamefastnesse, he is digne to have greet
mercy of God./ Swich was the confes-   985
sioun of the publican that wolde nat heven
up his eyen to hevene, for he hadde offended
God of hevene; for which shamefastnesse he
hadde anon the mercy of God./ And therof
seith Seint Augustyn that swich shamefast folk
been next foryevenesse and remissioun./ Another signe is humylitee in confessioun; of
which seith Seint Peter, "Humbleth yow under
the myght of God." The hond of God is
myghty in confessioun, for therby God foryeveth thee thy synnes, for he allone hath the
power./ And this humylitee shal been in herte,
and in signe outward; for right as he hath humylitee to God in his herte, right so sholde he
humble his body outward to the preest, that
sit in Goddes place./ For which in no manere, sith that Crist is sovereyn, and the preest
meene and mediatour bitwixe Crist and the
synnere, and the synnere is the laste by
wey of resoun,/ thanne sholde nat the   990
synnere sitte as heighe as his confessour,
but knele biforn hym or at his feet, but if maladie destourbe it. For he shal nat taken kep
who sit there, but in whos place that he sit-

teth./ A man that hath trespased to a lord,
and comth for to axe mercy and maken his accord, and set him doun anon by the lord, men
wolde holden hym outrageous, and nat worthy
so soone for to have remissioun ne mercy./ The
thridde signe is how that thy shrift sholde
be ful of teeris, if man may, and if man may
nat wepe with his bodily eyen, lat hym wepe
in herte./ Swich was the confession of Seint
Peter, for after that he hadde forsake Jhesu
Crist, he wente out and weep ful bitterly./
The fourthe signe is that he ne lette nat
for shame to shewen his confessioun./   995
Swich was the confessioun of the Magdalene, that ne spared, for no shame of hem
that weren atte feeste, for to go to oure Lord
Jhesu Crist and biknowe to hym hire synne./
The fifthe signe is that a man or a womman
be obeisant to receyven the penaunce that hym
is enjoyned for his synnes, for certes, Jhesu
Crist, for the giltes of o man, was obedient to
the deeth./

The seconde condicion of verray confession
is that it be hastily doon. For certes, if a man
hadde a deedly wounde, evere the lenger that
he taried to warisshe hymself, the moore wolde
it corrupte and haste hym to his deeth; and
eek the wounde wolde be the wors for to
heele./ And right so fareth synne that longe
tyme is in a man unshewed./ Certes, a man
oghte hastily shewen his synnes for manye
causes; as for drede of deeth, that cometh ofte
sodeynly, and no certeyn what tyme it shal be,
ne in what place; and eek the drecch-
ynge of o synne draweth in another;/ and   1000
eek the lenger that he tarieth, the ferther
he is fro Crist. And if he abide to his laste day,
scarsly may he shryven hym or remembre hym
of his synnes or repenten hym, for the grevous
maladie of his deeth./ And for as muche as he
ne hath nat in his lyf herkned Jhesu Crist
whanne he hath spoken, he shal crie to Jhesu
Crist at his laste day, and scarsly wol he
herkne hym./ And understond that this condicioun moste han foure thynges. Thi shrift
moste be purveyed bifore and avysed; for
wikked haste dooth no profit; and that a man
konne shryve hym of his synnes, be it of pride,
or of envye, and so forth with the speces and
circumstances;/ and that he have comprehended in hys mynde the nombre and the
greetnesse of his synnes, and how longe that
he hath leyn in synne;/ and eek that he be
contrit of his synnes, and in stidefast purpos,

by the grace of God, nevere eft to falle in synne; and eek that he drede and countrewaite hymself, that he fle the occasiouns of synne to whiche he is enclyned./ Also 1005 thou shalt shryve thee of alle thy synnes to o man, and nat a parcel to o man and a parcel to another; that is to understonde, in entente to departe thy confessioun, as for shame or drede; for it nys but stranglynge of thy soule./ For certes Jhesu Crist is entierly al good; in hym nys noon imperfeccioun; and therfore outher he foryeveth al parfitly or never a deel./ I seye nat that if thow be assigned to the penitauncer for certein synne, that thow art bounde to shewen hym al the remenaunt of thy synnes, of whiche thow hast be shryven of thy curaat, but if it like to thee of thyn humylitee; this is no departynge of shrifte./ Ne I seye nat, ther as I speke of divisioun of confessioun, that if thou have licence for to shryve thee to a discreet and an honest preest, where thee liketh, and by licence of thy curaat, that thow ne mayst wel shryve thee to him of alle thy synnes./ But lat no blotte be bihynde; lat no synne been untoold, as fer as thow hast remembraunce./ And whan thou shalt be 1010 shryven to thy curaat, telle hym eek alle the synnes that thow hast doon syn thou were last yshryven; this is no wikked entente of divisioun of shrifte./

Also the verray shrifte axeth certeine condiciouns. First, that thow shryve thee by thy free wil, noght constreyned, ne for shame of folk, ne for maladie, ne swiche thynges. For it is resoun that he that trespaseth by his free wyl, that by his free wyl he confesse his trespas;/ and that noon oother man telle his synne but he hymself; ne he shal nat nayte ne denye his synne, ne wratthe hym agayn the preest for his amonestynge to lete synne./ The seconde condicioun is that thy shrift be laweful, that is to seyn, that thow that shryvest thee, and eek the preest that hereth thy confessioun, been verraily in the feith of hooly chirche;/ and that a man ne be nat despeired of the mercy of Jhesu Crist, as Caym or Judas./ 1015 And eek a man moot accusen hymself of his owene trespas, and nat another; but he shal blame and wyten hymself and his owene malice of his synne, and noon oother./ But nathelees, if that another man be occasioun or enticere of his synne, or the estaat of a persone be swich thurgh which his synne is agregged, or elles that he may nat pleynly

shryven hym but he telle the persone with which he hath synned, thanne may he telle it,/ so that his entente ne be nat to bakbite the persone, but oonly to declaren his confessioun./

Thou ne shalt nat eek make no lesynges in thy confessioun, for humylitee, peraventure, to seyn that thou hast doon synnes of whiche thow were nevere gilty./ For Seint Augustyn seith, "If thou, by cause of thyn humylitee, makest lesynges on thyself, though thow ne were nat in synne biforn, yet artow thanne in synne thurgh thy lesynges."/ Thou 1020 most eek shewe thy synne by thyn owene propre mouth, but thow be woxe dowmb, and nat by no lettre; for thow that hast doon the synne, thou shalt have the shame therfore./ Thow shalt nat eek peynte thy confessioun by faire subtile wordes, to covere the moore thy synne; for thanne bigilestow thyself, and nat the preest. Thow most tellen it platly, be it nevere so foul ne so horrible./ Thow shalt eek shryve thee to a preest that is discreet to conseille thee; and eek thou shalt nat shryve thee for veyne glorie, ne for ypocrisye, ne for no cause but oonly for the doute of Jhesu Crist and the heele of thy soule./ Thow shalt nat eek renne to the preest sodeynly to tellen hym lightly thy synne, as whoso telleth a jape or a tale, but avysely and with greet devocioun./ And generally, shryve thee ofte. If thou ofte falle, ofte thou arise by confessioun./ 1025 And though thou shryve thee ofter than ones of synne of which thou hast be shryven, it is the moore merite. And, as seith Seint Augustyn, thow shalt have the moore lightly relessyng and grace of God, bothe of synne and of peyne./ And certes, oones a yeere atte leeste wey it is laweful for to been housled; for certes, oones a yeere alle thynges renovellen./

Now have I toold yow of verray Confessioun, that is the seconde partie of Penitence./

Explicit secunda pars Penitencie,
et sequitur tercia pars eiusdem.

The thridde partie of Penitence is Satisfaccioun, and that stant moost generally in almesse and in bodily peyne./ Now been ther thre manere of almesse: contricion of herte, where a man offreth hymself to God; another is to han pitee of defaute of his neighebores; and the thridde is in yevynge of good conseil and comfort, goostly and bodily, where men han nede, and namely in sustenaunce of mannes foode./ And tak kep that a man hath 1030 nede of thise thinges generally: he hath nede of foode, he hath nede of clothyng and herberwe, he hath nede of charitable conseil and visitynge in prisone and in maladie, and sepulture of his dede body./ And if thow mayst nat visite the nedeful with thy persone, visite hym by thy message and by thy yiftes./ Thise been general almesses or werkes of charitee of hem that han temporeel richesses or discrecioun in conseilynge. Of thise werkes shaltow heren at the day of doom./

Thise almesses shaltow doon of thyne owene propre thynges, and hastily and prively, if thow mayst./ But nathelees, if thow mayst nat doon it prively, thow shalt nat forbere to doon almesse though men seen it, so that it be nat doon for thank of the world, but oonly for thank of Jhesu Crist./ For, as 1035 witnesseth Seint Mathew, *capitulo quinto*, "A citee may nat been hyd that is set on a montayne, ne men lighte nat a lanterne and put it under a busshel, but men sette it on a candle-stikke to yeve light to the men in the hous./ Right so shal youre light lighten bifore men, that they may seen youre goode werkes, and glorifie youre fader that is in hevene."/

Now as to speken of bodily peyne, it stant in preyeres, in wakynges, in fastynges, in vertuouse techynges of orisouns./ And ye shul understonde that orisouns or preyeres is for to seyn a pitous wyl of herte, that redresseth it in God and expresseth it by word outward, to remoeven harmes and to han thynges espiritueel and durable, and somtyme temporele thynges; of whiche orisouns, certes, in the orison of the *Pater noster* hath Jhesu Crist enclosed moost thynges./ Certes, it is privyleged of thre thynges in his dignytee, for which it is moore digne than any oother preyere; for that Jhesu Crist hymself maked it;/ and it is short, for it sholde 1040 be koud the moore lightly, and for to withholden it the moore esily in herte, and helpen hymself the ofter with the orisoun;/ and for a man sholde be the lasse wery to seyen it, and for a man may nat excusen hym to lerne it, it is so short and so esy; and for it comprehendeth in it self alle goode preyeres./ The exposicioun of this hooly preyere, that is so excellent and digne, I bitake to thise maistres of theologie, save thus muchel wol I seyn;

that whan thow prayest that God sholde foryeve thee thy giltes as thou foryevest hem that agilten to thee, be ful wel war that thow ne be nat out of charitee./ This hooly orison amenuseth eek venyal synne, and therfore it aperteneth specially to penitence./

This preyere moste be trewely seyd, and in verray feith, and that men preye to God ordinatly and discreetly and devoutly; and alwey a man shal putten his wyl to be subget to the wille of God./ This orisoun moste eek 1045 been seyd with greet humblesse and ful pure; honestly, and nat to the anoyaunce of any man or womman. It moste eek been continued with the werkes of charitee./ It avayleth eek agayn the vices of the soule; for, as seith Seint Jerome, "By fastynge been saved the vices of the flessh, and by preyere the vices of the soule."/

After this, thou shalt understonde that bodily peyne stant in wakynge; for Jhesu Crist seith, "Waketh and preyeth, that ye ne entre in wikked temptacioun."/ Ye shul understanden also that fastynge stant in thre thynges: in forberynge of bodily mete and drynke, and in forberynge of worldly jolitee, and in forberynge of deedly synne; this is to seyn, that a man shal kepen hym fro deedly synne with al his myght./

And thou shalt understanden eek that God ordeyned fastynge, and to fastynge appertenen foure thinges:/ largenesse to 1050 povre folk; gladnesse of herte espiritueel, nat to been angry ne anoyed, ne grucche for he fasteth; and also resonable houre for to ete; ete by mesure; that is for to seyn, a man shal nat ete in untyme, ne sitte the lenger at his table to ete for he fasteth./

Thanne shaltow understonde that bodily peyne stant in disciplyne or techynge, by word, or by writynge, or in ensample; also in werynge of heyres, or of stamyn, or of haubergeons on hire naked flessh, for Cristes sake, and swiche manere penances./ But war thee wel that swiche manere penaunces on thy flessh ne make nat thyn herte bitter or angry or anoyed of thyself; for bettre is to caste awey thyn heyre, than for to caste awey the swetenesse of Jhesu Crist./ And therfore seith Seint Paul, "Clothe yow, as they that been chosen of God, in herte of misericorde, debonairetee, suffraunce, and swich manere of clothynge"; of whiche Jhesu Crist is moore apayed than of heyres, or haubergeouns, or hauberkes./

Thanne is discipline eek in knokkynge of thy brest, in scourgynge with yerdes, in knelynges, in tribulacions,/ in suffrynge 1055 paciently wronges that been doon to thee, and eek in pacient suffraunce of maladies, or lesynge of worldly catel, or of wyf, or of child, or othere freendes./

Thanne shaltow understonde whiche thynges destourben penaunce; and this is in foure maneres, that is, drede, shame, hope, and wanhope, that is, desperacion./ And for to speke first of drede; for which he weneth that he may suffre no penaunce;/ ther-agayns is remedie for to thynke that bodily penaunce is but short and litel at regard of the peyne of helle, that is so crueel and so long that it lasteth withouten ende./

Now again the shame that a man hath to shryven hym, and namely thise ypocrites that wolden been holden so parfite that they han no nede to shryven hem;/ agayns that 1060 shame sholde a man thynke that, by wey of resoun, that he that hath nat been shamed to doon foule thinges, certes hym oghte nat been ashamed to do faire thynges, and that is confessiouns./ A man sholde eek thynke that God seeth and woot alle his thoghtes and alle his werkes; to hym may no thyng been hyd ne covered./ Men sholden eek remembren hem of the shame that is to come at the day of doom to hem that been nat penitent and shryven in this present lyf./ For alle the creatures in hevene, in erthe, and in helle shullen seen apertly al that they hyden in this world./

Now for to speken of the hope of hem that been necligent and slowe to shryven hem, that stant in two maneres./ That 1065 oon is that he hopeth for to lyve longe and for to purchacen muche richesse for his delit, and thanne he wol shryven hym; and, as he seith, hym semeth thanne tymely ynough to come to shrifte./ Another is of surquidrie that he hath in Cristes mercy./ Agayns the firste vice, he shal thynke that oure lif is in no sikernesse, and eek that alle the richesses in this world ben in aventure, and passen as a shadwe on the wal;/ and, as seith seint Gregorie, that it aperteneth to the grete

rightwisnesse of God that nevere shal the peyne stynte of hem that nevere wolde withdrawen hem fro synne, hir thankes, but ay continue in synne; for thilke perpetueel wil to do synne shul they han perpetueel peyne./

Wanhope is in two maneres: the firste wanhope is in the mercy of Crist; that oother is that they thynken that they ne myghte nat longe persevere in goodnesse./ The 1070 firste wanhope comth of that he demeth that he hath synned so greetly and so ofte, and so longe leyn in synne, that he shal nat be saved./ Certes, agayns that cursed wanhope sholde he thynke that the passion of Jhesu Crist is moore strong for to unbynde than synne is strong for to bynde./ Agayns the seconde wanhope he shal thynke that as ofte as he falleth he may arise agayn by penitence. And though he never so longe have leyn in synne, the mercy of Crist is alwey redy to receiven hym to mercy./ Agayns the wanhope that he demeth that he sholde nat longe persevere in goodnesse, he shal thynke that the feblesse of the devel may nothyng doon, but if men wol suffren hym;/ and eek he shal han strengthe of the help of God, and of al hooly chirche, and of the proteccioun of aungels, if hym list./ 1075

Thanne shal men understonde what is the fruyt of penaunce; and, after the word of Jhesu Crist, it is the endelees blisse of hevene,/ ther joye hath no contrarioustee of wo ne grevaunce; ther alle harmes been passed of this present lyf; ther as is the sikernesse fro the peyne of helle; ther as is the blisful compaignye that rejoysen hem everemo, everich of otheres joye;/ ther as the body of man, that whilom was foul and derk, is moore cleer than the sonne; ther as the body, that whilom was syk, freele, and fieble, and mortal, is inmortal, and so strong and so hool that ther may no thyng apeyren it;/ ther as ne is neither hunger, thurst, ne coold, but every soule replenyssed with the sighte of the parfit knowynge of God./ This blisful regne may men purchace by poverte espiritueel, and the glorie by lowenesse, the plentee of joye by hunger and thurst, and the reste by travaille, and the lyf by deeth and mortificacion of synne./ 1080

Heere taketh the makere of this book his leve.

Now preye I to hem alle that herkne this litel tretys or rede, that if ther be any thyng in it that liketh hem, that therof they thanken oure Lord Jhesu Crist, of whom procedeth al wit and al goodnesse./ And if ther be any thyng that displese hem, I preye hem also that they arrette it to the defaute of myn unkonnynge, and nat to my wyl, that wolde ful fayn have seyd bettre if I hadde had konnynge./ For oure book seith, "Al that is writen is writen for oure doctrine," and that is myn entente./ Wherfore I biseke yow mekely, for the mercy of God, that ye preye for me that Crist have mercy on me and foryeve me my giltes;/ and namely of my translacions and enditynges of worldly vanitees, the whiche I revoke in my retracciouns:/ as is the book of Troi- 1085 lus; the book also of Fame; the book of the xxv. Ladies; the book of the Duchesse; the book of Seint Valentynes day of the Parlement of Briddes; the tales of Caunterbury, thilke that sownen into synne;/ the book of the Leoun; and many another book, if they were in my remembrance, and many a song and many a leccherous lay; that Crist for his grete mercy foryeve me the synne./ But of the translacion of Boece de Consolacione, and othere bookes of legendes of seintes, and omelies, and moralitee, and devocioun,/ that thanke I oure Lord Jhesu Crist and his blisful Mooder, and alle the seintes of hevene,/ bisekynge hem that they from hennes forth unto my lyves ende sende me grace to biwayle my giltes, and to studie to the salvacioun of my soule, and graunte me grace of verray penitence, confessioun and satisfaccioun to doon in this present lyf,/ thurgh the benigne grace of 1090 hym that is kyng of kynges and preest over alle preestes, that boghte us with the precious blood of his herte;/ so that I may been oon of hem at the day of doom that shulle be saved. *Qui cum patre et Spiritu Sancto vivit et regnat Deus per omnia secula. Amen.*

Heere is ended the book of the tales of Caunterbury, compiled by Geffrey Chaucer, of whos soule Jhesu Crist have mercy. Amen.

THE BOOK OF THE DUCHESS

It has long been recognized that Chaucer's earliest writings show French influence. The French literature with which he came chiefly in contact was not the great narrative poetry of the early Middle Ages, the Chanson de Roland or the Arthurian romances of the best period. Though he often displays a knowledge of the subjects treated in this older literature, no important use of the poems themselves has been traced in his writings. In the thirteenth and fourteenth centuries, while good metrical romances continued to be written, there was a change of literary fashion in France, and narratives of the earlier type were in large measure superseded by dreams and allegories. The great example of the new *genre* was the Roman de la Rose, which Chaucer himself says that he translated. The date of his translation is unknown, and it is not even certain that he wrote any part of the existing English fragments. But the influence of the Roman is apparent in his work from the beginning, and he found other models of the same general type of allegorical writing in the productions of Machaut, Froissart, and Deschamps, the chief French poets of his own century.

It is to Guillaume Machaut, the oldest of these writers, that Chaucer was particularly indebted in the *Book of the Duchess*, the earliest of his definitely dated works. There are no less than nine of Machaut's poems from which he may have derived suggestions, and of one of them, the Jugement dou Roy de Behaingne, he made extended use. He also drew upon love-visions by other French writers, and for the explanation and illustration of his text comparisons have been made especially with the Roman de la Rose, the Paradys d'Amours of Froissart, and the anonymous Songe Vert. For the incident of Ceyx and Alcione, though Chaucer apparently followed in some details the version of Machaut in the Dit de la Fontaine Amoureuse, he went straight to the Latin source in the Metamorphoses of Ovid, the clas-

sical poet to whom throughout his life he was most deeply indebted.

The *Book of the Duchess* is not only the earliest, but almost the only production of Chaucer that can with confidence be attached to an actual occurrence. According to a tradition recorded by John Stow and still accepted by nearly all critics, the poem was written in commemoration of the death of Blanche, duchess of Lancaster and first wife of John of Gaunt. Though recently called in question the tradition can be safely trusted. It is implied by the title, *The Deeth of Blaunche the Duchesse*, used by Chaucer himself in the *Legend of Good Women*, and is further supported by allusions in the poem to the names "Blanche" and "Lancaster" and "Richmond," the Yorkshire seat of John of Gaunt. The duchess died in September, 1369, and the *Book* was probably composed within the next few months.

It is at once an eulogy of Blanche and a consolation addressed to her bereaved husband. To fulfil the double purpose of the poem Chaucer had the happy idea of adapting a love-vision of the familiar kind to the uses of an elegy. Therein lies the chief originality of the work. Apart from its adaptation, the *Book of the Duchess* conforms strictly to its type. Indeed it sometimes follows one of its models, Machaut's Roy de Behaingne, so closely that the very description of Blanche seems to be drawn as much from Machaut as from life. The regular features of the love-vision, many of which reappear in the *House of Fame*, the *Parliament of Fowls*, and the *Prologue to the Legend of Good Women* — the discussion of sleeplessness and dreams, the setting on Mayday or in the spring-time, the vision itself, the guide (who in many poems takes the form of a helpful animal), the personified abstractions, Love, Fortune, Nature, and the like — all these are in evidence. For most modern readers the artificial conventions undoubtedly impair the effect of the story; and the young poet had not yet much thought to contribute or great mastery in expressing it. He was experimenting in style and meter, and the verse, in comparison with what he was soon to write, is both rough and lacking in flexibility. Yet already in this relatively crude work of Chaucer's youth there appears something of his vivid imagination. The hunting scene (which might be consulted as a document on the practice of the sport), the figure of the man in black, and the recital of his tragic story, — all possess a reality unusual in poems of the type. Even the dream itself is not a mere convention, as was often the case, but reflects the peculiar psychology of the sleeping state. And, what is most remarkable, the poem, in spite of the artificial tradition to which it belongs, expresses real feeling. A love-vision might have been ex-pected to serve, as this does so admirably, for an eulogy on the duchess. It is an evidence of the young Chaucer's power that the poem is also a moving narrative of the husband's grief and the dreamer's sympathy.

In a sense Chaucer was unfortunate in the models which the prevailing fashions of his youth forced upon him. For allegory was really foreign to his genius, and he had to work slowly out of it to find the more natural expression of his later years. His greatest and most representative work was undoubtedly in the realistic vein. Yet many of the best loved passages, even in his later writings, belong to the other tradition, commonly regarded as more characteristically mediæval; and English would be much poorer in the poetry of fancy if he had never practised in that school and become one of its masters.

The Book of the Duchess

I have gret wonder, be this lyght,
How that I lyve, for day ne nyght
I may nat slepe wel nygh noght;
I have so many an ydel thoght,
Purely for defaute of slep,   5
That, by my trouthe, I take no kep
Of nothing, how hyt cometh or gooth,
Ne me nys nothyng leef nor looth.
Al is ylyche good to me —
Joye or sorowe, wherso hyt be —   10
For I have felynge in nothyng,
But, as yt were, a mased thyng,
Alway in poynt to falle a-doun;
For sorwful ymagynacioun
Ys alway hooly in my mynde.   15
    And wel ye woot, agaynes kynde
Hyt were to lyven in thys wyse;
For nature wolde nat suffyse
To noon erthly creature
Nat longe tyme to endure   20
Withoute slep and be in sorwe.
And I ne may, ne nyght ne morwe,
Slepe; and thus melancolye
And drede I have for to dye.
Defaute of slep and hevynesse   25
Hath sleyn my spirit of quyknesse
That I have lost al lustyhede.

Suche fantasies ben in myn hede,
So I not what is best to doo.
    But men myght axe me why soo   30
I may not sleepe, and what me is.
But natheles, who aske this
Leseth his asking trewely.
Myselven can not telle why
The sothe; but trewly, as I gesse,   35
I holde hit be a sicknesse
That I have suffred this eight yeer,
And yet my boote is never the ner;
For there is phisicien but oon
That may me hele; but that is don.   40
Passe we over untill eft;
That wil not be mot nede be left;
Our first mater is good to kepe.
    So when I saw I might not slepe
Til now late, this other night,   45
Upon my bed I sat upright
And bad oon reche me a book,
A romaunce, and he it me tok
To rede, and drive the night away;
For me thoughte it beter play   50
Then play either at ches or tables.
And in this bok were written fables
That clerkes had in olde tyme,
And other poets, put in rime

To rede, and for to be in minde, 55
While men loved the lawe of kinde.
This bok ne spak but of such thinges,
Of quenes lives, and of kinges,
And many other thinges smale.
Amonge al this I fond a tale 60
That me thoughte a wonder thing.

This was the tale: There was a king
That highte Seys, and had a wif,
The beste that mighte bere lyf,
And this quene highte Alcyone. 65
So it befil, thereafter soone,
This king wol wenden over see.
To tellen shortly, whan that he
Was in the see, thus in this wise,
Such a tempest gan to rise 70
That brak her mast and made it falle,
And clefte her ship, and dreinte hem alle,
That never was founden, as it telles,
Bord ne man, ne nothing elles.
Right thus this king Seys loste his lif. 75
Now for to speken of his wif: —
This lady, that was left at hom,
Hath wonder that the king ne com
Hom, for it was a longe terme.
Anon her herte began to erme; 80
And for that her thoughte evermo
It was not wele [he dwelte] so,
She longed so after the king
That, certes, it were a pitous thing
To telle her hertely sorowful lif 85
That she had, this noble wif,
For him she loved alderbest.
Anon she sent bothe eest and west
To seke him, but they founde nought.
"Alas!" quoth shee, "that I was wrought! 90
And wher my lord, my love, be deed?
Certes, I nil never ete breed,
I make avow to my god here,
But I mowe of my lord here!"
Such sorowe this lady to her tok 95
That trewly I, which made this book,
Had such pittee and such rowthe
To rede hir sorwe, that, by my trowthe,
I ferde the worse al the morwe
Aftir, to thenken on hir sorwe. 100
So whan this lady koude here noo word
That no man myghte fynde hir lord,
Ful ofte she swouned, and sayed "Alas!"
For sorwe ful nygh wood she was,
Ne she koude no reed but oon; 105
But doun on knees she sat anoon
And wepte, that pittee was to here.
"A! mercy! swete lady dere!"

Quod she to Juno, hir goddesse,
"Helpe me out of thys distresse, 110
And yeve me grace my lord to se
Soone, or wite wher-so he be,
Or how he fareth, or in what wise,
And I shal make yow sacrifise,
And hooly youres become I shal 115
With good wille, body, herte, and al;
And but thow wolt this, lady swete,
Send me grace to slepe, and mete
In my slep som certeyn sweven
Wherthourgh that I may knowen even 120
Whether my lord be quyk or ded."
With that word she heng doun the hed
And fel a-swowne as cold as ston.
Hyr women kaught hir up anoon,
And broghten hir in bed al naked, 125
And she, forweped and forwaked,
Was wery, and thus the dede slep
Fil on hir, or she tooke kep,
Throgh Juno, that had herd hir bone,
That made hir to slepe sone. 130
For as she prayede, ryght so was don
In dede; for Juno ryght anon
Called thus hir messager
To doo hir erande, and he com ner.
Whan he was come, she bad hym thus: 135
"Go bet," quod Juno, "to Morpheus, —
Thou knowest hym wel, the god of slep.
Now understond wel, and tak kep!
Sey thus on my half, that he
Go faste into the grete se, 140
And byd hym that, on alle thyng,
He take up Seys body the kyng,
That lyeth ful pale and nothyng rody.
Bid hym crepe into the body,
And doo hit goon to Alcione 145
The quene, ther she lyeth allone,
And shewe hir shortly, hit ys no nay,
How hit was dreynt thys other day;
And do the body speke ryght soo,
Ryght as hyt was woned to doo 150
The whiles that hit was alyve.
Goo now faste, and hye the blyve!"
This messager tok leve and wente
Upon hys wey, and never ne stente
Til he com to the derke valeye 155
That stant betwixen roches tweye
Ther never yet grew corn ne gras,
Ne tre, ne [nothing] that ought was,
Beste, ne man, ne noght elles,
Save ther were a fewe welles 160
Came rennynge fro the clyves adoun,
That made a dedly slepynge soun,

And ronnen doun ryght by a cave
That was under a rokke ygrave
Amydde the valey, wonder depe.   165
There these goddes lay and slepe,
Morpheus and Eclympasteyr,
That was the god of slepes heyr,
That slep and dide noon other werk.
This cave was also as derk   170
As helle-pit overal aboute.
They had good leyser for to route,
To envye who myghte slepe best.
Somme henge her chyn upon hir brest,
And slept upryght, hir hed yhed,   175
And somme lay naked in her bed
And slepe whiles the dayes laste.
    This messager com fleynge faste
And cried, "O, ho! awake anoon!"
Hit was for noght; there herde hym non. 180
"Awake!" quod he, "whoo ys lyth there?"
And blew his horn ryght in here eere,
And cried "Awaketh!" wonder hyë.
This god of slep with hys oon yë
Cast up, axed, "Who clepeth ther?"   185
"Hyt am I," quod this messager.
"Juno bad thow shuldest goon" —
And tolde hym what he shulde doon,
As I have told yow here-to-fore;
Hyt ys no nede reherse hyt more —   190
And went hys wey, whan he had sayd.
Anoon this god of slep abrayd
Out of hys slep, and gan to goon,
And dyde as he had bede hym doon;
Took up the dreynte body sone   195
And bar hyt forth to Alcione,
Hys wif the quene, ther as she lay
Ryght even a quarter before day,
And stood ryght at hyr beddes fet,
And called hir ryght as she het   200
By name, and sayde, "My swete wyf,
Awake! let be your sorwful lyf!
For in your sorwe there lyth no red.
For, certes, swete, I nam but ded;
Ye shul me never on lyve yse.   205
But, goode swete herte, that ye
Bury my body, for such a tyde
Ye mowe hyt fynde the see besyde;
And farewel, swete, my worldes blysse!
I praye God youre sorwe lysse.   210
To lytel while oure blysse lasteth!"
    With that hir eyen up she casteth
And saw noght. "Allas!" quod she for sorwe,
And deyede within the thridde morwe.
But what she sayede more in that swow   215
I may not telle yow as now;

Hyt were to longe for to dwelle.
My first matere I wil yow telle,
Wherfore I have told this thyng
Of Alcione and Seys the kyng.   220
    For thus moche dar I saye wel,
I had be dolven everydel,
And ded, ryght thurgh defaute of slep
Yif I ne had red and take kep
Of this tale next before.   225
And I wol telle yow wherfore;
For I ne myghte, for bote ne bale,
Slepe, or I had red thys tale
Of this dreynte Seys the kyng,
And of the goddes of slepyng.   230
Whan I had red thys tale wel,
And overloked hyt everydel,
Me thoghte wonder yf hit were so;
For I had never herd speke, or tho,
Of noo goddes that koude make   235
Men to slepe, ne for to wake;
For I ne knew never god but oon.
And in my game I sayde anoon —
And yet me lyst ryght evel to pleye —
"Rather then that y shulde deye   240
Thorgh defaute of slepynge thus,
I wolde yive thilke Morpheus,
Or hys goddesse, dame Juno,
Or som wight elles, I ne roghte who,
To make me slepe and have som reste, —   245
I wil yive hym the alderbeste
Yifte that ever he abod hys lyve,
And here on warde, ryght now, as blyve,
Yif he wol make me slepe a lyte,
Of down of pure dowves white   250
I wil yive hym a fether-bed,
Rayed with gold, and ryght wel cled
In fyn blak satyn doutremer,
And many a pilowe, and every ber
Of cloth of Reynes, to slepe softe;   255
Hym thar not nede to turnen ofte.
And I wol yive hym al that falles
To a chambre; and al hys halles
I wol do peynte with pure gold
And tapite hem ful many fold   260
Of oo sute: this shal he have,
Yf I wiste where were hys cave,
Yf he kan make me slepe sone,
As did the goddesse quene Alcione.
And thus this ylke god, Morpheus,   265
May wynne of me moo feës thus
Than ever he wan; and to Juno,
That ys hys goddesse, I shal soo do,
I trow that she shal holde hir payd."
    I hadde unneth that word ysayd   270

Ryght thus as I have told hyt yow,
That sodeynly, I nyste how,
Such a lust anoon me took
To slepe, that ryght upon my book
Y fil aslepe, and therwith even   275
Me mette so ynly swete a sweven,
So wonderful, that never yit
Y trowe no man had the wyt
To konne wel my sweven rede;
No, not Joseph, withoute drede,   280
Of Egipte, he that redde so
The kynges metynge Pharao,
No more than koude the lest of us;
Ne nat skarsly Macrobeus,
(He that wrot al th'avysyoun   285
That he mette, kyng Scipioun,
The noble man, the Affrikan, —
Suche marvayles fortuned than)
I trowe, arede my dremes even.
Loo, thus hyt was, thys was my sweven. 290
   Me thoghte thus: that hyt was May,
And in the dawenynge I lay
(Me mette thus) in my bed al naked,
And loked forth, for I was waked
With smale foules a gret hep   295
That had affrayed me out of my slep,
Thorgh noyse and swetnesse of her song.
And, as me mette, they sate among
Upon my chambre roof wythoute,
Upon the tyles, overal aboute,   300
And songen, everych in hys wyse,
The moste solempne servise
By noote, that ever man, y trowe,
Had herd; for som of hem song lowe,
Som high, and al of oon acord.   305
To telle shortly, att oo word,
Was never herd so swete a steven, —
But hyt had be a thyng of heven, —
So mery a soun, so swete entewnes,
That certes, for the toun of Tewnes,   310
I nolde but I had herd hem synge;
For al my chambre gan to rynge
Thurgh syngynge of her armonye.
For instrument nor melodye
Was nowhere herd yet half so swete,   315
Nor of acord half so mete;
For ther was noon of hem that feyned
To synge, for ech of hem hym peyned
To fynde out mery crafty notes.
They ne spared not her throtes.   320
And sooth to seyn, my chambre was
Ful wel depeynted, and with glas
Were al the wyndowes wel yglased,
Ful clere, and nat an hoole ycrased,

That to beholde hyt was gret joye.   325
For holly al the story of Troye
Was in the glasynge ywroght thus,
Of Ector and of kyng Priamus,
Of Achilles and Lamedon,
And eke of Medea and of Jason,   330
Of Paris, Eleyne, and of Lavyne.
And alle the walles with colours fyne
Were peynted, bothe text and glose,
Of al the Romaunce of the Rose.
My wyndowes were shette echon,   335
And throgh the glas the sonne shon
Upon my bed with bryghte bemes,
With many glade gilde stremes;
And eke the welken was so fair, —
Blew, bryght, clere was the ayr,   340
And ful attempre for sothe hyt was;
For nother to cold nor hoot yt nas,
Ne in al the welken was no clowde.
   And as I lay thus, wonder lowde
Me thoght I herde an hunte blowe   345
T'assay hys horn, and for to knowe
Whether hyt were clere or hors of soun.
And I herde goynge, bothe up and doun,
Men, hors, houndes, and other thyng;
And al men speken of huntyng,   350
How they wolde slee the hert with strengthe,
And how the hert had, upon lengthe,
So moche embosed, y not now what.
   Anoon ryght, whan I herde that,
How that they wolde on-huntynge goon, 355
I was ryght glad, and up anoon
Took my hors, and forth I wente
Out of my chambre; I never stente
Til I com to the feld withoute.
Ther overtok y a gret route   360
Of huntes and eke of foresteres,
With many relayes and lymeres,
And hyed hem to the forest faste
And I with hem. So at the laste
I asked oon, ladde a lymere: 365
"Say, felowe, who shal hunte here?"
Quod I, and he answered ageyn,
"Syr, th'emperour Octovyen,"
Quod he, "and ys here faste by."
"A Goddes half, in good tyme!" quod I, 370
"Go we faste!" and gan to ryde.
Whan we came to the forest syde,
Every man dide ryght anoon
As to huntynge fil to doon.
The mayster-hunte anoon, fot-hot,   375
With a gret horn blew thre mot
At the uncouplynge of hys houndes.
Withynne a while the hert yfounde ys,

Yhalowed, and rechased faste
Longe tyme; and so at the laste   380
This hert rused, and staal away
Fro alle the houndes a privy way.
The houndes had overshote hym alle,
And were on a defaute yfalle.
Therwyth the hunte wonder faste   385
Blew a forloyn at the laste.
  I was go walked fro my tree,
And as I wente, ther cam by mee
A whelp, that fauned me as I stood,
That hadde yfolowed, and koude no good. 390
Hyt com and crepte to me as lowe
Ryght as hyt hadde me yknowe,
Helde doun hys hed and joyned hys eres,
And leyde al smothe doun hys heres.
I wolde have kaught hyt, and anoon   395
Hyt fledde, and was fro me goon;
And I hym folwed, and hyt forth wente
Doun by a floury grene wente
Ful thikke of gras, ful softe and swete.
With floures fele, faire under fete,   400
And litel used, hyt semed thus;
For both Flora and Zephirus,
They two that make floures growe,
Had mad her dwellynge ther, I trowe;
For hit was, on to beholde,   405
As thogh the erthe envye wolde
To be gayer than the heven,
To have moo floures, swiche seven,
As in the welken sterres bee.
Hyt had forgete the povertee   410
That wynter, thorgh hys colde morwes,
Had mad hyt suffre, and his sorwes,
All was forgeten, and that was sene.
For al the woode was waxen grene;
Swetnesse of dew had mad hyt waxe.   415
  Hyt ys no nede eke for to axe
Wher there were many grene greves,
Or thikke of trees, so ful of leves;
And every tree stood by hymselve
Fro other wel ten foot or twelve.   420
So grete trees, so huge of strengthe,
Of fourty or fifty fadme lengthe,
Clene withoute bowgh or stikke,
With croppes brode, and eke as thikke —
They were nat an ynche asonder —   425
That hit was shadewe overal under.
And many an hert and many an hynde
Was both before me and behynde.
Of founes, sowres, bukkes, does
Was ful the woode, and many roes,   430
And many sqwirelles, that sete
Ful high upon the trees and ete,

And in hir maner made festes.
Shortly, hyt was so ful of bestes,
That thogh Argus, the noble countour,   435
Sete to rekene in hys countour,
And rekened with his figures ten —
For by tho figures mowe al ken,
Yf they be crafty, rekene and noumbre,
And telle of every thing the noumbre —   440
Yet shoulde he fayle to rekene even
The wondres me mette in my sweven.
  But forth they romed ryght wonder faste
Doun the woode; so at the laste
I was war of a man in blak,   445
That sat and had yturned his bak
To an ook, an huge tree.
"Lord," thoght I, "who may that be?
What ayleth hym to sitten her?"
Anoon-ryght I wente ner;   450
Than found I sitte even upryght
A wonder wel-farynge knyght —
By the maner me thoghte so —
Of good mochel, and ryght yong therto,
Of the age of foure and twenty yer,   455
Upon hys berd but lytel her,
And he was clothed al in blak.
I stalked even unto hys bak,
And there I stood as stille as ought,
That, soth to saye, he saw me nought;   460
For-why he heng hys hed adoun,
And with a dedly sorwful soun
He made of rym ten vers or twelve
Of a compleynte to hymselve,
The moste pitee, the moste rowthe,   465
That ever I herde; for, by my trowthe,
Hit was gret wonder that Nature
Myght suffre any creature
To have such sorwe, and be not ded.
Ful pitous pale, and nothyng red,   470
He sayd a lay, a maner song,
Withoute noote, withoute song;
And was thys, for ful wel I kan
Reherse hyt; ryght thus hyt began:
"I have of sorwe so gret won   475
That joye gete I never non,
Now that I see my lady bryght,
Which I have loved with al my myght,
Is fro me ded and ys agoon.   479
  Allas, deth, what ayleth the,   481
That thou noldest have taken me,
Whan thou toke my lady swete,
That was so fair, so fresh, so fre,
So good, that men may wel se   485
Of al goodnesse she had no metel!"
  Whan he had mad thus his complaynte,

Hys sorwful hert gan faste faynte,
And his spirites wexen dede;
The blood was fled for pure drede   490
Doun to hys herte, to make hym warm —
For wel hyt feled the herte had harm —
To wite eke why hyt was adrad
By kynde, and for to make hyt glad;
For hit ys membre principal   495
Of the body; and that made al
Hys hewe chaunge and wexe grene
And pale, for ther noo blood ys sene
In no maner lym of hys.
Anoon therwith whan y sawgh this,   500
He ferde thus evel there he set,
I went and stood ryght at his fet,
And grette hym, but he spak noght,
But argued with his owne thoght,
And in hys wyt disputed faste   505
Why and how hys lyf myght laste;
Hym thoughte hys sorwes were so smerte
And lay so colde upon hys herte.
So, throgh hys sorwe and hevy thoght,
Made hym that he herde me noght;   510
For he had wel nygh lost hys mynde,
Thogh Pan, that men clepe god of kynde,
Were for hys sorwes never so wroth.
    But at the last, to sayn ryght soth,
He was war of me, how y stood   515
Before hym, and did of myn hood,
And had ygret hym as I best koude,
Debonayrly, and nothyng lowde.
He sayde, "I prey the, be not wroth.
I herde the not, to seyn the soth,   520
Ne I sawgh the not, syr, trewely."
"A, goode sir, no fors," quod y,
"I am ryght sory yif I have ought
Destroubled yow out of your thought.
Foryive me, yif I have mystake."   525
"Yis, th'amendes is lyght to make,"
Quod he, "for ther lyeth noon therto;
There ys nothyng myssayd nor do."
    Loo! how goodly spak thys knyght,
As hit had be another wyght;   530
He made hyt nouther towgh ne queynte.
And I saw that, and gan me aqueynte
With hym, and fond hym so tretable,
Ryght wonder skylful and resonable,
As me thoghte, for al hys bale.   535
Anoon ryght I gan fynde a tale
To hym, to loke wher I myght ought
Have more knowynge of hys thought.
"Sir," quod I, "this game is doon.
I holde that this hert be goon;   540
These huntes konne hym nowher see."

"Y do no fors therof," quod he;
"My thought ys theron never a del."
"By oure Lord," quod I, "y trow yow wel;
Ryght so me thinketh by youre chere.   545
But, sir, oo thyng wol ye here?
Me thynketh in gret sorowe I yow see.
But certes, sire, yif that yee
Wolde ought discure me youre woo,
I wolde, as wys God helpe me soo,   550
Amende hyt, yif I kan or may.
Ye mowe preve hyt be assay;
For, by my trouthe, to make yow hool,
I wol do al my power hool.
And telleth me of your sorwes smerte;   555
Paraunter hyt may ese youre herte,
That semeth ful sek under your syde."
    With that he loked on me asyde,
As who sayth, "Nay, that wol not be."
"Graunt mercy, goode frend," quod he,   560
"I thanke thee that thow woldest soo,
But hyt may never the rather be doo.
No man may my sorwe glade,
That maketh my hewe to falle and fade,
And hath myn understondynge lorn,   565
That me ys wo that I was born!
May noght make my sorwes slyde,
Nought al the remedyes of Ovyde,
Ne Orpheus, god of melodye,
Ne Dedalus with his playes slye;   570
Ne hele me may no phisicien,
Noght Ypocras, ne Galyen;
Me ys wo that I lyve houres twelve.
But whooso wol assay hymselve
Whether his hert kan have pitee   575
Of any sorwe, lat hym see me.
Y wreche, that deth hath mad al naked
Of al the blysse that ever was maked,
Yworthe worste of alle wyghtes,
That hate my dayes and my nyghtes!   580
My lyf, my lustes, be me loothe,
For al welfare and I be wroothe.
The pure deth ys so ful my foo
That I wolde deye, hyt wolde not soo;
For whan I folwe hyt, hit wol flee;   585
I wolde have hym, hyt nyl nat me.
This ys my peyne wythoute red,
Alway deynge and be not ded,
That Cesiphus, that lyeth in helle,
May not of more sorwe telle.   590
And whoso wiste al, by my trouthe,
My sorwe, but he hadde rowthe
And pitee of my sorwes smerte,
That man hath a fendly herte;
For whoso seeth me first on morwe   595

May seyn he hath met with sorwe,
For y am sorwe, and sorwe ys y.
"Allas! and I wol tel the why:
My song ys turned to pleynynge,
And al my laughtre to wepynge, 600
My glade thoghtes to hevynesse;
In travayle ys myn ydelnesse
And eke my reste; my wele is woo,
My good ys harm, and evermoo
In wrathe ys turned my pleynge 605
And my delyt into sorwynge.
Myn hele ys turned into seknesse,
In drede ys al my sykernesse;
To derke ys turned al my lyght,
My wyt ys foly, my day ys nyght, 610
My love ys hate, my slep wakynge,
My myrthe and meles ys fastynge,
My countenaunce ys nycete,
And al abaved, where so I be;
My pees, in pledynge and in werre. 615
Allas! how myghte I fare werre?
My boldnesse ys turned to shame,
For fals Fortune hath pleyd a game
Atte ches with me, allas the while!
The trayteresse fals and ful of gyle, 620
That al behoteth, and nothyng halt,
She goth upryght and yet she halt,
That baggeth foule and loketh faire,
The dispitouse debonaire,
That skorneth many a creature! 625
An ydole of fals portrayture
Ys she, for she wol sone wrien;
She is the monstres hed ywrien,
As fylthe over-ystrawed with floures.
Hir moste worshippe and hir flour ys 630
To lyen, for that ys hyr nature;
Withoute feyth, lawe, or mesure
She ys fals; and ever laughynge
With oon eye, and that other wepynge.
That ys broght up, she set al doun. 635
I lykne hyr to the scorpioun,
That ys a fals, flaterynge beste;
For with his hed he maketh feste,
But al amydde hys flaterynge
With hys tayle he wol stynge 640
And envenyme; and so wol she.
She ys th'envyouse charite
That ys ay fals, and semeth wel,
So turneth she hyr false whel
Aboute, for hyt ys nothyng stable, 645
Now by the fire, now at table;
For many oon hath she thus yblent.
She ys pley of enchauntement,
That semeth oon and ys not soo.

The false thef! what hath she doo, 650
Trowest thou? By oure Lord I wol the seye.
At the ches with me she gan to pleye;
With hir false draughtes dyvers
She staal on me, and tok my fers.
And whan I sawgh my fers awaye, 655
Allas! I kouthe no lenger playe,
But seyde, 'Farewel, swete, ywys,
And farewel al that ever ther ys!'
Therwith Fortune seyde 'Chek her!'
And 'Mat!' in myd poynt of the chekker, 660
With a poun errant, allas!
Ful craftier to pley she was
Than Athalus, that made the game
First of the ches, so was hys name.
But God wolde I had oones or twyes 665
Ykoud and knowe the jeupardyes
That kowde the Grek Pithagores!
I shulde have pleyd the bet at ches,
And kept my fers the bet therby.
And thogh wherto? for trewely 670
I holde that wyssh nat worth a stree!
Hyt had be never the bet for me.
For Fortune kan so many a wyle,
Ther be but fewe kan hir begile,
And eke she ys the lasse to blame; 675
Myself I wolde have do the same,
Before God, hadde I ben as she;
She oghte the more excused be.
For this I say yet more therto,
Had I be God and myghte have do 680
My wille, whan she my fers kaughte,
I wolde have drawe the same draughte.
For, also wys God yive me reste,
I dar wel swere she took the beste.
But through that draughte I have lorn 685
My blysse; allas! that I was born!
For evermore, y trowe trewly,
For al my wille, my lust holly
Ys turned; but yet, what to doone?
Be oure Lord, hyt ys to deye soone. 690
For nothyng I leve hyt noght,
But lyve and deye ryght in this thoght;
For there nys planete in firmament,
Ne in ayr ne in erthe noon element,
That they ne yive me a yifte echone 695
Of wepynge whan I am allone.
For whan that I avise me wel,
And bethenke me every del,
How that ther lyeth in rekenyng,
In my sorwe, for nothyng; 700
And how ther leveth no gladnesse
May glade me of my distresse,
And how I have lost suffisance,

And therto I have no plesance,
Than may I say I have ryght noght.   705
And whan al this falleth in my thoght,
Allas! than am I overcome!
For that ys doon ys not to come.
I have more sorowe than Tantale."

    And whan I herde hym tel thys tale   710
Thus pitously, as I yow telle,
Unnethe myght y lenger dwelle,
Hyt dyde myn herte so moche woo.
"A, goode sir," quod I, "say not soo!
Have som pitee on your nature   715
That formed yow to creature.
Remembre yow of Socrates,
For he ne counted nat thre strees
Of noght that Fortune koude doo."
"No," quod he, "I kan not soo."   720
"Why so? syr, yis parde!" quod y;
"Ne say noght soo, for trewely,
Thogh ye had lost the ferses twelve,
And ye for sorwe mordred yourselve,
Ye sholde be dampned in this cas   725
By as good ryght as Medea was,
That slough hir children for Jasoun;
And Phyllis also for Demophoun
Heng hirself, so weylaway!
For he had broke his terme-day   730
To come to hir. Another rage
Had Dydo, the quene eke of Cartage,
That slough hirself, for Eneas
Was fals; which a fool she was!
And Ecquo died, for Narcisus   735
Nolde nat love hir; and ryght thus
Hath many another foly doon;
And for Dalida died Sampson,
That slough hymself with a piler.
But ther is no man alyve her   740
Wolde for a fers make this woo!"
"Why so?" quod he, "hyt ys nat soo.
Thou wost ful lytel what thou menest;
I have lost more than thow wenest."
"Loo, [sey] how that may be?" quod y;   745
"Good sir, telle me al hooly
In what wyse, how, why, and wherfore
That ye have thus youre blysse lore."
"Blythely," quod he; "com sytte adoun!
I telle the upon a condicioun   750
That thou shalt hooly, with al thy wyt,
Doo thyn entent to herkene hit."
"Yis, syr." "Swere thy trouthe therto."
"Gladly." "Do thanne holde hereto!"
"I shal ryght blythely, so God me save,   755
Hooly, with al the wit I have,
Here yow, as wel as I kan."

"A Goddes half!" quod he, and began:
"Syr," quod he, "sith first I kouthe
Have any maner wyt fro youthe,   760
Or kyndely understondyng
To comprehende, in any thyng,
What love was, in myn owne wyt,
Dredeles, I have ever yit
Be tributarye and yiven rente   765
To Love, hooly with good entente,
And throgh plesaunce become his thral
With good wille, body, hert, and al.
Al this I putte in his servage,
As to my lord, and dide homage;   770
And ful devoutly I prayed hym to,
He shulde besette myn herte so
That hyt plesance to hym were,
And worship to my lady dere.

    "And this was longe, and many a yer,   775
Or that myn herte was set owher,
That I dide thus, and nyste why;
I trowe hit cam me kyndely.
Paraunter I was therto most able,
As a whit wal or a table,   780
For hit ys redy to cacche and take
Al that men wil theryn make,
Whethir so men wil portreye or peynte,
Be the werkes never so queynte.

    "And thilke tyme I ferde ryght so,   785
I was able to have lerned tho,
And to have kend as wel or better,
Paraunter, other art or letre;
But for love cam first in my thoght,
Therfore I forgat hyt noght.   790
I ches love to my firste craft;
Therfore hit ys with me laft,
For-why I tok hyt of so yong age
That malyce hadde my corage
Nat that tyme turned to nothyng   795
Thorgh to mochel knowlechyng.
For that tyme Yowthe, my maistresse,
Governed me in ydelnesse;
For hyt was in my firste youthe,
And thoo ful lytel good y couthe,   800
For al my werkes were flyttynge
That tyme, and al my thoght varyinge.
Al were to me ylyche good
That I knew thoo; but thus hit stood.

    "Hit happed that I cam on a day   805
Into a place ther that I say,
Trewly, the fayrest companye
Of ladyes that evere man with yë
Had seen togedres in oo place.
Shal I clepe hyt hap other grace   810
That broght me there? Nay, but Fortune,

That ys to lyen ful comune,
The false trayteresse pervers!
God wolde I koude clepe hir wers!
For now she worcheth me ful woo,   815
And I wol telle sone why soo.
  "Among these ladyes thus echon,
Soth to seyen y sawgh oon
That was lyk noon of the route;
For I dar swere, withoute doute,   820
That as the someres sonne bryght
Ys fairer, clerer, and hath more lyght
Than any other planete in heven,
The moone, or the sterres seven,
For al the world so hadde she   825
Surmounted hem alle of beaute,
Of maner, and of comlynesse,
Of stature, and of wel set gladnesse,
Of goodlyhede so wel beseye —
Shortly, what shal y more seye?   830
By God, and by his halwes twelve,
Hyt was my swete, ryght as hirselve,
She had so stedfast countenaunce,
So noble port and meyntenaunce.
And Love, that had wel herd my boone,   835
Had espyed me thus soone,
That she ful sone, in my thoght,
As helpe me God, so was ykaught
So sodenly, that I ne tok
No maner counseyl but at hir lok   840
And at myn herte; for-why hir eyen
So gladly, I trow, myn herte seyen,
That purely tho myn owne thoght
Seyde hit were beter serve hir for noght
Than with another to be wel.   845
And hyt was soth, for everydel
I wil anoon ryght telle thee why.
  "I sawgh hyr daunce so comlily,
Carole and synge so swetely,
Laughe and pleye so womanly,   850
And loke so debonairly,
So goodly speke and so frendly,
That, certes, y trowe that evermor
Nas seyn so blysful a tresor.
For every heer on hir hed,   855
Soth to seyne, hyt was not red,
Ne nouther yelowe, ne broun hyt nas,
Me thoghte most lyk gold hyt was.
And whiche eyen my lady hadde!
Debonaire, goode, glade, and sadde,   860
Symple, of good mochel, noght to wyde.
Therto hir look nas not asyde,
Ne overthwert, but beset so wel
Hyt drew and took up, everydel,
Al that on hir gan beholde.   865

Hir eyen semed anoon she wolde
Have mercy; fooles wenden soo;
But hyt was never the rather doo.
Hyt nas no countrefeted thyng;
Hyt was hir owne pure lokyng   870
That the goddesse, dame Nature,
Had mad hem opene by mesure,
And close; for, were she never so glad,
Hyr lokynge was not foly sprad,
Ne wildely, thogh that she pleyde;   875
But ever, me thoght, hir eyen seyde,
'Be God, my wrathe ys al foryive!'
  "Therwith hir lyste so wel to lyve,
That dulnesse was of hir adrad.
She nas to sobre ne to glad;   880
In alle thynges more mesure
Had never, I trowe, creature.
But many oon with hire lok she herte,
And that sat hyr ful lyte at herte,
For she knew nothyng of her thoght;   885
But whether she knew, or knew it nowght,
Algate she ne roughte of hem a stree!
To gete her love no ner nas he
That woned at hom, than he in Ynde;
The formest was alway behynde.   890
But goode folk, over al other,
She loved as man may do hys brother;
Of which love she was wonder large,
In skilful places that bere charge.
  "But which a visage had she thertoo!   895
Allas! myn herte ys wonder woo
That I ne kan discryven hyt!
Me lakketh both Englyssh and wit
For to undo hyt at the fulle;
And eke my spirites be so dulle   900
So gret a thyng for to devyse.
I have no wit that kan suffise
To comprehenden hir beaute.
But thus moche dar I sayn, that she
Was whit, rody, fressh, and lyvely hewed,   905
And every day hir beaute newed.
And negh hir face was alderbest;
For certes, Nature had swich lest
To make that fair, that trewly she
Was hir chef patron of beaute   910
And chef ensample of al hir werk,
And moustre; for be hyt never so derk,
Me thynketh I se hir ever moo.
And yet moreover, thogh alle thoo
That ever livede were now alyve,   915
Ne sholde have founde to discryve
Yn al hir face a wikked sygne;
For hit was sad, symple, and benygne.
  "And which a goodly, softe speche

Had that swete, my lyves leche!   920
So frendly, and so wel ygrounded,
Up al resoun so wel yfounded,
And so tretable to alle goode
That I dar swere wel by the roode,
Of eloquence was never founde   925
So swete a sownynge facounde,
Ne trewer tonged, ne skorned lasse,
Ne bet koude hele — that, by the masse
I durste swere, thogh the pope hit songe,
That ther was never yet throgh hir tonge   930
Man ne woman gretly harmed;
As for her [ther] was al harm hyd —
Ne lasse flaterynge in hir word,
That purely hir symple record
Was founde as trewe as any bond,   935
Or trouthe of any mannes hond.
Ne chyde she koude never a del;
That knoweth al the world ful wel.
    "But swich a fairnesse of a nekke
Had that swete that boon nor brekke   940
Nas ther non sene that myssat.
Hyt was whit, smothe, streght, and pure flat,
Wythouten hole; or canel-boon,
As be semynge, had she noon.
Hyr throte, as I have now memoyre,   945
Semed a round tour of yvoyre,
Of good gretnesse, and noght to gret.
    "And goode faire White she het;
That was my lady name ryght.
She was bothe fair and bryght;   950
She hadde not hir name wrong.
Ryght faire shuldres and body long
She had, and armes, every lyth
Fattyssh, flesshy, not gret therwith;
Ryght white handes, and nayles rede,   955
Rounde brestes; and of good brede
Hyr hippes were, a streight flat bak.
I knew on hir noon other lak
That al hir lymmes nere pure sewynge
In as fer as I had knowynge.   960
    "Therto she koude so wel pleye,
Whan that hir lyste, that I dar seye,
That she was lyk to torche bryght
That every man may take of lyght
Ynogh, and hyt hath never the lesse.   965
Of maner and of comlynesse
Ryght so ferde my lady dere;
For every wight of hir manere
Myght cacche ynogh, yif that he wolde,
Yif he had eyen hir to beholde.   970
For I dar swere wel, yif that she
Had among ten thousand be,
She wolde have be, at the leste,

A chef myrour of al the feste,
Thogh they had stonden in a rowe,   975
To mennes eyen that koude have knowe.
For wher-so men had pleyd or waked,
Me thoghte the felawsshyppe as naked
Withouten hir, that sawgh I oones,
As a corowne withoute stones.   980
Trewly she was, to myn yë,
The soleyn fenix of Arabye;
For ther livyth never but oon,
Ne swich as she ne knowe I noon.
    "To speke of godnesse, trewly she   985
Had as moche debonairte
As ever had Hester in the Bible,
And more, yif more were possyble.
And, soth to seyne, therwythal
She had a wyt so general,   990
So hool enclyned to alle goode,
That al hir wyt was set, by the rode,
Withoute malyce, upon gladnesse;
And therto I saugh never yet a lesse
Harmful than she was in doynge.   995
I sey nat that she ne had knowynge
What harm was; or elles she
Had koud no good, so thinketh me.
    "And trewly, for to speke of trouthe,
But she had had, hyt hadde be routhe.   1000
Therof she had so moche hyr del —
And I dar seyn and swere hyt wel —
That Trouthe hymself, over al and al
Had chose hys maner principal
In hir, that was his restyng place.   1005
Therto she hadde the moste grace,
To have stedefast perseveraunce,
And esy, atempre governaunce,
That ever I knew or wyste yit,
So pure suffraunt was hir wyt.   1010
And reson gladly she understood;
Hyt folowed wel she koude good.
She used gladly to do wel;
These were hir maners everydel.
    "Therwith she loved so wel ryght,   1015
She wrong do wolde to no wyght.
No wyght myghte do hir noo shame,
She loved so wel hir owne name.
Hyr lust to holde no wyght in honde,
Ne, be thou siker, she wolde not fonde   1020
To holde no wyght in balaunce
By half word ne by countenaunce,
But if men wolde upon hir lye;
Ne sende men into Walakye,
To Pruyse, and into Tartarye,   1025
To Alysaundre, ne into Turkye,
And byd hym faste anoon that he

Goo hoodles to the Drye Se
And come hom by the Carrenar,
And seye 'Sir, be now ryght war   1030
That I may of yow here seyn
Worshyp, or that ye come ageyn!'
She ne used no suche knakkes smale.
"But wherfore that y telle my tale?
Ryght on thys same, as I have seyd,   1035
Was hooly al my love leyd;
For certes she was, that swete wif,
My suffisaunce, my lust, my lyf,
Myn hap, myn hele, and al my blesse,
My worldes welfare, and my goddesse,   1040
And I hooly hires and everydel."
    "By oure Lord," quod I, "y trowe yow well!
Hardely, your love was wel beset;
I not how ye myghte have do bet."
"Bet? ne no wyght so wel," quod he.   1045
"Y trowe hyt, sir," quod I, "parde!"
"Nay, leve hyt wel!" "Sire, so do I;
I leve yow wel, that trewely
Yow thoghte that she was the beste,
And to beholde the alderfayreste,   1050
Whoso had loked hir with your eyen."
"With myn? nay, alle that hir seyen
Seyde and sworen hyt was soo.
And thogh they ne hadde, I wolde thoo
Have loved best my lady free,   1055
Thogh I had had al the beaute
That ever had Alcipyades,
And al the strengthe of Ercules,
And therto had the worthynesse
Of Alysaunder, and al the rychesse   1060
That ever was in Babyloyne,
In Cartage, or in Macedoyne,
Or in Rome, or in Nynyve;
And therto also hardy be
As was Ector, so have I joye,   1065
That Achilles slough at Troye —
And therfore was he slayn alsoo
In a temple, for bothe twoo
Were slayne, he and Antylegyus,
And so seyth Dares Frygius,   1070
For love of Polixena —
Or ben as wis as Mynerva,
I wolde ever, withoute drede,
Have loved hir, for I moste nede.
'Nede!' nay, trewly, I gabbe now;   1075
Noght 'nede,' and I wol tellen how,
For of good wille myn herte hyt wolde,
And eke to love hir I was holde
As for the fairest and the beste.
She was as good, so have I reste,   1080
As ever was Penelopee of Grece,

Or as the noble wif Lucrece,
That was the beste — he telleth thus,
The Romayn, Tytus Lyvyus —
She was as good, and nothyng lyk,   1085
Thogh hir stories be autentyk;
Algate she was as trewe as she.
    "But wherfore that I telle thee
Whan I first my lady say?
I was ryght yong, soth to say,   1090
And ful gret nede I hadde to lerne;
Whan my herte wolde yerne
To love, hyt was a gret empryse.
But as my wyt koude best suffise,
After my yonge childly wyt,   1095
Withoute drede, I besette hyt
To love hir in my beste wyse,
To do hir worship and the servise
That I koude thoo, be my trouthe,
Withoute feynynge outher slouthe;   1100
For wonder feyn I wolde hir se.
So mochel hyt amended me
That, whan I saugh hir first a-morwe,
I was warished of al my sorwe
Of al day after, til hyt were eve;   1105
Me thoghte nothyng myghte me greve,
Were my sorwes never so smerte,
And yet she syt so in myn herte,
That, by my trouthe, y nolde noght,
For al thys world, out of my thoght   1110
Leve my lady; noo, trewely!"
    "Now, by my trouthe, sir!" quod I,
"Me thynketh ye have such a chaunce
As shryfte wythoute repentaunce."
    "Repentaunce! nay, fy!" quod he,   1115
"Shulde y now repente me
To love? Nay, certes, than were I wel
Wers than was Achitofel,
Or Anthenor, so have I joye,
The traytor that betraysed Troye,   1120
Or the false Genelloun,
He that purchased the tresoun
Of Rowland and of Olyver.
Nay, while I am alyve her,
I nyl foryete hir never moo."   1125
    "Now, goode syre," quod I thoo,
"Ye han wel told me herebefore,
Hyt ys no nede to reherse it more,
How ye sawe hir first, and where.
But wolde ye tel me the manere   1130
To hire which was your firste speche,
Therof I wolde yow beseche;
And how she knewe first your thoght,
Whether ye loved hir or noght.
And telleth me eke what ye have lore,   1135

I herde yow telle herebefore."
   "Yee!" seyde he, "thow nost what thow
      menest;
I have lost more than thou wenest."
   "What los ys that?" quod I thoo;
"Nyl she not love yow? ys hyt soo?   1140
Or have ye oght doon amys,
That she hath left yow? ys hyt this?
For Goddes love, telle me al."
   "Before God," quod he, "and I shal.
I saye ryght as I have seyd,   1145
On hir was al my love leyd;
And yet she nyste hyt never a del
Noght longe tyme, leve hyt wel!
For be ryght siker, I durste noght,
For al this world, telle hir my thoght,   1150
Ne I wolde have wraththed hir, trewely.
For wostow why? She was lady
Of the body; she had the herte,
And who hath that, may not asterte.
But, for to kepe me fro ydelnesse,   1155
Trewly I dide my besynesse
To make songes, as I best koude,
And ofte tyme I song hem loude;
And made songes thus a gret del,
Althogh I koude not make so wel   1160
Songes, ne knewe the art al,
As koude Lamekes sone Tubal,
That found out first the art of songe;
For as hys brothres hamers ronge
Upon hys anvelt up and doun,   1165
Therof he took the firste soun, —
But Grekes seyn Pictagoras,
That he the firste fynder was
Of the art, Aurora telleth so, —
But therof no fors, of hem two.   1170
Algates songes thus I made
Of my felynge, myn herte to glade;
And, lo! this was the altherferste, —
I not wher hyt were the werste.
   'Lord, hyt maketh myn herte lyght,   1175
Whan I thenke on that swete wyght
That is so semely on to see;
And wisshe to God hit myghte so bee
That she wolde holde me for hir knyght,
My lady, that is so fair and bryght!'   1180
   "Now have I told thee, soth to say,
My firste song. Upon a day
I bethoghte me what woo
And sorwe that I suffred thoo
For hir, and yet she wyste hyt noght,   1185
Ne telle hir durste I nat my thoght.
'Allas!' thoghte I, 'y kan no red;
And but I telle hir, I nam but ded;

And yif I telle hyr, to seye ryght soth,
I am adred she wol be wroth.   1190
Allas! what shal I thanne do?'
   "In this debat I was so wo,
Me thoghte myn herte braste atweyne!
So at the laste, soth to sayne,
I bethoghte me that Nature   1195
Ne formed never in creature
So moche beaute, trewely,
And bounte, wythoute mercy.
In hope of that, my tale I tolde
With sorwe, as that I never sholde;   1200
For nedes, and mawgree my hed,
I most have told hir or be ded.
I not wel how that I began,
Ful evel rehersen hyt I kan;
And eke, as helpe me God withal,   1205
I trowe hyt was in the dismal,
That was the ten woundes of Egipte;
For many a word I over-skipte
In my tale, for pure fere
Lest my wordes mysset were.   1210
With sorweful herte, and woundes dede,
Softe and quakynge for pure drede
And shame, and styntynge in my tale
For ferde, and myn hewe al pale,
Ful ofte I wex bothe pale and red.   1215
Bowynge to hir, I heng the hed;
I durste nat ones loke hir on,
For wit, maner, and al was goon.
I seyde 'mercy!' and no more.
Hyt nas no game, hyt sat me sore.   1220
   "So at the laste, soth to seyn,
Whan that myn hert was come ageyn,
To telle shortly al my speche,
With hool herte I gan hir beseche
That she wolde be my lady swete;   1225
And swor, and hertely gan hir hete,
Ever to be stedfast and trewe,
And love hir alwey fresshly newe,
And never other lady have,
And al hir worship for to save   1230
As I best koude; I swor hir this —
'For youres is alle that ever ther ys
For evermore, myn herte swete!
And never to false yow, but I mete,
I nyl, as wys God helpe me soo!'   1235
   "And whan I had my tale y-doo,
God wot, she acounted nat a stree
Of al my tale, so thoghte me.
To telle shortly ryght as hyt ys,
Trewly hir answere hyt was this;   1240
I kan not now wel counterfete
Hir wordes, but this was the grete

Of hir answere: she sayde 'nay'
Al outerly. Allas! that day
The sorowe I suffred, and the woo   1245
That trewly Cassandra, that soo
Bewayled the destruccioun
Of Troye and of Ilyoun,
Had never swich sorwe as I thoo.
I durste no more say thertoo   1250
For pure fere, but stal away;
And thus I lyved ful many a day,
That trewely I hadde no ned
Ferther than my beddes hed
Never a day to seche sorwe;   1255
I fond hyt redy every morwe
For-why I loved hyr in no gere.
    "So hit befel, another yere,
I thoughte ones I wolde fonde
To do hir knowe and understonde   1260
My woo; and she wel understod
That I ne wilned thyng but god,
And worship, and to kepe hir name
Over alle thyng, and drede hir shame,
And was so besy hyr to serve;   1265
And pitee were I shulde sterve,
Syth that I wilned noon harm, ywis.
So whan my lady knew al this,
My lady yaf me al hooly
The noble yifte of hir mercy,   1270
Savynge hir worship, by al weyes, —
Dredles, I mene noon other weyes.
And therwith she yaf me a ryng;
I trowe hyt was the firste thyng;
But if myn herte was ywaxe   1275
Glad, that is no nede to axe!
As helpe me God, I was as blyve
Reysed, as fro deth to lyve,
Of al happes the alderbeste,
The gladdest, and the moste at reste.   1280
For trewely that swete wyght,
Whan I had wrong and she the ryght,
She wolde alway so goodly
Foryeve me so debonairly.
In al my yowthe, in al chaunce,   1285
She took me in hir governaunce.
Therwyth she was alway so trewe,
Our joye was ever ylyche newe;

Oure hertes wern so evene a payre,
That never nas that oon contrayre   1290
To that other, for no woo.
For sothe, ylyche they suffred thoo
Oo blysse, and eke oo sorwe bothe;
Ylyche they were bothe glad and wrothe;
Al was us oon, withoute were.   1295
And thus we lyved ful many a yere
So wel, I kan nat telle how."
    "Sir," quod I, "where is she now?"
"Now?" quod he, and stynte anoon.
Therwith he wax as ded as stoon,   1300
And seyde, "Allas, that I was bore!
That was the los that here-before
I tolde the that I hadde lorn.
Bethenke how I seyde here-beforn,
'Thow wost ful lytel what thow menest;   1305
I have lost more than thow wenest' —
God wot, allas! ryght that was she!"
    "Allas, sir, how? what may that be?"
    "She ys ded!" "Nay!" "Yis, be my trouthe!"
"Is that youre los? Be God, hyt ys routhe!"
And with that word ryght anoon   1311
They gan to strake forth; al was doon,
For that tyme, the hert-huntyng.
    With that me thoghte that this kyng
Gan homwardes for to ryde   1315
Unto a place, was there besyde,
Which was from us but a lyte.
A long castel with walles white,
Be seynt Johan! on a ryche hil
As me mette; but thus hyt fil.   1320
Ryght thus me mette, as I yow telle,
That in the castell ther was a belle,
As hyt hadde smyten houres twelve. —
Therwyth I awook myselve
And fond me lyinge in my bed;   1325
And the book that I hadde red,
Of Alcione and Seys the kyng,
And of the goddes of slepyng,
I fond hyt in myn hond ful even.
Thoghte I, "Thys ys so queynt a sweven   1330
That I wol, be processe of tyme,
Fonde to put this sweven in ryme
As I kan best, and that anoon."
This was my sweven; now hit ys doon.

Explicit the Bok of the Duchesse.

THE HOUSE OF FAME

THERE was probably a considerable interval between the composition of the *Book of the Duchess* and that of the *House of Fame*. Indeed the usual opinion has placed the *House of Fame* among the later of the minor poems, after the *Troilus* and not long before the *Legend of Good Women*. But there are sound reasons for questioning this date, and no decisive considerations in its support. The only positive evidence of the time of composition is furnished by Chaucer's reference to his daily "reckonings," which fixes the limit between 1374 and 1385, when he was controller of customs. For a more definite assignment within this period scholars have resorted to the interpretation of the poem itself. Allegorical explanations of its purpose and occasion, of which several have been proposed, are all very uncertain, and there remain only general literary considerations to fix the place of the poem in the sequence of Chaucer's writings.

In metrical form and literary type the *House of Fame* belongs with the *Book of the Duchess*. The device of the love-vision Chaucer continued to use until his later years, when he wrote and revised the *Legend of Good Women*. But he did not employ the octosyllabic couplet in any poem probably written after 1380, unless the *House of Fame* itself be an instance. As compared with the *Book of the Duchess*, the *House of Fame* shows a marked advance in technical mastery of style and meter. In both works the verse has something of the roughness or irregularity of the traditional English accentual type; but in the *House of Fame* it has become a freer instrument of expression. That poem also reveals much wider reading, and in particular the beginnings of Italian influence. Still there appears to be no reason why it should not be regarded as an early production. In it, as in the tragedies which were incorporated as the *Monk's Tale* in the Canterbury series, Chaucer draws upon Dante, who would very naturally have been the first Italian author to engage his attention. And the *House of Fame* is strikingly free from the influence of Boccaccio's long narrative poems, which so pervaded Chaucer's work in the decade of the eighties. Moreover, the undeniable independence, the experimental character, of the poem, though a mark of advancing craftsmanship, does not compel us to put it after the *Parliament of Fowls*, or even the *Anelida*. In view of all these considerations the *House of Fame* is here placed next to the *Book of the Duchess*, as the first specimen, among the longer works, of Chaucer's Italian period.

The poem, as already implied, is of a definitely transitional character. In structure a love-vision, it has many of the regular features of the type. It probably owes something to particular French visions such as Froissart's Paradys d'Amours and Temple d'Onnour and La Panthere d'Amours of Nicole de Margival. But no source or model has been found to which it is so much indebted as was the *Book of the Duchess* to the Jugement du Roy de Behaingne. And the dream convention is handled with great freedom and made the vehicle of many ideas quite remote from the usual allegories of love. Not only does Chaucer include a summary of the Æneid (which, because of the story of Dido, is appropriate enough in a love-vision), but he draws also upon several works of Ovid, upon the Somnium Scipionis, and upon mediæval Latin poets, historians, and men of science; and he makes so much use of Dante that the poem has been regarded — unjustifiably, to be sure — as an imitation of the Divine Comedy. The product of all these ingredients is a humorous, original, but rather heterogeneous work. For, though the thought of love is not lost sight of, and the purpose of the vision is declared to be that the poet may receive "tidings of Love's folk," yet the center of interest certainly shifts from the affairs of love to the vicissitudes of fame. Indeed by reason of this interest the *House of Fame* has been said to mark the transition from the Middle Ages to the Renaissance, and Chaucer has been hailed as a modern man. But his concern with the behavior of Fame and the circumstances of human reputation is something different from the craving for worldly immortality which is held, rightly or wrongly, to have distinguished the men of the Renaissance.

The primary purpose of the dream, if we may trust the words of the poem itself, was that Chaucer might be snatched away from the monotonous routine of his daily life and carried to the houses of Fame and Rumor, where he could hear tidings of love. This may be a sufficient motive and explanation of the work. But we never discover what the tidings were to be, and matters of love, as has been already remarked, by no means dominate the poem. Interpreters have consequently tried to read between the lines and find allegorical meanings related either to Chaucer's own life or to occasions in the life of his friends. According to autobiographical explanations, which long prevailed, Chaucer meant the poem to express his discontent with his dull and humble routine, or with his failure to win fame and recognition. Some have even seen in it a begging missive, addressed to those who might give him money or advancement. The expounders of the autobiographical allegory have been much influenced by parallels with the Divine Comedy, the importance of which has been overestimated, and their interpretations are at best very arbitrary. Of late these theories have fallen somewhat out of fashion, and in their place have been urged applications to various events at court. The tidings which Chaucer was to hear have been taken to refer to the marriage of Richard and Anne, or to the expected betrothal of Philippa, the daughter of John of Gaunt. Such explanations derive a certain support from the mention of the "man of gret auctoritee" at the end of the poem. But no good evidence has been found for the particular applications proposed, and if Chaucer had such an event in mind it seems likely to remain undiscovered. Professor Manly, relinquishing altogether the search for a definite historical occasion, suggested that the tidings were to be a series of tales, and the *House of Fame* was Chaucer's first attempt at a frame-story, which he abandoned for the *Legend of Good Women* and the *Canterbury Tales*. In spite of the popularity of the form and the variety of devices employed for enclosing tales within a tale, Manly's supposition is rather improbable in the case of the *House of Fame*. Certainly if Chaucer meant it as an introduction to a series of stories he allowed it to run to disproportionate length; and his reference to "this litel laste bok" (l. 1093) implies that he had no such continuation in mind. Perhaps the unknown tidings were to be as briefly related as the final tragic disclosure of the Black Knight in the *Book of the Duchess*.

Taken as it stands, without any allegorical interpretation or conjectured completion, the fragmentary *House of Fame* is a most entertaining specimen of the visions of which so many were written in Chaucer's time. If, when compared with the great tales of Chaucer's later years, it lacks the deeper interest of narrative and characterization, that is one reason for believing it to have been an early work. It is drawn, too, rather from books than from life. But it is rich in fancy, thought, and humor — the humor of situation and bright retort. It presents at least one comic character, the eagle, whose conversational powers are not unworthy of comparison with those of Chaunticleer. And, as a whole, it gives a lively impression of the intellectual interests of Chaucer and his contemporaries.

The House of Fame

Book I

Proem.

God turne us every drem to goode!
For hyt is wonder, be the roode,
To my wyt, what causeth swevenes
Eyther on morwes or on evenes;
And why th'effect folweth of somme,   5
And of somme hit shal never come;
Why that is an avisioun
And this a revelacioun,
Why this a drem, why that a sweven,
And noght to every man lyche even;   10
Why this a fantome, why these oracles,
I not; but whoso of these miracles
The causes knoweth bet then I,
Devyne he; for I certeinly
Ne kan hem noght, ne never thinke   15
To besily my wyt to swinke,
To knowe of hir signifiaunce
The gendres, neyther the distaunce
Of tymes of hem, ne the causes,
Or why this more then that cause is;   20
As yf folkys complexions
Make hem dreme of reflexions;
Or ellys thus, as other sayn,
For to gret feblenesse of her brayn,
By abstinence, or by seknesse,   25
Prison, stewe, or gret distresse,
Or ellys by dysordynaunce
Of naturel acustumaunce,
That som man is to curious
In studye, or melancolyous,   30
Or thus, so inly ful of drede,
That no man may hym botc bede;
Or elles that devocion
Of somme, and contemplacion
Causeth suche dremes ofte;   35
Or that the cruel lyf unsofte
Which these ilke lovers leden
That hopen over-muche or dreden,
That purely her impressions
Causen hem to have visions;   40
Or yf that spirites have the myght
To make folk to dreme a-nyght;
Or yf the soule, of propre kynde,
Be so parfit, as men fynde,
That yt forwot that ys to come,   45
And that hyt warneth alle and some

Of everych of her aventures
Be avisions, or be figures,
But that oure flessh ne hath no myght
To understonde hyt aryght,   50
For hyt is warned to derkly; —
But why the cause is, noght wot I.
Wel worthe, of this thyng, grete clerkys,
That trete of this and other werkes;
For I of noon opinion   55
Nyl as now make mensyon,
But oonly that the holy roode
Turne us every drem to goode!
For never, sith that I was born,
Ne no man elles me beforn,   60
Mette, I trowe stedfastly,
So wonderful a drem as I
The tenthe day now of Decembre,
The which, as I kan now remembre,
I wol yow tellen everydel.   65

The Invocation.

But at my gynnynge, trusteth wel,
I wol make invocacion,
With special devocion,
Unto the god of slep anoon,
That duelleth in a cave of stoon   70
Upon a strem that cometh fro Lete,
That is a flood of helle unswete,
Besyde a folk men clepeth Cymerie, —
There slepeth ay this god unmerie
With his slepy thousand sones,   75
That alwey for to slepe hir wone is.
And to this god, that I of rede,
Prey I that he wol me spede
My sweven for to telle aryght,
Yf every drem stonde in his myght.   80
And he that mover ys of al
That is and was and ever shal,
So yive hem joye that hyt here
Of alle that they dreme to-yere,
And for to stonden alle in grace   85
Of her loves, or in what place
That hem were levest for to stonde,
And shelde hem fro poverte and shonde,
And from unhap and ech disese,
And sende hem al that may hem plese,   90
That take hit wel and skorne hyt noght,

Ne hyt mysdemen in her thoght
Thorgh malicious entencion.
And whoso thorgh presumpcion,
Or hate, or skorn, or thorgh envye,   95
Dispit, or jape, or vilanye,
Mysdeme hyt, pray I Jesus God
That (dreme he barefot, dreme he shod),
That every harm that any man
Hath had, syth the world began,   100
Befalle hym therof, or he sterve,
And graunte he mote hit ful deserve,
Lo, with such a conclusion
As had of his avision
Cresus, that was kyng of Lyde,   105
That high upon a gebet dyde!
This prayer shal he have of me;
I am no bet in charyte!
Now herkeneth, as I have yow seyd,
What that I mette, or I abreyd.   110

Story.

Of Decembre the tenthe day,
Whan hit was nyght, to slepe I lay
Ryght ther as I was wont to done,
And fil on slepe wonder sone,
As he that wery was forgo   115
On pilgrymage myles two
To the corseynt Leonard,
To make lythe of that was hard.

But as I slepte, me mette I was
Withyn a temple ymad of glas;   120
In which ther were moo ymages
Of gold, stondynge in sondry stages,
And moo ryche tabernacles,
And with perre moo pynacles,
And moo curiouse portreytures,   125
And queynte maner of figures
Of olde werk, then I saugh ever.
For certeynly, I nyste never
Wher that I was, but wel wyste I,
Hyt was of Venus redely,   130
The temple; for in portreyture,
I sawgh anoon-ryght hir figure
Naked fletynge in a see.
And also on hir hed, pardee,
Hir rose garlond whit and red,   135
And hir comb to kembe hyr hed,
Hir dowves, and daun Cupido,
Hir blynde sone, and Vulcano,
That in his face was ful broun.

But as I romed up and doun,   140
I fond that on a wall ther was
Thus writen on a table of bras:

"I wol now singen, yif I kan,
The armes, and also the man
That first cam, thurgh his destinee,   145
Fugityf of Troy contree,
In Itayle, with ful moche pyne
Unto the strondes of Lavyne."
And tho began the story anoon,
As I shal telle yow echon.   150

First sawgh I the destruction
Of Troye, thurgh the Grek Synon,
[That] with his false forswerynge,
And his chere and his lesynge,
Made the hors broght into Troye,   155
Thorgh which Troyens loste al her joye.
And aftir this was grave, allas!
How Ilyon assayled was
And wonne, and kyng Priam yslayn
And Polytes, his sone, certayn,   160
Dispitously, of daun Pirrus.
And next that sawgh I how Venus,
Whan that she sawgh the castel brende,
Doun fro the heven gan descende,
And bad hir sone Eneas flee;   165
And how he fledde, and how that he
Escaped was from al the pres,
And took his fader, Anchises,
And bar hym on hys bak away,
Cryinge, "Allas! and welaway!"   170
The whiche Anchises in hys hond
Bar the goddes of the lond,
Thilke that unbrende were.
And I saugh next, in al thys fere,
How Creusa, daun Eneas wif,   175
Which that he lovede as hys lyf,
And hir yonge sone Iulo,
And eke Askanius also,
Fledden eke with drery chere,
That hyt was pitee for to here;   180
And in a forest, as they wente,
At a turnynge of a wente,
How Creusa was ylost, allas!
That ded, not I how, she was;
How he hir soughte, and how hir gost   185
Bad hym to flee the Grekes host,
And seyde he moste unto Itayle,
As was hys destinee, sauns faille;
That hyt was pitee for to here,
When hir spirit gan appere,   190
The wordes that she to hym seyde,
And for to kepe hir sone hym preyde.
Ther sawgh I graven eke how he,
Hys fader eke, and his meynee,
With hys shippes gan to saylle   195
Towardes the contree of Itaylle

As streight as that they myghte goo.
Ther saugh I thee, cruel Juno,
That art daun Jupiteres wif,
That hast yhated, al thy lyf,   200
Al the Troianysshe blood,
Renne and crye, as thou were wood,
On Eolus, the god of wyndes,
To blowen oute, of alle kyndes,
So lowde that he shulde drenche   205
Lord and lady, grom and wenche,
Of al the Troian nacion,
Withoute any savacion.
    Ther saugh I such tempeste aryse,
That every herte myght agryse   210
To see hyt peynted on the wal.
    Ther saugh I graven eke withal,
Venus, how ye, my lady dere,
Wepynge with ful woful chere,
Prayen Jupiter on hye   215
To save and kepe that navye
Of the Troian Eneas,
Syth that he hir sone was.
    Ther saugh I Joves Venus kysse,
And graunted of the tempest lysse.   220
Ther saugh I how the tempest stente,
And how with alle pyne he wente,
And prively tok arryvage
In the contree of Cartage;
And on the morwe, how that he   225
And a knyght, highte Achate,
Mette with Venus that day,
Goynge in a queynt array,
As she had ben an hunteresse,
With wynd blowynge upon hir tresse;   230
How Eneas gan hym to pleyne,
When that he knew hir, of his peyne;
And how his shippes dreynte were,
Or elles lost, he nyste where;
How she gan hym comforte thoo,   235
And bad hym to Cartage goo,
And ther he shulde his folk fynde,
That in the see were left behynde.
    And, shortly of this thyng to pace,
She made Eneas so in grace   240
Of Dido, quene of that contree,
That, shortly for to tellen, she
Becam hys love, and let him doo
Al that weddynge longeth too.
What shulde I speke more queynte,   245
Or peyne me my wordes peynte
To speke of love? Hyt wol not be;
I kan not of that faculte.
And eke to telle the manere
How they aqueynteden in fere,   250

Hyt were a long proces to telle,
And over-long for yow to dwelle,
    Ther sawgh I grave how Eneas
Tolde Dido every caas
That hym was tyd upon the see.   255
    And after grave was, how shee
Made of hym shortly at oo word
Hyr lyf, hir love, hir lust, hir lord,
And dide hym al the reverence,
And leyde on hym al the dispence,   260
That any woman myghte do,
Wenynge hyt had al be so
As he hir swor; and herby demed
That he was good, for he such semed.
Allas! what harm doth apparence,   265
Whan hit is fals in existence!
For he to hir a traytour was;
Wherfore she slow hirself, allas!
Loo, how a woman doth amys
To love him that unknowen ys!   270
For, be Cryste, lo, thus yt fareth:
"Hyt is not al gold that glareth."
For also browke I wel myn hed,
Ther may be under godlyhed
Kevered many a shrewed vice.   275
Therfore be no wyght so nyce,
To take a love oonly for chere,
Or speche, or for frendly manere,
For this shal every woman fynde,
That som man, of his pure kynde,   280
Wol shewen outward the fayreste,
Tyl he have caught that what him leste;
And thanne wol he causes fynde,
And swere how that she ys unkynde,
Or fals, or privy, or double was.   285
Al this seye I be Eneas
And Dido, and hir nyce lest,
That loved al to sone a gest;
Therfore I wol seye a proverbe,
That "he that fully knoweth th'erbe   290
May saufly leye hyt to his yë";
Withoute drede, this ys no lye.
    But let us speke of Eneas,
How he betrayed hir, allas!
And lefte hir ful unkyndely.   295
So when she saw al utterly,
That he wolde hir of trouthe fayle,
And wende fro hir to Itayle,
She gan to wringe hir hondes two.
"Allas!" quod she, "what me ys woo!   300
Allas! is every man thus trewe,
That every yer wolde have a newe,
Yf hit so longe tyme dure,
Or elles three, peraventure?

As thus: of oon he wolde have fame   305
In magnyfinge of hys name;
Another for frendshippe, seyth he;
And yet ther shal the thridde be
That shal be take for delyt,
Loo, or for synguler profit."   310
In suche wordes gan to pleyne
Dydo of hir grete peyne,
As me mette redely;
Non other auctour alegge I.
"Allas!" quod she, "my swete herte,   315
Have pitee on my sorwes smerte,
And slee mee not! goo noght awey!
O woful Dido, wel-away!"
Quod she to hirselve thoo.
"O Eneas, what wol ye doo?   320
O that your love, ne your bond
That ye have sworn with your ryght hond,
Ne my crewel deth," quod she,
"May holde yow stille here with me!
O haveth of my deth pitee!   325
Iwys, my dere herte, ye
Knowen ful wel that never yit,
As ferforth as I hadde wyt,
Agylte [I] yow in thoght ne dede.
O, have ye men such godlyhede   330
In speche, and never a del of trouthe?
Allas, that ever hadde routhe
Any woman on any man!
Now see I wel, and telle kan,
We wrechched wymmen konne noon art;   335
For certeyn, for the more part,
Thus we be served everychone.
How sore that ye men konne groone,
Anoon as we have yow receyved,
Certaynly we ben deceyvyd!   340
For, though your love laste a seson,
Wayte upon the conclusyon,
And eke how that ye determynen,
And for the more part diffynen.
"O, wel-awey that I was born!   345
For thorgh yow is my name lorn,
And alle myn actes red and songe
Over al thys lond, on every tonge.
O wikke Fame! for ther nys
Nothing so swift, lo, as she is!   350
O, soth ys, every thing ys wyst,
Though hit be kevered with the myst.
Eke, though I myghte duren ever,
That I have don, rekever I never,
That I ne shal be seyd, allas,   355
Yshamed be thourgh Eneas,
And that I shal thus juged be, —
'Loo, ryght as she hath don, now she

Wol doo eft-sones, hardely;'
Thus seyth the peple prively."   360
But that is don, is not to done;
Al hir compleynt ne al hir moone,
Certeyn, avayleth hir not a stre.
And when she wiste sothly he
Was forth unto his shippes goon,   365
She into hir chambre wente anoon,
And called on hir suster Anne,
And gan hir to compleyne thanne;
And seyde, that she cause was
That she first loved him, allas!   370
And thus counseylled hir thertoo.
But what! when this was seyd and doo,
She rof hirselve to the herte,
And deyde thorgh the wounde smerte.
And al the maner how she deyde,   375
And alle the wordes that she seyde,
Whoso to knowe hit hath purpos,
Rede Virgile in Eneydos
Or the Epistle of Ovyde,
What that she wrot or that she dyde;   380
And nere hyt to long to endyte,
Be God, I wolde hyt here write.
But wel-away! the harm, the routhe,
That hath betyd for such untrouthe,
As men may ofte in bokes rede,   385
And al day sen hyt yet in dede,
That for to thynken hyt, a tene is.
Loo, Demophon, duk of Athenys,
How he forswor hym ful falsly,
And traysed Phillis wikkidly,   390
That kynges doghtre was of Trace,
And falsly gan hys terme pace;
And when she wiste that he was fals,
She heng hirself ryght be the hals,
For he had doon hir such untrouthe.   395
Loo! was not this a woo and routhe?
Eke lo! how fals and reccheles
Was to Breseyda Achilles,
And Paris to Oenone;
And Jason to Isiphile,   400
And eft Jason to Medea;
And Ercules to Dyanira,
For he left hir for Yole,
That made hym cache his deth, parde.
How fals eke was he Theseus,   405
That, as the story telleth us,
How he betrayed Adriane;
The devel be hys soules bane!
For had he lawghed, had he loured,
He moste have ben al devoured,   410
Yf Adriane ne had ybe.
And, for she had of hym pite,

She made hym fro the deth escape,
And he made hir a ful fals jape;
For aftir this, withyn a while,   415
He lefte hir slepynge in an ile
Desert allone, ryght in the se,
And stal away, and let hir be,
And took hir suster Phedra thoo
With him, and gan to shippe goo.   420
And yet he had yswore to here
On al that ever he myghte swere,
That, so she saved hym hys lyf,
He wolde have take hir to hys wif;
For she desired nothing ellis,   425
In certeyn, as the book us tellis.
    But to excusen Eneas
Fullyche of al his grete trespas,
The book seyth Mercurie, sauns fayle,
Bad hym goo into Itayle,   430
And leve Auffrikes regioun,
And Dido and hir faire toun.
    Thoo sawgh I grave how to Itayle
Daun Eneas is goo to sayle;
And how the tempest al began,   435
And how he loste hys sterisman,
Which that the stere, or he tok kep,
Smot over bord, loo! as he slep.
    And also sawgh I how Sybile
And Eneas, besyde an yle,   440
To helle wente, for to see
His fader, Anchyses the free;
How he ther fond Palinurus,
And Dido, and eke Deiphebus,
And every turment eke in helle   445
Saugh he, which is longe to telle;
Which whoso willeth for to knowe,
He moste rede many a rowe
On Virgile or on Claudian,
Or Daunte, that hit telle kan.   450
    Tho saugh I grave al the aryvayle
That Eneas had in Itayle;
And with kyng Latyne hys tretee,
And alle the batayles that hee
Was at hymself, and eke hys knyghtis,   455
Or he had al ywonne his ryghtis;
And how he Turnus reft his lyf,
And wan Lavina to his wif;
And alle the mervelous signals
Of the goddys celestials;   460

How, mawgree Juno, Eneas,
For al hir sleight and hir compas,
Acheved al his aventure,
For Jupiter took of hym cure
At the prayer of Venus, —   465
The whiche I preye alwey save us,
And us ay of oure sorwes lyghte!
    When I had seen al this syghte
In this noble temple thus,
"A, Lord!" thoughte I, "that madest us,   470
Yet sawgh I never such noblesse
Of ymages, ne such richesse,
As I saugh graven in this chirche;
But not wot I whoo did hem wirche,
Ne where I am, ne in what contree.   475
But now wol I goo out and see,
Ryght at the wiket, yf y kan
See owhere any stiryng man,
That may me telle where I am."
    When I out at the dores cam,   480
I faste aboute me beheld.
Then sawgh I but a large feld,
As fer as that I myghte see,
Withouten toun, or hous, or tree,
Or bush, or grass, or eryd lond;   485
For al the feld nas but of sond
As smal as man may se yet lye
In the desert of Lybye;
Ne no maner creature
That ys yformed be Nature   490
Ne sawgh I, me to rede or wisse.
"O Crist!" thoughte I, "that art in blysse,
Fro fantome and illusion
Me save!" and with devocion
Myn eyen to the hevene I caste.   495
Thoo was I war, lo! at the laste,
That faste be the sonne, as hye
As kenne myghte I with myn yë,
Me thoughte I sawgh an egle sore,
But that hit semed moche more   500
Then I had any egle seyn.
But this as sooth as deth, certeyn,
Hyt was of gold, and shon so bryghte
That never sawe men such a syghte,
But yf the heven had ywonne   505
Al newe of gold another sonne;
So shone the egles fethers bryghte,
And somwhat dounward gan hyt lyghte.

Explicit liber primus.

Book II

Incipit liber secundus.

Proem.

Now herkeneth, every maner man
That Englissh understonde kan,   510
And listeneth of my drem to lere.
For now at erste shul ye here
So sely an avisyon,
That Isaye, ne Scipion,
Ne kyng Nabugodonosor,   515
Pharoo, Turnus, ne Elcanor,
Ne mette such a drem as this!
Now faire blisfull, O Cipris,
So be my favour at this tyme!
And ye, me to endite and ryme   520
Helpeth, that on Parnaso duelle,
Be Elicon, the clere welle.
O Thought, that wrot al that I mette,
And in the tresorye hyt shette
Of my brayn, now shal men se   525
Yf any vertu in the be,
To tellen al my drem aryght.
Now kythe thyn engyn and myght!

The Dream.

This egle, of which I have yow told,
That shon with fethres as of gold,   530
Which that so hye gan to sore,
I gan beholde more and more,
To se the beaute and the wonder;
But never was ther dynt of thonder,
Ne that thyng that men calle fouder,   535
That smot somtyme a tour to powder,
And in his swifte comynge brende,
That so swithe gan descende
As this foul, when hyt beheld
That I a-roume was in the feld;   540
And with hys grymme pawes stronge,
Withyn hys sharpe nayles longe,
Me, fleynge, in a swap he hente,
And with hys sours ayen up wente,
Me caryinge in his clawes starke   545
As lyghtly as I were a larke,
How high, I can not telle yow,
For I cam up, y nyste how.
For so astonyed and asweved
Was every vertu in my heved,   550
What with his sours and with my drede,
That al my felynge gan to dede;
For-whi hit was to gret affray.

Thus I longe in hys clawes lay,
Til at the laste he to me spak   555
In mannes vois, and seyde, "Awak!
And be not agast so, for shame!"
And called me tho by my name,
And, for I shulde the bet abreyde,
Me mette, "Awak," to me he seyde,   560
Ryght in the same vois and stevene
That useth oon I koude nevene;
And with that vois, soth for to seyn,
My mynde cam to me ageyn,
For hyt was goodly seyd to me,   565
So nas hyt never wont to be.
    And here-withal I gan to stere,
And he me in his fet to bere,
Til that he felte that I had hete,
And felte eke tho myn herte bete.   570
And thoo gan he me to disporte,
And with wordes to comforte,
And sayde twyes, "Seynte Marye!
Thou art noyous for to carye,
And nothyng nedeth it, pardee!   575
For, also wis God helpe me,
As thou noon harm shalt have of this;
And this caas that betyd the is,
Is for thy lore and for thy prow; —
Let see! darst thou yet loke now?   580
Be ful assured, boldely,
I am thy frend." And therwith I
Gan for to wondren in my mynde.
"O God!" thoughte I, "that madest kynde,
Shal I noon other weyes dye?   585
Wher Joves wol me stellyfye,
Or what thing may this sygnifye?
I neyther am Ennok, ne Elye,
Ne Romulus, ne Ganymede,
That was ybore up, as men rede,   590
To hevene with daun Jupiter,
And mad the goddys botiller."
Loo, this was thoo my fantasye!
But he that bar me gan espye
That I so thoughte, and seyde this: 595
"Thow demest of thyself amys;
For Joves ys not theraboute —
I dar wel putte the out of doute —
To make of the as yet a sterre,
But er I bere the moche ferre,   600
I wol the telle what I am,
And whider thou shalt, and why I cam
To do thys, so that thou take

Good herte, and not for fere quake."
"Gladly," quod I. "Now wel," quod he,   605
"First, I, that in my fet have the,
Of which thou hast a fere and wonder,
Am dwellynge with the god of thonder,
Which that men callen Jupiter,
That dooth me flee ful ofte fer   610
To do al hys comaundement.
And for this cause he hath me sent
To the; now herke, be thy trouthe!
Certeyn, he hath of the routhe,
That thou so longe trewely   615
Hast served so ententyfly
Hys blynde nevew Cupido,
And faire Venus also,
Withoute guerdon ever yit,
And never-the-lesse hast set thy wit —   620
Although that in thy hed ful lyte is —
To make bookys, songes, dytees,
In ryme, or elles in cadence,
As thou best canst, in reverence
Of Love, and of hys servantes eke,   625
That have hys servyse soght, and seke;
And peynest the to preyse hys art,
Although thou haddest never part;
Wherfore, also God me blesse,
Joves halt hyt gret humblesse,   630
And vertu eke, that thou wolt make
A-nyght ful ofte thyn hed to ake
In thy studye, so thou writest,
And ever mo of love enditest,
In honour of hym and in preysynges,   635
And in his folkes furtherynges,
And in hir matere al devisest,
And noght hym nor his folk dispisest,
Although thou maist goo in the daunce
Of hem that hym lyst not avaunce.   640
    "Wherfore, as I seyde, ywys,
Jupiter considereth this,
And also, beau sir, other thynges;
That is, that thou hast no tydynges
Of Loves folk yf they be glade,   645
Ne of noght elles that God made;
And noght oonly fro fer contree
That ther no tydynge cometh to thee,
But of thy verray neyghebores,
That duellen almost at thy dores,   650
Thou herist neyther that ne this;
For when thy labour doon al ys,
And hast mad alle thy rekenynges,
In stede of reste and newe thynges,
Thou goost hom to thy hous anoon;   655
And, also domb as any stoon,
Thou sittest at another book

Tyl fully daswed ys thy look,
And lyvest thus as an heremyte,
Although thyn abstynence ys lyte.   660
    "And therfore Joves, thorgh hys grace,
Wol that I bere the to a place
Which that hight the Hous of Fame,
To do the som disport and game,
In som recompensacion   665
Of labour and devocion,
That thou hast had, loo causeles,
To Cupido, the rechcheles!
And thus this god, thorgh his merite,
Wol with som maner thing the quyte,   670
So that thou wolt be of good chere.
For truste wel that thou shalt here,
When we be come there I seye,
Mo wonder thynges, dar I leye,
And of Loves folk moo tydynges,   675
Both sothe sawes and lesinges;
And moo loves newe begonne,
And longe yserved loves wonne,
And moo loves casuelly
That ben betyd, no man wot why,   680
But as a blynd man stert an hare;
And more jolytee and fare,
While that they fynde love of stel,
As thinketh hem, and over-al wel;
Mo discordes, moo jelousies,   685
Mo murmures, and moo novelries,
And moo dissymulacions,
And feyned reparacions;
And moo berdys in two houres
Withoute rasour or sisoures   690
Ymad, then greynes be of sondes;
And eke moo holdynge in hondes,
And also moo renovelaunces
Of olde forleten aqueyntaunces;
Mo love-dayes and acordes   695
Then on instrumentes be cordes;
And eke of loves moo eschaunges
Then ever cornes were in graunges, —
Unnethe maistow trowen this?"
Quod he. "Noo, helpe me God so wys!"   700
Quod I. "Noo? why?" quod he. "For hyt
Were impossible, to my wit,
Though that Fame had alle the pies
In al a realme, and alle the spies,
How that yet she shulde here al this,   705
Or they espie hyt." "O yis, yis!"
Quod he to me, "that kan I preve
Be reson worthy for to leve,
So that thou yeve thyn advertence
To understonde my sentence.   710
    "First shalt thou here where she duelleth,

And so thyn oune bok hyt tellith;
Hir paleys stant, as I shal seye,
Ryght even in myddes of the weye
Betwixen hevene, erthe, and see;   715
That what so ever in al these three
Is spoken, either privy or apert,
The way therto ys so overt,
And stant eke in so juste a place
That every soun mot to hyt pace,   720
Or what so cometh from any tonge,
Be hyt rouned, red, or songe,
Or spoke in suerte or in drede,
Certeyn, hyt moste thider nede.
   "Now herkene wel, for-why I wille   725
Tellen the a propre skille
And a worthy demonstracion
In myn ymagynacion.
   "Geffrey, thou wost ryght wel this,
That every kyndely thyng that is   730
Hath a kyndely stede ther he
May best in hyt conserved be;
Unto which place every thyng,
Thorgh his kyndely enclynyng,
Moveth for to come to,   735
Whan that hyt is awey therfro;
As thus: loo, thou maist alday se
That any thing that hevy be,
As stoon, or led, or thyng of wighte,
And bere hyt never so hye on highte,   740
Lat goo thyn hand, hit falleth doun.
Ryght so seye I be fyr or soun,
Or smoke, or other thynges lyghte;
Alwey they seke upward on highte.
While ech of hem is at his large,   745
Lyght thing upward, and dounward charge.
And for this cause mayst thou see
That every ryver to the see
Enclyned ys to goo by kynde,
And by these skilles, as I fynde,   750
Hath fyssh duellynge in flood and see,
And treës eke in erthe bee.
Thus every thing, by thys reson,
Hath his propre mansyon,
To which hit seketh to repaire,   755
Ther-as hit shulde not apaire.
Loo, this sentence ys knowen kouth
Of every philosophres mouth,
As Aristotle and daun Platon,
And other clerkys many oon;   760
And to confirme my resoun,
Thou wost wel this, that spech is soun,
Or elles no man myghte hyt here;
Now herke what y wol the lere.
   "Soun ys noght but eyr ybroken,   765

And every speche that ys spoken,
Lowd or pryvee, foul or fair,
In his substaunce ys but air;
For as flaumbe ys but lyghted smoke,
Ryght soo soun ys air ybroke.   770
But this may be in many wyse,
Of which I wil the twoo devyse,
As soun that cometh of pipe or harpe.
For whan a pipe is blowen sharpe,
The air ys twyst with violence   775
And rent; loo, thys ys my sentence;
Eke, whan men harpe-strynges smyte,
Whether hyt be moche or lyte,
Loo, with the strok the ayr tobreketh;
And ryght so breketh it when men speketh.   780
Thus wost thou wel what thing is speche.
   "Now hennesforth y wol the teche
How every speche, or noyse, or soun,
Thurgh hys multiplicacioun,
Thogh hyt were piped of a mous,   785
Mot nede come to Fames Hous.
I preve hyt thus — take hede now —
Be experience; for yf that thow
Throwe on water now a stoon,
Wel wost thou, hyt wol make anoon   790
A litel roundell as a sercle,
Paraunter brod as a covercle;
And ryght anoon thow shalt see wel,
That whel wol cause another whel,
And that the thridde, and so forth, brother,   795
Every sercle causynge other
Wydder than hymselve was;
And thus fro roundel to compas,
Ech aboute other goynge
Causeth of othres sterynge   800
And multiplyinge ever moo,
Til that hyt be so fer ygoo,
That hyt at bothe brynkes bee.
Although thou mowe hyt not ysee
Above, hyt gooth yet alway under,   805
Although thou thenke hyt a gret wonder.
And whoso seyth of trouthe I varye,
Bid hym proven the contrarye.
And ryght thus every word, ywys,
That lowd or pryvee spoken ys,   810
Moveth first an ayr aboute,
And of thys movynge, out of doute,
Another ayr anoon ys meved,
As I have of the watir preved,
That every cercle causeth other.   815
Ryght so of ayr, my leve brother;
Everych ayr another stereth
More and more, and speche up bereth,
Or voys, or noyse, or word, or soun.

Ay through multiplicacioun,   820
Til hyt be atte Hous of Fame, —
Take yt in ernest or in game.
    "Now have I told, yf thou have mynde,
How speche or soun, of pure kynde,
Enclyned ys upward to meve;   825
This, mayst thou fele, wel I preve.
And that same place, ywys,
That every thyng enclyned to ys,
Hath his kyndelyche stede:
That sheweth hyt, withouten drede,   830
That kyndely the mansioun
Of every speche, of every soun,
Be hyt eyther foul or fair,
Hath hys kynde place in ayr.
And syn that every thyng that is   835
Out of hys kynde place, ywys,
Moveth thidder for to goo,
Yif hyt aweye be therfroo,
As I have before preved the,
Hyt seweth, every soun, parde,   840
Moveth kyndely to pace
Al up into his kyndely place.
And this place of which I telle,
Ther as Fame lyst to duelle,
Ys set amyddys of these three,   845
Heven, erthe, and eke the see,
As most conservatyf the soun.
Than ys this the conclusyoun,
That every speche of every man,
As y the telle first began,   850
Moveth up on high to pace
Kyndely to Fames place.
    "Telle me this now feythfully,
Have y not preved thus symply,
Withoute any subtilite   855
Of speche, or gret prolixite
Of termes of philosophie,
Of figures of poetrie,
Or colours of rethorike?
Pardee, hit oughte the to lykel   860
For hard langage and hard matere
Ys encombrous for to here
Attones; wost thou not wel this?"
And y answered and seyde, "Yis."
    "A ha!" quod he, "lo, so I can   865
Lewedly to a lewed man
Speke, and shewe hym swyche skiles
That he may shake hem be the biles,
So palpable they shulden be.
But telle me this, now praye y the,   870
How thinketh the my conclusyon?"
[Quod he]. "A good persuasion,"
Quod I, "hyt is; and lyk to be

Ryght so as thou hast preved me."
"Be God," quod he, "and as I leve,   875
Thou shalt have yet, or hit be eve,
Of every word of thys sentence
A preve by experience,
And with thyne eres heren wel
Top and tayl, and everydel,   880
That every word that spoken ys
Cometh into Fames Hous, ywys,
As I have seyd; what wilt thou more?"
And with this word upper to sore
He gan, and seyde, "Be seynt Jame,   885
Now wil we speken al of game!"
    "How farest thou?" quod he to me.
"Wel," quod I. "Now see," quod he,
"By thy trouthe, yond adoun,
Wher that thou knowest any toun,   890
Or hous, or any other thing.
And whan thou hast of ought knowyng,
Looke that thou warne me,
And y anoon shal telle the
How fer that thou art now therfro."   895
    And y adoun gan loken thoo,
And beheld feldes and playnes,
And now hilles, and now mountaynes,
Now valeyes, now forestes,
And now unnethes grete bestes;   900
Now ryveres, now citees,
Now tounes, and now grete trees,
Now shippes seyllynge in the see.
    But thus sone in a while he
Was flowen fro the ground so hye   905
That al the world, as to myn yë,
No more semed than a prikke;
Or elles was the air so thikke
That y ne myghte not discerne.
With that he spak to me as yerne,   910
And seyde, "Seest thou any toun
Or ought thou knowest yonder doun?"
I sayde, "Nay." "No wonder nys,"
Quod he, "for half so high as this
Nas Alixandre Macedo;   915
Ne the kyng, Daun Scipio,
That saw in drem, at poynt devys,
Helle and erthe and paradys;
Ne eke the wrechche Dedalus,
Ne his child, nyce Ykarus,   920
That fleigh so highe that the hete
Hys wynges malt, and he fel wete
In myd the see, and ther he dreynte,
For whom was maked moch compleynte.
    "Now turn upward," quod he, "thy face,   925
And behold this large space,
This eyr; but loke thou ne be

Adrad of hem that thou shalt se;
For in this region, certeyn,
Duelleth many a citezeyn,   930
Of which that speketh Daun Plato.
These ben the eyryssh bestes, lo!"
And so saw y all that meynee
Boothe goon and also flee.
"Now," quod he thoo, "cast up thyn yë.   935
Se yonder, loo, the Galaxie,
Which men clepeth the Milky Wey,
For hit ys whit (and somme, parfey,
Kallen hyt Watlynge Strete)
That ones was ybrent with hete,   940
Whan the sonnes sone, the rede,
That highte Pheton, wolde lede
Algate hys fader carte, and gye.
The carte-hors gonne wel espye
That he koude no governaunce,   945
And gonne for to lepe and launce,
And beren hym now up, now doun,
Til that he sey the Scorpioun,
Which that in heven a sygne is yit.
And he, for ferde, loste hys wyt   950
Of that, and let the reynes gon
Of his hors; and they anoon
Gonne up to mounte and doun descende,
Til bothe the eyr and erthe brende;
Til Jupiter, loo, atte laste,   955
Hym slow, and fro the carte caste.
Loo, ys it not a gret myschaunce
To lete a fool han governaunce
Of thing that he can not demeyne?"
And with this word, soth for to seyne,   960
He gan alway upper to sore,
And gladded me ay more and more,
So feythfully to me spak he.
    Tho gan y loken under me
And beheld the ayerissh bestes,   965
Cloudes, mystes, and tempestes,
Snowes, hayles, reynes, wyndes,
And th'engendrynge in hir kyndes,
All the wey thrugh which I cam.
"O God!" quod y, "that made Adam,   970
Moche ys thy myght and thy noblesse!"
And thoo thoughte y upon Boece,
That writ, "A thought may flee so hye,
Wyth fetheres of Philosophye,
To passen everych element;   975
And whan he hath so fer ywent,
Than may be seen, behynde hys bak,
Cloude," — and al that y of spak.
    Thoo gan y wexen in a were,
And seyde, "Y wot wel y am here;   980
But wher in body or in gost

I not, ywys; but God, thou wostl"
For more clere entendement
Nas me never yit ysent.
And than thoughte y on Marcian,   985
And eke on Anteclaudian,
That sooth was her descripsion
Of alle the hevenes region,
As fer as that y sey the preve;
Therfore y kan hem now beleve.   990
    With that this egle gan to crye,
"Lat be," quod he, "thy fantasye!
Wilt thou lere of sterres aught?"
"Nay, certeynly," quod y, "ryght naught."
"And why?" "For y am now to old."   995
"Elles I wolde the have told,"
Quod he, "the sterres names, lo,
And al the hevenes sygnes therto,
And which they ben." "No fors," quod y.
"Yis, pardee!" quod he; "wostow why?   1000
For when thou redest poetrie,
How goddes gonne stellifye
Bridd, fissh, best, or him or here,
As the Raven, or eyther Bere,
Or Arionis harpe fyn,   1005
Castor, Pollux, or Delphyn,
Or Athalantes doughtres sevene,
How alle these arn set in hevene;
For though thou have hem ofte on honde,
Yet nostow not wher that they stonde."   1010
"No fors," quod y, "hyt is no nede.
I leve as wel, so God me spede,
Hem that write of this matere,
As though I knew her places here;
And eke they shynen here so bryghte,   1015
Hyt shulde shenden al my syghte,
To loke on hem." "That may wel be,"
Quod he. And so forth bar he me
A while, and than he gan to crye,
That never herde I thing so hye,   1020
"Now up the hed, for al ys wel;
Seynt Julyan, loo, bon hostel!
Se here the Hous of Fame, lo!
Maistow not heren that I do?"
"What?" quod I. "The grete soun,"   1025
Quod he, "that rumbleth up and doun
In Fames Hous, full of tydynges,
Bothe of feir speche and chidynges,
And of fals and soth compouned.
Herke wel; hyt is not rouned.   1030
Herestow not the grete swogh?"
"Yis, parde!" quod y, "wel ynogh."
"And what soun is it lyk?" quod hee.
"Peter! lyk betynge of the see,"
Quod y, "ayen the roches holowe,   1035

Whan tempest doth the shippes swalowe;
And lat a man stonde, out of doute,
A myle thens, and here hyt route;
Or elles lyk the last humblynge
After the clappe of a thundringe,   1040
Whan Joves hath the air ybete.
But yt doth me for fere swete!"
"Nay, dred the not therof," quod he;
"Hyt is nothing will byten the;
Thou shalt non harm have trewely."   1045
    And with this word both he and y
As nygh the place arryved were
As men may casten with a spere.
Y nyste how, but in a strete
He sette me fair on my fete,   1050
And seyde, "Walke forth a pas,
And tak thyn aventure or cas,
That thou shalt fynde in Fames place."
    "Now," quod I, "while we han space
To speke, or that I goo fro the,   1055
For the love of God, telle me —
In sooth, that wil I of the lere —
Yf thys noyse that I here
Be, as I have herd the tellen,
Of folk that doun in erthe duellen,   1060
And cometh here in the same wyse
As I the herde or this devyse;
And that there lives body nys

In al that hous that yonder ys,
That maketh al this loude fare."   1065
"Noo," quod he, "by Seynte Clare,
And also wis God rede me!
But o thing y will warne the
Of the whiche thou wolt have wonder.
Loo, to the Hous of Fame yonder,   1070
Thou wost now how, cometh every speche;
Hyt nedeth noght eft the to teche.
But understond now ryght wel this,
Whan any speche ycomen ys
Up to the paleys, anon-ryght   1075
Hyt wexeth lyk the same wight
Which that the word in erthe spak,
Be hyt clothed red or blak;
And hath so verray hys lyknesse
That spak the word, that thou wilt gesse   1080
That it the same body be,
Man or woman, he or she.
And ys not this a wonder thyng?"
"Yis," quod I tho, "by heven kyng!"
And with this word, "Farewel," quod he,   1085
"And here I wol abyden the;
And God of heven sende the grace
Some good to lernen in this place."
And I of him tok leve anon,
And gan forth to the paleys gon.   1090

Explicit liber secundus.

Book III

Incipit liber tercius.

Invocation.

O God of science and of lyght,
Appollo, thurgh thy grete myght,
This lytel laste bok thou gye!
Nat that I wilne, for maistrye,
Here art poetical be shewed;   1095
But for the rym ys lyght and lewed,
Yit make hyt sumwhat agreable,
Though som vers fayle in a sillable;
And that I do no diligence
To shewe craft, but o sentence.   1100
And yif, devyne vertu, thow
Wilt helpe me to shewe now
That in myn hed ymarked ys —
Loo, that is for to menen this,
The Hous of Fame for to descryve —   1105
Thou shalt se me go as blyve

Unto the nexte laure y see,
And kysse yt, for hyt is thy tree.
Now entre in my brest anoon!

The Dream.

Whan I was fro thys egle goon,   1110
I gan beholde upon this place.
And certein, or I ferther pace,
I wol yow al the shap devyse
Of hous and site, and al the wyse
How I gan to thys place aproche   1115
That stood upon so hygh a roche,
Hier stant ther non in Spayne.
But up I clomb with alle payne,
And though to clymbe it greved me,
Yit I ententyf was to see,   1120
And for to powren wonder lowe,

Yf I koude any weyes knowe
What maner stoon this roche was.
For hyt was lyk alum de glas,
But that hyt shoon ful more clere;   1125
But of what congeled matere
Hyt was, I nyste redely.
But at the laste aspied I,
And found that hit was every del
A roche of yse, and not of stel.   1130
Thoughte I, "By seynt Thomas of Kent!
This were a feble fundament
To bilden on a place hye.
He ought him lytel glorifye
That hereon bilt, God so me save!"   1135
    Tho sawgh I al the half ygrave
With famous folkes names fele,
That had iben in mochel wele,
And her fames wide yblowe.
But wel unnethes koude I knowe   1140
Any lettres for to rede
Hir names by; for, out of drede,
They were almost ofthowed so
That of the lettres oon or two
Was molte away of every name,   1145
So unfamous was woxe hir fame.
But men seyn, "What may ever laste?"
    Thoo gan I in myn herte caste
That they were molte awey with hete,
And not awey with stormes bete.   1150
For on that other syde I say
Of this hil, that northward lay,
How hit was writen ful of names
Of folkes that hadden grete fames
Of olde tyme, and yet they were   1155
As fressh as men had writen hem here
The selve day ryght, or that houre
That I upon hem gan to poure.
But wel I wiste what yt made;
Hyt was conserved with the shade   1160
Of a castel that stood on high —
Al this wrytynge that I sigh —
And stood eke on so cold a place
That hete myghte hit not deface.
Thoo gan I up the hil to goon,   1165
And fond upon the cop a woon,
That al the men that ben on lyve
Ne han the kunnynge to descrive
The beaute of that ylke place,
Ne coude casten no compace   1170
Swich another for to make,
That myght of beaute ben hys make,
Ne so wonderlych ywrought;
That hit astonyeth yit my thought,
And maketh al my wyt to swynke,   1175

On this castel to bethynke,
So that the grete craft, beaute,
The cast, the curiosite
Ne kan I not to yow devyse;
My wit ne may me not suffise.   1180
    But natheles al the substance
I have yit in my remembrance;
For whi me thoughte, be seynt Gyle!
Al was of ston of beryle,
Bothe the castel and the tour,   1185
And eke the halle and every bour,
Wythouten peces or joynynges.
But many subtil compassinges,
Babewynnes and pynacles,
Ymageries and tabernacles,   1190
I say; and ful eke of wyndowes,
As flakes falle in grete snowes.
And eke in ech of the pynacles
Weren sondry habitacles,
In which stoden, al withoute —   1195
Ful the castel, al aboute —
Of alle maner of mynstralles,
And gestiours, that tellen tales
Both of wepinge and of game,
Of al that longeth unto Fame.   1200
    Ther herde I pleyen on an harpe
That sowned bothe wel and sharpe,
Orpheus ful craftely,
And on his syde, faste by,
Sat the harper Orion,   1205
And Eacides Chiron,
And other harpers many oon,
And the Bret Glascurion;
And smale harpers with her gleës
Sate under hem in dyvers seës,   1210
And gunne on hem upward to gape,
And countrefete hem as an ape,
Or as craft countrefeteth kynde.
    Tho saugh I stonden hem behynde,
Afer fro hem, al be hemselve,   1215
Many thousand tymes twelve,
That maden lowde mynstralcies
In cornemuse and shalemyes,
And many other maner pipe,
That craftely begunne to pipe,   1220
Bothe in doucet and in rede,
That ben at festes with the brede;
And many flowte and liltyng horn,
And pipes made of grene corn,
As han thise lytel herde-gromes,   1225
That kepen bestis in the bromes.
Ther saugh I than Atiteris,
And of Athenes daun Pseustis,
And Marcia that loste her skyn,

Bothe in face, body, and chyn,   1230
For that she wolde envien, loo!
To pipen bet than Appolloo.
Ther saugh I famous, olde and yonge,
Pipers of the Duche tonge,
To lerne love-daunces, sprynges,   1235
Reyes, and these straunge thynges.
Tho saugh I in an other place
Stonden in a large space,
Of hem that maken blody soun
In trumpe, beme, and claryoun;   1240
For in fight and blod-shedynge
Ys used gladly clarionynge.
Ther herde I trumpen Messenus,
Of whom that speketh Virgilius.
There herde I trumpe Joab also,   1245
Theodomas, and other mo;
And alle that used clarion
In Cataloigne and Aragon,
That in her tyme famous were
To lerne, saugh I trumpe there.   1250
There saugh I sitte in other seës,
Pleyinge upon sondry gleës,
Whiche that I kan not nevene,
Moo than sterres ben in hevene,
Of whiche I nyl as now not ryme,   1255
For ese of yow, and los of tyme.
For tyme ylost, this knowen ye,
Be no way may recovered be.
Ther saugh I pleye jugelours,
Magiciens, and tregetours,   1260
And Phitonesses, charmeresses,
Olde wicches, sorceresses,
That use exorsisacions,
And eke these fumygacions;
And clerkes eke, which konne wel   1265
Al this magik naturel,
That craftely doon her ententes
To make, in certeyn ascendentes,
Ymages, lo, thrugh which magik
To make a man ben hool or syk.   1270
Ther saugh I the, quene Medea,
And Circes eke, and Calipsa;
Ther saugh I Hermes Ballenus,
Limote, and eke Symon Magus.
There saugh I, and knew hem by name,   1275
That by such art don men han fame.
Ther saugh I Colle tregetour
Upon a table of sycamour
Pleye an uncouth thyng to telle;
Y saugh him carien a wynd-melle   1280
Under a walsh-note shale.
   What shuld I make lenger tale
Of alle the pepil y ther say,

Fro hennes into domes day?
Whan I had al this folk beholde,   1285
And fond me lous, and nought yholde,
And eft imused longe while
Upon these walles of berile,
That shoone ful lyghter than a glas
And made wel more than hit was   1290
To semen every thing, ywis,
As kynde thyng of Fames is,
I gan forth romen til I fond
The castel-yate on my ryght hond,
Which that so wel corven was   1295
That never such another nas;
And yit it was be aventure
Iwrought, as often as be cure.
Hyt nedeth noght yow more to tellen,
To make yow to longe duellen,   1300
Of this yates florisshinges,
Ne of compasses, ne of kervynges,
Ne how they hatte in masoneries,
As corbetz, ful of ymageries.
But, Lord! so fair yt was to shewe,   1305
For hit was al with gold behewe.
But in I wente, and that anoon.
Ther mette I cryinge many oon,
"A larges, larges, hold up wel!
God save the lady of thys pel,   1310
Our oune gentil lady Fame,
And hem that wilnen to have name
Of us!" Thus herde y crien alle,
And faste comen out of halle
And shoken nobles and sterlynges.   1315
And somme corouned were as kynges,
With corounes wroght ful of losenges;
And many ryban and many frenges
Were on her clothes trewely.
   Thoo atte last aspyed y   1320
That pursevantes and heraudes,
That crien ryche folkes laudes,
Hyt weren alle; and every man
Of hem, as y yow tellen can,
Had on him throwen a vesture   1325
Which that men clepe a cote-armure,
Enbrowded wonderliche ryche,
Although they nere nought ylyche.
But noght nyl I, so mote y thryve,
Ben aboute to dyscryve   1330
Alle these armes that ther weren,
That they thus on her cotes beren,
For hyt to me were impossible;
Men myghte make of hem a bible
Twenty foot thykke, as y trowe.   1335
For certeyn, whoso koude iknowe
Myghte ther alle the armes seen

Of famous folk that han ybeen
In Auffrike, Europe, and Asye,
Syth first began the chevalrie.   1340
  Loo! how shulde I now telle al thys?
Ne of the halle eke what nede is
To tellen yow that every wal
Of hit, and flor, and roof, and al
Was plated half a foote thikke   1345
Of gold, and that nas nothyng wikke,
But, for to prove in alle wyse,
As fyn as ducat in Venyse,
Of which to lite al in my pouche is?
And they were set as thik of nouchis   1350
Ful of the fynest stones faire,
That men rede in the Lapidaire,
As grasses growen in a mede.
But hit were al to longe to rede
The names; and therfore I pace.   1355
  But in this lusty and ryche place,
That Fames halle called was,
Ful moche prees of folk ther nas,
Ne crowdyng for to mochil prees.
But al on hye, above a dees,   1360
Sitte in a see imperiall,
That mad was of a rubee all,
Which that a carbuncle ys ycalled,
Y saugh, perpetually ystalled,
A femynyne creature,   1365
That never formed by Nature
Nas such another thing yseye.
For alther-first, soth for to seye,
Me thoughte that she was so lyte
That the lengthe of a cubite   1370
Was lengere than she semed be.
But thus sone, in a whyle, she
Hir tho so wonderliche streighte
That with hir fet she erthe reighte,
And with hir hed she touched hevene,   1375
Ther as shynen sterres sevene.
And therto eke, as to my wit,
I saugh a gretter wonder yit,
Upon her eyen to beholde;
But certeyn y hem never tolde.   1380
For as feele eyen hadde she
As fetheres upon foules be,
Or weren on the bestes foure
That Goddis trone gunne honoure,
As John writ in th'Apocalips.   1385
Hir heer, that oundy was and crips,
As burned gold hyt shoon to see;
And, soth to tellen, also she
Had also fele upstondyng eres
And tonges, as on bestes heres;   1390
And on hir fet woxen saugh y

Partriches wynges redely.
  But, Lord! the perry and the richesse
I saugh sittyng on this godesse!
And, Lord! the hevenyssh melodye   1395
Of songes, ful of armonye,
I herde aboute her trone ysonge,
That al the paleys-walles ronge!
So song the myghty Muse, she
That cleped ys Caliope,   1400
And hir eighte sustren eke,
That in her face semen meke;
And ever mo, eternally,
They songe of Fame, as thoo herd y:
"Heryed be thou and thy name,   1405
Goddesse of Renoun or of Fame!"
  Tho was I war, loo, atte laste,
As I myne eyen gan up caste,
That thys ylke noble quene
On her shuldres gan sustene   1410
Bothe th'armes and the name
Of thoo that hadde large fame:
Alexander and Hercules,
That with a sherte hys lyf les!
Thus fond y syttynge this goddesse   1415
In nobley, honour, and rychesse;
Of which I stynte a while now,
Other thing to tellen yow.
  Tho saugh I stonde on eyther syde,
Streight doun to the dores wide,   1420
Fro the dees, many a peler
Of metal that shoon not ful cler;
But though they nere of no rychesse,
Yet they were mad for gret noblesse,
And in hem hy and gret sentence;   1425
And folk of digne reverence,
Of which I wil yow telle fonde,
Upon the piler saugh I stonde.
  Alderfirst, loo, ther I sigh
Upon a piler stonde on high,   1430
That was of led and yren fyn,
Hym of secte saturnyn,
The Ebrayk Josephus, the olde,
That of Jewes gestes tolde;
And he bar on hys shuldres hye   1435
The fame up of the Jewerye.
And by hym stoden other sevene,
Wise and worthy for to nevene,
To helpen him bere up the charge,
Hyt was so hevy and so large.   1440
And for they writen of batayles,
As wel as other olde mervayles,
Therfor was, loo, thys piler
Of which that I yow telle her,
Of led and yren bothe, ywys,   1445

For yren Martes metal ys,
Which that god is of bataylle;
And the led, withouten faille,
Ys, loo, the metal of Saturne,
That hath a ful large whel to turne.   1450

    Thoo stoden forth, on every rowe,
Of hem which that I koude knowe,
Though I hem noght be ordre telle,
To make yow to longe to duelle,
These of whiche I gynne rede.   1455
There saugh I stonden, out of drede,
Upon an yren piler strong
That peynted was, al endelong,
With tigres blod in every place,
The Tholosan that highte Stace,   1460
That bar of Thebes up the fame
Upon his shuldres, and the name
Also of cruel Achilles.
And by him stood, withouten les,
Ful wonder hy on a piler   1465
Of yren, he, the gret Omer;
And with him Dares and Tytus
Before, and eke he Lollius,
And Guydo eke de Columpnis,
And Englyssh Gaufride eke, ywis;   1470
And ech of these, as have I joye,
Was besy for to bere up Troye.
So hevy therof was the fame
That for to bere hyt was no game.
But yet I gan ful wel espie,   1475
Betwex hem was a litil envye.
Oon seyde that Omer made lyes,
Feynynge in hys poetries,
And was to Grekes favorable;
Therfor held he hyt but fable.   1480

    Tho saugh I stonde on a piler,
That was of tynned yren cler,
The Latyn poete, Virgile,
That bore hath up a longe while
The fame of Pius Eneas.   1485

    And next hym on a piler was,
Of coper, Venus clerk, Ovide,
That hath ysowen wonder wide
The grete god of Loves name.
And ther he bar up wel hys fame   1490
Upon his piler, also hye
As I myghte see hyt with myn yë;
For-why this halle, of which I rede,
Was woxen on highte, length, and brede,
Wel more, be a thousand del,   1495
Than hyt was erst, that saugh I wel.

    Thoo saugh I on a piler by,
Of yren wroght ful sternely,
The grete poete, daun Lucan,

And on hys shuldres bar up than,   1500
As high as that y myghte see,
The fame of Julius and Pompe.
And by him stoden alle these clerkes
That writen of Romes myghty werkes,
That yf y wolde her names telle,   1505
Al to longe most I dwelle.

    And next him on a piler stood
Of soulfre, lyk as he were wood,
Daun Claudian, the sothe to telle,
That bar up al the fame of helle,   1510
Of Pluto, and of Proserpyne,
That quene ys of the derke pyne.

    What shulde y more telle of this?
The halle was al ful, ywys,
Of hem that writen olde gestes,   1515
As ben on treës rokes nestes;
But hit a ful confus matere
Were alle the gestes for to here,
That they of write, or how they highte.

    But while that y beheld thys syghte,   1520
I herde a noyse aprochen blyve,
That ferde as been don in an hive
Ayen her tyme of out-fleynge;
Ryght such a maner murmurynge,
For al the world, hyt semed me.   1525
Tho gan I loke aboute and see
That ther come entryng into the halle
A ryght gret companye withalle,
And that of sondry regiouns,
Of alleskynnes condiciouns   1530
That dwelle in erthe under the mone,
Pore and ryche. And also sone
As they were come in to the halle,
They gonne doun on kneës falle
Before this ilke noble quene,   1535
And seyde, "Graunte us, lady shene,
Ech of us of thy grace a bone!"
And somme of hem she graunted sone,
And somme she werned wel and faire,
And somme she graunted the contraire   1540
Of her axyng outterly.
But thus I seye yow, trewely,
What her cause was, y nyste.
For of this folk ful wel y wiste,
They hadde good fame ech deserved,   1545
Although they were dyversly served;
Ryght as her suster, dame Fortune,
Ys wont to serven in comune.

    Now herke how she gan to paye
That gonne her of her grace praye;   1550
And yit, lo, al this companye
Seyden sooth, and noght a lye.
    "Madame," seyde they, "we be

Folk that here besechen the
That thou graunte us now good fame,   1555
And let our werkes han that name;
In ful recompensacioun
Of good werkes, yive us good renoun."
   "I werne yow hit," quod she anon;
"Ye gete of me good fame non,   1560
Be God! and therfore goo your wey."
"Allas!" quod they, "and welaway!
Telle us what may your cause be."
"For me lyst hyt noght," quod she;
"No wyght shal speke of yow, ywis,   1565
Good ne harm, ne that ne this."
And with that word she gan to calle
Her messager, that was in halle,
And bad that he shulde faste goon,
Upon peyne to be blynd anon,   1570
For Eolus the god of wynde, —
"In Trace, ther ye shal him fynde,
And bid him bringe his clarioun,
That is ful dyvers of his soun,
And hyt is cleped Clere Laude,   1575
With which he wont is to heraude
Hem that me list ypreised be.
And also bid him how that he
Brynge his other clarioun,
That highte Sklaundre in every toun,   1580
With which he wont is to diffame
Hem that me liste, and do hem shame."
   This messager gan faste goon,
And found where in a cave of ston,
In a contree that highte Trace,   1585
This Eolus, with harde grace,
Held the wyndes in distresse,
And gan hem under him to presse,
That they gonne as beres rore,
He bond and pressed hem so sore.   1590
   This messager gan faste crie,
"Rys up," quod he, "and faste hye,
Til thou at my lady be;
And tak thy clariouns eke with the,
And sped the forth." And he anon   1595
Tok to a man, that highte Triton,
Hys clarions to bere thoo,
And let a certeyn wynd to goo,
That blew so hydously and hye
That hyt ne lefte not a skye   1600
In alle the welken long and brod.
This Eolus nowhere abod
Til he was come to Fames fet,
And eke the man that Triton het;
And ther he stod, as stille as stoon,   1605
And her-withal ther come anoon
Another huge companye

Of goode folk, and gunne crie,
"Lady, graunte us now good fame,
And lat oure werkes han that name   1610
Now in honour of gentilesse,
And also God your soule blesse!
For we han wel deserved hyt,
Therfore is ryght that we ben quyt."
   "As thryve I," quod she, "ye shal faylle!   1615
Good werkes shal yow noght availle
To have of me good fame as now.
But wite ye what? Y graunte yow
That ye shal have a shrewed fame,
And wikkyd loos, and worse name,   1620
Though ye good loos have wel deserved.
Now goo your wey, for ye be served.
And thou, dan Eolus, let see,
Tak forth thy trumpe anon," quod she,
"That is ycleped Sklaundre lyght,   1625
And blow her loos, that every wight
Speke of hem harm and shrewednesse,
In stede of good and worthynesse.
For thou shalt trumpe alle the contrayre
Of that they han don wel or fayre."   1630
   "Allas!" thoughte I, "what aventures
Han these sory creatures!
For they, amonges al the pres,
Shul thus be shamed gilteles.
But what! hyt moste nedes be."   1635
   What dide this Eolus, but he
Tok out hys blake trumpe of bras,
That fouler than the devel was,
And gan this trumpe for to blowe,
As al the world shulde overthrowe,   1640
That thrughout every regioun
Wente this foule trumpes soun,
As swifte as pelet out of gonne,
Whan fyr is in the poudre ronne.
And such a smoke gan out wende   1645
Out of his foule trumpes ende,
Blak, bloo, grenyssh, swartish red,
As doth where that men melte led,
Loo, al on high fro the tuel.
And therto oo thing saugh I wel,   1650
That the ferther that hit ran,
The gretter wexen hit began,
As dooth the ryver from a welle,
And hyt stank as the pit of helle.
Allas, thus was her shame yronge,   1655
And gilteles, on every tonge!
   Tho come the thridde companye,
And gunne up to the dees to hye,
And doun on knes they fille anon,
And seyde, "We ben everychon   1660
Folk that han ful trewely

Deserved fame ryghtfully,
And praye yow, hit mote be knowe,
Ryght as hit is, and forth yblowe."
"I graunte," quod she, "for me list   1665
That now your goode werkes be wist,
And yet ye shul han better loos,
Right in dispit of alle your foos,
Than worthy is, and that anoon.
Lat now," quod she, "thy trumpe goon,   1670
Thou Eolus, that is so blak;
And out thyn other trumpe tak
That highte Laude, and blow yt soo
That thrugh the world her fame goo
Al esely, and not to faste,   1675
That hyt be knowen atte laste."
"Ful gladly, lady myn," he seyde;
And out hys trumpe of gold he brayde
Anon, and sette hyt to his mouth,
And blew it est, and west, and south,   1680
And north, as lowde as any thunder,
That every wight hath of hit wonder,
So brode hyt ran, or than hit stente.
And, certes, al the breth that wente
Out of his trumpes mouth it smelde   1685
As men a pot of bawme helde
Among a basket ful of roses.
This favour dide he til her loses.
    And ryght with this y gan aspye,
Ther come the ferthe companye —   1690
But certeyn they were wonder fewe —
And gunne stonden in a rewe,
And seyden, "Certes, lady bryght,
We han don wel with al our myght,
But we ne kepen have no fame.   1695
Hyde our werkes and our name,
For Goddys love; for certes we
Han certeyn doon hyt for bounte,
And for no maner other thing."
"I graunte yow alle your askyng,"   1700
Quod she; "let your werkes be ded."
    With that aboute y clew myn hed,
And saugh anoon the fifte route
That to this lady gunne loute,
And doun on knes anoon to falle;   1705
And to hir thoo besoughten alle
To hide her goode werkes ek,
And seyden they yeven noght a lek
For fame ne for such renoun;
For they for contemplacioun   1710
And Goddes love hadde ywrought,
Ne of fame wolde they nought.
"What?" quod she, "and be ye wood?
And wene ye for to doo good,
And for to have of that no fame?   1715

Have ye dispit to have my name?
Nay, ye shul lyven everychon!
Blow thy trumpes, and that anon,"
Quod she, "thou Eolus, y hote,
And ryng this folkes werk be note,   1720
That al the world may of hyt here."
And he gan blowe her loos so clere
In his golden clarioun
That thrugh the world wente the soun
Also kenely and eke so softe;   1725
But atte last hyt was on-lofte.
    Thoo come the sexte companye,
And gunne faste on Fame crie.
Ryght verraily in this manere
They seyden: "Mercy, lady dere!   1730
To tellen certeyn as hyt is,
We han don neither that ne this,
But ydel al oure lyf ybe.
But, natheles, yet preye we   1735
That we mowe han as good a fame,
And gret renoun and knowen name,
As they that han doon noble gestes,
And acheved alle her lestes,
As wel of love as other thyng.
Al was us never broche ne ryng,   1740
Ne elles noght, from wymmen sent,
Ne ones in her herte yment
To make us oonly frendly chere,
But myghten temen us upon bere;
Yet lat us to the peple seme   1745
Suche as the world may of us deme
That wommen loven us for wod.
Hyt shal doon us as moche good,
And to oure herte as moche avaylle
To countrepese ese and travaylle,   1750
As we had wonne hyt with labour;
For that is dere boght honour
At regard of oure grete ese.
And yet thou most us more plese:
Let us be holden eke therto   1755
Worthy, wise, and goode also,
And riche, and happy unto love.
For Goddes love, that sit above,
Thogh we may not the body have
Of wymmen, yet, so God yow save,   1760
Leet men gliwe on us the name!
Sufficeth that we han the fame."
"I graunte," quod she, "be my trouthe!
Now, Eolus, withouten slouthe,
Tak out thy trumpe of gold, let se   1765
And blow as they han axed me,
That every man wene hem at ese,
Though they goon in ful badde lese."
This Eolus gan hit so blowe

That thrugh the world hyt was yknowe. 1770
    Thoo come the seventh route anoon,
And fel on knees everychoon,
And seyde, "Lady, graunte us sone
The same thing, the same bone,
That [ye] this nexte folk han doon." 1775
"Fy on yow," quod she, "everychon!
Ye masty swyn, ye ydel wrechches,
Ful of roten, slowe techches!
What? false theves! wher ye wolde
Be famous good, and nothing nolde 1780
Deserve why, ne never ye roughte?
Men rather yow to hangen oughte!
For ye be lyke the sweynte cat
That wolde have fissh; but wostow what?
He wolde nothing wete his clowes, 1785
Yvel thrift come to your jowes,
And eke to myn, if I hit graunte,
Or do yow favour, yow to avaunte!
Thou Eolus, thou kyng of Trace,
Goo blowe this folk a sory grace," 1790
Quod she, "anon; and wostow how?
As I shal telle thee ryght now.
Sey: 'These ben they that wolde honour
Have, and do noskynnes labour,
Ne doo no good, and yet han lawde; 1795
And that men wende that bele Isawde
Ne coude hem noght of love werne,
And yet she that grynt at a querne
Ys al to good to ese her herte.'"
This Eolus anon up sterte, 1800
And with his blake clarioun
He gan to blasen out a soun
As lowde as beloweth wynd in helle;
And eke therwith, soth to telle,
This soun was so ful of japes, 1805
As ever mowes were in apes.
And that wente al the world aboute,
That every wight gan on hem shoute,
And for to lawghe as they were wod,
Such game fonde they in her hod. 1810
    Tho come another companye,
That had ydoon the trayterye,
The harm, the grettest wikkednesse
That any herte kouthe gesse;
And prayed her to han good fame, 1815
And that she nolde doon hem no shame,
But yeve hem loos and good renoun,
And do hyt blowe in a clarioun.
"Nay, wis," quod she, "hyt were a vice.
Al be ther in me no justice, 1820
Me lyste not to doo hyt now,
Ne this nyl I not graunte yow."
    Tho come ther lepynge in a route,

And gunne choppen al aboute
Every man upon the crowne, 1825
That al the halle gan to sowne,
And seyden: "Lady, leef and dere,
We ben suche folk as ye mowe here.
To tellen al the tale aryght,
We ben shrewes, every wyght, 1830
And han delyt in wikkednesse,
As goode folk han in godnesse;
And joye to be knowen shrewes,
And ful of vice and wikked thewes;
Wherefore we praye yow, a-rowe, 1835
That oure fame such be knowe
In alle thing ryght as hit ys."
"Y graunte hyt yow," quod she, "ywis.
But what art thow that seyst this tale,
That werest on thy hose a pale, 1840
And on thy tipet such a belle?"
"Madame," quod he, "soth to telle,
I am that ylke shrewe, ywis,
That brende the temple of Ysidis
In Athenes, loo, that citee." 1845
"And wherfor didest thou so?" quod she.
"By my thrift," quod he, "madame,
I wolde fayn han had a fame,
As other folk hadde in the toun,
Although they were of gret renoun 1850
For her vertu and for her thewes.
Thoughte y, as gret a fame han shrewes,
Though hit be for shrewednesse,
As goode folk han for godnesse;
And sith y may not have that oon, 1855
That other nyl y noght forgoon.
And for to gette of Fames hire,
The temple sette y al afire.
Now do our loos be blowen swithe,
As wisly be thou ever blythe!" 1860
"Gladly," quod she; "thow Eolus,
Herestow not what they prayen us?"
"Madame, yis, ful wel," quod he,
"And I wil trumpen it, parde!"
And tok his blake trumpe faste, 1865
And gan to puffen and to blaste,
Til hyt was at the worldes ende.
    With that y gan aboute wende,
For oon that stood ryght at my bak,
Me thoughte, goodly to me spak, 1870
And seyde, "Frend, what is thy name?
Artow come hider to han fame?"
"Nay, for sothe, frend," quod y;
"I cam noght hyder, graunt mercy,
For no such cause, by my hed! 1875
Sufficeth me, as I were ded,
That no wight have my name in honde.

I wot myself best how y stonde;
For what I drye, or what I thynke,
I wil myselven al hyt drynke,   1880
Certeyn, for the more part,
As fer forth as I kan myn art."
"But what doost thou here than?" quod he.
Quod y, "That wyl y tellen the,
The cause why y stonde here: 1885
Somme newe tydynges for to lere,
Somme newe thinges, y not what,
Tydynges, other this or that,
Of love, or suche thynges glade.
For certeynly, he that me made   1890
To comen hyder, seyde me,
Y shulde bothe here and se,
In this place, wonder thynges;
But these be no suche tydynges
As I mene of." "Noo?" quod he.   1895
And I answered, "Noo, parde!
For wel y wiste ever yit,
Sith that first y hadde wit,
That somme folk han desired fame
Diversly, and loos, and name.   1900
But certeynly, y nyste how
Ne where that Fame duelled, er now,
And eke of her descripcioun,
Ne also her condicioun,
Ne the ordre of her dom,   1905
Unto the tyme y hidder com."
"Whych than be, loo, these tydynges,
That thou now [thus] hider brynges,
That thou hast herd?" quod he to me;
"But now no fors, for wel y se   1910
What thou desirest for to here.
Com forth and stond no lenger here,
And y wil thee, withouten drede,
In such another place lede,
Ther thou shalt here many oon."   1915
     Tho gan I forth with hym to goon
Out of the castel, soth to seye.
Tho saugh y stonde in a valeye,
Under the castel, faste by,
An hous, that Domus Dedaly,   1920
That Laboryntus cleped ys,
Nas mad so wonderlych, ywis,
Ne half so queyntelych ywrought.
And ever mo, as swyft as thought,
This queynte hous aboute wente,   1925
That never mo hyt stille stente.
And therout com so gret a noyse
That, had hyt stonden upon Oyse,
Men myghte hyt han herd esely
To Rome, y trowe sikerly.   1930
And the noyse which that I herde,

For al the world, ryght so hyt ferde,
As dooth the rowtynge of the ston
That from th'engyn ys leten gon.
And al thys hous of which y rede   1935
Was mad of twigges, falwe, rede,
And grene eke, and somme weren white,
Swiche as men to these cages thwite,
Or maken of these panyers,
Or elles hottes or dossers;   1940
That, for the swough and for the twygges,
This hous was also ful of gygges,
And also ful eke of chirkynges,
And of many other werkynges;
And eke this hous hath of entrees   1945
As fele as of leves ben in trees
In somer, whan they grene been;
And on the roof men may yet seen
A thousand holes, and wel moo,
To leten wel the soun out goo.   1950
And be day, in every tyde,
Been al the dores opened wide,
And by nyght, echon, unshette;
Ne porter ther is noon to lette
No maner tydynges in to pace.   1955
Ne never rest is in that place
That hit nys fild ful of tydynges,
Other loude, or of whisprynges;
And over alle the houses angles
Ys ful of rounynges and of jangles   1960
Of werres, of pes, of mariages,
Of reste, of labour, of viages,
Of abood, of deeth, of lyf,
Of love, of hate, acord, of stryf,
Of loos, of lore, and of wynnynges,   1965
Of hele, of seknesse, of bildynges,
Of faire wyndes, and of tempestes,
Of qwalm of folk, and eke of bestes;
Of dyvers transmutacions
Of estats, and eke of regions;   1970
Of trust, of drede, of jelousye,
Of wit, of wynnynge, of folye;
Of plente, and of gret famyne,
Of chepe, of derthe, and of ruyne;
Of good or mys governement,   1975
Of fyr, and of dyvers accident.
     And loo, thys hous, of which I write,
Syker be ye, hit nas not lyte,
For hyt was sixty myle of lengthe.
Al was the tymber of no strengthe,   1980
Yet hit is founded to endure
While that hit lyst to Aventure,
That is the moder of tydynges,
As the see of welles and of sprynges;
And hyt was shapen lyk a cage.   1985

"Certys," quod y, "in al myn age,
Ne saugh y such an hous as this."
And as y wondred me, ywys,
Upon this hous, tho war was y
How that myn egle, faste by,   1990
Was perched hye upon a stoon;
And I gan streghte to hym gon,
And seyde thus: "Y preye the
That thou a while abide me,
For Goddis love, and lete me seen   1995
What wondres in this place been;
For yit, paraunter, y may lere
Som good thereon, or sumwhat here
That leef me were, or that y wente."

"Petre! that is myn entente,"   2000
Quod he to me; "therfore y duelle.
But certeyn, oon thyng I the telle,
That but I bringe the therinne,
Ne shalt thou never kunne gynne
To come into hyt, out of doute,   2005
So faste hit whirleth, lo, aboute.
But sith that Joves, of his grace,
As I have seyd, wol the solace
Fynally with these thinges,
Unkouthe syghtes and tydynges,   2010
To passe with thyn hevynesse,
Such routhe hath he of thy distresse,
That thou suffrest debonairly —
And wost thyselven outtirly
Diseserpat of alle blys,   2015
Syth that Fortune hath mad amys
The [fruit] of al thyn hertys reste
Languisshe and eke in poynt to breste —
That he, thrugh hys myghty merite,
Wol do the an ese, al be hyt lyte,   2020
And yaf expres commaundement,
To which I am obedient,
To further the with al my myght,
And wisse and teche the aryght
Where thou maist most tidynges here,   2025
Shaltow here anoon many oon lere."
With this word he ryght anoon
Hente me up bytweene hys toon,
And at a wyndowe yn me broghte,
That in this hous was, as me thoghte — 2030
And therwithalle, me thoughte hit stente,
And nothing hyt aboute wente —
And me sette in the flor adoun.
But which a congregacioun
Of folk, as I saugh rome aboute,   2035
Some wythin and some wythoute,
Nas never seen, ne shal ben eft;
That, certys, in the world nys left
So many formed be Nature,

Ne ded so many a creature;   2040
That wel unnethe in that place
Hadde y a fote-brede of space.
And every wight that I saugh there
Rouned everych in others ere
A newe tydynge prively,   2045
Or elles tolde al openly
Ryght thus, and seyde: "Nost not thou
That ys betyd, lo, late or now?"
"No," quod he, "telle me what."
And than he tolde hym this and that,   2050
And swor therto that hit was soth —
"Thus hath he sayd," and "Thus he doth,"
"Thus shal hit be," "Thus herde y seye,"
"That shal be founde," "That dar I leye" —
That al the folk that ys alyve   2055
Ne han the kunnynge to discryve
The thinges that I herde there,
What aloude, and what in ere.
But al the wondermost was this:
Whan oon had herd a thing, ywis,   2060
He com forth ryght to another wight,
And gan him tellen anon-ryght
The same that to him was told,
Or hyt a forlong way was old,
But gan somwhat for to eche   2065
To this tydynge in this speche
More than hit ever was.
And nat so sone departed nas
Tho fro him, that he ne mette
With the thridde; and or he lette   2070
Any stounde, he told him als;
Were the tydynge soth or fals,
Yit wolde he telle hyt natheles,
And evermo with more encres
Than yt was erst. Thus north and south 2075
Wente every tydyng fro mouth to mouth,
And that encresing ever moo,
As fyr ys wont to quyke and goo
From a sparke spronge amys,
Til al a citee brent up ys.   2080
And whan that was ful ysprongge,
And woxen more on every tonge
Than ever hit was, [hit] wente anoon
Up to a wyndowe out to goon;
Or, but hit myghte out there pace,   2085
Hyt gan out crepe at som crevace,
And flygh forth faste for the nones.
And somtyme saugh I thoo at ones
A lesyng and a sad soth sawe,
That gonne of aventure drawe   2090
Out at a wyndowe for to pace;
And, when they metten in that place,
They were achekked bothe two,

And neyther of hem moste out goo
For other, so they gonne crowde,   2095
Til ech of hem gan crien lowde,
"Lat me go first!" "Nay, but let me!
And here I wol ensuren the
Wyth the nones that thou wolt do so,
That I shal never fro the go,   2100
But be thyn owne sworen brother!
We wil medle us ech with other,
That no man, be they never so wrothe,
Shal han on [of us] two, but bothe
At ones, al besyde his leve,   2105
Come we a-morwe or on eve,
Be we cried or stille yrouned."
Thus saugh I fals and soth compouned
Togeder fle for oo tydynge.
    Thus out at holes gunne wringe   2110
Every tydynge streght to Fame,
And she gan yeven ech hys name,
After hir disposicioun,
And yaf hem eke duracioun,
Somme to wexe and wane sone,   2115
As doth the faire white mone,
And let hem goon. Ther myghte y seen
Wynged wondres faste fleen,
Twenty thousand in a route,
As Eolus hem blew aboute.   2120
    And, Lord, this hous in alle tymes,
Was ful of shipmen and pilgrimes,
With scrippes bret-ful of lesinges,
Entremedled with tydynges,
And eek allone be hemselve.   2125
O, many a thousand tymes twelve

Saugh I eke of these pardoners,
Currours, and eke messagers,
With boystes crammed ful of lyes
As ever vessel was with lyes.   2130
And as I alther-fastest wente
About, and dide al myn entente
Me for to pleyen and for to lere,
And eke a tydynge for to here,
That I had herd of som contre   2135
That shal not now be told for me —
For hit no nede is, redely;
Folk kan synge hit bet than I;
For al mot out, other late or rathe,
Alle the sheves in the lathe —   2140
I herde a gret noyse withalle
In a corner of the halle,
Ther men of love-tydynges tolde,
And I gan thiderward beholde;
For I saugh rennynge every wight,   2145
As faste as that they hadden myght;
And everych cried, "What thing is that?"
And somme sayde, "I not never what."
And whan they were alle on an hepe,
Tho behynde begunne up lepe,   2150
And clamben up on other faste,
And up the nose and yën kaste,
And troden fast on others heles,
And stampen, as men doon aftir eles.
Atte laste y saugh a man,   2155
Which that y [nevene] nat ne kan;
But he semed for to be
A man of gret auctorite. . ₀ ₀

[*Unfinished.*]

ANELIDA AND ARCITE

THE *Anelida* has long been a puzzle to the critics. It starts out with all the pomp and circumstance of an epic. After an invocation to Mars and Bellona, which would be a natural introduction to a poem of battle, it goes on to announce its subject as a very old Latin story of Queen Anelida and false Arcite. Then after a second invocation, this time to the Muses, it declares the name of its ancient authorities: Statius, the author of the Thebaid, and a mysterious Corinne, probably the Theban poetess Corinna, who was famous for having defeated the great Pindar in a competition. Then follows the story itself, which fails singularly to fulfill the promise of the proem. It does, to be sure, find its setting and point of departure in Statius' account of the war of the Seven against Thebes. But its actual source at this point is rather the Teseida of Boccaccio than the Thebaid. And the story of Anelida and Arcite, which is soon introduced, far from being an heroic tale of battle and of tournament (like the *Knight's Tale,* which has so similar a beginning) is a meager and ill-developed narrative of how a faithless knight abandoned one lady for another. It continues for only about a hundred lines, and is little more than an introduction to the lyric *Complaint* of the deserted Anelida. In contrast to the slender story, the *Complaint* is an elaborate specimen of its type. With a narrative fullness which is exceptional in such poems Anelida repeats many of the incidents mentioned earlier in the introduction. And the metrical structure of the piece, with its carefully balanced stanzas of varied form, is the most complicated that Chaucer is known to have employed. At the end of the *Complaint* the story is resumed, but only for seven lines. It relates that Anelida, after writing her lament, vowed sacrifice to Mars; and it stops abruptly before entering upon the description of his temple. Doubtless Chaucer meant to use at

this point the passage of the Teseida which at another time he made the basis of the description of the temple in the *Palemon and Arcite.*

Various have been the attempts to account for this strange fragment. Chaucer's acknowledgment of indebtedness to Statius and Corinne, it is agreed, is pure fiction, so far as concerns the story of Arcite's faithlessness. It is simply Chaucer's way of claiming ancient authority for his tale. He may even have had no literary source for the simple and conventional plot, and therefore no plan for continuing it beyond the *Complaint.* If he did not take the incident out of a book, there is the other possibility that it was suggested to him by some contemporary occurrence. For scholars are loath to credit anything to pure invention. So theories of personal allegory have been seriously urged. The historical counterpart of Arcite has been sought in the Earl of Oxford and in James Butler, second earl of Ormonde. Though Oxford did desert his wife for a Bohemian lady, his relations with Chaucer make a satirical attack on the part of the poet seem very improbable. And there is no striking parallelism between the incident and the poem to support the application. In the case of Butler the identification with Arcite rests entirely upon a few strange resemblances in proper names, — Ormonde and Ermonie, Arcite and d'Arcy (Butler's mother's maiden name), Anelida and Anne Welle (whom Butler married). Ormonde's marital infidelity is by no means proved, and his life with the Countess was certainly not such as to justify his representation as the faithless Arcite. Contemporary history, then, as well as literature, has failed to yield a satisfactory source or suggestion for the story. And it is possible that Chaucer never had any further plan than to frame a complaint of the French type in the setting furnished by Boccaccio's Teseida. This, in any case, is what he actually does in the fragment, which thus takes its place among the works of his period of transition from French to Italian influence.

The chronological position of the *Anelida* among the poems that show this two-fold influence can be only conjectured. The metrical form and the use of the Teseida suggest a date after the *House of Fame.* The treatment of the character of Arcite must be earlier than the heroic presentation of the same figure in the *Palemon.* In fact the *Anelida* bears every indication of having been Chaucer's first attempt to utilize the Teseida. It is therefore printed here before the *Parliament of Fowls,* which is at all events a more finished work in conception and execution.

In spite of its shortcomings the *Anelida* shows in some respects Chaucer's progressive mastery of his art. The great metrical proficiency he displays in the *Complaint* has already been mentioned. In the introductory story, too, thin as the substance is, there begins to appear the swift and flexible narrative style of Chaucer's later years. The characterization is poor and conventional; the expression of feeling and sentiment a little more adequate, perhaps because of Chaucer's reading of Ovid. In general, the *Anelida* testifies at once to Chaucer's enlarging literary knowledge and to the immaturity of his art. These conditions seem to be reflected even in the vocabulary of the poem, which is conspicuous among Chaucer's writings for a tendency to poetic diction.

Anelida and Arcite

The Compleynt of feire Anelida and fals Arcite.

Invocation.

Thou ferse god of armes, Mars the rede,
That in the frosty contre called Trace,
Within thy grisly temple ful of drede
Honoured art, as patroun of that place;
With thy Bellona, Pallas, ful of grace,   5
Be present, and my song contynue and guye;
At my begynnyng thus to the I crye.

For hit ful depe is sonken in my mynde,
With pitous hert in Englyssh to endyte
This olde storie, in Latyn which I fynde,   10
Of quene Anelida and fals Arcite,
That elde, which that al can frete and bite,
As hit hath freten mony a noble storie,
Hath nygh devoured out of oure memorie.

Be favorable eke, thou Polymya,   15
On Parnaso that with thy sustres glade,
By Elycon, not fer from Cirrea,
Singest with vois memorial in the shade,
Under the laurer which that may not fade,
And do that I my ship to haven wynne.   20
First folowe I Stace, and after him Corynne.

The Story.

Iamque domos patrias Cithice post aspera
    gentis
Prelia laurigero subeunte Thesea curru
Letifici plausus missusque ad sidera vulgi

When Theseus, with werres longe and grete,
The aspre folk of Cithe had overcome,
With laurer corouned, in his char gold-bete,
Hom to his contre-houses is he come;   25
For which the peple, blisful al and somme,
So cryëden that to the sterres hit wente,
And him to honouren dide al her entente.

Beforn this duk, in signë of victorie,
The trompes come, and in his baner large   30
The ymage of Mars; and, in token of glorie,
Men myghte sen of tresour many a charge,
Many a bright helm, and many a spere and
    targe,
Many a fresh knyght, and many a blysful route,
On hors, on fote, in al the feld aboute.   35

Ipolita his wif, the hardy quene
Of Cithia, that he conquered hadde,
With Emelye, her yonge suster shene,
Faire in a char of gold he with him ladde,
That al the ground about her char she spradde
With brightnesse of the beaute in her face,   41
Fulfilled of largesse and of alle grace.

With his tryumphe, and laurer-corouned thus,
In al the flour of Fortunes yevynge,
Let I this noble prince Theseus   45
Toward Athenes in his wey rydinge,
And founde I wol in shortly for to bringe
The slye wey of that I gan to write,
Of quene Anelida and fals Arcite.

Mars, which that through his furious cours of
ire,   50
The olde wrathe of Juno to fulfille,
Hath set the peples hertes bothe on fire
Of Thebes and Grece, everich other to kille
With blody speres, ne rested never stille,
But throng now her, now ther, among hem
bothe,   55
That everych other slough, so were they
wrothe.

For when Amphiorax and Tydeus,
Ipomedon, Parthonope also
Were ded, and slayn proude Campaneus,
And when the wrecched Thebans, bretheren
two,   60
Were slayn, and kyng Adrastus hom ago,
So desolat stod Thebes and so bare,
That no wight coude remedie of his care.

And when the olde Creon gan espye
How that the blood roial was broght a-doun, 65
He held the cite by his tyrannye,
And dyde the gentils of that regioun
To ben his frendes, and dwellen in the toun.
So, what for love of him, and what for awe,
The noble folk were to the toun idrawe.   70

Among al these Anelida, the quene
Of Ermony, was in that toun dwellynge,
That fairer was then is the sonne shene.
Thurghout the world so gan her name springe,
That her to seen had every wyght likynge;   75
For, as of trouthe, is ther noon her lyche,
Of al the women in this worlde riche.

Yong was this quene, of twenty yer of elde,
Of mydel stature, and of such fairenesse,

That Nature had a joye her to behelde;   80
And for to speken of her stidfastnesse,
She passed hath Penelope and Lucresse;
And shortly, yf she shal be comprehended,
In her ne myghte no thing been amended.

This Theban knyght [Arcite] eke, soth to seyn,
Was yong, and therwithal a lusty knyght,   86
But he was double in love and no thing pleyn,
And subtil in that craft over any wyght,
And with his kunnyng wan this lady bryght;
For so ferforth he gan her trouthe assure   90
That she him trusted over any creature.

What shuld I seyn? she loved Arcite so
That when that he was absent any throwe,
Anon her thoghte her herte brast a-two.
For in her sight to her he bar hym lowe,   95
So that she wende have al his hert yknowe;
But he was fals; hit nas but feyned chere, —
As nedeth not to men such craft to lere.

But nevertheles ful mykel besynesse
Had he, er that he myghte his lady wynne,   100
And swor he wolde dyen for distresse,
Or from his wit he seyde he wolde twynne.
Alas, the while! for hit was routhe and synne,
That she upon his sorowes wolde rewe;   104
But nothing thinketh the fals as doth the trewe.

Her fredom fond Arcite in such manere
That al was his that she hath, moche or lyte;
Ne to no creature made she chere
Ferther then that hit lyked to Arcite.
Ther nas no lak with which he myghte her
wite: 110
She was so ferforth yeven hym to plese,
That al that lyked hym hit dyde her ese.

Ther nas to her no maner lettre sent
That touched love, from any maner wyght, 114
That she ne shewed hit him, er hit was brent;
So pleyn she was, and dide her fulle myght
That she nyl hiden nothing from her knyght,
Lest he of any untrouthe her upbreyde.
Withoute bode his heste she obeyde.

And eke he made him jelous over here,   120
That what that any man had to her seyd,
Anoon he wolde preyen her to swere
What was that word, or make him evel apaid.
Then wende she out of her wyt have breyd;
But al this nas but sleght and flaterie;   125
Withoute love, he feyned jelousye.

And al this tok she so debonerly,
That al his wil, her thoghte hit skilful thing;
And ever the lenger she loved him tendirly,
And dide him honour as he were a kyng.   130
Her herte was to him wedded with a ring;
So ferforth upon trouthe is her entente,
That wher he gooth, her herte with him wente.

When she shal ete, on him is so her thoght,
That wel unnethe of mete tok she kep;   135
And when that she was to her reste broght,
On him she thoghte alwey til that she slep;
When he was absent, prevely she wep:
Thus lyveth feire Anelida the quene
For fals Arcite, that dide her al this tene.   140

This fals Arcite, of his newfanglenesse,
For she to him so lowly was and trewe,
Tok lesse deynte of her stidfastnesse,
And saw another lady, proud and newe,   144
And ryght anon he cladde him in her hewe —
Wot I not whethir in white, rede, or grene —
And falsed fair Anelida the quene.

But nevertheless, gret wonder was hit noon
Thogh he were fals, for hit is kynde of man,
Sith Lamek was, that is so longe agoon,   150
To ben in love as fals as evere he can;
He was the firste fader that began
To loven two, and was in bigamye;
And he found tentes first, but yf men lye.

This fals Arcite, sumwhat moste he feyne,   155
When he wex fals, to covere his traitorie,
Ryght as an hors, that can both bite and pleyne;
For he bar her on honde of trecherie,
And swor he coude her doublenesse espie,
And al was falsnes that she to him mente.   160
Thus swor this thef, and forth his way he wente.

Alas! what herte myght enduren hit,
For routhe or wo, her sorwe for to telle?
Or what man hath the cunnyng or the wit?
Or what man mighte within the chambre dwelle,   165
Yf I to him rehersen sholde the helle
That suffreth fair Anelida the quene
For fals Arcite, that dide her al this tene.

She wepith, waileth, swowneth pitously;
To grounde ded she falleth as a ston;   170
Craumpyssheth her lymes crokedly;

She speketh as her wit were al agon;
Other colour then asshen hath she noon;
Non other word speketh she, moche or lyte,
But "merci, cruel herte myn, Arcite!"   175

And thus endureth, til that she was so mat
That she ne hath foot on which she may sustene;
But forth languisshing evere in this estat,
Of which Arcite hath nouther routhe ne tene.
His herte was elleswhere, newe and grene,   180
That on her wo ne deyneth him not to thinke;
Him rekketh never wher she flete or synke.

His newe lady holdeth him so narowe
Up by the bridil, at the staves ende,
That every word he dredeth as an arowe;   185
Her daunger made him bothe bowe and bende,
And as her liste, made him turne or wende;
For she ne graunted him in her lyvynge
No grace, whi that he hath lust to singe,

But drof hym forth, unnethe liste her knowe   190
That he was servaunt unto her ladishippe;
But lest that he were proud, she held him lowe.
Thus serveth he, withoute fee or shipe;
She sent him now to londe, now to shippe;
And for she yaf him daunger al his fille,   195
Therfor she hadde him at her owne wille.

Ensample of this, ye thrifty wymmen alle,
Take her of Anelida and Arcite,
That for her liste him "dere herte" calle,
And was so meke, therfor he loved her lyte.   200
The kynde of mannes herte is to delyte
In thing that straunge is, also God me save!
For what he may not gete, that wolde he have.

Now turne we to Anelida ageyn,
That pyneth day be day in langwisshinge;   205
But when she saw that her ne gat no geyn,
Upon a day, ful sorowfully wepinge,
She caste her for to make a compleynynge,
And with her owne hond she gan hit write,
And sente hit to her Theban knyght, Arcite.   210

The compleynt of Anelida the quene upon fals Arcite.

Proem.

So thirleth with the poynt of remembraunce
The swerd of sorowe, ywhet with fals plesaunce,

Myn herte, bare of blis and blak of hewe,
That turned is in quakyng al my daunce,
My surete in awhaped countenaunce,   215
Sith hit availeth not for to ben trewe;
For whoso trewest is, hit shal hir rewe,
That serveth love and doth her observaunce
Alwey til oon, and chaungeth for no newe.

Strophe.

1.

I wot myself as wel as any wight;   220
For I loved oon with al myn herte and myght,
More then myself an hundred thousand sithe,
And called him myn hertes lif, my knyght,
And was al his, as fer as hit was ryght;
And when that he was glad, then was I blithe,   226
And his disese was my deth as swithe;
And he ayein his trouthe hath me plyght
For evermore, his lady me to kythe.

2.

Now is he fals, alas! and causeles,
And of my wo he is so routheles,   230
That with a word him list not ones deyne
To bringe ayen my sorowful herte in pes,
For he is caught up in another les.
Ryght as him list, he laugheth at my peyne,
And I ne can myn herte not restreyne,   235
For to love him alwey neveretheles;
And of al this I not to whom me pleyne.

3.

And shal I pleyne — alas! the harde stounde —
Unto my foo that yaf myn herte a wounde,
And yet desireth that myn harm be more?   240
Nay, certis, ferther wol I never founde
Non other helpe, my sores for to sounde.
My destinee hath shapen hit so ful yore;
I wil non other medecyne ne lore;
I wil ben ay ther I was ones bounde.   245
That I have seid, be seid for evermore!

4.

Alas! wher is become your gentilesse,
Youre wordes ful of plesaunce and humblesse,
Youre observaunces in so low manere,
And your awayting and your besynesse   250
Upon me, that ye calden your maistresse,
Your sovereyne lady in this world here?
Alas! is ther now nother word ne chere
Ye vouchen sauf upon myn hevynesse?
Alas! youre love, I bye hit al to dere.   255

5.

Now, certis, swete, thogh that ye
Thus causeles the cause be
Of my dedly adversyte,
Your manly resoun oghte hit to respite,
To slen your frend, and namely me,   260
That never yet in no degre
Offended yow, as wisly he,
That al wot, out of wo my soule quyte!
But for I shewed yow, Arcite,
Al that men wolde to me write,   265
And was so besy yow to delyte —
Myn honor save — meke, kynde, and fre,
Therfor ye put on me this wite.
Alas! ye rekke not a myte,
Thogh that the swerd of sorwe byte   270
My woful herte through your cruelte.

6.

My swete foo, why do ye so, for shame?
And thenke ye that furthered be your name
To love a newe, and ben untrewe? Nay!   274
And putte yow in sclaunder now and blame,
And do to me adversite and grame,
That love yow most — God, wel thou wost —
    alway?
Yet come ayein, and yet be pleyn som day,
And than shal this, that now is mys, be game,
And al foryive, while that I lyve may.   280

Antistrophe.

1.

Lo! herte myn, al this is for to seyne,
As whether shal I preye or elles pleyne?
Which is the wey to doon yow to be trewe?
For either mot I have yow in my cheyne,   284
Or with the deth ye mote departe us tweyne;
Ther ben non other mene weyes new.
For God so wisly upon my soule rewe,
As verrayly ye sleen me with the peyne;
That may ye se unfeyned on myn hewe.

2.

For thus ferforth have I my deth [y-]soght,   290
Myself I mordre with my privy thoght;
For sorowe and routhe of your unkyndenesse
I wepe, I wake, I faste; al helpeth noght;
I weyve joye that is to speke of oght,
I voyde companye, I fle gladnesse.   295
Who may avaunte her beter of hevynesse
Then I? And to this plyte have ye me broght,
Withoute gilt, — me nedeth no witnesse.

3.

And shal I preye, and weyve womanhede?
Nay! rather deth then do so foul a dede!   300
And axe merci, gilteles, — what nede?
And yf I pleyne what lyf that I lede,
Yow rekketh not; that knowe I, out of drede;
And if that I to yow myne othes bede
For myn excuse, a skorn shal be my mede.   305
Your chere floureth, but it wol not sede;
Ful longe agoon I oghte have taken hede.

4.

For thogh I hadde yow to-morowe ageyn,
I myghte as wel holde Aperill fro reyn,
As holde yow, to make yow be stidfast.   310
Almyghty God, of trouthe sovereyn,
Wher is the trouthe of man? Who hath hit
     slayn?
Who that hem loveth, she shal hem fynde as
     fast
As in a tempest is a roten mast.
Is that a tame best that is ay feyn   315
To renne away, when he is lest agast?

5.

Now merci, swete, yf I mysseye!
Have I seyd oght amys, I preye?
I noot; my wit is al aweye.
I fare as doth the song of *Chaunte-pleure*;   320
For now I pleyne, and now I pleye,
I am so mased that I deye;
Arcite hath born awey the keye
Of al my world, and my good aventure.
For in this world nis creature   325
Wakynge, in more discomfiture
Then I, ne more sorowe endure.
And yf I slepe a furlong wey or tweye,

Then thynketh me that your figure
Before me stont, clad in asure,   330
To profren eft a newe asure
For to be trewe, and merci me to preye.

6.

The longe nyght this wonder sight I drye,
And on the day for thilke afray I dye,
And of al this ryght noght, iwis, ye reche.   335
Ne nevere mo myn yen two be drie,
And to your routhe, and to your trouthe, I crie.
But welawey! to fer be they to feche;
Thus holdeth me my destinee a wreche.
But me to rede out of this drede, or guye,   340
Ne may my wit, so weyk is hit, not streche.

Conclusion.

Then ende I thus, sith I may do no more, —
I yeve hit up for now and evermore;
For I shal never eft putten in balaunce
My sekernes, ne lerne of love the lore.   345
But as the swan, I have herd seyd ful yore,
Ayeins his deth shal singen his penaunce,
So singe I here my destinee or chaunce,
How that Arcite Anelida so sore   349
Hath thirled with the poynt of remembraunce.

The Story continued.

When that Anelida, this woful quene,
Hath of her hand ywriten in this wise,
With face ded, betwixe pale and grene,
She fel a-swowe; and sith she gan to rise,
And unto Mars avoweth sacrifise   355
Withinne the temple, with a sorowful chere,
That shapen was as ye shal after here.

[*Unfinished.*]

THE PARLIAMENT OF FOWLS

❧

IN THE *Parliament of Fowls* Chaucer returned to the love-vision. Features made familiar by the *Book of the Duchess* and the *House of Fame* — the preliminary reading of a book, the ensuing sleep and dream, the supernatural guide, the vision itself, the allegorical abstractions — reappear in a somewhat different setting, adapted to a new purpose.

In the opening stanzas the poet declares himself to be without direct experience of the ways of the God of Love. "I knowe nat Love in dede." But, as he goes on to explain, he has learned of the subject from books, and to books he is wont to resort for all kinds of knowledge. Just lately he has been reading a most profitable work, the Somnium Scipionis, and he relates at some length how the elder Africanus appeared to Scipio the younger in a dream, and took him up into the heavens, where he showed him the mysteries of the future life. When night came on, the poet says, and put an end to his reading, he fell asleep and dreamed that Africanus came to him in turn and stood at his bedside. To reward him for the study of his "olde book totorn," the Roman took him to a beautiful park, where he saw the temple of Venus, and then to a hillside, where all the birds were assembled before the goddess of Nature on Saint Valentine's Day. They had come, in accordance with Nature's ordinance, to choose their mates, and then to fly away. The first choice belonged to the royal tercel eagle, who claimed the lovely formel eagle on the goddess's hand. Straightway a second and a third tercel, both of lower rank, disputed the first one's claim, and the three noble suitors pleaded their causes before Nature. Then the issue was debated by the general parliament of the birds. Finally Nature ruled that the choice should rest with the formel eagle herself, and she asked for a year's delay before making her decision.

Such, in very brief outline, is the story of the poem. In the familiar framework of the love-vision it presents the device, also familiar in mediæval literature, of a council or parliament of birds. But though it deals with well-known conventions, Chaucer's *Parliament* is a work of great freshness and originality. It has no definite source or model, but draws freely for its materials upon French, Latin, and Italian. Indeed in richness and aptness of literary quotation and allusion it may be compared with the best tales of Chaucer's latest period. And the natural and vivacious dialogue reveals in no small measure the dramatic power which afterward found full expression in the *Canterbury Tales*.

The *Parliament* is one of the most charming occasional poems in the language. But what was the occasion? The answer to this question has been the chief concern of the scholars who have studied the work in recent years. Like the *Complaint d'Amours* and the *Complaint of Mars*, the *Parliament* is definitely attached to Saint Valentine's Day, and perhaps a sufficient explanation of its origin is to be found in the celebration of that festival. Alceste says of Chaucer, in the *Prologue to the Legend of Good Women*, that he wrote "many an ympne for [Love's] holydayes." But, just as, in the case of the *Mars*, a tradition recorded in the fifteenth century explains the mythological episode as a personal allegory relating to an incident at court, so the modern commentators are many of them persuaded that the *Parliament* has an allegorical application. It is most commonly held to refer to the suit of Richard II for the hand of Anne of Bohemia in 1381. But since the situation in the poem does not agree very well with the actual events that led up to Richard's betrothal, other applications have been sought in Lancaster's plans for the marriage of his daughter Philippa, or even in Chaucer's own marriage as early as 1374. Most recently a new theory has been proposed which connects the *Parliament* with the negotiations, conducted in 1376 and 1377, for the marriage of the young prince Richard to the princess Marie of France. The soundness of such allegorical interpretations is very hard to judge. In the case of the *Book of the Duchess* and the Complaints of *Mars* and *Venus* personal applications are supported by early traditions, and modern scholarship has devised similar explanations for the *House of Fame*, the *Anelida*, the *Legend of Good Women*, and several of the *Canterbury Tales*. These theories of allegory are not unreasonable in themselves, and they find support in the literary practice of Chaucer's age. Yet the *Book of the Duchess* is the only one of all his works of which the personal application can be said to be generally accepted. The interpretations offered for some poems have been shown to be so out of accord with historical facts as to be totally unsatisfactory, and in other instances the parallels between Chaucer's story and the actual incidents are too slight or commonplace to be significant. Each case has to be judged on its merits. The *Parliament of Fowls* has perhaps received more such explanations than any other of Chaucer's writings. But none is without its difficulties. Even the application most recently proposed, to the negotiations for the betrothal of Richard and Marie, while less open to objection than earlier theories, is not supported by such strik-

ing parallels of incident as would make it convincing. It also implies a date of composition which seems a little too early. Moreover, an allegorical interpretation, though undeniably possible, is not necessary to the understanding of the poem. The central episode of the contending lovers has been shown to be a frequently recurring theme in literature and popular tradition, and the suspended judgment is the conventional ending.

Apart from theories of personal allegory, there is probably to be recognized in the *Parliament* a certain amount of political or social satire. As contrasted with the rival eagles, the other classes of birds — worm-fowl, water-fowl, and seed-fowl — clearly represent in a fashion the humbler orders of human society, and their speeches sometimes appear to reflect the discontent that produced the Peasants' Revolt. Certainly the ideals of courtly love, as expounded by the noble suitors, are treated with little respect by some of the spokesmen for the lower classes. How much Chaucer himself was concerned with the expression of such ideas we can only conjecture. Many of his writings testify to his sustained interest in the problems of courtly love. In the *Parliament*, at all events, he presents the issue dramatically, with the complete detachment of himself as author which is characteristic of the *Canterbury Tales*. He is so non-committal, in fact, that critics are even now disputing whether the poet took sides with seed-fowl or with "fowles of ravyne."

The Parliament of Fowls

Here begyneth the Parlement of Foules.

The lyf so short, the craft so long to lerne,
Th'assay so hard, so sharp the conquerynge,
The dredful joye, alwey that slit so yerne:
Al this mene I by Love, that my felynge
Astonyeth with his wonderful werkynge   5
So sore, iwis, that whan I on hym thynke,
Nat wot I wel wher that I flete or synke.

For al be that I knowe nat Love in dede,
Ne wot how that he quiteth folk here hyre,
Yit happeth me ful ofte in bokes reede   10
Of his myrakles and his crewel yre.
There rede I wel he wol be lord and syre;
I dar nat seyn, his strokes been so sore,
But "God save swich a lord!" — I can na moore.

Of usage — what for lust and what for lore — 15
On bokes rede I ofte, as I yow tolde.
But wherfore that I speke al this? Nat yoore
Agon, it happede me for to beholde
Upon a bok, was write with lettres olde,
And therupon, a certeyn thing to lerne,   20
The longe day ful faste I redde and yerne.

For out of olde feldes, as men seyth,
Cometh al this newe corn from yer to yere,
And out of olde bokes, in good feyth,
Cometh al this newe science that men lere.   25
But now to purpos as of this matere;
To rede forth hit gan me so delite,
That al that day me thoughte but a lyte.

This bok of which I make mencioun
Entitled was al thus as I shal telle: 30
"Tullyus of the Drem of Scipioun."
Chapitres sevene it hadde, of hevene and helle
And erthe, and soules that therinne dwelle,
Of whiche, as shortly as I can it trete,
Of his sentence I wol yow seyn the greete.   35

Fyrst telleth it, whan Scipion was come
In Affrike, how he meteth Massynisse,
That hym for joie in armes hath inome;
Thanne telleth it here speche and al the blysse
That was betwix hem til the day gan mysse,   40
And how his auncestre, Affrycan so deere,
Gan in his slep that nyght to hym apere.

Thanne telleth it that, from a sterry place,
How Affrycan hath hym Cartage shewed,
And warnede hym beforn of al his grace,   45
And seyde hym what man, lered other lewed
That lovede commune profyt, wel ithewed,
He shulde into a blysful place wende,
There as joye is that last withouten ende.

Thanne axede he if folk that here been dede   50
Han lyf and dwellynge in another place.
And Affrican seyde, "Ye, withouten drede,"
And that oure present worldes lyves space
Nis but a maner deth, what wey we trace,
And rightful folk shul gon, after they dye,   55
To hevene; and shewede hym the Galaxye.

Thanne shewede he hym the lytel erthe that
    here is,
At regard of the hevenes quantite;
And after shewede he hym the nyne speres,
And after that the melodye herde he   60
That cometh of thilke speres thryes thre,

That welle is of musik and melodye
In this world here, and cause of armonye.

Than bad he hym, syn erthe was so lyte,
And ful of torment and of harde grace,   65
That he ne shulde hym in the world delyte.
Thanne tolde he hym, in certeyn yeres space
That every sterre shulde come into his place
Ther it was first, and al shulde out of mynde
That in this world is don of al mankynde.   70

Thanne preyede hym Scipion to telle hym al
The wey to come into that hevene blisse.
And he seyde, "Know thyself first immortal,
And loke ay besyly thow werche and wysse
To commune profit, and thow shalt not mysse
To comen swiftly to that place deere   76
That ful of blysse is and of soules cleere.

"But brekers of the lawe, soth to seyne,
And likerous folk, after that they ben dede,
Shul whirle aboute th'erthe alwey in peyne,   80
Tyl many a world be passed, out of drede,
And than, foryeven al hir wikked dede,
Than shul they come into this blysful place,
To which to comen God the sende his grace."

The day gan faylen, and the derke nyght,   85
That reveth bestes from here besynesse,
Berafte me my bok for lak of lyght,
And to my bed I gan me for to dresse,
Fulfyld of thought and busy hevynesse;
For bothe I hadde thyng which that I nolde,   90
And ek I nadde that thyng that I wolde.

But fynally, my spirit at the laste,
For wery of my labour al the day,
Tok reste, that made me to slepe faste,
And in my slep I mette, as that I lay,   95
How Affrican, ryght in the selve aray
That Scipion hym say byfore that tyde,
Was come and stod right at my beddes syde.

The wery huntere, slepynge in his bed,
To wode ayeyn his mynde goth anon;   100
The juge dremeth how his plees been sped;
The cartere dremeth how his cartes gon;
The riche, of gold; the knyght fyght with his
    fon;
The syke met he drynketh of the tonne;
The lovere met he hath his lady wonne.   105

Can I not seyn if that the cause were
For I hadde red of Affrican byforn,

That made me to mete that he stod there;
But thus seyde he: "Thow hast the so wel born
In lokynge of myn olde bok totorn,　　110
Of which Macrobye roughte nat a lyte,
That sumdel of thy labour wolde I quyte."

Cytherea! thow blysful lady swete,
That with thy fyrbrond dauntest whom the lest,
And madest me this sweven for to mete,　　115
Be thow myn helpe in this, for thow mayst best!
As wisly as I sey the north-north-west,
Whan I began my sweven for to write,
So yif me myght to ryme and ek t'endyte!

This forseyde Affrican me hente anon,　　120
And forth with hym unto a gate broughte,
Ryght of a park walled with grene ston,
And over the gate, with lettres large iwroughte,
There were vers iwriten, as me thoughte,
On eyther half, of ful gret difference,　　125
Of which I shal now seyn the pleyn sentence:

"Thorgh me men gon into that blysful place
Of hertes hele and dedly woundes cure;
Thorgh me men gon unto the welle of grace,　　129
There grene and lusty May shal evere endure.
This is the wey to al good aventure.
Be glad, thow redere, and thy sorwe of-caste;
Al open am I — passe in, and sped thee faste!"

"Thorgh me men gon," than spak that other
　　side,
"Unto the mortal strokes of the spere　　135
Of which Disdayn and Daunger is the gyde,
Ther nevere tre shal fruyt ne leves bere.
This strem yow ledeth to the sorweful were
There as the fish in prysoun is al drye;
Th'eschewing is only the remedye!"　　140

These vers of gold and blak iwriten were,
Of whiche I gan astoned to beholde,
For with that oon encresede ay my fere,
And with that other gan myn herte bolde;　　144
That oon me hette, that other dide me colde:
No wit hadde I, for errour, for to chese,
To entre or flen, or me to save or lese.

Right as, betwixen adamauntes two
Of evene myght, a pece of yren set
Ne hath no myght to meve to ne fro —　　150
For what that oon may hale, that other let —
Ferde I, that nyste whether me was bet
To entre or leve, til Affrycan, my gide,
Me hente, and shof in at the gates wide,

And seyde, "It stondeth writen in thy face,　　155
Thyn errour, though thow telle it not to me;
But dred the not to come into this place,
For this writyng nys nothyng ment bi the,
Ne by non, but he Loves servaunt be:
For thow of love hast lost thy tast, I gesse,　　160
As sek man hath of swete and bytternesse.

"But natheles, although that thow be dul,
Yit that thow canst not do, yit mayst thow se.
For many a man that may nat stonde a pul,
It liketh hym at the wrastlyng for to be,　　165
And demeth yit wher he do bet or he.
And if thow haddest connyng for t'endite,
I shal the shewe mater of to wryte."

With that myn hand in his he tok anon,　　169
Of which I confort caughte, and wente in faste.
But, Lord, so I was glad and wel begoon!
For overal where that I myne eyen caste
Were treës clad with leves that ay shal laste,
Ech in his kynde, of colour fresh and greene
As emeraude, that joye was to seene.　　175

The byldere ok, and ek the hardy asshe;
The piler elm, the cofre unto carayne;
The boxtre pipere, holm to whippes lashe;
The saylynge fyr; the cipresse, deth to playne;
The shetere ew; the asp for shaftes pleyne;　　180
The olyve of pes, and eke the dronke vyne;
The victor palm, the laurer to devyne.

A gardyn saw I ful of blosmy bowes
Upon a ryver, in a grene mede,
There as swetnesse everemore inow is,　　185
With floures white, blewe, yelwe, and rede,
And colde welle-stremes, nothyng dede,
That swymmen ful of smale fishes lighte,
With fynnes rede and skales sylver bryghte.

On every bow the bryddes herde I synge,　　190
With voys of aungel in here armonye;
Some besyede hem here bryddes forth to
　　brynge;
The litel conyes to here pley gonne hye;
And ferther al aboute I gan aspye　　194
The dredful ro, the buk, the hert and hynde,
Squyrels, and bestes smale of gentil kynde.

Of instruments of strenges in acord
Herde I so pleye a ravyshyng swetnesse,
That God, that makere is of al and lord,
Ne herde nevere beter, as I gesse.　　200
Therwith a wynd, unnethe it myghte be lesse,

Made in the leves grene a noyse softe
Acordaunt to the foules song alofte.

Th'air of that place so attempre was   204
That nevere was ther grevaunce of hot ne cold;
There wex ek every holsom spice and gras;
No man may there waxe sek ne old;
Yit was there joye more a thousandfold
Than man can telle; ne nevere wolde it nyghte,
But ay cler day to any manes syghte.   210

Under a tre, besyde a welle, I say
Cupide, oure lord, his arwes forge and file;
And at his fet his bowe al redy lay;
And Wille, his doughter, temprede al this while
The hevedes in the welle, and with hire file   215
She touchede hem, after they shulde serve
Some for to sle, and some to wounde and kerve.

Tho was I war of Plesaunce anon-ryght,
And of Aray, and Lust, and Curteysie,   219
And of the Craft that can and hath the myght
To don by force a wyght to don folye —
Disfigurat was she, I nyl nat lye;
And by hymself, under an ok, I gesse,
Saw I Delyt, that stod with Gentilesse.

I saw Beute withouten any atyr,   225
And Youthe, ful of game and jolyte;
Foolhardynesse, Flaterye, and Desyr,
Messagerye, and Meede, and other thre —
Here names shul not here be told for me —
And upon pilers greete of jasper longe   230
I saw a temple of bras ifounded stronge.

Aboute that temple daunseden alwey
Women inowe, of whiche some ther weere
Fayre of hemself, and some of hem were gay;
In kertels, al dishevele, wente they there: 235
That was here offyce alwey, yer by yeere.
And on the temple, of dowves white and fayre
Saw I syttynge many an hundred peyre.

Byfore the temple-dore ful soberly
Dame Pees sat, with a curtyn in hire hond,   240
And by hire syde, wonder discretly,
Dame Pacience syttynge there I fond,
With face pale, upon an hil of sond;
And aldernext, withinne and ek withoute,
Byheste and Art, and of here folk a route.   245

Withinne the temple, of sykes hoote as fyr
I herde a swogh that gan aboute renne,
Whiche sikes were engendered with desyr,

That maden every auter for to brenne
Of newe flaume, and wel espyed I thenne   250
That al the cause of sorwes that they drye
Cam of the bittere goddesse Jelosye.

The god Priapus saw I, as I wente,
Withinne the temple in sovereyn place stonde,
In swich aray as whan the asse hym shente   255
With cri by nighte, and with hys sceptre in
          honde.
Ful besyly men gonne assaye and fonde
Upon his hed to sette, of sondry hewe,
Garlondes ful of freshe floures newe.

And in a prive corner in disport   260
Fond I Venus and hire porter Richesse,
That was ful noble and hautayn of hyre port.
Derk was that place, but afterward lightnesse
I saw a lyte, unnethe it myghte be lesse,
And on a bed of gold she lay to reste,   265
Til that the hote sonne gan to weste.

Hyre gilte heres with a golden thred
Ibounden were, untressed as she lay,
And naked from the brest unto the hed   269
Men myghte hire sen; and, sothly for to say,
The remenaunt was wel kevered to my pay,
Ryght with a subtyl coverchef of Valence —
Ther nas no thikkere cloth of no defense.

The place yaf a thousand savours sote,
And Bachus, god of wyn, sat hire besyde,   275
And Ceres next, that doth of hunger boote,
And, as I seyde, amyddes lay Cypride,
To whom on knees two yonge folk ther cryde
To ben here helpe. But thus I let hire lye,
And ferther in the temple I gan espie   280

That, in dispit of Dyane the chaste,
Ful many a bowe ibroke heng on the wal
Of maydenes swiche as gonne here tymes waste
In hyre servyse; and peynted overal
Of many a story, of which I touche shal   285
A fewe, as of Calyxte and Athalante,
And many a mayde of which the name I wante.

Semyramis, Candace, and Hercules,
Biblis, Dido, Thisbe, and Piramus,
Tristram, Isaude, Paris, and Achilles,   290
Eleyne, Cleopatre, and Troylus,
Silla, and ek the moder of Romulus:
Alle these were peynted on that other syde,
And al here love, and in what plyt they dyde.

Whan I was come ayeyn into the place   295
That I of spak, that was so sote and grene,
Forth welk I tho myselven to solace.
Tho was I war wher that ther sat a queene
That, as of lyght the somer sonne shene
Passeth the sterre, right so over mesure   300
She fayrer was than any creature.

And in a launde, upon an hil of floures,
Was set this noble goddesse Nature.
Of braunches were here halles and here boures
Iwrought after here cast and here mesure;   305
Ne there nas foul that cometh of engendrure
That they ne were prest in here presence,
To take hire dom and yeve hire audyence.

For this was on seynt Valentynes day,
Whan every foul cometh there to chese his
          make,   310
Of every kynde that men thynke may,
And that so huge a noyse gan they make
That erthe, and eyr, and tre, and every lake
So ful was, that unethe was there space
For me to stonde, so ful was al the place.   315

And right as Aleyn, in the Pleynt of Kynde,
Devyseth Nature of aray and face,
In swich aray men myghte hire there fynde.
This noble emperesse, ful of grace,
Bad every foul to take his owne place,   320
As they were woned alwey fro yer to yeere,
Seynt Valentynes day, to stonden theere.

That is to seyn, the foules of ravyne
Weere hyest set, and thanne the foules smale
That eten, as hem Nature wolde enclyne,   325
As worm or thyng of which I telle no tale;
And water-foul sat lowest in the dale;
But foul that lyveth by sed sat on the grene,
And that so fele that wonder was to sene.

There myghte men the royal egle fynde,   330
That with his sharpe lok perseth the sonne,
And othere egles of a lowere kynde,
Of whiche that clerkes wel devyse conne.
Ther was the tiraunt with his fetheres donne
And grey, I mene the goshauk, that doth pyne
To bryddes for his outrageous ravyne.   336

The gentyl faucoun, that with his feet dis-
          trayneth
The kynges hand; the hardy sperhauk eke,
The quayles foo; the merlioun, that payneth
Hymself ful ofte the larke for to seke;   340

There was the douve with hire yën meke;
The jelous swan, ayens his deth that syngeth;
The oule ek, that of deth the bode bryngeth;

The crane, the geaunt, with his trompes soun;
The thef, the chough; and ek the janglynge
          pye;   345
The skornynge jay; the eles fo, heroun;
The false lapwynge, ful of trecherye;
The stare, that the conseyl can bewrye;
The tame ruddok, and the coward kyte;
The kok, that orloge is of thorpes lyte;   350

The sparwe, Venus sone; the nyghtyngale,
That clepeth forth the grene leves newe;
The swalwe, mortherere of the foules smale
That maken hony of floures freshe of hewe;
The wedded turtil, with hire herte trewe;   355
The pekok, with his aungels fetheres bryghte;
The fesaunt, skornere of the cok by nyghte;

The waker goos; the cukkow ever unkynde;
The popynjay, ful of delicasye;
The drake, stroyere of his owene kynde;   360
The stork, the wrekere of avouterye;
The hote cormeraunt of glotenye;
The raven wys; the crowe with vois of care;
The throstil old; the frosty feldefare.

What shulde I seyn? Of foules every kynde   365
That in this world han fetheres and stature
Men myghten in that place assembled fynde
Byfore the noble goddesse of Nature,
And everich of hem dide his besy cure
Benygnely to chese or for to take,   370
By hire acord, his formel or his make.

But to the poynt: Nature held on hire hond
A formel egle, of shap the gentilleste
That evere she among hire werkes fond,
The moste benygne and the goodlieste.   375
In hire was everi vertu at his reste,
So ferforth that Nature hireself hadde blysse
To loke on hire, and ofte hire bek to kysse.

Nature, the vicaire of the almyghty Lord,   379
That hot, cold, hevy, lyght, moyst, and dreye
Hath knyt by evene noumbres of acord,
In esy voys began to speke and seye,
"Foules, tak hed of my sentence, I preye,
And for youre ese, in fortheryng of youre nede,
As faste as I may speke, I wol me speede.   385

"Ye knowe wel how, seynt Valentynes day,
By my statut and thorgh my governaunce,
Ye come for to cheese — and fle youre wey —
Youre makes, as I prike yow with plesaunce;
But natheles, my ryghtful ordenaunce   390
May I nat lete for al this world to wynne,
That he that most is worthi shal begynne.

"The tersel egle, as that ye knowe wel,
The foul royal, above yow in degre,
The wyse and worthi, secre, trewe as stel,   395
Which I have formed, as ye may wel se,
In every part as it best liketh me —
It nedeth not his shap yow to devyse —
He shal first chese and speken in his gyse.

"And after hym by ordre shul ye chese,   400
After youre kynde, everich as yow lyketh,
And, as youre hap is, shul ye wynne or lese.
But which of yow that love most entriketh,
God sende hym hire that sorest for hym
    syketh!"
And therwithal the tersel gan she calle,   405
And seyde, "My sone, the choys is to the falle.

"But natheles, in this condicioun
Mot be the choys of everich that is heere,
That she agre to his eleccioun,
Whoso he be that shulde be hire feere.   410
This is oure usage alwey, fro yer to yeere,
And whoso may at this tyme have his grace,
In blisful tyme he cam into this place!"

With hed enclyned and with ful humble cheere
This royal tersel spak, and tariede noght: — 415
"Unto my soverayn lady, and not my fere,
I chese, and chese with wil, and herte, and
    thought,
The formel on youre hond, so wel iwrought,
Whos I am al, and evere wol hire serve,
Do what hire lest, to do me lyve or sterve;   420

"Besekynge hire of merci and of grace,
As she that is my lady sovereyne;
Or let me deye present in this place.
For certes, longe may I nat lyve in payne,
For in myn herte is korven every veyne.   425
Havynge reward only to my trouthe,
My deere herte, have on my wo som routhe.

"And if that I to hyre be founde untrewe,
Disobeysaunt, or wilful necligent,
Avauntour, or in proces love a newe,   430
I preye to yow this be my jugement,

That with these foules I be al torent,
That ilke day that evere she me fynde
To hir untrewe, or in my gilt unkynde.

"And syn that non loveth hire so wel as I,   435
Al be she nevere of love me behette,
Thanne oughte she be myn thourgh hire mercy,
For other bond can I non on hire knette.
Ne nevere for no wo ne shal I lette
To serven hire, how fer so that she wende;   440
Say what yow list, my tale is at an ende."

Ryght as the freshe, rede rose newe
Ayeyn the somer sonne coloured is,
Ryght so for shame al wexen gan the hewe
Of this formel, whan she herde al this;   445
She neyther answerde wel, ne seyde amys,
So sore abasht was she, tyl that Nature
Seyde, "Doughter, drede yow nought, I yow
    assure."

Another tersel egle spak anon,   449
Of lower kynde, and seyde, "That shal nat be!
I love hire bet than ye don, by seint John,
Or at the leste I love hire as wel as ye,
And lenger have served hire in my degre,
And if she shulde have loved for long lovynge,
To me ful-longe hadde be the guerdonynge.   455

"I dar ek seyn, if she me fynde fals,
Unkynde, janglere, or rebel any wyse,
Or jelous, do me hangen by the hals!
And, but I bere me in hire servyse
As wel as that my wit can me suffyse,   460
From poynt to poynt, hyre honour for to save,
Take she my lif and al the good I have!"

The thridde tercel egle answerde tho,
"Now, sires, ye seen the lytel leyser heere;
For every foul cryeth out to ben ago   465
Forth with his make, or with his lady deere;
And ek Nature hireself ne wol not heere,
For taryinge here, not half that I wolde seye,
And but I speke, I mot for sorwe deye.

"Of long servyse avaunte I me nothing;   470
But as possible is me to deye to-day
For wo as he that hath ben languysshyng
This twenty wynter, and wel happen may,
A man may serven bet and more to pay
In half a yer, although it were no moore,   475
Than som man doth that hath served ful yoore.

"I seye not this by me, for I ne can
Don no servyse that may my lady plese;
But I dar seyn, I am hire treweste man
As to my dom, and faynest wolde hire ese.   480
At shorte wordes, til that deth me sese,
I wol ben heres, whether I wake or wynke,
And trewe in al that herte may bethynke."

Of al my lyf, syn that day I was born,
So gentil ple in love or other thyng   485
Ne herde nevere no man me beforn,
Who that hadde leyser and connyng
For to reherse hire chere and hire spekyng;
And from the morwe gan this speche laste   489
Tyl dounward drow the sonne wonder faste.

The noyse of foules for to ben delyvered
So loude rong, "Have don, and lat us wende!"
That wel wende I the wode hadde al to-
        shyvered.
"Com of!" they criede, "allas, ye wol us shende!
Whan shal youre cursede pletynge have an
        ende?   495
How sholde a juge eyther parti leve
For ye or nay, withouten any preve?"

The goos, the cokkow, and the doke also
So cryede, "Kek kek! kokkow! quek quek!" hye,
That thourgh myne eres the noyse wente
        tho.   500
The goos seyde, "Al this nys not worth a flye!
But I can shape herof a remedie,
And I wol seye my verdit fayre and swythe
For water-foul, whoso be wroth or blythe!"   504

"And I for worm-foul," seyde the fol kokkow,
"For I wol of myn owene autorite,
For comune spede, take on the charge now,
For to delyvere us is gret charite."
"Ye may abyde a while yit, parde!"
Quod the turtel, "If it be youre wille,   510
A wight may speke hym were as fayr be stylle.

"I am a sed-foul, oon the unworthieste,
That wot I wel, and litel of connynge.
But bet is that a wyghtes tonge reste
Than entermeten hym of such doinge,   515
Of which he neyther rede can ne synge;
And whoso hit doth, ful foule hymself acloyeth,
For office uncommytted ofte anoyeth."

Nature, which that alwey hadde an ere
To murmur of the lewednesse behynde,   520
With facound voys seyde, "Hold youre tonges
        there!

And I shal sone, I hope, a conseyl fynde
Yow to delyvere, and fro this noyse unbynde:
I juge, of every folk men shul oon calle
To seyn the verdit for yow foules alle."   525

Assented were to this conclusioun
The briddes alle; and foules of ravyne
Han chosen fyrst, by pleyn eleccioun,
The tercelet of the faucoun to diffyne
Al here sentence, and as him lest, termyne;   530
And to Nature hym gonne to presente,
And she accepteth hym with glad entente.

The terslet seyde thanne in this manere:
"Ful hard were it to preve by resoun
Who loveth best this gentil formel heere;   535
For everych hath swich replicacioun
That non by skilles may be brought adoun.
I can not se that argumentes avayle:
Thanne semeth it there moste be batayle."

"Al redy!" quod these egles tercels tho.   540
"Nay, sires," quod he, "if that I durste it seye,
Ye don me wrong, my tale is not ido!
For, sires, ne taketh not agref, I preye,
It may not gon, as ye wolde, in this weye;   544
Oure is the voys that han the charge in honde,
And to the juges dom ye moten stonde.

"And therfore pes! I seye, as to my wit,
Me wolde thynke how that the worthieste
Of knyghthod, and lengest had used it,
Most of estat, of blod the gentilleste,   550
Were sittyngest for hire, if that hir leste;
And of these thre she wot hireself, I trowe,
Which that he be, for it is light to knowe."

The water-foules han here hedes leid
Togedere, and of a short avysement,   555
Whan everych hadde his large golee seyd,
They seyden sothly, al by oon assent,
How that the goos, with here facounde gent,
"That so desyreth to pronounce oure nede,
Shal telle oure tale," and preyede "God hire
        spede!"   560

And for these water-foules tho began
The goos to speke, and in hire kakelynge
She seyde, "Pes! now tak kep every man,
And herkeneth which a resoun I shal forth
        brynge!
My wit is sharp, I love no taryinge;   565
I seye I rede hym, though he were my brother,
But she wol love hym, lat hym love another!"

"Lo, here a parfit resoun of a goos!"
Quod the sperhauk; "Nevere mot she thee!
Lo, swich it is to have a tonge loos!   570
Now, parde! fol, yit were it bet for the
Han holde thy pes than shewed thy nycete.
It lyth nat in his wit, ne in his wille,
But soth is seyd, 'a fol can not be stille.' "

The laughter aros of gentil foules alle,   575
And right anon the sed-foul chosen hadde
The turtle trewe, and gonne hire to hem calle,
And preyeden hire to seyn the sothe sadde
Of this matere, and axede what she radde.
And she answerde that pleynly hire entente   580
She wolde shewe, and sothly what she mente.

"Nay, God forbede a lovere shulde chaunge!"
The turtle seyde, and wex for shame al red,
"Though that his lady everemore be straunge,
Yit lat hym serve hire ever, til he be ded.   585
Forsothe, I preyse nat the goses red,
For, though she deyede, I wolde non other
    make;
I wol ben hires, til that the deth me take."

"Wel bourded," quod the doke, "by myn hat!
That men shulde loven alwey causeles,   590
Who can a resoun fynde or wit in that?
Daunseth he murye that is myrtheles?
Who shulde recche of that is recheles?
Ye quek!" yit seyde the doke, ful wel and fayre,
"There been mo sterres, God wot, than a
    payre!"   595

"Now fy, cherl!" quod the gentil tercelet,
"Out of the donghil cam that word ful right!
Thow canst nat seen which thyng is wel beset!
Thow farst by love as oules don by lyght: 599
The day hem blent, ful wel they se by nyght.
Thy kynde is of so low a wrechednesse
That what love is, thow canst nat seen ne
    gesse."

Tho gan the kokkow putte hym forth in pres
For foul that eteth worm, and seyde blyve: —
"So I," quod he, "may have my make in pes,
I reche nat how longe that ye stryve.   606
Lat ech of hem be soleyn al here lyve!
This is my red, syn they may nat acorde;
This shorte lessoun nedeth nat recorde."

"Ye, have the glotoun fild inow his paunche,
Thanne are we wel!" seyde the merlioun;   611
"Thow mortherere of the heysoge on the
    braunche

That broughte the forth, thow [rewthelees]
    glotoun!
Lyve thow soleyn, wormes corupcioun!
For no fors is of lak of thy nature —   615
Go, lewed be thow whil the world may dure!"

"Now pes," quod Nature, "I comaunde heer!
For I have herd al youre opynyoun,
And in effect yit be we nevere the neer.
But fynally, this is my conclusioun,   620
That she hireself shal han hir eleccioun
Of whom hire lest; whoso be wroth or blythe,
Hym that she cheest, he shal hire han as swithe.

"For sith it may not here discussed be
Who loveth hire best, as seyde the tercelet,   625
Thanne wol I don hire this favour, that she
Shal han right hym on whom hire herte is set,
And he hire that his herte hath on hire knet:
Thus juge I, Nature, for I may not lye;
To non estat I have non other yë.   630

"But as for conseyl for to chese a make,
If I were Resoun, certes, thanne wolde I
Conseyle yow the royal tercel take,
As seyde the tercelet ful skylfully,
As for the gentilleste and most worthi,   635
Which I have wrought so wel to my plesaunce,
That to yow hit oughte to been a suffisaunce."

With dredful vois the formel tho answerde,
"My rightful lady, goddesse of Nature!
Soth is that I am evere under youre yerde,   640
As is everich other creature,
And mot be youres whil my lyf may dure,
And therfore graunteth me my firste bone,
And myn entente I wol yow sey right sone."

"I graunte it yow," quod she; and right anon
This formel egle spak in this degre: 646
"Almyghty queen! unto this yer be gon,
I axe respit for to avise me,
And after that to have my choys al fre:
This al and som that I wol speke and seye.   650
Ye gete no more, although ye do me deye!

"I wol nat serve Venus ne Cupide,
Forsothe as yit, by no manere weye."
"Now, syn it may non otherwise betyde,"
Quod tho Nature, "heere is no more to seye.   655
Thanne wolde I that these foules were aweye,
Ech with his make, for taryinge lengere heere!"
And seyde hem thus, as ye shul after here.

"To yow speke I, ye tercelets," quod Nature,
"Beth of good herte, and serveth alle thre.   660
A yer is nat so longe to endure,
And ech of yow peyne him in his degre
For to do wel, for, God wot, quyt is she
Fro yow this yer; what after so befalle,
This entremes is dressed for yow alle."   665

And whan this werk al brought was to an ende,
To every foul Nature yaf his make
By evene acord, and on here way they wende.
And, Lord, the blisse and joye that they make!
For ech of hem gan other in wynges take,   670
And with here nekkes ech gan other wynde,
Thankynge alwey the noble goddesse of kynde.

But fyrst were chosen foules for to synge,
As yer by yer was alwey hir usaunce
To synge a roundel at here departynge,   675
To don to Nature honour and plesaunce.
The note, I trowe, imaked was in Fraunce,
The wordes were swiche as ye may heer fynde,
The nexte vers, as I now have in mynde.

"Now welcome, somer, with thy sonne softe,
That hast this wintres wedres overshake,   681
And driven away the longe nyghtes blake!

"Saynt Valentyn, that art ful hy on-lofte,
Thus syngen smale foules for thy sake:
Now welcome, somer, with thy sonne softe,   685
That hast this wintres wedres overshake.

"Wel han they cause for to gladen ofte,
Sith ech of hem recovered hath hys make,
Ful blissful mowe they synge when they wake:
Now welcome, somer, with thy sonne softe,   690
That hast this wintres wedres overshake,
And driven away the longe nyghtes blake!"

And with the shoutyng, whan the song was do
That foules maden at here flyght awey,
I wok, and othere bokes tok me to,   695
To reede upon, and yit I rede alwey.
I hope, ywis, to rede so som day
That I shal mete som thyng for to fare
The bet, and thus to rede I nyl nat spare.

Explicit parliamentum Auium in die sancti Valentini tentum, secundum Galfridum Chaucers. Deo gracias.

BOECE

THE De Consolatione Philosophiae of Boethius was fitly characterized by Gibbon, in an often quoted phrase, as "a golden volume not unworthy of the leisure of Plato or of Tully." Unhappily, as a result of the changing fashions in education, its elevated philosophy and fine Latinity — exceptionally classical for the sixth century — are little known today, even to students of Latin. But in the so-called Dark and Middle Ages it was among the most familiar of ancient classics. One of the earliest texts in Provençal is a fragment of a poem on the life and teachings of Boethius. The Consolation was translated into Old High German by the celebrated Notker Labeo of Saint-Gall. There are said to be as many as eight French translations which were made before the end of the fifteenth century, one of them by Jean de Meun, the author of the second part of the Roman de la Rose. In England, long before the time of any of these Continental versions, Boethius's treatise was selected by King Alfred as one of the four great works which he translated, or had translated, for the education of his people. And centuries later, after the Renaissance had enlarged men's knowledge of classical literature, the Consolation still held so important a place that another sovereign, Queen Elizabeth, undertook its "Englishing." Throughout all the generations from Alfred to Elizabeth it exerted a steady influence on poets and philosophers.

This extraordinary interest was due partly to the work itself and partly to the tragic career of the author. Boethius came of a Roman family long distinguished in the public service. His father held high offices under Odoacer, and was consul in 487. His father-in-law, Q. Aurelius Symmachus, also a consul, was long a leader of the Senate. Boethius himself, who was only a boy in 489 when Theodoric defeated Odoacer and established the Ostrogothic power in Italy, soon enjoyed the favor of the new ruler. Before he was thirty he was admitted to the Senate, and in 510 he served as sole consul. He continued to receive many honors under Theodoric and reached what he regarded as the height of his good fortune in 522, when his two sons were consuls together. But soon after this Theodoric became suspicious of the loyalty of his Italian subjects. Boethius, with others, was charged with plotting to maintain the power of the Senate and restore the liberties of Italy. He was imprisoned at Pavia, and in the year 524 was put to death.

The life which was thus brought to an end was even more important for its contributions to literature and learning than for its public services. From his youth Boethius was devoted to philosophical studies, and he set himself the task of translating into Latin all of the works of Plato and Aristotle, and then of harmonizing their doctrines. This vast programme he never carried out. But in spite of the demands of his public life he succeeded in translating Aristotle's Categories and De Interpretatione and writing commentaries on each, besides composing or translating treatises on the "quadrivium" and on various aspects of logic. He also took part, on the side of Catholic orthodoxy, in the theological controversies over Arianism and Nestorianism, and later ages even ascribed his death to martyrdom for the faith. Thus in one aspect of his work he has been called "the last of the pagan philosophers," and in another "the first of the schoolmen."

From Boethius's treatises and translations the early Middle Ages derived much of their knowledge of Greek thought. But his wider fame as a man of letters rests on the De Consolatione Philosophiae. The earlier writings were labors of scholarship; this was a work of imagination, produced less under the influence of Aristotle than of Plato and Seneca. The others were expositions of philosophical theory and method; this was applied philosophy — applied in the desperate circumstances of Boethius's fall. Written in prison in the last months of his life it was at once his *apologia* and the final statement of his philosophy.

It was inevitable that the Consolation should be familiar to Chaucer, and it is not remarkable that the Latin work deeply influenced his thought. As a matter of fact most of the sustained passages of philosophical reflection in his poetry can be traced to Boethius. The date of his translation was probably not far from 1380. The association of *Boece* and *Troilus* in the *Words to Adam Scriveyn* and the very heavy indebtedness of the *Troilus* to the Consolation indicate that Chaucer had the two works in hand at about the same time. The *Knight's Tale* (like the *Troilus*, probably a work of the early or middle eighties) also shows strong Boethian influence. On the other hand, in Chaucer's earlier poems very little material from Boethius has been detected, and in the later *Canterbury Tales*, while reminiscences of the Consolation are frequent, they are no longer of central importance. Everything goes to show that Boethius was "in his domination," along with Boccaccio, in the middle of Chaucer's so-called Italian period.

For literary excellence Chaucer's poetic adaptations of Boethius in the *Knight's Tale*

and the *Troilus* are far superior to his translation of the Consolation. Indeed his prose at its best (as in the freely composed introduction to the *Astrolabe*) shows no such mastery of style as his verse, and is hardly equal to that of the early Middle English Ancren Riwle or of King Alfred's Anglo-Saxon Boethius. Moreover in the case of the *Boece* the use of a French translation, heavily glossed, alongside of the Latin original contributed to looseness of structure and diffuseness of language. But in passing judgment upon a work of this sort one should remember that literal accuracy rather than the reproduction of stylistic excellence was a recognized ideal of translation in Chaucer's age. The freer method was also undoubtedly approved and practiced, and St. Jerome's rule, "Non verbum e verbo, sed sensum exprimere de sensu," carried high authority. But it was not always observed. Jean de Meun's French versions of Boethius and Vegetius were of the more literal kind, as had been Boethius's own translation of Aristotle. In fact Boethius, in his introduction to Porphyry's Isagoge, defended himself for having rendered "verbum verbo expressum comparatumque," and declared this method to be suitable in philosophical writings — "in his scriptis in quibus rerum cognitio quaeritur."

Boece

Incipit Liber Boecii de Consolacione Philosophie.

"Carmina qui quondam studio florente peregi." — Metrum 1

Allas! I wepynge, am constreyned to bygynnen vers of sorwful matere, that whilom in florysschyng studie made delitable ditees. For lo! rendynge Muses of poetes enditen to me thynges to ben writen, and drery vers of wretchidnesse weten my face with verray teres. At the leeste, no drede ne myghte overcomen tho Muses, that thei ne were felawes, and folowyden my wey (*that is to seyn, whan I was exiled*). They that weren glorie of   10
my youthe, whilom weleful and grene, conforten now the sorwful wyerdes of me, olde man. For eelde is comyn unwarly uppon me, hasted by the harmes that y have, and sorwe hath comandid his age to ben in me. Heeris hore arn schad overtymeliche upon myn heved, and the slakke skyn trembleth of myn emptid body.

Thilke deth of men is weleful that ne comyth noght in yeeris that ben swete,   19 but cometh to wrecches often yclepid. Allas! allas! with how deef an ere deth, cruwel, turneth awey fro wrecches, and nayteth to closen wepynge eien. Whil Fortune, unfeithful, favourede me with lyghte goodes, the sorwful houre (*that is to seyn, the deth*) hadde almoost dreynt myn heved. But now, for Fortune cloudy hath chaunged hir deceyvable chere to me-ward, myn unpietous lif draweth along unagreable duellynges.   29

O ye, my freendes, what, or wherto avaunted ye me to be weleful? For he that hath fallen stood noght in stedefast degre.

"Hec dum mecum tacitus." — Prosa 1

In the mene while that I, stille, recordede these thynges with myself, and merkid my weply compleynte with office of poyntel, I saw, stondynge aboven the heghte of myn heved, a womman of ful greet reverence by semblaunt, hir eien brennynge and cleer-seynge over the comune myghte of men; with a lifly colour and with swich vigour and strengthe that it ne myghte nat ben emptid, al were it so that sche was ful of so greet age that men   10 ne wolden not trowen in no manere that sche were of our elde. The stature of hire was of a doutous jugement, for somtyme sche constreyned and schronk hirselven lik to the comune mesure of men, and somtyme it semede that sche touchede the hevene with the heghte of here heved; and whan sche hef hir heved heyer, sche percede the selve hevene so that the sighte of men lokynge was in ydel. Hir clothes weren makid of right delye thredes   20 and subtil craft, of perdurable matere; the whiche clothes sche hadde woven with hir owene handes, as I knew wel aftir by hirselve declarynge and schewynge to me the beaute. The whiche clothes a derknesse of a forleten and despised elde hadde duskid and dirked, as it is wont to dirken besmokede ymages. In the nethereste hem or bordure of thise clothes, men redden ywoven in a Grekissch P (*that signifieth the lif actif*); and aboven that   30 lettre, in the heieste bordure, a Grekyssh T (*that signifieth the lif contemplatif*). And bytwixen thise two lettres ther were seyn degrees nobly ywrought in manere of laddres, by whiche degrees men myghten clymben fro the nethereste lettre to the uppereste. Natheles handes of some men hadden korve that cloth by violence or by strengthe, and everich man of hem hadde boren awey swiche peces as he myghte geten. And for sothe this for-   40 seide womman bar smale bokis in hir right hand, and in hir left hand sche bar a ceptre.

And whan she saugh thise poetical Muses aprochen aboute my bed and enditynge wordes to my wepynges, sche was a litil amoeved, and glowede with cruel eighen. "Who," quod sche, "hath suffred aprochen to this sike man thise comune strompettis of swich a place that men clepen the theatre; the whiche not oonly ne asswagen noght his sorwes with none rem-   50 edies, but thei wolden fedyn and noryssen hym with sweete venym. For sothe thise ben tho that with thornes and prikkynges of talentz or affeccions, whiche that ne bien nothyng fructifyenge nor profitable, destroyen the corn plentyvous of fruytes of resoun. For thei holden hertes of men in usage, but thei delyvre noght folk fro maladye. But yif ye Muses hadden withdrawen fro me with youre flateries any unkunnynge and unprofitable man, as men   60 ben wont to fynde comonly among the peple, I wolde wene suffre the lasse grevosly; forwhi, in swych an unprofitable man, myne ententes weren nothyng endamaged. But ye withdrawen me this man, that hath ben noryssed in the studies or scoles of Eleaticis and Achademycis in Grece. But goth now rather awey, ye mermaydenes, whiche that ben swete til it be at the laste, and suffreth this man to ben cured and heeled by myne muses   70 (*that is to seyn, by noteful sciences*)." And thus this companye of Muses, iblamed, casten wrothly the chere dounward to the erthe, and, schewing by rednesse hir schame, thei passeden sorwfully the thresschfold. And I, of whom the sighte, ploungid in teeres, was dirked so that y ne myghte noght knowen what that womman was of so imperial auctorite, I wax al abayssched and astoned, and caste my syghte doun to the erthe, and bygan, stille,   80 for to abide what sche woolde doon aftirward. Tho com sche ner, and sette her doun uppon the uttereste corner of my bed; and sche, byholdynge my chere that was cast to the erthe hevy and grevous of wepynge, compleynede, with thise wordis that I schal seyn, the perturbacion of my thought.

"Heu quam precipiti mersa profundo." — Metrum 2

"Allas how the thought of man, dreynt in overthrowynge depnesse, dulleth and forleteth

his propre clernesse, myntynge to gon into foreyne dirknesses as ofte as his anoyos bysynes
waxeth withoute mesure, that is dryven to and
fro with werldly wyndes. This man, that
whilom was fre, to whom the hevene was
opyn and knowen, and was wont to gon in
hevenliche pathes, and saugh the lyghtnesse of the rede sonne, and saugh the   10
sterres of the coolde mone, and which
sterre in hevene useth wandrynge recourses
iflyt by diverse speeris — this man, overcomere,
hadde comprehendid al this by nombres (*of
acontynge in astronomye*). And, over this, he
was wont to seken the causes whennes the soun-
ynge wyndes moeven and bysien the smothe
watir of the see; and what spirit turneth the
stable hevene; and why the sterre ariseth
out of the rede est, to fallen in the westrene   20
wawes; and what attemprith the lusty
houres of the firste somer sesoun, that hight-
eth and apparaileth the erthe with rosene
floures; and who maketh that plentyvous
autumpne in fulle yeris fletith with hevy
grapes. And eek this man was wont to tellen
the diverse causes of nature that weren yhidde.
Allas! now lyth he emptid of lyght of his
thoght, and his nekke is pressyd with hevy
cheynes, and bereth his chere enclyned   30
adoun for the grete weyghte, and is constreyned to loken on the fool erthe!

"Set medicine inquit tempus." — Prosa 2

"But tyme is now," quod sche, "of medicyne
more than of compleynte." Forsothe thanne
sche, entendynge to me-ward with al the lookynge of hir eien, seyde: — "Art nat thou he,"
quod sche, "that whilom, norissched with my
melk and fostred with myne metes, were escaped and comyn to corage of a parfit man?
Certes I yaf the swiche armures that, yif thou
thiselve ne haddest first cast hem awey,
they schulden han defended the in siker-   10
nesse that mai nat ben overcomyn. Knowestow me nat? Why arttow stille? Is it for
schame or for astonynge? It were me levere
that it were for schame, but it semeth me that
astonynge hath oppressid the." And whan sche
say me nat oonly stille, but withouten office
of tunge and al dowmb, sche leyde hir hand
sooftly uppon my breest, and seide: "Here nys
no peril," quod sche; "he is fallen into a
litargye, which that is a comune seknesse   20
to hertes that been desceyved. He hath a
litil foryeten hymselve, but certes he schal

lightly remembren hymself, yif so be that he
hath knowen me or now; and that he may so
doon, I will wipe a litil his eien that ben
dirked by the cloude of mortel thynges." Thise
woordes seide sche, and with the lappe of hir
garnement, yplited in a frownce, sche dryede
myn eien, that weren fulle of the wawes of
my wepynges.   30

"Tunc me discussa, &c." — Metrum 3

Thus, whan that nyght was discussed and
chased awey, dirknesses forleten me, and to
myn eien repeyred ayen hir firste strengthe.
And ryght by ensaumple as the sonne is hydd
whan the sterres ben clustred (*that is to seyn,
whan sterres ben covered with cloudes*) by a
swyft wynd that hyghte Chorus, and that the
firmament stant dirked with wete plowngy
cloudes; and that the sterres nat apeeren
upon hevene, so that the nyght semeth   10
sprad upon erthe: yif thanne the wynd that
hyghte Boreas, isent out of the kave of the
cuntre of Trace, betith this nyght (*that is to
seyn, chaseth it awey*), and discovereth the
closed day, thanne schyneth Phebus ischaken
with sodeyn light, and smyteth with his beemes
in merveylynge eien.

"Haut aliter tristicie." — Prosa 3

Ryght so, and noon other wise, the cloudes
of sorwe dissolved and doon awey, I took hevene, and resceyved mynde to knowe the face
of my fisycien; so that I sette myne eien on
hir and fastned my lookynge. I byholde my
noryce, Philosophie, in whoos hous I hadde
conversed and hauntyd fro my youthe; and
I seide thus: "O thou maystresse of alle vertues, descended from the sovereyne sete,
whi arttow comen into this solitarie place   10
of myn exil? Artow comen for thou art
maad coupable with me of false blames?" "O!"
quod sche, "my nory, schulde I forsake the
now, and schulde I nat parten with the, by
comune travaile, the charge that thow hast suffred for envye of my name? Certes it nere nat
leveful ne syttynge thyng to Philosophie, to
leten withouten companye the weye of hym
that is innocent. Schulde I thanne re-
dowte my blame, and agrysen as though   20
ther were byfallen a newe thyng? For
trowestow that Philosophie be now alderferst
assailed in periles by folk of wykkide maneris?
Have I noght stryven with ful greet strif in
olde tyme, byfor the age of my Plato, ayens

the foolhardynesse of folye? And eek, the same Plato lyvynge, his mayster Socrates desserved victorie of unryghtful deth in my presence. The heritage of the whiche Socrates (*the heritage is to seyn the doctryne of the whiche Socrates in his opinyoun of felicite, that I clepe welefulnesse*) whan that the peple of Epycuriens and Stoyciens and manye othre enforceden hem to gon ravyssche everych man for his part (*that is to seyn, that everych of hem wolde drawen to the deffense of his opinyoun the wordes of Socrates*), they as in partye of hir preye todrowen me, cryinge and debatyng ther-ayens, and korven and torente my clothes that I hadde woven with myn handes; and with tho cloutes that thei hadden arased out of my clothes, thei wenten awey wenynge that I hadde gon with hem every del. In whiche Epycuriens and Stoyciens for as myche as ther semede some traces or steppes of myn abyt, the folie of men wenynge tho Epycuryens and Stoyciens my familiers pervertede some thurw the errour of the wikkide or unkunnynge multitude of hem. (*This is to seyn, that, for they semeden philosophres, thei weren pursued to the deth and slayn.*) So yif thou ne hast noght knowen the exilynge of Anaxogore, ne the empoisonynge of Socrates, ne the turmentz of Zeno, for they weren straungiers, yit myghtestow han knowen the Senecciens, and the Canyos, and the Soranas, of whiche folk the renoun is neyther over-oold ne unsollempne. The whiche men nothyng elles ne broght hem to the deeth, but oonly for thei weren enformyd of myne maneris, and semyde moost unlyk to the studies of wykkid folk. And forthi thou oughtest noght to wondren though that I, in the byttere see of this lif, be fordryven with tempestes blowynge aboute. In the whiche tempestes this is my moste purpoos, that is to seyn to displesen to wikkide men. Of whiche schrewes al be the oost nevere so greet, it es to despise; for it nys nat governyd with no ledere (*of resoun*), but it es ravyssched oonly by fleetynge errour folyly and lyghtly; and yif they somtyme, makynge an oost ayens us, assayle us as strengere, our ledere draweth togidre his richesses into his tour, and they ben ententyf aboute sarpleris or sachelis, unprofitable for to taken. But we that ben heghe above, syker fro alle tumolte and wood noyse, warnstoryd and enclosed in swich a palis whider as that chaterynge or anoyinge folye ne may nat

atayne, we scorne swyche ravyneres and henteres of foulest thynges.

"Quisquis composito." — Metrum 4

"Whoso it be that is cleer of vertu, sad and wel ordynat of lyvynge, that hath put under fote the proude weerdes, and loketh, upright, upon either fortune, he may holden his chere undesconfited. The rage ne the manaces of the see, commoevynge or chasynge upward hete fro the botme, ne schal nat moeve that man. Ne the unstable mowntaigne that highte Visevus, that writhith out thurw his brokene chemeneyes smokynge fieres, ne the wey of thonder-leit, that is wont to smyten hye toures, ne schal nat moeve that man. Wharto thanne, o wrecches, drede ye tirauntz that ben wode and felenous withouten ony strengthe? Hope aftir no thyng, ne drede nat; and so schaltow desarmen the ire of thilke unmyghty tiraunt. But whoso that, qwakynge, dredeth or desireth thyng that nys noght stable of his ryght, that man that so dooth hath cast awey his scheeld, and is remoeved from his place, and enlaceth hym in the cheyne with which he mai ben drawen.

"Sentisne, inquit." — Prosa 4

"Felistow," quod sche, "thise thynges, and entren thei aught in thy corage? Artow like an asse to the harpe? Why wepistow, why spillestow teeris? Yif thou abidest after help of thi leche, the byhoveth discovre thy wownde."

Tho I, that hadde gaderyd strengthe in my corage, answeride and seide: "And nedeth it yit," quod I, "of rehersynge or of ammonicioun? And scheweth it nat ynogh by hymselve the scharpnesse of Fortune, that waxeth wood ayens me? Ne moeveth it nat the to seen the face or the manere of this place? Is this the librarye which that thou haddest chosen for a ryght certein sege to the in myn hous, there as thow disputedest ofte with me of the sciences of thynges touchynge dyvinyte and touchynge mankynde? Was thanne myn habit swych as it is now? Was my face or my chere swych as now whan I soghte with the the secretis of nature, whan thow enformedest my maneris and the resoun of al my lif to the ensaumple of the ordre of hevene? Is noght this the gerdouns that I referre to the, to whom I have ben obeisaunt?

Certes thou confermedest by the mouth of

Plato this sentence, that is to seyn that comune thynges or comunalites weren blisful yif they that hadden studied al fully to wysdom governeden thilke thynges; or elles yif it so befille that the governours of comunalites studieden to geten wysdom. Thou seidest eek by the mouth of the same Plato that it was a necessarie cause wise men to taken and desire the governance of comune thynges, for that the governementz of cites, ilefte in the handes of felonous turmentours citezeens, ne schulde noght bryngen in pestilence and destruccioun to goode folk. And therfore I, folwynge thilke auctorite, desired to putten forth in execucion and in act of comune administracioun thilke thynges that I hadde lernyd of the among my secre restyngwhiles.

Thow and God, that putte the in the thoughts of wise folk, ben knowynge with me that nothyng ne brought me to maistrie or dignyte but the comune studie of alle goodnesse. And therof cometh it that bytwixen wikkid folk and me han ben grevous discordes, that ne myghte nat ben relessed by preyeris; for this liberte hath fredom of conscience, that the wraththe of more myghty folk hath alwey ben despised of me for savacioun of right. How ofte have I resisted and withstonden thilke man that highte Conigaste, that made alwey assawtes ayens the prospere fortunes of pore feble folk! How ofte eek have I put of or cast out hym Trygwille, provost of the kyngis hous, bothe of the wronges that he hadde bygunne to doon, and ek fully performed! How ofte have I covered and defended by the auctorite of me put ayens perils (*that is to seyn, put myn auctorite in peril for*) the wrecche pore folk, that the covetise of straungiers unpunyschid tormentyde alwey with myseses and grevances out of nombre! Nevere man ne drow me yit fro right to wrong. Whan I say the fortunes and the richesses of the peple of the provinces ben harmed or amenused outher be pryve ravynes or by comune tributes or cariages, as sory was I as they that suffriden the harm. (*Glosa. Whan that Theodoric, the kyng of Gothes, in a dere yeer, hadde his gerneeris ful of corn, and comaundede that no man schulde byen no coorn til his corn were soold, and that at a grevous dere prys, Boece withstood that ordenaunce and overcom it, knowynge al this the kyng hymselve.*) *Textus.* Whan it was in the

sowre hungry tyme, ther was establissed or cryed grevous and unplitable coempcioun, that men sayen wel it schulde gretly tormenten and endamagen al the provynce of Campayne, I took stryf ayens the provost of the pretorie for comune profit; and, the kyng knowynge of it, Y overcom it, so that the coempcioun ne was nat axid ne took effect. (*Coempcioun is to seyn comune achat or beyinge togidre, that were establissed upon the peple by swich a manere imposicioun, as whoso boughte a busschel corn, he most yyve the kyng the fyfte part.*) Paulyn, a conseiller of Rome, the richesses of the whiche Paulyn the howndes of the paleys (*that is to seyn, the officeres*) wolden han devoured by hope and covetyse, yit drow I hym out of the jowes of hem that gapeden. And for as moche as the peyne of the accusacioun ajugid byforn ne schulde noght sodeynli henten ne punyssche wrongfully Albyn, a conseiller of Rome, I putte me ayens the hates and indignacions of the accusour Cyprian. Is it not thanne inogh isene, that I have purchaced grete discordes ayens myself? But I oughte be the more asseured ayens alle othere folk, that, for the love of rightwisnesse, I ne reservede nevere nothyng to myselve to hem-ward of the kyngis halle, by which I were the more syker. But thurw the same accusours accusynge I am condempned. Of the nombre of whiche accusours, oon Basilius, that whilom was chased out of the kyngis servyse, is now compelled in accusynge of my name for nede of foreyne moneye. Also Opilion and Gaudencius han accused me, al be it so that the justise regal hadde whilom demed hem bothe to gon into exil for hir trecheries and frawdes withouten nombre, to which juggement they nolden nat obeye, but defendeden hem by the sikernesse of holi houses (*that is to seyn, fledden into seyntuarie*); and whan this was aperceyved to the kyng, he comandide that, but they voydide the cite of Ravenne by certeyn day assigned, that men scholde marken hem on the forheved with an hoot iren and chasen hem out of the towne. Now what thyng semyth myghte ben likned to this cruelte? For certes thilke same day was resceyved the accusynge of myn name by thilke same accusours. What may ben seyd herto? Hath my studie and my kunnynge disserved thus? Or elles the forseyde dampnacioun of me — made that hem ryght-fulle accusours or no? Was noght Fortune aschamed of this? Certes, al hadde noght Fortune ben aschamed that innocence was accused, yit oughte sche han had schame of the fylthe of myn accusours.

But axestow in somme of what gylt I 140 am accused? Men seyn that I wolde saven the companye of the senatours. And desirestow to heren in what manere? I am accused that I schulde han disturbed the accusour to beren lettres, by whiche he scholde han maked the senatours gylty ayens the kynges real majeste. O Maystresse, what demestow of this? Schal I forsake this blame, that Y ne be no schame to the? Certes I have wold it (*that is to seyn the savacioun of the senat*), ne I schal 150 nevere letten to wilne it; and that I confesse and am aknowe; but the entente of the accusour to ben distorbed schal cese. For shal I clepe it thanne a felonye or a synne, that I have desired the savacioun of the ordre of the senat? And certes yit hadde thilke same senat don by me thurw hir decretz and hir jugementz as though it were a synne and a felonye (*that is to seyn, to wilne the savacioun of hem*). But folye, that lyeth alwey 160 to hymselve, may noght chaunge the merite of thynges, ne I trowe nat by the jugement of Socrates, that it were leveful to me to hide the sothe, ne assente to lesynges. But certes, how so evere it be of this, I putte it to gessen or prisen to the jugement of the and of wyse folk. Of which thyng all the ordenaunce and the sothe, for as moche as folk that been to comen aftir our dayes schullen knowen it, I have put it in scripture and in remem- 170 braunce. For touchynge the lettres falsly maked, by whiche lettres I am accused to han hoped the fredom of Rome, what aperteneth me to speken therof? Of whiche lettres the fraude hadde ben schewed apertely, yif I hadde had liberte for to han used and ben at the confessioun of myn accusours, the whiche thyng in alle nedes hath greet strengthe. For what other fredom mai men hopen? Certes I wolde that som other fredom myghte ben 180 hoped; I wolde thanne han answeryd by the wordys of a man that hyghte Canyus. For whan he was accused by Gaius Cesar, Germaynes sone, that he was knowynge and consentynge of a conjuracioun ymaked ayens hym, this Canyus answeride thus: 'Yif I hadde wyst it, thou haddest noght wyst it.' In which thyng sorwe hath noght so dullid my wyt, that I

pleyne oonly that schrewed folk apparailen felonyes ayens vertu; but I wondre gretly 190 how that thei may performe thynges that thei han hoped for to doon. For-why to wylne schrewydnesse — that cometh peraventure of our defaute; but it is lyk a monstre and a merveyle, how that, in the presente sight of God, may ben acheved and performed swiche thynges as every felonous man hath conceyved in his thoght ayens innocentz. For which thyng oon of thy familiers noght unskilfully axed thus: 'Yif God is, whennes comen wikkide 200 thyngis? And yif God ne is, whennes comen gode thynges?' But al hadde it ben leveful that felonous folk, that now desiren the blood and the deeth of alle gode men and ek of al the senat, han wilned to gon destroyen me, whom they han seyn alwey bataylen and defenden gode men and eek al the senat, yit hadde I nought disservyd of the faderes (*that is to seyn, of the senatours*) that they schulden wilne my destruccioun. 210

Thow remembrest wel, as I gesse, that whan I wolde doon or seyn any thyng, thow thiselve alwey present reuledest me. At the cite of Verone, whan that the kyng, gredy of comune slaughtre, caste hym to transporten upon al the ordre of the senat the gilt of his real majeste, of the whiche gilt that Albyn was accused, with how gret sykernesse of peril to me defended I al the senat! Thow woost wel that I sey sooth, ne I n'avawntede me 220 nevere in preysynge of myselve. For alwey whan any wyght resceyveth precious renoun in avauntynge hymselve of his werkes, he amenuseth the secre of his conscience. But now thow mayst wel seen to what eende I am comen for myn innocence; I resceyve peyne of fals felonye for guerdoun of verrai vertu. And what open confessioun of felonye hadde evere juges so accordaunt in cruelte (*that is to seyn, as myn accusynge hath*) that either 230 errour of mannys wit, or elles condicion of fortune, that is uncerteyn to alle mortel folk, ne submyttede some of hem (*that is to seyn, that it ne enclynede som juge to have pite or compassioun*)? For although I hadde ben accused that I wolde brenne holi houses and straungle preestis with wykkid sweerd, or that I hadde greythed deth to alle gode men, algates the sentence scholde han punysshed me present, confessed or convict. But now 240 I am remuwed fro the cite of Rome almost fyve hundred thowsand paas, I am withoute deffense dampnyd to proscripcion and to the deth for the studie and bountes that I have doon to the senat. But, O, wel ben thei wurthy of meryte! (*As who seith, nay.*) Ther myghte nevere yit noon of hem ben convict of swich a blame as myn is. Of which trespas myne accusours sayen ful wel the dignete; the whiche dignyte, for thei wolden derken it 250 with medlynge of some felonye, they bare me on hande, and lieden, that I hadde pollut and defouled my conscience with sacrilegie for covetise of dignyte. And certes thou thiselve, that art plaunted in me, chacedest out of the sege of my corage alle covetise of mortel thynges, ne sacrilege ne hadde no leve to han a place in me byforn thyne eien. For thow droppiddest every day in myn eris and in 260 my thought thilke commaundement of Pictagoras, that is to seyn, men schal serven to God, and noght to goddes. Ne it was noght convenient ne no nede to taken help of the fouleste spiritz — I, that thow hast ordeyned and set in swich excellence, that thou makedest me lyk to God. And over this, the right clene secre chaumbre of myn hous (*that is to seyn, my wif*), and the companye of myne honeste freendes, and my wyves fadir, as wel holi as worthy to ben reverenced thurw his 270 owene dedes, defenden me fro alle suspecioun of swich blame. But O malice! For they that accusen me taken of the, Philosophie, feith of so greet blame, for they trowen that I have had affinyte to malefice or enchauntement, bycause that I am replenysshid and fulfild with thy techynges, and enformed of thi maneris. And thus it suffiseth nat oonly that thi reverence ne avayle me nat, but yif that thow of thy free wil rather be blem- 280 essched with myne offencioun. But certes, to the harmes that I have, ther bytideth yit this encrees of harm, that the gessynge and the jugement of moche folk ne loken nothyng to the desertes of thynges, but oonly to the aventure of fortune; and jugen that oonly swiche thynges ben purveied of God, whiche that temporel welefulnesse commendeth. (*Glose. As thus: that yif a wyght have prosperite, he is a good man and worthy to han that* 290 *prosperite; and whoso hath adversite, he is a wikkid man, and God hath forsake hym, and he is worthy to han that adversite. This is the opinyoun of some folk.*) *Textus.* And therof cometh that good gessynge, first of alle thyng, forsaketh wrecches. Certes it greveth

me to thynke ryght now the diverse sentences that the peple seith of me. And thus moche I seie, that the laste charge of contrarious fortune is this: that whan that eny blame 300 is leid upon a caytif, men wenen that he hath desservyd that he suffreth. And I, that am put awey fro gode men, and despoyled of dignytes, and defouled of myn name by gessynge, have suffrid torment for my gode dedes. Certes me semyth that I se the felonous covynes of wykkid men habounden in joye and in gladnesse; and I se that every lorel schapeth hym to fynde out newe fraudes for to accuse goode folk; and I se that goode men ben 310 overthrowen for drede of my peril, and every luxurious turmentour dar doon alle felonye unpunysschyd, and ben excited therto by yiftes; and innocentz ne ben noght oonly despoiled of sikernesse, but of defense; and therfore me lyst to crie to God in this manere:

"O stelliferi conditor orbis." — Metrum 5

"O thow makere of the wheel that bereth the sterres, which that art festnyd to thi perdurable chayer, and turnest the hevene with a ravysschynge sweigh, and constreynest the sterres to suffren thi lawe; so that the moone somtyme, schynynge with hir fulle hornes metynge with alle the beemes of the sonne hir brothir, hideth the sterres that ben lasse; and somtyme, whan the moone pale with hir derke hornes aprocheth the sonne, leeseth 10 hir lyghtes; and that the eve sterre, Hesperus, which that in the first tyme of the nyght bryngeth forth hir colde arysynges, cometh eft ayen hir used cours, and is pale by the morwe at rysynge of the sonne, and is thanne clepid Lucyfer! Thow restreynest the day by schortere duellynge in the tyme of coold wynter, that maketh the leeves falle. Thow devydest the swyfte tydes of the nyght, whan the hote somer is comen. Thy myght attempreth 20 the variauntz sesouns of the yer, so that Zephirus, the debonere wynd, bryngeth ayen in the first somer sesoun the leeves that the wynd that hyghte Boreas hath reft awey in autumpne (*that is to seie, in the laste ende of somer*); and the seedes that the sterre that highte Arcturus saugh, ben waxen heye cornes whan the sterre Syrius eschaufeth hem. Ther nys no thyng unbounde from his olde lawe, ne forleteth the werk of his propre estat. 30 O thou governour, governynge alle thynges

by certein ende, whi refusestow oonly to governe the werkes of men by duwe manere?
Why suffrestow that slydynge Fortune turneth
so grete enterchaungynges of thynges; so that
anoyous peyne, that scholde duweliche pun-
ysche felons, punysscheth innocentz? And folk
of wikkide maneres sitten in heie chayeres; and
anoyinge folk treden, and that unright-
fully, on the nekkes of holi men; and vertu,   40
cleer and schynynge naturely, is hidde in
derke derknesses; and the rightful man bereth
the blame and the peyne of the feloun; ne the
forswerynge ne the fraude covered and kembd
with a fals colour, ne anoieth nat to schrewes?
The whiche schrewes, whan hem list to usen
hir strengthe, they rejoyssen hem to putten
undir hem the sovereyne kynges, whiche that
the peple withouten nombre dreden. O
thou, what so evere thou be that knyttest   50
alle boondes of thynges, loke on thise
wrecchide erthes. We men, that ben noght a
foul partie, but a fair partie of so greet a werk,
we ben turmented in this see of fortune. Thow
governour, withdraugh and restreyne the ravysschynge flodes, and fastne and ferme thise
erthes stable with thilke boond by which thou
governest the hevene that is so large."

"Hec ubi continuato dolore delatraui." —
Prosa 5

Whan I hadde, with a contynuel sorwe,
sobbyd or borken out thise thynges, sche, with
hir cheere pesible and nothyng amoeved with
my compleyntes, seide thus: "Whan I saugh
the," quod sche, "sorwful and wepynge, I
wiste anoon that thow were a wrecche and
exiled; but I wyste nevere how fer thyn exil
was yif thy tale ne hadde schewid it me. But
certes, al be thow fer fro thy cuntre, thou
n'art nat put out of it, but thow hast fayled   10
of thi weye and gon amys. And yif thou
hast levere for to wene that thow be put out
of thy cuntre, thanne hastow put out thyselve
rather than ony other wyght hath. For no
wyght but thyselve myghte nevere han doon
that to the. For yif thow remembre of what
cuntre thow art born, it nys nat governed by
emperoures, ne by governement of multitude,
as weren the cuntrees of hem of Atthenes;
but o lord and o kyng, and that is God, is   20
lord of thi cuntre, which that rejoisseth
hym of the duellynge of his citezeens, and nat

for to putten hem in exil; of the whiche lord
it is a sovereyn fredom to ben governed by the
brydel of hym and obeye to his justice. Hastow
foryeten thilke ryght oolde lawe of thi citee, in
the whiche cite it es ordeyned and estab-
lysschid, that what wyght that hath levere
founden therin his sete or his hous than
elleswhere, he may nat ben exiled by no   30
ryght fro that place? For whoso that is
contened in-with the palys and the clos of
thilke cite, ther nys no drede that he mai deserve to ben exiled; but who that leteth the
wil for to enhabyten there, he forleteth also
to deserve to ben citezen of thilke cite. So that
I seie that the face of this place ne moeveth
me noght so mochel as thyn owene face, ne
I ne axe nat rather the walles of thy librarye, apparayled and wrought with yvory   40
and with glas, than after the sete of thi
thought, in which I put noght whilom bookes,
but I putte that that maketh bokes wurthy
of prys or precyous, that is to seyn the sentence
of my bookes.

And certeynly of thy dessertes bystowed in
comune good thow hast seyd soth, but after the
multitude of thy gode dedes thou hast seyd
fewe. And of the honestete or of the falsnesse of thynges that ben opposed ayens   50
the, thow hast remembred thynges that ben
knowen to alle folk. And of the felonyes and
fraudes of thyn accusours, it semeth the have
touched it for sothe ryghtfully and schortly, al
myghten tho same thynges betere and more
plentevously ben couth in the mouth of the
peple that knoweth al this. Thow hast eek
blamed gretly and compleyned of the wrongful dede of the senat, and thow hast sorwyd
for my blame, and thow hast wepen for   60
the damage of thi renoun that is apayred;
and thi laste sorwe eschaufede ayens Fortune,
and compleyndest that guerdouns ne ben nat
eveneliche yolden to the dessertes of folk. And
in the lattre eende of thy wode muse, thow
preydest that thilke pees that governeth the
hevene schulde governe the erthe.

But for that many tribulacions of affeccions
han assailed the, and sorwe and ire and
wepynge todrawen the diversely, as thou   70
art now feble of thought, myghtyere remedies ne schullen noght yit touchen the. For
whych we wol usen somdel lyghtere medicynes,
so that thilke passiouns that ben waxen hard in
swellynge by perturbacions flowynge into thy
thought, mowen waxen esy and softe to re-

sceyven the strengthe of a more myghty and more egre medicyne, by an esyere touchynge.

"Cum Phebi radiis grave Cancri sidus inestuat." — Metrum 6

Whan that the hevy sterre of the Cancre eschaufeth by the bemes of Phebus (*that is to seyn, whan that Phebus the sonne is in the sygne of the Cancre*), whoso yeveth thanne largely his seedes to the feeldes that refusen to resceyven hem, lat hym gon, begiled of trust that he hadde to his corn, to accornes of okes. Yif thow wolt gadere vyolettes, ne go thow nat to the purpre wode whan the feeld, chirkynge, agryseth of cold by the felnesse 10 of the wind that hyghte Aquilon. Yif thou desirest or wolt usen grapes, ne seek thou nat with a glotonos hand to streyne and presse the stalkes of the vyne in the first somer sesoun; for Bachus, the god of wyn, hath rather yyven his yiftes to autumpne (*the lattere ende of somer*). God tokneth and assigneth the tymes, ablynge hem to hir propre offices, ne he ne suf- freth nat the stowndes whiche that hymself hath devyded and constreyned to ben 20 imedled togidre. And forthy he that forlet- eth certein ordenaunce of doynge by overthrow- ynge wey, he hath no glad issue or ende of his werkes.

"Primum igitur paterisne me pauculis rogacionibus." — Prosa 6

First wiltow suffre me to touche and assaye th'estaat of thi thought by a fewe demaundes, so that I may understande what be the man- ere of thi curacioun?"

"Axe me," quod I, "at thi wille what thou wolt, and I schal answere." Tho seyde sche thus: "Whethir wenestow," quod sche, "that this world be governed by foolyssche happes and fortunows, or elles wenestow that ther be inne it ony governement of resoun?" 10

"Certes," quod I, "I ne trowe nat in no manere that so certeyn thynges schulden be moeved by fortunows [folie]; but I woot wel that God, makere and maister, is governour of his werk, ne nevere nas yit day that myghte putte me out of the sothnesse of that sentence."

"So it is," quod sche, "for the same thyng songe thow a litil herebyforn, and bywayled- est and byweptest, that oonly men weren put out of the cure of God; for of alle othere 20

thynges thou ne doutedest the nat that they nere governed by resoun. But owgh! I wondre gretly, certes, whi that thou art sik, syn that thow art put in so holsom a sentence. But lat us seken depper; I conjecte that ther lakketh Y not what. But sey me this: syn that thow ne doutest noght that this world be governed by God, with whiche governayles takestow heede that it is governed?"

"Unnethes," quod I, "knowe I the sen- 30 tence of thy questioun, so that I ne may nat yit answeren to thy demandes."

"I nas nat desseyved," quod sche, "that ther ne faileth somwhat, by which the maladye of perturbacion is crept into thi thought, so as [thorw] the strengthe of the palys chynynge [and] open. But sey me this: remembrestow that is the ende of thynges, and whider that the entencion of alle kynde tendeth?"

"I have herd told it somtyme," quod I, 40 "but drerynesse hath dulled my memorie."

"Certes," quod sche, "thou wost wel whennes that alle thynges bien comen and proceded?"

"I woot wel," quod I, and answerede that God is bygynnynge of al.

"And how may this be," quod sche, "that, syn thow knowest the bygynnynge of thynges, that thow ne knowest nat what is the eende of thynges? But swiche ben the customes of perturbaciouns, and this power they han, 50 that they mai moeve a man from his place (*that is to seyn, fro the stabelnesse and perfec- cion of his knowynge*); but certes, thei mai nat al arrace hym, ne aliene hym in al. But I wolde that thou woldest answere to this: Remem- brestow that thow art a man?"

"Whi shulde I nat remembren that?" quod I.

"Maystow noght telle me thanne," quod sche, "what thyng is a man?"

"Axestow me nat," quod I, "whethir that 60 I be a resonable mortel beste? I woot wel, and I confesse wel that I am it."

"Wystestow nevere yit that thow were ony othir thyng?" quod sche.

"No," quod I.

"Now woot I," quod sche, "other cause of thi maladye, and that ryght greet: thow hast left for to knowen thyself what thou art. Thurw which I have pleynly fownde the cause of thi maladye, or elles the entree of recover- 70 ynge of thyn hele. For-why, for thow art confunded with foryetynge of thiself, forthi sor- westow that thow art exiled of thy propre goodes; and for thow ne woost what is the

eende of thynges, forthy demestow that feïonus
and wikkide men ben myghty and weleful; and
for thow hast foryeten by whiche governementz
the werld is governed, forthy weenestow that
thise mutacions of fortunes fleten withouten
governour. Thise ben grete causes, noght   80
oonly to maladye, but certes gret causes to
deth. But I thanke the auctour and the makere
of hele, that nature hath nat al forleten the.
I have gret noryssynge of thyn hele, and that is,
the sothe sentence of governance of the werld,
that thou bylevest that the governynge of it is
nat subgit ne underput to the folye of thise
happes aventurous, but to the resoun of God.
And therfore doute the nothing, for of this
litel spark thine heet of liif schal shine.   90

But for as moche as it is nat tyme yet of
fastere remedies, and the nature of thoughtes
desceyved is this, that, as ofte as they casten
awey sothe opynyouns, they clothen hem in
false opynyouns, of the whiche false opynyouns the derknesse of perturbacion waxeth up,
that confowndeth the verray insyghte — that
derknesse schal I assaie somwhat to maken
thynne and wayk by lyghte and meneliche
remedies; so that, aftir that the derknesse   100
of desceyvynge desyrynges is doon away,
thow mowe knowe the schynynge of verray
light.

"Nubibus atris condita." — Metrum 7

The sterres, covred with blake cloudes, ne
mowen yeten adoun no lyght. Yif the truble
wynd that hyghte Auster, turnynge and walwynge the see, medleth the heete (*that is to
seyn, the boylynge up fro the botme*), the
wawes, that whilom weren clere as glas and
lyk to the fayre bryghte dayes, withstande
anon the syghtes of men by the filthe and
ordure that is resolved. And the fleetynge
streem, that royleth doun diversely fro heye   10
montaygnes, is areestid and resisted ofte
tyme by the encountrynge of a stoon that is
departed and fallen fro som roche. And forthy,
yif thou wolt loken and demen soth with cleer
lyght, and hoolden the weye with a ryght path,
weyve thow joie, dryf fro the drede, fleme thow
hope, ne lat no sorwe aproche (*that is to seyn,
lat non of thise foure passiouns overcomen the
or blenden the*). For cloudy and derk is
thilke thoght, and bownde with bridelis,   20
where as thise thynges reignen."

EXPLICIT LIBER PRIMUS

"Postea paulisper conticuit." — Prosa 1

After this sche stynte a lytel; and after that
sche hadde gadred by atempre stillenesse myn
attencioun (*as who so myghte seyn thus: after
thise thynges sche stynte a litil, and whan sche
aperceyved by atempre stillenesse that I was
ententyf to herkne hire, sche bygan to speke in
this wyse*): "If I," quod sche, "have undirstonden and knowen outrely the causes and the
habyt of thy maladye, thow languyssest and
art deffeted for desir and talent of thi rather   10
fortune. Sche (that ilke Fortune) oonly,
that is chaunged, as thow feynest, to the-ward,
hath perverted the cleernesse and the estat of
thi corage. I undirstonde the felefolde colours
and desceytes of thilke merveylous monstre
Fortune and how sche useth ful flaterynge fa-
mylarite with hem that sche enforceth to bygyle, so longe, til that sche confounde with
unsuffrable sorwe hem that sche hath left
in despeer unpurveied. And yif thou re-   20
membrest wel the kynde, the maneris, and
the desserte of thilke Fortune, thou shalt wel
knowe that, as in hir, thow nevere ne haddest
ne hast ylost any fair thyng. But, as I trowe,
I schal nat greetly travailen to don the remembren on thise thynges. For thow were wont to
hurtlen and despysen hir with manly woordes
whan sche was blaundyssching and present,
and pursuydest hir with sentences that
weren drawen out of myn entre (*that is to   30
seyn, of myn enformacioun*). But no sodeyn mutacioun ne bytideth noght withouten
a manere chaungynge of corages; and so is it
byfallen that thou art a litil departed fro the
pees of thi thought.

But now is tyme that thou drynke and ataste
some softe and delitable thynges, so that
whanne thei ben entred withynne the, it
mowe maken wey to strengere drynkes of
medycines. Com now forth, therfore, the   40
suasyoun of swetnesse rethorien, which that
goth oonly the righte wey while sche forsaketh nat myn estatutz. And with Rethorice com
forth Musice, a damoysele of our hous, that
syngeth now lightere moedes or prolacions, now
hevyere. What eyleth the, man? What is it
that hath cast the into moornynge and into
wepynge? I trow that thou hast seyn some
newe thyng and unkouth. Thou wenest
that Fortune be chaunged ayens the; but   50
thow wenest wrong, yif thou that wene: al-

way tho ben hir maneres. Sche hath rather kept, as to the-ward, hir propre stablenesse in the chaungynge of hirself. Ryght swich was sche whan sche flateryd the and desseyved the with unleful lykynges of fals welefulnesse. Thou hast now knowen and ateynt the doutous or double visage of thilke blynde goddesse Fortune. Sche, that yit covereth and wympleth hir to other folk, hath schewyd hir 60 every del to the. Yif thou approvest here and thynkest that sche is good, use hir maneris and pleyne the nat; and yif thou agrisest hir false trecherie, despise and cast awey hir that pleyeth so harmfully. For sche, that is now cause of so mochel sorwe to the, scholde ben cause to the of pees and of joye. Sche hath forsaken the, forsothe, the whiche that nevere man mai ben siker that sche ne schal forsaken hym. (*Glose. But nathe-* 70 *les some bookes han the texte thus: forsothe sche hath forsaken the, ne ther nys no man siker that sche hath nat forsake.*) Holdestow thanne thilke welefulnesse precious to the, that schal passen? And is present Fortune dereworth to the, which that nys nat feithful for to duelle, and whan sche goth awey that sche bryngeth a wyght in sorwe? For syn she may nat ben withholden at a mannys wille, sche maketh hym a wrecche whan sche departeth 80 fro hym. What other thyng is flyttynge Fortune but a maner schewynge of wrecchidnesse that is to comen? Ne it ne suffiseth nat oonly to loken on thyng that is present byforn the eien of a man; but wisdom loketh and mesureth the ende of thynges. And the same chaungynge from oon into another (*that is to seyn, fro adversite into prosperite*), maketh that the manaces of Fortune ne ben nat for to dreden, ne the flaterynges of hir to ben 90 desired. Thus, at the laste, it byhoveth the to suffren wyth evene wil in pacience al that is doon inwith the floor of Fortune (*that is to seyn, in this world*), syn thou hast oonys put thy nekke undir the yok of hir. For yif thow wilt writen a lawe of wendynge and of duellynge to Fortune, which that thow hast chosen frely to ben thi lady, artow nat wrongful in that, and makest Fortune wroth and aspre by thyn impacience? And yit thow mayst 100 nat chaungen hir. Yif thou committest and betakest thi seyles to the wynd, thow shalt ben shoven, nat thider that thow woldest, but whider that the wynd schouveth the. Yif thow castest thi seedes in the feeldes, thou sholdest

han in mynde that the yeres ben amonges outherwhile plentevous and outherwhile bareyne. Thou hast bytaken thiself to the governaunce of Fortune and forthi it byhoveth the to ben obeisaunt to the maneris of 110 thi lady. Enforcestow the to aresten or withholden the swyftnesse and the sweigh of hir turnynge wheel? O thow fool of alle mortel foolis! Yif Fortune bygan to duelle stable, she cessede thanne to ben Fortune.

"*Hec cum superba, &c.*" — Metrum 1

Whan Fortune with a proud ryght hand hath turned hir chaungynge stowndes, sche fareth lyk the maneres of the boylynge Eurippe. (*Glosa. Eurippe is an arm of the see that ebbeth and floweth, and somtyme the streem is on o side, and somtyme on the tothir.*) *Textus.* She, cruel Fortune, casteth adoun kynges that whilom weren ydradd; and sche, desceyvable, enhaunceth up the humble chere of hym that is discounfited. Ne sche neither heer- 10 eth, ne rekketh of wrecchide wepynges; and she is so hard that sche laugheth and scorneth the wepynges of hem, the whiche sche hath maked wepe with hir free wille. Thus sche pleyeth, and thus sche proeveth hir strengthes, and scheweth a greet wonder to alle hir servauntz yif that a wyght is seyn weleful and overthrowe in an houre.

"*Vellem autem pauca.*" — Prosa 2

Certes I wolde pleten with the a fewe thynges, usynge the woordes of Fortune. Tak hede now thyselve, yif that sche asketh ryght: 'O thou man, wherfore makestow me gyltyf by thyne every dayes pleynynges? What wrong have I don the? What godes have I byreft the that weren thyne? Stryf or pleet with me byforn what juge that thow wolt of the possessioun of rychesses or of dignytees; and yif thou maist schewen me that ever any mor- 10 tel man hath resceyved ony of tho thynges to ben his in propre, thanne wil I graunte freely that thilke thynges weren thyne whiche that thow axest.

Whan that nature brought the foorth out of thi modir wombe, I resceyved the nakid and nedy of alle thynges, and I norissched the with my richesses, and was redy and ententyf thurw my favour to sustene the — and that maketh the now inpacient ayens me; and I 20 envyrounde the with al the habundaunce and schynynge of alle goodes that ben in my ryght. Now it liketh me to withdrawe myn hand. Thow hast had grace as he that hath used of foreyne goodes; thow hast no ryght to pleyne the, as though thou haddest outrely forlorn alle thy thynges. Why pleynestow thanne? I have doon the no wrong. Richesses, honours, and swiche othere thinges ben of my right. My servauntz knowen me for hir lady; they comen with me, and departen whan I wende. I dar wel affermen hardely that, yif tho thynges of whiche thow pleynest that thou hast forlorn [hem] hadden ben thyne, thow ne haddest nat lorn hem. Schal I thanne, oonly, be defended to usen my ryght?

Certes it is leveful to the hevene to maken clere dayes, and after that to coveren the same dayes with dirke nyghtes. The yeer hath eek leve to apparaylen the visage of the erthe, now with floures, and now with fruyt, and to confownden hem somtyme with reynes and with coldes. The see hath eek his ryght to ben somtyme calm and blaundyssch-yng with smothe watir, and somtyme to ben horrible with wawes and with tempestes. But the covetise of men, that mai nat be stawnched, — schal it bynde me to ben stedfast, syn that stidfastnesse is uncouth to my maneris? Swich is my strengthe, and this pley I pleye continuely. I torne the whirlynge wheel with the turnynge sercle; I am glad to chaungen the loweste to the heyeste, and the heyeste to the loweste. Worth up yif thow wolt, so it be by this lawe, that thow ne holden at that I do the wroong, though thow descende adown whan the resoun of my pley axeth it. Wystestow nat how Cresus, kyng of Lydyens, of which kyng Cirus was ful sore agast a lytil byforn, — that this rewliche Cresus was caught of Cirus and lad to the fyer to ben brend; but that a rayn descendede down fro hevene that rescowyde hym. And is it out of thy mynde how that Paulus, consul of Rome, whan he had taken the kyng of Percyens, weep pitously for the captivyte of the selve kyng. What other thyng bywaylen the cryinges of tragedyes but oonly the dedes of Fortune, that with unwar strook overturneth the realmes of greet nobleye? (*Glose. Tragedye is to seyn a dite of a prosperite for a tyme, that endeth in wrecchidnesse.*) *Textus.* Lernedest nat thow in Greek whan thow were yong, that in the entre or in the seler of Juppiter ther ben cowched two tonnes; the toon is ful of good, and the tother is ful of harm. What ryght

hastow to pleyne, yif thou hast taken more plentevously of the gode side (*that is to seyn of my richesses and prosperites*)? And what ek yif Y ne be nat al departed fro the? What eek yif my mutabilite yeveth the ryghtful cause of hope to han yit bettere thynges? Natheles dismaye the nat in thi thought; and thow that art put in the comune realme of alle, desire nat to lyven by thyn oonly propre ryght.

"Si quantas rapidis." — Metrum 2

Though Plente (*that is, goddesse of rych-esses*) hielde adoun with ful horn, and with-draweth nat hir hand, as many richesses as the see torneth upward sandes whan it is moeved with ravysshynge blastes, or elles as manye rychesses as ther schynen bryghte sterres in hevene on the sterry nyghtes; yit, for all that, mankynde nolde nat cese to wepe wrecchide pleyntes. And al be it so that God resceyv-eth gladly hir preiers, and yyveth hem, as fool-large, moche gold, and apparayleth coveytous folk with noble or cleer honours; yit semeth hem haven igeten nothyng, but alwey hir cruel ravyne, devourynge al that they han geten, scheweth othere gapynges (*that is to seyn, gapyn and desiren yit after mo rych-esses*). What brydles myghte withholden to any certeyn ende the disordene covetise of men, whan evere the rather that it fletith in large yiftes, the more ay brenneth in hem the thurst of havynge? Certes he that qwakynge and dredful weneth hymselven nedy, he ne lyveth nevermo ryche.

"Hiis igitur si pro se, &c." — Prosa 3

Therfore, yif that Fortune spake with the for hirself in this manere, forsothe thow ne haddest noght what thou myghtest answere. And yif thow hast any thyng wherwith thow mayst rightfully defenden thi compleynte, it behoveth the to schewen it, and I wol yyve the space to tellen it."

"Serteynly," quod I thanne, "thise ben faire thynges and enoynted with hony swet-nesse of Rethorik and Musike; and oonly whil thei ben herd thei ben delycious, but to wrecches it is a deppere felyng of harm. (*This is to seyn, that wrecches felen the harmes that thei suffren more grevously than the reme-dies or the delites of thise wordes mowen gladen or conforten hem.*) So that, whanne thise thynges stynten for to soune in eris, the sorwe that es inset greveth the thought."

"Right so it is," quod sche. "For thise ne ben yit none remedies of thy maladye, but they ben a maner norisschynges of thi sorwe, yit rebel ayen thi curacioun. For whan that tyme is, I schal moeve and ajuste swiche thynges that percen hemselve depe. But nathe-les that thow schalt noght wilne to leten thi-self a wrecche, hastow foryeten the nowmbre and the maner of thi welefulnesse? I holde me stille how that the sovereyn men of the city token the in cure and in kepynge, whan thow were orphelyn of fadir and of modir, and were chose in affynite of prynces of the cite; and thow bygonne rather to ben leef and deere than for to been a neyghebour, the whiche thyng is the moste precyous kinde of any propinquyte or alliaunce that mai ben. Who is it that ne seide tho that thow neere right weleful, with so gret a no-bleye of thi fadres-in-lawe, and with the chas-tete of thy wyf, and with the oportunyte and noblesse of thyne masculyn children (*that is to seyn, thy sones*)? And over al this — me list to passen of comune thynges — how thow haddest in thy youthe dignytees that weren wernd to oolde men. But it deliteth me to comen now to the synguler uphepynge of thi welefulnesse. Yif any fruyt of mortel thynges mai han any weyghte or pris of wele-fulnesse, myghtestow evere forgeten, for any charge of harm that myghte byfalle, the re-membraunce of thilke day that thow seye thi two sones maked conseileris, and iladde togidre fro thyn hous under so greet assemble of senatours and under the blithnesse of peple; and whan thow saye hem set in the court in hir chayeres of dignytes? Thow, rethorien or pronouncere of kynges preysynges, desservedst glorie of wit and of eloquence whan thow, syt-tynge bytwixen thi two sones conseylers, in the place that highte Circo, fulfildest the abyd-ynge of the multitude of peple that was sprad abouten the with so large preysynge and laude as men syngen in victories. Tho yave thow woordes to Fortune, as I trowe, (*that is to seyn, tho feffedestow Fortune with glos-ynge wordes and desceyvedest hir*) whan sche accoyede the and norysside the as hir owne delices. Thow bare awey of Fortune a yifte (*that is to seye, swich guerdoun*) that sche nevere yaf to prive man. Wiltow therfore leye a reknynge with Fortune? Sche hath

now twynkled first upon the with a wikkid eye. If thow considere the nowmbre and the maner of thy blisses and of thy sorwes, thou mayst noght forsaken that thow n'art yit blis-ful. For yif thou therfore wenest thiself nat weleful, for thynges that tho semeden joyeful ben passed, ther nys nat why thow sholdest wene thiself a wrecche; for thynges that semen now sory passen also. Artow now comen first, a sodeyn gest, into the schadowe or tabernacle of this lif? Or trowestow that any stedfastnesse be in mannes thynges, whan ofte a swyft hour dissolveth the same man (*that is to seyn, whan the soule departeth fro the body*)? For although that selde is ther any feith that fortunous thynges wollen dwellen, yet natheles the laste day of a mannes lif is a maner deth to Fortune, and also to thilke that hath dwelt. And therfore what wen-estow thar rekke, yif thow forleete hir in deyinge, or elles that sche, Fortune, for-leete the in fleynge awey?

"Cum primo polo." — Metrum 3

Whan Phebus, the sonne, bygynneth to spreden his clernesse with rosene charylettes, thanne the sterre, ydymmed, paleth hir white cheeres by the flambes of the sonne that over-cometh the sterre lyght. (*This to seyn, whan the sonne is rysen, the day-sterre waxeth pale, and leeseth hir lyght for the grete bryghtnesse of the sonne.*) Whan the wode waxeth rody of rosene floures in the fyrst somer sesoun thurw the breeth of the wynd Zephirus that waxeth warm, yif the cloudy wynd Auster blowe felliche, than goth awey the fairnesse of thornes. Ofte the see is cleer and calm without moevynge flodes, and ofte the hor-rible wynd Aquylon moeveth boylynge tem-pestes, and overwhelveth the see. Yif the forme of this world is so seeld stable, and yif it torn-eth by so manye entrechaungynges, wiltow thanne trusten in the tumblynge fortunes of men? Wiltow trowen on flyttynge goodes? It is certeyn and establissched by lawe per-durable, that nothyng that is engendred nys stedfast ne stable."

"Tum ego vera inquam." — Prosa 4

Thanne seide I thus: "O norice of alle ver-tues, thou seist ful sooth; ne I mai noght for-sake the ryght swyfte cours of my prosperite (*that is to seyn, that prosperite ne be comen to me wonder swyftli and sone*); but this is a

thyng that greetly smerteth me whan it remembreth me. For in alle adversites of fortune the moost unseely kynde of contrarious
fortune is to han been weleful."

"But that thow," quod sche, "abyest thus 10
the torment of thi false opynioun, that
maistow nat ryghtfully blamen ne aretten to
thynges. (*As who seith, for thow hast yit
manye habundances of thynges.*) *Textus.* For
al be it so that the ydel name of aventurous
welefulnesse moeveth the now, it is leveful that
thow rekne with me of how many grete thynges
thow hast yit plente. And therfore yif that
thilke thyng that thow haddest for moost
precyous in al thy rychesse of fortune be 20
kept to the yit by the grace of God unwemmed and undefouled, maistow thanne
pleyne ryghtfully upon the mescheef of Fortune, syn thow hast yit thi beste thynges?
Certes yit lyveth in good poynt thilke precyous
honour of mankynde, Symacus, thi wyves fader,
which that is a man maked al of sapience and
of vertu, the whiche man thow woldest byen
redyly with the pris of thyn owene lif. He
bywayleth the wronges that men don to 30
the, and nat for hymself; for he lyveth in
sikernesse of any sentences put ayens hym.
And yit lyveth thi wyf, that is atempre of wyt
and passynge othere wommen in clennesse of
chastete; and, for I wol closen schortly hir
bountes, sche is lyk to hir fadir. I telle the wel
that sche lyveth, loth of this lyf, and kepeth
to the oonly hir goost, and is al maat and overcomen by wepynge and sorwe for desir of
the; in the whiche thyng oonly I moot 40
graunten that thi welefulnesse is amenused.
What schal I seyn eek of thi two sones conseylours, of whiche, as of children of hir age,
ther shyneth the liknesse of the wit of hir fadir
or of hir eldefader! And syn the sovereyne
cure of al mortel folk is to saven hir owene
lyves, O how weleful artow, if thow knowe
thy goodes! For yit ben ther thynges dwelled
to the-ward that no man douteth that they
ne be more derworthe to the than thyn 50
owene lif. And forthy drye thi teeris, for
yit nys nat every fortune al hateful to the-
ward, ne overgreet tempest hath nat yit fallen
upon the, whan that thyne ancres clyven faste,
that neither wolen suffren the counfort of this
tyme present ne the hope of tyme comyng to
passen ne to faylen."

"And I preie," quod I, "that faste mote thei
halden; for, whiles that thei halden, how so

ever that thynges been, I shal wel fleetyn 60
forth and escapyn: but thou mayst wel seen
how grete apparailes and array that me lakketh, that ben passed awey fro me."

"I have somwhat avaunced and forthred
the," quod sche, "yif that thow anoye nat, or
forthynke nat of al thy fortune. (*As who seith,
I have somwhat comforted the, so that thou
tempeste the nat thus with al thy fortune, syn
thow hast yit thy beste thynges.*) But I mai
nat suffren thi delices, that pleynest so 70
wepynge and angwysschous for that ther
lakketh somwhat to thy welefulnesse. For what
man is so sad or of so parfit welefulnesse, that
he ne stryveth or pleyneth on som halve ayen
the qualite of his estat? Forwhy ful anguysschous thing is the condicioun of mannes
goodes; for eyther it cometh nat altogidre to
a wyght, or elles it ne last nat perpetuel. For
som man hath gret rychesse, but he is
aschamed of his ungentil lynage; and som 80
man is renomyd of noblesse of kynrede, but
he is enclosed in so greet angwyssche of nede
of thynges that hym were levere that he were
unknowe; and som man haboundeth bothe in
rychesse and noblesse, but yit he bewayleth his
chaste lyf, for he ne hath no wyf; and som man
is wel and selyly ymaried, but he hath no children, and norissheth his rychesses to the eyres
of straunge folk; and som man is gladed
with children, but he wepeth ful sory for 90
the trespas of his sone or of his doughter.
And for this ther ne accordeth no wyght lyghtly
to the condicioun of his fortune; for alwey to
every man ther is in somwhat that, unassayed,
he ne woot nat, or elles he dredeth that he hath
assaied. And adde this also, that every weleful
man hath a ful delicaat feelynge; so that, but
yif alle thynges byfalle at his owene wil, for
he is inpacient or is nat used to have noon
adversite, anoon he is throwen adoun for 100
every litil thyng. And ful litel thynges ben
tho that withdrawen the somme or the perfeccioun of blisfulnesse fro hem that been most
fortunat. How manye men trowestow wolde
demen hemself to ben almost in hevene, yif
thei myghten atayne to the leste partye of the
remenaunt of thi fortune? This same place
that thow clepest exil is contre to hem that
enhabiten here, and forthi nothyng [is]
wrecchid but whan thou wenest it. (*As* 110
*who seith, thow thiself, ne no wyght ellis,
nis a wrecche but whanne he weneth hymself
a wrechche by reputacion of his corage.*) And

ayenward, alle fortune is blisful to a man by
the aggreablete or by the egalyte of hym that
suffreth it. What man is that that is so weleful
that nolde chaunge his estat whan he hath lost
pacience? The swetnesse of mannes welefulnesse is spraynd with many bitternesses;
the whiche welefulnesse although it seme   120
swete and joieful to hym that useth it, yit
mai it nat ben withholden that it ne goth awey
whan it wole. Thanne is it wel seene how
wrecchid is the blisfulnesse of mortel thynges,
that neyther it dureth perpetuel with hem that
every fortune resceyven agreablely or egaly, ne
it deliteth nat in al to hem that ben angwyssous.

O ye mortel folk, what seeke ye thanne blisfulnesse out of yourself which that is put
in yowrself? Errour and folie confound-   130
eth yow. I schal schewe the schortly the
poynt of soverayn blisfulnesse. Is there anythyng more precyous to the than thiself? Thow
wolt answere, 'nay.' Thanne, yif it so be that
thow art myghty over thyself (*that is to seyn,
by tranquillite of thi soule*), than hastow thyng
in thi power that thow noldest nevere leesen,
ne Fortune may nat bynymen it the. And that
thow mayst knowe that blisfulnesse ne mai
nat standen in thynges that ben fortunous   140
and temporel, now undirstond and gadere
it togidre thus: yif blisfulnesse be the soverayn good of nature that lyveth by resoun,
ne thilke thyng nys nat soverayn good that
may ben taken awey in any wise (for more
worthy thyng and more dygne is thilke thyng
that mai nat ben take awey); than scheweth
it wel that the unstablenesse of fortune may
nat atayne to resceyven verray blisfulnesse.
And yit more over, what man that this   150
towmblynge welefulnesse ledeth, eyther
he woot that it is chaungeable, or elles he woot
it nat. And yif he woot it nat, what blisful
fortune may ther ben in the blyndnesse of ignoraunce? And yif he woot that it is chaungeable, he mot alwey ben adrad that he ne lese
that thyng that he ne douteth nat but that he
may leesen it (*as who seith he mot bien alwey
agast lest he lese that he woot wel he may
lese it*); for which the contynuel drede that   160
he hath, ne suffreth hym nat to ben weleful, or elles yif he lese it, he weneth to ben
despised and forleten. Certes eek that is a
ful litel good that is born with evene herte
whan it is lost (*that is to seyn, that men do no
more force of the lost than of the havynge*).
And for as moche as thow thiself art he to

whom it hath be schewed and proved by ful
many demonstracyons, as I woot wel, that
the soules of men ne mowen nat deyen in   170
no wyse; and ek syn it es cleer and certeyn
that fortunous welefulnesse endeth by the deth
of the body; it mai nat be douted that, yif that
deth may take awey blisfulnesse, that al the
kynde of mortel thynges ne descendeth into
wrecchidnesse by the ende of the deth. And
syn we knowe wel that many a man hath
sought the fruyt of blysfulnesse, nat oonly with
suffrynge of deeth, but eek with suffrynge
of peynes and tormentz, how myghte   180
thanne this present lif make men blisful,
syn that whanne thilke selve lif es ended it
ne maketh folk no wrechches?

"Quisquis volet perhennem cautus, &c." — Metrum 4

What maner man stable and war, that wol
fownden hym a perdurable seete, and ne wol
noght ben cast doun with the lowde blastes of
the wynd Eurus, and wole despise the see
manasynge with flodes; lat hym eschuwen to
bilde on the cop of the mountaigne, or in the
moyste sandes; for the felle wynd Auster tormenteth the cop of the mountaigne with alle
his strengthes, and the lause sandes refusen to beren the hevy weyghte. And   10
forthi, yif thou wolt fleen the perilous
aventure (*that is to seyn, of the werld*) have
mynde certeynly to fycchen thin hous of a
myrie site in a low stoon. For although the
wynd troublynge the see thondre with over-
throwynges, thou, that art put in quiete and
weleful by strengthe of thi palys, schalt leden
a cler age, scornynge the woodnesses and the
ires of the eyr.

"Set cum racionum iam in te, &c." — Prosa 5

But for as mochel as the norisschynges of
my resouns descenden now into the, I trowe it
were tyme to usen a litel strengere medicynes.
Now undirstand heere; al were it so that the
yiftes of Fortune ne were noght brutel ne transitorie, what is ther in hem that mai be thyn
in any tyme, or elles that it nys fowl, yif that
it be considered and lookyd perfitly? Richesses
ben they precious by the nature of hemself, or elles by the nature of the? What is   10
most worth of rychesses? Is it nat gold or

myght of moneye assembled? Certes thilke
gold and thilke moneye schyneth and yeveth
bettre renoun to hem that dispenden it than
to thilke folk that mokeren it; for avaryce maketh alwey mokereres to ben hated, and largesse
maketh folk cleer of renoun. For, syn that
swich thyng as is transferred fro o man to an
othir ne may nat duellen with no man,
certes thanne is thilke moneye precyous 20
whan it is translated into other folk and
stynteth to ben had by usage of large yyvynge
of hym that hath yeven it. And also yif al the
moneye that is overal in the world were gadryd
toward o man, it scholde make alle othere men
to be nedy as of that. And certes a voys al hool
(*that is to seyn, withouten amenusynge*) fulfilleth togydre the herynge of moche folk. But
certes your rychesses ne mowen noght
passen unto moche folk withouten amenus- 30
ynge; and whan they ben apassed, nedes
they maken hem pore that forgoon tho rychesses. O streyt and nedy clepe I this richesse,
syn that many folk ne mai nat han it al, ne al
mai it nat comen to o man withoute povert
of alle othere folk. And the schynynge of
gemmes (*that I clepe precyous stones*) draweth it nat the eighen of folk to hem-ward (*that
is to seyn, for the beautes*)? But certes, yif
ther were beaute or bountee in the schyn- 40
ynge of stones, thilke clernesse is of the
stones hemselve, and nat of men; for which I
wondre gretly that men merveylen on swiche
thynges. Forwhi what thyng is it that, yif it
wanteth moevynge and joynture of soule and
body, that by right myghte semen a fair creature to hym that hath a soule of resoun? For
al be it so that gemmes drawen to hemself a
litel of the laste beaute of the world thurw
the entente of hir creatour and thurw the 50
distinccioun of hemself, yit, for as mochel
as thei ben put under yowr excellence, thei ne
han nat desserved by no way that ye schulde
merveylen on hem. And the beaute of feeldes,
deliteth it nat mochel unto yow?"

Boece. "Why schulde it nat deliten us, syn
that it is a ryght fayr porcioun of the ryght
faire werk (*that is to seyn, of this world*)?
And right so ben we gladde somtyme of the
face of the see whan it es cleer; and also 60
merveylen we on the hevene, and on the
sterres, and on the sonne, and on the moone."

Philosophie. "Aperteneth," quod sche, "any
of thilke thynges to the? Why darstow glorifye
the in the shynynge of any swiche thynges?

Artow distyngwed and embelysed by the
spryngynge floures of the firste somer sesoun,
or swelleth thi plente in fruites of somer? Whi
artow ravyssched with idel joies? Why en-
bracest thow straunge goodes as they weren 70
thyne? Fortune ne schal nevere maken that
swiche thynges ben thyne that nature of thynges
hath maked foreyne fro the. Soth is that, withouten doute, the fruites of the erthe owen to
be to the noryssynge of beestis; and yif thow
wilt fulfille thyn nede after that it suffiseth to
nature, thanne is it no nede that thow seke
aftir the superfluyte of fortune. For with ful
fewe thynges and with ful litel thynges nature halt hir apayed; and yif thow wolt 80
achoken the fulfillynge of nature with su-
perfluytees, certes thilke thynges that thow
wolt thresten or powren into nature schulle
ben unjoyeful to the, or elles anoyous. Wenestow eek that it be a fair thyng to schyne with
divers clothynge? Of which clothynge yif the
beaute be aggreable to loken uppon, I wol
merveylen on the nature of the matiere of
thilke clothes, or elles on the werkman that
wroughte hem. But also a long route of 90
meyne, maketh that a blisful man? The
whiche servantes yif thei ben vicyous of con-
dyciouns, it is a gret charge and a destruccioun
to the hous, and a gret enemy to the lord hymself; and yif they ben gode men, how schal
straunge or foreyn goodnesse ben put in the
nowmbre of thi richesses? So that by alle thise
forseide thynges it es cleerly schewed, that nevere oon of thilke thynges that thou acount-
edest for thyne goodes nas nat thi good.   100

In the whiche thynges yif ther be no
beaute to ben desired, why scholdestow ben sory
yif thou leese hem, or whi scholdestow rejoysen
the for to holden hem? For yif thei ben faire
of hir owene kynde, what aperteneth that to
the? For al so wel scholde they han ben fayre
by hemselve, though thei were departed fro
alle thyne rychesses. Forwhy fair ne precyous
were thei nat for that thei comen among
thi rychesses; but for they semeden fair   110
and precyous, therfore thou haddest levere
rekne hem among thi rychesses. But what
desirestow of Fortune with so greet a noyse
and with so greet a fare? I trowe thou seeke
to dryve awey nede with habundaunce of
thynges, but certes it turneth to you al in the
contrarie. Forwhy certes it nedeth of ful manye
helpynges to kepyn the diversite of precious
ostelementz; and sooth it es that of many

thynges han they nede, that many thynges 120
han; and ayenward of litel nedeth hem
that mesuren hir fille after the nede of kynde,
and nat after the outrage of covetyse. Is it
thanne so, that ye men ne han no propre good
iset in yow, for which ye mooten seke outward
your goodes in foreyne and subgit thynges?
So is thanne the condicion of thynges turned
up-so-doun, that a man, that is a devyne beest
be meryte of his resoun, thynketh that
hymself nys neyther fair ne noble but it be 130
thurw possessioun of ostelementz that ne
han no soules. And certes alle othere thynges
been apayed of hir owene beautes, but ye men
that ben semblable to God by yowr resonable
thought, desiren to apparailen your excellent
kynde of the loweste thynges; ne ye undir-
standen nat how greet a wrong ye don to your
creatour. For he wolde that mankynde were
moost wurthy and noble of any othere
erthly thynges, and ye thresten adoun 140
yowre dignytes bynethen the loweste
thynges. For yif that al the good of every
thyng be more precyous than is thilke thyng
whos that the good es, syn ye demen that the
fowleste thynges ben your goodes, thanne sub-
mitten ye and putten yourselven undir the
fouleste thynges by your estimacioun; and
certes this betydeth nat withouten your desert.
For certes swich is the condicioun of alle
mankynde, that oonly whan it hath know- 150
ynge of itself, thanne passeth it in noblesse
alle othere thynges; and whan it forletith the
knowynge of itself thanne it is brought bynethen alle beestes. Forwhi alle othere lyvynge beestes han of kynde to knowe nat hemself; but whan that men leeten the knowynge
of hemself, it cometh hem of vice. But how
broode scheweth the errour and the folie of
yow men, that wenen that anythyng mai
ben apparailed with straunge apparaile- 160
mentz! But forsothe that mai nat be don.
For yif a wyght schyneth with thynges that ben
put to hym (*as thus, yif thilke thynges schynen
with whiche a man is aparayled*), certes thilke
thynges ben comended and preysed with
which he is apparayled; but natheles, the thyng
that is covered and wrapped under that duelleth in his filthe.

And I denye that thilke thyng be good
that anoyeth hym that hath it. Gabbe I of 170
this? Thow wolt sey 'nay.' Sertes rychesses han anoyed ful ofte hem that han tho
rychesses, syn that every wikkid schrewe, and

for his wikkidnesse is the more gredy aftir
othir folkes rychesses wher so evere it be in
ony place, be it gold or precyous stones; and
weneth hym oonly most worthy that hath hem.
Thow thanne, that so bysy dredest now the
swerd and the spere, yif thou haddest entred in the path of this lif a voyde weyfar- 180
ynge man, thanne woldestow syngen byfor
the theef. (*As who seith, a pore man that
bereth no rychesse on hym by the weie may
boldely synge byforn theves, for he hath nat
whereof to be robbed.*) O precyous and ryght
cleer is the blisfulnesse of mortel rychesses,
that, whan thow hast geten it, thanne hastow
lorn thi sikernesse!

"*Felix nimium prior etas.*" — Metrum 5

Blisful was the firste age of men. They
heelden hem apayed with the metes that the
trewe feeldes broughten forth. They ne de-
stroyeden ne desseyvede nat hemself with outrage. They weren wont lyghtly to slaken hir
hungir at even with accornes of ookes. They
ne coude nat medle the yift of Bachus to the
cleer hony (*that is to seyn, they coude make
no pyment or clarree*), ne they coude nat 10
medle the bryghte fleeses of the contre of
Seryens with the venym of Tyrie (*this is
to seyn, thei coude nat deyen white fleeses
of Syrien contre with the blood of a maner
schellefyssch that men fynden in Tirie, with
which blood men deyen purpre*). They
slepen holsome slepes uppon the gras, and
dronken of the rennynge watres, and layen
undir the schadwes of the heye pyn-trees. Ne
no gest ne straunger ne karf yit the heye
see with oores or with schipes; ne thei ne 20
hadden seyn yit none newe stroondes to
leden marchandise into diverse contrees. Tho
weren the cruele clariouns ful hust and ful
stille. Ne blood ischad by egre hate ne hadde
nat deyed yit armures. For wherto or which
woodnesse of enemys wolde first moeven
armes, whan thei seyen cruele wowndes, ne
none medes be of blood ishad? I wolde that
our tymes shold torne ayen to the oolde
maneris! But the anguysschous love of 30
havynge brenneth in folk more cruely than
the fyer of the mountaigne of Ethna that ay
brenneth. Allas! what was he that first dalf
up the gobbettes or the weyghtes of gold covered undir erthe and the precyous stones that
wolden han be hydd? He dalf up precious
periles. (*That is to seyn, that he that hem first

up dalf, he dalf up a precious peril; for-why,
for the preciousnesse of swich thyng hath
many man ben in peril.)   40

"Quid autem de dignitatibus." — Prosa 6

But what schal I seye of dignytes and of
powers, the whiche ye men, that neither
knowen verray dignyte ne verray power,
areysen hem as heyghe as the hevene? The
whiche dignytees and poweres yif thei comen
to any wikkid man, thei doon as greet damages and destrucciouns as dooth the flaumbe
of the mountaigne Ethna whan the flaumbe
walweth up, ne no deluge ne doth so cruele
harmes. Certes the remembreth wel, as I   10
trowe, that thilke dignyte that men clepyn
the imperie of consulers, the whiche that
whilom was begynnynge of fredom, yowr eldres
coveyteden to han don awey that dignyte for
the pride of the consulers. And ryght for the
same pride yowr eldres byforn that tyme hadden doon awey out of the cite of Rome the
kynges name (that is to seyn, thei nolden han
no lenger no kyng).

But now, if so be that dignytees and pow- 20
eris ben yyven to gode men, the whiche
thyng is ful selde, what aggreable thynges is
ther in tho dignytees or powers but oonly the
goodnesse of folk that usen hem? And therfore it is thus that honour ne cometh nat to
vertu for cause of dignyte, but, ayenward, honour cometh to dignyte for cause of vertu. But
which is thilke your derworthe power that is
so cleer and so requerable? O, ye erthliche
bestes, considere ye nat over which thyng   30
that it semeth that ye han power? Now yif
thou saye a mows among othere mys that chal-
anged to hymself-ward ryght and power over
alle othere mys, how gret scorn woldestow han
of it! (Glosa. So fareth it by men; the body
hath power over the body.) For yif thou looke
wel upon the body of a wyght, what thyng
shaltow fynde more freele than is mankynde;
the whiche men ful ofte ben slayn by bytynge of smale flyes, or elles with the en-   40
trynge of crepynge wormes into the pry-
vetees of mannes body? But wher schal men
fynden any man that mai exercen or haunten
any ryght upon another man, but oonly on his
body, or elles upon thynges that ben lowere
than the body, the whiche I clepe fortunous
possessiouns? Maystow evere have any comaundement over a free corage? Maystow re-
muwen fro the estat of his propre reste a

thought that is clyvynge togidre in hymself 50
by stedfast resoun? As whilom a tyraunt
wende to confownde a freman of corage, and
wende to constreyne hym by torment to maken
hym discoveren and accusen folk that wisten
of a conjuracioun (which I clepe a confederacye) that was cast ayens this tyraunt; but this
freman boot of his owene tonge, and caste it
in the visage of thilke wode tyraunt. So that
the tormentz that this tyraunt wende to han
maked matere of cruelte, this wise man   60
maked it matere of vertu. But what thing
is it that a man may doon to an other man,
that he ne may resceyven the same thyng of
other folk in hymself? (Or thus: what may a
man don to folk, that folk ne may don hym the
same?) I have herd told of Busyrides, that was
wont to sleen his gestes that herberweden in
his hous, and he was slayn hymself of Ercules
that was his gest. Regulus hadde taken in
bataile manye men of Affryke and cast hem   70
into feteres, but sone therafter he most yyve
his handes to ben bownde with the cheynes of
hem that he hadde whilom overcomen. Wenestow thanne that he be myghty that hath no
power to doon a thyng that othere ne mai doon
in hym that he doth in othere? And yit moreover, yif it so were that thise dygnytes or pow-
eris hadden any propre or naturel goodnesse
in hemself, nevere nolde they comen to
schrewes. For contrarious thynges ne ben   80
nat wont to ben ifelaschiped togydre. Nature refuseth that contrarious thynges ben
ijoyned. And so, as I am in certeyn that ryght
wykkyd folk han dignytees ofte tyme, thanne
scheweth it wel that dignytees and poweres
ne ben nat gode of hir owene kynde, syn that
they suffren hemselve to cleven or joynen hem
to schrewes. And certes the same thyng mai
I most digneliche juggen and seyn of alle
the yiftes of Fortune that most plente-   90
vously comen to schrewes. Of the whiche
yiftes I trowe that it oughte ben considered,
that no man douteth that he ne is strong in
whom he seeth strengthe; and in whom that
swyftnesse is, sooth it is that he is swyft; also
musyke maketh musicyens, and phisyk maketh
phisicyeens, and rethoryke, rethoriens. Forwhy
the nature of every thyng maketh his proprete,
ne it is nat entremedlyd with the effect of
contrarious thynges, and as of wil it chas- 100
eth out thynges that to it ben contrarie.
But certes rychesse mai nat restreyne avarice
unstaunched; ne power ne maketh nat a man

myghty over hymselve, which that vicyous lustes holden destreyned with cheynes that ne mowen nat ben unbownden. And dignytees that ben yyven to schrewide folk nat oonly ne maketh hem nat digne, but it scheweth rather al opynly that they been unworthy and undigne. And whi is it thus? Certes for 110 ye han joie to clepen thynges with false names, that beren hem al in the contrarie; the whiche names ben ful ofte reproved by the effect of the same thynges; so that thise ilke rychesses ne oughten nat by ryghte to ben cleped rychesses, ne swych power ne aughte nat ben clepyd power, ne swich dignyte ne aughte nat ben clepyd dignyte. And at the laste, I may conclude the same thyng of alle the yyftes of Fortune, in which ther 120 nys nothyng to ben desired, ne that hath in hymselve naturel bownte, as it es ful wel yseene. For neither thei ne joygnen hem nat alwey to gode men, ne maken hem alwey gode to whom they been ijoyned.

"Novimus quantas dederit." — Metrum 6

We han wel knowen how many grete harmes and destrucciouns weren idoon by the emperour Nero. He leet brennen the cite of Rome, and made sleen the senatours; and he cruel whilom slough his brothir, and he was maked moyst with the blood of his modir (*that is to seyn, he leet sleen and slitten the body of his modir to seen wher he was conceyved*); and he lookede on every halve uppon hir colde deede body, ne no teer ne wette his face, 10 but he was so hardherted that he myghte ben domesman or juge of hir dede beaute. And natheles yit governed this Nero by septre alle the peples that Phebus (*the sonne*) may seen, comynge fro his uttreste arysynge til he hide his bemes undir the wawes. (*That is to seyn he governede al the peples by ceptre imperial that the sonne goth aboute from est to west*). And ek this Nero governyde by ceptre all the peples that ben undir the colde sterres 20 that highten the Septem Tryones. (*This is to seyn he governede alle the peples that ben under the partye of the north.*) And eek Nero governede alle the peples that the vyolent wynd Nothus scorklith, and baketh the brennynge sandes by his drye heete (*that is to seyn, al the peple in the south*). But yit ne myghte nat al his heie power torne the woodnesse of this wikkid Nero. Allas! it is grevous for-

tune as ofte as wikkid sweerd is joyned to 30 cruel venym (*that is to seyn, venymows cruelte to lordschipe*)."

"Tum ego scis inquam." — Prosa 7

Thanne seyde I thus: "Thow woost wel thiselve that the covetise of mortel thynges ne hadde nevere lordschipe of me, but I have wel desired matere of thynges to done (*as who seith, I desirede to have matiere of governaunce over comunalites*), for vertu stille sholde nat elden (*that is to seyn that, list that, or he waxe oold, his vertu, that lay now ful stille, ne schulde nat perysshe unexercised in governaunce of comunes, for which men myghten speken 10 or wryten of his gode governement*)."

Philosophie. "For sothe," quod sche, "and that is a thyng that mai drawen to governaunce swiche hertes as ben worthy and noble of hir nature, but natheles it may nat drawen or tollen swiche hertes as ben ibrought to the fulle perfeccioun of vertu, that is to seyn, covetise of glorie and renoun to han wel adminystred the comune thynges, or doon gode desertes to profyt of the comune. For see now and 20 considere how litel and how voyde of alle prys is thylke glorye. Certeyn thyng is, as thou hast leerned by the demonstracioun of astronomye, that al the envyrounynge of the erthe aboute ne halt but the resoun of a prykke at regard of the gretnesse of hevene; that is to seyn that, yif ther were maked comparysoun of the erthe to the gretnesse of hevene, men wolde juggen in al that the erthe ne heelde no space. Of the whiche litel regioun of this 30 world, the ferthe partye is enhabited with lyvynge beestes that we knowen, as thou hast thyselve leerned by Tholome, that proveth it. And yif thow haddest withdrawen and abated in thy thought fro thilke ferthe partie as moche space as the see and the mareys contene and overgoon, and as moche space as the regioun of drowghte overstreccheth (*that is to seyn, sandes and desertes*), wel unnethe sholde ther duellen a ryght strevte place to the 40 habitacioun of men. And ye thanne, that ben envyrouned and closed withynne the leeste prykke of thilke prykke, thynken ye to manyfesten or publisschen your renoun and doon yowr name for to be born forth? But yowr glorye that is so narwe and so streyt ithrungen into so litel bowndes, how mochel conteneth it in largesse and in greet doynge? And also set this therto: that many a nacioun, diverse of

tonge and of maneris and ek of resoun 50
of hir lyvynge, ben enhabited in the cloos
of thilke lytel habitacle; to the whiche nacyons,
what for difficulte of weyes, and what for diversite of langages, and what for defaute of
unusage and entrecomunynge of marchandise,
nat oonly the names of synguler men ne may
nat strecchen, but eek the fame of citees ne
may nat strecchen. At the laste, certes, in the
tyme of Marcus Tulyus, as hymselve writ
in his book, that the renoun of the comune 60
of Rome ne hadde nat nat yit passid ne
clomben over the mountaigne that highte Caucasus; and yit was thilke tyme Rome wel waxen
and greetly redouted of the Parthes, and eek of
the othere folk enhabitynge aboute. Seestow
nat thanne how streyt and how compressid is
thilke glorie that ye travailen aboute to schewe
and to multeplye? May thanne the glorie of a
synguler Romeyn strecchen thider as the
fame of the name of Rome may nat clymben 70
ne passen? And ek seestow nat that the
maneris of diverse folk and ek hir lawes ben
discordaunt among hemselve, so that thilke
thyng that som men juggen worthy of preysynge, other folk juggen that it is worthy of torment? And therof comyth it that, though a
man delyte hym in preysynge of his renoun, he
ne mai nat in no wyse bryngen forth ne spreden
his name to many manere peples. And
therfore every maner man aughte to ben 80
apayed of his glorie, that is publysschid
among his owene neyghebours; and thilke noble
renoun schal ben restreyned withynne the
boundes of o manere folk. But how many a
man, that was ful noble in his tyme, hath the
wrecchid and nedy foryetynge of writeris put
out of mynde and doon awey; al be it so
that, certes, thilke wrytynges profiten litel, the
whiche writynges long and dirk eelde doth
awey, bothe hem and ek hir auctours! But 90
yow men semeth to geten yow a perdura-
blete, whan ye thynken that in tyme comynge
your fame schal lasten. But natheles yif thow
wolt maken comparysoun to the endles spaces
of eternyte, what thyng hastow by which thow
mayst rejoisen the of long lastynge of thi name?
For yif ther were makyd comparysoun of the
abydynge of a moment to ten thowsand wynter, for as mochel as bothe two spaces ben
endyd, for yit hath the moment som por- 100
cioun of it, although it litel be. But natheles thilke selve nowmbre of yeeris, and eek
as many yeris as therto mai be multiplyed, ne

mai nat certes be comparysoned to the per-
durablete that is endlees; for of thinges that
han ende may ben maked comparysoun, but of
thynges that ben withouten ende to thynges
that han ende may be makid no comparysoun.
And forthi is it that, although renome, of
as longe tyme as evere the list to thynken, 110
were thought to the regard of eternyte,
that is unstaunchable and infynyt, it ne sholde
nat only semen litel, but pleynliche ryght noght.
But ye men, certes, ne konne doon no thyng
aryght, but yif it be for the audience of the
peple and for idel rumours; and ye forsaken the
grete worthynesse of concience and of vertu,
and ye seeken yowr gerdouns of the smale
wordes of straunge folk. Have now (*here
and undirstand*) in the lyghtnesse of swich 120
pryde and veyne glorye how a man
scornede festyvaly and myriely swich vanyte.
Whilom ther was a man that hadde assaied
with stryvynge wordes another man, the
whiche, nat for usage of verray vertu but for
proud veyne glorie, had taken upon hym falsly
the name of a philosophre. This rather man
that I spak of thoughte he wolde assaie wher
he, thilke, were a philosophre or no; that
is to seyn, yif that he wolde han suffrid 130
lyghtly in pacience the wronges that weren
doon unto hym. This feynede philosophre took
pacience a litel while; and whan he hadde resceyved wordes of outrage, he, as in stryvynge
ayen and rejoysynge of hymself, seide at the
laste ryght thus: 'undirstondistow nat that I am
a philosophre?' The tother man answerede
ayen ful bytyngly and seyde: 'I hadde wel undirstonden it yif thou haddest holde thi
tonge stille.' But what is it to thise noble 140
worthy men (for, certes, of swyche folk
speke I) that seken glorie with vertu? What is
it?" quod sche; "what atteyneth fame to swiche
folk, whan the body is resolved by the deeth at
the laste? For if it so be that men dyen in all
(*that is to seyen, body and soule*), the whiche
thing our reson defendeth us to byleeven,
thanne is ther no glorie in no wyse; for what
schulde thilke glorie ben, whan he, of
whom thilke glorie is seyd to be, nys ryght 150
naught in no wise? And yif the soule,
which that hath in itself science of gode
werkes, unbownden fro the prysone of the
erthe, weendeth frely to the hevene, despiseth
it nat thanne al erthly ocupacioun; and, beynge
in hevene rejoyseth that it is exempt fro alle
erthly thynges? (*As who seith, thanne rekketh*

the soule of noon othir thyng, ne of renoun of this world.)

"Quicumque solam mente." — Metrum 7

Whoso that with overthrowynge thought oonly seketh glorie of fame, and weneth that it be sovereyn good, lat hym looke upon the brode schewynge contrees of the hevene, and upon the streyte sete of this erthe; and he schal be asschamed of the encres of his name, that mai nat fulfille the litel compas of the erthe. O! what coveyten proude folk to lyften up hir nekkes on idel in the dedly yok of this world? For although that renoun ysprad, 10 passynge to ferne peples, goth by diverse tonges; and although that greete houses or kynredes shynen with cleere titles of honours; yit natheles deth despiseth al hey glorie of fame, and deth wrappeth togidre the heyghe hevedes and the lowe, and maketh egal and evene the heygheste to the loweste. Where wonen now the bones of trewe Fabricius? What is now Brutus or stierne Caton? The thynne fame yit lastynge of here idel names 20 is marked with a fewe lettres. But although that we han knowen the fayre wordes of the fames of hem, it is nat yyven to knowen hem that ben dede and consumpt. Liggeth thanne stille, al outrely unknowable, ne fame maketh yow nat knowe. And yif ye wene to lyve the longer for wynd of yowr mortel name whan o cruel day schal ravyssche yow, than is the seconde deth duellynge unto yow."

(*Glose. The first deeth he clepeth here de- 30 partynge of the body and the soule, and the seconde deth he clepeth as here the styntynge of the renoun of fame.*)

"Set ne me inexorabile." — Prosa 8

"But for as mochel as thow schalt nat wenen," quod sche, "that I bere an untretable batayle ayens Fortune, yit somtyme it byfalleth that sche desceyvable desserveth to han ryght good thank of men. And that is whan sche hirself openeth, and whan sche discovereth hir frownt and scheweth hir maneris. Peraventure yit undirstandestow nat that I schal seie. It is a wonder that I desire to telle, and forthi unnethe may I unplyten my sentence with 10 wordes. For I deme that contrarious Fortune profiteth more to men than Fortune deb- onayre. For alwey, whan Fortune semeth deb- onayre, thanne sche lieth, falsly byhetynge the hope of welefulnesse; but forsothe contraryous

Fortune is alwey sothfast, whan sche scheweth hirself unstable thurw hir chaungynge. The amyable Fortune desceyveth folk; the contrarie Fortune techeth. The amyable Fortune byndeth with the beaute of false goodes 20 the hertes of folk that usen hem: the con- trarye Fortune unbyndeth hem by the know- ynge of freel welefulnesse. The amyable For- tune maystow seen alwey wyndy and flowynge, and evere mysknowynge of hirself; the con- trarie Fortune is atempre and restreyned and wys thurw exercise of hir adversite. At the laste, amyable Fortune with hir flaterynges draweth myswandrynge men fro the sover- eyne good; the contrarious Fortune ledeth 30 ofte folk ayen to sothfast goodes, and haleth hem ayen as with an hook. Wenestow than that thow auggtest to leeten this a litel thyng, that this aspre and horrible Fortune hath discovered to the the the thoughtes of thi trewe freendes. Forwhy this ilke Fortune hath departed and uncovered to the bothe the cer- tein visages and eek the doutous visages of thi felawes. Whan she departed awey fro the, she took awey hir freendes and lefte the 40 thyne freendes. Now whanne thow were ryche and weleful, as the semede, with how mochel woldestow han bought the fulle know- ynge of thys (*that is to seyn, the knowynge of thyne verray freendes*)? Now pleyne the nat thanne of rychesse ylorn, syn thow hast fownden the moste precyous kynde of rych- esses, that is to seyn, thi verray freendes.

"Quod mundus stabili fide." — Metrum 8

That the world with stable feyth varieth accordable chaungynges; that the contrarious qualites of elementz holden among hemself allyaunce perdurable; that Phebus, the sonne, with his goldene chariet bryngeth forth the rosene day; that the moone hath comaunde- ment over the nyghtes, whiche nyghtes Es- perus, the eve-sterre, hath brought; that the see, gredy to flowen, constreyneth with a certein eende his floodes, so that it is nat 10 leveful to strecche his brode termes or bowndes uppon the erthes (*that is to seyn, to coveren al the erthe*) — al this accordaunce of thynges is bounde with love, that governeth erthe and see, and hath also comandement to the hevene. And yif this love slakede the bridelis, alle thynges that now loven hem togidres wolden make batayle contynuely, and stryven to fordo the fassoun of this world,

the which they now leden in accordable 20
feith by fayre moevynges. This love halt
togidres peples joyned with an holy boond, and
knytteth sacrement of mariages of chaste loves;
and love enditeth lawes to trewe felawes. O
weleful were mankynde, yif thilke love that
governeth hevene governede yowr corages."

EXPLICIT LIBER SECUNDUS

INCIPIT LIBER TERTIUS

"Iam cantum illa, &c." — Prosa 1

By this sche hadde ended hir song, whan the
swetnesse of here dite hadde thurw-perced me,
that was desyrous of herknynge, and I astoned
hadde yit streyght myn eres (*that is to seyn, to
herkne the bet what sche wolde seye*). So that
a litel herafter I seide thus: "O thow that art
sovereyn confort of angwissous corages, so
thow hast remounted and norysshed me with
the weyghte of thi sentences and with delyt of thy syngynge; so that I trowe nat 10
now that I be unparygal to the strokes of
Fortune (*as who seith, I dar wel now suffren
alle the assautes of Fortune and wel defende
me fro hir*). And tho remedies whiche that
thou seydest herbyforn that weren ryght
scharpe, nat oonly that I ne am nat agrisen of
hem now, but I, desiros of herynge, axe gretly
to heren tho remedies."

Thanne seyde sche thus: "That feeled I
ful wel," quod sche, "whan thow ententyf 20
and stille ravysschedest my wordes, and I
abood til that thou haddest swich habit of thi
thought as thou hast now, or elles til that I myself hadde maked to the the same habit, which
that is a more verray thyng. And certes the
remenant of thynges that ben yet to seie ben
swiche, that first whan men tasten hem, they
ben bytynge; but whan they ben resceyved
withynne a wyght, thanne ben thei swete.
But for thou seyst that thow art so desyrous 30
to herkne hem, with how greet brennynge
woldestow glowen, yif thow wistest whider I
wol leden the!"

"Whider is that?" quod I.

"To thilke verray welefulnesse," quod sche,
"of which thyn herte dremeth; but forasmoche
as thi syghte is ocupyed and destourbed by
imagynacioun of erthly thynges, thow mayst
nat yit seen thilke selve welefulnesse."

"Do," quod I, "and schewe me what is 40
thilke verray welefulnesse, I preie the,
withoute taryinge."

"That wol I gladly do," quod sche, "for the
cause of the. But I wol first marken the by
woordes, and I wol enforcen me to enforme the
thilke false cause of blisfulnesse that thou more
knowest; so that whanne thow hast fully by-
hoolden thilke false goodes and torned thin
eighen to the tother syde, thow mowe
knowe the cleernesse of verray blisful- 50
nesse."

"Qui serere ingenuum." — Metrum 1

"Whoso wole sowe a feld plentevous, let hym
first delyvren it of thornes, and kerve asondir
with his hook the busschens and the feern, so
that the corn may comen hevy of erys and of
greynes. Hony is the more swete, if mouthes
han first tasted savours that ben wykke. The
sterres schynen more aggreablely whan the
wynd Nothus leteth his plowngy blastes; and
aftir that Lucifer, the day-sterre, hath
chased awey the dirke nyght, the day the 10
fairer ledeth the rosene hors of the sonne.
And ryght so thow, byhooldyng ferst the false
goodes, bygyn to withdrawe thy nekke fro the
yok of erthely affeccions; and afterward the
verray goodes schullen entren into thy corage."

"Cum defixo paululum." — Prosa 2

Tho fastnede sche a litel the syghte of hir
eyen, and withdrowgh hir ryght as it were into
the streyte seete of here thought, and bigan to
speke ryght thus: "Alle the cures," quod sche,
"of mortel folk, whiche that travailen hem in
many manere studies, gon certes by diverse
weyes; but natheles thei enforcen hem alle to
comyn oonly to oon ende of blisfulnesse. And
blisfulnesse is swich a good, that whoso
that hath geten it, he ne may over that 10
nothyng more desire. And this thyng forsothe is the soverayn good that conteneth in
hymself alle maner goodes; to the whiche good
if ther fayled any thyng, it myghte nat ben
sovereyn good, for thanne wer ther som good
out of this ilke sovereyn good, that myghte ben
desired. Now is it cleer and certeyn thanne,
that blisfulnesse is a parfyt estat by the congregacioun of alle goodes; the whiche blisfulnesse, as I have seyd, alle mortel folk en- 20
forcen hem to geten by diverse weyes.
Forwhy the covetise of verray good is naturely
iplauntyd in the hertes of men, but the myswandrynge errour mysledeth hem into false
goodes. Of the whiche men, some of hem
wenen that sovereyn good be to lyven withoute

nede of any thyng, and travaylen hem to ben habundaunt of rychesses. And some othere men demen that sovereyn good be for to be ryght digne of reverence, and enforcen 30 hem to ben reverenced among hir neyghebours by the honours that thei han igeten. And some folk ther ben that holden that ryght hey power be sovereyn good, and enforcen hem for to reignen or elles to joygnen hem to hem that reignen. And it semeth to some other folk, that noblesse of renoun be the sovereyn good, and hasten hem to geten hem gloryous name by the artz of werre or of pees. And many folk mesuren and gessen that the sovereyne 40 good be joye and gladnesse, and wenen that it be ryght blisful thyng to plowngen hem in voluptuous delyt. And ther ben folk that entrechaungen the causes and the endes of thyse forseyde goodes, as they that desiren rychesses to han power and delitz, or elles they desiren power for to have moneye or for cause of renoun. In thise thynges and in swiche other thynges is torned al the entencioun of desyrynges and werkes of men; as thus: 50 noblesse and favour of peple, which that yyveth to men, as it semeth hem, a maner cleernesse of renoun; and wyf and children, that men desiren for cause of delyt and myrynesse. But forsothe freendes schulde nat ben rekned among the goodes of fortune, but of vertu, for it is a ful hooly maner thyng; alle thise othere thinges forsothe ben taken for cause of power or elles for cause of delyt. Certes now am I redy to referren the 60 goodes of the body to thise forseide thynges aboven; for it semeth that strengthe and gretnesse of body yyven power and worthynesse, and that beaute and swyftnesse yyven noblesse and glorie of renoun; and heele of body semeth yyven delyt. In alle thise thynges it semeth oonly that blisfulnesse is desyred; forwhy thilke thing that every man desireth moost over alle thynges he demeth that it be the sovereyn good; but I have diffyned that blisfulnesse 70 is the sovereyn good; for which every wyght demeth that thilke estat that he desireth over alle thynges, that it be blisfulnesse.

Now hastow thanne byforn thyne eien almest al the purposede forme of the welefulnesse of mankynde: that is to seyn rychesses, honours, power, glorie, and delitz. The whiche delit oonly considered Epicurus, and juggid and establissyde that delyt is the soverayn good, for as moche as alle othere thynges, 80

as hym thoughte, byrefte awey joye and myrthe from the herte. But I retorne ayen to the studies of men, of whiche men the corage alwey reherceth and seketh the sovereyne good, al be it so that it be with a dyrkyd memorie; but he not by which path, ryght as a dronke man not nat by which path he may retourne hom to his hous. Semeth it thanne that folk foleyen and erren, that enforcen hem to have nede of nothyng? Certes ther nys 90 noon other thyng that mai so wel performe blisfulnesse, as an estat plentevous of alle godes, that ne hath nede of noon other thyng, but that it is suffisant of hymself unto hymself. And foleyen swiche folk, thanne, that wenen that thilke thyng that is ryght good, that it be eek ryght worthy of honour and of reverence? Certes, nay. For that thyng nys neither foul ne worthy to ben despysed that wel neygh al the entencioun of mortel folk travaylen for 100 to geten it. And power, aughte nat that ek to ben rekned among goodes? What elles? For it nys nat to wene that thilke thyng that is most worthy of alle thynges be feble and withoute strengthe. And cleernesse of renoun, aughte that to ben despysed? Certes ther may no man forsake, that alle thyng that is right excellent and noble, that it ne semeth to ben ryght cleer and renomed. For certes it nedeth nat to saie that blisfulnesse [ne] be angwyssous 110 ne drery, ne subgit to grevaunces ne to sorwes; syn that in ryght litele thynges folk seken to haven and to usen that may delyten hem. Certes thise ben thise thinges that men wolen and desiren to geten, and for this cause desiren they rychesses, dignytes, reignes, glorie, and delices; for therby wenen they to han suffysaunce, honour, power, renoun, and gladnesse. Thanne is it good that men seken thus, by so manye diverse studies. In 120 which desir it mai lyghtly be schewyd how greet is the strengthe of nature. For how so that men han diverse sentences and discordynge, algates men accorden alle in lovynge the eende of good.

"Quantas rerum flectat." — Metrum 2

It liketh me to schewe by subtil soong, with slakke and delytable sown of strenges, how that Nature, myghty, enclyneth and flytteth the governementz of thynges, and by whiche lawes sche, purveiable, kepith the grete world; and how sche, byndynge, restreyneth alle thynges by a boond that may nat be unbownde. Al be

it so that the lyouns of the contre of Pene beren
the fayre chaynes, and taken metes of the
handes of folk that yeven it hem, and   10
dreden hir stourdy maistres of whiche thei
ben wont to suffre betynges; yif that hir horrible mouthes ben bybled (*that is to seyn, of
beestes devoured*), hir corage of tyme passed,
that hath ben idel and rested, repeireth ayen,
and thei roren grevously, and remembren on
hir nature, and slaken hir nekkes from hir
cheynes unbownde; and hir mayster fyrst,
totorn with blody tooth, assaieth the wode
wratthes of hem (*this to seyn, thei freten*   20
hir maister). And the janglynge brid that
syngeth on the heghe braunches (*that is to
seyn, in the wode*), and after is enclosed in a
streyt cage, although that the pleyinge bysynes
of men yeveth hem honyed drynkes and large
metes with swete studye, yit natheles yif thilke
bryd skippynge out of hir streyte cage seith the
agreable schadwes of the wodes, sche defouleth
with hir feet hir metes ischad, and seketh
mornynge oonly the wode, and twytereth   30
desyrynge the wode with hir swete voys.
The yerde of a tree, that is haled adoun by
myghty strengthe, boweth redily the crop
adown; but yif the hand of hym that it bente
leet it goon ageyn, anoon the crop loketh upryght to hevene. The sonne, Phebus, that falleth at even in the westrene wawes, retorneth
ayen eftsones his carte, by a pryve path, there
as it is wont aryse. Alle thynges seken ayen
to hir propre cours, and alle thynges re-   40
joysen hem of hir retornynge ayen to hir
nature. Ne noon ordenaunce is bytaken to
thynges, but that that hath joyned the endynge
to the bygynnynge, and hath maked the cours
of itself stable (*that it chaunge nat from his
propre kynde*).

"Vos quoque terrena animalia." — Prosa 3

Certes also ye men, that ben erthliche
beestes, dremen alwey your bygynnynge, although it be with a thynne ymaginacioun; and
by a maner thought, al be it nat clerly ne parfitly, ye loken from afer to thilke verray fyn of
blisfulnesse. And therfore naturel entencioun
ledeth yow to thilke verray good, but many
maner errours mystorneth yow therfro. Considere now yif that by thilke thynges by
whiche a man weneth to geten hym blisful-   10
nesse, yif that he mai comen to thilke ende
that he weneth to come by nature. For yif that
moneye, or honours, or thise othere forseyde

thynges, brynge to men swich a thyng that no
good ne fayle hem ne semeth faile, certes
thanne wol I graunte that they ben maked blisful by thilke thynges that thei han geten. But
yif it so be that thilke thynges mowen nat performen that they byheten, and that there
be defaute of manye goodis, scheweth it   20
nat thanne clerly that false beute of blysfulnesse is knowen and atavnt in thilke thynges.
First and forward thow thiself, that haddest
haboundances of rychesses nat longe agoon, I
aske yif that, in the habowndance of alle thilke
rychesses, thow were nevere angwyssous ne
sory in thy corage of any wrong or grevance
that bytydde the on any side?"
   "Certes," quod I, "it ne remembreth me
nat that evere I was so fre of my thought   30
that I ne was alwey in angwyse of somwhat."
   "And was nat that," quod sche, "for that the
lakkide somwhat that thow woldest nat han
lakkid, or elles thou haddest that thow noldest
nat han had?"
   "Ryght so is it," quod I.
   "Than desiredest thow the presence of the
toon and the absence of the tothir?"
   "I graunte wel," quod I.   40
   "Forsothe," quod sche, "thanne nedeth
ther somwhat that every man desireth?"
   "Yee, ther nedeth," quod I.
   "Certes," quod sche, "and he that hath lak or
nede of aught nys nat in every wey suffisant to
hymself?"
   "No," quod I.
   "And thow," quod sche, "in al the plente of
thy richesses haddest thilke lak of suffisaunce?"   50
   "What elles?" quod I.
   "Thanne mai nat richesses maken that a man
nys nedy, ne that he be suffisaunt to hymself;
and yit that was it that thei byhighten, as it
semeth. And eek certes I trow that this be
gretly to considere, that moneye ne hath nat in
his owene kynde that it ne mai ben bynomen
of hem that han it, maugre hem."
   "I byknowe it wel," quod I.
   "Whi sholdestow nat byknowen it,"   60
quod sche, "whan every day the strengere
folk bynymen it fro the feblere, maugre hem?
For whennes comen elles thise foreyne compleyntes or quereles of pledynges but for that
men axen ayen hir moneye that hath ben bynomen hem by force or by gyle, and alwey
maugre hem?"

"Right so is it," quod I.

"Than," quod sche, "hath a man nede to seken hym foreyn help by which he may 70 defenden his moneye?"

"Who mai seie nay?" quod I.

"Certes," quod sche, "and hym nedide noon help yif he ne hadde no moneye that he myghte leese."

"That is douteles," quod I.

"Than is this thyng torned into the contrarie," quod sche; "for rychesses, that men wenen scholde maken suffisaunce, they maken a man rather have nede of foreyn 80 help. Which is the maner or the gyse," quod sche, "that rychesse mai dryve awey nede? Riche folk, mai they neyther han hungir ne thurst? Thise riche men, may they fele no cold on hir lymes in wynter? But thow wolt answeren that ryche men han inoghe wherwith thei mai staunchen hir hungir, and slaken hir thurst, and don awey cold. In this wise mai nede be conforted by richesses, but certes nede mai nat al outrely be doon awey; for 90 though this nede that is alwey gapynge and gredy, be fulfild with richesses, and axe any thyng, yit duelleth thanne a nede that myghte be fulfild. I holde me stille and telle nat how that litel thyng suffiseth to nature; but certes to avarice inowgh suffiseth nothyng. For syn that rychesse ne mai nat al doon awey nede, but richesses maken nede, what mai it thanne be that ye wenen that richesses mowen yyven yow suffisaunce? 100

"Quamvis fluente dives." — Metrum 3

Al weere it so that a riche coveytous man hadde a ryver or a goter fletynge al of gold, yit sholde it nevere staunchen his covetise; and though he hadde his nekke charged with precyous stones of the Rede See, and though he do ere his feeldes plentevous with an hundred oxen, nevere ne schal his bytynge bysynesse forleeten hym whil he lyveth, ne the lyghte richesses ne schal nat beren hym companye whan he is deed. 10

"Set dignitatibus." — Prosa 4

But dignytees, to whom thei ben comen, make they hym honourable and reverent? Han thei nat so gret strengthe that thei may putten vertus in the hertes of folk that usen the lordschipes of hem, or elles may they don awey the vices? Certes thei ben nat wont to don awey wikkidnesse, but thei ben wont rather to schewen wykkydnesse. And therof cometh it that Y have right gret disdayn that dignytes ben yyven ofte to wikkide men. For 10 which thyng Catullus clepid a consul of Rome that hyghte Nonyus 'postum' or 'boch' (*as who seith, he clepid hym a congregacioun of vices in his brest, as a postum is ful of corrupcioun*), al were this Nonyus set in chayere of dygnite. Sestow nat thanne how grete vylenye dignytes don to wikkide men? Certes unworthynesse of wikkide men schulde ben the lesse isene if thei neere renomed of none honours. Certes thou thiself ne myghtest 20 nat ben broght, with as many perils as thow myghtest suffren, that thow woldest beren the magistrat with Decorat (*that is to seyn, that for no peril that myghte byfallen the by offence of the kyng Theodorik, thou noldest nat be felawe in governaunce with Decorat*), whan thow seye that he hadde wikkid corage of a likerous schrewe and of an accusour. Ne I ne mai nat for swiche honours juggen hem worthy of reverence that I deme and holde 30 unworthy to han thilke same honours. Now yif thow seie a man that were fulfild of wysdom, certes thou ne myghtest nat deme that he were unworthy to the honour or elles to the wisdom of which he is fulfild?"

"No," quod I.

"Certes dignytees," quod sche, "aperteignen properly to vertu, and vertu transporteth dignyte anoon to thilke man to which sche hirself is conjoigned. And for as moche as 40 honours of peple ne mai nat maken folk digne of honour, it is wel seyn cleerly that thei ne han no propre beaute of dignyte. And yet men aughten taken more heede in this. For yif a wykkyd wyght be in so mochel the fowlere and the more outcast that he is despysed of moost folk, so as dignyte ne mai nat maken schrewes worthy of no reverence, than maketh dignyte schrewes rather so much more despised than preysed, the whiche schrewes 50 dignyte scheweth to moche folk; and forsothe nat unpunyssched (*that is for to seyn that schrewes revengen hem ayenward uppon dignytes*), for thei yelden ayen to dignytees as greet gerdoun, whan they byspotten and defoulen dignytes with hir vylenye. And for as mochel as thou now knowe that thilke verray reverence ne mai nat comen by thise schadwy transitorie dignytes, undirstond now thus: yif that a man hadde used and had manye 60 maner dignytees of consules, and weere comen peraventure among straunge nacions, scholde thilke honour maken hym worschipful and redouted of straunge folk? Certes yif that honour of peple were a natureel yifte to dignytes, it ne myghte nevere cesen nowhere amonges no maner folk to don his office; right as fyer in every contre ne stynteth nat to eschaufen and to ben hoot. But for as mochel as for to be holden honourable or 70 reverent ne cometh nat to folk of hir propre strengthe of nature, but oonly of the false opynyoun of folk (*that is to seyn, that weenen that dignytees maken folk digne of honour*), anoon therfore, whan that thei comen there as folk ne knowen nat thilke dignytees, hir honours vanysschen away, and that anoon. But that is amonges straunge folk, maystow seyn. Ne amonges hem ther thei weren born, ne duren nat thilke dignytes alwey? Certes 80 the dignyte of the provostrye of Rome was whilom a greet power; now nys it no thyng but an idel name, and the rente of the senatorie a greet charge. And yif a wyght whilom hadde the office to taken heede to the vitayles of the peple, as of corn and othere thynges, he was holden amonges grete; but what thyng is now more outcast than thilke provostrye? And, as I have seyd a litel herebyforn, that thilke thyng that hath no propre beute of hymself 90 resceyveth somtyme prys and schynynge, and somtyme leeseth it, by the opinyoun of usaunces. Now yif that dignytes thanne ne mowen nat make folk digne of reverence, and if that dignytees waxen foule of hir wil by the filthe of schrewes, and yif dignytees leesen hir schynynge by chaungynge of tymes, and yif thei waxen fowle by estimacion of peple, what is it that they han in hemself of beaute that oughte ben desired? (*As who seith* 100 *noon.*) Thanne ne mowen they yeven no beute of dignyte to noone othere.

"Quamvis se Tirio." — Metrum 4

Al be it so that the proude Nero, with al his wode luxurie, kembde hym and apparayled hym with faire purpres of Tyrie and with white peerles, algates yit throf he haatful to alle folk (*this is to seyn that, al was he byhated of alle folk, yit this wikkide Nero hadde gret lordschipe*), and yaf whilom to the reverentz senatours the unworschipful seetis of dignytees. (*Unworschipful seetes he clepeth here, for that Nero, that was so wikkide, yaf tho dig-* 10 *nytees.*) Who wolde thanne resonably

wenen that blisfulnesse were in swiche honours as ben yyven by vycious schrewes?

"An vero regna." — Prosa 5

But regnes and familiarites of kynges, mai thei maken a man to ben myghti? How elles, whan hir blisfulnesse dureth perpetuely? But certes the olde age of tyme passed, and ek of present tyme now, is ful of ensaumples how that kynges han chaungyd into wrecchidnesse out of hir welefulnesse. O, a noble thyng and a cleer thyng is power that is nat fownden myghty to kepe itself! And yif that power of remes be auctour and makere of blisful- 10 nesse, yif thilke power lakketh on any syde, amenuseth it nat thilke blisfulnesse and bryngeth in wrecchidnesse? But yit, al be it so that the remes of mankynde strecchen broode, yit moot ther nede ben moche folk over whiche that every kyng ne hath no lordschipe ne comaundement. And certes uppon thilke syde that power fayleth, which that maketh folk blisful, ryght on the same syde noun-power entreth undirnethe, that maketh hem 20 wrecches. In this manere thanne moten kynges han more porcioun of wrecchidnesse than of welefulnesse. A tyraunt, that was kyng of Sysile, that hadde assayed the peril of his estat, schewede by simylitude the dredes of remes by gastnesse of a swerd that heng over the heved of his familyer. What thyng is thanne this power, that mai nat don awey the bytynges of bysynesse, ne eschewe the prykkes of drede? And certes yit wolde 30 thei lyven in sykernesse, but thei may nat, and yit they glorifien hem in hir power. Holdestow thanne that thilke man be mighty, that thow seest that he wolde doon that he may nat doon? And holdestow thanne hym a myghti man, that hath envyrowned his sydes with men of armes or sergeantz, and dredeth more hem that he maketh agast thanne thei dreden hym, and that is put in the handes of his servauntz for he scholde seme myghty? But of 40 familiers or servantz of kynges, what scholde I telle the any thyng, syn that I myself have schewyd the that rewmes hemself ben ful of greet feblesse? The whiche famylieres, certes, the real power of kynges, in hool estat and in estaat abated, ful ofte throweth adoun. Nero constreynede Senek, his familver and his mayster, to chesen on what deeth he wolde deye. Antonyus comaundede that knyghtes slowen with here swerdes Papynian, his 50

famylier, which Papynian that had ben
long tyme ful myghty amonges hem of the
court. And yet certes thei wolden bothe han
renounced hir power; of whiche two Senek enforcede hym to yeven to Nero his richesses, and
also to han gon into solitarie exil. But whan the
grete weyghte (*that is to seyn, of lordes power
or of fortune*) draweth hem that schullen falle,
neither of hem ne myghte don that he
wolde. What thyng is thanne thilke power, 60
that though men han it, yit thei ben agast;
and whanne thou woldest han it, thou n'art nat
siker; and yif thou woldest forleeten it, thow
mayst nat eschuen it? But whethir swiche men
ben freendes at nede, as ben conseyled by fortune and nat be vertu? Certes swiche folk as
weleful fortune maketh frendes, contraryous
fortune maketh hem enemys. And what pestilence is more myghty for to anoye a wyght
than a famylier enemy?   70

"*Qui se volet esse potentem.*" — Metrum 5

Whoso wol ben myghti he moot daunten his
cruel corages, ne putte nat his nekke, overcomen, undir the foule reynes of leccherie. For
al be it so that thi lordschipe strecche so fer
that the contre of Ynde quaketh at thy comaundementz or at thi lawes, and that the laste
ile in the see that highte Tyle be thral to the,
yit yif thou maist nat putten away thi foule
dirke desires, and dryven out fro the
wrecchide compleyntes, certes it nys no   10
power that thow hast.

"*Gloria vero quam fallax.*" — Prosa 6

But glorie, how deceyvable and how foul is
it ofte! For which thyng nat unskilfully a tra-
gedien (*that is to seyn, a makere of dytees that
highten tragedies*) cride and seide: "O glorie,
glorie," quod he, "thow n'art nothyng elles to
thousandes of folk but a greet swellere of eres!"
For manye han had ful greet renoun by the
false opinyoun of the peple, and what thyng
mai ben thought foulere than swich preysynge? For thilke folk that ben preysed   10
falsly, they mote nedes han schame of hire
preysynges. And yif that folk han geten hem
thonk or preysynge by here dissertes, what
thyng hath thilke pris echid or encresed to the
conscience of wise folk, that mesuren hir good,
nat by the rumour of the peple, but by the
sothfastnesse of conscience? And yif it seme a
fair thyng a man to han encreced and sprad his
name, thanne folweth it that it is demed to

ben a foul thyng yif it ne be ysprad and   20
encreced. But, as I seide a litil herebyforn,
that syn ther moot nedes ben many folk to
whiche folk the renoun of a man ne mai nat
comen, it byfalleth that he that thow wenest be
glorious and renomed semeth in the nexte
partie of the erthes to ben withouten glorie and
withouten renoun. And certes amonges thise
thynges I ne trowe nat that the pris and the
grace of the peple nys neyther worthi to
ben remembred, ne cometh of wys juge-   30
ment, ne is ferme perdurably.

But now of this name of gentilesse, what
man is it that ne may wele seen how veyn and
how flyttynge a thyng it es? For yif the name
of gentilesse be referred to renoun and cleernesse of lynage, thanne is gentil name but a
foreyn thyng (*that is to seyn, to hem that glo-
ryfien hem of hir lynage.*) For it semeth that
gentilesse be a maner preisynge that cometh of the dessertes of auncestres; and yif   40
preisynge make gentilesse, thanne mote
they nedes ben gentil that been preysed. For
which thing it folweth that yif thou ne have no
gentilesse of thiself (*that is to seyn, prys that
cometh of thy desert*), foreyn gentilesse ne
maketh the nat gentil. But certes yif ther be
ony good in gentilesse, I trowe it be al only
this, that it semeth as that a maner necessite
be imposed to gentil men for that thei ne
schulde nat owtrayen or forlyven fro the   50
vertus of hir noble kynrede.

"*Omne hominum genus in terris.*" — Metrum 6

Alle the lynage of men that ben in erthe ben
of semblable byrthe. On allone is fadir of
thynges; On allone mynystreth alle thynges.
He yaf to the sonne his bemes, he yaf to the
moone hir hornes, he yaf the men to the erthe,
he yaf the sterres to the hevene. He encloseth
with membres the soules that comen from his
heye sete. Thanne comen alle mortel folk of
noble seed. Why noysen ye or bosten of
your eldres? For yif thow loke youre by-   10
gynnyng, and God your auctour and yowr
makere, thanne nis ther non forlyved wyght or
ongentil, but if he noryssche his corage unto
vices and forlete his propre byrthe.

"*Quid autem de corporibus.*" — Prosa 7

But what schal I seye of delyces of body, of
whiche delices the desirynges ben ful of an-

guyssch, and the fulfillynges of hem ben ful of penance? How grete seknesses and how grete sorwes unsuffrable, ryght as a maner fruyt of wykkidnesse, ben thilke delices wont to bryngen to the bodyes of folk that usen hem! Of whiche delices I not what joie mai ben had of here moevynge, but this woot I wel, that whosoevere wol remembren hym of his luxures, he schal wel undirstonden that the issues of delices ben sorweful and sorye. And yif thilke delices mowen maken folk blisful, thanne by the same cause moten thise beestis ben clepid blisful, of whiche beestes al the entencioun hasteth to fulfille here bodily jolyte. And the gladnesse of wyf and children were an honest thyng, but it hath ben seyd that it is overmochel ayens kynde that children han ben fownden tormentours to here fadris, I not how manye; of whiche children how bytynge is every condicioun, it nedeth nat to tellen it the that hast er this tyme assayed it, and art yit now angwysshous. In this approve I the sentence of my disciple Euripidis, that seide that he that hath no children is weleful by infortune.

"Habet hoc voluptas." — Metrum 7

Every delit hath this, that it angwisscheth hem with prykkes that usen it. It resembleth to thise flyenge flyes that we clepen ben; that, aftir that the be hath sched his agreable honyes, he fleeth awey, and styngeth the hertes of hem that ben ysmyte, with bytynge overlonge holdynge.

"Nichil igitur dubium." — Prosa 8

Now is it no doute thanne that thise weyes ne ben a maner mysledynges to blisfulnesse, ne that they ne mowen nat leden folk thider as thei byheten to leden hem. But with how grete harmes thise forseide weyes ben enlaced, I schal schewe the shortly. Forwhy yif thou enforcest the to assemble moneye, thow must byreven hym his moneye that hath it; and yif thow wolt schynen with dignytees, thow must bysechen and supplyen hem that yyven tho dignytees; and yif thow coveytest be honour to gon byfore othere folk, thow schalt defoule thiself thurw humblesse of axynge. Yif thou desirest power, thow schalt, be awaytes of thy subgetis, anoyously ben cast undir by manye periles. Axestow glorye? Thow shalt so bien distract by aspere thynges that thow schalt forgon sykernesse. And yif thou

wolt leden thi lif in delyces, every wyght schal despysen the and forleeten the, as thow that art thral to thyng that is right foul and brutyl (*that is to seyn, servaunt to thi body*). Now is it thanne wel yseyn how litil and how brotel possessioun thei coveyten that putten the goodes of the body aboven hir owene resoun. For maystow surmounten thise olifauntes in gretnesse or weighte of body? Or maistow ben strengere than the bole? Maystow ben swyftere than the tigre? Byhoold the spaces and the stablenesse and the swyft cours of the hevene, and stynt somtyme to wondren on foule thynges. The whiche hevene certes nys nat rather for thise thynges to ben wondryd upon, than for the resoun by which it is governed. But the schynynge of thi forme (*that is to seyn, the beute of thi body*), how swyftly passynge is it, and how transitorie!

Certes it es more flyttynge than the mutabilite of floures of the somer sesoun. For so as Aristotle telleth, that if that men hadden eyghen of a beeste that highte lynx, so that the lokynge of folk myghte percen thurw the thynges that withstonden it, whoso lokide thanne in the entrayles of the body of Alcibiades, that was ful fair in the superfice withoute, it schulde seme ryght foul. And forthi yif thow semest fair, thy nature ne maketh nat that, but the deceyvaunce of the feblesse of the eighen that loken. But preise the goodes of the body as mochil as evere the lyst, so that thow knowe algatis that, whatso it be (*that is to seyn, of the godes of the body*) which that thou wondrist uppon, mai ben destroied or dissolvid by the heete of a fevere of thre dayes. Of alle whiche forseide thynges Y mai reducen this schortly in a somme: that thise worldly goodes, whiche that ne mowen nat yeven that they byheeten, ne ben nat parfite by the congregacioun of alle goodis; that they ne ben nat weyes ne pathes that bryngen men to blisfulnesse, ne maken men to ben blisful.

"Heu que miseros tramite." — Metrum 8

Allas! which folie and which ignorance mysledeth wandrynge wrecchis fro the path of verray good! Certes ye ne seke no gold in grene trees, ne ye gadere nat precyous stones in the vynes, ne ye ne hiden nat yowr gynnes in heye mountaignes to kacchen fyssch of which ye mai maken riche festes. And if yow liketh to hunte to roos, ye ne gon nat to the foordes of the watir that highte Tyrene. And over

this, men knowen wel the krikes and the 10
cavernes of the see yhidde in the flodes,
and knowen ek which watir is moost plentevous
of white peerlis, and knowen which watir
haboundeth moost of reed purpre (*that is to
seyn, of a maner schellefyssch with which men
deien purpre*), and knowen whiche strondes
habounden most of tendre fysches or of scharpe
fyssches that hyghten echynnys. But folk suffren hemselve to ben so blynde, that hem
ne reccheth nat to knowe where thilke 20
goodes ben yhidd whiche that thei coveyten, but ploungen hem in erthe, and seken
there thilke good that surmounteth the hevene
that bereth the sterris. What preyere mai I
make, that be digne to the nyce thoughtes of
men? But I preie that thei coveyten rychesses
and honours, so that, whanne thei han geten
tho false goodes with greet travaile, that therby
they mowen knowen the verray goodes.

"Hactenus mendacis formam." — Prosa 9

It suffiseth that I have schewyd hiderto the
forme of fals welefulnesse, so that yif thou loke
now cleerly, the ordre of myn entencioun requireth from hennes forth to schewe the verray
welefulnesse."

"For sothe," quod I, "I se wel now that suffisaunce may nat comen by rychesse, ne power
by remes, ne reverence by dignites, ne gentilesse by glorie, ne joie be delices."

"And hastow wel knowen the causes," 10
quod sche, "whi it es?"

"Certes me semeth," quod I, "that y see hem
ryght as though it were thurw a litil clyfte, but
me were levere to knowen hem more opynly of
the."

"Certes," quod sche, "the resoun is al redy.
For thilke thyng that symply is o thyng withouten ony devysioun, the errour and folie of
mankynde departeth and divideth it, and
mysledeth it and transporteth from verray 20
and parfit good to godes that ben false and
inparfit. But seye me this. Wenestow that he
that hath nede of power, that hym ne lakketh
nothyng?"

"Nay," quod I.

"Certes," quod sche, "thou seyst aryght; for
if it so be that ther is a thyng that in ony partie
be feblere of power, certes, as in that, it moot
nedes be nedy of foreyn help."

"Ryght so is it," quod I. 30

"Suffisaunce and power ben thanne of
o kynde?"

"So semeth it," quod I.

"And demestow," quod sche, "that a thyng
that is of this manere (*that is to seyn, suffisaunt
and mighty*) oughte ben despised, or ellis that
it be right digne of reverence aboven alle
thynges?"

"Certes," quod I, "it nys no doute that it
nys right worthy to ben reverenced." 40

"Lat us," quod sche, "adden thanne reverence to suffisaunce and to power, so that we
demen that thise thre thynges be al o thyng?"

"Certes," quod I, "lat us adden it, yif we
wiln graunten the sothe."

"What demestow thanne," quod sche, "is
that a dirk thyng and nat noble that is suffisaunt, reverent, and myghty; or elles that it is
ryght noble and ryght cleer by celebrete of
renoun? Considere thanne," quod sche, "as 50
we han grauntid herbyfore, that he that ne
hath nede of no thyng and is moost myghty
and moost digne of honour, if hym nedeth ony
cleernesse of renoun, which clernesse he myght
nat graunten of hymself; so that for lak of
thilke cleernesse he myghte seme the feblere
on any side, or the more outcast." (*Glose. This
is to seyn, nay; for whoso that is suffisaunt,
mighty, and reverent, clernesse of renoun
folweth of the forseyde thynges; he hath it* 60
al redy of his suffysaunce.)

Boece. "I mai nat," quod I, "denye it, but I
moot granten, as it is, that this thyng be ryght
celebrable by clernesse of renoun and noblesse."

"Thanne folweth it," quod sche, "that we
adden clernesse of renoun to the thre forseyde
thynges, so that there ne be amonges hem no
difference."

"This is a consequence," quod I.

"This thyng thanne," quod sche, "that ne 70
hath nede of no foreyn thyng, and that
may don alle thynges by his strengthis, and
that is noble and honourable, nys nat that a
myry thyng and a joyful?"

Boece. "But whennes," quod I, "that any
sorwe myghte comen to this thyng that is
swich, certes I mai nat thynke."

Philosophie. "Thanne mote we graunten,"
quod sche, "that this thing be ful of gladnesse, if the forseide thynges ben sothe; 80
and certes also mote we graunten that suffisaunce, power, noblesse, reverence, and gladnesse be oonly diverse by names, but hir substaunce hath no diversite."

Boece. "It moot nedly ben so," quod I.

Philosophie. "Thilke thyng thanne," quod

sche, "that is oon and symple in his nature, the wikkidnesse of men departeth it and divideth it; and whanne thei enforcen hem to gete partie of a thyng that ne hath no part, thei 90 ne geten hem neyther thilke partie that is noon, ne the thyng al hool that thei ne desire nat."

Boece. "In which manere?" quod I.

Philosophie. "Thilke man," quod sche, "that seketh richesse to fleen poverte, he ne travaileth hym nat for to geten power, for he hath lever to ben dirk and vyl; and eek withdraweth from hymself manye naturel delites, for he nolde leese the moneie that he hath as- 100 sembled. But certes in this manere he ne geteth hym nat suffisance, that power forleteth, and that moleste prikketh, and that filthe maketh outcast, and that dirknesse hideth. And certes he that desireth oonly power, he wasteth and scatereth rychesse, and despyseth delices and eek honour that is withoute power, ne he ne preiseth glorie nothyng. Certes thus seestow wel that manye thynges failen to hym, for he hath som tyme defaute of manye neces- 110 sites, and manye anguysshes byten hym; and whan he ne mai nat do tho defautes awey, he forletith to ben myghty, and that is the thyng that he moost desireth. And ryght thus mai I make semblable resouns of honours, and of glorie, and of delyces; for so as every of thise forseide thinges is the same that thise othere thynges ben (*that is to seyn, al oon thyng*), whoso that evere seketh to geten that oon of thise, and nat that othir, he ne 120 geteth nat that he desireth."

Boece. "What seystow thanne, yif that a man coveyte to geten alle thise thynges togidre?"

Philosophie. "Certes," quod sche, "I wolde seye, that he wolde geten hym sovereyn blisfulnesse; but that schal he nat fynde in tho thynges that I have schewed that ne mowen nat yeven that thei byheeten?"

Boece. "Certes no," quod I. 130

"Thanne," quod sche, "ne sholde men nat by no weye seken blisfulnesse in swiche thynges as men wenen that they ne mowen yeven but o thyng sengly of al that men seken?"

Boece. "I graunte wel," quod I, "ne no sothere thyng ne may be seyd."

Philosophie. "Now hastow thanne," quod sche, "the forme and the causes of fals welefulnesse. Now torne and flytte the 140

eighen of thi thought, for ther shaltow seen anoon thilke verray blisfulnesse that I have behyght the."

Boece. "Certes," quod I, "it is cler and open, theygh it were to a blynd man; and that schewedestow me ful wel a litel herbyforn, whan thow enforcedest the to schewe me the causes of the false blisfulnesse. For, but if I be begiled, thanne is thilke the verray parfit blisfulnesse that parfitly maketh a man suf- 150 fisaunt, myghty, honourable, noble, and ful of gladnesse. And for thow schalt wel knowe that I have wel undirstonden thise thinges withynne myn herte, I knowe wel that thilke blisfulnesse that may verrayly yeven on of the forseyde thynges, syn thei ben alle oon — I knowe dowtelees that thilke thyng is the fulle blysfulnesse."

Philosophie. "O my nory," quod sche, "by this opynyoun I seie thow art blisful, 160 yif thow putte this therto that I schal seyn."

"What is that?" quod I.

"Trowestow that ther be any thyng in thise erthly, mortel, toumblynge thynges that may brynge this estat?"

"Certes," quod I, "y trowe it nought; and thow hast schewyd me wel that over thilke good ther nys no thyng more to ben de- sired." 170

Philosophie. "Thise thynges thanne," quod sche, (*that is to seyn, erthly suffysaunce, and power, and swiche thynges*) outher thei semen lyknesses of verray good, or elles it semeth that thei yeve to mortel folk a maner of goodes that ne be nat parfyt. But thilke good that is verray and parfyt that mai thei nat yeven."

Boece. "I accorde me wel," quod I.

Philosophie. "Thanne," quod sche, "for 180 as moche as thou hast knowen which is thilke verray blisfulnesse, and eek whiche thilke thynges ben that lyen falsly blisfulnesse (*that is to seyn, that be deceyte semen verray goodes*), now byhoveth the to knowe, whennes and where thow mowe seke thilke verrai blisfulnesse."

"Certes," quod I, "that desire I gretly and have abyden longe tyme to herkne it."

"But for as moche," quod sche, "as it 190 liketh to my disciple Plato, in his book of *In Thymeo,* that in ryght litel thynges men schulde byseche the help of God, what juggestow that be now to done, so that we may desserve to fynde the seete of thilke sovereyne good?"

"Certes," quod I, "Y deme that we schul clepe to the Fadir of alle goodes, for withouten hym is ther no thyng founded aryght.

"Thow seyst aryght," quod sche, and 200 bygan anoon to syngen right thus:

"O quam perpetua." — Metrum 9

"O thow Fadir, soowere and creatour of hevene and of erthes, that governest this world by perdurable resoun, that comaundest the tymes to gon from syn that age hadde bygynnynge; thow that duellest thiselve ay stedefast and stable, and yevest alle othere thynges to ben meved, ne foreyne causes necesseden the nevere to compoune werk of floterynge matere, but oonly the forme of sovereyn good iset within the withoute envye, that moevede 10 the frely. Thow, that art althir-fayrest, berynge the faire world in thy thought, formedest this world to the lyknesse semblable of that faire world in thy thought. Thou drawest alle thyng of thy sovereyn ensaumpler and comaundest that this world, parfytly ymakid, have frely and absolut his parfyte parties. Thow byndest the elementis by nombres proporcionables, that the coolde thinges mowen accorde with the hote thinges, and 20 the drye thinges with the moyste; that the fyr, that is purest, fle nat over-heye, ne that the hevynesse drawe nat adoun over-lowe the erthes that ben plongid in the watris. Thow knyttest togidere the mene soule of treble kynde moevynge alle thingis, and divydest it by membrys accordynge; and whan it es thus divyded [and] it hath assembled a moevynge into two rowndes, it gooth to torne ayen to hymself, and envyrouneth a ful deep 30 thought and turneth the hevene by semblable ymage. Thow by evene-lyke causes enhauncest the soules and the lasse lyves; and, ablynge hem heye by lyghte waynes or cartes, thow sowest hem into hevene and into erthe. And whan thei ben convertyd to the by thi benygne lawe, thow makest hem retourne ayen to the by ayen-ledynge fyer. O Fadir, yyve thou to the thought to steyen up into thi streyte seete; and graunte hym to envi- 40 roune the welle of good; and, the lyght ifounde, graunte hym to fycchen the clere syghtes of his corage in the; and skatere thou and tobreke the weyghtes and the cloudes of erthly hevynesse; and schyn thou by thi bryght-

nesse, for thou art cleernesse, thow art pesible reste to debonayre folk; thow thiself art bygynnynge, berere, ledere, path and terme; to looke on the, that is our ende.

"Quoniam igitur que sit." — Prosa 10

For as moche thanne as thow hast seyn which is the fourme of good that nys nat parfit, and which is the forme of good that is parfit, now trowe I that it were good to schewe in what this perfeccioun of blisfulnesse is set. And in this thing I trowe that we schulde first enquere for to witen, yf that any swich maner good as thilke good that thou hast dyffinysshed a litel herebyforn (*that is to seyn, sovereyn good*) may be founde in the nature of 10 thinges, for that veyn ymagynacioun of thought ne desceyve us nat, and put us out of the sothfastnesse of thilke thing that is summytted to us. But it may nat be denyed that thilke good ne is, and that it nys ryght as a welle of alle goodes. For alle thing that is cleped inparfyt is proevid inparfit be the amenusynge of perfeccioun or of thing that is parfit. And herof cometh it that in every thing general, yif that men seen any thing 20 that is inparfit, certes in thilke general ther moot ben som thing that is parfit. For yif so be that perfeccioun is don awey, men may nat thinke ne say fro whennes thilke thing is that is cleped inparfyt. For the nature of thinges ne took nat hir begynnynge of thinges amenused and inparfit, but it procedith of thinges that ben alle hole and absolut, and descendith so doun into uttereste thinges and into thinges empty and withouten fruyt. But, as I have 30 schewid a litel here byforn that yif ther be a blisfulnesse that be freel and veyn and inparfyt, ther may no man doute that ther nys som blisfulnesse that is sad, stedefast, and parfyt."

Boece. "This is concluded," quod I, "feermely and soothfastly."

Philosophie. "But considere also," quod sche, "in whom this blisfulnesse enhabiteth. The comune accordaunce and conceyt of the 40 corages of men proveth and graunteth that God, prince of alle thinges, is good. For, so as nothyng mai ben thought betere than God, mai nat ben douted thanne that he that no thing nys betere, that he nys good. Certes resoun scheweth that God is so good that it proeveth by verray force that parfyt good is in hym. For yif God nys swych, he ne mai nat be prince of alle thinges; for certes somthing possessyng in itself parfyt good schulde be 50 more worthy than God, and it scholde semen that thilke were first and eldere than God. For we han schewyd apertely that alle thinges that ben parfyt ben first er thynges that ben inparfit; and forthy, for as moche as that my resoun or my proces ne go nat awey withouten an ende, we owe to graunte that the sovereyn God is ryght ful of sovereyn parfit good. And we han establissched that the sovereyne good is verray blisfulnesse. 60 Thanne moot it nedis be that verray blisfulnesse is set in sovereyn God."

Boece. "This take I wel," quod I, "ne this ne mai nat be withseid in no manere."

"But I preye the," quod sche, "see now how thou mayst proeven holily and withoute corrupcioun this that I have seid, that the sovereyne God is ryght ful of sovereyn good."

"In which manere?" quod I.

"Wenestow aught," quod sche, "that the 70 fader of alle thynges have itake thilke sovereyne good anywher out of hymself, of which sovereyn good men proeveth that he is ful; ryght as thou myghtest thenken that God, that hath blisfulnesse in hymself, and thilke blisfulnesse that is in hym, were divers in substaunce? For yif thow wene that God have resseyved thilke good out of hymself, thow mayst wene that he that yaf thilke good to God be more worth than is God. But I am beknowe and 80 confesse, and that ryght dignely, that God is ryght worthy aboven alle thinges. And yif it so be that this good be in hym by nature, but that it is dyvers from him by wenynge resoun, syn we speke of God prynce of alle thynges, — feyne who so feyne mai — who was he that hath conjoyned thise divers thynges togidre? And eek at the laste se wel that a thing that is divers from any thing, that thilke thing nys nat that same thing fro which it es undir- 90 stonden to be divers. Thanne folweth it that thilke thing that be his nature is divers from sovereyn good, that that thyng nys nat sovereyn good. But certes it were a felenous cursydnesse to thinken that of hym that no thing nys more worth. For alwey, of alle thinges, the nature of hem may nat ben betere thanne hir begynnynge. For which I mai concluden by ryght verray resoun that thilke that is begynnynge of alle thinges, thilke 100 same thing is sovereyn good in his substaunce."

Boece. "Thow hast seyd ryghtfully," quod I.

Philosophie. "But we han graunted," quod sche, "that the sovereyn good is blisfulnesse."

"That is sooth," quod I.

"Thanne," quod sche, "moten we nedes granten and confessen that thilke same sovereyn good be God?"

"Certes," quod I, "y ne may nat denye 110 ne withstonde the resouns purposed; and I se wel that it folweth by strengthe of the premisses."

"Loke now," quod sche, "yif this be proevid yet more fermely thus that there ne mowen not ben two sovereyn goodis that ben divers among hemself. For certes the goodis that ben divers among hemself, the toon is nat that that the tothir is; thanne ne mowen neither of hem ben parfit, so as eyther of hem lakketh to 120 othir. But that that nys nat parfit, men mai seen apertely that it nys not sovereyn. The thinges thanne that ben sovereynly gode ne mowe by no weie be divers. But I have wel concluded that blisfulnesse and God ben the sovereyn good; for which it mote nedes be that sovereyn blisfulnesse is sovereyn devynite."

"No thing," quod I, "nys more sothfast than this, ne more ferme by resoun, ne a more worthy thing than God mai not ben con- 130 cluded."

"Upon thise thynges thanne," quod sche, "ryght as thise geometriens whan thei han schewed her proposicions ben wont to bryngen yn thinges that thei clepen porismes or declaracions of forseide thinges, right so wol I yeve the here as a corolarie or a meede of coroune. Forwhy, for as moche as by the getynge of blisfulnesse men ben makid blisful, and blisfulnesse is dyvinite, than is it manifest and 140 open that by the getynge of dyvinite men ben makid blisful. Right as by the getynge of justise [men ben maked just], and be the getynge of sapience thei ben maked wise, ryght so nedes by the semblable resoun, whan they han geten dyvinite thei ben maked goddes. Thanne is every blisful man God. But certes by nature ther nys but o God; but by the participacioun of dyvinite ther ne let ne distourbeth nothyng that ther ne ben many goddis." 150

"This ys," quod I, "a fair thing and a precious, clepe it as thou wilt, be it corolerie, or porisme, or mede of coroune, or declarynges."

"Certes," quod sche, "nothing nys fairere than is the thing that by resoun schulde ben addid to thise forseide thinges."

"What thing?" quod I.

"So," quod sche, "as it semeth that blisfulnesse conteneth many thinges, it weere for
to witen whether that alle thise thinges   160
maken or conjoynen as a maner body of
blisfulnesse by diversite of parties or membres,
or elles yif ony of alle thilke thinges ben swich
that it acomplise by hymself the substaunce of
blisfulnesse, so that alle thise othere thynges
ben referrid and brought to blisfulnesse (*that
is to seyn, as to the cheef of hem*)."

"I wolde," quod I, "that thow madest me
clerly to undirstonde what thou seist, and
that thou recordidest me the forseide   170
thinges."

"Have I not jugged," quod sche, "that blisfulnesse is good?"

"Yys for sothe," quod I, "and that sovereyne
good."

"Adde thanne," quod sche, "thilke good that
is maked [of] blisfulnesse to alle thise forseide
thinges. For thilke same blisfulnesse that is
demed to ben sovereyn suffisaunce, thilke
selve is sovereyn power, sovereyn rev-   180
erence, sovereyn clernesse or noblesse, and
sovereyn delyt. What seistow thanne of alle
thise thinges, that is to seyn, suffisaunce, power,
and thise othere thinges, — ben thei thanne as
membris of blisfulnesse, or ben they reffered
and brought to sovereyn good ryght as alle
thinges that ben brought to the cheef of hem?"

Boece. "I undirstonde wel," quod I, "what
thou purposest to seke, but I desire for
to herkne that thow schewe it me.   190

Philosophie. "Tak now thus the discrecioun of this questioun," quod sche; "yif alle thise
thinges," quod sche, "weren membris to felicite, thanne weren thei dyverse that on fro that
othir. And swich is the nature of parties or of
membres, that diverse membris compounen a
body."

"Certes," quod I, "it hath wel ben schewyd
here byforn that alle thise thinges
ben al o thyng."   200

"Thanne ben thei none membres," quod
sche, "for elles it schulde seme that blisfulnesse were conjoyned al of o membre allone;
but that is a thing that mai not ben don."

"This thing," quod I, "nys not doutous; but
I abide to herknen the remenaunt of the question."

"This is open and cler," quod sche, "that
alle othere thinges ben referrid and
brought to good. For therfore is suffi-   210

saunce requerid, for it is demyd to ben good;
and forthy is power requirid, for men trowen
also that it be good; and this same thing
mowen we thinken and conjecten of reverence,
and of noblesse, and of delyt. Thanne is sovereyn good the somme and the cause of al that
oughte ben desired; forwhy thilke thing that
withholdeth no good in itselve, ne sem-
balance of good, it ne mai not wel in no
manere be desired ne requerid. And the   220
contrarie; for though that thinges by here
nature ne ben not gode, algates yif men wene
that thei ben gode, yet ben thei desired as
though that thei were verrayliche gode; and
therefore is it that men oughte to wene by ryghte
that bounte be the sovereyn fyn and the cause
of alle the thinges that ben to requiren. But
certes thilke that is cause for which men
requiren any thing, it semeth that thilke
same thing be moost desired. As thus: yf   230
that a wyght wolde ryden for cause of hele,
he ne desireth not so mochel the moevyng to
ryden, as the effect of his hele. Now thanne,
syn that alle thynges ben required for the grace
of good, thei ne ben not desired of alle folk
more than the same good. But we han grauntid
that blisfulnesse is that thing for which that
alle thise othere thinges ben desired; thanne
is it thus that certes oonly blysfulnesse is
requered and desired. By which thing it   240
scheweth cleerly that of good and of blisfulnesse is al on and the same substaunce."

"I se nat," quod I, "wherfore that men
myghten discorden in this."

"And we han schewed that God and verray
blisfulnesse is al o thing."

"That is sooth," quod I.

"Thanne mowen we concluden sykerly, that
the substaunce of God is set in thilke same
good, and in noon other place.   250

"Nunc omnes pariter venite capti." —
Metrum 10

Cometh alle to-gidre now, ye that ben
ykaught and ybounde with wikkide cheynes by
the desceyvable delyt of erthly thynges enhabitynge in yowr thought! Her schal ben the
reste of your labours, her is the havene stable
in pesible quiete; this allone is the open refut
to wreches. (*Glose. This to seyn, that ye that
ben combryd and disseyvid with worldly affeccions, cometh now to this sovereyn
good, that is God, that is refut to hem*   10

that wolen come to hym.) Textus. Alle the
thinges that the ryver Tagus yyveth yow with
his goldene gravelis, or elles alle the thinges
that the ryver Hermus yeveth with his rede
brinke, or that Indus yyveth, that is next the
hote partie of the world, that medleth the grene
stones with the white, ne scholden not cleren
the lookynge of your thought, but hiden rather
your blynde corages withynne here derknesse. Al that liketh yow here, and ex- 20
citeth and moeveth your thoughtes, the
erthe hath norysschid it in his lowe caves. But
the schynynge by which the hevene is governed
and whennes that it hath his strengthe, that
eschueth the derke overthrowynge of the soule;
and whosoevere may knowen thilke light of
blisfulnesse, he schal wel seyn that the white
beemes of the sonne ne ben nat cleer."

"Assencior inquam cuncta." — Prosa 11

Boece. "I assente me," quod I, "for alle thise
thinges ben strongly bounden with ryght ferme
resouns."

"How mychel wiltow preysen it," quod sche,
"yif that thow knowe what thilke good is?"

"I wol preyse it," quod I, "be pris withouten
ende, yif it schal betyde me to knowe also togidre God that is good."

"Certes," quod sche, "that schal I do the
be verray resoun, yif that tho thinges that I 10
have concluded a litel herebyforn duellen
only in hir first grauntynge."

Boece. "Thei dwellen graunted to the,"
quod I. (*This to seyn as who seith, "I graunte
thi forseide conclusyouns."*)

"Have I nat schewed the," quod sche, "that
the thinges that ben required of many folk ne
ben not verray goodis ne parfite; for thei ben
divers that on fro that othir. And so as ich
of hem is lakkynge to othir, thei han no 20
power to bryngen a good that is ful and absolut. But thanne at erste ben thei verray good,
whan thei ben gadred togidre alle into o forme
and into oon werkynge. So that thilke thing
that is suffisaunce, thilke same be power, and
reverence, and noblesse, and myrthe. And for
sothe, but yif alle thise thinges ben alle o same
thing, thei ne han not wherby that thei mowen
be put in the nombre of thinges that
oughten ben required or desired." 30

Boece. "It is schewyd," quod I, "ne
herof mai ther no man douten."

Philosophie. "The thinges thanne," quod
sche, "that ne ben none goodis whan thei ben

diverse, and whanne thei bygynnen to ben al
o thing, thanne ben thei goodes, — ne cometh
it hem nat thanne by the getynge of unyte that
thei ben maked goodes?"

Boece. "So it semeth," quod I.

"But alle thing that is good," quod sche, 40
"grauntestow that it be good by the participacioun of good, or no?"

"I graunte it," quod I.

"Thanne mustow graunten," quod sche, "by
semblable resoun that oon and good be o same
thing; for of thinges of whiche that the effect
nys nat naturely divers, nedes the substaunce
moot be oo same thing."

"I ne may nat denye it," quod I.

"Hastow nat knowen wel," quod sche, 50
"that alle thing that is is hath so longe his
duellynge and his substaunce as longe as it es
oon? But whanne it forletith to be oon, it moot
nedys deien and corrumpen togidres?"

"In which manere?" quod I.

"Ryght as in beestis," quod sche, "whanne
the body and the soule ben conjoyned in oon
and dwellen togidre, it es cleped a beeste; and
whanne her unyte is destroyed be the disseveraunce the toon fro the tothir, thanne 60
scheweth it wel that it is a deed thing, and
that it nys no lenger no beeste. And the body
of a wyght, while it duelleth in oo fourme be
conjunccion of membris, it is wel seyn that it
is a figure of mankynde; and yif the parties of
the body ben so devyded and disseverid the
ton fro the tother that thei destroyen unite, the
body forletith to ben that it was beforn. And
whoso wolde renne in the same manere be
alle thinges, he scholde seen that withouten 70
doute every thing is in his substaunce as
longe as it is oon; and whanne it forletith to
ben oon, it dyeth and peryssheth."

Boece. "Whanne I considere," quod I,
"manye thinges, I se noon other."

"Is ther any thing thanne," quod sche, "that,
in as moche as it lyveth naturely, that forletith
the talent or the appetyt of his beynge and
desireth to come to deth and to corrupcioun?" 80

"Yif I considere," quod I, "the beestes
that han any maner nature of wyllynge and of
nyllynge, I ne fynde no beeste, but if it be
constreyned fro withoute-forth, that forletith or
despiseth the entencion to lyven and to duren;
or that wole, his thankes, hasten hym to dyen.
For every beest travaileth hym to defende and
kepe the savacion of his lif, and eschueth deeth

and destruccioun. But certes I doute me of
herbes and of trees (*that is to seyn, that I* 90
*am in a doute of swiche thinges as herbes
or trees*), that ne han no felyng soules (ne no
naturel werkynges servynge to appetites as
beestes han), whether thei han appetyt to
duellen and to duren."

"Certes," quod sche, "ne therof thar the nat
doute. Now looke upon thise herbes and thise
trees. They wexen first in suche places as ben
covenable to hem, in whiche places thei
mowen nat sone deye ne dryen, as longe 100
as hir nature mai defenden hem. For some
of hem waxen in feeldis, and some in mountaynes, and othere waxen in mareys, and othre
cleven on roches, and some wexen plentyvous
in soondes; and yif any wyght enforce hym to
bere hem into other places, thei wexen drye.
For nature yeveth to every thing that that is
convenient to hym, and travailleth that they ne
deie nat, as longe as thei han power to
duellen and to lyven. What wiltow seyn 110
of this, that thei drawen alle here norysschynges by here rootes, ryght as thei hadden
here mouthes yplounged withynne the erthes,
and sheden be hir maryes hir wode and hir
bark? And what wyltow seyn of this, that
thilke thing that is ryght softe, as the marie is,
that it is alwey hyd in the seete al withinne,
and that it is defended fro withoute by the stedfastnesse of wode; and that the outreste
bark is put ayens the distemperaunce 120
of the hevene as a deffendour myghty to
suffren harm? And thus certes maistow wel
seen how greet is the diligence of nature; for
alle thinges renovelen and publysschen hem
with seed ymultiplied, ne ther nys no man that
ne woot wel that they ne ben ryght as a foundement and edifice for to duren, noght oonly
for a tyme, but ryght as for to dure perdurably
by generacion. And the thinges eek that
men wenen ne haven none soules, ne de- 130
sire thei nat, ich of hem, by semblable
resoun to kepyn that that is hirs (*that is to
seyn, that is accordynge to hir nature in con-
servacioun of hir beynge and endurynge*)? For
wherfore ellis bereth lightnesse the flaumbes
up, and the weyghte presseth the erthe adoun,
but for as moche as thilke places and thilke
moevynges ben covenable to everych of hem?
And forsothe every thing kepeth thilke
that is accordynge and propre to hym, 140
ryght as thinges that ben contrarious and
enemys corrumpen hem. And yet the harde

thinges, as stones, clyven and holden here
parties togidere ryght faste and harde, and defenden hem in withstondynge that thei ne departe nat lyghtly atwynne. And the thinges
that ben softe and fletynge, as is watir and eyr,
thei departen lyghtly and yeven place to hem
that breken or divyden hem; but natheles
they retorne sone ageyn into the same 150
thinges fro whennes thei ben arraced; but
fyer fleeth and refuseth alle dyvisioun. Ne
I ne trete not now here of willeful moevynges
of the soule that is knowyng, but of the naturel
entencioun of thinges, as thus: ryght as we
swolwen the mete that we resseyven and
ne thinke nat on it, and as we drawen our
breeth in slepynge that we witen it nat while
we slepyn. For certes in the beestis the
love of hire lyvynges ne of hire beynges 160
ne cometh not of the wilnynges of the
soule, but of the bygynnynges of nature. For
certes, thurw constreynynge causes, wil desireth and embraceth ful ofte tyme the deeth that
nature dredeth. (*That is to seyn as thus: that
a man may be constreyned so, by som cause,
that his wille desireth and taketh the deeth
which that nature hateth and dredeth ful sore.*)
And somtyme we seen the contrarye, as
thus: that the wil of a wyght distourbeth 170
and constreyneth that that nature desireth
and requireth alwey, that is to seyn the werk of
generacioun, by which generacioun only duelleth and is susteyned the longe durablete of
mortel thinges. And thus this charite and this
love, that every thing hath to hymself, ne cometh not of the moevynge of the soule, but of the
entencioun of nature. For the purveaunce of
God hath yeven to thinges that ben creat
of hym this, that is a ful gret cause to 180
lyven and to duren, for which they desiren
naturely here lif as longe as evere thei mowen.
For which thou mayst not drede be no manere
that alle the thinges that ben anywhere, that
thei ne requiren naturely the ferme stablenesse
of perdurable duellynge, and eek the eschu-
ynge of destruccioun."

Boece. "Now confesse I wel," quod I, "that
Y see wel now certeynly withouten doutes
the thinges that whilom semeden uncer- 190
teyn to me."

Philosophie. "But," quod sche, "thilke thing
that desireth to be and to duelle perdurably,
he desireth to ben oon. For yif that oon were
destroyed, certes, beynge schulde ther noon
duellen to no wyght."

"That is sooth," quod I.

"Thanne," quod sche, "desiren alle thinges oon."

"I assente," quod I.   200

"And I have schewed," quod sche, "that thilke same oon is thilke that is good."

Boece. "Ye, forsothe," quod I.

"Alle thinges thanne," quod sche, "requiren good; and thilke good thow mayst descryven ryght thus: good is thilke thing that every wyght desireth."

"Ther ne may be thought," quod I, "no more verray thing. For eyther alle thinges ben referrid and brought to noght, and floteren   210 withouten governour, despoyled of oon as of hire propre heved; or elles, yif ther be any thing to which that alle thinges tenden and hyen to, that thing muste ben the sovereyn good of alle goodes."

Philosophie. Thanne seide sche thus: "O my nory," quod sche, "I have greet gladnesse of the, for thow hast fycched in thyn herte the myddel sothfastnesse, that is to seyn, the prykke. But this thing hath ben discov-   220 eryd to the in that thow seydest that thow wistest not a litel herbyforn."

"What was that?" quod I.

"That thou ne wistest noght," quod sche, "which was the ende of thinges. And certes that is the thyng that every wyght desireth; and for as mochel as we han gadrid and comprehendid that good is thilke thing that is desired of alle, thanne mote we nedys confessen that good is the fyn of alle thinges.   230

"Quisquis profunda." — Metrum 11

Whoso that seketh sooth by a deep thought, and coveyteth not to ben disseyvid by no mysweyes, lat hym rollen and trenden withynne hymself the lyght of his ynwarde sighte; and let hym gaderyn ayein, enclynynge into a compas, the longe moevynges of his thoughtes; and let hym techyn his corage that he hath enclosid and hid in his tresors, al that he compasseth or secheth fro withoute. And thanne thilke thing, that the blake cloude of errour   10 whilom hadde ycovered, schal lighte more clerly than Phebus hymself ne schyneth. (*Glosa. Whoso wol seke the depe ground of soth in his thought, and wil nat ben disseyvid by false proposiciouns that goon amys fro the trouthe, lat hym wel examine and rolle withynne hymself the nature and the propretes of*

the thing; and let hym yet eftsones examinen and rollen his thoghtes by good deliberacioun or that he deme, and lat hym techyn   20 his soule that it hath, by naturel principles kyndeliche yhyd withynne itself, al the trouthe the which he ymagineth to ben in thinges withoute. And thanne al the derknesse of his mysknowynge shall seen more evydently to the sighte of his undirstondynge than the sonne ne semeth to the sighte withoute-forth.) For certes the body, bryngynge the weighte of foryetynge, ne hath nat chased out of your thought al the cleernesse of your knowyng;   30 for certeynli the seed of soth haldeth and clyveth within yowr corage, and it is awaked and excited by the wyndes and by the blastes of doctrine. For wherfore elles demen ye of your owene wil the ryghtes, whan ye ben axid, but if so were that the norysschynges of resoun ne lyvede yplounged in the depe of your herte? (*This to seyn, how schulde men deme the sothe of any thing that were axid, yif ther nere a rote of sothfastnesse that were yplounged   40 and hyd in the naturel principles, the whiche sothfastnesse lyvede within the depnesse of the thought?*) And if it so be that the Muse and the doctrine of Plato syngeth soth, al that every wyght leerneth, he ne doth no thing elles thanne but recordeth, as men recorden thinges that ben foryeten."

"Tunc ego Platoni inquam." — Prosa 12

Thanne seide I thus: "I accorde me gretly to Plato, for thou recordist and remembrist me thise thinges yet the seconde tyme; that is to seye, first whan I loste my memorie be the contagious conjunccioun of the body with the soule, and eftsones aftirward, whan Y lost it confounded by the charge and be the burden of my sorwe."

And thanne seide sche thus: "Yif thow loke," quod sche, "first the thynges that   10 thou hast grauntid, it ne schal nat ben ryght fer that thow ne schalt remembren thilke thing that thou seidest that thou nystist nat."

"What thing?" quod I.

"By which governement," quod sche, "that this world is governed."

"Me remembreth it wel," quod I; "and I confesse wel that I ne wyste it nat. But al be it so that I see now from afer what thou purposist, algates I desire yit to herknen it of   20 the more pleynly."

"Thou ne wendest nat," quod sche, "a litel herebyforn, that men schulde doute that this world nys governed by God."

"Certes," quod I, "ne yet ne doute I it naught, ne I nyl nevere wene that it were to doute" (*as who seith, "but I woot wel that God gouverneth this world"*); "and I schal schortly answeren the be what resouns I am brought to this. This world," quod I, "of 30 so manye and diverse and contraryous parties, ne myghte nevere han ben assembled in o forme, but yif ther ne were oon that conjoyned so manye diverse thinges; and the same diversite of here natures, that so discorden the ton fro that other, most departen and unjoynen the thinges that ben conjoynid, yif ther ne were oon that contenyde that he hath conjoynid and ybounden. Ne the certein ordre of nature schulde not brynge forth so ordene moev- 40 ynges by places, by tymes, by doynges, by spaces, by qualites, yif ther ne were on, that were ay stedfast duellynge, that ordeynide and disponyde thise diversites of moevynges. And thilke thing, whatsoevere it be, by which that alle thinges ben ymaked and ilad, y clepe hym 'God,' that is a word that is used to alle folk."

Thanne seide sche: "Syn thou feelist thus thise thinges," quod sche, "I trowe that I have litel more to done that thou, myghty 50 of welefulnesse, hool and sound, ne see eftsones thi contre. But let us loken the thinges that we han purposed herebyforn. Have I nat nombrid and seid," quod sche, "that suffisaunce is in blisfulnesse? and we han accorded that God is thilke same blisfulnesse?"

"Yis, forsothe," quod I.

"And that to governen this world," quod sche, "ne schal he nevere han nede of noon help fro withoute? For elles, yif he hadde 60 nede of any help, he ne schulde nat have no ful suffisaunce?"

"Yys, thus it moot nedes be," quod I.

"Thanne ordeyneth he be hymself alone alle thinges?" quod sche.

"That may noght ben denyed," quod I.

"And I have schewyd that God is the same good?"

"It remembreth me wel," quod I.

"Thanne ordeigneth he alle thinges by 70 thilke good," quod sche, "syn he, which that we han accordid to ben good, governeth alle thinges by hymself; and he is as a keye and a styere, by which that the edifice of this world is kept stable and withouten corrumpynge?"

"I accorde me greetly," quod I. "And I aperceyvede a litil herebyforn that thow woldest seyn thus, al be it so that it were by a thynne suspecioun."

"I trowe it wel," quod sche; "for, as I 80 trowe, thou ledist now more ententyfliche thyn eyen to loken the verray goodes. But natheles the thing that I schal telle the yet ne scheweth not lesse to loken."

"What is that?" quod I.

"So as men trowen," quod sche, "and that ryghtfully, that God governeth alle thinges by the keye of his goodnesse, and alle thise same thinges, as I have taught the, hasten hem by naturel entencioun to come to good, 90 ther ne may no man douten that thei ne ben governed voluntariely, and that they ne converten hem of here owene wil to the wil of here ordeynour, as thei that ben accordynge and enclynynge to here governour and here kyng."

"It moot nedes be so," quod I, "for the reume ne schulde nat seme blisful yif ther were a yok of mysdrawynges in diverse parties, ne the savynge of obedient thynges ne scholde 100 nat be."

"Thanne is ther nothyng," quod sche, "that kepith his nature, that enforceth hym to gon ayen God."

"No," quod I.

"And yif that any thing enforcede hym to withstonde God, myghte it avayle at the laste ayens hym that we han graunted to ben almyghty be the ryght of blisfulnesse?"

"Certes," quod I, "al outrely it ne 110 myghte nat avaylen hym."

"Thanne is ther nothing," quod she, "that either wole or mai withstonden to this sovereyn good."

"I trowe nat," quod I.

"Thanne is thilke the sovereyn good," quod sche, that alle thinges governeth strongly and ordeyneth hem softly?"

Thanne seide I thus: "I delite me," quod I, "nat oonly in the eendes or in the 120 somme of resouns that thou hast concluded and proved, but thilke woordes that thou usest deliten me moche more. So that, at the laste, foolis that somtyme reenden grete thinges oughten ben asschamid of hemself! (*That is to seyn, that we foolis that reprehenden wikkidly the thinges that touchin Godis governaunce, we aughten ben asschamid of ourself; as I, that seide that God refuseth*

oonly the werkis of men and ne entremet- 130
tith nat of it.)

Philosophie. "Thow hast wel herd," quod
sche, "the fables of the poetis, how the geauntis
assaileden hevene with the goddis, but forsothe
the debonayre force of God disposide hem as it
was worthy (*that is to sey, destroyde the
geauntes, as it was worthy*). But wiltow that
we joynen togidres thilke same resouns, for
paraventure of swiche conjunccioun may
sterten up som fair sparcle of soth?" 140

"Do," quod I, "as the list."

"Wenestow," quod sche, "that God ne be
almyghty? — No man is in doute of it."

"Certes," quod I, "no wyght ne douteth it,
yif he be in his mynde."

"But he," quod sche, "that is almyghti — ther
nys no thyng that he ne may?"

"That is sooth," quod I.

"May God don evel?" quod sche.

"Nay, forsothe," quod I. 150

"Thanne is evel nothing," quod sche,
"syn that he ne may not don evel, that mai
doon alle thinges."

"Scornestow me," quod I, — (*or elles*, "Pley-
estow or disseyvistow me,") — "that hast so
woven me with thi resouns the hous of Dedalus,
so entrelaced that it is unable to ben unlaced —
thow that otherwhile entrist ther thow issist,
and other while issist ther thow entrest?
Ne fooldist thou nat togidre (*by replica-* 160
cioun of wordes) a manere wondirful cercle or envirounynge of the simplicite devyne?
For certes a litel herebyforn, whanne thou bygunne at blisfulnesse, thou seidest that it is
sovereyn good, and seidest that it is set in sovereyn God; and seidest that God hymself is
sovereyn good, and that good is the fulle blisfulnesse; for which thou yave me as a covenable yifte, that is to seyn, that no wyght is
blisful, but yif he be God also therwith. 170
And seidest eke that the forme of good is
the substaunce of God and of blisfulnesse; and
seidest that thilke same oon is thilke same good
that is required and desired of al the kynde of
thinges. And thou provedest in disputynge that
God governeth alle the thinges of the world by
the governementis of bounte; and seidest that
alle thinges wolen obeyen to hym; and seidest
that the nature of yvel nys no thing. And
thise thinges ne schewedest thou naught 180
with noone resouns ytaken fro withouten,
but by proeves in cercles and homliche knowen,
the whiche proeves drawen to hemself heer

feyth and here accord everich of hem of othir."

Thanne seide sche thus: "I ne scorne the nat,
ne pleie, ne disceyve the; but I have schewed
the the thing that is grettest over alle thinges,
by the yifte of God that we whilom prayeden.
For this is the forme of the devyne substaunce, that is swich that it ne slideth nat 190
into uttreste foreyne thinges, ne ne resceyveth noone straunge thinges in hym; but
ryght as Parmanydes seide in Greec of thilke
devyne substaunce — he seide thus: that thilke
devyne substaunce tornith the world and the
moevable cercle of thinges, while thilke devyne
substaunce kepith itself withouten moevynge.
(*That is to seyn, that it ne moeveth nevere mo,
and yet it moeveth alle othere thinges.*)
But natheles, yif I have styred resouns 200
that ne ben nat taken from withouten the
compas of the thing of which we treten, but
resouns that ben bystowyd withinne that compas, ther nys nat why that thou schuldest
merveillen, sith thow hast lernyd by the sentence of Plato that nedes the wordis moot be
cosynes to the thinges of whiche thei speken.

"Felix qui potuit." — Metrum 12

Blisful is that man that may seen the clere
welle of good! Blisful is he that mai unbynden
hym fro the boondes of the hevy erthe! The
poete of Trace (*Orpheus*), that whilom hadde
ryght greet sorwe for the deth of his wyf, aftir
that he hadde makid by his weeply songes the
wodes moevable to renne, and hadde makid
the ryveris to stonden stille, and hadde maked
the hertes and the hyndes to joynen dreed-
les here sydes to cruel lyouns (*for to herk-* 10
nen his song), and hadde maked that the
hare was nat agast of the hound, which was
plesed by his song; so, whanne the moste ardaunt love of his wif brende the entrayles of his
breest, ne the songes that hadden overcomen
alle thinges ne mighten nat asswagen hir lord
(*Orpheus*), he pleynid hym of the hevene
goddis that weren cruel to hym. He wente hym
to the houses of helle, and ther he tempride
his blaundysschinge songes by resounynge 20
strenges, and spak and song in wepynge al
that evere he hadde resceyved and lavyd out
of the noble welles of his modir (*Callyope*),
the goddesse. And he sang, with as mochel as
he myghte of wepynge, and with as moche as
love, that doublide his sorwe, myghte yeve hym
and teche hym, and he commoevede the helle,
and requyred and bysoughte by swete preyere

the lordes of soules in helle of relessynge (*that is to seyn, to yelden hym his wyf*). 30 Cerberus, the porter of helle, with his thre hevedes, was caught and al abasschid of the newe song. And the thre goddesses, furiis and vengeresses of felonyes, that tormenten and agasten the soules by anoy, woxen sorweful and sory, and wepyn teeris for pite. Tho was nat the heved of Ixion ytormented by the over-throwynge wheel. And Tantalus, that was de-stroied by the woodnesse of long thurst, despyseth the floodes to drynken. The foul 40 that highte voltor, that etith the stomak or the gyser of Tycius, is so fulfild of his song that it nil eten ne tiren no more. At the laste the lord and juge of soules was moevid to miseri-cordes, and cryede: 'We ben overcomen,' quod he; 'yyve we to Orpheus his wif to beren hym compaignye; he hath wel ybought hire by his faire song and his ditee. But we wolen putten a lawe in this and covenaunt in the yifte; that is to seyn that, til he be out of helle, 50 yif he loke byhynde hym, that his wyf schal comen ageyn unto us.' But what is he that may yeven a lawe to loverys? Love is a grettere lawe and a strengere to hymself (*thanne any lawe that men mai yyven*). Allas! whanne Orpheus and his wyf weren almest at the termes of the nyght (*that is to seyn, at the laste boundes of helle*), Orpheus lokede abak-ward on Erudyce his wif, and lost hire, and was deed. This fable apertenith to yow 60 alle, whosoevere desireth or seketh to lede his thought into the sovereyn day (*that is to seyn, into cleernesse of sovereyn good*). For whoso that evere be so overcomen that he ficche his eien into the put of helle (*that is to seyn, whoso sette his thoughtes in erthly thinges*), al that evere he hath drawen of the noble good celestial he lesith it, whanne he looketh the helles (*that is to seyn, into lowe thinges of the erthe*)." 70

EXPLICIT LIBER TERCIUS

INCIPIT LIBER QUARTUS

"Hec cum philosophia dignitate vultus."

— Prosa 1

Whanne Philosophie hadde songen softly and delitably the forseide thinges kepynge the dignyte of hir cheere and the weyghte of hir wordes, I, thanne, that ne hadde nat al outrely foryeten the wepynge and the moornynge that was set in myn herte, forbrak the entencioun of hir that entendede yit to seyn some othere thinges. "O," quod I, "thou that art gyderesse of verray light, the thinges that thou hast seid me hidirto ben to me so cleer and so 10 schewynge by the devyne lookynge of hem, and by thy resouns, that they ne mowen nat ben overcomen. And thilke thinges that thou toldest me, al be it so that I hadde whilom for-yeten hem for the sorwe of the wrong that hath ben don to me, yet natheles thei ne weren nat al outrely unknowen to me. But this same is namely a ryght gret cause of my sorwe: that so as the governour of thinges is good, yif that the eveles mowen ben by any weyes, or 20 elles yif that evelis passen withouten pun-ysschynge. The whiche thing oonly, how worthy it es to ben wondrid uppon, thou con-siderest it wel thiselve certeynly. But yit to this thing ther is yit another thing ijoyned more to ben wondrid uppon: for felonye is emperisse, and floureth ful of richesses, and vertu is nat al oonly withouten meedes, but it is cast undir and fortroden undir the feet of felonous folk, and it abyeth the tormentz in stede of 30 wikkide felouns. Of alle whiche thinges ther nys no wyght that may merveillen ynowgh, ne compleyne that swiche thinges ben don in the reigne of God, that alle thinges woot and alle thinges may and ne wole nat but oonly gode thinges."

Thanne seide sche thus: "Certes," quod sche, "that were a greet merveille and abaysschinge withouten ende, and wel more horrible than alle monstres, yif it were as thou wenest; 40 that is to seyn, that in the ryght ordene hous of so mochel a fadir and an ordeynour of meyne, that the vesselis that ben foule and vyl schulden ben honoured and heryed, and the precious vesselis schulden ben defouled and vyl. But it nys nat so. For yif the thinges that I have concluded a litel herebyforn ben kept hoole and unaraced, thou schalt wel knowe by the auctorite of God, of the whos reigne I speke, that certes the gode folk ben alwey 50 myghty and schrewes ben alwey outcast and feble; ne the vices ben neveremo with-outen peyne, ne the vertus ne ben nat with-outen mede; and that blisfulnesses comen alwey to goode folk, and infortune comith alwey to wikkide folk. And thou schalt wel knowe manye thinges of this kynde, that schullen cesen thi pleyntis and strengthen the with sted-fast sadnesse. And for thou hast seyn the

forme of the verray blisfulnesse by me that   60
have whilom yschewid it the, and thow
hast knowen in whom blisfulnesse is yset, alle
thingis ytreted that I trowe ben necessarie to
putten forth, I schal schewe the the weye that
schal bryngen the ayen unto thyn hous; and I
schal fycchen fetheris in thi thought, by whiche
it mai arisen in heighte; so that, alle tribulacioun idon awey, thow, by my gyding and by
my path and by my sledys, shalt mowen
retourne hool and sownd into thi contree.   70

"Sunt etenim penne volucres michi." — Metrum 1

"I have, forthi, swifte fetheris that surmounten the heighte of the hevene. Whanne
the swifte thoght hath clothid itself in tho
fetheris, it despiseth the hateful erthes, and surmounteth the rowndnesse of the gret ayr; and
it seth the clowdes byhynde his bak, and passeth the heighte of the regioun of the fir, that
eschaufeth by the swifte moevynge of the firmament, til that he areyseth hym into the
houses that beren the sterres, and joyneth   10
his weies with the sonne, Phebus, and
felawschipeth the weie of the olde colde Saturnus; and he, imaked a knyght of the clere
sterre (*that is to seyn, whan the thought is
makid Godis knyght by the sekynge of cleer
trouthe to comen to the verray knowleche of
God*) — and thilke soule renneth by the cercle
of the sterres in alle the places there as the
schynynge nyght is ypainted (*that is to
sey, the nyght that is cloudeles; for on*   20
*nyghtes that ben cloudeles it semeth as
the hevene were peynted with diverse ymages
of sterres*). And whan the thought hath don
there inogh, he schal forleten the laste hevene,
and he schal pressen and wenden on the bak
of the swifte firmament, and he schal be makid
parfit of the worschipful lyght of God. There
halt the lord of kynges the septre of his myght
and atemprith the governementz of the
world, and the schynynge juge of thinges,   30
stable in hymself, governeth the swifte
wayn (*that is to seyn, the circuler moevynge of
the sonne*). And yif this wey ledeth the ayein
so that thou be brought thider, thanne wiltow
seye that that is the contre that thou requerist,
of which thou ne haddest no mynde — 'but now
it remembreth me wel, here was I born, her
wol I fastne my degree (*here wol I duelle*).'
But yif the liketh thanne to looken on the

derknesse of the erthe that thou hast for-   40
leten, thanne shaltow seen that these fel-
ounous tirantz, that the wreechide peple dredeth now, schullen ben exiled fro thilke faire
contre."

"Tum ego pape ut magna." — Prosa 2

Thanne seide I thus: "Owh! I wondre me
that thow byhetist me so grete thinges. Ne I
ne doute nat that thou ne maist wel performe
that thow behetist; but I preie the oonly this,
that thow ne tarie nat to telle me thilke thinges
that thou hast moevid."

"First," quod sche, "thow most nedes knowen
that goode folk ben alwey strong and myghti,
and the schrewes ben feble, and desert and
naked of alle strengthes. And of thise   10
thinges, certes, everich of hem is declared
and schewed by othere. For so as good and
yvel ben two contraries, yif so be that good be
stedfast, thanne scheweth the feblesse of yvel
al opynly; and if thow knowe clerly the freel-
nesse of yvel, the stedfastnesse of good is
knowen. But for as moche as the fey of my
sentence schal ben the more ferme and haboun-
dant, I wil gon by the to weye and by the
tothir, and I wil conferme the thinges that   20
ben purposed, now on this side and now on
that side. Two thinges ther ben in whiche the
effect of alle the dedes of mankynde standeth,
that is to seyn, wil and power; and yif that oon
of thise two faileth, ther nys nothing that may
be doon. For yif that wille lakketh, ther nys no
wyght that undirtaketh to done that he wol nat
doon; and yif power faileth, the wil nys but in
idel and stant for naught. And therof cometh it that yif thou see a wyght that wolde   30
geten that he mai not geten, thow maist
nat douten that power ne faileth hym to have
that he wolde."

"This is open and cler," quod I, "ne it ne
mai nat be denyed in no manere."

"And yif thou se a wyght," quod sche, "that
hath doon that he wolde doon, thow nilt nat
douten that he ne hath had power to doon it?"

"No," quod I.

"And in that that every wyght may, in   40
that men may holden hym myghti?" (*As
who seith, in so moche as man is myghty to
doon a thing, in so mochel men halt hym
myghti; and in that he ne mai, in that men
demen hym to ben feble.*)

"I confesse it wel," quod I.

"Remembreth the," quod sche, "that I have

gaderid and ischewid by forseide resouns that
al the entencioun of the wil of mankynde,
which that is lad by diverse studies, hast-   50
eth to comen to blisfulnesse."

"It remembreth me wel," quod I, "that it
hath ben schewed."

"And recordeth the nat thanne," quod sche,
"that blisfulnesse is thilke same good that men
requiren? so that whanne that blisfulnesse is
required of alle, that good also is required and
desired of alle?"

"It ne recordeth me noght," quod I,
"for I have it gretly alwey ficched in my   60
memorie."

"Alle folk thanne," quod sche, "goode and
eek badde, enforcen hem withoute difference
of entencioun to comen to good."

"This is a verray consequence," quod I.

"And certein is," quod sche, "that by the
getynge of good men ben ymakid gode."

"This is certein," quod I.

"Thanne geten gode men that thei desiren?"   70

"So semeth it," quod I.

"But wikkide folk," quod sche, "yif thei
geten the good that thei desiren, thei ne mowe
nat ben wikkid."

"So is it," quod I.

"Than so as the ton and the tothir," quod
sche, "desiren good, and the gode folk geten
good and not the wikkide folk, than is it no
doute that the gode folk ne ben myghty
and wikkid folk ben feble."   80

"Whoso that evere," quod I, "douteth of
this, he ne mai nat considere the nature of
thinges ne the consequence of resouns."

"And over this," quod sche, "if that ther ben
two thinges that han o same purpos by kynde,
and that oon of hem pursuweth and performeth
thilke same thing by naturel office, and the
toother mai nat doon thilke naturel office, but
folweth, by other manere than is covenable
to nature, hym that acomplisseth his pur-   90
pos kyndely, and yit he ne acomplisseth
nat his owene purpos — whethir of thise two
demestow for more myghti?"

"Yif that I conjecte," quod I, "that thou wilt
seie, algates yit I desire to herkne it more
pleynly of the."

"Thou nilt nat thanne denye," quod sche,
"that the moevement of goynge nys in men by
kynde?"

"No, forsothe," quod I.   100

"Ne thou doutest nat," quod sche, "that

thilke naturel office of goinge ne be the office
of feet?"

"I ne doute it nat," quod I.

"Thanne," quod sche, "yif that a wight be
myghti to moeve, and goth uppon his feet, and
another, to whom thilke naturel office of feet
lakketh, enforceth hym to gone crepinge uppon
his handes, which of thise two oughte to
ben holden the more myghti by right?"   110

"Knyt forth the remenaunt," quod I,
"for no wight ne douteth that he that mai gon
by naturel office of feet ne be more myghti than
he that ne may nat."

"But the soverein good," quod sche, "that is
eveneliche purposed to the goode folk and to
badde, the gode folk seken it by naturel office
of vertus, and the schrewes enforcen hem to
getin it by divers coveytise of erthly
thinges, which that nys noon naturel office   120
to gete thilke same soverein good. Trowestow that it be any other wise?"

"Nai," quod I, "for the consequence is open
and schewynge of thinges that I have graunted,
that nedes goode folk moten be myghty, and
schrewes feble and unmyghti."

"Thou rennist aryght byforn me," quod sche,
"and this is the jugement (*that is to sein, I
juge of the*), ryght as thise leches ben
wont to hopin of sike folk, whan thei aper-   130
ceyven that nature is redressed and withstondeth to the maladye. But for I se the now
al redy to the undirstondynge, I schal schewe
the more thikke and contynuel resouns. For
loke now, how greetly schewyth the feblesse
and infirmite of wikkid folk, that ne mowen nat
comen to that hir naturel entencioun ledeth
hem; and yit almost thilke naturel entencioun
constreyneth hem. And what were to
demen thanne of schrewes, yif thilke nat-   140
urel help hadde forleten hem, the whiche
naturel help of entencioun goth alwey byforn
hem and is so gret that unnethe it mai ben
overcome. Considere thanne how gret defaute
of power and how gret feblesse ther is in wikkide felonous folk. (*As who seith, the gretter
thing that is coveyted and the desir nat acom-
plissed, of the lasse myght is he that coveyteth
it and mai nat acomplisse; and forthi philosophie seith thus be sovereyn good.*) Ne   150
schrewes ne requeren not lighte meedes ne
veyne games, whiche thei ne mai nat folwen ne
holden; but thei failen of thilke somme and of
the heighte of thinges (*that is to seyn, soverein
good*). Ne these wrecches ne comen nat to the

effect of sovereyn good, the whiche thei enforcen hem oonly to geten by nyghtes and by
dayes. In the getyng of which good the
strengthe of good folk is ful wel yseene.
For ryght so as thou myghtest demen hym   160
myghty of goinge that goth on his feet til
he myghte comen to thilke place fro the whiche
place ther ne laye no weie forthere to be gon,
ryght so mostow nedes demen hym for ryght
myghty, that geteth and atteyneth to the ende
of alle thinges that ben to desire, byyonde the
whiche ende ther nys no thing to desire. Of
the whiche power of goode folk men mai conclude that the wikkide men semen to be
bareyne and naked of alle strengthe. For   170
whi forleten thei vertus and folwen vices?
Nys it nat for that thei ne knowen nat the
godes? But what thing is more feble and more
caytif than is the blyndnesse of ignorance? Or
elles thei knowen ful wel whiche thinges that
thei oughten folwe, but lecherie and covetise
overthroweth hem mystorned. And certes so
doth distempraunce to feble men, that ne
mowen nat wrastlen ayen the vices. Ne
knowen thei nat thanne wel that thei for-   180
leten the good wilfully, and turnen hem
wilfully to vices? And in this wise thei ne forleten nat oonly to ben myghti, but thei forleten
al outrely in any wise for to been. For thei that
forleten the comune fyn of alle thinges that
ben, thei forleten also therwithal for to been.
And peraventure it scholde seme to som folk
that this were a merveile to seien, that schrewes,
whiche that contenen the more partie of
men, ne ben nat ne han no beynge; but   190
natheles it is so, and thus stant this thing.
For thei that ben schrewes I denye nat that
they ben schrewes, but I denye, and seie simply
and pleynly, that thei ne ben nat, ne han no
beynge. For right as thou myghtest seyn of the
careyne of a man, that it were a deed man, but
thou ne myghtest nat symply callen it a man;
so graunte I wel forsothe that vicyous folk ben
wikkid, but I ne may nat graunten abso-
lutly and symply that thei ben. For thilke   200
thing that withholdeth ordre and kepeth
nature, thilke thing es, and hath beinge; but
what thing that faileth of that (*that is to seyn,
he that forleteth naturel ordre*), he forleteth
thilke beinge that is set in his nature. But thow
wolt seyn that schrewes mowen. Certes, that
ne denye I nat; but certes hir power ne des-
scendeth nat of strengthe, but of feblesse. For
thei mowen don wikkydnesses, the whiche

thei ne myghten nat don yif thei myghten   210
duellen in the forme and in the doynge of
goode folk. And thylke power scheweth ful
evidently that they ne mowen ryght nat. For
so as I have gadrid and proevid a litil herebyforn that evel is nawght, and so as schrewes
mowen oonly but schrewednesses, this conclusion is al cler, that schrewes ne mowen ryght
nat, ne han no power. And for as moche as
thou undirstonde which is the strengthe
of this power of schrewes, I have diffin-   220
ysched a litil herbyforn that no thing is so
myghti as sovereyn good."
   "That is soth," quod I.
   "And thilke same sovereyn good may don
noon yvel?"
   "Certes, no," quod I.
   "Is ther any wyght thanne," quod sche, "that
weneth that men mowen don alle thinges?"
   "No man," quod I, "but yif he be out of
his wyt."   230
   "But certes schrewes mowen don evel?"
quod sche.
   "Ye; wolde God," quod I, "that thei ne
myghten don noon!"
   "Thanne," quod sche, "so as he that is
myghty to doon oonly but goode thinges mai
doon alle thinges, and thei that ben myghti to
doon yvele thinges ne mowen nat alle thinges,
thanne is it open thing and manyfest that
thei that mowen doon yvele ben of lasse   240
power. And yit to proeve this conclusioun
ther helpeth me this, that I have schewed herebyforn, that alle power is to be noumbred
among thinges that men oughten requere; and
I have schewed that alle thinges that oughten
ben desired ben referred to good, ryght as to a
maner heighte of hir nature. But for to mowen
don yvel and felonye ne mai nat ben referrid to
good. Thanne nys nat yvel of the nombre
of thinges that oughten ben desired. But   250
alle power aughte ben desired and requerid. Thanne is it open and cler that the
power ne the mowynge of schrewes nis no
power. And of alle thise thinges it scheweth
wel that the gode folk ben certeinli myghty,
and the schrewes doutelees ben unmyghty.
And it is cler and open that thilke sentence of
Plato is verray and soth, that seith that oonly
wise men may doon that thei desiren, and
schrewes mowen haunten that hem liketh,   260
but that thei desiren (*that is to seyn, to
come to sovereyn good*), thei ne han no power
to acomplissen that. For schrewes don that

hem lyst whan, by tho thinges in whiche thei deliten, thei wenen to ateynen to thilke good that thei desiren; but thei ne geten nat ne ateyne nat therto, for vices ne comen nat to blisfulnesse.

"*Quos vides sedere celsos.*" — Metrum 2

Whoso that the coverturis of hir veyn apparailes myghte strepen of thise proude kynges, that thow seest sitten an hy in here chayeres, gliterynge in schynynge purpre, envyrowned with sorwful armures, manasyng with cruel mowth, blowynge by woodnesse of herte, he schulde seen thanne that thilke lordis berin withynne hir corages ful streyte cheynes. For lecherye tormenteth hem on that o side with gredy venymes; and trowblable ire, 10 that areyseth in hem the floodes of trowblynges, tormenteth upon that othir side hir thought; or sorwe halt hem wery and icawght, or slidynge and desceyvynge hope turmenteth hem. And therfore, syn thow seest on heved (*that is to seyn, o tiraunt*) beren so manye tyranyes, than doth thilke tyraunt nat that he desireth, syn he is cast doun with so manye wikkide lordes (*that is to seyn, with so manye vices that han so wikkidly lord-* 20 *schipes over hym*).

"*Videsne igitur quanto.*" — Prosa 3

Seestow nat thanne in how greet filthe thise schrewes been iwrapped, and with which clernesse thise gode folk schynen? In this scheweth it wel that to goode folk ne lakketh neveremo hir meedes, ne schrewes ne lakken neveremo turmentes, for of alle thinges that ben idoon, thilke thing for which any thing is doon, it semeth as by ryght that thilke thing be the mede of that; as thus: yif a man renneth in the stadye (*or in the forlong*) for the 10 corone, thanne lith the mede in the coroune for which he renneth. And I have schewed that blisfulnesse is thilke same good for which that alle thinges ben doon; thanne is thilke same good purposed to the werkes of mankynde right as a comune mede, which mede ne may nat ben disseveryd fro goode folk. For no wight as by ryght, fro thennesforth that hym lakketh goodnesse, ne schal ben cleped good. For which thing folk of gode man- 20 eres, hir medes ne forsaken hem neveremo. For al be it so that schrewes waxen as wode as hem lyst ayein goode folk, yit natheles the coroune of wise men ne schal nat fallen ne faden; for foreyn schrewednesse ne bynymeth nat fro the corages of goode folk hir propre honour. But yif that any wyght rejoysede hym of goodnesse that he hadde taken fro withoute (*as who seith, yif any man hadde his goodnesse of any other man than of hymself*), 30 certes he that yaf hym thilke goodnesse, or elles som other wyght, myghte benymen it hym. But for as moche as to every wyght his owene propre bounte yeveth hym his mede, thanne at erste schal he failen of mede whan he forletith to ben good. And at the laste, so as alle medes ben requerid for men wenen that thei ben gode, who is he that nolde deme that he that is ryght myghti of good were partlees of the mede? And of what mede schal 40 he ben gerdoned? Certes of ryght fair mede and ryght greet aboven alle medes. Remembre the of thilke noble corrolarie that I yaf the a litel herebyforn, and gadre it togidre in this manere: so as God hymself is blisfulnesse, thanne is it cler and certein that alle gode folk ben imaked blisful for thei ben gode; and thilke folk that ben blisful it accordeth and is covenable to ben goddes. Thanne is the mede of goode folk swych that no day ne 50 schal empeiren it, ne no wikkidnesse schal derkne it, ne power of no wyght ne schal nat amenusen it, that is to seyn, to ben maked goddes. And syn it is thus (*that gode men ne failen neveremo of hir mede*), certes no wis man ne may doute of the undepartable peyne of schrewes (*that is to seyn, that the peyne of schrewes ne departeth nat from hemself neveremo*). For so as good and yvel, and peyne and mede ben contrarie, it moot nedes ben 60 that, ryght as we seen betyden in guerdoun of good, that also moot the peyne of yvel answere by the contrarie partie to schrewes. Now thanne, so as bounte and pruesse ben the mede to goode folk, also is schrewidnesse itself torment to schrewes. Thanne whoso that evere is entecchid or defouled with peyne, he ne douteth nat that he nys entecchid and defouled with yvel. Yi schrewes thanne wol preysen hemself, may it semen to hem that thei ben 70 withouten parti of torment, syn thei ben swiche that the uttreste wikkidnesse (*that is to seyn, wikkide thewes, which that is the uttereste and the worste kynde of schrewednesse*) ne defouleth ne enteccheth nat hem oonly, but enfecteth and envenymeth hem greetly? And also loke on schrewes, that ben the contrarie partie of gode men, how gret peyne felaw-

schipith and folweth hem! For thou hast
lerned a litil herebyforn that alle thing that   80
is and hath beynge is oon, and thilke same
oon is good: than is this the consequence, that
it semeth wel that al that is and hath beynge,
is good. (*This is to seyn, as who seith that
beinge and unite and goodnesse is al oon.*)
And in this manere it folweth thanne that alle
thing that fayleth to ben good, it stynteth for
to be and for to han any beynge. Wherfore it
es that schrewes stynten for to ben that
thei weeren. But thilke othir forme of man-   90
kynde (*that is to seyn, the forme of the
body withowte*) scheweth yit that thise
schrewes weren whilom men. Wherfore, whan
thei ben perverted and turned into malice,
certes, thanne have thei forlorn the nature of
mankynde. But so as oonly bownte and prowesse may enhawnsen every man over othere
men, than moot it nedes be that schrewes,
whiche that schrewednesse hath cast out of
the condicion of mankynde, ben put undir   100
the merit and the dissert of men. Than
betidith it that, yif thou seest a wyght that be
transformed into vices, thow ne mayst nat wene
that he be a man. For if he be ardaunt in
avaryce, and that he be a ravynour by violence
of foreyn richesse, thou schalt seyn that he is
lik to the wolf; and if he be felonows and
withoute reste, and exercise his tonge to chidynges, thow schalt likne hym to the
hownd; and if he be a pryve awaytour   110
yhid, and rejoiseth hym to ravyssche be
wiles, thou schalt seyn hym lik to the fox
whelpes; and yif he be distempre, and quak-
ith for ire, men schal wene that he bereth the
corage of a lyoun; and yif he be dredful and
fleynge, and dredith thinges that ne aughte nat
to ben dredd, men schal holden hym lik to the
hert; and yf he be slow, and astonyd, and
lache, he lyveth as an asse; yif he be lyght
and unstedfast of corage and chaungith ay   120
his studies, he is likned to briddes; and if
he be ploungid in fowle and unclene luxuris,
he is withholden in the foule delices of the
fowle sowe. Than folweth it that he that forleteth bounte and prowesse, he forletith to
ben a man; syn he ne may nat passe into the
condicion of God, he is torned into a beeste.

"*Vela Naricii ducis.*" — Metrum 3

Eurus, the wynd, aryved the sayles of Ulixes,
duc of the cuntre of Narice, and his wandrynge shippes by the see, into the ile theras

Cerces, the faire goddesse, dowhter of the
sonne, duelleth, that medleth to hir newe
gestes drynkes that ben touchid and makid
with enchauntementz. And aftir that hir hand,
myghti over the erbes, hadde chaunged hir
gestes into diverse maneres, that oon of
hem is coverid his face with forme of a   10
boor; the tother is chaungid into a lyoun
of the contre Marmoryke, and his nayles and
his teth waxen; that oother of hem is newliche
chaunged into a wolf, and howleth whan he
wolde wepe; that other goth debonayrely in
the hows as a tigre of Inde. But al be it so
that the godhede of Mercurie, that is cleped
the bridd of Arcadye, hath had merci of the
duc Ulixes, bysegid with diverse yveles,
and hath unbownden hym fro the pesti-   20
lence of his oostesse, algates the rowerys
and the maryneres hadden by this idrawen into
hir mouthes and dronken the wikkide drynkes.
Thei that weren woxen swyn, hadden by this
ichaunged hir mete of breed for to eten ak-
kornes of ookes. Noon of hir lymes ne duelleth with hem hool, but thei han lost the voys
and the body; oonly hir thought duelleth with
hem stable, that wepeth and bywayleth the
monstruous chaungynge that thei suffren.   30
O overlyght hand!" (*As who seith: "O
feble and light is the hand of Circes the en-
chaunteresse, that chaungith the bodyes of
folk into beestes, to regard and to comparysoun of mutacioun that is makid by vices!"*)
"Ne the herbes of Circes ne ben nat myghty.
For al be it so that thei mai chaungen the
lymes of the body, algates yit thei may nat
chaungen the hertes. For withinne is ihidd
the strengthe and the vygour of men, in the   40
secre tour of hir hertes, (*that is to seyn, the
strengthe of resoun*); but thilke venyms of vices
todrawen a man to hem more myghtely than
the venym of Circes. For vices ben so cruel
that they percen and thurw-passen the corage
withinne; and, though thei ne anoye nat the
body, yit vices woden to destroyen men by
wounde of thought."

"*Tum ego fateor inquam.*" — Prosa 4

Thanne seide I thus: "I confesse and I am
aknowe it," quod I, "ne I ne se nat that men
may seyn as by ryght that schrewes ne ben
chaunged into beestes by the qualite of hir
soules, al be it so that thei kepin yit the forme
of the body of mankynde; but I nolde nat of
schrewes, of whiche the thought crwel wood-

eth alwey into destruccion of gode men, that it were leveful to hem to don that."

"Certes," quod sche, "ne it is nat leveful 10 to hem, as I schal wel schewen the in covenable place. But natheles, yif so were that thilke that men wenen ben leveful to schrewes were bynomyn hem, so that they ne myghte nat anoyen or doon harm to gode men, certes a gret partie of the peyne to schrewes scholde ben alegged and releved. For al be it so that this ne seme nat credible thing peraventure to some folk, yit moot it nedes be that schrewes ben more wrecches and unsely, 20 whan thei mai doon and performe that thei coveyten, than yif that thei ne myghte nat acomplissen that thei coveiten. For yif it so be that it be wrecchidnesse to wilne to doon yvel, thanne is more wrecchidnesse to mowe don yvel, withoute which mowynge the wrecchid wil scholde langwisse withouten effect. Thanne syn that everich of thise thinges hath his wrecchidnesse (*that is to seyn, wil to don yvel and power to don yvel*), it moot nedes 30 be that thei (*schrewes*) ben constreyned by thre unselynesses, that wolen, and mowen, and performen felonyes and schrewednesses."

"I acorde me," quod I; "but I desire gretly that schrewes losten sone thilke unselynesse, that is to seyn, that schrewes weren despoyled of mowynge to don yvel."

"So schollen thei," quod sche, "sonner peraventure than thou woldest, or sonner than they hemselve wene. For ther nis noth- 40 ing so late, in so schorte bowndes of this lif, that is long to abyde, nameliche to a corage immortel. Of whiche schrewes the grete hope and the heye compassynges of schrewednesses is ofte destroyed by a sodeyn ende, or thei ben war; and that thing establisseth to schrewes the ende of hir schrewednesse. For yf that schrewednesse makith wrecchis, than mot he nedes ben moost wrecchid that lengest is a schrewe. The whiche wikkide 50 schrewes wolde I demen althermost unsely and kaytifs, yif that hir schrewednesse ne were fynissched at the leste weye by the owtreste deth; for yif I have concluded soth of the unselynesse of schrewednesse, thanne schewith it clerly that thilke wrecchidnesse is withouten ende the which is certein to ben perdurable."

"Certes," quod I, "this conclusion is hard and wondirful to graunte; but I knowe wel that it accordeth moche to the thinges that 60 I have grauntid herebiforn."

"Thou hast," quod sche, "the ryght estimacion of this. But whosoevere wene that it be an hard thing to accorde hym to a conclusioun, it is ryght that he schewe that some of the premysses ben false, or elles he mot schewe that the collacioun of proposicions is nat spedful to a necessarie conclusioun; and yif it ne be nat so, but that the premisses ben ygraunted, ther nys nat why he 70 scholde blame the argument. For this thing that I schal telle the now ne schal nat seme lesse wondirful, but of the thingis that ben taken also it is necessarie." (*As who seith, it folweth of that which that is purposed byforn.*)

"What is that?" quod I.

"Certes," quod sche, "that is that thise wikkid schrewes ben more blisful, or elles lasse wrecches, that abyen the tormentz 80 that thei han desservid, than if no peyne of justise ne chastisede hem. Ne this ne seie I nat now for that any man myghte thinke that the maneris of schrewes ben coriged and chastised by vengeaunce and that thei ben brought to the ryghte weye by the drede of the torment, ne for that they yeven to other folk ensaumple to fleen fro vices; but I undirstonde yit in another manere that schrewes ben more unsely whan thei ne ben nat punyssched, al 90 be it so that ther ne be had no resoun or lawe of correccioun, ne noon ensample of lokynge."

"And what manere schal that be," quod I, "other than hath ben told herbyforn?"

"Have we nat thanne graunted," quod sche, "that goode folk ben blisful and schrewes ben wrecches?"

"Yis," quod I.

"Thanne," quod sche, "yif that any good 100 were added to the wrecchidnesse of any wyght, nis he nat more blisful than he that ne hath no medlynge of good in his solitarie wrecchidnesse?"

"So semeth it," quod I.

"And what seistow thanne," quod sche, "of thilke wrecche that lakketh alle goodes (*so that no good nys medlyd in his wrecchidnesse*), and yit over al his wikkidnesse, for which he is a wrecche, that ther be yit another 110 yvel anexed and knyt to hym — schal nat men demen hym more unsely thanne thilke wrecche of which the unselynesse is relevid by the participacioun of som good?"

"Why sholde he nat?" quod I.

"Thannes certes," quod sche, "han schrewes, whan thei ben punyschid, somwhat of good anexid to hir wrecchidnesse, that is to seyn, the same peyne that thei suffren, which that is good by the resoun of justice; and whanne 120 thilke same schrewes ascapen withouten torment, than han they somwhat more of yvel yit over the wikkidnesse that thei han don, that is to seyn, defaute of peyne, which defaute of peyne thou hast grauntid is yvel for the dissert of felonye?"

"I ne may nat denye it," quod I.

"Moche more thanne," quod sche, "ben schrewes unsely whan thei ben wrong-fully delivred fro peyne, thanne whan thei 130 ben punyschid by ryghtful vengeaunce. But this is open thing and cleer, that it is ryght that schrewes ben punyschid, and it is wik-kidnesse and wrong that thei escapen unpun-yschid."

"Who myghte denye that?" quod I.

"But," quod sche, "may any man denye that al that is ryght nis good, and also the contra-rie, that al that is wrong is wikke?"

"Certes," quod I, "thise thinges ben 140 clere ynow, and that we han concluded a lytel herebyforn. But I preye the that thow telle me, yif thow accordest to leten no tor-ment to the soules aftir that the body is ended by the deeth?" (*This to seyn, "Undirstond-estow aught that soules han any torment aftir the deeth of the body?"*)

"Certes," quod sche, "ye, and that ryght greet. Of whiche soules," quod sche, "I trowe that some ben tormented by aspre- 150 nesse of peyne, and some soules, I trowe, ben exercised by a purgynge mekenesse; but my conseil nys nat to determyne of thise peynes. But I have travailed and told yit hid-erto for thou scholdest knowe the mowynge of schrewes, which mowynge that semeth to ben unworthy, nis no mowynge; and ek of schrewes, of whiche thou pleynedest that they ne were nat punysschid, that thow wold-est seen that thei ne were neveremo with- 160 outen the tormentz of hir wikkidnesse; and of the licence of mowynge to don yvel that thou preyedest that it myghte sone ben ended, and that thou woldest fayn lernen that it ne scholde nat longe endure; and that schrewes ben more unsely yif thei were of lengere dur-ynge, and most unsely yif thei weren perdur-able. And aftir this I have schewyd the that more unsely ben schrewes whan thei es-

capen withouten hir ryghtful peyne, 170 thanne whan thei ben punyschid by ryghtful venjaunce; and of this sentence fol-weth it that thanne ben schrewes constreyned at the laste with most grevous torment, whan men wene that thei ne ben nat punyssched."

"Whan I considere thi resouns," quod I, "I ne trowe nat that men seyn any thing more ver-rayly. And yif I turne ayein to the studies of men, who is he to whom it sholde seme, that he ne scholde nat oonly leven thise 180 thinges, but ek gladly herkne hem?"

"Certes," quod sche, "so it es. But men may nat, for they have hir eien so wont to the derk-nesse of erthly thinges that they ne may nat lyften hem up to the light of cler sothfastnesse, but thei ben lyk to briddes of whiche the nyght lightneth hir lokynge and the day blend-ith hem. For whan men loke nat the ordre of thinges, but hir lustes and talentz, they wene that either the leve or the mowynge 190 to don wikkidnesse, or elles the scapynge withouten peyne be weleful. But considere the jugement of the perdurable lawe. For yif thou conferme thi corage to the beste thinges, thow ne hast noon nede of no juge to yeven the prys or mede; for thow hast joyned thiself to the most excellent thing. And yif thow have en-clyned thi studies to the wikkide thinges, ne seek no foreyn wrekere out of thiself; for thow thiself hast thrist thiself into wikke 200 thinges: ryght as thow myghtest loken by diverse tymes the fowle erthe and the hevene, and that alle othere thinges stynten fro with-oute (*so that thow nere neyther in hevene ne in erthe, ne saye no thyng more*); thanne scholde it semen to the, as by oonly resoun of lokynge, that thow were now in the sterres, and now in the erthe. But the peple ne loketh nat on these thinges. What thanne? Schal we thanne approchen us to hem that I have 210 schewed that thei ben lyke to beestes? And what wyltow seyn of this: yif that a man hadde al forlorn his syghte, and hadde for-yeten that he evere sawh, and wende that no thing ne faylede hym of perfeccioun of man-kynde; now we that myghten sen the same thinges — wolde we nat wene that he were blynd? Ne also ne accordith nat the peple to that I schal seyn, the whiche thing is sus-tenyd by as stronge foundementz of re- 220 souns, that is to seyn, that more unsely ben they that doon wrong to othere folk, than they that the wrong suffren."

"I wolde here thilke same resouns," quod I.

"Denyestow," quod sche, "that alle schrewes ne ben worthy to han torment?"

"Nay," quod I.

"But," quod sche, "I am certein by many resouns that schrewes ben unsely."

"It accordeth," quod I.   230

"Thanne ne dowtestow nat," quod sche, "that thilke folk that ben worthy of torment, that they ne ben wrecches?"

"It accordeth wel," quod I.

"Yif thou were thanne iset a juge or a knowere of thinges, whethir trowestow that men scholden tormenten, hym that hath don the wrong or elles hym that hath suffred the wrong?"

"I ne doute nat," quod I, "that I nolde doon suffisaunt satisfaccioun to hym that   240 hadde suffrid the wrong, by the sorwe of hym that hadde doon the wrong."

"Thanne semeth it," quod sche, "that the doere of wrong is more wrecche than he that hath suffrid wrong?"

"That folweth wel," quod I.

"Than," quod sche, "by thise causes and by othere causes that ben enforced by the same roote, that filthe or synne be the propre nature of it maketh men wrecches; and it   250 scheweth wel that the wrong that men doon nis nat the wrecchidnesse of hym that resceyveth the wrong, but wrecchidnesse of hym that dooth the wrong. But certes," quod sche, "thise oratours or advocattes don al the contrarie; for thei enforcen hem to commoeve the juges to han pite of hem that han suffrid and resceyved the thinges that ben grevous and aspre, and yit men scholden more ryghtfully han pite of hem that doon the   260 grevances and the wronges; the whiche schrewes it were a more covenable thing that the accusours or advocattes, nat wroothe but pytous and debonayre, ledden the schrewes that han don wrong to the jugement, ryght as men leden syke folk to the leche, for that thei sholden seken out the maladyes of synne by torment. And by this covenant, eyther the entent of the deffendours or advocatz sholde fayle and cesen in al, or elles, yif the of-   270 fice of advocatz wolde betre profiten to men, it scholde be torned into the habyt of accusacioun. (*That is to seyn, thei scholden accuse schrewes, and nat excusen hem.*) And eek the schrewes hemself, yif it were leveful to hem to seen at any clifte the vertu that thei han forleten, and sawen that they scholden

putten adoun the filthes of hir vices by the tormentz of peynes, they ne aughten nat, ryght for the recompensacioun for to geten hem   280 bounte and prowesse which that thei han lost, demen ne holden that thilke peynes weren tormentz to hem; and eek thei wolden refuse the attendaunce of hir advocatz, and taken hemself to hir juges and to hir accusours. For which it betydeth that, as to the wise folk, ther nis no place yleten to hate (*that is to seyn, that hate ne hath no place among wise men*); for no wyght nil haten gode men, but yif he were overmochel a fool, and for to haten   290 schrewes it nis no resoun. For ryght so as langwissynge is maladye of body, ryght so ben vices and synne maladye of corage; and so as we ne deme nat that they that ben sike of hir body ben worthy to ben hated, but rather worthy of pite; wel more worthy nat to ben hated, but for to ben had in pite, ben thei of whiche the thoughtes ben constreyned by felonous wikkidnesse, that is more cruwel than any langwissynge of body.

"Quid tantos iuvat." — Metrum 4

What deliteth yow to exciten so grete moevynges of hatredes, and to hasten and bysien the fatal disposicioun of your deth with your propre handes (*that is to seyn, by batayles or contek*)? For yif ye axen the deth, it hasteth hym of his owene nil, ne deth ne taryeth nat his swifte hors. And the men that the serpentz, and the lyoun, and the tigre, and the bere, and the boor, seken to sleen with hir teeth, yit thilke same men seken to sleen   10 everich of hem oothir with swerd. Lo, for hir maneres ben diverse and discordaunt, thei moeven unryghtful oostes and cruel batayles, and wilnen to perise by entrechaungynge of dartes! But the resoun of cruelte nis nat inowh ryghtful. Wiltow hanne yelden a covenable gerdoun to the dissertes of men? Love ryghtfully goode folk, and have pite on schrewes."

"Hic ego video inquam." — Prosa 5

"Thus se I wel," quod I, "eyther what blisfulnesse or elles what unselynesse is establisshid in the dissertes of gode men and of schrewes. But in this ilke fortune of peple I se somwhat of good and somwhat of yvel. For no wis man hath nat levere ben exiled, pore and nedy and nameles, thanne for to duellen in his cyte, and flouren of rychesses, and be redowtable by honour and strong of power.

For in this wise more clerly and more wit- 10
nesfully is the office of wise men ytreted,
whanne the blisfulnesse and the pouste of
gouvernours is, as it were, ischad among peples that ben neyghbors and subgitz; syn that
namely prisown, lawe, and thise othere tormentz of laweful peynes ben rather owed to
felonus citezeins, for the whiche felonus citezeens tho peynes ben establisschid than for
good folk."

"Thanne I merveile me gretly," quod I,   20
"why that the thinges ben so mysentre-
chaunged that tormentz of felonyes pressen and
confounden goode folk, and schrewes rav-
ysschen medes of vertu (*and ben in honours
and in grete estatz*). And I desire eek for to
witen of the what semeth the to be the resoun
of this so wrongful a confusioun; for I wolde
wondre wel the lasse, yif I trowede that alle
thise thinges weren medled by fortunows
hap. But now hepith and encreseth myn   30
astonyenge God, governour of thinges, that,
so as God yeveth ofte tymes to gode men godes
and myrthes, and to schrewes yvelis and aspre thinges, and yeveth ayeinward to goode
folk hardnesses, and to schrewes he graunteth
hem hir wil and that they desiren — what difference thanne may ther be bytwixen that that
God doth and the hap of fortune, yif men ne
knowe nat the cause why that it is?"

"Ne it nis no merveile," quod sche,   40
"thowh that men wenen that ther be somwhat foolissh and confus, whan the resoun of
the ordre is unknowe. But although that thou
ne knowe nat the cause of so gret a disposicioun, natheles for as moche as God, the gode
governour, atempreth and governeth the world,
ne doute the nat that alle thinges ne ben don
aryght.

"*Si quis Arcturi sidera.*" — Metrum 5

"Whoso that ne knowe nat the sterres of
Arctour, ytorned neygh to the sovereyne centre or poynt (*that is to seyn, ytorned neygh to
the sovereyne pool of the firmament*), and wot
nat why the sterre Boetes passeth or gadreth
his waynes, and drencheth his late flaumbes in
the see, and whi that Boetes, the sterre, un-
fooldeth his overswifte arysynges, thanne schal
he wondryn of the lawe of the heye eyr.
And eek yif that he knowe nat why that   10
the hornes of the fulle mone waxen pale
and infect by bowndes of the derke nyght, and
how the mone derk and confus discovereth the

sterres that sche hadde covered by hir clere
vysage. The comune errour moeveth folk, and
maketh weery hir basyns of bras by thikke
strokes. (*That is to seyn, that ther is a maner
peple that hyghte Coribantes, that wenen that
whan the mone is in the eclips that it be
enchaunted, and therfore for to rescowe the   20
mone thei betyn hir basyns with thikke
strokes.*) Ne no man ne wondreth whanne the
blastes of the wynd Chorus beten the strondes
of the see by quakynge floodes; ne no man ne
wondrith whan the weighte of the snowh,
ihardid by the cold, is resolvyd by the brennynge hete of Phebus, the sonne; for her seen
men redily the causes. But the causes yhidd
(*that is to seyn, in hevene*) trowblen the
brestes of men. The moevable peple is   30
astoned of alle thinges that comen seelde
and sodeynly in our age; but yif the trubly errour of our ignoraunce departed fro us, so that
we wisten the causes why that swiche thinges
bytyden, certes thei scholde cesen to seme
wondres."

"*Ita est inquam.*" — Prosa 6

"Thus is it," quod I. "But so as thou hast
yeven or byhyght me to unwrappen the hidde
causes of thinges, and to discovere me the
resouns covered with derknes, I preie the that
thou devyse and juge me of this matere, and
that thou do me to undirstonden it. For this
miracle or this wonder trowbleth me ryght
gretly."

And thanne sche, a litel what smylinge,
seide: "Thou clepist me," quod sche, "to   10
telle thing that is gretteste of alle thingis
that mowen ben axed, and to the whiche questioun unnethes is ther aught inowgh to laven
it. (*As who seith, unnethes is ther suffisauntly
any thing to answeren parfitly to thy questioun.*) For the matere of it is swich, that
whan o doute is determined and kut awey, ther
waxen othere doutes withoute nombre, ryght
as the hevedes wexen of Idre (*the serpent
that Hercules slowh*). Ne ther ne were no   20
manere ne noon ende, but if that a wyght
constreynede tho doutes by a ryght lifly and
quyk fir of thought (*that is to seyn, by vigour and strengthe of wit*). For in this matere
men weren wont to maken questiouns of the
symplicite of the purveaunce of God, and of
the ordre of destyne, and of sodeyn hap, and
of the knowynge and predestinacioun devyne,
and of the liberte of fre wil; the whiche

thinges thou thiself aperceyvest wel of 30
what weighte thei ben. But for as moche
as the knowynge of thise thinges is a maner
porcioun of the medycyne to the, al be it so
that I have litil tyme to doon it, yit natheles
y wol enforcen me to schewe somwhat of it.
But although the noryssynges of dite of musyk
deliteth the, thou most suffren and forberen a
litel of thilke delit, whil that I weve to the resouns yknyt by ordre."

"As it liketh to the," quod I, "so do." 40
Tho spak sche ryght as by another bygynnynge, and seide thus: "The engendrynge
of alle thinges," quod sche, "and alle the progressiouns of muable nature, and al that moeveth in any manere, taketh his causes, his ordre,
and his formes, of the stablenesse of the devyne thought. And thilke devyne thought that
is iset and put in the tour (*that is to seyn, in
the heighte*) of the simplicite of God, stab-
lissith many maner gises to thinges that ben 50
to done; the whiche manere whan that
men looken it in thilke pure clennesse of the
devyne intelligence, it is ycleped purveaunce;
but whanne thilke manere is referred by men
to thinges that it moeveth and disponyth, than
of olde men it was clepyd destyne. The whiche
thinges yif that any wyght loketh wel in his
thought the strengthe of that oon and of that
oothir, he schal lyghtly mowen seen that
thise two thinges ben dyvers. For pur- 60
veaunce is thilke devyne resoun that is establissed in the sovereyn prince of thinges, the
whiche purveaunce disponith alle thinges; but,
certes, destyne is the disposicioun and ordenance clyvyng to moevable thinges, by the
whiche disposicion the purveaunce knytteth
alle thingis in hir ordres; for purveaunce enbraceth alle thinges to-hepe, althogh that thei
ben diverse and although thei ben infinit.
But destyne, certes, departeth and ordeyn- 70
eth alle thinges singulerly and devyded in
moevynges, in places, in formes, in tymes. As
thus: lat the unfoldynge of temporel ordenaunce, assembled and oonyd in the lokynge
of the devyne thought, be cleped purveaunce;
and thilke same assemblynge and oonynge, devyded and unfolden by tymes, lat that ben
called destyne. And al be it so that thise
thinges ben diverse, yit natheles hangeth
that oon of that oother; forwhi the ordre 80
destynal procedith of the simplicite of
purveaunce. For ryght as a werkman that aperceyveth in his thought the forme of the thing

that he wol make, and moeveth the effect of
the work, and ledith that he hadde lookid byforn in his thought symplely and presently, by
temporel ordenaunce; certes, ryght so God disponith in his purveaunce singulerly and stablely the thinges that ben to doone; but he
amynistreth in many maneris and in di- 90
verse tymes by destyne thilke same thinges
that he hath disponyd. Thanne, whethir that
destyne be exercised outhir by some devyne
spiritz, servantz to the devyne purveaunce, or
elles by som soule, or elles by alle nature servynge to God, or elles by the celestial moevynges of sterres, or elles by vertu of aungelis,
or elles by divers subtilite of develis, or elles
by any of hem, or elles by hem alle; the
destinal ordenaunce is ywoven and acom- 100
plissid. Certes, it es open thing that the
purveaunce is an unmoevable and symple
forme of thinges to doone; and the moevable
bond and the temporel ordenaunce of thinges
whiche that the devyne symplicite of purveaunce hath ordeyned to doone, that is destyne. For which it is that alle thinges that ben
put undir destyne ben certes subgitz to purveaunce, to which purveaunce destyne itself is subgit and under. But some thinges 110
ben put undir purveaunce, that sourmounten
the ordenance of destyne; and tho ben thilke
that stablely ben ifycchid neygh to the firste
godhede. They surmounten the ordre of destynal moevablete. For ryght as of cerklis that
tornen aboute a same centre or aboute a poynt,
thilke cerkle that is innerest or most withinne
joyneth to the symplesse of the myddle, and is,
as it were, a centre or a poynt to that
othere cerklis that tornen abouten hym; 120
and thilke that is utterest, compased by a
largere envyrownynge, is unfolden by largere
spaces, in so moche as it is ferthest fro the
myddel symplicite of the poynt; and yif ther
be any thing that knytteth and felawschipeth
hymself to thilke myddel poynt, it is constreyned into simplicite (*that is to seyn, into
unmoevablete*), and it ceseth to ben schad and
to fleten diversely; ryght so, by semblable
reson, thilke thing that departeth ferrest 130
fro the firste thought of God, it is unfolden
and summittid to grettere bondes of destyne;
and in so moche is the thing more fre and laus
fro destyne, as it axeth and hooldeth hym neer
to thilke centre of thingis (*that is to seyn, to
God*); and yif the thing clyveth to the stedfastnesse of the thought of God and be with-

oute moevynge, certes it surmounteth the
necessite of destyne. Thanne ryght swich
comparysoun as is of skillynge to un- 140
dirstondyng, and of thing that ys
engendrid to thing that is, and of tyme
to eternite, and of the cercle to the centre; ryght so is the ordre of moevable destyne to the stable symplicite of purveaunce.
Thilke ordenaunce moveth the hevene and the
sterres, and atemprith the elementz togidre
amonges hemself, and transformeth hem by entrechaungeable mutacioun. And thilke
same ordre neweth ayein alle thinges 150
growynge and fallynge adoun, by semblable progressions of sedes and of sexes (*that
is to seyn, male and femele*). And this ilke
ordre constreyneth the fortunes and the dedes
of men by a bond of causes nat able to ben
unbownde; the whiche destynal causes, whan
thei passen out fro the bygynnynges of the unmoevable purveaunce, it moot nedes be that
thei ne be nat mutable. And thus ben the
thinges ful wel igoverned yif that the sym- 160
plicite duellynge in the devyne thought
scheweth forth the ordre of causes unable to
ben ibowed. And this ordre constreyneth by
his propre stablete the moevable thingis, or
elles thei scholden fleten folyly. For which it
es that alle thingis semen to ben confus and
trouble to us men, for we ne mowen nat considere thilke ordenaunce. Natheles the propre
maner of every thing, dressynge hem to
gode, disponith hem alle; for ther nys no 170
thing doon for cause of yvel, ne thilke
thing that is doon by wikkid folk nys nat doon
for yvel, the whiche schrewes, as I have
schewed ful plentyvously, seken good, but wikkid errour mystorneth hem; ne the ordre comynge fro the poynt of sovereyn good ne de-
clyneth nat fro his bygynnynge.

But thou mayst seyn, "What unreste
may ben a worse confusioun than that
gode men han somtyme adversite and 180
somtyme prosperite, and schrewes also
han now thingis that they desiren and now
thinges that thei haten?" Whethir men lyven
now in swich holnesse of thought (*as who
seith, ben men now so wyse*) that swiche folk
as thei demen to ben gode folk or schrewes,
that it moste nedes ben that folk ben swiche as
thei wenen? But in this manere the domes of
men discorden, that thilke men that som
folk demen worthy of mede, other folk 190
demen hem worthy of torment. But lat us

graunten, I pose, that som man may wel demen
or knowen the goode folk and the badde; may
he thanne knowen and seen thilke innereste
atempraunce of corages as it hath ben wont
to ben seyd of bodyes? (*As who seith, may a
man speken and determinen of atempraunce in
corages, as men were wont to demen or speken
of complexions and atempraunces of bodies?*) Ne it ne is nat an unlik miracle to 200
hem that ne knowen it nat (*as who seith,
but it is lik a mervayle or miracle to hem that
ne knowen it nat*) whi that swete thinges ben
covenable to some bodies that ben hole, and
to some bodies byttere thinges ben covenable;
and also why that some syke folk ben holpen
with lyghte medicynes, and some folk ben
holpen with sharpe medicynes. But natheles
the leche, that knoweth the manere and
the atempraunce of hele and of maladye, 210
ne merveyleth of it nothyng. But what
othir thing semeth hele of corages but bounte
and prowesse? And what othir thing semeth
maladye of corages but vices? Who is elles
kepere of good or dryvere awey of yvel but
God, governour and lechere of thoughtes? The
whiche God, whan he hath byholden from the
hye tour of his purveaunce, he knoweth what
is covenable to every wight, and lenyth
hem that he woot that is covenable to 220
hem. Lo, herof comyth and herof is don
this noble miracle of the ordre destynal, whan
God, that al knoweth, dooth swich thing, of
which thing unknowynge folk ben astonyd.
But for to constreyne (*as who seith, but for to
comprehende and to telle*) a fewe thingis of
the devyne depnesse, the whiche that mannys
resoun may undirstonde, thilke man that thow
wenest to ben ryght just and ryght kepynge of equite, the contrarie of that sem- 230
eth to the devyne purveaunce, that al
woot. And Lucan, my famylier, telleth that the
victorious cause likide to the goddes, and the
cause overcomen likide to Catoun. Thanne
whatsoevere thou mayst seen that is doon in
this world unhopid or unwened, certes it es the
ryghte ordre of thinges; but as to thi wikkid
opynioun, it is a confusioun. But I suppose that
som man be so wel ithewed that the devyne jugement and the jugement of man- 240
kynde accorden hem togidre of hym; but
he is so unstidfast of corage that, yif any adversite come to hym, he wol forleten peraventure
to continue innocence, by the whiche he ne may
nat withholden fortune. Thanne the wise dis-

pensacion of God sparith hym, the whiche
man adversite myghte enpeyren; for that
God wol nat suffren hym to travaile, to whom
that travaile nis nat covenable. Another
man is parfit in alle vertus, and is an holi   250
man and neigh to God, so that the purveaunce of God wolde deme that it were a felonie that he were touched with any adversites;
so that he wol nat suffre that swich a man be
moeved with any bodily maladye. But so as
seyde a philosophre, the more excellent by
me, — he seyde in Grec that "vertues han edi-
fied the body of the holi man." And ofte tyme
it betydeth that the somme of thingis that
ben to done is taken to governe to goode   260
folk, for that the malice haboundaunt of
schrewes scholde ben abated. And God yeveth and departeth to other folk prosperites and
adversites, imedled to hepe aftir the qualite of
hir corages, and remordith some folk by adversite, for thei ne scholden nat waxen proude
by long welefulnesse; and other folk he suffreth
to ben travailed with harde thinges, for that
thei scholden confermen the vertues of corage by the usage and the exercitacioun of   270
pacience. And other folk dreden more
than thei oughten the whiche thei myghte wel
beren, and thilke folk God ledeth into experience of hemself by aspre and sorweful thingis.
And many other folk han bought honourable
renoun of this world by the prys of glorious
deth; and som men, that ne mowen nat ben
overcomen by torment, han yeven ensample
to other folk that vertu mai nat ben overcomyn by adversites.   280
And of alle thise thinges ther nis no
doute that thei ne ben doon ryghtfully and
ordeynly, to the profit of hem to whom we
seen thise thingis betyde. For certes, that adversite cometh somtyme to schrewes and somtyme that that they desiren, it comith of thise
forseyde causes. And of sorweful thinges that
betyden to schrewes, certes, no man ne wondreth; for alle men wenen that thei han
wel desservid it, and that thei ben of wyk-   290
kid meryt. Of whiche schrewes the torment somtyme agasteth othere to don felonyes,
and somtyme it amendeth hem that suffren
the tormentz; and the prosperite that is yeven
to schrewes scheweth a gret argument to goode
folk what thing thei scholde demen of thilke
welefulnesse, the whiche prosperite men seen
ofte serven to schrewes. In the whiche thing
I trowe that God dispenseth. For peraven-

ture the nature of som man is so over-   300
throwynge to yvel, and so uncovenable,
that the nedy poverte of his houshold myghte
rather egren hym to don felonyes; and to the
maladye of hym God putteth remedye to yeven
hym rychesses. And som othir man byholdeth
his conscience defouled with synnes, and makith comparysoun of his fortune and of hymself, and dredith peraventure that his blisfulnesse, of which the usage is joyeful to hym,
that the lesynge of thilke blisfulnesse ne   310
be nat sorwful to hym; and therfore he
wol chaunge his maneris, and, for he dredith
to lesen his fortune, he forletith his wikkidnesse. To other folk is welefulnesse iyeven
unworthely, the whiche overthroweth hem into
destruccioun, that thei han disservid; and to
som othir folk is yeven power to punysshen, for
that it schal be cause of contynuacioun and
exercisynge to goode folk, and cause of
torment to schrewes. For so as ther nis   315
noon alliaunce bytwixe goode folk and
schrewes, ne schrewes ne mowen nat acorden
among hemself. And whi nat? For schrewes
discorden of hemself by hir vices, the whiche
vices al toreenden her consciences, and doon
ofte time thinges the whiche thingis, whan thei
han doon hem, they demen that tho thinges ne
scholden nat han ben doon. For which thing
thilke sovereyne purveaunce hath makid
ofte tyme fair myracle, so that schrewes   320
han maked schrewes to ben gode men. For
whan that some schrewes seen that they suffren
wrongfully felonyes of othere schrewes, they
wexen eschaufed into hate of hem that anoyed
hem, and retornen to the fruyt of vertu, whan
thei studien to ben unlyke to hem that thei han
hated. Certis oonly this is the devyne myght
to the whiche myghte yvelis ben thanne gode
whan it useth the yvelis covenably and
draweth out the effect of any good. (*As*   325
who seith that yvel is good oonly to the
myght of God, for the myght of God ordeyn-
eth thilke yvel to good.)
For oon ordre enbraseth alle thinges, so that
what wyght that departeth fro the resoun of
thilke ordre which that is assigned to hym,
algatis yit he slideth into an othir ordre; so that
no thing is leveful to folye in the reaume of
the devyne purveaunce (*as who seith, no*
thing nis withouten ordenaunce in the   330
reame of the devyne purveaunce), syn that
the ryght stronge God governeth alle thinges
in this world. For it nis nat leveful to man

to comprehenden by wit, ne unfolden by word, alle the subtil ordenaunces and disposiciounis of the devyne entente. For oonly it owghte suffise to han lokid that God hymself, makere of alle natures, ordeineth and dresseth alle thingis to gode; whil that he hasteth to withholden the thingis that he hath makid 335 into his semblaunce (*that is to seyn, for to withholden thingis into gode, for he hymself is good*), he chasith out alle yvel fro the boundes of his comynalite by the ordre of necessite destinable. For which it folweth that, yif thou loke the purveaunce ordeynynge the thinges that men wenen ben outrageous or haboundaunt in erthis, thou ne schalt nat seen in no place no thing of yvel. But I se now that thou art charged with the weyghte of the 340 questioun, and wery with lengthe of my resoun, and that thou abydest som swetnesse of song. Take thanne this drawghte, and, whanne thou art wel reffressched and reflect, thou schalt be more stedfast to stye into heyere questions or thinges.

"Si vis celsi iura." — Metrum 6

Yif thou, wys, wilt demen in thi pure thought the ryghtes or the lawes of the heye thondrere (*that is to seyn, of God*), loke thou and byhoold the heightes of the sovereyn hevene. Ther kepin the sterres, be ryghtful alliaunce of thinges, hir oolde pees. The sonne, imoevid by his rody fyr, ne distorbeth nat the colde cercle of the mone. Ne the sterre yclepid the Bere, that enclyneth his ravysschynge coursis abowte the sovereyn heighte of the world 10 — ne the same sterre Ursa nis nevere mo wasschen in the depe westrene see, ne coveyteth nat to deeyen his flaumbes in the see of the occian, although it see othere sterres iplowngid in the see. And Hesperus the sterre bodith and telleth alwey the late nyghtes, and Lucyfer the sterre bryngeth ayein the clere day. And thus maketh Love entrechaungeable the perdurable courses; and thus is discord- 20 able bataile yput out of the contre of the sterres. This accordaunce atempryth by evenelyke maneres the elementz, that the moiste thingis, stryvynge with the drye thingis, yeven place by stoundes; and that the colde thingis joynen hem by feyth to the hote thingis; and that the lyghte fyr ariseth into heighte, and the hevy erthes avalen by her weyghtes. By thise same causes the floury yer yeldeth

swote smelles in the first somer sesoun 30 warmynge; and the hote somer dryeth the cornes; and autumpne comith ayein hevy of apples; and the fletyng reyn bydeweth the wynter. This atempraunce norysscheth and bryngeth forth alle thinges that brethith lif in this world; and thilke same attempraunce, ravysschynge, hideth and bynymeth, and drencheth undir the laste deth, alle thinges iborn.

Among thise thinges sitteth the heye 40 makere, kyng and lord, welle and bygynnynge, lawe and wys juge to don equite, and governeth and enclyneth the brydles of thinges. And tho thinges that he stireth to gon by moevynge, he withdraweth and aresteth, and affermeth the moevable or wandrynge thinges. For yif that he ne clepide nat ayein the ryght goynge of thinges, and yif that he ne constreynede hem nat eftsones into roundnesses enclyned, the thingis that ben now 50 contynued by stable ordenaunce, thei scholden departen from hir welle (*that is to seyn, from hir bygynnynge*), and failen (*that is to seyn, tornen into noght*). This is the comune love to alle thingis, and alle thinges axen to ben holden by the fyn of good. For elles ne myghten they nat lasten yif thei ne comen nat eftsones ayein, by love retorned, to the cause that hath yeven hem beinge (*that is to seyn, to God*).   60

"Iam ne igitur vides." — Prosa 7

Sestow nat thanne what thing folweth alle the thingis that I have seyd?"

"What thing?" quod I.

"Certes," quod sche, "al outrely that alle fortune is good."

"And how may that be?" quod I.

"Now undirstand," quod sche, "so as al fortune, whethir so it be joyeful fortune or aspre fortune, is yeven eyther bycause of gerdonynge or elles of exercisynge of goode 10 folk or elles bycause to punysschen or elles chastisen schrewes; thanne is alle fortune good, the whiche fortune is certeyn that it be either ryghtful or elles profitable."

"Forsothe this is a ful verray resoun," quod I; "and yif I considere the purveaunce and the destyne that thou taughtest me a litel herebyforn, this sentence is sustenyd by stedfast resouns. But yif it like unto the, lat us nombren hem amonges thilke thingis, of 20 whiche thow seydest a litel herebyforn that thei ne were nat able to ben wened to the peple."

"Why so?" quod sche.

"For that the comune word of men," quod I, "mysuseth this manere speche of fortune, and seyn ofte tymes that the fortune of som wyght is wikkid."

"Woltow thanne," quod sche, "that I ap- proche a litil to the wordis of the peple, 30 so that it seme nat to hem that I be over- moche departed as fro the usage of mankynde?"

"As thou wilt," quod I.

"Demestow nat," quod sche, "that alle thing that profiteth is good?"

"Yis," quod I.

"And certes thilke thing that exerciseth or corrigith profitith?"

"I confesse it wel," quod I.

"Thanne is it good," quod sche.   40

"Why nat?" quod I.

"But this is the fortune," quod sche, "of hem that eyther ben put in vertu and batayllen ayein aspre thingis, or elles of hem that es- chuen and declynen fro vices and taken the weye of vertu."

"This ne mai I nat denye," quod I.

"But what seistow of the merye fortune that is yeven to goode folk in gerdoun? Dem- eth aught the peple that it is wikkid?"   50

"Nay forsothe," quod I; "but thei demen, as it soth is, that it is ryght good."

"And what seistow of that othir fortune," quod sche, "that, although it be aspre and restreyneth the schrewes by ryghtful torment, weneth aught the peple that it be good?"

"Nay," quod I, "but the peple demeth that it is moost wrecchid of alle thingis that mai ben thought."

"War now and loke wel," quod sche, "lest 60 that we, in folwynge the opynioun of the peple, have confessid and concluded thing that is unable to be wened to the peple?"

"What is that?" quod I.

"Certes," quod sche, "it folweth or comith of thingis that ben grauntid that alle fortune, what so evere it be, of hem that ben eyther in pos- sessioun of vertu, or in the encres of vertu, or elles in the purchasynge of vertu, that thilke fortune is good; and that alle fortune is 70 ryght wikkid to hem that duellen in schrewidnesse." (As who seith: "And thus wen- eth nat the peple.")

"That is soth," quod I, "al be it so that no man dar confessen it ne byknowen it."

"Whi so?" quod sche; "for ryght as the stronge man ne semeth nat to abaissen or dis- daignen as ofte tyme as he herith the noyse of the bataile, ne also it ne semeth nat to the wise man to beren it grevously as ofte 80 as he is lad into the stryf of fortune. For, bothe to the to man and eek to the tothir thilke difficulte is the matere, to the to man of encres of his glorious renoun, and to the tothir man to confermen his sapience (that is to seyn, the asprenesse of his estat). For therfore it is called 'vertu,' for that it sustenith and enforceth by his strengthes that it nis nat overcomen by adversites. Ne certes thou, that art put in the encres or in the heyghte of vertu, ne 90 hast nat comen to fleten with delices, and for to welken in bodily lust; thou sowest or plawntest a ful egre bataile in thy corage ayeins every fortune. For that the sorwful fortune ne confownde the nat, ne that the myrie fortune ne corrumpe the nat, ocupye the mene by stide- fast strengthes. For al that evere is undir the mene, or elles al that overpasseth the mene, despyseth welefulnesse (as who seith, it is vycious), and ne hath no mede of his 100 travaile. For it is set in your hand (as who seith, it lyth in your power) what fortune yow is levest (that is to seyn, good or yvel). For alle fortune that semeth scharp or aspre, yif it ne exercise nat the goode folk ne chastiseth the wikkide folk, it punysseth.

"Bella bis quinis." — Metrum 7

The wrekere Attrides (that is to seyn, Aga- menon), that wroughte and contynued the bat- ailes by ten yer, recovered and purgide in wrekynge, by the destruccioun of Troye, the loste chaumbris of mariage of his brothir. (That is to seyn, that he, Agamenon, wan ayein Eleyne that was Menelaus wif his brothir.) In the mene while that thilke Agamenon de- sirede to yeven sayles to the Grykkyssche naveye, and boughte ayein the wyndes by 10 blood, he unclothide hym of pite of fadir; and the sory preest yeveth in sacrifyenge the wrecchide kuttynge of throte of the doughter. (That is to seyn that Agamenon leet kutten the throte of his doughter by the preest, to maken alliaunce with his goddes, and for to han wynd with which he myghte wenden to Troye.) Ytakus (that is to seyn, Ulixes) bywepte his felawes ilorn, the whiche felawes the fyerse Poliphemus, ligginge in his grete cave, had 20

fretyn and dreynt in his empty wombe. But
natheles Poliphemus, wood for his blynde visage, yald to Ulixes joye by his sorwful teres.
(*This is to seyn, that Ulixes smoot out the eye
of Poliphemus, that stood in his forheed, for
which Ulixes hadde joye whan he say Poliphemus wepynge and blynd*).

Hercules is celebrable for his harde travaile.
He dawntide the proude Centauris (*half
hors, half man*), and he byrafte the dispoil-   30
ynge fro the cruel lyoun (*that is to seyn, he
slough the lyoun and rafte hym his skyn*); he
smote the briddes that hyghten Arpiis with certein arwes; he ravysschide applis fro the wakynge dragoun, and his hand was the more hevy
for the goldene metal; he drowh Cerberus (*the
hound of helle*) by his treble cheyne; he, over-
comer, as it is seyd, hath put an unmeke lord
foddre to his crwel hors (*this to seyn, that
Hercules slowh Diomedes, and made his   40
hors to freten hym*); and he, Hercules,
slowh Idra the serpent, and brende the venym;
and Acheleous the flod, defowled in his forheed, dreynte his schamefast visage in his
strondes (*that is to seyn, that Achaleous coude
transfiguren hymself into divers liknesse, and,
as he faught with Hercules, at the laste he
torned hym into a bole, and Hercules brak oon
of his hornes, and he for schame hidde hym
in his ryver*); and he, Hercules, caste adoun   50
Antheus the geaunt in the strondes of
Libye; and Kacus apaysede the wratthes of
Evander (*this to seyn, that Hercules slouh the
monstre Kacus, and apaysed with that deth the
wratthe of Evander*); and the bristilede boor
markide with scomes the scholdres of Hercules, the whiche scholdres the heye cercle of
hevene sholde thriste; and the laste of his labours was that he susteynede the hevene
uppon his nekke unbowed; and he dis-   60
servide eftsones the hevene to ben the pris
of his laste travaile.

Goth now thanne, ye stronge men, ther as
the heye wey of the greet ensaumple ledith
yow. O nyce men! why nake ye your bakkes?
(*As who seith, 'O ye slowe and delicat men!
whi flee ye adversites, and ne fyghte nat ayeins
hem by vertu, to wynnen the mede of the hev-
ens?'*) For the erthe overcomen yeveth the
sterres. (*This to seyn, that whan that   70
erthly lust is overcomyn, a man is makid
worthy to the hevene.*)"

EXPLICIT LIBER QUARTUS

"Dixerat orationisque cursum." — Prosa 1

Sche hadde seyd, and tornede the cours of
hir resoun to some othere thingis to ben treted
and to ben ispedd. Than seide I, "Certes
ryghtful is thin amonestynge and ful digne by
auctorite. But that thou seydest whilom that
the questioun of the devyne purveaunce is enlaced with many othere questiouns, I undirstande wel and prove it by the same thing.
But I axe yif that thou wenest that hap be
anything in any weys; and yif thou wenest   10
that hap be anything, what is it?"

Thanne quod sche, "I haste me to yelden
and assoilen to the the dette of my byheste, and
to schewen and openen the wey, by which wey
thou maist comen ayein to thi contre. But al
be it so that the thingis whiche that thou
axest ben ryght profitable to knowe, yit ben
thei divers somwhat fro the path of my purpos;
and it is to douten that thou ne be makid
weery by mysweyes, so that thou ne maist   20
nat suffise to mesuren the ryghte weie."

"Ne doute the therof nothing," quod I; "for
for to knowen thilke thingis togidre, in the
whiche thinges I delite me gretly, — that schal
ben to me in stede of reste, syn it nis nat to
douten of the thingis folwynge, whan every
syde of thi disputesoun schal han ben stedfast to me by undoutous feyth."

"Thanne," seide sche, "that manere wol I
don the," and bygan to speken ryght thus: 30
"Certes," quod sche, "yif any wyght diffy-
nisse hap in this manere, that is to seyn that
'hap is a bytydynge ibrought forth by foolissh
moevynge and by no knyttynge of causes,' I
conferme that hap nis ryght naught in no wise;
and I deme al outrely that hap nis, ne duelleth
but a voys (*as who seith, but an idel word*),
withouten any significacioun of thing summitted to that voys. For what place myght
ben left or duellynge to folie and to dis-   40
ordenaunce, syn that God ledeth and constreyneth alle thingis by ordre? For this sentence is verray and soth, that 'no thing hath
his beynge of naught,' to the whiche sentence
noon of thise oolde folk ne withseide nevere;
al be it so that they ne undirstoden ne meneden
it nat by God, prince and bygynnere of wirkynge, but thei casten as a maner foundement
of subject material (*that is to seyn, of the
nature of alle resouns.*) And yif that any   50
thing is woxen or comen of no causes,

thanne schal it seme that thilke thing is comen or woxen of nawght; but yif this ne mai nat ben don, thanne is nat possible that hap be any swich thing as I have diffynysschid a litil herebyforn."

"How schal it thanne be?" quod I. "Nys ther thanne nothing that by right may ben clepid other hap or elles aventure of fortune; or is ther awght, al be it so that it is 60 hidd fro the peple, to which thing thise wordes ben covenable?"

"Myn Aristotles," quod sche, "in the book of his Phisic diffynysseth this thing by schort resoun, and nygh to the sothe."

"In which manere?" quod I.

"As ofte," quod sche, "as men don any thing for grace of any other thing, and an other thing than thilke thing that men entenden to don bytideth by some causes, it is clepid 70 'hap.' Ryght as a man dalf the erthe bycause of tylyinge of the feld, and founde ther a gobet of gold bydolven; thanne wenen folk that it is byfalle by fortunous bytydynge. But forsothe it nis nat of naught, for it hath his propre causes, of whiche causes the cours unforseyn and unwar semeth to han makid hap. For yif the tiliere of the feeld ne dulve nat in the erthe, and yif the hidere of the gold ne hadde hyd the gold in 80 thilke place, the gold ne hadde nat ben founde. Thise ben thanne the causes of the abregginge of fortuit hap, the whiche abreggynge of fortuit hap cometh of causes encontrynge and flowynge togidere to hemself, and nat by the entencioun of the doere. For neither the hidere of the gold ne the delvere of the feeld ne undirstoden nat that the gold sholde han ben founde; but, as I seide, it bytidde and ran togidere that he dalf there as that 90 oothir had hid the gold. Now mai I thus diffinysshen 'hap': hap is an unwar betydinge of causes assembled in thingis that ben doon for som oothir thing; but thilke ordre, procedinge by an uneschuable byndinge togidere, which that descendeth fro the welle of purveaunce, that ordeyneth alle thingis in hir places and in hir tymes, makith that the causes rennen and assemblen togidre.

"Rupis Achemenie." — Metrum 1

Tigrys and Eufrates resolven and springen of o welle in the cragges of the roche of the contre of Achemenye, ther as the fleinge bataile ficcheth hir dartes retorned in the breestis of hem that folwen hem. And sone aftir the same ryverys, Tigris and Eufrates, unjoignen and departen hir watres. And if thei comen togidre, and ben assemblid and clepid togidre into o course, thanne moten thilke thingis 10 fleten togidre whiche that the watir of the entrechaungynge flood bryngeth. The schippes and the stokkes, araced with the flood, moten assemblen; and the watris, imedled wrappeth or emplieth many fortunel happes or maneris; the whiche wandrynge happes natheles thilke enclynynge lowenesse of the erthe and the flowinge ordre of the slydinge watir governeth. Right so fortune, that semeth as it fletith with slakid or ungoverned bridles, it suffreth bridelis (*that is to seyn,* 20 *to ben governed*), and passeth by thilke lawe (*that is to seyn, by the devyne ordenaunce*)."

"Animadverto inquam." — Prosa 2

"This undirstonde I wel," quod I, "and I accorde me that it is ryght as thou seist, but I axe yif ther be any liberte of fre wille in this ordre of causes that clyven thus togidre in hemself. Or elles I wolde witen yif that the destinal cheyne constrenith the moevynges of the corages of men."

"Yis," quod sche, "ther is liberte of fre wil. Ne ther ne was nevere no nature of resoun that it ne hadde liberte of fre wil. For ev- 10 ery thing that may naturely usen resoun, it hath doom by which it discernith and demeth every thing; thanne knoweth it by itself thinges that ben to fleen and thinges that ben to desiren. And thilke thing that any wight demeth to ben desired, that axeth or desireth he; and fleeth thilke thing that he troweth be to fleen. Wherfore in alle thingis that resoun is, in hem also is liberte of willynge and of nillynge. But I ne ordeyne nat (*as who* 20 *seith, I ne graunte nat*) that this liberte be evenelyk in alle thinges. Forwhy in the sovereynes devynes substaunces (*that is to seyn, in spiritz*) jugement is more cleer, and wil nat icorrumped, and myght redy to speden thinges that ben desired. But the soules of men moten nedes be more fre whan thei loken hem in the speculacioun or lokynge of the devyne thought; and lasse fre whan thei slyden into the bodyes; and yit lasse fre whan thei ben gad- 30 rid togidre and comprehended in erthli membres. But the laste servage is whan that thei ben yeven to vices and han ifalle fro the possessioun of hir propre resoun. For aftir that thei han cast awey hir eyghen fro the lyght of the sovereyn sothfastnesse to lowe thingis and derke, anon thei derken by the cloude of ignoraunce and ben troubled by felonous talentz; to the whiche talentz whan thei approchen and assenten, thei hepen and en- 40 crecen the servage which thei han joyned to hemself; and in this manere thei ben caytifs fro hir propre liberte. The whiche thingis natheles the lokynge of the devyne purveaunce seth, that alle thingis byholdeth and seeth fro eterne, and ordeyneth hem everich in here merites as thei ben predestinat; and it is seid in Grek that 'alle thinges he seeth and alle thinges he herith.'

"Puro clarum lumine." — Metrum 2

Homer with the hony mouth (*that is to seyn, Homer with the swete ditees*) singeth that the sonne is cler by pure light; natheles yit ne mai it nat, by the infirme light of his bemes, breken or percen the inward entrayles of the erthe or elles of the see. So ne seth nat God, makere of the grete werld. To hym, that loketh alle thinges from an hey, ne withstondeth no thinges by hevynesse of erthe, ne the nyght ne withstondeth nat to hym by the 10 blake cloudes. Thilke God seeth in o strok of thought alle thinges that ben, or weren, or schollen comen; and thilke God, for he loketh and seeth alle thingis alone, thou maist seyn that he is the verrai sonne."

"Tum ego en inquam." — Prosa 3

Thanne seide I, "Now am I confowndid by a more hard doute than I was."

"What doute is that?" quod sche, "for certes I conjecte now by whiche thingis thou art trubled."

"It semeth," quod I, "to repugnen and to contrarien gretly, that God knoweth byforn alle thinges and that ther is any fredom of liberte. For yif it so be that God loketh alle thinges byforn, ne God ne mai nat ben desceyved in no manere, thanne moot it nedes ben that 10 alle thinges betyden the whiche that the purveaunce of God hath seyn byforn to comen. For which, yif that God knoweth byforn nat oonly the werkes of men, but also hir conseilles and hir willes, thanne ne schal ther be no liberte of arbitrie; ne certes ther ne may be noon other dede, ne no wil, but thilke which that the devyne purveaunce, that ne mai nat ben disseyved, hath felid byforn. For yif that thei

myghten writhen awey in othere manere 20 than thei ben purveyed, thanne ne sholde ther be no stedefast prescience of thing to comen, but rather an uncerteyn opynioun; the whiche thing to trowen of God, I deme felonye and unleveful. Ne I ne proeve nat thilke same resoun (*as who seith, I ne allowe nat, or I ne preyse nat, thilke same resoun*) by which that som men wenen that thei mowe assoilen and unknytten the knotte of this questioun. For certes thei seyn that 30 thing nis nat to comen for that the purveaunce of God hath seyn byforn that it is to comen, but rathir the contrarie; and that is this: that, for that the thing is to comen, that therfore ne mai it nat ben hidd fro the purveaunce of God; and in this manere this necessite slideth ayein into the contrarie partie: ne it ne byhoveth nat nedes that thinges betiden that ben ipurveied, but it byhoveth nedes that thinges that ben to comen ben ipurveied: 40 but, as it were, ytravailed (*as who seith, that thilke answere procedith ryght as though men travaileden or weren besy*) to enqueren the whiche thing is cause of the whiche thing, as whethir the prescience is cause of the necessite of thinges to comen, or elles that the necessite of thinges to comen is cause of the purveaunce. But I ne enforce me nat now to schewen it, that the bytidynge of thingis iwyst byforn is necessarie, how so or in what manere that 50 the ordre of causes hath itself; although that it ne seme naught that the prescience bringe in necessite of bytydinge to thinges to comen. For certes yif that any wyght sitteth, it byhoveth by necessite that the opynioun be soth of hym that conjecteth that he sitteth; and ayeinward also is it of the contrarie: yif the opynioun be soth of any wyght for that he sitteth, it byhoveth by necessite that he sitte. Thanne is here necessite in the toon and 60 in the tothir; for in the toon is necessite of syttynge, and certes in the tothir is necessite of soth. But therfore sitteth nat a wyght for that the opynioun of the sittynge is soth, but the opynioun is rather soth for that a wyght sitteth byforn. And thus, although that the cause of the soth cometh of that other side (*as who seith, that although the cause of soth cometh of the sittynge, and nat of the trewe opinioun*), algates yit is ther comune neces- 70 site in that oon and in that othir. Thus scheweth it that Y may make semblable skiles of the purveaunce of God and of thingis to comen.

For although that for that thingis ben to comen therfore ben thei purveied, and nat certes for thei be purveied therfore ne bytide thei nat; natheles byhoveth it by necessite that eyther the thinges to comen ben ipurveied of God, or elles that the thinges that ben ipurveyed of God betyden. And this thing oonly suf- 80 fiseth inow to destroien the fredom of oure arbitrie (*that is to seyn, of our fre wil*). But certes now scheweth it wel how fer fro the sothe and how up-so-doun is this thing that we seyn, that the betydynge of temporel thingis is cause of the eterne prescience. But for to wenen that God purveieth the thinges to comen for thei ben to comen, — what oothir thing is it but for to wene that thilke thinges that by- tiden whilom ben causes of thilke soverein 90 purveaunce that is in God? And herto I adde yit this thing: that ryght as whanne that I woot that a thing is, it byhoveth by neces- site that thilke selve thing be: and eek whan I have knowen that any thing schal betyden, so byhovith it by necessite that thilke same thing betide: so folweth it thanne that the be- tydynge of the thing that I wyste byforn ne may nat ben eschued. And at the laste, yif that any wyghte wene a thing to ben oothir 100 weyes than it is, it nis nat oonly unscience, but it is desceyvable opynioun ful divers and fer fro the sothe of science. Wherfore, yif any thing be so to comen that the betidynge of it ne be nat certein ne necessarie, who mai witen byforn that thilke thing is to comen? For ryght as science ne may nat ben medled with fals- nesse (*as who seith, that yif I woot a thing, it ne mai nat ben fals that I ne woot it*), ryght so thilke thing that is conceyved by 110 science may ben noon other weies than as it is conceyved. For that is the cause why that sci- ence wanteth lesynge (*as who seith, why that wytynge ne resceyveth nat lesynge of that it woot*); for it byhoveth by necessite that every thing be ryght as science comprehendeth it to be. What schal I thanne seyn? In which man- ere knoweth God byforn the thinges to comen, yif thei ne ben nat certein? For yif that he deme that thei ben to comen uneschew- 120 ably, and so may be that it is possible that thei ne schollen nat comen, God is dis- seyved. But not oonly to trowe that God is dis- seyved, but for to speke it with mouthe, it is a felonous synne. But yif that God woot that ryght so as thinges ben to comen, so schollen they comen, so that he wite egaly (*as who seith,*

indifferently) that thingis mowen ben doon or elles nat idoon, what is thilke prescience that ne comprehendeth no certein thing ne 130 stable? Or elles what difference is ther by- twixe the prescience and thilke japeworthi devynynge of Tyresie the divynour, that seide, 'Al that I seie,' quod he, 'either it schal be or elles it schal nat be?' Or elles how mochel is worth the devyne prescience more than the opinioun of mankynde, yif so be that it dem- eth the thinges uncertayn, as men doon, of the whiche domes of men the betydinge nis nat certein? But yif so be that noon uncer- 140 tein thing ne mai ben in hym that is right certein welle of alle thingis, than is the be- tydinge certein of thilke thingis whiche hath wist byforn fermely to comen. For which it folweth that the fredom of the conseiles and of the werkis of mankynde nis noon, syn that the thought of God, that seeth alle thinges withouten errour of falsnesse, byndeth and con- streyneth hem to a bytidynge by necessite. And yif this thing be oonys igrauntid and 150 resceyved (*this is to seyn, that ther nis no fre wil*), thanne scheweth it wel how gret de- struccioun and how gret damages ther folwen of thingis of mankynde. For in idel ben ther thanne purposed and byhyght medes to goode folk, and peynes to badde folk, syn that no moevynge of fre corage voluntarie ne hath nat disservid hem (*that is to seyn, neither mede ne peyne*). And it scholde seme thanne that thilke thing is alther-worst which that is 160 now demed for alther-moost just and moost ryghtful, that is to seyn that schrewes ben pun- ysschid or elles that goode folk ben iger- doned. The whiche folk, syn that hir propre wil ne sent hem nat to the toon ne to that othir (*that is to seyn, neither to good ne to harm*), but [ther] constreyneth hem certein necessite of thingis to comen; thanne ne schulle ther nevere be, ne nevere were, vice ne vertu, but it scholde rather ben confusion 170 of alle dissertes medlid withouten discre- cioun. And yit ther folweth anothir inconven- ient, of the whiche ther ne mai be thought no more felonous ne more wikke, and that is this: that, so as the ordre of thingis is iled and com- eth of the purveaunce of God, ne that nothing is leveful to the conseiles of mankynde (*as who seith that men han no power to don nothing ne wilne nothing*), thanne folweth it that oure vices ben referrid to the makere of alle 180 good (*as who seith, thanne folweth it that*

God oughte han the blame of our vices, syn he constreyneth us by necessite to doon vices).

Than nis ther no resoun to han hope in God, ne for to preien to God. For what scholde any wyght hopen to God, or why scholde he preien to God, syn that the ordenaunce of destyne, the whiche that mai nat ben enclyned, knytteth and streyneth alle thingis that men mai desiren? Thanne scholde ther be don 190 awey thilke oonly alliaunce bytwixen God and men, that is to seyn, to hopen and to preien. But by the pris of ryghtwisnesse and of verray mekenesse we disserven the gerdon of the devyne grace which that is inestimable (*that is to seyn, that it is so greet that it ne mai nat ben ful ipreysed*). And this is oonly the manere (*that is to seyn, hope and preieris*) for which it semeth that men mowen spekyn with God, and by resoun of supplica- 200 cacion be conjoyned to thilke cleernesse that nis nat aprochid no rather or that men byseken it and impetren it. And yif men ne wene nat that hope ne preieres ne han no strengthis by the necessite of thingis to comen iresceyved, what thing is ther thanne by which we mowen ben conjoyned and clyven to thilke sovereyne prince of thingis? For which it byhoveth by necessite that the lynage of mankynde, as thou songe a litil hereby- 210 forn, be departed and unjoyned from his welle, and failen of his bygynnynge (*that is to seyn, God*).

"Quenam discors." — Metrum 3

What discordable cause hath torent and unjoyned the byndynge or the alliaunce of thingis (*that is to seyn, the conjunccions of God and of man*)? Which God hath establisschid so gret bataile bytwixen these two sothfast or verrei thinges (*that is to seyn, bytwyxen the purveaunce of God and fre wil*) that thei ben singuler and dyvided, ne that they ne wole nat ben medled ne couplid togidre. But 10 ther nis no discord to the verray thinges, but thei clyven alwey certein to hemself. But the thought of man, confownded and overthrowen by the derke membres of the body, ne mai nat be fyr of his derked lookynge (*that is to seyn, by the vigour of his insyghte while the soule is in the body*) knowen the thynne subtile knyttynges of thinges. But wherfore eschaufeth it so by so gret love to fynden thilke notes of soth icovered? (*That is to seyn, wherfore eschaufeth the thought of* 20

man by so gret desir to knowen thilke notificaciouns that ben ihid undir the covertures of soth?*) Woot it aught thilke thing that it angwisshous desireth to knowe? (*As who seith, nay; for no man ne travaileth for to witen thingis that he wot. And therfore the texte seith thus:*) But who travaileth to wite thingis iknowe? And yif that he ne knoweth hem nat, what sekith thilke blynde thoght? What is he that desireth any thyng of which he wot 30 right naught? (*As who seith, whoso desireth any thing, nedes somwhat he knoweth of it, or elles he coude nat desiren it.*) Or who may folwen thinges that ne ben nat iwist? And though that he seke tho thingis, wher schal he fynde hem? What wyght that is al unkunnynge and ignoraunt may knowe the forme that is ifounde? But whanne the soule byholdeth and seeth the heye thought (*that is to seyn, God*), thanne knoweth it togidre the 40 somme and the singularites (*that is to seyn, the principles and everych by hymself*). But now, while the soule is hidd in the cloude and in the derknesse of the membres of the body, it ne hath nat al foryeten itself, but it withholdeth the somme of thinges and lesith the singularites. Thanne who so that sekith sothnesse, he nis in neyther nother habit, for he not nat al, ne he ne hath nat al foryeten; but yit hym remembreth the somme of 50 thinges that he withholdeth, and axeth conseil, and retretith deepliche thinges iseyn byforn (*that is to seyn, the grete somme in his mynde*). So that he mowe adden the parties that he hath foryeten to thilke that he hath withholden."

"Tum illa vetus inquit hec est." — Prosa 4

Than seide sche, "This is," quod sche, "the olde questioun of the purveaunce of God. And Marcus Tullius, whan he devyded the divynaciouns (*that is to seyn, in his book that he wrot of dyvynaciouns*), he moevede gretly this questioun; and thou thiself hast ysoght it mochel, and outrely, and longe. But yit ne hath it nat ben determined, ne isped fermely ne diligently of any of yow. And the cause of this derknesse and of this difficulte is, for that the 10 moevynge of the resoun of mankynde ne may nat moeven to (*that is to seyn, applien or joignen to*) the simplicite of the devyne prescience; the whiche symplicite of the devyne prescience, yif that men myghte thinken it in any manere (*that is to seyn, that yif men myghten thinken and comprehenden the thinges as God seeth hem*), thanne ne scholde ther duelle outrely no doute. The whiche resoun and cause of difficulte I schal assaye 20 at the laste to schewe and to speden, whan I have first ispendid and answered to the resouns by whiche thou art ymoeved. For I axe whi thou wenest that thilke resouns of hem that assoilen this questioun ne be nat speedful inow ne sufficient; the whiche solucioun, or the whiche resoun, for that it demeth that the prescience nis nat cause of necessite to thinges to comen, than weneth it nat that fredom of wil be distorbed or ylet be prescience. 30 For ne drawestow nat argumentz fro elleswhere of the necessite of thingis to comen (*as who seith, any oothir wey than thus*) but that thilke thinges that the prescience woot byforn ne mowen nat unbetyde? (*That is to seyn, that thei moten betide.*) But thanne, yif that prescience ne putteth no necessite to thingis to comen, as thou thiself hast confessed it and byknowen a litel herebyforn, what cause or what is it (*as who seith, ther may no cause 40 be*) by which that the endes voluntarie of thinges myghten be constreyned to certein bytydynge? For by grace of posicioun, so that thou mowe the betere undirstonde this that folweth, I pose that ther ne be no prescience. Thanne axe I," quod sche, "in as moche as aperteneth to that, scholden thanne thingis that comen of fre wil ben constreyned to bytiden by necessite?"

Boecius. "Nay," quod I. 50

"Thanne ayeinward," quod sche, "I suppose that ther be prescience, but that it ne putteth no necessite to thingis; thanne trowe I that thilke selve fredom of wil schal duellen al hool and absolut and unbounden. But thou wolt seyn, al be it so that prescience nis nat cause of the necessite of bytydynge to thingis to comen, algatis yit it is a signe that the thingis ben to bytyden by necessite. By this manere thanne, although the prescience ne 60 hadde nevere iben, yit algate, or at the leste wey, it is certein thing that the endes and bytydinges of thingis to comen scholden ben necessarie. For every signe scheweth and signifieth oonly what the thing is, but it ne makith nat the thing that it signifieth. For which it byhoveth first to schewen that nothing ne bytideth that it ne betideth by necessite, so that it mai apiere that the prescience is signe of this necessite; or elles, yif ther nere 70

no necessite, certes thilke prescience ne myghte nat ben signe of thing that nis nat. But certes, it is now certein that the proeve of this, ysusteyned by stedfast resoun, ne schal nat ben lad ne proeved by signes, ne by argumentz itaken fro withoute, but by causes covenable and necessarie. But thou mayst seyn, 'How may it be that the thingis ne betyden nat that ben ipurveied to comen?' But certes, ryght as we trowen that tho thingis 80 whiche that the purveaunce woot byforn to comen, ne ben nat to bytiden. But that ne scholde we nat demen; but rathir, although that thei schal betyden, yit ne have thei no necessite of hir kynde to betyden. And this maystow lyghtly aperceyven by this that I schal seyn. For we seen many thingis whan thei ben don byforn oure eyen, ryght as men seen the cartere worken in the tornynge or in atemprynge or adressynge of his cartes or chariottes. 90 And by this manere (*as who seith, maistow undirstonden*) of alle othere werkmen. Is ther thanne any necessite (*as who seith, in our lookynge*) that constreynith or compelleth any of thilke thingis to ben don so?"

Boece. "Nay," quod I, "for in idel and in veyn were al the effect of craft, yif that alle thingis weren moeved by constreynynge (*that is to seyn, by constreinynge of oure eyen or of our sighte*)." 100

Philosophie. "The thingis thanne," quod sche, "that, whan men doon hem, ne han no necessite that men doon hem, eek tho same thingis, first er thei ben don, thei ben to comen withoute necessite. Forwhy ther ben some thingis to betyden, of whiche the eendes and the bytydynges of hem ben absolut and quit of alle necessite. For certes I ne trowe nat that any man wolde seyn this: that tho thingis that men don now, that thei ne weren to 110 bytiden first or thei weren idoon; and thilke same thinges, although that men hadden iwyst hem byforn, yit thei han fre bytydynges. For right as science of thingis present ne bryngith in no necessite to thingis that men doon, right so the prescience of thinges to comen ne bryngith in no necessite to thinges to bytiden. But thou maist seyn that of thilke same it is idouted, as whethir that of thilke thingis that ne han noon issues and bytidynges 120 necessaries, yif therof mai ben any prescience; for certes thei semen to discorden. For thou wenest, yif that thingis ben iseyen byfore, that necessite folwith hem; and yif necessite

faileth hem, thei ne myghten nat ben wist byforn, and that nothing may be comprehended
by science but certein; and yif tho thinges that
ne han no certein bytydingis ben ipurveied
as certein, it scholde ben dirknesse of opinioun, nat sothfastnesse of science. And   130
thou wenest that it be dyvers fro the holnesse of science that any man scholde deme a
thing to ben otherwyse than it is itself. And
the cause of this errour is that of alle the thingis
that every wyght hath iknowe, thei wenen that
tho thingis ben iknowe al only by the strengthe
and by the nature of the thinges that ben iwyst
or iknowe. And it is al the contrarye; for al
that evere is iknowe, it is rather comprehendid and knowen, nat aftir his strengthe   140
and his nature, but aftir the faculte (*that
is to seyn, the power and the nature*) of hem
that knowen. And, for that this schal mowen
schewen by a schort ensaumple, the same
rowndnesse of a body, otherweys the sighte
of the eighe knoweth it, and otherweys the
touchynge. The lookynge, by castynge of his
bemys, waiteth and seeth fro afer al the body
togidre, withoute moevynge of itself; but
the touchynge clyveth and conjoyneth to   150
the rounde body, and moeveth aboute the
envyrounynge, and comprehendeth by parties
the roundnesse. And the man hymself, ootherweys wit byholdeth hym, and ootherweys
ymaginacioun, and otherweyes resoun, and
ootherweies intelligence. For the wit comprehendith withoute-forth the figure of the body
of the man that is establisschid in the matere
subgett; but the ymaginacioun comprehendith oonly the figure withoute the ma-   160
tere; resoun surmountith ymaginacioun
and comprehendith by an universel lokynge the
comune spece that is in the singuler peces; but
the eighe of the intelligence is heyere, for it
surmountith the envyrounynge of the universite, and loketh over that bi pure subtilte of
thought thilke same symple forme of man that
is perdurablely in the devyne thought. In
which this oughte gretly to ben considered,
that the heyeste strengthe to compre-   170
henden thinges enbraseth and contienith
the lowere strengthe; but the lowere strengthe
ne ariseth nat in no manere to the heyere
strengthe. For wit ne mai no thing comprehende out of matere ne the ymaginacioun loketh nat the universels speces, ne resoun ne
taketh nat the symple forme so as intelligence
takith it; but intelligence, that lookith al aboven,

whanne it hath comprehended the forme,
it knoweth and demyth alle the thinges   180
that ben undir that foorme. But sche
knoweth hem in thilke manere in the whiche it
comprehendeth thilke same symple forme that
ne may nevere ben knowen to noon of that
othere (*that is to seyn, to non of the thre forseyde strengthis of the soule*). For it knoweth
the universite of resoun, and the figure of ymaginacioun, and the sensible material conceyved
by wit; ne it ne useth nat nor of resoun ne
of ymaginacioun ne of wit withoute-forth;   190
but it byholdeth alle thingis, so as I schal
seie, by a strook of thought formely withoute
discours or collacioun. Certes resoun, whan it
lokith any thing universel, it ne useth nat of
ymaginacioun, nor of wit; and algates yit it comprehendith the thingis ymaginable and sensible.
For resoun is she that diffynyscheth the universel of here conceyte ryght thus: — Man is a
resonable two-foted beest. And how so
that this knowynge is universel, yit is ther   200
no wyght that ne wot wel that a man is a
thing ymaginable and sensible; and this same
considereth wel resoun; but that nis nat by
ymaginacioun nor by wit, but it lookith it by
resonable concepcioun. Also ymaginacioun,
albeit so that it takith of wit the bygynnynges to
seen and to formen the figures, algates although
that wit ne were nat present, yit it envyrowneth
and comprehendith alle thingis sensible;
nat by resoun sensible of demynge, but by   210
resoun ymaginatyf. Seestow nat thanne
that alle the thingis in knowynge usen more of
hir faculte or of hir power than thei don of the
faculte or power of thingis that ben iknowe?
Ne that nis nat wrong; for so as every jugement
is the dede or the doyng of hym that demeth,
it byhoveth that every wyght performe the
werk and his entencioun, nat of foreyn power,
but of his propre power.

"Quondam porticus attulit." — Metrum 4

The porche (*that is to seyn, a gate of the
toun of Athenis there as philosophris hadden
hir congregacioun to desputen*) — thilke porche
broughte somtyme olde men, ful dirke in hir
sentences (*that is to seyn, philosophris that
hyghten Stoyciens*), that wenden that ymages
and sensibilities (*that is to seyn, sensible ymaginaciouns or ellis ymaginaciouns of sensible
thingis*) weren enprientid into soules fro
bodyes withoute-forth (*as who seith that   10
thilke Stoyciens wenden that sowle had ben*

nakid of itself, as a mirour or a clene parche-
myn, so that alle figures most first comen fro
thingis fro withoute into soules, and ben em-
prientid into soules); ryght as we ben wont
somtyme by a swift poyntel to fycchen lettres
emprientid in the smothnesse or in the pleyn-
esse of the table of wex or in parchemyn that
ne hath no figure ne note in it. (*Glose. But*
now argueth Boece ayens that opynioun 20
and seith thus:) But yif the thryvynge soule
ne unpliteth nothing (*that is to seyn, ne doth*
nothing) by his propre moevynges, but suffrith and lith subgit to the figures and to the
notes of bodies withoute-forth, and yeldith ymages ydel and vein in the manere of a mirour,
whennes thryveth thanne or whennes comith
thilke knowynge in our soule, that discernith
and byholdith alle thinges? And whennes
is thilke strengthe that byholdeth the 30
singuler thinges? Or whennes is the
strengthe that devydeth thinges iknowe; and
thilke strengthe that gadreth togidre the thingis
devyded; and the strengthe that chesith his
entrechaunged wey? For somtyme it hevyth
up the heved (*that is to seyn, that it hevyth*
up the entencioun to ryght heye thinges), and
somtyme it descendith into ryght lowe thinges;
and whan it retorneth into hymself it
reproveth and destroyeth the false thingis 40
by the trewe thinges. Certes this strengthe
is cause more efficient, and mochel more
myghty to seen and to knowe thinges, than
thilke cause that suffrith and resceyveth the
notes and the figures empressid in manere
of matere. Algatis the passion (*that is to seyn,*
the suffraunce or the wit) in the quyke body
goth byforn, excitynge and moevynge the
strengthes of the thought. Ryght so as
whan that cleernesse smyteth the eyen and 50
moeveth hem to seen, or ryght so as voys or
soun hurteleth to the eres and commoeveth hem
to herkne; than is the strengthe of the thought
imoevid and excited, and clepith forth to semblable moevyngis the speces that it halt withynne itself, and addith tho speces to the notes
and to the thinges withoute-forth, and medleth
the ymagis of thinges withoute-forth to the
foormes ihidd withynne hymself.

"*Quod si in corporibus sentiendis.*"
     — Prosa 5

But what yif that in bodyes to ben feled
(*that is to seyn, in the takynge of knowlech-*

ynge of bodily thinges), and albeit so that
qualites of bodies that ben object fro withoute-
forth moeven and entalenten the instrumentz
of the wittes, and albeit so that the passioun
of the body (*that is to seyn, the wit or the suf-*
fraunce) goth toforn the strengthe of the wirkynge corage, the whiche passioun or suf-
raunce clepith forth the dede of the 10
thought in hymself and moeveth and exciteth in this menewhile the formes that resten
within-forth — and yif that in sensible bodies,
as I have seid, our corage nis nat ytaught or
empriented by passioun to knowe thise thinges,
but demeth and knoweth of his owne strengthe
the passioun or suffrance subject to the body,
moche more than tho thingis that ben absolut
and quit fro alle talentz or affecciouns of
bodyes (*as God or his aungelis*) ne folwen 20
nat in discernynge thinges object fro withoute-forth, but thei acomplissen and speden
the dede of hir thought. By this resoun,
thanne, ther comen many maner knowynges to
dyverse and to differynge substaunces. For the
wit of the body, the whiche wit is naked and
despoiled of alle oothre knowynges, — thilke
wit cometh to beestis that ne mowen nat
moeven hemself her and ther, as oistres
and muscles and oothir swich schelle-fyssch 30
of the see, that clyven and ben norisschid to
roches. But the ymaginacioun cometh to remuable bestis, that semen to han talent to fleen
or to desiren any thing. But resoun is al oonly
to the lynage of mankynde, ryght as intelligence is oonly the devyne nature. Of which
it folweth that thilke knowynge is more worth
than thise oothre, syn it knoweth by his propre
nature nat oonly his subget (*as who seith,*
it ne knoweth nat al oonly that apertenith 40
properly to his knowinge) but it knoweth
the subject of alle othre knowynges. But how
schal it thanne be, yif that wit and ymaginacioun stryven ayein resonynge, and seyn that,
of thilke universel thingis that resoun weneth to seen, that it nis ryght naught? For wit
and ymaginacioun seyn that that that is sensible or ymaginable, it ne mai nat ben universel. Thanne is either the jugement of
resoun soth, ne that ther nis no thing sen- 50
sible; or elles, for that resoun woot wel
that many thinges ben subject to wit and to
ymaginacioun, thanne is the concepcioun of
resoun veyn and fals, which that lokith and
comprehendith that that is sensible and singuler as universel. And yif that resoun wolde

answere ayein to thise two (*that is to seyn, to wit and to ymaginacioun*), and seyn that sothly sche hirselve (*that is to seyn, resoun*) lokith and comprehendith, by re- 60 soun of universalite, bothe that that is sensible and that that is ymaginable; and that thilke two (*that is to seyn, wit and ymaginacioun*) ne mowen nat strecchen ne enhaunsen hemself to knowynge of universalite, for that the knowynge of hem ne mai exceden ne surmounten the bodily figures: certes of the knowynge of thinges, men oughten rather yeven credence to the more stidfast and to the more parfit jugement. In this manere stryv- 70 ynge, thanne, we that han strengthe of resonynge and of ymagynynge and of wit (*that is to seyn, by resoun and by imagynacioun and by wit*) — we scholde rathir preise the cause of resoun (*as who seith, than the cause of wit and ymaginacioun*).

Semblable thing is it, that the resoun of mankynde ne weneth nat that the devyne intelligence byholdeth or knoweth thingis to comen, but ryght as the resoun of man- 80 kynde knoweth hem. For thou arguist and seist thus: that if it ne seme nat to men that some thingis han certeyn and necessarie bytydynges, thei ne mowen nat ben wist byforn certeinly to betyden, and thanne nis ther no prescience of thilke thinges; and yif we trowe that prescience be in thise thingis, thanne is ther nothing that it ne bytydeth by necessite. But certes yif we myghten han the jugement of the devyne thoght, as we ben 90 parsoners of resoun, ryght so as we han demyd that it byhovith that ymaginacioun and wit ben bynethe resoun, ryght so wolde we demen that it were ryghtfull thing, that mannys resoun oughte to summytten itself and to ben bynethe the devyne thought. For which yif that we mowen (*as who seith that, if that we mowen, I conseile that*) we enhaunse us into the heighte of thilke soverein intelligence; for ther schal resoun wel seen that that it 100 ne mai nat byholden in itself. And certes that is this, in what manere the prescience of God seeth alle thinges certeins and diffinyssched, although thei ne han no certein issues or bytydyngis; ne this nis noon opinioun, but it is rather the simplicite of the soverein science, that nis nat enclosed nor ischet withinne none boundes.

The beestes passen by the erthes be ful diverse figures. For some of hem han hir bodyes straught, and crepyn in the dust, and drawen aftir hem a traas or a furwe icontynued (*that is to sein, as naddres or snakes*); and oothre beestis, by the wandrynge lyghtnesse of hir wynges beten the wyndes, and oversywmmen the spaces of the longe eir by moyst fleynge; and oothere beestes gladen hemself to diggen hir traas or hir steppys in the erthe 10 with hir goinges or with hir feet, and to gon either by the grene feeldes, or elles to walken undir the wodes. And al be it so that thou seest that thei alle discorden by diverse foormes, algatis hir faces enclyned hevyeth hir dulle wittes. Only the lynage of man heveth heyest his heie heved, and stondith light with his upryght body, and byholdeth the erthes undir hym. And, but yif thou, erthly man, waxest yvel out of thi wit, this figure 20 amonesteth the, that axest the hevene with thi ryghte visage, and hast areised thi forheved to beren up an hy thi corage, so that thi thought ne be nat ihevyed ne put lowe undir fote, syn that thi body is so heyghe areysed.

Therfore thanne, as I have schewed a litel herebyforn that alle thing that is iwist nis nat knowen by his nature propre, but by the nature of hem that comprehenden it, lat us loke now, in as mochil as it is leveful to us (*as who seith, lat us loke now as we mowen*) which that the estat is of the devyne substaunce; so that we mowe eek knowen what his science is. The comune jugement of alle creatures resonables thanne is this: that God is eterne. 10 Lat us considere thanne what is eternite; for certes that schal schewen us togidre the devyne nature and the devyne science. Eternite, thanne, is parfit possessioun and altogidre of lif interminable. And that scheweth more cleerly by the comparysoun or collacioun of temporel thinges. For alle thing that lyveth in tyme, it is present, and procedith fro preteritz into futures (*that is to seyn, fro tyme passed into tyme comynge*), ne ther nis nothing 20 establisshed in tyme that mai enbrasen togidre al the space of his lif. For certis yit ne hath it nat taken the tyme of tomorwe, and it hath lost that of yisterday. And certes in the lif of this dai ye ne lyve namore but right as in this moevable and transitorie moment. Thanne thilke thing that suffreth temporel condicioun, although that it nevere bygan to be, ne though it nevere ne cese for to be, as Aristotile demed of the world, and althogh 30 that the lif of it be strecchid with infinite of tyme; yit algatis nis it no swich thing that men mighten trowen by ryghte that it is eterne. For although that it comprehende and embrase the space of lif infinit, yit algatis ne enbraseth it nat the space of the lif altogidre; for it ne hath nat the futuris that ne ben nat yit, ne it ne hath no lengere the preteritz that ben idoon or ipassed. But thilke thing, thanne, that hath and comprehendith togidre al the 40 plente of the lif interminable, to whom ther ne faileth naught of the future, and to whom ther nis noght of the preteryt escaped nor ipassed, thilke same is iwitnessed and iproevid by right to ben eterne; and yit it byhovith by necessite that thilke thing be alwey present to hymself, and compotent (*as who seith, alwey present to hymselve, and so myghty that al be right at his plesaunce*), and that he have al present the infinite of the moevable tyme. 50 Wherfore som men trowen wrongfully that, whan thei heren that it semede to Plato that this world ne hadde nevere bygynnynge of tyme, ne that it nevere schal han failynge, thei wenen in this manere that this world be makid coeterne with his makere. (*As who seith, thei wene that this world and God ben makid togidre eterne, and that is a wrongful wenynge.*) For other thing is it to ben ilad by lif interminable, as Plato grauntide to the 60 world, and oothir is it to enbrace togidre al the presence of the lif intermynable, the whiche thing it is cleer and manyfest that it is propre to the devyne thought. Ne it ne scholde nat semen to us that God is eldere than thinges that ben imaked by quantite of tyme, but rathir by the proprete of his simple nature. For this ilke infinit moevyng of temporel thinges folweth this presentarie estat of the lif unmoevable; and, so as it ne mai nat contrefetin it, ne feynen 70 it, ne be evene lik to it, for the immoevablete (*that is to sein, that is in the eternite of God*), it faileth and fallith into moevynge fro the simplicite of the presence of God, and discresith into the infinit quantite of futur and of preterit. And so as it ne mai nat han togidre al the plente of the lif, algates yit for as moche as it ne ceseth nevere for to ben in som manere, it semyth somdel to us that it folwith and resembleth thilke thing that it ne mai 80 nat atayne to, ne fulfillen; and byndeth itself to som maner presence of this litle and swifte moment, the whiche presence of this litle and swifte moment, for that it bereth a maner ymage or liknesse of the ai duellynge presence of God, it grauntith to swich manere thinges as it betydith to, that it semeth hem that thise thinges han iben and ben. And for that the presence of swich litil moment ne mai nat duelle, therfore it ravysschide and 90 took the infynit wey of tyme (*that is to seyn, by successioun*). And by this manere is it idoon, for that it sholde contynue the lif in goinge, of the whiche lif it myght nat enbrace the plente in duellinge. And forthi yif we wollen putten worthi names to thinges and folwen Plato, lat us seyen thanne sothly that God is 'eterne,' and that the world is 'perpetuel.' Thanne, syn that every jugement knoweth and comprehendith by his 100 owne nature thinges that ben subgect unto hym, ther is sothly to God alweys an eterne and presentarie estat; and the science of hym that overpasseth alle temporel moevement duelleth in the simplicite of his presence, and embraceth and considereth alle the infynit spaces of tymes preteritz and futures, and lokith in his simple knowynge alle thingis of preterit ryght as thei weren idoon presently ryght now. Yif thou wolt thanne thinken 110 and avise the prescience by which it knoweth alle thinges, thou ne schalt naught demen it as prescience of thinges to comen, but thou schalt demen more ryghtfully that it is science of presence or of instaunce that nevere ne faileth. For which it nis nat ycleped 'previdence,' but it sholde rathir ben clepid 'purveaunce,' that is establisshed ful fer fro ryght lowe thinges, and byholdeth fro afer alle thingis, right as it were fro the heye heighte of 120 thinges.

Why axestow thanne, or whi desputestow thanne, that thilke thingis ben doon by necessite whiche that ben yseyn and knowen by the devyne sighte, syn that forsothe men ne maken nat thilke thinges necessarie whiche that thei seen ben idoon in hir sighte? For addith thi byholdynge any necessite to thilke thinges that thou byholdest present?"

"Nay," quod I.   130

Philosophie. "Certes, thanne, yif men myghte maken any digne comparysoun or collacioun of the presence devyne and of the

presence of mankynde, ryght so as ye seen
some thinges in this temporel present, ryght
so seeth God alle thinges by his eterne present.

Wherfore this devyne prescience ne chaungeth nat the nature ne the proprete of thinges,
but byholdeth swiche thingis present to
hym-ward as thei shollen betyde to yow-   140
ward in tyme to comen. Ne it ne confowndeth nat the jugementz of thingis; but by
o sight of his thought he knoweth the thinges
to comen, as wel necessarie as nat necessarie.
Ryght so as whan ye seen togidre a man walke
on the erthe and the sonne arisen in the hevene, albeit so that ye seen and byholden the
ton and the tothir togidre, yit natheles ye
demen and discerne that the toon is voluntarie and the tother is necessarie. Ryght   150
so thanne the devyne lookynge, byholdynge alle thinges undir hym, ne trowbleth nat
the qualite of thinges that ben certeinly present to hym-ward; but, as to the condicioun of
tyme, forsothe thei ben futur. For which it folwith that this nis noon opynioun, but rathir a
stidfast knowynge istrengthid by soothnesse
that, whan that God knoweth any thing to be,
he ne unwot not that thilke thing wanteth
necessite to be. (*This is to sein that whan*   160
that God knoweth any thing to betide, he
wot wel that it ne hath no necessite to betyde.)
And yif thou seist here that thilke thing that
God seeth to betide, it ne may nat unbytide
(*as who seith, it moot bytide*), and thilke thing
that ne mai nat unbytide, it mot bytiden by
necessite, and that thou streyne me to this name
of necessite, certes I wol wel confessen and byknowen a thing of ful sad trouthe. But unnethe schal ther any wight mowe seen it   170
or come therto, but yif that he be byholdere of the devyne thought. For I wol answeren the thus: that thilke thing that is futur,
whan it is referred to the devyne knowynge,
than is it necesserie; but certis whan it is undirstonden in his owene kynde, men seen it
outrely fre and absolut fro alle necessite.

For certes ther ben two maneris of neces-
sites: that oon necessite is symple, as thus:
that it byhovith by necessite that alle men   180
ben mortal or dedly; anothir necessite is
condicionel, as thus: yif thou wost that a man
walketh, it byhovith by necessite that he walke.
Thilke thing, thanne, that any wight hath
iknowe to be, it ne mai ben noon oothir weys
thanne he knowith it to be. But this condicion
draweth nat with hir thilke necessite sim-

ple; for certes this necessite condicionel — the
propre nature of it ne makith it nat, but the
adjeccioun of the condicioun makith it.   190
For no necessite ne constreyneth a man to
gon that goth by his propre wil, al be it so that
whan he goth that it is necessarie that he goth.
Ryght on this same manere thanne, yif that
the purveaunce of God seeth any thyng present, than moot thilke thing ben by necessite,
althogh that it ne have no necessite of his owne
nature. But certes the futures that bytiden
by fredom of arbitrie, God seth hem alle
togidre presentz. Thise thinges thanne,   200
yif thei ben referrid to the devyne sighte,
than ben they maked necessarie by the condicioun of the devyne knowynge. But certes
yif thilke thingis ben considered by hemself,
thei ben absolut of necessite, and ne forleten
nat ne cesen nat of the liberte of hir owne nature. Thanne certes withoute doute alle the
thinges shollen ben doon whiche that God woot
byforn that thei ben to comen. But some of
hem comen and bytiden of fre arbitrie or   210
fre wil, that, al be it so that thei bytiden,
yit algates ne lese thei nat hir propre nature
in beinge; by the whiche first, or that thei
weren idon, thei hadden power noght to han
bytyd."

Boece. "What is this to seyn thanne," quod
I, "that thinges ne ben nat necessarie by hir
propre nature, so as thei comen in alle maneris in the liknesse of necessite by the condicioun of the devyne science?"   220

Philosophie. "This is the difference,"
quod sche, "that tho thinges that I purposide
the a litel herbyforn (*that is to seyn, the sonne*
arysynge and the man walkynge), that ther-
whiles that thilke thinges ben idoon, they ne
myghte nat ben undoon; natheles that oon of
hem, or it was idoon, it byhovide by necessite
that it was idoon, but nat that oothir. Ryght
so is it here, that the thinges that God hath
present, withoute doute thei shollen ben.   230
But som of hem descendith of the nature
of thinges (*as the sonne arysynge*); and som
descendith of the power of the doeris (*as the*
man walkynge). Thanne seide I no wrong
that, yif that thise thinges ben referred to the
devyne knowynge, thanne ben thei necessarie;
and yif thei ben considered by hemself, than
ben thei absolut fro the boond of necessite.
Right so as alle thingis that apiereth or
scheweth to the wittes, yif thou referre it   240
to resoun, it is universel; and yif thou loke

it or referre it to itself, than is it singuler. But
now yif thou seist thus: that, 'If it be in my power
to chaunge my purpos, than schal I voiden the
purveaunce of God, whan peraventure I schal
han chaungid the thingis that he knoweth byforn,' thanne schal I answeren the thus: 'Certes
thou maist wel chaungen thi purpos; but for as
mochel as the present sothnesse of the devyne purveaunce byholdeth that thou maist
chaunge thi purpos, and whethir thou wolt
chaunge it or no, and whider-ward that
thou torne it, thou ne maist nat eschuen the
devyne prescience, ryght as thou ne maist nat
fleen the sighte of the present eye, althogh that
thou torne thiself by thi fre wil into diverse
acciouns.' But thou maist sein ayein: 'How
schal it thanne be — schal nat the devyne science ben chaunged by my disposicioun
whan that I wol o thing now and now anothir? And thilke prescience — ne semeth it
nat to entrechaunge stoundis of knowynge?' "
(*As who seith, ne schal it nat seme to us that
the devyne prescience entrechaungith his diverse stoundes of knowynge, so that it knowe
somtyme o thing, and somtyme the contrarie?*)
"No, forsothe," quod I.
"For the devyne sighte renneth toforn, and
seeth alle futures, and clepith hem ayen,
and retorneth hem to the presence of his
propre knowynge; ne he ne entrechaungith
nat, so as thou wenest, the stoundes of fore-
knowynge, as now this, now that; but he ay
duellynge cometh byforn, and enbraseth at o
strook alle thi mutaciouns. And this presence
to comprehenden and to seen alle thingis —
God ne hath nat taken it of the bytidynge of

thinges to come, but of his propre symplicite.
And herby is assoiled thilke thing that
thou puttest a litel herebyforn, that is to
seyn, that it is unworthy thing to seyn that
our futures yeven cause of the science of God.
For certis this strengthe of the devyne science,
which that embraseth alle thinges by his presentarie knowynge, establissheth manere to alle
thinges, and it ne oweth nawht to lattere
thinges. And syn that thise thinges ben thus
(*that is to seyn, syn that necessite nis nat in
thinges by the devyne prescience*), thanne
is ther fredom of arbitrie, that duelleth
hool and unwemmed to mortal men; ne
the lawes ne purposen nat wikkidly medes and
peynes to the willynges of men, that ben unbownden and quyt of all necessite; and God,
byholdere and forwytere of alle thingis, duelleth above, and the present eternite of his
sighte renneth alwey with the diverse qualite
of our dedes, dispensynge and ordeynynge
medes to gode men and tormentz to wikkide men. Ne in ydel ne in veyn ne ben
ther put in God hope and preyeris that
ne mowen nat ben unspedful ne withouten
effect whan they been ryghtful.
Withstond thanne and eschue thou vices;
worschipe and love thou vertues; areise thi
corage to ryghtful hopes; yilde thou humble
preieres an heygh. Gret necessite of prowesse
and vertu is encharged and comaunded to yow,
yif ye nil nat dissimulen; syn that ye
worken and don (*that is to seyn, your
dedes or your werkes*) byforn the eyen of
the juge that seeth and demeth alle thinges."

Explicit liber Boecii

TROILUS AND CRISEYDE

❧

IN THE *Troilus and Criseyde* Chaucer reached the height of his powers. The later *Canterbury Tales,* to be sure, reveal new qualities — a wider range of interest, greater variety of style, perhaps a more modern tone, more independence of what we regard as mediæval sentiments and conventions. But there is no advance in narrative skill, or in characterization, or in the mastery of verse form. The *Troilus* is Chaucer's supreme example of sustained narration, the *Knight's Tale* alone being in any way comparable. And it remains unsurpassed in its kind in later English poetry.

The time of its composition is not definitely known, but it is hard to believe, as some have held, that so mature a performance can be early work. One or two indications — an apparent allusion to the Peasants' Revolt and a very probable compliment to Queen Anne — point to a date in the eighties; and if, as seems likely, the conjunction of Jupiter and Saturn in the sign of Cancer, described in Book III, was suggested by the actual occurrence of that very rare phenomenon in 1385, the completion of the poem cannot be put earlier than that year. This date would be entirely satisfactory from the point of view of literary considerations. The *Troilus* would immediately precede the *Prologue to the Legend of Good Women,* in which Chaucer represents himself as required to do penance for having, among other sins, related the story of the faithless Criseyde. It would surely be considerably later than the *House of Fame,* which we have seen to belong to the period of transition from French to Italian influence. And it would probably follow also the original version of the *Knight's Tale,* the *Palamon and Arcite,* though the two romances from Boccaccio, different as they are in method and treatment, cannot have been far apart in time of composition.

These two chief narrative poems of Chaucer, the *Troilus* and the *Knight's Tale,* are alike in having their immediate sources in long poems of Boccaccio, and in dealing with material drawn from the ancient cycles of romance. In the case of the *Knight's Tale* the main plot was apparently Boccaccio's invention, or at all events has not been traced beyond the Teseida But the history of the Troilus story is more complicated. In Homer, as might be expected, there is no trace of it. Though several great Homeric figures, Priam and Hector and Achilles and Diomedes, play their part in the *Troilus,* the chief actors in Chaucer's poem — Pandarus, and Criseyde (the Greek Chryseis in name only), and Troilus himself — count for little in the Iliad. Pandarus is mentioned only twice, as a leader of the Lycians and a great archer, slain by Diomedes; and Troilus is dismissed in a single line of lamentation for his death. The story of Troilus and Cressida does not even appear in Dares Phrygius or Dictys Cretensis, those ultimate "authorities" of the mediæval Trojan saga. But the way is prepared for it in Dares by the exaltation of Troilus to a place second only to Hector among the warriors of Troy. It was first related, so far as is known, by Benoit de Ste.-Maure, the author of the Roman de Troie. Some scholars have conjectured that he had a source for it in a longer version of Dares, now lost. But until more evidence is given of the existence of such a text, the invention of this French poet of the twelfth century must be credited with the story which became for the later Middle Ages and the Renaissance the most interesting episode of the Trojan War.

Benoit tells only the second part of the tale, beginning with the separation of the lovers on the departure of Criseyde from Troy. The heroine, in his version, is named Briseide, and not Criseyde, probably because Benoit found in Dares a portrait of Briseis, which may indeed have given him the first suggestion for the episode. But Troilus's Briseide has as little in common with the daughter of Briseus (or Brises) as Criseyde has with the Homeric Chryseis. According to the Iliad, it will be recalled, Briseis and Chryseis were Trojan girls taken captive by Achilles, and in the division of spoils Briseis was awarded to him and Chryseis to Agamemnon. Later, in obedience to Apollo, Chryseis was restored to her father, and Achilles was induced to relinquish Briseis to his superior commander. In resentment at the injustice Achilles long refrained from aiding the Greeks in battle. Now Briseis and Chryseis are of course patronymic forms, meaning, respectively, daughter of Briseus and daughter of Chryses. The real names of the girls, according to the scholiasts and later authorities, were Hippodamia and Astynome; and under the French equivalents of these (Ypodamia and Astinome) Benoit, in a passage later than the Troilus episode (ll. 26837–27037), tells the Homeric story, doubtless taken over from Dictys. He obviously failed to recognize the identity of his Briseide with Ypodamia, and was unaware that he had assigned two distinct rôles to the daughter of Briseus. In fact, in his ignorance of the meaning of Briseide's name, he made her the daughter of Calcas (Calchas), the Trojan seer.

The next author to tell the tale was Guido delle Colonne, in his Historia Trojana. Guido's work was merely a Latin prose redaction of Benoit's, which it largely superseded as an authority on the history of Troy. It had no independent value and contributed nothing to the development of the Troilus story. It did, however, help greatly to disseminate knowledge of the whole Trojan legend.

In the Roman de Troie the account of Troilus and Criseyde is only an episode, interrupted by other incidents, but well told and effective in pathetic appeal. In the hands of the next teller, Boccaccio, it becomes a complete poem, "with beginning, middle, and end," and charged with passionate interest. The intensity of feeling is largely due to the fact that Boccaccio wrote the Filostrato as an expression of devotion to Maria d'Acquino, and Troilo, in his ardent suit and final unhappiness, represents the author himself in his character of unaccepted lover. The entire first half of the poem, which recounts the wooing and winning of Criseida, was Boccaccio's invention, drawn partly from his personal experience and partly from the stories of Achilles and Polixena in the Roman de Troie and of Florio and Biancafiore in his own earlier romance, the Filocolo. Boccaccio added the essential figure of Pandaro, whose name alone he derived from earlier writers. For some reason also he changed the name of Troilus's beloved from Briseida to Criseida. Perhaps he simply adopted the altered form from Armannino, who mentions "Calchas, father to Criseide" in his Florita, written in 1325. Boccaccio doubtless knew from Ovid's Heroides of the true Homeric history of Briseis and Achilles; in fact he refers to it in the Ameto and the Filocolo. And if in substituting the name derived from Chryseis he was simply starting a new confusion, the story of Chryseis was in any event less familiar than the other. Moreover, Boccaccio, or whoever first made the change, may have been led by a misunderstanding of Ovid's Remedia Amoris (ll. 467–484) to think that Chryseis was the daughter of Calchas; and the fact that Calcas, in Benoit, is Briseide's father, would have supported the alteration.

The Filostrato was the immediate and principal source of Chaucer's *Troilus*. (This statement seems likely to prove essentially true in spite of the recent, still unpublished, discoveries of Professor Pratt concerning the relations of Chaucer's poem and the French prose translation of the Filostrato by Beauveau, Seneschal of Anjou. The exact nature and extent of Chaucer's possible indebtedness to Beauveau can not be judged until Mr. Pratt's study is completed.) The Filostrato and the Teseida, the source of the *Knight's Tale*, were models of narrative such as Chaucer had hardly encountered until he read Boccaccio; or if he knew specimens of equal excellence in the Latin poets, at all events his own first attempts of the kind were his adaptations of the Filostrato and the Teseida. The greatness of his debt to Boccaccio has been pointed out in the discussion of the *Knight's Tale*. But, much as he owed to his Italian models, neither of Chaucer's poems is a mere translation or servile redaction of its original; and the methods of adaptation in the two works are utterly dissimilar. In the *Knight's Tale*, as has been shown, a long, sometimes diffuse and digressive poem on the model of a classical epic has been reduced to a swiftly moving, highly dramatic romance of a quarter of its length; whereas in the *Troilus* a simple story of passion and sorrow has been expanded into what has often been called a psychological novel. In thus elaborating the Filostrato Chaucer improved the plot, and made the setting more vivid and more appropriate to its period. He gave the dialogue, which was good in the Italian original, his characteristic naturalness and humor, and sometimes a subtlety that is hardly matched in the best conversational passages in the *Canterbury Tales*. He enriched the whole narrative with moral and philosophical reflection. And above all, he transformed the characterization.

Troilus, the simplest character of the three protagonists, remains much the same as in Boccaccio. He is strong and brave — "Hector the secounde"; sentimental, it may be granted, and unpractical, but no weakling; gallant and generous to the end — the ideal courtly lover.

Boccaccio's Pandaro, though the character was his invention, is not highly individualized. He is Criseida's cousin and a young comrade of Troilo, the success of whose suit he serves without scruple. Chaucer, by making him a generation older — Criseyde's uncle — at once complicates his character. As an elder relative and supposed protector of Criseyde he has obligations of which he is not wholly unaware, while doing his best to further Troilus's suit. In his relations with Troilus he combines the rôles of a valiant friend, ready for any sacrifice, and of a philosophical adviser. His comments on life — often phrased in proverbial language, of which he is a master — are wise and humorous. They sometimes express disillusionment, for which experience and observation had given him plenty of occasion, but cynicism, which has been attributed to him, was not in his nature. And in his own rôle of an unsuccessful old suitor who has always "hopped on behind" in

the dance of love, he is an object of amused sympathy alike to fellow characters and to readers.

Boccaccio's Criseida, again, is a relatively simple personality. Widows, according to the assumption of Pandaro, are by nature amorous, and she yields to Troilo with less persuasion and intrigue than is needed to win Chaucer's Criseyde. With Diomed, also, after her separation from Troilo, she rather readily accepts consolation. She is, of course, no mere wanton, as she is sometimes called, and as she became in English tradition after Chaucer. Boccaccio makes the reader feel, as he makes Troilo praise, her qualities of a gentlewoman — her *atti altieri e signorali*. But on the whole her conduct and emotions are simple and easy to understand. Chaucer's Criseyde, on the other hand, is one of the most complex of his creations. This is made apparent by the very disagreements of the critics in their search for a key to her character. Some have found the explanation of her, or at least of Chaucer's treatment of her, in the idea of fate, which undoubtedly pervades the poem. For some she is merely selfish and designing, but these forget her sincere affection. For others she is simply weak, the helpless victim of intrigue and circumstances; yet to a great extent she makes her own decisions. In spite of her tenderness and passion, as is not seldom the case with women, she is less sentimental and more practical than either Pandarus or Troilus. She has in her even something of the skeptical or disillusioned woman, a type in which Chaucer felt enough interest to portray it again in the Pertelote of the *Nun's Priest's Tale*. In the end circumstances are too strong for her and destroy her happiness with Troilus. Troilus, undeceived, but loving to the end, meets death bravely in battle. Criseyde, also loving and — we must understand — sincere in her bitter self-reproach, has made a practical compromise with fate and gone to Diomed. For in her nature tenderness was allied with *slidynge corage*, and not with the loyalty that suffers and endures. This was her condemnation and, in the moral sense, her tragedy.

Where Chaucer got the suggestions for his

conception of Pandarus and Criseyde it would
be interesting to know. Perhaps there were
living models for them both, as there seem to
have been for several of the Canterbury pilgrims, at the by no means unsophisticated court
of Richard and Anne. The elderly Pandarus, it
has been shown, may also owe something to
the figure of Duke Ferramonte in Boccaccio's
Filocolo. If there is any literary model for
Criseyde, it is perhaps to be found in the Helen
of Ovid's *Heroides.*

It is now generally recognized by critics that
the *Troilus* is governed by the conventions of
courtly love. But the fact may properly be
emphasized here, it is so essential to the understanding of the poem. According to the ethics
of the system, neither Troilus nor Criseyde was
blameworthy for their union. It was expected
that love should be sought outside of marriage.
Even the offices of Pandarus as go-between
were not to be condemned, except as they con-
flicted with his duty to protect his niece's
honor. At that point, perhaps, the ordinary
code of morals was felt to intervene. Criseyde's
sin lay not in yielding to Troilus, but in "fals-
ing" Troilus for Diomed. The code, of course,
was absolutely un-Christian and doubtless out
of keeping with any stable system of social
morality. How far it was actually practiced in
mediæval society is a matter of dispute. But as
set forth in literature it was by no means without its ideal aspects. It deprecated coarseness
and mere sensuality. It was the very mark and
test of "gentilesse." The lover was expected to
acquire all the accomplishments and display all
the virtues — bravery, humility, honor, loyalty,
generosity. Love was a fine art, and its pursuit
was held to ennoble the character, so that any
courtly "servant" might have used of his lady
the familiar words of Sir Richard Steele, "To
love her is a liberal education." Beyond question the ideal of courtly love actually contributed to the refinement of life in the Middle
Ages and the Renaissance. There is no better
product or expression of the convention than
the *Troilus.* And when Chaucer has followed
the tragic story to the end his closing comment
is not, like Boccaccio's, a mere condemnation
of faithless women; nor is it strictly a reproba-

tion of the special ethics of courtly love. It is
a Christian counsel to fix the heart upon the
unfailing love of God. The earnestness of the
appeal and the elevation of its mood leave no
doubt of Chaucer's essentially religious spirit.
Moreover, it is not necessary to assume, as
some have held, that the Christian comment
was written long after the body of the poem,
in a moment of repentance such as called forth
the *Retracciouns* of the *Canterbury Tales.* It
expresses, on the contrary, exactly the feeling
by which Chaucer might have been possessed
at the moment when he was deeply moved by
his tale of "double sorwe."

As has been already indicated, and will be
shown in detail in the explanatory notes, Chaucer constantly went beyond the Filostrato for
the materials of the *Troilus.* It sometimes
seems as if a chronology of his poems might
almost be based upon the various degrees of
complication which they exhibit. His earliest
tales, such as the life of St. Cecilia (the *Second
Nun's Tale*) or the episode of Ceyx and Alcione
in *The Book of the Duchess,* tell a simple story
and depart very little from their sources. The
latest tales, on the other hand — even short
ones, like those of the Nun's Priest and the
Pardoner — are so overlaid with original elements and with borrowings from every quarter
that it matters little from what source the skel-
eton of the plot was derived. By this test the
individual legends of *Good Women* would be
classed with the earlier works. While the quality of complication is not susceptible of exact
measurement, the *Troilus* certainly shows it in
a high degree. Not only is the plot altered and
elaborated, apparently with the repeated use
of the Filocolo, the Roman de Troie, and the
Eneas; and the characterization improved, perhaps under the influence of Ovid; but songs are
derived from Petrarch and, probably, Machaut;
a series of portraits are taken from Joseph of
Exeter; and the whole poem is packed with
popular proverbs and allusions to literature,
both ancient and mediæval.

Among the authors who influenced the
thought of the poem, as distinguished from its
fable, should be mentioned particularly Boethius and Dante. To Boethius, for example,

may be traced Criseyde's discussion of false felicity in the third book — a speech similar to one of Arcite's in the *Knight's Tale*, which is derived from the same source. In the treatment of *gentilesse* and in many sentiments expressed by the lovers is reflected a knowledge of both Boethius and Dante, and possibly of some of Dante's fellow-poets of the *dolce stil nuovo*. And the influence of Boethius and Dante is again especially apparent, both in the *Troilus* and elsewhere, in Chaucer's discussions of fate.

In the *Troilus*, as has been already remarked, the idea of fate is pervasive. It is so fundamental, indeed, to the development of the story that one of the ablest investigators of Chaucer's scientific and philosophical background, Professor Walter Clyde Curry, has expounded the poem as a tragedy of complete and consistent determinism. The speech of Troilus on predestination, in the fourth book, expresses the doctrine, he maintains, which for Chaucer as a literary artist governed the whole action. The epilogue, which contains the comments of Chaucer as a Christian, is for Mr. Curry out of keeping with the rest of the poem and "dramatically a sorry performance." The artistic propriety of the epilogue may always be a matter of dispute, and its acceptability to the reader will depend in some measure upon his attitude toward explicit moralization. But it is not necessary to find any deep conflict between the epilogue and the story. The destinal forces, it is true, are recognized in the *Troilus* at every turn. But they are also fully described and analyzed by Boethius, as Mr. Curry himself sets forth; and he might have cited similar discussions in Dante. In Boethius and Dante the recognition of these forces is made to harmonize with a doctrine of responsibility and free-will, as it is in the daily assumptions of practical life. Chaucer's own attitude in relation to such matters was probably practical rather than deeply philosophical; and in any case it may be doubted whether he had worked out, even for dramatic purposes, a thorough-going determinism at variance with the teachings of his authorities.

Troilus and Criseyde

Book I

The double sorwe of Troilus to tellen,
That was the kyng Priamus sone of Troye,
In lovynge, how his aventures fellen
Fro wo to wele, and after out of joie,
My purpos is, er that I parte fro ye.   5
Thesiphone, thow help me for t'endite
Thise woful vers, that wepen as I write.

To the clepe I, thow goddesse of torment,
Thow cruwel Furie, sorwynge evere yn peyne,
Help me, that am the sorwful instrument,   10
That helpeth loveres, as I kan, to pleyne.
For wel sit it, the sothe for to seyne,
A woful wight to han a drery feere,
And to a sorwful tale, a sory chere.

For I, that God of Loves servantz serve,   15
Ne dar to Love, for myn unliklynesse,
Preyen for speed, al sholde I therfore sterve,
So fer am I from his help in derknesse.
But natheles, if this may don gladnesse
To any lovere, and his cause availle,   20
Have he my thonk, and myn be this travaille!

But ye loveres, that bathen in gladnesse,
If any drope of pyte in yow be,
Remembreth yow on passed hevynesse
That ye han felt, and on the adversite   25
Of othere folk, and thynketh how that ye
Han felt that Love dorste yow displese,
Or ye han wonne hym with to gret an ese.

And preieth for hem that ben in the cas
Of Troilus, as ye may after here,   30
That Love hem brynge in hevene to solas;
And ek for me preieth to God so dere

That I have myght to shewe, in som manere,
Swich peyne and wo as Loves folk endure,
In Troilus unsely aventure.   35

And biddeth ek for hem that ben despeired
In love that nevere nyl recovered be,
And ek for hem that falsly ben apeired
Thorugh wikked tonges, be it he or she;
Thus biddeth God, for his benignite,   40
So graunte hem soone owt of this world to pace,
That ben despeired out of Loves grace.

And biddeth ek for hem that ben at ese,
That God hem graunte ay good perseveraunce,
And sende hem myght hire ladies so to plese   45
That it to Love be worship and plesaunce.
For so hope I my sowle best avauntz,
To prey for hem that Loves servauntz be,
And write hire wo, and lyve in charite,

And for to have of hem compassioun,   50
As though I were hire owne brother dere.
Now herkneth with a good entencioun,
For now wil I gon streght to my matere,
In which ye may the double sorwes here
Of Troilus in lovynge of Criseyde,   55
And how that she forsook hym er she deyde.

    Yt is wel wist how that the Grekes, stronge
In armes, with a thousand shippes, wente
To Troiewardes, and the cite longe
Assegeden, neigh ten yer er they stente,   60
And in diverse wise and oon entente,
The ravysshyng to wreken of Eleyne,
By Paris don, they wroughten al hir peyne.

Now fel it so that in the town ther was
Dwellynge a lord of gret auctorite,   65
A gret devyn, that clepid was Calkas,
That in science so expert was that he
Knew wel that Troie sholde destroied be,
By answere of his god, that highte thus,
Daun Phebus or Appollo Delphicus.   70

So whan this Calkas knew by calkulynge,
And ek by answer of this Appollo,
That Grekes sholden swich a peple brynge,
Thorugh which that Troie moste ben fordo,
He caste anon out of the town to go;   75
For wel wiste he by sort that Troye sholde
Destroyed ben, ye, wolde whoso nolde.

For which for to departen softely
Took purpos ful this forknowynge wise,

And to the Grekes oost ful pryvely   80
He stal anon; and they, in curteys wise,
Hym diden bothe worship and servyse,
In trust that he hath konnynge hem to rede
In every peril which that is to drede.

The noise up ros, whan it was first aspied   85
Thorugh al the town, and generaly was spoken,
That Calkas traitour fled was and allied
With hem of Grece, and casten to be wroken
On hym that falsly hadde his feith so broken,
And seyden he and al his kyn at-ones   90
Ben worthi for to brennen, fel and bones.

Now hadde Calkas left in this meschaunce,
Al unwist of this false and wikked dede,
His doughter, which that was in gret penaunce,
For of hire lif she was ful sore in drede,   95
As she that nyste what was best to rede;
For bothe a widewe was she and allone
Of any frend to whom she dorste hir mone.

Criseyde was this lady name al right.
As to my doom, in al Troies cite   100
Nas non so fair, for passynge every wight
So aungelik was hir natif beaute,
That lik a thing inmortal semed she,
As doth an hevenyssh perfit creature,   104
That down were sent in scornynge of nature.

This lady, which that alday herd at ere
Hire fadres shame, his falsnesse and tresoun,
Wel neigh out of hir wit for sorwe and fere,
In widewes habit large of samyt broun,
On knees she fil biforn Ector adown   110
With pitous vois, and tendrely wepynge,
His mercy bad, hirselven excusynge.

Now was this Ector pitous of nature,
And saugh that she was sorwfully bigon,
And that she was so fair a creature;   115
Of his goodnesse he gladede hire anon,
And seyde, "Lat youre fadres treson gon
Forth with meschaunce, and ye youreself in
         joie
Dwelleth with us, whil yow good list, in Troie.

"And al th'onour that men may don yow have,
As ferforth as youre fader dwelled here,   121
Ye shul have, and youre body shal men save,
As fer as I may ought enquere or here."
And she hym thonked with ful humble chere,
And ofter wolde, and it hadde ben his wille,   125
And took hire leve, and hom, and held hir stille.

And in hire hous she abood with swich meyne
As til hire honour nede was to holde;
And whil she was dwellynge in that cite,
Kepte hir estat, and both of yonge and olde 130
Ful wel biloved, and wel men of hir tolde.
But wheither that she children hadde or noon,
I rede it naught; therfore I late it goon.

The thynges fellen, as they don of werre,
Bitwixen hem of Troie and Grekes ofte; 135
For som day boughten they of Troie it derre,
And eft the Grekes founden nothing softe
The folk of Troie; and thus Fortune on lofte,
And under eft, gan hem to whielen bothe 139
Aftir hir course, ay whil that thei were wrothe.

But how this town com to destruccion
Ne falleth naught to purpos me to telle;
For it were here a long digression
Fro my matere, and yow to long to dwelle.
But the Troian gestes, as they felle, 145
In Omer, or in Dares, or in Dite,
Whoso that kan may rede hem as they write.

But though that Grekes hem of Troie shetten,
And hir cite biseged al aboute,
Hire olde usage nolde they nat letten, 150
As for to honoure hir goddes ful devoute;
But aldirmost in honour, out of doute,
Thei hadde a relik, heet Palladion,
That was hire trist aboven everichon.

And so bifel, whan comen was the tyme 155
Of Aperil, whan clothed is the mede
With newe grene, of lusty Veer the pryme,
And swote smellen floures white and rede,
In sondry wises shewed, as I rede,
The folk of Troie hire observaunces olde, 160
Palladiones feste for to holde.

And to the temple, in al hir beste wise,
In general ther wente many a wight,
To herknen of Palladion the servyse;
And namely, so many a lusty knyght, 165
So many a lady fressh and mayden bright,
Ful wel arayed, both meste, mene, and leste,
Ye, bothe for the seson and the feste.

Among thise othere folk was Criseyda,
In widewes habit blak; but natheles, 170
Right as oure firste lettre is now an A,
In beaute first so stood she, makeles.
Hire goodly lokyng gladed al the prees.
Nas nevere yet seyn thyng to ben preysed derre,
Nor under cloude blak so bright a sterre 175

As was Criseyde, as folk seyde everichone
That hir behelden in hir blake wede.
And yet she stood ful lowe and stille allone,
Byhynden other folk, in litel brede,
And neigh the dore, ay undre shames drede, 180
Simple of atir and debonaire of chere,
With ful assured lokyng and manere.

This Troilus, as he was wont to gide
His yonge knyghtes, lad hem up and down
In thilke large temple on every side, 185
Byholding ay the ladies of the town,
Now here, now there; for no devocioun
Hadde he to non, to reven hym his reste,
But gan to preise and lakken whom hym leste.

And in his walk ful faste he gan to wayten 190
If knyght or squyer of his compaignie
Gan for to syke, or lete his eighen baiten
On any womman that he koude espye.
He wolde smyle and holden it folye,
And seye hym thus, "God woot, she slepeth
softe 195
For love of the, whan thow turnest ful ofte!

"I have herd told, pardieux, of youre lyvynge,
Ye loveres, and youre lewed observaunces,
And which a labour folk han in wynnynge 199
Of love, and in the kepyng which doutaunces;
And whan youre prey is lost, woo and pen-
aunces.
O veray fooles, nyce and blynde be ye!
Ther nys nat oon kan war by other be."

And with that word he gan caste up the browe,
Ascaunces, "Loo! is this naught wisely spoken?"
At which the God of Love gan loken rowe 206
Right for despit, and shop for to ben wroken.
He kidde anon his bowe nas naught broken;
For sodeynly he hitte hym atte fulle;
And yet as proud a pekok kan he pulle. 210

O blynde world, O blynde entencioun!
How often falleth al the effect contraire
Of surquidrie and foul presumpcioun;
For kaught is proud, and kaught is debonaire.
This Troilus is clomben on the staire, 215
And litel weneth that he moot descenden;
But alday faileth thing that fooles wenden.

As proude Bayard gynneth for to skippe
Out of the weye, so pryketh hym his corn,
Til he a lasshe have of the longe whippe; 220
Than thynketh he, "Though I praunce al byforn

First in the trays, ful fat and newe shorn,
Yet am I but an hors, and horses lawe
I moot endure, and with my feres drawe";

So ferde it by this fierse and proude knyght:
Though he a worthy kynges sone were,   226
And wende nothing hadde had swich myght
Ayeyns his wille that shuld his herte stere,
Yet with a look his herte wax a-fere,
That he that now was moost in pride above,   230
Wax sodeynly moost subgit unto love.

Forthy ensample taketh of this man,
Ye wise, proude, and worthi folkes alle,
To scornen Love, which that so soone kan
The fredom of youre hertes to hym thralle;   235
For evere it was, and evere it shal byfalle,
That Love is he that alle thing may bynde,
For may no man fordon the lawe of kynde.

That this be soth, hath preved and doth yit.
For this trowe I ye knowen alle or some,   240
Men reden nat that folk han gretter wit
Than they that han be most with love ynome;
And strengest folk ben therwith overcome,
The worthiest and grettest of degree:
This was, and is, and yet men shal it see.   245

And trewelich it sit wel to be so.
For alderwisest han therwith ben plesed;
And they that han ben aldermost in wo,
With love han ben comforted moost and esed;
And ofte it hath the cruel herte apesed,   250
And worthi folk maad worthier of name,
And causeth moost to dreden vice and shame.

Now sith it may nat goodly ben withstonde,
And is a thing so vertuous in kynde,
Refuseth nat to Love for to ben bonde,   255
Syn, as hymselven liste, he may yow bynde.
The yerde is bet that bowen wole and wynde
Than that that brest; and therfore I yow rede
To folowen hym that so wel kan yow lede.

But for to tellen forth in special   260
As of this kynges sone of which I tolde,
And leten other thing collateral,
Of hym thenke I my tale forth to holde,
Bothe of his joie and of his cares colde;
And al his werk, as touching this matere,   265
For I it gan, I wol therto refere.

Withinne the temple he wente hym forth
          pleyinge,
This Troilus, of every wight aboute,

On this lady, and now on that, lokynge,
Wher so she were of town or of withoute;   270
And upon cas bifel that thorugh a route
His eye percede, and so depe it wente,
Til on Criseyde it smot, and ther it stente.

And sodeynly he wax therwith astoned,
And gan hir bet biholde in thrifty wise.   275
"O mercy, God," thoughte he, "wher hastow woned,
That art so feyr and goodly to devise?"
Therwith his herte gan to sprede and rise,
And softe sighed, lest men myghte hym here,
And caught ayeyn his firste pleyinge chere.   280

She nas nat with the leste of hire stature,
But alle hire lymes so wel answerynge
Weren to wommanhod, that creature
Was nevere lasse mannyssh in semynge.
And ek the pure wise of hire mevynge   285
Shewed wel that men myght in hire gesse
Honour, estat, and wommanly noblesse.

To Troilus right wonder wel with alle
Gan for to like hire mevynge and hire chere,
Which somdel deignous was, for she let falle
Hire look a lite aside in swich manere,   291
Ascaunces, "What! may I nat stonden here?"
And after that hir lokynge gan she lighte,
That nevere thoughte hym seen so good a
          syghte.

And of hire look in him ther gan to quyken   295
So gret desir and such affeccioun,
That in his hertes botme gan to stiken
Of hir his fixe and depe impressioun.
And though he erst hadde poured up and
          down,
He was tho glad his hornes in to shrinke;   300
Unnethes wiste he how to loke or wynke.

Lo, he that leet hymselven so konnynge,
And scorned hem that Loves peynes dryen,
Was ful unwar that Love hadde his dwellynge
Withinne the subtile stremes of hir yen;   305
That sodeynly hym thoughte he felte dyen,
Right with hire look, the spirit in his herte.
Blissed be Love, that kan thus folk converte!

She, this in blak, likynge to Troilus
Over alle thing, he stood for to biholde;   310
Ne his desir, ne wherfore he stood thus,
He neither chere made, ne word tolde;
But from afer, his manere for to holde,

On other thing his look som tyme he caste,
And eft on hire, while that the servyse laste. 315

And after this, nat fullich al awhaped,
Out of the temple al esilich he wente,
Repentynge hym that he hadde evere ijaped
Of Loves folk, lest fully the descente   319
Of scorn fille on hymself; but what he mente,
Lest it were wist on any manere syde,
His woo he gan dissimulen and hide.

Whan he was fro the temple thus departed,
He streght anon unto his paleys torneth,
Right with hire look thorugh-shoten and
        thorugh-darted,   325
Al feyneth he in lust that he sojorneth;
And al his chere and speche also he borneth,
And ay of Loves servantz every while,
Hymself to wrye, at hem he gan to smyle,

And seyde, "Lord, so ye lyve al in lest,   330
Ye loveres! for the konnyngeste of yow,
That serveth most ententiflich and best,
Hym tit as often harm therof as prow.
Youre hire is quyt ayeyn, ye, God woot how!
Nought wel for wel, but scorn for good servyse.
In feith, youre ordre is ruled in good wise! 336

"In nouncerteyn ben alle youre observaunces,
But it a sely fewe pointes be;
Ne no thing asketh so gret attendaunces
As doth youre lay, and that knowe alle ye   340
But that is nat the worste, as mote I the!
But, tolde I yow the worste point, I leve,
Al seyde I soth, ye wolden at me greve.

"But take this: that ye loveres ofte eschuwe,
Or elles doon, of good entencioun,   345
Ful ofte thi lady wol it mysconstruwe,
And deme it harm in hire oppynyoun;
And yet if she, for other enchesoun,
Be wroth, than shaltow have a groyn anon.   349
Lord, wel is hym that may ben of yow oon!"

But for al this, whan that he say his tyme,
He held his pees; non other boote hym gayned;
For love bigan his fetheres so to lyme,
That wel unnethe until his folk he fayned
That other besy nedes hym destrayned;   355
For wo was hym, that what to doon he nyste,
But bad his folk to gon wher that hem liste.

And whan that he in chambre was allone,
He doun upon his beddes feet hym sette,

And first he gan to sike, and eft to grone, 360
And thought ay on hire so, withouten lette,
That, as he sat and wook, his spirit mette
That he hire saugh a-temple, and al the wise
Right of hire look, and gan it newe avise.

Thus gan he make a mirour of his mynde,   365
In which he saugh al holly hire figure;
And that he wel koude in his herte fynde,
It was to hym a right good aventure
To love swich oon, and if he dede his cure
To serven hir, yet myghte he falle in grace, 370
Or ellis for oon of hire servantes pace;

Imaginynge that travaille nor grame
Ne myghte for so goodly oon be lorn
As she, ne hym for his desir no shame,
Al were it wist, but in pris and up-born   375
Of alle lovers wel more than biforn;
Thus argumented he in his gynnynge,
Ful unavysed of his woo comynge.

Thus took he purpos loves craft to suwe,
And thoughte he wolde werken pryvely,   380
First to hiden his desir in muwe
From every wight yborn, al outrely,
But he myghte ought recovered be therby;
Remembryng hym that love to wide yblowe
Yelt bittre fruyt, though swete seed be sowe. 385

And over al this, yet muchel more he thoughte
What for to speke, and what to holden inne;
And what to arten hire to love he soughte,
And on a song anon-right to bygynne,
And gan loude on his sorwe for to wynne;   390
For with good hope he gan fully assente
Criseyde for to love, and nought repente.

And of his song naught only the sentence,
As writ myn auctour called Lollius,
But pleinly, save oure tonges difference,   395
I dar wel seyn, in al that Troilus
Seyde in his song, loo! every word right thus
As I shal seyn; and whoso list it here,
Loo, next this vers he may it fynden here.

Canticus Troili.

"If no love is, O God, what fele I so?   400
And if love is, what thing and which is he?
If love be good, from whennes cometh my woo?
If it be wikke, a wonder thynketh me,
When every torment and adversite   404
That cometh of hym, may to me savory thinke,
For ay thurst I, the more that ich it drynke.

"And if that at myn owen lust I brenne,
From whennes cometh my waillynge and my
          pleynte?
If harm agree me, wherto pleyne I thenne?
I noot, ne whi unwery that I feynte.   410
O quike deth, O swete harm so queynte,
How may of the in me swich quantite,
But if that I consente that it be?

"And if that I consente, I wrongfully
Compleyne, iwis. Thus possed to and fro,   415
Al sterelees withinne a boot am I
Amydde the see, bitwixen wyndes two,
That in contrarie stonden evere mo.
Allas! what is this wondre maladie?
For hete of cold, for cold of hete, I dye."   420

And to the God of Love thus seyde he
With pitous vois, "O lord, now youres is
My spirit, which that oughte youres be.
Yow thanke I, lord, that han me brought to
          this.
But wheither goddesse or womman, iwis,   425
She be, I not, which that ye do me serve;
But as hire man I wol ay lyve and sterve.

"Ye stonden in hir eighen myghtily,
As in a place unto youre vertu digne;
Wherfore, lord, if my service or I   430
May liken yow, so beth to me benigne;
For myn estat roial I here resigne
Into hire hond, and with ful humble chere
Bicome hir man, as to my lady dere."

In hym ne deyned spare blood roial   435
The fyr of love — the wherfro God me blesse —
Ne him forbar in no degree for al
His vertu or his excellent prowesse,
But held hym as his thral lowe in destresse,
And brende hym so in soundry wise ay newe,
That sexti tyme a day he loste his hewe.   441

So muche, day by day, his owene thought,
For lust to hire, gan quiken and encresse,
That every other charge he sette at nought.
Forthi ful ofte, his hote fir to cesse,   445
To sen hire goodly lok he gan to presse;
For therby to ben esed wel he wende,
And ay the ner he was, the more he brende.

For ay the ner the fir, the hotter is, —
This, trowe I, knoweth al this compaignye. 450
But were he fer or ner, I dar sey this:
By nyght or day, for wisdom or folye,

His herte, which that is his brestes ye,
Was ay on hire, that fairer was to sene
Than evere was Eleyne or Polixene.   455

Ek of the day ther passed nought an houre
That to hymself a thousand tyme he seyde,
"Good goodly, to whom serve I and laboure,
As I best kan, now wolde God, Criseyde,
Ye wolden on me rewe, er that I deyde!   460
My dere herte, allas! myn hele and hewe
And lif is lost, but ye wol on me rewe."

Alle other dredes weren from him fledde,
Both of th'assege and his savacioun;
N'yn him desir noon other fownes bredde,   465
But argumentes to this conclusioun,
That she of him wolde han compassioun,
And he to ben hire man, while he may dure.
Lo, here his lif, and from the deth his cure!

The sharpe shoures felle of armes preve,   470
That Ector or his othere brethren diden,
Ne made hym only therfore ones meve;
And yet was he, where so men wente or riden,
Founde oon the beste, and lengest tyme abiden
Ther peril was, and dide ek swich travaille 475
In armes, that to thynke it was merveille.

But for non hate he to the Grekes hadde,
Ne also for the rescous of the town,
Ne made hym thus in armes for to madde,
But only, lo, for this conclusioun: 480
To liken hire the bet for his renoun.
Fro day to day in armes so he spedde,
That the Grekes as the deth him dredde.

And fro this forth tho refte hym love his slep,
And made his mete his foo, and ek his sorwe
Gan multiplie, that, whoso tok kep,   486
It shewed in his hewe both eve and morwe.
Therfor a title he gan him for to borwe
Of other siknesse, lest men of hym wende
That the hote fir of love hym brende,   490

And seyde he hadde a fevere and ferde amys.
But how it was, certeyn, kan I nat seye,
If that his lady understood nat this,
Or feynede hire she nyste, oon of the tweye;
But wel I rede that, by no manere weye,   495
Ne semed it as that she of hym roughte,
Or of his peyne, or whatsoevere he thoughte.

But thanne felte this Troilus swich wo,
That he was wel neigh wood; for ay his drede

Was this, that she som wight hadde loved
   so,   500
That nevere of hym she wolde han taken hede.
For which hym thoughte he felte his herte
   blede;
Ne of his wo ne dorste he nat bygynne
To tellen hir, for al this world to wynne.

But whan he hadde a space from his care,   505
Thus to hymself ful ofte he gan to pleyne;
He seyde, "O fool, now artow in the snare,
That whilom japedest at loves peyne.
Now artow hent, now gnaw thin owen cheyne!
Thow were ay wont ech lovere reprehende   510
Of thing fro which thou kanst the nat defende.

"What wol now every lovere seyn of the,
If this be wist? but evere in thin absence
Laughen in scorn, and seyn, 'Loo, ther goth he
That is the man of so gret sapience,   515
That held us loveres leest in reverence.
Now, thanked be God, he may gon in the
   daunce
Of hem that Love list febly for to avaunce.

"But, O thow woful Troilus, God wolde,
Sith thow most loven thorugh thi destine,   520
That thow beset were on swich oon that sholde
Know al thi wo, al lakked hir pitee!
But also cold in love towardes the
Thi lady is, as frost in wynter moone,
And thow fordon, as snow in fire is soone.   525

"God wold I were aryved in the port
Of deth, to which my sorwe wol me lede!
A, Lord, to me it were a gret comfort;
Than were I quyt of languisshyng in drede.
For, be myn hidde sorwe iblowe on brede,   530
I shal byjaped ben a thousand tyme
More than that fol of whos folie men ryme.

"But now help, God, and ye, swete, for whom
I pleyne, ikaught, ye, nevere wight so faste!
O mercy, dere herte, and help me from   535
The deth, for I, while that my lyf may laste,
More than myself wol love yow to my laste.
And with som frendly lok gladeth me, swete,
Though nevere more thing ye me byheete."

Thise wordes, and ful many an other to,   540
He spak, and called evere in his compleynte
Hire name, for to tellen hire his wo,
Til neigh that he in salte teres dreynte.
Al was for nought: she herde nat his pleynte;

And whan that he bythought on that folie,   545
A thousand fold his wo gan multiplie.

Bywayling in his chambre thus allone,
A frend of his, that called was Pandare,
Com oones in unwar, and herde hym groone,
And say his frend in swich destresse and care.
"Allas," quod he, "who causeth al this fare?   551
O mercy, God! what unhap may this meene?
Han now thus soone Grekes maad yow leene?

"Or hastow som remors of conscience,
And art now falle in som devocioun,   555
And wailest for thi synne and thin offence,
And hast for ferde caught attricioun?
God save hem that biseged han oure town,
That so kan leye oure jolite on presse,
And bringe oure lusty folk to holynesse!"   560

Thise wordes seyde he for the nones alle,
That with swich thing he myght hym angry
   maken,
And with an angre don his wo to falle,
As for the tyme, and his corage awaken.
But wel he wist, as fer as tonges spaken,   565
Ther nas a man of gretter hardinesse
Thanne he, ne more desired worthinesse.

"What cas," quod Troilus, "or what aventure
Hath gided the to sen me langwisshinge,
That am refus of every creature?   570
But for the love of God, at my preyinge,
Go hennes awey, for certes my deyinge
Wol the disese, and I mot nedes deye;
Therfore go wey, ther is na more to seye.

"But if thow wene I be thus sik for drede,   575
It is naught so, and therfore scorne nought.
Ther is another thing I take of hede
Wel more than aught the Grekes han yet
   wrought,
Which cause is of my deth, for sorowe and
   thought.
But though that I now telle it the ne leste,   580
Be thow naught wroth; I hide it for the beste."

This Pandare, that neigh malt for wo and
   routhe,
Ful ofte seyde, "Allas! what may this be?
Now frend," quod he, "if evere love or trouthe
Hath ben, or is, bitwixen the and me,   585
Ne do thow nevere swich a crueltee
To hiden fro thi frend so gret a care!
Wostow naught wel that it am I, Pandare?

"I wol parten with the al thi peyne,
If it be so I do the no comfort,   590
As it is frendes right, soth for to seyne,
To entreparten wo as glad desport.
I have, and shal, for trewe or fals report,
In wrong and right iloved the al my lyve:
Hid nat thi wo fro me, but telle it blyve."   595

Than gan this sorwful Troylus to syke,
And seide hym thus: "God leve it be my beste
To telle it the; for sith it may the like,
Yet wol I telle it, though myn herte breste.
And wel woot I thow mayst do me no reste;
But lest thow deme I truste nat to the,   601
Now herke, frend, for thus it stant with me.

"Love, ayeins the which whoso defendeth
Hymselven most, hym alderlest avaylleth,
With disespeyr so sorwfulli me offendeth,   605
That streight unto the deth myn herte sailleth.
Therto desir so brennyngly me assailleth,
That to ben slayn it were a gretter joie
To me than kyng of Grece ben and Troye.

"Suffiseth this, my fulle frend Pandare,   610
That I have seyd, for now wostow my wo;
And for the love of God, my colde care,
So hide it wel — I tolde it nevere to mo.
For harmes myghten folwen mo than two,
If it were wist; but be thow in gladnesse,   615
And lat me sterve, unknowe, of my destresse."

"How hastow thus unkyndely and longe
Hid this fro me, thow fol?" quod Pandarus.
"Paraunter thow myghte after swich oon longe,
That myn avys anoon may helpen us."   620
"This were a wonder thing," quod Troilus.
"Thow koudest nevere in love thiselven wisse:
How devel maistow brynge me to blisse?"

"Ye, Troilus, now herke," quod Pandare;
"Though I be nyce, it happeth often so,   625
That oon that excesse doth ful yvele fare
By good counseil kan kepe his frend therfro.
I have myself ek seyn a blynd man goo
Ther as he fel that couthe loken wide;
A fool may ek a wis-man ofte gide.   630

"A wheston is no kervyng instrument,
But yet it maketh sharppe kervyng tolis.
And there thow woost that I have aught mys-
                went,
Eschuw thow that, for swich thing to the
      scole is;

Thus often wise men ben war by foolys.   635
If thow do so, thi wit is wel bewared;
By his contrarie is every thyng declared.

"For how myghte evere swetnesse han ben
      knowe
To him that nevere tasted bitternesse?
Ne no man may ben inly glad, I trowe,   640
That nevere was in sorwe or som destresse.
Eke whit by blak, by shame ek worthinesse,
Ech set by other, more for other semeth,
As men may se, and so the wyse it demeth.

"Sith thus of two contraries is o lore,   645
I, that have in love so ofte assayed
Grevances, oughte konne, and wel the more,
Counseillen the of that thow art amayed.
Ek the ne aughte nat ben yvel appayed,
Though I desyre with the for to bere   650
Thyn hevy charge; it shal the lasse dere.

"I woot wel that it fareth thus be me
As to thi brother, Paris, an herdesse,
Which that icleped was Oënone,
Wrot in a compleynte of hir hevynesse.   655
Yee say the lettre that she wrot, I gesse."
"Nay nevere yet, ywys," quod Troilus.
"Now," quod Pandare, "herkne, it was thus:

"'Phebus, that first fond art of medicyne,'
Quod she, 'and couthe in every wightes care   660
Remedye and reed, by herbes he knew fyne,
Yet to hymself his konnyng was ful bare;
For love hadde hym so bounden in a snare,
Al for the doughter of the kynge Amete,
That al his craft ne koude his sorwes bete.'   665

"Right so fare I, unhappily for me.
I love oon best, and that me smerteth sore;
And yet, peraunter, kan I reden the,
And nat myself; repreve me na more.
I have no cause, I woot wel, for to sore   670
As doth an hauk that listeth for to pleye;
But to thin help yet somwhat kan I seye.

"And of o thyng right siker maistow be,
That certein, for to dyen in the peyne,
That I shal nevere mo discoveren the;   675
Ne, by my trouthe, I kepe nat restreyne
The fro thi love, theigh that it were Eleyne
That is thi brother wif, if ich it wiste:
Be what she be, and love hire as the liste!

"Therfore, as frend, fullich in me assure,   680
And telle me plat now what is th'enchesoun

And final cause of wo that ye endure;
For douteth nothyng, myn entencioun
Nis nat to yow of reprehencioun,
To speke as now, for no wight may byreve   685
A man to love, tyl that hym list to leve.

"And witteth wel that bothe two ben vices,
Mistrusten alle, or elles alle leve.
But wel I woot, the mene of it no vice is,
For for to trusten som wight is a preve   690
Of trouth, and forthi wolde I fayn remeve
Thi wronge conseyte, and do the som wyght
     triste
Thi wo to telle; and tel me, if the liste.

"The wise seith, 'Wo hym that is allone,   694
For, and he falle, he hath non helpe to ryse';
And sith thow hast a felawe, tel thi mone;
For this nys naught, certein, the nexte wyse
To wynnen love, as techen us the wyse,
To walwe and wepe as Nyobe the queene,
Whos teres yet in marble ben yseene.   700

"Lat be thy wepyng and thi drerynesse,
And lat us lissen wo with oother speche;
So may thy woful tyme seme lesse.
Delyte nat in wo thi wo to seche,
As don thise foles that hire sorwes eche   705
With sorwe, whan thei han mysaventure,
And listen naught to seche hem other cure.

"Men seyn, 'to wrecche is consolacioun
To have another felawe in hys peyne.'
That owghte wel ben oure opynyoun,   710
For, bothe thow and I, of love we pleyne.
So ful of sorwe am I, soth for to seyne,
That certeinly namore harde grace
May sitte on me, for-why ther is no space.

"If God wol, thow art nat agast of me,   715
Lest I wolde of thi lady the bygyle!
Thow woost thyself whom that I love, parde,
As I best kan, gon sithen longe while.
And sith thow woost I do it for no wyle,   719
And seyst I am he that thow trustest moost,
Telle me somwhat, syn al my wo thow woost."

Yet Troilus for al this no word seyde,
But longe he ley as stylle as he ded were;
And after this with sikynge he abreyde,
And to Pandarus vois he lente his ere,   725
And up his eighen caste he, that in feere
Was Pandarus, lest that in frenesie
He sholde falle, or elles soone dye;

And cryde "Awake!" ful wonderlich and sharpe;
"What! slombrestow as in a litargie?   730
Or artow lik an asse to the harpe,
That hereth sown whan men the strynges plye,
But in his mynde of that no melodie
May sinken hym to gladen, for that he
So dul ys of his bestialite?"   735

And with that, Pandare of his wordes stente;
And Troilus yet hym nothyng answerde,
For-why to tellen nas nat his entente
To nevere no man, for whom that he so ferde.
For it is seyd, "man maketh ofte a yerde   740
With which the maker is hymself ybeten
In sondry manere," as thise wyse treten;

And namelich in his counseil tellynge
That toucheth love that oughte ben secree;
For of himself it wol ynough out sprynge,   745
But if that it the bet governed be.
Ek som tyme it is a craft to seme fle
Fro thyng whych in effect men hunte faste:
Al this gan Troilus in his herte caste.

But natheles, whan he hadde herd hym crye
"Awake!" he gan to syken wonder soore,   751
And seyde, "Frend, though that I stylle lye,
I am nat deef. Now pees, and crye namore,
For I have herd thi wordes and thi lore;
But suffre me my meschief to bywaille,   755
For thi proverbes may me naught availle.

"Nor other cure kanstow non for me.
Ek I nyl nat ben cured; I wol deye.
What knowe I of the queene Nyobe?   759
Lat be thyne olde ensaumples, I the preye."
"No," quod tho Pandarus, "therfore I seye,
Swych is delit of foles to bywepe
Hire wo, but seken bote they ne kepe.

"Now knowe I that ther reson in the failleth.
But telle me if I wiste what she were   765
For whom that the al this mysaunter ailleth.
Dorstestow that I tolde hir in hire ere
Thi wo, sith thow darst naught thiself for feere,
And hire bysoughte on the to han som routhe?"
"Why, nay," quod he, "by God and by my
     trouthe!"   770

"What? nat as bisyly," quod Pandarus,
"As though myn owene lyf lay on this nede?"
"No, certes, brother," quod this Troilus.
"And whi?" — "For that thow scholdest nevere
     spede."

"Wostow that wel?" — "Ye, that is out of
    drede,"   775
Quod Troilus; "for al that evere ye konne,
She nyl to noon swich wrecche as I ben
    wonne."

Quod Pandarus, "Allas! what may this be,
That thow dispeired art thus causeles?
What! lyveth nat thi lady, *bendiste*?   780
How wostow so that thow art graceles?
Swich yvel is nat alwey booteles.
Why, put nat impossible thus thi cure,
Syn thyng to come is oft in aventure.

"I graunte wel that thow endurest wo   785
As sharp as doth he Ticius in helle,
Whos stomak foughles tiren evere moo
That hightyn volturis, as bokes telle.
But I may nat endure that thow dwelle
In so unskilful an oppynyoun   790
That of thi wo is no curacioun.

"But oones nyltow, for thy coward herte,
And for thyn ire and folissh wilfulnesse,
For wantrust, tellen of thy sorwes smerte,
Ne to thyn owen help don bysynesse   795
As muche as speke a resoun moore or lesse,
But lyest as he that lest of nothyng recche.
What womman koude loven swich a wrecche?

"What may she demen oother of thy deeth,
If thow thus deye, and she not why it is,   800
But that for feere is yolden up thy breth,
For Grekes han biseged us, iwys?
Lord, which a thonk than shaltow han of this!
Thus wol she seyn, and al the town attones,   804
'The wrecche is ded, the devel have his bones!'

"Thow mayst allone here wepe and crye and
    knele,—
But love a womman that she woot it nought,
And she wol quyte it that thow shalt nat fele;
Unknowe, unkist, and lost, that is unsought.
What! many a man hath love ful deere ybought
Twenty wynter that his lady wiste,   811
That nevere yet his lady mouth he kiste.

"What? sholde he therfore fallen in dispayr,
Or be recreant for his owne tene,
Or slen hymself, al be his lady fair?   815
Nay, nay, but evere in oon be fressh and grene
To serve and love his deere hertes queene,
And thynk it is a guerdon, hire to serve,
A thousand fold moore than he kan deserve."

Of that word took hede Troilus,   820
And thoughte anon what folie he was inne,
And how that soth hym seyde Pandarus,
That for to slen hymself myght he nat wynne,
But bothe don unmanhod and a synne,
And of his deth his lady naught to wite;   825
For of his wo, God woot, she knew ful lite.

And with that thought he gan ful sore svke,
And seyde, "Allas! what is me best to do?"
To whom Pandare answered, "If the like,
The beste is that thow telle me al thi wo;   830
And have my trouthe, but thow it fynde so
I be thi boote, or that it be ful longe,
To pieces do me drawe, and sithen honge!"

"Ye, so thow seyst," quod Troilus tho, "allas!
But, God woot, it is naught the rather so.   835
Ful hard were it to helpen in this cas,
For wel fynde I that Fortune is my fo;
Ne al the men that riden konne or go
May of hire cruel whiel the harm withstonde;
For, as hire list, she pleyeth with free and
    bonde."   840

Quod Pandarus, "Than blamestow Fortune
For thow art wroth; ye, now at erst I see.
Woost thow nat wel that Fortune is comune
To everi manere wight in som degree?
And yet thow hast this comfort, lo, parde,   845
That, as hire joies moten overgon,
So mote hire sorwes passen everechon.

"For if hire whiel stynte any thyng to torne,
Than cessed she Fortune anon to be.
Now, sith hire whiel by no way may sojourne,
What woostow if hire mutabilite   851
Right as thyselven list, wol don by the,
Or that she be naught fer fro thyn helpynge?
Paraunter thow hast cause for to synge.

"And therfore wostow what I the biseche?   855
Lat be thy wo and tornyng to the grounde;
For whoso list have helyng of his leche,
To hym byhoveth first unwre his wownde.
To Cerberus yn helle ay be I bounde,
Were it for my suster, al thy sorwe,   860
By my wil she sholde al be thyn to-morwe.

"Look up, I seye, and telle me what she is
Anon, that I may gon about thy nede.
Knowe ich hire aught? For my love, telle me
    this.
Thanne wolde I hopen rather for to spede."   865

Tho gan the veyne of Troilus to blede,
For he was hit, and wax al reed for shame.
"A ha!" quod Pandare, "here bygynneth game."

And with that word he gan hym for to shake,
And seyde, "Thef, thow shalt hyre name telle."
But tho gan sely Troilus for to quake   871
As though men sholde han led hym into helle,
And seyde, "Allas! of al my wo the welle,
Thanne is my swete fo called Criseyde!"
And wel neigh with the word for feere he
        deide.   875

And whan that Pandare herde hire name
        nevene,
Lord, he was glad, and seyde, "Frend so deere,
Now far aright, for Joves name in hevene.
Love hath byset the wel; be of good cheere!
For of good name and wisdom and manere   880
She hath ynough, and ek of gentilesse.
If she be fayr, thow woost thyself, I gesse.

"Ne I nevere saugh a more bountevous
Of hire estat, n'a gladder, ne of speche
A frendlyer, n'a more gracious   885
For to do wel, ne lasse hadde nede to seche
What for to don; and al this bet to eche,
In honour, to as fer as she may strecche,
A kynges herte semeth by hyrs a wrecche.

"And forthy loke of good comfort thou be;   890
For certainly, the firste poynt is this
Of noble corage and wel ordayné,
A man to have pees with himself, ywis.
So oughtest thou, for nought but good it is
To loven wel, and in a worthy place;   895
The oughte nat to clepe it hap, but grace.

"And also thynk, and therwith glade the,
That sith thy lady vertuous is al,
So foloweth it that there is som pitee
Amonges alle thise other in general;   900
And forthi se that thow, in special,
Requere naught that is ayeyns hyre name;
For vertu streccheth naught hymself to shame.

"But wel is me that evere that I was born,
That thow biset art in so good a place;   905
For by my trouthe, in love I dorste have sworn
The sholde nevere han tid thus fayr a grace.
And wostow why? For thow were wont to
        chace
At Love in scorn, and for despit him calle
'Seynt Idyot, lord of thise foles alle.'   910

"How often hastow maad thi nyce japes,
And seyd that Loves servantz everichone
Of nycete ben verray Goddes apes;
And some wolde mucche hire mete allone,   914
Liggyng abedde, and make hem for to grone;
And som, thow seydest, hadde a blaunche
        fevere,
And preydest God he sholde nevere kevere.

"And some of hem tooke on hem, for the cold,
More than ynough, so seydestow ful ofte.
And som han feyned ofte tyme, and told   920
How that they waken, whan thei slepen softe;
And thus they wolde han brought hemself
        alofte,
And natheles were under at the laste.
Thus seydestow, and japedest ful faste.

"Yet seydestow, that for the moore part,   925
Thise loveres wolden speke in general,
And thoughten that it was a siker art,
For faylyng, for t'assayen overal.
Now may I jape of the, if that I shal;
But natheles, though that I sholde deye,   930
That thow art non of tho, I dorste saye.

"Now bet thi brest, and sey to God of Love,
'Thy grace, lord, for now I me repente,
If I mysspak, for now myself I love.'
Thus sey with al thyn herte in good entente."
Quod Troilus, "A, lord! I me consente,   936
And preye to the my japes thow foryive,
And I shal nevere more whyle I live."

"Thow seist wel," quod Pandare, "and now I
        hope
That thow the goddes wrathe hast al apesed;
And sithen thow hast wopen many a drope,   941
And seyd swych thyng wherwith thi god is
        plesed,
Now wolde nevere god but thow were esed!
And thynk wel, she of whom rist al thi wo
Hereafter may thy comfort be also.   945

"For thilke grownd that bereth the wedes wikke
Bereth ek thise holsom herbes, as ful ofte
Next the foule netle, rough and thikke,
The rose waxeth swoote and smothe and softe;
And next the valeye is the hil o-lofte;   950
And next the derke nyght the glade morwe;
And also joie is next the fyn of sorwe.

"Now loke that atempre be thi bridel,
And for the beste ay suffre to the tyde,

Or elles al oure labour is on ydel: 955
He hasteth wel that wisely kan abyde.
Be diligent and trewe, and ay wel hide;
Be lusty, fre; persevere in thy servyse,
And al is wel, if thow werke in this wyse.

"But he that parted is in everi place   960
Is nowher hol, as writen clerkes wyse.
What wonder is, though swich oon have no
     grace?
Ek wostow how it fareth of som servise,
As plaunte a tree or herbe, in sondry wyse,
And on the morwe pulle it up as blyve!   965
No wonder is, though it may nevere thryve.

"And sith that God of Love hath the bistowed
In place digne unto thi worthinesse,
Stond faste, for to good port hastow rowed;
And of thiself, for any hevynesse,   970
Hope alwey wel; for, but if drerinesse
Or over-haste oure bothe labour shende,
I hope of this to maken a good ende.

"And wostow why I am the lasse afered
Of this matere with my nece trete?   975
For this have I herd seyd of wyse lered,
Was nevere man or womman yet bigete
That was unapt to suffren loves hete,
Celestial, or elles love of kynde;
Forthy som grace I hope in hire to fynde.   980

"And for to speke of hire in specyal,
Hire beaute to bithynken and hire youthe,
It sit hire naught to ben celestial
As yet, though that hire liste bothe and kowthe;
But trewely, it sate hire wel right nowthe   985
A worthi knyght to loven and cherice,
And but she do, I holde it for a vice.

"Wherfore I am, and wol ben, ay redy
To peyne me to do yow this servyse;
For bothe yow to plese thus hope I   990
Herafterward; for ye ben bothe wyse,
And konne it counseil kepe in swych a wyse
That no man schal the wiser of it be;
And so we may ben gladed alle thre.

"And, by my trouthe, I have right now of the
A good conceyte in my wit, as I gesse,   996
And what it is, I wol now that thow se.
I thenke, sith that Love, of his goodnesse,
Hath the converted out of wikkednesse,
That thow shalt ben the beste post, I leve,
Of al his lay, and moost his foos to greve.   1001

"Ensample why, se now thise wise clerkes,
That erren aldermost ayeyn a lawe,
And ben converted from hire wikked werkes
Thorugh grace of God that list hem to hym
     drawe,   1005
Thanne arn they folk that han moost God in
     awe,
And strengest feythed ben, I undirstonde,
And konne an errowr alderbest withstonde."

Whan Troilus hadde herd Pandare assented
To ben his help in lovyng of Cryseyde,   1010
Weex of his wo, as who seith, untormented,
But hotter weex his love, and thus he seyde,
With sobre chere, although his herte pleyde:
"Now blisful Venus helpe, er that I sterve,
Of the, Pandare, I mowe som thank deserve.

"But, deere frend, how shal my wo be lesse   1016
Til this be doon? And good, ek telle me this:
How wiltow seyn of me and my destresse,
Lest she be wroth — this drede I moost, ywys —
Or nyl nat here or trowen how it is?   1020
Al this drede I, and eke for the manere
Of the, hire em, she nyl no swich thyng here."

Quod Pandarus, "Thow hast a ful gret care
Lest that the cherl may falle out of the moone!
Whi, Lord! I hate of the thi nyce fare!   1025
Whi, entremete of that thow hast to doone!
For Goddes love, I bidde the a boone:
So lat m'alone, and it shal be thi beste."
"Whi, frend," quod he, "now do right as the
     leste.

"But herke, Pandare, o word, for I nolde   1030
That thow in me wendest so gret folie,
That to my lady I desiren sholde
That toucheth harm or any vilenye;
For dredeles me were levere dye
Than she of me aught elles understode   1035
But that that myghte sownen into goode."

Tho lough this Pandare, and anon answerde,
"And I thi borugh? fy! no wight doth but so.
I roughte naught though that she stood and
     herde
How that thow seist! but farewel, I wol go.   1040
Adieu! be glad! God spede us bothe two!
Yef me this labour and this bisynesse,
And of my spede be thyn al that swetnesse."

Tho Troilus gan doun on knees to falle,
And Pandare in his armes hente faste,   1045

And seyde, "Now, fy on the Grekes alle!
Yet, pardee, God shal helpe us atte laste.
And dredelees, if that my lyf may laste,
And God toforn, lo, som of hem shal smerte;
And yet m'athinketh that this avant m'asterte!

"Now, Pandare, I kan na more seye,   1051
But, thow wis, thow woost, thow maist, thow
        art al!
My lif, my deth, hol in thyn hond I leye.
Help now!" Quod he, "Yis, by my trowthe, I
        shal."
"God yelde the, frend, and this in special," 1055
Quod Troilus, "that thow me recomande
To hire that to the deth me may comande."

This Pandarus, tho desirous to serve
His fulle frend, than seyde in this manere: 1059
"Farwell, and thenk I wol thi thank deserve!
Have here my trowthe, and that thow shalt wel
        here."
And went his wey, thenkyng on this matere,
And how he best myghte hire biseche of grace,
And fynde a tyme therto, and a place.

For everi wight that hath an hous to founde 1065
Ne renneth naught the werk for to bygynne
With rakel hond, but he wol bide a stounde,

And sende his hertes line out fro withinne
Aldirfirst his purpos for to wynne.
Al this Pandare in his herte thoughte,   1070
And caste his werk ful wisely or he wroughte.

But Troilus lay tho no lenger down,
But up anon upon his stede bay,
And in the feld he pleyde the leoun;
Wo was that Grek that with hym mette a-day!
And in the town his manere tho forth ay   1076
Soo goodly was, and gat hym so in grace,
That ecch hym loved that loked on his face.

For he bicom the frendlieste wight,
The gentilest, and ek the mooste fre,   1080
The thriftiest and oon the beste knyght,
That in his tyme was or myghte be.
Dede were his japes and his cruelte,
His heighe port and his manere estraunge,
And ecch of tho gan for a vertu chaunge.   1085

Now lat us stynte of Troilus a stounde,
That fareth lik a man that hurt is soore,
And is somdeel of akyngge of his wownde
Ylissed wel, but heeled no deel moore,
And, as an esy pacyent, the loore   1090
Abit of hym that gooth aboute his cure;
And thus he dryeth forth his aventure.

Explicit liber primus.

Book II

Incipit prohemium secundi libri.

Owt of thise blake wawes for to saylle,
O wynd, o wynd, the weder gynneth clere;
For in this see the boot hath swych travaylle,
Of my connyng, that unneth I it steere.
This see clepe I the tempestous matere   5
Of disespeir that Troilus was inne;
But now of hope the kalendes bygynne.

O lady myn, that called art Cleo,
Thow be my speed fro this forth, and my Muse,
To ryme wel this book til I have do;   10
Me nedeth here noon other art to use.
Forwhi to every lovere I me excuse,
That of no sentement I this endite,
But out of Latyn in my tonge it write.

Wherfore I nyl have neither thank ne blame 15
Of al this werk, but prey yow mekely,
Disblameth me, if any word be lame,
For as myn auctour seyde, so sey I.
Ek though I speeke of love unfelyngly,
No wondre is, for it nothyng of newe is;   20
A blynd man kan nat juggen wel in hewis.

Ye knowe ek that in forme of speche is
        chaunge
Withinne a thousand yeer, and wordes tho
That hadden pris, now wonder nyce and
        straunge
Us thinketh hem, and yet thei spake hem so,
And spedde as wel in love as men now do;   26
Ek for to wynnen love in sondry ages,
In sondry londes, sondry ben usages.

And forthi if it happe in any wyse,
That here be any lovere in this place   30
That herkneth, as the storie wol devise,
How Troilus com to his lady grace,
And thenketh, "so nold I nat love purchace,"
Or wondreth on his speche or his doynge,
I noot; but it is me no wonderynge.   35

For every wight which that to Rome went
Halt nat o path, or alwey o manere;
Ek in som lond were al the game shent,
If that they ferde in love as men don here,
As thus, in opyn doyng or in chere,   40
In visityng, in forme, or seyde hire sawes;
Forthi men seyn, ecch contree hath his lawes.

Ek scarsly ben ther in this place thre
That have in love seid lik, and don, in al;
For to thi purpos this may liken the,   45
And the right nought, yet al is seid or schal;
Ek som men grave in tree, some in ston wal,
As it bitit; but syn I have bigonne,
Myn auctour shal I folwen, if I konne.

Explicit prohemium secundi libri.

Incipit liber secundus.

In May, that moder is of monthes glade,   50
That fresshe floures, blew and white and rede,
Ben quike agayn, that wynter dede made,
And ful of bawme is fletyng every mede;
Whan Phebus doth his bryghte bemes sprede,
Right in the white Bole, it so bitidde,   55
As I shal synge, on Mayes day the thrydde,

That Pandarus, for al his wise speche,
Felt ek his part of loves shotes keene,
That, koude he nevere so wel of lovyng preche,
It made his hewe a-day ful ofte greene.   60
So shop it that hym fil that day a teene
In love, for which in wo to bedde he wente,
And made, er it was day, ful many a wente.

The swalowe Proigne, with a sorowful lay,
Whan morwen com, gan make hire wayment-
ynge,   65
Whi she forshapen was; and ever lay
Pandare abedde, half in a slomberynge,
Til she so neigh hym made hire cheterynge
How Tereus gan forth hire suster take,
That with the noyse of hire he gan awake,   70

And gan to calle, and dresse hym up to ryse,
Remembryng hym his erand was to doone

From Troilus, and ek his grete emprise;
And caste and knew in good plit was the moone
To doon viage, and took his weye ful soone   75
Unto his neces palays ther biside.
Now Janus, god of entree, thow hym gyde!

Whan he was come unto his neces place,
"Wher is my lady?" to hire folk quod he;
And they hym tolde, and he forth in gan pace,
And fond two othere ladys sete, and she,   81
Withinne a paved parlour, and they thre
Herden a mayden reden hem the geste
Of the siege of Thebes, while hem leste.

Quod Pandarus, "Madame, God yow see,   85
With al youre fayre book and compaignie!"
"Ey, uncle myn, welcome iwys," quod she;
And up she roos, and by the hond in hye
She took hym faste, and seyde, "This nyght
thrie,
To goode mot it turne, of yow I mette."   90
And with that word she doun on bench hym
sette.

"Ye, nece, yee shal faren wel the bet,
If God wol, al this yeer," quod Pandarus;
"But I am sory that I have yow let
To herken of youre book ye preysen thus.   95
For Goddes love, what seith it? telle it us!
Is it of love? O, som good ye me leere!"
"Uncle," quod she, "youre maistresse is nat
here."

With that thei gonnen laughe, and tho she
seyde,
"This romaunce is of Thebes that we rede;   100
And we han herd how that kyng Layus deyde
Thorugh Edippus his sone, and al that dede;
And here we stynten at thise lettres rede,
How the bisshop, as the book kan telle,   104
Amphiorax, fil thorugh the ground to helle."

Quod Pandarus, "Al this knowe I myselve,
And al th'assege of Thebes and the care;
For herof ben ther maked bookes twelve.
But lat be this, and telle me how ye fare.
Do wey youre barbe, and shewe youre face
bare;   110
Do wey youre book, rys up, and lat us daunce,
And lat us don to May som observaunce."

"I? God forbede!" quod she, "be ye mad?
Is that a widewes lif, so God yow save?

By God, ye maken me ryght soore adrad!   115
Ye ben so wylde, it semeth as ye rave.
It sate me wel bet ay in a cave
To bidde and rede on holy seyntes lyves;
Lat maydens gon to daunce, and yonge wyves."

"As evere thrive I," quod this Pandarus,   120
"Yet koude I telle a thyng to doon yow pleye."
"Now, uncle deere," quod she, "telle it us
For Goddes love; is than th'assege aweye?
I am of Grekes so fered that I deye."
"Nay, nay," quod he, "as evere mote I thryve,
It is a thing wel bet than swyche fyve."   126

"Ye, holy God," quod she, "what thyng is that?
What! bet than swyche fyve? I! nay, ywys!
For al this world ne kan I reden what
It sholde ben; some jape, I trowe, is this;   130
And but youreselven telle us what it is,
My wit is for t'arede it al to leene.
As help me God, I not nat what ye meene."

"And I youre borugh, ne nevere shal, for me,
This thyng be told to yow, as mote I
        thryve!"   135
"And whi so, uncle myn? whi so?" quod she.
"By God," quod he, "that wol I telle as blyve!
For proudder womman is ther noon on lyve,
And ye it wist, in al the town of Troye.
I jape nought, as evere have I joye!"   140

Tho gan she wondren moore than biforn
A thousand fold, and down hire eyghen caste;
For nevere, sith the tyme that she was born,
To knowe thyng desired she so faste;
And with a syk she seyde hym atte laste,   145
"Now, uncle myn, I nyl yow nought displese,
Nor axen more that may do yow disese."

So after this, with many wordes glade,
And frendly tales, and with merie chiere,
Of this and that they pleide, and gonnen wade
In many an unkouth glad and dep matere,   151
As frendes doon whan thei ben mette yfere;
Tyl she gan axen hym how Ector ferde,
That was the townes wal and Grekes yerde.

"Ful wel, I thonk it God," quod Pandarus,   155
"Save in his arm he hath a litel wownde;
And ek his fresshe brother Troilus,
The wise, worthi Ector the secounde,
In whom that alle vertu list habounde,
As alle trouth and alle gentilesse,   160
Wisdom, honour, fredom, and worthinesse."

"In good feith, em," quod she, "that liketh me;
Thei faren wel, God save hem bothe two!
For trewelich I holde it gret deynte,
A kynges sone in armes wel to do,   165
And ben of goode condiciouns therto;
For gret power and moral vertu here
Is selde yseyn in o persone yfere."

"In good faith, that is soth," quod Pandarus.
"But, by my trouthe, the kyng hath sones
        tweye, —   170
That is to mene, Ector and Troilus, —
That certeynly, though that I sholde deye,
Thei ben as voide of vices, dar I seye,
As any men that lyven under the sonne.
Hire myght is wyde yknowe, and what they
        konne.   175

"Of Ector nedeth it namore for to telle:
In al this world ther nys a bettre knyght
Than he, that is of worthynesse welle;
And he wel moore vertu hath than myght.
This knoweth many a wis and worthi wight.   180
The same pris of Troilus I seye;
God help me so, I knowe nat swiche tweye."

"By God," quod she, "of Ector that is sooth.
Of Troilus the same thyng trowe I;
For, dredeles, men tellen that he doth   185
In armes day by day so worthily,
And bereth hym here at hom so gentily
To every wight, that alle pris hath he
Of hem that me were levest preysed be."

"Ye sey right sooth, ywys," quod Pandarus;   190
"For yesterday, whoso hadde with hym ben,
He myghte han wondred upon Troilus;
For nevere yet so thikke a swarm of been
Ne fleigh, as Grekes fro hym gonne fleen,
And thorugh the feld, in everi wightes eere,
Ther nas no cry but 'Troilus is there!'   196

"Now here, now ther, he hunted hem so faste,
Ther nas but Grekes blood, — and Troilus.
Now hym he hurte, and hym al down he caste;
Ay wher he wente, it was arayed thus: 200
He was hir deth, and sheld and lif for us;
That, as that day, ther dorste non withstonde,
Whil that he held his blody swerd in honde.

"Therto he is the frendlieste man
Of gret estat, that evere I saugh my lyve,   205
And wher hym lest, best felawshipe kan
To swich as hym thynketh able for to thryve."

And with that word tho Pandarus, as blyve,
He took his leve, and seyde, "I wol gon henne."
"Nay, blame have I, myn uncle," quod she
  thenne.   210

"What aileth yow to be thus wery soone,
And namelich of wommen? wol ye so?
Nay, sitteth down; by God, I have to doone
With yow, to speke of wisdom er ye go."
And everi wight that was aboute hem tho,   215
That herde that, gan fer awey to stonde,
Whil they two hadde al that hem liste in honde.

Whan that hire tale al brought was to an ende,
Of hire estat and of hire governaunce,
Quod Pandarus, "Now is it tyme I wende.   220
But yet, I say, ariseth, lat us daunce,
And cast youre widewes habit to mischaunce!
What list yow thus youreself to disfigure,
Sith yow is tid thus fair an aventure?"   224

"A! wel bithought! for love of God," quod she,
"Shal I nat witen what ye meene of this?"
"No, this thing axeth leyser," tho quod he,
"And eke me wolde muche greve, iwys,
If I it tolde, and ye it toke amys.
Yet were it bet my tonge for to stille   230
Than seye a soth that were ayeyns youre wille.

"For, nece, by the goddesse Mynerve,
And Jupiter, that maketh the thondre rynge,
And by the blisful Venus that I serve,
Ye ben the womman in this world lyvynge,   235
Withouten paramours, to my wyttynge,
That I best love, and lothest am to greve,
And that ye weten wel youreself, I leve."

"Iwis, myn uncle," quod she, "grant mercy.
Youre frendshipe have I founden evere yit;   240
I am to no man holden, trewely,
So muche as yow, and have so litel quyt;
And with the grace of God, emforth my wit,
As in my gylt I shal yow nevere offende;
And if I have er this, I wol amende.   245

"But, for the love of God, I yow biseche,
As ye ben he that I love moost and triste,
Lat be to me youre fremde manere speche,
And sey to me, youre nece, what yow liste."
And with that word hire uncle anoon hire
  kiste,   250
And seyde, "Gladly, leve nece dere!
Tak it for good, that I shal sey yow here."

With that she gan hire eighen down to caste,
And Pandarus to coghe gan a lite,
And seyde, "Nece, alwey, lo! to the laste,   255
How so it be that som men hem delite
With subtyl art hire tales for to endite,
Yet for al that, in hire entencioun,
Hire tale is al for som conclusioun.

"And sithen th'ende is every tales strengthe,
And this matere is so bihovely,   261
What sholde I peynte or drawen it on lengthe
To yow, that ben my frend so feythfully?"
And with that word he gan right inwardly
Byholden hire and loken on hire face,   265
And seyde, "On swich a mirour goode grace!"

Than thought he thus: "If I my tale endite
Aught harde, or make a proces any whyle,
She shal no savour have therin but lite,
And trowe I wolde hire in my wil bigyle;   270
For tendre wittes wenen al be wyle
Thereas thei kan nought pleynly understonde;
Forthi hire wit to serven wol I fonde" —

And loked on hire in a bysi wyse,
And she was war that he byheld hire so,   275
And seyde, "Lord! so faste ye m'avise!
Sey ye me nevere er now — What sey ye, no?"
"Yis, yys," quod he, "and bet wole er I go!
But, be my trouthe, I thoughte, now if ye
Be fortunat, for now men shal it se.   280

"For to every wight som goodly aventure
Som tyme is shape, if he it kan receyven;
But if that he wol take of it no cure,
Whan that it commeth, but wilfully it weyven,
Lo, neyther cas ne fortune hym deceyven,   285
But ryght his verray slouthe and wrecched-
  nesse;
And swich a wight is for to blame, I gesse.

"Good aventure, o beele nece, have ye
Ful lightly founden, and ye konne it take;
And, for the love of God, and ek of me,   290
Cache it anon, lest aventure slake!
What sholde I lenger proces of it make?
Yif me youre hond, for in this world is noon,
If that yow list, a wight so wel bygon.

"And sith I speke of good entencioun,   295
As I to yow have told wel here-byforn,
And love as wel youre honour and renoun
As creature in al this world yborn,

By alle the othes that I have yow sworn,
And ye be wrooth therfore, or wene I lye,   300
Ne shal I nevere sen yow eft with yë.

"Beth naught agast, ne quaketh naught!
    Wherto?
Ne chaungeth naught for fere so youre hewe!
For hardely the werst of this is do,   304
And though my tale as now be to yow newe,
Yet trist alwey ye shal me fynde trewe;
And were it thyng that me thoughte unsit-
    tynge,
To yow wolde I no swiche tales brynge."

"Now, my good em, for Goddes love, I preye,"
Quod she, "come of, and telle me what it is!
For both I am agast what ye wol seye,   311
And ek me longeth it to wite, ywys;
For whethir it be wel or be amys,
Say on, lat me nat in this feere dwelle." —
"So wol I doon; now herkeneth! I shal telle:

"Now, nece myn, the kynges deere sone,   316
The goode, wise, worthi, fresshe, and free,
Which alwey for to don wel is his wone,
The noble Troilus, so loveth the,
That, but ye helpe, it wol his bane be.   320
Lo, here is al! What sholde I moore seye?
Do what yow lest, to make hym lyve or deye.

"But if ye late hym deyen, I wol sterve —
Have here my trouthe, nece, I nyl nat lyen —
Al sholde I with this knyf my throte kerve."
With that the teris bruste out of his yën,   326
And seide, "If that ye don us bothe dyen,
Thus gilteles, than have ye fisshed fayre!
What mende ye, though that we booth appaire?

"Allas! he which that is my lord so deere,   330
That trewe man, that noble gentil knyght,
That naught desireth but youre frendly cheere,
I se hym deyen, ther he goth upryght,
And hasteth hym with al his fulle myght
For to ben slayn, if his fortune assente.   335
Allas, that God yow swich a beaute sente!

"If it be so that ye so cruel be,
That of his deth yow liste nought to recche,
That is so trewe and worthi, as ye se,
Namoore than of a japer or a wrecche, —   340
If ye be swich, youre beaute may nat strecche
To make amendes of so cruel a dede.
Avysement is good byfore the nede.

"Wo worth the faire gemme vertulees!
Wo worth that herbe also that dooth no boote!
Wo worth that beaute that is routheeles!   346
Wo worth that wight that tret ech undir foote!
And ye, that ben of beaute crop and roote,
If therwithal in yow ther be no routhe,
Than is it harm ye lyven, by my trouthe!   350

"And also think wel that this is no gaude;
For me were levere thow and I and he
Were hanged, than I sholde ben his baude,
As heigh as men myghte on us alle ysee!
I am thyn em; the shame were to me,   355
As wel as the, if that I sholde assente,
Thorugh myn abet, that he thyn honour shente.

"Now understonde, for I yow nought requere
To bynde yow to hym thorugh no byheste,
But only that ye make hym bettre chiere   360
Than ye han doon er this, and moore feste,
So that his lif be saved atte leeste:
This al and som, and pleynly oure entente.
God help me so, I nevere other mente!

"Lo this requeste is naught but skylle, ywys,
Ne doute of reson, pardee, is ther noon.   366
I sette the worste, that ye dreden this:
Men wolde wondren sen hym come or goon.
Ther-ayeins answere I thus anoon,
That every wight, but he be fool of kynde,   370
Wol deme it love of frendshipe in his mynde.

"What? who wol demen, though he se a man
To temple go, that he th'ymages eteth?
Thenk ek how wel and wisely that he kan   374
Governe hymself, that he no thyng foryeteth,
That where he cometh, he pris and thank hym
    geteth;
And ek therto, he shal come here so selde,
What fors were it though al the town byhelde?

"Swych love of frendes regneth al this town;
And wry yow in that mantel evere moo;   380
And, God so wys be my savacioun,
As I have seyd, youre beste is to do soo.
But alwey, goode nece, to stynte his woo,
So lat youre daunger sucred ben a lite,
That of his deth ye be naught for to wite."   385

Criseyde, which that herde hym in this wise,
Thoughte, "I shal felen what he meneth, ywis."
"Now em," quod she, "what wolde ye devise?
What is youre reed I sholde don of this?"
"That is wel seyd," quod he, "certein, best is

That ye hym love ayeyn for his lovynge,   391
As love for love is skilful guerdonynge.

"Thenk ek how elde wasteth every houre
In ech of yow a partie of beautee;
And therfore, er that age the devoure,   395
Go love; for old, ther wol no wight of the.
Lat this proverbe a loore unto yow be:
'To late ywar, quod beaute, whan it paste';
And elde daunteth daunger at the laste.

"The kynges fool is wont to crien loude,   400
Whan that hym thinketh a womman berth hire
      hye,
'So longe mote ye lyve, and alle proude,
Til crowes feet be growen under youre yë,
And sende yow than a myrour in to prye,
In which that ye may se youre face a morwe!'
Nece, I bidde wisshe yow namore sorwe."   406

With this he stynte, and caste adown the heed,
And she began to breste a-wepe anoon,
And seyde, "Allas, for wo! Why nere I deed?
For of this world the feyth is al agoon.   410
Allas! what sholden straunge to me doon,
When he, that for my beste frend I wende,
Ret me to love, and sholde it me defende?

"Allas! I wolde han trusted, douteles,
That if that I, thorugh my disaventure,   415
Hadde loved outher hym or Achilles,
Ector, or any mannes creature,
Ye nolde han had no mercy ne mesure
On me, but alwey had me in repreve.
This false world, allas! who may it leve?   420

"What! is this al the joye and al the feste?
Is this youre reed? Is this my blisful cas?
Is this the verray mede of youre byheeste?
Is al this paynted proces seyd, allas!
Right for this fyn? O lady myn, Pallas!   425
Thow in this dredful cas for me purveye,
For so astoned am I that I deye."

Wyth that she gan ful sorwfully to syke.
"A! may it be no bet?" quod Pandarus,   429
"By God, I shal namore come here this wyke,
And God toforn, that am mystrusted thus!
I se ful wel that ye sette lite of us,
Or of oure deth! allas, I woful wrecche!
Might he yet lyve, of me is nought to recche.

"O cruel god, O dispitouse Marte,   435
O Furies thre of helle, on yow I crye!

So lat me nevere out of this hous departe,
If I mente harm or any vilenye!
But sith I se my lord mot nedes dye,
And I with hym, here I me shryve, and seye
That wikkedly ye don us bothe deye.   441

"But sith it liketh yow that I be ded,
By Neptunus, that god is of the see,
Fro this forth shal I nevere eten bred
Til I myn owen herte blood may see;   445
For certeyn I wol deye as soone as he." —
And up he sterte, and on his wey he raughte,
Til she agayn hym by the lappe kaughte.

Criseyde, which that wel neigh starf for feere,
So as she was the ferfulleste wight   450
That myghte be, and herde ek with hire ere
And saugh the sorwful ernest of the knyght,
And in his preier ek saugh noon unryght,
And for the harm that myghte ek fallen moore,
She gan to rewe, and dredde hire wonder
      soore,   455

And thoughte thus: "Unhappes fallen thikke
Alday for love, and in swych manere cas
As men ben cruel in hemself and wikke;
And if this man sle here hymself, allas!
In my presence, it wol be no solas.   460
What men wolde of hit deme I kan nat seye:
It nedeth me ful sleighly for to pleie."

And with a sorowful sik she sayde thrie,
"A! Lord! what me is tid a sory chaunce!
For myn estat lith now in jupartie,   465
And ek myn emes lif is in balaunce;
But natheles, with Goddes governaunce,
I shal so doon, myn honour shal I kepe,
And ek his lif," — and stynte for to wepe.

"Of harmes two, the lesse is for to chese;   470
Yet have I levere maken hym good chere
In honour, than myn emes lyf to lese.
Ye seyn, ye nothyng elles me requere?"
"No, wis," quod he, "myn owen nece dere."
"Now wel," quod she, "and I wol doon my
      peyne;   475
I shal myn herte ayeins my lust constreyne.

"But that I nyl nat holden hym in honde;
Ne love a man ne kan I naught, ne may,
Ayeins my wyl; but elles wol I fonde,
Myn honour sauf, plese hym fro day to day.
Therto nolde I nat ones han seyd nay,   481

But that I drede, as in my fantasye;
But cesse cause, ay cesseth maladie.

"And here I make a protestacioun,
That in this proces if ye depper go,   485
That certeynly, for no salvacioun
Of yow, though that ye sterven bothe two,
Though al the world on o day be my fo,
Ne shal I nevere of hym han other routhe." —
"I graunte wel," quod Pandare, "by my trowthe.

"But may I truste wel therto," quod he,   491
"That of this thyng that ye han hight me here,
Ye wole it holden trewely unto me?"
"Ye, doutelees," quod she, "myn uncle deere."
"Ne that I shal han cause in this matere,"   495
Quod he, "to pleyne, or ofter yow to preche?"
"Why, no, parde; what nedeth moore speche?"

Tho fillen they in other tales glade,
Tyl at the laste, "O good em," quod she tho,
"For his love, which that us bothe made,   500
Tel me how first ye wisten of his wo.
Woot noon of it but ye?" — He seyde, "No." —
"Kan he wel speke of love?" quod she; "I preye
Tel me, for I the bet me shal purveye."

Tho Pandarus a litel gan to smyle,   505
And seyde, "By my trouthe, I shal yow telle.
This other day, naught gon ful longe while,
In-with the paleis gardyn, by a welle,
Gan he and I wel half a day to dwelle,
Right for to speken of an ordinaunce,   510
How we the Grekes myghten disavaunce.

"Soon after that bigonne we to lepe,
And casten with oure dartes to and fro,
Tyl at the laste he seyde he wolde slepe,
And on the gres adoun he leyde hym tho;   515
And I afer gan rome to and fro,
Til that I herde, as that I welk alone,
How he bigan ful wofully to grone.

"Tho gan I stalke hym softely byhynde,
And sikirly, the soothe for to seyne,   520
As I kan clepe ayein now to my mynde,
Right thus to Love he gan hym for to pleyne:
He seyde, 'Lord, have routhe upon my peyne,
Al have I ben rebell in myn entente;
Now, *mea culpa*, lord, I me repente!   525

"'O god, that at thi disposicioun
Ledest the fyn, by juste purveiaunce,
Of every wight, my lowe confessioun

Accepte in gree, and sende me swich penaunce
As liketh the, but from disesperaunce,   530
That may my goost departe awey fro the,
Thow be my sheld, for thi benignite.

"'For certes, lord, so soore hath she me
            wounded,
That stood in blak, with lokyng of hire eyen,
That to myn hertes botme it is ysounded,   535
Thorugh which I woot that I moot nedes deyen.
This is the werste, I dar me nat bywreyen;
And wel the hotter ben the gledes rede,
That men hem wrien with asshen pale and
            dede.'

"Wyth that he smot his hed adown anon,   540
And gan to motre, I noot what, trewely.
And I with that gan stille awey to goon,
And leet therof as nothing wist had I,
And com ayein anon, and stood hym by,
And seyde, 'awake, ye slepen al to longe!   545
It semeth nat that love doth yow longe,

"'That slepen so that no man may yow wake.
Who sey evere or this so dul a man?'
'Ye, frend,' quod he, 'do ye youre hedes ake
For love, and lat me lyven as I kan.'   550
But though that he for wo was pale and wan,
Yet made he tho as fressh a countenaunce
As though he sholde have led the newe daunce.

"This passed forth til now, this other day,
It fel that I com romyng al allone   555
Into his chaumbre, and fond how that he lay
Upon his bed; but man so soore grone
Ne herde I nevere, and what that was his mone
Ne wist I nought; for, as I was comynge,
Al sodeynly he lefte his complaynynge.   560

"Of which I took somwat suspecioun,
And ner I com, and fond he wepte soore;
And God so wys be my savacioun,
As nevere of thyng hadde I no routhe moore.
For neither with engyn, ne with no loore,   565
Unnethes myghte I fro the deth hym kepe,
That yet fele I myn herte for hym wepe.

"And God woot, nevere, sith that I was born,
Was I so besy no man for to preche,
Ne nevere was to wight so depe isworn,   570
Or he me told who myghte ben his leche.
But now to yow rehercen al his speche,
Or alle his woful wordes for to sowne,
Ne bid me naught, but ye wol se me swowne.

"But for to save his lif, and elles nought,   575
And to noon harm of yow, thus am I dryven;
And for the love of God, that us hath wrought,
Swich cheer hym dooth, that he and I may
          lyven!
Now have I plat to yow myn herte shryven;
And sith ye woot that myn entent is cleene,
Take heede therof, for I non yvel meene.   581

"And right good thrift, I prey to God, have ye,
That han swich oon ykaught withouten net!
And, be ye wis as ye be fair to see,
Wel in the ryng than is the ruby set.   585
Ther were nevere two so wel ymet,
Whan ye ben his al hool, as he is youre:
Ther myghty God yet graunte us see that
          houre!"

"Nay, therof spak I nought, ha, ha!" quod she;
"As helpe me God, ye shenden every deel!"   590
"O, mercy, dere nece," anon quod he,
"What so I spak, I mente naught but wel,
By Mars, the god that helmed is of steel!
Now beth naught wroth, my blood, my nece
          dere."
"Now wel," quod she, "foryeven be it
          here!"   595

With this he took his leve, and hom he wente;
And, Lord, so he was glad and wel bygon!
Criseyde aros, no lenger she ne stente,
But streght into hire closet wente anon,
And set hire doun as stylle as any ston,   600
And every word gan up and down to wynde
That he had seyd, as it com hire to mynde;

And wax somdel astoned in hire thought,
Right for the newe cas; but whan that she
Was ful avysed, tho fond she right nought   605
Of peril, why she ought afered be.
For man may love, of possibilite,
A womman so, his herte may tobreste,
And she naught love ayein, but if hire leste.

But as she sat allone and thoughte thus,   610
Ascry aros at scarmuch al withoute,
And men cride in the strete, "Se, Troilus
Hath right now put to flighte the Grekes route!"
With that gan al hire meyne for to shoute,
"A, go we se! cast up the yates wyde!   615
For thorwgh this strete he moot to paleys ride;

"For other wey is fro the yate noon
Of Dardanus, there opyn is the cheyne."

With that com he and al his folk anoon
An esy pas rydyng, in routes tweyne,   620
Right as his happy day was, sooth to seyne,
For which, men seyn, may nought destourbed
          be
That shal bityden of necessitee.

This Troilus sat on his baye steede,
Al armed, save his hed, ful richely;   625
And wownded was his hors, and gan to blede,
On which he rood a pas ful softely.
But swich a knyghtly sighte, trewely,
As was on hym, was nought, withouten faille,
To loke on Mars, that god is of bataille.   630

So lik a man of armes and a knyght
He was to seen, fulfilled of heigh prowesse;
For bothe he hadde a body and a myght
To don that thing, as wel as hardynesse;
And ek to seen hym in his gere hym dresse,   635
So fressh, so yong, so weldy semed he,   636
It was an heven upon hym for to see.

His helm tohewen was in twenty places,
That by a tyssew heng his bak byhynde;
His sheeld todasshed was with swerdes and
          maces,   640
In which men myght many an arwe fynde
That thirled hadde horn and nerf and rynde;
And ay the peple cryde, "Here cometh oure
          joye,
And, next his brother, holder up of Troye!"

For which he wex a litel reed for shame,   645
Whan he the peple upon hym herde cryen,
That to byholde it was a noble game,
How sobrelich he caste down his yën.
Criscÿda gan al his chere aspien,
And leet it so softe in hire herte synke,   650
That to hireself she seyde, "Who yaf me
          drynke?"

For of hire owen thought she wex al reed,
Remembryng hire right thus, "Lo, this is he
Which that myn uncle swerith he moot be deed,
But I on hym have mercy and pitee."   655
And with that thought, for pure ashamed, she
Gan in hire hed to pulle, and that as faste,
Whil he and alle the peple forby paste;

And gan to caste and rollen up and down
Withinne hire thought his excellent prowesse,
And his estat, and also his renown,   661
His wit, his shap, and ek his gentilesse;

But moost hir favour was, for his distresse
Was al for hire, and thoughte it was a routhe
To sleen swich oon, if that he mente trouthe.

Now myghte som envious jangle thus: 666
"This was a sodeyn love; how myght it be
That she so lightly loved Troilus,
Right for the firste syghte, ye, parde?"
Now whoso seith so, mote he nevere ythe!   670
For every thyng, a gynnyng hath it nede
Er al be wrought, withowten any drede.

For I sey nought that she so sodeynly
Yaf hym hire love, but that she gan enclyne
To like hym first, and I have told yow whi;   675
And after that, his manhod and his pyne
Made love withinne hire herte for to myne,
For which, by proces and by good servyse,
He gat hire love, and in no sodeyn wyse.

And also blisful Venus, wel arrayed,   680
Sat in hire seventhe hous of hevene tho,
Disposed wel, and with aspectes payed,
To helpe sely Troilus of his woo.
And, soth to seyne, she nas not al a foo
To Troilus in his nativitee;   685
God woot that wel the sonner spedde he.

Now lat us stynte of Troilus a throwe,
That rideth forth, and lat us torne faste
Unto Criseyde, that heng hire hed ful lowe,
Ther as she sat allone, and gan to caste   690
Where on she wolde apoynte hire atte laste,
If it so were hire em ne wolde cesse,
For Troilus upon hire for to presse.

And, Lord! so she gan in hire thought argue
In this matere of which I have yow told,   695
And what to doone best were, and what eschue,
That plited she ful ofte in many fold.
Now was hire herte warm, now was it cold;
And what she thoughte, somwhat shal I write,
As to myn auctour listeth for t'endite.   700

She thoughte wel that Troilus persone
She knew by syghte, and ek his gentilesse,
And thus she seyde, "Al were it nat to doone,
To graunte hym love, ye, for his worthynesse,
It were honour, with pley and with gladnesse,   706
In honestee with swich a lord to deele,
For myn estat, and also for his heele.

"Ek wel woot I my kynges sone is he;
And sith he hath to se me swich delit,

If I wolde outreliche his sighte flee,   710
Peraunter he myghte have me in dispit,
Thorugh whicch I myghte stonde in worse plit.
Now were I wis, me hate to purchace,
Withouten nede, ther I may stonde in grace?

"In every thyng, I woot, there lith mesure.   715
For though a man forbede dronkenesse,
He naught forbet that every creature
Be drynkeles for alwey, as I gesse.
Ek sith I woot for me is his destresse,
I ne aughte nat for that thing hym despise,   720
Sith it is so, he meneth in good wyse.

"And eke I knowe, of longe tyme agon,
His thewes goode, and that he is nat nyce.
N'avantour, seith men, certein, he is noon;
To wis is he to doon so gret a vice;   725
Ne als I nyl hym nevere so cherice
That he may make avaunt, by juste cause;
He shal me nevere bynde in swich a clause.

"Now sette a caas: the hardest is, ywys,
Men myghten demen that he loveth me.   730
What dishonour were it unto me, this?
May ich hym lette of that? Why, nay, parde!
I knowe also, and alday heere and se,
Men loven wommen al biside hire leve;   734
And whan hem leste namore, lat hem byleve!

"I thenke ek how he able is for to have
Of al this noble town the thriftieste,
To ben his love, so she hire honour save.
For out and out he is the worthieste,
Save only Ector, which that is the beste;   740
And yet his lif al lith now in my cure.
But swich is love, and ek myn aventure.

"Ne me to love, a wonder is it nought;
For wel woot I myself, so God me spede,
Al wolde I that noon wiste of this thought,   745
I am oon the faireste, out of drede,
And goodlieste, whoso taketh hede,
And so men seyn, in al the town of Troie.
What wonder is though he of me have joye?

"I am myn owene womman, wel at ese,   750
I thank it God, as after myn estat,
Right yong, and stonde unteyd in lusty leese,
Withouten jalousie or swich debat:
Shal noon housbonde seyn to me "chek mat!"
For either they ben ful of jalousie,   755
Or maisterfull, or loven novelrie.

"What shal I doon? To what fyn lyve I thus?
Shal I nat love, in cas if that me leste?
What, par dieux! I am naught religious.
And though that I myn herte sette at reste   760
Upon this knyght, that is the worthieste,
And kepe alwey myn honour and my name,
By alle right, it may do me no shame."

But right as when the sonne shyneth brighte
In March, that chaungeth ofte tyme his
       face,   765
And that a cloude is put with wynd to flighte,
Which oversprat the sonne as for a space,
A cloudy thought gan thorugh hire soule pace,
That overspradde hire brighte thoughtes alle,
So that for feere almost she gan to falle.   770

That thought was this: "Allas! syn I am free,
Sholde I now love, and put in jupartie
My sikernesse, and thrallen libertee?
Allas! how dorst I thenken that folie?
May I naught wel in other folk aspie   775
Hire dredfull joye, hire constreinte, and hire
       peyne?
Ther loveth noon, that she nath why to pleyne.

"For love is yet the mooste stormy lyf,
Right of hymself, that evere was bigonne;
For evere som mystrust or nice strif   780
Ther is in love, som cloude is over that sonne.
Therto we wrecched wommen nothing konne,
Whan us is wo, but wepe and sitte and thinke;
Oure wrecche is this, oure owen wo to drynke.

"Also thise wikked tonges ben so prest   785
To speke us harm, ek men ben so untrewe,
That, right anon as cessed is hire lest,
So cesseth love, and forth to love a newe.
But harm ydoon is doon, whoso it rewe;
For though thise men for love hem first torende,
Ful sharp bygynnyng breketh ofte at ende.   791

"How ofte tyme hath it yknowen be,
The tresoun that to wommen hath ben do!
To what fyn is swich love I kan nat see,
Or wher bycometh it, whan it is ago.   795
Ther is no wight that woot, I trowe so,
Where it bycometh; lo, no wight on it sporneth:
That erst was nothing, into nought it torneth.

"How bisy, if I love, ek most I be   799
To plesen hem that jangle of love, and dremen,
And coye hem, that they seye noon harm of me!
For though ther be no cause, yet hem semen

Al be for harm that folk hire frendes quemen;
And who may stoppen every wikked tonge,   804
Or sown of belles whil that thei ben ronge?"

And after that, hire thought gan for to clere,
And seide, "He which that nothing under-
       taketh,
Nothyng n'acheveth, be hym looth or deere."
And with an other thought hire herte quaketh;
Than slepeth hope, and after drede awak-
       eth;   810
Now hoot, now cold; but thus, bitwixen tweye,
She rist hire up, and wente here for to pleye.

Adown the steyre anonright tho she wente
Into the garden, with hire neces thre,
And up and down ther made many a wente,
Flexippe, she, Tharbe, and Antigone,   816
To pleyen, that it joye was to see;
And other of hire wommen, a gret route,
Hire folowede in the garden al abowte.   819

This yerd was large, and rayled alle th' aleyes,
And shadewed wel with blosmy bowes grene,
And benched newe, and sonded alle the weyes,
In which she walketh arm in arm bitwene,
Til at the laste Antigone the shene
Gan on a Troian song to singen cleere,   825
That it an heven was hire vois to here.

She seyde: "O Love, to whom I have and shal
Ben humble subgit, trewe in myn entente,
As I best kan, to yow, lord, yeve ich al,
For everemo, myn hertes lust to rente.   830
For nevere yet thi grace no wight sente
So blisful cause as me, my lif to lede
In alle joie and seurte, out of drede.

"Ye, blisful god, han me so wel byset
In love, iwys, that al that bereth lif   835
Ymagynen ne kouthe how to be bet;
For, lord, withouten jalousie or strif,
I love oon which that is moost ententif
To serven wel, unweri or unfeyned,   839
That evere was, and leest with harm desteyned.

"As he that is the welle of worthynesse,
Of trouthe grownd, mirour of goodlihed,
Of wit Apollo, stoon of sikernesse,
Of vertu roote, of lust fynder and hed,
Thorugh which is alle sorwe fro me ded, —   845
Iwis, I love hym best, so doth he me;
Now good thrift have he, wherso that he be!

"Whom shulde I thanken but yow, god of Love,
Of al this blisse, in which to bathe I gynne?
And thanked be ye, lord, for that I love!   850
This is the righte lif that I am inne,
To flemen alle manere vice and synne:
This dooth me so to vertu for t'entende,
That day by day I in my wille amende.

"And whoso seith that for to love is vice,   855
Or thraldom, though he feele in it destresse,
He outher is envyous, or right nyce,
Or is unmyghty, for his shrewednesse,
To loven; for swich manere folk, I gesse,
Defamen Love, as nothing of him knowe.   860
Thei speken, but thei benten nevere his bowe!

"What is the sonne wers, of kynde right,
Though that a man, for feeblesse of his yen,
May nought endure on it to see for bright?
Or love the wers, though wrecches on it
          crien?   865
No wele is worth, that may no sorwe dryen.
And forthi, who that hath an hed of verre,
Fro cast of stones war hym in the werre!

"But I with al myn herte and al my myght,
As I have seyd, wol love unto my laste,   870
My deere herte, and al myn owen knyght,
In which myn herte growen is so faste,
And his in me, that it shal evere laste,
Al dredde I first to love hym to bigynne,
Now woot I wel, ther is no peril inne."   875

And of hir song right with that word she stente,
And therwithal, "Now nece," quod Cryseyde,
Who made this song now with so good en-
          tente?"
Antygone answerde anoon and seyde,
"Madame, iwys, the goodlieste mayde   880
Of gret estat in al the town of Troye,
And let hire lif in moste honour and joye."

"Forsothe, so it semeth by hire song,"
Quod tho Criseyde, and gan therwith to sike,
And seyde, "Lord, is ther swych blisse among
Thise loveres, as they konne faire endite?"   886
"Ye, wis," quod fresshe Antigone the white,
"For alle the folk that han or ben on lyve
Ne konne wel the blisse of love discryve.

"But wene ye that every wrecche woot   890
The parfite blisse of love? Why, nay, iwys!
They wenen all be love, if oon be hoot.
Do wey, do wey, they woot no thyng of this!

Men mosten axe at seyntes if it is
Aught fair in hevene (why? for they kan telle),
And axen fendes is it foul in helle."   896

Criseyde unto that purpos naught answerde,
But seyde, "Ywys, it wol be nyght as faste."
But every word which that she of hire herde,
She gan to prenten in hire herte faste,   900
And ay gan love hire lasse for t'agaste
Than it dide erst, and synken in hire herte,
That she wex somwhat able to converte.

The dayes honour, and the hevenes yë,   904
The nyghtes foo — al this clepe I the sonne —
Gan westren faste, and downward for to wrye,
As he that hadde his dayes cours yronne;
And white thynges wexen dymme and donne
For lak of lyght, and sterres for t'apere,
That she and alle hire folk in went yfeere.   910

So whan it liked hire to go to reste,
And voided weren thei that voiden oughte,
She seyde that to slepen wel hire leste.
Hire wommen soone til hire bed hire broughte.
Whan al was hust, than lay she stille and
          thoughte   915
Of al this thing; the manere and the wise
Reherce it nedeth nought, for ye ben wise.

A nyghtyngale, upon a cedir grene,
Under the chambre wal ther as she ley,
Ful loude song ayein the moone shene,   920
Peraunter, in his briddes wise, a lay
Of love, that made hire herte fressh and gay,
That herkned she so longe in good entente,
Til at the laste the dede slep hire hente.

And as she slep, anonright tho hire mette   925
How that an egle, fethered whit as bon,
Under hire brest his longe clawes sette,
And out hire herte he rente, and that anon,
And dide his herte into hire brest to gon,   929
Of which she nought agroos, ne nothyng
          smerte;
And forth he fleigh, with herte left for herte.

Now lat hire slepe, and we oure tales holde
Of Troilus, that is to paleis riden
Fro the scarmuch of the which I tolde,
And in his chaumbre sit, and hath abiden,   935
Til two or thre of his messages yeden
For Pandarus, and soughten hym ful faste,
Til they hym founde and broughte hym at the
          laste.

This Pandarus com lepyng in atones,
And seyde thus, "Who hath ben wel ibete   940
To-day with swerdes and with slynge-stones,
But Troilus, that hath caught hym an hete?"
And gan to jape, and seyde, "Lord, so ye swete!
But ris, and lat us soupe and go to reste."   944
And he answerde hym, "Do we as the leste."

With al the haste goodly that they myghte,
They spedde hem fro the soper unto bedde;
And every wight out at the dore hym dyghte,
And where hym liste upon his wey him spedde.
But Troilus, that thoughte his herte bledde   950
For wo, til that he herde som tydynge,
He seyde, "Frend, shal I now wepe or synge?"

Quod Pandarus, "Ly stylle, and lat me slepe,
And don thyn hood; thy nedes spedde be!
And ches if thow wolt synge or daunce or lepe!
At shorte wordes, thow shal trowen me: 956
Sire, my nece wol do wel by the,
And love the best, by God and by my trouthe,
But lak of pursuyt make it in thi slouthe.

"For thus ferforth I have thi werk bigonne,
Fro day to day, til this day by the morwe   961
Hire love of frendshipe have I to the wonne,
And also hath she leyd hire feyth to borwe.
Algate a foot is hameled of thi sorwe!"
What sholde I lenger sermon of it holde?   965
As ye han herd byfore, al he hym tolde.

But right as floures, thorugh the cold of nyght
Iclosed, stoupen on hire stalke lowe,
Redressen hem ayein the sonne bright,
And spreden on hire kynde cours by rowe,   970
Right so gan tho his eighen up to throwe
This Troilus, and seyde, "O Venus deere,
Thi myght, thi grace, yheried be it here!"

And to Pandare he held up bothe his hondes,
And seyde, "Lord, al thyn be that I have!   975
For I am hool, al brosten ben my bondes.
A thousand Troyes whoso that me yave,
Ech after other, God so wys me save,
Ne myghte me so gladen; lo, myn herte,
It spredeth so for joie, it wol tosterte!   980

"But, Lord, how shal I doon? How shal I lyven?
Whan shal I next my deere herte see?
How shal this longe tyme awey be dryven,
Til that thow be ayein at hire fro me?
Thow maist answer, 'abid, abid,' but he   985

That hangeth by the nekke, soth to seyne
In gret disese abideth for the peyne."

"Al esily, now, for the love of Marte,"
Quod Pandarus, "for every thing hath tyme.
So longe abid, til that the nyght departe;   990
For al so siker as thow list here by me,
And God toforn, I wyl be ther at pryme;
And forthi, werk somwhat as I shal seye,
Or on som other wight this charge leye.

"For, pardee, God woot I have evere yit   995
Ben redy the to serve, and to this nyght
Have I naught fayned, but emforth my wit
Don al thi lust, and shal with al my myght.
Do now as I shal seyn, and far aright;
And if thow nylt, wit al thiself thi care!   1000
On me is nought along thyn yvel fare.

"I woot wel that thow wiser art than I
A thousand fold, but if I were as thow,
God help me so, as I wolde outrely,
Of myn owen hond, write hire right now   1005
A lettre, in which I wold hire tellen how
I ferde amys, and hire biseche of routhe.
Now help thiself, and leve it nought for slouthe!

"And I myself wol therwith to hire gon;
And whan thow woost that I am with hire there,   1010
Worth thow upon a courser right anon,
Ye, hardily, right in thi beste gere,
And ryd forth by the place, as nought ne were,
And thow shalt fynde us, if I may, sittynge
At som wyndow, into the strete lokynge.   1015

"And if the list, than maystow us salue;
And upon me make thow thi countenaunce;
But, by thi lif, be war and faste eschue
To tarien ought, — God shilde us fro meschaunce!
Rid forth thi wey, and hold thi governaunce;   1020
And we shal speek of the somwhat, I trowe,
Whan thow art gon, to don thyn eris glowe!

"Towchyng thi lettre, thou art wys ynough.
I woot thow nylt it dygneliche endite,
As make it with thise argumentes tough;   1025
Ne scryvenyssh or craftily thow it write;
Biblotte it with thi teris ek a lite;
And if thow write a goodly word al softe,
Though it be good, reherce it nought to ofte.

"For though the beste harpour upon lyve   1030
Wolde on the beste sowned joly harpe
That evere was, with alle his fyngres fyve,
Touche ay o streng, or ay o werbul harpe,
Were his nayles poynted nevere so sharpe,
It sholde maken every wight to dulle,   1035
To here his glee, and of his strokes fulle.

"Ne jompre ek no discordant thyng yfeere,
As thus, to usen termes of phisik
In loves termes; hold of thi matere
The forme alwey, and do that it be lik;   1040
For if a peyntour wolde peynte a pyk
With asses feet, and hede it as an ape,
It cordeth naught, so nere it but a jape."

This counseil liked wel to Troilus,
But, as a dredful lovere, he seyde this: 1045
"Allas, my deere brother Pandarus,
I am ashamed for to write, ywys,
Lest of myn innocence I seyde amys,
Or that she nolde it for despit receyve;
Than were I ded, ther myght it nothyng
      weyve."   1050

To that Pandare answerid, "If the lest,
Do that I seye, and lat me therwith gon;
For by that Lord that formede est and west,
I hope of it to brynge answere anon
Right of hire hond; and if that thow nylt noon,
Lat be, and sory mote he ben his lyve,   1056
Ayeins thi lust that helpeth the to thryve."

Quod Troilus, "Depardieux, ich assente!
Sith that the list, I wil arise and write;
And blisful God prey ich with good entente,
The viage, and the lettre I shal endite,   1061
So spede it; and thow, Minerva, the white,
Yif thow me wit my lettre to devyse."
And sette hym down, and wrot right in this
      wyse.

First he gan hire his righte lady calle,   1065
His hertes lif, his lust, his sorwes leche,
His blisse, and ek thise other termes alle
That in swich cas thise loveres alle seche;
And in ful humble wise, as in his speche,
He gan hym recomaunde unto hire grace;   1070
To telle al how, it axeth muchel space.

And after this, ful lowely he hire preyde
To be nought wroth, thogh he, of his folie,
So hardy was to hire to write, and seyde
That love it made, or elles most he die;   1075

And pitousli gan mercy for to crye;
And after that he seyde, and leigh ful loude,
Hymself was litel worth, and lasse he koude;

And that she sholde han his konnyng excused,
That litel was, and ek he dredde hire soo;   1080
And his unworthynesse he ay acused;
And after that, than gan he telle his woo;
But that was endeles, withouten hoo;
And seyde he wolde in trouthe alwey hym
      holde, —
And radde it over, and gan the lettre folde.

And with his salte teris gan he bathe   1086
The ruby in his signet, and it sette
Upon the wex deliverliche and rathe.
Therwith a thousand tymes, er he lette,
He kiste tho the lettre that she shette,   1090
And seyde, "Lettre, a blisful destine
The shapyn is: my lady shal the see!"

This Pandare tok the lettre, and that bytyme
A-morwe, and to his neces paleis sterte,   1094
And faste he swor that it was passed prime,
And gan to jape, and seyde, "Ywys, myn herte,
So fressh it is, although it sore smerte,
I may naught slepe nevere a Mayes morwe;
I have a joly wo, a lusty sorwe."

Criseyde, whan that she hire uncle herde,   1100
With dredful herte, and desirous to here
The cause of his comynge, thus answerde:
"Now, by youre fey, myn uncle," quod she,
      "dere,
What manere wyndes gydeth yow now here?
Tel us youre joly wo and youre penaunce.   1105
How ferforth be ye put in loves daunce?"

"By God," quod he, "I hoppe alwey byhynde!"
And she to laughe, it thoughte hire herte brest.
Quod Pandarus, "Loke alwey that ye fynde
Game in myn hood; but herkneth, if yow
      lest!   1110
Ther is right now come into town a gest,
A Greek espie, and telleth newe thinges,
For which I come to telle yow tydynges.

"Into the gardyn go we, and ye shal here,
Al pryvely, of this a long sermoun."   1115
With that they wenten arm in arm yfeere
Into the gardyn from the chaumbre down;
And whan that he so fer was that the sown
Of that he spake, no man heren myghte,   1119
He seyde hire thus, and out the lettre plighte:

"Lo, he that is al holy youres free
Hym recomaundeth lowely to youre grace,
And sente yow this lettre here by me.
Avyseth yow on it, whan ye han space,   1124
And of som goodly answere yow purchace;
Or, helpe me God, so pleynly for to seyne,
He may nat longe lyven for his peyne."

Ful dredfully tho gan she stonden stylle,
And took it naught, but al hire humble chere
Gan for to chaunge, and seyde, "Scrit ne
          bille,   1130
For love of God, that toucheth swich matere,
Ne brynge me noon; and also, uncle deere,
To myn estat have more reward, I preye,
Than to his lust! What sholde I more seye?

"And loketh now if this be resonable,   1135
And letteth nought, for favour ne for slouthe,
To seyn a sooth; now were it covenable
To myn estat, by God and by youre trouthe,
To taken it, or to han of hym routhe,
In harmyng of myself, or in repreve?   1140
Ber it ayein, for hym that ye on leve!"

This Pandarus gan on hire for to stare,
And seyde, "Now is this the grettest wondre
That evere I seigh! Lat be this nyce fare!
To dethe mot I smyten be with thondre,   1145
If for the citee which that stondeth yondre,
Wold I a lettre unto yow brynge or take
To harm of yow! What list yow thus it make?

"But thus ye faren, wel neigh alle and some,
That he that most desireth yow to serve,   1150
Of hym ye recche leest wher he bycome,
And whethir that he lyve or elles sterve.
But for al that that ever I may deserve,
Refuse it naught," quod he, and hente hire
          faste,
And in hire bosom the lettre down he thraste,

And seyde hire, "Now cast it awey anon,   1156
That folk may seen and gauren on us tweye."
Quod she, "I kan abyde til they be gon";
And gan to smyle, and seyde hym, "Em, I
          preye,
Swich answere as yow list youreself purveye,
For trewely I nyl no lettre write."   1161
"No? than wol I," quod he, "so ye endite."

Therwith she lough, and seyde, "Go we dyne."
And he gan at hymself to jape faste,
And seyde, "Nece, I have so gret a pyne   1165

For love, that everich other day I faste — "
And gan his beste japes forth to caste,
And made hire so to laughe at his folye,
That she for laughter wende for to dye.

And whan that she was comen into halle,   1170
"Now, em," quod she, "we wol go dyne anon."
And gan some of hire wommen to hire calle,
And streght into hire chambre gan she gon;
But of hire besynesses this was on,
Amonges othere thynges, out of drede,   1175
Ful pryvely this lettre for to rede.

Avysed word by word in every lyne,
And fond no lak, she thoughte he koude good;
And up it putte, and wente hire in to dyne.
But Pandarus, that in a studye stood,   1180
Er he was war, she took hym by the hood,
And seyde, "Ye were caught er that ye wiste."
"I vouche sauf," quod he, "do what you liste."

Tho wesshen they, and sette hem down, and
          ete;
And after noon ful sleighly Pandarus   1185
Gan drawe hym to the wyndowe next the strete,
And seyde, "Nece, who hath araied thus
The yonder hous, that stant aforyeyn us?"
"Which hous?" quod she, and gan for to by-
          holde,   1189
And knew it wel, and whos it was hym tolde;

And fillen forth in speche of thynges smale,
And seten in the windowe bothe tweye.
Whan Pandarus saugh tyme unto his tale,
And saugh wel that hire folk were alle aweye,
"Now, nece myn, tel on," quod he, "I seye,
How liketh yow the lettre that ye woot?   1196
Kan he theron? For, by my trouthe, I noot."

Therwith al rosy hewed tho wex she,
And gan to homme, and seyde, "So I trowe."
"Aquite hym wel, for Goddes love," quod he;
"Myself to medes wol the lettre sowe."   1201
And held his hondes up, and sat on knowe;
"Now, goode nece, be it nevere so lite,
Yif me the labour it to sowe and plite."

"Ye, for I kan so writen," quod she tho;   1205
"And ek I noot what I sholde to hym seye."
"Nay, nece," quod Pandare, "sey nat so.
Yet at the leeste thonketh hym, I preye,
Of his good wille, and doth hym nat to deye.
Now, for the love of me, my nece deere,   1210
Refuseth nat at this tyme my prayere!"

"Depardieux," quod she, "God leve al be wel!
God help me so, this is the firste lettre
That evere I wroot, ye, al or any del."
And into a closet, for t'avise hire bettre,   1215
She wente allone, and gan hire herte unfettre
Out of desdaynes prison but a lite,
And sette hire down, and gan a lettre write,

Of which to telle in short is myn entente
Th'effect, as fer as I kan understonde.   1220
She thanked hym of al that he wel mente
Towardes hire, but holden hym in honde
She nolde nought, ne make hireselven bonde
In love; but as his suster, hym to plese,   1224
She wolde ay fayn, to doon his herte an ese.

She shette it, and in to Pandare gan goon,
Ther as he sat and loked into the strete,
And down she sette hire by hym on a stoon
Of jaspre, upon a quysshyn gold-ybete,
And seyde, "As wisly help me God the grete,
I nevere dide thing with more peyne   1231
Than writen this, to which ye me constreyne";

And took it hym. He thonked hire and seyde,
"God woot, of thyng ful often looth bygonne
Comth ende good; and nece myn, Criseyde,
That ye to hym of hard now ben ywonne   1236
Oughte he be glad, by God and yonder sonne;
For-whi men seith, 'impressiounes lighte
Ful lightly ben ay redy to the flighte.'   1239

"But ye han played the tirant neigh to longe,
And hard was it youre herte for to grave.
Now stynte, that ye no lenger on it honge,
Al wolde ye the forme of daunger save,
But hasteth yow to doon hym joye have;
For trusteth wel, to longe ydoon hardnesse
Causeth despit ful often for destresse."   1246

And right as they declamed this matere,
Lo, Troilus, right at the stretes ende,
Com rydyng with his tenthe som yfere,
Al softely, and thiderward gan bende   1250
Ther as they sete, as was his way to wende
To paleis-ward; and Pandarus hym aspide,
And seyde, "Nece, ysee who comth here ride!

"O fle naught in (he seeth us, I suppose),   1254
Lest he may thynken that ye hym eschuwe."
"Nay, nay," quod she, and wex as red as rose.
With that he gan hire humbly to saluwe,
With dredful chere, and oft his hewes muwe;
And up his look debonairly he caste,
And bekked on Pandare, and forth he paste.

God woot if he sat on his hors aright,   1261
Or goodly was biseyn, that ilke day!
God woot wher he was lik a manly knyght!
What sholde I drecche, or telle of his aray?
Criseyde, which that alle thise thynges say,
To telle in short, hire liked al in-fere,   1266
His person, his aray, his look, his chere,

His goodly manere, and his gentilesse,
So wel that nevere, sith that she was born,
Ne hadde she swych routh of his des-
    tresse;   1270
And how so she hath hard ben here-byforn,
To God hope I, she hath now kaught a thorn,
She shal nat pulle it out this nexte wyke.
God sende mo swich thornes on to pike!

Pandare, which that stood hire faste by,   1275
Felte iren hoot, and he bygan to smyte,
And seyde, "Nece, I pray yow hertely,
Telle me that I shal axen yow a lite.
A womman, that were of his deth to wite,   1279
Withouten his gilt, but for hire lakked routhe,
Were it wel doon?" Quod she, "Nay, by my
    trouthe!"

"God help me so," quod he, "ye sey me soth.
Ye felen wel youreself that I nought lye.
Lo, yond he rit!" "Ye," quod she, "so he doth!"
"Wel," quod Pandare, "as I have told yow
    thrie,   1285
Lat be youre nyce shame and youre folie,
And spek with hym in esyng of his herte;
Lat nycete nat do yow bothe smerte."

But theron was to heven and to doone.
Considered al thing it may nat be;   1290
And whi, for shame; and it were ek to soone
To graunten hym so gret a libertee.
For pleynly hire entente, as seyde she,
Was for to love hym unwist, if she myghte,
And guerdon hym with nothing but with
    sighte.   1295

But Pandarus thought, "It shal nought be so,
Yif that I may; this nyce opynyoun
Shal nought be holden fully yeres two."
What sholde I make of this a long sermoun?
He moste assente on that conclusioun,   1300
As for the tyme; and whan that it was eve,
And al was wel, he roos and tok his leve.

And on his wey ful faste homward he spedde,
And right for joye he felte his herte daunce;

And Troilus he fond allone abedde,   1305
That lay, as do thise lovers, in a traunce
Bitwixen hope and derk disesperaunce.
But Pandarus, right at his in-comynge,
He song, as who seyth, "Somwhat I brynge,"

And seyde, "Who is in his bed so soone   1310
Iburied thus?" "It am I, frend," quod he.
"Who, Troilus? Nay, help me so the moone,"
Quod Pandarus, "thow shalt arise and see
A charme that was sent right now to the,
The which kan helen the of thyn accesse,
If thow do forthwith al thi bisynesse."   1316

"Ye, thorugh the myght of God," quod Troilus.
And Pandarus gan hym the lettre take,
And seyde, "Parde, God hath holpen us!
Have here a light, and loke on al this blake."
But ofte gan the herte glade and quake   1321
Of Troilus, whil that he gan it rede,
So as the wordes yave hym hope or drede.

But finaly, he took al for the beste   1324
That she hym wroot, for somwhat he byheld,
On which hym thoughte he myghte his herte
        reste,
Al covered she the wordes under sheld.
Thus to the more worthi part he held,
That, what for hope and Pandarus byheste,
His grete wo foryede he at the leste.   1330

But as we may alday oureselven see,
Thorugh more wode or col, the more fir,
Right so encrees of hope, of what it be,
Therwith ful ofte encresseth ek desir;
Or as an ook comth of a litel spir,   1335
So thorugh this lettre, which that she hym
        sente,
Encressen gan desir, of which he brente.

Wherfore I seye alwey, that day and nyght
This Troilus gan to desiren moore
Thanne he did erst, thorugh hope, and did his
        myght   1340
To preessen on, as by Pandarus loore,
And writen to hire of his sorwes soore.
Fro day to day he leet it nought refreyde,
That by Pandare he wroot somwhat or seyde;

And dide also his other observaunces   1345
That til a lovere longeth in this cas;
And after that thise dees torned on chaunces,
So was he outher glad or seyde "allas!"
And held after his gistes ay his pas;

And after swiche answeres as he hadde,   1350
So were his dayes sory outher gladde.

But to Pandare alwey was his recours,
And pitously gan ay to hym to pleyne,
And hym bisoughte of reed and som socours:
And Pandarus, that sey his woode peyne,   1355
Wex wel neigh ded for routhe, sooth to seyne,
And bisily with al his herte caste
Som of his wo to slen, and that as faste;

And seyde, "Lord, and frend, and brother dere,
God woot that thi disese doth me wo.   1360
But wiltow stynten al this woful cheere,
And, by my trouthe, er it be dayes two,
And God toforn, yet shal I shape it so,
That thow shalt come into a certeyn place,
There as thow mayst thiself hire preye of grace.

"And certeynly, I noot if thow it woost,   1366
But tho that ben expert in love seye,
It is oon of the thynges forthereth most,
A man to han a layser for to preye,
And siker place his wo for to bywreye;   1370
For in good herte it mot som routhe impresse,
To here and see the giltlees in distresse.

"Peraunter thynkestow: though it be so,
That Kynde wolde don hire to bygynne
To have a manere routhe upon my woo,   1375
Seyth Daunger, 'Nay, thow shalt me nevere
        wynne!'
So reulith hire hir hertes gost withinne,
That though she bende, yeet she stant on roote;
What in effect is this unto my boote?   1379

"Thenk here-ayeins: whan that the stordy ook,
On which men hakketh ofte, for the nones,
Receyved hath the happy fallyng strook,
The greete sweigh doth it come al at ones,
As don thise rokkes or thise milnestones;   1384
For swifter cours comth thyng that is of wighte,
Whan it descendeth, than don thynges lighte.

"And reed that boweth down for every blast,
Ful lightly, cesse wynd, it wol aryse;
But so nyl nought an ook, whan it is cast;
It nedeth me nought the longe to forbise.   1390
Men shal rejoissen of a gret empryse
Acheved wel, and stant withouten doute,
Al han men ben the lenger theraboute.

"But, Troilus, yet telle me, if the lest,
A thing which that I shal now axen the: 1395

Which is thi brother that thow lovest best,
As in thi verray hertes privetee?"
"Iwis, my brother Deiphebus," quod he.
"Now," quod Pandare, "er houres twyes twelve,
He shal the ese, unwist of it hymselve.   1400

"Now lat m'alone, and werken as I may,"
Quod he; and to Deiphebus wente he tho,
Which hadde his lord and grete frend ben ay;
Save Troilus, no man he loved so.
To telle in short, withouten wordes mo,   1405
Quod Pandarus, "I pray yow that ye be
Frend to a cause which that toucheth me."

"Yis, parde," quod Deiphebus, "wel thow
                woost,
In al that evere I may, and God tofore,
Al nere it but for man I love moost,   1410
My brother Troilus; but sey wherfore
It is; for sith that day that I was bore,
I nas, ne nevere mo to ben I thynke,
Ayeins a thing that myghte the forthynke."

Pandare gan hym thank, and to hym seyde,
"Lo, sire, I have a lady in this town,   1416
That is my nece, and called is Criseyde,
Which some men wolden don oppressioun,
And wrongfully han hire possessioun;
Wherfore I of youre lordship yow biseche   1420
To ben oure frend, withouten more speche."

Deiphebus hym answerde, "O, is nat this,
That thow spekest of to me thus straungely,
Criseÿda, my frend?" He seyde, "Yis."
"Than nedeth," quod Deiphebus, "hardyly,   1426
Namore to speke, for trusteth wel that I
Wol be hire champioun with spore and yerde;
I roughte nought though alle hire foos it herde.

"But telle me, thow that woost al this matere,
How I myght best avaylen." — "Now lat se,"
Quod Pandarus; "if ye, my lord so dere,   1431
Wolden as now do this honour to me,
To preyen hire to-morwe, lo, that she
Come unto yow, hire pleyntes to devise,
Hire adversaries wolde of it agrise.   1435

"And yif I more dorste preye yow as now,
And chargen yow to han so gret travaille,
To han som of youre bretheren here with yow,
That myghten to hire cause bet availle,
Than wot I wel she myghte nevere faille   1440
For to ben holpen, what at youre instaunce,
What with hire other frendes governaunce."

Deiphebus, which that comen was of kynde
To alle honour and bounte to consente,
Answerd, "It shal be don; and I kan fynde   1445
Yet grettere help to this, in myn entente.
What wiltow seyn, if I for Eleyne sente
To speke of this? I trowe it be the beste,
For she may leden Paris as hire leste.   1449

"Of Ector, which that is my lord, my brother,
It nedeth naught to preye hym frend to be;
For I have herd hym, o tyme and ek oother,
Speke of Cryseyde swich honour, that he
May seyn no bet, swich hap to hym hath she.
It nedeth naught his helpes for to crave;   1455
He shal be swich, right as we wol hym have.

"Spek thow thiself also to Troilus
On my byhalve, and prey hym with us dyne."
"Syre, al this shal be don," quod Pandarus,
And took his leve, and nevere gan to fyne,   1460
But to his neces hous, as streyght as lyne,
He com; and fond hire fro the mete arise,
And sette hym down, and spak right in this
                wise.

He seide, "O verray God, so have I ronne!
Lo, nece myn, se ye nought how I swete?   1465
I not wheither ye the more thank me konne.
Be ye naught war how false Poliphete
Is now aboute eftsones for to plete,
And brynge on yow advocacies newe?"
"I? no," quod she, and chaunged al hire hewe.   1469

"What is he more aboute, me to drecche
And don me wrong? What shal I doon, allas?
Yet of hymself nothing ne wolde I recche,
Nere it for Antenor and Eneas,
That ben his frendes in swich manere cas.   1475
But, for the love of God, myn uncle deere,
No fors of that, lat hym han al yfeere.

"Withouten that I have ynough for us."
"Nay," quod Pandare, "it shal nothing be so.
For I have ben right now at Deiphebus,   1480
At Ector, and myn oother lordes moo,
And shortly maked ech of hem his foo,
That, by my thrift, he shal it nevere wynne,
For aught he kan, whan that so he bygynne."

And as thei casten what was best to doone,
Deiphebus, of his owen curteisie,   1486
Com hire to preye, in his propre persone,
To holde hym on the morwe compaignie

At dyner; which she nolde nought denye,
But goodly gan to his preier obeye.   1490
He thonked hire, and went upon his weye.

Whan this was don, this Pandare up anon,
To telle in short, and forth gan for to wende
To Troilus, as stille as any ston;
And al this thyng he tolde hym, word and
     ende,   1495
And how that he Deiphebus gan to blende,
And seyde hym, "Now is tyme, if that thow
     konne,
To bere the wel tomorwe, and al is wonne.

"Now spek, now prey, now pitously compleyne;
Lat nought for nyce shame, or drede, or
     slouthe!   1500
Somtyme a man mot telle his owen peyne.
Bileve it, and she shal han on the routhe:
Thow shalt be saved by thi feyth, in trouthe.
But wel woot I that thow art now in drede,
And what it is, I leye, I kan arede.   1505

"Thow thynkest now, 'How sholde I don al this?
For by my cheres mosten folk aspie
That for hire love is that I fare amys;
Yet hadde I levere unwist for sorwe dye.'
Now thynk nat so, for thow dost gret folie;
For I right now have founden o manere   1511
Of sleyghte, for to coveren al thi cheere.

"Thow shalt gon over nyght, and that bylyve,
Unto Deiphebus hous, as the to pleye,
Thi maladie awey the bet to dryve, —   1515
For-whi thow semest sik, soth for to seye.
Sone after that, down in thi bed the leye,
And sey, thow mayst no lenger up endure,
And ly right there, and byd thyn aventure.

"Sey that thi fevre is wont the for to take,   1520
The same tyme, and lasten til a-morwe;
And lat se now how wel thow kanst it make,
For, parde, sik is he that is in sorwe.
Go now, farwel! and Venus here to borwe,
I hope, and thow this purpos holde ferme,   1525
Thi grace she shal fully ther conferme."

Quod Troilus, "Iwis, thow nedeles
Conseilest me that siklich I me feyne,
For I am sik in ernest, douteles,
So that wel neigh I sterve for the peyne."   1530
Quod Pandarus, "Thow shalt the bettre pleyne,
And hast the lasse nede to countrefete,
For hym men demen hoot that men seen swete.

"Lo, hold the at thi triste cloos, and I
Shal wel the deer unto thi bowe dryve."   1535
Therwith he took his leve al softely,
And Troilus to paleis wente blyve.
So glad ne was he nevere in al his lyve,
And to Pandarus reed gan al assente,   1539
And to Deiphebus hous at nyght he wente.

What nedeth yow to tellen al the cheere
That Deiphebus unto his brother made,
Or his accesse, or his sikliche manere,
How men gan hym with clothes for to lade,
Whan he was leyd, and how men wolde hym
     glade?   1545
But al for nought; he held forth ay the wyse
That ye han herd Pandare er this devyse.

But certayn is, er Troilus hym leyde,
Deiphebus had hym preied over-nyght
To ben a frend and helpyng to Criseyde.   1550
God woot that he it graunted anon-right,
To ben hire fulle frend with al his myght;
But swich a nede was to preye hym thenne,
As for to bidde a wood man for to renne.

The morwen com, and neighen gan the tyme
Of meeltide, that the faire queene Eleyne   1556
Shoop hire to ben, an houre after the prime,
With Deiphebus, to whom she nolde feyne;
But as his suster, homly, soth to seyne,
She com to dyner in hire pleyne entente.   1560
But God and Pandare wist al what this mente.

Com ek Criseyde, al innocent of this,
Antigone, hire suster Tarbe also.
But fle we now prolixitee best is,
For love of God, and lat us faste go   1565
Right to th'effect, withouten tales mo,
Whi al this folk assembled in this place;
And lat us of hire saluynges pace.

Gret honour did hem Deiphebus, certeyn,   1569
And fedde hem wel with al that myghte like;
But evere mo "Allas!" was his refreyn,
"My goode brother Troilus, the syke,
Lith yet" — and therwithal he gan to sike;
And after that, he peyned hym to glade
Hem as he myghte, and cheere good he made.

Compleyned ek Eleyne of his siknesse   1576
So feythfully, that pite was to here,
And every wight gan waxen for accesse
A leche anon, and seyde, "In this manere

Men curen folk." — "This charme I wol yow
    leere."   1580
But ther sat oon, al list hire nought to teche,
That thoughte, "Best koud I yet ben his leche."

After compleynte, hym gonnen they to preyse,
As folk don yet, whan som wight hath bygonne
To preise a man, and up with pris hym
    reise   1585
A thousand fold yet heigher than the sonne:
"He is, he kan, that fewe lordes konne."
And Pandarus, of that they wolde afferme,
He naught forgat hire preisynge to conferme.

Herde al this thyng Criseyde wel inough,   1590
And every word gan for to notifie;
For which with sobre cheere hire herte lough.
For who is that ne wolde hire glorifie,
To mowen swich a knyght don lyve or dye?
But al passe I, lest ye to longe dwelle;   1595
For for o fyn is al that evere I telle.

The tyme com, fro dyner for to ryse,
And as hem aughte, arisen everichon.
And gonne a while of this and that devise.
But Pandarus brak al this speche anon,   1600
And seide to Deiphebus, "Wol ye gon,
If it youre wille be, as I yow preyde,
To speke here of the nedes of Criseyde?"

Eleyne, which that by the hond hire held,
Took first the tale, and seyde, "Go we blyve";
And goodly on Criseyde she biheld,   1606
And seyde, "Joves lat hym nevere thryve,
That doth yow harm, and brynge hym soone
    of lyve,
And yeve me sorwe, but he shal it rewe,
If that I may, and alle folk be trewe!"   1610

"Telle thow thi neces cas," quod Deiphebus
To Pandarus, "for thow kanst best it telle."
"My lordes and my ladys, it stant thus:
What sholde I lenger," quod he, "do yow
    dwelle?"
He rong hem out a proces lik a belle   1615
Upon hire foo, that highte Poliphete,
So heynous, that men myghte on it spete.

Answerde of this ech werse of hem than other,
And Poliphete they gonnen thus to warien:
"Anhonged be swich oon, were he my brother!
And so he shal, for it ne may nought varien!"
What shold I lenger in this tale tarien?   1622

Pleynliche, alle at ones, they hire highten
To ben hire helpe in al that evere they
    myghten.

Spak than Eleyne, and seyde, "Pandarus,   1625
Woot ought my lord, my brother, this matere,
I meene Ector? or woot it Troilus?"
He seyde, "Ye, but wole ye now me here?
Me thynketh this, sith that Troilus is here,
It were good, if that ye wolde assente,   1630
She tolde hireself hym al this, er she wente.

"For he wol have the more hir grief at herte,
By cause, lo, that she a lady is;
And, by youre leve, I wol but in right sterte
And do yow wyte, and that anon, iwys,   1635
If that he slepe, or wol ought here of this."
And in he lepte, and seyde hym in his ere,
"God have thi soule, ibrought have I thi beere!"

To smylen of this gan tho Troilus,
And Pandarus, withouten rekenynge,   1640
Out wente anon to Eleyne and Deiphebus,
And seyde hem, "So ther be no taryinge,
Ne moore prees, he wol wel that ye brynge
Criseÿda, my lady, that is here;
And as he may enduren, he wol here.   1645

"But wel ye woot, the chaumbre is but lite,
And fewe folk may lightly make it warm;
Now loketh ye (for I wol have no wite,
To brynge in prees that myghte don hym harm,
Or hym disesen, for my bettre arm)   1650
Wher it be bet she bide til eft-sonys,
Now loketh ye, that knowen what to doon is.

"I sey for me, best is, as I kan knowe,
That no wight in ne wente but ye tweye,
But it were I, for I kan in a throwe   1655
Reherce hire cas unlik that she kan seye;
And after this, she may hym ones preye
To ben good lord, in short, and take hire leve.
This may nought muchel of his ese hym reve.

"And ek, for she is straunge, he wol for-
    bere   1660
His ese, which that hym thar nought for yow;
Ek oother thing, that toucheth nought to here,
He wol yow telle — I woot it wel right now —
That secret is, and for the townes prow."   1664
And they, that nothyng knewe of his entente,
Withouten more, to Troilus in they wente.

Eleyne, in al hire goodly softe wyse,
Gan hym salue, and wommanly to pleye,

And seyde, "Iwys, ye moste alweies arise!
Now, faire brother, beth al hool, I preye!" 1670
And gan hire arm right over his shulder leye,
And hym with al hire wit to reconforte;
As she best koude, she gan hym to disporte.

So after this quod she, "We yow biseke,
My deere brother, Deiphebus, and I, 1675
For love of God — and so doth Pandare eke —
To ben good lord and frend, right hertely,
Unto Criseyde, which that certeynly
Receyveth wrong, as woot weel here Pandare,
That kan hire cas wel bet than I declare." 1680

This Pandarus gan newe his tong affile,
And al hire cas reherce, and that anon.
Whan it was seyd, soone after in a while,
Quod Troilus, "As sone as I may gon, 1684
I wol right fayn with al my myght ben oon,
Have God my trouthe, hire cause to sustene."
"Good thrift have ye!" quod Eleyne the queene.

Quod Pandarus, "And it youre wille be,
That she may take hire leve, er that she go?"
"O, elles God forbede it," tho quod he, 1690
"If that she vouche sauf for to do so."
And with that word quod Troilus, "Ye two,
Deiphebus and my suster lief and deere,
To yow have I to speke of o matere, 1694

To ben avysed by youre reed the bettre — "
And fond, as hap was, at his beddes hed,
The copie of a tretys and a lettre,
That Ector hadde hym sent to axen red
If swych a man was worthi to ben ded,
Woot I nought who; but in a grisly wise 1700
He preyede hem anon on it avyse.

Deiphebus gan this lettre for t'onfolde
In ernest greet; so did Eleyne the queene;
And romyng outward, faste it gonne byholde,
Downward a steire, into an herber greene. 1705
This ilke thing they redden hem bitwene,
And largely, the mountance of an houre,
Thei gonne on it to reden and to poure.

Now lat hem rede, and torne we anon
To Pandarus, that gan ful faste prye 1710
That al was wel, and out he gan to gon
Into the grete chaumbre, and that in hye,
And seyde, "God save al this companye!

Come, nece myn; my lady queene Eleyne
Abideth yow, and ek my lordes tweyne. 1715

"Rys, take with yow youre nece Antigone,
Or whom yow list; or no fors; hardyly
The lesse prees, the bet; com forth with me,
And loke that ye thonken humblely
Hem alle thre, and whan ye may goodly 1720
Youre tyme se, taketh of hem youre leeve,
Lest we to longe his restes hym byreeve."

Al innocent of Pandarus entente,
Quod tho Criseyde, "Go we, uncle deere";
And arm in arm inward with hym she wente,
Avysed wel hire wordes and hire cheere; 1726
And Pandarus, in ernestful manere,
Seyde, "Alle folk, for Godes love, I preye,
Stynteth right here, and softely yow pleye.

"Aviseth yow what folk ben hire withinne, 1730
And in what plit oon is, God hym amende!"
And inward thus, "Ful softely bygynne,
Nece, I conjure and heighly yow defende,
On his half which that soule us alle sende,
And in the vertu of corones tweyne, 1735
Sle naught this man, that hath for yow this
    peyne!

"Fy on the devel! thynk which oon he is,
And in what plit he lith; com of anon!
Thynk al swich taried tyde, but lost it nys.
That wol ye bothe seyn, whan ye ben oon.
Secoundely, ther yet devyneth noon 1741
Upon yow two; come of now, if ye konne!
While folk is blent, lo, al the tyme is wonne.

"In titeryng, and pursuyte, and delayes,
The folk devyne at waggyng of a stree; 1745
And though ye wolde han after mirye dayes,
Than dar ye naught; and whi? for she, and she
Spak swych a word; thus loked he, and he!
Lest tyme I loste, I dar nought with yow dele.
Com of, therfore, and bryngeth hym to hele!"

But now to yow, ye loveres that ben here, 1751
Was Troilus nought in a kankedort,
That lay, and myghte whisprynge of hem here,
And thoughte, "O Lord, right now renneth my
    sort
Fully to deye, or han anon comfort!" 1755
And was the firste tyme he shulde hire preye
Of love; O myghty God, what shal he seye?

Explicit liber secundus.

Book III

Incipit prohemium tercii libri.

O blisful light, of which the bemes clere
Adorneth al the thridde heven faire!
O sonnes lief, O Joves doughter deere,
Plesance of love, O goodly debonaire,
In gentil hertes ay redy to repaire!   5
O veray cause of heele and of gladnesse,
Iheryed be thy myght and thi goodnesse!

In hevene and helle, in erthe and salte see
Is felt thi myght, if that I wel descerne;
As man, brid, best, fissh, herbe, and grene tree
Thee fele in tymes with vapour eterne.   11
God loveth, and to love wol nought werne;
And in this world no lyves creature
Withouten love is worth, or may endure.

Ye Joves first to thilk effectes glade,   15
Thorugh which that thynges lyven alle and be,
Comeveden, and amorous him made
On mortal thyng, and as yow list, ay ye
Yeve hym in love ese or adversitee;
And in a thousand formes down hym sente   20
For love in erthe, and whom yow liste, he
        hente.

Ye fierse Mars apaisen of his ire,
And as yow list, ye maken hertes digne;
Algates hem that ye wol sette a-fyre,   24
They dreden shame, and vices they resygne;
Ye do hem corteys be, fresshe and benigne;
And heighe or lowe, after a wight entendeth,
The joies that he hath, youre myght him send-
        eth.

Ye holden regne and hous in unitee;
Ye sothfast cause of frendshipe ben also;   30
Ye knowe al thilke covered qualitee
Of thynges, which that folk on wondren so,
Whan they kan nought construe how it may jo
She loveth hym, or whi he loveth here,
As whi this fissh, and naught that, comth to
        were.   35

Ye folk a lawe han set in universe,
And this knowe I by hem that lovers be,
That whoso stryveth with yow hath the werse.
Now, lady bryght, for thi benignite,
At reverence of hem that serven the,   40
Whos clerc I am, so techeth me devyse
Som joye of that is felt in thi servyse.

Ye in my naked herte sentement
Inhielde, and do me shewe of thy swetnesse. —
Caliope, thi vois be now present,   45
For now is nede; sestow nought my destresse,
How I mot telle anonright the gladnesse
Of Troilus, to Venus heryinge?
To which gladnesse, who nede hath, God hym
        brynge!

Explicit prohemium tercii libri.

Incipit liber tercius.

Lay al this mene while Troilus,   50
Recordyng his lesson in this manere:
"Mafay," thoughte he, "thus wol I sey, and
        thus;
Thus wol I pleyne unto my lady dere;
That word is good, and this shal be my cheere;
This nyl I nought foryeten in no wise."   55
God leve hym werken as he kan devyse!

And, Lord, so that his herte gan to quappe,
Heryng hire come, and shorte for to sike!
And Pandarus, that ledde hire by the lappe,
Com ner, and gan in at the curtyn pike,   60
And seyde, "God do boot on alle syke!
Se who is here yow comen to visite;
Lo, here is she that is youre deth to wite."

Therwith it semed as he wepte almost.
"Ha, a," quod Troilus so reufully,   65
"Wher me be wo, O myghty God, thow woost!
Who is al ther? I se nought trewely."
"Sire," quod Criseyde, "it is Pandare and I."
"Ye, swete herte? allas, I may nought rise,
To knele and do yow honour in som wyse."   70

And dressed hym upward, and she right tho
Gan bothe hire hondes softe upon hym leye.
"O, for the love of God, do ye nought so
To me," quod she, "I! what is this to seye?
Sire, comen am I to yow for causes tweye: 75
First, yow to thonke, and of youre lordshipe eke
Continuance I wolde yow biseke."

This Troilus, that herde his lady preye
Of lordshipe hym, wax neither quyk ne ded,
Ne myghte o word for shame to it seye,   80
Although men sholde smyten of his hed.
But, Lord, so he wex sodeynliche red,
And sire, his lessoun, that he wende konne
To preyen hire, is thorugh his wit ironne.

Criseyde al this aspied wel ynough,   85
For she was wis, and loved hym nevere the
    lasse,
Al nere he malapert, or made it tough,
Or was to bold, to synge a fool a masse.
But whan his shame gan somwhat to passe,
His resons, as I may my rymes holde,   90
I wol yow telle, as techen bokes olde.

In chaunged vois, right for his verray drede,
Which vois ek quook, and therto his manere
Goodly abaist, and now his hewes rede,
Now pale, unto Criseyde, his lady dere,   95
With look down cast and humble iyolden chere,
Lo, the alderfirste word that hym asterte
Was, twyes, "Mercy, mercy, swete herte!"

And stynte a while, and whan he myghte out
    brynge,
The nexte word was, "God woot, for I have,
As ferforthly as I have had konnynge,   101
Ben youres al, God so my soule save,
And shal, til that I, woful wight, be grave!
And though I dar, ne kan, unto yow pleyne,
Iwis, I suffre nought the lasse peyne.   105

"Thus muche as now, O wommanliche wif,
I may out brynge, and if this yow displese,
That shal I wreke upon myn owen lif
Right soone, I trowe, and do youre herte an ese,
If with my deth youre wreththe I may
    apese.   110
But syn that ye han herd me somwhat seye,
Now recche I nevere how soone that I deye."

Therwith his manly sorwe to biholde,
It myghte han mad an herte of stoon to rewe;
And Pandare wep as he to water wolde,   115
And poked evere his nece new and newe,
And seyde, "Wo bygon ben hertes trewe!
For love of God, make of this thing an ende,
Or sle us both at ones, er ye wende."

"I! what?" quod she, "by God and by my
    trouthe,   120
I not nat what ye wilne that I seye."
"I! what?" quod he, "that ye han on hym
    routhe,
For Goddes love, and doth hym nought to
    deye."
"Now thanne thus," quod she, "I wolde hym
    preye
To telle me the fyn of his entente.   125
Yet wist I nevere wel what that he mente."

"What that I mene, O swete herte deere?"
Quod Troilus, "O goodly, fresshe free,
That with the stremes of youre eyen cleere
Ye wolde somtyme frendly on me see,   130
And thanne agreen that I may ben he,
Withouten braunche of vice on any wise,
In trouthe alwey to don yow my servise,

"As to my lady right and chief resort,
With al my wit and al my diligence;   135
And I to han, right as yow list, comfort,
Under yowre yerde, egal to myn offence,
As deth, if that I breke youre defence;
And that ye deigne me so muche honoure,
Me to comanden aught in any houre;   140

"And I to ben youre verray, humble, trewe,
Secret, and in my paynes pacient,
And evere mo desiren fresshly newe
To serve, and ben ay ylike diligent,
And with good herte al holly youre talent   145
Receyven wel, how sore that me smerte, —
Lo, this mene I, myn owen swete herte."

Quod Pandarus, "Lo, here an hard requeste,
And resonable, a lady for to werne!
Now, nece myn, by natal Joves feste,   150
Were I a god, ye sholden sterve as yerne,
That heren wel this man wol nothing yerne
But youre honour, and sen hym almost sterve,
And ben so loth to suffren hym yow serve."

With that she gan hire eyen on hym caste   155
Ful esily and ful debonairly,
Avysyng hire, and hied nought to faste
With nevere a word, but seyde hym softely,
"Myn honour sauf, I wol wel trewely,
And in swich forme as he gan now devyse,   160
Receyven hym fully to my servyse,

"Bysechyng hym, for Goddes love, that he
Wolde, in honour of trouthe and gentilesse,
As I wel mene, eke menen wel to me,
And myn honour with wit and bisynesse   165
Ay kepe; and if I may don hym gladnesse,
From hennesforth, iwys, I nyl nought feyne.
Now beth al hool, no lenger ye ne pleyne."

"But natheles, this warne I yow," quod she,
"A kynges sone although ye be, ywys,   170
Ye shal namore han sovereignete
Of me in love, than right in that cas is;
N'y nyl forbere, if that ye don amys,
To wratthe yow; and whil that ye me serve,
Chericen yow right after ye disserve.   175

"And shortly, deere herte and al my knyght,
Beth glad, and draweth yow to lustinesse,
And I shal trewely, with al my myght,
Youre bittre tornen al into swetenesse;
If I be she that may yow do gladnesse,   180
For every wo ye shal recovere a blisse."
And hym in armes took, and gan hym kisse.

Fil Pandarus on knees, and up his eyen
To heven threw, and held his hondes highe,
"Immortal god," quod he, "that mayst nought
        deyen,   185
Cupid I mene, of this mayst glorifie;
And Venus, thow mayst maken melodie!
Withouten hond, me semeth that in towne,
For this merveille, ich here ech belle sowne.

"But ho! namore as now of this matere;   190
For-whi this folk wol comen up anon,
That han the lettre red; lo, I hem here.
But I conjure the, Criseyde, and oon,
And two, thow Troilus, whan thow mayst goon,
That at myn hous ye ben at my warnynge,   195
For I ful well shal shape youre comynge;

"And eseth there youre hertes right ynough;
And lat se which of yow shal bere the belle,
To speke of love aright!" — therwith he lough —
"For ther have ye a leiser for to telle."   200
Quod Troilus, "How longe shal I dwelle,
Er this be don?" Quod he, "Whan thow mayst
        ryse,
This thyng shal be right as I yow devyse."

With that Eleyne and also Deiphebus   204
Tho comen upward, right at the steires ende;
And Lord, so thanne gan gronen Troilus,
His brother and his suster for to blende.
Quod Pandarus, "It tyme is that we wende.
Tak, nece myn, youre leve at alle thre,
And lat hem speke, and cometh forth with me."

She took hire leve at hem ful thriftily,   211
As she wel koude, and they hire reverence
Unto the fulle diden, hardyly,
And wonder wel speken, in hire absence,
Of hire, in preysing of hire excellence,   215
Hire governaunce, hire wit; and hire manere
Comendeden, it joie was to here.

Now lat hire wende unto hire owen place,
And torne we to Troilus ayein,
That gan ful lightly of the lettre pace   220
That Deiphebus hadde in the gardyn seyn;

And of Eleyne and hym he wolde feyn
Delivered ben, and seyde that hym leste
To slepe, and after tales have reste.

Eleyne hym kiste, and took hire leve blyve,   225
Deiphebus ek, and hom wente every wight;
And Pandarus, as faste as he may dryve,
To Troilus tho com, as lyne right,
And on a paillet al that glade nyght
By Troilus he lay, with mery chere,   230
To tale; and wel was hem they were yfeere.

Whan every wight was voided but they two,
And alle the dores weren faste yshette,
To telle in short, withouten wordes mo,
This Pandarus, withouten any lette,   235
Up roos, and on his beddes syde hym sette,
And gan to speken in a sobre wyse
To Troilus, as I shal yow devyse:

"Myn alderlevest lord, and brother deere,
God woot, and thow, that it sat me so soore,
When I the saugh so langwisshyng to-yere   241
For love, of which thi wo wax alwey moore,
That I, with al my myght and al my loore,
Have evere sithen don my bisynesse
To brynge the to joye out of distresse,   245

"And have it brought to swich plit as thow
        woost,
So that thorugh me thow stondest now in weye
To faren wel; I sey it for no bost,
And wostow whi? for shame it is to seye:
For the have I bigonne a gamen pleye,   250
Which that I nevere do shal eft for other,
Although he were a thousand fold my brother.

"That is to seye, for the am I bicomen,
Bitwixen game and ernest, swich a meene
As maken wommen unto men to comen;   255
Al sey I nought, thow wost wel what I meene.
For the have I my nece, of vices cleene,
So fully maad thi gentilesse triste,
That al shal ben right as thiselven liste.

"But God, that al woot, take I to witnesse,   260
That nevere I this for coveitise wroughte,
But oonly for t'abregge that distresse
For which wel neigh thow deidest, as me
        thoughte.
But, goode brother, do now as the oughte,
For Goddes love, and kep hire out of blame,
Syn thow art wys, and save alwey hire
        name.   266

"For wel thow woost, the name as yet of here
Among the peeple, as who seyth, halwed is;
For that man is unbore, I dar wel swere,
That evere wiste that she dide amys.   270
But wo is me, that I, that cause al this,
May thynken that she is my nece deere,
And I hire em, and traitour eke yfeere!

"And were it wist that I, thorugh myn engyn,
Hadde in my nece yput this fantasie,   275
To doon thi lust and holly to ben thyn,
Whi, al the world upon it wolde crie,
And seyn that I the werste trecherie
Dide in this cas, that evere was bigonne,
And she forlost, and thow right nought ywonne.

"Wherfore, er I wol ferther gon a pas,   281
Yet eft I the biseche and fully seye,
That privete go with us in this cas,
That is to seyn, that thow us nevere wreye;
And be nought wroth, though I the ofte preye
To holden secree swich an heigh matere,   286
For skilfull is, thow woost wel, my praiere.

"And thynk what wo ther hath bitid er this,
For makyng of avantes, as men rede;
And what meschaunce in this world yet ther
        is,   290
Fro day to day, right for that wikked dede;
For which thise wise clerkes that ben dede
Han evere thus proverbed to us yonge,
That 'firste vertu is to kepe tonge.'

"And nere it that I wilne as now t'abregge   295
Diffusioun of speche, I koude almoost
A thousand olde stories the allegge
Of wommen lost through fals and foles bost.
Proverbes kanst thiself ynowe and woost,
Ayeins that vice, for to ben a labbe,   300
Al seyde men soth as often as thei gabbe.

"O tonge, allas! so often here-byforn
Hath mad ful many a lady bright of hewe
Seyd 'weilaway, the day that I was born!'
And many a maydes sorwe for to newe;   305
And for the more part, al is untrewe
That men of yelpe, and it were brought to
        preve.
Of kynde non avauntour is to leve.

"Avauntour and a lyere, al is on;
As thus: I pose, a womman graunte me   310
Hire love, and seith that other wol she non,

And I am sworn to holden it secree,
And after I go telle it two or thre;
Iwis, I am avauntour at the leeste,
And lyere, for I breke my biheste.   315

"Now loke thanne, if they be nought to blame,
Swich manere folk — what shal I clepe hem?
        what? —
That hem avaunte of wommen, and by name,
That nevere yet bihyghte hem this ne that,
Ne knewe hem more than myn olde hat!   320
No wonder is, so God me sende hele,
Though wommen dreden with us men to dele.

"I sey nought this for no mistrust of yow,
Ne for no wise men, but for foles nyce,
And for the harm that in the werld is now,   325
As wel for folie ofte as for malice;
For wel woot I, in wise folk that vice
No womman drat, if she be wel avised;
For wyse ben by foles harm chastised.

"But now to purpos; leve brother deere,   330
Have al this thyng that I have seyd in mynde,
And kep the clos, and be now of good cheere,
For at thi day thow shalt me trewe fynde.
I shal thi proces set in swych a kynde,
And God toforn, that it shal the suffise,   335
For it shal be right as thow wolt devyse.

"For wel I woot, thow menest wel, parde;
Therfore I dar this fully undertake.
Thow woost ek what thi lady graunted the,
And day is set, the chartres up to make.   340
Have now good nyght, I may no lenger wake;
And bid for me, syn thow art now in blysse,
That God me sende deth or soone lisse."

Who myghte tellen half the joie or feste
Which that the soule of Troilus tho felte,   345
Heryng th'effect of Pandarus byheste?
His olde wo, that made his herte swelte,
Gan tho for joie wasten and tomelte,
And al the richesse of his sikes sore
At ones fledde; he felte of hem namore.   350

But right so as thise holtes and thise hayis,
That han in wynter dede ben and dreye,
Revesten hem in grene, when that May is,
Whan every lusty liketh best to pleye;
Right in that selve wise, soth to seye.   355
Wax sodeynliche his herte ful of joie,
That gladder was ther nevere man in Troie.

And gan his look on Pandarus up caste
Ful sobrely, and frendly for to se,
And seyde, "Frend, in Aperil the laste, —   360
As wel thow woost, if it remembre the, —
How neigh the deth for wo thow fownde me,
And how thow dedest al thi bisynesse
To knowe of me the cause of my destresse.

"Thow woost how longe ich it forbar to seye
To the, that art the man that I best triste;   366
And peril non was it to the bywreye,
That wist I wel, but telle me, if the liste,
Sith I so loth was that thiself it wiste,
How dorst I mo tellen of this matere,   370
That quake now, and no wight may us here?

"But natheles, by that God I the swere,
That, as hym list, may al this world governe, —
And, if I lye, Achilles with his spere
Myn herte cleve, al were my lif eterne,   375
As I am mortal, if I late or yerne
Wolde it bewreye, or dorst, or sholde konne,
For al the good that God made under sonne —

"That rather deye I wolde, and determyne,
As thynketh me, now stokked in prisoun,   380
In wrecchidnesse, in filthe, and in vermyne,
Caytif to cruel kyng Agamenoun;
And this in all the temples of this town
Upon the goddes alle, I wol the swere
To-morwe day, if that it like the here.   385

"And that thow hast so muche ido for me
That I ne may it nevere more diserve,
This know I wel, al myghte I now for the
A thousand tymes on a morwe sterve.
I kan namore, but that I wol the serve   390
Right as thi sclave, whider so thow wende,
For evere more, unto my lyves ende.

"But here, with al myn herte, I the biseche
That nevere in me thow deme swich folie
As I shal seyn; me thoughte by thi speche   395
That this which thow me dost for compaignie,
I sholde wene it were a bauderye.
I am nought wood, al if I lewed be!
It is nought so, that woot I wel, parde!

"But he that gooth, for gold or for ricchesse,
On swich message, calle hym what the list;   401
And this that thow doost, calle it gentilesse,
Compassioun, and felawship, and trist.
Departe it so, for wyde-wher is wist

How that ther is diversite required   405
Bytwixen thynges like, as I have lered.

"And, that thow knowe I thynke nought, ne
        wene,
That this servise a shame be or jape,
I have my faire suster Polixene,
Cassandre, Eleyne, or any of the frape,   410
Be she nevere so fair or wel yshape,
Telle me which thow wilt of everychone,
To han for thyn, and lat me thanne allone.

"But sith thow hast idon me this servyse,
My lif to save, and for non hope of mede,   415
So, for the love of God, this grete emprise
Perfourme it out, for now is moste nede;
For heigh and lough, withouten any drede,
I wol alwey thyn hestes alle kepe.
Have now good nyght, and lat us bothe slepe."

Thus held hym ech of other wel apayed,   421
That al the world ne myghte it bet amende;
And on the morwe, whan they were arayed,
Ech to his owen nedes gan entende.
But Troilus, though as the fir he brende   425
For sharp desir of hope and of plesaunce,
He nought forgat his goode governaunce.

But in hymself with manhod gan restreyne
Ech racle dede and ech unbridled cheere,
That alle tho that lyven, soth to seyne,   430
Ne sholde han wist, by word or by manere,
What that he mente, as touchyng this matere.
From every wight as fer as is the cloude
He was, so wel dissimulen he koude.

And al the while which that I yow devyse,   435
This was his lif: with all his fulle myght,
By day, he was in Martes heigh servyse,
This is to seyn, in armes as a knyght;
And for the more part, the longe nyght   439
He lay and thoughte how that he myghte serve
His lady best, hire thonk for to deserve.

Nil I naught swere, although he lay ful softe,
That in his thought he nas somwhat disesed,
Ne that he torned on his pilwes ofte,   444
And wold of that hym missed han ben sesed.
But in swich cas man is nought alwey plesed,
For aught I woot, namore than was he;
That kan I deme of possibilitee.

But certeyn is, to purpos for to go,
That in this while, as writen is in geeste,   450

He say his lady somtyme, and also
She with hym spak, whan that she dorst and
    leste;
And by hire bothe avys, as was the beste,
Apoynteden full warly in this nede,
So as they durste, how they wolde procede.   455

But it was spoken in so short a wise,
In swich await alwey, and in swich feere,
Lest any wight devynen or devyse
Wolde of hem two, or to it laye an ere,
That al this world so leef to hem ne were   460
As that Cupide wolde hem grace sende
To maken of hire speche aright an ende.

But thilke litel that they spake or wroughte,
His wise goost took ay of al swych heede,
It semed hire he wiste what she thoughte   465
Withouten word, so that it was no nede
To bidde hym ought to doon, or ought for-
    beede;
For which she thought that love, al come it
    late,
Of alle joie hadde opned hire the yate.

And shortly of this proces for to pace,   470
So wel his werk and wordes he bisette,
That he so ful stood in his lady grace,
That twenty thousand tymes, er she lette,
She thonked God that evere she with hym
    mette.
So koude he hym governe in swich servyse,   475
That al the world ne myght it bet devyse.

For whi she fond hym so discret in al,
So secret, and of swich obëisaunce,
That wel she felte he was to hire a wal
Of stiel, and sheld from every displesaunce;
That to ben in his goode governaunce,   481
So wis he was, she was namore afered, —
I mene, as fer as oughte ben required.

And Pandarus, to quike alwey the fir,
Was evere ylike prest and diligent;   485
To ese his frend was set al his desir.
He shof ay on, he to and fro was sent;
He lettres bar whan Troilus was absent;
That nevere man, as in his frendes nede,
Ne bar hym bet than he, withouten drede.   490

But now, paraunter, som man wayten wolde
That every word, or soonde, or look, or cheere
Of Troilus that I rehercen sholde,
In al this while unto his lady deere.

I trowe it were a long thyng for to here;   495
Or of what wight that stant in swich disjoynte,
His wordes alle, or every look, to poynte.

For sothe, I have naught herd it don er this
In story non, ne no man here, I wene;
And though I wolde, I koude nought, ywys;
For ther was som epistel hem bitwene,   501
That wolde, as seyth myn autour, wel contene
Neigh half this book, of which hym liste nought
    write.
How sholde I thanne a lyne of it endite?

But to the grete effect. Than sey I thus,   505
That stondyng in concord and in quiete,
Thise ilke two, Criseyde and Troilus,
As I have told, and in this tyme swete, —
Save only often myghte they nought mete,
Ne leiser have hire speches to fulfelle, —   510
That it bifel right as I shal yow telle,

That Pandarus, that evere dide his myght
Right for the fyn that I shal speke of here,
As for to bryngen to his hows som nyght
His faire nece and Troilus yfere,   515
Wheras at leiser al this heighe matere,
Touchyng here love, were at the fulle up-
    bounde,
Hadde out of doute a tyme to it founde.

For he with gret deliberacioun
Hadde every thyng that herto myght availle
Forncast and put in execucioun,   521
And neither left for cost ne for travaile.
Come if hem list, hem sholde no thyng faille;
And for to ben in ought aspied there,
That, wiste he wel, an impossible were.   525

Dredeles, it cler was in the wynd
From every pie and every lette-game;
Now al is wel, for al the world is blynd
In this matere, bothe fremed and tame.
This tymbur is al redy up to frame;   530
Us lakketh nought but that we witen wolde
A certeyn houre, in which she comen sholde.

And Troilus, that al this purveiaunce
Knew at the fulle, and waited on it ay,
Hadde hereupon ek mad gret ordinaunce,
And found his cause, and therto his aray,   536
If that he were missed, nyght or day,
Ther-while he was aboute this servyse,
That he was gon to don his sacrifise,

And moste at swich a temple allone wake,   540
Answered of Apollo for to be;
And first to sen the holy laurer quake,
Er that Apollo spake out of the tree,
To telle hym next whan Grekes sholde flee, —
And forthy lette hym no man, God forbede,   545
But prey Apollo helpen in this nede.

Now is ther litel more for to doone,
But Pandare up, and shortly for to seyne,
Right sone upon the chaungynge of the moone,
Whan lightles is the world a nyght or
          tweyne,   550
And that the wolken shop hym for to reyne,
He streght o morwe unto his nece wente;
Ye han wel herd the fyn of his entente.

Whan he was com, he gan anon to pleye
As he was wont, and of hymself to jape;   555
And finaly he swor and gan hire seye,
By this and that, she sholde hym nought es-
          cape,
Ne lenger don hym after hire to cape;
But certeynly she moste, by hire leve,
Come soupen in his hous with hym at eve.   560

At which she lough, and gan hire faste excuse,
And seyde, "It reyneth; lo, how sholde I gon?"
"Lat be," quod he, "ne stant nought thus to
          muse.
This moot be don! Ye shal be ther anon."
So at the laste herof they fille aton,   565
Or elles, softe he swor hire in hire ere,
He nolde nevere comen ther she were.

Soone after this, she gan to hym to rowne,
And axed hym if Troilus were there.
He swor hire nay, for he was out of towne,   570
And seyde, "Nece, I pose that he were;
Yow thurste nevere han the more fere;
For rather than men myghte hym ther aspie,
Me were levere a thousand fold to dye."

Nought list myn auctour fully to declare   575
What that she thoughte whan he seyde so,
That Troilus was out of towne yfare,
As if he seyde therof soth or no;
But that, withowten await, with hym to go,
She graunted hym, sith he hire that bisoughte,
And, as his nece, obeyed as hire oughte.   581

But natheles, yet gan she hym biseche,
Although with hym to gon it was no fere,
For to ben war of goosish poeples speche,

That dremen thynges whiche that nevere
          were,   585
And wel avyse hym whom he broughte there;
And seyde hym, "Em, syn I most on yow triste,
Loke al be wel, and do now as yow liste."

He swor hire yis, by stokkes and by stones,
And by the goddes that in hevene dwelle,   590
Or elles were hym levere, soule and bones,
With Pluto kyng as depe ben in helle
As Tantalus! — what sholde I more telle?
Whan al was wel, he roos and took his leve,
And she to soper com, whan it was eve,   595

With a certein of hire owen men,
And with hire faire nece Antigone,
And other of hire wommen nyne or ten.
But who was glad now, who, as trowe ye,
But Troilus, that stood and myght it se   600
Thoroughout a litel wyndow in a stewe,
Ther he bishet syn mydnyght was in mewe,

Unwist of every wight but of Pandare?
But to the point; now whan that she was come,
With alle joie and alle frendes fare,   605
Hire em anon in armes hath hire nome,
And after to the soper, alle and some,
Whan tyme was, ful softe they hem sette.
God woot, ther was no deynte for to fette!

And after soper gonnen they to rise,   610
At ese wel, with hertes fresshe and glade,
And wel was hym that koude best devyse
To liken hire, or that hire laughen made.
He song; she pleyde; he tolde tale of Wade.
But at the laste, as every thyng hath ende,   615
She took hire leve, and nedes wolde wende.

But O Fortune, executrice of wyrdes,
O influences of thise hevenes hye!
Soth is, that under God ye ben oure hierdes,
Though to us bestes ben the causes wrie.   620
This mene I now, for she gan homward hye,
But execut was al bisyde hire leve
The goddes wil; for which she moste bleve.

The bente moone with hire hornes pale,
Saturne, and Jove, in Cancro joyned were,   625
That swych a reyn from heven gan avale,
That every maner womman that was there
Hadde of that smoky reyn a verray feere;
At which Pandare tho lough, and seyde thenne,
"Now were it tyme a lady to gon henne!   630

"But goode nece, if I myghte evere plese
Yow any thyng, than prey ich yow," quod he,
"To don myn herte as now so gret an ese
As for to dwelle here al this nyght with me,
For-whi this is youre owen hous, parde.   635
For, by my trouthe, I sey it nought a-game,
To wende as now, it were to me a shame."

Criseyde, which that koude as muche good
As half a world, took hede of his preiere;
And syn it ron, and al was on a flod,   640
She thoughte, "As good chep may I dwellen
          here,
And graunte it gladly with a frendes chere,
And have a thonk, as grucche and thanne abide;
For hom to gon, it may nought wel bitide."

"I wol," quod she, "myn uncle lief and deere;
Syn that yow list, it skile is to be so.   646
I am right glad with yow to dwellen here;
I seyde but a-game, I wolde go."
"Iwys, graunt mercy, nece," quod he tho,
"Were it a game or no, soth for to telle,   650
Now am I glad, syn that yow list to dwelle."

Thus al is wel; but tho bigan aright
The newe joie and al the feste agayn.
But Pandarus, if goodly hadde he myght,
He wolde han hyed hire to bedde fayn,   655
And seyde, "Lord, this is an huge rayn!
This were a weder for to slepen inne;
And that I rede us soone to bygynne.

"And, nece, woot ye wher I wol yow leye,
For that we shul nat liggen far asonder,   660
And for ye neither shullen, dar I seye,
Heren noyse of reynes nor of thonder?
By God, right in my litel closet yonder.
And I wol in that outer hous allone
Be wardein of youre wommen everichone.   665

"And in this myddel chaumbre that ye se
Shul youre wommen slepen, wel and softe;
And there I seyde shal youreselven be;
And if ye liggen wel to-nyght, com ofte,
And careth nought what weder is alofte.   670
The wyn anon, and whan so that yow leste,
So go we slepe; I trowe it be the beste."

Ther nys no more, but hereafter soone,
The voide dronke, and travers drawe anon,   674
Gan every wight that hadde nought to done
More in the place out of the chaumbre gon.
And evere mo so sterneliche it ron,

And blew therwith so wondirliche loude,
That wel neigh no man heren other koude.   679

Tho Pandarus, hire em, right as hym oughte,
With wommen swiche as were hire most aboute,
Ful glad unto hire beddes syde hire broughte,
And took his leve, and gan ful lowe loute,
And seyde, "Here at this closet dore withoute,
Right overthwart, youre wommen liggen alle,
That, whom yow list of hem, ye may here
          calle."   686

So whan that she was in the closet leyd,
And alle hire wommen forth by ordinaunce
Abedde weren, ther as I have seyd,
There was nomore to skippen nor to traunce,
But boden go to bedde, with meschaunce,   691
If any wight was steryng anywhere,
And lat hem slepen that abedde were.

But Pandarus, that wel koude ech a deel
The olde daunce, and every point therinne,   695
Whan that he sey that alle thyng was wel,
He thought he wolde upon his werk bigynne,
And gan the stuwe doore al softe unpynne,
And stille as stoon, withouten lenger lette,
By Troilus adown right he hym sette.   700

And, shortly to the point right for to gon,
Of al this werk he tolde hym word and ende,
And seyde, "Make the redy right anon,
For thow shalt into hevene blisse wende."
"Now, blisful Venus, thow me grace sende!"
Quod Troilus, "For nevere yet no nede   706
Hadde ich er now, ne halvendel the drede."

Quod Pandarus, "Ne drede the nevere a deel,
For it shal be right as thow wolt desire;
So thryve I, this nyght shal I make it weel,   710
Or casten al the gruwel in the fire."
"Yet, blisful Venus, this nyght thow me en-
          spire,"
Quod Troilus, "As wys as I the serve,
And evere bet and bet shal, til I sterve.

"And if ich hadde, O Venus ful of myrthe,   715
Aspectes badde of Mars or of Saturne,
Or thow combust or let were in my birthe,
Thy fader prey al thilke harm disturne
Of grace, and that I glad ayein may turne,   719
For love of hym thow lovedest in the shawe,
I meene Adoun, that with the boor was slawe.

"O Jove ek, for the love of faire Europe,
The which in forme of bole away thow fette,

Now help! O Mars, thow with thi blody cope,
For love of Cipris, thow me nought ne lette!   725
O Phebus, thynk whan Dane hireselven shette
Under the bark, and laurer wax for drede,
Yet for hire love, O help now at this nede!

"Mercurie, for the love of Hierse eke,
For which Pallas was with Aglawros wroth,   730
Now help! and ek Diane, I the biseke,
That this viage be nought to the looth.
O fatal sustren, which, er any cloth
Me shapen was, my destine me sponne,
So helpeth to this werk that is bygonne!"   735

Quod Pandarus, "Thow wrecched mouses herte,
Artow agast so that she wol the bite?
Why, don this furred cloke upon thy sherte,
And folwe me, for I wol have the wite.
But bid, and lat me gon biforn a lite."   740
And with that word he gan undon a trappe,
And Troilus he brought in by the lappe.

The sterne wynd so loude gan to route
That no wight oother noise myghte heere;
And they that layen at the dore withoute,   745
Ful sikerly they slepten alle yfere;
And Pandarus, with a ful sobre cheere,
Goth to the dore anon, withouten lette,
There as they laye, and softely it shette.

And as he com ayeynward pryvely,   750
His nece awook, and axed, "Who goth there?"
"My dere nece," quod he, "it am I.
Ne wondreth nought, ne have of it no fere."
And ner he com, and seyde hire in hire ere,
"No word, for love of God, I yow biseche!   755
Lat no wight risen and heren of oure speche."

"What! which wey be ye comen, *benedicite?*"
Quod she, "and how thus unwist of hem alle?"
"Here at this secre trappe-dore," quod he.   759
Quod tho Criseyde, "Lat me som wight calle!"
"I! God forbede that it sholde falle,"
Quod Pandarus, "that ye swich folye wroughte!
They myghte demen thyng they nevere er
   thoughte.

"It is nought good a slepyng hound to wake,
Ne yeve a wight a cause to devyne.   765
Youre wommen slepen alle, I undertake,
So that, for hem, the hous men myghte myne,
And slepen wollen til the sonne shyne.
And whan my tale brought is to an ende,
Unwist, right as I com, so wol I wende.   770

"Now, nece myn, ye shul wel understonde,"
Quod he, "so as ye wommen demen alle,
That for to holde in love a man in honde,
And hym hire lief and deere herte calle,
And maken hym an howve above a calle,   775
I meene, as love another in this while,
She doth hireself a shame, and hym a gyle.

"Now, wherby that I telle yow al this:
Ye woot yourself, as wel as any wight,
How that youre love al fully graunted is   780
To Troilus, the worthieste knyght,
Oon of this world, and therto trouthe yplight,
That, but it were on hym along, ye nolde
Hym nevere falsen while ye lyven sholde.

"Now stant it thus, that sith I fro yow wente,
This Troilus, right platly for to seyn,   786
Is thorugh a goter, by a pryve wente,
Into my chaumbre come in al this reyn,
Unwist of every manere wight, certeyn,
Save of myself, as wisly have I joye,   790
And by that feith I shal Priam of Troie.

"And he is come in swich peyne and distresse
That, but he be al fully wood by this,
He sodeynly mot falle into wodnesse,
But if God helpe; and cause whi this is,   795
He seith hym told is of a frend of his,
How that ye sholde loven oon that hatte
   Horaste;
For sorwe of which this nyght shal ben his
   laste."

Criseyde, which that al this wonder herde,
Gan sodeynly aboute hire herte colde,   800
And with a sik she sorwfully answerde,
"Allas! I wende, whoso tales tolde,
My deere herte wolde me nought holde
So lightly fals! Allas! conceytes wronge,
What harm they don, for now lyve I to longe!

"Horaste! allas, and falsen Troilus?   806
I knowe hym nought, God helpe me so," quod
   she.
"Allas, what wikked spirit tolde hym thus?
Now certes, em, tomorwe, and I hym se,
I shal therof as ful excusen me,   810
As evere dide womman, if hym like."
And with that word she gan ful soore sike.

"O God!" quod she, "so worldly selynesse,
Which clerkes callen fals felicitee,
Imedled is with many a bitternesse!   815

Ful angwissous than is, God woot," quod she,
"Condicioun of veyn prosperitee;
For either joies comen nought yfeere,
Or elles no wight hath hem alwey here.

"O brotel wele of mannes joie unstable!   820
With what wight so thow be, or how thow
     pleye,
Either he woot that thow, joie, art muable,
Or woot it nought; it mot ben oon of tweye.
Now if he woot it nought, how may he seye
That he hath verray joie and selynesse,   825
That is of ignoraunce ay in derknesse?

"Now if he woot that joie is transitorie,
As every joie of worldly thyng mot flee,
Than every tyme he that hath in memorie,
The drede of lesyng maketh hym that he   830
May in no perfit selynesse be;
And if to lese his joie he sette a myte,
Than semeth it that joie is worth ful lite.

"Wherfore I wol diffyne in this matere,
That trewely, for aught I kan espie,   835
Ther is no verray weele in this world heere.
But O thow wikked serpent, jalousie,
Thow mysbyleved and envyous folie,
Why hastow Troilus mad to me untriste,
That nevere yet agylt hym, that I wiste?"   840

Quod Pandarus, "Thus fallen is this cas —"
"Why, uncle myn," quod she, "who tolde hym
     this?
Why doth my deere herte thus, allas?"
"Ye woot, ye, nece myn," quod he, "what is.
I hope al shal be wel that is amys;   845
For ye may quenche al this, if that yow leste.
And doth right so, for I holde it the beste."

"So shal I do to-morwe, ywys," quod she,
And God toforn, so that it shal suffise."
"To-morwe? allas, that were a fair!" quod he.
"Nay, nay, it may nat stonden in this wise.   851
For, nece myn, thus writen clerkes wise,
That peril is with drecchyng in ydrawe;
Nay, swiche abodes ben nought worth an hawe.

"Nece, alle thyng hath tyme, I dar avowe,   855
For whan a chaumbre afire is, or an halle,
Wel more nede is, it sodeynly rescowe
Than to dispute and axe amonges alle
How this candele in the strawe is falle.
A, *benedicite!* for al among that fare   860
The harm is don, and fare-wel feldefare!

"And nece myn — ne take it naught agrief —
If that ye suffre hym al nyght in this wo,
God help me so, ye hadde hym nevere lief, —
That dar I seyn, now ther is but we two.   865
But wel I woot that ye wol nat do so;
Ye ben to wys to doon so gret folie,
To putte his lif al nyght in jupertie."

"Hadde I hym nevere lief? by God, I weene
Ye hadde nevere thyng so lief!" quod she.   870
"Now by my thrift," quod he, "that shal be
     seene!
For syn ye make this ensaumple of me,
If ich al nyght wolde hym in sorwe se,
For al the tresour in the town of Troie,
I bidde God I nevere mote have joie.   875

"Now loke thanne, if ye that ben his love
Shul putte his lif al night in jupertie
For thyng of nought, now, by that God above,
Naught oonly this delay comth of folie,
But of malice, if that I shal naught lie.   880
What! platly, and ye suffre hym in destresse,
Ye neyther bounte don ne gentilesse."

Quod tho Criseyde, "Wol ye don o thyng,
And ye therwith shal stynte al his disese?   884
Have heere, and bereth hym this blewe ryng,
For ther is nothyng myghte hym bettre plese,
Save I myself, ne more hys herte apese;
And sey my deere herte, that his sorwe
Is causeles, that shal be sene to-morwe."

"A ryng?" quod he, "ye, haselwodes shaken!
Ye, nece myn, that ryng moste han a stoon   891
That myhte dede men alyve maken;
And swich a ryng trowe I that ye have non.
Discrecioun out of youre hed is gon;
That fele I now," quod he, "and that is routhe.
O tyme ilost, wel maistow corsen slouthe!   896

"Woot ye not wel that noble and heigh corage
Ne sorweth nought, ne stynteth ek, for lite?
But if a fool were in a jalous rage,
I nolde setten at his sorwe a myte,   900
But feffe hym with a fewe wordes white
Anothir day, whan that I myghte hym fynde;
But this thyng stant al in another kynde.

"This is so gentil and so tendre of herte,   904
That with his deth he wol his sorwes wreke;
For trusteth wel, how sore that hym smerte,
He wol to yow no jalous wordes speke.
And forthi, nece, er that his herte breke,

So speke youreself to hym of this matere;
For with o word ye may his herte stere.   910

"Now have I told what peril he is inne,
And his comynge unwist is to every wight;
Ne, parde, harm may ther be non, ne synne;
I wol myself be with yow al this nyght.
Ye knowe ek how it is youre owen knyght,   915
And that bi right ye moste upon hym triste,
And I al prest to fecche hym whan yow liste."

This accident so pitous was to here,
And ek so like a sooth, at prime face,
And Troilus hire knyght to hir so deere,   920
His prive comyng, and the siker place,
That, though that she did hym as thanne a grace,
Considered alle thynges as they stoode,
No wonder is, syn she did al for goode.

Criseyde answerde, "As wisly God at reste   925
My soule brynge, as me is for hym wo!
And, em, iwis, fayn wolde I don the beste,
If that ich hadde grace to do so.
But whether that ye dwelle or for hym go,
I am, til God me bettre mynde sende,   930
At dulcarnoun, right at my wittes ende."

Quod Pandarus, "Yee, nece, wol ye here?
Dulcarnoun called is 'flemyng of wrecches.'
It semeth hard, for wrecches wol nought lere,
For verray slouthe or other wilfull tecches;   935
This seyd by hem that ben nought worth two fecches.
But ye ben wis, and that we han on honde
Nis neither hard, ne skilful to withstonde."

"Than, em," quod she, "doth herof as yow list.
But er he com, I wil up first arise,   940
And, for the love of God, syn al my trist
Is on yow two, and ye ben bothe wise,
So werketh now in so discret a wise
That I honour may have, and he plesaunce;
For I am here al in youre governaunce."   945

"That is wel seyd," quod he, "my nece deere.
Ther good thrift on that wise gentil herte!
But liggeth stille, and taketh hym right here;
It nedeth nought no ferther for hym sterte.
And ech of yow ese otheres sorwes smerte,   950
For love of God; and Venus, I the herye;
For soone hope I we shul ben alle merye."

This Troilus ful soone on knees hym sette
Ful sobrely, right be hyre beddes hed,

And in his beste wyse his lady grette.   955
But, Lord, so she wex sodeynliche red!
Ne though men sholde smyten of hire hed,
She kouthe nought a word aright out brynge
So sodeynly, for his sodeyn comynge.

But Pandarus, that so wel koude feele   960
In every thyng, to pleye anon bigan,
And seyde, "Nece, se how this lord kan knele!
Now, for youre trouthe, se this gentil man!"
And with that word he for a quysshen ran,   964
And seyde, "Kneleth now, while that yow leste,
There God youre hertes brynge soone at reste!"

Kan I naught seyn, for she bad hym nought rise,
If sorwe it putte out of hire remembrance,
Or elles that she took it in the wise
Of dewete, as for his observaunce;   970
But wel fynde I she dede hym this plesaunce,
That she hym kiste, although she siked sore,
And bad hym sitte adown withouten more.

Quod Pandarus, "Now wol ye wel bigynne.
Now doth hym sitte, goode nece deere,   975
Upon youre beddes syde al ther withinne,
That ech of yow the bet may other heere."
And with that word he drow hym to the feere,
And took a light, and fond his contenaunce,
As for to looke upon an old romaunce.   980

Criseyde, that was Troilus lady right,
And cler stood on a ground of sikernesse,
Al thoughte she hire servant and hire knyght
Ne sholde of right non untrouthe in hire gesse,
Yet natheles, considered his distresse,   985
And that love is in cause of swich folie,
Thus to hym spak she of his jalousie:

"Lo, herte myn, as wolde the excellence
Of love, ayeins the which that no man may
Ne oughte ek goodly make resistence;   990
And ek bycause I felte wel and say
Youre grete trouthe and servise every day,
And that youre herte al myn was, soth to seyne,
This drof me for to rewe upon youre peyne.

"And youre goodnesse have I founde alwey yit,
Of which, my deere herte and al my knyght,   996
I thonke it yow, as fer as I have wit,
Al kan I nought as muche as it were right;
And I, emforth my connyng and my might,
Have and ay shal, how sore that me smerte,   1000
Ben to yow trewe and hool with al myn herte;

"And dredeles, that shal be founde at preve.
But, herte myn, what al this is to seyne
Shal wel be told, so that ye nought yow greve,
Though I to yow right on youreself compleyne.
For therwith mene I fynaly the peyne 1006
That halt youre herte and myn in hevynesse
Fully to slen, and every wrong redresse.

"My goode myn, noot I for-why ne how
That jalousie, allas! that wikked wyvere, 1010
Thus causeles is cropen into yow,
The harm of which I wolde fayn delyvere.
Allas, that he, al hool, or of hym slyvere,
Shuld han his refut in so digne a place,
Ther Jove hym soone out of youre herte arace!

"But O, thow Jove, O auctour of nature, 1016
Is this an honour to thi deyte,
That folk ungiltif suffren hire injure,
And who that giltif is, al quyt goth he?
O, were it leful for to pleyn on the, 1020
That undeserved suffrest jalousie,
Of that I wolde upon the pleyne and crie!

"Ek al my wo is this, that folk now usen
To seyn right thus, 'Ye, jalousie is love!'
And wolde a busshel venym al excusen, 1025
For that o greyn of love is on it shove.
But that woot heighe God that sit above,
If it be likkere love, or hate, or grame;
And after that, it oughte bere his name.

"But certeyn is, som manere jalousie 1030
Is excusable more than som, iwys;
As whan cause is, and som swich fantasie
With piete so wel repressed is
That it unnethe doth or seyth amys,
But goodly drynketh up al his distresse; 1035
And that excuse I, for the gentilesse.

"And som so ful of furie is and despit
That it sourmounteth his repressioun.
But, herte myn, ye be nat in that plit,
That thonke I God; for which youre passioun
I wol nought calle it but illusioun, 1041
Of habundaunce of love and besy cure,
That doth youre herte this disese endure.

"Of which I am right sory, but nought wroth;
But, for my devoir and youre hertes reste, 1045
Wherso yow list, by ordal or by oth,
By sort, or in what wise so yow leste,
For love of God, lat preve it for the beste;
And if that I be giltif, do me deye!
Allas, what myght I more don or seye?" 1050

With that a fewe brighte teris newe
Owt of hire eighen fille, and thus she seyde,
"Now God, thow woost, in thought ne dede
  untrewe
To Troilus was nevere yet Criseyde. 1054
With that here heed down in the bed she leyde,
And with the sheete it wreigh, and sighte soore,
And held hire pees; nought o word spak she
  more.

But now help God to quenchen al this sorwe!
So hope I that he shal, for he best may.
For I have seyn, of a ful misty morwe 1060
Folowen ful ofte a myrie someris day;
And after wynter foloweth grene May.
Men sen alday, and reden ek in stories,
That after sharpe shoures ben victories.

This Troilus, whan he hire wordes herde, 1065
Have ye no care, hym liste nought to slepe;
For it thought hym no strokes of a yerde
To heere or seen Criseyde, his lady, wepe;
But wel he felt aboute his herte crepe,
For everi tere which that Criseyde asterte, 1070
The crampe of deth, to streyne hym by the
  herte.

And in his mynde he gan the tyme acorse
That he com there, and that he was born;
For now is wikke torned into worse,
And al that labour he hath don byforn, 1075
He wende it lost; he thoughte he nas but lorn.
"O Pandarus," thoughte he, "allas, thi wile
Serveth of nought, so weylaway the while!"

And therwithal he heng adown the heed,
And fil on knees, and sorwfully he sighte. 1080
What myghte he seyn? He felte he nas but
  deed,
For wroth was she that sholde his sorwes lighte.
But natheles, whan that he speken myghte,
Than seyde he thus, "God woot that of this
  game, 1084
Whan al is wist, than am I nought to blame."

Therwith the sorwe so his herte shette,
That from his eyen fil ther nought a tere,
And every spirit his vigour in knette,
So they astoned or oppressed were.
The felyng of his sorwe, or of his fere, 1090
Or of aught elles, fled was out of towne;
And down he fel al sodeynly a-swowne.

This was no litel sorwe for to se;
But al was hust, and Pandare up as faste, —

"O nece, pes, or we be lost!" quod he,   1095
"Beth naught agast!" but certeyn, at the laste,
For this or that, he into bed hym caste,
And seyde, "O thef, is this a mannes herte?"
And of he rente al to his bare sherte;

And seyde, "Nece, but ye helpe us now,   1100
Allas, youre owen Troilus is lorn!"
"Iwis, so wolde I, and I wiste how,
Ful fayn," quod she; "Allas, that I was born!"
"Yee, nece, wol ye pullen out the thorn
That stiketh in his herte," quod Pandare,   1105
"Sey 'al foryeve,' and stynt is al this fare!"

"Ye, that to me," quod she, "ful levere were
Than al the good the sonne aboute gooth."
And therwithal she swor hym in his ere,
"Iwys, my deere herte, I am nought wroth,   1110
Have here my trouthe!" and many an other oth;
"Now speke to me, for it am I, Criseyde!"
But al for nought; yit myght he nought
          abreyde.

Therwith his pous and paumes of his hondes
They gan to frote, and wete his temples
          tweyne;   1115
And to deliveren hym fro bittre bondes,
She ofte hym kiste; and shortly for to seyne,
Hym to revoken she did al hire peyne.
And at the laste, he gan his breth to drawe,
And of his swough sone after that adawe,   1120

And gan bet mynde and reson to hym take,
But wonder soore he was abayst, iwis.
And with a sik, whan he gan bet awake,
He seyde, "O mercy, God, what thyng is this?"
"Why do ye with youreselven thus amys?"   1125
Quod tho Criseyde, "Is this a mannes game?
What, Troilus, wol ye do thus for shame?"

And therwithal hire arm over hym she leyde,
And al foryaf, and ofte tyme hym keste.
He thonked hire, and to hire spak, and seyde
As fil to purpos for his hertes reste;   1131
And she to that answerde hym as hire leste,
And with hire goodly wordes hym disporte
She gan, and ofte his sorwes to comforte.

Quod Pandarus, "For aught I kan aspien,   1135
This light, nor I, ne serven here of nought.
Light is nought good for sike folkes yën!
But, for the love of God, syn ye ben brought
In thus good plit, lat now no hevy thought

Ben hangyng in the hertes of yow tweye" —
And bar the candele to the chymeneye.   1141

Soone after this, though it no nede were,
Whan she swiche othes as hire leste devyse
Hadde of hym take, hire thoughte tho no fere,
Ne cause ek non, to bidde hym thennes rise.
Yet lasse thyng than othes may suffise   1146
In many a cas; for every wyght, I gesse,
That loveth wel, meneth but gentilesse.

But in effect she wolde wit anon
Of what man, and ek wheer, and also why   1150
He jalous was, syn ther was cause non;
And ek the sygne that he took it by,
She badde hym that to telle hire bisily;
Or elles, certeyn, she bar hym on honde
That this was don of malice, hire to fonde.

Withouten more, shortly for to seyne,   1156
He most obeye unto his lady heste;
And for the lasse harm, he moste feyne.
He seyde hire, whan she was at swich a feste,
She myght on hym han loked at the leste, —   1160
Noot I nought what, al deere ynough a rysshe,
As he that nedes most a cause fisshe.

And she answerde, "Swete, al were it so,
What harm was that, syn I non yvel mene?
For, by that God that bought us bothe two,
In alle thyng is myn entente cleene.   1166
Swiche argumentes ne ben naught worth a
          beene.
Wol ye the childissh jalous contrefete?
Now were it worthi that ye were ybete."

Tho Troilus gan sorwfully to sike;   1170
Lest she be wroth, hym thoughte his herte
          deyde;
And seyde, "Allas, upon my sorwes sike
Have mercy, swete herte myn, Criseyde!
And if that in tho wordes that I seyde
Be any wrong, I wol no more trespace.   1175
Doth what yow list, I am al in youre grace."

And she answerde, "Of gilt misericorde!
That is to seyn, that I foryeve al this.
And evere more on this nyght yow recorde,
And beth wel war ye do namore amys."   1180
"Nay, dere herte myn," quod he, "iwys!"
"And now," quod she, "that I have don yow
          smerte,
Foryeve it me, myn owene swete herte."

This Troilus, with blisse of that supprised,
Putte al in Goddes hand, as he that mente   1185
Nothyng but wel; and sodeynly avysed,
He hire in armes faste to hym hente.
And Pandarus, with a ful good entente,
Leyde hym to slepe, and seyde, "If ye be wise,
Swouneth nought now, lest more folk arise!"

What myghte or may the sely larke seye,   1191
Whan that the sperhauk hath it in his foot?
I kan namore, but of thise ilke tweye, —
To whom this tale sucre be or soot, —
Though that I tarie a yer, somtyme I moot,
After myn auctour, tellen hire gladnesse,   1196
As wel as I have told hire hevynesse.

Criseyde, which that felte hire thus itake,
As writen clerkes in hire bokes olde,
Right as an aspes leef she gan to quake,   1200
Whan she hym felte hire in his armes folde.
But Troilus, al hool of cares colde,
Gan thanken tho the blisful goddes sevene.
Thus sondry peynes bryngen folk to hevene.

This Troilus in armes gan hire streyne,   1205
And seyde, "O swete, as evere mot I gon,
Now be ye kaught, now is ther but we tweyne!
Now yeldeth yow, for other bote is non!"
To that Criseyde answerde thus anon,   1209
"Ne hadde I er now, my swete herte deere,
Ben yold, ywis, I were now nought heere!"

O, sooth is seyd, that heled for to be
As of a fevre, or other gret siknesse,
Men moste drynke, as men may ofte se,   1214
Ful bittre drynke; and for to han gladnesse,
Men drynken ofte peyne and gret distresse;
I mene it here, as for this aventure,
That thorugh a peyne hath founden al his cure.

And now swetnesse semeth more swete,
That bitternesse assaied was byforn;   1220
For out of wo in blisse now they flete;
Non swich they felten syn that they were born.
Now is this bet than bothe two be lorn.
For love of God, take every womman heede
To werken thus, if it comth to the neede.   1225

Criseyde, al quyt from every drede and tene,
As she that juste cause hadde hym to triste,
Made hym swich feste, it joye was to seene,
Whan she his trouthe and clene entente wiste;
And as aboute a tree, with many a twiste,   1230

Bytrent and writh the swote wodebynde,
Gan ech of hem in armes other wynde.

And as the newe abaysed nyghtyngale,
That stynteth first whan she bygynneth to
     synge,
Whan that she hereth any herde tale,   1235
Or in the hegges any wyght stirynge,
And after siker doth hire vois out rynge,
Right so Criseyde, whan hire drede stente,
Opned hire herte, and tolde hym hire entente.

And right as he that seth his deth yshapen,   1240
And dyen mot, in ought that he may gesse,
And sodeynly rescous doth hym escapen,
And from his deth is brought in sykernesse,
For al this world, in swych present gladnesse
Was Troilus, and hath his lady swete.   1245
With worse hap God lat us nevere mete!

Hire armes smale, hire streghte bak and softe,
Hire sydes longe, flesshly, smothe, and white
He gan to stroke, and good thrift bad ful ofte
Hire snowisshe throte, hire brestes rounde and
     lite: 1250
Thus in this hevene he gan hym to delite,
And therwithal a thousand tyme hire kiste,
That what to don, for joie unnethe he wiste.

Than seyde he thus, "O Love, O Charite!
Thi moder ek, Citherea the swete,   1255
After thiself next heried be she,
Venus mene I, the wel-willy planete!
And next that, Imeneus, I the grete;
For nevere man was to yow goddes holde
As I, which ye han brought fro cares colde.   1260

"Benigne Love, thow holy bond of thynges,
Whoso wol grace, and list the nought honouren,
Lo, his desir wol fle withouten wynges.
For noldestow of bownte hem socouren
That serven best and most alwey labouren,   1265
Yet were al lost, that dar I wel seyn certes,
But if thi grace passed oure desertes.

"And for thow me, that leest koude disserve
Of hem that noumbred ben unto thi grace,
Hast holpen, ther I likly was to sterve,   1270
And me bistowed in so heigh a place
That thilke boundes may no blisse pace,
I kan namore; but laude and reverence
Be to thy bounte and thyn excellence!"

And therwithal Criseyde anon he kiste,   1275
Of which certein she felte no disese.

And thus seyde he, "Now wolde God I wiste,
Myn herte swete, how I yow myght plese!
What man," quod he, "was evere thus at ese
As I, on which the faireste and the beste   1280
That evere I say, deyneth hire herte reste?

"Here may men seen that mercy passeth right;
Th'experience of that is felt in me,
That am unworthi to so swete a wight.
But herte myn, of youre benignite,   1285
So thynketh, though that I unworthi be,
Yet mot I nede amenden in som wyse,
Right thorugh the vertu of youre heigh servyse.

"And for the love of God, my lady deere,
Syn God hath wrought me for I shall yow
          serve, —   1290
As thus I mene, he wol ye be my steere,
To do me lyve, if that yow liste, or sterve, —
So techeth me how that I may disserve
Youre thonk, so that I thorugh myn ignoraunce,
Ne do no thing that yow be displesaunce.   1295

"For certes, fresshe wommanliche wif,
This dar I seye, that trouth and diligence,
That shal ye fynden in me al my lif;
N'y wol nat, certein, breken youre defence;
And if I do, present or in absence,   1300
For love of God, lat sle me with the dede,
If that it like unto youre wommanhede."

"Iwys," quod she, "myn owen hertes list,
My ground of ese, and al myn herte deere,
Gramercy, for on that is al my trist!   1305
But lat us falle awey fro this matere,
For it suffiseth, this that seyd is heere,
And at o word, withouten repentaunce,
Welcome, my knyght, my pees, my suffisaunce!"

Of hire delit, or joies oon the leeste,   1310
Were impossible to my wit to seye;
But juggeth ye that han ben at the feste
Of swich gladnesse, if that hem liste pleye!
I kan namore, but thus thise ilke tweye,
That nyght, bitwixen drede and sikernesse,   1316
Felten in love the grete worthynesse.

O blisful nyght, of hem so longe isought,
How blithe unto hem bothe two thow weere!
Why nad I swich oon with my soule ybought,
Ye, or the leeste joie that was theere?   1320
Awey, thow foule daunger and thow feere,
And lat hem in this hevene blisse dwelle,
That is so heigh that al ne kan I telle!

But soth is, though I kan nat tellen al,
As kan myn auctour, of his excellence,   1325
Yet have I seyd, and God toforn, and shal
In every thyng, al holy his sentence;
And if that ich, at Loves reverence,
Have any word in eched for the beste,
Doth therwithal right as youreselven leste.   1330

For myne wordes, heere and every part,
I speke hem alle under correccioun
Of yow that felyng han in loves art,
And putte it al in youre discrecioun
To encresse or maken dymynucioun   1335
Of my langage, and that I yow biseche.
But now to purpos of my rather speche.

Thise ilke two, that ben in armes laft,
So loth to hem asonder gon it were,
That ech from other wenden ben biraft,   1340
Or elles, lo, this was hir mooste feere,
That al this thyng but nyce dremes were;
For which ful ofte ech of hem seyde, "O swete,
Clippe ich yow thus, or elles I it meete?"

And Lord! so he gan goodly on hire se,   1345
That nevere his look ne bleynte from hire face,
And seyde, "O deere herte, may it be
That it be soth, that ye ben in this place?"
"Yee, herte myn, God thank I of his grace,"
Quod tho Criseyde, and therwithal hym kiste,
That where his spirit was, for joie he nyste.   1351

This Troilus ful ofte hire eyen two
Gan for to kisse, and seyde, "O eyen clere,
It weren ye that wroughte me swich wo,
Ye humble nettes of my lady deere!   1355
Though ther be mercy writen in youre cheere,
God woot, the text ful hard is, soth, to fynde!
How koude ye withouten bond me bynde?"

Therwith he gan hire faste in armes take,
And wel an hondred tymes gan he syke,   1360
Naught swiche sorwfull sikes as men make
For wo, or elles when that folk ben sike,
But esy sykes, swiche as ben to like,
That shewed his affeccioun withinne;
Of swiche sikes koude he nought bilynne.   1365

Soone after this they spake of sondry thynges,
As fel to purpos of this aventure,
And pleyinge entrechaungeden hire rynges,
Of whiche I kan nought tellen no scripture;
But wel I woot, a broche, gold and asure,   1370

In which a ruby set was lik an herte,
Criseyde hym yaf, and stak it on his sherte.

Lord, trowe ye a coveytous or a wrecche,
That blameth love, and halt of it despit,
That of tho pens that he kan mokre and
      krecche   1375
Was evere yit yyeven hym swich delit
As is in love, in o poynt, in som plit?
Nay, douteles, for also God me save,
So perfit joie may no nygard have.

They wol seyn "yis," but Lord! so that they lye,
Tho besy wrecches, ful of wo and drede!   1381
Thei callen love a woodnesse or folie,
But it shall falle hem as I shal yow rede;
They shal forgon the white and ek the rede,
And lyve in wo, ther God yeve hem mes-
      chaunce,   1385
And every lovere in his trouthe avaunce!

As wolde God tho wrecches that dispise
Servise of love hadde erys also longe
As hadde Mida, ful of coveytise,
And therto dronken hadde as hoot and stronge
As Crassus dide for his affectis wronge,   1391
To techen hem that they ben in the vice,
And loveres nought, although they holde hem
      nyce.

Thise ilke two, of whom that I yow seye,
Whan that hire hertes wel assured were,   1395
Tho gonne they to speken and to pleye,
And ek rehercen how, and whan, and where
Thei knewe hem first, and every wo and feere
That passed was; but al swich hevynesse,
I thank it God, was torned to gladnesse.   1400

And evere mo, when that hem fel to speke
Of any wo of swich a tyme agoon,
With kissyng al that tale sholde breke,
And fallen in a newe joye anoon;
And diden al hire myght, syn they were oon,
For to recoveren blisse and ben at eise,   1406
And passed wo with joie contrepeise.

Resoun wol nought that I speke of slep,
For it acordeth nought to my matere.
God woot, they took of that ful litel kep!   1410
But lest this nyght, that was to hem so deere,
Ne sholde in veyn escape in no manere,
It was byset in joie and bisynesse
Of al that souneth into gentilesse.

But whan the cok, comune astrologer,   1415
Gan on his brest to bete and after crowe,
And Lucyfer, the dayes messager,
Gan for to rise, and out hire bemes throwe,
And estward roos, to hym that koude it knowe,
Fortuna Major, that anoon Criseyde,   1420
With herte soor, to Troilus thus seyde:

"Myn hertes lif, my trist, and my plesaunce,
That I was born, allas, what me is wo,
That day of us moot make disseveraunce!
For tyme it is to ryse and hennes go,   1425
Or ellis I am lost for evere mo!
O nyght, allas! why nyltow over us hove,
As longe as whan Almena lay by Jove?

"O blake nyght, as folk in bokes rede,
That shapen art by God this world to hide   1430
At certeyn tymes wyth thi derke wede,
That under that men myghte in reste abide,
Wel oughten bestes pleyne, and folk the chide,
That there as day wyth labour wolde us breste,
That thow thus fleest, and deynest us nought
      reste.   1435

"Thow doost, allas, to shortly thyn office,
Thow rakle nyght, ther God, maker of kynde,
The, for thyn haste and thyn unkynde vice,
So faste ay to oure hemysperie bynde,
That nevere more under the ground thow
      wynde!   1440
For now, for thow so hiest out of Troie,
Have I forgon thus hastili my joie!"

This Troilus, that with tho wordes felte,
As thoughte hym tho, for piëtous distresse,
The blody teris from his herte melte,   1445
As he that nevere yet swich hevynesse
Assayed hadde, out of so gret gladnesse,
Gan therwithal Criseyde, his lady deere,
In armes streyne, and seyde in this manere:

"O cruel day, accusour of the joie   1450
That nyght and love han stole and faste iwryen,
Acorsed be thi comyng into Troye,
For every bore hath oon of thi bryghte yën!
Envyous day, what list the so to spien?   1454
What hastow lost, why sekestow this place,
Ther God thi light so quenche, for his grace?

"Allas! what have thise loveris the agylt,
Dispitous day? Thyn be the peyne of helle!
For many a lovere hastow slayn, and wilt;
Thy pourynge in wol nowher lat hem dwelle.

What profrestow thi light here for to selle?   1461
Go selle it hem that smale selys grave;
We wol the nought, us nedeth no day have."

And ek the sonne, Titan, gan he chide,
And seyde, "O fool, wel may men the dispise,
That hast the dawyng al nyght by thi syde,   1466
And suffrest hire so soone up fro the rise,
For to disese loveris in this wyse.
What! holde youre bed ther, thow, and ek thi
    Morwe!
I bidde God, so yeve yow bothe sorwe!"   1470

Therwith ful soore he syghte, and thus he
    seyde:
"My lady right, and of my wele or wo
The welle and roote, O goodly myn, Criseyde,
And shal I rise, allas, and shal I so?
Now fele I that myn herte moot a-two.   1475
For how sholde I my lif an houre save,
Syn that with yow is al the lyf ich have?

"What shal I don? For, certes, I not how,
Ne whan, allas! I shal the tyme see
That in this plit I may ben eft with yow.   1480
And of my lif, God woot how that shal be,
Syn that desir right now so biteth me,
That I am ded anon, but I retourne.
How sholde I longe, allas, fro yow sojourne?

"But natheles, myn owen lady bright,   1485
Yit were it so that I wiste outrely
That I, youre humble servant and youre knyght,
Were in youre herte iset as fermely
As ye in myn, the which thyng, trewely,
Me levere were than thise worldes tweyne,
Yet sholde I bet enduren al my peyne."   1491

To that Criseyde answerde right anon,
And with a sik she seyde, "O herte deere,
The game, ywys, so forforth now is gon,
That first shal Phebus fallen fro his spere,   1495
And everich egle ben the dowves feere,
And everi roche out of his place sterte,
Er Troilus out of Criseydes herte.

"Ye ben so depe in-with myn herte grave,
That, though I wolde it torne out of my
    thought,   1500
As wisly verray God my soule save,
To dyen in the peyne, I koude nought.
And, for the love of God that us hath wrought,
Lat in youre brayn non other fantasie
So crepe, that it cause me to dye!   1505

"And that ye me wolde han as faste in mynde
As I have yow, that wolde I yow biseche;
And if I wiste sothly that to fynde,
God myghte nought a poynt my joies eche.
But herte myn, withouten more speche,   1510
Beth to me trewe, or ellis were it routhe;
For I am thyn, by God and by my trouthe!

"Beth glad, forthy, and lyve in sikernesse!
Thus seyde I nevere er this, ne shal to mo;
And if to yow it were a gret gladnesse   1515
To torne ayeyn soone after that ye go,
As fayn wolde I as ye that it were so,
As wisly God myn herte brynge at reste!"
And hym in armes tok, and ofte keste.

Agayns his wil, sith it mot nedes be,   1520
This Troilus up ros, and faste hym cledde,
And in his armes took his lady free
An hondred tyme, and on his wey hym spedde;
And with swiche voys as though his herte
    bledde,
He seyde, "Farewel, dere herte swete,   1525
Ther God us graunte sownde and soone to
    mete!"

To which no word for sorwe she answerde,
So soore gan his partyng hire distreyne;
And Troilus unto his paleys ferde,
As wo-bygon as she was, soth to seyne.   1530
So harde hym wrong of sharp desir the peyne,
For to ben eft there he was in plesaunce,
That it may nevere out of his remembraunce.

Retorned to his real paleys soone,
He softe into his bed gan for to slynke,   1535
To slepe longe, as he was wont to doone.
But al for nought; he may wel ligge and wynke,
But slep ne may ther in his herte synke,
Thynkyng how she, for whom desir hym
    brende,
A thousand fold was worth more than he
    wende.   1540

And in his thought gan up and down to wynde
Hire wordes alle, and every countenaunce,
And fermely impressen in his mynde
The leeste point that to him was plesaunce;
And verraylich, of thilke remembraunce,   1545
Desir al newe hym brende, and lust to brede
Gan more than erst, and yet took he non hede.

Criseyde also, right in the same wyse,
Of Troilus gan in hire herte shette

His worthynesse, his lust, his dedes wise,   1550
His gentilesse, and how she with hym mette,
Thonkynge Love he so wel hire bisette;
Desiryng eft to han hire herte deere
In swich a plit, she dorste make hym cheere.

Pandare, o-morwe which that comen was   1555
Unto his nece and gan hire faire grete,
Seyde, "Al this nyght so reyned it, allas,
That al my drede is that ye, nece swete,
Han litel laiser had to slepe and mete.
Al nyght," quod he, "hath reyn so do me wake,
That som of us, I trowe, hire hedes ake."   1561

And ner he com, and seyde, "How stant it now
This mury morwe? Nece, how kan ye fare?"
Criseyde answerde, "Nevere the bet for yow,
Fox that ye ben! God yeve youre herte kare!
God help me so, ye caused al this fare,   1566
Trowe I," quod she, "for al youre wordes white.
O, whoso seeth yow, knoweth yow ful lite."

With that she gan hire face for to wrye
With the shete, and wax for shame al reed;   1570
And Pandarus gan under for to prie,
And seyde, "Nece, if that I shal be ded,
Have here a swerd and smyteth of myn hed!"
With that his arm al sodeynly he thriste   1574
Under hire nekke, and at the laste hire kyste.

I passe al that which chargeth nought to seye.
What! God foryaf his deth, and she al so
Foryaf, and with here uncle gan to pleye,
For other cause was ther noon than so.
But of this thing right to the effect to go,   1580
Whan tyme was, hom to here hous she wente,
And Pandarus hath fully his entente.

Now torne we ayeyn to Troilus,
That resteles ful longe abedde lay,
And pryvely sente after Pandarus,   1585
To hym to com in al the haste he may.
He com anon, nought ones seyde he nay;
And Troilus ful sobrely he grette,
And down upon his beddes syde hym sette.

This Troilus, with al th'affeccioun   1590
Of frendes love that herte may devyse,
To Pandarus on knowes fil adown,
And er that he wolde of the place arise,
He gan hym thonken in his beste wise   1594
An hondred sythe, and gan the tyme blesse
That he was born, to brynge hym fro destresse.

He seyde, "O frend of frendes the alderbeste
That evere was, the sothe for to telle,
Thow hast in hevene ybrought my soule at
     reste
Fro Flegetoun, the fery flood of helle;   1600
That, though I myght a thousand tymes selle,
Upon a day, my lif in thi servise,
It myghte naught a moote in that suffise.

"The sonne, which that al the world may se,
Saugh nevere yet my lif, that dar I leye,   1605
So inly fair and goodly as is she,
Whos I am al, and shal, tyl that I deye.
And that I thus am hires, dar I seye,
That thanked be the heighe worthynesse
Of Love, and ek thi kynde bysynesse.   1610

"Thus hastow me no litel thing yyive,
For which to the obliged be for ay
My lif, and whi? For thorugh thyn help I lyve,
Or elles ded hadde I ben many a day."
And with that word down in his bed he lay,
And Pandarus ful sobrely hym herde   1616
Til al was seyd, and than he thus answerde:

"My deere frend, if I have don for the
In any cas, God wot, it is me lief;
And am as glad as man may of it be,   1620
God help me so; but tak it nat a-grief
That I shal seyn, be war of this meschief,
That, there as thow now brought art in thy
     blisse,
That thow thiself ne cause it nat to misse.

"For of fortunes sharpe adversitee   1625
The worste kynde of infortune is this,
A man to han ben in prosperitee,
And it remembren, whan it passed is.
Th'art wis ynough, forthi do nat amys:
Be naught to rakel, theigh thow sitte warme;
For if thow be, certeyn, it wol the harme.   1631

"Thow art at ese, and hold the wel therinne;
For also seur as reed is every fir,
As gret a craft is kepe wel as wynne.
Bridle alwey wel thi speche and thi desir,   1635
For worldly joie halt nought but by a wir.
That preveth wel it brest al day so ofte;
Forthi nede is to werken with it softe."

Quod Troilus, "I hope, and God toforn,
My deere frend, that I shal so me beere,   1640
That in my gylt ther shal nothyng be lorn,

N'y nyl nought rakle as for to greven heere.
It nedeth naught this matere ofte stere;
For wystestow myn herte wel, Pandare,
God woot, of this thow woldest litel care."   1645

Tho gan he telle hym of his glade nyght,
And wherof first his herte dred, and how,
And seyde, "Frend, as I am trewe knyght,
And by that feyth I shal to God and yow,
I hadde it nevere half so hote as now;   1650
And ay the more that desir me biteth
To love hire best, the more it me deliteth.

"I not myself naught wisly what it is;
But now I feele a newe qualitee,
Yee, al another than I dide er this."   1655
Pandare answerd, and seyde thus, that "he
That ones may in hevene blisse be,
He feleth other weyes, dar I leye,
Than thilke tyme he first herde of it seye."

This is o word for al; this Troilus   1660
Was nevere ful to speke of this matere,
And for to preisen unto Pandarus
The bounte of his righte lady deere,
And Pandarus to thanke and maken cheere.
This tale was ay span-newe to bygynne,   1665
Til that the nyght departed hem atwynne.

Soon after this, for that Fortune it wolde,
Icomen was the blisful tyme swete
That Troilus was warned that he sholde,
There he was erst, Criseyde his lady mete;   1670
For which he felte his herte in joie flete,
And feithfully gan alle the goddes herie;
And lat se now if that he kan be merie!

And holden was the forme and al the wise
Of hire commyng, and eek of his also,   1675
As it was erst, which nedeth nought devyse.
But pleynly to th'effect right for to go,
In joie and suerte Pandarus hem two
Abedde brought, whan that hem bothe leste,
And thus they ben in quyete and in reste.   1680

Nought nedeth it to yow, syn they ben met,
To axe at me if that they blithe were;
For if it erst was wel, tho was it bet
A thousand fold; this nedeth nought enquere.
Agon was every sorwe and every feere;   1685
And bothe, ywys, they hadde, and so they
          wende,
As muche joie as herte may comprende.

This is no litel thyng of for to seye;
This passeth every wit for to devyse;
For ech of hem gan otheres lust obeye.   1690
Felicite, which that thise clerkes wise
Comenden so, ne may nought here suffise;
This joie may nought writen be with inke;
This passeth al that herte may bythynke.

But cruel day, so wailaway the stounde!   1695
Gan for t'aproche, as they by sygnes knewe;
For which hem thoughte feelen dethis wownde.
So wo was hem that changen gan hire hewe,
And day they gonnen to despise al newe,
Callyng it traitour, envyous, and worse,   1700
And bitterly the dayes light thei corse.

Quod Troilus, "Allas, now am I war
That Pirous and tho swifte steedes thre,
Which that drawen forth the sonnes char,
Han gon som bi-path in dispit of me;   1705
That maketh it so soone day to be;
And, for the sonne hym hasteth thus to rise,
Ne shal I nevere don him sacrifise."

But nedes day departe hem moste soone,   1709
And whan hire speche don was and hire cheere,
They twynne anon, as they were wont to doone,
And setten tyme of metyng eft yfeere.
And many a nyght they wroughte in this
          manere,
And thus Fortune a tyme ledde in joie
Criseyde, and ek this kynges sone of Troie.   1715

In suffisaunce, in blisse, and in singynges,
This Troilus gan al his lif to lede.
He spendeth, jousteth, maketh festeynges;
He yeveth frely ofte, and chaungeth wede,
And held aboute hym alwey, out of drede,   1720
A world of folk, as com hym wel of kynde,
The fresshest and the beste he koude fynde;

That swich a vois was of hym and a stevene
Thorughout the world, of honour and largesse,
That it up rong unto the yate of hevene.   1725
And, as in love, he was in swich gladnesse,
That in his herte he demed, as I gesse,
That ther nys lovere in this world at ese
So wel as he; and thus gan love hym plese.

The goodlihede or beaute which that kynde
In any other lady hadde yset   1731
Kan nought the montance of a knotte unbynde,
Aboute his herte, of al Criseydes net.
He was so narwe ymasked and yknet,

That it undon on any manere syde,　1735
That nyl naught ben, for aught that may bitide.

And by the hond ful ofte he wolde take
This Pandarus, and into gardyn lede,
And swich a feste and swich a proces make
Hym of Criseyde, and of hire womanhede,　1740
And of hire beaute, that, withouten drede,
It was an hevene his wordes for to here;
And thanne he wolde synge in this manere:

"Love, that of erthe and se hath governaunce,
Love, that his hestes hath in hevenes hye,　1745
Love, that with an holsom alliaunce
Halt peples joyned, as hym lest hem gye,
Love, that knetteth lawe of compaignie,
And couples doth in vertu for to dwelle,
Bynd this acord, that I have told and telle.　1750

"That that the world with feith, which that is
　　stable,
Diverseth so his stowndes concordynge,
That elementz that ben so discordable
Holden a bond perpetuely durynge,　1754
That Phebus mote his rosy day forth brynge,
And that the mone hath lordshipe over the
　　nyghtes, —
Al this doth Love, ay heried be his myghtes!

"That that the se, that gredy is to flowen,
Constreyneth to a certeyn ende so
His flodes that so fiersly they ne growen　1760
To drenchen erthe and al for evere mo;
And if that Love aught lete his bridel go,
Al that now loveth asondre sholde lepe,
And lost were al that Love halt now to-hepe.

"So wolde God, that auctour is of kynde,　1765
That with his bond Love of his vertu liste
To cerclen hertes alle, and faste bynde,
That from his bond no wight the wey out wiste;
And hertes colde, hem wolde I that he twiste
To make hem love, and that hem liste ay
　　rewe　1770
On hertes sore, and kepe hem that ben
　　trewe!" —

In alle nedes, for the townes werre,
He was, and ay, the first in armes dyght,
And certeynly, but if that bokes erre,
Save Ector most ydred of any wight;　1775

And this encrees of hardynesse and myght
Com hym of love, his ladies thank to wynne,
That altered his spirit so withinne.

In tyme of trewe, on haukyng wolde he ride,
Or elles honte boor, beer, or lyoun;　1780
The smale bestes leet he gon biside.
And whan that he com ridyng into town,
Ful ofte his lady from hire wyndow down,
As fressh as faukoun comen out of muwe,
Ful redy was hym goodly to saluwe.　1785

And moost of love and vertu was his speche,
And in despit hadde alle wrecchednesse;
And douteles, no nede was hym biseche
To honouren hem that hadde worthynesse,
And esen hem that weren in destresse.　1790
And glad was he if any wyght wel ferde,
That lovere was, whan he it wiste or herde.

For, soth to seyne, he lost held every wyght,
But if he were in Loves heigh servise, —
I mene folk that oughte it ben of right.　1795
And over al this, so wel koude he devyse
Of sentement, and in so unkouth wise,
Al his array, that every lovere thoughte
That al was wel, what so he seyde or wroughte.

And though that he be come of blood roial,　1800
Hym liste of pride at no wight for to chace;
Benigne he was to ech in general,
For which he gat hym thank in every place.
Thus wolde Love, yheried be his grace,
That Pride, Envye, and Ire, and Avarice　1805
He gan to fle, and everich other vice.

Thow lady bryght, the doughter to Dyone,
Thy blynde and wynged sone ek, daun Cupide,
Yee sustren nyne ek, that by Elicone
In hil Pernaso listen for t'abide,　1810
That ye thus fer han deyned me to gyde,
I kan namore, but syn that ye wol wende,
Ye heried ben for ay withouten ende!

Thorugh yow have I seyd fully in my song
Th'effect and joie of Troilus servise,　1815
Al be that ther was som disese among,
As to myn auctour listeth to devise.
My thridde bok now ende ich in this wyse,
And Troilus in lust and in quiete
Is with Criseyde, his owen herte swete.　1820

Explicit liber tercius.

Book IV

Incipit prohemium quarti libri

But al to litel, weylaway the whyle,
Lasteth swich joie, ythonked be Fortune,
That semeth trewest whan she wol bygyle,
And kan to fooles so hire song entune,   4
That she hem hent and blent, traitour comune!
And whan a wight is from hire whiel ythrowe,
Than laugheth she, and maketh hym the mowe.

From Troilus she gan hire brighte face
Awey to writhe, and tok of hym non heede,
But caste hym clene out of his lady grace,   10
And on hire whiel she sette up Diomede;
For which right now myn herte gynneth blede,
And now my penne, allas! with which I write,
Quaketh for drede of that I moste endite.

For how Criseyde Troilus forsook,   15
Or at the leeste, how that she was unkynde,
Moot hennesforth ben matere of my book,
As writen folk thorugh which it is in mynde.
Allas! that they sholde evere cause fynde
To speke hire harm, and if they on hire lye,   20
Iwis, hemself sholde han the vilanye.

O ye Herynes, Nyghtes doughtren thre,
That endeles compleignen evere in pyne,
Megera, Alete, and ek Thesiphone;
Thow cruel Mars ek, fader to Quyryne,   25
This ilke ferthe book me helpeth fyne,
So that the losse of lyf and love yfeere
Of Troilus be fully shewed heere.

Explicit prohemium quarti libri.

Incipit liber quartus.

Liggyng in oost, as I have seyd er this,
The Grekys stronge aboute Troie town,   30
Byfel that, whan that Phebus shynyng is
Upon the brest of Hercules lyoun,
That Ector, with ful many a bold baroun,
Caste on a day with Grekes for to fighte,
As he was wont, to greve hem what he myghte.

Not I how longe or short it was bitwene   36
This purpos and that day they fighten mente;
But on a day wel armed, brighte, and shene,
Ector and many a worthi wight out wente,
With spere in honde and bigge bowes bente;   40
And in the berd, withouten lenger lette,
Hire fomen in the feld anon hem mette.

The longe day, with speres sharpe igrounde,
With arwes, dartes, swerdes, maces felle,
They fighte and bringen hors and man to
    grounde,   45
And with hire axes out the braynes quelle.
But in the laste shour, soth for to telle,
The folk of Troie hemselven so mysledden
That with the worse at nyght homward they
    fledden.

At which day was taken Antenore,   50
Maugre Polydamas or Monesteo,
Santippe, Sarpedon, Polynestore,
Polite, or ek the Trojan daun Rupheo,
And other lasse folk as Phebuseo;
So that, for harm, that day the folk of Troie   55
Dredden to lese a gret part of hire joie.

Of Priamus was yeve, at Grekes requeste,
A tyme of trewe, and tho they gonnen trete,
Hire prisoners to chaungen, meste and leste,
And for the surplus yeven sommes grete.   60
This thing anon was couth in every strete,
Bothe in th'assege, in town and everywhere,
And with the firste it com to Calkas ere.

Whan Calkas knew this tretis sholde holde,
In consistorie, among the Grekes soone   65
He gan in thringe forth with lordes olde,
And sette hym there as he was wont to doone;
And with a chaunged face hem bad a boone,
For love of God, to don that reverence,
To stynte noyse, and yeve hym audience.   70

Than seyde he thus, "Lo, lordes myn, ich was
Troian, as it is knowen out of drede;
And, if that yow remembre, I am Calkas,
That alderfirst yaf comfort to youre nede,
And tolde wel how that ye shulden spede.   75
For dredeles, thorugh yow shal in a stownde
Ben Troie ybrend, and beten down to grownde.

"And in what forme, or in what manere wise,
This town to shende, and al youre lust t'acheve,
Ye han er this wel herd me yow devyse: 80
This knowe ye, my lordes, as I leve.
And, for the Grekis weren me so leeve,
I com myself, in my propre persone,
To teche in this how yow was best to doone,

"Havyng unto my tresor ne my rente   85
Right no resport, to respect of youre ese.

Thus al my good I lefte and to yow wente,
Wenyng in this yow, lordes, for to plese.
But al that los ne doth me no disese.
I vouchesauf, as wisly have I joie,   90
For yow to lese al that I have in Troie,

"Save of a doughter that I lefte, allas!
Slepyng at hom, whanne out of Troie I sterte.
O sterne, O cruel fader that I was!
How myghte I have in that so hard an herte? 95
Allas, I ne hadde ibrought hire in hire sherte!
For sorwe of which I wol nought lyve to-
        morwe,
But if ye lordes rewe upon my sorwe.

"For, by that cause I say no tyme er now
Hire to delivere, ich holden have my pees;   100
But now or nevere, if that it like yow,
I may hire have right soone, douteles.
O help and grace! amonges al this prees,
Rewe on this olde caytyf in destresse,
Syn I thorugh yow have al this hevynesse.   105

"Ye have now kaught and fetered in prisoun
Troians ynowe; and if youre willes be,
My child with oon may han redempcioun,
Now, for the love of God and of bounte,
Oon of so fele, allas, so yive hym me!   110
What nede were it this preiere for to werne,
Syn ye shul bothe han folk and town as yerne?

"On peril of my lif, I shal nat lye,
Appollo hath me told it feithfully;
I have ek founde it be astronomye,   115
By sort, and by augurye ek, trewely,
And dar wel say, the tyme is faste by
That fire and flaumbe on al the town shal
        sprede,
And thus shal Troie torne to asshen dede.

"For certein, Phebus and Neptunus bothe,   120
That makeden the walles of the town,
Ben with the folk of Troie alwey so wrothe,
That they wol brynge it to confusioun,
Right in despit of kyng Lameadoun.
Bycause he nolde payen hem here hire,   125
The town of Troie shal ben set on-fire."

Tellyng his tale alwey, this olde greye,
Humble in his speche, and in his lokyng eke,
The salte teris from his eyen tweye
Ful faste ronnen down by either cheke.   130
So longe he gan of socour hem biseke
That, for to hele hym of his sorwes soore,
They yave hym Antenor, withouten moore.

But who was glad ynough but Calkas tho?
And of this thyng ful soone his nedes leyde 135
On hem that sholden for the tretis go,
And hem for Antenor ful ofte preyde
To bryngen hom kyng Toas and Criseyde.
And whan Priam his save-garde sente,
Th'embassadours to Troie streight they wente.

The cause itold of hire comyng, the olde   141
Priam, the kyng, ful soone in general
Let her-upon his parlement to holde,
Of which th'effect rehercen yow I shal.
Th'embassadours ben answerd for fynal,   145
Th'eschaunge of prisoners and al this nede
Hem liketh wel, and forth in they procede.

This Troilus was present in the place,
Whan axed was for Antenor Criseyde;
For which ful soone chaungen gan his face,   150
As he that with tho wordes wel neigh deyde.
But natheles he no word to it seyde,
Lest men sholde his affeccioun espye;
With mannes herte he gan his sorwes drye,

And ful of angwissh and of grisly drede   155
Abod what lordes wolde unto it seye;
And if they wolde graunte, as God forbede,
Th'eschaunge of hire, than thoughte he thynges
        tweye,
First, how to save hire honour, and what weye
He myghte best th'eschaunge of hire with-
        stonde;   160
Ful faste he caste how al this myghte stonde.

Love hym made al prest to don hire byde,
And rather dyen than she sholde go;
But resoun seyde hym, on that other syde,
"Withouten assent of hire ne do nat so,   165
Lest for thi werk she wolde be thy fo,
And seyn that thorugh thy medlynge is iblowe
Youre bother love, ther it was erst unknowe."

For which he gan deliberen, for the beste,
That though the lordes wolde that she wente,
He wolde lat hem graunte what hem leste,   171
And telle his lady first what that they mente;
And whan that she hadde seyd hym hire en-
        tente,
Therafter wolde he werken also blyve,
Theigh al the world ayeyn it wolde stryve.   175

Ector, which that wel the Grekis herde,
For Antenor how they wolde han Criseyde,
Gan it withstonde, and sobrely answerde:

"Syres, she nys no prisonere," he seyde;
"I not on yow who that this charge leyde,   180
But, on my part, ye may eftsone hem telle,
We usen here no wommen for to selle."

The noyse of peple up stirte thanne at ones,
As breme as blase of straw iset on-fire;
For infortune it wolde, for the nones,   185
They sholden hire confusioun desire.
"Ector," quod they, "what goost may yow en-
        spyre,
This womman thus to shilde, and don us leese
Daun Antenor — a wrong wey now ye chese —

"That is so wys and ek so bold baroun?   190
And we han nede of folk, as men may se.
He is ek oon the grettest of this town.
O Ector, lat tho fantasies be!
O kyng Priam," quod they, "thus sygge we,
That al oure vois is to forgon Criseyde."   195
And to deliveren Antenor they preyde.

O Juvenal, lord! trewe is thy sentence,
That litel wyten folk what is to yerne
That they ne fynde in hire desir offence;
For cloude of errour lat hem nat discerne   200
What best is. And lo, here ensample as yerne:
This folk desiren now deliveraunce
Of Antenor, that brought hem to meschaunce.

For he was after traitour to the town
Of Troye; allas, they quytte hym out to rathe!
O nyce world, lo, thy discrecioun!   206
Criseyde, which that nevere dide hem scathe,
Shal now no lenger in hire blisse bathe;
But Antenor, he shal com hom to towne,
And she shal out; thus seyden here and howne.

For which delibered was by parlement,   211
For Antenor to yelden out Criseyde,
And it pronounced by the president,
Altheigh that Ector "nay" ful ofte preyde.
And fynaly, what wight that it withseyde,   215
It was for nought; it moste ben and sholde,
For substaunce of the parlement it wolde.

Departed out of parlement echone,
This Troilus, withouten wordes mo,
Unto his chambre spedde hym faste allone,   220
But if it were a man of his or two,
The which he bad out faste for to go,
Bycause he wolde slepen, as he seyde,
And hastily upon his bed hym leyde.

And as in wynter leves ben biraft,   225
Ech after other, til the tree be bare,
So that ther nys but bark and braunche ilaft,
Lith Troilus, byraft of ech welfare,
Ibounden in the blake bark of care,
Disposed wood out of his wit to breyde,   230
So sore hym sat the chaungynge of Criseyde.

He rist hym up, and every dore he shette
And wyndow ek, and tho this sorwful man
Upon his beddes syde adown hym sette,
Ful lik a ded ymage, pale and wan;   235
And in his brest the heped wo bygan
Out breste, and he to werken in this wise
In his woodnesse, as I shal yow devyse.

Right as the wylde bole bygynneth sprynge,
Now her, now ther, idarted to the herte,   240
And of his deth roreth in compleynynge,
Right so gan he aboute the chaumbre sterte,
Smytyng his brest ay with his fistes smerte;
His hed to the wal, his body to the grounde
Ful ofte he swapte, hymselven to confounde.

His eyen two, for piete of herte,   246
Out stremeden as swifte welles tweye;
The heighe sobbes of his sorwes smerte
His speche hym refte; unnethes myghte he
        seye,
"O deth, allas! why nyltow do me deye?   250
Acorsed be that day which that Nature
Shop me to ben a lyves creature!"

But after, whan the furie and al the rage
Which that his herte twiste and faste threste,
By lengthe of tyme somwhat gan aswage,   255
Upon his bed he leyde hym down to reste.
But tho bygonne his teeris more out breste,
That wonder is the body may suffise
To half this wo, which that I yow devyse.

Than seyde he thus, "Fortune, allas the while!
What have I don? What have I the agylt?   261
How myghtestow for rowthe me bygile?
Is ther no grace, and shal I thus be spilt?
Shal thus Creiseyde awey, for that thow wilt?
Allas! how maistow in thyn herte fynde   265
To ben to me thus cruwel and unkynde?

"Have I the nought honoured al my lyve,
As thow wel woost, above the goddes alle?
Whi wiltow me fro joie thus deprive?
O Troilus, what may men now the calle   270
But wrecche of wrecches, out of honour falle

Into miserie, in which I wol bewaille
Criseyde, allas! til that the breth me faille?

"Allas, Fortune! if that my lif in joie
Displesed hadde unto thi foule envye,　　275
Why ne haddestow my fader, kyng of Troye,
Byraft the lif, or don my bretheren dye,
Or slayn myself, that thus compleyne and crye,
I, combre-world, that may of nothyng serve,
But evere dye and nevere fulli sterve?　　280

"If that Criseyde allone were me laft,
Nought roughte I whider thow woldest me
　　steere;
And hire, allas! than hastow me biraft.
But everemore, lo, this is thi manere,
To reve a wight that most is to hym deere,　　285
To preve in that thi gerful violence.
Thus am I lost, ther helpeth no diffence.

"O verrey lord, O Love! O god, allas!
That knowest best myn herte and al my
　　thought,
What shal my sorwful lif don in this cas,　　290
If I forgo that I so deere have bought?
Syn ye Criseyde and me han fully brought
Into youre grace, and bothe oure hertes seled,
How may ye suffre, allas! it be repeled?

"What shal I don? I shal, while I may dure　295
On lyve in torment and in cruwel peyne,
This infortune or this disaventure,
Allone as I was born, iwys, compleyne;
Ne nevere wol I seen it shyne or reyne,
But ende I wol, as Edippe, in derknesse　　300
My sorwful lif, and dyen in distresse.

"O wery goost, that errest to and fro,
Why nyltow fleen out of the wofulleste
Body that evere myghte on grounde go?
O soule, lurkynge in this wo, unneste,　　305
Fle forth out of myn herte, and lat it breste,
And folowe alwey Criseyde, thi lady dere.
Thi righte place is now no lenger here.

"O woful eyen two, syn youre disport
Was al to sen Criseydes eyen brighte,　　310
What shal ye don but, for my discomfort,
Stonden for naught, and wepen out youre
　　sighte,
Syn she is queynt, that wont was yow to lighte?
In vayn fro this forth have ich eyen tweye
Ifourmed, syn youre vertu is aweye.　　315

"O my Criseyde, O lady sovereigne
Of thilke woful soule that thus crieth,
Who shal now yeven comfort to my peyne?
Allas! no wight; but whan myn herte dieth,
My spirit, which that so unto yow hieth,　　320
Receyve in gree, for that shal ay yow serve;
Forthi no fors is, though the body sterve.

"O ye loveris, that heigh upon the whiel
Ben set of Fortune, in good aventure,
God leve that ye fynde ay love of stiel,　　325
And longe mote youre lif in joie endure!
But whan ye comen by my sepulture,
Remembreth that youre felawe resteth there;
For I loved ek, though ich unworthi were.

"O oold, unholsom, and myslyved man,　　330
Calkas I mene, allas! what eileth the,
To ben a Grek, syn thow art born Troian?
O Calkas, which that wolt my bane be,
In corsed tyme was thow born for me!
As wolde blisful Jove, for his joie,　　335
That I the hadde, wher I wolde, in Troie!"

A thousand sikes, hotter than the gleede,
Out of his brest ech after other wente,
Medled with pleyntes new, his wo to feede,
For which his woful teris nevere stente;　　340
And shortly, so his peynes hym torente,
And wex so mat, that joie nor penaunce
He feleth non, but lith forth in a traunce.

Pandare, which that in the parlement
Hadde herd what every lord and burgeys
　　seyde,　　345
And how ful graunted was by oon assent
For Antenor to yelden so Criseyde,
Gan wel neigh wood out of his wit to breyde,
So that, for wo, he nyste what he mente,
But in a rees to Troilus he wente.　　350

A certeyn knyght, that for the tyme kepte
The chambre door, undide it hym anon;
And Pandare, that ful tendreliche wepte,
Into the derke chambre, as stille as ston,
Toward the bed gan softely to gon,　　355
So confus that he nyste what to seye;
For verray wo his wit was neigh aweye.

And with his chiere and lokyng al totorn,
For sorwe of this, and with his armes folden,
He stood this woful Troilus byforn,　　360
And on his pitous face he gan byholden.
But, Lord, so ofte gan his herte colden,

Seyng his frend in wo, whos hevynesse
His herte slough, as thoughte hym, for des-
    tresse.

This woful wight, this Troilus, that felte   365
His frend Pandare ycomen hym to se,
Gan as the snow ayeyn the sonne melte;
For which this sorwful Pandare, of pitee,
Gan for to wepe as tendreliche as he;
And specheles thus ben thise ilke tweye,   370
That neither myghte o word for sorwe seye.

But at the laste this woful Troilus,
Neigh ded for smert gan bresten out to rore,
And with a sorwful noise he seyde thus,
Among hise sobbes and his sikes sore: 375
"Lo, Pandare, I am ded, withouten more.
Hastow nat herd at parlement," he seyde,
"For Antenor how lost is my Criseyde?"

This Pandarus, ful ded and pale of hewe,
Ful pitously answerde and seyde, "Yis!   380
As wisly were it fals as it is trewe,
That I have herd, and woot al how it is.
O mercy, God, who wolde have trowed this?
Who wolde have wend that in so litel a throwe
Fortune oure joie wold han overthrowe?   385

"For in this world ther is no creature,
As to my dom, that ever saw ruyne
Straunger than this, thorugh cas or aventure.
But who may al eschue, or al devyne?
Swich is this world! forthi I thus diffyne,   390
Ne trust no wight to fynden in Fortune
Ay propretee; hire yiftes ben comune.

"But telle me this, whi thow art now so mad
To sorwen thus? Whi listow in this wise,
Syn thi desir al holly hastow had,   395
So that, by right, it oughte ynough suffise?
But I, that nevere felte in my servyse
A frendly cheere, or lokyng of an eye,
Lat me thus wepe and wailen til I deye.

"And over al this, as thow wel woost thiselve,
This town is ful of ladys al aboute;   401
And, to my doom, fairer than swiche twelve
As evere she was, shal I fynde in som route,
Yee, on or two, withouten any doute.
Forthi be glad, myn owen deere brother!   405
If she be lost, we shal recovere an other.

"What! God forbede alwey that ech plesaunce
In o thyng were, and in non other wight!

If oon kan synge, an other kan wel daunce;
If this be goodly, she is glad and light;   410
And this is fair, and that kan good aright.
Ech for his vertu holden is for deere,
Both heroner and faucoun for ryvere.

"And ek, as writ Zanzis, that was ful wys,
'The newe love out chaceth ofte the olde;'   415
And upon newe cas lith newe avys.
Thenk ek, thi lif to saven artow holde.
Swich fir, by proces, shal of kynde colde;
For syn it is but casuel plesaunce,
Som cas shal putte it out of remembraunce.   420

"For also seur as day comth after nyght,
The newe love, labour, or oother wo,
Or elles selde seynge of a wight,
Don olde affecciouns alle over-go.
And, for thi part, thow shalt have oon of tho
T'abregge with thi bittre peynes smerte;   426
Absence of hire shal dryve hire out of herte."

Thise wordes seyde he for the nones alle,
To help his frend, lest he for sorwe deyde;
For douteles, to don his wo to falle,   430
He roughte nought what unthrift that he seyde.
But Troilus, that neigh for sorwe deyde,
Took litel heede of al that evere he mente;
Oon ere it herde, at tothir out it wente.

But at the laste he answerde, and seyde, "Frend,   435
This lechecraft, or heeled thus to be,
Were wel sittyng, if that I were a fend,
To traysen hire that trewe is unto me!
I pray God lat this conseil nevere ythe;
But do me rather sterve anon-right here,   440
Er I thus do as thow me woldest leere!

"She that I serve, iwis, what so thow seye,
To whom myn herte enhabit is by right,
Shal han me holly hires til that I deye.
For, Pandarus, syn I have trouthe hire hight,
I wol nat ben untrewe for no wight;   446
But as hire man I wol ay lyve and sterve,
And nevere other creature serve.

"And ther thow seist thow shalt as faire fynde
As she, lat be, make no comparisoun   450
To creature yformed here by kynde!
O leve Pandare, in conclusioun,
I wol nat ben of thyn opynyoun,
Touchyng al this; for which I the biseche,
So hold thi pees; thow sleest me with thi
    speche!   455

"Thow biddest me I shulde love another
Al fresshly newe, and lat Criseyde go!
It lith nat in my power, leeve brother;
And though I myght, I wolde nat do so.
But kanstow playen raket, to and fro, 460
Nettle in, dok out, now this, now that, Pandare?
Now foule falle hire for thi wo that care!

"Thow farest ek by me, thow Pandarus,
As he that, whan a wight is wo bygon, 464
He cometh to hym a paas, and seith right thus,
'Thynk nat on smert, and thow shalt fele non.'
Thow moost me first transmewen in a ston,
And reve me my passiones alle,
Er thow so lightly do my wo to falle.

"The deth may wel out of my brest departe 470
The lif, so longe may this sorwe myne;
But fro my soule shal Criseydes darte
Out nevere mo; but down with Proserpyne,
Whan I am ded, I wol go wone in pyne,
And ther I wol eternaly compleyne 475
My wo, and how that twynned be we tweyne.

"Thow hast here made an argument, for fyn,
How that it sholde a lasse peyne be
Criseyde to forgon, for she was myn,
And lyved in ese and in felicite. 480
Whi gabbestow, that seydest thus to me
That 'hym is wors that is fro wele ythrowe,
Than he hadde erst noon of that wele yknowe?'

"But telle me now, syn that the thynketh so
light
To changen so in love ay to and fro, 485
Whi hastow nat don bisily thi myght
To chaungen hire that doth the al thi wo?
Why nyltow lete hire fro thyn herte go?
Whi nyltow love an other lady swete,
That may thyn herte setten in quiete? 490

"If thou hast had in love ay yet myschaunce,
And kanst it not out of thyn herte dryve,
I, that levede in lust and in plesaunce
With here, as muche as creature on lyve,
How sholde I that foryete, and that so blyve?
O, where hastow ben hid so longe in muwe, 496
That kanst so wel and formaly arguwe?

"Nay, God wot, nought worth is al thi red,
For which, for what that evere may byfalle,
Withouten wordes mo, I wol be ded. 500
O deth, that endere art of sorwes alle,
Com now, syn I so ofte after the calle;

For sely is that deth, soth for to seyne,
That, ofte ycleped, cometh and endeth peyne.

"Wel wot I, whil my lyf was in quyete, 505
Er thow me slowe, I wolde have yeven hire;
But now thi comynge is to me so swete
That in this world I nothing so desire.
O deth, syn with this sorwe I am a-fyre,
Thow other do me anoon in teeris drenche, 510
Or with thi colde strok myn hete quenche.

"Syn that thou sleest so fele in sondry wyse
Ayens hire wil, unpreyed, day and nyght,
Do me at my requeste this servise:
Delyvere now the world, so dostow right, 515
Of me, that am the wofulleste wyght
That evere was; for tyme is that I sterve,
Syn in this world of right nought may I serve."

This Troylus in teris gan distille,
As licour out of a lambic ful faste; 520
And Pandarus gan holde his tunge stille,
And to the ground his eyen doun he caste.
But natheles, thus thought he at the laste:
"What! parde, rather than my felawe deye,
Yet shal I somwhat more unto hym seye." 525

And seyde: "Frend, syn thow hast swych dis-
tresse,
And syn thee list myn arguments to blame,
Why nylt thiselven helpen don redresse,
And with thy manhod letten al this grame?
Go ravisshe here ne kanstow nat for shame! 530
And other lat here out of towne fare,
Or hold here stille, and leve thi nyce fare.

"Artow in Troie, and hast non hardyment
To take a womman which that loveth the,
And wolde hireselven ben of thyn assent? 535
Now is nat this a nyce vanitee?
Ris up anon, and lat this wepyng be,
And kith thow art a man; for in this houre
I wol ben ded, or she shal bleven oure."

To this answerde hym Troilus ful softe, 540
And seyde, "Parde, leve brother deere,
Al this have I myself yet thought ful ofte,
And more thyng than thow devysest here.
But whi this thyng is laft, thow shalt wel here;
And whan thow me hast yeve an audience, 545
Therafter maystow telle al thi sentence.

"First, syn thow woost this town hath al this
werre
For ravysshyng of wommen so by myght,

It sholde nought be suffred me to erre,
As it stant now, ne don so gret unright.   550
I sholde han also blame of every wight,
My fadres graunt if that I so withstoode,
Syn she is chaunged for the townes goode.

"I have ek thought, so it were hire assent,
To axe hire at my fader, of his grace;   555
Than thynke I, this were hire accusement,
Syn wel I woot I may hire nought purchace.
For syn my fader, in so heigh a place
As parlement, hath hire eschaunge enseled,
He nyl for me his lettre be repeled.   560

"Yet drede I moost hire herte to perturbe
With violence, if I do swich a game;
For if I wolde it openly desturbe,
It mooste be disclaundre to hire name.
And me were levere ded than hire diffame,   565
As nolde God but if I sholde have
Hire honour levere than my lif to save!

"Thus am I lost, for aught that I kan see.
For certeyn is, syn that I am hire knyght,
I moste hire honour levere han than me   570
In every cas, as lovere ought of right.
Thus am I with desir and reson twight:
Desir for to destourben hire me redeth,
And reson nyl nat, so myn herte dredeth."

Thus wepyng that he koude nevere cesse,   575
He seyde, "Allas! how shal I, wrecche, fare?
For wel fele I alwey my love encresse,
And hope is lasse and lasse alway, Pandare.
Encressen ek the causes of my care.
So weilaway, whi nyl myn herte breste?   580
For, as in love, ther is but litel reste."

Pandare answerde, "Frend, thow maist, for me,
Don as the list; but hadde ich it so hoote,
And thyn estat, she sholde go with me,
Though al this town cride on this thyng by   585
    note.
I nolde sette at al that noys a grote!
For whan men han wel cryd, than wol they
    rowne;
Ek wonder last but nyne nyght nevere in
    towne.

"Devyne not in resoun ay so depe
Ne corteisly, but help thiself anon.   590
Bet is that othere than thiselven wepe,
And namely, syn ye two ben al on.
Ris up, for by myn hed, she shal not goon!

And rather be in blame a lite ifounde
Than sterve here as a gnat, withouten wounde.

"It is no shame unto yow ne no vice,   596
Hire to witholden that ye love moost.
Peraunter, she myghte holde the for nyce,
To late hire go thus to the Grekis oost.
Thenk ek Fortune, as wel thiselven woost,   600
Helpeth hardy man to his enprise,
And weyveth wrecches for hire cowardise.

"And though thy lady wolde a lite hire greve,
Thow shalt thiself thi pees hereafter make,
But as for me, certeyn, I kan nat leve   605
That she wolde it as now for yvel take.
Whi sholde thanne of ferd thyn herte quake?
Thenk ek how Paris hath, that is thi brother,
A love; and whi shaltow nat have another?

"And Troilus, o thyng I dar the swere,   610
That if Criseyde, which that is thi lief,
Now loveth the as wel as thow dost here,
God help me so, she nyl nat take a-grief,
Theigh thow do boote anon in this meschief.
And if she wilneth fro the for to passe,   615
Thanne is she fals; so love hire wel the lasse.

"Forthi tak herte, and thynk right as a knyght,
Thorugh love is broken al day every lawe.
Kith now somwhat thi corage and thi myght;
Have mercy on thiself, for any awe.   620
Lat nat this wrecched wo thyn herte gnawe,
But manly sette the world on six and sevene;
And if thow deye a martyr, go to hevene!

"I wol myself ben with the at this dede,
Theigh ich and al my kyn, upon a stownde,   625
Shulle in a strete as dogges liggen dede,
Thorough-girt with many a wid and blody
    wownde,
In every cas I wol a frend be founde.
And if the list here sterven as a wrecche,
Adieu, the devel spede hym that it recche!"   630

This Troilus gan with tho wordes quyken,
And seyde, "Frend, graunt mercy, ich assente.
But certeynly thow maist nat so me priken,
Ne peyne non ne may me so tormente,
That, for no cas, it is nat myn entente,   635
At shorte wordes, though I deyen sholde,
To ravysshe hire, but if hireself it wolde."

"Whi, so mene I," quod Pandarus, "al this day.
But telle me thanne, hastow hire wil assayed,

That sorwest thus?" And he answerde hym,
      "Nay."   640
"Wherof artow," quod Pandare, "thanne
      amayed,
That nost nat that she wol ben yvele appayed
To ravysshe hire, syn thow hast nought ben
      there,
But if that Jove told it in thyn ere?

"Forthi ris up, as nought ne were, anon,   645
And wassh thi face, and to the kyng thow
      wende,
Or he may wondren whider thow art goon.
Thow most with wisdom hym and othere
      blende,
Or, upon cas, he may after the sende,
Er thow be war; and shortly, brother deere,   650
Be glad, and lat me werke in this matere.

"For I shal shape it so, that sikerly
Thow shalt this nyght som tyme, in som
      manere,
Come speken with thi lady pryvely
And by hire wordes ek, and by hire cheere,   655
Thow shalt ful sone aperceyve and wel here
Al hire entente, and of this cas the beste.
And far now wel, for in this point I reste."

The swifte Fame, which that false thynges
Egal reporteth lik the thynges trewe,   660
Was thoroughout Troie yfled with preste wynges
Fro man to man, and made this tale al newe,
How Calkas doughter, with hire brighte hewe,
At parlement, withouten wordes more,
Ygraunted was in chaunge of Antenore.   665

The whiche tale anon-right as Criseyde
Hadde herd, she, which that of hire fader
      roughte,
As in this cas, right nought, ne whan he deyde,
Ful bisily to Jupiter bisoughte
Yeve hem meschaunce that this tretis broughte.
But shortly, lest thise tales sothe were,   671
She dorst at no wight asken it, for fere.

As she that hadde hire herte and al hire mynde
On Troilus iset so wonder faste,
That al this world ne myghte hire love un-
      bynde,   675
Ne Troilus out of hire herte caste,
She wol ben his, while that hire lif may laste.
And thus she brenneth both in love and drede,
So that she nyste what was best to reede.

But as men seen in towne, and al aboute,   680
That wommen usen frendes to visite,
So to Criseyde of wommen com a route,
For pitous joie, and wenden hire delite;
And with hire tales, deere ynough a myte,   684
Thise wommen, which that in the cite dwelle,
They sette hem down, and seyde as I shall telle.

Quod first that oon, "I am glad, trewely,
Bycause of yow, that shal youre fader see."
Another seyde, "Ywis, so nam nat I;
For al to litel hath she with us be."   690
Quod tho the thridde, "I hope, ywis, that she
Shal bryngen us the pees on every syde,
That, whan she goth, almyghty God hire gide!"

Tho wordes and tho wommanysshe thynges,
She herde hem right as though she thennes
      were;   695
For, God it woot, hire herte on othir thyng is.
Although the body sat among hem there,
Hire advertence is alwey elleswhere;
For Troilus ful faste hire soule soughte;   699
Withouten word, on hym alwey she thoughte.

Thise wommen, that thus wenden hire to plese,
Aboute naught gonne alle hire tales spende.
Swich vanyte ne kan don hire non ese,
As she that al this mene while brende
Of other passioun than that they wende,   705
So that she felte almost hire herte dye
For wo and wery of that compaignie.

For which no lenger myghte she restreyne
Hir teeris, so they gonnen up to welle,
That yaven signes of the bittre peyne   710
In which hir spirit was, and moste dwelle;
Remembryng hir, fro heven into which helle
She fallen was, syn she forgoth the syghte
Of Troilus, and sorwfully she sighte.

And thilke fooles sittynge hire aboute   715
Wenden that she wepte and siked sore
Bycause that she sholde out of that route
Departe, and nevere pleye with hem more.
And they that hadde yknowen hire of yore
Seigh hire so wepe, and thoughte it kynde-
      nesse,   720
And ech of hem wepte eke for hire destresse.

And bisyly they gonnen hire comforten
Of thyng, God woot, on which she litel
      thoughte;
And with hire tales wenden hire disporten,

And to be glad they often hire bysoughte.   725
But swich an ese therwith they hire wroughte,
Right as a man is esed for to feele,
For ache of hed, to clawen hym on his heele!

But after al this nyce vanyte
They toke hire leve, and hom they wenten alle.
Criseyde, ful of sorweful pite,   731
Into hire chambre up went out of the halle,
And on hire bed she gan for ded to falle,
In purpos nevere thennes for to rise;   734
And thus she wroughte, as I shal yow devyse.

Hire ownded heer, that sonnyssh was of hewe,
She rente, and ek hire fyngeres longe and smale
She wrong ful ofte, and bad God on hire rewe,
And with the deth to doon boote on hire bale.
Hire hewe, whilom bright, that tho was
     pale,   740
Bar witnesse of hire wo and hire constreynte;
And thus she spak, sobbyng in hire com-
     pleynte:

"Allas!" quod she, "out of this regioun
I, woful wrecche and infortuned wight,
And born in corsed constellacioun,   745
Moot goon, and thus departen fro my knyght.
Wo worth, allas! that ilke dayes light
On which I saugh hym first with eyen tweyne,
That causeth me, and ich hym, al this peyne!"

Therwith the teris fro hire eyen two   750
Down fille, as shour in Aperil ful swithe;
Hire white brest she bet, and for the wo
After the deth she cryed a thousand sithe,
Syn he that wont hire wo was for to lithe,
She moot forgon; for which disaventure   755
She held hireself a forlost creature.

She seyde, "How shal he don, and ich also?
How sholde I lyve, if that I from hym twynne?
O deere herte eke, that I love so,
Who shal that sorwe slen that ye ben inne?   760
O Calkas, fader, thyn be al this synne!
O moder myn, that cleped were Argyve,
Wo worth that day that thow me bere on lyve!

"To what fyn sholde I lyve and sorwen thus?
How sholde a fissh withouten water dure?   765
What is Criseyde worth, from Troilus?
How sholde a plaunte or lyves creature
Lyve withouten his kynde noriture?
For which ful ofte a by-word here I seye,
That 'rooteles moot grene soone deye.'   770

"I shal doon thus, syn neither swerd ne darte
Dar I noon handle, for the crueltee,
That ilke day that I from yow departe,
If sorwe of that nyl nat my bane be,
Thanne shal no mete or drynke come in me   775
Til I my soule out of my breste unshethe;
And thus myselven wol I don to dethe.

"And, Troilus, my clothes everychon
Shul blake ben in tokenyng, herte swete,
That I am as out of this world agon,   780
That wont was yow to setten in quiete;
And of myn ordre, ay til deth me mete,
The observance evere, in youre absence,
Shal sorwe ben, compleynt, and abstinence.

"Myn herte and ek the woful goost therinne
Byquethe I, with youre spirit to compleyne   786
Eternaly, for they shal nevere twynne.
For though in erthe ytwynned be we tweyne,
Yet in the feld of pite, out of peyne,
That highte Elisos, shal we ben yfeere,   790
As Orpheus with Erudice, his fere.

"Thus, herte myn, for Antenor, allas!
I soone shal be chaunged, as I wene.
But how shul ye don in this sorwful cas;
How shal youre tendre herte this sustene?   795
But, herte myn, foryete this sorwe and tene,
And me also; for, sothly for to seye,
So ye wel fare, I recche naught to deye."

How myghte it evere yred ben or ysonge,
The pleynte that she made in hire destresse?
I not; but, as for me, my litel tonge,   801
If I discryven wolde hire hevynesse,
It sholde make hire sorwe seme lesse
Than that it was, and childisshly deface
Hire heigh compleynte, and therfore ich it
     pace.   805

Pandare, which that sent from Troilus
Was to Criseyde — as ye han herd devyse
That for the beste it was acorded thus,
And he ful glad to doon hym that servyse —
Unto Criseyde, in a ful secree wise,   810
Ther as she lay in torment and in rage,
Com hire to telle al hoolly his message,

And fond that she hireselven gan to trete
Ful pitously; for with hire salte teris
Hire brest, hire face, ybathed was ful wete.   815
The myghty tresses of hire sonnysshe heeris,
Unbroiden, hangen al aboute hire eeris;

Which yaf hym verray signal of martire
Of deth, which that hire herte gan desire.   819

Whan she hym saugh, she gan for sorwe anon
Hire tery face atwixe hire armes hide;
For which this Pandare is so wo-bygon
That in the hous he myghte unnethe abyde,
As he that pite felt on every syde.   824
For if Criseyde hadde erst compleyned soore,
Tho gan she pleyne a thousand tymes more.

And in hire aspre pleynte thus she seyde:
"Pandare first of joies mo than two
Was cause causyng unto me, Criseyde,
That now transmewed ben in cruel wo.   830
Wher shal I seye to yow welcom or no,
That alderfirst me broughte unto servyse
Of love, allas! that endeth in swich wise?

"Endeth thanne love in wo? Ye, or men lieth!
And alle worldly blisse, as thynketh me.   835
The ende of blisse ay sorwe it occupieth;
And whoso troweth nat that it so be,
Lat hym upon me, woful wrecche, ysee,
That myself hate, and ay my burthe acorse,
Felyng alwey, fro wikke I go to worse.   840

"Whoso me seeth, he seeth sorwe al atonys,
Peyne, torment, pleynte, wo, distresse!
Out of my woful body harm ther noon is,
As angwissh, langour, cruel bitternesse,
Anoy, smert, drede, fury, and ek siknesse.   845
I trowe, ywys, from hevene teeris reyne
For pite of myn aspre and cruel peyne."

"And thow, my suster, ful of discomfort,"
Quod Pandarus, "what thynkestow to do?
Whi ne hastow to thyselven som resport?   850
Whi wiltow thus thiself, allas, fordo?
Leef al this werk, and tak now heede to
That I shal seyn; and herkne of good entente
This, which by me thi Troilus the sente."

Tornede hire tho Criseyde, a wo makynge   855
So gret that it a deth was for to see.
"Allas!" quod she, "what wordes may ye
     brynge?
What wol my deere herte seyn to me,
Which that I drede nevere mo to see?
Wol he han pleynte or teris, er I wende?   860
I have ynough, if he therafter sende!"

She was right swich to seen in hire visage
As is that wight that men on beere bynde;
Hire face, lik of Paradys the ymage,

Was al ychaunged in another kynde.   865
The pleye, the laughter, men was wont to
     fynde
In hire, and ek hire joies everichone,
Ben fled, and thus lith now Criseyde allone.

Aboute hire eyen two a purpre ryng
Bytrent, in sothfast tokenyng of hire peyne,
That to biholde it was a dedly thyng;   871
For which Pandare myghte nat restreyne
The teeris from his eighen for to reyne.
But natheles, as he best myghte, he seyde
From Troilus thise wordes to Criseyde: 875

"Lo, nece, I trowe wel ye han herd al how
The kyng with othere lordes, for the beste,
Hath mad eschaunge of Antenor and yow,
That cause is of this sorwe and this unreste.
But how this cas dooth Troilus moleste,   880
That may non erthely mannes tonge seye;
For verray wo his wit is al aweye.

"For which we han so sorwed, he and I,
That into litel bothe it hadde us slawe;
But thorugh my conseyl this day, finaly,   885
He somwhat is fro wepynge now withdrawe,
And semeth me that he desireth fawe
With yow to ben al nyght, for to devyse
Remedie in this, if ther were any wyse.

"This, short and pleyn, th'effect of my message,
As ferforth as my wit kan comprehende;   891
For ye, that ben of torment in swich rage,
May to no long prologe as now entende.
And hereupon ye may answere hym sende;
And, for the love of God, my nece deere,   895
So lef this wo er Troilus be here!"

"Gret is my wo," quod she, and sighte soore,
As she that feleth dedly sharp distresse;
"But yit to me his sorwe is muchel more,
That love hym bet than he hymself, I gesse.   900
Allas! for me hath he swich hevynesse?
Kan he for me so pitously compleyne?
Iwis, this sorwe doubleth al my peyne.

"Grevous to me, God woot, is for to twynne,"
Quod she, "but yet it harder is to me   905
To sen that sorwe which that he is inne;
For wel woot I it wol my bane be,
And deye I wol in certeyn," tho quod she;
"But bid hym come, er deth, that thus me
     threteth,
Dryve out that goost which in myn herte
     beteth."   910

Thise wordes seyd, she on hire armes two
Fil gruf, and gan to wepen pitously.
Quod Pandarus, "Allas! whi do ye so,
Syn wel ye woot the tyme is faste by,
That he shal come? Aris up hastily,   915
That he yow nat bywopen thus ne fynde,
But ye wole have hym wood out of his mynde.

"For wiste he that ye ferde in this manere,
He wolde hymselven sle; and if I wende
To han this fare, he sholde nat come here   920
For al the good that Priam may dispende.
For to what fyn he wolde anon pretende,
That knowe ich wel; and forthi yet I seye,
So lef this sorwe, or platly he wol deye.

"And shapeth yow his sorwe for t'abregge,   925
And nought encresse, leeve nece swete!
Beth rather to hym cause of flat than egge,
And with som wisdom ye his sorwe bete.
What helpeth it to wepen ful a strete,
Or though ye bothe in salte teeris dreynte?   930
Bet is a tyme of cure ay than of pleynte.

"I mene thus: whan ich hym hider brynge,
Syn ye be wise, and bothe of oon assent,
So shapeth how destourbe youre goynge,
Or come ayeyn, soon after ye be went.   935
Women ben wise in short avysement;
And lat sen how youre wit shal now availle,
And what that I may helpe, it shal nat faille."

"Go," quod Criseyde, "and uncle, trewely,
I shal don al my myght me to restreyne   940
From wepyng in his sighte, and bisily,
Hym for to glade I shal don al my peyne,
And in myn herte seken every veyne.
If to this sore ther may be fonden salve,
It shal nat lakke, certeyn, on my halve."   945

Goth Pandarus, and Troilus he soughte,
Til in a temple he fond hym al allone,
As he that of his lif no lenger roughte;
But to the pitouse goddes everichone   949
Ful tendrely he preyed, and made his mone,
To doon hym sone out of this world to pace;
For wel he thoughte ther was non other grace.

And shortly, al the sothe for to seye,
He was so fallen in despeir that day,
That outrely he shop hym for to deye.   955
For right thus was his argument alway:
He seyde, he nas but lorn, so weylaway!

"For al that comth, comth by necessitee:
Thus to ben lorn, it is my destinee.

"For certeynly, this wot I wel," he seyde,   960
"That forsight of divine purveyaunce
Hath seyn alwey me to forgon Criseyde,
Syn God seeth every thyng, out of doutaunce,
And hem disponyth, thorugh his ordinaunce,
In hire merites sothly for to be,   965
As they shul comen by predestyne.

"But natheles, allas! whom shal I leeve?
For ther ben grete clerkes many oon,
That destyne thorugh argumentes preve;
And som men seyn that, nedely, ther is noon,
But that fre chois is yeven us everychon.   971
O, welaway! so sleighe arn clerkes olde,
That I not whos opynyoun I may holde.

"For som men seyn, if God seth al biforn,
Ne God may nat deceyved ben, parde,   975
Than moot it fallen, theigh men hadde it sworn,
That purveiance hath seyn before to be.
Wherfore I sey, that from eterne if he
Hath wist byforn oure thought ek as oure dede,
We han no fre chois, as thise clerkes rede.   980

"For other thought, nor other dede also,
Myghte nevere ben, but swich as purveyaunce,
Which may nat ben deceyved nevere mo,
Hath feled byforn, withouten ignoraunce.
For yf ther myghte ben a variaunce   985
To writhen out fro Goddis purveyinge,
Ther nere no prescience of thyng comynge,

"But it were rather an opynyoun
Uncerteyn, and no stedfast forseynge.
And certes, that were an abusioun,   990
That God sholde han no parfit cler wytynge
More than we men that han doutous wenynge.
But swich an errour upon God to gesse
Were fals and foul, and wikked corsednesse.

"Ek this is an opynyoun of some   995
That han hire top ful heighe and smothe
     yshore:
They seyn right thus, that thyng is nat to come
For that the prescience hath seyn byfore
That it shal come; but they seyn that therfore
That it shal come, therfore the purveyaunce
Woot it byforn, withouten ignoraunce;   1001

"And in this manere this necessite
Retorneth in his part contrarie agayn.

For nedfully byhoveth it nat to bee
That thilke thynges fallen in certayn   1005
That ben purveyed; but nedly, as they sayn,
Byhoveth it that thynges whiche that falle,
That they in certayn ben purveyed alle.

"I mene as though I laboured me in this,
To enqueren which thyng cause of which thyng
          be: 1010
As wheither that the prescience of God is
The certeyn cause of the necessite
Of thynges that to comen ben, parde;
Or if necessite of thyng comynge
Be cause certeyn of the purveyinge.   1015

"But now n'enforce I me nat in shewynge
How the ordre of causes stant; but wel woot I
That it byhoveth that the byfallynge
Of thynges wiste byforen certeynly
Be necessarie, al seme it nat therby   1020
That prescience put fallynge necessaire
To thyng to come, al falle it foule or faire.

"For if ther sitte a man yond on a see,
Than by necessite bihoveth it
That, certes, thyn opynyoun sooth be,   1025
That wenest or conjectest that he sit.
And further over now ayeynward yit,
Lo, right so is it of the part contrarie,
As thus, — nowe herkne, for I wol nat tarie:

"I sey, that if the opynyoun of the   1030
Be soth, for that he sitte, than sey I this,
That he mot siten by necessite;
And thus necessite in eyther is.
For in hym nede of sittynge is, ywys,
And in the nede of soth; and thus, forsothe,
There mot necessite ben in yow bothe.   1036

"But thow mayst seyn, the man sit nat therfore,
That thyn opynyoun of his sittynge soth is;
But rather, for the man sit ther byfore,
Therfore is thyn opynyoun soth, ywis.   1040
And I seye, though the cause of soth of this
Comth of his sittyng, yet necessite
Is entrechaunged both in hym and the.

"Thus in this same wise, out of doutaunce,
I may wel maken, as it semeth me,   1045
My resonyng of Goddes purveyaunce
And of the thynges that to comen be;
By which resoun men may wel yse
That thilke thynges that in erthe falle,
That by necessite they comen alle.   1050

"For although that, for thyng shal come, ywys,
Therfore is it purveyed, certeynly,
Nat that it comth for it purveyed is;
Yet natheles, bihoveth it nedfully,
That thing to come be purveyd, trewely;   1055
Or elles, thynges that purveyed be,
That they bitiden by necessite.

"And this suffiseth right ynough, certeyn,
For to destruye oure fre chois every del.
But now is this abusioun, to seyn   1060
That fallyng of the thynges temporel
Is cause of Goddes prescience eternel.
Now trewely, that is a fals sentence,
That thyng to come sholde cause his prescience.

"What myght I wene, and I hadde swich a
          thought,   1065
But that God purveyeth thyng that is to come
For that it is to come, and ellis nought?
So myghte I wene that thynges alle and some,
That whilom ben byfalle and overcome,
Ben cause of thilke sovereyne purveyaunce
That forwoot al withouten ignoraunce.   1071

"And over al this, yet sey I more herto,
That right as whan I wot ther is a thyng,
Iwys, that thyng moot nedfully be so;
Ek right so, whan I woot a thyng comyng,   1075
So mot it come; and thus the bifallyng
Of thynges that ben wist bifore the tyde,
They mowe nat ben eschued on no syde."

Thanne seyde he thus: "Almyghty Jove in
          trone,
That woost of al this thyng the sothfastnesse,
Rewe on my sorwe, and do me deyen sone,   1081
Or bryng Criseyde and me fro this destresse!"
And whil he was in al this hevynesse,
Disputyng with hymself in this matere,   1084
Com Pandare in, and seyde as ye may here.

"O myghty God," quod Pandarus, "in trone,
I! who say evere a wis man faren so?
Whi, Troilus, what thinkestow to doone?
Hastow swich lust to ben thyn owen fo?
What, parde, yet is nat Criseyde ago!   1090
Whi list the so thiself fordoon for drede,
That in thyn hed thyne eyen semen dede?

"Hastow nat lyved many a yer byforn
Withouten hire, and ferd ful wel at ese?
Artow for hire and for noon other born?   1095
Hath Kynde the wrought al only hire to plese?

Lat be, and thynk right thus in thi disese:
That, in the dees right as ther fallen chaunces,
Right so in love ther come and gon plesaunces.

"And yet this is my wonder most of alle,   1100
Whi thow thus sorwest, syn thow nost nat yit,
Touchyng hire goyng, how that it shal falle,
Ne yif she kan hireself destourben it.
Thow hast nat yet assayed al hire wit.
A man may al bytyme his nekke beede   1105
Whan it shal of, and sorwen at the nede.

"Forthi tak hede of that I shal the seye:
I have with hire yspoke, and longe ybe,
So as acorded was bitwixe us tweye;
And evere mo me thynketh thus, that she   1110
Hath somwhat in hire hertes privete,
Wherwith she kan, if I shal right arede,
Destourbe al this of which thow art in drede.

"For which my counseil is, whan it is nyght,
Thow to hire go, and make of this an ende;   1115
And blisful Juno, thorugh hire grete myght,
Shal, as I hope, hire grace unto us sende.
Myn herte seyth, 'Certeyn, she shal nat wende.'
And forthi put thyn herte a while in reste,
And hold thi purpos, for it is the beste."   1120

This Troilus answerd, and sighte soore:
"Thow seist right wel, and I wol don right so."
And what hym liste, he seyde unto it more.
And whan that it was tyme for to go,
Ful pryvely hymself, withouten mo,   1125
Unto hire com, as he was wont to doone;
And how they wroughte, I shal yow tellen
                                        soone.

Soth is, that whan they gonnen first to mete,
So gan the peyne hire hertes for to twiste,
That neyther of hem other myghte grete,   1130
But hem in armes toke, and after kiste.
The lasse woful of hem bothe nyste
Wher that he was, ne myghte o word out
                                       brynge,
As I seyde erst, for wo and for sobbynge.

Tho woful teeris that they leten falle   1135
As bittre weren, out of teris kynde,
For peyne, as is ligne aloes or galle.
So bittre teeris weep nought, as I fynde,
The woful Mirra thorugh the bark and rynde;
That in this world ther nys so hard an herte,   1140
That nolde han rewed on hire peynes smerte.

But whan hire wofulle weri goostes tweyne
Retourned ben ther as hem oughte to dwelle,
And that somwhat to wayken gan the peyne
By lengthe of pleynte, and ebben gan the welle
Of hire teeris, and the herte unswelle,   1146
With broken vois, al hoors forshright, Criseyde
To Troilus thise ilke wordes seyde:

"O Jove, I deye, and mercy I beseche!
Help, Troilus!" and therwithal hire face   1150
Upon his brest she leyde, and loste speche;
Hire woful spirit from his propre place,
Right with the word, alwey o poynt to pace.
And thus she lith with hewes pale and grene,
That whilom fressh and fairest was to sene.   1155

This Troilus, that on hire gan biholde,
Clepyng hire name, — and she lay as for ded,
Withoute answere, and felte hire lymes colde,
Hire eyen throwen upward to hire hed, —
This sorwful man kan now noon other red,   1160
But ofte tyme hire colde mowth he kiste.
Wher hym was wo, God and hymself it wiste!

He rist hym up, and long streght he hire leyde;
For signe of lif, for aught he kan or may,
Kan he non fynde in nothyng on Criseyde,   1165
For which his song ful ofte is "weylaway!"
But whan he saugh that specheles she lay,
With sorweful vois, and herte of blisse al bare,
He seyde how she was fro this world yfare.   1169

So after that he longe hadde hire compleyned,
His hondes wrong, and seyd that was to seye,
And with his teeris salt hire brest byreyned,
He gan tho teeris wypen of ful dreye,
And pitously gan for the soule preye,   1174
And seyde, "O Lord, that set art in thi trone,
Rewe ek on me, for I shal folwe hire sone!"

She cold was, and withouten sentement,
For aught he woot, for breth ne felte he non;
And this was hym a pregnant argument
That she was forth out of this world agon.   1180
And whan he say ther was non other woon
He gan hire lymes dresse in swich manere
As men don hem that shal ben layd on beere.

And after this, with sterne and cruel herte,   1184
His swerd anon out of his shethe he twighte,
Hymself to slen, how sore that hym smerte,
So that his soule hire soule folwen myghte
Ther as the doom of Mynos wolde it dighte;

Syn Love and cruel Fortune it ne wolde,
That in this world he lenger lyven sholde.   1190

Than seyde he thus, fulfild of heigh desdayn:
"O cruel Jove, and thow, Fortune adverse,
This al and som, that falsly have ye slayn
Criseyde, and syn ye may do me no werse,
Fy on youre myght and werkes so dyverse!   1195
Thus cowardly ye shul me nevere wynne;
Ther shal no deth me fro my lady twynne.

"For I this world, syn ye have slayn hire thus,
Wol lete, and folwe hire spirit low or hye.
Shal nevere lovere seyn that Troilus   1200
Dar nat, for fere, with his lady dye;
For, certeyn, I wol beere hire compaignie.
But syn ye wol nat suffre us lyven here,
Yet suffreth that oure soules ben yfere.

"And thow, cite, which that I leve in wo,   1205
And thow, Priam, and bretheren al yfeere,
And thow, my moder, farwel! for I go;
And Atropos, make redy thow my beere.
And thow, Criseyde, o swete herte deere,
Receyve now my spirit!" wolde he seye,   1210
With swerd at herte, al redy for to deye.

But, as God wolde, of swough therwith
                              sh'abreyde,
And gan to sike, and "Troilus" she cride;
And he answerde, "Lady myn, Criseyde,
Lyve ye yet?" and leet his swerd down glide.
"Ye, herte myn, that thonked be Cipride!"   1216
Quod she, and therwithal she soore syghte,
And he bigan to glade hire as he myghte;

Took hire in armes two, and kiste hire ofte,
And hire to glade he did al his entente;   1220
For which hire goost, that flikered ay on lofte,
Into hire woful herte ayeyn it wente.
But at the laste, as that hire eye glente
Asyde, anon she gan his swerd espie,
As it lay bare, and gan for fere crye,   1225

And asked hym, whi he it hadde out drawe.
And Troilus anon the cause hire tolde,
And how hymself therwith he wolde han slawe;
For which Criseyde upon hym gan biholde,
And gan hym in hire armes faste folde,   1230
And seyde, "O mercy, God, lo, which a dede!
Allas, how neigh we weren bothe dede!

"Than if I nadde spoken, as grace was,
Ye wolde han slayn yourself anon?" quod she.

"Yee, douteles"; and she answerde, "Allas!   1235
For, by that ilke Lord that made me,
I nolde a forlong wey on lyve have be,
After youre deth, to han ben crowned queene
Of al the lond the sonne on shyneth sheene.

"But with this selve swerd, which that here is,
Myselve I wolde han slawe," quod she tho.   1241
"But hoo, for we han right ynough of this,
And lat us rise, and streght to bedde go,
And there lat us speken of oure wo.
For, by the morter which that I se brenne,   1245
Knowe I ful wel that day is nat far henne."

Whan they were in hire bed, in armes folde,
Naught was it lik tho nyghtes here-byforn.
For pitously ech other gan byholde,
As they that hadden al hire blisse ylorn,   1250
Bywaylinge ay the day that they were born;
Til at the laste this sorwful wight, Criseyde,
To Troilus thise ilke wordes seyde:

"Lo, herte myn, wel woot ye this," quod she,
"That if a wight alwey his wo complevne,   1255
And seketh nought how holpen for to be,
It nys but folie and encrees of peyne;
And syn that here assembled be we tweyne
To fynde boote of wo that we ben inne,
It were al tyme soone to bygynne.   1260

"I am a womman, as ful wel ye woot,
And as I am avysed sodeynly,
So wol I telle yow, whil it is hoot.
Me thynketh thus, that nouther ye nor I
Ought half this wo to maken, skilfully;   1265
For ther is art ynough for to redresse
That yet is mys, and slen this hevynesse.

"Soth is, the wo, the which that we ben inne,
For aught I woot, for nothyng ellis is
But for the cause that we sholden twynne.   1270
Considered al, ther nys namore amys.
But what is thanne a remede unto this,
But that we shape us soone for to meete?
This al and som, my deere herte sweete.

"Now, that I shal wel bryngen it aboute,   1275
To come ayeyn, soone after that I go,
Therof am I no manere thyng in doute.
For, dredeles, withinne a wowke or two,
I shal ben here; and that it may be so
By alle right, and in a wordes fewe,   1280
I shal yow wel an heep of weyes shewe.

"For which I wol nat make long sermoun,
For tyme ylost may nought recovered be;
But I wol gon to my conclusioun,
And to the beste, in aught that I kan see.   1285
And, for the love of God, foryeve it me,
If I speke aught ayeyns youre hertes reste;
For trewely, I speke it for the beste;

"Makyng alwey a protestacioun,
That now thise wordes, which that I shal seye,
Nis but to shewen yow my mocioun   1291
To fynde unto oure help the beste weye;
And taketh it non other wise, I preye.
For in effect, what so ye me comaunde,
That wol I don, for that is no demaunde.   1295

"Now herkneth this: ye han wel understonde,
My goyng graunted is by parlement
So ferforth that it may nat be withstonde
For al this world, as by my jugement.
And syn ther helpeth non avisement   1300
To letten it, lat it passe out of mynde,
And lat us shape a bettre wey to fynde.

"The soth is this: the twynnyng of us tweyne
Wol us disese and cruelich anoye;
But hym byhoveth somtyme han a peyne,   1305
That serveth Love, if that he wol have joye.
And syn I shal no ferther out of Troie
Than I may ride ayeyn on half a morwe,
It oughte lesse causen us to sorwe;

"So as I shal not so ben hid in mewe,   1310
That day by day, myn owne herte deere,
Syn wel ye woot that it is now a trewe,
Ye shal ful wel al myn estat yheere.
And er that trewe is doon, I shal ben heere;
And thanne have ye both Antenore ywonne   1315
And me also. Beth glad now, if ye konne,

"And thenk right thus, 'Criseyde is now agon.
But what! she shal come hastiliche ayeyn!'
And whanne, allas? By God, lo, right anon,
Er dayes ten, this dar I saufly seyn.   1320
And than at erste shal we be so feyn,
So as we shal togideres evere dwelle,
That al this world ne myghte oure blisse telle.

"I se that ofte tyme, there as we ben now,
That for the beste, oure counseyl for to hide,
Ye speke nat with me, nor I with yow   1326
In fourtenyght, ne se yow go ne ride.
May ye naught ten dayes thanne abide,

For myn honour, in swich an aventure?
Iwys, ye mowen ellis lite endure!   1330

"Ye knowe ek how that al my kyn is heere,
But if that onliche it my fader be;
And ek myn othere thynges alle yfeere,
And nameliche, my deere herte, ye,
Whom that I nolde leven for to se   1335
For al this world, as wyd as it hath space;
Or ellis se ich nevere Joves face!

"Whi trowe ye my fader in this wise
Coveyteth so to se me, but for drede
Lest in this town that folkes me despise   1340
Because of hym, for his unhappy dede?
What woot my fader what lif that I lede?
For if he wiste in Troie how wel I fare,
Us neded for my wendyng nought to care.

"Ye sen that every day ek, more and more,   1345
Men trete of pees; and it supposid is
That men the queene Eleyne shal restore,
And Grekis us restoren that is mys.
So, though ther nere comfort non but this,
That men purposen pees on every syde,   1350
Ye may the bettre at ese of herte abyde.

"For if that it be pees, myn herte deere,
The nature of the pees moot nedes dryve
That men moost entrecomunen yfeere,
And to and fro ek ride and gon as blyve   1355
Alday as thikke as been fleen from an hyve,
And every wight han liberte to bleve
Whereas hym liste the bet, withouten leve.

"And though so be that pees ther may be non,
Yet hider, though ther nevere pees ne were,
I moste come; for whider sholde I gon,   1361
Or how, meschaunce, sholde I dwelle there
Among tho men of armes evere in feere?
For which, as wisly God my soule rede,
I kan nat sen wherof ye sholden drede.   1365

"Have here another wey, if it so be
That al this thyng ne may yow nat suffise.
My fader, as ye knowen wel, parde,
Is old, and elde is ful of coveytise;
And I right now have founden al the gise,   1370
Withouten net, wherwith I shal hym hente.
And herkeneth now, if that ye wol assente.

"Lo, Troilus, men seyn that hard it is
The wolf ful, and the wether hool to have;
This is to seyn, that men ful ofte, iwys,   1375

Mote spenden part the remenant for to save.
For ay with gold men may the herte grave
Of hym that set is upon coveytise;
And how I mene, I shal it yow devyse.

"The moeble which that I have in this town
Unto my fader shal I take, and seye,   1381
That right for trust and for savacioun
It sent is from a frend of his or tweye,
The whiche frendes ferventliche hym preye
To senden after more, and that in hie,   1385
Whil that this town stant thus in jupartie.

"And that shal ben an huge quantite, —
Thus shal I seyn, — but lest it folk espide,
This may be sent by no wight but by me.
I shal ek shewen hym, yf pees bytyde,   1390
What frendes that ich have on every syde
Towardes the court, to don the wrathe pace
Of Priamus, and don hym stonde in grace.

"So, what for o thyng and for other, swete,
I shal hym so enchaunten with my sawes,   1395
That right in hevene his sowle is, shal he meete.
For al Appollo, or his clerkes lawes,
Or calkulyng, avayleth nought thre hawes;
Desir of gold shal so his soule blende,
That, as me lyst, I shal wel make an ende.   1400

"And yf he wolde ought by hys sort it preve,
If that I lye, in certayn I shal fonde
Distroben hym, and plukke hym by the sleve,
Makynge his sort, and beren hym on honde
He hath not wel the goddes understonde;   1405
For goddes speken in amphibologies,
And, for a sooth, they tellen twenty lyes.

"Eke drede fond first goddes, I suppose, —"
Thus shal I seyn, — and that his coward herte
Made hym amys the goddes text to glose,   1410
Whan he for fered out of Delphos sterte.
And but I make hym soone to converte,
And don my red withinne a day or tweye,
I wol to yow oblige me to deye."

And treweliche, as writen wel I fynde,   1415
That al this thyng was seyd of good entente;
And that hire herte trewe was and kynde
Towardes hym, and spak right as she mente,
And that she starf for wo neigh, whan she
          wente,
And was in purpos evere to be trewe: 1420
Thus writen they that of hire werkes knewe.

This Troilus, with herte and erys spradde,
Herde al this thyng devysen to and fro;
And verrayliche him semed that he hadde
The selve wit; but yet to late hire go   1425
His herte mysforyaf hym evere mo.
But fynaly, he gan his herte wreste
To trusten hire, and took it for the beste.

For which the grete furie of his penaunce
Was queynt with hope, and therwith hem bi-
          twene   1430
Bigan for joie th'amorouse daunce.
And as the briddes, whanne the sonne is shene,
Deliten in hire song in leves grene,
Right so the wordes that they spake yfeere
Delited hem, and made hire hertes clere.   1435

But natheles, the wendyng of Criseyde,
For al this world, may nat out of his mynde;
For which ful ofte he pitously hire preyde
That of hire heste he myghte hire trewe fynde,
And seyde hire, "Certes, if ye be unkynde,   1440
And but ye come at day set into Troye,
Ne shal I nevere have hele, honour, ne joye.

"For also soth as sonne uprist o-morwe,
And God, so wisly thow me, woful wrecche,
To reste brynge out of this cruel sorwe,   1445
I wol myselven sle if that ye drecche!
But of my deeth though litel be to recche,
Yet, er that ye me causen so to smerte,
Dwelle rather here, myn owen swete herte.

"For trewely, myn owne lady deere,   1450
Tho sleghtes yet that I have herd yow stere
Ful shaply ben to faylen alle yfeere.
For thus men seyth, 'that on thenketh the
          beere,
But al another thenketh his ledere.'
Youre syre is wys; and seyd is, out of drede   1455
'Men may the wise atrenne, and naught atrede.'

"It is ful hard to halten unespied
Byfore a crepel, for he kan the craft;
Youre fader is in sleght as Argus eyed;
For al be that his moeble is hym biraft,   1460
His olde sleighte is yet so with hym laft,
Ye shal nat blende hym for youre womman-
          hede,
Ne feyne aright; and that is al my drede.

"I not if pees shal evere mo bitide;
But pees or no, for ernest ne for game,   1465
I woot, syn Calkas on the Grekis syde

Hath ones ben, and lost so foule his name,
He dar nomore come here ayeyn for shame;
For which that wey, for aught I kan espie,
To trusten on, nys but a fantasie.   1470

"Ye shal ek sen, youre fader shal yow glose
To ben a wif, and as he kan wel preche,
He shal som Grek so preyse and wel alose,
That ravysshen he shal yow with his speche,
Or do yow don by force as he shal teche;   1475
And Troilus, of whom ye nyl han routhe,
Shal causeles so sterven in his trouthe!

"And over al this, youre fader shal despise
Us alle, and seyn this cite nys but lorn,
And that th'assege nevere shal aryse,   1480
For-whi the Grekis han it alle sworn,
Til we be slayn, and down oure walles torn.
And thus he shal yow with his wordes fere,
That ay drede I, that ye wol bleven there.

"Ye shal ek seen so many a lusty knyght   1485
Among the Grekis, ful of worthynesse,
And ech of hem with herte, wit, and myght
To plesen yow don al his bisynesse,
That ye shul dullen of the rudenesse
Of us sely Troians, but if routhe   1490
Remorde yow, or vertu of youre trouthe.

"And this to me so grevous is to thynke,
That fro my brest it wol my soule rende;
Ne dredeles, in me ther may nat synke
A good opynyoun, if that ye wende;   1495
For whi youre fadres sleghte wol us shende.
And if ye gon, as I have told yow yore,
So thenk I n'am but ded, withoute more.

"For which, with humble, trewe, and pitous
    herte,
A thousand tymes mercy I yow preye;   1500
So rueth on myn aspre peynes smerte,
And doth somwhat as that I shal yow seye,
And lat us stele awey bitwixe us tweye;
And thynk that folie is, whan man may chese,
For accident his substaunce ay to lese.   1505

"I mene thus: that syn we mowe er day
Wel stele awey, and ben togidere so,
What wit were it to putten in assay,
In cas ye sholden to youre fader go,
If that ye myghten come ayeyn or no?   1510
Thus mene I, that it were a gret folie
To putte that sikernesse in jupertie.

"And vulgarly to speken of substaunce
Of tresour, may we bothe with us lede
Inough to lyve in honour and plesaunce,   1515
Til into tyme that we shal ben dede;
And thus we may eschuen al this drede.
For everich other wey ye kan recorde,
Myn herte, ywys, may therwith naught acorde.

"And hardily, ne dredeth no poverte,   1520
For I have kyn and frendes elleswhere
That, though we comen in oure bare sherte,
Us sholde neyther lakken gold ne gere,
But ben honured while we dwelten there.
And go we anon; for, as in myn entente,   1525
This is the beste, if that ye wole assente."

Criseyde, with a sik, right in this wise,
Answerde, "Ywys, my deere herte trewe,
We may wel stele awey, as ye devyse,
And fynden swich unthrifty weyes newe;   1530
But afterward, ful soore it wol us rewe.
And helpe me God so at my mooste nede,
As causeles ye suffren al this drede!

"For thilke day that I for cherisynge
Or drede of fader, or of other wight,   1535
Or for estat, delit, or for weddynge,
Be fals to yow, my Troilus, my knyght,
Saturnes doughter, Juno, thorugh hire myght,
As wood as Athamante do me dwelle
Eternalich in Stix, the put of helle!   1540

"And this on every god celestial
I swere it yow, and ek on ech goddesse,
On every nymphe and deite infernal,
On satiry and fawny more and lesse,
That halve goddes ben of wildernesse;   1545
And Attropos my thred of lif tobreste,
If I be fals! now trowe me if yow leste!

"And thow, Symois, that as an arwe clere
Thorugh Troie rennest ay downward to the se,
Ber witnesse of this word that seyd is here,   1550
That thilke day that ich untrewe be
To Troilus, myn owene herte fre,
That thow retourne bakward to thi welle,
And I with body and soule synke in helle!

"But that ye speke, awey thus for to go   1555
And leten alle youre frendes, God forbede,
For any womman, that ye sholden so!
And namely syn Troie hath now swich nede
Of help. And ek of o thyng taketh hede:

If this were wist, my lif lay in balaunce,   1560
And youre honour; God shilde us fro mes-
      chaunce!

"And if so be that pees heere-after take,
As alday happeth after anger game,
Whi, Lord, the sorwe and wo ye wolden make,
That ye ne dorste come ayeyn for shame!   1565
And er that ye juparten so youre name,
Beth naught to hastif in this hoote fare;
For hastif man ne wanteth nevere care.

"What trowe ye the peple ek al aboute
Wolde of it seye? It is ful light t'arede.   1570
They wolden seye, and swere it, out of doute,
That love ne drof yow naught to don this dede,
But lust voluptuous and coward drede.
Thus were al lost, ywys, myn herte deere,
Youre honour, which that now shyneth so clere.

"And also thynketh on myn honeste,   1576
That floureth yet, how foule I sholde it shende,
And with what filthe it spotted sholde be,
If in this forme I sholde with yow wende.
Ne though I lyved unto the werldes ende,   1580
My name sholde I nevere ayeynward wynne.
Thus were I lost, and that were routhe and
      synne.

"And forthi sle with resoun al this hete!
Men seyn, 'the suffrant overcomith,' parde;
Ek 'whoso wol han lief, he lief moot lete.'   1585
Thus maketh vertu of necessite
By pacience, and thynk that lord is he
Of Fortune ay, that naught wole of hire recche;
And she ne daunteth no wight but a wrecche.

"And trusteth this, that certes, herte swete,   1590
Er Phebus suster, Lucina the sheene,
The Leoun passe out of this Ariete,
I wol ben here, withouten any wene.
I mene, as helpe me Juno, hevenes quene,
The tenthe day, but if that deth m'assaile,   1595
I wol yow sen, withouten any faille."

"And now, so this be soth," quod Troilus,
"I shal wel suffre unto the tenthe day,
Syn that I se that nede it mot be thus.
But, for the love of God, if it be may,   1600
So late us stelen privelich away;
For evere in oon, as for to lyve in reste,
Myn herte seyth that it wol be the beste."

"O mercy, God, what lif is this?" quod she.
"Allas, ye sle me thus for verray tene!   1605

I se wel now that ye mystrusten me,
For by youre wordes it is wel yseene.
Now, for the love of Cinthia the sheene,
Mistrust me nought thus causeles, for routhe,
Syn to be trewe I have yow plight my trouthe.

"And thynketh wel, that somtyme it is wit   1611
To spende a tyme, a tyme for to wynne.
Ne, parde, lorn am I naught fro yow yit,
Though that we ben a day or two atwynne.
Drif out the fantasies yow withinne,   1615
And trusteth me, and leveth ek youre sorwe,
Or here my trouthe, I wol naught lyve tyl
      morwe.

"For if ye wiste how soore it doth me smerte,
Ye wolde cesse of this; for, God, thow wost,
The pure spirit wepeth in myn herte   1620
To se yow wepen that I love most,
And that I mot gon to the Grekis oost.
Ye, nere it that I wiste remedie
To come ayeyn, right here I wolde dye!

"But certes, I am naught so nyce a wight   1625
That I ne kan ymaginen a wey
To come ayeyn that day that I have hight.
For who may holde a thing that wol awey?
My fader naught, for al his queynte pley!
And by my thrift, my wendyng out of Troie
Another day shal torne us alle to joie.   1631

"Forthi with al myn herte I yow biseke,
If that yow list don ought for my preyere,
And for that love which that I love yow eke,
That er that I departe fro yow here,   1635
That of so good a confort and a cheere
I may yow sen, that ye may brynge at reste
Myn herte, which that is o poynt to breste.

"And over al this I prey yow," quod she tho,
"Myn owene hertes sothfast suffisaunce,   1640
Syn I am thyn al hol, withouten mo,
That whil that I am absent, no plesaunce
Of oother do me fro youre remembraunce.
For I am evere agast, forwhy men rede
That love is thyng ay ful of bisy drede.   1645

"For in this world ther lyveth lady non,
If that ye were untrewe (as God defende!),
That so bitraised were or wo-bigon
As I, that alle trouthe in yow entende.
And douteles, if that ich other wende,   1650
I ner but ded, and er ye cause fynde,
For Goddes love, so beth me naught unkynde!"

To this answerde Troilus and seyde,
"Now God, to whom ther nys no cause ywrye,
Me glade, as wys I nevere unto Criseyde,   1655
Syn thilke day I saugh hire first with yë,
Was fals, ne nevere shal til that I dye.
At shorte wordes, wel ye may me leve:
I kan na more, it shal be founde at preve."

"Grant mercy, goode myn, iwys!" quod she,
"And blisful Venus lat me nevere sterve   1661
Er I may stonde of plesaunce in degree
To quyte hym wel, that so wel kan deserve.
And while that God my wit wol me conserve,
I shal so don, so trewe I have yow founde,   1665
That ay honour to me-ward shal rebounde.

"For trusteth wel, that youre estat roial,
Ne veyn delit, nor only worthinesse
Of yow in werre or torney marcial,
Ne pompe, array, nobleye, or ek richesse   1670
Ne made me to rewe on youre destresse;
But moral vertu, grounded upon trouthe,
That was the cause I first hadde on yow routhe!

"Eke gentil herte and manhod that ye hadde,
And that ye hadde, as me thoughte, in despit
Every thyng that souned into badde,   1676
As rudenesse and poeplissh appetit,

And that youre resoun bridlede youre delit;
This made, aboven every creature,
That I was youre, and shal while I may
     dure.   1680

"And this may lengthe of yeres naught fordo,
Ne remuable Fortune deface.
But Juppiter, that of his myght may do
The sorwful to be glad, so yeve us grace,
Or nyghtes ten, to meten in this place,   1685
So that it may youre herte and myn suffise!
And fareth now wel, for tyme is that ye rise."

And after that they longe ypleyned hadde,
And ofte ykist, and streite in armes folde,
The day gan rise, and Troilus hym cladde,   1690
And rewfullich his lady gan byholde,
As he that felte dethes cares colde,
And to hire grace he gan hym recomaunde.
Wher him was wo, this holde I no demaunde.

For mannes hed ymagynen ne kan,   1695
N'entendement considere, ne tonge telle
The cruele peynes of this sorwful man,
That passen every torment down in helle.
For whan he saugh that she ne myghte dwelle,
Which that his soule out of his herte rente,   1700
Withouten more, out of the chaumbre he
     wente.

Explicit liber quartus.

Book V

Incipit liber quintus.

Aprochen gan the fatal destyne
That Joves hath in disposicioun,
And to yow, angry Parcas, sustren thre,
Committeth, to don execucioun;
For which Criseyde moste out of the town,   5
And Troilus shal dwellen forth in pyne
Til Lachesis his thred no lenger twyne.

The gold-ytressed Phebus heighe on-lofte
Thries hadde alle with his bemes clene
The snowes molte, and Zepherus as ofte   10
Ibrought ayeyn the tendre leves grene,
Syn that the sone of Ecuba the queene
Bigan to love hire first for whom his sorwe
Was al, that she departe sholde a-morwe.

Ful redy was at prime Diomede,   15
Criseyde unto the Grekis oost to lede,
For sorwe of which she felt hire herte blede,
As she that nyste what was best to rede.
And trewely, as men in bokes rede,
Men wiste nevere womman han the care,   20
Ne was so loth out of a town to fare.

This Troilus, withouten reed or loore,
As man that hath his joies ek forlore,
Was waytyng on his lady evere more
As she that was the sothfast crop and more   25
Of al his lust or joies herebifore.
But Troilus, now far-wel al thi joie,
For shaltow nevere sen hire eft in Troie!

Soth is that while he bood in this manere,

He gan his wo ful manly for to hide,   30
That wel unnethe it sene was in his chere;
But at the yate ther she sholde out ride,
With certeyn folk he hoved hire t'abide,
So wo-bigon, al wolde he naught hym pleyne,
That on his hors unnethe he sat for peyne.   35

For ire he quook, so gan his herte gnawe,
Whan Diomede on horse gan hym dresse,
And seyde to hymself this ilke sawe:
"Allas!" quod he, "thus foul a wrecchednesse,
Whi suffre ich it? Whi nyl ich it redresse?   40
Were it nat bet atones for to dye
Than evere more in langour thus to drye?

"Whi nyl I make atones riche and pore
To have inough to doone, er that she go?
Why nyl I brynge al Troie upon a roore?   45
Whi nyl I slen this Diomede also?
Whi nyl I rather with a man or two
Stele hire away? Whi wol I this endure?
Whi nyl I helpen to myn owen cure?"

But why he nolde don so fel a dede,   50
That shal I seyn, and whi hym liste it spare:
He hadde in herte alweyes a manere drede
Lest that Criseyde, in rumour of this fare,
Sholde han ben slayn; lo, this was al his care.
And ellis, certeyn, as I seyde yore,   55
He hadde it don, withouten wordes more.

Criseyde, whan she redy was to ride,
Ful sorwfully she sighte, and seyde "allas!"
But forth she moot, for aught that may bitide,
And forth she rit ful sorwfully a pas.   60
Ther is non other remedie in this cas.
What wonder is, though that hire sore smerte,
Whan she forgoth hire owen swete herte?

This Troilus, in wise of curteysie,   64
With hauk on honde, and with an huge route
Of knyghtes, rood and did hire companye,
Passyng al the valeye fer withoute;
And ferther wolde han riden, out of doute,
Ful fayn, and wo was hym to gon so sone;
But torne he moste, and it was ek to done.   70

And right with that was Antenor ycome
Out of the Grekis oost, and every wight
Was of it glad, and seyde he was welcome.
And Troilus, al nere his herte light,
He peyned hym with al his fulle myght   75
Hym to withholde of wepyng atte leeste,
And Antenor he kiste, and made feste.

And therwithal he moste his leve take,
And caste his eye upon hire pitously,
And neer he rood, his cause for to make,   80
To take hire by the honde al sobrely.
And Lord! so she gan wepen tendrely!
And he ful softe and sleighly gan hire seye,
"Now holde youre day, and do me nat to deye."

With that his courser torned he aboute   85
With face pale, and unto Diomede
No word he spak, ne non of al his route;
Of which the sone of Tideus took hede,
As he that koude more than the crede
In swich a craft, and by the reyne hire hente;   90
And Troilus to Troie homward he wente.   91

This Diomede, that ledde hire by the bridel,
Whan that he saugh the folk of Troie aweye,
Thoughte, "Al my labour shal nat ben on ydel,
If that I may, for somwhat shal I seye.   95
For at the werste it may yet shorte oure weye.
I have herd seyd ek tymes twyes twelve,
'He is a fool that wole foryete hymselve.'"

But natheles, this thoughte he wel ynough,
That "certeynlich I am aboute nought,   100
If that I speke of love, or make it tough;
For douteles, if she have in hire thought
Hym that I gesse, he may nat ben ybrought
So soon awey; but I shal fynde a meene,   104
That she naught wite as yet shal what I mene."

This Diomede, as he that koude his good,
Whan this was don, gan fallen forth in speche
Of this and that, and axed whi she stood
In swich disese, and gan hire ek biseche,
That if that he encresse myghte or eche   110
With any thyng hire ese, that she sholde
Comaunde it hym, and seyde he don it wolde.

For treweliche he swor hire, as a knyght,
That ther nas thyng with which he myghte hire
      plese,
That he nolde don his peyne and al his myght
To don it, for to don hire herte an ese;   116
And preyede hire, she wolde hire sorwe apese,
And seyde, "Iwis, we Grekis kan have joie
To honouren yow, as wel as folk of Troie."

He seyde ek thus, "I woot yow thynketh
      straunge, —   120
Ne wonder is, for it is to yow newe, —
Th'aquayntaunce of thise Troianis to chaunge

For folk of Grece, that ye nevere knewe.
But wolde nevere God but if as trewe
A Grek ye sholde among us alle fynde   125
As any Troian is, and ek as kynde.

"And by the cause I swor yow right, lo, now,
To ben youre frend, and helply, to my myght,
And for that more aquayntaunce ek of yow   129
Have ich had than another straunger wight,
So fro this forth, I pray yow, day and nyght,
Comaundeth me, how soore that me smerte,
To don al that may like unto youre herte;

"And that ye me wolde as youre brother trete;
And taketh naught my frendshipe in de-
            spit;   135
And though youre sorwes be for thynges grete,
Not I nat whi, but out of more respit,
Myn herte hath for t'amende it gret delit.
And if I may youre harmes nat redresse,
I am right sory for youre hevynesse.   140

"For though ye Troians with us Grekes wrothe
Han many a day ben, alwey yet, parde,
O god of Love in soth we serven bothe.
And, for the love of God, my lady fre,   144
Whomso ye hate, as beth nat wroth with me;
For trewely, ther kan no wyght yow serve,
That half so loth youre wratthe wold disserve.

"And nere it that we ben so neigh the tente
Of Calcas, which that sen us bothe may,
I wolde of this yow telle al myn entente;   150
But this enseled til anothir day.
Yeve me youre hond; I am, and shal ben ay,
God helpe me so, while that my lyf may dure,
Youre owene aboven every creature.

"Thus seyde I nevere er now to womman born;
For, God myn herte as wisly glade so,   156
I loved never womman here-biforn
As paramours, ne nevere shal no mo.
And, for the love of God, beth nat my fo,
Al kan I naught to yow, my lady deere,   160
Compleyne aright, for I am yet to leere.

"And wondreth nought, myn owen lady bright,
Though that I speke of love to yow thus blyve;
For I have herd er this of many a wight,
Hath loved thyng he nevere saigh his lyve.   165
Ek I am nat of power for to stryve
Ayeyns the god of Love, but hym obeye
I wole alwey; and mercy I yow preye.

"Ther ben so worthi knyghtes in this place,
And ye so fayr, that everich of hem alle   170
Wol peynen hym to stonden in youre grace.
But myghte me so faire a grace falle,
That ye me for youre servant wolde calle,
So lowely ne so trewely yow serve
Nil non of hem, as I shal, til I sterve."   175

Criseyde unto that purpos lite answerde,
As she that was with sorwe oppressed so
That, in effect, she naught his tales herde
But her and ther, now here a word or two.
Hire thoughte hire sorwful herte brast a-two;
For whan she gan hire fader fer espie,   181
Wel neigh down of hire hors she gan to sye.

But natheles she thonked Diomede
Of al his travaile and his goode cheere,
And that hym list his frendshipe hire to bede;
And she accepteth it in good manere,   186
And wol do fayn that is hym lief and dere,
And trusten hym she wolde, and wel she
            myghte,
As seyde she; and from hire hors sh'alighte.

Hire fader hath hire in his armes nome,   190
And twenty tyme he kiste his doughter sweete,
And seyde, "O deere doughter myn, welcome!"
She seyde ek, she was fayn with hym to mete,
And stood forth muwet, milde, and mansuete.
But here I leve hire with hire fader dwelle,
And forth I wol of Troilus yow telle.   196

To Troie is come this woful Troilus,
In sorwe aboven alle sorwes smerte,
With feloun look and face dispitous.
Tho sodeynly doun from his hors he sterte,   200
And thorugh his paleis, with a swollen herte,
To chaumbre he wente; of nothyng took he
            hede,
Ne non to hym dar speke a word for drede.

And ther his sorwes that he spared hadde
He yaf an issue large, and "deth!" he criede;
And in his throwes frenetik and madde   206
He corseth Jove, Appollo, and ek Cupide,
He corseth Ceres, Bacus, and Cipride,
His burthe, hymself, his fate, and ek nature,
And, save his lady, every creature.   210

To bedde he goth, and walweth ther and torn-
            eth
In furie, as doth he Ixion in helle;
And in this wise he neigh til day sojorneth.

But tho bigan his herte a lite unswelle
Thorugh teris, which that gonnen up to welle;
And pitously he cryde upon Criseyde,   216
And to hymself right thus he spak, and seyde:

"Wher is myn owene lady, lief and deere?
Wher is hire white brest? wher is it, where?
Wher ben hire armes and hire eyen cleere,   220
That yesternyght this tyme with me were?
Now may I wepe allone many a teere,
And graspe aboute I may, but in this place,
Save a pilowe, I fynde naught t'enbrace.

"How shal I do? whan shal she come ayeyn?
I not, allas! whi lete ich hire to go.   226
As wolde God, ich hadde as tho ben sleyn!
O herte myn, Criseyde, O swete fo!
O lady myn, that I love and na mo!
To whom for evermo myn herte I dowe,   230
Se how I dey, ye nyl me nat rescowe!

"Who seth yow now, my righte lode-sterre?
Who sit right now or stant in youre presence?
Who kan conforten now youre hertes werre?
Now I am gon, whom yeve ye audience?   235
Who speketh for me right now in myn absence?
Allas, no wight; and that is al my care!
For wel woot I, as yvele as I ye fare.

"How sholde I thus ten dayes ful endure,
Whan I the firste nyght have al this tene?   240
How shal she don ek, sorwful creature?
For tendernesse, how shal she ek sustene
Swich wo for me? O pitous, pale, and grene
Shal ben youre fresshe, wommanliche face
For langour, er ye torne unto this place."   245

And whan he fil in any slomberynges,
Anon bygynne he sholde for to grone,
And dremen of the dredefulleste thynges
That myghte ben; as, mete he were allone
In place horrible, makyng ay his mone,   250
Or meten that he was amonges alle
His enemys, and in hire hondes falle.

And therwithal his body sholde sterte,
And with the stert al sodeynliche awake,
And swich a tremour fele aboute his herte,   255
That of the fere his body sholde quake;
And therwithal he sholde a noyse make,
And seme as though he sholde falle depe
From heighe o-lofte; and thanne he wolde
       wepe.

And rewen on hymself so pitously,   260
That wonder was to here his fantasie.
Another tyme he sholde myghtyly
Conforte hymself, and sein it was folie,
So causeles swich drede for to drye;
And eft bygynne his aspre sorwes newe,   265
That every man myght on his sorwes rewe.

Who koude telle aright or ful discryve
His wo, his pleynt, his langour, and his pyne?
Naught alle the men that han or ben on lyve.
Thow, redere, maist thiself ful wel devyne   270
That swich a wo my wit kan nat diffyne.
On ydel for to write it sholde I swynke,
Whan that my wit is wery it to thynke.

On hevene yet the sterres weren seene,
Although ful pale ywoxen was the moone;   275
And whiten gan the orisonte shene
Al estward, as it wont is for to doone;
And Phebus with his rosy carte soone
Gan after that to dresse hym up to fare
Whan Troilus hath sent after Pandare.   280

This Pandare, that of al the day biforn
Ne myghte han comen Troilus to se,
Although he on his hed it hadde sworn,
For with the kyng Priam alday was he,
So that it lay nought in his libertee   285
Nowher to gon, — but on the morwe he wente
To Troilus, whan that he for hym sente.

For in his herte he koude wel devyne
That Troilus al nyght for sorwe wook;
And that he wolde telle hym of his pyne,   290
This knew he wel ynough, withoute book.
For which to chaumbre streght the wey he took,
And Troilus tho sobrelich he grette,
And on the bed ful sone he gan hym sette.

"My Pandarus," quod Troilus, "the sorwe   295
Which that I drye, I may nat longe endure.
I trowe I shal nat lyven til to-morwe.
For which I wolde alweys, on aventure,
To the devysen of my sepulture
The forme; and of my moeble thow dispone,   301
Right as the semeth best is for to done.

"But of the fir and flaumbe funeral
In which my body brennen shal to glede,
And of the feste and pleyes palestral
At my vigile, I prey the, tak good hede   305
That that be wel; and offre Mars my steede.

My swerd, myn helm, and, leve brother deere,
My sheld to Pallas yef, that shyneth cleere.

"The poudre in which myn herte ybrend shal
    torne,
That preye I the thow take and it conserve 310
In a vessell that men clepeth an urne,
Of gold, and to my lady that I serve,
For love of whom thus pitouslich I sterve,
So yeve it hire, and do me this plesaunce,
To preyen hire kepe it for a remembraunce.

"For wele I fele, by my maladie,   316
And by my dremes now and yore ago,
Al certeynly that I mot nedes dye.
The owle ek, which that hette Escaphilo,
Hath after me shright al thise nyghtes two. 320
And, god Mercurye! of me now, woful wrecche,
The soule gyde, and, whan the liste, it fecche!"

Pandare answerde and seyde, "Troilus,
My deere frend, as I have told the yore,
That it is folye for to sorwen thus,   325
And causeles, for which I kan namore.
But whoso wil nought trowen reed ne loore,
I kan nat sen in hym no remedie,
But lat hym worthen with his fantasie.

"But, Troilus, I prey the, tel me now   330
If thow trowe, er this, that any wight
Hath loved paramours as wel as thow?
Ye, God woot! and fro many a worthi knyght
Hath his lady gon a fourtenyght,
And he nat yet made halvendel the fare.   335
What nede is the to maken al this care?

"Syn day by day thow maist thiselven se
That from his love, or ellis from his wif,
A man mot twynnen of necessite,
Ye, though he love hire as his owene lif;   340
Yet nyl he with hymself thus maken strif.
For wel thou woost, my leve brother deere,
That alwey frendes may nat ben yfeere.

"How don this folk that seen hire loves wedded
By frendes myght, as it bitit ful ofte,   345
And sen hem in hire spouses bed ybedded?
God woot, they take it wisly, faire, and softe,
Forwhi good hope halt up hire herte o-lofte.
And, for they kan a tyme of sorwe endure,
As tyme hem hurt, a tyme doth hem cure.   350

"So sholdestow endure, and laten slide
The tyme, and fonde to ben glad and light.

Ten dayes nys so longe nought t'abide.
And syn she the to comen hath bihyght,
She nyl hire heste breken for no wight.   355
For dred the nat that she nyl fynden weye
To come ayein; my lif that dorste I leye.

"Thy swevenes ek and al swich fantasie
Drif out, and lat hem faren to meschaunce;
For they procede of thi malencolie,   360
That doth the fele in slep al this penaunce.
A straw for alle swevenes signifiaunce!
God helpe me so, I counte hem nought a bene!
Ther woot no man aright what dremes mene.

"For prestes of the temple tellen this,   365
That dremes ben the revelaciouns
Of goddes, and as wel they telle, ywis,
That they ben infernals illusiouns;
And leches seyn, that of complexiouns
Proceden they, or fast, or glotonye.   370
Who woot in soth thus what thei signifie?

"Ek oother seyn that thorugh impressiouns,
As if a wight hath faste a thyng in mynde,
That therof comen swiche avysiouns;
And other seyn, as they in bokes fynde,   375
That after tymes of the yer, by kynde,
Men dreme, and that th'effect goth by the
    moone.
But leve no drem, for it is nought to doone.

"Wel worthe of dremes ay thise olde wives,
And treweliche ek augurye of thise fowles,   380
For fere of which men wenen lese here lyves,
As revenes qualm, or shrichyng of thise owles.
To trowen on it bothe fals and foul is.
Allas, allas, so noble a creature
As is a man shal dreden swich ordure!   385

"For which with al myn herte I the biseche,
Unto thiself that al this thow foryyve;
And ris now up withowten more speche,
And lat us caste how forth may best be dryve
This tyme, and ek how fresshly we may
    lyve   390
Whan that she comth, the which shal be right
    soone.
God helpe me so, the beste is thus to doone.

"Ris, lat us speke of lusty lif in Troie
That we han led, and forth the tyme dryve;
And ek of tyme comyng us rejoie,   395
That bryngen shal oure blisse now so blyve;
And langour of thise twyes dayes fyve

We shal therwith so foryete or oppresse,
That wel unneth it don shal us duresse.

"This town is ful of lordes al aboute,   400
And trewes lasten al this mene while.
Go we pleye us in som lusty route
To Sarpedoun, nat hennes but a myle;
And thus thow shalt the tyme wel bygile,
And dryve it forth unto that blisful morwe,   405
That thow hire se, that cause is of thi sorwe.

"Now ris, my deere brother Troilus,
For certes, it non honour is to the
To wepe, and in thi bedde to jouken thus.
For trewelich, of o thyng trust to me,   410
If thow thus ligge a day, or two, or thre,
The folk wol wene that thow, for cowardise,
The feynest sik, and that thow darst nat rise!"

This Troilus answerde, "O brother deere,
This knowen folk that han ysuffred peyne, 415
That though he wepe and make sorwful cheere,
That feleth harm and smert in every veyne,
No wonder is; and though ich evere pleyne,
Or alwey wepe, I am no thyng to blame,
Syn I have lost the cause of al my game.   420

"But syn of fyne force I mot arise,
I shal arise as soone as evere I may;
And God, to whom myn herte I sacrifice,
So sende us hastely the tenthe day!
For was ther nevere fowel so fayn of May   425
As I shal ben, whan that she comth in Troie,
That cause is of my torment and my joie.

"But whider is thi reed," quod Troilus,
"That we may pleye us best in al this town?"
"By God, my conseil is," quod Pandarus,   430
"To ride and pleye us with kyng Sarpedoun."
So longe of this they speken up and down,
Til Troilus gan at the laste assente
To rise, and forth to Sarpedoun they wente.

This Sarpedoun, as he that honourable   435
Was evere his lyve, and ful of heigh largesse,
With al that myghte yserved ben on table,
That deynte was, al coste it gret richesse,
He fedde hem day by day, that swich noblesse,
As seyden bothe the mooste and ek the leeste,
Was nevere er that day wist at any feste.   441

Nor in this world ther is non instrument
Delicious, thorugh wynd or touche of corde,
As fer as any wight hath evere ywent,

That tonge telle or herte may recorde,   445
That at that feste it nas wel herd acorde;
Ne of ladys ek so fair a compaignie
On daunce, er tho, was nevere iseye with ië.

But what availeth this to Troilus,
That for his sorwe nothyng of it roughte?   450
For evere in oon his herte pietous
Ful bisyly Criseyde, his lady, soughte.
On hire was evere al that his herte thoughte,
Now this, now that, so faste ymagenynge,
That glade, iwis, kan hym no festeyinge.   455

Thise ladies ek that at this feste ben,
Syn that he saugh his lady was aweye,
It was his sorwe upon hem for to sen,
Or for to here on instruments so pleye.
For she, that of his herte berth the keye,   460
Was absent, lo, this was his fantasie,
That no wight sholde maken melodie.

Nor ther nas houre in al the day or nyght,
Whan he was there as no wight myghte hym
      heere,
That he ne seyde, "O lufsom lady bryght, 465
How have ye faren syn that ye were here?
Welcome, ywis, myn owne lady deere!"
But weylaway, al this nas but a maze.
Fortune his howve entended bet to glaze!

The lettres ek that she of olde tyme   470
Hadde hym ysent, he wolde allone rede
An hondred sithe atwixen noon and prime,
Refiguryng hire shap, hire wommanhede,
Withinne his herte, and every word or dede
That passed was; and thus he drof t'an
      ende   475
The ferthe day, and seyde he wolde wende.

And seyde, "Leve brother Pandarus,
Intendestow that we shal here bleve
Til Sarpedoun wol forth congeyen us?
Yet were it fairer that we toke oure leve.   480
For Goddes love, lat us now soone at eve
Oure leve take, and homward lat us torne;
For treweliche, I nyl nat thus sojourne."

Pandare answerde, "Be we comen hider
To fecchen fir, and rennen hom ayein?   485
God help me so, I kan nat tellen whider
We myghte gon, if I shal sothly seyn,
Ther any wight is of us more feyn
Than Sarpedoun; and if we hennes hye
Thus sodeynly, I holde it vilanye,   490

"Syn that we seyden that we wolde bleve
With hym a wowke; and now, thus sodeynly,
The ferthe day to take of hym owre leve,
He wolde wondren on it, trewely!
Lat us holde forth oure purpos fermely.   495
And syn that ye bihighten hym to bide,
Holde forward now, and after lat us ride."

Thus Pandarus, with alle peyne and wo,
Made hym to dwelle; and at the wikes ende,
Of Sarpedoun they toke hire leve tho,   500
And on hire wey they spedden hem to wende.
Quod Troilus, "Now Lord me grace sende,
That I may fynden, at myn hom-comynge
Criseyde comen!" and therwith gan he synge.

"Ye, haselwode!" thoughte this Pandare,   505
And to hymself ful softeliche he seyde,
"God woot, refreyden may this hote fare,
Er Calkas sende Troilus Criseyde!"
But natheles, he japed thus, and pleyde,   509
And swor, ywys, his herte hym wel bihighte,
She wolde come as soone as evere she myghte.

Whan they unto the paleys were ycomen
Of Troilus, they doun of hors alighte,
And to the chambre hire wey than han they
          nomen.
And into tyme that it gan to nyghte,   515
They spaken of Criseÿde the brighte;
And after this, whan that hem bothe leste,
They spedde hem fro the soper unto reste.

On morwe, as soone as day bygan to clere,
This Troilus gan of his slep t'abrayde,   520
And to Pandare, his owen brother deere,
"For love of God," ful pitously he sayde,
"As go we sen the palais of Criseyde;
For syn we yet may have namore feste,
So lat us sen hire paleys atte leeste."   525

And therwithal, his meyne for to blende,
A cause he fond in towne for to go,
And to Criseydes hous they gonnen wende.
But Lord! this sely Troilus was wo!   529
Hym thoughte his sorwful herte braste a-two.
For, whan he saugh hire dores spered alle,
Wel neigh for sorwe adoun he gan to falle.

Therwith, whan he was war and gan biholde
How shet was every wyndow of the place,   534
As frost, hym thoughte, his herte gan to colde;
For which with chaunged dedlich pale face,
Withouten word, he forthby gan to pace,

And, as God wolde, he gan so faste ride,
That no wight of his contenance espide.

Than seide he thus: "O paleys desolat,   540
O hous of houses whilom best ihight,
O paleys empty and disconsolat,
O thow lanterne of which queynt is the light,
O paleys, whilom day, that now art nyght,
Wel oughtestow to falle, and I to dye,   545
Syn she is went that wont was us to gye!

"O paleis, whilom crowne of houses alle,
Enlumyned with sonne of alle blisse!
O ryng, fro which the ruby is out falle,   549
O cause of wo, that cause hast ben of lisse!
Yet, syn I may no bet, fayn wolde I kisse
Thy colde dores, dorste I for this route;
And farwel shryne, of which the seynt is oute!

Therwith he caste on Pandarus his yë,   554
With chaunged face, and pitous to biholde;
And whan he myghte his tyme aright aspie,
Ay as he rood, to Pandarus he tolde
His newe sorwe, and ek his joies olde,
So pitously and with so ded an hewe,
That every wight myghte on his sorwe rewe.

Fro thennesforth he rideth up and down,   561
And every thyng com hym to remembraunce
As he rood forby places of the town
In which he whilom hadde al his plesaunce.
"Lo, yonder saugh ich last my lady daunce;
And in that temple, with hire eyen cleere,   566
Me kaughte first my righte lady dere.

"And yonder have I herd ful lustyly
My dere herte laugh; and yonder pleye
Saugh ich hire ones ek ful blisfully.   570
And yonder ones to me gan she seye,
'Now goode swete, love me wel, I preye;'
And yond so goodly gan she me biholde,
That to the deth myn herte is to hire holde.

"And at that corner, in the yonder hous,   575
Herde I myn alderlevest lady deere
So wommanly, with vois melodious,
Syngen so wel, so goodly, and so clere,
That in my soule yet me thynketh ich here
The blisful sown; and in that yonder place   580
My lady first me took unto hire grace."

Thanne thoughte he thus, "O blisful lord Cu-
          pide,
Whan I the proces have in my memorie,

How thow me hast wereyed on every syde,
Men myght a book make of it, lik a storie.   585
What nede is the to seke on me victorie,
Syn I am thyn, and holly at thi wille?
What joie hastow thyn owen folk to spille?

"Wel hastow, lord, ywroke on me thyn ire,
Thow myghty god, and dredefull for to greve!
Now mercy, lord! thow woost wel I desire   591
Thi grace moost of alle lustes leeve,
And lyve and dye I wol in thy byleve;
For which I n'axe in guerdoun but o bone,
That thow Criseyde ayein me sende sone.   595

"Distreyne hire herte as faste to retorne,
As thow doost myn to longen hire to see,
Than woot I wel that she nyl naught sojorne.
Now blisful lord, so cruel thow ne be
Unto the blood of Troie, I preye the,   600
As Juno was unto the blood Thebane,
For which the folk of Thebes caughte hire
     bane."

And after this he to the yates wente
Ther as Criseyde out rood a ful good paas,   604
And up and down ther made he many a wente,
And to hymself ful ofte he seyde, "Allas!
Fro hennes rood my blisse and my solas!
As wolde blisful God now, for his joie,
I myghte hire sen ayein come into Troie!

"And to the yonder hille I gan hire gyde,   610
Allas, and ther I took of hire my leve!
And yond I saugh hire to hire fader ride,
For sorwe of which myn herte shal tocleve.
And hider hom I com whan it was eve,
And here I dwelle out cast from alle joie,   615
And shal, til I may sen hire eft in Troie."

And of hymself ymagened he ofte
To ben defet, and pale, and waxen lesse
Than he was wont, and that men seyden softe,
"What may it be? Who kan the sothe gesse
Whi Troilus hath al this hevynesse?"   621
And al this nas but his malencolie,
That he hadde of hymself swich fantasie.

Another tyme ymaginen he wolde
That every wight that wente by the weye   625
Hadde of hym routhe, and that they seyen
     sholde,
"I am right sory Troilus wol deye."
And thus he drof a day yet forth or tweye,

As ye have herd; swich lif right gan he lede,
As he that stood bitwixen hope and drede.   630

For which hym likede in his songes shewe
Th'enchesoun of his wo, as he best myghte,
And made a song of wordes but a fewe,
Somwhat his woful herte for to lighte.
And whan he was from every mannes syghte,
With softe vois he of his lady deere,   636
That absent was, gan synge as ye may heere.

Canticus Troili.

"O sterre, of which I lost have al the light,
With herte soor wel oughte I to biwaille,   639
That evere derk in torment, nyght by nyght,
Toward my deth with wynd in steere I saille;
For which the tenthe nyght, if that I faille
The gydyng of thi bemes bright an houre,
My ship and me Caribdis wol devoure."

This song whan he thus songen hadde, soone
He fil ayeyn into his sikes olde;   646
And every nyght, as was his wone to doone,
He stood the brighte moone to byholde,
And al his sorwe he to the moone tolde,
And seyde, "Ywis, whan thow art horned newe,
I shal be glad, if al the world be trewe!   651

"I saugh thyn hornes olde ek by the morwe,
Whan hennes rood my righte lady dere,
That cause is of my torment and my sorwe;
For which, O brighte Latona the clere,   655
For love of God, ren faste aboute thy spere!
For whan thyne hornes newe gynnen sprynge,
Than shal she come that may my blisse brynge."

The dayes moore, and lenger every nyght,   659
Than they ben wont to be, hym thoughte tho,
And that the sonne went his cours unright
By lenger weye than it was wont to do;
And seyde, "Ywis, me dredeth evere mo,
The sonnes sone, Pheton, be on lyve,
And that his fader carte amys he dryve."   665

Upon the walles faste ek wolde he walke,
And on the Grekis oost he wolde se,
And to hymself right thus he wolde talke:
"Lo, yonder is myn owene lady free,
Or ellis yonder, ther the tentes be.   670
And thennes comth this eyr, that is so soote,
That in my soule I fele it doth me boote.

"And hardily this wynd, that more and moore
Thus stoundemele encresseth in my face,

Is of my ladys depe sikes soore.   675
I preve it thus, for in noon othere place
Of al this town, save onliche in this space,
Fele I no wynd that sowneth so lik peyne:
It seyth, 'Allas! whi twynned be we tweyne?' "

This longe tyme he dryveth forth right thus,
Til fully passed was the nynthe nyght;   681
And ay bisyde hym was this Pandarus,
That bisily did al his fulle myght
Hym to conforte, and make his herte light,   684
Yevyng hym hope alwey, the tenthe morwe
That she shal come, and stynten al his sorwe.

Upon that other syde ek was Criseyde,
With wommen fewe, among the Grekis stronge;
For which ful ofte a day "Allas!" she seyde,   689
"That I was born! Wel may myn herte longe
After my deth; for now lyve I to longe.
Allas! and I ne may it nat amende!
For now is wors than evere yet I wende.

"My fader nyl for nothyng do me grace
To gon ayeyn, for naught I kan hym queme;
And if so be that I my terme pace,   696
My Troilus shal in his herte deme
That I am fals, and so it may wel seme:
Thus shal ich have unthonk on every side.
That I was born, so weilaway the tide!   700

"And if that I me putte in jupartie,
To stele awey by nyght, and it bifalle
That I be kaught, I shal be holde a spie;
Or elles — lo, this drede I moost of alle —
If in the hondes of som wrecche I falle,   705
I nam but lost, al be myn herte trewe.
Now, myghty God, thow on my sorwe rewe!"

Ful pale ywoxen was hire brighte face,
Hire lymes lene, as she that al the day   709
Stood, whan she dorste, and loked on the place
Ther she was born, and ther she dwelt hadde
    ay;
And al the nyght wepyng, allas, she lay.
And thus despeired, out of alle cure,
She ladde hire lif, this woful creature.

Ful ofte a day she sighte ek for destresse,   715
And in hireself she wente ay purtrayinge
Of Troilus the grete worthynesse,
And al his goodly wordes recordynge
Syn first that day hire love bigan to springe.
And thus she sette hire woful herte afire   720
Thorugh remembraunce of that she gan desire.

In al this world ther nys so cruel herte
That hire hadde herd compleynen in hire sorwe,
That nolde han wepen for hire peynes smerte,
So tendrely she wepte, bothe eve and morwe.
Hire nedede no teris for to borwe!   726
And this was yet the werste of al hire peyne,
Ther was no wight to whom she dorste hire
    pleyne.

Ful rewfully she loked upon Troie,
Biheld the toures heigh and ek the halles: 730
"Allas!" quod she, "the plesance and the joie,
The which that now al torned into galle is,
Have ich had ofte withinne tho yonder walles!
O Troilus, what dostow now?" she seyde.
"Lord! wheyther thow yet thenke upon Cri-
    seyde?   735

"Allas, I ne hadde trowed on youre loore,
And went with yow, as ye me redde er this!
Than hadde I now nat siked half so soore.
Who myghte have seyd that I hadde don amys
To stele awey with swich oon as he ys?   740
But al to late comth the letuarie,
Whan men the cors unto the grave carie.

"To late is now to speke of that matere.
Prudence, allas, oon of thyne eyen thre
Me lakked alwey, er that I come here!   745
On tyme ypassed wel remembred me,
And present tyme ek koud ich wel ise,
But future tyme, er I was in the snare,
Koude I nat sen; that causeth now my care.

"But natheles, bityde what bityde,   750
I shal to-morwe at nyght, by est or west,
Out of this oost stele on som manere syde,
And gon with Troilus where as hym lest.
This purpos wol ich holde, and this is best.
No fors of wikked tonges janglerie,   755
For evere on love han wrecches had envye.

"For whoso wol of every word take hede,
Or reulen hym by every wightes wit,
Ne shal he nevere thryven, out of drede;
For that that som men blamen evere yit,   760
Lo, other manere folk comenden it.
And as for me, for al swich variaunce,
Felicite clepe I my suffisaunce.

"For which, withouten any wordes mo,
To Troie I wole, as for conclusioun."   765
But God it wot, er fully monthes two,
She was ful fer fro that entencioun!

For bothe Troilus and Troie town
Shal knotteles thoroughout hire herte slide;
For she wol take a purpos for t'abyde.   770

This Diomede, of whom yow telle I gan,
Goth now withinne hymself ay arguynge
With al the sleghte, and al that evere he kan,
How he may best, with shortest taryinge,
Into his net Criseydes herte brynge.   775
To this entent he koude nevere fyne;
To fisshen hire, he leyde out hook and lyne.

But natheles, wel in his herte he thoughte,
That she nas nat withoute a love in Troie;   779
For nevere, sythen he hire thennes broughte,
Ne koude he sen hire laughe or maken joie.
He nyst how best hire herte for t'acoye.
"But for t'asay," he seyde, "it naught ne
      greveth;
For he that naught n'asaieth, naught n'achev-
      eth."

Yet seide he to hymself upon a nyght,   785
"Now am I nat a fool, that woot wel how
Hire wo for love is of another wight,
And hereupon to gon assaye hire now?
I may wel wite, it nyl nat ben my prow.
For wise folk in bookes it expresse,   790
'Men shal nat wowe a wight in hevynesse.'

But whoso myghte wynnen swich a flour
From hym for whom she morneth nyght and
      day,
He myghte seyn he were a conquerour."
And right anon, as he that bold was ay,   795
Thoughte in his herte, "Happe how happe may,
Al sholde I dye, I wol hire herte seche!
I shal namore lesen but my speche."

This Diomede, as bokes us declare,
Was in his nedes prest and corageous,   800
With sterne vois and myghty lymes square,
Hardy, testif, strong, and chivalrous
Of dedes, lik his fader Tideus.
And som men seyn he was of tonge large;
And heir he was of Calydoigne and Arge.   805

Criseyde mene was of hire stature,
Therto of shap, of face, and ek of cheere,
Ther myghte ben no fairer creature.
And ofte tyme this was hire manere,
To gon ytressed with hire heres clere   810
Doun by hire coler at hire bak byhynde,
Which with a thred of gold she wolde bynde.

And, save hire browes joyneden yfere,
Ther nas no lak, in aught I kan espien.
But for to speken of hire eyen cleere,   815
Lo, trewely, they writen that hire syen,
That Paradis stood formed in hire yën.
And with hire riche beaute evere more
Strof love in hire ay, which of hem was more.

She sobre was, ek symple, and wys withal,   821
The best ynorisshed ek that myghte be,
And goodly of hire speche in general,
Charitable, estatlich, lusty, and fre;
Ne nevere mo ne lakked hire pite;
Tendre-herted, slydynge of corage;   825
But trewely, I kan nat telle hire age.

And Troilus wel woxen was in highte,
And complet formed by proporcioun
So wel that kynde it nought amenden myghte;
Yong, fressh, strong, and hardy as lyoun;   830
Trewe as stiel in ech condicioun;
Oon of the beste entecched creature
That is, or shal, whil that the world may dure.

And certeynly in storye it is yfounde,
That Troilus was nevere unto no wight,   835
As in his tyme, in no degree secounde
In durryng don that longeth to a knyght.
Al myghte a geant passen hym of myght,
His herte ay with the first and with the beste
Stood paregal, to durre don that hym leste.   840

But for to tellen forth of Diomede:
It fel that after, on the tenthe day
Syn that Criseyde out of the citee yede,
This Diomede, as fressh as braunche in May,
Com to the tente, ther as Calkas lay,   845
And feyned hym with Calkas han to doone;
But what he mente, I shal yow tellen soone.

Criseyde, at shorte wordes for to telle,
Welcomed hym, and down hym by hire sette;
And he was ethe ynough to maken dwelle!
And after this, withouten longe lette,   851
The spices and the wyn men forth hem fette;
And forth they speke of this and that yfeere,
As frendes don, of which som shal ye heere.

He gan first fallen of the werre in speche   855
Bitwixe hem and the folk of Troie town;
And of th'assege he gan hire ek biseche
To telle hym what was hire opynyoun.
Fro that demaunde he so descendeth down
To axen hire, if that hire straunge thoughte   860
The Grekis gise, and werkes that they wroughte;

And whi hire fader tarieth so longe
To wedden hire unto som worthy wight.
Criseyde, that was in hire peynes stronge
For love of Troilus, hire owen knyght,   865
As ferforth as she konnyng hadde or myght,
Answerde hym tho; but, as of his entente,
It semed nat she wiste what he mente.

But natheles, this ilke Diomede
Gan in hymself assure, and thus he seyde: 870
"If ich aright have taken of yow hede,
Me thynketh thus, O lady myn, Criseyde,
That syn I first hond on youre bridel leyde,
Whan ye out come of Troie by the morwe,
Ne koude I nevere sen yow but in sorwe.   875

"Kan I nat seyn what may the cause be,
But if for love of som Troian it were,
The which right sore wolde athynken me,
That ye for any wight that dwelleth there
Sholden spille a quarter of a tere,   880
Or pitously youreselven so bigile;
For dredeles, it is nought worth the while.

"The folk of Troie, as who seyth, alle and some
In prisoun ben, as ye youreselven se;
Nor thennes shal nat oon on-lyve come   885
For al the gold atwixen sonne and se.
Trusteth wel, and understondeth me,
Ther shal nat oon to mercy gon on-lyve,
Al were he lord of worldes twiës fyve!

"Swiche wreche on hem, for fecchynge of
    Eleyne,   890
Ther shal ben take, er that we hennes wende,
That Manes, which that goddes ben of peyne,
Shal ben agast that Grekes wol hem shende.
And men shul drede, unto the worldes ende,
From hennesforth to ravysshen any queene,
So cruel shal oure wreche on hem be seene.   896

"And but if Calkas lede us with ambages,
That is to seyn, with double wordes slye,
Swiche as men clepen a word with two visages,
Ye shal wel knowen that I naught ne lye,   900
And al this thyng right sen it with youre yë,
And that anon, ye nyl nat trowe how sone.
Now taketh hede, for it is for to doone.

"What! wene ye youre wise fader wolde
Han yeven Antenor for yow anon,   905
If he ne wiste that the cite sholde
Destroied ben? Whi, nay, so mote I gon!
He knew ful wel ther shal nat scapen oon

That Troian is; and for the grete feere,
He dorste nat ye dwelte lenger there.   910

"What wol ye more, lufsom lady deere?
Lat Troie and Troian fro youre herte pace!
Drif out that bittre hope, and make good
    cheere,
And clepe ayeyn the beaute of youre face,
That ye with salte teris so deface.   915
For Troie is brought in swich a jupartie,
That it to save is now no remedie.

"And thenketh wel, ye shal in Grekis fynde
A moore parfit love, er it be nyght,
Than any Troian is, and more kynde,   920
And bet to serven yow wol don his myght.
And if ye vouchesauf, my lady bright,
I wol ben he to serven yow myselve,
Yee, levere than be lord of Greces twelve!"

And with that word he gan to waxen red,   925
And in his speche a litel wight he quok,
And caste asyde a litle wight his hed,
And stynte a while; and afterward he wok,
And sobreliche on hire he threw his lok,
And seyde, "I am, al be it yow no joie,   930
As gentil man as any wight in Troie.

For if my fader Tideus," he seyde,
"Ilyved hadde, ich hadde ben, er this,
Of Calydoyne and Arge a kyng, Criseyde!
And so hope I that I shal yet, iwis.   935
But he was slayn, allas! the more harm is,
Unhappily at Thebes al to rathe,
Polymytes and many a man to scathe.

"But herte myn, syn that I am youre man, —
And ben the first of whom I seche grace, —
To serve yow as hertely as I kan,   941
And evere shal, whil I to lyve have space,
So, er that I departe out of this place,
Ye wol me graunte that I may to-morwe,
At bettre leyser, tellen yow my sorwe."   945

What sholde I telle his wordes that he seyde?
He spak inough, for o day at the meeste.
It preveth wel, he spak so that Criseyde
Graunted, on the morwe, at his requeste,
For to speken with hym at the leeste,   950
So that he nolde speke of swich matere.
And thus to hym she seyde, as ye may here,

As she that hadde hire herte on Troilus
So faste, that ther may it non arace;

And strangely she spak, and seyde thus: 955
"O Diomede, I love that ilke place
Ther I was born; and Joves, for his grace,
Delyvere it soone of al that doth it care!
God, for thy myght, so leve it wel to fare!

"That Grekis wolde hire wrath on Troie wreke,
If that they myght, I knowe it wel, iwis.   961
But it shal naught byfallen as ye speke,
And God toforn! and forther over this,
I woot my fader wys and redy is;
And that he me hath bought, as ye me tolde,
So deere, I am the more unto hym holde.   966

"That Grekis ben of heigh condicioun,
I woot ek wel; but certeyn, men shal fynde
As worthi folk withinne Troie town,
As konnyng, and as parfit, and as kynde,   970
As ben bitwixen Orkades and Inde.
And that ye koude wel yowre lady serve,
I trowe ek wel, hire thank for to deserve.

"But as to speke of love, ywis," she seyde,
"I hadde a lord, to whom I wedded was,   975
The whos myn herte al was, til that he deyde;
And other love, as help me now Pallas,
Ther in myn herte nys, ne nevere was.
And that ye ben of noble and heigh kynrede,
I have wel herd it tellen, out of drede.   980

"And that doth me to han so gret a wonder,
That ye wol scornen any womman so.
Ek, God woot, love and I ben fer ysonder!
I am disposed bet, so mot I go,
Unto my deth, to pleyne and maken wo.   985
What I shal after don, I kan nat seye;
But trewelich, as yet me list nat pleye.

"Myn herte is now in tribulacioun,
And ye in armes bisy day by day.
Herafter, whan ye wonnen han the town,   990
Peraunter, thanne so it happen may,
That whan I se that nevere yit I say,
Than wol I werke that I nevere wroughte!
This word to yow ynough suffisen oughte.   994

"To-morwe ek wol I speken with yow fayn,
So that ye touchen naught of this matere.
And whan yow list, ye may come here ayayn;
And er ye gon, thus muche I sey yow here:
As help me Pallas with hire heres clere,
If that I sholde of any Grek han routhe,   1000
It sholde be youreselven, by my trouthe!

"I say nat therfore that I wol yow love,
N'y say nat nay; but in conclusioun,
I mene wel, by God that sit above!"
And therwithal she caste hire eyen down,   1005
And gan to sike, and seyde, "O Troie town,
Yet bidde I God, in quiete and in reste
I may yow sen, or do myn herte breste."

But in effect, and shortly for to seye,
This Diomede al fresshly newe ayeyn   1010
Gan pressen on, and faste hire mercy preye;
And after this, the sothe for to seyn,
Hire glove he took, of which he was ful feyn.
And finaly, whan it was woxen eve,
And al was wel, he roos and tok his leve.   1015

The brighte Venus folwede and ay taughte
The wey ther brode Phebus down alighte;
And Cynthea hire char-hors overraughte
To whirle out of the Leoun, if she myghte;
And Signifer his candels sheweth brighte,   1020
Whan that Criseyde unto hire bedde wente
Inwith hire fadres faire brighte tente,

Retornyng in hire soule ay up and down
The wordes of this sodeyn Diomede,
His grete estat, and perel of the town,   1025
And that she was allone and hadde nede
Of frendes help; and thus bygan to brede
The cause whi, the sothe for to telle,
That she took fully purpos for to dwelle.

The morwen com, and gostly for to speke,   1030
This Diomede is come unto Criseyde;
And shortly, lest that ye my tale breke,
So wel he for hymselven spak and seyde,
That alle hire sikes soore adown he leyde.
And finaly, the sothe for to seyne,   1035
He refte hire of the grete of al hire peyne.

And after this the storie telleth us
That she hym yaf the faire baye stede,
The which he ones wan of Troilus;   1039
And ek a broche — and that was litel nede —
That Troilus was, she yaf this Diomede.
And ek, the bet from sorwe hym to releve,
She made hym were a pencel of hire sleve.

I fynde ek in the stories elleswhere,   1044
Whan thorugh the body hurt was Diomede
Of Troilus, tho wepte she many a teere,
Whan that she saugh his wyde wowndes blede;
And that she took, to kepen hym, good hede;

And for to helen hym of his sorwes smerte,
Men seyn — I not — that she yaf hym hire
    herte.   1050

But trewely, the storie telleth us,
Ther made nevere woman moore wo
Than she, whan that she falsed Troilus.
She seyde, "Allas! for now is clene ago
My name of trouthe in love, for everemo! 1055
For I have falsed oon the gentileste
That evere was, and oon the worthieste!

"Allas! of me, unto the worldes ende,
Shal neyther ben ywriten nor ysonge
No good word, for thise bokes wol me shende.
O, rolled shal I ben on many a tonge! 1061
Thoroughout the world my belle shal be ronge!
And wommen moost wol haten me of alle.
Allas, that swich a cas me sholde falle!

"Thei wol seyn, in as muche as in me is, 1065
I have hem don dishonour, weylaway!
Al be I nat the first that dide amys,
What helpeth that to don my blame awey?
But syn I se ther is no bettre way,
And that to late is now for me to rewe, 1070
To Diomede algate I wol be trewe.

"But, Troilus, syn I no bettre may,
And syn that thus departen ye and I,
Yet prey I God, so yeve yow right good day,
As for the gentileste, trewely, 1075
That evere I say, to serven feythfully,
And best kan ay his lady honour kepe"; —
And with that word she brast anon to wepe.

"And certes, yow ne haten shal I nevere;
And frendes love, that shal ye han of me, 1080
And my good word, al sholde I lyven evere.
And, trewely, I wolde sory be
For to seen yow in adversitee;
And gilteles, I woot wel, I yow leve. 1084
But al shal passe; and thus take I my leve."

But trewely, how longe it was bytwene
That she forsok hym for this Diomede,
Ther is non auctour telleth it, I wene.
Take every man now to his bokes heede;
He shal no terme fynden, out of drede. 1090
For though that he bigan to wowe hire soone,
Er he hire wan, yet was ther moore to doone.

Ne me ne list this sely womman chyde
Forther than the storye wol devyse.

Hire name, allas! is punysshed so wide, 1095
That for hire gilt it oughte ynough suffise.
And if I myghte excuse hire any wise,
For she so sory was for hire untrouthe,
Iwis, I wolde excuse hire yet for routhe.

This Troilus, as I byfore have told, 1100
Thus driveth forth, as wel as he hath myght.
But often was his herte hoot and cold,
And namely that ilke nynthe nyght,
Which on the morwe she hadde hym bihight
To com ayeyn: God woot, ful litel reste 1105
Hadde he that nyght; nothyng to slepe hym
    leste.

The laurer-crowned Phebus, with his heete,
Gan, in his course ay upward as he wente,
To warmen of the est see the wawes weete,
And Nysus doughter song with fressh entente,
Whan Troilus his Pandare after sente; 1111
And on the walles of the town they pleyde,
To loke if they kan sen aught of Criseyde.

Tyl it was noon, they stoden for to se
Who that ther come; and every maner wight
That com fro fer, they seyden it was she, 1116
Til that thei koude knowen hym aright.
Now was his herte dul, now was it light.
And thus byjaped stonden for to stare
Aboute naught this Troilus and Pandare. 1120

To Pandarus this Troilus tho seyde,
"For aught I woot, byfor noon, sikirly,
Into this town ne comth nat here Criseyde.
She hath ynough to doone, hardyly,
To wynnen from hire fader, so trowe I. 1125
Hire olde fader wol yet make hire dyne
Er that she go; God yeve hys herte pyne!"

Pandare answerede, "It may wel be, certeyn.
And forthi lat us dyne, I the byseche, 1129
And after noon than maystow come ayeyn."
And hom they go, withoute more speche,
And comen ayeyn; but longe may they seche
Er that they fynde that they after gape.
Fortune hem bothe thenketh for to jape!

Quod Troilus, "I se wel now that she 1135
Is taried with hire olde fader so,
That er she come, it wol neigh even be.
Com forth, I wole unto the yate go.
Thise porters ben unkonnyng evere mo,
And I wol don hem holden up the yate 1140
As naught ne were, although she come late."

The day goth faste, and after that com eve,
And yet com nought to Troilus Criseyde.
He loketh forth by hegge, by tre, by greve,
And fer his hed over the wal he leyde,   1145
And at the laste he torned hym and seyde,
"By God, I woot hire menyng now, Pandare!
Almoost, ywys, al newe was my care.

"Now douteles, this lady kan hire good;
I woot, she meneth riden pryvely.   1150
I comende hire wisdom, by myn hood!
She wol nat maken peple nycely
Gaure on hire whan she comth; but softely
By nyghte into the town she thenketh ride.
And, deere brother, thynk not longe t'abide.

"We han naught elles for to don, ywis.   1156
And Pandarus, now woltow trowen me?
Have here my trouthe, I se hire! yond she is!
Heve up thyn eyen, man! maistow nat se?"
Pandare answerede, "Nay, so mote I the!   1160
Al wrong, by God! What saistow, man, where arte?
That I se yond nys but a fare-carte."

"Allas! thow seyst right soth," quod Troilus.
"But, hardily, it is naught al for nought
That in myn herte I now rejoysse thus.   1165
It is ayeyns som good I have a thought.
Not I nat how, but syn that I was wrought,
Ne felte I swich a comfort, dar I seye;
She comth to-nyght, my lif that dorste I leye!"   1169

Pandare answerde, "It may be, wel ynough,"
And held with hym of al that evere he seyde.
But in his herte he thoughte, and softe lough,
And to hymself ful sobreliche he seyde,
"From haselwode, there joly Robyn pleyde,
Shal come al that that thow abidest heere.
Ye, fare wel al the snow of ferne yere!"   1176

The warden of the yates gan to calle
The folk which that withoute the yates were,
And bad hem dryven in hire bestes alle,
Or al the nyght they moste bleven there.   1180
And fer withinne the nyght, with many a teere,
This Troilus gan homward for to ride;
For wel he seth it helpeth naught t'abide.

But natheles, he gladed hym in this:
He thought he misacounted hadde his day,
And seyde, "I understonde have al amys.   1186
For thilke nyght I last Criseyde say,

She seyde, 'I shal ben here, if that I may,
Er that the moone, O deere herte swete,
The Leoun passe, out of this Ariete.'   1190

"For which she may yet holde al hire byheste."
And on the morwe unto the yate he wente,
And up and down, by west and ek by este,
Upon the walles made he many a wente;   1194
But al for nought; his hope alwey hym blente.
For which at nyght, in sorwe and sikes sore
He wente hym hom, withouten any more.

His hope al clene out of his herte fledde;
He nath wheron now lenger for to honge;
But for the peyne hym thoughte his herte bledde,   1200
So were his throwes sharpe and wonder stronge.
For whan he saugh that she abood so longe,
He nyste what he juggen of it myghte,
Syn she hath broken that she hym bihighte.

The thridde, ferthe, fifte, sexte day   1205
After tho dayes ten of which I tolde,
Bitwixen hope and drede his herte lay,
Yet somwhat trustyng on hire hestes olde.
But whan he saugh she nolde hire terme holde,
He kan now sen non other remedie   1210
But for to shape hym soone for to dye.

Therwith the wikked spirit, God us blesse,
Which that men clepeth the woode jalousie,
Gan in hym crepe, in al this hevynesse;
For which, by cause he wolde soone dye,   1215
He ne et ne drank, for his malencolye,
And ek from every compaignye he fledde:
This was the lif that al the tyme he ledde.

He so defet was, that no manere man
Unneth hym myghte knowen ther he wente;
So was he lene, and therto pale and wan,   1221
And feble, that he walketh by potente;
And with his ire he thus hymselve shente.
And whoso axed hym wherof hym smerte,   1224
He seyde, his harm was al aboute his herte.

Priam ful ofte, and ek his moder deere,
His bretheren and his sustren gonne hym freyne
Whi he so sorwful was in al his cheere,
And what thyng was the cause of al his peyne;
But al for naught. He nolde his cause pleyne,
But seyde he felte a grevous maladie   1231
Aboute his herte, and fayn he wolde dye.

So on a day he leyde hym doun to slepe,
And so byfel that in his slep hym thoughte

That in a forest faste he welk to wepe   1235
For love of here that hym these peynes
    wroughte;
And up and doun as he the forest soughte,
He mette he saugh a bor with tuskes grete,
That slepte ayeyn the bryghte sonnes hete.

And by this bor, fast in his armes folde,   1240
Lay, kissyng ay, his lady bryght, Criseyde.
For sorwe of which, whan he it gan byholde,
And for despit, out of his slep he breyde,
And loude he cride on Pandarus, and seyde:
"O Pandarus, now know I crop and roote.   1245
I n'am but ded; ther nys non other bote.

"My lady bryght, Criseyde, hath me bytrayed,
In whom I trusted most of any wight.
She elliswhere hath now here herte apayed.
The blysful goddes, thorugh here grete myght,
Han in my drem yshewed it ful right.   1251
Thus yn my drem Criseyde have I byholde" —
And al this thing to Pandarus he tolde.

"O my Criseyde, allas! what subtilte,   1254
What newe lust, what beaute, what science,
What wratthe of juste cause have ye to me?
What gilt of me, what fel experience,
Hath fro me raft, allas! thyn advertence?
O trust, O feyth, O depe aseuraunce,   1259
Who hath me reft Criseyde, al my plesaunce?

"Allas! whi leet I you from hennes go,
For which wel neigh out of my wit I breyde?
Who shal now trowe on any othes mo?
God wot, I wende, O lady bright, Criseyde,
That every word was gospel that ye seyde!
But who may bet bigile, yf hym lyste,   1266
Than he on whom men weneth best to triste?

"What shal I don, my Pandarus, allas?
I fele now so sharp a newe peyne,
Syn that ther is no remedye in this cas,   1270
That bet were it I with myn hondes tweyne
Myselven slow than thus alwey to pleyne.
For thorugh my deth my wo shold han an ende,
Ther every day with lyf myself I shende."

Pandare answerde and seyde, "Allas the while
That I was born! Have I nat seyd er this,   1276
That dremes many a maner man bigile?
And whi? For folk expounden hem amys.
How darstow seyn that fals thy lady ys,   1279
For any drem, right for thyn owene drede?
Lat be this thought; thow kanst no dremes rede.

"Peraunter, ther thow dremest of this boor,
It may so be that it may signifie,
Hire fader, which that old is and ek hoor,
Ayeyn the sonne lith, o poynt to dye,   1285
And she for sorwe gynneth wepe and crie,
And kisseth hym, ther he lith on the grounde:
Thus sholdestow thi drem aright expounde!"

"How myghte I than don," quod Troilus,   1289
"To knowe of this, yee, were it nevere so lite?"
"Now seystow wisly," quod this Pandarus.
"My red is this, syn thow kanst wel endite,
That hastily a lettre thow hire write,
Thorugh which thow shalt wel bryngyn it
    aboute,
To know a soth of that thow art in doute.   1295

"And se now whi; for this I dar wel seyn,
That if so is that she untrewe be,
I kan nat trowen that she wol write ayeyn.
And if she write, thow shalt ful sone yse,
As wheither she hath any liberte   1300
To come ayeyn; or ellis in som clause,
If she be let, she wol assigne a cause.

"Thow hast nat writen hire syn that she wente,
Nor she to the; and this I dorste laye,
Ther may swich cause ben in hire entente,
That hardily thow wolt thiselven saye   1306
That hire abod the best is for yow twaye.
Now writ hire thanne, and thow shalt feele
    sone
A soth of al; ther is namore to done."

Acorded ben to this conclusioun,   1310
And that anon, thise ilke lordes two;
And hastily sit Troilus adown,
And rolleth in his herte to and fro,
How he may best discryven hire his wo.
And to Criseyde, his owen lady deere,   1315
He wrot right thus, and seyde as ye may here:

Litera Troili.

"Right fresshe flour, whos I ben have and shal,
Withouten part of elleswhere servyse,
With herte, body, lif, lust, thought, and al,
I, woful wyght, in everich humble wise   1320
That tonge telle or herte may devyse,
As ofte as matere occupieth place,
Me recomaunde unto youre noble grace.

"Liketh yow to witen, swete herte,
As ye wel knowe, how longe tyme agon   1325

That ye me lefte in aspre peynes smerte,
Whan that ye wente, of which yit boote non
Have I non had, but evere wors bigon
Fro day to day am I, and so mot dwelle,   1329
While it yow list, of wele and wo my welle.

"For which to yow, with dredful herte trewe,
I write, as he that sorwe drifth to write,
My wo, that everich houre encresseth newe,
Compleynyng, as I dar or kan endite.
And that defaced is, that may ye wite   1335
The teris which that fro myn eyen reyne,
That wolden speke, if that they koude, and
     pleyne.

"Yow first biseche I, that youre eyen clere,
To loke on this, defouled ye nat holde;
And over al this, that ye, my lady deere,   1340
Wol vouchesauf this lettre to byholde.
And by the cause ek of my cares colde,
That sleth my wit, if aught amys m'asterte,
Foryeve it me, myn owen swete herte!

"If any servant dorste or oughte of right   1345
Upon his lady pitously compleyne,
Thanne wene I that ich oughte be that wight,
Considered this, that ye thise monthes tweyne
Han taried, ther ye seyden, soth to seyne,
But dayes ten ye nolde in oost sojourne, —
But in two monthes yet ye nat retourne.   1351

"But for as muche as me moot nedes like
Al that yow liste, I dar nat pleyne moore,
But humblely, with sorwful sikes sike,
Yow write ich myn unresty sorwes soore,   1355
Fro day to day desiryng evere moore
To knowen fully, if youre wille it weere,
How ye han ferd and don whil ye be theere;

"The whos welfare and hele ek God encresse
In honour swich, that upward in degree   1360
It growe alwey, so that it nevere cesse.
Right as youre herte ay kan, my lady free,
Devyse, I prey to God so moot it be,
And graunte it that ye soone upon me rewe,
As wisly as in al I am yow trewe.   1365

"And if yow liketh knowen of the fare
Of me, whos wo ther may no wit discryve,
I kan namore but, chiste of every care,
At wrytyng of this lettre I was on-lyve,
Al redy out my woful gost to dryve;   1370
Which I delaye, and holde hym yet in honde,
Upon the sighte of matere of youre sonde.

"Myn eyen two, in veyn with which I se,
Of sorwful teris salte arn woxen welles;
My song, in pleynte of myn adversitee;   1375
My good, in harm; myn ese ek woxen helle is;
My joie, in wo; I kan sey yow naught ellis,
But torned is, for which my lif I warie,
Everich joie or ese in his contrarie.   1379

"Which with youre comyng hom ayeyn to Troie
Ye may redresse, and more a thousand sithe
Than evere ich hadde, encressen in me joie.
For was ther nevere herte yet so blithe
To han his lif as I shal ben as swithe   1384
As I yow se; and though no manere routhe
Commeve yow, yet thynketh on youre trouthe.

"And if so be my gilt hath deth deserved,
Or if yow list namore upon me se,
In guerdoun yet of that I have yow served,
Byseche I yow, myn hertes lady free,   1390
That hereupon ye wolden write me,
For love of God, my righte lode-sterre,
That deth may make an ende of al my werre.

"If other cause aught doth yow for to dwelle,
That with youre lettre ye me recomforte;   1395
For though to me youre absence is an helle,
With pacience I wol my wo comporte,
And with youre lettre of hope I wol desporte.
Now writeth, swete, and lat me thus nat pleyne;
With hope, or deth, delivereth me fro peyne.

"Iwis, myne owene deere herte trewe,   1401
I woot that, whan ye next upon me se,
So lost have I myn hele and ek myn hewe,
Criseyde shal nought konne knowen me.
Iwys, myn hertes day, my lady free,   1405
So thursteth ay myn herte to byholde
Youre beute, that my lif unnethe I holde.

"I say namore, al have I for to seye
To yow wel more than I telle may.
But wheither that ye do me lyve or deye,   1410
Yet praye I God, so yeve yow right good day!
And fareth wel, goodly, faire, fresshe may,
As ye that lif or deth may me comande!
And to youre trouthe ay I me recomande,

"With hele swich that, but ye yeven me   1415
The same hele, I shal non hele have.
In yow lith, whan yow liste that it so be,
The day in which me clothen shal my grave;
In yow my lif, in yow myght for to save

Me fro disese of alle peynes smerte;   1420
And far now wel, myn owen swete herte!
                    le vostre T."

This lettre forth was sent unto Criseyde,
Of which hire answere in effect was this:
Ful pitously she wroot ayeyn, and seyde,
That also sone as that she myghte, ywys,   1425
She wolde come, and mende al that was mys.
And fynaly she wroot and seyde hym thenne,
She wolde come, ye, but she nyste whenne.

But in hire lettre made she swich festes
That wonder was, and swerth she loveth hym
          best;   1430
Of which he fond but botmeles bihestes.
But Troilus, thow maist now, est or west,
Pipe in an ivy lef, if that the lest!
Thus goth the world. God shilde us fro mes-
          chaunce,
And every wight that meneth trouthe avaunce!

Encressen gan the wo fro day to nyght   1436
Of Troilus, for tarying of Criseyde;
And lessen gan his hope and ek his myght,
For which al down he in his bed hym leyde.
He ne eet, ne dronk, ne slep, ne no word seyde,
Ymagynyng ay that she was unkynde;   1441
For which wel neigh he wex out of his mynde.

This drem, of which I told have ek byforn,
May nevere come out of his remembraunce.
He thought ay wel he hadde his lady lorn,
And that Joves, of his purveyaunce,   1446
Hym shewed hadde in slep the signifiaunce
Of hire untrouthe and his disaventure,
And that the boor was shewed hym in figure.

For which he for Sibille his suster sente,   1450
That called was Cassandre ek al aboute,
And al his drem he tolde hire er he stente,
And hire bisoughte assoilen hym the doute
Of the stronge boor with tuskes stoute;
And fynaly, withinne a litel stounde,   1455
Cassandre hym gan right thus his drem ex-
          pounde.

She gan first smyle, and seyde, "O brother
          deere,
If thow a soth of this desirest knowe,
Thow most a fewe of olde stories heere,
To purpos, how that Fortune overthrowe   1460
Hath lordes olde; thorugh which, withinne a
          throwe,

Thow wel this boor shalt knowe, and of what
          kynde
He comen is, as men in bokes fynde.

"Diane, which that wroth was and in ire
For Grekis nolde don hire sacrifise,   1465
Ne encens upon hire auter sette afire,
She, for that Grekis gonne hire so despise,
Wrak hire in a wonder cruel wise;
For with a boor as gret as ox in stalle   1469
She made up frete hire corn and vynes alle.

"To sle this boor was al the contre raysed,
Amonges which ther com, this boor to se,
A mayde, oon of this world the beste ypreysed;
And Meleagre, lord of that contree,
He loved so this fresshe mayden free,   1475
That with his manhod, er he wolde stente,
This boor he slough, and hire the hed he sente;

"Of which, as olde bokes tellen us,
Ther ros a contek and a gret envye;
And of this lord descended Tideus   1480
By ligne, or ellis olde bookes lye.
But how this Meleagre gan to dye
Thorugh his moder, wol I yow naught telle,
For al to longe it were for to dwelle."

She tolde ek how Tideus, er she stente,   1485
Unto the stronge citee of Thebes,
To cleymen kyngdom of the citee, wente,
For his felawe, daun Polymytes,
Of which the brother, daun Ethiocles,
Ful wrongfully of Thebes held the strengthe;
This tolde she by proces, al by lengthe.   1491

She tolde ek how Hemonydes asterte,
Whan Tideus slough fifty knyghtes stoute.
She tolde ek alle the prophecyes by herte,
And how that seven kynges with hire route
Bysegeden the citee al aboute;   1496
And of the holy serpent, and the welle,
And of the furies, al she gan hym telle;

Of Archymoris burying and the pleyes,
And how Amphiorax fil thorugh the grounde,
How Tideus was sleyn, lord of Argeyes,   1501
And how Ypomedoun in litel stounde
Was dreynt, and ded Parthonope of wownde;
And also how Capaneus the proude   1504
With thonder-dynt was slayn, that cride loude.

She gan ek telle hym how that eyther brother,
Ethiocles and Polymyte also,

At a scarmuche ech of hem slough other,
And of Argyves wepynge and hire wo;   1509
And how the town was brent, she tolde ek tho.
And so descendeth down from gestes olde
To Diomede, and thus she spak and tolde.

"This ilke boor bitokneth Diomede,
Tideüs sone, that down descended is
Fro Meleagre, that made the boor to blede.
And thy lady, wherso she be, ywis,   1516
This Diomede hire herte hath, and she his.
Wep if thow wolt, or lef! For, out of doute,
This Diomede is inne, and thow art oute."

"Thow seyst nat soth," quod he, "thow sor-
      ceresse,   1520
With al thy false goost of prophecye!
Thow wenest ben a gret devyneresse!
Now sestow nat this fool of fantasie
Peyneth hire on ladys for to lye?   1524
Awey!" quod he, "ther Joves yeve the sorwe!
Thow shalt be fals, peraunter, yet tomorwe!

"As wel thow myghtest lien on Alceste,
That was of creatures, but men lye,
That evere weren, kyndest and the beste!
For whan hire housbonde was in jupertye 1530
To dye hymself, but if she wolde dye,
She ches for hym to dye and gon to helle,
And starf anon, as us the bokes telle."

Cassandre goth, and he with cruel herte
Foryat his wo, for angre of hire speche; 1535
And from his bed al sodeynly he sterte,
As though al hool hym hadde ymad a leche.
And day by day he gan enquere and seche
A sooth of this with al his fulle cure;
And thus he drieth forth his aventure.   1540

Fortune, which that permutacioun
Of thynges hath, as it is hire comitted
Thorugh purveyaunce and disposicioun
Of heighe Jove, as regnes shal be flitted 1544
Fro folk in folk, or when they shal be smytted,
Gan pulle awey the fetheres brighte of Troie
Fro day to day, til they ben bare of joie.

Among al this, the fyn of the parodie
Of Ector gan aprochen wonder blyve.   1549
The fate wolde his soule sholde unbodye,
And shapen hadde a mene it out to dryve,
Ayeyns which fate hym helpeth nat to stryve;
But on a day to fighten gan he wende,
At which, allas! he caught his lyves ende.

For which me thynketh every manere wight
That haunteth armes oughte to biwaille   1556
The deth of hym that was so noble a knyght;
For as he drough a kyng by th'aventaille,
Unwar of this, Achilles thorugh the maille 1559
And thorugh the body gan hym for to ryve;
And thus this worthi knyght was brought of
      lyve.

For whom, as olde bokes tellen us,
Was mad swich wo, that tonge it may nat telle;
And namely, the sorwe of Troilus,
That next hym was of worthynesse welle. 1565
And in this wo gan Troilus to dwelle,
That, what for sorwe, and love, and for unreste,
Ful ofte a day he bad his herte breste.

But natheles, though he gan hym dispaire,
And dradde ay that his lady was untrewe,
Yet ay on hire his herte gan repaire.   1571
And as thise loveres don, he soughte ay newe
To get ayeyn Criseyde, brighte of hewe;
And in his herte he wente hire excusynge,
That Calkas caused al hire tariynge.   1575

And ofte tyme he was in purpos grete
Hymselven lik a pilgrym to desgise,
To seen hire; but he may nat contrefete
To ben unknowen of folk that weren wise,
Ne fynde excuse aright that may suffise, 1580
If he among the Grekis knowen were;
For which he wep ful ofte and many a tere.

To hire he wroot yet ofte tyme al newe
Ful pitously, — he lefte it nought for slouthe, —
Bisechyng hire, syn that he was trewe,   1585
That she wol come ayeyn and holde hire
      trouthe.
For which Criseyde upon a day, for routhe, —
I take it so, — touchyng al this matere,
Wrot hym ayeyn, and seyde as ye may here:

Litera Criseydis.

"Cupides sone, ensample of goodlyheede, 1590
O swerd of knyghthod, sours of gentilesse,
How myght a wight in torment and in drede
And heleles, yow sende as yet gladnesse?
I herteles, I sik, I in destresse!   1594
Syn ye with me, nor I with yow, may dele,
Yow neyther sende ich herte may nor hele.

"Youre lettres ful, the papir al ypleynted,
Conceyved hath myn hertes pietee.

I have ek seyn with teris al depeynted   1599
Youre lettre, and how that ye requeren me
To come ayeyn, which yet ne may nat be.
But whi, lest that this lettre founden were,
No mencioun ne make I now, for feere.

"Grevous to me, God woot, is youre unreste,
Youre haste, and that the goddes ordinaunce
It semeth nat ye take it for the beste.   1606
Nor other thyng nys in youre remembraunce,
As thynketh me, but only youre plesaunce.
But beth nat wroth, and that I yow biseche;
For that I tarie is al for wikked speche.   1610

"For I have herd wel moore than I wende,
Touchyng us two, how thynges han ystonde;
Which I shal with dissymulyng amende.
And beth nat wroth, I have ek understonde
How ye ne do but holden me in honde.   1615
But now no force, I kan nat in yow gesse
But alle trouthe and alle gentilesse.

"Come I wole; but yet in swich disjoynte
I stonde as now, that what yer or what day
That this shal be, that kan I naught apoynte.
But in effect I pray yow, as I may,   1621
Of youre good word and of youre frendship ay.
For trewely, while that my lif may dure,
As for a frend ye may in me assure.

"Yet preye ich yow, on yvel ye ne take   1625
That it is short which that I to yow write;
I dar nat, ther I am, wel lettres make,
Ne nevere yet ne koude I wel endite.
Ek gret effect men write in place lite;
Th'entente is al, and nat the lettres space.   1630
And fareth now wel, God have yow in his grace!
La vostre C."

This Troilus this lettre thoughte al straunge,
Whan he it saugh, and sorwfullich he sighte.
Hym thoughte it lik a kalendes of chaunge.
But fynaly, he ful ne trowen myghte   1635
That she ne wolde hym holden that she hyghte;
For with ful yvel wille list hym to leve,
That loveth wel, in swich cas, though hym
greve.

But natheles, men seyen that at the laste,
For any thyng, men shal the soothe se.   1640
And swich a cas bitidde, and that as faste,
That Troilus wel understod that she
Nas nought so kynde as that hire oughte be.

And fynaly, he woot now, out of doute,
That al is lost that he hath ben aboute.   1645

Stood on a day in his malencolie
This Troilus, and in suspecioun
Of hire for whom he wende for to dye.
And so bifel that thorughout Troye town,
As was the gise, iborn was up and down   1650
A manere cote-armure, as seith the storie,
Byforn Deiphebe, in signe of his victorie;

The whiche cote, as telleth Lollius,
Deiphebe it hadde rent fro Diomede
The same day. And whan this Troilus   1655
It saugh, he gan to taken of it hede,
Avysyng of the lengthe and of the brede,
And al the werk; but as he gan byholde,
Ful sodeynly his herte gan to colde,

As he that on the coler fond withinne   1660
A broche, that he Criseyde yaf that morwe
That she from Troie moste nedes twynne,
In remembraunce of hym and of his sorwe.
And she hym leyde ayeyn hire feith to borwe
To kepe it ay! But now ful wel he wiste,   1665
His lady nas no lenger on to triste.

He goth hym hom, and gan ful soone sende
For Pandarus; and al this newe chaunce,
And of this broche, he tolde hym word and
ende,
Compleynyng of hire hertes variaunce,   1670
His longe love, his trouthe, and his penaunce.
And after deth, withouten wordes moore,
Ful faste he cride, his reste hym to restore.

Than spak he thus, "O lady myn, Criseyde,
Where is youre feith, and where is youre bi-
heste?   1675
Where is youre love? where is youre trouthe?"
he seyde.
"Of Diomede have ye now al this feeste!
Allas! I wolde han trowed atte leeste
That, syn ye nolde in trouthe to me stonde,
That ye thus nolde han holden me in honde!

"Who shal now trowe on any othes mo?   1681
Allas! I nevere wolde han wend, er this,
That ye, Criseyde, koude han chaunged so;
Ne, but I hadde agilt and don amys,   1684
So cruel wende I nought youre herte, ywis,
To sle me thus! Allas, youre name of trouthe
Is now fordon, and that is al my routhe.

"Was ther non other broche yow liste lete
To feffe with youre newe love," quod he,
"But thilke broch that I, with teris wete,   1690
Yow yaf, as for a remembraunce of me?
Non other cause, allas, ne hadde ye
But for despit, and ek for that ye mente
Al outrely to shewen youre entente.

"Thorugh which I se that clene out of youre
          mynde   1695
Ye han me cast; and I ne kan nor may,
For al this world, withinne myn herte fynde
To unloven yow a quarter of a day!
In corsed tyme I born was, weilaway,
That yow, that doon me al this wo endure,
Yet love I best of any creature!   1701

"Now God," quod he, "me sende yet the grace
That I may meten with this Diomede!
And trewely, if I have myght and space,
Yet shal I make, I hope, his sydes blede.   1705
O God," quod he, "that oughtest taken heede
To fortheren trouthe, and wronges to punyce,
Whi nyltow don a vengeaunce of this vice?

"O Pandarus, that in dremes for to triste
Me blamed hast, and wont art oft upbreyde,
Now maistow se thiself, if that the liste,   1711
How trewe is now thi nece, bright Criseyde!
In sondry formes, God it woot," he seyde,
"The goddes shewen bothe joie and tene
In slep, and by my drem it is now sene.   1715

"And certeynly, withouten moore speche,
From hennesforth, as ferforth as I may,
Myn owen deth in armes wol I seche.
I recche nat how soone be the day!
But trewely, Criseyde, swete may,   1720
Whom I have ay with al my myght yserved,
That ye thus doon, I have it nat deserved."

This Pandarus, that al thise thynges herde,
And wiste wel he seyde a soth of this,
He nought a word ayeyn to hym answerde;
For sory of his frendes sorwe he is,   1726
And shamed for his nece hath don amys,
And stant, astoned of thise causes tweye,
As stille as ston; a word ne kowde he seye.

But at the laste thus he spak, and seyde: 1730
"My brother deer, I may do the namore.
What sholde I seyen? I hate, ywys, Cryseyde;
And, God woot, I wol hate hire evermore!
And that thow me bisoughtest don of yoore,

Havyng unto myn honour ne my reste   1735
Right no reward, I dide al that the leste.

"If I dide aught that myghte liken the,
It is me lief; and of this tresoun now,
God woot that it a sorwe is unto me!
And dredeles, for hertes ese of yow,   1740
Right fayn I wolde amende it, wiste I how.
And fro this world, almyghty God I preye
Delivere hire soon! I kan namore seye."

Gret was the sorwe and pleynte of Troilus;
But forth hire cours Fortune ay gan to holde.
Criseyde loveth the sone of Tideüs,   1746
And Troilus moot wepe in cares colde.
Swich is this world, whoso it kan byholde:
In ech estat is litel hertes reste.
God leve us for to take it for the beste!   1750

In many cruel bataille, out of drede,
Of Troilus, this ilke noble knyght,
As men may in thise olde bokes rede,
Was seen his knyghthod and his grete myght.
And dredeles, his ire, day and nyght,   1755
Ful cruwely the Grekis ay aboughte;
And alwey moost this Diomede he soughte.

And ofte tyme, I fynde that they mette
With blody strokes and with wordes grete,
Assayinge how hire speres weren whette;   1760
And, God it woot, with many a cruel hete
Gan Troilus upon his helm to bete!
But natheles, Fortune it naught ne wolde,
Of oothers hond that eyther deyen sholde.

And if I hadde ytaken for to write   1765
The armes of this ilke worthi man,
Than wolde ich of his batailles endite;
But for that I to writen first bigan
Of his love, I have seyd as I kan, —
His worthi dedes, whoso list hem heere,   1770
Rede Dares, he kan telle hem alle ifeere —

Bysechyng every lady bright of hewe,
And every gentil womman, what she be,
That al be that Criseyde was untrewe,
That for that gilt she be nat wroth with me.
Ye may hire giltes in other bokes se;   1776
And gladlier I wol write, yif yow leste,
Penelopeës trouthe and good Alceste.

N'y sey nat this al oonly for thise men,
But moost for wommen that bitraised be   1780
Thorugh false folk; God yeve hem sorwe, amen!

That with hire grete wit and subtilte
Bytraise yow! And this commeveth me
To speke, and in effect yow alle I preye,
Beth war of men, and herkneth what I seye! —

Go, litel bok, go, litel myn tragedye,   1786
Ther God thi makere yet, er that he dye,
So sende myght to make in som comedye!
But litel book, no makyng thow n'envie,
But subgit be to alle poesye;   1790
And kis the steppes, where as thow seest pace
Virgile, Ovide, Omer, Lucan, and Stace.

And for ther is so gret diversite
In Englissh and in writyng of oure tonge,
So prey I God that non myswrite the,   1795
Ne the mysmetre for defaute of tonge,
And red wherso thow be, or elles songe,
That thow be understonde, God I biseche!
But yet to purpos of my rather speche. —

The wrath, as I bigan yow for to seye,   1800
Of Troilus the Grekis boughten deere.
For thousandes his hondes maden deye,
As he that was withouten any peere,
Save Ector, in his tyme, as I kan heere.
But weilawey, save only Goddes wille!   1805
Despitously hym slough the fierse Achille.

And whan that he was slayn in this manere,
His lighte goost ful blisfully is went
Up to the holughnesse of the eighthe spere,
In convers letyng everich element;   1810
And ther he saugh, with ful avysement,
The erratik sterres, herkenyng armonye
With sownes ful of hevenyssh melodie.

And down from thennes faste he gan avyse
This litel spot of erthe, that with the se   1815
Embraced is, and fully gan despise
This wrecched world, and held al vanite
To respect of the pleyn felicite
That is in hevene above; and at the laste,   1819
Ther he was slayn, his lokyng down he caste.

And in hymself he lough right at the wo
Of hem that wepten for his deth so faste;
And dampned al oure werk that foloweth so
The blynde lust, the which that may nat laste,
And sholden al oure herte on heven caste.   1825

And forth he wente, shortly for to telle,
Ther as Mercurye sorted hym to dwelle.

Swich fyn hath, lo, this Troilus for love!
Swich fyn hath al his grete worthynesse!
Swich fyn hath his estat real above,   1830
Swich fyn his lust, swich fyn hath his noblesse!
Swych fyn hath false worldes brotelnesse!
And thus bigan his lovyng of Criseyde,
As I have told, and in this wise he deyde.

O yonge, fresshe folkes, he or she,   1835
In which that love up groweth with youre age,
Repeyreth hom fro worldly vanyte,
And of youre herte up casteth the visage
To thilke God that after his ymage   1839
Yow made, and thynketh al nys but a faire
This world, that passeth soone as floures faire.

And loveth hym, the which that right for love
Upon a crois, oure soules for to beye,
First starf, and roos, and sit in hevene above;
For he nyl falsen no wight, dar I seye,   1845
That wol his herte al holly on hym leye.
And syn he best to love is, and most meke,
What nedeth feynede loves for to seke?

Lo here, of payens corsed olde rites,   1849
Lo here, what alle hire goddes may availle;
Lo here, thise wrecched worldes appetites;
Lo here, the fyn and guerdoun for travaille
Of Jove, Appollo, of Mars, of swich rascaille!
Lo here, the forme of olde clerkis speche
In poetrie, if ye hire bokes seche.   1855

O moral Gower, this book I directe
To the and to the, philosophical Strode,
To vouchen sauf, ther nede is, to correcte,
Of youre benignites and zeles goode.   1859
And to that sothefast Crist, that starf on rode,
With al myn herte of mercy evere I preye,
And to the Lord right thus I speke and seye:

Thow oon, and two, and thre, eterne on lyve,
That regnest ay in thre, and two, and oon,
Uncircumscript, and al maist circumscrive,
Us from visible and invisible foon   1866
Defende, and to thy mercy, everichon,
So make us, Jesus, for thi mercy digne,
For love of mayde and moder thyn benigne.
        Amen.

Explicit liber Troili et Criseydis.

THE LEGEND OF GOOD WOMEN

NEXT to the description of April "with his shoures sote" at the beginning of the *Canterbury Tales*, probably the most familiar and best loved lines of Chaucer are those in the Prologue to the *Legend of Good Women* which tell of his adoration of the daisy. Both passages are notable examples of the freshness and simplicity — the "vernal spirit which soothes and refreshes" — long ago praised by Lowell as characteristic of Chaucer. The quality is truly Chaucerian, and by no means restricted to descriptions of outward nature. But the secret of it is hard to discover. It is partly, without doubt, the effect of the language, — not of the "quaintness" falsely ascribed to Chaucer's speech by those to whom it is simply unfamiliar, but of a real simplicity of structure in early English, found also in Old French and comparable to that which distinguishes Homeric Greek from the later Attic. In part, too, the freshness of Chaucer's poetry is a reflection of his age, of a certain youthful directness in its relation to life. And in great measure it is an expression of his own mind and temperament. In any case it is not to be set down to naïve simplicity on the part of the poet or his contemporaries. Nor in the two poems which have been mentioned is the effect in question due to the avoidance of literary material or, it must be granted, to the direct observation of nature. The passage in the *General Prologue* follows an established convention, in which, to be sure, it surpasses all its models; and the panegyric on the daisy is almost a cento of quotations or imitations of contemporary poetry, French and perhaps Italian. Indeed the whole *Prologue* to the *Legend* is steeped in literary associations. The truth of its description and sentiment is not for that reason to be denied or disparaged. But the reader cannot understand the *Prologue* aright without knowing something of the conventions which underlie it and the fund of poetry on which it has drawn for its enrichment.

Like the *Book of the Duchess*, the *House of Fame*, and the *Parliament of Fowls*, the *Legend of Good Women* is a love-vision. But before the relation of the actual dream, the scene is set by an account of the poet's worship of the daisy on the first of May. In that passage, besides the simple delight in nature which has endeared it to generations of readers, must be recognized the skilful use of literary and social conventions. The relative merits of the flower and the leaf were a subject of poetic debate in Chaucer's time, as they were in the next century, when the poem entitled the Flower and the Leaf was composed. The ladies and gentlemen of the court — so the *Prologue* to the *Legend* indicates — divided themselves into two orders, devoted one to the Leaf and the other to the Flower. Similarly there is evidence, in both French and English poetry, of the existence of a cult of the marguerite. Both these courtly fashions are reflected in the *Prologue*. In the controversy of Flower against Leaf Chaucer refuses to take sides. But he proclaims his utter devotion to the daisy, and his celebration of this queen of flowers contains many lines and phrases paralleled in Deschamps, Machaut, and Froissart, and some perhaps from Boccaccio. To complete the glorification of the daisy he invents a happy metamorphosis, worthy of the old mythologies, and represents the flower as a transformation of the queen Alceste, the leader of his "good women," who appears in his vision as an attendant of the god of Love.

According to the central fiction of the *Prologue*, Chaucer is condemned by the god of Love for having written heresies against his law — in particular, for having defamed women by composing the *Troilus* and translating the Roman de la Rose. As a penalty for his misconduct he is commanded to write a legendary of Cupid's saints — that is, of women who were good according to the standard of the religion of Love. The *Legend* thus falls at once into the ancient category of palinodes, known in literary history from the time of Stesichorus, who first wrote an ode against Helen of Troy, and then composed his Palinodia in her praise. Perhaps the most familiar Latin example of the type is Horace's "O matre pulchra filia pulchrior," and among classical writings known to Chaucer Ovid's Ars Amatoria, Book III, and his Remedia Amoris form a kind of double palinode. In mediæval French literature the fashion was revived. Jean le Fèvre, who translated the strongly antifeminist Lamentationes Matheoli, composed his Leesce as a *contrepeise*, and Nicholas de Bozon atoned for his Char d'Orgeuil by his counterplea De la Bonté des Femmes. Machaut's Jugement dou Roy de Navarre was not only a palinode, but may also have furnished an actual suggestion for Chaucer's *Legend*. Again in the fifteenth century, in English, the Dialogue with a Friend by Hoccleve, Chaucer's disciple, still continues the convention. In writing such a recantation, then, Chaucer was following a familiar custom. And perhaps the occasion of his palinode was not wholly fictitious. Just as Ovid's Remedia Amoris is held to have been his apology to the gossiping critics of the Amores, so, it has been not unreasonably suggested, Chaucer's defense of good women may have been called forth by actual condemnation of his *Troilus*.

The form of the work imposed upon Chaucer as a penance is that of a legendary, or collection of lives of saints. The good women whose tragic stories he relates are heroines of classical antiquity who suffered or died out of devotion to their lovers. They are represented as saints or martyrs on Cupid's calendar. So the *Legend* may be regarded, in the words of a recent critic, as "a cross between the Heroides of Ovid and the Legenda Aurea." In an age which produced a lover's manual of sins — the Confessio Amantis, the Ten Commandments of love, matins and lauds of love sung by the birds, paternosters and credos of love, and masses of Venus, the *Legend* affords another

striking example of the adaptation of Christian ideas and institutions to the affairs of love.

Such are the varied origins and antecedents of the *Legend of Good Women*. In spite of Chaucer's uncommon skill in combining diverse elements in a simple and artistic design, he was not altogether successful in achieving unity or consistency in the *Prologue*. He doubtless realized this himself, and for that reason gave the poem a careful revision. Even in what appears to be the later version, preserved in a single manuscript, the inconsistencies are not wholly removed, though the structure is improved and made more logical. Some of the most delightful poetry is sacrificed in the revision, so that many critics prefer the earlier version. And in fact the charm of the *Prologue* lies not so much in the orderly development of the argument as in the pleasant description and the happy expression of poetic feeling and fancy.

The legends themselves, regarded as narratives, are much inferior to the stories of Chaucer's latest period. They lack the variety, brilliancy, and dramatic reality of the *Troilus* or the best of the *Canterbury Tales*. Yet if compared with any contemporary narrative poems except Chaucer's own, they would be reckoned among the masterpieces of the age. They were very likely written, at least in part, earlier than the *Prologue*, and represent an important stage in Chaucer's literary development. Composed largely under the influence of Virgil and Ovid, they show a definite advance in narrative structure over the poems of the so-called French period of Chaucer's youth; and though they have not the interest of his more independent works, yet if read attentively and compared with their sources they reveal great care in translation and no small degree of artistry. From his painstaking study and imitation of Ovid Chaucer profited in the niceties of observation and expression.

The monotonous theme of the legend — the praise of faithful women — and its conventional treatment make the stories tiresome to the modern reader; and Chaucer himself appears to have lost interest in them, though he may never have deliberately abandoned them. The introduction to the *Man of Law's Tale* implies that while occupied with the *Canterbury Tales* he still had in mind the composition of more lives of good women, and he appears to have revised the *Prologue* as late as 1394. But he did not actually bring the series to completion, and we may well suppose that it was simply superseded in his interest by the *Canterbury Tales.* Indeed critics have questioned whether Chaucer could ever have felt real enthusiasm for the *Legend*; whether it was ever anything more than a concession to contemporary taste, or perhaps to a royal command. One scholar has gone so far as to suggest that Chaucer composed the work from the outset with satirical purpose — writing, so to speak, with his tongue in his cheek. Some of the good women, this writer reminds us, were anything but good, being guilty of murder and other crimes. Chaucer selected them and praised them, he argues, precisely for the purpose of making his ostensible defense of women ridiculous, and so of perpetrating a huge joke upon critics and patrons. This attempt to find unrecognized humor in the *Legend*, and so to rescue it from the charge of dullness, even if it seemed needful, is ill-advised. For there can be no doubt that in the mind of Chaucer and his contemporaries the heroines he celebrates were good in the only sense that counted for the purpose in hand — they were faithful followers of the god of Love. The rubric "Explicit Legenda Cleopataras Martiris" has a humor for us that it would hardly have had for the readers at the court of Richard II.

Attempts have been made to date the two versions of the *Prologue* on the evidence of historical allegory. But there is so much doubt about the assumed applications that the arguments are unconvincing. Recent theories on the subject are mentioned in the Explanatory Notes.

Apart from the real interest of its substance, the *Legend of Good Women* is an important landmark in versification. Chaucer, always an experimenter in meter, here employed — for the first time in English, so far as is known — the decasyllabic couplet, the principal verse-form of the *Canterbury Tales* and the "heroic couplet" of a long line of English poets.

The Legend of Good Women

THE PROLOGUE

Text F

A thousand tymes have I herd men telle
That ther ys joy in hevene and peyne in helle,
And I acorde wel that it ys so;
But, natheles, yet wot I wel also
That ther nis noon dwellyng in this contree,   5
That eyther hath in hevene or helle ybe,
Ne may of hit noon other weyes witen,
But as he hath herd seyd, or founde it writen;
For by assay ther may no man it preve.
But God forbede but men shulde leve   10
Wel more thing then men han seen with ye!
Men shal not wenen every thing a lye
But yf himself yt seeth, or elles dooth;

Text G

A thousand sythes have I herd men telle
That there is joye in hevene and peyne in helle,
And I acorde wel that it be so;
But natheles, this wot I wel also,
That there ne is non that dwelleth in this con-
    tre,   5
That eyther hath in helle or hevene ybe,
Ne may of it non other weyes witen,
But as he hath herd seyd or founde it writen;
For by assay there may no man it preve.
But Goddes forbode, but men shulde leve   10
Wel more thyng than men han seyn with ye!
Men shal nat wenen every thyng a lye,

For, God wot, thing is never the lasse sooth,
Thogh every wight ne may it nat ysee.   15
Bernard the monk ne saugh nat all, pardee!
  Than mote we to bokes that we fynde,
Thurgh whiche that olde thinges ben in mynde,
And to the doctrine of these olde wyse,
Yeve credence, in every skylful wise,   20
That tellen of these olde appreved stories
Of holynesse, of regnes, of victories,
Of love, of hate, of other sondry thynges,
Of whiche I may not maken rehersynges.
And yf that olde bokes were aweye,   25
Yloren were of remembraunce the keye.
Wel ought us thanne honouren and beleve
These bokes, there we han noon other preve.
  And as for me, though that I konne but lyte,
On bokes for to rede I me delyte,   30
And to hem yive I feyth and ful credence,
And in myn herte have hem in reverence
So hertely, that ther is game noon
That fro my bokes maketh me to goon,
But yt be seldom on the holyday,   35
Save, certeynly, whan that the month of May
Is comen, and that I here the foules synge,
And that the floures gynnen for to sprynge,
Farewel my bok, and my devocioun!
  Now have I thanne eek this condicioun,   40
That, of al the floures in the mede,
Thanne love I most thise floures white and
      rede,
Swiche as men callen daysyes in our toun.
To hem have I so gret affeccioun,
As I seyde erst, whanne comen is the May,   45
That in my bed ther daweth me no day
That I nam up and walkyng in the mede
To seen this flour ayein the sonne sprede,
Whan it upryseth erly by the morwe.
That blisful sighte softneth al my sorwe,   50
So glad am I, whan that I have presence
Of it, to doon it alle reverence,
As she that is of alle floures flour,
Fulfilled of al vertu and honour,
And evere ilyke faire, and fressh of hewe;
And I love it, and ever ylike newe,
And evere shal, til that myn herte dye.
Al swere I nat, of this I wol nat lye;
Ther loved no wight hotter in his lyve.
And whan that hit ys eve, I renne blyve,   60
As sone as evere the sonne gynneth weste,
To seen this flour, how it wol go to reste,
For fere of nyght, so hateth she derknesse.

Hire chere is pleynly sprad in the brightnesse

For that he say it nat of yore ago.
God wot, a thyng is nevere the lesse so,
Thow every wyght ne may it nat yse.   15
Bernard the monk ne say nat al, parde!
  Thanne mote we to bokes that we fynde,
Though whiche that olde thynges ben in
      mynde,
And to the doctryne of these olde wyse
Yeven credence, in every skylful wyse,   20
And trowen on these olde aproved storyes
Of holynesse, of regnes, of victoryes,
Of love, of hate, of othere sondry thynges,
Of which I may nat make rehersynges.
And if that olde bokes weren aweye,   25
Yloren were of remembrance the keye.
Wel oughte us thanne on olde bokes leve,
There as there is non other assay by preve.
  And as for me, though that my wit be lite,
On bokes for to rede I me delyte,   30
And in myn herte have hem in reverence,
And to hem yeve swich lust and swich credence
That there is wel unethe game non
That fro my bokes make me to gon,
But it be other upon the halyday,   35
Or ellis in the joly tyme of May,
Whan that I here the smale foules synge,
And that the floures gynne for to sprynge.
Farwel my stodye, as lastynge that sesoun!
  Now have I therto this condicioun,   40
That, of alle the floures in the mede,
Thanne love I most these floures white and
      rede,
Swyche as men calle dayesyes in oure toun.
To hem have I so gret affeccioun,
As I seyde erst, whan comen is the May,   45
That in my bed there daweth me no day
That I n'am up and walkynge in the mede
To sen these floures agen the sonne sprede,
Whan it up ryseth by the morwe shene,
The longe day thus walkynge in the grene.   50

And whan the sonne gynneth for to weste,
Thanne closeth it, and draweth it to reste,
So sore it is afered of the nyght,
Til on the morwe, that it is dayes lyght.
This dayesye, of alle floures flour,   55
Fulfyld of vertu and of alle honour,

Of the sonne, for ther yt wol unclose.   65
Allas, that I ne had Englyssh, ryme or prose,
Suffisant this flour to preyse aryght!
But helpeth, ye that han konnyng and myght,
Ye lovers that kan make of sentement;
In this cas oghte ye be diligent   70
To forthren me somwhat in my labour,
Whethir ye ben with the leef or with the flour.
For wel I wot that ye han her-biforn
Of makyng ropen, and lad awey the corn,
And I come after, glenyng here and there,   75
And am ful glad yf I may fynde an ere
Of any goodly word that ye han left.
And thogh it happen me rehercen eft
That ye han in your fresshe songes sayd,
Forbereth me, and beth nat evele apayd,   80
Syn that ye see I do yt in the honour
Of love, and eke in service of the flour
Whom that I serve as I have wit or myght.

[Cf. ll. 188–196, below]

She is the clernesse and the verray lyght   84
That in this derke world me wynt and ledeth.
The hert in-with my sorwfull brest yow dredeth
And loveth so sore that ye ben verrayly
The maistresse of my wit, and nothing I.
My word, my werk ys knyt so in youre bond
That, as an harpe obeieth to the hond   90
And maketh it soune after his fyngerynge,
Ryght so mowe ye oute of myn herte bringe
Swich vois, ryght as yow lyst, to laughe or
      pleyne.
Be ye my gide and lady sovereyne!
As to myn erthly god to yow I calle,   95
Bothe in this werk and in my sorwes alle.
   But wherfore that I spak, to yive credence
To olde stories and doon hem reverence,
And that men mosten more thyng beleve   99
Then men may seen at eye, or elles preve, —
That shal I seyn, whanne that I see my tyme;
I may not al at-ones speke in ryme.
My besy gost, that thursteth alwey newe
To seen this flour so yong, so fressh of hewe,
Constreyned me with so gledy desir   105
That in myn herte I feele yet the fir
That made me to ryse, er yt were day —

And evere ylike fayr and fresh of hewe,
As wel in wynter as in somer newe,
Fayn wolde I preysen, if I coude aryght;
But wo is me, it lyth nat in my myght!   60
For wel I wot that folk han here-beforn
Of makyng ropen, and lad awey the corn;
And I come after, glenynge here and there,
And am ful glad if I may fynde an ere
Of any goodly word that they han left.   65
And if it happe me rehersen eft
That they han in here freshe songes said,
I hope that they wole nat ben evele apayd,
Sith it is seyd in fortheryng and honour
Of hem that eyther serven lef or flour.   70
For trusteth wel, I ne have nat undertake
As of the lef agayn the flour to make,
Ne of the flour to make ageyn the lef,
No more than of the corn agen the shef,
For, as to me, is lefer non, ne lother.   75
I am witholde yit with never nother;
I not who serveth lef, ne who the flour.
That nys nothyng the entent of my labour.
For this werk is al of another tonne,
Of olde story, er swich strif was begonne.   80

   But wherfore that I spak, to yeve credence
To bokes olde and don hem reverence,
Is for men shulde autoritees beleve,
There as there lyth non other assay by preve.
For myn entent is, or I fro yow fare,   85
The naked text in English to declare
Of many a story, or elles of many a geste,
As autours seyn; leveth hem if yow leste!

And this was now the firste morwe of May —
With dredful hert and glad devocioun,
For to ben at the resureccioun   110
Of this flour, whan that yt shulde unclose
Agayn the sonne, that roos as red as rose,
That in the brest was of the beste, that day,
That Agenores doghtre ladde away.

[Cf. ll. 197–210, below]

And doun on knes anoon-ryght I me sette,   115
And, as I koude, this fresshe flour I grette,
Knelyng alwey, til it unclosed was,
Upon the smale, softe, swote gras,
That was with floures swote enbrouded al,
Of swich swetnesse and swich odour overal,   120
That, for to speke of gomme, or herbe, or tree,
Comparisoun may noon ymaked bee;
For yt surmounteth pleynly alle odoures,
And of riche beaute alle floures.
Forgeten hadde the erthe his pore estat   125
Of wynter, that hym naked made and mat,
And with his swerd of cold so sore greved;
Now hath th'atempre sonne all that releved,
That naked was, and clad him new agayn.
The smale foules, of the sesoun fayn,   130
That from the panter and the net ben scaped,
Upon the foweler, that hem made awhaped
In wynter, and distroyed hadde hire brood,
In his dispit hem thoghte yt did hem good
To synge of hym, and in hir song despise   135
The foule cherl that, for his coveytise,
Had hem betrayed with his sophistrye.
This was hire song, "The foweler we deffye,
And al his craft."   And somme songen clere
Layes of love, that joye it was to here,   140
In worship and in preysinge of hir make;
And for the newe blisful somers sake,
Upon the braunches ful of blosmes softe,
In hire delyt they turned hem ful ofte,
And songen, "Blessed be Seynt Valentyn,   145
For on this day I chees yow to be myn,
Withouten repentyng, myn herte swete!"
And therwithalle hire bekes gonnen meete,
Yeldyng honour and humble obeysaunces
To love, and diden hire other observaunces   150
That longeth onto love and to nature;
Construeth that as yow lyst, I do no cure.
And thoo that hadde doon unkyndenesse —

Whan passed was almost the month of May,
And I hadde romed, al the someres day,   90
The grene medewe, of which that I yow tolde,
Upon the freshe dayseie to beholde,
And that the sonne out of the south gan weste,
And closed was the flour, and gon to reste,
For derknesse of the nyght, of which she
      dredde,   95
Hom to myn hous ful swiftly I me spedde,
And in a lytel herber that I have,
Ybenched newe with turves, fresshe ygrave,
I bad men shulde me my couche make;
For deynte of the newe someres sake,   100
I bad hem strowe floures on my bed.
Whan I was layd, and hadde myn eyen hed,
I fel aslepe withinne an hour or two.
Me mette how I was in the medewe tho,
And that I romede in that same gyse,   105
To sen that flour, as ye han herd devyse.
Fayr was this medewe, as thoughte me, overal;
With floures sote enbrouded was it al.
As for to speke of gomme, or herbe, or tre,
Comparisoun may non ymaked be;   110
For it surmountede pleynly alle odoures,
And of ryche beaute alle floures.
Forgeten hadde the erthe his pore estat
Of wynter, that hym naked made and mat,
And with his swerd of cold so sore hadde
      greved.   115
Now hadde th'atempre sonne al that releved,
And clothed hym in grene al newe ageyn.
The smale foules, of the seson fayn,
That from the panter and the net ben skaped,
Upon the foulere, that hem made awhaped   120
In wynter, and distroyed hadde hire brod,
In his dispit hem thoughte it dide hem good
To synge of hym, and in here song despise
The foule cherl that for his coveytyse
Hadde hem betrayed with his sophistrye.   125
This was here song, "The foulere we defye."
Some songen [layes] on the braunches clere
Of love and [May], that joye it was to here,
In worshipe and in preysyng of hire make;
And for the newe blysful somers sake,   130
[They] sungen, "Blyssed be Seynt Valentyn!
For on his day I ches yow to be myn,
Withoute repentynge, myn herte swete!"
And therwithal here bekes gonne mete,
[Yelding] honour and humble obeysaunces;
And after diden othere observaunces   136
Ryht [longing] onto love and to nature;
So ech of hem [doth wel] to creature.
This song to herkenen I dide al myn entente,

As dooth the tydif, for newfangelnesse —
Besoghte mercy of hir trespassynge,   155
And humblely songen hire repentynge,
And sworen on the blosmes to be trewe,
So that hire makes wolde upon hem rewe,
And at the laste maden hire acord.
Al founde they Daunger for a tyme a lord,   160
Yet Pitee, thurgh his stronge gentil myght,
Forgaf, and made Mercy passen Ryght,
Thurgh innocence and ruled Curtesye.
But I ne clepe nat innocence folye,
Ne fals pitee, for vertu is the mene,   165
As Etik seith; in swich maner I mene.
And thus thise foweles, voide of al malice,
Acordeden to love, and laften vice
Of hate, and songen alle of oon acord,
"Welcome, somer, oure governour and lord!"   170
     And Zepherus and Flora gentilly   171
Yaf to the floures, softe and tenderly,
Hire swoote breth, and made hem for to
          sprede,
As god and goddesse of the floury mede;
In which me thoghte I myghte, day by day,
Duellen alwey, the joly month of May,   176
Withouten slep, withouten mete or drynke.
Adoun ful softely I gan to synke,
And lenynge on myn elbowe and my syde,
The longe day I shoop me for t'abide   180
For nothing elles, and I shal nat lye,
But for to loke upon the dayesie,
That wel by reson men it calle may
The "dayesye," or elles the "ye of day,"
The emperice and flour of floures alle.   185
I pray to God that faire mote she falle,
And alle that loven floures, for hire sake!
But natheles, ne wene nat that I make
In preysing of the flour agayn the leef,
No more than of the corn agayn the sheef;   190
For, as to me, nys lever noon ne lother.
I nam withholden yit with never nother;
Ne I not who serveth leef, ne who the flour.
Wel browken they her service or labour;
For this thing is al of another tonne,   195
Of olde storye, er swich stryf was begonne.
     Whan that the sonne out of the south gan
          weste,
And that this flour gan close and goon to reste
For derknesse of the nyght, the which she
          dredde,
Hom to myn hous ful swiftly I me spedde   200
To goon to reste, and erly for to ryse,
To seen this flour to sprede, as I devyse.
And in a litel herber that I have,
That benched was on turves fressh ygrave,

For-why I mette I wiste what they mente,   140

[Cf. ll. 71-80, above]

[Cf. ll. 93-106, above]

I bad men sholde me my couche make;   205
For deyntee of the newe someres sake,
I bad hem strawen floures on my bed.
Whan I was leyd, and had myn eyen hed,
I fel on slepe within an houre or twoo.
Me mette how I lay in the medewe thoo,   210
To seen this flour that I so love and drede;
And from afer com walkyng in the mede
The god of Love, and in his hand a quene,
And she was clad in real habit grene.
A fret of gold she hadde next her heer,   215
And upon that a whit corowne she beer
With flourouns smale, and I shal nat lye;
For al the world, ryght as a dayesye
Ycorouned ys with white leves lyte,   219
So were the flowrouns of hire coroune white.
For of o perle fyn, oriental,
Hire white coroune was ymaked al;
For which the white coroune above the grene
Made hire lyk a daysie for to sene,
Considered eke hir fret of gold above.   225
    Yclothed was this myghty god of Love
In silk, enbrouded ful of grene greves,
In-with a fret of rede rose-leves,
The fresshest syn the world was first bygonne.
His gilte heer was corowned with a sonne,   230
Instede of gold, for hevynesse and wyghte.
Therwith me thoghte his face shoon so bryghte
That wel unnethes myghte I him beholde;
And in his hand me thoghte I saugh him holde
Twoo firy dartes, as the gledes rede,   235
And aungelyke hys wynges saugh I sprede.
And al be that men seyn that blynd ys he,
Algate me thoghte that he myghte se;
For sternely on me he gan byholde,
So that his loking dooth myn herte colde.   240
And by the hand he held this noble quene,
Corowned with whit, and clothed al in grene,
So womanly, so benigne, and so meke,
That in this world, thogh that men wolde seke,
Half hire beaute shulde men nat fynde   245
In creature that formed ys by kynde.

[Cf. ll. 276-296, below]

Tyl at the laste a larke song above:
"I se," quod she, "the myghty god of Love.
Lo! yond he cometh! I se his wynges sprede."
Tho gan I loken endelong the mede,   144
And saw hym come, and in his hond a quene
Clothed in real habyt al of grene.
A fret of goold she hadde next hyre her
And upon that a whit corone she ber
With many floures, and I shal nat lye;
For al the world, ryght as the dayesye   150
Ycorouned is with white leves lite,
Swiche were the floures of hire coroune white.
For of o perle fyn and oryental
Hyre white coroun was ymaked al;
For which the white coroun above the grene
Made hire lyk a dayesye for to sene,   156
Considered ek the fret of gold above.
    Yclothed was this myghty god of Love
Of silk, ybrouded ful of grene greves,
A garlond on his hed of rose-leves,   160
Stiked al with lylye floures newe.
But of his face I can not seyn the hewe;
For sikerly his face shon so bryghte
That with the glem astoned was the syghte;
A furlong-wey I myhte hym not beholde.   165
But at the laste in hande I saw hym holde
Two firy dartes, as the gleedes rede,
And aungellych hys winges gan he sprede.
And al be that men seyn that blynd is he,
Algate me thoughte he myghte wel yse;   170
For sternely on me he gan beholde,
So that his lokynge doth myn herte colde.
And by the hond he held the noble quene,
Corouned with whit, and clothed al in grene,
So womanly, so benygne, and so meke,   175
That in this world, thogh that men wolde
    seke,
Half hire beaute shulde men nat fynde
In creature that formed is by kynde.
Hire name was Alceste the debonayre.
I preye to God that evere falle she fayre!   180
For ne hadde confort been of hire presence,
I hadde be ded, withouten any defence,
For dred of Loves wordes and his chere,
As, whan tyme is, hereafter ye shal here.
    Byhynde this god of Love, upon this grene,
I saw comynge of ladyes nyntene   186
In real habyt, a ful esy pas,
And after hem come of wemen swich a tras
That, syn that God Adam had mad of erthe,

And therfore may I seyn, as thynketh me,
This song in preysyng of this lady fre.

Balade

Hyd, Absolon, thy gilte tresses clere;
Ester, ley thou thy meknesse al adown;   250
Hyd, Jonathas, al thy frendly manere;
Penalopee and Marcia Catoun,
Make of youre wifhod no comparysoun;
Hyde ye youre beautes, Ysoude and Eleyne:
My lady cometh, that al this may disteyne.   255

Thy faire body, lat yt nat appere,
Lavyne; and thou, Lucresse of Rome toun,
And Polixene, that boghten love so dere,
And Cleopatre, with al thy passyoun,
Hyde ye your trouthe of love and your re-
            noun;   260
And thou, Tisbe, that hast for love swich peyne:
My lady cometh, that al this may disteyne.

Herro, Dido, Laudomia, alle yfere,
And Phillis, hangyng for thy Demophoun,
And Canace, espied by thy chere,   265
Ysiphile, betrayed with Jasoun,
Maketh of your trouthe neythir boost ne soun;
Nor Ypermystre or Adriane, ye tweyne:
My lady cometh, that al this may dysteyne.

This balade may ful wel ysongen be,   270
As I have seyd erst, by my lady free;
For certeynly al thise mowe nat suffise
To apperen wyth my lady in no wyse.
For as the sonne wole the fyr disteyne,
So passeth al my lady sovereyne,   275
That ys so good, so faire, so debonayre,
I prey to God that ever falle hire faire!
For, nadde comfort ben of hire presence,
I hadde ben ded, withouten any defence,
For drede of Loves wordes and his chere,   280
As, when tyme ys, herafter ye shal here.

The thridde part, of wemen, ne the ferthe,   190
Ne wende I not by possibilite
Hadden evere in this wyde world ybe;
And trewe of love these wemen were echon.

Now whether was that a wonder thyng, or
            non,
That ryght anon as that they gonne espye   195
This flour, which that I clepe the dayesye,
Ful sodeynly they stynten alle atones,
And knelede adoun, as it were for the nones.
And after that they wenten in compas,
Daunsynge aboute this flour an esy pas,   200
And songen, as it were in carole-wyse,
This balade, which that I shal yow devyse.

Balade

Hyd, Absalon, thy gilte tresses clere;
Ester, ley thow thy meknesse al adoun;
Hyd, Jonathas, al thyn frendly manere;   205
Penelope and Marcia Catoun,
Mak of youre wyfhod no comparisoun;
Hyde ye youre beautes, Ysoude and Eleyne:
Alceste is here, that al that may desteyne.

Thy fayre body, lat it nat apeere,   210
Laveyne; and thow, Lucresse of Rome toun,
And Polixene, that boughte love so dere,
Ek Cleopatre, with al thy passioun,
Hide ye youre trouth in love and youre renoun;
And thow, Tysbe, that hast for love swich
            peyne: 215
Alceste is here, that al that may desteyne.

Herro, Dido, Laodomya, alle in-fere,
Ek Phillis, hangynge for thy Demophoun,
And Canace, espied by thy chere,
Ysiphile, betrayed with Jasoun,   220
Mak of youre trouthe in love no bost ne soun;
Nor Ypermystre or Adriane, ne pleyne:
Alceste is here, that al that may disteyne.

Whan that this balade al ysongen was,

[Cf. ll. 179–198, above]

Behynde this god of Love, upon the grene,
I saugh comyng of ladyes nyntene,
In real habit, a ful esy paas, 284
And after hem coome of wymen swich a traas
That, syn that God Adam hadde mad of erthe,
The thridde part, of mankynde, or the ferthe,
Ne wende I not by possibilitee
Had ever in this wide world ybee; 289
And trewe of love thise women were echon.
  Now wheither was that a wonder thing, or non,
That ryght anoon as that they gonne espye
Thys flour, which that I clepe the dayesie,
Ful sodeynly they stynten al attones,
And kneled doun, as it were for the nones, 295
And songen with o vois, "Heel and honour
To trouthe of womanhede, and to this flour
That bereth our alder pris in figurynge!
Hire white corowne bereth the witnessynge."
And with that word, a-compas enviroun, 300
They setten hem ful softely adoun.
First sat the god of Love, and syth his quene
With the white corowne, clad in grene,
And sithen al the remenaunt by and by,
As they were of estaat, ful curteysly; 305
Ne nat a word was spoken in the place
The mountaunce of a furlong wey of space.
  I, knelyng by this flour, in good entente,
Abood to knowen what this peple mente,
As stille as any ston; til at the laste 310
This god of Love on me hys eyen caste,
And seyde, "Who kneleth there?" and I answerde
Unto his askynge, whan that I it herde,
And seyde, "Sir, it am I," and com him ner,
And salwed him. Quod he, "What dostow her
So nygh myn oune floure, so boldely? 316
Yt were better worthy, trewely,
A worm to neghen ner my flour than thow."
"And why, sire," quod I, "and yt lyke yow?"
"For thow," quod he, "art therto nothing able.
Yt is my relyke, digne and delytable, 321
And thow my foo, and al my folk werreyest,
And of myn olde servauntes thow mysseyest,
And hynderest hem with thy translacioun,
And lettest folk from hire devocioun 325
To serve me, and holdest it folye
To serve Love. Thou maist yt nat denye,
For in pleyn text, withouten nede of glose,
Thou hast translated the Romaunce of the Rose,
That is an heresye ayeins my lawe, 330
And makest wise folk fro me withdrawe;

Upon the softe and sote grene gras 225
They setten hem ful softely adoun,
By order alle in compas, enveroun.
Fyrst sat the god of Love, and thanne this queene
With the white corone, clad in grene,
And sithen al the remenant by and by, 230
As they were of degre, ful curteysly;
Ne nat a word was spoken in that place
The mountaunce of a furlong-wey of space.
  I, lenynge faste by under a bente,
Abod to knowe what this peple mente, 235
As stille as any ston, til at the laste
The god of Love on me his eye caste
And seyde "Who restith there?" and I answerde
Unto his axynge, whan that I hym herde
And seyde, "Sire, it am I," and cam hym ner, 240
And salewede hym. Quod he, "What dost thow her
In my presence, and that so boldely? 241
For it were better worthi, trewely,
A worm to comen in my syght than thow."
"And why, sire," quod I, "and it lyke yow?" 245
"For thow," quod he, "art therto nothyng able.
My servaunts ben alle wyse and honourable.
Thow art my mortal fo and me werreyest,
And of myne olde servauntes thow mysseyest,
And hynderest hem with thy translacyoun, 250
And lettest folk to han devocyoun
To serven me, and holdest it folye
To truste on me. Thow mayst it nat denye,
For in pleyn text, it nedeth nat to glose,
Thow hast translated the Romauns of the Rose,
That is an heresye ageyns my lawe, 256
And makest wise folk fro me withdrawe;

And of Creseyde thou hast seyd as the lyste,
That maketh men to wommen lasse triste,
That ben as trewe as ever was any steel.
Of thyn answere avise the ryght weel;   335

And thynkest in thy wit, that is ful col,
That he nys but a verray propre fol
That loveth paramours, to harde and hote.   260
Wel wot I therby thow begynnyst dote
As olde foles, whan here spiryt fayleth;
Thanne blame they folk, and wite nat what hem
    ayleth.
Hast thow nat mad in Englysh ek the bok
How that Crisseyde Troylus forsok,   265
In shewynge how that wemen han don mis?
But natheles, answere me now to this,
Why noldest thow as wel han seyd goodnesse
Of wemen, as thow hast seyd wikednesse?
Was there no good matere in thy mynde,   270
Ne in alle thy bokes me coudest thow nat fynde
Som story of wemen that were goode and
    trewe?
Yis, God wot, sixty bokes olde and newe
Hast thow thyself, alle ful of storyes grete,
That bothe Romayns and ek Grekes trete   275
Of sundry wemen, which lyf that they ladde,
And evere an hundred goode ageyn oon badde.
This knoweth God, and alle clerkes eke,
That usen swiche materes for to seke.
What seith Valerye, Titus, or Claudyan?   280
What seith Jerome agayns Jovynyan?
How clene maydenes, and how trewe wyves,
How stedefaste widewes durynge alle here
    lyves,
Telleth Jerome, and that nat of a fewe,
But, I dar seyn, an hundred on a rewe;   285
That it is pite for to rede, and routhe,
The wo that they endure for here trouthe.
For to hyre love were they so trewe
That, rathere than they wolde take a newe,
They chose to be ded in sondry wyse,   290
And deiden, as the story wol devyse;
And some were brend, and some were cut the
    hals,
And some dreynt, for they wolden not be fals.
For alle keped they here maydenhede,
Or elles wedlok, or here widewehede.   295
And this thing was nat kept for holynesse,
But al for verray vertu and clennesse,
And for men schulde sette on hem no lak;
And yit they were hethene, al the pak,
That were so sore adrad of alle shame.   300
These olde wemen kepte so here name
That in this world I trowe men shal nat fynde
A man that coude be so trewe and kynde
As was the leste woman in that tyde.
What seyth also the epistel of Ovyde   305
Of trewe wyves and of here labour?
What Vincent in his Estoryal Myrour?

Ek al the world of autours maystow here,
Cristene and hethene, trete of swich matere;
It nedeth nat al day thus for to endite.   310
But yit, I seye, what eyleth the to wryte
The draf of storyes, and forgete the corn?
By Seynt Venus, of whom that I was born,
Althogh thow reneyed hast my lay,
As othere olde foles many a day,   315

For thogh thou reneyed hast my lay,
As other wrecches han doon many a day,
By Seynt Venus, that my moder ys,
If that thou lyve, thou shalt repenten this
So cruelly that it shal wel be sene!"   340
Thoo spak this lady, clothed al in grene,
And seyde, "God, ryght of youre curtesye,
Ye moten herken yf he can replye
Agayns al this that ye have to him meved.
A god ne sholde nat thus be agreved,   345
But of hys deitee he shal be stable,
And therto gracious and merciable.
And yf ye nere a god, that knowen al,
Thanne myght yt be as I yow tellen shal:
This man to yow may falsly ben accused,   350
Ther as by right him oughte ben excused.
For in youre court ys many a losengeour,
And many a queynte totelere accusour,
That tabouren in youre eres many a sown,
Ryght after hire ymagynacioun,   355
To have youre daliance, and for envie.
Thise ben the causes, and I shal not lye.
Envie ys lavendere of the court alway,
For she ne parteth, neither nyght ne day,   359
Out of the hous of Cesar; thus seith Dante;
Whoso that gooth, algate she wol nat wante.
[Cf. ll. 350–351, above]

And eke, peraunter, for this man ys nyce,
He myghte doon yt, gessyng no malice,
But for he useth thynges for to make;
Hym rekketh noght of what matere he take.

Or him was boden maken thilke tweye   366
Of som persone, and durste yt nat withseye;
Or him repenteth outrely of this.
He ne hath nat doon so grevously amys,
To translaten that olde clerkes writen,   370
As thogh that he of malice wolde enditen
Despit of love, and had himself yt wroght.
This sholde a ryghtwis lord have in his thoght,
And nat be lyk tirauntz of Lumbardye,
That han no reward but at tyrannye,   375
For he that kynge or lord ys naturel,
Hym oghte nat be tiraunt ne crewel,
As is a fermour, to doon the harm he kan.
He moste thinke yt is his lige man,

Thow shalt repente it, so that it shal be sene!"
Thanne spak Alceste, the worthyeste queene,
And seyde, "God, ryght of youre curteysye,
Ye moten herkenen if he can replye
Ageyns these poynts that ye han to hym meved.
A god ne sholde not thus been agreved,   321
But of his deite he shal be stable,
And therto ryghtful, and ek mercyable.
He shal nat ryghtfully his yre wreke,
Or he have herd the tother partye speke.   325
Al ne is nat gospel that is to yow pleyned;
The god of Love hereth many a tale yfeyned.
For in youre court is many a losengeour,
And many a queynte totelere accusour,
That tabouren in youre eres many a thyng   330
For hate, or for jelous ymagynyng,
And for to han with you som dalyaunce.
Envye — I preye to God yeve hire mys-
      chaunce! —
Is lavender in the grete court alway,
For she ne parteth, neyther nyght ne day,   335
Out of the hous of Cesar; thus seyth Dante;
Whoso that goth, alwey she mot nat wante.
This man to yow may wrongly ben acused,
There as by ryght hym oughte ben excusid.
Or elles, sire, for that this man is nyce,   340
He may translate a thyng in no malyce,
But for he useth bokes for to make,
And taketh non hed of what matere he take,
Therfore he wrot the Rose and ek Crisseyde
Of innocence, and nyste what he seyde.   345
Or hym was boden make thilke tweye
Of som persone, and durste it not withseye;
For he hath write many a bok er this.
He ne hath not don so grevously amys
To translate that olde clerkes wryte,   350
As thogh that he of maleys wolde endyte
Despit of love, and hadde hymself ywrought.
This shulde a ryghtwys lord han in his thought,
And not ben lyk tyraunts of Lumbardye,
That usen wilfulhed and tyrannye.   355
For he that kyng or lord is naturel,
Hym oughte nat be tyraunt and crewel,
As is a fermour, to don the harm he can.
He moste thynke it is his lige man,

And is his tresour, and his gold in cofre.   380
This is the sentence of the philosophre,
A kyng to kepe his liges in justice;
Withouten doute, that is his office.

Al wol he kepe his lordes hire degree,
As it ys ryght and skilful that they bee   385
Enhaunced and honoured, and most dere —
For they ben half-goddes in this world here —
Yit mot he doon bothe ryght, to poore and
     ryche,
Al be that hire estaat be nat yliche,
And han of poore folk compassyoun.   390
For loo, the gentil kynde of the lyoun!
For whan a flye offendeth him or biteth,
He with his tayl awey the flye smyteth
Al esely; for, of hys genterye,
Hym deyneth not to wreke hym on a flye,   395
As dooth a curre, or elles another best.
In noble corage ought ben arest,
And weyen every thing by equytee,
And ever have reward to his owen degree.
For, syr, yt is no maistrye for a lord   400
To dampne a man without answere of word,
And, for a lord, that is ful foul to use.
And if so be he may hym nat excuse,
But asketh mercy with a sorweful herte,
And profereth him, ryght in his bare sherte,
To ben ryght at your owen jugement,   406
Than oght a god, by short avysement,
Consydre his owne honour and hys trespas.
For, syth no cause of deth lyeth in this caas,
Yow oghte to ben the lyghter merciable;   410
Leteth youre ire, and beth sumwhat tretable.
The man hath served yow of his kunnynge,
And furthred wel youre lawe in his makynge.

Al be hit that he kan nat wel endite,
Yet hath he maked lewed folk delyte   415
To serve yow, in preysinge of your name.
He made the book that hight the Hous of
     Fame,
And eke the Deeth of Blaunche the Duchesse,
And the Parlement of Foules, as I gesse,
And al the love of Palamon and Arcite   420
Of Thebes, thogh the storye ys knowen lyte;
And many an ympne for your halydayes,
That highten balades, roundels, virelayes;

And that hym oweth, of verray duetee,   360
Shewen his peple pleyn benygnete,
And wel to heren here excusacyouns,
And here compleyntes and petyciouns,
In duewe tyme, whan they shal it profre.
This is the sentence of the philosophre,   365
A kyng to kepe his lyges in justice;
Withouten doute, that is his office.
And therto is a kyng ful depe ysworn
Ful many an hundred wynter herebeforn;
And for to kepe his lordes hir degre,   370
As it is ryght and skylful that they be
Enhaunsed and honoured, and most dere —
For they ben half-goddes in this world here —
This shal be don bothe to pore and ryche,
Al be that her estat be nat alyche,   375
And han of pore folk compassioun.
For lo, the gentyl kynde of the lyoun!
For whan a flye offendeth hym or byteth,
He with his tayl awey the flye smyteth
Al esyly; for, of his genterye,   380
Hym deyneth nat to wreke hym on a flye,
As doth a curre, or elles another best.
In noble corage oughte ben arest,
And weyen every thing by equite,
And evere han reward to his owen degre.   385
For, sire, it is no maystrye for a lord
To dampne a man withoute answere of word,
And, for a lord, that is ful foul to use.
And if so be he may hym nat excuse,
But axeth mercy with a sorweful herte,   390
And profereth hym, ryght in his bare sherte,
To been ryght at youre owene jugement,
Than ought a god, by short avisement,
Considere his owene honour and his trespas.
For syth no cause of deth lyth in this cas,   395
Yow oughte to ben the lyghter merciable;
Leteth youre yre, and beth somwhat tretable.
The man hath served yow of this konnynge,
And forthered wel youre lawe with his mak-
     ynge.
Whil he was yong, he kepte youre estat;   400
I not wher he be now a renegat.
But wel I wot, with that he can endyte
He hath maked lewed folk delyte
To serven yow, in preysynge of youre name.
He made the bok that highte the Hous of
     Fame,   405
And ek the Deth of Blaunche the Duchesse,
And the Parlement of Foules, as I gesse,
And al the love of Palamon and Arcite
Of Thebes, thogh the storye is knowen lite;
And many an ympne for youre halydayes,   410
That highten balades, roundeles, vyrelayes;

And, for to speke of other holynesse,
He hath in prose translated Boece,   425

And maad the lyf also of Seynt Cecile.
He made also, goon ys a gret while,
Origenes upon the Maudeleyne.
Hym oughte now to have the lesse peyne;
He hath maad many a lay and many a thing.
    Now as ye be a god, and eke a kyng,   431
I, your Alceste, whilom quene of Trace,
Y aske yow this man, ryght of your grace,
That ye him never hurte in al his lyve,
And he shal sweren to yow, and that as blyve,
He shal no more agilten in this wyse,   436
But he shal maken, as ye wol devyse,
Of wommen trewe in lovyng al hire lyve,
Wherso ye wol, of mayden or of wyve,
And forthren yow, as muche as he mysseyde
Or in the Rose or elles in Creseyde."   441
    The god of Love answerede hire thus anoon:
"Madame," quod he, "it is so long agoon
That I yow knew so charitable and trewe,
That never yit, syn that the world was newe,
To me ne fond y better noon than yee.   446
If that I wol save my degree,
I may, ne wol, nat werne your requeste.
Al lyeth in yow, dooth wyth hym what yow
    leste;
I al foryeve, withouten lenger space;   450
For whoso yeveth a yifte, or dooth a grace,
Do it by tyme, his thank ys wel the more.
And demeth ye what he shal doo therfore.
Goo thanke now my lady here," quod he.
    I roos, and doun I sette me on my knee,   455
And seyde thus, "Madame, the God above
Foryelde yow, that ye the god of Love
Han maked me his wrathe to foryive,
And yeve me grace so longe for to lyve,
That I may knowe soothly what ye bee,   460
That han me holpe and put in this degree.
But trewly I wende, as in this cas,
Naught have agilt, ne doon to love trespas.
For-why a trewe man, withouten drede,
Hath nat to parten with a theves dede;   465
Ne a trewe lover oght me not to blame,
Thogh that I speke a fals lovere som shame.
They oghte rather with me for to holde,
For that I of Creseyde wroot or tolde,
Or of the Rose; what so myn auctour mente,
Algate, God woot, yt was myn entente   471
To forthren trouthe in love and yt cheryce,
And to ben war fro falsnesse and fro vice

And, for to speke of other besynesse,
He hath in prose translated Boece,
And of the Wreched Engendrynge of Man-
    kynde,
As man may in pope Innocent yfynde;   415
And mad the lyf also of Seynt Cecile.
He made also, gon is a gret while,
Orygenes upon the Maudeleyne.
Hym oughte now to have the lesse peyne;
He hath mad many a lay and many a thyng.
    Now as ye ben a god, and ek a kyng,   421
I, youre Alceste, whilom quene of Trace,
I axe yow this man, ryght of youre grace,
That ye hym nevere hurte in al his lyve;
And he shal swere to yow, and that as blyve,
He shal no more agilten in this wyse,   426
But he shal maken, as ye wol devyse,
Of women trewe in lovynge al here lyve,
Wherso ye wol, of mayden or of wyve,
And fortheren yow, as muche as he mysseyde
Or in the Rose or elles in Crisseyde."   431
    The god of Love answerede hire thus anon:
"Madame," quod he, "it is so longe agon
That I yow knew so charytable and trewe,
That nevere yit, sith that the world was newe,
To me ne fond I betere non than ye;   436
That, if that I wol save my degre,
I may, ne wol, not warne youre requeste.
Al lyth in yow, doth with hym what yow
    leste;
And al foreyve, withoute lenger space.   440
For whoso yeveth a yifte, or doth a grace,
Do it by tyme, his thank is wel the more.
And demeth ye what he shal do therfore.
Go thanke now my lady here," quod he.
    I ros, and doun I sette me on my kne,   445
And seyde thus, "Madame, the God above
Foryelde yow, that ye the god of Love
Han maked me his wrathe to foryive,
And yeve me grace so longe for to live,
That I may knowe sothly what ye be,   450
That han me holpen and put in swich degre.
But trewely I wende, as in this cas,
Naught have agilt, ne don to love trespas.
For-why a trewe man, withoute drede,
Hath nat to parte with a theves dede;   455
Ne a trewe lovere oghte me nat to blame,
Thogh that I speke a fals lovere som shame.
They oughte rathere with me for to holde,
For that I of Crisseyde wrot or tolde,
Or of the Rose; what so myn auctour mente,
Algate, God wot, it was myn entente   461
To forthere trouthe in love and it cheryce,
And to be war fro falsnesse and fro vice

By swich ensample; this was my menynge."
And she answerde, "Lat be thyn arguynge,   475
For Love ne wol nat countrepleted be
In ryght ne wrong; and lerne that at me!
Thow hast thy grace, and hold the ryght therto.
Now wol I seyn what penance thou shalt do
For thy trespas, and understonde yt here: 480
Thow shalt, while that thou lyvest, yer by yere,
The moste partye of thy tyme spende
In makyng of a glorious legende
Of goode wymmen, maydenes and wyves,
That weren trewe in lovyng al hire lyves;   485
And telle of false men that hem bytraien,
That al hir lyf ne do nat but assayen
How many women they may doon a shame;
For in youre world that is now holde a game.
And thogh the lyke nat a lovere bee,   490
Speke wel of love; this penance yive I thee.
And to the god of Love I shal so preye
That he shal charge his servantz, by any weye,
To forthren thee, and wel thy labour quyte.
Goo now thy wey, this penaunce ys but
     lyte.   495
And whan this book ys maad, yive it the quene,
On my byhalf, at Eltham or at Sheene."
    The god of Love gan smyle, and than he
     sayde:
"Wostow," quod he, "wher this be wyf or
     mayde,
Or queene, or countesse, or of what degre,   500
That hath so lytel penance yiven thee,
That hast deserved sorer for to smerte?
But pite renneth soone in gentil herte;
That maistow seen, she kytheth what she ys."
And I answered, "Nay, sire, so have I blys,   505
No moore but that I see wel she is good."
"That is a trewe tale, by myn hood!"
Quod Love, "and that thou knowest wel, par-
     dee,
If yt be so that thou avise the.
Hastow nat in a book, lyth in thy cheste,   510
The grete goodnesse of the quene Alceste,
That turned was into a dayesye;
She that for hire housbonde chees to dye,
And eke to goon to helle, rather than he,
And Ercules rescowed hire, parde,   515
And broght hir out of helle agayn to blys?"
And I answerd ageyn, and sayde, "Yis,
Now knowe I hire. And is this good Alceste,
The dayesie, and myn owene hertes reste?
Now fele I weel the goodnesse of this wyf,   520
That both aftir hir deth and in hir lyf
Hir grete bounte doubleth hire renoun.
Wel hath she quyt me myn affeccioun,

By swich ensaumple; this was my menynge."
    And she answerde, "Lat be thyn arguynge,
For Love ne wol nat counterpletyd be   466
In ryght ne wrong; and lerne this at me!
Thow hast thy grace, and hold the ryght therto.
Now wol I seyn what penaunce thow shalt do
For thy trespas, and understond it here: 470
Thow shalt, whil that thow livest, yer by yere,
The moste partye of thy tyme spende
In makynge of a gloryous legende
Of goode women, maydenes and wyves,
That were trewe in lovynge al here lyves;   475
And telle of false men that hem betrayen,
That al here lyf ne don nat but assayen
How manye wemen they may don a shame;
For in youre world that is now holden game.
And thogh the lesteth nat a lovere be,   480
Spek wel of love; this penaunce yeve I thee.
And to the god of Love I shal so preye
That he shal charge his servaunts, by any weye,
To fortheren the, and wel thy labour quite.
Go now thy wey, thy penaunce is but
     lyte."   485
    The god of Love gan smyle, and thanne he
     seyde:
"Wostow," quod he, "wher this be wif or
     mayde,
Or queen, or countesse, or of what degre,
That hath so lytel penaunce yiven the,
That hast deserved sorer for to smerte?   490
But pite renneth sone in gentil herte;
That mayst thow sen, she kytheth what she is."
And I answerde, "Nay, sire, so have I blys,
No more but that I se wel she is good."
"That is a trewe tale, by myn hood!"   495
Quod Love, "and that thow knowest wel,
     parde,
Yif it be so that thow avise the.
Hast thow nat in a bok, lyth in thy cheste,
The grete goodnesse of the queene Alceste,
That turned was into a dayesye;   500
She that for hire husbonde ches to dye,
And ek to gon to helle rather than he,
And Ercules rescued hire, parde,
And broughte hyre out of helle ageyn to blys?"
And I answerde ayen, and seyde, "Yis,   505
Now knowe I hire. And is this goode Alceste,
The dayesye, and myn owene hertes reste?
Now fele I wel the goodnesse of this wif,
That bothe after hire deth and in hire lyf
Hire grete bounte doubleth hire renoun.   510
Wel hath she quit me myn affeccioun,

That I have to hire flour, the dayesye.
No wonder ys thogh Jove hire stellyfye,   525
As telleth Agaton, for hire goodnesse!
Hire white corowne berith of hyt witnesse;
For also many vertues hadde shee
As smale florouns in hire corowne bee.
In remembraunce of hire and in honour   530
Cibella maade the daysye and the flour
Ycrowned al with whit, as men may see;
And Mars yaf to hire corowne reed, pardee,
In stede of rubyes, sette among the white."
  Therwith this queene wex reed for shame a
    lyte,   535
Whan she was preysed so in hire presence.
Thanne seyde Love, "A ful gret necli-
    gence
Was yt to the, that ylke tyme thou made
'Hyd, Absolon, thy tresses,' in balade,
That thou forgate hire in thi song to sette,   540
Syn that thou art so gretly in hire dette,
And wost so wel that kalender ys shee
To any woman that wol lover bee.
For she taught al the craft of fyn lov-
    ynge,
And namely of wyfhod the lyvynge,   545
And al the boundes that she oghte kepe.
Thy litel wit was thilke tyme aslepe.
But now I charge the, upon thy lyf,
That in thy legende thou make of thys wyf,
Whan thou hast other smale ymaad before;   550
And far now wel, I charge the namore.
But er I goo, thus muche I wol the telle:
Ne shal no trewe lover come in helle.
Thise other ladies sittynge here arowe   554
Ben in thy balade, yf thou kanst hem knowe,
And in thy bookes alle thou shalt hem fynde.
Have hem now in thy legende al in mynde;
I mene of hem that ben in thy knowynge.
For here ben twenty thousand moo sittynge
Than thou knowest, goode wommen alle,   560
And trewe of love, for oght that may byfalle.
Make the metres of hem as the lest —
I mot goon hom (the sonne draweth west)
To paradys, with al this companye —
And serve alwey the fresshe dayesye.
At Cleopatre I wol that thou begynne,   565
And so forth, and my love so shal thou wynne.
For lat see now what man that lover be,
Wol doon so strong a peyne for love as she.
I wot wel that thou maist nat al yt ryme,   570
That swiche lovers diden in hire tyme;
It were to long to reden and to here.
Suffiseth me thou make in this manere,
That thou reherce of al hir lyf the grete,

That I have to hire flour, the dayesye.
No wonder is thogh Jove hire stellifye,
As telleth Agaton, for hyre goodnesse!   515
Hire white coroun bereth of it witnesse;
For also manye vertues hadde she
As smale flourys in hyre coroun be.
In remembraunce of hire and in honour
Cibella made the dayesye and the flour
Ycoroned al with whit, as men may se;   520
And Mars yaf to hire corone red, parde,
In stede of rubies, set among the white."
  Therwith this queene wex red for shame a
    lyte,
Whan she was preysed so in hire presence.   524
Thanne seyde Love, "A ful gret neglygence
Was it to the, to write unstedefastnesse
Of women, sith thow knowest here goodnesse
By pref, and ek by storyes herebyforn.
Let be the chaf, and writ wel of the corn.
Why noldest thow han writen of Alceste,   530
And laten Criseide ben aslepe and reste?
For of Alceste shulde thy wrytynge be,
Syn that thow wost that calandier is she
Of goodnesse, for she taughte of fyn lovynge,
And namely of wifhod the lyvynge,   535
And alle the boundes that she oughte kepe.
Thy litel wit was thilke tyme aslepe.
But now I charge the, upon thy lyf,
That in thy legende thow make of this wif,
Whan thow hast othere smale mad byfore;   540
And far now wel, I charge the no more.

At Cleopatre I wol that thow begynne,
And so forth, and my love so shalt thow
    wynne."

After thise olde auctours lysten for to trete. 575
For whoso shal so many a storye telle,
Sey shortly, or he shal to longe dwelle."
And with that word my bokes gan I take,
And ryght thus on my Legende gan I make.

And with that word, of slep I gan awake,
And ryght thus on my Legende gan I make. 545

Explicit prohemium.

I

THE LEGEND OF CLEOPATRA

Incipit legenda Cleopatrie, Martiris, Egipti regine.

After the deth of Tholome the kyng, 580
That al Egipt hadde in his governyng,
Regned his queene Cleopataras;
Tyl on a tyme befel there swich a cas,
That out of Rome was sent a senatour,
For to conqueren regnes and honour 585
Unto the toun of Rome, as was usaunce,
To han the world at hire obeÿsaunce,
And soth to seyne, Antonius was his name.
So fil it, as Fortune hym oughte a shame,
Whan he was fallen in prosperite, 590
Rebel unto the toun of Rome is he.
And over al this, the suster of Cesar,
He lafte hire falsly, or that she was war,
And wolde algates han another wyf;
For which he tok with Rome and Cesar stryf.
Natheles, for sothe, this ilke senatour 596
Was a ful worthy gentil werreyour,
And of his deth it was ful gret damage.
But love hadde brought this man in swich a
        rage,
And hym so narwe bounden in his las, 600
Al for the love of Cleopataras,
That al the world he sette at no value.
Hym thoughte there nas nothyng to hym so
        due
As Cleopatras for to love and serve;
Hym roughte nat in armes for to sterve 605
In the defence of hyre and of hire ryght.
This noble queene ek lovede so this knyght,
Thourgh his desert, and for his chyvalrye;
As certeynly, but if that bokes lye,
He was, of persone and of gentillesse, 610
And of discrecioun and hardynesse,
Worthi to any wyght that liven may;
And she was fayr as is the rose in May.

And, for to make shortly is the beste,
She wax his wif, and hadde hym as hire leste.
    The weddynge and the feste to devyse, 616
To me, that have ytake swich empryse
Of so many a story for to make,
It were to longe, lest that I shulde slake
Of thyng that bereth more effect and charge;
For men may overlade a ship or barge. 621
And forthy to th'effect thanne wol I skyppe,
And al the remenaunt, I wol lete it slippe.
    Octovyan, that wod was of this dede,
Shop hym an ost on Antony to lede 625
Al uterly for his destruccioun.
With stoute Romeyns, crewel as lyoun,
To ship they wente, and thus I lat hem sayle.
Antonius was war, and wol nat fayle
To meten with these Romeyns, if he may; 630
Tok ek his red, and bothe, upon a day,
His wif and he, and al his ost, forth wente
To shipe anon, no lengere they ne stente;
And in the se it happede hem to mete.
Up goth the trompe, and for to shoute and
        shete, 635
And peynen hem to sette on with the sunne.
With grysely soun out goth the grete gonne,
And heterly they hurtelen al atones,
And from the top doun come the grete stones.
In goth the grapenel, so ful of crokes; 640
Among the ropes renne the sherynge-hokes.
In with the polax preseth he and he;
Byhynde the mast begynnyth he to fle,
And out ageyn, and dryveth hym overbord;
He styngeth hym upon his speres ord; 645
He rent the seyl with hokes lyke a sithe;
He bryngeth the cuppe, and biddeth hem be
        blythe;

He poureth pesen upon the haches slidere;
With pottes ful of lyme they gon togidere;
And thus the longe day in fyght they spende,
Tyl at the laste, as every thyng hath ende,   651
Antony is schent, and put hym to the flyghte,
And al his folk to-go, that best go myghte.

Fleth ek the queen, with al hire purpre sayl,
For strokes, whiche that wente as thikke as
    hayl;   655
No wonder was she myghte it nat endure.
And whan that Antony saw that aventure,
"Allas," quod he, "the day that I was born!
My worshipe in this day thus have I lorn."
And for dispeyr out of his wit he sterte,   660
And rof hymself anon thourghout the herte,
Or that he ferther wente out of the place.
His wif, that coude of Cesar have no grace,
To Egipt is fled for drede and for destresse.
But herkeneth, ye that speken of kyndenesse,
Ye men that falsly sweren many an oth   666
That ye wol deye, if that youre love be wroth,
Here may ye sen of wemen which a trouthe!
This woful Cleopatre hath mad swich routhe
That ther is tonge non that may it telle.   670
But on the morwe she wolde no lengere dwelle,
But made hire subtyl werkmen make a shryne
Of alle the rubyes and the stones fyne
In al Egypte, that she coude espie,
And putte ful the shryne of spicerye,   675
And let the cors enbaume, and forth she fette
This dede cors, and in the shryne it shette.

And next the shryne a pit thanne doth she
    grave,
And alle the serpentes that she myghte have,
She putte hem in that grave, and thus she
    seyde: 680
"Now, love, to whom my sorweful herte obeyde
So ferforthly that from that blisful houre
That I yow swor to ben al frely youre —
I mene yow, Antonius, my knyght —
That nevere wakynge, in the day or nyght,   685
Ye nere out of myn hertes remembraunce,
For wel or wo, for carole or for daunce;
And in myself this covenaunt made I tho,
That ryght swich as ye felten, wel or wo,
As fer forth as it in my power lay,   690
Unreprovable unto my wyfhod ay,
The same wolde I fele, lyf or deth, —
And thilke covenant, whil me lasteth breth,
I wol fulfille; and that shal ben wel sene,   694
Was nevere unto hire love a trewer quene."
And with that word, naked, with ful good herte,
Among the serpents in the pit she sterte,
And there she ches to have hire buryinge.
Anon the nadderes gonne hire for to stynge,
And she hire deth receyveth with good cheere,
For love of Antony that was hire so dere.   701
And this is storyal soth, it is no fable.
Now, or I fynde a man thus trewe and stable,
And wol for love his deth so frely take,
I preye God let oure hedes nevere ake!
    Amen.   705

Explicit Legenda Cleopatre, martiris.

II

THE LEGEND OF THISBE

Incipit Legenda Tesbe Babilonie, martiris.

At Babiloyne whylom fil it thus,
The whyche toun the queen Semyramus
Let dychen al aboute, and walles make
Ful hye, of hard tiles wel ybake:
There were dwellyng in this noble toun   710
Two lordes, whiche that were of gret renoun,
And woneden so nygh, upon a grene,
That there nas but a ston-wal hem betweene,

As ofte in grete tounes is the wone.
And, soth to seyne, that o man hadde a sone,
Of al that lond oon of the lustyeste.   716
That other hadde a doughter, the fayreste
That tho was in that lond estward dwellynge.
The name of everych gan to other sprynge
By women that were neighebores aboute.   720
For in that contre yit, withouten doute,

Maydenes been ykept, for jelosye,
Ful streyte, lest they diden som folye.
This yonge man was called Piramus,   724
And Tysbe hight the maide, Naso seyth thus;
And thus by report was hire name yshove
That, as they wex in age, wex here love.
And certeyn, as by resoun of hire age,
There myghte have ben bytwixe hem maryage,
But that here fadres nolde it nat assente;   730
And bothe in love ylyke sore they brente,
That non of alle hyre frendes myght it lette,
But pryvyly som tyme yit they mette
By sleyghte, and spoken som of here desyr;
As, wry the glede, and hotter is the fyr;   735
Forbede a love, and it is ten so wod.

    This wal, which that bitwixe hem bothe stod,
Was clove a-two, ryght from the top adoun,
Of olde tyme of his fundacioun;
But yit this clyfte was so narw and lyte,   740
It nas nat sene, deere ynogh a myte.
But what is that that love can nat espye?
Ye loveres two, if that I shal nat lye,
Ye founden first this litel narwe clifte;
And with a soun as softe as any shryfte,   745
They lete here wordes thorough the clifte pace,
And tolden, whil that they stode in the place,
Al here compleynt of love, and al here wo,
At every tyme whan they durste so.
Upon that o syde of the wal stod he,   750
And on that other side stod Thesbe,
The swote soun of other to receyve.
And thus here wardeyns wolde they deceyve,
And every day this wal they wolde threte,   754
And wisshe to God that it were doun ybete.
Thus wolde they seyn: "Alas, thow wikkede
         wal!
Thorgh thyn envye thow us lettest al.
Why nylt thow cleve, or fallen al a-two?
Or at the leste, but thou woldist so,
Yit woldest thow but ones lat us mete,   760
Or ones that we myghte kyssen swete,
Thanne were we covered of oure cares colde.
But, natheles, yit be we to thee holde,
In as muche as thow sufferest for to gon   764
Oure wordes thourgh thy lym and ek thy ston.
Yit oughte we with the been wel apayd."
And whan these ydele wordes weren sayd,
The colde wal they wolden kysse of ston,
And take here leve and forth they wolden gon.
And this was gladly in the eve-tyde,   770
Or wonder erly, lest men it espyde.
And longe tyme they wroughte in this manere,
Tyl on a day, whan Phebus gan to cleere —
Aurora with the stremes of hire hete   774

Hadde dreyed up the dew of herbes wete —
Unto this clyft, as it was wont to be,
Com Piramus, and after com Thysbe,
And plyghten trouthe fully in here fey
That ilke same nyght to stele awey,
And to begile here wardeyns everichon,   780
And forth out of the cite for to goon;
And, for the feldes ben so brode and wide,
For to mete in o place at o tyde,
They sette mark here metynge sholde be
There kyng Nynus was grave, under a tre, —
For olde payens, that idoles heryed,   786
Useden tho in feldes to ben beryed, —
And faste by this grave was a welle.
And, shortly of this tale for to telle,   789
This covenaunt was affermed wonder faste;
And longe hem thoughte that the sonne laste,
That it nere gon under the se adoun.

    This Tisbe hath so gret affeccioun
And so gret haste Piramus to se,
That whan she say hire tyme myghte be,   795
At nyght she stal awey ful pryvyly,
With hire face ywympled subtyly;
For alle hire frendes — for to save hire trouthe —
She hath forsake; allas! and that is routhe
That evere woman wolde ben so trewe   800
To truste man, but she the bet hym knewe!
And to the tre she goth a ful good pas,
For love made hire so hardy in this cas,
And by the welle adoun she gan hyre dresse.
Allas! than cometh a wilde lyonesse   805
Out of the wode, withoute more arest,
With blody mouth, of strangelynge of a best,
To drynken of the welle there as she sat.
And whan that Tisbe hadde espyed that,
She rist hire up, with a ful drery herte,   810
And in a cave with dredful fot she sterte,
For by the mone she say it wel withalle.
And as she ran, hire wympel let she falle,
And tok non hed, so sore she was awhaped,
And ek so glad of that she was escaped;   815
And thus she sit, and darketh wonder stylle.
Whan that this lyonesse hath dronke hire fille,
Aboute the welle gan she for to wynde,
And ryght anon the wympel gan she fynde,
And with hire blody mouth it al torente.   820
Whan this was don, no lengere she ne stente,
But to the wode hire weye thanne hath she
         nome.
    And at the laste this Piramus is come,
But al to longe, allas! at hom was he.
The mone shon, and he myghte wel yse,   825
And in his wey, as that he com ful faste,
His eyen to the ground adoun he caste,

And in the sond, as he byheld adoun,
He sey the steppes brode of a lyoun,
And in his herte he sodeynly agros,   830
And pale he wex; therwith his heer aros,
And ner he com, and fond the wimpel torn.
"Allas," quod he, "the day that I was born!
This o nyght wol us lovers bothe sle!
How shulde I axe mercy of Tisbe,   835
Whan I am he that have yow slayn, allas!
My biddyng hath yow slayn, as in this cas.
Allas! to bidde a woman gon by nyghte
In place there as peril falle myghte!
And I so slow! allas, I ne hadde be   840
Here in this place a furlong wey or ye!
Now what lyoun that be in this forest,
My body mote he renten, or what best
That wilde is, gnawe mote he now myn herte!"
And with that word he to the wympel sterte,
And kiste it ofte, and wep on it ful sore,   846
And seyde, "Wympel, allas! there is no more
But thow shalt feele as wel the blod of me
As thow hast felt the bledyng of Thisbe!"   849
And with that word he smot hym to the herte.
The blod out of the wounde as brode sterte
As water, whan the condit broken is.
   Now Tisbe, which that wiste nat of this,
But sittynge in hire drede, she thoughte thus:
"If it so falle that my Piramus   855
Be comen hider, and may me not yfynde,
He may me holde fals and ek unkynde."
And out she cometh and after hym gan espien,
Bothe with hire herte and with hire yen,
And thoughte, "I wol hym tellen of my drede,
Bothe of the lyonesse and al my deede."   861
And at the laste hire love thanne hath she
        founde,
Betynge with his heles on the grounde,
Al blody, and therwithal a-bak she sterte,
And lik the wawes quappe gan hire herte,   865
And pale as box she was, and in a throwe
Avisede hire, and gan hym wel to knowe,
That it was Piramus, hire herte deere.
Who coude wryte which a dedly cheere   869
Hath Thisbe now, and how hire heer she rente,
And how she gan hireselve to turmente,
And how she lyth and swouneth on the
        grounde,
And how she wep of teres ful his wounde;
How medeleth she his blod with hire com-
        pleynte;
How with his blod hireselve gan she peynte;
How clyppeth she the deede cors, allas!   876

How doth this woful Tisbe in this cas!
How kysseth she his frosty mouth so cold!
"Who hath don this, and who hath been so
        bold
To sle my leef? O spek, my Piramus!   880
I am thy Tisbe, that the calleth thus."
And therwithal she lifteth up his hed.
   This woful man, that was nat fully ded,
Whan that he herde the name of Tisbe cryen,
On hire he caste his hevy, dedly yen,   885
And doun agayn, and yeldeth up the gost.
Tysbe ryst up withouten noyse or bost,
And saw hire wympel and his empty shethe,
And ek his swerd, that hym hath don to dethe.
Thanne spak she thus: "My woful hand," quod
        she,   890
"Is strong ynogh in swich a werk to me;
For love shal yeve me strengthe and hardy-
        nesse
To make my wounde large ynogh, I gesse.
I wol thee folwe ded, and I wol be
Felawe and cause ek of thy deth," quod
        she.   895
"And thogh that nothing, save the deth only,
Mighte thee fro me departe trewely,
Thow shalt no more departe now fro me
Than fro the deth, for I wol go with thee.
And now, ye wrechede jelos fadres oure,   900
We that whilom were children youre,
We preyen yow, withouten more envye,
That in o grave yfere we moten lye,
Sith love hath brought us to this pitous ende.
And ryghtwis God to every lovere sende,   905
That loveth trewely, more prosperite
Than evere yit had Piramus and Tisbe!
And lat no gentil woman hyre assure
To putten hire in swich an aventure.
But God forbede but a woman can   910
Ben as trewe in lovynge as a man!
And for my part, I shal anon it kythe."
And with that word his swerd she tok as
        swythe,
That warm was of hire loves blod, and hot,
And to the herte she hireselven smot.   915
And thus are Tisbe and Piramus ygo.
Of trewe men I fynde but fewe mo
In alle my bokes, save this Piramus,
And therfore have I spoken of hym thus.
For it is deynte to us men to fynde   920
A man that can in love been trewe and kynde.
Here may ye se, what lovere so he be,
A woman dar and can as wel as he.

Explicit Legenda Tesbe.

III

THE LEGEND OF DIDO

Incipit Legenda Didonis martiris, Cartaginis Regine.

Glorye and honour, Virgil Mantoan,
Be to thy name! and I shal, as I can,   925
Folwe thy lanterne, as thow gost byforn,
How Eneas to Dido was forsworn.
In Naso and Eneydos wol I take
The tenor, and the grete effectes make.
Whan Troye brought was to destruccioun   930
By Grekes sleyghte, and namely by Synoun,
Feynynge the hors offered unto Mynerve,
Thourgh which that many a Troyan moste
          sterve;
And Ector hadde, after his deth, apeered;
And fyr, so wod it myghte nat been steered,
In al the noble tour of Ylioun,   936
That of the cite was the chef dongeoun;
And al the contre was so lowe ybrought,
And Priamus the kyng fordon and nought;
And Enyas was charged by Venus   940
To fleen awey, he tok Ascanius,
That was his sone, in his ryght hand, and
          fledde;
And on his bak he bar, and with hym ledde,
His olde fader ycleped Anchises,
And by the weye his wif Creusa he les.   945
And moche sorwe hadde he in his mynde,
Or that he coude his felaweshipe fynde.
But at the laste, whan he hadde hem founde,
He made hym redy in a certeyn stounde,
And to the se ful faste he gan him hye,   950
And sayleth forth with al his companye
Toward Ytayle, as wolde his destinee.
But of his aventures in the se
Nis nat to purpos for to speke of here,
For it acordeth nat to my matere.   955
But, as I seyde, of hym and of Dido
Shal be my tale, til that I have do.
  So longe he saylede in the salte se
Tyl in Libie unnethe aryvede he,
With shipes sevene and with no more navye;
And glad was he to londe for to hye,   961
So was he with the tempest al toshake.
And whan that he the haven hadde ytake,
He hadde a knyght, was called Achates,
And hym of al his felawshipe he ches   965
To gon with hym, the cuntre for t'espie.
He tok with hym no more companye,

But forth they gon, and lafte his shipes ryde,
His fere and he, withouten any gyde.
So longe he walketh in this wildernesse,   970
Til at the laste he mette an hunteresse.
A bowe in hande and arwes hadde she;
Hire clothes cutted were unto the kne.
But she was yit the fayreste creature
That evere was yformed by Nature;   975
And Eneas and Achates she grette,
And thus she to hem spak, whan she hem
          mette:
"Saw ye," quod she, "as ye han walked wyde,
Any of my sustren walke yow besyde
With any wilde bor or other best,   980
That they han hunted to, in this forest,
Ytukked up, with arwes in hire cas?"
"Nay, sothly, lady," quod this Eneas;
"But by thy beaute, as it thynketh me,
Thow myghtest nevere erthly woman be,   985
But Phebus syster art thow, as I gesse.
And, if so be that thow be a goddesse,
Have mercy on oure labour and oure wo."
"I n'am no goddesse, sothly," quod she tho;
"For maydens walken in this contre here,   990
With arwes and with bowe, in this manere.
This is the reyne of Libie, there ye ben,
Of which that Dido lady is and queen" —
And shortly tolde hym al the occasyoun
Why Dido cam into that regioun,   995
Of which as now me lesteth nat to ryme;
It nedeth nat, it were but los of tyme.
For this is al and som, it was Venus,
His owene moder, that spak with him thus,
And to Cartage she bad he sholde hym dighte,
And vanyshed anon out of his syghte.   1001
I coude folwe, word for word, Virgile,
But it wolde lasten al to longe while.
  This noble queen, that cleped was Dido,
That whilom was the wif of Sytheo,   1005
That fayrer was than is the bryghte sonne,
This noble toun of Cartage hath bigonne;
In which she regneth in so gret honour,
That she was holden of alle queenes flour,
Of gentillesse, of fredom, of beaute;   1010
That wel was hym that myghte hire ones se;
Of kynges and of lordes so desyred,

That al the world hire beaute hadde yfyred;
She stod so wel in every wightes grace.
  Whan Eneas was come unto that place,   1015
Unto the mayster temple of al the toun,
Ther Dido was in hire devocyoun,
Ful pryvyly his weye than hath he nome.
Whan he was in the large temple come,
I can nat seyn if that it be possible,   1020
But Venus hadde hym maked invysible —
Thus seyth the bok, withouten any les.
And whan this Eneas and Achates
Hadden in this temple ben overal,
Thanne founde they, depeynted on a wal,   1025
How Troye and al the lond destroyed was.
"Allas, that I was born!" quod Eneas;
"Thourghout the world oure shame is kid so
          wyde,
Now it is peynted upon every syde.
We, that weren in prosperite,   1030
Been now desclandred, and in swich degre,
No lenger for to lyven I ne kepe."
And with that word he brast out for to wepe
So tenderly that routhe it was to sene.
This fresshe lady, of the cite queene,   1035
Stod in the temple, in hire estat real,
So rychely and ek so fayr withal,
So yong, so lusty, with hire eyen glade,
That, if that God, that hevene and erthe made,
Wolde han a love, for beaute and good-
          nesse,   1040
And womanhod, and trouthe, and semelynesse,
Whom shulde he loven but this lady swete?
Ther nys no woman to hym half so mete.
Fortune, that hath the world in governaunce,
Hath sodeynly brought in so newe a chaunce
That nevere was ther yit so fremde a cas.   1046
For al the companye of Eneas,
Which that he wende han loren in the se,
Aryved is nat fer from that cite;
For which, the gretteste of his lordes some   1050
By aventure ben to the cite come,
Unto that same temple, for to seke
The queene, and of hire socour to beseke,
Swich renoun was there sprongen of hire good-
          nesse.
And whan they hadden told al here distresse,
And al here tempest and here harde cas,   1056
Unto the queen apeered Eneas,
And openly biknew that it was he.
Who hadde joye thanne but his meyne,
That hadde founde here lord, here gover-
          nour?   1060
The queen saugh that they dide hym swych
          honour,

And hadde herd ofte of Eneas er tho,
And in hire herte she hadde routhe and wo
That evere swich a noble man as he
Shal ben disherited in swich degre;   1065
And saw the man, that he was lyk a knyght,
And suffisaunt of persone and of myght,
And lyk to been a verray gentil man;
And wel his wordes he besette can,
And hadde a noble visage for the nones,   1070
And formed wel of braunes and of bones.
For after Venus hadde he swich fayrnesse
That no man myghte be half so fayr, I gesse;
And wel a lord he semede for to be.
And, for he was a straunger, somwhat she   1075
Likede hym the bet, as, God do bote,
To som folk ofte newe thyng is sote.
Anon hire herte hath pite of his wo,
And with that pite love com in also;
And thus, for pite and for gentillesse,   1080
Refreshed moste he been of his distresse.
She seyde, certes, that she sory was
That he hath had swych peryl and swich cas;
And, in hire frendly speche, in this manere
She to hym spak, and seyde as ye may here:
  "Be ye nat Venus sone and Anchises?   1086
In good feyth, al the worshipe and encres
That I may goodly don yow, ye shal have.
Youre shipes and youre meyne shal I save."
And many a gentil word she spak hym to,   1090
And comaunded hire messageres to go
The same day, withouten any fayle,
His shippes for to seke, and hem vitayle.
Ful many a beste she to the shippes sente,   1094
And with the wyn she gan hem to presente,
And to hire royal paleys she hire spedde,
And Eneas alwey with hire she ledde.
What nedeth yow the feste to descrive?
He nevere beter at ese was in his lyve.   1099
Ful was the feste of deyntees and rychesse,
Of instruments, of song, and of gladnesse,
Of many an amorous lokyng and devys.
This Eneas is come to paradys
Out of the swolow of helle, and thus in joye
Remembreth hym of his estat in Troye.   1105
  To daunsynge chaumberes ful of paramentes,
Of riche beddes, and of ornementes,
This Eneas is led, after the mete.
And with the quene, whan that he hadde sete,
And spices parted, and the wyn agon,   1110
Unto his chambres was he led anon
To take his ese and for to have his reste,
With al his folk, to don what so hem leste.
There nas courser wel ybrydeled non,
Ne stede, for the justing wel to gon,   1115

Ne large palfrey, esy for the nones,
Ne jewel, fretted ful of ryche stones,
Ne sakkes ful of gold, of large wyghte,
Ne ruby non, that shynede by nyghte,
Ne gentil hawtein faucoun heroner,   1120
Ne hound, for hert or wilde bor or der,
Ne coupe of gold, with floreyns newe ybete,
That in the land of Libie may be gete,
That Dido ne hath it Eneas ysent;
And al is payed, what that he hath spent.   1125
Thus can this quene honurable hire gestes calle,
As she that can in fredom passen alle.
Eneas sothly ek, withouten les,
Hadde sent unto his ship, by Achates,
After his sone, and after riche thynges,   1130
Bothe sceptre, clothes, broches, and ek rynges,
Some for to were, and some for to presente
To hire, that alle thise noble thynges hym
          sente;
And bad his sone how that he shulde make
The presenting, and to the queen it take.   1135
Repeyred is this Achates agayn,
And Eneas ful blysful is and fayn
To sen his yonge sone Ascanyus.
But natheles, oure autour telleth us,
That Cupido, that is the god of love,   1140
At preyere of his moder hye above,
Hadde the liknesse of the child ytake,
This noble queen enamored to make
On Eneas; but, as of that scripture,
Be as be may, I take of it no cure.   1145
But soth is this, the queen hath mad swich
          chere
Unto this child, that wonder is to here;
And of the present that his fader sente
She thanked hym ful ofte, in good entente.

     Thus is this queen in plesaunce and in joye,
With alle these newe lusty folk of Troye.   1151
And of the dedes hath she more enquered
Of Eneas, and al the story lered
Of Troye, and al the longe day they tweye
Entendeden to speken and to pleye;   1155
Of which ther gan to breden swich a fyr,
That sely Dido hath now swich desyr
With Eneas, hire newe gest, to dele,
That she hath lost hire hewe, and ek hire hele.

     Now to th'effect, now to the fruyt of al,   1160
Whi I have told this story, and telle shal.
Thus I begynne: it fil upon a nyght,
Whan that the mone up reysed hadde his lyght,
This noble queene unto hire reste wente.   1164
She siketh sore, and gan hyreself turmente;
She waketh, walweth, maketh many a breyd,
As don these lovers, as I have herd seyd.

And at the laste, unto hire syster Anne
She made hire mone, and ryght thus spak she
          thanne:
"Now, dere sister myn, what may it be   1170
That me agasteth in my drem?" quod she.
"This newe Troyan is so in my thought,
For that me thynketh he is so wel ywrought,
And ek so likly for to ben a man,
And therwithal so moche good he can,   1175
That al my love and lyf lyth in his cure.
Have ye nat herd him telle his aventure?
Now certes, Anne, if that ye rede it me,
I wolde fayn to hym ywedded be;
This is th'effect; what sholde I more seye?   1180
In hym lyth al, to do me live or deye."
Hyre syster Anne, as she that coude hire good,
Seyde as hire thoughte, and somdel it withstod.
But herof was so long a sermounynge,
It were to long to make rehersynge.   1185
But finaly, it may nat ben withstonde:
Love wol love, for nothing wol it wonde.

     The dawenyng up-rist out of the se.
This amorous queene chargeth hire meyne
The nettes dresse, and speres brode and kene;
An huntyng wol this lusty freshe queene,   1191
So priketh hire this newe joly wo.
To hors is al hir lusty folk ygo;
Into the court the houndes been ybrought;
And upon coursers, swift as any thought,   1195
Hire yonge knyghtes hoven al aboute,
And of hire women ek an huge route.
Upon a thikke palfrey, paper-whit,
With sadel red, enbrouded with delyt,
Of gold the barres up enbosede hye,   1200
Sit Dido, al in gold and perre wrye;
And she as fair as is the bryghte morwe,
That heleth syke folk of nyghtes sorwe.
Upon a courser stertlynge as the fyr —
Men myghte turne hym with a litel wyr —   1205
Sit Eneas, lik Phebus to devyse,
So was he fressh arayed in his wyse.
The fomy brydel with the bit of gold
Governeth he, ryght as hymself hath wold.
And forth this noble queen thus lat I ride   1210
On huntynge, with this Troyan by hyre side.

     The herde of hertes founden is anon,
With "Hay! go bet! pryke thow! lat gon, lat
          gon!
Why nyl the leoun comen, or the bere,   1214
That I myghte ones mete hym with this spere?"
Thus sey these yonge folk, and up they kylle
These bestes wilde, and han hem at here wille.
Among al this to rumbelen gan the hevene;
The thunder rored with a grisely stevene;

Doun cam the reyn, with hayl and slet, so faste,
With hevenes fyr, that it so sore agaste	1221
This noble queen, and also hire meyne,
That ech of hem was glad awey to fle.
And shortly, from the tempest hire to save,
She fledde hireself into a litel cave,	1225
And with hire wente this Eneas also.
I not, with hem if there wente any mo;
The autour maketh of it no mencioun.
And here began the depe affeccioun	1229
Betwixe hem two; this was the firste morwe
Of hire gladnesse, and gynning of hire sorwe.
For there hath Eneas ykneled so,
And told hire al his herte and al his wo,
And swore so depe to hire to be trewe,	1234
For wel or wo, and chaunge hire for no newe,
And as a fals lovere so wel can pleyne,
That sely Dido rewede on his peyne,
And tok hym for husbonde, and becom his wyf
For everemo, whil that hem laste lyf.	1239
And after this, whan that the tempest stente,
With myrthe out as they comen, hom they
	wente.
	The wikke fame upros, and that anon,
How Eneas hath with the queen ygon
Into the cave; and demede as hem liste.
And whan the kyng, that Yarbas highte, it
	wiste,	1245
As he that hadde hir loved evere his lyf,
And wowede hyre, to han hire to his wyf,
Swich sorwe as he hath maked, and swich
	cheere,
It is a routhe and pite for to here.
But, as in love, alday it happeth so,	1250
That oon shal laughen at anothers wo.
Now laugheth Eneas, and is in joye
And more richesse than evere he was in Troye.
	O sely wemen, ful of innocence,
Ful of pite, of trouthe, and conscience,	1255
What maketh yow to men to truste so?
Have ye swych routhe upon hyre feyned wo,
And han swich olde ensaumples yow beforn?
Se ye nat alle how they ben forsworn?	1259
Where sen ye oon, that he ne hath laft his leef,
Or ben unkynde, or don hire som myscheef,
Or piled hire, or bosted of his dede?
Ye may as wel it sen, as ye may rede.
Tak hede now of this grete gentil-man,
This Troyan, that so wel hire plesen can,	1265
That feyneth hym so trewe and obeysynge,
So gentil, and so privy of his doinge,
And can so wel don alle his obeysaunces,
And wayten hire at festes and at daunces,
And whan she goth to temple and hom ageyn,

And fasten til he hath his lady seyn,	1271
And beren in his devyses, for hire sake,
Not I not what; and songes wolde he make,
Justen, and don of armes many thynges,	1274
Sende hire lettres, tokens, broches, rynges —
Now herkneth how he shal his lady serve!
There as he was in peril for to sterve
For hunger, and for myschef in the se,
And desolat, and fled from his cuntre,
And al his folk with tempest al todryven,	1280
She hath hire body and ek hire reame yiven
Into his hand, there as she myghte have been
Of othere land than of Cartage a queen,
And lyved in joye ynogh; what wole ye more?
This Eneas, that hath so depe yswore,	1285
Is wery of his craft withinne a throwe;
The hote ernest is al overblowe.
And pryvyly he doth his shipes dyghte,
And shapeth hym to stele awey by nyghte.
	This Dido hath suspecioun of this,	1290
And thoughte wel that it was al amys.
For in his bed she lyth a-nyght and syketh;
She axeth hym anon what hym myslyketh —
"My dere herte, which that I love most?"
	"Certes," quod he, "this nyght my faderes
	gost	1295
Hath in my slep so sore me tormented,
And ek Mercurye his message hath presented,
That nedes to the conquest of Ytayle
My destine is sone for to sayle;	1299
For which, me thynketh, brosten is myn herte!"
Therwith his false teres out they sterte,
And taketh hire withinne his armes two.
	"Is that in ernest?" quod she, "wole ye so?
Have ye nat sworn to wyve me to take?
Allas! what woman wole ye of me make?	1305
I am a gentil woman and a queen.
Ye wole nat from youre wif thus foule fleen?
That I was born, allas! What shal I do?"
To telle in short, this noble quen Dydo,
She seketh halwes and doth sacryfise;	1310
She kneleth, cryeth, that routhe is to devyse;
Conjureth hym, and profereth hym to be
His thral, his servant in the leste degre;
She falleth hym to fote and swouneth ther,
Dischevele, with hire bryghte gilte her,	1315
And seyth, "Have mercy! and let me with yow
	ryde!
These lordes, which that wonen me besyde,
Wole me distroyen only for youre sake.
And, so ye wole me now to wive take,	1319
As ye han sworn, thanne wol I yeve yow leve
To slen me with youre swerd now sone at eve!
For thanne yit shal I deyen as youre wif.

I am with childe, and yeve my child his lyf!
Mercy, lord! have pite in youre thought!"
    But al this thing avayleth hire ryght nought,
For on a nyght, slepynge, he let hire lye,   1326
And stal awey unto his companye,
And as a traytour forth he gan to sayle
Toward the large contre of Ytayle.
Thus he hath laft Dido in wo and pyne,   1330
And wedded ther a lady, hyghte Lavyne.
    A cloth he lafte, and ek his swerd stondynge,
Whan he from Dido stal in hire slepynge,
Ryght at hire beddes hed, so gan he hie,
Whan that he stal awey to his navye;   1335
Which cloth, whan sely Dido gan awake,
She hath it kyst ful ofte for his sake,
And seyde, "O swete cloth, whil Juppiter it
        leste,
Tak now my soule, unbynd me of this unreste!
I have fulfild of fortune al the cours."   1340
And thus, allas! withouten his socours,
Twenty tyme yswouned hath she thanne.
And whanne that she unto hire syster Anne
Compleyned hadde — of which I may nat
        wryte,

So gret a routhe I have it for t'endite —   1345
And bad hire norice and hire sister gon
To fechen fyr and other thyng anon,
And seyde that she wolde sacryfye, —
And whan she myghte hire tyme wel espie,
Upon the fir of sacryfice she sterte,   1350
And with his swerd she rof hyre to the herte.
    But, as myn auctour seith, yit thus she seyde;
Or she was hurt, byforen or she deyde,
She wrot a lettre anon that thus began:
"Ryght so," quod she, "as that the white swan
Ayens his deth begynnyth for to synge,   1356
Right so to yow make I my compleynynge.
Not that I trowe to geten yow ageyn,
For wel I wot that it is al in veyn,
Syn that the goddes been contraire to me.   1360
But syn my name is lost thorugh yow," quod
        she,
"I may wel lese on yow a word or letter,
Al be it that I shal ben nevere the better;
For thilke wynd that blew youre ship awey,
The same wynd hath blowe awey youre fey."
But who wol al this letter have in mynde,   1366
Rede Ovyde, and in hym he shal it fynde.

Explicit Legenda Didonis martiris, Cartaginis Regine.

IV

THE LEGEND OF HYPSIPYLE AND MEDEA

Incipit Legenda Ysiphile et Medee, martirum.

Thow rote of false lovers, Duc Jasoun,
Thow sly devourere and confusioun
Of gentil wemen, tendre creatures,   1370
Thow madest thy recleymyng and thy lures
To ladyes of thy statly aparaunce,
And of thy wordes, farced with plesaunce,
And of thy feyned trouthe and thy manere,
With thyn obeÿsaunce and humble cheere,
And with thy contrefeted peyne and wo.   1376
There othere falsen oon, thow falsest two!
O, often swore thow that thow woldest dye
For love, whan thow ne feltest maladye
Save foul delyt, which that thow callest love!
Yif that I live, thy name shal be shove   1381
In English that thy sekte shal be knowe!
Have at thee, Jason! now thyn horn is blowe!
But certes, it is bothe routhe and wo

That love with false loveres werketh so;   1385
For they shal have wel betere love and chere
Than he that hath abought his love ful dere,
Or hadde in armes many a blody box.
For evere as tendre a capoun et the fox,   1389
Thow he be fals and hath the foul betrayed,
As shal the good-man that therfore hath payed.
Al have he to the capoun skille and ryght,
The false fox wol have his part at nyght.
On Jason this ensaumple is wel ysene
By Isiphile and Medea the queene.   1395

1. *The Legend of Hypsipyle*

    In Tessalie, as Guido tellith us,
There was a kyng that highte Pelleus,
That hadde a brother which that highte Eson;

And whan for age he myghte unnethes gon,
He yaf to Pelleus the governyng 1400
Of al his regne, and made hym lord and kyng.
Of which Eson this Jason geten was,
That in his tyme in al that land there nas
Nat swich a famous knyght of gentilesse, 1404
Of fredom, and of strengthe and lustynesse.
After his fadres deth he bar hym so
That there nas non that liste ben his fo,
But dide hym al honour and companye.
Of which this Pelleus hadde gret envye,
Imagynynge that Jason myghte be 1410
Enhaunsed so, and put in swich degre
With love of lordes of his regioun,
That from his regne he may ben put adoun.
And in his wit, a-nyght, compassed he
How Jason myghte best distroyed be 1415
Withoute sclaunder of his compassement,
And at the last he tok avysement
To senden hym into som fer contre,
There as this Jason may destroyed be.
This was his wit, al made he to Jasoun 1420
Gret chere of love and of affeccioun,
For drede lest his lordes it espide.
So fyl it, so as fame renneth wide,
There was swich tydyng overal and swich loos,
That in an yle that called was Colcos, 1425
Beyonde Troye, estward in the se,
That therin was a ram, that men mighte se,
That hadde a fles of gold, that shon so bryghte
That nowher was swich anothir syghte;
But it was kept alwey with a dragoun, 1430
And many other merveyles, up and doun,
And with two boles, maked al of bras,
That spitten fyr, and moche thyng there was.
But this was ek the tale, natheles,
That whoso wolde wynne thylke fles, 1435
He moste bothe, or he it wynne myghte,
With the boles and the dragoun fyghte.
And kyng Oetes lord was of that yle.
This Pelleus bethoughte upon this wile,
That he his neveu Jason wolde enhorte 1440
To saylen to that lond, hym to disporte,
And seyde, "Nevew, if it myghte be
That swich a worshipe myghte fallen the,
That thow this famous tresor myghtest wynne,
And bryngen it my regioun withinne, 1445
It were to me gret plesaunce and honour.
Thanne were I holde to quyte thy labour;
And al the cost I wol myselven make.
And chees what folk that thow wilt with the take;
Lat sen now, darst thow take this viage?" 1450
Jason was yong, and lusty of corage,

And undertok to don this ilke empryse.
Anon Argus his shipes gan devyse;
With Jason wente the stronge Ercules,
And many another that he with hym ches. 1455
But whoso axeth who is with hym gon,
Lat hym go rede Argonautycon,
For he wole telle a tale long ynogh.
Philotetes anon the sayl up drogh,
Whan that the wynd was good, and gan hym hye 1460
Out of his contre called Thessalye.
So longe he seyled in the salte se,
Til in the yle of Lemnon aryvede he —
Al be this nat rehersed of Guido,
Yit seyth Ovyde in his Epistels so — 1465
And of this ile lady was and quene
The fayre yonge Ysiphele, the shene,
That whylom Thoas doughter was, the kyng.
  Isiphile was gon in hire pleying,
And, romynge on the clyves by the se, 1470
Under a banke anon aspied she
Where that the ship of Jason gan aryve.
Of hire goodnesse adoun she sendeth blythe
To witen if that any straunge wight 1474
With tempest thider were yblowe a-nyght,
To don him socour, as was hire usaunce
To fortheren every wight, and don plesaunce
Of verrey bounte and of curteysye.
This messangeer adoun hym gan to hye,
And fond Jason and Ercules also, 1480
That in a cog to londe were ygo,
Hem to refreshen and to take the eyr.
The morwenynge attempre was and fayr,
And in his weye this messanger hem mette.
Ful cunnyngly these lordes two he grette, 1485
And dide his message, axinge hem anon
If they were broken, or ought wo begon,
Or hadden nede of lodman or vitayle;
For of socour they sholde nothyng fayle,
For it was outrely the quenes wille. 1490
  Jason answerde mekely and stylle:
"My lady," quod he, "thanke I hertely
Of hire goodnesse; us nedeth, trewely,
Nothyng as now, but that we wery be,
And come for to pleye, out of the se, 1495
Tyl that the wynd be better in oure weye."
  This lady rometh by the clyf to pleye,
With hire meyne, endelong the stronde,
And fynt this Jason and this other stonde
In spekynge of this thyng, as I yow tolde. 1500
This Ercules and Jason gan beholde
How that the queen it was, and fayre hire grette,
Anon-ryght as they with this lady mette.

And she tok hed, and knew by hyre manere,
By hire aray, by wordes, and by chere, 1505
That it were gentil-men of gret degre,
And to the castel with hire ledeth she
These straunge folk, and doth hem gret honour,
And axeth hem of travayle and labour
That they han suffered in the salte se; 1510
So that, withinne a day, or two, or thre,
She knew, by folk that in his shipes be,
That it was Jason, ful of renome,
And Ercules, that hadde the grete los,
That soughten the aventures of Colcos; 1515
And dide hem honour more than before,
And with hem deled evere lenger the more,
For they ben worthy folk, withouten les.
And namely, most she spak with Ercules;
To hym hire herte bar, he shulde be 1520
Sad, wys, and trewe, of wordes avyse,
Withouten any other affeccioun
Of love, or evyl ymagynacyoun.

This Ercules hath so this Jason preysed 1524
That to the sonne he hath hym up areysed,
That half so trewe a man there nas of love
Under the cope of heven that is above;
And he was wis, hardy, secre, and ryche.
Of these thre poyntes there nas non hym liche:
Of fredom passede he, and lustyhede, 1530
Alle tho that lyven or been dede;
Therto so gret a gentilman was he,
And of Thessalye likly kyng to be.
There nas no lak, but that he was agast
To love, and for to speke shamefast. 1535
He hadde lever hymself to morder, and dye,
Than that men shulde a lovere hym espye.
"As wolde almighty God that I hadde yive
My blod and flesh, so that I myghte live,
With the nones that he hadde owher a wif
For hys estat; for swich a lusty lyf 1541
She shulde lede with this lusty knyght!"

And al this was compassed on the nyght
Bytwixe hym Jason and this Ercules.
Of these two here was a shrewed lees, 1545
To come to hous upon an innocent!
For to bedote this queen was here assent.
And Jason is as coy as is a mayde;
He loketh pitously, but nought he sayde,
But frely yaf he to hire conseyleres 1550
Yiftes grete, and to hire officeres.
As wolde God I leyser hadde and tyme
By proces al his wowyng for to ryme!
But in this hous if any fals lovere be, 1554
Ryght as hymself now doth, ryght so dide he,
With feynynge, and with every subtil dede.
Ye gete namore of me, but ye wole rede

Th'orignal, that telleth al the cas.

The somme is this, that Jason wedded was
Unto this queen, and tok of hir substaunce 1560
What so hym leste, unto his purveyaunce;
And upon hire begat he children two,
And drogh his sayl, and saw hir nevere mo.
A letter sente she to hym, certeyn,
Which were to longe to wryten and to sen, 1565
And hym reprevith of his grete untrouthe,
And preyeth him on hire to have som routhe.
And of his children two she seyde hym this:
That they ben lyk of alle thyng, ywis,
To Jason, save they coude nat begile; 1570
And preyede God, or it were longe while,
That she, that hadde his herte yraft hire fro,
Moste fynden hym untrewe to hir also,
And that she moste bothe hire chyldren spylle,
And alle tho that sufferede hym his wille. 1575
And trewe to Jason was she al hire lyf,
And evere kepte hire chast, as for his wif;
Ne nevere hadde she joye at hire herte,
But deyede, for his love, of sorwes smerte.

2. The Legend of Medea

To Colcos comen is this duc Jasoun, 1580
That is of love devourer and dragoun.
As mater apetiteth forme alwey,
And from forme into forme it passen may,
Or as a welle that were botomles,
Ryght so can false Jason have no pes. 1585
For, to desyren, thourgh his apetit,
To don with gentil women his delyt,
This is his lust and his felicite.

Jason is romed forth to the cyte,
That whilom cleped was Jaconitos, 1590
That was the mayster-toun of al Colcos,
And hath ytold the cause of his comyng
Unto Oetes, of that contre kyng,
Preyinge hym that he moste don his assay
To gete the fles of gold, if that he may; 1595
Of which the kyng assenteth to his bone,
And doth hym honour, as it was to done,
So fer forth that his doughter and his eyr,
Medea, which that was so wis and fayr
That fayrer say there nevere man with ye, 1600
He made hire don to Jason companye
At mete, and sitte by hym in the halle.

Now was Jason a semely man withalle,
And lyk a lord, and hadde a gret renoun,
And of his lok as real as a leoun, 1605
And goodly of his speche, and familer,
And coude of love al the art and craft pleyner
Withoute bok, with everych observaunce.

And, as Fortune hire oughte a foul myschaunce,
She wex enamoured upon this man.   1610
   "Jason," quod she, "for ought I se or can,
As of this thyng the whiche ye ben aboute,
Ye han youreself yput in moche doute.
For whoso wol this aventure acheve,
He may nat wel asterten, as I leve,   1615
Withouten deth, but I his helpe be.
But natheles, it is my wylle," quod she,
"To fortheren yow, so that ye shal nat die,
But turnen sound hom to youre Tessalye."
   "My ryghte lady," quod this Jason tho,   1620
"That ye han of my deth or of my wo
Any reward, and don me this honour,
I wot wel that my myght ne my labour
May nat disserve it in my lyves day.
God thanke yow, there I ne can ne may!   1625
Youre man I am, and lowely yow beseche
To ben my helpe, withoute more speche;
But, certes, for my deth shal I nat spare."
   Tho gan this Medea to hym declare
The peril of this cas, from poynt to poynt,   1630
And of his batayle, and in what disjoynt
He mote stonde, of which no creature,
Save only she, ne myghte his lyf assure.
And, shortly to the poynt ryght for to go,
They been acorded ful bytwixe hem two   1635
That Jason shal hire wedde, as trewe knyght;
And terme set, to come sone at nyght
Unto hire chamber and make there his oth
Upon the goddes, that he for lef or loth
Ne sholde nevere hire false, nyght ne day,   1640
To ben hire husbonde whil he lyve may,
As she that from his deth hym saved here.
And hereupon at nyght they mette in-feere,
And doth his oth, and goth with hire to bedde;

And on the morwe upward he hym spedde,
For she hath taught hym how he shal nat fayle
The fles to wynne, and stynten his batayle;
And saved hym his lyf and his honour;   1648
And gat hym a name ryght as a conquerour,
Ryght thourgh the sleyghte of hire enchaunte-
   ment.   1650
   Now hath Jason the fles, and hom is went
With Medea, and tresor ful gret won;
But unwist of hire fader is she gon
To Tessaly, with Duk Jason hire lef,
That afterward hath brought hire to myschef.
For as a traytour he is from hire go,   1656
And with hire lafte his yonge children two,
And falsly hath betraysed hire, allas!
As evere in love a chef traytour he was;
And wedded yit the thridde wif anon,   1660
That was the doughter of the kyng Creon.
   This is the mede of lovynge and guerdoun
That Medea receyved of Jasoun
Ryght for hire trouthe and for hire kyndenesse,
That lovede hym beter than hireself, I gesse,
And lafte hire fader and hire herytage.   1666
And of Jason this is the vassellage,
That, in his dayes, nas ther non yfounde
So fals a lovere goinge on the grounde.
And therfore in hire letter thus she seyde   1670
Fyrst, whan she of his falsnesse hym upbreyde:
"Whi lykede me thy yelwe her to se
More than the boundes of myn honeste?
Why lykede me thy youthe and thy fayrnesse,
And of thy tonge, the infynyt graciousnesse?
O, haddest thow in thy conquest ded ybe,   1676
Ful mikel untrouthe hadde ther deyd with the!"
Wel can Ovyde hire letter in vers endyte,
Which were as now to long for me to wryte.

Explicit Legenda Ysiphile et Medee, martirum.

V

THE LEGEND OF LUCRECE

Incipit Legenda Lucrecie Rome, martiris.

Now mot I seyn the exilynge of kynges   1680
Of Rome, for here horible doinges,
And of the laste kyng Tarquinius,
As seyth Ovyde and Titus Lyvius.
But for that cause telle I nat this storye,

But for to preyse and drawe to memorye   1685
The verray wif, the verray trewe Lucresse,
That, for hyre wifhod and hire stedefastnesse,
Nat only that these payens hire comende,
But he that cleped is in oure legende

The grete Austyn, hath gret compassioun   1690
Of this Lucresse, that starf at Rome toun;
And in what wise, I wol but shortly trete,
And of this thyng I touche but the grete.

     Whan Ardea beseged was aboute   1694
With Romeyns, that ful sterne were and stoute,
Ful longe lay the sege, and lytel wroughten,
So that they were half idel, as hem thoughten;
And in his pley Tarquinius the yonge
Gan for to jape, for he was lyght of tonge,
And seyde that it was an ydel lyf,   1700
No man dide there no more than his wif.
"And lat us speke of wyves, that is best;
Preyse every man his owene, as hym lest,
And with oure speche lat us ese oure herte."

     A knyght, that highte Colatyn, up sterte,
And seyde thus: "Nay, sire, it is no nede   1706
To trowen on the word, but on the dede.
I have a wif," quod he, "that, as I trowe,
Is holden good of alle that evere hire knowe.
Go we to-nyght to Rome, and we shal se."   1710
Tarquinius answerde, "That liketh me."
To Rome be they come, and faste hem dyghte
To Colatynes hous and doun they lyghte,
Tarquinius, and ek this Colatyn.
The husbonde knew the estris wel and fyn,
And prively into the hous they gon,   1716
Nor at the yate porter nas there non,
And at the chambre-dore they abyde.
This noble wif sat by hire beddes side
Dischevele, for no malyce she ne thoughte;
And softe wolle oure bok seyth that she
     wroughte   1721
To kepen hire from slouthe and idelnesse;
And bad hire servaunts don hire besynesse,
And axeth hem, "What tydyngs heren ye?
How seyth men of the sege, how shal it be?
God wolde the walles were falle adoun!   1726
Myn husbonde is to longe out of this toun,
For which the drede doth me so to smerte
That with a swerd it stingeth to myn herte
Whan I thynke on the sege or on that place.
God save my lord, I preye hym for his grace!"
And therwithal ful tenderly she wep,   1732
And of hire werk she tok no more kep,
And mekely she let hyre eyen falle;
And thilke semblaunt sat hire wel withalle,
And eek hire teres, ful of honeste,   1736
Embelished hire wifly chastite,
Hyre contenaunce is to hire herte dygne,
For they acorde bothe in dede and sygne.
And with that word hire husbonde Colatyn,
Or she of him was war, com stertynge in,   1741
And seyde, "Drede the nat, for I am here!"

And she anon up ros, with blysful chere,
And kiste hym, as of wives is the wone.

     Tarquinius, this proude kynges sone,   1745
Conceyved hath hire beaute and hyre cheere,
Hire yelwe her, hire shap, and hire manere,
Hire hew, hire wordes, that she hath com-
     pleyned
(And by no craft hire beaute nas nat feyned),
And caughte to this lady swich desyr   1750
That in his herte brende as any fyr
So wodly that his wit was al forgeten.
For wel thoghte he she wolde nat ben geten;
And ay the more that he was in dispayr,
The more he coveyteth and thoughte hire fayr.
His blynde lust was al his coveytynge.   1756

     A-morwe, whan the brid began to synge,
Unto the sege he cometh ful privily,
And by hymself he walketh soberly,   1759
Th'ymage of hire recordynge alwey newe:
"Thus lay hire her, and thus fresh was hyre
     hewe;
Thus sat, thus spak, thus span; this was hire
     chere;
Thus fayr she was, and this was hire manere."
Al this conseit hys herte hath newe ytake.
And as the se, with tempest al toshake,   1765
That after, whan the storm is al ago,
Yit wol the water quappe a day or two,
Ryght so, thogh that hire forme were absent,
The plesaunce of hire forme was present;
But natheles, nat plesaunce but delit,   1770
Or an unrightful talent, with dispit —
"For, maugre hyre, she shal my leman be!
Hap helpeth hardy man alday," quod he.
"What ende that I make, it shal be so."   1774
And girte hym with his swerd, and gan to go,
And forth he rit til he to Rome is come,
And al alone his wey than hath he nome
Unto the hous of Colatyn ful ryght.
Doun was the sonne, and day hath lost his
     lyght;
And in he cometh into a prive halke,   1780
And in the nyght ful thefly gan he stalke,
Whan every wight was to his reste brought,
Ne no wight hadde of tresoun swich a thought.
Were it by wyndow or by other gyn,
With swerd ydrawe, shortly he com in   1785
There as she lay, this noble wif Lucresse.
And as she wok, hire bed she felte presse.
"What beste is that," quod she, "that weyeth
     thus?"
"I am the kynges sone, Tarquinius,"
Quod he, "but, and thow crye or noyse make,
Or if there any creature awake,   1791

By thilke God that formed man alyve,
This swerd thourghout thyn herte shal I ryve."
And therwithal unto hire throte he sterte,   1794
And sette the poynt al sharp upon hire herte.
No word she spak, she hath no myght therto.
What shal she seyn? hire wit is al ago.
Ryght as a wolf that fynt a lomb alone,   1798
To whom shal she compleyne, or make mone?
What! shal she fyghte with an hardy knyght?
Wel wot men that a woman hath no myght.
What! shal she crye, or how shal she asterte
That hath hire by the throte, with swerd at
      herte?
She axeth grace, and seyth al that she can.
"Ne wilt thow nat," quod he, this crewel man,
"As wisly Jupiter my soule save,   1806
As I shal in the stable slen thy knave,
And ley hym in thy bed, and loude crye
That I the fynde in swich avouterye.
And thus thow shalt be ded, and also lese   1810
Thy name, for thow shalt non other chese."
    These Romeyn wyves lovede so here name
At thilke tyme, and dredde so the shame,
That, what for fer of sclaunder and drede of
      deth,
She loste bothe at ones wit and breth,   1815
And in a swogh she lay, and wex so ded,
Men myghte smyten of hire arm or hed;
She feleth no thyng, neyther foul ne fayr.
    Tarquinius, that art a kynges eyr,
And sholdest, as by lynage and by ryght,   1820
Don as a lord and as a verray knyght,
Whi hastow don dispit to chivalrye?
Whi hastow don this lady vilanye?
Allas! of the this was a vileyns dede!
    But now to purpos; in the story I rede,   1825
Whan he was gon, and this myschaunce is falle,
This lady sente after hire frendes alle,
Fader, moder, husbonde, alle yfeere;
And al dischevele, with hire heres cleere,
In habit swich as women used tho   1830
Unto the buryinge of hire frendes go,
She sit in halle with a sorweful sighte.
Hyre frendes axen what hire eylen myghte,
And who was ded; and she sit ay wepynge;
A word, for shame, forth ne myght she brynge,
Ne upon hem she durste nat beholde.   1836
But atte last of Tarquyny she hem tolde

This rewful cas and al thys thing horryble.
The woo to tellen were an impossible,
That she and al hir frendes made attones.   1840
Al hadde folkes hertes ben of stones,
Hyt myght have maked hem upon hir rewe,
Hir herte was so wyfly and so trewe.
She sayde that, for hir gylt ne for hir blame,
Hir husbonde shulde nat have the foule name,
That wolde she nat suffre, by no wey.   1846
And they answerden alle, upon hir fey,
That they forgave yt hyr, for yt was ryght;
It was no gilt, it lay not in hir myght;
And seyden hir ensamples many oon.   1850
But al for noght; for thus she seyde anoon:
"Be as be may," quod she, "of forgyvyng,
I wol not have noo forgyft for nothing."
But pryvely she kaughte forth a knyf,
And therwithal she rafte hirself hir lyf;   1855
And as she fel adoun, she kaste hir lok,
And of hir clothes yet she hede tok.
For in hir fallynge yet she had a care,
Lest that hir fet or suche thyng lay bare;
So wel she loved clennesse and eke trouthe.
Of hir had al the toun of Rome routhe,   1861
And Brutus by hir chaste blood hath swore
That Tarquyn shulde ybanysshed be therfore,
And al hys kyn; and let the peple calle,
And openly the tale he tolde hem alle,   1865
And openly let cary her on a bere
Thurgh al the toun, that men may see and here
The horryble dede of hir oppressyoun,
Ne never was ther kyng in Rome toun
Syn thilke day; and she was holden there   1870
A seynt, and ever hir day yhalwed dere
As in hir lawe; and thus endeth Lucresse,
The noble wyf, as Tytus bereth witnesse.
    I telle hyt, for she was of love so trewe,
Ne in hir wille she chaunged for no newe;   1875
And for the stable herte, sadde and kynde,
That in these wymmen men may alday fynde.
Ther as they kaste hir herte, there it dwelleth.
For wel I wot that Crist himselve telleth
That in Israel, as wyd as is the lond,   1880
That so gret feyth in al that he ne fond
As in a woman; and this is no lye.
And as of men, loke ye which tirannye
They doon alday; assay hem whoso lyste,
The trewest ys ful brotel for to triste.   1885

Explicit Legenda Lucrecie Rome, martiris.

VI

THE LEGEND OF ARIADNE

Incipit Legenda Adriane de Athenes.

Juge infernal, Mynos, of Crete kyng,
Now cometh thy lot, now comestow on the
    ryng.
Nat for thy sake oonly write I this storye,
But for to clepe ageyn unto memorye
Of Theseus the grete untrouthe of love;   1890
For which the goddes of the heven above
Ben wrothe, and wreche han take for thy synne.
Be red for shame! now I thy lyf begynne.
    Mynos, that was the myghty kyng of Crete,
That hadde an hundred citees stronge and
    grete,   1895
To scole hath sent hys sone Androgeus,
To Athenes; of the which hyt happed thus,
That he was slayn, lernynge philosophie,
Ryght in that citee, nat but for envye.
The grete Mynos, of the which I speke,   1900
Hys sones deth ys come for to wreke.
Alcathoe he besegeth harde and longe;
But natheles, the walles be so stronge,
And Nysus, that was kyng of that citee,
So chevalrous, that lytel dredeth he.   1905
Of Mynos or hys ost tok he no cure,
Til on a day befel an aventure,
That Nysus doughter stod upon the wal,
And of the sege saw the maner al.
So happed it that, at a scarmishyng,   1910
She caste hire herte upon Mynos the kyng,
For his beaute and for his chyvalrye,
So sore that she wende for to dye.
And, shortly of this proces for to pace,
She made Mynos wynnen thilke place,   1915
So that the cite was al at his wille,
To saven whom hym leste, or elles spille.
But wikkedly he quitte hire kyndenesse,
And let hire drenche in sorwe and distresse,
Nere that the goddes hadde of hire pite;   1920
But that tale were to long as now for me.
Athenes wan thys kyng Mynos also,
As Alcathoe, and other tounes mo.
And this th'effect, that Mynos hath so driven
Hem of Athenes, that they mote hym yiven
From yer to yer hire owene children dere   1926
For to be slayn, right thus as ye shal here.
    This Mynos hadde a monstre, a wiked best,
That was so crewel that, withoute arest,   1929

Whan that a man was brought in his presence,
He wolde hym ete; ther helpeth no defence.
And every thridde yeer, withouten doute,
They caste lot, and as it com aboute
On riche or pore, he moste his sone take,
And of his child he moste present make   1935
Unto Minos, to save hym or to spylle,
Or lete his best devoure hym at his wille.
And this hath Mynos don, ryght in dispit;
To wreke his sone was set al his delyt,
And maken hem of Athenes his thral   1940
From yer to yer, whil that he liven shal;
And hom he sayleth, whan this toun is wonne.
This wiked custom is so longe yronne,
Til that of Athenes kyng Egeus
Mot senden his owene sone, Theseus,   1945
Sith that the lot is fallen hym upon,
To ben devoured, for grace is there non.
And forth is lad this woful yonge knyght
Unto the court of kyng Mynos ful ryght,
And into a prysoun, fetered, cast is he   1950
Tyl thilke tyme he sholde freten be.
    Wel maystow wepe, O woful Theseus,
That art a kynges sone, and dampned thus.
Me thynketh this, that thow were depe yholde
To whom that savede thee from cares colde!
And if now any woman helpe the,   1956
Wel oughtestow hire servaunt for to be,
And ben hire trewe lovere yer be yere!
But now to come ageyn to my matere.
The tour, there as this Theseus is throwe   1960
Doun in the botom derk and wonder lowe,
Was joynynge in the wal to a foreyne;
And it was longynge to the doughtren tweyne
Of Mynos, that in hire chaumbers grete
Dwellten above, toward the mayster-strete
Of Athenes, in joye and in solas.   1966
Noot I not how, it happede par cas,
As Theseus compleynede hym by nyghte,
The kynges doughter, Adryane that highte,
And ek hire syster Phedra, herden al   1970
His compleynynge, as they stode on the wal,
And lokeden upon the bryghte mone.
Hem leste nat to go to bedde so sone;
And of his wo they hadde compassioun.
A kynges sone to ben in swich prysoun,   1975

And ben devoured, thoughte hem gret pite.
This Adryane spak to hire syster fre,
And seyde, "Phedra, leve syster dere,
This woful lordes sone may ye nat here,
How pitously compleyneth he his kyn,   1980
And ek his povre estat that he is in,
And gilteles? Now, certes, it is routhe!
And if ye wol assenten, by my trouthe,
He shal ben holpen, how so that we do."
Phedra answerde, "Ywis, me is as wo   1985
For hym as evere I was for any man;
And, to his help, the beste red I can
Is that we do the gayler prively
To come and speke with us hastily,
And don this woful man with hym to come.
For if he may this monstre overcome,   1991
Thanne were he quyt; ther is non other bote.
Lat us wel taste hym at his herte-rote,
That if so be that he a wepen have,
Wher that he dar, his lyf to kepe and save,   1995
Fyghten with the fend, and hym defende.
For in the prysoun, ther he shal descende,
Ye wote wel that the beste is in a place
That nys nat derk, and hath roum eek and
    space
To welde an ax, or swerd, or staf, or knyf;   2000
So that, me thynketh, he shulde save his lyf.
If that he be a man, he shal do so.
And we shul make hym balles ek also
Of wex and tow, that whan he gapeth faste,
Into the bestes throte he shal hem caste   2005
To slake his hunger and encombre his teth;
And right anon, whan that Theseus seth
The beste achoked, he shal on hym lepe
To slen hym, or they comen more to-hepe.
This wepen shal the gayler, or that tyde,   2010
Ful prively withinne the prysoun hyde;
And for the hous is krynkeled to and fro,
And hath so queynte weyes for to go —
For it is shapen as the mase is wrought —
Therto have I a remedye in my thought,   2015
That, by a clewe of twyn, as he hath gon,
The same weye he may returne anon,
Folwynge alwey the thred, as he hath come.
And whan that he this beste hath overcome,
Thanne may he flen awey out of this drede,
And ek the gayler may he with hym lede,   2021
And hym avaunce at hom in his cuntre,
Syn that so gret a lordes sone is he.
This is my red, if that he dar it take."
What sholde I lenger sarmoun of it make?   2025
This gayler cometh, and with hym Theseus.
Whan these thynges ben acorded thus,
Adoun sit Theseus upon his kne: —

"The ryghte lady of my lyf," quod he,
"I, sorweful man, ydampned to the deth,   2030
Fro yow, whil that me lasteth lyf or breth,
I wol nat twynne, after this aventure,
But in youre servise thus I wol endure,
That, as a wreche unknowe, I wol yow serve
For everemo, til that myn herte sterve.   2035
Forsake I wol at hom myn herytage,
And, as I seyde, ben of youre court a page,
If that ye vouche-sauf that in this place
Ye graunte me to han so gret a grace   2039
That I may han nat but my mete and drynke.
And for my sustenaunce yit wol I swynke,
Ryght as yow leste, that Mynos ne no wight —
Syn that he saw me nevere with eyen syght —
Ne no man elles, shal me conne espye;
So slyly and so wel I shal me gye,   2045
And me so wel disfigure and so lowe,
That in this world ther shal no man me knowe,
To han my lyf, and for to han presence
Of yow, that don to me this excellence.
And to my fader shal I sende here   2050
This worthy man, that is now youre gaylere.
And, hym so gwerdone, that he shal wel be
Oon of the gretteste men of my cuntre.
And if I durste seyn, my lady bryght,
I am a kynges sone, and ek a knyght.   2055
As wolde God, if that it myghte be
Ye weren, in my cuntre, alle thre,
And I with yow, to bere yow compaignye,
Thanne shulde ye se if that I therfore lye.
And if I profre yow in low manere   2060
To ben youre page and serven yow ryght here,
But I yow serve as lowly in that place,
I preye to Mars to yeve me swich a grace
That shames deth on me ther mote falle,
And deth and poverte to my frendes alle;   2065
And that my spirit by nyghte mote go,
After my deth, and walke to and fro,
That I mote of traytour have a name,
For which my spirit go, to do me shame!
And if I evere cleyme other degre,   2070
But if ye vouche-sauf to yeve it me,
As I have seyd, of shames deth I deye!
And mercy, lady! I can nat elles seye."

A semely knyght was Theseus to se,
And yong, but of a twenty yer and thre.   2075
But whoso hadde seyn his contenaunce,
He wolde have wept, for routhe of his pen-
    aunce;
For which this Adryane in this manere
Answerde hym to his profre and to his chere:
"A kynges sone, and ek a knyght," quod she,
"To ben my servaunt in so low degre,   2081

God shilde it, for the shame of wemen alle,
And lene me nevere swich a cas befalle!
But sende yow grace of herte and sleyghte also,
Yow to defende, and knyghtly slen youre fo,
And leve hereafter that I may yow fynde 2086
To me and to my syster here so kynde,
That I repente nat to yeve yow lyf!
Yit were it betere that I were youre wyf,
Syn that ye ben as gentil born as I, 2090
And have a reaume, nat but faste by,
Than that I suffered, gilteles, yow sterve,
Or that I let yow as a page serve.
It nys no profre as unto youre kynrede;
But what is that that man nyl don for drede?
And to my syster, syn that it is so 2096
That she mot gon with me, if that I go,
Or elles suffre deth as wel as I,
That ye unto youre sone as trewely
Don hire ben wedded at youre hom-comyng.
This is the final ende of al this thyng; 2101
Ye swere it here, upon al that may be sworn."
"Ye, lady myn," quod he, "or ellis torn
Mote I be with the Mynotaur to-morwe!
And haveth hereof myn herte blod to borwe,
If that ye wole; if I hadde knyf or spere, 2106
I wolde it laten out, and theron swere,
For thanne at erst I wot ye wole me leve.
By Mars, that is the chef of my beleve,
So that I myghte liven and nat fayle 2110
To-morwe for t'acheve my batayle,
I wolde nevere from this place fle,
Til that ye shulde the verray preve se.
For now, if that the sothe I shal yow say,
I have yloved yow ful many a day, 2115
Thogh ye ne wiste it nat, in my cuntre,
And aldermost desired yow to se
Of any erthly livynge creature.
Upon my trouthe, I swere, and yow assure
This sevene yer I have youre servaunt be. 2120
Now have I yow, and also have ye me,
My dere herte, of Athenes duchesse!"

This lady smyleth at his stedefastnesse,
And at his hertely wordes, and his chere,
And to hyre sister seyde in this manere, 2125
Al softely: "Now, syster myn," quod she,
"Now be we duchesses, bothe I and ye,
And sekered to the regals of Athenes,
And bothe hereafter likly to ben quenes;
And saved from his deth a kynges sone, 2130
As evere of gentil women is the wone
To save a gentyl man, emforth hire myght,
In honest cause, and namely in his ryght.
Me thynketh no wight oughte herof us blame,
Ne beren us therfore an evil name." 2135

And shortly of this mater for to make,
This Theseus of hire hath leve take,
And every poynt was performed in dede,
As ye han in this covenaunt herd me rede.
His wepne, his clewe, his thyng, that I have
    sayd, 2140
Was by the gayler in the hous yleyd,
Ther as the Mynotaur hath his dwellynge,
Ryght faste by the dore, at his entrynge.
And Theseus is lad unto his deth,
And forth unto this Mynotaur he geth, 2145
And by the techynge of this Adryane
He overcom this beste, and was his bane;
And out he cometh by the clewe agayn
Ful prively, whan he this beste hath slayn;
And by the gayler geten hath a barge, 2150
And of his wyves tresor gan it charge,
And tok his wif, and ek hire sister fre,
And ek the gayler, and with hem alle thre,
Is stole awey out of the lond by nyghte,
And to the contre of Ennopye hym dyghte 2155
There as he hadde a frend of his knowynge.
There feste they, there daunce they and synge;
And in his armes hath this Adryane,
That of the beste hath kept hym from his bane;
And gat hym there a newe barge anon, 2160
And of his contre-folk a ful gret won,
And taketh his leve, and homward sayleth he.
And in an yle, amyd the wilde se,
Ther as there dwelled creature non
Save wilde bestes, and that ful many oon, 2165
He made his ship a-londe for to sette;
And in that yle half a day he lette,
And seyde that on the lond he moste hym reste.
His maryners han don ryght as hym leste;
And, for to tellen shortly in this cas, 2170
Whan Adryane his wif aslepe was,
For that hire syster fayrer was than she,
He taketh hire in his hond, and forth goth he
To shipe, and as a traytour stal his wey,
Whil that this Adryane aslepe lay, 2175
And to his contre-ward he sayleth blyve —
A twenty devel-wey the wynd hym dryve! —
And fond his fader drenched in the se.
    Me lest no more to speke of hym, parde.
These false lovers, poysoun be here bane! 2180
But I wol turne ageyn to Adryane,
That is with slep for werynesse atake.
Ful sorwefully hire herte may awake.
Allas, for thee myn herte hath now pite!
Ryght in the dawenyng awaketh she, 2185
And gropeth in the bed, and fond ryght nought.
"Allas," quod she, "that evere that I was
    wrought!

I am betrayed!" and hire her torente,
And to the stronde barefot faste she wente,
And cryed, "Theseus! myn herte swete!   2190
Where be ye, that I may nat with yow mete,
And myghte thus with bestes ben yslayn?"
The holwe rokkes answerde hire agayn.
No man she saw, and yit shyned the mone,
And hye upon a rokke she wente sone,   2195
And saw his barge saylynge in the se.
Cold wex hire herte, and ryght thus seyde she:
"Meker than ye fynde I the bestes wilde!"
Hadde he nat synne, that hire thus begylde?
She cryed, "O turn ageyn, for routhe and
          synne!   2200
Thy barge hath nat al his meyne inne!"
Hire coverchef on a pole up steked she,
Ascaunce that he shulde it wel yse,
And hym remembre that she was behynde,
And turne ageyn, and on the stronde hire
          fynde.   2205
But al for nought; his wey he is ygon.

Adoun she fyl aswoune upon a ston;
And up she rist, and kyssed, in al hire care,
The steppes of his fet, ther he hath fare,   2209
And to hire bed ryght thus she speketh tho:
"Thow bed," quod she, "that hast receyved two,
Thow shalt answere of two, and nat of oon!
Where is thy gretter part awey ygon?
Allas! where shal I, wreche wight, become?
For thogh so be that ship or boot here come,
Hom to my contre dar I nat for drede.   2216
I can myselven in this cas nat rede."
What shulde I more telle hire compleynyng?
It is so long, it were an hevy thyng.
In hire Epistel Naso telleth al;   2220
But shortly to the ende I telle shal.
The goddes han hire holpen for pite,
And in the signe of Taurus men may se
The stones of hire corone shyne clere.
I wol no more speke of this mateere;   2225
But thus this false lovere can begyle
His trewe love, the devel quyte hym his while!

Explicit Legenda Adriane De Athenes.

VII

THE LEGEND OF PHILOMELA

Incipit Legenda Philomene.

Deus dator formarum.

Thow yevere of the formes, that hast
          wrought
This fayre world, and bar it in thy thought
Eternaly, er thow thy werk began,   2230
Why madest thow, unto the slaunder of man,
Or, al be that it was nat thy doing,
As for that fyn, to make swich a thyng,
Whi sufferest thow that Tereus was bore,
That is in love so fals and so forswore,   2235
That fro this world up to the firste hevene
Corrumpeth, whan that folk his name nevene?
And, as to me, so grisely was his dede
That, whan that I his foule storye rede,
Myne eyen wexe foule and sore also.   2240
Yit last the venym of so longe ago,
That it enfecteth hym that wol beholde
The storye of Tereus, of which I tolde.

Of Trace was he lord, and kyn to Marte,   2244
The crewel god that stant with blody darte;
And wedded hadde he, with a blysful cheere,
Kyng Pandiones fayre doughter dere,
That highte Progne, flour of hire cuntre,
Thogh Juno lyst nat at the feste to be,
Ne Imeneus, that god of wedyng is;   2250
But at the feste redy ben, ywis,
The Furies thre, with al here mortal brond.
The oule al nyght aboute the balkes wond,
That prophete is of wo and of myschaunce.
This revel, ful of song and ek of daunce,   2255
Laste a fortenyght, or lytel lasse.
But, shortly of this story for to passe,
For I am wery of hym for to telle,
Fyve yer his wif and he togeder dwelle,
Til on a day she gan so sore longe   2260

To sen hire sister, that she say nat longe,
That for desyr she nyste what to seye.
But to hire husbonde gan she for to preye,
For Godes love, that she moste ones gon
Hyre syster for to sen, and come anon,   2265
Or elles, but she moste to hire wende,
She preyde hym that he wolde after hire sende;
And this was, day by day, al hire preyere,
With al humblesse of wifhod, word and chere.
   This Tereus let make his shipes yare,   2270
And into Grece hymself is forth yfare.
Unto his fadyr-in-lawe gan he preye
To vouche-sauf that, for a month or tweye,
That Philomene, his wyves syster, myghte
On Progne his wyf but ones han a syghte —
"And she shal come to yow ageyn anon.   2276
Myself with hyre I wol bothe come and gon,
And as myn hertes lyf I wol hire kepe."
   This olde Pandion, this kyng, gan wepe
For tendernesse of herte, for to leve   2280
His doughter gon, and for to yeve hire leve;
Of al this world he loveth nothyng so;
But at the laste leve hath she to go.
For Philomene, with salte teres eke,
Gan of hire fader grace to beseke   2285
To sen hire syster, that she loveth so;
And hym embraseth with hire armes two.
And therwithal so yong and fayr was she
That, whan that Tereus saw hire beaute,   2289
And of aray that there was non hire lyche,
And yit of beaute was she two so ryche,
He caste his fyry herte upon hyre so
That he wol have hir, how so that it go;
And with his wiles kneled and so preyde,
Tyl at the laste Pandyon thus seyde: 2295
"Now, sone," quod he, "that art to me so dere,
I the betake my yonge doughter here,
That bereth the keye of al myn hertes lyf.
And gret me wel my doughter and thy wif,
And yif hire leve somtyme for to pleye,   2300
That she may sen me ones er I deye."
And sothly, he hath mad hym riche feste,
And to his folk, the moste and ek the leste,
That with hym com; and yaf hym yiftes grete,
And hym conveyeth thourgh the mayster-strete
Of Athenes, and to the se hym broughte,   2306
And turneth hom; no malyce he ne thoughte.
   The ores pullen forth the vessel faste,
And into Trace aryveth at the laste,
And up into a forest he hire ledde,   2310
And to a cave pryvely hym spedde;
And in this derke cave, yif hir leste,
Or leste nat, he bad hire for to reste;
For which hire herte agros, and seyde thus:

"Where is my sister, brother Tereus?"   2315
And therwithal she wepte tenderly,
And quok for fere, pale and pitously,
Ryght as the lamb that of the wolf is biten;
Or as the culver, that of the egle is smiten,
And is out of his clawes forth escaped,   2320
Yit it is afered and awhaped,
Lest it be hent eft-sones; so sat she.
But utterly, it may non other be.
By force hath he, this traytour, don that dede,
That he hath reft hire of hire mayden-
     hede,   2325
Maugre hire hed, by strengthe and by his
     myght.
Lo! here a dede of men, and that a ryght!
She cryeth "syster!" with ful loud a stevene,
And "fader dere!" and "help me, God in
     hevene!"
Al helpeth nat; and yit this false thef   2330
Hath don this lady yit a more myschef,
For fere lest she shulde his shame crye,
And don hym openly a vilenye,
And with his swerd hire tonge of kerveth he,
And in a castel made hire for to be   2335
Ful pryvely in prisoun everemore,
And kepte hire to his usage and his store,
So that she myghte hym neveremore asterte.
O sely Philomene, wo is thyn herte!
God wreke thee, and sende the thy bone!   2340
Now is it tyme I make an ende sone.
   This Tereus is to his wif ycome,
And in his armes hath his wif ynome,
And pitously he wep, and shok his hed,
And swor hir that he fond hir sister ded;   2345
For which this sely Progne hath swich wo
That nygh hire sorweful herte brak a-two.
And thus in terys lete I Progne dwelle,
And of hire sister forth I wol yow telle.
   This woful lady lerned hadde in youthe   2350
So that she werken and enbroude couthe,
And weven in hire stol the radevore
As it of wemen hath be woned yore.
And, sothly for to seyne, she hadde hire fille
Of mete and drynk, and clothyng at hire
     wille.   2355
She coude eek rede, and wel ynow endyte,
But with a penne coude she nat wryte.
But letters can she weve to and fro,
So that, by that the yer was al ago,
She hadde ywoven in a stamyn large   2360
How she was brought from Athenes in a barge,
And in a cave how that she was brought;
And al the thyng that Tereus hath wrought,
She waf it wel, and wrot the storye above,

How she was served for hire systers love.   2365
And to a knave a ryng she yaf anon,
And preyed hym, by signes, for to gon
Unto the queen, and beren hir that cloth,
And by signes swor hym many an oth,   2369
She wolde hym yeven what she geten myghte.
This knave anon unto the quene hym dyghte,
And tok it hire, and al the maner tolde.
And whan that Progne hath this thing beholde,
No word she spak, for sorwe and ek for rage,
But feynede hire to gon on pilgrymage   2375
To Bacus temple; and in a litel stounde
Hire dombe sister sittynge hath she founde,
Wepynge in the castel, here alone.
Allas! the wo, the compleynt, and the mone

That Progne upon hire doumbe syster maketh!   2380
In armes everych of hem other taketh,
And thus I late hem in here sorwe dwelle.
    The remenaunt is no charge for to telle,
For this is al and som: thus was she served,
That nevere harm agilte ne deserved   2385
Unto this crewel man, that she of wiste.
Ye may be war of men, if that yow liste.
For al be it that he wol nat, for shame,
Don as Tereus, to lese his name,
Ne serve yow as a morderour or a knave,   2390
Ful lytel while shal ye trewe hym have —
That wol I seyn, al were he now my brother —
But it so be that he may have non other.

Explicit Legenda Philomene.

VIII

THE LEGEND OF PHYLLIS

Incipit Legenda Phillis.

By preve as wel as by autorite,
That wiked fruit cometh of a wiked tre,   2395
That may ye fynde, if that it like yow.
But for this ende I speke this as now,
To tellen yow of false Demophon.
In love a falser herde I nevere non,
But if it were his fader Theseus.   2400
"God, for his grace, fro swich oon kepe us!"
Thus may these women preyen that it here.
Now to the effect turne I of my matere.
    Destroyed is of Troye the cite;
This Demophon com seylynge in the se   2405
Toward Athenes, to his paleys large.
With hym com many a ship and many a barge
Ful of his folk, of whiche ful many oon
Is wounded sore, and sek, and wo begon,
As they han at th'asege longe yleyn.   2410
Byhynde hym com a wynd and ek a reyn
That shof so sore, his sayl ne myghte stonde;
Hym were levere than al the world a-londe,
So hunteth hym the tempest to and fro.
So derk it was, he coude nowher go;   2415
And with a wawe brosten was his stere.
His ship was rent so lowe, in swich manere,
That carpenter ne coude it nat amende.

The se, by nyghte, as any torche it brende
For wod, and possith hym now up, now doun,
Til Neptune hath of hym compassioun,   2421
And Thetis, Chorus, Triton, and they alle,
And maden hym upon a lond to falle,
Wherof that Phillis lady was and queene,
Ligurges doughter, fayrer on to sene   2425
Than is the flour ageyn the bryghte sonne.
Unnethe is Demophon to londe ywonne,
Wayk, and ek wery, and his folk forpyned
Of werynesse, and also enfamyned,
That to the deth he almost was ydriven.   2430
His wise folk to conseyl han hym yiven
To seken help and socour of the queen,
And loke what his grace myghte been,
And maken in that lond som chevysaunce,
To kepen hym fro wo and fro myschaunce.
For syk he was, and almost at the deth;   2436
Unnethe myghte he speke or drawe his breth,
And lyth in Rodopeya hym for to reste.
Whan he may walke, hym thoughte it was the
        beste
Unto the court to seken for socour.   2440
Men knewen hym wel, and diden hym honour;
For of Athenes duk and lord was he,

As Theseus his fader hadde be,
That in his tyme was of gret renoun,
No man so gret in al the regyoun,   2445
And lyk his fader of face and of stature,
And fals of love; it com hym of nature.
As doth the fox Renard, the foxes sone,
Of kynde he coude his olde faders wone,
Withoute lore, as can a drake swimme   2450
Whan it is caught and caryed to the brymme.
This honurable Phillis doth hym chere;
Hire liketh wel his port and his manere.
But, for I am agroted herebyforn
To wryte of hem that ben in love forsworn,
And ek to haste me in my legende,   2456
(Which to performe God me grace sende!)
Therfore I passe shortly in this wyse.
Ye han wel herd of Theseus devyse
In the betraysynge of fayre Adryane,   2460
That of hire pite kepte him from his bane.
At shorte wordes, ryght so Demophon
The same wey, the same path hath gon,
That dide his false fader Theseus.
For unto Phillis hath he sworen thus,   2465
To wedden hire, and hire his trouthe plyghte,
And piked of hire al the good he myghte,
Whan he was hol and sound, and hadde his
       reste;
And doth with Phillis what so that hym leste,
As wel coude I, if that me leste so,   2470
Tellen al his doynge to and fro.

He seyde, unto his contre moste he sayle,
For there he wolde hire weddynge aparayle,
As fel to hire honour, and his also.
And openly he tok his leve tho,   2475
And hath hire sworn he wolde nat sojorne,
But in a month he wolde ageyn retorne;
And in that lond let make his ordenaunce
As verray lord, and tok the obeysaunce
Wel and homly, and let his shipes dighte,   2480
And hom he goth the nexte wey he myghte.
For unto Phillis yit ne com he nought;
And that hath she so harde and sore abought,
Allas! that, as the storyes us recorde,   2484
She was hire owene deth ryght with a corde,
Whan that she saw that Demophon hire
       trayed.
But to hym first she wrot, and faste him prayed
He wolde come, and hire delyvere of peyne,
As I reherce shal a word or tweyne.
Me lyste nat vouche-sauf on hym to swynke,
Ne spende on hym a penne ful of ynke,   2491
For fals in love was he, ryght as his syre.
The devil sette here soules bothe afyre!
But of the letter of Phillis wol I wryte

A word or two, althogh it be but lyte.   2495
"Thyn hostesse," quod she, "O Demophon,
Thy Phillis, which that is so wo begon,
Of Rodopeye, upon yow mot compleyne
Over the terme set bytwixe us tweyne,
That ye ne holde forward, as ye seyde.   2500
Youre anker, which ye in oure haven leyde,
Hyghte us that ye wolde comen, out of doute,
Or that the mone wente ones aboute.
But tymes foure the mone hath hid hire face,
Syn thilke day ye wente from this place,   2505
And foure tymes lyghte the world ageyn.
But for al that, yif I shal soothly seyn,
Yit hath the strem of Sytho nat ybrought
From Athenes the ship; yit cometh it noght.
And if that ye the terme rekene wolde,   2510
As I or as a trewe lovere shulde,
I pleyne nat, God wot, byforn my day."
But al hire letter wryten I ne may
By order, for it were to me a charge;
Hire letter was ryght long and therto large.
But here and ther in rym I have it layd,   2516
There as me thoughte that she wel hath sayd.
She seyde, "Thy sayles come nat agen,
Ne to thy word there is no fey certeyn;
But I wot why ye come nat," quod she,   2520
"For I was of my love to yow to fre.
And of the goddes that ye han forswore,
Yif hire vengeaunce falle on yow therfore,
Ye be nat suffisaunt to bere the peyne.
To moche trusted I, wel may I pleyne,   2525
Upon youre lynage and youre fayre tonge,
And on youre teres falsly out yronge.
How coude ye wepe so by craft?" quod she.
"May there swiche teres feyned be?
Now certes, yif ye wol have in memorye,   2530
It oughte be to yow but lyte glorye
To han a sely mayde thus betrayed!
To God," quod she, "preye I, and ofte have
       prayed,
That it mot be the grettest prys of alle,   2534
And most honour that evere the shal befalle!
And whan thyne olde auncestres peynted be,
In which men may here worthynesse se,
Thanne preye I God thow peynted be also
That folk may rede, forby as they go,
'Lo! this is he, that with his flaterye   2540
Bytraised hath and don hire vilenye
That was his trewe love in thought and dede!'
But sothly, of oo poynt yit may they rede,
That ye ben lyk youre fader as in this,
For he begiled Adriane, ywis,   2545
With swich an art and with swich subtilte
As thow thyselven hast begyled me.

As in that poynt, althogh it be nat fayr,
Thow folwest hym, certayn, and art his ayr.
But syn thus synfully ye me begile,   2550
My body mote ye se, withinne a while,
Ryght in the haven of Athenes fletynge,
Withoute sepulture and buryinge,
Thogh ye ben harder than is any ston."

And whan this letter was forth sent anon,   2555
And knew how brotel and how fals he was,
She for dispeyr fordide hyreself, allas!
Swych sorwe hath she, for she besette hire so.
Be war, ye wemen, of youre subtyl fo,
Syn yit this day men may ensaumple se;   2560
And trusteth, as in love, no man but me.

Explicit Legenda Phillis.

IX

THE LEGEND OF HYPERMNESTRA

Incipit Legenda Ypermystre.

In Grece whilom weren brethren two,
Of whiche that oon was called Danao,
That many a sone hath of his body wonne,
As swiche false lovers ofte conne.   2565
Among his sones alle there was oon
That aldermost he lovede of everychoon.
And whan this child was born, this Danao
Shop hym a name, and callede hym Lyno.
That other brother called was Egiste,   2570
That was of love as fals as evere hym liste,
And many a doughter gat he in his lyf;
Of whiche he gat upon his ryghte wyf
A doughter dere, and dide hire for to calle
Ypermystra, yongeste of hem alle.   2575
The whiche child, of hire natyvyte,
To alle thewes goode yborn was she,
As likede to the goddes, er she was born,
That of the shef she sholde be the corn.
The Wirdes, that we clepen Destine,   2580
Hath shapen hire that she mot nedes be
Pyëtous, sad, wis, and trewe as stel,
As to these wemen it acordeth wel.
For thogh that Venus yaf hire gret beaute,
With Jupiter compouned so was she   2585
That conscience, trouthe, and drede of shame,
And of hyre wifhod for to kepe hire name,
This, thoughte hire, was felycite as here.
The rede Mars was that tyme of the yeere
So feble that his malyce is hym raft;   2590
Repressed hath Venus his crewel craft,
That, what with Venus and other oppressioun
Of houses, Mars his venim is adoun,
That Ypermystra dar nat handle a knyf
In malyce, thogh she shulde lese hire lyf.   2595

But natheles, as hevene gan tho turne,
To badde aspectes hath she of Saturne,
That made hire for to deyen in prisoun,
As I shal after make mencioun.
   To Danao and Egistes also —   2600
Althogh so be that they were brethren two,
For thilke tyme was spared no lynage —
It lykede hem to make a maryage
Bytwixen Ypermystre and hym Lyno,
And casten swich a day it shal be so,   2605
And ful acorded was it utterly;
The aray is wrought, the tyme is faste by.
And thus Lyno hath of his faders brother
The doughter wedded, and ech of hem hath
      other.
The torches brennen, and the laumpes bryghte;
The sacryfices ben ful redy dighte;   2611
Th'encens out of the fyre reketh sote;
The flour, the lef is rent up by the rote
To maken garlondes and crounes hye.
Ful is the place of soun of minstralsye,   2615
Of songes amorous of maryage,
As thylke tyme was the pleyne usage.
And this was in the paleys of Egiste,
That in his hous was lord, ryght as hym lyste.
And thus the day they dryve to an ende;   2620
The frendes taken leve, and hom they wende;
The nyght is come, the bryd shal go to bedde.
Egistus to his chamber faste hym spedde,
And prively he let his doughter calle.   2624
Whan that the hous was voyded of hem alle,
He loketh on his doughter with glad chere,
And to hire spak, as ye shal after here:
"My ryghte doughter, tresor of myn herte,

Syn fyrst that day that shapen was my sherte,
Or by the fatal systren had my dom,   2630
So nygh myn herte nevere thyng ne com
As thow, myn Ypermystre, doughter dere.
Tak hed what I, thy fader, seye the here,
And werk after thy wiser evere mo.
For alderfirst, doughter, I love the so   2635
That al the world to me nis half so lef;
Ne I nolde rede the to thy myschef
For al the good under the colde mone.
And what I mene, it shal be seyd right sone,
With protestacioun, as in this wyse,   2640
That, but thow do as I shal the devyse,
Thow shalt be ded, by hym that al hath
    wrought!
At shorte wordes thow ne scapest nought
Out of my paleys, or that thow be ded,
But thow consente and werke after my red;
Tak this to thee for ful conclusioun."   2646
   This Ypermystre caste hire eyen doun,
And quok as doth the lef of aspe grene,
Ded wex hire hew, and lyk an ash to sene,
And seyde, "Lord and fader, al youre wille,
After my myght, God wot, I shal fulfille,   2651
So it to me be no confusioun."
"I nele," quod he, "have non excepcioun";
And out he caught a knyf, as rasour kene.
"Hyd this," quod he, "that it be nat ysene;
And, whan thyn husbonde is to bedde go,   2656
Whil that he slepeth, kit his throte atwo.
For in my dremes it is warned me
How that my nevew shal my bane be,
But which I noot, wherfore I wol be siker.   2660
If thow sey nay, we two shul have a biker,
As I have seyd, by hym that I have sworn!"
   This Ipermystre hath nygh hire wit forlorn;
And, for to passen harmles of that place,
She graunteth hym; ther is non other grace.
And therwithal a costret taketh he,   2666
And seyde, "Herof a draught, or two, or thre,
Yif hym to drynke, whan he goth to reste,
And he shal slepe as longe as evere thee leste,
The narcotyks and opies ben so stronge.   2670
And go thy wey, lest that him thynke longe."
Out cometh the bryd, and with ful sobre cheere,
As is of maydens ofte the manere,
To chaumbre is brought with revel and with
    song.
And shortly, lest this tale be to long,   2675

This Lyno and she sone ben brought to bedde,
And every wight out at the dore hym spedde.
   The nyght is wasted, and he fyl aslepe.
Ful tenderly begynneth she to wepe;   2679
She rist hire up, and dredfully she quaketh,
As doth the braunche that Zepherus shaketh,
And hust were alle in Argon that cite.
As cold as any frost now waxeth she;
For pite by the herte hire streyneth so,
And drede of deth doth hire so moche wo,   2685
That thryes doun she fyl in swich a were.
She rist yit up, and stakereth her and there,
And on hire hondes faste loketh she.
"Allas! and shal myne hondes blody be?
I am a mayde, and, as by my nature,   2690
And bi my semblaunt and by my vesture,
Myne handes ben nat shapen for a knyf,
As for to reve no man fro his lyf.
What devel have I with the knyf to do?
And shal I have my throte korve a-two?   2695
Thanne shal I blede, allas! and me beshende!
And nedes-cost this thyng moste have an ende;
Or he or I mot nedes lese oure lyf.
Now certes," quod she, "syn I am his wif,
And hath my feyth, yit is it bet for me   2700
For to be ded in wifly honeste
Than ben a traytour lyvynge in my shame.
Be as be may, for ernest or for game,
He shal awake, and ryse, and gon his way,
Out at this goter, or that it be day" —   2705
And wep ful tenderly upon his face,
And in hyre armes gan hym to enbrace,
And hym she roggeth and awaketh softe.
And at a wyndow lep he fro the lofte,
Whan she hath warned hym, and don hym
    bote.   2710
This Lyno swift was, and lyght of fote,
And from his wif he ran a ful good pas.
This sely woman is so weik, allas!
And helples so, that, or that she fer wente,
Hire crewel fader dide hire for to hente.   2715
Allas! Lyno! whi art thow so unkynde?
Why ne haddest thow remembred in thy mynde
To taken hire, and lad hire forth with the?
For, whan she saw that gon awey was he,
And that she myghte nat so faste go,   2720
Ne folwen hym, she sat hire doun ryght tho,
Til she was caught and fetered in prysoun.
This tale is seyd for this conclusioun —

[*Unfinished.*]

SHORT POEMS

IT IS supposed that in addition to the narrative poems by which Chaucer is chiefly known he also composed lyrics in considerable number. This is altogether probable in itself. He would be likely, as a young courtier, to have possessed and practised such accomplishments as he ascribes to the Squire in the *General Prologue,* who, it will be recalled, "koude songes make and wel endite." In the Prologue to the *Legend of Good Women* Alceste pleads on Chaucer's behalf that he has made

Many an ympne for Loves halidayes

That highte balades, roundels, virelayes,

and her testimony — lest it should be dismissed as fiction — is confirmed by that of Gower and Lydgate. But of all these songs, if they ever existed, very few have come down to us under Chaucer's name. Only about a score of his short poems are now known, and of these not more than ten, including some of doubtful authorship, could be reckoned as hymns for the God of Love. The others, which are nearly all ballades in form, are either humorous epistles or poems on moral or religious subjects.

Hardly any of Chaucer's short poems can be precisely dated. The Envoy of the *Complaint to His Empty Purse* was certainly written after the accession of Henry IV, and so may be the latest piece of his composition that is preserved. But the *Complaint* itself is possibly of earlier date. The *A B C,* if the association with the Duchess Blanche of Lancaster is trustworthy, may be the earliest of the poet's surviving works. In any case there is every probability that he composed it in his youth. The *Envoy to Bukton* can be attached with considerable confidence to an expedition of the year 1396, and the *Envoy to Scogan,* less confidently, to the floods of 1393. But the events which underlie the other pieces are either entirely doubtful or of uncertain date, and the poems can be arranged only in an approximate order, based

partly upon the evidence of their relation to Chaucer's longer works.

It is only in the looser sense of the word that most of Chaucer's short poems can be called lyrics. In so far as lyrical poetry is an intensely individual expression of thought or feeling, it would seem not to have been natural to Chaucer's temperament. Even among narrative poets he is exceptionally objective and impersonal; and for that matter, the individual "lyric cry" was not characteristic of his age. His few love-poems, to be sure, are written in the first person, and have been held by biographers to give evidence of a "long, early, and hopeless" attachment. But they sound rather like exercises in a conventional style of composition. The more mature pieces are in a didactic or satirical vein. Whether any poems of the whole series are lyrics in the particular sense of having been composed as songs, is hard to judge. The roundel in the *Parliament of Fowls* — "Now welcom somer with thy sonne softe" — proves that Chaucer could write verse that sings itself, and several of the short poems have a comparable movement. Chaucer may very well have written some of them for music, if he did not, like a number of his contemporaries, himself compose the melodies. But very few of them would find a place in a song-book.

They do show, however, that Chaucer, from his early years, was concerned with metrical technique and given to experimentation, and they are consequently of much interest to the historian of English verse. The *Complaint unto Pity* and *Complaint to his Lady* furnish what are probably the earliest English examples of the seven-line stanza known as rime royal, and the latter contains also the first attempt in English at the imitating of Dante's *terza rima.* Most striking of all, Chaucer found, apparently at the very outset, the measure which he practically introduced into English versification, and which he employed in all of his greatest works — the five-accent, or decasyllabic, line. Only a few inconspicuous examples of it have been shown to occur earlier in English. Chaucer is commonly said to have derived it, at least in the couplet arrangement, from Machaut, but his persistent use of it must have been largely due to the *endecasillabi* of his Italian masters. He employed it in his earliest short poems, even in the *A B C*, of which the French original was in octosyllabics. It not only remained the favorite measure of his later works, but became, in the stanzaic combinations and couplets which he made current, and afterwards in blank verse, the most characteristic line of English prosody.

An A B C. — According to a statement in Speght's edition of Chaucer, the *A B C*, or La Prière de Nostre Dame, was made "at the request of Blanche, Duchess of Lancaster, as a prayer for her private use, being a woman in her religion very devout." The Duchess died in 1369, and there is no reason for hesitating to date the poem in or before that year. It is a rather free rendering, with the metrical modification already mentioned, of a prayer in Deguilleville's Pèlerinage de la Vie Humaine. A complete translation of the French poem, with the exception of the prayer, was afterward made by Lydgate. It is interesting to note that Deguilleville's work, used by the young Chaucer, was a forerunner, if not in some measure an actual model, of Bunyan's Pilgrim's Progress.

The *A B C* being only a translation, reveals very little about Chaucer. If the tradition about the Duchess Blanche is true, it is not possible even to credit him with the choice of the subject, and to draw inferences therefrom. But the poem itself, if not an evidence of Chaucer's piety, is a characteristic expression of the piety of his age, and is by no means an unworthy specimen of the hymns and prayers evoked by the veneration of the Blessed Virgin.

The Complaint unto Pity. — The three pieces that follow, together with the *Complaynt d'Amours* and the complaints of Mars, Venus, and Anelida, belong to a type of poetry that was very much cultivated in mediæval France

and England. As a literary term, "complaint," or its Latin equivalent "planctus," had a variety of applications. The De Planctu Naturae of Alanus de Insulis is a kind of poetic treatise, in which Nature is represented as deploring the sins and shortcomings of mankind. Similarly, in various languages, the title was given to religious lyrics, and there are complaints of Christ and of the Virgin; complaints of the Soul and of the Flesh. The term was applied also to poems of lamentations on particular catastrophes, as when Geoffrey of Vinsauf "complained the death so sore" of Richard I. Indeed the idea of a formal lament became so familiar that Chaucer puts more or less elaborate complaints into the mouths of the characters in a number of his stories, and in the *Physician's Tale* Virginia asks her father, before killing her to preserve her honor, to grant her a respite in which she may "complain her death."

The theme of love-poetry, from antiquity down, has often been the sorrow or grievance of the unaccepted lover, and this sentiment found natural expression in the complaint. It is to the type of amorous complaint that nearly all of Chaucer's lyrics, so entitled, belong, and the first of them, the *Complaint unto Pity*, is an excellent specimen. No definite source is known for it, though parallels have been pointed out for the ideas, which are for the most part familiar and conventional. As in the following *Complaint to his Lady* and the *Complaynt d'Amours*, the poet speaks in the first person and appears to be the lover. But there is little likelihood that the poems reflect a serious experience of Chaucer's.

A Complaint to his Lady. — The piece usually printed as the *Complaint to his Lady* is fragmentary, and it is not certain that the three parts constitute a single poem. But they are bound together by the common theme of unrequited love. For this complaint, again, no source is known, but the attempt at *terza rima* points to the influence of Dante. The ideas are thoroughly conventional, and the poem is chiefly interesting for the versification.

The Complaint of Mars. — In *The Complaint of Mars* the speaker is no longer the poet, but the Roman divinity, and the cause of his lament, as in the case of the *Complaint of Anelida,* is explained in an introductory narrative. The simple incident of the separation of Mars and Venus by the coming of Phebus is told with various complications of detail which have been shown to refer, not properly to the gods, but to the positions and movements of the corresponding planets. So the whole poem may be regarded as a treatment, in personal or human terms, of a conjunction of Mars and Venus. Whether it has further meaning, as an allegory of an intrigue at court, is a matter of disagreement. Shirley, in a note at the end of his copy of the poem, recorded the belief that it referred to a *liaison* between John Holland, Lord Huntingdon, and Isabel, Duchess of York. He added that the French original of the so-called *Complaint of Venus* (here printed among Chaucer's late poems) was written by Otes de Granson for Isabel, in the character of Venus. Most editors of Chaucer have accepted the tradition, at least as regards the *Complaint of Mars.* Chaucer's recent biographer, Mr. Cowling, would interpret the *Mars* as referring rather to the seduction of Elizabeth, daughter of John of Gaunt, by the same John Holland. But both these personal applications are altogether doubtful, and the astronomical interpretation would account sufficiently for the poem. It seems clear in any case that the *Complaint of Venus,* traditionally so entitled because of Shirley's explanation, had originally no connection with the *Complaint of Mars.*

ROSEMOUNDE. — The metrical form which Chaucer chiefly employed in his later lyrics was the ballade. In origin a dance-song, the ballade came to be written in various measures and stanzaic arrangements. In Chaucer's hand it usually consisted of seven-line or eight-line stanzas, followed by an envoy. In substance, very commonly, the ballade was a love-lyric. But its uses, like those of the English sonnet in the time of Milton, were extended to cover a great variety of subjects, conspicuously by Chaucer's French contemporary, Eustache Deschamps, who wrote innumerable poems of the type dealing with moral philosophy and social satire. In treating a similar range of subjects, in his later ballades, Chaucer may have been consciously following Deschamp's example.

The poem to *Rosemounde,* the following one, entitled *Womanly Noblesse,* and the one *Against Women Inconstant* (here included among pieces of doubtful authorship) appear to be the earliest of Chaucer's ballades that are preserved. The *Rosemounde,* addressed to an unknown lady, is a typical complimentary poem in the spirit of courtly love. But in its grace and humor it is distinctively Chaucerian.

WOMANLY NOBLESSE. — Although called a ballade in the manuscript and accompanied by the usual envoy, *Womanly Noblesse* has a difficult rime scheme not elsewhere adopted by Chaucer in poems of the type. In spite of the scribe's ascription to Chaucer, his authorship has been questioned. The poem is less characteristic of him than the *Rosemounde,* but there seems to be no good reason for rejecting it from the canon.

ADAM SCRIVEYN. — The lines to Adam Scriveyn, which read like one of the personal epigrams of the ancients, reveal some of the anxieties which beset an author before the invention of printing. The poem could hardly be more vivid if the record searchers should succeed in discovering Adam's family name. Some of their conjectures on the subject are recorded in the explanatory notes.

THE FORMER AGE. — The following five ballades, all on moral or philosophical subjects, are associated by a common, though unequal, indebtedness to the De Consolatione Philosophiae. They are here printed in a series because of this relationship to Boethius. But it is not necessarily to be inferred that they were written in close sequence. The date of none of them is certain, but such doubtful references to contemporary events as have been noted in them point to their composition at intervals of several years.

The *Former Age* cannot be attached to any definite occasion, though the reflections on the happiness of man's primeval state might well

have been prompted by the troubled conditions of the reign of Richard II. The central
idea of the poem is familiar in literature —
classical, early Christian, mediæval, and modern. Chaucer must have known many expressions of it, but his actual sources were apparently few. In addition to Boethius he made
use of Ovid and the Roman de la Rose, and
possibly of Virgil.

FORTUNE. — Chaucer's general conception
and doctrine of Fortune are derived primarily
from Boethius. In the Consolation, as in Chaucer's ballade sequence, there is a complaint
against Fortune, a defense of the goddess, and
a discussion of her significance. But the influence of other authors, certainly Jean de
Meun and probably Dante, is also apparent.
It is noteworthy that here, as in some of his
other references to Fortune, Chaucer, following the teaching of Boethius and Dante, so to
speak adopts the pagan divinity into the system
of Christian theology, and makes her the executor of the will of God.

The occasion of the poem is unknown. It is
clearly an appeal for favor, and the poet's
"beste frend" might be either John of Gaunt or
the King. Some critics, favoring on literary
grounds a date in the eighties, hold the reference to be to Lancaster. But the three princes
addressed in the Envoy seem to be the Dukes
of Lancaster, York, and Gloucester, who were
given control, in 1390, over gifts made at the
cost of the King. Unless the Envoy, then, was
attached to an earlier poem, the appeal was
apparently intended for the King himself.

TRUTH. — To judge by the twenty-two manuscript copies that are preserved, *Truth,* or the
Balade de Bon Conseyl, would seem to have
been the best known or most admired of Chaucer's short poems. The interest in it may have
been increased by the belief that it was the
parting counsel of the poet, composed upon his
deathbed. Reasons have been found for doubting that tradition, but the poem is none the
less an epitome of a wise practical philosophy,
expressed in a Christian spirit. In its general
thought *Truth* shows the influence of Boethius,
though it does not closely follow particular

passages. Biblical influence is also apparent in
both thought and language, most notably in
the refrain, which echoes the Gospel of John:
"Ye shall know the truth, and the truth shall
make you free."

According to the traditional opinion, as has
just been said, Chaucer's good counsel was intended to be general, and was written at the
end of his life. But an acute observer has recognized in the puzzling word "vache" in the
Envoy the name of Sir Philip de la Vache, who
married the daughter of Chaucer's intimate
friend, Sir Lewis Clifford. The question again
arises whether the ballade proper was composed
independently of the envoy. But it is highly
probable that Chaucer wrote the poem to give
advice or encouragement to his young friend.
And though the immediate occasion is unknown, a date before 1390 seems best to fit
the circumstances of Sir Philip's life.

GENTILESSE. — Chaucer's teaching concerning "gentilesse," like that concerning Fortune,
is compounded of ideas derived from Boethius,
Dante, and Jean de Meun. He repeats it in
very similar terms in the *Wife of Bath's Tale,*
where Dante is quoted by name. The sentiments he expresses are sometimes treated by
critics as if they were bold utterances, far in
advance of the social philosophy of the age.
But on the contrary the doctrine that gentility
depends on character, not inheritance — *virtus,
non sanguis* — was commonly received opinion.
It might be described as the Christian democ-
racy regularly taught by the church, though
not regularly exemplified in Christian society.

LAK OF STEDFASTNESSE. — The title *Lak of
Stedfastnesse* is now commonly used for the
poem described by Shirley as a "Balade Royal
made by our Laureal poete of Albyon in hees
laste yeres." The envoy, in Shirley's copy, is
headed "Lenvoye to Kyng Richard." Another
manuscript also says that Chaucer sent the
poem to the King, and there is no reason for
discrediting the statement. But Shirley's assignment of the poem to Chaucer's last years
is more open to question, especially since doubt
has been cast upon his similar dating of *Truth.*
The complaint of lack of steadfastness in the

state of England would certainly have been appropriate in the period from 1386 to 1390, to which reasons have been given for assigning some of the other ballades of the Boethian group.

THE COMPLAINT OF VENUS. — The inappropriate title of the *Complaint of Venus*, and the allegorical interpretation which applies it to the Duchess of York, have already been explained in the account of the *Complaint of Mars*. The series of ballades which compose the *Venus* are freely translated from ballades of Otes de Granson, and appear to have no relation to the *Mars*. Nor is it necessary to see in either the *Mars* or the *Venus* a reference to the love-affairs of Isabel of York. Some critics who reject the allegory still hold that Chaucer probably translated the ballades for Isabel. But this also is rendered doubtful by the well-supported reading *Princes*, for *Princess*, in the envoy. On the whole the purpose and destination of the poem must be regarded as entirely uncertain. The date is likewise unknown. The French ballades are held by M. Piaget, who edited them, to have been written in Granson's youth, but Chaucer's envoy contains a reference to old age which has led to the classification of his translation with his later poems.

LENVOY DE CHAUCER A SCOGAN. — In the envoys to Scogan and Bukton Chaucer employs, not the ballade form with its continuous rime scheme and recurrent refrain, but a free sequence of seven-line or eight-line stanzas. In each case, however, the last stanza, with its personal message, has somewhat the effect of the envoy of a regular ballade.

The serious purpose of the letter to Scogan, in so far as it had any, was apparently to ask for the good offices of a friend at court. This appears in the final stanza. In the body of the epistle Chaucer rallies Scogan humorously on his disloyalty to Venus, and warns him against the vengeance of the goddess. Thus the poem takes its place among the documents cited in exposition of Chaucer's treatment of courtly love.

Scogan is probably to be identified as Henry Scogan, an avowed disciple of Chaucer, who wrote a Moral Ballade, addressed to the sons of Henry IV. Chaucer's *Envoy* is supposed to have been written in 1393.

LENVOY DE CHAUCER A BUKTON. — The *Envoy to Bukton*, from its reference to capture "in Fryse," can be confidently dated in 1396, the year of an expedition against Friesland. It may have been addressed to either Sir Peter Bukton, of Holderness in Yorkshire, or Sir Robert Bukton, of Goosewold in Suffolk. Both men were associated with Chaucer's circle, but Sir Peter's close relations with the house of Lancaster make it seem probable that the *Envoy* was intended for him.

Like the *Envoy to Scogan*, it is a humorous epistle. But this time the humor takes a different turn. Bukton's approaching marriage is the occasion of the bantering address, in which Chaucer, in gay spirit, rehearses some of the time-honored attacks upon matrimony. It ought not to be necessary to add, but some remarks of the commentators invite the observation, that the *Envoy* is not to be taken seriously as evidence that Chaucer either disapproved his friend's marriage or regretted his own!

THE COMPLAINT OF CHAUCER TO HIS PURSE. — The envoy of the *Complaint to his Purse* must have been written immediately after the coronation of Henry IV, on September 30, 1399. From the fact that the *Complaint* is preserved in some manuscripts without the envoy, it is conjectured that Chaucer wrote it earlier, perhaps as a petition to Richard II. But in the date of its actual use, or what might be called its publication, it is the last work known to have come from the author's hand. It is interesting to see the elderly Chaucer reverting to the type of poem which he wrote in his youth, the lover's complaint, here skillfully travestied in the appeal to his new lady, his empty purse. And the petition was not only skillful, but also effective. At all events, on October 3, 1399, Chaucer received a grant from Henry IV.

Short Poems of Doubtful Authorship

A few poems have been here classified by themselves as of doubtful authorship, either because they are not ascribed to Chaucer in the manuscripts, or because something in their language or style makes their authenticity questionable. Of this group the ballades *Against Women Unconstant* and *Complaynt d'Amours* and the roundel *Merciles Beaute* are almost certainly Chaucer. The *Balade of Complaint* and the *Proverbs* are very doubtful indeed.

AGAINST WOMEN UNCONSTANT. — This ballade bears a general resemblance to one of Machaut's, which has the same refrain. But Chaucer's poem is not a translation of the French one, and no source for it has been discovered. Its occasion is also unknown. Its mood, as Skeat observed, is somewhat like that of *Lak of Stedfastnesse,* but the subject is more personal.

COMPLAYNT D'AMOURS. — This is a typical complaint for unrequited love, and was perhaps written merely as a poetic exercise for St. Valentine's Day. If genuine it is probably to be assigned to Chaucer's early period, along with several other poems on the same theme.

MERCILES BEAUTE. — The roundel appropriately entitled *Merciles Beaute* in the single manuscript which contains it, treats its conventional subject in characteristically Chaucerian spirit and style. No definite source has been found for it, though several passages which Chaucer may well have had in mind have been pointed out in French poetry.

A BALADE OF COMPLAINT. — This is an undistinguished specimen of the familiar type. There is no strong reason for attributing it to Chaucer.

PROVERBS. — The *Proverbs* are ascribed to Chaucer in two manuscripts, and may be his in spite of one suspicious rime. The brevity of the piece and its complete unlikeness to Chaucer's other work make the question of authorship hard to decide. The structure of the quatrains, which begin with descriptive or illustrative matter and lead up to the literal words of the proverb, is traditional in gnomic poetry in various languages.

An A B C

Incipit carmen secundum ordinem litterarum alphabeti.

Almighty and al merciable queene,
To whom that al this world fleeth for socour,
To have relees of sinne, of sorwe, and teene,
Glorious virgine, of alle floures flour,
To thee I flee, confounded in errour.   5
Help and releeve, thou mighti debonayre,
Have mercy on my perilous langour!
Venquisshed me hath my cruel adversaire.

Bountee so fix hath in thin herte his tente,
That wel I wot thou wolt my socour bee;   10
Thou canst not warne him that with good en-
        tente
Axeth thin helpe, thin herte is ay so free.
Thou art largesse of pleyn felicitee,
Haven of refut, of quiete, and of reste.

Loo, how that theeves sevene chasen mee!   15
Help, lady bright, er that my ship tobreste!

Comfort is noon but in yow, ladi deere;
For, loo, my sinne and my confusioun,
Which oughten not in thi presence appeere,
Han take on me a greevous accioun   20
Of verrey right and desperacioun;
And, as bi right, thei mighten wel susteene
That I were wurthi my dampnacioun,
Nere merci of you, blisful hevene queene!   24

Dowte is ther noon, thou queen of misericorde,
That thou n'art cause of grace and merci heere;
God vouched sauf thurgh thee with us to ac-
        corde.

For, certes, Crystes blisful mooder deere,
Were now the bowe bent in swich maneere
As it was first, of justice and of ire,   30
The rightful God nolde of no mercy heere;
But thurgh thee han we grace, as we desire.

Evere hath myn hope of refut been in thee,
For heer-biforn ful ofte, in many a wyse,
Hast thou to misericorde receyved me.   35
But merci, ladi, at the grete assyse,
Whan we shule come bifore the hye justyse!
So litel fruit shal thanne in me be founde
That, but thou er that day me wel chastyse,
Of verrey right my werk wol me confounde.

Fleeinge, I flee for socour to thi tente   41
Me for to hide from tempeste ful of dreede,
Biseeching yow that ye you not absente,
Thouh I be wikke. O help yit at this neede!
Al have I ben a beste in wil and deede,   45
Yit, ladi, thou me clothe with thi grace.
Thin enemy and myn — ladi, tak heede! —
Unto my deth in poynt is me to chace!

Glorious mayde and mooder, which that nevere
Were bitter, neither in erthe nor in see,   50
But ful of swetnesse and of merci evere,
Help that my Fader be not wroth with me.
Spek thou, for I ne dar not him ysee,
So have I doon in erthe, allas the while!
That certes, but if thou my socour bee,   55
To stink eterne he wole my gost exile.

He vouched sauf, tel him, as was his wille,
Bicome a man, to have oure alliaunce,
And with his precious blood he wrot the bille
Upon the crois, as general acquitaunce,   60
To every penitent in ful creaunce;
And therfore, ladi bright, thou for us praye.
Thanne shalt thou bothe stinte al his grevaunce,
And make oure foo to failen of his praye.

I wot it wel, thou wolt ben oure socour,   65
Thou art so ful of bowntee, in certeyn.
For, whan a soule falleth in errour,
Thi pitee goth and haleth him ayein.
Thanne makest thou his pees with his sovereyn,
And bringest him out of the crooked strete.   70
Whoso thee loveth, he shal not love in veyn;
That shal he fynde, as he the lyf shal lete.

Kalenderes enlumyned ben thei
That in this world ben lighted with thi name;

And whoso goth to yow the righte wey,   75
Him thar not drede in soule to be lame.
Now, queen of comfort, sith thou art that same
To whom I seeche for my medicyne,
Lat not my foo no more my wounde entame;
Myn hele into thin hand al I resygne.   80

Ladi, thi sorwe kan I not portreye
Under the cros, ne his greevous penaunce.
But for youre bothes peynes I yow preye,
Lat not oure alder foo make his bobaunce
That he hath in his lystes of mischaunce   85
Convict that ye bothe have bought so deere.
As I seide erst, thou ground of oure substaunce,
Continue on us thi pitous eyen cleere!

Moises, that saugh the bush with flawmes rede
Brenninge, of which ther never a stikke brende,
Was signe of thin unwemmed maidenhede.   91
Thou art the bush on which ther gan descende
The Holi Gost, the which that Moyses wende
Had ben a-fyr; and this was in figure.
Now, ladi, from the fyr thou us defende   95
Which that in helle eternalli shal dure.

Noble princesse, that nevere haddest peere,
Certes, if any comfort in us bee,
That cometh of thee, thou Cristes mooder deere.
We han noon oother melodye or glee   100
Us to rejoyse in oure adversitee,
Ne advocat noon that wole and dar so preye
For us, and that for litel hire as yee,
That helpen for an Ave-Marie or tweye.

O verrey light of eyen that ben blynde,   105
O verrey lust of labour and distresse,
O tresoreere of bountee to mankynde,
Thee whom God ches to mooder for humblesse!
From his ancille he made the maistresse   109
Of hevene and erthe, oure bille up for to beede.
This world awaiteth evere on thi goodnesse,
For thou ne failest nevere wight at neede.

Purpos I have sum time for to enquere
Wherfore and whi the Holi Gost thee soughte,
Whan Gabrielles vois cam to thin ere.   115
He not to werre us swich a wonder wroughte,
But for to save us that he sithen boughte;
Thanne needeth us no wepen us for to save,
But oonly ther we dide not, as us oughte,
Doo penitence, and merci axe and have.   120

Queen of comfort, yit whan I me bithinke
That I agilt have bothe him and thee,
And that my soule is worthi for to sinke,
Allas! I caityf, whider may I flee?
Who shal unto thi Sone my mene bee?   125
Who, but thiself, that art of pitee welle?
Thou hast more reuthe on oure adversitee
Than in this world might any tonge telle.

Redresse me, mooder, and me chastise,
For certeynly my Faderes chastisinge,   130
That dar I nouht abiden in no wise,
So hidous is his rightful rekenynge.
Mooder, of whom oure merci gan to springe,
Beth ye my juge and eek my soules leche;
For evere in you is pitee haboundinge   135
To ech that wole of pitee you biseeche.

Soth is that God ne granteth no pitee
Withoute thee; for God, of his goodnesse,
Foryiveth noon, but it like unto thee.
He hath thee maked vicaire and maistresse   140
Of al this world, and eek governouresse
Of hevene, and he represseth his justise
After thi wil; and therfore in witnesse
He hath thee corowned in so rial wise.   144

Temple devout, ther God hath his woninge,
Fro which these misbileeved deprived been,
To you my soule penitent I bringe.
Receyve me — I can no ferther fleen!
With thornes venymous, O hevene queen,
For which the eerthe acursed was ful yore,   150
I am so wounded, as ye may wel seen,
That I am lost almost, it smert so sore.

Virgine, that art so noble of apparaile,
And ledest us into the hye tour
Of Paradys, thou me wisse and counsaile
How I may have thi grace and thi socour,
All have I ben in filthe and in errour.   157
Ladi, unto that court thou me ajourne
That cleped is thi bench, O freshe flour!
Ther as that merci evere shal sojourne.   160

Xristus, thi sone, that in this world alighte
Upon the cros to suffre his passioun,
And eek that Longius his herte pighte,
And made his herte blood to renne adoun,
And al was this for my salvacioun;   165
And I to him am fals and eek unkynde,
And yit he wole not my dampnacioun —
This thanke I yow, socour of al mankynde!

Ysaac was figure of his deth, certeyn,
That so fer forth his fader wolde obeye   170
That him ne roughte nothing to be slayn;
Right soo thi Sone list, as a lamb, to deye.
Now, ladi ful of merci, I yow preye,
Sith he his merci mesured so large,
Be ye not skant; for alle we singe and seye   175
That ye ben from vengeaunce ay oure targe.

Zacharie yow clepeth the open welle
To wasshe sinful soule out of his gilt.
Therfore this lessoun oughte I wel to telle,
That, nere thi tender herte, we were spilt.   180
Now, ladi bryghte, sith thou canst and wilt
Ben to the seed of Adam merciable,
Bring us to that palais that is bilt
To penitentes that ben to merci able. Amen.

Explicit carmen.

The Complaint unto Pity

Pite, that I have sought so yore agoo,
With herte soore, and ful of besy peyne,
That in this world was never wight so woo
Withoute deth, — and, yf I shal not feyne,
My purpos was to Pite to compleyne   5
Upon the crueltee and tirannye
Of Love, that for my trouthe doth me dye.

And when that I, be lengthe of certeyne yeres,
Had evere in oon a tyme sought to speke,

To Pitee ran I, al bespreynt with teres,   10
To prayen hir on Cruelte me awreke.
But er I myghte with any word outbreke,
Or tellen any of my peynes smerte,
I fond hir ded, and buried in an herte.

Adoun I fel when that I saugh the herse,   15
Ded as a ston, while that the swogh me laste;
But up I roos, with colour ful dyverse,
And pitously on hir myn eyen I caste,

And ner the corps I gan to presen faste,
And for the soule I shop me for to preye.   20
I nas but lorn; ther was no more to seye.

Thus am I slayn, sith that Pite is ded.
Allas, that day! that ever hyt shulde falle!
What maner man dar now hold up his hed?
To whom shal any sorwful herte calle?   25
Now Cruelte hath cast to slee us alle,
In ydel hope, folk redeless of peyne, —
Syth she is ded, to whom shul we compleyne?

But yet encreseth me this wonder newe,
That no wight woot that she is ded, but I —   30
So many men as in her tyme hir knewe —
And yet she dyed not so sodeynly;
For I have sought hir ever ful besely
Sith first I hadde wit or mannes mynde;
But she was ded er that I koude hir fynde.   35

Aboute hir herse there stoden lustely,
Withouten any woo, as thoughte me,
Bounte parfyt, wel armed and richely,
And fresshe Beaute, Lust, and Jolyte,
Assured Maner, Youthe, and Honeste,   40
Wisdom, Estaat, Drede, and Governaunce,
Confedred both by bonde and alliaunce.

A compleynt had I, writen, in myn hond,
For to have put to Pittee as a bille;
But when I al this companye ther fond,   45
That rather wolden al my cause spille
Then do me help, I held my pleynte stille;
For to that folk, withouten any fayle,
Withoute Pitee ther may no bille availe.

Then leve I al these vertues, sauf Pite,   50
Kepynge the corps, as ye have herd me seyn,
Confedered alle by bond of Cruelte,
And ben assented when I shal be sleyn.
And I have put my complaynt up ageyn;
For to my foes my bille I dar not shewe,   55
Th'effect of which seith thus, in wordes fewe: —

The Bill of Complaint

Humblest of herte, highest of reverence,
Benygne flour, coroune of vertues alle,
Sheweth unto youre rial excellence
Youre servaunt, yf I durste me so calle,   60
Hys mortal harm, in which he is yfalle;
And noght al oonly for his evel fare,
But for your renoun, as he shal declare.

Hit stondeth thus: your contraire, Crueltee,
Allyed is ayenst your regalye,   65
Under colour of womanly Beaute, —
For men shulde not, lo, knowe hir tirannye, —
With Bounte, Gentilesse, and Curtesye,
And hath depryved yow now of your place
That hyghte "Beaute apertenant to Grace."   70

For kyndely, by youre herytage ryght,
Ye ben annexed ever unto Bounte;
And verrayly ye oughte do youre myght
To helpe Trouthe in his adversyte.
Ye be also the corowne of Beaute;   75
And certes, yf ye wanten in these tweyne,
The world is lore; ther is no more to seyne.

Eke what availeth Maner and Gentilesse
Withoute yow, benygne creature?
Shal Cruelte be your governeresse?   80
Allas! what herte may hyt longe endure?
Wherfore, but ye the rather take cure
To breke that perilouse alliaunce,
Ye sleen hem that ben in your obeisaunce.

And further over, yf ye suffre this,   85
Youre renoun ys fordoo than in a throwe;
Ther shal no man wite well what Pite is.
Allas, that your renoun sholde be so lowe!
Ye be than fro youre heritage ythrowe
By Cruelte, that occupieth youre place;   90
And we despeyred, that seken to your grace.

Have mercy on me, thow Herenus quene,
That yow have sought so tendirly and yore;
Let som strem of youre lyght on me be sene
That love and drede yow, ever lenger the
more.   95
For, sothly for to seyne, I bere the soore;
And, though I be not konnynge for to pleyne,
For Goddis love, have mercy on my peyne!

My peyne is this, that what so I desire
That have I not, ne nothing lyk therto;   100
And ever setteth Desir myn hert on fire.
Eke on that other syde, where so I goo,
What maner thing that may encrese my woo,
That have I redy, unsoght, everywhere;
Me [ne] lakketh but my deth, and than my
bere.   105

What nedeth to shewe parcel of my peyne?
Syth every woo that herte may bethynke
I suffre, and yet I dar not to yow pleyne;

For wel I wot, although I wake or wynke,
Ye rekke not whether I flete or synke.   110
But natheles, yet my trouthe I shal sustene
Unto my deth, and that shal wel be sene.

This is to seyne, I wol be youres evere;

Though ye me slee by Crueltee, your foo,
Algate my spirit shal never dissevere   115
Fro youre servise, for any peyne or woo.
Sith ye be ded — allas, that hyt is soo! —
Thus for your deth I may wel wepe and pleyne
With herte sore, and ful of besy peyne.

Explicit.

A Complaint to his Lady

I

The longe nightes, whan every creature
Shulde have hir rest in somwhat, as by kynde,
Or elles ne may hir lif nat longe endure,
Hit falleth most into my woful mynde
How I so fer have broght myself behynde,   5
That, sauf the deeth, ther may nothyng me
      lisse,
So desespaired I am from alle blisse.

This same thoght me lasteth til the morwe,
And from the morwe forth til hit be eve;
Ther nedeth me no care for to borwe,   10
For bothe I have good leyser and good leve;
Ther is no wyght that wol me wo bereve
To wepe ynogh, and wailen al my fille;
The sore spark of peyne now doth me spille.

II

This Love, that hath me set in swich a place
That my desir he nevere wol fulfille,
For neither pitee, mercy, neither grace,
   Can I nat fynde; and yit my sorwful herte,
   For to be deed, I can hit nought arace.
The more I love, the more she doth me smerte,
   Thourgh which I see, withoute remedye   21
   That from the deeth I may no wyse asterte.

III

Now sothly, what she hight I wol reherse.
Hir name is Bountee, set in womanhede,   24
Sadnesse in youthe, and Beautee prydelees
And Plesaunce, under governaunce and
      drede;
Hir surname is eek Faire Rewthelees,
   The Wyse, yknit unto Good Aventure,
   That, for I love hir, she sleeth me giltelees.

Hir love I best, and shal, whyl I may dure,   30
   Bet than myself an hundred thousand deel,
   Than al this worldes richesse or creature.
Now hath not Love me bestowed weel
   To love ther I never shal have part?
   Allas! right thus is turned me the wheel,   35
Thus am I slayn with Loves fyry dart.
   I can but love hir best, my swete fo;
   Love hath me taught no more of his art
But serve alwey, and stinte for no wo.

IV

In my trewe and careful herte ther is   40
So moche wo, and [eek] so litel blis
   That wo is me that ever I was bore;
For al that thyng which I desyre I mis,
And al that ever I wolde not, ywis,
   That finde I redy to me evermore;   45
And of al this I not to whom me pleyne.
   For she that mighte me out of this brynge
   Ne reccheth nought whether I wepe or
      synge;
So litel rewthe hath she upon my peyne.

Allas! whan slepyng-tyme is, than I wake;   50
Whan I shulde daunce, for fere, lo, than I
      quake;
This hevy lif I lede for your sake,
Thogh ye therof in no wyse hede take,
My hertes lady, and hool my lyves quene!
   For trewly dorste I seye, as that I fele,   55
   Me semeth that your swete herte of stele
Is whetted now ageynes me to kene.

My dere herte and best beloved fo,
Why lyketh yow to do me al this wo,
   What have I doon that greveth yow, or sayd,
But for I serve and love yow and no mo?   61

And whilst I lyve I wol ever do so;
  And therfor, swete, ne beth nat yvel apayd.
For so good and so fair as ye be
  Hit were right gret wonder but ye hadde 65
  Of alle servantes, bothe of goode and badde;
And leest worthy of alle hem, I am he.

But nevertheles, my righte lady swete,
Thogh that I be unconnyng and unmete
  To serve, as I coude best, ay your hynesse;
Yit is ther fayner noon, that wolde I hete, 71
Than I, to do yow ese, or elles bete
  What so I wiste that were to you [distresse];
And hadde I myght as good as I have wille,
  Than shulde ye fele wher it were so or
      noon; 75
  For in this world than livyng is ther noon
That fayner wolde your hertes wil fulfille.

For bothe I love and eek drede yow so sore,
And algates moot, and have doon yow, ful
      yore,
  That bettre loved is noon, ne never shal; 80
And yit I wolde beseche yow of no more,
But leveth wel, and be not wrooth therfore,
  And lat me serve yow forth; lo, this is al!
For I am not so hardy, ne so wood,
  For to desire that ye shulde love me; 85
  For wel I wot, allas! that may nat be;
I am so litel worthy, and ye so good.

For ye be oon the worthiest on-lyve
And I the most unlykly for to thryve;
  Yit, for al this, witeth ye right wele 90
That ye ne shul me from your servyce dryve
That I nil ay, with alle my wittes fyve,
  Serve yow trewly, what wo so that I fele.

For I am set on yow in swich manere,
  That, thogh ye never wil upon me rewe, 95
  I moste yow love, and been ever as trewe
As any man can, or may, on-lyve [here].

But the more that I love yow, goodly free,
The lasse fynde I that ye loven me;
  Allas! whan shal that harde wit amende?
Wher is now al your wommanly pitee, 101
Your gentilesse and your debonairtee?
  Wil ye nothyng therof upon me spende?
And so hool, swete, as I am youres al,
  And so gret wil as I have yow to serve, 105
  Now, certes, and ye lete me thus sterve,
Yit have ye wonne theron but a smal.

For at my knowyng, I do nought why,
And this I wol beseche yow hertely,
  That, ther ever ye fynde, whyl ye lyve, 110
A trewer servant to yow than am I,
Leveth thanne, and sleeth me hardely,
  And I my deeth to yow wol al foryive.
And if ye fynde no trewer verrayly,
  Wil ye suffre than that I thus spille, 115
  And for no maner gilt but my good wille?
As good were thanne untrewe as trewe to be.

But I, my lyf and deeth, to yow obeye,
And with right buxom herte hooly I preye,
  As [is] your moste plesure, so doth by me;
Wel lever is me liken yow and deye 121
Than for to anythyng or thynke or seye
  That yow myghte offende in any tyme.
And therfor, swete, rewe on my peynes smerte,
  And of your grace graunteth me som drope;
  For elles may I laste no blis ne hope, 126
Ne dwelle within my trouble careful herte.

The Complaint of Mars

The Proem

GLADETH, ye foules, of the morowe gray!
Lo! Venus, rysen among yon rowes rede!
And floures fressh, honoureth ye this day;
For when the sunne uprist, then wol ye sprede.
But ye lovers, that lye in any drede, 5
Fleeth, lest wikked tonges yow espye!
Lo! yond the sunne, the candel of jelosye!

Wyth teres blewe, and with a wounded herte,

Taketh your leve; and with seint John to bor-
      owe,
Apeseth sumwhat of your sorowes smerte. 10
Tyme cometh eft that cese shal your sorowe:
The glade nyght ys worth an hevy morowe! —
Seynt Valentyne, a foul thus herde I synge
Upon thy day, er sonne gan up-sprynge.

Yet sang this foul — I rede yow al awake, 15
And ye that han not chosen in humble wyse,
Without repentynge cheseth yow your make;
And ye that han ful chosen as I devise,

Yet at the leste renoveleth your servyse;
Confermeth hyt perpetuely to dure,   20
And paciently taketh your aventure.

And for the worship of this highe feste,
Yet wol I, in my briddes wise, synge
The sentence of the compleynt, at the leste,
That woful Mars made atte departyng   25
Fro fresshe Venus in a morwenynge,
Whan Phebus, with his firy torches rede,
Ransaked every lover in hys drede.

The Story

Whilom the thridde hevenes lord above,
As wel by hevenysh revolucioun   30
As by desert, hath wonne Venus his love,
And she hath take him in subjeccioun,
And as a maistresse taught him his lessoun,
Commaundynge him that nevere, in her servise,
He nere so bold no lover to dispise.   35

For she forbad him jelosye at al,
And cruelte, and bost, and tyrannye;
She made him at her lust so humble and tal,
That when her deyned to cast on hym her ye,
He tok in pacience to lyve or dye.   40
And thus she brydeleth him in her manere,
With nothing but with scourging of her chere.

Who regneth now in blysse but Venus,
That hath thys worthy knyght in governaunce?
Who syngeth now but Mars, that serveth thus
The faire Venus, causer of plesaunce?   46
He bynt him to perpetuall obeisaunce,
And she bynt her to loven him for evere,
But so be that his trespas hyt desevere.

Thus be they knyt, and regnen as in hevene
Be lokyng moost; til hyt fil, on a tyde,   51
That by her bothe assent was set a stevene,
That Mars shal entre, as fast as he may glyde,
Into hir nexte paleys, and ther abyde,
Walkynge hys cours, til she had him atake,   55
And he preide her to haste her for his sake.

Then seyde he thus: "Myn hertes lady swete,
Ye knowe wel my myschef in that place;
For sikerly, til that I with yow mete,
My lyf stant ther in aventure and grace;   60
But when I se the beaute of your face,
Ther ys no drede of deth may do me smerte,
For al your lust is ese to myn herte."

She hath so gret compassioun of her knyght,
That dwelleth in solitude til she come —   65
For hyt stod so that thilke tyme no wight
Counseyled hym ther, ne seyde to hym wel-
    come —
That nygh her wit for wo was overcome;
Wherfore she sped her as faste in her weye
Almost in oo day as he dyde in tweye.   70

The grete joye that was betwix hem two,
When they be mette, ther may no tunge telle.
Ther is no more, but unto bed thei go;
And thus in joy and blysse I lete hem duelle.
This worthi Mars, that is of knyghthod
    welle,   75
The flour of feyrnesse lappeth in his armes,
And Venus kysseth Mars, the god of armes.

Sojourned hath this Mars, of which I rede,
In chambre amyd the paleys prively
A certeyn tyme, til him fel a drede,   80
Throgh Phebus, that was comen hastely
Within the paleys yates sturdely,
With torche in honde, of which the stremes
    bryghte
On Venus chambre knokkeden ful lyghte.

The chambre, ther as ley this fresshe quene,
Depeynted was with white boles grete,   86
And by the lyght she knew, that shon so shene,
That Phebus cam to brenne hem with his hete.
This sely Venus nygh dreynt in teres wete,
Enbraceth Mars, and seyde, "Alas, I dye!   90
The torche is come that al this world wol wrie."

Up sterte Mars; hym liste not to slepe,
When he his lady herde so compleyne;
But, for his nature was not for to wepe,
In stede of teres, from his eyen tweyne   95
The firi sparkes brosten out for peyne;
And hente his hauberk, that ley hym besyde.
Fle wolde he not, ne myghte himselven hide.

He throweth on his helm of huge wyghte,   99
And girt him with his swerd, and in his hond
His myghty spere, as he was wont to fyghte,
He shaketh so that almost hit towond.
Ful hevy was he to walken over lond;
He may not holde with Venus companye,
But bad her fleen, lest Phebus her espye.   105

O woful Mars! alas! what maist thou seyn,
That in the paleys of thy disturbaunce
Art left byhynde, in peril to be sleyn?

And yet therto ys double thy penaunce,
For she that hath thyn herte in governaunce
Is passed half the stremes of thin yen;   111
That thou nere swift, wel maist thou wepe and
    crien.

Now fleeth Venus unto Cilenios tour,
With voide cours, for fere of Phebus lyght.
Alas! and ther ne hath she no socour,   115
For she ne found ne saugh no maner wyght;
And eke as ther she hath but litil myght;
Wherfor, herselven for to hyde and save,
Within the gate she fledde into a cave.   119

Derk was this cave, and smokyng as the helle;
Not but two pas within the yate hit stod.
A naturel day in derk I lete her duelle.
Now wol I speke of Mars, furious and wod.
For sorow he wolde have sen his herte blod;
Sith that he myghte don her no companye,   125
He ne roghte not a myte for to dye.

So feble he wex, for hete and for his wo,
That nygh he swelte; he myghte unnethe en-
    dure;
He passeth but o steyre in dayes two.
But nathelesse, for al his hevy armure,   130
He foloweth her that is his lyves cure,
For whos departyng he tok gretter ire
Then for al his brennyng in the fire.

After he walketh softely a paas,
Compleynyng, that hyt pite was to here.   135
He seyde, "O lady bryght, Venus, alas!
That evere so wyd a compas ys my spere!
Alas! when shal I mete yow, herte dere?
This twelfte daye of April I endure,
Throgh jelous Phebus, this mysaventure."   140

Now God helpe sely Venus allone!
But, as God wolde, hyt happed for to be,
That, while that Venus weping made her mone,
Cilenius, rydinge in his chevache,
Fro Venus valaunse myghte his paleys se,   145
And Venus he salueth and doth chere,
And her receyveth as his frend ful dere.

Mars dwelleth forth in his adversyte,
Compleynyng ever on her departynge;
And what his compleynt was, remembreth me;
And therfore, in this lusty morwenynge,   151
As I best can, I wol hit seyn and synge,
And after that I wol my leve take;
And God yeve every wyght joy of his make!

The Compleynt of Mars

The Proem

The ordre of compleynt requireth skylfully   155
That yf a wight shal pleyne pitously,
Ther mot be cause wherfore that men pleyne;
Or men may deme he pleyneth folily
And causeles; alas! that am not I!
Wherfore the ground and cause of al my peyne,
So as my troubled wit may hit atteyne,   161
I wol reherse; not for to have redresse,
But to declare my ground of hevynesse.

I

The firste tyme, alas! that I was wroght,
And for certeyn effectes hider broght   165
Be him that lordeth ech intelligence,
I yaf my trewe servise and my thoght
For evermore — how dere I have hit boght! —
To her that is of so gret excellence
That what wight that first sheweth his pres-
    ence,   170
When she is wroth and taketh of hym no cure,
He may not longe in joye of love endure.

This is no feyned mater that I telle;
My lady is the verrey sours and welle
Of beaute, lust, fredom, and gentilnesse,   175
Of riche aray — how dere men hit selle! —
Of al disport in which men frendly duelle,
Of love and pley, and of benigne humblesse,
Of soun of instrumentes of al swetnesse;
And therto so wel fortuned and thewed   180
That thorogh the world her goodnesse is
    yshewed.

What wonder ys it then, thogh I besette
My servise on such on that may me knette
To wele or wo, sith hit lyth in her myght?
Therfore myn herte forever I to her hette;   185
Ne truly, for my deth, I shal not lette
To ben her truest servaunt and her knyght.
I flater noght, that may wete every wyght;
For this day in her servise shal I dye.
But grace be, I se her never wyth ye.   190

II

To whom shal I than pleyne of my distresse?
Who may me helpe? Who may my harm re-
    dresse?
Shal I compleyne unto my lady fre?
Nay, certes, for she hath such hevynesse,
For fere and eke for wo, that, as I gesse,   195

In lytil tyme hit wol her bane be.
But were she sauf, hit were no fors of me.
Alas! that ever lovers mote endure,
For love, so many a perilous aventure!

For thogh so be that lovers be as trewe   200
As any metal that is forged newe,
In many a cas hem tydeth ofte sorowe.
Somtyme her lady wil not on hem rewe;
Somtyme, yf that jelosie hyt knewe,   204
They myghten lyghtly leye her hed to borowe;
Somtyme envyous folk with tunges horowe
Depraven hem; alas! whom may they plese?
But he be fals, no lover hath his ese.

But what availeth such a long sermoun
Of aventures of love, up and doun?   210
I wol returne and speken of my peyne.
The poynt is this of my distruccioun:
My righte lady, my savacyoun,
Is in affray, and not to whom to pleyne.
O herte swete, O lady sovereyne!   215
For your disese wel oughte I swowne and
        swelte,
Thogh I non other harm ne drede felte.

III

To what fyn made the God that sit so hye,
Benethen him, love other companye,
And streyneth folk to love, malgre her hed?
And then her joy, for oght I can espye,   221
Ne lasteth not the twynkelyng of an ye,
And somme han never joy til they be ded.
What meneth this? What is this mystihed?
Wherto constreyneth he his folk so faste   225
Thing to desyre, but hit shulde laste?

And thogh he made a lover love a thing,
And maketh hit seme stedfast and during,
Yet putteth he in hyt such mysaventure
That reste nys ther non in his yeving.   230
And that is wonder, that so juste a kyng
Doth such hardnesse to his creature.
Thus, whether love breke or elles dure,
Algates he that hath with love to done
Hath ofter wo then changed ys the mone.   235

Hit semeth he hath to lovers enmyte,
And lyk a fissher, as men alday may se,
Baiteth hys angle-hok with som plesaunce,
Til many a fissh ys wod til that he be
Sesed therwith; and then at erst hath he   240
Al his desir, and therwith al myschaunce;
And thogh the lyne breke, he hath penaunce;

For with the hok he wounded is so sore
That he his wages hath for evermore.

IV

The broche of Thebes was of such a kynde,
So ful of rubies and of stones of Ynde,   246
That every wight, that sette on hit an ye,
He wende anon to worthe out of his mynde;
So sore the beaute wolde his herte bynde,
Til he hit had, him thoghte he moste dye;   250
And whan that hit was his, then shulde he
        drye
Such woo for drede, ay while that he hit hadde,
That wel nygh for the fere he shulde madde.
And whan hit was fro his possessioun,
Then had he double wo and passioun   255
For he so feir a tresor had forgo;
But yet this broche, as in conclusioun,
Was not the cause of his confusioun;
But he that wroghte hit enfortuned hit so
That every wight that had hit shulde have wo;
And therfore in the worcher was the vice,   261
And in the covetour that was so nyce.

So fareth hyt by lovers and by me;
For thogh my lady have so gret beaute
That I was mad til I had gete her grace,   265
She was not cause of myn adversite,
But he that wroghte her, also mot I the,
That putte such a beaute in her face,
That made me coveyten and purchace
Myn oune deth; him wite I that I dye,   270
And myn unwit, that ever I clamb so hye.

V

But to yow, hardy knyghtes of renoun,
Syn that ye be of my devisioun,
Al be I not worthy to so gret a name,
Yet, seyn these clerkes, I am your patroun;   275
Therfore ye oghte have som compassioun
Of my disese, and take hit not a-game.
The proudest of yow may be mad ful tame;
Wherfore I prey yow, of your gentilesse,
That ye compleyne for myn hevynesse.   280

And ye, my ladyes, that ben true and stable,
Be wey of kynde, ye oughten to be able
To have pite of folk that be in peyne.
Now have ye cause to clothe yow in sable;
Sith that youre emperise, the honurable,   285
Is desolat, wel oghte ye to pleyne;
Now shulde your holy teres falle and reyne.
Alas! your honour and your emperise,
Negh ded for drede, ne can her not chevise.

Compleyneth eke, ye lovers, al in-fere,   290
For her that with unfeyned humble chere
Was evere redy to do yow socour;
Compleyneth her that evere hath had yow
dere;

Compleyneth beaute, fredom, and manere;
Compleyneth her that endeth your labour;   295
Compleyneth thilke ensample of al honour,
That never dide but al gentilesse;
Kytheth therfore on her sum kyndenesse.

To Rosemounde

A Balade

MADAME, ye ben of al beaute shryne
As fer as cercled is the mapemounde,
For as the cristal glorious ye shyne,
And lyke ruby ben your chekes rounde.
Therwith ye ben so mery and so jocounde   5
That at a revel whan that I see you daunce,
It is an oynement unto my wounde,
Thogh ye to me ne do no daliaunce.

For thogh I wepe of teres ful a tyne,
Yet may that wo myn herte nat confounde;   10
Your semy voys, that ye so smal out twyne,
Maketh my thoght in joy and blis habounde.
So curtaysly I go, with love bounde,

That to myself I sey, in my penaunce,
"Suffyseth me to love you, Rosemounde,   15
Thogh ye to me ne do no daliaunce."

Nas never pyk walwed in galauntyne
As I in love am walwed and ywounde,
For which ful ofte I of myself devyne
That I am trewe Tristam the secounde.   20
My love may not refreyde nor affounde;
I brenne ay in an amorous plesaunce.
Do what you lyst, I wyl your thral be founde,
Thogh ye to me ne do no daliaunce.

TREGENTIL.   CHAUCER.

Womanly Noblesse

Balade That Chaucier Made

So hath myn herte caught in remembraunce
Your beaute hoole and stidefast governaunce,
Your vertues alle and your hie noblesse,
That you to serve is set al my plesaunce.
So wel me liketh your womanly contenaunce,
Your fresshe fetures and your comlynesse,   6
That whiles I live, myn herte to his maystresse
You hath ful chose in trewe perséveraunce
Never to chaunge, for no maner distresse.

And sith I shal do [you] this observaunce   10
Al my lif, withouten displesaunce,
You for to serve with al my besynesse,

.   .   .   .

And have me somwhat in your souvenaunce.
My woful herte suffreth greet duresse;
And [loke how humblely], with al symplesse,
My wyl I cónforme to your ordynaunce   16
As you best list, my peynes for to redresse.

Considryng eke how I hange in balaunce,
In your service, such, lo! is my chaunce,
Abidyng grace, whan that your gentilnesse,   20
Of my grete wo listeth don alleggeaunce,
And wyth your pite me som wise avaunce,
In ful rebatyng of myn hevynesse,
And thynketh by resoun that wommanly no-
blesse
Shulde nat desire for to do the outrance   25
Ther as she fyndeth non unbuxumnesse.

Lenvoye

Auctour of norture, lady of plesaunce,
Soveraigne of beautee, flour of wommanhede,
Take ye non hede unto myn ignoraunce,
But this receyveth of your goodlihede,   30
Thynkyng that I have caught in remembraunce,
Your beaute hole, your stidefast governaunce.

Chaucers Wordes unto Adam, His Owne Scriveyn

ADAM scriveyn, if ever it thee bifalle
Boece or Troylus for to wryten newe,
Under thy long lokkes thou most have the
    scalle,

But after my makyng thou wryte more trewe;
So ofte a-daye I mot thy werk renewe,   5
It to correcte and eek to rubbe and scrape;
And al is thorugh thy negligence and rape.

The Former Age

A BLISFUL lyf, a paisible and a swete,
Ledden the peples in the former age.
They helde hem payed of the fruites that they
    ete,
Which that the feldes yave hem by usage;
They ne were nat forpampred with outrage.   5
Unknowen was the quern and eek the melle;
They eten mast, hawes, and swich pounage,
And dronken water of the colde welle.

Yit nas the ground nat wounded with the
    plough,
But corn up-sprong, unsowe of mannes hond,
The which they gnodded, and eete nat half
    ynough.   11
No man yit knew the forwes of his lond;
No man the fyr out of the flint yit fond;
Unkorven and ungrobbed lay the vyne,
No man yit in the morter spyces grond   15
To clarre, ne to sause of galantyne.

No mader, welde, or wood no litestere
Ne knew; the flees was of his former hewe;
No flesh ne wiste offence of egge or spere; 19
No coyn ne knew man which was fals or trewe;
No ship yit karf the wawes grene and blewe;
No marchaunt yit ne fette outlandish ware;
No trompes for the werres folk ne knewe,
Ne toures heye and walles rounde or square.

What sholde it han avayled to werreye?   25
Ther lay no profit, ther was no richesse,
But cursed was the tyme, I dare wel seye,
That men first dide hir swety bysinesse
To grobbe up metal, lurkinge in derknesse,
And in the riveres first gemmes soghte.   30
Allas! than sprong up al the cursednesse
Of coveytyse, that first our sorwe broghte!

Thise tyraunts putte hem gladly nat in pres
No wildnesse ne no busshes for to winne;
Ther poverte is, as seith Diogenes,   35
Ther as vitaile is eek so skars and thinne
That noght but mast or apples is therinne.
But, ther as bagges been and fat vitaile,
Ther wol they gon, and spare for no sinne
With al hir ost the cite for t'assaile.   40

Yit were no paleis-chaumbres, ne non halles;
In caves and [in] wodes softe and swete
Slepten this blissed folk withoute walles,
On gras or leves in parfit quiete.
Ne doun of fetheres, ne no bleched shete   45
Was kid to hem, but in seurtee they slepte.
Hir hertes were al oon, withoute galles;
Everich of hem his feith to other kepte.

Unforged was the hauberk and the plate;
The lambish peple, voyd of alle vyce,   50
Hadden no fantasye to debate,
But ech of hem wolde other wel cheryce;
No pryde, non envye, non avaryce,
No lord, no taylage by no tyrannye;   54
Humblesse and pees, good feith, the em-
    perice,

•   •   •

Yit was not Jupiter the likerous,
That first was fader of delicacye,
Come in this world; ne Nembrot, desirous
To regne, had nat maad his toures hye.
Allas, allas! now may men wepe and crye!   60
For in oure dayes nis but covetyse,
Doublenesse, and tresoun, and envye,
Poyson, manslauhtre, and mordre in sondry
    wyse.

Finit Etas Prima. Chaucers.

Fortune

Balades de Visage sanz Peinture

I. *Le Pleintif countre Fortune*

THIS wrecched worldes transmutacioun,
As wele or wo, now povre and now honour,
Withouten ordre or wys discrecioun
Governed is by Fortunes errour.
But natheles, the lak of hir favour   5
Ne may nat don me singen, though I dye,
"Jay tout perdu mon temps et mon labour;"
For fynally, Fortune, I thee defye!

Yit is me left the light of my resoun,
To knowen frend fro fo in thy mirour.   10
So muchel hath yit thy whirling up and doun
Ytaught me for to knowen in an hour.
But trewely, no force of thy reddour
To him that over himself hath the maystrye!
My suffisaunce shal be my socour;   15
For fynally, Fortune, I thee defye!

O Socrates, thou stidfast champioun,
She never mighte be thy tormentour;
Thou never dreddest hir oppressioun,
Ne in hir chere founde thou no savour.   20
Thou knewe wel the deceit of hir colour,
And that hir moste worshipe is to lye.
I knowe hir eek a fals dissimulour;
For fynally, Fortune, I thee defye!

II. *La respounse de Fortune au Pleintif*

No man is wrecched, but himself it wene,   25
And he that hath himself hath suffisaunce.
Why seystow thanne I am to thee so kene,
That hast thyself out of my governaunce?
Sey thus: "Graunt mercy of thyn habound-
          aunce
That thou hast lent or this." Why wolt thou
          stryve?   30
What wostow yit how I thee wol avaunce?
And eek thou hast thy beste frend alyve.

I have thee taught divisioun bitwene
Frend of effect, and frend of countenaunce;
Thee nedeth nat the galle of noon hyene,   35
That cureth eyen derked for penaunce;
Now seestow cleer, that were in ignoraunce.
Yit halt thyn ancre, and yit thou mayst arryve
Ther bountee berth the keye of my substaunce;
And eek thou hast thy beste frend alyve.   40

How many have I refused to sustene,
Sin I thee fostred have in thy plesaunce!
Woltow than make a statut on thy quene
That I shal been ay at thyn ordinaunce?
Thou born art in my regne of variaunce,   45
Aboute the wheel with other most thou dryve.
My lore is bet than wikke is thy grevaunce;
And eek thou hast thy beste frend alyve.

III. *La respounse du Pleintif countre Fortune*

Thy lore I dampne, it is adversitee.   49
My frend maystow nat reven, blind goddesse
That I thy frendes knowe, I thanke hit thee.
Tak hem agayn, lat hem go lye on presse!
The negardye in keping hir richesse
Prenostik is thou wolt hir tour assayle;
Wikke appetyt comth ay before syknesse: 55
In general, this reule may nat fayle.

La respounse de Fortune countre le Pleintif

Thou pinchest at my mutabilitee,
For I thee lente a drope of my richesse,
And now me lyketh to withdrawe me.
Why sholdestow my realtee oppresse?   60
The see may ebbe and flowen more or lesse;
The welkne hath might to shyne, reyne, or
          hayle;
Right so mot I kythen my brotelnesse:
In general, this reule may nat fayle.

Lo, th'execucion of the majestee   65
That al purveyeth of his rightwysnesse,
That same thing "Fortune" clepen ye,
Ye blinde bestes, ful of lewednesse!
The hevene hath propretee of sikernesse,
This world hath ever resteles travayle;   70
Thy laste day is ende of myn intresse:
In general, this reule may nat fayle.

Lenvoy de Fortune

Princes, I prey you, of your gentilesse,
Lat nat this man on me thus crye and pleyne,
And I shal quyte you your bisinesse   75

At my requeste, as three of you or tweyne;
And, but you list releve him of his peyne,

Preyeth his beste frend, of his noblesse,
That to som beter estat he may atteyne.

Explicit.

Truth

Balade de Bon Conseyl

FLEE fro the prees, and dwelle with sothfast-
nesse,
Suffyce unto thy good, though it be smal;
For hord hath hate, and climbing tikelnesse,
Prees hath envye, and wele blent overal;
Savour no more than thee bihove shal;   5
Reule wel thyself, that other folk canst rede;
And trouthe thee shal delivere, it is no drede.

Tempest thee noght al croked to redresse,
In trust of hir that turneth as a bal:
Gret reste stant in litel besinesse;   10
Be war also to sporne ayeyns an al;
Stryve not, as doth the crokke with the wal.
Daunte thyself, that dauntest otheres dede;
And trouthe thee shal delivere, it is no drede.

That thee is sent, receyve in buxumnesse;   15

The wrastling for this world axeth a fal.
Her is non hoom, her nis but wildernesse:
Forth, pilgrim, forth! Forth, beste, out of thy
stal!
Know thy contree, look up, thank God of al;
Hold the heye wey, and lat thy gost thee
lede;   20
And trouthe thee shal delivere, it is no drede.

Envoy

Therfore, thou Vache, leve thyn old wrecched-
nesse;
Unto the world leve now to be thral;
Crye him mercy, that of his hy goodnesse
Made thee of noght, and in especial   25
Draw unto him, and pray in general
For thee, and eek for other, hevenlich mede;
And trouthe thee shal delivere, it is no drede.

Explicit Le bon counseill de G. Chaucer.

Gentilesse

Moral Balade of Chaucier

THE firste stok, fader of gentilesse —
What man that claymeth gentil for to be
Must folowe his trace, and alle his wittes dresse
Vertu to sewe, and vyces for to flee.
For unto vertu longeth dignitee,   5
And noght the revers, saufly dar I deme,
Al were he mytre, croune, or diademe.

This firste stok was ful of rightwisnesse,
Trewe of his word, sobre, pitous, and free,
Clene of his gost, and loved besinesse,   10
Ayeinst the vyce of slouthe, in honestee;

And, but his heir love vertu, as dide he,
He is noght gentil, thogh he riche seme,
Al were he mytre, croune, or diademe.

Vyce may wel be heir to old richesse;   15
But ther may no man, as men may wel see,
Bequethe his heir his vertuous noblesse
(That is appropred unto no degree
But to the firste fader in magestee,
That maketh hem his heyres that him queme),
Al were he mytre, croune, or diademe.   21

Lak of Stedfastnesse

Balade

SOMTYME the world was so stedfast and stable
That mannes word was obligacioun;
And now it is so fals and deceivable
That word and deed, as in conclusioun,
Ben nothing lyk, for turned up-so-doun   5
Is al this world for mede and wilfulnesse,
That al is lost for lak of stedfastnesse.

What maketh this world to be so variable
But lust that folk have in dissensioun?
For among us now a man is holde unable,   10
But if he can, by som collusioun,
Don his neighbour wrong or oppressioun.
What causeth this but wilful wrecchednesse,
That al is lost for lak of stedfastnesse?

Trouthe is put doun, resoun is holden fable;

Vertu hath now no dominacioun;   16
Pitee exyled, no man is merciable;
Through covetyse is blent discrecioun.
The world hath mad a permutacioun
Fro right to wrong, fro trouthe to fikelnesse,
That al is lost for lak of stedfastnesse.   21

Lenvoy to King Richard

O prince, desyre to be honourable,
Cherish thy folk and hate extorcioun!
Suffre nothing that may be reprevable
To thyn estat don in thy regioun.   25
Shew forth thy swerd of castigacioun,
Dred God, do law, love trouthe and worthi-
    nesse,
And wed thy folk agein to stedfastnesse.

Explicit.

The Complaint of Venus

THER nys so high comfort to my pleasaunce,
When that I am in any hevynesse,
As for to have leyser of remembraunce
Upon the manhod and the worthynesse,
Upon the trouthe and on the stidfastnesse   5
Of him whos I am al, while I may dure.
Ther oghte blame me no creature,
For every wight preiseth his gentilesse.

In him is bounte, wysdom, governaunce,
Wel more then any mannes wit can gesse;   10
For grace hath wold so ferforth hym avaunce
That of knyghthod he is parfit richesse.
Honour honoureth him for his noblesse;
Therto so wel hath formed him Nature
That I am his for ever, I him assure;   15
For every wight preyseth his gentilesse.

And notwithstondyng al his suffisaunce,
His gentil herte is of so gret humblesse
To me in word, in werk, in contenaunce,
And me to serve is al his besynesse,   20

That I am set in verrey sikernesse.
Thus oghte I blesse wel myn aventure,
Sith that him list me serven and honoure;
For every wight preiseth his gentilesse.

II

Now certis, Love, hit is right covenable   25
That men ful dere abye thy nobil thing,
As wake abedde, and fasten at the table,
Wepinge to laughe, and singe in compleynyng,
And doun to caste visage and lokyng,
Often to chaunge hewe and contenaunce,   30
Pleyne in slepyng, and dremen at the daunce,
Al the revers of any glad felyng.

Jelosie be hanged be a cable!
She wolde al knowe thurgh her espying.
Ther doth no wyght nothing so resonable,   35
That al nys harm in her ymagenyng.
Thus dere abought is Love in yevyng,
Which ofte he yiveth withouten ordynaunce,
As sorwe ynogh, and litil of plesaunce,
Al the revers of any glad felyng.   40

A lytel tyme his yift ys agreable,
But ful encomberous is the usyng;
For subtil Jelosie, the deceyvable,
Ful often tyme causeth desturbyng.
Thus be we ever in drede and sufferyng;   45
In nouncerteyn we languisshe in penaunce,
And han ful often many an hard mischaunce,
Al the revers of any glad felyng.

III

But certes, Love, I sey not in such wise
That for t'escape out of youre las I mente;   50
For I so longe have ben in your servise
That for to lete of wil I never assente;
No fors thogh Jelosye me turmente!
Sufficeth me to sen hym when I may;
And therfore certes, to myn endyng day,   55
To love hym best ne shal I never repente.

And certis, Love, when I me wel avise
On any estat that man may represente,
Then have ye maked me, thurgh your fraun-
            chise,
Chese the best that ever on erthe wente.   60
Now love wel, herte, and lok thou never stente;
And let the jelous putte it in assay

That, for no peyne, wol I not sey nay;
To love him best ne shal I never repente.

Herte, to the hit oughte ynogh suffise   65
That Love so high a grace to the sente,
To chese the worthieste in alle wise
And most agreable unto myn entente.
Seche no ferther, neythir wey ne wente,
Sith I have suffisaunce unto my pay.   70
Thus wol I ende this compleynt or this lay;
To love hym best ne shal I never repente.

Lenvoy

Princesse, receyveth this compleynt in gre,
Unto your excelent benignite
Direct after my litel suffisaunce.   75
For elde, that in my spirit dulleth me,
Hath of endyting al the subtilte
Wel nygh bereft out of my remembraunce;
And eke to me it ys a gret penaunce,
Syth rym in Englissh hath such skarsete,   80
To folowe word by word the curiosite
Of Graunson, flour of hem that make in
            Fraunce.

Here endith the Compleynt of Venus.

Lenvoy de Chaucer a Scogan

Tobroken been the statutz hye in hevene
That creat were eternally to dure,
Syth that I see the bryghte goddis sevene
Mowe wepe and wayle, and passion endure,
As may in erthe a mortal creature.   5
Allas, fro whennes may thys thing procede,
Of which errour I deye almost for drede?

By word eterne whilom was yshape
That fro the fyfte sercle, in no manere,
Ne myghte a drope of teeres doun escape.   10
But now so wepith Venus in hir spere
That with hir teeres she wol drenche us here.
Allas! Scogan, this is for thyn offence;
Thow causest this diluge of pestilence.   14

Hastow not seyd, in blaspheme of the goddes,

Thurgh pride, or thrugh thy grete rekelnesse,
Swich thing as in the lawe of love forbode is,
That, for thy lady sawgh nat thy distresse,
Therfore thow yave hir up at Michelmesse?
Allas! Scogan, of olde folk ne yonge   20
Was never erst Scogan blamed for his tonge.

Thow drowe in skorn Cupide eke to record
Of thilke rebel word that thou hast spoken,
For which he wol no lenger be thy lord.
And, Scogan, though his bowe be nat broken,
He wol nat with his arwes been ywroken   26
On the, ne me, ne noon of oure figure;
We shul of him have neyther hurt ne cure.

Now certes, frend, I dreede of thyn unhap,   29
Lest for thy gilt the wreche of Love procede

On alle hem that ben hoor and rounde of shap,
That ben so lykly folk in love to spede.
Than shal we for oure labour han no mede;
But wel I wot, thow wolt answere and saye:
"Lo, olde Grisel lyst to ryme and playe!" 35

Nay, Scogan, say not so, for I m'excuse —
God helpe me so! — in no rym, dowteles,
Ne thynke I never of slep to wake my muse,
That rusteth in my shethe stille in pees.
While I was yong, I put hir forth in prees; 40

But al shal passe that men prose or ryme;
Take every man hys turn, as for his tyme.

Envoy

Scogan, that knelest at the stremes hed
Of grace, of alle honour and worthynesse,
In th'ende of which strem I am dul as ded, 45
Forgete in solytarie wildernesse, —
Yet, Scogan, thenke on Tullius kyndenesse;
Mynne thy frend, there it may fructyfye!
Far-wel, and loke thow never eft Love dyffye.

Lenvoy de Chaucer a Bukton

My maister Bukton, whan of Crist our kyng
Was axed what is trouthe or sothfastnesse,
He nat a word answerde to that axing,
As who saith, "No man is al trewe," I gesse.
And therfore, though I highte to expresse 5
The sorwe and wo that is in mariage,
I dar not writen of it no wikkednesse,
Lest I myself falle eft in swich dotage.

I wol nat seyn how that yt is the cheyne
Of Sathanas, on which he gnaweth evere; 10
But I dar seyn, were he out of his peyne,
As by his wille he wolde be bounde nevere.
But thilke doted fool that eft hath levere
Ycheyned be than out of prison crepe,
God lete him never fro his wo dissevere, 15
Ne no man him bewayle, though he wepe!

But yet, lest thow do worse, take a wyf;
Bet ys to wedde than brenne in worse wise.
But thow shal have sorwe on thy flessh, thy lyf,
And ben thy wives thral, as seyn these wise;
And yf that hooly writ may nat suffyse, 21
Experience shal the teche, so may happe,
That the were lever to be take in Frise
Than eft to falle of weddynge in the trappe.

Envoy

This lytel writ, proverbes, or figure 25
I sende yow, take kepe of yt, I rede;
Unwys is he that kan no wele endure.
If thow be siker, put the nat in drede.
The Wyf of Bathe I pray yow that ye rede
Of this matere that we have on honde. 30
God graunte yow your lyf frely to lede
In fredam; for ful hard is to be bonde.

Explicit.

The Complaint of Chaucer to his Purse

To yow, my purse, and to noon other wight
Complayne I, for ye be my lady dere!
I am so sory, now that ye been lyght;
For certes, but ye make me hevy chere,
Me were as leef be layd upon my bere; 5
For which unto your mercy thus I crye:
Beth hevy ageyn, or elles mot I dye!

Now voucheth sauf this day, or yt be nyght,
That I of yow the blisful soun may here,
Or see your colour lyk the sonne bryght, 10
That of yelownesse hadde never pere.
Ye be my lyf, ye be myn hertes stere,
Quene of comfort and of good companye:
Beth hevy ageyn, or elles moot I dye!

Now purse, that ben to me my lyves lyght   15
And saveour, as doun in this world here,
Out of this toune helpe me thurgh your myght,
Syn that ye wole nat ben my tresorere;
For I am shave as nye as any frere.
But yet I pray unto your curtesye: 20
Beth hevy agen, or elles moot I dye!

Lenvoy de Chaucer

O conquerour of Brutes Albyon,
Which that by lyne and free eleccion
Been verray kyng, this song to yow I sende;
And ye, that mowen alle oure harmes amende,
Have mynde upon my supplicacion!   26

SHORT POEMS OF DOUBTFUL AUTHORSHIP

Against Women Unconstant

Balade

MADAME, for your newefangelnesse,
Many a servaunt have ye put out of grace.
I take my leve of your unstedfastnesse,
For wel I wot, whyl ye have lyves space,
Ye can not love ful half yeer in a place,   5
To newe thing your lust is ay so kene;
In stede of blew, thus may ye were al grene.

Right as a mirour nothing may enpresse,
But, lightly as it cometh, so mot it pace,
So fareth your love, your werkes bereth wit-
    nesse.   10

Ther is no feith that may your herte enbrace;
But, as a wedercok, that turneth his face
With every wind, ye fare, and that is sene;
In stede of blew, thus may ye were al grene.

Ye might be shryned, for your brotelnesse,   15
Bet than Dalyda, Creseyde or Candace;
For ever in chaunging stant your sikernesse;
That tache may no wight fro your herte arace.
If ye lese oon, ye can wel tweyn purchace;   19
Al light for somer, ye woot wel what I mene,
In stede of blew, thus may ye were al grene.

Explicit.

Complaynt D'Amours

An Amorous Complaint, Made at Windsor

I, WHICH that am the sorwefulleste man
That in this world was ever yit livinge,
And leest recoverer of himselven can,
Beginne right thus my deedly compleininge
On hir, that may to lyf and deeth me bringe,
Which hath on me no mercy ne no rewthe   6
That love hir best, but sleeth me for my
    trewthe.

Can I noght doon ne seye that may yow lyke?
Nay, certes! Now, allas! allas, the whyle!
Your plesaunce is to laughen whan I syke,   10
And thus ye me from al my blisse exyle.
Ye han me cast in thilke spitous yle
Ther never man on lyve mighte asterte;
This have I for I love you best, swete herte!

Sooth is, that wel I woot, by lyklinesse,   15
If that it were a thing possible to do
For to acompte youre beautee and goodnesse,
I have no wonder thogh ye do me wo;
Sith I, th'unworthiest that may ryde or go,
Durste ever thinken in so hy a place,   20
What wonder is, thogh ye do me no grace?

Allas! thus is my lyf brought to an ende;
My deeth, I see, is my conclusioun.
I may wel singe, "In sory tyme I spende
My lyf;" that song may have confusioun!   25
For mercy, pitee, and deep affeccioun,
I sey for me, for al my deedly chere,
Alle thise diden, in that, me love yow dere.

And in this wyse and in dispayr I live
In love; nay, but in dispayr I dye!   30
But shal I thus yow my deeth foryive,
That causeles doth me this sorwe drye?
Ye, certes, I! For she of my folye
Hath nought to done, although she do me
    sterve;
Hit is nat with hir wil that I hir serve!   35

Than sithen I am of my sorwe the cause,
And sithen I have this, withoute hir reed,
Than may I seyn, right shortly in a clause,
It is no blame unto hir womanheed
Though swich a wrecche as I be for hir deed.
Yet alwey two thinges doon me dye,   41
That is to seyn, hir beautee and myn yë;

So that, algates, she is verray rote
Of my disese, and of my deth also;
For with oon word she mighte be my bote,   45
If that she vouched sauf for to do so.
But than is hir gladnesse at my wo?
It is hir wone plesaunce for to take,
To seen hir servaunts dyen for hir sake!

But certes, than is al my wonderinge,   50
Sithen she is the fayrest creature
As to my doom, that ever was livinge,
The benignest and beste eek that Nature
Hath wrought or shal, whyl that the world may
    dure,

Why that she lefte pite so behinde?   55
It was, ywis, a greet defaute in Kinde.

Yit is al this no lak to hir, pardee,
But God or Nature sore wolde I blame.
For, though she shewe no pite unto me,
Sithen that she doth othere men the same,   60
I ne oughte to despyse my ladyes game;
It is hir pley to laughen whan men syketh,
And I assente, al that hir list and lyketh!

Yet wolde I, as I dar, with sorwful herte
Biseche unto your meke womanhede   65
That I now dorste my sharpe sorwes smerte
Shewe by word, that ye wolde ones rede
The compleynte of me, which ful sore I drede
That I have seid here, through myn unkon-
    ninge,
In any word to your displesinge.   70

Lothest of anything that ever was loth
Were me, as wisly God my soule save!
To seyn a thing through which ye might be
    wroth;
And, to that day that I be leyd in grave,
A trewer servaunt shulle ye never have;   75
And, though that I have pleyned unto you
    here,
Foryiveth it me, myn owne lady dere!

Ever have I been, and shal, how-so I wende,
Outher to live or dye, your humble trewe;
Ye been to me my ginning and myn ende,   80
Sonne of the sterre bright and clere of hewe;
Alwey in oon to love yow freshly newe,
By God and by my trouthe, is myn entente;
To live or dye, I wol it never repente!

This compleynte on seint Valentynes day,   85
Whan every foughel chesen shal his make,
To hir, whos I am hool, and shal alwey,
This woful song and this compleynte I make,
That never yit wolde me to mercy take;
And yit wol I evermore her serve   90
And love hir best, although she do me sterve.

Explicit.

Merciles Beaute

A Triple Roundel

YOUR yen two wol slee me sodenly;
I may the beautee of hem not sustene,
So woundeth hit thourghout my herte kene.

And but your word wol helen hastily
My hertes wounde, while that hit is grene, 5
  Your yen two wol slee me sodenly;
  I may the beautee of hem not sustene.

Upon my trouthe I sey you feithfully
That ye ben of my lyf and deeth the quene;
For with my deeth the trouthe shal be sene. 10
  Your yen two wol slee me sodenly;
  I may the beautee of hem not sustene,
   So woundeth it thourghout my herte kene.

II

So hath your beautee fro your herte chaced
Pitee, that me ne availeth not to pleyne; 15
For Daunger halt your mercy in his cheyne.

Giltles my deeth thus han ye me purchaced;
I sey you sooth, me nedeth not to feyne;
  So hath your beautee fro your herte chaced
  Pitee, that me ne availeth not to pleyne. 20

Allas! that Nature hath in you compassed
So greet beautee, that no man may atteyne
To mercy, though he sterve for the peyne.
  So hath your beautee fro your herte chaced
  Pitee, that me ne availeth not to pleyne; 25
   For Daunger halt your mercy in his cheyne.

III

Sin I fro Love escaped am so fat,
I never thenk to ben in his prison lene;
Sin I am free, I counte him not a bene.

He may answere, and seye this and that; 30
I do no fors, I speke right as I mene.
  Sin I fro Love escaped am so fat,
  I never thenk to ben in his prison lene.

Love hath my name ystrike out of his sclat,
And he is strike out of my bokes clene 35
For evermo; [ther] is non other mene.
  Sin I fro Love escaped am so fat,
  I never thenk to ben in his prison lene;
   Sin I am free, I counte him not a bene.

Explicit.

A Balade of Complaint

COMPLEYNE ne koude, ne might myn herte
  never
My peynes halve, ne what torment I have,
Though that I sholde in your presence ben ever,
Myn hertes lady, as wisly he me save 4
That bountee made, and beautee list to grave
In your persone, and bad hem bothe in-fere
Ever t'awayte, and ay be wher ye were.

As wisly he gye alle my joyes here
As I am youres, and to yow sad and trewe,
And ye, my lyf and cause of my gode chere,

And deeth also, whan ye my peynes newe, 11
My worldes joye, whom I wol serve and sewe,
Myn heven hool, and al my suffisaunce,
Whom for to serve is set al my plesaunce.

Beseching yow in my most humble wyse 15
T'accepte in worth this litel pore dyte,
And for my trouthe my servyce not despyse,
Myn observaunce eke have not in despyte,
Ne yit to longe to suffren in this plyte;
I yow beseche, myn hertes lady, here, 20
Sith I yow serve, and so wil yeer by yere.

Proverbs

I

WHAT shul thise clothes thus manyfold,
  Lo! this hote somers day? —
After greet hete cometh cold;
  No man caste his pilche away.

II

Of al this world the large compas   5
  Hit wol not in myn armes tweyne, —
Whoso mochel wol embrace,
  Litel therof he shal distreyne.

A TREATISE ON THE ASTROLABE

It is no longer customary, as it was in the days of Leland and Speght, to speak of "learned Chaucer." Recent critics, on the contrary, have often concerned themselves with pointing out the limitations of his scholarship — his occasional mistranslations and other inaccuracies, his use of French and Italian versions of Latin texts, or even his tendency to show familiarity with the beginnings of works which he may not have read to the end. And it is true that Chaucer's attitude toward books and learning was that of the man of letters rather than of the professional scholar. Nevertheless the range of his knowledge and the quality of his intelligence were such that the old epithet, "learned," is not without justification. His wide reading of literature, in classical and mediæval Latin, French, and Italian as well as in English, is apparent everywhere in his writings. Though he nowhere finds occasion for extended discourse on legal science, his various references to the subject tend to confirm the tradition that he had some professional training in law. His knowledge of philosophy may have been mostly derived from Boethius, but his serious interest in its problems is shown by frequent discussions in his poetry as well as by his translation of the De Consolatione. And he had considerable acquaintance with the natural science of his age. His familiarity with the processes of alchemy may have been acquired, as some suppose, at the cost of unhappy personal experience. But he shows also some knowledge of the literature of the subject, which was not merely a pesudo-science. In the *House of Fame* he discusses problems of the science which we should now call physics. Throughout his works he makes free use of medical lore, and though his discussions cannot usually be traced to particular authorities they have been shown to conform very well to the teachings of the treatises on medicine and physiognomy. And finally, his references to astronomy and astrology are so numerous and important that their elucidation has been a principal part of the work of his commentators.

It is not surprising, in view of all his knowledge and intellectual curiosity, that Chaucer should have left a specimen of scientific writing. His interest in science was probably not exceptional among educated men of his time, though his reading in this as in other fields was extraordinary, and he certainly would not himself have claimed to be an authority in any of the sciences. The *Treatise on the Astrolabe*, in particular, is not so much an evidence of Chaucers' attainments in astronomy as of his opinion of its importance in education. For he describes himself modestly as an "unlearned compiler of the labors of old astrologiens," and the treatise itself, so far as completed, is a very elementary work, translated for a little boy not yet able to use Latin. The later, unwritten sections, though they were to deal in part with more advanced problems of astronomy and astrology, were apparently also to be adapted to the intelligence of a child. It is not clear whether the title *Bread and Milk for Children*, which the work bears in some manuscripts, was due to Chaucer or to the scribes. Of course if the recently discovered and published *Equatorie of the Planetis* should be proved to be a work of Chaucer's, it would give evidence of his more serious application to astronomical study.

The two parts of the treatise which were completed contain a description of the astrolabe and a series of simple "conclusions," or problems, which can be solved with its aid. Nearly all the material is translated or adapted from the Compositio et Operatio Astrolabii of Messahala, an Arabian astronomer of the eighth century, whose work was of course accessible to Chaucer in Latin. But a few definitions and explanations correspond in substance to passages in the De Sphaera of John de Sacrobosco, and several sections have not been traced to any source. It is not unlikely that among the numerous unpublished astronomical treatises in mediæval manuscripts may be found the exact compilation, based upon Messahala, that Chaucer used.

The boy for whom the English translation was made is addressed in the beginning as "little Lewis, my son," and it has usually been inferred that Chaucer had a son by that name. In the absence of positive information on the subject Professor Kittredge has suggested that the person referred to may be Lewis Clifford, the younger, the son of Chaucer's friend Sir Lewis Clifford and possibly a godson of the poet. The younger Clifford is known to have died in October, 1391, the year in which the treatise was apparently compiled; and the death of the boy might well explain the unfinished state of the work. But Professor Manly has recently found a record which includes the name of Lewis Chaucer in association with that of Thomas Chaucer, and the latter is probably Geoffrey's son. So the old opinion gains likelihood that Chaucer translated the *Astrolabe* for his own child.

The treatise, simple as it is, has some interest for students of the history of English science. According to Mr. R. T. Gunther, the author of Early Science at Oxford, it is "the oldest work written in Englissh upon an elaborate scientific instrument." And there must have been very few comparable textbooks of any sort in the language in an age when Latin was the usual medium of higher instruction. For students of Chaucer's poetry the *Astrolabe* has of course the interest that attaches to any piece of his workmanship. Occasionally it helps explain technical passages in his literary writings. What is more important, it reveals in some measure the mind and spirit of the man, his modesty and his painstaking seriousness in intellectual work. The introduction deserves special notice as being the only piece of Chaucer's prose, of any length, that is not rather close translation. It is a short specimen, but it indicates that if Chaucer had written any considerable amount of freely composed prose it would have been superior in form to the *Boece* and the *Melibee*.

A Treatise on the Astrolabe

Lyte Lowys my sone, I aperceyve wel by certeyne evydences thyn abilite to lerne sciences touching nombres and proporciouns; and as wel considre I thy besy praier in special to lerne the tretys of the Astrelabie. Than for as mochel as a philosofre saith, "he wrappith him in his frend, that condescendith to the rightfulle praiers of his frend," therfore have I yeven the a suffisant Astrolabie as for oure orizonte, compowned after the latitude of Oxenforde; upon which, 10 by mediacioun of this litel tretys, I purpose to teche the a certein nombre of conclusions aperteynyng to the same instrument. I seie a certein of conclusions, for thre causes. The first cause is this: truste wel that alle the conclusions that han be founde, or ellys possibly might be founde in so noble an instrument as is an Astrelabie ben unknowe parfitly to eny mortal man in this regioun, as I suppose. Another cause is this, that sothly in any tretis of the Astrelabie 20 that I have seyn, there be somme conclusions that wol not in alle thinges parformen her bihestes; and somme of hem ben to harde to thy tendir age of ten yeer to conceyve.

This tretis, divided in 5 parties, wol I shewe the under full light reules and naked wordes in Englissh, for Latyn ne canst thou yit but small, my litel sone. But natheles suffise to the these trewe conclusions in Englissh as wel as sufficith to these noble clerkes Grekes these 30 same conclusions in Grek; and to Arabiens in Arabik, and to Jewes in Ebrew, and to the

Latyn folk in Latyn; whiche Latyn folk had hem first out of othere dyverse langages, and writen hem in her owne tunge, that is to seyn, in Latyn. And God woot that in alle these langages and in many moo han these conclusions ben suffisantly lerned and taught, and yit by diverse reules; right as diverse pathes leden diverse folk the righte way to Rome. 40 Now wol I preie mekely every discret persone that redith or herith this litel tretys to have my rude endityng for excusid, and my superfluite of wordes, for two causes. The first cause is for that curious endityng and hard sentence is ful hevy at onys for such a child to lerne. And the secunde cause is this, that sothly me semith better to writen unto a child twyes a god sentence, than he forgete it onys.

And Lowys, yf so be that I shewe the in 50 my light Englissh as trewe conclusions touching this mater, and not oonly as trewe but as many and as subtile conclusiouns, as ben shewid in Latyn in eny commune tretys of the Astrelabie, konne me the more thank. And preie God save the king, that is lord of this langage, and alle that him feith berith and obeieth, everich in his degre, the more and the lasse. But considre wel that I ne usurpe not to have founden this werk of my labour 60 or of myn engyn. I n'am but a lewd compilator of the labour of olde astrologiens, and have it translatid in myn Englissh oonly for thy doctrine. And with this swerd shal I sleen envie.

Prima pars. — The firste partie of this tretys shal reherse the figures and the membres of thyn Astrelabie by cause that thou shalt have the gretter knowing of thyn owne instrument.

Secunda pars. — The secunde partie shal techen the worken the verrey practik of 70

the forseide conclusiouns, as ferforth and as narwe as may be shewed in so small an instrument portatif aboute. For wel woot every astrologien that smallist fraccions ne wol not be shewid in so small an instrument as in subtile tables calculed for a cause.

Tertia pars. — The thirde partie shal contene diverse tables of longitudes and latitudes of sterres fixe for the Astrelabie, and tables of the declinacions of the sonne, and tables 80 of longitudes of citees and townes; and tables as well for the governaunce of a clokke, as for to fynde the altitude meridian; and many anothir notable conclusioun after the kalenders of the reverent clerkes, Frere J. Somer and Frere N. Lenne.

Quarta pars. — The fourthe partie shal ben a theorike to declare the moevyng of the celestiall bodies with the causes. The whiche fourthe partie in speciall shal shewen a table 90 of the verrey moeving of the mone from houre to houre every day and in every signe after thyn almenak. Upon which table there folewith a canoun suffisant to teche as wel the manere of the worchynge of the same conclusioun as to knowe in oure orizonte with which degre of the zodiak that the mone arisith in any latitude, and the arisyng of any planete after his latitude fro the ecliptik lyne.

Quinta pars. — The fifthe partie shal be 100 an introductorie, after the statutes of oure doctours, in which thou maist lerne a gret part of the generall rewles of theorik in astrologie. In which fifthe partie shalt thou fynden tables of equaciouns of houses after the latitude of Oxenforde; and tables of dignitees of planetes, and othere notefull thinges, yf God wol vouche saaf and his Moder the Maide, moo than I behete.

Part I

Here begynneth the descripcioun of thin Astralabie.

1. Thyn Astrolabie hath a ring to putten on the thombe of thi right hond in taking the height of thinges. And tak kep, for from henes forthward I wol clepen the heighte of any thing that is taken by the rewle "the altitude," withoute moo wordes.

2. This ryng renneth in a maner toret fast to the moder of thyn Astrelabie in so rown a

space that it distourbith not the instrument to hangen after his right centre.

3. The moder of thin Astrelabye is thikkest plate, perced with a large hool, that resceiveth in hir wombe the thynne plates compowned for diverse clymates, and thy reet shapen in manere of a nett or of a webbe of a loppe.

4. This moder is dividid on the bakhalf with

a lyne that cometh descending fro the ring doun to the netherist bordure. The whiche lyne, fro the forseide ring unto the centre of the large hool amidde, is clepid the south lyne, or ellis the lyne meridional. And the remenaunt of this lyne doun to the bordure is clepid the north lyne, or ellis the lyne of midnyght.

5. Overthwart this forseide longe lyne ther crossith him another lyne of the same lengthe from eest to west. Of the whiche lyne, from a litel cros (+) in the bordure unto the centre of the large hool, is clepid the est lyne, or ellis the lyne orientale. And the remenaunt of this lyne, fro the forseide centre unto the bordure, is clepid the west lyne, or ellis the lyne occidentale. Now hast thou here the foure quarters of thin Astrolabie divided after the 10 foure principales plages or quarters of the firmament.

6. The est syde of thyn Astrolabie is clepid the right syde, and the west syde is clepid the left syde. Forget not thys, litel Lowys. Put the ryng of thyn Astrolabie upon the thombe of thi right hond, and than wol his right side be toward thi lift side, and his left side wol be toward thy right side. Tak this rewle generall, as wel on the bak as on the wombe syde. Upon the ende of this est lyne, as I first seide, is marked a litel cros (+), where as evere 10 moo generaly is considerid the entring of the first degre in which the sonne arisith.

7. Fro this litel cros (+) up to the ende of the lyne meridionall, under the ryng, shalt thou fynden the bordure divided with 90 degrees; and by that same proporcioun is every quarter of thin Astrolabie divided. Over the whiche degrees ther ben noumbres of augrym that dividen thilke same degres fro 5 to 5, as shewith by longe strikes bitwene. Of whiche longe strikes the space bitwene contenith a myle wey, and every degre of the bor- 10 dure conteneth 4 minutes, this is to seien, mynutes of an houre.

8. Under the compas of thilke degrees ben writen the names of the Twelve Signes: as Aries, Taurus, Gemini, Cancer, Leo, Virgo, Libra, Scorpio, Sagittarius, Capricornus, Aquarius, Pisces. And the nombre of the degrees of thoo signes be writen in augrym above, and with longe divisiouns fro 5 to 5, dyvidid fro the tyme that the signe entrith unto the last ende. But understond wel that these degres of signes ben everich of hem consid- 10

red of 60 mynutes, and every mynute of 60 secundes, and so furth into smale fraccions infinite, as saith Alkabucius. And therfore knowe wel that a degre of the bordure contenith 4 minutes, and a degre of a signe conteneth 60 minutes, and have this in mynde.

9. Next this folewith the cercle of the daies, that ben figured in manere of degres, that contenen in nombre 365, dividid also wtih longe strikes fro 5 to 5, and the nombre in augrym writen under that cercle.

10. Next the cercle of the daies folewith the cercle of the names of the monthes, that is to say, Januarius, Februarius, Marcius, Aprilis, Maius, Junius, Julius, Augustus, September, October, November December. The names of these monthes were clepid thus, somme for her propirtees and somme by statutes of lordes Arabiens, somme by othre lordes of Rome. Eke of these monthes, as liked to Julius Cesar and to Cesar Augustus, somme were 10 compouned of diverse nombres of daies, as Julie and August. Than hath Januarie 31 daies, Februarie 28, March 31, Aprill 30, May 31, Junius 30, Julius 31, Augustus 31, September 30, October 31, November 30, December 31. Natheles, all though that Julius Cesar toke 2 daies out of Feverer and putte hem in his month of Juyll, and Augustus Cesar clepid the month of August after his name and ordeined it of 31 daies, yit truste wel that the 20 sonne dwellith therfore nevere the more ne lasse in oon signe than in another.

11. Than folewen the names of the holy daies in the Kalender, and next hem the lettres of the A B C on whiche thei fallen.

12. Next the forseide cercle of the A B C, under the cross lyne, is marked the skale in manere of 2 squyres, or ellis in manere of laddres, that serveth by his 12 pointes and his dyvisiouns of ful many a subtil conclusioun. Of this forseide skale fro the cross lyne unto the verrey angle is clepid Umbra Versa, and the nethir partie is clepid Umbra Recta, or ellis Umbra Extensa.

13. Than hast thou a brod reule, that hath on either ende a square plate perced with certein holes, somme more and somme lasse, to resceyve the stremes of the sonne by day, and eke by mediacioun of thin eye to knowe the altitude of sterres by night.

14. Than is there a large pyn in manere of an extre, that goth thorugh the hole that halt the tables of the clymates and the riet in the

wombe of the moder; thorugh which pyn ther
goth a litel wegge, which that is clepid the
hors, that streynith all these parties to-hepe.
Thys forseide grete pyn in manere of an extre
is ymagyned to be the Pool Artik in thyn
Astralabie.

15. The wombe syde of thyn Astrelabie is
also divided with a longe croys in 4 quarters
from est to west, fro southe to northe, fro
right syde to left side, as is the bakside.

16. The bordure of which wombe side is
divided fro the point of the est lyne unto the
point of the south lyne under the ring, in 90
degrees; and by that same proporcioun is every
quarter divided, as is the bakside. That
amountith 360 degrees. And understond wel
that degres of this bordure ben aunswering and
consentrike to the degrees of the equinoxiall,
that is dividid in the same nombre as
every othir cercle is in the highe hevene. 10
This same bordure is divided also with 23
lettres capitals and a small crosse (+) above
the south lyne, that shewith the 24 houres
equals of the clokke. And, as I have seid, 5
of these degres maken a myle wey, and 3 milewei maken an houre. And every degre of thys
bordure contenith 4 minutes, and every minute 60 secundes. Now have I told the twyes.

17. The plate under the riet is discrived
with 3 principal cercles, of whiche the leest
is clepid the cercle of Cancre by cause that
the heved of Cancre turnith evermo consentrik upon the same cercle. In this heved
of Cancer is the grettist declinacioun northward of the sonne, and therfore is he clepid
solsticium of somer; which declinacioun, after
Ptholome, is 23 degrees and 50 minutes as
wel in Cancer as in Capricorn. This signe 10
of Cancer is clepid the tropik of somer, of
tropos, that is to seien "ageynward." For than
beginneth the sonne to passen from us-ward.

The myddel cercle in wydnesse, of these 3,
is clepid the cercle equinoxiall, upon which
turnith evermo the hevedes of Aries and Libra.
And understond wel that evermo thys cercle
equinoxiall turnith justly from verrey est to verrey west as I have shewed the in the speer
solide. This same cercle is clepid also 20
Equator, that is the weyer of the day; for
whan the sonne is in the hevedes of Aries and
Libra, than ben the dayes and the nightes ylike
of lengthe in all the world. And therfore ben
these 2 signes called the equinoxiis. And all
that moeveth withinne the hevedes of these

Aries and Libra, his moevyng is clepid northward; and all that moevith withoute these
hevedes, his moevyng is clepid southward,
as fro the equinoxiall. Tak kep of these 30
latitudes north and south, and forget it nat.
By this cercle equinoxiall ben considred the
24 houres of the clokke; for evermo the arisyng
of 15 degrees of the equinoxiall makith an
houre equal of the clokke. This equinoxiall is
clepid the gurdel of the first moeving, or ellis
of the first moevable. And note that the first
moevyng is clepid moevyng of the first moevable of the 8 speer, which moeving is from
est into west, and eft ageyn into est. Also 40
it is clepid girdel of the first moeving for it
departith the first moevable, that is to seyn
the spere, in two like partyes evene distantz
fro the poles of this world.

The widest of these 3 principale cercles is
clepid the cercle of Capricorne, by cause that
the heved of Capricorne turneth evermo consentrik upon the same cercle. In the heved of
this forseid Capricorne is the grettist declinacioun southward of the sonne, and ther- 50
fore it is clepid the solsticium of wynter.
This signe of Capricorne is also clepid the
tropic of wynter, for than begynneth the sonne
to come ageyn to us-ward.

18. Upon this forseide plate ben compassed
certeyn cercles that highten almycanteras, of
whiche somme of hem semen parfit cercles and
somme semen inparfit. The centre that stondith amyddes the narwest cercle is clepid the
cenyth. And the netherist cercle, or the first
cercle, is clepid the orizonte, that is to seyn,
the cercle that divideth the two emysperies,
that is, the partie of the hevene above the
erthe and the partie bynethe. These almy- 10
kanteras ben compowned by 2 and 2, all
be it so that on diverse Astrelabies somme
almykanteras ben divided by oon, and somme
by two, and somme by thre, after the quantite
of the Astrelabie. This forseide cenyth is
ymagined to ben the verrey point over the
crowne of thin heved. And also this cenyth
is the verray pool of the orizonte in every regioun.

19. From this cenyth, as it semeth, there
comen a maner croked strikes like to the clawes
of a loppe, or elles like the werk of a wommans calle, in kervyng overthwart the almykanteras. And these same strikes or divisiouns
ben clepid azimutz, and thei dividen the orisounte of thin Astrelabie in 24 divisiouns. And

these azymutz serven to knowe the costes of
the firmament, and to othre conclusions, as
for to knowe the cenyth of the sonne and   10
of every sterre.

20. Next these azymutz, under the cercle
of Cancer, ben there 12 divisiouns embelif,
muche like to the shap of the azemutz, that
shewen the spaces of the houres of planetes.

21. The riet of thin Astrelabie with thy zodiak, shapen in manere of a net or of a lopwebbe
after the olde descripcioun, which thou maist
turnen up and doun as thiself liketh, contenith
certein nombre of sterres fixes, with her longitudes and latitudes determinat, yf so be that the
maker have not errid. The names of the sterres
ben writen in the margyn of the riet there as thei
sitte, of whiche sterres the smale point is
clepid the centre. And understond also that   10
alle the sterres sitting within the zodiak of
thin Astrelabie ben clepid sterres of the north, for
thei arise by northe the est lyne. And all the remenaunt fixed oute of the zodiak ben clepid sterres
of the south. But I seie not that thei arisen alle
by southe the est lyne; witnesse on Aldeberan
and Algomeyse. Generaly understond this rewle,
that thilke sterres that ben clepid sterres of the
north arisen rather than the degre of her
longitude, and alle the sterres of the south   20
arisen after the degre of her longitude —
this is to seyn, sterres fixed in thyn Astrelabie. The mesure of the longitude of sterres is
taken in the lyne ecliptik of hevene, under
which lyne, whan that the sonne and the mone
be lyne-right, or ellis in the superficie of this
lyne, than is the eclipse of the sonne or of the
mone, as I shal declare, and eke the cause
why. But sothly the ecliptik lyne of thy
zodiak is the utterist bordure of thy zodiak   30
there the degrees be marked.

Thy zodiak of thin Astrelabie is shapen as
a compas which that contenith a large brede
as after the quantite of thyn Astrelabie, in ensample that the zodiak in hevene is ymagyned
to ben a superfice contenyng a latitude of 12
degrees, whereas alle the remenaunt of cercles
in the hevene ben ymagyned verrey lynes
withoute eny latitude. Amiddes this celestial
zodiak is ymagined a lyne which that is   40
clepid the ecliptik lyne, under which lyne
is evermo the wey of the sonne. Thus ben
there 6 degres of the zodiak on that oo syde

of the lyne and 6 degrees on that othir. This
zodiak is dividid in 12 principale divisiouns that
departen the 12 signes, and, for the streitnesse
of thin Astrolabie, than is every smal divisioun
in a signe departed by two degrees and two, I
mene degrees contenyng 60 mynutes. And
this forseide hevenysshe zodiak is clepid   50
the cercle of the signes, or the cercle of the
bestes, for "zodia" in langage of Grek sowneth
"bestes" in Latyn tunge. And in the zodiak
ben the 12 signes that han names of bestes,
or ellis for whan the sonne entrith into eny
of tho signes he takith the propirte of suche
bestes, or ellis that for the sterres that ben
ther fixed ben disposid in signes of bestes or
shape like bestes, or elles whan the planetes
ben under thilke signes thei causen us by   60
her influence operaciouns and effectes like
to the operaciouns of bestes.

And understond also that whan an hot planete cometh into an hot signe, than encrescith
his hete; and yf a planete be cold, than amen-
usith his coldnesse by cause of the hoote sygne.
And by thys conclusioun maist thou take ensample in alle the signes, be thei moist or drie,
or moeble or fixe, reknyng the qualite of the
planete as I first seide. And everich of   70
these 12 signes hath respect to a certeyn
parcel of the body of a man, and hath it in
governaunce; as Aries hath thin heved, and
Taurus thy nekke and thy throte, Gemini thin
armholes and thin armes, and so furth, as shall
be shewid more pleyn in the 5 partie of this
tretis.

This zodiak, which that is part of the 8 speer,
over-kervith the equinoxial, and he over-
kervith him ageyn in evene parties; and   80
that oo half declineth southward; and that
othir northward, as pleinly declarith the Tretys
of the Speer.

Than hast thou a label that is shapen like
a reule, save that it is streit and hath no plates
on either ende with holes. But with the smale
point of the forseide label shalt thou calcule
thin equaciouns in the bordure of thin Astralabie, as by thin almury.

Thin almury is clepid the denticle of   90
Capricorne, or ellis the calculer. This same
almury sitt fix in the heved of Capricorne, and
it serveth of many a necessarie conclusioun in
equacions of thinges as shal be shewid.

Here endith the descripcioun of the Astrelabie and here begynne the
conclusions of the Astrelabie.

Part II

1. *To fynde the degre in which the sonne is day by day, after his cours aboute.*

Rekne and knowe which is the day of thy month, and ley thy rewle up that same day, and than wol the verrey poynt of thy rewle sitten in the bordure upon the degre of thy sonne.

Ensample as thus: — The yeer of oure Lord 1391, the 12 day of March at midday, I wolde knowe the degre of the sonne. I soughte in the bakhalf of myn Astrelabie and fond the cercle of the daies, the whiche I knowe by 10 the names of the monthes writen under the same cercle. Tho leyde I my reule over this foreseide day, and fond the point of my reule in the bordure upon the firste degre of Aries, a litel within the degre. And thus knowe I this conclusioun.

Anothir day I wolde knowen the degre of my sonne, and this was at midday in the 13 day of December. I fond the day of the month in manere as I seide; tho leide I my 20 rewle upon this foreseide 13 day, and fond the point of my rewle in the bordure upon the firste degre of Capricorne a lite within the degre. And than had I of this conclusioun the ful experience.

2. *To knowe the altitude of the sonne or of othre celestial bodies.*

Put the ryng of thyn Astrelabie upon thy right thombe, and turne thi lift syde ageyn the light of the sonne; and remewe thy rewle up and doun til that the stremes of the sonne shine thorugh bothe holes of thi rewle. Loke than how many degrees thy rule is areised fro the litel crois upon thin est lyne, and tak there the altitude of thi sonne. And in this same wise maist thow knowe by night the alti- tude of the mone or of brighte sterres. 10

This chapitre is so generall evere in oon that there nedith no more declaracioun; but forget it not.

3. *To knowe every tyme of the day by light of the sonne; and every tyme of the nyght by the sterres fixe; and eke to knowe by nyght or by day the degre of eny signe that ascendith on the est orisonte, which that is clepid co- mounly the ascendent, or ellis horoscopum.*

Tak the altitude of the sonne whan the list, as I have seid, and set the degre of the sonne, in caas that it be beforn the myddel of the day, among thyn almykanteras on the est syde of thin Astrelabie; and if it be after the myddel of the day, set the degre of thy sonne upon the west syde. Take this manere of settyng for a general rule, ones for evere. And whan thou hast set the degre of thy sonne upon as many almykanteras of height as was the al- 10 titude of the sonne taken by thy rule, ley over thi label upon the degre of the sonne; and than wol the point of thi labell sitte in the bordure upon the verrey tyde of the day.

Ensample as thus: — The yeer of oure lord 1391, the 12 day of March, I wolde knowe the tyde of the day. I tok the altitude of my sonne, and fond that it was 25 degrees and 30 of min- utes of height in the bordure on the bak side. Tho turned I myn Astrelabye, and by 20 cause that it was beforn mydday, I turned my riet and sette the degre of the sonne, that is to seyn the first degre of Aries, on the right side of myn Astrelabye upon 25 degrees and 30 mynutes of height among myn almykanteras. Tho leide I my label upon the degre of my sonne, and fond the point of my label in the bordure upon a capital lettre that is clepid an X. Tho rekned I alle the capitale lettres fro the lyne of mydnight unto this foreseide 30 lettre X, and fond that it was 9 of the clokke of the day. Tho loked I doun upon the est orizonte, and fond there the 20 degre of Geminis ascendyng, which that I tok for myn ascendent. And in this wise had I the expe- rience for evermo in which manere I shulde knowe the tyde of the day and eke myn as- cendent.

Tho wolde I wite the same nyght folew- yng the houre of the nyght, and wroughte 40 in this wise: — Among an heep of sterres fixe it liked me for to take the altitude of the faire white sterre that is clepid Alhabor, and fond hir sittyng on the west side of the lyne of midday, 12 degrees of heighte taken by my rewle on the bak side. Tho sette I the centre of this Alhabor upon 12 degrees among myn almykanteras upon the west side, by cause that she was founde on the west side. Tho leyde I my label over the degre of the 50 sonne, that was discendid under the west orisounte, and rekned all the lettres capitals fro the lyne of midday unto the point of my label in the bordure, and fond that it was passed 9 of the clokke the space of 10 degrees. Tho lokid I doun upon myn est orisounte, and fond there 10 degrees of Scorpius ascendyng, whom I tok for myn ascendent. And thus lerned I to knowe onys for ever in which manere I shuld come to the houre of the 60 nyght, and to myn ascendent, as verrely as may be taken by so smal an instrument.

But natheles this rule in generall wol I warne the for evere: — Ne make the nevere bold to have take a just ascendent by thin Astrelabie, or elles to have set justly a clokke, whan eny celestial body by which that thou wenyst governe thilke thinges be nigh the south lyne. For trust wel, whan the sonne is nygh the meridional lyne, the degre of the sonne 70 renneth so longe consentrik upon the almykanteras that sothly thou shalt erre fro the just ascendent. The same conclusion sey I by the centre of eny sterre fix by nyght. And more over, by experience I wot wel that in our orisounte, from xi of the clokke unto oon of the clokke, in taking of a just ascendent in a portatif Astrelabie it is to hard to knowe — I mene from xi of the clokke before the houre of noon til oon of the clokke next 80 folewyng.

4. A special declaracioun of the ascendent.

The ascendent sothly, as wel in alle nativites as in questions and eleccions of tymes, is a thing which that these astrologiens gretly observen. Wherfore me semeth convenyent, syth that I speke of the ascendent, to make of it speciall declaracioun.

The ascendent sothly, to take it at the largest, is thilke degre that ascendith at eny of these forseide tymes upon the est orisounte. And therfore, yf that eny planete ascende 10 at thatt same tyme in thilke forseide degre, than hath he no latitude fro the ecliptik lyne, but he is than in the degre of the ecliptik which that is the degre of his longitude. Men sayn that thilke planete is *in horoscopo.*

But sothly the hous of the ascendent, that is to seyn, the first hous or the est angle, is a thing more brod and large. For, after the statutes of astrologiens, what celestial body that is 5 degrees above thilke degre that 20 ascendith, or withinne that nombre, that is to seyn neer the degree that ascendith, yit

rekne they thilke planete in the ascendent. And what planete that is under thilke degre that ascendith the space of 25 degres, yit seyn thei that thilke planete is "like to him that is the hous of the ascendent." But sothly, if he passe the boundes of these forseide spaces, above or bynethe, thei seyn that the planete is "fallyng fro the ascendent." Yit saien 30 these astrologiens that the ascendent and eke the lord of the ascendent may be shapen for to be fortunat or infortunat, as thus: — A "fortunat ascendent" clepen they whan that no wicked planete, as Saturne or Mars or elles the Tayl of the Dragoun, is in the hous of the ascendent, ne that no wicked planete have noon aspect of enemyte upon the ascendent. But thei wol caste that thei have a fortunat planete in hir ascendent, and yit in his fe- 40 licite; and than sey thei that it is wel. Further over thei seyn that the infortunyng of an ascendent is the contrarie of these forseide thinges. The lord of the ascendent, sey thei that he is fortunat whan he is in god place fro the ascendent, as in an angle, or in a succident where as he is in hys dignite and comfortid with frendly aspectes of planetes and wel resceyved; and eke that he may seen the ascendent; and that he be not retro- 50 grad, ne combust, ne joyned with no shrewe in the same signe; ne that he be not in his discencioun, ne joyned with no planete in his descencioun, ne have upon him noon aspect infortunat; and than sey thei that he is well.

Natheles these ben observaunces of judicial matere and rytes of payens, in whiche my spirit hath no feith, ne knowing of her *horoscopum.* For they seyn that every 60 signe is departid in thre evene parties by 10 degrees, and thilke porcioun they clepe a face. And although that a planete have a latitude fro the ecliptik, yit sey somme folk, so that the planete arise in that same signe with eny degre of the forseide face in which his longitude is rekned, that yit is the planete *in horoscopo,* be it in nativyte or in eleccion, etc.

5. To knowe the verrey equacioun of the degre of the sonne yf so be that it falle bitwene two almykanteras.

For as muche as the almykanteras in thin Astrelabie ben compowned by two and two, where as somme almykanteras in sondry astrelabies be compowned by 1 and 1, or elles by 3 and 3, it is necessarie to thy lernyng to teche the first to knowe and worke with thin owne instrument. Wherfore whan that the degre of thi sonne fallith bytwixe 2 almykanteras, or ellis yf thin almykanteras ben graven with over-gret a poynt of a compas (for bothe 10 these thinges may causen errour as wel in knowing of the tide of the day, as of the verrey ascendent), thou must worken in this wise: —

Set the degre of thy sonne upon the hyer almykanteras of bothe, and wayte wel where as thin almury touchith the bordure and set there a prikke of ynke. Sett doun agayn the degre of the sunne upon the nether almykanteras of bothe, and sett there another pricke. Remeve than thin almury in 20 the bordure evene amiddes bothe prickes, and this wol lede justly the degre of thi sonne to sitte atwixe bothe almykanteras in his right place. Ley than thy label over the degre of thi sonne, and fynd in the bordure the verrey tyde of the day, or of the night. And as verraily shalt thou fynde upon thin est orisonte thin ascendent.

6. *To knowe the spryng of the dawenyng and the ende of the evenyng, the whiche ben called the two crepuscules.*

Set the nadir of thy sonne upon 18 degrees of height among thyn almykanteras on the west syde; and ley thy label on the degre of thy sonne, and than shal the point of thy label shewen the spryng of the day. Also set the nader of thy sonne upon 18 degrees of height among thin almykanteras on the est side, and ley over thy label upon the degre of the sonne, and with the point of thy label fynd in the bordure the ende of the evenyng, that is 10 verrey nyght.

The nader of the sonne is thilke degre that is opposyt to the degre of the sonne, in the 7 signe, as thus: — every degre of Aries by ordir is nadir to every degre of Libra by ordre, and Taurus to Scorpioun, Gemini to Sagittarie, Cancer to Capricorne, Leo to Aquarie, Virgo to Pisces. And if eny degre in thy zodiak be derk, his nadir shal declare hym.

7. *To knowe the arch of the day, that some folk callen the day artificiall, fro sonne arisyng tyl it go to reste.*

Set the degre of thi sonne upon thin est orisonte, and ley thy label on the degre of the sonne, and at the point of thy label in the bordure set a pricke. Turne than thy riet aboute tyl the degre of thy sonne sitte upon the west orisonte, and ley thy label upon the same degre of the sonne, and at the poynt of thy label set there another pricke. Rekne than the quantite of tyme in the bordure bitwixe bothe prickes, and tak there thyn arch of 10 the day. The remenaunt of the bordure under the orisonte is the arch of the nyght. Thus maist thou rekne bothe arches, or every porcioun, of whether that the liketh. And by this manere of worching maist thou se how longe that eny sterre fix dwelleth above the erthe, fro tyme that he riseth til he go to reste. But the day naturall, that is to seyn 24 hours, is the revolucioun of the equinoxial with as muche partie of the zodiak as the sonne of 20 his propre moeving passith in the mene while.

8. *To turne the houres inequales in houres equales.*

Know the nombre of the degrees in the houres inequales, and depart hem by 15, and tak there thin houres equales.

9. *To knowe the quantite of the day vulgar, that is to seyn fro spryng of the day unto verrey nyght.*

Know the quantite of thy crepuscles, as I have taught in the 2 chapitre bifore, and adde hem to the arch of thy day artificial, and tak there the space of all the hool day vulgar unto verrey night. The same manere maist thou worche to knowe the quantite of the vulgar nyght.

10. *To knowe the quantite of houres inequales by day.*

Understond wel that these houres inequales ben clepid houres of planetes. And understond wel that som tyme ben thei lenger by day than by night, and som tyme the contrarie. But understond wel that evermo generaly the houre inequal of the day with the houre inequal of the night contenen 30 degrees of the bordure, which bordure is evermo answeryng to the degrees of the equinoxial. Wherfore departe the arch of the day arti- 10 ficial in 12, and tak there the quantite of the houre inequale by day. And if thou abate the quantite of the houre inequale by day out

of 30, than shal the remenaunt that levith par-
forme the houre inequale by night.

11. *To knowe the quantite of houres equales.*

The quantite of houres equales, that is to
seyn the houres of the clokke, ben departid by
15 degrees alredy in the bordure of thin Astre-
laby, as wel by night as by day, generaly for
evere. What nedith more declaracioun?

Wherfore whan the list to knowe how many
houres of the clokke ben passed, or eny part
of eny of these houres that ben passed, or ellis
how many houres or parties of houres ben
to come fro such a tyme to such a tyme by   10
day or by night, know the degre of thy
sonne, and ley thy label on it. Turne thy ryet
aboute joyntly with thy label, and with the
poynt of it rekne in the bordure fro the sonne
ariste unto that same place there thou desirist,
by day as by nyght. This conclusioun wol I declare in the last chapitre of the 4 partie of this
tretys so openly that ther shal lakke no word
that nedith to the declaracioun.

12. *Special declaracioun of the houres of planetes.*

Understond wel that evermo, fro the arisyng of the sonne til it go to reste, the nadir of
the sonne shal shewe the houre of the planete;
and fro that tyme forward al the night til the
sonne arise, than shal the verrey degre of the
sonne shewe the houre of the planete.

Ensample as thus: — The xiij day of March
fyl upon a Saturday, peraventure, and atte risyng of the sonne I fond the secunde degre
of Aries sittyng upon myn est orisonte, all   10
be it that it was but litel. Than fond I the
2 degre of Libra, nadir of my sonne, discending
on my west orisonte, upon which west orisonte
every day generaly, atte sonne arist, entrith the
houre of every planete, after which planete the
day berith his name, and endith in the next
strike of the plate under the forseide west
orisonte. And evere as the sonne clymbith upper and upper, so goth his nadir downer
and downer, teching by suche strikes the   20
houres of planetes by ordir as they sitten
in the hevene. The firste houre inequal of
every Saturday is to Saturne, and the seconde
to Jupiter, the thirde to Mars, the fourthe to
the sonne, the fifte to Venus, the sixte to Mercurius, the seventhe to the mone. And then
ageyn the 8 houre is to Saturne, the 9 is to
Jupiter, the 10 to Mars, the 11 to the sonne,

the 12 to Venus. And now is my sonne gon
to reste as for that Saturday. Than shewith   30
the verrey degre of the sonne the houre
of Mercurie entring under my west orisonte at
eve; and next him succedith the mone, and
so furth by ordir, planete after planete in houre
after houre, all the nyght longe til the sonne
arise. Now risith the sonne that Sonday by
the morwe, and the nadir of the sonne upon
the west orisonte shewith me the entring of the
houre of the forseide sonne. And in this
manere succedith planete under planete fro   40
Saturne unto the mone, and fro the mone up
ageyn to Saturne, houre after houre generaly.
And thus have I this conclusyoun.

13. *To knowe the altitude of the sonne in myddes of the day that is clepid the altitude meridian.*

Set the degre of the sonne upon the lyne
meridional, and rekne how many degrees of
almykanteras ben bitwyxe thin est orisonte and
the degre of thy sonne; and tak there thin altitude meridian, this to seyn, the highest of the
sonne as for that day. So maist thou knowe in
the same lyne the heighest cours that eny sterre
fix clymbeth by night. This is to seyn that whan
eny sterre fix is passid the lyne meridional,
than begynneth it to descende; and so doth   10
the sonne.

14. *To knowe the degre of the sonne by thy ryet, for a maner curiosite.*

Sek besily with thy rule the highest of the
sonne in mydde of the day. Turne than thin
Astrelabie, and with a pricke of ynke marke
the nombre of that same altitude in the lyne
meridional; turne than thy ryet aboute tyl thou
fynde a degre of thy zodiak according with the
pricke, this is to seyn, sitting on the pricke.
And in soth thou shalt finde but 2 degrees in
all the zodiak of that condicioun; and yit
thilke 2 degrees ben in diverse signes.   10
Than maist thou lightly, by the sesoun of
the yere, knowe the signe in which that is the
sonne.

15. *To knowe which day is lik to which day as of lengthe.*

Loke whiche degrees ben ylike fer fro the
hevedes of Cancer and Capricorne, and loke
when the sonne is in eny of thilke degrees;
than ben the dayes ylike of lengthe. This is
to seyn that as longe is that day in that month,

as was such a day in such a month; there varieth but litel.

Also, yf thou take 2 dayes naturales in the
yere ylike fer fro either point of the equinoxiall in the opposyt parties, than as longe   10
is the day artificiall of that oon day as is the
night of that othir, and the contrarie.

16. *This chapitre is a maner declaracioun to
conclusiouns that folewen.*

Understond wel that thy zodiak is departed
in two halve circles, as fro the heved of Capricorne unto the heved of Cancer, and ageynward fro the heved of Cancer unto the heved
of Capricorne. The heved of Capricorne is
the lowest point where as the sonne goth in
wynter, and the heved of Cancer is the heighist
point in which the sonne goth in somer. And
therfore understond wel that eny two degrees that ben ylike fer fro eny of these two   10
hevedes, truste wel that thilke two degrees
ben of ilike declinacioun, be it southward or
northward, and the daies of hem ben ilike of
lengthe and the nyghtes also, and the shad-
ewes ilyke, and the altitudes ylike atte midday
for evere.

17. *To knowe the verrey degre of eny maner
sterre, straunge or unstraunge, after his longitude; though he be indetermynat in thin Astra-
labye, sothly to the trouthe thus he shal be
knowe.*

Tak the altitude of this sterre whan he is on
the est syde of the lyne meridionall, as neigh
as thou mayst gesse; and tak an ascendent anon
right by som manere sterre fix which that thou
knowist; and forget not the altitude of the firste
sterre ne thyn ascendent. And whan that this
is don, aspye diligently whan this same firste
sterre passith eny thyng the south westward;
and cacche him anon right in the same
nombre of altitude on the west syde of this   10
lyne meridional, as he was kaught on the
est syde; and tak a newe ascendent anon-ryght
by som manere sterre fix which that thou knowist, and forget not this secunde ascendent. And
whan that this is don, rekne than how many
degrees ben bitwixe the first ascendent and
the secunde ascendent; and rekne wel the myddel degre bitwene bothe ascendentes, and set
thilke myddel degre upon thyn est orizonte;
and wayte than what degre that sitte upon   20
the lyne meridional, and tak there the verrey degre of the ecliptik in which the sterre

stondith for the tyme. For in the ecliptik is the
longitude of a celestiall body rekned, evene
fro the heved of Aries unto the ende of Pisces;
and his latitude is rekned after the quantite of
his declynacioun north or south toward the
polys of this world.

As thus: — Yif it be of the sonne or of
eny fix sterre, rekne hys latitude or his   30
declinacioun fro the equinoxiall cercle; and
if it be of a planete, rekne than the quantite
of his latitude fro the ecliptik lyne, all be it
so that fro the equinoxiall may the declinacioun
or the latitude of eny body celestiall be rekned
after the site north or south and after the quantite of his declinacioun. And right so may the
latitude or the declinacioun of eny body celestiall, save oonly of the sonne, after hys site
north or south and after the quantite of his   40
declinacioun, be rekned fro the ecliptik
lyne; fro which lyne alle planetes som tyme
declinen north or south save oonly the forseide
sonne.

18. *To knowe the degrees of longitudes of
fixe sterres after that they be determynat in
thin Astrelabye, yf so be that thei be trewly
sette.*

Set the centre of the sterre upon the lyne
meridionall, and tak kep of thy zodiak, and
loke what degre of eny signe that sitte upon
the same lyne meridionall at that same tyme,
and tak there the degre in which the sterre
stondith; and with that same degre cometh that
same sterre unto that same lyne fro the orisonte.

19. *To knowe with which degre of the zodiak eny sterre fix in thin Astrelabie arisith
upon the est orisonte, all though his dwellyng
be in another signe.*

Set the centre of the sterre upon the est
orisonte, and loke what degre of eny signe that
sitt upon the same orisonte at that same tyme.
And understond wel that with that same degre
arisith that same sterre.

And thys merveylous arisyng with a straunge
degre in another signe is by cause that the
latitude of the sterre fix is either north or south
fro the equinoxiall. But sothly the latitudes
of planetes be comounly rekened fro the   10
ecliptyk, by cause that noon of hem declyn-
eth but fewe degrees out fro the brede of the
zodiak. And tak god kep of this chapitre of
arisyng of celestialle bodies; for truste wel that
neyther mone ne sterre, as in our embelif

orisonte, arisith with that same degre of his longitude save in oo cas, and that is whan they have no latitude fro the ecliptyk lyne. But natheles som tyme is everich of these planetes under the same lyne. 20

20. *To knowe the declinacioun of eny degre in the zodiak fro the equinoxiall cercle.*

Set the degre of eny signe upon the lyne meridionall, and rekne hys altitude in the almykanteras fro the est orisonte up to the same degre set in the forseide lyne, and set there a prikke; turne up than thy riet, and set the heved of Aries or Libra in the same meridionall lyne, and set there a nother prikke. And whan that this is don, considre the altitudes of hem bothe; for sothly the difference of thilke altitudes is the declinacioun of thilke degre fro the 10 equinoxiall. And yf it so be that thilke degre be northward fro the equinoxiall, than is his declinacyoun north; yif it be southward, than is it south.

21. *To knowe for what latitude in eny regioun the almykanteras of eny table ben compowned.*

Rekene how many degrees of almykanteras in the meridionall lyne ben fro the cercle equinoxiall unto the cenyth, or elles from the pool artyk unto the north orisonte; and for so gret a latitude, or for so smal a latitude, is the table compowned.

22. *To know in speciall the latitude of oure countre, I mene after the latitude of Oxenford, and the height of oure pool.*

Understond wel that as fer is the heved of Aries or Libra in the equinoxiall fro oure orisonte as is the cenyth fro the pool artik; and as high is the pool artik fro the orisonte as the equinoxiall is fer fro the cenyth. I prove it thus by the latitude of Oxenford: understond wel that the height of oure pool artik fro oure north orisonte is 51 degrees and 50 mynutes; than is the cenyth fro oure pool artik 38 degrees and 10 mynutes; than is the equinox- 10 ial from oure cenyth 51 degrees and 50 mynutes; than is oure south orisonte from oure equinoxiall 38 degrees and 10 mynutes. Understond wel this rekenyng. Also forget not that the cenyth is 90 degrees of height from oure orisonte, and oure equinoxiall is 90 degres from oure pool artik. Also this shorte rule is soth, that the latitude of eny place in a regioun is the distaunce fro the cenyth unto the equinoxiall. 20

23. *To prove evidently the latitude of eny place in a regioun by the preve of the height of the pool artik in that same place.*

In som wynters nyght whan the firmament is cler and thikke sterred, wayte a tyme til that eny sterre fix sitte lyne-right perpendiculer over the pool artik, and clepe that sterre A; and wayte another sterre that sitte lyne right under A, and under the pool, and clepe that sterre F. And understond wel that F is not considrid but oonly to declare that A sitte evene over the pool. Tak than anoon-right the altitude of A from the orisonte, and for- 10 get it not; let A and F goo fare wel tyl ageynst the dawenyng a gret while, and com than ageyn, and abid til that A is evene under the pool, and under F; for sothly than wol F sitte over the pool, and A wol sitte under the pool. Tak than eftsonys the altitude of A from the orisonte, and note as wel his secunde altitude as hys first altitude. And whan that this is doon, rekene how many degrees that the first altitude of A excedith his secunde alti- 20 tude, and tak half thilke porcioun that is excedid and adde it to his secunde altitude, and tak there the elevacioun of thy pool, and eke the latitude of thy regioun; for these two ben of oo nombre, this is to seyn, as many degres as thy pool is elevat, so muche is the latitude of the regioun.

Ensample as thus: — peraventure the altitude of A in the evenyng is 56 degrees of height; than wol his secunde altitude or the dawen- 30 yng be 48 degres, that is 8 degrees lasse than 56, that was his first altitude att even. Tak than the half of 8 and adde it to 48 that was his secunde altitude, and than hast thou 52. Now hast thou the height of thy pool and the latitude of the regioun. But understond wel that to prove this conclusioun and many another faire conclusioun, thou must have a plomet hangyng on a lyne, heygher than thin heved, on a perche; and thilke lyne 40 must hange evene perpendiculer bytwixe the pool and thin eye; and than shalt thou seen yf A sitte evene over the pool, and over F atte evene; and also yf F sitte evene over the pool and over A or day.

24. *Another conclusioun to prove the height of the pool artik fro the orisonte.*

Tak eny sterre fix that never discendith under the orisonte in thilke regioun, and considre his heighist altitude and his lowist altitude fro the orisonte, and make a nombre of
bothe these altitudes; tak than and abate half
that nombre, and take there the elevacioun of
the pool artik in that same regioun.

25. *Another conclusioun to prove the latitude of the regioun.*

Understond wel that the latitude of eny
place in a regioun is verrely the space bytwexe
the cenyth of hem that dwellen there and the
equinoxiall cercle north or south, takyng the
mesure in the meridional lyne, as shewith in
the almykanteras of thin Astrelabye. And thilke
space is as much as the pool artike is high in
that same place fro the orisonte. And than is
the depressioun of the pool antartik, that
is to seyn, than is the pool antartik, by-   10
nethe the orisonte the same quantite of
space neither more ne lasse.

Than if thou desire to knowe this latitude
of the regioun, tak the altitude of the sonne
in the myddel of the day, whan the sonne is
in the hevedes of Aries or of Libra; for than
moeveth the sonne in the lyne equinoxiall;
and abate the nombre of that same sonnes
altitude out of 90 degrees, and than is
the remenaunt of the nombre that lev-   20
eth the latitude of that regioun. As
thus: — I suppose that the sonne is thilke
day at noon 38 degrees of height; abate than
38 oute of 90; so leveth there 52; than is 52
degrees the latitude. I say not this but for
ensample; for wel I wot the latitude of Oxenford is certeyn minutes lasse, as thow might
preve.

Now yf so be that the semeth to longe a
tarieng to abide til that the sonne be in the   30
hevedes of Aries or of Libra, than wayte
whan the sonne is in eny othir degre of the
zodiak, and considre the degre of his declinacioun fro the equinoxiall lyne; and if it so be
that the sonnes declinacioun be northward fro
the equinoxiall, abate than fro the sonnes altitude at non the nombre of his declinacioun,
and than hast thou the height of the hevedes
of Aries and Libra. As thus: — My sonne
is peraventure in the first degre of Leoun,   40
58 degrees and 10 minutes of height at
non, and his declinacioun is almost 20 degrees
northward fro the equinoxiall; abate than thilke
20 degrees of declinacioun out of the altitude

at non; than leveth there 38 degrees and odde
minutes. Lo there the heved of Aries or Libra
and thin equinoxiall in that regioun. Also if
so be that the sonnes declinacioun be southward fro the equinoxiall, adde than thilke
declinacioun to the altitude of the sonne at   50
noon, and tak there the hevedes of Aries
and Libra and thin equinoxial; abate than the
height of the equinoxial out of 90 degrees;
than leveth there the distance of the pool of
that regioun fro the equinoxiall. Or elles, if
the list, tak the highest altitude fro the equinoxial of eny sterre fix that thou knowist, and
tak the netherest elongacioun (lengthing) fro
the same equinoxial lyne, and work in the
manere forseid.   60

26. *Declaracioun of the ascensioun of signes.*

The excellence of the spere solide, amonges
othir noble conclusiouns, shewith manyfest the
diverse ascenciouns of signes in diverse places,
as wel in the right cercle as in the embelif
cercle. These auctours writen that thilke signe
is cleped of right ascensioun with which more
part of the cercle equinoxiall and lasse part of
the zodiak ascendith; and thilke signe ascendith embelif with which lasse part of the
equinoxiall and more part of the zodiak   10
ascendith. Ferther-over, they seyn that in
thilke cuntrey where as the senith of hem that
dwellen there is in the equinoxial lyne, and
her orisonte passyng by the two poles of this
world, thilke folk han this right cercle and
the right orisonte; and evermore the arch of
the day and the arch of the night is there ilike
longe; and the sonne twies every yer passing
thorugh the cenith of hir heed, and two
someres and two wynters in a yer han these   20
forseide peple. And the almycanteras in
her Astrelabyes ben streight as a lyne, so as
it shewith in the figure.

The utilite to knowe the ascensions of signes
in the right cercle is this: — Truste wel that
by mediacioun of thilke ascensions these astrologiens, by her tables and her instrumentes,
knowen verreily the ascensioun of every degre
and minute in all the zodiak in the embelif
cercle, as shal be shewed. And *nota* that   30
this forseide right orisonte, that is clepid
Orison Rectum, dividith the equinoxial into
right angles; and the embelif orisonte, where
as the pool is enhaunced upon the orisonte,
overkervith the equinoxiall in embilif angles,
as shewith in the figure.

27. *This is the conclusioun to knowe the ascensions of signes in the right cercle, that is circulus directus.*

Set the heved of what signe the lyst to knowe his ascendyng in the right cercle upon the lyne meridionall, and wayte where thyn almury touchith the bordure, and set there a prikke; turne than thy riet westward til that the ende of the forseide signe sitte upon the meridional lyne and eftsonys wayte where thin almury touchith the bordure, and set there another pricke. Rekene than the nombre of degres in the bordure bitwixe bothe prikkes, and 10 tak the ascensioun of the signe in the right cercle. And thus maist thou werke with every porcioun of thy zodiak.

28. *To knowe the ascensions of signes in the embelif cercle in every regioun, I mene, in circulo obliquo.*

Set the heved of the signe which as the list to knowe his ascensioun upon the est orisonte, and wayte where thin almury touchith the bordure, and there set a prikke. Turne than thy riet upward til that the ende of the same signe sitte upon the est orisonte, and wayte eftsonys where as thin almury touchith the bordure, and set there a nother prikke. Rekene than the nombre of degrees in the bordure bitwyxe bothe prikkes and tak there the as- 10 censioun of the signe in the embelif cercle. And understond wel that alle the signes in thy zodiak, fro the heved of Aries unto the ende of Virgo, ben clepid signes of the north fro the equinoxiall. And these signes arisen bitwyxe the verrey est and the verrey north in oure orisonte generaly for evere. And alle the signes fro the heved of Libra unto the ende of Pisces ben clepid signes of the south fro the equinoxial; and these signes arisen 20 evermore bitwexe the verrey est and the verrey south in oure orisonte. Also every signe bitwixe the heved of Capricorne unto the ende of Geminis arisith on oure orisonte in lasse than 2 houres equales. And these same signes fro the heved of Capricorne unto the ende of Geminis ben cleped tortuose signes, or croked signes, for thei arise embelyf on oure orisonte. And these croked signes ben obedient to the signes that ben of right ascensioun. 30 The signes of right ascencioun ben fro the heved of Cancer unto the ende of Sagittarie; and these signes arisen more upright, and thei

ben called eke sovereyn signes and everich of hem arisith in more space than in 2 houres. Of whiche signes Gemini obeieth to Cancer, and Taurus to Leo, Aries to Virgo, Pisces to Libra, Aquarius to Scorpioun, and Capricorne to Sagittarie. And thus evermore 2 signes that ben ilike fer fro the heved of Capricorne 40 obeyen everich of hem til othir.

29. *To knowe justly the 4 quarters of the world, as Est, West, North, and South.*

Tak the altitude of thy sonne whan the list, and note wel the quarter of the world in which the sonne is for the tyme by the azymutz. Turne than thin Astrelabie, and set the degre of the sonne in the almykanteras of his altitude on thilke syde that the sonne stant, as is the manere in takyng of houres, and ley thy label on the degre of the sonne; and rekene how many degrees of the bordure ben bitwixe the lyne meridional and the point of thy 10 label, and note wel that nombre. Turne than ageyn thin Astrelabie, and set the point of thy gret rule there thou takist thin altitudes upon as many degrees in his bordure fro his meridional as was the point of thy label fro the lyne meridional on the wombe side. Take than thin Astrelabie with bothe hondes sadly and slighly, and lat the sonne shyne thorugh bothe holes of thy rule, and slighly in thilke shynyng lat thin Astrelabie kouche adoun 20 evene upon a smothe ground, and than wol the verrey lyne meridional of thin Astrelabie lye evene south, and the est lyne wol lye est, and the west lyne west, and the north lyne north, so that thou worke softly and avysely in the kouching. And thus hast thou the 4 quarters of the firmament.

30. *To knowe the altitude of planetes fro the wey of the sonne, whethir so they be north or south fro the forseide wey.*

Loke whan that a planete is in the lyne meridional, yf that hir altitude be of the same height that is the degre of the sonne for that day, and than is the planete in the verrey wey of the sonne and hath no latitude. And if the altitude of the planete be heigher than the degre of the sonne, than is the planete north fro the wey of the sonne such a quantite of latitude as shewith by thin almykanteras. And if the altitude of the planete be lasse 10 than the degre of the sonne, than is the planete south fro the wey of the sonne such a quantite of latitude as shewith by thin almykanteras. This is to seyn, fro the wey where as the sonne went thilke day, but not fro the wey of the sonne in every place of the zodiak.

31. *To knowe the cenyth of the arising of the sonne, this is to seyn, the partie of the orisonte in which that the sonne arisith.*

Thou must first considere that the sonne arisith not alwey verrey est, but somtyme by northe the est and somtyme by south the est. Sothly the sonne arisith nevere moo verrey est in oure orisonte, but he be in the heved of Aries or Libra. Now is thin orisonte departed in 24 parties by thin azimutes in significacioun of 24 parties of the world; al be it so that shipmen rekene thilke parties in 32. Than is there no more but wayte in which azimut that thy 10 sonne entrith at his arisyng, and take there the cenith of the arisyng of the sonne.

The manere of the divisioun of thin Astrelabie is this, I mene as in this cas: — First it is divided in 4 plages principalis with the lyne that goth from est to west; and than with another lyne that goth fro south to north; than is it divided in smale parties of azymutz, as est, and est by south, where as is the first azymut above the est lyne; and so furth fro 20 partie to partie til that thou come ageyn unto the est lyne. Thus maist thou understonde also the cenyth of eny sterre, in which partie he riseth.

32. *To knowe in which partie of the firmament is the conjunccyoun.*

Considere the tyme of the conjunccyoun by the kalender, as thus: — Loke hou many houres thilke conjunccioun is fro the midday of the day precedent, as shewith by the canon of thy kalender. Rekene than thilke nombre of houres in the bordure of thin Astrelabie, as thou art wont to do in knowyng of the houres of the day or of the nyght, and ley thy label over the degre of the sonne, and than wol the point of thy label sitte upon the houre 10 of the conjunccioun. Loke than in which azymut the degre of thy sonne sittith, and in that partie of the firmament is the conjunccioun.

33. *To knowe the cenyth of the altitude of the sonne.*

This is no more to seyn but eny tyme of the day tak the altitude of the sonne, and by the azymut in which he stondith maist thou seen in which partie of the firmament he is. And in the same wise maist thou seen by night, of eny sterre, whether the sterre sitte est or west, or north or south, or eny partie bitwene, after the name of the azimut in which the sterre stondith.

34. *To knowe sothly the degre of the longitude of the mone, or of eny planete that hath no latitude for the tyme fro the ecliptik lyne.*

Tak the altitude of the mone, and rekne thy altitude up among thyn almykanteras on which syde that the mone stondith, and set there a prikke. Tak than anon-right upon the mones syde the altitude of eny sterre fix which that thou knowist, and set his centre upon his altitude among thyn almykanteras there the sterre is founde. Wayte than which degre of the zodiak touchith the prykke of the altitude of the mone, and tak there the degre 10 in which the mone stondith. This conclusioun is verrey soth, yf the sterres in thin Astrelabie stonden after the trouthe. Comoun tretes of the Astrelabie ne maken non excepcioun whether the mone have latitude or noon, ne on wheyther syde of the mone the altitude of the sterre fixe be taken.

And *nota* that yf the mone shewe himself by light of day, than maist thou worche this same conclusioun by the sonne, as wel 20 as by the fixe sterre.

35. *This is the worchynge of the conclusioun to knowe yf that eny planete be direct or retrograd.*

Tak the altitude of any sterre that is clepid a planete, and note it wel; and tak eke anon the altitude of any sterre fix that thou knowist, and note it wel also. Com than ageyn the thridde or the fourthe nyght next folewing, for than shalt thou perceyve wel the moeving of a planete, whether so he moeve forward or bakward. Awayte wel than whan that thy sterre fixe is in the same altitude that she 10 was whan thou toke hir firste altitude. And tak than eft-sones the altitude of the forseide planete and note it wel; for truste wel yf so be that the planete be on the right syde of the meridional lyne, so that his secunde altitude be lasse than hys first altitude was, than is the planete direct; and yf he be on the west syde in that condicioun, than is he retrograd.

And yf so be that this planete be upon the est side whan his altitude is ytaken, so that his secunde altitude be more than his first altitude, than is he retrograd. And if he be on the west syde, than is he direct. But the contrarie of these parties is of the cours of the mone; for certis the mone moeveth the contrarie from othre planetes as in hir epicicle, but in noon othir manere.

36. *The conclusioun of equaciouns of houses after the Astrelabie.*

Set the begynnyng of the degre that ascendith upon the ende of the 8 houre inequal; than wol the begynnyng of the 2 hous sitte upon the lyne of mydnight. Remeve than the degre that ascendith, and set him on the ende of the 10 houre inequal, and than wol the begynnyng of the 3 hous sitte up on the mydnight lyne. Bring up ageyn the same degre that ascended first, and set him upon the est orisonte, and than wol the begynnyng of the 4 hous sitte 10 upon the lyne of mydnight. Tak than the nader of the degre that first ascendid, and set him in the ende of the 2 houre inequal; and than wol the begynnyng of the 5 hous sitte upon the lyne of mydnight. Set than the nader of the ascendent in the ende of the 4 houre inequal, and than wol the begynnyng of the 6 hous sitte on the mydnight lyne. The begynnyng of the 7 hous is nader of the ascendent, and the begynnyng of the 8 hous 20 is nader of the 2 hous, and the begynnyng of the 9 hous is nader of the 3, and the begynnyng of the 10 hous is nader of the 4, and the begynnyng of the 11 hous is nader of the 5, and the begynnyng of the 12 hous is nader of the 6.

37. *Another maner of equaciouns of houses by the Astrelabie.*

Tak thin ascendent, and than hast thou thy 4 angles; for wel thou wost that the opposit of thin ascendent, that is to seyn, the begynnyng of the 7 hous, sitt upon the west orisonte, and the begynnyng of the 10 hous sitt upon the lyne meridional, and his opposyt upon the lyne of mydnight. Than ley thy label over the degre that ascendith, and rekne fro the point of thy label alle the degrees in the bordure tyl thou come to the meridional lyne; and 10 departe alle thilke degrees in 3 evene parties, and take there the evene equacions of 3 houses; for ley thy label over everich of these 3 parties, and than maist thou se by thy label, lith in the zodiak, the begynnyng of everich of these same houses fro the ascendent; that is to seyn the begynnyng of the 12 hous next above thin ascendent, the begynnyng of the 11 hous, and than the 10 upon the meridional lyne, as I first seide. The same wise 20 worch thou fro the ascendent doun to the lyne of mydnyght, and thus hast thou othre 3 houses; that is to seyn, the begynnyng of the 2, and the 3, and the 4 hous. Than is the nader of these 3 houses the begynnyng of the 3 houses that folewen.

38. *To fynde the lyne meridional to dwelle fix in eny certeyn place.*

Tak a round plate of metal; for werpyng, the brodder the better; and make there upon a just compas a lite within the bordure. And ley this rounde plate upon an evene ground, or on an evene ston, or on an evene stok fix in the ground; and ley it evene by a level. And in the centre of the compas styke an evene pyn, or a wyr, upright, the smaller the better; set thy pyn by a plom-rule evene upright, and let this pyn be no lenger than 10 a quarter of the dyametre of thy compas, fro the centre amiddes. And wayte bisely aboute 10 or 11 of the clokke, whan the sonne shineth, whan the shadewe of the pyn entrith enythyng within the cercle of thy compas an heer-mele; and marke there a pricke with inke. Abid than stille waityng on the sonne til after 1 of the clokke, til that the shadwe of the wyr, or of the pyn, passe enything out of the cercle of the compas, be it nevere so lyte, 20 and set there another pricke of ynke. Tak than a compas, and mesure evene the myddel bitwixe bothe prickes, and set there a prikke. Tak me than a rule and draw a strike evene a-lyne, fro the pyn unto the middel prikke; and tak there thi lyne meridional for evermore, as in that same place. And yif thou drawe a cross-lyne overthwart the compas justly over the lyne meridional, than hast thou est and west and south, and par consequens, than 30 the nader of the south lyne is the north lyne.

39. *The descripcion of the meridional lyne, of longitudes and latitudes of citees and townes, as wel as of climates.*

Thys lyne meridional is but a maner descripcioun, or lyne ymagined, that passith upon the

poles of this world and by the cenyth of oure
heved. And it is cleped the lyne meridional,
for in what place that eny man ys at any tyme
of the yer, whan that the sonne, by mevynge
of the firmament, cometh to his verrey meridian
place, than is it verrey mydday, that we clepen
oure non, as to thilke man. And therefore
is it clepid the lyne of mydday. And *nota* 10
that evermore of eny 2 cytes or 2 townes,
of which that oo town approchith more toward the est than doth that othir town, truste
wel that thilke townes han diverse meridians.
Nota also that the arch of the equinoxial that
is contened or bownded bitwixe the 2 meridians is clepid the longitude of the toun. And
yf so be that two townes have ilike meridian
or oon meridian, than is the distaunce of
hem both ilike fer fro the est, and the con- 20
trarie; and in this manere thei change not
her meridian. But sothly thei chaungen her
almykanteras, for the enhaunsyng of the pool
and the distance of the sonne.

The longitude of a climat is a lyne ymagined fro est to west ilike distant fro the equinoxiall. And the latitude of a climat may be
cleped the space of the erthe fro the begynnyng of the first clymat unto the verrey
ende of the same clymat evene direct 30
ageyns the pool artyke. Thus sayn somme
auctours; and somme of hem sayn that yf men
clepe the latitude of a cuntrey the arch meridian that is contened or intercept bitwix the
cenyth and the equinoxial, than say they that
the distance fro the equinoxial unto the ende
of a climat evene ageynst the pool artik is the
latitude of a climat forsoothe.

40. *To knowe with which degre of the zodiak that eny planete ascendith on the orisonte, whether so that his latitude be north or
south.*

Know by thin almenak the degre of the
ecliptik of eny signe in which that the planete
is rekned for to be, and that is clepid the
degre of his longitude. And know also the
degre of his latitude fro the ecliptik north or
south. And by these ensamples folewynge in
speciall maist thou worche forsothe in every
signe of the zodiak: —

The degree of the longitude peraventure
of Venus or of another planete was 6 of 10
Capricorne, and the latitude of hir was

northward 2 degrees fro the ecliptik lyne. Than
tok I a subtil compas, and clepid that oo point
of my compas A, and that other point F. Than
tok I the point of A and sette it in the ecliptik lyne in my zodiak in the degre of the longitude of Venus, that is to seyn, in the 6 degre
of Capricorne; and than sette I the point of
F upward in the same signe by cause that
latitude was north upon the latitude of 20
Venus, that is to seyn, in the 6 degre fro the
heved of Capricorne; and thus have I 2 degrees
bitwixe my two prickes. Than leide I down
softly my compas, and sette the degre of the
longitude upon the orisonte; tho tok I and
waxed my label in manere of a peire tables to
receyve distinctly the prickes of my compas.
Tho tok I thys forseide label, and leyde it fix
over the degre of my longitude; tho tok I
up my compas and sette the point of A in 30
the wax on my label, as evene as I koude
gesse, over the ecliptik lyne in the ende of the
longitude, and sette the point of F endelong
in my label upon the space of the latitude,
inward and over the zodiak, that is to seyn
northward fro the ecliptik. Than leide I doun
my compas, and loked wel in the wey upon
the prickes of A and of F; tho turned I my ryet
til that the pricke of F satt upon the orisonte; than saw I wel that the body of 40
Venus in hir latitude of 2 degrees septem-
trionals ascendid, in the ende of the 6 degre,
in the heved of Capricorne.

And *nota* that in this manere maist thou
worche with any latitude septemtrional in alle
signes. But sothly the latitude meridional of
a planete in Capricorne ne may not be take by
cause of the litel space bitwixe the ecliptyk
and the bordure of the Astrelabie; but
sothly in all othre signes it may. 50

2 pars hujus conclusio.

Also the degre peraventure of Jupiter, or of
another planete, was in the first degre of Piscis
in longitude, and his latitude was 2 degrees
meridional; tho tok I the point of A and sette
it in the first degre of Piscis on the ecliptik;
and than sette I the point of F dounward in
the same signe by cause that the latitude was
south 2 degres, that is to seyn, fro the heved
of Piscis; and thus have 2 degres bitwexe
bothe prikkes. Than sette I the degre of 60
the longitude upon the orisonte; tho tok I
my label, and leide it fix upon the degre of the
longitude; tho sette I the point of A on my

label evene over the ecliptik lyne in the ende of the degre of the longitude, and sette the point of F endlong in my label the space of 2 degres of the latitude outward fro the zodiak (this is to seyn southward fro the ecliptik toward the bordure), and turned my riet til that the pricke of F saat upon the ori- 70 sonte. Than say I wel that the body of Jupiter in his latitude of 2 degrees meridional ascendid with 8 degres of Piscis *in horoscopo*.

And in this manere maist thou worche with any latitude meridional, as I first seide, save in Capricorne. And yif thou wilt pleye this craft with the arisyng of the mone, loke thou rekne wel hir cours houre by houre, for she ne dwel- lith not in a degre of hir longitude but litel while, as thow wel knowist. But natheles 80 yf thou rekne hir verrey moevyng by thy tables houre after houre, [thou shalt do wel ynow].

Supplementary Propositions

41. *Umbra Recta.*

Yif it so be that thou wilt werke by *umbra recta*, and thou may come to the bas of the tour, in this maner thou shalt werke. Tak the altitude of the tour by bothe holes, so that thy rewle ligge even in a poynt. Ensample as thus: I see him thorw at the poynt of 4; than mete I the space between me and the tour, and I finde it 20 feet; than beholde I how 4 is to 12, right so is the space betwixe thee and the tour to the altitude of the tour. 10 For 4 is the thridde part of 12, so is the space between thee and the tour the thridde part of the altitude of the tour; than thryes 20 feet is the heyghte of the tour, with adding of thyn owne persone to thyn eye. And this rewle is so general in *umbra recta*, fro the poynt of oon to 12. And yif thy rewle falle upon 5, than is 5 12-partyes of the heyght the space be- tween thee and the tour; with adding of thyn owne heyghte. 20

42. *Umbra Versa.*

Another maner of the werkinge, by *umbra versa*. Yif so be that thou may nat come to the bas of the tour, I see him thorw the nom- bre of 1; I sette ther a prikke at my fot; than go I neer to the tour, and I see him thorw at the poynt of 2, and there I sette another prikke; and I beholde how 1 hath him to 12, and ther finde I that it hath him twelfe sythes; than beholde I how 2 hath him to 12, and thou shalt finde it sexe sythes; than thou shalt 10 finde that as 12 above 6 is the numbre of 6, right so is the space between thy two prikkes the space of 6 tymes thyn altitude. And note, that at the ferste altitude of 1, thou settest a

prikke; and afterward, whan thou seest him at 2, ther thou settest another prikke; than thou findest between two prikkys 60 feet; than thou shalt finde that 10 is the 6-party of 60. And then is 10 feet the altitude of the tour. For other poyntis, yif it fille in *umbra versa*, as 20 thus: I sette caas it fill upon 2, and at the secunde upon 3; than schalt thou finde that 2 is 6 partyes of 12; and 3 is 4 partyes of 12; than passeth 6 4, by nombre of 2; so is the space between two prikkes twyes the heyghte of the tour. And yif the differens were thryes, than shulde it be three tymes; and thus mayst thou werke fro 1 to 12; and yif it be 4, 4 tymes; or 5, 5 tymes; *et sic de ceteris*.

43. *Umbra Recta.*

Another maner of wyrking, by *umbra recta*. Yif it so be that thou mayst nat come to the baas of the tour, in this maner thou schalt werke. Set thy rewle upon 1 till thou see the altitude, and set at thy foot a prikke. Than set thy rewle upon 2, and behold what is the differense between 1 and 2, and thou shalt finde that it is 1. Than mete the space be- tween two prikkes, and that is the 12 par- tie of the altitude of the tour. And yif ther 10 were 2, it were the 6 partye; and yif ther were 3, the 4 partye; *et sic deinceps*. And note, yif it were 5, it were the 5 party of 12; and 7, 7 party of 12; and note, at the altitude of thy conclusioun, adde the stature of thyn heyghte to thyn eye.

* * * * * *

44. *Another maner conclusion, to knowe the mene mote and the argumentis of any planete.*

To know the mene mote and the argumentis of every planete fro yere to yere, from day to day, from houre to houre, and from smale fraccionis infinite.

In this maner shalt thou worche; consider thy rote first, the whiche is made the beginning of the tables fro the yer of oure Lord 1397, and enter hit into thy slate for the laste meridie of December; and than consider the yer of oure Lord, what is the date, and behold whether thy date be more or lasse than the yer 1397. And yf hit so be that hit be more, loke how many yeres hit passeth, and with so many enter into thy tables in the first 10 lyne theras is writen *anni collecti et expansi.* And loke where the same planet is writen in the hed of thy table, and than loke what thou findest in direct of the same yer of oure Lord which is passid, be hit 8, or 9, or 10, or what nombre that evere it be, til the tyme that thou come to 20, or 40, or 60. And that thou findest in direct wryt in thy slate under thy rote, and adde hit togeder, and that is thy mene mote, for the laste meridian of 20 the December, for the same yer which that thou hast purposed. And if hit so be that hit passe 20, consider wel that fro 1 to 20 ben *anni expansi,* and fro 20 to 3000 ben *anni collecti;* and if thy nomber passe 20, than tak that thou findest in direct of 20, and if hit be more, as 6 or 18, than tak that thou findest in direct thereof, that is to sayen, signes, degrees, minutes, and secoundes, and adde togedere unto thy rote; and thus to make rotes. And 30 note, that if hit so be that the yer of oure Lord be lasse than the rote, which is the yer of oure Lord 1397, than shalt thou wryte in the same wyse furst thy rote in thy slate, and after enter into thy table in the same yer that be lasse, as I taught before; and than consider how many signes, degrees, minutes, and secoundes thyn entringe conteyneth. And so be that ther be 2 entrees, than adde hem togeder, and after withdraw hem from the 40 rote, the yer of oure Lord 1397; and the residue that leveth is thy mene mote for the laste meridie of December, the whiche thou hast purposed; and if hit so be that thou wolt weten thy mene mote for any day, or for any fraccioun of day, in this maner thou shalt worche. Make thy rote fro the laste day of December in the maner as I have taught, and afterward behold how many monethes,

dayes, and houres ben passid from the 50 meridie of December, and with that enter with the laste moneth that is ful passed, and take that thou findest in direct of him, and wryt hit in thy slate; and enter with as mony dayes as be more, and wryt that thou findest in direct of the same planete that thou worchest for; and in the same wyse in the table of houres, for houres that ben passed, and adde alle these to thy rote; and the residue is the mene mote for the same day and the same 60 houre.

45. Another manere to knowe the mene mote.

Whan thou wolt make the mene mote of eny planete to be by Arsechieles tables, tak thy rote, the whiche is for the yer of oure Lord 1397; and if so be that thy yer be passid the date, wryt that date, and than wryt the nomber of the yeres. Than withdraw the yeres out of the yeres that ben passed that rote. Ensampul as thus: the yer of oure Lord 1400, I wolde witen, precise, my rote; than wroot I furst 1400. And under that number I 10 wrot a 1397; than withdrow I the laste nomber out of that, and than fond I the residue was 3 yer; I wiste that 3 yer was passed fro the rote, the whiche was writen in my tables. Than afterward soghte I in my tables the *annis collectis et expansis,* and among myn expanse yeres fond I 3 yeer. Than tok I alle the signes, degrees, and minutes, that I fond direct under the same planete that I wroghte for, and wroot so many signes, 20 degrees, and minutes in my slate, and afterward added I to signes, degrees, minutes, and secoundes, the whiche I fond in my rote the yer of oure Lord 1397; and kepte the residue; and than had I the mene mote for the laste day of December. And if thou woldest wete the mene mote of any planete in March, April, or May, other in any other tyme or moneth of the yer, loke how many monethes and dayes ben passed from the laste day of De- 30 cember, the yer of oure Lord 1400; and so with monethes and dayes enter into thy table ther thou findest thy mene mote ywriten in monethes and dayes, and tak alle the signes, degrees, minutes, and secoundes that thou findest ywrite in direct of thy monethes, and adde to signes, degrees, minutes, and secoundes that thou findest with thy rote the yer of oure Lord 1400, and the residue that leveth is the

mene mote for that same day. And note, 40
if hit so be that thou woldest wete the mene
mote in any yer that is lasse than thy rote,
withdraw the nomber of so many yeres as hit
is lasse than the yer of oure Lord a 1397, and
kep the residue; and so many yeres, monethes,
and dayes enter into thy tabels of thy mene
mote. And tak alle the signes, degrees, and
minutes, and secoundes, that thou findest in
direct of alle the yeres, monethes, and
dayes, and wryt hem in thy slate; and 50
above thilke nomber wryt the signes, degrees, minutes, and secoundes, the whiche thou
findest with thy rote the yer of oure Lord a
1397; and withdraw alle the nethere signes
and degrees fro the signes and degrees, minutes, and secoundes of other signes with thy
rote; and thy residue that leveth is thy mene
mote for that day.

46. *For to knowe at what houre of the day,
or of the night, shal be flod or ebbe.*

First wite thou certeinly, how that haven
stondeth, that thou list to werke for; that is
to say in which place of the firmament the
mone being, maketh full see. Than awayte
thou redily in what degree of the zodiak that
the mone at that tyme is inne. Bring furth
than the label, and set the point therof in
that same cost that the mone maketh flod, and
set thou there the degree of the mone according with the egge of the label. Than 10
afterward awayte where is than the degree

of the sonne, at that tyme. Remeve thou than
the label fro the mone, and bring and set it
justly upon the degree of the sonne. And the
point of the label shal than declare to thee, at
what houre of the day or of the night shal
be flod. And there also maist thou wite by the
same point of the label, whether it be, at that
same tyme, flod or ebbe, or half flod, or
quarter flod, or ebbe, or half or quarter 20
ebbe; or ellis at what houre it was last, or
shal be next by night or by day, thou than
shalt esely knowe, &c. Furthermore, if it so
be that thou happe to worke for this matere
aboute the tyme of the conjunccioun, bring
furth the degree of the mone with the label
to that coste as it is before seyd. But than thou
shalt understonde that thou may not bringe
furth the label fro the degree of the mone
as thou dide before; for-why the sonne is 30
than in the same degree with the mone.
And so thou may at that tyme by the point of
the label unremeved knowe the houre of the
flod or of the ebbe, as it is before seyd, &c.
And evermore as thou findest the mone passe
fro the sonne, so remeve thou the label than
fro the degree of the mone, and bring it to
the degree of the sonne. And work thou than
as thou dide before, &c. Or elles know
thou what houre it is that thou art inne, 40
by thyn instrument. Than bring thou furth
fro thennes the label and ley it upon the degree of the mone, and therby may thou wite
also whan it was flod, or whan it wol be next,
be it night or day; &c.

THE ROMAUNT OF THE ROSE

The older editions of Chaucer included many works now held to be of other or doubtful authorship. Of the more important pieces which make up this body of Chaucerian apocrypha the *Romaunt of the Rose* alone continues to be printed with the acknowledged writings of the poet, and for excellent reasons. We have Chaucer's own testimony in the *Legend of Good Women* that he made a translation of the French poem. Although the greater part of the English version can hardly be by him, there is nothing in the style or dialect of another portion to make his authorship impossible; and the whole work, if not Chaucer's, is conspicuously Chaucerian. The original Roman, moreover, of which about one third is represented in the English translation, probably exerted on Chaucer a more lasting and more important influence than any other work in the vernacular literature of either France or England.

This last fact is not surprising in view of the position which the Roman de la Rose held in French literature for some two hundred years. It was begun, probably about 1237, by Guillaume de Lorris, and the part that he wrote (ending at l. 4432 of the English translation) set the fashion for numberless allegorical love-visions. Guillaume was a young poet and wrote in honor, or, as he would have said in the "service," of a lady. Whatever the facts of his personal experiences, in his writing he adhered to the conventions of courtly love. He relates how, in his twentieth year, he had a vision of a beautiful garden, where the God of Love and all his train were making merry. Among the flowers he was shown a Rosebud (the symbol of his lady), and wounded by Cupid's arrows he was overcome by the desire to possess it. His suit was opposed by Chastity, Danger (Offishness, Disdain), Shame, and Wicked-Tongue, and helped by Franchise, Pity, and Belacueil (Fair-Welcoming). Once, through the interposition of Venus herself, Belacueil allowed him to kiss the Bud. But Belacueil was punished by imprisonment, and the lover banished from the garden.

In this situation, before the lover gains his object, Guillaume's fragment comes to an end. His work was cut short, probably by death, when he had brought the slender plot of his poem almost to its termination. Forty years later the Roman was continued by a different poet in a totally different spirit. Jean de Meun, apparently in mature age, a scholar, philosopher, and moralist — the translator of Vegetius, Boethius, Giraldus Cambrensis, and Ailred of Rievaux — delayed the conclusion of the story till he had added about eighteen thousand lines, and made Guillaume's simple framework the vehicle of an elaborate treatise on the life and thought of the age. Science, theology, social philosophy, satire all find their place in his voluminous, but entertaining discourse. Love still remains the central subject. But it is no longer discussed in the courtly spirit of Guillaume. It is rather analyzed rationalistically as a feeling implanted by Nature to ensure the propagation of the race. And woman, idealized by Guillaume as an object of worship, becomes, along with friars, knights, lawyers, and doctors, the subject of Jean de Meun's most biting satire. The story, to be sure, is brought to a happy termination. The lover finally gains possession of the Rosebud. But the interest of Jean de Meun, like that of his readers, lay less in finishing the tale than in expounding the philosophy which has gained him the name, not without appropriateness, of "the Voltaire of the thirteenth century."

The later reputation and influence of the Roman was chiefly determined by Jean de

Meun's continuation. His free-thinking criticism precipitated a long controversy known to historians of French literature as the "querelle du Roman de la Rose." In particular his attacks upon women were taken up in a debate between feminists and anti-feminists which was at its height in the time of Christine de Pisan, at the end of the fourteenth century. So to Chaucer and his contemporaries the Roman was a book of heresy against the God of Love, and Chaucer's translation of it, according to the delightful fiction of the *Prologue to the Legend of Good Women,* was one of the sins for which he had to do penance by composing a book of the lives of Cupid's saints.

The English *Romaunt,* strangely enough, contains very little to justify this accusation against Chaucer. The second fragment alone (ll. 1705–5810), which includes Jean de Meun's discussion of the nature of love, might

conceivably fall under the reprehension of Cupid. Fragment A (ll. 1–1704) stops in the middle of Guillaume de Lorris's portion of the Roman, and fragment C, which is mainly concerned with the sin of Hypocrisy, as represented in the figure of False-Semblant, has very little bearing on women and the affairs of love. Jean de Meun's really abusive satire on women and his cynical exposition of the art of love, on which Chaucer drew freely in the *Wife of Bath's Prologue,* are nowhere included in the translation. And of the three fragments only the first and most inoffensive can with any probability be ascribed to Chaucer. Fragment C, though accepted as authentic by some scholars, departs considerably from his usage, and fragment B seems to have been the work of a follower and imitator of Chaucer who wrote under the influence of the Northern dialect.

The Romaunt of the Rose

Fragment A

Many men sayn that in sweveninges
Ther nys but fables and lesynges;
But men may some swevenes sen
Whiche hardely that false ne ben,
But afterward ben apparaunt.   5
This may I drawe to warrant
An authour that hight Macrobes,
That halt nat dremes false ne lees,
But undoth us the avysioun
That whilom mette kyng Cipioun.   10
And whoso saith or weneth it be
A jape, or elles nycete,
To wene that dremes after falle,
Let whoso lyste a fol me calle.
For this trowe I, and say for me,   15
That dremes signifiaunce be
Of good and harm to many wightes,
That dremen in her slep a-nyghtes
Ful many thynges covertly,
That fallen after al openly.   20
  Within my twenty yer of age,

Whan that Love taketh his cariage
Of yonge folk, I wente soone
To bedde, as I was wont to done,
And faste I slepte; and in slepyng   25
Me mette such a swevenyng
That lyked me wonders wel.
But in that sweven is never a del
That it nys afterward befalle,
Ryght as this drem wol tel us alle.   30
  Now this drem wol I ryme aright
To make your hertes gaye and lyght,
For Love it prayeth, and also
Commaundeth me that it be so.
And if there any aske me,   35
Whether that it be he or she,
How this book, [the] which is here,
Shal hatte, that I rede you here:
It is the Romance of the Rose,
In which al the art of love I close.   40
  The mater fayre is of to make;
God graunt me in gree that she it take
For whom that it begonnen is!
And that is she that hath, ywis,

So mochel pris; and therto she   45
So worthy is biloved to be,
That she wel ought, of pris and ryght,
Be cleped Rose of every wight.
    That it was May me thoughte tho —
It is fyve yer or more ago —   50
That it was May, thus dremed me,
In tyme of love and jolite,
That al thing gynneth waxen gay,
For ther is neither busk nor hay
In May, that it nyl shrouded ben,   55
And it with newe leves wren.
These wodes eek recoveren grene,
That drie in wynter ben to sene;
And the erthe wexith proud withalle,
For swote dewes that on it falle,   60
And the pore estat forget
In which that wynter had it set.
And than bycometh the ground so proud
That it wole have a newe shroud,
And makith so queynt his robe and faire   65
That it hath hewes an hundred payre
Of gras and flouris, ynde and pers,
And many hewes ful dyvers.
That is the robe I mene, iwis,
Through which the ground to preisen is.   70
    The byrdes that han left her song,
While thei suffride cold so strong,
In wedres gryl and derk to sighte,
Ben in May, for the sonne brighte,
So glade that they shewe in syngyng   75
That in her hertis is sich lykyng
That they mote syngen and be light.
Than doth the nyghtyngale hir myght
To make noyse and syngen blythe.
Than is blisful many sithe   80
The chelaundre and papyngay.
Than yonge folk entenden ay
Forto ben gay and amorous,
The tyme is than so saverous.
Hard is the hert that loveth nought   85
In May, whan al this mirth is wrought,
Whan he may on these braunches here
The smale briddes syngen clere.
Her blisful swete song pitous.
And in this sesoun delytous,   90
Whan love affraieth alle thing,
Me thought a-nyght, in my sleping,
Right in my bed, ful redily,
That it was by the morowe erly,
And up I roos, and gan me clothe.   95
Anoon I wissh myn hondis bothe;
A sylvre nedle forth y drough
Out of an aguler queynt ynough,

And gan this nedle threde anon;
For out of toun me list to gon   100
The song of briddes forto here,
That in thise buskes syngen clere.
And in the swete seson that leef is,
With a thred bastyng my slevis,
Alone I wente in my plaiyng,   105
The smale foules song harknyng,
That peyned hem, ful many peyre,
To synge on bowes blosmed feyre,
Jolif and gay, ful of gladnesse,
Toward a ryver gan I me dresse,   110
That I herd renne faste by;
For fairer plaiyng non saugh I
Than playen me by that ryver.
For from an hill that stood ther ner,
Cam doun the strem ful stif and bold.   115
Cleer was the water, and as cold
As any welle is, soth to seyne;
And somdel lasse it was than Seyne,
But it was strayghter wel away.
And never saugh I, er that day,   120
The watir that so wel lyked me;
And wondir glad was I to se
That lusty place and that ryver.
And with that watir, that ran so cler,
My face I wyssh. Tho saugh I well   125
The botme paved everydell
With gravel, ful of stones shene.
The medewe softe, swote and grene,
Beet right on the watir syde.
Ful cler was than the morowtyde,   130
And ful attempre, out of drede.
    Tho gan I walke thorough the mede,
Dounward ay in my pleiyng,
The ryver syde costeiyng.
and whan I had a while goon,   135
I saugh a gardyn right anoon,
Ful long and brood, and everydell
Enclosed was, and walled well
With highe walles enbatailled,
Portraied without and wel entailled   140
With many riche portraitures.
And bothe the ymages and peyntures
Gan I biholde bysyly;
And I wole telle you redyly
Of thilk ymages the semblaunce,   145
As fer as I have in remembraunce.
    Amydde saugh I Hate stonde,
That for hir wrathe, yre, and onde,
Semede to ben a moveresse,
An angry wight, a chideresse;   150
And ful of gyle and fel corage,
By semblaunt, was that ilk ymage.

And she was nothyng wel arraied,
But lyk a wod womman afraied.
Yfrounced foule was hir visage,   155
And grennyng for dispitous rage;
Hir nose snorted up for tene.
Ful hidous was she for to sene,
Ful foul and rusty was she, this.
Hir heed ywrithen was, ywis,   160
Ful grymly with a greet towayle.
    An ymage of another entayle
A lyft half was hir faste by.
Hir name above hir heed saugh I,
And she was called Felonye.   165
    Another ymage, that Vilanye
Yclepid was, saugh I and fond
Upon the wal on hir right hond.
Vilany was lyk somdell
That other ymage, and, trustith wel,   170
She semede a wikked creature.
By countenaunce, in portrayture,
She semed be ful dispitous,
And eek ful proud and outragious.
Wel coude he peynte, I undirtake,   175
That sich ymage coude make;
Ful foul and cherlyssh semed she,
And eek vylayneus for to be,
And litel coude of norture,
To worshipe any creature.   180
    And next was peynted Coveitise,
That eggith folk, in many gise,
To take and yeve right nought ageyn,
And gret tresouris up to leyn.
And that is she that for usure   185
Leneth to many a creature
The lasse for the morwe wynnyng,
So coveitous is her brennyng.
And that is she, for penyes fele,
That techith for to robbe and stele   190
These theves and these smale harlotes;
And that is routh, for by her throtes
Ful many oon hangith at the laste.
She makith folk compasse and caste
To taken other folkis thyng   195
Thorough robberie or myscounting.
And that is she that makith trechoures,
And she makith false pleadoures,
That with hir termes and hir domes
Doon maydens, children, and eek gromes   200
Her heritage to forgo.
Ful croked were hir hondis two,
For coveitise is evere wod
To gripen other folkis god.
Coveityse, for hir wynnyng,   205
Ful leef hath other mennes thing.

    Another ymage set saugh I
Next Coveitise faste by,
And she was clepid Avarice.
Ful foul in peyntyng was that vice;   210
Ful fade and caytif was she eek,
And also grene as ony leek.
So yvel hewed was hir colour,
Hir semed to have lyved in langour.
She was lyk thyng for hungre deed,   215
That ladde hir lyf oonly by breed
Kneden with eisel strong and egre,
And therto she was lene and megre.
And she was clad ful porely
Al in an old torn courtepy,   220
As she were al with doggis torn;
And bothe bihynde and eke biforn
Clouted was she beggarly.
A mantyl heng hir faste by,
Upon a perche, weik and small;   225
A burnet cote heng therwithall
Furred with no menyver,
But with a furre rough of her,
Of lambe-skynnes hevy and blake;
It was ful old, I undirtake.   230
For Avarice to clothe hir well
Ne hastith hir never a dell;
For certeynly it were hir loth
To weren ofte that ilke cloth;
And if it were forwered, she   235
Wolde have ful gret necessite
Of clothyng, er she bought hir newe,
Al were it bad of woll and hewe.
This Avarice hild in hir hand
A purs that heng [doun] by a band,   240
And that she hidde and bond so stronge,
Men must abyde wondir longe
Out of that purs er ther come ought.
For that ne cometh not in hir thought;
It was not, certein, hir entente   245
That fro that purs a peny wente.
    And by that ymage, nygh ynough,
Was peynted Envye, that never lough,
Nor never wel in hir herte ferde,
But if she outher saugh or herde   250
Som gret myschaunce or gret disese.
Nothyng may so moch hir plese
As myschef and mysaventure;
Or whan she seeth discomfiture
Upon ony worthy man falle,   255
Than likith hir wel withalle.
She is ful glad in hir corage,
If she se any gret lynage
Be brought to nought in shamful wise.
And if a man in honour rise,   260

Or by his wit or by his prowesse,
Of that hath she gret hevynesse.
For, trustith wel, she goth nygh wod
Whan any chaunce happith god.
Envie is of such crueltee   265
That feith ne trouthe holdith she
To freend ne felawe, bad or good.
Ne she hath kyn noon of hir blood,
That she nys ful her enemy;
She nolde, I dar seyn hardely,   270
Hir owne fadir ferde well.
And sore abieth she everydell
Hir malice and hir maltalent;
For she is in so gret turment,
And hath such [wo,] whan folk doth good, 275
That nygh she meltith for pure wood.
Hir herte kervyth and so brekith,
That God the puple wel awrekith.
Envie, iwis, shal nevere lette
Som blame upon the folk to sette.   280
I trowe that if Envie, iwis,
Knewe the beste man that is
On this side or biyonde the see,
Yit somwhat lakken hym wolde she;
And if he were so hende and wis   285
That she ne myght al abate his pris,
Yit wolde she blame his worthynesse,
Or by hir wordis make it lesse.
I saugh Envie, in that peyntyng,
Hadde a wondirful lokyng;   290
For she ne lokide but awry
Or overthwart, all baggyngly.
And she hadde a foul usage;
She myght loke in no visage
Of man or womman forth-right pleyn, 295
But shette hir oon eie for disdeyn;
So for envie brenned she
Whan she myght any man se
That fair or worthi were, or wis,
Or elles stod in folkis prys.   300
   Sorowe was peynted next Envie
Upon that wall of masonrye.
But wel was seyn in hir colour
That she hadde lyved in langour;
Hir semede to have the jaunyce.   305
Nought half so pale was Avarice,
Nor nothyng lyk of lenesse;
For sorowe, thought, and gret distresse
That she hadde suffred day and nyght,
Made hir ful yelow, and nothyng bright, 310
Ful fade, pale, and megre also.
Was never wight yit half so wo
As that hir semede for to be,
Nor so fulfilled of ire as she.

I trowe that no wight myght hir please 315
Nor do that thyng that myght hir ease;
Nor she ne wolde hir sorowe slake,
Nor comfort noon unto hir take,
So depe was hir wo bigonnen,
And eek hir hert in angre ronnen.   320
A sorowful thyng wel semed she,
Nor she hadde nothyng slowe be
For to forcracchen al hir face,
And for to rent in many place
Hir clothis, and for to tere hir swire, 325
As she that was fulfilled of ire;
And al totorn lay eek hir her
Aboute hir shuldris here and ther,
As she that hadde it al torent
For angre and for maltalent.   330
And eek I telle you certeynly
How that she wep ful tendirly.
In world nys wight so hard of herte
That hadde sen her sorowes smerte,
That nolde have had of her pyte,   335
So wo-begon a thyng was she.
She al todassht herself for woo,
And smot togyder her hondes two.
To sorowe was she ful ententyf,
That woful recheles caytyf;   340
Her roughte lytel of playing,
Or of clypping or kissyng;
For whoso sorouful is in herte,
Him luste not to play ne sterte,
Ne for to dauncen, ne to synge,   345
Ne may his herte in temper bringe
To make joye on even or morowe,
For joy is contrarie unto sorowe.
   Elde was paynted after this,
That shorter was a foot, iwys,   350
Than she was wont in her yonghede.
Unneth herself she mighte fede;
So feble and eke so old was she
That faded was al her beaute.
Ful salowe was waxen her colour; 355
Her heed, for hor, was whyt as flour.
Iwys, great qualm ne were it non,
Ne synne, although her lyf were gon.
Al woxen was her body unwelde,
And drie and dwyned al for elde. 360
A foul, forwelked thyng was she,
That whylom round and softe had be.
Her eeres shoken faste withalle,
As from her heed they wolde falle;
Her face frounced and forpyned, 365
And bothe her hondes lorne, fordwyned.
So old she was that she ne wente
A foot, but it were by potente.

The tyme, that passeth nyght and day,
And resteles travayleth ay,   370
And steleth from us so prively
That to us semeth sykerly
That it in oon poynt dwelleth ever,
And certes, it ne resteth never,
But goth so faste, and passeth ay,   375
That ther nys man that thynke may
What tyme that now present is
(Asketh at these clerkes this);
For [er] men thynke it, redily
Thre tymes ben passed by —   380
The tyme, that may not sojourne,
But goth, and may never retourne,
As watir that doun renneth ay,
But never drope retourne may;
Ther may nothing as tyme endure,   385
Metall, nor erthely creature,
For alle thing it fret and shall;
The tyme eke, that chaungith all,
And all doth waxe and fostred be,
And alle thing distroieth he;   390
The tyme, that eldith our auncessours,
And eldith kynges and emperours,
And that us alle shal overcomen,
Er that deth us shal have nomen;
The tyme, that hath al in welde   395
To elden folk, had maad hir elde
So ynly that, to my witing,
She myghte helpe hirsilf nothing,
But turned ageyn unto childhede.
She had nothing hirsilf to lede,   400
Ne wit ne pithe in hir hold,
More than a child of two yeer old.
But natheles, I trowe that she
Was fair sumtyme, and fresh to se,
Whan she was in hir rightful age;   405
But she was past al that passage,
And was a doted thing bicomen.
A furred cope on had she nomen;
Wel had she clad hirsilf and warm,
For cold myght elles don hir harm.   410
These olde folk have alwey cold;
Her kynde is sich, whan they ben old.
    Another thing was don there write,
That semede lyk an ipocrite,
And it was clepid Poope-Holy.   415
That ilk is she that pryvely
Ne spareth never a wikked dede,
Whan men of hir taken noon hede;
And maketh hir outward precious,
With pale visage and pitous,   420
And semeth a simple creature;
But ther nys no mysaventure

That she ne thenkith in hir corage.
Ful lyk to hir was that ymage,
That makid was lyk hir semblaunce.   425
She was ful symple of countenaunce,
And she was clothed and eke shod,
As she were, for the love of God,
Yolden to relygioun,
Sich semede hir devocioun.   430
A sauter held she fast in honde,
And bisily she gan to fonde
To make many a feynt praiere
To God, and to his seyntis dere.
Ne she was gay, fresh, ne jolyf,   435
But semede to be ful ententyf
To gode werkis and to faire;
And therto she had on an haire.
Ne, certis, she was fatt nothing,
But semed wery for fasting;   440
Of colour pale and deed was she.
From hir the gate ay werned be
Of paradys, that blisful place;
For sich folk maketh lene her face,
As Crist seith in his evangile,   445
To gete hem prys in toun a while,
And for a litel glorie veine,
They lesen God and eke his reigne.
    And alderlast of everychon
Was peynted Povert al aloon,   450
That not a peny hadde in wolde,
All though she hir clothis solde,
And though she shulde anhonged be;
For nakid as a worm was she.
And if the wedir stormy were,   455
For cold she shulde have deyed there.
She nadde on but a streit old sak,
And many a clout on it ther stak;
This was hir cote and hir mantell;
No more was there, never a dell,   460
To clothe hir with; I undirtake,
Gret leyser hadde she to quake.
And she was putt, that I of talke,
Fer fro these other, up in an halke.
There lurked and there coured she,   465
For pover thing, whereso it be,
Is shamefast and dispised ay.
Acursed may wel be that day
That povere man conceyved is;
For, God wot, al to selde, iwys,   470
Is ony povere man wel yfed,
Or wel araied or wel cled,
Of wel biloved, in sich wise
In honour that he may arise.
    Alle these thingis, well avised,   475
As I have you er this devysed,

With gold and asure over all,
Depeynted were upon the wall.
Square was the wall, and high sumdell;
Enclosed and ybarred well,   480
In stede of hegge, was that gardyn;
Com nevere shepherde theryn.
Into that gardyn, wel [y]wrought,
Whoso that me coude have brought,
By laddre, or elles by degre,   485
It wolde wel have liked me.
For sich solas, sich joie, and play,
I trowe that nevere man ne say,
As was in that place delytous.
The gardeyn was not daungerous   490
To herberwe briddes many oon.
So riche a yerd was never noon
Of briddes song, and braunches grene;
Therynne were briddes mo, I wene,
Than ben in all the rewme of Fraunce.   495
Ful blisful was the accordaunce
Of swete and pitous song thei made,
For all this world it owghte glade.
And I mysilf so mery ferde,
Whan I her blisful songes herde,   500
That for an hundred pound nolde I,
If that the passage openly
Hadde be unto me free,
That I nolde entren for to se
Th'assemble — God kepe it fro care! —   505
Of briddis, whiche therynne ware,
That songen thorugh her mery throtes
Daunces of love and mery notes.

Whan I thus herde foules synge,
I fel fast in a weymentynge,   510
By which art, or by what engyn,
I myght come into that gardyn;
But way I couthe fynde noon
Into that gardyn for to goon.
Ne nought wist I if that ther were   515
Eyther hole or place [o-] where,
By which I myght have entre;
Ne ther was noon to teche me.
For I was al aloone, iwys,
Ful wo and angwishus of this,   520
Til atte last bithought I me
That by no weye ne myght it be
That ther nas laddre, or wey to passe,
Or hole, into so faire a place.
Tho gan I go a full gret pas   525
Envyronyng evene in compas
The closing of the square wall,
Tyl that I fond a wiket small
So shett, that I ne myght in gon,
And other entre was ther noon.   530

Uppon this dore I gan to smyte,
That was fetys and so lite;
For other wey coude I not seke.
Ful long I shof, and knokkide eke,
And stood ful long and oft herknyng,   535
If that I herde ony wight comyng,
Til that the dore of thilk entre
A mayden curteys openyde me.
Hir heer was as yelowe of hewe
As ony basyn scoured newe;   540
Hir flesh [as] tendre as is a chike,
With bente browis smothe and slyke;
And by mesure large were
The openyng of hir yen clere;
Hir nose of good proporcioun,   545
Hir yen grey as is a faucoun,
With swete breth and wel savoured;
Hir face whit and wel coloured,
With litel mouth and round to see;
A clove chynne eke hadde she.   550
Hir nekke was of good fasoun
In lengthe and gretnesse, by resoun,
Withoute bleyne, scabbe, or royne;
Fro Jerusalem unto Burgoyne
Ther nys a fairer nekke, iwys,   555
To fele how smothe and softe it is;
Hir throte, also whit of hewe
As snowe on braunche snowed newe.
Of body ful wel wrought was she;
Men neded not in no cuntre   560
A fairer body for to seke.
And of fyn orfrays hadde she eke
A chapelet; so semly oon
Ne werede never mayde upon.
And faire above that chapelet   565
A rose gerland had she sett.
She hadde [in honde] a gay mirrour,
And with a riche gold tressour
Hir heed was tressed queyntely;
Hir sleves sewid fetisly.   570
And for to kepe hir hondis faire
Of gloves white she had a paire.
And she hadde on a cote of grene
Of cloth of Gaunt; withouten wene,
Wel semyde by hir apparayle   575
She was not wont to gret travayle.
For whan she kempt was fetisly,
And wel arayed and richely,
Thanne had she don al hir journe;
For merye and wel bigoon was she.   580
She ladde a lusty lyf in May:
She hadde no thought, by nyght ne day,
Of nothyng, but if it were oonly
To graythe hir wel and uncouthly.

Whan that this dore hadde opened me   585
This mayde semely for to see,
I thanked hir as I best myghte,
And axide hir how that she highte,
And what she was, I axide eke.
And she to me was nought unmeke,   590
Ne of hir answer daungerous,
But faire answerde, and seide thus:
"Lo, sir, my name is Ydelnesse;
So clepe men me, more and lesse.
Ful myghty and ful riche am I,   595
And that of oon thyng namely,
For I entende to nothyng
But to my joye and my pleyng,
And for to kembe and tresse me.
Aqueynted am I and pryve   600
With Myrthe, lord of this gardyn,
That fro the land Alexandryn
Made the trees hidre be fet,
That in this gardyn ben yset.
And whan the trees were woxen on highte,   605
This wall, that stant heere in thi sighte,
Dide Myrthe enclosen al aboute;
And these ymages, al withoute,
He dide hem bothe entaile and peynte,
That neithir ben jolyf ne queynte,   610
But they ben ful of sorowe and woo,
As thou hast seen a while agoo.
And ofte tyme, hym to solace,
Sir Myrthe cometh into this place,
And eke with hym cometh his meynee,   615
That lyven in lust and jolite.
And now is Myrthe therynne to here
The briddis, how they syngen clere,
The mavys and the nyghtyngale,
And other joly briddis smale.   620
And thus he walketh to solace
Hym and his folk; for swetter place
To pleyen ynne he may not fynde,
Although he sought oon in-tyl Ynde.
The alther-fairest folk to see   625
That in this world may founde be
Hath Mirthe with hym in his route,
That folowen hym always aboute."
    Whan Ydelnesse had told al this,
And I hadde herkned wel, ywys,   630
Thanne seide I to dame Ydelnesse:
"Now, also wisly God me blesse,
Sith Myrthe, that is so faire and fre,
Is in this yerde with his meyne,
Fro thilk assemble, if I may,   635
Shal no man werne me to-day,
That I this nyght ne mote it see.
For wel wene I there with hym be

A fair and joly companye
Fulfilled of alle curtesie."   640
And forth, withoute wordis mo,
In at the wiket went I tho,
That Ydelnesse hadde opened me,
Into that gardyn fair to see.
    And whan I was inne, iwys,   645
Myn herte was ful glad of this,
For wel wende I ful sikerly
Have ben in paradys erthly.
So fair it was that, trusteth wel,
It semede a place espirituel.   650
For certys, as at my devys,
Ther is no place in paradys
So good inne for to dwelle or be
As in that gardyn, thoughte me.
For there was many a bridd syngyng,   655
Thoroughout the yerd al thringyng;
In many places were nyghtyngales,
Alpes, fynches, and wodewales,
That in her swete song deliten
In thilke places as they habiten.   660
There myghte men see many flokkes
Of turtles and laverokkes.
Chalaundres fele sawe I there,
That wery, nygh forsongen were;
And thrustles, terins, and mavys,   665
That songen for to wynne hem prys,
And eke to sormounte in her song
That other briddes hem among.
By note made fair servyse
These briddes, that I you devise;   670
They songe her song as faire and wel
As angels don espirituel.
And trusteth wel, whan I hem herde,
Ful lustily and wel I ferde;
For never yitt sich melodye   675
Was herd of man that myghte dye.
Sich swete song was hem among
That me thought it no briddis song,
But it was wondir lyk to be
Song of mermaydens of the see,   680
That, for her syngyng is so clere,
Though we mermaydens clepe hem here
In English, as is oure usaunce,
Men clepe hem sereyns in Fraunce.
    Ententif weren for to synge   685
These briddis, that nought unkunnynge
Were of her craft, and apprentys,
But of song sotil and wys.
And certis, whan I herde her song,
And saw the grene place among,   690
In herte I wex so wondir gay
That I was never erst, er that day,

So jolyf, nor so wel bigoo,
Ne merye in herte, as I was thoo.
And than wist I, and saw ful well, 695
That Ydelnesse me served well,
That me putte in sich jolite.
Hir freend wel ought I for to be,
Sith she the dore of that gardyn
Hadde opened, and me leten in. 700
    From hennes forth hou that I wroughte,
I shal you tellen, as me thoughte.
First, whereof Myrthe served there,
And eke what folk there with hym were,
Withoute fable I wol discryve. 705
And of that gardyn eke as blyve
I wole you tellen aftir this
The faire fasoun all, ywys,
That wel wrought was for the nones.
I may not telle you all at ones; 710
But, as I may and can, I shall
By ordre tellen you it all.
Ful fair servise and eke ful swete
These briddis maden as they sete.
Layes of love, ful wel sownyng, 715
They songen in hir jargonyng;
Summe high and summe eke lowe songe
Upon the braunches grene yspronge.
The swetnesse of her melodye
Made al myn herte in reverdye. 720
And whan that I hadde herd, I trowe,
These briddis syngyng on a rowe,
Than myght I not withholde me
That I ne wente inne for to see
Sir Myrthe; for my desiryng 725
Was hym to seen, over alle thyng,
His countenaunce and his manere;
That sighte was to me ful dere.
    Tho wente I forth on my right hond
Doun by a lytel path I fond 730
Of mentes full, and fenell grene;
And faste by, without wene,
Sir Myrthe I fond, and right anoon
Unto Sir Myrthe gan I goon,
There as he was, hym to solace. 735
And with hym in that lusty place
So fair folk and so fresh had he
That whan I saw, I wondred me
Fro whennes siche folk myght come,
So faire they weren, alle and some; 740
For they were lyk, as to my sighte,
To angels that ben fethered brighte.
This folk, of which I telle you soo,
Upon a karole wenten thoo.
A lady karolede hem that hyghte 745
Gladnesse, [the] blissful and the lighte;

Wel coude she synge and lustyly,—
Noon half so wel and semely,—
And make in song sich refreynynge,
It sat hir wondir wel to synge. 750
Hir vois ful clere was and ful swete.
She was nought rude ne unmete
But couthe ynow of sich doyng
As longeth unto karolyng;
For she was wont in every place 755
To syngen first, folk to solace.
For syngyng moost she gaf hir to;
No craft had she so leef to do.
    Tho myghtist thou karoles sen,
And folk daunce and mery ben, 760
And made many a fair tournyng
Upon the grene gras springyng.
There myghtist thou see these flowtours,
Mynstrales, and eke jogelours,
That wel to synge dide her peyne. 765
Somme songe songes of Loreyne;
For in Loreyn her notes bee
Full swetter than in this contre.
There was many a tymbestere,
And saillouris, that I dar wel swere 770
Couthe her craft ful parfitly.
The tymbres up ful sotilly
They caste and hente full ofte
Upon a fynger fair and softe,
That they failide never mo. 775
Ful fetys damyseles two,
Ryght yonge, and full of semelyhede,
In kirtles, and noon other wede,
And faire tressed every tresse,
Hadde Myrthe doon, for his noblesse, 780
Amydde the karole for to daunce;
But herof lieth no remembraunce,
Hou that they daunced queyntely.
That oon wolde come all pryvyly
Agayn that other, and whan they were 785
Togidre almost, they threwe yfere
Her mouthis so, that thorough her play
It semed as they kiste alway.
To dauncen well koude they the gise;
What shulde I more to you devyse? 790
Ne bede I never thennes go,
Whiles that I saw hem daunce so.
    Upon the karoll wonder faste
I gan biholde, til atte laste
A lady gan me for to espie, 795
And she was cleped Curtesie,
The worshipfull, the debonaire;
I pray to God evere falle hir faire!
Ful curteisly she called me,
"What do ye there, beau ser?" quod she: 800

"Come, and if it lyke you
To dauncen, dauncith with us now."
And I, withoute tariyng,
Wente into the karolyng,
I was abasshed never a dell, 805
But it to me liked right well
That Curtesie me cleped so,
And bad me on the daunce go.
For if I hadde durst, certeyn
I wolde have karoled right fayn, 810
As man that was to daunce right blithe.
Thanne gan I loken ofte sithe
The shap, the bodies, and the cheres,
The countenaunce and the maneres
Of all the folk that daunced there, 815
And I shal telle what they were.
    Ful fair was Myrthe, ful long and high;
A fairer man I nevere sigh.
As round as appil was his face,
Ful rody and whit in every place. 820
Fetys he was and wel beseye,
With metely mouth and yen greye;
His nose by mesure wrought ful right;
Crisp was his heer, and eek ful bright;
His shuldris of a large brede, 825
And smalish in the girdilstede.
He semed lyk a portreiture,
So noble he was of his stature,
So fair, so joly, and so fetys,
With lymes wrought at poynt devys, 830
Delyver, smert, and of gret myght;
Ne sawe thou nevere man so lyght.
Of berd unnethe hadde he nothyng,
For it was in the firste spryng.
Ful yong he was, and mery of thought, 835
And in samet, with briddis wrought,
And with gold beten ful fetysly,
His body was clad ful richely.
Wrought was his robe in straunge gise,
And al toslytered for queyntise 840
In many a place, lowe and hie.
And shod he was with gret maistrie,
With shoon decoped, and with laas.
By druery and by solas,
His leef a rosyn chapelet 845
Hadde mad, and on his heed it set.
    And wite ye who was his leef?
Dame Gladnesse there was hym so leef,
That syngith so wel with glad courage,
That from she was twelve yeer of age, 850
She of hir love graunt hym made.
Sir Mirthe hir by the fynger hadde
Daunsyng, and she hym also;
Gret love was atwixe hem two.

Bothe were they faire and bright of hewe; 855
She semed lyk a rose newe
Of colour, and hir flesh so tendre,
That with a brere smale and slendre
Men myght it cleve, I dar wel seyn.
Hir forheed frounceles al pleyn; 860
Bente were hir browis two,
Hir yen greye, and glad also,
That laugheden ay in hir semblaunt,
First or the mouth, by covenaunt.
I not what of hir nose descryve; 865
So fair hath no womman alyve.
Hir heer was yelowe, and clere shynyng;
I wot no lady so likyng.
Of orfrays fresh was hir gerland;
I, which seyen have a thousand, 870
Saugh never, ywys, no gerlond yitt
So wel wrought of silk as it.
And in an overgilt samit
Clad she was, by gret delit,
Of which hir leef a robe werde, 875
The myrier she in hir herte ferde.
    And next hir wente, on hir other side,
The God of Love, that can devyde
Love, and as hym likith it be.
But he can cherles daunten, he, 880
And maken folkis pride fallen,
And he can wel these lordis thrallen,
And ladyes putt at lowe degre,
Whan he may hem to proude see.
    This God of Love of his fasoun 885
Was lyk no knave, ne quystroun;
His beaute gretly was to pryse.
But of his robe to devise
I drede encombred for to be;
For nought yclad in silk was he, 890
But all in floures and in flourettes,
Ypaynted al with amorettes,
And with losenges, and scochouns,
With briddes, lybardes, and lyouns,
And other beestis wrought ful well. 895
His garnement was everydell
Yportreied and ywrought with floures,
By dyvers medlyng of coloures.
Floures there were of many gise
Ysett by compas in assise. 900
Ther lakkide no flour, to my dom,
Ne nought so mych as flour of brom,
Ne violete, ne eke pervynke,
Ne flour noon that man can on thynke;
And many a rose-leef ful long 905
Was entermedled theramong.
And also on his heed was set
Of roses reed a chapelett.

But nyghtyngales, a ful gret route,
That flyen over his heed aboute,   910
The leeves felden as they flyen;
And he was all with briddes wryen,
With popynjay, with nyghtyngale,
With chalaundre, and with wodewale,
With fynch, with lark, and with archaungell.
He semede as he were an aungell   916
That doun were comen fro hevene cler.
    Love hadde with hym a bacheler,
That he made alweyes with hym be;
Swete-Lokyng cleped was he.   920
This bacheler stod biholdyng
The daunce, and in his hond holdyng,
Turke bowes two had he.
That oon of hem was of a tree
That bereth a fruyt of savour wykke;   925
Ful crokid was that foule stikke,
And knotty here and there also,
And blak as bery or ony slo.
That other bowe was of a plante
Withoute wem, I dar warante,   930
Ful evene and by proporcioun,
Treitys and long, of ful good fasoun;
And it was peynted wel and thwyten,
And overal diapred and writen
With ladyes and with bacheleris,   935
Ful lyghtsom and glad of cheris.
These bowes two held Swete-Lokyng,
That semede lyk no gadelyng.
And ten brode arowis hild he there,
Of which fyve in his right hond were.   940
But they were shaven wel and dight,
Nokked and fethered aright;
And all they were with gold bygoon,
And stronge poynted everychoon,
And sharpe for to kerven well.   945
But iren was ther noon ne steell;
For al was gold, men myght it see,
Out-take the fetheres and the tree.
    The swiftest of these arowis fyve
Out of a bowe for to dryve,   950
And best fethered for to flee,
And fairest eke, was clepid Beaute.
That other arowe, that hurteth lesse,
Was clepid, as I trowe, Symplesse.
The thridde cleped was Fraunchise,   955
That fethred was in noble wise
With valour and with curtesye.
The fourthe was cleped Compaignye,
That hevy for to sheten ys.
But whoso shetith right, ywys,   960
May therwith doon gret harm and wo.
The fifte of these, and laste also,

Faire-Semblaunt men that arowe calle,
The leeste grevous of hem alle.
Yit can it make a ful gret wounde;   965
But he may hope his soris sounde,
That hurt is with that arowe, ywys;
His wo the bet bistowed is.
For he may sonner have gladnesse,
His langour oughte be the lesse.   970
    Five arowis were of other gise,
That ben ful foule to devyse;
For shaft and ende, soth for to telle,
Were also blak as fend in helle.
The first of hem is called Pride;   975
That other arowe next hym biside,
It was cleped Vylanye;
That arowe was al with felonye
Envenymed, and with spitous blame.
The thridde of hem was cleped Shame;   980
The fourthe Wanhope cleped is;
The fifte, the Newe-Thought, ywys.
    These arowis that I speke of heere,
Were alle fyve on oon maneere,
And alle were they resemblable.   985
To hem was wel sittyng and able
The foule croked bowe hidous,
That knotty was, and al roynous.
That bowe semede wel to shete
These arowis fyve that ben unmete   990
And contrarye to that other fyve.
But though I telle not as blyve
Of her power, ne of her myght,
Herafter shal I tellen right
The soothe, and eke signyfiaunce,   995
As fer as I have remembraunce.
All shal be seid, I undirtake,
Er of this book an ende I make.
    Now come I to my tale ageyn.
But aldirfirst I wol you seyn   1000
The fasoun and the countenaunces
Of all the folk that on the daunce is.
The God of Love, jolyf and lyght,
Ladde on his hond a lady bright,
Of high prys and of gret degre.   1005
This lady called was Beaute,
As an arowe, of which I tolde.
Ful wel thewed was she holde,
Ne she was derk ne broun, but bright,
And clere as the mone lyght,   1010
Ageyn whom all the sterres semen
But smale candels, as we demen.
Hir flesh was tendre as dew of flour;
Hir chere was symple as byrde in bour;
As whyt as lylye or rose in rys,   1015
Hir face gentyl and tretys.

Fetys she was, and smal to se;
No wyndred browis hadde she,
Ne popped hir, for it neded nought
To wyndre hir, or to peynte hir ought.   1020
Hir tresses yelowe, and longe straughten,
Unto hir helys doun they raughten;
Hir nose, hir mouth, and eye, and cheke
Wel wrought, and all the remenaunt eke.
A ful gret savour and a swote   1025
Me toucheth in myn herte rote,
As helpe me God, whan I remembre
Of the fasoun of every membre.
In world is noon so fair a wight;
For yong she was, and hewed bright,   1030
Sore plesaunt, and fetys withall,
Gente, and in hir myddill small.
    Biside Beaute yede Richesse,
An high lady of gret noblesse,
And gret of prys in every place.   1035
But whoso durste to hir trespace,
Or til hir folk, in word or dede,
He were full hardy, out of drede.
For bothe she helpe and hyndre may;
And that is nought of yisterday   1040
That riche folk have full gret myght
To helpe, and eke to greve a wyght.
The leste and the grettest of valour
Diden Rychesse ful gret honour,
And besy weren hir to serve,   1045
For that they wolde hir love deserve.
They cleped hir lady, gret and small;
This wide world hir dredith all;
This world is all in hir daunger.
Hir court hath many a losenger,   1050
And many a traytour envyous,
That ben ful besy and curyous
For to dispreisen and to blame
That best deserven love and name.
Bifore the folk, hem to bigilen,   1055
These losengeris hem preyse, and smylen,
And thus the world with word anoynten;
And aftirward they prikke and poynten
The folk right to the bare boon,
Bihynde her bak whan they ben goon,   1060
And foule abate the folkis prys.
Ful many a worthy man and wys
Han hyndrid and ydon to dye
These losengers thorough flaterye;
And make folk ful straunge be,   1065
There hem oughte be pryve.
Wel yvel mote they thryve and thee,
And yvel aryved mote they be,
These losengers, ful of envye!
No good man loveth her companye.   1070

Richesse a robe of purpur on hadde, —
Ne trowe not that I lye or madde, —
For in this world is noon it lyche,
Ne by a thousand deell so riche,
Ne noon so fair; for it ful well   1075
With orfrays leyd was everydeell,
And portraied in the ribanynges
Of dukes storyes, and of kynges;
And with a bend of gold tasseled,
And knoppis fyne of gold ameled.   1080
Aboute hir nekke of gentyl entayle
Was shet the riche chevesaile,
In which ther was full gret plente
Of stones clere and bright to see.
    Rychesse a girdell hadde upon,   1085
The bokel of it was of a stoon
Of vertu gret and mochel of myght;
For whoso bar the stoon so bright,
Of venym durst hym nothing doute,
While he the stoon hadde hym aboute.   1090
That stoon was gretly for to love,
And tyl a riche mannes byhove
Worth all the gold in Rome and Frise.
The mourdaunt wrought in noble wise
Was of a stoon full precious,   1095
That was so fyn and vertuous
That hol a man it koude make
Of palasie and of toth-ake.
And yit the stoon hadde such a grace
That he was siker in every place,   1100
All thilke day, not blynd to ben,
That fastyng myghte that stoon seen.
The barres were of gold ful fyn,
Upon a tyssu of satyn,
Full hevy, gret, and nothyng lyght;   1105
In everich was a besaunt wight.
    Upon the tresses of Richesse
Was sette a cercle, for noblesse,
Of brend gold, that full lyghte shoon;
So fair, trowe I, was never noon.   1110
But he were kunnyng for the nonys,
That koude devyse all the stonys
That in that cercle shewen clere.
It is a wondir thing to here;
For no man koude preyse or gesse   1115
Of hem the valewe or richesse.
Rubyes there were, saphires, jagounces,
And emeraudes, more than two ounces;
But all byfore, ful sotilly,
A fyn charboncle set saugh I.   1120
The stoon so clere was and so bright
That, also soone as it was nyght,
Men myghte seen to go, for nede,
A myle or two in lengthe and brede.

Sich lyght sprang out of the ston 1125
That Richesse wondir brighte shon,
Bothe hir heed and all hir face,
And eke aboute hir al the place.
    Dame Richesse on hir hond gan lede
A yong man ful of semelyhede, 1130
That she best loved of ony thing.
His lust was moch in housholding.
In clothyng was he ful fetys,
And loved well to have hors of prys.
He wende to have reproved be 1135
Of theft or moordre, if that he
Hadde in his stable on hakeney.
And therfore he desired ay
To be aqueynted with Richesse;
For all his purpos, as I gesse, 1140
Was forto make gret dispense,
Withoute wernyng or diffense.
And Richesse myght it wel sustene,
And hir dispence well mayntene,
And hym alwey sich plente sende 1145
Of gold and silver for to spende
Withoute lakking or daunger,
As it were poured in a garner.
    And after on the daunce wente
Largesse, that sette al hir entente 1150
For to be honourable and free.
Of Alexandres kyn was she;
Hir most joye was, ywys,
Whan that she yaf, and seide, "Have this."
Not Avarice, the foule caytyf, 1155
Was half to gripe so ententyf,
As Largesse is to yeve and spende;
And God ynough alwey hir sende,
So that the more she yaf awey
The more, ywys, she hadde alwey. 1160
Gret loos hath Largesse and gret pris;
For bothe wys folk and unwys
Were hooly to hir baundon brought,
So wel with yiftes hath she wrought.
And if she hadde an enemy, 1165
I trowe that she coude craftely
Make hym full soone hir freend to be,
So large of yift and free was she.
Therfore she stod in love and grace
Of riche and pover in every place. 1170
A full gret fool is he, ywys,
That bothe riche and nygard is.
A lord may have no maner vice
That greveth more than avarice.
For nygart never with strengthe of hond 1175
May wynne him gret lordship or lond;
For freendis all to fewe hath he
To doon his will perfourmed be.

And whoso wole have freendis heere,
He may not holde his tresour deere. 1180
For by ensample I telle this;
Right as an adamaunt, iwys,
Can drawen to hym sotylly
The iren that is leid therby,
So drawith folkes hertis, ywis, 1185
Silver and gold that yeven is.
Largesse hadde on a robe fresh
Of riche purpur Sarsynesh.
Wel fourmed was hir face and cleer,
And opened hadde she hir coler; 1190
For she right there hadde in present
Unto a lady maad present
Of a gold broche, ful wel wrought.
And certys, it myssat hir nought;
For thorough hir smokke, wrought with silk, 1195
The flesh was seen as whit as mylk.
Largesse, that worthy was and wys,
Hild by the hond a knyght of prys,
Was sib to Artour of Britaigne,
And that was he that bar the ensaigne 1200
Of worship and the gounfanoun.
And yit he is of sich renoun
That men of hym seye faire thynges
Byfore barouns, erles, and kynges.
This knyght was comen all newely 1205
Fro tourneiynge faste by;
There hadde he don gret chyvalrie
Thorough his vertu and his maistrie;
And for the love of his lemman
He caste doun many a doughty man. 1210
    And next hym daunced dame Fraunchise,
Arayed in full noble gyse.
She was not broun ne dun of hewe,
But whit as snow yfallen newe.
Hir nose was wrought at poynt devys, 1215
For it was gentyl and tretys;
With eyen gladde, and browes bente;
Hir heer doun to hir helis wente.
And she was symple as dowve on tree;
Ful debonaire of herte was she. 1220
She durst never seyn ne do
But that that hir longed to;
And if a man were in distresse,
And for hir love in hevynesse,
Hir herte wolde have full gret pite, 1225
She was so amiable and free.
For were a man for hir bistad,
She wolde ben right sore adrad
That she dide over-gret outrage,
But she hym holpe his harm to aswage; 1230
Hir thought it elles a vylanye.
And she hadde on a sukkenye,

That not of hempene heerdis was;
So fair was noon in all Arras.
Lord, it was ridled fetysly!   1235
Ther nas nat a poynt, trewely,
That it nas in his right assise.
Full wel yclothed was Fraunchise;
For ther is no cloth sittith bet
On damysell, than doth roket.   1240
A womman wel more fetys is
In roket than in cote, ywis.
The whyte roket, rydled faire,
Bitokeneth that full debonaire
And swete was she that it ber.   1245

  Bi hir daunced a bacheler;
I can not telle you what he highte,
But faire he was and of good highte,
All hadde he be, I sey no more,
The lordis sone of Wyndesore.   1250

  And next that daunced Curtesye,
That preised was of lowe and hye;
For neither proud ne fool was she.
She for to daunce called me
(I pray God yeve hir right good grace!),   1255
Whanne I com first into the place.
She was not nyce, ne outrageous,
But wys, and war, and vertuous,
Of fair speche, and of fair answere;
Was never wight mysseid of here;   1260
She bar no rancour to no wight.
Clere broun she was, and therto bright
Of face, of body avenaunt;
I wot no lady so plesaunt.
She were worthy for to bene   1265
An emperesse or crowned quene.

  And by hir wente a knyght dauncyng,
That worthy was and wel spekyng,
And ful wel koude he don honour.
The knyght was fair and styf in stour,   1270
And in armure a semely man,
And wel biloved of his lemman.

  Faire Idilnesse thanne saugh I,
That alwey was me faste by.
Of hir have I, withoute fayle,   1275
Told yow the shap and apparayle;
For (as I seide) loo, that was she
That dide to me so gret bounte
That she the gate of the gardyn
Undide, and let me passen in.   1280

  And after daunced, as I gesse,
[Youthe], fulfilled of lustynesse,
That nas not yit twelve yeer of age,
With herte wylde, and thought volage.
Nyce she was, but she ne mente   1285
Noon harm ne slight in hir entente,

But oonly lust and jolyte;
For yonge folk, wel witen ye,
Have lytel thought but on her play.
Hir lemman was biside alway   1290
In sich a gise that he hir kyste
At alle tymes that hym lyste,
That all the daunce myght it see.
They make no force of pryvete;
For who spake of hem yvel or well,   1295
They were ashamed never a dell,
But men myght seen hem kisse there,
As it two yonge dowves were.
For yong was thilke bacheler;
Of beaute wot I noon his per;   1300
And he was right of sich an age
As Youthe his leef, and sich corage.

  The lusty folk thus daunced there,
And also other that with hem were,
That weren alle of her meyne;   1305
Ful hende folk and wys and free,
And folk of faire port, truëly,
There weren alle comunly.

  Whanne I hadde seen the countenaunces
Of hem that ladden thus these daunces,   1310
Thanne hadde I will to gon and see
The gardyn that so lyked me,
And loken on these faire loreres,
On pyntrees, cedres, and olmeris.
The daunces thanne eended were;   1315
For many of them that daunced there
Were with her loves went awey
Undir the trees to have her pley.

  A! Lord, they lyved lustyly!
A gret fool were he, sikirly,   1320
That nolde, his thankes, such lyf lede!
For this dar I seyn, oute of drede,
That whoso myghte so wel fare,
For better lyf durst hym not care;
For ther nys so good paradys   1325
As to have a love at his devys.

  Oute of that place wente I thoo,
And in that gardyn gan I goo,
Pleyyng along full meryly.
The God of Love full hastely   1330
Unto hym Swete-Lokyng clepte;
No lenger wolde he that he kepte
His bowe of gold, that shoon so bright.
He bad hym bende [it] anoon ryght;
And he full soone [it] sette an-ende,   1335
And at a braid he gan it bende,
And tok hym of his arowes fyve,
Full sharp and redy for to dryve.
Now God, that sittith in mageste,
Fro deedly woundes he kepe me,   1340

If so be that he hadde me shette!
For if I with his arowe mette,
It hadde me greved sore, iwys.
But I, that nothyng wist of this,
Wente up and doun full many a wey,   1345
And he me folwed fast alwey;
But nowhere wold I reste me,
Till I hadde in all the gardyn be.
   The gardyn was, by mesuryng,
Right evene and square in compassing;   1350
It as long was as it was large.
Of fruyt hadde every tree his charge,
But it were any hidous tree,
Of which ther were two or three.
There were, and that wot I full well,   1355
Of pome-garnettys a full gret doll;
That is a fruyt full well to lyke,
Namely to folk whanne they ben sike.
And trees there were, gret foisoun,
That baren notes in her sesoun,   1360
Such as men notemygges calle,
That swote of savour ben withalle.
And alemandres gret plente,
Fyges, and many a date-tree
There wexen, if men hadde nede,   1365
Thorough the gardyn in length and brede.
Ther was eke wexyng many a spice,
As clowe-gelofre, and lycorice,
Gyngevre, and greyn de parys,
Canell, and setewale of prys,   1370
And many a spice delitable
To eten whan men rise fro table.
And many homly trees ther were
That peches, coynes, and apples beere,
Medlers, plowmes, perys, chesteynes,   1375
Cherys, of which many oon fayn is.
Notes, aleys, and bolas,
That for to seen it was solas.
With many high lorer and pyn
Was renged clene all that gardyn,   1380
With cipres and with olyveres,
Of which that nygh no plente heere is.
There were elmes grete and stronge,
Maples, assh, ok, asp, planes longe,
Fyn ew, popler, and lyndes faire,   1385
And othere trees full many a payre.
   What shulde I tel you more of it?
There were so many trees yit,
That I shulde al encombred be
Er I had rekened every tree.   1390
   These trees were set, that I devyse,
Oon from another, in assyse,
Fyve fadome or sixe, I trowe so;
But they were hye and great also,

And for to kepe out wel the sonne,   1395
The croppes were so thicke yronne,
And every braunche in other knet,
And ful of grene leves set,
That sonne myght there non discende,
Lest [it] the tender grasses shende.   1400
There myght men does and roes yse,
And of squyrels ful great plente
From bowe to bowe alway lepynge.
Conies there were also playinge,
That comyn out of her clapers,   1405
Of sondrie colours and maners,
And maden many a tourneying
Upon the fresshe grass spryngyng.
   In places saw I welles there,
In whiche there no frogges were,   1410
And fayr in shadowe was every welle.
But I ne can the nombre telle
Of stremys smal that by devys
Myrthe had don come through condys,
Of whiche the water, in rennyng,   1415
Gan make a noyse ful lykyng.
   About the brinkes of these welles,
And by the stremes overal elles,
Sprang up the grass, as thicke yset
And softe as any veluët,   1420
On which men myght his lemman leye,
As on a fetherbed, to pleye;
For the erthe was ful softe and swete.
Through moisture of the welle wete
Sprong up the sote grene gras   1425
As fayre, as thicke, as myster was.
But moche amended it the place,
That th'erthe was of such a grace
That it of floures hath plente,
That bothe in somer and wynter be.   1430
   There sprang the vyolet al newe,
And fressh pervynke, riche of hewe,
And floures yelowe, white, and rede;
Such plente grew there never in mede.
Ful gay was al the ground, and queynt,   1435
And poudred, as men had it peynt,
With many a fressh and sondri flour,
That casten up ful good savour.
   I wol nat longe holde you in fable
Of al this garden dilectable.   1440
I mot my tonge stynten nede,
For I ne may, withouten drede,
Naught tellen you the beaute al,
Ne half the bounte therewithal.
   I went on right hond and on left   1445
About the place; it was nat left,
Tyl I had [in] al the garden ben,
In the estres that men myghte sen.

And thus while I wente in my play,
The God of Love me folowed ay,   1450
Right as an hunter can abyde
The beest, tyl he seeth his tyde
To shoten at good mes to the der,
Whan that hym nedeth go no ner.
    And so befyl, I rested me   1455
Besydes a wel, under a tree,
Which tree in Fraunce men cal a pyn.
But sithe the tyme of kyng Pepyn,
Ne grew there tree in mannes syghte
So fayr, ne so wel woxe in highte;   1460
In al that yard so high was non.
And springyng in a marble ston
Had Nature set, the sothe to telle,
Under that pyn-tree a welle.
And on the border, al withoute,   1465
Was written in the ston aboute,
Letters smal, that sayden thus,
"Here starf the fayre Narcisus."
    Narcisus was a bacheler,
That Love had caught in his danger,   1470
And in his net gan hym so strayne,
And dyd him so to wepe and playne,
That nede him must his lyf forgo.
For a fayr lady, that hight Echo,
Him loved over any creature,   1475
And gan for hym such payne endure
That on a tyme she him tolde
That if he her loven nolde,
That her behoved nedes dye,
There laye non other remedye.   1480
    But natheles, for his beaute,
So feirs and daungerous was he,
That he nolde graunten hir askyng,
For wepyng ne for fair praiyng;
And whanne she herde hym werne her soo,   1486
She hadde in herte so gret woo,
And took it in so gret dispit,
That she, withoute more respit,
Was deed anoon. But er she deide,
Full pitously to God she preide   1490
That proude-hertid Narcisus,
That was in love so daungerous,
Myght on a day ben hampred so
For love, and ben so hoot for woo,
That never he myght to joye atteyne;   1495
Than shulde he feele in every veyne
What sorowe trewe lovers maken,
That ben so vilaynsly forsaken.
    This prayer was but resonable;
Therfore God held it ferme and stable.   1500
For Narcisus, shortly to telle,
By aventure com to that welle

To reste hym in the shadowing
A day whanne he com fro huntyng.
This Narcisus hadde suffred paynes   1505
For rennyng alday in the playnes,
And was for thurst in gret distresse
Of heet, and of his werynesse
That hadde his breth almost bynomen.
Whanne he was to that welle ycomen,   1510
That shadowid was with braunches grene,
He thoughte of thilke water shene
To drynke, and fresshe hym wel withalle;
And doun on knees he gan to falle,
And forth his heed and necke out-straughte   1515
To drynken of that welle a draughte.
And in the water anoon was seene
His nose, his mouth, his yen sheene,
And he therof was all abasshed;
His owne shadowe had hym bytrasshed.   1520
For well wende he the forme see
Of a child of gret beaute.
Well kouthe Love hym wreke thoo
Of daunger and of pride also,
That Narcisus somtyme hym beer.   1525
He quytte hym well his guerdoun ther;
For he musede so in the welle
That, shortly all the sothe to telle,
He lovede his owne shadowe soo,
That atte laste he starf for woo.   1530
For whanne he saugh that he his wille
Myght in no maner wey fulfille,
And that he was so faste caught
That he hym kouthe comfort nought,
He loste his wit right in that place,   1535
And diede withynne a lytel space.
And thus his warisoun he took
For the lady that he forsook.
    Ladyes, I preye ensample takith,
Ye that ageyns youre love mistakith;   1540
For if her deth be yow to wite,
God kan ful well youre while quyte.
    Whanne that this lettre, of which I telle,
Hadde taught me that it was the welle
Of Narcisus in his beaute,   1545
I gan anoon withdrawe me,
Whanne it fel in my remembraunce
That hym bitidde such myschaunce.
But at the laste thanne thought I
That scatheles, full sykerly,   1550
I myght unto the welle goo.
Wherof shulde I abasshen soo?
Unto the welle than wente I me,
And doun I loutede for to see
The clere water in the stoon,   1555
And eke the gravell, which that shoon

Down in the botme as silver fyn;
For of the well this is the fyn,
In world is noon so cler of hewe.
The water is evere fresh and newe, 1560
That welmeth up with wawis brighte
The mountance of two fynger highte.
Abouten it is gras spryngyng,
For moiste so thikke and wel likyng,
That it ne may in wynter dye, 1565
No more than may the see be drye.
    Down at the botme set saw I
Two cristall stonys craftely
In thilke freshe and faire welle.
But o thing sothly dar I telle, 1570
That ye wole holde a gret mervayle
Whanne it is told, withouten fayle.
For whanne the sonne, cler in sighte,
Cast in that well his bemys brighte,
And that the heete descendid is, 1575
Thanne taketh the cristall stoon, ywis,
Agayn the sonne an hundrid hewis,
Blew, yelow, and red, that fresh and newe is.
Yitt hath the merveilous cristall
Such strengthe that the place overall, 1580
Bothe flour, and tree, and leves grene,
And all the yerd in it is seene.
And for to don you to undirstonde,
To make ensample wole I fonde.
Ryght as a myrrour openly 1585
Shewith all thing that stondith therby,
As well the colour as the figure,
Withouten ony coverture;
Right so the cristall stoon, shynyng,
Withouten ony disseyvyng, 1590
The estrees of the yerd accusith
To hym that in the water musith.
For evere, in which half that he be,
He may well half the gardyn se;
And if he turne, he may right well 1595
Sen the remenaunt everydell.
For ther is noon so litil thyng
So hid, ne closid with shittyng,
That it ne is sene, as though it were
Peyntid in the cristall there. 1600
    This is the mirrour perilous,
In which the proude Narcisus
Saw all his face fair and bright,
That made hym sithe to ligge upright.
For whoso loketh in that mirrour, 1605
Ther may nothyng ben his socour
That he ne shall there sen somthyng
That shal hym lede into lovyng.
Full many a worthy man hath it
Yblent, for folk of grettist wit 1610

Ben soone caught heere and awayted;
Withouten respit ben they baited.
Heere comth to folk of-newe rage;
Heere chaungith many wight corage;
Heere lith no red ne wit therto; 1615
For Venus sone, daun Cupido,
Hath sowen there of love the seed,
That help ne lith there noon, ne red,
So cerclith it the welle aboute.
His gynnes hath he sette withoute, 1620
Ryght for to cacche in his panters
These damoysels and bachelers.
Love will noon other briddes cacche,
Though he sette oither net or lacche.
And for the seed that heere was sowen, 1625
This welle is clepid, as well is knowen,
The Welle of Love, of verray right,
Of which ther hath ful many a wight
Spoken in bookis dyversely.
But they shull never so verily 1630
Descripcioun of the welle heere,
Ne eke the sothe of this matere,
As ye shull, whanne I have undo
The craft that hir bilongith too.
    Allway me liked for to dwelle, 1635
To sen the cristall in the welle,
That shewide me full openly
A thousand thinges faste by.
But I may say, in sory houre
Stode I to loken or to poure; 1640
For sithen [have] I sore siked;
That mirrour hath me now entriked.
But hadde I first knowen in my wit
The vertu and [the] strengthe of it, 1645
I nolde not have mused there.
Me hadde bet ben elliswhere;
For in the snare I fell anoon,
That hath bitrasshed many oon.
    In thilke mirrour saw I tho,
Among a thousand thinges mo, 1650
A roser chargid full of rosis,
That with an hegge aboute enclos is.
Tho had I sich lust and envie,
That for Parys ne for Pavie
Nolde I have left to goon and see 1655
There grettist hep of roses be.
Whanne I was with this rage hent,
That caught hath many a man and shent,
Toward the roser gan I go;
And whanne I was not fer therfro, 1660
The savour of the roses swote
Me smot right to the herte-rote,
As I hadde all enbawmed be.
And if I ne hadde endouted me

To have ben hatid or assailed,   1665
My thankis, wolde I not have failed
To pulle a rose of all that route
To beren in myn hond aboute,
And smellen to it where I wente;
But ever I dredde me to repente,   1670
And lest it grevede or forthoughte
The lord that thilke gardyn wroughte.
Of roses ther were gret won;
So faire waxe never in ron.
Of knoppes clos some sawe I there;   1675
And some wel beter woxen were;
And some ther ben of other moysoun,
That drowe nygh to her sesoun,
And spedde hem faste for to sprede.
I love well sich roses rede,   1680
For brode roses and open also
Ben passed in a day or two;
But knoppes wille [al] freshe be
Two dayes, atte leest, or thre.
The knoppes gretly liked me,   1685
For fairer may ther no man se.
Whoso myght have oon of alle,
It ought hym ben full lief withalle.
Might I [a] gerlond of hem geten,
For no richesse I wolde it leten.   1690
Among the knoppes I ches oon
So fair, that of the remenaunt noon
Ne preise I half so well as it,
Whanne I avise it in my wit.
For it so well was enlumyned   1695
With colour reed, [and] as well fyned
As nature couthe it make faire.
And it hath leves wel foure paire,
That Kynde hath sett, thorough his knowyng,
Aboute the rede Rose spryngyng.   1700
The stalke was as rishe right,
And theron stod the knoppe upright,
That it ne bowide upon no side.
The swote smelle sprong so wide
That it dide all the place aboute —   1705

Fragment B

Whanne I hadde smelled the savour swote,
No will hadde I fro thens yit goo,
Bot somdell neer it wente I thoo,
To take it; but myn hond, for drede,
Ne dorste I to the Rose bede,   1710
For thesteles sharpe, of many maneres,
Netles, thornes, and hokede breres;
For mych they distourbled me,
For sore I dradde to harmed be.
    The God of Love, with bowe bent,   1715

That all day set hadde his talent
To pursuen and to spien me,
Was stondyng by a fige-tree.
And whanne he saw hou that I
Hadde chosen so ententifly   1720
The botoun, more unto my pay
Than ony other that I say,
He tok an arowe full sharply whet,
And in his bowe whanne it was set,
He streight up to his ere drough   1725
The stronge bowe, that was so tough,
And shet att me so wondir smerte
That thorough myn ye unto myn herte
The takel smot, and depe it wente.
And therwithall such cold me hente   1730
That, under clothes warme and softe,
Sithen that day I have chevered ofte.
    Whanne I was hurt thus, in [a] stounde
I felle doun plat unto the grounde.
Myn herte failed and feynted ay,   1735
And longe tyme a-swoone I lay.
But whanne I come out of swonyng,
And hadde witt, and my felyng,
I was all maat, and wende full well
Of blood have loren a full gret dell.   1740
But certes, the arowe that in me stod
Of me ne drew no drope of blod,
For-why I found my wounde all dreie.
Thanne tok I with myn hondis tweie
The arowe, and ful fast out it plighte,   1745
And in the pullyng sore I sighte.
So at the last the shaft of tree
I drough out with the fethers thre.
But yet the hokede heed, ywis,
The which [that] beaute callid is,   1750
Gan so depe in myn herte passe,
That I it myghte nought arace;
But in myn herte still it stod,
Al bledde I not a drope of blod.
I was bothe anguyssous and trouble   1755
For the perill that I saw double:
I nyste what to seye or do,
Ne gete a leche my woundis to;
For neithir thurgh gras ne rote
Ne hadde I help of hope ne bote.   1760
But to the botoun evermo
Myn herte drew; for all my wo,
My thought was in noon other thing.
For hadde it ben in my kepyng,
It wolde have brought my lyf agayn.   1765
For certeynly, I dar wel seyn,
The sight oonly and the savour
Alegged mych of my langour.
Thanne gan I for to drawe me

Toward the botoun faire to se; 1770
And Love hadde gete hym, in a throwe,
Another arowe into his bowe,
And for to shete gan hym dresse;
The arowis name was Symplesse.
And whanne that Love gan nygh me nere, 1775
He drow it up, withouten were,
And shet at me with all his myght,
So that this arowe anoon-right
Thourghout [myn] eigh, as it was founde,
Into myn herte hath maad a wounde. 1780
Thanne I anoon dide al my craft
For to drawen out the shaft,
And therwithall I sighed eft.
But in myn herte the heed was left,
Which ay encreside my desir 1785
Unto the botoun drawe ner;
And evermo that me was woo,
The more desir hadde I to goo
Unto the roser, where that grew
The freysshe botoun so bright of hew. 1790
Betir me were to have laten be;
But it bihovede nedes me
To don right as myn herte bad.
For evere the body must be lad
Aftir the herte, in wele and woo; 1795
Of force togidre they must goo.
But never this archer wolde fyne
To shete at me with all his pyne.
And for to make me to hym mete,
The thridde arowe he gan to shete, 1800
Whanne best his tyme he myght espie,
The which was named Curtesie;
Into myn herte it dide avale.
A-swoone I fell bothe deed and pale;
Long tyme I lay and stired nought, 1805
Till I abraide out of my thought.
And faste thanne I avysede me
To drawe out the shaft of tree;
But evere the heed was left bihynde,
For ought I couthe pulle or wynde. 1810
So sore it stikid whanne I was hit,
That by no craft I myght it flit;
But anguyssous and full of thought,
I felte sich woo my wounde ay wrought,
That somonede me alway to goo 1815
Toward the Rose that plesede me soo.
But I ne durste in no maner,
Bicause the archer was so ner;
"For evermore gladly," as I rede,
"Brent child of fir hath myche drede." 1820
And, certis yit, for al my peyne,
Though that I sigh yit arwis reyne,
And grounde quarels sharpe of steell,

Ne for no payne that I myght feell,
Yit myght I not mysilf witholde 1825
The faire roser to biholde;
For Love me yaf sich hardement
For to fulfille his comaundement.
Upon my fete I ros up than,
Feble as a forwoundid man, 1830
And forth to gon [my] myght I sette,
And for the archer nolde I lette.
Toward the roser fast I drow,
But thornes sharpe mo than ynow
Ther were, and also thisteles thikke, 1835
And breres, brymme for to prikke,
That I ne myghte gete grace
The rowe thornes for to passe,
To sen the roses fresshe of hewe.
I must abide, though it me rewe, 1840
The hegge aboute so thikke was,
That closide the roses in compas.
But o thing lyked me right well;
I was so nygh, I myghte fel
Of the botoun the swote odour, 1845
And also se the fresshe colour;
And that right gretly liked me,
That I so neer myghte it se.
Sich joie anoon therof hadde I
For the richesse among the thoppes 1850
To sen I hadde sich delit,
Of sorwe and angre I was al quyt,
And of my woundes that I hadde thore;
For nothing liken me myght more
Than dwellen by the roser ay, 1855
And thennes never to passe away.
But whanne a while I hadde be thar,
The God of Love, which al toshar
Myn herte with his arwis kene,
Cast hym to yeve me woundis grene. 1860
He shet at me full hastily
An arwe named Company,
The whiche takell is full able
To make these ladies merciable.
Thanne I anoon gan chaungen hewe 1865
For grevaunce of my wounde newe,
That I agayn fell in swonyng,
And sighede sore in compleynyng.
Soore I compleyned that my sore
On me gan greven more and more. 1870
I hadde noon hope of allegeaunce;
So nygh I drow to desperaunce,
I roughte of deth ne of lyf,
Wheder that Love wolde me dryf.
Yf me a martir wolde he make, 1875
I myght his power nought forsake.
And while for anger thus I wok,

The God of Love an arowe tok;
Ful sharp it was and pugnaunt,
And it was callid Faire-Semblaunt,   1880
The which in no wise wole consente
That ony lover hym repente
To serve his love with herte and alle,
For ony perill that may bifalle.
But though this arwe was kene grounde   1885
As ony rasour that is founde,
To kutte and kerve, at the poynt
The God of Love it hadde anoynt
With a precious oynement,
Somdell to yeve aleggement   1890
Upon the woundes that he had
Through the body in myn herte maad,
To helpe her sores, and to cure,
And that they may the bet endure.
But yit this arwe, withoute more,   1895
Made in myn herte a large sore,
That in full gret peyne I abod.
But ay the oynement wente abrod;
Thourghout my woundes large and wide
It spredde aboute in every side,   1900
Thorough whos vertu and whos myght
Myn herte joyfull was and light.
I hadde ben deed and al toshent,
But for the precious oynement.
The shaft I drow out of the arwe,   1905
Rokyng for wo right wondir narwe;
But the heed, which made me smerte,
Lefte bihynde in myn herte
With other foure, I dar wel say,
That never wole be take away;   1910
But the oynement halp me wel.
And yit sich sorwe dide I fel
Of my woundes fresshe and newe
That al day I chaunged hewe
As men myght se in my visage.   1915
The arwis were so full of rage,
So variaunt of diversitee,
That men in everich myghte se
Bothe gret anoy and eke swetnesse,
And joie meynt with bittirnesse.   1920
Now were they esy, now were they wod;
In hem I felte bothe harm and good;
Now sore without alleggement,
Now softenyng with oynement;
It softnede heere and prikkith there: 1925
Thus ese and anger togidre were.
  The God of Love delyverly
Com lepande to me hastily,
And seide to me in gret rape,
"Yeld thee, for thou may not escape!   1930
May no defence availe thee heer;

Therfore I rede make no daunger.
If thou wolt yelde thee hastily,
Thou shalt rather have mercy.
He is a fool in sikernesse,   1935
That with daunger or stoutnesse
Rebellith there that he shulde plese;
In sich folye is litel ese.
Be meke, where thou must nedis bow;
To stryve ageyn is nought thi prow.   1940
Com at oones, and have ydoo,
For I wol that it be soo.
Thanne yeld thee heere debonairly."
And I answerid ful hombly,
"Gladly, sir, at youre biddyng,   1945
I wole me yelde in alle thyng.
To youre servyse I wol me take;
For God defende that I shulde make
Ageyn youre biddyng resistence;
I wole not don so gret offence;   1950
For if I dide, it were no skile.
Ye may do with me what ye wile,
Save or spille, and also sloo.
Fro you in no wise may I goo.
My lyf, my deth is in youre hond;   1955
I may not laste out of youre bond.
Pleyn at youre lyst I yelde me,
Hopyng in herte that sumtyme ye
Comfort and ese shull me sende;
Or ellis, shortly, this is the eende;   1960
Withouten helthe I mot ay dure,
But if ye take me to youre cure.
Comfort or helthe how shuld I have,
Sith ye me hurt, but ye me save?
The helthe of love mot be founde   1965
Where as they token first her wounde.
And if ye lyst of me to make
Youre prisoner, I wol it take
Of herte and will, fully at gree.
Hoolly and pleyn Y yelde me,   1970
Withoute feynyng or feyntise,
To be governed by youre emprise.
Of you I here so myche pris,
I wole ben hool at youre devis,
For to fulfille youre lykyng,   1975
And repente for nothyng,
Hopyng to have yit in som tide
Mercy, of that I abide."
And with that covenaunt yelde I me
Anoon, down knelyng upon my kne,   1980
Proferyng for to kisse his feet;
But for nothyng he wolde me let,
And seide, "I love thee bothe and preise,
Sen that thyn aunswar doth me ease,
For thou answerid so curteisly.   1985

For now I wot wel uttirly,
That thou art gentyll by thi speche.
For though a man fer wolde seche,
He shulde not fynden, in certeyn,
No sich answer of no vileyn;   1990
For sich a word ne myghte nought
Isse out of a vilayns thought.
Thou shalt not lesen of thi speche,
For [to] thy helpyng wole I eche,
And eke encresen that I may.   1995
But first I wole that thou obay
Fully, for thyn avauntage,
Anoon to do me heere homage.
And sithe kisse thou shalt my mouth,
Which to no vilayn was never couth   2000
For to aproche it, ne for to touche;
For sauff of cherlis I ne vouche
That they shull never neigh it ner.
For curteis, and of faire maner,
Well taught, and ful of gentilnesse   2005
He muste ben that shal me kysse,
And also of full high fraunchise,
That shal atteyne to that emprise.
And first of o thing warne I thee,
That peyne and gret adversite   2010
He mot endure, and eke travaile,
That shal me serve, withouten faile.
But ther-ageyns, thee to comforte,
And with thi servise to desporte,
Thou mayst full glad and joyfull be   2015
So good a maister to have as me,
And lord of so high renoun.
I bere of love the gonfanoun,
Of curtesie the banere;
For I am of the silf manere,   2020
Gentil, curteys, meke, and fre;
That who ever ententyf be
Me to honoure, doute, and serve,
And also that he hym observe
Fro trespas and fro vilanye,   2025
And hym governe in curtesie
With will and with entencioun.
For whanne he first in my prisoun
Is caught, thanne must he uttirly
Fro thennes forth full bisily   2030
Caste hym gentyll for to bee,
If he desire help of me."
   Anoon withouten more delay,
Withouten daunger or affray,
I bicom his man anoon,   2035
And gaf hym thankes many a oon,
And knelide doun, with hondis joynt,
And made it in my port full queynt;
The joye wente to myn herte rote.

Whanne I hadde kissed his mouth so swote,
I hadde sich myrthe and sich likyng,   2041
It cured me of langwisshing.
He askide of me thanne hostages: —
"I have," he seide, "taken fele homages
Of oon and other, where I have ben   2045
Disceyved ofte, withouten wen.
These felouns, full of falsite,
Have many sithes biguyled me,
And thorough falshed her lust achieved,
Wherof I repente and am agreved.   2050
And I hem gete in my daunger,
Her falshede shull they bie full der.
But for I love thee, I seie thee pleyn,
I wol of thee be more certeyn;
For thee so sore I wole now bynde   2055
That thou away ne shalt not wynde
For to denyen the covenaunt,
Or don that is not avenaunt.
That thou were fals it were gret reuthe,
Sith thou semest so full of treuthe."   2060
  "Sire, if thee lyst to undirstande,
I merveile the askyng this demande.
For why or wherfore shulde ye
Ostages or borwis aske of me,
Or ony other sikirnesse,   2065
Sith ye wot, in sothfastnesse,
That ye have me susprised so,
And hol myn herte taken me fro,
That it wole do for me nothing,
But if it be at youre biddyng?   2070
Myn herte is youres, and myn right nought,
As it bihoveth, in dede and thought,
Redy in all to worche youre will,
Whether to turne to good or ill,
So sore it lustith you to plese,   2075
No man therof may you disseise.
Ye have theron sette sich justice,
That it is werreid in many wise;
And if ye doute it nolde obeye,
Ye may therof do make a keye,   2080
And holde it with you for ostage."
  "Now, certis, this is noon outrage,"
Quod Love, "and fully I acord.
For of the body he is full lord
That hath the herte in his tresor;   2085
Outrage it were to asken more."
  Thanne of his awmener he drough
A litell keye, fetys ynowgh,
Which was of gold polisshed clere,
And seide to me, "With this keye heere   2090
Thyn herte to me now wole I shette.
For all my jowelles, loke and knette,
I bynde undir this litel keye,

That no wight may carie aweye.
This keye is full of gret poeste."   2095
With which anoon he touchide me
Undir the side full softely,
That he myn herte sodeynly
Withouten anoy hadde spered,
That yit right nought it hath me dered.   2100

Whanne he hadde don his will al oute,
And I hadde putte hym out of doute,
"Sire," I seide, "I have right gret wille
Youre lust and plesaunce to fulfille.
Loke ye my servise take at gree,   2105
By thilke feith ye owe to me.
I seye nought for recreaundise,
For I nought doute of youre servise.
But the servaunt traveileth in vayne,
That for to serven doth his payne   2110
Unto that lord, which in no wise
Kan hym no thank for his servyse."

Love seide, "Dismaie thee nought.
Syn thou for sokour hast me sought,
In thank thi servise wol I take,   2115
And high of degre I wol thee make,
If wikkidnesse ne hyndre thee;
But, as I hope, it shal nought be.
To worshipe no wight by aventure
May come, but if he peyne endure.   2120
Abid and suffre thy distresse;
That hurtith now, it shal be lesse.
I wot mysilf what may thee save,
What medicyne thou woldist have.
And if thi trouthe to me thou kepe,   2125
I shal unto thy helpyng eke,
To cure thy woundes and make hem clene,
Where so they be olde or grene;
Thou shalt be holpen, at wordis fewe.
For certeynly thou shalt well shewe   2130
Wher that thou servest with good wille
For to complysshen and fulfille
My comaundementis, day and nyght,
Whiche I to lovers yeve of right."

"A sire, for Goddis love," seide I,   2135
"Er ye passe hens, ententyfly
Youre comaundementis to me ye say,
And I shall kepe hem, if I may;
For hem to kepen is all my thought.
And if so be I wot hem nought,   2140
Thanne may I [erre] unwityngly.
Wherfore I pray you enterely,
With all myn herte, me to lere,
That I trespasse in no manere."

The God of Love thanne chargide me   2145
Anoon, as ye shall here and see,
Word by word, by right emprise.

So as the Romance shall devise.

The maister lesith his tyme to lere,
Whanne the disciple wol not here.   2150
It is but veyn on hym to swynke,
That on his lernyng wol not thinke.
Whoso luste love, lat hym entende,
For now the Romance bigynneth to amende.
Now is good to here, in fay,   2155
If ony be that can it say,
And poynte it as the resoun is
Set; for other-gate, ywys,
It shall nought well in alle thyng
Be brought to good undirstondyng.   2160
For a reder that poyntith ille
A good sentence may ofte spille.
The book is good at the eendyng,
Maad of newe and lusty thyng;
For whoso wol the eendyng here,   2165
The craft of love he shall mowe lere,
If that he wol so long abide,
Tyl I this Romance may unhide,
And undo the significance
Of this drem into Romance.   2170
The sothfastnesse that now is hid,
Without coverture shall be kid
Whanne I undon have this dremyng,
Wherynne no word is of lesyng.

"Vilanye, at the bigynnyng,   2175
I wole," sayde Love, "over alle thyng,
Thou leve if thou wolt [not] be
Fals, and trespasse ageynes me.
I curse and blame generaly
All hem that loven vilany;   2180
For vilanye makith vilayn,
And by his dedis a cherl is seyn.
Thise vilayns arn withouten pitee,
Frendshipe, love, and all bounte.
I nyl resseyve unto my servise   2185
Hem that ben vilayns of emprise.
But undirstonde in thyn entent
That this is not myn entendement,
To clepe no wight in noo ages
Oonly gentill for his lynages.   2190
But whoso is vertuous,
And in his port nought outrageous,
Whanne sich oon thou seest thee biforn,
Though he be not gentill born,
Thou maist well seyn, this is in soth,   2195
That he is gentil by cause he doth
As longeth to a gentilman;
Of hem noon other deme I can.
For certeynly, withouten drede,
A cherl is demed by his dede,   2200
Of hie or lowe, as we may see,

Or of what kynrede that he bee.
Ne say nought, for noon yvel wille,
Thyng that is to holden stille;
It is no worshipe to myssey.   2205
Thou maist ensample take of Key,
That was somtyme, for mysseiyng,
Hated bothe of olde and ying.
As fer as Gaweyn, the worthy,
Was preised for his curtesy,   2210
Kay was hated, for he was fell,
Of word dispitous and cruell.
Wherfore be wise and aqueyntable,
Goodly of word, and resonable
Bothe to lesse and eke to mare.   2215
And whanne thou comest there men are,
Loke that thou have in custome ay
First to salue hem, if thou may;
And if it fall that of hem som
Salue thee first, be not domm,   2220
But quyte hem curteisly anoon,
Without abidyng, er they goon.
    For nothyng eke thy tunge applye
To speke wordis of rebaudrye,
To vilayn speche in no degre   2225
Lat never thi lippe unbounden be.
For I nought holde hym, in good feith,
Curteys, that foule wordis seith.
And alle wymmen serve and preise,
And to thy power her honour reise;   2230
And if that ony myssaiere
Dispise wymmen, that thou maist here,
Blame hym, and bidde hym holde hym stille.
And set thy myght and all thy wille
Wymmen and ladies for to please,   2235
And to do thyng that may hem ese,
That they ever speke good of thee,
For so thou maist best preised be.
    Loke fro pride thou kepe thee wel;
For thou maist bothe perceyve and fel   2240
That pride is bothe foly and synne,
And he that pride hath hym withynne
Ne may his herte in no wise
Meken ne souplen to servyse.
For pride is founde in every part   2245
Contrarie unto loves art.
And he that loveth, trewely,
Shulde hym contene jolily
Withouten pride in sondry wise,
And hym disgysen in queyntise.   2250
For queynt array, withouten drede,
Is nothyng proud, who takith hede;
For fresh array, as men may see,
Withouten pride may ofte be.
    Mayntene thysilf aftir thi rent,   2255

Of robe and eke of garnement;
For many sithe fair clothyng
A man amendith in myche thyng.
And loke alwey that they be shape,
What garnement that thou shalt make,   2260
Of hym that kan best do,
With all that perteyneth therto.
Poyntis and sleves be well sittand,
Right and streght on the hand;
Of shon and bootes, newe and faire,   2265
Loke at the leest thou have a paire,
And that they sitte so fetisly
That these rude may uttirly
Merveyle, sith that they sitte so pleyn,
How they come on or off ageyn.   2270
Were streite gloves, with awmenere
Of silk; and alwey with good chere
Thou yeve, if thou have richesse;
And if thou have nought, spende the lesse.
Alwey be mery, if thou may;   2275
But waste not thi good alway.
Have hat of floures as fresh as May,
Chapelett of roses of Whitsonday;
For sich array ne costeth but lite.
Thyn hondis wassh, thy teeth make white,
And let no filthe upon thee bee.   2281
Thy nailes blak if thou maist see,
Voide it awey delyverly,
And kembe thyn heed right jolily.
Fard not thi visage in no wise,   2285
For that of love is not th' emprise;
For love doth haten, as I fynde,
A beaute that cometh not of kynde.
Alwey in herte I rede thee
Glad and mery for to be,   2290
And be as joyfull as thou can;
Love hath no joye of sorowful man.
That yvell is full of curtesie
That laughith in his maladie;
For ever of love the siknesse   2295
Is meynd with swete and bitternesse.
The sore of love is merveilous;
For now the lover [is] joyous,
Now can he pleyne, now can he grone,
Now can he syngen, now maken mone.   2300
To-day he pleyneth for hevynesse,
To-morowe he pleyeth for jolynesse.
The lyf of love is full contrarie,
Which stoundemele can ofte varie.
But if thou canst mirthis make,   2305
That men in gre wole gladly take,
Do it goodly, I comaunde thee;
For men shulde, wheresoevere they be,
Do thing that hem sittyng is,

For therof cometh good loos and pris.   2310
Whereof that thou be vertuous,
Ne be not straunge ne daungerous.
For if that thou good ridere be,
Prike gladly, that men may se.
In armes also if thou konne,   2315
Pursue til thou a name hast wonne.
And if thi voice be faire and cler,
Thou shalt maken [no] gret daunger
Whanne to synge they goodly preye;
It is thi worship for t' obeye.   2320
Also to you it longith ay
To harpe and gitterne, daunce and play;
For if he can wel foote and daunce,
It may hym greetly do avaunce.
Among eke, for thy lady sake,   2325
Songes and complayntes that thou make;
For that wole meven in hir herte,
Whanne they reden of thy smerte.
Loke that no man for scarce thee holde,
For that may greve thee many folde.   2330
Resoun wole that a lover be
In his yiftes more large and fre
Than cherles that can not of lovyng.
For who therof can ony thyng,
He shal be leef ay for to yeve,   2335
In Loves lore whoso wolde leve;
For he that, thorough a sodeyn sight,
Or for a kyssyng, anoonright
Yaff hool his herte in will and thought,
And to hymsilf kepith right nought,   2340
Aftir swich gift it is good resoun
He yeve his good in abandoun.
    Now wol I shortly heere reherce,
Of that I have seid in verce,
Al the sentence by and by,   2345
In wordis fewe compendiously,
That thou the better mayst on hem thynke,
Whether so it be thou wake or wynke.
For the wordis litel greve
A man to kepe, whanne it is breve.   2350
Whoso with Love wole goon or ride,
He mot be curteis, and voide of pride,
Mery, and full of jolite,
And of largesse alosed be.
    First I joyne thee, heere in penaunce,   2355
That evere, withoute repentaunce,
Thou sette thy thought in thy lovyng
To laste withoute repentyng;
And thenke upon thi myrthis swete,
That shall folowe aftir, whan ye mete.   2360
    And for thou trewe to love shalt be,
I wole, and comaunde thee,
That in oo place thou sette, all hool,

Thyn herte, withoute halfen dool
Of trecherie and sikernesse;   2365
For I lovede nevere doublenesse.
To many his herte that wole depart,
Everich shal have but litel part;
But of hym drede I me right nought,
That in oo place settith his thought.   2370
Therfore in oo place it sette,
And lat it nevere thannys flette.
For if thou yevest it in lenyng,
I holde it but a wrecchid thyng;
Therfore yeve it hool and quyt,   2375
And thou shalt have the more merit.
If it be lent, than aftir soon,
The bounte and the thank is doon;
But, in love, fre yeven thing
Requyrith a gret guerdonyng.   2380
Yeve it in yift al quyt fully,
And make thi yift debonairly;
For men that yift holde more dere,
That yeven is with gladsom chere.
That yift nought to preisen is,   2385
That man yeveth maugre his.
Whanne thou hast yeven thyn herte, as I
Have seid thee heere openly,
Thanne aventures shull thee falle,
Which harde and hevy ben withalle.   2390
For ofte whan thou bithenkist thee
Of thy lovyng, whereso thou be,
Fro folk thou must departe in hie,
That noon perceyve thi maladie;
But hyde thyne harm thou must alone,   2395
And go forth sool, and make thy mone.
Thou shalt no whyle be in o stat,
But whylom cold and whilom hat;
Now reed as rose, now yelowe and fade.
Such sorowe, I trowe, thou never hade;   2400
Cotidien, ne quarteyne,
It is nat so ful of peyne.
For often tymes it shal falle
In love, among thy paynes alle,
That thou thyself al holly   2405
Foryeten shalt so utterly
That many tymes thou shalt be
Styl as an ymage of tree,
Domm as a ston, without steryng
Of fot or hond, without spekyng.   2410
Than, soone after al thy payn,
To memorye shalt thou come agayn,
As man abasshed wonder sore,
And after syghen more and more.
For wyt thou wel, withouten wen,   2415
In such astat ful ofte have ben
That have the yvel of love assayd

Wherthrough thou art so dismayd.
　After, a thought shal take the so,
That thy love is to fer the fro.   2420
Thou shalt saye, 'God! what may this be,
That I ne may my lady se?
Myn herte alone is to her go,
And I abyde al sol in wo,
Departed fro myn owne thought,   2425
And with myne eyen se right nought.
Alas! myne eyen sende I ne may
My careful herte to convay!
Myn hertes gyde but they be,
I prayse nothyng, whatever they se.   2430
Shul they abyde thanne? nay;
But gon and visyten without delay
That myn herte desyreth so.
For certainly, but if they go,
A fool myself I may wel holde,   2435
Whan I ne se what myn herte wolde.
Wherfore I wol gon her to sen,
Or eased shal I never ben,
But I have som tokenyng.'
Than gost thou forth without dwellyng;   2440
But ofte thou faylest of thy desyr,
Er thou mayst come her any ner,
And wastest in vayn thi passage.
Thanne fallest thou in a newe rage;
For want of sight thou gynnest morne,   2445
And homward pensyf thou dost retorne.
In greet myscheef thanne shalt thou bee,
For thanne agayn shall come to thee
Sighes and pleyntes, with newe woo,
That no ycchyng prikketh soo.   2450
Who wot it nought, he may go lere
Of hem that bien love so dere.
　Nothyng thyn herte appesen may,
That ofte thou wolt goon and assay
If thou maist seen, by aventure,   2455
Thi lyves joy, thin hertis cure;
So that, bi grace, if thou myght
Atteyne of hire to have a sight,
Thanne shalt thou don noon other dede,
But with that sight thyne eyen fede.   2460
That faire fresh whanne thou maist see,
Thyne herte shall so ravysshed be
That nevere thou woldest, thi thankis, lete,
Ne remove, for to see that swete.
The more thou seest in sothfastnesse,   2465
The more thou coveytest of that swetnesse;
The more thin herte brenneth in fir,
The more thin herte is in desir.
For who considreth everydeell,
It may be likned wondir well,   2470
The peyne of love, unto a fer;

For evermore thou neighest ner,
Thou, or whooso that it bee,
For verray sothe I tell it thee,
The hatter evere shall thou brenne,   2475
As experience shall thee kenne.
Whereso [thou] comest in ony coost,
Who is next fyr, he brenneth moost.
And yitt forsothe, for all thin hete,
Though thou for love swelte and swete,   2480
Ne for nothyng thou felen may,
Thou shalt not willen to passen away.
And though thou go, yitt must thee nede
Thenke all day on hir fairhede
Whom thou biheelde with so good will,   2485
And holde thisilf biguyled ill,
That thou ne haddest noon hardement
To shewe hir ought of thyn entent.
Thyn herte full sore thou wolt dispise,
And eke repreve of cowardise,   2490
That thou, so dul in every thing
Were domm for drede, withoute spekyng.
Thou shalt eke thenke thou didest foly,
That thou were hir so faste by,
And durst not auntre thee to saye   2495
Somthyng, er thou cam awaye;
For thou haddist no more wonne,
To speke of hir whanne thou bigonne.
But yif she wolde, for thy sake,
In armes goodly thee have take,   2500
It shulde have be more worth to thee
Than of tresour gret plente.
Thus shalt thou morne and eke compleyn,
And gete enchesoun to goon ageyn
Unto thi walk, or to thi place,   2505
Where thou biheelde hir fleshly face.
And never, for fals suspeccioun,
Thou woldest fynde occasioun
For to gon unto hire hous.
So art thou thanne desirous   2510
A sight of hir for to have,
If thou thin honour myghtist save,
Or ony erande myghtist make
Thider, for thi loves sake,
Full fayn thou woldist; but for drede   2515
Thou gost not, lest that men take hede.
Wherfore I rede, in thi goyng,
And also in thyn ageyn-comyng,
Thou be well war that men ne wit.
Feyne thee other cause than it   2520
To go that weye, or faste by;
To hele wel is no foly.
And if so be it happe thee
That thou thi love there maist see,
In siker wise thou hir salewe,   2525

Wherewith thi colour wole transmewe,
And eke thy blod shal al toquake,
Thyn hewe eke chaungen for hir sake.
But word and wit, with chere full pale,
Shull wante for to tell thy tale.   2530
And if thou maist so fer forth wynne
That thou [thy] resoun durst bigynne,
And woldist seyn thre thingis or mo,
Thou shalt full scarsly seyn the two.
Though thou bithenke thee never so well,   2535
Thou shalt foryete yit somdell,
But if thou dele with trecherie.
For fals lovers mowe all folye
Seyn, what hem lust, withouten drede,
They be so double in her falshede;   2540
For they in herte cunne thenke o thyng,
And seyn another in her spekyng.
And whanne thi speche is eendid all,
Ryght thus to thee it shall byfall:
If ony word thanne come to mynde,   2545
That thou to seye hast left bihynde,
Thanne thou shalt brenne in gret martir;
For thou shalt brenne as ony fir.
This is the stryf, and eke the affray,
And the batell that lastith ay.   2550
This bargeyn eende may never take,
But if that she thi pees will make.
And whanne the nyght is comen, anoon
A thousand angres shall come uppon.
To bedde as fast thou wolt thee dight,   2555
Where thou shalt have but smal delit;
For whanne thou wenest for to slepe,
So full of peyne shalt thou crepe,
Sterte in thi bed aboute full wide,
And turne full ofte on every side;   2560
Now dounward groff, and now upright,
And walowe in woo the longe nyght;
Thine armys shalt thou sprede a-bred,
As man in werre were forwerreyd.
Thanne shall thee come a remembraunce   2565
Of hir shap and hir semblaunce,
Whereto non other may be pere.
And wite thou wel, withoute were,
That thee shal seme, somtyme that nyght,
That thou hast hir, that is so bright,   2570
Naked bitwene thyne armes there,
All sothfastnesse as though it were.
Thou shalt make castels thanne in Spayne,
And dreme of joye, all but in vayne,
And thee deliten of right nought,   2575
While thou so slombrest in that thought,
That is so swete and delitable,
The which, in soth, nys but a fable;
For it ne shall no while laste.

Thanne shalt thou sighe and wepe faste,   2580
And say, 'Dere God, what thing is this?
My drem is turned all amys,
Which was full swete and apparent;
But now I wake, it is al shent!
Now yede this mery thought away!   2585
Twenty tymes upon a day
I wolde this thought wolde come ageyn,
For it aleggith well my peyn.
It makith me full of joyfull thought;
It sleth me, that it lastith noght.   2590
A, Lord! why nyl ye me socoure?
Fro joye I trowe that I langoure.
The deth I wolde me shulde sloo,
While I lye in hir armes twoo.
Myn harm is hard, withouten wene;   2595
My gret unese full ofte I meene.
   But wolde Love do so I myght
Have fully joye of hir so bright,
My peyne were quyt me rychely.
Allas, to gret a thing aske I!   2600
Hit is but foly and wrong wenyng,
To aske so outrageous a thyng;
And whoso askith folily,
He mot be warned hastily.
And I ne wot what I may say,   2605
I am so fer out of the way;
For I wolde have full gret likyng,
And full gret joye of lasse thing.
For wolde she, of hir gentylnesse,
Withouten more, me oonys kesse,   2610
It were to me a gret guerdoun,
Relees of all my passioun.
But it is hard to come therto;
All is but folye that I do,
So high I have myn herte set,   2615
Where I may no comfort get.
I not wher I seye well or nought,
But this I wot wel in my thought,
That it were better of hir alloone,
For to stynte my woo and moone,   2620
A lok of hir ycast goodly,
Than for to have al utterly
Of an other all hool the pley.
A, Lord! wher I shall byde the day
That evere she shall my lady be?   2625
He is full cured that may hir see.
A, God! whanne shal the dawnyng spring?
To liggen thus is an angry thyng;
I have no joye thus heere to ly,
Whanne that my love is not me by.   2630
A man to lyen hath gret disese,
Which may not slepe ne reste in ese.
I wolde it dawed, and were now day,

And that the nyght were went away;
For were it day, I wolde uprise.   2635
A, slowe sonne! shewe thin enprise!
Sped thee to sprede thy beemys bright,
And chace the derknesse of the nyght,
To putte away the stoundes stronge,
Whiche in me lasten all to longe.'   2640
    The nyght shalt thou contene soo,
Withoute rest, in peyne and woo.
If evere thou knewe of love distresse,
Thou shalt mowe lerne in that siknesse,
And thus enduryng shalt thou ly,   2645
And ryse on morwe up erly
Out of thy bedde, and harneyse thee,
Er evere dawnyng thou maist see.
All pryvyly thanne shalt thou goon,
What weder it be, thisilf alloon,   2650
For reyn or hayl, for snow, for slet,
Thider she dwellith, that is so swet,
The which may fall a-slepe be,
And thenkith but lytel upon thee.
Thanne shalt thou goon, ful foule afeered,   2655
Loke if the gate be unspered,
And waite without, in woo and peyn,
Full yvel a-coold, in wynd and reyn.
Thanne shal thou go the dore bifore,
If thou maist fynde ony score,   2660
Or hool, or reeft, whatevere it were;
Thanne shalt thou stoupe, and lay to ere,
If they withynne a-slepe be,—
I mene, all save thy lady free,
Whom wakyng if thou maist aspie,   2665
Go putte thisilf in jupartie,
To aske grace, and thee bimene,
That she may wite, withouten wene,
That thou [a-] nyght no rest hast had,
So sore for hir thou were bystad.   2670
Wommen wel ought pite to take
Of hem that sorwen for her sake.
And loke, for love of that relyk,
That thou thenke noon other lyk;
For whom thou hast so gret annoy   2675
Shall kysse thee, er thou go away,
And holde that in full gret deynte.
And for that no man shal thee see
Bifore the hous, ne in the way,
Loke thou be goon ageyn er day.   2680
Such comyng, and such goyng,
Such hevynesse, and such wakyng,
Makith lovers, withouten ony wene,
Under her clothes pale and lene.
For Love leveth colour ne cleernesse;   2685
Who loveth trewe hath no fatnesse.
Thou shalt wel by thysilf see

That thou must nedis assayed be.
For men that shape hem other wey
Falsly her ladyes for to bitray,   2690
It is no wonder though they be fatt;
With false othes her loves they gatt.
For oft I see suche losengours
Fatter than abbatis or priours.
    Yit with o thing I thee charge,   2695
That is to seye, that thou be large
Unto the mayde that hir doth serve;
So best hir thank thou shalt deserve.
Yeve hir yiftes, and get hir grace;
For so thou may thank purchace,   2700
That she thee worthy holde and free,
Thi lady, and all that may thee see.
Also hir servauntes worshipe ay,
And please as mychel as thou may;
Gret good thorough hem may come to thee,   2705
Bicause with hir they ben pryve.
They shal hir telle hou they thee fand
Curteis, and wys, and well doand,
And she shall preise well the mare.
Loke oute of londe thou be not fare,   2710
And if such cause thou have that thee
Bihoveth to gon out of contree,
Leve hool thin herte in hostage,
Till thou ageyn make thi passage.
Thenk long to see the swete thyng   2715
That hath thin herte in hir kepyng.
    Now have I told thee in what wise
A lovere shall do me servise.
Do it thanne, if thou wolt have
The meede that thou aftir crave."   2720
    Whanne Love all this hadde boden me,
I seide hym: "Sire, how may it be
That lovers may in such manere
Endure the peyne ye have seid heere?
I merveyle me wonder faste   2725
How ony man may lyve or laste
In such peyne and such brennyng,
In sorwe, and thought, and such sighing,
Ay unrelesed woo to make,
Whether so it be they slepe or wake,   2730
In such annoy contynuely,—
As helpe me God, this merveile I
How man, but he were maad of stele,
Myght lyve a month, such peynes to fele."
    The God of Love thanne seide me: 2735
"Freend, by the feith I owe to thee,
May no man have good, but he it by.
A man loveth more tendirly
The thyng that he hath bought most dere.
For wite thou well, withouten were,   2740
In thank that thyng is taken more,

For which a man hath suffred sore.
Certis, no wo ne may atteyne
Unto the sore of loves peyne;
Noon yvel therto ne may amounte,   2745
No more than a man [may] counte
The dropes that of the water be.
For drye as well the greete see
Thou myghtist, as the harmes telle
Of hem that with love dwelle   2750
In servyse; for peyne hem sleeth,
And yet ech man wolde fle the deeth.
And trowe thei shulde nevere escape,
Nere that hope couthe hem make
Glad, as man in prisoun sett,   2755
And may not geten for to et
But barly breed, and watir pure,
And lyeth in vermyn and in ordure;
With all this yitt can he lyve,
Good hope such comfort hath hym yive,   2760
Which maketh wene that he shall be
Delyvered, and come to liberte.
In fortune is [his] fulle trust;
Though he lye in strawe or dust,
In hoope is all his susteynyng.   2765
And so for lovers, in her wenyng,
Whiche Love hath shit in his prisoun,
Good hope is her salvacioun.
Good hope, how sore that they smerte,
Yeveth hem bothe will and herte   2770
To profre her body to martire;
For hope so sore doth hem desire
To suffre ech harm that men devise,
For joye that aftirward shall aryse.
    Hope in desir caccheth victorie;   2775
In hope of love is all the glorie;
For hope is all that love may yive;
Nere hope, ther shulde no lover lyve.
Blessid be hope, which with desir
Avaunceth lovers in such maner!   2780
Good hope is curteis for to please,
To kepe lovers from all disese.
Hope kepith his bond, and wole abide,
For ony perill that may betyde;
For hope to lovers, as most cheef,   2785
Doth hem endure all myscheef;
Hope is her helpe, whanne myster is.
    And I shall yeve thee eke, iwys,
Three other thingis that gret solas
Doth to hem that be in my las.   2790
The firste good that may be founde
To hem that in my las be bounde,
Is Swete-Thought, for to recorde
Thing wherwith thou canst accorde
Best in thyn herte, where she be.   2795

Thenkyng in absence is good to thee.
Whanne ony lover doth compleyne,
And lyveth in distresse and in peyne,
Thanne Swete-Thought shal come, as blyve,
Awey his angre for to dryve: 2800
It makith lovers to have remembraunce
Of comfort, and of high plesaunce,
That Hope hath hight hym for to wynne.
For Thought anoon thanne shall bygynne,
As fer, God wot, as he can fynde,   2805
To make a mirrour of his mynde;
For to biholde he wole not lette.
Hir persone he shall afore hym sette,
Hir laughing eyen, persaunt and clere,
Hir shape, hir forme, hir goodly chere,   2810
Hir mouth, that is so gracious,
So swete, and eke so saverous;
Of all hir fetures he shall take heede,
His eyen with all hir lymes fede.
    Thus Swete-Thenkyng shall aswage   2815
The peyne of lovers and her rage.
Thi joye shall double, withoute gesse,
Whanne thou thenkist on hir semlynesse,
Or of hir laughing, or of hir chere,
That to thee made thi lady dere.   2820
This comfort wole I that thou take;
And if the next thou wolt forsake,
Which is not lesse saverous,
Thou shuldist ben to daungerous.
    The secounde shal be Swete-Speche,   2825
That hath to many oon be leche,
To bringe hem out of woo and wer,
And holpe many a bachiler;
And many a lady sent socour,
That have loved paramour,   2830
Thorough spekyng whanne they myghte heere
Of hir lovers, to hem so dere.
To [hem] it voidith all her smerte,
The which is closed in her herte.
In herte it makith hem glad and light,   2835
Speche, whanne they [ne] mowe have sight.
And therfore now it cometh to mynde,
In olde dawes, as I fynde,
That clerkis writen that hir knewe,
Ther was a lady fresh of hewe,   2840
Which of hir love made a song
On hym for to remembre among,
In which she seyde, 'Whanne that I here
Speken of hym that is so dere,
To me it voidith all [my] smert,   2845
Iwys, he sittith so ner myn hert.
To speke of hym, at eve or morwe,
It cureth me of all my sorwe.
To me is noon so high plesaunce

As of his persone dalyaunce.'   2850
She wist full well that Swete-Spekyng
Comfortith in full myche thyng.
Hir love she hadde full well assayed;
Of him she was full well apaied;
To speke of hym hir joye was sett.   2855
Therfore I rede thee that thou gett
A felowe that can well concele,
And kepe thi counsell, and well hele,
To whom go shewe hoolly thine herte,
Bothe wele and woo, joye and smerte;   2860
To gete comfort to hym thou goo,
And pryvyly, bitwene yow twoo,
Yee shall speke of that goodly thyng
That hath thyn herte in hir kepyng;
Of hir beaute, and hir semblaunce,   2865
And of hir goodly countenaunce.
Of all thi stat thou shalt hym sey,
And aske hym counseill how thou may
Do ony thyng that may hir plese;
For it to thee shall do gret ese,   2870
That he may wite thou trust hym soo,
Bothe of thi wele and of thi woo.
And if his herte to love be sett,
His companye is myche the bett.
For resoun wole, he shewe to thee   2875
All uttirly his pryvyte;
And what she is he loveth so,
To thee pleynly he shal undo,
Withoute drede of ony shame,
Bothe tell hir renoun and hir name.   2880
Thanne shall he forther, fer and ner,
And namely to thi lady der,
In syker wise; yee, every other
Shall helpen as his owne brother,
In trouthe, withoute doublenesse,   2885
And kepen cloos in sikernesse.
For it is noble thing, in fay,
To have a man thou darst say
Thy pryve counsell every deell;
For that wole comforte thee right well,   2890
And thou shalt holde thee well apayed,
Whanne such a freend thou hast assayed.
    The thridde good of gret comfort,
That yeveth to lovers most disport,
Comyth of sight and biholdyng,   2895
That clepid is Swete-Lokyng,
The whiche may noon ese do
Whanne thou art fer thy lady fro;
Wherfore thou prese alwey to be
In place where thou maist hir see.   2900
For it is thyng most amerous,
Most delytable and saverous,
For to aswage a mannes sorowe,

To sen his lady by the morwe.
For it is a full noble thing,   2905
Whanne thyne eyen have metyng
With that relike precious,
Wherof they be so desirous.
But al day after, soth it is,
They have no drede to faren amys;   2910
They dreden neither wynd ne reyn,
Ne noon other maner peyn.
For whanne thyne eyen were thus in blis,
Yit of hir curtesie, ywys,
Alloone they can not have her joye,   2915
But to the herte they [it] convoye;
Part of her blisse to hym they sende,
Of all this harm to make an ende.
The eye is a good messanger,
Which can to the herte in such maner,   2920
Tidyngis sende that [he] hath sen,
To voide hym of his peynes clen.
Wherof the herte rejoiseth soo,
That a gret party of his woo
Is voided, and put awey to flight.   2925
Right as the derknesse of the nyght
Is chased with clernesse of the mone,
Right so is al his woo full soone
Devoided clene, whanne that the sight
Biholden may that freshe wight   2930
That the herte desireth soo,
That al his derknesse is agoo.
For thanne the herte is all at ese,
Whanne the eyen sen that may hem plese.
    Now have I declared thee all oute,   2935
Of that thou were in drede and doute;
For I have told thee feithfully
What thee may curen utterly,
And alle lovers that wole be
Feithfull and full of stabilite.   2940
Good-Hope alwey kep bi thi side,
And Swete-Thought make eke abide,
Swete-Lokyng and Swete-Speche;
Of all thyne harmes thei shall be leche;
Of every thou shalt have gret plesaunce.   2945
If thou canst bide in sufferaunce,
And serve wel withoute feyntise,
Thou shalt be quyt of thyn emprise
With more guerdoun, if that thou lyve;
But at this tyme this I thee yive."   2950
    The God of Love whanne al the day
Had taught me, as ye have herd say,
And enformed compendiously,
He vanyshide awey all sodeynly;
And I alloone lefte, all sool,   2955
So full of compleynt and of dool,
For I saw no man there me by.

My woundes me greved wondirly;
Me for to curen nothyng I knew,
Save the botoun bright of hew,   2960
Wheron was sett hoolly my thought.
Of other comfort knew I nought,
But it were thorugh the God of Love;
I knew not elles to my bihove
That myght me ease or comfort gete,   2965
But if he wolde hym entermete.
      The roser was, withoute doute,
Closed with an hegge withoute,
As ye toforn have herd me seyn;
And fast I bisiede, and wolde fayn   2970
Have passed the hay, if I myghte
Have geten ynne by ony slighte
Unto the botoun so faire to see.
But evere I dradde blamed to be,
If men wolde have suspeccioun   2975
That I wolde of entencioun
Have stole the roses that there were;
Therfore to entre I was in fere.
But at the last, as I bithought
Whether I shulde passe or nought,   2980
I saw come with a glad cher
To me, a lusty bacheler,
Of good stature and of good highte,
And Bialacoil forsothe he highte.
Sone he was to Curtesy;   2985
And he me grauntide full gladly
The passage of the outter hay,
And seide: "Sir, how that yee may
Passe, if youre wille be
The freshe roser for to see,   2990
And yee the swete savour fele.
Youre warrant may [I be] right wele;
So thou thee kepe fro folye,
Shall no man do thee vylanye.
If I may helpe you in ought,   2995
I shall not feyne, dredeth nought;
For I am bounde to youre servise,
Fully devoide of feyntise."
      Thanne unto Bialacoil saide I,
"I thanke you, sir, full hertely,   3000
And youre biheeste take at gre,
That ye so goodly profer me.
To you it cometh of gret fraunchise,
That ye me profer youre servise."
      Thanne aftir, full delyverly,   3005
Thorough the breres anoon wente I,
Wherof encombred was the hay.
I was wel plesed, the soth to say,
To se the botoun faire and swote
So freshe spronge out of the rote.   3010
      And Bialacoil me served well,

Whanne I so nygh me myghte fel
Of the botoun the swete odour,
And so lusty hewed of colour.
But thanne a cherl (foule hym bityde!)   3015
Biside the roses gan hym hyde,
To kepe the roses of that roser,
Of whom the name was Daunger.
This cherl was hid there in the greves,
Kovered with gras and with leves,   3020
To spie and take whom that he fond
Unto that roser putte an hond.
He was not sool, for ther was moo;
For with hym were other twoo
Of wikkid maners and yvel fame.   3025
That oon was clepid, by his name,
Wykked-Tonge, God yeve hym sorwe!
For neither at eve ne at morwe,
He can of no man [no] good speke;
On many a just man doth he wreke.   3030
Ther was a womman eke that hight
Shame, that, who can reken right,
Trespas was hir fadir name,
Hir moder Resoun; and thus was Shame
Brought of these ilke twoo.   3035
And yitt hadde Trespas never adoo
With Resoun, ne never ley hir by,
He was so hidous and so ugly,
I mene, this that Trespas highte;
But Resoun conceyved of a sighte   3040
Shame, of that I spak aforn.
And whanne that Shame was thus born,
It was ordeyned that Chastite
Shulde of the roser lady be,
Which, of the botouns more and las,   3045
With sondry folk assailed was,
That she ne wiste what to doo.
For Venus hir assailith soo,
That nyght and day from hir she stal
Botouns and roses overal.   3050
To Resoun thanne praieth Chastite,
Whom Venus hath flemed over the see,
That she hir doughter wolde hir lene,
To kepe the roser fresh and grene.
Anoon Resoun to Chastite   3055
Is fully assented that it be,
And grauntide hir, at hir request,
That Shame, by cause she is honest,
Shall keper of the roser be.
And thus to kepe it ther were three,   3060
That noon shulde hardy be ne bold,
Were he yong or were he old,
Ageyn hir will awey to bere
Botouns ne roses that there were.
I hadde wel sped, hadde I not ben   3065

Awayted with these three and sen.
For Bialacoil, that was so fair,
So gracious, and debonair,
Quytt hym to me full curteisly,
And, me to plese, bad that I   3070
Shulde drawe me to the botoun ner;
Prese in, to touche the roser
Which bar the roses, he yaf me leve;
This graunt ne myght but lytel greve.
And for he saw it liked me,   3075
Ryght nygh the botoun pullede he
A leef all grene, and yaff me that,
The whiche ful nygh the botoun sat.
I made [me] of that leef full queynt;
And whanne I felte I was aqueynt   3080
With Bialacoil, and so pryve,
I wende all at my will hadde be.
Thanne wax I hardy for to tel
To Bialacoil hou me bifel
Of Love, that tok and wounded me,   3085
And seide, "Sir, so mote I thee,
I may no joye have in no wise,
Uppon no side, but it rise.
For sithe (if I shall not feyne)
In herte I have had so gret peyne,   3090
So gret annoy, and such affray,
That I ne wot what I shall say;
I drede youre wrath to disserve.
Lever me were that knyves kerve
My body shulde in pecys smale,   3095
Than in any wise it shulde falle,
That ye wratthed shulde ben with me."
"Sey boldely thi will," quod he,
"I nyl be wroth, if that I may,
For nought that thou shalt to me say."   3100
     Thanne seide I, "Ser, not you displease
To knowen of my gret unese,
In which oonly Love hath me brought;
For peynes gret, disese, and thought,
Fro day to day he doth me drye;   3105
Supposeth not, sir, that I lye.
In me fyve woundes dide he make,
The soore of whiche shall nevere slake,
But ye the botoun graunte me,
Which is moost passaunt of beaute,   3110
My lyf, my deth, and my martire,
And tresour that I moost desire."
     Thanne Bialacoil, affrayed all,
Seyde, "Sir, it may not fall;
That ye desire, it may not arise.   3115
What? Wolde ye shende me in this wise?
A mochel fool thanne I were,
If I suffride you awey to bere
The fresh botoun so faire of sight.

For it were neither skile ne right,   3120
Of the roser ye broke the rynde,
Or take the Rose aforn his kynde.
Ye are not curteys to aske it.
Late it still on the roser sitt,
And growe til it amended be,   3125
And parfytly come to beaute.
I nolde not that it pulled were
Fro the roser that it bere,
To me it is so leef and deer."
     With that sterte oute anoon Daunger,   3130
Out of the place were he was hid.
His malice in his chere was kid;
Full gret he was and blak of hewe,
Sturdy and hidous, whoso hym knewe;
Like sharp urchouns his her was growe;   3135
His eyes reed sparclyng as the fyr glowe;
His nose frounced, full kirked stood.
He com criand as he were wood,
And seide, "Bialacoil, telle me why
Thou bryngest hider so booldely   3140
Hym that so nygh [is] the roser?
Thou worchist in a wrong maner.
He thenkith to dishonoure thee;
Thou art wel worthy to have maugree
To late hym of the roser wit.   3145
Who serveth a feloun is yvel quit.
Thou woldist have doon gret bounte,
And he with shame wolde quyte thee.
Fle hennes, felowe! I rede thee goo!
It wanteth litel I wole thee sloo.   3150
For Bialacoil ne knew thee nought,
Whanne thee to serve he sette his thought;
For thou wolt shame hym, if thou myght,
Bothe ageyns resoun and right.
I wole no more in thee affye,   3155
That comest so slyghly for t'espye;
For it preveth wonder well,
Thy slight and tresoun, every deell."
I durst no more there make abod
For the cherl, he was so wod;   3160
So gan he threte and manace,
And thurgh the haye he dide me chace.
For feer of hym I tremblyde and quok,
So cherlishly his heed he shok,
And seide, if eft he myght me take,   3165
I shulde not from his hondis scape.
     Thanne Bialacoil is fled and mat,
And I, all sool, disconsolat,
Was left aloone in peyne and thought;
For shame to deth I was nygh brought.   3170
Thanne thought I on myn high foly,
How that my body utterly
Was yeve to peyne and to martire;

And therto hadde I so gret ire,
That I ne durst the haye passe.   3175
There was noon hope, there was no grace.
I trowe nevere man wiste of peyne,
But he were laced in loves cheyne;
Ne no man [wot], and sooth it is,
But if he love, what anger is.   3180
Love holdith his heest to me right wel,
Whanne peyne he seide I shulde fel;
Noon herte may thenke, ne tunge seyn,
A quarter of my woo and peyn.
I myght not with the anger laste;   3185
Myn herte in poynt was for to braste,
Whanne I thought on the Rose, that soo
Was thurgh Daunger cast me froo.
A long while stod I in that stat,
Til that me saugh so mad and mat   3190
The lady of the highe ward,
Which from hir tour lokide thiderward.
Resoun men clepe that lady,
Which from hir tour delyverly
Com doun to me, withouten mor.   3195
But she was neither yong ne hoor,
Ne high ne lowe, ne fat ne lene,
But best, as it were in a mene.
Hir eyen twoo were cleer and light
As ony candell that brenneth bright;   3200
And on hir heed she hadde a crowne
Hir semede wel an high persoune;
For round enviroun, hir crownet
Was full of riche stonys frett.
Hir goodly semblaunt, by devys,   3205
I trowe were maad in paradys;
For Nature hadde nevere such a gras,
To forge a werk of such compas.
For certeyn, but if the letter ly,
God hymsilf, that is so high,   3210
Made hir aftir his ymage,
And yaff hir sith sich avauntage
That she hath myght and seignorie
To kepe men from all folye;
Whoso wole trowe hir lore,   3215
Ne may offenden nevermore.
    And while I stod thus derk and pale,
Resoun bigan to me hir tale.
She seide, "Al hayl, my swete freend!
Foly and childhood wol thee sheend,   3220
Which the have putt in gret affray.
Thou hast bought deere the tyme of May,
That made thyn herte mery to be.
In yvell tyme thou wentist to see
The gardyn, whereof Ydilnesse   3225
Bar the keye, and was maistresse,
Whanne thou yedest in the daunce

With hir, and haddest aqueyntaunce.
Hir aqueyntaunce is perilous,
First softe, and aftir noious;   3230
She hath [thee] trasshed, withoute wen.
The God of Love hadde the not sen,
Ne hadde Ydilnesse thee conveyed
In the verger, where Myrthe hym pleyed.
If Foly have supprised thee,   3235
Do so that it recovered be;
And be wel ware to take nomore
Counsel, that greveth aftir sore.
He is wis, that wol hymsilf chastise.
And though a yong man in ony wise   3240
Trespace among, and do foly,
Late hym not tarye, but hastily
Late hym amende what so be mys.
And eke I counseile thee, iwys,
The God of Love hoolly foryet,   3245
That hath thee in sich peyne set,
And thee in herte tourmented soo.
I can nat sen how thou maist goo
Other weyes to garisoun;
For Daunger, that is so feloun,   3250
Felly purposith thee to werreye,
Which is ful cruel, the soth to seye.
    And yitt of Daunger cometh no blame,
In reward of my doughter Shame,
Which hath the roses in hir ward,   3255
As she that may be no musard.
And Wikked-Tunge is with these two,
That suffrith no man thider goo;
For er a thing be do, he shal,
Where that he cometh, overall,   3260
In fourty places, if it be sought,
Seye thyng that nevere was don ne wrought;
So moche tresoun is in his male
Of falsnesse, for to seyne a tale.
Thou delest with angry folk, ywis;   3265
Wherfore to thee bettir is
From these folk awey to fare,
For they wole make thee lyve in care.
This is the yvell that love they call,
Wherynne ther is but foly al;   3270
For love is foly everydell.
Who loveth in no wise may do well,
Ne sette his thought on no good werk.
His scole he lesith, if he be a clerk;
Of other craft eke if he be,   3275
He shal not thryve therynne; for he
In love shal have more passioun
Than monk, hermyte, or chanoun.
The peyne is hard, out of mesure;
The joye may eke no while endure;   3280
And in the possessioun

Is myche tribulacioun.
The joye it is so short lastyng,
And but in hap is the getyng;
For I see there many in travaille,   3285
That atte laste foule fayle.
I was nothyng thi counseler,
Whanne thou were maad the omager
Of God of Love to hastily;
Ther was no wisdom, but foly.   3290
Thyn herte was joly, but not sage,
Whanne thou were brought in sich a rage,
To yelde thee so redily,
And to leve of is gret maistry.
    I rede thee Love awey to dryve,   3295
That makith thee recche not of thi lyve.
The foly more fro day to day
Shal growe, but thou it putte away.
Tak with thy teeth the bridel faste,
To daunte thyn herte; and eke thee caste,   3300
If that thou maist, to gete thee defence
For to redresse thi first offence.
Whoso his herte alwey wol leve,
Shal fynde among that shal hym greve."
    Whanne I hir herd thus me chastise,   3305
I answerd in ful angry wise.
I prayed hir ceessen of hir speche,
Outher to chastise me or teche,
To bidde me my thought refreyne,
Which Love hath caught in his demeyne: 3310
"What? wene ye Love wol consent,
That me assailith with bowe bent,
To drawe myn herte out of his hond,
Which is so qwikly in his bond?
That ye counseyle may nevere be;   3315
For whanne he first arestide me,
He took myn herte so hool hym till,
That it is nothyng at my wil;
He taught it so hym for to obeye,
That he it sparrede with a keye.   3320
I pray yow, late me be all stille.
For ye may well, if that ye wille,
Youre wordis waste in idilnesse;
For utterly, withouten gesse,
All that ye seyn is but in veyne.   3325
Me were lever dye in the peyne,
Than Love to me-ward shulde arette
Falsheed, or tresoun on me sette.
I wole me gete prys or blame,
And love trewe, to save my name.   3330
Who that me chastisith, I hym hate."
    With that word Resoun wente hir gate,
Whanne she saugh for no sermonynge
She myght me fro my foly brynge.
Thanne dismaied, I lefte all sool,   3335

Forwery, forwandred as a fool,
For I ne knew no chevisaunce.
Thanne fell into my remembraunce
How Love bad me to purveye
A felowe, to whom I myghte seye   3340
My counsell and my pryvete,
For that shulde moche availe me.
With that bithought I me that I
Hadde a felowe faste by,
Trewe and siker, curteys and hend,   3345
And he was called by name a Freend;
A trewer felowe was nowher noon.
In haste to hym I wente anoon,
And to hym all my woo I tolde;
Fro hym right nought I wold witholde.   3350
I tolde hym all, withoute wer,
And made my compleynt on Daunger,
How for to see he was hidous,
And to me-ward contrarious,
The whiche thurgh his cruelte   3355
Was in poynt to have meymed me.
With Bialacoil whanne he me sey
Withynne the gardeyn walke and pley,
Fro me he made hym for to go,
And I bilefte aloone in woo;   3360
I durst no lenger with hym speke,
For Daunger seide he wolde be wreke,
Whanne that he saw how I wente
The freshe botoun for to hente,
If I were hardy to come neer   3365
Bitwene the hay and the roser.
    This freend, whanne he wiste of my thought,
He discomforted me right nought,
But seide, "Felowe, be not so mad,
Ne so abaysshed nor bystad.   3370
Mysilf I knowe full well Daunger,
And how he is feers of his cheer,
At prime temps, Love to manace;
Ful ofte I have ben in his caas.
A feloun first though that he be,   3375
Aftir thou shalt hym souple se.
Of longe passed I knew hym well;
Ungoodly first though men hym feel,
He wol meke aftir in his beryng
Been, for service and obeyssyhing.   3380
I shal thee telle what thou shalt doo.
Mekely I rede thou go hym to,
Of herte pray hym specialy
Of thy trespas to have mercy,
And hote wel, hym here to plese,   3385
That thou shalt nevermore hym displese.
Who can best serve of flatery,
Shall please Daunger most uttirly."
    Mi freend hath seid to me so wel

That he me esid hath somdell,   3390
And eke allegged of my torment;
For thurgh hym had I hardement
Agayn to Daunger for to go,
To preve if I myght meke hym soo.
    To Daunger came I all ashamed,   3395
The which aforn me hadde blamed,
Desiryng for to pese my woo;
But over hegge durst I not goo,
For he forbed me the passage.
I fond hym cruel in his rage,   3400
And in his hond a gret burdoun.
To hym I knelide lowe adoun,
Ful meke of port, and symple of chere,
And seide, "Sir, I am comen heere
Oonly to aske of you mercy.   3405
That greveth me full gretly
That evere my lyf I wratthed you;
But for to amenden I am come now,
With all my myght, bothe loude and stille,
To doon right at youre owne wille.   3410
For Love made me for to doo
That I have trespassed hidirto;
Fro whom I ne may withdrawe myn hert.
Yit shall I never, for joy ne smert,
What so bifalle, good or ill,   3415
Offende more ageyn youre will.
Lever I have endure disese,
Than do that shulde you displese.
    I you require and pray that ye
Of me have mercy and pitee,   3420
To stynte your ire that greveth soo,
That I wol swere for ever mo
To be redressid at youre likyng,
If I trespasse in ony thyng;
Save that I pray thee graunte me   3425
A thyng that may not warned be,
That I may love, all oonly;
Noon other thyng of you aske I.
I shall doon [al your wyl], iwys,
If of youre grace ye graunte me this.   3430
And ye may not letten me,
For wel wot ye that love is free,
And I shall loven, sith that I will,
Who ever like it well or ill;
And yit ne wold I, for all Fraunce,   3435
Do thyng to do you displesaunce."
    Thanne Daunger fil in his entent
For to foryeve his maltalent;
But all his wratthe yit at laste
He hath relesed, I preyde so faste.   3440
Shortly he seide, "Thy request
Is not to mochel dishonest,
Ne I wole not werne it thee;

For yit nothyng engreveth me.
For though thou love thus evermor,   3445
To me is neither softe ne soor.
Love where that the list; what recchith me,
So [thou] fer fro my roses be?
Trust not on me, for noon assay,
If ony tyme thou passe the hay."   3450
    Thus hath he graunted my praiere.
Thanne wente I forth, withouten were,
Unto my freend, and tolde hym all,
Which was right joyful of my tall.
He seide, "Now goth wel thyn affaire.   3455
He shall to thee be debonaire;
Though he aforn was dispitous,
He shall heere aftir be gracious.
If he were touchid on som good veyne,
He shuld yit rewen on thi peyne.   3460
Suffre, I rede, and no boost make,
Till thou at good mes maist hym take.
By sufferaunce and wordis softe
A man may overcome ofte
Hym that aforn he hadde in drede,   3465
In bookis sothly as I rede."
    Thus hath my freend with gret comfort
Avaunced me with high disport,
Which wolde me good as mych as I.
And thanne anoon full sodeynly   3470
I tok my leve, and streight I went
Unto the hay, for gret talent
I hadde to sen the fresh botoun
Wherynne lay my salvacioun;
And Daunger tok kep if that I   3475
Kepe hym covenaunt trewely.
So sore I dradde his manasyng,
I durst not breke his biddyng;
For, lest that I were of hym shent,
I brak not his comaundement,   3480
For to purchase his good wil.
It was [nat] for to come ther-til;
His mercy was to fer bihynde.
I wepte for I ne myght it fynde.
I compleyned and sighed sore,   3485
And langwisshed evermore,
For I durst not over goo
Unto the Rose I loved soo.
Thurghout my demyng outerly
Than he had knowlege certanly   3490
That Love me ladde in sich a wise
That in me ther was no feyntise,
Falsheed, ne no trecherie.
And yit he, full of vylanye,
Of disdeyn, and cruelte,   3495
On me ne wolde have pite,
His cruel will for to refreyne,

Though I wepe alwey, and me compleyne.
  And while I was in this torment,
Were come of grace, by God sent,   3500
Fraunchise, and with hir Pite.
Fulfild the bothen of bounte,
They go to Daunger anoon-right
To forther me with all her myght,
And helpe in worde and in dede,   3505
For well they saugh that it was nede.
First, of hir grace, dame Fraunchise
Hath taken [word] of this emprise.
She seide, "Daunger, gret wrong ye do,
To worche this man so myche woo,   3510
Or pynen hym so angerly;
It is to you gret villany.
I can not see why, ne how,
That he hath trespassed ageyn you,
Save that he loveth; wherfore ye shulde   3515
The more in cherete of hym holde.
The force of love makith hym do this;
Who wolde hym blame he dide amys?
He leseth more than ye may do;
His peyne is hard, ye may see, lo!   3520
And Love in no wise wolde consente
That he have power to repente;
For though that quyk ye wolde hym sloo,
Fro love his herte may not goo.
Now, swete sir, is it youre ese   3525
Hym for to angre or disese?
Allas! what may it you avaunce
To don to hym so gret grevaunce?
What worship is it agayn hym take,
Or on youre man a werre make,   3530
Sith he so lowly, every wise,
Is redy, as ye lust devise?
If Love hath caught hym in his las,
You for t'obeye in every caas,
And ben youre suget at youre will,   3535
Shuld ye therfore willen hym ill?
Ye shulde hym spare more, all out,
Than hym that is bothe proud and stout.
Curtesie wol that ye socoure
Hem that ben meke undir youre cure.   3540
His herte is hard that wole not meke,
Whanne men of mekenesse hym biseke."
  "That is certeyn," seide Pite;
"We se ofte that humilite
Bothe ire, and also felonye,   3545
Venquyssheth, and also malencolye,
To stonde forth in such duresse,
This cruelte and wikkidnesse.
Wherfore I pray you, sir Daunger,
For to mayntene no lenger heer   3550
Such cruel werre agayn youre man,

As hoolly youres as ever he can;
Nor that ye worchen no more woo
Upon this caytif, that langwisshith soo,   3555
Which wole no more to you trespasse,
But putte hym hoolly in youre grace.
His offense ne was but lite;
The God of Love it was to wite,
That he youre thrall so gretly is,   3560
And if ye harme hym, ye don amys.
For he hath had full hard penaunce,
Sith that ye refte hym th'aqueyntaunce
Of Bialacoil, his moste joye,
Which alle his peynes myght acoye.   3565
He was biforn anoyed sore,
But thanne ye doubled hym well more;
For he of blis hath ben full bare,
Sith Bialacoil was fro hym fare.
Love hath to hym do gret distresse,   3570
He hath no nede of more duresse.
Voideth from hym youre ire, I rede;
Ye may not wynnen in this dede.
Makith Bialacoil repeire ageyn,
And haveth pite upon his peyn;   3575
For Fraunchise wole, and I, Pite,
That mercyful to hym ye be;
And sith that she and I accorde,
Have upon hym misericorde.
For I you pray and eke moneste   3580
Nought to refusen oure requeste;
For he is hard and fell of thought,
That for us twoo wole do right nought."
  Daunger ne myght no more endure;
He mekede hym unto mesure.
  "I wole in no wise," seith Daunger,   3585
Denye that ye have asked heer;
It were to gret uncurtesie.
I wole ye have the companye
Of Bialacoil, as ye devise;
I wole hym lette in no wise."   3590
  To Bialacoil thanne wente in hy
Fraunchise, and seide full curteisly:
"Ye have to longe be deignous
Unto this lover, and daungerous,
Fro him to withdrawe your presence,   3595
Which hath do to him gret offence,
That ye not wolde upon him se;
Wherfore a sorouful man is he.
Shape ye to paye him, and to please,
Of my love if ye wol have ease.   3600
Fulfyl his wyl, sith that ye knowe
Daunger is daunted and brought lowe
Through help of me and of Pyte.
You dar no more afered be."
  "I shal do right as ye wyl,"   3605

Saith Bialacoil, "for it is skyl,
Sithe Daunger wol that it so be."
Than Fraunchise hath him sent to me.

Byalacoil at the begynnyng
Salued me in his commyng. 3610
No straungenesse was in him sen,
No more than he ne had wrathed ben.
As fayr semblaunt than shewed he me,
And goodly, as aforn dyd he;
And by the hond, withouten doute, 3615
Within the haye, right al aboute
He ladde me, with right good cher,
Al envyron the verger,
That Daunger hadde me chased fro.
Now have I leave overal to go; 3620
Now am I raysed, at my devys,
Fro helle unto paradys.
Thus Bialacoil, of gentylnesse,
With al his payne and besynesse,
Hath shewed me, only of grace, 3625
The estres of the swote place.

I saw the Rose, whan I was nygh,
Was greatter woxen and more high,
Fressh, roddy, and fayr of hewe,
Of colour ever yliche newe. 3630
And whan I hadde it longe sen,
I saw that through the leves gren
The Rose spredde to spaunysshing;
To sene it was a goodly thyng.
But it ne was so spred on bred 3635
That men within myght knowe the sed;
For it covert was and close,
Bothe with the leves and with the rose.
The stalke was even and grene upright,
It was theron a goodly syght; 3640
And wel the better, withoute wene,
For the seed was nat sene.
Ful fayre it spradde (God it blesse!),
For such another, as I gesse,
Aforn ne was, ne more vermayle. 3645
I was abawed for marveyle,
For ever the fayrer that it was,
The more I am bounden in Loves laas.

Longe I abod there, soth to saye,
Tyl Bialacoil I gan to praye, 3650
Whan that I saw him in no wyse
To me warnen his servyse,
That he me wolde graunt a thyng,
Which to remembre is wel syttyng;
This is to sayn, that of his grace 3655
He wolde me yeve leysar and space,
To me that was so desyrous,
To have a kyssynge precious
Of the goodly fresshe Rose,

That so swetely smelleth in my nose. 3660
"For if it you displeased nought,
I wolde gladly, as I have sought,
Have a cos therof freely,
Of your yefte; for certainly,
I wol non have but by your leve, 3665
So loth me were you for to greve."

He sayde, "Frend, so God me spede,
Of Chastite I have such drede;
Thou shuldest nat warned be for me,
But I dar nat, for Chastyte. 3670
Agayn her dar I nat mysdo,
For alway byddeth she me so
To yeve no lover leave to kys;
For who therto may wynnen, ywis,
He of the surplus of the pray 3675
May lyve in hoope to get som day.
For whoso kyssynge may attayne,
Of loves payne hath (soth to sayne)
The beste and most avenaunt,
And ernest of the remenaunt." 3680

Of his answere I sighed sore;
I durst assaye him tho no more,
I hadde such drede to greve him ay.
A man shulde nat to moche assay
To chafe hys frend out of measure, 3685
Nor putte his lyf in aventure;
For no man at the firste strok
Ne may nat felle down an ok;
Nor of the reysyns have the wyn,
Tyl grapes be rype, and wel afyn 3690
Be sore empressid, I you ensure,
And drawen out of the pressure.
But I, forpeyned wonder stronge,
Thought that I abood right longe
Aftir the kis, in peyne and woo, 3695
Sith I to kis desired soo;
Till that, rewyng on my distresse,
Ther to me Venus the goddesse,
Which ay werreyeth Chastite,
Cam of hir grace to socoure me, 3700
Whos myght is knowe fer and wide,
For she is modir of Cupide,
The God of Love, blynde as stoon,
That helpith lovers many oon.
This lady brought in hir right hond 3705
Of brennyng fyr a blasyng brond;
Wherof the flawme and hoote fir
Hath many a lady in desir
Of love brought, and sore het,
And in hir servise her hertes set. 3710
This lady was of good entaile,
Right wondirfull of apparayle.
Bi hir atyr so bright and shen

Men myght perceyve well and sen
She was not of religioun. 3715
Nor I nell make mencioun
Nor of robe, nor of tresour,
Of broche, neithir of hir riche attour;
Ne of hir girdill aboute hir side,
For that I nyll not longe abide. 3720
But knowith wel that certeynly
She was araied richely.
Devoyd of pryde certeyn she was;
To Bialacoil she wente apas,
And to hym shortly, in a clause, 3725
She seide, "Sir, what is the cause
Ye ben of port so daungerous
Unto this lover and deynous,
To graunte hym nothyng but a kis?
To warne it hym ye don amys, 3730
Sith well ye wote, how that he
Is Loves servaunt, as ye may see,
And hath beaute, wherthrough [he] is
Worthy of love to have the blis.
How he is semely, biholde and see, 3735
How he is fair, how he is free,
How he is swoote and debonair,
Of age yong, lusty, and fair.
Ther is no lady so hawteyn,
Duchesse, ne countesse, ne chasteleyn, 3740
That I nolde holde hir ungoodly
For to refuse hym outterly.
His breth is also good and swete,
And eke his lippis rody, and mete
Oonly to pleyen and to kesse. 3745
Graunte hym a kis, of gentilnesse!
His teth arn also white and clene;
Me thinkith wrong, withouten wene,
If ye now warne hym, trustith me,
To graunte that a kis have he. 3750
The lasse to helpe hym that ye haste,
The more tyme shul ye waste."
Whanne the flawme of the verry brond,
That Venus brought in hir right hond,
Hadde Bialacoil with hete smete, 3755
Anoon he bad, withouten lette,
Graunte to me the Rose kisse.
Thanne of my peyne I gan to lysse,
And to the Rose anoon wente I,
And kisside it full feithfully. 3760
Thar no man aske if I was blithe,
Whanne the savour soft and lythe
Strok to myn herte withoute more,
And me alegged of my sore,
So was I full of joye and blisse. 3765
It is fair sich a flour to kisse,
It was so swoote and saverous.

I myght not be so angwisshous
That I [ne] mote glad and joly be,
Whanne that I remembre me. 3770
Yit ever among, sothly to seyne,
I suffre noy and moche peyne.
 The see may never be so stille
That with a litel wynde it nille
Overwhelme and turne also, 3775
As it were wood, in wawis goo.
Aftir the calm the trouble sone
Mot folowe and chaunge as the moone.
Right so farith Love, that selde in oon
Holdith his anker; for right anoon 3780
Whanne they in ese wene best to lyve,
They ben with tempest all fordryve.
Who serveth Love, can telle of woo;
The stoundemele joie mot overgoo.
Now he hurteth, and now he cureth; 3785
For selde in oo poynt Love endureth.
 Now is it right me to procede,
How Shame gan medle and take hede
Thurgh whom fele angres I have had;
And how the stronge wall was maad, 3790
And the castell of brede and lengthe,
That God of Love wan with his strengthe.
All this in romance will I sette,
And for nothyng ne will I lette,
So that it lykyng to hir be, 3795
That is the flour of beaute;
For she may best my labour quyte,
That I for hir love shal endite.
 Wikkid-Tunge, that the covyne
Of every lover can devyne 3800
Worst, and addith more somdell
(For Wikkid-Tunge seith never well),
To me-ward bar he right gret hate,
Espiyng me erly and late,
Till he hath sen the grete chere 3805
Of Bialacoil and me ifeere.
He myghte not his tunge withstond
Worse to reporte than he fond,
He was so full of cursed rage.
It sat hym well of his lynage, 3810
For hym an Irish womman bar;
His tunge was fyled sharp and squar,
Poignaunt, and right kervyng,
And wonder bitter in spekyng.
For whanne that he me gan espie, 3815
He swoor, affermyng sikirlye,
Bitwene Bialacoil and me
Was yvel aquayntaunce and pryve.
He spak therof so folily
That he awakide Jelousy, 3820
Which, all afrayed in his risyng,

Whanne that he herde janglyng,
He ran anoon, as he were wood,
To Bialacoil, there that he stod,
Which hadde lever in this caas   3825
Have ben at Reynes or Amyas;
For foot-hoot, in his felonye,
To hym thus seide Jelousie:
"Why hast thou ben so necligent
To kepen, whanne I was absent,   3830
This verger heere left in thi ward?
To me thou haddist no reward,
To truste (to thy confusioun!)
Hym thus, to whom suspeccioun
I have right gret, for it is nede;   3835
It is well shewed by the dede.
Gret faute in thee now have I founde.
By God, anoon thou shalt be bounde,
And faste loken in a tour,
Withoute refuyt or socour.   3840
For Shame to longe hath be thee froo;
Over-soone she was agoo.
Whanne thou hast lost bothe drede and feere,
It semede wel she was not heere.
She was bisy in no wyse   3845
To kepe thee and [to] chastise,
And for to helpen Chastite
To kepe the roser, as thenkith me.
For thanne this boy-knave so booldely
Ne shulde not have be hardy,   3850
In this verger hadde such game,
Which now me turneth to gret shame."
     Bialacoil nyste what to sey;
Full fayn he wolde have fled awey,
For feere han hid, nere that he   3855
All sodeynly tok hym with me.
And whanne I saugh he hadde soo,
This Jelousie, take us twoo,
I was astoned, and knew no red,
But fledde awey for verrey dred.   3860
     Thanne Shame cam forth full symply
(She wende have trespaced full gretly),
Humble of hir port, and made it symple,
Weryng a vayle in stide of wymple,
As nonnys don in her abbey.   3865
By cause hir herte was in affray,
She gan to speke withynne a throwe
To Jelousie right wonder lowe.
First of his grace she bysought,
And seide, "Sire, ne leveth nought   3870
Wikkid-Tunge, that false espie,
Which is so glad to feyne and lye.
He hath you maad, thurgh flateryng,
On Bialacoil a fals lesyng.
His falsnesse is not now a-new;   3875

It is to long that he hym knew.
This is not the firste day;
For Wikkid-Tunge hath custome ay
Yonge folkis to bewreye,
And false lesynges on hem leye.   3880
     Yit nevertheles I see among,
That the loigne it is so long,
Of Bialacoil, hertis to lure,
In Loves servyse for to endure,
Drawyng suche folk hym to,   3885
That he hath nothyng with to doo.
But in sothnesse I trowe nought
That Bialacoil hadde ever in thought
To do trespas or vylonye;
But, for his modir Curtesie   3890
Hath taught hym ever to be
Good of aqueyntaunce and pryve.
For he loveth noon hevynesse,
But mirthe, and pley, and all gladnesse;
He hateth alle trecherous,   3895
Soleyn folk, and envyous;
For ye witen how that he
Wol ever glad and joyfull be
Honestly with folk to pley.
I have be negligent, in good fey,   3900
To chastise hym; therfore now I
Of herte crye you heere mercy,
That I have been so recheles
To tamen hym, withouten lees.
Of my foly I me repente;   3905
Now wole I hool sette myn entente
To kepe, bothe lowde and stille,
Bialacoil to do youre wille."
     "Shame, shame," seyde Jelousy,
"To be bytrasshed gret drede have I.   3910
Leccherie hath clombe so hye
That almoost blered is myn ye;
No wonder is, if that drede have I.
Overall regnyth Lecchery,
Whos myght growith nyght and day.   3915
Bothe in cloistre and in abbey
Chastite is werreyed overall.
Therfore I wole with siker wall
Close bothe roses and roser.
I have to longe in this maner   3920
Left hem unclosid wilfully;
Wherfore I am right inwardly
Sorowfull, and repente me.
But now they shall no lenger be
Unclosid; and yit I drede sore,   3925
I shall repente ferthermore,
For the game goth all amys.
Counsell I must newe, ywys.
I have to longe tristed thee,

But now it shal no lenger be,   3930
For he may best, in every cost,
Disceyve, that men tristen most.
I see wel that I am nygh shent,
But if I sette my full entent
Remedye to purveye.   3935
Therfore close I shall the weye
Fro hem that wole the Rose espie,
And come to wayte me vilonye,
For, in good feith and in trouthe,
I wole not lette, for no slouthe,   3940
To lyve the more in sikirnesse,
To make anoon a forteresse,
T'enclose the roses of good savour.
In myddis shall I make a tour
To putte Bialacoil in prisoun;   3945
For evere I drede me of tresoun.
I trowe I shal hym kepe soo
That he shal have no myght to goo
Aboute to make companye
To hem that thenke of vylanye;   3950
Ne to no such as hath ben heere
Aforn, and founde in hym good chere,
Which han assailed hym to shende,
And with her trowandyse to blende.
A fool is eythe to bigyle;   3955
But may I lyve a litel while,
He shal forthenke his fair semblaunt."
     And with that word came Drede avaunt,
Which was abasshed, and in gret fere,
Whanne he wiste Jelousie was there.   3960
He was for drede in sich affray
That not a word durste he say,
But quakyng stod full still aloon,
Til Jelousie his weye was gon,
Save Shame, that him not forsok.   3965
Bothe Drede and she ful sore quok;
That atte laste Drede abreyde,
And to his cosyn Shame seide:
"Shame," he seide, "in sothfastnesse,
To me it is gret hevynesse   3970
That the noyse so fer is go,
And the sclaundre of us twoo.
But sithe that it is byfalle,
We may it not ageyn calle,
Whanne onys sprongen is a fame.   3975
For many a yeer withouten blame
We han passed, not ashamed,
For many an Aprill and many a May
We han passed, not ashamed,
Till Jelousie hath us blamed   3980
Of mystrust and suspecioun,
Causeles, withoute enchesoun.
Go we to Daunger hastily,

And late us shewe hym openly
That he hath not aright wrought,   3985
Whanne that he sette nought his thought
To kepe better the purprise;
In his doyng he is not wise.
He hath to us do gret wrong,
That hath suffred now so long   3990
Bialacoil to have his wille,
All his lustes to fulfille,
He must amende it utterly,
Or ellys shall he vilaynesly
Exiled be out of this lond;   3995
For he the werre may not withstond
Of Jelousie, nor the greef,
Sith Bialacoil is at myscheef."
     To Daunger, Shame and Drede anoon
The righte weye ben [a-]goon.   4000
The cherl thei founden hem aforn,
Liggyng undir an hawethorn;
Undir his heed no pilowe was,
But in the stede a trusse of gras.
He slombred, and a nappe he tok,   4005
Tyll Shame pitously hym shok,
And grete manace on hym gan make.
"Why slepist thou, whanne thou shulde wake?"
Quod Shame; "thou doist us vylanye!
Who tristith thee, he doth folye,   4010
To kepe roses or botouns,
Whanne thei ben faire in her sesouns.
Thou art woxe to familiere,
Where thou shulde be straunge of chere,
Stout of thi port, redy to greve.   4015
Thou doist gret folye for to leve
Bialacoil hereinne to calle
The yonder man to shenden us alle.
Though that thou slepe, we may here
Of Jelousie gret noyse heere.   4020
Art thou now late? Ris up in hy,
And stop sone and delyverly
All the gappis of the haye.
Do no favour, I thee praye.
It fallith nothyng to thy name   4025
To make faire semblaunt, where thou maist
        blame.
Yf Bialacoil be sweete and free,
Dogged and fell thou shuldist be,
Froward and outrageous, ywis;
A cherl chaungeth that curteis is.   4030
This have I herd ofte in seiyng,
That man [ne] may, for no dauntyng,
Make a sperhauk of a bosard.
Alle men wole holde thee for musard,
That debonair have founden thee;   4035
It sittith thee nought curteis to be.

To do men plesaunce or servise,
In thee it is recreaundise.
Let thi werkis fer and ner
Be like thi name, which is Daunger."   4040
    Thanne, all abawid in shewing,
Anoon spak Drede, right thus seiyng,
And seide, "Daunger, I drede me
That thou ne wolt bisy be
To kepe that thou hast to kepe;   4045
Whanne thou shuldist wake, thou art aslepe.
Thou shalt be greved, certeynly,
If the aspie Jelousy,
Or if he fynde thee in blame.
He hath to-day assailed Shame,   4050
And chased awey with gret manace
Bialacoil out of this place,
And swereth shortly that he shall
Enclose hym in a sturdy wall;
And all is for thi wikkednesse,   4055
For that thee faileth straungenesse.
Thyn herte, I trowe, be failed all;
Thou shalt repente in speciall,
If Jelousie the soothe knewe;
Thou shalt forthenke and sore rewe."   4060
    With that the cherl his clubbe gan shake,
Frounyng his eyen gan to make,
And hidous chere; as man in rage
For ire he brente in his visage.
Whanne that he herd hym blamed soo,   4065
He seide, "Out of my wit I goo!
To be discomfyt I have gret wrong.
Certis, I have now lyved to long,
Sith I may not this closer kepe.
All quyk I wolde be dolven deepe,   4070
If ony man shal more repeire
Into this gardyn, for foule or faire.
Myn herte for ire goth a-fere,
That I let ony entre heere.
I have do folie, now I see,   4075
But now it shall amended bee.
Who settith foot heere ony more,
Truly he shall repente it sore;
For no man moo into this place
Of me to entre shal have grace.   4080
Lever I hadde with swerdis tweyne
Thurghoute myn herte, in every veyne,
Perced to be, with many a wounde,
Thanne slouthe shulde in me be founde.
From hennes forth, by nyght or day,   4085
I shall defende it, if I may,
Withouten ony excepcioun
Of ech maner condicioun;
And if I it eny man graunt,
Holdeth me for recreaunt."   4090

Thanne Daunger on his feet gan stond,
And hente a burdoun in his hond.
Wroth in his ire, ne lefte he nought,
But thurgh the verger he hath sought.
If he myght fynde hole or trace,   4095
Wherethurgh that me mot forth-by pace,
Or ony gappe, he dide it close,
That no man myghte touche a rose
Of the roser all aboute.
He shitteth every man withoute.   4100
    Thus day by day Daunger is wers,
More wondirfull and more dyvers,
And feller eke than evere he was.
For hym full ofte I synge "allas!";
For I ne may nought, thurgh his ire,   4105
Recovere that I moost desire.
Myn herte, allas, wole brest a-twoo,
For Bialacoil I wratthed soo.
For certeynly, in every membre
I quake, whanne I me remembre   4110
Of the botoun, which I wolde
Full ofte a day sen and biholde.
And whanne I thenke upon the kiss,
And how myche joye and bliss
I hadde thurgh the savour swete,   4115
For want of it I grone and grete.
Me thenkith I fele yit in my nose
The swete savour of the Rose;
And now I woot that I mot goo
So fer the freshe floures froo,   4120
To me full welcome were the deth.
Absens therof, allas! me sleeth.
For whilom with this Rose, allas!
I touched nose, mouth, and face;
But now the deth I must abide.   4125
But Love consente another tyde
That onys I touche may and kisse,
I trowe my peyne shall never lisse;
Theron is all my coveitise,
Which brent myn herte in many wise.   4130
Now shal repaire agayn sighinge,
Long wacche on nyghtis, and no slepinge,
Thought in wisshing, torment and woo,
With many a turnyng to and froo,
That half my peyne I can not telle.   4135
For I am fallen into helle
From paradys, and wel the more
My turment greveth; more and more
Anoieth now the bittirnesse,
That I toforn have felt swetnesse.   4140
And Wikkid-Tunge, thurgh his falshede,
Causeth all my woo and drede.
On me he leieth a pitous charge,
Bicause his tunge was to large.

Now it is tyme, shortly, that I   4145
Telle you som thyng of Jelousy,
That was in gret suspecioun.
Aboute hym lefte he no masoun,
That stoon coude leye, ne querrour;
He hirede hem to make a tour.   4150
And first, the roses for to kep,
Aboute hem made he a diche deep,
Right wondir large, and also brood;
Upon the whiche also stod
Of squared stoon a sturdy wall,   4155
Which on a cragge was founded all,
And right gret thikkenesse eke it bar.
Aboute, it was founded squar,
An hundred fademe on every sid;
It was all liche longe and wid.   4160
Lest ony tyme it were assayled,
Ful wel aboute it was batayled,
And rounde enviroun eke were set
Ful many a riche and fair touret.
At every corner of this wall   4165
Was set a tour full pryncipall;
And everich hadde, withoute fable,
A porte-colys defensable
To kepe of enemyes, and to greve,
That there her force wolde preve.   4170
And eke amydde this purprise
Was maad a tour of gret maistrise;
A fairer saugh no man with sight,
Large and wid, and of gret myght.
They [ne] dredde noon assaut   4175
Of gyn, gunne, nor skaffaut.
The temperure of the morter
Was maad of lycour wonder der;
Of quykke lym, persant and egre,
The which was tempred with vynegre.   4180
The stoon was hard, of ademant,
Wherof they made the foundement.
The tour was round, maad in compas;
In all this world no riccher was,
Ne better ordeigned therwithall.   4185
Aboute the tour was maad a wall,
So that bitwixt that and the tour
Rosers were sette of swete savour,
With many roses that thei bere;
And eke withynne the castell were   4190
Spryngoldes, gunnes, bows, and archers;
And eke above, atte corners,
Men seyn over the wall stonde
Grete engynes, who were nygh honde.
And in the kernels, heere and there,   4195
Of arblasters gret plente were;
Noon armure myght her strok withstonde;
It were foly to prece to honde.

Withoute the diche were lystes maad,
With wall batayled large and brad,   4200
For men and hors shulde not atteyne
To neigh the dyche, over the pleyne.
Thus Jelousie hath enviroun
Set aboute his garnysoun
With walles rounde and diche dep,   4205
Oonly the roser for to kep.
And Daunger, erly and late,
The keyes kepte of the utter gate,
The which openeth toward the eest.
And he hadde with hym atte leest   4210
Thritty servauntes, echon by name.
That other gate kepte Shame,
Which openede, as it was couth,
Toward the partie of the south.
Sergeauntes assigned were hir to   4215
Ful many, hir wille for to doo.
Thanne Drede hadde in hir baillie
The kepyng of the conestablerye
Toward the north, I undirstond,
That openyde upon the lyft hond;   4220
The which for nothyng may be sure,
But if she do bisy cure,
Erly on morowe and also late,
Strongly to shette and barre the gate.
Of every thing that she may see   4225
Drede is aferd, wherso she be;
For with a puff of litell wynd
Drede is astonyed in hir mynd.
Therfore, for stelyng of the Rose,
I rede hir nought the yate unclose.   4230
A foulis flight wol make hir flee,
And eke a shadowe, if she it see.
Thanne Wikked-Tunge, ful of envye,
With soudiours of Normandye,
As he that causeth all the bate,   4235
Was keper of the fourthe gate,
And also to the tother three
He wente full ofte, for to see.
Whanne his lot was to wake anyght,
His instrumentis wolde he dight,   4240
For to blowe and make sown
Ofte thanne he hath enchesoun;
And walken oft upon the wall,
Corners and wikettis overall
Full narwe serchen and espie;   4245
Though he nought fond, yit wolde he lye.
Discordaunt ever fro armonye,
And distoned from melodie,
Controve he wolde, and foule fayle,
With hornepipes of Cornewaile.   4250
In floytes made he discordaunce,
And in his musyk, with myschaunce!

He wolde seyn, with notes newe,
That he fond no womman trewe,
Ne that he saugh never in his lyf   4255
Unto hir husbonde a trewe wyf,
Ne noon so ful of honeste
That she nyl laughe and mery be,
Whanne that she hereth, or may espie,
A man speken of leccherie.   4260
Everich of hem hath som vice:
Oon is dishonest, another is nyce;
If oon be full of vylanye,
Another hath a likerous ye;
If oon be full of wantonesse,   4265
Another is a chideresse.
  Thus   Wikked-Tunge — God   yeve   him
    shame! —
Can putt hem everychon in blame,
Withoute desert and causeles;
He lieth, though they ben giltles.   4270
I have pite to sen the sorwe
That waketh bothe eve and morwe,
To innocentis doith such grevaunce.
I pray God yeve him evel chaunce,
That he ever so bisy is   4275
Of ony womman to seyn amys!
Eke Jelousie God confound,
That hath maad a tour so round,
And made aboute a garisoun,
To sette Bealacoil in prisoun,   4280
The which is shet there in the tour,
Ful longe to holde there sojour,
There for to lyve in penaunce.
And for to do hym more grevaunce,
Ther hath ordeyned Jelousie   4285
An olde vekke, for to espye
The maner of his governaunce;
The whiche devel, in hir enfaunce,
Hadde lerned of loves art,
And of his pleyes tok hir part;   4290
She was expert in his servise.
She knew ech wrench and every gise
Of love, and every wile;
It was [the] harder hir to gile.
Of Bealacoil she tok ay hede,   4295
That evere he lyveth in woo and drede.
He kepte hym koy and eke pryve,
Lest in hym she hadde see
Ony foly countenaunce,
For she knew all the olde daunce.   4300
And aftir this, whanne Jelousie
Hadde Bealacoil in his baillie,
And shette hym up that was so fre,
For seur of hym he wolde be,
He trusteth sore in his castell;   4305

The stronge werk hym liketh well.
He dradde not that no glotouns
Shulde stele his roses or botouns.
The roses weren assured all,
Defenced with the stronge wall.   4310
Now Jelousie full well may be
Of drede devoid in liberte,
Whether that he slepe or wake,
For of his roses may noon be take.
  But I, allas! now morne shall;   4315
Bicause I was withoute the wall,
Full moche dool and moone I made.
Who hadde wist what woo I hadde,
I trowe he wolde have had pite.
Love to deere hadde soold to me   4320
The good that of his love hadde I.
I wende a bought it all queyntly;
But now, thurgh doublyng of my peyn,
I see he wolde it selle ageyn,
And me a newe bargeyn leere,   4325
The which all-oute the more is deere,
For the solas that I have lorn,
Thanne I hadde it never aforn.
Certayn, I am ful lik in deed
To hym that cast in erthe his seed,   4330
And hath joie of the newe spryng,
Whanne it greneth in the gynnyng,
And is also fair and fresh of flour,
Lusty to seen, swoote of odour;
But er he it in sheves shere,   4335
May falle a weder that shal it dere,
And make it to fade and falle,
The stalke, the greyn, and floures alle;
That to the tylyer is fordon
The hope that he hadde to soon.   4340
I drede, certeyn, that so fare I;
For hope and travaile sikerly
Ben me byraft all with a storm;
The flour nyl seeden of my corn.
For Love hath so avaunced me,   4345
Whanne I bigan my pryvite
To Bialacoil all for to tel,
Whom I ne fond froward ne fel,
But tok a-gree all hool my play.
But Love is of so hard assay,   4350
That al at oonys he reved me,
Whanne I wende best aboven to have be.
It is of Love, as of Fortune,
That chaungeth ofte, and nyl contune;
Which whilom wol on folk smyle,   4355
And glowmbe on hem another while;
Now freend, now foo, [thow] shalt hir feel;
For [in] a twynklyng turneth hir wheel;
She can writhe hir heed awey;

This is the concours of hir pley.   4360
She can areise that doth morne,
And whirle adown, and overturne
Who sittith hyest, but as hir lust.
A fool is he that wole hir trust;
For it is I that am come down,   4365
Thurgh change and revolucioun!
Sith Bealacoil mot fro me twynne,
Shet in the prisoun yond withynne,
His absence at myn herte I fele;
For all my joye and all myn hele   4370
Was in hym and in the Rose,
That but yon wal, which hym doth close,
Opene that I may hym see,
Love nyl not that I cured be
Of the peynes that I endure,   4375
Nor of my cruel aventure.
    A, Bialacoil, myn owne deer!
Though thou be now a prisoner,
Kep atte leste thyn herte to me,
And suffre not that it daunted be;   4380
Ne lat not Jelousie, in his rage,
Putten thin herte in no servage.
Although he chastice thee withoute,
And make thy body unto hym loute,
Have herte as hard as dyamaunt,   4385
Stedefast, and nought pliaunt.
In prisoun though thi body be,
At large kep thyn herte free;
A trewe herte wole not plie
For no manace that it may drye.   4390
If Jelousie doth thee payn,
Quyte hym his while thus agayn,
To venge thee, atte leest in thought,
If other way thou maist nought;
And in this wise sotilly   4395
Worche, and wynne the maistry.
But yit I am in gret affray,
Lest thou do not as I say.
I drede thou canst me gret maugre,
That thou enprisoned art for me;   4400
But that [is] not for my trespas,
For thurgh me never discovred was
Yit thyng that oughte be secree.
Wel more anoy is in me,
Than is in thee, of this myschaunce;   4405
For I endure more hard penaunce,
Then ony can seyn or thynke,
That for the sorwe almost I synke.
Whanne I remembre me of my woo,
Full nygh out of my witt I goo.   4410
Inward myn herte I feele blede,
For comfortles the deth I drede.
Owe I not wel to have distresse,

Whanne false, thurgh hir wikkednesse,
And traitours, that arn envyous,   4415
To noyen me be so corajous?
A, Bialacoil, full wel I see
That they hem shape to disceyve thee,
To make thee buxom to her lawe,
And with her corde thee to drawe,   4420
Where so hem lust, right at her will.
I drede they have thee brought thertill.
Withoute comfort, thought me sleeth;
This game wole brynge me to my deeth.
For if youre goode wille I leese,   4425
I mot be deed; I may not chese.
And if that thou foryete me,
Myn herte shal nevere in likyng be;
Nor elleswhere fynde solas,
If I putt out of youre gras,   4430
As it shal never been, I hope;
Thanne shulde I falle in wanhope.
    Allas, in wanhope? nay, pardee!
For I wole never dispeired be.
If hope me faile, thanne am I   4435
Ungracious and unworthy.
In hope I wole comforted be;
For Love, whanne he bitaught hir me,
Seide that Hope, whereso I goo,
Shulde ay be relees to my woo.   4440
But what and she my baalis beete,
And be to me curteis and sweete?
She is in nothyng full certeyn.
Lovers she putt in full gret peyn,
And makith hem with woo to deele.   4445
Hir faire biheeste disceyveth feele;
For she wole byhote, sikirly,
And failen aftir outrely.
A! that is a full noyous thyng!
For many a lover, in lovyng,   4450
Hangeth upon hir, and trusteth faste,
Whiche leese her travel at the laste.
Of thyng to comen she woot right nought;
Therfore, if it be wysely sought,
Hir counseill foly is to take.   4455
For many tymes, whanne she wole make
A full good silogisme, I dreede
That aftirward ther shal in deede
Folwe an evell conclusioun.
This put me in confusioun;   4460
For many tymes I have it seen,
That many have bigyled been
For trust that they have set in Hope,
Which fell hem aftirward a-slope.
    But nevertheles, yit gladly she wolde   4465
That he, that wole hym with hir holde,
Hadde alle tymes his purpos cler,

Withoute deceyte or ony wer.
That she desireth sikirly;
Whanne I hir blamed, I dide foly.   4470
But what avayleth hir good wille,
Whanne she ne may staunche my stounde ille?
That helpith litel, that she may doo,
Out-take biheest unto my woo.
And heeste certeyn, in no wise,   4475
Withoute yift, is not to prise.
Whanne heest and deede asunder varie,
They doon [me have] a gret contrarie.
Thus am I possed up and doun
With dool, thought, and confusioun;   4480
Of my disese ther is no noumbre.
Daunger and Shame me encumbre,
Drede also, and Jelousie,
And Wikked-Tunge, full of envie,
Of whiche the sharpe and cruel ire   4485
Full ofte me putte in gret martire.
They han my joye fully let,
Sith Bialacoil they have bishet
Fro me in prisoun wikkidly,
Whom I love so entierly   4490
That it wole my bane bee
But I the sonner may hym see.
And yit moreover, wurst of alle,
Ther is set to kepe, foule hir bifalle!
A rympled vekke, fer ronne in age,   4495
Frownyng and yelowe in hir visage,
Which in awayt lyth day and nyght,
That noon of him may have a sight.
    Now mote my sorwe enforced be;
Full soth it is that Love yaf me   4500
Three wonder yiftes of his grace,
Whiche I have lorn now in this place,
Sith they ne may, withoute drede,
Helpen but lytel, who taketh heede.
For here availeth no Swete-Thought,   4505
And Sweete-Speche helpith right nought.
The thridde was called Swete-Lokyng,
That now is lorn, without lesyng.
    Yiftes were faire, but not forthy
They helpe me but symply,   4510
But Bialacoil loosed be,
To gon at large and to be free.
For hym my lyf lyth all in doute,
But if he come the rather oute.
Allas! I trowe it wole not ben!   4515
For how shuld I evermore hym sen?
He may not out, and that is wrong,
By cause the tour is so strong.
How shulde he out? by whos prowesse,
Out of so strong a forteresse?   4520
By me, certeyn, it nyl be doo;

God woot, I have no wit therto!
But, wel I woot, I was in rage,
Whonne I to Love dide homage.
Who was in cause, in sothfastnesse,   4525
But hirsilf, Dame Idelnesse,
Which me conveied, thurgh my praier,
To entre into that faire verger.
She was to blame me to leve,
The which now doth me soore greve.   4530
A foolis word is nought to trowe,
Ne worth an appel for to lowe;
Men shulde hym snybbe bittirly,
At pryme temps of his foly.
I was a fool, and she me leeved,   4535
Thurgh whom I am right nought releeved.
She accomplisshid all my will,
That now me greveth wondir ill.
Resoun me seide what shulde falle.
A fool mysilf I may well calle,   4540
That love asyde I had nat leyd,
And trowed that Dame Resoun seid.
Resoun hadde bothe skile and ryght,
Whanne she me blamed, with all hir myght,
To medle of love, that hath me shent;   4545
But certeyn, now I wole repent.
    And shulde I repente? Nay, parde!
A fals traitour thanne shulde I be.
The develes engynnes wolde me take,
If I my lord wolde forsake,   4550
Or Bialacoil falsly bitraye.
Shulde I at myscheef hate hym? Nay,
Sith he now, for his curtesie,
Is in prisoun of Jelousie.
Curtesie certeyn dide he me,   4555
So mych that may not yolden be,
Whanne he the hay passen me let,
To kisse the Rose, faire and swet.
Shulde I therfore cunne hym mawgre?
Nay, certeynly, it shal not be;   4560
For Love shal nevere, yif God wille,
Here of me, thurgh word or wille,
Offence or complaynt, more or lesse,
Neither of Hope nor Idilnesse.
For certis, it were wrong that I   4565
Hated hem for her curtesy.
Ther is not ellys but suffre and thynke,
And waken whanne I shulde wynke;
Abide in hope, til Love, thurgh chaunce,
Sende me socour or allegeaunce,   4570
Expectant ay till I may mete
To geten mercy of that swete.
    Whilom I thenke how Love to me
Seide he wolde take att gree
My servise, if unpacience   4575

Caused me to don offence.
He seide, "In thank I shal it take,
And high maister eke thee make,
If wikkednesse ne reve it thee;
But sone, I trowe, that shall not be."   4580
These were his wordis, by and by;
It semede he lovede me trewely.
Now is ther not but serve hym wel,
If that I thenke his thank to fel.
My good, myn harm lyth hool in me;   4585
In Love may no defaute be.
For trewe Love ne failide never man;
Sothly the faute mot nedys than —
As God forbede! — be founde in me;
And how it cometh, I can not see.   4590
Now late it goon as it may goo;
Whether Love wole socoure me or sloo,
He may do hool on me his will.
I am so sore bounde hym till,
From his servise I may not fleen;   4595
For lyf and deth, withouten wen,
Is in his hand; I may not chese;
He may me doo bothe wynne and leese.
And sith so sore he doth me greve,
Yit, if my lust he wolde acheve,   4600
To Bialacoil goodly to be,
I yeve no force what felle on me.
For though I dye, as I mot nede,
I praye Love, of his goodlyhede,
To Bialacoil do gentylnesse,   4605
For whom I lyve in such distresse,
That I mot deyen for penaunce.
But first, withoute repentaunce,
I wole me confesse in good entent,
And make in haste my testament,   4610
As lovers doon that feelen smert:
To Bialacoil leve I myn hert
All hool, withoute departyng,
Or doublenesse of repentyng.

Coment Raisoun vient a l'amant.

Thus, as I made my passage   4615
In compleynt and in cruel rage,
And I not where to fynde a leche
That couthe unto myn helpyng eche,
Sodeynly agayn comen doun
Out of hir tour I saugh Resoun,   4620
Discret and wis and full plesaunt,
And of hir port full avenaunt.
The righte weye she took to me,
Which stod in gret perplexite,
That was posshed in every side,   4625
That I nyst where I myght abide,

Till she, demurely sad of cher,
Seide to me, as she com ner: —
"Myn owne freend, art thou yit greved?
How is this quarell yit acheved   4630
Of Loves side? anoon me telle.
Hast thou not yit of love thi fille?
Art thou not wery of thy servise,
That the hath [greved] in sich wise?
What joye hast thou in thy lovyng?   4635
Is it swete or bitter thing?
Canst thou yit chese, lat me see,
What best thi socour myghte be?
   Thou servest a full noble lord,
That maketh thee thrall for thi reward,   4640
Which ay renewith thy turment,
With foly so he hath thee blent.
Thou fell in myscheef thilke day,
Whanne thou didist, the sothe to say,
Obeysaunce and eke homage.   4645
Thou wroughtest nothyng as the sage,
Whanne thou bicam his liege man;
Thou didist a gret foly than;
Thou wistest not what fell therto,
With what lord thou haddist to do.   4650
If thou haddist hym wel knowe,
Thou haddist nought be brought so lowe;
For if thou wistest what it wer,
Thou noldist serve hym half a yeer,
Not a weke, nor half a day,   4655
Ne yit an hour, withoute delay,
Ne never yloved paramours,
His lordshipp is so full of shours.
Knowest hym ought?"
      L'amaunt   "Ye, dame, parde!"
      Raisoun "Nay, nay."
      L'amaunt   "Yis, I."
      Raisoun   "Wherof? late se."   4660
      L'amaunt "Of that he seide I shulde be
Glad to have sich lord as he,
And maister of sich seignorie."
      Raisoun "Knowist hym no more?"
      L'amaunt   "Nay, certis, I,
Save that he yaf me rewles there,   4665
And wente his wey, I nyste where,
And I abood, bounde in balaunce."
      Raisoun "Lo, there a noble conisaunce!
But I wille that thou knowe hym now,
Gynnyng and eende, sith that thou   4670
Art so anguisshous and mat,
Disfigured out of astat;
Ther may no wrecche have more of woo,
Ne caytyf noon enduren soo.
It were to every man sittyng   4675
Of his lord have knowleching;

For if thou knewe hym, out of doute,
Lightly thou shulde escapen oute
Of the prisoun that marreth thee."

    L'amant "Ye, dame, sith my lord is he, 4680
And I his man, maad with myn hond,
I wolde right fayn undirstond
To knowe of what kynde he be,
If ony wolde enforme me."

    Raisoun "I wolde," seide Resoun, "thee ler,
Sith thou to lerne hast sich desir, 4686
And shewe thee, withouten fable,
A thyng that is not demonstrable.
Thou shalt [wite], withouten science,
And knowe withouten experience, 4690
The thyng that may not knowen be,
Ne wist, ne shewid, in no degre.
Thou maist the sothe of it not witen,
Though in thee it were writen.
Thou shalt not knowe therof more, 4695
While thou art reuled by his lore;
But unto hym that love wole flee,
The knotte may unclosed bee,
Which hath to thee, as it is founde,
So long be knet and not unbounde. 4700
Now set wel thyn entencioun,
To here of love discripcioun.

    Love, it is an hatefull pees,
A free acquitaunce, withoute relees,
A trouthe, fret full of falsheede, 4705
A sikernesse all set in drede.
In herte is a dispeiryng hope,
And full of hope, it is wanhope;
Wis woodnesse, and wod resoun;
A swete perell, in to droun; 4710
An hevy birthen, lyght to bere;
A wikked wawe, awey to were.
It is Caribdis perilous,
Disagreable and gracious.
It is discordaunce that can accorde, 4715
And accordaunce to discorde.
It is kunnyng withoute science,
Wisdom withoute sapience,
Wit withoute discrecioun,
Havior withoute possessioun. 4720
It is sike hele and hool seknesse,
A thurst drowned in dronkenesse,
And helthe full of maladie,
And charite full of envie,
And hunger full of habundaunce, 4725
And a gredy suffisaunce;
Delit right full of hevynesse,
And drerihed full of gladnesse;
Bitter swetnesse and swete errour,
Right evell savoured good savour; 4730

Sin that pardoun hath withynne,
And pardoun spotted withoute [with] synne.
A peyne also it is joious,
And felonye right pitous;
Also pley that selde is stable, 4735
And stedefast [stat], right mevable;
A strengthe, weyked to stonde upright,
And feblenesse full of myght;
Wit unavised, sage folie,
And joie full of turmentrie; 4740
A laughter it is, weping ay;
Reste, that traveyleth nyght and day;
Also a swete helle it is,
And a soroufull paradys;
A pleasant gayl, and esy prisoun, 4745
And, full of froste, somer sesoun;
Pryme temps full of frostes whit,
And May devoide of al delit,
With seer braunches, blossoms ungrene,
And newe fruyt, fillid with wynter tene. 4750
It is a slowe, may not forbere
Ragges, ribaned with gold, to were;
For also wel wol love be set
Under ragges, as riche rochet;
And eke as wel be amourettes 4755
In mournyng blak, as bright burnettes.
For noon is of so mochel pris,
Ne no man founden so wys,
Ne noon so high is of parage,
Ne no man founde of wit so sage, 4760
No man so hardy ne so wight,
Ne no man of so mochel myght,
Noon so fulfilled of bounte,
That he with love may daunted be.
All the world holdith this wey; 4765
Love makith all to goon myswey,
But it be they of yvel lyf,
Whom Genius cursith, man and wyf,
That wrongly werke ageyn nature.
Noon such I love, ne have no cure 4770
Of sich as Loves servauntes ben,
And wole not by my counsel flen.
For I ne preise that lovyng
Wherthurgh men, at the laste eendyng,
Shall calle hem wrecchis full of woo, 4775
Love greveth hem and shendith soo.
But if thou wolt wel Love eschewe,
For to escape out of his mewe,
And make al hool thi sorwe to slake,
No bettir counsel maist thou take 4780
Than thynke to fleen wel, iwis;
May nought helpe elles, for wite thou this,
If thou fle it, it shal flee thee;
Folowe it, and folowen shal it thee."

L'amant Whanne I hadde herde all Resoun
    seyn, 4785
Which hadde spilt hir speche in veyn,
"Dame," seide I, "I dar wel sey,
Of this avaunt me wel I may
That from youre scole so devyaunt
I am, that never the more avaunt 4790
Right nought am I thurgh youre doctrine.
I dulle under youre discipline;
I wot no more than [I] wist er,
To me so contrarie and so fer
Is every thing that ye me ler; 4795
And yit I can it all *par cuer.*
Myn herte foryetith therof right nought,
It is so writen in my thought;
And depe greven it is so tendir
That all by herte I can it rendre, 4800
And rede it over comunely;
But to mysilf lewedist am I.
But sith ye love discreven so,
And lak and preise it, bothe twoo,
Defyneth it into this letter, 4805
That I may thenke on it the better;
For I herde never diffyne it er,
And wilfully I wolde it ler."
    Raisoun "If love be serched wel and sought,
It is a syknesse of the thought 4810
Annexed and knet bitwixe tweyne,
Which male and female, with oo cheyne,
So frely byndith that they nyll twynne,
Whether so therof they leese or wynne.
The roote springith, thurgh hoot brennyng
Into disordinat desiryng 4816
For to kissen and enbrace,
And at her lust them to solace.
Of other thyng love recchith nought,
But setteth her herte and all her thought
More for delectacioun 4821
Than ony procreacioun
Of other fruyt by engendring;
Which love to God is not plesyng;
For of her body fruyt to get 4825
They yeve no force, they are so set
Upon delit to pley in-feere.
And somme have also this manere,
To feynen hem for love sek;
Sich love I preise not at a lek. 4830
For paramours they do but feyne;
To love truly they disdeyne.
They falsen ladies traitoursly,
And swern hem othes utterly,
With many a lesyng and many a fable, 4835
And all they fynden deceyvable.
And whanne they han her lust geten,

The hoote ernes they al foryeten.
Wymmen, the harm they bien full sore;
But men this thenken evermore, 4840
That lasse harm is, so mote I the,
Deceyve them than deceyved be;
And namely, where they ne may
Fynde non other mene wey.
For I wot wel, in sothfastnesse, 4845
[What man] doth now his bisynesse
With ony womman for to dele
For ony lust that he may fele,
But if it be for engendrure,
He doth trespas, I you ensure. 4850
For he shulde setten all his wil
To geten a likly thyng hym til,
And to sustene, if he myght,
And kepe forth, by kyndes right,
His owne lyknesse and semblable; 4855
For bycause al is corrumpable,
And faile shulde successioun,
Ne were ther generacioun
Oure sectis stren for to save.
Whanne fader or moder arn in grave, 4860
Her children shulde, whanne they ben deede,
Full diligent ben, in her steede,
To use that werk on such a wise
That oon may thurgh another rise.
Therfore sette Kynde therynne delit, 4865
For men therynne shulde hem delit,
And of that deede be not erk,
But ofte sithes haunt that werk.
For noon wolde drawe therof a draught,
Ne were delit, which hath hym kaught. 4870
Thus hath sotilled dame Nature;
For noon goth right, I thee ensure,
Ne hath entent hool ne parfit;
For her desir is for delyt,
The which fortened crece and eke 4875
The pley of love for-ofte seke,
And thrall hemsilf, they be so nyce,
Unto the prince of every vice.
For of ech synne it is the rote,
Unlefull lust, though it be sote, 4880
And of all yvell the racyne,
As Tulius can determyne,
Which in his tyme was full sage,
In a bok he made 'Of Age,'
Where that more he preyseth eelde, 4885
Though he be croked and unweelde,
And more of commendacioun
Than youthe in his discripcioun.
For youthe set bothe man and wyf
In all perell of soule and lyf; 4890
And perell is, but men have grace,

The tyme of youthe for to pace
Withoute ony deth or distresse,
It is so full of wyldenesse;
So ofte it doth shame or damage   4895
To hym or to his lynage.
It ledith man now up, now doun,
In mochel dissolucioun,
And makith hym love yvell company,
And lede his lyf disrewlily,   4900
And halt hym payed with noon estat.
Withynne hymsilf is such debat,
He chaungith purpos and entent,
And yalt [him] into som covent,
To lyven aftir her emprise,   4905
And lesith fredom and fraunchise,
That Nature in hym hadde set,
The which ageyn he may not get,
If he there make his mansioun,
For to abide professioun.   4910
Though for a tyme his herte absente,
It may not fayle, he shal repente,
And eke abide thilke day
To leve his abit, and gon his way,
And lesith his worshipp and his name,   4915
And dar not come ageyn for shame;
But al his lyf he doth so mourne,
By cause he dar not hom retourne,
Fredom of kynde so lost hath he
That never may recured be,   4920
But if that God hym graunte grace
That he may, er he hennes pace,
Conteyne undir obedience
Thurgh the vertu of pacience.
For Youthe sett man in all folye,   4925
In unthrift and ribaudie,
In leccherie and in outrage,
So ofte it chaungith of corage.
Youthe gynneth ofte sich bargeyn,
That may not eende withouten peyn.   4930
In gret perell is sett youthede,
Delit so doth his bridil leede.
Delit thus hangith, dred thee nought,
Bothe mannys body and his thought,
Oonly thurgh Youthe, his chaumberere,   4935
That to don yvell is customere,
And of nought elles taketh hede
But oonly folkes for to lede
Into disport and wyldenesse,
So is [she] froward from sadnesse.   4940
    But Eelde drawith hem therfro;
Who wot it nought, he may wel goo
Demande of hem that now arn olde,
That whilom Youthe hadde in holde,
Which yit remembre of tendir age,   4945

Hou it hem brought in many a rage,
And many a foly therynne wrought.
But now that Eelde hath hem thourgh-sought,
They repente hem of her folye,
That Youthe hem putte in jupardye,   4950
In perell, and in myche woo,
And made hem ofte amys to do,
And suen yvell companye,
Riot and avouterie.
    But Eelde can ageyn restreyne   4955
From sich foly, and refreyne,
And sette men by her ordinaunce
In good reule and in governaunce.
But yvell she spendith hir servise,
For no man wole hir love neither prise;   4960
She is hated, this wot I wel.
Hir acqueyntaunce wolde no man fel,
Ne han of Elde companye;
Men hate to be of hir alye.
For no man wolde bicomen old,   4965
Ne dye, whanne he is yong and bold.
And Eelde merveilith right gretly,
Whanne thei remembre hem inwardly
Of many a perelous emprise,
Which that they wrought in sondry wise,   4970
Houevere they myght, withoute blame,
Escape awey withoute shame,
In youthe, withoute damage
Or repreef of her lynage,
Loss of membre, shedyng of blod,   4975
Perell of deth, or los of good.
Wost thou nought where Youthe abit,
That men so preisen in her wit?
With Delit she halt sojour,
For bothe they dwellen in oo tour.   4980
As longe as Youthe is in sesoun,
They dwellen in oon mansioun.
Delit of Youthe wole have servise
To do what so he wole devise;
And Youthe is redy evermore   4985
For to obey, for smert of sore,
Unto Delit, and hym to yive
Hir servise, while that she may lyve.
    Where Elde abit, I wol thee telle
Shortly, and no while dwelle,   4990
For thidir byhoveth thee to goo.
If Deth in youthe thee not sloo,
Of this journey thou maist not faile.
With hir Labour and Travaile
Logged ben, with Sorwe and Woo,   4995
That never out of hir court goo.
Peyne and Distresse, Syknesse and Ire,
And Malencoly, that angry sire,
Ben of hir paleys senatours;

Gronyng and Grucchyng, hir herberjours,
The day and nyght, hir to turmente,   5001
With cruell Deth they hir presente,
And tellen hir, erliche and late,
That Deth stont armed at hir gate.
Thanne brynge they to her remembraunce
The foly dedis of hir infaunce,   5006
Whiche causen hir to mourne in woo
That Youthe hath hir bigiled so,
Which sodeynly awey is hasted.
She wepeth the tyme that she hath wasted,
Compleynyng of the preterit,   5011
And the present, that not abit,
And of hir olde vanite,
That, but aforn hir she may see
In the future som socour,   5015
To leggen hir of hir dolour,
To graunte hir tyme of repentaunce,
For her synnes to do penaunce,
And at the laste so hir governe
To wynne the joy that is eterne,   5020
Fro which go bakward Youthe hir made,
In vanite to droune and wade.
For present tyme abidith nought;
It is more swift than any thought.
So litel while it doth endure   5025
That ther nys compte ne mesure.
But hou that evere the game go,
Who list to have joie and mirth also
Of love, be it he or she,
High or lowe, who it be,   5030
In fruyt they shulde hem delyte;
Her part they may not elles quyte,
To save hemsilf in honeste.
And yit full many on I se
Of wymmen, sothly for to seyn,   5035
That desire and wolde fayn
The pley of love, they be so wilde,
And not coveite to go with childe.
And if with child they be, perchaunce,
They wole it holde a gret myschaunce;   5040
But whatsomever woo they fele,
They wole not pleyne, but concele;
But if it be ony fool or nyce,
In whom that Shame hath no justice.
For to delyt echon they drawe,   5045
That haunte this werk, bothe high and lawe,
Save sich that arn worth right nought,
That for money wole be bought.
Such love I preise in no wise,
Whanne it is goven for coveitise.   5050
I preise no womman though she be wood,
That yeveth hirsilf for ony good.
For litel shulde a man telle

Of hir, that wole hir body selle,
Be she mayde, be she wyf,   5055
That quyk wole selle hir, bi hir lif.
Hou faire chere that evere she make,
He is a wrecche, I undirtake,
That loveth such on, for swete or sour,
Though she hym calle hir paramour,   5060
And laugheth on hym, and makith hym feeste.
For certeynly no such beeste
To be loved is not worthy,
Or bere the name of druery.
Noon shulde hir please, but he were wood,
That wole dispoile hym of his good.   5066
Yit nevertheles, I wol not sey
But she, for solas and for pley,
May a jewel or other thyng
Take of her loves fre yevyng;   5070
But that she aske it in no wise,
For drede of shame of coveitise.
And she of hirs may hym, certeyn,
Withoute sclaundre yeven ageyn,
And joyne her hertes togidre so   5075
In love, and take and yeve also.
Trowe not that I wolde hem twynne,
Whanne in her love ther is no synne;
I wol that they togedre go,
And don al that they han ado,   5080
As curteis shulde and debonaire,
And in her love beren hem faire,
Withoute vice, bothe he and she,
So that alwey, in honeste,
Fro foly love they kepe hem cler,   5085
That brenneth hertis with his fer;
And that her love, in ony wise,
Be devoide of coveitise.
Good love shulde engendrid be
Of trewe herte, just, and secre,   5090
And not of such as sette her thought
To have her lust and ellis nought, —
So are they caught in Loves las,
Truly, for bodily solas.
Fleshly delit is so present   5095
With thee, that sette all thyn entent
Withoute more (what shulde I glose?)
For to gete and have the Rose;
Which makith thee so mat and wood
That thou desirest noon other good.   5100
But thou art not an inche the nerre,
But evere abidist in sorwe and werre,
As in thi face it is sene;
It makith thee bothe pale and lene;
Thy myght, thi vertu goth away.   5105
A sory gest, in goode fay,
Thou herberedest than in thyn inn,

The God of Love whanne thou let inn!
Wherfore I rede, thou shette hym oute,
Or he shall greve thee, out of doute;　5110
For to thi profit it wol turne,
If he nomore with thee sojourne.
In gret myscheef and sorwe sonken
Ben hertis, that of love arn dronken,
As thou peraventure knowen shall,　5115
Whanne thou hast lost thy tyme all,
And spent thy youthe in ydilnesse,
In waste, and wofull lustynesse.
If thou maist lyve the tyme to se
Of love for to delyvered be,　5120
Thy tyme thou shalt biwepe sore,
The whiche never thou maist restore;
For tyme lost, as men may see,
For nothyng may recovered be.
And if thou scape yit, atte laste,　5125
Fro Love, that hath thee so faste
Knytt and bounden in his las,
Certeyn I holde it but a gras.
For many oon, as it is seyn,
Have lost and spent also in veyn,　5130
In his servise, withoute socour,
Body and soule, good and tresour,
Wit, and strengthe, and eke richesse,
Of which they hadde never redresse."

　　Thus taught and preched hath Resoun,
But Love spilte hir sermoun,　5136
That was so ymped in my thought,
That hir doctrine I sette at nought.
And yitt ne seide she never a del
That I ne undirstod it wel,　5140
Word by word, the mater all;
But unto Love I was so thrall,
Which callith overall his pray,
He chasith so my thought alway,
And holdith myn herte undir his sel　5145
As trust and trew as ony stel;
So that no devocioun
Ne hadde I in the sermoun
Of dame Resoun, ne of hir red;
It tok no sojour in myn hed.　5150
For all yede out at oon ere
That in that other she dide lere.
Fully on me she lost hir lore;
Hir speche me greved wondir sore.

　　Than unto hir for ire I seide,　5155
For anger, as I dide abraide:
"Dame, and is it youre wille algate
That I not love, but that I hate
Alle men, as ye me teche?
For if I do aftir youre speche,　5160
Sith that ye seyn love is not good,

Thanne must I nedis say with mood,
If I it leve, in hatrede ay
Lyven, and voide love away
From me, [and ben] a synfull wrecche　5165
Hated of all [that love] that tecche.
I may not go noon other gate,
For other must I love or hate.
And if I hate men of-newe
More than love, it wol me rewe,　5170
As by youre preching semeth me,
For Love nothing ne preisith thee.
Ye yeve good counsel, sikirly,
That prechith me alday that I
Shulde not Loves lore alowe.　5175
He were a fool, wolde you not trowe!
In speche also ye han me taught
Another love, that knowen is naught,
Which I have herd you not repreve,
To love ech other; by youre leve,　5180
If ye wolde diffyne it me,
I wolde gladly here, to se,
At the leest, if I may lere
Of sondry loves the manere."

　　Raisoun "Certis, freend, a fool art thou,
Whan that thou nothyng wolt allow　5186
That I for thi profit say.
Yit wole I sey thee more in fay;
For I am redy, at the leste,
To accomplisshe thi requeste,　5190
But I not where it wole avayle;
In veyn, perauntre, I shal travayle.
Love ther is in sondry wise,
As I shal thee heere devise.
For som love leful is and good,　5195
I mene not that which makith thee wood,
And bringith thee in many a fit,
And ravysshith fro thee al thi wit,
It is so merveilous and queynt;
With such love be no more aqueynt.　5200

Comment Raisoun diffinist amiste

Love of freendshipp also ther is,
Which makith no man don amys,
Of wille knytt bitwixe two,
That wole not breke for wele ne woo;
Which long is likly to contune,　5205
Whanne wille and goodis ben in comune;
Grounded by Goddis ordinaunce,
Hool, withoute discordaunce;
With hem holdyng comunte
Of all her good in charite,　5210
That ther be noon excepcioun
Thurgh chaungyng of entencioun;

That ech helpe other at her neede,
And wisely hele bothe word and dede;
Trewe of menyng, devoide of slouthe,   5215
For witt is nought withoute trouthe;
So that the ton dar all his thought
Seyn to his freend, and spare nought,
As to hymsilf, without dredyng
To be discovered by wreying.   5220
For glad is that conjunccioun,
Whanne ther is noon susspecioun
[Ne lak in hem], whom they wolde prove
That trewe and parfit weren in love.
For no man may be amyable,   5225
But if he be so ferme and stable
That fortune chaunge hym not, ne blynde,
But that his freend allwey hym fynde,
Bothe pore and riche, in oo stat.
For if his freend, thurgh ony gat,   5230
Wole compleyne of his poverte,
He shulde not bide so long til he
Of his helpyng hym requere;
For good dede, don thurgh praiere,
Is sold and bought to deere, iwys,   5235
To hert that of gret valour is.
For hert fulfilled of gentilnesse
Can yvel demene his distresse;
And man that worthy is of name
To asken often hath gret shame.   5240
A good man brenneth in his thought
For shame, whanne he axeth ought.
He hath gret thought and dredeth ay
For his disese, whanne he shal pray
His freend, lest that he warned be,   5245
Til that he preve his stabilte.
But whanne that he hath founden oon
That trusty is and trewe as ston,
And assaied hym at all,
And founde hym stedefast as a wall   5250
And of his freendshipp be certeyn,
He shal hym shewe bothe joye and peyn,
And all that [he] dar thynke or sey,
Withoute shame, as he wel may.
For how shulde he ashamed be   5255
Of sich on as I tolde thee?
For whanne he woot his secre thought,
The thridde shal knowe therof right nought;
For tweyne of noumbre is bet than thre
In every counsell and secre.   5260
Repreve he dredeth never a deel,
Who that bisett his wordis wel;
For every wise man, out of drede,
Can kepe his tunge til he se nede;
And fooles can not holde her tunge;   5265
A fooles belle is soone runge.

Yit shal a trewe freend do more
To helpe his felowe of his sore,
And socoure hym, whanne he hath neede,
In all that he may don in deede;   5270
And gladder [be] that he hym plesith,
Than his felowe that he esith.
And if he do not his requeste,
He shal as mochel hym moleste
As his felow, for that he   5275
May not fulfille his volunte
Fully, as he hath requered.
If bothe the hertis Love hath fered,
Joy and woo they shull depart,
And take evenly ech his part.   5280
Half his anoy he shal have ay,
And comfort [him] what that he may;
And of his blisse parte shal he,
If love wel departed be.
And whilom of this amyte   5285
Spak Tulius in a ditee:
'Man shulde maken his request
Unto his freend, that is honest;
And he goodly shulde it fulfille,
But it the more were out of skile,   5290
And otherwise not graunte therto,
Except oonly in causes twoo:
If men his freend to deth wolde drive,
Lat hym be bisy to save his lyve;
Also if men wolen hym assayle,   5295
Of his wurshipp to make hym faile,
And hyndren hym of his renoun,
Lat hym, with full entencioun,
His dever don in ech degre
That his freend ne shamed be,   5300
In thise two caas with his myght,
Taking no kep to skile nor right,
As fer as love may hym excuse;
This oughte no man to refuse.'
This love that I have told to thee   5305
Is nothing contrarie to me;
This wole I that thou folowe wel,
And leve the tother everydel.
This love to vertu all entendith,
The tothir fooles blent and shendith.   5310
    Another love also there is,
That is contrarie unto this,
Which desir is so constreyned
That [it] is but wille feyned.
Awey fro trouthe it doth so varie   5315
That to good love it is contrarie;
For it maymeth, in many wise,
Sike hertis with coveitise.
All in wynnyng and in profit
Sich love settith his delit.   5320

This love so hangeth in balaunce
That, if it lese his hope, perchaunce,
Of lucre, that he is sett upon,
It wole faile and quenche anoon;
For no man may be amerous,   5325
Ne in his lyvyng vertuous,
But he love more, in mood,
Men for hemsilf than for her good.
For love that profit doth abide
Is fals, and bit not in no tyde.   5330
[This] love cometh of dame Fortune,
That litel while wol contune;
For it shal chaungen wonder soone,
And take eclips, right as the moone,
Whanne she is from us lett   5335
Thurgh erthe, that bitwixe is sett
The sonne and hir, as it may fall,
Be it in partie, or in all.
The shadowe maketh her bemys merke,
And hir hornes to shewe derke,   5340
That part where she hath lost hir lyght
Of Phebus fully, and the sight;
Til, whanne the shadowe is overpast,
She is enlumyned ageyn as fast,
Thurgh the brightnesse of the sonne bemes,
That yeveth to hir ageyn hir lemes.   5346
That love is right of sich nature;
Now is faire, and now obscure,
Now bright, now clipsi of manere,
And whilom dym, and whilom clere.   5350
As soone as Poverte gynneth take,
With mantel and wedis blake
Hidith of love the light awey,
That into nyght it turneth day.
It may not see richesse shyne   5355
Till the blake shadowes fyne.
For, whanne Richesse shyneth bright,
Love recovereth ageyn his light;
And whanne it failith he wol flit,
And as she groweth, so groweth it.   5360
Of this love — here what I sey! —
The riche men are loved ay,
And namely tho that sparand ben,
That wole not wasshe her hertes clen
Of the filthe nor of the vice   5365
Of gredy brennyng avarice.
The riche man full fonned is, ywys,
That weneth that he loved is.
If that his herte it undirstod,
It is not he, it is his good;   5370
He may wel witen in his thought,
His good is loved, and he right nought.
For if he be a nygard ek,
Men wole not sette by hym a lek,

But haten hym; this is the soth.   5375
Lo, what profit his catell doth!
Of every man that may hym see
It geteth hym nought but enmyte.
But he amende hym of that vice,
And knowe hymsilf, he is not wys.   5380
Certys, he shulde ay freendly be,
To gete hym love also ben free,
Or ellis he is not wise ne sage
Nomore than is a goot ramage.
That he not loveth, his dede proveth,   5385
Whan he his richesse so wel loveth
That he wole hide it ay and spare,
His pore freendis sen forfare,
To kepen ay his purpos,
Til for drede his yen clos,   5390
And til a wikked deth hym take.
Hym hadde lever asondre shake,
And late alle his lymes ryve,
Than leve his richesse in his lyve.
He thenkith parte it with no man;   5395
Certayn, no love is in hym than.
How shulde love withynne hym be,
Whanne in his herte is no pite?
That he trespasseth, wel I wat,
For ech man knowith his estat;   5400
For wel hym ought to be reproved
That loveth nought, ne is not loved.
    But sithe we arn to Fortune comen,
And han oure sermoun of hir nomen,
A wondir will y telle thee now,   5405
Thou herdist never sich oon, I trow.
I not where thou me leven shall,
Though sothfastnesse it be all,
As it is writen, and is soth,
That unto men more profit doth   5410
The froward Fortune and contraire,
Than the swote and debonaire.
And if thee thynke it is doutable,
It is thurgh argument provable;
For the debonaire and softe   5415
Falsith and bigilith ofte;
For lyche a moder she can cherish,
And mylken as doth a norys,
And of hir goode to hem deles,
And yeveth hem part of her joweles,   5420
With gret richeses and dignite;
And hem she hoteth stabilite
In a stat that is not stable,
But chaungynge ay and variable;
And fedith hem with glorie veyn,   5425
And worldly blisse noncerteyn.
Whanne she hem settith on hir whel,
Thanne wene they to be right wel,

And in so stable stat withalle,
That never they wene for to falle.   5430
And whanne they sette so highe be,
They wene to have in certeynte
Of hertly freendis so gret noumbre,
That nothyng myght her stat encombre.
They trust hem so on every side,   5435
Wenyng with hem they wolde abide
In every perell and myschaunce,
Withoute chaunge or variaunce,
Bothe of catell and of good;
And also for to spende her blood,   5440
And all her membris for to spille,
Oonly to fulfille her wille.
They maken it hool in many wise,
And hoten hem her full servise,
How sore that it do hem smerte,   5445
Into her very naked sherte!
Herte and all so hool they yive,
For the tyme that they may lyve,
So that with her flaterie
They maken foolis glorifie   5450
Of her wordis spekyng;
And han therof a rejoysyng,
And trowe hem as the Evangile;
And it is all falsheede and gile,
As they shal aftirwardes se,   5455
Whanne they arn falle in poverte,
And ben of good and catell bare;
Thanne shulde they sen who freendis ware.
For of an hundred, certeynly,
Nor of a thousand full scarsly,   5460
Ne shal they fynde unnethis oon,
Whanne poverte is comen upon.
For this Fortune that I of telle,
With men whanne hir lust to dwelle,
Makith hem to leese her conisaunce,   5465
And norishith hem in ignoraunce.
    But froward Fortune and pervers,
Whanne high estatis she doth revers,
And maketh hem to tumble doun
Of hir whel, with sodeyn tourn,   5470
And from her richesse doth hem fle,
And plongeth hem in poverte,
As a stepmoder envyous,
And leieth a plastre dolorous
Unto her hertis, wounded egre,   5475
Which is not tempred with vynegre,
But with poverte and indigence,
For to shewe, by experience,
That she is Fortune verely,
In whom no man shulde affy,   5480
Nor in hir yeftis have fiaunce,
She is so full of variaunce. —

Thus kan she maken high and lowe,
Whanne they from richesse arn throwe,
Fully to knowen, withoute were,   5485
Freend of effect and freend of chere,
And which in love weren trewe and stable,
And whiche also weren variable,
After Fortune, her goddesse,
In poverte, outher in richesse.   5490
For all she yeveth here, out of drede,
Unhap bereveth it in dede;
For Infortune lat not oon
Of freendis, whanne Fortune is gon;
I mene tho freendis that wole fle   5495
Anoon as entreth poverte.
And yit they wole not leve hem so,
But in ech place where they go
They calle hem 'wrecche,' scorne, and blame,
And of her myshappe hem diffame;   5500
And namely siche as in richesse
Pretendid moost of stablenesse,
Whanne that they sawe hym sett on lofte,
And weren of hym socoured ofte,
And most yholpe in all her neede;   5505
But now they take no maner heede,
But seyn in voice of flaterie,
That now apperith her folye,
Overall where so they fare,
And synge, 'Go, farewel, feldefare.'   5510
All suche freendis I beshrewe,
For of trewe ther be to fewe.
But sothfast freendis, what so bitide,
In every fortune wolen abide;
Thei han her hertis in such noblesse   5515
That they nyl love for no richesse,
Nor for that Fortune may hem sende
Thei wolen hem socoure and defende,
And chaunge for softe ne for sore;
For who is freend, loveth evermore.   5520
Though men drawe swerd his freend to slo,
He may not hewe her love a-two.
But, in cas that I shall sey,
For pride and ire lese it he may,
And for reprove by nycete,   5525
And discovering of privite,
With tonge woundyng, as feloun,
Thurgh venemous detraccioun.
Frend in this cas wole gon his way,
For nothyng greve hym more ne may;   5530
And for nought ellis wole he fle,
If that he love in stabilite.
And certeyn, he is wel bigon,
Among a thousand that fyndith oon.
For ther may be no richesse   5535
Ageyns frendshipp, of worthynesse;

For it ne may so high atteigne
As may the valour, soth to seyne,
Of hym that loveth trew and well.
Frendshipp is more than is catell.   5540
For freend in court ay better is
Than peny in purs, certis;
And Fortune myshappyng
Whanne upon men she is fallyng,
Thurgh mysturnyng of hir chaunce,   5545
And casteth hem out of balaunce,
She makith, thurgh hir adversite,
Men full clerly for to se
Hym that is freend in existence
From hym that is by apparence.   5550
For Ynfortune makith anoon
To knowe thy freendis fro thy foon,
By experience, right as it is.
The which is more to preise, ywis,
Than is myche richesse and tresour.   5555
For more doth profit and valour
Poverte and such adversite
Bifore, than doth prosperite;
For the toon yeveth conysaunce,
And the tother ignoraunce.   5560
    And thus in poverte is in dede
Trouthe declared fro falsheede;
For feynte frendis it wole declare,
And trewe also, what wey they fare.
For whanne he was in his richesse,   5565
These freendis, ful of doublenesse,
Offrid hym in many wise
Hert, and body, and servise.
What wolde he thanne ha yove to ha bought
To knowen openly her thought,   5570
That he now hath so clerly seen?
The lasse bigiled he shulde have ben,
And he hadde thanne perceyved it;
But richesse nold not late hym wit.
Wel more avauntage doth hym than,   5575
Sith that it makith hym a wise man,
The gret myscheef that he receyveth,
Than doth richesse that hym deceyveth.
Richesse riche ne makith nought
Hym that on tresour set his thought;   5580
For richesse stont in suffisaunce
And nothyng in habundaunce;
For suffisaunce all oonly
Makith men to lyve richely.
For he that at mycches tweyne   5585
Ne valued is in his demeigne,
Lyveth more at ese, and more is riche,
Than doth he that is chiche,
And in his berne hath, soth to seyn,
An hundred mowis of whete greyn,   5590

Though he be chapman or marchaunt,
And have of gold many besaunt.
For in the getyng he hath such woo,
And in the kepyng drede also,
And set evermore his bisynesse   5595
For to encrese, and not to lesse,
For to aument and multiply.
And though on hepis it lye hym by,
Yit never shal make his Richesse
Asseth unto his gredynesse.   5600
But the povre that recchith nought,
Save of his lyflode, in his thought,
Which that he getith with his travaile,
He dredith nought that it shall faile,
Though he have lytel worldis good,   5605
Mete, and drynke, and esy food,
Upon his travel and lyvyng,
And also suffisaunt clothyng.
Or if in syknesse that he falle,
And lothe mete and drynke withalle,   5610
Though he have noght his mete to by,
He shal bithynke hym hastily,
To putte hym oute of all daunger,
That he of mete hath no myster;
Or that he may with lytel ek   5615
Be founden, while that he is sek;
Or that men shull hym beren in hast,
To lyve til his syknesse be past,
To som maysondew biside;
He cast nought what shal hym bitide.   5620
He thenkith nought that evere he shall
Into ony syknesse fall.
    And though it falle, as it may be,
That all betyme spare shall he
As mochel as shal to hym suffice,   5625
While he is sik in ony wise,
He doth [it] for that he wole be
Content with his poverte
Withoute nede of ony man.
So myche in litel have he can,   5630
He is apaied with his fortune;
And for he nyl be importune
Unto no wight, ne onerous,
Nor of her goodes coveitous,
Therfore he spareth, it may wel ben,   5635
His pore estat for to susten.
    Or if hym lust not for to spare,
But suffrith forth, as noght ne ware,
Atte last it hapneth, as it may,
Right unto his laste day,   5640
And taketh the world as it wolde be;
For evere in herte thenkith he,
The sonner that deth hym slo,
To paradys the sonner go

He shal, there for to lyve in blisse,   5645
Where that he shal noo good misse.
Thider he hopith God shal hym sende
Aftir his wrecchid lyves ende.
Pictagoras hymsilf reherses
In a book that 'The Golden Verses'   5650
Is clepid, for the nobilite
Of the honourable ditee: —
'Thanne, whanne thou gost thy body fro,
Fre in the eir thou shalt up go,
And leven al humanite,   5655
And purely lyve in deite.'
He is a fool, withouten were,
That trowith have his countre heere.
'In erthe is not oure countre,'
That may these clerkis seyn and see   5660
In Boece of Consolacioun,
Where it is maked mencioun
Of oure contre pleyn at the ye,
By teching of philosophie,
Where lewid men myght lere wit,   5665
Whoso that wolde translaten it.
If he be sich that can wel lyve
Aftir his rente may hym yive,
And not desireth more to have
Than may fro poverte hym save,   5670
A wise man seide, as we may seen,
Is no man wrecched, but he it wen,
Be he kyng, knyght, or ribaud.
And many a ribaud is mery and baud,
That swynkith, and berith, bothe day and
         nyght,   5675
Many a burthen of gret myght,
The whiche doth hym lasse offense
For he suffrith in pacience.
They laugh and daunce, trippe and synge,
And ley not up for her lyvynge,   5680
But in the taverne all dispendith
The wynnyng that God hem sendith.
Thanne goth he, fardeles for to ber,
With as good chere as he dide er;
To swynke and traveile he not feynith,   5685
For for to robben he disdeynith;
But right anoon aftir his swynk
He goth to taverne for to drynk.
All these ar riche in abundaunce,
That can thus have suffisaunce   5690
Wel more than can an usurere,
As God wel knowith, withoute were.
For an usurer, so God me se,
Shal nevere for richesse riche be,
But evermore pore and indigent;   5695
Scarce and gredy in his entent.
    For soth it is, whom it displese,

Ther may no marchaunt lyve at ese;
His herte in sich a were is sett
That it quyk brenneth [more] to get,   5700
Ne never shal ynogh have geten,
Though he have gold in gerners yeten,
For to be nedy he dredith sore.
Wherfore to geten more and more
He set his herte and his desir;   5705
So hote he brennyth in the fir
Of coveitise, that makith hym wood
To purchace other mennes good.
He undirfongith a gret peyne,
That undirtakith to drynke up Seyne;   5710
For the more he drynkith, ay
The more he leveth, the soth to say.
Thus is thurst of fals getyng,
That last ever in coveityng,
And the angwisshe and distresse   5715
With the fir of gredynesse.
She fightith with hym ay, and stryveth,
That his herte asondre ryveth;
Such gredynesse hym assaylith
That whanne he most hath, most he failith.
Phisiciens and advocates   5721
Gon right by the same yates;
They selle her science for wynnyng,
And haunte her craft for gret getyng.
Her wynnyng is of such swetnesse   5725
That if a man falle in siknesse,
They are full glad, for her encres;
For by her wille, withoute lees,
Everich man shulde be sek,
And though they die, they sette not a lek.   5730
After, whanne they the gold have take,
Full litel care for hem they make.
They wolde that fourty were seke at onys,
Ye, two hundred, in flesh and bonys,
And yit two thousand, as I gesse,   5735
For to encrecen her richesse.
They wole not worchen, in no wise,
But for lucre and coveitise;
For fysic gynneth first by *fy*,
The physicien also sothely;   5740
And sithen it goth fro *fy* to *sy*:
To truste on hem, it is foly;
For they nyl, in no maner gre,
Do right nought for charite.
    Eke in the same secte ar sett   5745
All tho that prechen for to get
Worshipes, honour, and richesse.
Her hertis arn in gret distresse,
That folk lyve not holily.
But aboven all, specialy,   5750
Sich as prechen [for] veynglorie,

And toward God have no memorie,
But forth as ypocrites trace,
And to her soules deth purchace,
And outward shewen holynesse,   5755
Though they be full of cursidnesse.
Not liche to the apostles twelve,
They deceyve other and hemselve;
Bigiled is the giler than.
For prechyng of a cursed man,   5760
Though [it] to other may profite,
Hymsilf it availeth not a myte;
For ofte good predicacioun
Cometh of evel entencioun.
To hym not vailith his preching,   5765
All helpe he other with his teching;
For where they good ensaumple take,
There is he with veynglorie shake.

But late us leven these prechoures,
And speke of hem that in her toures   5770
Hepe up hir gold, and faste shette,
And sore theron her herte sette.
They neither love God ne drede;
They kepe more than it is nede,
And in her bagges sore it bynde,   5775
Out of the sonne and of the wynde;
They putte up more than nede ware,
Whanne they seen pore folk forfare,
For hunger die, and for cold quake;
God can wel vengeaunce therof take!   5780
Three gret myscheves hem assailith,
And thus in gadring ay travaylith;
With myche peyne they wynne richesse,
And drede hem holdith in distresse,
To kepe that they gadre faste;   5785
With sorwe they leve it at the laste;
With sorwe they bothe dye and lyve,
That unto richesse her hertis yive;
And in defaute of love it is.
As it shewith ful wel, iwys.   5790
For if thise gredy, the sothe to seyn,
Loveden and were loved ageyn,
And good love regned overall,
Such wikkidnesse ne shulde fall;
But he shulde yeve that most good had 5795
To hem that weren in nede bistad,
And lyve withoute false usure,
For charite full clene and pure.
If they hem yeve to goodnesse,
Defendyng hem from ydelnesse,   5800
In all this world thanne pore noon
We shulde fynde, I trowe, not oon.
But chaunged is this world unstable;
For love is overall vendable.
We se that no man loveth now,   5805

But for wynnyng and for prow;
And love is thralled in servage,
Whanne it is sold for avauntage.
Yit wommen wole her bodyes selle;
Suche soules goth to the devel of helle!" 5810

Fragment C

Whanne Love hadde told hem his entente,
The baronage to councel wente.
In many sentences they fille,
And dyversely they seide hir wille;
But aftir discord they accorded,   5815
And her accord to Love recorded.
"Sir," seiden they, "we ben at on,
Bi evene accord of everichon,
Out-take Richesse al oonly,
That sworen hath ful hauteynly,   5820
That she the castel nyl not assaile,
Ne smyte a strok in this bataile,
With darte, ne mace, spere, ne knyf,
For man that spekith or berith the lyf,
And blameth youre emprise, iwys,   5825
And from oure hoost departed is,
Atte leste wey, as in this plyt,
So hath she this man in dispit.
For she seith he ne loved hir never,
And therfore she wole hate hym evere. 5830
For he wole gadre no tresor,
He hath hir wrath for evermor.
He agylte hir never in other caas,
Lo, heere all hoolly his trespas!
She seith wel that this other day   5835
He axide hir leve to gon the way
That is clepid To-Moche-Yevyng,
And spak full faire in his praiyng;
But whanne he praiede hir, pore was he,
Therfore she warned hym the entre.   5840
Ne yit is he not thryven so
That he hath geten a peny or two,
That quytly is his owne in hold.
Thus hath Richesse us alle told;
And whanne Richesse us this recorded, 5845
Withouten hir we ben accorded.
    And we fynde in oure accordaunce
That Fals-Semblant and Abstinaunce,
With all the folk of her bataille,
Shull at the hyndre gate assayle,   5850
That Wikkid-Tunge hath in kepyng,
With his Normans, full of janglyng.
And with hem Curtesie and Largesse,
That shull shewe her hardynesse
To the olde wyf that kepte so harde   5855
Fair-Welcomyng withynne her warde.

Thanne shal Delit and Wel-Heelynge
Fonde Shame adown to brynge;
With all her oost, erly and late,
They shull assailen that ilke gate.   5860
Agaynes Drede shall Hardynesse
Assayle, and also Sikernesse,
With all the folk of her ledyng,
That never wist what was fleyng.
    Fraunchise shall fight, and eke Pite,   5865
With Daunger, full of cruelte.
Thus is youre hoost ordeyned wel.
Doun shall the castell every del,
If everich do his entent,
So that Venus be present,   5870
Youre modir, full of vasselage,
That can ynough of such usage.
Withouten hir may no wight spede
This werk, neithir for word ne deede;
Therfore is good ye for hir sende,   5875
For thurgh hir may this werk amende."
    "Lordynges, my modir, the goddesse,
That is my lady and my maistresse,
Nis not [at] all at my willyng,
Ne doth not all my desiryng.   5880
Yit can she som tyme don labour,
Whanne that hir lust, in my socour,
Al my nedes for to acheve;
But now I thenke hir not to greve.
My modir is she, and of childhede   5885
I bothe worshipe hir, and eke drede;
For who that dredith sire ne dame,
Shal it abye in body or name.
And, natheles, yit kunne we
Sende aftir hir, if nede be;   5890
And were she nygh, she comen wolde;
I trowe that nothyng myght hir holde.
    Mi modir is of gret prowesse;
She hath tan many a forteresse,
That cost hath many a pound, er this,   5895
There I nas not present, ywis.
And yit men seide it was my dede;
But I com never in that stede,
Ne me ne likith, so mote I the,
That such toures ben take withoute me.   5900
For-why me thenkith that, in no wise,
It may ben clepid but marchandise.
    Go bye a courser, blak or whit,
And pay therfore; than art thou quyt.
The marchaunt owith thee right nought,   5905
Ne thou hym, whanne thou [hast] it bought.
I wole not sellyng clepe yevyng,
For sellyng axeth no guerdonyng:
Here lith no thank ne no merit;
That oon goth from that other al quyt.   5910

But this sellyng is not semblable;
For whanne his hors is in the stable,
He may it selle ageyn, parde,
And wynnen on it, such hap may be;
All may the man not leese, iwys,   5915
For at the leest the skyn is his.
Or ellis, if it so bitide
That he wole kepe his hors to ride,
Yit is he lord ay of his hors.
But thilke chaffare is wel wors,   5920
There Venus entremetith ought.
For whoso such chaffare hath bought,
He shal not worchen so wisely
That he ne shal leese al outerly
Bothe his money and his chaffare;   5925
But the seller of the ware
The prys and profit have shall.
Certeyn, the bier shal leese all;
For he ne can so dere it bye
To have lordship and full maistrie,   5930
Ne have power to make lettyng,
Neithir for yift ne for prechyng,
That of his chaffare, maugre his,
Another shal have as moche, iwis,
If he wol yeve as myche as he,   5935
Of what contrey so that he be;
Or for right nought, so happe may,
If he can flater hir to hir pay.
Ben thanne siche marchauntz wise?
No, but fooles in every wise,   5940
Whanne they bye sich thyng wilfully,
There as they leese her good fully.
But natheles, this dar I saye,
My modir is not wont to paye,
For she is neither so fool ne nyce   5945
To entremete hir of sich vice.
But truste wel, he shal pay all,
That repent of his bargeyn shall,
Whanne poverte putte hym in distresse,
All were he scoler to Richesse,   5950
That is for me in gret yernyng,
Whanne she assentith to my willyng.
    But [by] my modir, seint Venus,
And by hir fader Saturnus,
That hir engendride by his lyf —   5955
But not upon his weddid wyf! —
Yit wole I more unto you swer,
To make this thyng the sikerer;
Now by that feith and that leaute
That I owe to all my britheren fre,   5960
Of which ther nys wight undir heven
That kan her fadris names neven,
So dyverse and so many ther be
That with my modir have be prive!

Yit wolde I swere, for sikirnesse,   5965
The pol of helle to my witnesse,
Now drynke I not this yeer clarre,
If that I lye or forsworn be!
(For of the goddes the usage is
That whoso hym forswereth amys   5970
Shal that yeer drynke no clarre.)
Now have I sworn ynough, pardee,
If I forswere me, thanne am I lorn,
But I wole never be forsworn.
Syth Richesse hath me failed heere,   5975
She shal abye that trespas ful dere,
Atte leeste wey, but [she] hir arme
With swerd, or sparth, or gysarme.
For certis, sith she loveth not me,
Fro thilke tyme that she may se   5980
The castell and the tour toshake,
In sory tyme she shal awake.
If I may grype a riche man,
I shal so pulle hym, if I can,
That he shal in a fewe stoundes   5985
Lese all his markis and his poundis.
I shal hym make his pens outslynge,
But they in his gerner sprynge;
Oure maydens shal eke pluk hym so
That hym shal neden fetheres mo,   5990
And make hym selle his lond to spende,
But he the bet kunne hym defende.
     Pore men han maad her lord of me;
Although they not so myghty be
That they may fede me in delit,   5995
I wol not have hem in despit.
No good man hateth hem, as I gesse,
For chynche and feloun is Richesse,
That so can chase hem and dispise,
And hem defoule in sondry wise.   6000
They loven full bet, so God me spede,
Than doth the riche, chynchy gnede,
And ben, in good feith, more stable
And trewer and more serviable;
And therfore it suffisith me   6005
Her goode herte and her leaute.
They han on me set all her thought,
And therfore I forgete hem nought.
I wolde hem bringe in gret noblesse,
If that I were god of richesse,   6010
As I am god of love sothly,
Sich routhe upon her pleynt have I.
Therfor I must his socour be,
That peyneth hym to serven me;
For if he deide for love of this,   6015
Thanne semeth in me no love ther is."
"Sir," seide they, "soth is every deel
That ye reherce, and we wote wel

Thilk oth to holde is resonable;
For it is good and covenable   6020
That ye on riche men han sworn.
For, sir, this wote we wel biforn:
If riche men don you homage,
That is as fooles don outrage;
But ye shull not forsworn be,   6025
Ne lette therfore to drynke clarre,
Or pyment makid fresh and newe.
Ladies shull hem such pepir brewe,
If that they fall into her laas,
That they for woo mowe seyn 'allas!'   6030
Ladyes shullen evere so curteis be
That they shal quyte youre oth all free.
Ne sekith never othir vicaire,
For they shal speke with hem so faire
That ye shal holde you paied full wel,   6035
Though ye you medle never a del.
Late ladies worche with her thyngis,
They shal hem telle so fele tidynges,
And moeve hem eke so many requestis
Bi flateri, that not honest is,   6040
And therto yeve hem such thankynges,
What with kissyng, and with talkynges,
That, certis, if they trowed be,
Shal never leve hem lond ne fee
That it nyl as the moeble fare,   6045
Of which they first delyverid are.
Now may ye telle us all youre wille,
And we youre heestes shal fulfille.
     But Fals-Semblant dar not, for drede
Of you, sir, medle hym of this dede,   6050
For he seith that ye ben his foo;
He not if ye wole worche hym woo.
Wherfore we pray you alle, beau sire,
That ye forgyve hym now your ire,
And that he may dwelle, as your man,   6055
With Abstinence, his dere lemman;
This oure accord and oure wille now."
     "Parfay," seide Love, I graunte it yow.
I wole wel holde hym for my man;
Now late hym come" — and he forth ran.   6060
"Fals-Semblant," quod Love, "in this wise
I take thee heere to my servise,
That thou oure freendis helpe alway;
And hyndre hem neithir nyght ne day,
But do thy myght hem to releve;   6065
And eke oure enemyes that thou greve.
Thyn be this myght, I graunte it thee,
My kyng of harlotes shalt thou be;
We wole that thou have such honour.
Certeyn, thou art a fals traitour,   6070
And eke a theef; sith thou were born,
A thousand tyme thou art forsworn.

But natheles, in oure heryng,
To putte oure folk out of doutyng,
I bidde thee teche hem, wostow how,   6075
Bi som general signe now,
In what place thou shalt founden be,
If that men had myster of thee;
And how men shal thee best espye,
For thee to knowe is gret maistrie.   6080
Telle in what place is thyn hauntyng."
     "Sir, I have fele dyvers wonyng,
That I kepe not rehersed be,
So that ye wolde respiten me.
For if that I telle you the sothe,   6085
I may have harm and shame bothe.
If that my felowes wisten it,
My talis shulden me be quytt;
For certeyn, they wolde hate me,
If ever I knewe her cruelte.   6090
For they wolde overall holde hem stille
Of trouthe that is ageyne her wille;
Suche tales kepen they not here.
I myght eftsoone bye it full deere,
If I seide of hem ony thing   6095
That ought displesith to her heryng.
For what word that hem prikke or biteth,
In that word noon of hem deliteth,
Al were it gospel, the evangile,
That wolde reprove hem of her gile,   6100
For they are cruel and hauteyn.
And this thyng wot I well, certeyn,
If I speke ought to peire her loos,
Your court shal not so well be cloos
That they ne shall wite it atte last.   6105
Of good men am I nought agast,
For they wole taken on hem nothyng,
Whanne that they knowe al my menyng;
But he that wole it on hym take,
He wole hymsilf suspecious make,   6110
That he his lyf let covertly
In Gile and in Ipocrisy
That me engendred and yaf fostryng."
     "They made a full good engendryng,"
Quod Love, "for whoso sothly telle,   6115
They engendred the devel of helle!
But nedely, howsoevere it be,"
Quod Love, "I wole and charge thee
To telle anoon thy wonyng places,
Heryng ech wight that in this place is;   6120
And what lyf that thou lyvest also,
Hide it no lenger now; wherto?
Thou most discovere all thi wurchyng,
How thou servest, and of what thyng,
Though that thou shuldist for thi soth-sawe
Ben al tobeten and todrawe;   6126

And yit art thou not wont, pardee.
But natheles, though thou beten be,
Thou shalt not be the first that so
Hath for sothsawe suffred woo."   6130
"Sir, sith that it may liken you,
Though that I shulde be slayn right now,
I shal don youre comaundement,
For therto have I gret talent."
     Withouten wordis mo, right than,   6135
Fals-Semblant his sermon bigan,
And seide hem thus in audience:
"Barouns, take heede of my sentence!
That wight that list to have knowing
Of Fals-Semblant, full of flatering,   6140
He must in worldly folk hym seke,
And, certes, in the cloistres eke.
I wone nowhere but in hem tweye,
But not lyk even, soth to seye;
Shortly, I wole herberwe me   6145
There I hope best to hulstred be;
And certeynly, sikerest hidyng
Is undirnethe humblest clothing.
Religiouse folk ben full covert;
Seculer folk ben more appert.   6150
But natheles, I wole not blame
Religious folk, ne hem diffame,
In what habit that ever they go.
Religioun umble, and trewe also,
Wole I not blame ne dispise;   6155
But I nyl love it, in no wise.
I mene of fals religious,
That stoute ben and malicious,
That wolen in an abit goo,
And setten not her herte therto.   6160
     Religious folk ben al pitous;
Thou shalt not seen oon dispitous.
They loven no pride ne no strif,
But humbly they wole lede her lyf;
With swich folk wole I never be,   6165
And if I dwelle, I feyne me.
I may wel in her abit go;
But me were lever my nekke a-two,
Than lete a purpos that I take,
What covenaunt that ever I make.   6170
I dwelle with hem that proude be,
And full of wiles and subtilte,
That worship of this world coveiten,
And grete nedes kunnen espleiten,
And gon and gadren gret pitaunces,   6175
And purchace hem the acqueyntaunces
Of men that myghty lyf may leden;
And feyne hem pore, and hemsilf feden
With gode morcels delicious,
And drinken good wyn precious,   6180

And preche us povert and distresse,
And fisshen hemsilf gret richesse
With wily nettis that they caste.
It wole come foule out at the laste.
They ben fro clene religioun went;　　6185
They make the world an argument
That hath a foul conclusioun.
'I have a robe of religioun,
Thanne am I all religious.'
This argument is all roignous;　　6190
It is not worth a croked brere.
Abit ne makith neithir monk ne frere,
But clene lyf and devocioun
Makith gode men of religioun.
Natheles, ther kan noon answere,　　6195
How high that evere his heed he shere
With rasour whetted never so kene,
That Gile in braunches kut thrittene;
Ther can no wight distincte it so,
That he dar sey a word therto.　　6200
　　But what herberwe that ever I take,
Or what semblant that evere I make,
I mene but gile, and folowe that;
For right no mo than Gibbe oure cat,
That awayteth mys and rattes to kyllen,　　6205
Ne entende I but to bigilen.
Ne no wight may by my clothing
Wite with what folk is my dwellyng,
Ne by my wordis yit, parde,
So softe and so plesaunt they be.　　6210
Bihold the dedis that I do;
But thou be blynd, thou oughtest so;
For, varie her wordis fro her deede,
They thenke on gile withoute dreede,
What maner clothing that they were,　　6215
Or what estat that evere they bere,
Lered or lewd, lord or lady,
Knyght, squyer, burgeis, or bayly."
　　Right thus while Fals-Semblant sermoneth,
Eftsones Love hym aresoneth,　　6220
And brak his tale in his spekyng,
As though he had hym told lesyng,
And seide, "What, devel, is that I here?
What folk hast thou us nempned heere?
May men fynde religioun　　6225
In worldly habitacioun?"
　　"Ye, sir; it folowith not that they
Shulde lede a wikked lyf, parfey,
Ne not therfore her soules leese,
That hem to worldly clothes chese;　　6230
For, certis, it were gret pitee.
Men may in seculer clothes see
Florishen hooly religioun.
Full many a seynt in feeld and toun,

With many a virgine glorious,　　6235
Devout, and full religious,
Han deied, that comun cloth ay beeren,
Yit seyntes nevere the lesse they weren.
I cowde reken you many a ten;
Ye, wel nygh, al these hooly wymmen,　　6240
That men in chirchis herie and seke,
Bothe maydens and these wyves eke,
That baren full many a fair child heere,
Wered alwey clothis seculere,
And in the same dieden they,　　6245
That seyntes weren, and ben alwey.
The eleven thousand maydens deere
That beren in heven hir ciergis clere,
Of whiche men rede in chirche and synge,
Were take in seculer clothinge,　　6250
Whanne they resseyved martirdom,
And wonnen hevene unto her hom.
Good herte makith the goode thought;
The clothing yeveth ne reveth nought.
The goode thought and the worching,　　6255
That makith the religioun flowryng,
Ther lyth the good religioun,
Aftir the right entencioun.
　　Whoso took a wethers skyn,
And wrapped a gredy wolf theryn,　　6260
For he shulde go with lambis whyte,
Wenest thou not he wolde hem bite?
Yis, neverthelasse, as he were wood,
He wolde hem wery and drinke the blood,
And wel the rather hem disceyve;　　6265
For, sith they cowde not perceyve
His treget and his cruelte,
They wolde hym folowe, al wolde he fle.
　　If ther be wolves of sich hewe
Amonges these apostlis newe,　　6270
Thou hooly chirche, thou maist be wailed!
Sith that thy citee is assayled
Thourgh knyghtis of thyn owne table,
God wot thi lordship is doutable!
If thei enforce [hem] it to wynne,　　6275
That shulde defende it fro withynne,
Who myght defense ayens hem make?
Withoute strok it mot be take
Of trepeget or mangonel;
Without displaiyng of pensel.　　6280
And if God nyl don it socour,
But lat [hem] renne in this colour,
Thou most thyn heestis laten be.
Thanne is ther nought but yelde thee,
Or yeve hem tribut, doutelees,　　6285
And holde it of hem to have pees,
But gretter harm bitide thee,
That they al maister of it be.

Wel konne they scorne thee withal;
By day stuffen they the wall,   6290
And al the nyght they mynen there.
Nay, thou planten most elleswhere
Thyn ympes, if thou wolt fruyt have;
Abid not there, thisilf to save.

But now pees! heere I turne ageyn.   6295
I wole nomore of this thing seyn,
If I may passen me herby;
I myghte maken you wery.
But I wole heten you alway
To helpe youre freendis what I may,   6300
So they wollen my company;
For they be shent al outerly,
But if so falle that I be
Ofte with hem, and they with me.
And eke my lemman mote they serve,   6305
Or they shull not my love deserve.
Forsothe, I am a fals traitour;
God jugged me for a theef trichour.
Forsworn I am, but wel nygh non
Wot of my gile, til it be don.   6310

Thourgh me hath many oon deth resseyved,
That my treget nevere aperceyved;
And yit resseyveth, and shal resseyve,
That my falsnesse shal nevere aperceyve.
But whoso doth, if he wis be,   6315
Hym is right good be war of me,
But so sligh is the deceyvyng
[That to hard is the aperceyving;]
For Protheus, that cowde hym chaunge
In every shap, homly and straunge,   6320
Cowde nevere sich gile ne tresoun
As I; for I com never in toun
There as I myghte knowen be,
Though men me bothe myght here and see.
Full wel I can my clothis chaunge,   6325
Take oon, and make another straunge.
Now am I knyght, now chasteleyn,
Now prelat, and now chapeleyn,
Now prest, now clerk, and now forster;
Now am I maister, now scoler,   6330
Now monk, now chanoun, now baily;
Whatever myster man am I.
Now am I prince, now am I page,
And kan by herte every langage.
Som tyme am I hor and old;   6335
Now am I yong, stout, and bold;
Now am I Robert, now Robyn;
Now Frere Menour, now Jacobyn;
And with me folwith my loteby,
To don me solas and company,   6340
That hight Dame Abstinence-Streyned,
In many a queynte array feyned.

Ryght as it cometh to hir lykyng,
I fulfille al hir desiryng.
Somtyme a wommans cloth take I;   6345
Now am I a mayde, now lady.
Somtyme I am religious;
Now lyk an anker in an hous.
Somtyme am I prioresse,
And now a nonne, and now abbesse;   6350
And go thurgh alle regiouns,
Sekyng alle religiouns.
But to what ordre that I am sworn,
I take the strawe, and lete the corn.
To [blynde] folk [ther] I enhabit,   6355
I axe nomore but her abit.
What wole ye more in every wise?
Right as me lyst, I me disgise.
Wel can I wre me undir wede;
Unlyk is my word to my dede.   6360
Thus make I into my trappis falle,
Thurgh my pryveleges, alle
That ben in Cristendom alyve.
I may assoile, and I may shryve,
That no prelat may lette me,   6365
All folk, where evere thei founde be.
I not no prelat may don so,
But it the pope be, and no mo,
That made thilk establisshing.
Now is not this a propre thing?   6370
But, were my sleightis aperceyved
[Ne shulde I more ben receyved,]
As I was wont, and wostow why?
For I dide hem a tregetry.
But therof yeve I lytel tale;   6375
I have the silver and the male.
So have I prechid, and eke shriven,
So have I take, so have me yiven,
Thurgh her foly, husbonde and wyf,
That I lede right a joly lyf,   6380
Thurgh symplesse of the prelacye;
They knowe not al my tregettrie.

But forasmoche as man and wyf
Shulde shewe her paroch-prest her lyf,
Onys a yeer, as seith the book,   6385
Er ony wight his housel took,
Thanne have I pryvylegis large,
That may of myche thing discharge.
For he may seie right thus, parde:
'Sir preest, in shrift I telle it thee,   6390
That he, to whom that I am shryven,
Hath me assoiled, and me yiven
Penaunce, sothly, for my synne,
Which that I fond me gilty ynne,
Ne I ne have nevere entencioun   6395
To make double confessioun,

Ne reherce eft my shrift to thee;
O shrift is right ynough to me,
This oughte thee suffice wel;
Ne be not rebel never a del.   6400
For certis, though thou haddist it sworn,
I wot no prest ne prelat born,
That may to shrift eft me constreyne;
And if they don, I wole me pleyne,
For I wot where to pleyne wel.   6405
Thou shalt not streyne me a del,
Ne enforce me, ne not me trouble,
To make my confessioun double.
Ne I have non affeccioun
To have double absolucioun.   6410
The firste is right ynough to me;
This latter assoilyng quyte I thee.
I am unbounde; what maist thou fynde
More of my synnes me to unbynde?
For he, that myght hath in his hond,   6415
Of all my synnes me unbond.
And if thou wolt me thus constreyne,
That me mot nedis on thee pleyne,
There shall no jugge imperial,
Ne bisshop, ne official,   6420
Don jugement on me; for I
Right wel shamme on thee crye,
Shal gon and pleyne me openly
Unto my shrifte-fadir newe,
(That hight not Frere Wolf untrewe!)
And he shal cheveys hym for me,   6425
For I trowe he can hampre thee.
But, Lord! he wolde be wrooth withalle,
If men hym wolde Frere Wolf calle!
For he wolde have no pacience,
But don al cruel vengeaunce.   6430
He wolde his myght don at the leeste,
Nothing spare for Goddis heeste.
And, God so wys be my socour,
But thou yeve me my Savyour
At Ester, whanne it likith me,   6435
Withoute presyng more on thee,
I wole forth, and to hym gon,
And he shal housel me anoon.
For I am out of thi grucching;
I kepe not dele with thee nothing."   6440
    Thus may he shryve hym, that forsaketh
His paroch-prest, and to me taketh.
And if the prest wole hym refuse,
I am full redy hym to accuse,
And hym punysshe and hampre so   6445
That he his chirche shal forgo.
    But whoso hath in his felyng
The consequence of such shryvyng,
Shal sen that prest may never have myght
To knowe the conscience aright   6450

Of hym that is undir his cure.
And this ageyns holy scripture,
That biddith every heerde honest
Have verry knowing of his beest.
But pore folk that gone by strete,   6455
That have no gold, ne sommes grete,
Hem wolde I lete to her prelates,
Or lete her prestis knowe her states,
For to me right nought yeve they."
"And why?"
                    "It is for they ne may,   6460
They ben so bare; I take no kep,
But I wole have the fatte sheep;
Lat parish prestis have the lene.
I yeve not of her harm a bene!
And if that prelates grucchen it,   6465
That oughten wroth be in her wit,
To leese her fatte beestes so,
I shal yeve hem a strok or two,
That they shal leesen with force,
Ye, bothe her mytre and her croce.   6470
Thus jape I hem, and have do longe,
My pryveleges ben so stronge."
    Fals-Semblant wolde have stynted heere,
But Love ne made hym no such cheere
That he was wery of his sawe;   6475
But for to make hym glad and fawe,
He seide, "Telle on more specialy
Hou that thou servest untrewly.
Telle forth, and shame thee never a del;
For, as thyn abit shewith wel,   6480
Thou semest an hooly heremyte."
    "Soth is, but I am an ypocrite."
"Thou gost and prechest poverte."
"Ye, sir, but richesse hath pouste."
"Thou prechest abstinence also."   6485
"Sir, I wole fillen, so mote I go,
My paunche of good mete and wyn,
As shulde a maister of dyvyn;
For how that I me pover feyne,
Yit alle pore folk I disdeyne.   6490
    I love bettir th'acqueyntaunce,
Ten tymes, of the kyng of Fraunce
Than of a pore man of mylde mod,
Though that his soule be also god.
For whanne I see beggers quakyng,   6495
Naked on myxnes al stynkyng,
For hungre crie, and eke for care,
I entremete not of her fare.
They ben so pore and ful of pyne,
They myght not oonys yeve me dyne,   6500
For they have nothing but her lyf.
What shulde he yeve that likketh his knyf?
It is but foly to entremete,

To seke in houndes nest fat mete.
Lete bere hem to the spitel anoon,   6505
But, for me, comfort gete they noon.
But a riche sik usurer
Wolde I visite and drawe ner;
Hym wole I comforte and rehete,
For I hope of his gold to gete.   6510
And if that wikkid deth hym have,
I wole go with hym to his grave.
And if ther ony reprove me,
Why that I lete the pore be,
Wostow how I mot ascape?   6515
I sey, and swere hym ful rape,
That riche men han more tecches
Of synne than han pore wrecches,
And han of counsel more mister;
And therfore I wole drawe hem ner.   6520
But as gret hurt, it may so be,
Hath a soule in right gret poverte
As soule in gret richesse, forsothe,
Al be it that they hurten bothe.
For richesse and mendicitees   6525
Ben clepid two extremytees;
The mene is cleped suffisaunce;
Ther lyth of vertu the aboundaunce.
For Salamon, full wel I wot,
In his Parablis us wrot,   6530
As it is knowe to many a wight,
In his thrittethe chapitre right,
'God thou me kepe, for thi pouste,
Fro richesse and mendicite;
For if a riche man hym dresse   6535
To thenke to myche on richesse,
His herte on that so fer is set
That he his creatour foryet;
And hym that begging wole ay greve,
How shulde I bi his word hym leve?   6540
Unnethe that he nys a mycher
Forsworn, or ellis God is lyer.'
Thus seith Salamones sawes.
Ne we fynde writen in no lawis,
And namely in oure Cristen lay,   6545
(Whoso seith 'ye,' I dar sey 'nay')
That Crist, ne his apostlis dere,
While that they walkide in erthe heere,
Were never seen her bred beggyng,
For they nolden beggen for nothing.   6550
And right thus were men wont to teche,
And in this wise wolde it preche
The maistres of divinite
Somtyme in Parys the citee.
    And if men wolde ther-geyn appose   6555
The nakid text, and lete the glose,
It myghte soone assoiled be;

For men may wel the sothe see,
That, parde, they myght aske a thing
Pleynly forth, without begging.   6560
For they weren Goddis herdis deere,
And cure of soules hadden heere,
They nolde nothing begge her fode;
For aftir Crist was don on rode,
With her propre hondis they wrought,   6565
And with travel, and ellis nought,
They wonnen all her sustenaunce,
And lyveden forth in her penaunce,
And the remenaunt yave awey
To other pore folkis alwey.   6570
They neither bilden tour ne halle,
But ley in houses smale withalle.
A myghty man, that can and may,
Shulde with his hond and body alway
Wynne hym his fode in laboring,   6575
If he ne have rent or sich a thing,
Although he be religious,
And God to serven curious.
Thus mot he don, or do trespas,
But if it be in certeyn cas,   6580
That I can reherce, if myster be,
Right wel, whanne the tyme I se.
    Sek the book of seynt Austyn,
Be it in papir or perchemyn,
There as he writ of these worchynges   6585
Thou shalt seen that noon excusynges
A parfit man ne shulde seke
Bi wordis ne bi dedis eke,
Although he be religious,
And God to serven curious,   6590
That he ne shal, so mote I go,
With propre hondis and body also,
Gete his fode in laboryng,
If he ne have proprete of thing.
Yit shulde he selle all his substaunce,   6595
And with his swynk have sustenaunce,
If he be parfit in bounte.
Thus han tho bookes told me.
Fro he that wole gon ydilly,
And usith it ay besily   6600
To haunten other mennes table,
He is a trechour, ful of fable;
Ne he ne may, by god resoun,
Excuse hym by his orisoun.
For men bihoveth, in som gise,   6605
Blynne somtyme in Goddis servise
To gon and purchasen her nede.
Men mote eten, that is no drede,
And slepe, and eke do other thing;
So longe may they leve praiyng.   6610
So may they eke her praier blynne,

While that they werke, her mete to wynne.
Seynt Austyn wole therto accorde,
In thilke book that I recorde.
Justinian eke, that made lawes,   6615
Hath thus forboden, by olde dawes:
'No man, up peyne to be ded,
Mighty of body, to begge his bred,
If he may swynke it for to gete;
Men shulde hym rather mayme or bete,   6620
Or don of hym apert justice,
Than suffren hym in such malice.'
They don not wel, so mote I go,
That taken such almesse so,
But if they have som pryvelege,   6625
That of the peyne hem wole allege.
But how that is, can I not see,
But if the prince disseyved be;
Ne I ne wene not, sikerly,
That they may have it rightfully.   6630
But I wole not determine
Of prynces power, ne defyne,
Ne by my word comprende, iwys,
If it so fer may strecche in this.
I wole not entremete a del;   6635
But I trowe that the book seith wel,
Who that takith almessis, that be
Dewe to folk that men may se
Lame, feble, wery, and bare,
Pore, or in such maner care, —   6640
That konne wynne hem never mo,
For they have no power therto,
He etith his owne dampnyng,
But if he lye, that made al thing.
And if ye such a truaunt fynde,   6645
Chastise hym wel, if ye be kynde.
But they wolde hate you, percas,
And, if ye fillen in her laas,
They wolde eftsoonys do you scathe,
If that they myghte, late or rathe;   6650
For they be not full pacient,
That han the world thus foule blent.
And witeth wel that [ther] God bad
The good-man selle al that he had,
And folowe hym, and to pore it yive,   6655
He wolde not therfore that he lyve
To serven hym in mendience,
For it was nevere his sentence;
But he bad wirken whanne that neede is,
And folwe hym in goode dedis.   6660
Seynt Poul, that loved al hooly chirche,
He bad th'appostles for to wirche,
And wynnen her lyflode in that wise,
And hem defended truandise,
And seide, 'Wirketh with youre honden.'   6665

Thus shulde the thing be undirstonden:
He nolde, iwys, have bidde hem begging,
Ne sellen gospel, ne prechyng,
Lest they berafte, with her askyng,
Folk of her catel or of her thing.   6670
For in this world is many a man
That yeveth his good, for he ne can
Werne it for shame; or ellis he
Wolde of the asker delyvered be,
And, for he hym encombrith so,   6675
He yeveth hym good to late hym go.
But it can hem nothyng profite;
They lese the yift and the meryte.
The goode folk, that Poul to preched,
Profred hym ofte, whan he hem teched,   6680
Som of her good in charite.
But therof right nothing tok he;
But of his hondwerk wolde he gete
Clothes to wryen hym, and his mete."
    "Telle me thanne how a man may lyven,
That al his good to pore hath yiven,   6686
And wole but oonly bidde his bedis
And never with hondes labour his nedes.
May he do so?"
                              "Ye, sir."
                                        "And how?"
"Sir, I wole gladly telle yow: 6690
Seynt Austyn seith a man may be
In houses that han proprete,
As Templers and Hospitelers,
And as these Chanouns Regulers,
Or White Monkes, or these Blake —   6695
I wole no mo ensamplis make —
And take therof his sustenyng,
For therynne lyth no begging;
But other weyes not, ywys,
Yif Austyn gabbith not of this.   6700
And yit full many a monk laboureth,
That God in hooly chirche honoureth;
For whanne her swynkyng is agon,
They rede and synge in chirche anon.
    And for ther hath ben gret discord,   6705
As many a wight may bere record,
Upon the estat of mendience,
I wole shortly, in youre presence,
Telle how a man may begge at nede,
That hath not wherwith hym to fede,   6710
Maugre his felones jangelyngis,
For sothfastnesse wole none hidyngis.
And yit, percas, I may abeye
That I to yow sothly thus seye.
    Lo, heere the caas especial: 6715
If a man be so bestial
That he of no craft hath science,

And nought desireth ignorence,
Thanne may he go a-begging yerne,
Til he som maner craft kan lerne,   6720
Thurgh which withoute truaundyng,
He may in trouthe have his lyvyng.
Or if he may don no labour,
For elde, or syknesse, or langour,
Or for his tendre age also,   6725
Thanne may he yit a-begging go.
Or if he have, peraventure,
Thurgh usage of his noriture,
Lyved over deliciously,
Thanne oughten good folk comunly   6730
Han of his myscheef som pitee,
And suffren hym also that he
May gon aboute and begge his breed,
That he be not for hungur deed.
Or if he have of craft kunnyng,   6735
And strengthe also, and desiryng
To wirken, as he hadde what,
But he fynde neithir this ne that,
Thanne may he begge til that he
Have geten his necessite.   6740
Or if his wynnyng be so lite
That his labour wole not acquyte
Sufficiantly al his lyvyng,
Yit may he go his breed begging;
Fro dore to dore he may go trace,   6745
Til he the remenaunt may purchace.
Or if a man wolde undirtake
Ony emprise for to make
In the rescous of oure lay,
And it defenden as he may,   6750
Be it with armes or lettrure,
Or other covenable cure,
If it be so he pore be,
Thanne may he begge til that he
May fynde in trouthe for to swynke,   6755
And gete hym clothes, mete, and drynke,
Swynke he with hondis corporell,
And not with hondis espirituell.
In al thise caas, and in semblables,
If that ther ben mo resonables,   6760
He may begge, as I telle you heere,
And ellis nought, in no manere;
As William Seynt Amour wolde preche,
And ofte wolde dispute and teche
Of this mater all openly   6765
At Parys full solempnely.
And, also God my soule blesse,
As he had, in this stedfastnesse,
The accord of the universite
And of the puple, as semeth me.   6770
  No good man oughte it to refuse,

Ne ought hym therof to excuse,
Be wroth or blithe whoso be;
For I wole speke, and telle it thee,
Al shulde I dye, and be putt doun,   6775
As was Seynt Poul, in derk prisoun;
Or be exiled in this caas
With wrong, as maister William was,
That my moder, Ypocrysie,
Banysshed for hir gret envye.   6780
  Mi modir flemed hym Seynt Amour;
The noble dide such labour
To susteyne evere the loyalte,
That he to moche agilte me.
He made a book, and lete it write,   6785
Wherein his lyf he dide al write,
And wolde ich reneyed begging,
And lyved by my traveylyng,
If I ne had rent ne other good.
What? Wened he that I were wood?   6790
For labour myght me never plese.
I have more wille to ben at ese,
And have wel lever, soth to seye,
Bifore the puple patre and preye,
And wrie me in my foxerie   6795
Under a cope of papelardie."
  Quod Love, "What devel is this that I heere?
What wordis tellest thou me heere?"
  "What, sir?"
            "Falsnesse, that apert is;
Thanne dredist thou not God?"
                        "No, certis;   6800
For selde in gret thing shal he spede
In this world, that God wole drede.
For folk that hem to vertu yiven,
And truly on her owne lyven,
And hem in goodnesse ay contene,   6805
On hem is lytel thrift ysene.
Such folk drinken gret mysese;
That lyf may me never plese.
But se what gold han usurers,
And silver eke in [hir] garners,   6810
Taylagiers, and these monyours,
Bailifs, bedels, provost, countours;
These lyven wel nygh by ravyne.
The smale puple hem mote enclyne,
And they as wolves wole hem eten.   6815
Upon the pore folk they geten
Full moche of that they spende or kepe.
Nis non of hem that he nyl strepe
And wrien himsilf wel atte fulle;
Withoute scaldyng they hem pulle.   6820
The stronge the feble overgoth;
But I, that were my symple cloth,
Robbe bothe robbed and robbours

And gile giled and gilours.
By my treget I gadre and threste   6825
The gret tresour into my cheste,
That lyth with me so faste bounde.
Myn highe paleys do I founde,
And my delites I fulfille
With wyn at feestes at my wille,   6830
And tables full of entremees.
I wole no lyf but ese and pees,
And wynne gold to spende also.
For whanne the grete bagge is go,
It cometh right with my japes.   6835
Make I not wel tumble myn apes?
To wynnen is alwey myn entente;
My purchace is bettir than my rente.
For though I shulde beten be,
Overal I entremete me;   6840
Withoute me may no wight dure.
I walke soules for to cure.
Of al the world [the] cure have I
In brede and lengthe; boldely
I wole bothe preche and eke counceilen;   6845
With hondis wille I not traveilen;
For of the Pope I have the bulle;
I ne holde not my wittes dulle.
I wole not stynten, in my lyve,
These emperoures for to shryve,   6850
Or kyngis, dukis, and lordis grete;
But pore folk al quyte I lete.
I love no such shryvyng, parde,
But it for other cause be.
I rekke not of pore men —   6855
Her astat is not worth an hen.
Where fyndest thou a swynker of labour
Have me unto his confessour?
But emperesses and duchesses,
Thise queenes, and eke countesses,   6860
Thise abbessis, and eke bygyns,
These grete ladyes palasyns,
These joly knyghtis and baillyves,
Thise nonnes, and thise burgeis wyves,
That riche ben and eke plesyng,   6865
And thise maidens welfaryng,
Wherso they clad or naked be,
Uncounceiled goth ther noon fro me.
And, for her soules savete,
At lord and lady, and her meyne,   6870
I axe, whanne thei hem to me shryve,
The proprete of al her lyve,
And make hem trowe, bothe meest and leest,
Hir paroch-prest nys but a beest
Ayens me and my companye,   6875
That shrewis ben as gret as I;
Fro whiche I wole not hide in hold

No pryvete that me is told,
That I by word or signe, ywis,
Nil make hem knowe what it is,   6880
And they wolen also tellen me;
They hele fro me no pryvyte.
And for to make yow hem perceyven,
That usen folk thus to disceyven,
I wole you seyn, withouten drede,   6885
What men may in the gospel rede
Of seynt Mathew, the gospelere,
That seith, as I shal you seye heere:
'Uppon the chaire of Moyses' —
Thus is it glosed, douteles,   6890
That is the Olde Testament,
For therby is the chaire ment —
'Sitte Scribes and Pharisen;'
That is to seyn, the cursid men
Whiche that we ypocritis calle.   6895
'Doth that they preche, I rede you alle,
But doth not as they don a del;
That ben not wery to seye wel,
But to do wel no will have they.
And they wolde bynde on folk alwey,   6900
That ben to be begiled able,
Burdons that ben importable;
On folkes shuldris thinges they couchen,
That they nyl with her fyngris touchen.' "
    "And why wole they not touche it?"
                              "Why?   6905
For hem ne lyst not, sikirly;
For sadde burdons that men taken
Make folkes shuldris aken.
And if they do ought that good be,
That is for folk it shulde se.   6910
Her bordurs larger maken they,
And make her hemmes wide alwey,
And loven setes at the table,
The firste and most honourable;
And for to han the first chaieris   6915
In synagogis, to hem full deere is;
And willen that folk hem loute and grete,
Whanne that they passen thurgh the strete,
And wolen be cleped 'maister' also.
But they ne shulde not willen so;   6920
The gospel is ther-ageyns, I gesse,
That shewith wel her wikkidnesse.
    Another custome use we:
Of hem that wole ayens us be,
We hate hem deedly everichon,   6925
And we wole werrey hem, as oon.
Hym that oon hatith, hate we alle,
And congecte hou to don hym falle.
And if we seen hym wynne honour,
Richesse, or preis, thurgh his valour,   6930

Provende, rent, or dignyte,
Ful fast, iwys, compassen we
Bi what ladder he is clomben so;
And for to maken hym doun to go,
With traisoun we wole hym defame,   6935
And don hym leese his goode name.
Thus from his ladder we hym take,
And thus his freendis foes we make;
But word ne wite shal he noon,
Till alle his freendis ben his foon.   6940
For if we dide it openly,
We myght have blame redily;
For hadde he wist of oure malice,
He hadde hym kept, but he were nyce.
    Another is this, that if so falle   6945
That ther be oon amonge us alle
That doth a good turn, out of drede,
We seyn it is oure alder deede.
Ye, sikerly, though he it feyned,
Or that hym list, or that hym deyned   6950
A man thurgh hym avaunced be;
Therof all parseners be we,
And tellen folk, whereso we go,
That man thurgh us is sprongen so.
And for to have of men preysyng,   6955
We purchace, thurgh oure flateryng,
Of riche men of gret pouste
Lettres to witnesse oure bounte,
So that man weneth, that may us see,
That alle vertu in us be.   6960
And alwey pore we us feyne;
But how so that we begge or pleyne,
We ben the folk, without lesyng,
That all thing have without havyng.
Thus be we dred of the puple, iwis.   6965
And gladly my purpos is this:
I dele with no wight, but he
Have gold and tresour gret plente;
Her acqueyntaunce wel love I;
This is moche my desir, shortly.   6970
I entremete me of brokages,
I make pees and mariages,
I am gladly executour,
And many tymes procuratour;
I am somtyme messager,   6975
That fallith not to my myster;
And many tymes I make enquestes —
For me that office not honest is.
To dele with other mennes thing,
That is to me a gret lykyng.   6980
And if that ye have ought to do
In place that I repeire to,
I shal it speden, thurgh my witt,
As soone as ye have told me it.

So that ye serve me to pay,   6985
My servyse shal be youre alway.
But whoso wole chastise me,
Anoon my love lost hath he;
For I love no man, in no gise,
That wole me repreve or chastise.   6990
But I wolde al folk undirtake,
And of no wight no teching take;
For I, that other folk chastie,
Wole not be taught fro my folie.
    I love noon hermitage more;   6995
All desertes and holtes hore,
And grete wodes everichon,
I lete hem to the Baptist John.
I quethe hym quyt and hym relesse
Of Egipt all the wildirnesse.   7000
To fer were alle my mansiounes
Fro alle citees and goode tounes.
My paleis and myn hous make I
There men may renne ynne openly,
And sey that I the world forsake,   7005
But al amydde I bilde and make
My hous, and swimme and pley therynne,
Bet than a fish doth with his fynne.
    Of Antecristes men am I,
Of whiche that Crist seith openly,   7010
They have abit of hoolynesse,
And lyven in such wikkednesse.
Outward, lambren semen we,
Fulle of goodnesse and of pitee,
And inward we, withouten fable,   7015
Ben gredy wolves ravysable.
We enviroune bothe lond and se;
With all the world werreyen we;
We wole ordeyne of alle thing,
Of folkis good, and her lyvyng.   7020
    If ther be castel or citee,
Wherynne that ony bouger be,
Although that they of Milayn were
(For therof ben they blamed there);
Or if a wight out of mesure   7025
Wolde lene his gold, and take usure,
For that he is so coveitous;
Or if he be to leccherous,
Or theef [or] haunte symonye,
Or provost full of trecherie,   7030
Or prelat lyvyng jolily,
Or prest that halt his quene hym by,
Or olde horis hostilers,
Or other bawdes or bordillers,
Or elles blamed of ony vice   7035
Of which men shulden don justice:
Bi all the seyntes that me pray,
But they defende them with lamprey,

With luce, with elys, with samons,
With tendre gees and with capons,   7040
With tartes, or with cheses fat,
With deynte flawnes brode and flat,
With caleweis, or with pullaylle,
With conynges, or with fyn vitaille,
That we, undir our clothes wide,   7045
Maken thourgh oure golet glide;
Or but he wole do come in haste
Roo-venysoun, bake in paste;
Whether so that he loure or groyne,
He shal have of a corde a loigne,   7050
With whiche men shal hym bynde and lede,
To brenne hym for his synful deede,
That men shull here hym crie and rore
A myle-wey aboute, and more;
Or ellis he shal in prisoun dye,   7055
But if he wole oure frendship bye,
Or smerten that that he hath do,
More than his gilt amounteth to.
But, and he couthe thurgh his sleght,
Do maken up a tour of height,   7060
Nought rought I whethir of ston, or tree,
Or erthe, or turves though it be,
Though it were of no vounde ston,
Wrought with squyre and scantilon,
So that the tour were stuffed well   7065
With alle richesse temporell,
And thanne that he wolde updresse
Engyns, bothe more and lesse,
To cast at us by every side,
To bere his goode name wide,   7070
Such sleghtes [as] I shal yow nevene,
Barelles of wyn, by sixe or sevene,
Or gold in sakkis gret plente,
He shulde soone delyvered be.
And if he have noon sich pitaunces,   7075
Late hym study in equipolences,
And late lyes and fallaces,
If that he wolde deserve oure graces;
Or we shal bere hym such witnesse
Of synne and of his wrecchidnesse,   7080
And don his loos so wide renne,
That al quyk we shulden hym brenne;
Or ellis yeve hym such penaunce,
That is wel wors than the pitaunce.
    For thou shalt never, for nothing,   7085
Kon knowen aright by her clothing
The traitours fulle of trecherie,
But thou her werkis can aspie.
And ne hadde the goode kepyng be
Whilom of the universite,   7090
That kepith the key of Cristendom,
We had ben turmented al and som.

Suche ben the stynkyng prophetis;
Nys non of hem that good prophete is,
For they thurgh wikked entencioun,   7095
The yeer of the Incarnacioun,
A thousand and two hundred yeer,
Fyve and fifty, ferther [ne neer],
Broughten a book, with sory grace,
To yeven ensample in comune place,   7100
That seide thus, though it were fable:
'This is the gospel perdurable,
That fro the Holy Goost is sent.'
Wel were it worth to ben brent!
Entitled was in such manere   7105
This book, of which I telle heere.
Ther nas no wight in all Parys,
Biforne Oure Lady, at parvys,
That he ne myghte bye the book,
To copy if hym talent tok.   7110
There myght he se, by gret tresoun,
Full many fals comparisoun:
'As moche as, thurgh his grete myght,
Be it of hete or of lyght,
The sonne sourmounteth the mone,   7115
That troublere is, and chaungith soone,
And the note-kernell the shelle
(I scorne not that I yow telle),
Right so, withouten ony gile,
Sourmounteth this noble evangile   7120
The word of ony evangelist.'
And to her title they token Crist;
And many a such comparisoun,
Of which I make no mencioun,
Mighte men in that book fynde,   7125
Whoso coude of hem have mynde.
    The universite, that tho was aslep,
Gan for to braide, and taken kep;
And at the noys the heed upcaste,
Ne never sithen slept it faste,   7130
But up it stert, and armes tok
Ayens this fals horrible bok,
Al redy bateil for to make,
And to the juge the book to take.
But they that broughten the bok there   7135
Hent it anoon awey, for fere;
They nolde shewe it nevere a del,
But thenne it kept, and kepen will,
Til such a tyme that they may see
That they so stronge woxen be   7140
That no wyght may hem wel withstonde;
For by that book they durst not stonde.
Awey they gonne it for to bere,
For they ne durste not answere
By exposicioun ne glose   7145
To that that clerkis wole appose

Ayens the cursednesse, iwys,
That in that book writen is.
Now wot I not, ne I can not see
What maner eende that there shal be　　7150
Of al this [bok] that they hyde;
But yit algate they shal abide
Til that they may it bet defende.
This, trowe I best, wol be her ende.

　　Thus, Antecrist abiden we,　　7155
For we ben alle of his meyne;
And what man that wole not be so,
Right soone he shal his lyf forgo.
We wole a puple upon hym areyse,
And thurgh oure gile don hym seise,　　7160
And hym on sharpe speris ryve,
Or other weyes brynge hym fro lyve,
But if that he wole folowe, iwis,
That in oure book writen is.

　　Thus mych wole oure book signifie,　　7165
That while Petre hath maistrie,
May never John shewe well his myght.
Now have I you declared right
The menyng of the bark and rynde,
That makith the entenciouns blynde;　　7170
But now at erst I wole bigynne
To expowne you the pith withynne: —
　　*　　*　　*　　*　　*　　*　　*

And the seculers comprehende,
That Cristes lawe wole defende,
And shulde it kepen and mayntenen　　7175
Ayenes hem that all sustenen,
And falsly to the puple techen.
[And] John bitokeneth hem [that] prechen
That ther nys lawe covenable
But thilke gospel perdurable,　　7180
That fro the Holy Gost was sent
To turne folk that ben myswent.

　　The strengthe of John they undirstonde
The grace, in which they seie they stonde,
That doth the synfull folk converte,　　7185
And hem to Jesus Crist reverte.
Full many another orribilite
May men in that book se,
That ben comaunded, douteles,
Ayens the lawe of Rome expres;　　7190
And all with Antecrist they holden,
As men may in the book biholden.
And thanne comaunden they to sleen
Alle tho that with Petre been;
But they shal nevere have that myght,　　7195
And, God toforn, for strif to fight,
That they ne shal ynowe fynde
That Petres lawe shal have in mynde,
And evere holde, and so mayntene,

That at the last it shal be sene　　7200
That they shal alle come therto,
For ought that they can speke or do.
And thilke lawe shal not stonde,
That they by John have undirstonde,
But, maugre hem, it shal adown,　　7205
And ben brought to confusioun.
But I wole stynt of this matere,
For it is wonder longe to here;
But hadde that ilke book endured,
Of better estat I were ensured;　　7210
And freendis have I yit, pardee,
That han me sett in gret degre.

　　Of all this world is emperour
Gyle my fadir, the trechour,
And emperisse my moder is,　　7215
Maugre the Holy Gost, iwis.
Oure myghty lynage and oure rowte
Regneth in every regne aboute;
And well is worthy we maistres be,
For all this world governe we,　　7220
And can the folk so wel disceyve
That noon oure gile can perceyve;
And though they don, they dar not seye;
The sothe dar no wight bywreye.
But he in Cristis wrath hym ledith,　　7225
That more than Crist my britheren dredith.
He nys no full good champioun,
That dredith such simulacioun;
Nor that for peyne wole refusen
Us to correcte and accusen.　　7230
He wole not entremete by right,
Ne have God in his eye-sight,
And therfore God shal hym punyshe.
But me ne rekketh of no vice,
Sithen men us loven comunably,　　7235
And holden us for so worthy
That we may folk repreve echoon,
And we nyl have repref of noon.
Whom shulden folk worshipen so
But us, that stynten never mo　　7240
To patren while that folk may us see,
Though it not so bihynde hem be.

　　And where is more wod folye,
Than to enhaunce chyvalrie,
And love noble men and gay,　　7245
That joly clothis weren alway?
If they be sich folk as they semen,
So clene, as men her clothis demen,
And that her wordis folowe her dede,
It is gret pite, out of drede,　　7250
For they wole be noon ypocritis!
Of hem, me thynketh, gret spit is;
I can not love hem on no side.

But beggers with these hodes wide,
With sleighe and pale faces lene,   7255
And greye clothis not full clene,
But fretted full of tatarwagges,
And highe shoos, knopped with dagges,
That frounce lyke a quaile pipe,
Or botis rivelyng as a gype;   7260
To such folk as I you dyvyse
Shulde princes, and these lordis wise,
Take all her londis and her thingis,
Bothe werre and pees, in governyngis;
To such folk shulde a prince hym yive,   7265
That wolde his lyf in honour lyve.
    And if they be not as they seme,
That serven thus the world to queme,
There wolde I dwelle, to disceyve
The folk, for they shal not perceyve.   7270
But I ne speke in no such wise,
That men shulde humble abit dispise,
So that no pride ther-undir be.
No man shulde hate, as thynkith me,
The pore man in sich clothyng.   7275
But God ne preisith hym nothing,
That seith he hath the world forsake,
And hath to worldly glorie hym take,
And wole of siche delices use.
Who may that begger wel excuse,   7280
That papelard, that hym yeldith so,
And wole to worldly ese go,
And seith that he the world hath left,
And gredily it grypeth eft?
He is the hound, shame is to seyn,   7285
That to his castyng goth ageyn.
    But unto you dar I not lye;
But myght I felen or aspie
That ye perceyved it no thyng,
Ye shulde have a stark lesyng   7290
Right in youre honde thus, to bigynne;
I nolde it lette for no synne."
    The god lough at the wondir tho,
And every wight gan laugh also,
And seide, "Lo, heere a man aright   7295
For to be trusty to every wight!"
"Fals-Semblant," quod Love, "sey to me,
Sith I thus have avaunced thee,
That in my court is thi dwellyng,
And of ribawdis shalt be my kyng,   7300
Wolt thou wel holden my forwardis?"
"Ye, sir, from hennes forwardis;
Hadde never youre fadir heere-biforn
Servaunt so trewe, sith he was born."
"That is ayenes all nature."   7305
"Sir, putte you in that aventure.
For though ye borowes take of me,

The sikerer shal ye never be
For ostages, ne sikirnesse,
Or chartres, for to bere witnesse.   7310
I take youresilf to recorde heere,
That men ne may in no manere
Teren the wolf out of his hide,
Til he be flayn, bak and side,
Though men hym bete and al defile.   7315
What! wene ye that I nil bigile
For I am clothed mekely?
Ther-undir is all my trechery;
Myn herte chaungith never the mo
For noon abit in which I go.   7320
Though I have chere of symplenesse,
I am not wery of shrewidnesse.
My lemman, Streyned-Abstinaunce,
Hath myster of my purveaunce;
She hadde ful longe ago be deed,   7325
Nere my councel and my red.
Lete hir al!one, and you and me."
And Love answerde, "I truste thee
Withoute borowe, for I wole noon."
And Fals-Semblant, the theef, anoon,   7330
Ryght in that ilke same place,
That hadde of tresoun al his face
Ryght blak withynne and whit withoute,
Thankyng hym, gan on his knees loute.
    Thanne was ther nought but, "Every man
Now to assaut, that sailen can,"   7336
Quod Love, "and that full hardyly."
Thanne armed they hem communly
Of sich armour as to hem fel.
Whanne they were armed, fers and fel,   7340
They wente hem forth, alle in a route,
And set the castel al aboute.
They will nought away, for no drede,
Till it so be that they ben dede,
Or til they have the castel take.   7345
And foure batels they gan make,
And parted hem in foure anoon,
And toke her way, and forth they gon,
The foure gates for to assaile,
Of whiche the kepers wole not faile;   7350
For they ben neithir sike ne dede,
But hardy folk, and stronge in dede.
    Now wole I seyn the countynaunce
Of Fals-Semblant and Abstynaunce,
That ben to Wikkid-Tonge went.   7355
But first they heelde her parlement,
Whether it to done were
To maken hem be knowen there,
Or elles walken forth disgised.
But at the laste, they devysed   7360
That they wolde gon in tapinage,

As it were in a pilgrimage,
Lyke good and hooly folk unfeyned.
And Dame Abstinence-Streyned
Tok on a robe of kamelyne,   7365
And gan hir graithe as a Bygyne.
A large coverechief of thred
She wrapped all aboute hir heed,
But she forgat not hir sawter;
A peire of bedis eke she ber   7370
Upon a las, all of whit thred,
On which that she hir bedes bed.
But she ne bought hem never a del,
For they were geven her, I wot wel,
God wot, of a full hooly frere,   7375
That seide he was hir fadir dere,
To whom she hadde ofter went
Than ony frere of his covent.
And he visited hir also,
And many a sermoun seide hir to;   7380
He nolde lette, for man on lyve,
That he ne wolde hir ofte shryve.
And with so great devocion
They made her confession,
That they had ofte, for the nones,   7385
Two heedes in oon hood at ones.

    Of fayre shap I devysed her the,
But pale of face somtyme was she;
That false traytouresse untrewe
Was lyk that salowe hors of hewe,   7390
That in the Apocalips is shewed,
That signifyeth tho folk beshrewed,
That ben al ful of trecherye,
And pale, through hypocrisye;
For on that hors no colour is,   7395
But only deed and pale, ywis.
Of such a colour enlangoured
Was Abstynence, iwys, coloured;
Of her estat she her repented,
As her visage represented.   7400

    She had a burdoun al of Thefte,
That Gyle had yeve her of his yefte;
And a skryppe of Faynt Distresse,
That ful was of elengenesse;
And forth she walked sobrely.   7405
And Fals-Semblant saynt, *je vous die*,
[Had], as it were for such mister,
Don on the cope of a frer,
With chere symple and ful pytous;
Hys lokyng was not disdeynous,   7410
Ne proud, but meke and ful pesyble.

    About his necke he bar a byble,
And squierly forth gan he gon,
And, for to rest his lymmes upon,
He had of Treason a potente;   7415

As he were feble, his way he wente.
But in his sleve he gan to thringe
A rasour sharp and wel bytynge,
That was forged in a forge,
Which that men clepen Coupe-Gorge.   7420
    So longe forth her way they nomen,
Tyl they to Wicked-Tonge comen,
That al his gate was syttyng,
And saw folk in the way passyng.
The pilgrymes saw he faste by,   7425
That beren hem ful mekely,
And humbly they with him mette.
Dame Abstinence first him grette,
And sythe him Fals-Semblant salued,
And he hem; but he not remued,   7430
For he ne dredde hem not a del.
For whan he saw her faces wel,
Alway in herte him thoughte so,
He shulde knowe hem bothe two;
For wel he knew Dame Abstynaunce,   7435
But he ne knew not Constreynaunce.
He knew nat that she was constrayned,
Ne of her theves lyve fayned,
But wende she com of wyl al free,
But she com in another degree,   7440
And if of good wyl she began,
That wyl was fayled her than.

    And Fals-Semblant had he sayn als,
But he knew nat that he was fals.
Yet fals was he, but his falsnesse   7445
Ne coude he nat espye nor gesse;
For Semblant was so slye wrought,
That Falsnesse he ne espyed nought.
    But haddest thou knowen hym beforn,
Thou woldest on a bok have sworn,   7450
Whan thou him saugh in thylke aray,
That he, that whilom was so gay,
And of the daunce joly Robyn,
Was tho become a Jacobyn.
But sothly, what so men hym calle,   7455
Freres preachours ben good men alle;
Her order wickedly they beren,
Suche mynstrelles if they weren.
So ben Augustyns and Cordyleres,
And Carmes, and eke Sacked Freeres,   7460
And alle freres, shodde and bare
(Though some of hem ben great and square)
Ful hooly men, as I hem deme;
Everych of hem wolde good man seme.
But shalt thou never of apparence   7465
Sen conclude good consequence
In non argument, ywis,
If existens al fayled is.
For men may fynde alway sophyme

The consequence to envenyme, 7470
Whoso that hath the subtelte
The double sentence for to se.
　Whan the pylgrymes commen were
To Wicked-Tonge, that dwelled there,
Her harneys nygh hem was algate; 7475
By Wicked-Tonge adown they sate,
That bad hem ner him for to come,
And of tidynges telle him some,
And sayd hem: "What cas maketh you
To come into this place now?" 7480
　"Sir," sayde Strayned-Abstynaunce,
"We, for to drye our penaunce,
With hertes pytous and devoute
Are commen, as pylgrimes gon aboute.
Wel nygh on fote alwey we go; 7485
Ful dusty ben our heeles two;
And thus bothe we ben sent
Throughout this world, that is miswent,
To yeve ensample, and preche also.
To fysshen synful men we go, 7490
For other fysshynge ne fysshe we.
And, sir, for that charyte,
As we be wonte, herborowe we crave,
Your lyf to amende, Christ it save!
And, so it shulde you nat displease, 7495
We wolden, if it were youre ease,
A short sermon unto you sayn."
And Wicked-Tonge answered agayn:
"The hous," quod he, "such as ye see,
Shal nat be warned you for me. 7500
Say what you lyst, and I wol here."
　"Graunt mercy, swete sire dere!"
Quod alderfirst Dame Abstynence,
And thus began she her sentence:
　"Sir, the firste vertu, certayn, 7505
The greatest and moste soverayn
That may be founde in any man,
For havynge, or for wyt he can,
That is his tonge to refrayne;
Therto ought every wight him payne. 7510
For it is better stylle be
Than for to speken harm, parde!
And he that herkeneth it gladly,
He is no good man, sykerly.
　And, sir, aboven al other synne, 7515
In that art thou most gylty inne.
Thou spake a jape not longe ago,
(And, sir, that was ryght yvel do)
Of a young man that here repayred,
And never yet this place apayred. 7520
Thou saydest he awayted nothyng
But to disceyve Fayr-Welcomyng,
Ye sayde nothyng soth of that;

But, sir, ye lye, I tel you plat.
He ne cometh no more, ne goth, parde! 7525
I trowe ye shal him never se.
Fayr-Welcomyng in prison is,
That ofte hath played with you, er this,
The fayrest games that he coude,
Withoute fylthe, stylle or loude. 7530
Now dar he nat himself solace;
Ye han also the man do chace,
That he dar neyther come ne go.
What meveth you to hate him so,
But properly your wicked thought, 7535
That many a fals leasyng hath thought
That meveth your foole eloquence,
That jangleth ever in audyence,
And on the folk areyseth blame,
And doth hem dishonour and shame, 7540
For thyng that may have no prevyng,
But lyklynesse, and contryvyng?
　For I dar sayn that Reason demeth
It is nat al soth thyng that semeth,
And it is synne to controve 7545
Thyng that is to reprove;
This wote ye wel, and sir, therfore
Ye arn to blame the more.
And nathelesse, he recketh lyte;
He yeveth nat now therof a myte. 7550
For if he thoughte harm, parfay,
He wolde come and gon al day;
He coude himselve nat abstene.
Now cometh he nat, and that is sene,
For he ne taketh of it no cure, 7555
But if it be through aventure,
And lasse than other folk, algate.
And thou her watchest at the gate,
With speare in thyn arest alway;
There muse, musard, al the day. 7560
Thou wakest night and day for thought;
Iwis, thy traveyle is for nought;
And Jelousye, withouten fayle,
Shal never quyte the thy traveyle.
And skathe is that Fayr-Welcomyng, 7565
Withouten any trespassyng,
Shal wrongfully in prison be,
There wepeth and languyssheth he.
And though thou never yet, ywis,
Agyltest man no more but this, 7570
(Take nat a-gref) it were worthy
To putte the out of this bayly,
And afterward in prison lye,
And fettre the tyl that thou dye;
For thou shalt for this synne dwelle 7575
Right in the devels ers of helle,
But if that thou repente thee."

"Ma fay, thou liest falsly!" quod he.
"What? welcome with myschaunce now!
Have I therfore herbered yow,   7580
To seye me shame, and eke reprove?
With sory hap, to youre bihove,
Am I to day youre herberger!
Go herber yow elleswhere than heer,
That han a lyer called me!   7585
Two tregetours art thou and he,
That in myn hous do me this shame,
And for my soth-sawe ye me blame,
Is this the sermoun that ye make?
To all the develles I me take,   7590
Or elles, God, thou me confounde,
But, er men diden this castel founde,
It passid not ten daies or twelve,
But it was told right to myselve,
And as they seide, right so tolde I,   7595
He kyst the Rose pryvyly!
Thus seide I now, and have seid yore;
I not wher he dide any more.
Why shulde men sey me such a thyng,
If it hadde ben gabbyng?   7600
Ryght so seide I, and wol seye yit;
I trowe, I lied not of it.
And with my bemes I wole blowe
To alle neighboris a-rowe,
How he hath bothe comen and gon."   7605
    Tho spak Fals-Semblant right anon:
"All is not gospel, out of doute,
That men seyn in the town aboute.
Ley no deef ere to my spekyng;
I swere yow, sir, it is gabbyng!   7610
I trowe ye wote wel, certeynly,
That no man loveth hym tenderly
That seith hym harm, if he wot it,
All he be never so pore of wit.
And soth is also, sikerly   7615
(This knowe ye, sir, as wel as I),
That lovers gladly wole visiten
The places there her loves habiten.
This man yow loveth and eke honoureth;
This man to serve you laboureth,   7620
And clepith you his freend so deere:
And this man makith you good chere,
And everywhere that [he] you meteth,
He yow saloweth, and he you greteth.
He preseth not so ofte that ye   7625
Ought of his come encombred be;
Ther presen other folk on yow
Full ofter than he doth now.
And if his herte hym streyned so
Unto the Rose for to go,   7630
Ye shulde hym sen so ofte nede,

That ye shulde take hym with the dede.
He cowde his comyng not forbere,
Though me hym thrilled with a spere;
It nere not thanne as it is now.   7635
But trusteth wel, I swere it yow,
That it is clene out of his thought.
Sir, certis, he ne thenkith it nought;
No more ne doth Fair-Welcomyng,
That sore abieth al this thing.   7640
And if they were of oon assent,
Full soone were the Rose hent;
The maugre youres wolde be.
And sir, of o thing herkeneth me,
Sith ye this man that loveth yow   7645
Han seid such harm and shame now,
Witeth wel, if he gessed it,
Ye may wel demen in youre wit
He nolde nothyng love you so,
Ne callen you his freend also,   7650
But nyght and day he wolde wake
The castell to destroie and take,
If it were soth as ye devise;
Or som man in som maner wise
Might it warne hym everydel,   7655
Or by hymsilf perceyven wel.
For sith he myght not come and gon,
As he was whilom wont to don,
He myght it sone wite and see;
But now all other wise doth he.   7660
Thanne have [ye], sir, al outerly,
Deserved helle, and jolyly
The deth of helle, douteles,
That thrallen folk so gilteles."
    Fals-Semblant proveth so this thing   7665
That he can noon answeryng,
And seth alwey such apparaunce
That nygh he fel in repentaunce,
And seide hym: — "Sir, it may wel be.
Semblant, a good man semen ye,   7670
And, Abstinence, full wise ye seme.
Of o talent you bothe I deme.
What counceil wole ye to me yiven?"
    "Ryght heere anoon thou shalt be shryven,
And sey thy synne withoute more;   7675
Of this shalt thou repente sore.
For I am prest and have pouste
To shryve folk of most dignyte
That ben, as wide as world may dure.
Of all this world I have the cure,   7680
And that hadde never yit persoun,
Ne vicarie of no maner toun.
And, God wot, I have of thee
A thousand tymes more pitee
Than hath thi preest parochial,   7685

Though he thy freend be special.
I have avauntage, in o wise,
That youre prelatis ben not so wise
Ne half so lettred as am I.
I am licenced boldely   7690
In divynite for to rede,

And to confessen, out of drede.
If ye wol you now confesse,
And leave your synnes, more and lesse,
Without abode, knele down anon,   7695
And you shal have absolucion."

Explicit.

APPENDIX

BIBLIOGRAPHY

GENERAL REFERENCES

THE general bibliography given here and the more specific references in the notes that follow are to be understood everywhere to be selected and not exhaustive lists. It is impossible to give complete bibliographical information within the limits of a library edition of Chaucer.

Miss E. P. Hammond's admirable Chaucer, A Bibliographical Manual, New York, 1908, is supplemented for the period since its publication by the following bibliographies:

J. E. Wells, A Manual of the Writings in Middle English, New Haven, 1916; Supplements, 1919, 1923, 1926, 1929, 1932, 1935, 1938, 1941; and 1945 (by Beatrice D. Brown, Eleanor K. Heningham, and F. L. Utley).
Martha H. Shackford, Chaucer, Selected References, Wellesley, Mass., 1918.
D. D. Griffith, A Bibliography of Chaucer, Seattle, 1926.
W. S. Martin, A Chaucer Bibliography, Durham, N. Carolina, 1935.
A. C. Baugh, Fifty Years of Chaucer Scholarship, Speculum, XXVI, 659 ff.
D. D. Griffith, Bibliography of Chaucer, 1908–1953, Seattle, 1955.
> (A comprehensive, well classified list of books and articles on Chaucer since the publication of Miss Hammond's bibliography. It is very inclusive, even recording numerous unpublished theses, and its full registration of reviews will be of great use to researchers. Since it did not appear until the present revised commentary was already in typescript prepared for the press, the editor has been able to make only slight use of Professor Griffith's work.)

Annual lists of publications relating to Chaucer are included in the Year's Work in English Studies, Oxford, 1919—, the Annual Bibliography of the Modern Language Association of America, published in PMLA, and that of the Modern Humanities Research Association, Cambridge, 1920—. This last was suspended during the Second World War, and though publication has been resumed, the series extends only to 1942 at this time. The Jahresbericht . . . der Germanischen Philologie suspended publication with the 1935 number, but has recently resumed with the 1936 bibliography, published 1954.

The publications of the Chaucer Society, to which frequent reference is made in the notes, are listed by Miss Hammond, pp. 523–41.

For an excellent brief introduction to the study of Chaucer, with selected bibliography, reference may be made to R. D. French, A Chaucer Handbook, 2nd ed. New York, 1947.

LIFE OF CHAUCER

Early biographies are noted and described by Miss Hammond, pp. 1–39. The first work of critical value is that of Sir Harris Nicolas, The Life of Chaucer, London, 1843, also prefixed to the Aldine Chaucer, London, 1845. There is a good survey and discussion in T. R. Lounsbury's Studies in Chaucer, 3 v., New York, 1892 (ch. 1, The Life of Chaucer, ch. 2, The Chaucer Legend). Other lives of recent date are:

W. W. Skeat's biographical introduction in the Oxford Chaucer, I, ix–lxi.
J. W. Hales, Chaucer, Dictionary of National Biography, 1887.
A. W. Pollard, Chaucer, Encyclopædia Britannica, 11th ed., 1910, et seq.
A. W. Ward, Chaucer, English Men of Letters, London, 1879.
G. H. Cowling, Chaucer, London, 1927.
W. Clemen, Der Junge Chaucer, Kölner Anglistiche Arbeiten, No. 33, 1938.
Marchette Chute, Geoffrey Chaucer of England, New York, 1946 (with a useful bibliography).

Biographical sketches are prefixed to many editions of selected works, the most valuable being that in J. M. Manly's selections from the Canterbury Tales, New York, 1928. There is also a good brief outline in French's Chaucer Handbook, ch. 2.

The following studies of special topics are important:

A. A. Kern, The Ancestry of Chaucer, Baltimore, 1906.
J. R. Hulbert, Chaucer's Official Life, Menasha, Wisc., 1912.
M. B. Ruud, Thomas Chaucer, Univ. of Minn. Studies in Lang. and Lit., no. 9, Minneapolis, 1926.
Edith Rickert, Was Chaucer a Student at the Inner Temple?, Manly Anniversary Studies, Chicago, 1923.
Russell Krauss, Chaucerian Problems: Especially The Petherton Forestership and The Question of Thomas Chaucer, in Three Chaucer Studies, New York, 1932.

Many documents themselves relating to Chaucer were made accessible in Life-Records of Chaucer, published in four parts by the Chaucer Society, 1875–1900. There is a useful index by E. P. Kuhl in MP, X (1912–13), 527 ff.

A very large number of additional records have been found in recent years. See the bibliographies of Wells and Griffith; also Manly's sketch, where account was taken of such new data. A selection of the life-records relating to Thomas Chaucer, collected but not printed by R. E. G. and E. F. Kirk, with additional items, has been published by A. C. Baugh in PMLA, XLVII (1932), 461 ff. Cf. also Krauss's study, cited above. Since the death of both Professors Manly and Rickert the work of collecting life-records has been steadily pursued, chiefly under the direction of Miss Lilian Redstone. A description of the material assembled by her and her corps of researchers is given by Professor M. M. Crow, Univ. of Texas Studies in English XXXI, 1 ff. Hundreds of new records, either referring specifically to Chaucer or illustrating his activities, still await publication. For an account of the project, as well as a survey of earlier biographies, see Mr. Crow's co-editor, Professor C. C. Olson, The Emerging Biography of a Poet (College of the Pacific, 1953). The numerous special articles on Chaucer's life published in recent years are listed in Professor Griffith's Bibliography (1955), pp. 13–27.

On the portraits of Chaucer there is a special study by M. H. Spielmann, Chaucer Society, 1900. See also Miss Hammond's Manual, p. 49, and her English Verse between Chaucer and Surrey, Durham, N.C., 1927, p. 408; Manly, selections from the *Canterbury Tales*, pp. 37–39; A. Brusendorff, The Chaucer Tradition, London, 1925, pp. 13–27; Manly-Rickert, Canterbury Tales, I, 587–590, where Miss Margaret Rickert makes a careful comparison of the Ellesmere and Hoccleve miniatures. On the Plimpton portrait, see R. Call, Speculum, XXII, 135 ff. with a useful fund of information about other representations of Chaucer. See also G. L. Lam and W. N. Smith, MLQ, V, 303 ff. (on Vertue's drawings of Chaucer).

EDITIONS

The early editions of Chaucer are listed and described by Miss Hammond, pp. 114 ff., 202 ff., 350, 395. Of modern editions, that of Thomas Tyrwhitt (*Canterbury Tales*, 5 v., London, 1775–78) is still interesting for its introduction and commentary. Knowledge of Middle English grammar had not advanced far enough in Tyrwhitt's time to make possible the establishment of a correct text. Only two of the complete editions before the present one represent at all closely Chaucer's linguistic usage, that of Skeat and that of the Globe editors.

W. W. Skeat, Oxford Chaucer, 6 v. and Supplement, Oxford, 1894–97; The Student's Chaucer, Oxford, 1895.
The Globe Chaucer, London, 1898: *Canterbury Tales* and *Legend of Good Women*, ed. A. W. Pollard; Minor Poems, ed. H. F. Heath; *Boece*, *Astrolabe*, and *Romaunt*, ed. M. H. Liddell; *Troilus*, ed. W. S. McCormick.

There have been various reprints of Skeat's text, in whole or in part, most notably that of the Kelmscott Press, ed. T. S. Ellis, 1896.

References to important editions of selected works, and also to investigations of the MSS. will be given in the Textual Notes.

But a reference to the monumental Chicago edition of the *Canterbury Tales* may be added here.

John M. Manly and Edith Rickert, The Text of the Canterbury Tales, studied on the basis of all known manuscripts, 6 v., University of Chicago Press, 1940.

Mention should also be made of the recently discovered Equatorie of the Planetis, conjecturally ascribed to Chaucer by some authorities, and edited by Derek J. Price, Cambridge University Press, 1955. The work contains a linguistic analysis by R. M. Wilson and a discussion of the question of authorship by the editor.

CANON AND CHRONOLOGY

Studies of the authenticity and date of the various works will be taken up at appropriate places in the notes. General references on the subject are given by Miss Hammond, pp. 51–72. The following treatments of the subject are of special importance:

John Koch, The Chronology of Chaucer's Writings, Chaucer Society, 1890.
W. W. Skeat, The Chaucer Canon, Oxford, 1900.
J. S. P. Tatlock, The Development and Chronology of Chaucer's Works, Chaucer Society, 1907.
Aage Brusendorff, The Chaucer Tradition, London, 1924.

The following studies of special topics may also be noted here because of their bearing on general problems:

J. L. Lowes, The Prologue to the "Legend of Good Women" as Related to the French "Marguerite" Poems and the "Filostrato," PMLA, XIX (1904), 593 ff.; The Prologue to the "Legend of Good Women" Considered in its Chronological Relations, PMLA, XX (1905), 749 ff.
G. L. Kittredge, The Date of Chaucer's Troilus, Chaucer Society, 1909.

No such convenient chronological test has been found for Chaucer's writings as the familiar classification of Shakespeare's plays by end-stopped and run-on lines. But a certain regularity of change in Chaucer's practice with regard to the apocopation of final -e was pointed out by Charlotte F. Babcock in A Study of the Metrical Use of the Inflectional -e in Middle English, an unpublished Radcliffe dissertation, 1912; results summarized in PMLA, XXIX (1914), 59 ff. Mr. G. H. Cowling (in Rev. of Engl. Stud., II (1926), 311 ff., and again in his Chaucer, London, 1927, pp. 67 ff.) tried to find a criterion of date in the place of the pause, or *volta*, in the Chaucerian stanza. But his results are very uncertain.

LITERARY SOURCES

Detailed facts with regard to the sources of Chaucer's writings are given in the various introductions and notes. Passages cited by reference will often be found quoted at length in Skeat's notes. A convenient general list of the writings used by Chaucer is given by Miss Hammond, pp. 73–105; and Lounsbury's chapter on "The Learning of Chaucer" (Studies, ch. 5) gives an excellent survey of the subject. For valuable observations on the subject see also R. A. Pratt, Progress of Mediæval Studies in the U.S. and Canada, Bulletin No. 20, 1949, pp. 40 ff. But recent investigations have brought to light information not included in either of these works. The following studies of Chaucer's relations to special authors or writings may be noted:

Vulgate: Grace W. Landrum, Chaucer's Use of the Vulgate, unpublished Radcliffe dissertation, 1921; results summarized in PMLA, XXXIX (1924), 75 ff.
Latin Poets: E. F. Shannon, Chaucer and the Roman Poets, Cambridge, Mass., 1929.
   John Koch, Chaucers Belesenheit in den Römischen Klassikern, ESt, LVII (1923), 8 ff.
Statius: B. A. Wise, The Influence of Statius upon Chaucer, Baltimore, 1911.
Horace: C. L. Wrenn, MLR, XVIII, 286 ff.

Claudian: R. A. Pratt, Spec., XXII, 419 ff.
Seneca: H. M. Ayres, Rom. Rev., X, 1 ff.
Goliardic verse: J. A. S. McPeek, Chaucer and the Goliards, Spec., XXVI, 332.
Boethius: B. L. Jefferson, Chaucer and the Consolation of Philosophy of Boethius, Princeton, 1917.
Dante: J. L. Lowes, Chaucer and Dante's Convivio, MP, XIII (1915–16), 19 ff.; Chaucer and Dante, MP, XIV (1916–17), 705 ff.
   C. Looten, Chaucer et Dante, Rev. de Lit. Comp., V (1925), 545 ff.
   J. P. Bethel, The Influence of Dante on Chaucer's Thought and Expression, unpublished Harvard dissertation, 1927.
Boccaccio: H. M. Cummings, The Indebtedness of Chaucer's Works to the Italian Works of Boccaccio, Univ. of Cincinnati Studies, X, 1916.
   R. A. Pratt, Chaucer's Use of the Teseida, PMLA, LXII, 598 ff.
Roman de la Rose: Lisi Cipriani, Studies in the Influence of the Romance of the Rose on Chaucer, PMLA, XXII (1907), 552 ff.
   D. S. Fansler, Chaucer and the Roman de la Rose, New York, 1914.
Machaut: G. L. Kittredge, Guillaume de Machaut and the Book of the Duchess, PMLA, XXX (1915), 1 ff.
Deschamps: J. L. Lowes, Chaucer and the Miroir de Mariage, MP, VIII (1910–11), 165 ff., 305 ff.; Illustrations of Chaucer, drawn chiefly from Deschamps, Rom. Rev., II (1911), 113 ff.
Graunson: Haldeen Braddy, Chaucer and the French Poet Graunson, Louisiana State University, 1947.
Proverbs: Willi Haeckel, Das Sprichwort bei Chaucer, Erlanger Beiträge, II, viii, 1890.
   W. W. Skeat, Early English Proverbs, Oxford, 1910.
   B. J. Whiting, Studies in the Middle English Proverb, Harvard dissertation, 1932. A portion published under the title Chaucer's Use of Proverbs, Harvard University Press, 1934.

For parallels to Chaucer's writings in popular literature—ballads, folk-tales, sagas, etc.—a general reference should be added here to Stith Thompson, Motif-Index of Folk-Literature, Bloomington, Ind., 1932–6; revised and enlarged edition now appearing, Ind. Univ. Press, 1955—.

MEDIÆVAL HISTORY, LIFE, AND THOUGHT

L. G. Paetow, A Guide to the Study of Mediæval History, rev. ed., New York, 1931.
Charles Gross, Sources and Literature of English History, 2d ed., London, 1915.
The Political History of England, general editors, W. Hunt and R. L. Poole: vol. III, by T. F. Tout, London, 1905; vol. IV, by C. Oman, London, 1906.
G. M. Trevelyan, England in the Age of Wycliffe, 4th ed., London, 1909; Illustrated English Social History, London, 1949. The first volume is especially useful for illustrations taken from mediæval manuscripts.
W. W. Capes, The English Church in the Fourteenth and Fifteenth Centuries, London, 1900.
H. W. C. Davis, Mediæval England, Oxford, 1924.
H. S. Bennett, Chaucer and the Fifteenth Century, Oxford, 1947.
J. W. Thompson, The Middle Ages, 300–1500, New York, 1931; Reference Studies in Mediæval History, rev. ed., Chicago, 1923.
Eileen Power, Mediæval People, London, 1924.
Edith Rickert, Chaucer's World, ed. C. C. Olson and M. M. Crow, New York and London, 1948.
L. Thorndike, A History of Magic and Experimental Science during the First Thirteen Centuries of our Era, New York, 1923.
W. C. Curry, Chaucer and the Mediæval Sciences, New York, 1926.
T. O. Wedel, The Mediæval Attitude toward Astrology, New Haven, 1920.
J. J. Jusserand, English Wayfaring Life in the Middle Ages (XIVth Century), rev. ed., London, 1925.
G. G. Coulton, Chaucer and his England, 3d ed., London, 1921; Social Life in Britain from the Conquest to the Reformation, Cambridge Univ. Press, 1918; Mediæval Panorama, New York and Cambridge, 1938.
H. S. Ward, The Canterbury Pilgrimages, London, 1904.
Francis Watt, Canterbury Pilgrims and their Ways, London, 1917.

HISTORY OF MIDDLE ENGLISH LITERATURE

B. ten Brink, Geschichte der Englischen Litteratur, 2 v., 2d ed., Strassburg, 1899–1912; 1st ed. tr., History of English Literature, 2 v. in 3, New York, 1883–96.
Cambridge History of English Literature, II, Cambridge, 1908.
W. H. Schofield, English Literature from the Norman Conquest to Chaucer, London, 1906.
J. J. Jusserand, Histoire Littéraire du Peuple Anglais, des Origines à la Renaissance, Paris, 1894; tr., A Literary History of the English People, I, 3d ed., London, 1925.

GENERAL CRITICISM

J. R. Lowell, Chaucer, North American Rev., CXI (1870), 155 ff.; reprinted in My Study Windows, Boston, 1871.
B. ten Brink, Chaucer Studien, Münster, 1870.
T. R. Lounsbury, Studies in Chaucer, 3 v., New York, 1892.
George Saintsbury, CHEL, II, ch. 7 (1908).
R. K. Root, The Poetry of Chaucer, rev. ed., Boston, 1922.
G. L. Kittredge, Chaucer and his Poetry, Cambridge, Mass., 1915.
Émile Legouis, Geoffroy Chaucer, Paris, 1910; tr., London, 1913.
Aage Brusendorff, The Chaucer Tradition, London, 1925.
J. M. Manly, Some New Light on Chaucer, New York, 1926; Chaucer and the Rhetoricians, Proceedings of the British Academy, XII (1926), Warton Lecture.

J. L. Lowes, The Art of Geoffrey Chaucer, London, 1930.

C. F. E. Spurgeon, Five Hundred Years of Chaucer Criticism and Allusion, 1357–1900, Chaucer Society, 7 parts, 1914–24; also 3 v., Cambridge, 1925; Supplement, Additional Entries, 1868–1900, London, 1920; Chaucer devant la Critique en Angleterre et en France depuis son temps jusqu'à nos jours, Paris, 1911. For comments on Miss Spurgeon's work see Earle Birney, JEGP, XLI, 303 ff.

Germaine C. Dempster, Dramatic Irony in Chaucer, Stanford Univ. Publications in Languages and Literature, IV, No. 3, 1932.

W. Héraucourt, Die Wertwelt Chaucers, Heidelberg, 1939.

Percy Van Dyke Shelly, The Living Chaucer, Philadelphia, 1940.

Nevill Coghill, The Poet Chaucer, London, 1947.

C. S. Lewis, The Allegory of Love: A Study of Mediæval Tradition, Oxford, 1936.

H. R. Patch, On Rereading Chaucer, Harvard Univ. Press, 1939.

W. W. Lawrence, Chaucer and the Canterbury Tales, New York, 1950.

K. Malone, Chapters on Chaucer, Baltimore, 1951.

J. S. P. Tatlock, The Mind and Art of Chaucer, Syracuse, N.Y., 1950.

J. Speirs, Chaucer the Maker, London, 1951.

Sister M. Madeleva, C.S.C., A Lost Language, New York, 1951.

Gordon Hall Gerould, Chaucerian Essays, Princeton, 1952.

Clair C. Olson, Chaucer and the Music of the Fourteenth Century, Spec., XV, 64 ff.

Dorothy Everett, Some Reflections on Chaucer's "Art Poetical," Proceedings of the British Academy, XXXVI, 131 ff.

F. Mossé, Chaucer et le Métier de l'Écrivain, Études Anglaises, VII, 395 ff.

LANGUAGE AND METER

The foundations of a scientific knowledge of Chaucer's grammar were laid in the memorable essay of Francis James Child, Observations on the Language of Chaucer (Memoirs of the American Academy of Arts and Sciences, new ser., VIII (1861–63), 445 ff.). Child's study was based upon Wright's printed text of the Canterbury Tales (Percy Society, 3 v., 1847–51). After many years the same method was extended by Professor Kittredge to the Troilus (Observations on the Language of Chaucer's Troilus, Chaucer Society, 1894), and by Professor Manly to that of the Legend of Good Women ([Harv.] Stud. and Notes in Phil, and Lit., II (1893), 1 ff.). A similar study of the Ellesmere text of the Canterbury Tales by A. C. Garrett (Harvard dissertation, 1892) was never published. The results of Child's investigation were used in A. J. Ellis's Early English Pronunciation, Chaucer Society, 5 v., 1869–89.

The earliest authoritative treatment of Chaucer's language in the form of a systematic grammar is B. ten Brink's Chaucers Sprache und Verskunst, Leipzig, 1884, 3d ed., Leipzig, 1920. Schematic summaries of the grammar have been given in most of the modern editions of Chaucer's works, the most

useful being those in Skeat's Oxford Chaucer, in Liddell's edition of the General Prologue, etc., London, 1901, and in Manly's selections from the Canterbury Tales. For a valuable study of the linguistic usage in Chaucerian MSS., see Friedrich Wild, Die Sprachlichen Eigentümlichkeiten der Wichtigeren Chaucer-handschriften und die Sprache Chaucers, Wiener Beiträge, XLIV, 1915.

The following grammars are standard authorities for Middle English:

Lorenz Morsbach, Mittelenglische Grammatik, Halle, 1896.

Max Kaluza, Historische Grammatik der Englischen Sprache, 2 v., Berlin, 1900–01.

Joseph Wright, An Elementary Middle English Grammar, 2d ed., Oxford, 1928.

Richard Jordan, Handbuch der Mittelenglischen Grammatik, Heidelberg, 1925.

Karl Luick, Historische Grammatik der Englischen Sprache, Leipzig, 1914–29.

There is a convenient summary by Samuel Moore, Historical Outlines of English Phonology and Morphology, Ann Arbor, Mich., 1925, revised by A. H. Marckwardt as Historical Outlines of Engish Sounds and Inflections, Ann Arbor, 1951. The older grammars of E. Mätzner (1880–85) and C. F. Koch (2d ed., 1882–91) are still valuable to consult, chiefly for their illustrations of syntax and usage. See also F. Karpf, Studien zur Syntax an den Werken Geoffrey Chaucers, Wiener Beiträge zur englischen Philologie, I teil, 55, 1930. Special mention should also be made of A Guide to Chaucer's Pronunciation, by H. Kökeritz, Stockholm and New Haven, 1954.

The study of Chaucer's meter has been closely associated with that of his grammar, and many observations will be found in the works of Child, Kittredge, and Ten Brink, cited above. Systematic treatment of the subject appears in most modern editions, as in those, for example, of Skeat, Liddell, and Manly. The metrical forms employed by Chaucer are of course treated in the standard works on English versification. General reference may be made to the following:

Jakob Schipper, Englische Metrik in Historischer und Systematischer Entwickelung Dargestellt, 2 pts. in 3 v., Bonn, 1881–88; also his account of "Fremde Metra" in Paul's Grundriss der Germanischen Philologie, II, ii, 7, 2d ed., Strassburg, 1905, pp. 181 ff.

G. Saintsbury, A History of English Prosody from the Twelfth Century to the Present Day, 3 v., London, 1906–10 (particularly vol. I, pp. 43 ff.).

There is a good brief discussion of the sources of Chaucer's decasyllabic verse-forms in R. M. Alden's English Verse, New York, 1903, pp. 177 ff. Interesting observations on Chaucer's artistic methods and effects are made by Miss Hammond, English Verse between Chaucer and Surrey, pp. 17 ff.

It should be added that the generally accepted theory of Chaucer's pronunciation of final -e and his metrical use of it has been disputed by Mrs. Ruth Buchanan McJimsey, Chaucer's Irregular -E, New York, 1942, and by J. G. Southworth, PMLA, LXII, 910 ff. and Verses of Cadence, Oxford, 1954.

DICTIONARIES

Many editions of Chaucer are provided with glossaries. The most extensive of these is that of Skeat, in his Oxford Chaucer, Vol. VI. There is also a Chaucer concordance: John S. P. Tatlock and Arthur G. Kennedy, A Concordance to the Complete Works of Geoffrey Chaucer and the Romaunt of the Rose, Washington, 1927.

For Middle English in general the existing lexicons have been very inadequate. The most important are:

A Middle-English Dictionary, by Francis Henry Stratmann, revised by Henry Bradley, Oxford, 1891.

E. Mätzner, Altenglische Sprachproben nebst einem Wörterbuche, Berlin, 1878 —. (More extensive than Bradley-Stratmann, but incomplete. Continuations cease with the letter M.)

There are many citations from Middle English in the Oxford Dictionary (NED). But neither the vocabulary of the period nor the occurrence of words is fully registered.

A comprehensive Middle English Dictionary, edited by Hans Kurath and Sherman M. Kuhn (Ann Arbor, 1952 —) is now appearing. But at the time of writing only a few fascicles, including a Plan and Bibliography, had been published.

There is also a valuable gazetteer of Chaucer's geographical names by Professor F. P. Magoun, Jr., published in three instalments: Chaucer's Ancient and Biblical World, Med. Stud., XV, 107 ff.; Chaucer's Great Britain, ibid., XVI, 131 ff.; Chaucer's Mediæval World outside Great Britain, ibid., XVII, 117 ff. This work analyzes in detail Chaucer's treatment of the various localities and peoples. Frequent use of Mr. Magoun's material has been made in the Explanatory Notes and Glossary of Proper Names below.

DICTIONARIES

Many editions of Chaucer are provided with glossaries. The most extensive of these is that of Skeat, in his Oxford Chaucer, Vol. VI. There is also a Chaucer concordance: John S. P. Tatlock and Arthur G. Kennedy, *A Concordance to the Complete Works of Geoffrey Chaucer and the Romaunt of the Rose*, Washington, 1927.

For Middle English in general the existing lexicons have been very inadequate. The most important are:

A Middle-English Dictionary, by Francis Henry Stratmann, revised by Henry Bradley, Oxford, 1891.

E. Mätzner, Altenglische Sprachproben nebst einem Wörterbuche, Berlin, 1878– . (More extensive than Bradley-Stratmann, but incomplete. Continuations cease with the letter M.)

There are many citations from Middle English in the Oxford Dictionary (NED). But neither the vocabulary of the period nor the occurrence of words is fully registered.

A comprehensive Middle English Dictionary edited by Hans Kurath and Sherman M. Kuhn (Ann Arbor, 1952–) is now appearing. But at the time of writing only a few fascicles, including a Plan and Bibliography, had been published.

There is also a valuable gazetteer of Chaucer's geographical names by Professor F. P. Magoun, Jr., published in three installments: Chaucer's Ancient and Biblical World, Med. Stud. XV, 107 ff.; Chaucer's Great Britain, ibid., XVI, 131 ff.; Chaucer's Medieval World outside Great Britain, ibid., XVII, 117 ff. This work analyzes in detail Chaucer's treatment of the various localities and peoples. Frequent use of Mr. Magoun's material has been made in the Explanatory Notes and Glossary of Proper Names below.

ABBREVIATIONS

I. CHAUCER'S WORKS

Adam	*Adam Scriveyn*
Anel	*Anelida and Arcite*
Astr	*A Treatise on the Astrolabe*
Bal Compl	*A Balade of Complaint*
BD	*The Book of the Duchess*
Bo	*Boece*
Buk	*Lenvoy de Chaucer a Bukton*
CkT	*The Cook's Tale*
ClT	*The Clerk's Tale*
Compl d'Am	*Complaynt d'Amours*
CT	*The Canterbury Tales*
CYT	*The Canon's Yeoman's Tale*
Form Age	*The Former Age*
Fort	*Fortune*
FranklT	*The Franklin's Tale*
FrT	*The Friar's Tale*
Gen Prol	*The General Prologue*
Gent	*Gentilesse*
HF	*The House of Fame*
KnT	*The Knight's Tale*
Lady	*A Complaint to his Lady*
LGW	*The Legend of Good Women*
MancT	*The Manciple's Tale*
Mars	*The Complaint of Mars*
Mel	*The Tale of Melibee*
MercB	*Merciles Beaute*
MerchT	*The Merchant's Tale*
MillT	*The Miller's Tale*
MkT	*The Monk's Tale*
MLT	*The Man of Law's Tale*
NPT	*The Nun's Priest's Tale*
PardT	*The Pardoner's Tale*
ParsT	*The Parson's Tale*
PF	*The Parliament of Fowls*
PhysT	*The Physician's Tale*
Pity	*The Complaint unto Pity*
PrT	*The Prioress's Tale*
Purse	*The Complaint of Chaucer to his Purse*
Rom	*The Romaunt of the Rose*
RvT	*The Reeve's Tale*
Scog	*Lenvoy de Chaucer a Scogan*
SecNT	*The Second Nun's Tale*
ShipT	*The Shipman's Tale*
SqT	*The Squire's Tale*
Sted	*Lak of Stedfastnesse*
SumT	*The Summoner's Tale*
Thop	*Sir Thopas*
Tr	*Troilus and Criseyde*
Ven	*The Complaint of Venus*
WBT	*The Wife of Bath's Tale*
Wom Nob	*Womanly Noblesse*
Wom Unc	*Against Women Unconstant*

II. EDITIONS OF CHAUCER (TEXT AND NOTES)

Bell	Works, 8 v., London, 1854–56
Gl., Globe	Globe Chaucer, London, 1898
Koch	*Canterbury Tales*, Heidelberg, 1915; Kleinere Dichtungen, Heidelberg, 1928
Manly	*Canterbury Tales* [selections], New York, 1928
Manly-Rickert. M-R CT	The Text of the *Canterbury Tales*, Studied on the Basis of All Known Manuscripts, Chicago, 1940
Morris	Works, rev. ed., 6 v., London, 1872 (Aldine Poets)
Root	*Troilus and Criseyde*, Princeton, 1926
Sk., Skeat	Oxford Chaucer, 6 v. and Supplement, Oxford, 1894–97
Th., Thynne	Works, London, 1532
Tyrwhitt	*Canterbury Tales*, 5 v. London, 1775–78
Urry	Works, London, 1721

III. JOURNALS, PUBLICATIONS, STUDIES, AND TEXTS

Acad.	The Academy, London
Angl.	Anglia, Zeitschrift für Englische Philologie
Angl. Beibl.	Beiblatt zur Anglia
Athen.	The Athenæum, London
Boethius	De Consolatione Philosophiae, ed. R. Peiper, Leipzig, 1871
Bowden	A Commentary on the General Prologue of the *Canterbury Tales*, New York, 1948
Brusendorff	The Chaucer Tradition, London, 1925
CHEL	Cambridge History of English Literature
Ch. Soc.	Publications of the Chaucer Society
Curry	Chaucer and the Mediæval Sciences, New York, 1926
CZ	Zeitschrift für Celtische Philologie
DNB	Dictionary of National Biography
EETS	Publications of the Early English Text Society
ELH	English Literary History
ESt	Englische Studien
Eng. Stud.	English Studies
Fansler	Chaucer and the Roman de la Rose, New York, 1914
FF Com.	Folklore Fellows Communications
Fil.	Boccaccio, Il Filostrato, ed. Moutier, Opere Volgari, XIII, Florence, 1831
Haeckel	Das Sprichwort bei Chaucer, Erlanger Beiträge, II, viii, 1890
Hammond	Chaucer, a Bibliographical Manual, New York, 1908

Herrig's Arch.	Archiv für das Studium der Neueren Sprachen und Literaturen	Rom.	Romania
Hinckley	Notes on Chaucer, Northampton, Mass., 1907	Rom. Rev.	Romanic Review
		RR	Roman de la Rose, ed. Langlois, 5 v., SATF, 1914–24
JEGP	Journal of English and Germanic Philology	SA	Sources and Analogues of Chaucer's *Canterbury Tales*, Chicago, 1941
Litblt.	Literaturblatt für Germanische und Romanische Philologie	SATF	Publications de la Société des Anciens Textes Français
Med. Aev.	Medium Aevum	SP	Studies in Philology
Med. Stud.	Mediæval Studies	Spec.	Speculum
MLN	Modern Language Notes	Stud. Phil.	Studies in Philology
MLQ	Modern Language Quarterly	Tes.	Boccaccio, Teseide, ed. Moutier, Opere Volgari, IX, Florence, 1831
MLR	Modern Language Review		
MP	Modern Philology		
N & Q	Notes and Queries		
NED	New English Dictionary	Theb.	Statius, Thebaid
Neuph. Mit.	Neuphilologische Mitteilungen	TLS	London Times Literary Supplement
Orig. and Anal.	Originals and Analogues, Chaucer Society, London, 1872–87		
PMLA	Publications of the Modern Language Association of America	Vulg.	Vulgate Bible
		Wells	A Manual of the Writings in Middle English, New Haven, 1916; Supplements, 1919, 1923, 1926, 1929, 1932, 1935, 1938, 1941, 1945
PQ	Philological Quarterly		
QF	Quellen und Forschungen zur Sprach- und Culturgeschichte der Germanischen Völker		
		ZRPh	Zeitschrift für Romanische Philologie
Rev. Celt.	Revue Celtique		

The Canterbury Tales

REFERENCES to publications on the sources, literary relations, and date of composition of the various parts of the *Canterbury Tales* are given in the notes to the *General Prologue* and to the separate tales.

The reason for Chaucer's choice of a pilgrimage as a setting for his stories is unknown. It has been commonly held that he described, at least in part, a pilgrimage on which he himself was present, perhaps in 1387, and Skeat has shown (Oxford Chaucer, III, 373 f.) that the dates mentioned in the narrative would fit well enough with the calendar of that year. Mr. Walter Rye has argued that Chaucer got the idea from Lynn pilgrimages to the shrine of St. Thomas. See TLS, 1927, p. 126.

On the route, time, and other arrangements of actual pilgrimages to Canterbury see, besides the books of Ward and Watt mentioned in the "General Criticism" section of the Bibliography, H. Little-hales, Some Notes on the Road from London to Canterbury in the Middle Ages, Ch. Soc., 1898; J. S. P. Tatlock, PMLA, XXI, 478 ff., Charles A. Owen, Jr., PMLA, LXVI, 820 ff. Mr. Owen argues for an extensive rearrangement of the tales, putting groups IX, III, IV, V, VI, and X on the homeward journey. See also his paper on the aesthetic design in the first day's stories, Eng. Stud., XXXV, 49 ff., and cf. W. C. Stokoe, Jr., Univ. of Toronto Quart., XXI, 120 ff. On the localities see further F. P. Magoun, Jr., Med. Stud., XVI, 137 ff. On mediæval pilgrimages in general there is interesting material in Jusserand's English Wayfaring Life (cited above). See also S. H. Heath, Pilgrim Life in the Middle Ages, London, 1911, and an article dealing primarily with Celtic Britain by G. Hartwell Jones, Y Cymm-rodor, XXIII.

A fresh impulse to discussion of the order of the tales was given by the appearance of the Manly-Rickert edition with its exhaustive presentation of the manuscript evidence. Manly's own general observations on the subject will be found in Vol. II, pp. 475 ff. of that work. A detailed and exhaustive examination of the question would hardly serve the purposes of the present edition, but opinions as to the authenticity and placing of the various tales and groups will be cited in relevant places. General references may be given here to the more important discussions of the question. Earlier articles: G. L. Kittredge, MP, IX, 435 ff.; W. W. Lawrence, MP, XI, 247 ff.; J. S. Kenyon, JEGP, XV, 282 ff.; S. B. Hemingway, MLN, XXXI, 479 ff.; C. Brown, Stud. Phil., XXXIV, 8 ff.; C. R. Kase, Three Chaucer Studies, New York, 1932; J. S. P. Tatlock, PMLA, L, 100 ff.

Since the M-R edition several articles by Mrs. G. Dempster should be cited as particularly valuable for clarifying both Manly's results and the various problems involved. See PMLA, LXI, 379 ff.; MLN, LXIII, 325 ff.; PMLA, LXIII, 456 ff.; PMLA, LXIV, 1123 ff.; PMLA, LXVII, 1177 (in reply to

A. E. Hartung, ibid., 1173 ff.); and PMLA, LXVIII, 1142 ff. Cf. also C. A. Owen, Jr., JEGP, LIV, 104 ff.

On the important editorial problem, the adoption of the so-called "Bradshaw Shift," references are given in the notes to the *Man of Law's Epilogue*. The most important survey is that of R. A. Pratt, PMLA, LXVI, 1141 ff. See also W. W. Lawrence, Chaucer and the *Canterbury Tales*, pp. 90 ff. The present edition, like that of Manly and Rickert, still follows the order of the manuscripts. But it is generally agreed that this cannot represent any final intention of Chaucer, and Professor Pratt has argued most plausibly that Chaucer was practically committed to the Bradshaw order. Mention should also be made of the discussion of the framework of the *Tales* by W. H. Clawson in the Univ. of Toronto Quarterly, XX, 137 ff.

Various literary parallels have been pointed out which may have afforded Chaucer suggestions for the general plan of the *Tales*. It has been commonly held that the Decameron of Boccaccio in particular furnished a model. Parallel passages in that work have been pointed out by R. K. Root (ESt, XLIV, 1 ff.), W. E. Farnham (MLN, XXXIII, 193 ff.), and Miss H. Korten (Chaucers Literarische Beziehungen zu Boccaccio, Rostock, 1920). But Chaucer's knowledge and use of the Decameron have not been placed beyond a doubt. See the observations of Karl Young (Kittredge Anniv. Papers, Boston, 1913, p. 405), W. E. Farnham (PMLA, XXXIX, 123 ff.), and J. W. Spargo (FF Com. No. 91, 11 ff.). On the possibility that Chaucer was influenced by other works of Boccaccio see J. S. P. Tatlock, in Angl., XXXVII, 69 ff.

Numerous references to studies of the "frame story" are given in SA, p. 3, n., and the type is discussed at pp. 6 ff. See also W. H. Clawson, U. of Toronto Quarterly XX, 137 ff. On a special form of framed or boxed narrative perhaps illustrated by the (unknown) source of the *SqT* see H. Braddy, JEGP, XLI, 279 ff.

An especially interesting analogue to the *Canterbury Tales*, because it is another collection of stories told on a pilgrimage, and because it may have been known to Chaucer, is furnished by the Novelle of Giovanni Sercambi. See H. B. Hinckley, Notes on Chaucer, Northampton, Mass., 1907, pp. 2 f., and Young, Kittredge Anniv. Papers, pp. 406 ff. Sercambi's Proemio and Intermezzi, together with a minute analysis of the work, are printed in SA, pp. 32 ff. The editors of the chapter, Messrs. Pratt and Young, express doubt about Chaucer's indebtedness to it. For interesting comments on Sercambi's profession as a stationer and publisher see R. A. Pratt, Italica XXV, 12 ff. For a thirteenth century analogue involving stories told on a pilgrimage see Beatrice D. Brown, MLN, LII, 28 ff. For a study of the relationship of the tales to the framework of the pilgrimage see W. W. Lawrence, Chaucer and the Canterbury Tales, pp. 9 ff.

For discussion of the relation of Chaucer the poet to Chaucer the pilgrim and narrator of the tales see B. Kimpel, ELH, XX, 77 ff. and E. T. Donaldson, PMLA, LXIX, 928 ff. On the adaptation of the individual tales to their narrators see J. R. Hulbert, SP, XLV, 565 ff.

Attempts have been made, especially by Professor Frederick Tupper, to find an underlying unity in the subject-matter of the *Canterbury Tales.* In a communication to the [New York] Nation (XCVII, 354 ff.) Mr. Tupper argued that the central principle was to be found in the celebration or service of Venus, the dominating influence of the pilgrimage. But this statement, while recognizing the obvious importance of love as a motif in the secular tales, does not take sufficient account of the tales of religious, even of ascetic, spirit. In a later and more elaborate study, Mr. Tupper tried to show that the tales were intended to treat in a systematic way the Seven Deadly Sins. According to Chaucer's scheme, as he interpreted it, each pilgrim represents in his person a sin which he condemns in his tale. This holds true, without doubt, for the Pardoner, and perhaps for some of the other pilgrims. But the system breaks down when applied to the whole series of tales. Mr. Tupper's extended exposition of it will be found in PMLA, XXIX, 93 ff.; for special observations see also his articles in JEGP, XIII, 553 ff.; XIV, 256 ff.; XV, 56 ff. The arguments against this interpretation were very fully presented by Professor Lowes in PMLA, XXX, 237 ff.

Two collective works of greatest importance on the background of the *Canterbury Tales* should be noted here: The Chaucer Society Originals and Analogues of the Canterbury Tales (London, 1872–87), and Sources and Analogues of the Canterbury Tales, W. F. Bryan, ed., and Mrs. G. Dempster, assoc. ed. (Chicago, 1941), which has already been cited as SA in these preliminary notes.

FRAGMENT I

General Prologue

The composition of the *Prologue* is generally put in or about 1387. If it refers to an actual pilgrimage the few data that are given would fit well enough the calendar of that year. (See the various calculations recorded by Miss Hammond, pp. 265–67, and Skeat, Oxford Chaucer, III, 373 ff.) In any case Chaucer probably began work on the Canterbury series at about that date, and the *Prologue* was presumably written before the main body of the tales. Of course Chaucer may have returned to it from time to time to make additions and revisions. For the theory that several characters (specifically the Reeve, the Miller, the Summoner, the Pardoner, and the Manciple) were added after the first draught, see Miss Hammond, p. 254. She further suggests that the description of the Wife of Bath was probably not composed in its present form until after the Wife's special Prologue was written. Mr. C. Camden, Jr., in PQ, VII, 314 ff, argues that the group of Guildsmen may have been a late addition.

The antecedents of the *Prologue* as a literary type have been discussed in the introductory note, pp. 2 ff., above. For further illustration see H. R. Patch, MLN, XL, 1 ff.; Frederick Tupper, Types of Society in Medieval Literature, New York, 1926, pp. 32 ff. (with special reference to the figures described in the chess-book of Jacobus de Cessolis); and Manly, Warton Lecture (No. XVII) on Chaucer and the Rhetoricians, Proceedings of the British Acad., 1926; and cf. *Tr*, v, 799 ff., n.

For the interpretation of the text of the *Canterbury Tales* as a whole the present editor would acknowledge his indebtedness to Skeat's notes in the Oxford Chaucer, Mr. H. B. Hinckley's Notes, Professor Koch's Anmerkungen in his edition of Hertzberg's translation (Berlin, 1925), and to Professor Manly's selections. Manly's material on the *Prologue*, both in his notes and in his New Light, is especially full and valuable. He emphasizes the individuality of the portraits and suggests historical counterparts. Typical features, on the other hand, are pointed out by W. C. Curry, Chaucer and the Mediæval Sciences, and F. Tupper, Types of Society. There is an excellent commentary in Mr. Pollard's separate edition, London, 1903. Valuable illustrative material was collected also by E. Flügel in Angl., XXIII, 225 ff. See also Le Chanoine Camille Looten, Chaucer, ses modèles, ses sources, sa religion, in the Mémoires et travaux publiés par des professeurs des facultés catholiques de Lille, XXVIII, especially pp. 99 ff. The literary tradition behind the portraits is discussed in SA, pp. 3 ff. See further J. V. Cunningham, MP, XLIX, 172 ff. (who finds parallels to the general form of the *Prologue* in the dream-vision tradition).

It has been the common practice of Chaucer critics now for two generations or more to emphasize the dramatic character of the *Canterbury Tales.* Their comment has ranged all the way from simple observations on the adaptation of the tales to tellers or to the situations on the pilgrimage to the comparison of Chaucer's art to that of Molière. This dramatic aspect of the *Tales* has recently been made the subject of an extended study by R. M. Lumiansky in his volume Of Sondry Folk: The Dramatic Principle in the Canterbury Tales (Austin, U. of Texas Press, 1955). The work completes and supersedes Professor Lumiansky's discussion of the subject in several earlier articles. It also surveys conveniently the opinions expressed by other critics. On the closely related matter, the function of Chaucer as both pilgrim and narrator of the Canterbury pilgrimage, there is a recent discussion by Professor Edgar H. Duncan in Essays in honor of Walter Clyde Curry (Nashville, Tenn., 1955).

A very full commentary, embodying most important discussion up to the date of its publication, has been compiled by Miss Muriel Bowden, A Commentary on the General Prologue of the Canterbury Tales (New York, 1948). It contains more illustrative material than there is room for in the notes to an edition. For articles on special passages, see Wells, pp. 876–77, 1030, 1146–47, 1237–38, 1326, 1424, 1537, 1645, 1737–8, 1931. The Ellesmere MS. contains miniature representations of those pilgrims who tell tales, which are photographically reproduced in the Chaucer Society reprint of MS. El. and again (more accurately) in the facsimile of the Ellesmere Chaucer (Manchester, 1911); drawings based on the miniatures are given in color in the Six-Text print, and uncolored in the separate prints of the MSS. See also, for detailed descriptions and discussion, E. F. Piper, PQ, III, 241 ff.; E. Markert, Chaucer's Canterbury-Pilger und ihre Tracht, Würzburg diss., 1911, p. 3.

1 ff. Several passages have been pointed out as possible sources of the introductory lines on spring. Cf. especially Guido delle Colonne, Historia Trojana, fol. b 4 recto (Strassburg, 1489); Boccaccio's Ameto, Moutier, pp. 23–24; his Filocolo, Bk. v, Moutier, pp. 238–39; his Teseida, iii, st. 6, 7; Petrarch's Sonnet 9, In Vita di Madonna Laura; Boethius, i, m. 5 and ii, m. 3; and Virgil's Georgics, ii, 323 ff., and the Pervigilium Veneris. From any of these places Chaucer may have received suggestions. Taken together they show that he was dealing with a conventional theme, in the treatment of which commonplace features inevitably reappeared. Such descriptions were especially frequent at the beginning of poems, not only of romances such as the Fulk Fitz Warine, but also in a chronicle such as Creton's account of the fall of Richard II (Histoire du Roy d'Angleterre Richard, ed. and tr. in Archæologia, XX, 1 ff.). Of the passages cited above those in the Filocolo and the Historia Trojana offer, perhaps, the closest verbal resemblances to the *Prologue;* and these works were almost certainly familiar to Chaucer. He also knew the Teseida. It is not so clear that he had read the Ameto or the Georgics. (For full discussion of the parallels, with references to other articles, see A. S. Cook, Trans. Conn. Acad. of Arts and Sciences, XXIII, 1 ff.; and cf. Cummings, MLN, XXXVII, 86, J. E. Hankins, MLN, XLIX 80 ff., Miss R. Tuve, MLN, LII, 9ff., and Miss Bowden, Commentary, pp. 20, 40.)

1 The final e in *Aprille,* if intended by the Ellesmere writing of ll joined by a ligature, may be merely scribal. Though usually kept by editors (as in the first edition of the present work), it is not etymologically justified, and there is no evidence that it was pronounced.

On the variant forms of this adjective, *swete, swote, sote,* etc., see J. H. Fisher, JEGP I, 326 ff., who argues for a distinction in meaning or connotation.

3 *veyne,* probably "vessels of sap," rather than "veins of the earth."

6 *Inspired,* either "breathed upon" the tender twigs, or "quickened" them, made them grow. The former meaning is more usual, but the latter is equally natural here. Professor Baum (PMLA, LXXI, 229) suggests a kind of word-play involving both meanings.

7 *the yonge sonne,* the sun in the early part of its annual course, just emerging from Aries, the first sign of the zodiac. Cf. *SqT,* V, 385.

8 This might refer, if taken by itself, to the beginning of April. But in *ML Prol,* II, 5–6, April 18th is explicitly named, probably as the second day of the pilgrimage. To fit that date the *halve cours* in the Ram must be interpreted as the second half. The sun entered Aries on March 12 (*Astr,* ii, 1; and see ESt, XXXI, 288), and the first half course would be completed toward the end of the month. By April 18th the sun would have travelled a number of degrees in Taurus, the second sign.

Chaucer shows considerable fondness for definitions of time in terms of astronomy or mythology. For other examples in the *Canterbury Tales* cf. *MerchT,* IV, 1795, 1885 ff., 2219 ff.; *SqT,* V, 48 ff.,

263 ff., 385 ff., 671 f.; *FranklT,* V, 1245 ff.; *Pars Prol,* X, 2 ff.; and note particularly the humorous turn in *FranklT,* V, 1018 (and *Tr,* ii, 904–05). The device is employed frequently in the *Troilus.* Chaucer was perhaps influenced by the Teseida, which in turn imitated similar figures in the Thebaid of Statius. The example of Dante, with whom the practice was common, doubtless also had its effect upon both Boccaccio and Chaucer (See Harv. Stud. in Class. Phil., XXVIII, 118–20).

10 For this striking line no parallel before Chaucer has been suggested. The idea is found later in the romance of the Sowdone of Babilone, ed. Hausknecht (EETS, 1881), ll. 45–46. Manly notes that the birds were probably nightingales, and cites the Book of the Knight of La Tour Landry (EETS, 1868), p. 156, and Pliny, Hist. Nat., x, 43.

11 Perhaps *nature* should be capitalized here. Chaucer may have had in mind the familiar conception of the goddess Nature, of which he made striking use in the *Parlement of Foules.* See especially the note to *P.F.* 298.

17 Thomas à Becket was murdered in 1170 and canonized three years later. The scene of his martyrdom was the object of many pilgrimages for centuries.

17–18 "Identical rime," as in *seke : seeke,* was permitted, or even sought, in Old French and Middle English.

20 *the Tabard.* The sign of the inn was a tabard, or short sleeveless coat, embroidered with armorial bearings. The word came also to be applied to the laborer's blouse or smock. There was an actual hostelry of the name in Southwark in Chaucer's time. It became the property of Hyde Abbey, near Westminster, in 1306, and was surrendered by the Abbot of Hyde at the dissolution of the monasteries in 1548. Details about its history, from a cartulary of the Abbey lands (MS. Harl. 1761 of the British Museum), were collected by Professor Manly; see also his note on the present passage. For a general account of the inn see the Surrey Archæological Society, Collections, XIII, London, 1897, pp. 28 ff.; also the Victoria County History of Surrey, IV, London, 1912, p. 127; and for Southwark hostelries in general, W. Rendle and P. Norman, The Inns of Old Southwark, London, 1888. The original building was burned in 1676. It was afterwards rebuilt, and the name was corrupted to the Talbot. This survived until 1875–76. At present a part of the site is occupied by a small public house called by the old name.

24 The discrepancy between twenty-nine and the actual number of the pilgrims has been reconciled by commentators in various ways. Cf. Carleton Brown, MLN, XLIX, 216 ff. He holds the Squire to have been a late addition to the group. See also N. Nathan, MLN, LXVII, 533–4.

33 The subject of *made* is *we* implied in l. 32. In Middle English the pronominal subject of a verb is frequently omitted if indirectly expressed in the context. Cf., for other examples, *Gen Prol,* I, 529, 786, 810; *KnT,* I, 1642, 1755, 2433, and for occurrences of the same construction in Chaucer's prose, P. Pintelon, Chaucer's Treatise on the Astrolabe, p. 106.

37 *resoun,* here probably in the sense of "order," "suitable arrangement." On its use as a technical term in rhetoric see MLR, XXI, 13–18.

The Knight

For full discussion of the historical background of the description see J. M. Manly in Trans. of the Am. Phil. Association, 1907, pp. 89 ff., and A. S. Cook, Trans. of the Conn. Acad. of Arts and Sciences, XX, 165 ff.

It is not likely that any single historical figure is represented by Chaucer's Knight. But the career which is sketched is typical, and the events referred to might all have been witnessed by a contemporary of the poet. Besides fighting in the King's service (*in his lordes werre*, l. 47), the Knight might have gone to Granada (*Gernade*) with Henry, Earl of Derby, in 1343, remaining till the capture of Algezir in 1344. About the same time he could have seen fighting in *Belmarye* (i.e., Benmarin, Morocco) and *Tramyssene* (i.e., Tlemcen, Western Algeria) in Northern Africa; but there were also campaigns in those regions in the sixties and the eighties. Between 1345 and 1360 the wars with France might well have kept the Knight occupied nearer home. But after the Peace of Brétigny, in 1360, he would have been free for the campaigns of Pierre de Lusignan (King Peter of Cyprus), one of the most brilliant leaders of chivalric warfare in the fourteenth century. King Peter made a tour through Europe, during which he visited the English court, in 1362–63. He captured *Satalye* (the ancient Attalia, on the southern coast of Asia Minor) in 1361, conquered Alexandria (*Alisaundre*) in 1365, and partially reduced *Lyeys* (Lyas, Ayas, in Armenia) in 1367. He was assassinated at¹ Rome in 1369 (See Chaucer's stanza on his death in *MkT*, VII, 2391 ff.). The reference to the Knight's service with the lord of *Palatye* (probably Turkish Balat, on the site of the ancient Miletus) is not definite. But since, according to Strambaldi (ed. René de Mas Latrie, Paris, 1893, p. 66, in Collection de Doc. Inédits, Première Série) the lord of Palatye, in 1365, was a heathen bound in friendly treaty to King Peter, the episode should probably be brought into connection with the campaigns of the sixties. To a later period may be assigned the Knight's campaigns in Lithuania and Russia, in the service of the Teutonic Order (ll. 52 ff.). Professor Manly, whose reconstruction of the Knight's career is here followed, remarks that in 1386 the Lithuanians turned Christians, and that the Knight may have been conceived as making the Canterbury pilgrimage immediately upon his return to England from Lithuania. Professor Cook, on the other hand, argues that Chaucer had in mind an expedition of the Earl of Derby (afterwards Henry IV), who took part in the siege of Vilna in 1390–91. He even suggests that it was from Henry of Derby, after his return to England in July, 1393, that Chaucer learned about the institution of the "table of honor." But the theory which thus connects the description of the Knight with the Earl of Derby implies a later date for the *Prologue* than seems probable on other grounds.

Professor Manly argues, quite reasonably, that the Knight's career is not merely typical. From the very specific details he infers that Chaucer may have had in mind some contemporary knight, or more probably several. And he points out that three members of the Scrope family — Sir William, Sir Stephen, and Sir Geoffrey — took part in campaigns mentioned in the description of the Knight. Chaucer's acquaintance with the Scropes is well attested.

Efforts have been made to find literary as well as historical counterparts for the Knight, but Chaucer's description of the character, if not of the career, is simple and typical, and he can hardly be shown to have followed any model. Professor Schofield pointed out to the editor that a good illustrative parallel is afforded by the characterization of the brave knight in a dit (Du Preu Chevalier) of Watriquet (ed. Scheler, Bruxelles, 1868, pp. 187 ff.). See also Professor Tupper's observations, Types of Society, pp. 33 ff.

It is worthy of note that Chaucer presents in the Knight a completely ideal figure. Although chivalry in the fourteenth century was in its decline and had a very sordid side, Chaucer has wholly refrained from satirizing the institution. It has been suggested, indeed, that in this very ideal presentation the keenest satire was concealed. But it may be doubted if such was Chaucer's intention. Professor Loomis (Essays and Studies in honor of Carleton Brown, N.Y. 1940, pp. 136–7) argues that in emphasizing the Knight's service in religious wars, Chaucer betrays pacificism and a lack of sympathy for the Hundred Years' War. For objections to this view see Stillwell and Webb, MLN, LIX, 45 ff.

46 *honour*, here coupled with *trouthe*, probably means "sense of honor, honorable dealing" rather than "fame."

52 *he hadde the bord bigonne*, he had sat at the head of the table. The reference need not be particularly to the "table of honor," which was held only on stated occasions by the Teutonic Knights. For a list of recorded instances of this celebration see Cook's article, Trans. Conn. Acad., XX, 209–12.

57 Belmarye, usually explained as the Moorish kingdom in Africa ruled by The Ben-Marin and corresponding approximately to modern Morocco. See Magoun, Med. Stud., XVII, 121. Dr. A. R. Nykl has expressed (orally) to the editor doubt about this derivation from a dynastic name, and suggested a preference for identifying *Belmarye* with *Almeria*. But for forms in French and English, see Professor Magoun's discussion.

59 *the Grete See*, the Mediterranean.

60 *armee*, armed expedition, armada (Lat. "armata"). The reading *aryve* (MSS. Hg, Ha, Gg, En¹) "arrival or disembarkation" is more difficult since the word is not found elsewhere in English.

68 "Though he was brave, he was prudent." Tupper (Types, p. 34 f.) quotes de Cessolis to prove that "sapientia" in a knight means skill and prudence. The contrast here, he argues, is between "fortitudo" or "audacia" and "sapientia" ("ars et prudentia"). Cf. Chanson de Roland, lxxxvii: "Rolanz est proz e Oliver est sage."

The subjunctive (*were*) implies no doubt of the Knight's worthiness. It is the mood commonly employed by Chaucer in simple concession.

72 "A true and perfect gentle knight." Manly notes that Chaucer apparently never uses "very" (*verray*) as an intensive adverb.

The Squire

On the training and duties of squires cf. John Saunders, Cabinet Pictures of English Life: Chaucer, Lond., 1845, pp. 70 ff. Chaucer's description exhibits the qualities and accomplishments that were regularly expected of a young courtly lover. Much stress was laid on the virtue of "joy." The whole passage is well illustrated by RR, 2175–2210. It is possible, as several scholars have suggested, that in making the portrait Chaucer had in mind his own youth. See E. Legouis, Chaucer, Paris, 1910, p. 5; and O. F. Emerson, Rom. Rev., III, 321–61. Chaucer had been trained as a page in the household of Prince Lionel. He had even taken part himself, in 1369, in a campaign in Artois and Picardy. But in the case of the Squire the reference is doubtless to the so-called crusade of Henry Le Despenser, Bishop of Norwich, in 1383.

80 *Lovyere*, Southern dialect for the more usual *lovere*. *Bacheler*, a probationer for the honor of knighthood. Cf. the academic use of the title for the first degree in arts.

85 On the uses of *chyvachye* in French and English see A. A. Prins, Eng. Stud., XXX, 42 ff.

88 In the Ellesmere miniature of the Squire his coat and cap are both much decorated with embroidery. Cf. also the garment of the God of Love in *Rom*, ll. 896–98 (RR, 876 ff.). But it is possible that Chaucer's line refers to the pink and white of the Squire's complexion.

91 *floytynge*, either "whistling" or "playing the flute." See Flügel, JEGP, I, 125. Manly suggests that the Bohemian flute may have become fashionable in Queen Anne's time.

95 *songes make*, i.e., the music; *endite* meant "compose the words."

97–8 For the belief that during the mating season nightingales sing all night see, besides the references given in the note on l. 10, above, Flügel, JEGP, I, 122. The comparison between them and the lover is closely paralleled in a couplet of the Welsh poet Dafydd Nanmor (ed. Roberts and Williams, London, 1923, p. 88): "Ni chysgaf tra vo haf hir Mwy nog eos vain gywir."

100 Carving was a regular duty of a squire in his lord's house. Cf. *SumT*, III, 2243–44; *MerchT*, IV, 1772–73.

The Yeoman

A Yeoman ranked in service next above a "garson" or groom. The term was later loosely applied to small landholders, some of whom had considerable substance. The Ellesmere MS. has no picture of the Yeoman since he tells no tale. It is conjectured that Chaucer intended to rewrite for him the Tale of Gamelyn, found in a number of MSS. of the *Canterbury Tales*.

101 *he*, namely, the Knight, who was accompanied by the Yeoman as well as the Squire.

104 For references to the use of peacock-feathered arrows see, besides Skeat's note, E. S. Krappe in MLN, XLIII, 176.

107 On drooping feathers Manly refers to Ascham's Toxophilus, ed. Arber, London, 1868, 128–33.

115 Small images of the saints were worn as talismans, and Christopher was the patron saint of foresters.

The Prioress

For general comment on the Prioress see particularly J. L. Lowes in Angl., XXXIII, 440 ff. A somewhat different interpretation of her character is given by Sister Madeleva, Chaucer's Nuns and Other Essays, New York, 1925. On the convent of St. Leonard's see Manly, New Light, pp. 202 ff., and the notes in his selections; also E. P. Kuhl, PQ, II, 306 ff. There is a good general account of the life and discipline of such institutions in Eileen Power's Mediæval English Nunneries, Cambridge (Eng.), 1922; see also her Mediæval People, Boston, 1924, pp. 59 ff.

Chaucer's characterization of the Prioress is extremely subtle, and his satire — if it can be called satire at all — is of the gentlest and most sympathetic sort. The closing remark about her brooch and motto has often been misunderstood, and the whole spirit of the passage consequently misrepresented. The inscription *Amor vincit omnia* (Love overcometh all things) was applicable alike to religious and to romantic love, and carries no implication that the Prioress was "acquainted with the gallantries of her age." She is treated, throughout the *Canterbury Tales*, with the utmost respect. Yet the ambiguity of the motto suggests, in Professor Lowes's phrase, the "delightfully imperfect submergence of the woman in the nun," and the same implication appears in many other elements of the description. The very adjectives *symple and coy*, at the beginning, are part of the regular vocabulary of romantic poetry; the name *Madame Eglentyne* has similar associations; the description of the Prioress's personal beauty is quite in the style of the romances; and the account of her dainty manners at table is based upon a passage in the Roman de la Rose which was meant as a kind of prescription for young ladies of fashion. Throughout the whole description there is a curious mingling of *love celestial* and *cheere of court*.

But if Chaucer did not mean to disparage the character of the Prioress, there are certain laxities in conduct — matters of discipline rather than morals — which he does imply in her case as well as in that of other ecclesiastical figures among the pilgrims. Perhaps the brooch was objectionable as a bit of worldly vanity. The wimple, possibly, should not have been fluted, and the broad forehead should have been veiled. The pet dogs were clearly against the rules. The very presence of the Prioress on a pilgrimage was a violation of orders promulgated at various times (791, 1195, 1318), though it does not appear that this regulation was consistently enforced. For specific references on these matters see E. Power, as cited above; also E. P. Kuhl, PQ, II, 305 f. Sister Madeleva — who takes issue not only with the critics who have seen moral disparagement in Chaucer's portrayal of the Prioress, but even with Professor Lowes in his more sympathetic interpretation of the character — tries to explain away these various breaches of discipline. She holds the Prioress to have been an elderly sister, perhaps a woman of fifty. Her interpretation is not convincing, though her knowledge of the life of a religious makes it worth consideration. Sister Madeleva's views appear more recently in A Lost Language, pp. 31 ff. For further observations on the Prioress, especially in the light of Benedictine tradition, see M. J. Brennan, MLQ, X, 451 ff.

119 *coy,* "quiet," without the modern implication of coquetry.

120 *Seinte,* MS. Pt; the rest, *seint.* The meter calls for a dissyllable, and *seinte* is more probable than *seint.* The weak form of adjectives is not infrequently found with proper names. See the Introduction, above.

The reason for the selection of St. Loy (Eloi, Eligius) here has been much discussed. The rime with *coy* doubtless had something to do with it, and the ladylike sound of the oath may have confirmed the choice. But there were probably other reasons. Mr. J. W. Hales, Folia Literaria, New York, 1893, pp. 102 ff., on the basis of a story that Eloi once refused to take an oath, proposed to interpret Chaucer's line as meaning that the Prioress swore after the same manner, that is, that she never swore at all. But this explanation is altogether far-fetched. Miss Hammond's suggestion (MLN, XXII, 51), that the saint was invoked as a patron of journeys, lacks good support, and besides gives the line too restricted an application. Professor Lowes (Rom. Rev., V, 368 ff.) has shown that the character and person of St. Loy were such as might naturally have appealed to the Prioress. Beginning life as a goldsmith's apprentice, Eligius rose, by reason of his integrity and the excellence of his work, to become the intimate counsellor of King Dagobert, and after important service in government and diplomacy he was finally made Bishop of Noyon. He was famed for his personal beauty and courtesy as well as for his craftsmanship, and his whole character is delightfully consonant with that of the Prioress herself. Cf. further the observations of B. B. Wainwright, MLN, XLVIII, 34 ff.

Professor Manly notes that there may have been a special cult of St. Loy at the English court at this time. The Countess of Pembroke gave an image of him to the high altar of the Grey Friars. Moreover, Queen Philippa came from a district where he was especially popular.

For the association of St. Eligius with horses and carters, on the basis of an episode in his legend, see *FrT,* III, 1564, n.

121 *madame Eglentyne.* This romantic sounding name ("Lady Sweetbriar") has a curious resemblance, as Professor Manly has noted, to that of Madame Argentine ("Domina Argentyn"), a nun known to have been at Stratford in 1375. But the identification is improbable, as Mr. Manly also grants, because the prioress when Chaucer wrote was Mary Syward (or Suhard). See TLS, 1927, p. 817. On *Eglentyne* see further Bennett in Essays and Studies, XXXI, 34 ff. Also E. P. Kuhl (MLN, LX, 325), who argued for a religious association, and R. T. Davies (MLN, LXVII, 400) who questions Kuhl's argument and cites an historic *Idoine* as a nun with a romantic name.

123 *Entuned in hir nose.* This mode of nasal intonation is traditional with the recitative portions of the church service. Sister Madeleva observes that the Prioress would have intoned the office only in the convent, not on a journey. So the passage implies that Chaucer, perhaps through ties of kinship, was familiar with her community.

125 The traditional interpretation of the reference to *Stratford atte Bowe* appears to be the right one. The Prioress's French was only such as she could have heard in an English nunnery. The comparison with the *Frenssh of Parys* is disparaging, for the latter was the standard and had long been recognized as such. Chaucer can hardly mean that she spoke a dialect that was just as good. (For a defense of the contrary opinion see Skeat's note on the passage.) Evidence that the French spoken in England was regarded as inferior to "French of Paris" is cited by Hinckley, pp. 10–11, and in Manly's note. See also J. E. Matzke, MP, III, 47 ff. But it is possible, as Manly remarks, that the French of Stratford is disparaged because it was the dialect of Hainaut, introduced there by the sister of Queen Philippa; and incidentally, Chaucer's wife came from Hainaut!

By *Stratford atte Bowe* is undoubtedly meant the Benedictine nunnery of St. Leonard's, at Bromley, Middlesex, adjoining Stratford-Bow. It was founded in the time of William the Conqueror. Elizabeth of Hainaut, sister of Queen Philippa, was a nun there for many years and died there in 1375. Elizabeth, countess of Ulster, visited it in 1356, when Chaucer was in her train. St. Leonard's was never rich, like the house of the same order at Barking, and its occupants were on the whole of lower station. Elizabeth Chaucy, supposed to be Chaucer's sister or daughter, became a nun at Barking in 1381. Professor Kuhl (PQ, II, 308 f.) raises the question whether the slur on the Prioress's French was partly a reflection on the inferior convent, and whether in counterfeiting *cheere of court* the Stratford nuns were aping Windsor or their more aristocratic neighbors at Barking. For further comments see Miss M. P. Hamilton, Philologica: The Malone Anniversary Studies (Baltimore, 1945) pp. 179 ff.

127–36 Cf. RR, 13408–32.

137 The Prioress's elegant manners, like her French, are gently satirized. But *countrefete* means simply "imitate," without the implication of dishonesty.

142, 150 *conscience,* "tender feeling," "sensitiveness," rather than "moral conscience."

146 *Of smale houndes,* an old partitive construction. For evidence that nuns were forbidden to keep dogs see E. Power, Med. Eng. Nunneries, p. 305 ff.; Dugdale, Monasticon, London, 1846, II, 619, no. xi; Kuhl, PQ, II, 303 f.

147 *wastel breed.* Though the word *wastel* is of the same origin as the Fr. "gateau," *wastel breed* seems to have been rather a fine white wheat bread than what would now be called cake. The Liber Albus (1419) describes four grades of bread; first "demeine" ("panis dominicus"), the lord's bread, doubtless the *payndemayn* of *Thop,* VII, 725; second *wastel breed;* third a light bread, also called "Fraunceis" and "pouf"; and fourth "tourte," perhaps identical with "bis" bread or brown. Exact references on the subject are given by Professor E. P. Kuhl, PQ, II, 302 f. He finds no evidence that wastel bread was sweetened.

149 *men,* probably not plural, but the weakened form of *man,* used in the indefinite sense. Cf. *men seyth* (German, "man sagt").

151 According to Mr. G. G. Coulton (in a letter to the editor) the wimple should have been plain, not fluted. But Sister Madeleva (Chaucer's Nuns, pp. 16 f.) explains it as a Benedictine collar accordeon-pleated in concentric circles.

152 The meaning of *greye* is disputed. It probably included blue (sky-blue) as well as the shades verging on green or yellow which it would now suggest. For illustrative passages, see M. Kinney, Rom. Rev., X, 320 ff. and A. K. Moore, PQ, XXVI, 307 ff.

154 For evidence that the *fair forheed* should not have been exposed Mr. Coulton (in the letter referred to above) cites Alnwich's Visitations, Lincoln Record Soc., XIV, 3, 118, 130 f., 176; also Olivier Maillard, Quadrigesimale, Serm. xlv (Petit, Paris, 1512, fol. 114a). On the admiration of high and broad foreheads in Chaucer's age see Manly's note. Mr. T. B. Clark (PQ, IX, 312 ff.) brings evidence from the physiognomists that an extremely broad forehead was sometimes regarded as a sign of stupidity and folly. But he observes that, in view of l. 156, the Prioress's forehead was probably proportionate to her height. Both characteristics are so individualizing as to suggest strongly that Chaucer had in mind an actual person.

159 *peire of bedes*, a rosary. The "gauds," or large beads were of green. See B. Boyd, MLQ, XI, 404 ff.

161 On the *crowned A*, apparently a capital A surmounted by a crown, see Miss Hammond, in Angl., XXVII, 393 and XXX, 320, and H. Braddy, in MLN, LVIII, 18 ff.

162 Proverbial: cf. Haeckel, p. 2, no. 6.

164 *chapeleyne*, "capellana," a kind of secretary and personal assistant to the Prioress. For references to the office in English records see M. Förster, Herrig's Archiv, CXXXII, 399 ff.; Kuhl, PQ, II, 304; and Manly's note.

The three priests have been the subject of much discussion. They would bring the total number of pilgrims up to thirty-one, instead of twenty-nine, as given in l. 24. This discrepancy in itself need disturb no one, in view of other inconsistencies that were allowed to stand in the uncompleted *Canterbury Tales*. But there is every reason to doubt the presence of more than one priest with the Prioress. Only one is mentioned later. It is altogether improbable that she would have been attended by three. Moreover, the confessor of the convent would have been the priest of the parish. Chaucer very likely started to describe the Second Nun and stopped with the word *chapeleyne*; then somebody else completed the line, perhaps adding, as Miss Rickert suggested (M-R CT, III, 423), *and the preest is three.* Emendation seems unnecessary. For various proposals, none of which is satisfactory, see O. F. Emerson, PQ, II, 89 ff. Professor Emerson's own suggestion that Chaucer meant at first to include the Monk and the Friar in a "church group" with the Prioress and her priest, is improbable. Mr. W. P. Lehmann's suggestion (MLN, LXVII 317 ff.) that Chaucer meant *three* to include the Prioress and the *chapeleyne* is rather debatable. See Professor Spitzer in reply, MLN LXVII, 502. Miss M. P. Hamilton, in Philologica (Malone Festschrift), pp. 179 ff. cites records from the nunnery of St. Leonard's to support the statement that three priests actually accompanied the Prioress. See also A. Sherbo, PMLA LXIV, 236 ff.

The Monk

The character of the hunting monk is well illustrated in the articles of the Visitation of Selborne Abbey held by William of Wykeham, Bishop of Winchester, in 1387. (See the appendix to Gilbert White's Natural History and Antiquities of Selborne, ed. Buckland, London 1875, p. 512.) Not only the hunting, but also the love of fine horses and dogs and rich food and clothing, is there condemned. It should be added that the secular clergy, as well as the regulars, were blamed by the reforming party for such luxurious living. Cf. Wyclif, English Works, ed. F. D. Matthew, EETS, 1880, pp. 149, 151, 212–13, 434, and Select English Works, ed. Arnold, Oxford, 1869–71, III, 519 f.

Miss R. Bressie (MLN, LIV, 477 ff.) suggests that Chaucer may have had in mind one particular hunting monk, William de Cloun, Abbot of Leicester (1345–78), though he was an Augustinian Canon rather than a Benedictine monk. Objections were urged by Tatlock (MLN, LV, 350 ff.) and answered by Miss Bressie (MLN, LVI, 161) and E. P. Kuhl (MLN, LV, 480). See also Mrs. Frank, MLN, LV, 760 f., and Tatlock again, MLN, LVI, 80.

165 *for the maistrie* (Fr. "pour la maistrye") surpassing all others; hence an adverbial phrase meaning "extremely."

166 *outridere*, a monk whose duty it was to look after the estates of the monastery. Cf. *ShipT*, VII, 65 f.

170 Skeat's note cites a number of passages to show that it was fashionable to have bells on the bridles and harness of horses. See also Child's note on Thomas Rymer, Engl. and Scot. Pop. Ball., Boston, 1882–98, I, 320.

172 *celle*, a subordinate monastery.

173 St. Benedict, the father of western monasticism, established his central monastery at Monte Cassino in 529. St. Maurus was his disciple.

175 To avoid the anacoluthon here Professor Liddell made *olde thynges pace* parenthetical, and took *reule* to be the object of *leet*. But the resulting construction, though logical, is unnatural.

176 Skeat interpreted *heeld . . . the space*, "held his course" and is supported by Tatlock, MLN, L, 293. Manly, being doubtful about this use of *space*, took it adverbially, "meanwhile, for the time." A. A. Prins (Eng. Stud., XXX, 83 ff.), interprets the passage "This same monk let old people (*thynges*) observe (*pace*) the rule, whereas he allowed himself greater liberty (*heeld . . . the space*). But the meaning of the words is rather forced. The explanation proposed by F. T. Visser (Eng. Stud., XXX, 133–4), "The Monk regarded (*leet*) the rule as a precept (*pace*) of old-fashioned people," is no less difficult.

177 The text referred to may be the following canon recorded in the Decretum of Gratian (i, 86, Lyons, 1560, col. 411), and based on the Breviarium in Psalmo attributed to St. Jerome: "Esau venator erat: quoniam peccator erat: et penitus non invenimus in Scripturis sanctis sanctum aliquem venatorem. Piscatores invenimus sanctos" (Psalm xc, Migne, Pat. Lat., XXVI, Col. 1163A). For further discussion see O. F. Emerson, MP, I, 105 ff. Professor S. J. Crawford (TLS, 1930, p. 942) quotes a passage in condemnation of Nimrod from St. Augustine, De Civ. Dei (xvi, 4). But it is by no means clear that Chaucer had this in mind.

A pulled hen, and *an oystre,* l. 182, are examples of the numerous comparisons to denote worthlessness with which the language swarmed in the Middle English period. They were often homely or vivid, and were commonly used to enforce a simple negation — "not a nut, a straw, a button," etc. For discussion of their vogue see Dreyling, in Ausgaben und Abhandlungen, LXXXII; J. Hein, Angl., XV, 41 ff., 396 ff.; F. H. Sykes, The French Elements in Middle English, Oxford, 1899, pp. 24 ff. Other examples in Chaucer are collected by Haeckel, pp. 60 ff.

179 Various emendations (*restelees, rewlelees, cloysterles* — the last from MS. Harl., 7334) have been proposed for *recchelees,* but no change is necessary. The word means "reckless," "careless," here "neglectful of duty and discipline," and is more particularly explained by l. 181. (See Emerson, MP, I, 110 ff.) A second text from Gratian's Decretum (ii, 16, 1, Lyons, 1560, col. 1076) is probably referred to in the passage: "Sicut piscis sine aqua caret vita, ita sine monasterio monachus." The comparison was a commonplace. Skeat notes several examples, the earliest being from the Life of St. Anthony, attributed to St. Athanasius.

181–82 The language and rime here are closely similar to the Testament of Jean de Meun, ll. 1064–67 (ed. Méon, Le Roman de la Rose, 1814, IV, p. 60), though the sense is reversed.

184 *What,* why.

187 St. Augustine was the reputed author of a famous monastic rule, which was in reality deduced from one of his letters (Epist. 211, Migne, Pat. Lat., XXXIII, 958 ff.) and certain sermons on his community in Hippo (Serm. 355, 356, De vita et moribus clericorum suorum, Migne, XXXIX, 1568 ff. For the text of the rule, see Dugdale, Monasticon, London, 1846, VI, 42 ff.). His teachings on monastic labor were set forth in his treatise De Opere Monachorum (Migne, XL, 547 ff.), written for Aurelius, bishop of Carthage. It was a regular charge of the Lollard reformers against the "possessioners" that they avoided hard work. See H. B. Workman, John Wyclif, Oxford, 1926, II, 94.

Bit, contr. of *biddeth.*

The question *How shal the world be served?* has reference to the fact that many secular positions of trust were held by the clergy. Cf. Gower's Mirour de l'Omme, 20245 ff. Chaucer ironically asks how these valuable services are to be rendered if the clergy confine themselves to their religious duties and manual labor.

191 *prikyng,* "the tracking of a hare by its pricks or footprints" (NED, s.v. pricking, 2).

201 *stepe,* "large, prominent" (rather than "bright," as sometimes explained).

202 His eyes gleamed like a furnace under a cauldron.

The Friar

With the description of the Friar here should be compared the story of another friar told by the Summoner (*SumT,* III, 1709 ff.). Both characters are made to represent the corrupt condition of the mendicant orders, which in Chaucer's time had departed from the ideals of their founders. His treatment of them reflects current attacks on them. For a convenient summary of the relevant literature see

Arnold Williams in Spec., XXVIII, 499 ff., and MP, LIV, 117 ff. Professor Williams cites illustrative parallels at considerable length (especially from the De Periculis of William de St. Amour and the Defensio Curatorum of Richard FitzRalph), and holds that Chaucer's attacks are not to be particularly associated with the Wycliffite movement, though of course that was also opposed to the mendicants.

Though there are a number of individualizing traits in the Friar's portrait, no model has been identified. For suggestions (without positive conclusion) on the order to which he belonged see Tatlock, MLN, L, 289 ff. Professor Manly notes that *Huberd* (l. 269) is an uncommon name in English records of the fourteenth century.

208 *wantowne,* gay; cf. *wantownesse,* l. 264, used of an attractive mannerism. Chaucer's description clearly implies that the Friar was "wanton" also in the modern sense.

The final *-e* on *wantowne,* unpronounced in any case before *and,* may be merely a scribal error. But it is possibly to be regarded as the ending of the weak adjective, standing without a noun.

209 *lymytour;* see ll. 252 a–b.

solempne, in this context, apparently, "festive." It ranges in meaning from this sense to those of "grand, imposing, pompous, solemn."

210 The four orders were Dominicans, Franciscans, Carmelites, and Augustinians.

212–13 He found husbands, and perhaps dowries, for women whom he had himself seduced. Flügel's explanation (JEGP, I, 133 ff.), that the Friar married runaway couples free of charge, misses or avoids an innuendo which Chaucer surely intended. See K. Young, MLN, L, 83.

214 Cf. the phrase, "a pillar of the church."

216 On franklins see ll. 331 ff., which explains sufficiently why the Friar liked to frequent their houses. Their scale of living is further illustrated by the rimed bill of fare, entitled "A fest for a franklen," in John Russell's Book of Nurture (The Babees Book, ed. F. J. Furnivall, EETS, 1868, pp. 170–71).

218 ff. He had received from his order a license to hear confessions. The Franciscans and other friars had privileges which enabled them to confess the members of a parish without leave of the local ordinaries, and to give absolution for more serious offenses than they could deal with. The rivalry between friars and parish priests turned largely upon this practice. The friars were often charged with laxity in the imposition of penance. For illustrations from contemporary literature and ecclesiastical documents see E. Flügel, Angl., XXIII, 225 ff.; F. Tupper, JEGP, XIV, 258 f.; H. B. Workman, John Wyclif, II, 106–07.

227 f. "For if a man gave, the Friar dared to assert he knew the man was repentant."

238 For citations from the physiognomists showing that the soft white neck and the lisping were regarded as marks of licentiousness or depravity see O. E. Horton, MLN, XLVIII, 31 ff.

241 f. In *tappestere* and probably in *beggestere* the suffix *-stere* (AS. "-estre") has its proper feminine signification, as in the Mod. Eng. "spinster"; so also doubtless in *hoppesteres* (*KnT,* I, 2017), *chidestere* (*MerchT,* IV, 1535), and *tombesteres* and *frutesteres* (*PardT,* VI, 477 f.). But the distinction of gender was often lost in early English.

243 ff. With his avoidance of *poraille* cf. Wyclif, Eng. Works, ed. Matthew, EETS, 1880, pp. 15, 17; Select Eng. Works, ed. Arnold, 3 v., Oxford, 1869-71, III, 374; also RR, 11366 ff. (*Rom*, 6491 ff.). The character of Fals-Semblant is reproduced partly in the Friar and partly in the Pardoner.

252 a-b This couplet, which is found in only a few MSS., is probably genuine, though it may have been deliberately canceled. (See the Textual Notes.) The *ferme* was rent paid by the friar for the privilege of begging within assigned limits.

254 *In principio*, from John i, 1. The opening words of St. John's Gospel (vv. 1-14) were regarded with peculiar reverence and even held to have a magical virtue. Cf. Tyndale's reference to the "limiter's saying of 'In principio erat verbum' from house to house" (Answer to More, ed. H. Walter, Parker Soc., 1850, p. 62). On the superstitious use of the passage see E. G. C. F. Atchley, Trans. of the St. Paul's Ecclesiological Soc., IV, 161 ff.; J. S. P. Tatlock, MLN, XXIX, 141 f.; R. A. Law, PMLA, XXXVII, 208 ff.; and (for the same practice in Wales) J. Jenkins, Trans. of the Soc. of Cymmrodorion, 1919-20, p. 111. On the use of Leabhar Eóin as a charm in Ireland see Seán Ó Suilleabháin, A Handbook of Irish Folklore, pp. 307, 403. Professor Reisner has called the editor's attention to a similar custom among the Soudanese Mohammedans who give bread to a man for reciting the Surah el-Ihlās (No. 112) of the Koran.

256 What he picked up amounted to more than his income. Sometimes interpreted: the proceeds of his begging were greater than the rent or *ferme* which he turned in to his convent. (See Flügel in Angl., XXIII, 233 ff.) But the phrase was proverbial in the other sense. Cf. the *FrT*, III, 1451, and RR, 11566; and other references in MLN, XXIII, 144, 200. The word *purchas* was commonly applied to illegal gains.

258 On *love-dayes* see J. W. Spargo, Spec., XV, 36 ff. They were days appointed for settlement of disputes out of court, and the clergy took an active part as arbiters, at first with the approval of the Church. Later, when the institution became corrupt, they were forbidden to take part.

261 The Master's degree was one of considerable dignity and was obtained only after lavish expenditure of money.

263 *presse*, probably the mould of the bell, rather than the clothes-press. Cf. the Old French phrase "a fons de cuve," i.e., "en forme de cuve renversée (de cloche)," and for examples of its use see Ste.-Palaye, Dict. Historique, Paris, 1877, s.v. "cuve," and a note by Lowes, Rom. Rev., II, 118. See R. W. Frank, Jr. (MLN, LXVIII, 524 ff.) for the suggestion that the comparison may be due to the fact that Chaucer's house in Aldgate was in the midst of the London bell-founders.

269 The reason for the choice of the name *Huberd* is unknown. Miss Bowden, p. 119, suggests the possibility of a personal allusion. Mr. Charles Muscatine (MLN, LXX, 169 ff.) sees in it rather a reminiscence of Hubert, the kite, in the Roman de Renart.

The Merchant

The character of the Merchant is admirably illustrated from contemporary documents by T. Knott,

PQ, I, 1 ff. See also Manly, New Light, pp. 181 ff., and his notes.

It has generally been held by scholars, including Mr. Knott, that the Merchant is to be regarded as one of the merchants of the Staple, whose business was primarily the export of wool, woolfells, and skins. But since Chaucer makes no mention of wool, Professor Manly argues that he may have had in mind rather one of the Merchant Adventurers. They were originally organized in the thirteenth century for trade with the Low Countries. They were especially concerned with the importation of English cloth into the foreign cities where they were established. The fact that they were known as "The Fraternity of St. Thomas of Canterbury" may be a reason for the presence of the Merchant on the pilgrimage. Whether an Adventurer or a Stapler, he represented a class that was very rich and powerful in England in the fourteenth century. The merchants traded most successfully on the necessities of Edward III and Richard II, and from the secretiveness of Chaucer's Merchant Mr. Knott infers that he was involved in the national finances. The description sounds very personal, and the subject of the sketch, if there was one, may have been easily recognized. Mr. Knott suggests that it was some merchant of Ipswich, of which Orwell was the seaport, and Professor Manley adds the reminder that Chaucer's father was born in the town and owned property there. Miss Rickert has even ventured to suggest an historical counterpart in the Merchant-Adventurer Gilbert Maghfield, whose account book she published in MP, XXIV, 111 ff., 249 ff. Whether or not Maghfield was Chaucer's actual model, his career illustrates admirably the sketch of the merchant.

271 *mottelee*, motley, cloth woven with a figured design, often parti-colored. Liveries of such material were in regular use for members of various gilds and companies, and there is evidence that the Merchants of the Staple wore a distinctive dress.

hye on horse, seated in a very high saddle.

272 On the Flemish hat trade see F. P. Magoun, Jr. in Med. Stud., XVII, 126 f.

274 *resons*, opinions, remarks.

solempnely, impressively, pompously.

275 *Sownynge*, proclaiming, making known; probably not equivalent to *Sownynge in* [*to*], l. 307.

276-77 "He wished the sea to be guarded at all hazards, between Middelburg and Orwell." With regard to the keeping of the sea, to protect foreign trade, see Manly's note on the passage.

Orewelle, the old port of Orwell, close by Harwich. Since Harwich is not known to have been a wool port, whereas Ipswich is repeatedly named as a staple in fourteenth century records, Mr. Knott holds the Merchant to have belonged to Ipswich. This would also be likely enough if he was a Merchant Adventurer. *Middelburgh*, a port on the island of Walcheren on the Dutch coast, nearly opposite Orwell. The wool-staple was at Middelburg instead of at Calais from 1384 till 1388; whence it has been inferred that Chaucer must have written these lines between those years. (See J. W. Hales, Folia Litteraria, New York, 1893, pp. 100 f.) But it is certainly not impossible that, writing a few years later, he could have recalled the circumstances. Oddly enough, the date also fits if the reference is to the Merchant Adventurers, who appear to have been established in Middelburg in 1384, and for some time after.

278 By selling French *sheeldes* ("écus") at a profit the Merchant was breaking the statute which forbade anyone except the royal money changers to make a profit on exchange (25 Edw. III, Stat. 5, ch. 12, Ruffhead, Statutes at Large, Lond., 1763, I, 265). Possibly Chaucer means further to imply that the merchant took usury under color of exchange. For illustrations of both fraudulent money-changing and the concealment of debts — which were perhaps stock charges against the merchants — see also Tupper, Types, pp. 43 ff.

282 *chevysaunce*, which properly referred to borrowing and lending, or dealing for profit, was constantly used (like the word *bargayn*) for dishonest practices. It was sometimes a term for usury, and this implication may be intended here. Or the Merchant may have been a farmer of the revenue who failed to make honest returns to the Exchequer; or again, he may have bargained unscrupulously with the King's creditors. Mr. Knott (pp. 10 ff.) shows that Richard Lyons, a London merchant of the time was charged with buying the King's obligations at a discount and then obtaining full payment of them. The same man was also prosecuted for making profits on foreign exchange.

284 The last line has been held to convey contempt for the merchant class, or at least the condescension of a court poet writing for persons of higher station. But it may well be that Chaucer merely wishes to disavow any such personal identification of the Merchant as his readers might be led to make.

The Clerk

The term "clerk" was applied to any ecclesiastical student as well as to a man in holy orders. Chaucer's Clerk, though he had long since proceeded to logic (l. 286), was still pursuing his studies, perhaps in preparation for the Master's degree. On the curriculum and related matters see Jones, PMLA, XXVII, 106 ff. In the prologue to his own tale of Griselda the Clerk represents himself as having been at Padua, then the seat of a famous university.

Professor Manly is surely right in rejecting the supposition that Chaucer meant to describe his own education in that of the Clerk. Neither here nor in the Clerk's own prologue, where he speaks of his meeting with Petrarch, is there reason for supposing that his experiences represent those of the poet.

For the suggestion that the Clerk is to be identified with Walter Dissy (or Disse), mentioned in the will of William Mowbray (d. 1391) as "jadys clerk de Oxenford," see M. E. Richardson, TLS, 1932, pp. 331, 390; and comments by R. B. Turton, p. 368. To prove Chaucer's acquaintance with Disse, it is pointed out that Disse was a confessor of John of Gaunt from 1375 till 1386; also that Mowbray's daughter married Thomas Ingleby, and that the Inglebys probably knew Chaucer. But the grounds for the identification are very slight. Disse's relation to John of Gaunt really counts against it.

292 *to have office*, to accept secular employment. This was a common practice with men of clerical training. Cf. the reference to it in the account of the Monk (note to l. 187 above).

294 *Twenty bookes. Twenty* is here of course a round number, and it is not to be supposed that Chaucer had in mind literally twenty volumes of Aristotle, though the works of the philosopher accessible in Latin to Englishmen of that generation might have filled a score of manuscripts, not to speak of the numerous mediæval commentaries from Boethius down. But private libraries of that size were very uncommon at the time, and if the Clerk had bought one it is not strange that he had no money left for food or clothing. Coulton (Chaucer and his England, p. 99) calculated that the twenty books might have cost the equivalent of two or three burghers' houses. See also W. L. Schramm, MLN, XLVIII, p. 139.

297 Puns are relatively unusual in Chaucer, and it is not always easy to determine whether they are intentional. But there is here an unquestionable play on the word *philosophre* in its ordinary meaning and in the cant sense of "alchemist." Other more or less clear cases of word-play are found in l. 514, below, *SumT*, III, 1916 f., 1934, *WB Prol*, III, 837–38, *SqT*, V, 105–06, *CYT*, VIII, 730, *Tr*, i, 71, and *Purse*, 3–4. For discussion of these and other instances see J. S. P. Tatlock, in the Flügel Memorial Volume, Palo Alto, Cal., 1916, pp. 228–32, and H. Kökeritz, PMLA, LXIX, 937 ff. Professor Kökeritz extends his inquiry to other types of paranomasia. See also C. Jones, MLN, LII, 570, and for judicious comment on previous discussion, with additional examples of word-play (some of them uncertain), P. F. Baum, PMLA, LXXI, 225 ff.

299 The beggar student, or at least the student who was aided by contributions from friends and others, was a familiar figure in mediæval England. For references on the subject, and data with regard to the expenses of life at the universities, see H. S. V. Jones, PMLA, XXVII, 106 ff.; also Manly's note.

301 *gan* ("began"), at first primarily ingressive in meaning, came to be used in Middle English as a colorless preterite auxiliary like Modern English "did" (which had in Chaucer a causative sense). For a collection of cases of *gan* in Chaucer, with an interesting attempt to show various shades of meaning, see Miss E. R. Homann, JEGP, LIII, 389 ff.

305 "With due formality and respect."

307 *Sownynge in*, tending towards, consonant with (from Med. Lat. "sonare in" or "ad"). Cf. *PhysT*, VI, 54; *Mk Prol*, VII, 1967; *Tr*, iii, 1414, iv, 1676; *SqT*, V, 517; and see NED, s.v. "sound," v¹ 5.

The Sergeant of the Law

On the rank and status of sergeants of the law and the possible identification of Chaucer's Man of Law see Manly, New Light, pp. 131 ff., and his notes on the passage; also E. H. Warren, Virginia Law Review, May, 1942, reprinted as Serjeants-at-Law; the Order of the Coif, Cambridge, Mass., 1942.

The Sergeants-at-Law ("servientes ad legem") were the King's legal servants, selected from barristers of sixteen years' standing. From their number were chosen the judges of the King's courts and the chief baron of the Exchequer. Those who were not regular judges sometimes went on circuit as "justices in assize" (l. 314). They were few in number—about twenty when Chaucer wrote—and the most eminent members of the profession. They were addressed in the King's writ by the respectful plural "vos," and had the privilege of wearing their headcovering, the coif, in the royal presence. Professor Manly cites from Fortescue and Dugdale accounts of the elaborate ceremonies and feasts connected with their creation.

Among the lawyers known to have held the rank of sergeant in Chaucer's time Professor Manly finds only one — Thomas Pynchbek — who seems to fit the portrait of the Man of Law. He was admitted sergeant as early as 1376, and often served as justice in assize between 1376 and 1388. April 24, 1388, he was appointed chief baron of the Exchequer, from which office he was removed in 1389. From 1391 to 1396 he was justice of Common Pleas. He died by 1397. He was of a new, landless family, and appears in the records as acquiring land. His village was near the chief manor of Katherine Swynford. He and Chaucer were apparently on opposite sides politically, and Pynchbek offended Chaucer's friend Sir William Beauchamp by denying his claim to the Pembroke estates. One of the writs to arrest Chaucer for a small debt, in 1388, was signed by Pynchbek as chief baron of the Exchequer. So Chaucer might have had some personal motive for his satire. Finally, there is a possible pun on Pynchbek's name in l. 326.

The characterization of the lawyer is of especial interest in view of the probability recently established that Chaucer himself had a legal education. See the biographical introduction, above.

310 *at the Parvys.* Hitherto explained as the porch of St. Paul's, where lawyers met their clients for consultation. But Professor Manly questions whether this custom goes back to the fourteenth century. He suggests that the *parvys* was either a "*paradisus*" at Westminster, used (according to later records, to be sure) for the court of the Exchequer, or an afternoon exercise or moot of the students at the Inns of Court. The last explanation is that of John Selden, in his Notes on Fortescue's De Laudibus Legum Angliae, London, 1672, p. 50 (see also NED, s.v. Parvis, 2). But Fortescue's own text, it may be observed, rather supports the traditional interpretation of Chaucer's line. He says of the suitors ("Placitantes") that in the afternoon, when the courts are closed, they resort "ad pervisum, & alibi, consulentes cum servientibus ad legem & aliis consiliariis suis" (p. 124). For further discussion see G. L. Frost, MLN, XLIV, 469 ff., and E. H. Warren, Reprint, p. 24, both of whom argue (Warren says "probably but not surely") that the *parvys*, as used by Chaucer, included the nave as well as the porch of St. Paul's.

315 *By patente*, by the King's letters patent making the appointment as judge; *pleyn commissioun*, a letter addressed to the appointee giving him jurisdiction over all kinds of cases.

317 The *fees* and *robes* were gifts of clients.

318 *purchasour*, rather a buyer of land for himself than a conveyancer. He wished to become himself a landed gentleman. Moreover, he always succeeded in getting unrestricted possession (*fee symple*). Cf. Gower's Mirour de l'Omme, 24541 ff., and Wyclif's Thre Thingis (Eng. Works, ed. Matthew, EETS, 1880, pp. 180 ff.).

323 He knew accurately all the cases and judgments since the Conquest. He was versed in the common law and decisions of the courts as well as in the statutes (see l. 327).

328 *medlee*, medley, cloth of mixed weave, sometimes parti-colored. The official robes of the Sergeant-at-Law were of brown and green stripes. See further M. C. Linthicum, JEGP, XXXIV, 39 ff.

The Franklin

On the status and character of the Franklin see G. H. Gerould, PMLA, XLI, 262 ff., and R. M. Lumiansky, Univ. of Toronto Quar. XX, 344 ff. A possible identification is proposed by Manly, New Light, pp. 159 ff.

The word "franklin" sometimes designates a mere "free man" ("libertinus"); sometimes, as here, a landholder of free but not of noble birth. The exact social status of franklins is a matter of dispute. According to Henry Bradley (NED, s.v.), they ranked below the gentry, and Chaucer's Franklin has been taken by some commentators to be a kind of parvenu, with an excessive interest in *gentilesse* and an uncomfortable consciousness of his inferiority to the gentle members of the party. But Professor Gerould has collected considerable evidence that franklins were not merely men of substance, but were regarded as gentlemen, with a social position similar to that of knights, esquires, and sergeants of the law. Certainly Chaucer's Franklin is described as a person of wealth and dignity; his traveling companion is the Sergeant, a figure of consequence; and he held offices to which a man below the rank of gentleman was not ordinarily eligible. He corresponds in general to the country squire of a later period. His remarks about *gentilesse* may have been prompted, not by a sense of social inferiority, but the knowledge that he had less experience of courtly society than some of his fellow-pilgrims from the city.

Professor Manly suggests that the subject of the sketch was Pynchbek's neighbor Sir John Bussy of Kesteven in Lincolnshire. The identifying traits are perhaps not so striking as those which Pynchbek shares with the Man of Law. But Bussy was sheriff of Lincolnshire in 1384 and 1385; he was repeatedly knight of the shire; and he often sat on commissions of the peace, sometimes with Pynchbek. The fact that he was knighted as early as 1384 would not exclude him, Professor Manly argues, for he was not a knight banneret, the probable rank of Chaucer's Knight. Objections against the identification with Bussy are urged by K. L. Wood-Legh in RES, IV, 145 ff. She suggests instead Stephen de Hales of Norfolk, who was also associated with Pynchbek.

333 *complexioun*, doubtless used here in its older sense of "temperament," "combination of humours." A ruddy face was only one of the signs of a "complexioun" in which blood predominated. The other "complexiouns" commonly mentioned were the choleric, melancholy, and phlegmatic, characterized respectively by the predominance of choler, black bile, and phlegm.

336 ff. He was, as we should say, an epicure. The philosophy of Epicurus was associated (somewhat unjustly) then as now with luxurious living. With the present passage cf. *Bo*, iii, pr. 2, 78 ff., and *MerchT*, IV, 2021 ff.

340 St. Julian, the patron of hospitality, was a figure more legendary than historical, said to have died about 313 A.D.

341 *after oon*, according to one standard, uniformly good.

347-8 On the changing of diet in different seasons, see J. A. Bryant, Jr., MLN, LXIII, 318 ff.

353 *table dormant*, a table fixed in its place, as distinguished from a movable one. The Franklin was always ready for company.

355 He presided over the sessions of the Justices of the Peace.

356 *knyght of the shire*, member of Parliament for his county.

359 As sheriff he was the King's administrative officer in his county and ranked next to the Lord Lieutenant. *Countour*, a term of various applications. Selden, Titles of Honour (Works, London, 1726, III, 1027), defines it as "a sergeant at law," and Professor Manly cites evidence that it was used also of non-professional pleaders in court. But it may also mean "accountant," and refer to the Franklin's services as auditor in the shire.

360 *vavasour*, usually explained as a "vassal's vassal" (from "vassus vassorum"), that is, a tenant who did not hold directly from the King. But both the etymology and the theory of tenure have been called in question. See Pollock and Maitland, History of Engl. Law, 2d ed., Cambridge (Eng.), 1898, I, 546, n. 1. The term was loosely used in both France and England for substantial landholders, below the rank of barons. Professor Manly notes that the term was not in common use in southern England in the fourteenth century. In fact, he argues in support of his identification of Bussy, it appears to have been especially frequent in Lincolnshire.

The Five Gildsmen

On the mediæval English gilds see Charles Gross, The Gild Merchant, Oxford, 1890, and Westlake, Parish Gilds, New York, 1919.

For an account of the companies here represented and for notes on Chaucer's text, see E. P. Kuhl, Trans. Wisconsin Acad. of Sciences, XVIII, 652 ff. Professor Kuhl suggests that Chaucer had reasons of policy for the selection of these five. They all belonged to the non-victualing trades, which were under the protection of John of Gaunt. But these particular companies were neutral on the whole in the struggle between victualers and non-victualers for the control of the city. They did not join in the denunciation of Mayor Brembre in the Parliament of 1386. Mr. C. Camden, Jr. (PQ, VII, 314 ff.), draws from these facts the bold inference that the Gildsmen were added to the *Prologue* late, after the political strife had subsided. In Chaucer's original draught, he thinks, the Cook belonged with the Man of Law and the Franklin.

364 Since the five pilgrims belonged to different trades, the fraternity of which they all wore the livery must have been a social and religious gild. Professor Manly notes (New Light, p. 259) that St. Thomas of Canterbury was the patron saint of the Mercers, a craft closely related to the Weavers, Dyers, and Tapicers. For further discussion see T. A. Kirby, MLN, LIII, 504 ff.; Miss A. B. Fuller-

ton, MLN, LXI, 515 ff.; Miss Sarah Herndon, Florida State Univ. Stud., No. 5, 33–44; and P. Lisca, MLN, LXX, 321 ff.

369-70 "Each of them seemed a good burgess to sit on the raised platform in a gildhall." The mayor and aldermen sat on the dais, the common councilors on the floor. The reference here and in l. 372 (*alderman*) seems to be rather to the municipal magistrates than to officers of the gilds.

373 To become an alderman a burgess was required by law to have a certain amount of property.

375 *to blame*, "deserving of blame." In modern English the phrase "to blame" usually fixes responsibility on a person; here it rather defines the character of the act.

377 *vigilies*, celebrations held the evening before the gild festival. The term was also used for services on the vigils of saints' days. On such occasions the wives of the aldermen would have precedence. For lists of actual precedences in the livery companies see W. Herbert, The History of The Twelve Great Livery Companies, London, 1834, I, 100 f.

The Cook

For further information about this character see the introduction to his tale.

379 *for the nones*, probably "for the occasion," to cook their meals on the pilgrimage. But the phrase might mean "especially skilful" (of the cook). See the Glossary. Chaucer's uses of the phrase are collected and discussed by R. M. Lumiansky in Neophilologus, XXXV, 29 ff. He holds that the primary meaning, "for that time, purpose, etc." is usually discernible. But a number of the cases seem more indefinite.

384 *mortreux*. It is hard to be sure of the early English pronunciation of the -*x* in certain words where it represents etymologically an -*s* or -*us*. In the case of *mortreux* spellings like *mortrels*, *mortrewes*, point to a final -*s*. In *Burdeux* (see l. 397) the same pronunciation is probable and is supported by the spelling "Burdios" in fifteenth-century Welsh. But the sound of -*x* is indicated as occurring, at least sporadically, by recorded English spellings like "Burdeukes." *Lybeux* (*Thop*, VII, 900), Fr. "li biaus," doubtless also had an -*s*. For *Amphiorax* (*WB Prol*, III, 741; *Anel*, 57; *Tr*, ii, 105; v, 1500) Chaucer must have been familiar with the Latin form "Amphiaraus," though there may have been a corrupt English pronunciation in -*x*.

386 *a mormal* (Lat. "male mortuum"), a species of dry-scabbed ulcer. For medical theories on the subject see Curry, pp. 47 ff. There is a contemporary account of the treatment of an ulcerated leg in John Arderne's Treatises, ed. Power, EETS, 1910, pp. 52–54 (printed also by A. S. Cook, Trans. Conn. Acad., XXIII, 27 ff.). See further H. Braddy, MLQ, VII, 265 ff.

The Shipman

On the Shipman see P. Q. Karkeek, in Essays on Chaucer (Ch. Soc., 1884), Part V, no. 15; Manly, New Light, pp. 169 ff. Dr. Karkeek long ago pointed out that a vessel named the "Magdaleyne," from Dartmouth, paid customs duties in 1379 and 1391. In the former year the master was named

George Cowntree; in the latter, Peter Risshenden. Scholars have recognized the possibility that one of these men was the original of the Shipman, and Professor Manly has produced new arguments which make probable the identification with Risshenden. He notes a number of records of cases between 1385 and 1389, where Dartmouth ships were charged with unlawfully attacking others at sea. John Hawley, the chief shipowner of Dartmouth (also mayor of the city and collector of customs for Devon and Cornwall) is mentioned in several such prosecutions. (The records of one case are summarized and several documents translated, by Florence E. White, MP, XXVI, 249 ff., 379 ff.; XXVII, 123 ff.) In 1386 Piers Riesselden (apparently the same man as Risshenden) commanded a Dartmouth balinger that joined a barge of Hawley's in the capture of three Breton crayers.

In MLR, XXXIV, 497 ff., Miss M. Galway proposed the identification of the Shipman with John Piers, a naturalized Englishman from Biscay, who lived "fer by weste" in Teignmouth and whose career offers striking parallels to Chaucer's sketch. In 1383, for example, Piers captured an English vessel named "Maudeleyne." She even went on to suggest (in TLS, Oct. 3, 1942) that *phisylas*, in *M. L. Endlink*, II, 1189, is from a Basque word. For an account of some criticisms of her theory see her rejoinder in TLS, Apr. 10, 1943.

390 It is hard to decide whether *rouncy* here means a poor hackney, a nag (as usually assumed), or a great, strong horse. Mr. Hinckley, who argues for the latter interpretation, gives evidence of both meanings of the term.

As he kouthe implies that the Shipman's riding was poor.

391 On *faldyng* see M. C. Linthicum, JEGP, XXXIV, 39 ff.

395 *a good felawe*, often used with an implication of rascality. For examples see Manly's note on l. 649.

396 f. The Shipman stole wine which he was carrying for a merchant (*chapman*) from Bordeaux. Brusendorff's interpretation (pp. 481 f.), that the Shipman captured many a cargo (*draughte*), is less probable. On the laws governing the supply of wine to a crew by the merchant for whom it was carried see Miss M. R. Stobie, PMLA, LXIV, 565. With *Fro Burdeux-ward* cf. *To Caunterbury-ward*, l. 793 below; *To Thebes-ward, KnT*, I, 967. On the pronunciation of *Burdeux* see the note on *mortreux*, l. 384 above.

398 *conscience*, tender feeling, sympathy; cf. ll. 142, 150, above.

400 He drowned his prisoners — apparently not an unusual practice at the time. Instances in 1350, in the battle of L'Espagnols sur mer, and in 1403 are cited in Mr. Pollard's note.

404 *Cartage*, probably one of the Spanish ports, Cartagena, or Cartaya, rather than the ancient Carthage.

408 *Gootlond*, probably the island of Gotland, off the coast of Sweden. Visby, its capital, was a very important trading town. For the opinion that the spelling with long o (*Gootlond*) points rather to Jutland, see K. Malone, MLR, XX, 6. E. V. K. Dobbie, cited in Bowden, p. 197, argues for Gotland, as does Professor Magoun, Med. Stud., XVII, 128.

Fynystere could refer to either Finisterre in Brittany or, more probably, as Professor Magoun argues, (Med. Stud., XVII, 128), Cape Finisterra, Galicia, Spain.

409 *Britaigne*, Brittany.

The Doctor of Physic

On the character of the Physician see E. E. Morris in An English Miscellany [Furnivall], Oxford, 1901, pp. 338 ff.; Curry, pp. 3 ff. (a revision of PQ, IV, 1 ff.); F. Tupper, Types of Society, pp. 45 ff.; H. H. Bashford, Nineteenth Cent. and After, CIV, 237 ff. (with especial reference to Bernard, Gilbert, and Gaddesden). For further treatment of physiological and medical science in Chaucer's age reference may be made to Sir Robert Steele, Mediæval Lore, London, 1893; P. A. Robin, The Old Physiology in English Literature, London, 1911; L. Thorndike, History of Magic and Experimental Science, N.Y., 1923, II; Gunther, Early Science in Oxford, III, Oxford, 1925. Some illustration of Chaucer's own acquaintance with the subject is given by Lowes, MP, XI, 491 ff.

Chaucer gives here an admirable account of the mediæval practice of medicine, as he did earlier of the practice of law. Some traits in the description seem to be individual, but no model is known. The old supposition that Chaucer had especially in mind John Gaddesden (*Gatesden*), who died in 1361, is improbable. Miss Bowden's suggestion (Commentary, pp. 208 ff.) that Chaucer had in mind John Arderne is advanced tentatively, but is not impossible.

413 *To speke of*, having regard to (that is, on the author's part). Professor Curry is surely mistaken in taking the line to imply that the Physician's superiority consisted only in his ability to talk about his profession.

414 *astronomye*, rather what would now be called astrology. Its importance to medical science appears in the lines that follow. See also *Astr*, i, 21, 71 ff. The Physician watched (*kepte*) his patient and chose the astrological hours which would be most favorable to the treatment; he was skillful in taking the advantageous time for making talismanic figures. Cf. *HF*, 1265 ff. For further development of the idea that the physician should be *grounded in astronomye* see the medical treatise (ascribed in the title to Hippocrates) in the Brussels MS. of the *Astrolabe*, fols. 42–46 (cited by Pintelon, Chaucer's Treatise on the Astrolabe, p. 39).

The images referred to may have been either representations of the patient, like the wax figures made by sorcerers with maleficent purpose, or talismans representing the constellations or signs of the Zodiac, or symbolically associated with them. That both sorts were used by physicians is made clear in Professor Kittredge's discussion of image magic, Witchcraft in Old and New England, Cambridge, Mass., 1929, pp. 73 ff. Their virtue depended upon the aspects of the planets at the time when they were made. The supposed relations between planetary influences and disease, and the whole procedure of the manufacture and use of images, are illustrated at length in Professor Curry's chapter (cited above). See also Thorndike, History of Magic, I, 672 ff. For a figure representing the association of the sign of the Zodiac see the photograph of the Brussels MS., fol. 67, in Pintelon's treatise (just cited).

416 *magyk natureel.* "Natural magic," which was regarded as legitimate science (and indeed still had that application in Bacon's Advancement of Learning), must always be distinguished from "black magic" or necromancy. For a similar distinction in Eastern science, cf. D. B. McDonald in Encyclopedia of Islam, s.v. *sihr.* See also D. B. Emrich's unpublished Harvard dissertation on Avicenna.

417 *fortunen,* find or place in a favorable position (Lat. "fortunare"). This involved much more than merely selecting a favorable ascendant. The planet known as the lord of the ascending sign, and also the Moon, must be favorably situated, and the malefic planets must be in positions where their influence would be slight. See the elaborate directions quoted by Curry (p. 21) from Thebit ibn Corat.

420 The four elementary qualities or contraries, which by combination in pairs produced the four elements: — earth (cold and dry), air (hot and moist), water (cold and moist), fire (hot and dry) Similarly the fundamental contraries were held to combine in the four humours: blood (hot and moist), phlegm (cold and moist), yellow bile (hot and dry), black bile (cold and dry). See Galen, De Placitis Hippocratis et Platonis, Bk. viii, ed. I. Müller, Leipzig, 1874, pp. 667 ff.

425 With this familiar fling at doctors and druggists cf. Gower, Mirour de l'Omme, 25621 ff. Professor Curry (pp. 31 ff.) cites evidence from the seventeenth century of collusion between men of the two callings. Druggists are charged with foisting incompetent practitioners ("apothecaries' physicians") upon patients, and doctors with causing patients to be imposed upon by their particular druggists ("covenant apothecaries"). There were doubtless similar practices in the fourteenth century. But Chaucer's repetition of a current joke on the medical profession hardly justifies Professor Curry in setting down the Doctor among apothecaries' quacks.

429 The names which Chaucer here parades are those of eminent authorities in medicine. Five of them appear in a similar, but shorter list in RR, 15959 ff. Aesculapius, the legendary father of medicine, was supposed to be the author of works current in the Middle Ages. Dioscorides, a Greek writer on the materia medica, flourished about 50 A.D. *Rufus* of Ephesus lived in the second century. Hippocrates (*Olde Ypocras*), the founder of Greek medical science, was born at Cos about 460 B.C. *Haly* is probably the Persian Hali ibn el Abbas (d. 994), an eminent physician of the Eastern Caliphate; but the name might also refer to Hali filius Rodbon (born c. 980). Galen (commonly spelled *Galyen*) was the famous authority of the second century. The name *Serapion* was borne by three medical writers, an Alexandrian Greek, probably of the second century B.C., a Christian physician of Damascus, probably of the ninth century, and an Arabian of the eleventh or twelfth. Probably the last of these, author of the Liber de Medicamentis Simplicibus, is referred to. Rhazes (*Razis*) of Baghdad lived in the ninth and tenth centuries. Avicenna and Averroes were famous Arabian philosophers, as well as medical authorities, of the eleventh and twelfth centuries respectively. Chaucer refers to the Canon of Avicenna in *PardT*, VI, 889–90. *Damascien* is of less certain identification. St. John of Damascus (676–754) was concerned rather with philosophy and theology than

with medicine, but the name Johannes (or Jannus) Damascenus was also attached to the writings of two ninth-century medical authorities, Mesuë (Yuhannā ibn Māsawaih) and the elder Serapion. Constantinus Afer (*Constantyn*), a monk of Carthage, brought Arabian learning to Salerno in the eleventh century. He is the *daun Constantyn* of *MerchT*, IV, 1810. The three who end the list, all of British origin, wrote medical compendiums of wide influence. Bernard Gordon, a Scot, was professor of medicine at Montpellier about 1300. John of Gaddesden (or *Gatesden*), of Merton College, Oxford, died in 1361. His reputation for thrift was such that Chaucer has been supposed to refer to him in ll. 441 ff. Gilbertus Anglicus (*Gilbertyn*) lived in the latter part of the thirteenth century.

It is perhaps useless to seek a single source for such a list of medical authorities. But Miss Bowden, p. 200, citing Miss Pauline Aiken, notes that they are all to be found in the Speculum Majus of Vincent of Beauvais.

438 For the implication of irreligion in this line comparison has often been made with the proverb, "Ubi tres medici, duo athei." There is plenty of evidence that doctors were commonly regarded as skeptical, especially if they were avowed followers of the Arabian or Averroist school. See Tupper, Types, pp. 47 ff. Cf. also Curry, pp. 29 ff., citing John of Salisbury's condemnation of physicians who "attribute too much to Nature, cast aside the Author of Nature" (Polycraticus, ii, 29).

441 *esy of dispence,* slow to spend money.

443–44 He loved gold, Chaucer observes ironically, because "aurum potabile" was so good a remedy. Professor Curry (pp. 34 f.) finds in the sentence the further suggestion that the Doctor put "aurum potabile" into his medicines to raise their price.

The Wife of Bath

On the Wife of Bath see especially W. E. Mead, PMLA, XVI, 388 ff.; Curry, pp. 91 ff.; Manly, New Light, pp. 225 ff.

The portrait of the Wife here is supplemented by her own account of herself in the *Prologue* to her tale. For the latter work Chaucer drew freely on the satirical anti-feminist literature of his age. See the notes to *WB Prol*, pp. 801 ff. below. Whether the brief description in the *General Prologue* was written early, or added (or revised) later when Chaucer's conception of the Wife had been fully worked out, is uncertain. Cf. Miss Hammond, pp. 296–97.

Various opinions have been advanced as to the origin of the conception. Literary imitation of the description of La Vieille in the Roman de la Rose (ll. 12761 ff.) is apparent, but this is not enough to account for the character. Professor Curry, whose study has reference particularly to the *Wife's Prologue*, has shown that many of her characteristics are such as were regularly associated with a person born when Taurus is in the ascendant and Mars and Venus are in conjunction in that sign (*WB Prol*, III, 605 ff.). But he admits that the figure is no mere abstract construction and may have been drawn from life. Professor Manly, without attempting an identification, argues strongly that the wife is an individual. He points out as traits that are rather personal than typical her love of travel, her rather unfashionable dress and equipment, and the fact that she was deaf and gat-toothed. Her name *Alisoun* (*WB Prol*, III, 804) would of course prove nothing. But Mr. Manly notes that it is of frequent occurrence in the records of Bath in the fourteenth century. Moreover, Chaucer gives a singularly precise statement as to the locality from which she came. *Biside Bathe* doubtless refers to the parish of "St. Michael's juxta Bathon," a suburb of the town largely given over to weaving. Chaucer would have had occasion, perhaps frequently, to pass through St. Michael's on his journeys to North Petherton where he was forester in 1391 and the following years.

446 For the occasion of the Wife's deafness see her *Prol*, III, 668.

448 Ypres and Ghent were important seats of the Flemish wool trade, and Flemish weavers emigrated to England in large numbers in the fourteenth century. The line, which Professor Kittredge has paraphrased "She beat the Dutch" (Chaucer and his Poetry, Cambridge, Mass., 1915, p. 32) is perhaps to be taken ironically, for the reputation of the cloth made in Bath was not of the best. See Manly, New Light, pp. 225 ff. (quoting Alton and Holland, The King's Customs)

449–52 The people went up in order of precedence when they made their offerings. Cf. Deschamps, Miroir de Mariage, 3376–81. If Chaucer used that work here, the passage was probably written late. But strife over precedence at the offering was apparently a stock illustration of the sin of pride. See *ParsT*, X, 407, and cf. Le Fèvre, Lamentations de Matheolus (ed. Van Hamel, I, Paris, 1892), ii, 1430 ff.

453 Professor Manly (New Light, pp. 230 f.) notes that the kerchief had not been in style since the middle of the century. For illustrations of heavy head-dress he refers to Fairholt, Costume in England, ed. Dillon, London, 1885, I, figs. 125, 129, 130, 151. But Cf. D. E. Wretlind (MLN, LXIII, 381 f.), who cites evidence that heavy headdress came in fashion with Queen Anne.

459 The form *lyve* is exceptional in the accusative, which would be the natural case in this construction. The final *-e* is probably due to the influence of the "petrified" dative (*on-*)*lyve*, (*by-*)*lyve*, etc.

460 The celebration of marriage *at chirche dore* was usual in Western Christendom from the 10th till the 16th century. The service was in two parts — the marriage proper, conducted "ante ostium ecclesiae," and the nuptial mass, celebrated afterward at the altar. It is a matter of dispute whether the first part was a survival of the Roman "sponsalia" or of the Germanic "gifta." On this whole matter see G. E. Howard, A History of Matrimonial Institutions, I, Chicago, 1904, 291–363.

461 Besides, not to speak of, other company in youth. This interpretation is supported by the description of La Vieille (RR, 12781).

462 *as nowthe*, as now, for the present. *As* was commonly used in such phrases (*as now, as then, as in my lyf*, etc.), where it would now be regarded as pleonastic. "As yet" is still sometimes heard. In such combinations *as* had a restrictive sense, "having regard only to the time or circumstances mentioned."

For another kind of "pleonastic as" see *KnT*, I, 2302, n.

463 *Jerusalem*, probably to be pronounced *Jerusalem*, as it was sometimes spelled. For some account of the shrines here mentioned and other objects of interest at the localities see Bowden, pp. 221 ff.

465 *Boloigne*, probably Boulogne-sur-mer, where a fragmentary image of the Blessed Virgin is still venerated. *Galice* (Galicia) refers to the shrine of St. James at Compostella. At Cologne was the shrine of the Three Kings. All these places were much resorted to by pilgrims. The long pilgrimages of the Wife, it should be remembered, would have been by no means unusual, nor were they in any way inconsistent with her character. Her motives, as she intimated in her *Prologue* (III, 551 ff.), were not entirely religious. In fact, the pilgrimage in Chaucer's day was a favorite form of traveling for pleasure. Such provision was made for the safety and comfort of the pilgrims that it corresponded, in a way, to the modern personally conducted party. It even fell under condemnation as offering occasion for temptation to vice. Evidence of this might be multiplied indefinitely. Cf., for illustrative examples, H. B. Workman, John Wyclif, II, 18; C. Langlois, La Vie en France au Moyen Âge, II (D'Après des moralistes du temps), Paris, 1925, p. 259; Heath, Pilgrim Life in the Middle Ages, London, 1911, pp. 33 f.; Van Hamel's note to Le Fèvre's Lamentations de Matheolus (ii, 947 ff.), II, Paris, 1905, p. 166; Lowes (citing Deschamps), Rom. Rev., II, 120; Crescini, Atti del R. Istit. Veneto, LX, 455, Bowden, pp. 19 ff.

468 *Gat-tothed*, with teeth set wide apart (gap-toothed or gate-toothed). Skeat notes that this has been regarded as a sign a person will be "lucky and travel." But the Wife herself, in her *Prologue*, seems to connect the feature with her amorous nature (III, 603); and Professor Curry has shown that the physiognomists regarded it as a sign of boldness, falseness, gluttony, and lasciviousness (see PMLA, XXXVII, 45). See also A. J. Barnouw, The Nation, CIII, 540. To accord with this interpretation the unlikely etymology, "goat-toothed" has been proposed.

470 On her hat see D. E. Wretlind, MLN, LXIII, 381.

472 *A foot-mantel*, which ordinarily meant "saddle-cloth," here seems to be an outer skirt. In the Ellesmere miniature the Wife is represented as riding astride. The custom of sitting sidewise is said to have been introduced by Queen Anne.

475 *remedies of love*, cures of love, with an allusion to Ovid's Remedia Amoris.

476 *the olde daunce*; she knew all the rules of the game. Cf. *PhysT*, VI, 79, and for a vivid application of the figure, *Tr*, iii, 694–95. Chaucer perhaps got the phrase from the Roman de la Rose. But it was a current figure in French, meaning "to be artful, knowing," and not restricted to the affairs of love. See RR, 3936, and Langlois's note.

The Parson

The sketch of the Parson is an ideal portrait of a good parish priest. It should not be taken to represent Wyclif or one of his followers. To be sure, it praises the virtues on which the Wycliffites laid emphasis and condemns certain abuses which they were always attacking. The Parson, too, is contemptuously addressed as a Lollard in the *Man of Law's Epilogue* (II, 1173). Probably Chaucer would not have described him in just the terms he uses if reform had not been in the air. The poet himself was in intimate relations, it should also be remembered, with some of the most influential patrons of the Lollards. But the Parson is not represented as holding some of the most distinguishing beliefs of the Lollard party. Moreover Wyclif, who died in 1384, presumably three or four years before the *Prologue* was written, was repudiated as a heretic in his last days. On the whole question see Lounsbury, Studies, II, 459 ff., Tatlock, MP, XIV, 257 ff., and R. S. Loomis, Essays and Studies in Honor of Carleton Brown (New York, 1940), pp. 141 ff.; also the introduction to the Explanatory Notes on the *ParsT*.

478 f. Cf. Prov. xiii, 7.

486 The penalty of excommunication was often imposed for the non-payment of tithes. The Parson himself of course could not pronounce the greater excommunication, but he could report the offense, exclude the offender from the sacraments, and declare him liable to the excommunication, which would be actually pronounced by the bishop. In the implied condemnation of this method of enforcing payment there is very likely an echo of Wyclif's protests against the abuse of the power of the keys. See his Eng. Works, ed. Matthew, EETS, 1880, pp. 36, 146, 150, 277. Cf. also l. 661 below, and n.

493–95 With this description of the Parson's visits Mayor and Lumby, in their notes on Bede's Eccl. Hist., iii, 5 (Cambridge, Eng., 1881, p. 227) compare Bede's account of Aidan.

494 *muche and lite*, high and low, cf. note to l. 534 below.

497 f. The primary allusion here is to Matt. v, 19. For the idea Mayor and Lumby again quote Bede, iii, 5: "Non aliter quam vivebat cum suis ipse docebat" (p. 226). Cf. also Gower, Conf. Am., v, 1825, and for other parallels see Cook, Trans. Conn. Acad., XXIII, 29.

500 For the figures of gold and iron, and the *shiten shepherde* and the *clene sheep* cf. the Roman de Carité, of the Renclus de Moiliens (late twelfth century), which also offers other less striking parallels to Chaucer's sketch. See particularly A. G. Van Hamel's edition, Paris, 1885, stanzas 56, 58, 62, 69, 71. Chaucer may have followed the Roman, or both may be indebted to a common source or to ideas generally current. The figure of rusted gold was often used by Biblical commentators. The ultimate source may be Lamentations 4:1. See Kittredge, MLN, XII, 113, and Flügel, Angl., XXIV, 500 and n.

507 On absenteeism see H. B. Workman, John Wyclif, II, 110 ff. "Some livings rarely saw a resident rector."

510 *a chaunterie* was a provision for a priest to sing mass daily for the repose of a soul. The usual remuneration about 1380 was seven marks a year. According to Dugdale (History of St. Paul's Cathedral, Lond., 1818, p. 29) there were thirty-five chantries at St. Paul's. In 1391 these were restricted to the minor canons of the Cathedral.

511 Or to be retained, engaged for service (*withholde*), by a gild (*bretherhed*) to act as their chaplain. For illustration of the practice see Tatlock, MLN, XXXI, 139 ff.

514 Cf. John, x, 12. There is perhaps further reference to the title "chappelain mercenaire," which was applied to priests who made their living entirely by saying mass.

517 *daungerous*, severe, arrogant; *digne*, haughty. *Daunger* (from Fr. "daungier," LL *"dominarium") meant originally "dominion," "power," "control." Cf. l. 663 below. *Daungerous*, in Chaucer, has the related senses of "arrogant," "severe," "difficult," "fastidious," and very commonly meant "difficile," "offish," in the affairs of love.

518 *discreet*, apparently here and in a few other passages in Chaucer, with the suggestion of "courteous, civil." See P. E. Dustoon, RES, XIII, 206 ff.

523 f. The rime of two words with one (*nonys: noon ys*), which is a characteristic freedom of comic verse in Mod. Eng., was regularly admissible in serious passages in Mid. Eng. For other Chaucerian examples see ll. 671 f. below (*Rome: to me*); KnT, I, 1323 f. (*dyvynys: pyne ys*); SqT, V, 675 f. (*yowthe: allow the*); Tr, i, 2, 4, 5 (*Troye: joie: fro ye*); v, 1374, 1376, 1377 (*welles: helle is: ellis*).

525 He demanded no reverence.

526 *spiced*, seasoned, hence highly refined, over-scrupulous; possibly with the suggestion that he was not sophisticated, versed in anise and cummin, and negligent of weightier matters. Hinckley's interpretation, "unctuous, over complaisant" seems less appropriate. The Parson was reasonable and not too fastidious in his dealings with his flock. The phrase occurs again in *WB Prol*, III, 435. Skeat's derivation of *spiced* from Fr. "espices," fees or dues paid to a judge, is improbable.

The Plowman

The Plowman was apparently a small tenant farmer or a holder of Lammas lands (village lands let out from year to year). Like his brother, the Parson, he is represented as an ideal Christian. Professor Tupper (Types, pp. 40 ff.) notes the occurrence of the same convention in the Chess-Book. But on the whole the treatment of the peasant in mediæval literature was more likely to be satirical or contemptuous. See P. Meissner, Der Bauer in der Eng. Lit., Bonner Studien, 1922; G. M. Vogt, The Peasant in Mid. Eng. Lit., unpublished Harvard dissertation, 1923, G. Stilwell in ELH, VI, 285 ff., and J. Horrell, Spec., XIV, 82 ff. With Chaucer's idealized portrait may be compared the description in Iolo Goch's Cywyddy Llafurwr, in Cywyddau Iolo Goch ac Eraill, Ed. Henry Lewis and others, 1937, no. 27; tr. by H. I. Bell in Trans. of the Cymmrodorion Society, 1942, p. 137. On Chaucer's attitude toward the common people there is a brief, but admirably judicial, discussion by H. R. Patch in JEGP, XXIX, 376 ff.

529 In Mid. Eng. the relative pronoun was frequently omitted when subject, as well as when object, of a verb. Cf., for examples, *Cl Prol*, IV, 3; *ShipT*, VII, 105; *Mel*, VII, 1593; *NPT*, VII, 2849, 2900, 3175; *Tr*, i, 203; *LGW*, 704.

533 Cf. Matt. xxii, 37–39.

534 *thogh him gamed or smerte,* in pleasure or pain; one of a number of phrases current in early English to denote "under all circumstances," "in all respects." Cf. *in heigh and lough,* l. 817, below; *in (for) ernest nor (ne) in (for) game, ClT,* IV, 609, 733; *For foul ne fair, MLT,* II, 525; *for lief ne looth, ShipT,* VII, 132.

541 The mare was a humble mount.

The Miller

On the Miller see Curry, pp. 71 ff. (materials published earlier in PMLA, XXXV, 189 ff.), and Tupper, Types, pp. 52 ff. For an interesting speculation about a possible model for the Miller, for Robin in the *Mill T,* and for Simkin in the *RvT* see Manly, New Light, pp. 94 ff. Miss Galway, N & Q, CXCV, 486 ff., and the comments of C. A. Owen, Jr., MLN, LXVII, 336.

To the description in the *Prologue* may be added the later reference to the Miller's powerful voice (*Mill Prol,* I, 3124). It is likely, too, that the account of Simkin, in the *Reeve's Tale,* contained hits on the fellow-pilgrim at whose story the Reeve had taken offense.

The Miller's physical characteristics are such as were regularly associated by the physiognomists with men of his nature. His short-shouldered, stocky figure, his fat face with red bushy beard, his flat nose with a wart on top — these variously denoted a shameless, loquacious, quarrelsome, and lecherous fellow. Many curious observations on the subject, drawn from such works as the pseudo-Aristotelian Secreta Secretorum and the treatise of Rhazes, De Re Medecina, are brought together by Professor Curry. The influence of similar ideas is apparent in the description of the Reeve, the Pardoner, the Summoner, and the Wife of Bath. But whether Chaucer went directly to the learned treatises on the subject (as Dr. Curry implies), or simply made use of familiar current notions, it is hard to say.

545 *for the nones,* here apparently in the intensive sense.

548 Cf. *Thop,* VII, 740 f. With the ram cf. the fighting for the *maout* in modern Brittany, Bleuniou Breiz, Poésies Anciennes et Modernes de la Bretagne, (Quimperlé, 1888) p. 16.

550 On the Miller's head see B. J. Whiting, MLN, LII, 417 ff, A. N. Wiley, MLN, LIII, 505 ff., F. L. Utley, MLN, LVI, 534 ff., and B. J. Whiting, MLN, LXIX, 309. A New England door-smasher of the sort is the Negro Abe the Bunter, made historic by Carroll Perry in his Professor of Life, pp. 43–46.

560 *goliardeys,* coarse buffoon. In its origin the word is related to the so-called "goliardic" poetry, satirical and convivial verse, chiefly in Latin, composed by vagabond clerics in the twelfth and thirteenth centuries. For illustrations of this literature see Latin Poems commonly attributed to Walter Mapes, ed. T. Wright, London, 1841 (Camden Soc.), and the Carmina Burana, ed. J. A. Schmeller, Breslau, 1894; J. A. Symonds, Wine, Women, and Song, London, 1925; cf. also J. H. Hanford, Speculum, I, 38 f. *Goliardic* lost its literary association and came to be applied, as in the case of the Miller, to tellers of coarse tales and jests. Cf. Piers Plowman, B-Prologue, 139: "a goliardeys, a glotoun of

wordes" (which illustrates another association of the term with "gula," gluttony, etc.). The origin of the word, in relation to "Golias," on the one hand and "gula" on the other, is uncertain. For two theories see Manly, MP, V, 201–09, and J. W. Thompson, Stud. Phil., XX, 83–98.

563 He was honest, as millers go. The reference is to the proverb, "An honest miller hath a golden thumb."

The Manciple

A manciple was a servant who purchased provisions for a college or an inn of court. The temple referred to would have been the Inner or Middle Temple near the Strand, both of which were occupied in Chaucer's time by societies of lawyers.

The inclusion in the company of so inconspicuous a character as the Manciple tends to support the theory that Chaucer had been educated in the Inns of Court.

570 *by taille,* on credit. The "tally" was a stick on which the amount of a debt was recorded by notches. Cf. Jenkinson, Archæologia, LXXIV, 289 ff.

579 On the steward's office see the note on the Reeve, below.

581 To make him live on his income.

586 *sette hir aller cappe,* make fools of them all. *Aller (alder)* is the old genitive plural (AS. "ealra"). Cf. ll. 710, 799, below, and see the Introduction on Language and Meter.

The Reeve

There is some uncertainty as to the exact office of the Reeve. The chief manager of an estate, under the lord of the manor, was the steward (or seneschal). Subordinate to him was the bailiff, and below the bailiff was the provost, who was elected by the peasants and had immediate care of the stock and grain. Normally the reeve was subordinate to the bailiff, but many manors did not have a full complement of officers, and titles were more or less interchanged. Chaucer's Reeve was apparently superior to a bailiff, and even exercised some of the functions of a steward. He is represented as dealing directly with his lord, ruling under-bailiffs and hinds, outwitting auditors, and accumulating property. On these officials see F. Tupper, JEGP, XIV, 265, who follows the Anglo-French Seneschaucie in Miss Lamond's edition of Walter of Henley's Husbandry (London, 1890, pp. 83 ff.); F. H. Cripps-Day, The Manor Farm, London, 1931, pp. 56 ff., 71, 86 ff., 96 f.; H. Y. Moffett, PQ, IV 208 ff.; also the accounts of Robert Oldman, bailiff of Cuxham, in Roger's History of Agriculture and Prices in England, I, Oxford, 1866, pp. 506 ff.

With the personal description of the Reeve should be compared that given in his own *Prologue* (I, 3855 ff.). On his physical characteristics, which were regularly associated by the physiognomists with the choleric complexion and denoted sharpness of wit, irascibility, and wantonness, see Curry, pp. 71 ff. (the chapter already cited for the Miller).

Though the personal appearance of the Reeve is in some respects typical, several details of the description suggest that Chaucer had in mind an actual official, whose dwelling he had seen and whose character might be recognized. Professor Manly (New Light, pp. 84 ff.) shows reason for suspecting that the portrait applied to a Norfolk reeve, probably the manager of some of the estates of John Hastings, second earl of Pembroke. *Baldeswelle* (l. 620; the modern Bawdswell, in the northern part of Norfolk) was the property of the Pembrokes. Hastings came of age in 1368, and was abroad nearly all the time till his death in 1375. When, in 1378, the custody of his estates in Kent was granted to his cousin, Sir William de Beauchamp, Chaucer was one of Beauchamp's mainpernors. There is evidence that some of the Pembroke estates were mismanaged, and Sir William de Beauchamp's management had to be officially investigated in 1386–87. Professor Manly concedes that he has found no evidence of maladministration of the Norfolk properties, which were in the custody of the Countess of Pembroke. But he suggests that Chaucer may have served as a deputy to view the waste of the Pembroke lands, and may have thus learned about the rascally Norfolk Reeve. For objections to some of Mr. Manly's inferences, including his low estimate of the Reeve's character, see E. B. Powley, TLS, 1932, p. 516. Mr. Powley would explain Chaucer's acquaintance with Baldeswelle on the ground that it was part of the Manor of Clare, which belonged in 1360 to Prince Lionel. Chaucer had entered service with Lionel's wife, Elizabeth de Burgh, in 1357. But these associations were remote at the probable time of the writing of the *Prologue*. Moreover, as Miss L. V. Redstone has shown in TLS, 1932, pp. 789–90, the interest of the lords of Clare in Baldeswelle was very indirect. She argues in support of Professor Manly's application of the description to the Pembroke estate. She suggests that Chaucer may have known Baldeswelle through Sir Richard Burley, who married, in or about 1385, Beatrice, the widow of Thomas Lord Roos and the holder of the manor of Whitewell. The Burleys were large landowners in Kent and Chaucer is known to have sat on the bench with Sir Simon Burley, Richard's brother.

A further bit of possible evidence that Chaucer had connections with Baldeswelle is furnished by the fact that one of his mainpernors in the great customs of 1382 was Richard Baldewell, perhaps from that locality. See TLS, 1928, p. 684. For further discussion of the character with special reference to Chaucer's treatment of old age see G. R. Coffman, Spec., IX, 273 ff. and B. Forehand, PMLA, LXIX, 984 ff.

589 His close-cropped hair was a sign of his servile station.

594 The bailiff was required to make a careful accounting to his auditors.

605 *the deeth,* probably "death," in general, rather than "the death, the pestilence." The definite article was occasionally used in Middle English in constructions similar to French, "la mort." Cf. *the feere, FranklT,* V, 893.

606 ff. A dwelling at the cost of the lord and a robe (cf. the *cote and hood* below) were apparently regular perquisites of the bailiff, in addition to his salary. Miss Redstone, in the communication cited above, notes that there is still a heath at Bawdswell shadowed by the trees of Bylaugh wood. It appears to have belonged in Pembroke's manor of Foxby.

611 He could please his lord by lending him some

of his (the lord's) own possessions, and thus obtain thanks and a reward besides.

613–14 Professor Tupper (Types, pp. 54 f.) suggests that Chaucer introduced the couplet on the Reeve's trade to provide a motive for his later quarrel with the Miller.

616 *Scot,* still a common name of horses in Norfolk, according to Bell's note. Professor Manly refers to its occurrence in John de Berington's inventory (1389).

618 Perhaps rusty because long out of use, as suggested by Mr. Forehand, p. 985.

621 *Tukked,* having his long coat hitched up and held by a girdle.

622 Whether the Reeve rode last out of cowardice or out of instinctive craftiness, he at any rate chose the place farthest away from the Miller, with whom he had an altercation early in the journey. The quarrel between the two may even have been conceived as having begun before they met on the pilgrimage. On the traditional enmity of millers and reeves see Tupper, Types, pp. 52 ff.

The Summoner

The Summoner (or Apparitor) was an officer who cited delinquents to appear before the ecclesiastical court. The abuses practiced by such officials are further illustrated in the *FrT,* III, 1299 ff. The Archdeacon is also represented here as not above bribes.

For an examination of ecclesiastical records and other documents for evidence with regard to the office and character of the Summoner, see L. A. Haselmayer, Spec., XII, 43 ff., who concludes that Chaucer's description is more unfavorable than historical testimony seems to warrant. But he shows that Chaucer was following literary tradition, and suggests further that the bitterness of the description may be due to the fact that the application was personal, as seems probable in the case of other pilgrims.

For an account of the Summoner's disease see Curry, pp. 37 ff. It was technically known as "alopicia," a form of leprosy. The causes mentioned by Chaucer, and the remedies, correspond closely to those named in the medical treatises. Professor Curry cites Lanfranc, Science of Cirurgie (EETS, 1894, pp. 193 ff.) and Guy de Chauliac, La Grande Chirurgie; ed. Nicaise, Paris, 1890, p. 413. See also Miss P. Aiken (Stud. Phil., XXXIII, 40 ff.) who argues for special indebtedness to the Speculum Majus of Vincent of Beauvais.

624 The cherubim were usually depicted with faces as red as fire. The form *cherubyn* or *cherubim,* though properly corresponding to the Hebrew plural, has been occasionally used as singular both in early and in modern English.

626 The sparrow, called *Venus sone* in *PF,* 351, was traditionally associated with lecherousness; cf. Pliny, Hist. Nat., x, 36; Juvenal, Sat., ix, 54 ff.

627 *piled,* scanty, with hair falling out. Cf. *RvT,* I, 3935, n. Manly cites Lanfranc's Cirurgie to show that this was regarded as a symptom of "allopix."

637–38 Cf. the proverbial couplet:
Post sumptum vinum loquitur mea lingua Latinum.
Et bibo cum bis ter, sum qualibet arte magister.
For other references to the idea see Manly's note and

H. B. Hinckley, MP, XIV, 317. Perhaps its origin is to be found in the Biblical account of the gift of tongues (Acts ii, 1 ff.).

642 Jays were taught to cry *Watte* (Walter) as parrots now call "Poll." Cf. Gower's Vox Clamantis, Liber I, cap. ix, Macaulay, Works of Gower, IV, pp. 40–41.

644–45 If anyone should question him, test him further, then his philosophy was all spent. Cf. *SumT*, III, 1816 f.

646 "The question is, what portion of the law (applies)." On this phrase, apparently a tag repeated in the courts, see J. W. Spargo, MLN, LXII, pp. 119 ff.

650 *good felawe*, here used in the colloquial sense of "rascal." The reference is probably to priests who lived with concubines.

652 This line, commonly misinterpreted, refers to the Summoner's own indulgences in the same sin for which he is said just before to have excused others. See Kittredge, MP, VII, 475 ff. and H. B. Woolf, MLN, LXVIII, 118 ff.

656 f. A recurring fling at the venality of the ecclesiastical courts. Cf., for example, Gower, Mirour de l'Omme, 20198 f., and Vox Clamantis, iii, 3, 189 ff.

661 *assoillyng*, either canonical absolution, i.e. the removal of the sentence of excommunication, or the ordinary sacramental absolution. Whichever is meant, the passage implies an unmistakable doubt of its efficacy — a hint which perhaps comes as near to downright heresy as anything in Chaucer. In fact, Lounsbury (Studies, II, 517 ff.) took the remark as evidence that Chaucer was a kind of agnostic — an extreme and unwarranted inference. Professor Tatlock, MP, XIV, 266, argues, more reasonably, that the Summoner's scoff at excommunication perhaps reflects the influence of Wyclif's teachings concerning the "power of the keys." But the doubt is so guardedly expressed that it would hardly amount to heresy, and it need imply no more than a condemnation of the abuses of an avaricious clergy. Cf. the note on l. 486 above.

662 "Significavit nobis venerabilis pater" were the opening words of a writ remanding to prison an excommunicated person. Mr. H. B. Workman (John Wyclif, II, 26) notes that some ten thousand of these writs are preserved in the Public Record Office. A few deal with heresy, but most of them with tithes and other money matters.

663 *daunger*, "control." He had the young men and women at his mercy. *Girles* might apply to both sexes. For the opinion that the reference here is only to young women see M. W. Bloomfield, PQ, XXVIII, 503 ff.

The Pardoner

Pardoners (or quaestors) were sellers of papal indulgences. Many were forbidden to preach, and some were even laymen. Many who travelled as pardoners were wholly unauthorized, and the tricks and abuses they practiced were condemned by ecclesiastical authority. The *noble ecclesiaste* of the *Prologue* seems to have been at least in minor orders. But his conduct as a pardoner, by his own showing, was fraudulent, and his pardons are very likely to be regarded as spurious. On the class as a whole see

J. J. Jusserand, Chaucer's Pardoner and the Pope's Pardoners, in Chaucer Society Essays, Part v, no. 13; and Manly, New Light, pp. 122 ff. Other references are given on p. 729 below.

The personal description of the Pardoner in the *Prologue* is supplemented by the remarkable confession with which he introduces his *Tale* (VI, 329 ff.). For general discussion of his character and behavior see Kittredge, Atlantic Monthly, LXXII, 829 ff., Chaucer and his Poetry, pp. 211 ff.; and Curry, pp. 54 ff. (earlier in JEGP, XVIII, 593 ff.). Professor Kittredge's essay will receive further notice in the notes on the *Pardoner's Tale*. Professor Curry shows that the physical and moral type of the Pardoner was well recognized in the mediæval treatises on physiognomy. As a parallel he cites especially the account of Favorinus of Arles by Polemon Laodicensis. For some objections to Curry's theory see G. G. Sedgwick, MLQ, I, 431 ff.

The character of Fals-Semblant in RR doubtless furnished Chaucer with suggestions for the Pardoner's confession. See D. S. Fansler, Chaucer and the Roman de la Rose, New York, 1914, p. 162.

670 *Rouncivale*, the hospital of the Blessed Mary of Rouncivalle, near Charing Cross. This was a cell of the convent of Nuestra Señora de Roncesvalles in Navarre, and was founded by William Marshall, Earl of Pembroke, at Charing in 1229. John of Gaunt was one of its patrons. A number of incidents in the history of the house are noted by Professor Manly, New Light, pp. 122 ff., with references to Sir James Galloway, The Story of St. Mary Roncevall, and Canon Westlake, History of Parish Gilds. See also S. Moore, in MP, XXV, 59 ff. and Miss M. P. Hamilton, JEGP, XL, 48 ff.

Pardoners of Rouncivale were commonly satirized. There is evidence that in 1382, and again in 1387, unauthorized sales of pardons were made by persons professing to collect for the hospital. It is possible that Chaucer had in mind some definite Pardoner whose portrait he expected his readers to recognize.

Professor Tatlock (Flügel Memorial volume, Palo Alto, Calif., 1916, p. 232, n. 15) has suggested, hesitatingly, that a pun is intended on "rouncival," a mannish woman, or "rouncy," a riding-horse. Even if this were involved, which is unlikely, the primary reference would still be to the hospital of that name.

671 This, at least, would have been the Pardoner's claim.

672 The first line or the refrain of some popular song. Professor Gollancz has compared the Pearl, ll. 763–64 (stanza 64): "Cum hyder to me, my lemman swete, For mote ne spot is non in the," for which he suggests the Song of Solomon iv, 7–8, as a source. (See his second edition of the Pearl, p. 154.) But Chaucer's line is dissimilar in rhyme and movement, and such invitations are very common in love poetry.

On the rime *Rome: to me* see the note to l. 523 above.

673 *burdoun*, ground melody. See E. P. M. Dieckmann, MP, XXVI, 279 ff.

685 *vernycle* (diminutive of "veronica"), a small copy of the handkerchief of St. Veronica, which she is said to have lent Christ as he was bearing his cross to Calvary. According to the tradition, it received the imprint of his face.

692 *fro Berwyk into Ware*, apparently, from the north of England to the South. The choice of Ware (in Hertfordshire) as the southern limit is strange. It was perhaps mentioned as the first town of importance north of London. Possibly Wareham, in the south of Dorsetshire is intended. Or *Berwyk* might conceivably stand for Barwick in Somerset, which is on the other side of London in relation to Ware. But many passages in mediæval poetry suggest that in such phrases place-names were chosen mainly for the convenience of the rime. Cf. Le Vair Palefroi, ed. Långfors, Paris, 1912, ll. 658, 660, 1020. For further discussion see F. P. Magoun, Jr., Med. Stud., XVI, 134, 150.

696 Cf. Matt. xiv, 29.

706 "He made fools of the parson and the people"; cf. *MillT*, I, 3389; *Intr. to PrT*, VII, 440; *CYT*, VIII, 1313; Haeckel, p. 40, no. 136.

708 Perhaps with special reference to his preaching. See F. Mossé, Revue Germanique, XIV, 285. Note also his comments on the order of the service. He argues that the sermon never followed the offertory, and makes *that song* refer to earlier songs in the service. For an opinion on this matter the editor has turned to the distinguished liturgiologist, the Rev. Dr. Gerald Ellard, S.J., who has kindly pointed out that in Chaucer's time it was customary for the priest, after the offertory, to read the so-called Bidding Prayer in the vernacular to the people. He concludes that "it is quite clear that the Pardoner preached in connection with the Bidding Prayer after the offertory was sung. Dr. Ellard gives references to T. E. Bridgett, History of the Holy Eucharist in Great Britain, ed. H. Thurston, 1908, p. 194; T. F. Simmons, The Lay Folks Mass Book, EETS, London, 1879, p. 63.

709 f. The *lessoun* was the prescribed portion of the Scripture, the "lectio" of the Canonical Office. *Storie*, probably the liturgical "historia," a series of lessons covering parts of the Bible or the life of a saint. *Offertorie*, the "offertorium" of the Mass, said or sung after the Creed.

710 *alderbest*, best of all. See l. 586, n.

714 *murierly*. This formation, in which the adverbial -*ly* is added to the comparative ending, is very unusual. For a few parallels see Maetzner's English Grammar, tr. C. J. Grece, I, London, 1874, p. 398. It is more likely to be due to Chaucer than to a scribe. For variant readings see the Textual Notes.

719 *the Belle*. A Southwark inn of uncertain identification. References to nine taverns of the name (not necessarily all different inns) are given by Rendle and Norman (The Inns of Old Southwark, London, 1888, Index, p. 420). They take Chaucer's Bell to have been situated on Borough High Street, on the opposite side from the Tabard. The existence of such a tavern seems to be inferred from the Bell Yard, which appears on an eighteenth-century map. But there is no evidence of its presence before 1600. Professor Baum, who has listed and discussed the various Bells in MLN, XXXVI, 307 ff., suggests that Chaucer had in mind one of the "allowed stewhouses" mentioned by Stow, Survey of London (ed. Kingsford, Oxford, 1908, II, 54 f.), whose licenses dated back to Edward III's reign.

725 ff. The excuse here is similar to those offered by Jean de Meun, RR, 15159 ff., and by Boccaccio in the "Conclusione dell'Autore" of the Decameron. For a second apology, which relates to subject matter and not merely to language, see *Mill Prol*, I, 3167 ff. See also RR, 7108 ff.

742 The reference is to the Timaeus 29 B; Chaucer's knowledge of the passage may have come from Boethius, iii, pr. 12, or from RR, 7099 ff., 15190 ff. Cf. *MancT*, IX, 208; Haeckel, p. 15, no. 47.

The Host

Of all the Canterbury pilgrims the Host is the one who has been identified with most assurance. In the *Cook's Prologue* (I, 4358) he is addressed as *Herry Bailly*, and there is clear evidence of the existence of an innkeeper of that name in Southwark in 1380–81. In the Subsidy Rolls for Southwark for that year stands the entry: "Henri Bayliff ostyler Christian uxor eius — ijs." It further appears from the rolls that Bailif was himself one of the four controllers of the subsidy for Southwark. Several other records referring to Henry Bailly, very probably the same person, have been discovered. They show that he represented Southwark in Parliament in 1376–77 and 1378–79; that he witnessed a deed of gift at Lesnes, near Greenwich, in 1387; and that he served repeatedly as tax collector, assessor, or coroner between 1377 and 1394. In a Custom House memorandum of 1384 he is recorded as carrying money from the Custom House to the Treasurer of the Household. In an Issue Roll of the same period he is entered as carrying money from the Exchequer to the Keeper of the Wardrobe. In a roll of the Clerk of the Market for 1375–76 he is fined for violating the assize of ale and bread. For exact references see Manly, New Light, pp. 77 ff., and TLS, 1928, p. 707. For arguments against the identification see K. Malone, Eng. Stud., XXXI, 209 ff.

754 The *Chepe*, Cheapside, one of the principal London streets.

771 *By the weye*. Perhaps specific for the Canterbury Road. See *Manc Prol*, IX, 3, n., and Professor Magoun's comments in Med. Stud., XVI, 137.

785 *to make it wys*, to make it a matter of wisdom, to hold off and deliberate. For similar idioms cf. *make it... tough*, *Tr*, ii, 1025 and n.; *queynt*, *Rom*, 2038; *towgh ne queynte*, *BD*, 531; *straunge*, *RvT*, I, 3980; *FranklT*, V, 1223; *symple*, *Rom*, 3863. They perhaps had their origin in the imitation of Fr. constructions with "faire."

791 "With which to shorten our journey" ("to shorten our journey with"). The order, with the preposition immediately after the verb instead of at the end of the phrase, is regular in Mid. Eng. Cf. *Mill Prol*, I, 3119; *Pard Prol*, VI, 345; *ShipT*, VII, 273; *CYT*, VIII, 1055.

792 This program, which calls for four tales from each pilgrim, was never carried out. Chaucer did not actually get round the circle once. Evidence that he modified his original plan is furnished by the *Pars Prol* (X, 16 ff.), and the *Retractation* (X, 1081 ff.).

810–11 *we* must be supplied as the subject of *preyden*, and possibly of *swore* in l. 810, though that is more probably a past participle. See the note to l. 33, above.

817 *In heigh and lough*, in all respects. The phrase translates the Latin legal formula "in alto et basso." See PMLA, XLVI, 98 f. On other similar expressions, cf. l. 534, and n.

819 For the custom of drinking a cup of wine before retiring cf. *Tr*, iii, 671 ff.

826 *the wateryng of Seint Thomas*, according to Nares' Glossary (s.v. Watering) a brook at the second milestone on the Kent road.

829 "I recall it to you": or (if *I* is omitted, as in some of the best MSS.) "you recall it" (with reflex. pron.).

830 The expression is apparently proverbial and means "if you feel in the morning as you did the night before."

835 ff. The imperatives in *-eth* (*draweth, cometh, studieth*) were the full plural forms, used in courteous address. Contrast the more peremptory *ley hond to*, *every man* in l. 841, and see *NP Prol*, VII, 2810, n. For examples of cases departing from the strict pattern see H. Koziol, ESt, LXXV, 170 ff.

844 No very definite distinction was probably meant in the use of *aventure, sort*, and *cas*. For similar balancing of alternatives see *ClT*, IV, 812; *MerchT*, IV, 1967; *Tr*, i, 568. Chaucer's use of such formulas has been attributed to the influence of Dante. Cf. Inf. xv, 46; xxi, 82; xxxii, 76.

854 *a Goddes name*, in God's name.

The Knight's Tale

The Knight's Tale is a free adaptation of the Teseida of Boccaccio. In early editions of Boccaccio's poem, and in early essays and studies concerning it, the title regularly used was La Teseide. But recent editions, on the authority of Boccaccio's own manuscript, have adopted the form Il Teseida, which seems clearly to have been used by the poet. In the revision of the present work it is the editor's intention to cite the poem as Il (or the) Teseida, except in references to earlier publications.

A reference in the *Prologue of the Legend of Good Women* (G, 408) to *the love of Palamon and Arcite* shows that Chaucer had made a version of Boccaccio's poem, in some form, before the Canterbury period. But the exact relation of this to the existing tale is unknown. The opinion, supported by Ten Brink, Koch, and Skeat, that the *Palamon* was in seven-line stanzas has been questioned by several recent critics and was opposed in a detailed argument by Professor Tatlock, Dev. and Chron., pp. 45 ff. (Cf. also Langhans, Angl. XLIV, 226 ff., and for further references see Miss Hammond, pp. 271–72; Wells, pp. 692, 877; for Koch's reassertion of the theory see Angl. Beibl., XX, 133 ff.) The stanzaic hypothesis is, to say the least, unnecessary, and there is no strong reason for holding that the *Knight's Tale* is essentially different in form or substance from Chaucer's first version. Some revision was doubtless necessary to fit the *Palamon* for its place in the Canterbury collection. But in one passage at least (*But of that storie list me nat to write*, l. 1201) even this slight adaptation seems to have been neglected.

The stanzaic *Palamon*, by those who have believed in it, has usually been dated early in Chaucer's Italian period (between 1372 and 1376). But if the first redaction of the poem was practically identical with the *Knight's Tale*, a later date is more probable, and there are reasons for putting the completed text not earlier than 1382. In l. 884 there is perhaps a complimentary allusion to the landing in England of Anne of Bohemia, and several passages in the account of the marriage of Palamon and Emelye have been plausibly interpreted as referring to the marriage of Richard and Anne and the Bohemian alliance. It is even possible that the poem was written, or adapted, to celebrate the royal wedding. In that case it probably preceded the *Troilus*, which there are reasons for dating about 1386. It is natural to suppose that Chaucer had in hand the two great Italian poems at about the same time. But no decisive evidence has yet been found in the works themselves to show which was the earlier. (On the date of the *Troilus* see the introduction to the Explanatory Notes to that poem. On the references to Anne and the Bohemian alliance see Lowes, MLN, XIX, 240 ff.; O. F. Emerson, Studies in Lang. and Lit. in Celebration of the Seventieth Birthday of James Morgan Hart, N.Y., 1910, pp. 203 ff.)

On the assumption that the indications of date in ll. 1462 ff. would correspond to the actual calendar of the year of composition, Skeat showed that the tale (that is, the revised *Knight's Tale*) might be assigned to 1387. In that year May 5 fell on Sunday. (See Oxf. Chau., V, 70, 75–76.) Professor Mather, applying the same argument to the original *Palamon*, preferred the year 1381. (Furnivall Miscellany, pp. 308–10.) Professor Manly, taking the date of the duel to have been Saturday, May 4, would put the assembly on Sunday, May 4, of the following year. This would point to 1382, a reasonable date for the poem. But in none of these cases is the inference secure. See the note to l. 1462, below, and for further discussion cf. Tatlock, Dev. and Chron., pp. 70 ff. For arguments in favor of a later date for the *KnT*, also for a more extensive revision of an earlier *Palamon* than has been usually assumed, see Johnstone Parr, PMLA, LX, 307 ff. Mr. Parr's paper is discussed and his conclusions are rejected (with good reason, in the opinion of the present editor) by R. A. Pratt, PMLA, LXIII, 726 ff.; see also W. E. Weese, MLN, LXIII, 331 ff. Mr. Parr has a brief rejoinder following Mr. Pratt's article.

For a theory which would imply for part of the story a date as late as 1393, see the note on the portrait of Emetreus, l. 2155.

Chaucer's main source was the Teseida of Boccaccio (Opere Volgari, ed. Moutier, IX, Florence, 1831), critical editions by S. Battaglia, Florence, 1938, and Roncaglia, Bari, 1941. For a detailed summary of the poem see SA, pp. 93 ff. Professor Pratt (Stud. Phil., XLII, 745 ff.) discusses the question of the classification of the particular MS. of the Teseida which Chaucer used. The sources of the Teseida have never been fully determined. According to an early theory, now generally abandoned, Boccaccio followed a lost Greek romance. In the opinion of recent authorities he made an independent compilation from various sources. He certainly used Statius freely, and perhaps also some version of the Roman de Thèbes. But neither of these works supplied him with his central plot of the rival lovers. See G. Koerting, Boccaccio's Leben und Werke, in Geschichte der Litteratur Italiens im Zeitalter der Renaissance, II, Leipzig, 1880, pp. 620 ff. (supporting the theory of the Greek romance); V. Crescini, Contributo agli Studi sul Boccaccio, Turin, 1887, pp. 220 ff., and Atti del Reale Istituto Veneto, LX, 449 ff.; J. Schmitt, La Théséide de Boccace et la

Théséide Grecque, in Études de Philologie Néo-Grecque, ed. J. Psichari, Bibl. de l'École des Hautes Études, 1892, pp. 279 ff.; P. Savj-Lopez, Giornale Storico della Lit. Ital., XXXVI, 57 ff.

The Teseida is a long poem in twelve books. For the nearly ten thousand lines of the Italian Chaucer has but 2250 lines, of which only about 700 correspond, even loosely, to Boccaccio's. The relation of the two was indicated by H. L. Ward by marginal marks in the Six-Text edition, also used in Pollard's edition of the *Canterbury Tales*. The main correspondences are shown by the following table, based upon one drawn up by Skeat. Arabic numerals in the case of the Teseida refer to stanzas.

Knight's Tale	Teseida
865–883	i, ii
893–1027	ii, 2–5, 25–95
1030–1274	iii, 1–11, 14–20, 47, 51–54, 75
1361–1448	iv, 26–29, 59
1451–1479	v, 1–3, 24–27, 33
1545–1565	iv, 13, 14, 31, 85, 84, 17, 82
1638–1641	vii, 106, 119
1668–1739	v, 77–91
1812–1860	v, 92–98
1887–2022	vii, 108–110, 50–64, 29–37
2102–2206	vi, 71, 14–22, 65–70, 8
2222–2593	vii, 43–49, 68–93, 23–41, 67, 95–99, 7–13, 131, 132, 14, 100–102, 113–118, 19
2275–2360	vii, 71–92
2600–2683	viii, 2–131
2684–2734	ix, 4–61
2735–2739	xii, 80, 83
2743–2808	x, 12–112
2809–2962	xi, 1–67
2967–3102	xii, 3–19, 69–83

For general comparisons of the two narratives see F. J. Mather's edition of the *Gen Prol, KnT*, and *NPT*, Boston, 1899, pp. lxii ff., and H. M. Cummings, The Indebtedness of Chaucer's Works to the Italian Works of Boccaccio, Univ. of Cincinnati Studies, X, Pt. 2, 1916, pp. 123 ff. On Chaucer's MS. of the Teseida see R. A. Pratt, SP, XLII, 745 ff. Of Chaucer's additions and modifications the more significant will be pointed out in the notes. Attention will also be called to his literary sources outside of the Teseida. He apparently had direct recourse to Statius, and perhaps to the Roman de Thèbes (here cited by references to the edition of Constans, SATF, 1890). See Wise, The Influence of Statius Upon Chaucer, Baltimore, 1911, pp. 46 ff., 78 ff., 129 ff. Chaucer also made important use of the Consolation of Boethius. On parallels between the *KnT* and a Middle English version of Partonope of Blois see R. M. Smith, MLN, LI, 320, and J. Parr, MLN, LX, 486 ff.

On Chaucer's adaptation of the story to contemporary customs, see Dr. Stuart Robertson, JEGP, XIV, 226 ff.; and on his striking use of astrology, see Curry, ch. vi. Mr. H. N. Fairchild, in JEGP, XXVI, 285 ff., has suggested the interpretation of Arcite and Palamon as types, respectively, of the active and the contemplative life. But the allegory is somewhat forced. Professor J. R. Hulbert (Stud. Phil., XXVI, 375 ff.) argues that the real

purpose of the tale was to set forth a typical "question of love" as to "which of two young men, of equal worth and with almost equal claims, shall (or should) win the lady." This problem is doubtless involved in the story, and would have been more apparent in the Middle Ages than it is today. But the *Knight's Tale* would never have engaged, as it does, the sympathy of the reader if it had been written primarily as a discussion of such an academic problem. And the Teseida, we are assured, grew out of Boccaccio's own emotional experience.

For general observations on the tales see Charles Muscatine, PMLA, LXV, 911 ff., W. H. French, JEGP, XLVIII, 320 ff., William Frost, RES, XXV, 295 ff., A. H. Marckwardt, U. of Michigan Contributions in Modern Philology No. 5 (April, 1947), C. A. Owen, Jr., Eng. Stud., XXXV, 49 ff., R. M. Lumiansky, Tulane Stud. in Eng., III, 47 ff., and Dorothy Everett, Essays on Middle English Literature (Oxford, 1955), pp. 164 ff. (reprinted from the Proc. of the Brit. Academy, 1950). On the underlying institution of courtly love references are given in the introductory note on the *Troilus*, p. 812 below.

Explanatory notes of value, besides those of Skeat, are to be found in the editions of Pollard, Mather, Liddell, and Manly, and in Mr. Hinckley's Notes on Chaucer, to all of which the following brief commentary is indebted.

The Motto, "Iamque domos" is from Statius, Theb., xii, 519 f. The whole introduction, ll. 859–1004, draws upon the Thebaid as well as the Teseida. From the former comes apparently the mention of the night march of Theseus (l. 970), of the Minotaur (l. 980), and, perhaps, of Fortune (l. 915).

860 Theseus was, properly speaking, King of Athens, though here called "duke," by a characteristic anachronism. On the existence of the title "Duke of Athens" in Chaucer's time see Liebermann, Herrig's Arch., CXLV, 101 f. See also Patch, ESt, LXV, 354, n.

877 *Femenye*, the land of the Amazons. On the geographical localization in Chaucer and Old French see F. P. Magoun, Jr., Med. Stud., XV, 128.

884 In this rapid summary of Boccaccio's first book and part of his second, Chaucer has found room for one additional incident. There is no mention in the Teseida of a tempest at the home-coming of Theseus and Hippolyta. Professor Curry (MLN, XXXVI, 272 f.) has suggested that Chaucer's line refers only to the popular excitement on the arrival of the royal bride. His interpretation is supported by W. J. Wager (MLN, L, 296), and J. Parr (PMLA, LX, 315). But this is an unnatural interpretation of *tempest*. It is far more likely, as Professor Lowes has argued (MLN, XIX, 240 ff.), that Chaucer introduced this line as a complimentary allusion to the arrival of Queen Anne in England. On that occasion, according to Walsingham's Historia Anglicana (ed. Riley, London, 1863–64), II, 46, there was a great commotion of the sea which destroyed the vessel in which she had come.

It should be added that the rhetorical figure here employed — the refusal to describe or narrate, technically known as "occupatio" — is very common with Chaucer. In the present tale it usually indicates that he is actually omitting materials in his source, as is the case in what is one of the most protracted examples anywhere to be found, namely, the account of Arcite's funeral in ll. 2919 ff. Elsewhere the figure is sometimes merely a rhetorical device for speeding up the narrative. Examples of its occurrence are numerous, and only a few need be cited. Cf. *KnT*, I, 2197 ff., *MLT*, II, 701 ff., *SqT*, V, 34 ff., 63 ff., 283 ff.

890   *aboute*, in turn.

894   According to both Boccaccio and Statius the temple of Clemence was in the city.

908   Probably "that (ye)," with omission of pronominal subject, rather than "who."

925–26   The general idea and the figure of the wheel are both common. Cf. *Bo*, ii, pr. 2, and see H. R. Patch, The Goddess Fortuna in Mediæval Literature, Cambridge, 1927, Index, s.v. "wheel."

932   Capaneus, one of the "Seven against Thebes." He was killed by Zeus with a thunderbolt. See *Tr*, v, 1501 ff., and n.

938   The adjective *old* is applied to Creon as a kind of fixed epithet in the Rom. de Thèbes: "Creon li vieuz," ll. 5190, 5799, 8341, 10008, etc.

949 ff.   Here again a few details may come from the Rom. de Thèbes; for example, the riding of Theseus on a horse instead of in a chariot. Cf. with *KnT*, I, 949, Thèbes, 9944 ff.; with *KnT*, I, 950, Thèbes, 9994; with *KnT*, I, 952, Thèbes, 9946; with *KnT*, I, 957, Thèbes, 9997 ff.

977   *feeldes*, rather the lands over which they marched than the "grounds" of their banners (as understood by Skeat). Cf. Theb., xii, 656 ff.; Thèbes, 9914 ff.; and, for illustrative parallels, Hinckley, p. 58, and Kittredge, MLN, XXV, 28.

979   *ybete*, which might mean "hammered," seems here, as in *Tr*, ii, 1229, and *Rom*, 836 ff., to mean "embroidered." See Emerson, PQ, II, 85, and cf. the notes of Hinckley and Manly on this passage.

980   The Minotaur was the Cretan monster which Theseus had slain.

983 ff.   In Boccaccio's account of the victory of Theseus (Tes., ii, 53–73) the Theban forces flee to the woods and mountains and the Athenians enter the city unopposed. Chaucer, in representing Thebes as won by assault, substitutes a familiar feature of mediæval warfare. See S. Robertson, JEGP, XIV, 227 ff. Of numerous instances in Froissart, Dr. Robertson cites particularly the battle of Cadsant, Bk. i, ch. 31 (tr. Johnes, London, 1839, I, 44) and the capture of Limoges, Bk. i, ch. 290 (I, 453–54).

989   For the destruction of the city cf. Rom. de Thèbes, 10073 ff. (where it is said to have taken place before Creon's death).

1007   According to Boccaccio (ii, 84) Theseus sent out men to care for the dead and wounded, and to bring in the spoils for proper distribution. Chaucer refers only to pillagers (*pilours*).

1010   Almost identical with *Tr*, iv, 627.

1011   *by and by*, side by side.

1012   *in oon armes*, in one kind of arms; that is, bearing the same heraldic device.

1013   The names *Arcita* and *Palamon* are from Boccaccio. Where he found them is unknown. Palamon occurs in Statius and in the Rom. de Thèbes as the name of a Theban warrior. Mr. Hinckley suggests that Boccaccio had in mind the Greek philosopher Polemon and, for Arcite, the Archytas of Cicero's De Senectute. But this seems unlikely.

1024   The mention of ransom here, as also in ll. 1032, 1176, 1205, and 1849, is not paralleled in Boccaccio. Dr. Robertson (p. 229) notes it as another bit of mediæval realism introduced by Chaucer.

1033 ff.   Chaucer's account of the lovers' first sight of Emily differs considerably from Boccaccio's. The dialogue, which corresponds in part to the later debate in the Teseida, where Palamon and Arcite meet in the grove, is far more vivacious than in the Italian, and lays more stress upon the rivalry of the lovers. It is possible, as Professor Kittredge has suggested, that Chaucer's modification of the narrative was due to his memory of the rival lovers in the *Parliament of Fowls*, whose arguments are in part similar to those of Palamon and Arcite.

1035   Cf. *LGW*, 2425. *To sene*, the inflected infinitive; see the Introduction on Language and Meter.

1047   On May-day observances see, besides Skeat's note, Hazlitt, Faiths and Folklore, London, 1905, II, 397; Chambers, Book of Days, Edinburgh, 1863–64, I, 570 ff.; W. Hone, Every-day Book, London, 1826–27, I, 543 ff., II, 570 ff.; Table Book, London, 1827, I, 541, 557, 628 f.; Year Book, London, 1832, 521 ff.

1072   His words, in direct quotation, were "Alas, that I was born."

1084   "That art so pale and deathly to behold."

1088   On Saturn as a planet of evil influence cf. ll. 2453 ff. below, and *Astr*, ii, 4, 35 ff. *Constellacioun*, disposition or arrangement of heavenly bodies. Cf. *SqT*, V, 129; *FranklT*, V, 581.

1089   "Although we had sworn to the contrary." Cf. *ClT*, IV, 403; *SqT*, V, 325; *Tr*, iv, 976. In this idiom the negative idea is usually implied rather than expressed. But see ll. 1666 f. below.

1091   *this is*, monosyllabic, as often elsewhere; sometimes written simply *this* (as in l. 2761). *Playn*, either "plain" or "full"; in this formula, probably "plain," "clear."

1096   Cf. l. 1567; also *MercB*, 1 ff., and *Compl d'Am*, 41 ff. The idea that a lover is wounded or slain by his lady's eyes is so familiar that illustrations need not be multiplied. They could be collected in endless number from both European and Oriental literature. Boccaccio uses the figure in the Filocolo (Opere Volgari, VII, 6) and the Fiametta (Opere, VI, 10). For examples in Old French see J. L. Lowes, MLR, V, 34 ff., and for further discussion, Miss M. V. Young, MLN, XXII, 232, and H. R. Patch, ESt, LXV, 352. The ancient Greeks had the same conception. Cf. Sophocles, Antigone, 795, with Jebb's references, including Plato's Phædrus, 251 B (κάλλους ἀπορροή). Cf. also the Greek romance of Achilles Tatius, with M. B. Ogle's comments in American Journal of Philology, XXXIV, 136 ff. The idea, indeed, was not merely a conceit of the poets, but may fairly be called an old scientific hypothesis. According to the regular explanation, an effluence, sometimes figured as a spear or arrow, passed from the lady's eyes through those of the lover into his heart. A similar theory has been held about the "ejaculation" from the evil eye. See Bacon's essay Of Envy.

Arabic literature offers many parallels to this, as to most devices of mediæval erotic poetry. For examples, with comparison of the effluence to a sword-

blade or an arrow, see Beha-ed-Din Zoheir, ed.
E. H. Palmer (Cambridge, 1876–7), I, pp. 37, 42,
44, 53; English translation, ibid., II, pp. 43, 49, 50,
61. Further illustration of the conception is supplied
by A. R. Nykl, Hispano-Arabic Poetry (Baltimore,
1946), pp. 48, 207, 247, 249.

1101 With the expression of uncertainty whether
Emily is a woman or a goddess cf. *Tr*, i, 425 (Fil., i,
38) and Aen., i, 327.

Wher, whether; a common contraction.

1108 *shapen*, shaped, determined; frequently
used in early English with reference to destiny.

1122 "I am not but (no better than) dead."
Cf. the Northern English "nobbut."

1127 "So help me God, I have little desire to jest."

1132 Palamon and Arcite were not only cousins,
but also "sworn brothers." The institution here
referred to has been of almost world-wide diffusion.
See Hamilton-Grierson's article on Brotherhood
(Artificial) in Hastings's Encyclopædia of Religion
and Ethics; and, for special consideration of the
early Teutons and Celts, J. C. Hodges, MP, XIX,
384 ff., and Rev. Celt., XLIV, 109 ff. (with many
references). Ancient examples of sworn brothers are
Theseus and Pirithous (see ll. 1191 ff. below),
Achilles and Patroclus, Orestes and Pylades, Nysus
and Euryalus. Among savage or semi-civilized
peoples the union is accompanied by various formali-
ties, often the drinking or mingling of blood. In
the English romances and ballads, where frequent
reference is made to the custom, the usual ceremony
is simply an oath. For instances in Chaucer see
ShipT, VII, 40–42; *PardT*, VI, 697 f., and *FrT*,
III, 1405 ff. Good examples are also furnished by the
romances of Athelston and Amis and Amiloun.

1133 *for to dyen in the peyne*, though we had to
die by torture. The use of *for* with an infinitive in a
concessive sense was common in Middle English.
Cf. *ClT*, IV, 364; *Tr*, i, 674. The construction was
perhaps modeled upon French; cf. "pur murir,"
Chanson de Roland (ed. T. Müller, Göttingen, 1878),
l. 1048. On the torture known as the "peine forte
et dure" see Hinckley, pp. 64 f.

1155 *Paramour*, lit. "by love, in the way of
love." The phrase was regularly applied to romantic or passionate love. Cf. l. 2112, below. Arcite
bases his claim to priority on the distinction between
human passion and religious adoration (*affeccioun
of hoolynesse*).

1162 *I pose*, I suppose, grant for the sake of
argument.

1164 From Boethius, iii, m. 12, (*Bo*, iii, m. 12,
52 f.). Cf. also *Tr*, iv, 618, and *Rom*, 3432 ff.

1167 *positif lawe*, a technical term. "Lex posi-
tiva," as opposed to natural law, is that which rests
solely upon man's decree. Gower, Mirour de
l'Omme, 18469 ff., applies the term to the ecclesiastical restriction on marriage which Chaucer perhaps had in mind. In that case *in ech degree* may
refer to degrees of kinship; otherwise it means
simply "in every rank." (See MLR, IV, 17.)

1177 The fable is practically the same as that
of Æsop on The Lion and the Bear (no. 247 in
Halm's edition, Leipzig, 1854; Croxall's translation,
London, 1792, p. 238, no. 141). Cf. also La Fontaine,
"Les Voleurs et l'Ane." (Book i, Fable 13; ed.
Robert, Paris, 1825, I, 66.) The source of Chaucer's
version is unknown.

1182 Proverbial. Cf. "A la cort le roi chascun9
i est por soi," Morawski, Proverbes Français, Paris,
1925, p. 2, no. 45. See also Skeat, EE Prov., pp. 89 f.,
no. 213.

1194 On the visit of Pirithous to Athens see also
Tes., iii, 47–51.

1196 Cf. *LGW*, 2282.

1198 Chaucer's reference is probably to RR,
8148 ff. The account there corresponds to his statement. Strictly speaking, Theseus accompanied
Pirithous on his search for Proserpina. See Plutarch's Theseus, c. xxxi.

1201 Probably an unaltered line of the original
Palamon, inappropriate to the Knight as teller of
the story.

1210 *hym Arcite*. Though *Arcite* is grammatically in apposition with *hym*, the modern punctuation with commas misrepresents the Mid. Eng.
idiom, in which the personal pronoun has the effect
of a demonstrative (Lat. "ille," "iste"). For other
examples see *MLT*, II, 940; *MerchT*, IV, 1734:
MkT, VII, 2673. Mr. H. B. Hinckley (MP, XVI,
43) compares similar constructions in the Scandinavian languages and Middle Welsh. For further
discussion see H. R. Patch, ESt, LXV, 355.

1212 *oo stounde*, a single hour, has the support
of only one of the published MSS. But the alternative reading, *or stounde*, somewhat desperately
rendered "or at any hour," seems hardly possible.

1218 *to wedde*, for a pledge; hence, in jeopardy.

1223 Cf. *LGW*, 658.

1238 The figure from dice was commonly applied
to the vicissitudes of Fortune. Cf. *MkT*, VII, 2661,
and *Tr*, ii, 1347, and see Patch, The Goddess
Fortuna, p. 81.

1242 Proverbial; see Haeckel, p. 5, no. 16.

1247 On the four elements see *Gen Prol*, I, 420, n.

1251 ff. In these reflections on the vanity of
human wishes Chaucer followed Boethius, iii, pr. 2;
cf. also Dante, Inf., vii, 67 ff.

1260 Cf. Romans, viii, 26.

1261 *dronke is as a mous*, a common comparison
in older English. Cf. *WB Prol*, III, 246; Skeat,
EE Prov., p. 90, no. 214; Haeckel, p. 60.

1262 f. The illustration is from a gloss to the
passage in Boethius. See *Bo*, iii, pr. 2, 86 f. But
l. 1264 is apparently Chaucer's own.

1279 *pure*, very; cf. *BD*, 583. *Grete*, perhaps to
be taken with *fettres*. The fetters seem to be added
in Chaucer's account.

1303–12 Cf. Boethius, i, m. 5; Eccl. iii, 18 ff.
(quoted in Innocent, De Contemptu Mundi, i, 2,
Migne, Pat. Lat., CCXVII, 703).

1315–21 For the familiar idea that brutes are
happier than men Mr. Hinckley cites the Dialogus
inter Corpus et Animam, ll. 227–30 (Lat. Poems
attrib. to W. Mapes, ed. Wright, Camden Soc.,
1841, p. 103).

1317 *to letten of his wille*, to refrain from his
desire.

1329 The anger of Juno against Thebes was
caused by Jupiter's relations with Semele and
Alcmena. It is repeatedly referred to by Boccaccio
and Statius; see Tes., iii, 1; iv. 14; v, 56; ix, 44;
x, 39; and Theb., i, 12, 250; x, 74, 126, 162, 282.
Cf. also Ovid, Met., iii, 253 ff.; iv, 416; and (for
phraseology) Dante, Inf., xxx, 1 f., 22 f.

1331 Cf. Theb., xii, 704.

1344 *upon his heed*, on pain of losing his head (OF. "sur sa teste").

1347 This is a typical love-problem ("demande d'amour" or "questione d'amore"), such as were familiar in French, Provençal, and Italian. Other examples from the *Canterbury Tales* are found in *WBT*, III, 905, 1219 ff., and *FranklT*, V, 1621 ff., to which may be added the whole underlying conception of the so-called Marriage Group of Tales. For numerous parallels from European and Oriental literature see Rajna, Rom., XXXI, 28 ff., and cf. Manly, Morsbach Festschrift, Halle, 1913, pp. 282 ff. A series of similar questions, in most cases attached to an illustrative story, were propounded in Boccaccio's Filocolo (Opere Volgari, VIII, 27 ff.).

1369 On the various kinds of spirits recognized by the old physiology see the note to l. 2749 below.

1372-76 The name *Hereos*, for the "lover's malady," has a long and curious history, as Professor Lowes has shown (MP, XI, 491 ff.). Derived ultimately from ἔρως, the word became distorted in Latin into various forms, such as "ereos," "hereos," "heroys," and "hercos"; and from these were made the adjectival derivatives "hereosus," "herosus," "hereseus," "heresius," and "heroicus." Numerous examples of the use of the term from the Viaticum of Constantinus Africanus (11th century) down to Burton's Anatomy of Melancholy, are cited by Mr. Lowes. As a result of the change of form in Latin, *hereos* came to be sometimes associated with "herus" ("erus") and sometimes with "heros" (ἥρως), and was defined accordingly. But it usually refers to the mania or mad desire of a lover for the object of his affection. The disease was discussed by a long series of mediæval physicians, and into their treatment of it entered various conceptions derived from the Arabic "al-ishq." The symptoms described by Chaucer — sleeplessness, lack of appetite, loss of flesh and color, weeping and wailing, and aversion to music — can all be paralleled in the medical treatises. Indeed it is hard to determine how far the whole conception of love-sickness, so common in mediæval saga and romance, was of scientific origin, and how far it was due merely to the naïve observation of the extravagances of lovers. For Celtic doctrine on the subject see Winifred Wulf, Eriu, XI, 174 ff. The treatment of love in Arabic literature offers, as might be expected in view of the references already given to Arabic science, striking parallels to that in mediæval Europe. See S. Singer, Abhandlungen der Preussischen Akademie der Wissenschaften, 1918, No. 13, pp. 24-25. A good example is afforded by the poem of Omar ben Fâredh printed in Grangeret de Lagrange, Anthologie Arabe (Paris, 1828), pp. 39, 49. The representatives systematic treatise on the subject was Tauk-al-Hamâma of Ibn Hazm, edited by D. K. Pétrof (St. Pétersbourg, Leide, 1914) and translated by A. R. Nykl, The Dove's Neck-Ring (Paris, 1931). It is also summarized at length in Nykl's Hispano-Arabic Poetry, pp. 78 ff. The symptoms of love-sickness are discussed at length in the Tauk, ed. Pétrof, p. 12 (Nykl's trans. p. 15; see also p. 344).

1374 According to both Bernard Gordon and Arnaldus (quoted by Lowes, p. 526), unless *hereos* is cured, the sufferers fall into mania or die.

1376 This has reference to the old division of the brain into three cells, the front one commonly as-

signed to fantasy, the middle one to reason, and the back one to memory. Mania was described as an affection of the first. Cf. the Collectio Salernitana (ed. De Renzi, Naples, 1852-59, II, 124) cited by Lowes (p. 527, note 6): "Mania est infectio anterioris cellulae capitis cum privatione imaginationis. Melancholia est infectio mediae cellulae capitis cum privatione rationis." The reading of l. 1376 is doubtful. The best MSS., including Ellesmere, have *Biforn his (owene) celle fantastik.* MS. Ha⁴ reads *Byforne in his selle fantastyk.* The former is defended by Professor Manly on the ground that, according to Bernard, fantasy is seated in the hinder part of the first cell. But Chaucer — like Arnaldus, in a passage quoted by Lowes (p. 527) — apparently referred to the entire front cell as the *celle fantastik.* Mania was localized *in* this cell, and not *before* it. So the Ha⁴ reading, adopted by Skeat, corresponds more accurately to the authorities. Professor Lowes would omit the comma after *biforen*, apparently on the ground that the disease affected the front part of the cell. But this is not clear from the text he cites.

1385 ff. Skeat suggested as a source of this passage Claudian, De Raptu Proserpinae, i, 78, but the description of Mercury in Ovid's Met., i, 671-72, is also similar and is followed a littler later by an account of Argus. The *slepy yerde* ("somniferam virgam") was the caduceus of Mercury.

1390 *Argus*, Argus of the hundred eyes. For the story how Mercury put him to sleep before slaying him see Ovid, Met., i, 714 ff.

1401 Cf. *Tr*, iv, 864 f.

1409 In Tes. (iv, 22) the disguise is that of a poor valet ("in maniera di pover valetto").

1422 A biblical phrase; cf. Jos., ix, 21.

1426-43 In making Arcite first a *page of the chaumbre* of a lady and then a *squyer* of the duke's chamber, Chaucer adds details, possibly autobiographical, not found in Boccaccio. (See Lowes, MP, XV, 692, n.)

1428 In the Tes. the name assumed by Arcite is Penteo; Chaucer took *Philostrate* from Boccaccio's "Filostrato," the title of the poem which was the primary source of the *Troilus.* From its Greek derivation Filostrato ought properly to mean "army-lover," but Boccaccio connected the second element with the Latin "stratus," and understood it to mean, "vanquished by love," in which sense it is admirably appropriate to Arcite. Two other proper names in Boccaccio are based upon a similar misunderstanding of φίλος, as a noun meaning "love," — Filocolo, which, through confusion of χόλος and κόπος, he interprets as "fatica d'amore" (Opere Volgari, VII, 354), and Filostropo (in his fifteenth eclogue), which he explains as coming from "phylos, quod est amor, et tropos, quod est conversio." See Epist. xxiii, A Fra Martino Da Signa, Opere Latine Minori, ed. Massèra, Bari, 1928, p. 220.

1439 *neer*, usually comparative in Chaucer, is here positive, as in Modern English.

1444 *honestly and slyly*, suitably and prudently. Both words have changed their meaning in modern English.

1462 ff. The indications of date here given are entirely independent of Boccaccio, and it is not clear how Chaucer came to insert them. Palamon, according to the usual understanding of the passage, escaped from prison on the night of May 3, discovered Arcite on the 4th, and on the 5th fought the duel which Theseus interrupted. The assembly for the tournament, if held exactly a year later, was consequently also on May 5, and it is distinctly said (l. 2188) to have taken place on a Sunday. Now in 1387 May 5 actually fell on Sunday, and Skeat found in the fact an argument for dating the *Knight's Tale* in that year. But, as Mr. Mather argued, the dates also fitted in 1381, the year to which he assigned the original Palamon and Arcite. If, as Professor Manly holds, the *thridde nyght* (l. 1463) refers to the night preceding May 3, then the date of the duel would have been Saturday, May 4, and the assembly would have fallen on Sunday, May 4, of the following year. This would point to 1382. But it may be doubted whether there is any significance in these correspondences of calendar. For further references on the matter see Manly's note to l. 1850 and the introduction to the Explanatory Notes on the *KnT*.

The reason is not certain for the selection of May 3 as a starting point. The day of the month is not an essential part of the astrological scheme which follows (ll. 2217 ff.). Curiously enough the same date is given in *NPT* (VII, 3187 ff.) for the tragic seizure of Chanticleer, and in *Tr* (ii, 55 ff.) it is the day on which Pandarus suffers from a misfortune (*teene*) in love. Again in The Cuckoo and the Nightingale (l. 55, Oxf. Chau., VII, 349), where there may of course be a reminiscence of Chaucer, it is associated with a lover's ill success. Various reasons have been suggested for Chaucer's repeated mention of the date. Miss Hammond (English Verse between Chaucer and Surrey, Durham, N.C., 1927, p. 472) notes that May 1–3 were the regular days of the Maytime festival. But that would hardly account for the association of May 3 with tragic occurrences; nor (as Mr. Root observes) is it explained by the fact that in the ecclesiastical calendar May 3 is the feast of the Invention of the Holy Cross. Both Mr. Root, in his note on *Tr*, ii, 56, and Mr. Manly, in his discussion of the *KnT*, I, 1850, point out that May 3 was recognized as one of the "dismal" or unlucky days of the year. There is also a reference to *the dismal* in *BD*, 1206, in explanation of misfortunes. Mr. Manly prints two lists of such dates, and May 3 appears in both. In one of them are also included May 6 and June 8, the dates, respectively, of Dorigen's promise to Aurelius in the *FranklT* (V, 906), and of the assignation in the garden in the *MerchT* (IV, 2132 f.). It may be that Chaucer had only this reason for the selection of all three dates. But since there were numerous days of ill omen in the calendar, and many of them are designated as "very unlucky," whereas May 3 is simply "unlucky," one cannot help wondering whether Chaucer had some personal reason, not yet discovered, for his repeated references to that day. Professor R. M. Smith (MLN, LI, 316) cites evidence from Anglo-Saxon that May 3 was an unlucky day.

1465 Cf. *Gen Prol*, I, 844, and n.

1466 Proverbial; see Skeat, EE Prov., p. 90, no. 215

1471 *claree*, a mixed drink of wine, honey, and spices. Directions for making it are quoted in Skeat's note.

1472 The reference is to Egyptian Thebes. For

its association with opium see the references collected by Professor Emerson, MP, XVII, 287 ff. He notes that drugs and narcotics were a recognized remedy for the "lover's malady of hereos," a fact which makes Palamon's possession of them plausible. In Boccaccio the wine is not definitely said to be drugged.

1477 *nedes cost*, of necessity; lit. in the way of necessity (AS. "cost," ON. "kostr," distinct from the Mod. Eng. "cost," OF. "cost").

1479 *dredeful*, full of fear. *Stalketh*, walks stealthily; cf. *ClT*, IV, 525; *LGW*, 1781; *Tr*, ii, 519.

1494 From Dante, Purg., i, 20.

1495 *greves*, probably "bushes" here and in 1641; in l. 1507 it means "branches," "boughs."

1502 Cf. *LGW*, 1204.

1509 Cf. *Tr*, ii, 920.

1512 Professor Manly sees here an allusion to the controversy of "the flower and the leaf." See *LGW Prol F*, 72 ff., and n.

1522 The proverb also occurs in the Latin form: "Campus habet lumen, et habet nemus auris acumen." Cf. further Skeat, EE Prov., pp. 90 f., no. 216; Haeckel, p. 22, no. 71; and Morawski, Proverbes Français, Paris, 1925, p. 81, no. 2236.

1524 Also a proverb; cf. Sir Eglamour, l. 1282 f. (Thornton Romances, Camden Soc., 1844, p. 174), and Skeat, EE Prov., p. 91, no. 217. The form *men*, as in *men seyth* (Ger. "man sagt"), is probably the singular *man*, in the indefinite sense. Cf. *Gen Prol*, I, 149, and n.

1531 *thise loveres*, lovers (in general). For the use of *thise* in a generalizing sense cf. *RvT*, I, 4100; *MkT*, VII, 2121; *WBT*, III, 1004; *Astr*, ii, 26.

1533 For the proverbial figure of the bucket see Patch, The Goddess Fortuna, pp. 53 f., and ESt, LXV, 352 f.; Skeat, EE Prov., pp. 91 f., no. 218.

1539 This saying, still current in various forms, means that Friday is an off-day, different from the rest of the week. Skeat quotes a Devonshire version, "Fridays in the week are never aleek." Cf. also the Transactions of the National Eisteddfod of Wales, 1895, p. 332, and (for a mediæval explanation of the belief) Alexander Neckam, De Naturis Rerum, i, 7 (Rolls Series, p. 42). See further Lowes, MLR, IX, 94; Koch, Angl. Beibl., XXV, 337; Haeckel, p. 34, no. 115, and for a modern Irish version, Arland Ussher, Cainnt an t-Sean Shaoghail (Baile atha Cliath, 1942), p. 7.

1566 Cf. *Tr*, iii, 733 f.; iv, 1208, 1546; v, 3–7; *LGW*, 2629 f. Miss Hibbard (Mrs. Laura Hibbard Loomis) suggested that the figure has reference to a "transcendental garment, symbolic of life and destiny," and cites instances of such magic shirts. (PQ, I, 222.) But Chaucer does not represent the shirt as made by the Parcae. His meaning seems to be simply that a man's fate is determined before his first garment is made for him in infancy.

With the use of *erst*, superlative, where the comparative would be more natural in Mod. Eng., cf. *NPT*, VII, 3281; *ClT*, IV, 336.

1587 *be deed*, die. The phrase is frequently so used in early English. Cf. *PardT*, VI, 710; *ClT*, IV, 364.

1604 "I disavow the assurance and the bond."

1606 Proverbial; cf. *Tr*, iv, 618; Haeckel, pp. 1 f., nos. 3–5.

1609 *to darreyne hire*, to decide the right to her

(OF. "deraisnier," Lat. "derationare"). Cf. l. 1853;
in l. 2097 the phrase is, *The bataille to darreyne.*

1622 *to borwe,* for a pledge; cf. *to wedde,* l. 1218.
1624 Cf. Theb., i, 127 f.
1625 From Tes., v, 13: "signoria nè amore sta
bene in compagnia." Skeat cites RR, 8451 ff., and
Ovid, Met., ii, 846 f., which Chaucer may have had
in mind, though both passages say that Love and
Lordship cannot dwell together, whereas he seems to
mean that neither of them will endure any rival or
partner. A closer parallel is furnished by Ovid's Ars
Amat., iii, 564, cited by Matthieu de Vendôme, Ars
Versificatoria, iii, 10 (E. Faral, Les Arts Poétiques
du xiie et du xiiie Siècle, Paris, 1924, p. 170); cf.
also Seneca, Agamemnon, 259; Skeat, EE Prov.,
pp. 92 f., no. 220; Haeckel, p. 2, no. 7. The idea of
the sovereignty of love is also emphasized in Arabic
courtly literature. See Ibn Hazm, Tauk-al-Hamâma,
ch. 7 (Nykl, Hispano-Arabic Poetry, p. 86).
1626 *his thankes,* willingly; adv. gen. of *thank,*
in the primary sense of "thought," hence "will,"
"wish." Cf. ll. 2107, 2114 below; *Rom,* 2463.
1636 ff. The single combat of Palamon and Arcite
is conducted quite differently in Boccaccio. In his
account Palamon unhorses Arcite with a blow on the
head which makes him unconscious. When Arcite re-
covers he demands that the fight proceed, but it is
almost immediately interrupted by Theseus.
Chaucer's version, as Mr. Robertson has noted
(JEGP, XIV, 232), in which the combatants begin
fighting with the spear and turn later to the sword,
corresponds to the usual procedure in Froissart.
1638 Cf. Tes., vii, 106, 119; Theb., iv, 494 ff.
1660 With the exaggeration here (which is,
after all, characteristic of saga and romance) editors
have compared the Rom. de Troie, 24372 f.; Richard
Cœur-de-Lion, 5856 ff., Havelok, 2684 ff., and the
Icelandic saga of Gunnlaugr Ormstunga. See also,
for the simile of wild boars, Theb., xi, 530 ff.
1663 ff. Destiny, like the pagan goddess Fortuna,
was adopted into the system of Christian philosophy
and poetry, and was conceived as the executor of the
will of God. Cf. *Tr,* iii, 617 ff. On the development
of the idea, especially by Boethius and Dante, see
Patch, The Goddess Fortuna, pp. 17 ff., and MLR,
XXII, 377 ff. The *locus classicus* for the conception
is Dante, Inf., vii, 73 f., which Chaucer may have
recalled here. For further discussion see V. Cioffari,
The Conception of Fortune and Fate in the works of
Dante (Cambridge, Mass., 1940), Fortune in
Dante's Fourteenth Century Commentators (Cambridge, Mass., 1944), and Fortune and Fate from
Democritus to St. Thomas Aquinas (New York,
1935). For the Greek conception, the standard
treatise is that of W. C. Greene, Moira: Fate, Good
and Evil, in Greek Thought (Cambridge, Mass.,
1944). It is interesting to note that the necessity for
adjusting the conception of fate to that of an overruling God was also of concern to the thinkers of
Islam. The old Arabian idea of time or destiny was
condemned by Mohammed, who forbade men to
revile fate because it is by the will of God that evils
are brought to pass. Professor William Thomson
has referred the editor to the Koran, Surah XLV, 23,
and the commentaries. Later literary instances of
the subordination of Fate to Allah could be easily
collected. See, for example, Palmer's edition of
Beha-ed-Din-Zoheir, I, p. 4 (trans., II, pp. 4–5).

1666–67 Cf. l. 1089 above, and n.
1668 From Tes., v, 77; but also proverbial. Cf.
"C'avient en un jour que n'avient en cent ans"
(Morawski, p. 12, no. 315), and for further parallels
see Cook, MLN, XXII, 207; Skeat, EE Prov., p. 93,
no. 221.
1675, 1681 *the grete hert,* a great hart and old,
worthy game for the hunt. The term occurs frequently in books on hunting. See O. F. Emerson,
Rom. Rev., XIII, 140.
1678 *hunte,* huntsman (AS. "hunta").
1697 *Under the sonne.* Theseus looked under a
low-lying sun, perhaps (as Professor Child used to
suggest) shielding his eyes as he swept the field in
his observation. See J. S. P. Tatlock, MLN,
XXXVII, 377, and S. B. Hustvedt, MLN, XLIV,
182. For further examples see R. M. Smith, MLN,
LI, 318. The same phrase occurs in Flemish, apparently in a similar sense, in a ballad cited by G. L.
van Roosbroeck, MLN, XXXVIII, 59; cf. also the
Flemish Reinaert de Vos, 759. (See MP, XIV, 318).
The interpretation "all about," "in every direction,"
supported in MLN, XXXVII, 120 and 376, is less
probable.
1702 With the intervention of the duke cf. that
of Adrastus in the fight between Tydeus and
Polynices, Theb., i, 438 ff. In the Tes., Palamon and
Arcite are first discovered by Emily, who sends word
of them to Theseus.
1710 *what myster men,* what kind of men (OF.
"mester," Mod. Fr. "métier," properly, "business,
calling").
1721 The form *seinte* (with final -*e*) in this phrase,
might be explained as a case of inflected adjective
with a proper name, or as a dative, or as a French
feminine. On these inflections see the Introduction
on Language and Meter.
1736 *it am I,* the usual Middle English idiom.
Cf. the German, "Ich bin es."
1746 *to pyne yow with the corde,* i.e., "to force
confession by torture."
1747 The epithet *red,* as applied to Mars, may
have been particularly suggested to Chaucer by the
third stanza of the Tes. ("Marte rubicondo"). It
was also familiar, however, in the Latin poets. Cf.
Aen., xii, 332 ("sanguineus"); Ovid, Rem. Amoris,
153 ("sanguinei"); Theb., viii, 231 ("cruenti").
1748 Boccaccio does not mention the intercession
of the queen. Possibly Chaucer had in mind the release by Edward III of six citizens of Calais at the
entreaty of Queen Philippa. This incident, related
by Froissart (Bk. i, ch. 145; tr. Johnes, London,
1839, I, 188) has been questioned by historians, and
Professor Manly suggests that Chaucer is more
likely to have been thinking of various occasions of
intercession by Queen Anne. He refers especially to
her plea for all offenders in 1382 (Knighton, Chronicon, ed. Lumby, London, 1889–95, II, 151). Professor Parr (PMLA, LX, 307) would apply the
passage to Queen Anne's intercession for Burley in
1388.
1761 This line, which is not in Boccaccio, is repeated in almost identical form in *MerchT,* IV, 1986;
in *SqT,* V, 479; and in *LGW Prol F,* 503; and the
idea recurs in *MLT,* II, 660. It expresses a favorite
sentiment of Chaucer's, which recalls the familiar
doctrine of the poets of the "dolce stil nuovo" that
Love repairs to the gentle heart. See especially

Dante, Inf., v, 100; Vita Nuova, xx (Sonetto x); Guido Guinicelli's famous canzone: "Al core gentile ripara sempre Amore" (ed. D'Ancona, Bologna, 1877, p. 6); and cf. *Tr*, iii, 5. It should be observed, however, that the association of pity with nobility is also Ovidian. See Tristia, iii, 5, 31–32.

1781 *after oon*, alike, according to one standard.

1785 ff. The Duke's speech is almost wholly Chaucer's invention. In Boccaccio, Theseus refers to the madness ("gran follia," v, 91) of the lovers, and admits that he himself has been foolish because of love ("per amor ... folleggiai," v, 92). But the humor, even flippancy of tone, is Chaucer's. It has been suggested that he intended a serious attack on courtly love. But this is making "ernest of game." For the commonplace sentiment of the opening lines cf. *Rom*, 878 ff. Theseus' speech was apparently influenced by RR, 4229 ff. Such mockery of love is common in Old French poetry. See, for example, the poems "Contre l'Amour" collected by Jeanroy and Långfors in Chansons Satiriques et Bachiques du xiiie Siècle (Paris, 1921), pp. 20 ff.; and particularly the couplet,

Biaus sires Deus, un pou me dout
Cil ne soit fous qui Amors croit (p. 35).

Benedicite, a common exclamation, often in a deprecatory use. Cf. "Bless me!", "God save the mark," etc. For other examples in Chaucer, see *KnT*, I, 2115, and n.; *FrT*, III, 1456, 1584; *Thop*, VII, 784; *Tr*, i, 780. *Benedicite* here has its full five syllables. In most of the other cases the verse shows the pronunciation to have been trisyllabic — always, Professor Manly thinks, when the expression was used to ward off evil.

1799 "Who can be a fool unless he is in love?" Love is the one royal road to folly. The reading of some editions, *Who may (nat) be a fool, if that he love*, has poor authority, and is really less emphatic. For the sentiment the editors compare Publilius Syrus, Sententiae (ed. Meyer, Leipzig, 1880), no. 22: "Amare et sapere vix deo conceditur." It is really proverbial. See Haeckel, p. 3, no. 11. For an expression of the same idea in Arabic poetry see the quotation from Ibn Quzmân in Nykl's Hispano-Arabic Poetry, p. 285.

1808 *Kan hem ... thank*, thanks them, owns an obligation; lit. "knows thanks." *Thank* is a substantive, as in "danksagen."

1810 Both reading and interpretation are doubtful. MSS. El Hg Cp read *of*, and there may have been a proverb to the effect that the cuckoo knows little of the hare. But *of*, as Mr. Manly remarks, may be a mistake for *or*, which has the support of good MSS.

1814 *servant*, lover. Cf l. 2787, below. According to the courtly code the lover was a servant of the lady, and also of the god of Love.

1817 Cf. l. 1951, below; *LGW* 600; RR, 15108 f.

1835 The argument is in Tes. (v, 95), but the tone is different.

1838 "He may as well go whistle (for consolation)." Cf. *Tr*, v, 1433 (with Root's parallels); also *blowe the bukkes horn*, *MillT*, I, 3387, and "go blow one's flute" (proverbial). See also Skeat, EE Prov., p. 85, no. 204; Haeckel, p. 49, no. 169.

1850 *fer ne ner*, farther nor nearer; an exact year is probably intended ("un anno intero," Tes., v, 98). With regard to the dates see the note to l. 1462 above.

1877 *namely*, especially; cf. "namentlich."

1884 For a detailed analysis of the description of the stadium, with comparison of other structures, see F. P. Magoun, Jr., Med. Stud. XV, 111. On the relation of Chaucer's theater to that in the Teseida, see R. A. Pratt, PMLA, LXII, 617–18. The rules for the construction of lists, as laid down by Thomas, Earl of Gloucester, uncle of Richard II, are quoted by Skeat from Strutt, Sports and Pastimes, London, 1801, Bk. iii, ch. 1, § 23.

1910 With this use of coral cf. the romance of Guy of Warwick, 15th cent. version, ed. Zupitza, EETS, ll. 11399 ff.; also the Land of Cockaygne (in Mätzner, Alteuglische Sprachproben, Berlin, 1867, I, 150, ll. 67–70; Heuser, Die Kildare-Gedichte, Bonn, 1904, p. 146). For the suggestion that the material referred to was really red porphyry see Hinckley, p. 78.

1912 *Dyane of chastitee*, the chaste Diana. The phrase with *of* is equivalent to an adjective, as frequently in Shakespeare. Cf. *MkT*, VII, 2137; also the similar use of the bare genitive in *lyves creature*, l. 2395 below; *shames deeth*, *MLT*, II, 819; *LGW*, 2064.

1913 *Doon wroght*, caused (to be) made. The causative *don* is ordinarily used with the infinitive, but for parallels to this construction with the participle see *MLT*, II, 171; *ClT*, IV, 1098; *HF*, 155.

1918 ff. The account of the temple of Venus is a condensed version, with a few additions, of Tes., vii, 53 ff. A closer imitation of the same passage was made by Chaucer in *PF*, 183–294, and there is a third (brief) description of the temple in *HF*, 119–39. For a comparison of the passages in *KnT* and *PF* see Skeat, Oxf. Chau., III, 390. A classical model for the whole account of the pictures in the temple is of course furnished by Virgil's description of the temple of Juno, Aen., i, 446 ff.

1929 *gooldes*, marigolds. Cf. the description of jealousy in RR, 21772–73. With the color symbolism here (yellow for jealousy) cf. the use of red for anger, l. 1997, below; blue for fidelity, *SqT*, V, 644, *Anel*, 330 (*asure*); green for disloyalty, *SqT*, V, 646; and white for virtue, *SecNT*, VIII, 115; *Tr*, ii, 1062, 887.

1936–37 The error by which Chaucer confuses the island Cythera with the mountain Cithaeron, not properly associated with Venus, is found also in the "Cytheron" of RR, 15663, and in the "Citerea" of Boccaccio's Ameto (Opere Volgari, XV, 133). It may be partly due to Aen., x, 51 or 86.

1940 In making Idleness the porter of the garden of Love Chaucer follows RR, 515–82 (*Rom*, 528 ff.). Cf. *SecN Prol*, VIII, 2 f.; *ParsT*, X, 714.

1941 On Narcissus see Ovid, Met., iii, 407 ff.; on the *folye of ... Salamon*, I Kings xi, 1 ff.

1944 Possibly a reminiscence of RR, 14404–06, where Medea and Circe are mentioned successively.

1945 On Turnus see Virgil, Aen., viii, 1 and passim; on Croesus, *MkT*, VII, 2727 ff., and n.

1952 Cf. *Rom*, 6030, though no source need be sought for such a formula.

1953–54 Cf. ll. 2039–40, below; see also RR, 13263–64, 16689–90.

1955 With the description of Venus cf. that of Albricus Philosophus, De Deorum Imaginibus, ch. v (Mythographi Latini, Amsterdam, 1681, II, 304 ff.).

Chaucer probably drew upon some such mythological treatise here and in the description of Mars; see the note to l. 2041 below. Professor Patch has reminded the editor that there is a description of a "simulacrum" of Venus in Boccaccio's De Gen. Deor., iii, ch. 23.

1967–2050 The account of the temple of Mars mainly follows Boccaccio (Tes., vii, 29–37), though an occasional detail appears to go back to his source in Theb., vii, 34–73. Some lines (for example, the vivid description of treachery, l. 1999) are additions or variations of Chaucer's.

1979 f. Cf. Dante, Inf., ix, 64–70.

1982 *armypotente*, from Boccaccio's "armipotente" (Tes., vii, 32).

1985 *veze*, rush, blast; glossed "impetus" in some MSS., doubtless with reference to Theb., vii, 47 ("Impetus amens").

1987 *The northren lyght*, probably suggested by Theb., vii, 45 ("aduersum Phoebi iubar"). The reference would then not be to the Aurora Borealis.

1990 *adamant*, properly speaking, an indestructible substance (from α privative, and δαμάω); finally applied to the diamond. It was also used of the loadstone and incorrectly associated with the Latin "ad-amare." See *PF*, 148.

1991 *overthwart and endelong*, crosswise and lengthwise.

1995 *saugh I*. This formula, which recurs seven or eight times in the description of the temples, is not appropriate to the Knight and may have been carried over from the original version of the *Palamon*. But it was hardly more appropriate to Chaucer there. In the Teseida, where the personified prayers of Palamon, Arcite, and Emelye are represented as describing the temples, similar expressions are used with dramatic propriety. Chaucer (as Mr. Manly suggests) probably allowed them to stand, like the direct address in l. 1918, as mere devices for vividness of expression.

1999 Possibly influenced by RR, 12093–94 (*Rom*, 7419–20).

2001 Perhaps a reference to the story of Hypermnestra. See *LGW*, 2562 ff.

2002 Cf. Tes., vii, st. 35.

2004 For the meaning of *chirkyng* cf. *Bo*, I m. 6, 10, where it translates "stridens."

2007 Doubtless an allusion to Judges iv, 17 ff.

2014 Those who died of pestilence (*qualm*) were subject to the influence of Saturn. See l. 2469 below.

2017 *the shippes hoppesteres*, the dancing ships (AS. "hoppestre," dancing girl; on the suffix *-estre* see *Gen Prol*, I, 241, n.). Boccaccio has "navi bellatrici" (Tes., vii, 37), and Statius "bellatricesque carinae" (Theb., vii, 57). Chaucer apparently translated "ballatrici" or "ballatrices." For the association of the burning of the ships with the evil influence of Mars, Skeat compares Ptolemy's Centum Dicta, 55.

2020 ff. The catastrophes here mentioned, some of them scarcely of epic dignity, were such as were attributed to the influence of Mars. Wright and Skeat quote illustrative passages from the Compost of Ptolemy and another astrological treatise. See also Cornelius Agrippa, De Occulta Philosophia, Bk. i, cap. 22. It is not necessary to assume, with Tyrwhitt, that Chaucer meant the passage to be satirical.

2021 *by*, with reference to.

2025 Tyrwhitt (having in mind considerations of decorum) adopted the emendation *th' armerer, and the bowyer* for *the barbour, and the bocher*. But barbers and butchers belonged properly to "Mars' division."

2028 ff. The figure of the sword of Damocles was probably suggested to Chaucer by Boethius, iii, p. 5, where it is also brought into connection with conquest.

2031–34 Cf. the lines of Bernard Sylvester's Megacosmus cited in the note to *MLT*, II, 197.

2035 *by figure*, perhaps a technical reference to the horoscope.

2039 *oon ensample*. The reference is inexact. Three examples are cited in ll. 2031 ff.

2041 The figure of Mars, like that of Venus above, seems to have been influenced by some mythological treatise. Skeat quotes a passage from Albricus Philosophus, De Deorum Imaginibus, ch. iii (Amsterdam, 1681, II, 302), which derives the name *Mavors* (Mars) from "mares vorans" (devouring males). It is altogether likely that this etymology underlies the picture of the wolf devouring a man.

2045 *Puella* and *Rubeus* are figures in geomancy. On this method of divination see L. Thorndike, History of Magic, II, 110 ff., and Speculum, II, 326 ff. Cf. also Cornelius Agrippa, De Occulta Philosophia, ii, cap. 48. The process is essentially as follows: Four rows of dots are hurriedly made, without regard to their number. Then they are counted. If a row is of an odd number a single dot is set down, if even, two dots; and the results are arranged in a perpendicular column. Sixteen possible figures may thus be formed, of which the following three are concerned in the present passage.

1	2	3
•	• •	•
•	• •	• •
• •	•	• •
• •	• •	•
Puella	**Rubeus**	**Puer**

Authorities differ as to both the forms and the assignment of Puer and Puella. According to Cornelius Agrippa Puella (fig. 1, above) was dedicated to Venus, and Puer (fig. 3) to Mars. Skeat inferred that Chaucer had confused Puer and Puella. But Mr. Manly has found contemporary authority in which the names of figs. 1 and 3 are interchanged, with the consequent assignment of Puella to Mars. He cites particularly a treatise in MS. Bodley 581, which was prepared for Richard II. For a photograph of a page of the MS., and for further references on the whole matter, see Manly's note on l. 2045.

2049 *soutil*, subtile; perhaps suggested by "sottil" (Tes., vii, 38).

2053 ff. The temple of Diana is not described by Boccaccio.

2056 ff. *Calistopee*, Callisto. There seems to be confusion in regard to both her name and her story. The form *Calistopee* may be due to association with Calliope. According to the usual account (Ovid, Fasti, ii, 153 ff.), Callisto was transformed into Arctus, the Great Bear, and her son, Arcas, into the constellation Boötes. Indeed the gloss "Ursa Major" appears in several MSS., at the present passage. But the *loode-sterre,* or Polestar, is in Ursa Minor. Chaucer appears to have known a different version of the story, such as that cited by Mr. Manly from Boccaccio's De Gen. Deor. (v, 49): "Calisto autem ursa minor dicta est, ubi major vocatus est Arcas." But in either account Arcas is rather a constellation than a *sterre.* R. A. Pratt (Stud Phil, XLII, 758) suggests that Chaucer may have been influenced by Ovid's version, Met, II, 401–530.

2062 On the transformation of Daphne see Ovid, Met., i, 548 ff. With the form *Dane,* cf. Lat. "Dana" for "Daphne" which occurs in a poem published in the Neues Archiv., XV, 401, l. 9. But the influence of old French is more probable. Professor R. M. Smith (MLN, LXVI, 27) cites the form *Dane* from several passages in Froissart, in one of which she is associated with *Diane.*

2063 With the Knight's insistence on being correctly understood cf. the Pardoner's careful distinction between Samuel and Lemuel (*PardT,* VI, 585). See also *MLT,* II, 261, n., on the use of *I mene, I seye,* etc.

2065 *Attheon,* Actaeon; see Met., iii, 138 ff. for his story. Cf. also, for the phraseology, R. de Thèbes, MSS. B and C, 9127 ff. (ed. Constans, SATF, 1890, II, 78–79), and Froissart, L'Espinette and Le Buisson de Jeunesse (both cited by R. M. Smith, MLN, LXVI, 28).

2070–71 On Meleager and Atalanta (there referred to by Ovid as Tegeaea) see Met. viii, 298 ff.

2075 *seet,* an unusual form for the third singular (sat), probably due to the analogy of the plural *seeten.*

2085 *Lucyna,* Lucina, a title given to Juno and Diana in their character as goddesses of child-birth. There are frequent references to Lucina in Ovid, cf. Fasti, ii, 449; iii, 255; Her., vi, 122, xi, 55; Ars Amat., iii, 785; Met., v, 304, ix, 294 f., 698, x, 507.

2086 *thou mayst best,* thou art best able, hast most power.

2087 Cf. RR, 163 f. (*Rom,* 175 f.).

2095 ff. In the description of the opposing companies Chaucer has departed from Boccaccio. The entire sixth book of the Tes. is taken up with the accounts of the individual knights. But Chaucer has concentrated his attention upon the figures of Ligurge and Emetreus. The descriptions are full of mediæval realism, as has been shown in detail by Professor Cook; see the note to ll. 2155–86.

2100 *at alle rightes,* completely, in all respects. The phrase, of obscure origin, also occurs in the forms *to alle rightes, at hire right,* and *at right(s).*

2103 *of hir hond,* of the deeds of their hand; so, of valor or prowess; more commonly plural (*hands*) in later use. Cf. Merry Wives of Windsor, i, 4, 27.

2115 *benedicitee,* here, as usually, trisyllabic (*ben-ciie* or *bendiste*). In l. 1785, above, it has its full five syllables. See further the note to that line.

2119 *Som,* one (singular). Cf. ll. 2187, 2761.

2125 "There is no new fashion that has not been old"; cf. Skeat, EE Prov., p. 93, no. 222.

2129 *Lygurge,* "re Licurgo" Tes., vi, 14; Lycurgus, father of Opheltes, called "ductor Nemeae" in Theb., v, 733. In making him king of Thrace Chaucer apparently confused him with another Lycurgus, mentioned in Theb., iv, 386, vii, 180. The description of him resembles in part Boccaccio's description of Agamemnon and Evandro (Tes., vi, 21 ff., 35 ff.)

2141 This refers to the ancient practice of gilding an animal's claws when its hide was worn as a cloak. Cf. Tes., vi, 36. Chaucer may also have had in mind the description of a tiger's skin in Theb., vi, 722 ff.

2142–44 *for old* and *for blak,* usually printed with hyphens as compound adjectives, are probably to be taken as phrases, meaning "because of age, blackness." This construction is well attested for Chaucer and his period. Cf. *for wod, HF,* 1747; *for pure wood, Rom.* 276; *for syk, WB Prol,* III, 394; *for bright, Tr,* ii, 864; *for pure ashamed, Tr,* ii, 656; *For wo and wery, Tr,* iv, 707; and the instances from other Mid. Eng. writers listed by Kittredge, [Harv.] Stud. and Notes, I, 16; by Zupitza, ed. of Lydgate's Fabula Duorum Mercatorum, l. 532, n. (QF, LXXXIII, 56); and by Macaulay, Works of Gower, Oxford, 1899–1902, II, 505 f. The sense of *for* varies somewhat in the different examples, which might easily be multiplied. But *for* as a prefix of emphasis in adjectives, though not common, is also found in English and Scandinavian. Anglo-Saxon shows the formation in a number of intensive adjectives and adverbs. Some of them are not quite parallel to Chaucer's forms, because the accent appears from metrical evidence to have fallen on the prefix (as in the case of the related prefix *fore-,* which occasionally alternates with *for-* in the same compound). But others (like the adverbs *fornean, forswithe, forwel*) are shown by occurrences in verse to have had unaccented *for-.* And the NED cites from Middle and early Modern English what appear to be clear cases of the intensive formation in the adjectives "forcold," "forgret," "forwery," "fordead," and "fordull." The use of *for* as a prefix must therefore be regarded as possible in *for old* and *for blak,* though the other idiom seems more probable. Strangely enough several passages in Chaucer present the same difficulty of choice between the two constructions. Cf. *for hor, Rom,* 356; *for wery, PF,* 93; *for drye, SqT,* V, 409; *forwaked, MLT,* II, 596; and *for dronken, Mill Prol,* I, 3120 (where the sense seems to favor the preposition, though the verbal prefix *for-* would be very natural with the participle).

For further discussion of the construction see F. Mossé, Études Anglaises, V, 289 ff.

2148 The *alaunt* was a tall, heavy hunting dog. For a full account see Cook, Trans. Conn. Acad., XXI, 128; XXIII, 30.

2155–86 Emetreus is not mentioned by either Boccaccio or Statius. The name may have been derived by some misunderstanding from Demetrius. H. B. Hinckley (MLN, XLVIII, 148 ff.) connected it with Demetrius, a Græco-Bactrian prince, who was known as the "king of the Indians." Professor Manly remarks that the description is somewhat suggestive of Richard II. Professor Cook (Trans. Conn. Acad., XX, 166 ff.) argued that the real original of the portrait was the Earl of Derby on the occasion of his return to London from the continent on July 5, 1393. He showed that the description was not inapplicable to Henry personally and that many of the trappings and treasures mentioned are known to have been such as he possessed at one time or another. There is even evidence that Henry brought home a leopard from the East. But many of the features of the description emphasized by

Cook do not seem particularly significant, and in other cases (as where he would explain *frakenes* by "pock-marks") his argument is forced. On the whole the indentification seems not to be justified. Moreover, it would imply for the passage in question a date much later than is probably to be assigned to the *Knight's Tale*.

Professor Curry (pp. 130 ff.) offers an entirely different explanation of Lycurgus and Emetreus. He holds them to be types, respectively, of the Saturnalian and Martian figure, appropriately introduced here since Arcite was under the protection of Mars, and Saturn had taken up the cause of Palamon. Although the descriptions of the Martian and the Saturnalian man, cited by Mr. Curry from the astrological authorities, are not altogether consistent, the correspondences between them and Chaucer's figures are striking enough. Even the yellow eyes are noted by Alchabitius ("croceos"), and the freckles by Albohazen Haly. In this passage, just as in some of the descriptions of the pilgrims in the *General Prologue*, it is hard to judge how definitely Chaucer had such scientific lore in mind. But in view of the conspicuous use of astrology throughout the *Knight's Tale*, Mr. Curry's theory deserves serious consideration.

2160 *clooth of Tars*, a rich stuff, apparently of silk. The word is of uncertain origin. The NED identifies *Tars* with Mandeville's mythical Tarsia or Tharsia, in the borders of China. Mr. Hinckley (MP, XIV, 318) argued for the derivation from Tarsus, and this explanation is supported by Professor Magoun, Med. Stud., XVII, 140.

2178 Since white eagles are unknown, probably a falcon is here meant. Cf. Chaucer's uses of the term *egle* in *PF*, 332 ff.

2187 *alle and some*, all and each, one and all. Cf. l. 2761: *this al and som*, this is the whole and every particular. *Som* is the indefinite pronoun. The phrase was common. See *FranklT*, V, 1606; *Tr*, iv, 1193, 1274.

2200 Not in Boccaccio. Dr. Robertson (JEGP, XIV, 235) shows that it is a mediæval touch.

2202 For *dauncen*, which has the overwhelming support of the manuscripts, Manly (M-R CT, III, p. 432) offers the tempting emendation *chanten*.

2217 *And in hir houre*. The astrological system of the hours of the planets is explained at length in the *Astrolabe*, ii, § 12. Each day is divided into twelve hours, reckoned from sunrise to sunset, and twelve more, reckoned from sunset to sunrise. The first hour from sunrise belongs to the planet for which the day is named, and subsequent hours, throughout the twenty-four, are assigned according to the following series: Saturn, Jupiter, Mars, Sun, Venus, Mercury, Moon. Thus on Sunday the hour after sunrise was dedicated to the Sun, the second to Venus, and the twenty-third (when Palamon rose) also to Venus. The twenty-fourth was Mercury's, and the first hour of Monday, when Emily rose and went to Diana's temple (l. 2273), belonged to the Moon. *The nexte houre of Mars folwynge this* (l. 2367) was the fourth after sunrise, and it was then that Arcite offered his sacrifice.

2221-60 The prayer of Palamon corresponds closely to that in Tes. (vii, 43-49).

2224 On Venus and Adonis cf. Ovid, Met., x, 519 ff.

2236 Cf. RR, 21096.

2238 "I care not to boast of arms."

2239 *Ne I ne axe*, to be read "N'I n'axe."

2252 *wher I ride or go*, whether I ride or walk.

2271 *The thridde houre inequal*. Since the day and the night are each divided into twelve planetary hours, the hours of the day and those of the night were unequal except just at the equinoxes.

2275-2360 Cf. Tes., vii, 71-92.

2281 *Smokynge the temple*. Boccaccio (Tes., vii, 72) reads, "Fu mondo il tempio," the temple was clean. But Chaucer apparently translated "Fumando il tempio."

2288 Either "it is well for a man to be unhampered in his story," or "it is well for a man to preserve his freedom (to keep out of prison)." The purport of the whole passage is doubtful. The Knight may mean that he is restrained by modesty from continuing the description. Yet what he actually omits of Boccaccio's text is the detailed account of the rites after washing. Professor Child used to suggest that the Knight thought it best not to seem to know too much about heathen religion. This was one of the charges brought against the Templars in the prosecution of the order at the beginning of Chaucer's century.

2293-94 Of course Emilia's sacrifice is described by Boccaccio (Tes., vii, 76 ff.), and not by Statius. But Boccaccio's model was doubtless the account in Theb., iv, 455 ff., of the rites performed by Tiresias and his daughter Manto. Chaucer's citation of Statius here may be an acknowledgment of that ultimate source; or it may be merely a claim of ancient authority for his story, even where such authority was really lacking.

2298 *sene*, the adjective (AS. "gesiene"), not the participle. It consequently takes the preposition "to," instead of "by."

2302 *As keep*; cf. *As sende*, l. 2317. *As* is freely employed in Mid. Eng., in a sense which now seems pleonastic, with the imperative or subjunctive in commands, entreaties, or exhortations. Cf. *as beth of bettre cheere*, *Cl Prol*, IV, 7. The construction apparently developed out of the strictly logical use of *as* in adjurations: "as help me God," etc. For another type of "pleonastic as" see *Gen Prol*, I, 462, n.

2313 The three forms are those of Luna, in heaven; Diana, on earth; and Proserpina, in the lower world.

2340 The conception of the bleeding twigs (Tes., vii, 92) doubtless goes back ultimately to the Polydorus episode in the Æneid (iii, 19 ff.). Cf. also Ovid, Met., ii, 325 ff., especially 360; Dante, Inf., xiii, 31-34.

2356 *Shulle thee declaren*. The declaration has already been made in ll. 2331 ff. In the Teseida the omen follows Diana's speech.

2365 *the nexte weye*, the nearest way.

2373 ff. With Arcite's prayer cf. Tes., vii, 24-28.

2388-90 Boccaccio's reference to Mars and Venus is somewhat expanded by Chaucer, who may have recalled Ovid (Ars Amat., ii, 561-600; Met., iv, 171 ff.) or RR, 13838 ff., 14157 ff., 18061 ff.

2395 *lyves creature*, living creature. See the note to l. 1912 above.

2397 Cf. *Anel*, 182, and *Lady*, 52.

2399 *in the place*, in the lists.

2410–17 The vows of Arcite (which Chaucer got from the Teseida) have several parallels also in Statius; cf. Theb., ii, 732 ff., vi, 193 ff., 607; viii, 491. The dedication of hair and beard was an actual custom in antiquity. On its significance see Sir J. G. Frazer, Golden Bough, 3d ed., London, 1911, I, 25, 28; Farnell, Greek Hero Cults, Oxford, 1921, pp. 64 ff.

2413 *fynde*, provide.

2432 ff. For *murmurynge Ful lowe and dym*, Tes. (vii, 40, 6) has "con dolce romore," and Professor Lowes (MP, XV, 708 f.) has suggested that Chaucer's paraphrase was due to the recollection of "un tacito mormorio" in Filocolo (Opere, VII, 208), where Florio and Ascalione visit the temple of Mars.

2433 "And (the voice) said." For the omission of the subject cf. the *Gen Prol*, I, 33, and n.

2437 With this proverbial expression cf. *ShipT*, VII, 51, and *CYT*, VIII, 1342; also *Tr*, v, 425; *Rom*, 74 f. See Skeat, EE Prov., p. 94, no. 223; Haeckel, p. 50, no. 178.

2443 In astrology the aspect of Saturn was cold. Cf. Ptolemy, De Judiciis, Lib. ii (ed. Basel, 1551, p. 399): "Saturnus, ubi solus dominationem fuerit sortitus, corrumpit generaliter frigore."

2447–48 Cf. RR, 12818, ff.

2449 Proverbial. "Men may the old outrun but not outwit." Dryden, Palamon and Arcite, iii, 387 f. misinterpreted *at-rede* as "outride." In *Tr*, iv, 1456, the same proverb is applied to the wise. See further Skeat, EE Prov., p. 81, no. 195; Haeckel, p. 21, nos. 66, 67.

2452 In making Venus daughter of Saturn Chaucer was very likely following RR, 5541, 10827 ff. In l. 2222 above she is called *Doughter to Jove*. Perhaps, as Professor Cleanth Brooks suggests (MLN, XLIX, 459 ff.), Chaucer uses "daughter" loosely for a granddaughter, a female descendant.

2454 *My cours*, the course or orbit of the planet Saturn. This was the largest known orbit before the discovery of Neptune and Uranus. For a similar list of calamities ascribed to the influence of Saturn see Ptolemy, De Judiciis, Lib. ii (ed. Basel, 1551, p. 399). But the distinction between the *infortune of Marte* and that of Saturn was not very consistently maintained, and in the same chapter Mars is associated with "tumultibus plebeis."

2456 The disasters mentioned are such as were regularly ascribed to Saturn by astrology.
The adjective *wan* is applicable either to the sea or to the drowned body.

2459 *cherles rebellynge*, doubtless an allusion to the Peasants' Revolt of 1381. For an explicit reference to that occurrence see *NPT*, VII, 3393; and cf. also *ClT*, IV, 995 ff., and *Tr*, iv, 183 f. But see Johnston Parr (MLN, LXIX, 393–4) for an argument against this application, and W. E. Weese (PMLA, LX, 307 ff.) for support of the usual application.

2462 According to a paraphrase of the Tetrabiblos of Ptolemy, quoted by Professor Liddell (note to l. 2456), it was especially when in the signs of the quadrupeds (hence, when in Leo) that Saturn caused destruction by falling buildings ("necem ex ruina"). See also Hinckley, pp. 101 f.

2466 Probably to be read as a headless line. The participle in *-inge* very seldom keeps its final *-e*

within the verse, and the initial accent on *I* suits the sense.

2467 *colde*, perhaps here in the sense of "destructive." See *NPT*, VII, 3256, and n.

2475 *compleccioun*, temperament, constitution. The reference is primarily to the mixture of the humors. See *Gen Prol*, I, 420 and n.

2491 ff. The description of the royal entrance and the fight is largely Chaucer's. The rules for the tournament differ somewhat from those in the Teseida (where, for example, the use of the lance is forbidden). Nearly all the details can be paralleled in Froissart. Dr. Robertson (JEGP, XIV, 239 ff.) draws illustrations especially from a tournament held by Richard II in 1390. See Froissart's account, Bk. iv, ch. 22–23 (tr. Johnes, London, 1839, II, 474 ff.). Such group-combats were of frequent occurrence, the number of contestants, in those mentioned by Froissart, varying from three on a side to forty or sixty. Sometimes they were fought "in the gyse of mortal bataille," as in the case of the famous contest, in 1351, between thirty Bretons and thirty Englishmen. (See Dom P. H. Morice, Hist. de Bretagne, Paris, 1750, I, 280; A. de la Borderie, Hist. de Bretagne, III, Rennes, 1899, pp. 510 ff.) In other instances, as in the *Knight's Tale*, provision was made to avoid the loss of life. To the combats discussed or mentioned by Dr. Robertson may be added the fight of thirty on a side at Perth in 1396 (R. C. MacLagan, The Perth Incident of 1396, etc., Edinburgh, 1905). A tournament of twenty against twenty was also proposed, but never held, by Eustace de Renti in his challenge to John, Lord Wells, in 1383. (See Speculum, II, 107 ff.) General information about the regulations of such contests is given in Strutt's Sports and Pastimes, Bk. iii, ch. 1, §§ 16 ff. For further comment on the realism of Chaucer's description see W. H. Schofield, Chivalry in English Literature, Cambridge, 1912, pp. 38 ff. Professor Johnston Parr argues that many features of Chaucer's tournament were suggested by the London affair of 1390. See PMLA, LX, 317 ff.

2503 *Nailynge the speres*, fastening the heads to the shafts.

2504 *Giggynge*, fitting the shields with straps (OF. "guige").

2511 *nakers*, probably kettledrums, though the rest of the list are wind instruments. Arabic has two words, "naqqārah," drum, and "nāqūr," also "naqīr," horn, trumpet, but the English *naker* seems always to mean a kind of drum.

2519 *he... and he... He*, this man... and that, etc. For the indefinite use of the pronoun cf. ll. 2614 ff.

2546 *bitynge*, piercing (without the modern figurative reference to the bite of a tooth).

2563–64 These lines, which correspond very closely to Boccaccio, Dr. Robertson (pp. 236–37) holds to be out of keeping with the actual sentiment of the crowds at mediæval tournaments.

2568 For the contrast between *sarge* and more precious cloth cf. Chrétien de Troyes, Erec (ed. Foerster, Halle, 1909, p. 185), 6667 ff., and the Roman de Fauvel by Gervais de Bus, ll. 1923 ff. (ed. Långfors, SATF, 1914–19, p. 72).

2601 ff. This passage and the description of the battle of Actium in *LGW*, 635 ff., may be compared for the striking use of alliteration with the combat in the romance of Ywain and Gawain, ll. 3525 ff.

(ed. Schleich, Oppeln, 1887, pp. 89 ff.). The device was doubtless suggested to both poets by the English alliterative poetry which flourished, particularly in the West Midland dialect, in the fourteenth century. Striking parallels from the Ipomedon and the Partonope of Blois are cited by Professor R. M. Smith, MLN, LI, 320 ff. See also the comments of Miss Dorothy Everett, Essays on Middle English Literature (Oxford, 1955), p. 141 — a paper reprinted from RES, XXIII, 201 ff. Chaucer skillfully suggests the effect of the meter, without reproducing its structure or conforming strictly to the rules of alliteration. Good fourteenth-century examples of the verse-form are the romance of Gawain and the Green Knight, and Piers Plowman. On metrical details see J. Schipper, Hist. of English Versification, Oxf., 1910, ch. iv. Tennyson's use of the device in the Passing of Arthur was doubtless an imitation of Chaucer, though he had some acquaintance with the regular alliterative verse in early English.

2602 "In go the spears full firmly into the rest"; that is, they were couched for the attack.

2621 *dooth hem... to reste,* causes them to rest. This is the usual meaning of the auxiliary *do* in Middle English.

2624 *and wroght his felawe wo,* and done each other harm (lit. and done his opponent harm). The construction is inconsequent.

2626 *Galgopheye,* probably the Vale of Gargaphia, where Actaeon was turned into a stag (Met., iii, 156).

2628 *hunte,* huntsman, as in l. 2018 above.

2630 *Belmarye,* i.e., Benmarin, Morocco; cf. *Gen Prol,* I, 57, and the introductory note on the description of the Knight in *Gen Prol.*

2636 Proverbial. Cf. l. 3026 below; *Tr,* iii, 615, and n.

2663–70 Not paralleled in the Teseida. Mr. Hinckley (p. 109) suggests the influence of Aen., i, 223 ff.

2675 *Which a,* what a, how great a. *Which* commonly had the sense of "qualis."

2681–82 These lines, which are omitted in the best MSS., seem to be by Chaucer, though he may have intended to cancel them.

2683 The reading and interpretation are both doubtful. See Textual Notes. Probably to be understood (with Skeat): "she was all his delight, as regarded his heart." Mr. Liddell, reading *in chiere,* interprets: "He saw no one else, just as he loved no one else." But the text is emended and the meaning seems forced.

2685 The Fury here and in Tes. (ix, 4) is borrowed from Statius (Theb., vi, 495 ff.).

2689 Skeat cites from Walsingham's Historia Anglicana (ed. Riley, London, 1863–64, II, 177) an account of an accident very similar to Arcite's, which occurred in Cambridge in 1388.

2694 ff. In the description of Arcite's death after his last interview with Emilia both Chaucer and Boccaccio may have had in mind Statius' account of the death of Atys in the presence of Ismene (Theb., viii, 636 ff.).

2710 *That... was thirled his brest boon,* whose breastbone was pierced. The use of a general relative "that," followed by a personal pronoun to define its exact relation (*that... his* for *whose, that... him* for *whom,* etc.), is still familiar in childish or illiterate speech. In Middle English the construction was regular. For other instances in Chaucer see *MLT,* II, 271 (with ellipsis of *that*); *PrT,* VII, 504; *ClT,* IV, 88 f.; *Tr,* ii, 318; *HF,* 76.

2712 *charmes,* incantations. These were regularly recognized among remedies in Chaucer's age.

2713 *save,* usually explained as "salvia," "sage" (so NED). But it was rather a decoction of herbs to be drunk. Skeat printed from MS. Sloane 1314 a recipe for making it, and showed that the ingredients numbered from thirty to forty. He suggested further the derivation from Lat. "sapa," defined by Ducange as "mustum coctum." See MLQ, II, 132–34, and cf. Schöffler, Beiträge zur Mittelenglischen Medizinliteratur, Sächsische Forschungsinstitute in Leipzig, III, i, Halle, 1919, pp. 104–08; Henslow, Medical Werkes of the 14th Centurye, London, 1899, pp. 55, 126.

2731 *leet crye,* caused to be proclaimed. *Leten,* like *don,* was commonly used as a causative auxiliary.

2733 *gree,* rank, superiority (Lat. "gradus").

2747 *veyne-blood,* drawing off the venous blood; *ventusynge,* letting blood by means of a cupping glass. Mr. Manly notes (ll. 2743 ff.) that French physicians also use ventousing "to reduce congestion by setting up a counter-irritation, without blood-letting."

2749 ff. According to the old physiology there were three kinds of "virtues" (sometimes called "spirits") which controlled the processes of life: the natural, seated primarily in the liver; the vital, localized chiefly in the heart; and the animal, operating through the brain. The "virtus animalis," controlling the muscular motions, was the expulsive force; but in Arcite's case it was unable to expel the poison from (or for) the natural virtue. Professor Manly prefers the reading *For,* but *Fro* seems equally appropriate and has much better support in the printed MSS. In MS. Gg, which has *For,* the whole line is corrupt.

On the doctrine of virtues see L. Thorndike, Hist. of Magic, New York, 1923, I, 658. For a full discussion of the present passage, with citations from the medical authorities, see Curry, pp. 139 ff. Mr. Curry shows that astrology was also involved in that the "retentive virtue" which prevented the expulsion of the poison, was under the control of Saturn.

2759–60 Bohn (Hand-book of Proverbs, London, 1882, p. 124) cites as a proverb: "If physic do not work, prepare for the kirk," but does not indicate how early it was current.

2761 See l. 2187, n.

2775 In the Teseida (ix, 83) there is an actual marriage of Arcita to Emilia. But Chaucer's *wyf* may be merely a term of devotion.

2779 The phrase, which recurs in *MillT,* I, 3204, and *Mel,* VII, 1560, was a regular formula in both French and English. To the examples collected by Miss Hammond, English Verse between Chaucer and Surrey, p. 471, may be added "soule sens compaignon," in the pastourelle of the Lamb and the Wolf (Bartsch, Altfr. Romanzen und Pastourellen, Leipzig, 1870, II, 122); "toz seus sanz compaignie," Gautier d'Aupais, ed. E. Faral, Paris, 1919, l. 15; Jugement d'Amour, l. 44, in Fabliaux et Contes, ed. Barbazan et Méon, Paris, 1808, IV, 355.

2780 *my swete foo;* on the use of this and similar phrases in love-poetry see *Tr,* i, 411, n.

2800 For the suggestion that Chaucer was indebted to Vincent of Beauvais for some portion of his account of Arcite's illness see Miss Pauline Aiken, PMLA, LI, 361 ff.

2801 *And yet mooreover*, and still further. Tes., "ed ancor" (x, iii). Cf. *Bo*, ii, pr. 6, 76 ff.; where *moreover* translates "ad haec," and *Rom*, 4493, where it corresponds to Fr. "enseurquetout.")

2803 The heart is represented as the seat of the intellect. This doctrine, taught by Empedocles, Aristotle, and others, was familiar but not undisputed. Galen, for example, assigned the rational faculty rather to the brain.

2805 ff. This observation on the destination of Arcite's soul replaces a rather long description by Boccaccio of its journey through the spheres (Tes., xi, 1 ff.). Chaucer used the Italian passage in his account of the death of Troilus (*Tr*, v, 1807–27). If the *Troilus* was written before the *Knight's Tale*, the omission of the same description here would be easy to understand. It is quite possible, on the other hand, that the passage was rejected in the *Knight's Tale* as unsuitable to the spirit of the poem, and was afterwards recalled by Chaucer and turned to account in the *Troilus*.

In any case, the flippancy of the remark about Arcite's soul should not be taken as evidence that Chaucer was doubtful either about human immortality in general or (as Dryden's rendering implies) about the destiny of virtuous pagans. It was characteristic of Chaucer, as of Horace, to seek in a jest relief from the strain of pathos.

2809 For the figure, which may be scriptural, Miss Landrum has cited II Cor. v, 1.

2810 *As I cam nevere*, (there) where I never came. *As* is apparently not used by Chaucer in a causal sense.

2815 *ther Mars his soule gye*, "where (or there) may Mars guide his soul." For the use of *ther* as an expletive in optative clauses of blessing or cursing cf. *FrT*, III, 1561; *MerchT*, IV, 1308; *Tr*, iii, 947, 966, 1437, 1456; v, 1787. The primary sense seems to have been "in that (or which) case," "under which circumstances"; hence, "therewith," "wherewith," and perhaps "wherefore."

2835 A common sentiment in popular "keens" or laments. Cf. also Aen., ix, 481 ff., and see the comment of Professor F. B. Gummere, Beginnings of Poetry, New York, 1901, p. 222, n. 1.

2837 Chaucer made a skillful shift of speeches at this point. The Teseida says here simply that nobody could console Theseus or Egeus (xi, 9). Later on, when proposing the marriage of Palamon, Theseus expresses the commonplace sentiments attributed by Chaucer to Egeus (ll. 2843–49). By transferring the remarks Chaucer created the character of the platitudinous Egeus. Then, in their place, he gave Theseus, very appropriately, an elevated philosophical speech based upon Boethius (ll. 2987 ff.).

2841 Cf. l. 3068 below; and for parallels see Haeckel, p. 7, no. 22; Skeat, EE Prov., p. 95, no. 225.

2847 The familiar figure of the pilgrimage is perhaps scriptural. See Heb. xi, 13 f. Cf. also *Truth*, 20. For further discussion see R. M. Smith, MLN, LXV, 443 ff. and J. Parr, MLN, LXVII, 340–1.

2849 Professor Mather (edn., p. 104) compares Seneca, Consolatio ad Marciam, 19, 5; but the sentiment is commonplace.

2853–2962 The description of Arcite's funeral is closely modelled upon Boccaccio, who followed in turn Statius' description of the funeral of Archemorus (Theb., vi). For an analysis of the two accounts see Wise, Influence of Statius on Chaucer, Baltimore, 1911, pp. 107 ff. It is not clear that Chaucer made much direct use here of Statius, but a few parallel passages are noted below.

2858 There is a discrepancy between this statement and l. 1862, where the theater is said to have been erected on the scene of the combat in the woods. In the earlier passage Chaucer departed from Boccaccio. Here, in the account of the pyre, he returned to his source.

2863 ff. With the tree-list here may be compared that given in *PF*, 176 ff. See the note on that passage.

2871 ff. Professor Cook (Rom. Rev., IX, 317) suggests that Boccaccio drew from observation in his description of the bier covered with the cloth of gold. He compares the accounts of Petrarch's funeral (Rom. Rev., VIII, 223).

2874 The line is defective in most manuscripts. For *hadde he* or *were* Manly proposes *putte he* for better continuity. The white gloves were appropriate at the funeral of an unmarried person. See Hazlitt, Faiths and Folklore, London, 1905, I, 249.

2895 Turkish bows, also mentioned in *Rom*, 923 ff., were regarded as especially good. For mediæval references to them see the NED, s.v. Turkeys, and cf. C. M. Webster, MLN, XLVII, 260.

2902 *maister strete*, chief street. For this use of *maister* cf. *maister-tour*, *SqT*, V, 226; *mayster-toun*, *LGW*, 1591; *maister-temple*, *LGW*, 1016; and the modern "master-key."

2921 Chaucer transfers to his account of the pyre the list of trees which Boccaccio gives, at greater length and with full characterization, in his description of the grove. There is a similar list in Theb., vi, 98–106. For further examples see *PF*, 176, n.

2925 ff. There is perhaps an echo here of Theb., vi, 110 ff., as well as of the immediate source, Tes., xi, 25. Cf. also Met., i, 192–93, 680–91.

2933 Cf. Theb., vi, 56 ff.

2967 ff. The account here differs from Boccaccio's in several details, notably in the reference to foreign alliances. For the suggestion that Chaucer, in departing from his source, had in mind the marriage of Richard and Anne and the alliance of England with Bohemia and the Papal States, see Professor O. F. Emerson, Studies in Language and Literature in Celebration of the Seventieth Birthday of James Morgan Hart, N.Y., 1910, pp. 203 ff.

2987 ff. This passage, which replaces the speech transferred by Chaucer from Theseus to Egeus (ll. 2843–49), is based upon Boethius, ii, m. 8; iv, pr. 6; m. 6; and iii, pr. 10. For the figure of the chain, or bond, cf. also RR, 16785–88. It goes back ultimately to the story of Homer (Iliad, viii, 19), and the history of the conception has been elaborately set forth by Professor Arthur O. Lovejoy in The Great Chain of Being (Cambridge, Mass., 1950).

3016 *at ye*, at a glance (lit. "at eye").

3026 Cf. l. 2636, above, and n.

3034 Proverbial; cf. Haeckel, p. 44, no. 150.

3041–42 This phrase, which occurs in Tes., xii, 11, was already proverbial. Cf. *SqT*, V, 593, and *Tr*, iv, 1586; also RR, 14015–16. It is as old as St.

Jerome, Adv. Rufinum, iii, 2 (Migne, Pat. Lat., XXIII, 458). See Haeckel, p. 30, no. 96; Skeat, EE Prov., pp. 83 f., no. 199.

3063 *loved.* The better supported reading, *loveth*, might refer, as Manly points out (M-R CT, III 435), to Arcite's continued love of them after his death.

3064 The idea that overmuch mourning is an affliction to the departed is traditional and widespread. Cf. the ballad of The Unquiet Grave, with Child's comments (English and Scottish Ballads, II, 234).

3084 *kynges brother sone.* Professor Emerson, in the article just cited (p. 248 f.), argues that Chaucer used this term because of its applicability to Richard II.

3089 "Mercy ought to prevail over justice." The lover is dependent upon the lady's grace, or unmerited favor. Cf. the similar phrase of Troilus to Criseyde (*Tr*, iii, 1282), also Haeckel, p. 47, no. 159; Skeat, EE Prov., p. 77, no. 184. The underlying idea is of course the Christian doctrine of grace. In fact, the theology, ritual, and polity of the Church were freely drawn upon in the mediæval literature of courtly love. For general illustration of the tradition see W. A. Neilson, The Origins and Sources of the Court of Love, [Harv.] Stud. and Notes, 1899, pp. 33, 48, 137, 220 ff. Gower's Confessio Amantis is a manual of sins as expounded by the priest of Venus to a penitent lover. Similarly Chaucer's *Legend of Good Women* is a legendary or martyrology of Cupid's Saints (*The Seintes Legende of Cupyde*). For other instances of theological or ecclesiastical imagery in Chaucer see *Tr*, i, 15 ff., and n.

The Miller's Prologue

The continuation of Fragment I from the *Miller's Prologue* through the Cook's fragment is a consecutive composition clearly written for the place it occupies after the *Knight's Tale*. There is no definite evidence of its date, but it is probably not to be assigned to the beginning of the Canterbury period. The narrative skill of the *Miller's Tale* and the *Reeve's Tale*, their subject matter and tone, all point to the last decade of Chaucer's life. It has also been suggested that the Miller and the Reeve themselves, together with the rest of the group of pilgrims mentioned in the *General Prologue* (ll. 542–44), were added to the company by way of afterthought and did not belong in the original scheme. But if the tales in question are not among the earliest, there are also reasons for not putting them at the very end of Chaucer's activity. They seem to precede the so-called Marriage Group, and show little or no acquaintance with the literature which Chaucer there turned to account. And they must have been put in shape before the collection as a whole was arranged in very systematic order. For though the manuscripts show various stages of revision and rearrangement, Fragment I is found in all of them or at least in all the different classes. A reasonable conjecture for its date seems therefore to be the early nineties. See further the section on Chronology in the Introduction, and for detailed discussion, Miss Hammond, pp. 254 ff. On aesthetic design in the stories of the first day, see C. A. Owen, Jr., Eng. Stud., XXXV, 49 ff.

3115 *unbokeled is the male,* the bag is unbuckled, that is, the wares are displayed.

3119 "Something to match the *Knight's Tale* with." On the order see *Gen Prol*, I, 791, n.

3120 *for dronken,* because of being drunken. See also l. 4150. In both cases it is doubtful whether the reading should be *for dronken* or *fordronken* (AS. "fordruncen"). Compare the similar question with regard to *for old* and *for blak*, *KnT*, I, 2142 ff., n.

3124 *Pilates voys,* a voice like that of the ranting Pilate in the mystery plays. For another suggestion see L. Ellinwood, Spec., XXVI, 482.

3125 "By the arms, blood, and bones of Christ." See *PardT*, VI, 651, n.

3131 *thriftily,* profitably. Cf. *thrifty tale*, *ML Headlink*, II, 46, and *ML Epil*, II, 1165.

3134 *a devel wey,* "originally an impatient strengthening of *away* — further intensified as *a twenty devel way*, etc. —... In later times it appears to have been taken more vaguely, as an expression of impatience, and sometimes equals 'in the devil's name.'" (NED, s.v. Devil.) Here clearly imprecatory; cf. also l. 3713.

3139 *mysspeke or seye.* The prefix *mis-* goes in sense with both verbs. Cf. the *Mk Prol*, VII, 1922.

3143 Cf. *Gen Prol*, I, 586; also *Rv Prol*, I, 3911.

3152 The idea is proverbial. Cf. also RR, 9129 ff.

3154–56 Closely parallel to *LGW Prol G*, 276–78. It is uncertain which passage was written first. With both may be compared Deschamps, Miroir de Mariage, 9097–9100.

3161 *that I were oon,* i.e., a cuckold; or perhaps an ox (which, being horned, might stand for a cuckold).

3164 For the religious part of this counsel cf. ll. 3454, 3558 below.

3165 *Goddes foyson,* God's plenty.

3170 *M'athynketh,* etc., "I regret that I must rehearse it here." Boccaccio makes a very similar apology for the Decameron, in the Conclusione dell' Autore (ed. Moutier, V, Florence, 1828, 148 f.). There also the author says he is not responsible, and the reader may skip. See R. K. Root, Engl. Stud., XLIV, 1 ff., for a discussion of the passages. In spite of their close resemblance it seems unlikely that Chaucer knew the Decameron. Cf. the introduction to the Explanatory Notes on the *CT*. For another parallel with that work see *Rv Prol*, I, 3878–79 and n.

3186 Proverbial; cf. Haeckel, p. 36, no. 122.

The Miller's Tale

On the date of the *Miller's Tale* see the introductory note on the *Prologue* just preceding.

The source is unknown. There are two episodes in the story, that of the man who is made to fear a second flood, and that of the misdirected kiss. The second of these occurs separately in an Italian novel (no. 29) of Masuccio (about 1470) and in several later versions, and the two are combined, not only in tales of Hans Sachs and Schumann (sixteenth century) and other versions later than Chaucer, but also in a Middle Flemish "boerde" or jest of the fourteenth century. Chaucer doubtless found the combination in his source, which is likely to have been a French fabliau. The story is no. 1361 in A. Aarne, Types of the Folk-Tale, tr. Stith Thompson (FF Com., no. 74, Helsinki, 1928), pp. 168–69.

For discussion of the various analogues see especially
Varnhagen, Angl., VII, Anz., 81 ff.; Zupitza, Herrig's
Arch., XCIV, 444–45 (with a genealogy of versions);
Bolte, ed. of Schumann's Nachtbüchlein, Stuttgart
Lit. Verein, CXCVII, Tübingen, 1893, p. 384 f.; and
Barnouw, Zesde Nederlandsche Philologencongress
(1910), 125 ff., and MLR, VII, 145 ff. Other references are given by Miss Hammond, p. 275; to which
may be added Angl., XXVI, 273; Angl. Beibl., XIII,
307, and XXVII, 61 f. The results of previous
discussion are printed in SA, pp. 106 ff., where texts
are printed of Masuccio's novella, the Flemish
fabliau, the Nachtbüchlein version, and one by
Hans Sachs.

On the fabliau as a type see J. Bédier, Les Fabliaux, 4th ed., Paris, 1925. The two great French
collections are those of Barbazan and Méon, 4 v.,
Paris, 1808, and Montaiglon and Raynaud, 6 v.,
Paris, 1872–90. Chaucer's use of the *genre* is discussed by Professor W. M. Hart, PMLA, XXIII,
329 ff., and [Kittredge] Anniv. Papers, Boston, 1913,
pp. 209 ff. See also L. A. Haselmayer, RES, XIV,
310 (on the portraits in the fabliaux); C. A. Owen,
Jr., College English, XVI, p. 226; W. W. Heist,
Papers of Michigan Acad. of Science, Arts, and
Letters, XXXVI, 251 ff.; and G. Stillwell, JEGP,
LIV, 693 ff.

Professor Pratt (MLN, LIX, 47 ff.) conjectures
that there may have been some factual background
for the episode in the Miller's own life. This might
explain the Reeve's fury, but it is only a surmise.

3187 ff. Professor G. R. Coffman (MLN, LXVII,
329 ff.) argues that there is in this passage deliberate
burlesquing of the Seven Liberal Arts.

3188 *gnof*, churl, fellow; a slang term of doubtful
origin. Skeat took it from Hebrew "ganāv," thief
(Ex. xxii, 1), but the NED would connect it rather
with the Germanic root represented by East Fris.
"knufe," lump, "gnuffig," coarse, rough, etc.

3189 He is a carpenter like the Reeve on the
pilgrimage, at whom the *Miller's Tale* is in a measure
aimed.

3193 *a certeyn*. A certain number or quantity.
Cf. *Tr*, iii, 596; *CYT*, VIII, 776.

conclusiouns, propositions or problems. Cf. the
Astrolabe, passim. But here the reference is to
astrological operations undertaken to obtain answers
to horary questions. In the course of the story
Nicholas's skill is employed to predict a rain greater
than "Noah's flood."

3199, 3272, 3386 ff. The combination *hende
Nicholas* is perhaps the nearest approach in Chaucer
to the fixed epithet common in popular poetry and
the classical epic. The repetition of *fals* in *PhysT*
(*this false juge*) and *Anel* (*fals Arcite*) though similar,
is not quite parallel.

It should be observed that the association of
astrology with Noah's flood was traditional. Interesting notes on Noah's reputation as a philosopher
have been collected by Professor J. J. O'Connor in
an article awaiting publication.

3204 Identical with *KnT*, I, 2779, and *Mel*, VII,
1560.

3208 *Almageste*, Arabic "al majisti," from Greek
μεγίστη (for μεγίστη σύνταξις, "greatest composition"), the name given to Ptolemy's astronomical
treatise, and then applied loosely to works on
astrology.

3209 *His Astrelabie*; see Chaucer's *Treatise of
the Astrolabe*.

3210 *augrym stones*, stones or counters marked
with the numerals of algorism and intended for use
upon an abacus. "Algorism" (*augrym*) is derived
from the name of Al-Khowārizmī, an Arab mathematician of the ninth century. His treatise on numbers was translated into Latin, "De Numero Indo-
rum," early in the twelfth century. A second version
was entitled "Liber Algorismi," and the name
"algorism" came to be transferred to the science
itself. See MLN, XXVII, 206 ff., and for a full
description of the counters and the method of their
use see Florence A. Yeldham, Story of Reckoning in
the Middle Ages, London, 1926, pp. 36 ff.

3216 *Angelus ad virginem*, a hymn on the An-
nunciation beginning

Angelus ad virginem subintrans in conclaue,
Virginis formidinem demulcens inquit, "Aue!"

It is printed in the Chaucer Society reprint of MS.
Harl. 7334, p. 695 f.

3217 *the kynges noote*, conjecturally identified by
Ritson (Ancient Songs, London, 1829, I, lix) with
the song called "Kyng Villzamis Note" in the Complaint of Scotland (1549); by Edward Jones (Musical, Poetical, and Historical Relics of the Welsh
Bards, London, 18–?, III, 1) with the Welsh air
called Ton y Brenhin, "The King's Tune." The
music of the latter is published by Jones, who observes that the song known in the time of Henry
VIII as "The King's Ballad" (printed in Chappell's
Old English Popular Music, Wooldridge's revision,
London, 1893, I, 42–45), is entirely different from
Ton y Brenhin. Since "Pastime with good company"
is mentioned in the Complaint of Scotland in the
same list with "Kyng Villzamis Note," those two
songs are not likely to have been identical; and there
appears to be no evidence beyond the titles themselves for connecting either of them with Ton y
Brenhin or with Chaucer. Mr. Fletcher Collins, in
Spec., VIII, 195 ff., suggests that the reference is to a
sequence on St. Edmund beginning *Ave rex gentis
Anglorum*.

3225 The Oxford carpenter is an example of the
familiar figure of the "senex amans." See the introductory note to the *MerchT*, Chaucer's most
noteworthy treatment of the theme.

3227 *Catoun*, Dionysius Cato, the supposed
author of a collection of Latin maxims, usually called
Disticha de Moribus ad Filium. The collection was
probably written in the third or fourth century and
was widely current in the Middle Ages. An English
translation was published by Caxton. For the
original text see the edition of F. Hauthal, Berlin,
1869; Baehrens, Poetae Latini Minores, Leipzig,
1879, III, 205 ff.; and G. Nemethy, Budapest, 1895.
The proverb here referred to is found, not in the
Disticha proper, but in a supplement called Facetus.
It runs:

Duc tibi prole parem morumque vigore venustam,
Si cum pace velis vitam deducere iustam.

See C. Schroeder, Der deutsche Facetus, Berlin, 1911
(Palaestra, LXXXVI), p. 16.

3235 *barred*, adorned with bars (cross stripes).
Cf. *Gen Prol*, I, 329.

3248 *pere-jonette*, early-ripe pear. Etymology
uncertain; Skeat compared "gennitings" (jennet-
ings) and suggested a connection with "Jean" be-

cause the fruit ripened about St. John's Day, or with "jaune" because of its yellow color. The former interpretation is supported by the French name "pomme de St. Jean." See NED, s.v. Jenneting.

3251 *perled with latoun*, with pearls (knobs or buttons) made of the mixed metal called *latoun.*

3256 The noble was a gold coin worth 6s. 8d. The principal London mint was in the Tower.

3258 Cf. *Pard Prol*, VI, 397.

3261 *bragot*, bragget (Welsh "bragawd"), a drink made of ale and honey.

3268 *piggesnye*, pigsnie (lit. "pig's eye"), the name of a flower, used as a term of endearment, as also in Elizabethan English. In Essex it is applied to the cuckoo-flower; in some parts of America to trillium. See Manly's note. The form *nye, neye* for "eye" arose by false division of "an eye."

3274 There was an abbey of Augustinian canons at Oseney, near Oxford.

3286 On the custom of crying "harrow" see M. Henshaw, Folklore Quarterly, XIV, 158 ff.

3291 St. Thomas à Becket.

3299 "A clerk would have employed his time ill."

3312 ff. On Absalom as a traditional type of beauty, see Rev. P. E. Beichner, Med. Stud., XII, 222 ff.

3318 The leather of his shoes was cut with designs resembling the windows in St. Paul's. Such shoes were called in Latin "calcei fenestrati" (see Du Cange, s.v. calceus). For illustrations see F. W. Fairholt's Costume in England, 3d ed., London, 1885, II, 64 f. For the doubtful suggestion that the decorations were intended to suggest devices on shoes worn by prostitutes and libertines, and that word-play is to be recognized on *Poules* and *poulaine*, see L. Whitbread, N & Q, CLXXXIII, 158.

3322 *poyntes*, tagged laces.

3329 Cf. *Gen Prol*, I, 125, and n. It is not clear that the reference to Oxford dancing, like that to Stratford French, is to be taken satirically.

3332 On the *quynyble*, a very high voice, an octave above the treble, see W. Chappell, N & Q, Ser. 4, VI, 117.

3338 *daungerous*, fastidious? or sparing (Skeat)? Cf. *Gen Prol*, I, 517, and n.

3382 Some MSS. have the marginal note: "Unde Ovidius: Ictibus agrestis." But the quotation has not been identified. Professor Lowes suggests (orally) that Jerome against Jovinian was really in Chaucer's mind.

3384 He took the part of Herod in a mystery play.

3387 Cf. the phrase "to pipe in an ivy-leaf." See *KnT*, I, 1838, and n.

3389 Cf. *Gen Prol*, I, 706, and n.

3392 f. Gower's version, Conf. Am., iii, 1899 ff., is similar. Cf. also the modern "Out of sight, out of mind"; Skeat, EE Prov., p. 95, no. 226; Haeckel, p. 48, no. 166.

3396 The figure is also proverbial.

3427 "God forbid that he should die suddenly!"

3430 *That... hym*, whom. Cf. *KnT*, I, 2710, and n.

3441 The reference is to a so-called cathole. See NED s.v. and Supplement. Both the word and the thing are familiar in parts of the United States. See also Angl. Beibl., XXVII, 62; XIII, 307.

3449 There was a priory of St. Frideswide at Oxford. For evidence that she was held to have healing power see Miss R. H. Cline, MLN, LX, 480.

3451 The corrupt form *astromye* for *astronomye* is supported by the meter here and in l. 3457. It was doubtless intended as a specimen of the carpenter's speech. Cf. *Nowelis flood*, l. 3818; also *procutour*, *FrT*, III, 1596 (not so clearly an error), perhaps *cardynacle*, *Words of Host*, VI, 313, and certainly the Host's Latin.

3456 "That knows nothing but his creed."

3457 A familiar fable, related by Plato of Thales in the Theaetetus, 174 A; also in Diogenes Laertius, i, 34. Cf. Æsop's Fables, ed. James, Philadelphia, 1851, no. 193; also Cento Novelle Antiche, no. 38.

3480-86 The *nyght-spel*, which is rough in meter and not wholly clear in sense, is based upon an actual popular charm. It refers to a prayer familiarly known as the White Paternoster. A French prose version (Petite Patenôtre Blanche) is quoted in the (apocryphal) Enchiridion Leonis Papae (Rome, 1660, p. 145 f.), and similar prayers have been collected in various languages. See besides Skeat's note, W. J. Thoms in the Folk Lore Record, I, 145 ff.; E. Carrington, ibid., II, 127 ff.; D. Hyde, Religious Songs of Connacht, London, 1906, I, 362 ff.; and Rois ni Ogain, Duanaire Gaedhilge, Dublin, 1921, pp. 84, 115. The child's hymns

Matthew, Mark, Luke and John
Bless the bed that I lie on,

and

Now I lay me down to sleep

belong to the same general tradition.

The significance of "St. Peter's sister" is uncertain. In one of the English charms cited by Skeat the White Paternoster is associated with St. Peter's brother. Skeat says that the person originally intended was St. Peter's daughter, i.e., St. Petronilla, who was invoked to cure the quartain ague. But it looks as if the White Paternoster was itself personified as St. Peter's brother or sister, perhaps because of its supposed power to admit the petitioner to heaven. For the personification of the regular Paternoster see the Anglo-Saxon Salomon and Saturnus, ed. Kemble, London, 1848, p. 136.

With the use of "white" cf. the remarks on "White things" in Pater's Marius the Epicurean, ch. ii (London, 1897, pp. 9 ff.). The "white Mass" was celebrated by candidates for the priesthood with an unconsecrated host, by way of rehearsal. Cf. further F. B. Gummere, On the Symbolic Use of the Colors Black and White, Haverford Coll. Stud. no. 1, 1889.

On the form *seinte* see *Gen Prol*, I, 120, n.

3485 *verye*, interpreted by Skeat as "evil spirits" (AS. "werigum"). Thoms suggested a connection with "Wera, Werre," the name of an old witch or sorceress, the devil's grandam, and cited Kuhn and Schwartz, Norddeutsche Sagen, Märchen, und Gebräuche (see p. 508). But all this is entirely uncertain. The reading *mare*, of Tyrwhitt and the early editors, has very little support. For the proposal to read *nerye*, "save, protect," see E. T. Donaldson, MLN, LXIX, 310 ff. The resulting interpretation, "may the white Paternoster save [us] from the [perils of the] night," is not very easy.

3507 "If you betray me, you shall go mad."

3512 *hym*, Christ. The Harrowing of Hell was one of the most familiar episodes in the Christian literature of the Middle Ages. On the source of the story, the apocryphal Gospel of Nicodemus, see R. P. Wülcker, Das Evangelium Nicodemi in der Abendländischen Literatur, Paderborn, 1872, and cf. Wells, pp. 326, 814, 1014, 1118, 1268, 1308. For a version contemporary with Chaucer, see Piers Plowman, C, xxi, 338 ff. (B, xviii, 313 ff.)

3515 On prognostication by the moon, or "the days of the moon," see W. Farnham in Stud. Phil., XX, 70 ff. Cf. also *MLT*, II, 306 ff., and *Tr*, ii, 74, and n. Sometimes recourse was had to astronomical calculations as to the position of the moon. Sometimes the mere day of the moon was considered as being favorable or unfavorable for certain undertakings. On mediæval moon-books, or *lunaria*, cf. Thorndike, Magic and Exp. Science, I, 680 ff. A rhymed guide to popular beliefs on the subject, dating probably from the beginning of the fifteenth century, is printed by Mr. Farnham (pp. 73 ff.).

3518 *Noe*, Noah; the Vulgate form. A few MSS. have *Nowelles*, which Chaucer perhaps intended to be a blunder of the Miller's.

3530 See Ecclus, xxxii, 19 (attributed not to Solomon but to Jesus son of Sirach). Cf. *Mel*, VII, 1003; *MerchT*, IV, 1485 f.; Haeckel, p. 28, no. 90; also parallels noted by C. F. Bühler, Spec., XXIV, 410 ff.

3539 The reference is to the comic accounts of Noah's wife in the mystery plays. See L. T. Smith, York Plays, Oxford, 1885, pp. 45 ff.

3550 *swymme*, float.

3554 *pryme*, 9 A.M.

3576 *his* (drake), a well-supported reading, can be kept only on the assumption that it means "its."

3598 Apparently a proverb of similar sense to "A word to the wise," cf. Haeckel, p. 49, no. 172.

3611 *affeccioun*, rather "feeling," "impression" (the state of being affected) than "affection" in the modern sense.

3624 *His owene hand*, with his own hand. For the idiom cf. Gower, Conf. Am., iv, 2436; v, 5455; it is perhaps a survival of an original instrumental.

3637 *a furlong way*; see *MLT*, II, 557 n.

3638 "Now say a Paternoster, and then mum's the word!"

3645 *corfew-tyme*, probably 8 P.M.

3655 *laudes*, the service that follows nocturns. According to l. 3731 the night was still pitch-dark; *at cokkes crowe*, l. 3675, then refers to the first cock's crow, also in the dead of night. Skeat quotes Tusser's Husbandrie, sect. 74 (EDS, 1878, p. 165) for the statement that cocks crow "At midnight, at three, and an hower ere day."

3682 Divination from itching hands or face, or burning ears is an old and common popular practice. Examples are collected in Angl. Beibl., XXVII, 61 f.

3692 *trewe love*, probably leaves of herb-paris, which grew in the form of a fourfold true-love knot.

3697 In view of the existence of Lat. *semisonus* it is tempting to print *semy-soun* as a compound. But the MSS. favor separating the words, and there is clear evidence for an adj. *semy*, "thin, small" in Middle English. See H. Kökeritz, MLN, LXIII, 313 ff.

3699 With the rime *cynamome: to me* cf. *pa me: blame* just below; also *Gen Prol*, I, 672 n.

3708 *Jakke*, Jack; here an epithet of contempt.

3709 "*com pa me*," come-kiss-me; perhaps the name or refrain of a song.

3713 Cf. l. 3134 and n.

3725 Cf. RR, 3403 f. (*Rom*, 3674 ff.); Ovid, Ars Amat., i, 669.

3728 "Have done; come off (desist)." Cf. *FrT*, III, 1602, n.

3756 Proverbial. Cf. Skeat, EE Prov., p. 96, no. 227.

3762 For evidence that blacksmiths actually worked at night in Chaucer's London see E. P. Kuhl, MLN, XXIX, 156.

3770 *viritoot*; meaning unknown. Skeat conjectures "upon the move," "astir," and suggests a connection with Fr. "virer," turn, and "tout," all. For further conjecture see L. Spitzer, Language, XXVI, 389 ff.

3771 *seinte Note*, St. Neot (9th cent.). On the form *seinte* see *Gen Prol*, I, 120 and n.

3774 "He had more business on hand," — a proverbial phrase. Cf. Skeat, EE Prov., p. 96, no. 228.

3782 *foo*, probably for *foot*; an intentional substitution, such as is common in oaths. Cf. for substitutions of another sort *Manc Prol*, IX, 9; *Pars Prol*, X, 29.

3785 *stele*, handle.

3818 *Nowelis flood*, a confusion of "Noe" and "Nowel," Christmas. See the note to l. 3451.

3821 "He did not stop to trade on the way" — probably a current expression. Cf. the French fabliau of Aloul, in Barbazan's ed., III, p. 344, l. 591 f.

3822 *celle*, sill, flooring; a Kentish form.

3823 *floor*, earth, ground.

The Reeve's Prologue

3857 A recurring formula. Cf. *MLT*, II, 211; *MerchT*, IV, 1469; *SqT*, V, 202; and RR, 10683 f. Fansler (p. 121) adds Dante, Par., ii, 139 f.

3860 Professor Manly notes that Oswald appears to have been a rare name in Norfolk in the fourteenth century.

3864 *So thee'k*, so may I prosper. The northern *ik*, which Chaucer makes the Reeve use several times, was appropriate to a Norfolk man.

3865 "To blear the eye" meant to hoodwink, to delude. Cf. l. 4049, below; also *MancT*, IX, 252; *CYT*, VIII, 730.

3868 "I have left the pasture for the stable."

3869 "My gray head declares my age."

3876 Cf. Luke, vii, 32.

3877 *nayl*, nail; here figuratively for a hindrance.

3878 The comparison, which occurs also in the Decameron, Introduction to the Fourth Day (ed. Moutier, II, 146), was doubtless proverbial. Cf. Dekker and Webster, Northward Ho, iv, 1, and the note in Dyce's ed. of Webster's Works, London, 1859, p. 270.

3881–82 Cf. Alanus de Insulis, Parabolae, cap. i, ll. 61–62 (Migne, Pat. Lat., CCX, 582).

3882 "Still, in our old ashes, is fire raked."

3883 ff. For the figure cf. Jean de Meun, Testament, 1734 ff. (in RR, ed. Méon, Paris, 1814, IV).

3888 Proverbial; cf. *WB Prol*, III, 602, and *MerchT*, IV, 1847; Skeat, EE Prov., pp. 96 f., no.

229. See further Professor B. J. Whiting (Med. Stud. in Honor of J. D. M. Ford, Cambridge, Mass., 1948, pp. 321 ff. He suggests that Chaucer may be responsible for the rather extensive use of the term.

3891 ff. Cf. again Jean de Meun, Testament, 165 (not so close).

3901 "What does all this wisdom amount to?"

3902 *What shul*, why must.

3904 Cf. "Ex sutore medicus," Phaedrus, Fables, i, 14.

3906 *Depeford*, Deptford. *half-wey pryme*, half-past seven o'clock.

3907 There may be some special point in the fling at Greenwich. Chaucer was probably living there when he wrote the passage.

3911 Cf. *Gen Prol*, I, 586.

3912 "To shove off force by force"; glossed in MS. E, "vim vi repellere," a well-known legal maxim. See F. Montgomery, PQ, X, 404, where an illustrative passage is quoted from the Digesta of Justinian (Paulus, ix, 2, 45, 4; ed. Mommsen, Berlin, 1870, I, 291), also L. M. Myers, MLN, XLIX, 222 ff. For other legal maxims cf. ll. 4180 ff. below, also *Intro. to MLT*, II, 43 f.

3919 *stalke*, small piece of a stick. Cf. Matt. vii, 3 (Vulg. "festucam"); Haeckel, p. 17, no. 54.

The Reeve's Tale

On the date of the *Reeve's Tale* see the introduction to the Explanatory Notes on the *Miller's Prologue*. The story is of the same type as the Miller's, and is probably derived from a lost fabliau. Several analogues have been found, the closest being a French fabliau preserved in two versions: A, in a Berne MS., printed in Wright's Anecdota Literaria, London, 1844, pp. 15 ff.; in the Chaucer Society's Originals and Analogues, pp. 93 ff.; and in the Recueil des Fabliaux of Montaiglon and Raynaud, 6 v., Paris, 1872-90, V, 83 ff.; and B, in a Berlin MS., printed by H. Varnhagen, ESt, IX, 240 ff. Varnhagen took A to be the better representative of Chaucer's source. But for an argument that that source must have contained some features of B, see G. Dempster, JEGP, XXIX, 473 ff. Both versions are printed in SA, pp. 126 ff. The cradle-trick was a favorite subject of popular tales. See A. Aarne's Types of the Folk-Tale, tr. S. Thompson (FF Com., no. 74, Helsinki, 1928), p. 169, no. 1363. For further discussion of the group, see Ebeling, Tobler Festschrift, Halle, 1895, pp. 335 ff.; W. Stehmann, Die Mittelhochdeutsche Novelle vom Studentenabenteuer, Palaestra, LXVII, Berlin, 1909. To the examples cited by them may be added an Irish analogue printed in ČZ, II, 156 ff., and Mr. Robin Flower informs the editor that he has found a variant in the Blasket Islands.

3921 ff. The topographical details here are apparently accurate. Skeat notes that a mill once stood at the spot, near Trumpington, now marked "Old Mills" on the ordnance-map, and that there was an old bridge about a quarter of a mile below it. The *fen*, l. 4065, he suggests may be either Lingay Fen or a field between the Old Mills and the road. See also F. P. Magoun, Jr., Med. Stud., XVI, 149.

Professor Manly (New Light, pp. 97 ff.) speculates on the reasons for Chaucer's choice of the neighborhood of Trumpington. Sir Roger de Trumpington, he notes, was in the King's household, and his wife, like Chaucer's (as Skeat pointed out, Oxf. Chau., V, 116), was a lady-in-waiting to Constance of Padilla. So Chaucer would easily have known about the locality. But it may have been chosen merely because it was near Cambridge and fitted the story of the clerks. An Oxford clerk figures in the companion story of the Miller, and both university towns were of interest to court circles in 1388, when the King's Council met at Oxford and Parliament at Cambridge.

3925 ff. The description corresponds in some details with that of the Miller in the company, whom the Reeve wished to annoy. See *Gen Prol*, I, 545 ff.

3928 *turne coppes*, make wooden cups in a turning-lathe.

3931 *poppere*, dagger (from "poppen," thrust).

3933 Sheffield was famous then as now for its cutlery.

3935 *piled*, probably "bald, scanty." Cf. *Gen Prol*, I, 627, n., and see NED, s.v. Pilled. Professor Curry (pp. 82 f.) would interpret it here rather as "thick, bristly" (NED, s.v. Piled, ppl. a. 3: "Covered with pile, hair, or fur").

3936 *market-betere*, a quarrelsome frequenter of markets.

3938 *abegge*, a Kentish form of *abygge*, *abye*, a-buy, pay for.

3941 *Symkyn*, diminutive of Simond. The word is perhaps trisyllabic (Symekyn) here and in l. 3959, though the MSS. favor *Symkyn*. Skeat's reading *dëynous* (like *sëynt* in *Gen Prol*, I, 120) is very hard. See O. F. Emerson, Rom. Rev., VIII, 74 f.

3943 She was an illegitimate daughter of the parson, who consequently paid money for her marriage. For information on concubinage among priests in the fourteenth century, see H. C. Lea, History of Sacerdotal Celibacy, 3d ed., N.Y., 1907, I, 418 ff.; H. B. Workman, John Wyclif, Oxford, 1926, II, 116-17.

3954 *gyte* (Fr. "guite"), of uncertain meaning. In Old French, according to Godefroy, it referred to head-dress; in English it seems rather to mean some kind of robe or gown.

3963 *smoterlich*, besmirched; probably an allusion to her illegitimacy.

3964 *digne*, dignified, haughty. The comparison, "digne as ditch-water," was proverbial. Cf. the Plowman's Crede, ed. Skeat, EETS, 1867, l. 375.

3966 *spare*, show her consideration.

3972 *a propre page*, a fine-looking baby.

3980 "And made difficulties about her marriage." With the idiom cf. *Gen Prol*, I, 785.

3989 *collegge*, academic building.

3990 *Soler Halle*, another name for King's Hall, founded by Edward III in 1337 and afterward merged in Trinity College. On its history see F. P. Magoun, Jr., Med. Stud., XVI, 148. The name *soler* would refer to the upper rooms (sun-chambers) of the house. Professor Kuhl (PMLA, XXXVIII, 123) has noted that Soler Hall came into "prominence in 1388 when the members of Parliament (which met at Barnwell Abbey) were entertained at the College."

3999 *made fare*, made a to-do.

4001 *craketh boost*, talks loudly.

4014 *Strother* seems to refer to the place, no longer existent, which gave its name to the famous Northumbrian family. Castle Strother, the family seat, was apparently near Kirknewton, about five miles west of Wooler. Whether Chaucer, in using the name "Aleyn," meant to make a joking allusion to the important historic personage Aleyn (or Alan) de Strother, Constable of Roxburgh, can be only a matter of conjecture. Aleyn de Strother died in 1381, and had a son John. Professor Manly, in his note on this passage, mentions various possible points of contact between the family and Chaucer. Cf. also Miss Rickert, in TLS, 1928, p. 707. She suggests that Chaucer not only knew these Northumbrians but even "mimicked their speech for an audience who also knew them."

4022 The speech of the students is full of Northern forms, though not consistently transposed into that dialect. The most important features to be noted are: ā for Chaucer's usual ō (as in *gas, swa, ham*); indicative present in *-es,* or *-s; s* for *sh* (*sal*); the forms *thair, til* (for *to*), *ymel, heythen* (for *hennes*), *gif,* (for *if*) *pit* (for *put*); and the words *boes, lathe, fonne, hethyng, taa.*

For a description of the dialect forms in various MSS. see J. R. R. Tolkien, Transactions of the Philological Society, 1934, pp. 1 ff.

4026 Cf. "Necessity knows no law." See Skeat, EE Prov., p. 97, no. 231; Haeckel, p. 29, no. 95.

4027 *boes,* behooves (Northern *bos* or *bus*). Chaucer apparently has in mind a proverb (perhaps in Latin); cf. Haeckel, p. 53.

4029 *hope,* expect.

4030 *werkes,* aches (lit. "works").

4054 Proverbial; cf. Skeat, EE Prov., p. 98, no. 233; Haeckel, p. 20, no. 64. A very ancient statement of the idea is credited to Heraclitus: πολυμαθίη νόον [ἔχειν] οὐ διδάσκει (ed. Deils, Berlin, 1901, fragment 40 [16]).

4055 The mare told the wolf, who wanted to buy her foal, that the price was written on her hind foot. When he tried to read it she kicked him. See Willem's Reinaert, ii, 3994 ff. (ed. Martin, Paderborn, 1874, pp. 215 ff.); Caxton's Esope, v, 10 (ed. J. Jacobs, London, 1889, I, 254, II, 157). Versions of the story are numerous and the central *motif,* that of the kick, has been combined with different incidents. For full discussion see P. F. Baum, MLN, XXXVII, 350 ff., and cf. Aarne's Types of Folk-Tales, tr. S. Thompson (FF Com., no. 74, Helsinki, 1928), p. 27, no. 47B.

4096 "Make his beard," another phrase for cheating. Cf. *WB Prol,* III, 361; *HF,* 689–91; Haeckel, pp. 39 f., no. 135.

4101 *jossa,* down here; *warderere,* look out behind.

4127 *Cutberd,* St. Cuthbert, bishop of Lindisfarne (d. 686). Miss R. H. Cline (MLN, LX, 480) notes that he was an apparent saint to invoke in an appeal for hospitality.

4129 f. "A man must take what he finds or what he brings." Apparently another proverb. See Skeat, EE Prov., p. 98, no. 234; Haeckel, p. 53.

4134 Also proverbial; repeated in *WB Prol,* III, 415. Cf. RR, 7518–20; also John of Salisbury, Policraticus, v, 10 (ed. Webb, 2 v., Oxford, 1909, I, 565). See Skeat, EE Prov., p. 98 f., no. 235; Haeckel, pp. 9 f., no. 32.

4140 *chalons,* blankets; named from Chalons, France, the place of manufacture. See F. P. Magoun, Jr., Med. Stud., XVII, 124.

4155 This figure is still current and needs no illustration.

4171 The reading of most MSS. is *complyng,* of uncertain meaning. *Complyn* may be an emendation or the original reading corrupted in nearly all copies.

4172 *wilde fyr,* erysipelas. Cf. "maus feus," RR, 7400, 8279, 10724.

4174 *the flour of il endyng,* the best (i.e., the worst) of a bad end.

4181 In the margin of MS. Ha is noted the legal maxim: "Qui in uno gravatur in alio debet relevari."

4194 *upright,* supine; a common meaning in early English.

4210 A proverb like "Nothing venture, nothing have." See *Thop,* VII, 831 and n.; also *Tr,* iv, 600 ff.; Skeat, EE Prov., pp. 78 f., no. 189; Haeckel, p. 5, no. 18.

4233 *the thridde cok,* near dawn (about five o'clock). See l. 3655, n.

4264 Cf. *ShipT,* VII, 227.

4286 A supposed relic of the true cross, known as the Rood of Bromeholm, was brought from the East to Norfolk in 1223. On the appropriateness of its mention here see R. A. Pratt, MLN, LXX.

4287 *In manus tuas,* the beginning of the common religious formula, "Into thy hands I commend my spirit." See Luke xxiii, 46.

4320–21 It was a common rhetorical convention to end a tale with a proverb or general idea, and in particular with a moral application. Cf., for other examples, *ShipT,* and *MancT.* In the present ending two proverbs are combined. For the first, "He must not expect good who does evil" see *PrT,* VII, 632, and n.; Haeckel, p. 40, nos. 137, 138; Skeat, EE Prov., p. 99, no. 236. *Hym thar* is impersonal, lit. "it needs him" (from AS. "thearf"). For the second proverb, which is current in many languages, see Skeat, ibid., no. 237, and cf. especially RR, 7342 f. (Rom., 5759), 7387, 11551 f., and Gower, Conf. Am., vi, 1379 ff.

The Cook's Prologue

There is an apparent inconsistency between the *Cook's Prologue* and that of the Manciple (IX, 1 ff.) where the Host speaks to the Cook as if he were then first taking notice of him, and asks him for a tale. It may be that Chaucer had in mind in the later passage the plan that each pilgrim should tell two tales on the outward journey. But it is more probable that he meant to cancel the existing Cook's fragment and not to introduce the Cook until near the end of the series. Possibly, too, the *Manciple's Prologue* was written before the continuation of Fragment I and represents an earlier plan. For the discussion of the question see F. Tupper, PMLA, XXIX, 113 f.; R. K. Root, Poetry of Chaucer, Boston, 1922, p. 179 f.; E. D. Lyon in SA, pp. 148 ff.

4331 From Ecclus. xi, 29.

4336 *Hogge,* Hodge, a nickname for Roger. *Ware,* in Hertfordshire. It has long been suspected that Roger of Ware was a real person, and Miss Rickert has recently reported the discovery of several records which confirm the suspicion. In a plea of debt, of 1377, there appears, in a list of attorneys, "Roger Ware of London, Cook." He may be the same person as "Roger Knight de Ware, Cook," named in another plea of debt of the year 1384–85. There is also a record of a Roger Ware, who sold wood to the King's household, but he may have been a different person. For detailed references to these documents see TLS, 1932, p. 761. For a very unlikely explanation of *Roger Hogge* (hog) as a play upon Roger Bacon see L. Whitbread, N & Q, CLXXXIII, pp. 157–8.

4345 There is a hint here, as Professor Tupper notes (JEGP, XIV, 263 f.) of a clash of trades between cooks and hostelers. Originally innkeepers were permitted to furnish only lodging for man and beast, without food and drink. But apparently this rule was not in force in Southwark, and the City Cook might well have felt hostility to the Southwark innkeeper.

The pilgrims expected to need the services of the Cook along the road.

4347 *Jakke of Dovere*, usually explained as a twice-cooked pie. Skeat cites "Jak of Paris" in this sense, from Thomas More, Works, London, 1557, p. 675 E, and the French "jaques," which is so defined in Roquefort's Glossaire de la Langue Romane (Paris, 1808), s.v. "Jaquet"; also the use of "Jack of Dover" for an old story or jest. It is possible (as Professor Kittredge suggested to the editor) that the name was applied, like "Poor John," "John Dory," etc., to some kind of fish. "Poor John" is used for dried hake in Congreve's Love for Love, Mermaid ed., London, n.d., p. 229. In any case the reference seems to be to warmed-over food. For evidence that in 1287–89 cooks and pasty-makers warmed up pies and meats on the second and third days see Tancock, in N & Q, Ser. 8, III, 366, quoting Hudson, Leet Jurisdiction in Norwich (Selden Soc., no. 5, London, 1891, p. 13). Brusendorff's suggestion (p. 480) that *Jakke of Dovere* means "fool," and that *that* in the following line means "what" ("that which"), is altogether improbable.

4351 *stubbel goos*, fatted goose, so called because fed on stubble.

4355 Proverbial, cf. *Mk Prol*, VII, 1964; Haeckel, p. 36, nos. 120, 121; Skeat, EE Prov., p. 107, no. 253.

4357 "A true jest is a bad jest." Cf. "True jest is no jest," "Sooth boord is no boord," etc., Skeat, EE Prov., p. 100, no. 238; Haeckel, pp. 36 f., no. 123. Chaucer may have known the proverb in Flemish form. The adjective *quaad* corresponds to Flem. "quaad," Du. "kwaad," whereas the usual Middle English form was "cwed" (from AS. "cwead"). But cf. *quade yeer*, *Pr Prol*, VII, 438. In the form *Waer spot, quaet spot*, the saying is cited by J. Graels and J. F. Vanderheijden in Rev. Belge de Philol. et d'Hist., XIII, 748. They suggest that it may have been current with *spel* instead of *spot*, which would account for the variant *spel* for the second *pley* in certain Chaucer MSS. Another Flemish proverb is quoted in *MancT*, IX, 349–50. Not only were there many Flemings in London, from whom Chaucer could have learned their sayings, but his own wife was the daughter of a Flemish knight.

4358 The name of *Herry Bailly*, the host, corresponds to that of an actual innkeeper of Southwark, referred to as "Henri Bayliff, Ostyler," in the Subsidy Rolls, 4 Rich. II (1380–81). For further information about him see *Gen Prol*, I, 751 ff., n.

The Cook's Tale

The Cook's fragment is long enough to show that the tale was to be of the same general type as the Miller's and the Reeve's, but too short to disclose the plot or, consequently, the source. For conjectures as to the nature of the story see E. D. Lyon, SA, pp. 148 ff. He suggests that Chaucer may have had no literary source, but may have started out to fictionalize contemporary persons and events. On certain spurious endings found in a few MSS. and early editions see Miss Hammond, pp. 276–77.

A number of MSS. have inserted after the *Cook's Tale* the Tale of Gamelyn, also ascribed to the Cook. It is printed from six MSS. by the Chaucer Society as an appendix to Group A (Fragment I) of the Six-Text Edition, and by Skeat, Oxf. Chau., IV, 645 ff. For references to other editions see Miss Hammond, pp. 425–26. The general plot is the "expulsion and return" story which underlies As You Like It. The piece is certainly not by Chaucer, though he may very well have intended to work it over for one of the pilgrims. If so, it would have been more appropriate to the Yeoman than to the Cook.

4368 Cf. *Gen. Prol.* I, 207.

4377 *Chepe*, Cheapside, which was a favorite scene of festivals and processions. For an account of "ridings," processions, see Wm. Kelly, Notices . . . of Leicester, London, 1865, pp. 38 ff.; W. Herbert, Hist. of the Twelve Great Livery Companies, London, 1834, I, 90 ff.

4383 *setten stevene*, made an appointment. Cf. *KnT*, I, 1524.

4397 "Revelling and honesty, in a man of low rank, are always angry with each other," i.e., incompatible.

4402 Disorderly persons, when carried off to prison, were preceded by minstrels, to proclaim their disgrace. See the Liber Albus, Munimenta Gildhallae Londoniensis, Rolls Series, 1859–62, I, 459 f. (tr. III, 180 f).

4404 *his papir*, probably his certificate of service and release. See R. Blenner-Hassett, MLN, LVII, 34 f., H. Braddy, MLN, LVIII, 18, and R. Call, MLQ, IV, 167.

4406 f. The idea is familiar. For various forms of the proverb cf. Hazlitt's Eng. Proverbs, London, 1907, p. 436; Düringsfeld, Sprichwörter, no. 354 (Leipzig, 1872–75, I, 178); Dan Michel's Ayenbite of Inwyt (ed. Morris, EETS, 1866), p. 205; Haeckel, p. 23, no. 74.

4415 Proverbial; cf. Haeckel, p. 32, no. 105.

4417 *brybe*, to steal.

FRAGMENT II

Introduction to the Man of Law's Tale

The Man of Law's *Introduction* and *Tale* regularly stand in the manuscrips after the unfinished Fragment I. The time, according to the Host's explicit statement, was ten o'clock on the morning of April 18, which is usually taken to be the second day of the pilgrimage. For the conjecture that it was the first day see Koch, The Chron. of Chaucer's Writings, pp. 56–57, and Miss Hammond, pp. 258, 281 ff.

Compare also the references on the length of the pilgrimage in the introduction to the Explanatory Notes on the *Canterbury Tales*. In view of the incomplete condition of the *Canterbury Tales*, the satisfactory settlement of such questions is hardly possible.

Several puzzling problems are raised by the *Introduction*.

It contains a list of the heroines celebrated in the *Legend of Good Women*. But eight of the women named are not actually treated in the *Legend* and two whose story is there told (Cleopatra and Philomela) are not mentioned by the Man of Law. Various attempts have been made to construct from the passage, with the aid of the ballade in the *Prologue* to the *Legend*, Chaucer's complete plan for the work. See particularly Skeat's note, Oxf. Chau., V, 137. The conclusions are doubtful, but one thing seems clear: when Chaucer wrote the Man of Law's *Introduction* he planned to continue working on the *Legend*.

In lines 77 ff. the Man of Law is made to condemn such tales of incest as those of Canace and Apollonius of Tyre. Both stories are told in the Confessio Amantis, and Chaucer very probably intended the passage as a fling at Gower. It has even been inferred that Gower took offense at the criticism, and consequently canceled a compliment to Chaucer which stood in the first recension of the Epilogue to the Confessio. But there is no positive evidence of this estrangement of the two poets. For a summary of opinions on the subject, with references, see Miss Hammond, pp. 278 ff., and Miss M. Schlauch, Chaucer's Constance and Accused Queens, p. 132. Cf. also *LGW Prol G*, 315, n. If the passage in the Man of Law's *Introduction* is correctly interpreted as an allusion to Gower, it was probably not written much before 1390, generally accepted as the year of the publication of the Confessio. The date 1390 is not positive, however, for the "first edition" of the Confessio. See H. Spies, ESt, XXXII, 259. Some allowance must also be made for the possibility that Chaucer had personal knowledge of Gower's work before it was put into general circulation. For further discussion of the headlink, both as regards Gower and as regards the order and chronology of the tales, see C. Brown, Stud. Phil., XXXIV, 8 ff.

The Man of Law's declaration, *I speke in prose* (l. 96), probably indicates that the *Introduction* was not written to precede the Tale of Constance. Skeat's explanation, that it means: "I speak usually, customarily, in prose," is wholly unlikely. The statement is rather to be understood like the similar remarks in the *Monk's Prologue*, the *Prologue* to *Melibee*, and the *Parson's Prologue*, and was almost certainly intended to introduce a prose tale. Both the *Melibee* and the translation of Innocent's De Contemptu Mundi have been suggested as tales that might have been at one time meant for the Man of Law. See especially Lowes, PMLA, XX, 795 f., Miss Hammond, p. 280 (with further references), and in support of the assignment of Constance to the Man of Law, Dr. E. C. Knowlton, JEGP, XXIII, 83 ff.

2 The *artificial day* is the time while the sun is above the horizon, as distinguished from the natural day of twenty-four hours. See the *Astr*, ii, § 7, where it is explained how "to know the arch of the day."

In the present instance the reckoning is as follows. On April 18 the sun was in the 6th degree of Taurus, which crossed the horizon at 22° north of the east point, or 112° from the South. The middle of this distance is the 56th degree, over which the sun would seem to stand at twenty minutes past nine. The Host's second observation was that the sun's altitude was 45°, a point which it reached at exactly two minutes before ten. See Brae's calculations in his edition of the *Astrolabe*, London, 1870, pp. 68 ff.

10 *took his wit*, made his calculation.

20 These observations on the passage of time, often with the comparison to the river, were commonplace or even proverbial. Cf. *ClT*, IV, 118 f.; also RR, 361 ff. (*Rom.* 369 ff.); Ovid, Met., xv, 179 ff.; Ars Am., iii, 62 ff.; Seneca, Ep., I, i, 1; XIX, viii, 32; and the Latin proverb, "Transit ut aqua fluens tempus et hora ruens."

25 ff. The comparison with virginity was also familiar. See St. Thomas Aquinas, Summa Theologica, iii, 89, 3, 1 (Opera, Rome, 1882–1930, XII, 329). That it was still conventional in the seventeenth century appears from Francis Beaumont's Elegy on the Lady Markham, ll. 1 ff. (Chalmers' Eng. Poets, London, 1810, VI, 183.)

30 *Malkyn*, a wanton woman (proverbial).

37 *Acquiteth yow*, acquit, absolve yourself. The Host speaks, and the Man of Law replies, in legal terms. While the slight use of technical language here would not constitute proof of Chaucer's legal knowledge, it is nevertheless interesting in view of the tradition, recently defended, that he studied at the Inns of Court. See the Biographical Introduction.

39 *depardieux*, in God's name (Fr "de par," a double preposition).

41 *Biheste is dette* is proverbial in various languages. Cf. O'Rahilly, Miscellany of Irish Proverbs, Dublin, 1922, p. 81; H. E. Rollins, Paradise of Dainty Devices, Harv. Univ. Press, 1927, p. 192; Skeat, EE Prov., p. 101, no. 241; Haeckel, p. 15, no. 48; Archer Taylor, The Proverb, Cambridge, Mass., 1931, p. 138.

43 ff. A legal maxim, which survives as a proverb in various languages. Cf. "Patere legem quam ipse tulisti." See also Haeckel, p. 24, no. 78; Skeat, EE Prov., p. 101 f., no. 242. By *oure text* Chaucer appears to mean some actual textbook of the lawyers, and the Digesta of Justinian states the principle in words closely resembling his: "Quod quisque iuris in alterum statuerit, ut ipse eodem iure utatur" (ii, 2, rubric; ed. Mommsen, Berlin, 1870, I, 42).

46 *thrifty*, profitable. Cf. *Mill Prol*, I, 3131; *ML Epil*, II, 1165; *WB Prol*, III, 238; and for a different extension of the meaning, *Tr*, i, 275, and n.

47 ff. It has been suggested that these lines were written to occupy a place after Chaucer's failure in *Sir Thopas*. But, as Skeat notes, there are remarks in the same strain in *Gen Prol*, I, 746, and in *HF*, 621.

49 *Hath*; *Nath* (or *But* for *That* in l. 47) might be expected. But the illogical construction is probably to be regarded as an idiom; cf. *Tr*. i, 456 f.; also *Rom*, 3774, where the MS. reads *wylle*, and *Rom*, 4764.

54 *made of mencioun*, made mention of; cf. *Gen. Prol*, I, 791, and n.

55 *Episteles*, Ovid's Heroides.

57 *Ceys and Alcion*. The story of Ceyx and Alcione is told in the *Book of the Duchess*. From the form of the title here and in Lydgate's list in the Falls of Princes (i, 304) it has been inferred, though it does not necessarily follow, that the episode once constituted an independent poem.

61   *the Seintes Legende of Cupide,* the *Legend of Good Women,* which was conceived as a legendary or martyrology of the saints of the God of Love. This is one of the numerous instances of the treatment of Love in theological or ecclesiastical terms. See *KnT,* I, 3089, n.

63   *Babilan Tesbee,* Babylonian Thisbe.

64   *The swerd of Dido,* the sword with which she killed herself. See *LGW,* 1351, and Aen., iv, 646.

65   *tree,* either the tree on which Phyllis hanged herself, or that into which she was transformed. See *LGW,* 2485; Gower, Conf. Am., iv, 856 ff., 866 f.

66–67   *The pleinte of Dianire,* etc., the epistles of Deianira, Hermione, Ariadne, and Hypsipyle, in Ovid's Heroides.

68   *The bareyne yle,* said to have been Naxos, on which Ariadne was abandoned. See *LGW,* 2163; Her., x, 59.

71   *Brixseyde,* Briseis (acc. Briseida). Briseis was the heroine of the Troilus story in the Roman de Troie of Benoît de Ste. Maure. Chaucer followed Boccaccio in making her Criseyde. The present passage shows that he had it in mind to tell the ancient story of Briseis in *LGW.*

72–74   Possibly the idea that the children were hanged was derived by Chaucer from Jean de Meun's statement that Medea strangled them ("estrangla," RR, 13259). No such incident is mentioned in the Legend of Medea (*LGW,* 1580 ff.), which has consequently been dated by some scholars after the *Man of Law's Introduction.* See Lounsbury, Studies, I, 418, and Root, PMLA, XXIV, 124 ff., XXV, 228 ff. But the inference is by no means secure. See Kittredge, PMLA, XXIV, 343 ff.

75   *Alceste,* Alcestis. Her story is not in the Heroides. Chaucer sketches it briefly in the *Prologue* to the *LGW* (G, 499 ff., F 511 ff.), and probably meant to devote to it a separate legend.

78   *Canacee,* Canace. See Heroides, xi, and Conf. Am., iii, 143 ff. On the probable allusion to Gower, see the introduction to the Explanatory Notes on Fragment II.

81   *Tyro Appollonius,* Apollonius of Tyre (Apollonius de Tyro). See Conf. Am., viii, 271 ff.; also Gesta Romanorum, no. cliii. The specific detail mentioned in l. 85 does not appear in Gower, and the editor has not found it in any other version of the Apollonius. Professor Tatlock (Dev. and Chron., p. 173 n.) suggests that Chaucer may have had a confused recollection of a horrible touch in the original Latin version (ed. Riese, Leipzig, 1871, pp. 2–3) or of an episode in Gower's Canacee story (Conf. Am., iii, 307 ff.). The former passage would sufficiently explain Chaucer's line. In fact it is used by E. Klebs (Die Erzählung von Apollonius aus Tyrus, Berlin, 1899, pp. 471 f.) as evidence that Chaucer referred definitely to the Latin version of the story.

89   *if that I may,* so far as it is in my power; hence, if I can help it. Cf. *FranklT,* V, 1418; *Rom,* 3099; also RR, 626 ("se je puis"); and for the same negative implication cf. Henry V, Prol. (l. 39) to Act ii; also the formula *though we* (*men,* etc.) *hadde it sworn, KnT,* I, 1089; *Tr,* iv, 976. Other parallels are cited by Kittredge, [Harv.] Stud. and Notes, I, 20.

92   *Pierides,* the Muses, so named from Pieria, their birthplace, or Pierus, their father. But Chaucer has in mind those other Pierides, daughters of King Pierus of Emathia, who contended with the Muses and were changed into magpies. See Ovid, Met., v, 302.

93   *Metamorphosios,* genitive (Metamorphoseos), dependent upon Liber, Libri, in the full title. Strictly speaking, the form should be Metamorphoseon, plural, but the singular was in constant use. See E. F. Shannon, Chaucer and the Rom. Poets, Cambridge, Mass., 1929 pp. 307 ff. For the use of the construction in citations cf. further *Eneydos, NPT,* VII, 3359; *Judicium, MkT,* VII, 2046; *Argonauticon, LGW,* 1457. See also K. Young, Spec. XIX, 1 ff.

95   *with hawebake,* with plain fare (lit. "baked haw")

96   *I speke in prose.* See the introduction to the Explanatory Notes on Fragment II.

The Man of Law's Prologue

The *Man of Law's Prologue,* as far as line 121, is practically a paraphrase of Pope Innocent's De Contemptu Mundi, i, 16 (Migne, Pat. Lat., CCXVII, 708 f.). Passages from the same work are used in the *Man of Law's Tale,* ll. 421 ff., 771 ff., 925 ff., and 1132 ff. If, as seems probable, Chaucer made his translation from Innocent between 1386 and 1394 (i.e., between the two *Prologues* to the *Legend*), the use of material here would favor the assignment of the *Man of Law's Prologue* and *Tale* to the same interval.

The connection between the end of the *Prologue* and the *Tale* is rather far-fetched, and looks like an afterthought. If the translation from Innocent (in prose?) was originally intended to be the Man of Law's Tale (as Lowes has argued, PMLA, XX, 794 ff.), the Poverty stanzas may have been written to introduce it and afterwards patched up to fit the tale of Constance. Manly (M-R CT, III, 448) points out that the passage is quoted in both the Latin and the French of the tale of Melibeus. For the suggestion that the impatient Poverty of the *Prologue* was a vice especially associated with lawyers, see F. Tupper, PMLA, XXIX, 118; N.Y. Nation, XCIX, 41. Voluntary Poverty was differently regarded, and is praised at length in the *Wife of Bath's Tale,* III, 1177–1206. Mr. Tupper has also suggested that Chaucer intended the tale of Constance itself as an exposure of Detraction (Envy). See PMLA, XXIX, 110 ff.; and cf. the comments on his general theory in the introduction to the Explanatory Notes on the *Canterbury Tales.*

The significance of the astrological element in the story is well set forth by Professor Curry (pp. 164 ff.), though his detailed explanations are open to question.

99   *poverte,* pronounced *povértë* to rime with *herte.*

103   For the rime of two words with one (*woundid: wounde hid*) cf. *Gen Prol,* I, 523, n.

114   From Jesus son of Sirach, Ecclus, xl, 28; cf. *Mel,* VII, 1571 f.; Haeckel, p. 44, nos. 151, 152.

115   Prov. xiv, 20.

118   Prov. xv, 15 (Vulg., "Omnes dies pauperis mali").

120 Cf. Prov. xix, 7; Ovid, Tristia, i, 9, 5; and for further parallels, Skeat, EE Prov., p. 102, no. 243; Haeckel, p. 8, no. 27.

123 *as in this cas*, in respect to this matter (a rime-tag).

124 f. *ambes as*, the double ace. The allusion is apparently to the game of hazard in which the double ace is always a losing cast and the *sys cynk* (a six and a five) often a winning one. Skeat briefly summarizes the rules of the game, as given in the English Cyclopædia, suppl. vol., div. Arts and Sciences. The caster "calls a main," or names one of the numbers five, six, seven, eight, or nine — most commonly seven. "If he then throws either seven or eleven (Chaucer's *sys cynk*) he wins; if he throws aces (Chaucer's *ambes as*), or deuce-ace (two and one), or double sixes, he loses. If he throws some other number, that number is called the caster's *chaunce*, and he goes on playing till either the main or the chance turns up. In the first case he loses, in the second he wins." This explains the technical meaning of *chaunce* in l. 125 and in *PardT*, VI, 653.

The Man of Law's Tale

In the opinion of Skeat and other commentators the tale of Constance was first written before the Canterbury period, and afterwards revised and adapted for its place in the series. The moral and philosophical comments, according to this view, were added in revision. But there is no real evidence that any part of the text was added or interpolated, and such positive clues as have been detected all point to a rather late date (about 1390) for the composition of the whole poem. The moralizing passages are largely based on the De Contemptu Mundi, with the translation of which Chaucer was probably occupied between 1386 and 1394. There are apparently allusions, in the *Tale* as well as in the *Introduction*, to Gower's Confessio Amantis, which was not published till 1390. And the fact that in the first *Prologue* to the *Legend of Good Women*, written in or about 1386, the tale of Constance is not mentioned among Chaucer's works in defense of women also implies — though the argument should not be pressed too seriously — that the story was not yet written. For a detailed discussion of the evidence see Tatlock, Dev. and Chron., pp. 172 ff. A minute comparison of MLT with Trivet is made by E. A. Block in PMLA, LXVIII, 572 ff. On the possibility that Trivet's version was influenced by the story of the King of Tars see Lillian H. Hornstein, MLN, LV, 354 ff. For the suggestion that Chaucer realized the applicability of some features to the actual history of Constance of Padilla, and made changes to forefend such an identification, see R. M. Smith, JEGP, XLVII, 343 ff. On historical precursors of Constance see Miss M. Schlauch, PQ, XXIX, 402 ff.

The primary source of the tale is in the Anglo-Norman Chronicle of Nicholas Trivet, written about 1335 (printed in the Originals and Analogues, Ch. Soc., 1872, pp. 2 ff. and again, from a different MS. in SA, pp. 165 ff.). This was also the source of Gower's version of the story in the Confessio Amantis, ii, 587 ff. It seems probable, as noted above in the discussion of the date, that Chaucer made some use of Gower's tale. For Gower's version, see, besides collected editions, SA, pp. 181 ff. But

on this point there is difference of opinion. See, besides Tatlock, cited above, Skeat, Oxf. Chaucer, III, 409 ff.; Lücke, Angl., XIV, 77 ff.; Macaulay, Works of Gower, Oxford, 1899–1902, II, 483; and M. Schlauch, Chaucer's Constance and Accused Queens, New York, 1927, pp. 132 ff. Aside from the three versions mentioned, which stand in close literary relation, there are numerous tales which deal with the same general situation. Of the Constance saga, so called, alone there have been collected many versions, popular or literary, and they constitute only one group in the larger cycle of stories of the calumniated wife. There is an excellent account of the general type in Miss Schlauch's work, cited above; see also O. Siefken, Das Geduldige Weib in der Englischen Literatur bis auf Shakspere, Rathenow, 1903. For the Constance group in particular see H. Suchier, Œuvres de Philippe de Beaumanoir, Paris, 1884, I, xxiii ff.; A. B. Gough, The Constance Saga, Palaestra, XXIII, Berlin, 1902; E. Rickert, MP, II, 355 ff. To the versions, over threescore in number, discussed by Suchier and Gough, many other analogues, complete or partial, have been added by H. Däumling, Studie über den Typus des "Mädchens ohne Hände" innerhalb des Konstanzezyklus, München, 1912, and Bolte-Polívka, Anmerkungen zu den Kinder-u. Hausmärchen, I, Leipzig, 1913, No. 31: Das Mädchen ohne Hände. The distribution and ultimate origin of the saga is discussed by J. Schick, Die Urquelle der Offa-Konstanze-Saga, in Britannica, Festschrift for Max Foerster, Leipzig, 1929, pp. 31 ff. Professor Schick concludes that the story certainly did not originate in England, as held by Gough and others, and probably not in India, as maintained by Clouston (Orig. and Anal., p. 414) and Cosquin (Contes populaires de Lorraine, Paris, 1886, II, 323 ff.). He argues that it is closely related to the Crescentia saga, and that both cycles have their ultimate roots in the romantic part of the Clementine Recognitions. Cf. further S. Teubert, Crescentia-Studien, Halle, 1916. A. H. Krappe, Anglia, LXI, 361 ff., also the elaborate study by J. W. Knedler, The Girl without Hands (unpubl. Harvard dissertation, 1937), and Miss Schlauch's discussion in SA, pp. 155 ff.; and Maria Wickert, Anglia, LXIX, 89 ff.

134 *Surrye*, Syria; Serazine in Trivet.

136 *spicerye*, spices, oriental goods. Manly, p. 632, notes that the term included foreign fruits, cloths, and other products.

144 *message*, messenger (as often).

145 Here, and in l. 255, we may read either *this the ende* (contracting *this is*) or *this is th' ende*.

151 Gower gives the emperor's name as Tiberius Constantine. He was actually emperor at Constantinople, not Rome, in 578, and was succeeded, in 582, by Maurice of Cappadocia, to whom he gave his daughter Constantina in marriage. Since Chaucer found the name *Custance* in his sources, it is not necessary to assume that he intended any special compliment to Constance of Padilla, the second wife of John of Gaunt.

171 *han doon fraught*, have caused (to be) laden. See *KnT*, I, 1913, n.

181 *leere*, learn; properly *leeren* (AS. "láeran"), should mean "teach" and *lernen* (AS. "leornian"), "learn," but the two words are freely confused in Middle English.

185 *ceriously*, minutely, in detail (one meaning of Low Latin "seriose").

197 ff. From the Megacosmos of Bernardus Silvester (twelfth century). Four lines of the Latin are quoted in the margins of several MSS.

201 On the death of Turnus see Aen., xii, 901 ff.

211 Cf. *Rv Prol*, I, 3857, and n.

218 ff. On the treatment of the religious impediment here see P. E. Beichner, Spec., XXIII, 70. He sees in the Man of Law's display of legal knowledge an instance of the adaptation of the tale to the teller.

224 *Mahoun*, Mahomet; called *Makomete* below. Note also the common noun "maumet," idol, derived from the name. Mahomet is not mentioned in Trivet, and his introduction by Chaucer (as Skeat notes) is an anachronism. He was but twelve years old in 582.

236 *mawmettrie*, very likely "idolatry." The mediæval Christians held the Mahometans to be idolaters — quite unjustly, since the Koran expressly condemns the practice.

243 *founden*, provided (pp.).

261 On the use of *I seye, I mene*, and similar expressions in early English poetry, see Miss E. P. Hammond, Engl. Verse between Chaucer and Surrey, Durham, N.C., 1927, p. 447. Sometimes they seem to serve merely for emphatic repetition, sometimes they are rather a kind of scholastic formula (like Dante's use of "dico" in Inf., iv, 66, and elsewhere).

271 "Whose character she does not know." The general relative *that* is omitted. On the full construction see *KnT*, I, 2710, n.

273–87 Not in Trivet.

277 "Except Christ on high."

286 Cf. Gen., iii, 16.

289 *Ilion*; cf. *LGW*, 936, n.

295–315 Here, as in the *Legend of Hypermnestra* (*LGW*, 2576 ff.), Chaucer introduces an astrological explanation not taken from the source of his story. In the margin of MS. E, ll. 295 ff., is a reference to Ptholomeus, lib. I, cap. 8 (i.e., the Almagest). But the ideas were of course familiar. The passage perhaps contains reminiscences of Boethius, i, met. 5, and iv, met. 1. For extended accounts of the old astronomy see the articles "Astronomy, History of" and "Ptolemy" in the Encyclopædia Britannica, 11th ed. (in the latter an analysis of the Almagest). There is also a good description of the Ptolemaic universe in Masson, Milton's Poetical Works, 3 v., London, 1874, I, 89 ff. The earth was conceived as a fixed globe at the center of a series of concentric spheres. The ninth, or outermost, sphere was called the Primum Mobile (first moving). Next within it came the sphere of the Fixed Stars, and within that successively those of the seven planets. The Primum Mobile was held to have a swift diurnal motion from east to west, which accounted for the daily apparent revolution of the sun in a direction opposite to that of its "natural" motion along the zodiac. The revolution of the Primum Mobile carried everything with it, and was thus responsible for the unfavorable position of Mars at the time of Constance's marriage.

The astrological situation — if Chaucer himself had an exact one in mind — is not wholly clear. It has even been discussed whether the calculation was intended as an election or a nativity. But the general sense of the passage is plainly that the position

of the stars was unfavorable to Constance's voyage and marriage. If an election had been made by an astrologer, it would have revealed the conditions described, and of course an important element in the calculation would have been the position of the stars at the birth of Constance.

Professor Curry (pp. 172 ff.), following Skeat's note, worked out a detailed explanation of the passage on the theory that the unfavorable astrological situation was due to the individual motions of the planets. His main points are that the horoscope is in Aries; Mars is cadent in Scorpio, the eighth house, and hence an unfavorable sign succedent; Luna is also cadent, and in conjunction with Mars in Scorpio. Then he shows by citation from numerous authorities that a nativity in Aries predestinates a "rather checkered and precarious life"; that the presence of Scorpio in the eighth house is unfavorable; that the position of the Moon in Scorpio, in conjunction with Mars, was peculiarly unfortunate for marriage or for a journey; and that the presence of Mars in his darker mansion, Scorpio, presaged definite misfortune.

Although Professor Curry has no difficulty in making his construction fit Constance's case, Mr. Manly (in his notes) raises the valid objection that Chaucer explicitly attributes the astrological situation to the Primum Mobile. He argues, therefore, that the reference is to the "mundane houses" (fixed divisions of the firmament), and not to the "mansions" of the planets in the zodiacal signs. He concludes that Mars, the lord of the ascendant sign Aries, has been thrust from his angle, "probably the ascendant itself, into the darkest of the mundane houses, a cadent (perhaps the twelfth house, which adjoined the ascendant)." The Moon is also said to have been forced (*weyved*, l. 308), apparently by the Primum Mobile, into a position where it is not "in reception" with a favorable planet; that is (as Mr. Manly explains), "that none of the planets which have 'dignities' where she is situated are situated where she has any 'dignity.'"

For further criticism of Mr. Curry's theory see J. T. Curtiss, JEGP, XXVI, 24 ff.

In l. 295 the punctuation (*O firste moevyng!*) follows Manly, who is probably right in taking the phrase to be substantival (Primum Mobile) rather than adjectival.

302 *tortuous*, a term applied to the six signs nearest the point of the vernal equinox; so called because they ascend more obliquely than the other signs. The reference here is probably to Aries, of which Mars was the "lord."

305 *atazir*, from Arabic "at-ta'thīr" ("al ta'thīr," influence; cf. "athar," mark, trace), Sp., OF. "atazir," commonly Latinized "athazir." In the astrological treatises the term is sometimes used to denote the process of calculating planetary positions and influences, sometimes for the influences, and sometimes, apparently, for the particular planet concerned. Chaucer seems to refer to Mars as atazir *as in this cas*. For citations from the authorities see Curry, pp. 182 ff., and Manly's note.

312 *eleccioun*, an astrological term, meaning the choice of a favorable time for an undertaking. Chaucer appears to have had in mind a particular work, the Liber Electionum of Zael, from which a quotation is copied in the margin of MSS. El and Hg.

Zael, or Zahel, Judaeus (Sahl ben Bishr ben Habîb) was an astronomer in the service of the governor of Chorâzân in the early ninth century. See H. Suter, Die Mathematiker und Astronomen der Araber (Suppl. to Zt. für Math. und Physik, Leipzig, XLV, 1900), pp. 15 f.

314 *roote*, the "epoch" from which a reckoning is made. The exact moment of the princess's birth being known, there was absolutely no excuse for the Emperor's negligence.

332 *Alkaron*, the Koran; formerly called in English "the Alcoran," with retention of the Arabic article "al."

352 *Coold water*; this contemptuous jest about baptism is not in Trivet.

358 Here and elsewhere in the *Canterbury Tales* is a marginal note *auctor* in many MSS. See, for example, ll. 925 ff., below, and *ClT*, IV, 995 ff. This is not to be taken as indicating that Chaucer meant to intervene as author in the discourse of the Man of Law and other pilgrims. The note sometimes occurs against passages added by Chaucer to his primary sources. But it may be doubted whether the scribes, as has been supposed, meant to designate such additions. Their purpose seems rather to have been simply to call attention to sententious or otherwise noteworthy utterances — to such quotable texts as were regularly called *auctoritees*. See *WB Prol*, III, 1, and n.

358 f. The comparison of the *sowdanesse* to Semiramis may be due (as Lowes has suggested, MP, XIV, 706 ff.) to Dante's Inf., v, 58–60.

360 The serpent who tempted Eve in Eden is sometimes described as having a woman's head. See Comestor, Historia Scholastica, Libri Genesis, cap. xxi (with a reference to Bede).

361 See also l. 634, below. For the chaining of the fallen angels there is scriptural authority in II Peter ii, 4, Jude 6, and Rev. xx, 1–2. But the popular conception of the bound Satan was probably influenced rather by the apocryphal Gospel of Nicodemus. (See B. H. Cowper, Apocryphal Gospels, 5th ed., London, 1881, p. 307). On the doctrine in general much information will be found in S. Bugge's Studier over de Nordiske Gude- og Heltesagns Oprindelse, Christiania, 1881, I, 53 ff., and the review by George Stephens in Mémoires des Antiquaires du Nord, 1878–83, pp. 331 ff.; 1884, 1 ff. A few references to mediæval treatments of the subject are given by T. Spencer in Speculum, II, 187 f.

376 *lay* (Fr. "lai") and *lawe* (AS. "lagu"), "law," were both used for "religion."

400 No such triumph is mentioned by Lucan, who laments that Caesar had none (Pharsalia, iii, 79). Professor Shannon (Chaucer and the Rom. Poets, Cambridge, Mass., 1929, p. 335) remarks that Chaucer may have got the hint from Pharsalia, iv, 358 ff., and v, 328 ff. Professor Lowes has suggested to the editor that he had in mind rather the French version of Lucan by Jehan de Tuim, in which triumphs are elaborately described at both the beginning and the end. See Li Hystore de Julius Cesar, ed. F. Settegast, Halle, 1881, pp. 8 ff., 244 ff.

404 The scorpion was the symbol of treachery. Cf. *MerchT*, IV, 2058 ff.; also the Ayenbite of Inwyt (ed. Morris, EETS, 1866, p. 62): "the scorpioun, thet maketh uayr mid the heauede, and enueymeth mid the tayle." *Wikkid goost*, evil spirit.

421 ff. From the De Contemptu Mundi, i, 23 (Migne, Pat. Lat., CCXVII, 713), which in turn embodies sentences from Boethius, ii, pr. 4, Prov. xiv, 13, and Ecclus. xi, 25. For similar commonplaces see *NPT*, VII, 3205; *Tr*, iv, 836.

422 *spreynd*, Boethius "respersa" (l. 62; so rendered also in *Bo*, ii, pr. 4, 119).

438 The punishment of being cast adrift — twice visited on Custance and common in the related tales — is often referred to in mediæval texts as an actual legal penalty. For examples from Irish and Icelandic, including cases of the exposure of wives charged with infidelity and of illegitimate children, see Miss M. E. Byrne, Eriu, XI, 97 ff. *Foot-hoot*, hastily; so also "hot fot," Debate of Body and Soul (Emerson, Mid. Eng. Reader, New York, 1915, p. 63, l. 29, variant), and OF. "chalt pas."

448 On the relation of fortune to divine Providence see *KnT*, I, 1663, n.

449–462 Not in Trivet. Skeat refers to similar addresses to the Cross in the hymn "Lustra sex qui iam peregit" of Venantius Fortunatus (Dreves, Analecta Hymnica, Leipzig, 1886–1922, II, 44 f.), and in the Ancren Riwle, ed. Morton, Camden Soc., 1853, p. 34. See also Miss M. V. Rosenfeld, MLN, LV, 359 f.

451 *cleere*, probably "shining" (Lat. "clarus").

460 "Banisher of fiends from man and woman over whom thine arms faithfully extend" (i.e., upon whom the sign of the cross has been made).

464 f. *the Strayte of Marrok*, the strait of Gibraltar.

470–504 Not in Trivet.

480 The reference is probably to Boethius, iv, pr. 6.

486 Chaucer here substitutes Jonah for Trivet's reference to Noah.

488 ff. See Ex. xiv, 21–31.

491 ff. See Rev. vii, 1–3.

500 St. Mary of Egypt, after a youth of wantonness, lived for forty-seven years in the wilderness. See the Legenda Aurea, cap. lvi.

502 ff. See Matt. xiv, 15 ff.

508 *Northhumberlond*, strictly speaking, the Anglo-Saxon kingdom of Deira (the modern counties of Yorkshire, Nottinghamshire, Derbyshire, and Lancashire). See F. P. Magoun, Jr., Med. Stud. XVI, 145.

510 *of al a tyde*, Skeat interprets, "for the whole of an hour." But a "tide" of the sea makes better sense. For the exceptional use of *of* in the sense of "during" see NED, s.v. Of, 53.

512 The constable is called Elda in Trivet and Gower.

519 According to Trivet she spoke to Elda in Saxon ("en sessoneys"). Chaucer's *maner Latyn corrupt* has a curiously precise air, as if he were consciously characterizing late popular Latin. Indeed the whole account of Roman Britain in the tale conforms to historic fact to a degree unusual in mediæval stories. Cf., however, Mr. T. H. McNeal, in MLN, LIII, 257 ff., who notes that in a tale with similar incident in the Decameron (Fifth Day, Second Tale) the heroine Gostanza speaks Latin when rescued from her ship.

532 Cf. *ClT*, IV, 413.

557 *a furlong wey*, used as a measure of time; two and a half minutes, if Chaucer's reckoning in the

Astrolabe (i, 16) — *Thre milewei maken an houre* —
be followed exactly; cf. *MillT*, I, 3637; *RvT*, I,
4199; *ClT*, IV, 516; *Anel*, 328; *Tr*, iv, 1237; *HF*,
2064; *LGW*, 841.

578 *Alla*, Aella, king of Deira (d. 588).

609 Cf. *Tr*, iv, 357.

620 *Berth hire on hond*, accuses her falsely. Cf.
WB Prol, III, 393; *ParsT*, X, 505; *Anel*, 158; *Bo*,
i, pr. 4, 251 f. In *WB Prol*, III, 232, 380, the phrase
means rather to "persuade falsely." The source and
original meaning of the idiom are uncertain. The
NED compares Fr. "maintenir," which is not strictly
parallel; nor is the phrase "prendre a main,
prendre en main," discussed by Tobler in Herrig's
Arch., CII, 176. More nearly equivalent is ON.
"bera á hendr," suggested as the source of the English idiom by A. Trampe Bødtker, Videnskabs
Selskabets Skrifter, Christiania, 1905, no. 6, p. 5.

628 "Has caught a great idea, suggestion, from
this witness."

631-58 Not in Trivet.

631 One regular way of establishing the innocence of an accused woman would have been by
ordeal of battle. Cf. the story of the Erl of Toulous,
ed. Lüdtke, Berlin, 1881; also Child, Eng. and Scott.
Ballads, the introduction to Sir Aldingar (Boston,
1882–98, II, 33 ff.); and Siefken's general account
of the Calumniated Wife, cited above.

634 See the note to l. 361, above.

639 See the History of Susannah in the Apocrypha.

641 On St. Anne, the mother of the Virgin, see
the apocryphal Gospel of James (B. H. Cowper,
Apocryphal Gospels, 5th ed., London, 1881, p. 4 ff.).
The rime with *Hosanne*, here and in *SecN Prol*,
VIII, 69–70, may be a reminiscence of Dante's
Paradiso, xxxii, 133–35.

660 See *KnT*, I, 1761, and n.

666 According to Trivet the witness was a Christian; hence the use of the British gospel book.

676 In Trivet, "Hec fecisti et tacui." Skeat
suggested the possible emendation *held* for *holde*.
The words are perhaps due to the Vulgate, Psalm
XLIX (Auth. Vers. L), v. 21.

695 *Donegild*; the original form of the name is
doubtful. Gower has "Domilde"; Trivet shows
variants: "Domulde," "Domylde," "Dommylde."
namo, no other (lit. "nomore"); cf. *ClT*, IV, 1039.

701-02 Cf. *LGW Prol G*, 311–12.

729 *to doon his avantage*, to secure his own profit.

736 *lettres*; with the plural cf. the common use
of Lat. "literae."

754 *elf*, an evil spirit; strictly speaking, a fairy,
a woman of the "other world." The union of mortal
men with elf-women was a common episode in romance. Cf. especially the cycle of Melusine Tales,
J. Kohler, Ursprung der Melusinensage, Leipzig,
1895.

770 *to doone*, an inflected infinitive. See the
Grammatical Introduction.

771-77 Based upon the De Contemptu Mundi,
ii, 19 (which is quoted in the margin of several MSS.;
Migne, Pat. Lat., CCXVII, 724). Ll. 776 f. are also
proverbial; cf. *Mel*, VII, 1194; Skeat, EE Prov.,
pp. 102 f., no. 244.

784 There is very likely here a reminiscence of
Dante's account of the punishment of traitors in
Tolomea (Inf., xxxiii, 121 ff.). See MLN, XXIX, 97.

But the idea was familiar. A similar conception
underlies *LGW*, 2066 ff. Cf. further John of Salisbury, Policraticus, iii, 8 (ed. Webb, 2 v., Oxford,
1909, I, 190); A. Graf, Miti, Leggende e Super-
stizioni del Medio Evo, Turin, 1892–93; II, 99 f.;
Lives of Saints from the Book of Lismore, ed. W.
Stokes, Anecdota Oxoniensia, V, 1890, p. 161;
Caesarius Heisterbacensis, Dialogus Miraculorum,
xii, 4, Cologne, 1851, II, 317 f.; also the vision of the
monk of Wenlock, related in a letter of Boniface, in
Jaffé, Monumenta Moguntina, Berlin, 1866, pp. 59 f.
Biblical authority was found in John xiii, 27, and
Ps. lv, 15.

798 Here, as in l. 510, the question arises whether
tyde means "hour" (so Skeat) or the "tide" of the
sea. The latter seems more appropriate in both
places.

813-26 Not in Trivet. With ll. 813–16 cf.
Bo, i, m. 5, 31–37; Ps. civ, 2 ff.

819 *shames deeth*; with the construction cf.
lyves creature, *KnT*, I, 2395, and n.

833 *steere*, rudder. So "remigium" is applied to
the Virgin in the Analecta Hymnica, ed. Dreves,
Leipzig, 1886–1922, XXXI, 178.

835-75 Almost wholly Chaucer's addition. The
description has been compared (of course with no
suggestion of indebtedness) to Simonides' account of
the exposure of Danae and the infant Perseus. See
Simonides, no. 37; in Bergk's Anthologia Lyrica,
Leipzig, 1868, p. 444; Smyth's Melic Poets, London,
1900, pp. 59 f.

868 *She blisseth hire*, probably "she makes the
sign of the cross." *Blissen* and *blessen* were freely
interchanged.

885 The French text makes no mention of torture.

894 The account is fuller in Trivet.

896 *with meschance*, probably to be taken as an
imprecation, like *God yeve hym meschance* in l. 914,
below.

905 Trivet says simply, "un chastel dun Admiral
de paens."

925-31 From De Contemptu Mundi, ii, 21
(Migne, Pat. Lat., CCXVII, 725). On the marginal
note *Auctor*, see the note to l. 358, above.

932-45 Not in Trivet.

934 *Golias*, Goliath of Gath, I Sam. xvii, 4.

940 See the Book of Judith in the Apocrypha;
also *MkT*, VII, 2551 ff. On the use of *hym* cf. *KnT*,
I, 1210, and n.

947 *Jubaltare*, Gibraltar; *Septe*, usually explained as Ceuta, an ancient seaport at the foot of
the ridge on the African coast opposite Gibraltar.
For the suggestion that Chaucer had in mind rather
the ridge itself, Septem Fratres, from which Ceuta
derived its name, see F. P. Magoun, Med. Stud.,
XVII, 139.

967 In Trivet the senator's name is Arsemius,
and his wife was Helen, daughter of Sallustius, the
emperor's brother.

981 *aunte*, really her cousin, as Trivet makes
clear. Chaucer may have misunderstood Fr.
"nece," used for cousin.

982 *she*, Helen. Constance, on the other hand,
knew her, according to Trivet.

988 King Alla's visit to Rome probably has
reference to the practice of "reserving" certain sins
to the Pope. See Taunton, Law of the Church,

London, 1906, s.v. Reserved Cases, and Catholic Encyclopædia, s. v. Censures, Ecclesiastical.

1009 *Som men wolde seyn.* Probably a reference to Gower, both here and in l. 1086. Skeat notes that the matters in question are also treated by Trivet. But there seems to be more point in an allusion to Gower, especially in view of the supposed fling at him in the *Introduction.* In strict accuracy it should be observed, as Manly remarks, that Trivet and Gower "merely say that Constance instructed the child how he should act at the feast."

1038–71 Chaucer does not follow Trivet closely.

1090 *As he that,* as one who; a common Middle English idiom, perhaps due to OF. "com cil que."

1091 *Sente,* as to send ("as that he should send"); an unusual ellipsis, but not unparalleled. Cf. *Rom,* 3850–53; Owl and Nightingale, ll. 1093 ff. Professor Kittredge has pointed out to the editor a somewhat similar construction in Shakespeare's King John, iv, 2, 241 ff.

1121 The historic emperor Maurice of Cappadocia was not descended from Tiberius, whom he succeeded in 582.

1126 *olde Romayn geestes,* apparently Roman history in general, as again in *WB Prol,* III, 642, where the same phrase is used of a story taken from Valerius Maximus. Cf. also *MerchT,* IV, 2284. The life of Mauricius is not in the Gesta Romanorum, or, to judge from Loesche's analysis, in the vast unpublished French compilation, Li Faits des Romains, mentioned in Manly's notes. See J. Loesche, Die Abfassung der Faits des Romains, Halle, 1907.

1132–38 From the De Contemptu Mundi, i, 22 (Migne, Pat. Lat., CCXVII, 713). Cf. also Ecclus. xviii, 26; Job xxi, 12 ff.

1142 Proverbial; cf. *ParsT,* X, 762; Haeckel, p. 45, nos. 154, 155

1143 According to Trivet Aella died nine months later. Then, after half a year, Constance returned to Rome. Tiberius lived only thirteen days after her arrival, and a year later she herself died and was buried in St. Peter's.

The Man of Law's Epilogue

On the order of the tales at this point see the introduction to the Textual Notes on the *Canterbury Tales.* Other references are given in the Explanatory Notes, p. 649, above. Most of the recent editions have adopted the arrangement proposed by Bradshaw and adopted by the Six-Text editor, who brought forward Fragment VII (*ShipT* to *NPT,* inclusive) from its regular position near the end of the series and attached it to the *Man of Law's Epilogue,* which immediately follows the *Man of Law's Tale.* But since the Six-Text order has really no MS. support, it has seemed best to the present editor to return to the Ellesmere arrangement. It is not to be supposed, however, that this order represents any final decision of the author. Chaucer had obviously not arrived at any final arrangement, and if he had written additional tales he might have altered such plans as he had in mind. The best discussion of this special problem is that of Professor R. A. Pratt, PMLA, LXVI, 1141 ff. Mr. Pratt makes a good case for the theory that Chaucer was working toward the arrangement of the "Bradshaw shift."

Apart from the general question of order, the *Man of Law's Epilogue,* usually known as the *Shipman's Prologue,* itself presents troublesome problems. The different arrangements and the more important variant readings are recorded in the Textual Notes and more fully in the Manly-Rickert edition. In many MSS. the speech is assigned to the Squire and the Squire's tale follows the Man of Law's. Some MSS. have this assignment and this order, but name the Summoner in the text (l. 1179). In one copy there is no assignment, but the Summoner is named in the text, and the Wife's tale follows! In a single copy only (MS. Arch. Seld.) is the *Shipman's Tale* preceded by the so-called *Shipman's Prologue,* and in that case the *Man of Law's Tale* is brought down to join it, after the *Squire's Tale.* In the Ellesmere group of MSS., the most authoritative, the passage is omitted entirely. The explanation of these inconsistencies is altogether uncertain. But it is very probable that the *Epilogue* was written to follow the tale of the Man of Law. (Compare the repetition of *thrifty* in ll. 46 and 1165.) The speech seems unsuited to the Squire, and may have been intended for either the Shipman or the Summoner. Skeat suggests that it was meant for the Shipman, but not to precede his present tale, which was probably written for the Wife of Bath. Then, he conjectures further, when Chaucer wrote a new tale for the Wife he handed over her first one, unrevised, to the Shipman and put it, late in the series, before the *Prioress's Tale.* The old Prologue, thus rendered useless, he first transferred, and adjusted, to the Squire, and afterwards canceled altogether. Miss Hammond suggests rather that the passage was first written for the Summoner, who was meant to follow the Man of Law. But when Chaucer constructed Fragment III he shifted the Summoner and erased his name in the old Prologue. The assignments to the Squire and the Shipman in various MSS. and the combination with the Shipman's Tale in MS. Arch. Seld. she takes to be purely scribal. The cancellation of the passage in the Ellesmere group she holds to represent Chaucer's final intention. Her theory has this advantage over Skeat's, that it does not assume Chaucer to have been responsible for the inappropriate assignment of the speech to the Squire. For further discussion see Miss Hammond, pp. 277 f.; Skeat in MLR, V, 430 ff.; and Tatlock, Dev. and Chron., p. 218 n.

Professor Brusendorff suggested (pp. 70 ff.) that the *ML Epil* was intended by Chaucer for the Yeoman, marked *Squire* in the margin of the MS. to indicate that the Squire's Yeoman and not the Canon's Yeoman was intended. Then, he conjectures, some scribe copied *Squire* into the body of the text. This theory also relieves Chaucer of any responsibility for the inappropriate assignment. But there seems to be no actual support for it in the MSS.

Professor Pratt would follow Bradshaw in assigning the *Epilogue* to the Shipman. But he also accepts as probable the suggestion of Professor R. F. Jones (JEGP, XLIV, 512 ff.) that Chaucer originally wrote it for the Wife of Bath. The *Shipman's Tale,* it will be remembered, must have been first written for a woman. The phrase "my joly body" in the

Epilogue supports the conjecture, though the general tone of the speech is not so clearly feminine as Mr. Pratt holds. But it might be replied that the Wife herself is none too feminine.

Although the MSS. strongly support the theory that Chaucer abandoned the *Epilogue*, there can be no doubt of its genuineness or of its interest to the reader of the *Canterbury Tales*. It is therefore included, but bracketed, in the present text.

On two spurious Pardoner-Shipman links see the Textual Notes on the *PardT*.

1165 Cf. l. 46, above. Professor Manly observes that the word *thrifty* is as appropriate to the *Melibee*, supposed by some to have been originally assigned to the Man of Law, as to the tale of Constance; and that ll. 1188–89 describe the *Melibee* very well and are entirely unsuited to the Constance story.

1168 The reference here to *lerned men in lore* has been taken as an indication that more than one professional man — perhaps, consequently, the Doctor and the Pardoner, as well as the Lawyer — had already told a tale. See the introduction to the Explanatory Notes on Fragment VI.

1169 *Can moche good*, lit. "know much good"; a phrase of general application, meaning to be capable or competent, to know one's profit or advantage. Cf. *WB Prol.* III, 231; *BD*, 998, 1012; *LGW*, 1175. Essentially the same idiom occurs in English as early as the Beowulf (nát hé þára góda, l. 681).

1171 The condemnation of swearing is not particularly characteristic of Wyclif's writings. But it appears to have been a favorite issue with the Lollard group. See the Twenty-Five Points (1388–89), in Wyclif, Select English Works, ed. Arnold, Oxford, 1869–71, III, 483.

1172 *Jankin*, a derisive name for a priest, often referred to as Sir John. See *NP Prol*, VII, 2810.

1173 *Lollere*, a contemptuous term, like the more familiar "Lollard," for the followers of Wyclif. The corresponding Dutch form, "lollaerd," was used early in the fourteenth century for the members of the Alexian fraternity, who cared for the poor and the sick; and the name was also applied to other orders on the continent. The ultimate derivation is probably from "lollen," mutter, mumble. Skeat suggests that there is in the present passage a play upon a second word "loller," meaning lounger, loafer. However that may be, there is a clear allusion in l. 1183, in connection with the parable of the tares (Matt. xiii, 24–30), to a traditional pun on Lollard and the Latin "lol[l]ium" (tares, cockel). Contemporary instances of the use of the same figure are given by H. B. Workman, John Wyclif, Oxford, 1926, II, 162, 400 f. For early occurrences of the whole group of related words see also Workman, I, 327.

1178 From the oath *by my fader sowle* some scholars have inferred that the speaker could not be the Squire, whose father was alive and present. But Professor B. J. Whiting, by citing numerous cases of oaths by living parents, has shown the argument to be inconclusive. See JEGP, XLIV, 1 ff., XLVI, 297.

1180 *glosen*, interpret, expound. Cf. *SumT*, III, 1792 ff., for a hint of the wide range of much of the preacher's comment.

1185 *body*, self; cf. for the colorless use of the word, "nobody," "anybody."

1189 *phislyas* (so numerous MSS.; variants, *phisilias*, *phillyas*, *fisleas*, etc.) is of uncertain ex-

planation. Some late MSS. read (*of*) *physik*, adopted by Globe. Skeat suggested that the original reading was *physices*, a Greek genitive such as might be used in titles. (Cf. *ML Intro*, II, 93 n.) The strange Greek form would explain the scribal corruptions, but it is unlikely that Chaucer would have put it into the mouth of the Shipman. Dr. Shipley (MLN, X, 134 f.) tried to support the MS. reading by an Anglo-Saxon gloss "phisillos: leceas" (i.e., leeches, physicians); but this would serve rather to illustrate the scribal corruption. Later proposals have been to connect the word with law instead of medicine. Mr. R. C. Goffin (MLR, XVIII, 335 f.) suggested that the original reading was "filas" (Anglo-Fr. "filas," files or cases). Professor Manly thinks this was probably the underlying word, but that Chaucer intentionally represented the ignorant speaker as using a corrupted form like those he often ascribed to the Host. Miss M. Galway, in keeping with her conjecture that the Shipman is to be identified with the Biscayan, John Piers, would derive the word from the Basque *phizlea*, "edifier." For discussion of this explanation see particularly TLS, Oct. 3 and 24, 1942, and Jan. 23 and Apr. 10, 1943.

FRAGMENT III

The Wife of Bath's Prologue

Fragment III begins abruptly with the *Wife of Bath's Prologue*, and has no link to attach it to a preceding tale. Mrs. Dempster (PMLA, LXVIII, 1149 ff.) suggests that the abrupt interruption was deliberately intended. (For spurious links connecting it with the *Merchant's Tale* and the *Squire's Tale* see the Textual Notes on the *Merch Epil* and the *SqT*. It stands in various positions in the different MSS.; see the introduction to the Textual Notes on the *Canterbury Tales*. But in the best copies it begins a sequence, III, IV, V, which clearly represents Chaucer's final arrangement. For the opinion that it is also sufficiently connected, as it stands, with the *Nun's Priest's Tale*, see Kenyon, JEGP, XV, 282 ff.)

The tales and the links in the sequence mentioned, from the *Wife's Prologue* through the *Franklin's Tale* are usually referred to as the Marriage Group. This name was given them by Professor Kittredge, who pointed out that, apart from certain dramatic interruptions, they deal continuously with the problem of conjugal relations presented at the outset by the Wife. It is true that love and marriage form the theme of other tales in the series, so much so that Professor Tupper has proposed to interpret the whole Canterbury collection as a systematic exposition of the subject. (See the introduction to the Explanatory Notes on the *Canterbury Tales*.) The particular question of the wife's wisdom and proper authority is also broached outside this group, in the *Melibee* and the *Nun's Priest's Tale*. But nowhere else is the subject clearly defined and discussed with so much coherence. Even if Professor Kittredge has been over-schematic in his interpretation of the *Franklin's Tale*, the fact remains that the Wife gives the keynote to the Clerk and the Merchant and that the Franklin clearly alludes to the matter at issue. On the general question see Kittredge, MP, IX,

435 ff.; W. W. Lawrence, MP, XI, 247 ff.; Koch, ESt, XLVI, 112 f.; S. B. Hemingway, MLN, XXXI, 479 ff.; H. B. Hinckley, PMLA, XXXII, 292 ff. (rejecting the classification entirely).

On the whole, scholarly opinion has accepted Kittredge's main conclusions about the Marriage Group, and recent discussion has been chiefly concerned with attempting to discover the stages of Chaucer's procedure. Among the more important notes and articles on the subject are the following: Carleton Brown, PMLA, XLVIII, 1041; MLN, LV, 606 ff. (review of Manly-Rickert); MLN, LVI, 163 ff.; PMLA, LVII, 29; Dorothy Everett, YWES, XXIII, 50 ff. (a summary of discussion); M. Schlauch, PMLA, LXI, 416 ff.; Mrs. G. Dempster, PMLA, LXIII, 456 ff.; PMLA, LXVIII, 1142. In the last article Mrs. Dempster argues for the extension of the idea of the Marriage Group to the *Mel*, the *Mel-Mk* link, and the *NPT*.

The date of the Marriage Group is most fully discussed by Professor Tatlock, Dev. and Chron., pp. 198 ff., 156 ff. Cf. also Lowes, MP, VIII, 305 ff., and S. Moore, MLN, XXVI, 172 ff. A reference to the Wife of Bath in the *Envoy to Bukton* fixes the composition of her *Prologue*, almost with certainty, before 1396. Beyond this, the evidences that have been noted are not precise, and serve to do little more than indicate the probable order of the related tales. By the influence of Deschamps' Miroir de Mariage and of Jerome's Epistola Adversus Jovinianum the Marriage Group is associated with the second (G) *Prologue to the Legend*, and a date about 1393–94 is made probable. Within the group it seems likely that the *Wife's Prologue* was composed first, and followed shortly by her own tale and that of the Merchant. The quarrel of the Summoner and the Friar was probably devised and worked out at about the same time. But there is little evidence to indicate the exact order of these and the related tales of the Clerk, Squire, and Franklin. Professors Tatlock and Lowes agree in putting the *Melibee* between the *Wife's Prologue* and the *Merchant's Tale*. It certainly preceded the latter, and probably without a long interval. But its relation to the *Wife's Prologue* is not so clear.

The *Wife's Prologue* is derived from no single source. Like the *General Prologue* and that of the Pardoner, it is highly original in its conception and structure. But it shows the influence of a whole series of satires against women. Whether, as Ten Brink suggests, the Wife of Bath was a proverbial character before Chaucer treated her, is not definitely known. Some elements in his description of her are undoubtedly derived from the account of La Vieille and from the speeches of the jealous husband, Le Jaloux, in the Roman de la Rose, and the influence of that work is apparent in many passages throughout her *Prologue*. Chaucer drew further, for the material of his discussion, upon the Miroir de Mariage of Eustache Deschamps, the Epistola Adversus Jovinianum of St. Jerome (Migne, Pat. Lat., XXIII, 211 ff.), the Liber Aureolus de Nuptiis of Theophrastus (which Jerome quotes, Adv. Jov., 276), and the Epistola Valerii ad Rufinum de non Ducenda Uxore of Walter Map (De Nugis Curialium, iv, 3–5; ed. M. R. James, Anecdota Oxoniensia, XIV, 1914, pp. 143 ff.; also in works falsely attributed to St. Jerome, Migne, XXX, 254 ff.). The three Latin

treatises are all named in the text (ll. 671 ff.), together with other writings of which less use was made. Parallels from the works named, and from others, are cited in the notes below; but it is not to be assumed that they represent Chaucer's actual sources. Much of the Wife's discourse was common talk, and need not be traced to any literary origin. And in any case Chaucer had so thoroughly assimilated the anti-feminist literature of his age that it is impossible to identify his allusions. The principal passages in question from Jerome, Map, the Roman de la Rose, and Deschamps are assembled by Professor B. J. Whiting in SA, pp. 207 ff. For fuller discussion and detailed references see especially Mead, PMLA, XVI, 391 ff.; Lounsbury, Studies, II, 292; Lowes, MP, VIII, 305 ff. The Corbaccio of Boccaccio was suggested as a possible source of the *Prologue* by Rajna, Rom., XXXII, 248; cf., however, the opposing argument of H. M. Cummings, The Indebtedness of Chaucer to Boccaccio, Univ. of Cincinnati Stud., X, 43 ff. A number of parallels in the Lamentations of Matheolus (ed. Van Hamel, 2 v., Paris, 1892–1905) were noted years ago by the editor, and others are cited by Manly from the 14th-century French translation of Le Fèvre (in Van Hamel). On Matheolus see also A. K. Moore, N & Q, CXC, 245 ff. But it is not clear that Chaucer had read either of these works. For a general account of the satires on women in the earlier Middle Ages see A. Wulff, Die frauenfeindlichen Dichtungen in den romanischen Literaturen des Mittelalters bis zum ende des XIII Jahrhunderts, Halle, 1914. For an index to the treatment of the subject in Middle English and Scottish literature see F. L. Utley, The Crooked Rib (Columbus O., 1944). Professor R. A. Pratt has in preparation an edition of an antifeminist compilation under the title of the Jankyn Book.

With those passages of the *Prologue* which deal with the personal description of the Wife should be compared the account of her in the *General Prologue* and the notes thereon. Special reference may be made again here to the discussion of Mr. W. C. Curry, PMLA, XXXVII, 30 ff.

In spite of all the literary influences which have been detected in the *Prologue*, it is hard to believe that the Wife herself was not, at least in some measure, drawn from life.

1–2 Imitated from RR, 12802 ff.

auctoritee, authoritative text. Cf. III, 1276, below.

6 Cf. *Gen Prol*, I, 460. There is an apparent inconsistency between I, 461 ff., and the statement here that the Wife was married at twelve. See the comments of Professor Tatlock, Angl., XXXVII, 97, n.

7 That is, if so many marriages could really be valid.

11 John ii, 1. The argument here is from St. Jerome, Adv. Jov., i, 14 (Migne, Pat. Lat., XXIII, 233).

14 ff. John iv, 6 ff.

28 Gen. i, 28. This text and Matt. xix, 5 (quoted in ll. 30–31) are both used by St. Jerome at the beginning of his letter (i, 3, Migne, 213; i, 5, Migne, 215).

33 Bigamy, according to the canonists, was applied to successive marriages. Octogamy, marriage with eight husbands; the word is taken from St. Jerome, i, 15 (Migne, 234).

35 ff. *Heere,* glossed "audi," hear, in MS. El. *Salomon,* 1 Kings, xi, 3.

44 a–f These lines are certainly genuine, though Chaucer may have meant to cancel them. Cf. *MerchT,* IV, 1427.

44 f. *Scoleiyng,* probably "schooling," "training"; Skeat reads *scolering* and interprets, "young scholar."

46 I Cor. vii, 9. From St. Jerome, i, 9 (Migne, 222); the succeeding Biblical allusions are also taken from him.

47 I Cor. vii, 39. St. Jerome, i, 10 (Migne, 224); i, 14 (Migne, 232).

51 I Cor. vii, 28.

54 Cf. Gen. iv, 19–23. St. Jerome says: "Primus Lamech sanguinarius et homicida, unam carnem in duas divisit uxores" (i, 14, Migne, 233). See also *SqT,* V, 550; *Anel,* 150.

61 Cf. Jerome, i, 12 (Migne, 227).

65 I Cor. vii, 25.

71–72 For the serious use of this argument in defense of marriage cf. Jerome, Ep. xxii, ad Eustochium, § 20, Migne, XXII, 406 (Laudo nuptias,… sed quia mihi virgines generant).

75 *The dart,* apparently a prize in a running contest. It corresponds to "bravium" in St. Jerome (i, 12, Migne, 228), which comes in turn from I Cor. ix, 24 (βραβεῖον). Cf. the use of *spere* in Lydgate's Falls of Princes, i, 5108 f.

77 Perhaps suggested by Matt. xix, 11 f.

81 I Cor. vii, 7.

84 I Cor. vii, 6.

84–86 "There is no sin in wedding me, not excepting that of bigamy."

87 I Cor. vii, 1.

89 Proverbial; see Skeat, EE Prov., pp. 110 f., no. 262; Haeckel, p. 18, no. 57.

91 Again from St. Jerome (ii. 22).

96 *preferre,* be preferable to.

101 Cf. II Tim. ii, 20.

103 f. I Cor. vii, 7.

105 Cf. Rev. xiv, 1–4, phrases from which are quoted in the margin of MS. El.

107 ff. Matt. xix, 21. The appeal to Scripture is exactly paralleled by Faux-Semblant in RR, 11375 ff. Cf. also Jerome, i, 34 (Migne, 256); ii, 6 (Migne, 294).

112 Almost identical in phrasing with *Mel,* VII, 1088, and *MerchT,* IV, 1456.

115 ff. With the argument here cf. St. Jerome, i, 36 (Migne, 260); also RR, 4401–24.

130 I Cor. vii, 3; cf. also *ParsT,* X, 940; *MerchT,* IV, 2048.

135 ff. Cf. Jerome, i, 36 (Migne, 260).

145 Not Mark (vi, 38), but John vi, 9. The comparison is again from Jerome (i, 7, Migne, 219).

147 I Cor. vii, 20.

155 Cf. Jerome, i, 12 (Migne, 230).

156 I Cor. vii, 28.

158 I Cor. vii, 4.

161 Eph. v, 25.

164 ff. With the Pardoner's remark here about marriage cf. *Pard Prol,* VI, 416, n. For discussion of the part the Pardoner's interruption plays in the Wife's motivation, see A. K. Moore, MLQ, X, 49 ff. He also discusses the general theme of the man *qui sapit uxorem* in MLN, LIX, 481 ff.

168 *to-yere,* usually with the meaning "this year." But in the present passage, with the negative, it may have the sense "never," "not at all." See Gollancz, The Pearl, Lond., 1921, note to l. 588.

170 ff. Probably, as Brusendorff suggests (p. 484), a colloquial expression rather than a literary allusion to RR, 6813 ff., 10631 ff., or Boethius, ii, pr. 2. He notes that it occurs again in *LGW Prol G,* 79 (*F,* 195), and remarks that a similar colloquialism is still current in Danish.

180 The saying referred to is given in Latin in the margin of MS. Dd: "Qui per alios non corigitur, alii per ipsum corigentur." It is not in the Almagest; nor is the quotation in l. 326 f. below. But both sayings have been found in a collection of apophthegms ascribed to Ptolemy, and published after his life in Gerard of Cremona's translation of the Almagest, Venice, 1515. See Flügel, Angl., XVIII, 133 ff. Boll, Angl., XXI, 222 ff., shows that the author of the life was "Albuguafe" (i.e., Emir abu 'l Wafā Mutaskshir ben Fatik, 12th century). On the Almagest see *MillT,* I, 3208, n. Cf. also Skeat, EE Prov., p. 111, no. 263.

197 Professor Tatlock (Angl., XXXVII, 97) remarks that the senile husband of the nymph Agapeo in Boccaccio's Ameto may have furnished a suggestion for the three old husbands here. But the type has been common in literature. See the introduction to the Explanatory Notes on the *MerchT.*

198–202 With these lines and ll. 213–16, cf. the Miroir de Mariage, 1576–84 (Deschamps, Œuvres, IX, SATF).

204–06 For the idea cf. *MerchT,* IV, 1303–04.

207–10 Cf. RR, 13269–72.

208 *tolde no deyntee of,* set no value on.

218 At Dunmow, near Chelmsford in Essex, a flitch of bacon was offered to any married couple who lived a year without quarrelling or repenting of their union. Tyrwhitt (III, 319) quotes Blount, Antient Tenures of Land, and Jocular Customs of Some Mannors, London, 1679, p. 162 f., and cites a similar institution in French Brittany, near Rennes. See also Robt. Chambers, Book of Days, Edinburgh, 1862–64, I, 748 ff., and cf. Piers Plowman, C, xi, 276 ff., with Skeat's note; Francis W. Steer, Essex Record Office Publication 13 (Chelmsford, 1951); C. L. Shaver, MLN, L, 322 ff. There is an amusing account of the Dunmow competition in 1949 by A. L. Hench in the Southern Folklore Quarterly, XVI, 128 ff. For the substitution of war-bonds for the prize of bacon see the Christian Science Monitor (Boston), July 15, 1944, p. 9.

226 For the phrase *to bere hem on honde* cf. ll. 232, 380, below, and see *MLT,* II, 620, n.

227–28 Almost literally from RR, 18136 f.

229 For the apologetic formula cf. RR, 9917, 11017 ff.

231 *if that she can hir good,* if she knows what is best for her. See *MLT,* II, 1169, n.

232 "Will testify, or convince him, that the chough is mad." The allusion is to the bird that tells a jealous husband of his wife's misconduct with her lover. The wife persuades him that the bird is lying. See Chaucer's version of the story in the *Manciple's Tale,* and cf. Clouston's paper on the Tell-Tale Bird, Orig. and Anal., Ch. Soc., pp. 439 ff.

233 For the collusion of the maid cf. Miroir, 3634 f., 3644–55; also most versions of the story of the Tell-Tale Bird.

235-47 This passage shows the influence of both the Liber de Nuptiis (Migne, Pat. Lat., XXIII, 276) and the Miroir, 1589–1611 (very close). Cf. also Matheolus, Lamentations, ed. Van Hamel, 2 v., Paris, 1892–1905, ll. 1107 ff. (tr. Le Fèvre, ii, 1452 ff.).

236 ff. With these lines and ll. 265–70 cf. *ClT*, IV, 1207–10.

246 Cf. *KnT*, I, 1261, n.

248-75 Cf. Liber de Nuptiis (Migne, 277); apparently supplemented by the use of RR, 8579–8600 and Miroir, 1625–48, 1732–41, 1755–59.

257 ff. Chaucer apparently misunderstood his Latin text ("alius liberalitate sollicitat," etc., Migne, 277) and made *richesse* a ground of the lover's desires rather than a means of his wooing.

265 *foul*, ugly.

268 *hire to chepe*, to bargain, do business, with her (gerundive); or, for a trade for her (dative substantive).

269 f. "Every Jack his Jill," apparently proverbial; cf. Haeckel, p. 31 f., no. 104; Skeat, EE Prov., pp. 111 f., no. 264.

272 *his thankes*, willingly. See *KnT*, I, 2107, n. *Helde*, hold. Chaucer regularly has *holde*.

278 On this saying see *Mel*, VII, 1086, n.

282-92 Cf. Liber de Nuptiis (Migne, 277); also Miroir, 1538–75, and RR, 8667–82. The idea is also developed by Matheolus, 2425 ff. (Le Fèvre, iii, 265), 800–11 (Le Fèvre, ii, 399–418).

293-302 Cf. Liber de Nuptiis (Migne, 277); apparently supplemented again by Miroir, 1760–77.

303-06 A marginal note in MS. El ("et procurator calamistratus"), indicates that Chaucer was still following Theophrastus (Migne, 277).

308-10 Cf. *MerchT*, IV, 1300.

311 Cf. the Miroir, 3225. *Oure dame*, the mistress, i.e., myself. On the so-called domestic "our" see *ShipT*, VII, 69, n.

312 On St. James see *Gen Prol*, I, 465, n.

316-22 Cf. Miroir, 3520–25, 3871 ff.

320 *Alis*, Alice.

326 See the note to l. 180 above. In MS. El, the saying is quoted in Latin: "Intra omnes alcior existit, qui non curat in cuius manu sit mundus." Cf. Skeat, EE Prov., p. 112, no. 265; Haeckel, p. 20, no. 65.

333-36 Cf. *BD*, 963 ff. (from RR, 7410 ff.). The idea, which became proverbial, occurs in Ennius (quoted by Cicero, De Officiis i, 16). Cf. also Ars Amat., iii, 93 f.

337-39 Cf. Miroir, 1878–84, 8672–91.

342 ff. I Tim. ii, 9.

348-56 Cf. Miroir, 3207–15. Matheolus, 1939 ff. (Le Fèvre, ii, 3071 ff.) also has the figure; for other parallels see Van Hamel's introduction to Matheolus, II, cxliv.

354 *caterwawed*, "caterwauling." On the form see *Pard Prol*, VI, 406, n.

357-61 From RR, 14381–84, 14393–94. Cf. also Matheolus, 1880 f. (Le Fèvre, ii, 2979–80); and the proverb "Fous est cis qui feme weut gaitier," Morawski, Proverbes Français, Paris, 1925, p. 28, no. 769, and p. 29, no. 800.

361 *make his berd*, outwit or delude him. Cf. *RvT*, I, 4096, and n.

362-70 From St. Jerome, Adv. Jov., i, 28 (Migne, 250). The ultimate source is Prov. xxx, 21–23.

371 ff. From St. Jerome, i, 28 (Migne, 250). Cf. Prov. xxx, 16.

373 *wilde fyr*, an inflammable preparation that could not be quenched by water.

376 From St. Jerome, i, 28 (Migne, 249). Cf. Prov. xxv, 20 (Vulg.).

378 From St. Jerome, i, 28 (Migne, 249).

386 Cf. *Anel*, 157.

387-92 Cf. Miroir, 3600–08, 3620–22, 3629–32.

389 Lat. "Ante molam primus qui venit non molat imus." Cf. "First come first served"; and Skeat, EE Prov., p. 112, no. 266; and Haeckel, p. 24, no. 79.

393 Cf. RR, 13828–30; also Miroir, 3920 ff.

401 MSS. Cp Pw La have in the margin the Latin line of unknown source: "Fallere, flere, nere, dedit (Pw statuit) deus in muliere." See Skeat, EE Prov., p. 113, no. 267.

407-10 From RR, 9091–96.

414 "Let him profit who may, for everything has its price"; cf. Haeckel, p. 49, no. 168.

415 For this proverb see *RvT*, I, 4134, and n.

416 For *wynning* in the old sense of gaining money, making profit, see *Gen Prol*, I, 275.

418 *bacoun*, old meat; and so here for old men.

432 *mekely* is probably trisyllabic; otherwise *oure* must have two syllables, which is against Chaucer's usual practice.

435 *spiced conscience*, scrupulous, fastidious conscience. See *Gen Prol*, I, 526, and n.

446 *Peter*, an oath by St. Peter.

450 *to blame*, to be blamed. On its use see *Gen Prol*, I, 375, n.

455-56 Cf. *MerchT*, IV, 1847–48.

460 From Valerius Maximus, vi, c. 3, 9. (Pliny, Hist. Nat., xiv, 13, also has the story.) For further use of the same chapter see 642, 647 below.

464 ff. Cf. Ovid, Ars Amat., i, 229–44.

466 Proverbial; cf. Haeckel, p. 50, no. 177.

467-68 Cf. RR, 13452–63 (closely similar); also Ars Amat., iii, 765 ff.

469-73 Cf. RR, 12924–25, 12932 ff.

483 *Joce*, Judocus, a Breton saint. But the reference is probably to the Testament of Jean de Meun, 461 ff. (in RR, ed. Méon, Paris, 1814, IV).

487 The phrase "to fry in his own grease" or "to stew in his own juice" is still proverbial. See Skeat, EE Prov., pp. 113 f., no. 269.

489 For the figure of purgatory, as for many of the jibes against women and marriage, no single source is probably to be sought. But comparison may be made with the following lines from one of the Latin poems attributed to Walter Map (ed. Wright, Camden Soc., London, 1841, p. 84):

> Quid dicam breviter esse coniugium?
> Certe vel tartara, vel purgatorium.

Perhaps the most striking use of the idea is found in the Lamentations of Matheolus (ll. 3024 ff.), where God is represented as defending himself for having instituted matrimony as a purgatory on earth, because he desired not the death of the sinful:

> O! peccatorum quia mortem nolo, redemptor
> Et pugil ipsorum, cum res non debeat emptor
> Emptas tam care pessundare, jamque parare
> Iccirco volui sibi purgatoria plura,
> Ut se purgarent; egros sanat data cura;
> Inter que majus est conjugium.

See also Le Fèvre, iii, 1673 ff. For a similar comparison with hell, instead of purgatory, see l. 1067, and the references in Angl., XXXVII, 107, n. Contrast the *paradys terrestre*, *MerchT*, IV, 1332. The figure of purgatory also recurs in that tale, IV, 1670, and Lydgate has it (very likely from Chaucer) in his Hertford Mumming, l. 87 (Angl., XXII, 369). In a Welsh poem of Tudur Aled (ed. T. Gwynn Jones, Cardiff, 1926, II, 475) the "Purgatory of Ovid" ("Dyn wyf ym mhurdan Ofydd") is applied, quite differently, to the pain of unrequited love.

492 Cf., for the figure of the shoe, St. Jerome, Adv. Jov., i, 48 (Migne, 279). It occurs again in *MerchT*, IV, 1553. See Skeat, EE Prov., pp. 117 f., no. 277; Haeckel, p. 6, no. 20.

495 See *Gen Prol*, I, 463.

496 *roode-beem*, the beam, usually between the chancel and the nave, on which was placed a crucifix.

498 On the use of *him*, practically like a demonstrative, see *KnT*, I, 1210, n. On the tomb of Darius cf. Gualtier de Chatillon, Alexandreis, vii, 381 ff. (ed. Mueldener, Leipzig, 1863; summarized by Lounsbury, Studies, II, 354).

503–14 Cf. the experience of La Vieille, RR, 14472 ff.

514 *daungerous*, offish, "difficile"; so *daunger*, in l. 521, means "holding off" to enhance the price. Cf. *Gen Prol*, I, 517, and n.

516–24 Cf. RR, 13697–708.

517 *Wayte what*, whatever. Cf. Cook, MLN, XXXI, 442, and Derocquigny, MLR, III, 72.

522 Proverbial. Cf. Haeckel, p. 33, no. 109.

534 ff. Cf. RR, 16347–64; but the idea was a commonplace.

552 There is a strikingly close parallel to this line, though probably not a source of it, in the rubric to chap. xliii of the Miroir de Mariage: "Comment femmes procurent aler aux pardons, non pas pour devocion qu'elles aient, mais pour veoir et estre veues." See also RR, 9029–30 and Ovid, Ars Amat., i, 99.

555–58 Cf. RR, 13522–28; Matheolus, 988 ff. (Le Fèvre, ii, 947 ff.).

557 Cf. l. 657 below. The habit of making pilgrimages from other than religious motives is illustrated by Professor Lowes, Rom. Rev., II, 120 f., by several citations from the Miroir. See also *Gen Prol*, I, 465, n.

559 For the peculiar use of *upon* without an object cf. ll. 1018 (*on*), 1382 below. Cf. Mod. Eng. "What did she have on?" *Gytes* (apparently) gowns. See *RvT*, I, 3954, and n.

560 On the use of *thise* in a generalizing sense (as also in l. 1004, below) cf. *KnT*, I, 1531, n.

572–74 The mouse with one hole is proverbial. Cf. Morawski, Proverbes Français, Paris, 1925, p. 16, no. 449, "Dahez ait la soriz qui ne set c'un pertuis"; and Skeat, EE Prov., p. 114, no. 270. Cf. also RR, 13150 (with Langlois' note). As a possible literary source for Chaucer, Manly (Chaucer and the Rhetoricians, Brit. Acad., 1926, p. 12) cites Matthieu de Vendôme.

575 For "enchanted" in this sense cf. RR, 13691.

576, 583 *My dame* was identified by Koeppel as La Vieille of the Roman de la Rose, but the chapters of the Miroir which contain the love of "la mère" seem more likely to have been in Chaucer's mind if there was any definite source for the phrase. That it was proverbial and of general application is suggested by its use in the *PardT*, VI, 684. Cf. also

Matheolus, 1362 ff. (Le Fèvre, ii, 1807–1992). Curry's interpretation of it (PMLA, XXXVII, 32, n.) as a reference to Venus is hardly to be accepted.

581 It was a regular doctrine that in the interpretation of dreams gold and blood are related, each signifying the other. See Arnaldus de Villa Nova, Expositiones Visionum, etc., in Opera, Basel, 1524, i, 4, and ii, 2 (cited by Curry, pp. 212 and 265).

593–99, 627–31 With the account of the Wife's easy consolation cf. Miroir, 1966–77, also Ars. Amat., iii, 431.

602 Cf. *Rv Prol*, I, 3888, n., and *MerchT*, IV, 1847.

603 On *gat-tothed* see *Gen Prol*, I, 468, and n.

604 f. *seel*, birthmark. She was subject to Venus and Mars (*Venerien*, l. 609, *Marcien*, l. 610). On the characteristics derived from these planets and, particularly, on the bodily marks they produced, see Curry, pp. 104 ff.

613 At the time of her birth Taurus, the nighthouse of Venus, was ascendant, and Mars was in it. In MS. El there is a reference to the treatise called Almansoris Propositiones, which is printed in the volume entitled Astrologia Aphoristica Ptolomaei, Hermetis, . . . Almansoris, &c., Ulm, 1641 (Skeat).

618 Cf. RR, 13336, with Langlois' note.

624 Cf. RR, 8516.

630 ff. On Jankyn's motive for tormenting his wife see E. H. Slaughter, MLN, LXV, 530 ff.

636 Cf. *Gen Prol*, I, 446.

640 "Although he had sworn to the contrary." See *KnT*, I, 1089, n.

642 *Romayn geestes*, stories of Roman history. Cf. *MLT*, II, 1126, n. The incidents referred to here and in l. 647 are in Valerius Maximus, vi, 3.

647 *another Romayn*, P. Sempronius Sophus, whose story is told in the same chapter of Valerius.

651 ff. Ecclus. xxv, 25; cf. Haeckel, p. 49, no. 170.

655 ff. Proverbial; see Skeat, EE Prov., pp. 114 f., no. 271; Haeckel, p. 49, no. 171.

657 *seken halwes*, make pilgrimages to saints' shrines. Cf. *Gen Prol*, I, 14.

659 With *hawe* as a symbol of worthlessness cf. *pulled hen*, *oystre*, *Gen Prol*, I, 177, n.

662 Cf. RR, 9980.

670 ff. The works first mentioned as contained in Jankyn's volume are the three Latin treatises of which Chaucer has been shown to have made use in this *Prologue*: the Epistola Valerii ad Rufinum de non Ducenda Uxore of Walter Map, the Liber de Nuptiis of Theophrastus, and the Epistola Adversus Jovinianum of St. Jerome. *Tertulan* is interpreted as Tertullian, whose treatises De Exhortatione Castitatis, De Monogamia, and De Pudicitia may be referred to. *Crisippus* is probably the person mentioned by St. Jerome (Adv. Jov., i, 48, Migne, Pat. Lat., XXIII, 280) in the statement: "Ridicule Chrysippus ducendam uxorem sapienti praecipit, ne Jovem Gamelium et Genethlium violet." The reference is unknown, and Chaucer may have had no further information. (For the suggestion that he had in mind the discussion of the Stoic Chrysippus in Cicero's De Divinatione, see G. L. Hamilton, Chaucer's Indebtedness to Guido delle Colonne, New York, 1903, p. 109, n.).

Trotula is traditionally regarded as a distinguished female doctor of Salerno, who lived about the middle of the 11th century. She was credited with the authorship of a treatise on the diseases of women and the care of children (variously entitled Trotulae De Aegritudinibus Muliebribus, De Passionibus Mulierum, etc., and known as Trotula Major) and one on cosmetics (De Ornatu Mulierum, known as Trotula Minor). She has been conjecturally identified as of the family de Ruggieri, and as the wife of Johannes Platearius of Salerno, and the mother of Johannes Platearius the second and of Matthaeus Platearius. See Salvatore de Renzi, Collectio Salernitana, 5 v., Naples, 1852–59, I, 149 ff.; G. L. Hamilton, MP, IV, 377 ff. (citing French and German translations of the Latin treatises and references to Trotula in Old French literature); P. Meyer, Rom., XXXII, 87 ff. (part of the text of an Old French version). Recent investigators, however, have questioned not only Trotula's authorship of the Latin treatises, but also her standing as a medical authority. In one study (Charles and Dorothea Singer, in History, N. S. X, 244) doubt is even thrown upon her existence, and Trotula is explained as the title of the compilations of Trottus, a doctor of Salerno. A more reasonable suggestion, perhaps, is that of H. R. Spitzner (Die Salernitanische Gynäkologie und Geburtshilfe unter dem Namen der Trotula, Leipzig diss., 1921), that Trotula was a famous Salernitan midwife, whose name was given to the gynecological treatise.

Helowys is the famous Heloise, wife of Abelard. The reference may be due to the account of her in RR, 8760 ff.

688 *an inpossible*, an impossibility. Cf. *SumT*, III, 2231.

692 The allusion is to the Æsopic fable of the Man and the Lion. See Jacobs's ed., London, 1889, I, 251; II, 121.

696 *the mark of Adam*, the likeness of Adam, i.e., all males.

697 *The children of Mercurie and of Venus*, men and women born under their domination.

699 ff. According to the teachings of astrology the exaltation of one planet, the sign in which its influence is greatest, is the dejection (Lat. "casus") of another planet of contrary nature (of *diverse disposicioun*). Thus Aries is the exaltation of the Sun and the dejection of Saturn; Pisces the exaltation of Venus and the dejection of Mercury. Mercury, moreover, signifies science and philosophy, whereas Venus causes lively joys and whatever is agreeable to the body. The matter is explained in Almansoris Propositiones, § 2 (Skeat), to which there is a marginal reference in MS. El.

713 *sire*, husband.

715 ff. Most of the instances that follow are mentioned in the Epistola Valerii. Cf. also RR, 9195 ff. (Dianyre), 9203 ff. (Sampson); and *MkT*, VII, 2015 ff. (Sampson), 2095 ff. (Hercules).

727–46 From Jerome, Adv. Jov., i, 48 (Migne, 278 ff.), which preserves in part Seneca's De Matrimonio. Chaucer apparently added details from his general knowledge of the Theban story (perhaps derived from Statius' Thebaid, iv).

732 Proverbial; cf. Haeckel, p. 8, no. 26.

733 On Pasiphaë see Ovid, Ars Amat., i, 295 ff.

741 *Amphiorax*, Amphiaraus. On the form in -*x* see *Gen Prol*, I, 384, n.

747 *Lyvia* and *Lucye* come from the Epistola Valerii (De Nugis Curialium, iv, 3; ed. James,

Anecdota Oxoniensia, XIV, 153). But the first (spelled *Luna* in the MS. of the Epistola cited by Tyrwhitt) is a corruption of Livia, who poisoned Drusus, at the instigation of Sejanus, A.D. 23. *Lucye* is Lucilia, wife of the poet Lucretius. See Lounsbury, II, 369 f.

757 Doubtless from the Epistola Valerii (ed. James, p. 151) though the story, or one like it, is told in various places. Cf. the Gesta Romanorum, cap. 33; Cicero, De Oratore, ii, 69 (where only one wife is mentioned); Eramus, Apophthegms, Paris, 1533, pp. 157–58 (attributed to Diogenes). The origin of the name *Latumyus* is uncertain. It may be a corruption of Pacuvius, which is the form in the Epistola. In another text of Valerius, quoted by Tyrwhitt, the name is Pavorinus, and in the Gesta Romanorum, which refers to Valerius, it is Paletinus or Peratinus.

766 Skeat refers to the story of the Matron of Ephesus (in Petronius, Satyricon, cxi), which, as he observes, is not quite parallel. For a parallel in the Polycraticus of John of Salisbury see R. A. Pratt, MLN, LXV, 243 ff.

769 The allusion is probably to the story of Jael and Sisera, Judges iv, 21. Cf. *KnT*, I, 2007.

770 The particular allusion, if one was intended, is again doubtful.

775 f. Ecclus. xxv, 16; cf. Haeckel, p. 51, no. 183.

778 ff. Cf. Prov. xxi, 9–10; Haeckel, p. 51, no. 184.

782 f. From Jerome, Adv. Jov., i, 48 (Migne, 279 f.); ultimately from Herodotus, i, 8; cf. Haeckel, p. 45, no. 156.

784 f. Prov. xi, 22; cf. *ParsT*, X, 156; Haeckel, p. 46, no. 157.

800 ff. Mr. Tatlock suggests (MLN, XXIX, 143) that Chaucer got the idea of these lines from a passage in Map's De Nugis Curialium (ii, 26; ed. James, p. 99) where a wounded man begs another to come and take a kiss to bear to his wife and children, and then, as the other is about to kiss him, stabs him in the belly. But the situation is rather different.

816 Dr. Fansler (p. 173) compares the lay of Guigemar, by Marie de France (ed. Warnke, 3d ed., Halle, 1925), ll. 234 ff., for "a rather curious literary precedent" to this passage.

835 f. Proverbial; cf. Haeckel, p. 50, no. 176.

847 *Sidyngborne*, Sittingbourne, about forty miles from London. It is nearer Canterbury than Rochester, which is mentioned in *Mk Prol*, VII, 1926. The order of the best MSS., which puts Fragment III before Fragment VII, is thus unsatisfactory. Mr. Greenfield's attempt (MLR, XLVIII, 51 ff.) to get rid of the discrepancy by assuming that Sittingbourne is here mentioned as "a future destination" is hardly convincing.

856 *Yis*, the emphatic form, "yes, indeed," "by all means."

The Wife of Bath's Tale

On the date of the *Wife of Bath's Tale* see the introduction to the Explanatory Notes on her *Prologue*.

The exact source is unknown, but the theme of the Transformed Hag, or Loathly Lady, appears in numerous tales, both literary and popular. On their relations see W. Stokes, Acad., XLI, 399; G. H. Maynadier, The Wife of Bath's Tale, Its Sources and Analogues, London, 1901; J. W. Beach, The Loathly Lady: A Study in the Popular Elements of the Wife of Bath's Tale, an unpublished Harvard dissertation, 1907. Dr. Maynadier's volume deals fully with the literary versions. His results are supplemented, and in some details corrected, by Dr. Beach's exhaustive study of the related folktales. For the theory that the story is based ultimately on a nature myth see H. Kern, Verslagen d. Konin. Akad., Ser. 4, IX, 346 ff. The most important analogues in English are Gower's tale of Florent (Conf. Am., i, 1407 ff.); the romance, The Wedding of Sir Gawayn and Dame Ragnell; and the ballads, The Marriage of Gawain, and King Henry (all in Orig. and Anal., 483 ff.). Gower's version and Chaucer's appear to be mutually independent, that of Gower being probably the earlier. It is also in some respects more primitive than that of Chaucer. The hag is represented as a victim of enchantment, and the choice offered to Florent, of having her fair by day and foul by night or foul by day and fair by night, is an old feature of popular tales. In both versions the transformation is conditioned on the submission of the husband. Each story is an exemplum: in Gower, to illustrate obedience, in Chaucer to prove the Wife's doctrine of the sovereignty of women. Gower's tale, the Marriage of Sir Gawaine, the Weddynge of Sir Gawen, and various subsidiary sources of *WBT* are printed in SA, pp. 223 ff., where there is also a general discussion of the problem by Professor Whiting. An Irish origin for the opening incident of the tale has been suggested by G. R. Coffman, MLN, LIX, 271 ff.

According to the theory suggested by Stokes and developed by Dr. Maynadier, the tales of both Chaucer and Gower and some other analogues are indirectly derived from an Irish story, preserved in several forms and related of different heroes. In the oldest Irish version, recorded in a twelfth-century manuscript it is applied to Niall of the Nine Hostages. The hag is visited by several princes who are competing for the kingship, and the fulfilment of her request for a kiss becomes the test of their fitness for sovereignty; which only one (in this instance, Niall) successfully undergoes. In the Irish tale, as in Chaucer's, the hag appears to be acting independently and is not said to be the victim of enchantment. The emphasis, in both stories, on "sovereignty" is also cited as evidence that they are closely related. But, as Dr. Beach pointed out, "sovereignty" in the Irish story means "royal rule," whereas in Chaucer it refers to domestic supremacy. At this point, then, the parallel is not very significant. The close connexion of Chaucer's tale with the Irish has hardly been proved, though a Celtic, and specifically Irish, derivation for the English group remains a reasonable theory. The possibility of a French intermediary — such as the lost French "lai breton" assumed long ago by Gaston Paris (Hist. Litt., XXX, Paris, 1888, p. 102) — must also still be recognized. Cf. P. Rajna, Rom., XXXII, 233, n.

Additional observations and suggestions of importance have been made by Miss Margaret Schlauch, PMLA, LXI, 416 ff. She shows that Chaucer's "marital dilemma," the choice between beauty and fidelity, belongs rather to the tradition of Roman satire and ecclesiastical discussion of marriage than to that of the Celtic sagas and mediæval romances, and she comments on the significance of this for the conception of the Marriage Group.

On ironical elements in the tale see C. A. Owen, Jr., JEGP, LII, 301 ff. On the character and behavior of the "nameless knight" see F. G. Townsend, MLR, XLIX, 1 ff. On the relation of the tale to courtly love conventions see B. F. Huppé, MLN, LXIII, 378 ff. On the converted-knight theme see J. F. Roppolo, College English, XII, 263 ff. and W. P. Albrecht, ibid., p. 459.

857 The scene of Gower's story is not laid at King Arthur's court.

860 *elf-queene*, the fairy queen; cf. *Thop*, VII, 788.

875 *undermeles*, afternoon. Usually in Chaucer *undern* refers to the morning.

876 Cf. *ShipT*, VII, 91.

881 The meaning apparently is: The friar brought only dishonor upon a woman; the incubus always caused conception.

884 *fro ryver*, from hawking (or the hawking-ground) by the river. Cf. *Thop*, VII, 737, n.

887 *maugree hir heed*, in spite of her head, in spite of her very life.

904 For parallels to the Sphinx motif, or the life-question, see Maynadier, pp. 124 ff.

929–30 Cf. RR, 9945 ff.

939 ff. The meaning is probably: "There is no one of us that will not kick if anybody scratches us on a sore spot." Some MSS. read *like* (or, corruptly, *loke*) for *kike*, and the phrase *to clawe on the galle* might mean to stroke or rub the sore spot soothingly. But the other reading and interpretation better suits the context. Moreover, the phrase was clearly proverbial. Cf. the Italian expression "Mi tocca dove mi prude" (of a keen thrust in argument).

950 From RR, 19220.

951 Cf. Ovid, Met., xi, 174 ff., where the story is told, however, of Midas' barber, not of his wife. Professor Shannon remarks (Chau. and the Rom. Poets, Cambridge, Mass., 1929, p. 319) that the Wife probably got the perverted form of the tale from her fifth husband, and repeated it innocently! For Gower's version of the tale see Conf. Am., v, 141 ff. On the Italian-looking form of the name, *Myda*, see *MkT*, VII, 2345, n.

961 Cf. RR, 16521–30.

968 Cf. RR, 16367–68.

990 The dancing ladies correspond to a typical "fairy-ring" such as is repeatedly described in Celtic folk-tales.

1004 Old folks know many things. The idea is proverbial, if not the exact language.

1009 The troth was plighted in this instance by joining hands.

1018 *wereth on*, wears upon (her). See the note to l. 559 above.

1028 Bell noted that the assembly here, with the queen as presiding justice, resembles the courts of love actually held in the Middle Ages. On this institution see W. A. Neilson, Origins and Sources of the Court of Love, [Harv.] Studies and Notes, VI. Of course the life penalty was not usually involved in its deliberations.

1067 With the antithesis here Professor Tatlock (Angl., XXXVII, 107 n.) compares Ameto, p. 61, and Il Corbaccio, p. 234; and for the same rhetorical device he notes (more remotely) Ameto, p. 30, and Decameron, viii, 1. Is not the figure equally characteristic of Dante? Cf. "Non donna di provincie, ma bordello" (Purg., vi, 78).

1068 *nacioun*, perhaps used here in the sense of *naissance*, birth.

1090 *dangerous*, fastidious, "difficile."

1109 ff. With this whole discussion cf. the ballade on *Gentilesse*. Chaucer's treatment of the subject seems to have been influenced by Dante's Convivio, which affords a parallel not only to the recurring phrase *old richesse* ("antica ricchezza"), but also to the general development of the argument. The passages of the Convivio concerned are the canzone prefixed to the fourth Tractate and chaps. 3, 10, 14, and 15 of this Tractate. In ll. 1126 ff. Chaucer refers definitely to Purg., vii, 121 ff., and there can be little doubt that he also drew upon RR, 6579–92, 18607–896. See Lowes, MP, XIII, 19 ff. Professor Lumiansky, in Italica, XXXI, 4 ff., points out that there is also a parallel situation in Boccaccio's Filostrato, VII, stanzas 86 ff., though hardly a source for the discussion of *gentilesse*. On the doctrine in general cf. Vogt, JEGP, XXIV, 102 ff.; Miss S. Resnikow, JEGP, XXXVI, 391 ff. It was a commonplace of Christian literature and in no sense an evidence of radical or advanced opinion on the part of Chaucer.

1113 *Looke who*, probably to be understood as equivalent to "whoever"; cf. *Looke what*, *FranklT*, V, 992; *Looke whan*, *PardT*, VI, 826; *Wayte what*, l. 517, above.

1118–24 Cf. RR, 18620–34.

1133–38 Cf. particularly Convivio, iv, 15, 19–38, where Dante argues that mere lapse of time, or continuance of a single condition, cannot constitute nobility.

1139–45 This comparison with fire is made, in general terms, in Boethius, iii, pr. 4. It also occurs in Macrobius (Comm. in Somn. Scip., II, xvi, 6) and in Servius (Comm. in Vergilii Carmina, ed. Thilo and Hagen, Leipzig, 1883–84, II, 101, ll. 15–21), and certain detailed correspondences make it appear probable that Chaucer used Servius, or perhaps his source. (See Lowes, MP, XV, 199.)

1140 *the mount of Kaucasous*, perhaps from Bo, ii, pr. 7, 58 ff.

1142 *lye*, blaze.

1152–58 Cf. Dante's canzone (prefixed to Convivio, iv) ll. 34–37, and the prose comment in Convivio, iv, 7, 87–92.

1158 Cf. RR, 2083 (*Rom*, 2181 f.).

1159 For the suggestion that *For* in l. 1159 and *They* in l. 1162 should be interchanged see J. S. Kenyon, MLN, LIV, 133 ff.

1162–63 Cf. Dante's canzone, 112–16 and the comment in Convivio, iv, 20, 24–28, 47–57. For the argument that *thy* should be applied generally, and not to the Knight, see Mrs. Dempster, MLN, LIX, 173 ff.

1165 See Valerius Maximus, iii, c. 4.

1168 See Seneca, Epist. xliv.

1170 Cf. RR, 18802–05.

1178 f. Cf. II Cor. viii, 9.

1183 ff. Mainly from Seneca, Epist. xvii. See also Haeckel, p. 8, no. 28.

1187 Cf. RR, 18566.

1191–94 The quotation from Juvenal (Sat., x, 21) also occurs in Dante's discussion of "gentilesse" (Convivio, iv, 13, 101–10). Chaucer also alludes to it in *Bo*, ii, pr. 5, 179 ff., perhaps because of a gloss which he was using.

1195 The source is indicated in the margin of MS. El: — "Secundus philosophus: Paupertas est odibile bonum, sanitatis mater, curarum remocio, sapientie reparatrix, possessio sine calumpnia." This is from a collection of Gnomae, preserved in both Greek and Latin, and attributed to Secundus. See Fabricius, Bibl. Graeca, lib. vi, cap. x (XIII, Hamburg, 1726, p. 573). The passage quoted is in Vincent of Beauvais, Spec. Historiale, x, 71.

1200 The following marginal note in MS. El (from Jerome, Adv. Jov., ii, 9, Migne, 298) probably indicates that Chaucer meant to add lines on Crates: "Unde et Crates ille Thebanus, projecto in mari non paruo auri pondere, Abite inquit pessime male cupiditates: ego vos mergam, ne ipse mergar a vobis."

1203 f. Cf. RR, 4953–56 (*Rom*, 5551 f.); also *Bo*, ii, pr. 8, 32 ff.; and *Fortune*, 9 f., 32, 34.

1208 *auctoritee*, text. Cf. *WB Prol*, III, 1.

1210 Cf. *PardT*, VI, 743.

1245 *to seene*, the so-called inflected infinitive. See the Grammatical Introduction.

1249 *curtyn*, curtain. Cf. *MerchT*, IV, 1817; *Tr*, iii, 674.

1258 ff. Cf. *ShipT*, VII, 175 ff.

The Friar's Prologue

The *Friar's Prologue* and *Tale* were probably written shortly after those of the Wife, with which they are brought into close connection. On the dates of the whole series see the introduction to the Explanatory Notes on the *Wife of Bath's Prologue* (p. 698 above).

The quarrel between the Friar and the Summoner is probably to be understood as an old one, which began long before the pilgrimage. In fact, as Professor Tupper has remarked (Types, p. 56 f.), it reflects the traditional enmity of mendicants and possessioners. For interesting speculation about the two pilgrims and the persons and localities in their stories see E. P. Kuhl, PMLA, XXXVIII, 123, and MLN, XL, 321 ff., and Manly, New Light, pp. 103 ff. The friar in the *Summoner's Tale*, Professor Manly reasons, was not a Cistercian but of the same order as the Canterbury Friar, who must have been a Franciscan on the evidence of the scurrilous anecdote in the *Summoner's Prologue*. The only Franciscan house was at Beverley, the seat of the archdeacon of the East Riding. Greyfriars of Beverley were actually collecting funds for a building when Chaucer was writing. The archdeacon in the *Friar's Tale* Mr. Manly identifies conjecturally with Richard de Ravenser (or de Beverley), one of the canons of Beverley Minster and archdeacon of Lincoln (1368–1386). His name appears often in the Life Records of Chaucer. Mr. Kuhl (MLN, XL, 325 ff.) saw in the character rather a reference to Walter Skirlawe, archdeacon of Holderness. The claims of the two are compared by Mr. Manly, pp. 112 ff.

Both tales have a northern complexion. The Summoner's is definitely put at Holderness. The language in both, though not out-and-out dialect, as in the speech of the Cambridge students in the *Reeve's Tale*, points to a northerly locality. Mr. Manly (New Light, p. 106) cites, for example, *Brock, Scot, hayt, tholed, caples, thou lixt.*

1276 *auctoritees*, texts, quotations; a reference to l. 1208 above.

1284 *mandementz*, summonses to the archdeacon's court.

1295-96 In MS. Ha these lines follow what is here printed as l. 1308. Koch suggests that they should be canceled entirely (ESt, XLVII, 366).

The Friar's Tale

No definite source of the *Friar's Tale* has been found, or is likely to be. The chief interest lies in Chaucer's vivid description and his brilliant presentation of character and situation. The story itself, told here at the expense of a summoner, is known in a number of versions, applied to various functionaries — a seneschal, a judge, a lawyer, and the like. The devil's trick turns, of course, on the popular belief that a curse is effective when it comes from the heart. Two versions of the tale from fifteenth-century collections are printed in the Originals and Analogues (Ch. Soc.), pp. 103 ff.; also in SA, pp. 269 ff., where Professor Archer Taylor has added several other analogues and discussed their relations. Another version, in Caesarius Heisterbacensis, Lib. VIII Miraculorum, Römische Quartalschrift, Suppl. XIII, Rome, 1901, pp. 90 f., is cited by Förster in Herrig's Arch., CX, 427. For further information cf. J. A. Herbert, Ward's Catalogue of Romances, III, London, 1910, p. 592; R. Th. Christiansen, The Norwegian Fairytales, FF Com., no. 46, Helsinki, 1922, p. 34, no. 1185; A. Taylor, PMLA, XXXVI, 35 ff.; Andrae, Angl. Beibl., XXVII, 85 ff. References to a number of modern analogues are given in Koch's notes to Hertzberg's translation of the Canterbury Tales, Berlin, 1925, p. 527.

1309 *usure*, the taking of interest, which was forbidden by the Canon Law. *Symonye*, the buying or selling of ecclesiastical preferment; so named from Simon, in Acts viii, 18 ff.

1314 Skeat interprets: "No fine could save the accused from punishment." Probably it means rather: "No fine ever escaped him," i.e., he never failed to impose one. Cf. *Gen Prol*, I, 656–58.

1317 The bishop's crosier is shaped at the end like a hook.

1322 On *sly* cf. *KnT*, I, 1444, n. Here it perhaps has its modern connotation.

1323 *espiaille*, set of spies (collective).

1327 Cf. "as mad as a March hare." See Skeat, EE Prov., p. 115, no. 272. Professor Tatlock (Flügel Memorial Volume, Stanford Univ., 1916, p. 230) also discerns a pun on *hare* and *harlotrye*. But this is doubtful.

1329 The mendicant orders were not subject to the bishops.

1332 *Peter*, by Saint Peter. *Styves*, houses of ill-fame. These were licensed and exempted from ecclesiastical control.

1334 *with myschance and with mysaventure*, an imprecation. Cf. *MLT*, II, 896, and n.

1340 Cf. *WB Prol*, III, 415. The *lure* was a piece of leather furnished with feathers to resemble a small bird. It was used to recall the falcon which had flown at its prey.

1349 *atte nale*, at the ale-house; for *atten ale*, with transposed *n*.

1350 f. John xii, 6.

1356 *sir Robert* and *sir Huwe* were probably priests. See the note on *Sir John*, *NP Prol*, VII, 2810.

1365 "You need not take any more trouble in this case."

1369 *dogge for the bowe*, a dog to follow up a deer.

1373 "And because that was the substance of his income." Cf. the contrast between fruit and chaff.

1377 *ribibe*; cf. *rebekke*, l. 1573. Both forms, meaning literally a fiddle, were used as cant terms for "old woman." Skeat suggests a pun on *rebekke* and Rebecca who is named in the marriage service. A further play on the Latin words "vetula" and "vidula" is probably also involved.

1380 ff. The description is strikingly like that of the *Yeoman* in the *Gen Prol*, I, 101 ff. It has been suggested that the green clothing of the Summoner's companion has a further significance here as revealing his supernatural, i.e., devilish, origin. See Garrett, JEGP, XXIV, 129, with a reference to the Green Knight, whose color connects him with the Celtic underworld.

1413 In the mention of the *north contree* there is a veiled revelation of the Yeoman's character. For both in biblical tradition and in Germanic mythology the North is associated with the infernal regions. See Isaiah xiv, 13, 14; also Gregory's Commentary on Job, Bk. xvii, c. 24 (Migne, Pat. Lat., LXXVI, 26). Cf. further F. B. Gummere, Founders of England, New York, 1930, p. 418, n., and Haverford College Studies, I (1889), 118 ff. Professor Manly cites also the proverb, "Ab Aquilone omne malum."

1436 Still proverbial; cf. Skeat, EE Prov., pp. 115 f., no. 273.

1451 Cf. *Gen Prol*, I, 256, and n.

1467 *jogelour*, originally "joculator," minstrel; here "juggler." The word degenerated in meaning.

1475 Cf. Eccl. iii, 1; also *Cl Prol*, IV, 6; *MerchT*, IV, 1972; *Tr*, ii, 989; iii, 855; Haeckel, p. 43, no. 145.

1491 Job i, 12; ii, 6.

1502-03 It is uncertain what incident in St. Dunstan's life Chaucer may have had in mind. For the story of how he thrust burning tongs into the Devil's nose, see the metrical legend in Mätzner's Altenglische Sprachproben, I, Berlin, 1867, p. 171 ff. Skeat refers also to the "Lay of St. Dunstan" in the Ingoldsby Legends; and Sister Mary Immaculate, in PQ, XXI, 240 ff., cites from lives of the saint incidents in which a fiend became subject to his will. For instances of fiends in the service of the apostles Skeat cites the Lives of Saints, ed. Horstmann, EETS, 1887, pp. 36, 368. Cf. also Acts xix, 15.

1510-11 *Phitonissa*, the name commonly applied to the Witch of Endor. See I Chron. x, 13 (Vulg.) and cf. "mulier pythonem habens," I Sam. xxviii, 7. According to a common theory the spirit of Samuel was not raised, but he was personated by the Devil. This was cited in discussion of witchcraft to prove that the Devil could represent a good man.

1518 The summoner, he declares, will be better fitted for a professorial chair in the subject than such authorities on the lower world as Virgil and Dante.

1528 Cf. *KnT*, I, 1131 ff.

1543 *Hayt*, a cry used by drivers to make their horses go. Skeat's note cites a number of instances. *Brok* (lit. badger) was applied to gray horses. *Scot* is said to be still a common name for horses in East Anglia. Cf. *Gen Prol*, I, 616.

1553 Such appearances of the Devil to seize what has been assigned to him are not uncommon. Cf. Child's English and Scottish Popular Ballads, I (Boston, 1882), 219 f.; and for further references see the introduction to the Explanatory Notes on the *FrT*.

1560 It is doubtful whether one should read *to stoupe*, with change of construction, or *to-stoupe*, an emphatic compound. See the note on *to swinke*, *PardT*, VI, 519.

1561 With this use of *ther* as an expletive in clauses of blessing or cursing cf. *KnT*, I, 2815, and n.

1564 *Seinte Loy*, St. Eligius. Cf. *Gen Prol*, I, 120, and n. Here St. Loy is invoked as the patron of blacksmiths and carriers. On this aspect of his cult cf. Lowes, Rom. Rev., V, 382 ff. A story there cited is included, under the title "Christ and the Smith," in Aarne's Types of the Folk-Tale, tr. S. Thompson (FF Com., no. 74, Helsinki, 1928), p. 118, no. 753. For further parallels see C. Marstrander, in the Miscellany Presented to Kuno Meyer, Halle, 1912, pp. 371 ff.

1568 Cf. RR, 10299 f.

1570 *upon cariage*, by way of quitting any claim to his cart and team. Cf. *ParsT*, X, 752; *Bo*, i, pr. 4, 72.

1573 *rebekke*, old woman. See the note on l. 1377, above.

1576 Twelve pence was equivalent to twenty-five shillings or more today.

1582 *virytrate*, another contemptuous term for an old woman; perhaps related to "trot" or "trat," often used in the same sense.

1595 *a libel*, a copy of the indictment.

1602 *Com of*. The expression was probably first applied to calling off the dogs from game; cf. *MillT*, I, 3728; *PF*, 494.

1613 *seinte Anne*, the mother of the Blessed Virgin. See the Gospel of the Nativity of Mary (B. H. Cowper's Apocryphal Gospels, 5th ed., London, 1881, pp. 85 ff.) or Legenda Aurea (ed. Graesse, 2d ed., Leipzig, 1850) cap. ccxxii, p. 934.

1630 *stot*, usually stallion or bullock; here a term of abuse for the old woman.

1645 ff. For the suggestion that the warning remarks of the Friar at this point owe something to the office of Compline in the Breviary, see R. C. Sutherland, PQ, XXXI, 436 ff.

1647 *Poul*, possibly to be read as a dissyllable, *Powel*. Otherwise the line is defective. The editors supply *and*.

1652 For the somewhat unusual reference to hell as a *hous*, Mr. Spencer (Speculum, II, 197 f.) cites parallels in the Middle Engl. Vision of St. Paul (l. 140; ed. R. Morris, An Old English Miscellany, EETS, 1872, p. 227) and the romance of the Holy Grail (ed. Furnivall, EETS, 1875, ch. xxxiii, 108 ff.).

Cf. also *infernos domos*, Boethius, iii, m. 12, and the Homeric Ἄϊδος δόμον (or δόμους).

1657 Ps. x, 9.

1661 1 Cor. x, 13.

The Summoner's Prologue

No literary source has been found for the Summoner's account of the last abode of friars, but the punishment itself was certainly not invented by Chaucer. The mention of it in the *Romaunt* (l. 7575 f.) where it is not restricted to friars, may be due to the present passage. But a number of other references to it, usually in vulgar jests or curses, have been collected. See Kaluza, Chau. und der Rosenroman, Berlin, 1893, p. 237; Fansler, p. 165; Kittredge, [Harv.] Stud. and Notes, I, 21; Brusendorff, p. 411. To the examples given by these scholars may be added Merlin Cocaie, I, 135 (cited in Littré's dictionary, s.v. "cul," from Lacurne de Sainte-Palaye). The same repulsive conception is also represented in ecclesiastical art. See T. Spencer, in Speculum, II, 196 f., who cites particularly the fresco of hell in the Campo Santo at Pisa and Giotto's Last Judgment in the Arena Chapel at Padua. The particular form of the jest in the *Summoner's Prologue* may have originated as a vulgarization of the tale, of contrary import, about a Cistercian monk, who found that his brethren in heaven dwelt under the pallium of the Blessed Virgin. See Caesarius Heisterbacensis, Dialogus Miraculorum, vii, 59 (Cologne, 1851, II, 79 f.), and cf. Tatlock, MLN, XXIX, 143.

1685 *Yis*, the emphatic form of assent, used here in response to the negative implication of the question, that no friars go to hell. "Yes, on the contrary, many million" is the answer.

1688 Cf. Dante's description of the wings of Satan, Inf., xxxiv, 48.

1692 *furlong-wey*, applied to time; cf. *MLT*, II, 557, and n.

1693 On this figure of the bees, which Chaucer has again in *Tr*, ii, 193, and iv, 1356, see Angl., XIV, 243 f.

The Summoner's Tale

The *Summoner's Tale* is mainly a description of the methods of a begging friar. The jest which makes the point of the story was doubtless a current anecdote. A somewhat similar story, entitled Le Dis de la Vescie a Prestre (The Story of the Priest's Bladder), by Jakes de Basiu or Baisieux, is printed in the Originals and Analogues (Ch. Soc.), pp. 137 ff., and again in SA, pp. 275 ff., where Professor W. M. Hart has introductory comments. Another tale is recorded of a bequest of Jean de Meun to the Jacobin friars. See Koeppel, Angl., XIV, 256; Oxf. Ch., III, 452. On special literary influences see F. Tupper, JEGP, XV, 74 f.

1710 *Holdernesse*, in the southeast corner of Yorkshire. On the possibility that Chaucer may have been interested in the place partly because of his acquaintance with Sir Peter Bukton, see E. P. Kuhl, PMLA, XXXVIII, 115 ff., and cf. the introduction to the Explanatory Notes on the *Envoy to Bukton*. Professor Manly (New Light, pp. 119 ff.)

prefers to identify the *lord of that village* (l. 2165) as Michael de la Pole. Until 1386, he observes, the de la Poles were the greatest lords in Holderness. Chaucer also seems pretty surely to have known the family. Mr. Manly queries whether Ravenser, whom he takes to be the original of the archdeacon, owed his preferment to Michael de la Pole and was ungrateful, and so incurred Chaucer's satire.

1717 A trental was an office of thirty masses for souls in purgatory. Cf. The Trentals of St. Gregory, in Political, Religious, and Love Poems, ed. Furnivall, EETS (1866), pp. 83 ff. (1903), pp. 114 ff. Cf. Wells, 172, 789, 956, 1007, 1051, 1108. The masses were usually said on thirty successive days. But sometimes they were all said in one day, and the friar suggests below (l. 1726) that this is better because it delivers the soul sooner.

1722 *possessioners*, the regular monastic orders and the beneficed clergy. Later references in the tale seem to apply particularly to the latter. The friars, in contrast to the possessioners, were supposed to have no endowments and no private property.

1723 *Thanked be God.* This ejaculation, which Skeat attributes to the Summoner, is rather a bit of pious hypocrisy on the part of the friar.

1727 "A secular priest, without incurring condemnation for being jolly or gay, will sing only one mass in a day."

1730 The punishments mentioned are found in many of the mediæval descriptions of hell. Cf. particularly Dante's Inferno. Burning is commonly associated with both hell and purgatory; the torture with fleshhooks and awls, in the hands of devils, more commonly with hell. But it is mentioned in various accounts of St. Patrick's Purgatory. See JEGP, XIX, 377 ff. On the meaning of *oules* see T. Spencer, Speculum, II, 196.

1734 The full formula is "qui cum Patre et Spiritu Sancto vivit et regnat per omnia secula seculorum."

1745 *Ascaunces*, as if, as though; cf. *CYT*, VIII, 838; also *Tr*, i, 205, and 292 (where it corresponds to the Italian "quasi dicesse," introducing a quotation). It was explained by Skeat as a compound of "as" and the OF. "quanses," as if. But this hybrid combination has been questioned by Professor C. H. Livingston, who prefers to assume an unrecorded OF. "escaunces" as the source. See MLR, XX, 71 f.

1747 *A Goddes kechyl*, lit. "a little cake of God." Cf. *a Goddes halfpeny*, l. 1749, and the French phrases, "un bel écu de Dieu," "une bénite aumône de Dieu" cited by Tyrwhitt. He explains them (quoting M. de la Monnoye, Contes de B. D. Periers, II, 107) as expressions of the common people, who piously attribute everything to God.

1751 For the suggestion that *blanket* refers not to a woolen blanket but to a cut or dressing of meat see J. G. Southworth, Explicator, XI, No. 29. This seems more consistent with the context. The term is still current in America, usually "blanket of veal." But more evidence is needed of its use in Middle English, and *dag*, *dagoun*, etc. seem to be associated with cloth.

1755 *hostes man*, servant to the guests. ME. "hoste" occurs rarely in the sense of "guest," which is common in the case of OF. "hoste."

1760 Cf. RR, 11332 ("sert de fable").

1770 *Deus hic*, God be here.

1778 *go walked*, gone a-walking. *Walked* is probably for *a-walked*, like *a-blakeberyed*, *Pard Prol*, VI, 406.

1792 *glose*, interpretation, comment. Cf. *ML Epil*, II, 1180; *MkT*, VII, 2140.

1794 II Cor. iii, 6.

1803 *narwe*, tightly. Professor Manly is doubtless right in holding that the kiss was a usual mode of salutation. But the tight embrace and the *chirkyng* are not altogether in keeping with the office and character of the priest. See further A. L. Kellogg, Scriptorium, VII, 115.

1810 *God amende defautes*, God mend my defects, a deprecatory reply to his compliments.

1817 *grope*, examine at confession.

1820 Cf. Luke v, 10; Matt. iv, 19.

1824 On the form *seinte* see *Gen Prol*, I, 120, n.

1834 *Ire* is the third in the regular list of the Seven Deadly Sins.

1838 *Je vous dy sanz doute*, I tell you without doubt. Cf. l. 1832 above. These French phrases were in familiar use and do not necessarily indicate that Chaucer was following a French source.

1845 Cf. John iv, 34; Job xxiii, 12.

1854 ff. This is a typical example of the "somnium coeleste" or dream which was supposed to be a divine *revelacioun*. On the belief in such visions see Curry, p. 214, citing especially St. Augustine, De Genesi ad Litteram, lib. xii, cap. 7 (Migne, Pat. Lat., XXXIV, 459), and De Spiritu et Anima, caps. 24, 25 (Migne, XL, 796 ff.).

1859 *fermerer*, for *enfermerer*, the friar in charge of the infirmary.

1862 One of the privileges of friars who, after fifty years of service, "made their jubilee" was to go about alone instead of in pairs.

1866 In acknowledgment of the miraculous vision they sang a song of thanksgiving, "Te deum laudamus," and nothing else.

1872 *burel folk*, the laity; perhaps so called from the material of their clothing.

1876 The following passage about friars, as Professor Tupper has noted (MLN, XXX, 8 f.) seems to contain several reminiscences of Jerome, Adv. Jovinianum. With ll. 1876 ff. he compares lib. ii, caps. 11, 17; with ll. 1885 ff., 1915 ff., cap. 15 (Migne, Pat. Lat., XXIII, 300, 310, 305).

1877 See Luke xvi, 19 ff

1880 In MS. El is the marginal note: "Melius est animam saginare quam corpus," of uncertain source. Cf. also Jean de Meun, Testament, l. 345: "Amegrient leurs ames plus que leurs cors n'engressent" (in RR, ed. Méon, Paris, 1814, IV).

1881 f. Cf. I Tim. vi, 8.

1885 ff. Exod. xxxiv, 28.

1890 ff. I Kings xix, 8.

1898 f. Levit. x, 9.

1916–17 It is possible, but by no means certain, that a pun is intended here on the words *chaced* and *chaast*. On word-play in Chaucer cf. *Gen Prol*, I, 297, n.

1922 *by*, concerning.

1923 Matt. v, 3.

1928 *diffye*, distrust.

1929 In view of the use of St. Jerome's treatise Adversus Jovinianum in the early part of Fragment III and of the parallels noted in the present tale, it is clear that the reference here is to Jerome's adversary rather than to the mythical emperor of the Gesta Romanorum (as suggested in the Globe ed.).

1930 Skeat notes St. Jerome's description of Jovinian (i, 40, Migne, Pat. Lat., XXIII, 268): "iste formosus monachus, crassus, nitidus, dealbatus, et quasi sponsus semper incedens."

1934 Ps. xliv, 2 (Vulg.): "Eructavit cor meum verbum bonum." The summoner is playing on the literal meaning of "eructare," to belch. Chaucer apparently used, or adapted, a current joke. Mr. J. A. McPeek has called the editor's attention to a similar representation of a drunken man's repetition of a psalm in a Latin prose satire under the name of Golias (The Latin Poems attributed to Walter Mapes, ed. Thos. Wright, Camden Soc., London, 1841, p. xliv): ". . . eructitando inchoat, 'Laudate Dominum, *puf*, omnis gens, laudate, *puf*, et omnis spiritus laudet, *puf*.' " But in this case there is no pun on the text of the psalm. Miss M. P. Hamilton (MLN, LVII, 655 ff.) suggests that the humor of the passage lies also in the inappropriateness of the *Cor meum eructavit* as a psalm for the Dead.

1937 James i, 22.

1943 St. Yve, probably the patron saint of Brittany. See *ShipT*, VII, 227 (identical with this line), and n.

1944 On the practice of admitting lay brothers and sisters to a religious fraternity (a favorite means of obtaining gifts) see H. B. Workman, John Wyclif, Oxford, 1926, II, 107.

1958 *confusioun*, ruin.

1968 In the margin of MS. El is the note: "Omnis virtus unita fortior est seipsa dispersa." The quotation is unidentified; for the idea cf. Æsop's fable of the bundle of sticks; also Boethius, iii, pr. 11.

1973 Luke x, 7. Cf. Haeckel, p. 13, no. 43.

1980 "In the life of St. Thomas of India." St. Thomas the Apostle is said to have preached in India and built many churches. See Legenda Aurea (ed. Graesse, 2d ed., Leipzig, 1850), cap. v, pp. 32 ff.; and cf. A. Dickson, Valentine and Orson, N.Y., 1929, p. 230. On the order of words cf. *ClT*, IV, 1170, n.

1989 Ecclus. iv, 30.

1994 f. Imitated from RR, 16591 ff. Virgil's "snake in the grass" (Eclogue iii, 93) is referred to.

2001–03 From RR, 9800–04, which goes back to Ovid, Ars Amat., ii, 376. Cf. also Aen., v, 6, and Seneca, Medea, 579 ff.

2004 MS. Ha adds:

Schortly may no man by rym and vers
Tellen her thoughtes thay ben so dyvers.

from RR, 16334–36. On spurious couplets inserted after ll. 2012, 2037, 2048, see the textual note.

2005 "One of the chief of the Seven (Deadly Sins)." With the homily on Ire, which follows, cf. *ParsT*, X, 533 ff.

2018 *Senek*, Seneca. The three anecdotes are found in the De Ira, but may have been taken by Chaucer from some secondary source. For the first see Bk. i, ch. 18. All three are printed in SA, pp. 286 ff.

2042 *dide doon sleen*, the repetition of the causative *do* is unusual. Cf. *leet . . . Doon* in *SqT*, V, 45 f.

2043 See the De Ira, iii, 14.

2075 "Placebo Domino in regione vivorum,"

Ps. cxiv, 9 (Vulg.). This begins an anthem in the office for the dead. *Placebo*, "I will please," came to be used proverbially for flattering complaisance. Cf. *ParsT*, X, 617; also Dan Michel, Ayenbite of Inwyt, ed. Morris, EETS, 1866, p. 60; Bacon's Essay of Counsel; also the modern term "placebos" for the sugar pills given by physicians to patients who insist on having a remedy.

2079 See the De Ira, iii, 21.

2080 *Gysen*, a name of uncertain origin. Seneca and Herodotus (i, 189, 202; v, 52) call the river Gyndes; so also Orosius (ii, 6). On the corruption of the name, see F. P. Magoun, Jr., Med. Stud., XV, 119.

2085 *he*, Solomon. See Prov. xxii, 24, 25.

2090 "As exact as a carpenter's square"; cf. Skeat, EE Prov., p. 116, no. 274.

2107 On Christ's harrowing of hell see *MillT*, I, 3512, n.

2113 Koeppel would derive the comparison of the friars with the sun from Cicero's similar figure for friendship (De Amicitia, xiii, 47). The passage is cited in Peraldus's Summa de Virtutibus. See Herrig's Arch., CXXVI, 180 f.

2116 *Elye*, Elias, Elijah; *Elise*, Eliseus, Elisha. The Carmelites claimed that their order was founded by Elijah on Mt. Carmel. See I Kings xviii, 19, 20.

2126 Cf. l. 1944 above, and n.

2162 *the court*, the manor-house.

2173 Apparently a proverbial comparison.

2186 He had received the degree of Master of Divinity.

2187 Matt. xxiii, 7 f.; Mark xii, 38 f.

2196 Matt. v, 13.

2215 *with meschaunce*, an imprecation. So also is *with harde grace*, l. 2228, probably to be taken.

2231 *an impossible*; Cf. *WB Prol*, III, 688, and n.

2233 f. Cf. the long exposition of the theory of sound in *HF*, 765 ff.

2244 Cf. *Gen Prol*, I, 100.

2253 For the mention of a similar gratuity to a minstrel, see Cerddi Rhydd Cynnar, ed. T. H. Parry-Williams, Caerdydd, 1932, p. 179.

2289 *Ptholomee*, corruptly spelled *Protholomee* in nearly all MSS. This might account for the loss of *dide* or the second *as*, supplied by Skeat. The mistake in the name can hardly be Chaucer's unless he meant it humorously as a blunder of the Summoner. For the association of Euclid and Ptolemy cf. RR, 16171.

2294 *at towne*, probably at Sittingbourne. But cf. S. B. Greenfield, MLR, XLVIII, 51.

FRAGMENT IV

Fragment IV, consisting of the *Clerk's Prologue* and *Tale* and the *Merchant's Prologue* and *Tale*, is not definitely connected at the beginning with the *Summoner's Tale*. But its position in the best MSS. is between Fragments III and V, and there can be little doubt that Chaucer intended that order. In fact, IV and V are really connected, as they stand, and might be regarded as one group.

On the position of Fragment IV in the different classes of MSS. see Miss Hammond, p. 302.

The Clerk's Prologue

2 f. Cf. *Gen Prol*, I, 840 f.; RR, 1000.

6 Eccl. iii, 1. Cf. *FrT*, III, 1475, and n.

7 *as beth*; on this use of *as* (pleonastic) see *KnT*, I, 2302, n.

10 f. Cf. the Fr. proverb, "ki en jeu entre jeu consente"; and Skeat, EE Prov., p. 116, no. 275.

12 This reference to friars fits the preceding tale, whether or not it was written with that in mind.

16 *colours*, rhetorical ornaments, a term frequently employed by Geoffroi de Vinsauf. Cf. his Nova Poetria, 1094 ff. (ed. Faral, Les Arts Poétiques du xiie et du xiiie Siècle, Paris, 1924, pp. 231 ff.), his De Modo et Arte Dictandi et Versificandi, ii, 3 (Faral, pp. 284 ff.), and his De Coloribus Rhetoricis (Faral, pp. 321 ff.). See H. B. Hinckley, MP, XVI, 39; cf. further C. S. Baldwin, PMLA, XLII, 106 ff. For general discussion of Chaucer's knowledge of the rhetoricians see Manly, Chaucer and the Rhetoricians, Brit. Acad., 1926.

18 *Heigh style* (also in l. 41), apparently derived from the misreading "stylo . . . alto" for "stylo . . . alio" in the letter which accompanied Petrarch's version of the tale of Griselda (Ch. Soc. Orig. and Anal., p. 170).

26 Many have inferred from this passage that Chaucer himself met Petrarch in Italy. But there is no real evidence of the meeting, and the chances are against it. The Clerk's statement, of course, proves nothing. It is more likely to be an acknowledgment, in a traditional form, of literary indebtedness, than testimony to a personal experience. See, for some account of the convention, Professor G. L. Hendrickson, MP, IV, 179 ff., and cf. M. Praz, Monthly Criterion, VI, 144 f. For evidence that Chaucer had little opportunity to visit Petrarch, see the discussion of his first Italian journey by Professor F. J. Mather, MLN, XI, 210 ff., XII, 1 ff. For a conjectural construction of a route of travel which might have made the meeting possible see G. B. Parks, ELH, XVI, 174 ff. Further references on the whole subject are given by Miss Hammond, pp. 305 ff.; see also Wells, pp. 611, 726, and a recent article by E. H. Wilkins, ELH, XVI, 167, reprinted in The Making of the Canzoniere, Rome, 1951, pp. 305 ff., which comments on Chaucer's acquaintance with Italian.

29 Petrarch died July 18, 1374. Professor A. S. Cook notes (Rom. Rev., VIII, 222 f.) that he was never literally *nayled in his cheste*, but that his body was laid uncoffined in a sarcophagus. Of course, Chaucer's phrase meant no more than that Petrarch was "dead and buried."

31 With this tribute to Petrarch Professor Lowes (PMLA, XIX, 641, n.) compares Deschamps's famous lines on Chaucer. Both here and in *MkT*, VII, 2325, the best MSS. support the spelling *Petrak* rather than *Petrark*. There are parallels for it in French, Latin, and Italian documents, and Petrarch's father was regularly called "Petracco." But the best authorized spelling for the poet's own name was "Petrarca" or "Petrarcha." See Tatlock, Dev. and Chron., p. 159; G. L. Hamilton, MLN, XXIII, 171 f ; and A. S. Cook, Rom. Rev., VIII, 218.

34 *Lynyan*, Giovanni da Lignaco (or Legnano) (circa 1310–1383), the eminent Professor of Canon Law at Bologna. He wrote on law, ethics, theology, and astronomy. For an account of his life, see A. S. Cook, Rom. Rev., VIII, 353 ff.

Professor Cook argues that Chaucer used the term *philosophie* here with special reference to natural philosophy.

41 ff. The explicit reference here to the written form of Petrarch's tale rather counts against the supposition of a personal meeting between him and Chaucer.

43 *prohemye*, proem, introduction. The reference is really to the first section of the tale.

Except for *Mount Vesulus* (which is Petrarch's Latin form for Mt. Viso), Chaucer gives the places in the story their French names. This has been taken as an indication that he was following a French translation of Petrarch.

51 *To Emele-ward*, towards Æmilia.

54 *impertinent*, irrelevant.

55 *conveyen his mateere*, introduce (lit. "escort") his matter.

The Clerk's Tale

The source of the *Clerk's Tale*, as definitely acknowledged in the *Prologue*, is Petrarch's Latin story, De Obedientia ac Fide Uxoria Mythologia. This is in turn a translation from Boccaccio, Decamerone, x, 10. The Italian and Latin texts are both printed in the Chaucer Society's Originals and Analogues, pp. 153 ff. Chaucer's version corresponds so closely in many places to Petrarch's, that he is generally held to have followed the Latin text. Whether he also used other redactions of the story has been the subject of considerable discussion. Dr. W. E. Farnham (MLN, XXXIII, 193 ff.) has pointed out a number of passages which appear to have been influenced by Boccaccio's Italian. They are possibly to be explained by the existence of marginal quotations in the MS. of Petrarch's Latin. At all events, neither these parallels nor those noted in other tales suffice to prove that Chaucer was acquainted with the Decameron. There can be no doubt, however, that the story of Griselda was known to him in a French translation. Professor Cook (Rom. Rev., VIII, 210 ff.) argued that Chaucer consulted the version which is preserved in Le Ménagier de Paris (ed. Pichon, 2 v., Paris, 1846), or one nearly like it. But Dr. J. B. Severs, in an article of which he has kindly given the editor a copy (since published in PMLA, XLVII, 431 ff.), has shown that another French translation (in MS. Fr. 1165, Bibliothèque Nationale) stands much closer to Chaucer's text. Some of the more significant parallels pointed out by Dr. Severs are recorded in the following notes. Dr. Severs has also collated the published text of Petrarch's Latin, reprinted in the Originals and Analogues from the Basel edition of 1581 with that of three MSS. (Bibl. Nat. Lat., 11291, 16232, and 17165). Both the Latin original and the French translation are printed by Professor Severs in SA, pp. 296 ff. with detailed discussion of Chaucer's use of his sources. For further treatment see his volume, The Literary Relationships of Chaucer's Clerkes Tale, New Haven, 1944. His conclusions as to the exact type of MS. used by Chaucer have been disputed by Mrs. Dempster, MP, XLI, 6 ff.

The question whether Chaucer ever revised the *ClT* is discussed in M-R CT, II, 244, 500–1; by

Severs in Spec., XXI, 295 ff.; by Mrs. Dempster in PMLA, LXI, 384 ff. and PMLA, LXVIII, 1144 ff.

With Chaucer's use of a French version of the *Clerk's Tale* may be compared what is known or surmised concerning his recourse to French translations of Lucan, and Ovid, and Boethius. See *MLT*, II, 400, n.; *MkT*, VII, 2671, n.; and the introductions to the Explanatory Notes on *LGW* and *Bo*.

On the general history of the Griselda story, see Landau, Quellen des Dekameron, Stuttgart, 1884, pp. 156 ff.; R. Köhler, Kleinere Schriften, Berlin, 1900, II, 501 ff.; Westenholz, Die Griseldis-sage in der Literaturgeschichte, Heidelberg, 1888; Käte Laserstein, Der Griseldisstoff in der Weltliteratur, Weimar, 1926. Elie Golenistcheff-Koutouzoff, L'Histoire de Griseldis en France au XIVme et au XVme siècle, Paris, 1933; W. Küchler, Die Neueren Sprachen, XXXIII, 354 ff. Further references are given in Aarne's Types of the Folk-Tale, tr. S. Thompson, FF Com., no. 74, Helsinki, 1928, p. 133, no. 887, and p. 68, no. 425 A; and (especially for modern versions) in Koch's notes to Hertzberg's translation of the *Canterbury Tales*, Berlin, 1925, pp. 531 ff.

The Griselda story is one of the most familiar and popular in European literature. Most treatments of the subject, like Chaucer's, are based directly or indirectly on the Decameron. So Boccaccio may be called, in a real sense, the creator of the type. He at least gave it the literary form by which it has been known all over the world, and no source of his version has ben discovered. But Petrarch, in the letter which accompanied his Latin translation, implies that Boccaccio drew upon Italian popular tradition, and modern investigation has found the elements of the story to be widely dispersed in folklore. Four Griselda *märchen* published by R. Köhler in Gosche's Archiv, I, 409 ff., have been shown to represent versions probably older than Boccaccio's. (See E. Castle, in Archivum Romanicum, VIII, 281 ff.) And in two recent investigations the general body of related folk-tales has been fully examined. Dr. D. D. Griffith (The Origin of the Griselda Story, Univ. of Washington Pub. in Lang. & Lit., VIII, Seattle, 1931), following a suggestion made some time ago by Professor Kittredge, has shown that Boccaccio's story is ultimately derived from a combination of the Cupid and Psyche tale with another of the type of the Lai le Fraisne or the ballad of Fair Annie. Mr. W. A. Cate has collected evidence to prove that the two elements were not first combined by Boccaccio. On the contrary he finds that the entire Griselda story is accounted for by what he calls the "western version" of the Cupid and Psyche type — represented by upwards of forty tales in western Europe (see p. 394, n.). Mr. Cate has very kindly supplied the editor with information about the progress and results of his study. His conclusions are also briefly indicated in his published article (Stud. Phil., XXIX, 389 ff.), which gives an excellent statement of the whole problem.

In its ultimate origin, the story of Griselda is doubtless a fairy-tale. For an attempt to discern some survivals of a supernatural character in the heroine in Chaucer's version, see W. H. Schofield, Eng. Lit. from the Norman Conquest to Chaucer, London, 1906, pp. 193 f. Cf. also Le Moyen Age, III, 182 f. The husband was originally an other-world visitant, and persecutions like those of Griselda were not infrequently made to serve supernatural or magic ends. Cf., for a single example, the Irish tale of disenchantment (of partly dissimilar plot) in Dr. Douglas Hyde's An Sgeuluidhe Gaodhalach, ii, 123, no. 17 (trans. by Dottin, Annales de Bretagne, XII, 245 ff.).

The extravagant, not to say "monstrous" behavior of both Walter and Griselda has been the subject of much discussion. Ultimately it must probably be explained as a reflection of the underlying folk-tale. For varying estimates of Chaucer's use of the story see the studies of Griffith and Cate, already cited; K. Malone, Chapters on Chaucer, pp. 210 ff., 222 ff.; and J. Sledd, MP, LI, 78 ff.

The *Clerk's Tale* has usually been regarded as one of Chaucer's earlier works, written shortly after his first Italian journey. Thus Skeat put it about 1373, and Mr. Pollard accepted a date in the seventies (see Oxf. Chau., III, 454; Pollard, Chaucer Primer, London, 1893, p. 68). These scholars of course recognized that certain modifications were made to fit the tale to its place in the Canterbury series. Recently there has been a disposition to put the whole composition of the piece in the Canterbury period. See particularly Professor Tatlock's discussion, Dev. and Chron., pp. 156 ff. He shows that, as in the case of the *Man of Law's Tale*, general arguments from the stanzaic meter or from the mediæval character of the poem are by no means conclusive as to early composition. For further discussion, with a reasonable statement of the grounds for assigning the work to the Canterbury period, see Professor K. Sisam's separate edition of the tale (Oxford, 1923).

58 *roote*, "foot"; Petrarch, "ad radicem Vesuli" (p. 153).

76 "Save in some things in which he was at fault." On the sense of *to blame* see *Gen Prol*, I, 375, n.

88 f. *that . . . he*, equivalent to a relative. On such loose constructions cf. *KnT*, I, 2710, n.

107 *and evere han doon*. Skeat interprets: "and (both you and your doings) have ever brought it about." But it is simpler, and quite in accord with Middle English construction, to understand the passage: "So well you and all your works please us, and ever have." *Us lyketh yow* is itself inconsistent in construction, the pronoun *yow* apparently standing as object of the impersonal *us lyketh*.

113 ff. Cf. Barbour's Bruce, i, 266–68.

118 f. Cf. *ML Intro*, II, 20, n.

155 ff. With the discussion of heredity here cf. the treatment of *gentilesse* in *WBT*, III, 1109 ff., and in *Gentilesse*.

157 *Bountee*, goodness. Petrarch: "Quicquid in homine boni est" (p. 155).

206 f. A reference to the Nativity; Luke ii, 7.

212 *oon the faireste*; cf. *FranklT*, V, 734; also *oon the beste, Tr*, i, 1081; *oon the leeste, Tr*, iii, 1310; *oon . . . the beste ypreysed, Tr*, v, 1473. For this construction, which was regular in AS. and Mid. Eng., Mod. Eng. has substituted "one of the fairest, best," etc. (followed by a plural). Some passages show a confusion of the two constructions. Cf. *oon of the gretteste . . . thyng, Mel*, VII, 1678; *Oon of the gretteste auctour, NPT*, VII, 2984; also *FranklT*, V, 932, and *Tr*, v, 832. For further discussion of the idiom see L. Kellner, Historical Outlines of Eng. Syntax,

London, 1892, pp. 110 ff.; Hinckley, MP, XVI, 46; C. Stoffel, ESt, XXVII, 253 ff.

215-17 Chaucer's addition.

220 *rype and sad corage,* "a mature and steadfast heart"; "courage meur et ancien," MS. 1165 (Severs, PMLA, XLVII, 438).

227 *shredde and seeth for hir lyvinge,* sliced and boiled for their sustenance.

229 *kepte . . . on-lofte,* kept aloft, sustained.

237 *in sad wyse,* seriously.

253 *hath doon make,* has caused (somebody) to make, has had made. Cf. l. 1098, below, and *KnT,* I, 1913, n.

260-94 Considerably expanded in Chaucer.

260 *undren,* 9 A.M. Petrarch, "hora . . . prandii" (pp. 156 f.).

262 ff. On the structure and internal arrangements of houses in Chaucer's time see H. M. Smyser, Speculum, XXXI, 297 ff.

266 Either "to farthest Italy" or "as far as Italy extends" (*last,* the contracted form of *lasteth*).

276 Professor Manly notes that the well here mentioned perhaps preserves a trace of a spring or lake which marked the entrance to the other world in the original version.

336 *nevere erst,* never before. On this use of the superlative, see *KnT,* I, 1566, n.

350 *yow avyse,* deliberate, with the implication of refusal. The editors compare the formula "le roy s'avisera," used in withholding the royal consent to a proposed measure.

364 *For to be deed,* though I were to die. See *KnT,* I, 1133, n., and 1587, n.

375-76 The disinclination of the ladies to handle Griselda's clothing is mentioned in MS. 1165, but not in Petrarch's Latin or the French version in the Ménagier (Severs, p. 439).

381 *corone,* nuptial garland. Cf. *SecNT,* VIII, 220, n.; *Tr,* ii, 1735, n.

403 *dorste han swore,* i.e., the contrary. Cf. *KnT,* I, 1089, n.

413 Cf. *MLT,* II, 532; *Tr,* i, 1078.

422 *honestetee,* honor, nobility. Cf. the gloss in MSS. El Hg Dd: "Sic Walterus humili quidem set insigni ac prospero matrimonio honestatis summa dei in pace," etc. Professor Hendrickson (MP, IV, 191) points out that "honestatis" (so in Orig. and Anal., p. 159) is probably an error for Petrarch's original reading, "honestatus."

429 "Knew all a wife's domestic work."

431 *The commune profit* (repeated ironically in l. 1194) has been called a "favorite phrase of fourteenth-century Socialism." It certainly recurs often in works on social questions or on the duties of a prince. For instances of its use see NED, s. vv. Common, Profit; also H. R. Patch, JEGP, XXIX, 381 f. (with references to other articles), and Miss M. Schlauch, Spec., XX, 133 ff.

432 ff. Cook notes (PQ, IV, 27) that the corresponding passage in Petrarch rests upon Pilatus' Latin translation of Odyssey, vii, 73 f.

444 *Al had hire levere,* a confusion of *hire were levere* and *she had levere.*

452 *tempte,* test, prove.

459-62 Chaucer's addition.

460 *yvele it sit,* it ill befits (Fr. "il sied mal").

483 Here and in the following stanza, Walter employs the disrespectful *thou,* perhaps (as Skeat

suggested) "under pretence of reporting the opinion of others." But it recurs in ll. 1031, 1053, 1056, where it may be taken simply as a mark of intimacy.

516 *a furlong wey;* cf. *MLT,* II, 557, n.

533-36 Chaucer's description of the cruel conduct of the sergeant is closer to MS. 1165 than to Petrarch or the Ménagier (Severs, p. 440).

554-67 Chaucer's addition.

570 f. *That . . . burieth;* the construction is inconsequent. Cf. *PardT,* VI, 826.

588 *whenne,* whence (AS. "hwanon").

590 *Panik;* Petrarch, "de Panico" (p. 161); Boccaccio, "de Panago" (p. 166). This place has not been identified with certainty, but an actual Panico, near Bologna, is noted by R. B. Pearsall in MLN, LXVII, 529 ff. See also F. P. Magoun, Jr., who cites evidence of the existence of *conti di Panico* near Bologna, in Med. Stud. XVII, p. 133.

602 *evere in oon ylike,* always alike, consistently.

607 *Noon accident for noon adversitee,* no outward sign of any adversity she suffered. In this apparently technical use of *accident* Chaucer departs from both Petrarch ("sive ex proposito sive incidenter," p. 161) and MS. 1165 ("de purpose ou par accident"; Severs, p. 447).

609 *in ernest nor in game,* under any circumstances. On this and similar phrases see *Gen Prol,* I, 534, n.

621-23 Chaucer's addition.

625 *sikly berth,* dislike, take it ill; Petrarch, "aegre . . . ferre" (p. 162).

687 "Wondered the more, the longer (he thought of it)." Cf. "the longer, the better."

719 *for no worldly unreste,* on account of no earthly discomfort.

738 *message,* messenger, or collectively, messengers; Petrarch, "nuncios" (p. 164). Cf. also l. 947, below.

743 *countrefete,* in early English, meant literally "imitate." But passages like this and *MerchT,* IV, 2121, show how it acquired its modern sense.

811-12, 837-40, 851-61 Chaucer's additions.

871 f. Cf. Job i, 21.

880-82 Chaucer's addition; cf. RR, 445. *Lyk a worm,* i.e., naked; a stock comparison (Fr. "nu comme un ver").

902 From Job iii, 3.

903 On *lyves creature* see *KnT,* I, 1912, n.

911 Professor Manly notes that "the preservation of the old clothing is a feature of the original folk-tale."

915-17 This realistic detail, not mentioned in Petrarch or the Ménagier, appears in MS. 1165 (Severs, p. 439).

916 There is strong MS. support for the reading *and she more of age.* This is accepted by Manly and may be right, though it clogs the meter.

932-38 Chaucer's addition.

932 Cf. Job xl, 4; xlii, 1–6. Also *WB Prol,* III, 436.

934 f. Cf. *WB Prol.,* III, 706, 688 ff.

938 *but it be falle of newe,* "unless it has happened recently."

965 *yvel biseye,* ill provided.

981 *undren,* 9 A.M.; Petrarch "hora tertia" (p. 167).

990-91 Not in Petrarch.

995-1008 Chaucer's addition. Skeat held that

the passage was written later than the body of the tale, and Ten Brink (Hist. of Eng. Lit., New York, 1893–96, II, 123) suggested that it referred to the reception of Richard II in 1387. Brusendorff (p. 161, n.) compared Petrarch, Trionfo del Tempo, ll. 132–34. Though the passages are similar, there is no evidence that Chaucer had Petrarch in mind. On the scribal note *Auctor*, in the margin of several MSS., which is not to be taken here as indicating that Chaucer interrupts the Clerk, see *MLT*, II, 358, n.

999 "Dear enough at a jane," a Genoese coin worth a half-penny; used also in Provençal as a comparison for worthlessness. See a poem of Raimbaut de Vaqueires in V. Crescini, Studi Romanzi, Padua, 1892, p. 50, ll. 71 f.;

> Jujar, to proenzalesco,
> s'eu ja gauz aja de mi,
> non prezo un genoi.

1039 *mo*, others (lit. "more"); Petrarch, "alteram" (p. 168).

1049 *gan his herte dresse*, prepared his heart.

1079–1106 Much expanded in Chaucer's version.

1109 *feeste maketh*, "does her honor" (Fr. "faire fête à").

1138–40 Cf. *The Former Age*.

1141–62 The moral is taken from Petrarch, the *auctour* referred to in the text.

1151 *Receyven . . . in gree*, receive in good spirit, in good part.

1152 "For it is very reasonable that He should test that which He created."

1153 f.   James i, 13.

1162 ff.   See note at l. 1212 in text and explanatory note to l. 1212ᵃ.

1163 The second application of the tale, which follows, is the Clerk's direct reply, in satirical vein, to the Wife of Bath. It was obviously written when the plan of the Marriage Group was well under way. Whether any considerable time elapsed between the writing of the tale and the addition of this ending is unknown.

1170 "For the love of the Wife of Bath." For the order of words cf. *the Grekes hors Synoun*, *SqT*, V, 209; *The kynges metynge Pharao*, *BD*, 282; *Eleyne that was Menelaus wif his brothir*, *Bo*, iv, m. 7, 7. Other examples are given by Skeat in his note on the passage in the *SqT*. In the earlier form of the construction the proper name was put in the genitive ("the Kinges sone Henries," AS. Chron., s.a., 1140), and there was therefore no ambiguity.

1171 *secte*, either "Sect" or "Sex." The former meaning is established for Chaucer, and Kittredge, in his discussion of the Marriage Group, took it in that sense here. The Clerk, he held, was describing the Wife as a heresiarch. For objections see H. Kökeritz, PQ, XXVI, 147 ff., who argues for the meaning "Sex."

1177 The song, as the scribe's heading, *Lenvoy de Chaucer*, indicates, is Chaucer's independent composition. But it belongs dramatically to the Clerk, and is entirely appropriate. (For the opposing view see Koch, Angl., L, 65 f.)

The meter changes to six-line stanzas, with only three rimes throughout the series (*-ence, -aille, -inde*).

1188 *Chichevache* (lit. "lean cow," perhaps a corruption of *chiche face* "lean face"), a cow which fed only on patient wives, and consequently had little to eat; sometimes contrasted with Bicorne, which lived on patient husbands, and fared better. See Jubinal, Mystères Inédits du xvᵉ Siècle, Paris, 1837, I, 248, 390; Lydgate, Bycorne and Chichevache, Minor Poems, ed. Halliwell-Phillips, Percy Soc., 1840, p. 129; Bolte, Herrig's Arch., CVI, 1, CXIV, 80; Zt. für Volkskunde, XIX, 58 ff. For a good account of the recorded forms of the name see Miss Hammond, English Verse between Chaucer and Surrey, pp. 113 ff.

1204 *aventaille*, ventail, the lower half of the movable part of a helmet. Cf. G. L. Hamilton, MP, III, 541 ff.

1207–10 Cf. *WB Prol*, III, 253–56, 265–70.

1211 A proverbial comparison. See Piers Plowman, B, i, 154; Skeat, EE Prov., p. 117, no. 276.

1212ᵃ ff. The Host's stanza, which breaks the continuity of the tale, is generally held to have been written early and rejected in favor of the present ending. But it held its place in the MSS. On the question of the author's revision of the Envoy see M-R CT, II, 243 ff., 265 ff., III, 473; and J. B. Severs, MLN, LXIX, 472. For a plausible reconstruction of the successive stages in the adaptation of the tale to the Marriage Group, see Mrs. Dempster, PMLA, LXVIII, 1142 ff.

The Merchant's Prologue

On the date of the *Merchant's Prologue* and *Tale* see the introduction to the Explanatory Notes on the *Wife of Bath's Prologue*. The repetition of l. 1212 in l. 1213 and the mention of Griseldis in l. 1224 unmistakably link the *Merchant's Prologue* to the *Clerk's Tale*. But in a number of MSS. the two tales are separated. See the Textual Notes on the *Host's Stanza* (IV, 1212ᵃ⁻ᵍ). In several MSS. the *Merchant's Tale* is followed by the *Wife of Bath's*. For a spurious link connecting the two see the Textual Notes on *Merch Epil*.

1226–27 Cf. *Bukton*, 13–16.

1230 On *Seint Thomas of Ynde* see *SumT*, III, 1980, n.

The Merchant's Tale

The story of January and May is one of the most original of Chaucer's narratives. For the earlier part of the poem he drew on his own *Melibee*, from which he took a number of passages. For the trick played at the end on the old dotard he used a jest — the so-called Pear-Tree episode — current in many popular tales. His exact source is unknown, but close parallels are afforded by an Italian tale and a German poem, both printed by Holthausen, Eng. Stud., XLIII, 168 ff. On other analogues and their relation, see Originals and Analogues (Ch. Soc.), pp. 177 ff., 341 ff., 544; Varnhagen, Anglia, VII, Anz., 155 ff.; Koeppel, Angl., XIV, 257; Angl. Beibl., XXVII, 61; J. Bédier, Les Fabliaux, 4th ed., Paris, 1925, p. 469 f.; Koch's notes to Hertzberg's translation of the *Canterbury Tales*, Berlin, 1925, pp. 535 f. and Miss M. Schlauch, MLN, XLIX, 229 ff. and ELH, IV, 201 ff. The Pear-Tree story is no. 1423 in Aarne's Types of the Folk-Tale, tr. S. Thompson, FF. Com., no. 74, Helsinki, 1928, p. 175. Beyond the plot, or strictly narrative portion, the tale contains much descriptive and satirical matter, derived largely from the same sources that Chaucer used in the earlier parts of the Marriage Group: The Miroir de Mariage, St. Jerome against Jovinian, Theophrastus, and the *Parson's Tale*. Reminiscences of Boethius and of Albertano's Liber de Amore have also been pointed out. Parallel passages in these and other works are noted below. For further details see Skeat, Oxf. Ch., III, 458; Koeppel, Herrig's Arch., LXXXVI, 34 ff.; Lowes, MP, VIII, 165 ff.; and the references in Miss Hammond, p. 309; Wells, pp. 880, 1032, 1148, 1240, 1328, 1426, 1541, 1647, 1741, 1934. Parallels from Deschamps and Boccaccio as well as analogues of the Pear-Tree (or better, Fruit-Tree) episode are assembled by Mrs. Dempster in SA, 333 ff. She gives added references on the history of the story. Professor J. C. McGalliard, in PQ, XXV, 193, notes additional parallels, both verbal and structural, in the Miroir, and argues for more influence of Deschamps on Chaucer's thought than has been previously recognized. For an extended comparison of Chaucer's method of characterization with that of Ben Jonson and Molière, see again McGalliard, PQ, XXV, 343. On the relations of Pope's January and May to Chaucer's poem see A. Schade, ESt, XXV, 1 ff.

The figure of the aged or feeble lover is so frequent in literature that it is not necessary to multiply references on the subject. It appears in the *Shipman's Tale* and the *Wife of Bath's Prologue*, but Chaucer's most noteworthy treatment of it is here in the *Merchant's Tale*. No particular model has been pointed out for the character of January. Examples of the general type in both European and oriental literature are cited by L. C. Stern in CZ, V, 200, 310, n. He includes Ovid's Amores, iii, 7, and Boccaccio's Decameron, ii, 10, both of which might have been known to Chaucer. But neither of them is really similar to the *Merchant's Tale*. There is more chance that Chaucer was influenced by the description of the aged husband of Agapes in the Ameto, since he probably knew that work. See SA, 333, 339 ff. Illustrations of the character as it appears in mediæval lyrics (especially in the "chansons des malmariées") are cited by T. Chotzen, Recherches sur la Poésie de Dafydd ab Gwilym, Amsterdam, 1927, p. 246. One of the most brilliant poems in Modern Irish, the Cúirt an Mheadhon Oidhche of Brian Merriman, deals with the *senex amans*.

Professor Tatlock (Dev. and Chron., pp. 205 ff.) conjectured that the *Merchant's Tale* was originally intended by Chaucer as a reply to the *Shipman's Tale*, then the Wife of Bath's. It is highly probable that the *Shipman's Tale* was written for the Wife, and possible enough (in spite of Brusendorff's objection, pp. 119 f.) that Chaucer at one time planned an altercation between her and the Merchant. But Professor Manly has pointed out (*CT*, p. 624) that there are also indications of a shift of assignment in the case of the *Merchant's Tale*. Certain passages (ll. 1251, 1322, 1389–90, and perhaps ll. 1347, 1384) imply that the speaker was a member of a religious order, and it is possible that in Chaucer's first plan it was the Monk, and not the Merchant, who was to oppose the Wife. Professor A. C. Baugh, who reviews the discussion of the problem in MP, XXXV, 16 ff., argues rather for an original assignment to the Friar. But cf. Mrs. Dempster, MP, XXXVI, 1 ff.,

who argues strongly that the tale was intended from the outset for the Merchant.

For critical observations on the tale see G. G. Sedgwick, University of Toronto Quarterly, XVII, 337 ff., and C. A. Owen, Jr., JEGP, LII, 297 ff.

1230 Miss R. H. Cline (in MLN, LX, 482 ff.) argues that St. Thomas is appropriately invoked here because of his incredulity.

1245 The localization in Lombardy may be due to some unidentified source of the story.

The account of the old man at the beginning has a number of parallels in the Miroir de Mariage. With ll. 1245–51 cf. Miroir, 278–83 (Deschamps, Œuvres, IX, SATF).

1251 *seculeer*, either secular clergy or laity. Professor McGalliard (PQ, XXV, 194) argues for the latter interpretation.

1260 Identical with *FranklT*, V, 805.

1267–1392 The Merchant's long praise of marriage is of course bitterly ironical. The whole passage is taken by Professor Koch to be a continuation of January's speech.

1268–74 Cf. Miroir, 369–70, 377–79, 394–98, 1074 ff.

1270 *the fruyt of his tresor*, i.e. (according to Skeat) purchased with his own wealth. But it may mean rather "the choicest part, and flower of his possessions." Cf. the proverbial contrast between *fruit* and *chaff*.

1277 *it sit wel*, it is fitting. *Sit* is the contracted form for *sitteth*.

1281 ff. Cf. Miroir, 528–33.

1287–92 Cf. Miroir, 221–30.

1294 *Theofraste*, the author of the Liber Aureolus de Nuptiis, quoted by St. Jerome (Adv. Jov., i, 47). See the introduction to the Explanatory Notes on *WB Prol*. With ll. 1296–1304 cf. Theophrastus's discussion "an vir sapiens ducat uxorem," quoted by Jerome (Migne, Pat. Lat., XXIII, 276), and in John of Salisbury's Policraticus, viii, 11 (ed. Webb, Oxford, 1909, II, 296). On the construction *he Theophraste*, see *KnT*, I, 1210, n. Cf. also ll. 1368, 1373, 1720, 1734, below.

1300 Cf. *WB Prol*, III, 308–10, 204–06.

1305–06 On the variant readings see the textual note. It is probable that Chaucer never completed the couplet.

1311 In MSS. El Hg is written the Latin source, from Albertano of Brescia, Liber de Amore Dei, De Uxore Diligenda (appended to De Arte Loquendi et Tacendi, Cuneo, 1507), fol. 40 recto. For the ultimate source cf. Prov. xix, 14.

1315 Cf. *ShipT*, VII, 9, and *ParsT*, X, 1068.

1319 Cf. *ParsT*, x, 918; also Eph. v, 32 (Vulg.).

1323–35 Again from Albertano, De Amore Dei, fol. 39 verso, whose text is followed in marginal glosses in MSS. El Hg.

1325–29 Gen. ii, 18, 21 f.

1332 With *paradys terrestre* contrast *purgatorie* in l. 1670, below, and *WB Prol*, III, 489.

1334–36 Cf. RR, 16438–42; also Miroir, 217–20.

1335 Gen. ii, 23 f.

1341 Cf. *Tr*. v, 445, 1321; RR, 2965 f., 20375 f.

1343–56 Cf. Miroir, ll. 231–34, 239–40, 245–47, 211–16, 248–51, 418, 423–24, 435–37.

1345 Cf. *ClT*, IV, 355.

1356–80 Chaucer here draws upon Albertano, Liber Consolationis (ed. Sundby, Chau. Soc., 1873, pp. 17 f.), in part directly and in part through his own *Melibee* (see VII, 1098 ff., and n.). Incidental use of the Miroir appears in ll. 1371–74 (cf. ll. 9143–49), and perhaps also in ll. 1366–68 (cf. ll. 9111–16).

1364 The reference to the *kydes skyn*, which does not appear in Albertano or the Fr. Melibée, seems due to direct recollection of Gen. xxvii, 16.

1376 The passage ascribed to Seneca is really from Albertano (Liber Consol., p. 18). Sundby traces it to Fulgentius, Mythologiarum, i, 22 (ed. Helm, Leipzig, 1898).

1377 *bit*, biddeth. From Dionysius Cato, Disticha, iii, no. 23.

1381–82 Eccl. xxxvi, 27: "Ubi non est mulier, ingemiscit egens." Quoted by Albertano, with variant readings *eger* ("sick") and *egens* (De Amore Dei, fol. 40 recto). Chaucer must have followed the former.

1384 ff. See Eph. v, 25, 28, 29, 31; quoted by Albertano, De Amore Dei, fol. 39 verso, et seq., whose text is followed in marginal glosses in MSS. El Hg.

1387 ff. Cf. *FranklT*, V, 749 ff.; *WB Prol*, III, 437 ff.

1393–96 Cf. Miroir, 9150–52, 9156–59, 9006–07, and (perhaps) 741, 745, 754.

1401 Cf. Ps. xxx, 3, 9.

1405–17 From Albertano, De Amore Dei, fol. 40 recto.

Professor Tatlock (Angl., XXXVII, 73, n.) has noted a similarity with the discussion of Feramonte in the "Questioni d'amore" in the Filocolo. But although Chaucer knew that work, it is hardly likely that he had it in mind here.

1415–17 Cf. Miroir, 722, 725, 727.

1417 Most MSS. read *sixteen*, which Manly defends as "in harmony with the humor of the tale. But he prints *twenty*, perhaps regarding it as an emendation or author's revision.

1418 Proverbial; see Haeckel, p. 35, no. 116.

1424 "Wade's boat." In *Tr*, iii, 614, there is another reference to the "tale of Wade." Speght's comment on the passage in the *Merchant's Tale* (in his edition of 1598) has often been called the most exasperating note ever written on Chaucer. He says: "Concerning Wade and his bote called Guingelot, as also his strange exploits in the same, because the matter is long and fabulous, I passe it over." If Speght really knew the story and understood the point of the allusion he was more fortunate than later editors. For though there are a number of references in mediæval literature which indicate that Wade was a famous hero, they do not suffice for the reconstruction of the narrative as it was known to Chaucer. The earliest mention of Wade is in the Anglo-Saxon poem Widsith, l. 22, where he is said to have ruled the Haelsings. In the Middle High German Kudrun and the Alexanderlied he is associated with Hagen, and in numerous romances he is referred to as a famous warrior. A Middle English fragment (c. 1300) connects him with sea-creatures but is altogether obscure. Only the Scandinavian Thidrekssaga (ed. Bertelsen, 2 v., Copenhagen, 1905–11, I, 73 ff.) and the related Rabenschlacht (ed. Martin, Deutsches Heldenbuch, II, Berlin, 1866, st. 964 ff.) give any extended account of him. According to the Thidrekssaga he was a giant, the son of King Vilkinus and a sea-woman. He was the father of

Wayland, whom he took to the dwarfs to be educated. It was agreed that after two years they might kill Wayland if Wade did not return. Wade was killed, but Wayland made his escape, and when checked in his flight by a great river he built himself a remarkable boat and sailed down to the sea. Possibly in the story known to Chaucer this boat was transferred from Wayland to Wade. Professor W. G. Howard reminds the editor that Wate, in the Kudrun, also has a boat, on which he abducts Hilde before her espousal to Hetel, and suggests that Chaucer, if he had in mind any similar incident in the story of Wade, may mean simply that *olde wyves* know too much about the tricks of wedlock. A boat figures, too, in Walter Map's De Gadone Milite (De Nugis Curialium, ii, 17), which has an altogether different story. Gado is a Vandal warrior and traveler who defends Offa's realm against the Romans. He is brought to England in a boat against his will.

For full discussion of the subject see, besides Skeat's note, an early article by Müllenhoff in the Zt. f. Deut. Alterthum, VI, 62 ff. (explaining Wade as a sea-divinity); R. W. Chambers, ed. Widsith, Cambridge, Eng., 1912, pp. 95 ff.; E. J. Bashe, PQ, II, 282 ff.

1425 *broken harm*, of uncertain meaning; Skeat explains it as "petty annoyances." Professor Magoun (Anglia, LIII, 223 f.) cites the similar phrase "broken sorowe" in Skelton's Magnificence (ed. Ramsay, EETS, 1908, l. 1587), of which the meaning is also doubtful. For the proposal to take *broken* as an infinitive, "to make use of" (A. S. *brúcan*), see F. G. Cassidy, MLN, LVIII, 23 ff.

1427–28 Cf. *WB Prol*, III, 44c ff.

1429–40 Cf. Miroir, 730–33, 423–430, 91, 103–04.

1441–51 Cf. *ParsT*, X, 938 ff.; also Miroir, 106–16.

1456 Cf. *WB Prol*, III, 112, and *Mel*, VII, 1088. The following lines also recall *WB Prol*, III, 113 ff.

1461–66 Cf. Miroir, ll. 117–25.

1476 On *Placebo*, the appropriate name for the complaisant adviser, see *SumT*, III, 2075, n.

1485 Cf. *MillT*, I, 3530, and n.

1516 "Your heart is merry." The figure is that of hanging on a peg.

1523–25 The idea here expressed is discussed in a general way by Seneca in De Beneficiis, i, 14–15. It is combined with the second counsel, which follows in ll. 1526–29, in a passage of Walter Map's Epistola Valerii, which Chaucer may have had in mind. See De Nugis Curialium, iv, 3 (ed. James, Anecdota Oxoniensia, XIV, 1914, p. 146, ll. 17 f.).

1531–36 Cf. Miroir, 1538–45.

1535 On the feminine suffix in *chidestere*, see *Gen Prol*, I, 241 f., n.

1536 *mannysh wood*, perhaps a fierce virago (lit. "mannish mad"). But the interpretation "lustful, mad for men," is defended by F. L. Utley, MLN, LIII, 359 ff.

1537–42 Cf. Albertano, De Amore Dei, fol. 40 verso; also Miroir, 1553–75.

1543 Cf. Miroir, 509, and the heading to Chapter vii.

1544–48 Cf. Miroir, 1576–84.

1553 For this allusion, see *WB Prol*, III, 492 n.

1560–61 Cf. RR, 13851 f.

1582 Cf. Boethius, *Bo*, v, m. 4, 26; *Tr*, i, 365.

1598 Proverbial; see Skeat, EE Prov., p. 118, no. 278; Haeckel, p. 1, no. 2.

1601-04 Cf. Miroir, ll. 1202–06, which comes, in turn, from the beginning of Jerome's excerpt from Theophrastus, (Migne, Pat. Lat., XXIII, 276).

1621 Cf. Miroir, 422.

1640 On the seven deadly sins see the *Parson's Tale* and Dan Michel's Ayenbite of Inwyt (ed. Morris, EETS, 1866, pp. 15 ff.). The classification by "branches" and "twigs" was customary. Cf. *ParsT*, X, 389.

1659 If there is no other obstacle than wedded happiness, he argues, in the way of your salvation, God of his mercy can remove that.

1662 *er ye have youre right of hooly chirche*, before you receive the blessing of the Church, i.e. before your wedding is really solemnized.

1670 Cf. *WB Prol*, III, 489, and n.

1682 This line is metrically defective in all MSS. Tyrwhitt inserted *but* before *thynne*, and other emendations can be easily devised. But since there are a few other lines in which an unaccented syllable is apparently lacking, it seems best to keep the reading of the MSS. and recognize that Chaucer occasionally allowed himself this freedom. Because of the frequency of such lines in Lydgate the type is sometimes called "Lydgation." For other possible examples see *FrT*, III, 1647; *Prol Mel*, VII, 951; *NPT*, VII, 3418 (see textual note).

1684-87 This reference to the Wife of Bath, if regarded as a comment of the Merchant's, is dramatically appropriate, though it is inserted a little strangely before the last line of Justin's speech. To avoid a complicated punctuation, and also to save the better accredited reading *ye* in l. 1686, Professor Tatlock suggests that Chaucer adopted the bold device of making Justin himself quote the Wife. There is admittedly a choice of difficulties. But Mr. Tatlock's interpretation seems the harder of the two. See his Dev. and Chron., p. 204; and the textual note on l. 1686. Koch (Eng. Stud., XLVII, 372) treats the passage as a late addition to the tale. See also Angl., L, 65 f. Manly (M-R CT, III, 475) suggests, rather desperately, that the line might be an intrusion from a memorandum set down by Chaucer for use in his *Envoy to Bukton*.

1693 *Mayus*, as Skeat notes, is a masculine form because the name of the month is so.

1701 ff. "A composite of . . . significant bits from the order for matrimony and from the nuptial mass which would follow" (Tatlock, MLN, XXXII, 373). The *hooly sacrement* may refer either to the sacrament of matrimony or the receiving of the Eucharist. For considerations in favor of the former interpretation see Sister Mary Immaculate, MLQ, II, pp. 62 ff.

1703-07 Cf. Miroir, 275–77.

1716 On *Orpheus*, the ancient musician, see Ovid, Met., x, 1–85; xi, 1–66; and on Amphion (pronounced *Amphioún*) who helped by his music to build the city of Thebes, Met., vi, 177 ff., 224 ff., 271 ff., 402 ff.; xv, 427. There are also several references to Amphion in Statius (Theb., i, 9 f.; viii, 232; x, 873). Orpheus, Joab, and Theodamas are mentioned in *HF*, 1203, 1245, 1246.

1719 See II Sam. ii, 28; xviii, 16; xx, 22.

1720 *Theodomas*, Theodamas, the Theban augur. The episode referred to is uncertain. In the Thebaid

Theodamas is not represented as a trumpeter, though his invocation is said to have been followed by a sound of trumpets (viii, 343).

1727 *fyrbrond*, the torch of the marriage procession. Cf. RR, 3424 ff.

1730 Cf. *LGW*, 2250.

1732 Martianus Capella (5th cent.), the author of De Nuptiis Philologiae et Mercurii.

With the phraseology here cf. Inf., xxv, 94–98 ("Taccia Lucano omai," etc.); and for the idea, see also Inf., xxxiv, 22; Par., xix, 7 ff.

1745 Esther ii and v.

1754 Cf. *BD*, 331, *PF*, 290 f.

1763 Mr. Hinckley (PQ, VI, 313) compares Catullus, v, 5–6. But the idea is a commonplace in love-poetry, especially of the "Tagelied" type.

1772 f. Cf. *Gen Prol*, I, 100, n.

1777 Cf. *PF*, 114; RR, 15778 f.

1783 Here and at ll. 1869, 2057, 2107, 2125, MS. El (and occasionally others) again has *Auctor* written in the margin. Cf. *MLT*, II, 358, n.

1785 *false hoomly hewe*, "false domestic servant."

1786 Cf. Phaedrus, lib. iv, fab. 18; Gesta Romanorum, ch. 174.

1793 From Boethius, *Bo*, iii, pr. 5, 68 ff. The whole passage treats the [same general subject as ll. 1783 ff.

1795 Cf. *Astr*, ii, 7.

1807 *ypocras*, a cordial drink made of wine, with spices and sugar. See *Pard Prol*, VI, 306, n.

clarree, see *KnT*, I, 1471, n.

vernage, a strong and sweet kind of Italian wine ("vernaccia").

1810 On *Constantyn*, see *Gen Prol*, I, 429 ff., n.

1817 For the *travers*, or curtain, cf. *Tr*, iii, 674.

1819 ff. Cf. *LGW*, 2677. On the ritual "Benedictio thalami" see Tatlock, MLN, XXXII, 374; and for further illustrative notes on the marriage customs here referred to see Karl Schmidt, Jus Primae Noctis, Freiburg, 1881, pp. 146 ff.; W. Hertz, Spielmannsbuch, 3d ed., Berlin, 1905, pp. 405 f. For an interesting parallel to Chaucer's whole account see the lay of *Le Fraisne* by Marie de France, ll. 369 ff. (ed. Warnke, 3d ed., Halle, 1925).

1840 Cf. *ParsT*, X, 859.

1847-48 Cf. *WB Prol*, III, 455–56.

1862 From RR, 19731 f.; cf. *SqT*, V, 349; Haeckel, p. 13, no. 42.

1881 *compleynt*, a technical name for a form of poetical composition. Cf. Chaucer's own complaints, and the introduction to the *Short Poems*.

1887 In the four days the Moon passed from the second degree of Taurus, through Gemini, into Cancer.

1942 The use of the subjunctive with *that* in direct commands or entreaties is rare in Chaucer. Cf. *BD*, 206.

1962 *precious*, over-fastidious (Fr. "précieux").

1967 Cf. *Gen Prol*, I, 844, and n.

1972 The sentence is proverbial; cf. *FrT*, III, 1475, n. But the application here is astrological. See the reference to "elections," *MLT*, II, 312, and n.

1986 Cf. *KnT*, I, 1761, and n.

1987 ff. The sentiment is familiar in the love-poetry of the period.

2014 See *FrT*, III, 1369, n.

2021 Cf. *Gen Prol*, I, 335 ff.

2028 ff. Professor McGalliard (PQ, XXV, 204)

suggests that this garden may owe something to the one in the Miroir, but the parallels are not very striking.

2032 The reference is to Guillaume de Lorris, author of the first part of the Roman de la Rose.

2034 On *Priapus* see Ovid, Fasti, i, 415 ff.

2038 The classical divinities of the lower world are here brought into association with the fairies of northern tradition. Skeat (on l. 2227, below) observes that the notion of identifying Pluto with the King of Fairyland occurs again in the romance, or lay, of Sir Orfeo (Ritson, Met. Rom., rev. ed., Edinburgh, 1885, III, 4). Sir Orfeo (Orpheus) redeems Eurydice from "the Kyng of fayri." This conception might carry with it the identification of Proserpina with the fairy queen, which is not peculiar to Chaucer. Cf., for example, the romance of Arthur of Little Britain, translated by Lord Berners from a lost French source of the fourteenth century (ed. Utterson, Lond., 1814, pp. 47 ff.). On a similar confusion between fairy-land and the lower world of Christian eschatology cf. Dr. T. Spencer, Speculum, II, 183, n. 7.

In *HF*, 1511 f., Proserpina appears in her proper classical character as *quene . . . of the derke pyne*.

2048 Cf. *WB Prol*, III, 130. But the phrase was a commonplace; see *ParsT*, X, 940.

2055 Cf. *MLT*, II, 421 ff., 1133, 1140 f.

2058 For this conception of the scorpion cf. Vincent of Beauvais, Spec. Nat., xx, 160.

2080 *Soul*, sole.

2088-91 Cf. Miroir, 734–40.

2111 Cf. Ovid, Met., i, 625 ff. Argus is again referred to in *KnT*, I, 1390.

2121 *countrefeted*; cf. *ClT*, IV, 743, n.

2128 See Met., iv, 55 ff.

2126 f. Cf. *LGW*, 742.

2132 f. This roundabout expression means "on June 8." Cf. l. 2222, below.

2133 Manly notes that *Juyl*, the reading of all the manuscripts, must be an error of the archetype; according to line 2222 the sun was in Gemini, which would have covered the period from May 11 to June 11.

2138-48 The passage is full of phrases from the Song of Solomon (cited also in Jerome, Adv. Jov., i, 30, Migne, Pat. Lat., XXIII, 251 ff.). Cf. particularly ii, 10–12; i, 15; iv, 7–16.

2146 *spot*, fault.

2222 The Sun was in Gemini, near Cancer, which he entered about June 12. Cancer was the declination of the Sun, and the exaltation of Jupiter.

2232 Claudius Claudianus (4th cent.). See his unfinished poem De Raptu Proserpinae. The plural *stories*, which has overwhelming manuscript support, may well be an error of the first copy.

2247 Cf. *Mel*, VII, 1057, and n.

2250 *Jhesus, filius Syrak*, the reputed author of Ecclesiasticus.

2252 Cf. *RvT*, I, 4172, and n.

2265 *by my moodres sires soule*, i.e., by the soul of Saturn. See Ovid, Fasti, vi, 285 f.

2268-75 Cf. Miroir, 2949–56, 2959–64.

2277-90 The passage seems to combine reminiscences of Albertano and Deschamps, with probably a reference to Jerome. Cf. *Mel*, VII, 1076–79, Miroir, 9051–57, 9063–70; and Jerome's chapter on Mulieres Romanae Insignes (Adv. Jov., i, 46, Migne,

Pat. Lat., XXIII, 275 f.). On *Romayn geestes* (l. 2284) for Roman history, see *MLT*, II, 1126, n.

2290 Cf. Mark x, 18, *neither he nor she*, neither man nor woman.

2300 I Kings xi, 12.

2315 Cf. Arthur's words to Gawain, in Chrestien de Troyes, Erec, 61 f. (ed. Foerster, Halle, 1896):

> Ja na doit estre contredite
> Parole puis que rois l'a dite.

2321-22 Cf. RR, 10097 f.

2335 With this belief about the longings of pregnant women cf. the ballad The Cherry-Tree Carol, and Professor Child's notes (Eng. and Scott. Ballads, Boston, 1882–98, no. 54, II, 1 ff.). Mr. McGalliard (PQ, XXV, 203) notes that though the motif does not appear in any of the collected analogues of the *MerchT*, it is treated at length in the *Miroir* (ll. 3782 ff.) There was of course a special point in May's assertion that she was pregnant. See M. Miller, PQ, XXIX, 437 ff.

2349 *by a twiste*, by a branch.

2365 Cf. Ovid, Rem. Am., 127–30; referred to in *Mel*, VII, 976.

2367 *stoore*, bold (AS. "stór," great); the vocative form of the adjective.

2393 *I wende han seyn*, I supposed (myself) to have seen.

2410 Proverbial. See Haeckel, p. 28, no. 91.

The Merchant's Epilogue

2426 For another account of the Host's wife see the *Mk Prol*, VII, 1889 ff.

2435 *cause why*, apparently preserved in the modern vulgar "cause why" (usually understood as "because why").

2437 The reference to the Wife of Bath is sufficiently clear.

FRAGMENT V

Fragment V, comprising the *Squire's Prologue* and Tale and the *Franklin's Prologue* and *Tale*, regularly follows the *Merchant's Epilogue* in the best MSS. Although the *Squire's Prologue* does not contain any reference to the preceding piece, it makes a satisfactory transition therefrom. Consequently it has been argued by several scholars that Fragments IV and V should properly be considered as forming a single consecutive group. In fact in MS. El the whole passage from IV, 2419, through V, 8, is written continuously and headed *The Prologe of the Squieres Tale*. See Ten Brink, Gesch. der Eng. Lit., II (2d ed., Strassburg, 1912), 171, 620 ff. (Eng. tr., II, i, New York, 1893, 164 f.; ii, New York, 1896, 268); Skeat, MLR, V, 431; Tatlock, MLN, XXIX, 141, n. 3. On the position of Fragment V in the different classes of MSS. see Miss Hammond, pp. 310 f.; and MP, III, 167 ff.; Wells, p. 680.

In some MSS. the *Squire's Tale* is followed by the *Wife of Bath's*. See the Textual Notes on the *SqT*, where the spurious link is given. Similarly, in certain MSS., as noted in the Textual Notes on the *Host's Stanza* (IV, 1212[a-g]), the *Franklin's Tale* is preceded by the *Clerk's* and connected with it by a spurious link. In Tyrwhitt's edition the *Franklin's Tale* is followed by the Physician's. For the spurious link there used see the Textual Notes on the *FranklT*.

The Squire's Prologue

2 On the character of the Squire, and the appropriateness of the request here made, see *Gen Prol*, I, 79 ff.

7-8 The Squire's remark, if it is more than a conventional protest of modesty, may be, as Dr. Baum has suggested, a disapproving allusion to the *MerchT*, which precedes (MLN, XXXII, 376).

The Squire's Tale

The *Squire's Tale* is a typical romance. Interrupting, as it does, the discussion of sovereignty, it is recognized as forming a kind of interlude in the Marriage Group. For an argument that it is really a bridge between the tales of the Merchant and the Franklin see Miss M. Neville, JEGP, L, 167 ff.

It has not been traced to a definite source, and perhaps its incompleteness is due to the fact that Chaucer, having no story before him, never worked out a plot of his own. Or possibly he intended — for his plan was obviously elaborate — to piece together episodes of different origin. A few passages, at all events, rather imply that he was following an original. See ll. 65 ff., 655, and compare the note on l. 29 ff.

Various parallels have been noted to different parts of the narrative. The oriental setting Skeat attributed to the influence of the travels of Marco Polo. His evidence, however, was not enough to prove special indebtedness to that author. Several other accounts of the Mongol empire, by travelers such as Carpini, Simon de St. Quentin, Guillaume de Rubriquis, Friar Ricold, Hayton the Armenian, and Odoric of Pordenone, were current in western Europe in the thirteenth and fourteenth centuries, and may have been known to Chaucer. He may also have drawn on general information about the Tartar courts, or have found his material ready to hand in the unknown source of his romance. For detailed accounts of the literature in question see, besides Skeat's notes, Pollard's edition of the *Squire's Tale*, London, 1899, pp. x, ff.; J. M. Manly, in PMLA, XI, 349 ff.; J. L. Lowes, MP, III, 1 ff., and Wash. Univ. Studies, I, ii, 3 ff. In the latter place Professor Lowes showed that for the setting, though not for the plot, Chaucer (or his source) may have drawn material from the Epistola Presbyteri Johannis (ed. F. Zarncke, Berichte der Kgl. Sächs. Gesellschaft, Phil.-Hist. Classe, XXIX, 111 ff., XXX, 41 ff.). In a version of English origin, Prester John, the King of India and Arabia, sends to Frederick, "imperator Romanus," three gifts, one of which is a magic ring. Prester John is also possessed of a magic mirror like Canacee's. He celebrates a birthday feast, and has a marvelous chapel associated with the day. Other details — strange food, the dry tree, etc. — afford parallels more or less significant. Relevant passages from the Prester John texts are published by H. S. V. Jones in SA, 357 ff. Other illustrations of the magical features of the story were collected, chiefly from Oriental litera-

ture, by W. A. Clouston, Magical Elements in the Squire's Tale, Ch. Soc., 1889.

The episode of Algarsyf and Theodora (mentioned in ll. 663–65) was apparently to be of the general type of the tale of the Ebony Horse in the Arabian Nights. See Bolte-Polívka, Anmerkungen, II, Leipzig, 1915, 134 f. A mediæval western version, to which Chaucer was possibly indebted, is the romance of Cléomadès, by Adenès le Roi (about 1285). See Clouston, pp. 382 ff.; H. S. V. Jones, PMLA, XX, 346 ff.; JEGP, VI, 221 ff.; MLN, XXIV, 158. For pertinent passages see again Jones, SA, 364 ff. The influence of the Cléomadès is questioned by Mr. Hinckley in MLN, XXIV, 95, and Notes, p. 212, and by Mr. Pollard in his separate edition of the *SqT*, p. xvi.

Parallel features in narrative and setting between the *Squire's Tale* and Gawain and the Green Knight are pointed out by C. O. Chapman, MLN, LXVIII, 521 ff.

In the Falcon episode there is a striking resemblance, as Skeat noted, to the situation in Chaucer's own *Anelida*. Professor Tupper, who interprets the *Anelida* as an allegory of the married life of the Earl and Countess of Ormonde, would make the same application of the story of the Falcon (PMLA, XXXVI, 196 ff.). But his whole theory is improbable. See the introduction to the Explanatory Notes on *Anelida*. Another and more elaborate allegorical interpretation of the whole *Squire's Tale* was proposed by Brandl, ESt, XII, 161 ff. (also Ch. Soc. Essays, Part vi) and disproved by Kittredge, ESt, XIII, 1 ff. Analogues to the Canacee and Falcon episode have been discussed by H. Braddy (MLR, XXXI, 17 ff.). He emphasizes the oriental character of the story (see also SA, 372 ff.). In a later article (JEGP, XLI, 279 ff.) Mr Braddy argues that Chaucer's source was an oriental tale of a recognized type of frame or boxed story. If completed, the *SqT* would have contained intercalary episodes between the beginning and ending of the story of Canacee. In view of the possible implication in l. 667 that Canacee married her brother, and of the presence of incest in oriental analogues, Mr. Braddy even suggests that it was because of these unpleasant features that Chaucer abandoned the *SqT*.

The date of the tale is generally held to be late, though decisive evidences are lacking. The "note of time" in l. 73 suggests that Chaucer was writing with the Canterbury scheme in mind.

The tale ends abruptly after the second line of the third part. The genuineness of the final couplet is disputed. For a brief conclusion, undoubtedly spurious, found in MS. La, see the Textual Notes on the *SqT*. Continuations were written by Spenser, in Book iv of the Faerie Queene, and by John Lane, whose work was licensed in 1614–15, though first printed by the Chaucer Society in 1888.

For comments on the way Chaucer introduced humor and realism into romance in the *SqT* see G. Stillwell, RES, XXIV, 177 ff., who perhaps goes too far in attributing comic or ironic purpose to Chaucer.

9 *Sarray*, the modern Tzarev, near Stalingrad in southeastern Russia. Founded by Batu Khan in the 13th century, it became a flourishing capital of the Tartar empire. For the identification see Yule's Marco Polo, 2 v., London, 1903, I, 4 f.; II, 494; also Magoun, Med. Stud., XVII, p. 138.

12 The MSS. vary between *Cambyuskan* and *Cambinskan*. But the form with *u* has better support on the whole and corresponds to the Latin Camius Khan. The name has been identified, though the correspondence is imperfect, with that of Genghis (or Chingis) Khan (1162–1227), the founder of the Mongol Empire. Skeat holds that the description applies better to Kublai Khan, his grandson, who ruled at Cambaluc, the modern Pekin. But the resemblances are mostly conventional traits. Moreover, it was another grandson of Genghis Khan, namely, Batu Khan, who *werreyed Russye* and held court at *Sarray*. It is uncertain whether Chaucer had any distinct knowledge of these historical figures. On the whole subject see Manly, PMLA, XI, 349 ff. and Magoun, Med. Stud., XVII, 138.

22 *centre*, a fulcrum or pivot about which anything turns; especially, the center of the earth; hence, an emblem of stability.

29 ff. The names *Elpheta*, *Algarsyf*, *Cambalo*, and *Canacee* are all unexplained. Skeat thought *Cambalo* was suggested by Cambaluc (Pekin), the capital of Kublai Khan. But the Tartar personal name "Kambala," the grandson of Kublai, is closer. (See Yule's Marco Polo, I, 361.) On Chaucer's tendency to use Italian-looking forms in *-o* see *MkT*, VII, 2345, n. *Elpheta* and *Algarsyf* look like oriental forms, and are unlikely to have been invented by Chaucer. Professor Manly suggests that Chaucer took the former from some list of the principal stars. He notes its occurrence in the Liber Astronomicus, qui dicitur Albion, ascribed to Richard de Wallingford (MS. Harl. 80, fol. 51ᵃ). But Professor Braddy (JEGP, XLI, 284) cites a literary occurrence of the name in a Catalan Chanson. See also MLN, LVIII, 21. *Canacee* (Gr. Κανάκη) is familiar enough as occurring in the tale (told by Ovid and Gower) condemned in the *Man of Law's Prologue*, II, 77 ff. But there seems to be no reason why Chaucer should have taken it over from there. Probably all four names come from an undiscovered source, or sources, of the *Squire's Tale*. Professor F. W. Cleaves, in reply to an inquiry by Professor Magoun, has kindly written that he cannot identify any of them with Mongolian names in accounts of the Golden Horde.

39 Cf. *Frankl Prol*, V, 723 ff.

45 f. *leet . . . Doon*, the double causative is unusual.

For descriptions of the birthday festivals of the Khan see Yule's Marco Polo, I, 386 ff.

47 *The last Idus of March*, March 15, when the sun was in the fourth degree of Aries. The sign Aries, specifically the the 19th degree, was the "exaltation" of the Sun. Aries was also the "mansion" of Mars, the first "face" (degrees 1–10) being known as the "face of Mars."

51 Skeat cites other references to Aries as hot and dry, or choleric and fiery.

52–55 Cf. RR, 67–73.

57 Cf. *LGW Prol F*, 127, n.

59 *sit*, "sits," a contracted present; so also *halt*, l. 61; *stant*, l. 171; *bit*, l. 291; *hit*, l. 512.

63 ff. On the rhetorical figure of occupatio see *KnT* I, 884. Mr. Wager (MLN, L, 306 f.) suggests that Chaucer resorted to it here by way of adapting the *SqT* to the Canterbury scheme.

67 *sewes*, broths (AS. "séaw"). With this reference to strange meats Professor Lowes (Wash. Univ.

Stud., I, ii, 13) compares passages from the accounts of Prester John's land. Miss J. W. Bennett cites also a parallel from Mandeville's *Travels*. See MLN, LXVIII, 531 ff.

73 *pryme*, the first division of the day, from 6 to 9 A.M. In Chaucer the reference is usually to the end of that period.

75 *firste*, first subject or purpose.

80 Skeat notes several instances of the riding of a horse into a hall. See also Clouston, Magical Elements, p. 276 ff.; F. J. Child, Eng. and Scott. Pop. Ballads, Boston, 1882–98, II, 51 (on King Estmere).

95 Sir Gawayn, King Arthur's nephew, was the pattern of courtesy. See B. J. Whiting, Med. Stud., IX, 189 ff. and F. P. Magoun, Jr., MLN, LXVII, 183 ff.

96 "Though he should come back from Fairyland." The association of the Knights of the Round Table with *Fairye* was natural, in view of the many tales of enchantment and other-world adventure in the Arthurian romances. Cf. *WBT*, III, 857 ff. Moreover, in the case of King Arthur there was a definite tradition that after he was wounded in his last battle he was carried away to the land of the fairies, whence he would some day return to rule his people. That there was a similar tradition about Gawayn is pointed out by R. S. Loomis, MLN, LII, 413 ff.

103 Cf. *Tr*, i, 12–14. The doctrine that the action should be suited to the words was a commonplace of the rhetoricians from Horace down. Cf. particularly Ars Poetica, 105 ff.; Geoffroi de Vinsauf, De Modo et Arte Dictandi et Versificandi, ed. Faral, Les Arts Poétiques du xiiᵉ et du xiiiᵉ Siècle, Paris, 1924, pp. 318 ff.

105–06 Whether the repetition of *style* was felt as a pun, or was merely a case of identical rime, it is hard to judge. On Chaucer's puns, *Gen Prol*, I, 297, n.

115 ff. For parallels to the steed of brass, the mirror, the ring, and the sword, see W. A. Clouston, Magical Elements; also Lowes, Wash. Univ. Stud., I, ii, 3 ff.

116 *day natureel*, the day of twenty-four hours, as distinguished from the *day artificial*, which lasted from sunrise to sunset. See *ML Prol*, II, 2, n.

129 *constellacioun*, here employed not in the common modern sense, but rather with reference to the shifting positions of the heavenly bodies. "He watched for a favorable arrangement, or combination, of the planets." For a similar practice of physicians, in their use of natural magic, cf. *Gen Prol*, I, 414 ff., and n.

131 The use of seals was common in ancient and mediæval magic. One of the most famous in oriental tradition was Solomon's seal, with which he controlled the Jinns. See Burton's Arabian Nights, I, ch. 2, and G. Salzberger, Die Salomosage in der Semitischen Literatur, Berlin, 1907, pp. 96 ff. Skeat refers to a mediæval treatise on seals in MS. Arundel 295, fol. 265. Cf. also L. Thorndike, History of Magic and Experimental Science, New York, 1923, II, 858 (with citations from Arnaldus de Villanova).

Bond probably refers to some means of imprisoning or controlling a spirit, though no special use of the term in magic is recorded by the NED.

132 The most famous mirror of the sort here described was that which Virgil was supposed to have set up in Rome. See l. 231, below, and cf. Gower, Conf. Am., v, 2031 ff., and the Seven Sages, 9th tale (ed. K. Campbell, Boston, 1907, pp. 75 ff.). For further illustration see Clouston, pp. 299 ff.; Lowes, Wash. Univ. Stud., I, ii, 7 ff.

146 On magic rings, which conferred various powers on their owners, see also Clouston, pp. 334 ff. In only one of the stories cited (p. 348, from Wolff's Deutsche Hausmärchen) is the wearer enabled to understand the language of birds. But this power is often referred to in Eastern tales, and was especially attributed to Solomon. For other magic devices to enable men to understand birds and beasts, see Édelstand du Méril, Études d'Archéologie, Paris, 1862, pp. 448 f. Professor Kittredge has called the editor's attention to the fact that in the account of the trial of Alice Perrers (1376) mention is made of the use of magic rings. See Chronicon Angliae, 1328–88, Rolls Ser., 1874, p. 98.

156 The weapon, which possessed the power of healing the wound it inflicted, is compared below (ll. 236 ff.) with that with which Achilles wounded Telephus. For other references see *Tr*, iv, 927; Dante, Inf., xxxi, 4–6; Ovid, Met., xii, 112; xiii, 171–72; Trist. v, 2, 15; Rem. Am., 44–48. Examples of similar conceptions are given by Clouston, pp. 372 ff.

162 *the plat*, the flat side.

184 "By no device of windlass or pulley."

185 *cause why*; cf. *Merch Epil*, IV, 2435.

195 *Poilleys*, Apulian. Lombardy and Apulia were celebrated for their horses.

203 Proverbial; cf. "Quot homines, tot sententiae"; Skeat, EE Prov., p. 118, no. 279; Haeckel, p. 34, no. 114.

207 *the Pegasee*, Pegasus, the winged horse of Bellerophon and the Muses. Chaucer's form is due to the Latin adjective "Pegaseus," as indicated by the gloss ("equs Pegaseus") in several MSS.

209 "The horse of the Greek, Sinon," i.e., the Wooden Horse used by the Greeks at Troy. See Aen., ii, 15, 195. Skeat notes that according to Guido delle Colonne the Trojan horse was of brass. On the order of words see *ClT*, IV, 1170, n.

211 *olde geestes*. In Chaucer's age the chief authorities on Troy, besides Virgil, were Guido delle Colonne and Benoît de Ste.-Maure. See the introductory note on the *Troilus*.

218 For instances of such feats of jugglers see *FranklT*, V, 1139 ff., and *HF*, 1277 ff. Skeat (Oxf. Ch., III, 473) cites further illustrations from Marco Polo.

220 ff. Cf. Ovid, Tristia, iv, 2, 25–26.

221 *demeth*, the Southern plural in *-th*, which occurs rarely in Chaucer. MSS. Dd and Pw have here the more regular *demen*.

226 *maister-tour*, chief tower; cf. *KnT*, I, 2902, n.

228 ff. Cf., for various parallels of ideas or phraseology, RR, 18031–60, 18176, 18187, 18247 ff. Alhazen and Aristotle are mentioned, but not Vitello.

231 See the note to l. 132, above.

232 *Alocen*, Abū 'Alī al-Hasan ibn al-Hasan ibn al-Haitham (ca. 965–1039); commonly called in Latin Alhazen and in Arabic Ibn al-Haitham. He was a distinguished Moslem physicist and astronomer and one of the greatest authorities on optics.

Vitulon, Witelo (latinized Vitello), a Polish physicist of the thirteenth century, who translated Alhazen's optics. Tyrwhitt cited an edition of their combined works, Alhazeni et Vitellonis Opticæ Thesaurus, ed. F. Risner, Basel, 1572.

233 Aristotle, the Greek philosopher (384–322 B.C.). *Writen*, preterite plural.

238 Telephus, king of Mysia, was wounded by Achilles, and then healed by the rust from his spear. See note to l. 156 above.

250 In ancient and mediæval tradition Moses and Solomon were both regarded as great magicians. Reference has already been made to their rings in the note to l. 146. The ring of Moses was held to cause forgetfulness, and was known as the Ring of Oblivion. See Clouston, p. 340; Peter Comestor, on Exodus vi (Migne, Pat. Lat., CXCVIII, 1144).

On the construction *he Moyses* see *KnT*, I, 1210, n.

252 Cf. Aen., ii, 39.

254 Ashes of ferns were used as an ingredient in making glass. Chaucer's reference here to the process, and also to the cause of thunder and mist, is borrowed from RR, 16096–105. See F. P. Magoun, Rom. Rev., XVII, 69 f. and F. de Tollenaere, Eng. Stud., XXXI, 97 ff.

263 ff. On this method of indicating time see *Gen Prol*, I, 8, n. The data here given, though more elaborate than usual, simply mean that it was nearly two hours past noon. The heavens were divided into twelve equal parts, called "mansions" or "houses," of which the 1st, 4th, 7th, and 10th were known as "angles." The *angle meridional*, or tenth mansion, was bounded by the meridian and by a semicircle passing through the north and south points of the horizon and lying 30° east of the meridian. On March 15 the Sun would pass through this house between 10 A.M. and noon. About noon, also, the constellation Leo (*the beest roial*) began to ascend, and would not have completely risen until about a quarter before three. There is doubt about the identification of *Aldiran*. Skeat held it to refer to the star now called θ Hydrae, situated near the Lion's forepaws. Though itself insignificant, this star heralded the rising of the brilliant α Leonis, called Regulus or Calbalesed (i.e., Cor Leonis). Professor Manly (p. 135) suggests that the reference may have been directly to the brighter star. Mr. Hinckley takes Aldiran to mean rather Castor and Pollux (α and β of Gemini). See his Notes, p. 227, with a reference to R. H. Allen, Star Names and Their Meanings, New York, 1899, p. 234.

269 *chambre of paramentz*, the Presence Chamber.

271 Cf. l. 558 below; also *Tr*, ii, 637.

272 *Venus children*, followers or subjects of Venus, lovers.

273 Cf. *WB Prol*, III, 704: *In Pisces, wher Venus is exaltat*. Purg., i, 19–21, which Chaucer used in *KnT*, I, 1494, and perhaps in *Tr*, iii, 1257, is less likely to have been in mind here.

277 Clouston (Magical Elements, p. 272, n. 1) observes that this was hardly an oriental practice.

279 The Squire seems here modestly to disclaim the qualities which Chaucer ascribes to him in the *General Prologue*. Or were these lines written without regard to his delivery of them?

287 *Launcelot*, the famous knight of the Round Table, and the lover of Queen Guinevere.

294 ff. Cf. the closely similar passage in *Tr*, v, 852 ff.

296 *as reson was*, as was right, proper. Cf. Fr. "raison."

299–300 The readings vary here, perhaps because Chaucer, as Manly suggested, confused two constructions. But *hath* may be used in the sense of Fr. [*il*] *y a*.

302 *At after-soper*; see *ShipT*, VII, 255, n.

316 On the omitted relative cf. *Gen Prol*, I, 529, n.

325 Cf. *KnT*, I, 1089, and n.

340 The magical power of making the horse move, or indeed of summoning him, lay in the bridle, which was carefully preserved.

347 On the relation of sleep to digestion, as conceived in Chaucer's age, Curry (pp. 204 f.) cites Avicenna, iii, fen 1, tract. 1, cap. 7.

349 Cf. *MerchT*, IV, 1862, n.

352 On the four humors see *Gen Prol*, I, 420, n. Authorities differed as to when each was in *domynacioun*, or chief power. According to the De Natura, ascribed to Galen, the domination of blood lasted from the ninth hour of the night till the third hour of the day. The Kalender of Shepherdes (ed. Sommer, London, 1892, III, 117) says: "Syxe houres after mydnyght blode hath the maystry."

357 *for me*, so far as I am concerned.

358 On the fumes that arise from wine-drinking cf. *PardT*, VI, 567.

360 *pryme large*, 9 A.M.

362 *mesurable*, temperate. Cf. *Gen Prol*, I, 435.

374 *maistresse*, governess, as in *PhysT*, VI, 72.

376 The sentence was carelessly constructed. It means: "Her governess, like these old women who are usually inquisitive, answered at once." For the use of *thise* to designate a class cf. *KnT*, I, 1531, n. For the special meaning of *gladly* ("usually") cf. *NPT*, VII, 3224, n.

383 *a ten or twelve*, some ten or twelve. Cf. *a certain*, "a certain number (or amount) of," *ShipT*, VII, 334, and n.; *MkT*, VII, 2177.

385 *the yonge sonne*, the sun at the beginning of its annual course. Cf. *Gen Prol*, I, 7.

387 The sun had not risen more than four degrees above the horizon; i.e., it was about a quarter past six.

388 *esily a pas*, at a slow pace.

401 *knotte*, "point." Mr. Manly compares the Latin "nodus" in Horace, Ars Poetica, 191.

409 It is doubtful whether we should read *fordrye*, "very dry," or *for drye*, "because dry, for dryness." See *KnT*, I, 2142, n.

Skeat refers to the "Arbre Sec" or "Dry Tree" mentioned by mediæval travelers, which may have furnished a suggestion to Chaucer or to his source. See Yule's Marco Polo, I, 127 ff.; Lowes, Wash. Univ. Stud., I, ii, 14.

425 *of fairnesse*, in respect of beauty. Cf. *PF*, 298 f.

428 *A faucoun peregryn*. According to Le Tresor of Brunetto Latini, quoted by Tyrwhitt, the falcon peregrin is so called because no one finds its nest, but it is taken elsewhere as if on pilgrimage. He adds that it is very easy to bring up, very courteous, and brave, and of good manner.

435 *leden*, language (AS. "læden," lit. "Latin"). Cf., for the same use of Ital. "latino," Dante's Ballata, iv, 10 f.:

"E cantinne gli augelli
Ciascuno in suo latino."

OF. "latin" has the same application in RR, 8408.

461 *ferde with hymself*, treated himself (lit. "fared with himself").

467 *disese*, distress.

471 "To heal your hurts with quickly." On the order see *Gen Prol*, I, 791, n.; cf. also l. 641 below.

474 *aswowne*, apparently a dative phrase *on swowne*, the noun "swoon" itself being derived by misunderstanding from the past participle "geswogen," Mid. Eng. "yswowen," "aswowen."

479 On the other occurrences of this line see *KnT*, I, 1761, n.

483 For Chaucer's full discussion of "gentilesse" see *WBT*, III, 1109 ff.; cf. also *Rom*, 2187 ff.

491 "As the lion is chastised by means of the dog." The reference is to the proverb, "Beat the dog before the lion." Cf. Othello, ii, 3, 275. For various forms of the saying see, besides Skeat's note, Anglia, XIV, 320; Herrig's Arch., CXXIV, 132; and MLN, XXXVIII, 506 f. For evidence that lion-tamers of the 13th century did actually beat dogs to intimidate the lions see C. S. Brown, Jr., and R. H. West in MLN, LV, 209 f. For further illustrations of the practice and the saying see Mrs. G. Frank, ibid., p. 481.

496 "As if she would (turn) to water."

504 *tercelet*, the male falcon, so-called because it is usually a third smaller than the female.

506 *Al were he*, although he was. On the use of the subjunctive in concessive clauses see *Gen Prol*, I, 68, n.

511 *in greyn*, in a fast color; see *Thop*, VII, 727. On *colours*, for ornaments of rhetoric, see *ClT*, IV, 16, n.

512 *hit*, hideth. Cf. the proverbial "snake in the grass"; also Virgil, Ecl., iii, 93.

517 *sownen into*, are consonant with. See *Gen Prol*, I, 307, n.

518 Cf. Matt. xxiii, 27.

526 *crouned*, consummate.

527 *Forfered*, "afraid"; perhaps to be read *for fered*, "because afraid," cf. *Tr*, iv, 1411.

537 "An honest man and a thief do not think alike." Although this is clearly given as a proverb, no close parallels except *Anel*, 105, seem to have been noted.

548 ff. Jason deserted Medea, and Paris Oenone. On *Lameth* (Lamech) *and his bigamye* see *WB Prol*, III, 53 f.

555 An allusion to Mark i, 7. Modern taste might impose a restraint in such use of a scriptural passage, though the comparison had become proverbial (cf. Haeckel, p. 47, no. 160). In Chaucer's age men spoke freely of sacred persons and things. Cf. *LGW*, 1038; *BD*, 237, 679; *PF*, 199 f.; *Buk*, 1 ff.; and the somewhat startling application of the proverb, *God foryaf his deth*, in *Tr*, iii, 1577. Even the illustration drawn from the Gospels in *Prol Mel*, VII, 943, would be less natural today. This kind of liberty was by no means peculiar to Chaucer. Examples from other writers might be indefinitely multiplied. Lounsbury (Studies, II, 505 ff.) noted the occurrence of such "irreverence" in the miracle plays. Gower's comparison of Jason to "God's brother" (Conf. Am., v, 3824) will serve as a further illustration; also the couplet of Dafydd ap Gwilym in no. ccxxi (as found in some MSS.):

Anodd im gysgu unhun
Be canai Dduw huw ei hun

("I could hardly sleep a wink though God were to sing a lullaby"). This was apparently altered later, perhaps from scruples about irreverence, by the substitution of St. David for God. See the edition of Jones and Pughe, London, 1789, p. 438. Dafydd's appeal, in another place (ed. 1789, p. 154), to St. Dwynwen to be his messenger (llattai) to his (married) lady-love seems rather audacious, even if the saint was, as Chutzen suggested, "la patronesse des amoureux" in the local tradition of Mon (Anglesey).

Of course such passages do not necessarily indicate lack of proper reverence. Sometimes they seem to show affectionate familiarity with objects of worship. But the examples cited from Provençal poets in Spec., XIII, 387 appear to involve real disrespect for sacred things.

558 Cf. *Tr*, ii, 637.

559 *Til*, to.

571 "Always guarding my honor."

579 *Wher*, whether.

593 Proverbial. Cf. *KnT*, I, 3041, n.

596 *to borwe*, for a security (AS. "borh," pledge).

601 "When he has well said everything, he has finished (and does not keep his word)"; "when he has talked well, then he acts (shamefully)."

602 Proverbial; see Skeat, EE Prov., pp. 119 f., no. 282; Haeckel, p. 22, no. 70.

607 From Boethius, iii, m. 2. This is also the source of ll. 611 ff. Chaucer uses the example again in *MancT*, IX, 163.

611 The number shifts from the plural to the singular.

619 Cf. *Tr*, ii, 756.

624 The kite was a cowardly kind of hawk, typifying baseness.

640 Canacee's ring gave her knowledge of the medicinal herbs.

644 For the symbolism of the colors ("true blue") cf. *KnT*, I, 1929, n.

648 The *tidyf* is again mentioned as inconstant in *LGW Prol F*, 154. On the identification (doubtful) of the bird see U. T. Holmes, PQ, XVI, 65 ff. and F. P. Wilson, ibid., p. 216 ff.

655 This reference supports the theory that Chaucer was following some source for his story.

663–66 On the name *Algarsif* see the note to l. 29 ff., above. The episode about him and Theodora was apparently to be similar in plot to the romance of Cléomadès and the story of the Ebony Horse in the Arabian Nights. See the introduction to the Explanatory Notes on the *SqT*.

667 The plot, as here sketched, is obscure. The editors usually assume that *Cambalo* in l. 667 is Canacee's lover and a different person from her brother *Cambalus* in l. 656 (called also *Cambalo* in l. 31). But the identity of names would be strange. If *Cambalo* was not inserted by a scribal error, Chaucer may have intended that Canacee should be abducted by two brothers, and then won back by Cambalo. Mr. Braddy (JEGP, XLI, 287) takes *win* in the sense of "marry." See the introductory note above, p. 717, above. Spenser (F. Q., iv, 3) represents three brothers as suitors for Canacee, fighting against Cambello her brother.

On the occurrence of the "two-brothers motive" in the accounts of Prester John, see J. L. Lowes, Wash. Univ. Stud., I, ii, 17.

671–72 These lines, though sometimes rejected as spurious, have good support in the MSS. The method of indicating time, moreover, is Chaucerian. See l. 263, above, and n.

The sun, the uncompleted sentence seems to indicate, was in Gemini, the mansion of Mercury. In other words, the action of the third part was to begin about the middle of May.

With the order of words in *the god Mercurius hous the slye*, "The mansion of the god Mercury, the cunning," compare l. 209, above, and n.

The Introduction to the Franklin's Tale

676 *allow the*, commend thee (Lat. "allaudare"). With the rime *yowthe: allow the* cf. *Gen Prol*, I, 523, n.

683 That is, land having an annual rental value of twenty pounds.

687 *vertuous*, rather "accomplished, capable," than "innocent."

The Franklin's Prologue and Tale

No definite evidence has been found to fix precisely the date of the *Franklin's Tale*. Its connection with the "Marriage Group" and the incidental use of Jerome against Jovinian (in ll. 1367–1458) both favor a late assignment, as do certain parallels to the revised (*G*) *Prologue to the Legend*. (See Lowes, MP, VIII, 324 f.) But other parallel passages pointed out by Professor Lowes (MP, XV, 690 ff.) associate it with the Teseida and the *Knight's Tale*. Possibly it was written early and then adapted for its place in the Canterbury collection.

With regard to the source there has been much discussion, largely on the question whether Chaucer is to be taken literally in his statement that he followed a Breton lay. The affirmative opinion was defended by Professor Schofield, in PMLA, XVI, 405 ff. Schofield showed that the tale corresponded closely in character to the so-called "Breton lays" in French and English, and he sought to prove that the elements of the plot were of Celtic origin. But he failed to find in Celtic any significant analogue. Later writers have emphasized Chaucer's indebtedness to Boccaccio, who has the same story in the Filocolo (iv, 4, ed. Moutier, Florence, 1829, II, 48 ff.) and the Decamerone, x, 5. The Filocolo version affords striking parallels to the Franklin's, and the Italian work as a whole was almost certainly known to Chaucer. See the introductory note on the *Troilus*, and for detailed discussion of the problem, P. Rajna, Rom., XXXII, 204–67; K. Young, Orig. and Dev. of the Story of Troilus and Criseyde, Ch. Soc., 1908, p. 181; J. S. P. Tatlock, The Scene of the Franklin's Tale Visited, Ch. Soc., 1914, p. 554; J. L. Lowes, MP, XV, 689–728; J. M. Manly, New Light, p. 281; Mrs. G. Dempster and J. S. P. Tatlock in SA, pp. 377 ff., where pertinent parallels from Boccaccio, Geoffrey of Monmouth, and the Breton lays are assembled. All these writers support the derivation from Boccaccio, though Professors Young and Lowes admit the possibility that a Breton lay on the subject also existed. In any case, as Mr. Lowes insists, the pretence of following a lay would have been a natural literary artifice, and Chaucer's veracity, in the ordinary sense, is in no way involved. Since certain features of the tale are derived from the Teseida, there can be no doubt — lay or no lay — of the complex character of the composition. For the suggestion that Chaucer made use of the lays in the Auchinleck MS, may indeed have drawn his knowledge of the literary type mainly from them, see Mrs. R. S. Loomis, SP, XXXVIII, 14 ff.

The underlying story is far older than Chaucer's poem or his immediate source, whatever that may have been. It is a *märchen* of wide dissemination, sometimes referred to by folk-lorists under the title, "The Damsel's Rash Promise." Numerous oriental versions are known, of which the most ancient form appears to be that preserved in the Vetāla-Stories in Sanskrit. In occidental literature, besides the closely similar tales of Chaucer and Boccaccio, there are well-known versions in Bojardo's Orlando Innamorato, in the Conde Lucanor of Juan Manuel, and in the Chevalier à la Manche of Jean de Condé. On these various analogues and their relations see M. Landau, Quellen des Dekameron, 2d ed., Stuttgart, 1884, pp. 93 ff.; Clouston, in Originals and Analogues, Ch. Soc., pp. 291 ff.; Aman, Die Filiation der Frankeleynes Tale, Erlangen, 1912; and, for a convenient brief statement, Koch's notes to Hertzberg's translation of the *Canterbury Tales*, Berlin, 1925, pp. 544–46. Schofield, in arguing for the derivation of the *Franklin's Tale* from a Breton lay, showed that faithfulness in keeping a rash promise appears repeatedly as a motif in Celtic literature and Arthurian romance. Examples are furnished by the Irish Tochmarc Etaine, the Welsh Mabinogi of Pwyll, the lay of Sir Orfeo, and various versions of the Tristan romance. But none of these can be regarded as a source, even indirect, of Chaucer's tale. For further discussion of the Celtic stories see G. Schoepperle, Tristan and Isolt, London, 1913, II, 528 ff. For a distant analogue to the removal of rocks by enchantment Professor Magoun, of course with no suggestion of any relationship to Chaucer's tale, has called the editor's attention to the Finnish Kalevala, XL, 41–60, 83–88.

The local setting of the *Franklin's Tale* is carefully studied by Professor Tatlock in the Chaucer Society volume cited above. There is also a good description of the region in Frank Cowper's Sailing Tours: Yachtman's Guide to the Cruising Waters of the English Coast, Part III: Coasts of Brittany (London, 1894), pp. 156 ff. On the narrative method see W. M. Hart, in Haverford Essays, Haverford, Pa., 1909, pp. 185–234, and on ironical elements see C. A. Owen, Jr., JEGP, LII, 295 ff. For an attempt to find, both in the character of the Franklin and in his tale, especially in the use of technical legal terms, echoes of Chaucer's own training and official life, see R. Blenner-Hassett, Spec., XXVIII, 791 ff.

A general parallel (probably not a source) for the Franklin's discussion of marriage is cited from the Enfances Gauvain by R. S. Loomis, Philologica: The Malone Anniversary Studies, pp. 191 ff.

The Franklin's Prologue

709 *Britouns*, Bretons, inhabitants of French Brittany.
710 The usual meaning of *lay*, as of OF. "lai," was "song" or "lyric." In the sense which it here

bears, a short narrative poem of romantic character, it is not known to occur before the time of Marie de France (circa 1170). Her famous series of Lais she professed to derive from Breton sources, and there is no reason for doubting the Celtic origin of her material. But no lays in the Breton language have been preserved, and their form, if they ever existed, is quite unknown. The literary type was perhaps the creation of Marie, who had a number of successors in French and English. It is uncertain, as was pointed out in the introductory note above, whether Chaucer followed an actual lay of Breton origin. He may simply be repeating the customary ascription which he found in the poems of Marie and her imitators. It is even doubtful whether he had direct knowledge of the writings of Marie, though the *Franklin's Tale* is held by some scholars to show the influence of her lay of Equitan. Chaucer could have got full knowledge of the type from the English lays of the 13th and 14th centuries. On the history of the term "lay" see Foulet, Zt. f. Rom. Phil., XXX, 698 ff. For the Lais of Marie de France see the edition of Roquefort, Paris, 1820, and Warnke, Halle, 3d ed., 1925. On the Middle English lays compare Wells, pp. 124 ff.

716 The "modesty prologue" is a conventional literary type. For parallels see Miss Hammond, English Verse between Chaucer and Surrey, Durham, N.C., 1927, pp. 392 ff.
721 From the Satires of Persius, Prol., 1–3.
722 *Scithero*, Cicero. On the confusion between Cicero and Cithero, in which Mt. Cithaeron is also sometimes involved, see Miss Hammond, cited above, p. 458. Professor R. A. Pratt notes occurrences of *Cithero* in Latin MSS of Chaucer's time and before in Progress of Medieval and Renaissance Studies in U.S. and Canada, Bull. 20, p. 48.
726 *Colours of rethoryk*. See *ClT*, IV, 16, n.

The Franklin's Tale

729 *Armorik*, Armorica, "Ar vor" (the land by the sea); another name for Brittany.
734 *oon the faireste*. On the idiom see *ClT*, IV, 212, n.
749 ff. Cf. *MerchT*, IV, 1377–79.
752 *for shame of his degree*, out of regard for his rank (as husband).
764–66 Cf. *KnT*, I, 1624–26, from Tes., v, 13, 7–8, a passage which may have suggested the phraseology here and in *Tr*, ii, 756. Chaucer seems also to have had in mind the RR (see ll. 9424 ff.). Other parallels are Ovid, Met., ii, 846–47, and the Ovide Moralisée, ii, 4977–87 (ed. C. de Boer, in the Verhandelingen of the Amsterdam Academy, Afdeeling Letterkunde, Nieuwe Reeks, XV, 277).
768 ff. Cf. *MancT*, IX, 147 ff.; also RR, 13959 ff.
771 ff. See also *Tr*, IV, 1584. The idea — "vincit qui patitur" — is a commonplace. Dionysius Cato, Disticha, i, 38, — may have been in Chaucer's mind. For other parallels see Skeat's note. Professor Lowes has pointed out a similar passage in Machaut's Dit dou Lyon (Œuvres, ed. Hoepffner, SATF, II, ll. 2040–44, 2066–76), with which Chaucer is known to have been familiar. Cf. further Haeckel, p. 14, no. 46.
786 *kan on*, has skill in.

792-96 Cf. RR, 9449-54.

801 *Pedmark*, doubtless the modern Breton Penmarc'h, a commune in the southwest corner of the department of Finistère, though the name may apply rather to the cape than to the village. Professor Tatlock points out that the coast is still characterized by dangerous outlying rocks. The village is now small, but there is every indication that it was rich and populous in the fourteenth century. The shore just at the cape is not so bold as Chaucer's description implies, and the nearest point which combines high headlands with outlying rocks is Concarneau, about thirty-five kilometers away. It seems most likely that Penmarc'h, with its perilous ledges, is really meant, and that the description of the shore itself is a little inaccurate.

803-05 For similar language, in a satirical passage, see *MerchT*, IV, 1259 ff. Cf. also IV, 1650 ff.

808 *Kayrrud* seems clearly to correspond to the modern Breton Kerru (Welsh Caerrudd). There are several places of the name in modern Brittany, but none of them fits the conditions of the tale. The meaning of the name would be "red house" or "red village," and the adjective probably refers to the color of the old Roman brick. Remains of Roman building abound in the department of Finistère, and have been found directly facing the Rochers de Penmarc'h. The form *Kayrrud* does not correspond exactly to either the natural Breton or the natural French form in Chaucer's time. The former would be more normally spelled "Ker (or Kaer-) ruz," and the latter "Karru" (or "Carru"). Mr. Tatlock (p. 15) suggests that Chaucer's spelling represents the Breton pronunciation ("Kaerrud" or "-ruz") as heard by an Englishman. But it may be an old Breton spelling taken over from Chaucer's source. For further discussion see F. P. Magoun, Jr., Med. Stud., XVII, 130.

Arveragus, a Latinized Celtic name, spelt "Arviragus" in Juvenal, Sat., iv, 127, and in Geoffrey of Monmouth, Hist. Brit., iv, 12. On Geoffrey's account of Arviragus and Geniussa see Schofield, PMLA, XVI, 409 ff.

815 *Dorigen*, also a name of Celtic appearance. Tyrwhitt noted that Droguen, or Dorguen, was the wife of Alain I (G. A. Lobineau, Histoire de Bretagne, 2 v., Paris, 1707, I, 70). Cf. also the series "Dorgen," "Dorien" (*Dubrogenos?) — all masculine. The source and pronunciation of Chaucer's *Dorigen* are both uncertain. If it comes from a Breton form in *gu*, the *g* was probably sounded as in "get."

829-31 Cf. Boccaccio, Filocolo (ed. Moutier, Florence, 1829, II, 49), alluding to Ovid, Ex Ponto, iv, 10, 5 ("gutta cavat lapidem"). But Chaucer's figure is not quite the same.

861 Cf. *Anel*, 177.

865-67 Possibly a reminiscence of Tes., ix, 52-53. Cf. also Boethius, i, m. 5.

867 *In ydel*, in vain.

875 *anoyeth*, injures, does harm.

877 ff. Cf. Boethius, iii, m. 9.

880 *merk*, image (Gen. i, 27). It was used of the impression upon a coin.

885 Dorigen leaves the problem of evil to the experts, much as Palamon does in the *KnT*, I, 1323 f., or as the Nun's Priest dismisses the question of God's foreordination, *NPT*, VII, 3251.

886 Cf. Rom. viii, 28, and (for a philosophical statement of the case) Boethius, iv, p. 6.

889 *this*, this is.

893 *for the feere*, for fear. Cf. *the deeth*, Gen *Prol*, I, 605, n.

899 *delitables*, a French plural form in -*s*. See the Grammatical Introduction.

900 *tables*, backgammon.

901 ff. The garden corresponds to one in the Filocolo (II, 23 ff.), which Rajna held to be the main source of the description. But Chaucer also drew upon recollections of Emilia's garden in the Teseida (iii, 5-7), with which he combined a passage from the Dit dou Vergier of Machaut (Œuvres, ed. Hoeppfner, SATF, I, ll. 52-66; quoted in full in PMLA, XVI, 446). Cf. further *LGW Prol G*, 104 ff.

918 *At after-dyner*. See *ShipT*, VII, 255, n.

927 Cf. *Gen Prol*, I, 91 f.

932 *beste farynge*, handsomest. This meaning of *faring* is clearly established in Mid. Eng., as in Old Norse. See NED, s.v. Farrand; and cf. Patch, ESt, LXV, 355 f.

For the confused construction with *man* (sg.) cf. *NPT*, VII, 2984; see also *ClT*, IV, 212, n.

938 *Aurelius*, a name of Roman origin, but known to have been in use among the Britons. Compare Gildas, De Excidio Brit., ch. 30; Geoffrey of Monmouth, Hist. Brit., vi, 5.

In the account of Aurelius's unrevealed love, as Mr. Lowes has shown (MP, XV, 689 ff.) Chaucer was influenced by the similar description of the love of Arcite in the Teseida (iv, 40 ff.). The reminiscences seem sometimes to go directly back to the Italian poem, and sometimes to Chaucer's English version in *The Knight's Tale*. The following parallel passages are most significant; others also are noted by Mr. Lowes.

V   925-32: Tes., iv, 62, 1-6.
V   933-34: *KnT*, I, 1423-43.
V   935-43: Tes., iv, 60, 5-6, and 63.
V   940   : *KnT*, I, 1446.
V   944-45: Tes., iv, 66, 6-8.
V   946   : Tes., iv, 68, 2.
V   947-49: Tes., iv, 78, 1-2.
V   959   : Tes., iv, 62, 7-8.
V   1031-37: Tes., iv, 43 (with incidental use of Tes., iii, 6, a passage which also influenced *Tr*, ii, 50-56, and *LGW Prol F*, 103-14.

942 *Withouten coppe*, under difficulties, or perhaps, in full draught. Cf. the Tale of Beryn, Ch. Soc., 1887, 306, 460. For the general idea of drinking woe, punishment, etc., cf. *HF*, 1879 f.; *Tr*, ii, 784, iii, 1035, 1214 f.; RR, 11535, 12640; and the French proverb, "Qui fait folie, si la boive" (Morawski, Prov. Fr., Paris, 1925, p. 71, no. 1939). See also Kittredge, [Harv.] Stud. and Notes, I, 32; Hinckley, MP, XVI, 47, and W. H. French, MLN, LX, 477.

943 *He was despeyred*. The corresponding line in the Teseida reads "Ed isperava, e non sapea in che cosa." Professor Wilkins suggests that Chaucer may have read "E disperava." See Lowes, MP, XV, 692, n. 5.

947-48 *layes*, used here in its ordinary sense of "songs," "lyrics." See the note to l. 710 above. The term *compleintes*, which had reference to subject-matter, was applied to both love-lyrics and religious poems. Chaucer regularly uses it in the former sense, and sometimes treats *lay* and *compleint* as synonymous. See the introduction to the *Short Poems*.

950 *langwissheth*, endures pain. Cf. the account of the Furies in *Tr*, iv, 22 ff. See also *Tr*, i, 1, n.

951-52 In this reference to the death of Echo, Chaucer seems to have been following Ovid, Met., iii, 394 ff., rather than RR, 1439 ff., which doubtless suggested the reference in *BD*, 735 f.

963 "And [she] had known him a long time." For the omission of the subject cf. *Gen Prol*, I, 33, n.

981 *Nevere erst*, never before. On this use of *erst* see *KnT*, I, 1566, n.

999-1000 Most MSS. and probably the archetype have these lines where they stand in the text, but Manly holds them to have been erroneously inserted from the margin. He would transfer them to follow l. 1006.

1015 After an interval dancing is resumed. It is hardly necessary to assume (with Rajna and Tatlock) the influence of the Filocolo, where the festivities are begun afresh in Fiammetta's garden after the heat of the day has passed.

1016-17 Mr. Lowes (MP, XV, 695) suggests that these lines go back to the May morning scene in the Teseida (particularly to iii, 12, 1–2), with a simultaneous reminiscence of Tes., vii, 68, 1–2, and probably also of a line of Dante (Purg., vii, 60) which Boccaccio doubtless also recalled. With the use of *reft* he compares also Tes., iii, 43, 1–2; and in general Tes., iv, 72, 5–6; x, 14, 5–6.

1018 The astronomical mode of defining times and persons, here satirized, was very characteristic of Chaucer and his time. Cf. *Gen Prol*, I, 8, n. A close parallel to Chaucer's humorous comment is cited by Miss Hammond (MLN, XXVII, 91 f.) from Fulgentius, Mitologiarum Libri Tres, Opera, ed. Helm, Leipzig, 1898, p. 13. After eleven flowery lines of verse, Fulgentius returns to prose with the remark, "et, ut in uerba paucissima conferam, nox erat." Professor Manly (Chaucer and the Rhetoricians, British Acad., 1926, p. 13) compares also the comments of Geoffroi de Vinsauf on the opening lines of the Aeneid, and on the meter of Boethius, "O qui perpetua mundum ratione gubernas — Quod nihil aliud est quam 'O Deus'" (De Modo et Arte Dictandi et Versificandi, ed. E. Faral, Les Arts Poétiques du xiie et du xiiie Siècle, Paris, 1924, p. 273).

1033 *after thy declinacioun*, according to thy distance from the celestial equator.

1045 ff. With Aurelius's procedure here in begging Apollo to invoke in turn the aid of Lucina (a rather unusual complication) Lowes (MP, XV, 721 f.) compares the prayer of Florio in the Filocolo, I, 166. For the suggesion that Aurelius had to seek the intervention of Apollo because Lucina was the goddess of chastity, see MLN, LXVIII, 174.

1049-50 Possibly suggested by the Anticlaudianus of Alanus de Insulis, ii, 3 (Migne, Pat. Lat., CCX, 501). But a particular source is hardly needed to explain so simple a reference to the dependence of lunar upon solar light.

1053 *as she that is*. The nominative is retained, where the accusative might be expected, in this stereotyped phrase. For the idiom compare l. 1088, below, and *KnT*, I, 964.

1055 ff. The highest tides occur when the sun and moon are in conjunction or in opposition. Aurelius prays that when the sun is next in Leo, its own mansion, and the Moon in opposition, the moon may move for two years at the same apparent rate as the sun. Then it will remain at the full, and the spring-flood will last all the while

1074 Luna is here conceived in her character as Proserpina, goddess of the lower world. Cf. *KnT*, I, 2081 f.

1077 *Delphos*, Chaucer's form for Delphi, from the Lat. acc.

1084 *thoght*. anxiety, grief.

1086 *for me*, so far as I am concerned ("for all of me"). *Wheither*, pronounced *whe'r*.

1094 *ymaginatyf*, full of imaginings; here suspicious.

1110 *Pamphilus*, the hero of the mediæval Latin poem, Pamphilus de Amore. See *Mel*, VII, 1556, n.

1113 *sursanure*, a wound healed only on the surface; here used with reference to the first line of the De Amore: "Vulneror, et clausum porto sub pectore telum" (ed. Baudouin, Paris, 1874).

1118 *Orliens*, Orleans, the seat of an ancient university. On Wright's dubious suggestion, quoted by Skeat, that as a result of its rivalry with the University of Paris it came to be regarded as a seat of occult sciences, see Tatlock, Scene of the Franklin's Tale, Ch. Soc., 1911, p. 43. Professor Lowes printed in Rom. Rev., II, 125 ff., notes on student life at Orleans; see also J. F. Royster, Stud. Phil., XXIII, 383 f.

1125 On *magyk natureel* see *Gen Prol*, I, 416, n.

1130 The twenty-eight mansions, or stations, of the moon correspond to the twenty-eight days of a lunation. For their positions, Skeat refers to Ideler, Untersuchungen über den Ursprung und die Bedeutung der Sternnamen, Berlin, 1809, pp. 287 ff., and for their astrological significance, to Joannes Hispalensis, Epitome Astrologiae, Nürnberg, 1548, i, 11; iv, 18.

1133 Cf. l. 1293 below. For a discussion of Chaucer's attitude and that of the church in his time toward judicial astrology see Tatlock, Scene of the Franklin's Tale, pp. 27 ff.; Kittredge Anniversary Papers, Boston, 1913, p. 348; and T. O. Wedel, The Mediæval Attitude toward Astrology, Yale Stud. in Eng., 1920, 142 ff.

1141 *tregetoures*, jugglers. Skeat notes that there are accounts of jugglery in Marco Polo (Yule, I, 314 ff., 386). Mandeville also reports magic at the court of the Great Khan (ed. Hamelius, EETS, 1919, I, 156). But this feature of the story is not necessarily oriental. For Celtic parallels cf. Schofield, PMLA, XVI, 417 ff.; also the early Irish saga of Muirchertach mac Erca, in the Yellow Book of Lecan, cols. 313 ff. (published in Rev. Celt., XXIII, 395 ff.) and the modern folktale, Mac an Sgoloige ocus an Gearra Glas, published by Douglas Hyde in An Sgeuluidhe Gaodhalach ii, 85, no. 12. In the last instance the magical performances are made the condition of a marriage.

1174 *thriftily*, suitably, or perhaps, heartily, well. The meanings of the word are often hard to define precisely.

1180 *dawes*, a variant of *dayes*, pl. of *day*. Cf. *fawe(n)*, beside *fayn*, and *slawe(n)*, beside *slayn*.

1196 *Thise*, used in a generalizing sense, as in ll. 376, 818, above. Cf. *KnT*, I, 1531, n. With *ryver* in the sense of "hawking-ground" cf. *WBT*, III, 884, n.; *Thop*, VII, 737, n.

1203 For the clapping of hands to break a spell cf. the Epilogue to The Tempest.

1204 For this extension of the use of the possessive — the familiar or "domestic" *our* — see *ShipT*, VII, 69, n.

1219 See *ShipT*, VII, 255, n.

1222 *Gerounde*, the Gironde. *Sayne*, the Seine.

1223 *made it straunge*, held off, made difficulties about it. Cf. *to make it wys*, *Gen Prol*, I, 785, and n.

1228 It was the regular scientific teaching of the Middle Ages that the earth was round.

1232–44 Rajna (Rom., XXXII, 239) and Lowes (MP, XV, 715 f.) note a striking parallel in both words and situation between this passage and the Filocolo, II, 53.

1245 *hewed lyk latoun*, copper-colored.

1246 *in his hoote declynacioun*, in Cancer.

1248 The sun entered Capricorn on Dec. 13.

1250–51 Cf. Tes., iii, 44, 2 f.

1252 *Janus . . . with double berd* stands for January. In MS. El is the marginal gloss "Janus biceps," referring to "Iane biceps," Ovid's Fasti, i, 65. For a calculation of the approximate date of the clerk's operation — Jan. 3–4, when the full moon would be in the fourth term of Cancer and in its own "face," a position of extraordinary potency — see Tatlock, Kitt. Anniv. Papers, pp. 343 ff.

1255 *Nowel*, Noel, Christmas.

1263 *conclusioun*: cf. the frequent use of the word in Chaucer's *Astrolabe* for problems or exercises in astronomy.

1273 *tables Tolletanes*, Toledan Tables (with French plural adjective). The term applied originally to astronomical tables compiled by Al-Zarḡālī in the eleventh century. But these were superseded by later ones prepared under the direction of Alfonso el Sabio, King of Castile and Leon, about 1272. Chaucer, in so far as he considered the matter at all, would have had in mind the later, Alfonsine tables, which in their Latin form had a wide circulation in the fourteenth century. In fact the tables in the Equatorie of the Planetis, conjecturally ascribed by some authorities to Chaucer himself, are based upon the Alfonsine, with adaptations to the longitude of London. See G. Sarton, Introduction to the History of Sciences (Baltimore, 1931), II, 837; Derek J. Price, The Equatorie of the Planetis (Cambridge, 1955), pp. 79–80; and F. P. Magoun, Jr., Med. Stud., XVII, 141.

1274 *corrected*, either adapted to a given locality, or purged of errors. For testimony on the inaccuracy of the tables see Tatlock, Kitt. Anniv. Papers, p. 346, n.

1275 *Expans yeeris*, computations of the changes of a planet's position in single years or short periods up to 20 years; *collect yeeris*, computations for round periods from 20 to 3000 years. See *Astr*, ii, 44.

1276 *rootes*, data for a given time or period, which serve as the basis of a computation. Cf. *MLT*, II, 314, and *Astr*, ii, 44.

1277 *centris*, "the end of the small brass projection on the 'rete' of an astrolabe which denoted the position of a fixed star" (Skeat). *Argumentz*, "the angle, arc, or other mathematical quantity, from which another required quantity may be deduced, or on which its calculation depends" (NED).

1278 *proporcioneles convenientz*, tables of proportional parts for computing the motions of planets during fractions of a year. For the adjectival plural in -s cf. *delitables*, l. 899 above.

1279 *equacions*, possibly allowances for minor motions, though the NED does not record this meaning before the seventeenth century. The reference here may be rather to the equations, or divisions, of the sphere into "houses" for astrological purposes.

1280 ff. *his eighte speere*, the sphere of the fixed stars. The true equinoctial point (the head of the "fixed Aries") was conceived as situated in the ninth sphere, i.e., the Primum Mobile. The amount of the precession of the equinoxes was ascertained by observing the distance between the true equinoctial point and the star Alnath (α Arietis) in the head of Aries (in the eighth sphere).

1285 *his firste mansioun*, the first mansion of the moon, called Alnath from the name of the star.

1288 Each sign of the zodiac was divided into equal parts, of ten degrees each, called *faces*, and unequal parts, *termes*. The faces and terms were all assigned to one or another of the planets.

1289–90 The association of the moon with magic is of course familiar from antiquity down. For illustrations see Tatlock, Kitt. Anniv. Papers, pp. 341–49. According to his calculations, the mansion here concerned was probably the eighth. See p. 347.

1311 The speeches of Aurelius (ll. 1311 ff.) and Dorigen (ll. 1355 ff.), as Chaucer notes in the case of the second, are formal "complaints." Skeat points out the similarity of the whole passage in style to the *Complaint of Anelida*, comparing especially l. 1318 with *Anel*, 288, l. 1340 with *Anel*, 173, l. 1348 with *Anel*, 169.

1325 *but youre grace*, but only your favor. This conception, that the lover's only hope lay in the unmerited favor of the lady, was the counterpart, in the religion of love, of the Christian doctrine of grace. Cf. *KnT*, I, 3089, n.

1355–1456 This complaint rehearses the six chapters of Jerome against Jovinian which precede the extract from Theophrastus. Cf. the briefer summing-up by the God of Love in *LGW Prol G*, 281–304. In ll. 1412–14 there is perhaps also a reminiscence of Deschamps, Miroir de Mariage, l. 9153.

1356 Possibly suggested by "si strigneano le catene," Tes., iii, 32, 5.

1357–58 Cf. Filocolo (ed. Moutier), II, 59.

1360 *have I levere*, I had rather. On this idiom cf. Am. Jour. Philol., II, 281 ff.

1366 Most of the passages from Jerome are quoted at length in Skeat's notes. The persons and places are briefly identified, when necessary, here below.

1367 ff. The accumulation of *exempla* here was in accord both with the recommendations of the rhetoricians and with the practice of other mediæval poets, conspicuously with Machaut's. See Manly, Chaucer and the Rhetoricians, Brit. Acad., 1926, p. 12; Œuvres de Machaut, ed. Hoepffner, SATF, I, lxxiii. In M-R CT, IV, 487, Manly suggests that Chaucer had become weary of *exempla* and wished to make them absurd. See also, on Chaucer's possible procedure, Mrs. Dempster, MLN, LII, 16 ff. and LIV, 137.

1367 The Thirty Tyrants were put down in 403 B.C.

1380 *Lacedomye*, Lacedaemonia.

1387 f. *Aristoclides,* tyrant of Orchomenos in Arcadia. *Stymphalides,* properly *Stymphalis* (acc. *Stymphalidem*).

1399 A reference to the story of Hasdrubal's wife in the third Punic War (146 B.C.). Cf. also *NPT,* VII, 3363.

1405 Cf. the legend of Lucretia, *LGW,* 1680 ff.

1409 *Milesie,* Miletus. A reference to the sack of Miletus by the Gauls (or Galatians) in 276 B.C.

1414 *Habradate,* Abradates, King of the Susi. Jerome took the story from Xenophon's Cyropaedia, vii, 3.

1418 *if I may,* if I have power (to prevent it). For this negative implication cf. *ML Prol,* II, 89, n.

1426 The virgin daughter of Demotion, when she learned of the death of the man to whom she was betrothed, killed herself lest she should be compelled to marry another, "cum priori mente nupsisset."

1428 *Cedasus,* Scedasus of Bœotia. Plutarch (Amatoriae Narrationes) relates that his daughters, after being violated, killed each other from shame.

1432 *Nichanore,* Nicanor, an officer of Alexander at the capture of Thebes (B.C. 336).

1437 Nicerates was put to death by the Thirty Tyrants, and his wife killed herself lest she should become their victim.

1439 The concubine of Alcibiades, who buried his dead body, was Timandra. See Plutarch, Life of Alcibiades.

1442 On Alcestis see *LGW Prol F,* 510 ff., and n.

1443 *Penalopee,* Penelope, the faithful wife of Odysseus.

1445 On Laodamia, who refused to survive her husband Protesilaus, see Ovid, Heroides, xiii.

1448 On the death of Portia, the wife of Brutus, see the end of Plutarch's Life of Brutus.

1451 *Arthemesie,* Artemisia, wife of King Mausolus, who built for him the famous "mausoleum."

1453 *Teuta,* queen of Illyria.

1455 *Bilyea,* Bilia, wife of Duillius, who won a naval victory over the Carthaginians, B.C. 260 (see Florus, Epitome, i, 18). Her story, under the name Ulie, is told by Hoccleve, De Regimine Principum (EETS, p. 135), quoting Jerome, Adv. Jov., i, 46 (Migne, Pat. Lat., XXIII, 275).

Ll. 1455-6 and 1493-8 occur only in MSS. El. and Ad³. Since the second passage sounds "Chaucerian," it is hard to reject the first.

1456 *Rodogone,* Rhodogune, daughter of Darius. She killed her nurse, who tried to persuade her to a second marriage. *Valeria,* wife of Servius, refused to marry a second time.

The following marginal notes in MS. El, doubtless due to Chaucer, indicate both the source of the passage and a plan, at some time in his mind, to add further instances of unfortunate wives. "Memorandum Strato regulus. Vidi & omnes pene Barbares capitulo, xxvi° primi. Item Cornelia &c. Imitentur ergo nupte Theanam Cleobiliam Gorgim (or Gorgun) Thymodiam Claudias atque Cornelias in fine libri primi."

"Singulas has historias & plures hanc materiam concernentes recitat beatus Ieronimus contra Iovinianum in primo suo libro, capitulo 39°."

1461 Cf. Filocolo (ed. Moutier), II, 58.

1470 *as wys,* as (is) certain.

1471 *and,* if (an unusual meaning in Chaucer).

1472 Cf. the proverb, "Let sleeping dogs lie."

1479 *Trouthe,* troth, pledged word. This is the first moral of the tale. Professor Manly compares the motto on the tomb of King Edward I, "Pactum serva."

1483 *telle,* imperative. The construction is broken after *That.*

1503 *bown,* ready, prepared, bound (ON. "buinn").

1531 Cf. the note to l. 1360, above.

1532 "Than that I should part." The ellipsis of *that* was common in this situation.

1533 Professor Blenner-Hassett (Spec., XXVIII, 797 ff.) notes that the language of the release of Dorigen resembles that of Cecilia Chaumpayne to Chaucer "de meo raptu."

1540 In nearly all MSS. ll. 1541-4 are included in Dorigen's speech. But Professor Baum (MLN, XXXII, 377) pointed out that they are more suitable to the Franklin, and Manly (M-R CT, IV, p. 488) agrees, but would transfer them to a later place (after l. 1550). Cf. also F. P. Magoun, Jr., MLN, LXX, p. 173.

1543-44 The second virtue inculcated is *gentilesse.*

1547 *sayd,* an unusual use of the past participle. See A. Graef, Das Perfectum bei Chaucer, Frankenhausen, 1888, p. 93.

1549 *wryte* seems to be used here by oversight. Cf. *KnT,* I, 1201, and n.

1575 *dayes,* days (of respite).

1580 *a-begged,* a-begging. On the form see *PardT,* VI, 406, n.

1614 "As if you had just crept out of the ground," had just made your first appearance.

1624 The closing question is a common device at the end of a story or an episode. Cf. *KnT,* I, 1347, and n., and Filocolo (ed. Moutier), II, 60; also Giovanni da Prato, Il Paradiso degli Alberti, ed. A. Wesselofsky, 3 v., Bologna, 1867, III, 152, 225. For a question similar to the one here, but propounded under different circumstances, see J. F. Campbell's Tales from the West Highlands, Paisley, 1890-93, II, 24 ff.

FRAGMENT VI

Fragment VI, comprising the *Physician's Tale,* the *Words of the Host,* and the *Pardoner's Prologue* and *Tale,* is a floating fragment which is not connected at either end with the rest of the tales. In the Ellesmere group of MSS. it stands after Fragment V, in most other MSS. after VIII, and in most recent editions after VII. This last arrangement, which was adopted by the Six-Text editor to fill out the tales of the second day, has no real authority, and recent discussion has favored either the Ellesmere order or one which puts Fragment VI immediately after Fragment II. See the general discussion of the subject in the introduction to the Textual Notes on the *Canterbury Tales.*

Three spurious prologues to the *Physician's Tale* are preserved in the MSS. and early editions. Note Manly's analysis of the different versions (M-R CT, IV, 488-9). Cf. also J. B. Severs in Spec., XXIX, 512 ff. who concludes that Chaucer made no systematic revision of either *PhysT.* or *PardT,* but did make important changes in the link that joins them. See the Textual Notes on the *CYT* and the *FranklT*.

The Physician's Tale

The *Physician's Tale* is generally held to have been written as early as the beginning of the Canterbury period. In spirit and narrative method it resembles the stories that make up the *Legend of Good Women*, so much so, in fact, that some scholars have suggested that it was originally intended to stand, with the similar tale of Lucretia, in that collection. For this surmise there is no real evidence, but it is altogether probable that the story of Virginia was closely contemporary with the legends. From the fact that it is not mentioned in the list of Chaucer's works in the *Prologue* to the *Legend*, a date later than 1386 has been inferred, and from the fact that it shows no influence of Gower's version in the Confessio Amantis, a date earlier than 1390. As has been suggested by Professor Tatlock, the passage about duennas (ll. 72 ff.) has reference to a scandalous affair in the family of John of Gaunt, the most likely time of composition would be between 1386 and 1388. See the note to l. 72 below, and compare, for the historical details, G. L. Kittredge, MP, I, 5, n. 7, and Tatlock, Dev. and Chron., pp. 150 ff.

Opinions differ as to the suitability of the tale to the Physician. It is defended by Professor Tupper (JEGP, XV, 59 ff.). Professor Kittredge (Atlantic, LXXII, 829) also observes that the prosy discourse at the beginning is appropriate to the speaker. The same may be said of the advice to parents and governesses. And though the direct address to *maistresses* and *fadres* and *moodres* is not especially suited to the pilgrims, it is a natural rhetorical figure and may be disregarded as evidence. On the whole the situation is puzzling. The passages especially appropriate to the Physician might have been added in revision, and it is doubtful whether the tale was originally composed with him in mind.

The ultimate source of the story of Virginia is Livy's History, Bk. iii. Chaucer refers to Livy as his authority, but he certainly made use of the version in the Roman de la Rose (5589 ff.). Whether the French or the Latin was his primary source is a matter of disagreement. See Fansler, Chaucer and the RR., New York, 1914, pp. 31 ff., and E. F. Shannon in SA, 398 ff., where the account in the Roman and parallel passages from Livy are printed. Chaucer's version and that of Gower (Conf. Am., vii, 5131 ff.) appear to be mutually independent. See O. Rumbaur, Die Geschichte von Appius und Virginia in der englischen Litteratur, Breslau, 1890.

6 Other authorities say simply that Virginia was an only daughter. In making her an only child, Miss Grace W. Landrum suggests, Chaucer was influenced by the story of Jephthah's daughter (Judges xi, 34), mentioned in l. 240. (See her unpub. Radcliffe diss., Chaucer's Use of the Vulgate, 1921.)

9 It was a common device, in the description of beautiful women, to represent the goddess Nature as having given special attention to their creation. Cf. *Anel.* 80; *BD,* 871 ff.; *PF,* 374 ff.; and see E. C. Knowlton, MP, XX, 310 f.

14 ff. On Pygmalion see Ovid, Met., x, 242 ff. For treatment in Old French see The Pearl, ed. C. G. Osgood, p. 84. But Chaucer was doubtless follow-

ing RR, 16177 ff., where Pygmalion, Apelles, and Zeuxis are all mentioned in a similar argument. On *Apeles* and *Zanzis* (a corruption of Zeuxis) MSS. El and Hg have the marginal note: "Appeles fecit mirabile opus in tumulo Darii. Vide in Alexandri libro 1°, (Hg 6°) de Zanze in libro Tullii." According to the Alexandreis of Philippe Gualtier de Chatillon (ca. 1200), vii, 384 ff. (ed. Mueldener, Leipzig, 1863) the tomb of Darius was the work of a Jewish artist named Apelles. The famous Athenian painter, Zeuxis, is mentioned, along with Apelles, in Cicero's De Oratore, iii, 26, to which reference is doubtless intended in the marginal note above. But Cicero's Apelles was the historic painter of ancient Athens, and not the fictitious figure of the Alexander romance.

20 *vicaire general;* with this epithet of Nature cf. *PF,* 379; also RR, 16782, 19505 ff., and earlier, Alanus de Insulis, De Planctu Naturae (Migne, Pat. Lat., CCX, 453).

32–34 Cf. RR, 16242 ff.

35–120 This passage is Chaucer's addition.

41 ff. The description of Virginia's maidenly virtues, which is not derived from the Roman de la Rose, contains much that was commonplace in treatises on virginity. Professor Tupper (MLN, XXX, 5 ff.) has shown that good illustrations of the passage, if not its actual source, may be found in the Libri Tres de Virginibus of St. Ambrose (Migne, Pat. Lat., XVI, 187–232). He compares especially l. 43 with Ambrose, ii, §7; l. 48 with Ambrose, iii, 9; ll. 58–59 with Ambrose, iii, 5; l. 61 ff. with Ambrose, iii, 25; ll. 72 ff. with Ambrose, iii, 31; ll. 117 ff. with Ambrose, ii, 10; and ll. 118 ff. with Ambrose, ii, 9, 14. The pathetic speech in which Virginia chooses death rather than dishonor is modeled on such examples of the self-sacrifice of virgin martyrs as are found in the stories cited from St. Jerome by the Franklin (V, 1367 ff.). But for this also, Mr. Tupper points out, a good parallel is furnished by the account of St. Pelagia in the treatise of Ambrose (Bk. iii, ch. 7). The relevant passages from Ambrose are assembled in SA, 407 f. Parallels from the De Eruditione Filiorum Nobilium of Vincent of Beauvais were assembled by K. Young in Spec., XVI, 340 ff. He argued that they were closer to Chaucer than those from Ambrose. But he did not reject the possibility, whatever literary source Chaucer may have had, that there was also an application to Katherine Swynford.

54 *Sownynge in,* conducing to. See *Gen Prol,* I, 307 n.

59 Cf. Ovid, Ars Amat., i, 243 f.

60 A proverbial phrase; cf. Horace, Sat., ii, 3, 321; and see Skeat, EE Proverbs, p. 109, no. 258.

65 Cf. Ars Amat., i, 229 ff.

72 ff. In inserting this rather extraordinary digression on the responsibilities of governesses and parents it has been supposed that Chaucer had in mind the family of John of Gaunt. Katherine Swynford, the governess of Lancaster's children, was for many years his mistress, and in 1396 became his third wife. Moreover, Elizabeth, his second daughter, who was married to the Earl of Pembroke as a mere child in 1380, was introduced at court in 1386, and shortly afterward had a liaison with John Holland. Pembroke secured a divorce and Holland married Elizabeth and took her to Spain. In June,

1388, or perhaps earlier, they returned to England. (For further details see Tatlock, Dev. and Chron., pp. 153 ff.).

Mr. Cowling (Chaucer, London, 1927, p. 166) would connect the passage not only with the affair of Elizabeth of Lancaster, but also with the abduction of Isabella atte Halle in 1387. Chaucer was commissioned to attend the inquiry.

79 Cf. *Gen Prol*, I, 476, and n.

85 Cf. the modern proverb, "Set a thief to catch a thief"; and Skeat, EE Prov., p. 109, no. 259.

91 f. Cf. *Bo*, iii, pr. 5, 68 ff., and *MerchT*, IV, 1793 f.

98 Prov. xiii, 24.

101 Proverbial; cf. Alanus de Insulis, Liber Parabolarum, i, 31 (Migne, Pat. Lat., CCX, 581).

Sub molli pastore capit (var. rapit) lanam lupus,
   et grex

Incustoditus dilaceratur eo.

See also Skeat, EE Prov., p. 110, no. 260; Haeckel, p. 48, no. 165.

107–08 Cf. II Cor. iii, 2.

117 *The doctour*, St. Augustine (not the Physician who tells the tale). Cf. *NPT*, VII, 3241, and *ParsT*, X, 484. It is unnecessary to assume (with Brusendorff, p. 129, n. 3) a word-play on the profession of the Physician.

135 ff. Chaucer here returns to his source.

140 The MSS. are divided between *cherl* and *clerk*, the former being perhaps an intentional rendering of the Fr. *ribauz* (Rom. de la Rose, 5599).

153 ff. The judge's name was Appius Claudius and the churl's Marcus Claudius. But Jean de Meun calls the former simply Apius and the latter Claudius.

168 ff. Cf. RR, 5612 ff.

207–53 The account of the speech is original with Chaucer.

240 Judges xi, 37–38.

255–76 Cf. RR, 5635–58. The bringing in of the head is narrated in RR and not in Livy. See Langlois, Origines et Sources du Roman de la Rose, Paris, 1891, p. 118.

277 Proverbial; cf. Haeckel, p. 41, no. 141.

286 With this formula, which was proverbial, cf. *ParsT*, X, 93.

The Words of the Host

The version of the *Words* here printed really combines two forms of the passage, as shown in detail by Manly, M-R CT, IV, 490 ff. Since all the lines are doubtless genuine, the traditional "standard" version is given here, though ll. 297–8 may have been cancelled by Chaucer. For a reconstruction of the two versions see Manly's discussion.

288 *by nayles and by blood*, the familiar oath, by the nails of the Cross and the blood of Christ. See l. 651, and n.

291 *advocatz*, spelled *advocas* (e) in several MSS., seems to have been pronounced with a silent *t*. Otherwise there is only assonance with *allas*.

295 The distinction between gifts of Fortune and gifts of Nature (both powers being more or less personally conceived) was familiar in mediæval literature. See Dan Michel, Ayenbite of Inwit, ed., Morris, EETS, pp. 24–25, following Frère Lorens, Somme des Vices et des Vertus. In general the en-

dowments of the body and the soul are attributed to Nature, and the advantages of outer circumstance — honor, rank, prosperity — to Fortune. But the distinction was not consistently maintained, and physical beauty, for example, was sometimes counted among the gifts of Fortune. See Deschamps, Œuvres, SATF, III, 386 (no. 544). In *ParsT*, X, 450 there is a three-fold classification of gifts of Fortune, of Nature, and of Grace.

304 *cors*, body, self. Cf. *ML Epil*, II, 1185.

306 *Ypocras*, a beverage composed of red wine, spices, and sugar, said to have been so named because a strainer was known as "Hippocrates' sleeve." See Halliwell's Dictionary, s.v. Hippocras, Ipocras, from which Skeat's note quotes a receipt for making the drink. For an example of its use see *MerchT*, IV, 1807.

Galiones, apparently (Skeat suggests) drinks or remedies named after Galen. But there seems to be no other occurrence of the word, and it may be a blunder of the Host's.

310 *Seint Ronyan. Ronyan* here has three syllables and rimes with *man*; in l. 320, *Ronyon* is dissyllabic and rimes with *anon*. It was taken by Skeat to be a corruption of Ronan, well known to readers of "St. Ronan's Well." But later commentators have questioned the identification. Professor Tupper has proposed another explanation. In JEGP, XIV, 257, n., he suggested the possibility of ribald ambiguity, with word-play upon "runnion"; and later (JEGP, XV, 66 f.) developing the theory more fully, he took the name to be a coinage from French "rognon," kidney. This suggestion is supported by G. L. Frost, MLN, LVIII, 177 ff. See further J. Sledd, Med. Stud., XIII, 226 ff. and R. P. Miller, Spec., XXX, 194. Professor Manly points out that "runian" occurs in fifteenth-century English documents as a term for a farm servant. A double meaning with reference to one or more of these terms may have been in Chaucer's mind, but the hypothesis is not necessary. For "Ronyan" and "Rinian" were current, as Professor G. L. Hamilton has pointed out to the editor, as corruptions of the name of St. Ninian, the celebrated founder of Candida Casa. See J. Dowden, Proc. of the Soc. of Ant. of Scotland, 3d. Ser., V, 198 ff.

313 *cardynacle*, for "cardiacle," pain about the heart. It is hard to say whether this reading (in the Ellesmere MS. and several others) was merely an error of the scribe or blunder intentionally attributed to the Host. In support of the latter assumption (which may apply to *galiones* and *jurdones*) see Mrs. Dempster, PMLA, LXVIII, 1152. In either case, of course, the form is due to confusion with "cardinal."

314 *By corpus bones*; see *Mk Prol*, VII, 1906, n.

327 Obviously the Pardoner is not really put to it to think of a decent story. He is simply making an excuse for a drink. Moreover, the association between taking a drink and telling a tale is ancient and proverbial. Cf. O'Rahilly, Miscellany of Irish Proverbs, Dublin, 1922, pp. 118 f.

The Pardoner's Prologue and Tale

The Pardoner's Prologue and *Tale* form a consecutive composition clearly written in the period of the *Canterbury Tales*. There is no definite indication of a more precise date. If, as some commentators suggest, the Pardoner was not in the original group of pilgrims, his tale was probably not among the earliest of the stories. On the other hand, there is no reason for putting it among the very latest, in the period of the so-called Marriage Group. The frequent quotation from Innocent's *De Contemptu Mundi* associates it with the *Man of Law's Tale*, which has been conjecturally dated about 1390.

The story is a typical exemplum or "example," skillfully worked up in what the Pardoner presents as a customary sermon. It is of oriental origin, the earliest known analogue being one of the Jatakas, or birth-tales of Buddha, and one of the most recent being the story of the King's Ankus in Kipling's *Second Jungle Book*. Chaucer's source is unknown, but the version which most nearly resembles his is that in the Libro di Novelle e di Bel Parlar Gentile, Florence, 1572, no. lxxxii; also printed in the Originals and Analogues (Ch. Soc.) Pt. II, p. 131; and by Skeat, Oxf. Chau., III, 440–42, and again, along with several other parallels, by F. Tupper in SA, 415 ff. For further information see A. d'Ancona, Studj di Critica e Storia Letteraria, 2d ed., Bologna, 1912, II, 136–38; Miss Hammond, p. 296; T. F. Crane, MP, X, 310; W. Wells, MP, XXV, 163–64; A. L. Friend, JEGP, LIII, 387. Numerous current anecdotes have been cited as analogues. See, for example, H. B. Woolf, MLN, LXVI, 267 ff., and T. A. Kirby, ibid., 269. The *märchen* type is no. 763 in A. Aarne's Types of the Folk-Tale, tr. S. Thompson, Helsinki, 1928. Besides what may have been derived from its main source, the *Pardoner's Tale* contains numerous literary borrowings of an incidental character. The quotations from Innocent have been already mentioned, and there are also a number of passages derived from, or parallel with, portions of Chaucer's own *Parson's Tale*. For the character of the Old Man, which is largely original with Chaucer, use was almost certainly made of an elegy of Maximian. See G. L. Kittredge, Am. Jour. Philol., IX, 84 f. Further references in the character are given below in the note to ll. 713 ff. Miss Petersen (Sources of the Nonne Prestes Tale, Boston, 1898, p. 100, n.), suggests that the same character owes something to the Liber de Apibus, by Thomas of Cantimpré, in which she also finds parallels to the localization in Flanders and to the descriptions of dicing, swearing, and reveling.

Both the *Prologue* and the *Tale* of the Pardoner are apparently delivered while the pilgrims are still at the tavern (l. 321). At least there is no indication that they take the road before the Pardoner begins. So a story which is in large part an attack upon gluttony and revelry is told in a tavern by a man notoriously addicted to the vices he condemns. Professor Tupper has laid emphasis upon the humor of the situation. On his further contention that a similar method is carried out generally in the *Canterbury Tales* see the introduction to the Explanatory Notes on the *CT*.

On the pardoners of Chaucer's age as a class and the abuses they practiced, see J. J. Jusserand, Chaucer's Pardoner and the Pope's Pardoners, Chaucer Soc. Essays, xiii (Pt. v); cf. also G. R. Owst, Preaching in Mediæval England, Cambridge, 1926, pp. 99 ff., and A. L. Kellogg and L. A. Haselmayer, PMLA, LXVI, 251 ff. The character and conduct of Chaucer's Pardoner, in particular the problem of his

self-betrayal, are discussed by Professor G. L. Kittredge in the Atlantic Monthly, LXXII, 829 ff.; Chaucer and his Poetry, pp. 211–18. See also R. M. Lumiansky, Tulane Studies in English, I, 1 ff.; J. Swart, Neophilologus, XXXVI, 45 ff.

The Confession of Faux-Semblant in the Roman de la Rose (ed. Langlois, III, 183 ff.) has long been recognized as a passage which probably influenced Chaucer. The parallel lines are printed by Mrs. Dempster in SA, pp. 409 ff.

Professor A. L. Kellogg (Spec., XXVI, 465) has tried to show Chaucer's dependence on St. Augustine for the concept of sin and deterioration in the Pardoner's character. In view of the slight use of St. Augustine that has been found elsewhere in Chaucer, such a definite source may be questioned here. But the Augustinian conceptions were undoubtedly current and accessible to Chaucer, and Mr. Kellogg's study illustrates the theological background of the character. The discussion has been continued by Mr. R. P. Miller (Spec., XXX, 180 ff.) who argues that spiritual imagery about eunuchry was utilized by Chaucer both in the portrait of the Pardoner and in his tale.

The Pardoner's Prologue

333 *theme*, text. The regular mediæval sermon was in six parts: (1) theme; (2) protheme, a kind of introduction; (3) dilatation, exposition of the text; (4) exemplum, illustration by anecdote; (5) peroration, or application; (6) closing formula. The Pardoner's sermon seems to have only three or four of these divisions: (1) l. 334; (4) ll. 463–903; (5) ll. 904–15; and perhaps (6) ll. 916–18. See Professor Manly's note, with references to Lecoy de la Marche, La Chaire Française au Moyen Âge, Paris, 1868, and J. M. Neale, Mediæval Preachers and Mediæval Preaching, London, 1856; also a study of the passages in Chaucer which relate to preaching, by C. O. Chapman, PMLA, XLIV, 178 ff.

334 I Tim. vi, 10 (omitting *omnium*, which would be hypermetrical). Cf. *Mel*, VII, 1130, n.

337 *Oure lige lordes seel*, the seal of some bishop. Cf. Piers Plowman, A Prol, 66 ff.

345 "To give color and flavor to my preaching." On the position of *with* immediately after the infinitive see *Gen Prol*, I, 791, n.

347 *cristal stones*, glass cases.

351 The *hooly Jew* was presumably of the Old Testament era, possibly Jacob. See Gen. xxx, 31 ff., and cf. l. 364 below. The superstitious use of a sheep's shoulderbone mentioned in *ParsT*, X, 603, is quite different. The reference there seems to be to spatulomancy, a recognized form of divination.

355 "That hath eaten any worm, or any worm hath stung." The strange repetition of *worm* is due to the fact that in the first case it is the object of *ete*, in the second the subject of (*hath*) *ystonge*. The diseases of cattle were often attributed to the eating of injurious worms. Cf. the taint-worm in Milton's Lycidas, l. 46.

377 ff. For analogues to the Pardoner's *gaude* of declaring that great sinners must not offer to his relics see B. J. Whiting, MLN, LI, 322 ff. and SA, pp. 411 ff.

390 *An hundred mark*. The mark was worth 13*s*. 4*d*. (two-thirds of a pound). But the purchasing value of money then was at least twenty-five or thirty times what it would be today, after two World Wars and the ensuing inflation.

392 Professor Manly observes that this passage and Gower's Mirour de l'Omme, ll. 5245 ff., prove the use of some kind of seats in English churches. He cites further evidence as to French churches from Lecoy de la Marche, La Chaire Française, pp. 197 ff.

403 Cf. RR, 11565 (*Rom*, 6837). Professor Brusendorff (pp. 402 ff.) argued that the English *Romaunt*, rather than the French original, was followed here and in ll. 407 f., 443 f., below.

406 "Though their souls go a-blackberrying," i.e., wandering at large. The form *blakeberyed*, as Skeat explained, is formed on the analogy of such nouns as *hunted*, *fished*, from AS. nouns in -ath, -th ("huntoth," "fiscath," etc.). The Middle English ending, properly -*eth*, came to be assimilated to that of the preterite participle. Cf. *a-caterwawed*, *WB Prol*, III, 354. Other examples are given in Skeat's note.

407 ff. Cf. RR, 5113 f. (*Rom*, 5763 f.), and perhaps 5071–5118.

416 Here and in ll. 441 ff., the Pardoner speaks as if he belonged to a mendicant order. On the other hand, his reference, in *WB Prol*, III, 166, to taking a wife—if it is not a mere outburst of facetiousness—implies that he was a layman or one of the lower clergy.

435 *ensamples*, "exempla," the term regularly applied to the illustrative anecdotes of preachers.

443 ff. Cf. RR, 12504 (Michel). The basket-maker was Paul the Hermit, not St. Paul, as some of the commentators have supposed. Cf. Piers Plowman, B, xv, 281 ff., and see St. Jerome's Life of Paul the Hermit, §16 (Migne, Pat. Lat., XXIII, 28). Whether Chaucer himself was confused (note the *apostles*, l. 447) is not clear.

447 *counterfete*, imitate.

The Pardoner's Tale

463 ff. Reasons for associating drinking with Flanders were given by Manly, Cant. T., p. 619. For further discussion of the attitude of fourteenth-century Englishmen toward Flanders see Miss D. M. Norris, PMLA, XLVIII, 636 ff.

472 ff. With this familiar characterization of swearing cf. *ParsT*, X, 591. Further illustration is given in Skeat's note on the present passage, by Professor Lowes in Rom. Rev., II, 113 ff., and by R. Brotanek, Mittelenglische Dichtungen aus der Handschrift 432, etc. (Halle, 1940), pp. 102 ff. In the idea there is perhaps a reminiscence of Heb. vi, 6. The oaths were commonly by the parts of the body of Christ (as in ll. 651 ff. below). Professor Magoun has called the editor's attention to an instance of the appearance of the conception in Christian art. See the account of a fifteenth-century church window in Norfolk in The Times (London), 7 April, 1956, p. 7, col. 7.

477 *tombesteres*, female dancers. On the suffix -*stere* (AS. "-estre"), here used with its proper feminine significance, see *Gen Prol*, I, 241, n.

479 On the bad reputation of *wafereres* see Skeat's note.

483 Eph. v, 18.

487 Gen. xix, 33.

488 *the stories*, usually taken to be a reference to the Historia Evangelica (published with Hist. Scholastica) of Peter Comestor, which tells the story of Herod and John the Baptist in chap. lxxiii. But Comestor's account is very brief and says nothing about drunkenness. For the biblical narrative see Matt. xiv; Mark vi. Miss Landrum (diss., II, 134) notes also the Breviarium Romanum, Pars Aestiva, pp. 713–19.

492 ff. See Seneca, Epist. lxxxiii, 18. The Senecan reminiscences seem to continue through l. 548. Cf. especially Epist. lx, 4; lxxxiii, 27; xcv, 15, 19, 25, 26, 28–29; cxiv, 26. (See Rom. Rev., X, 5–7.)

495 *dronkelewe*, drunken. On the rare suffix -*lewe* see NED, VI, 232; Angl. Beibl., XIII, 235 f.

499 *confusioun*, ruin.

501 *boght . . . agayn* exactly translates "redimit."

505 ff. From Jerome, Adversus Jovinianum, ii, 15 (Migne, Pat. Lat., XXIII, 305).

512 ff. Cf. Ecclus. xxxvii, 29–31.

517 *the shorte throte*, the brief pleasure of swallowing. See again Jerome, Adv. Jov., bk. ii, §8: "Propter brevem gulae voluptatem, terrae lustrantur et maria" (Migne, 297). Cf. also Innocent, De Cont. Mundi, bk. ii, ch. 17: "Tam brevis est gulae voluptas" (Migne, CCXVII, 723).

519 *to swynke*, taken by Skeat and the NED as a compound *to-swynke*. But the existence of the word is very doubtful, and it seems easier to assume (with Manly) a change of construction.

522 I Cor. vi, 13.

526 *white and rede*, white wine and red. See *NPT*, VII, 2842.

529 ff. Phil. iii, 18 f.

537 ff. With the discourse on gluttony cf. the De Contemptu Mundi, bk. ii, ch. 17 (Migne, 723) especially the clause "substantiam convertit in accidens" (translated in l. 539). Substance and accident are used in their philosophical senses, the real essence of a thing, and the outward qualities (color, weight, texture, etc.) by which it is apprehended. For another passage where the same terms are applied to cooking see the Latin Poems commonly attributed to Walter Map, ed. T. Wright, p. xlii.

Chaucer can hardly have used this phrase without thinking of the current controversy about the Eucharist. Cf. Wyclif's joke about the friar's treatment of a lord's cask of wine (Sermones, Wyclif Soc., III, 194).

547 f. I Tim. v, 6.

549 Prov. xx, 1, cited by St. Jerome (Adv. Jov., ii, 10, Migne, XXIII, 299).

555 Judges xiii, 4 f.; Num. vi, 3.

557 *honeste cure*, care for one's honor, sense of decency, self-respect.

558 ff. Proverbial: cf. *MLT*, II, 771 f., n.

563 *Lepe*, a town near Cadiz, which was known for its strong wines.

564 *Fysshstrete*, now Fish Hill Street, leads out of Lower Thames Street, near London Bridge. Chaucer's father was a Thames Street vintner. *Chepe*, either Cheapside, where there were numerous taverns, or, as Professor Magoun suggests, the present Eastcheap, at right angles with upper Fish Street Hill.

565 Doubtless an allusion to the illicit mixing of wines by the vintners. Professor Manly cites evidence (from Letter Book H, p. 145) that Spanish wines were cheaper than French — which would explain why they tended to creep subtly in! For further evidence on the mixture of wines see A. L. Hench, MLN, LII, 27.

567 On *fumositee*, see *NPT*, VII, 2924, n.

579 On the death of Attila (A.D. 453) see Jordanes, De Getarum . . . Gestis, ch. xlix; Paulus Diaconus, De Gestis Romanorum, lib. xv.

585 *Lamuel*, Lemuel; Prov. xxxi, 4 ff.

590 ff. Cf. *ParsT*, X, 793.

591 ff. From John of Salisbury's Polycraticus i, ch. 5.

603 The story is apparently taken from the Polycraticus, but Chaucer has substituted *Stilbon* for *Chilon*, possibly under the influence of Seneca, Epist. ix, 18–19; x, 1. (See Rom. Rev., X, 5, n. 15.) For discussion of the identity of Stilbon, see N & Q, Ser. 8, IV, 175.

614 For *othere wise* Koch (edn. of *ParsT*, 1902) reads *otherwyse*, which he interprets as an adjective meaning "different," "otherwise minded" — a difficult and unnecessary alteration.

629 With the whole passage on swearing cf. *ParsT*, X, 587 ff.

633 Cf. Matt. v, 34 (cited in the margin of MSS. Hg Dd and 5 others), and James v, 12.

635 ff. Jer. iv, 2.

639 *the firste table*. The first tablet of the Ten Commandments, which have been variously subdivided. For the argument that Chaucer would have had in mind the patristic division into three and seven see Sister Mary Immaculate, MLQ, II, 64.

641 *the seconde heeste*, reckoned by Protestants as the third commandment. The first two commandments, according to the Protestant division, are regarded by the Catholic Church as one, and the tenth divided into two.

643 *rather*, earlier, sooner (the literal sense).

649 f. Ecclus. xxiii, 11.

651 The oath by God's nails is ambiguous in English, and might refer to the nails of his body ("ungues") or the nails of the cross ("claves"). In favor of the second application see Lowes, Rom. Rev., II, 115. He cites, among other examples, "par les cloux Dieu" from a ballade of Arnaud de Corbie (Œuvres de Deschamps, SATF, I, 273, no. 146). Probably, as Skeat suggests, swearers were not particular in making the distinction. The nails of the body are more appropriate to the present context.

652 A portion of Christ's blood was supposed to be preserved in a phial at Hayles in Gloucestershire. For accounts of it see Holinshed's Chronicle, London, 1807, II, p. 475; Southey, Book of the Church, ch. xii (3d edn., London, 1825, II, 70 f.); and Horstmann, Altenglische Legenden, Heilbronn, 1881, p. 275.

653 A reference to the game of hazard, on which see *ML Prol*, II, 124, n.

656 *bicched bones*, dice. *Bicched*, explained by Tyrwhitt and others as connected with "bichel," a name for dice (compare Du. "bikkel," cockal), is probably to be regarded rather as an opprobrious epithet derived from "bitch" and employed in Mid. Engl., as it is today, in the sense of "cursed, execrable." Professor Carleton Brown (MLN, XXIII, 126) cites as a parallel phrase the Lat. "ossibus caninis, id est deciis," Vincent of Beauvais, Spec.

Morale, iii, 8, 4. It is not clear whether the adjective "caninis" refers to the material of which the dice were made or is a mere equivalent of the English epithet of abuse.

667 *Go bet*, go better, faster; a call to the dogs in the chase.

673 *to-nyght*, referring, as commonly in older English, to the previous night.

674 *Fordronke*; doubtless the compound with *for-* in this case. See *KnT*, I, 2142, n.

679 *this pestilence*, during this plague. There were four serious plagues, as Skeat notes, in the reign of Edward III, in 1348–49, 1361–62, 1369, 1375–76. But since Chaucer's tale is later, and his source unknown, it is not possible to connect the reference definitely with any one of them.

684 *my dame*, my mother. Cf. *MancT*, IX, 317.

698 On the institution of sworn brotherhood, here referred to, see *KnT*, I, 1132, n.

710 *be deed*, die; cf. *KnT*, I, 1587, n.

713 ff. The old man here described seems to be almost entirely Chaucer's invention. In the Italian tale in the Cento Novelle Antiche there is a hermit ("romito") represented as fleeing from Death. The figure in Chaucer becomes rather a symbol of Death itself, or possibly of Old Age, conceived as Death's messenger. Mr. W. J. B. Owen, in RES (New Series) II, 49 ff., argues against such symbolistic interpretations. Miss Petersen (Sources of the Nonne Prestes Tale, p. 100 n.) suggests that a hint for the character may have been furnished by the old man in the Liber de Apibus. The Wandering Jew is a similar figure and may have furnished hints. See N. S. Bushnell, Stud. Phil., XXVIII, 450 ff. For part of the speech that follows (ll. 727 ff.) Professor Kittredge (Am. Jour. Philol., IX, 84 f.) has pointed out a very probable source in the first elegy of Maximianus, ll. 1–4, 223–28 (ed. Petschenig, Berliner Studien für class. Phil. u. Arch., XI, ii; also by R. Webster, Princeton, 1900, pp. 25 ff.). Cf. also the Middle English poem on Maximian, in Böddeker's Altenglische Dichtungen, Berlin, 1878, pp. 245 f. With the general sentiment may be compared Boethius, i, m. 1, used by Chaucer in *Tr*, iv, 501 ff. See further Miss M. P. Hamilton, SP, XXXVI, 571 ff. for a collection of interpretations; Mr. R. Miller, in his recent article in Spec., XXX, 188 ff., would identify the Old Man with St. Paul's *vetus homo*, the unregenerate image of the fallen Adam.

717 *with sory grace*, an imprecation, as again in l. 876.

722 On the use of India as a limit of remoteness, which was common in Middle English, see Kittredge, [Harv.] Stud. and Notes, I, 21 f.

734 *cheste*, not coffin, but clothes-chest.

736 *to wrappe in me*; on the order see *Gen Prol*, I, 791, n.

743 Levit. xix, 32.

745 ff. Cf. Ecclus. viii, 6.

748 *go or ryde*, lit. "walk or ride."

771 *an eighte*; for this use of the indefinite article cf. *ShipT*, VII, 334, and n.; also *LGW*, 2075.

774 The value of an English florin was 6s. 8d.

781 Cf. the proverb, "Lightly come, lightly go"; and Skeat, EE Prov., p. 110, no. 261.

782 *wende*, would have supposed (pret. subj.).

789 *theves stronge*, violent thieves, highwaymen.

792 *slyly*, practically synonymous with *wysly* in

older English. In the present case the wisdom consisted in what might now be called slyness.

793 For drawing *cuts* cf. *Gen Prol*, I, 835 ff.

847 With the theology, or demonology, of this passage cf. Job i, 12, ii, 6, and Chaucer's discussion in the *FrT*, III, 1482 ff.

851-78 There is no similar account of the purchase of the poison in the Italian tale.

858 *destroyed*, disturbed, harassed. Cf. *SumT*, III, 1847.

889 f. *Avycen*, Avicenna. See *Gen Prol*, I, 432. His chief work was entitled The Book of the Canon in Medicine (Kitâb-al-Qânûn fi'l-Tibb). For a full account of the work and a translation of the first book see O. Cameron Gruner, A Treatise on the Canon of Medicine of Avicenna, London, 1930. The *fen* was properly a section or subdivision of the work. Skeat held *canoun* to be a mistaken use of the general title for a subdivision of the work. But Professor Manly points out that the term is used repeatedly in chapter headings to denote "rule of procedure." The discussion of poisons is in Lib. iv, Fen vi (Venice, 1582).

891 *signes*, symptoms.

895 ff. The moralizing passages here and elsewhere are marked *Auctor* by the scribe of MS. El. See *MLT*, II, 358, n.

907 *nobles*, coins first struck by Edward III about 1339 and valued at 6s. 8d.

sterlynges, silver pennies.

915 *and lo, sires, thus I preche*. This definitely marks the end of the sermon. The men and women mentioned in the preceding lines are part of the imaginary congregation. What follows is addressed to the Canterbury pilgrims.

For a detailed discussion of the Pardoner's behavior here, and throughout his *Prologue* and *Tale*, see G. L. Kittredge, Atlantic, LXXII, 829 ff.; Chau. and his Poetry, pp. 211–18. Professor Kittredge's interpretation, very briefly stated, is as follows: The Pardoner entered upon his confession, not because he was overcome by drink, but because he was proud of his successful rascality. He trusted the company, too, not to betray his confidence. At the end of the sermon he suffered a revulsion of feeling. His better nature asserted itself, and he spoke in deepest earnestness when he invoked upon the pilgrims the true pardon of Christ. But this mood lasted only a moment, and he relapsed at once into impudent jocularity as he addressed the Host. The Host replied with bitter offensiveness, and the Pardoner, who might ordinarily have been expected to match abuse with abuse, was reduced to silence because of the moral struggle within him. Then the Host, perceiving the intensity of his anger, desisted, and the Knight intervened as peacemaker.

916 Cf. Ps. cxlvii, 3.

935 *Paraventure*, trisyllabic here; often spelled "paraunter."

939 *moore and lasse*, high and low.

947 *so thee'ch*, so may I prosper (*thee ich*).

951 *Seint Eleyne*, St. Helen, the mother of Constantine, held to have been the finder of the true Cross. See A. Butler, Lives of the Saints, Dublin, 1833, Aug. 18th.

952 ff. There is possibly an echo here of RR, 7108 ff., a passage of quite different general import, part of which seems to underlie *Gen Prol*, I, 738 ff.

953 *seintuarie*, here sacred object or relic, rather than sacred place. Cf. Roman de Troie, 25515, Cligés, 1194–96, Yvain, 6630–33.

In certain MSS. the *Pardoner's Tale* is followed by the *Shipman's*. For two spurious links connecting the tales see the Textual Notes on the *PardT*.

FRAGMENT VII

On the position of Fragment VII (formerly called Group B² in editions of the *Tales*) see the introduction to the Explanatory Notes on the *Man of Law's Epilogue* and the introduction to the Textual Notes on the *Canterbury Tales*. For spurious Pardoner-Shipman links see the Textual Notes on the *Pardoner's Tale*.

The Shipman's Tale

It is clear from ll. 12–19 that the *Shipman's Tale* was written for a woman, presumably for the Wife of Bath. Furnivall and Skeat thought it was perhaps to be her second tale, but it was more probably meant to be her first one and was then transferred to the Shipman after the plan of Fragment III was devised. Professor Tatlock has conjectured, from the evidence of some copies of the *Prologue*, that the tale may have been temporarily shifted to the Summoner, before its final assignment to the Shipman. He suggests further that Chaucer originally intended, by this story of a merchant duped, to set on foot a quarrel between the Wife and the Merchant. Professor Manly (p. 624) notes further that the *Merchant's Tale* bears indications of having been first intended for a member of a religious order, and that Chaucer may have meant the Monk to retaliate there for the satire on monks in the Wife of Bath's tale (now the Shipman's). If either of these plans ever existed, it was abandoned in favor of the marriage debate in Fragment III. In any case, the composition of the *Shipman's Tale* probably somewhat antedates that of the *Wife of Bath's Prologue and Tale*. See Tatlock, Dev. and Chron., pp. 205 ff.

The story belongs to a familiar group of folk-tales, which have in common the motif of the "Lover's Gift Regained." Similar anecdotes are still current in the United States, told at the expense of nationalities proverbially famed for parsimony or shrewdness. Chaucer's exact source is unknown. It can hardly have been Decameron, viii, 1, or viii, 2, both of which have features in common with the Shipman's story. The setting and the French phrase in l. 214 make it seem probable that Chaucer was following a French *fabliau*. But the Old French Le Boucheur d'Abbeville, though a similar story, cannot be the source for either Chaucer or Boccaccio. Sercambi's version, Novella 19 (ed. Renier, Turin, 1889), stands close to Decam., viii, 1. Numerous other analogues, ranging from the Ancient Indian Śukasaptati (Parrot-Book) to modern stories current in Western Europe are discussed by J. W. Spargo, Chaucer's Shipman's Tale, The Lover's Gift Regained, FF Com., no. 91, Helsinki, 1930 (part of a Harvard dissertation, Studies in the Transmission of the Mediæval Popular Tale, 1926). Dr. Spargo observes that Chaucer's tale, as compared with Boccaccio's, shows a minimum of plot and a maximum of characterization. The analogues from Boccaccio and Sercambi are published by Spargo in SA, pp. 441 ff. Professor R. A. Pratt (MLN, LV, 142), while recognizing the variations between Chaucer and the Italian versions, argues that they may have been deliberate improvements.

1 *Seint-Denys*, St. Denis, near Paris.

4–19 Cf. *WB Prol*, III, 337–56. The parallelism of thought, as well as the use of feminine pronouns, suggests that Chaucer was writing for the Wife. See also the note to ll. 173 ff. below.

9 Cf. *MerchT*, IV, 1315; both perhaps from *ParsT*, X, 1068. See also Job xiv, 2.

38 For this proverbial comparison see l. 51 below; also *KnT*, I, 2437, and n.

41 This suggests the institution of sworn brotherhood, though not explicitly described as such. See *KnT*, I, 1132, n.

55 *Brugges*, Bruges.

65 Cf. *Gen Prol*, I, 166, and n.

69 *Oure deere cosyn*. With the use of *oure* here, indicating a point of view not literally that of the speaker or writer, cf. ll. 107, 356, 363 below; also *NPT*, VII, 3383; *WB Prol*, III, 311, 432, 595, 713, 793; *SumT*, III, 1797, 1829, 2128; and *FranklT*, V, 1204. Professor Tatlock, who has collected the instances, has appropriately termed the construction "the domestic *our*." "The colloquialism," he observes, "is an extension of an ordinary possessive to cases where it involves taking the point of view of the person addressed, and finally becomes stereotyped." See Stud. Phil., XVIII, 425 ff.

70 *malvesye*, Malmsey; wine of Malvasia (now Napoli di Malvasia), on the eastern coast of the Peloponnesus.

71 *vernage*, red wine from Italy (Ital. "vernaccia," the name of a grape).

72 *volatyl*, wild fowl (Lat. "volatilia"; Fr. "volaille").

88 *pryme*, 9 A.M.

91 *his thynges*, the things he had to say, namely, the divine office in the Breviary.

97 *under the yerde*, under the rod, i.e., subject to discipline.

103 *dare*, lie still, crouch.

104 "As a weary hare sits on its lair."

105 "Which should happen to be distracted." For the omission of the relative subject see *Gen Prol*, I, 529, n.

With *forstraught* cf. *distraught*, both formed as if from "strecchen," to stretch.

131 *porthors*, breviary (Fr. "porte-hors"; Lat. "portiforium").

137 *for to goon*, though I had to go. For the idiom see *KnT*, I, 1133, and n.

148 *Seint Martyn*, St. Martin of Tours.

151 *Seint Denys*, St. Dionysius, the patron saint of France (d. 272).

173 Cf. *WBT*, III, 1258 ff. For Irish lists of six most desirable things, with the suggestion that Chaucer may have had a source, doubtless indirect, see R. M. Smith, Journal of Celtic Studies, I, 98 ff.

194 *Genyloun*, Ganelon, the traitor who betrayed Charlemagne's army at Roncesvalles. In punishment he was torn to death by wild horses. See the Chanson de Roland, 3735 ff. Cf. *MkT*, VII, 2389, and *BD*, 1121.

206 *chilyndre*, a portable sun-dial (lit. "cylin-

der"). For a description see Hoveden's Practica Chilindri, ed. E. Brock, in Essays on Chaucer, II, iii, Ch. Soc., 1874.

For the practice, regular in Chaucer's time, of dining soon after prime, cf. *Tr*, ii, 1557; v, 1126.

214 *Quy la*, glossed *Who ther* in MSS. El and Hg. *Peter*, an oath, by St. Peter.

225 *curious*, involving elaborate care. Cf. the active sense, "especially careful," l. 243.

227 The line is repeated in *SumT*, III, 1943. *Seint Yve* is identified by Skeat with St. Ives of Huntingdonshire, a very mythical Persian bishop who preached in England in the seventh century. Yves (or Yve) the familiar patron saint of Brittany, canonized in 1347, would also naturally have been known to Chaucer. Still a third saint, a twelfth-century bishop of Chartres, bore the same name. (See Migne, Pat. Lat., CLXI, xviii ff.) See further Miss R. H. Cline (MLN, LX, 482), who favors identification with the Bishop of Chartres.

228 For *tweye* (*two*) the superior MSS. read *ten*, which would be a high proportion of successful merchants. It is conceivable that Chaucer wrote *ten* and meant the sentence to be ironical. But it seems more likely that a scribe substituted *ten* for *twey(n)e* under the influence of the recurring phrase "ten or twelve." Or, finally, could the Shipman's humor be like that of the Cape Cod farmer (often quoted by Professor Kittredge, though not in his Chaucerian capacity!) who complained that of a dozen chickens "all but them ten died on me"?

233 "Seek relaxation on a pilgrimage." Cf. the general remarks on the mediæval pilgrimage, *Gen Prol*, I, 465, n.

255 *At after-dyner*, printed by Skeat and other editors *at-after dinner*, as in the similar phrases in *MerchT*, IV, 1921, *SqT*, V, 302, *FranklT*, V, 918, 1219. There is support for the combination of *at* with *after*, *under*, etc. But in view of the frequent occurrence of the compounds *after-dinner*, *after-supper*, etc., and of phrases like *at afternoon*, the simple preposition seems more natural.

259 *seint Austyn*, St. Augustine.

272 *beye*, buy. Chaucer uses two forms, *beye* and *bye* (like *deye* and *dye*).

276 *a mile-wey*, here a measure of time. Cf. *furlong wey*, *MLT*, II, 557.

316 *upright*, supine, flat on the back.

334 "A certain (number) of francs." Cf. *MkT*, VII, 2177; *Tr*, iii, 596. Somewhat similar is the use of cardinal numerals after *a*, as *an eighte busshels*, *PardT*, VI, 771; *a twenty wynter*, *WB Prol*, III, 600.

355 *seint Jame*, probably St. James of Compostella.

367 The Lombards were famous moneylenders.

369 Cf. *MerchT*, IV, 2322, and RR, 10098.

379 *maketh it ... tough*; on the various meanings of the phrase see *Tr*, ii, 1025, n.

402 *Marie*, an oath by the Virgin.

403 "I care not a bit for his tokens."

416 "Score it on my tally"; charge it to my account. Cf. *Gen Prol*, I, 570.

434 *Taillynge*, dealing by tally, on credit; hence, incurring or paying a debt. A few MSS. read *talyng*, "telling tales," but it is unlikely that Chaucer wrote this and a scribe substituted the less familiar word. Here, as in many of the *Tales*, the final blessing is adapted to the story which precedes. In view of the likelihood that the *Shipman's Tale* was composed for the *Wife of Bath* the passage should doubtless be interpreted in the light of *WB Prol*, III, 130, 153, etc. Note also the comments of A. H. Silverman, PQ, XXXII, 329 ff.

The Introduction to the Prioress's Tale

435 *corpus dominus*, the Host's blunder for "Corpus Domini," the body of the Lord.

438 *a thousand last quade yeer*, a thousand cart-loads of bad years (*last* uninflected because used as a measure). Cf. *Mk Prol*, VII, 1893.

440 The monk made dupes of the man and his wife. Cf. *MillT*, I, 3389, and *CYT*, VIII, 1313.

442 *in*, "inn," originally used of a private house.

The Prioress's Prologue and Tale

The *Prioress's Tale*, although in the stanzaic meter which Chaucer used chiefly in the early eighties, is by common consent assigned to the period of the *Canterbury Tales*. The artistic perfection of the poem and its complete appropriateness to the Prioress are both evidence of a late date. Even the trifling oversight, *quod she*, in l. 581 betrays the fact that the tale was written with the teller in mind.

In type the story is a legend, or more precisely a miracle of the Virgin. The exact source is unknown, but from twenty-seven analogues which have been collected and examined by Professor Carleton Brown it is possible to construct pretty definitely what Chaucer had before him. In one group of legends the little martyr is a choir-boy, but in the greater number, as in Chaucer's tale, he is a school-boy. In most versions, and apparently in the original form of the story, the ending is happy and the murdered child is miraculously restored. For full information see C. Brown, The Miracle of Our Lady, Ch. Soc., 1910; and later, in SA, pp. 447 ff., where the ten known analogues of Chaucer's version are printed or fully described. The earliest of these is a manuscript of Corpus Christi College, Oxford, which was reported by Dr. Friend in PMLA, LI, 621 ff., proves that the story cannot be later than the early years of the thirteenth century. Note further the re-examination of Brown's classification of analogues by Miss M. H. Statler, PMLA, LXV, 896 ff. Additional analogues have been noted by W. O. Ross, MLN, L, 307 ff., LII, 23 ff. An excellent study of the miracle of Our Lady as a literary type — primarily an analysis of the Old French collection by Gautier de Coincy — was contributed by W. M. Hart to the Charles Mills Gayley Anniversary Papers, Berkeley, 1922, pp. 31 ff. For an interesting miniature illustration of Mielot's 15th century version of the legend (printed by Brown, pp. 29 ff.) see Warner's edition, Roxburghe Club, Westminster, 1885, fol. 15 verso, from MS. Douce 374, Bodleian; and Miracles de Notre Dame, Miniatures du MS. Fr. 9199, Bib. Nat., Paris, 19—, II, plate 19.

It appears that Chaucer followed closely the simple plot of his original. He also reproduced, though with far superior workmanship, the style and spirit of the numerous miracles of the Virgin current in his day. Even the tragic ending, which Skeat suggested might be due to him, has been found in several analogues. Brown was at first inclined to attribute this feature to the influence of the independent tale of Hugh of Lincoln, and when it appeared necessary to date the tragic version earlier than the time of Hugh, he still suggested, very reasonably, that the modification might have been due to older tales of child-murder at the hands of Jews. See SA, p. 455. Apart from the faultless beauty of the verse, Chaucer's own contribution, in this tale as in many others, was largely in developing the setting and the personal characterization. The *litel clergeoun* he changed from a boy of ten years or more to a child of seven in the beginning of his schooling, and the older *felawe* seems to have been entirely Chaucer's invention.

The legend took shape, according to Professor Brown, before 1200, and although the earliest version discovered belongs to the tragic type, he adhered to his opinion that the older form of the story had the happy ending. The general tradition of the murder of Christian children by Jews is much more ancient than this particular story, beginning as early as the time of the Church historian Socrates (fifth century), and it is still alive. See the protest against its revival in the [London] Spectator, XCVI, 97. On the history of the whole matter cf. F. J. Child's introduction to the ballad of Sir Hugh or the Jew's Daughter, English and Scottish Ballads, Boston, 1882–98, III, 233 (no. 155); also the Life of William of Norwich, ed. Jessopp and James, Cambridge, 1896, pp. lxii ff.; H. L. Strack, The Jew and Human Sacrifice, London, 1909, pp. 169 ff.; and J. Trachtenberg, The Devil and the Jews, New Haven, 1943.

Professor Magoun has called the editor's attention to a case of child-murder perpetrated in England in 1860, in which the gruesome details of the Prioress's story are closely paralleled. The victim was the little Francis Savile Kent, aged three years and ten months. A full account of the case, with thorough documentation, is given by Mrs. Yseult Bridges, The Tragedy at Road Hill House, New York, 1955. Mr. Magoun observes that it was never suggested that any of the suspects had any familiarity with Chaucer. If there is any relief to be found in the horror occasioned by the revolting recital, it might be in the fact that religious animosity no longer figures as a motive.

For the opinion, certainly mistaken, that Chaucer meant the *Prioress's Tale* as a satire on childish legends, see A. Brandl, in Paul's Grundriss der Germ. Phil., Strassburg, 1889–93, II, i, 680.

The Prioress's Prologue

453 ff. The *Prioress's Prologue*, like that of the Second Nun (VIII, 1 ff.), has been shown to contain many ideas and expressions drawn from the Scriptures, the services of the church, and other religious poetry. It recalls in particular, as was most appropriate to the Prioress, certain passages in the Office (and Little Office) of the Blessed Virgin. The first stanza paraphrases Ps. viii, 1–2, the opening psalm of Matins in that service. The figure of the burning bush (which was of course a familiar symbol of the Virgin) occurs in the antiphon Rubum quem vidit. This is given for the sixth hour in the Middle-English Prymer or Lay Folks' Prayer Book, where it is translated: "Bi the buysch that Moises sigh unbrent, we knowen that thi preisable maydenhede is kept" (ed. H. Littlehales, EETS, 1895–97, p. 24).

Cf. F. Tupper, MLN, XXX, 9 ff., and Sister Made-leva, Chaucer's Nuns, New York, 1925, pp. 30 ff. Less exact parallels in thought or phraseology are further noted by Sister Madeleva, who compares the second stanza with the antiphon of Matins, "Dignare me laudare te, Virgo sacrata"; and the fourth stanza with the prayer and absolution of Matins: "Sancta et immaculata virginitas, quibus te laudibus efferam nescio," and "Precibus et meritis beatae Mariae semper Virginis et omnium Sanctorum, perducat nos Dominus ad regna caelorum." In ll. 474 ff. there seems clearly to be a reminiscence of Dante's address to the Virgin in Par., xxxiii, 16–21, which Chaucer translated more fully in the proem to the *Second Nun's Tale*. For the suggestion that he followed in part his own previous translation see R. A. Pratt, MLQ, VII, 259 ff.

It was a regular literary convention to prefix to a miracle or saint's legend an invocation to Christ or the Blessed Virgin.

461 The white lily and the burning bush were familiar symbols of the Virgin Mother. For the latter, already noted as occurring in an antiphon, cf. also *ABC*, 89 ff. (where Chaucer is following De-guilleville). The figure of the lily, Professor Manly points out, is said by Alanus de Insulis to be derived from the Song of Solomon, ii, 2.

470 *th'alighte*. The vowel of *thee*, like that of the article *the*, was sometimes elided.

471 *lighte*, either "cheered" or "illuminated."

472 See I Cor. i, 24.

The Prioress's Tale

488 It is unknown what suggested to Chaucer the localization in Asia, which has not been found in any other version of the legend. The conditions described remind one of the situation in Norwich, England, where the Jewish colony was under the special protection of the King. See the introduction to the Life of William of Norwich, cited above.

491 *usure*, interest, the taking of which was for-bidden by the Church in the Middle Ages.
lucre of vileynye, "filthy lucre" (gl. "turpe lucrum" in MS. El); cf. I Tim. iii, 8. For the construction (adjectival phrase with *of*) cf. *KnT*, I, 1912, n.

495 ff. The *litel scole* was taken by Skeat to be a school of choir-boys. But it is more probable, as Professor Brown has shown, that Chaucer had in mind a regular village school. This may be inferred from the large number of children, from the lack of strict discipline, and from the hint (l. 536) that some of the pupils were learning grammar. Moreover, the *litel clergeoun* was clearly not a choir-boy but a child in his first year of regular schooling. Neither in French nor in English does *clergeoun* mean primarily a chorister, and the little boy is not represented as singing with those who *lerned hire antiphoner*. Pro-fessor Brown shows by contemporary documents that the learning of anthems was part of the regular instruction in mediæval English schools.

It is true that in one group of versions of the legend the victim is a little chorister. But Chaucer's version belongs to another group.

497 *an heep*, possibly to be read *an* (= on) *hepe* (dat.), "in a crowd." See J. Derocquigny, Rev. Anglo-Américaine, V, 160 f.

500 *to rede*, probably with special reference to reading Latin. See Brown, pp. 132 ff.

504 *That . . . his*, whose; see *KnT*, I, 2710, n.

512 Cf. "Sely chyld is sone ylered," Proverbs of Hendyng, st. 9; and see Skeat, EE Prov., p. 103, no. 245; Haeckel, p. 49, no. 173.

514 It is related of St. Nicholas that he sucked only once on Wednesdays and Fridays when an in-fant at the breast (Breviarium Romanum, Dec. 6).

517 The primer was a prayer-book compiled for the use of both young and old, at first in Latin, though English versions came into use in the four-teenth century. See The Prymer or Lay Folks' Prayer Book, ed. H. Littlehales, cited above. Such compilations were regularly used in schools as late as the time of the Reformation. Very likely the copies prepared for the youngest pupils would have had prefixed an alphabet and such pieces as the Lord's Prayer, the Ave Maria, the Creed, and the Confes-sion. See Brown, pp. 126 ff.

518 The anthem referred to occurs in the Roman Breviary and begins:
Alma redemptoris mater, quae pervia caeli
Porta manes, et stella maris, succurre cadenti.
The text is given in full in one of the versions of the legend. See Brown, pp. 39, 120 ff.; also his frontis-piece, where the musical notation is reproduced from an early MS.

In most versions of the legend the hymn men-tioned is the "Gaude Maria." The "Alma Re-demptoris" appears only in the small group most closely related to the *Prioress's Tale*.

520 *ner and ner*, nearer and nearer.

523 *to seye*, to be interpreted (the gerundial infinitive); he did not know what the Latin meant. Cf. *to mene*, *MkT*, VII, 2751.

561 *honest*, honorable.

564 There is strong manuscript support for *oure lawes*, and Chaucer may have intended to make Satan identify himself with the Jews.

572 *wardrobe*, here obviously in the sense of "privy" (called "cloaca" or "latrina" in the Latin versions nearest to Chaucer's). For evidence that the same room was often used for a clothes-room and a privy (hence the extension of the term "ward-robe") see J. W. Draper, ESt, LX, 238 ff.

576 The familiar proverb, "Murder will out," occurs also in *NPT*, VII, 3052, 3057. Cf. Haeckel, p. 42, no. 143, and Skeat, EE Prov., pp. 103 f., no. 246.

578 Cf. Gen. iv, 10.

579 ff. See Rev. xiv, 3, 4. For a note on the tradi-tion that "any child who resembled the Holy Inno-cents in youthful martyrdom . . . might be assigned to the blessed company" see The Pearl, ed. E. V. Gordon (Oxford, 1953) pp. xxv–xxvi.

583 *Pathmos*, doubtless pronounced *Patmos* (with *th* like *t*, as in "Thomas").

585 *fleshly*, here an adverb.

627 See Matt. ii, 18. Mr. Joseph Dwight has pointed out to the editor that this passage, along with the psalm Domine, Dominus noster, occurs among the portions of Scripture read at Mass on the Feast of the Holy Innocents. This might account for their association in Chaucer's mind, though the comparison of the bereaved mother to Rachel would have been natural in itself. But it is an interesting general question how far Chaucer's Scriptural quotations were suggested by the services of the Church rather than the consecutive reading of the Bible.

632 With the proverbial formula cf. *RvT*, I, 4320, and n.; *Bo*, iv, pr. 1, 46 ff.; Skeat, EE Prov., p. 104, no. 247; Skeat's note to Piers Plowman, C, v, 140; Haeckel, p. 40, no. 138.

662 In four versions of the legend the miracle is wrought with the aid of a magical object placed in the child's mouth. According to one account it was a lily, according to two others, a precious stone which replaced the tongue which the Jews had cut out. In Chaucer's version the tongue is not removed, and the *grain* which was laid upon it has usually been taken to be a vegetable grain or kernel. Skeat suggested that the idea might have come from the story of Seth, who places three kernels or pippins under Adam's tongue at his burial. (See Legends of the Holy Rood, ed. Morris, EETS, 1871, pp. 26, 70; and Cursor Mundi, ed. Morris, EETS, 1874–93, 1366 ff.) But there is very little similarity between the two stories. Probably Chaucer's *grain* is to be understood after all as a precious stone, a grain of pearl. For this meaning of the Middle English word see Wright, Specimens of Lyric Poetry, Percy Soc., 1842, p. 38. Other possible interpretations of the *grain*, suggested by Sister Madeleva (pp. 39–40), are a particle of the consecrated Host, or a prayer-bead. But in view of the precious stone in other versions of the legend, the explanation "pearl" is probably to be preferred. The pearl, moreover, was a recognized symbol of the Virgin.

669 Cf. John xiv, 18; Heb. xiii, 5.

684 According to the Annals of Waverley, Hugh of Lincoln was murdered by Jews in 1255. For a list of contemporary documents relating to the case see Brown, p. 87. The story is preserved in the ballad of Sir Hugh, or The Jew's Daughter, edited, with valuable introduction, by F. J. Child, English and Scottish Ballads, III, 233 ff. Professor Manly (Essays and Studies, XIII, 53), apparently on the authority of A. P. Leach (Proc. Brit. Acad. 1913–1914, p. 444, and Schools of Mediæval England, p. 192) noted that a miracle-play on the subject was performed at Lincoln in 1316. But Professor Loomis (MLN, LXIX, 31 ff.) shows that there is no evidence of such a performance.

Prologue to Sir Thopas

This *Prologue* is noteworthy as conforming in meter to the rime-royal stanza of the preceding tale. The regular meter of the headlinks, or talks by the way, is the heroic couplet, even when they connect tales in stanzaic form or in prose.

691 *miracle*, probably in the technical sense of "legend," "story of a miracle."

694 On the phrase *thanne at erst*, probably "then for the first time" or "then (and not till then)," see J. P. Roppolo, MLN, LXIII, 365 ff.

696 There has been much discussion as to the seriousness with which Chaucer's portrait of himself should be taken. The hint that his figure was corpulent is confirmed by the *Lenvoy a Scogan*, l. 31. The aloofness with which he is taxed by the Host seems quite inconsistent with his own account of his conduct in the *General Prologue*. Yet reticence may well have been his social habit, as it was one of his marked literary characteristics. It should be remem-

bered, however, that the Host's description applied particularly to his aspect and behavior after listening to the Prioress's moving tale. See the comments of Dr. Thomas Knott, MP, VIII, 135 ff.

703 *elvyssh*, elf-like; hence, aloof, belonging to another world.

711 *deyntee*, excellent, superior, rare. The word, which is related in origin to Lat. "dignitas," has become less dignified in meaning.

Sir Thopas

Sir Thopas was probably intended as a twofold satire, literary and social.

It has long been recognized as a burlesque of the metrical romance. Richard Hurd (Letters on Chivalry and Romance, ed. Morley, London, 1911, p. 147), quoting an unnamed person, declared that Chaucer wrote the poem with the intention of exposing "the leading impertinences of books of chivalry"; and commentators have collected many parallels of language or episode. No particular romance seems to have been singled out by Chaucer for imitation or attack. But the Libeus Desconus presents a rather striking similarity of situation. Professor Magoun (PMLA, XLII, 833 ff.) has called attention to the "virtual identity of setting, actors, and action in the Ile d'Or episode" and in *Sir Thopas*, and concludes that Chaucer had this definitely in mind. The Middle English romance of Guy of Warwick is also a good example of the general type, and contains many of the features which Chaucer reproduces. Both Libeus and Guy, it may be observed, are mentioned in the list of heroes in ll. 897 ff. A number of similarities between *Sir Thopas* and Sir Thomas of Erceldoune were noted by Sir J. A. H. Murray in his edition of the latter romance (EETS, 1875); and still others, involving plot as well as language, have been pointed out to the editor by Dr. J. R. Caldwell. Passages from the three romances mentioned, and from other texts, are cited in the following notes merely to illustrate the satire in *Sir Thopas*, but with no intention either to establish a source for Chaucer or to give extensive collections of parallels. For further discussion of the features satirized, with references to numerous romances, see C. J. Bennewitz, Chaucer's Sir Thopas (Halle diss., 1879); E. Kölbing, ESt, XI, 495–511; Miss C. Strong, MLN, XXIII, 73 ff., 102 ff., and Miss Hammond, p. 288. With special reference to the meter see Miss Strong, Manly, MP, VIII, 141 ff., and A. M. Trounce, Medium Aevum, vols i–iii. The most extensive collection of illustrative parallels, incorporating the results of previous studies, has been brought together by Mrs. R. S. Loomis in SA, pp. 486 ff. She makes the interesting and plausible suggestion that Chaucer may have had in hand the famous Auchinleck MS., now in the Advocates' Library, Edinburgh, and perhaps some fourteenth century prototype of MS. Cotton Caligula A, II, now in the British Museum. See also her article on Chaucer and the Auchinleck MS. in Essays and Studies in honor of Carleton Brown (N.Y., 1940).

Doubts have been expressed from time to time as to the presence or extent of literary satire in the tale, especially on the ground that Chaucer admired the romances and wrote excellent ones himself. But this would not have prevented him from recognizing or burlesquing their many absurdities, and it is hard to believe that such was not his intention. At the same time two recent studies of *Sir Thopas* have made it seem very probable that Chaucer had another purpose, perhaps his primary one, namely, to poke fun at the Flemish knighthood. This opinion is set forth by Miss L. Winstanley in her edition of the *Prioress's Tale* and *Sir Thopas*, Cambridge, Eng., 1922, and by Professor Manly in Essays and Studies, XIII, pp. 52 ff. They find plenty of evidence of the contemptuous attitude of the French and English aristocracy toward the Flemish bourgeoisie. It is especially apparent in Froissart's account of the treatment of Flemish embassies at court. The interpretation proposed by these scholars gives point to many of the jokes about Sir Thopas' equipment and behavior. Whether, as Miss Winstanley maintains, Chaucer meant Sir Thopas to represent Philip van Artevelde himself, is more doubtful. The parallels she draws between Philip's career and Chaucer's tale are not very convincing, but attention will be called to them below. Her theory was opposed by Professor W. W. Lawrence in PMLA, L, 81 ff. Dr. Carroll Camden, RES, XI, 326 ff., argues that Chaucer meant to represent Thopas as cowardly and effeminate and collects features of the description which the physiognomists regarded as signs of such a character. The notes are intended to supply only a very brief explanation of the points of the satire, nearly all of which have been discussed in the books and articles cited above.

The tale contains no definite indication of date. It is usually held to have been written during the Canterbury period, and even to have been planned for the dramatic situation in which it is so effectively introduced. But if, as Professor Manly suggests, it was composed at the time of the Flemish embassy to London in 1383, it would have been just as available for Chaucer's purposes in the Canterbury series.

The following are the full titles and editions of the romances cited below, usually by abbreviations:

Amis, Amis and Amiloun, ed. Kölbing, Heilbronn, 1884.

Bevis, Sir Beves of Hamptoun, ed. Kölbing, EETS, 1894.

Cleges, Sir Cleges, ed. Treichel, ESt, XXII (1896), 345 ff.

Degare, Sire Degarre, ed. Schleich, Heidelberg, 1929.

Eglam., Sir Eglamour of Artois, Cambridge MS., ed. Halliwell, Thornton Romances, Camden Soc., 1844.

G. G. Kn., Sir Gawain and the Green Knight, ed. Tolkien and Gordon, Oxford, 1925.

Guy, Sir Guy of Warwick, Auchinleck MS., ed. Zupitza, EETS, 1883–91.

Horn Childe, Horn Childe and Maiden Rimnild, ed. Hall in King Horn, Oxford, 1901, pp. 179 ff.

Ipom., The lyfe of Ipomydon, Harleian MS., in Ipomedon, ed. Kölbing, Breslau, 1889, pp. 257 ff.

Isumb., Sir Isumbras, ed. Schleich, Berlin, 1907.

K. Alis., King Alisaunder, in Metrical Romances, ed. Weber, Edinburgh, 1810, I, 1 ff.

K. Horn, King Horn, ed. Hall, Oxford, 1901.

K. Tars, The King of Tars, ed. Krause, ESt, XI (1887), 1 ff.

Lib. Des., Libeaus Desconus, ed. Kaluza, Leipzig, 1890.

Oct., Octavian, Southern version, ed. Sarrazin, Heilbronn, 1885.

Perc., Sir Perceval of Gales, ed. Campion and Holthausen, Heidelberg, 1913.

Rich. L., Richard Cœur-de-Lion, ed. Brunner, Vienna, 1913.

Sq. L. Deg., The Squire of Low Degree, ed. Mead, Boston, 1904.

Sev. Sages, The Seven Sages of Rome, ed. Campbell, Boston, 1907.

T. E., Thomas of Erceldoune, ed. Murray, EETS, 1875.

Tristr., Sir Tristrem, ed. Kölbing, Heilbronn, 1882.

712 ff. A typical beginning. Skeat cites Sir Bevis and Sir Degare; cf. also, for various forms of the opening address to the hearers, Chronicle of England (in Ritson, Metrical Romances, Edinburgh, 1884–85, II, 270), Horn Childe, T. E., Cleges, Ipom., Amis, and Sev. Sages. See also Mrs. Loomis, SA, pp. 496 ff.

712 *entent*; Chaucer's form, where it can be tested, is almost invariably *entente*, but the rime here calls for *entent*. In several other instances in *Sir Thopas* the rimes are irregular or unusual, such as would cast doubt on the authenticity of a poem not frankly written as a burlesque. Cf. *deer: river*, 736–37 (*ryvere*, *Tr*, iv, 413, but *ryver*, *WBT*, III, 884); *plas: solas*, 781–82; *Thopas: gras*, 830–31; *cote-armour: flour*, 866–67; *chivalry: drury*, 894–95 (possibly a mere spelling); *Gy: chivalry*, 899–902; *well: Percyvell*, 915–16; *wilde: childe*, 803–06 (where the irregularity seems to consist in adding an unhistoric -*e* to the nom. *child*).

717 *Thopas*, obviously topaz, the gem; "an excellent name for such a gem of a knight" (Skeat). There may have been the further symbolism of purity, inasmuch as the topaz was worn by young girls as a charm against luxury. See Manly's note, and cf. ll. 745 ff., also The English Mediaeval Lapidaries, ed. J. Evans and M. E. Sargeantson (EETS orig. 190, 1933), pp. 19, 107. Professor R. M. Smith (MLN, LI, 314) finds Topaz to have been used as a feminine name, and takes it to carry a hint of effeminacy. For a different explanation, which involves rather too many conjectures, see H. Lange, Deutsche Literaturzeitung, XXXVII, 1299 ff., 1669 ff., 1827 ff. Mr. Lange holds that Chaucer was playing upon Froissart's "Méliador, ou le chevaleir au soleil d'or"; that he took Méliador to mean "honeygold" (as he took Meliboeus to mean "mel bibens," VII, 1410); and that he adopted *Thopas* as an equivalent because in heraldry the topaz corresponds to the blazon "or" and to the planet Sol. It was suitable, Mr. Lange adds, for "Ritter Honiggold" to have had a golden shield and saffron hair!

720 *At Poperyng, in the place*. Miss Winstanley, in support of the theory that Sir Thopas represents Philip van Artevelde, notes that Philip's father, Jacques van Artevelde, "had devoted himself in a quite special way to the interests of Poperinghe." But this would not be an obvious reason for making it the birthplace of Sir Thopas. Professor Manly looks for the explanation in a tradition, which he infers from the contemporary Cronycke van Nederlent, that the men of Poperinghe were regarded as stupid. He observes further that the actual lord of Poperinghe, as Chaucer might well have known, was the Abbot of St. Bertin — a most improper father for the pattern knight! (See F. H. d'Hoop, Recueil des Chartes du Prieuré de Saint-Bertin, à Poperinghe, Bruges, 1870, Introd., p. xiv.)

In the place, interpreted by Skeat "in the mansion, manorhouse"; but it may be a mere rime-tag, meaning "right there." Other more typical tags are in ll. 723, 749, 766, 793, 796, 831, 887, 917.

722 Cf. Amis, 25; Ipom., 11; Eglam., 934 ff.

724–35 The following description, with its ridiculous comparisons, as Professor Manly observes, fits a burgher rather than a knight of aristocratic lineage. See also Mrs. Loomis, SA, pp. 504 ff.

725 *Payndemayn*, very fine white bread. The name "panis dominicus" is explained by Chambers, Book of Days, Edinburgh, 1862–64, I, 119, as derived from the figure of the Saviour or the Virgin imprinted on each loaf. But R. F. Patterson in MLR, VII, 376, compares rather the classical Latin "vinum dominicum" (Petronius, Satiricon, § 31) used for the superior wine which was served to the master. There is an Old French adj. "demaine," "qui appartient au seigneur," perhaps derived from the rare Lat. adj. "dominus." "Panis domina" would exactly correspond to *payndemayn*. See E. Blau, Angl. Beibl., XXXI, 237.

727 *scarlet in grayn*, i.e., cloth dyed with grain, with cochineal. Cf. *NP Epil*, VII, 3459.

731 Cf. Lib. Des., 139 f. The long beard (compared absurdly to saffron, used in cooking for coloring and flavoring) was an antiquated fashion.

734 *Syklatoun*, a costly cloth (OF. "ciclaton"). On the history of the name see G. F. Moore, Ciclatoun-Scarlet, Kittredge Anniversary Papers, Boston, 1913, pp. 25 ff.

735 *jane*, see *ClT*, IV, 999, n.

736 ff. Cf. Guy (Auchinleck MS.), 2797 ff.; Amis, 136 ff.; Perc., 209 ff.

737 *for river*, Skeat renders "towards the river" (Fr. "en riviere"); but the preposition is strange. In *Tr*, iv, 413, *for ryvere* might mean either "for waterfowl" or "for hawking"; the former would make better sense here. For the use of the term for "hawking" cf. *fro ryver*, *WBT*, III, 884; and see NED, s.v. River 2.

738 The *goshauk* was appropriate to a yeoman rather than a knight.

740 Archery belonged to the yeomen, and in Chaucer's time wrestling was also not a knightly accomplishment. Cf. *Gen Prol*, I, 548 (where the ram is mentioned as a prize).

742 ff. Cf. Guy, 237 ff. (thirty maidens in love with the hero). Miss Winstanley, in drawing the parallel with Philip van Artevelde, compares the elf-queen here with the "demoiselle" said by Froissart to have accompanied Philip in the field.

743 *Paramour*, passionately. See *KnT*, I, 1155, n.

745 For this rhetorical device — the reinforcement of a word by adding the negative of its opposite — see also l. 882, below, and cf. *Intro to MancT*, IX, 20, *Rom*, 310, *BD*, 143. Many examples from Middle English verse are given by Kittredge, [Harv.] Stud. and Notes, I, 62 f.

750 With *out ride* cf. *Gen Prol*, I, 45.

751 Cf. Ipom., 1489. *Worth upon*, got upon; lit. "became upon" (AS. "wearþ").

752 *launcegay*, a short lance, originally a Moorish halfpike (from Span. "azagaya"); not a weapon for severe encounters.

754 Cf. Oct. Imp., 283–84. *Priketh*, spurs his horse. Chaucer rings the changes on the word through the tale.

756 The *bukke and hare*, Mr. Manly suggests, are wild beasts such as might be expected in the forests of Flanders.

759 Skeat, comparing Amis (ll. 979 ff.), suggests that the accident which nearly befell him was killing his horse. But Professor Manly is probably right in holding that the *sory care* refers to the events that follow.

760 There follow a series of catalogues of birds, trees, food, clothing, etc., such as were endlessly spun out in the later romances. Cf. particularly, for trees and birds, K. Alis., 6790 ff.; T. E., 29 ff.; and the late romance, Sq. L. Deg., 27 ff., with Mead's note. On such catalogues see Mrs. Loomis, SA, pp. 550 ff. Chaucer's list of herbs and spices is again appropriate to the tradesman. His description of the songs of the birds is of course intentionally absurd — including, possibly, the feminine pronoun *hir* (which appears in good MSS.) after *thrustelcok*.

772 ff. For the association of *longynge* with the song of the birds cf. Guy, 4519 ff., T. E., 33 ff., especially the latter. Thomas of Erceldoune, after hearing the birds, "lay in longinge" and had a dream or vision of an elf-queen. He set out with all his might to meet her at "Eldoune tree." If, as has been suggested, Chaucer had this story in mind, he managed the affair of Sir Thopas rather differently, and with comic effect. There is also a similar dream in the Sev. Sages, ll. 3235 ff. But it may be doubted whether Chaucer was parodying any particular piece. In general, no episodes were more familiar or delightful in the romances, especially in the Arthurian cycle, than the adventures of knights with ladies of the "other world." But it was usual for the fairy to seek or summon her mortal lover, whereas here is no indication that the elf-queen is in pursuit of Sir Thopas.

Part of the humor of the situation, as suggested long ago by Bennewitz, may lie in the fact that Sir Thopas has never seen the object of his passion. Love for an unknown person, or one known only by report — love before sight — is common in saga and romance, so common, indeed, in Celtic saga that Irish has a technical name for it, "grád écmaise."

782 Mrs. Loomis (SA, pp. 508, 514) cites several parallels to the "forest nap" of the hero.

783 Professor Manly notes that *forage* was properly "dry fodder" — another intentional absurdity?

797 A knight would surely have leapt or vaulted, not climbed, into his saddle.

805 This line is in so few MSS. that Manly suspects it to have been supplied by the scribes.

807 The giant guardian, commonly a herdsman, was one of the regular figures in the "other world." See A. C. L. Brown, [Harv.] Stud. and Notes, VIII, 70 ff. Cf. further, for giants in romances, K. Horn, 801; Lib. Des., 1324; Oct., 920; Tristr., 2333, 2712; Guy, 10590 ff. (the famous fight with Colbrand), and others noted by Mrs. Loomis, pp. 530 ff. Miss Winstanley makes the bold conjecture that the giant in *Sir Thopas*, described later as three-headed (l. 842) stands for the threefold army of Charles VI, the Count of Flanders, and the Duke of Burgundy, which opposed Philip van Artevelde.

808 *Sire Olifaunt,* Sir Elephant. Miss Winstanley, because "Olifaunt" was the name of Roland's horn in the Chanson de Roland, takes the giant to represent the French chivalry opposed to Philip. But the name is appropriate enough without any such far-fetched explanation.

810 *Termagaunt,* supposed by the mediæval Christians to be a god or idol of the Saracens. The origin of the name (Fr. "Tervagan(t)," Ital. "Tervagante" or "Trivigante") is uncertain. The oath occurs five times in Guy.

815 For the musical instruments cf. Guy, st. 17 (pp. 394, 396); Cleges, 99 ff.; Oct., 67 ff. They also surround the elf-queen in T. E., 257 ff.

symphonye, used vaguely in Middle English as the name for several kinds of instruments, sometimes pipes and sometimes strings.

826 *slawe,* slain. With the form *slawe(n),* a dialectal variant of *slayn,* may be compared *fawe(n)* beside *fayn.*

829 For the suggestion that the sling-shot is a reminiscence of the combat of David and Goliath see Mrs. Loomis, MLN, LI, 311 ff.

830-32 Here the satire turns upon a commonplace sentiment of saga and romance, that Heaven helps the brave, "Fortuna fortes adjuvat." Cf. *LGW,* 1773. For the negative statement of the same doctrine, *Unhardy is unseely,* see *RvT,* I, 4210, and n. Cf. also Haeckel, p. 5, no. 17[b].

Child, a term commonly applied to knights and squires. Cf. *Horn child,* l. 898 below; also Byron's, Childe Harold and Browning's Child Roland.

833-35 Perhaps an imitation of Bevis, 1–4.

836 *sydes smale,* hardly appropriate to a knight. Dr. Caldwell suggests that Thopas was deliberately made effeminate, in imitation of the elf-queen in T. E. The *white leere,* l. 857 (cf. T. E., 68, Camb. MS.) and the ambling war-horse (*dappul gray,* l. 884, like the palfrey in T. E., 41) certainly give a feminine turn to the description. But the parallel passages are not decisive enough to establish imitation. For further illustration of the feminine fashion see Mrs. Loomis, SA, pp. 504 ff.

843 *For paramour,* for love. The French phrase has here become a noun, as in the modern "paramour," but the sense is abstract, not personal.

845 *Do come,* cause to come, summon.

846 *geestours,* tellers of gestes, that is, tales of history or adventure.

847 ff. The festivities here have been regarded as altogether out of place, mentioned purely for satire. This may be doubted, since feasts and ceremonies were not unusual at the dubbing of a knight or before he set out on some exploit. But the description of Sir Thopas' arming, short as it is, Chaucer contrived to make tedious in effect. It is also pretentious and absurd, with the list of dainties and spices, and the tales of popes and cardinals linked up with *love-likynge.* It should be noted, however, that the inclusion of these prelatical figures has been explained by the fact that the Trentals of St. Gregory (called a pope) and a life of St. Jerome (commonly regarded as a cardinal) appeared alongside of romances in certain manuscripts. See Mrs. Loomis, SA, p. 488.

848 *roiales,* the French pluralization of the adjective is unusual in Chaucer except in his translations. But cf. *delitables, FranklT,* V, 899.

851 ff. The account of the actual arming of Sir Thopas has usually been taken by modern authorities — as, for example, by Fairholt, Costume in England, London, 1885, I, 154–55, Cutts, Scenes and Characters of the Middle Ages, 5th ed., London, 1925, pp. 350 f., and Mr. O. Barron in the article on Arms and Armour (English) in the Encyc. Brit. (11th ed., II, 587) — as a serious document on the practice of the period. Professor Manly (Ess. and Stud., XIII, 70) argued that it is full of absurdities which were intended by Chaucer as part of his burlesque. Instead of a linen shirt and breech, he maintained, the knight would put on a padded jerkin; he would not have worn an aketon at all; and it would have been absurd for him to wear a habergeon above an aketon and a hauberk outside of that. But this is by no means all clear. The *aketoun* doubtless refers to the padded jacket or jerkin worn under the armor. It was usual for a knight to have the threefold protection of an aketon, a coat of chain mail, and body plates. The *haubergeoun* (properly a diminutive of *hauberk*) refers to the coat of mail. The *hawberk* (which meant originally a protection for neck and shoulders, and was later applied to a long coat of mail) seems to stand here for the breastplate and backplate (cf. l. 865), though this use of the word is exceptional. It is also probable that the knight might have worn a breech and shirt of fine cloth next his skin. Mr. Barron (p. 586) cites the use, at an earlier period, of a "gambeson" of linen, not necessarily quilted. Cf. also Schultz, Das Höfische Leben, Leipzig, 1889, II, 33–39, and Fairholt, I, 155 (with an illustration showing a knight in shirt and breech about to put on his armor). Libeus (Lib. Des., 223, in Cotton MS., ed. Ritson, II) puts on a "scherte of selk," and Gawain (G. G. Kn., 571) wears a "dublet of a dere Tars." For other parallels from the romances see I. Linn, MLN, LI, 300 ff.; S. J. Herben, Spec., XII, 479 ff.; Mrs. Loomis, SA, pp. 526 ff. Perhaps, as Mr. Manly suggested, there is a joke in the description of the *cote-armour* as lily-white, when it should have displayed the knight's armorial bearings, though this comparison is also paralleled in Launfal, 742 (Ritson, Met. Rom., I, 202). Further improprieties may be recognized in the spear of cypress (l. 881) instead of the customary ash, and in the war-horse softly ambling *In londe* (ll. 885 ff.). For accounts of the armor of the period see, besides the works of Fairholt and Schultz already cited, J. Quicherat, Histoire du Costume en France, Paris, 1877, Viollet-le-Duc, Dictionnaire Raisonné du Mobilier Français, vols. 5 and 6, Paris, 1874–75, A. Demmin, Die Kriegswaffen, Leipzig, 1893.

862 *For percynge,* for fear of, to prevent, piercing. The preposition "for" frequently has this sense in early English. For other examples see *NPT,* VII, 3117, *Astr,* ii, 38.

864 *Jewes werk.* For an interesting collection of evidence that the Jews have been famous as armorers and workers in metal from the beginning of their history see H. S. Ficke, PQ, VII, 82 ff. They were of course also the principal dealers in armor and weapons in the Middle Ages. It is unlikely that the term *Jewes werk* is used by Chaucer here in ridicule (as it is interpreted by Kölbing, ESt, XI, 510, and Brusendorff, p. 483). Cf. further Kr. S. Jensen, Nationalfølelsen, Copenhagen, 1910, p. 41 (cited by

Brusendorff). For the suggestion that Chaucer took *Jewes* from the romance of Sir Guy see Mrs. Loomis, SA, p. 528 n.

869–70 Cf. Lib. Des., 1657–58; Degare, 998 ff.; Oct., 1033.

872 Sir Thopas swears by homely fare. His oath is doubtless a burlesque of solemn oaths by the peacock, the swan, the heron, etc. Cf. the celebrated episode at the court of Edward III related in the poem called The Vows of the Heron (La Curne de Ste. Palaye, Mémoires sur l'ancienne chevalerie, Paris, 1826, II). For further references on the custom see Wells, pp. 99, 105 f., 242, Miss Hammond, English Verse between Chaucer and Surrey, Durham, N.C., 1927, pp. 414–15, and Mrs. Loomis, pp. 541 ff.

875 *quyrboilly*, leather softened in hot water and afterwards dried (Fr. "cuir bouilli"). On its use Skeat refers to Cutts, Scenes and Characters, p. 344.

878 *rewel boon*, whale ivory (OF. "rohal," probably from a Scandinavian word ending in "hval," whale). With the description of saddle and bridle cf. T. E., 49, 63.

884 Cf. T. E., 41.

888–90 For the same expression cf. Eglam., 344, 634, 905; Sir Degrevant, ed. Luick, Vienna, 1917, p. 27; T. E., 307 f. On the history of the term *fit* see M. Förster in the Berichte der Sächsischen Akad. der Wissenschaften, Leipzig, Phil.-Hist. Kl., LXXI, iv, 85, n.

891 ff. The minstrels' appeals for silence sometimes approached the bluntness of Chaucer's lines here. Cf. K. Alis., 29, 39, 2047; Rich. L., 4069.

897 For references to such stereotyped lists of romances see Miss H. E. Allen, PMLA, XXXII, 140, and Mrs. Loomis, pp. 556 ff. Cf. also the beginning of Rich. L. On *Horn child* there are two Mid. Eng. romances: King Horn, ed. Lumley, EETS, 1866, and Hall, Oxford, 1901; and Horn Child and Maiden Rimnild, printed in Ritson's Metrical Romances, Edinburgh, 1884–85, II, 216 ff., and in Hall's King Horn. *Ypotys* is rather a legend than a romance, and was perhaps included in the list for the purpose of burlesque. It has been pointed out, however, by Miss Dorothy Everett (RES, VI, 446 ff.) that the Ypotys is found together with Sir Lybeux in two late MSS., and she suggests that Chaucer may have associated Ypotys with romances simply because he recalled a MS. of similar contents. It is edited in Horstmann's Altenglische Legenden, Neue Folge, Heilbronn, 1881, pp. 341–48, 511–26. Sir *Beves* of Hampton and *sir Guy* of Warwick were constantly associated. For editions of these and of Libeus Desconus (*sir Lybeux*) see the introductory note. The name *Lybeux* is from "Li Biaux Desconneus," the Fair Unknown. *Pleyndamour*, obviously from "plein d'amour," is unidentified. Skeat notes that a Sir Playne de Amours is mentioned in Malory's Morte Darthur, ix, ch. 7; also that Spenser's Sir Blandamour (Faerie Queene, iv, 1, 32) may be derived from Chaucer's *Pleyndamour*. The name appears to have been in actual use in the fifteenth century. It occurs as that of one of the scribes of the Cambridge MS. Ff. 1. 6: "Nomen scriptoris Nicholaus plenus amoris" (perhaps a Latinization of Pleyndamour or Fullalove, though it may be a mere rime-tag). See Athen., 1909, I, 557, and Brusendorff, p. 188, n. Dr. Eccles has called

the editor's attention to the occurrence of "Robertus Plenus Amoris" as the name of the scribe of another fifteenth-century MS. (Bodleian Summary Catalogue of Western MSS., II, 211); and "Thomas plenus amoris," is given as the name of the writer of a fifteenth-century addition to the Fr. romance of Alixandre (Summary Catalogue, II, 381). Professor Magoun, who noted this last occurrence, suggests that Pleyndamour in *Sir Thopas* is really due to a confused memory of Bevis's *amie*, "la dame d'amour." For parallels to the utterly conventional praise of the hero see Mrs. Loomis, pp. 545 ff.

905 A stock comparison. See Lib. Des., 669; Isumb., 458; K. Tars, 194.

916 See Perc., 5 ff., 2204 ff. The first reference, however, is to Percival's father.

917 *worthy under wede*, well-looking in his clothing, a common alliterative expression like "goodly under gore," or the AS. "heard under helme."

The Prologue to Melibee

923 *drasty*, filthy (AS. "draestig," which glosses Lat. "feculentus"). The early editions printed *drafty*, erroneously.

933 The use of *geeste* is peculiar. It regularly means either "exploit" or "narrative of exploits," "tale," "romance" (usually in verse). The sense here may be "tell a real story," as distinguished from mere "rime doggerel." But the term seems rather to designate a form of writing distinct from prose or rime. Similarly in the *Pars Prol* (X, 43) the corresponding verb is used with reference to alliterative verse: *I kan nat geeste, "rum, ram, ruf," by lettre*. See further G. D. Bone, Med. Aev., VII, 226.

943 On Gospel harmonies such as Chaucer might have known, see Margaret Deanesly, The Lollard Bible, Cambridge, 1920, p. 55, n. 1.

947 *as in hire sentence*, so far as their meaning is concerned. The particle *as* is not quite pleonastic here, but retains some restrictive force. In l. 954 it is more nearly superfluous. On the construction see *Gen Prol*, I, 462, n.

951 It would mend the meter to supply *and* after *Monk*, but the irregularity may be due to the pause in the list.

955 Chaucer's remark about proverbs is odd, as Professor Tatlock has observed, for the French version of Melibee which he followed was considerably more condensed than the Latin original.

958 On the order of words see *Gen Prol*, I, 791, n.

The Tale of Melibee

The *Melibee* is a close translation of the French Livre de Melibée et de Dame Prudence, attributed sometimes to Jean de Meun but now by general agreement to Renaud de Louens, which is in turn a condensed paraphrase of the Liber Consolationis et Consilii by Albertanus of Brescia (?1193–?1270). The Latin original, edited by Thor Sundby, was published by the Chaucer Society in 1873. The French version was embodied in the Ménagier de Paris, compiled in 1392–94, and is accessible in the edition of that work by J. Pichon, 2 v., Paris, 1846. It has now been re-edited from the manuscripts, with an attempt to restore as fully as possible the text which Chaucer followed, by Professor J. B.

Severs in SA, pp. 560 ff. See also E. Koeppel, in Herrig's Arch., LXXXVI, 29 ff.; G. Gröber, Grundriss der Rom. Philologie, Strassburg, 1888–92, II, i, 746, 1025. Chaucer's tale was edited separately, with valuable notes, by E. Mätzner, Altenglische Sprachproben, Berlin, 1867–1900, I, ii, 373 ff.

Dr. Severs, in his introduction, discusses fully the relation of the French version to the Latin and of Chaucer's to both. He shows that Renaud handled his Latin source "very boldly and freely." Chaucer's translation of the French, on the other hand, is extremely close, and his few departures do not even make clear whether he used the Latin text.

For additional notes see M-R CT, IV, pp. 500 ff.

Since the French translation of Albertanus is earlier than the compilation of the Ménagier, the date of that work proves nothing with regard to the date of Chaucer's *Melibee*; and other precise evidence is lacking. Skeat held the tale to have been written early (1372–77) and afterwards revised; and Dr. F. J. Mather (ed. *Gen Prol*, *KnT*, and *NPT*, Boston, 1899, xiv f.) pronouncing it a "stupid piece," also assigned it to the seventies. But in such a critical judgment large allowance must be made for change of taste, and the *Melibee* in its own age seems to have been highly esteemed. Moreover, Chaucer apparently wrote the translation of Innocent's De Contemptu Mundi between 1386 and 1394, and the *Parson's Tale*, another treatise of distinctly mediæval character, is usually assigned to his later years. In the case of the *Melibee* the few clues that have been pointed out are all uncertain or indefinite. They are discussed by Professor Tatlock, Dev. and Chron., pp. 188 ff. From the absence in the English text (after l. 1199) of a passage of the French in condemnation of boy sovereigns Mr. Tatlock infers that Chaucer made a deliberate omission to avoid giving offense to Richard II. In that case he must have written after 1376. Then Mr. Tatlock tries to determine the date more closely from the literary relations of the *Melibee* to Chaucer's other works. He shows that it probably preceded the *Man of Law's Prologue* and *Tale*, the *Nun's Priest's Tale*, the *Pardoner's Tale*, and the *Merchant's Tale*, in all of which there is pretty clear evidence of its influence; and on the basis of less conclusive parallels he argues that it followed the *Troilus* and the *Knight's Tale*. All the literary associations favor an assignment to the Canterbury period.

Another historical argument, which, if valid, would fix the date about 1386, has been set forth by Professor J. L. Hotson in an ingenious article (Stud. Phil., XVIII, 429–52), on the *Tale of Melibee* and John of Gaunt. Mr. Hotson shows the striking parallels between the situation of Melibeus and that of John of Gaunt when he contemplated going to war to enforce his claim to the throne of Castile, and he suggests that Chaucer made the translation to dissuade his patron from that undertaking. The argument would be stronger if the data concerned were not nearly all present in Chaucer's French original.

For further comments on the political bearings of the tale see G. Stillwell, Spec., XIX, 433 ff.

The passages quoted from various authors have been mostly identified by Sundby and Skeat. They are registered in the following notes for the reader's convenience. But it should be understood that in nearly every case Chaucer was simply following his French original. Professor P. F. Baum (JEGP, XLV, 38 ff.) points out that Chaucer's prose at the beginning of the *Melibee* can be almost continuously scanned as decasyllabic verse. The number of metrical lines falls off rapidly after the first few pages. Mr. Baum suggests that Chaucer began with an attempt at metrical prose.

967 *Melibeus*, explained below (l. 1410) as meaning *a man that drynketh hony* ("mel bibens"). *Prudence*, taken by Albertanus from Cassiodorus, Variarum, lib. ii, epist. 15: "Superavit cuncta infatigabilis et expedita prudentia." *Sophie*, wisdom (σοφία), not mentioned in either the French or the Latin text.

970 According to l. 1421 the three *olde foes* represent allegorically the world, the flesh, and the devil, known as the three enemies of man. Cf. the Middle English Debate of the Body and Soul (Emerson, Mid. Eng. Reader, New York, 1915, pp. 56 f.), and see P. Meyer, Rom., XVI, 2 ff.

976 Ovid, Rem. Am., 127 ff.

984 From Seneca, Epist. 74, § 30. References to the Epistles are to Hense's ed., Leipzig, 1914.

987 See John xi, 35.

989 See Rom. xii, 15.

991 Seneca, Epist. 63, § 1.

993 Cf. also Epist. 63, § 11.

995 Not from Jesus son of Sirach, or Ecclesiasticus, but from Prov. xvii, 22. This text and the next were quoted in the opposite order by Albertanus; hence Chaucer's confusion.

996 Ecclus. xxx, 22–24.

997 Prov. xxv, 20 (Vulg.). Chaucer added *in the shepes flees*, perhaps through confusion of the French "l'artuison," moth, with "toison."

998 *goodes temporels*; the French adjectival plural in -(e)s is rare in Chaucer except in his translated works. See the Grammatical Introduction.

1000 Job i, 21.

1003 Cf. *MillT*, I, 3530, and n.

1017 *by vengeaunce*, omitted by Tyrwhitt, with Lounsbury's approval (Studies, I, 320), is in all the eight published MSS. and the French text.

1028 *to moeve werre*, Fr. "de mouvoir guerre."

1030 Skeat notes that the Latin text has here three phrases for Chaucer's proverb. The closest is "Ad paenitendum properat, cito qui iudicat," from Publilius Syrus, Sententiae (ed. Meyer, Leipzig, 1880), no. 32. Mätzner quotes also from Publilius Syrus (p. 59): "Velox consilium sequitur poenitentia." This is quoted later by Albertanus (p. 39). Cf. l. 1135, below; and Haeckel, p. 28, no. 92.

1031 Proverbial; cf. Haeckel, p. 29, no. 93.

1036 Proverbial; cf. *Tr*, ii, 1276; Haeckel, pp. 24 f., no. 80; Skeat, EE Prov., p. 71, no. 169.

1045 Ecclus. xxii, 6.

1047 Ecclus. xxxii, 6 (Vulg.).

1048 From Publilius Syrus, Sent., 594. See also Haeckel, p. 27, no. 89.

1053 *Piers Alfonce*, Petrus Alphonsus (or Alfonsi) a Spanish Jew who was baptized in 1106, author of the Disciplina Clericalis. The reference is to Ex. xxiv (ed. Hilka and Söderhjelm, Heidelberg, 1911, p. 37).

1054 This proverb, which is not given in the French or Latin, corresponds exactly to *Tr*, i, 956; Tatlock argues that it was taken from that poem. Cf. also *Tr*, iv, 1567 f.; Haeckel, p. 25, no. 83, and

p. 26, no. 85; Skeat, EE Prov., pp. 64 f., no. 155. On *wikked haste* cf. *ParsT*, X, 1003; Haeckel, p. 26, no. 84.

1057 Eccl. vii, 28.

1059 Ecclus. xxv, 30 (Vulg.).

1060 Ecclus. xxxiii, 19–21.

1062 From Marcus Annaeus Seneca, Controversiarum, Lib. ii, 5 (13), 12. Cf. *WBT*, III, 950.

1063 From Publilius Syrus, Sent., 324.

1067 Cf. Seneca, De Beneficiis, iv, 38, 1. *Turneth his corage*, changes his mind.

1070 *save youre grace*, Lat. "salua reverentia tua." *The book*; the Latin text gives no further reference.

1071 The reference is apparently to the Formula Honestae Vitae of Martinus Dumiensis, cap. iii (Migne, Pat. Lat., LXXII, 26), though the parallel is loose. The work is attributed to Seneca by Albertanus.

1075 See Mark xvi, 9.

1077–79 Cf. *MerchT*, IV, 2277–90.

1079 Cf. Matt. xix, 17; Luke xviii, 19.

1086 This proverb, which Chaucer here takes from Albertanus, is found again in *WB Prol*, III, 278 ff. It was of common occurrence, and Chaucer may well have known, among other versions, that of Innocent III in the De Contemptu Mundi (Migne, Pat. Lat., CCXVII, 710) and that of the Goliardic poem De Coniuge non Ducenda (T. Wright, Latin Poems Commonly Attributed to Walter Mapes, Camden Soc., 1841, p. 83). In a shorter form, which mentions only the leaking roof and the chiding wife, it is quoted in the *ParsT*, X, 631 This corresponds to Prov. xxvii, 15, which is doubtless the source of the whole group of sayings. Cf. also Prov. xix, 13 and x, 26. On the many variants and their diffusion in European literature see Archer Taylor, Hessische Blätter für Volkskunde, XXIV, 130 ff.; Skeat, EE Prov., pp. 105 f., no. 249; Haeckel, p. 46, no. 158.

1087 See Prov. xxi, 9; cf. *WB Prol*, III, 775 ff.

1098 ff. For these examples cf. also *MerchT*, IV, 1362 ff. See Gen. xxvii; Judith viii et seq.; I Sam. xxv; Esther vii et seq.

1104 "It is not good for a man to be alone." For the idiom cf. *ParsT*, X, 456, 469, 666, 849, 935. See Gen. ii, 18.

1106 Cf. *NPT*, VII, 3164.

1107 The verses, as quoted in the Latin text, are: "Quid melius auro? Jaspis. Quid jaspide? Sensus.
     Quid sensu? Mulier. Quid muliere? Nihil."
With these Sundby compares the following variant from Ebrardi Bituniensis Graecismus, cum comm. Vincentii Metulini, fol. C, 1 verso:
"Quid melius auro? Jaspis. Quid jaspide? Sensus.
     Quid sensu? Ratio. Quid ratione? Deus."
Skeat adds, from MS. Harl. 3362, fol. 67, as printed in T. Wright's Reliquiae Antiquae, London, 1845, I, 91:
"Vento quid levius? Fulgur. Quid fulgure? Flamma.
     Flamma quid? Mulier. Quid muliere? Nichil."

1113 Prov. xvi, 24.

1115–18 At this point the Latin text has ten pages (Sundby, pp. 20–30) which are omitted in the French and the English.

1118 Tobit iv, 19.

1119 *If any of yow*. This corrects the first pers. ("nostrum") of Albertano (p. 31), perhaps from recollection of James i, 5.

1121 f. Cf. ll. 1246 f., below, and see Haeckel, p. 27, no. 88.

1127 Not from Seneca, but from Publilius Syrus, Sent., 281:
"Iratus nihil non criminis loquitur loco."

1130 I Tim. vi, 10. Cf. l. 1840, below; *Pard Prol*, VI, 334; *ParsT*, X, 739; and see Haeckel, pp. 11 f., no. 38.

1135 From Publilius Syrus, Sent., 32. Cf. ll. 1030, 1054 above.

1141 Ecclus. xix, 8, 9.

1144 *The book*, not definitely quoted in the Latin text. Cf. Petrus Alphonsus, Disc. Cler., Ex. ii (p. 6); Ecclus. viii, 22.

1147 Not from Seneca, but from Martinus Dumiensis, De Moribus (Migne, Pat. Lat., LXXII, 29).

1153 Apparently cited as proverbial. Albertanus (Sundby, p. 41) has something similar.

1158 Prov. xxvii, 9.

1159 Ecclus. vi, 15.

1161 Ecclus. vi, 14.

1162 Cf. Prov. xxii, 17; Tobit iv, 19; Ecclus. ix, 14.

1164 Cf. Job xii, 12.

1165 De Senectute, vi, 17.

1167 Ecclus. vi, 6.

1171 Prov. xi, 14.

1173 Ecclus. viii, 20 (Vulg.).

1174 From Cicero, Disput. Tusc., iii, 30, 73.

1176 From Cicero, Laelius, xxv, 91.

1177 Cf. Martinus Dumiensis, Formula Honestae Vitae, iii: "Non acerba, sed blanda, timebis verba." See also Prov. xxviii, 23.

1178 Prov. xxix, 5; perhaps also the basis of l. 1179.

1180 From De Officiis, i, 26, 91.

1181 From Dionysius Cato, Disticha, iii, 4.

1183 From Publilius Syrus, Sent., 91.

1184 The Latin text quotes from "Ysopus":
"Ne confidatis secreta nec hiis detegatis,
Cum quibus egistis pugnae discrimina tristis."

1185 Not from Seneca, but from Publilius Syrus, Sent., 389.

1186 Ecclus, xii, 10.

1189 From the Disc. Cler., Ex. ii (p. 6). In the last clause, "Que enim male egeris, notabunt; que uero bona fuerint, deuitabunt," there is a reading "deuiabunt," which may account for Chaucer's *perverten*.

1191 *a philosophre*, unidentified. Latin text reads: "ut quidam philosophus dixit, nemo ei satis fidus est, quem metuit."

1192 Loosely quoted from the De Officiis, ii, 7, 25.

1194 Prov. xxxi, 4 (Vulg.). See also *MLT*, II, 771 ff., n.

1196 The passage in Cassiodorus is Variarum, lib. x, epist. 18.

1197 Cf. Prov. xii, 5. Sundby notes that the quotation in the Latin text closely resembles Publilius Syrus, Sent., 354.

1198 Ps. i, 1.

1199 After l. 1199 there are omitted in the French and English about two pages of Latin original (Sundby, 53–55). After l. 1210 another passage is omitted (Sundby, 57–58). The English version also omits, after l. 1199, a passage of the French on the lack of wisdom of young princes. See the introductory note above.

1201–10 Based upon the De Officiis, ii, 5, 18.
1215 Cf. Chaucer's *Proverbs*, and Haeckel, p. 12, no. 39.
1216 From Dionysius Cato, Disticha, iii, 14.
1218 From the Disc. Cler., Ex. iv (ed. cit., p. 11).
1219 Proverbial; cf. *PF*, 511; Haeckel, pp. 15 f., nos. 49, 50.
1221 From the De Officiis, i, 9.
1225 Apparently a legal aphorism, quoted from no particular source.
1226 Not identified in Seneca.
1229 Cf. the Digesta of Justinian, xlv, 1, 26 (ed. Mommsen, Berlin, 1870, II, 653).
1231 Cf. Publilius Syrus, Sent., 362.
1246 Cf. ll. 1121 ff. above.
1257 *there been ye condescended*, to that you have yielded.
1264 For this sentiment, which became proverbial, Sundby compares St. Chrysostom, Adhortatio ad Theodorum Lapsum (i, 15, Paris, 1839); Vincent of Beauvais, Spec. Hist., xvii, c. 45. See also Haeckel, p. 41, no. 140.
1269 From the Decretals of Gregory IX (Frankfort, 1586), lib. i, tit. 37, cap. 3 (but applied to priests, not physicians).
1292 See Rom. xii, 17, quoted in the Latin text. Skeat suggests that Chaucer had in mind also I Pet. iii, 9. Cf. also I Thess. v, 15; I Cor. iv, 12.
1304 Ps. cxxvii, 1 (cxxvi, 1, Vulg.).
1306 f. From Dionysius Cato, Disticha, iv, 13. Cf. Haeckel, p. 4, no. 14.
1309 From the Disc. Cler., Ex. xvii (p. 27).
1315 *lete the kepyng*, neglect the protection.
1316 f. Prov. xxviii, 14.
1319 *espiaille*, rather collective, "companies of spies," than abstract, according to Skeat. See NED, s.v. Espial 2.
1320 Not from Seneca but from Publilius Syrus; the Latin text quotes Sent., 542, 607, 380, 116.
1324 Again from Publilius Syrus, Sent., 255.
1325 f. From Ovid, Rem. Am., 421–22:
"Parua necat morsu spatiosum uipera taurum;
  a cane non magno saepe tenetur aper."
The reference to the thorn is inserted by Chaucer, and occurs neither in Albertanus nor in the Ménagier. From the attribution to *the book* (the Bible?) of the statements about the thorn and the dog, Koeppel argued that Chaucer cannot have been following Albertanus's Latin text. (See Herrig's Arch., LXXXVI, 29–30.)
Wesele, weasel, seems due to a confusion of Fr. "vivre" = Lat. "uipera," with Lat. "uiuerra."
1328 From Seneca, Epist. 3, § 3.
1330 Albertanus here quoted his own De Arte Loquendi et Tacendi (ed. Sundby, in Brunetto Latinos Levnet og Skrifter, Copenhagen, 1869, p. cviii).
1339 f. Not from Cicero, but from Seneca, De Clementia, i, 19, 6.
1344 From Cicero, De Officiis, i, 21, 73.
1347 Not identified in Cicero. Mätzner quotes Publilius Syrus, Sent., 125: "Diu apparandum est bellum, ut vincas celerius."
1348 From Cassiodorus, Variarum, lib. i, epist. 17.
1355 The reference is to the De Officiis, ii, 5;

cf. ll. 1200 ff. above, where the points mentioned by Cicero are enumerated.
1360 *consentynge*, consistent with, conducive to; Cicero, "quid consentaneum cuique."
1380 Cf. Justinian's Codex, viii, 4, 1.
1383 *that nay*, Fr. "que non."
1392 Fr. "de la vengence se engendrera autre vengence" (variant reading, not in Ménagier text).
1395 *Oriens*, which is not mentioned in the Latin text, seems to be used as the equivalent of "longinqua." Dr. H. O. White suggests that Chaucer may have misread the French: "Deux causes ouvrières et efficiens." Manly (M-R CT, IV, 504) suggests that Chaucer may himself have been responsible for the Latin terms.
1401 *letted nat*, delayed not; Lat. "nec per eos remansit."
1404 From the Decretum Gratiani, Pars ii, causa i, qu. 1, c. 25.
1406 Perhaps from I Cor. iv, 55, and Rom. xi, 33.
1410 The Latin text interprets Melibeus as "mel bibens."
1415 From Amores, i, 8, 104: "Impia sub dulci melle venena latent." The application is not there.
1416 Prov. xxv, 16. See also Skeat, EE Prov., p. 106, no. 250.
1424 On the Seven Deadly Sins see the *Parson's Tale. Fyve wittes*, five senses.
1437 Fr. "Cellui nuist aux bons, qui espargne les mauvais"; from Martinus Dumiensis, De Moribus, v: "Bonis nocet qui malis parcit." Chaucer's MS. was apparently corrupt.
1438 From Cassiodorus, Variarum, lib. i, epist. 4.
1439 From Publilius Syrus, Sent., 528.
1440 Rom. xiii, 4. *Spere* is a mistake for *swerd*, Fr. "glaive," Lat. "gladium."
1449 From Publilius Syrus, Sent., 320.
1450 From Publilius Syrus, Sent., 189.
1455 From Publilius Syrus, Sent., 172.
1460 Rom. xii, 19.
1463 From Publilius Syrus, Sent., 645.
1466 From Publilius Syrus, Sent., 487.
1473 From Caecilius Balbus, De Nug. Phil. (ed. Woelfflin, Basel, 1855), p. 33, no. xli, 4.
1477 *putte*, suppose; Fr. "posons."
1481 From Seneca, De Ira, ii, 34, 1.
1485 Prov. xx, 3.
1488 From Publilius Syrus, Sent., 483.
1489 From Dionysius Cato, Disticha, iv, 39.
1496 *the poete*, Fr. "le poëte"; not mentioned in the Latin text, and unidentified. Skeat compares Luke xxiii, 41. Mr. J. R. Kreuzer (MLN, LXIII, 54) suggests that he was a versifier of the De Duodecim Utilitatibus Tribulationis ascribed to Peter of Blois.
1497 *Seint Gregorie*; Harl. MS. *Seint Paul*; not mentioned in the Latin text. The passage has not been traced.
1502 From I Pet. ii, 21 ff.
1510 Cf. II Cor. iv, 17.
1512 Prov. xix, 11 (Vulg.).
1513 Prov. xiv, 29 (Vulg.).
1514 Prov. xv, 18.
1515 Prov. xvi, 32.
1517 Cf. James i, 4.
1528 From Cassiodorus, Variarum, lib. i, epist. 30.
1531 Not from Seneca; cf. Martinus Dumiensis, De Moribus, vi: "Nunquam scelus scelere vincendum est."

1539 Prov. xix, 19.

1541 Cf. the Digesta of Justinian, l, 17, 36.

1542 Prov. xxvi, 17.

1550 Eccl. x, 19; cf. Haeckel, p. 10, no. 35.

1553 The Latin text quotes I Tim. iv, 4.

1554 Skeat notes that on the fly-leaf of a MS. is written: "Homo sine pecunia est quasi corpus sine anima." The source is unknown.

1556 *Pamphilles*, Pamphilus, hero of a Latin poetic dialogue, Pamphilus de Amore (ed. A. Baudouin, Paris, 1874). The lines (53–54) referred to are:
"Dum modo sit dives cuiusdam nata bubulci,
Eliget ex mille quem libet [or, volet] illa virum."
Cf. *FranklT*, V, 1110.

1558 Not from Pamphilus. Skeat compares Ovid, Tristia, i, 9, 5 f.

1559 Proverbial; cf. *ML Prol*, II, 120, n.

1561 Also not from Pamphilus. Cf. Petrus Alphonsus, Disc. Cler., Ex. iv (p. 10): "ut ait versificator: Glorificant [var. Clarificant] gaze priuatos nobilitate." The author is unknown.

1562 Cf. Horace, Epist. i, 6, 37, quoted by Albertanus, ed. Sundby, p. 98.

1564 See Cassiodorus, Variarum, lib. ix, epist. 13. The Latin reads "mater criminum," and the French "mère des crimes." Chaucer's text is based on a misreading "ruines."

1566 From the Disc. Cler., Ex. ii (pp. 6 f.).

1568 See the De Contemptu Mundi, i, 16. The same passage underlies *ML Prol*, II, 99 ff.

1571 Ecclus. xl, 28. Cf. *ML Prol*, II, 114, and n.

1572 Ecclus. xxx, 17. Chaucer's version corresponds to the French: "mieulx vault la mort amère que telle vie."

1575 *hou ye shul have yow*, how you should behave yourself.

1578 Prov. xxviii, 20.

1579 Prov. xiii, 11.

1583 The quotation is not in the Latin. The source is unknown.

1585 From Cicero, De Officiis, iii, 5, 21.

1589 Ecclus. xxxiii, 27. Cf. Haeckel, p. 12, no. 40.

1590 f. Prov. xxviii, 19.

1593 Cf. Prov., xx, 4.

1594 From Dionysius Cato, Disticha, i, 2.

1595 The reference to St. Jerome has not been traced. The idea is attributed to him also in the Ayenbite of Inwyt (ed. Morris, EETS, 1866, p. 206), and in Jehan de Vignay's introduction to his French translation of the Legenda Aurea. Chaucer quotes it again, following de Vignay, in *SecN Prol*, VIII, 6–7.

1602 From Dionysius Cato, Disticha, iv, 16.

1605 From Dionysius Cato, Disticha, iii, 21.

1612 The quotation, which is not in the Latin, is unidentified.

1617 Cf. Prov. xxvii, 20.

1621 From De Officiis, ii, 15, 55.

1628 Prov. xv, 16.

1630 Ps. xxxvii, 16. *Prophete*: Fr. "philosophe."

1634 II Cor. i, 12.

1635 Ecclus. xiii, 24.

1638 Prov. xxii, 1.

1639 Ecclus. xli, 12. The reading *freind* is apparently due to a French MS. which had *ami* instead of *nom*. See Manly, M-R CT, IV, 506.

1642 From Cassiodorus, Variarum, lib. i, epist.

4: "Est enim indigni [var. digni] animi signum, famae diligere commodum." Albertanus inserts this sentence, as if it were his own, between two other quotations from Cassiodorus (iii, 12, and ix, 22). But for "indigni" (or "digni") he substitutes "ingenui," which explains *gentil* in the Fr. version and in Chaucer's.

1643 From St. Augustine, Sermo ccclv, 1 (Migne, Pat. Lat., XXXIX, 1568 f.). This is not in Albertanus.

1644 This explanation is perhaps Chaucer's addition.

1651 The author is unidentified; Latin text: "quidam philosophus."

1653 Eccl. v, 11. Not in Albertanus.

1661 I Macc. iii, 18, 19.

1664 Eccl. ix, 1 (Vulg.).

1668 II Sam. xi, 25. I Sam. and II Sam. are called Liber Primus and Liber Secundus Regum in the Vulgate.

1671 Not from Solomon, but from Jesus son of Sirach, Ecclus. iii, 26; cf. Haeckel, p. 17, no. 55.

1676 *Seint Jame*, an error for *Senek* (Fr. "Sénèque"). See Seneca, Epist. 94, 46, which quotes Sallust, Jugurtha, 10, 6.

1678 For the construction cf. *ClT*, IV, 212, n. The English text adds *unitee* where the French has only *paix*. Manly suggests (M-R CT, IV, 506) that this was due to the interest in unity in fourteenth-century England.

1680 Matt. v, 9.

1686 Cf. "Familiarity breeds contempt"; also Skeat, EE Prov., pp. 106 f., no. 251.

1691 From Martinus Dumiensis, De Moribus, iii (where, however, it is an injunction): "Dissensio ab alio incipiat, a te autem reconciliatio."

1692 Ps. xxxiv, 14.

1696 Prov. xxviii, 14.

1701 The source of the quotation is unknown. Skeat compares the French proverb, "À l'œil malade la lumière nuit."

1704 Prov. xxviii, 23.

1707 ff. Eccl. vii, 4–6 (Vulg.).

1719 Prov. xvi, 7.

1735 Ps. xx, 4 (Vulg.).

1740 Ecclus. vi, 5 (Vulg.).

1753 ff. Ecclus. xxxiii, 18 ff.

1757 *that man sholde nat yeven*; the negative is perhaps due to the French construction. Cf. *Bo*, iii, pr. 10, 14. But for similar constructions in English see *Tr*, ii, 716, n.

1775 f. From Martinus Dumiensis, De Moribus, iv: "Locum tenet innocentiae proximum confessio. Ubi confessio, ibi remissio."

1777 This quotation does not quite correspond to that given by Albertanus: "Peccatum extenuat qui celeriter corrigit" (Publilius Syrus, Sent., 489). On the manuscript confusion see M-R CT, IV, 506.

1783 From the Digesta of Justinian, l, 17, 35.

1794 Proverbial; cf. *LGW Prol F*, 452, n.

1815 ff. From this point onward Chaucer's text is a much freer paraphrase of the French.

1840 From I Tim. vi, 10.

1842 From Publilius Syrus, Sent., 479.

1846 From Publilius Syrus, Sent., 293.

1850 From the Decretals of Gregory cf. 1269, p. 849, IX, lib. 3, tit. 31, cap. 18.

1858 Cf. Seneca, De Clementia, i, 24, 1.

1859 From Publilius Syrus, Sent., 64.
1860 De Officiis, i, 25, 88.
1866 From Publilius Syrus, Sent., 366.
1869 James ii, 13.
1884–88 Not in the Lat. or the Fr. (See Tatlock, Dev. and Chron., p. 191, n. 2.) It is obviously a free translation of I John i, 9.

The Monk's Prologue

The opening words of the Host in the *Monk's Prologue* correspond closely to a single stanza (usually cited as "Verba Hospitis") which appears in some MSS. at the end of the *Clerk's Tale* (see IV, 1162 ff., and n.). Apparently Chaucer first wrote the speech for the latter position, and then transferred it to the *Monk's Prologue* when he developed at length the characterization of the Host's wife. Professor Tupper (Types, pp. 50 f.) reminds us that the shrewish hostess has been a conventional type in English literature. He compares Mrs. Towwowse in Joseph Andrews.

The address to the Monk (ll. 1932 ff.) is similarly repeated, in substance, in the so-called Nun's Priest's Epilogue (VII, 3447–62), which is preserved in only four published MSS. and was doubtless meant to be canceled.

Mrs. Dempster (PMLA, LXVII, 1143) argues that Chaucer was consciously leading up to the Marriage Group when he revised the *Monk's Prologue*. She also makes a point (p. 1151) of the comic characterization of the Host here and in the Monk's end-link, the Shipman-Prioress link, and the Physician-Pardoner link, all of which she would date near together.

1891 *As I am feithful man,* "upon my faith as a Christian."

1892 *corpus Madrian,* the body of Madrian, a saint who seems to be otherwise unknown, — probably one of the characteristic blunders of the Host. The name may be a corruption of St. Materne or St. Mathurin. For the story of the latter, with references to his "precious body," see the Legenda Aurea, tr. Caxton, Temple Classics, 1900, IV, 1 ff. Professor G. L. Frost (MLN, LVII, 177 ff.) suggests that the name of the saint may carry a reference to the confection of grape and lye known as *madrian.* He compares January's use of *spices hoote* in MerchT, IV, 1808. Neither this nor the suggestion of Miss D. M. Norris (MLN, XLVIII, 146) that the name is a corruption of the Italian *madre* is very convincing.

1893 *barel ale;* for the construction cf. *Intro to PrT,* VII, 438, and n.

1894 *Goodelief,* printed *gode lief* in previous editions. But Miss Rickert has shown that it occurs as a proper name in numerous Kentish records, and it is doubtless to be so taken here. It is written as one word in several MSS., and spelled with a capital in two. The name of Henry Bailly's wife appears as "Christian" in the Subsidy Roll for Southwark (4 Rich., II), and we can only conjecture whether he is here concealing her real name or referring to a second wife. See TLS, 1926, p. 935, and MP, XXV, 79 ff. Further examples of the name, dating as far back as the 12th century, are given by H. G. Richardson, TLS, 1927, p. 44. *Goode lief* occurs again in *WB Prol,* III, 431, where it may conceivable be a man's

name (like the German "Gottlieb"), but it seems more likely to be the epithet.

1901 Cf. *Gen Prol,* I, 449 ff.

1906 *By corpus bones,* the blundering phrase, characteristic of the speech of the Host, is here attributed to his wife.

1917 "She will make me kill some neighbor and then suffer the death penalty" (or perhaps, "go my way in flight"?).

1922 The prefix *mys-* goes with both *dooth* and *seith.* Cf. *Mill Prol,* I, 3139.

1926 Rochester is thirty miles from London. Since Sittingbourne, mentioned in *WB Prol,* III, 847, is ten miles farther on the road towards Canterbury, the order of tales in the MSS., which puts Fragment III before Fragment VII, is unsatisfactory. See the introduction to the Textual Notes on the *CT.*

It is uncertain whether Chaucer meant Rochester to be the lodging-place of the pilgrims on their first or their second night.

1933 Cf. Jean de Meun, Testament, 1072 (RR, ed. Méon, Paris, 1814, IV, 55), for a reference to the good pastures of the friars.

1936 *sexteyn,* "sacristan," the officer in charge of the monastic buildings and church vessels and ornaments; *celerer,* in charge of kitchen and cellar, and of the provision of food and drink.

1940 *governour* might refer either to a place of authority in an ecclesiastical establishment or to a secular position, like that of a governor in a royal palace.

1956 Proverbial; cf. *LGW,* 2395; Haeckel, p. 33, no. 111.

1962 *Lussheburghes,* spurious light coins imported into England from Luxemburg during the reign of Edward III.

To take the Host's banter here as serious theological argument would clearly be to "maken ernest of game." From one point of view it is simply a variation on the old theme of the Goliardic poets, that "clerus scit diligere uirginem plus milite." Nevertheless it should be observed that sacerdotal celibacy was much discussed in England at the end of the fourteenth century. Wyclif's opinion on the subject is a matter of dispute. Though he has some passages, especially in his later writings, in defence of the marriage of the clergy, he appears to have been in general sympathy with the practice, if not the requirement, of celibacy. But in the decade or two following his death the Lollards made an open attack on the regulation. The particular argument of the Host, however, seems to have been seldom used. In the century-long controversy about compulsory celibacy the opponents of the law have laid emphasis chiefly on the weakness of human nature and the licentiousness of the clergy when living under unnatural restraint. They have rarely referred to the effect on the population of the withdrawal of the clergy from parenthood. A striking parallel to the Host's remarks is furnished by a passage, also in a humorous vein, in the brilliant Irish satirical poem of Brian Merriman, The Midnight Court (especially ll. 805 ff., see the edition of L. C. Stern, CZ, V, 225). On the opinions of Wyclif and the Lollards see H. C. Lea, History of Sacerdotal Celibacy, New York, 1907, I, 473 ff.; H. B. Workman, John Wyclif, Oxford, 1926, II, 45.

1964 Proverbial; cf. *Ck Prol*, I, 4355, and n.

1967 Cf. l. 2158, below, and see *Gen Prol*, I, 307, and n.

1970 St. Edward, probably Edward the Confessor.

1973 ff. A closely similar definition of tragedy is given in a gloss inserted in *Bo*, ii, pr. 2, 70. In fact the terms "tragedy" and "comedy" in mediæval literature have reference chiefly to writing in epic or narrative form rather than in dramatic. Thus Chaucer calls his *Troilus* a tragedy (v, 1786), and Dante's great poem, which begins in Hell and ends in Heaven, is known as the Divine Comedy. On the history of the terms see Wilhelm Cloetta, Komödie und Tragödie im Mittelalter (Vol. I of Beiträge zur Litteraturgeschichte des Mittelalters, Halle, 1890). References will be found there to works in hexameter and the other forms of which Chaucer speaks. Since the Aeneid, the Thebaid, and the Pharsalia were all reckoned tragedies in this looser sense of the term, Chaucer may have had them particularly in mind. In mediæval works of the sort the elegiac meter was chiefly employed. The De Casibus and De Claris Mulieribus of Boccaccio were in prose.

1984 ff. The Monk's excuse for departing from chronological order is usually held to apply to the position of the Modern Instances. But the ancient tragedies themselves, with Cæsar before Crassus and Nero before Alexander, are not strictly arranged.

The Monk's Tale

On the date of the *Monk's Tale* and the probable circumstances of its composition see particularly Tatlock, Dev. and Chron., pp. 164 ff., and Kittredge, The Date of Chaucer's Troilus, Chau. Soc., 1909, pp. 41 ff. This tale, like that of the Second Nun, has usually been taken to be one of Chaucer's early writings. The Bernabò stanza, which cannot have been written before 1386 (Bernabò died Dec. 19, 1385), has been recognized as a later interpolation, and the other so-called Modern Instances — the two Pedros and Ugolino — have been similarly regarded by Skeat and most authorities. Professor Tatlock, who opposes the theory of interpolation and appears to take the whole tale as a product of the Canterbury period, gives no decisive reason in support of the late date. In fact positive evidence is lacking on both sides, but the general character of the tragedies favors an assignment to the beginning of Chaucer's Italian period (about 1374). Professor Kittredge shows that even the accounts of Ugolino and the Pedros may very well have been written at that time. They emphasize the Fortune moral and conform in general to the plan of the series, whereas the Bernabò stanza has every appearance of being an afterthought.

The general plan of the tale is due to the Roman de la Rose (5839 ff.) and, perhaps, to Boccaccio's De Casibus (apparently acknowledged in Chaucer's sub-title). From the Roman doubtless came the Fortune motif, in the illustration of which the French poem also makes use of contemporary instances. The single tragedies are many of them so brief and general that it is hard to establish particular sources for them, and usually not important except for the light they would throw on Chaucer's reading. The Adam, Hercules, Nero, and Samson

have commonly been held to show the influence of the De Casibus, and the Zenobia that of the De Claris Mulieribus. The Hercules comes in part from Boethius (IV, m. 7); Ugolino from Dante's Inferno XXXIII, perhaps with collateral use of an Italian Chronicle; and Lucifer, Samson, Nebuchadnezzar, Belshazzar, Holofernes, and Antiochus all derive in substance from the Old Testament or the Apocrypha. For evidence that the Samson and the Nero and perhaps the Cæsar (for which Chaucer himself cites Lucan, Valerius and Suetonius) may have been influenced by the Speculum Historiale of Vincent of Beauvais see Miss Pauline Aiken in Spec., XVII, 56 ff. There are also possible, though hardly demonstrable, borrowings from the Speculum in the Adam, Belshazzar, Alexander, and Croesus. Mr. Dudley R. Johnson, in PMLA, LXVI, 827 ff., has suggested another possible source for some of Chaucer's variations from Boccaccio and the Vulgate in the Bible Historiale of Guyart Desmoulins. For the accounts of the two Pedros and of Bernabò, Chaucer doubtless drew on his own knowledge and recollections. Other parallels to the various tragedies that have been noted will be mentioned in the notes that follow. The more important material has been assembled and printed by R. K. Root in SA, pp. 615 ff.

On the general conception of Fortune as the ruling motif of the tragedies reference may be made to H. R. Patch, The Goddess Fortuna, Cambridge, Mass., 1927. Cf. also the note to *KnT*, I, 1663 above. An extensive list of similar stories and collections, Roman and mediæval, has been drawn up and discussed by R. W. Babcock, PMLA, XLVI, 205 ff. It exhibits very well the development of the tradition before Chaucer. For a detailed comparison of the passages on Fortuna with their sources see E. M. Socola, JEGP, XLIX, 159 ff. He argues that there is a developing conception — a progressive personalization — of Fortune which involves positive alteration of a number of the tragedies and which, incidentally, supports the placing of the Modern Instances between Zenobia and Nero.

The position of the Modern Instances differs in various MSS. In the best group (Ellesmere and most of its nearest relatives) they stand at the end. But in most copies they come between Zenobia and Nero. The following head-link, the *Nun's Priest's Prologue*, with its reference (l. 2782) to the closing line of Croesus, suggests that Chaucer's final purpose was to put the Modern Instances in the middle. There is a natural ending of the whole tale, moreover, in the definition of tragedy with which Croesus closes. But whether the Ellesmere order is simply due to an officious scribe, desirous of mending the chronology, or preserves the form of an early copy of the tale, it is perhaps impossible to determine. The Monk's own apology for the chronological confusion unfortunately does not settle the matter, for it might have reference to the ancient instances alone. There is a slight inconsistency, on any assumption, in the final state of the text. If the Croesus stands at the end, as the following head-link appears to require, then the tale has so good a formal conclusion that the Knight's interruption seems out of place. The question is still further complicated by the head-link itself, which exists in several MSS. in a short form omitting all reference to the Croesus passage. Here again there is doubt whether the shorter link represents a first version by Chaucer or is simply due to a scribe's omission of twenty lines. To account for all the facts one might imagine some such procedure as the following: Chaucer may have first written the ancient tragedies, ending with Croesus, and then have appended the tragedies of the two Pedros and Ugolino, which were probably written at the same period. Bernabò was doubtless added in 1386, perhaps just when Chaucer was considering the use of the whole series for the Canterbury collection. If the Modern Instances stood at that moment at the end, Chaucer may have observed the unfinished character of the series and therefore have planned the interruption of the Knight (or Host, as a few MSS. say). He may first have written the shorter link, without any reference to Croesus, and afterwards expanded it, having decided to restore the original conclusion. If he transferred the Modern Instances to the middle, he may at the same time have inserted the Monk's apology for the order of the tragedies. All this is possible, but it involves a complicated series of assumptions; and it is simpler, to say the least, to regard the order with Croesus at the end as the one intended by Chaucer from the outset. Then the shift in the Ellesmere group of MSS. can be attributed to a scribe and the Knight's interruption is natural enough if Chaucer forgot for the moment the inconspicuous though formal conclusion of the Croesus, and conceived of the tale simply as an indefinitely extensible series of tragedies. This was certainly his conception of it when he made the Monk say, in his Prologue, that he had a hundred such stories in his cell. For further discussion of the whole question see Miss Hammond, p. 258; Bradshaw, cited in Furnivall's Temporary Preface to the Six-Text edn., Ch. Soc., 1868, pp. 23-24; Tatlock, Dev. and Chron., pp. 171 f.; Koch, ESt, XLI, 127 ff.; Brusendorff, pp. 77 f.; and Manly, M-R CT, IV, p. 511, who suggests as a possible solution that the Modern Instances belonged to a pre-Canterbury Tale stage of the tragedies, and were cancelled by Chaucer when he assigned the story to the Monk. The later arrangements would then be scribal or editorial.

1999 *Lucifer,* "light-bringer," the name of the morning star. It was applied to Satan as a result of a common interpretation of Is. xiv, 12.

2007 The statements about Adam are so general as to give no sure indication of a source. *The feeld of Damyssene* has been traced to the De Casibus, but it is paralleled also in Petrus Comestor, Hist. Schol., Genesis, cap. xiii, and in the Speculum Historiale, I, c. xli. See Miss Aiken, Spec., XVII, 57.

2009 Perhaps suggested by the De Contemptu Mundi, ii, 1: "Formatus est homo . . . de spurcissimo spermate." But the idea was familiar.

2015 The account of Samson seems to be mainly derived from Judges xiii-xvi. But the influence of Speculum Historiale and RR, 16677-88, should probably be recognized.

2018 *whil he myghte see,* until he became blind.

2035 *cornes,* crops (Vulg. "segetes," "fruges").

2046 *Judicum,* for Liber Judicum, the Book of Judges. Cf. *Metamorphosios, Intro to MLT,* II, 93, n.

2047 *Gazan,* apparently due to the accusative "Gazam" in Judges xvi, 1.

2063 The form *Dalida* for Delilah, held by Fansler

(p. 31) to be due to RR, occurs as Miss Landrum has noted (PMLA, XXXIX, 89) in the Speculum Historiale, the Cursor Mundi, the Confessio Amantis, and Deguilleville's Pèlerinage.

2091 The moral, which differs from the usual references to Fortune in the other tragedies, closely resembles the comment in De Casibus and RR, 16541-16700.

2095 The chief source of the Hercules is Boethius, iv, m. 7. Certain details may be due to Ovid, Met., ix and Heroides, ix, and Boccaccio, De Clar. Mul., xxii. See Shannon, Ch. and the Roman Poets, Cambridge, Mass., 1929, pp. 312 ff.

2098 ff. In the references to the labors of Hercules the names of Cerberus and Cacus are clear. The *leoun* is the Nemean lion. *Centauros,* the exact form found in Boethius, refers to Pholus and Nessus. The *dragoun* is Ladon. *Busirus* is a distortion of Busiris, whose story is confused with that of Diomedes, king of Thrace. The error was perhaps due to Heroides, ix, 67-70. The *serpent* is the Lernaean hydra. *Acheloys,* i.e., Achelous. *Antheus,* i.e., Antaeus. The *boor,* i.e., the Erymanthian boar.

2105 It is hard to choose between the reading *firy,* found in a few MSS., some of them superior, and *verray,* which has better support. Manly argues that there is no evidence that Hydra was conceived of as a fiery serpent.

2117 *bothe the worldes endes,* the eastern and western ends of the world. The Pillars of Hercules at Gibraltar were familiar to everybody, and there was also a tradition that Hercules set up pillars at the limits of the oriental world. The latter are mentioned by Gower in the Conf. Am. (iv, 2054 ff.), and by Benoît de Ste. Maure in the Roman de Troie (ed. Constans, SATF, ll. 805 ff.), and accounts of them are given in several versions of the Alexander Legend. See particularly Julius Valerius, Res Gestae Alexandri, iii, 49 (ed. Kübler, Leipzig, 1888), and the so-called Pseudo-Callisthenes, iii, 27, Codex A (ed. Müller, in Arrianus, Anabasis, etc., Paris, 1846, p. 139 n.). For other references and further discussion of the tradition, which is connected with the ancient story of the pillars of Dionysus, consult G. L. Kittredge, The Pillars of Hercules and Chaucer's Trophee, in Putnam Anniversary Volume, Cedar Rapids, Iowa, 1909, pp. 545 ff.

The identification of *Trophee* is uncertain. The gloss (in MSS. El and Hg) *Ille vates Chaldeorum Tropheus,* "Tropheus, the well-known prophet of the Chaldees," simply explains *ignotum per ignotius;* and the problem is further complicated by a reference in Lydgate's Fall of Princes, i, 283-87 (ed. Bergen, EETS, 1924), where the name is applied not to a person, but to the source of Chaucer's *Troilus:*

In youthe he [i.e., Chaucer] made a translacioun
Off a book which callid is Trophe
In Lumbard tunge, as men may reede and see;
And in our vulgar, long or that he deide,
Gaff it the name off Troilus and Cresseide.

For various explanations see Skeat, Oxf. Ch., II, lvi, n.; Miss Hammond, p. 98, and Engl. Verse between Chaucer and Surrey, Durham, N.C., 1927, pp. 440-41; Kittredge, Putnam Vol., pp. 557 ff.; F. Tupper, MLN, XXXI, 11 ff.; and O. F. Emerson, ibid., p. 142 ff. The most likely conjectures are those of Professor Kittredge, that the common noun "tropaea," "trophea," for the pillars, came somehow to be misunderstood as the name of an author or a book; and that of Skeat, supported by Professors Tupper and Emerson, that the same word was applied to Guido, because of his epithet "delle Colonne" ("de Columpnis"). In favor of this latter identification is urged the fact that Guido's Historia Trojana may have been the source of Chaucer's passage about the pillars of Hercules, and was also one of the principal forerunners, and probably an actual source, of the *Troilus*. But Lydgate, it should be kept in mind, applies the name *Trophee* to Chaucer's Italian source. The Chaldaean prophet remains a puzzle, which Professor Tupper would explain away by dividing the gloss. He suggests that two notes, *Tropheus* on the present passage, and "Ille vates Chaldeorum" on Daniel in l. 2154, stood on contiguous inner margins of a MS. and were consequently combined. It would be a relief to accept this explanation, but certain difficulties stand in the way. Glosses were less usual on inner margins of MSS.; the chances are against these two having stood side by side and having been combined in reversed order; and Daniel was not a prophet of the Chaldees.

2121 *thise clerkes*, scholars, authorities (in general). For the use of *thise* cf. *KnT*, I, 1531, and n. Below, in l. 2127, *somme clerkes* seems to refer specifically to Ovid and Boccaccio. See Ovid's Met., ix, and Heroides, ix, and Boccaccio's De Casibus, i, 18, and De Clar. Mul., xxii.

2136 *any throwe*, for any time.

2137 *world of prees*, world of turmoil, turbulent world. For the construction cf. *KnT*, I, 1912, and n. The grammatical inconsistency, *For hym . . . is . . . yleyd*, may be noted.

2139 Proverbial; cf. Haeckel, p. 52.

2140 *glose*, deceive, beguile. From the original sense of "gloss," "interpret," the word passes to the idea of an irrelevant or misleading comment, and so to outright deception.

2143 The accounts of Nebuchadnezzar and Belshazzar were paired as a double tragedy, and the Fortune moral is introduced at the end of the second. They are taken from Dan. i–v. On possible use of Guyart Desmoulins see D. R. Johnson, PMLA, LXVI, 827 ff.

2147 See II Kings xxiv, xxv.

2148 *The vessel*, the plate; used collectively like Fr. "vaisselle."

2152 *leet do gelde*, caused to be castrated. The verbs *leet* and *do*, commonly used separately in a causative sense, are here combined.

The statement itself, which is not in the biblical account, may be due to Vincent's statement (Spec. Hist., ii, c. cxxi): "Fuit adeo castus: ut a contribulibus suis spado putaretur."

2166 *tweye*; an error for *three*, namely, Shadrach, Meshech, and Abednego. The idea that Daniel himself was in the fiery furnace may be due to a misunderstanding of Vincent. See Miss Aiken, Spec., XVII, p. 60.

2177 *a certeyn yeres*, a certain number of years; cf. *ShipT*, VII, 334, and n.

2239 *Lordynges*, a common term of address with minstrels and poets. It has been taken here to indicate that the line was written with the oral delivery of the Monk definitely in mind; but the assumption is unnecessary.

2244–46 See Skeat, EE Prov., p. 102, no. 243,

and p. 107, no. 254; Haeckel, p. 6, no. 19, for parallels.

2247 The account of Zenobia comes from the De Clar. Mul., xcviii, with some use, apparently, of the De Casibus, viii, 6.

Palymerie, Palmyra.

2252 Boccaccio, on the contrary, says she was of the race of the Ptolemies.

2253 f. *fairnesse*, beauty in general, seems to be contrasted with *shap*, beauty of figure.

2256 *Office of wommen*, a close rendering of De Clar. Mul.: "muliebribus officiis."

2271 *Odenake*, Odenatus or Odenathus, the ruler of Palmyra.

2307 She was acquainted with Egyptian literature and studied Greek under the famous philosopher Longinus.

2320 *Sapor*, Shapur I, king of Persia, 241–272 A.D.

2325 *Petrak*. Why Chaucer refers here to Petrarch rather than to Boccaccio is unknown. From the fact that he never names Boccaccio it has even been inferred that he attributed to Petrarch (or to Lollius) all the writings of Boccaccio that he knew. See the remarks on Lollius in the introduction to the Explanatory Notes on the *Troilus*. On the spelling *Petrak* see *ClT*, IV, 31, n.

2335 Claudius Gothicus, emperor, 268–70 A.D. He was preceded by Gallienus (253–68) and followed by Aurelianus (270–75).

2345 In Boccaccio the names are "Heremianus" and "Timolaus." Probably *Hermanno* should be emended to *Heremanno* or *Hermianno*, which would scan better, though the headless line was common enough. Chaucer's forms in -o might be thought to indicate that he had a source or intermediary in Italian. But he changed a number of names in various works to an Italian form. Cf. *Cambalo*, *SqT*, V, 31, 667; *Danao*, *LGW*, 2563; *Iulo*, *HF*, 177; *Lyno*, *LGW*, 2569; *Myda*, *WBT*, III, 951; *Sytheo*, *LGW*, 1005; *Vulcano*, *HF*, 138; and *Pernaso*, *Parnaso*, passim. Some of the instances in *LGW* have been explained as due to Chaucer's use of an Italian translation of Ovid. See the introduction to the Explanatory Notes on *LGW*.

2347 Proverbial; see Skeat, EE Prov., p. 108, no. 255.

2372 *vitremyte*, usually explained (in accordance with a suggestion of Skeat's) as a coined word, formed on the Latin "vitream mitram," and meaning a glass head-dress. There are a number of phrases in which a head of glass or a cap of glass is a symbol of weakness or discomfiture. Cf. *Tr*, ii, 867; v, 469; Debate of Body and Soul (Emerson, Mid. Eng. Reader, New York, 1915, p. 56, l. 14); also the following passage quoted by Tatlock (MLN, XXI, 62) from Boccaccio's De Gen. Deor., xiv, 18: "Verum si hi imbecilles sunt atque tractabiles sibi caueant memores prouerbii ueteris, quo prohibetur hos certamen lapidum non intrare, quibus sit galea uitrea." Düringsfeld, Sprichwörter, Leipzig, 1872, I, 311, cites Italian proverbs very similar to Chaucer: "Chi ha testa di vetro, non faccia a' sassi," "Chi ha cervelliera di vetro, non vada a battaglia di sassi." Skeat's interpretation of *vitremyte* thus gives a meaning in itself not unsatisfactory. But it is to be observed that there is no such idea in Boccaccio's De Casibus, which Chaucer was probably following.

The corresponding sentence there runs: "Haec nunc galeata concionari militibus assueta, nunc velata cogitur muliercularum audire fabellas." In view of the antithesis between "galeata" and "velata" Professor T. A. Jenkins has proposed a derivation of *vitremyte* from Old French "vite" or "vete" (L. "vitta") and Old French "mite" (L. "mitra"), perhaps by metathesis from "vitemitre" or "mitrevite." He gives evidence that "vitta" and "mitra" were used more or less interchangeably in the sense of "veil" or "band," and suggests that Zenobia's *vitremyte* was a hood with two horns (like a mitre); to which a veil was attached. If the word was actually employed for such a head-dress, some instance of its use may be expected to be found. For Professor Jenkins's argument see his article in Mélanges de Linguistique et de Littérature offerts à M. Alfred Jeanroy, Paris, 1928, pp. 140 ff. Professor K. Young (Stud. Phil., XL, 494 ff.) supports Skeat's derivation with the citation of *taenam* (for *taeniam*) *vitream* from the sentence pronounced in 1385 against Henry Crompe. But he points out that the "glass head-dress there suggested the deceiving of the wearer," and queries whether the same implication may not be intended in the case of Zenobia.

2374 The *distaf*, Skeat notes, is mentioned in the De Casibus.

2375 ff. For the brief account of the two Pedros and of Bernabò no written sources need be assumed.

Pedro, King of Castile and Leon, 1350–69, was killed by his brother, Don Enrique, March 23, 1369. *The feeld of snow*, etc. refers to the arms of Bertrand du Guesclin, who lured Pedro to Enrique's tent. The *wikked nest* has been identified as Oliver Mauny (OF. "mau ni"), who helped Enrique when the struggle first went against him. He was not, the Monk continues, like Charlemagne's Oliver, the friend of Roland, but was a kind of Genilon-Oliver, a traitor like Genilon.

Chaucer had various reasons for interest in Pedro of Spain. The Black Prince fought with him against Enrique in 1367. Then John of Gaunt married Constance, Pedro's daughter, in 1371, and assumed in her right the title of King of Castile and Leon. And for about two years after Constance came to England Chaucer's wife, Philippa, appears to have been attached to her household. Professor Brusendorff (p. 489) pointed out a ballade on Bertrand du Guesclin, attributed to Deschamps and written after Bertrand's death in 1380, which refers to the coat of arms in language closely similar to Chaucer's. It begins: "Lescu dargent a une aigle de sable A deux testes et un roge baton Portoit le preuz le vaillant connestable, Le bon Bertran de Clesquin ot surnon." If it were certain, as Brusendorff held, that Chaucer imitated the ballade, the Pedro stanzas (and with them probably the Modern Instances as a whole) would have to be dated after 1380.

For a detailed examination of the recorded history of the death of Pedro see H. L. Savage, Spec., XXIV, 359 ff. Mr. Savage holds Chaucer's source to have been oral communication, and suggests that Don Fernando de Castro was most likely his informant. He would date the original composition shortly after the marriage of John of Gaunt to Blanche in 1371. Professor Braddy (PMLA, L, 74 ff.) had suggested Sir Guichard d'Angle as Chaucer's probable inform-

ant. For objections to this theory see Savage, p. 361, n., and compare further Braddy, MLQ, XIII, 3 ff.

2378 Manly notes that many MSS. read *Thy bastard brother made thee to fle*, perhaps an earlier reading which was changed after the reconciliation affected in 1386 by the marriage of Pedro's granddaughter Katherine to Henri, grandson of Henri of Tratamare.

2391 King Peter of Cyprus, otherwise known as Pierre de Lusignan, was assassinated in 1369. On his conquest of Alexandria and some of his other campaigns see the note on Chaucer's Knight in the Explanatory Notes on the *Gen Prol*. Like Peter of Spain he was well known to the English court, having been entertained by Edward III in 1363 and having numbered many Englishmen among his followers. His reputation for chivalry, as Chaucer says, was of the highest, but his murder can hardly be ascribed to jealousy of his fame. It was due rather to resentment at his personal misconduct and his oppressive rule. See N. Jorga, Philippe de Mézières, Paris, 1896, pp. 385–91. See further H. Braddy, PMLA, L, 78 ff., who points out that Chaucer's account of the death of Peter is at variance with historical fact, and suggests that it may have been derived from the Prise d'Alexandrie of Machaut.

2399 Bernabò Visconti fell from power on May 6, 1385, when he was treacherously arrested by Gian Galeazzo. On Dec. 19 of the same year he died suddenly in prison, and the current opinion attributed his death to poison. Chaucer very likely wrote this stanza as soon as the news reached England, and the uncertainty of the last line is paralleled curiously by a marginal entry in Malverne's continuation of Higden's Chronicle (Rolls Ser., IX, 78, n.): "Quo in tempore dominus Barnabos moriebatur in carcere, qua morte an gladio aut fame seu veneno ignoratur." For an account of the occurrence, with references to the authorities, see Kittredge, The Date of Chaucer's Troilus, pp. 46–50. Professor Kittredge even conjectures that the news may have been brought to England by a particular member of Sir John Hawkwood's company, who came from Lombardy, according to Malverne, early in January, 1386.

Bernabò, like the two Peters, was a character of special interest to Chaucer and the English court. His niece, Violanta, married Lionel Duke of Clarence; Bernabò had offered one daughter, Katerina, to Richard II, and had married another, Donnina, to Sir John Hawkwood; and Chaucer himself had been on an embassy to Milan in 1378. For evidence that he met Hawkwood see R. A. Pratt, ELH, XVI, 188 ff.

2407 ff. Chaucer's account of Ugolino comes from Dante's Inferno, xxxiii, but differs in some details from its source. (See T. Spencer, Spec., IX, 295 ff.) In Dante there is no explicit statement about the *fals suggestioun* of Ruggieri, and the number of the children is four. Possibly Chaucer's variations in these points are to be explained by his use of some Italian chronicle. See N. & Q., Ser. 8, XI, 205 f., 369 f. Chaucer omits all reference to Ugolino's dream. On the other hand he expands the narrative in places, adding, for example, ll. 2433–38. The references to Fortune, which bring the story into accord with the general scheme of the Monk's Tale, are likewise his own.

2463 It is questionable whether Chaucer actually

used Suetonius for the Nero. See Fansler, pp. 24 ff. All the incidents, except perhaps those mentioned in the second stanza, would be accounted for by RR, 6185 ff., 6414 ff., and Boethius, ii, m. 6; iii, m. 4. The reference to Suetonius itself may have been taken from RR, 6458. For the second stanza Dr. Fansler (p. 26, n. 7) doubtfully suggests the use of Eutropius's Breviarium, vii, 9 (14 in modern editions). Professor Root, in SA, 640, cites also possible sources in the De Casibus, Suetonius, and Boethius. But Miss Aiken (pp. 61–2) holds that all details not accounted for by the Roman de la Rose appear in the Speculum Historiale.

2467   *south* is supplied by the editors for *north*, the reading of the MSS., since that quarter is represented by *septemtrioun*. The blunder seems more likely to be a scribe's than Chaucer's.

2477   Cf. Dante, Inf., v, 56: "Che libito fe' licito in sua legge."

2479 ff.   Closely similar to Boethius, ii, m. 6.

2495   *a maister*, i.e., Seneca.

2552   For the story of Holofernes see the Book of Judith.

2560   *For lesynge*, for fear of losing.

2565   On the identification of Bethulia, perhaps Shechem or Sichem, see R. H. Pfeiffer, The History of New Testament Times, p. 247, n. 15.

2575 ff.   On Antiochus see II Maccabees ix.

2631 ff.   The story of Alexander was the more *commune* in the Middle Ages because he was the hero of a favorite cycle of romances. In the *House of Fame* (ll. 914 f.) Chaucer shows acquaintance with the legendary material. But in the Monk's tragedy he follows rather historical tradition, as represented, for example, by Quintus Curtius (see his Historiarum Alexandri Magni, ed. Hedicke, Leipzig, 1908). Chaucer's knowledge may have come from the popular Alexandreis of Gautier de Chatillon. Cf. also Vincent of Beauvais, Spec. Hist., iv, capp. i ff. The tragedy is so brief and general as not to be easily assigned to a particular source. For an excellent account of the Alexander cycle as a whole, with full bibliography, see F. P. Magoun, Jr., The Gests of King Alexander of Macedon, Harvard Univ. Press, 1929.

2644   There is a brief reference to his *luxuria* in the Spec. Hist., iv, 31.

2653   *write*, pret. subjunctive.

2655   See I Macc. i, 7.

2660   This account of Alexander's death, given as an alternative tradition by Diodorus Siculus, xvii, 118, and adopted by Quintus Curtius, is usually followed by mediæval writers. See, for example, Vincent, Spec. Hist. (ed. Douai, 1624), iv, 64–65.

2661   I.e., Fortune hath turned thy high throw (at dice) into the lowest throw. For the figure cf. Gower, Mirour de l'Omme, 23399, 22102–03.

Another instance of the poetical use of Alexander as a victim of Fortune occurs in Boccaccio's Amorosa Visione, XXXV.

2671   For an argument that Chaucer's Caesar is really based upon Lucan, Suetonius, and Valerius, as suggested in ll. 2719–20, see E. F. Shannon, Chau. and Rom. Poets, pp. 335 ff. Professor Lowes has called the editor's attention to the fact that certain features of the tragedy — the triumph, the epithet *lauriat*, the account of Pompey's death — are closely paralleled in the French Hystore de Julius Cesar of

Jehan de Tuim (ed. Settegast, Halle, 1881). President MacCracken, in his edition of Lydgate's Serpent of Division (London, 1911), pp. 42 f., suggests that Chaucer followed Vincent of Beauvais, Spec. Hist., vi, 35–42, and Miss Aiken (pp. 63–4) supports the argument. Boccaccio's account, De Casibus, vi, 9, Chaucer appears not to have used. For further discussion see Root, SA, pp. 642–3.

2673   For the use of *he* cf. *KnT*, I, 1333.

2680   For the statement that Pompey was Caesar's father-in-law cf. Higden's Polychronicon, where the same error occurs twice (Rolls Series, IV, 188, 192). The ultimate source of this mistake is perhaps the statement in Suetonius, ch. xxvii, that Caesar proposed for the hand of Pompey's daughter. He was refused, but this fact is not added by Suetonius. See MacCracken, p. 43.

2697   *Brutus Cassius*, an error in which Lydgate followed Chaucer at least four times (Falls of Princes, vi, 2877 ff.; Serpent of Division; Coronation Address to Henry VI; Minor Poems, Percy Soc., 1840, p. 125). It occurs also in the Anglo-Saxon translation of Boethius, ch. xix (where the original, Bk. ii, m. 7, really refers to the elder Brutus, who drove out the kings). Still an earlier example of the error, in an anonymous commentary on Virgil written not later than the ninth century (preserved in MS. 358, École de Méd. de Montpellier), was pointed out by H. T. Silverstein, MLN, XLVII, 148 ff. The misunderstanding was perhaps due originally to the omission of *et* between Brutus and Cassius in some Latin epitome — in a phrase, for example, like "dolo Bruti et Cassii" in Vincent of Beauvais, Spec. Hist., vi, 42. Cf. MacCracken's ed. of The Serpent of Division, pp. 39 ff.; Miss Hammond, Engl. Verse between Chaucer and Surrey, p. 450.

2721   *word and ende*, a modification of the older formula, *ord and ende*, beginning and end; cf. *Tr*, ii, 1495; v, 1669.

2727   The tragedy of Croesus seems to be based upon the longer account in RR, 6489 ff. In l. 2728 Chaucer drew upon Boethius, ii, pr. 2 (perhaps indirectly through Vincent, who prefixes the same quotation to his account of Croesus). See W. K. Wimsatt, Jr., Spec., XII, 379 ff. and Miss Aiken, p. 68.

2751   *to meene*, to be interpreted. Cf. *PrT*, VII, 523.

2761   With the definition here cf. ll. 1973 ff. and 1991 ff. above; also Boethius, ii, pr. 2, just after the passage about Croesus.

The Nun's Priest's Prologue

The *Nun's Priest's Prologue* is preserved in several MSS. in a shorter form which omits, among other passages, the Host's reference to the tragedy of Croesus (ll. 2782–87). In two copies, moreover, the interruption in l. 2767 is ascribed to the Host instead of the Knight. These variants suggest that Chaucer wrote the *Nun's Priest's Prologue* and *Tale* for another position and that later, upon transferring them to the end of Fragment VII, he introduced the Croesus passage, and also removed what would have been a monotonous repetition of the Host's interruption of Chaucer just before the Melibee. See Miss Hammond, pp. 241 ff.; also the Textual Notes on the *NP Prol*; also the recent discussion by Manly, M-R CT, IV, 513–4. Cf. also Mrs. Dempster, PMLA, LXVIII, 1147 ff.

2779 "By St. Paul's bell" (in London).

2782 Cf. *MkT*, VII, 2766, 1993, 2762.

2800 Cf. Ecclus. xxxii, 6 (Vulg.): "Ubi auditus non est, non effundas sermonem"; also *Mel*, VII, 1047.

2810 *sir John*, a common nickname for a priest, but apparently the Nun's Priest's actual name. See l. 2820. The familiarity of the Host's address is shown in the use of the second person singular.

2816 *Yis*, the emphatic form of assent. The modern "yes" is equivalent rather to Chaucer's *ye*.

The Nun's Priest's Tale

It is probable that the *Nun's Priest Tale* was composed with the narrator in mind. Certainly the homiletic material and method are highly appropriate to the teller. Whether, as has been suggested, Chaucer intended the story from the outset for the place it occupies after the *Monk's Tale*, is more doubtful. It supplies an effective contrast to the Monk's "tragedies," which it has been thought to burlesque. (See S. B. Hemingway, MLN, XXXI, 479 ff.) Yet the examples of Croesus and Nero (ll. 3138, 3370) are introduced without any such backward references as would have been natural if Chaucer had meant his readers to recall the Monk's accounts of them. On the whole it seems clear that the *Nun's Priest's Tale* was composed when the scheme of the Canterbury pilgrimage was well under way. The maturity of the workmanship favors this supposition. But beyond these considerations, and the reference in l. 3394 to the Peasants' Revolt of 1381, there is no positive evidence as to its date.

The tale would have to be assigned to Chaucer's very last years if an allegorical interpretation, recently proposed by Professor J. L. Hotson (PMLA, XXXIX, 762 ff.) could be established as true. According to Mr. Hotson's theory, *daun Russell* is represented as a *col-fox*, instead of the usual red fox of the Renard cycle, because he stands for Nicholas Colfax, a follower of Mowbray, who was associated with him in the murder of Gloucester at Calais in September, 1397. But the fox's colors (ll. 2902 ff.) correspond to those of Mowbray's truncheon as Earl Marshal. Hence he represents Mowbray himself as well as Colfax, and the quarrel with the cock stands for the duel of Mowbray and Bolingbroke. Chaunticleer's colors correspond to Henry's arms. The fox is ruined by talking, as Mowbray was ruined by his slander of the King. Mowbray's duel with Bolingbroke took place on September 16, 1398, and Mr. Hotson would date Chaucer's tale shortly after the exile of the principals on Oct. 3. The allegory, as appears even from this bare summary, is not altogether consistent. Mr. Hotson complicates it still further by making the fox, already a composite of Colfax and Mowbray, represent also, through his name *daun Russell* (l. 3334), Sir John Russell, a minion of Richard II Some of the parallels — for example, that between the cock's colors and Henry's arms — do not seem very significant. The whole interpretation is extremely conjectural. Yet it deserves to be recorded, along with the same scholar's theory about the *Melibeus* and Professor Tupper's

explanation of the *Anelida*, among the ingenious attempts to find political or social allegory in Chaucer's poems. Obviously it cannot be used with any confidence to establish a date for the *Nun's Priest's Tale*. On the other hand there is no difficulty in assuming that the tale, standing as it does at the end of a fragment, was added by Chaucer at a late stage of the composition of the Canterbury series.

For another attempt, also more ingenious than convincing, at an allegorical interpretation of the *NPT* see C. R. Dahlberg, JEGP, LIII, 277 ff. In his primary allegory the fox represents the friars, the cock the secular clergy, and the poor widow the Church. On higher levels Chaunticleer is a figure of Christ and Pertelote of the Church eternal. The whole method seems more applicable to the allegorical exegesis of the Bible or the Divine Comedy than to Chaucer's tale, and even in those fields the inconsistency of the symbolism would make it dubious.

Still another symbolistic interpretation of *NPT* is proposed by M. J. Donovan, JEGP, LII, 498 ff. He holds the widow to represent the Church, the cock the alert Christian, and the fox the devil-heretic. As a reconstruction of Chaucer's intention this is all very dubious, but the paper contains relevant material on the character of the fox in mediæval literature.

In still another interpretation, J. Speirs (Chaucer the Maker, pp. 185 ff.) views the tale as an allegory of the fall of Adam.

The source of the story of the Cock and the Fox was held by Tyrwhitt to be the fable of Marie de France, Dou Coc et dou Werpil (see Ch. Soc. Orig. and Anal., p. 116; Die Fabeln der Marie de France, ed. K. Warnke, Halle, 1898, pp. 198 ff.; Eng. tr., Oxf. Chau., III, 432 f.). Later investigators have compared it rather with the Roman de Renart, and Miss K. O. Petersen, by a careful analysis of many forms of the tale, showed that Chaucer's version belongs rather with the epic than with the fable and corresponds pretty closely to the original of Goethe's Reinecke Fuchs. Specifically, she concludes that it goes back to a lost source which combines features from the Roman and from the Reinhart Fuchs of Heinrich Glichezare (12th century). See her study On the Sources of the Nonne Prestes Tale, Radcliffe College Monographs, no. 10, Boston, 1898. Later investigators, while accepting her general conclusion as to the epic connections of the story, have expressed varying opinions about its exact relation to the Roman. See especially L. Foulet, Rom., XXVIII, 296 ff.; I. C. Lecompte, MP, XIV, 737 ff.; and K. Sisam, in his separate edition of the tale, Oxford, 1927, pp. xxiii ff. All these scholars reject Miss Petersen's hypothetical version. The first two would account for Chaucer's variations as due to invention or independent combination of sources. Professor Sisam holds that the tale is in the direct line of descent from the Roman, but was separated from that source by an uncertain number of intermediate versions, probably some of them oral. That the epic form of the story is ultimately derived from the fable is maintained by E. P. Dargan, MP, IV, 38 ff. For further discussion see J. R. Hulbert in SA, pp. 645 ff., where the episode from the Roman de Renart is printed.

Only a small part of Chaucer's tale is taken up

with the central episode. The narrative is expanded
with anecdotes and moral applications suitable to
the Priest, and is enriched by literary allusions. The
homiletic material is discussed by Miss Petersen and
fully illustrated by citations from sermon books of
the period. She concludes that Chaucer made particular use of the commentary of Robert Holkot
(d. 1349), Super Libros Sapientiae. See the note to
l. 2984 below. On the sermon books in general, which
hold an important place in mediæval fiction, see,
besides Miss Petersen's interesting discussion, H. B.
Workman, John Wyclif, Oxford, 1926, II, 213 ff.
The homiletic elements in the tale may be partly due
to examples of "apostrophe" in the Nova Poetria of
Geoffrey de Vinsauf. On Chaucer's acknowledged
use of that poem see the note to l. 3347.

Chaucer's conception of the person and character
of the Nun's Priest has been recently the subject of
interesting discussion. See A. Sherbo, PMLA,
LXIV, 236 ff., and R. M. Lumiansky, PMLA,
LXVIII, 896 ff., If the Host's remarks in NPEpil
are taken as literal description the Priest was a more
robust figure than his speech and behavior elsewhere
imply, and it has even been suggested that Chaucer
cancelled the Epilogue because he was aware of the
inconsistency (see Manly, M-R CT, IV, 516). Mr.
Lumiansky, who reviews the whole discussion, argues
that the Host's remarks are cynical. He analyzes
the episodes at length, showing the bearing of NPT
on the dramatic development of the pilgrimage.

The following notes are indebted to the excellent
introduction and commentary in Professor Sisam's
separate edition.

2821 *stape in age*, advanced (lit. "stepped") in
years. Cf. *MerchT*, IV, 1514, and the Elizabethan
"stept in years." For a similar expression cf. "ferre
ronne in age," Lydgate's letter to Gloucester, l. 46
(Minor Poems, Percy Soc., 1840, p. 51).

2829 "She found herself," provided for herself.

2832 The "hall" and the "bower" were old
Anglo-Saxon terms for the main banquet hall and
the inner apartments, respectively, of a great house.
On their survival in mediæval England, particularly
in relation to the royal court ("aula" and "camera")
see Liebermann, Herrig's Arch., CXLIII, 248. There
is humorous exaggeration in their application by
Chaucer to the humble cottage of the widow, who
would doubtless have had only one room, or a single
room with a loft above.

2842 *whyt ne reed*: cf. *PardT*, VI, 562 ff.; *Tr*,
iii, 1384.

2844 Either "with which she found no fault" or
"of which she had plenty." Probably the former;
cf. *lakken*, "blame," *Tr*, i, 189.

2845 *seynd bacoun*; the usual interpretation,
"singed, broiled bacon," has been questioned by
Professor Bruce Dickens (Leeds Studies in English,
No. 4), who compares Fr. *saindoux*, "lard."

2849 *hight*, 3 sg. pt. or pp. For the omission of
the subject relative see *Gen Prol*, I, 529 n.

2850 ff. Chaunticleer's colors, as noted above,
have been taken to represent the arms of Bolingbroke. But the significance of the comparison is
made doubtful by the similar description of a cock
in the song (perhaps, to be sure, of later date)
printed in CHEL, II, 391. Miss L. P. Boone (MLN,
LXIV, 78 ff.) suggests that Chaucer was describing
an actual type of cock now known as the Golden

Spangled Hamburg. Mr. Dahlberg, in his allegorical
interpretation of the tale cited above, would explain
the colors as symbolic of the clergy.

2851 *orgon*, apparently felt as a plural, like Lat.
"organa"; cf. the plural verb *gon*.

2856 *equynoxial*, the equinoctial circle, a great
circle of the heavens in the plane of the earth's
equator. According to the old astronomy it made a
complete daily revolution, so that fifteen degrees
would pass, or "ascend," every hour. For the belief
that the cock crew exactly on the hour cf. Gawain
and the Green Knight, l. 2008, and Hinckley, p. 128.

2875 *loken in every lith*, locked in every limb.

2879 Cf the stanza printed by Skeat, Athen.,
1896, II, 566 (from Trin. Coll. Camb. MS. R. 3. 19),
and Hinckley, p. 130:

> My lefe ys faren in lond;
> Allas! why ys she so?
> And I am so sore bound
> I may nat com her to.
> She hath my hert in hold
> Where euer she ryde or go,
> With trew loue a thousand-fold.

2881 For mediæval references to this belief or
tradition see E. du Méril, Poésies Inédites du Moyen
Âge, Paris, 1854, pp. 5, 7, etc.

2896 *recche aright*, interpret favorably, bring to
good issue.

2908 *hertelees*, lacking in courage.

2914 ff. The qualities mentioned were those
regularly demanded of lovers in the works on
Courtly Love. See W. G. Dodd, Courtly Love in
Chaucer and Gower, Harv. Stud. in Eng., I, 1913,
pp. 246 f. Cf. also *ShipT*, VII, 173 and n. *Avauntours*, men who boast of the favors they receive,
were held in especial contempt. Cf. *Tr*, iii, 288 ff.,
and see W. A. Neilson, The Origins and Sources of
the Court of Love, [Harv.] Stud. and Notes, VI, 169.
Avauntours were similarly regarded in Arabic courtly
literature. Ibn Hazm has a section on them in his
Tauk-al-hamāma (cap. xiii; see Nykl, Hispano-
Arabic Poetry, p. 89).

2922 ff. Chaucer's writings give abundant evidence of his interest in dreams. Several pieces —
BD, HF, PF, LGW Prol — purport to be the records
of dreams, and though this might be a mere case of
conformity to literary fashion, the poems themselves
show more than a passing consideration of the dream
experience. Then in at least three passages of some
length — HF, 1–65, Tr, v. 358 ff., and the present
debate of Chaunticleer and Pertelote — the mediæval theories on the subject are explicitly discussed.
Macrobius's Commentary on the Somnium Scipionis
has been long recognized as the source of much of
Chaucer's information on the matter. He expressly
refers to Macrobius several times and professes to
have been reading the Dream of Scipio when he fell
asleep and had the vision which he records in PF,
and commentators have regarded the discussion in
HF, 1–65, as a recapitulation of Macrobius's chapter.
But in that passage and elsewhere Chaucer has many
observations not derived from Macrobius. Some
may be traced with probability to the Roman de la
Rose (see particularly ll. 1–20). And beyond that it
is probable that Chaucer knew the medical treatises
on the subject, or at least drew on the general information and opinion current in his age. A convenient description of this body of doctrine will be

found in W. C. Curry's Chaucer and the Medieval Sciences, pp. 195 ff.

Pertelote, like Pandarus in *Tr*, v, 358 ff., goes pretty far in her skeptical denial of the significance of dreams. But she was quite in accord with current learned opinion in so far as she denied any prophetic import in the so-called "somnium naturale," which originates with the bodily complexions and humors. Cf. Curry, p. 220 ff., citing Galen, Avicenna, Albohazen Haly, Arnoldus de Villa Nova, and others. See specifically Avicenna, lib. iii, fen 1, tract. 4, cap. 18; lib. i, fen 2, doc. 3, cap. 7.

2924 *fume*, vapor rising from the stomach. Cf. the explanation of drunkenness in *PardT*, VI, 567.

2925 ff. On the humors see the notes to *Gen Prol*, I, 333, 420. For the doctrine that they affect the colors of objects cf. Burton, Anatomy of Melancholy, i, 3, 3.

2926 *to-night*, this night just past, a common meaning in older English; cf. *RvT*, I, 4253; *PardT*, VI, 673. Chaucer also uses the phrase for the present night (now passing), *Tr*, iii, 669; v, 1169; and for the night following the present day, *FrT*, III, 1636; *MerchT*, IV, 2253; *ShipT*, VII, 278; *LGW*, 1710.

2940 *Catoun*, Dionysius Cato. See *MillT*, I, 3227, n. The reference here is to his Disticha, ii, 31.

2941 *Ne do no fors*, "attach no importance"; cf. Fr. "faire fors." Cato says, "Somnia ne cures."

2942 ff. Pertelote's prescriptions, like her diagnosis, are in complete accord with the authorities. They agree that *digestyves*, medicines for absorbing or dissipating melancholy and choler, should be administered before purgatives, and the remedies named by Pertelote all have a recognized place in the *materia medica*. Curry (p. 225) cites especially the accounts of them by Dioscorides (*Deyscorides*, *Gen Prol*, I, 432). For the digestives he refers particularly to Richard Saunders. The Astrological Judgment and Practice of Physic, London, 1677, remarking that of course nothing will be found there about *digestyves Of wormes*. But, as Professor Lowes has pointed out to the editor, Dioscorides has a chapter on the use of earthworms (Περὶ τῶν τῆς λῆς ἐντέρων) in the treatment of tertian fever and other diseases (ii, 72, in Sprengel's ed., Leipzig, 1829–30; ii, 67, in Willmann's ed., Berlin, 1907–14). For the suggestion that Chaucer may have drawn on Vincent's Speculum Majus for his account of Pertelote's knowledge of medicine see Miss P. Aiken, Spec., X, 281 ff.

2959 The *Fevere terciane*, which recurred every third (i.e., alternate) day, was attributed by the medical authorities to the predominance of red and black bile, either pure or mixed with other humors. See the passages cited by Curry, pp. 226 ff. He suggests that Chaunticleer was in danger of a particularly severe type of malady, known as "causon" or "febris ardens."

2966 *mery*, pleasant; referring to the garden rather than to the nauseous *herbe yve* (coronopus). Liddell interprets: "in our garden where the marrow is."

2967 The conversational effect of the meter is surely intentional, and it is not necessary to regularize the line by omitting *hem* or *up*.

2984 *Oon of the gretteste auctour*; see *ClT*, IV, 212, n. The term here used might have been applied to either Cicero or Valerius Maximus, both of whom

have the stories (Cicero, De Divinatione, i, 27; Valerius, i, 7). Miss Petersen, p. 109 f.; argues that the latter is meant, but that Chaucer got the stories second-hand from Holkot, where they are quoted from Valerius. In MLN, XLVII, 150, Miss S. Sakanishi notes that Giraldus Cambrensis, in his Expugnatio Hibernica, cites the anecdotes from Valerius and has them in the order given by Chaucer (Opera, V, 294 ff., Rolls Ser., 1867).

2990 *o* can be either the unstressed article or the numeral "one."

3050 *Auctor* is written in the margin of MS. El. On its meaning see *MLT*, II, 358, n.

3052, 3057 Cf. *PrT*, VII, 576, and n.

3065 This statement does not apply strictly to Cicero or Valerius Maximus or Holkot. Professor Manly remarks that Chaunticleer is perhaps "deceiving Pertelote by a pretense of scrupulous accuracy." In l. 3164 he is certainly not above taking advantage of her ignorance of Latin!

3076 Most manuscripts read *But herkneth* which overloads the line. Manly suggests that Chaucer may have inserted *herkneth* for dramatic effect in reading.

3092 *owles* are commonly regarded as birds of ill omen. The *apes*, it has been suggested, are mentioned simply for the sake of the rime. But for other cases of the association of owls and apes see C. L. Shaver, MLN, LVIII, 105.

3110 On the death of *Kenulphus* (Cēnwulf), King of Mercia, in 821, his son *Kenelm* (Cēnhelm), a child of seven, became heir to the crown. He was put under the tutelage of his aunt, Quenedreda (Cwēnthryth), who procured his murder. Shortly before his death the child dreamed that he climbed to the top of a noble tree, whereupon one of his best friends cut it down and he flew to heaven in the form of a little bird. See Alban Butler, Lives of the Saints, Dublin, 1833, Dec. 13, Caxton's Golden Legend, ed. Ellis (Temple Classics), IV, 60 ff.

3117 *For traisoun*, for fear of, to prevent, treason. Cf. l. 862 above, and n.

3123 The Somnium Scipionis of Cicero, originally a chapter of the De Republica, Bk. vi, was edited with an elaborate commentary by Macrobius about 400 A.D., and the work in this form was well known in the Middle Ages. See also *PF*, 31, and n.

3128 Dan. vii, 1 ff.

3130–35 Gen. xxxvii, xl, xli.

3138 On the dream of Croesus cf. *MkT*, VII, 2740 ff.

3141 On Andromache's dream, for which there appears to be no ancient "authority," see Dares Phrygius, De Excidio Trojae Historia, ch. xxiv; Roman de Troie, 15263 ff.; Guido, Hist. Trojana, sig. i 4ᵛ (Strassburg, 1489).

3160 Cf. *Mars*, 61 (almost identical).

3163 "As surely as gospel truth" ("In principio" being the first words of the gospel of St. John), or "as surely as in the beginning" (when woman first tempted man). The first explanation is probably right. See *Gen Prol*, I, 254, n.

3164 "Woman is man's ruin"; a common sentiment in mediæval literature, for which no single source need be cited. A number of variations on the theme will be found in Vincent of Beauvais's Spec. Hist., x, 71. Cf. MLN, XXXV, 479 ff.; Skeat, EE Prov., p. 108, no. 256. The late Dr. G. G. Coulton called the editor's attention to a citation of the usual string of abusive comparisons in Fr. Bartolommeo da S. Concordio, Ammaestramenti degli Antichi, cap. 35, rub. i (Milan, 1808). Bartolommeo is quoting Chrysostom, sup. Matth. X and Secundus Philosophus. Since Bartolommeo died in 1347, Dr. Coulton raised the question whether Chaucer could have known the work. But, as for Secundus, see Carleton Brown's article (MLN, XXXV, 479 ff.) cited above.

3187 According to a common opinion the creation took place at the time of the vernal equinox. See Bede, De Temporum Ratione, c. 66.

3190 The date intended is apparently May 3. March was complete and there had passed, besides March, thirty days of April and two of May. According to the calculations of Brae (*Astrolabe*, London, 1870, pp. 99 ff.) and Skeat (n. to l. 4045) the sun would have passed 21° of Taurus on May 3 and its altitude at 9 o'clock would be 41° or a fraction more.

Chaunticleer's catastrophe falls on the same date as the fight of Palamon and Arcite and an experience of Pandarus. See the notes to *KnT*, I, 1462, and *Tr*, ii, 55.

3205 Cf. *MLT*, II, 421 ff., and n.

3208 The name "Petrus Comestor" is written here in the margin of MSS. El and Hg, but the reference to him, if one is intended, has not been traced.

3212 *Lancelot de Lake*, the knight of Arthur's court. Mr. Hinckley (p. 141) cites the reputation of Walter Map, the supposed author of the original Lancelot, for untruthfulness.

3217 *heigh ymaginacioun*, i.e., by divine foreknowledge. Cf. *worthy forwityng*, l. 3243. Mr. V. M. Hamm (MLN, LXIX, 394) would apply it rather to Chaunticleer's own dream.

3222 *undren*, perhaps nine o'clock, though the term was applied to different hours. See Glossary.

3224 *gladly*, usually, habitually. For this extension of meaning cf. *SqT*, V, 376; *ParsT*, X, 887; *LGW*, 770; and perhaps *SqT*, V, 224; *BD*, 1010, 1012; also Gr. φιλεῖν meaning both "to love" and "to be accustomed."

3227 *Scariot*, Judas Iscariot. *Genylon*, the traitor in the Chanson de Roland. Cf. *MkT*, VII, 2389.

3228 *Synoun*, the deviser of the Trojan horse. See the Aeneid, ii, 259.

3241 The problems of foreordination and freedom, of divine grace and human merit, were much discussed in Chaucer's age. St. Augustine was the great representative of orthodox doctrine on the subject in the early church. Boethius treats it in his De Consolatione Philosophiae, bk. iv, pr. 6, and bk. v. The passage illustrates the distinction, mentioned just below, between "simple necessity" and "conditional necessity." Thomas Bradwardyne, lecturer at Oxford in the reign of Edward III and archbishop of Canterbury at his death in 1349, was author of a treatise De Causa Dei, which was an important contribution to the controversy, on the Augustinian side. For a long discussion of the subject by Chaucer see *Tr*, iv, 953–1078. The distinction between contingency and necessity was also several times treated by Wyclif. See his Logic, iii, 194; Misc. Phil., i, 71; De Dom. Div., 166 ff.

3256 *colde*, baneful, fatal. The line is proverbial. Cf. *Mel*, VII, 1096; also "Cold red is quene red," Proverbs of Alfred, l. 336 (ed Skeat, Oxford, 1907, p. 32); and Skeat, EE Prov., pp. 108 f., no. 257.

The Icelandic form, "Köld eru opt kvenna-ráth," comes even closer to Chaucer's line.

3260 Cf. RR, 15195 ff.

3271 *Phisiologus*, the Latin bestiary, entitled Physiologus de Natura XII Animalium, and attributed to Theobaldus. This contains a passage De Sirenis. For the text and translation see A. W. Rendell, Physiologus, London, 1928.

3280 According to the old philosophy every object or creature had its contrary toward which it felt a natural antipathy. As late as the 17th century the term was used with reference to magnetism. Cf. Bacon, Introduction to the History of the Sympathy and Antipathy of Things.

3281 On the use of *erst*, where Mod. Eng. would more natually employ the comparative, see *KnT*, I, 1566, and n.

3294 Boethius wrote a treatise De Musica. See Skeat's reference to it in his note to *HF*, 788.

3306 *wynke* in older English meant to close the eyes, and so not to see.

3312 See the poem of Nigellus Wireker (or Witeker) entitled Burnellus seu Speculum Stultorum (in T. Wright's Anglo-Latin Satirical Poets of the Twelfth Century, Rolls Ser., 1872, I, 54 ff.). A young man named Gundulfus broke a cock's leg by throwing a stone at it. Later, when Gundulfus was to be ordained and receive a benefice, the cock crowed so late that Gundulfus overslept and lost his living.

3320 On *seinte* see *KnT*, I, 1721, n.

3321 *counterfete*, imitate.

3325 f. Cf. RR, 1034 f. (*Rom*, 1050 ff.); *LGW Prol F*, 352 f. Mr. Sisam cites *ye lordes* here, along with *maistresses* in *PhysT*, VI, 72, and *chanouns religious*, *CYT*, VIII, 992, as examples of direct address not dramatically appropriate to the Canterbury pilgrims. They are all natural rhetorical figures.

3329 Ecclus. xii, 10 ff., xxvii, 26. Or the reference may be to Solomon as the author of Proverbs (xxix, 5).

3345 Cf. RR, 4385 ff.

3347 *Gaufred*, Geoffrey de Vinsauf, author of the Poetria Nova, which was published soon after the death of Richard I. It was long recognized as an authoritative treatise on poetry. The passage referred to is an example of a lamentation, and deals with Richard's death. Cf. particularly the lines on Friday, the day on which Richard was wounded:

O Veneris lacrimosa dies! O sidus amarum!

Illa dies tua nox fuit et Venus illa venenum.

(ed. E. Faral, Les Arts Poétiques du xiie et du xiiie Siècle, Paris, 1924, p. 208). The relevant passages of the Nova Poetria have been published by K. Young in MP, XLI, 172 ff. Young called attention to the exceptional vogue of the poem and suggested that other parts of the work may have contributed to the sermonistic element in *NPT*.

3357 *streite swerd*, drawn sword ("acies stricta," Aen., ii, 333 f.)

3358 f. See Aen. ii, 550 ff. With the form *Eneydos* (gen. sg.) cf. *Metamorphosios*, *ML Prol*, II, 93, and n. Professor Pratt, in MLN, LXIV, 76–78, points out that Chaucer may have got the hint for his references to Troy, Carthage, and Rome from lines of the Nova Poetria just preceding those he ridiculed above. Cf. Nova Poetria, ll. 363–8 (ed. Faral, p. 208).

3363 Hasdrubal was the king of Carthage when the Romans burnt it in 146 B.C. For the suicide of his wife see Orosius, iv, 23, and St. Jerome, Adversus Jovinianum, i, 43.

3370 Cf. *MkT*, VII, 2479.

3375 ff. The chase of the fox was a stock scene in mediæval poetry of peasant life. Cf. The False Fox, in T. Wright's Reliquiæ Antiquæ, London, 1845, I, 4–5. Other examples are cited by Dr. G. M. Vogt in his unpublished Harvard dissertation (1923) on The Peasant in Middle English Literature. Representations of the chase from carvings of the 14th and 15th centuries are reproduced in Professor Sisam's edition, frontispiece and p. xxi.

3380 On the custom of crying "harrow" see M. Henshaw, Folk-lore Quarterly, XIV, 158 f.

3383 *Colle oure dogge*; on the "domestic" *our* see *ShipT*, VII, 69, n. For the dog's name Talbot cf. a song printed in CHEL, II, 393. There is a long list of names of hounds in the Roman de Renart (ed. E. Martin, Strassburg, 1882–87), V, 1187 ff.

3393 *benedicitee*, to be pronounced in three syllables; see *KnT*, I, 1785, n.

3394 The reference is to the Peasants' Revolt of 1381. The hostility to the Flemings was due to their competition in labor. See Oman, The Great Revolt of 1381, Oxford, 1906.

3426 Cf. *WBT*, III, 1062.

3438 Cf. *Pars Prol*, X, 31 ff.

3442 Rom. xv, 4.

3443 For the familiar figure cf. RR, 11216; also Jean de Meun's Testament, 2167 ff. (in RR, ed. Méon, Paris, 1814, IV, 115), and *MLT*, II, 701 f.

3445 *As seith my lord*. It is uncertain who is meant or why he is mentioned at this point. Writers of stories commonly ended them with a prayer, as may be seen in many of the Canterbury tales, and it is not clear in what respect the form here used is peculiar. If the ascription applies especially to the phrase *if that it be thy wille*, there may be an allusion to the prayer of Jesus in Gethsemane (Matt. xxvi). But in that case *oure lord* would be more natural than *my lord*. A marginal note, of uncertain authority, in MS. El identifies the *lord* as "Dominus archiepiscopus Cantuariensis," and a considerable search has been made, without success, to find a similar form of benediction associated with that prelate. From 1381 to 1396 the Archbishop of Canterbury was William Courtenay. Professor Manly observes that the actual "lord" of the Nun's Priest was the Bishop of London, then Robert Braybrooke.

The Nun's Priest's Epilogue

Manly rejects this as genuine, but cancelled. Mrs. Dempster (PMLA, LXVIII, 1149) suggests that it may have been discarded "because it dropped a Marriage Group theme which Chaucer, on second thought, wanted picked up by the next speaker. Then, she goes on to suggest, Chaucer decided to let the Wife of Bath break in uninvited. For the suggestion that Chaucer originally meant to use the lines to introduce the Wife see R. F. Gibbons, SP, LI, 21 ff.

3459 *brasile*, a wood used for a bright red dye. The name was afterwards applied to Brazil in South America, because a similar wood was found in that region.

Greyn of Portyngale, the coccus grain imported from Portugal. For information about both the dyes and the names *brasile* and *greyn*, see Magoun, Med. Stud., XVII, 121, 135. He would print no comma after *brasile*, because both dyes were exported by the Portuguese. But *greyn of Portyngale* may have been used to distinguish this use of *greyn*.

3461–2 These lines, with the indefinite reference to *another*, may be a spurious attempt at patchwork.

FRAGMENT VIII

Fragment VIII comprises the *Second Nun's Prologue* and *Tale* and the *Prologue* and *Tale* of the Canon's Yeoman. The two stories are clearly connected (see l. 554), but the fragment as a whole has neither head-link nor end-link. In the Ellesmere group of MSS. it stands between Fragments VII and IX; in the others it is separated from IX by VI, or both VI and VII. In the modern editions, as explained in the introduction to the Explanatory Notes on the *ML Epil*, VII and VI have been transferred to an earlier position. The Ellesmere order, VIII, IX, X, although attributed by some authorities to a redactor later than Chaucer, has been adopted in the Six-Text print and recent editions. It is supported by the indication, in l. 556, that the Canon's Yeoman joined the company at Boghton-under-Blee, which is five miles beyond Ospring, on the way to Canterbury.

For details with regard to the MSS. see Miss Hammond, pp. 172, 315; Wells, p. 737. In certain MSS., in which the *Second Nun's Tale* follows the *Nun's Priest's Tale*, a spurious link has been added to the latter tale. See the Textual Notes on the *NP Epil*. Two spurious links which appear in many MSS. and connect the *Canon's Yeoman's Tale* with the *Physician's Tale* will be found in the Textual Notes on the *CYT*.

The Second Nun's Prologue and Tale

The *Second Nun's Prologue and Tale* are held generally, and with the highest probability, to be early writings of Chaucer, which he took over, but never really adapted, for the *Canterbury Tales*. Even the ascription to the Second Nun appears only in the rubrics, while in the text of the *Prologue* (l. 62) the narrator is referred to as an *unworthy sone of Eve*. Yet there seems no reason for doubting that Chaucer meant to assign the tale to the Nun who attended the Prioress as her *chapeleyne* (*Gen Prol*, I, 163 f.). According to Griffith's Bibliography, p. 240, Mr. J. P. MacManus, in an unpublished dissertation, would explain away the "sone of Eve" as a phrase of the liturgy regularly sung by the nuns.

Except for the mention of the *Lyf of Seint Cecile* in the *Prol LGW*, there is no definite indication of the date of composition. The immaturity of style and the closeness of the translation are generally accepted as evidences of early work. But the passages from Dante in the *Invocatio ad Mariam* are not likely to have been written before the first Italian journey. Unless the *Invocatio* was composed separately and added later (as Professor Carleton Brown has inconclusively argued), a safe date for the whole work would be shortly after 1373.

The *Prologue* consists of four parts: (1) four stanzas on Idleness (ll. 1–28), (2) the *Invocatio ad Mariam* (ll. 29–77), (3) a brief Envoy to the Reader (ll. 78–84), (4) the *Interpretatio nominis Cecilie*, also addressed to the Reader (ll. 85–119).

The idea of the stanzas on Idleness Skeat held to have been taken from Jehan de Vignay's Introduction to his French translation of the Legenda Aurea. But there are no very significant correspondences between the passages of Chaucer and of de Vignay, and the "Idleness-Prologue" has been shown to be a conventional type of introduction used in many works. See C. Brown, MP, IX, 1–16, and F. Tupper, MLN, XXX, 10, n. 6.

On Mr. Tupper's inference that the story was intended as part of a schematic treatment of the Deadly Sins, see the general observations in the introduction to the Explanatory Notes on the *Canterbury Tales*.

The *Invocatio ad Mariam* is a fabric made up of elements from the Paradiso of Dante, several Latin hymns, or anthems, the Anticlaudianus of Alanus de Insulis, and the Commentary of Macrobius on the Somnium Scipionis. Stanzas 2, 3, and 4 are in large part translated from the address of St. Bernard to the Virgin at the beginning of Canto xxxiii of the Paradiso. But several lines and phrases from Alanus are interwoven with Dante. The fifth stanza is indebted to the Salve Regina, and lines 43–47 echo the Quem Terra (and perhaps also another canto of the Paradiso). Both these Latin hymns occur in the Hours of the Virgin, whence Chaucer probably derived the passages here used. The often repeated *motif* of ll. 47–49 occurs in the anthems for Evensong, Post Partum and Beata es Virgo. For the familiar phrase *ful of grace* (l. 67) the Ave Maria is a sufficient source. The sixth stanza recalls another place in the Paradiso (xxxii, 133–35) and part of the seventh (ll. 71–74) is almost certainly based upon a passage in Macrobius. For the full discussion of these parallels see Skeat's notes; Holthausen, in Herrig's Arch., LXXXVII, 265 ff.; Carleton Brown, in MP, IX, 1 ff., MLN, XXX, 231–32; F. Tupper, in MLN, XXX, 9–10; Lowes in MP, XV, 193 ff.; and Sister Madeleva, Chaucer's Nuns and Other Essays, N.Y., 1925, pp. 34–35. Mr. Tupper remarks that the composition of such a prelude to a miracle of the Virgin or a life of a saint was a literary convention even commoner than the "Idleness-Prologue," which precedes. It seems probable, therefore, that the *Invocatio* was composed at the same time as the tale of Cecilia, and that the combination of the two was not made especially for the *Canterbury Tales*. For a discussion of the relation of the *Invocatio* to the *Prioress's Prologue* see R. A. Pratt, MLQ, VII, 259 ff.

The *Interpretatio nominis Cecilie* Chaucer himself, or a scribe's rubric (in MSS. El Hg), credits to Jacobus Januensis (i.e., a Voragine) in the Legenda Aurea.

The source of the tale proper has been assumed to be also the version in the Golden Legend (ed. Graesse, 2d ed., Leipzig, 1850, pp. 771 ff.; also in the Ch. Soc. Orig. and Anal., p. 192 ff.). But in certain features Chaucer's account is closer to a version which follows the Greek life by Simeon Metaphrastes. For this Latin text see Historiæ Aloysii Lipomani de Vitis Sanctorum, Pars ii, Lovanii, 1571, p. 32

(Kölbing); Surius, De Probatis Sanctorum Vitis, November, Cologne, 1617–18, pp. 478 ff., revised as Historiae seu Vitae Sanctorum, Turin, 1875–80, XI, 638 ff. A careful comparison of Chaucer's version with both was printed by Kölbing, ESt, I, 215 ff. Nearly all the features which Ten Brink held to be original with Chaucer are paralleled in the Metaphrastes text. The version of Metaphrastes is itself derived from early Latin Acta, represented in modified form in the Acta compiled by G. Laderchi, Sanctae Caeciliae . . . Acta, etc., Rome, 1722, and in the Sanctuarium of Mombritius, Paris, 1910, I, 332 ff. Chaucer's version is compared with these Latin texts by Holthausen, Herrig's Arch., LXXXVII, 265 ff. It appears that Chaucer either had an original which combined materials from the Legenda Aurea and the old Latin Acta or that he made such a combination himself. Professor Tatlock, in MLN, XLV, 297 f., argues for the latter conclusion. For the conjecture that Chaucer's copy of the Legenda Aurea contained a fuller version of this legend than that in Graesse's text see G. H. Gerould in SA, pp. 664 ff. He prints the version from MS. Bodley 236 and the text of the Passio by Mombritius.

On the origin and early history of the legend the most important authorities are Laderchi, G. B. de Rossi, Roma Sotterranea Cristiana, Rome, 1864–77, II, xxxii ff., and H. Delehaye, Étude sur le Légendier Romain; les saints de Novembre et de Décembre (Bruxelles, 1936). For further references see the Catholic Encyclopædia, s.v. Cecilia, St.

The Second Nun's Prologue

1 ff. For this characterization of Idleness cf. Jehan de Vignay's Introduction, where the idea is attributed to St. Bernard. See Orig. and Anal., p. 190 f. Professor Tatlock (Angl., XXXVII, 106, n. 2) has noted a parallel in the Ameto, ed. Moutier, Florence, 1834, p. 58 f.

2 f. Cf. KnT, I, 1940, and n.

7 The idea, which is common enough, is also in Jehan de Vignay's Introduction, where it is ascribed to St. Jerome.

8 ff. For the comparison of Idleness to the devil's net ("panter") Skeat cites Wyclif, Select Eng. Works, ed. Arnold, Oxford, 1869–71, III, 200.

15 "Even if men never feared to die," i.e., if they considered this life only.

19 Sloth holds Idleness in a leash. Idleness was recognized as a brand of Sloth (Accidia) in the classification of the Deadly Sins.

25 *the legende*, the regular name for the life of a saint; also a short title for the most popular collection of such lives, the Legenda Aurea of Jacobus a Voragine.

30 St. Bernard was celebrated for his devotion to the Virgin. In the Paradiso, xxxi, 102, he calls himself "il suo fedel Bernardo," and the address to her in Canto xxxiii, of which Chaucer makes use in the *Invocatio* below, is put in Bernard's mouth. For some account of his writings in her honor see Mrs. Jameson, Legends of the Monastic Orders, 5th edn., London, 1872, pp. 142, 144, 145.

36–56 These lines follow in general the prayer of St. Bernard in the Paradiso, xxxiii, 1 ff., as indicated by line numbers below:

l. 36. Vergine Madre, figlia del tuo Figlio,
l. 39. Umile ed alta più che creatura,
     Termine fisso d'eterno consiglio,
     Tu se' colei che l'umana natura
ll. 40, 41. Nobilitasti sì, che il suo Fattore
ll. 41, 42. Non disdegnò di farsi sua fattura.
l. 43. Nel ventre tuo si raccese l'amore,
l. 44. Per lo cui caldo nell' eterna pace
     Così è germinato questo fiore.
     Qui sei a noi meridiana face
     Di caritate, e giuso intra i mortali
     Sei di speranza fontana vivace.
     Donna, sei tanto grande e tanto vali,
     Che qual vuol grazia ed a te non ricorre,
     Sua disianza vuol volar senz' ali.
ll. 53, 54. La tua benignità non pur soccorre
ll. 53, 54. A chi domanda, ma molte fiate
ll. 55, 56. Liberamente al domandar precorre.
l. 51. In te misericordia, in te pietate,
l. 50. In te magnificenza, in te s'aduna
     Quantunque in creatura è di bontate.

On other passages reminiscences of which Chaucer apparently combined with these lines from Dante, see the introductory note above. With ll. 37–38 cf. the Anticlaudianus, v, 9 (Migne, Pat. Lat., CCX, 538 ff.); ll. 13–14, 26; with l. 42, the same chapter, ll. 14–16; and with l. 56, perhaps, l. 66, ibid. But some of these phrases were commonplaces of the Marian hymns. With ll. 45–49 cf. the opening lines of a hymn of Venantius Fortunatus (Dreves, Analecta Hymnica, Leipzig, 1886–1922, II, 38, no. 27):

     Quem terra, pontus, aethera,
     Colunt, adorant, praedicant,
     Trinam regentem machinam,
     Claustrum Mariae bajulat.

The *cloistre blisful* of l. 43 may be an echo of this passage as well as of the "beato chiostro" of the Paradiso, xxv, 127.

Against Skeat's opinion that the Dante passage (ll. 36–56) was a late insertion, Professor Carleton Brown has argued effectively for the unity of the *Invocatio*. But his own suggestion that the whole *Invocatio* was late is also unlikely.

46 *out of relees*, without ceasing.

52 Skeat (reading *hir*) notes that in Chaucer's time the gender of *sonne* was still felt to be feminine. Cf. *Astr*, ii, rubric 1, also Piers Plowman, B, xviii, 243.

Dr. Paget Toynbee (Athen., 1904, II, 518) proposed the emendation *somme*, "sum," in order to bring the line nearer to Dante's "Quantunque . . . di bontate." But Professor Brown argued that the figure of the sun was commonly enough applied to the Virgin to make such an emendation unnecessary. And in fact another phrase, in the same underlying passage from Dante, "meridiana face di caritate" (ll. 10–11), is interpreted by the Italian commentators as referring to the noonday sun at the height of its power.

57–63 The fifth stanza departs from Dante and seems to have been influenced by the antiphon, "Salve regina." (See Daniel, Thes. Hymnol., Leipzig, 1855–56, II, 321.)

58 *flemed wrecche*, banished exile (the original sense of AS. "wraecca"). Lounsbury (Studies, II, 389) compares St. Bernard, Tractatus ad Laudem Gloriosae Virginis, Migne, Pat. Lat., CLXXXII, 1148: "Respice ergo beatissima Virgo, ad nos pro-

scriptos in exsilio filios Evae." The conception of this life as an exile was not unusual, but the parallel to *sone of Eve* (l. 62) is striking. *Galle*, bitterness; perhaps with an allusion to the name *Mary*, and to the Hebrew "mar," bitter. Cf. *ABC*, 50.

59 See Matt. xv, 22 ff.

62 On the inappropriateness of this line to the Second Nun see the introductory note, above.

64–70 This stanza perhaps contains a reminiscence of Paradiso, xxxii, 133–35:
     Di contro a Pieta vedi sedere Anna,
     Tanto contenta di mirar sua figlia.
     Che non move occhi per cantare Osanna.
With l. 64 cf. James ii, 17.

67 *ful of grace*: cf. "Ave Maria, gratia plena," and Luke i, 28.

69 *Osanne*, Hosanna.

70 On Anna, the mother of the Virgin, see *FrT*, III, 1613, n.

71–74 These lines, which have a general resemblance to the sense of Bernard's prayer (ll. 31–33, 35–37), correspond much more closely to passages in the commentary of Macrobius on the Somnium Scipionis (i, 10, 9; 11, 2, 3, 11; 8, 8, 9). This contains the figures of the prison, the contagion of the body, and the weight of earthly desire. The remoter source of both Chaucer and Macrobius, as Mr. Lowes points out, may be found in the Aeneid, vi, 730–34, and in Servius's commentary on this passage occurs again the figure of the contagion of the body. Perhaps Chaucer knew and recalled this comment. Possibly, too, as Mr. Lowes further shows, Chaucer may have found the passages from Servius and Macrobius both in Albericus the Mythographer, where they are brought together in the long chapter on Pluto (Bode, Scriptores Rerum Mythicarum, Cellis, 1834, I, 178, 180). For further conjectures as to the transmission of the quotations see Lowes, MP, XV, 200–01.

75 *havene of refut*: cf. Ps. xlvi, 1; xlviii, 3; cvii, 30. But the epithet was common in the hymns to the Virgin. See also *MLT*, II, 852; *ABC*, 14.

85 ff. The *Interpretatio*, in the original Latin of Jacobus Januensis, forms part of the legend. Similar etymological explanations, as Skeat observes, are found in other chapters. He compares particularly the account of St. Valentine, chap. xlii. In the case of St. Cecilia all the etymologies proposed are wrong. The word is really a "gentile" name, borne by members of the "Caecilia gens." Their common ancestor, according to tradition, was Caeculus, whose name was doubtless a diminutive of "caecus," blind. For an attempt to prove that St. Cecilia actually belonged to the patrician family in question see De Rossi, Roma Sotterranea, II, xxxii–xliii, 133–61. The derivations given by Jacobus Januensis and adopted by Chaucer are the following: (1) "coeli lilia," *hevenes lilie*; (2) "caecis via," *wey to blynde*; (3) "caelo et lya," *hevene and Lia* (representative of the active life); (4) "caecilia quasi caecitate carens," *Wantynge of blyndnesse* (on the principle, "lucus a non lucendo"); (5) "coelo et leos" (i.e., Gk. λεώς, Attic λαός, people), *hevene of people*.

113 ff. The Latin which corresponds to this stanza belongs to the third derivation. Chaucer has transferred it to the fifth.

114 *swift and round* refer to the Primum Mobile, *brennynge*, to the Empyrean.

The Second Nun's Tale

120 Most of the traditional account of St. Cecilia is included in Chaucer's tale. Her martyrdom has been variously assigned to the reigns of Marcus Aurelius, Alexander Severus, and Diocletian. Her remains, along with those of Valerianus and Tibertius, are supposed to have been buried in the catacombs of St. Calixtus, and removed thence, in 821, by Pope Paschal I to a church called after her name (Santa Cecilia in Trastevere). In 1589, when the church was rebuilt by Cardinal Sfondrati, her coffin was found there. (See Baronino, Annales, Mainz, 1623, ad ann. 821.) In 1851, De Rossi discovered what was probably her original crypt next to the papal crypt in the cemetery of Calixtus. See his Roma Sotterranea.

134 *the organs* (Lat. "cantantibus organis"), the archaic plural, for which "organ" came to be used later. In *NPT*, VII, 2851, *orgon* is construed as plural. On the history of the word, see Chappell, Hist. of Music, London, 1874, I, 327.

The association of music with St. Cecilia is held to be due to this passage in her legend. Its earliest occurrence in art seems to be the picture by Raphael now in Bologna, painted in 1513.

139 A mistranslation of the Latin, "et biduanis et triduanis jejuniis."

152 Sister Madeleva (Chaucer's Nuns, pp. 40–41) explains the angel as the "guardian angel" of Christian teaching, and refers to Psalm xci, 1.

172 *Via Apia*, the Appian Way, which led from Rome to Capua and Brundisium. The Latin text, which Chaucer mistranslates, says that Valerian is to go along the Via Appia to the third milestone.

177 *Urban*, Pope Urban I, who succeeded Calixtus, A.D. 222, and was beheaded May 25, 230. For his legend, see the Legenda Aurea, cap. lxxvii.

181 *purged*, i.e., by baptism.

186 *seintes buryeles*, Lat. "sepulchra martium." The reference is to the catacombs. The form *buryeles* is here plural, though originally the singular ended in -s (AS. "byrigels"). The modern singular, "burial," arose from misunderstanding of the ending. Cf. "girdle," "prickle," "riddle," all of which were formed by the same suffix.

lotynge, lying hid (Lat. "latitantem").

201 *An oold man*, doubtless St. Paul. The passage Valerian reads in his book (ll. 207 ff.) is a close translation of Eph. iv, 5, 6.

208 *cristendom*, baptism.

218 *fynt*, findeth.

220 ff. The roses and lilies are symbols, respectively, of martyrdom and purity. Skeat, following an explanation in Mrs. Jameson's Sacred and Legendary Art (8th edn., London, 1879, pp. 35 f.), held the roses to typify love or divine fervor. But the other interpretation has been clearly established by numerous parallels. As early as the third century St. Cyprian, in an epistle to martyrs and confessors, speaks of white and purple crowns as rewards for the children of God; the white, "de opere" (i.e., for Christian living); the purple, "de passione" (Migne, Pat. Lat., IV, 249 f.). St. Jerome, in a letter to Eustochium, written about the year 404, associates crowns of roses and violets with actual martyrdom ("effusio sanguinis") and crowns of lilies with the purity which he describes as a "quotidianum mar-

tyrium" (Migne, XXII, 905, §31). Again, in an epistle to Furia (557, §14), he ascribes lilies to virgins and roses to martyrs, as does also St. Ambrose in his commentary on the Song of Songs (Migne, XV, 1871, §3). On these and other uses of the same symbolism from the early centuries till the age of Chaucer, see J. L. Lowes, in PMLA, XXVI, 315 ff., XXIX, 129 ff.; H. N. MacCracken, in MLN, XXVII, 63; F. Holthausen, in Herrig's Arch., LXXXVII, 271; O. F. Emerson, in PMLA, XLI, 252 ff.; and R. D. Cornelius, PMLA, XLII, 1055 ff. Other references are given in Wells's Manual, pp. 880, 1032, 1149, 1241, 1328, and the whole subject is further discussed by Professor Tatlock in PMLA, XLV, 169 ff. To the same study the following notes are indebted for a number of references.

Apart from the symbolism of the flowers there is a question as to the exact significance of the crowns. In most of the instances that have been noted they were undoubtedly conceived, like the "crown of life" or "crown of glory" repeatedly mentioned in the New Testament, as tokens of victory or rewards of faithful struggle. This is the case also in the so-called Pseudo-Linus version of the martyrdom of St. Peter, to whom angels bring crowns of roses and lilies as he hangs upon the cross. (Martyrium Beati Petri apostoli a Lino episcopo conscriptum, ed. Lipsius and Bonnet, in Acta Apostolorum Apocrypha, Leipzig, 1891, I, 15.) Moreover this legend of St. Peter, which is cited by Mr. Tatlock (pp. 170 f.), is probably roughly coeval with the life of St. Cecilia. In the case of St. Cecilia, however, another interpretation is at least equally possible. The crowns are brought to her and her husband, not at the moment of martyrdom, but as soon as they determine to live a life of virginity in marriage. The situation is closely parallel to that recorded in the life of St. Amator, bishop of Auxerre, who died in 418. Amator was compelled by his parents to marry a virgin. "Sed cum tempus copulationis urgeret, se mutuo exhortantes, votum virginitatis fecerunt. Et ecce Angelus adfuit, qui duas eis coronas attulit, propositum laudans, & ad perseverandum exhortans" (Bollandist Acta Sanctorum, May, I, 51). The flowers in the crowns of Amator and his wife are not specified, but the circumstances of the presentation are similar to those in the legend of St. Cecilia. In both cases, husband and wife each receive a garland. It seems natural to regard the crowns as celestial substitutes for the nuptial crowns of an earthly marriage. The coronation of bride and groom was a conspicuous part of the ancient wedding ceremonies among both Greeks and Romans, as the στεφάνωμα is to this day in the Eastern Church.

For further discussion of nuptial crowns see *Tr*, ii, 1735, n.

236 Cf. *KnT*, I, 1196.

248 *Of rose and lilies*. The Lat. "roseus hic odor et liliorum" explains the strange change of number.

270–83 Skeat notes that this passage, though present in the Latin and French texts of the legend, is lacking in three other English versions. He accepts Tyrwhitt's suggestion that it was originally a marginal observation, which crept into the Latin text.

271 The reference is to the proper "preface" to the mass for St. Cecilia's day in the Ambrosian liturgy. This explanation of the passage, which is not given in previous editions, has — curiously enough — been several times discovered and forgotten. Professor Child, as Professor Tatlock reminded the present editor, long ago pointed it out orally to his classes, but apparently neither he nor any of his students ever printed the observation. Then in 1891 Professor Holthausen (Herrig's Arch., LXXXVII, 269) indicated the same source. And recently it was independently rediscovered by Mr. M. Henshaw, who printed the passage from the praefatio in MP, XXVI, 15 f. See Tatlock, PMLA, XLV, 169, n. 3.

274 *palm of martirdom*, literally translated from the Legenda ("martirii palmam"), which takes it in turn from the Ambrosian preface. Emerson has noted the use of the same symbol in St. Ambrose's Sermo xx (Migne, Pat. Lat., XVII, 642–43), and in Tertullian's De Spectaculis, cap. xxix (Opera, ed. Oehler, Leipzig, 1853, I, 61). See PMLA, XLI, 260.

276 *hire chambre*, i.e., marriage.

277 *Valerians*, a probable correction for the reading *Ceciles* of nearly all MSS.

shrifte, confession. Lat. "testis est Valeriani conjugis et Tiburtii prouocata confessio."

283 *Devocioun of chastitee to love*, chaste devotion to (spiritual) love. The Latin original (both in the Legenda and in the Ambrosian preface) has simply: "Mundus agnovit, quantum valeat devotio castitatis." Skeat's rendering, "To love such devotion to chastity," and that of Emerson, "Devotion to chastity as against love," both seem unnatural, though the grammatical construction in either case is possible enough. For the use of *to* to indicate opposition or hostility Emerson cites NED, s.v. To, 25, b.

315 *we*, in the nominative, anticipates l. 318.

319 *Cecile*. In the French translation Valerian answers, not Cecilia.

322 "If this were the only life," Lat. "si haec sola esset uita."

329 *Hath sowled*, Lat. "animauit."

338–39 This does not quite correspond to the Latin: "Sicut in una hominis sapientia sunt tria, scilicet ingenium, memoria et intellectus."

347 *colde*, baneful, destructive. See *NPT*, VII, 3256, and n.

349 From this point forward Chaucer's version corresponds rather to that derived from Simeon Metaphrastes than to the Legenda Aurea.

351 *That*, who.

352-3 For the argument that those lines refer to the sacrament of Confirmation as well as of Baptism see C. A. Reilly, MLN, LXIX, 37 f.

369 *corniculer*, subordinate officer, assistant (Lat. "corniculario"). The designation does not occur in the Legenda Aurea, and Skeat held that Chaucer used at this point the lives of Valerian and Tiburtius (Bollandist Acta Sanctorum, April, II, 203 ff.). But Kölbing (p. 221) shows that it occurs in the Metaphrastes version (corrupted into "cubiculario").

386-91 From II Tim. iv, 7, 8.

413 *Juppiter encense*, offer incense to Jupiter.

420 Possibly a reminiscence of Job xiii, 15.

442 *bigonne*, the full form of the strong preterite, second person singular. The final -e here was only rarely preserved in Chaucer's verse.

443-67 Chaucer here departs considerably from his original. A close parallel from the Sarum Breviary to the speech in ll. 463–5 has been noted by Miss M.-V. Rosenfeld, MLN, LV, 358.

467 "He stares and raves in uttering his judgment." Compare the modern phrase "staring mad."

489-97 Not in the Legenda Aurea. Cecilia, in Chaucer's narrative, has not yet said anything to justify this remark of Almachius. But in the Latin text from Metaphrastes she attacks the heathen gods in a short speech just preceding. The speech may have been omitted in the copy Chaucer followed.

498 *outter eyen*, outer (bodily) eyes.

503 *taste*, test, try.

539 "whom she had fostered." Lat. "omnes quos ad fidem conuerterat."

550 The Church of St. Cecilia, at the end of the Trastevere, is supposed to occupy the site of the saint's house. It is doubtful whether any part of the present building is older than 1599.

The Canon's Yeoman's Prologue and Tale

The first line of the *Canon's Yeoman's Prologue* indicates that it was to follow the *Second Nun's Tale*. Otherwise there is no connection between either *Prologue* or *Tale* and that which precedes.

The whole episode of the Canon and his Yeoman is generally held to have been written late. But whether it was actually an afterthought on Chaucer's part, there is no way of telling. For in any case the characters would not have been mentioned in the *General Prologue*. That Chaucer introduced them out of resentment against some alchemist who had cheated him (as Tyrwhitt suggested, IV, 181) is pure supposition, but the conjecture has led recently to interesting speculation.

Mr. H. E. Richardson, in the Transactions of the Royal Historical Society, Ser. 4, V, 38 f., called attention to a contemporary of Chaucer's who was both an alchemist and a canon, William Shuchirch, canon of the King's Chapel at Windsor. In 1374, one William de Brumley, "chaplain, lately dwelling with the Prior of Harmandsworth," confessed that he had made counterfeit gold pieces according to the teaching ("per doctrinam") of Shuchirch. It is not known whether Shuchirch was still practicing his "science" at Windsor in 1390, when Chaucer was charged with repairing the royal chapel. If he was, Chaucer would almost inevitably have known about him, and may have had personal dealings with him. Mr. Richardson even suggests — and Professor Manly joins him in the tempting conjecture — that the poet was a victim of Shuchirch and wrote the *Canon's Yeoman's Tale* in resentment at his deception. Professor Manly calls attention to the repeated occasions in his later years on which Chaucer borrowed small sums of money, and raises the question whether his need of ready cash may not have been due to the pursuit of Elixir, the Philosopher's Stone (New Light, pp. 244 ff.).

For Mr. Manly's further suggestions that the *Canon's Yeoman's Tale* was originally composed, not for the Canterbury series, but to be read to an audience which included some canons of the church — perhaps even for the canons at Windsor — see the note to l. 992, below.

No source has been discovered for the *Tale*. In the first part the Yeoman describes his life with his master; in the second he tells of the tricks of a London canon — a quite different person, he definitely protests. The story was doubtless a current anecdote, or combination of anecdotes. But in working it up Chaucer may have drawn on personal observation, for he displays considerable practical acquaintance with alchemy. Whatever his actual experience, his attitude toward the science, if any inference can be drawn from the Yeoman's exposures, would seem to have been skeptical.

A number of parallels to the *Tale* are pointed out by Professor Kittredge in Petrarch's Dialogue De Alchimia (No. 111 in De Remediis, Lib. i). He gives these merely as illustrations and not as sources of Chaucer's story. See Trans. Royal Soc. of Lit., XXX, 92 ff. The first trick of the Canon is closely paralleled later in Erasmus's Colloquium Πτωχολογία, and there are slighter resemblances to the tale in his Colloquium Alcumistica. See H. de Vocht, ESt, XLI, 385 ff. For another anecdote of the same character see the Centifolium Stultorum, Vienna, 1709, p. 147 (noted by Andrae, Angl. Beibl., XXVII, 84 f.). A very similar modern case of swindling is also recorded in the [London] Spectator, LXVI, 646. The most important literary analogue to the whole episode is Ben Jonson's Alchemist.

There is an excellent general discussion of alchemy in Chaucer's time, with extensive references to the relevant literature, by J. W. Spargo in SA, pp. 685 ff. A collection of alchemical treatises known to Chaucer or illustrative of *CYT* is in preparation by Professor Edgar H. Duncan. Miss Pauline Aiken, it should be noted, has questioned the extent of Chaucer's knowledge of alchemy, arguing that much of his information could have been derived from Vincent of Beauvais. See SP, XLI, 371 ff.

On the interpretation of the tale and the character of the Yeoman see G. L. Kittredge, Trans. Royal Soc. of Lit., XXX, 87 ff.; and S. F. Damon, PMLA, XXXIX, 782 ff. For the argument that the Canon was a "Black Canon," a Canon Regular of St. Augustine, see Miss M. P. Hamilton, Spec., XVI, 103 ff. The alchemical terms and processes are discussed at length in Skeat's notes, to which the brief explanations below are largely indebted. For fuller information reference may be made to Ashmole's Theatrum Chemicum, London, 1652. There is a convenient historical sketch of alchemy in the introduction to C. M. Hathaway's edition of Jonson's Alchemist, N.Y., 1903, pp. 15 ff.

The Canon's Yeoman's Prologue

556 *Boghtoun under Blee.* Boughton, which was five miles from Ospring, a regular stopping-place on the Canterbury Road. See the references on the duration of the pilgrimage in the introduction to the Explanatory Notes on the *CT*. On the name *under Blee*, "under the Blean forest," see F. P. Magoun, Jr., Med. Stud., XVI, 134.

557 *A man*, the Canon. Skeat quotes from Rock, Church of Our Fathers, London, 1903–04, II, 69, the statement that some families of canons regularly required their members, when outside of the house, to wear over their cassock a linen surplice, and above that a black cape. Whether Chaucer's Canon was

regular or secular is not clearly stated, but he manifestly enjoyed considerable freedom.

565 "He (i.e., the Canon) was spotted with foam, so that he looked like a magpie." But see G. R. Coffman, in MLN, LIX, 269 ff., who would apply the lines to the horse.

566 *male tweyfoold*, a double bag. Perhaps *tweyfoold* implies that it was folded over because nearly empty.

578 *For swoot*, to prevent sweat.

581 *Were ful*, (that) might be full. The relative is omitted, as frequently.

587 On the function of the Yeoman as a "setter," see the remarks of Professor Kittredge, Trans. Royal Soc. of Lit., XXX, 89 f. At the outset he speaks respectfully enough of the Canon. If there is mockery in his extravagant praise, it is not made too apparent. But the Host shrewdly leads him on to turn against his master.

602 *knewë*. The *-e* is apparently preserved in hiatus, though the emendation *knewen* would be easy.

611 *leye in balaunce*, put in the balance, wager.

632 *worshipe*, dignity; hence, respectable appearance.

633 f. "His upper garment is not worth a mite, in reality, for a man like him."

So moot I go, so may I have the power to walk; a frequent adjuration.

645 Cf. "Omne quod est nimium uertitur in uitium," of which the first words are quoted in the margin of MS. El. A number of similar proverbs are cited in Skeat's note.

655 *crafty* and *sly* here do not carry their present evil connotation. Cf. l. 1253, below.

658 *blynde*, without opening at the farther end; compare the modern "blind alley."

659 *by kynde*, by nature.

665 *Peter*, by St. Peter.

Harde grace, ill-favor.

669 *multiplie*, the technical term for transmuting the metals into gold. Perhaps a pun is involved on the multiplication of gold, in this sense, and the original chemical sense of multiplication, which referred to the fact that the strength of an elixir could be multiplied by repeated operations. See L. Zetzner's Theatrum Chemicum, Strassburg, 1659–61, "Multiplicatio praedicti sulphuris," III, 301, and "De multiplicatione," III, 818.

681 Cf. *KnT*, I, 1089, and n.

682 *slit*, slideth; contracted form.

688 f. From Dionysius Cato, Disticha de Moribus, i, 17.

The Canon's Yeoman's Tale

721 *neer*, nearer.

726 Mr. E. F. Piper (PQ, III, 253) queries whether Chaucer, and also the artist who represents the Yeoman in the Ellesmere miniature, knew the proverb: "A man's a man though he wear a hose upon his head."

731 *which*, what sort of; Lat. "qualis."

739 *ydo*, done with, ended.

743 *jupartye*, jeopardy, hazard; literally, "jeu parti," a game in which the chances are even. In French and Provençal the term was used for certain debates in verse. See L. Selbach, Das Streitgedicht in der Altprovenzalischen Lyrik, in Ausgaben und Abhandlungen, LVII; Knobloch, Streitgedichte im Prov. und Altfranzösichen, Breslau, 1886. Also Ducange, s.v. "Jocus Partitus."

746–47 "Misery loves company." MS. El has the marginal quotation, "Solacium miseriorum &c.," with which Skeat compares the proverb quoted in Marlowe's Faustus, ii, 1, 42: "Solamen miseris socios habuisse doloris." For the idea, cf. further Seneca, De. Cons. ad Polybium, xii, 2; *Tr*, i, 708 f.

764 *lampe*, plate, sheet; for *lambe*, OF. "lame," Lat. "lamina."

770 *sublymynge*, sublimating, vaporizing by heat.

772 *mercurie crude*, crude Mercury, ordinary quicksilver, as distinguished from the real Mercury (the "Greene Lyon"), which the alchemists professed to make. Skeat refers to Ashmole's Theatrum Chemicum, p. 280.

778 *spirites*, gases or vapors. Four "spirits" in particular were ordinarily recognized in alchemy: sulphur, sal ammoniac, quicksilver, and arsenic (or, according to some authorities, orpiment). See ll. 820 ff.

782 Cf. *Mill Prol*, I, 3134, and n.

790 *armonyak*, a corruption of *armeniak*, Armenian. "Bolearmenie" or "Bol Oriental" was a medicinal red earth or clay. (Cf. *armonyak*, l. 798.)

797 *Watres rubifiyng*, reddening of waters (i.e. fluids which transmute to gold). Contrast the process called *albificacioun*, or whitening, of waters (fluids which transmute to silver), in l. 805. See Zetzner's Theatrum Chemicum, III, 41, 110, 634 ff.

798 *sal armonyak*, properly *sal ammoniac* (also called *sal armeniac*). Salt of Ammon, in Libya; a crystalline salt. The form *armonyak* may be due either to association with Gk. ἁρμονία, joining, since the gum ammoniac was used as a cement, or to confusion with *armeniak*, the proper form in *boole armonyak*, above.

808 *Cered pokets*, bags or pockets closed with wax.

814 *enbibynge*, moistening, soaking; see Wilson, Osiris, II, 323.

816 *citrinacioun*, turning to citron color. When the materials of the philosopher's stone were in a state favorable to the success of the experiment, they were supposed to assume the color of a citron.

817 *cementyng*, "combining two solids at high temperatures in such a way as to change the proportion of one of the substances before melting takes place." See Spargo, SA, p. 688.

820 On the four spirits and the seven bodies see also Gower's Conf. Am., iv, 2462 ff.

838 *Ascaunce*, as if perhaps. See *SumT*, III, 1745, and n.

842 *elvysshe nyce loore*, strange and foolish lore. With the use of *elvish* here compare *Prol Thop*, VII, 703.

844 *lerne*, teach. On the confusion of *leren* and *lernen* see *MLT*, II, 181, n.

860 f. The list of names would be enough to raise a devil. For an example of this kind of conjuration see The Bugbears, Herrig's Arch., XCIX, 29 f.

874 *to seken evere*, always to seek; i.e., never found.

875 *temps*, tense. The reference of the gerund *to seken* is future.

877 *sadde*, sated.

878 *bitter sweete*, bitter-sweet; here, a dangerous allurement.

897 Compare *PhysT*, VI, 92.

921 *chit*, chideth; *halt*, holdeth.

922 *Somme seyde*, one said. The tense changes from a general present to a definite past, as if a particular instance came to mind.
long on, attributable to, owing to (mod. dial. "along of"; AS. "gelang").

929 *so theech*, "so thee ich," so may I prosper.

934 *crased*, cracked.

941 *many a throwe*, many a time.

962 ff. Proverbial. Cf. the following couplet from the Parabolae of Alanus de Insulis (iii, 1 f., Migne, Pat. Lat., CCX, 585), of which the beginning is quoted in the margin of MS. El —
Non teneas aurum totum quod splendet ut aurum,
Nec pulchrum pomum quodlibet esse bonum.
See also *HF*, 272; Haeckel, p. 38, nos. 130, 131; Skeat, EE Prov., p. 86, no. 206; p. 121, no. 284.

972 The story begins at this point. *Chanoun of religioun*, i.e., a regular canon, not a secular one. See ll. 992 ff.

979 *of falshede*, in respect to falseness. Cf. *NPT*, VII, 2850.

989 *governaunce*, conduct.

992 The address to *chanouns religious* here has been criticized as inappropriate to the Canterbury pilgrimage, and Professor Manly has suggested the bold inference that the tale was actually read to the canons of King's Chapel at Windsor. See the introductory note above for his theory about the personal application of the tale. The speculations are all interesting, but l. 992 would not be inexplicable as a merely rhetorical apostrophe. Cf. *PhysT*, VI, 72; *NPT*, VII, 3325.

1005 *By yow*, with reference to you.

1012 *an annueleer*, a priest employed solely in singing annual masses for the dead.

1018 *spendyng silver*, spending-money.

1024 *a certeyn*, a certain sum.

1026 The mark was 13*s*. 4*d*.; the noble, 6*s*. 8*d*.

1039 *condicioun*, character.

1048 *in good tyme*, at a seasonable time; hence, fortunately; a formula used to avert evil consequences from a boast or a compliment.

1055 For the order of words, compare *Gen Prol*, I, 791, and n.; also l. 1151, below.

1062 *Marie*, an oath by the Virgin.

1066 Skeat notes several parallels to the proverb, "Proffered service stinketh," EE Prov., p. 121, no. 285; cf. Haeckel, p. 47, no. 161.

1122 For this meaning of *philosofre* compare *Gen Prol*, I, 297, and n.

1126 *mortifye*, lit. "kill," i.e., change from quicksilver (argentum vivum) into silver; cf. l. 1431.

1175 *abit*, abideth; contracted form.

1185 *Seint Gile*, St. Ægidius. See the Legenda Aurea, cap. cxxx.

1189 *with harde grace*, a plague upon him; a mild imprecation.

1230 The *teyne*, or plate, which is here concealed from the priest, is to be used in the third trick.

1313 *ape*, dupe. Cf. *Gen Prol*, I, 706, and n.

1319 *heyne*, wretch; primarily, niggard (origin unknown; possibly connected with *heyne*, spare, save, ON. "hegna").

1320 *Unwityng,* like *knowynge* in l. 1324, is an absolute participle.

1327 "You are blameworthy." On the change in the use of "to blame" see *Gen Prol,* I, 375, n.

1342 For this proverbial comparison see *KnT,* I, 2437, n.

1348 Cf. *Gen Prol,* I, 88.

1362 *nere the freendshipe,* if the friendship were not; or, by the modern idiom, if it were not for the friendship.

1371 *and,* if; an uncommon use in Chaucer.

1389 *debaat,* strife.

1391 *blent,* blinds (contracted form of *blendeth).*

1407 Cf. the proverb, "The burnt child fears the fire"; and Skeat, EE Prov., pp. 121 f., no. 286.

1410 "Better late than never"; cf. Haeckel, p. 23, no. 76.

1411 "Never is a long term"; see Skeat, EE Prov., p. 122, no. 287.

1413 *Bayard,* a common name for a horse. "As bold as blind Bayard" was a proverbial comparison; see Skeat, EE Prov., pp. 122 f., no. 288.

1418 f. Cf. *MLT,* II, 552 f.

1422 *rape and renne,* seize and lay hold of (?); an alliterative phrase of uncertain origin, which occurs in various forms: *rap(e) and ren(ne), rap and rend* (or *wring), rive and rend.* It is sometimes regarded as a corruption of AS. "hreapian and hrinan." But the NED derives *rape* rather from Lat. "rapere," OF. "raper."

1428 Arnoldus de Villa Nova (c. 1235–1314) was the author of a treatise on alchemy entitled Rosarium Philosophorum. Skeat quotes a reference to the saying of Arnold in a tract printed in Zetzner's Theatrum Chemicum, III, 285. But the passage which Chaucer appears to have used is in Arnold's treatise De Lapide Philosophorum. It is cited in full by Lowes, MLN, XXVIII, 229, with a reference to Arnaldus de Villanova, Opera, Lyons, 1532, fol. 304, recto. See also SA, p. 698, E. H. Duncan, MLN, LVII, 31 ff., and J. Ruska, Anglia, LXI, 136 ff.

On the Newe Toun, probably Villeneuve-Loubet in Provence, see F. P. Magoun, Jr., Med. Stud., XVII, 132.

1432 The "brother" of mercury was sulphur.

1434 Hermes Trismegistus was the supposed author of many works on magic and alchemy. The name was given by the Greeks to the Egyptian god Thoth, whose wisdom was held to be preserved in certain "Hermetical Books" dating from the second, third, and fourth centuries. See W. Scott, Hermetica, I, Oxford, 1924; also Pauly-Wissowa, Real-encyclopädie, s.v. Hermes Trismegistos, and the recent edition, translation, and commentary of Nock and Festugière, Corpus Hermeticum, Paris, 1945. For some account of his reputation in the Middle Ages see L. Thorndike, History of Magic and Experimental Science, London, 1923, II, 214 ff. A specimen of the works ascribed to him is printed in Zetzner's Theatrum Chemicum, IV, 592 ff.

1440 *Sol and Luna,* gold and quicksilver.

1447 *the secree of secrees,* commonly explained as an allusion to the treatise Secreta Secretorum, attributed to Aristotle (ed. Robert Steele, in Opera hactenus inedita, Rogeri Baconi, Fasc. v, Oxford, 1920). It is the main source of the seventh book of Gower's Confessio Amantis, and was translated into English by Lydgate and Burgh (ed. R. Steele,

EETS, 1894). But Manly (Canterbury Tales, New York, 1928, p. 653) took the phrase to mean simply "the best of secrets," and Young (MLN, LVIII, 98 ff.) argued convincingly in support of this interpretation. The idiom is of course familiar in biblical language.

1450 This reference is to the work printed in Zetzner's Theatrum Chemicum (V, 191 ff.) under the title Senioris Zadith Tabula Chimica. The story which Chaucer tells of Plato is in the Tabula related of Solomon (p. 224). The Arabic philosopher known as Senior was Muhammad ibn Umail, called Al-Ṣadiḳ, "the true" (probably the source of *Zadith*). On his Tabula see Ruska in Isis, XXIV, 310, and Spargo in SA, p. 686 n.

1457 *ignotum per ignocius,* explaining the unknown by the more unknown.

1460 On the four elements see *Gen Prol,* I, 420, n.

1470 *deffende,* forbid.

1479 *terme of his lyve,* for the duration of his life.

1481 *boote of his bale,* remedy for his evil.

FRAGMENT IX

The *Manciple's Prologue* and *Tale* constitute a separate group in the Six-Text print. Although the *Prologue* is not definitely linked to the *Canon's Yeoman's Tale,* the action is said to take place under the Blean Forest, at a point identified as either Harbledown or Up-and-Down Field in Thannington. It has usually been assumed, then, that the pilgrims had passed Boughton on their last day's journey toward Canterbury. But the possibility, long ago suggested by Ten Brink, that the *Manciple's Tale* was intended to start the homeward journey from Canterbury, has been recently urged again, with valid arguments, by Professor Root. See MLN, XLIV, 493 ff.; cf. *Pars Prol,* X, 16, n. The position of Fragment IX in the various classes of manuscripts is regularly just before the final Fragment X.

The Host's remarks to the Cook in the *Prologue* are puzzling, in view of the fact that the Cook had already taken part in the discussion and had told a (fragmentary) tale. See the introduction to the Explanatory Notes on the *Cook's Prologue.* Perhaps Chaucer meant to cancel the *Cook's Prologue* and *Tale,* and introduce the Cook for the first time in the *Manciple's Prologue.* Or, on the other hand, the *fabliaux* which finish Fragment I may have been written later than the *Manciple's Prologue,* and the discrepancy between the two left unadjusted. Both possibilities are supported by Skeat, in different places. See Oxf. Ch., III, 399, and V, 436.

A separate edition of the *Manciple's Tale,* or rather a reprint of it from the Lansdowne and Ellesmere MSS., accompanied by facsimiles of the Lansdowne text, was published by Dr. G. Plessow, Berlin, 1929. Though intended primarily as an introduction to palæography and textual criticism, the edition contains a phonetic transcription of the Ellesmere text, notes on sources, and an analysis of the formal rhetorical devices employed in the tale.

The date of Fragment IX is undetermined. Miss Hammond (pp. 254–57), although suggesting that the Manciple was one of several pilgrims added by afterthought to the *General Prologue,* nevertheless reckons his *Tale* among the earlier of the Canterbury series. Dr. Plessow also argues for an early date, finding evidence in the formal rhetorical type of narration and the free use of the Roman de la Rose. There is no close connection between the *Prologue* and the *Tale*, or indication that the latter was written with the particular situation in mind. Neither of them contributes particularly to the dramatic interplay of the pilgrimage. But Professor Severs in JEGP, LI, 1 ff., argues plausibly that Chaucer in his modifications of the story had the Manciple in mind.

The source of the *Tale* is Ovid's account of Apollo and Coronis (Met., ii, 531–632), which Gower also followed for his briefer version in the Confessio Amantis, iii, 768–817. The use of *my sone* in the opening and closing exhortations in Gower and in the Manciple's moral application has been taken as evidence that Chaucer recalled Gower's treatment of the story. But since the formula recurs constantly throughout the Confessio in the remarks of the priest, whereas the Manciple attributes it to his mother (*my dame*), any influence of Gower at this point must remain doubtful. Neither Chaucer nor Gower has been clearly shown to have used the other's version, and Chaucer's was in all probability the earlier in date.

The general theme, of the Tell-Tale Bird, was the subject of one of the stories in the romance of the Seven Sages, and Professor Tatlock has argued from an allusion in *WB Prol*, III, 232 f., that Chaucer perhaps knew that version of the tale. But in the *Manciple's Tale*, which is not very similar, he followed rather Ovid. See Tatlock, Dev. and Chron., p. 203, n. 3, and Plessow's edition, Beilage 2 (a detailed comparison of Chaucer's tale with Ovid's, in parallel columns). On the various analogues, European and oriental, see Clouston, in the Ch. Soc. Orig. and Anal., pp. 437 ff.; Skeat, Oxf. Ch., III, 501; V, 439; Killis Campbell, Seven Sages, Boston, 1907, p. xcvii ff.; Plessow's edition, pp. 94 ff. Mr. H. B. Hinckley has called the editor's attention to a version in Machaut's Livre du Voir-Dit, ed. P. Paris, Paris, 1875, pp. 317–330. Several versions, including that of Ovid and that of the Seven Sages, are printed by J. A. Work in SA, pp. 699 ff.

Chaucer's narrative is considerably expanded by moralizing comments, drawn from the *Parson's Tale*, probably from the De Arte Loquendi et Tacendi of Albertano de Brescia, and from other sources. References for particular passages are given below.

The Manciple's Prologue

2 *Bobbe-up-and-doun*, usually identified with Harbledown (spelled also *Herbaldoun* and *Hebbadonne*). For references to this place in early accounts of journeys to Canterbury see Furnivall, Temp. Pref. to Six-Text edn., Ch. Soc., 1868, pp. 31, 124, 127, 131. Another identification, with Up-and-Down Field, in Thannington, was proposed by J. M. Cowper, Athen., 1868, II, 886.

3 *Canterbury Weye*, later called the Canterbury Road. It is often difficult to tell whether references to the *wey* are specific or general. See *Gen Prol*, I, 771 n.

5 *Dun*, like *Bayard*, was a general name for a horse. The reference here is to a rural game, described in Brand's Popular Antiquities, ed. Hazlitt,

London, 1870, II, 308 f., and in Nares' Glossary, London, 1822, s.v. Dun. A heavy log was brought into a room, and the cry was raised "Dun is in the mire," the horse is stuck in the mud. Then two members of the company would try to move the log, and if they failed, the rest, one after another, would come to their aid. A number of allusions to the game are noted by Skeat. Cf. Haeckel, p. 50, no. 180.

9 *for cokkes bones*, a corruption of the oath "for Goddes bones." Cf. *Pars Prol*, X, 29.

12 *Do hym come forth*, make him come forth.

14 *a botel hey*, a small bundle of hay; here a symbol of worthlessness. For the construction, compare *a barel ale*, *Mk Prol*, VII, 1893; also *galon wyn*, l. 24, below.

18 *quene*, quean, wench (AS. "cwene").

23 "I had rather sleep (*slepe*, infin.) than (have) the best gallon of wine in Cheapside."

25 ff. For evidence that the enmity of cooks and manciples was traditional see F. Tupper, Types of Society, New York, 1926, p. 100.

29 *as now*, for the present. On the so-called pleonastic *as* see *Gen Prol*, I, 462, n.

33 *nat wel disposed*, i.e., indisposed in health.

38 A curse; apparently with reference to the belief that the devil entered through the open mouth. See Angl. Beibl., XIII, 306, for a story of a lad who was held to be possessed. He had the habit of keeping his mouth open, and the women said he did so in order that the Devil might easily pass in and out.

42 *atte fan*, at the vane of the quintain. On the game see Nares' Glossary, s.v. Quintain, and Strutt, Sports and Pastimes, ed. Hone, London, 1876, pp. 182 ff. (bk. iii, ch. 2); also the notes on Ben Jonson's Love's Welcome at Welbeck, ed. Cunningham, London, 1875, VIII, 125, 132. The vane or board was at one end of a cross-bar, which swung round on a pivot. At the other end hung a bag or a club. The jouster had to strike the fan and avoid the stroke of the bag.

44 *wyn ape*, ape-wine. The different stages of drunkenness, or its effects upon different men, were compared to various animals. According to the Kalendrier et Compost des Bergiers (Troyes [1480?], facsimile reprint, Paris, 1925, sig. F., xli f.), the choleric man has "vin de lyon"; the sanguine, "vin de cinge"; the phlegmatic, "vin de mouton"; and the melancholic, "vin de pourceau." Another tradition, found earliest in Rabbinical literature, says that when a man begins to drink he is like the lamb; then he becomes successively like the lion, the ape, and the sow. A number of references on the subject are collected in Skeat's note, and to them may be added the tractate De Generibus Ebriosorum et Ebrietate Vitanda, printed in Zarncke's Deutschen Universitäten, Leipzig, 1857, I, 116 ff. Classification in the last-named text is into "ebrietas asinina," "canina," "ebrii ut oves," "ut vituli et simiae," "sues." For other references to the use of the idea in stories and riddles see V. Hull and A. Taylor, Collection of Welsh Riddles (Calif. Pub. in Mod. Phil., XXVI, No. 3, Berkeley, 1942), p. 298 n.

The cook is satirically described as ape-drunk. Instead of being foolishly playful, he is really surly and dull.

50 *chyvachee*, exploit of horsemanship. Miss Rickert, noting the possibility that the cook's name was Roger Knight, has suggested that *chyvachee* may be one of the few cases of word-play in Chaucer. See *TLS*, 1932, p. 761.

51 "Alas that he did not stick to his ladle!"

57 *dominacioun*, a common term in both physiology and astrology. See *KnT*, I, 2749 ff., and n.

72 *Reclayme*, a technical term, meaning to bring back a hawk by holding out a *lure*.

85 *if I may*, if I have power (to make him). On the formula see *ML Intro*, II, 89, n.

90 *pouped*, blown. There is a play here upon the double meaning of horn, drinking horn and wind instrument.

The Manciple's Tale

105 Chaucer may have got his idea of Phoebus's life on earth from two or three passages in Ovid: Ars Amat., ii, 239–40; Met., i, 438 ff., ii, 679 ff.

109 *Phitoun*, the Python. See Ovid, Met., i, 438 ff.

116 *Amphioun*, Amphion. Cf. *MerchT*, IV, 1716, and n. The story of Amphion was so familiar that no particular source need be assumed for it. Passages which Chaucer may have known are Horace, Ars Poetica, 394 ff.; Statius, Thebaid, i, 9 ff.; Boccaccio, De Gen. Deorum, v, 30.

133 Ovid likens the crow to doves, geese, and swans. Chaucer and Gower mention only the swan.

139 Coronis of Larissa, according to Ovid.

148 ff. The sentiment here expressed was a commonplace in literature and popular proverbs. Cf. the parallels cited in *WB Prol*, III, 357–61, n. But the present passage, as indicated by a marginal note in MS. Hg, is based upon the Liber Aureolus de Nuptiis of Theophrastus (quoted in Jerome, Adversus Jovinianum, i, 47, Migne, Pat. Lat., XXIII, 277). On Chaucer's other use of this work see the introduction to the Explanatory Notes on the *WB Prol*.

160 ff. Cf. RR, 14027–30, which is preceded by the illustration of the caged bird (ll. 13941–58). Chaucer doubtless also had in mind Horace, Epist. i, 10, 24, on which Jean de Meun comments. It is quoted again in John of Salisbury's Polycraticus, iii, 8 (ed. Webb, Oxford, 1909, I, 191). For a similar idea compare further *LGW*, 2446 ff.; *Tr*, i, 218 ff.

163 ff. The illustration by the caged bird is found in Boethius as well as in the *Roman de la Rose*. See SA, pp. 719 f. Chaucer employed it again in the *Squire's Tale* (V, 610 ff.), where he clearly followed Boethius; here in the *Manciple's Tale*, however, he seems rather to have used the French version. Compare Angl., XIV, 261 f., for a chronological theory.

175 ff. The parallels of the cat and the she-wolf are from RR, 14039–52, 7761–66. For further information on this animal lore see O. F. Emerson, Rom. Rev., XIII, 146 f.

183 *vileyns*, properly the genitive of *vileyn*, though it came to be felt as an adjective and developed the adverb *vileynsly* (*ParsT*, X, 154).

187 *by*, with reference to.

193 *with meschaunce*, a mild curse.

195 *sowneth into*, is consonant with. See *Gen Prol*, I, 307, and n.

207–08 Cf. *Gen Prol*, I, 742, n.

210–37 With the Manciple's excuse Fansler (p. 222) compares that of Reason, RR, 6987–7184.

226 This anecdote about Alexander was familiar. See Cicero, De Republica, iii, 12; St. Augustine, De Civ. Dei, iv, c. 4; Gesta Romanorum, c. 146; John of Salisbury, Polycraticus, iii, 14 (ed. Webb, Oxford, 1909, I, 224 f.); Higden, Polychronicon, III, 422 (Rolls Series).

235 *textueel*, familiar with texts, learned in the authorities.

258 *sadde tokenes*, sure signs.

265 Both Chaucer and Gower omit the pathetic circumstances related by Ovid, that Coronis begs Phoebus not to slay her unborn child.

279 *trouble wit*, troubled, clouded mind. With the whole passage on *ire* compare *ParsT*, X, 537 ff., and *SumT*, III, 2005 ff.

292 ff. There is a whole class of tales, known to folk-lorists as "les pourquois," which account similarly for the appearance or other characteristics of animals.

301 Cf. *PF*, 363.

307 *which*, to whom.

314 f. Prov. xxi, 23.

317 With this formula cf. *WP Prol*, III, 576.

318 *My sone*. The repetition of this form of address, though appropriate enough to the Manciple's *dame*, was perhaps actually due in part to its recurrence in the Proverbs of Solomon (cf. xxiii, 15, 19, 26). Professor Tatlock (MLN, L, 296) also called attention to the occurrence of the phrase in gnomic collections.

318 ff. The counsels which follow are mostly familiar or proverbial, and in several cases of biblical origin. Koeppel (Herrig's Arch., LXXXVI, 44 ff.) argued that Chaucer's immediate source was the De Arte Loquendi et Tacendi of Albertano of Brescia, in which nearly all the ideas and some of the exact quotations are found. But his parallels are widely scattered in Albertano and are not always close to Chaucer. Dr. Fansler, who questions the influence of Albertano, cites (pp. 201 f.) alternative passages from RR. The more important parallels are noted below. References to Albertano are to the ed. of Thor Sundby, in Brunetto Latinos Levenet og Skrifter, Copenhagen, 1869, pp. lxxxv–cxix.

320 Proverbial; cf. Haeckel, p. 52.

325–28 Cf. Dionysius Cato (i, 12): "Nam nulli tacuisse nocet nocet, esse locutum" (quoted by Albertano, p. xcviii).

329 Cf. RR, 7037 ff. Albertano, p. cx, is not so close.

332 f. Cf. Dionysius Cato (i, 3): "Virtutem primam esse puto, conpescere linguam" (quoted by Albertano, p. xcvi); also RR, 12179 ff., and *Tr*, iii, 294.

335 ff. Cf. Albertano, p. cxv.

338 Prov. x, 19 (quoted by Albertano, p. cxv).

340 Ps. lvii, 4.

343 Prov. vi, 17.

345 Cf. Prov. x, 19, and 31; xvii, 20; xxvi, 28. Among passages on the subject in the Psalms, Skeat notes Ps. x, 7; xii, 3; lii, 2; lxiv, 3–8; cxx, 2–3. By *Senekke* is probably meant Seneca's treatise De Ira, used by Chaucer in the *Summoner's Tale* (III, 2018 ff.). But, as Skeat notes, *Senek* is often used in the *Melibee* for the Sententiae of Publilius Syrus

350 For parallels to the proverb, "of little medlyng cometh rest," see Skeat, EE Prov., p. 124, no. 290; and H. E. Rollins, ed. Paradise of Dainty Devices, Harv. Univ. Press, 1927, p. 251. A Flemish form of it, "Luttel onderwinds maakt groote rust," is cited by Grauls and Vanderheijden in the Revue Belge de Phil. et Hist., XIII, 746. For a similar reference, also unexplained, see the *Ck Prol*, I, 4357.

355 ff. Another commonplace. Cf. Albertano, p. xcviii (quoting Horace, Epist. i, 18, 71); RR, 16545 f.; Haeckel, p. 53; and A. Dickson, MLN, LXII, 562.

357 Koeppel and Skeat compare Albertano, p. cvi (not quite parallel).

359 Cf. Dionysius Cato (i, 12): "Rumores fuge, neu studeas novus auctor haberi."

FRAGMENT X

Fragment X, which is regularly the final fragment in the MSS., comprises the *Parson's Prologue* and *Tale*, and the author's *Retractation*. The *Parson's Prologue* seems to be perfectly linked by its first line to the *Manciple's Tale*, which precedes, and Fragments IX and X might consequently be regarded as a single fragment. But there is some doubt about the reading *Manciple* in l. 1. In the Hengwrt MS. the word is written over an erasure, and in MS. Christ Church the Yeoman is named instead, and his tale precedes. Possibly Chaucer left the space blank, and the Manciple's name was inserted by the scribe or editor who finally combined the fragments. Aside from the questionable reading in l. 1, there is reason to doubt whether Chaucer meant Fragment X to follow as it stands. The *Manciple's Tale* was begun in the morning (IX, 16), and cannot have lasted till four in the afternoon (X, 2 ff.). Chaucer must have planned other stories for the interval; perhaps one by the Cook, whose place the Manciple generously took for the moment; possibly, as Mr. Hinckley has suggested to the editor, one in alliterative verse, which would have given special point to the Parson's remark in l. 43. But the Parson's reference to alliteration was natural enough without this explanation. Skeat held that Chaucer wished to recognize the Vision of Piers the Plowman.

The Parson's Prologue

1 *Maunciple.* On the reading, see the introductory note just preceding.

2 *south lyne.* The altitude of the sun was 29°, which means, for April 20th, that the time was about 4 P.M. With the sun at that angle an object six feet high would cast a shadow eleven feet long. For the same method of calculating time, see also *ML Prol*, II, 7 ff.

10 The Moon's exaltation was Taurus, whereas Libra was the exaltation of Saturn. Since Libra would be actually ascending at the time indicated, this must be the sign intended. Chaucer either forgot his astrology for the moment, or confused the "exaltation" with the "face" of the Moon, which was the first ten degrees of Libra. For the reading *in mene Libra*, see the Textual Notes. Skeat was apparently right in rejecting it, and with it the calculations of the date of *CT* which had been based upon

it. See his notes, p. 445, and also Wells, p. 681.

16 Whatever tales were still to be written, Chaucer apparently intended the Parson's to be either the last on the journey to Canterbury, or the last on the return to Southwark. For the query whether it was perhaps to be saved for the latter place see Manly, p. 655; and cf. the suggestion that the *Manciple's Tale* was also meant for the return from Canterbury, in the introduction to the Explanatory Notes on Fragment IX.

23 *arte, artow* with reduced stress on the last syllable.

29 *for cokkes bones*; see *Manc Prol*, IX, 9, n.

32 I Tim. i, 4; iv, 7; II Tim. iv, 4.

39 The conjunction *that* is occasionally employed in Mid. Eng. to repeat *if, when, as,* etc. See *ParsT*, X, 740; *PF*, 312; *Bo*, i, m. 3, 7; and cf. similar uses of Fr. "que."

42 The alliterative verse of Chaucer's century was written mainly in the Northern and West Midland dialects. Hence a southern man could not be expected to be familiar with it.

43 *geeste*, the usual sense is "to tell a tale, a geste." Skeat remarks that it has here no reference to the form of the story. But in the *Prol Mel* (VII, 933) the corresponding noun seems to designate a form of writing distinct from either prose or rime. It looks as if Chaucer applied the term especially to alliteration, and Skeat himself notes that one important alliterative poem bore the title "Gest Hystoriale" (of Troy). In support of the application to alliteration see G. Bone (Med. Aev., VII, 226) citing Knighthode and Bataile, l. 1276.

The nonsense-words *rum-ram-ruf*, which here simply indicate the consonantal repetition, were current in both French and English in similar uses. For examples see Skeat's note.

49 See, for the same idea, the opening paragraph of the *ParsT*. Miss K. O. Petersen, The Sources of the Parson's Tale, Radcliffe College Monograph No. 12, Boston, 1901, p. 3, n. 5, compares also the last chapter of L'Ymage du Monde, by St. Pierre de Luxembourg.

51 See Rev. xxi, 2.

57 *textueel*, learned in the texts, hence exact, accurate. Cf. *MancT*, IX, 316.

58 *sentence*, substance, essential meaning. For the same distinction see the *Prol Mel*, VII, 947.

67 *hadde the wordes*, was the spokesman (Fr. "avoit les paroles").

The Parson's Tale

The *Parson's Tale* is a sermon on Penitence, in which is embodied a long treatise, originally separate, on the Deadly Sins. Its authorship has been much disputed, some critics denying it to Chaucer altogether, and others maintaining that it is heavily interpolated. Both style and subject-matter, in places, have been suspected as un-Chaucerian. According to one theory, developed in an elaborate essay by H. Simon, the original tale was a Wyclifite treatise, to which orthodox additions were made in the first decade of the fifteenth century. By other scholars other methods have been used for detecting supposed interpolations. But, in spite of all their attacks, present opinion is decidedly in favor of the authenticity of the whole work. The supposition that Chaucer was a Wyclifite and meant the Parson to represent Wyclif or one of his followers, is now generally abandoned (See the note on the Parson in the Explanatory Notes on the *Gen Prol*.) Many portions of the tale which were suspected to be interpolations have been found to correspond to passages in texts which presumably represent Chaucer's source. And althout the treatise is undeniably dull, as compared with Chaucer's original tales in verse, it nevertheless contains many characteristically Chaucerian terms of expression. Moreover Chaucer appears to have used in his recognized works numerous passages of the tale. For a full discussion of the question of authorship and interpolation, with a digest of earlier opinions, see H. Spies, Festschrift für L. Morsbach, Halle, 1913, pp. 626 ff. Simon's essay, Chaucer a Wyclifite, is published in the Chaucer Society Essays, Pt. iii, 1876, and a dissertation of W. Eilers, supporting a different theory of interpolation, was translated and printed in the same series of Essays, Pt. v, 1884. The principle arguments before Spies, in defense of the unity and authenticity of the tale were those of Furnivall, Trial Forewords, Ch. Soc., 1871, p. 113; Koch, Angl., II, 540 ff.; V, Anz., 130 ff.; Herrig's Arch., LXIX, 464; and Litblt., 1885, Sp. 326; and Koeppel, Herrig's Arch., LXXXVII, 33 ff.

Chaucer's immediate source has not been found. It was long supposed that he derived the material on the Deadly Sins from the Somme des Vices et des Vertus of Frère Lorens. But that portion of the treatise is now held to come from an untraced version of the Summa seu Tractatus de Viciis, of Guilielmus Peraldus (before 1261), and the sermon on Penitence, from some version of Raymund of Pennaforte's Summa Casuum Poenitentiae (before 1243) See Miss Petersen, Sources of the *ParsT*; Spies, p. 647; and Koeppel, Herrig's Arch., LXXXVII, 47 ff. (where it is argued, from certain parallel passages, that Chaucer also made some use of Frère Lorens). For a detailed comparison of Chaucer's treatise with that of Frère Lorens, see Eilers. A list of related texts is given by Miss Petersen, p. 80, n. 1. See also, on one Middle English analogue, the Clensyng of Mannes Sowle (in MS. Bod. 923), M. H. Liddell, in An English Miscellany presented to Dr. Furnivall, Oxford, 1901, pp. 255 ff., and Spies, Neue Philologische Rundschau, 1902, pp. 115 ff. On Gaytringe's Sermon on Shrift, see F. Tupper, MLN, XXX, 11; and on still another similar treatise (in MS. Bod. 90), see Liddell, Acad., XLIX, 447, 509. A good general account of religious manuals of the type is given by H. G. Pfander, JEGP, XXXV, 243 ff. See also Mrs. G. Dempster in SA, pp. 723 ff. She prints passages from Pennaforte and Peraldus, from an Anglo-Norman Compileisun, and from Frère Lorens. D. R. Johnson, in PMLA, LVII, 51 ff., discusses the passage on homicide, which he traces to Pennaforte. A. L. Kellogg, Traditio, VIII, 424 ff., has questioned Chaucer's use of Peraldus because his order of the sins correponds rather to that of Gregory. On quotations from St. Bernard in the tale see G. Sanderlin, MLN, LIV, 447 ff.

Professor Tupper's theory that Chaucer meant the *Canterbury Tales* as a whole to be a more or less systematic exposition of the Seven Deadly Sins has been discussed in the introduction to the Explanatory Notes on the *CT*. It does not derive any strong support from parallels between the *Parson's Tale* and those of the other pilgrims.

Since the exact original of the *Parson's Tale* is unknown, the relation of this text to its sources cannot be traced in detail, and the meaning of some passages cannot be explained to complete satisfaction. But account is taken in the following notes of the parallels pointed out by Miss Petersen and by Spies. References are also given, where the editor found it possible, to the ultimate source of quotations from the Bible and other authors, and to significant parallel passages in Chaucer's other works. Most of this material was of course brought together by Skeat and his predecessors. Miss G. W. Landrum, in an unpublished Radcliffe dissertation on Chaucer's Use of the Vulgate, has pointed out a number of biblical quotations where Chaucer is closer to the original text than the intermediate sources he is supposed to have followed. In the following notes references are not always given for familiar biblical persons and events; of course such citations might be indefinitely multiplied. Unless otherwise noted, references are to the English Authorized Version.

Whether Chaucer was the first to bring together the Sermon and the Treatise on the Sins or found them already combined in his source, has not been proved. Miss Petersen expressed the latter opinion (p. 80). Koeppel (Herrig's Arch., LXXXVII, 48), and Spies (p. 720) both argue that Chaucer made the combination. The language of Chaucer's source, or sources, is also uncertain. Miss Petersen says "perhaps Latin." But certain indications — adjectival plurals in -*s*, adjectives placed after nouns, the quotation in v. 248, for example — point rather to French. On this point, and on the general relation of the tale to similar manuals, see also H. G. Pfander, JEGP, XXXV, 243 ff.

The date of the tale is also undetermined. Skeat, Oxf. Ch., III, 503, put it before 1380 — along with the *Melibee*. Koch (Chronol. of Chaucer's Writings, Ch. Soc., 1890, p. 79) and Ten Brink (Litgesch., II, 189 f.) assigned it to Chaucer's last years. For references to other estimates see Miss Hammond, p. 320. The question is bound up, of course, with that of Chaucer's exact relation to his sources. If he made his translation at one time and from a single source, the date was probably early. For many passages from the Treatise on Sins appear to have been used in tales generally assigned to the eighties. But if the two portions of the *Parson's Tale* came separately to Chaucer's hands, it is possible to assume, with Koeppel (p. 50), that he translated the Treatise on Sins early, and then wrote the Sermon on Penitence, in which he incorporated the older work, toward the end of his life. Positive evidence, however, is lacking of date of composition even for the Sermon on Penitence.

For an analysis of the structure of the *Parson's Tale*, showing its accordance with the principles of mediæval sermon writing, see C. O. Chapman, MLN, XLIII, 229 ff. On the characteristics of Chaucer's prose see references given in the introduction to the notes on *Boece*, p. 797.

Verse numbers refer to the subdivisions (usually sentences or clauses) made in the Six-Text print and carried over to later editions.

Correspondence between the *Tale* and the Summa of Pennaforte, Miss Petersen points out (p. 3), "begins with the first paragraph . . . and runs on pretty consecutively, with the exception of the break at the digression on sin . . ., almost to the end of the *Tale*."

The scripture text is from Jer. vi, 16 (Vulg.).

75 *perisse*, perhaps in the active sense, "destroy." The order of words is against Skeat's rendering, "that wishes no one to perish." But the reference is to II Pet. iii, 9, "nolens aliquos perire"; cf. Ez. xviii, 23, 32; and xxxiii, 11; I Tim. ii, 4.

79 *espirituels*, the French plural in *-s*, which is rare in Chaucer's verse, occurs frequently in *Mel* and *ParsT*. This suggests that the direct source of the latter, as of the former, was French.

80 Cf. *Pars Prol*, X, 49 ff.

82 *whennes it is cleped Penitence*; not taken up in Chaucer's text, though treated regularly by Pennaforte.

84 See St. Ambrose, Sermo xxv, §1 (Migne, Pat. Lat., XVII, 655).

85 Skeat quotes a sentence with similar meaning from the passage of St. Ambrose just cited. But Pennaforte refers to St. Augustine.

89 Skeat cites St. Isidore, Sententiarum, lib. ii, c. 13 (Migne, Pat. Lat., LXXXIII, 615) — a passage which is not precisely parallel.

92 See St. Gregory, In Septem Psalmos Poenitentiales Expositio, Ps. xxxvii, v. 8 (Migne, Pat. Lat., LXXIX, 572).

93 Cf. *PhysT*, VI, 286.

96 ff. *The firste . . . accioun of Penitence* (96) . . . *Another defaute* (99) . . . *The thridde defaute* (100).

The statement here is confusing, and Skeat suggested that the original must have described three *actions* of Penitence, and afterwards three *defects*. But no such lacuna is indicated by a comparison with Pennaforte's Latin. Pennaforte lists three actions of Penitence, and makes no mention of defects:

"Una est, quae novum hominem parturit, et fit ante baptismum. . . Altera vero poenitentia est, sive actio poenitentiae, quam quis post baptismum facit de mortalibus peccatis. Tertia est, quae fit de peccatis venialibus quotidianis."

97 See St. Augustine, Sermo cccli, c. 2 (Migne, Pat. Lat., XXXIX, 1537).

100 See St. Augustine, Epist. cclxv, §8 (Migne, Pat. Lat., XXXIII, 1089).

103 *slaughtre of children*, probably a reference to the accidental overlaying of them by nurses. See v. 575, below.

105 *naked*, thinly clad.

108 St. John Chrysostom. The exact passage is not identified. Skeat quotes a reference to "confessio" and "cordis contritio" in the 20th Homily on Genesis, c. iv (Migne, Pat. Gr., LIII, 170).

112 ff. The figure is not in Pennaforte. But Miss Petersen compares Bonaventura, De Dieta Salutis, tit. ii, De Poenitentia, and Spies (Morsbach Festschrift, p. 664) refers to the Clensing of Mannes Sowle, described by Liddell, Furnivall Miscellany, p. 265.

115 Really the words of John the Baptist, Matt. iii, 8.

116 Matt. vii, 20; cf. Haeckel, p. 34, no. 112.

119 Prov. xvi, 6.

125 Ps. cxix, 113.

126 Dan. iv, 10 ff.

127 Cf. Prov. xxviii, 13.

130 St. Bernard of Clairvaux. The quotation has not been identified. Skeat compares Sermo xi, §5 (Migne, Pat. Lat., CLXXXIII, 649).

134 Pennaforte has "Res dignas *confusione* agunt," and though he and Chaucer both cite Job, the reference seems to be really to Prov. xii, 4 (Vulg.).

135 *Ezechie*, Hezekiah. See Is. xxxviii, 15.

136 Rev. ii, 5.

138 Cf. II Pet. ii, 22.

141 Ezek. xx, 43.

142 II Pet. ii, 19. Both Chaucer and Pennaforte cite St. Peter, but the words are closer to John viii, 34, to which there is a marginal reference in the Latin MS.

143 Probably a reference to Job xlii, 6.

144 The quotation is not identified.

145 Also unidentified; it is attributed by Pennaforte simply to Philosophus.

150 See St. Augustine, Sermo ix, §16 (Migne, Pat. Lat., XXXVIII, 87).

151 This sentence, as Miss Petersen notes, seems to be a part of the quotation. *Take reward of*, have regard to.

156 Prov. xi, 22; cf. *WB Prol*, III, 784, n.

159 A marginal gloss in Pennaforte refers to Jerome, ad cap. 7, Oseae. Skeat refers to the Regula Monachorum, falsely attributed to St. Jerome (Migne, Pat. Lat., XXX, 319 ff.).

162 Rom. xiv, 10.

166 See St. Bernard, Sermo ad Prelatos in Concilio, §5 (Migne, Pat. Lat., CLXXXIV, 1098).

168 Cf. Prov. i, 28.

166 ff. A number of parallels between the following passages and the Pricke of Conscience are noted by Miss Petersen (pp. 12 ff.).

169 From St. Anselm, Meditatio Secunda (Migne, Pat. Lat., CLVIII, 724). The paraphrase is loose at the end.

174 Not identified in St. Jerome; probably based ultimately upon Ps. xcvii, 3, 4.

175 ff. Vv. 175–230 deal with the pains of Hell. They are not paralleled in Pennaforte. Miss Petersen notes that the primary source of some of them is St. Gregory's Moralia, ix, c. 63–66 (Migne, Pat. Lat., LXXV, 910–18). There is a similar account in the Pricke of Conscience, ll. 6552 ff., to which reference is given by Miss Petersen.

176 Job x, 20–22.

180 *at regard of*, in comparison with.

182 For the "dark light" Professor A. L. Kellogg has noted a parallel conception in the Moralia, ix, c. 65.

183 *shal turne hym al to peyne*, shall all turn to pain for him.

186 ff. *agayn, agayns*, over against, in place of.

189 I Sam. ii, 30; not from Jeremiah.

191 The reference is to Job xx, 25: "vadent et venient super eum horribiles" (Vulg.). Skeat notes that this is quoted in the Pricke of Conscience, l. 8592, with "demones" supplied before "horribiles"; also that Wyclif's version has "orrible fendis."

defouled, trampled upon.

193 Ps. lxxv, 6 (Vulg., somewhat expanded). *oneden . . . to*, united to, centered upon.

195 Deut. xxxii, 24, 33.

196 *forther over*, a frequent connective in the *Tale*. On Chaucer's use of it see Spies, Morsbach Festschrift, p. 719.

198 Is. xiv, 11.

201 Micah vii, 6.

202 *flesshly*, carnally.

204 Ps. x, 6 (Vulg.).

208 Matt. xiii, 42; xxv, 30.

209 Is. xxiv, 9.

210 Is. lxvi, 24.

211 Job x, 22.

214 From St. Gregory, Moralium, lib. ix c. 66 (Migne, Pat. Lat., LXXV, 915).

216 Rev. ix, 6.

217 Cf. "et nullus ordo," Job x, 22.

220 Ps. cvii, 34 (loosely quoted).

221 St. Basil the Great, bishop of Caesarea (329–79). See his Homilies on the Psalms, on Ps. xxviii, 7, §6 (Migne, Pat. Gr., XXIX, 298).

223 "sempiternus horror inhabitat," Job x, 22.

227 Prov. xi, 7.

229 Quotation unidentified. Cf. Eccl. i, 18.

230 The quotation from St. Augustine is also unidentified.

231 At this point Chaucer returns to the subject-matter of Pennaforte.

236 Ezek. xviii, 24.

238 The reference to St. Gregory has not been traced.

248 Again quoted, as verse, in *Fortune*, l. 7. Its appearance here favors the supposition that Chaucer's original was in French.

252 "to pay his debt with." On the order see *Gen Prol*, I, 791, n.

253 The passage in St. Bernard is unidentified. It is also referred to in the Pricke of Conscience, 5653.

256–82 This passage does not correspond exactly to anything in Pennaforte.

256 This quotation has also not been traced.

269 The quotation from St. Augustine is not identified.

273 Probably a reference to Ps. lxix, which was commonly applied to the sufferings of Christ.
And therfore . . . manere; this and other shorter clauses were apparently supplied by the scribes, who felt the need of an introductory sentence.

274 Quotation unidentified.

281 Is. liii, 5.

284 John xix, 19.

286 Matt. i, 21.

287 Acts iv, 12.

288 For the etymology compare Dan Michel, Ayenbite of Inwyt, ed. Morris, EETS, 1866, p. 118. It apparently rests upon association with Heb. "netzer," branch, sprout, as in Is. xi, 1; xiv, 19; lx, 21.

289–90 Rev. iii, 20.

300 *and nat repente*, and not to repent (infinitive used coördinately with the noun *repentaunce*).

303 St. Augustine, De Vera et Falsa Poenitentia, 24 (Migne, Pat. Lat., XL, 1121).

307 Ps. xcvii, 10.

309 Ps. xxxii, 5. Chaucer seems to be following Pennaforte's exact words: " 'Dixi,' id est, firmiter in animo proposui."

313 Cf. Eph. ii, 3. Miss Petersen notes that

Pennaforte has at this point a column and a half of quotations not taken over by Chaucer.

317 Chaucer omits the consideration of the second point, *wheither it oghte nedes be doon or noon*. The discussion of the third point, *whiche thynges been covenable to verray Confessioun*, he defers until after a threefold digression on Sin, vv. 321–981.

320 *and noght avaunte thee*, and he must not boast. The change of subject is confusing.

321–981 The tract on Sin, which interrupts the course of the sermon on Penitence, falls into three parts: (1) vv. 321–86, a general introduction, which corresponds to scattered passages in Pennaforte (collected by Miss Petersen, p. 34, n. 2; (2) vv. 387–955, the systematic account of the Seven Deadly Sins, based ultimately on Peraldus; and (3) vv. 960–81, a discussion of the circumstances which aggravate Sin, expounded by Pennaforte as the fifth topic of Confession.

322 Rom. v, 12.

325 Cf. Gen. iii, 1–7.

331 Cf. Pennaforte, quoted by Miss Petersen, p. 30. He cites St. Augustine.

334 *contract*, contracted (short form of the participle).

336 Cf. I John ii, 16; also Pennaforte, quoted by Miss Petersen, p. 27.

337–40 Skeat notes the close agreement with the Ninth of the Articles of Religion.

342 Gal. v, 17.

343 II Cor. xi, 25–27.

344 Rom. vii, 24.

345 Cf. St. Jerome, Epistola xxii ad Eustachium, De Virginitate, §7 (Migne, Pat. Lat., XXII, 398).

348 James i, 14.

349 I John i, 8.

351 *subjeccioun*, suggestion, i.e., temptation. MSS. En¹ Se La read *suggestion*. But this was a recognized sense of the Lat. "subiectio."
bely, bellows.

355 *by the devel*, concerning the Devil. The source of this supposed utterance of Moses is unidentified.

357 Cf. v. 331, above, and n.

362–64 Miss Petersen (p. 7, n. 1) quotes a parallel passage from Pennaforte, based upon St. Augustine. The proverb occurs there in the form: "Levia multa faciunt unum grande." Cf. "Many littles make a mickle," Skeat, EE Prov., pp. 124 f., no. 292; Haeckel, p. 14, no. 45.

365 *The love of* is inserted by Koch; an attractive emendation, but without manuscript support.

368 Quotation not traced in St. Augustine; other occurrences of it are noted by Miss Petersen, p. 34, n. 2.

371–81 A close rendering of a passage of St. Augustine cited by Pennaforte. See Miss Petersen, p. 34, n. 2.

376 Cf. Matt. xxv, 43.

383 The quotation from St. Augustine has not been traced. For another occurrence of it see Miss Petersen, p. 35, n.

385–86 Cf. Pennaforte, quoted by Miss Petersen, p. 30.

387–955 Correspondences between this section and the Tractatus de Viciis of Peraldus are given in parallel columns by Miss Petersen, pp. 36 ff.

387 *spryng*, source (or perhaps *spryngen*, pl.). If

taken as a verb, *sprynge(n)* gives a sense opposite to the one expected.

388 Cf. Ecclus. x, 15, quoted by Peraldus.

390 The number of branches assigned to Pride varies considerably in different treatises. See Miss Petersen's note, p. 36, n. 3; also Liddell, Acad., XLIX, 509.

406 *clappen as a mille;* doubtless a stock comparison. See *ClT*, IV, 1200.

407 This reference to precedence seems not to occur in the recognized sources of the *Parson's Tale.* Lowes (MP, VIII, 322 n.) has pointed out the possibility that Chaucer had in mind Deschamps (Miroir de Mariage, ll. 3376–81, 3292–93, 3305–07, 3311–20). In a matter of popular custom like this, however, it is hardly safe to assign a particular literary source. Cf. *Gen Prol,* I, 449 ff.

Kisse pax, to kiss the "pax," a small piece of wood or metal used at the Mass for the "kiss of peace."

411 *leefsel,* arbor. Cf. *RvT,* I, 4061.

413 Luke xvi, 19.

414 See St. Gregory, Homiliarum in Evangelia, ii, 40, §3 (Migne, Pat. Lat., LXXVI, 1305).

415 *costlewe,* costly. For the suffix, cf. *dronkelewe, PardT,* VI, 495, n.

423–31 Chaucer's discussion here is more detailed than that of Peraldus. Liddell (Acad., XLIX, 509) notes a parallel in this respect in the sermon in MS. Bodl. 90.

427 *fir of seint Antony,* erysipelas, which St. Anthony was supposed to cure. Mr. J. U. Nicolson (The Complete Works of Villon, tr., N.Y., 1931, pp. 256 f.) explains the name by the fact that the order of St. Anthony in the Dauphiné nursed the sick in an epidemic of the disease in the 13th century.

429 *honestitee,* decency; in vv. 431, 436, it seems rather to mean "dignity."

434 Zech. x, 5.

435 See Matt. xxi, 7. The reference to the disciples' garments is not in Peraldus.

440 *hostilers,* servants (ostlers); so perhaps also in *Gen Prol,* I, 241.

442 Ps. lv, 15.

443 See Gen. xxxi; xlvii, 7.

445 The illustrations are not in Peraldus.

Wilde fir, some burning spirit, like the flaming brandy around Christmas pudding.

452 *delivernesse,* "agilitas" (Peraldus); *franchise,* "libertas."

457 Cf. *Words of Host,* VI, 299 f.

459 Cf. Gal. v, 17.

460 *causeth ful ofte many a man to peril,* bringeth . . . to peril. The idiom seems not to be exactly paralleled elsewhere.

461 ff. For the argument cf. *WBT,* III, 1109 ff.; also *Gentilesse.*

467–68 From Seneca, De Clementia, i, 3, 3, and i, 19, 2, quoted by Peraldus.

472 Cf. *KnT,* I, 1255–56.

473 Cf. *ClT,* IV, 1000.

475–83 There is no close agreement to be noted between the first six "remedia" of *ParsT,* and the tract of Peraldus. See Miss Petersen, p. 45, n. 3.

483 *to stonde . . . to,* to abide by.

484 The *philosophre* is not identified. For the quotation from St. Augustine, see his treatise on Ps. civ, 25 (Migne, Pat. Lat., XXXVII, 1399). Cf. also *PhysT,* VI, 114 ff.

485 On the general conception of the sin against the Holy Ghost, cf. Matt. xii, 32.

500 Ps. xxxvii, 7.

502 John xii, 4–6 (where the reference is not to the Magdalen, but to Mary, the sister of Martha).

504 Luke vii, 39.

506 Peraldus cites Matt. xx, 11 (Petersen, p. 48).

512 Matt. xxii, 37 ff.; Mark xii, 30 f.

526 Matt. v, 44.

532 *The speces of this paas,* the kinds of this grade or degree.

535 From St. Augustine, De Civ. Dei, bk. xiv, c. 15, §2 (Migne, Pat. Lat., XLI, 424).

536 The *philosophre* not identified. Skeat quotes Horace, Ep. i, 2, 62: "Ira furor breuis est." But neither this nor the passage from Peraldus cited by Miss Petersen (p. 49) is quite parallel to Chaucer.

537 *trouble,* troubled (adj.).

539 Eccl. vii, 4 (Vulg.): "Melior est ira risu."

540 Ps. iv, 5 (Vulg.).

544 Cf. *SumT,* III, 2005 ff.

549–56 Not paralleled in Miss Petersen's citations from Peraldus.

551 See St. Isidore, Etymol., xvii, c. 7 (Migne, Pat. Lat., LXXXII, 615). The story is told of the "juniper," which Isidore derives from the Gk. πῦρ, fire. In v. 552 the allusion is clearly to the kindling of the New Fire on Holy Saturday. This was noted (as Professor Karl Young has brought to the editor's attention) by Mr. J. N. Dalton, The Collegiate Church of Ottery St. Mary, Cambridge, 1917, p. 244. On the custom of kindling an Easter fire see J. E. Frazer, The Golden Bough, X (Balder the Beautiful, I), 3d ed., London, 1913, pp. 120 ff.

562 *oold wratthe,* "via inveterata," ultimately from. St. Augustine, Sermo lviii, 7 (Migne, Pat. Lat., XXXVIII, 397).

564 Cf. *SumT,* III, 2009 ff.

565 *sixe,* an error for three. The reference is to I John iii, 15.

566 Probably from Prov. xxv, 18.

568 Prov. xxviii, 15.

shepe, an unusual word glossed by either Chaucer or a scribe.

569 Prov. xxv, 21.

570–79 Not closely paralleled in Peraldus.

572 *in his defendaunt,* in his (own) defense. The unusual construction suggests that Chaucer was following a French original ("en se defendant"?).

574 Num. xxv, 17.

582 Ps. cxlv, 9.

588–90 Exod. xx, 7; Matt. v, 34–37.

591 ff. Cf. *PardT,* VI, 472 ff., and n., 635, 651, 708.

592 Jer. iv, 2.

593 Ecclus. xxiii, 11.

594–97 This passage again departs from Peraldus.

597 Acts iv, 12.

598 Phil. ii, 10. The manuscripts have a broken construction which should perhaps be retained. See M-R CT, IV, pp. 419, 532.

599 Cf. James ii, 19.

601–07 Not paralleled in Peraldus.

603 ff. Cf. *Pard Prol,* VI, 350. The references that follow are to various sorts of magic or divination. Basins of water or swords were sometimes use instead of mirrors in catoptromancy. Circles were drawn on the ground, to confine the spirit invoked by sorcerers. The use of fire gave its name to "pyromancy," that of the shoulder-bone to "spatulomancy." Divination by birds is the familiar Roman augury. The commonest form of divination by beasts was by the inspection of its entrails after a sacrifice. The use of lots (*sort*) was familiar in the Middle Ages. On *geomancie*, divination by dots in the dust, see *KnT*, I, 2045, n. Divination by dreams and by strange noises is still familiar. References to these various practices are given by Skeat. They are nearly all described in Brand's Popular Antiquities (ed. Hazlitt, London, 1870). See also W. J. Thoms, Folk Lore Record, I, 176–79.

611 *he*, loosely used for "a man," "the person implied" (in the preceding clause).

614 Prov. xvi, 29, is cited by Peraldus.

617 Cf. *SumT*, III, 2075, n.; also the personal name *Placebo* in *MerchT*, IV, 1476.

619 I Cor. vi, 10.

620 Proverbial. "Curses, like chickens, come home to roost." Skeat notes Southey's use of it, in Greek, as a motto for the Curse of Kehama; cf. EE Prov., p. 125, no. 293. Peraldus quotes Prov. xxvi, 2, which was apparently interpreted in the same sense.

623 Matt. v, 22.

627 Matt. xii, 34; cf. Haeckel, p. 37, no. 124.

629 Prov. xv, 4.

Deslavee, lit. unwashed, foul (Fr. "deslaver"); used here to translate "immoderata."

630 The passage in St. Augustine (also quoted by Peraldus) is not identified. For the idea, cf. *WB Prol*, III, 244. The second reference is to II Tim. ii, 24.

631 Prov. xxvii, 15. Cf. *Mel*, VII, 1086, n.

633 Prov. xvii, 1. Cf. Haeckel, p. 9, no. 29.

634 Col. iii, 18. Cf. *WB Prol*, III, 160 f.

636 Wine was considered an antidote to the poison of the toad.

639 See II Sam. xvii, 1.

640 Cf. Ecclus. xxvii, 29 (quoted by Peraldus). *Fals lyvynge*, evil liver. This form (from "vivant"?) is perhaps another sign of a French original. See the introductory note.

642 Cf. Eph. ii, 14.

643 *is aboute to*, sets out to, is on the point of.

647 In Peraldus this idea is credited to St. Jerome, without a particular reference.

648 Cf. Matt., xii, 36 (quoted by Peraldus).

649 Eccl. v, 3.

650 *a philosophre*, "quidam philosophus" in Peraldus; not identified.

651 With *the develes apes* cf. *Goddes apes, Tr*, i, 913. *deffendeth*, forbids; see Eph. v, 4.

654–76 Not paralleled in Peraldus.

657 Cf. I Cor. xiii, 4, 5. The reference in St. Jerome has not been traced.

658 The *philosophre* is unidentified.

660 This reference has also not been traced. Cf. for the idea, Boethius, *Bo*, ii, pr. 7, 141 ff.

661 Matt. v, 9. Cf. *FranklT*, V, 773 ff. *The wise man*, Dionysius Cato. See the Disticha de Moribus, i, 38: "Quem superare potes, interdum vince ferendo."

664 Prov. xxix, 9.

665 Matt. xxvii, 35.

670 Skeat cites a story of similar purport from Seneca, De Ira, i, 15, 3. But Chaucer's anecdote is different.

677–85 Only the introductory sentence corresponds to Peraldus.

678 For the quotation from St. Augustine see v. 484, above, where it is applied, more properly, to envy.

679 Eccl. ix, 10.

680 Jer. xlviii, 10 (where the Vulgate has "fraudulenter" for *necligently*).

687 Probably a reference to Rev. iii, 16.

688 Cf. Prov. xviii, 9; xx, 4; xxi, 25.

690 The reference to St. Bernard has not been traced.

692 Quotation from St. Gregory also unidentified.

694 Skeat compares St. Augustine, De Natura et Gratia, c. 35 (Migne, Pat. Lat., XLIV, 266), and Sermo xx, §3 (Migne, XXXVIII, 140).

698 *seith* "creant," surrenders, owns himself beaten. On *creant*, a cry for mercy, apparently meaning "entrusting oneself to the enemy," see Ducange, s.v. Recredere; Godefroy, s.v. Recreant; NED, s.v. Creant.

700–01 Luke xv, 7, 24.

702–03 Luke xxiii, 42, 43.

705 Matt. vii, 7; John, xvi, 24.

709 Prov. viii, 17.

710 With this and v. 714 compare *SecN Prol*, VIII, 1–3.

712 Eccl. vii, 19 (Vulg.).

714 Cf. *KnT*, I, 1940, and n.

716 Perhaps a reference to Matt. xi, 12, and, for the words of David, Ps. lxxiii, 5.

721 It has been suggested that the *newe sheepherdes*, who do not appear in Peraldus, as cited by Miss Petersen, may have been intended by Chaucer as a reference to the government being taken over by Gloucester in 1388.

723 Skeat refers to St. Bernard's Vitis Mystica, c. xix, §66 (Migne, Pat. Lat., CLXXXIV, 674–75). But the correspondence is not very close between that passage and the citation from St. Bernard in Peraldus.

725 II Cor. vii, 10.

728–37 Not paralleled in Peraldus, De Viciis. But Miss Petersen compares his treatment of Fortitude in the Summa Virtutum, i, 4.

734 *arn*, the Northern form of the plural (Mod. Eng. *are*), which is unusual in Chaucer.

739 I Tim. vi, 10. Cf. *Mel*, VII, 1130, n.

740 On the repetition of *when, if*, etc., by *that* see *Pars Prol*, X, 39, n.

741 St. Augustine, Enarratio in Psalmum, xxxi, part ii, §5 (Migne, Pat. Lat., XXXVI, 260).

748 Eph. v, 5.

751 Ex. xx, 3, 4.

752 *taylages*, taxes (lit. "taking by tally"). *Cariage* was a service of carrying, or a payment in lieu of the same. Cf. *FrT*, III, 1570. *Amercimentz*, fines inflicted "at the mercy" of an affixor.

753–74 Not paralleled in Peraldus. With ideas on gentility cf. *WBT*, III, 1109–76.

754 The reference should be to St. Augustine's De Civ. Dei., bk. xix, c. 15 (Migne, Pat. Lat., XLI, 643).

755 Gen. ix, 18–27 (not Gen. v).

759–63 From Seneca, Epist. xlvii (loosely rendered).

762   Cf. *MLT*, II, 1141, n.

766   Gen. ix, 26.

778   One *that* is superfluous, but the repetition is found in all the published MSS. except Ha. Compare v. 941, below. Perhaps correction should be made in both cases.

781 ff.   On Simon Magus see Acts viii, 17 ff.

788   *Damasie*, Pope Damasus I (336–84). Cf. St. Jerome, Contra Hierosolymitanum, §8 (Migne, Pat. Lat., XXIII, 361).

793   Cf. *PardT*, VI, 590 ff.

794–803   Not in Peraldus.

797   See Dan. xiii (Vulg.), or the apocryphal Book of Susannah.

804–17   These verses have only a slight correspondence to Peraldus.

819–20   From Phil. iii, 18, 19. Cf. *PardT*, VI, 505 ff., 529 ff.

822   Cf. *PardT*, VI, 549, 558.

828   See St. Gregory, Moralium, Lib. xxx, c. xviii, §60 (Migne, Pat. Lat., LXXVI, 556).

831–35   Not paralleled in Peraldus.

831   *Galien*, Galen. The references to him and to St. Augustine have not been traced.

837 ff.   Ex. xx, 14; Lev. xx, 10; xix, 20 (Vulg., "non morientur"); Deut. xxii, 21; Lev. xxi, 9.

839   See Gen. xix, 24 f.; Is. xix, 18.

841   Rev. xxi, 8.

842 ff.   See Matt. xix, 5; Gen. ii, 24; Eph. v, 25; Ex. xx, 17; Matt. v, 28.

843–51, 853–64   Not paralleled in Peraldus.

844   The reference to St. Augustine has not been traced.

850   The reference to *the prophete* is unidentified.

852   *that oother*, the second; for the first, see v. 830, above.

853   *basilicok*, the basilisk, or cockatrice, which was supposed to kill by a glance.

854   See Prov. vi, 26–29; vii, 26; Ecclus. xii, 13, 14; xiii, 1; xxvi, 10; and Skeat, EE Prov., pp. 125 f., no. 294.

858   *bushes*, which seems to be the right reading, has no published authority before Tyrwhitt (MSS. *beautees*, Thynne, *benches*).

859   Cf. *MerchT*, IV, 1839 ff.

861   Cf. St. Jerome, Contra Jovinianum, i, §11 (Migne, Pat. Lat., XXIII, 226).

864   Cf. Mark ix, 44.

867   See Gal. v, 19–21; Rev. xxi, 8.

869   See Matt. xiii, 8. The states of virginity, widowhood, and matrimony were likened, respectively, to the bringing forth of fruit a hundredfold, sixtyfold, and thirtyfold. Cf. St. Jerome, Contra Jovinianum, i, §3 (Migne, Pat. Lat., XXIII, 213).

The Latin citation at this point has been held to indicate that Chaucer's original was in Latin. But he may of course have found the words quoted in a French text.

879   I Cor. iii, 17.

880 f.   Gen. xxxix, 8, 9.

883   Cf. Gen. i, 28.

889   John viii, 11 (Vulg.).

894   Cf. *SumT*, III, 1869 ff.

895   II Cor. xi, 14.

897–98   See I Sam. ii, 12 (Vulg. "Liber Primus Regum"). Belial is explained in Judges xix, 22 (Vulg.), as meaning "absque iugo." Chaucer may have found this in French as "sans joug," and mis-

interpreted it as "sans juge" (Skeat). On the "free bull," who roamed with the herd, see G. C. Homans, RES, XIV, 447 ff.

900   *mysterie*, office (from Lat. "ministerium"); in I Sam. ii, 13 (Vulg.), the word is "officium."

904   Cf. St. Jerome, Contra Jovinianum, i, §49 (Migne, Pat. Lat., XXIII, 281).

906   See Tobias vi, 17 (Vulg.).

910   Cf. Rom. i, 26, 27.

911   Proverbial; see Skeat, EE Prov., p. 126, no. 295.

915–55   This last Remedium, unlike the other six, has a number of correspondences with Peraldus, as noted by Miss Petersen.

918   Eph. v, 32 (Vulg.); Gen. ii, 24.

919   John ii, 1–11.

921   The reference to St. Augustine has not been traced.

922   Eph. v, 23 ff.; I Cor. xi, 3.

923–38   Not paralleled in Peraldus. Sister Mariella (MLN, LIII, p. 251 ff.) points out the resemblance of the passage to the general argument of the Marriage Group and suggests that Chaucer may have been adding to his sources at this point. In any case, however, as she shows, the doctrine here presented was a commonplace of mediæval religious literature.

929   Eph. v, 25.

930   I Pet. iii, 1.

931   *the decree*, perhaps an untraced reference to the Decretals of Gratian.

932   Perhaps a reference to I Pet. iii, 3.

933   The passage in St. Jerome has not been traced. Perhaps the question about St. John refers to Rev. xvii, 4; xviii, 16.

934   See the ref. to St. Gregory in v. 414, above.

941–50   Not paralleled in Peraldus.

947   Matt. xxvi, 7; John xii, 3.

948   "She is the life of angels," i.e., she lives like them. The phrase does not seem natural, and may be due to some misunderstanding of the source. Sister Mary Immaculate, in MLQ, II, 65, suggests emending *lyf* to *lyk*, comparing as an ultimate source Mark xii, 25; but in a later personal note to the editor she queries whether the right reading may be *lyf* in the sense of "beloved."

949   Manly notes that *ne herte thynke* may be an addition of the Ellesmere group of MSS.

955   The comparison to Samson, David, and Solomon occurs in both Peraldus and Frère Lorens. Such lists were in fact proverbial, as pointed out by A. C. Friend (MP, XLVI, 117 ff.), who collects numerous literary uses of these and other examples.

957   *I lete to divines*, cf. *KnT*, I, 1323, where the remark is dramatically more appropriate, though the Parson may mean by *divines* the authorities in theology, as distinguished from a humble priest like himself. But Chaucer very likely wrote the passage without having him in mind. The general sentiment reappears several times in Chaucer's works, and may be taken as a characteristic expression of the author. Cf. *NPT*, VII, 3240 ff.; *HF*, 12 ff., 52 ff.

960–81   This section, on the circumstances which aggravate Sin, corresponds to the fifth topic of Confession in the Summa of Raymund de Pennaforte. (See the note to v. 321, above.) Miss Petersen notes (p. 35) that the substance of it is found in Frère Lorens and many other authors.

958 The passage in St. Augustine has not been traced. For other places where it is quoted see Miss Petersen, p. 35, n. Against v. 959 MS. El has the marginal note: "Memorandum mors intravit per fenestras."

971 *eschew*, reluctant (lit. "shy").

982 At this point Chaucer returns to the regular course of Pennaforte's treatise, taking up the third point mentioned in v. 317.

983 *Ezechias*, Hezekiah. See Is. xxxviii, 15.

985 Liber de Vera et Falsa Poenitentia, X, 25 (see K. Guinagh, MLN, LV, 211 f.).

986 See Luke xviii, 13.

988 I Pet. v, 6.

994 Matt. xxvi, 75.

996 Luke vii, 37.

998 The comparison to the wound is not found at this point in Pennaforte, though he has it in another connection. See Miss Petersen, p. 26. She cites other parallels on p. 20, n. 1.

1000 Cf. Luke xii, 46.

1003–05 On certain additions to Pennaforte's discussion here and in vv. 1008–11, see Miss Petersen, p. 24, n.

1003 Cf. *Mel*, VII, 1054, and n.

1005 Between vv. 1005 and 1006 Pennaforte has a passage corresponding to vv. 1025–27.

1015 *Caym*, Cain; see Gen. iv, 14. On Judas, see Matt. xxvii, 5.

1020 From St. Augustine, Sermo clxxxi, §4 (Migne, Pat. Lat., XXXVIII, 981).

1025–27 In Pennaforte the corresponding passage comes earlier. Cf. the note to v. 1005, above.

1025 The quotation from St. Augustine is not identified.

1028 The rubric *Explicit secunda pars Penitencie* also stands after v. 386, before the digression on the Seven Deadly Sins. But it is really in place here, after the conclusion of the third subdivision of Confession.

1032 Cf. Matt. xxv, 40 ff.

1036–37 Matt. v, 14–16.

1040–44 Not in Pennaforte. Miss Petersen (p. 28, n.) cites several parallels.

1043 Cf. note to v. 957, above. In this case, of course, the Parson might naturally not include himself among *maistres of theologie*.

1047 The quotation from St. Jerome has not been traced.

1048 Matt. xxvi, 41.

1054 Col. iii, 12.

1057 Pennaforte also names "timor" (*drede*) first and "pudor" (*shame*) second. But he proceeds to treat them in the reversed order.

1062 Cf. Ps. xliv, 20, 21; Heb. iv, 13.

1068 Cf. *ShipT*, VII, 9, and *MerchT*, IV, 1315. There is perhaps an allusion to Job xiv, 2.

1069 Cf. St. Gregory, Moralium, lib. xxxiv, c. 19, §36 (Migne, Pat. Lat., LXXVI, 738).

1073 Skeat suggests emending *seconde* to *same*, because the second kind of *wanhope* is discussed in v. 1074. But the confusion seems to lie in Chaucer's relation to his source. *The seconde wanhope* here corresponds to a second division of the first kind of despair ("desperatio veniae") in Pennaforte. With the second sentence of v. 1073, compare Ps. ciii, 17 (cited by Pennaforte).

1076–80 The peroration is not in Pennaforte.

Chaucer's Retractation

At the end of the *Parson's Tale*, in every MS. which has that tale complete, stands the so-called *Retractation* of the author. Its authenticity has been often questioned. But it has good support in the MSS., and the testimony of Gascoigne, in his Dictionarium Theologicum (printed by J. W. Hales, Athen., 1888, I, 404 f., and again in his Folia Litteraria, New York, 1893, pp. 110–11) shows that the story of Chaucer's death-bed repentance was believed in the fifteenth century. Instances more or less parallel have been noted by Kittredge, MP, I, 12 f.; Tatlock, PMLA, XXVIII, 521 ff.; and Wells, p. 747; and the list they give — which includes, among others, St. Augustine, Bede, Giraldus Cambrensis, Jean de Meun, Sir Lewis Clifford, Spenser, Herrick, Dryden, Ruskin, Ibsen, Tolstoi — might be easily extended. Henry Vaughan — while still young, to be sure — repented of the frivolous poetry of his earliest years. In Chaucer's own age Boccaccio is said to have turned, because of conviction of sin, from his licentious writing in Italian to the learned Latin treatises of his later years. (See E. Hutton, Giovanni Boccaccio, London, 1909, pp. 198 ff.) One other name may be added here, because it is also that of a contemporary of Chaucer: the Welsh poet, Llewelyn Goch, who repudiates in his Awdl i Dduw (Ode to God) his love-song to Lleucu Llwyd. See the Myvyrian Archaiology of Wales, London, 1801–07, I, 534; ed. Denbigh, London, 1870, p. 352. On the whole there is no sufficient reason for rejecting the *Retractation*. For detailed discussion see the references given by Miss Hammond, pp. 321–22; to which should be added H. Spies, in the Tobler-Festschrift, Braunschweig, 1905, pp. 383 ff.; Sister Madeleva, A Lost Language, New York, 1951, pp. 105 ff. Conjectures as to the date of the passage, and the manner of its insertion into the MSS., are discussed by Miss Hammond, pp. 262 f; see also R. M. Lumiansky, Tulane St. in Eng., VI, 5ff.

On the headings of the *Retractation* see the Textual Notes. It has reference primarily, of course, to the *Parson's Tale* itself, described as *this litel tretys* in v. 1081. The passage from v. 1084 to the middle of v. 1090 has been suspected to be an interpolation, but may have been inserted by Chaucer himself.

1083 Cf. II Tim. iii, 16.

1086 *The book of the ·xxv· Ladies*, the *Legend of Good Women*. Most MSS. read *xxv*, which was certainly in the archetype, o¹, according to Manly. Skeat emended to *xix*, or *nynetene*, to accord with the facts. The inaccuracy might be due to various causes, and is surely not reason enough for rejecting Chaucer's authorship of the *Retractation*. For further discussion see Miss E. P. Hammond, MLN, LXVIII, 514 f.

1087 *The book of the Leoun*, now lost; usually held to have been a redaction of Machaut's Dit dou Lyon (Œuvres, ed. Hoepffner, SATF, II).

Professor Manly questions whether Chaucer would have been likely to translate that work, and even suggests that the Wife of Bath's query (III, 692), *Who peyntede the leoun, tel me who?*, may have led somebody to infer that Chaucer wrote a book of this title. Professor Brusendorff, who also doubted that Chaucer translated Machaut's poem, suggested

(p. 429 f.) that the work here referred to was a re-daction of Deschamps's La Fiction (or Le Dict) du Lyon (Œuvres, SATF, VIII, 247 ff.), a satire on the political situation in France about 1380–82. But the case for Machaut's Dit dou Lyon has been reasonably restated by Langhans, Angl., LII, 113 ff. Chaucer gives evidence, in the *Book of the Duchess* and the *Troilus*, of having known the Dit, and if he made a version of it he would have been likely to

include it among the love-poems repudiated in the *Retractation*. For the suggestion that the book of the Leoun was adapted freely from Deschamps to compliment Prince Lionel on the occasion of his marriage see F. M. Dear, Med. Aev., VII, 105 ff.

1092 The full form of the invocation is, "Qui cum Patre et Spiritu Sancto vivit et regnat in saecula saeculorum."

The Book of the Duchess

Although the *Book of the Duchess* is not assigned to Chaucer by any of the copyists, its authenticity is sufficiently attested by *LGW* (*Prol F*, 418; *Prol G*, 406), and the Prologue to Bk. i of Lydgate's Falls of Princes. The Man of Law also, in the introduction to his *Tale* (II, 57), says of Chaucer, *In youthe he made of Ceys and Alcione*, having reference, apparently, to the passage in *BD* about Ceyx and Alcione. It is possible, however, that the episode was originally treated in an independent poem.

A note, said to be in the hand of John Stow, in the Fairfax MS., declares that Chaucer wrote the *Book of the Duchess* at the request of the Duke of Lancaster, "pitiously complaynynge the deathe of the sayd dutchesse blanche." Blanche of Lancaster, the first wife of John of Gaunt, died Sept. 12, 1369, and the poem, if it is an elegy upon her, was probably written soon after that date. Lancaster was remarried in 1372. For an argument against Stow's interpretation, see Langhans, Untersuchungen, pp. 280 ff. and Angl., LI, 350. Cf. also Samuel Schoenbaum, MLN, LXVIII, 121 f. Although there are difficulties in the way of the application to John of Gaunt, still the traditional view is probably right. For a biographical account of Blanche of Lancaster see M. Anderson, MP, XLV, 152 ff.

Opinions differ as to the presence of autobiographical material in the *Book of the Duchess*. It is hardly possible that the whole poem refers, as Langhans maintains, to Chaucer's unsuccessful love for a lady of high rank. But certain references in the poem (ll. 30 ff.), taken together with the *Complaint to Pity*, have often been interpreted as evidence of a long and hopeless love on the part of the poet. See Furnivall, Trial Forewords, pp. 35 ff.; Ten Brink, Geschichte der Eng. Lit., II (2d ed., Strassburg, 1912), 49 f. According to another theory, proposed by Fleay (Guide to Chaucer and Spenser, London, 1877, pp. 36–37), Chaucer's eight-year sickness was his unhappy married life. But in view of the conventional character of the passages in question their autobiographical value is very dubious. See the note to ll. 30 and 37 below, and cf. Lounsbury, Studies, I, 211 ff., and Sypherd, MLN, XX, 240 ff. For an attempt to show that Chaucer's lady was the Princess Joan, see Miss Margaret Galway, MLN, LX, 431 ff.; but cf. R. S. Loomis, MLN, LIX, 178 ff.

The literary influences behind the *Book of the Duchess* are almost wholly French. Parallels with the Roman de la Rose and with poems of Machaut and Froissart have long been recognized. Although

the opinion expressed by Sandras in his Étude sur Chaucer, Paris, 1859, that Chaucer's poem is a servile imitation of Machaut's Dit de la Fonteinne Amoureuse, is badly mistaken, yet the Dit may have furnished some hints for the general situation, and it apparently served, beside Ovid, as a subsidiary source for the Alcione episode. Chaucer's especial indebtedness to Machaut's Jugement dou Roy de Behaingne has been shown in detail. See, besides Skeat's introduction and notes, Max Lange, Untersuchungen über Chaucers Boke of the Duchesse, Halle, 1883; G. L. Kittredge in ESt, XXVI, 321 ff., MP, VII, 465 ff., and PMLA, XXX, 1 ff.; and Miss Anna T. Kitchel, Chaucer and Machaut's Dit de la Fontaine Amoureuse, Vassar Medieval Studies, New Haven, 1923, pp. 219 ff. Resemblances between the *Book of the Duchess* and Machaut's Dit dou Lyon are noted by Langhans, Angl., LII, 117 f. Possible influence of Le Regret of Jean de la Mote was pointed out by Constance L. Rosenthal, in MLN, XLVIII, 511 ff., and two complaints of Otes de Graunson are suggested by H. Braddy, MLN, LII, 487 ff.

On the type of vision to which both the *Book of the Duchess* and the *House of Fame* belong, see W. O. Sypherd, Studies in Chaucer's Hous of Fame, Chaucer Soc., 1907; also MLN, XXIV, 46, where special comparison is made of Le Songe Vert. There is a full collection and classification of the dreams in Anglo-Saxon and Middle English literature in an unpublished Harvard doctoral dissertation (1921) by E. C. Ehrensperger. For a noteworthy critical discussion of the *Book of the Duchess* see G. L. Kittredge, Chaucer and his Poetry, Cambridge, 1915, ch. 2. On the rhetorical artificiality of its structure see Manly, Chaucer and the Rhetoricians, Brit. Acad., 1926, pp. 8 ff. The character of the dreamer as related to that of the author has been recently the subject of considerable discussion. See J. R. Kreuzer, PMLA, LXVI, 543 ff.; H. R. Patch, MLN, LXVIII, 554 ff.; B. H. Bronson, PMLA, LXVII, 863; D. C. Baker, PMLA, LXX, 279 ff.; and especially K. Malone, Chapters on Chaucer, pp. 19–41, and H. R. Patch, On Re-reading Chaucer, pp. 33 ff.

1–15 Imitated from Froissart, Paradys d'Amours, ll. 1 ff. (Œuvres, ed. Scheler, Brussells, 1870, I). Froissart was long supposed to be the borrower. For evidence that his poem preceded Chaucer's see Kittredge, ESt, XXVI, 321 ff. Professor Kittredge (p. 336) also notes that the opening passage of the Paradys was suggested by several passages in Machaut's Dit de la Fonteinne Amoureuse.

The conditions here described are just such as, according to mediæval theory or general human experience, would have led to dreams. See Curry's remarks on the "somnium animale," pp. 233 ff.; also Kittredge, Chaucer and his Poetry, p. 58 ff.

16–21 Cf. the beginning of Machaut's first Complainte (Poésies Lyriques, ed. Chichmaref, Paris, 1909, I, 241).

23 Cf. Paradys d'Amours, l. 1.

23–29 With these lines and l. 42 cf. Machaut's Jugement dou Roy de Navarre, Œuvres, ed. Hoepffner, SATF, I, Paris, 1908, ll. 109–12.

30 On the inferences which have been drawn from this and related passages as to an unfortunate love affair of Chaucer's youth, see the introductory note, just above. Since the situation and the sentiments are paralleled again and again in the French poets of the period, it is safest to regard the account as pure convention. It is to be noted, however, that Chaucer assumes a different attitude in the *Troilus*, where he represents himself as an absolute outsider in the affairs of love.

31 *what me is*, what the matter is with me.

32 *who aske* (subjunctive), whoever may ask.

37 The specific mention of eight years has been taken as evidence of actual experience on Chaucer's part. But Prof. Loomis (MLN, LIX, 178 ff.) has pointed out that even this may have come from Machaut. Cf. further M. Galway, MLN, LX, 431 ff.

39–43 The comparison of the lady to a physician is a commonplace. Particular use may have been made here, however, of two passages in Machaut: Remede de Fortune (Œuvres, SATF, II), ll. 1467–69, and Dit dou Lyon, ll. 57–61 (Œuvres, SATF, II).

40 *but that is don*, i.e., no more of that.

44 ff. The introductory device of reading a book was held by Sypherd to be a regular convention of love-visions. For the argument that it did not become such until after Chaucer see M. W. Stearns, MLN, LVII, 28 ff.

45 Cf. Paradys d'Amours, l. 13.

48 The romance was Ovid's Metamorphoses. For the story of Ceyx and Alcione see xi, 410 ff.

68 *To tellen shortly*. The storm and shipwreck are described at length in Ovid (ll. 480–557). Machaut does not mention them.

73 *telles*. The third singular present indicative in *-es* (properly of the Northern or West Midland dialect) occurs very rarely in Chaucer. Here and in l. 257 below it is clearly established by the rime.

136 *Go bet*, literally, go better, i.e., faster; a common phrase.

142 *Seys body the kyng*, the body of Seys the king. On the order of words see ClT, IV, 1170, n.

153–65 This seems to combine Ovid (ll. 592 ff.) and Statius (Theb., x, 84 ff., 95 ff.).

154 *hys*. The messenger in Ovid is Iris; Chaucer substitutes a male.

155–56 Imitated from Machaut's Dit de la Fonteinne Amoureuse, ll. 591 f. (Œuvres, SATF, III).

164 The phrase *under a rokke* corresponds to the MS. variant reading "sub rupe" (in place of "sub nube") in Met., xi, 591. (See Shannon, Chaucer and the Rom. Poets, Cambridge, Mass., 1929, pp. 6 f.)

167 *Eclympasteyr*. In Froissart's Paradys d'Amours (l. 28) Enclimpostair is one of the sons of the "noble dieu dormant." The source of the name

is uncertain. Derivation has been suggested from Icelon plastera (Gk. πλαστήρ), or from Icelon and Phobetora (corrupted into Pastora), which occur in Met., xi, 640.

171 On Chaucer's references to the "pit of hell" see T. Spencer, Speculum, II, 179 ff. They have sometimes been attributed to the influence of Dante, but the conception was familiar in the Middle Ages. In addition to the examples given by Mr. Spencer see those cited from Celtic literature in Rev. Celt., XLVI, 138 ff.

173 *To envye*, in rivalry (Fr. "à l'envi").

184 *oon yë* corresponds to Machaut's "l'un de ses yeus" (Fonteinne Amoureuse, l. 632); Ovid has "oculos" (l. 619).

189–90 For this commonplace formula, which recurs in *FranklT*, V, 1465 f., 1593 f., *PhysT*, VI, 229 f., cf. RR, 7244 f.

222–23 Cf. Paradys d'Amours, ll. 19–22.

242–69 Chaucer seems to be following the Dit de la Fonteinne Amoureuse (ll. 807–10), where the poet promises the god a hat and a feather bed. Cf. also Paradys d'Amours, ll. 15–18. Froissart there prays to Morpheus, Juno, and Oleus, the last of whom may be represented by Chaucer's *som wight elles*.

248 *on warde*, in his keeping, custody.

255 *cloth of Reynes*, a kind of linen made at Rennes, in Brittany.

272–75 Cf. Paradys d'Amours, ll. 14, 31.

282 *The kynges metynge Pharao*, the dream of King Pharaoh. For the idiom see l. 142, and n.; for the story of the dream see Gen. xli.

284 ff. The reference to Macrobius is perhaps really second-hand and due to a similar citation in RR, 7–10. On the Somnium Scipionis, which was written by Cicero and edited by Macrobius, see PF, 31, n.

291 ff. The whole description at the beginning of the dream is largely indebted to the Roman de la Rose, and there is a kind of acknowledgment of this fact in ll. 332–34. For particular resemblances cf. ll. 291–92 with RR, 45–47, 88; 304–05 with RR, 705, 484–85; 306–08 with RR, 667–68; 309–11 with RR, 487–92; 318 with RR, 74 f., 101; 331–32 with RR, 20831–32; 339–43 with RR, 124–25 (though in this case the Dit du Roy de Behaigne, ll. 13–14, is closer).

293 Chaucer represents himself as sleeping without a night-shirt. But for references to night attire see Tr III, 738, 1099, 1372, IV, 92 ff.

304 *som* is probably singular, as often elsewhere in this construction. Cf. KnT, I, 3031–32.

309 *entewnes*, usually taken as a noun, "tunes." Emerson suggested (PQ, II, 81 f.) that it is the Northern form of the verb, 3 sg. pr., substituted for the preterite in rime. For other Northern forms see ll. 73, 257.

310 "Certainly, even to gain the town of Tunis, I would not have given up hearing them sing." The choice of Tunis was probably due to the rime.

326 ff. In mentioning these subjects related to the tale of Troy Chaucer doubtless had in mind either Benoît or Guido delle Colonne, probably the former. The Roman de la Rose does not associate Medea with the Trojan story.

333 *bothe text and glose*, perhaps simply a formula meaning "the whole story." Possibly, as Professor Rand has suggested to the editor, Chaucer may have had in mind some manuscript in which both text and commentary were illustrated by pictures. An excellent specimen of such illustration is the famous Bible Moralisée, of which a "reproduction intégrale" was published in Paris, 1911–27 (Soc. Française de Reproductions de MSS. à Peintures). No similar MS. of the Roman de la Rose is known.

334 On the Roman de la Rose see the introduction to the *Romaunt*.

348 ff. With this scene Professor Lowes (PMLA, XIX, 648) compares the huntsmen of the god of Love in the Paradys d'Amours, ll. 916 ff. Chaucer's description of the hunt here and in ll. 1311 ff. is quite in accord with the actual practice of his age. For full explanations of the technical terms see O. F. Emerson, Rom. Rev., XIII, 115 ff.

351 *slee ... with strengthe*, kill in regular chase with horses and hounds (Fr. "à force").

353 *embosed*, become exhausted (lit. "covered with bosses or flecks of foam"). See Emerson, pp. 117 ff.

357-8 Mr. Claes Schaar (in Eng. Stud., XXXV, 16), finding the *hysteron proteron* in these lines troublesome, would emend to read:

Out of my chamber forth I wente;
I took my hors, and never stente.

368 *th' emperour Octovyen*, probably the Roman emperor Octavian, a favorite figure in the Charlemagne romances, who married Florence, daughter of Dagobert, king of France. There is a Middle English romance, Octovian (or Octavian Imperator), ed. Sarrazin, Heilbronn, 1885.

It has been held that the character introduced here is a flattering allegory of Edward III. Professor Cook, who accepts this application, takes the comparison to have been with the historical Octavianus, the Emperor Augustus. See Trans. Conn. Acad., XXIII, 31 f.

Professor S. P. Damon has suggested orally to the editor that both Octavian and the Black Knight, into whom he is changed by dream substitution, stand for John of Gaunt. Thus Chaucer begins by complimenting the Duke as a warrior, and proceeds to console him for his bereavement. This interpretation rests upon Mr. Damon's opinion that the poem represents an actual dream of Chaucer's. In view of the prevalence of the dream convention such an inference is very dubious. But an examination of the poems of the type to determine their agreement with the facts of dream psychology might yield interesting results. The *Book of the Duchess*, Mr. Damon argues, has all the natural features of a dream. Professor Kittredge (Chaucer and his Poetry, pp. 67 ff.) has also called attention to this aspect of the poem.

370 *A goddys half, in good tyme!* Phrases employed in the expression of a favorable wish or good omen.

384 *on a defaute yfalle*, checked by the loss of the scent.

386 *A forloyn*, lit. "very far off"; a signal that the dogs were far off from the game. It would be followed by the coupling of the hounds.

387 *I was go walked*. The construction of *walked* appears to correspond to that of the past participle in German ("kam gelaufen," etc.). But there may be involved a confusion with nouns in *-ed*, earlier *-eth*, *-ath*. See the note on *a-blakeberyed*, Pard Prol, VI, 406.

388-97 The description of the lost whelp contains resemblances to that of the little dog in Machaut's Dit du Roy de Behaingne, ll. 1204 ff., and that of the lion who is compared to a dog in the Dit dou Lyon, ll. 325 ff.

390 *koude no good*, did not know any good or advantage; hence, knew not what to do. On this recurring idiom cf. *ML Epil*, II, 1169, n.

402-03 These lines are perhaps reminiscent of RR, 8411 ff., though Flora and Zephirus were naturally associated. See *LGW Prol F*, 171; for other resemblances with RR, cf. ll. 405–09 with *RR*, 8427 ff.; 410–15 with RR, 53 ff. (also with *LGW Prol F*, 125 ff.); 416–42 with RR, 1361–82, 12790–96.

408 *swiche seven*, seven times as many. On the idiom see Klaeber, MLN, XVII, 323 f.

419-22 From RR, 1367–69. For a different rendering see *Rom*, 1391–94.

435 *Argus*, more commonly called Algus, which is in turn an Old French adaptation of the Arabic surname Al-Khwārizmī (native of Khwārizm) of the mathematician Abū 'Abdallāh Muhammad ibn Mūsa. See *MillT*, I, 3210, n. The form "Argus" occurs in RR, 13731 (Michel), a passage which Chaucer may have had in mind.

438 *ken*, i.e., kin, mankind. The form *ken* (riming with *ten*) is properly Kentish.

442 From this point forward Chaucer draws largely, as Professor Kittredge has shown (MP, VII, 465 ff.; PMLA, XXX, 7 ff.), on several poems of Machaut, and especially on the Jugement dou Roy de Behaingne. With the complaint cf. Behaingne 193–200. There the lady faints after her lament (208 ff., as the Black Knight comes near doing (ll. 487 ff.).

445 ff. The young knight, according to the usual interpretation of the poem, represents John of Gaunt, who was, however, twenty-nine years old when his wife died. This discrepancy in age is used by Professor Langhans (Untersuchungen zu Chaucer, Halle, 1918, pp. 281 ff.) as an argument against the identification. It is possible that *foure and twenty* is a scribal error, perhaps due to the omission of *v* in *xxviiij*.

490 *pure*, very, as in *KnT*, I, 1279. Cf. also ll. 583, 1212 below.

502-04 Cf. Roy de Behaingne, ll. 56 ff.

512 Professor Kittredge has suggested (in an unpublished note) that Chaucer's information about *Pan, the god of kynde*, came ultimately from Servius, who calls Pan "totius Naturae deus" (Comm. on Virgil, Ecl. ii, 31). The statements of Servius, as he shows, are repeated, with variations, by Isidore, Etym., viii, 11, 81–83 (Migne, Pat. Lat., LXXXII, 323); Vincent of Beauvais, Spec. Doctrinale, xvii, 10 (Douai, 1624); and by several of the mythographers. See Bode, Scriptores Rerum Mythicarum, Cellis, 1834, I, 40–41, 91, 200; and Van Staveren, Auctores Mythographi Latini, Leyden, 1742, pp. 914 f.

519-25 Cf. Roy de Behaingne, ll. 70 ff.

526-28 "Yes, indeed, the amends are easily made, for none are really due."

526-66 These lines show resemblances to the Roy de Behaingne, ll. 75–101.

531 *He made hyt nouther towgh ne queynte*, he did not make it a matter of difficulty or elaborate formality. On this idiom see *Gen Prol*, I, 785, n.

568 The allusion is to Ovid's Remedia Amoris.

569 ff. The music of Orpheus had power to bring rest to the tortured in the lower world. Cf. Ovid, Met., x, 40 ff. Daedalus represents the skillful mechanician; his story is also told in Met., viii, 183 ff. On *Ypocras* (Hippocrates) and *Galyen* see *Gen Prol*, I, 429, n.

583 Cf. Roy de Behaingne, ll. 196–97.

589 *Cesiphus*, Sisyphus, mentioned along with Orpheus in Met., x, 44. But *that lyeth in helle* is applicable rather to Tityus, who is referred to (but not named) by Ovid in the same place. Perhaps Chaucer's memory was confused for the moment.

591–94 Possibly an echo of *Rom*, 333 ff.

599–616 Apparently based upon the Roy de Behaingne, ll. 177–87 (Œuvres, SATF, I), which may in turn have been suggested by RR, 4293 ff. With l. 600 cf. Machaut's Remede de Fortune, l. 1198. K. Hammerle (Anglia LXVI, 70 ff.) suggests also that Chaucer may have recalled the opening couplet of the Liber de Planctu Naturae of Alanus de Insulis.

617–709 The tirade against Fortune contains reminiscences of at least four of Machaut's poems, the Remede de Fortune, the Roy de Behaingne, the eighth Motet, and the Lay de Confort. Cf. particularly the Remede de Fortune, ll. 918, 1052–56, 1138, 1162; 1167–68; Behaingne, ll. 1072–74, 1078–80, the eighth Motet (Poésies Lyriques, ed. Chichemaref, Paris, 1909, II, 497 f.) ll. 5–9, 16–18; and Confort (Poésies Lyriques, II, 415), ll. 10–13 (for the unusual remark, in ll. 693 ff., that the planets and elements give the Black Knight a "gift of weeping"). The allegory of the game of chess is probably taken from RR, 6620 ff. The figure from checkmating is also found in the Remede de Fortune, ll. 1190–91. But such comparisons were common; cf., for example, Rutebeuf's Miracle de Theophile, ll. 1–8 (Œuvres, ed. Jubinal, Paris, 1874–75, II, 231 f.). With the figure of the scorpion, Kittredge (PMLA, XXX, 11), compares Machaut's ninth Motet (Poésies Lyriques, II, 500). See also RR, 6744–46; *MLT*, II, 361, 404; and *MerchT*, IV, 2058–64.

628 f. Cf. RR, 8907 ff.

653 ff. *draughtes*, moves at chess. *Fers*, properly "wise man, counsellor" (Pers. "ferzēn"), the piece next to the king, now called the queen, which appears to be the meaning here. In mediæval chess, as Mr. D. C. McKenna has noted in an unpublished discussion of this passage, the queen did not have the importance that the piece has in the modern game. Chaucer may have had in mind the power of a real queen. But Mr. F. D. Cooley, in MLN, LXIII, 30 ff., suggests that the mediæval strategy in chess was "to keep the queen" in close attendance on the king, to protect him from checkmating, so that her loss was tantamount to the loss of the game. The rules and problems of chess in the Middle Ages are treated by Mr. H. J. R. Murray, A History of Chess, Oxford, 1913. See also Mr. S. W. Stevenson, ELH, XV, 247–260, and W. H. French, MLN, LXIV, 261 ff.

660 The *myd poynt of the chekker* apparently refers to the four central squares of the board, where the checkmate often took place. See Murray, pp. 605, 474.

661 *poun errant*, lit. "traveling pawn." According to Mr. Murray (p. 751) the expression was frequently used for the mating pawn.

663 *Athalus*, Attalus III, Philometor, King of Pergamos, called in RR, 6691 f., the inventor of chess. See Murray, p. 502.

667 *Pithagores*, Pythagoras, called *Pictagoras* in l. 1167.

699 f. "There is nothing owing me in the way of sorrow."

707 Proverbial; cf. *Tr*, ii, 789, and n.

709 *Tantale*, Tantalus, who is mentioned along with Ixion and Sisyphus in Met., x, 41. Cf. the note to l. 589 above. Ixion, Tantalus, and Sisyphus are also named near together in RR, 19279–99.

710–58 In the following conversation Chaucer made considerable use of the Roman de la Rose; cf., for example, ll. 717–19 with RR, 5847–56; 726–34 with RR, 13174 ff. (for the same stock examples); 735–37 with RR, 1439 ff. (= *Rom*, 1469 ff.); 738–39 with RR, 9203–06 (and 16677 ff.).

722 ff. *ferses twelve*, all the pieces except the king. Mr. Murray (p. 452) shows that by the mediæval rules "a game was won by checkmating the opponent's king, or by robbing or denuding him of his forces — an ending called Bare King." But the use of *fers* for "piece in general" is difficult. Mr. Cooley (cited above) would omit the article and interpret the line "though you had lost twelve queens (i.e. twelve games)."

735 *Ecquo*, Echo.

749–52 Cf. Roy de Behaingne, ll. 253–56.

759 ff. The following account of the service of the God of Love is thoroughly conventional. It contains reminiscences of the Roy de Behaingne, ll. 125–33, 261–73, the Remede de Fortune, ll. 23–60, and RR, 1881–2022, 12889–92.

797 John of Gaunt was only nineteen when he married Blanche.

805 ff. Cf. Roy de Behaingne, ll. 281 ff.; Dit dou Vergier (Œuvres, SATF, I), ll. 155–58.

813 Practically a translation of Machaut's eighth Motet, l. 17.

816–1040 For the long description of the lady Chaucer drew very largely upon the Roy de Behaingne, with frequent incidental use of the Remede de Fortune, and occasional reminiscences from the Lay de Confort and the Roman de la Rose. Even some of the most individualizing traits in the picture are paralleled in the French sources. Yet it is hard to believe that the passage does not contain real portrayal of the Duchess of Lancaster. Cf. ll. 817 ff. with Behaingne 286 ff.; 833–45 with Fortune 71–72, 95–99, 102–03, 197–99 (and also with RR, 1681–83); 844–45 with Confort 164–66; 848–74 with Behaingne 297–330; 871–72 with *Rom* 543 f. and Behaingne 321–22; 904–06 with Behaingne 356–58 and Fortune 1629–30; 907–11 with Behaingne 397–403, 582; 912–13 with Behaingne 411–14; 918 with Behaingne 580–81; 919–37 with Fortune 217–38; 939–47 with Behaingne 361–63; 948–51 with Fortune 54–56; 952–60 with Behaingne 364–83; 966–74 with Fortune 167–74; 985–87 with Fortune 123–24; 1035–40 with Behaingne 148–53, 156–58.

This mode of describing a lady feature by feature was conventional in mediæval love poetry. A rhetorician's specimen doubtless known to Chaucer was furnished by Geoffroi de Vinsauf, Poetria Nova, ll. 563 ff. (Faral, Les Arts Poétiques du xiiᵉ et du xiiie Siècle, Paris, 1924, pp. 214 ff.) For a number of other examples see Faral, pp. 80 f.; and Miss Hammond, Engl. Verse between Chaucer and Surrey, pp. 405, 452. Cf. also, with regard to formal portraits, *Tr*, v, 799, n.

824 *the sterres seven.* This phrase usually meant the planets; but since these have been mentioned just before, some other reference must have been intended, possibly the seven stars of the Ursa Major, or the Pleiades.

831 "By Christ and the twelve Apostles."

893 "She was free in giving human affection where it could be reasonably and worthily bestowed" (lit. "in reasonable cases that carry weight").

905 In the margin of the Fairfax MS. beside this line, and also ll. 942 and 948, is written, apparently by John Stow, the word "blanche," intended doubtless to identify the lady as the Duchess Blanche of Lancaster.

945 f. Cf. Song of Songs vii, 4.

963-65 For the figure of the torch, which was a common illustration, cf. RR, 7410 ff.

982 *The soleyn fenix.* The ancient tradition about the Phœnix was of course familiar in both learned and popular writings of the Middle Ages. Passages which Chaucer may have had in mind are Met., xv, 392 ff., and RR, 15977 ff., both of which emphasize the solitariness of the bird. Cf. also Gower's Balade no. 35 (Works, ed. Macaulay, Oxford, 1899-1902, I, 365 f.).

1019 *to holde . . . in honde,* to cajole, to put off with false promises. Cf. Shakespeare's phrase "to bear in hand." See also *MLT*, II, 620, n.

1021 *in balaunce,* in suspense.

1024 ff. Cf., for the general tenor of this passage, the Dit dou Lyon, ll. 1368 ff.; RR, 17563 ff.; and Gower's Conf. Am., iv, 1615 ff. For illustrations of the young knight's wanderings see Lowes, Rom. Rev., II, 121 ff. *Tartarye,* probably used here loosely for Outer Mongolia. See F. P. Magoun, Jr., Med. Stud, XVII, 140.

1028-29 *the Drye Se,* probably the great Desert of Gobi in Central Asia; *the Carrenar* (or *Carrenare*), the Kara-Nor, or Black Lake, on its eastern side. This region lay on a main trade route between China and the West. That it was known to mediæval Europeans is proved by the mention of it by Marco Polo (ed. Yule, 3d ed., London, 1903, I, 196 ff.). Chaucer and his contemporaries may have confused it with great shoals at the mouths of the Dwina and the Petchora in Russia, which bore similar names and lay along the course of another Asiatic trade route. On the whole subject see Lowes, MP, III, 1 ff.; for other explanations, see pp. 2-5.

1054-74 With this list of worthies cf. the Remede de Fortune, ll. 107 ff.; and also Machaut's thirty-eighth Balade Notée (Poésies Lyriques, II, 560 f.), and Behaingne, ll. 421-25. The sentiment was a commonplace.

1069 *Antylegyus,* a corruption of Antilogus (Antilochus), which is in turn a mistake for Archilochus. Achilles and Antilogus were slain by ambush in the temple of Apollo, whither they had resorted in order that Achilles might marry Polyxena. The plot was laid against them in revenge for the death of Hector and Troilus. This episode is briefly related by Dares, ch. 34; but Chaucer may have got it rather from Benoît, Roman de Troie,

ll. 21838 ff. (where Dares is cited), or from Joseph of Exeter, De Bello Trojano, vi, 402 ff. It is also in Guido delle Colonne (Strassburg, 1489, sig. l. 3, verso).

1070 On Dares Phrygius and his place in the history of the Trojan legend, see the introduction to the *Troilus*.

1080-85 Probably from RR, 8605-12, where "Titus Livius" is cited by name. Cf. *PhysT*, VI, 1.

1088 ff. Cf. Remede de Fortune, ll. 64-65, 89-94, 135 ff., 295-302.

1089 f. The rime *say* (pret. ind.) and *say* (a clipped form of the infin.) is very unusual in Chaucer. Possibly, as Skeat suggested, the former should be *seye* (pret. subj.), though the indicative seems more natural.

1108-11 Cf. Dit dou Lyon, ll. 207-12.

1115-25 Perhaps a development of Behaingne, ll. 1140-47.

1117 On Ahithophel see II Sam. xvii. Antenor betrayed Troy by sending the Palladium to Ulysses. Cf. *Tr*, iv, 202 ff., Benoît, Roman de Troie, ll. 24397 ff. (where both Dares and Dictys are referred to), and Guido delle Colonne, Historia Trojana, Strassburg, 1489, sigg. m 1 ff. *Genelloun,* the celebrated traitor of the Chanson de Roland. See *MkT*, VII, 2375 ff., n. Roland and Oliver, whose friendship was proverbial, were the most famous of Charlemagne's knights.

1146-50 Cf. Remede de Fortune, ll. 357-66.

1152-53 Cf. RR, 1996-97: "Il est assez sires dou cors Qui a le cuer en sa comande." This is turned about in l. 1154: "and if any one has that (his heart), a man may not escape."

1155-57 Cf. Remede de Fortune, ll. 401-03. The making of complaints in song was of course the regular procedure under such circumstances.

1162 ff. In Gen. iv, 21 it is Jubal, not Tubal, who is called the "father of all such as handle the harp and the organ." The ascription to Tubal, however, is not peculiar to Chaucer. It occurs in Peter Comestor's Historia Scholastica (Lib. Gen. cap. XXVIII) and Vincent's Speculum Doctrinale (Lib. XVII, cap. xxv), as well as in the Aurora of Petrus de Riga, which Chaucer in l. 1169 acknowledges as his source. All these passages were printed by K. Young in Spec., XII, 299 ff. They all mention also the Greek attribution of the invention of music to Pythagoras (Pictagoras).

1180-1312 In the following passages Chaucer again makes frequent use of the Roy de Behaingne and the Remede de Fortune. Cf. ll. 1181-82 with Fortune 681-82; 1183-91 with Behaingne 453-56; 1192 with Behaingne 466; 1195-98 with Behaingne 461-62 and Fortune 1671-83; 1203-18 with Behaingne 467-76; 1216 with Fortune 696; 1219 with Behaingne 504-05; 1226-28 with Behaingne 656-58; 1236-38 with Behaingne 509-12; 1239-44 with Behaingne 541-48; 1250-51 with Fortune 751-52; 1258-67 with Behaingne 610; 1273 with Fortune 4074-75; 1275-78 with Behaingne 642-43; 1285-86 with Fortune 139-40; 1289 ff. with Behaingne 166-76.

1200 *With sorwe,* probably imprecatory rather than descriptive. For the construction see *MLT*, II, 896, n.

1206 *the dismal,* the evil days; Anglo-Fr. "dismal," Lat. "dies mali." These were two special days each month in the mediæval calendars. They were also called Egyptian Days ("dies Aegyptiaci"). See Vincent of Beauvais, Speculum Naturale, xv, 83 (Douai, 1624). Chaucer very likely interpreted the word as meaning "ten evils" (taking it from the French "dix"). The English adjective "dismal" is derived from this source.

1212 *Pure*, very. See note on l. 490 above.

1234 *but I mete*, unless I am dreaming.

1246 ff. For the lamentation of Cassandra see Benoît, Roman de Troie, ll. 26113 ff.

1248 On *Ilyoun* see *LGW*, 936, n.

1270 This phrase occurs twice in Behaingne, ll. 641, 670.

1318 f. The *ryche hil* was doubtless Richmond, or Richemont, in Yorkshire, which came into the possession of John of Gaunt at the age of two, when he was created Earl of Richmond, and belonged to him until his second marriage in 1372. For the historical details see Professor F. Tupper, MLN, XXXI, 250. The *long castel* probably refers to "Lancaster" (also called "Loncastel," "Longcastel"), and there may be further reference in the *walles white* and *seynt Johan* to the names of Blanche and John of Gaunt. See Skeat's letter in Acad., XLV, 191, and Tupper's note in MLN, XXXII, 54.

1324 ff. At the end of the poem Chaucer reverts to the Paradys d'Amours, from which he took the suggestion of his opening lines. With ll. 1324–25 cf. the Paradys, ll. 1685–92; with 1330–34, Paradys 1693–95 and 1722–23.

The House of Fame

The *House of Fame*, like the *Book of the Duchess*, is not ascribed to Chaucer in the MSS., but its authenticity is sufficiently vouched for by Chaucer's own reference in the *Prologue to the Legend of Good Women* (F, 417, G, 405) and in the *Retractation* at the end of the *Canterbury Tales*. In the poem itself, moreover, the Eagle addresses the narrator as *Geffrey* (l. 729).

From the fact that Lydgate, in the Fall of Princes, does not name the *House of Fame* among Chaucer's works the inference has been drawn that the piece is there indirectly referred to as "Dante in Inglissh," and several scholars have striven to show that it is a kind of parody of the Divine Comedy. Chaucer undoubtedly used a number of passages from Dante, and was under his influence at the time of writing. But there is no organic or structural relation between the two works, and Lydgate's phrase, "Dante in Inglissh," is best interpreted as a complimentary characterization of Chaucer himself. (The application of the term to the Ugolino story, as proposed by Miss Hammond, pp. 374 f., or to the *Wife of Bath's Tale*, III, 1125 ff., as suggested by Professor Brusendorff, p. 151, seems less probable.) For extreme statements of the theory of Dantean influence on the *House of Fame* see A. Rambeau in ESt, III, 209–68, and C. Chiarini, Di una imitazione inglese della Divina Commedia, La Casa della Fama di Chaucer, Bari, 1902; and for dissenting criticism cf. Lounsbury's Studies in Chaucer, New York, 1892, II, 242 ff., and a review of Chiarini in the Journ. of Comp. Lit., I, 292–97. In the following notes are registered only those parallels from Dante which seem probably significant.

Primarily and essentially the *House of Fame* belongs to the type of love-visions which abounded in French literature for a century after the Roman de la Rose. The best general account of its literary relations is Professor W. O. Sypherd's Studies in Chaucer's *Hous of Fame*, Ch. Soc., 1907. See also ESt, XLI, 113 ff. Among the French parallels or sources the Panthère d'Amours of Nicole de Margival (ed. H. A. Todd, SATF, 1883) is particularly important. See H. R. Patch, MLN, XXXIV, 321–28. Le Temple d'Onnour of Froissart, taken by Brusendorff (pp. 158 ff.) to be a primary source, may also have given Chaucer a few hints, but certainly did not supply him with his general plot or plan. It was written to celebrate a marriage (of unidentified persons), and some critics, as will be indicated below, hold Chaucer to have had a similar purpose. The Corbaccio of Boccaccio, a work of the same genre, has been suggested as a partial source of the *House of Fame* by Miss M. L. Brown in MLN, XXXII, 411–15. But the resemblances she cites are not convincing.

Many special literary influences on the *House of Fame* have been pointed out, particularly by Skeat in his notes and by Ten Brink in his Chaucer Studien, Münster, 1870. The debt to Virgil and Ovid, which was perhaps not sufficiently emphasized by Professor Sypherd, has been studied by Professor E. F. Shannon, Chaucer and the Roman Poets, Cambridge, 1929, pp. 48 ff. On the possible use of the Old French Roman d'Eneas see Lowes, PMLA, XXXII, liv; on the use of Theodulus see Holthausen in Angl., XVI, 264–66. The influence of the Amorosa Visione of Boccaccio on this and other works of Chaucer is doubtful. It is asserted by Professor Koeppel in Anglia, XIV, 233 ff., and by Professor C. G. Child in MLN, X, 190 ff., and questioned by Dr. H. M. Cummings, Indebtedness of Chaucer's Works to the Italian Works of Boccaccio, Univ. of Cincinnati Studies, 1916, p. 26. On the evidence of the general similarity of the two works and of the special testimony of a single passage (ll. 1136 ff.) Professor Brusendorff (p. 161, n.) has argued unconvincingly for Chaucer's knowledge and use of Petrarch's Trionfo della Fama. Parallels between the *HF* and the Book of Revelation (in most cases not verbally close) are noted by L. J. Henkin in MLN, LVI, 583 ff.

The *HF* belongs of course to the literary type which describes an intellectual or mental flight. Numerous examples of this type are cited by F. Cumont, Le Mysticisme astral dans l'antiquité, Acad. Roy. de Belgique, Bull. (Lettres), 4th series, 1909, pp. 258 ff., 278 ff. For additional references see Nock and Festugière, Corpus Hermeticum (Hermès Trismégiste), I, p. 66.

Many critics have found in the poem a more or less elaborate allegory of Chaucer's own life. For an account of various theories see Sypherd, pp. 156 ff.; Koch, ESt, XLI, 113-21; Wells, pp. 656 ff., and V. Langhans, Untersuchungen zu Chaucer, Halle, 1918, pp. 71-74. These interpretations are mostly arbitrary and fanciful, and Professor Sypherd is probably right in rejecting them. But some scholars who have abandoned the autobiographical theories still insist that Chaucer must have had a purpose beyond the mere writing of a love-vision. Thus Professor R. Imelmann (ESt., XLV, 397 ff.) and Professor Brusendorff (pp. 162 ff.) hold that the poem was to celebrate the marriage of Richard and Anne. Professor Koch (ESt., L, 369 ff.) would refer it to John of Gaunt's (finally unsuccessful) plans for the marriage of his daughter Philippa in 1384. And Mr. F. C. Riedel (JEGP, XXVII, 441 ff.) would explain it as Chaucer's veiled rebuke to John of Gaunt for having outraged decency by appearing in public with his mistress, Catherine Swynford, in the summer of 1378. Chaucer's own indignation, he holds, was aroused because he had reason to suspect Lancaster of illicit relations with his own wife. Mr. Riedel's theory involves a series of arbitrary interpretations and hazardous conjectures. His fundamental assumption about Lancaster and Philippa Chaucer, though recently supported anew by Dr. Russell Krauss (Chaucerian Problems: especially the Petherton Forestership and the Question of Thomas Chaucer, in Three Chaucer Studies, New York, 1932), is by no means proved or even made probable. For the personal allegories assumed by the other scholars there is also no secure basis in the text, and the poem seems at best inappropriate to the celebration of a marriage or betrothal. One thing only—the mention of the *man of gret auctorite* in l. 2158 — leads the reader to suspect that the completed poem was to be connected somehow with a person of consequence such as Richard or John of Gaunt. But the identity of the person and the nature of the connection seem now beyond the range of conjecture. Professor Manly (Kittredge Anniv. Papers, Boston, 1913, pp. 73 ff.), giving up the allegorical explanation, has argued that the vision was meant to introduce a collection of tales, but that the scheme was abandoned in favor of the Canterbury pilgrimage. For discussion of this suggestion, with some reasonable objections, see Sypherd, MLN, XXX, 65-68. For other hypotheses about the interpretation of the poem see B. H. Bronson, U. of California Publications in English, III, Nº. 4, pp. 171 ff.; P. F. Baum, ELH, VIII, 248 ff.; Ingeborg Besser, Chaucer's *Hous of Fame*: eine Interpretation (Hamburg 1941), Britannica, Heft 20.

In view of the probability that Chaucer was once a member of one of the Inns of Court, mention should be made of the suggestion of Mr. R. J. Schoeck (Univ. of Toronto Quarterly, XXIII, 185 ff.) that he may have written the *House of Fame* for the Christmas Revels at the Temple. This is based on an allusion in a sixteenth-century heraldry book to Chaucer's having built "a house called Fame" for Pegasus (the arms of The Inner Temple).

The *House of Fame* contains no precise indication of date. Inferences drawn from the biographical and allegorical interpretations are all uncertain. Those based upon literary relations are also not very secure. The assumption, for example, that the poem is the "Comedy" announced by Chaucer at the end of the *Troilus* is both unwarranted and improbable. The possible use by Chaucer of the Temple d'Onnour and the imitation of Chaucer by Gower in the Mirrour de l'Omme (see the note to l. 1547) afford slight clues, and are both consistent with a date about 1379-80. In general, the probabilities favor the early years of the Italian period, before the composition of the *Palamon* or the *Troilus*. The use of the octosyllabic couplet would have been more natural at that time than later. This date would account also for the transitional character of the poem — a French love-vision in type, but clearly written under the influence of Dante. See Wells, pp. 659-60, and for fuller discussion Tatlock, Dev. and Chron., Ch. Soc., 1907, pp. 34 ff.; Lowes, PMLA, XX, 819, 854 ff.; and Kittredge, The Date of Chaucer's Troilus, Ch. Soc., 1909, pp. 53-55.

For further general comments on the *House of Fame* see Paul G. Ruggiers, SP, L, 16-29; and K. Brunner, Rivista di Letteratura Moderna, XI, 344-50.

1 ff. Rhetorical preliminaries — sixty-five lines on dreams, forty-five of invocation, and about three hundred and fifty in the outline of the Aeneid — occupy nearly all the first book. See Manly, Chaucer and the Rhetoricians, Brit. Acad., 1926, p. 8.

For the opening passage on dreams Chaucer seems to have been chiefly indebted to suggestions from the Roman de la Rose (particularly ll. 1 ff., and 18499 ff.). Resemblances may be noted between *HF*, 11 and RR, 18181, 18424; *HF*, 12 and RR, 18208; *HF*, 15-18 and RR, 18247 ff.; *HF*, 24-31 and RR, 18342-49; *HF*, 33-35 and RR, 18357-60; *HF*, 36-40 and RR, 18394-402; and *HF*, 41-42 and RR, 18365-66. For part of this material, not closely paralleled in RR, Chaucer may have drawn on various authorities. The subject was much discussed in the literature current in the Middle Ages. The classification of dreams in ll. 7-11 seems most likely to go back to Macrobius (Som. Scip., i, 3), who distinguishes five kinds: "somnium," "visio," "oraculum," "insomnium," and "visum" (also called "phantasma"). Again, in l. 18 the *gendres* perhaps have reference to Macrobius's division of the "somnium" into five species ("proprium," "alienum," "commune," "publicum," "generale"), though this is not certain. Other discussions which Chaucer may have had in mind, or which at all events illustrate his doctrine, are those of John of Salisbury, Policraticus, ii, 15 (ed. Webb, Oxford, 1909, I, 88 ff.); Vincent of Beauvais, Speculum Naturale, xxvi, 32 ff. (Douai, 1624); Bartholomaeus Anglicus, De Proprietatibus Rerum, vi, 24-27 (De Somno); and Robert Holkot, Liber Sapientiae, Lectio ccii. For a tabulation of pertinent passages see Sypherd, pp. 74-76; cf. also Curry, pp. 202 ff.

It is not clear just how seriously Chaucer meant his own classification to be taken. There does not seem to be any regularly recognized distinction between *drem* and *sweven* (l. 9). Ten Brink's suggestion that the former corresponds to "somnium" and the latter to "insomnium" (Chaucer Studien, p. 101) is at all events not borne out by Chaucer's usage elsewhere.

21 On the complexions see *Gen Prol*, I, 333, n.

48 *figures*, if not used in its ordinary sense of figurative or symbolic representations, may refer to the images ("simulacra") supposed to originate in the imagination of a dreamer. See Curry (pp. 206–07). For the process assumed he refers to Vincent of Beauvais, Spec. Nat., xxvi, 41 (Douai, 1624); Antonius Gaizo, De Somno, etc., Basel, 1539, c. vii.

53–54 "Let this thing be the affair of great scholars." Cf. *Tr*, v, 379; also the modern (bookish) construction, "Woe worth the day," in which "worth" is a verb (AS. "weorþan," to become).

55–56 Cf. RR, 18513.

63 The reason for the date is unknown. Professor Imelmann explains it as referring to Dec. 10, 1381, when (he estimates) the news came of Ann's approaching arrival in England. Professor Brusendorff (pp. 163 ff.), who also held the poem to celebrate the royal marriage, would date the dream Dec. 10, 1380, two days before the appointment of the ambassadors who were to make the arrangements. This, he suggested, was the actual date of the decision of the King and Council. According to Professor Koch, who would explain the *House of Fame* as referring to John of Gaunt's efforts to arrange a marriage for his daughter Philippa, Chaucer may have received a premature report of a betrothal in December, 1384, and may thereupon have written the poem. The later failure of the negotiations would account for the fact that he never finished it. In none of these three cases, it is to be observed, has December tenth been shown to have been actually a significant day, and the allegorical interpretations of the poem are themselves altogether doubtful.

66 ff. There has been considerable discussion as to the source of the three invocations. The second and third (ll. 518–28, 1091–1109) clearly come from Dante, and it has been held that the whole idea of invocations was suggested by the Divine Comedy. But their use was common in poetry of various kinds and not unexampled in love-visions. In fact the particular address to Morpheus in the present passage seems to have been suggested by Froissart's Trésor Amoureux (ll. 615 ff.; Œuvres, ed. Scheler, Brussels, 1870–72, III, 71). The description of the god and his habitat is based upon Ovid, Met., xi, 592 ff. With the lines on Lethe Dr. T. Spencer compares Claudian, De Raptu Pros., i, 282 (Speculum, II, 182).

76 *That . . . hir*, equivalent to "whose." On this construction see *KnT*, I, 2710, n.

81 From Dante, Par., i, 1.

82 With this echo of the Gloria Patri cf. *Tr*, i, 245.

99 *That*, a repetition of *That* in l. 98.

105 For the story of Crœsus' dream and his death upon the gallows see *MkT*, VII, 2740 ff. Chaucer's source was RR, 6489 ff., which he doubtless had in mind when writing this passage.

112–14 Cf. *Rom*, 23–25.

115 *forgo*, ordinarily explained as "overwearied by walking," but no other instances of this use of the word seem to be recorded. Possibly we should read *for go* (two words) and interpret "for gone," i.e., because of having walked. On this construction with *for* cf. *KnT*, I, 2142, and n.

117–18 Cf. RR, 8833–38. St. Leonard was the patron saint of captives and might therefore be expected to release the wretched who were in the

prison of married life. For a somewhat similar use of the figure cf. *MercB*, 28. See also H. M. Smyser, MLN, LVI, 205 ff. (noting that Chaucer lived two miles from St. Leonard's convent).

120 This line furnished Lydgate with the title of his Temple of Glas.

130 The temple of Venus here resembles her temple, which is much more fully described, in the *Knight's Tale*. No model has been found for either description. For the idea of the paintings on the walls there would have been sufficient suggestion in the temple of Juno in the Aeneid, i, 446 ff. Mediæval poetry provides numerous other examples, and Chaucer must have been familiar with many actual decorations of the sort. (See Sypherd, pp. 81 ff.) For some of the details of the description of Venus and Cupid Chaucer may have drawn on the De Deorum Imaginibus of Albricus Philosophus (printed in Van Staveren's Auctores Mythographi Latini, Leyden, 1742) or some similar treatise. See Lounsbury's Studies, II, 381 f.

134–5 E. P. Kuhl (PQ, XXIV, 34) suggests that there is an allusion here to the white and red roses of the Mortimers and Lancastrians. The evidence is very slight.

141–42 Perhaps reminiscent of Dante's Inf., iii, 10–11.

143 Here follows at some length a summary of the earlier portion of Virgil's Æneid. The opening lines are translated.

152 *Synoun*, Sinon.

155 *Made the hors broght*, caused the horse to be brought. For the idiom cf. *KnT*, I, 1913, n.

158 *Ilyoun*, Ilium, properly only a poetical name for Troy, but apparently used by Chaucer, as elsewhere in mediæval writings, in the restricted sense of the citadel of Troy. Cf. *LGW*, 936, n.

177 *Iulo*, Iulus, who was the same person as Ascanius. The blunder, if it be one, may be due to the wording of Aen., iv, 274, or possibly to a misinterpretation (by Chaucer or a predecessor) of the Historia Miscella (formerly ascribed to Paulus Diaconus), i, 2: after Aeneas, "regnum suscepit Ascanius, qui et Iulus, eiusdem Aeneae filius" (ed. Eyssenhardt, Berlin, 1869, p. 2). For evidence of a confusion in the Latin tradition itself see E. K. Rand, Speculum, I, 222 ff.

184 Virgil does not tell how Creusa met her death.

198 From here to l. 225 Chaucer follows the first book of the Aeneid. But according to Virgil the storm is quieted by Neptune, and it is not until Aeneas has landed that Venus appeals to Jupiter to protect him. Perhaps Chaucer's variation, usually referred to as an inaccuracy, was a deliberate alteration to emphasize the activity of Venus. (See E. K. Rand, Speculum, I, 222.) Professor A. C. Friend (Spec., XXVIII, 317 ff.) calls attention to similarities between Chaucer's account of Aeneas and the Ilias of Simon Aurea Capra.

219 *Joves*, Jupiter. This peculiar form, which seems to be formed on an Old French nominative, occurs again in ll. 586, 597, 630, and in *Tr*, ii, 1607; iii, 15.

240 ff. Virgil's account of Aeneas is here considerably enlarged upon in the form of a love-story. This development was due, as Professor Shannon (pp. 55 ff.) has shown, to the influence of Ovid, who is cited with Virgil in l. 379. Chaucer also drew upon Ovid in his legend of Dido in the *Legend of Good Women*.

265-66 Cf. RR, 12139–42 (*Rom.* 7467 ff.).

269-85 For these reflections on men as deceivers Professor Shannon (pp. 364 ff.) has suggested a possible source in Catullus, Carmen lxiv, 143–48. But Mr. J. A. S. McPeek, in MLN, XLVI, 295 ff., argues that they are sufficiently accounted for by Heroides, xvi (xvii), 191 ff., and RR, 4391 ff. On Chaucer's use of Catullus see further *LGW*, 1891 ff., n.

272 On this proverb see *CYT*, VIII, 962, n.

273 "So may I have the use of my head." Cf. *MerchT*, IV, 2308; *NPT*, VII, 3300; *LGW Prol F*, 194.

286 *be Eneas*, by, with reference to Aeneas.

290 Skeat quotes from Cotgrave's Dictionary, s. v. "Herbe," the similar French proverb: "L'herbe qu'on cognoist on la doit lier à son doigt." See his EE Prov., pp. 86 f., no. 207; also Haeckel, p. 22, no. 69.

315 ff. With Dido's plea, which has no exact parallel in the Aeneid, Professor C. G. Child compares the Amorosa Visione, c. xxviii (MLN, X, 191 f.). See also R. M. Estrich (MLN, LV, 342 ff.) who suggests a parallel from Daude de Pradas.

350 Cf. Aen., iv, 174, which is quoted (incorrectly) on the margin of MSS. F and B.

351 Cf. Luke xii, 2, also quoted in MSS. F and B; cf. Haeckel, pp. 41 f., no. 142.

355-56 *seyd . . . Yshamed be*, said to be put to shame.

359 The MSS. cite here the line, "Cras poterunt turpia fieri sicut heri." With "turpia" and "fieri" transposed this is a rimed pentameter from the so-called Versus Magistri Hildeberti, a short elegiac poem on Troy. The text is printed by Hauréau, Notices et Extraits, XXVIII, ii, 438–40, and by Du Méril, Poésies Populaires Latines Antérieures au xiie Siècle, Paris, 1843, pp. 309–13. Fourteen lines are quoted at the end of Caxton's Recuyell of the Historyes of Troye (ed. Sommer, London, 1894, II, 703). For further references see G. L. Hamilton, MLN, XXIII, 63.

361 Proverbial. Cf. *Tr*, ii, 789, and n.

378 On the form *Eneydos* (genitive) see *ML Prol*, II, 93, n.

379 The reference is to the Heroides, vii (Dido to Aeneas).

388 ff. The examples of untrue lovers come from the Heroides, ii, iii, v, vi, ix, x, xii. See Shannon, Chaucer and Rom. Poets, pp. 62 ff., and (on the possible supplementary use of the Italian translation attributed to Filippo Ceffi) S. B. Meech, PMLA, XLV, 110 ff. Here and there Chaucer seems to have drawn on other versions of the stories. Thus the lines on Phyllis combine information from Ovid with the account in RR. They have also been compared by Professor C. G. Child with the Amorosa Visione, c. xxv (MLN, X, 191). The account of Theseus and Ariadne corresponds in a number of details to that in Machaut's Jugement dou Roy de Navarre, ll. 2741 ff. But it is uncertain whether Chaucer was following Machaut or the Ovide Moralisé, which has been shown to have been in turn Machaut's source. See Lowes, PMLA, XXXIII, 322 ff. Professor Shannon (pp. 66 ff.), who ques-

tions Chaucer's use of Machaut, would derive the whole account from Ovid except the introduction of Phaedra, which he thinks probably due to the De Gen. Deorum. Chaucer's information about Phaedra may also have come from the Amorosa Visione (c. xxii) or from Filippo's Italian translation of Ovid.

391 On the parentage of Phyllis see *LGW*, 2423, n. In Boccaccio's De Gen. Deor., xi, 25, she is called "Lycurgi filia."

392 This phrase is closely similar to RR, 13213; also to Ovid's statement in Her., ii, 1 f.

405-26 Certain details in this account of Theseus are not found in Ovid. Chaucer may be following the Jugement dou Roy de Navarre or the Ovide Moralisé. See Lowes, PMLA, XXXIII, 320 ff., and Meech, PMLA, XLVI, 182 ff.

409 "Whether he had laughed or lowered," i.e., in any case. For expressions of this type see *Gen Prol*, I, 534, n.

411 The modern idiom is "if it had not been for Ariadne."

416 *in an ile*, i e., on the isle of Naxos.

426 On the Northern (and West Midland) form *tellis* see *BD*, 73, n.

429 *The book*, etc., the Aeneid (iv, 252 ff.).

435 f. For the tempest see Aen., v, 8 ff., and for the death of Palinurus, the *sterisman*, the end of Bk. v.

439 For the account of Aeneas's consultation of the Sibyl and visit to the lower world see Aen., vi.

449 Claudius Claudianus, the author of the De Raptu Proserpinae (about 400 A.D.), is mentioned along with Virgil and Dante as an authority on the lower world. Cf. also l. 1509 below; *LGW Prol G*, 280; and *MerchT*, IV, 2232.

451 ff. Chaucer's summary of the last six books of the Aeneid is very brief.

458 *Lavina*, Lavinia. The form of the name (which occurs again as *Lavyne* in *BD*, 331) may be due to either French or Italian. Cf. RR, 20831, and Dante's Purg., xvii, 37.

482 The desolate places in the Panthère and the Corbaccio are not actual deserts of sand. For this feature Chaucer's description may be reminiscent of Inf., i, 64, or xiv, 8–13. In the latter passage Dante refers to the desert of Libya, also described by Lucan in Pharsalia, ix. Chaucer may have drawn directly upon Lucan or (as Professor Lowes has suggested to the editor) upon the French Hystore de Julius Cesar of Jehan de Tuim (ed. Settegast, Halle, 1881), which shows closer resemblances. Another desert which may have been in Chaucer's mind is that in the Lay du Desert d'Amours of Deschamps (Œuvres, SATF, II, 182 ff.). Various symbolic interpretations of the desert have been suggested by the commentators. See Sypherd, pp. 49, 52. In the imagery of the love-vision, as Professor Patch has shown, it may well represent the state of the despairing lover. See MLN, XXXIV, 321 ff.

493 The *fantome*, or "phantasm," was often explained as produced by the operation of demons upon the mind of the sleeper, and the term *illusioun* was applied to their false revelations. See Curry, pp. 209, 214, with especial citation of Vincent of Beauvais, Spec. Nat., xxvi, 56 (Douai, 1624).

499 ff. These lines are perhaps an imitation of Purg., ix, 19–20, and ll. 502 ff. may go back to Purg., ii, 17–24. How far the suggestion for the eagle came

from Dante and how far from the description of
Ganymede in both Virgil and Ovid is a matter of
dispute.

504–6 These lines seem to echo Dante's Paradiso,
I, 61–3. See Miss D. A. Dilts, MLN, LVII, 26 ff.

Book II

514 ff. For the dream of Isaiah see either ch. i or
ch. vi of his prophecy. That of Scipio is related in
the Somnium Scipionis of Cicero; cf. Chaucer's account of it at the beginning of the *Parliament of
Fowls*. On Nebuchadnezzar see Daniel i–iv, and
MkT, VII, 2143 ff.; and on Pharaoh, see Gen. xli,
1–7. The mention of Turnus is not so clear. Skeat
took it to refer to the visit of Iris, Aen., ix, 1 ff.; but
Professor Tatlock (MLN, XXXVI, 95, n.), suggests
rather the visit of the Fury Alecto, vii, 413 ff.
Elcanor is of uncertain identification. Professor
Bright (MLN, IX, 241) suggested Hamilcar, whose
dream of the fall of Syracuse is mentioned by
Valerius Maximus, Facta et Dicta Memorabilia, i,
7, 8. Dr. Heath (Globe edn., p. 564), suggested
Elkanah (Vulg., Elcana), the father of Samuel. But
though the names are similar, it is not recorded that
Elkanah had any dream; and the same is true of
Alcanor (Aen., ix, 672, x, 338), who is mentioned by
Skeat. Other characters who have been suggested
are Elpenor (Odyssey, x, 552; xi, 51; xii, 10),
Acanor (prose Merlin, SATF, 1886, I, 209), Elpinor
(Roman de Troie, SATF, 12327), and Escanor (in
the romance of Escanor by Girard d'Amiens, Stuttgart Litt. Ver., CLXXVIII). But none of these appears to have been associated with a vision. A more
likely explanation than any of the preceding is that
proposed by Professor Tatlock, MLN, XXXVI, 95–
97. He refers to the Old French Cassidorus, a continuation of the prose redaction of the Sept Sages
de Rome. (This romance is unprinted, but some
account of it is given in Alton's edition of the Mar-
ques de Rome, Stuttgart Litt. Ver., CLXXXVII,
pp. v–vii, xiii.) Helcana, the heroine of the story,
is forced to live in man's disguise, and takes the name
Helcanor. When her lover is counselled not to marry,
she appears to him twelve times in dreams and
tells him stories to show that he should. As Professor
Tatlock remarks, there is a difficulty in the identification in the fact that Helcana-Helcanor is not herself the dreamer. But Chaucer may have forgotten
this, or may have thought the inaccuracy added to
the humor of the allusion. Mr. Tatlock thinks there
was intentional anticlimax in the addition of this
rather absurd figure to the list of famous dreamers
of antiquity.

518–19 This invocation to Cipris is almost certainly reminiscent of Tes., i, 3. Throughout the
passage memories of Boccaccio are mingled with
those of Dante. See the note on ll. 520 ff. The form
Cipris occurs again in *Tr*, iii, 725, and *Cypride* in
PF, 277. On the relation of the passage to *PF*,
113 ff., see R. A. Pratt, MLQ, VII, 259 ff.

519 *favour*, apparently in the unusual sense of
"help" or "helper."

520 ff. The address to the Muses is clearly an
imitation of Inf., ii, 7. With the following lines cf.
also Inf., ii, 8–9; Par., i, 11; xviii, 87. The Italian
spellings of *Parnaso* and *Elicon* are probably due to
recollections of Tes., xi, 63, or of Par., i, 16 and

Purg., xxix, 40. The dubious language of the last-
named passage may explain, Skeat suggests, why
Chaucer took Helicon to be a well rather than a
mountain. But in the Teseida it is definitely called a
fountain ("fonte"), and Guido's Historia Trojana,
sig. a 5, recto, col. 1 ("imbibens Elicona") carries the
same implication. In *Anel*, 16, and *Tr*, iii, 1810,
Elicon is also described as *in* (or *on*) *Parnaso*, hence
doubtless to be understood as a spring. The mountains, Helicon and Parnassus, were in reality not
near together. But they were often so represented
by post-classical writers. On the whole matter see
Lowes, MP, XIV, 725 ff., and Root's note on *Tr*,
iii, 1807–10.

534 The descent of the eagle is partly imitated
from Dante (Purg., ix, 28–30) and partly from Machaut's Jugement dou Roy de Navarre, Œuvres, ed.
Hoeffner, SATF, I, ll. 301 f., and Confort d' Ami,
Œuvres, III, ll. 1899 n.

557 Skeat compares Inf., ii, 122, and Purg., ix,
46, but the correspondence is not close, and no source
seems necessary.

573 The form *Seynte* can be easily explained here
and in l. 1066 below as the feminine form of the adjective (from the French). On certain cases where
it is masculine and a different explanation seems
necessary see the *Gen Prol*, I, 120, n.

586 "Will Jupiter turn me into a constellation?"

588 On Enoch see Gen. v, 24; on Elijah, II
Kings ii, 11; on Romulus, who was carried to heaven
by Mars, Met., xiv, 816 ff.; and on Ganymede,
whom Jupiter bore up in the form of an eagle Aen.,
i, 28, and Met., x, 159–60. Enoch and Elijah were
constantly associated, and they, as well as Ganymede, are mentioned in the Ecloga Theoduli (ll. 65–
68, 217–19, 77–80; ed. Osternacher, Ripariae prope
Lentiam, 1902), a poem which was known to Chaucer. (See Holthausen, Angl., XVI, 264 ff.) The
whole passage may have been suggested by Inf., ii,
32, where Dante says that he is neither Aeneas nor
Paul. In that case Chaucer substituted names of
characters more appropriate to his peculiar situation.

597 *ther-aboute*, busy about that, having it in
intention.

600 ff. Possibly influenced by Inf., ii, 49 ff.

623 The meaning of *cadence* here is uncertain.
Skeat suggested that perhaps *ryme* is used for couplets, and *cadence* for longer stanzas. From the contrast with rime one might also infer that the reference is to unrimed or alliterative verse, or even to
the rhythm of prose. Examples of the application
of the word to rhythmic prose are cited from the
fifteenth century by Miss Hammond, Eng. Verse
between Chaucer and Surrey, p. 457. See further
P. F. Baum, JEGP, XLV, 38 n., and Miss M.
Schlauch, PMLA, LXV, 578. Possibly no precise
contrast was intended. Cf. the note on *drem* and
sweven, ll. 1 ff., above; also that on *sort, cas*, and
aventure in *Gen Prol*, I, 844 ff. Saintsbury (History
of Eng. Prosody, London, 1906–10, I, 160, n.), citing
Gower, Conf. Am., iv, 2414, and Andrew of Wyn-
toun, Chronicle, v, 4341 ff. (ed. Amours, Scot. Text
Soc., 1903–14, IV, 22), argues for the "ordinary
sense" of the word.

637 "And describest everything in relation to
them" (i.e., to lovers).

639 f. For this figure of the "dance of love" cf.
Tr, i, 517 f., and *Gen Prol*, I, 476, n

652 This has reference obviously to Chaucer's labors as comptroller of the Custom.

662 Cf. Inf., i, 113.

678 *long yserved*, served for a long period. On the use of "serve" in relation to love see *KnT*, I, 1814, n.

681 Proverbial; cf. Skeat, EE Prov., p. 87, no. 208.

689 "To make the beard" meant to cheat, delude. Cf. *RvT*, I, 4096, and n.

692 "Holding in hand," cajoling, putting off with false hopes. See *MLT*, II, 620, and n.

695 On *love-dayes*, "days of reconciliation," see *Gen Prol*, I, 258, n.

696 *cordes*, probably "cords, strings" rather than "musical chords." See J. B. Colvert, MLN, LXIX, 239 ff.

698 *cornes*, usually interpreted as grains of corn.

706 *yis*, the emphatic affirmative. See *NP Prol*, VII, 2816, n.

712 *thyn oune book*, i.e., Ovid's Metamorphoses. The description of the House of Fame is in Bk. xii, 39–63.

719 "And [it, the house] stands in so exactly determined a place."

730 The doctrine (stated again in ll. 826 ff. below) that every natural object has a natural place which it tries to reach, and in which it tries to remain, was the predecessor of the law of gravitation. It survives in the familiar hymn, "Rivers to the ocean run." It is not easy to assign Chaucer's statement to a definite source. But he very likely had in mind the similar discussion in Boethius, *Bo*, iii, pr. 11, 96 ff., and perhaps also a passage in the Paradiso (i, 103 ff.). Cf. further Purg., xviii, 28 (for the remarks on fire); the Convivio, iii, 3 ("loco proprio"); RR, 16761–67; and the De Planctu Naturae of Alanus de Insulis (Migne, Pat. Lat., CCX, 453). An earlier statement than any of these, as Professor Patch reminds us in ESt., LXV, 357, is to be found in St. Augustine's Confessions, xiii, 9 (Migne, XXXII, 848).

745 "While each of them is free ('at large'), a light thing seeks to go up and a heavy thing down."

765 Cf. *SumT*, III, 2233 ff. The doctrine was familiar. The statement of it which Chaucer probably knew, and which contains the illustration given in ll. 788 ff., will be found in Boethius' De Musica, Bk. i (especially chaps. 3 and 14). Another statement, which is perhaps still closer to Chaucer's, is that of Vincent of Beauvais in Spec. Nat. (Douai, 1624), iv, 14–18 (partly quoted by Sypherd, pp. 97–99, with a parallel passage from Macrobius); cf. also xxv, 58.

798 *fro roundel to compas*, from small circle to large.

811 *an ayr*, a surrounding circle or sphere of air.

822 *Take yt in ernest or in game*, take it seriously or as a joke; i.e., in any way you choose. For another occurrence of the same formula see *ClT*, IV, 609. A number of phrases of similar import were current in Middle English. Cf. *foul or fair*, 1. 833, below, and see *Gen Prol*, I, 534, n.

824 *Of pure kynde*, lit., of pure nature; by its very nature.

845–46 Cf. Met., xii, 39–40.

847 *conservatyf the soun*. This construction, in which the adjective takes an object like a participle, is most peculiar. Cf. the occasional treatment of verbal nouns in Plautus: "quid tibi nos tactiost?", Aulularia, 423.

888 Cf. Dante, Par., xxii, 128; but the similarities of language may be due only to the similarity of situation.

907 The comparison of the distant earth to a *prikke* is natural enough and calls for no explanation. Chaucer may, however, have had in mind a similar passage in the Somnium Scipionis (vi, 16) or one in Boethius, *Bo*, ii, pr. 7, 22 ff.

915 The reference is to the account, in the romances of Alexander, of how he was carried in a car in the air by four gigantic griffins. See the Mid. Eng. Wars of Alexander, ed. Skeat, EETS, 1886, ll. 5515 ff.; the Latin version, De Preliis, ed. Landgraf, Erlangen, 1885, p. 131; the Ethiopic version, in E. A. T. W. Budge, Life and Exploits of Alexander, London, 1896, pp. 277 f. (where the reference is to an eagle) and 474 f.; and, for further references, F. P. Magoun, The Gests of King Alexander of Macedon, Cambridge, Mass., 1929, p. 41, n. 3.

916–18 This brief reference to Scipio may be due to RR, 18367–69, though the Somnium Scipionis was doubtless known to Chaucer at the time of writing.

919 Daedalus and Icarus are likewise mentioned in RR, 5226–27. But Chaucer certainly knew Ovid's version of the familiar story (Met., viii, 183 ff.) and the brief reference here points to no special source. Comparisons have been made with Inf., xvii, 109–14, the Ecloga Theoduli, ll. 101–03, and Boccaccio's Amorosa Visione, xxxv.

930 ff. By *many a citezeyn* and *eyryssh bestes* are probably meant the daemons of the air. Skeat took the "beasts" to be the signs of the zodiac. But with the term "citizen" he compared several passages in the Anticlaudianus of Alanus de Insulis, where the reference is to the aerial powers. See iv, 5 (Migne, Pat. Lat., CCX, 525), "aerios cives"; v, 7 (Migne, 537), "cives superi"; v, 9 (Migne, 538), "superos cives." Since Chaucer clearly identifies the two, the same interpretation probably applies to the beasts. It is supported, as Professor W. P. Ker has shown, by the term "animalia . . . corpore aeria" in St. Augustine's De Civ. Dei, viii, 16; in viii, 15, Plato is acknowledged as an authority on the powers in question. (See Migne, Pat. Lat., XLI, 240 f. The reference to Plato in Dante's Par., iv, 22–24, seems to be irrelevant here.) Ker further suggested that the discussion of the subject by Apuleius, in his De Deo Socratis, which was one of Augustine's sources, may also have been known to Alanus and to Chaucer. He compared particularly ll. 925 ff., 965 ff., with sentences in Apuleius. For full discussion see his note, Mod. Quart., I (= MLQ, II), no. 5, pp. 38–39.

In support of Skeat's earlier explanation Mr. W. N. Francis (MLN, LXIV, 339 ff.) points out that Ovid in the Phaethon story (Met. II, 47 ff.), briefly mentioned in ll. 941 ff. just below, clearly refers to the signs of the zodiac as *formas ferarum* and *simulacra ferarum*.

939 *Watlynge Strete*, a famous old road, which probably ran from Kent to the Firth of Forth. The Milky Way was called "Watling street" or "Walsingham way" in England, just as it was known in southern Europe as "la via di San Jacopo" (the way to Santiago), and "la strada di Roma" (the way to Rome). Cf. Dante's Convito, ii, 15, and H. F. Cary's note on Par., xxv, 18 (his translation).

942 For the story of Phaethon see Met., ii, 31 ff.

948 *the Scorpioun*, the zodiacal sign.

950 *for ferde*, for fear. In this phrase *ferd(e)* seems to be a substantive, but its original construction is uncertain. Possibly it was a participle after *for*, but this again would be easily confused with the compound *forfered*.

966 ff. Cf. Anticlaudianus, iv, 6 (Migne, 526); also Apuleius, De Deo Socratis, x.

972 See Boethius, iv, m. 1.

981 Cf. II Cor. xii, 2.

985 *Marcian*, Martianus Capella (fifth century). His treatise De Nuptiis inter Philologiam et Mercurium contained an extended discussion of astronomy. Chaucer refers to him again, in a quite different context, in *MerchT*, IV, 1732 ff.

986 *Anteclaudian*, the Anticlaudianus of Alanus de Insulis.

1004 *the Raven*, the constellation Corvus. *Eyther Bere*, Ursa Major and Ursa Minor.

1005 *Arionis harpe*, Lyra.

1006 *Castor, Pollux*, Gemini; *Delphyn*, Delphinus.

1007 "The seven daughters of Atlas," the Pleiades.

1008 The unusual form *arn* for the regular *be(n)* of Chaucer's dialect may be noted.

1022 On St. Julian, the patron saint of hospitality, see *Gen Prol*, I, 340, n.

1034 For this oath by St. Peter cf. l. 2000 below; also *ShipT*, VII, 214; *WB Prol*, III, 446; *FrT*, III, 1332.

1044 Cf. *Tr*, iii, 737.

1063 On the idiom *lives body* for "living body" (genitive for adjective) see *KnT*, I, 1912, n.

1066 *Seynte Clare* (1194–1253), an abbess and a disciple of St. Francis. See Catholic Encyclopædia, IV, 4–6.

1068 ff. Three sources have been suggested for this explanation of the conversion of words into images. Mr. J. T. Williams (MLN, LXII, 488 ff.) points out a similar device in the thirteenth century Hebrew Zohar. Mr. J. Ziegler (MLN, LXIV, 73 ff.) sees a possible source in the De Consolatione Philosophiae, iv, pr. 1 and met. 1, a passage used just above in ll. 972 ff. Mr. P. G. Ruggiers (MLN, LXIX, 34 ff.) argues that Chaucer is more likely to have been influenced by the words of Beatrice in Dante's Paradiso (IV, 37 ff.), explaining the appearance of spirits on the various planets.

Book III

1091 ff. The invocation is imitated from Par., i, 13–27.

1098 This seems to be a definite acknowledgement on Chaucer's part of his practice of writing verses without the full number of syllables. He may have in mind particularly those which begin with an accented syllable, — the seven-syllable lines in the octosyllabic, and the nine-syllable lines in the decasyllabic, measure. Or is it simply a prayer for indulgence with imperfect verses?

1099 On the use of *that* to repeat *though, if*, etc., see *Pars Prol*, X, 39, n.

1116 Cf. Met., xii, 43.

1117 Professor R. M. Smith (MLN, LX, 39 ff.)

notes that the reference to Spain may be due to the Roman de la Rose, 243 ff. This seems to be the earliest extant reference to "castles in Spain."

1130 Various sources have been suggested for the idea of a mountain of ice. The commentators who have emphasized Dante's influence on the poem have compared the mountain of Purgatory. See particularly Rambeau, ESt, III, 249–50. Dr. A. C. Garrett proposed to trace the conception to folk-tale accounts of glass mountains. See [Harv.] Stud. and Notes, V, 157 ff. But the most probable suggestion is that of Professor Sypherd (pp. 114 ff.), who shows that the whole conception of the goddess of Fame and her abode was influenced by descriptions of Fortune and her house, and who cites particularly the account of the dwelling of Fortune on a rock of ice in La Panthère d'Amours by Nicole de Margival.

1131 *seynt Thomas of Kent*, St. Thomas à Becket.

1136 *half*, i.e., side. With the names carved on ice and melted by heat Professor Brusendorff (p. 161, n.) has compared Petrarch's Trionfo del Tempo, ll. 127 ff.

1147 Proverbial; cf. Haeckel, p. 44, no. 149.

1170 *compace*, riming with *place*, ought to be the infinitive, and not the noun "compass." It is probable, therefore, that we should either emend the MS. reading *no* to *ne* or interpret *no* as "nor" (for which there is slight authority). See Kenyon, The Syntax of the Infinitive in Chaucer; Ch. Soc., 1909, p. 91, n. 1.

1181 ff. With the description here Professor Whiting in MP, XXXI, 196 ff., compares a similar one in Li Biaus Desconneus of Renaud de Beaujeu.

1183 *seynt Gyle*, St. Aegidius. See *CYT*, VIII, 1185, n.

1184 *beryle*, Professor Sypherd suggests (p. 133, n. 2), was an appropriate material for a palace of Love. He quotes from L'Intelligenza (ed. Gellrich, Breslau, 1883, st. 25), "Per sua vertute fa crescer l'amore." The word was sometimes employed in a transferred sense for crystal or glass. See NED, s.v., II, 3, which assumes this meaning in l. 1288 below. But the reference there, as here, seems to be to the gem. For further notes on the symbolism of the beryl see H. R. Patch, MLN, L, 312 ff.

1203 *Orpheus*, the famous minstrel. Chaucer doubtless knew Ovid's account of him in Met., x and xi.

1205 *Orion*, apparently Chaucer's spelling for Arion. See Ovid's Fasti, ii, 79–118, for his story.

1206 *Eacides Chiron*, Achilles' tutor, Chiron the centaur. Achilles was the grandson of Aeacus. The combination seems to have come from Ovid's Ars Amat., i, 17, "Aeacidae Chiron."

1208 *Glascurion*, a British bard. He is probably the same as the Glasgerion of a well-known ballad (Child, Engl. and Scottish Ballads, Boston, 1882–98, III, 136, no. 67). The name may go back to the Welsh "y Bardd Glas Keraint (or Geraint)," the Blue Bard Keraint, supposed to have lived in the tenth century. This identification was proposed by T. Price, Literary Remains, Llandovery, 1854–55, I, 151–52, and has been received favorably by most commentators both on Chaucer and on the ballad. Unfortunately the accounts of the Welsh bard thus far pointed out are modern and of very little authority. According to the Iolo MSS. (ed. Taliesin Williams, Llandovery, 1848, pp. 623–25) he was a brother of Morgan Hên, King of Glamorgan; he collected ancient records of poetry and bardism and compiled the laws of the chair and the Gorsedd. He is also credited with having compiled the first Welsh grammar. A few pieces of prose and verse, attributed to him, are published in the Myvyrian Archaiology of Wales, London, 1801–07, III, 100 ff. The Iolo MSS. also record that he went to King Alfred to London as his domestic bard; they say that many other Welsh bards accompanied him, and that to them was due an improvement in learning and knowledge among the Saxons. As a result of these statements some scholars have been disposed to identify the Bardd Glas with Bishop Asser, the biographer of Alfred. Cf. W. Owen Pughe, Cambrian Biography, London, 1803, pp. 19, 128–29; T. Price, Lit. Remains, I, 151; T. Williams, Iolo MSS., p. 624. But there is no real support for the hypothesis. Cf. J. H. Parry, The Cambrian Plutarch, London, 1834, pp. 95 f. Nothing is known of the Blue Bard to account for Chaucer's mention of him here, and the source of Chaucer's information is undiscovered. Possibly he got it from some of his Welsh friends. See the note on l. 1925, below.

1212–13 Cf. RR, 16029–31.

1221 "Both on dulcet (or doucet) and on reed." The former was "a wind instrument resembling a flute." See NED, s.v. Doucet, 2.

1224 *pipes made of grene corn*, i.e., the simple pipes made by the rustics. See *Rom*, 4250.

1227 f. *Atiteris* and *Pseustis* (variants of Cytherus and Presentus) are of doubtful identity. The former has been taken as a corruption of Tyrtaeus, or of Tityrus (in Virgil's Eclogues). Pseustis has been explained as the shepherd who debates with Alithia in the Ecloga Theoduli.

1229 *Marcia*, Marsyas, the satyr whom Apollo first defeated in a musical contest and then flayed. Chaucer's form of the name and his treatment of it as feminine are doubtless due to the fact that he was misled by the Italian "Marsia," which occurs in Dante's Paradiso, i, 20, and in the Teseida, xi, 62. (For Chaucer's earlier use of this passage see the note to l. 1091 above.) Elements from Ovid's account (Met., vi, 382 ff.) seem to be combined here with those from Dante.

1243 *Messenus*, Misenus, trumpeter to Hector and to Aeneas. See Aen., iii, 239; vi, 162 ff.

1245 *Joab* is mentioned as trumpeting in II Sam. ii, 28; xviii, 16; xx, 22. *Theodomas*, doubtless Thiodamas, the augur of Thebes. In Theb., viii, 342 ff., as Skeat observes, his invocation is followed by trumpeting, though he is not actually mentioned as himself blowing a trumpet. Perhaps Chaucer had in mind some mediæval version of the Theban story. Cf. also *MerchT*, IV, 1720.

1247–48 For evidence that trumpet playing was a great feature of ceremonial life in Catalonia and Aragon, at least in the thirteenth century, the editor is indebted to his friend and colleague, Mr. Walter Whitehill, who has referred him to Higini Anglès, La Musica a Catalunya fins al segle XIII (Barcelona, 1935) p. 88. For a note on several passages in the *House of Fame* [dealing with "*mynstralcye and noyse*" see R. M. Smith, MLN, LXV, 521 ff.

1257 f. Cf. RR, 4623 f. (*Rom*, 5123); Haeckel, p. 42, no. 144; *Intro* to *MLT*, II, 20 ff., and n.

1260 On *tregetours* see *FranklT*, V, 1141, and n.

1266 On natural magic and the treatment of diseases by images cf. *Gen Prol*, I, 414, n.

1268 The ascendant is that part of the zodiacal circle which ascends above the horizon at a given moment.

1271–74 Skeat has compared with this passage RR, 14397 ff., where Balenus, Medea, and Circe are mentioned together.

Quene Medea, Medea, who by magic restored Aeson to youth. See Met., vii, 162 ff.

1272 *Circes*, Circe; cf. Met., xiv. Chaucer's form with -s may be due to the frequent occurrence of the genitive "Circes" in Ovid.

Calipsa, Calypso, the nymph who detained Odysseus on an island (Odyssey, i). Cf. also Ovid, Ex Ponto, iv, 10, 13.

1273 *Hermes Ballenus*, Belinous (Balanus), the disciple of Hermes Trismegistus. *Hermes* is apparently either a possessive genitive or an epithet. On Hermes Trismegistus see *CYT*, VIII, 1434, n. On *Ballenus* see Professor Langlois's note to RR, 14399. He cites de Sacy's identification of Belinous, Belenos, etc., with Apollonius of Tyana; also the mention of a Liber Beleni de horarum opere, in the Speculum Astronomie of Albertus Magnus. The usual Arabic form of the name is Balinas. For a list of works attributed to him see M. Steinschneider, Apollonius von Thyana (oder Balinas) bei den Arabern, Zt. d. Deutschen Morgenländ. Gesellschaft, XLV, 439 ff.

1274 *Limote*, probably Elymas, the sorcerer mentioned in Acts xiii, 8. On *Symon Magus* see Acts viii, 9.

1277 *Colle tregetour*, probably an English magician mentioned in a French manual of conversation composed in 1396, and declared to have practiced his art recently at Orléans. He is described as "un Englois qu' estoit fort nigromancien qui est a nom Colin T. qui savoit faire beaucoup des mervailles par voie de nigromancie." The manual is attributed, doubtfully, to an Englishman, M. T. Coyfurelly. Professor J. F. Royster, who proposed the identification, suggested very reasonably that "T." in the French may stand for Tregetour. He called to mind further the reference in *FranklT* to Orléans as a seat of magic arts. For further references see his article in Stud. Phil., XXIII, 380 ff.

Lady Guest (Mabinogion, London, 1838–49, II, 176) long ago noted that the name of *Colle* is similar to that of "Coll mab Collfrewi," described in one of the Welsh Triads (no. 90) as a famous magician. This identification was repeated by J. Loth, Les Mabinogion, 2d ed., Paris, 1913, II, 271, n., and has been noted again recently in TLS, 1931, p. 28. In TLS, 1931, p. 79, Miss K. M. Buck argues that the reference is rather to Collfrewi than to Coll, his son, and cites her Wayland-Dietrich Saga, London, 1924–29, VIII, 384, for further information.

1303 Adopting *hatte* (Skeat's conjecture), we may render the sentence: "Nor how they are named in masonry, as for example corbels full of carved work."

1311 ff. At this point and in the description of the goddess which follows, Professor Emil Koeppel found certain resemblances to Boccaccio's Amorosa Visione. See Angl., XIV, 235 ff. The actual parallels between the two descriptions are of little significance, and it has never been established that Chaucer knew the Visione. If he did, however, the fact that

Boccaccio presents a goddess of Renown ("La Gloria del Popol Mondano") may help to account for Chaucer's modification of the traditional character of Fame as a goddess merely of rumor or report. Whether or not Chaucer was influenced by Boccaccio's poem, his portrayal of the goddess was chiefly affected by the current conceptions of the divinities of Fortune and Love. (See Sypherd, pp. 16-17, 112-32.) The association of the ideas of fame and fortune in Boethius may, as Sypherd suggests, have helped determine the course of Chaucer's thought.

1316 *kynges*, i.e., kings-of-arms.

1329-35 Cf. RR, 6738-40.

1352 *the Lapidaire*, the Lapidarium, a metrical treatise in Latin on precious stones, composed in the eleventh century by Abbot Marbodus.

1361 *see*, seat.

1368 ff. With the description here cf. Boethius, *Bo*, i, pr. 1, 4 ff., and Aen., iv, 173 ff. The curious mention of *Partriches wynges* (l. 1392) seems to be due to a mistranslation of Virgil's "pernicibus alis" (or Chaucer may have had a MS. which read "perdicibus"). The Latin phrase is correctly rendered in *Tr*, iv, 661, *with preste wynges*.

1376 *sterres sevene*, the planets.

1380 *tolde*, counted.

1383 ff. See Rev. iv, 6. It is hardly necessary to assume the influence of Purg., xxix, 92 ff., as suggested by Rambeau.

1395-1405 Comparison has been suggested with Par., xxiii, 97-111.

1414 For the story of the shirt see *MkT*, VII, 2119 ff.

1432 ff. *Josephus*, author of the Historia Judaeorum, probably said to be of the *secte saturnyn* because of the astrological doctrine that the Jewish religion, as the root of all others, is signified by "the father of the planets." See Miss A. H. Miller, MLN, XLVII, 99 ff. She cites Roger Bacon, Opus Majus, tr. Burke, Philadelphia, 1928, I, 277 f.

1437 The *other sevene*, presumably Jewish historians, are not named.

1455 *gynne*, here apparently merely a colorless auxiliary, as was commonly the case with the pret. *gan, gunnen*.

1459 An allusion to the story of the two tigers in Theb., vii. By killing three Greeks they led to the renewal of hostilities at Thebes.

1460 *Stace*, Statius (d. 96 A.D.), the author of the Thebaid and of the Achilleid. He was incorrectly supposed to have been a native of Toulouse. Thus Dante calls him "Tolosano" (Purg., xxi, 89), and Boccaccio "Stazio di Tolosa" (Amorosa Visione, v, 34). Though Chaucer appears to be following Dante just here, it is not probable that he derived the persons on the pillars from any single source. The great poets who receive Dante upon his entrance into hell are not quite the same. They include Horace and omit Statius and Claudian. See Inf., iv, 88 ff. The Amorosa Visione has no parallel list.

1466 *Omer*, Homer.

1467 ff. *Dares*, Dares Phrygius. *Tytus*, doubtless a corruption of Dictys (Cretensis), whom Chaucer calls *Dite* in *Tr*, i, 146. It is barely possible, as Professor Rand has argued (Speculum, I, 224) that Chaucer meant to include Livy (the *Tytus Lyvyus* of *BD*, 1084, and *PhysT*, VI, 1) among the authorities

on the Trojan story. *Lollius*, supposed by Chaucer to be the name of an authority on the Trojan war and adopted as the author of the pretended source of the Troilus. For a full discussion of the Lollius question see Professor Kittredge's article in the Harv. Stud. in Class. Philol., XXVIII, 47-133. *Guydo ... de Columpnis* (or Guido delle Colonne), author of the Latin Historia Trojana, which was based upon the Roman de Troie of Benoît de Ste.-Maure. On all these writers and their part in the transmission of the mediæval Trojan legend see the introduction to the *Troilus*.

1470 *Gaufride*, Geoffrey of Monmouth (d. 1154), author of the celebrated Historia Regum Britanniae, which is the source of a great body of literary material on the legendary history of Britain. Since he deals with the tradition which makes the Britons the descendants of Aeneas, he is properly reckoned among the writers who "bore up Troy." It is unlikely that Chaucer, as Professor Rand has suggested (Speculum, I, 225), meant himself to be recognized as the *Englyssh Gaufride*.

1479-80 Perhaps an echo of Benoît, ll. 45-70, 110-16.

1482 The significance of the *tynned yren* of Virgil's pillar is not quite clear. Miss Elizabeth Nitchie, Vergil and the English Poets, New York, 1919, pp. 57-59, points out that tin was the metal of Jupiter ("a plate of Jupiter"), and interprets "tinned iron" to imply Mars controlled and directed by Jupiter in the Aeneid. Copper, as the metal sacred to Venus, was a natural choice for Ovid, and the sulphur in Claudian's case is associated with the lower world.

1499 *Lucan*, the author of the Pharsalia, which narrates the wars between Caesar and Pompey.

1508 *lyk as he were wood*, explained by Professor Shannon (pp. 357 f.) with reference to Claudian's own mention of the poetic "furor" in De Raptu Pros., i, 5.

1511 f. Cf. Inf., ix, 44.

1526 ff. In the description of the groups of suppliants and the awards that they receive there may be reminiscences of Dante. Rambeau notes particularly (p. 259) the sound of bees in Inf., xvi, 3. The passage on Providence in Boethius, iv, pr. 6, may also have been in Chaucer's mind. But the whole conception of the arbitrary goddess seems to have been most influenced, as Sypherd has argued (pp. 117 ff.), by the characteristics of the divinities of Love and Fortune.

Other bee-similes in Chaucer are noted by Koeppel in Angl., XIV, 243.

1530 *alleskynnes*, really a genitive singular, dependent upon *condiciouns*.

1547 There seems to be no definite authority for the statement that Fame and Fortune are sisters, but the frequent association of the two, and the obvious derivation of much of Chaucer's description of Fame from the accounts of Fortune, make it natural for him to invent the relationship (if he did).

Ll. 1547 f. and 1573-82 have a rather striking parallel in Gower's Mirour de l'Omme, ll. 22129-52. Professor Tatlock, who pointed out the resemblance (Dev. and Chron., pp. 38 ff.), held Gower to have been probably the borrower and inferred a date "about 1379" for the *House of Fame*. But Professor Patch questions this inference and has called the editor's attention to a similar conception of the trumpets (in this case called "Eur" and "Malheur") in the Dance aux Aveugles of Pierre Michault (ed. Douxfils, Lille, 1748, pp. 32 f.). He holds Gower's version to represent an earlier form of the idea than Chaucer's.

1571 With the phrase *the god of wynde* Skeat compares RR, 18006, but no source is needed for this commonplace epithet. The representation of Aeolus with two trumpets is ascribed by Lounsbury (Studies, II, 382) to Albricus Philosophus, De Deorum Imaginibus (Van Staveren, Auct. Myth. Lat., Leyden, 1742, 920 f.). The connection with Thrace Professor Shannon (p. 341 f.) would explain by reference to Valerius Flaccus, Argonauticon, i, 597 ff. Skeat notes also Ovid's phrase "Threicio Borea" (Ars Amat., ii, 431).

1596 *Triton*, mentioned in recollection of Ovid's Met., i, 333. He is referred to as a trumpeter twice in the Aeneid (vi, 171 ff.; x, 209).

1598 The use of *to* after *let* is unusual, and Skeat suggests the possibility of reading *togoo* here (and *to-glyde* in *FranklT*, V, 1415) as a compound.

1643 *pelet*, a stone ball, such as were used with the earliest kind of cannon.

1702 *clew*, a strong preterite of *clawen*, "to claw, rub." Chaucer elsewhere has the weak form *clawed*.

1708 For the use of *a lek* in a comparison to denote worthlessness, see *Gen Prol*, I, 177, n.

1710–11 Cf. RR, 17443–44, though no literary source need be assumed.

1742 "They did not once intend in their heart to show us friendliness; on the contrary [they] could (i.e., would gladly) see us dead" (lit. "bring us on our bier").

1747 *for wod*, like mad. Cf. *for pure wood, Rom*, 276, and on this use of *for* with an adjective see *KnT*, I, 2142, n.

1758–62 Cf. RR. 9855–58.

1768 For the figure of the pasture cf. *Tr*, ii, 752.

1783 The proverb of the cat who would eat fish but would not wet her feet was widely current. Skeat cites, among other versions, the mediæval Latin line, "Catus amat piscem, sed non vult tingere plantam." He compares also Conf. Am., iv, 1108–09, and Macbeth, i, 7, 45. Cf. his EE Prov., pp. 87 f., no. 209; and Haeckel, p. 9, no. 31.

1794 *noskynnes labour*, labor of no kind. Cf. note to l. 1530.

1796 *bele Isawde*, the fair Isolde (or Iseult), mentioned as a type of beauty, contrasted with the menial that grinds at a handmill.

1803 Cf. Inf., v, 28–33, where "mugghia" corresponds to Chaucer's *beloweth*. Other mediæval references to the wind of hell are collected by T. Spencer, Speculum, II, 192 ff.

1810 "Such amusement they found in their hoods," i.e., so much fun did they make of them. For the idiom cf. the phrase "to put an ape in a man's hood," *Intro* to *PrT*, VII, 440, and n.

1840 *pale*, stripe. He wore the garb of a fool.

1844 *Ysidis*, Isis ("Isidis" being the Latin genitive). The reference is generally taken to be to Herostratus, who in desire for fame set fire to the temple of Diana at Ephesus. Why the temple of Isis in Athens is substituted is unknown.

1879–80 A proverbial expression. Cf. Conf. Am., iii, 1626–27.

1908 The form *brynges* (for *bryngest*), supported by the rime, is without parallel in Chaucer (though there are cases of the Northern third person singular in *-es*). It seems better to let the irregularity stand than to remove it by emendation.

1920 For the "house of Daedalus" see Met., viii, 158 ff. The name "labyrinthus" is applied to it in Aen., v, 588, and in Boethius, iii, pr. 12, where a gloss identifies it as "Domus Dedali." See *Bo*, iii, pr. 12, 156. The syntactical construction of this sentence is loose. It seems to mean "a house [such that] the Domus Dedali was not so wonderfully wrought. For a different treatment of the passage see F. P. Magoun, Jr., Med. Stud., XVI, 153.

1925 ff. For many features of the House of Rumor Chaucer is indebted to Ovid's account of the dwelling of Fame (Met., xii, 39–63). But in two striking particulars he departs from his classical source. He describes it as a revolving house, made of interwoven twigs. The conception of a whirling house was common in the romances, and entrance was often gained by the aid of a guide, sometimes a helpful animal. (Cf. La Mule sanz Frain, ed. Hill, Baltimore, 1911, ll. 440 ff.; the Welsh Seint Greal, ed. Robert Williams, Hengwrt MSS. I, London, 1876, p. 325; and the prose Perceval, ed. Potvin, Perceval le Gallois, Mons, 1866–71, I, 195 f.; and for other instances see Sypherd, pp. 144 ff.) But buildings of wicker or wattle were more unusual in the literature familiar to Chaucer, and it seems probable that he may have known by observation or report of such actual houses among the Irish and Welsh. For information about them again consult Sypherd, pp. 141 ff. The question whether Chaucer ever lived in Ireland has been briefly discussed in the biographical introduction. His possible interest in Wales through his friends Sir John Clanvowe and Lewis Johan has been pointed out by Professor Kittredge in MP, I, 16, and PMLA, XVI, 450–52. It may be noted further that *the Bret Glascurion* (l. 1208) also suggests some knowledge of Welsh lore on Chaucer's part.

1926 Possibly a reminiscence of Inf., iii, 53–54.

1928 *Oyse*, a river which flows into the Seine near Paris. It was doubtless chosen here for the rime.

1940 *hottes*, baskets. Skeat's emendation for *hattes* seems reasonably sure to be right.

1943 With *chirkynges* cf. *KnT*, I, 2004.

2011 "To drive away thy heaviness with." For the order of words cf. *Gen Prol*, I, 791, n.

2016–18 Reading and interpretation are both uncertain. "Since Fortune has made the fruit (object, effect?), or the root (cause, source?) of thy heart's rest to languish," etc. (?).

2034 ff. Cf. Inf., iii, 55–57.

2053 *Thus shal hit be*, probably in the sense, "Thus is it reported to be." This use of *shal*, like Ger. "soll," is known in early English. *LGW*, 1725 appears to be another example.

2060 There is a discussion of the spreading of report in Dante's Convivio, i, 3.

2101 On sworn brotherhood see *KnT*, I, 1132, n.

2108–09 This conception of the compact of truth and falsehood is developed from a bare suggestion in Ovid: "Mixtaque cum veris passim commenta vagantur Millia rumorum" (Met., xii, 54–55).

2119 Cf. *Sum Prol*, III, 1695.

2122 Shipmen and pilgrims might both be naturally associated with travelers' yarns. On the reputation of pilgrims, in particular, for untruthfulness, see the note in Hall's edition of King Horn, Oxford, 1901, p. 153.

2152 The reading is uncertain. The line means either "And lifted up their noses on high" or "And lifted up their noses and eyes."

2154 "And stamp as men do in trying to catch eels." Editors have in general refrained from commenting on this line, either because its meaning seems clear or because the custom was familiar. But Professor Magoun has had the curiosity to collect instances of catching eels by "stamping" or by "treading," and the editor is indebted to him for the following references. From Dr. Alfred C. Redfield of the Woods Hole Oceanographic Institution he cites the information, on the testimony of Mr. Harold Backus, chief engineer at Woods Hole, that the custom still exists in Norfolk Broads, England, where the term for treading is "stomping." Mr. Jan Halin, of the publicity department at Woods Hole, testifies that the fishermen in the Zuider Zee have a similar method of driving eels into nets.

The one published reference Mr. Magoun has found is in Mourt's Relation or Journal of the Plymouth Plantation (ed. H. M. Dexter, Boston, 1865, p. 97) where Squanto (an Indian) is described as treading eels out with his feet.

2158 The *man of gret auctorite* has been conjecturally identified with Richard II (Snell, Age of Chaucer, London, 1901, p. 185), Thomas of Gloucester (von Westenholz, Angl. Beibl., XII, 172), and John of Gaunt (Riedel, JEGP, XXVII, 447 ff.). But in our complete ignorance of what was to follow, speculation is idle.

The fragment ends in the middle of a sentence. Caxton's copy breaks off at l. 2094, after which he adds twelve lines of his own; see the Textual Notes. Thynne prints ll. 2095–2158 and then appends Caxton's ending slightly altered. What Chaucer's own intentions were with regard to continuing the poem is entirely unknown. Professor Brusendorff argued (p. 156) that the unfinished form is due merely to bad MS. tradition. He held Chaucer to have composed a very short ending, which has been lost. This appears to be also Professor Manly's opinion (Kittredge Anniv. Papers, p. 79).

Anelida and Arcite

The *Anelida*, which is ascribed to Chaucer by Lydgate (Prologue to Bk. i of the Falls of Princes) and marked as his in three MSS., is of undoubted authenticity.

The question of its date is bound up with that of the date of the other works in which use is made of the *Teseida*. It may well have been the earliest of the group, and it almost certainly preceded the *Knight's Tale*. See the Introduction on Chronology, and cf. Tatlock, Dev. and Chron., Ch. Soc., 1907, pp. 83 ff. Professor Langhans (Angl., XLIV, 239) rightly recognizes the inferiority of the *Anelida* to the *Knight's Tale*, the *Troilus*, and the *Parliament of Fowls*. But his date, 1373–74, rests upon an unproved assignment of the *Parliament* to 1374.

Two attempts have been made to connect the poem with episodes in court society. Professor Bilderbeck (N & Q, 8th Ser., IX, 301 f.) took it to refer to Robert de Vere, Earl of Oxford, who repudiated his wife, Philippa de Coucy, in 1387. But there is little reason for the identification, which is generally regarded as improbable because of Chaucer's friendly relation to the Earl. See Tatlock, as cited above, and Miss Hammond, ESt, XLIII, 26. A more elaborate theory, proposed by Professor F. Tupper (PMLA, XXXVI, 186 ff.) must also, in spite of certain curious resemblances in proper names, be rejected for lack of real evidence. Mr. Tupper would identify Anelida, Queen of Ermonie, as the Countess of Ormonde (born Anne Welle), the wife of James Butler, the third earl. Ormonde, he shows, was sometimes Latinized Ermonia. Butler, being a d'Arcy on his mother's side, was represented by Arcite. From the fact that he had two illegitimate sons, Thomas and James le Botiller, born sometime in the eighties, it is inferred that he was

guilty of such infidelity as the poem condemns. But bastardy was not so rare in the English court of Chaucer's time as to give one much confidence in the selection of this particular instance. Moreover, there is no evidence whether Thomas and James le Botiller were born before or after Ormonde's marriage to Anne; and, as Mr. Tupper himself points out, the Earl lived honorably and happily with his wife for many years. The parallel between Arcite's behavior and that of d'Arcy, or Ormonde, is after all not very striking, and with the acceptance or rejection of this central identification stand or fall Mr. Tupper's interpretations of other details of the story. Scythia, according to his explanation, represents Ireland; Thebes, the English Pale; Theseus stands for Lionel; Hippolyta for Elizabeth de Burgh, Countess of Ulster; Emily for Maud Ufford, half-sister of Elizabeth and wife of Thomas de Vere, Earl of Oxford; Creon possibly for the Earl of Desmond, Lionel's successor as viceroy. The resemblances are slight between these characters and the historical counterparts named; and the fact that their story follows Boccaccio in all essentials makes the whole allegorical explanation as unnecessary as it is unlikely.

The source of the plot (if the allegorical theories are rejected) is unknown. For similar situations Skeat (Oxf. Chaucer, I, 78, 534) compares the story of the falcon in the *Squire's Tale*, and the *Complaint to His Lady*. On the former parallel see also Tupper (pp. 196 ff.), who would identify the falcon, as well as Anelida, with Anne Welle. Chaucer himself, in his Proem, professes to follow *Stace* and *Corynne*, and he actually uses for the setting and beginning of his narrative both Statius and the *Teseida* of Boccaccio. See Ten Brink, Chaucer Studien,

Münster, 1870, pp. 48 ff., B. A. Wise, The Influence of Statius upon Chaucer, Baltimore, 1911, pp. 66 ff., and R. A. Pratt, Chaucer's Use of the Teseida, PMLA, LXII, 598 ff. The explanation of *Corynne* is a matter of dispute. Of the various persons suggested — Corinna, Corinnus, Corippus, Ovid (Corinna's poet), Boccaccio — the Theban poetess Corinna seems most appropriate. There is no good reason for a reference to Corinnus or Corippus. The theory of Professor Shannon (Chaucer and the Roman Poets, Cambridge, Mass., 1929, pp. 15 ff.) that Chaucer meant to acknowledge indebtedness to the Heroides, would be easier to accept if the use of Corrinna as a name for Ovid could be really established. Moreover, Mr. Shannon somewhat overestimates the influence of Ovid on the *Anelida*. Dr. Wise's suggestion, that Chaucer was constructing a synonym for "Boccaccio" out of the Italian "corina" ("wry-mouthed"), like Professor Bright's similar explanation of "Lollius" (PMLA, XIX, xxii f.) is altogether improbable. For fuller discussion of the whole subject see Lounsbury, Studies in Chaucer, New York, 1892, II, 403-04; Wise, p. 67; and Shannon, as cited.

The suggestion recently made by Professor T. Vallese (Goffredo Chaucer, etc., Milan, 1930, pp. 43 ff.), that the real source of the *Anelida* was Boccaccio's Fiammetta, cannot be accepted. The resemblances on which it is based are either too general or too conventional to be significant.

The *Complaint* proper belongs to a genre much practiced in Chaucer's time, and represented by several of his other poems. On this type in general, known as the "complainte d'amour" or the "salut d'amour," see P. Meyer, Bibl. de l'École de Chartes, 1867, pp. 124-70, and Bull. de la SATF, 1887, pp. 94 ff.; also Faral's ed. of Gautier d'Aupais, Paris, 1919, p. ix. The specimen in the *Anelida* has been compared particularly with the second of two complaints of Machaut, entitled Le Lay de Plour (Poésies Lyriques, ed. Chichmaref, Paris, 1909, II, 434, 459), and with his Lay de la Souscie (II, 443). See Legouis, Chaucer, Paris, 1910, p. 45, and Miss M. Fabin, MLN, XXXIV, 266 ff. But none of these pieces closely resembles it. For comparisons with Ovid's Heroides see Shannon, pp. 38 ff. Professor Shannon, whose discussion of the genre is interesting, shows that Anelida's complaint, like the *Complaint of Mars*, differs from most poems of the sort in being more specific and embodying more narrative elements.

The name of *Arcite* was taken over from the Teseida; the source of *Anelida*, unless Professor Tupper's theory be accepted, must be regarded as undiscovered. The derivation by Bradshaw and Cowell (Proc. Camb. Philol. Soc., xiii-xv, 14 f.; Ch. Soc. Essays, pp. 615 ff.) from the ancient Persian goddess Anâhita ('Aναîτις, Latinized in the accusative Anaetidem or Anaetida, whence Anelida) is far-fetched. On the occurrence of the name *Anelida* in Arthurian romance see J. Schick, Lydgate's Temple of Glas, EETS, 1891, p. cxx. Professor Koeppel (ESt, XX, 156) suggested that Chaucer took it from L'Intelligenza (ed. Gellrich, Breslau, 1883), st. 75. But conclusive evidence is lacking of his knowledge of that work. (See Kittredge, MP, VII, 478.)

1-70 The chief sources of the first ten stanzas

are as follows: 1-3 from Tes., i, 3, 2, and 1; 4-7 from Theb., xii, 519 ff. (with use of Tes., ii, 22 in st. 6); 8-10 from Tes., ii, 10-12.

1 On the epithet red as applied to Mars see *KnT*, I, 1747, n. Here it is doubtless due to Tes., i, 3, "Marte rubicondo."

2 A reference to the temple of Mars on Mt. Haemus in Thrace, described by Statius, Theb., vii, 40 ff.

5 Chaucer here confuses Bellona and Pallas (unless, as is possible, the names are not in apposition). The two are kept distinct in the Thebaid (cf. ii, 704, 715 ff.). But the confusion appears in Boccaccio, De Gen. Deor., v, 48, where Bellona is also called sister of Mars, and his charioteer. Examples of the same error are cited by R. A. Pratt from the glosses in the Achilleid. See Prog. of Med. and Ren. Studies in U.S. and Canada, Bull. No. 20, p. 49.

8-14 This stanza contains, alongside the main source in Boccaccio, echoes of Dante's Paradiso, i, 8-9; cf. also Boethius, ii, pr. 7. (See Lowes, MP, XIV, 729.)

10 Oddly enough the Teseida at this point declares that the story there related is *not* treated by a Latin author. Chaucer implies that the tale of Anelida is in Statius, whom he cites below by name (l. 21). But as a matter of fact he derived it neither from Statius nor from Boccaccio, and his statement must be regarded simply as a literary fiction. He is only making the conventional claim to ancient classical authority.

15-20 With the opening stanza of the Teseida Chaucer has here interwoven reminiscences of Bk. xi, st. 63, and of Par., i, 31, 36, and xxiii, 55-59. The reference to *Cirrea*, the epithet *glade*, and the specific mention of the laurel and of Polyhymnia all seem to be due to Dante. (See Lowes, MP, XIV, 725 ff.) The adjective *memorial* may even be due to Dante's "memoria" (Par., i, 9), though it is appropriate on general grounds to the character of Polyhymnia. On the idea that Helicon was a well see *HF*, 521, n. and on the geographical relations of the passage see F. P. Magoun, Jr., Med. Stud., XV, 114.

20 For the figure cf. Tes., xii, 86, Theb., xii, 809, and Filostrato, ix, 3. It recurs in *Tr*, ii, 1 ff., where Chaucer was clearly following Purg., i, 1.

22 The beginning of this passage from Statius (Theb., xii, 519 ff.), inserted before l. 22, is also quoted in several MSS. of the *Canterbury Tales* at the head of the *Knight's Tale*. Ll. 22-42 closely follow the Thebaid, and have also striking similarities with the *Knight's Tale*. For example, with l. 25 cf. KnT, I, 869; l. 24, I, 1027, 979; ll. 30-31, I, 975-76; ll. 36-37, I, 881-82; ll. 43-46, I, 872-73, 1027; ll. 64 ff., I, 938 ff. L. 38 repeats I, 972. *Emelye* is the Emilia of the Teseida (and the *Knight's Tale*); she does not appear in Statius.

25 *contre houses*, homes ("domos patriae").

50 ff. The following summary of the earlier part of the Thebaid is based upon Boccaccio.

51 Juno was angry with Thebes because it had been the scene of Jupiter's amours with Europa, Alcmena, and Semele. Cf. Theb., i, 250 ff.

57 ff. The persons here named took part in the famous war of the Seven against Thebes. For a further account of them see *Tr*, v, 1485 ff., and n.

Chaucer's spelling of *Amphiorax* (Amphiaraus) is noteworthy. The final *-x* is the French spelling for *-us*, but was perhaps pronounced here as *x*. Cf. *Gen Prol*, I, 384 f., n.

72 *Ermony*, apparently Armenia. (Professor Tupper's identification with Ormonde is discussed above.) The reason for the choice of Armenia is unknown. Possibly it was suggested by Scythia, the land of Emilia's sister; possibly by a visit of the King of Armenia to England in 1384, though this assumption implies a rather late date for the poem. Professor Lowes (Washington Univ. Studies, I, ii, 17 f.) collects references to the presence of Armenians in England, and suggests further that Chaucer's interest in Peter of Cyprus implies an interest in other eastern visitors. Dr. Wise (p. 70) would connect Ermony with Harmonia, who possessed the brooch of Thebes (see Theb., ii, 265 ff.). But this involves an unnatural confusion of personal and local names. Moreover, Dr. Wise himself remarks (p. 136) that a French Theban romance might have represented an Armenian queen as residing in the city. He compares the Roman de Thèbes, 3872, for a similar statement about the son of Hergart, King of Ermine.

80 Such references to the satisfaction of Nature were conventional in the description of beautiful women. Cf. *PhysT*, VI, 9, and n.

82 Penelope and Lucretia are also named as examples of constancy in *BD*, 1081–82, a passage which seems to go back to RR, 8605 ff.

85 The name of Arcite, which does not occur here in any of the MSS., seems necessary to both sense and meter.

105 For this proverbial expression cf. *SqT*, V, 537. Skeat and Tupper note, besides the general similarity of the situation to that of the falcon and the false tercelet, several other more or less significant parallels of detail. With l. 99 here cf. V, 523; with l. 119, V, 569; with l. 141, V, 610; with l. 146, V, 644; with l. 150, V, 550; with l. 162, V, 462, 632; with l. 166, V, 448; and with l. 169, V, 412, 417, 430, 631.

146 Blue is not included since that was the color of constancy. Cf. l. 330 below, and *SqT*, V, 644.

150 See Gen. iv, 19–20. It is really Jabal, Lamech's son, who is called "the father of such as dwell in tents."

157 Cf. *WB Prol*, III, 386, where the line is repeated, with the substitution of *whyne* for *pleyne*. The idea is that a treacherous horse can both bite and whinny.

158 *bar her on honde*, accused her. Cf. *MLT*, II, 620, and n.

182 Cf. *KnT*, I, 2397.

184 *at the staves ende*, "at a distance, away from close quarters or familiarity, on unfriendly terms" (NED, s.v. Staff, 5b). In Chaucer the figure seems to be drawn from riding or driving. For further discussion see N & Q, Ser. 8, VII, 344, 418 f., 471 f.

186 For the various uses of *daunger* cf. *Gen Prol*, I, 517, n. Here it refers, as commonly, to the offishness or fastidiousness of the lady.

194 The custom is illustrated in *BD*, 1024 ff.

201–03 Cf. Ovid's Amores, ii, 19, 3; iii, 4, 17, 25–26.

207 With the account of Anelida here and in

the opening lines of the *Compleynt*, Shannon (pp. 38 f.) compares Her., x, 137–40 (Ariadne).

211 The metre of the *Compleynt* is very elaborate. The introductory stanza, riming aabaabbab, is exactly matched by the last stanza, ll. 342–50, the words of the first line of the *Compleynt* being repeated at the end. The next six stanzas form a kind of strophe, and are matched by the six stanzas of antistrophe which follow. In each series the first four are in the measure of the introductory stanza. The fifth is more complicated, containing sixteen lines, of which the fourth, eighth, twelfth, and sixteenth have five accents and the rest four; their rimes approach the arrangement of a virelay, aaabaaabbbbabbba. The sixth stanza of each returns to the decasyllabic measure, with final rimes aabaabbab as in the introductory stanza; but there are internal rimes in every line. The correspondences are indicated by numbers in the text.

The device of internal rime was a "colour" taught by the rhetoricians. For early English examples of it, mainly in poets who were imitators of Chaucer, see Miss Hammond, Engl. Verse between Chaucer and Surrey, Durham, N.C., 1927, pp. 466–67.

211 With the *poynt of remembraunce* cf. "la puntura della rimembranza," Purg., xii, 20.

214 ff. Parallels to the *Complaint to his Lady* are as follows: 214 and *Lady*, 55; 216 and *Lady*, 123; 222 and *Lady*, 35; 237 and *Lady*, 50; 247 and *Lady*, 107–08.

229 ff. With ll. 229–34 Professor Shannon (pp. 39 f.) compares Her., xii, 175–78 (Medea); and with ll. 247 ff., Her., ii, 49. But the ideas are commonplace and the parallels, like some of the others he cites, are of doubtful significance.

265 Cf. ll. 113–15 above.

272 On *swete foo* and similar cases of oxymoron see *Tr*, i, 411, n.

273 ff. With ll. 273–77 Professor Shannon (pp. 40 f.) compares Her., ii, 63–66 (Phyllis) and iii, 144 (Briseis), and with 284–89, Her., iii, 139–41 (Briseis).

286 *mene weyes*, middle courses.

299 *weyve womanhede*, cast aside womanhood by taking the man's part as suitor.

306 "Your demeanor flowers but does not seed"; that is, there is promise but no performance.

315 Cf. RR, 9913–14.

320 *Chaunte-pleure*; a French moral poem of the 13th century, entitled La Pleurechante, warns those who sing but will weep hereafter: "Mult vaut meuz plure chante, ke ne fet chaunte et plure." The expression became proverbial for joy that ends in woe. See Rom., VI, 26 f.; XIII, 510 f.; A. Thomas in Medieval Studies in memory of Gertrude Schoeperle Loomis, Paris and New York, 1927, pp. 329 ff.; Morawski, Proverbes Français, Paris, 1925, p. 47, no. 1279.

328–34 With the appearance of the lover in a dream Professor Shannon (p. 41) compares Heroides, xv, 123 ff. (Sappho).

346 Cf. *PF*, 342, n. In Heroides, vii, 3 ff., Dido similarly compares her lament to a swan-song.

357 Here, if the poem had not broken off, was obviously to follow the description of the temple of Mars which Chaucer actually used in *KnT*, I, 1967 ff.

The Parliament of Fowls

Both Chaucer and Lydgate testify to the genuineness of the *Parliament*. See *LGW Prol G*, 407, and the *Retractation* at the end of the *CT*; also the Prologue to Bk. i of the Falls of Princes.

On the date and possible occasion of the poem see Tyrwhitt's edition of the *CT*, I, xxvii, note e; Saturday Review, XXXI, 468; J. Koch, ESt, I, 287 ff., and his Chronology of Chaucer's Writings, Ch. Soc., 1890, pp. 37 f.; J. B. Bilderbeck, Selections from Chaucer's Minor Poems, London, 1895, pp. 71 ff.; O. F. Emerson, MP, VIII, 45 ff., MLN, XXVI, 109 ff., and JEGP, XIII, 566 ff.; S. Moore, MLN, XXVI, 8 ff.; H. Lange, Angl., XL, 394 ff.; J. M. Manly, Studien zur Eng. Phil. (L. Morsbach Festschrift), 279 ff.; V. Langhans, Untersuchungen zu Chaucer, Halle, 1918, pp. 19 ff., and Angl., LIV, 25 ff.; Edith Rickert, MP, XVIII, 1 ff.; M. E. Reid, Wisconsin Stud. in Lang. and Lit., XVIII, 60 ff.; T. W. Douglas, MLN, XLIII, 378 ff. (with a convenient summary of recent discussion); H. Braddy, PMLA, XLVI, 1007 ff. (and in Three Chaucer Studies, New York, 1932, part ii), and MLN, LXVIII, 232 ff.

Tyrwhitt's conjecture that the *Parliament* refers to the marriage of John of Gaunt with Blanche of Lancaster, and that of the Saturday Review, connecting it with the courtship of Ingelbert de Couci and Isabel Plantagenet (in 1364), are now both abandoned. Recent opinion has generally associated the poem with the betrothal of Richard II and Anne of Bohemia in 1381. This theory, as originally presented by Professor Koch, identified the three tercels as Richard, William of Hainault, and Frederick of Meissen. Later Emerson showed that William was not a suitor for Anne in 1381; consequently he put Frederick of Meissen in the second place, and identified the third suitor as Charles VI of France. But even in its amended form the theory proved to be open to serious objections. There is ground for believing that the engagement with Frederick was broken by Anne's relatives in 1377; in which case he could hardly have been regarded as a rival of Richard in 1381; and the evidence of the suit of Charles VI is very slight. These and other difficulties were urged by Professor Manly and Miss Rickert, the former rejecting the personal allegory altogether, and the latter proposing a new set of identifications. According to Miss Rickert's interpretation, the formel represents Philippa of Lancaster, eldest daughter of John of Gaunt, and the suiters are Richard, William of Hainault, and John of Blois. She has shown that in 1381, the year of Richard's betrothal to Anne, John of Gaunt apparently had in mind all three men as possible husbands for Philippa. But the evidence does not indicate that they were in any proper sense suitors or rivals. Some of the general objections, too, which were urged by Professor Manly against the Richard-Anne theory, hold against Miss Rickert's suggestion. Recently Miss Reid and Mr. Douglas, in the articles cited above, have restated the argument for the application to Richard and Anne. The former sees in the passage from the Somnium Scipionis the poet's counsel to the young king, and several scholars have found in the closing lines a veiled appeal to Richard for favor. But these interpretations, doubtful in themselves, do not particularly strengthen the case for the allegory. Mr. Douglas, admitting that it is hard to fit the fiction to the historical facts, goes so far as to maintain that the poem would be even more of a compliment if Richard was the only suitor and the rival birds were pure inventions! It must be conceded that these conjectures are far from satisfactory, and it is not surprising that the most recent writers on the subject have searched in new directions for an interpretation. Professor Langhans (in Angl., LIV, 25 ff.) abandons entirely the application to Richard and propounds a new theory, that Chaucer wrote the poem for his own marriage (dated conjecturally in 1374). But this again is pure surmise, unsupported by any real evidence in the text, and involves, moreover, an improbably early date of composition. Mr. Haldeen Braddy (in the article cited above), after restating the general argument for an allegorical interpretation, brings Richard again into the discussion. He suggests that the poem alludes to the negotiations, conducted in 1376 and 1377, for the marriage of Richard to the Princess Marie of France. Marie died suddenly in May, 1377, and the treaty was never ratified. Since, at the time of the negotiations, she was already affianced to William of Bavaria, Mr. Braddy takes him to be the second tercel. For the third eagle he has no historical identification to propose. The circumstances of the negotiations fit several features of the *Parliament*, and the theory offers fewer difficulties than those previously proposed. But it is not supported by such striking parallels of incident as would make it convincing. On the whole the question of a topical interpretation must still be left open. The *Parliament* looks, without doubt, like an occasional piece. But St. Valentine's Day in itself was perhaps a sufficient occasion. After all the discussion, a personal application of the poem, though undeniably possible, still seems to be by no means necessary.

If the theories of allegory in the *Parliament* are rejected, the principal evidence usually relied on for dating the poem about 1381–82 disappears. There remains the uncertain astronomical clue in l. 117, which seems to point to 1382 (though the conditions were also fulfilled in 1374). General considerations of literary relationship also favor a date in the early eighties, and the social satire which is probably to be recognized in the speeches of the birds may reflect the "class consciousness" of the period of the Peasants' Revolt. On various interpretations of these speeches see the note to l. 323.

On its face the *Parliament* is a poem for St. Valentine's Day. It belongs to the well-known mediæval literary genre, the love debate, and the subject discussed is a typical "question of love" ("demande d'amour"). See Manly, p. 282, and W. A. Neilson, The Origin and Sources of the Court of Love, [Harv.] Stud. and Notes, VI, ch. 3. The particular plot or situation is paralleled by a wide-spread tale of The Contending Lovers, which is discussed by Dr. W. E. Farnham in PMLA, XXXII, 492 ff., XXXV, 247 ff., and Wisc. Stud. in Lang. and Lit., no. 2 (1918), 340 ff. Chaucer may even have known a version of the story in which the rival suitors were birds, though he may have made this modification himself to suit his immediate purposes. The idea of a counsel cr parliament of birds was familiar. The one described by Gower (Balade xxxv) as held on St. Valentine's Day may have been suggested by Chaucer's poem. For other examples see, besides the articles of Manly and Farnham, W. Seelmann, Die Vogelsprachen (Vogelparlamente), in Jahrbuch des Vereins für Niederdeutsche Sprachforschung, XIV, 101 ff. Instances of bird allegory in Machaut and Deschamps are cited by Miss Rickert, MP, XVIII, 4. For the dream device or framework, comparison may be made with the *Book of the Duchess* and the *House of Fame*, and the works cited as sources and analogues in the introductions to the Explanatory Notes on these poems.

Reference should be made to the suggestion of Professor Brusendorff (p. 286, n.) that Chaucer may have been influenced by an Old Czech poem, the New Council (Nová Rada) of Smil Flaška. Knowledge of this, Brusendorff observed, could have reached Chaucer through some of the Bohemian followers of Anne at the English court. But as Mr. George Gibian has kindly pointed out to the editor, Brusendorff's suggestion is disproved by the generally accepted dates of the two works. Moreover they are not similar enough to make indebtedness probable in either direction. See Langhans, Angl., LIV, 25 ff. (with a full summary of Smil's poem at pp. 47–56). Professor Magoun has called the editor's attention to an earlier comparison of the two poems by A. Kraus, in the Listy Filologické, XXXI, 199 ff. There is a German rendering of the Nová Rada (Der Neue Rath) by J. Wenzig, Leipzig, 1855.

Definite literary borrowings are to be noted in the *Parliament* from the Somnium Scipionis, at the beginning of the poem; from the Teseida in ll. 183–294; and from the De Planctu Naturae of Alanus de Insulis in the description of Nature (ll. 298 ff.). Perhaps Alanus furnished also the immediate hint for the parliament itself (see the note to l. 298). Further literary indebtedness is indicated in the notes. On the use of Dante see particularly Lowes, MP, XIV, 706 ff. Reminiscences of the Roman de la Rose are few and unimportant; cf. Fansler, pp. 134 ff. Parallels to the assembly of birds in the Pavo of Jordanus of Osnabruck are cited by P. W. Damon in MLN, LXVII, 520 ff.

Recent discussion of the *Parlement* has dealt chiefly with its moral or philosophical purpose. See especially B. Bronson, U. of California Publ. in English, III, no. 5, 193 ff.; G. Stillwell, JEGP, XLIX, 470 ff., and LIII, 546 ff.; R. C. Goffin, MLR, XXI, 493 ff.; C. H. Owen, Jr., College English, XIV, 264 ff.; and R. M. Lumiansky, RES, XXIV, 81 ff.; H. Braddy, MLN, LXVIII, 232 ff.; and Dorothy Everett, Essays on Middle English Literature (Oxford, 1955), pp. 97 ff. The principal suggested interpretations are listed conveniently by Mr. Lumiansky, who presents his own theory that the poem is a philosophical unit, Chaucer's subject being his unsuccessful search for a way of reconciling true and false felicity. If this view were accepted it would afford a parallel to other cases where the poet reproaches himself for writing about earthly love. Mr. Owen finds the deepest meaning of the poem in the struggle between instinct and moral choice. Very

recently the editor had the opportunity to read in manuscript an interpretation of the *Parlement* by Charles O. McDonald of Yale University (now published in Spec., XXX, 444 ff.). He finds the central meaning to lie in the conflict between courtly love and love according to Nature for "commun profit," namely, procreation. His arguments are sometimes pushed too far, but on the whole he shows an understanding of the elements in the poem. All these studies have some value in showing the moral and social background of Chaucer's work. But all moral, allegorical, and anagogical interpretations are bound to be conjectural unless supported by some such evidence as was afforded in the case of the Divine Comedy by Dante's letter to Can Grande della Scala.

Valuable notes on the text, supplementary to those of Skeat, will be found in the editions of Bilderbeck (Selections from Chaucer's Minor Poems, London, 1895), and Emerson (Poems of Chaucer, London, 1911). Professor Koch's notes (Chaucers Kleinere Dichtungen, Heidelberg, 1928) deal chiefly with textual variants.

1 The familiar aphorism, "Ars longa, vita brevis," which goes back to Hippocrates. Cf. Skeat, EE Prov., p. 57, no. 135.

Professor Manly (Chaucer and the Rhetoricians, Brit. Acad., 1926, p. 8) notes that the passage is a typical instance of the rhetorical method of beginning a poem with a "sententia" — here expanded into two stanzas. Further rhetorical devices follow in the preliminary narrative, which occupies 119 lines, before the story proper begins.

8 With Chaucer's claim to be an outsider in affairs of love may be compared his attitude in the *Troilus*. For comment on his disclaimer see further Tatlock, The Mind and Art of Chaucer, p. 65.

10–13 With these lines, which express a familiar sentiment, Professor Shannon (Chaucer and the Rom. Poets, Cambridge, 1927, pp. 13 f.), compares Ovid, Amor., i, 1, 21–26; ii, 1; iii, 1; Ars Amat., i, 9; and Rem. Am., 1–40.

15 ff. Cf. *Prol LGW*, 29–39.

31 The Somnium Scipionis of Cicero originally formed part of the De Re Publica, Bk. vi. It was preserved by Macrobius (about 400 A.D.), who illustrated it with a long commentary. The combined work of Cicero and Macrobius was of great influence on mediæval literature. Chaucer refers to it in *BD*, 284, *HF*, 514, and *NPT*, VII, 3123 (where Macrobius appears to be credited with the authorship of the Somnium). The Scipio referred to is the younger Africanus, who visited Massinissa, king of Numidia, in 150 B.C. They talked all day of the elder Africanus, and the younger dreamed of him at night.

An edition of the Somnium Scipionis, with an attempt to determine the text used by Chaucer, is in preparation by Professor C. W. Barlow for the Chaucer Library of the Modern Language Association. For the suggestion that Chaucer's use of the Somnium Scipionis here involved a veiled petition for remuneration or reward see S. Moore, MLN, XXVI, ii, and Braddy, PMLA, XLVI, 1018.

56 *galaxye*, the Milky Way, apparently thought of here as a path to heaven. On various popular names for it, "Watling street," "Walsingham Way," etc., see *HF*, 939, n.

59–63 The nine spheres are those of the seven

planets, that of the fixed stars, and the primum mobile. Chaucer refers to their music again in *Tr*, v, 1812–13. Cicero and Macrobius distinctly recognize only seven notes of the spheres, excluding the primum mobile altogether, and giving the same note to the sphere of the fixed stars and to that of one planet (probably Saturn). Macrobius gives a single note to Venus and Mercury (Commentary, ii, 4, 9).

64 The reference is to the so-called Great or Mundane Year, the period in which all the heavenly bodies should depart from and return to a given position. The time has been variously estimated. Macrobius makes it 15,000 ordinary solar years (ii, 11, 11); the Roman de la Rose, 36,000 years (l. 16816); the Complaynt of Scotland (ed. Murray, EETS, 1872, p. 33), 37,000 years.

80 The resemblance of this passage in Cicero to the doctrine of purgatory doubtless gave it special interest for Christian writers. It was imitated by Dante in Inf., v, 31–36.

82 *dede,* possibly an old plural in *-e,* though Chaucer's regular ending is *-es.*

85 ff. Based on Dante, Inf., ii, 1 ff. Cf. also Aen., ix, 224–25.

90 f. Cf. Boethius, *Bo,* iii, pr. 3, 33 ff.; also Chaucer's *Pity,* ll. 99 ff.

93 It is uncertain whether there was an adjective *forwery,* or whether all cases of this apparent compound are to be printed as two words. On the idiomatic use of *for* with adjectives see *KnT,* I, 2142, n.

97 The explanation of the dream here suggested by Chaucer is quite in keeping with the theory of the "somnium animale," i.e., a dream caused by some activity or disturbance of the mind. Cf. Curry, pp. 234 ff.

99 The theme of this stanza is familiar; a close parallel is found in Claudian, De VI Consulatu Honorii Augusti, Praefatio, ll. 3–10 (Leipzig, 1876–79, II, 29). See R. A. Pratt, Spec., XXII, 419 ff. Cf. also Macrobius's Commentary, i, 3, 4. Skeat notes other passages on the subject; to his list may be added Petronius, Fragm. xxx (ed. Buecheler, Berlin, 1922), and Boccaccio, De Gen. Deor., i, 31.

109 Cf. Dante, Inf., i, 83 ff.

111 Macrobius concludes his Commentary with the words: "Vere igitur pronunciandum est nihil hoc opere perfectius quo universa philosophiae continetur integritas."

113 *Cytherea,* Venus. Professor Pratt (MLQ, VII, 259 ff.) points out the similarity between these lines and *HF*, 518 ff., and argues that Chaucer was here "borrowing" from his earlier work.

114 Cf. *MerchT,* IV, 1777, and n.

117 *North-north-west.* This passage affords a possible clue to the date of the poem. Though Venus can never be seen exactly in the position named, she might be so described when she is at or near her greatest distance north from the equator, and the sun is about 45° east of the vernal equinox. Early in May, 1382, as Professor Koch pointed out (Chronology, pp. 37–38), she was visible as evening star slightly north of the northwest point, and Professor Manly (Morsbach Festschrift, pp. 288–89) has shown that the conditions were also fulfilled in 1374 and 1390. Of these three years, 1382 alone seems a probable time for the composition of the *Parliament.* For further discussion see Koch, ESt,

LV, 224–25 (where the writer withdraws an earlier conjecture, based upon the reading *north nor west,* that the date should be 1381, when Venus, as morning star from January to June, was visible south and east). Mr. Braddy (PMLA, XLVI, 1019) argues that Venus was near enough to the position indicated in April or May, 1377.

Of course, as Professor Manly remarks, the phrase *north-north-west* may not have been used with exact astronomical significance. It may mean only "in an unpropitious position." He compares Hamlet's "I am but mad north-north-west" (ii, 2, 396). For the suggestion that the phrase meant "hardly at all" see B. Bronson, U. of California Publ. in Engl., III, no. 5, pp. 204 ff.

122 *grene ston,* mossy stone. The description here has been supposed to refer to Woodstock. (See Hales, Folia Litteraria, New York, 1893, ch. 7.) If this could be proved it would not necessarily mean that Chaucer resided there when he wrote the poem. Koeppel (Angl., XIV, 234) argues that Chaucer was following a description in Boccaccio's Amorosa Visione, ii, 20–35. Cf. also RR, 130 f.

127 ff. Here the indebtedness to Dante, Inf., iii, 1 ff., is obvious. Possibly some features of the description — the contrasted parks and streams, for example — are reminiscences of RR, 20279–636, 20651 ff.

140 Cf. RR, 16616; Skeat, EE Prov., p. 57, no. 136; Haeckel, p. 24, no. 77; though no particular source need be sought for the proverbial statement.

141 The first inscription was in gold, the second in black.

146, 156 *errour,* ignorance, doubt (lit. "wandering").

148 *adamauntes,* loadstones. The primary meaning was "diamond" (ἀδάμας, indestructible), but in mediæval Latin the word was applied to the loadstone, and thus associated by confusion with "adamans."

155–56 These lines, which echo a commonplace of the Divine Comedy, seem to have been most definitely influenced by Par., iv, 10–12. With ll. 157–58 cf. Inf., iii, 127–29.

155 Perhaps *It* should be taken here as the equivalent of "there" (like the German introductory "es"), in which case there should be no comma after *face.*

159 On the use of "servant" for lover see *KnT,* I, 1814, n.

169 Cf. Inf., iii, 19.

176–82 Lists of trees, such as the one here given, are a well-known convention in classical and modern poetry. There is another in *KnT,* I, 2921 ff., suggested by Tes., xi, 22–24; and others probably known to Chaucer occur in Met., x, 90 ff., in Pharsalia, iii, 440 ff., in Theb., vi, 98 ff., in De Raptu Proserp., ii, 107 ff., and in Joseph of Exeter's Iliad (the metrical Dares), i, 505 ff. Spenser imitated Chaucer in the Faerie Queene, i, 1, st. 8, 9, and later poets have carried on the convention. For notes on the continuity of the literary tradition from Ennius to modern times see Lane Cooper, Class. Weekly, XXII, 166, and W. B. Sedgwick, ibid., p. 184; cf. also Fleckeisen's Neue Jahrbücher, XCVII, 65.

The list here in *PF* is modeled in part, as Professor

Root has shown, on the passage in Joseph of Exeter. The following epithets employed by Joseph are similar to Chaucer's: "fraxinus audax," *the hardy asshe*; "cantatrix buxus," the *boxtre pipere*; "cupressus flebilis," *the cipresse, deth to playne*; "oliva concilians," *the olyve of pes*; "ebria vitis," *the dronke vyne*; "interpres laurus," *the laurer to devyne*. Several of these characterizations have parallels in the other lists. *The saylynge fyr*, also, is matched by Claudian's "apta fretis abies," and *the victor palm*, in any case an obvious commonplace, is paralleled in both Ovid and Boccaccio. But the remaining five characterizations seem to be Chaucer's. For a detailed comparison of the different lists see Root, MP, XV, 18 ff.

The epithets are all clear except perhaps the *piler elm*, which doubtless refers to the tree's support of the vine (Spenser's "vine-propp elme"). The association of elm and vine recurs in several of the lists.

183–294 A close imitation of Tes., vii, st. 51–60, 63–66, 61–62. The Italian passage in turn goes back here and there to the Roman de la Rose; and it is hard to judge whether Chaucer recalled the French poem directly or only followed it at one remove. With 190–96 cf. RR, 1375–82, 661–70; with 204–10, RR, 20395 ff., 20559 ff., 20655 f. (possibly, as Fansler, p. 135, suggests, the recollection in 204–05 was simply carried over from *BD*, 340–42). 201–03, which depart from Boccaccio, perhaps contain a reminiscence of Dante's Earthly Paradise (Purg., xxviii, 9–15); and 204–07 may be from the Anticlaudianus, i, 3, 20–22. (See O. F. Emerson, PQ, II, 83 ff.) Chaucer's use of the Teseida passage is also discussed by R. A. Pratt, PMLA, LXII, 605 ff. Mr. McDonald, in the paper cited above, argues that Chaucer's departure from Boccaccio served the deliberate purpose of exalting love according to Nature.

199 On the mediæval freedom in referring to sacred persons and things see *SqT*, V, 555, n.

214 *Wille* may be due to a misreading of "voluntade" for "voluptade," an easy scribal error which Dante actually mentions in his Convivio, iv, 6 (as noted by Miss Hammond, MLN, XXXI, 121). For evidence of the reading *voluntá* in an Italian MS. see R. A. Pratt, SP, XLII, 745 ff. But, as Professor Malone has pointed out (MLR, XLV, 63), *Wille* was used in the sense of *voluttá* (*voluptas*).

217 Cf. Met., i, 468–71.

228 What Chaucer means by the unnamed *other thre* is not clear. Skeat takes them to refer to "il folle Ardire Lusinghe e Ruffianie" (Foolish Boldness, Flatteries, and Pimps) with which Boccaccio's list ends. But the first two correspond well enough to *Foolhardynesse* and *Flaterye*, and the "Ruffianie" are suggested by *Messagerye* and *Meede* (the sending of messages and giving of bribes). Chaucer's *Beute* represents Boccaccio's "Bellezza," his *Youthe*, "Giovinezza," and his *Desyr* may stand for "Piacevolezza," to which it is not so exactly equivalent. No other figures are mentioned in Boccaccio's stanza.

231 *bras*. Boccaccio says copper, the metal appropriate to Venus. But, as Professor Pratt points out, there was considerable confusion about copper and its alloys in the Middle Ages.

243 The hill of sand, with its appropriate symbolism, is Chaucer's addition.

245 *Byheste and Art*, Boccaccio's "Promesse ed arte," artful behests (hendiadys).

246 ff. Cf. *KnT*, I, 1920 ff.

253 In referring to the *god Priapus* Chaucer may have had in mind, besides the Teseida, Ovid, Fasti, i, 415.

256 With the use of *sceptre*, cf. the Carmina Priapea, especially no. 25, in Petronii Saturae et Liber Priapeorum (Berlin, 1904), p. 144.

261 In *KnT*, I, 1940, the porter of Venus is Idleness; so also in *Rom*, 582.

272 *Valence*, probably Valence, near Lyons, in France. The name survives in the modern "valance," for hangings or curtains.

275 Cf. the proverb: "Sine Cerere et Libero friget Venus," Terence, Eunuchus, iv, 5, 732.

277 *Cypride*, from Cypris (Cypridis), an epithet of Venus, having reference to her worship in Cyprus. Chaucer may have taken the form from Alanus; it occurs again in *Tr*, v, 208.

283 ff. This list of lovers is a combination of Boccaccio's stanzas 61–62 and Dante's Inf., v, 58–69. L. 294 was apparently suggested by the last line in Dante's passage. On *Calyxte* (Callisto) see Ovid, Fasti, ii, 156; Met., ii, 409 ff. Chaucer lacked the name of the mother of Parthenopaeus, mentioned by Boccaccio as "that other proud one" ("quell' altra altiera," st. 61), namely, the second Atalanta. R. A. Pratt, in Stud. Phil., XLII, 759 ff., observes that Boccaccio's commentary, if Chaucer had possessed it, would have supplied the information. The others are mostly familiar and need no explanation. On *Biblis* see Ovid, Met., ix, 453 ff.; on *Silla* (Scylla), Met., viii, 6–151, xiii, 730–34, and xiv, 18 ff.; and on Rhea Silvia (*the moder of Romulus*), Livy, i, 3–4, and Ovid, Fasti, iii, 9–45. *Candace* was the Indian queen of the Alexander romances. On the trick by which she got Alexander into her power see the Pseudo-Callisthenes and Julius Valerius, ed. Müller, in Arriani Anabasis, etc., Paris, 1846, pp. 126 ff.; also the Mid. Eng. alliterative Wars of Alexander, ll. 5075 ff. (EETS, 1886, pp. 257 ff.). Professor R. M. Smith (MLN, LXVI, 28 ff.) notes that she is mentioned in Froissart's L'Espinette, where her trick is also described. The Mid. Eng. Romance of Sir Tristrem has been edited by Sir Walter Scott (Edinburgh, 1804), by Kölbing (Heilbronn, 1882), and by G. P. McNeill (Scottish Text Soc., 1886). The stories of Dido, Pyramus and Thisbe, and Cleopatra are all told in the *Legend of Good Women*.

298 The account of Nature and the birds is based upon a much longer passage in the De Planctu Naturae of Alanus de Insulis, a poet of the twelfth century. (For the Latin text see Migne, Pat. Lat., CCX, 431 ff.) The birds are said by Alanus to be depicted upon the wonderful garments of Nature. Chaucer represents them, more naturally, as gathered around the goddess. But many of his characterizations correspond to those of Alanus. For others he perhaps drew upon RR, 643 ff. It is not necessary, however, to assume direct literary sources for what may have come from common belief or personal observation.

It should be noted that Alanus compares the birds to an "animalium concilium" (Migne, 435) which perhaps gave Chaucer the immediate suggestion for his *Parliament*.

299 This comparison is proverbial and particularly common in mediæval literature. Examples are cited by Miss Hammond, Eng. Verse between Chaucer and Surrey, p. 452.

309 In the fourteenth century the ancient popular cult of St. Valentine was taken up by courtiers and made the subject of literary treatment. Chaucer's *Complaint of Venus* and the *Complaynt d' Amours* (of doubtful authorship) were both Valentine poems, and other examples by Gower, Lydgate, Granson, and Charles d'Orléans are mentioned by Manly (Morsbach Festschrift, p. 286). Some Valentine's Day celebration may have been the sole outward occasion of the *Parliament*.

312 On the use of *that* in clauses where *when* or *if* might be expected to be repeated see *Pars Prol*, X, 39, n.

323 Skeat remarks that this classification of birds into birds of prey, seed-fowl, worm-fowl, and water-fowl can hardly be Chaucer's own. He cites a somewhat similar division attributed to Aristotle by Vincent of Beauvais, Speculum Naturale, xvi, 14 (Douai, 1624). The groups are usually taken to represent the different classes of society, the birds of prey standing for the nobles, the worm-fowl for the bourgeoisie, the seed-fowl for the agricultural class (or, according to some, for the clergy), and the water-fowl for the great merchants. Some such application is likely to have been intended, whether or not the *Parliament* referred to any particular courtship or marriage. Miss Rickert, supporting her application of the poem to Philippa of Lancaster, argues that the utterances of worm-fowl and water-fowl reflect the opinions of the merchants and the citizens, two groups who were hostile toward John of Gaunt. But it is not necessary to see in them anything except the natural reaction of the middle classes against the sentiments of courtly love. Holding this to be the real issue involved, two recent writers have offered opposite interpretations of the poet's purpose. According to Mr. Douglas (MLN, XLIII, 381 f.) Chaucer was poking fun at the inability of the lower classes to appreciate the fine points of courtly love. According to Mr. David Patrick (PQ, IX, 61 ff.) his sympathies were with the common birds. But Mr. Patrick exaggerates the satire on courtly love in various works of Chaucer.

For the suggestion that the passages about worm-fowl contain veiled comments by Chaucer on the social discontent at the time of the Peasants' Revolt, see Bilderbeck, Chaucer's Minor Poems, pp. 74 ff.

331 For the belief that the eagle looks straight at the sun when it is brightest cf. the Mid. Eng. Bestiary, ll. 68 ff. (Mätzner's Altenglische Sprachproben, I, Berlin, 1867, p. 59); also the etymology of Isidore, "Aquila ab acumine oculorum vocata" (Migne, Pat. Lat., LXXXII, 460).

333 Cf. Pliny, Hist. Nat., x, 3, where six kinds of eagles are enumerated.

337 Cf. *SqT*, V, 428.

339 The merlin preys upon smaller birds like the lark.

341 The dove seems to be distinguished from the *turtil* in l. 355 below. Perhaps the ring-dove or wood-pigeon is meant.

342 Alanus refers to the swan, "sui funeris praeco" (Migne, 435). But the idea is of course familiar. Skeat compares Pliny, Hist. Nat., x, 23, and Vincent of Beauvais, Spec. Nat., xvi, 49–50 (Douai, 1624). Cf. *Anel*, 346 f.; *LGW*, 1355 f.;

Skeat, EE Prov., p. 58, no. 137; Haeckel, p. 44, no. 153.

343 For the ill-boding owl see, besides Alanus (Migne, 436), Aen., iv, 462; Theb., iii, 511–12; and particularly Met., v, 533 ff., where the story is told of the transformation of Ascalaphus (*Escaphilo* in *Tr*, v, 319).

345 On the supposed thievishness of the chough (mentioned by Alanus, Migne, 436) see C. Swainson, Folk Lore and Provincial Names of British Birds, London, 1886, p. 75. Skeat also refers to Pliny, Hist. Nat., x, 29. The Bohn translator of Pliny refers in a note (London, 1855–57, II, 508) to parallel stories.

346 *The skornynge jay*, so called, probably with reference to its mocking imitation of the sounds of other birds.

351 The epithet, *Venus sone*, is probably due to the proverbial reputation of the sparrow for lecherousness. Cf. *Gen Prol*, I, 626, n. An allusion to Lesbia's sparrow in Catullus, suggested by K. P. Harrington, Catullus and his Influence, Boston, 1923, p. 142, is rightly questioned by J. A. S. McPeek, MLN, XLVI, 294.

353 For *foules* two MSS. read *flyes*, which Skeat adopted. But Professor Cook has shown (MLN, XXI, 111; XXII, 146) that bees were classified as birds ("aves") by patristic and mediæval authorities.

357 Chaucer perhaps confused Alanus' description of the pheasant with that of the "gallus silvestris, domestici galli deridens desidiam" a few lines below (Migne, 436). Or he may have had in mind the fact that a pheasant will breed with the common hen (for which Skeat cites Stanley's History of Birds, 1880, p. 279).

358 The proverbial watchfulness of the goose is illustrated by the story of the saving of the Roman Capitol in 389 B.C. The cuckoo is called unnatural (*unkynde*) because of its behavior to the hedgesparrow; cf. King Lear, i, 4, 235. See also l. 612.

360 This refers either to the belief that the drakes destroy the young ducks (Bell), or that they sometimes kill the female in the fury of their wantonness. For the latter idea see Vincent, Spec. Nat., xvi, 27 (Douai, 1624).

361 Skeat cites numerous authorities for the belief that the stork destroys its female if he finds it unfaithful. See Vincent, Spec. Nat., xvi, 48 (Douai, 1624); Bartholomaeus, De Proprietatibus Rerum, xii, 8 (citing Aristotle); Oesterley's notes (p. 725) to Gesta Romanorum, c. 82, Berlin, 1872. The allusion might also be to the story that a stork struck out the eyes of a servant who committed adultery with his master's wife (Aelian, De Natura Animalium, viii, 20).

363 The raven is called wise because of its predictions. For the crow *with vois of care* see Georgics, i, 388: "Tum cornix plena pluviam vocat improba voce" (not quite accurately translated, if it is the source); cf. also Batman's translation of Bartholomew, xii, 9: "with an eleinge voyce" (London, 1582, fol. 181 verso).

364 The throstle was apparently supposed to live to great age.

371 *formel*, applied to the female of a fowl, seems to mean primarily "mate, fit companion." On proposed identifications of the formel here see the introduction to the Explanatory Notes on the *PF*.

376 *at his reste*, at home.

379 The term *vicaire* Chaucer doubtless took from Alanus, where it occurs in cols. 453, 476, and 479 (Migne). It is also found in RR, 16782, 19507. Cf. further *PhysT*, VI, 20.

380 f. This familiar idea appears in Alanus, col. 443 (Migne). See also RR, 16961, and Boethius, iii, m. 9; and cf. *Gen Prol*, I, 420, n.

388 The break in the construction is unusual, even for Chaucer's period.

393 ff. The commentators who support the allegorical interpretation of the poem insist, reasonably enough, on the superiority of Richard in rank and birth. But in view of the fact that he was only fifteen years old in 1382, the latest date suggested for the poem, these lines seem extravagant and inappropriate. Certainly Professor Bilderbeck's interpretation of *secre* as a reference to Richard's secretive nature is not warranted. The adjective refers rather to the virtue of secrecy in love, the opposite of "avaunting." See l. 430 below; also *Tr*, i, 744, and *NPT*, VII, 2917.

411 *This is*, to be read as a monosyllable ("this"), and frequently so written.

452 f. On the applicability of these lines to William of Bavaria see H. Braddy, PMLA, XLVI, 1015.

477 f. Professor Emerson sees in these lines allusions to the youth of Charles VI and his helplessness in the hands of his uncles. Miss Rickert remarks, on the other hand, that they are especially appropriate to John of Blois, who was in prison and consequently unable to offer his lady any service. But neither application is necessary; the speech may be no more than a modest profession of unworthiness suitable to any lover.

485 Note the use of legal terms (*ple, pletynge*, etc.) in this and the following stanzas.

489 *this speche*, the speaking in general, rather than the plea of the third tercel.

494 On this colloquialism see *FrT*, III, 1602, n.

510–11 The meaning and punctuation are uncertain. Skeat interpreted: "If it be *your* wish for any one to speak, it would be as good for him to be silent." Possibly it means rather: "If you please (with your permission), a man may say what he might as well keep silent about." Cf. *Mel*, VII, 1219, n. The elliptical construction is of course difficult, and Professor Bronson (in a letter to the editor) suggests another possible interpretation. He would move the comma from *wille* to *speke* and make the speech mean "If a body have your permission [i.e. the hearers'] to speak, [I would say] that it would be a good thing if he [i.e. the cuckoo] kept his mouth shut."

518 A proverb equivalent to "Proffered service stinketh"; cf. *CYT*, VIII, 1066, n.; for a verbal parallel cf. Dante's "offizio non commesso," Purg., x, 57.

564 *which a resoun*, what sort of a reason.

574 Cf. RR, 4733–34. But the sentence is proverbial; see Skeat, EE Prov., pp. 58 f., no. 139; Haeckel, p. 19, no. 62.

592 Apparently proverbial. Cf. Lydgate, Dance Macabre, l. 392, 511 f. (in Hammond, English Verse between Chaucer and Surrey, Durham, N.C., 1927).

595 Also proverbial. Cf. "There's as good fish in the sea as ever was caught"; Skeat, EE Prov., p. 59, no. 140; Haeckel, p. 11, no. 37.

599 Cf. Boethius, *Bo*, iv, pr. 4, 185 ff.

612 See l. 358, n.

630 Interpreted by Skeat: "I have no other [i.e., no wrongful] regard to any rank."

632 *If I were Resoun*. This seems to refer to the function of a counselor, commonly discharged by Reason in the allegorical writings of the period. (It should be noted, however, that several MSS. read: *If hit were resoun*.)

636 With this remark of Nature cf. *PhysT*, VI, 9 ff., and n.

647 ff. These lines are usually taken to refer to the negotiations preceding Richard's marriage with Anne. Mr. Braddy (PMLA, XLVI, 1017 ff.) has shown that they are at least equally applicable to the earlier plans for his betrothal to Marie. But the delay was common enough as a matter of literary convention, and makes a natural ending for a poem of the type of the "demande d'amour."

657 *for taryinge*, to prevent tarrying, to avoid delay.

675 A *roundel*, or triolet, is a short poem in which the first line or lines recur as a refrain in the middle and at the end. The usual form in Machaut, Deschamps, and Chaucer is abb abR abbR (in which R represents one or more of the first three lines). The length of the poem varies from fourteen lines, when both refrains repeat three lines in full, to nine, when one refrain is omitted entirely and the other consists of a single line. The MSS. do not make clear in the present instance, and in Chaucer's *Merciles Beaute*, how many lines should be repeated in each refrain, but the form adopted by Skeat and here printed has good support and fits the meaning of the lines.

677 *The note*, the tune. The words "Qui bien aime a tard oublie," written in several MSS., probably indicate the French tune, though (as Skeat observes) it is hard to see how Chaucer's line could be matched by a tune which goes with a line of four accents. Octosyllabic pieces of Moniot de Paris and Machaut beginning with these words, and a ballade of Deschamps having nearly the same burden, are cited by Skeat, who also notes scattered occurrences of the line. It is recorded as a proverb by Morawski, Proverbes Français, Paris, 1925, p. 67, no. 1835; and Haeckel, p. 3, no. 10.

680 On the use of *somer* for the warm season in general, including spring (for which *lenten* had passed out of use) see A. K. Moore, N & Q, 19 Feb., 1949, p. 82.

697 Some commentators see in these closing lines an appeal for royal favor. Professor Jones (MLN, XXVII, 95) compares rather the sentiment of Inf., i, 83.

Boece

Although the *Boece* is ascribed to Chaucer in only one MS. (Shirley's Add., 16165, British Museum) it is generally accepted as authentic. Chaucer acknowledges the authorship of such a work in *Adam Scriveyn*, the *Prologue* to the *Legend of Good Women*, and the *Retractation* at the end of the *Canterbury Tales*, and Lydgate includes it in his list of Chaucer's writings in the Prologue to Bk. i of the Falls of Princes.

The exact date is unknown. But from the fact that *Boece* and *Troilus* are coupled by Chaucer in *Adam Scriveyn* it is commonly held that the works were written in the same period, and the *Boece* is put shortly after 1380. Though the influence of Boethius is discernible in works probably written by Chaucer before that year, it is most marked in the *Troilus*, the *Knight's Tale*, and other *Canterbury Tales*, all presumably of later date.

Chaucer's translation, though painstaking, is diffuse and sometimes very free, and it is heavily glossed. He unquestionably used, alongside of the Latin original, the Latin commentary of Nicholas Trivet and a French prose version ascribed to Jean de Meun. Unfortunately neither Trivet's commentary nor the French translation is accessible as a whole in print. But the English text, in those passages where the French work is available for comparison, has been shown to correspond sometimes to the French and sometimes to Boethius's Latin. Dr. E. T. Silk, of Yale University, in an uncompleted study of which he kindly communicated the results to the editor at the time of the publication of the first edition of this work, has made a comparison of Chaucer's text with Trivet's which leaves no doubt of Chaucer's use of the commentary.

For some account of the French version, to serve until the publication of the complete text, reference may be made to M. H. Liddell, Acad., XLVIII, 227; Nation [New York], LXIV, 125; also his notes to the Globe text (from which are derived most of the French citations given below). The French version is preserved in MSS. Fr. 1079, Lat. 8654, and Lat. 18424, in the Bibliothèque Nationale. MS. 18424 contains also the Latin original and Trivet's commentary, but was almost certainly not the copy used by Chaucer. Jean de Meun's authorship, which is not certain, is defended by E. Langlois in Rom., XLII, 331 ff., in opposition to the opinion which ascribes to him the version in mixed prose and verse preserved in MS. Fr. 17272 and numerous other MSS.

The glosses, which are freely interspersed in the course of both the French and the English translations, Professor Liddell held to be derived from the commentary wrongly ascribed to St. Thomas Aquinas. But Miss K. O. Petersen (PMLA, XVIII, 173 ff.) showed that in nearly every case Chaucer's glosses correspond more closely to those of Trivet, whose work was probably a source of this Pseudo-Aquinas. For further discussion see J. L. Lowes, Rom. Rev., VIII, 383 ff.; and for a convenient and judicious exposition of the whole question, B. L. Jefferson, Chaucer and the Consolation of Philosophy of Boethius, Princeton, 1917, pp. 1–15. Good editions of the Latin text are those of Obbarius (Jena, 1843), Peiper (Leipzig, 1871), and Stewart and Rand (London, 1918). The last named contains the English translation of "I. T." (1609), revised and corrected. V. L. Dedeck-Héry, in PMLA, LIX, 18 ff., attempted, on the basis of an examination of seventeen MSS. of the French translation, to determine the type to which Chaucer's copy belonged, and he expressed the hope that the actual MS. used by Chaucer may yet come to light. Cf. also his earlier work on the relations of the MSS. in Spec., XV, 432 ff. The Chaucer Group in the Modern Language Association has in hand a projected edition of the Latin text closest to Chaucer, to be prepared by Professor Barnet Kottler. For exposition and criticism of the Consolatio see H. F. Stewart, Boethius, an Essay, Edinburgh, 1891, and E. K. Rand, in Harv. Stud. in Class. Phil., XV, 1 ff.

In the notes that follow, no systematic comparison of Chaucer's text with either the Latin or the French is presented. Passages from one or the other, and from the glosses, are cited simply to elucidate the English version. Errors in the translation are noted when they seem significant. They are more fully discussed in Mr. Stewart's Boethius, pp. 222–25, and in Dr. Jefferson's monograph, pp. 16 ff. Glosses clearly intended to be recognized as such are printed in italics. But no attempt has been made to indicate the numerous words and phrases throughout the translation which also rest upon glosses. The Latin glosses which appear frequently in the English MSS. are also not included in the text, though attention is called to some of them in the notes.

Miss L. Cipriani (PMLA, XXII, 565) has argued — very dubiously — that Chaucer's translation was influenced by the Roman de la Rose. But the parallels she cites are mostly without significance. See Dr. Fansler's comments, Chaucer and the Roman de la Rose, New York, 1914, pp. 180 ff.

On the characteristics of Chaucer's prose see P. F. Baum, JEGP, XLV, 38 ff., and M. Schlauch, PMLA, LXV, 568 ff. Note also the account of the *Astrolabe* by Sister Madeleva, A Lost Language (New York, 1951), pp. 87 ff.

Title

It may be noted that the "Consolatio" was a recognized literary type in Greek and Latin. For examples, cf. the address to Apollonius, who had lost a son (a work attributed to Plutarch, but now held to be spurious; see the Moralia, Leipzig, 1925, I, 248 ff.) and the consolation of Seneca, addressed to Marcia, daughter of Cremutius Cordus, when suffering a similar bereavement.

Book I
Meter 1

4 *rendynge*, "lacerae," rent or tattered.

12 *wyerdes*, "fata." In the Latin the adjective "maesti" (*sorwful*) goes with "senis."

20 *to wrecches*, a mistranslation of "maestis," which refers to "annis," in sad years.

20　*yclepid,* "uocata," invoked (referring to *deth*).
24　*lyghte,* "leuibus"; correctly glossed *temporels,* transitory, in MS. A¹.
28　*unpietous,* "impia."
29　*unagreable duellynges,* "ingratas moras."
30　*what,* why; "Quid."
32　*in stedefast degre,* "stabili gradu."

Prose 1

2　*and merkid,* etc., wrote down by the use of a stilus.
4　The woman here described is Philosophy.
8　*with swich vigour,* etc., "inexhausti uigoris."
24　*the beaute,* "Quarum speciem," which begins the next sentence in the Latin.
29 ff.　By the Greek P and T are meant Π and Θ, the initials of Πρακτική and Θεωρητική, Practical (or Active) and Theoretical (or Contemplative). On this distinction in Philosophy see Boethius, In Porphyrium Dial., i, and on the corresponding distinction between the active and the contemplative life see *SecNT,* VIII, 85, n.
46　*cruel,* "toruis," stern, severe.
47 f.　The translation here is a conflation of Fr. "ces communes putereles abandonnees au peuple," and Lat. "has scenicas meretriculas."
54　*nothyng fructifyenge,* "infructuosis."
55　*destroyen the corne,* "segetem necant," gl. "destruunt" (Triv.).
56 f.　This follows the French: "Tiennent les pensees des hommes en costume et ne les delivrent pas de maladie." (Lat., "hominumque mentes assuefaciunt morbo, non liberant.")
58 ff.　"At si quem profanum, uti uulgo solitum uobis, blanditiae uestrae detraherent." Chaucer follows Jean de Meun in mistranslating "uti uulgo solitum uobis."
65　*me,* i.e., from me.
66–67　"eleaticis atque academicis studiis." The Eleatic philosophers were followers of Zeno of Elea; the Academic, of Plato.
68　*mermaydenes,* "Sirenes."
69　*til it be at the laste,* Chaucer apparently was translating "usque in exitum" (as in Peiper). The better reading appears to be "exitium" (Rand).
73　*wrothly,* rather "sadly"; Lat. "maestior."
84　Freely rendered from Lat. "uultum luctu grauem atque in humum maerore deiectum."

Meter 2

1　*dreynt in overthrowynge depnesse,* "praecipiti mersa profundo."
5　*dryven,* "aucta"; perhaps Chaucer read "acta."
11　*the sterres of the coolde mone,* "gelidae sidera lunae," possibly with reference to the constellations seen by moonlight but invisible by day.
12–13　*recourses,* courses, orbits. *Iflyt by diverse speeris,* moved, or whirled, by different spheres. "Et quaecumque uagos stella recursus Exercet uarios flexa per orbes." According to the Ptolemaic system of astronomy each planet was fixed in a revolving sphere which carried it about in its orbit. The reference here is particularly to the theory of direct and retrograde motions. Cf. the *Astr.,* ii, 35.
14　*by nombres,* etc. "Conprensam numeris uictor

habebat." Trivet adds an astronomical demonstration.
32　*fool,* "stolidam"; Fr. "la fole terre."

Prose 2

28　*yplited in a frownce,* "contracta in rugam ueste."

Meter 3

5　*clustred,* "glomerantur."
7, 8　On the repetition of *when* by *that* cf. *Pars Prol,* X, 39, n.; *firmament,* "polus," gl. "firmamentum" (Triv.).
8　*plowngy,* "nimbosis."
12　*Boreas,* Boreas, the north wind.
13　*betith,* "Verberet."
15　*ischaken,* "uibratus."

Prose 3

2　*took hevene,* apparently from Fr. "je pris le ciel" rather than Lat. "hausi caelum."
4　*so that I sette,* "ubi . . . deduxi."
5　*byholde,* "respicio."
21　MS. C¹ inserts *quasi diceret, non* above *newe;* so in Trivet.
25　Reference may be here intended to such philosophers as Solon, Anaxagoras, and Pythagoras, all of whom lived before Plato and met with opposition in their time.
47　MS. C¹ inserts *persequendo* above *pervertede;* so in Trivet.
52　*So yif,* "quod si," but if.
53　*Anaxogore,* Anaxagoras (B.C. 500–428) was exiled from Athens on the charge of impiety.
54　Zeno of Elea (Velia) in Italy, born about B.C. 488, the inventor of Dialectic. The accounts of his torments vary. See Diogenes Laertius, ix, 26 ff.; Cicero, De Nat Deor., iii, 82; Tusc., ii, 22; Valerius Maximus, iii, 3.
56　*the Seneciens, and the Canyos, and the Soranas,* "at Canios at Senecas at Soranos," meaning men like Seneca, Canius, and Soranus. The form *Seneciens,* which might more naturally be taken to mean followers of Seneca, is probably due, as Liddell suggests, to the Fr. "Senecciens." On the familiar story of Seneca see *MkT,* VII, 2495 ff. Julius Canius (or Canus) was a Stoic philosopher, condemned to death by Caligula. His death is described by Seneca, De Tranquillitate, cap. xiv. Soranus, another Stoic, was condemned to death under Nero. See Tacitus, Annales, xvi, 23.
63　*the byttere see,* etc., "in hoc uitae salo"; gl. "in hac uita que salum, id est, mare dicitur" (Triv.).
78　*palis,* spelled *paleys* in some MSS.; in either case it means "rampart" (Lat. "uallo").

Meter 4

1　*cleer of vertu,* "serenus," gl. "clarus virtute."
6　*hete,* "aestum," surge. Cf. Chaucer's own gloss on *heete* in m. 7, below.
8　*Visevus,* Vesuvius.
18　*stable of his ryght,* "stabilis suique iuris"; Fr. "estables de son droit."

Prose 4

3 *an asse to the harpe*; proverbial. Boethius has it in Greek, ὄνος λύρας (in some MSS. ὄνος πρὸς λύραν); in MS. C², "asinus ad liram." For another case of its use by Chaucer see *Tr*, i, 731. A number of occurrences of the Greek proverb are cited in the edition of Boethius by A. Fortescue, London, 1925, p. 11.

4 Chaucer omits the quotation, Ἔξαυδα, μὴ κεῦθε νόῳ, "speak out, conceal not in mind" (Homer, Il., i, 363). Jefferson (p. 17) notes that several words of the Latin are omitted in this Prose.

With 4–6 cf. *Tr*, i, 857.

10 *And scheweth it nat ynogh by hymselve*, "nec per se satis eminet."

22 *enformedest*, "formares."

23 *ordre of hevene*, "ad caelestis ordinis exempla"; a reference to Plato's Republic, ix, the end.

26 *confermedest*, "sanxisti." See the Republic, v, 473 D.

33 See the Republic, vi.

37 *felonous turmentours citezeens*, "improbis flagitiosisque ciuibus."

40 MS. C¹ inserts *sc. Platonis* after *auctorite*; "sc. quam . . . ex traditione Platonis" (Triv.).

46 *knowynge with me*, "mihi . . . conscii"; Fr. consachables avecques moi."

50 *that ne myghte nat ben relessed by preyeris*, "inexorabiles." gl. "que exoratione relaxari non possent" (Triv.).

56 *Conigaste*, Conigastus (or Cunigastus). This passage is the only authority for the facts. Conigastus is mentioned in Cassiodorus, Epist. viii, 28.

59 *Trygwille*, Triguilla.

66 *myseses and grevances*, "calumniis," slanders.

72 *cariages*, "uectigalibus," taxes. See *FrT*, III, 1570.

73 ff. This gloss is divided by Skeat, and the second part put after l. 101. But the French text has it combined, as in the English MSS. See Jefferson, p. 14.

82 *unplitable*, "inexplicabilis."

86 On the phrase *comune profit*, which here translates "communis commode ratione," see *ClT*, IV, 431, n.

87 *so that*, etc., "ne coemptio exigeretur" (purpose, not result).

93 *Paulyn*, Decius Paulinus, consul in 498. Skeat refers to Cassiodorus, Epist. i, 23; iii, 29.

101 *Albyn*, probably Decius Albinus. Skeat refers to a letter addressed to him by Theodoric; see Cassiodorus, Epist. iv, 30.

103 On *Cyprian* see also two letters in Cassiodorus, Epist. v, 40, 41, and cf. H. F. Stewart's Essay on Boethius, pp. 42–52.

108 *to hem-ward*, "apud aulicos"; Fr. "vers ceus du paliz roial."

112 On *Basilius*, see Stewart's Essay, p. 48.

115 *for nede of foreyne moneye*, "alienae aeris necessitate."

Opilion, Opilio, brother of Cyprian. See Cassiodorus, Epist. v, 41; viii, 16.

116 *Gaudencius*, otherwise unknown.

123 *aperceyved*, "compertum," made known.

124 *The kyng*, Theodoric, King of Italy, 493–526. Ravenna was his capital.

128 *likned*; rather "added"; "astrui."

140 *axestow in somme*, "summam quaeris?", will you have it in a word?

148 *forsake*, deny.

149 ff. "At uolui nec umquam uelle desistam. Fatebimur?, sed impediendi delatoris opera cessabit," (or "cessauit"). Chaucer's rendering is inaccurate.

162 See Republic, vi, 485 C.

165 *to gessen or prisen*, "aestimandum."

178 *nedes*, "negotiis," "besoingnes" (mistaken by Chaucer for "besoings"?).

183 *Germaynes sone*, Caligula, son of Germanicus.

199 Epicurus, in Lactantius's De Ira Dei, xiii.

216 *the gilt*, etc., "maiestatis crimen," "le blasme de la royal maieste."

224 *secre*, in the Lat. not a substantive but an adjective modifying "pretium" understood. "Minuit . . . conscientiae secretum, quotiens ostentando quis factum recepit famae pretium." The French has the same mistake.

233 *submyttede*, "summitteret," subdued.

241 Boethius was imprisoned in a tower at Pavia.

246 The gloss points out that the remark is ironical.

251 *bare me on hande*, accused me. See *MLT*, II, 620, n.

257 *sacrilege*, "sacrilegio"; gl. "sorcerie."

260 *Pittagoras*, Pythagoras. The saying is given by Boethius in Greek, ἕπου θεῷ (MSS. θεόν). See Iamblichus, De Vita Pythag., xviii (86); Seneca, De Vita Beata, xv.

264 *I*, for me; an unusual use of the nominative.

266 *right clene secre chaumbre*, "penetral innocens domus"; referring to his innocent private life. Chaucer's explanation rests upon a gloss, "uxor."

274 *feith of so greet blame*, "de te tanti criminis fidem capiunt."

280 *of thy free wil*, "ultro"; "de ton gre"; of thy part.

282 *bytideth*, "accedit" (mistranslated as "accidit").

295 *good gessynge*, "existimatio bona." So again

296 Loosely translated.

299 *charge*, "sarcinam," burden.

304 *by gessynge*, "existimatione."

Meter 5

1 *wheel*, etc., "stelliferi . . . orbis," "la roe qui porte les estoiles," i.e., the Primum Mobile.

2 *festnyd*, "nexus" variant for "nixus," (Obbarius).

6 *fulle hornes*, i.e., at full moon.

10 *derke hornes*, the faint horns of the crescent. Cf. *Tr*, iii, 624.

13 *cometh eft*, etc., "Solitas iterum mutet habenas," should change again his accustomed reins, i.e., change chariot, become again a morning-star. Skeat quotes Cicero, De Nat. Deor., ii, 20, 53: "dicitur Lucifer, cum antegreditur solem, cum subsequitur autem, Hesperus. Skeat's emendation, *torneth* for *cometh*, seems unnecessary.

16 *restreynest*, shortenest; "stringis."

19 *swyfte tydes*, "Agiles . . . horas."

27 *Arcturus*, Arcturus, α Bootis, in Libra.

28 *Syrius*, α Canis Maioris, the Dog-Star, in Cancer.

34 *slydynge Fortune*, "lubrica . . . Fortuna."

43 *the blame and the peyne of the feloun,* "Crimen iniqui," gl. "penam criminis iniqui."
44 *covered and kembd,* "compta."
52 *erthes,* lands; "terras."
57 *boond,* i.e., the chain of love, described in ii, m. 8. Cf. also *KnT,* I, 2987 ff.

Prose 5

17 *by emperoures,* etc., "multitudinis imperio," "par empire ne par commandement."
20 In the original the quotation is in Greek: εἰς κοίρανός ἐστιν εἷς, βασιλεύς (Il., ii, 204, with ἔστω changed to ἐστίν).
37 *face,* the look of this place; "loci huius . . . facies."
50 *thynges . . . opposed,* accusations, "obiectorum."
65 *thy wode muse,* "Musae saeuientis." See m. 5, above.
74 *thilke passiouns,* etc., "ut quae in tumorem perturbationibus influentibus induruerunt."
78 *by an esyere touchynge,* "tactu blandiore."

Meter 6

1 *the hevy sterre,* "graue Cancri sidus." The sun is in Cancer in June.
6 *lat hym gon,* etc., "Quernas pergat ad arbores."
10 *chirkynge,* hoarse, raucous; "Stridens campus inhorruit." Cf. *KnT,* I, 2004.
22 *by overthrowynge wey,* "praecipiti uia."

Prose 6

13 *fortunows* [*folie*] (MSS. *fortunows fortune*), "fortuita temeritate," "fortunele folie." Perhaps the MSS. are right, and the translation is due to "fortuitis casibus," two lines above.
17 See m. 5, above.
22 *owgh!* "Pape."
23 *whi that thou art sik,* etc., "cur in tam salubri sententia locatus aegrotes."
25 *I conjecte,* etc., "nescio quid abesse coniecto," "ie ne sce quoi."
31 *so that,* "nedum," much less.
35 *so as* [*thorw*] *the strengthe,* etc., "uelut hiante ualli robore." On the reading see the Textual Notes.
53 *thei mai nat al arrace,* etc., "conuellere autem sibique totum exstirpare non possint."
69 *pleynly,* "plenissime," "pleinement."
70 *the entree of recoverynge,* "aditum reconciliandae."
71 *For-why, for . . . forthi,* wherefore, since . . . therefore.
73 *exiled fro thy propre goodes,* "exsulem te et expoliatum propriis bonis." Cf. *KnT,* I, 1272.
84 *noryssynge,* "fomitem," furtherance; perhaps misread as "fomentum." Cf. iii, m. 11, 36.
92 *fastere,* "firmioribus." *of thoughtes desceyved,* "mentium" (confused with "mentior"?).
99 *meneliche,* "mediocribus."

Meter 7

2 *yeten adoun,* "Fundere."
truble, adj., "Turbidus."
4 *medleth the heete,* "Misceat aestum." See m. 4, 6, above.
6 f. *clere as glas,* "Vitrea." Cf. *KnT,* I, 1958.

7 *withstande,* "Mox resoluto Sordida caeno Visibus obstat." (Possibly the reading *withstant,* sg., as in Lat., is correct.)
10 *royleth,* "uagatur."
15 *hoolden the weye,* etc., "Tramite recto Carpere callem."

Book II

Prose 1

2 *by atempre stillenesse,* "modesta taciturnitate." Chaucer seems to apply this to Boethius, Boethius to Philosophy.
14 *colours and desceytes,* "fucos," gl. "id est, deceptiones."
16 ff. Cf. *Tr.,* iv, 2–3.
27 *hurtlen and despysen,* "incessere," "assaillir."
30 *entre,* "adyto," sanctuary; confused by Chaucer with "aditu" (as also in the gloss of the Pseudo-Aquinas quoted by Liddell).
40 ff. *Com,* etc., "Adsit igitur rhetoricae suadela dulcedinis."
45 *moedes or prolacions,* "modos." For an explanation of the double translation of *modos* the editor is indebted to a letter of Mr. John Hollander, Junior Fellow in Harvard University, who says: "*Prolatio* here is a technical term in medieval music, not in the sense of 'pronunciation' or 'articulation,' but referring to one of the three rhythmic modes or meters. . . . Chaucer translated *modus,* or melodic mode, into *prolacion,* or rhythmic mode." See *MLN,* LXXI, 397 ff.
49 ff. Cf. *Fortune.*
51 *alway tho ben hir maneres;* "ista natura" is omitted in translation.
62 *use hir maneris,* "utere moribus."
70 ff. Chaucer's note is apparently due to an alternative reading such as is recorded in MS. C²; "uel quam non relictam, secundum alios libros."
93 *floor,* "aream," domain.
106 *amonges,* from time to time; "inter se."
114 Cf. *Tr,* i, 848.

Meter 1

3 *Eurippe,* Euripus, the channel between Boeotia and Euboea, which was famous for its strong current.
12 Cf. *Tr,* iv, 7.

Prose 2

Cf. *Fort,* 25 ff.
24 "habes gratiam uelut usus alienis."
54 *Worth up,* "Ascende"; imperative of *worthen* (AS. "weorðan").
57 "An tu mores ignorabas meos?" omitted in translation.
58 *Cresus,* Croesus. See Herodotus, i, 86, 87; and cf. *MkT,* VII, 2727 ff.
65 *Percyens,* "Persi regis," of King Perseus; Fr. "le roy de Perse." The reference is to the defeat of Perseus (or Perses) III, of Macedonia, by L. Æmilius Paulus in 168 B.C. See Livy, xlv, 8.
70 ff. Cf. *Mk Prol,* VII, 1973 ff., and n.
74–76 *in the entre or in the seler of Juppiter,* "in Iouis limine"; Fr. "ou sueil, c'est dire en l'entree de la meson Jupiter." In Boethius the quotation runs, δοιοὺς πίθους τὸν μὲν ἕνα κακῶν τὸν δὲ ἕτερον ἑάων.

See Il., xxiv, 527. For the use of *tonne*, cf. also *WB Prol*, III, 170; *LGW Prol F*, 195. *Seler* is possibly a mistake for *selle*, "seuil."

Meter 2

2 *hielde*, "fundat."
6 *bryghte*, "edita," lofty.
10 *as fool large*, "Multi prodigus auri."
15 *scheweth othere gapynges*, "Alios pandit hiatus" (some MSS. read "altos").
17 *to any certeyn ende*, "Certo fine," within a certain limit.

Prose 3

32 *prynces*, Festus and Symmachus. Boethius married Rusticiana, Symmachus's daughter.
34 *the whiche thyng*, i.e., *affynite*.
41 *over al this*, "Praetereo," I pass over; mistranslated as "praeterea."
53 *under the blithnesse of peple*, "sub plebis alacritate."
59 *Circo*, the Circus (properly ablative, Lat. "in circo").
61 *preysynge and laude*, "largitione," largesse.
66 *as hir owne delices*, "ut delicias suas," as her darling.
74 *forsaken*, "negare."
80 *schadowe or tabernacle*, "scaenam," "en la cortine et en l'ombre."
87 See *Fort*, 71.
88 *and also*, etc., "fortunae . . . etiam manentis."
89 *what . . . thar rekke*, what need you care?

Meter 3

16 *overwhelveth*, "Verso concitat aequore."
19 *tumblynge*, "caducis"; as also in pr. 4, l. 151, below, and iii, pr. 9, l. 165.

Prose 4

7 ff. Cf. *Tr*, iii, 1625–28; Dante, Inf., v, 121 ff.
15 *al be it*, "si," if.
26 Symmachus was put to death by Theodoric soon after the execution of Boethius.
33 *thi wyf*, Rusticiana, daughter of Symmachus.
42 *conseylours*, "consulares," of consular rank. *of whiche*, "quorum," "es quiex."
48 *ben . . . dwelled*, "suppetunt."
54 Cf. *Fortune*, 38.
70 *thi delices*, "delicias tuas," here "effeminacy."
75 ff. Cf. *Tr*, iii, 816 ff.
82 *angwyssche of nede*, "angustia rei familiaris," "angoisse de povrete."
93 ff. *for alwey*, etc., "inest enim singulis, quod inexpertus ignoret, expertus exhorreat."
109 *nothyng wrecchid*, "adeo nihil est miserum."
115 *aggreablete*, "aequanimitate."
118 ff. Cf. *Tr*, iii, 813 ff.; *MLT*, II, 421 ff.
151 ff. *ledeth*, "uehit." Cf. *Tr*, iii, 820–33.
159–60 *that . . . it*, what. See *KnT*, I, 2710, n.
165 *lost*, loss (sbst.).
174 *al the kynde of mortel thynges*, "omne mortalium genus."

Meter 4

9 *lause*, loose (ON. "lauss").
11 ff. Freely translated. "Fugiens periculosam Sortem sedis amoenae Humili domum memento Certus figere saxo."
18 *a cler age*, "Duces serenus aeuum."

Prose 5

4 *Now undirstand heere*, "Age"; "Or entens ici."
14 *to hem that dispenden*, "effundendo," strictly "by spending." So also "coaceruando," by hoarding.
26 *al hool*, "tota."
46 *semen a fair creature*; rather "semen fair to a creature"; "naturae pulchrum esse . . . uideatur."
49 *of the laste beaute of the world*, "postremae aliquid pulchritudinis," something of the basest beauty. Peiper reads "postremo."
75 *of beestis*, "animantium" (not "animalium").
84 *to the*; not in Boethius, where the sense is rather "to her."
126 *subgit*, "sepositis," separate (misread as "suppositis"?).
128 *beest*, "animal."
155 *han . . . to knowe* etc., "sese ignorare naturae est."
157 *cometh hem of vice*, "hominibus uitio venit," "leur vint."
173 *and for his wikkidnesse*; obscure. Perhaps "even for his wickedness"; "cum pessimus quisque eoque alieni magis auidus quidquid usquam auri gemmarumque est se solum qui habeat dignissimum putat."
181 From Juvenal, Sat. x, 22. Cf. *WBT*, III, 1191 ff.

Meter 5

1 The French version of this meter (from MS. Lat. 18424), the Latin original, and Trivet's comments are all printed in full by Miss Petersen, pp. 190 ff. With the passage as a whole cf. *The Former Age*.
9 *pyment* and *clarree* are associated in RR, 8379, a passage, based upon this meter, which may in turn have influenced Chaucer's translation.
10 f. *fleeses of the contre*, etc., "uellera Serum," referring to the Seres, the Chinese; the French translation, "les toisons de Sirians," might appear to mean Syria. Cf. Virgil, Georg., ii, 121. *venym of Tyrie*, "Tyrio . . . ueneno" (rather "dye" than *venym*; cf. Georg., ii, 465).

Prose 6

6 *as greet damages*, etc. The Latin has a rhetorical question.
12 *the imperie of consulers*, "consulare imperium." See Livy, iii, 32.
28 *which*, what.
29 *so requerable*, "expetibilis."
51 *As whilom*, etc., "Cum . . . putaret"; translation perhaps due to Fr. "comme." *A tyraunt*, Nicocreon, king of Cyprus. *A fre man of corage*, "liberum," gl. "sc. animo." The reference is to Anaxarchus of Abdera. See Valerius Maximus, iii, 3, Diog. Laert., ix, 59.

58 ff.   *So that the torments*, etc.; Fr. "les torments . . . li sages homs le fist estre." But the Latin
is also closely similar.
66 *Busyrides*, Busiris (called *Busirus* in *MkT*,
VII, 2103), a king of Egypt who sacrificed all strangers, until he was slain by Hercules. See Virgil,
Georg., iii, 5; Ovid, Tristia, iii, 11, 39.
69 *Regulus*, Marcus Regulus, B.C. 255. See
Cicero, De Officiis, iii, 99.
73 ff.   *Wenestow*, etc. Obscure. Cf. the Lat.:
"Vllamne igitur eius hominis potentiam putas, qui
quod ipse in alio potest, ne id in se alter ualeat,
efficere non possit?" Probably *a thyng* should be
shifted to follow the second *doon*.
100   *and as of wil*, "ultro."
106   *And dignytees*, etc. The number is confused.
Lat. "collata improbis dignitas."
112   *that beren hem*, i.e., *thynges*.
113   *reproved*, disproved; Lat. "redarguuntur."

Meter 6

1   *We han wel knowen*, "nouimus." This passage, as Mr. Lowes has noted, is a conflation of
Boethius's Latin and Jean de Meun's French.
3 ff.   Cf. *MkT*, VII, 2463 ff.
4   *made sleen*, Fr. "fist ocire."
5   *his brothir*, Britannicus. See Tacitus, Ann.,
xiii, 16; Suetonius, Nero, 33.
12   "Censor extincti . . . decoris." Cf. Tacitus,
Ann., xiv, 9; Suetonius, Nero, 34.
16   After translating the Latin, Chaucer here
inserts as a gloss his translation of the French.
21   *Septem Tryones*, the seven chief stars in Ursa
Minor; hence, the North.
25   *Nothus*, Notus, the south wind.
29 ff.   "Heu grauem sortem quotiens iniquus
Additur saeuo gladius ueneno." In MS. C² (Latin)
are the glosses: "gladius, i. potestas exercendi gladium; ueneno, i. venenose crudelitati."

Prose 7

4   *matere of thynges to done*, "materiam gerendis
rebus."
7   *list that . . . ne schulde*, lest that his virtue should
perish, etc. The *ne* seems due to French idiom.
13   *drawen to governaunce*, "allicere," allure.
25   *ne halt but the resoun of a prykke*, etc., "ad
caeli spatium puncti constat optinere rationem."
33   *Tholome*, Ptolemy; see his Megale Syntaxis,
ii (beginning).
54 ff.   *what for defaute*, etc., apparently a conflation of Lat. "tum commercii insolentia" and Fr.
"par faute de acoustumance de mercheandise."
59   *Marcus Tulyus*; see Somnium Scipionis, vi.
60   *that* introduces a direct quotation.
64   *Parthes*, Parthians.
100   *endyd*, "definitum," finite.
111 ff.   *were thought*, etc., "si cum inexhausta
aeternitate cogitetur."
115   *audience of the peple*, "populares auras" (not
"aures").
119   *Have now* (here and *undirstand*), "Accipe,"
"Or recoit et entent."
127   *rather*, former.
132   *took pacience*, "patientiam . . . adsumpsit,"
" il prist un petit en soi pacience."

Meter 7

1   *overthrowynge*, "praecipit."
4   *schewynge*, "patentes."
11   *ferne*, distant; "remotos."
18   *Fabricius*, consul 282 B.C., and conqueror of
Pyrrhus.
19   *Brutus*, either Lucius Junius Brutus, consul
509 B.C., the founder of the Republic, or the later
Brutus who killed Julius Caesar.
Caton, either Marcus Portius Cato, consul
195 B.C., or Cato Uticensis (B.C. 95–46).
24   *Liggeth*, "Iacetis"; Fr. "Donques gesiez vous"
(which probably accounts for the imperative).
28   *cruel*, "sera" (mistaken for "seua," i.e.,
"saeua").

Prose 8

2   *bere an untretable batayle*, "inexorabile . . . gerere
bellum."
4   *desceyvable*, "fallax . . . nihil"; negative omitted.
10   *unplyten*, "explicare."
27   *exercise*, "exercitatione," experience.
36 ff.   Cf. *Fortune*.

Meter 8

1   *Tr*, iii, 1744–64 is based upon this meter.
Varieth accordable chaungynges, "Concordes uariat
uices."
10   *eende*, limit; Lat., "fine."
13   Cf. *KnT*, I, 2991–93.
15   *hath also commandement to the hevene*, "caelo
imperitans," "commandant au ciel."
17 f.   *loven hem togidres*, "Quidquid nunc amat
inuicem," "s'entreaiment."
18   *Contynuely*, "continuo," straightway.

Book III

Prose 1

4   *streyghte*, pp. (apparently pl.); Lat. "arrectis
. . . auribus."
7   *so*, "quantum."
11   *unparygal*, "inparem."
16   *agrisen*, pp., filled with terror; Lat "perhor-
resco."
40   *Do . . . and schewe*, "Fac . . . et . . . demonstra,"
"Fai . . . et demonstre."
43 f.   *for the cause of the*, "tibi causa." *Marken
the*, Fr. "je te senefierai."

Meter 1

1   *plentevous*, Lat. "ingenuum."
5 ff.   Cf. *Tr*, i, 638 f.; iii, 1219 f.
if mouthes, etc., "Si malus ora prius sapor
edat."
11   *hors*, horses.

Prose 2

3   *streyte seete*, "augustam . . . sedem" (misread
"angustam"). See also m. 9, 40, below.
4   *cures*, efforts; Lat. "cura."
16   *out of this ilke sovereyn good*, "extrinsecus."

22 ff. With this whole passage cf. *KnT*, I, 1255, 1266 ff.

49 *is torned*, "uersatur," resides.

55 *freendes*, "amicorum ... genus"; hence *it*, below.

74 "Habes igitur ante oculos propositam fere formam," etc.

77 ff. Cf. *Gen Prol*, I, 336 ff.; *MerchT*, IV, 2021; *Tr*, iii, 1691.

81 *byrefte awey*, "afferre" (confused with "auferre"?).

83 ff. *studies*, "studia," efforts. *reherceth and seketh*, "repetit." Cf. *KnT*, I, 1262 ff.

103 *it nys nat to wene*, "num ... aestimandum est."

124 *lovynge*, "diligendo" (var. lect., "deligendo").

Meter 2

1 *with slakke*, etc., "Fidibus lentis"; Fr. "par sons delitables." Liddell suggests that *slakke* is a mistake for *wakke (waike)*, soft.

3 *enclyneth and flytteth*, "flectat."

5 *purveiable*, "prouida."

8 *Pene*, "poeni ... leones," lions of North Africa.

11 *stourdy*, "trucem," cruel.

19 *assaieth*, "imbuit." Liddell suggests emending to *apaieth*.

21 ff. Cf. *SqT*, V, 611 ff.; *MancT*, IX, 163 ff.

21 *janglynge*, "garrula."

24 *pleyinge bysynes*, "Ludens ... cura."

38 *by a pryve path*, "secreto tramite." Cf. *Tr*, iii, 1705.

Prose 3

21 *false beaute*, "falsa ... beatitudinis species," a false semblance of happiness.

33 ff. Cf. *PF*, 90–91; *Pity*, 99 ff.; *Lady*, 44 ff.

63 *foreyne*, "forenses," public; Fr. "complaintez de plaiz."

90 ff. *for thoughe this nede*, etc., "nam si haec hians semper atque aliquid poscens opibus expletur."

98 *what mai ... be*, "quid est quod," why is it.

Meter 3

1 ff. Inaccurately translated. "Quamuis fluente diues auri gurgite Non expleturas cogat auarus opes," etc.

4 f. *precyous stones*, pearls; "bacis." *Rede See*, "rubri litoris." On the Red Sea pearls see Pliny, Nat. Hist., xii, 18.

7 *bytynge bysynesse*, "cura mordax."

Prose 4

2 ff. Inaccurately translated. "Num uis ea est magistratibus, ut utentium mentibus uirtutes ... depellant?"

12 *Nonyus*, Nonius, called "struma" by Catullus, Carmen lii.

22 *beren the magistrat*, hold office; "gerere magistratum."

23 *Decorat*, Decoratus, quaestor circa 508. See Cassiodorus, Epist. v, 3 and 4

47 *so as*, since; "cum ... nequeat."

51 *and forsothe nat unpunyssched*, "uerum non impune."

58 *comen by*, "contingere." Cf. *Gent*, 5.

60 *manye maner*, etc.; a mistranslation of "multiplici consulatu." Boethius had been often consul.

79 *weren born*, "ortae sunt."

81 *provostrye*, "praefectura."

92 *of usaunces*, properly "of those using them"; Lat. "utentium"; Fr. "des usans" (perhaps mistaken for "usances").

Meter 4

Cf. *MkT*, VII, 2463 ff.

3 *Tyrie*, Tyre; Lat. "tyrio" (adj.).

7 f. *reverentz*, French plural form.
    Unworschipful seetis, "indecores curules."

Prose 5

2 *How elles*, etc., gl. *yronice* in MS. C[1].

19 *noun-power entreth undirnethe*, "inpotentia subintrat."

23 *tyraunt*, Dionysius of Syracuse. The reference is to the familiar story of the sword of Damocles. See Cicero, Tusc., v, 21, 6.

41 *familiers or servantes*, "familiaribus" (confused with "famularibus"?); Fr. "familieres."

45 *in hool*, etc., "saepe incolumis saepe autem lapsa."

47 ff. See *MkT*, VII, 2495 ff.

49 *Antonyus*, a mistake for Antoninus, i.e. Caracalla. See Spartianus, Caracallus, 8 (Scriptores Historiae Augustae, xiii, ed. E. Hohl, Leipzig, 1927).

54 ff. See Tacitus, Ann., xiv.

58 *hem that schullen falle*, "ruituros"; gl. "ipsos casuros."

64 ff. Loosely translated. "An praesidio (or "auxilio" as in some MSS.) sunt amici, quos non uirtus sed fortuna conciliat?" (Confusion between *conseyled* and *conciled*?)

66 ff. Cf. *MkT*, VII, 2244 f.

68 ff. Cf. *MerchT*, IV, 1784, 1793–94.

Meter 5

2 *cruel corages*, "Animos ... feroces."

7 *Tyle*, "ultima Thyle," identified as Iceland or one of the Shetland Isles.

Prose 6

4 From Euripides, Andromache, 319 f. Quoted in Greek in the original: ὦ δόξα δόξα, μυρίοισι δὴ βροτῶν οὐδὲν γεγῶσι βίοτον ὤγκωσας μέγαν. MS. C[2] has: "O gloria, gloria, in milibus hominum nichil aliud facta nisi auribus inflatio magna."

28 ff. *I ne trowe*, etc. The Lat. "ne commemoratione quidem dignam puto" perhaps explains the extra negative.

32 ff. See *WBT*, III, 1109 ff.; also *Gentilesse*.

50 *owtrayen or forlyven*, "degenerent." (Peiper: "degeneret.")

Meter 6

10 *thow ... youre*, etc., "si primordia uestra ... spectes."

12 *forlyved*, "degener."

Prose 7

1 *delyces*, "uoluptatibus."
16 *jolyte*, translating "lasciuiam," for which most MSS. read "lacunam."
18 ff. Mistranslated: "sed nimis e natura dictum est nescio quem filios inuenisse tortores: quorum quam sit mordax quaecumque condicio, neque alias expertum te neque nunc anxium necesse est ammonere."
25 *Euripidis*, in the genitive form, as in the Latin. The reference is to the Andromache, 418-20.

Meter 7

6 *with bytynge overlonge haldynge*, "nimis tenaci . . . morsu."

Prose 8

1 *that thise weyes ne ben*, "quin hae ad beatitudinem uiae . . . sint."
10 *supplyen*, supplicate; Lat. "danti supplicabis."
14 ff. Mistranslated from the Lat. "subiectorum insidiis obnoxius periculis subiacebis."
17 *distract*, "distractus."
39 f. *of the somer sesoun*, "uernalium." *Aristotle.* No such passage has been found in Aristotle, and Messrs. Rand and Stewart emend to "Aristophanes" in the Latin original. Cf. Plut., 210, βλέποντ' ἀποδείξω σ'ὀξύτερον τοῦ Λυγκέως. Boethius refers to Lynceus, rather than to the lynx. For his story (to which may be due the tradition about the lynx's sharp vision) see Pindar, Nem., x, 61 ff. The Fr., like Chaucer, refers to the animal ("de lins").

Meter 8

8 *the foordes*, etc., "Tyrrhena . . . uada." Cf. Aen., i, 67.
24 *What preyere*, etc., "Quid . . . inprecer"; Fr. "Quelle priere puis je faire," etc.

Prose 9

13 *litil clyfte*, "rimula."
16 *al redy*, "promptissima."
22 ff. *Wenestow*, etc., "an tu arbitraris quod nihilo indigeat egere potentia?"
51 *that* is superfluous. The sense is: Consider whether he who needs nothing, etc., needs fame.
66 *adden*, "fateamur." According to Liddell the free translation is also in the French.
102 *that*, whom; Lat. "quem ualentia deserit," etc.
127 *that schal he nat fynde*, "num . . . reperiet" (interrogative instead of negative).
140 Lat. "in aduersum" omitted in translation after *torne*.
159 *nory*, "alumne."
183 *that lyen*, "quae autem beatitudinem mentiantur."
192 See the Timaeus, 27 C.

Meter 9

This meter is an abridgment of the first part of the Timaeus. The beginning of the translation seems to echo the Apostles' Creed.
8 *floterynge matere*, "Materiae fluitantis."

10 *that moevede the frely*, from Trivet's gloss, "non necessitando sed libere movendo te."
12 *berynge . . . in thyn thought*, "mente gerens." Cf. *LGW*, 2229.
14 *Thou drawest . . . ensaumpler*, precedes *Thow, that art althir-fayrest*, etc., in Lat and Fr.
25 *the mene soule*, etc., the soul in the midst of threefold nature; Lat. "Tu triplicis mediam naturae cuncta mouentem Conectens animam per consona membra resoluis."
32 ff. *Thow by evene-lyke causes*, etc., "Tu causis animas paribus uitasque minores Prouehis et leuibus sublimes curribus aptans In caelum terramque seris quas lege benigna Ad te conuersas reduci facis igne reuerti."
34 It is doubtful whether Chaucer means *heye* to be an inf. or an adj.
40 *streyte seete*; see pr. 2, 3, above.
enviroune, "lustrare," behold; Fr. "avirouner."
48 *berere*, "uector."

Prose 10

11 *for that*, in order that.
15 *ne is* With the negative after *denye* cf. ll. 33 f., 45 f., below, and see *Tr*, ii, 716, n.
ryght as a welle of alle goodes, "ueluti quidam omnium fons bonorum."
17 *be the amenusynge of perfeccioun*, "imminutione perfecti," i.e., by the lack of perfection.
19 *in every thing general*, "in quolibet genere."
25 ff. Cf. *KnT*, I, 3003 ff. *descendith*, "dilabitur."
44 *that no thing nys beter*, "quo melius nihil est."
54 *first er thynges that ben inparfit*, "minus integris priora."
55 *that my resoun . . . ne go nat awey withouten an ende*, "ne in infinitum ratio prodeat."
63 *take*, "accipio"; Fr. "recoif."
80 *am beknowe*, acknowledge.
86 *feyne*, etc., "fingat qui potest."
119 ff. *thanne ne mowen neither of hem ben parfit*, etc., "quare neutrum poterit esse perfectum, cum alterutri alterum deest."
132 *Upon*, besides; "super haec."
135 *porismes*, "porismata," deductions.
137 *corolarie*, from Lat. "corolla," garland, hence gift; in mathematics, an additional inference or deduction.
Meede of coroune, gift of a garland; Fr. "loier de coroune."
143 *men ben maked just*, supplied from the Lat., "uti iustitiae adeptione iusti sapientes sapientes fiunt," and from the Fr.
192 *the discrecioun of this questioun*, the settlement of this matter; "Cuius discretionem rei sic accipe."
227 *the sovereyn fyn and the cause*, "summa, cardo atque causa."
233 *the moevyng to ryden*, "equitandi motum."

Meter 10

12 On the river *Tagus* (in Spain and Portugal) and its golden sands see Ovid, Am., i, 15, 34; Met., ii, 251.
14 f. *Hermus* (some MSS., *Herynus, Herinus*!), a river in Lydia; "auro turbidus Hermus," Georg.,

ii, **137.** *Rede brinke*, "rutilante ripa." *Indus*, in northwestern India.

16 *grene stones … white*, gl. *smaragdus* (emeralds) and *margarites* (pearls) in C¹ C² A². Lat. "Candidis miscens uirides lapillos."

25 *eschueth*, etc., "Vitat obscuras animae ruinas."

Prose 11

4 *How mychel … preysen*, "quanti … aestimabis."

7 *also togidre*, at the same time; Fr. "aussi ensemble."

10 *yif that tho thinges*, etc., "maneant modo quae paulo ante conclusa sunt."

36 *ne cometh it hem nat*, etc., "nonne … contingit"; Fr. "leur avient."

65 *figure of mankynde*, "humana … species"; Fr. "humaine figure."

75 *I se noon other*, "minime aliud uidetur."

89 Lat. "Sed uide quod de herbis arboribusque, quid de inanimatis omnino consentiam rebus prorsus dubito." Chaucer erroneously makes "inanimatis rebus" identical with "herbis arboribusque." Boethius distinguishes between vegetable growths and lifeless objects. See 129 ff., below.

114 *sheden*, diffuse, "per medullas robur corticemque diffundunt."

121 *myghty to suffren harm*, "mali patiens," gl. by Pseudo-Aq., "potens mala sustinere."

124 *renovelen and publysschen hem*; combining Lat. "propagentur" and Fr. "renouuellent."

132 *hirs*, MS. C²; rest *his*; Fr. "leur."

153 *willeful moevynges*, etc., "de uoluntariis animae cognoscentis motibus."

162 *the bygynnynges of nature*, "ex naturae principiis."

211 *despoyled of oon*, etc., "uno ueluti uertice destituta."

218 *the myddel sothfastnesse*, "mediae ueritatis notam."

220 *But this thing … in that*; Liddell would emend, *But in this thing … that that*, to conform to Lat. and Fr.

Meter 11

2 f. *by no mysweyes*, "nullis … deuiis." *rollen and trenden*, "reuoluat."

10 Cf. *Tr*, iv, 200.

11 *lighte*, "lucebit."

13 After translating eight lines of Boethius, Chaucer here retranslates the passage from Trivet's commentary. The corresponding glosses of Trivet and the Pseudo-Aquinas are printed in full by Miss Petersen, pp. 181 ff. and Dr. Jefferson, p. 12.

25 *seen*, appear, with which Liddell compares *LGW Prol F*, 224, *G*, 156; Gen. and Exod., 1923 (ed. Morris, EETS, 1865). MS. B has *be*; Skeat reads *seme*, with Thynne. Lat. "lucebit," translated *lighte*, above; glossed "lucebit" in Ps.-Aq.

27 *to the sighte withoute-forth*, "uisui exteriori" (Triv.). Cf. v, pr. 4, 189.

36 *norysschynges*, "fomes" (mistranslated as "fomentum"). Cf. i, pr. 6, 84.

44 ff. For one statement of the Platonic doctrine of anamnesis see the Phaedo, 72 E.

Prose 12

22 ff. *Thou ne wendest nat*, etc., "Mundum, inquit, hunc, deo regi paulo ante minime dubitandum putabas."

24 *nys*, negative, as frequently, after *doute*.

29 *answeren*, "exponam"; Fr. "espondrai" (mistaken for "respondrai"?).

33 *but yif ther ne were oon*, "nisi unus esset."

40 *brynge forth*, "disponeret." The sentence is loosely translated.

47 *used to alle folk*, "usitato cunctis."

67 *the same good*, "ipsum bonum."

73 *a keye and a styere*, "ueluti quidam clauus atque gubernaculum." Here, and in 96, Chaucer apparently confused "clauus" and "clauis."

83 *ne scheweth*, etc., "non minus ad contuendum patet."

97 ff. *for the reume*, etc., "nec beatum regimen esse uideretur, si quidem detrectantium iugum foret, non obtemperantium salus." The English here departs from the original.

123 ff. *So that, at the laste*, etc., "ut tandem aliquando stultitiam magna lacerantem sui pudeat."

132 Cf. Ovid, Met., i, 151 ff.; Virgil, Georg., i, 277 ff.

134 *with the goddis*, against the gods; explained by Liddell from the confusion of Fr. "ou les dieux" with "aux diex."

156 *the hous of Didalus*, Lat. "labyrinthum." See Aeneid, vi, 27 ff.; v, 588.

168 *as a covenable yifte*, "quasi munusculum," referring to the "corollarium," which Chaucer translated *a meede of coroune* (pr. x, 137, above). Liddell suggests that Fr. "coronable (don)" was here misread as "covenable."

177 *governementis*, "gubernaculis."

182 *in cercles and*, inserted by Chaucer; Lat. "sed ex altero fidem trahente insitis domesticisque probationibus." Liddell notes that *in cercles* is due to a gloss in Ps.-Aq., and that *knowen* is from Fr. "conneus," translating "domesticis."

185 *scorne*, etc., "ludimus," gl. "deludere uel decipere (Trivet)."

193 For the line of Parmenides (corruptly quoted in the Boethius MSS.) see Plato's Sophistes, 244 E: πάντοθεν εὐκύκλου σφαίρης ἐναλίγκιον ὄγκῳ, "like the mass of a sphere well-rounded on all sides." Skeat suggests that Boethius' explanation, "rerum orbem mobilem rotat, dum se immobilem ipsa conseruat," may be due to the succeeding verses: μεσσόθεν ἰσοπαλὲς πάντῃ, τὸ γὰρ οὔτε τι μεῖζον οὔτε βεβαιότερον πέλει.

200 *styred*, "agitauimus."

205 See Timaeus, 29 B: ὡς ἄρα τοὺς λόγους, ὦνπέρ εἰσιν ἐξηγηταί, τούτων αὐτῶν καὶ συγγενεῖς ὄντας. Cf. *Gen Prol*, I, 741–42; *MancT*, IX, 207–10.

Meter 12

4 *Orpheus*; see Virgil, Georg., iv, 454–527; Ovid, Met., x, 1–85.

6 ff. *the wodes moevable*, etc., "Postquam flebilibus modis Siluas currere mobiles Amnes stare coegerat." Dr. Jefferson (p. 22) following Peiper takes "mobiles" with "amnes." But Chaucer's rendering seems preferable.

22 f. *resceyved and lavyd*, "hauserat"; Fr. "puisie." Cf. iv, pr. 6, 13. *Callyope*, the chief of the Muses.

Orpheus' father was Oeagrus, King of Thrace. See Ovid, Ibis, 482.

29 *of relessynge,* "ueniam."

31 On Cerberus, the three-headed dog, see Virgil, Aen., vi, 417; Ovid, Met., iv, 450.

34 Loosely translated from "Quae sontes agitant metu."

37 On Ixion's wheel see Ovid, Met., iv, 461; Virgil, Georg., iii, 38; iv, 484.

overthrowynge, turning over. "Non Ixionium caput Velox praecipitat rota."

38 On *Tantalus,* see Ovid, Met., iv, 458; x, 41.

42 On *Tycius,* Tityus, see Virgil, Aen., vi, 595; Ovid, Met., iv, 457.

48 *But we wolen putten,* etc., "Sed lex dona coerceat," gl. "sed apponemus conditionem quam vocat legem" (Trivet).

52 Cf. *KnT,* I, 1164.

59 *and was deed;* "Orpheus Eurydicen suam Vidit perdidit occidit." "Occidit" apparently means "was undone" (cf. Georg., iv, 491–92), but Chaucer took it to mean "died."

62 Chaucer's gloss here combines that of Trivet, "in superna bona," and that of the Pseudo-Aquinas, "in supernam claritatem."

69 *helles,* "inferos."

Book IV

Prose 1

6 *forbrak,* interrupted; "abrupi."

18 f. *so as,* since, "cum." *yif that,* that; "quod."

30 *abyeth the tormentes,* etc., "in locum facinorum (i.e., crimes) supplicia luit."

35 *and alle thinges may,* "potentis omnia."

48 *unaraced,* "inconuulsa."

58 *cesen,* transitive; "sopitis querelis."

62 *alle thingis ytreted,* "decursis omnibus" (ablative absolute).

66 *fetheris,* wings, "pinnas." So again in m. i, 1.

69 *sledys,* sledges; Lat. "uehiculis"; Fr. "voiturez."

Meter 1

2 ff. See *HF,* 973 ff.

7 The region of fire was supposed to be next outside that of the air. Beyond this were the spheres of the planets, next that of the fixed stars, and then the Primum Mobile. *That eschaufeth,* etc., "Quique agili motu calet aetheris."

12 *the weie of the olde colde Saturnus,* "iter gelidi senis."

13 *and he, imaked a knyght of the clere sterre,* "Miles corusci sideris." Perhaps, as Skeat suggests, Boethius imagines thought to become a companion of the planet Mars, and there to be made a knight. Both Trivet and the Pseudo-Aquinas explain the star as God ("sc. dei").

22 *ymages of sterres,* constellations.

·38 *fastne my degree,* take my stand; "sistam gradum."

Prose 2

This prose and the following are based upon Plato's Gorgias.

1 *Owh!* "Papae!"

10 *naked of alle strengthes,* "cunctis uiribus . . . desertos." Liddell explains *naked* by Fr. "desunez," mistaken for "desnuez."

17 *the fey of my sentence,* the certainty of my opinion; "nostrae sententiae fides."

40 *And in that that every wyght may,* "Quod uero quisque potest."

50 *studies,* desires; "studiis."

94 *Yif that,* "Etsi," even though.

111 *Knyt forth,* "Contexe."

128 *jugement.* Chaucer evidently misread "indicium" as "iudicium." Lat. "idque, uti medici sperare solent, indicium est erectae iam resistentisque naturae."

133 *I schal schewe the,* etc., "crebras coaceruabo rationes."

137 *to that,* i.e., to that to which (a customary ellipsis).

150 *be,* by, in respect to.

151 *lighte meedes ne veyne games,* "leuia aut ludicra praemia."

177 *mystorned,* "transuersos."

184 *for to been,* to exist. So also in 204, and later.

201 *withholdeth ordre,* "ordinem retinet."

206 *mowen,* "possunt."

258 *Plato,* in the Gorgias (especially, 507 C).

Meter 2

Boethius drew the subject of this meter from Plato's Republic, Book x.

4 *envyrowned,* etc., "saeptos tristibus armis."

6 *blowynge,* etc., "rabie cordis anhelos."

10 *gredy venymes,* "auidis . . . uenenis."

14 *slidynge and desceyvynge hope,* "spes lubrica."

Prose 3

10 *forlong,* Chaucer's gloss on *stadye,* "stadio."

15 *purposed,* "propositum."

25 *foreyn schrewednesse,* "aliena . . . improbitas."

39 *partlees of the mede,* devoid of reward, "praemii . . . expertem."

65 *also,* even so.

75 ff. *ne defouleth,* etc., "non affecit modo uerum etiam uehementer infecit."

100 *undir,* below, "infra."

106 *of foreyn richesse,* "alienarum opum."

118 *slow, and astonyd, and lache,* "segnis ac stupidus torpit."

121 *studies,* "studia," purposes.

Meter 3

1 *aryved,* in transitive sense; Lat. "appulit."

2 *duc of the cuntre of Narice,* "neritii ducis." Neritos was a mountain of Ithaca. *Ulixes* (and *Cerces,* below) are explanatory glosses.

6 *drynkes,* etc., "Tacta carmine pocula"; Fr. "beuvages fez par enchantemens."

12 *Marmoryke,* strictly speaking, northern Africa between Egypt and the great Syrtis.

17 *the godhede of Mercurie, that is cleped the bridd of Arcadye,* "Numen Arcadis alitis." Mercury was born on Mt. Cyllene in Arcadia.

30 *the monstruous chaungynge,* "Monstra quae patitur," gl. "monstruosam mutationem quam sustinet."

Prose 4

1 *I confesse and I am aknowe it,* "Fateor."
32 *by thre unselynesses,* "triplici infortunio" (i.e., "uelle," "posse," "perficere").
36 *thilke unselynesse,* "hoc infortunio," namely, the second of the three.
75 *taken,* "sumpta," assumed.
93 *ne noon ensample of lokynge,* "nullus respectus ... exempli." Chaucer has inverted the order of both Lat. and Fr.
125 *for the dissert of felonye,* in view of the deserts of wickedness; "quam iniquitatis merito malum esse confessus es."
138 *nis;* negative, as commonly, after *denye.* See also l. 226, below.
144 *to leten,* "relinquis."
150 ff. *some ben tormented,* etc., "quorum alia poenali acerbitate alia uero purgatoria clementia exerceri puto."
164 *and that thou woldest fayn lernen; and* is added by error here and in one Fr. MS.
178 *studies of men,* "hominum iudicia."
186 *briddes,* i.e., owls.
198 *ne seek,* etc., "extra ne quaesieris ultorem."
201 *ryght as,* just as if.
203 *that* repeats the particle *as.* Cf. *Pars Prol,* X, 39, n.
217 *wolde we nat wene that he were blynd?,* "num uidentes eadem caecos putaremus." Chaucer follows the Fr. in taking "uidentes" with the subject of "putaremus."
246 *That folweth wel,* "Consequitur"; Fr. "ce s'ensuit bien."
250 *and it scheweth,* etc.; *and* is not in the Latin.
276 *at any clifte,* "aliqua rimula."

Meter 4

1 *What,* why; "Quid tantos iuuat excitare motus."
2 f. *hasten and bysien,* combining Lat. "sollicitare" and Fr. "hastir." *The fatal disposicioun of your deth,* "fatum," gl. "fatalem dispositionem sive mortem."
7 *serpentz,* "serpens"; Liddell emends to the singular.
15 *But the resoun,* etc., "Non est iusta satis saeuitiae ratio."

Prose 5

4 *fortune of peple,* "fortuna populari."
11 *wise men,* "sapientiae."
14 *subgitz,* not in Lat. or Fr.
30 *hepith,* "exaggerat."
32 *so as,* "cum," since.

Meter 5

2 *Arctour,* Arcturus, properly the chief star in Bootes; here used as a name for the constellation. *neygh to the sovereyne centre or poynt,* "Propinqua summo cardine."
5 *sterre,* constellation.
5 ff. The reference is to the rising and setting of Bootes. Lat. "Cur legat tardus plaustra Bootes Mergatque seras aequore flammas, Cum nimis celeres explicet ortus."

11 ff. This refers to an eclipse of the moon. Lat. "Palleant plenae cornua lunae Infecta metis noctis opacae." At such a time, Boethius says, a vulgar error ("publicus error") leads people to beat upon brass with frequent strokes ("crebris pulsibus"). On this practice, the purpose of which was apparently to drive away the evil spirit that had taken control of the moon, see Tylor, Primitive Culture, 4th ed., London, 1903, I, 328 ff. Cf. also Tacitus, Ann., i, 28; Pliny, ii, 9 (12); Juvenal, Sat. vi, 440 ff. Chaucer follows Trivet and the French in attributing the custom to the Corybantes, who were really priests of Cybele and worshiped her with noisy rites.
16 *thikke,* "crebris," gl. "spissis vel frequentibus."
32 *trubly,* "nubilus."

Prose 6

9 *a litel what,* a little bit.
13 *laven,* exhaust; "cui uix exhausti quicquam satis sit."
19 *Idre,* the Hydra. See m. 7, below.
20 *no manere ne noon ende,* "nec ullus fuerit modus." ("Modus" means here "limit," not "manner," as also in v, pr. 6, 285, below.)
38 *whil that I weve to the,* etc., "dum nexas sibi ordine contexo rationes." Chaucer apparently read, with some MSS., "tibi" for "sibi."
40 *As it liketh to the ... so do,* "Vt libet ... ," gl. "supple, fac, ut tibi placet."
56 *olde men,* ancients.
85 ff. *ledith,* etc., "per temporales ordines ducit."
94 *or elles by som soule,* "seu anima" (gl. "anima mundi"). For the idea Skeat cites Plato, De Legibus, x.
134 *it axeth,* "petit," seeks, tends toward.
152 *of sexes,* "fetuum"; Fr. "sexes." Was there a variant "sexuum"?
156 *whan,* "cum," because.
162 *unable to ben ibowed,* "indeclinabilem."
178 f. *But thou mayst seyn,* etc., "Quae uero, inquies, potest ulla iniquior esse confusio." Chaucer, as Liddell suggests, seems first to have translated "Mais tu diras" from the French, and then to have taken "inquies" as a noun. Skeat notes that the reading "inquiescior" for "iniquior" (as in MS. C²) may underlie Chaucer's error.
183 *Whethir,* "num."
212 *hele of corages,* "animorum salus."
216 *lechere,* leech-er, "medicator."
225 ff. *for to constreyne,* etc., "ut pauca ... perstringam."
232 *my famylier,* servant, disciple; "familiaris noster Lucanus." See Pharsalia, i, 128.
237 *wikkid,* "peruersa" (with "confusio," not "opinioni").
244 *continue,* "colere"; Fr. "coutiuer" (apparently misread by Chaucer as "continuer").
245 *withholden,* retain, "retinere."
256 *the more excellent by me,* "quidam me quoque excellentior," more excellent than I. Boethius apparently forgot that Philosophy, not the author, is speaking. Chaucer's version, which seems to mean "more excellent through me, by my aid," may be due to the gloss (as in MS. C¹) "philosophus per me." The Greek quotation, 'Ανδρὸς δὴ ἱεροῦ δέμας

αἰθέρες οἰκδόμησαν, is from an unknown source. Chaucer doubtless followed the Latin gloss in MS. C¹: "Viri sacri corpus aedificauerunt uirtutes."
260 *taken*, "deferatur," entrusted.
273 *into experience of hemself*, "hos in experimentum sui tristibus ducit." "Sui" is usually taken to refer to "hos," and this gives a sense more in keeping with the context.
290 *of wykkid meryt*, "male meritos"; Fr. "de mauvaise merite."
298 *In the whiche thing I trowe that god dispenseth*, "In qua re illud etiam dispensari credo," in which thing also this is to be allowed for.
300 f. *overthrowynge to yvel*, "praeceps." *Uncovenable*, "inportuna" (misread as inop(p)ortuna?).
303 *egren*, "exacerbare."
313 *contynuacioun and exercisynge*, "exercitii," Fr. "coutumance." Chaucer combined both, misreading the latter as "continuance."
331 *syn that*, etc. Boethius here quotes: Ἀργαλέον δέ με ταῦτα θεὸν ὡς πάντ' ἀγορεύειν. From Homer, Il., xii, 176 (with ἀγορεύειν for ἀγορεῦσας). Chaucer seems to have followed the Latin gloss (as in MS. C²): "Fortissimus in mundo Deus omnia regit."

Meter 6

9 *ravysschynge coursis*, "rapidos ... meatus."
13 *deeyen*, dye; "tinguere."
26 *joynen hem by feyth*, "Iungantque fidem," join alliance.
40 *Among thise thinges*, "interea," meanwhile.
49 *roundnesses enclyned*, "Flexos ... orbes"; Fr. "rondeces flechiez."
51 *contynued*, "continet," read as "continuit," or translated in the light of the Fr. "contenuez par ordenance estable."

Prose 7

22 *nat able to ben wened to the peple*, "inopinabiles." So again in 63.
26 *and seyn*; subject, "they," omitted.
60 *War now and loke wel*, "Vide," gl. "cave."
65 *it folweth or comith*, "euenit," gl. "sequitur."
79 *semeth*, "debet" (perhaps misread as "decet," which occurs just below).
85 *confermen* (Skeat *confirme*), Lat. "conformandae."
86 Boethius means that "uirtus" is derived from "uires." The accepted etymology, from "uir," is given by Cicero in 2 Tusc., xviii.
90 *in the encres or in the heyghte*, combining Lat. "prouectu" and Fr. "hautece."
91 ff. *to fleten with delices*, etc., "diffluere deliciis et emarescere uoluptate."
94 *For that the sorwful fortune*, etc. This purpose clause, in the Latin, belongs in the previous sentence.
96 *ocupye the mene*, "medium ... occupate."

Meter 7

3 *recovered and purgide*, combining Fr. "recouvra" and Lat. "piauit."
7 *Menelaus wif his brothir*. For the construction cf. *the Grekes hors Sinon*, SqT, V, 209, and n.
11 *unclothide hym*, etc., "Exuit patrem," gl. "pietatem paternam."

13 *doughter*, Iphigenia. On her sacrifice, see Ovid, Met., xii, 27 ff.
21 *empty*, rather "great"; Lat. "inmani" (perhaps mistaken for "inani").
28 ff. The following passage, on the labors of Hercules, was used by Chaucer in the *MkT*, vii, 2095 ff. See, for most of the incidents, Ovid, Met., ix, 190 ff.
29 On Hercules and the Centaurs cf. further Ovid, Met., xii, 536.
30 *dispoilynge*, "spolium," spoil. On the Nemean lion see also Heroides, ix, 61.
34 The apples of the Hesperides, guarded by a dragon.
42 *Idra*, Hydra.
51 *Antheus*, Antaeus. For his story, see also Lucan, Pharsalia, iv, 590–660.
54 On *Kacus*, Cacus, see Ovid, Fasti, i, 543 ff.
55 *the bristilede boor*, the boar of Erymanthus. See Ovid, Heroides, ix, 87.
65 *why nake' ye your bakkes?* "Cur ... terga nudatis?" Why do you expose your backs (in flight)?

Book V
Prose 1

2 *resoun*, "orationis" (misread as "rationis"?).
3 "Recta quidem, inquam, exhortatio tuaque prorsus auctoritate dignissima." (We should expect *thyn* before *auctorite*.)
12 ff. *I haste me*, etc., "Festino ... debitum promissionis absoluere uiamque tibi ... aperire."
19 *and it is to douten*, "uerendumque est."
23 *to knowen ... togidre*, etc., "nam quietis mihi loco fuerit ea quibus maxime delector agnoscere, simul cum omne disputationis tuae latus indubitata fide constiterit, nihil de sequentibus ambigatur." (Chaucer seems to have taken "simul" with "agnoscere.")
37 *voys*, "uocem" (in the sense of "word," as the gloss indicates).
38 *thing summitted*, "subiectae rei."
40 *left or duellynge*, "reliquus."
43 Cf. the proverb, "Ex nihilo nihil fit."
47 *prince and bygynnere*, "principio" (beginning).
48 *but thei casten*, etc., "quamquam id illi non de operante principio, sed de materiali subiecto: hoc omnium de natura rationum quasi quoddam iecerint fundamentum."
63 See Aristotle, Physics, ii, 4–5.
68 *for grace*, "gratia," for the sake of.
82 *the causes of the abregginge of fortuit hap*, "fortuiti causa compendii," the causes of fortuitous gain. Chaucer follows the French ("l'abregement du cas fortunel") in translating "compendii."
88 *undirstoden*, "intendit," intended; mistake perhaps due to Fr. "entendirent."

Meter 1

Mr. Lowes has noted that Chaucer follows the French closely at the beginning of this meter.
3 *Achemenye*, properly Persia (from Achæmenes, the grandfather of Cyrus); here extended to include Armenia, where the sources of the Tigris and the Euphrates are near together though not identical.

the fleinge bataile, the fleeing troop, battalion; or perhaps a literal rendering of the Latin "pugna fugax." The reference is to the Parthians, who shot arrows at their pursuers. Cf. Virgil, Georg., iii, 31.

13 *and the watris*, etc., "Mixtaque fortuitos implicet unda modos."

21 *passeth*, "meat," moves.

Prose 2

9 *nature of resoun*, "rationalis natura."

22 *sovereynes*, the French plural form of the adjectives, seldom used by Chaucer except in his translations from French. But see *FranklT*, V, 899, and the Grammatical Introduction.

24 *wil*, "uoluntas."

25 *myght*, "potestas."

27 *loken hem*, "se . . . conservant," keep themselves; Fr. "se gardent" (misunderstood by Chaucer?).

42 *caytifs*, "captiuae." For the idea of the following sentence cf. *Tr*, iv, 963 ff.

48 Cf. Homer, Il., iii, 277; Ἥέλιός θ', ὃς πάντ' ἐφορᾷς καὶ πάντ' ἐπακούεις; also Od., xii, 323. In Peiper's Boethius and earlier editions the line stands at the end of Prose 2: Πάντ' ἐφορῶν καὶ πάντ' ἐπακούων, and this was obviously the arrangement known to Chaucer. Stewart and Rand, following Engelbrecht, transfer it to the beginning of m. 3 (reading ἐφορᾶν and ἐπακούειν, infinitives, with "Phoebum" as subject).

Meter 2

1 The explanation of the epithet "mellifui oris" follows the French.

3 "Puro clarum lumine Phœbum." Cf. the Homeric phrase, λαμπρὸν φάος ἠελίοιο, Il., i, 605.

11 *strok of thought*, "Vno mentis cernit in ictu." Cf. v, pr. 4, 192.

Prose 3

With this whole discussion cf. *Tr*, iv, 967 ff.

20 *writhen awey*, "detorqueri."

25 *proeve*, "probo," in the sense of "approve," as indicated by Chaucer's gloss.

36 ff. *and in this manere*, etc., "eoque modo necessarium hoc in contrariam relabi partem."

41 *but, as it were, ytravailed*, "quasi uero . . . laboretur," as though this were the problem. The meaning is brought out by the gloss, where the Fr. has "nous travaillons."

48 *But I ne enforce me nat now to schewen it*, "Ac non illud demonstrare nitamur." Some read "nos" for "non."

66 ff. *although that the cause of the soth cometh of that other side*, "ita cum causa ueritatis ex altera parte procedat," though the cause of truth proceed from *one* part. Chaucer's translation and gloss rest upon a misunderstanding of "altera."

113 *wanteth lesynge*, "mendacio . . . careat."

134 See Horace, Sat., ii, v, 59.

155 *purposed and byhyght*, "proponuntur."

172 *And yit ther folweth*, etc.; from the French; Lat. "Quoque nihil sceleratius excogitari potest." *inconvenient*, Fr. "desconvenue," disadvantage.

176 *ne that no thing is leveful*, etc., "nihilque

consiliis liceat humanis," and nothing is permitted to human counsels.

200 ff. A loose rendering of the Latin: "illique inaccessae luci prius quoque quam impetrent ipsa supplicandi ratione coniungi."

205 *by the necessite of thingis to comen iresceyved*, "recepta futurorum necessitate," the necessity of future events being granted.

210 See iv, m. 6, above.

Meter 3

3 *the conjunccions of God and of man*. But the reference seems to be rather to foreknowledge and free will, as indicated in the next gloss.

4 *Which God*, "quis . . . deus."

9 *But ther nis no discord*; a question in the Latin: "An discordia nulla est ueris Semperque sibi certa cohaerent?" ("An" misread as "Ac"?)

14 *be fyr*, etc., "oppressi luminis igne."

18 *to fynden thilke notes of soth icovered*, "Veri tectas reperire notas."

38 *But whanne*, etc.; again a question in the Latin.

45 *withholdeth*, "tenet."

48 *neyther nother*, lit. "ne either ne other"; Lat. "Neutro est habitu."

52 *retretith*, "retractans"; Fr. "retraite."

Prose 4

3 See Cicero, De Divinatione, ii, 60. *devyded*, "distribuit."

22 *ispendid*, spent; for Lat. "expendero," in the sense of "weighed," "considered"; Fr. "respondu."

38 *confessed . . . and byknowen*, "fatebare," gl. "concedendo, fassus es."

41 *endes*, "exitus," outcomes.

43 *by grace of posicioun*, "positionis gratia," by way of supposition.

45 Cf. the use of *pose* in *KnT*, I, 1162, MS. C² glosses, per impossibile.

79 ff. *But certes ryght as we trowen*, etc., "quasi uero nos ea quae prouidentia futura esse praenoscit non esse euentura credamus ac non illud potius arbitremur, licet eueniant, nihil tamen ut euenirent sui natura necessitatis habuisse."

89 ff. *in the tornynge*, etc., "in quadrigis moderandis atque flectendis."

143 *And, for that this schal mowen schewen*, etc., "Nam ut hoc breui liqueat exemplo."

145 *otherweys . . . otherweys*, "aliter . . . aliter."

154 *wit*, sense.

165 *the envyrounynge of the universite*, "uniuersitatis ambitum," the compass of the universal. The reference here is to the Platonic doctrine of forms.

170 *strengthe*, power; "uis." So also in m. 4, below.

189 *nor . . . ne . . . ne*, neither . . . nor . . . nor.

192 *by a strook of thought formely*, "illo uno ictu mentis formaliter." Cf. iv, m. 2, 11.

Meter 4

1 *The porche*, "porticus," in Athens, where Zeno taught and whence the Stoics had their name (Gk. στοά).

22 *unpliteth*, "explicat."

34 *that chesith his entrechaunged wey,* "Alternumque legens iter."
46 *passion,* "passio," feeling, sensation.

Prose 5

1 *But what yif . . . and albeit so,* But if . . . even though; Lat. "Quod si . . . quamuis."
5 *entalenten,* "afficiant."
14 *ytaught or emprinted,* "insignitur."
32 *remuable bestis,* "mobilibus beluis."
49 ff. *Thanne is either the jugement of resoun soth ne that ther nis no thing sensible; or elles,* etc., "aut igitur rationis uerum esse iudicium nec quidquam esse sensibile, aut —." Either the judgment of reason is true and sensible things do not exist, or the conception of reason is false, which treats the sensible as if it were universal.
91 *parsoners of resoun,* "rationis participes."

Meter 5

1 *passen by,* "permeant"; Fr. "passent . . . par."
3 "Continuumque trahunt ui pectoris incitata sulcum." Chaucer omits "ui pectoris incitata."
8 *by moyst fleynge,* "liquido . . . uolatu" (in smooth flight). *and oothere bestes,* etc., "Haec pressisse solo uestigia gressibusque gaudent."
16 Cf. *Truth,* 19.
21 *axest,* "petis," seekest.

Prose 6

14 *parfit possessioun and al togidre,* "tota simul et perfecta possessio"; Fr. "parfaite possession et toute ensemble."
30 Aristotle, De Caelo, i (especially 279 B, ff.).
45 ff. *and yit it byhovith,* etc., "idque necesse est et sui compos praesens sibi semper adsistere." Cf. Trivet's gloss: "compos enim dicitur cui nichil deest sed assequitur omnia ad uotum."
52 Skeat notes that this is rather the doctrine of Proclus and Plotinus, Plato himself having taught the contrary in the Timaeus.
59, 61 *other . . . oothir,* one thing . . . another; "aliud . . . aliud."
68 *folweth,* "imitatur."
74 *discresith,* "decrescit"; Fr. "descraist."
93 ff. *for that it sholde contynue,* etc., "ut continuaret eundo uitam cuius plenitudinem complecti non ualuit permanendo."
103 *the science of hym,* i.e., his knowledge.

132 *comparysoun or collacioun,* "digna collatio," gl. "collatio vel comparatio" (Trivet).
133 *presence,* "praesentis," present, the present instant; Fr. "present."
152 *trowbleth,* "perturbat"; Fr. "trouble" (var. "destourbe").
169 *of ful sad trouthe,* "solidissimae ueritatis."
200 *presentz,* the Fr. plural form of the adjective.
213 *by the whiche,* etc., "qua prius quam fierent etiam non euenire potuissent."
218 *so as,* since; "cum . . . eueniet."
238 *absolut fro the boond of necessite,* "necessitatis . . . nexibus absoluta."
239 *alle thingis,* Fr. "tout," by which Liddell would explain *it* in l. 268, and later.
257–311 are printed by Lowes alongside of the Latin original and Jean de Meun's translation in Rom. Rev., VIII, 386 ff. The correspondence between the English and the French is shown to be very close.
262 *to entrechaunge stoundis of knowynge,* "noscendi uices alternare." Cf. the gloss, which follows the Fr., "que elle entrechaunge aussi ses divers fais de cognoistre."
269 *clepith hem ayen, and retorneth hem,* "retorquet ac reuocat."
275 *And this presence,* etc., "quam comprehendendi omnia uisendique praesentiam."
279 ff. See v, pr. 3, above.
285 *manere,* "modum," measure, limit; Fr. "propre maniere."
288 ff. The gloss, attributed by Miss Petersen to Trivet, is shown by Mr. Lowes to be a literal translation of the French.
292 *wikkidly,* "iniquae" (spelled "inique"); Fr. "feloneosement."
293 *to the willynges,* "uoluntatibus."
295 *byholdere and forwytere,* "spectator . . . praescius"; Fr. "regardeur et cognoisseur."
297 *diverse;* not in the Latin; translated from the French (which probably followed Trivet).
306 *yilde,* "porrigite."
311 A final ascription in the terms of a Christian doxology (*To whom be g[l]o[r]ye and worshipe bi Infynyt tymes. Amen.*) is added in MS. C². It is not in the text of Boethius, though added in the Latin copy in MS. C² (Skeat). It is also in Trivet's commentary. See PMLA, XVIII, 188.

Troilus and Criseyde

On the date of the *Troilus* opinions have differed considerably. For a statement of the views of the older authorities see Tatlock, Development and Chronology, Ch. Soc., 1907, p. 10. Professor Tatlock himself (chap. i, §2, and previously in MP, I, 317 ff.) argued for a date not later than 1377. He maintained that the passage about Troilus in Gower's Mirour de l'Omme (ll. 5245–56), probably written in 1376 or 1377, alluded to Chaucer's version of the story; and he tried to show that the general character of the *Troilus* indicates early composition. But the evidence drawn from the Mirour is inconclusive, and general critical considerations, in the opinion of most scholars, count rather in favor of a later date. This conclusion is supported by a few bits of definite evidence, in no single case perhaps decisive. In Bk. iv, 169–210, a passage largely original with Chaucer, there may be allusion to Jack Straw's rebellion of 1381. The reference in Bk. i, 171, to the letter A ("Right as oure firste lettre is *now* an A") is almost certainly a compliment to Queen Anne, married Jan. 14, 1382. And the planetary situation described in Bk. iii, 624 ff. — Saturn, Jupiter, and the crescent Moon all in conjunction in Cancer — corresponds with surprising closeness to the actual conditions on or about May 13, 1385. Moreover, there had been no conjunction of Saturn and Jupiter in Cancer since 769 A.D., so that the occurrence would inevitably have been a matter of interest to Chaucer and his circle. In fact it was actually recorded, with a reference to its astrological significance ("quam secuta est maxima regnorum commotio"), in Walsingham's *Historia Anglicana*, ed. Riley, London, 1863-64, II, 126. It is uncertain at what stage in the composition of the *Troilus* the description of the storm was introduced, though it clearly stood in the first or unrevised edition. In any case, if the passage refers to the conjunction of 1385, the poem cannot have been completed before that year. And this date is satisfactory on literary grounds. The *Troilus* would then be clearly later than the *House of Fame*, and probably also than the *Palamon and Arcite*; and it would be separated by only a short interval from the *Prologue* to the *Legend of Good Women*, which there is reason for dating in 1386-87.

For detailed discussion see Lowes, PMLA, XXIII, 285 ff.; Kittredge, The Date of Chaucer's Troilus, Ch. Soc., 1909; C. Brown, MLN, XXVI, 208 ff.; R. K. Root and H. N. Russell, PMLA, XXXIX, 48 ff., and J. J. O'Connor (questioning the astronomical argument), JEGP, LV, 585.

A special problem is presented by the relation of the *Troilus* to Usk's Testament of Love. Several passages in the Testament are based upon the *Troilus*, and in fact show knowledge on Usk's part of widely separate portions of Chaucer's poem. There is no difficulty in explaining this indebtedness if the Testament is dated as late as 1387. But if, as has been recently argued, the Testament is composed by Usk during his period of imprisonment between December, 1384, and June, 1385, it may be necessary to assume that he knew the *Troilus* in the making. For the discussion of the matter see R. Bressie, MP, XXVI, 28-29.

The text of the *Troilus* was clearly revised by Chaucer, in some places possibly twice. See the introduction to the Textual Notes. Although many passages were changed, the alterations were not so significant as in the case of the *Prologue to the Legend*, and there is no sure evidence of the date of the second edition.

The main source of the *Troilus*, as has been long recognized, was Boccaccio's Filostrato (Opere Volgari, ed. Moutier, Florence, 1827-34, XIII). The Italian poem (Moutier's text) has been published separately to accompany the English prose translation by N. E. Griffin and A. B. Myrick (Philadelphia, 1929), and another text has appeared in the Bibliotheca Romanica, ed. P. Savj-Lopez, Strassburg, 1912. An English metrical rendering in a modified form of ottava rima, by Hubertis M. Cummings, was published at Princeton in 1924. The sources and occasion of Boccaccio's poem, and his treatment of the material, are fully discussed by Professor Griffin in his introduction to the prose translation. Cf. also the early article by P. Savj-Lopez in Romania, XXVII, 442 ff., and the recent

discussion by R. M. Lumiansky, in Italica, XXXI, 1 ff., suggesting that Boccaccio's account of the wooing of Troilo was influenced by Benoît's account of the wooing of Diomedes.

The relation of Chaucer's work to that of Boccaccio was first exhibited at length by W. M. Rossetti, who made for the Chaucer Society in 1873-83 a parallel edition of the *Troilus* and the corresponding passages of the Filostrato. A detailed comparison of the two poems was made by R. Fischer, Zu den Kunstformen des mittelalterlichen Epos, Wiener Beiträge, IX, 1899, pp. 217-370. For a comprehensive study of the sources of the *Troilus* see Karl Young, The Origin and Development of the Story of Troilus and Criseyde (Ch. Soc., 1908); and cf. his earlier article in MP, IV, 169 ff. Professor Young showed that for certain parts of the poem, especially Bk. iii, ll. 512-1190, Chaucer probably utilized Boccaccio's Filocolo (Opere Volgari, VII-VIII). Of the Troilus story proper, Chaucer doubtless knew both of the versions which precede Boccaccio's, those of Benoît de Sainte-Maure and Guido delle Colonne. He made considerable use of the former, and probably followed the latter in occasional details. It is not clear that he used either Dictys or Dares, though he drew upon the poetical paraphrase of Dares by Joseph of Exeter. Incidental borrowings from various authors — most notably from Ovid, Statius, Boethius, Dante, and Petrarch — have been pointed out by scholars and will be recorded in the notes. It has long been recognized that the De Consolatione Philosophiae deeply influenced the philosophical thought in the poem. For an attempt to show that the narrative and characterization also owe much to Boethius and that Chaucer conceived the *Troilus* as a counterpart of the *Boece*, see T. L. Stroud, MP, XLIX, 1 ff. For additional information or discussion see N. E. Griffin, Dares and Dictys, Baltimore, 1907; also his introduction to the prose translation of the Filostrato already mentioned, and his edition of Guido's Latin text (Med. Acad. of America, 1936); G. L. Hamilton, The Indebtedness of Chaucer's Troilus and Criseyde to Guido delle Colonne's Historia Trojana, New York, 1903; G. L. Kittredge, Chaucer's Troilus and Guillaume de Machaut, MLN, XXX, 69; and Chaucer's Lollius, Harv. Stud. in Class. Phil., XXVIII, pp. 47 ff. (with an appendix on the use of the Teseida); H. N. Cummings, The Indebtedness of Chaucer's Works to the Italian Works of Boccaccio, Univ. of Cincinnati Studies, X, 50 ff. (in which the influence of the Filocolo is denied); B. A. Wise, The Influence of Statius upon Chaucer, Baltimore, 1911; R. K. Root, Chaucer's Dares, MP, XV, 1 ff.; M. Praz, Chaucer and the Great Italian Writers of the Trecento, in The Monthly Criterion, VI, 18 ff., 131 ff.; E. F. Shannon, Chaucer and the Roman Poets, Cambridge, Mass., 1929, pp. 157 ff. (a comparison of Criseyde with the Helen of Ovid's Heroides). Professor Lumiansky, in Spec., XXIX, 727 ff., makes a useful comparison of the versions of the story in Guido and in Benoît. The notes that follow are indebted to all these studies, as well as to Skeat's edition and the various articles registered by Miss Hammond, pp. 395 ff., and Wells, pp. 872 f., and appendixes. The editor wishes to acknowledge especially the use he has made of the very full notes in Professor Root's edition. The

Troilus episode in the Roman de Troie comprises ll. 13065–21782. The poem is here cited from the edition of L. Constans, SATF, 6 v., 1904–12. A convenient summary of the episode is given by Professor Kittredge, The Date of Chaucer's Troilus, pp. 62–65. The Historia Trojana of Guido is cited from the Strassburg edition of 1489. For a detailed analysis of the time-scheme of the *Troilus* see H. W. Sams, MLN, LVI, 94 ff.

All these findings on the relation of the *Troilus* to the Filostrato must be re-examined in the light of new discoveries of Professor Pratt, of which he kindly sent the editor an account in advance of publication. (See now his preliminary statement in SP, LIII, 509 ff.) It has long been known to Chaucerians that there was a French prose version of the Filostrato by Beauveau, Seneschal of Anjou, entitled Le Roman de Troyle et de Criseide. But since Beauveau was supposed to have lived in the fifteenth century, his Roman was not considered to be a possible source for Chaucer. Professor Pratt has now made a comparison of the three works, the Filostrato, the Roman, and the *Troilus*, and has found an astonishing number of parallels peculiar to the English and the French. Even the preliminary body of evidence which he has communicated privately to several Chaucer scholars seems to prove that Chaucer at least made subsidiary use of the French text, like his use of French versions of Boethius and of Petrarch's story of Griseldis. If this is true, the Roman will of course have to be assigned to an earlier author than the fifteenth-century seneschal, and Mr. Pratt is also investigating this biographical problem. He hopes, too, to be able to identify the type of manuscript of the Roman which Chaucer used. Until his evidence is all in, opinion must be reserved both on the authorship of the French work and on the fact and the extent of Chaucer's indebtedness.

Chaucer's own attribution of his original to *myn auctour called Lollius* (i, 394) has been the subject of much discussion. See the references in Miss Hammond, pp. 94 ff., and Wells, p. 872, and especially Kittredge, Harv. Stud. in Class. Phil., XXVIII, 47 ff.; also Lange, in Anglia, XLII, 345 ff. and Imelmann, ESt., XLV, 406 f. The theories that Lollius stands for Boccaccio or Petrarch must be rejected. The passages in connection with which he is mentioned, or Chaucer's source referred to, come sometimes from one of these authors and sometimes from neither. But in none of them does Chaucer mean to acknowledge indebtedness to an Italian contemporary. He professes to be following an ancient Latin authority to whom he attributes the whole substance of his story, from whatever source derived. This authority he calls Lollius, most probably because he believed that there was actually an ancient historian of Troy who bore that name. This supposition is borne out by the mention of Lollius alongside of Dictys (*Tytus*) and Dares in the *House of Fame* (l. 1468). Where Chaucer got his supposed information about Lollius is unknown, but it is likely, as was long ago suggested by R. G. Latham (Athen., 1868, II, 433), that the whole notion originated, with him or with some predecessor, in a mistaken inference from Horace's "Trojani belli scriptorem, maxime Lolli" (Epist., i, 2, 1). Chaucer may even have known the line only as it is quoted in John of Salisbury's Polycraticus, vii, 9 (ed. Webb, Oxford, 1909, II, 128). In support of the Horatian theory Professor Pratt (MLN, LXV, 183 ff.) cites the reading *scriptorum* from a late twelfth-century copy of the Polycraticus and a statement from Foullechat's translation of the Polycraticus that Horace says "que Lolli fu principal écrivain de la bataille de Troie."

Two recent identifications of Lollius deserve mention. H. J. Epstein (MLQ, III, 391 ff.) suggests that Chaucer was mystifying his readers by citing Lollius Bassus (c. 19 A.D.). But there is no evidence that he was known in Chaucer's England or ever associated with Troilus. Mrs. L. H. Hornstein (PMLA, LXIII, 64 ff.) argues for the identification of Lollius with Lellius, the friend whom Petrarch addressed as Laelius. She suggests that Chaucer may have seen his name in a manuscript of the Filostrato and have taken him to be the author. The possibility is not to be denied, but it remains a mere supposition unless there is evidence connecting Laelius with the Trojan story, and the corruption of Lellius to Lollius remains a difficulty.

Another baffling name for the source of the *Troilus* is preserved by Lydgate, who speaks of the poem as "a translacioun off a book which callid is Trophe in Lumbard tunge." See his list of Chaucer's works, Prologue to the Fall of Princes. Chaucer also cites *Trophee*, either as an author or as a work, in the account of Hercules in the *Monk's Tale* (VII, 2117), and various interpretations are discussed in the notes to that passage.

Of fundamental importance in all the mediæval treatments of the Troilus story are the conventions of courtly love. The general history and underlying philosophy of that institution have been treated in scholarly publications too voluminous to be cited here. But for recent discussion reference may be made to a series of articles by the Rev. Dr. Alexander J. Denomy in Med. Stud., VI, 175 ff.; VII, 139 ff.; VIII, 107 ff.; and Spec., XXVIII, 44 ff. See also the critical survey of J. Silverstein in MP, XLVII, 117 ff. For a convenient survey of Chaucer's use of the system, see W. G. Dodd, Courtly Love in Chaucer and Gower (Boston, 1913); cf. also Thomas A. Kirby, Chaucer's Troilus: a Study in Courtly Love, Louisiana State Univ. Press, 1940; C. S. Lewis, The Allegory of Love, London, 1946; Dorothy Everett, Essays on Middle English Literature, Oxford, 1955. For a brief discussion of the treatment of courtly conceptions in the *fabliaux* see G. Stillwell, JEGP, LIV, 693 ff., and on its treatment in *MerchT* and *FranklT*, see Miss M. Schlauch, ELH, IV, 201 ff., and C. H. Holman, ELH, XVIII, 241 ff. On the relation between courtly love and Christian teaching, as presented in the *Troilus*, see E. E. Slaughter, Essays in Honor of Walter Clyde Curry (Nashville, 1955), pp. 61 ff.

A good study of "The Domestic Background of *Troilus and Criseyde*," which includes the consideration of the architectural design of houses and their furniture and internal arrangements in other works of Chaucer, has been written by Professor H. M. Smyser, Spec., April, 1956. Frequent reference to the courtly love background of the *Troilus* will be made in the following notes.

In the table which follows are indicated the main parallels between the *Troilus* and the Filostrato. The correspondences are often not close, even in the passages noted, and in many places not listed, lines and phrases were taken over from the Italian. Such details, when they seem significant, will be mentioned in the Notes. In the case of the *Troilus* numbers refer to lines, in that of the Filostrato, to stanzas (with lines occasionally added after commas).

Troilus	Filostrato
I, 21–30	I, 5–6
57–140	7–16
148–231	17–25
267–273	26
281–329	27–32, 6
354–392	32, 7–37
421–546	38–57
547–553	II, 1
568–630	2–10
646–647	11, 1
666–667	13, 7–8
673–686	11, 7–8; 12
701–703, 708–714	13
722–724	15, 1–2
856–865; 874–889	16–17; 20–22
967–994	24–25; 27–28
1009–1064	29–34
II, 274–291	35–36; 44
316–320	46
393–399	54–55
407–420	47–48
501–509, 519–522	55–57
540–541	61, 1–2
554–578	62–64
584–588	43
596–604	68
659–665; 704–707	72
733–735	71–70
746–763; 768–788	69; 73; 75–77
960–981	79–81; 89
995–1009	90–91
1044–1064	93–95
1065–1092	97; 105; 107
1100–1104	108–109
1120–1158	109–113
1173–1178	114
1195–1200	118
1205–1209	119
1212–1226	120–128; 134
1321–1351	128–131
III, 1–38	III, 74–79
239–287	5–10
330–336	9–10
344–441	11–20
1310–1323	31–33
1338–1365	34–37
1373–1386	38–39
1394–1426	40–43
1443–1452	44
1471–1493	44–48
1499–1555	49–56, 1
1588–1624	56–60
1639–1680	61–65
1695–1701	70
1709–1743	71–73
1772–1806	90–93
IV, 1–10	III, 94
29–35	IV, 1
47–112	2–11
127–168	12–16
211–322	17; 22; 26–36

Troilus	Filostrato
IV, 330–357	IV, 38–41; 43
365–385	44–46
393–406	47–48
415	49
439–451	50
452–628	52; 54–58; 60–75
631–637	76
645–795	77–93
799–821	95–96
841–926	97–107
939–948	108–109
1083–1095	109–110
1108–1253	110; 112–127
1303–1306; 1324–27	133
1331–1348	131–134
1359–1372	135–136
1422–1446	137–140
1464–1542	141–146
1555–1659	147–163
1667–1701	164–167
V, 15–90	V, 1–6; 10–13
190–261	14–21; 24–28
280–295	22–23
323–336; 353–364	29–32
386–686	33–38; 40–61; 67–71
687–693; 708–743	VI, 1–6
750–755	7
766–805	8; 10–11; 33; 24
841–847	9
855–942	12–25
953–958	26–27
967–991	28–31
1100–1354	VII, 1–32; 40–41; 48–55
1373–1421	60; 62; 72; 75
1422–1439	76; 105; 77
1513–1522	27; 89–90
1523–1537	100–102; 104
1562–1586	VIII, 1–5
1632–1764	6–26
1800–1806	27
1828–1836	28–29

Book I

1 ff. The opening stanzas of the Filostrato were inconsistent with Chaucer's attitude as an outsider in love (cf. ii, 13), and he therefore did not use them.

The invocation to Tisiphone instead of one of the Muses may be due to Theb., i, 56 ff. Cf. further ibid., ll. 85–87, viii, 65–71, 686. A mediæval parallel is afforded by the Lamentationes Matheoli (ed. Van Hamel, I, Paris, 1892, p. 6; Lat., l. 60, Fr., l. 214) which would hardly have been in Chaucer's mind here. Chaucer's conception of the Furies appears to be a blending of the classical notion of the goddesses who inflict torment with Dante's description of them as eternally suffering (Inf., ix, 37–51). The idea of their "eterno pianto" is emphasized again in the invocation to Bk. iv (ll. 22–24). Cf. further *SqT*, V, 448; *FranklT*, V, 949–50, 1101, and see MP, XIV, 720 ff. It should be added that the conception of sorrowing Furies is not without classical authority. Mr. T. Spencer (in Speculum, II, 185) cites Claudian, De Raptu Pros., i, 225 and Boethius, iii, m. 12, 31 ff.

1 *double sorwe.* Cf. "Della doppia tristizia di

Jocasta," in Purg., xxii, 56 — a phrase which Chaucer may have recalled, though the passages are otherwise quite dissimilar.

2 "The son of King Priam of Troy." For the order of words cf. *the Grekes hors Sinon*, *SqT*, V, 209, and n.

5 In the *Troilus* the poet represents himself as reading or telling the story to an audience. Similar references to hearers are of course naturally to be expected in the *Canterbury Tales*, which purport to have been orally narrated on a pilgrimage. But they also occur in Chaucer's other works, where they doubtless reflect the actual practice of the poets of reading their works aloud to a company. See *Anel*, 162 ff.; *LGW Prol G*, 85 ff.; *F*, 97 ff.; *LGW*, 1554 ff., 2559 ff.; *HF*, 245 ff., 1255 ff., 1299 f., 1453 ff. For further illustration of the custom see the note to ii, 80, below.

With the rime *Troye*: *fro ye* cf. *Rome*: *to me*, *Gen Prol*, I, 523, n.

7 Cf. Fil., i, 6: "Ciò che dirà 'l mio verso lagrimoso"; also Boethius, De Cons. Phil. I, m. 1, which was perhaps also in Chaucer's mind.

12–14 A commonplace of the rhetoricians. See *SqT*, V, 103, and n.

15 ff. Chaucer's service of the god of Love is more fully described in *HF*, 615 ff.

Line 15 was probably intended as a paraphrase of the papal title, "servus servorum Dei." (Cf. *ParsT*, X, 773; also Dante's Inf., xv, 112). In fact the poem as a whole combines the conventions of pagan epic with the mediæval conception of the religion of love. Lines 29 ff., as Root notes, recall the liturgical "form of a 'bidding prayer,' when the priest exhorts the congregation to pray successively for various categories of persons." And l. 42 refers in strict theological terms to the sin of despairing of the mercy of God, which was held to be the "sin against the Holy Ghost." So the lover is said to be *despeired out of Loves grace*. (See also ii, 530 ff., and *ParsT*, X, 693 ff.). This conception of the Church of Love, which is of structural importance in the *LGW*, as in Gower's Confessio Amantis, appears only incidentally in the *Troilus*. For other references to it see i, 336; ii, 523 ff., 1503; iii, 15–17, 1267, 1282. Cf. also *KnT*, I, 3089, and n., and W. G. Dodd, Courtly Love in Chaucer and Gower, Harv. Stud. in Eng., I, 1913, pp. 191 ff.

21 From Fil., i, 5: "Tuo sia l'onore, e mio si sia l'affanno." But Boccaccio is addressing his lady, whereas the subject in Chaucer's line is the god of Love.

58, 60 The *thousand shippes* and *ten yer* may have been suggested by Aen., ii, 198; cf. also Ovid, Her., xiii, 97.

66 Homer's Calchas (Iliad, i, 69 ff.) was a Greek. In Guido he is represented as a Trojan and takes the place of Chryses.

68–70 Cf. iv, 1409 ff. This consultation of the Delphic oracle is not mentioned in the Filostrato. Chaucer could have got the suggestion either from Benoît (Roman de Troie, ll. 5817 ff.) or Guido (Historia, sig. e 6 recto, col. 1).

71 *calkulynge*, astrological computation? It is hard to believe that Chaucer was unconscious here of word-play on the name of Calchas. On the infrequency of his puns see *Gen Prol*, I, 297, n.

77 *wolde whoso nolde*, whether anybody wished it or not. Compare "willy-nilly" (will he, nill he).

88 With the omission of the subject of *casten* cf. *Gen Prol*, I, 33, and n.

99 *Criseyde*. On the development of the name see E. H. Wilkins, in MLN, XXIV, 65 ff. Boccaccio's original spelling was probably "Criseida," although "Griseida" is common in MSS. and editions of the Filostrato. The change from a learned form in "Cr" to a more popular one in "Gr" is paralleled in other Italian words, and in the present case it would have been assisted by the analogy of "Griselda." The name is derived from the Greek "Chryseida," acc. of "Chryseis." But between the Homeric daughter of Chryses and the mediæval Criseyde there is otherwise little connection. In fact, as has been shown in the Introduction to the *Troilus*, Criseida is Boccaccio's substitute for Briseida, who is the heroine of the story in the Roman de Troie, and she in turn has little in common with the Briseis of the Iliad. The story of Troilus and Criseyde is wholly of post-classical invention. The steps by which it came to be attached to Criseyde are discussed by President Wilkins, in the article just cited, and by Professor Kittredge, The Date of Chaucer's Troilus, pp. 13 ff.

126 *and hoom*, and (went) home.

132–33 Boccaccio (st. 15) says that Griseida had neither son nor daughter, and Benoît (l. 13111) refers to her as "la pucele."

146 On the part played by Dares and Dictys in the development of the Trojan story see the Introduction to the *Troilus*. The form *Dite* is perhaps due to Guido, who cites "Ditem Grecum et Phrigium Daretem" (sig. a 1 recto, col. 2); apparently through misunderstanding of Benoît, l. 92 (variant reading), "Et en lengue greçoise dite" — past participle). Since, however, Benoît regularly employs the form "Dithis" or "Ditis" the assumption of Guido's influence is not absolutely necessary.

153 *Palladion*, the Palladium or image of Pallas. See Aen., ii, 166 ff.

162 ff. The account of the "inamoramento" of Troilus (Fil., i, 17–31) is Boccaccio's, for the story in Benoît begins later with the separation of the lovers. Boccaccio apparently drew suggestions for his invention from another episode in the Roman de Troie, the love of Achilles for Polyxena (ll. 17489 ff.), from the Filocolo, and from his personal experience with Maria d'Aquino. Chaucer's account, while based upon that in the Filostrato, adds details which suggest that he may have independently resorted to the Filocolo or the Polyxena episode. For a detailed comparison of all these passages see Young, Origin, pp. 35 ff., 167 ff. Cf. also E. H. Wilkins, MP, XI, 39 ff. The situation itself, the meeting of lovers at a religious service, is distinctly mediæval. Interesting examples, including Dante's sight of Beatrice in a church at Florence and Petrarch's first sight of Laura at a service in Avignon, are mentioned by Professor Griffin in the introduction to his translation of the Filostrato, p. 15.

170 Professor Griffin notes further (intr., p. 55) that the black habit was not only appropriate to Criseyde's widowhood, but also corresponded to the "bruna vesta" which Maria d'Aquino apparently wore when Boccaccio first saw her.

171 This line, which replaces Boccaccio's statement that Griseida surpassed other women as the rose does the violet, has been very plausibly explained by Professor Lowes as a compliment to Queen Anne. See the Introductory Note above.

193 The cynical remarks of Troilus are taken from the Filostrato, and there perhaps reflect the opinions of Boccaccio, born of his early experience in love. See Griffin, intr., pp. 53 f.

203 Cf. iii, 329, and n.

205 *Ascaunces*, as if (Ital. "quasi dicesse"). Cf. *SumT*, III, 1745; *CYT*, VIII, 838; also l. 292, below.

208 If any literary allusion is intended here, beyond the familiar figure of Cupid's bow, the reference might be to Met., i, 456 ff.

210 For the stock comparison, "proud as a peacock," see Haeckel, p. 60.

214 An elaboration of the proverbial saying, "Pride will have a fall." See Apperson, Engl. Proverbs, London, 1929, p. 512.

217 Cf. the Scotch proverb, "All fails that fools think." See Skeat, EE Prov., p. 63, no. 148.

218 *Bayard*, the name of the famous bay-colored steed given by Charlemagne to Renaud; hence a poetic or allusive name for any horse.

219 *so pryketh hym his corn*, he "feels his oats."

221 *Though I praunce al byforn*; the figure is that of a tandem team.

228 *stere*, probably "steer, control" (as in iii, 910). See JEGP, XX, 397 f.

229 *a-fere*, afire (Kentish form).

232–66 These lines are in general Chaucer's own. For the reflections on the power of Love, which are too commonplace to be traced to a particular source, comparison has been made with the Rom. de Troie, 18443–59; Filocolo, I, 5–6 and 96–98; and Confessio Amantis, vi, 78 ff.

234 *To scornen*, "with regard to scorning."

236–38 Cf. *KnT*, I, 1163 ff.

241 ff. Cf. *WB Prol*, III, 721 ff.; also Gower, Conf. Am., vi, 78 ff. Solomon, Virgil, and Aristotle were familiar examples of wise men, overcome by love. Samson and Hercules of strong men, overcome by love.

245 The language echoes the Gloria Patri. Cf. also *HF*, 82.

250 Comparison has been made with Ovid, Amores, i, 9, 46. But the doctrine of the ennobling effect of love was a commonplace of the courtly literature of the Middle Ages and the Renaissance. See, for example, iii, 22–28, 1786–1806. The idea also appears, though less conspicuously, in the Arabic poets. Cf., for example, Behā Ed-Dîn Zoheir, ed. E. H. Palmer, p. 151 (Arabic text), p. 174 (translation) and for general comments, the Tauk of Ibn Hazm, ed. Petrof, pp. 12–13 (Nykl's translation, p. 16), p. 39 (Nykl, p. 60).

257 The figure is of course proverbial. Cf. ii, 1387 ff.; and also the Aesopic fable of the Oak and the Reed. See Haeckel, p. 23, no. 75; Skeat, EE Prov., p. 62, no. 149.

274 ff. Cf., besides Fil., i, 28, Guido's Historia, sig. 2 k, verso, and Filocolo, i, 4–7.

275 *in thrifty wise*, thoroughly, attentively. Cf. *thriftily*, iii, 211, and see *ML Prol*, II, 46, and n.

281 This statement, which corresponds to Boccaccio's "Ell' era grande" (i, 27), is not quite consistent with Chaucer's later description in Book v, ll. 806 ff. The formal portrait there given was influenced, as will be seen, by other sources.

285 "Her very bearing, the mere movements of her body."

295–98 Cf. ll. 365–66 and iii, 1499. The idea, which is conventional, occurs also in Fiammetta, Opere Volgari, ed. Moutier, VI, 9, and in the Roman de Troie, ll. 17552 ff. Root notes also the philosophical statement in *Bo*, v, m. 4, 1 ff.

300 "To draw in his horns," to become less presumptuous. Proverbial, alluding to the action of the snail.

307 *the spirit in his herte*, the vital spirit. *KnT*, I, 2749 ff., and n.

336 The allusion is to the religious orders, which lived under a "rule." With the whole speech in mockery of lovers cf. the words of Theseus, *KnT*, I, 1785 ff.

338 *a sely fewe*, either "a few simple points" or "a very few"; probably the latter. *Sely*, "trifling, insignificant," was sometimes merely used for emphasis.

363 *a temple*, in the temple.

386 The use of *wynne* is strange. It is usually taken to mean here "overcome, triumph over." The suggestion of Professor D. C. Fowler (MLN, LXIX, 313 ff.) that it means "complain" is hard to support.

394 On Lollius see the Introductory Note above. He is the Latin author from whom Chaucer professes to have derived his story and whom he pretends faithfully to follow.

400–20 The *Canticus Troili* is a fairly close rendering of Petrarch's Sonnet 88 (In Vita), "S'amor non è." A few variants seem due to Chaucer's misunderstanding of the Italian. See E. H. Wilkins, ELH, XVI, 176 ff. (reprinted in The Making of the Canzoniere (Rome, 1951), pp. 305 ff.

409 *If harm agree me*; Petrarch, "S'a mal mio grado" (if against my will), for which Root suggests Chaucer's MS. may have read, "Se mal mi agrada."

411 *quike deth*, living death. For the use of such contradictory terms, cf. ii, 1099; v, 228. The rhetorical figure of oxymoron in the description of love has been common in both ancient and modern literature. Cf. RR, 4293 ff., derived from Alanus de Insulis, De Planctu Naturae (Migne, Pat. Lat., CCX, 445 f.). For further illustration see Romeo and Juliet, i, 1, 169, with Farmer's note (Furness, Variorum edn., p. 22); and cf. the remarks on the subject in the Tatler, No. 90. The Ovidian use of the figure is noted by Miss Hammond, Eng. Verse between Chaucer and Surrey, Durham, N.C., 1927, p. 524. Though perhaps not so much of a commonplace as in mediæval literature, the oxymoron of love is found in familiar passages of the Palatine Anthology. Cf. Meleager's γλυκύπικρος and the observations of J. W. Mackail, Select Epigrams (New York, 1911), p. 36.

449 Proverbial; cf. RR, 2358 (*Rom*, 2478), and see Haeckel, p. 17, no. 56.

455 Polyxena, the daughter of Priam and Hecuba.

456 f. For the illogical construction, cf. *ML Prol*, II, 49, n.

457 The omission of the negative was idiomatic. See Zupitza's edition of the Mid. Eng. Guy of Warwick, EETS, 1875–76, p. 368.

464 *savacioun* (Ital. "salute," Fil., i, 44) is perhaps here, as W. M. Rossetti suggested, in the sense of well-being or safety. The usual theological application, even if transferred to love, seems inappropriate.

465 *fownes,* fawns, i.e., young desires. The figure is not in Boccaccio.

470 *of armes preve,* "proof, test of prowess."

483 *the deth,* the plague.

484 ff. For these regular symptoms of love-sickness cf. *KnT,* I, 1372 ff., and n.

517 Cf. *HF,* 639–40, also *Gen Prol,* I, 476, and n.

532 This line, for which the Italian has simply "più ch' altro" (Fil., i, 54, 8), sounds proverbial. No particular reference has been recognized in it.

548 *Pandare.* For general remarks on the character of Pandarus, especially as modified by Chaucer, see the introduction to the *Troilus.* Cf. also E. E. Slaughter, in JEGP, XLVIII, 186 ff., who gives a summary of opinions on the subject, and in his own interpretation emphasizes Chaucer's purpose to represent Pandarus as conforming consistently to the classical character of an ideal friend. Boccaccio may have taken the name Pandaro from Benoît's "Pandarus de Sezile," which in turn goes back to Homer's Pandarus of Zeleia, the Lydian archer who shot an arrow in violation of a truce, and who was killed by Diomed (Iliad, iv, 125–26; v, 95 ff.). But beyond the bare name Boccaccio's Pandaro has no connection with these figures. For the development of the character of the go-between — of which Pandarus has become *par excellence* the representative in European literature — various models have been suggested: Governale, the friend of Tristan, in the Italian Tristano; Galehout, in the French Lancelot du Lac, who arranges a meeting between Lancelot and Guinevere; the *ami* of Achilles, who negotiates with Hecuba for the hand of Polyxena; and four characters in the Filocolo — Duke Feramonte, Ascolione, Glorizia, and the "fedelissimo servidore" who carries letters between Florio and Biancofiore. (For detailed references see Young, pp. 43 ff., and Griffin, intr., pp. 42 ff.). From any or all of these figures single features in the character and conduct of Pandaro may have been derived. But no one of them can be regarded as his original. In fact the type of procurer (or more commonly procuress) was so well established in both Latin and mediæval literature that the places are very numerous from which Boccaccio might have derived hints. It has even been suggested that he drew upon personal experience with such an intermediary in his relations with Maria d'Aquino.

For information about feminine counterparts of Pandarus in classical and mediæval literature reference may be made to the commentators on La Celestina, perhaps the most famous example of the type. See particularly Menéndez y Pelayo, Orígenes de la Novela, III (Nueva Biblioteca de Autores Españoles, XIV), Madrid, 1910, pp. xlii–xciii; and cf. Bonilla y San Martín, Revue Hispanique, XV, 372 ff., and F. Castro Guisasola, Observaciones sobre las Fuentes Literarias de La Celestina, Madrid, 1924.

550 ff. With this dialogue and the corresponding passage in the Filostrato (ii, 1–20) has been compared the scene in the Filocolo (I, 214–22) in which Duke Feramonte extorts from Florio a confession of his love.

557 *for ferde,* "for fear." *Attricioun* was imperfect sorrow for sin; something less than "contrition."

559 *leye . . . on presse,* "lay away, put aside" (rather than "compress, diminish," as suggested by Skeat).

560 *holynesse,* piety. (See Tatlock, Stud. Phil., XVIII, 422 ff.)

568 With the alternatives here cf. *Gen Prol,* I, 844, and n.

628 ff. Apparently proverbial; Elizabethan variants are cited by H. E. Rollins, Paradise of Dainty Devices, Harv. Univ. Press, 1927, pp. 267 ff. Pandarus makes frequent use of proverbs throughout the poem. On their function is the portrayal of the characters, especially Pandarus and Troilus, see R. M. Lumiansky, Tulane Stud. in English, II, 5–48.

630 Proverbial. See Skeat, EE Prov., p. 62, no. 150; Haeckel, p. 20, no. 63.

631 ff. The comparison to the whetstone is also proverbial. See Rollins, p. 268. Chaucer may have known its occurrence in the Ars Poetica, ll. 304–05. This whole passage, which does not follow the Filostrato, contains echoes of the Roman de la Rose. Cf. particularly l. 637 with RR, 21573 ff., and ll. 638–44 with RR, 21559 ff. The proverbial statement in l. 637 is also paralleled by *Bo,* iii, m. 1 and the gloss, "Namque per oppositum noscitur omne bonum." See further Haeckel, p. 35, no. 118. Possibly ll. 646–47 were suggested by Fil., ii, 11, 1.

637 Proverbial; cf. Haeckel, p. 35, no. 118.

652–700 The citation of "ensamples" here, for which there is no parallel in the Filostrato, may be due to the similar use of exempla by Duke Feramonte in the Filocolo, I, 219 ff.

659–65 From Heroides, v, 151 f. (now regarded as spurious), expanded, probably, by the use of glosses or of the Italian translation attributed to Filippo Ceffi. (See PMLA, XLV, 112 f.) Perhaps Chaucer was also influenced by Tes., iii, 25. The conception of the physician who cannot heal himself was of course proverbial. Cf., e.g., Luke iv, 23.

674 For the phrase cf. *KnT,* I, 1133 and n.

687–88 Cf. Seneca, Epist. Mor., i, 3, 4: "Utrumque enim vitium est, et omnibus credere et nulli" (quoted in a gloss to Boethius, iii, m. 8).

694 Eccl. iv, 10; cf. Skeat, EE Prov., pp. 62 f., no. 151.

700 This bit of local color, not found in the Filostrato, is a characteristic Chaucerian addition, doubtless suggested by Ovid, Met., vi, 312.

704–07 A gloss in MS. R ("Require in Metamorphosios") makes it probable that Chaucer was following Ovid in these lines, and Root suggests doubtfully that he had in mind Met., ix, 142 f. A passage in the account of Procris (Met., vii, 720) is perhaps closer: "Quaerere quod doleam statuo" (var. "studeo," which fits better Chaucer's passage). But the parallel is not conclusive and the counsel against over-indulgence in grief was a commonplace of moral philosophy.

704 Cf. Seneca, Epist. xvi, 4, 26 ("Quid enim est turpius quam captare in ipso luctu voluptatem?"); also the OF. proverb, "Nul duel sordoleir ne nule joye sorjoyr" (Morawski, Proverbes Français, Paris, 1925, p. 51, no. 1403).

708 For the proverb "Misery loves company" cf. *CYT,* VIII, 746 f., and see Skeat, EE Prov., p. 63, no. 152.

712–14 A gloss in MS. R again refers to Ovid, and Professor Kittredge has observed to the editor that Chaucer was probably following the Epist. Ex Ponto, ii, 7, 41–42: "Sic ego continuo Fortunae vulneror ictu, vixque habet in nobis iam nova plaga locum." Cf. also iv, 16, 51–52.

715 *If God wol,* a phrase of emphasis; "in God's name."

731 This phrase is taken literally from *Bo,* i, pr. 4, 2. Cf. also Haeckel, p. 33, no. 108. The passage as a whole has been compared by Mr. Young with Filocolo, I, 238.

738–39, 755, 806, etc. With these references to solitary complaint cf. Fil., ii, 1, 6, 13, 16, etc.

740 Skeat compares "He makes a rod for his own breech." For other parallels see his EE Prov., pp. 63 f., no. 153; Haeckel, pp. 6 f., no. 21; H. B. Hinckley, MP, XVI, 39. Chaucer's version resembles those in Provençal given in Cnyrim's Sprichwörter, Marburg, 1888, nos. 779–85.

747 f.   Cf. RR, 7557–58.

780–82 With this consolation may be compared Filocolo, I, 220.

786 On *Ticius* (Titius) see Boethius, iii, m. 12. Cf. also Aen., vi, 595; Met., iv, 457; x, 43.

809 *Unknowe, unkist.* Proverbial. Cf. Haeckel, p. 10, no. 33. The idea is also expressed in the proverb, "Spare to speak, and spare to speed," discussed by H. E. Rollins, The Paradise of Dainty Devices, Harv. Univ. Press, 1927, p. 266 f.

810–12 Cf. RR, 20889–92 (closely similar).

813–19 Cf. Machaut's Remede de Fortune, 1636–51, 1662.

834–56 With this passage, of which there is no hint in the Filostrato, Dr. Fansler compares the discourse of Reason, RR, 5842 ff. The argument is also paralleled, as Root notes, in Boethius at the beginning of Bk. ii.

846–47 Cf. Boethius, *Bo,* ii, pr. 3, 75–79.

848 ff.   Cf. the Remede de Fortune, 2531–38, and Boethius, *Bo,* ii, pr. 1, 111 ff.

856 Cf. *Rom,* 2560–61.

857–58 Cf. Boethius, *Bo,* i, pr. 4, 4 f.; also Ovid, Rem. Am., 125–26.

860–61 Cf. iii, 407 ff.

890–966 Mainly Chaucer's, with occasional echoes of Boccaccio.

891–93 Cf. Seneca, Epist. i, 2, 1; Boethius, *Bo,* ii, pr. 4, 134–38.

894–95 For the doctrine that the love of a good object is good cf. Dante, Purg., xvii, 94 ff., xviii, 34 ff. (not necessarily Chaucer's source).

897–900 Cf. the Remede de Fortune, 1671–83. Fil., ii, 23, is partly parallel, though the argument is different.

900 Among all the other virtues she must have Pity.

916 " 'Fievres blanches.' The agues wherwith maidens that haue the greene sicknesse are troubled; and hence; 'Il a les fievres blanches,' either he is in loue, or sicke of wantonnesse." (Cotgrave, s.v. Fievre.) Cf. The Cuckoo and the Nightingale, l. 41 (Oxf. Chau., VII, 349), and Conf. Am., vi, 239.

918 *tooke on hem,* either "complained" or "put on clothing."

927 f.   Cf. RR, 21551–52.

928 *For faylynge,* to avoid failure.

932–38 Cf. ll. 421–27, above.

946–49 From Ovid, Rem. Am., 45–46.   Cf.

Alanus de Insulis, Liber Parabolarum, Migne, Pat. Lat., CCX, 582.

948–52 Cf. for elaborate series of such antitheses Alanus de Insulis, Liber Parabolarum, loc. cit. Other examples are cited by Skeat, EE Prov., p. 64, no. 154; Haeckel, p. 67; Morawski, p. 5; and Miss Hammond, Eng. Verse between Chaucer and Surrey, p. 467.

950 Cf. Filocolo, ii, 276.

953 f.   Possibly a reminiscence of Fil., ii, 23, 7–8: "possi tu soffrire, Ben raffrenando il tuo caldo disire." Cf. also *Bo,* v, m. 1, 18 ff. (for the figure of the bridle).

954 "Yield to the time (or occasion)." This use of *suffre to* has no exact parallel in NED. It suggests the Latin proverb, "Vincit qui patitur." But Chaucer's choice of the word here may be due merely to the Italian ("soffrire").

956 This proverb is familiar in many variants. Cf. "The more haste, the worse speed." See Haeckel, p. 25, no. 83; Skeat, EE Prov., pp. 64 f., no. 155. Chaucer has it in exactly the same form in *Mel,* VII, 1054, and Tatlock (Dev. and Chron., p. 193) has suggested that it is there quoted from *Tr.* Cf. also Bk. iv, l. 1567 f., below.

960–61 Cf. RR, 2245–46 (*Rom,* 2367 f.); also Seneca, Epist. i, 2, 2–3, and Boethius, *Bo,* iii, pr. 11, 62 ff.

964 Cf. Albertanus of Brescia, De Amore Dei, iii (quoting Seneca Ad Lucilium, Epist. i, 2, 3): "Etiam Seneca dixit, Non convalescit planta que sepe transfertur" (Coni, 1507, fol. 60 verso).

969 Cf. *Anel,* 20, and RR, 12759–60.

976 It is unknown who are meant by the *wyse lered.* Chaucer may have had in mind Virgil's statement in the Purg., xvii, 91–93. Cf. also xviii, 19. No such authority is cited in the corresponding passage of Fil. (ii, 27), where Pandaro's argument is frankly cynical. "Io credo certo, ch'ogni donna in voglia Viva amorosa," and "La mia cugina è vedova, e disia." Professor Young (Wisconsin Studies in Lang. and Lit., no. 2, pp. 367 ff.) has shown how the sensual theory of Boccaccio is refined away by Chaucer. Perhaps the change was due in part to Dantean influence.

1000 "The best pillar of his religion and (the one) to disturb his enemies most." For the figure of a "pillar of the church" cf. *Gen Prol,* I, 214.

1001 The zeal of converts is proverbial.

1004–05 Cf. Ephes. i, 4 f., though no special text is needed on the doctrine of salvation by grace.

1021 *for the manere,* from considerations of propriety, good behavior.

1024 On the notion that the spots on the moon represented an old man with a bundle of sticks see S. Baring-Gould, Curious Myths of the Middle Ages, Philadelphia, 1869, pp. 190 ff.; also R. Köhler, in Anglia, II, 137 ff. There is a Middle English poem on the subject printed in T. Wright's Specimens of Lyric Poetry, Percy Soc., 1842, pp. 110 ff., in Ritson's Ancient Songs, London, 1829, I, 68, and Böddeker's Altenglische Dichtungen, Berlin, 1878, pp. 176 ff. Cf. also Inf., xx, 126; Par., ii, 49.

1038 "And I thy surety!" A strong affirmation, here perhaps with the ironical suggestion, "How could there be anything wrong?"

1065–92 These lines do not correspond to the Filostrato, though they perhaps echo later passages in the Italian poem. Cummings (Indebtedness to Boccaccio, p. 53), compares particularly iii, 90 and vii, 80.

1065 ff. The figure is taken almost literally from the Nova Poetria of Geoffrey de Vinsauf, ll. 43–45: "Si quis habet fundare domum, non currit ad actum Impetuosa manus: intrinseca linea cordis Praemetitur opus" (Les Arts Poétiques, ed. E. Faral, Paris, 1924, p. 198). *Sende . . . out* (l. 1068) is apparently a translation of "praemittitur" (or "praemittetur"), instead of "praemetitur."

1092 *dryeth forth*, endures, goes through with; cf. v, 1540.

Book II

1–3 Almost surely a reminiscence of Dante, Purg., i, 1–3, although the figure is familiar. Cummings (p. 53) compares Boccaccio, Ninfale Fiesolano, vii, 65, and Sonnet 95; Tes., xi, 12; Fil., ix, 3; and Petrarch's Canzone viii (In Morte). See also Ovid, Ars Amat., i, 772; iii, 26, 748; Rem. Am., 811–12.

3–4 *The boot . . . Of my connyng*, "la navicella del mio ingegno," Purg., i, 2.

7 *kalendes*, beginning; literally, the first day of the month.

8 With the invocation to Clio, the Muse of history, cf. the Thebaid, i, 41.

14 According to Chaucer's fiction the source of the Troilus was in Latin. See the Introductory Note above. There is no reason for understanding the reference here to be to Italian ("Latino volgare"), as Skeat explained it.

21 A proverb of wide currency: "Caecus non judicat de coloribus." See Haeckel, p. 29, no. 94; Skeat, EE Prov., p. 66, no. 157. It is used with a similar application in Dante's De Vulgari Eloquentia, II, vi, 27, and in L'Intelligenza, (ed. Gellrich, Breslau, 1883), st. 5; and both passages have been suggested as possible sources for Chaucer. (See Kittredge, MP, VII, 477 f., and Lowes, MP, XIV, 710–11.)

22 ff. Ultimately from Horace, Ars Poetica, 70–71, with perhaps further debt to Seneca, Epist. xix, 5, 13; Chaucer's immediate source for the Horatian passage may have been John of Salisbury, Metalogicon, i, 16; iii, 3 (ed. Webb, Oxford, 1929, pp. 42, 134); or Dante's Convivio, ii, 14, 83–89 (cf. also i, 5, 55–66).

28 Proverbial. Cf. l. 42 below; also the Proverbs of Hendyng, l. 29 (Mätzner's Altenglische Sprachproben, I, 305). See Skeat, EE Prov., p. 66, no. 158.

36 Cf. Alanus de Insulis, Liber Parabolarum, Migne, Pat Lat., CCX, 591; "Mille viae ducunt homines per saecula Romam." See also Haeckel, p. 69.

42 Also proverbial. Cf. Haeckel, p. 34, no. 113.

50–56 Cf. Tes., iii, 6–7; RR, 45–66.

55 *Bole*, Taurus. On May 3 the sun would have reached about the twentieth degree of Taurus. The epithet *white* has been traced to Ovid's description of the snow-white bull in the form of which Jupiter visited Europa (Met., ii, 852). But the reason for the association is not obvious.

It is uncertain why Chaucer chose May 3 specifically as the date of this occurrence. The same question arises, it will be remembered, in the *Knight's*

Tale and the *Nun's Priest's Tale*. See KnT, I, 1462, n.

64–71 The passage is somewhat similar to Tes., iv, 73. Cf. also Purg., ix, 13 ff., and Petrarch's Sonnet 42, In Morte, "Zefiro torna." For the transformation of Progne see Ovid, Met., vi, 412 ff.

74 Cf. MillT, I, 3515 f. An instance where the Moon was in unfavorable "plight" is described in MLT, II, 302 ff. For an account of the astrological calculations involved see the note on that passage. Troilus's "casting," as Root suggests, might have consisted simply in consulting a moon-book (Lunarium). See L. Thorndike, Hist. of Magic, New York, 1929, I, 680 ff.

80 ff. This scene, in which the maiden reads aloud to the three ladies, is not taken from the Filostrato. It doubtless represents a common practice of Chaucer's age. See Miss Ruth Crosby's (unpublished) Radcliffe dissertation, Chaucer and the Custom of Oral Delivery, 1929, especially pp. 43 ff. She notes (pp. 28 ff.) that similar groups are described in the Yvain (ed. Foerster, Halle, 1912), ll. 5360 ff., and Li Chevaliers as Deus Espees (ed. Foerster, Halle, 1877), ll. 4266 ff., 8951 ff. Cf. also the familiar story of Robert Bruce reading Fierabras to his men as they were ferried across Loch Lomond (Barbour's Bruce, ed. Skeat, EETS, 1870–89, iii, 435 ff.). For further references to the custom see Havelock (ed. Skeat-Sisam, Oxford, 1915), l. 2327, and Sir Tristrem, ii, st. 13 (with Sir W. Scott's note, Edinburgh, 1804, pp. 285 ff.); and cf. the discussion by Miss R. Crosby in Spec., XI, 88, and Spec., XIII, 413; also B. H. Bronson, Univ. of California Publications in English, I, 53.

84 ff. Chaucer's classical authority for the story of Thebes was the Thebaid of Statius, of which a Latin summary is inserted in the Troilus MSS. after v, 1498. See the note to v, 1485 ff. Although the term "romance" (l. 100) is not altogether applicable to the Latin poem, still the mention of *bookes twelve* (l. 108) indicates that Chaucer had it in mind.

104 The use of *bisshop* here may have been suggested by "evesque" in the Roman de Thebes, 5053, though it was natural enough as a bit of unconscious modernization. The description of the geste of the *assege of Thebes* here is applicable in general to the Thebaid.

110 The *barbe*, a piece of white pleated linen passed over or under the chin and reaching midway to the waist, was worn by widows. See the NED, and DuCange, s.v. Barbuta.

113–19 Cummings compares Fil., ii, 49. The whole scene of Pandarus's visit to Criseyde, he suggests, is borrowed from Fil., ii, 108.

134 And I your surety, i.e., I will warrant, guarantee.

151 "Many a strange matter, joyous and solemn." Skeat gives *unkouth* an adverbial force, "very" (Scottish "unco"), but this use, as Root observes, seems to be late.

157–61 Cf. the Roman de Troie, 3991–92, 5393–96.

158 Perhaps an echo of Guido's phrase "alius Hector vel secundus ab ipso" (Historia, sig. e 2 verso, col. 1. For the comparison with Hector see also iii, 1775.

167–68 Cf. RR. 5660–62, which in turn goes back to Lucan, Pharsalia, viii, 494–95.

191-203 These lines have no counterpart in the Filostrato, and Chaucer does not seem to be referring to any particular episode in Benoît or Guido.

193 For the figure cf. iv, 1356; also RR, 8721 f. Other parallels in Chaucer are noted in Angl., XIV, 243 f.

197 ff. Apparently influenced by Tes., viii, 81.

225-26 Cf. Fil., ii, 37. The next fifty lines are mainly independent of Boccaccio.

236 *Withouten paramours*; either "except sweethearts," or "except by way of passionate love."

260 Proverbial. Root quotes, "The last word byndeth the tale." Cf. also "La fin loe l'œuvre" (Morawski, p. 37, no. 1002).

315-85 The speech of Pandarus is mainly Chaucer's, though suggestions for it are found in various passages in Boccaccio. Cf. particularly Fil., ii, 42, 43, 44, 46.

343 Proverbial; cf. Skeat, EE Prov., pp. 66 f., no. 159.

344 *vertulees*, lacking in such virtue or efficacy as a gem ought to possess. For a representative mediæval account of the virtues of precious stones see Marbodus (bishop of Rennes, 11th century), De Lapidibus Preciosis Enchiridion, Paris, 1531. Cf. also L. Pannier, Les Lapidaires Français du Moyen Âge, Paris, 1882.

366 *doute of reson*, reasonable fear.

398 Hazlitt records two somewhat similar proverbs: "Too late to grieve when the chance is past" (London, 1907, p. 501), and "He is wise that is ware in time" (p. 193). See also Skeat, EE Prov., p. 67, no. 160. Archer Taylor, The Proverb (Cambridge, Mass., 1931), p. 203, cites Chaucer's form of this proverb as a "Wellerism."

400 ff. Cf. Ars Amat., ii, 117-18.

409-27 With Criseyde's speeches here cf. that of Helen in Ovid's Her., xvi (xvii), 111 ff.

424 *paynted proces*, dishonest procedure, colored so as to appear what it is not.

425 Skeat suggests that Pallas is invoked here with reference to the Palladion (i, 153), and notes also that she was a virgin goddess. Criseyde calls upon her again in v, 977, 999.

428-500 In these lines, which are mainly Chaucer's own, a few parallels with the Filostrato have been noted; see Fil., i, 52, 66, and 121.

435-36 Cf. Tes., i, 58, and iii, 1.

470 Proverbial. See Haeckel, p. 23, no. 73; Skeat, EE Prov., p. 67, no. 161.

477 On holding in hand see iii, 773 ff., and HF, 692, n.

479 f. With Criseyde's reservation as regards her honor cf. ii, 468, 762, and iii, 941 ff.; also Fil., ii, 121. Professor Shannon has noted as a parallel the words of Helen in Her., xvi (xvii), 17 f. See also ll. 727-28 below.

483 Proverbial medical doctrine. Cf. Gen Prol, I, 423-24.

484 ff. Mr. C. L. Wrenn, in MLR, XVIII, 289 ff., suggests that this stanza was influenced by Horace, Odes, iii, 3, 1-8. But the two passages are not very similar.

513 On the game of throwing darts or spears see Strutt, Sports and Pastimes, ed. Cox, London, 1903, pp. 62 ff.

525 *mea culpa*, a familiar phrase from the Confiteor, or the form of confession. Professor Hutson,

in a letter to the editor, notes further that the muttering and smiting of the head would correspond to the act of contrition. Thus Chaucer develops the situation of the penitent before his confessor. Cf. MLN, LXIX, 468 ff. The whole speech of Troilus here illustrates the application of religious conceptions to the affairs of love.

527 *Ledest the fyn*, directest the end. With the thought in general cf. Boethius, Bo, iv, pr. 6, 217 ff.

530 On the sin of *disesperaunce* or "wanhope," see i, 15, n.

533 ff. Cf. KnT, I, 1096, and n.

538-39 Cf. Ovid, Met., iv, 64; also LGW, 735-36. See Skeat, EE Prov., p. 68, no. 162.

542-50 Certain details of this episode, for which Fil. (ii, 61-62) offers no parallels, were possibly suggested by Filocolo (I, 238).

553 With *the newe daunce* Root compares "the newefot," Conf. Am., vi, 145.

611-44 The description of Troilus's triumphant entry has no counterpart in the Filostrato. The original hint for the passage, and for the second ride of Troilus (ii, 1247 f.), Chaucer perhaps got from Fil., ii, 82, where Criseida stands at her window and Troilo and Pandaro pass by, apparently on foot. For certain features of the triumph he may have drawn upon Benoît's account of Hector's return from battle (Roman de Troie, 10201 ff.). Cf. also the lines which describe the return of Troilus from a later fight (20597 ff.); and further similarities of detail may be noted in ll. 3147-48, 10283 ff., and 20620 ff. But the best parallel to the episode as a whole (as pointed out by Professor Lowes in an unpublished study) is afforded by the account of Aeneas and Lavinia in the OF. Roman d'Eneas, ll. 8047 ff.; cf. also ll. 8381 ff.

615 *cast up*, open. The adoption of the reading *latis* for *yates*, against MS. authority, is unnecessary. (See MP, VII, 479.)

616-18 Cf. Benoît (ll. 3143 ff.) and Guido (sig. c 1 verso, col. 2). Both relate that Hector ordered the gate Dardanides to be opened to allow his army to issue forth. According to Guido the city had six gates, the first of which was Dardanides. The name Dardanus was originally that of an ancestor of Priam.

622-23 Cf. Boethius, Bo, v, pr. 6, 168 ff.

637 Cf. SqT, V, 558.

651 *Who yaf me drynke?* Who has given me a love-potion?

656 *for pure ashamed*, for very shame. On this idiomatic use of "for" with an adjective or participle see KnT, I, 2142, n.

659 ff. With Criseyde's reflections here cf. those of Helen in Her., xvi (xvii), n.

671 Proverbial. See Skeat, EE Prov., p. 68, no. 163; also Düringsfeld, I, 50, no. 102.

681 The term *hous* here (as Skeat remarks) probably refers not to the zodiacal sign, but rather to one of the twelve divisions of the celestial sphere made by great circles passing through the north and south points of the horizon. See Chaucer's Astrolabe, ii, 37, on the equations of houses. The first and seventh, the one just below the eastern horizon and the one just above the western, were deemed fortunate.

684-85 Venus had also not been in an entirely unfavorable position at the time of Troilus's birth.

715 ff. Proverbial. See Haeckel, p. 27, no. 87, and p. 49, no. 174.

716-18 Cf. RR, 5744 f. The negative *drynkeles* seems at first to contradict the natural meaning of the sentence. But after "forbid" and other verbs with a negative implication it was not uncommon in early English to repeat the negative idea, usually by the particle *ne*, in a dependent clause. Cf. *n'art*, *ABC*, 26 (after *dowte*); *that no man make*, *Mel*, VII, 1584 (after *deffendeth* and *forbedeth*); *sholde nat*, *Mel*, VII, 1757 (after *deffendeth*); *nys*, *Bo*, iii, pr. 10, 14 ff. (after *denyed*); 34 f. (after *doute*); also Layamon's Brut, ed. Madden, London, 1847, ll. 13179, 22067; and see, for examples from AS., J. E. Wülfing, Die Syntax in den Werken Alfreds des Grossen, Bonn, 1894-1901, II, 93 ff. In the present passage the negative idea is expressed by the idea *drynkeles*. But such substitution for the clause with *ne* was rare.

724 For the vehement condemnation of *avauntours*, men who boast of favors received, see iii, 306 ff. Cf. also *NPT*, VII, 2914 ff., and n.

754 The figure from chess, which has been referred to RR, 6652 ff., occurs also in *BD*, 659 ff. It was a common trope, used by Rutebeuf, Deschamps, and Machaut.

756 Cf. *KnT*, I, 1625, and n.; *SqT*, V, 619.

759 *naught religious*, that is, not a nun, not vowed to celibacy.

766-67 Cf. Boethius, *Bo*, 1, m. 3, 4 ff.

784 For this phrase, cf. *FranklT*, V, 942, and n.

786-88 Cf. Ovid, Her. xvi (xvii), 39 f.

789 Proverbial. See Haeckel, p. 31, no. 103, and cf. *HF*, 361; *BD*, 708.

791 Apparently also proverbial. MS. S¹ has the gloss: "Acriores in principi(o) franguntur in fine." For sayings of similar tenor cf. Haeckel, p. 52.

797 *sporneth*, stumbles: it is too insubstantial to make anybody stumble.

798 "Ex nihilo nihil fit." Cf. Haeckel, p. 10, no. 34.

807-08 "Nothing venture, nothing win." Cf. v, 784; and see Skeat, EE Prov., pp. 68 f., no. 164; pp. 78 f., no. 189; Haeckel, p. 9, no. 30.

811 Cf. RR, 2277-78.

813 ff. The garden scene and Antigone's song are added by Chaucer. The setting may have been suggested by a later passage in the Filostrato (iii, 73 ff.) where Troilo leads Pandaro into a garden and sings a lovesong in some respects similar. But the real source of Antigone's song appears to be Machaut's Paradis d'Amour (ed. Chichmaref, Poésies lyriques, Paris, 1909, II, 345 ff.). See Young, Origin, pp. 173-76, and Kittredge in MLN, XXV, 158. Koeppel, in ESt, XX, 156, compared Gower's 46th Balade. But the resemblance is slight.

816 The origin of the names of Criseyde's nieces is unknown. Antigone is of course familiar in the story of Thebes. Hamilton, Chaucer's Indebtedness to Guido, pp. 94 ff., would derive *Tharbe* from "rex Thabor" in Guido's Historia (sig. f. 5 verso, col. 2), and *Flexippe* from Ovid's Plexippus, the uncle of Meleager (Met., viii, 440).

841 ff. Cf. *Venus*, 1-24.

861 Cf. the proverb, "Many talk of Robin Hood, that never shot in his bow." See Hazlitt, p. 311. Root notes that two of the scribes (those of MSS. Hl⁴ and Ph) recognize the saying and supply glosses referring to Robin Hood.

867 For the figure of a glass head or a glass cap, as a symbol of insecurity, see *MkT*, VII, 2372, n. (*vitremyte*), and cf. v, 469. The present passage of course corresponds to the modern proverb, "Those who live in glass houses should not throw stones." Cf. Skeat, EE Prov., pp. 69 f., no. 166.

884-86 The assonance here (*sike: endite*) is perhaps the only clear case in Chaucer. Skeat suggested emending to *syte*, "be anxious."

905 Cf., for the humorous turn, *FranklT*, V, 1017 f.

908 Cf. Dante, Par., xxii, 93.

920 Cf. *KnT*, I, 1509; *SqT*, V, 53 ff.; *LGW Prol G*, 49.

925 On a possible relation between this dream of the eagle and Fil., vii, 23-24, with further influence of Dante's Purg., xxix, 108 (and following cantos), see M. Praz, Monthly Criterion, VI, 29-31.

954 "Put on your hat and go."

964 *hameled*, hambled, mutilated. The term was used of both dogs and deer. It is probably here to be applied to the sorrow of Troilus, conceived as a pursuing hound. For the suggestion that it may refer rather to Criseyde, conceived as the game in flight but now half captured, see O. F. Emerson, Rom. Rev., XIII, 147-48.

967-71 Cf., besides Fil., ii, 80, Dante's Inf., ii, 127-32, which Boccaccio followed.

986-87 The homely comparison sounds proverbial.

989 Cf. *FrT*, III, 1475, n.

1001 "I am not to blame for your ill-success." For the idiomatic use of *long*, *along*, see *CYT*, VIII, 922, n.

1022 It is still a familiar belief that men's ears glow when they are talked about.

1023 The suggestion of the letter comes doubtless from Fil., ii, 91. For the directions about how to write it cf. Ovid, Ars Amat., i, 467 ff.

1025 "Don't make a display by using arguments." *Thise* is employed here, as often, in the generalizing sense. *Make it ... tough* has a meaning not recognized by the NED, but clearly established by several passages to which Professor Kittredge has called the editor's attention. The NED gives two senses: (a) "to make it difficult, to show reluctance" (the probable meaning in *BD*, 531); (b) "to be persistent or obstinate." A third sense (c), "to bear one's self jauntily or with self-assurance, to put on style or airs, to swagger," is found in A Treatise of a Galaunt, 138-39 (Hazlitt, Early Pop. Poetry, London, 1866, III, 157):

"Tryppynge with small shankes/as lyght as lefe on lynde/
To make it toughe and fresshe/as it were the newe yere."

Cf. also Rowlande and Ottuell, l. 118, and Hoccleve, Reg. of Princes, 3516 ff., both put by the NED under (a). This meaning best fits the present passage and iii, 87; probably also v, 101. Further developments of sense (c) are: "to make merry," as in The Kyng and the Hermyt, 308 (Hazlitt, I, 24); "to use eager blandishments," as in A Penni Worth of Witte, ed. Laing, Edinburgh, 1857, l. 329; "to act lustily" — sensu obscoeno — as in *ShipT*, VII, 379. The meaning "vigorous," "assiduous," or "energetic" may underlie all these special idioms.

1027 Cf. Ovid, Her., iii, 3.

1030 ff. The phrase "to harp on one string" was doubtless proverbial, but Chaucer may have known the parallel passage in Horace, Ars Poetica, 355–56. Cf. Skeat, EE Prov., p. 70, no. 167.

1041-43 Cf. Horace, Ars Poetica, 1–5, partly quoted in John of Salisbury's Policraticus, ii, 18 (ed. Webb, I, 103).

1093 ff. The services of Pandarus in the *Troilus* and the Filostrato in bearing letters between the lovers have been compared to those of the "fedelissimo servidore" in the Filocolo (I, 267–75). The sentimental performance of Troilus in moistening the seal with tears has also a parallel in the Filocolo, I, 274.

1099 Cf. "the jolif wo," Conf. Am., vi, 84; and see i, 411, n., above.

1107 On the figure of the dance of love see *Gen Prol*, I, 476, n.

1108 Skeat and Root read *to-laugh*, "laughed exceedingly" (pret. 3 sing.). NED under To-prefix² 2, records numerous examples of the use of "to-" merely for emphasis. But it gives no case of the prefix with "laugh" or verbs of similar meaning. In the absence of such parallels it seems safer to read *to laughe* (inf.), though the construction is doubtful. There is little support in Chaucer for the historical infinitive. *LGW* 635 and 653 may be examples. Cf. also Conf. Am., viii, 1393, and Macaulay's note. In the present passage *to laughe* is possibly to be taken in a causal sense: "And she, for laughter, thought, 'it seemed'') her heart would break." See J. S. Kenyon, The Syntax of the Infinitive in Chaucer, Chaucer Society, 1909, pp. 80–81.

1109-10 "*fynde Game in myn hood*," make a joke of me. Root compares *Intro* to *PrT*, VII, 440.

1120 ff. Cf. the similar situation in Fil., ii, 109.

1145 This was the fate of Capaneus. Cf. v, 1504 f., and Thebaid, x, 888 ff.

1178 *he koude good*, he knew how to act (in the circumstances in question). See *ML Epil*, II, 1169, n.

1201 The reference is to the old custom of sewing together the pieces of parchment on which a letter was written.

1213 f. Cf. Her., xvi (xvii), 143 f.

1229 *ybete*, embroidered. See *KnT*, I, 979, n.

1234 f. Apparently proverbial; cf. Haeckel, p. 54.

1239 Also a proverb. Skeat, EE Prov., p. 71, no. 168, cites Hazlitt, "Soon learnt, soon forgotten." But the Latin gloss in MS. Hl⁴ is closer: "Levis impressio, levis recessio."

1240-1304 Chaucer's own elaboration of the narrative.

1249 *with his tenthe som*, with a party of ten. The idiom is common in Mid. Eng. Sometimes the number includes the leader (as in AS.), and frequently not. *Som* is the indefinite pronoun, not the noun "sum." See Bosworth-Toller, Anglo-Saxon Dictionary, s.v. *sum*, i, 1, b.

1274 "God send others such thorns to pick on!" This pious wish is perhaps aimed at Pandarus's unresponsive mistress. For the use of *mo* cf. *ClT*, IV, 1039.

1276 "Strike while the iron is hot." Cf. *Mel*, VII, 1036, n.

1298 On two years as a recognized period for widowhood see T. A. Kirby, MLR, XXIX, 67, and XXXIII, 402; and M. G. Ellsworth, ibid., XLII, 358.

1332 Cf. Skeat, EE Prov., p. 71, no. 170.

1335 Cf. Skeat, EE Prov., pp. 71 f., no. 171. Koeppel (Herrig's Arch., XC, 151) compares Alanus de Insulis, Liber Parabolarum, Migne, Pat. Lat., CCX, 583: "De nuce fit corylus: de glande fit ardua quercus."

1347 For the use of dice in divination to foretell success in love see Macaulay's note on Conf. Am., iv, 2792; also Cicero, De Divinatione, i, 13, 23; ii, 21, 48; ii, 59, 121.

1349 *After his gistes*, according to his plan or itinerary. *Gistes* almost certainly means "stations or stages of a journey" (NED *Gist*¹, *Gest*⁴). Professor Root's interpretation, "casts (of dice)," would fit the context, but the word seems not to be recorded in this sense.

1380-83 Proverbial: "A great tree has a great fall"; cf. Skeat, EE Prov., p. 72, no. 172. The lines are imitated by Usk in the Testament of Love, iii, 7, 99–101.

1387 ff. Cf. i, 257 f., and n.

1394-1757 This episode as a whole is Chaucer's invention. The intimacy of Deifebo and Troilo in the Filostrato (see especially vii, 78 ff.) may well enough have given him the hint for it. The idea of Criseyde's insecurity in Troy, used by Pandarus as a pretext for his intercession with Deiphebus, is sufficiently suggested by her appeals to Hector at the beginning of the poem (*Tr*, i, 106 ff.; Fil., i, 12–13). A few lines near the end of the episode, as noted by Professor Patch (MLN, LXX, 9), appear to have been suggested by lines in an earlier dialogue of Criseida and Pandaro in Fil., ii, stanzas 134 ff.

For the suggestion that Chaucer may have been indebted for the device of feigned illness to the Biblical story of Amnon and Tamar (II Sam. xiii, 1–20) see C. Muscatine, MLN, LXIII, 372 ff.

1467 *false Poliphete* does not appear in the Filostrato. Hamilton (Chaucer's Indebtedness to Guido, p. 97, n. 3) suggests that Chaucer had in mind the Trojan priest, "Cererique sacrum Polyphoeten," of Aen., vi, 484. Two characters in the Roman de Troie are named Polibetes, but they are both Greeks.

1495 *word and ende*; see *MkT*, VII, 2721, n.

1503 Another instance of the application of theological terms to love. Cf. Luke viii, 48.

1533 This sounds proverbial.

1534 *triste*, the hunter's station in a deer hunt.

1554 An absurd request, since running was proverbially associated with madness. Cf. "to run mad"; also, "Dote renne aboute and breyde wod," Body and Soul (Emerson, Mid. Eng. Reader, New York, 1915, p. 50, l. 30).

1557 *an houre after the prime*, ten in the morning, the hour of dinner. See v, 1126.

1564 A literal equivalent of RR, 18298. Cf. *SqT*, V, 401 ff.

1610 Cf. v, 651.

1735 The significance of the *corones tweyne* is uncertain. Skeat explained them as the crowns of roses and lilies brought by an angel to the virgin couple in the *Second Nun's Tale* (VIII, 270). Pandarus, he says, thus boldly insinuates that the proposed meeting is to be of the most innocent character. But such an allusion is out of place here, unless Chaucer meant by the very anachronism to heighten the cynical humor of Pandarus's speech. And it is hard to believe that Chaucer's readers, without some further hint, would have thought, at this point, of the crowns of Cecilia and Valerius. The meaning or implication of the line may be what Skeat suggests, and the allusion in *corones tweyne* be rather to nuptial crowns as symbols of innocent or honorable love. Another explanation, offered by Bell (III, 115), is that the crowns were those of Priam and Hecuba. But this lacks point, and is not supported by anything in the context.

Other scholars still have proposed allegorical interpretations of the passage. Mr. G. C. Macaulay (in Acad., 1895, I, 339), taking his hint from the dialogue just preceding in the Filostrato (ii, 134), in which Criseida refers to "la corona dell onestà mea" and Pandaro in reply speaks of "questa corona," suggests that Chaucer's Pandarus is referring symbolically to Love and Mercy. But this application, though possible, is entirely arbitrary, whereas the crown has often served as a symbol of honor ("onestà"), and especially the honor of chastity. If an explanation is to be sought in this passage of the Filostrato, it would seem safer to take the crowns as symbolizing the honor of both parties, Criseyde and Troilus. Mr. Root, in his note on this line, hesitatingly suggests that the crowns stand for either Pity and Bountee (see *Pity*, 58, 71–77), or Justice and Mercy, represented in Christ and the Virgin (see *ABC*, 137–44). These interpretations also are possible. But if Chaucer intended either of them, he certainly left his readers to search for it.

The explanation of the *corones tweyne* as nuptial crowns would seem altogether the most natural if it were clear that Chaucer had any knowledge of their ancient use. The garland of the bride was of course familiar to him. In fact he refers to it in *ClT*, IV, 381. But the double crowning of brides and grooms was a regular custom of the Greeks and Romans (apparently also of the Hebrews) and of the early Christian Church. To this day it is so conspicuous a part of the marriage service in the Orthodox Eastern Church that the whole ceremony is known as the "crowning" (στεφάνωμα). In the Western church it was discontinued early as a general practice, though it is recognized in a Latin ritual printed for Poland and Lithuania as late as 1691. And according to L. Gautier (La Chevalerie, Paris, 1884, pp. 416, 420) it survived as a social custom in mediæval France (though he fails to cite clear evidence of the crowning of the groom). On the whole it is not unreasonable to suppose that Chaucer and his readers would have associated a pair of crowns with the marriage service. And if Chaucer knew of the ancient Greek custom, he may conceivably have been trying for "local color" here as in a number of other passages in the *Troilus*.

On nuptial crowns in general see G. E. Howard, A History of Matrimonial Institutions, Chicago, 1904, I, 295. References to Hebrew usage were collected by Selden, Uxor Hebraica (ed. Becmann, Frankfurt am Oder, 1673) lib. ii, cap. 15, and to that of the Greeks and Romans by Carlo Pasquali, Coronae, Leyden, 1671, pp. 126 ff.; see also Smith-Cornish, Concise Dictionary of Greek and Roman Antiquities, London, 1898, s.v. Matrimonium, and J. Köchling, De Coronarum apud Antiquos Vi atque

Usu (Religionsgeschichtliche Versuche, XIV, pt. ii, Giessen, 1914). On the Christian marriage ritual see, besides Howard's chapter cited above, Martene, De Antiquis Ecclesiae Ritibus, Antwerp, 1763–64, II, 124 f.; and for other references consult the Catholic Encyclopaedia, s.v. Marriage (Ritual of). Professor Patch (MLN, LXX, 8 ff.) has recently reverted to the old suggestion about the angelic crowns in *SecNT*, but with a difference. He points out that in an earlier dialogue between Criseida and Pandaro in Filostrato, not utilized by Chaucer in the scene at the house of Deiphebus, she refers to the "crown of her virtue (la corona dell' onestà mia, Fil. ii, st. 134), and notes several other lines in the passage which strikingly resemble passages in *Tr*, ii, 1735–49. On the basis of these parallels he suggests that Criseyde's crown of virtue may have reminded Chaucer of the crown of chastity in the *SecNT*, "and that thus these other crowns of roses and of lilies flashed into the poet's mind long enough to suggest a reference to two crowns by way of emphasis." Although the explanation is by no means obvious or convincing, in view of the uncertainty of other suggestions it deserves careful consideration.

1738 *com of.* On this figure from falconry or hunting see the Glossary.

1745 *waggyng of a stree*, proverbial for "the slightest movement."

1752 *kankedort*, an unexplained word which seems to refer to a state of discomfort or anxiety. Comparison has been made with Swedish "kanka" (to be unsteady) and "ort" (place); also with "canker" (cancer) and "dort" (Lowland Scottish = sulkiness); and also with Old French "quant que dort" (whenever he sleeps). The derivation from Fr. *calembourd*, proposed by L. Spitzer (MLN, LXIV, 503) involves a series of changes difficult to accept. None of these derivations seems likely to be right. More plausible, if still uncertain, is the derivation of Spargo from *kankered-ort*, "place of hesitation," in MLN, LXIV, 264. Root notes the occurrence of what appears to be a corruption of the word, in the form "crank dort," in Henry Medwall's Nature, Tudor Facsimile Text reproduction of the British Museum copy, London, 1908, sig. e 1 recto.

1750 See the Textual Notes for an extra stanza inserted at this point by a single MS. R. It is apparently genuine, but Chaucer doubtless meant to cancel it. As Root remarks, it may have been originally intended to follow l. 1736.

Book III

1–49 The proem is an invocation to Venus, based mainly upon Filostrato, iii, 74–79, where a similar address to the goddess forms a portion of the song of Troilo. At that point (ll. 1744 ff., below) Chaucer substitutes a different song derived from Boethius. Perhaps the added appeal to Calliope (l. 45) is due to Statius, Theb., iv, 34 f., or Dante, Purg., i, 9.

The whole passage affords an excellent example of the mediæval practice of "astrologizing the gods." (See *KnT*, I, 2217 ff., n.) Venus is addressed first as the planet of the third sphere (l. 2), companion of the sun (l. 3), and then as the daughter of Jove, the goddess of love. By love, moreover, is meant both sexual attraction and the cosmic "love" which binds together the universe. In fact several lines in both

Boccaccio and Chaucer are clearly colored by the Christian conception of the love of God.

A number of passages, classical and Christian, on Venus, Love, etc., which illustrate Boccaccio's stanzas and indicate some of his sources, are collected by A. S. Cook in Herrig's Arch., CXIX, 40 ff. Professor Cook lays especial stress on the influence of Dante. See also M. W. Bloomfield, Class. Phil., XLVII, 162 ff.

5 Closer to this than Fil., iii, 74 ("Benigna donna d'ogni gentil core") or Inf., v, 100 ("Amor, che al cor gentil ratto s'apprende") is Guido Guinizelli's line, "Al cor gentil ripara sempre Amore" (Canzone, ed. d'Ancona, Bologna, 1877, p. 13, l. 1.) If Chaucer had not read Guido's poem, he might have known this single line from Dante's citation of it in the Convivio, iv, 20. The idea that only the gentle heart was capable of love was of course fundamental to the courtly system.

8–14 For a fuller statement of this doctrine see ll. 1744–71, below, and *KnT*, I, 2988, both of which go back to Boethius, ii, m. 8.

11 *vapour*, influence, emanation (Bocc. "vapor"). Perhaps from Purg., xi, 6, where the early commentators understood "vapore" to refer to the divine Love. It is now interpreted as Wisdom. Cf. Wisdom of Solomon, vii, 25.

15–17 Behind the names of pagan divinities Mr. Root is doubtless right in recognizing the Christian doctrine that the vivifying power in creation was the Holy Spirit, which impersonates the Love of God. He cites Thomas Aquinas, Summa, pars i, qu. 45, art. 6.

17–21 Chaucer seems to have in mind only the amorous adventures of Jupiter, whereas Boccaccio speaks of Venus in terms applicable to Mercy as an attribute of God.

22 ff. Cf. i, 250, and n.

22 For the influence of Venus upon Mars see also *Mars*, 36–42.

33 *jo*, a word otherwise unknown in English, was derived by Skeat from Old French "joer," to play, to move. Here he would interpret it as "come about, come to pass." Mr. Root suggests doubtfully a connection with Mod. Eng. "gee," to fit, suit, agree.

35 Cf. the saying, "There are as good fish in the sea as ever were caught."

39–42 The language here seems to echo that often addressed to the Virgin. Cf. *Pr Prol*, VII, 478, and Dante, Par., xxxiii, 16.

43 Cf. ii, 13.

45 The invocation of Calliope, the Muse of epic poetry, was perhaps influenced by Dante's Purg., i, 7–9.

50–238 Largely original with Chaucer, though suggestions are furnished by the Filostrato, especially iii, 23–29. With the vows of Troilus (ll. 127–47) may be compared also passages in the letter to Criseida, Fil., ii, 96–106. But the similarities are mostly of too commonplace a character to prove indebtedness.

63 *that is youre deth to wite*, that is to blame for your death.

81 A recurring expression. Cf. l. 957, below; also *LGW*, 1817, and *Gen Prol*, I, 782 (Harl. 7334 variant).

87 f. Criseyde liked him none the less for being

abashed — (1) for not being malapert, (2) for not bearing himself with jaunty self-assurance, (3) for not being over-bold in flattery or in professions of love — in such "fair words" as, according to the proverb, "make fools fain."

For this interpretation, which gives a consistent meaning to a difficult passage, the editor is indebted to an unpublished note of Professor Kittredge. On *made it tough* see ii, 1025, n. The phrase "to sing a fool a mass" was undoubtedly proverbial, though no exact parallel seems to have been found to its use in the present passage. Lydgate (Chorl and Bird, Minor Poems, Percy Soc., 1840, p. 191) associates it, as an act of mad futility, with teaching an ass to play on the harp. Both examples he may have got from the *Troilus* (see i, 731), though there is a very similar combination of ideas in the proverb, "Surdis frustra canitur: nec asinus cithara gaudet" (Bebel, Proverbia Germanica, ed. Suringar, Leyden, 1879, no. 79, p. 28). "Surdo canere" ("narrare," etc.) is a common Latin saying, which in Low German regions is elaborated by the mention of the mass. Cf. "Men en sal ghenen doven twee missen singhen." (Hoffmann von Fallersleben, Altniederländische Sprichwörter, no. 495, p. 32, in Horae Belgicae, IX, Hanover, 1854. See also Antonius Tunnicius, ed. H. von Fallersleben, Die Älteste Niederdeutsche Sprichwörtersammlung, Berlin, 1870, no. 722, p. 65; P. J. Harrebomée, Spreekwoordenboek der Nederlandsche Taal, Utrecht, 1858, I, 147.) Lydgate's use of the English phrase "to sing a fool a mass" indicates that it was probably current in the same sense. But this meaning does not suit the passage about Troilus. Here, Professor Kittredge suggests, the reference is rather to "fine and flattering speeches such as a confident suitor might use to beguile a silly woman." She would take them all on faith, not understanding their true import any better than a fool understands the mass.

For the idiom *to bold, to synge*, "overbold in singing," see Kenyon, Syntax of the Infinitive in Chaucer, Chau. Soc., 1909, p. 67; and cf. Macbeth, iv, 2, 69.

114 For the proverbial comparison see *LGW*, 1841; Haeckel, p. 47, no. 163.

115 Cf. *SqT*, V, 496.

150 *natal Joves feste*, probably (as Skeat suggests) the feast of Jupiter, who presides over nativities. Cf. l. 1016 below. Mr. Root's interpretation, "Jove's natal feast," "the pagan equivalent of Christmas," does not seem the natural meaning of the words.

188–89 There are numerous instances in ballad and romance where bells are said to have been thus rung "without hand" to mark an event of special joy or solemnity. See, for example, Child, English and Scottish Ballads, Boston, 1882–98, I, 173, 231; III, 235, 244, 519 f.; also Hinckley in MP, XVI, 40; Tatlock in MLN, XXIX, 98, and P. Barry in MLN, XXX, 28 f. Mr. Barry suggests that many stories of the sort had their origin in a single instance related by St. Willibrord (eighth century) about the monks of Fulda. See Vitae S. Bonifatii, ed. W. Levison, Hanover, 1905, p. 53.

198 *bere the belle*, usually explained as meaning "lead the flock," hence "take precedence." For the suggestion that the reference is rather to taking the prize in a race see JEGP, VI, 115. See also Skeat, EE Prov., pp. 72 f., no. 173; Haeckel, p. 48, no. 167

294 From Dionysius Cato, Bk. i, Dist. 3. Cf. *MancT*, IX, 332 f.; also RR, 7037, 7041–45, 7055–57. Several similar proverbial expressions are cited by Haeckel, p. 16, no. 52.

309 Also proverbial. See Haeckel, p. 32, no. 106, and Skeat, EE Prov., p. 73, no. 175.

329 Cf. the Latin proverb: "Felix quem faciunt aliena pericula cautum"; also RR, 8003–04; and for other variants see Skeat, EE Prov., p. 73 f., no. 176.

340 *the chartres. up to make*, to draw up the charters, i.e., to put in writing the exact terms that she has granted you.

349 *richesse*, abundance (Ital. "dovizia," Fil., iii, 11, 5).

351–54 Besides the immediate source, Fil., iii, 12, cf. RR, 47–54 and 78–80.

404 *Departe*, make the distinction. Root notes that Troilus is making "a common distinction of scholastic philosophy between *likeness* and *identity of substance*." He cites Duns Scotus, Expositio in Metaphy. Arist., lib. x, sum. 2, cap. 1, no. 30 (Paris, 1891–95, VI, 385), and Thomas Aquinas, Summa, pars i, qu. 31, art. 2.

413 *and lat me thanne allone*, "and then leave me to arrange it alone." Ital. "Poi mi lascia operar con qual sia l'una" (Fil., iii, 18).

445 *sesed*, seized, possessed (in the legal sense).

451–52 Perhaps an echo of Fil., ii, 84, 7–8.

502 *as seyth myn autour*, i.e., the fictitious Lollius; the statement is not in the Filostrato. The same applies also to l. 575.

510 *fulfelle*, Kentish for *fulfille*.

512–1190 The account of the way by which the lovers are brought together differs widely from the corresponding part of the Filostrato. Professor Young (Origin, pp. 139 ff.) has argued that Chaucer probably derived many suggestions for his plan from the passage in Boccaccio's Filocolo where a meeting is arranged between Florio and Biancofiore (II, 165–83). In both stories are to be noted the concealment of the lover by a go-between, the motif of jealousy, the lady's exaction of oaths, the use of rings, and the interchange of more or less formal vows. The whole suggestion of Troilus's jealousy of Horaste, for which there is no basis in the Filostrato, may be due to the account of Florio's jealousy, in an episode in the early part of the Filocolo (I, 247–89). Dr. Cummings, who rejects the theory of the influence of the Filocolo, has pointed out (Indebtedness to Boccaccio, p. 65) a number of parallel features in the Filostrato. But some of these are insignificant, and the rest are not sufficient to account for the development of the plot. On the whole question see further Professor Root's comments in his edition, pp. xxix–xxx, and Professor Griffin's introduction to the prose translation of the Filostrato, p. 101, n. 1. The nocturnal visit, as Mr. Griffin argues, was undoubtedly a stereotyped situation.

526 f. "Beyond a doubt it was free in the wind from every magpie and every spoilsport," i.e., there were no birds to windward to give an alarm.

542 For *the holy laurer* Skeat cites Met., i, 566 f. But, as Root observes, Ovid does not represent Apollo as speaking from out the tree.

549 *the chaungynge of the moone*, the phase when the moon is invisible.

587 "Since I trust you most."

593 For the story of Tantalus see Met., iv, 548 ff., and cf. Boethius, *Bo*, iii, m. 12, 38 ff.

596 *a certein*; cf. *ShipT*, VII, 334, n.

609 No dainty was lacking.

614 On Wade see the *MerchT*, IV, 1424, and n.

615 Proverbial: "Every thing hath an end" — to which is sometimes added in English and several other languages, "and a pudding (sausage) hath two." Cf. *KnT*, I, 2636; *LGW*, 651; Skeat, EE Prov., p. 94, no. 224; Haeckel, p. 43, nos. 147, 148.

617–20 Cf. Boethius, *Bo*, iv, pr. 6, 43–195; v, m. 1, 18 ff.; and *KnT*, I, 1663 ff., n. Chaucer may also have been influenced here and elsewhere by Dante's discussion of the heavenly spheres in Convivio, ii, 4.

624 The rain was caused by the conjunction of the crescent Moon, Saturn, and Jupiter in Cancer, which was the Moon's mansion. On the actual occurrence of such a conjunction in May, 1385, and its bearing on the date of the *Troilus* see the introduction to the Explanatory Notes on *Tr*. According to the calculations of Professor Russell, there cited, Jupiter and Saturn were in exact conjunction in Gemini on April 13, and remained in "platic" conjunction (i.e., less than nine degrees apart) until the end of June. Jupiter entered Cancer on May 1, and Saturn on May 14. By May 13 the crescent moon appeared close to both planets. Venus, which had been in conjunction with Saturn May 3, and with Jupiter May 5, had moved on some ten degrees. Chaucer transferred Venus to the morning (see ll. 1415 ff. below, and n.).

It is worth noting, though it has no bearing on the calculation of the date, that the conjunction of Jupiter and Saturn was regarded by most astrologers as the portent which foretold Noah's flood. See Pico della Mirandola, Disput. advers. Astrol. Divinatricem, ed. Garin (Forence, 1946) Bk. V, ch. 1, p. 520. The editor is indebted for this reference to Mr. J. J. O'Connor.

671 For the custom of drinking wine just before going to bed see *Gen Prol*, I, 819–21.

694–95 Cf. *ii*, 1106, and *Gen Prol*, I, 476, n.

711 Proverbial, like "the fat is in the fire." See Skeat, EE Prov., p. 74, no. 177.

716 Mars and Saturn both had an evil influence. Cf. *KnT*, I, 1995 ff., 2456 ff., for illustrations of the misfortunes they caused. Venus, when "combust" by being too near the Sun, lost its influence. See *Astr*, ii, §4. On the combination of astrology and mythology see the note to ll. 1 ff., above.

720–21 Possibly suggested by Tes., vii, 43, though no source need be assumed. See Chaucer's translation of the passage in *KnT*, I, 2221–25. Cf. also Ovid, Met., x, 715.

722 On Jupiter and Europa see Met., ii, 833 ff., and cf. *LGW*, *Prol F*, 113, and n.

725 For the form *Cipris*, see also *HF*, 518. With the adjuration of Mars by his love of Venus cf. *KnT*, I, 2383 ff.

726 On *Dane* (Daphne) see Met., i, 452 ff., and cf. *KnT*, I, 2062 ff.

729 See Met., ii, 708–832.

731 Cf. Ovid, Ars Amat., i, 261 f.

733 With *fatal sustren* cf. v, 3; also, for the application of the term "sorores" to the Parcae, Theb., i, 632; viii, 59; ix, 323. For the idea that the child's fate is spun before his first garment is made see *KnT*, I, 1566, and n.

741 *trappe*, probably a trap-door in the floor or possibly a secret entrance in the paneling.

764 Proverbial. See Haeckel, pp. 22 f., no. 72; Skeat, EE Prov., p. 74, no. 178.

773 See *HF*, 692, and n.

775 "Make him a hood above a cap," apparently meaning to cover up the eyes, hoodwink, deceive. For similar phrases see *Gen Prol*, I, 586, n.

797 The motif of jealousy is suggested in the Filocolo (II, 175), where brief reference is made to the episode cited in the note on l. 512. The character of Horaste is Chaucer's invention, and the name is apparently taken from that of Orestes ("Horestes" in Guido, "Horeste" in the Conf. Am., iii, 2176). See Kittredge, Language, p. 347, and Hamilton, Indebtedness to Guido, p. 97.

808 With this expression may be compared Biancofiore's reference to the "iniquo spirito" of Florio's jealousy (Filocolo, I, 259–60). But the Filostrato (vii, 18, 3–4) has the phrase "e 'l nemico Spirto di gelosia."

813–33 Cf. *Bo*, ii, pr. 4, 75–78, 118–127. The sentiments were commonplaces. Cf. *MLT*, II, 421 ff.; *NPT*, VII, 3205.

837 Apparently a stock comparison. See also l. 1010, below. Root refers to Gower, Mirour, ll. 2641 ff., and Ovid, Met., ii, 768 ff.

850 *a fair*: "a fine thing (to do)." Root suggests that the word is rather *fair*, "market," with some such sense as "bad bargain."

853 Glossed in MSS. Hl¹ Hl⁴, "Mora trahit periculum" ("delays are dangerous"). Cf. Skeat, EE Prov., pp. 74 f., no. 179.

855 From Eccl. iii, 1.

861 *fare-wel feldefare*; the bird is flown, all is over. Cf. *Rom*, 5510, where the phrase is used of false friends who desert one in misfortune. According to Skeat and the NED the phrase expresses good riddance, with allusion to the fieldfare's welcome departure northward at the end of winter. Professor Kittredge suggests to the editor that the emphasis here is rather on folly, and that the phrase might be paraphrased "Away, you fools." But in the *Troilus* passage, as he agrees, there is surely no such implication. For further examples see the NED; and Hazlitt, Proverbs, London, 1907, p. 149.

885 "True blue" was the color of constancy. Cf. *Anel*, 146, n.

890 "Hazel-bushes shake." A proverbial saying of which the application is not entirely clear. Skeat takes it to be simply a useless truism, to indicate the futility of sending the ring. In two later passages (v, 505, 1174) references to hazelwood seem to be mere expressions of incredulity or derision, and that may be the meaning here. Professor Kittredge has called the editor's attention to the expression, "Thou sitest on hasel bou," apparently in the sense, "You talk idly," in The Thrush and the Nightingale, 106 (Hazlitt, Early Pop. Poetry, London, 1864–66, I, 54); and he compares also "Thou maist of haselwode singe" (Dan Topias, in Wright's Political Poems, Rolls Ser., 1859–61, II, 79).

896 Apparently proverbial.

901 *white*, "specious, plausible." Cf. l. 1567, below; also NED, s.v. White, †10, and for a parallel

use of Fr. "blanche," the Testament of Jean de Meun, l. 1473 (in RR, ed. Méon, Paris, 1814, IV, 75).

919 *at prime face*, "prima facie."

920–45 The account here of Criseyde's acceding to Troilus's desire perhaps goes back to earlier passages in the Filostrato. Cummings (Indebtedness to Boccaccio, pp. 67 f.), compares particularly Fil., ii, 133, 139, 121.

931 *dulcarnoun*, a name for the 47th proposition of the first book of Euclid; hence a term for difficulty or perplexity. The word is originally an Arabic epithet of Alexander the Great ("Dhu 'l Karnayn," the two-horned), who claimed descent from Jupiter Ammon, the horned god. The application to the proposition in Euclid probably came from the resemblance of the diagram to a figure with horns. In l. 933 Pandarus says Dulcarnon is called *flemyng of wrecches*. But that is a translation of "Fuga miserorum" which corresponds in turn to "Eleufuga," a name which was actually applied to the fifth proposition. See Skeat, Athenaeum, 1871, II, p. 393; and for *at my wittes ende*, his EE Prov., pp. 75 f., no. 181.

936 *fecches*, "beans," one of Chaucer's numerous comparisons to denote worthlessness. See *Gen Prol*, I, 177, n.

947 For the use of *ther* in clauses which express blessing or cursing cf. ll. 966, 1437, 1456, below, and see *KnT*, I, 2815, n.

978 *feere*, fire (Kentish).

979 *fond his contenaunce*, "assumed the attitude or appearance." Cf. "to make a countenance," NED, under Countenance, 1b, 2d.

989–90 Cf. *KnT*, I, 1169, 1785 ff.

1016 ff. Cf. *KnT*, I, 1313, and *Bo*, i, m. 5.

1021 *suffrest*, permittest.

1035 Cf. ii, 784.

1046 ff. On ordeal and purgation by oath Root refers to Pollock and Maitland, Hist. of Engl. Law (Cambridge, 1898, II, 598 ff.). On sortilege, one of the most primitive and widespread of all forms of divination, see Tylor, Primitive Culture, 4th ed., London, 1903, I, 78 ff.

1060–61 Proverbial. Cf. Haeckel, pp. 7 f., no. 25; Skeat, EE Prov., p. 76, no. 182.

1064 *shoures*, assaults; the Middle English "shour" (AS. "scúr") referred often to the storm of battle.

1072–92 Similar to earlier scenes in the Filostrato (ii, 1–3, 62).

1088 See *KnT*, I, 2749, n.

1092 ff. This episode appears to be partly imitated from Fil., iv, 18, 19, where Troilo faints on learning that the Trojans are willing to give up Criseida. The swoon is not repeated by Chaucer in the corresponding passage in Bk. iv.

1104 For the figure, cf. ii, 1272 f.

1141 ff. In the Filocolo there is also a formal marriage before the image of Cupid.

1154 *bar hym on honde*, accused him. See MLT, II, 620, n.

1161 See *Gen Prol*, I, 177, n.

1192 For a similar comparison see Filocolo, II, 165–66.

1194 For the bitterness of soot, which was proverbial, cf. RR, 10633–34; also NED, s.v. Soot

1200 Proverbial; cf. *LGW*, 2648; Haeckel, p. 32, no. 107.

1203 "The seven planets." Cf. *Scogan*, 3.

1215 "Bitter pills may have sweet effects." Cf. Skeat, EE Prov., p. 76, no. 183.

1219–20 Cf. *Bo*, iii, m. 1, 5–6; also Alanus de Insulis, Liber Parabolarum, Migne, Pat. Lat., CCX, 592.

1235 "When she hears any shepherd speak."

1255 The application of the name *Cithera* to the planet is paralleled, as Root notes, in Dante (Purg., xxvii, 95).

1257 Comparison has been made with Dante, Purg., i, 19. But the conception of Venus as a beneficent planet was usual.

1258 *Imeneus*, Hymenaeus, Hymen, the divinity of marriage.

1261 Cf. Dante, Par., xxxiii, 14 ff. On the bond, or chain, of love cf. ll. 1762 ff. below. See also *KnT*, I, 2987 ff., and n.

1267 Note the use of this familiar Christian doctrine here in the prayer to Venus, and also in l. 1282. On its application to the affairs of lovers see *KnT*, I, 3089, n.

1316 Whether intentionally or through misunderstanding, Chaucer here departs from the Italian: "D'amor sentiron l'ultimo valore" (Fil., iii, 32).

1324–37 On the position of these stanzas see the Textual Notes.

1365 ff. The interchange of rings is one of the features which Young (Origin, p. 146) attributes to the influence of the Filocolo (II, 181 f.).

1368 ff. This gift of Criseyde's is Chaucer's addition. Boccaccio (Fil., viii, 9–10) simply tells of a "fermaglio" or "fibbiaglio" given by Troilo to Griseida. By *scripture* Chaucer may mean either the motto or posy on the ring or the written authority for the story.

1384 *the white and ek the rede.* In NPT, VII, 2842, and *PardT*, VI, 526, *white ne (and) rede* refers to wine, and the same meaning is possible here. But in view of the Italian "denari perderanno" (Fil., iii, 39) "white silver and red gold" seems more likely to be intended. For illustrations of this meaning see NED, s.v. White, 10.

1387–93 These lines, which depart from Boccaccio, seem to have been suggested by Dante's Purg., xx, 106–08, 116–17, where Midas and Crassus are likewise associated in a discussion of avarice. See Lowes in MP, XIV, 711 ff. The use of *affectis*, a characteristically Dantean word, indicates Chaucer's assimilation of Dante's moral doctrine. On Midas cf. further Ovid, Met., xi, 100 ff. M. Crassus was slain in battle against the Parthians in 53 B.C. The Parthian King Orodes had molten gold poured into the mouth of his fallen enemy. Mr. Lowes (p. 712) suggests that Chaucer's account may contain reminiscences of Li Hystore de Julius Cesar, by Jehan de Tuim. On the other hand Professor Shannon (Chaucer and the Rom. Poets, pp. 133, and n.), holds that the De Casibus, vi, 7 is a sufficient source for what Chaucer tells about Crassus.

1415–26 Primarily from Fil., iii, 42–43. In elaborating the passage Chaucer probably had in mind Purg., xix, 1–6, with its reference to the rising of "maggior fortuna." For the epithet *comune astrologer* cf. Alanus de Insulis, De Planctu Naturae, Migne, Pat. Lat., CCX, 436 ("vulgaris astrologus").

By *Lucyfer*, the morning star, is meant the planet Venus. For similar references to *the dayes messanger* cf. Amores, i, 6, 65 f., ii, 11, 55 f.; Her., xvii (xviii), 112. For *Fortuna Maior* various explanations have been offered. Skeat interpreted it as Jupiter, and cited Gavin Douglas's notes to his translation of the Aeneid (ed. Small, Edinburgh, 1874, II, 288). But he later rejected this application for Chaucer's time. (See Acad., XLVI, 352, and Oxf. Chau., VI, 404; also W. C. Curry, MLN, XXXVIII, 94 ff.). In the first instance *Fortuna Maior* had reference to geomancy, the occult art which is described in *KnT*, I, 2045, n. The figure so named had the form

$$x\ x$$
$$x\ x$$
$$x$$
$$x,$$

and in the arbitrary assignments of the geomancers it was referred to the Sun as its planet. So Professor Curry would interpret the passage as meaning simply "the sun rose." But according to the commentators on Dante the name was sometimes applied to a group of six stars in the constellations of Aquarius and Pisces, and "maggior fortuna" in the Purgatorio is held to refer to this figure. Skeat (Acad., XLVI, 352) identified the stars concerned as θ Pegasi and α, π, γ, ζ, η Aquarii; and Professors Root and Russell (in PMLA, XXXIX, 56–58) calculated that in the latter part of the fourteenth century, in the middle of May, at the first appearance of dawn the group would have been about halfway between the eastern horizon and the zenith, and was still rising *estward*.

1427–42 These lines, which have no counterpart in the Filostrato, recall the sentiment of the "aubade" or "Tagelied" and lead up to the dawn-song proper in ll. 1450–70. Filocolo, I, 173, has an address to Night in some respects similar. Cf. also Amores, i, 13. The "aube" was not so common in mediæval English poetry as in French and German. Examples of later English songs on the night visit are given by C. R. Baskervill, in PMLA, XXXVI, 593 ff. As might be expected, Arabic poetry offers parallels to the lovers' earnest lament on the shortness of the night. See Singer, Berlin Abhandlung. d. Akademie der Wissenschaften, 1918, no. 13, pp. 25–6. With the night of Jupiter and Alcmena cf. particularly the prayer of the Arabic poet in Grangeret de Lagrange, Anthologie Arabe, no. xlvii, that the "night of Alkadr" might descend on the pleasure of love. Of that night the Koran, Surah xcvii, says that it was better than a thousand months. According to tradition it was the night on which the Koran was revealed to Mohammed.

1428 Alcmena (*Almena*) was the mother of Hercules by Jupiter. For the story that the moon passed through three courses on the night when the child was begotten see Theb., vi, 288 f.; xii, 300 f.; Roman de Thèbes, ed. Constans, SATF, Paris, 1890, ii, 88. Another account which may have been known to Chaucer is in Boccaccio, De Gen. Deor., lib. xiii, cap. 1. There are references to the incident in Amores, i, 13, 45 f., and Tes., iv, 14.

1433–35 Cf. Ovid, Amores, i, 13, 11 f., 17 ff.

1450–70 There is a bare suggestion for this passage in a single couplet of Fil. (iii, 44). But the passage cited above from the Amores (i, 13) seems the more likely source.

1462 The light would be necessary to the work of engravers of seals.

1464-70 The confusion between Titan and Tithonus may be due to Boccaccio's "Titon" in Tes., iv, 72, or in Filocolo, II, 222. Cf. further Ovid, Heroides, xvii (xviii), 111 ff.; Dante, Purg., ix, 1–3; Petrarch, Sonnet 23, In Morte; and Servius on Georg., iii, 48.

1490 *thise worldes tweyne*, "two worlds such as this"? (Root.) The Filostrato has "che 'l troian regno" (iii, 47). Perhaps Chaucer meant "the realms of both Troy and Greece."

1495-97 Cf. Virgil, Eclogue i, 60–64 (very general resemblance).

1502 Cf. *KnT*, I, 1133, and n.

1514 With this use of *mo* ("others") cf. ii, 1274; also *ClT*, IV, 1039, and n.

1546 *brede*, "arise." Cf. *LGW*, 1156.

1555-89 The visit of Pandarus to Criseyde here is not paralleled in the Filostrato.

1577 "Christ forgave his crucifixion." The ultimate reference is doubtless to Luke xxiii, 34. But the phrase had become proverbial, to express the limit to which forgiveness might be carried. Cf. "Dieu pardonna sa mort," Morawski, Proverbes Français, Paris, 1925, p. 21, no. 585.

1600 Cf. Aen., vi, 550 f. For the alternative readings which substitute *Cocytus* for *Flegetoun* see the Textual Notes.

1625-28 Cf. Dante, Inf., v, 121–23; also *Bo*, ii, pr. 4, 7–9, and Thomas Aquinas, Summa, Secunda Secundae, qu. 36, art. 1.

1634 Cf. RR, 8261–64; ultimately from Ovid, Ars Amat., ii, 11–13.

1642 *rakle*, here a verb, "behave rashly."

1688-94 Comparison has been suggested with Par., xix, 7 ff., xxiv, 25 ff. But surely no source need be sought for so familiar a formula.

1691 f. Cf. *Bo*, iii, pr. 2, 8–11; also Dante's Convivio, iv, 22.

1693 Cf. Par., xix, 8.

1703 *Pirous*, Pyrois, one of the four horses of the sun. The other three, according to Ovid, Met., ii, 153 ff., were Eous, Aethon, and Phlegon.

1716-19 A combination of Fil., iii, 72, and ii, 84.

1744 For Troilo's song, as given here by Boccaccio, Chaucer substitutes a song based upon Boethius, ii, m. 8. Five and a half stanzas of the Italian song were used earlier in the *Proem* of this book. The fact that this whole passage (ll. 1744–71) is omitted in MS. Hl² and the first form of MS. Ph has led to the plausible inference that Chaucer added it some time after he wrote the rest of the book. (See Root's note.) See, however, the comments of Mr. J. V. Hagopian, Explicator, X, item 2.

1762 ff. See the note to l. 1261, above.

1784 In the figure of the falcon Chaucer followed Boccaccio (Fil., iii, 91), and Boccaccio, Dante (Par., xix, 34). But in the Filostrato the application is to Troilo instead of Criseida.

1807-10 These lines combine reminiscences of Tes., i, 3, and xi, 63, and Dante, Par., viii, 7–8. The reference to Venus as daughter of Dione might be due to Aen., iii, 19, or to various passages in Ovid (Ars Amat., ii, 593; iii, 3, 769; Amores, i, 14, 33).

1809-10 On the erroneous conception of Helicon as a fountain or spring on Mt. Parnassus see *HF*, 521, n.

Book IV

1-11 For the commonplace sentiments of the opening stanzas cf., besides Fil., iii, 94, Boethius, ii, pr. 1 and m. 1; RR, 8039 ff.; and Machaut, Remede de Fortune (Œuvres, SATF, II), 1049–62, and Jugement dou Roy de Behaingne (Œuvres, I), 684–91. See also Chaucer's very similar phraseology in *MLT*, II, 1132 f., 1140 f.

22 ff. On the term *Herynes* see *Pity*, 92, n., and for the character of the Furies as suffering pain cf. i, 1, n., above. Both passages seem to contain reminiscences of Inf., ix, 45 ff. Perhaps the form *Alete* is due to the Italian "Aletto." For the idea that the Furies are *Nyghtes doughtren thre* cf. Met., iv, 451–52; Aen., xii, 845–47; and Boccaccio, De Gen. Deor., iii, 6–9. For the invocation as a whole comparisons have been suggested with Met., viii, 481 ff., Heroides, xi, 103, and Theb., xi, 57 ff., 344 ff. But these passages have no evident bearing on Chaucer's lines.

25 *Quyryne*, Quirinus, a name given to Romulus. See Ovid, Fasti, ii, 475–76. For the statement that he was a son of Mars see Fasti, ii, 419; Aen., i, 274 ff.; Met., xv, 863; and cf. Par., viii, 131–32. With the epithet *cruel* cf. "saevi" in Theb., vii, 703.

32 *Hercules lyoun*, the sign Leo, associated with Hercules because that hero killed the Nemean lion. Cf. "Herculei terga leonis," Ars Amat., i, 68. The Sun was in Leo during the latter part of July and the first part of August.

38-42 With these lines, which do not correspond to anything in the Filostrato, cf. Rom. de Troie, ll. 11996–12006.

50 ff. Except for *Phebuseo*, who appears to have been invented by Chaucer, all these men are named in Fil., iv, 3. According to Boccaccio they were all taken prisoners, but there is no authority for this statement in Benoît or Guido, and Chaucer's account (with *Maugre* in l. 51) is in accord with theirs. The reading of a single MS., Hl³ (*Palidomas and also Menestes*), suggests, as Root points out, that Chaucer's earliest draft may have agreed with Boccaccio. Antenor, Polydamas, Sarpedon, and Polymnestor are familiar names in the Trojan cycle. *Santippe* (Ital. "Santippo") is doubtless Antipus, or Xantipus, King of Frisia. The spelling with X, which occurs in the 1489 edition of Guido (sig. h 6 recto, col. 1), would account for Boccaccio's form. *Polite* (Polites, Aen., ii, 526), *Monesteo* (Mnestheus, Aen., v, 116 ff.), and *Rupheo* (Ripheus or Rhipeus, Aen., ii, 339) Boccaccio may have taken over from Virgil.

57-58 Boccaccio here says that Priam asked for the truce ("Chiese Priamo triegua, e fugli data," Fil., iv, 4, 1). But both Benoît and Guido say that the Greeks sent Ulysses and Diomedes as legates to seek a cessation of fighting for the burial of the dead. See Roman de Troie, ll. 12822–13120, and Historia, sig. i 1 recto, col. 1. Chaucer's statement differs in the different MSS., as may be seen from the Textual Notes. Perhaps the first version agreed with Boccaccio, and was revised later under the influence of Guido or Benoît.

96 *in hire sherte*, in her smock; that is, without rich apparel.

115 *astronomye*, what would be rather called "astrology" today. Calchas's prediction has the four-fold support of an oracle, astrological calculations, the casting of lots, and divination by augury with birds.

120 ff. The reference to Neptune and Apollo is not in the Filostrato. Benoît (Rom. de Troie, 25920 ff.) says that Neptune built the walls of Troy and Apollo consecrated them, but he does not tell of Laomedon's refusal to pay their wages. This part of the story Chaucer might have learned from Ovid (Met., xi, 194 ff.; cf. also Her., xv (xvi), 181 f.). The "locus classicus" for the legend is Iliad, xxi, 441 ff. For other accounts of it see Hyginus, Fab. 89 (ed. Bunte, Leipzig, 1857, p. 82); Servius, Comm. in Aeneida, ii, 610; Boccaccio, De Gen. Deor., vi, 6; Bode, Scriptores Rerum Mythicarum, Cellis, 1834, I, 43–44, 138, 174.

138 Thoas is not mentioned in the Filostrato. In including him in the exchange Chaucer may have been following either Benoît, Rom. de Troie, ll. 13079 ff., or Guido, Historia, sig. i 1 verso, col. 1. The account in Guido bears the closer resemblance to Chaucer's.

143 *parlement*, used by Chaucer in the English sense, though the Italian "parlamento" in the corresponding passage apparently means "parley." Guido's term is "consilium."

169–210 In this passage, which is largely independent of the Filostrato, Chaucer seems again to be indebted to Benoît or Guido. The speech of Hector may have been suggested by Benoît's account of his protest against the truce with the Greeks (ll. 12965 ff.), and the popular outcry it arouses recalls the outburst against Calchas when he asked for his daughter, as related by Guido (sig. i 1 verso, col. 1). If Chaucer had these incidents in mind, he chose to alter the story. According to the Historia, the Trojans opposed the surrender of Criseyde, but were overruled by Priam, whereas in Chaucer's account they urge the exchange of Criseyde for Antenor. For a detailed comparison of the different versions of the episode see C. Brown, in MLN, XXVI, 208 ff. Professor Brown suggests further that Chaucer's stanzas in condemnation of the *noyse of peple* (ll. 183 ff.) allude to the Peasants' Revolt, and that the *blase of straw* (l. 184) may even contain a pun on the name of Jack Straw. In spite of the infrequency of word-play in Chaucer, it is not unlikely here. Gower, as Mr. Brown notes, has two puns, in Latin, on the same name in the Vox Clamantis (i, 652, 655). The whole tone of the present passage, moreover, is similar to that of a stanza of the *Clerk's Tale* (IV, 995–1001) which has long been regarded as an allusion to the uprising of the peasants.

197 ff. From Juvenal, Sat., x, 2–4.

198 *what is to yerne*, what is to be desired.

202–06 For the treason of Antenor, which does not appear in the Filostrato, compare Benoît (ll. 24397 ff.) and Guido (Historia, sig. m 1 recto, col. 1, et seq.). It consisted in contriving the removal of the Palladium.

210 *here and howne*, an unexplained phrase, which seems to mean "people of all sorts, everybody." The interpretation "hare and hound," as Skeat shows, does not fit the form of either word (though the NED cites late occurrences of "hound" without the d, and Professor Kittredge has called the editor's attention to "masterles howne" in G. Harvey's Letter-Book, ed. Scott, p. 42). Skeat's

own suggestion, "gentle and savage" (from AS. "heóre" and "húna") is possible, but lacks support. Root offers another explanation — *howne* from ON. "hún," young bear, hence urchin, and *here* from ON. "herra," lord, master — but recognizes that it is equally unconvincing. The proposal to emend to *her randoun*, "their harangue" (R. C. Goffin, MLR, XL, 208) is also rather desperate.

225–27 Imitated from Dante, Inf., iii, 112 ff.

239 The figure here, which is in Boccaccio (Fil., iv, 27), goes back to Inf., xii, 22–24, and this in turn to Aen., ii, 222 ff.

251–52 Cf. *ClT*, IV, 902–03, and also, for the adjectival use of the genitive *lyves*, KnT, I, 1912, n.

271–72 Cf. *Mk Prol*, VII, 1976 f.

279 There is possibly an echo here of some of the passages in Statius about the living death of Oedipus. Cf. especially Theb., i, 46–48; xi, 580–82 and 698 ("quantum miser incubo terrae"). The comparison to Oedipus is made explicit in l. 300. The epithet *combre-world* occurs in Hoccleve's Lament for Chaucer, De Regimine Princ., l. 2091 (ed. Furnivall, EETS, p. 76).

300 Oedipus blinded himself on finding that he had killed his father Laius and married his mother Jocasta. See Statius, Theb., i, 46–48, and Tes., x, 96.

305 *unneste*, correctly glossed in MS. Hl[1] by "go out of thi nest."

316 For the term *lady sovereigne* cf. *LGW Prol* F, 94, 275. (Fil. has "o dolce bene," iv, 36.)

323–29 Perhaps there is a reminiscence here of Tes., xi, 91, for which Boccaccio in turn may have got a hint from Ovid's epitaph, Tristia, iii, 3, 73–76.

327–29 The reference to Troilus's burial-place, for which there is no parallel in the Filostrato, was possibly suggested by the Filocolo (I, 266).

330 *unholsom*, Ital. "insano" (Fil., iv, 38), probably in the ordinary sense of "insane."

351–55 The attendant knight is a new figure introduced by Chaucer.

356–57 Cf. Fil., iv, 43, 8. The lines of the *Troilus* are nearly repeated in *MLT*, II, 608 f.

386–92 Cf. Boethius, *Bo*, ii, pr. 2, 9–13; also RR, 8023–26.

407 ff. With the sentiment expressed here cf. Ovid, Amores, ii, 4, 10 ff.

413 *ryvere*, either "the sport of hawking" or "water-fowl." See *Thop*, VII, 737, n.

415 The real source of this line, quoted as a saying by Boccaccio and attributed by Chaucer to *Zanzis* or *Zauzis*, was perhaps Ovid's Rem. Am., 462 or 484. For evidence of its later currency as a proverb see Haeckel, p. 3, no. 9; Skeat, EE Prov., p. 77, no. 186. Chaucer's passage shows, besides the use of Fil., iv, 59, further reminiscences of the Remedia, particularly ll. 135–210, 214–39. (See Kittredge, Harv. Stud. in Class. Philol., XXVIII, 70.) *Zanzis* is of uncertain identity. If the form is a corruption of Zeuxis, Chaucer may have had in mind the sage of that name in the Alexander story. See Julius Valerius (ed. Kuebler, Leipzig, 1888), i, 9. Zeuxis the painter is referred to, also as *Zanzis*, in PhysT, VI, 16.

416 The added line of Pandarus was also apparently proverbial. Professor Kittredge (in a letter) cited the expression of the idea by Cicero (Pro Lege Manilia, 20): "Semper ad novos casus temporum novorum consiliorum rationes adcommodasse." The Irish proverb, "Dotéit meas fo aimsera (aimseraib?)," Revue Celtique, XXII, 34, is closely similar, and cf. "Necessity is the mother of invention."

431 *unthrift*, foolish, unprofitable stuff. Cf. *ML Epil*, II, 1165, and i, 275, above.

432–34 There seems to be a verbal reminiscence here of RR, 4640–41 (*Rom*, 5151 f.); which suggests that Chaucer somewhat associated Pandarus with the character of Reason. The resemblances, however, are unimportant, and in any case l. 434 was proverbial. See Haeckel, pp. 12 f., no. 41.

461 *Nettle in, dok out*, nettle in, dock out; that is, first one thing and then another. The phrase comes from a charm for curing the sting of a nettle. The wound is rubbed with the juice of a dock-leaf, while the charm is repeated. The words, as given in Notes and Queries, 1st Ser., III, 133, are as follows:

Nettle in, dock out, Dock in, nettle out;
Nettle in, dock out, Dock rub nettle out.

For other forms, with references, see Skeat's note on the passage; also his EE Prov., p. 78, no. 187, and Notes and Queries, same vol., pp. 205, 368, 463; Grendon, in Journ. of Am. Folklore, XXII, 214, n. 6; and Haeckel, p. 50, no. 179. Chaucer's lines here are imitated by Usk, Testament of Love, Bk. i, chap. 2, l. 167 (Oxf. Chau., VII, 13).

462 "Now evil befall her that may care for thy woe!"

466 Cf. Seneca, Epist. 78, 13; though the idea is so familiar that no source is certain. It occurs also in Boethius, *Bo*, ii, pr. 4, 109–13.

470–76 The mention of Proserpina, which is not found in the corresponding passage in the Filostrato (iv, 54), may well be due to the lines of the Inf. (ix, 43 ff.) which seem also to have influenced Chaucer's conception of the Furies. See the note to i, 1 ff., above. Perhaps there is a further echo of the same Dantean passage in iv, 785 ff.

477 *for fyn*, probably to be taken in the sense "finally." Professor Magoun suggests the possible reading *for-fyn*, "very ingenious." On such adjectival compounds with *for-* see *KnT*, I, 2142, n.

503 f. From Boethius, *Bo*, i, m. 1, 19–21.

506 *hire*, a bribe. Troilus says that while he was happy he would have bribed Death to let him alone, but now he would be glad to be killed.

519–20 The figure was probably suggested by RR, 6382–83.

548 *ravysshyng of wommen*. Hesione, sister of Priam, was carried away to Greece by Telamon, and when the Greeks refused to surrender her, Helen was seized by Paris in reprisal. See Benoît, ll. 2793 ff., 3187 ff., 4059 ff.

556 "This would constitute an accusation against her."

557 "Moreover I know very well that I can not obtain her." The Filostrato (iv, 69) has: "Nè spero ancora ch'el dovesse darla."

585 *by note*, apparently "in song, music"; though the NED (s.v. Note, sb.², 3ᶜ) cites no case of this idiom before 1436.

588 Skeat compares "a nine days' wonder," also the Latin "novendiale sacrum," Livy, i, 31; see also his EE Prov., p. 78, no. 188; and NED, s.v. Nine, adj. 3ᵃ and 4ᵇ.

600–01 On this favorite commonplace ("Fortes Fortuna adiuvat") see *Thop*, VII, 830, n.

607 *of ferd*, "because of being frightened"(?). Root suggests also "frightened off," which is less likely. The construction with *of* and the participle seems to be a variant of the more familiar idiom with *for* discussed in the note to *KnT*, I, 2142–44, above. For further illustration see the articles of Professor T. F. Mustanoja there cited. Skeat's reading *for ferd*, "for fear," has some MS. support.

618 Not so close to Filostrato (iv, 75) as to *KnT*, I, 1163–68. Chaucer may have recalled his own lines (if written earlier) or their source in Boethius, iv, m. 6. For the currency of the idea as a proverb see Haeckel, p. 2, no. 5.

622 For the proverbial phrase "on six and seven" (or "at sixes and sevens") see Skeat, EE Prov., pp. 79 f., no. 190; Haeckel, p. 50, no. 175; and NED, s.v. Six, B. 5. Professor Root, who would interpret the present passage "risk everything on the cast of the dice," shows how the term may have been applied in the game of hazard. "A player throws two dice, and the sum of the numbers which fall is the 'main.' If the 'main' is 6, the caster may win by throwing at the next cast either 6 or 12. If he throws 2, 3, or 11, he loses. If his second throw is a number other than these, that number becomes his 'chance'. . . . If 6 is the 'main' and 7 the 'chance,' probability favors the caster at the odds of six to five. The chances are correspondingly against the 'setter,' who bets against him. To 'set' one's all on six and seven is, therefore, to venture with the odds against one." This explanation of the original application of the phrase is very likely correct. But it developed another meaning, "in confusion, disorder, state of upheaval," which would also make good sense in the present passage. The NED does not recognize this sense as occurring before the sixteenth century, though it is very likely the meaning of the passage there cited from the Towneley Plays (EETS, 1897, xvi, 128).

623 There is clearly an allusion here to the teaching of the Church that a martyr's death ensured immediate entrance into heaven, of which the ultimate source was perhaps Rev. vii, 14. It appears in the Divine Comedy, Par., x, 128, and Par., xv, 148. The belief was especially emphasized in the time of the Crusades. Pope Urban, at the Council of Clermont in 1095, gave assurance of remission of sins to those who should lose their lives either on the journey to the Holy Land or in battle against the Saracens. See the Historia Hierosolymitana of Fulcher of Chartres, ed. Hagenmeyer, Heidelberg, 1913, p. 135. For illustrations of the belief cf. Hagenmeyer's notes; also Fulcher's account of the speech of Baldwin, pp. 411–12; and the striking incident related on pp. 476–77. A crusader rides to meet certain death in the Turkish hosts, crying, "si quis vestrum in Paradiso cenare desiderat, nunc mecum veniat et mecum prandeat. iam iam enim abibo." On the prevalence of the belief in the early Christian centuries see Harnack, Lehrbuch der Dogmengeschichte, Freiburg, 1894, I, 425 ff. For modern statements of the doctrine the Rev. A. J. Denomy has referred the editor to Tanquerey, Synopsis Theologiae Dogmaticae Specialis, II, 262–64, and Billuart, Theologia Dogmatica, Tractatus de Fortitudine, diss. i, art. ii. It is interesting to note that the Mohammedans had a similar belief, which is given a curious turn by Beha-ad-Din Zoheir (ed. Palmer, text, I, p. 303, trans., II, p. 337) into consolation for a lover slain (i.e. martyred) by unrequited love. The conception of death from love as martyrdom was common to the amatory poetry of East and West.

661 *with preste wynges*, with swift wings (Ital. "con prestissim' ale," Fil., iv, 78); ultimately from Virgil's "pernicibus alis" (Aen., iv, 180) which Chaucer, in *HF*, 1392, rendered *partriches wynges*, obviously by confusion with "perdix."

683 *pitous joie*, Ital. "pietosa allegrezza" (Fil., iv, 80). In his account of the women's talk Chaucer follows Boccaccio closely.

707 *wo and wery* are probably both to be construed as adjectives after *for*. On the construction see *KnT*, I, 2142, n.

728 The Italian says "itch," not "ache" ("ove 'l capo prudea," Fil., iv, 85).

736 ff. On the order of the stanzas at this point see the Textual Notes.

736 *ownded*, wavy; cf. *oundy*, *HF*, 1386; also *RR*, 21135–36.

737 For the detail about the fingers, which does not occur in the Filostrato, comparison has been made with Guido (Historia, sig. i 2 recto, col. 2), where the parallel is not exact. Filocolo, I, 176, which has also been cited, is hardly closer ("dilicate mani").

745 *in corsed constellacioun*, when the planets were in unfavorable combination.

762 The name of Criseyde's mother is not given by Boccaccio, and Chaucer's authority (if he had one) is unknown. *Argyve* occurs below, in the Latin summary of the Thebaid, as the equivalent of Argia, the name of Polynices's wife. See v, 1509, and Theb., ii, 297.

765 Cf. *Gen Prol*, I, 97–110.

767–68 Cf. *Bo*, iii, pr. 11, 97–110.

769 *by-word*, proverb. Root cites from Le Roux de Lincy (Proverbes Français, Paris, 1859, I, 83): "Seiche racine de l'arbre la ruyne." See also Skeat, EE Prov., p. 80, no. 192.

776 *unshethe*, unsheath; perhaps a reminiscence of Dante's lines about the flaying of Marsyas, Par., i, 20–21. The same passage doubtless underlies *HF*, 1229–32, where, however, the striking figure does not appear.

782 *ordre*, religious order.

785–87 Cf. ll. 470 ff., above. The language here recalls again the *KnT*, I, 2768; cf. the note to l. 618, above.

788 ff. Chaucer's conception of Elysium may have been influenced by Dante, especially Inf., iv. The particular definition, *feld of pite*, if not merely an adaptation of Ovid's "arva piorum" (Met., xi, 62), was perhaps due to an association of Elysos with "eleison" in the familiar κύριε ἐλεῖσον of the liturgy. See MLN, XXIX, 97; Harv. Stud. in Class. Philol., XXVIII, 53, n. 10.

791 For the story of Orpheus and Eurydice see Virgil, Georg., iv, 453 ff.; Ovid, Met., x, 1 ff., xi, 1 ff.

813 ff. Besides the corresponding passage in Filostrato, Chaucer may have had in mind Guido's similar description (Historia, sig. i 2 recto, col. 2); also possibly Filocolo (I, 188).

829 *cause causyng*, the "causa causans" or primary cause, as distinguished from a "causa causata" or secondary cause.

836 From Prov. xiv, 13. Cf. *MLT*, II, 421 f., and n.; *NPT*, VII, 3205; also Boethius, ii, pr. 4.

841 In Fil. (iv. 97), this stanza is spoken by Pandaro.

865 Cf. *KNT*, I, 1400 f.

884 *into litel*, nearly.

918 ff. With Pandarus's argument here (and in Fil., iv, 106 f.) has been compared that of Glorizia to Biancofiore in Filocolo, I, 117 f.

927 "Be to him a cause rather of the flat than of the edge"; that is, rather of healing than of hurting. For the conception see *SqT*, V, 156 ff., and the note, 239 ff. In the present passage Root suggests a possible verbal echo of Dante's Inf., xxxi, 4–6.

934–38 Cf. Fil., iv, 107, where Pandaro merely advises Griseida to control her own grief so as to be able to alleviate Troilo's sorrow. Chaucer substitutes lines which advise more positive action; and in ll. 1254 the advice is carried out.

953–1085 This long discussion of predestination is derived from Boethius, v, pr. 2 and 3. It is not found in the *α* MSS. of the *Troilus*, and seems to have been inserted by Chaucer after the main body of the narrative was composed. See Root's discussion of the MSS., Textual Tradition, pp. 216 ff., and the Introduction to his edition, pp. lxxi ff. Stanzas 136 and 156, which precede and follow the soliloquy, are based upon a single stanza (iv, 109) of the Filostrato.

The philosophical doctrine of the passage, and the appropriateness of its insertion in the *Troilus*, have both been much discussed by the commentators. See especially W. C. Curry, PMLA, XLV, 129 ff., and H. R. Patch, JEGP, XVII, 399 ff., MLR, XXII, 384 ff., and Speculum, VI, 225 ff. The argument of Troilus closely follows that of Boethius, but whereas in the De Consolatione, Philosophy makes a reply and defends human freedom, Chaucer (or Troilus) stops with the fatalistic conclusion. It is not to be inferred that Chaucer himself was a fatalist. The speech, as Mr. Patch argues, expresses not Chaucer's moral, but Troilus's emotional reaction, and is therefore completely relevant. At the same time it is to be observed that more than once in the *Troilus* the reader is made to feel a deep sense of overruling Destiny. See v, 1085, and n.

958 Proverbial. See Haeckel, p. 31, no. 102.

968 For the *grete clerkes* cf. the *NPT*, VII, 3241 f., where St. Augustine, Boethius, and Bishop Bradwardine are mentioned.

976 For the idiom see *KnT*, I, 1089, n.

996 The reference is to the tonsure of the clergy.

1016 *n'enforce I me nat in shewynge*, Lat. "Ac non illud demonstrare nitamur" (Boethius, *Bo*, v, pr. 3, 48). Skeat suggests that Chaucer's negative, which occurs also in his *Boece*, was due to a misreading of "nitamur" as "vitamus."

1098 Cf. ii, 1347, and n.

1116 There is no reference to Juno at this point in the Filostrato (iv, 111 f.).

1128 ff. In the part of the Filostrato which deals with the separation of the lovers there are many features and incidents which Boccaccio appears to have taken over from his Filocolo. Griseida's promise to return on the tenth day, which is not found in Benoît, seems to have come from that source. See Young, *Origin*, pp. 66–103.

1135 The simile is Chaucer's.

1136 *out of teris kynde*, unlike the nature of tears.

1139 On Myrrha, the daughter of Cinyras, King of Cyprus, who was changed into a myrrh tree, see *Met.*, x, 311 ff.

1142 *hire wofulle weri goostes*, apparently the souls of the lovers, though the corresponding phrase in *Fil.*, iv, 116 ("gli spiriti affannati") refers rather to the "spiriti," in the old technical sense, which control the functions of their bodies. On this matter see *KnT*, I, 2749, n.

1159 Filostrato, iv, 117, reads "E gli occhi suoi velati." Chaucer's copy, as Root suggests, may have had the variant reading "levati."

1174 Not in Filostrato. Cf. *Gen Prol*, I, 301.

1181 *woon*, hope, resource (apparently from AS. "wắn").

1187–88 Boccaccio does not mention Minos at this point. Chaucer may have been thinking of Dante's Minos, or of the pagan judge of the dead, as described by Virgil, Statius, and Claudian, or of both combined. Although the pagan conception would be more strictly appropriate in the case of Troilus, Christian ideas cannot be dismissed as anachronistic in a poem which refers to "Amphiorax" as a "bishop."

1208 Atropos was the Fate who cut the thread of life. Cf., besides the regular Latin sources, *RR*, 20364–65. See also l. 1546, below.

1216 *Cipride*, the Cyprian Venus. Cf. v, 208.

1237 *a forlong wey*, see *MLT*, II, 557, n.

1283 Proverbial. Cf. *ML Prol*, II, 27–28.

1295 *for that is no demaunde*, there is no question about it. Cf. l. 1694, below.

1305–06 Cf., for the sentiment, *RR*, 2601–02 (*Rom*, 2740–42).

1356 On this familiar comparison see ii, 193, n.

1366–1414 The use of the avarice of Calchas, merely suggested by Boccaccio (*Fil.*, iv, 136, 7) is most skillfully developed by Chaucer.

1373 f. Apparently proverbial, in the sense that one cannot "have it both ways," or "have one's cake and eat it too." See Skeat, *EE Prov.*, p. 81, no. 194, for similar sayings.

1397–98, 1404–11 These passages about the gods have no exact equivalent in the Filostrato. They are more nearly paralleled in Benoît (Roman de Troie, 13768–73) and better still in Guido (Historia, sig. i. 3 recto, col. 1). Both these authors represent Criseyde as making such reproaches to her father. In Chaucer, though she expresses the intention of speaking thus, she is actually *muwet, milde, and mansuete* at the time of meeting (see v, 194); and the account in the Filostrato is similar (v, 14, 3). For the skepticism (real or pretended) of Criseyde Dr. Wise (Influence of Statius, p. 16 ff.) has suggested another possible source in Statius's portrayal of Capaneus, "superum contemptor." See *Theb.*, iii, 611 ff., 648 ff.; ix, 550; etc.

1406 *amphibologies*, ambiguities; from Lat. "amphibologia," itself a corruption of "amphibolia" which is used with reference to the ambiguous answers of oracles by Isidorus, *Etymol.*, i, 34, 13 (Migne, Pat. Lat., LXXXII, 109), and Cicero, *De Div.*, ii, 56.

1408 The marginal gloss in Hl⁴, "Timor invenit

deos," may record the exact words of Chaucer's Latin source. But various statements of the doctrine were accessible to him. The most familiar version is the line, "Primus in orbe deos fecit timor," which occurs in a fragment attributed to Petronius (ed. Buecheler, Berlin, 1922, no. 27), and was probably taken over from him by Statius, Theb., iii, 661. It is quoted, in slightly differing forms, as from Petronius by Fulgentius, Mitologiarum, i, 32 (*Opera*, ed. Helm, Leipzig, 1898, p. 17); Petrus Cantor, Verbum Abbreviatum, cap. 93 (Migne, Pat. Lat., CCV, 271); and Holkot, Super Libros Sapientiae, lect. 164 (Reuthlingen, 1489, fol. H 3 recto); and as from Virgil by Johannes de Alta Silva, Dolopathos (ed. Hilka, Heidelberg, 1913, p. 102, l. 9). The association with Virgil may be due to Servius's quotation of the line from Statius in his Comm. in Aen., ii, 715. Chaucer had thus a number of possible sources for the idea, which had become a commonplace in Latin and mediæval literature. For still other variations on the theme see Lucretius, i, 151; v, 1218 ff.; vi, 52; Cicero, De Fin., i, 19, 64; Juvenal, x, 365 (with special reference to Fortuna); Orosius, vi, 1; and for the Epicurean doctrine behind some of the Romans, Diog. Laertius, x, 79, 81, 142. Lucan's "Quae finxere timent" (Pharsalia, i, 486), which was doubtless known to Chaucer, is sometimes cited as a source of Petronius. But Lucan refers, not to the invention of gods, but to the imagined terrors of Caesar's advance on Rome. (See also G. L. Kittredge, MP, VII, 480; and B. A. Wise, Influence of Statius, p. 17.)

1411 For the occasion see Benoît, Rom. de Troie, 5817–5927. Calchas, sent to Delphi by the Trojans, met Achilles, who was consulting the oracle on behalf of the Greeks. When the oracle gave warning of the fall of Troy, Calchas went over to the enemy.

On the form Delphos cf. *FranklT*, V, 1077, n.

1415 ff. These declarations of Criseyde's sincerity are not paralleled at this point in the Filostrato. But see v, 7, and *Tr*, v, 19–21, and cf. Benoît, Rom. de Troie, 13495–97 and Guido, Historia, sig. i 2 recto, col. 2.

1453 The bear and his leader are of different opinions. Obviously a proverbial observation, with which Root compares, as of similar purport, "Man proposes, God disposes."

1456 For a variant of the same proverb cf. *KnT*, I, 2449, and n.

1457–58 Another proverb. Cf. "Clochier ne faut devant boiteux" (Leroux de Lincy, Proverbes Français, I, 211); also Skeat, EE Prov., p. 82, no. 196.

1459 Argus had a hundred eyes. See Ovid, Met., i, 625; cf. Haeckel, p. 48, no. 164.

1478–82 Chaucer seems at this point to have used Benoît (ll. 13803 ff.) or Guido (sig. i 3 recto, col. 1) as well as the Filostrato.

1483 *Fere*, terrify.

1505 On the philosophical distinction between substance and accident see *PardT*, VI, 537 ff., n. Root suggests that Troilus is also playing with the more popular meaning of accident, "uncertainty" as opposed to *sikernesse*. This is possible, though Chaucer is not much given to playing upon words. See *Gen Prol*, I, 297, n.

1534 ff. Criseyde's oath by Athamas is probably

due to Dante's Inf., xxx, 1 ff., where the punishment of "falsatori" is described. Ovid's account of Athamas (Met., iv, 420 ff.), may also have been in Chaucer's mind. Juno, he relates, crossed the Styx into hell to persuade Tisiphone to haunt him. This may have suggested the mention of the Styx. But the characterization of it as the "pit of hell" is rather mediæval than classical. Numerous references to the conception are cited by T. Spencer in Speculum, II, 180 f. Dante's description of the Styx as "una palude" (Inf., vii, 106) is not quite parallel, though a pit and a marsh are easily associated.

1541–45 From Met., i, 192 f. Cf. also Theb., vi, 112–13.

1548 Probably a reminiscence of Ovid, Amores, i, 15, 10 ("Dum rapidas Simois in mare volvet aquas"). L. 1553 doubtless goes back to the similar statement about the Xanthus in the Heroides, v, 29–30, repeated in RR, 13225 f. Cf. also Theb., vii, 553, and Met., xiii, 324 (where, however, the application is not to love). On the geographical inaccuracy of the reference to Simois, see Med. Stud., XV, 129.

1554 Cf. the fate of Amphiaraus, ii, 105.

1562 *take*, "take place," recorded by NED (s.v. Take, 27 b) as the only occurrence of the word in this sense.

1568 Proverbial. A number of sayings of similar purport are noted by Haeckel, p. 26, no. 85. Cf. i, 956, n.

1584 Another proverb, "Vincit qui patitur." Cf. FranklT, V, 771 ff., and n.

1585 "He who will have what he likes must give up what he likes." Root compares "Nought lay down, nought take up," Hazlitt's Proverbs, p. 340. See also Skeat, EE Prov., p. 83, no. 198.

1586 With this (which is again proverbial) cf. Tes., xii, 11, 1–2, and see KnT, I, 3041–42, n.

1590 ff. The astrology here, as so often, is Chaucer's addition to his source.

1591 Before Lucina (the moon) pass out of Aries and beyond Leo, that is, before the tenth day.

1608 *Cinthia*, Cynthia, the moon.

1620 *pure*, very; cf. KnT, I, 1279.

1628 Proverbial. Cf. Haeckel, p. 30, no. 98.

1645 Cf. Ovid, Heroides, i, 12; Skeat, EE Prov., p. 84, no. 200.

1667–82 The corresponding passage in the Filostrato (iv, 164–66) is spoken by Troilo to Criseida.

1677 *poeplissh*, popular, vulgar; Ital. "popolesco" (Fil., iv, 165).

1695 Cf. MerchT, IV, 1341, and n., for the recurring formula. The fuller form here is perhaps influenced by I Cor. ii, 9.

Book V

1 Cf. Tes., ix, 1, 1.

2 The Fates are conceived as subject to Jupiter. Cf. Theb., i, 212 f. For the same idea, in Christian terms, see KnT, I, 1663 ff.

3 *Parcas*, the Latin accusative of "Parcae," the Fates. The *sustren thre* are Clotho, who spins, Lachesis, who apportions, and Atropos, who cuts the thread of life. Cf. RR, 19768 ff.; Purg., xxv, 79; xxi, 25, though no single source need be sought for so familiar an allusion. See also iii, 733 ff.

8 ff. From Tes., ii, 1; cf. also Theb., iv, 1 f. On the use of astronomical and mythological definitions of time see Gen Prol, I, 8, n. For *gold-ytressed* MS. Hl² has *Auricomus tressed*, doubtless incorporating a gloss which shows the Latin original of the epithet. Chaucer's source is unknown. The Latin adjective is applied to the sun in Valerius Flaccus, Argonauticon, iv, 92, and in Martianus Capella, De Nuptiis Phil. et Merc., i, 12 (ed. Kopp, Frankfurt am Main, 1836, p. 44).

12 Troilus was the son of Hecuba.

25 *crop and more*, "twig and root"; hence "altogether, from top to bottom."

41 *atones for to dye*, "to die once for all."

53 *in rumour of this fare*, "upon hearing of this behavior."

67 *valeye*, a mistranslation of Boccaccio's "vallo," rampart (Fil., v, 10).

88–175 The account of Diomedes's conversation with Criseyde has some basis in Fil., vi, 10–12; 14–25; but it shows also the influence of the Rom. de Troie, 13529 ff.

90 *by the reyne hire hente*. W. M. Rossetti (MS. Hl², Chau. Soc., p. 235) suggested that Chaucer misunderstood the Italian "di colei si piglia," which means "takes a fancy to her."

98 A proverbial expression. Cf. Skeat, EE Prov., p. 84, no. 201, and Haeckel, p. 16, no. 53.

101 *make it tough*, act over-boldly in making love. See ii, 1025, n., above.

106 *koude his good*, knew what was best for him, knew what he was about. See ML Epil, II, 1169, and n.

113–16 Cf. Rom. de Troie, 13602–610.

143 *O god of love*, one god of love.

155–58 Cf. Rom. de Troie, 13591–96.

158 *As paramours*, by way of passionate love. Cf. KnT, I, 1155.

164–65 Cf. Rom. de Troie, 13552–55.

176–92 This description of Criseyde's conduct seems influenced by passages from the Rom. de Troie (ll. 13617 ff., 13637 ff., 13676 ff., 13713 ff.). L. 189 may perhaps be an echo of Guido (Historia, sig. i 2 verso, col. 1).

212 The punishment of Ixion, bound to an everturning wheel in hell, was of course a matter of familiar knowledge. For references to it cf. Georgics, iii, 38; Met., iv, 461; x, 42; Boethius, Bo, iii, m. 12, ll. 36 ff.

223–24 Chaucer is here following Fil., v, 20. Boccaccio in turn may have been echoing Ovid, Her., x, 12. Cf. LGW, 2186.

249 *mete*, "dream."

270 The address to the reader has been ascribed to the influence of Dante. Similar expressions are certainly characteristic of the Divine Comedy. Cf. Inf., viii, 94; xxv, 46; xxxiv, 22; Par., v, 109; x, 7. But it is hardly necessary to assume that Chaucer had any literary model for so natural a device.

274 ff. An imitation, sometimes almost literal, of Tes., vii, 94. Cf. also Boethius, ii, m. 3, 1–4, and (more remotely) Theb., xii, 1 ff.

280 ff. This passage combines with its immediate source in the Filostrato (v, 22–23) a number of elements from the account of Arcite's death in the Teseida. Perhaps Chaucer had also in mind the pyre and funeral games of Archemorus in Theb., vi. For various parallels, some of them not very significant, see Tes., vii, 4, 27; x, 37, 89, 93–98; xi, 13, 14, 35, 50, 52–62, 69, 90. See also the corresponding episode in the *KnT*, I, 2809–2966.

319 On the evil foreboding of the owl cf. *LGW*, 2253 f. The name *Escaphilo* (or *Ascaphilo*) is clearly a transformation of Ascalaphus, whom Proserpina changed into an owl. See Met., v, 539 ff.; vi, 432; x, 453; xv, 791. The Italian-looking form in *-o* is puzzling, since there is no mention of the name in the Filostrato. But for similar formations see *MkT*, VII, 2345, n.

321 It was Mercury's function to act as the guide of souls (Psychopompus). Cf. l. 1827, below.

332 *paramours*, adverbial, as in l. 158, above.

337 ff. Cowling (Chaucer, p. 16) observes that Chaucer himself must have lived apart from his wife much of the time when she was in the service of Constance of Padilla.

350 Proverbial. Cf. Haeckel, p. 53.

358 ff. Pandarus argues that Troilus's dream is without import, because it is a mere "somnium naturale," proceeding from the melancholic humor. With the discussion here, which is much fuller than Boccaccio's (Fil., v, 32), cf. *NPT*, VII, 2922 ff., and n.

365 ff. Cf., besides Fil., v, 32, RR, 18509 ff.

376 On the belief that dreams vary with the seasons of the year see Curry, p. 211. He cites especially Vincent of Beauvais, Spec. Nat., XXVI, 63.

379 "May it be well with old women in this matter of dreams," i.e., "let old women concern themselves with dreams." For *Wel worth, wo worth*, cf. *HF*, 53, and n. For the generalizing *thise* see *KnT*, I, 1531, n.

387 *foryyve*, Ital. "a te stesso pardona" (Fil., v, 33), which means rather "spare thyself."

403 According to iv, 52, Sarpedon had been taken prisoner by the Greeks. Neither Chaucer nor Boccaccio explains his return to Troy.

421 *of fyn force*, of very necessity.

445 Cf. l. 1321, below; and see *MerchT*, IV, 1341, and n.

451 *piteous* or *pietous*, with three syllables, seems called for by the meter. Chaucer's usual form is *pitous*, and Skeat suggests that the Ital. "pietoso" had some influence here.

460 The figure of the key, here taken from Fil., v, 43, was of frequent occurrence. Cf. *Anel*, 323–24; also RR, 1999 ff.; Ivain (ed. Foerster, Halle, 1891), 4632 ff.; Perceval (ed. Hilke, Halle, 1932), 2634 ff.; Machaut, Livre du Voir Dit, ll. 3883 ff. (Soc. des Bibliophiles Fr., Paris, 1875, pp. 161 f.).

469 On the figure, cf. ii, 867, and n.

484 A man who borrows fire must hurry home with it. Cf. the proverbial phrase "to come to fetch fire" (Hazlitt, Proverbs, London, 1907, p. 468).

505 *Ye, haselwode*, an expression of incredulity. Cf. l. 1174, below. See also iii, 890, n.

523 Chaucer's use of the term *palais* for Criseyde's house, which Boccaccio calls simply "la casa" or "la magione" is striking. Professor Young (Origin, p. 172) has suggested that it is due to the influence of passages in the Filocolo which refer to the "palagio" of Biancofiore.

549 The figure of the ruby is not in the Filostrato.

551 f. For the detail of kissing the doors, which the Filostrato does not mention, comparison may be made with RR, 2538, and the Filocolo, I, 124.

The latter seems more likely to have influenced Chaucer at this point.

561–81 The corresponding passage in the Filostrato (v, 54 f.), as Professor Griffin has observed (intro., p. 56), apparently reflects Boccaccio's own experience as described in his Proemio, p. 4. Cf. also Filocolo, I, 120, 263. For the suggestion that Filostrato v, 54 ff. contains reminiscences of Petrarch's Sonnet No. 112 see E. H. Wilkins, MLN, XXXII, 196 ff., and MP, XLVI, 3.

601 On the fury of Juno against Thebes see *KnT*, I, 1329, and n. Perhaps the language here echoes especially Inf., xxx, 1–2.

638 The figure of a voyage may be due, as suggested by Rossetti, to a misreading of Fil., v, 62, "disii porto di morte," "I carry desires of death." Chaucer perhaps took "porto" to be the noun for "port, harbor." Even if the figure here is primarily due to mistranslation of the Italian, Chaucer in developing it may have recalled another passage in the Filostrato (iv, st. 143), pointed out by Professor Patch in MLN, LXX, 11.

644 Charybdis, the famous whirlpool, opposite Scylla's rock, on the straits of Messina. Cf. Aen., iii, 420, 558; Met., xiv, 75.

655–58 All the MSS. read *Lat(h)ona*, which Caxton and Thynne emended to *Lucyna*, perhaps correctly. The scribes could easily have corrupted the latter into the former, and Chaucer shows elsewhere an acquaintance with Lucina's name and function. See *KnT*, I, 2085. But in view of the epithet "Latonia" applied to Diana in Virgil and Ovid, it seems at least equally possible that the slip was Chaucer's.

662 Chaucer tells the Phaethon story in *HF*, 940–56, following Met., ii, 31 f. Here no definite classical source need be assumed.

671–72 Cf., besides Fil., v, 70, Boccaccio's Proemio, p. 4; also Filocolo, I, 120, and Tes., iv, 32.

694–707 Criseyde's scheme of playing upon her father's covetousness is here taken up again. See the note to iv, 1366.

741–42 Proverbial. Root cites from Düringsfeld (Sprichwörter, Leipzig, 1872–75, II, no. 122), as the version nearest to Chaucer's, "Dopo la morte non val medicina."

744–49 The figure of the three eyes of Prudence Chaucer may have derived from Purg., xxix, 130–32. The underlying idea, that Prudence regards past, present, and future, is explained in several of the commentaries. Cf. also Cicero, De Inventione, ii, 53; Thomas Aquinas, Summa, Prima Secundae, qu. 57, art. 6; Dante's Convivio, iv, 27; and the Pseudo-Seneca (Martinus Dumiensis) Formula Honestae Vitae, chapter i, quoted by Albertanus, Liber Consolationis et Consilii, ed. Sundby, Chau. Soc., 1873, pp. 57–58 (in a passage omitted in Chaucer's *Melibee* and the French source).

757–61 With these lines, not derived from Boccaccio, Root compares the proverb, "Tous se mêlent de donner des avis, un sot est celui qui les tous suit" (Düringsfeld, Sprichwörter, II, no. 235).

763 Cf. the discussion of *suffisaunce* in *Bo*, ii, pr. 2, 3, and 4.

769 *knotteles*; the figure is that of a thread which slips smoothly, without a knot.

784 Proverbial. Cf. ii, 807, and n.

790–91 The exact source of this quotation seems

not to have been found. For the idea cf. Ars Amat., i, 361 f.: "Pectora dum gaudent nec sunt adstricta dolore, Ipsa patent; blanda tum subit arte Venus."

799 ff. The portraits of Diomede, Criseyde, and Troilus, which here interrupt the narrative, are examples of a literary type cultivated chiefly by the later Greek and Roman writers and in the Middle Ages. Striking examples are the personal descriptions of Alexander in the documents which relate his legendary life (see Pseudo-Callisthenes and Julius Valerius, i, 13, ed. Müller, Paris, 1846, pp. 12 f., in Arrianus, Anabasis, etc.) and the early Christian portraits of Christ and Antichrist. For some account of the vogue of this type in Greek and Roman, as well as Christian, literature see E. von Dobschütz, Christusbilder, Leipzig, 1899, especially II, 293** ff. Similar in literary method is the feature-by-feature description of ladies which is extremely common in mediæval love-poetry, and was recognized as one of the regular "colours of rhetorik." For references to the rhetoricians see BD, 816 ff., n.; and cf. further L. A. Haselmayer, Chaucer and Mediæval Verse Portraiture (Yale dissertation, 1937), and his paper in RES, XIV, 310.

There are portraits of Diomede, Criseyde, and Troilus in Dares, Benoît, and Guido, and all of them Chaucer doubtless had in mind. But his primary source, as indicated by marginal quotations in MSS. J and Gg, and fully set forth by Professor Root, was the Frigii Daretis Ylias of Joseph of Exeter. For discussion of the parallel passages see Mr. Root's notes and his earlier article in MP, XV, 1–22. (Lines and references given below follow his citations from MSS. and sometimes differ from the text of the Delphin Classics, London, 1825.) On Joseph of Exeter cf. further G. B. Riddehough, JEGP, XLVI, 254 ff. Certain features in Chaucer's descriptions seem to be due to Boccaccio or Benoît.

With the account of Diomede cf. particularly Joseph of Exeter, iv, 124–27. Lines 804–05 probably go back to Fil., vi, 33 and 24, though *heir ... of Calydoigne* may be due to a misreading of Joseph's "(Calydonius) heros" (iv, 349) as "heres." See also F. P. Magoun, Jr., Med. Stud., XV, 117.

806 ff. Again a composite of Joseph (iv, 156–62) and Benoît (ll. 5275 ff.). Lines 818–19, in particular, seem due to a misreading of Joseph's line, "Diviciis forme certant insignia morum," of which the last word is wrongly copied as "amorum" in the margin of MS. J.

With the statement about Criseyde's stature in l. 806 contrast i, 281, where Chaucer was following Boccaccio. The present passage is in agreement with Joseph, Benoît, and Guido (sig. e 2 recto, col. 2). The analysis of Criseyde's character has been to such an extent a favorite subject of Chaucerian criticism that a list of references would have to include most of the critical works mentioned in the general bibliography on p. 643 f., above. But mention may be made here of two articles dealing specifically with the comparison of Criseyde and the Prioress: A. C. Cawley, MLR, XLIII, 74 ff., and F. M. Smith, W. Va. Univ. Bulletin, Philol. Papers, VI, 1 ff.

809–12 The description of Criseyde's hair departs from Joseph: "nodatur in equos Flavicies crinita sinus." The corresponding passages in Benoît and Guido do not mention the subject.

Possibly Chaucer recalled Tes., vii, 65, or xii, 54; but compare also his earlier reference in Tr, iv, 816–17.

813 f. Criseyde's joined brows are mentioned by Dares, Joseph, Benoît, and Guido, but only the last two regard the trait as a *lak*. In ancient Greece it was held to be a mark of beauty, and sometimes as the sign of a passionate nature. See Curry, The Middle English Ideal of Personal Beauty, Baltimore, 1916, p. 48; Griffin, JEGP, XX, 39 ff.

817 With this striking line have been compared Fil., i, 27, 3–4, 28, 8, and iv, 100, 3; also Par., xviii, 21 (which is the closest parallel). See Professor A. S. Cook in Rom. Rev., VIII, 226, where the Dante passage was noted and other parallels discussed.

825 Cf. Benoît, l. 5286, and Guido, sig. e 2 recto, col. 2, ll. 22 f.

827–40 Partly from Joseph of Exeter, iv, 61–64; cf. also Benoît, especially ll. 5393–5446.

832 For the construction, with *creature* in the singular number, cf. ClT, IV, 212, n.

837 "In daring to do what belongs to a knight." Cf. Joseph of Exeter: "nullique secundus Audendo virtutis opus" (ll. 61 f.).

852 Cf. SqT, V, 294 (closely similar).

892 Either the gods of retribution, or the departed spirits of the slain Trojans, shall be in terror of the Greeks, so cruel a vengeance will be inflicted. Though Chaucer's definition of Manes seems explicit enough, his application of it is uncertain, and the source of the definition is also unknown. In classical Latin the term referred sometimes to departed spirits, sometimes to the gods of the lower world, and in a few instances to punishment conceived impersonally (as in Aen., vi, 743, where it is glossed by Servius "supplicia"). In the present passage, Dr. Wise suggests (Influence of Statius, p. 24), the spirits of the Trojans may be represented as the agents of retribution. For the idea that the Manes torment those who inflict violent death he cites Aen., iv, 387; Theb., iii, 75, iv, 606, v, 163, 312, vii, 770, and other passages. But Mr. Root's interpretation of Chaucer's words is simpler and more natural: "The Greeks will strike terror even to the deities of hell."

897 *ambages*, ambiguities; Ital. "ambage" (Fil., vi, 17, 3).

904–10 With the argument here drawn from Fate cf. that used by Paris with Helen, Her., xv (xvi), 17 f., 41 f.

932 Tydeus, the father of Diomedes, was one of the chief heroes on the side of Polynices in the Theban struggle. See Fil., vi, 24, and Theb., vii, 538 ff.

971 *Orkades*, the Orkneys, representing the western limit of the world, as India did the eastern.

975 Cf. i, 97.

999 "Flavus" is the customary Latin adjective for Pallas's hair. Cf. Theb., iii, 507; Met., ii, 749, viii, 275, etc.

1000–04 In these lines Chaucer appears to have combined the accounts of Benoît and Guido. Cf. Rom. de Troie, 13676–78 (for ll. 1000–01) and Guido, sig. i 2 verso, col. 1 (for ll. 1002–04).

1010–11 Cf. Rom. de Troie, 15053 ff.

1013 For the incident of the glove, which is lacking in the Filostrato, cf. Rom. de Troie, 13709–11, and Guido, sig. i 2 verso, col. 1–2.

1018 Criseyde had promised to return before the moon should pass out of Leo. See iv, 1590 ff.

1020 *Signifer*, the zodiac; so called by Claudian, In Rufinum, i, 365.

1023–29 Cf. Fil., vi, 33, 6–8. But *this sodeyn Diomede* is apparently Chaucer's.

1030 *gostly for to speke*, "to speak truly," lit. "religiously," "devoutly." Cf. the modern phrase "the gospel truth." This use of *gostly* seems to have been rare. Dr. Theodore Spencer has called the editor's attention to two instances in Handlyng Synne, ed. Furnivall, EETS, 1901–03, ll. 2372, 2418.

1033–36 Cf. Fil., vi, 34.

1037–39 *he ... wan*, that is, Diomede won it in battle (Thynne reads *she ... wan*, incorrectly). This occurrence, which is not mentioned by Boccaccio and of which Guido gives only a partial account, is related in the Rom. de Troie, 14286 ff.

1040–44 The *broche* corresponds to the "fer-maglio" which Boccaccio says Troilo noticed on a garment which Deifebo captured from Diomede (Fil., viii, 8–10). The *pencel of hire sleve*, however, is due to Benoît, Rom. de Troie, 15176 ff.

1044–50 Apparently based upon Benoît's account (Rom. de Troie, 20202 ff.). Cf. also Guido, sig. k 6 verso, col. 2.

1054 ff. Criseyde's soliloquy, for which Boccaccio and Guido offer no parallel, follows in part the soliloquy of Briseida in the Rom. de Troie, 20238–340.

1057–64 Cf. Helen's words to Paris in Her., xvi (xvii), 207 ff., which do not, however, include the reflection *And women moost wol haten me of alle*. Many readers of Chaucer must have recalled Helen's self-reproach in Iliad iii, 411–412: τρωαὶ δέ μ'ὀπίσσω / πᾶσαι μωμήσονται.

1062 "My bell shall be rung," that is, my story shall be told, my dishonor proclaimed. A proverbial phrase, for which Mr. Root cites parallels in Conf. Am., ii, 1727 ff., and Lydgate's Compl. of the Bl. Knight, 262 (Oxf. Chau., VII, 253).

This prophecy of the condemnation of Cressida is amply fulfilled in later English poetry. But the degradation of her character in Shakespeare is due not so much to Chaucer as to his successors, beginning with Henryson. See H. E. Rollins, The Troilus-Cressida Story from Chaucer to Shakespeare, PMLA, XXXII, 383 ff.

1067 f. The idea, "Sie ist die Erste nicht" (Faust, Part i, "Trüber Tag"), arises naturally enough in the situation. But Chaucer may have had in mind the words of Paris and Helen in Her., xvi (xvii), 41, 47 f.

1071 Criseyde's pathetic declaration of her purpose to be faithful to Diomede occurs also in Benoît (ll. 20277 f.).

1085 Note here the implication of Fate, the influence of which is repeatedly recognized in the course of the poem.

1086 From the indications given by Benoît, Root shows that the elapsed time can hardly have been less than two years.

1107 Cf. "laurigero ... Phoebo," Ovid, Ars Amat., iii, 389.

1109 *The est-see* according to R. A. Pratt (MLN, LXI, 541 ff.) was probably a vague non-existent body of water east of Troy. Professor Magoun (Med. Stud., XV, 117) would place it farther east and perhaps identify it with the Indian Ocean.

1110 *Nisus' doughter*, Scylla, who was changed into the bird "ciris." See *LGW*, 1908 ff. Professor Meech (PMLA, XLVI, 189) shows that Chaucer might have found the explanation of "ciris" as "lark" in a gloss or in the Ovide Moralisé.

1140 *the yate*, the portcullis.

1141 *as naught ne were*, as if there were nothing; that is, without giving any special reason for doing so.

1174 In the Filostrato Pandaro's expression of incredulity is different: "From Mongibello the fellow expects the wind!" (vii, 10). With Chaucer's phrase here cf. l. 505, above. It seems to mean, "Your happiness will come out of the wood if it come at all." *Joly Robyn* was a common name for a shepherd or rustic. Skeat cites instances of its occurrence in Adam de la Halle's Jeu de Robin (Théâtre Français au Moyen-Âge, ed. Monmerqué and Michel, Paris, 1870, pp. 26 ff., 102 ff.), in *Rom* (l. 7453), in Twelfth Night (iv, 2, 744), and in Hamlet (iv, 5, 181).

1176 Last year's snow is a familiar symbol of the irrevocable past, as in Villon's refrain, "Mais où sont les neiges d'antan?" (Ballade des Dames du Temps Jadis.)

1177–80 From Fil., vii, 11.

1190 Troilus tries to persuade himself that Criseyde meant that the moon should pass wholly out of Leo, which would give her another day. It was in Aries when she made the promise. See iv, 1592.

1277 Cf. RR, 1 ff., and see, with reference to theories of dreams, *NPT*, VII, 2922, n.

For the incident of Troilus's dream and the encouraging advice of Pandarus, Boccaccio may have obtained a hint from the similar account of Governale and Tristan in the Italian Tristano (ed. E. G. Parodi, Bologna, 1896, p. 187) or from the advice of Ascalione to Florio in the Filocolo (II, 26 f.).

1368 *chiste of every care*, "receptacle of every sorrow."

1375–79 With these lines, which are not from Boccaccio, Root compares *BD*, 599–616, and RR, 4293–4330.

1433 Cf. *KnT*, I, 1838, and n.

1443–49 A resumption of ll. 1240–53.

1450–1519 Chaucer substitutes the divination of Cassandra for the altercation between her and Troilo in Fil., vii, 86 ff. In Boccaccio's account Troilo interprets his own dream (Fil., vii, 25–28). *Sibille*, which was properly an epithet ("prophetess"), Chaucer seems to take as a second name of Cassandra. Other cases of the same confusion or misunderstanding are cited in Root's note.

It is unnecessary to seek a particular source for the conception of Cassandra as a prophetess of evil. Chaucer may have got it from Benoît (ll. 4143 ff., 4881 ff., 10417 ff., 27183 ff., etc.) or from Ovid (Her., v, 113 ff.; xvi, 121 ff.).

1464–84 Cf. Met., viii, 260–546; and Boccaccio, De Gen. Deor., ix, cap. 15 and 19.

1480 According to ancient authorities Tydeus was the half-brother, and not a descendant, of Meleager. Chaucer was probably misled by "l'avolo" in Fil., vii, 27, which he translated below in ll. 1512 ff. Root notes that Boccaccio gives the relationship correctly in De Gen. Deor., ix, 21.

1485 ff. A summary of the Thebaid of Statius. A Latin argument is inserted in the MSS. after

l. 1498 and printed by Skeat after l. 1484. In this edition it will be found in the Textual Notes. On its probable source, in the metrical arguments, perhaps as old as the sixth century, which preceded the single books of the Thebaid, see G. L. Hamilton, in MLN, XXIII, 127. These arguments are accessible in Statius, Opera, ed. Amar and Lemaire, Paris, 1825–27, II–III. Chaucer's outline goes far beyond the meager Latin summary and shows familiar knowledge of Statius. Some details, as Professor Magoun pointed out to the editor before the publication of the first edition of the present work, he seems to have taken directly from the arguments prefixed to the separate books. A few examples of such indebtedness are pointed out in the notes below. Very recently, in Traditio, V, 409 ff. Mr. Magoun has printed the Latin text of the relevant arguments, with English translations and detailed comparisons with Chaucer's outline. For a detailed comparison of the whole passage with the Thebaid see Wise, Influence of Statius, pp. 26 ff. The story is treated more briefly in *KnT*, I, 931 ff. and *Anel*, 50 ff.

Polynices (*Polymytes*) and Eteocles (*Ethiocles*), sons of Oedipus, were to rule Thebes alternately, but the latter expelled his brother. Adrastus, king of Argos, took up the cause of Polynices and conducted the famous war of "The Seven against Thebes." With Adrastus and Polynices were associated Tydeus, Amphiaraus (*Amphiorax*), Capaneus (or *Campaneus*), Hippomedon (*Ypomedoun*), and Parthenopaeus (*Parthonope*). All of the seven except Adrastus were slain, and Creon, who seized control of the city, refused to allow the burial of their bodies. This led to the expedition of Theseus, King of Athens, which is mentioned at the beginning of the *KnT*.

1488 Tydeus and Polynices were *felawes* by formal compact. See Theb., i, 468 ff., and cf. the "sworn brotherhood" of Palamon and Arcite (*KnT*, I, 1132, and n.).

1492 *Hemonydes*, Maeon, the son of Haemon, one of the fifty warriors sent by Eteocles to waylay Tydeus. Tydeus killed the other forty-nine and sent Maeon back to Eteocles.

1494 The reference may be to the prophecies of Maeon (Theb., iii, 71 ff.), or of Amphiaraus (Theb., iii, 640 ff.), or of Laius (Theb., iv, 637 ff.). Mr. Magoun compares the *presagia* in Arg. ad III, i, 8.

1497 A serpent, sent by Jove, stung the infant Archemorus to death, while the child's nurse, Hypsipyle, was guiding the Argive host to the river Langia (Theb., v, 505 ff.). The epithet *holy* seems due to the "sacro serpente" of the metrical argument to Theb., v.

1498 *the furies*; the women of Lemnos, incited by the Furies, killed all the males but one on the island.

1499 The funeral rites of Archemorus occupy Theb. vi.

1500 On the death of Amphiaraus see Theb., vii, 794 ff. On the spelling *Amphiorax* see *Gen Prol*, I, 384, n.

1501 ff. On the death of Tydeus see Theb., viii, 716 ff.; on that of Hippomedon, ix, 526 ff.; on that of Parthenopaeus, ix, 841 ff.; and on that of Capaneus, x, 907 ff. The drowning of Hippomedon is mentioned in only one MS. of the brief Latin sum-

mary, namely Hl², which has the additional line "Fervidus Ypomedon timidique (read "tumidoque") in gurgite mersus," which comes from the twelve-line argument to Bk. ix.

1508 The first combat of Eteocles and Polynices is described in Theb., xi, 389 ff.

1509 *Argyve*, Argia, the wife of Polynices ("Argiva," variant in the argument to Bk. xii). This seems to be Chaucer's source for the name of Criseyde's mother, though the reason for the choice is not apparent. See iv, 762, n.

1511 The statement that Thebes was burned is not definitely made in the Thebaid, though there are a number of references to the possibility of destruction by fire. Chaucer may have got the hint from these, or from the Teseide or the Roman de Thèbes (cf. l. 10131).

1513–19 The interpretation of Troilus's dream, here transferred to Cassandra's mouth, corresponds to that in Fil., vii, 27.

1520–26 Cf. Fil., vii, 89. In the Filostrato Cassandra taunts Troilo for loving Griseida (vii, 86, 87); in the *Troilus* she angers her brother by her interpretation of the dream.

1523 *sestow*, a rhetorical question, not addressed to Cassandra. *Fool of fantasie*, fantastic fool.

1527–33 *Alceste*, Alcestis, the heroine of the *LGW*, and the model of wifely devotion. Her husband was Admetus, King of Pherae in Thessaly.

1541–47 Cf. Inf., vii, 68–82; also the discussion in Boethius, iv, pr. 6.

1548 *parodie*, glossed "duracioun" in MSS. Hl¹ Hl⁴ Cp, seems to be merely a corrupt form of *periode*.

1558 On *aventaille* see G. L. Hamilton, MP, III, 541.

1558–61 Boccaccio's account of the death of Hector is supplemented by that of Benoît (Rom. de Troie, 16185 ff.). Cf. also Guido's Historia, sig. i 6 recto, col. 1.

1577 On the use of pilgrim's dress as a disguise see F. P. Magoun, Jr. in MLN, LIX, 176 ff. (instances from literature), and B. J. Whiting, MLN, LX, 47 ff. (historical cases).

1589 ff. Criseyde's letter at this point is found only in Chaucer. But Boccaccio's poem indicates some kind of communication between Troilo and Griseida. See Fil., viii, 5–6. For the contents, moreover, Chaucer drew on earlier letters in Fil., ii, 96, 122, 126.

1597–1600 Cf. Fil., ii, 122, 4–8.

1611–13 Cf. Her., xvii (xvi), 149–51.

1634 *kalendes*, beginning, as in ii, 7. Root observes that Chaucer seems to be playing upon the phrase "Calends of exchange," explained conjecturally by NED, s.v., Calends 3a as meaning a money-changer's calendar, reckoning, or account.

1644–66 Cf. Fil., viii, 8–10.

1660 This brooch was not mentioned earlier in the account of the parting of the lovers. But according to iii, 1370 ff., Criseyde gave Troilus a brooch of gold and azure.

1669 *word and ende*; see *MkT*, VII, 2721, n.

1689 "To fief your love with." On the order of words see *Gen Prol*, I, 791, n.

1705 This detail of the bleeding sides, not mentioned in the Filostrato (viii, 16, 4–7), may have been added from Benoît (l. 20075).

1751–56 These lines allude to combats which

are fully described by both Benoît and Guido. See the Rom. de Troie, 19281–21189, and the Historia, sig. k 5 verso — sig. l 2 verso. Boccaccio dismisses the matter with a single line (Fil., viii, 25, 7).

1758 ff. These lines, which correspond to Fil., viii, 26, 1–5 are perhaps influenced by the account of Troilus in the Rom. de Troie, 19955–21189.

1765 ff. Lounsbury (Studies, II, 315) suggested that Chaucer was thinking rather of Guido than of Dares. Anyhow it is very doubtful if he made direct use of Dares's prose Historia. Root has shown that the material here referred to is to be found in the Metrical "Dares" of Joseph of Exeter, which also furnished hints for the portraits in ll. 799 ff., above.

1772 ff. The conclusion, or epilogue, of the poem is carefully analyzed and fully discussed by Professor Tatlock in MP, XVIII, 625 ff. Ll. 1772–85, in which Chaucer makes his first moral application of the *Troilus,* suggest that he already had in mind the plan of the *Legend of Good Women.*

1786 ff. *Go, litel bok*; in the use of this formula, Chaucer follows a long literary tradition. For examples from Ovid, Martial, Statius, and various mediæval writers in French, Provençal, and Italian, see Tatlock, pp. 627 ff. Nearly all the cases he cites occur in collections of short poems. Boccaccio employs the device also at the end of longer works, and Chaucer probably had his usage in mind. The envoi in the Filocolo (II, 376–78) seems most likely to have influenced him. Boccaccio there mentions Virgil, Lucan, Statius, Ovid, and Dante, for the last of whom Chaucer may have deliberately substituted Homer as more appropriate to a tale of Troy. But too much significance should not be attached to the similarity of the lists. The same poets, with the addition of Claudian, are represented in the pillars in *HF,* 1455 ff. and they correspond also, with the single exception of Statius (who takes the place of Horace), to the group whom Dante joined in Limbo (Inf., iv, 82 ff.).

In ll. 1789–90 may be recognized a variation on another literary convention, that of the so-called "envy-postscript." Cf. *Astr, Prol,* 64, and see F. Tupper, JEGP, XVI, 551 ff., where numerous examples are cited, both ancient and mediæval, of prologues and epilogues in deprecation of envy. The idea, and in l. 1791 the language, repeats Statius, Theb., xii, 816 f. ("vestigia semper adora").

1787 On this use of *ther* see *KnT,* I, 2815, n.

1788 On the interpretation of *make* see R. C. Boys (MLN, LII, 351), who suggests that it is an early instance of its use in the sense of "match." This is more satisfactory than "compose (poetry)."

1793 ff. With the solicitude here expressed cf. *Adam Scriveyn.* That there was plenty of occasion for the caution is fully shown by the condition of Chaucer MSS. The *diversite,* which Chaucer rightly recognized as a cause of corruption, consisted partly in dialectical variations and partly in growing disregard of final -e. See the Grammatical Introduction.

1807–27 From Tes., xi, 1–3, where the flight of Arcite's soul is described. Chaucer did not use the passage in the *KnT.* On the reasons for its omission see *KnT,* I, 2805 ff., n. Boccaccio's stanzas are supposed to have been suggested by the Somnium Scipionis (De Re Publica, lib. vi), to which Chaucer also may have independently reverted. His knowledge of it is well attested by the *PF.* A second

source, if not the primary suggestion, for the passage in the Teseida (as pointed out in a long-neglected note of Tyrwhitt's, to which the editor's attention was called by Professor Lowes), is certainly to be recognized in Lucan's account of the death of Pompey (Pharsalia, ix, 1 ff.). For further comment see H. R. Patch, ESt, LXV, 357 ff. Both Boccaccio and Chaucer may well have had in mind the passage in Dante's Paradiso (xxii, 151) also noted by Professor Patch, when Dante looks down upon the threshing-floor of earth and smiles.

1809 Nearly all the MSS. read *seventhe* for *eighthe.* But Boccaccio has "ottava" and the reference seems clearly to the concavity (or inner surface) of the eighth sphere. It is not made clear by either Chaucer or Boccaccio whether the spheres are numbered from that of the Moon outward or from that of the Fixed Stars inward. Professor Root argues in favor of the latter order, which is followed in the Somnium Scipionis (cap. xvii), and it seems probable on the whole that the station of Troilus was conceived as in the sphere of the Moon. For the suggestion that Chaucer deliberately departed from Boccaccio and followed Dante's order of numbering, see J. L. Cope, MLN, LXVII, 245 f.

1810 *In convers letyng,* leaving on the other side. Boccaccio has "convessi," convex surfaces, which Chaucer either misread or deliberately altered. The reference is of course to the terrestrial elements: earth, water, air, and fire.

1812 The erratic stars are the planets. On the music of the spheres see Somnium, cap. xviii, and *PF,* 59 ff.

1814 ff. Cf. Somnium, cap. xix–xx.

1819–21 Cf. Pharsalia, ix, 11–14, especially "risitque sui ludibria trunci."

1835–55 On this repudiation of earthly love see Tatlock, MP, XVIII, 635 ff. The contrast between earthly and heavenly affection was of course one of the most familiar commonplaces of the age, and is more than once brought out by Chaucer. The expression of it here has been taken by some to be merely conventional. (Cf. Fansler, Chaucer and the RR, p. 228, n. 12.) But the whole spirit of the passage is that of religious sincerity. How far it is merely an utterance of personal feeling on Chaucer's part, and how far it reflects a more general conflict of pagan and Christian ideals, as Professor Tatlock suggests, is difficult to judge. A similar conflict or contrast in the De Amore of Andreas Capellanus is cited by Professor Young in MLN, XL, 274 ff. Cf. also T. A. Stroud, MP, XLIX, 1 ff. Regarding the poem as a whole as a kind of application of the philosophy of Boethius, Mr. Stroud finds the retractation less out of harmony than have certain other scholars. For further discussion see J. Speirs, Chaucer the Maker, pp. 51 ff.; K. Malone, Chapters on Chaucer, pp. 135 ff.; H. R. Patch MLN, LXVIII, 555; Sister Madeleva, A Lost Language, pp. 119 ff.; A. J. Denomy, Trans. Royal Soc. of Canada, XLIV, Ser. III, Sec. 2 (1950), p. 43; D. W. Robertson, Jr., ELH, XIX, 1 ff.; J. L. Shanley, ELH, VI, 271 ff.; J. W. Clark, JEGP, L, 1 ff.; Dorothy Everett, Essays on Middle English Literature (Oxford, 1955), pp. 134 ff.; and E. E. Slaughter, Essays in Honor of Walter Clyde Curry (Nashville, 1955), pp. 61 ff.

1837 Cf. *KnT,* I, 2847, and n.

1840-41   A proverbial comparison. See Skeat, EE Prov., pp. 85 f., no. 205.   Cf. also Ps. ciii, 15 f.

1848   The attack on heathen worship seems to be no less earnest than that on pagan love. Professor Tatlock (pp. 652 ff.) notes that there is a parallel disowning of paganism at the end of Boccaccio's De Genealogia Deorum. For the terms of the invective comparison has been made with Guido's denunciation of idolatry, Historia, sig. e 4 verso, col. 2; Hecuba's outburst, Rom. de Troie, 21715 ff., 21732 ff.; and Emilia's, in Tes., xi, 42.

1856 ff.   The request for criticism or correction is in accordance with usage, though less common than the general device of the envoi. Professor Tatlock (pp. 631 ff.) notes instances in the life of St. Dunstan by "B," the Ormulum, Deguilleville's Pèlerinage, and various works of Boccaccio, whose example Chaucer probably followed. The selection of Gower and Strode, Tatlock suggests, had particular reference to the moral and religious issues involved in the paganism of the poem.

On Gower and his personal relations to Chaucer see the Biographical Introduction. With the term "moral," which has become a kind of fixed epithet for Gower, cf. the characterization of him in the metrical prologue to John Walton's translation of the Consolation of Philosophy (ed. M. Science, EETS, 1927, p. 2, st. 5).

The *philosophical Strode* is doubtless to be identified with Ralph Strode, fellow of Merton College before 1360, an opponent of Wyclif, though apparently on friendly terms with the reformer. Strode was an eminent Thomist philosopher and authority on logic. His Logica is lost, but fragments of his system are preserved in his Consequentiae and Obligationes. His theological treatises all appear to have perished, and for a statement of his opinions we are dependent on Wyclif's rejoinders: Responsio ad decem Questiones Magistri R. Strode (Opera Minora, London, 1913, pp. 398-404) and Responsiones ad Argumenta Radulphi Strode (Opera Minora, pp. 175-200). It is clear that one feature of Wyclif's philosophy to which Strode objected was his necessitarianism, and Professor Tatlock (p. 656, n. 2) observes that he might for the same reason have disapproved of the philosophy of the *Troilus*. See iv, 953, n.

In the Vetus Catalogus of the fellows of Merton, written in 1422, there is added to the name of "Strood" the statement: "Nobilis poeta fuit et versificavit librum elegiacum vocatum Phantasma Radulphi" (DNB). On this evidence it has been suggested that Strode was the author of the fourteenth-century elegiac poem The Pearl, and consequently of the associated poems, Clennesse, Patience, and Sir Gawayn and the Green Knight. But the identification of The Pearl with the Phantasma

Radulphi is at best an unsupported conjecture, and there is some difficulty in the assumption that the Middle English author, who wrote in a northerly (West Midland) dialect, was fellow of Merton, a southern college. Another work, not yet identified, an Itinerarium Terrae Sanctae, was attributed to Strode by Bale on the authority of a lost treatise of Nicholas Brigham, De Venatione Rerum Memorabilium. The list of Strode's compositions is still further amplified by Pits and Dempster. But his authorship of literary works, as distinguished from philosophical or theological, must be regarded as doubtful.

There is more to be said for the identification of Strode the philosopher with the Radulphus Strode who was prominent as a London lawyer from 1373 until his death in 1387. Notices of Ralph Strode of London do not appear until after references to Strode cease in the Merton records. In 1373 he became Common Pleader (Common Serjeant), and in 1386 Standing Counsel for the City. Reasons for identifying him with Strode of Merton have been found in two records, one of which was only lately discovered. In 1374 Wyclif and Ralph Strode of London appear together as mainpernors for a parson. And in 1377, according to a document preserved at Merton College and copied in the Calendar of Fine Rolls (for 1377-1383) IX, London, 1926, p. 8, Ralph Strode of the City of London and Robert Rygge, parson of the church of St. Stephen, Bristol, were mainpernors in the commitment of certain land in the suburb of Oxford to John Bloxham, warden of "Mertonhalle." Finally, he is brought into relation with Chaucer by the fact that he was granted a mansion over Aldersgate in 1375, the year after Chaucer received his Aldgate residence; and especially by the recent discovery in the Coram Rege rolls that he and Chaucer were fellow sureties in 1382 for the peaceful behavior of John Hende, a wealthy London draper.

For more complete data on Strode see Sir I. Gollancz in DNB; C. Brown, PMLA, XIX, 146; E. P. Kuhl, PMLA, XXIX, 272 ff.; H. B. Workman, John Wyclif, London, 1926, II, 125 ff.; and, for discussion of the lately discovered records, Miss Rickert, TLS, Oct. 4, 1928, p. 707; H. W. Garrod, ibid., Oct. 11, p. 736; Sir I. Gollancz, ibid., Oct. 25, p. 783. Mr. J. T. T. Brown (Scottish Antiquary, XII, pp. 5 ff.) suggested the possibility that the literary works ascribed to Strode by Bale and his successors were really by David Rate, the confessor of James I of Scotland. But his identifications of the various titles are not convincing.

On a reference, late and perhaps untrustworthy, to N. (or R.) Strode as tutor of Chaucer's "little son" Lewis, see the Explanatory Notes to the *Astrolabe*.

1863-65   From Dante, Par., xiv, 28-30.

The Legend of Good Women

On the various forms of the title see the Textual Notes. The authenticity of the *Legend* is well established, not only by the MS. attributions, but also by internal evidence and by Chaucer's acknowledgment of the *Seintes Legende of Cupyde* in the *Introduction to the Man of Law's Tale*. Chaucer refers to the work again as the *Book of the XIX* (or *XXV*) *Ladies* in his *Retractation* (probably genuine) at the end of the *Canterbury Tales*. Lydgate includes it in his list in the Prologue to Bk. i of the Fall of Princes, describing it as a "legende off parfit hoolynesse," and declaring that it was written at the request of the Queen. But the authority for this last assertion, and for Speght's similar statement in his 1598 edition ("Argument" to the *Legend*), is entirely uncertain. In its support see Professor Carleton Brown, ESt, XLVII, 61 f., and Tatlock, Development and Chronology, Ch. Soc., 1907, pp. 111 ff. Dr. V. Langhans (Untersuchungen zu Chaucer, Halle, 1918, p. 186) makes the unlikely suggestion that the queen referred to by Lydgate was Alceste rather than Anne.

Whether or not the work was written at the Queen's request, there is a kind of dedication to her in *Prologue F* (ll. 496–97). This serves to date at least the *Prologue* in question between Richard's marriage, June 14, 1382, and the death of Anne, June 7, 1394. Within these limits no exact date has been established. Ten Brink (Chaucer Studien, Münster, 1870, pp. 147 ff.) suggested that the poem expresses Chaucer's gratitude to the Queen for the appointment of his deputy in the custom house in February, 1385. But the petition for this assistance was signed by the King's favorite, the Earl of Oxford, and the intervention of the Queen, though not impossible, is entirely unproved. (See Life Records, Ch. Soc., 1875–1900, Pt. iv, p. 251, and Tatlock's comments in MP, I, 325 ff.) More secure evidence for an approximate date is furnished by the literary relations of the *Prologue*. Following a suggestion of Tyrwhitt, Professor Lowes argued (PMLA, XIX, 593 ff.) that it was indebted to Deschamps's Lay de Franchise and other French poems on the "marguerite." Now Deschamps's lay was written for May 1, 1385, and may have been brought, Lowes suggested, to Chaucer by Sir Lewis Clifford in the spring or summer of 1386. At all events, Deschamps declares, in a ballade addressed to Chaucer, that he sent some of his poems to Chaucer by Clifford's hand; and while the communication cannot be proved, the relation between the *Prologue* to the *Legend* and the French poems in question led Lowes to propose 1386 as the year for Chaucer's composition. (Deschamps's ballade has been several times printed. See, besides the editions of Deschamps [no. 285, SATF, II, 138 ff.], Paget Toynbee, Specimens of Old French, Oxford, 1892, pp. 314 f., 482 ff., and especially T. A. Jenkins, MLN, XXXIII, 268 ff., with text, translation, and full commentary.) But this whole argument has been questioned by recent investigators. Miss Marian Lossing (Stud. Phil., XXXIX, 15 ff.) has thrown serious doubt on Chaucer's use of the Lay de Franchise. This makes an earlier date than 1385 possible for the *Prologue*, and Carleton Brown, in MLN, LVIII, 274 ff., pointed out that Clifford would have been unlikely to deliver Deschamp's verses to Chaucer after May, 1385. He consequently argued for a date not later than 1384 for the composition of Chaucer's poem.

The *Prologue* exists in two versions, about whose relative dates scholars disagree. The form here designated G (usually A) is preserved in only one MS. (Cambridge Univ., Gg. 4. 27), and was first printed by Furnivall, in 1871. All the other MSS. have the form here called F (usually B), from MS. Fairfax. The G-version has generally been regarded as the earlier draft, and was so represented by Skeat and the Globe editor. But Ten Brink (ESt, XVII, 13 ff.) questioned the traditional view and dated G later than F, probably not before 1393. Since his argument, opinions have been rather evenly divided on the subject. In favor of the priority of G see especially E. Legouis, Quel fut le premier composé par Chaucer des deux prologues de la Légende des Femmes Exemplaires?, Le Havre, 1900; J. B. Bilderbeck, Chaucer's Legend of Good Women, London, 1902; J. C. French, The Problem of the Two Prologues to Chaucer's Legend of Good Women, Baltimore, 1905; and John Koch, ESt, XXXVI, 142 ff., XXXVII, 232 ff., Angl., L, 62 ff. For the opposite order see (besides Ten Brink) Lowes, PMLA, XIX, 593 ff., XX, 749 ff., and in Kittredge Anniversary Papers, Boston, 1913, pp. 95 ff.; Tatlock, Dev. and Chron., ch. 4; and H. Lange, Angl., XLIX, 173 ff., LII, 123 ff. Dr. Langhans, in his Untersuchungen, pp. 77 ff., argued that G alone is genuine and that F is a revision of Chaucer's text by another author. See also his later articles in ESt, LVI, 36 ff., Angl., L, 70 ff. (with a brief review of the history of opinion), and LIV, 99 ff. Less important articles and reviews are listed by Miss Hammond, pp. 381 ff., and by Wells, pp. 873, 1030, 1145, 1235 f., 1325, 1422, 1534, 1643, 1735, 1930.

Although neither theory may be susceptible of absolute demonstration, the probabilities, in the opinion of the present editor, strongly favor the priority of the F-version. Arguments based upon a literary preference for either version, or upon the problematic interpretation of Alceste as an allegorical figure representing Queen Anne, are of necessity indecisive. But such considerations as have been advanced by Professor Lowes, in the articles listed above, are less colored and consequently safer. After pointing out certain French and Italian sources of the *Prologue*, as already noted, he showed that F is closer to the originals, both verbally and structurally, than G. This relation is hard to understand on the theory that G is the original version. Then from an examination of passages shifted in revision, Mr. Lowes also showed that the purely mechanical "joiner-work," is easier to explain on the assumption that G is the later text. A number of the altered passages point clearly to this conclusion, and none of them seem inconsistent with it. Indeed the chief objection to regarding G as the revision is probably the fact that some excellent poetry in F has been sacrificed in the rearrangement. But this will not surprise anybody who recalls how Chaucer appears to have canceled some of the best links in the *Canterbury Tales*. And fortunately the special beauties of version F need not be lost to the reader. For it is the wise practice of most modern editors to print the two texts side by side.

More or less involved in the whole problem of the *Prologue*, as already remarked, is the particular question whether Alceste represents Queen Anne. In support of this identification, which according to the usual understanding carries with it the identification of Love as King Richard, see Ten Brink, Geschichte der Eng. Lit., Strassburg, 1912, II, 116; Skeat, Oxf. Chau., III, xxiv; the works of Bilderbeck and French cited above; H. Lange, Angl., XXXIX, 347 ff. (with detailed argument from heraldry); and Koch, ESt, LV, 174 ff., and Angl., L, 62 ff. R. Bressie, in MP, XXVI, 28 f., argues that Usk's Testament of Love, and even the Pearl, are to be associated with a marguerite cult in honor of the Queen. For adverse criticism of the allegorical interpretation of the *Prologue* see Lowes, PMLA, XX, 773 ff.; Kittredge, MP, VI, 435 ff.; and Langhans, Untersuchungen, pp. 182 ff., and Angl., L, 70 ff. The possibility of a compliment to Queen Anne in the panegyric on the daisy is perhaps not to be denied, though very little is known of the literary "cults" actually in vogue at her court. But in the opinion of the present editor an allegorical equation between Alceste and Anne, and still more, between Richard and the God of Love, involves too many difficulties and improprieties to be probable. Nor is such an interpretation of the characters required by anything in the text of the *Prologue*. Passages in which evidence of the allegory has been sought will be considered in the notes that follow.

A different identification for Alceste was proposed by Professor Tupper in JEGP, XXI, 308 ff. He took her to represent Alice Chester (or de Cestre), whom he held to be a lady-in-waiting of the Queen and a life-long friend of the poet. But Professor Manly, in MP, XXIV, 257 ff., produced evidence from the household books to show that she was an elderly laundress. Still another identification has been proposed by Miss Margaret Galway in MLR, XXXIII, 145 ff., XLIV, 161 ff., and MLN, LX, 431 ff., namely with the Princess Joan of Kent, widow of the Black Prince and mother of Richard II. (See also MLR, XLIII, 383 ff., and, for further biographical information about Joan, Miss Galway's article on her relation to the Order of the Garter, Univ. of Birmingham Hist. Journal, I, 13 ff.) Since Joan died on August 7, 1385, the *Prologue* would have been unlikely to refer to her if written after the Lay de Franchise. But this chronological difficulty would be removed by the acceptance of an earlier date for the poem. The identification is accepted as probable by Brown in MLN, LVIII, 278. For arguments against it see B. F. Huppe, MLN, XLIII, 393 (with reply by Miss Galway at p. 399), and W. E. Weese, MLN, LXIII, 474 ff. For the suggestion that *Prologue G* was written by Chaucer for Princess Isabel of France see Miss Galway, Rev. Eng. Stud., XXIV, 273 ff.

In the fundamental idea of the *LGW* — a martyrology of Cupid's saints — there is involved the application of theological conceptions to the affairs of love. It is therefore not surprising that Queen Alceste, the intercessor, should bear some resemblance in character and office to the Blessed Virgin. The God of Love, too, is not quite the ordinary Cupid, but has the character of a pitying lord. This religious parallelism was pointed out by Professor Lange in Angl., XLIX, 173 ff., 267 ff. It is set forth in detail by Dr. D. D. Griffith, Manly Anniversary Studies, Chicago, 1923, pp. 32 ff. Dr. Griffith shows that the Christian coloring is less marked in version G than in version F. But Professor Brusendorff (p. 144, n.) questioned whether this was the result of deliberate purpose.

The date of the *Prologues*, either or both, does not determine the time of composition of the individual legends; and on this subject there is also a wide diversity of opinion. Professor Lowes (PMLA, XX, 802 ff.) showed reason for holding most of the legends to be earlier than the *Prologue*; see also Tatlock, Dev. and Chron., pp. 122–31. Professor Root, basing his discussion particularly on the Medea, argued for a later date (PMLA, XXIV, 124 ff.; XXV, 228 ff.); against his view, see Kittredge, PMLA, XXIV, 343 ff.

The sources of the *Prologue* have been most fully exhibited in Professor Lowes's articles. For the first part — the panegyric of the daisy (F, 1–196) — the principal suggestion came apparently from Deschamps's Lay de Franchise, but there are also reminiscences of a number of other French poems on the "marguerite." The second part — the vision of Love, with the accusation and defense of the offender against his law (F, 197–end) — is indebted for its framework and many details to the Paradys d'Amours of Froissart. The more important parallels in these various sources are pointed out in the notes that follow. Other literary influences on the *Prologue*, less important structurally, have been observed by several scholars. Professor Kittredge in MP, VII, 471 ff., noted a possible relation to Machaut's Jugement dou Roy de Navarre. The striking parallelism of the general situation between the *Prologue* and the woodland fight of Palamon and Arcite in the *KnT* has been noted by Professor Tatlock (Stud. Phil., XVIII, 419 ff.). Dr. Fansler (pp. 69 ff.) calls attention to a few resemblances to Machaut's Dit du Vergier. He also compares with Alceste's defense of the poet the defense of the lover by Fals-Semblant in RR, 12277 ff. But on the whole the influence of the Roman de la Rose was slight (cf. Fansler, p. 256). For the underlying fiction of Chaucer's heresy against Love there are various literary parallels. See Brusendorff, p. 140, citing, besides Machaut's two Jugement poems, Jean de Meun's excuses (RR, 15135 ff.), and Brantôme's story of Jean in the Vies des Dames Galantes. Cf. F. Guillon, Jean Clopinel, Paris, 1903, pp. 169 f.

For the general conception of the legends Chaucer was indebted on the one hand to the lives of the saints, and on the other to Ovid's Heroides and Boccaccio's De Claris Mulieribus and De Casibus Virorum et Feminarum Illustrium. The nine individual stories seem to have been based on various authorities, chiefly Ovid and Virgil. Those sources which can be recognized with some probability are indicated in the notes. Cf. Bech, Angl., V, 313 ff., and Skeat's introduction and notes; and especially E. F. Shannon, Chaucer and the Roman Poets, Harv. Univ. Press, 1929, pp. 169 ff. Professor Shannon makes detailed comparison of Chaucer's text with the Latin texts, in particular with Ovid. Here, as in the case of several of Chaucer's other works, the question arises as to his use of vernacular translations of his Latin sources. Professor Lowes has shown (PMLA, XXXIII, 302 ff.), in an examination of the Philomela, that in that legend Chaucer utilized the French Ovide Moralisé alongside of Ovid's Latin; and Mr. S. B. Meech (PMLA, XLV, 117; XLVI, 182 ff.) has pointed out the influence of the same French work in the *Legend of Ariadne*. Mr. Meech has found no trace of the Ovide Moralisé in the other *Legends* or in the *Canterbury Tales*. But in the first article cited he shows that in a number of passages, noted below, Chaucer probably utilized the Italian translation of the Heroides, ascribed to Filippo Ceffi. On the general question of Chaucer's use of vernacular versions of Latin texts see the introductions to the Explanatory Notes on the *Clerk's Tale* and on *Boece*. Professor Shannon (Ch. and the Roman Poets, pp. 282–83) dismisses the subject a little too summarily.

Professor H. C. Goddard's articles (JEGP, VII, no. 4, 87; VIII, no. 1, 47) should be mentioned, in support of the theory that the *Legend* was really a satire upon women, to be understood in a sense opposite to its apparent meaning. Against this opinion see the cogent argument of Lowes (JEGP, VIII, 513 ff.). Professor R. M. Garrett, in JEGP, XXII, 64 ff., has restated the satirical interpretation in a less extreme form, but he also appears to the editor to carry it too far. The general problem of Chaucer's satirical purpose is also discussed by P. F. Baum in MLN, LX, 377 ff.

Special acknowledgment should be made here, as in the case of all Chaucer's writings, of the editor's indebtedness to Skeat's notes. The two later editions, by Pollard (in the Globe Chaucer) and by Koch (in [Chaucer's] Kleinere Dichtungen),' are sparsely annotated, though Koch gives extensive lists of variant readings.

Prologue

(References are to the line-numbers of *Prologue F*, unless the G-version is specially designated. Corresponding passages in the two versions will be found in the parallel columns of the text, except where the order was changed in revision.)

1 On the rhetorical character of the beginning — a combination of the methods of "sententia" and "exemplum" — see Manly, Chaucer and the Rhetoricians, Brit. Acad., 1926, p. 8. There is a striking parallel to the opening lines in Froissart's Joli Buisson de Jonece, ll. 786–92 (Œuvres, ed. Scheler, Bruxelles, 1870–72, II, 24; see Kittredge, ESt, XXVI, 336, n.).

11 *Wel more thing*, many more things.

16 Evidently a proverb, the Latin form of which is noted in the margins of some MSS.: "Bernardus monachus non uidit omnia." It is by Tyrwhitt and most later commentators taken to refer to St. Bernard of Clairvaux (1091–1153). Skeat (following Tyrwhitt) cites J. J. Hoffmann, Lexicon Universale (Leyden, 1698), s.v. S. Bernardus, Burgundus: "Nullos habuit praeceptores praeter quercus & fagos. Hinc proverb. Neque enim Bernardus vidit omnia." A writer signing himself E. S. A., in N & Q, 8th Ser., III, 433, argues that the reference was rather to Bernard of Morlaix, whose De Contemptu Mundi describes heaven and hell. Professor Tatlock

(MLN, XLVI, 21 ff.) has proposed a third identification, with Bernard the traveler (sometimes called "Bernardus Sapiens"), who with two other monks made a journey to the Holy Land about the year 870, and left an account in his brief Itinerarium (T. Tobler, Descriptiones Terrae Sanctae, Leipzig, 1874, pp. 85–99, 393 ff.; Migne, Pat. Lat., CXXI, 569–74). Mr. Tatlock cites several references to him as "Bernardus Monachus." Professor G. L. Hamilton, who was at the time preparing an argument in favor of the traditional identification with Bernard of Clairvaux, called the editor's attention to a variant of the proverb — "Multa sunt quae bonus Bernardus nec vidit, nec audivit" — used by Cowper in a letter written July 25, 1792 (Correspondence, ed. Johnson, London, 1824, II, 294). Mr. Hamilton would connect the saying with a treatise attributed to St. Bernard and entitled Meditationes, or De Interiori Homine. See Migne, Pat. Lat., CLXXXIV, 485 ff. In support of the identification with Bernard of Clairvaux see also R. M. Smith, MLN, LXI, 38 ff., and Marie P. Hamilton, MLN, LXII, 190 ff. (with examples of the proverb in Thynne).

27 ff. For a comparison of the two versions at this point, with the purpose of illustrating Chaucer's methods in revision, see K. Malone, Proc. Am. Philosophical Society, XCIV, 317 ff.

40–65 These lines, as Lowes has pointed out, contain numerous echoes of the French "marguerite" poems. Cf. in particular ll. 40–43 with Froissart's Paradys d'Amours (Œuvres, I, 1 ff.), ll. 1633–35, 1621–22, and his Prison Amoureuse (Œuvres, I, 211 ff.), ll. 898–99; ll. 44–49 with Deschamps's Lay de Franchise (Œuvres, SATF, II, 203 ff.), ll. 14, 27–30, and Froissart's Dittié de la Flour de la Margherite (Œuvres, II, 209 ff.), ll. 162–66; ll. 50–52 with Machaut's Dit de la Marguerite, ed. Tarbé, Rheims, 1849, p. 124; ll. 53–55 with Froissart's Le Joli Mois de May (Œuvres, II, 194 ff.), ll. 289–90, and Deschamps's ballade no. 532 (Œuvres, SATF, III, 368 ff.), ll. 15–16; ll. 56–59 with Froissart's Dittié, ll. 81–82, 159–62; and ll. 60–65 with Deschamps's Lay de Franchise, ll. 44–50. Line 43 may reflect Chaucer's consciousness that he was substituting the English name of the daisy for the French "marguerite" of his sources. Cf. also ll. 182–85, below. The phrase *flower of flowers* in l. 53 and again in l. 185 is a commonplace. Cf. *A B C*, 4.

43 With this use of *our* cf. l. 1689, below; also *ShipT*, VII, 69, and n. (The reading *her*, which is peculiar to MS. F, is clearly an error.)

45 ff. Closely similar to *KnT*, I, 1675 ff. As Professor Tatlock has noted, the resemblances between the *Prologue* to *LGW* and *KnT* are not merely verbal. There is also a parallel between the situation here and that where Duke Theseus separates Palamon and Arcite, and then pardons them at the queen's request. See Stud. Phil., XVIII, 419 ff.

G 58 With this line, which is true to actual fact, Professor Lowes compares, among other passages, Froissart's Dittié, ll. 96 ff., and his Paradys d'Amours, ll. 1636–38.

68–77 This is addressed to contemporary poets, such as Machaut, Froissart, and Deschamps, and may be regarded as an acknowledgment on Chaucer's part of his debt to their poems on the "marguerite."

72 Court society in both England and France was apparently divided into two parties or amorous orders devoted respectively to the Flower and to the Leaf. Cf. Gower, Conf. Am., viii, 2462 ff., and Deschamps, Balades, nos. 764–67 (Œuvres, SATF, IV, 257 ff.). In England Philippa of Lancaster was the great patroness of the Flower. The English poem, The Flower and the Leaf, formerly attributed to Chaucer, is now held to be of the 15th century. On the literature of the Flower and the Leaf see Kittredge, MP, I, 1 ff.; G. L. Marsh, MP, IV, 121 ff., 281 ff.

74 *makyng*, poetry; "ye have reaped the field of poetry, and carried away the grain." The figure of gleaning after the reapers may be an echo of Ruth ii (if any literary suggestion was necessary), which was used in the Introduction to Higden's Polychronicon. The reference to reaping in Usk's Testament of Love (Prol., 97 ff.), generally associated with Chaucer's lines, has more resemblance to the passage in Higden. (See MP, XXVI, 19 ff.)

G 71–80 These lines correspond to F, 188–96. Professor Lowes has shown (Kittredge Anniv. Papers, pp. 96 ff.) that the verbal changes are best explained on the theory that G is the revised form. He argues similarly with regard to two other shifted passages, G, 93–106 (= F, 197–211) and G, 179–202 (= F, 276–99).

G 76 "I am not retained by either party." With the use of *withholde(n)* here (and in F, 192) cf. *Gen Prol*, I, 511.

84–96 Chaucer here follows closely the opening stanzas of the Filostrato, a passage which he did not use in the *Troilus*. At the same time several phrases still echo the French "marguerite" poetry. With ll. 86–87, for example, may be compared Machaut's Dit de la Marguerite, pp. 126–27; with the phrase *erthly god* (l. 95) cf. "la déesse mondaine" in Deschamps's Lay de Franchise, l. 52; and the simile of the harp suggests the title of Machaut's Dit de la Harpe, until lately inaccessible. But Professor Karl Young's recent edition of the Dit (Essays in honor of Albert Feuillerat, New Haven, 1943, pp. 1 ff.) does not reveal any use of the French by Chaucer. Indeed Professor Lowes conjectures that Chaucer's transition to the Filostrato was itself due to certain lines near the close of the Dit de la Marguerite (p. 128) which are similar in language and sentiment to the passage in Boccaccio.

100 *seen at eye*, see clearly, before the eyes.

103 *besy gost*, active spirit.

108 Note the change of date from the first of May, in the F-version, to the end of the month in the G-version (l. 89).

113–14 These lines contain an echo of Tes., iii, 5. Europa is there called by her own name; in calling her *Agenores doghtre* Chaucer may have recalled "Agenore nata," Met., ii, 858 (where her story is told), or the Filocolo (ed. Moutier, II, 149). The sun, as the passage indicates, was in the middle of Taurus on the first of May.

G 96 The G-version introduces at this point the poet's return to the house and his dream, which do not occur in F until l. 200. Professor Lowes argues that G has thus more unity and avoids verbal repetitions, and is therefore the revised form. The remark about the house with the arbor (which occurs in both texts) perhaps furnishes an indication of the date of composition. It seems hardly applicable to Chaucer's house over the city gate, and he is

known to have surrendered his lease in October, 1386, perhaps for the purpose of attending to new duties, either as Member of Parliament, or as Justice of the Peace in Kent.

G 113 ff. From RR, 57 ff. The Fr. has "povreté," rendered *pore estat* here and in *Rom*, 61. Brusendorff (p. 398) suggested that Chaucer recalled his own translation. |In *BD*, 410, he rendered the same passage more literally.

115 ff. There is here a complex interweaving of Machaut (Dit, ll. 17–23), Guillaume de Lorris, Baudouin de Condé, and perhaps Boccaccio (Tes., iii, 6–7).

123 In the attribution of fragrance to the daisy (against the truth of fact) Chaucer again follows the tradition of the "marguerite" poets. Cf., for example, Machaut's Dit de la Marguerite, pp. 123, 125; Froissart's Pastourelle, xvii (Œuvres, II, 341 ff.), l. 66; and Deschamps's Marguerite ballade, no. 539 (Œuvres, SATF, III, 379 f.), l. 16. It is probable that in this particular the poets simply transferred to the daisy a quality which they were continually celebrating in the rose.

127 For the figure of the cold sword of winter cf. *SqT*, V, 57. Chaucer may have got it from Machaut, Roy de Navarre (Œuvres, SATF, I), ll. 34–36, or from RR, 5942 ff., or from the Anticlaudianus of Alanus de Insulis, vii, 8 (Migne, Pat. Lat., CCX, 557). With the passage as a whole cf. also (as noted above) *BD*, 410 ff. and RR, 55 ff., 124–25.

137 *sophistrye*, cf. "sofime" in RR, 21498, and the De Planctu Naturae of Alanus, "perdix . . . nunc venatorum sophismata . . . abhorrebat (Migne, CCX, 436; pointed out by E.S.A., N & Q, 8th Ser., III, 249–50.

139–40 Cf. RR, 703–04.

145 Cf. *PF*, 683.

153–74 This paragraph on the birds is replaced in G by the five lines (139–43) in which the lark heralds the approach of the God of Love. The passage in F is in the manner of the Roman de la Rose, and contains a number of verbal parallels of more or less uncertain significance. (See Miss Cipriani, PMLA, XXII, 594–95.) With ll. 139–40 of G Professor Lowes compares *SqT*, V, 399–400, on which he suggests Chaucer may have been occupied at about the same time. See also note to l. 127, above.

160 On *Daunger*, here used in the sense of the fastidiousness, offishness, of the Lady, see *Gen Prol*, I, 517, n.

162 The reference here is to the Christian doctrine of grace. On the application of this and other theological ideas to the affairs of love, see *KnT*, I, 3089, n., and *Tr*, i, 15 ff., n.

166 *Etik* (or *Étike*) here might refer either to a book or to a person. The term is several times applied to Horace by John of Salisbury, who, in Policraticus, viii, 13 (ed., Webb, Oxford, 1909, II, 317), introduces a quotation from the Satires (i, 2, 24) and a paraphrase from the Epistles (i, 18, 9) with "ut enim ait ethicus." Chaucer's quotation doubtless comes, directly or indirectly, from the latter passage. The version in Dante's Convivio, Canz., iii, 81 ff., may also have been in his mind. See further Lowes, MLN, XXV, 87–89.

171 ff. For the association of Flora and Zephyrus cf. RR, 8411 ff.

184 Chaucer's etymology of "daisy," from "day's eye," is entirely correct. The Anglo-Saxon is "dægeseage" ("dægesege"). The flower was probably so called because of its resemblance to the sun, to which the term primarily applied.

G 141 ff. Mr. Praz compares Purg., ii, 26 ff. See Monthly Criterion, VI, 22.

213 Cupid leads in Alceste, clothed in the likeness of a daisy. Her name is disclosed in F, 432, but through apparent inadvertence in composition Chaucer represents himself later (until l. 518) as failing to recognize her. This slip is common to both texts of the *Prologue*. In the G-version Alceste is named in l. 422, but the passage may possibly be regarded as an aside to the reader, and hence not inconsistent with what follows. On her story see the note to l. 510, below.

215 *fret*, a caul of gold wire; below, l. 228, it means rather an ornamental border. The origin of the word is uncertain; cf. OF. "frete," trellis-work, and AS. "frætwe," adornment.

217, 220 The rare word *flouroun*, here used in the sense of "petal," must have been taken by Chaucer from Froissart's Dittié, where it is twice employed in the same sense (ll. 166, 187). Professor Lowes argues that its use in the F-version, over against the more familiar *floures* in the G-version, is evidence of the priority of the former. But it is not quite certain that we are dealing here with an alteration by the poet. *Floures* (as Mr. Lowes himself notes) is the reading of part of the MSS. of the F-version, and its appearance in G may simply perpetuate a scribal blunder. *Flouroun* seems anyhow to have been Chaucer's first form.

221 *o perle*, a single stone. *Oriental*, eastern, means (as commonly, when applied to gems) of superior quality. For an allegorical interpretation of the crown see the note to l. 504, below.

227 *greves*, sprays, boughs; explained by some commentators as referring to the branches of the broom ("planta genesta"), worn by Richard as a badge. See the next note. *Rose-leves*, rose petals.

G 161 The *lylye flouris* in G replace a sun-crown in F. Those commentators who hold the *Prologue* to be allegorical understand both, as they do the *grene greves* above, to refer to Richard. On his monument there is a representation of the sun ascending behind clouds; and the lilies, it is pointed out, may betoken his claim to the French throne. Professor Bilderbeck, on the theory that F is the revised version, held that the lily crown was appropriate in 1385, when the war with France broke out, but that in 1390, in time of peace, the sun was substituted. Professor Lange, holding F to be the earlier version, argued that the sun was appropriate in 1385–86, and that the lilies were substituted in 1396 to symbolize Richard's marriage to the young French princess Isabella. But Lange also recognized Christian symbolism in the sun-crown, and compared the title "sol justitiae" given to Christ by Albertus Magnus. And again changing the symbol, he suggested that the sun, serving as a crown of gold, represents pure, heavenly love as opposed to the earthly passion celebrated in the *Troilus*. See Bilderbeck, Chaucer's Legend of Good Women, pp. 85 ff.; Lange, Angl., XLIV, 72 ff., XLIX, 173 ff., 267 ff.; and for critical comment, Langhans, Untersuchungen, pp. 216 ff., and Angl. L, 97 ff.; Koch, Angl., L, 64. Professor

E. P. Kuhl (PQ, XXIV, 35) has also argued for an allegorical interpretation of the fleur-de-lys. But the presence of any of this allegory in the passage is dubious, and the particular interpretations suggested are arbitrary and more or less inconsistent.

231 *for hevynesse*, to avoid heaviness. With this use of *for* cf. *Tr*, i, 928, and n.

232 ff. Cf. Dante, Purg., ii, 34, 37–39, and (more doubtfully) Inf., iii, 52–54. See M. Praz, Monthly Criterion, VI, 22 f.

G 179-202 These lines correspond to F, 276–99. If the former was the revised version the shift had the advantage of bringing closely together the sternness of the God of Love and the comfort of Alceste. The new order may also have suggested the transfer of the ballade from the dreamer to the Ladies.

247 In the F-version the ballade is sung by the poet, like the corresponding song in the Paradys d'Amours. The change in G makes it form a distinct part of the action. Froissart's ballade sings the praises of the daisy, and agrees in substance and language with other parts of the *Prologue*. Both pieces, with their lists of proper names, belong to a type of poetry common in the period. Cf., for example, Machaut's Voir-Dit (Soc. des Bibl. Fr., Paris, 1875), ll. 6753 ff. (also ll. 6045 ff.); Deschamps, nos. 313 (Œuvres, SATF, II, 335 ff.), 546 (III, 389 f.), 651 (IV, 110), 778 (IV, 279 f.), 1274 (VII, 13 ff.), and no. 42 of the Pièces attribuables à Deschamps (X, xlix f.). Professor R. M. Smith (MLN, LXVI, 29 ff.) notes that in some respects Froissart's ballade vi is closer to Chaucer's.

249 ff. Though Absalom's beauty was proverbial, the line about him seems to be derived from RR, 13870. *Marcia Catoun*, Marcia, the wife of Cato Uticensis. Chaucer may have had in mind Dante's references to her (Inf., iv, 128; Purg., i, 78 ff.). "Martia . . . Catonis" is mentioned, however, also by Geoffroi de Vinsauf, Poetria Nova, l. 1780 (ed. E. Faral, Les Arts Poétiques, etc., Paris, 1924, p. 251); cf. also Lucan, Pharsalia, ii, 326 ff. (which gives some account of her); and note Dante's comment on this passage in Convivio, iv, 28. See Kittredge, MP, VII, 482 f. The other characters in the ballade are easily recognizable, and the stories of several are told in the Legends that follow. Probably Chaucer intended to include all the women in the series (see F, 554), though the variation between the list here and those names in *ML Prol* suggests that his purpose was never exactly defined.

255, 262, 269 *My lady*, of version F, corresponds to "ma dame," in Froissart and ballade no. 42, attributed to Deschamps, cited in the note to l. 247, above, and is probably the original reading, for which G substituted *Alceste*.

265 *espied by thy chere*, whose condition is disclosed by thy appearance.

285 Such a multitude that not even the third or fourth part of it had ever been in this world, of all mankind; that is, simply, three or four times the whole population of the world since the time of Adam. The passage is probably an echo of Inf., iii, 55–57. See M. Praz, Monthly Criterion, VI, 21.

298 *in figurynge*, in emblem, symbol.

307 *furlong wey of space*, the time required to walk a furlong. See *MLT*, II, 557, and n.

308 ff. With the general situation here — the

accusation by the king, the queen's intercession, her reminder to her lord of his duty to be merciful, the pardon of the offender, and the imposition of a task — cf. the scene in *KnT*, I, 1696 ff., where Duke Theseus comes upon Palamon and Arcite fighting in the woods. It is likely that Chaucer carried over some or all of these features from his earlier work. In both cases, too, they are largely his invention, or at least not derived from his recognized sources.

314 *it am I;* for the idiom cf. *KnT*, I, 1736. *Ner,* nearer (the comparative of *neigh*).

321 *relyke,* treasure, precious possession; applied primarily to the relics of a saint. The use of the word as a term of endearment is striking, but not unnatural. It occurs in both English and French (see *Rom*, 2673, 2907), and the Welsh word, "crair," is commonly used in the same sense. Cf. Barddoniaeth Dafydd ab Gwilym, London, 1789, xii, 43; xxxi, 12; xxxii, 11.

329 Chaucer here testifies clearly that he translated the Roman de la Rose. Whether he ever completed it, or left it unfinished like so many of his works, is unknown; and it is also a matter of dispute whether he made any part of the existing Middle English translation. On this question see the Introduction and Explanatory Notes to that work. It happens that none of the three fragments contains such passages as would have given most offense to the God of Love.

G **260** *paramours,* doubtless adverbial here, "by way of romantic love." See *KnT*, I, 1155, and n.

332 The reference is of course to Chaucer's *Troilus*.

G **268–312** This passage on books occurs only in the G-version. By some commentators it is condemned as a digression and its omission from the F-version deemed an evidence of revision in that text. By others (who take G to be the later version) it is defended as germane to the argument and held to have been added in revision. In support of this latter opinion is the fact that some of the authors cited are those whom Chaucer used in his later writings.

The identity of *Valerye* is doubtful. Skeat (following Tyrwhitt) took the name to refer to the Epistola Valerii ad Rufinum ne uxorem ducat, printed among the works of Jerome, but now ascribed to Walter Map. (See Migne, Pat. Lat., XXX, 254 ff.; also Thomas Wright's edition of Map's De Nugis Curialium, Camden Soc., London, 1850, pp. 142 ff., the edition by M. R. James, in Anecdota Oxoniensia, XIV, 1914, pp. 143 ff., and the translation by Tupper and Ogle, Courtiers' Trifles, London, 1924, pp. 183 ff.) The mention of Jerome just below supports this identification, and although the work is primarily denunciatory, it does speak in praise of Penelope, Lucretia, and the Sabine women. Lounsbury and others take *Valerye* to be Valerius Maximus, who praises Portia, Julia, Lucretia, and the wives of Scipio, Q. Lucretius, and Lentulus. (See Tatlock, Dev. and Chron., p. 100, for a brief defense of this view.) A third possibility (in spite of Tatlock's flat denial) is Valerius Flaccus, whose Argonautica tells the stories of Hypsipyle and Medea (Bks. ii and vii). It is quoted by name in the Legend of Hypsipyle (l. 1457). But since Valerius is mentioned there quite incidentally, and only as authority for the names of the Argonauts

rather than for the story of Hypsipyle, he hardly seems to belong in the present list.

The other names are easily identified. *Titus* is Titus Livius — cited below (l. 1683) as an authority for the Legend of Lucretia; and *Claudyan* is the late Roman poet, author of the De Raptu Proserpinae. (On Chaucer's knowledge and use of him see R. A. Pratt, Spec., XXII, 19 ff.) *Jerome agayns Jovynyan* refers to a celebrated attack on marriage by St. Jerome (Migne, Pat. Lat., XXIII, 211 ff.). By the *epistel of Ovyde* is meant the Heroides, one of the chief sources of the individual legends that follow. The *Estoryal Myrour* is the Speculum Historiale, part of the encyclopaedic work of Vincent of Beauvais (first printed in Strassburg, 1469–73; there is no modern edition, but the Histoire Littéraire de la France, XVIII, contains a good synopsis).

Chaucer makes extensive use of the antifeminist satire of Jerome in the *Wife of Bath's Prologue* and the *Merchant's Tale*. The God of Love cites him here, and (probably) Valerius ad Rufinum, because they both give some testimony about good women. Cf. the *Franklin's Tale*, which derives from a long list of examples of chastity (V, 1364–1456). Valerius Maximus also is used in the *Wife of Bath's Prologue* (III, 642) and *Tale* (III, 1165).

Besides the preceding authorities, acknowledged by name, Chaucer may have remembered in writing the present passage Deschamps's Miroir de Mariage (Œuvres, SATF, IX), which, like Jerome, influenced the works of his last period. With G, 268–69 cf. Miroir, 9081 ff.; with ll. 276–77, Miroir, 9097–9100; and with ll. 301–04, Miroir, 9063–67. Furthermore, ll. 261–63 recall *WB Prol*, III, 707–10, a passage which was very likely written first.

G **273** There has been some discussion as to whether *sixty* indicates the actual size of Chaucer's library. On the use of sixty as a round number, generally implying magnitude, see Sister Mary Immaculate, MLQ, II, 59 ff. and Miss S. J. Tucker, RES, XXV, 152 ff.

G **277** There is possibly an echo of this line (and hence of the G-version) in Lydgate's Troy-Book, iii, 4362. (See C. Brown, ESt, XLVII, 59).

G **315** Possibly there is to be recognized here a friendly fling at Gower, who suggested, at the end of the Confessio Amantis (viii, 2941* ff., ed. G. C. Macaulay, III, 466), that Chaucer, like himself, was too old for the service of Love. This might explain the substitution, for *wrecches* of the F-version, of the more vivacious *olde foles* of the G-version. Cf. the probable reference to Gower in the *Introduction* to the *Man of Law's Tale* (II, 77–89) and the introduction to the Explanatory Notes on that passage. For the theory that the old age lines were removed in revision, also because of the passage in Gower, see Bilderbeck, pp. 105–06. (Professor Bilderbeck reasons, of course, on the assumption that F was the revised version.) The whole matter of a literary quarrel, and perhaps personal estrangement, between Chaucer and Gower is very dubious. The passages cited in evidence should not be taken too seriously.

338 With *Seynt Venus* cf. RR, 10827, 21086. The use of the term here was probably traditional rather than the result of deliberate adaptation to the device of the *Legend*. Cf. *WB Prol*, III, 604.

341 ff. A number of commentators have seen in

this speech a serious lecture on the duties of a king, addressed to Richard II by Anne in the person of Alceste. Cf. particularly Bilderbeck, *Legend of Good Women*, pp. 94 ff.; S. Moore, MLR, VII, 488 ff.; and Lowes's criticism of the view in PMLA, XX, 773 ff. For the objections to regarding Alceste as a symbol of the Queen see the introduction to the Explanatory Notes on *LGW*. The speech itself, it may be readily granted, can easily be applied to the circumstances of Richard's reign. In fact such an application is supported by a passage of similar import in *Lak of Stedfastnesse*, and Chaucer's sympathy with the sentiment expressed may perhaps be inferred from the *Parson's Tale* (X, 761 ff.). But this interpretation by no means carries with it the allegorical identification of Love with Richard. The political counsel, if intended, is quite incidental. Alceste's advice is intelligible and consistent throughout if understood to be addressed, as on its face it appears to be, to the God of Love. Even such incongruity as may be felt in the reference to *tirauntz of Lumbardye* serves a humorous purpose. The first suggestion for the whole exhortation may have come from the account of Theseus in the *KnT*, I, 1773 ff. Miss M. Galway (MLN, LX, 434) would trace the speech to the advice which Princess Joan, according to Malverne, addressed to Richard II when she effected a reconciliation between him and John of Gaunt in 1385. For extended illustration of the political doctrines of the speech, drawn from mediæval political writings, see Miss M. Schlauch, Spec., XX, 151 ff.

G 326   For the phraseology, which was doubtless proverbial, cf. RR. 12277 f.

352   Cf. RR, 1034.

353   *totelere*, tattler, properly a substantive; here used as a modifier in apposition.

381   *the philosophre*, probably Aristotle. See his advice to Alexander on the subject of kings, cited at length by Gower in Conf. Am., vii, 2149 ff. The treatment of the matter in the Nicomachean Ethics, Bk. v, may have been indirectly known to Chaucer. Cf. also Seneca, De Clementia, i, 3, 3 and 5, 4. For a repetition of the language and the rime, see *Intro.* to *MLT*, II, 25 f.

G 400-1   For the argument that these lines indicate Chaucer's advancing years when he wrote the G-version, see T. Kaut, MLN, XLIX, 87.

411   Cf. RR, 10923 f.

412-13   With the plea here made cf. the close of Deschamps's Lay Amoureux, ll. 275–end (Œuvres, SATF, II, 202), and Ovid's defense of himself at the beginning of the Remedia Amoris (except that Ovid declares himself to have been always a lover, whereas Chaucer usually maintained the attitude of an outsider in the service of lovers).

417 ff.   The references to *HF, BD, PF* and RR are clear enough. In the case of Palamon and Arcite it is a matter of dispute whether the poem so named was substantially identical with the *KnT*, or a quite different earlier version of the Teseida, probably in stanzas. On this matter see the introduction to the Explanatory Notes on the *KnT*. The remark (l. 421) that the story is little known refers to the Palamon and Arcite tale in general, not to Chaucer's English poem. It simply echoes a statement in Tes., i, 2. Most of the *balades, roundels,* and *virelayes* mentioned in l. 423 are lost. Indeed Professor Brusen-

dorff (pp. 432 f.) argued that the reference here is too conventional to prove that Chaucer ever composed any considerable number. But Chaucer's testimony is confirmed by Lydgate (Prologue to Bk. i of the Fall of Princes), though perhaps only on the authority of this passage (which his statement resembles in phraseology), and by Gower (Conf. Am., viii, 2943* ff.). Songs and lays are also included in the list of sinful works repudiated in the *Retractation*. But only a few of Chaucer's lyrical compositions seem to be preserved. No real virelay of his is known, and only two roundels (*Merciles Beaute*, and *PF* 680 ff.); and of the twelve ballades or ballade-groups attributed to him only three or four could properly be described as hymns for the God of Love. Professor Manly (Cant. Tales, p. 503) suggests that Chaucer, who was working in the technique of Machaut, probably composed the music as well as the words of his songs.

The *lyf . . . of Seynt Cecile* (l. 426) is doubtless the *Second Nun's Tale*, which bears every mark of being an early work. *Origenes upon the Maudeleyne* (l. 428), which is lost, is supposed to have been a translation of the homily De Maria Magdalena, commonly attributed to Origen. This identification was suggested by Tyrwhitt, Glossary, s.v. Origenes, with a reference to Opera Origenis (Paris, 1604, II, 291 ff.).

The term *other holynesse* (l. 424) apparently means "another religion"; the works that follow belong rather to Christianity than to the religion of the God of Love.

G 414   *the Wreched Engendrynge of Mankynde*, apparently a lost translation, complete or partial, of the Latin prose treatise of Pope Innocent III, De Contemptu Mundi sive De Miseria Conditionis Humanae (Migne, Pat. Lat., CCXVII, 701 ff.). The form and extent of Chaucer's version are unknown. From the fact that passages from Innocent appear in *ML Prol* and *Tale*, Skeat inferred that Chaucer made a translation in seven-line stanzas; but the citations would have been adapted in any case to the form of the work in which they were used. Professor Lowes suggested that the rendering was in prose, and that Chaucer at one time meant to assign it to the Man of Law, who protests that he cannot tell his tale in verse. (See II, 96, and the introductory note to *ML Headlink*.) This is possible, though entirely uncertain. On the date of the translation positive proof is also lacking. But the use of the material in *ML Prol* and *Tale* favors the supposition that Chaucer was occupied with Innocent about 1390; and this would also explain the mention of the work in the revised version of the *LGW Prol.* Professor Carleton Brown, in PMLA, L, 997 ff., proposed to identify the *Wreched Engendrynge* with *An Holy Medytacion*, ascribed to Lydgate and printed in H. N. McCracken's Minor Poems of John Lydgate, I, pp. 43–48. The identification was questioned by Tatlock, MLN, LI, 275 ff., and reasserted by Brown, ibid., pp. 296 ff.

432   *Quene of Trace.* On the confusion here between Thrace and Thessaly see F. P. Magoun, Jr., Med. Stud., XV, 132.

452   A common proverb: "Bis dat qui cito dat." Cf. *Mel*, VII, 1794 ff.; Skeat, EE Prov., p. 88, no. 210; Haeckel, p. 25, nos. 81, 82.

464-65   That is, an honest man has no participation in the deed of a thief. Cf. Haeckel, p. 37, no. 126.

490 Chaucer takes here his habitual attitude of an outsider in love.

496–97 *Eltham,* seven miles from London; *Sheene,* now Richmond. These lines are found in the F-version only. Their addition there, if F is the later version, is hard to explain. Both Koch and Langhans, holding that opinion, explain away the couplet as an interpolation, which Langhans ascribes to Lydgate. (See ESt, LV, 178; Angl., L, 74.) If, however, G is the revised form, the excision of the passage is natural. After the death of Anne, in 1394, Richard at once forsook the royal residence of Shene and ordered its destruction. Chaucer might well have preferred not to keep lines which would perpetuate the association of the poem with the place. (References to Shene in chronicles later than the time of the supposed destruction of the manor house appear to show that the King's command was not fully carried out. For such passages, see Lowes, MP, VIII, 331, n. and 334, n.)

503 On this line, which Chaucer repeats in five places in nearly identical form, see *KnT,* I, 1761, n.

504 Professor Lange finds in this line an allusion to the allegorical character of Alceste. According to his general theory she stands for the Queen, whose name, "Anna," signifies (in Hebrew) "gratia," grace, mercy. So she discloses by her action *what* she is. She wears a crown of pearl (l. 221, above) because in the symbolism of precious stones the pearl stands for "gratia," mercy. See Angl., XLIV, 213 ff.; and for objections, Langhans, ibid., pp. 337 ff., and L, 87 ff.; Koch, ibid., L, 62.

510 Alcestis was the wife of Admetus, king of Pherae in Thessaly. To prolong her husband's life she consented to die in his stead. Afterwards she was brought back to him from the lower world by Hercules. As an ancient type of wifely devotion she was a natural choice for the chief heroine of the *Legend;* but the work was broken off before her separate story was reached. The source from which Chaucer derived the brief account of her given here is unknown; it might have been from Hyginus, Fable li, or from Boccaccio, De Gen. Deor., xiii, 1, though the statements of neither correspond precisely to his. The story of the transformation into a daisy (l. 512) seems to have been Chaucer's own invention. Ovid's Metamorphoses, in which Clytie, Daphne, Narcissus, Crocus, and Hyacinthus were all changed into flowers, perhaps furnished a suggestion; and a further hint may have come from Froissart's Dittié, ll. 69 ff., which tells how the tears of Herès for her husband Cepheï were turned into daisies.

518 The discrepancy between this line and l. 432, where Alceste has already told her name, cannot be quite explained away. It is probably due to the fact that Chaucer was following Froissart (Paradys d'Amours, ll. 358–60) so closely that he overlooked for the moment what had gone before in his own poem. The blunder was not corrected in revision. Professor Langhans would adjust matters by omitting the comma after *Alceste* and interpreting, "Is this good Alceste the daisy, etc.?" But this is hardly consistent with the rest of the speech.

526 *Agaton,* apparently Agatho, an Athenian tragic poet and friend of Plato. The reason for his association with Alcestis may be that Plato's Symposium, which tells her story, was known as Agatho's Feast. (It is called Agathonis Convivium by Macrobius, Saturnalia, ii, 1. See Hales, MLQ, I, 5 ff.) The direct source of Chaucer's information is unknown. His spelling, *Agaton,* suggests an Italian original, and instances of the occurrence of the name in Dante (Purg., xxii, 107), and Boccaccio (Amorosa Visione, v, 50) have been pointed out; yet neither of these passages would have led Chaucer to associate Agatho with Alcestis.

531 *Cibella,* Cybela or Cybele, a Phrygian goddess of fertility; possibly suggested to Chaucer by the mention of Ceres in Froissart's Dittié, ll. 105 ff.

533 "And Mars gave redness to her crown"; with reference to the red tips of the petals. For the association of Mars with the color red see *KnT,* I, 1747, n.

540 In the F-version of the ballade (ll. 249 ff.) Alceste is not mentioned by name. In the G-text she appears in the refrain, and this reproach of the God of Love was therefore canceled.

542 *kalender,* almanac; hence guide, example, model.

562 In putting these words into the mouth of the God of Love Chaucer may have had in mind, and have expected his readers to recall, the similar situation in Machaut's Jugement dou Roy de Navarre and the Trésor Amoureux (ascribed to Froissart, Œuvres, III, 52 ff., but of doubtful authority), where very special meters are prescribed (see Kittredge, MP, VII, 471 ff.).

The Legend of Cleopatra

Chaucer apparently used the account of Cleopatra in Boccaccio's De Casibus, vi, 15, or that in the De Claris Mulieribus, cap. lxxxvi, or both. Whether he had other literary sources is uncertain. Bech (Angl., V, 314 ff.) thought he followed Florus (Epitome Rerum Romanorum, iv, 11; modern editions, ii, 21) for certain details, but the only striking parallel is that of the "purple sails," and these are mentioned, as Professor Shannon has pointed out (pp. 186 f.), in both of Boccaccio's accounts. Skeat noted other parallel features in Plutarch, and suggested that Chaucer might possibly have known him in a Latin translation. In any case Chaucer appears to have handled his sources freely, and the description of the battle of Actium is thoroughly mediæval. Perhaps also the serpent-pit, in the account of Cleopatra's death, may have been taken by Chaucer from contemporary life or story. Gower's reference to Cleopatra, in Conf. Am., viii, 2573 ff., is probably based upon Chaucer.

580 *Tholome,* Ptolemy, the name of Cleopatra's father and two brothers. The reference here is probably to the elder brother, in conjunction with whom she was appointed queen after her father's death (B.C. 51). He perished in the Alexandrine War, and she then reigned in conjunction, nominally, with her younger brother, a mere child. In less than four years she procured his murder, and became sole ruler.

583 *on a tyme,* soon after the battle of Philippi (B.C. 42).

589 For this commonplace doctrine about Fortune cf. *MkT,* especially VII, 2136 ff., 2763 ff.

592 After the death of his first wife, Fulvia,

Antony married Octavia, the sister of Augustus, whom he deserted for Cleopatra.

600 Cf. *KnT*, I, 1817, and n.

614 ff. The general idea here, *for to make shortly is the beste*, is of course common in Chaucer. The particular figure in l. 621, a variation on more familiar phrases, may have been suggested by a description of Cleopatra's barge in the source of the story.

624 *Octovyan*, Octavianus, better known as the Emperor Augustus.

629 ff. Nearly all the features of this account of the battle of Actium were apparently taken by Chaucer from descriptions of sea battles of his own time. In 1901 Professor W. P. Ker, in his introduction to Berners's translation of Froissart (Tudor Translations, London, 1901–03, I, lxxviii), pointed to Froissart's account of the battle of La Rochelle (1372) as possibly the original of this passage. Schofield (Kittredge Anniversary Papers, pp. 139 ff.) collected excellent illustrations from Froissart's description of the battles of Sluys (1340) and Espagnols-sur-Mer (1350), and from the English romance of Richard Coeur de Lion (ed. Brunner, Wiener Beiträge, XLII), ll. 2639 ff. The relevant passages in Froissart are bk. i, chaps. 50 and 303–05 of Johnes's translation, London, 1839 (Berners, ch. 50, 297–99), and the addition, printed in Johnes, I, 197 ff. Schofield, supposing the *Legend* to have been written between 1385 and 1387, showed that there was an intense interest in naval affairs in England during those years. But nothing in his argument stands in the way of the theory that the Cleopatra was written at an earlier date. Froissart's first book was finished about 1373. And in any case it need not be assumed that Chaucer used him as a literary source.

The employment of alliteration is noteworthy through a large part of this description. The same device is used with similar effect in the account of the tournament in *KnT* (I, 2601 ff.). See the note on that passage.

634 With the general situation here cf. that when Edward III set out to meet the Spaniards in the battle of Espagnols-sur-Mer (Froissart, tr. Johnes, I, 197 ff.; not in Berners's version). On the *see*, the Sinus Ambracius or modern Gulf of Arta, see Magoun, Med. Stud., XV, 109.

636 "And try to attack with the sun at their back." The English followed precisely this method in the battle of Sluys (Froissart, chap. 50; Johnes, I, 72).

637 The *gonne* certainly means "cannon," and not (as Skeat held) the "missile" hurled therefrom. With *out gooth*, in the sense "goes off, is discharged," Professor Webster (MP, XXV, 292) compares "russhe out" in Skelton's Garland of Laurel, l. 623.

639 For the use of great stones in attempts to sink the enemy cf. the battle of Espagnols and La Rochelle (Johnes, I, 197 ff., 472 f.).

640 The grapnels (hooks for laying hold of vessels) and the shearing-hooks (used to cut their ropes) are mentioned in the description of Sluys, Espagnols, and La Rochelle.

642 For a similar boarding exploit cf. Espagnols (Johnes, I, 199); and also an account of a battle between the French and English in 1217 (Nicolas, History of the Royal Navy, London, 1847, I, 177–81).

645 For the use of spears in sea-fights cf. a battle off Guernsey (Johnes, bk. i, chap. 91), and La Rochelle (chap. 305).

648 The *pesen* are explained by Skeat as "peas," poured on the hatches to make them too slippery for the boarding party. Because of the lack of evidence of this practice, Schofield took the passage to refer rather to the use of pitch, which, according to Jean de Meun's Art de Chevalerie (a translation of Vegetius's De Re Militari), ed. Robert, SATF, 1897, p. 174, was poured on the decks of enemies' ships for the purpose of spreading wild fire (or "Greek fire"). Such use of burning oil is mentioned in an account of a sea fight with the Saracens in 1190 (Itinerarium Regis Ricardi, ed. Stubbs, Rolls Series, 1864, p. 81). Cf. also the romance of Richard Coeur de Lion, ll. 2643 ff. A more remote example, in which "Greek fire" figures, is afforded by the description of a battle between Greeks and Russes (c. 940) in the Russian Primary Chronicle, tr. S. H. Cross, [Harv.] Stud. and Notes, XII, 158. This explanation implies a misunderstanding by Chaucer of some written source; for *pesen* can hardly have been an English word for pitch. The French "pois" (pitch) on the other hand could easily have been mistaken for "pois" (peas). But Professor Webster (MP, XXV, 291) found two passages which he presented in support of the older interpretation that peas were poured on the decks to make them slippery. In both cases, to be sure, soap or grease is the substance employed or recommended. His first citation is from an account of a sea-fight off Naples in 1283, given in Saba Malaspina's chronicle (Rosario Gregorio, Bibl. Scriptorum qui Res in Sicilia Gestas sub Aragonum Imperio Retulere, Panormi, 1791–92, II, 407). The second is from Aegidius Romanus, De Regimine Principum, bk. iii, part 3, ch. 23. Mr. Webster notes that the grease was poured on the enemy's deck, not on one's own. Finding the attempts to explain *pesen* desperate, Professor F. J. Mather, Jr., proposed to emend to *resyn* (JEGP, XLIII, 375 ff.), and Professor R. M. Smith to *peires*, = *pierres*, "stones" (JEGP, XLIV, 56 ff.). See also W. T. Furniss, MLN, LXVIII, 115 ff., for a parallel passage from Gascoigne which actually refers to a similar use of peas at the battle of Lepanto.

649 The quicklime was carried to be thrown into the enemies' eyes. See N & Q, 5th Ser., X, 188; Strutt, Manners and Customs, London, 1774–76, II, 11; and Aegidius Romanus, in the chapter cited.

651 Proverbial, cf. *Tr*, iii, 615, n.

653 It is not certain whether *to-go* is to be regarded as a third plural present indicative of a compound with *to-*, meaning "scatter," or as the infinitive of the simple verb. On the whole the compound makes the best sense here, and the historical or narrative use of the infinitive has slight support in Chaucer. Cf. *to laughe, Tr*, ii, 1108; and see J. S. Kenyon, The Syntax of the Infinitive in Chaucer, Ch. Soc., 1909, pp. 82 f.

654 With the *purpre sayl* cf. Boccaccio's De Claris Mulieribus, "ornata purpureis velis et aurea classe," and his De Casibus, "cum aurata naui, velisque purpureis"; and also the Epitome of Florus, "cum aurea puppe veloque purpureo."

655 For the comparison, which was a commonplace, see RR, 15621–22.

662 Antony really stabbed himself a year later

at Alexandria. In hastening the action Chaucer perhaps followed Florus.

672 The description of the shrine again shows a resemblance to Florus.

678-80, 696-702 This account of Cleopatra's death in a pit of snakes seems to be peculiar to Chaucer and Gower (Conf. Am., viii, 2573–75). The earlier authorities, ancient and mediæval, usually say that she died from the bite of an asp or serpent in the mausoleum of Antony (in case they mention any place at all), and some of them record an alternative tradition that she died by poison. According to the Old French Histoire de Jules César (of Jehan de Tuim), she went naked into a pit to meet her death; but there is no mention of the serpents. References to confinement in a serpent-pit are by no means uncommon, however, in mediæval literature. There is a familiar instance in the romance of Bevis of Hampton, and other examples in considerable number have been collected by Tatlock (MLN, XXIX, 99 f.), C. Brown (ibid., pp. 198–99), and Griffith (Manly Anniversary Studies, p. 38). Dr. F. E. Faverty, in an unpublished Harvard dissertation (1930) on Legends of Joseph, adds references to the Gesta Romanorum, ed. Oesterley, Berlin, 1872, pp. 556, 739; G. H. Gerould, North-English Homily Collection, Oxford diss., 1902, pp. 41–42; E. Hull, The Cuchullin Saga, London, 1898, p. 283. Many of these instances occur in the lives of saints, and Chaucer, as Dr. Griffith suggests, may have been led to think of them by his representation of Cleopatra as a martyr. Or, as Professor Tatlock observes, he may have devised this horrible form of death simply because he knew serpent-pits to be common in Africa. This would be one of the most striking cases of his use of local color.

The Legend of Thisbe

Chaucer's version is based on Ovid's Met., iv, 55–166. His rendering is at once close in substance and free and natural in form. The omission of all mention of the mulberry-tree is noteworthy. See Shannon, pp. 190 ff. Gower has the same story in the Conf. Am., iii, 1331 ff. For a comparison of his version with Chaucer's see Macaulay, Works of Gower, Oxford, 1899–1902, II, 497 f., and Meech, PMLA, XLVI, 201, n. Professor Meech includes the Ovide Moralisé in a triangular comparison, but finds it impossible to determine whether either English version was influenced by the French. The versions of Chaucer and Gower appear to be related, but it is hard to say which poet was the borrower.

707 *Semyramus*, Semiramis, the mythical queen who was said to have built the walls of Babylon.

719-20 The gossip of the matchmaking women is an addition of Chaucer's.

725 *Naso*, Publius Ovidius Naso.

735 "Cover [imperative] the coal, and the fire becomes hotter." Cf. *Tr*, ii, 538 f., n.

736 *ten so wod*, ten times as mad. Cf. l. 2291, below.

741 *deere ynogh a myte*, to the slightest extent; see Glossary, s.v. *myte*. With the phrase, which is rather strangely employed, cf. *CYT*, VIII, 795.

745 The comparison to the confessional is Chaucer's. Ovid has simply "murmure . . . minimo" (l. 70).

762 *covered*, recovered. *Colde*, destructive, fatal; for this use cf. *NPT*, VII, 3256, and n.

785 *Nynus*, the husband of Semiramis and founder of Nineveh.

797 *Ywympled*, wearing a covering over her neck and about her face, like the wimple of a nun.

811 *with dredful fot*, "timido pede" (l. 100). The phrase occurs again in *KnT*, I, 1479.

917-18 Cf. RR, 14145 (not closely parallel).

The Legend of Dido

The main source is Virgil's Aeneid, with incidental use of the Heroides, vii. In the treatment of the character of Dido the influence of Ovid is especially to be recognized. See Shannon, pp. 196 ff. The Old French Roman d'Eneas, which combines Virgil and Ovid in a somewhat similar fashion, was probably known to Chaucer and may have been utilized in the legend.

For an earlier rendering by Chaucer of the story of Dido see HF, 151–382.

924 Mantua was Virgil's birthplace. With ll. 924–7 C. O. Chapman compares Dante, Purg., xxii, 64–9. See TLS, Aug. 29, 1952, p. 565.

926 With the figure of the lantern cf. Dante, Purg., i, 43.

931 For Sinon's stratagem of the wooden horse see Aen., ii, 57–267.

934 Hector's ghost advised Aeneas to take flight (Aen., ii, 270 ff.).

936 *Ylioun*, Ilium, properly only another name for Troy, but taken by mediæval writers to mean the royal palace or citadel. Cf. *MLT*, II, 289.

939 The death of Priam at the hands of Pyrrhus is related in Aen., ii, 533 ff.

940 Cf. Aen., ii, 594 ff.

941 Cf. Aen., ii, 723.

945 Cf. Aen., ii, 738.

947 He had gone back to seek Creusa. (But Chaucer omits the incident of Creusa's ghost.)

950 ff. Chaucer passed rapidly over the contents of Bk. iii of the Aeneid.

959 *Libie*, Libya, on the northern coast of Africa.

958-1102 These lines correspond in general to Aen., i, 305–642.

971 *an hunteresse*, Venus in the disguise of an huntress.

978-82 From Aen., i, 321–24.

982 *Ytukked up*, with robe tucked up; "succinctam."

983-93 From Aen., i, 325–40.

994-1014 Cf. Aen., i, 341–414.

1005 *Sytheo*, Sichaeus. The confusion of c and t is common in MSS. The ending in -o is perhaps due to Italian influence: cf. Inf., v. 62, "Sicheo."

1022 Cf. Aen., i, 412, 516.

1039 The audacity of this comparison is not to be explained away on the ground that Jupiter was in Chaucer's mind or that Virgil compares Dido to Diana. Mediæval taste differed from modern in speaking of sacred persons and things. Cf. *SqT*, V, 555, and n.

1047-60 Cf. Aen., i, 509–612.

1048 *wende han loren*, supposed he had lost.

1061-65 From Aen., i, 613–14.

1066-74 From Aen., i, 588–91.

1072 *after Venus,* taking after Venus, his mother.

1086–1102 From Aen., i, 617–42.

1103–27 Chaucer here departs from Virgil and gives the description a decidedly mediæval cast.

1104 *swolow,* probably "whirlpool," though the "mouth" of hell would make good sense.

1110 Cf. *SqT,* V, 294.

1114 ff. In this description of Dido's gift Chaucer again departs from Virgil. Mr. E. B. Atwood (in Spec., XIII, 454 ff.) suggested that he utilized Aen., v, 570–92 and vii, 274–79.

1122 *with floreyns newe ybete,* together with florins newly struck.

1128–49 From Aen., i, 643–722.

1153 With this brief remark Chaucer passes over Virgil's second book.

1162–1351 These lines cover the ground of the fourth book of the Aeneid.

1170–81 From Aen., iv, 9–29.

1182 *coude hire good,* see *ML Epil,* II, 1169, n., and Glossary under *can.*

1183 In the Aeneid Anna does not definitely advise against marriage. But, as Professor Shannon observes, her long series of rhetorical questions might be taken as indicating opposition.

1187 Proverbial; see Haeckel, p. 1, no. 1.

1188–1211 From Aen., iv, 129 ff.

1191 *An huntyng,* on hunting, a-hunting (as also in l. 1211). The omission of the verb of motion after *wol* is idiomatic.

1198 The comparison to paper was unusual. Dafydd ap Gwilym applies it once to the fair skin of a lady ("lliw papir," London, 1789, p. 298).

1204 This line is nearly the same as *KnT,* I, 1502.

1205 *A litel wyr,* a small bit.

1212–31 From Aen., iv, 154–70.

1213 Terms of stimulation and encouragement. *Go bet,* go faster, hurry up; *pryke thow,* use the spurs; *lat gon,* let (the dogs) go.

1218 ff. Chaucer ignores the fact that according to the Aeneid the storm was prearranged by Juno and Venus.

1231 *gladnesse;* perhaps Chaucer mistook Virgil's "leti" (iv, 169) for "letitie" or some form of the adj. "laetus" ("letus").

1232–37 Chaucer adds this scene. He emphasizes the falseness and fickleness of Æneas, and again ignores, or minimizes the importance of the intervention of the gods.

1242 Virgil's description of Fame, which Chaucer used in *HF,* 1360 ff., is here omitted.

1244 On the omission of the subject, implied in what precedes, see *Gen Prol,* I, 33, n.

1245 *Yarbas,* Iarbas (Aen., iv, 196).

1254–84 Original with Chaucer.

1272 *devyses,* heraldic decorations.

1295–99 Cf. Aen., iv, 351–59.

1305 *what woman,* what sort of woman.

1310 The sacrifice is in Virgil (iv, 452 ff.); the saints' shrines (*halwes*) are Chaucer's mediæval addition.

1311–24 There is little of all this in Virgil.

1323 The appeal of pregnancy is suggested by Ovid, though Virgil intimates that there was no child.

1329 For the statement that Aeneas stole away while Dido was asleep — another departure from

Virgil's account — Mr. Atwood (in Spec., XIII, 456) suggests that Chaucer was influenced by the Excidium Troie (MS. Rawl. D. 893, fol. 85 r. b.).

1331 *Lavyne,* Lavinia (Aen., vii, 359). For the form, cf. *HF,* 458, and n.

1332 On the *cloth* and the *swerd* see Aen., iv, 648 and 646.

1338–40 From Aen., iv, 651–53.

1346 *kire norice,* Barce, the nurse of Sichaeus (Aen., iv, 632).

1352 *myn auctour,* Ovid. The *lettre* is based upon Heroides, vii, 1–8. Ll. 1357 and 1360 are so closely paralleled in Filippo's translation of Ovid that it appears probable that Chaucer consulted the Italian version. See PMLA, XLV, 114–15.

1355 f. Proverbial; cf. *PF,* 342, n.

The Legend of Hypsipyle and Medea

For the stories of Hypsipyle and Medea Chaucer went to Ovid's Metamorphoses, vii, and his Heroides, vi and xii, and to Guido Delle Colonne's Historia Trojana, Bk. i. He made most use of Guido. He seems incidentally to have consulted the Argonautica of Valerius Flaccus, which he cites by name; and he may also have used Statius, Thebaid, v, and Hyginus, Fables, xiv and xv. For detailed comparisons see Shannon, pp. 208 ff. The character of Medea, which (as Professor Shannon observes) bears some resemblance to that of Criseyde, was particularly influenced by Ovid's portrayal of her in the Heroides.

1368–95 The introductory lines on Jason are not in the sources. With ll. 1371–72 may be compared Dante's Inf., xviii, 85, 91 ff.

1371 *recleymyng,* enticement; used primarily of calling back a hawk.

1383 The figure of the horn possibly comes from Inf., xix, 5, where it refers to the public crying of the misdeeds of condemned criminals. But the phrase *Have at thee* suggests that Chaucer had in mind rather the hunter's horn, sounded to start the pursuit of the game.

1389 *et,* eateth (contr. pres.).

1396 *Guido* is clearly the right reading here, and not *Ovyde.* The Historia Trojana begins with the story of Jason, and Chaucer follows it, at least as far as l. 1455.

1397 *Pelleus,* Guido's spelling ("Peleus"), properly Pelias.

1398 *Eson,* Aeson, the father of Jason.

1416 "Without incurring blame in the accomplishment of his purpose."

1425 *Colcos,* Colchis. Though not really an island it is so called ("insula") by Guido.

1438 *Oetes,* Guido's form for Aeetes, king of Colchis and father of Medea.

1453 *Argus,* the builder of the Argo.

1457 The Argonautica of Valerius Flaccus, Bk. i, contains a long list of the Argonauts. Possibly Chaucer took this reference at second hand from Dares (De Excidio Trojae Historia, i): "sed qui vult eos cognoscere, Argonautas legat." But the accurate citation of the title supports the theory that he knew Valerius Flaccus at first hand, and the influence of the Argonautica is perhaps to be recognized also in *HF,* 1572 and *Tr,* v, 8. On the whole question see Shannon, pp. 340 ff.

1459 *Philotetes,* Guido's spelling for Philoctetes.

1463 *Lemnon,* Lemnos. Cf. Heroides, vi, 50, 117, 136.

1467 *Ysiphele,* Hypsipyle, daughter of Thoas and queen of Lemnos. The account of her which follows contains circumstances not derived from Ovid and not in agreement with the narratives of Statius, Valerius Flaccus, or Hyginus. Chaucer may have invented them. He characteristically develops the rôle of Hercules.

1479 In the ancient tradition the messenger was a woman (Iphinoe, according to Valerius Flaccus, ii, 327). The Lemnian women had killed all the men on the island except Thoas, whom Hypsipyle saved.

1509 Cf. Argonautica, ii, 351.

1524 With Chaucer's use of Hercules as an ally and messenger of Jason, which is not paralleled in the authorities, Professor Shannon compares the part played by Achates in the story of Dido in the Aeneid. The substitution of a male messenger in ll. 1479 ff., above, he suggests may be due to the fact that Chaucer had the same incident in mind.

1526 ff. This is a conventional description of a courtly lover. Cf., for closely similar phraseology, *NPT,* VII, 2913 ff.

1529 The "three points" follow in ll. 1530–33.

1538 "Would God that I had given my blood and flesh, provided that I might still live, if only he had a worthy wife." This seems to mean: "I would gladly give my flesh and blood to get him a worthy wife, if only I could live to see the outcome."

1546 *To come to hous upon,* to become familiar with.

1558 *Th'origynal,* probably Heroides, vi, which is the letter referred to in l. 1564. But it remains uncertain how much knowledge Chaucer had of the other accounts mentioned above.

1580–1655 The account here is mainly based upon Guido's Historia, Bk. ii.

1582 Cf. Guido, "sicut appetit materia semper formam." But in Guido the application is made to the dissoluteness of woman. For further citations illustrating the general doctrine, see W. R. Moses, MLN, XLIX, 226 ff.

1590 *Jaconitos,* Iaconites.

1603–06 The description of Jason may be reminiscent of Dante's Inf., xviii, 85 ff.

1609 *as* seems here to be employed in the unusual causal sense, "inasmuch as," "since"; perhaps however, it means "as if." For the reference to *Fortune,* or fate, cf. Her., xii, 35.

1661 Creon's daughter was named Creusa. See Her., xii, 53–54.

1667 *vassellage,* prowess (here used ironically).

1670 Cf. Her., xii, particularly ll. 11 ff. Here again certain of Chaucer's phrases (ll. 1673, 1675) point to the use of Filippo's Italian translation.

The Legend of Lucrece

Chaucer refers both to Livy (i, 57–59) and to Ovid (Fasti, ii, 685–852), but seems to have made use of the latter only. He probably cited Livy merely for the authority of his name, as in the *Physician's Tale,* where the actual source was the Roman de la Rose. For a detailed comparison of the authorities see Shannon, pp. 220 ff.

1680–93 These lines form Chaucer's introduction to the story.

1682 *the laste kyng Tarquinius,* Tarquinius Superbus.

1690 *The grete Austyn,* St. Augustine, who comments on the story in his De Civitate Dei, i, 19. *Oure legende* (l. 1689) is doubtless the Legenda Aurea, which because of its familiar use would be not unnaturally accompanied by the "domestic our." The reference is wholly in keeping with the treatment of St. Augustine by Jacobus Januensis.

1694 From this point Chaucer closely follows Ovid, Fasti, ii, 721. *Ardea,* capital of the Rutuli, in Latium.

1696 *and lytel wroughten,* and accomplished little.

1698 "Tarquinius iuuenis," Tarquinius Sextus, son of Tarquinius Superbus. He did not occupy the throne.

1705 *Colatyn,* not directly named in Ovid's account. Chaucer may have taken the name from Livy or Augustine.

1710 The location at Rome instead of Collatia may be due to a misunderstanding of Ovid, who is not very clear. Livy is explicit about Collatia.

1721 *oure bok,* Ovid, who mentions the wool at l. 742.

1725 *how shal it be,* apparently in the sense, "How is it said to be?" Cf. the use of "soll" in German, and see *HF,* 2053, n.

1729 This line (as Skeat noted) is possibly due to a misunderstanding of Ovid's ll. 751–52: "sed enim temerarius ille Est meus et stricto quolibet ense ruit."

1771 "Or an evil inclination, with malice."

1773 For this proverbial expression, which is in the source (l. 782), and occurs in numerous forms, cf. *Tr,* iv, 600–01, and *Thop,* VII, 830–32, n.

1778 ff. The statement that Tarquin came secretly into the house of Lucrece is not consistent with either Ovid or Livy. Professor Shannon suggests that Chaucer may have wished to emphasize her innocence.

1781 *stalke,* move stealthily; cf. *KnT,* I, 1479; *ClT,* V, 525; and Shakespeare's Lucrece, l. 365.

1812–26 These lines are Chaucer's; Ovid says simply: "Succubuit famae victa puella metu" (l. 810).

1839–49 This also does not exactly correspond to anything in Ovid. Ll. 1847–49 are rather closely paralleled in Livy (i, 58), and perhaps afford the strongest argument for the view that Chaucer made use of that version of the story.

1841 f. Proverbial; cf. *Tr,* iii, 114, n.

1871 Lucretia's canonization here is not simply part of the device of the Legend. As Skeat observes, it was probably suggested to Chaucer by the fact that Ovid tells her tale in the Fasti under the date (Feb. 24) which was commemorated as "Fuga Tarquinii Superbi." Thus she appeared to have a place on the calendar, like a Christian saint. Professor Shannon notes further, as affording a kind of suggestion of the veneration of saints, that Brutus took oath by Lucretia's spirit, which would become a divinity to him ("perque tuos manes, qui mihi numen erunt"), to drive out the Tarquins.

1881 The reference is to the Syro-Phoenician woman (Matt. xv, 28), unless Chaucer confused her story with that of the centurion (Matt. viii, 10; Luke vii, 9).

The Legend of Ariadne

The sources have been pretty definitely ascertained. The beginning is from Ovid, Met., vii, 456–58; viii, 6 ff., and the conclusion from his Heroides, x. For the main narrative Bech (Angl., V, 337 ff.) and Skeat long ago noted parallels in Plutarch's Theseus, of which Chaucer might have known a Latin version; in Boccaccio's De Gen. Deor., xi, 27, 29, 30; in Aen., vi, 20–30; and in Hyginus, Fables, xli–xliii. (Cf. also C. G. Child, MLN, XI, 482 ff., and Shannon, pp. 228 ff.) But Mr. Meech (PMLA, XLV, 116 ff., and, especially, XLVI, 182 ff., both cited here below by pages) has shown that most of Chaucer's modifications and expansions of Ovid's narrative can be explained by the Ovide Moralisé or Filippo's Italian translation of the Heroides (the introduction to the Epistle of Phaedra). To the former source he ascribes, besides various details, the account of the Athenian tribute and of Theseus' adventures in Crete, the introduction of Phaedra, and "the general content of some of the speeches of Theseus and the daughters of Minos." From the latter he would derive the reference to Daedalus, the betrothal of Phaedra to Hippolytus, and the drowning of Aegeus. Various details, as Mr. Meech suggests, may have come from glosses on Ovid. He is perhaps too positive in excluding all influence of Boccaccio's De Gen. Deor. A contemporary source for the prison scene was recognized by Lowes in the Teseida (PMLA, XX, 803 ff.). See the note to ll. 1960 ff. On the use of Catullus, suggested by Professor Shannon but highly improbable, see the note to ll. 1891 f.

1886 The confusion of Minos, the judge of the lower world, with Minos, the king of Crete, who was usually regarded as his grandson, has been traced to the De Gen. Deor., xi, 26. Mr. Meech (p. 185) notes that the identification is made in numerous glosses on the Metamorphoses, and suggests that Chaucer found it in his copy.

1887 The mention of the lot was perhaps due to Aen., vi, 431.

1891 f. Professor Shannon (pp. 368 f.) suggests that the idea of retribution sent upon Theseus by the gods (which is not clearly expressed by Ovid), may have come from Catullus, Carmen lxiv, 188–248, a poem which he thinks also influenced HF, 269–85. But it is Minos, not Theseus, upon whom the gods are here said to take vengeance, and Chaucer does not develop at all Catullus's idea of poetic justice in the fate of Theseus. See J. A. S. McPeek, MLN, XLVI, 299 ff. (quoting G. L. Kittredge). Mr. McPeek shows also (pp. 295 ff.) that the passage in the *House of Fame* is sufficiently explained by other parallels in Ovid and the Roman de la Rose. Chaucer's knowledge of Catullus must be regarded as doubtful.

1895 For the hundred cities of Crete cf. Her., x, 67, and Aen., iii, 106. Possibly Chaucer had in mind the mention of them in the Filocolo (I, 297), where they are immediately associated with Minos.

1896 ff. Cf. Ovid, Met., vii, 456 ff. According to the ancient authorities Androgeus was killed because of envy of his victory in the Pan-Athenaic games. Chaucer implies that it was from jealousy of his attainments in philosophy, an idea which he may have derived either from glosses or from the

Ovide Moralisé. The statement in the De Gen. Deor., xi, 26 f., cited by Child (MLN, XI, 484) and Shannon (p. 231), is not so explicit. See Meech, pp. 186 f., where reference is made to another account of the same tradition by Geoffroi de Vinsauf in his Documentum de Modo et Arte Dictandi et Versificandi (ed. Faral, Les Arts Poétiques, etc., Paris, 1924, p. 269).

1900–21 Here Chaucer abbreviates Met., viii, 6–151. As Mr. Meech observes (p. 187), he reshapes the story to make Scylla a good woman.

1902 *Alcathoe*, the citadel of Megara; from Alcathoüs, founder of the city. The name occurs in Met., vii, 443.

1904 *Nysus*, king of Megara, had a daughter, Scylla, who became enamored of Minos, and in order to gain his love cut off the purple lock of her father's hair, on which the safety of his kingdom depended. Chaucer omits the details of the transformation of Nisus and Scylla.

1919–20 Perhaps due to the Ovide Moralisé (quoted by Meech, p. 188).

1922–47 At this point Chaucer departs from Ovid. Many of the deviations can be explained by the De Gen. Deorum. But they are also paralleled in Machaut's version of the story in his Jugement dou Roy de Navarre, ll. 2707 ff., and the Ovide Moralisé, which has been shown to be Machaut's source, and was probably Chaucer's. On the French version see de Boer, Rom., XLIII, 342 f.; Lowes, PMLA, XXXIII, 320 ff.; Meech, pp. 189 ff. The full text of the Ovide Moralisé is not yet available in print for comparison, but Mr. Meech gives extensive citations.

1928 The monster was the Minotaur, half bull and half man, that dwelt in the Labyrinth. Cf. Met., viii, 155 ff.

1932 *every thridde yeer*; the usual statement is that seven children were sent yearly, and this perhaps underlies l. 1926. Chaucer may have got his idea of the three-year period from a misunderstanding of Ovid ("tertia sors annis domuit repetita novenis," Met., viii, 171), or of Servius on Aen., vi, 14. The Jugement dou Roy de Navarre makes the tribute annual; in the Ovide Moralisé the period is left indefinite.

1933 The statement about casting lots also appears to rest ultimately upon a misunderstanding of the line of Ovid just cited. The word "sors" there means "tribute," but it was misunderstood as "lot" in some of the glosses, and this conception reappears in various mediæval writings, including the Ovide Moralisé. See Meech, pp. 190, 194 f.

1944 *Egeus*, Aegeus, king of Athens.

1960 ff. In this device of Theseus' imprisonment, the entrance of Ariadne into the action, and the proposal that Theseus shall enter her service in disguise, Chaucer seems clearly to have been following the account of Palamon and Arcite in Tes., iii, 11 ff. (Lowes, PMLA, XX, 803 ff.). Cf. also KnT, I, 1056 ff.

1962 *foreyne*, probably "privy," the ordinary sense of *chambre foreine*. Skeat argues for the sense of "outer chamber," but this lacks support. Theseus was apparently imprisoned "in an oubliette that may have served also as the pit for the garderobe tower, the upper part of which belonged to the princesses' suite." See J. W. Draper, ESt, LX, 250 f.

1966 All but two MSS. here read *Of Athenes*, for which Skeat, on the basis of MSS. Addit. 9832 and R. 3. 19 only, reads *In mochel mirthe*. It is likely that the slip was Chaucer's own, and that it was due, as Lowes has suggested, to the fact that the description here is really based upon the Teseida.

1969 *Adryane*, Ariadne. For the spelling cf. *HF*, 407, and *ML Prol*, II, 67.

1985 Note the mixture of the two constructions *I am woe* and *Woe is me*.

2004 The device of the ball of wax or pitch which occurs also in Conf. Am., v, 5349, is derived from the commentators on Ovid (Meech, p. 118, n.). Bell compared the story of Daniel and the dragon (Dan. xiv, 26, in the Vulgate, or Bel and the Dragon, 27, in the Apocrypha).

2010 ff. The *gayler* does not appear in the Metamorphoses or the Ovide Moralisé. Mr. Meech (pp. 117 f.) suggests that he was Daedalus, the builder of the Labyrinth, who, according to a tradition not recorded in Ovid, gave Theseus "instruments for conquering the beast and the intricacies of its dwelling." The reference to the matter in Filippo's preface is not explicit, and Chaucer must have had some other source. The escape by ship may have been his invention, for according to the ancient tradition Daedalus fled from Crete on wings. See Met., viii, 183 ff.

2012 *the hous*, the labyrinth.

2064 *shames deth*, shameful death. Cf. *KnT*, I, 1912, and n.; and *Tr*, iii, 13.

2066 ff. This punishment was particularly associated with traitors. See the striking passage about Donegild in *MLT*, II, 784, and n.

2070 *other degre*, higher rank than that of page.

2075 *a twenty*, cf. *a ten or twelve*, *SqT*, V, 383; *A certeyn frankes*, *ShipT*, VII, 334, and n. The idiom does not seem to be restricted to indefinite round numbers.

2099 *youre sone*, Hippolytus. This suggestion seems hardly consistent with the statement in l. 2075 that Theseus was only twenty-three. Skeat thought Ariadne was jesting. But there is mediæval authority for the betrothal. Cf. De Gen. Deor., xi, 29. Mr. Meech (p. 117, n.) cites also Giovanni dei Bonsignori's paraphrase of the Metamorphoses (viii, 11), and Filippo's double preface to the Epistles of Ariadne and Phaedra. The incident is not found in the Ovide Moralisé.

2122 *of Athenes duchesse*; Theseus is called by Chaucer *duc . . . Of Atthenes* (*KnT*, I, 860 f.).

2130 *And saved*, and (have) saved. The construction changes.

2145 *geth*, goeth; the archaic form corresponding to AS. "gæþ."

2146–49 Cf. Her., x, 71–72, 103; Met., viii, 172–73.

2155 *Ennopye*, Oenopia, another name for Aegina. Aeacus, the king, was an old ally of the Athenians. Cf. Met., vii, 472–89.

2163 *yle*, usually said to be Naxos. But by Chaucer's account Theseus had passed Aegina. For the description see Ovid, Her., x, 59 ff., 83 ff. The end of the legend is taken mainly from that epistle.

2171–74 Cf. De Gen. Deor., x, 49; xi, 29.

2178 The reference to Aegeus's death might come from De Gen. Deor. (x, 48), or from Filippo's

preface. See Meech, pp. 118–19. Chaucer does not tell the familiar incident of the black sail.

2185–2217 Chaucer here follows rather closely Her., x. The exact correspondences are noted by Shannon, pp. 255 ff., and Meech, p. 116, n.

2186 From Her., x, 12. Cf. also *Tr*, v, 223–24, where Chaucer follows Fil., v, 20.

2208–09 A mistranslation of Her., x, 53–54.

2223–24 "In the sign of Taurus" clearly means when the sun is in that sign; for the constellation Corona Borealis is almost opposite Taurus and comes to the meridian with Scorpio. Similar instances of roughly locating a constellation are given by Tatlock (MLN, XXIX, 100–01). For the story that Bacchus, out of pity, placed the crown of Ariadne in the heavens see Ovid, Fasti, iii, 461–516, and Met., viii, 176–82.

The Legend of Philomela

The primary source is Ovid's Met., vi, 424 ff. Alongside of this Chaucer probably used the Ovide Moralisé. (See Lowes, PMLA, XXXIII, 302 ff., many of whose parallels are questioned by Shannon, pp. 259 ff.) The French story in question was identified by Gaston Paris (Rom., XIII, 399) as the Muance de la hupe et de l'aronde et del rossignol of Chrétien de Troyes, incorporated by the author of the Ovide Moralisé. It has been separately edited under the title Philomena by de Boer, Paris, 1909. Chaucer used Ovid's Latin as the basis of his narrative, supplementing it at many points by vivid details introduced from the French; some of the more significant of these additions are noted below. The psychological discussion and elaboration peculiar to Chrétien, Chaucer did not take over.

Gower's version (Conf. Am., v, 5551 ff.) shows no use of the French text.

The form of the name with *n* — *Philomena* for Philomela — is common to Chaucer and Chrétien; but it was also found in mediæval MSS. of Ovid.

2228 In MS. B the words "Deus dator formarum" follow the title. They doubtless come from some unidentified source which Chaucer was translating in the opening lines. The general Platonic doctrine of the passage can be found in many writers accessible to Chaucer. Of works known to him Boethius iii, m. 9 or Rom. de la Rose 15995 ff. have been cited as possible sources. Professor Young (Spec., XIX, 1 ff.) showed that the idea is also expressed in the opening passage of the Ovide Moralisé (i, 71–97) and in several prefaces ("accessus") to the Metamorphoses, of which he prints five specimens. The precise words of Chaucer's gloss do not appear in any of the passages printed by Young, but it is altogether probable that Chaucer was drawing from some such commentary. See further W. R. Moses, MLN, XLIX, 226 ff., J. A. Bryant, MLN, LVIII, 194 ff., and Clementine Wien, ibid., LVIII, 605 ff.

2236 From this world, regarded as the center of the universe, up to the outermost heaven (the Primum Mobile).

2244 At this point begins the account based on Ovid.

2247 *Pandion*, king of Athens.

2250 For the spelling *Imeneus* cf. RR, 22004 (ed. Michel).

2252 The reference to the Furies is in Ovid (l. 430).

2261 *say nat longe*, had not seen for a long time.

2291 For *Beaute*, the better supported reading, which corresponds to Ovid's "Divitior forma," MSS. FB have *bounte (bounde)*, with which Professor Lowes compares Chrétien, "Ne fu pas mains sage que bele" (l. 172). *Two so ryche*, twice as rich. Cf. l. 736, above.

2307 In saying that Pandion suspected no malice Chaucer follows Chrétien's account (ll. 544 ff.). Ovid says: "timuitque suae praesagia mentis" (l. 510).

2350 This statement that Philomela had learned to embroider in her youth is derived, or inferred, from Chrétien. It appears, at an earlier point in the French poem (ll. 188 ff.), in a long description of which Chaucer used only this significant detail.

2352 *radevore* is uncertain both in meaning and in derivation. Skeat's explanation, that it comes from "ras de Vaur," stuff of Vaur, is open to the twofold objection that "ras" is not known before the sixteenth century and that the proper form of the place-name seems to have been Lavaur. The final *-e*, required by the rime with *yore*, is also unexplained. Lowes, who discusses the word in PMLA, XXXIII, 314, n., is even doubtful whether it refers to a stuff or to a design. He also expresses uncertainty about the meaning of *stol*, usually interpreted as "frame."

2360 *a stamyn large* (Ovid, l. 576, has "stamina") a large piece of stamin or woolen cloth, such as was used for shirts. Cf. *ParsT*, X, 1051.

2361 ff. The description of the embroidery was probably added from Chrétien (ll. 1120 ff.), but his version is much fuller.

2366 In Chrétien the messenger is a woman, and in some MSS. Ovid has the feminine pronoun "illa" (Met., vi, 579). But, as Professor Shannon (pp. 279 f.) points out, "ille" has the better authority and was doubtless the reading followed by Chaucer.

2382 ff. Chaucer omits the account of the vengeance taken on Tereus and of the transformation of Progne and Philomela.

The Legend of Phyllis

Most of the material comes from the Heroides, ii. But apparently both Chaucer and Gower, who tells the story in Conf. Am., iv, 731 ff., used some other source. Certain features thought by Professors Child and Shannon to have been derived from Boccaccio's De Gen. Deorum are held by Mr. Meech (pp. 119 ff.) to be due rather to Filippo's translation.

2395 Cf. Matt. vii, 17; also *Mk Prol*, VII, 1956, and n.

2398 *Demophon*, usually known as Demophoön, son of Theseus and Phaedra.

2400 The reference here and in ll. 2446 ff. to the treachery of Theseus is due to Ovid's allusion to the desertion of Ariadne (Her., ii, 75–76), which is made more explicit in Filippo's translation.

2404 ff. The statement that Demophoön came to Rhodope on his return from the siege of Troy may have been derived from Filippo's introduction to the Letter. It is recorded also in introductions to the Latin Epistle and in the De Gen. Deorum. For references see Meech, pp. 119–20.

2420 *For wod*, for mad, "like mad." On this use of *for* with an adjective see *KnT*, I, 2142, n.

2422 Neither *Thorus* (the MS. reading) nor *Chorus* (Thynne's reading) is known as a sea-god. Skeat suggested, very plausibly, that Chaucer was writing from misunderstanding or confused recollection of Aen., v, 823 ff.:

... Et senior Glauci chorus Inousque Palaemon
    Tritonesque citi Phorcique exercitus omnis;
    Laeva tenent Thetis et Melite Panopeaque
    virgo. . . .

2423 Phyllis's *lond* was Thrace; the ancient authorities disagree as to the name of her father. Both Chaucer and Gower make her the daughter of Ligurgus (Lycurgus), perhaps on the authority of Boccaccio, De Gen. Deor., xi, 25. But Mr. Meech (pp. 119 f.) shows that the same account appears in glosses on Ovid and in Filippo's preface to his Italian version of the letter. The idea may have originally arisen by inference from Her., ii, 111.

2434 *chevysaunce*, apparently here in the sense of "provision, substance."

2438 *Rodopeya*, the country near Rhodope, a mountain range in Thrace.

2448 "As doth Reynard the fox, so doth the fox's son." For the general idea that animals stick to the nature of their kind cf. *MancT*, IX, 160 ff., and RR, 14027 ff.

2496 From this point onward Chaucer follows Her., ii. Mr. Meech shows (pp. 120 ff.) that there are verbal correspondences with Filippo's Italian translation in ll. 2511, 2522, 2524, 2528, 2544 ff.

2536 Ovid represents the ancestors as sculptured, but Mr. Meech cites two glosses which refer rather to painting. Ovid's "Aegidas," descendants of Aegeus, Chaucer renders *thyne olde auncestres*, which corresponds to Filippo's translation ("tuoi antichi").

The Legend of Hypermnestra

The main source is again Ovid's Heroides, xiv. But Chaucer confines his story to Hypermnestra and Lynceus, disregarding the murder of the other brothers. He also departs from his original in a number of details. Some of these have parallels in Boccaccio's De Gen. Deor., ii, 22, but Mr. Meech (pp. 123 ff.) argues that they are all derived rather from Filippo's translation of Ovid.

2563 ff. Danaus and Aegyptus were twin brothers. The former had fifty daughters, the latter fifty sons. Fearing his nephews, Danaus fled with his daughters to Argos, but the sons of Aegyptus followed and asked for the girls in marriage. Danaus consented, but gave each daughter a dagger with which to kill her husband. Hypermnestra, however, spared her husband, who killed Danaus. In Chaucer's version Aegyptus and Danaus change places. The forms *Danao* and *Lyno* seem to be due to Filippo's Italian, though "Lino," for "Lynceo," also occurs in Lat. MSS. of Ovid, and both forms are given in the De Gen. Deor. *Egiste* (*Egistes*, l. 2600) and *Ypermystre* may well enough come from either the Italian or the Latin.

The opening lines correspond closely to Filippo's translation.

2575 Filippo also says that Hypermnestra was the youngest of many daughters.

2576 ff. The nativity here described seems to have been introduced by Chaucer. For a detailed discussion of it, with citation of authorities, see Curry, pp. 164 ff. To summarize briefly, the influence of Venus accounts for Hypermnestra's beauty and for the partial suppression of the malice of Mars; the conjunction with Jupiter caused her gentleness and fidelity; and the unfavorable position of Saturn was ultimately the influence that brought about her death.

2580 *Wirdes*; the AS. "wyrd" meant "fate"; the Middle English plural *wierdes* was occasionally used to translate Lat. "Parcae."

2582 The forms of these adjectives are puzzling. Skeat's text, following some of the MSS., reads *Pitouse, sadde, wise and trewe*. *Trewe* is properly entitled to its final -e from AS., and *wise* (properly *wis* from AS. "wis") seems to have acquired a Mid. Eng. -e (perhaps from the weak form), which accounts for the modern pronunciation of *wise*. But *pitous* and *sad* regularly had no -e in the strong nominative singular. Skeat's suggestion that the -e here is due to the treatment of the adjectives like French feminine forms is very dubious. The trisyllabic form *pyëtous* (or *piteous*) keeps the rhythm without requiring any irregular -e's.

2584 Venus, Jupiter, Mars, and Saturn are here the planets rather than the gods.

2593 *Mars his venim*. This form of the possessive is familiar in Elizabethan English. On its development see L. Kellner, Hist. Outlines of Engl. Syntax, London, 1892, § 308.

2597 For the association of Saturn with imprisonment see *KnT*, I, 2457.

2602 *was spared no lynage*, no consanguinity was a bar to marriage. Chaucer seems to have had no authority for saying that the union was within the prohibited degrees.

2603 Ovid tells of the marriage of the fifty pairs of cousins.

2610 Verbal resemblances between Chaucer's

poem and Filippo's Italian are noted by Mr. Meech (pp. 124 ff.) in ll. 2610–12, 2616, 2682, 2706.

2629 "Since my first shirt was made for me"; a familiar formula. Cf. *KnT*, I, 1566, and n.

2634 *after thy wiser*, according to thy superior in wisdom. Cf. l. 2645.

2638 This line has been held to come from Dante, Inf., vii, 64; but the parallelism is not striking unless *good* be emended to *gold*.

2648 Cf. *Tr*, iii, 1200.

2649 Ovid reads, in modern texts, "mentemque calor corpusque relinquit." Chaucer's translation renders the variant "color," as does also Filippo's.

2654 The *knyf* corresponds to Filippo's "coltello" rather than to Ovid's "ensis." Here Chaucer is also in agreement with Boccaccio in both the De Gen. Deor. (ii, 22) and the De Clar. Mul. (ch. xiii).

2656 ff. The dream is not mentioned by Ovid. Professor Shannon (p. 294) holds Chaucer to have followed the De Gen. Deor., but Mr. Meech (p. 126) shows that the information is supplied by Filippo's prefatory note.

2668 ff. Ovid (Her., xiv, 42) makes only general mention of soporific wines. With Chaucer's lines cf. *KnT*, I, 1472. Professor Emerson (MP, XVII, 288) suggested that he used the plural *opies* because he knew of the two kinds of opium, meconium (μηκώνειον) and opium proper (ὀπός, ὄπιον).

2694 *devel*; this idiomatic expletive has no correspondent in Ovid.

2697 *nedes-cost*, necessarily (lit., "by a choice of necessity"). Cf. *KnT*, I, 1477.

2705 The details of the escape seem to be Chaucer's addition.

2723 It is a little surprising that the legend should have been left incomplete, when the story was finished and a very few lines would have sufficed to make the application. Possibly the ending was written and lost. More probably Chaucer left it to be added when he should continue the series.

Short Poems

The poems here brought together are miscellaneous in character and have little in common except that they are short. They also belong obviously to different periods of Chaucer's life. But very few can be exactly dated, and the order in which they are printed is only approximately chronological. Information about the MS. copies and early prints of each piece will be found in the Textual Notes. A convenient table of the MSS. and early editions, showing which of the short poems (and also which of the longer works of Chaucer) are contained in each, is given by Professor Koch, [Chaucer's] Kleinere Dichtungen, pp. 17 ff. Most of the authorities for the texts have been made accessible in the Chaucer Society's prints of the Minor Poems (Series 1, nos. 21–24, 57–61, 77). Of modern editions of the poems (or of selections) the following deserve special mention: J. Koch, A Critical Edition of some of Chaucer's "Minor Poems," Berlin, 1883; Skeat, Minor Poems, Oxford, 1888, afterwards included in

the Oxford Chaucer; the Globe edition, London, 1898, in which the short pieces were edited by Mr. Heath; J. B. Bilderbeck, Selections from Chaucer's Minor Poems, London, 1895; O. F. Emerson, Poems of Chaucer, New York, 1911; H. N. MacCracken, The College Chaucer, New Haven, 1913; M. Kaluza, Chaucer-Handbuch für Studierende, Leipzig, 1919; and J. Koch, [Chaucer's] Kleinere Dichtungen, Heidelberg, 1928. There is also an important discussion of the short poems in Brusendorff's Chaucer Tradition. The present editor has made use of all of these works, but he is especially indebted, both in his textual notes and his commentary, to the editions of Skeat, Heath, and Koch, and to Professor Brusendorff's volume.

On the supposed "lost songs" of Chaucer see A. K. Moore, JEGP, XLVIII, 196 ff. He argues that the short poems which we have preserved, either separately or embedded in longer works, are enough to account for Chaucer's own testimony and that of his contemporaries about his composition of songs. He insists especially that "no lost songs with music need be sought."

An A B C

The *A B C* is translated from Le Pèlerinage de la Vie Humaine, by Guillaume Deguilleville. It is ascribed to Chaucer in four copies. Lydgate also testified, in his version of Deguilleville, that Chaucer made such a translation, and left a space for it in his own text. But the gap was never filled. The piece has various titles in the MSS. (See the Textual Notes.) It is called *Chaucer's A B C* in the Fairfax MS. (*A. b. c.*) and by Speght, who has the following heading in his 1602 edition (fol. 347): "Chaucers A.B.C. called *La Priere de nostre Dame*: made, as some say, at the request of Blanch, Duchesse of Lancaster, as a praier for her priuat vse, being a woman in her religion very deuout." For the statement with regard to the Duchess Blanche no confirmation has been found. If it is true, the poem must be dated between 1359 and 1369. In any case it is probably to be regarded as one of the earliest poems of Chaucer that are preserved. It is thus noteworthy as a very early specimen of the English decasyllabic line. See the comments of Sir G. Young, An English Prosody on Inductive Lines, Cambridge, Eng., 1928, p. 16. For comments on the *A B C* in connection with other prayers in Chaucer's writings see Sister Madeleva, A Lost Language (New York, 1951), pp. 11 ff.

The French original, which was written about 1330, was published in the One-Text Print of the Chaucer Society, pp. 84 ff., and again in Skeat's Oxford Chaucer, I, 261 ff.

4 For the familiar phrase "flower of flowers," which is not in Deguilleville, cf. *LGW ProlF*, 185.

14 Cf. *MLT*, II, 852.

15 *theeves sevene*, the Seven Deadly Sins.

20 *accioun*, legal action, accusation. For the idea of the stanza comparison has been suggested with I John iii, 20–21.

24 *Nere merci*, were it not for mercy (lit. if mercy were not, did not exist). Cf. l. 180, below.

26 *n'art*; on the use of *ne* after words indicating doubt, fear, etc., see *Tr*, ii, 716 ff., n.

29 "Were the bow of justice and of wrath now bent" — as it was before the Incarnation. For the figure, cf. Ps. vii, 12.

38 The biblical figure of fruit is added by Chaucer. Cf. Rom. vii, 4.

50 *bitter*, Fr. "amère." There is here an allusion to the association of the name "Maria" with the Hebrew "mārāh," bitterness.

54–56 The conception of hell as a place of stench recurs in *HF*, 1654. Cf. Dante, Inf., vi, 12; vii, 127; xi, 5. The idea was common in mediæval literature. See the examples cited by T. Spencer in Speculum, II, 191 f.

59–61 Not closely paralleled in De Guilleville. Cf. Col. ii, 14.

73 The high festivals of the Church are written in the Calendar with illuminated letters.

81 De Guilleville, "La douceur de toy pourtraire Je ne puis." Perhaps Chaucer's MS. read "douleur."

84–86 "Let not the foe of us all make his boast that he has, by his wiles of misfortune, convicted [the soul] that you have so dearly purchased."

89–91 For this familiar symbol of the virgin birth cf. *PrT*, VII, 468. The construction here appears to be confused.

100 *melodye or glee*. Chaucer took the Fr. "tirelire" in the sense of "melody," though in the original it means "money-box."

109 Cf. Luke i, 38 (Vulg., "ancilla Domini").

110 "To offer our petition."

116 *to werre*, Fr. "pour guerre": it was not in hostility that he wrought such a miracle for us.

132 Reading and interpretation uncertain. See the textual note.

149–50 Cf. Gen. iii, 18.

159 Chaucer introduces the English term, as in King's Bench, Common Bench.

161 *Xristus*. The initial here, as in the French, is of course really the Greek Chi and not X.

163 *Longius*, more commonly called Longinus, the blind centurion who was supposed to have pierced the side of Christ. Cf. the Legenda Aurea, ch. xlvii (ed. Graesse, p. 202). There is no reference to Longinus in De Guilleville.

169 Cf. Gen. xxii; Heb., xi, 19.

177 Zech. xiii, 1.

The Complaint unto Pity

Entitled *A Complaint of Pitee* by Shirley in MS. Harley 78, and attributed by him to Chaucer. There is no conclusive evidence of date, but all the indications point to early composition, perhaps at the beginning of Chaucer's Italian period. See the introduction to the Explanatory Notes to the *Complaint to his Lady*, immediately following.

The source, if Chaucer had one, is unknown. Skeat suggested that the notion of personifying Pity came from Statius, and he compared the struggle between Pity and Cruelty in the Thebaid, xi. But the parallel is remote. In Statius Pietas checks the Furies in their attempt to bring on war; and in Chaucer Pity is concerned with the affairs of love. And a lady's Pity or Mercy toward her lover was commonly personified in the allegorical verse of Chaucer's age. For instances where it is represented as destroyed or dead see Flügel in Angl., XXIII, 196. Professor Brusendorff (p. 270), on the evidence of rather dubious parallel passages, argued for the influence of Dante and Petrarch.

The *Complaint unto Pity*, like the *Book of the Duchess*, is held by some to refer to Chaucer's personal experience in love. On this interpretation see the introduction and Explanatory Notes to the *Book of the Duchess*.

The meter is the familiar rime royal, a seven-line stanza riming *ababbcc*. The *Pity* may be the earliest example of this verse-form in English. The general structure of the poem, a narrative introduction followed by the *Bille* (or complaint proper), resembles that of the *Mars* and the *Anelida and Arcite*.

14 For the figure of Pity "buried in an herte" Professor Brusendorff compared Petrarch's Canzoniere, Sonn., cxx. But the conception of the death of Pity was not unfamiliar. See the article of Flügel cited above.

15 *the herse*, the bier. The body is conceived as lying in state.

37 ff. The figures named are personifications of various qualities of the lady. It is of no use to appeal to them since Pity is dead within her.

54 *put . . . up*, put by.

57 The *Bille* is divided into three terns or groups of three stanzas, each group ending with the same rime (*seyne*, l. 77: *peyne*, l. 98: *peyne*, l. 119).

In this reference to the humble and reverential character of Pity Skeat finds a hint of the Thebaid, xi, 493, 467. But, as already remarked, the whole comparison with Statius's *Pietas* seems far-fetched.

59 *Sheweth*; the word regularly employed in petitions. For illustrations from documents in Chancery and rolls of Parliament see Angl., XXIII, 204. Cf. also *PhysT*, VI, 179.

60 *servaunt*; apart from its general suitability as applied to a petitioner, the term is especially appriate here in the sense of "lover."

64 ff. The allegory here is not quite clear. The conception seems to be that Cruelty, under color of Womanly Beauty (i.e., in the lady's guise), has made alliance with Bounty, Gentilesse, and Courtesy, and usurped the place of Pity, which ought rightly to dwell in Gracious Beauty.

76 "If Beauty and Bounty are not accompanied by Pity, the world is lost."

92 *Herenus quene.* For the variant readings see the textual note. *Herenus*, which has the best MS. support, is usually taken to be an error or corruption for *Herines*, the Erinyes, the three Furies (cf. *Tr*, iv, 22). Chaucer's reason for calling Pity the queen of the Furies is uncertain. Skeat took it to mean that she alone was supposed to be able to control them, and he referred again to the struggle between Pietas and Tisiphone in Statius. Professor Lowes (MP, XIV, 723) has sought an explanation in the Inferno, ix, 44 ff., where Proserpine is represented as the "queen of everlasting lamentation," and the Furies ("le feroci Erine") as her handmaids. In *Tr*, iv, 789, he points out, the Elysian Fields are called *the feld of pite*, and Chaucer may thus have connected the figure of Pity with the queen of Elysium. The association of ideas is possible, though by no means obvious. Flügel (Angl., XXIII, 205) rejected *Herenus* altogether, and favored the emendation *my hertes quene*. The Globe edition reads *serenous*, Professor Liddell's emendation. Koch adopts the reading *vertuouse* (MSS. Harl. 78 and 7578, Add. 34360).

110 Cf. *Anel*, 182.

119 This repeats l. 2. Cf. *Anel*, 211, 350; also *Wom Nob*, 1 f., 31 f.

A Complaint to his Lady

In Shirley's MS. Harley 78 and in MS. Add. 34360, which is apparently derived from it, this poem is entitled *The Balade of Pytee* and treated as a continuation of the *Complaint unto Pity*. The two complaints are similar in thought and spirit. The second certainly, and perhaps the first, shows Italian influence, and both may be dated with probability very early in Chaucer's Italian period. Cf. Lowes, MP, XIV, 724.

The *Complaint to his Lady* is a series of metrical experiments. Indeed it may be regarded as three distinct poems (or drafts of poems), and Professor Brusendorff (p. 273) would have the parts printed

separately, entitled simply *Complaints*, and numbered I–III. But since there is a certain continuity in the thought, the traditional arrangement and Skeat's title have been here retained. The first two stanzas are in rime royal. These are followed by a passage (really two fragments) in *terza rima*, the earliest known example of that meter in English. Then the last division is in ten-line stanzas (also apparently the first instances in the language), resembling in structure the nine-line stanza of the Complaint in *Anelida*; the poems are also occasionally similar in language and thought.

The subject of all the fragments, like that of the *Complaint unto Pity*, is unrequited love.

A number of emendations and conjectural restorations, sometimes of whole lines, have been made by previous editors. For references to them see the Textual Notes.

18 The construction is doubtful. Apparently the sentence means, "And yet, though I were to die, I cannot tear it (i.e., love) out of my sorrowful heart." Skeat's emendation *fro* for *yit* (or *and*) may be right.

31 Cf. *Anel*, 222.

37 *my swete fo*; cf. l. 58, below; *Anel*, 272; *Tr*, v, 228, and for the use of oxymoron in general, *Tr*, i, 411, n.

40 Cf. *KnT*, I, 1565.

43–45 For this commonplace reflection cf. *Pity*, 99 ff.; *PF*, 90–91; *Bo*, iii, pr. 3.

I mis; Chaucer very seldom apocopates the verbal inflection in rime. To avoid the irregularity Koch would emend *is mis*.

46 Cf. *Anel*, 237.

51 Cf. *Anel*, 214.

112 The conception of the lover as slain by his lady's cruelty was familiar. Cf. *Compl. d'Am*, 30 ff. Examples from various literatures are cited by T. Chotzen, Recherches sur la Poésie de Dafydd ab Gwilym, Amsterdam, 1927, pp. 327 ff.

118 ff. The last stanza is found only in MS. Add. 34360. Its authenticity is questioned by the Globe editor.

124 Cf. *KnT*, I, 2392, and *FranklT*, V, 974.

The Complaint of Mars

Chaucer's authorship of the *Complaint of Mars* is attested by Shirley in MS. R. 3.20, Trinity College, Cambridge, and also by Lydgate (Prologue to Bk. i of The Falls of Princes), who refers to it as "the broche which that Vulcanus At Thebes wrouhte." In MS. Harl. 7333 it is entitled "The Broche of Thebes."

Shirley's heading further testifies that the poem was written at the command of John of Gaunt; and in a note at the close he adds that some men say the complaint "was made by [that is, with respect to] my lady of York doughter to the kyng of Spaygne and my lord of Huntyngdoun some tyme Duc of Excestre." Then follows the *Complaint of Venus*, at the end of which Shirley records the tradition that Granson made this ballade (that is, the French original) "for Venus resembled to my lady of York, aunswering the complaynt of Mars." In five other copies (two in Pepys 2006, and one each in Fairfax 16, Tanner 346, and Selden B 24) the *Venus* follows the *Mars*, and the two are treated as a connected whole. But each piece is also preserved separately, *Mars* in MSS. Harl. 7333 and Longleat 258, and *Venus* in MSS. Ashmole 59 and Camb. Univ. Lib. Ff. 1. 6. The printed editions from Thynne down combined the poems, until Furnivall argued for their separation in his Trial-Forewords (Ch. Soc., 1871), and published them apart from each other in the Chaucer Society reprints. Later editors have followed Furnivall's example. Neither the English *Venus* nor the series of French ballades of Granson of which it is an adaptation appears to have any connection with the *Mars* or with the Lady Isabel of York.

It is very doubtful whether even the *Mars* should be brought into association with the personal affairs of Isabel, though there can be little doubt about her character; for we have, besides Shirley's rubric, the almost contemporary report in Thomas of Walsingham's Ypodigma Neustriae (written about 1420) that she was "mulier mollis et delicata, sed in fine, prout fertur, satis pœnitens et conversa" (ed. Riley, Rolls Series, 1876, p. 366). The association is accepted, somewhat hesitatingly, by Furnivall (Trial-Forewords, p. 80), and Skeat (Oxf. Chau., I, 65), and more confidently by Ten Brink (Litteraturgeschichte, II, 76). For argument against it, see Manly, [Harv.] Stud. and Notes, V, 124 ff., and Langhans, Untersuchungen, pp. 237 ff. It was recently reasserted, for both the *Mars* and the *Venus*, by Professor Brusendorff, who found in Holland's seduction of Elizabeth, the daughter of John of Gaunt, an explanation of the Duke's hostility. Though he showed several passages in the description of Mars to be conceivably applicable to Holland, the whole theory remains very doubtful. Mr. Cowling (Chaucer, pp. 60 ff.), who rejects Shirley's application to Holland and Isabella of York, would explain both poems as referring to the affair with Elizabeth of Lancaster.

Of course no secure evidence as to the date of the *Mars* is furnished by the allegorical interpretations, and other indications are hardly more decisive. Professor Koch (Angl., IX, 582–84), on the basis of Turein's calculations of the conjunctions of Mars and Venus, decided upon 1379 as the year of composition. But Professor Manly (pp. 107 ff.) proved the astronomical conclusions to be erroneous, and showed further that the exact conditions demanded by the poem were not fulfilled at any time between 1369 and 1400. The nearest approach to the situation described he found in the year 1385, but he concluded that it would be hazardous to draw any inferences from the astronomical data.

For the mythological story of Mars and Venus, see Ovid, Met., iv, 171–89. The astronomical data which underlie Chaucer's narrative have been carefully worked out by Skeat and Manly, to whose commentaries the following notes are largely indebted. The story of the Brooch of Thebes (ll. 245 ff.) comes from the Thebaid of Statius (ii, 265 ff.). Skeat conjectured that Chaucer introduced it into his poem by way of allusion to a tablet of jasper which the king of Armonie (Armenia) gave to Isabel and which she, in a will dated Dec. 6, 1382, bequeathed to John of Gaunt. The name Armonie, he remarked, is suggestive of Harmonia, the first possessor of the brooch. In view of the doubt about the connection of the poem with Isabel, the identification of the brooch with a tablet in her possession is doubly difficult.

For comments on Chaucer's individual treatment of conventional elements in the *Complaint*, together with comparison of a previously unnoticed analogue in the Ovide Moralisé, see G. Stillwell, PQ, XXXV, 69 ff.

The proem and the story (ll. 1–154) are in Chaucer's customary seven-line stanza. The complaint consists of sixteen nine-line stanzas, one introductory stanza and five terns, or sets of three stanzas, on different subjects.

1 Proverbial: "As fain as fowl of a fair morrow"; cf. *KnT*, I, 2437.

Professor Baskervill (PMLA, XXXVI, 594) has pointed out that the opening stanzas contain elements characteristic of the "aube" or "Tagelied"; cf. further *Tr*, iii, 1422 ff., and n.

2 *Venus*, the planet, regarded as a morning star. *Rowes rede*, streaks or rays of light.

7 The epithet, *candel of jelosye*, is especially appropriate here, since it was Phoebus who discovered the amour of Mars and Venus and reported it to Vulcan.

8 *blewe*, livid, pale. This seems to be the only instance in Chaucer of the common Middle English confusing of *blew* (OF. "bleu"), "blue," and *blo* (ON. "blá[r]"), "gray," "livid."

9 "With St. John for a surety"; cf. *SqT*, V, 596.

12 Proverbial; cf. Haeckel, p. 52.

13 With the reference here to St. Valentine's Day and the choosing of mates cf. *PF*, 309, and n.

29 The third heaven is the sphere of Mars; the outermost sphere (that of Saturn) being reckoned first. In *Tr*, iii, 2, Chaucer counts from the earth outward, and the third heaven is that of Venus.

30–31 These lines appear to mean that Mars had approached Venus, perhaps that he had come into a trine or sextile aspect with her (a friendly relation). From the mention of *hevenysh revolucioun* rather than planetary motion Professor Manly (p. 114) draws the possible inference that mundane rather than zodiacal aspects are here referred to. This supposition might explain how the nature of Mars is changed by Venus (ll. 32–42). And the phrase *as in hevene* (l. 50) might be intended to direct the reader's attention, from that point onward, to the zodiacal or celestial aspects or relations.

51 *lokyng*, aspect; probably used with reference to the favorable aspects, trine and sextile.

54 *hir nexte paleys*, the nearer of her two houses, Taurus and Libra. Mars was to pass out of Aries into Taurus, the nocturnal mansion of Venus.

55 The apparent motion of Venus is about twice as swift as that of Mars. Cf. ll. 69–70 and 129.

58 Cf. ll. 107–08. The situation of Mars is bad because he is in a detrimental house and in solitude. Taurus was in particular an unfortunate sign for Mars; and according to ll. 66–67 no other planet welcomed him, that is, no planet in one of whose dignities he stood was in trine or sextile aspect with him.

61 The same line occurs in *NPT*, VII, 3160 — Chauntecleer addressing Dame Pertelote!

66–67 Professor Brusendorff (pp. 265–66) argued that these lines fit the situation of Holland in 1385, when he was in disgrace for having killed the son of the Earl of Stafford.

72 *When they be mette*, that is, when Venus enters Taurus.

79 The *chambre* mentioned here and in l. 85 may refer to some subdivision of the sign regarded as a house. Manly (p. 118) suggests very doubtfully that it means the second dodecatemorion ($17\frac{1}{2}$°–20°) of Venus in Taurus. For the rays of the sun are said to strike the chamber lightly as he enters the palace gate, and according to some authorities a planet is under the sun's beam when within seventeen degrees of that body.

81 The sun enters the sign of Taurus. In Chaucer's time the sun entered Taurus on April 12, the date mentioned below, in l. 139.

86 The colors of Taurus are red and citron. The bulls were probably white because that is one of the colors of Venus.

89 Venus, *dreynt in teres*, was a cold and wet planet, whereas Mars was hot and dry. Cf. ll. 94–96.

97 ff. The description of Mars is traditional in astrological works. Professor Manly (p. 119) compares the armed figure given by Schöner, Isagogae Astrologiae Iudiciariae, Nürnberg, 1551, p. xxxiv.

111 Venus had passed half the rays of Mars; that is, according to Manly's calculation (p. 119), she had separated from Mars by about four degrees.

113 *Cilenios*, Mercury. Venus was in the first two degrees of Gemini, which is the mansion of Mercury. The meaning of *tour* is uncertain. It does not seem to be a mere synonym for "mansion" (as Skeat suggests), and Manly (p. 119) explains it as perhaps equivalent to "chariot" or "throne" as in the following passage from Ptolemy: "Each planet is also said to be in its proper chariot, or throne, or otherwise triumphantly situated, when it holds familiarity with the place which it occupies by two, or more, of the prescribed modes of connection." Gemini is Mercury's mansion; and the first six degrees form a term which belongs to Mercury; thus these degrees are his by a twofold right.

114 *With voide cours*, that is, Venus passed through the sign without coming into familiarity with any planet. Emerson (PQ, II, 83) argues for the meaning "cunning, artful," a recognized sense of Fr. "voide." The astrological explanation is the safer, but a play upon the double meaning of the word is possible.

117 Venus is said to have *litel myght* because in her situation in Gemini she has few "dignities" and many "debilities." In technical language, she is peregrine (i.e., in a place where she has no essential dignities) as well as solitary. Consequently she flees into a cave (Lat. "puteus"). Skeat notes that the "putei" in Gemini are the degrees numbered 2, 12, 17, 26, 30.

120 *Derk* and *smokyng* seem to correspond to the terms "gradus tenebrosi" and "gradus fumosi." But Professor Manly (p. 121), finding no such degrees assigned to Gemini, concludes that either Chaucer forgot the astrological details or allowed himself a poetic license. Skeat took *derk* to mean merely "inauspicious." In any case there seems to be no implication that the light of Venus was diminished; the first four degrees of Gemini were all light ("lucidi").

Darkness is a characteristic common to hell and the classical Hades. Smoke seems to belong more particularly to mediæval tradition. References to

both conceptions are collected by Dr. T. Spencer, Speculum, II, 189 ff.

122 Venus is said to remain "a natural day" in the cave because her mean daily motion is 59′ 08″ — just a little less than a degree.

127-28 The feebleness of Mars is due to the approach of the sun.

129 *steyre*, degree.

144 *chevache*, journey by horse, ride. Here it may refer simply to the swift course of Mercury; or (as Manly suggests, p. 122) it may have carried the meaning of "knightly expedition." Mercury is returning home after a year's absence, and welcomes the distressed lady to his castle.

145 *valaunse*, explained by Skeat as an error for *falance* (*fallance*), more usually spelled *faillance*. The word is found in Old French, but is not known to occur elsewhere in English. It is apparently a translation of the astrological term "detrimentum." The "detrimenta" of Venus (the signs opposite to her mansions) were Scorpio and Aries, and the latter is probably here intended. From that sign Mercury could see his mansion, Gemini.

164 ff. These rather obscure lines are probably to be understood in the light of two passages in Dante's Convivio, ii, 5, 8, 9. The "Intelligences" are there compared variously with the angels, the heathen gods, and the Platonic ideas, and their effects ("effetti") are explained as love ("amore"). Their lord ("sire") is declared to be God. Thus Chaucer's lines would mean that Mars was created by his lord (*the God that sit so hye*, l. 218) to fulfill the end of love. See Lowes, MP, XIII, 30 ff.

185 *hette*, promised (instead of the usual form *heet*, perhaps by confusion with the passive, AS. "hátte").

190 "Unless I receive favor, I shall never look upon her."

205 "They could readily give their head (their life) as a pledge."

219 *other*, or.

245 The *broche* of Thebes, in the ancient account, is really a bracelet, made by Vulcan for Harmonia, a daughter of Mars and Venus. It brought misfortune upon all women who wore it or coveted it.

273 *of my devisioun*, subject to my influence. For the phrase cf. *KnT*, I, 2024.

To Rosemounde

The single known copy of *Rosemounde* follows the *Troilus* in MS. Rawl. Poet. 163. At the end of both poems stand the names Tregentil and Chaucer; the former has usually been taken to be the signature of the scribe, and the latter his ascription to the poet. But for the opinion that *Tregentil* was simply a complimentary adjective to be applied to Chaucer, see H. N. MacCracken, Athenaeum, 1908, I, 258, and H. Kökeritz, MLN, LXII, 312 f. Professor Kökeritz's article contains valuable notes, both textual and explanatory. Professor Brusendorff (p. 439) questioned the value of the ascription to Chaucer, which he regarded as a mere imitation of the colophon of the *Troilus*. The title, *Rosemounde*, was adopted by Skeat, who first printed the ballade in Athen., 1891, I, 440. There are no definite indications of date, but the general temper of the poem is recognized as suitable to the period of the *Troilus* (1380–88). No source is known. For the conjecture that the poem may have been written for the child-wife of Richard II see E. Rickert, MP, XXV, 255.

11 *semy*, apparently an adjective, "thin, small." Skeat em. *seemly*. Cf. Kökeritz, p. 313.

20 *Tristam*, Tristram, the ideal lover. Professor Lowes (Rom. Rev., II, 128) compares Froissart, Œuvres, ed. Scheler, Brussels, 1870–72, II, 367: "Nom ai Amans, et en surnom Tristrans."

21 Kökeritz (p. 316) is probably right in following NED and interpreting *affounde* as "be numb with cold," rather than "founder, perish."

Womanly Noblesse

The single copy, in MS. Add. 34360 (perhaps derived from Shirley), is headed *Balade that Chauncier made*, and there is no strong reason for doubting his authorship. The title, *Womanly Noblesse*, was given by Skeat. Professor Brusendorff (p. 277) expressed a preference for "Envoy to a Lady." In thought and sentiment the poem is conventional; and it contains no particular indication of date. The skillful handling of a difficult meter suggests Chaucer's middle period, probably after 1380.

12 After this line, to supply the missing rime and complete the stanza, Furnivall composed, *Taketh me, lady, in your obeisaunce* (Oxf. Chau., IV, xxvi).

31–32 For the repetition of an opening line at the end of a poem cf. *Pity*, 119, and n.

Adam Scriveyn

In Shirley's MS. R. 3. 20 this poem bears the superscription: *Chauciers wordes · a · Geffrey vnto Adame his owen scryveyne*. The lines themselves show clearly enough that Chaucer is addressing his own copyist. But further information about Adam seems to be lacking. Professor Brusendorff (p. 57), having found a record that a certain Adam Chaucer held the lease of a tenement in Smithfield, conjectured that the scribe was a relative of the poet, which would explain, in his opinion, "the familiar strength of the curse!" It has also been suggested (MP, XI, 223) that *Scriveyn* was a proper name, but this is unlikely. Nor does the marginal entry "lechares," in Shirley's MS., seem to indicate Adam's surname, as suggested by Miss Hammond. (See her Manual, p. 405, and MLN, XIX, 36.) Professor Brusendorff observed that the word is added in a late hand (about 1500). In the absence of definite knowledge of his family name several scholars have sought to identify Adam with one or another of the scribes known to have lived in London at the period. Miss Ramona Bressie (TLS, 1929, p. 383) cites one Adam Stedeman, who was practicing as a law scrivener in 1384, but is not known to have been a copyist of MSS. Professor Manly (TLS, 1929, p. 403) mentions Adam Acton, but points out that he was apparently a limner. And Mr. B. M. Wagner (TLS, 1929, p. 474) adds a third possibility in the person of Adam Pinckhurst, mentioned in the records of the Scriveners' Company among some forty men who appear to have been of the Brotherhood of Writers of the Court Letter of the city of London between 1392 and 1404. If

Pinckhurst was a member of the Brotherhood in 1392, Mr. Wagner observes, he would have been working as an apprentice as early as 1385, which was about the time of Chaucer's occupation with the *Troilus*.

The mention of the *Troilus* fixes the probable date of the poem about the middle of the eighties.

2 *Boece*, Chaucer's translation of Boethius; *Troylus*, his *Troilus and Criseyde*.

2–4 Skeat, following in part Dr. Koch's first edition, omits *for* (l. 2), *long* (l. 3), *more* (l. 4), as overloading the meter.

The Former Age

The Former Age and the four poems which follow it are all ascribed to Chaucer in the MSS., and his authorship is generally accepted. They have been assigned to various dates between 1380 and the end of his life. They all show indebtedness to Boethius, and it is probable that they were written after Chaucer's translation of the Consolation, and while he was still very much under its influence. But that influence persisted for many years. A few references, all rather indefinite, to contemporary events are perhaps to be recognized in the poems, and some of these indicate a date considerably later than that usually assumed for the *Boece*. See the notes to *The Former Age* (ll. 58 ff.), *Fortune* (l. 73), *Truth* (l. 22), and *Lak of Stedfastnesse* (introductory references).

The Former Age was first printed by Morris in the Aldine Chaucer (revised edition), 1870, under the title *Aetas Prima* (which is found in MS. Hh. 4.12). The present title, usually adopted in later editions, was taken from the second line of the poem.

The tradition of the Golden Age has been familiar in literature from antiquity. A thorough study of it is to be found in A Documentary History of Primitivism and Related Ideas, by Professor A. O. Lovejoy and a group of associated scholars (Baltimore, 1935). However many expressions of the doctrine Chaucer knew, his actual sources for *The Former Age* were apparently few. He drew chiefly upon Boethius, ii, m. 5, and made use also of Ovid's Met., i, 89–112; of RR, 8355 ff.; and possibly of Virgil's Fourth Eclogue, 32 f. For detailed comparisons see Skeat's notes and B. L. Jefferson, Chaucer and the Consolation of Philosophy of Boethius, Princeton, 1917, p. 134. References to the passages in Boethius, which can easily be compared either in the Latin or in Chaucer's *Boece*, are not given below.

5 *forpampred with outrage*, spoilt by pampering with excess.

6 ff. Cf. RR, 8364–78.

9–10 Cf. Met., i, 101–02 and RR, 8381–84.

11 Cf. RR, 8373.

12, 23 f. These lines, which are not exactly paralleled in the corresponding passages of Boethius or RR, may contain reminiscences of Virgil's Fourth Eclogue, 32–33. But the ideas are expressed also in Met., i, 97–102, 109; and it is not certain that Chaucer knew any work of Virgil except the Aeneid.

15–18 Cf. RR, 8379–80, 8388 f.

23–24 Cf. Met., i, 97–100.

27–29 Cf. Met., i, 137–40.

30 Cf. Boethius, *Bo*, iii, m. 10, 15–17.

33 ff. From John of Salisbury's Policraticus,

viii, 6 (ed. Webb, II, 255), or Jerome, Adv. Jov., ii, 11 (Migne, Pat. Lat., XXIII, 300).

42–46 Cf. RR, 8393 ff.

48–63 Expanded in part from Ovid. Cf. particularly Met., i, 128–31 (lack of faith), 113–15 (Jupiter), 151–53 (giants). For the characterization of Jupiter see also RR, 20095 ff.

52 f. Cf. RR, 9522–34.

54 Cf. RR, 8445–48.

55 To follow l. 55, Skeat skilfully composed a concluding line to this stanza: *Fulfilled erthe of olde curtesye.* Other proposals are: *Yit hadden in this worlde the maistrie* (Koch); *Of alle yfere, wolde hem lede and gye* (Brusendorff, p. 293, n. 4).

58 f. According to mediæval tradition Nimrod built the tower of Babel. Cf. the Cursor Mundi, ll. 2212 ff. It has been suggested that he is introduced here as a type of the ambitious Gloucester, whose ascendancy in the years 1386 to 1389 was disastrous to many friends of the King. See Bilderbeck's edition of the Minor Poems, pp. 118, 120.

61–63 Cf. RR, 9561–68.

Fortune

Several MSS. use the title *Balades de vilage* (doubtless an error for *visage*) *sanz peinture.*

The primary source of the poem is again Boethius, with incidental use of the Roman de la Rose and probably of Dante. For detailed analysis, with citations from Boethius, see Jefferson, pp. 57–60, 134–35; cf. also Lowes, MP, XIII, 27, where borrowings from Deschamps are noted. A double ballade of Deschamps, as Professor Brusendorff has observed (p. 242), presents a dialogue between Franche Volonté and Fortune, and may have afforded Chaucer a model. (See his Œuvres, II, 140 ff., nos. cclxxxvi–vii). The use of Machaut's Remède de Fortune, mentioned by Dr. Jefferson, is more doubtful, as is also that of the dialogue between "Auctor" and "Fortune" in the prologue to Book vi of Boccaccio's De Casibus. On Chaucer's possible indebtedness to the latter passage, and also to a "Complaint against Fortune" (perhaps by Usk), see Brusendorff, pp. 244, n., 439. On the general idea of Fortune in Chaucer and Dante see H. R. Patch in the Thirty-Third Report of the [Cambridge] Dante Society, Boston, 1916, and in MLR, XXII, 377 ff.; also his Goddess Fortuna, pp. 18 ff., 30 ff.

The parts of the Consolation used in the poem are Book ii, pr. 1–4 and 8. Only the closer parallels are listed below.

On the date of the poem see the note to l. 73, below.

1–4 On the variability of Fortune Skeat compares Boethius, ii, m. 1, and Rom, 5479–82 (RR, 4901–04).

7 The same line is quoted, as a *newe Frenshe song*, in ParsT, X, 248.

9 ff. Cf. Boethius, *Bo*, ii, pr. 8, 36–41; RR, 4949–52, 5045–46, 4975–78; Rom, 5551–52, 5671–72, 5579–81. The idea is of course proverbial; cf. Whiting, p. 31.

13 f. Cf. Boethius, *Bo*, ii, pr. 4, 134–38.

17 ff. Socrates was familiarly regarded as a champion against Fortune. Cf. RR, 5845–50, 6887–90.

25 ff. Fortune is similarly represented as defending herself in Boethius, ii, pr. 2. With ll. 25–26 cf. particularly Boethius, *Bo*, ii, pr. 4, 109–10.

29–31 Cf. Boethius, *Bo*, ii, pr. 2, 19–23, 72 f.

32 On *Thy beste frend* see the note to l. 73, below. For the idea, cf. RR, 8019–22.

33 Cf. Boethius, *Bo*, ii, pr. 8, 36–41; RR, 4905–07 ff. (*Rom*, 5486 ff. and 5549 ff.)

38 Cf. Boethius, *Bo*, ii, pr. 4, 51–57.

43 f. Cf. Boethius, *Bo*, ii, pr. 1, 95–100.

45 f. Cf. Boethius, *Bo*, ii, pr. 2, 54–57.

47 "My teaching benefits you more than your affliction injures you."

51 Cf. Boethius, *Bo*, ii, pr. 8, 36–41.

56 Cf. RR, 18979 f.

57–63 Cf. Boethius, *Bo*, ii, pr. 2, 4–51.

65 ff. Cf. Boethius, *Bo*, iv, pr. 6, 51–56; v, m. 1, 18–23. It is to be observed that the Christian (and Dantesque) conception of Fortune appears here, as in *Tr*, iii, 617 ff.; v, 1541 ff. Destiny is described in similar terms in KnT, I, 1663 ff. For further information see the note to that passage.

71 Cf. Boethius, *Bo*, ii, pr. 3, 87 ff.

73 The three princes are most naturally understood as the Dukes of Lancaster, York, and Gloucester. In an ordinance of the Privy Council, passed on March 8, 1390, it was provided that no gift or grant at the cost of the King should be authorized without the consent of the three dukes, or of two of them. In l. 76 allusion seems to be made to the exact terms of the order. The *beste frend*, in ll. 32, 40, 48, 78, therefore appears to be the King himself. If these allusions are correctly interpreted, the date of the poem can hardly be before 1390. Professor Brusendorff (p. 439) put it as late as 1393–94, when he believed Clifford to have brought Chaucer the ballades of Deschamps. If it were not for the evidence of the *Envoy*, Professor Patch, in view of the combined use of Boethius and Deschamps, would date the *Fortune* shortly after the *Boece* and near the *Prologue to the Legend*. He appears to harbor the suspicion that the *Envoy* was a late addition. See his discussion in MLR, XXII, 381 ff. If the poem refers to the earlier period, and is interpreted without the *Envoy*, the *beste frend* might of course be John of Gaunt (as argued by Koch, Kleinere Dichtungen, p. 15).

For the suggestion that the occasion of the poem may have been the double robbery suffered by Chaucer in 1390 see Miss Margaret Galway, TLS, Apr. 20, 1946, p. 187.

Truth

The poem here called *Truth* bears the title "Balade de bon Conseyl" (or some similar designation) in most MSS. and early prints. According to Shirley's statement (in MS. R. 3.20) it was made by Chaucer on his deathbed; and although the value of this testimony has been questioned, the ballade has usually been assigned to Chaucer's last years. But there are considerations in favor of its earlier composition. The puzzling word *Vache* in the envoy, as Miss Rickert has acutely observed (MP, XI, 209 ff.) may be a proper name or a punning reference to one. If, as she suggests, the poem was addressed to Sir Philip (de) la Vache, a date between 1386 and 1390 appears probable. (See the note on l. 22.)

It should be added, however, that the envoy, which is preserved in only one MS. (Addit., 10340), is held by some to be spurious and by others to have been written later than the rest of the ballade. See the observations of H. R. Patch, MP, XXII, 33; also Brusendorff, pp. 246 ff.

In its general thought *Truth* shows the influence of Boethius, though it does not follow closely any particular passages, and Dr. Jefferson goes rather too far in calling it an epitome of the Consolation. In his careful comparison of the poem with the Latin treatise (Chaucer and the Consolation, pp. 104 ff., 136) he designates as passages which had most influence on the ideas Bk. ii, pr. 4, 96–101 and m. 4; iii, pr. 11, 161–70, and m. 11; and iv, pr. 6 and m. 6. But in some of these cases the resemblances are too general to be surely significant. Other parallels, which illustrate particular passages in the poem, are mentioned below. Biblical influence, direct or indirect, is also to be noted in both language and thought. Professor Brusendorff (pp. 251–52) prints two other specimens of ballades "de bon(e) counseyl(e)," one in English and one in French. The latter (from Shirley's MS. R. 3. 20) contains a few phrases which resemble Chaucer's.

Valuable explanatory notes on the text were published by E. Flügel in Angl., XXIII, 209 ff.

1 *prees*, apparently used here with special reference to the ambitious throng of the Court. Flügel cites similar applications of Fr. "la presse," which he equates with MHG. "gedranc." Cf. also the French ballade printed by Brusendorff (p. 252).

2 The unusual personal use of *Suffyce* is probably due to the following Latin: "Si res tue tibi non sufficiant, fac ut rebus tuis sufficias" (quoted by Gower, Conf. Am., v, 7735 ff., marginal gloss, as from Seneca, but actually from Caecilius Balbus, De Nugis Philosophorum, xi, 3, ed. Woelfflin, Basel, 1855, p. 22). See Flügel, pp. 212 ff. He suggests further that the variant reading of three MSS., which gives *suffyce* its ordinary meaning, is due to Chaucer's own revision. But this is unlikely. The passage in Gower, which affords parallels to two or three of Chaucer's lines, was held by Professor Brusendorff (p. 205) to have given the primary suggestion for the ballade.

For the general doctrine of contentment, cf. Boethius, *Bo*, ii, pr. 5, 78–80; iii, pr. 3, 96–100.

3 Cf. Boethius, *Bo*, ii, pr. 5, 15 f.

7 John viii, 32. Professor Brusendorff (p. 252, n.) cites a number of mediæval works which celebrate the supremacy of Truth.

8-9 Cf. *Bo*, ii, pr. 4, 66–69; and for the familiar figure of the wheel of Fortune, Boethius, *Bo*, ii, pr. 2, 51–57.

11 Cf. Acts ix, 5; Skeat, EE Prov., pp. 59 f., no. 143; Haeckel, p. 18, no. 59.

12 Apparently a variant of the fable of the earthen and brazen pots; see Fables of Aesop, ed. Jacobs, London, 1889, I, 260; II, 227.

15 Cf. Boethius, *Bo*, ii, pr. 1, 91–94.

17 ff. Cf. Boethius, *Bo*, i, pr. 5, 8–25; iii, pr. 12, 51 ff.; iv, pr. 1, m. 1, and pr. 4; v, pr. 1 and 2, m. 4 and 5.

The conception of life as a pilgrimage is of course a commonplace of biblical and Christian literature: cf., e.g., Ps. cxix, 54; Heb. xi, 13; I Pet. ii, 11.

18 *beste*, perhaps an anticipation of *Vache* in

the Envoy. The comparison of man's lower nature with the beasts is altogether natural. It occurs several times in Boethius; see *Bo*, iv, pr. 3, 101–127; iv, m. 3; v, m. 5. Cf. also similar expressions of Chaucer's in *Tr*, iii, 620; *Fort*, 68; *KnT*, I, 1309.

20 *the heye wey*, the main, sure road to the destination. Cf. Boethius, *Bo*, i, m. 7, 13 ff.; iv, pr. 1, 64 f.

Lat thy gost thee lede; cf. Rom. viii, 4; Gal. vi, 16.

22 *thou Vache*. The word *vache*, if taken as a common noun, seems strange and unnatural. Miss Edith Rickert in MP, XI, 209 ff., made the convincing suggestion that it is a proper name, and that the envoy is addressed to Chaucer's contemporary, Sir Philip (de) la Vache (1346–1408). She cites from official records many facts of his personal and family history. His association with Chaucer is sufficiently established by his marriage to the daughter of Chaucer's intimate friend, Sir Lewis Clifford. During most of his life he enjoyed prosperity and preferment, but from 1386 till 1389 (perhaps because of Gloucester's control of the government) he was apparently in disfavor. He surrendered his office of Keeper of the King's manor and park of Chiltern Langley, and accepted some foreign post. From 1390 onward he was again prosperous. He received lucrative appointments from the King, recovered the keepership of Chiltern Langley in 1396, and in 1399 was made Knight of the Garter. If the ballade was written to bring him encouragement or consolation in misfortune, the most probable date is shortly before 1390.

27 *mede* is usually taken to mean "meed, reward." But Mr. J. F. Ragan (MLN, LXVIII, 534) suggests that "mead, meadow" was humorously intended as a suitable reward for *vache*. The suggestion is worth considering, though Mr. Ragan's argument from rime is not conclusive, since Chaucer did not consistently avoid riming close and open -*e*'s and -*o*'s.

Gentilesse

The entire text of *Gentilesse* is quoted as Chaucer's by Henry Scogan in his Moral Balade (MS. Ashmole 59), and the ascription is repeated by Shirley in MSS. Ashmole 59 and R. 3.20, and by MS. Harley 7333 (probably derived from Shirley). Even in the absence of such testimony the genuineness of the poem could hardly be doubted. It is thoroughly Chaucerian in style and meter, and the doctrine it sets forth is expounded in closely similar terms in *WBT*, III, 1109–64. See the note to that passage.

The ultimate source of both passages is Boethius, iii, pr. 6, and m. 6. But, just as in the case of *Fortune*, Chaucer was also influenced by Dante and the Roman de la Rose, and it is hardly possible to determine what he took from each authority. See Lowes, MP, XIII, 19–27, and Jefferson, pp. 94 ff. It is noteworthy that for the discussion of *gentilesse* Chaucer drew on the Convivio of Dante, as well as on the Divine Comedy. The chief treatment of the subject in the Roman de la Rose is ll. 18607–896; it is more briefly discussed in ll. 6579–92. Passages parallel to Chaucer (some of them not very close) are listed by Fansler, Chaucer and the Roman de la Rose, p. 221.

1 *The firste stok*, surely to be taken (as by Scogan) as referring to Christ or God. Cf. *WBT*, III, 1117 ff. Professor Brusendorff (p. 257), on the evidence of a passage in Lydgate's Thoroughfare of Woe, applied the term to Adam and Eve. The reading *stock-fader*, suggested by C. Brown, Register of ME Rel. and Didact. Verse (Oxford, 1916–20), II, p. 320, is very tempting.

5–7 Cf. Boethius, *Bo*, ii, pr. 6, 20–27; iii, pr. 4, 37 ff.; Dante's Convivio, iv, Canz. 3, 101–04; and perhaps the Filostrato, vii, 99 (noted by Brusendorff, p. 256).

15 ff. *old richesse*, probably from Dante's "antica richezza" several times repeated in the Convivio (e.g., iv, 3, 45, 50, 54; iv, 14, 5), though "richeces anciens" in RR, 20313 is closely similar. The phrase also occurs in WBT, III, 1110, 1118 (see the note on l. 1110). The idea of riches is prominent in Dante's discussion. For the general argument that gentility cannot be bequeathed cf. Boethius, *Bo*, iii, pr. 6, 32–51; Purg., vii, 121–23 (quoted in *WBT*, III, 1128 ff.); Convivio, iv, chaps. 13, 14; RR, 18619 ff.

19–20 Cf. *WBT*, III, 1162–64. The idea is common to Boethius (iii, m. 6) and Dante (Convivio, iv, Canz. 3, 112–19, and the commentary, iv, 20, 47–57).

Lak of Stedfastnesse

In Shirley's MS. R. 3. 20 *Lak of Stedfastnesse* is entitled "Balade Royal made by oure laureal poete of Albyon in hees laste yeeres," and the envoy is headed "Lenvoye to Kyng Richard." This is defended by Professor Brusendorff (pp. 274 f.) as the best title, but *Lak of Stedfastnesse*, long ago adopted by Furnivall, has become current, and is conveniently descriptive of the ballade. According to MS. Harley 7333 Chaucer sent the poem to Richard, "thane being in his Castell of Windesore." On the basis of this statement and Shirley's heading most scholars have assigned the ballade to the last years of Richard's reign (1397–99). But the immediate occasion is quite uncertain, and both the characterization of the age and the admonition to the sovereign would have been equally appropriate between 1386 and 1390. In fact there is a familiar passage of similar import in the *Prologue to the Legend* (F, 373 ff., G, 353 ff.). The association of *Lak of Stedfastnesse* with the Boethius group also counts somewhat in favor of the earlier date. The relation to the Consolation is not close, however, as in the case of the preceding pieces. Boethius's description of the "bond of love" which establishes faith and order in the universe (ii, m. 8) serves as a mere starting-point for Chaucer's denunciation of his unsteadfast age. The contrasted picture of the Former Age (Boethius, ii, m. 5) seems also to have been in his mind. The parallel passages are discussed in detail by Jefferson, pp. 106 f., 136.

Professor Brusendorff (p. 487) calls attention to several ballades of Deschamps (31, Œuvres, SATF, I, 113; 209, II, 31; 234, II, 63) that have some similarity to Chaucer's poem. Professor Haldeen Braddy (JEGP, XXXVI, 481 ff.) who favors the late date for the poem, also argued for association with Deschamps rather than Boethius. For a minor change in Professor Braddy's views, based on the re-attribution to Granson of a ballade formerly assigned to Deschamps, see Chaucer and the French Poet Graunson, pp. 67 ff., 88 f.

Chaucer's attitude toward "tyrants" is discussed at length, with many citations from political literature by Miss M. Schlauch, Spec., XX, 133 ff.

4 f. Cf. perhaps Boethius, *Bo*, iii, pr. 12, 205–08.

5 Cf. Boethius, *Bo*, ii, pr. 5, 27–28.

7 *al is lost*; the words recur (with variations) in *Tr*, iii, 1266, 1764, passages which go back, like this ballade, to Boethius, ii, m. 8. This is a more probable source than the refrain of Deschamps's ballade, 234 ("Tout se destruit et par default de garde," Œuvres, II, 63), suggested by Brusendorff (p. 487).

21 For a spurious fourth stanza, from the Bannatyne MS., see Oxf. Chau., I, 556.

The Complaint of Venus

The Complaint of Venus is a free translation or adaptation of three French ballades by Otes de Granson. The title is wholly inappropriate, and originated, perhaps with Shirley, in the belief that the piece was a pendant to the *Complaint of Mars*. According to the tradition which Shirley records, the *Mars* was written with reference to an intrigue of Isabel, Duchess of York, and the Duke of Exeter, and the French ballades of Granson were composed for Isabel in the character of Venus. This interpretation of the *Mars* has already been shown to be very dubious; see the introduction to the Explanatory Notes on that poem. As for the *Venus*, two of the original French ballades are explicitly written about a lady and do not at all fit the supposed situation. The whole theory should therefore probably be rejected. Yet Skeat, who denied the connection of the *Venus* with the *Mars*, still argued in the Oxford Chaucer (I, 87) for the possibility that Chaucer made the translation from Granson for Isabel. The title *Princesse* in the first line of the envoy, he pointed out, would have been appropriate to her as daughter of Pedro, King of Castile. But the variant reading *Princes* introduces a new element of uncertainty. It is possible that the *Venus*, like the *Fortune*, was addressed to a group of princes, perhaps to the Dukes of Lancaster, York, and Gloucester. The subject matter, however, it must be granted, is not particularly fitted for this destination.

The date of the *Venus* is unknown. If it was intended for Isabel of York, it must have been written before her death in 1392. On November 17, 1393, Granson received from Richard II an annuity of £126, 13s. 4d., and about this time he and Chaucer may have been in personal contact. Chaucer's reference to his own advancing years (ll. 75 ff.), though not to be interpreted too precisely, would have been most natural in the nineties. In the lack of decisive evidence these indications have led to the classification of the *Venus* with the later minor poems.

The ballades of Granson were printed by Piaget in Rom., XIX, 411–16, and again by Skeat in the Oxford Chaucer, I, 400 ff. (below the English text). The date of their composition is unknown, but Piaget shows reason for assigning them to Granson's early years. Chaucer's version of the first is hardly a translation at all. Only five or six lines are adapted and those very freely. The second and third ballades are followed more closely.

Skeat inserted the following titles to indicate the subject of each part: 1. The Lover's worthiness, 2. Disquietude caused by Jealousy, 3. Satisfaction in Constancy.

22–23 The rime *aventure: honoure* is not in accord with Chaucer's regular usage.

27 ff. With the "symptoms" of love here mentioned cf. *KnT*, I, 1372 ff., and n.

82 "Granson, flower of the poets of France." The use of *make, maker* (like ποιεῖν, ποιήτης) with reference to poetry was apparently not current until late in the Middle English period.

Otes (or Oton) de Granson was a knight of Savoy who had sworn allegiance to the King of England. According to Froissart he fought on the side of the English on several occasions. In 1391 he was charged with complicity in the death of Amadeus VII, Count of Savoy. In 1393 his estates in Savoy were confiscated, and he received a pension from Richard II. Then to prove his innocence he fought a judicial duel in France, in 1397, and was killed. For an account of him see Piaget, Rom., XIX, 237 ff., and Braddy's Chaucer and the French Poet Graunson (Louisiana State Univ., 1947).

Lenvoy de Chaucer a Scogan

The *Envoy* is attributed to Chaucer in all three MSS., Gg. 4. 27, Fairfax 16, and Pepys 2006, and generally accepted as authentic.

Scogan is generally held to have been Henry Scogan (1361?–1407), lord of the manor of Haviles after the death of his brother, John Scogan, in 1391. He became tutor to the sons of Henry IV, and his only literary work is the "Moral Balade" addressed to them and written after the death of Chaucer. In that poem he quotes the entire text of *Gentilesse*, and refers to Chaucer several times as his "maistre."

Chaucer's *Envoy* is supposed to have been written in 1393, toward the end of the year (after Michaelmas, l. 19). The *diluge of pestilence* (l. 14) may well refer to the great floods of rain which fell in September and October. See Stowe's Annales, London, 1631, p. 308 (quoted in Skeat's notes), and Walsingham, Historia Anglicana, ed. Riley, London, 1863–64, II, 213. At that time Scogan was only thirty-two years of age, and Chaucer's association of him with those that are too old for love must not be taken very seriously. On this matter, and on the (erroneous) attribution of the Court of Love to Scogan, see Kittredge, [Harv.] Stud. and Notes, I, 109 ff.

Both the identity of Scogan and the date of the *Envoy*, it should be added, have been called in question by Professor Brusendorff (pp. 289 ff.). He proposed to explain the deluge as a reference to a prolonged period of dampness and pestilence· recorded by Walsingham (II, 202 f.) for the summer of 1391. Scogan, he held, was not Henry but his elder brother John, who died in 1391, perhaps a victim of the pestilence. But there is no strong reason for applying the poem to the conditions of 1391 rather than 1393, and the argument that John Scogan's age fits the description (ll. 31–32) better than Henry's counts for little in view of the mani-

festly humorous tone of the passage. Moreover there is no such evidence of John Scogan's association with Chaucer as is furnished in Henry's case by his Moral Balade.

1–2 With these lines have been compared two passages in Dante's Purgatorio (i, 46 and 76). But it may be questioned whether the broken statutes here were suggested by the "leggi rotte" of the pit.

3 *the bryghte goddis sevene*, the planets. On their relation to the floods see R. K. Root, PMLA, XXXIX, 59.

7 *errour*, probably the aberration or abnormality of the weather rather than the ignorance of the poet (as suggested by Skeat).

9 *the fyfte sercle*, the sphere of Venus.

14 *diluge of pestilence*, pestilential deluge. For the construction cf. *KnT*, I, 1912, n.

15 *the goddes*; Skeat reads *this goddes*, "this goddess," i.e., Venus. But the form *goddes* for *goddesse* in rime is hardly Chaucerian.

21 *erst*, before. For this idiomatic use of the superlative see *KnT*, I, 1566, n.

28 Cf. RR, 1876 ff.

35 *Grisel*, "the old gray-haired man"; or, if the reading *renne* be adopted for *ryme*, "the gray horse."

38–39 The figure is perhaps from the Anticlaudianus of Alanus de Insulis, close of the prose preface and l. 3 of the verse preface (Migne, Pat. Lat., CCX, 487–88). Alanus, Professor Kittredge has pointed out to the editor, may in turn have been echoing Ovid's Tristia, v, 12, 21 f.

43 *the stremes hed*, marked "Windesore" in the MSS. Similarly, against l. 45 is written "Grenewich" (Chaucer's residence). But Professor Manly (New Light, pp. 40 f.) argues that Chaucer was probably living at North Petherton in 1393. The marginal reference to Windsor, he suggests, may date from the time of Henry VI, who spent much time there.

47 It is uncertain what is meant by what the editors have taken to be a reference to Cicero. They have referred to Epist. vi, ad Caecinam, and to the De Amicitia. But it is possible, as Professor R. C. Goffin has pointed out (MLR, XX, 318 ff.), that Chaucer was quoting "Tullius" at second hand and really had in mind the citations on "love of friendship" in RR, 4747 ff. (*Rom*, 5285 ff.). For the not improbable suggestion that Chaucer is referring to the generosity of Tullius Hostilius, see T. M. Phipps, MLN, LVIII, 108.

Lenvoy de Chaucer a Bukton

The *Envoy to Bukton* is preserved in one MS., Fairfax 16, and there ascribed to Chaucer. It was printed by Notary, 1499–1501. In the early editions of the collected works it was placed after the *Book of the Duchess* and the name Bukton omitted in the heading and the first line. Urry inferred that the poem was addressed to John of Gaunt. But Tyrwhitt corrected the error (V, xiv), and most later editions have placed the *Envoy* among the minor poems. (For details on this matter see Miss Hammond, pp. 366–67.)

Of the various Buktons whose names are preserved in records of Chaucer's time, two have been identified by scholars with the friend to whom Chaucer addressed the *Envoy*: Sir Peter Bukton, of

Holderness, in Yorkshire, and Sir Robert Bukton, of Goosewold, in Suffolk. The former was suggested by Tyrwhitt, and his claims have been fully presented by Professor E. P. Kuhl in PMLA, XXXVIII, 115 ff.; see also A. S. Cook, Trans. Conn. Acad., XX, 191. The case for Sir Robert has been stated by Professor Tatlock, Dev. and Chron., pp. 210 f., and Professor J. R. Hulbert, Chaucer's Official Life, Menasha, Wis., 1912, pp. 54 f. From the fact that on March 14, 1397, indults were granted in Rome to "Robert Bukton, donsel, nobleman, and Anne his wife, noblewoman, of the diocese of Norwich," to have a portable altar and mass before daybreak, Mr. Tatlock reasonably infers that the young man cannot have been married later than Jan., 1397. And since the *Envoy* was written not earlier than October, 1396, he conjectures that the marriage was after that date. But the second inference of course rests upon the assumption that the poem was addressed to Sir Robert. No external evidence has been found of the date of his marriage, or, for that matter, of Sir Peter's, and the identification must consequently rest on other grounds. Both men were prominent at court and may well have been known to Chaucer.

Robert Bukton (d. 1408) was an esquire of Queen Anne in 1391, and later an esquire of the King; also an "armiger" and "scutifer" of Thomas de Percy. He received royal grants of land in Suffolk and in 1394 was made constable (for life) of the castle of Eye. He may have been one of the four King's justices of South Wales in 1390. He was several times member of Parliament from Suffolk between 1390 and 1401. In 1402–03 he was given a commission of array in Suffolk. In 1405 he became deputy in Ipswich and Colchester to Thomas Chaucer, the King's chief butler.

Peter Bukton (1350–1414) was a native and resident of Holderness in Yorkshire. He served in John of Gaunt's army in 1369, and in that of the Earl of Buckingham in 1380 and 1384. By 1381 he was a knight of King Richard. In 1386 he testified, as did Chaucer and several friends, in the famous Scrope-Grosvenor suit. He accompanied the Earl of Derby to Prussia on his two expeditions in 1390–91 and 1392–93. During Henry's exile in 1398–99 he was one of the two managers of the Earl's estate, and upon Henry's accession he received various favors and honors. He was a guardian of the King's son, Thomas de Lancastre; member of the King's council (1401 and 1404); escort of the Queen on a visit to Denmark (1406); and twice mayor of Bordeaux (1411 and 1412). His long and close contact with the Lancasters brings him into association with Chaucer, and it may not be without significance, as Professor Kuhl has had the keenness to observe, that his native region of Holderness is the scene of the *Summoner's Tale.*

The evidence as to the date of Chaucer's *Envoy* would permit its association with either Peter or Robert Bukton. The reference to the *Wife of Bath's Prologue* (l. 29) points at once to Chaucer's last years. And the mention, in l. 23, of capture *in Frise* is very probably to be connected with the expedition against Friesland between August 24 and the end of September, 1396. The ballade can therefore be dated with considerable confidence in that year. Although the exact date of Robert Bukton's mar-

riage is unknown and no evidence has been found concerning Peter's, the approaching marriage of one of them — probably of Peter — was doubtless the occasion of the *Envoy.*

The allegations against marriage in the poem were, of course, familiar and traditional, and are not to be taken too seriously. For references to poems of Deschamps in the same vein, with comments on their lack of biographical significance, see Kittredge, MLN, XXIV, 14 f. He notes especially Balades 271 (Œuvres, SATF, II, 116), 340 (III, 54), 823 (IV, 343), and 977 (V, 217), to which Brusendorff (p. 487) adds 888 (V, 73). The passages cited are not necessarily to be regarded as having actually suggested Chaucer's *Envoy,* though no. 823, "Contre ceux qui se remarient," affords striking parallels.

1 Bukton is possibly addressed as *maister* because he was a lawyer. See Miss E. Rickert, Manly Anniv. Stud., p. 31.

2 John xviii, 38. With this use of a passage of Scripture in a humorous poem cf. *SqT,* V, 555, n.

8 *eft,* again. Chaucer's wife Philippa is supposed to have died in 1387.

10 On the bound Satan see *MLT,* II, 361, n. For the figure of gnawing one's chain cf. *Tr,* i, 509.

14 The comparison of marriage with prison occurs also in *MercB,* 28. For the particular figure of returning to fetters after release cf. John of Salisbury, Policraticus, viii, 11 (ed. Webb, II, 299, ll. 5–6). See Tatlock, MLN, XXIX, 98.

18 I Cor. vii, 9.

19 Cf. *WB Prol,* III, 154–60. Brusendorff (p. 487) calls especial attention also to Deschamps's Balade no. 823, st. 2 (Œuvres, SATF, IV, 343 f.).

23 On the expedition against Friesland in 1396 see Froissart, Chronicles, tr. Johnes, Hafod, 1803–05, IV, ch. 98–99. According to him the Frieslanders refused to ransom their countrymen when captured, and put their own prisoners to death.

Chaucer's *Envoy,* on the evidence of this allusion to Friesland, has usually been dated after August, 1396, when the expedition began. But Professor Lowes (in MLN, XXVII, 45 ff.) produces evidence that capture *in Frise* was a commonplace comparison, and argues that it was "the state of mind which accompanied the *preparations* for the expedition . . . which gave the allusion point." He would therefore put the poem before, rather than after, the month of August.

25 *proverbes,* series of proverbs. The use of the plural is peculiar.

27 Proverbial; see Haeckel, p. 51, no. 187.

28 Proverbial; see Skeat, EE Prov., p. 60, no. 144; Haeckel, p. 26, no. 86.

29 Cf. *WB Prol.* There is a similar reference to the Wife's discourse in *MerchT,* IV, 1685.

The Complaint of Chaucer to his Purse

The Envoy to Chaucer's *Complaint to his Purse* can be very precisely dated. It must have been written between September 30, 1399, when Henry was received as king by the parliament, and October 3, when Chaucer received the royal grant of an additional stipend of forty marks. The poem itself, which is preserved without the Envoy in several MSS., was probably written earlier and may have been originally intended for Richard II. The historical circumstances attending the deposition of Richard II and the accession of Henry IV are set forth, with citations of contemporary documents and chronicles, by Miss M. D. Legge in MLN, LXVIII, 19 ff.

For the suggestion that the reading *this night*, found in the Morgan MS. (l. 17), may represent an early text written before May 4, 1398, when Richard II took Chaucer "into his special protection," see G. B. Pace, Papers of Bibl. Soc. of U. of Virginia, I, 119.

The *Complaint* belongs to a familiar type of begging poem. Skeat cited an example by Machaut, addressed to John II of France (ed. Tarbé, Paris, 1849, p. 78) and another by Deschamps, written to Charles VI in 1381 (no. 247, Œuvres, SATF, II, 81). The latter somewhat resembles Chaucer's poem in thought and structure, though Skeat goes too far in calling it his model. Other examples of the type will be found in Miss Hammond's English Verse between Chaucer and Surrey; see especially pp. 68, 149 f., 174 ff. Professor A. S. Cook (Trans. Conn. Acad., XXIII, 33 ff.) noted several poems of Deschamps in a similar vein, and called attention in particular to a well-known poem of the Chatelain

de Coucy, "A vos, amant, plus k'a nule autre gent Est bien raisons, ke ma dolor complaigne" (ed. Fath, Heidelberg, 1883, pp. 36 ff.) — a genuine love-lyric, and not a begging missive — to which he held Chaucer's *Complaint* to allude. But the parallels he notes are not convincing. Another striking parallel, to Froissart's Ballade XXXI, is noted by R. M. Smith, MLN, LXVI, 31-32. By whatever poem or poems it was suggested, Chaucer's complaint, with its humorous adaptation of the language of a lover's appeal to his mistress, is certainly one of the happiest variations on the well-worn theme.

10 *colour*, the yellow of gold coins.

12 *stere*, rudder.

17 As Skeat and others have observed, this line implies that Chaucer wished to get away from London, perhaps to some cheaper place.

19 *shave as nye as any frere*, "as bare of money as the tonsure of a friar is of hair" (Bell).

22 *Brutes Albyon*, the Albion of Brutus, the descendant of Aeneas who, according to the old chronicles, was the eponymous hero of the Britons. See Geoffrey of Monmouth, i, 16; (ed. Griscom, London, 1929, p. 249); Layamon's Brut, ll. 1243 ff.

Short Poems of Doubtful Authorship

The pieces here classified as doubtful are, with the exception of the *Proverbs*, not ascribed to Chaucer in the MSS., and the *Proverbs*, in Shirley's copy, have no ascription. The different poems vary in excellence and in conformity to Chaucerian usage. But none of them can be positively excluded from the canon on grounds of language or meter.

A considerable number of other short poems are ascribed to Chaucer in MSS. or have been printed among his works. They are included in the lists of doubtful or rejected writings in Skeat's Oxford Chaucer, I, pp. 27-48, and in Miss Hammond's Manual, pp. 406-63, and a number of them are published in Skeat's supplementary volume of Chaucerian and Other Pieces. The question of their authenticity is treated by Skeat in both the volumes cited, and Miss Hammond gives references to other discussions; cf. also Professor Brusendorff's section on Spurious Poems in his Chaucer Tradition, pp. 433 ff. The present edition includes all the pieces not rejected by the common consent of recent scholarship except two which should have special mention out of respect to the distinguished Chaucerians who have defended their authenticity. These are the "Balade of a Reeve" and the "Balade of the Plough." They are both preserved in Shirley's MS. Add. 16165, and there is a second copy of the former in MS. Harl. 7578. In the Shirley MS. the page which contains the end of the "Reeve" and the beginning of the "Plough" bears the super-scription "Balade by Chaucer." Miss Hammond takes this to refer to the second ballade and argues in favor of Chaucer's authorship. See MLN, XIX, 37 f., where she prints both poems. Professor Brusendorff (p. 279) has shown that the heading is more likely to refer to the "Reeve," which he regards

as authentic. He prints both texts of the poem, with a facsimile of Shirley's page which bears the superscription. Both ballades were published in 1871 by Furnivall, who thought they might be Chaucer's. See his edition of Jyl of Brentford's Testament, Ballad Soc., London, 1871, pp. 34 ff. The language of neither poem is positively incompatible with the theory that Chaucer was the author. But both are so unlike his acknowledged works in tone and subject, and (as Professor Brusendorff admitted in the case of the "Reeve") so inferior in style and technique, that the present editor has not even admitted them to the limbo of "Doubtful Poems."

Against Women Unconstant

The ballade *Against Women Unconstant* (entitled by Koch *Newe Fangelnesse*) is ascribed to Chaucer on unknown authority in Stowe's edition (1561). In the three MS. copies no author is named, but in two of them (Cotton Cleopatra D. vii and Harley 7578) the ballade is closely associated with several genuine poems. Professor Brusendorff (pp. 203, 225, 441) declared it to be spurious. But the language, meter, and subject-matter are all consistent with the theory of Chaucer's authorship. Skeat notes particularly the resemblance of mood between *Women Unconstant* and *Lak of Stedfastnesse*.

The general idea of the poem is similar to that of a ballade of Machaut (Voir-Dit, Soc. des Bibliophiles Fr., Paris, 1875, p. 309). The French refrain, "Qu'en lieu de bleu, Dame, vous vestez vert," is almost identical with Chaucer's, but beyond this the two poems have little verbal resemblance. Moreover, the line of the refrain, in a close variant, occurs elsewhere in Machaut (Voir-Dit, l. 4929), and may have been proverbial.

7 Blue is the symbol of constancy and green of fickleness.

8 Skeat compares James i, 23–24, which is hardly parallel. Tatlock suggested (in a letter to the editor) that the similar use of the figure in *MerchT.*, IV, 1582, is perhaps an evidence of the genuineness of the ballade.

12 Proverbial, see Skeat, EE Prov., p. 61, no. 147.

15 *shryned*, enshrined (like a saint).

16 *Dalýda*, Delilah. *Creseyde*, Cressida. *Candáce*, Queen Candace of the Alexander romances. See *PF*, 283 ff., n.

20 *Al light for somer*, apparently with the implication of fickleness or wantonness. The phrase occurs, in a wholly different context, in *CY Prol*, VIII, 568.

Complaynt d'Amours

The *Complaynt d'Amours* or *Amorous Complaint* was discovered by Skeat and first described and printed in part by him in Acad., XXXIII, 307. It is preserved in three MSS. (Harl. 7333, Fairfax 16, and Bodley 638), all of which contain Chaucerian material, and the language is in general consistent with Chaucer's usage. Occasional defects of meter might be due either to scribal mistakes (the copies are not very good) or to early composition. Chaucerian turns of thought and expression (pointed out by Skeat and noted below) of course prove nothing as to authorship. Professor Brusendorff (p. 437) declares the piece spurious.

If genuine, the poem was probably early. An unintelligible heading in MS. H declares that it was made "at wyndesore in the laste May tofore Novembre." Nothing can be made of this date, but the reference to Windsor falls in very well with the fact that Chaucer became valet of the King's Chamber in 1367. The last stanza indicates that the immediate occasion of the poem was St. Valentine's Day.

The piece is a typical complaint for unrequited love. Skeat notes a general resemblance to the complaint of Aurelius in *FranklT*, V, 1311 ff., and to various complaints in the *Troilus*. Ll. 85–86 are closely similar to ll. 309–10 of the *Parliament of Foules*. If either of these passages is derived from the other, the chances are that the *Parliament* is the later.

1 Cf. *Tr*, iv, 516.

6 Cf. *Lady*, 49.

7 Cf. *Lady*, 29; *FranklT*, V, 1322.

12 *thilke spitous yle*, the island of Naxos, where Ariadne was deserted by Theseus; here used as a symbol of despair. Cf. *ML Prol*, II, 68; *HF*, 416; *LGW*, 2163.

17 ff. Cf. *Lady*, 88 ff.

24 Cf. *Fort*, 5–7.

31 Cf. *Lady*, 113.

57 For the idea cf. *Mars*, 264 ff.

70 Cf. *FranklT*, V, 1313.

72 The formula is similar to that in *Tr*, iii, 1501; *LGW*, 1806; and *Bal Compl*, 4.

81 "Sun of the bright star," etc.; that is, source of light to Venus, the lover's star.

85 ff. See the introductory note, above, and cf. further *PF*, 419; *KnT*, I, 1143–44.

Merciles Beaute

In view of the Chaucerian contents of MS. Pepys 2006, and of the thoroughly Chaucerian style and meter of the poem, *Merciles Beaute* may be accepted as authentic. The title, used by Skeat and earlier by Todd (Illustrations of Chaucer, London, 1810, p. 117), is found in the index to the MS.

No definite source is known, though parallels to several passages have been pointed out in French. Skeat remarks that the suggestion may have come from a roundel of Guillaume d'Amiens, printed in Bartsch-Wiese, Chrestomathie de l'Ancien Français, no. 67a (Leipzig, 1920, pp. 224 f.). The similarity, however, does not extend beyond the opening lines, and consists in a commonplace sentiment. A more significant parallel to the first section is furnished by a virelay or chançon baladée of Deschamps (no. 541, Œuvres, SATF, III, 382). For a detailed comparison see Lowes, MLR, V, 33 ff., where it is further suggested that Chaucer may have caught the word *sodenly* in l. 1 from a marguerite ballade immediately preceding (no. 540). The third section of the roundel Mr. Lowes regards as a humorous paraphrase of another poem of Deschamps, the rondeau which begins "Puis qu'Amour ay servi trestout mon temps" (no. 570, Œuvres, IV, 29). But though the general theme of the two poems is the same, they differ totally in figures and phraseology. Moreover, as several commentators have observed, the striking line, *Sin I fro Love escaped am so fat* (l. 27), is exactly matched in another French ballade. The response of the Duc de Berry to the Cent Balades begins "Puiz qu'a Amours suis si gras eschapé." His poem is otherwise quite unlike Chaucer's, but the resemblance between the two lines can hardly be accidental. Either one poet is echoing the other, or both are quoting a common source. De Berry's ballade is definitely dated by the editor between Oct. 31 and Nov. 6, 1389. (See Les Cent Ballades, ed. G. Raynaud, SATF, 1905, p. 213.)

On the structure of the roundel see *PF*, 675, n. The first refrain of each part is printed here with two lines, as by Skeat and the Globe editor.

1 For the idea, which was a familiar conceit in love poetry, cf. *KnT*, I, 1096, and n.

16 *Daunger*, disdain, fastidiousness.

23 Cf. Deschamps's Balade no. 540, l. 15 (Œuvres, III, 382).

27 On this line see the introductory note, above. For the proverbial leannesss of lovers Skeat cites *Rom*, 2681 ff. (RR, 2543 ff.).

28 It is possible, as Skeat suggests (MLR, V, 194) to omit *in* and take *prison* as "prisoner." For the recurring figure of imprisonment cf. *Buk*; also Machaut, ed. Tarbé, Rheims, 1849, p. 133. Two examples may also be cited from Welsh poetry: D. Lloyd-Jenkins, Cerddi Rhydd Cynnar (Llandysul, Cardiganshire, n.d.) p. 85, and T. N. Parry-Williams, Canu Rhydd Cynnar (Caerdydd, 1932), p. 44.

A Balade of Complaint

The authorship of the *Balade of Complaint* must be regarded as very doubtful. Skeat, who discovered the poem and printed it as Chaucer's in Acad.,

XXXIII, 292, afterwards denied its authenticity (Canon, pp. 63–64, 147). It was rejected by Professor Brusendorff (p. 437) and not included in Koch's Kleinere Dichtungen. Though smooth and correct in language and meter, it is loose in structure and wholly without distinction. Skeat notes a few resemblances in phraseology between it and some of the genuine poems, but they are not particularly significant.

20 *here*, if retained, means "to hear." The emendation *dere* may be right.

Proverbs

The *Proverbs* are ascribed to Chaucer in MSS. Fairfax 16 and Harley 7578, though not in Shirley's copy (Add. 16165). They may be his, though the rime *compas* (sbst.): *embrace* (inf.) is suspicious. For discussion on the question see Bradshaw, cited by Furnivall in Temp. Pref. to Six-Text Edn., p. 108; Koch, Chronology, Ch. Soc., 1890, p. 78; Skeat, Canon, Oxford, 1900, pp. 145 f.; and Brusendorff, pp. 284 ff. (citing a proverbial quatrain of similar structure from Deschamps).

To the eight lines which may be Chaucer's are appended in MS. Harley 7578 and in some modern editions two additional seven-line stanzas, which are certainly spurious. See Bell's edn., London, 1854–56, VIII, 149; Morris's (Aldine) edn., London, 1872, VI, 303; and cf. Angl., XXVIII, 16 f., 21. On the general subject of the proverb in Chaucer, see the works of Haeckel, Skeat, and Whiting, cited above in the General Bibliography, p. 643.

4 Probably a saying of wide currency. Cf. Li Proverbe au Vilain, ed. Tobler, Leipzig, 1895, p. 20, no. 44. On other parallels see Kittredge, MP, VII, 479; Brusendorff, p. 286; Langhans, Angl., LIV, 25 ff. Brusendorff's suggestion that Chaucer may have known a Bohemian version preserved among the sayings ascribed to Smil of Pardubic is interesting in view of the Bohemian relations of Queen Anne. But of course in the case of proverbs such a connection is hard to establish.

7 Cf. the familiar French proverb, "Qui trop embrasse, mal étreint." Skeat notes its occurrence at the head of a ballade of Deschamps (ed. Tarbé, Rheims, 1849, I, 132; cf. SATF, V, 383, with a similar proverb), and also its use by Chaucer in *Mel*, VII, 1215.

A Treatise on the Astrolabe

Among the works ascribed to Chaucer by Lydgate in the Prologue to Bk. i of The Fall of Princes is "a tretis, full noble & off gret pris, upon thastlabre," which he made "to his sone, that callid was Lowis." The exact title is not given, but the subject is indicated as astronomy and astrology. The *Treatise on the Astrolabe*, which is assigned to Chaucer in at least seven MSS. (Dd. 3. 53, in a late hand, E Museo 54, Corpus Christi Coll., Camb., 424, Ashmole 391, Sloane 261, Egerton 2622 and Ashmole 360), is by general consent identified as the work in question. "Little Lowis" is commonly supposed to have been Chaucer's own son. According to the colophon in MS. Dd. 3. 53, he was under the instruction of N. (or R.) Strode at Oxford, and this statement has some support in the facts that the problems are adapted to the latitude of Oxford, and that one MS. (Bod. 619) was apparently written by an astronomer of Merton College.

But "Little Lewis's" relation to Chaucer is not completely established. Apart from the testimony of Lydgate and the MSS. of the *Astrolabe* no conclusive evidence has been found that Chaucer had a child of that name. The word *sone* ("filium" in the Latin colophon) might apply to a godson or pupil, or even to a younger friend. So Professor Kittredge has suggested that the *Astrolabe* was written for the son and namesake of Chaucer's intimate friend, Sir Lewis Clifford. The date of the younger Lewis Clifford's birth is uncertain, but he is known to have died on October 22, 1391 — a fact which may explain why the *Astrolabe* was left unfinished. (For further support of this conjecture see Professor Kittredge's article, MP, XIV, 513 ff.; also, on Sir Lewis Clifford and his family, an earlier article by the same scholar in MP, I, 6 ff., and W. T.

Waugh's account of the "Lollard Knights," Scottish Hist. Rev., XI, 55 ff.) Very recently a record has been discovered which includes the names of Lewis Chaucer and Thomas Chaucer, "scutiferi," among the garrison of the royal castle of Carmarthen in 1403. Professor Manly draws the plausible inference that Lewis was the younger brother of Thomas, and the poet's son, and conjectures further that he was a godson and namesake of Sir Lewis Clifford. (The document has been printed in the West Wales Hist. Rec., IV, 4 ff. For further discussion see Manly's article in TLS, 1928, p. 430. In TLS, 1928, p. 486, Mr. Walker Rye argues against the identification of either Lewis or Thomas as Geoffrey Chaucer's son. But his suppositions are quite as conjectural.)

The composition of the *Astrolabe* may safely be put in 1391, the year referred to in Part ii, § 1. (Against Professor Samuel Moore, who argues for 1392 in MP, X, 203 ff., see Kittredge, MP, XIV, 513.)

Chaucer's exact source has not been determined. Most of the "conclusions" go back, directly or indirectly, to the Compositio et Operatio Astrolabii of Messahala, an Arabian astronomer of the 8th century. The description of the instrument is also little more than an amplification of Messahala's. Chaucer's indebtedness to the Arabian was recognized long ago by John Selden (Preface to Drayton's Polyolbion, Drayton's Works, London, 1876, I, xliii) and clearly established by Skeat. For the definitions and descriptive astronomy Professor Liddell holds Chaucer to have drawn on the De Sphaera of John de Sacrobosco, where a good deal of the material, at least in substance, is to be found. But there is little correspondence in language or arrangement between Chaucer's treatise and Sacrobosco's, and it seems probable that Chaucer worked with some other compilation. The second part of Messahala's work (the portion which is parallel to Chaucer's) is printed in Skeat's edition of the *Astrolabe*, Ch. Soc., 1872, pp. 88 ff., to which references are made. A collotype facsimile of Camb. Univ. MS. Ii. 3. 3 of Messahala's Latin text, accompanied by an English translation, may be found in Gunther, *Chaucer and Messahala on the Astrolabe*, Oxford, 1929 (Early Science in Oxford, V). There are numerous editions of the *De Sphaera*. References are made here to that printed in Venice in 1478. On Sacrobosco cf. further L. Thorndike, The Sphere of Sacrobosco and its Commentators (Chicago, 1949); reviewed in Isis, XL, 254 ff. Numerous works on the astrolabe are extant in MS., among them one ascribed to Sacrobosco and one to Nicholas Lynne. For a list see Houzeau et Lancaster, Bibliographie Générale de l'Astronomie, I, Brussels, 1887, nos. 3069–3320. Cf. also R. T. Gunther, Early Science in Oxford, II, Oxford, 1923, 202 ff. (with photographic plates of various instruments), and O. Neugebauer, The Early History of the Astrolabe (with bibliography), Isis, XL, 240 ff.

In the notes which follow the editor has made free use of the valuable commentaries in the editions of Brae (London, 1870) and Skeat, and, for the revised edition, of the study of P. Pintelon, Chaucer's Treatise of the Astrolabe, MS. 4862–4869 of the Royal Library in Brussels (published posthumously in Antwerp, 1940; Rijksuniversiteit te Gent, Werken uitgegeven door de Faculteit van de Wysbegeerte en Letteren (89e. Aflevering). Pintelon gives a useful bibliography on pp. xi–xiv.

On the characteristics of Chaucer's prose see Miss M. Schlauch, PMLA, LXV, 586 ff. She contrasts the "straightforward exposition" of the *Astrolabe* with the more rhythmic and rhetorical prose of the *Melibee* and the *Boece*. Note also the account of the work by Sister Madeleva, A Lost Language, pp. 87 ff.

For a general discussion of Chaucer's use of astronomy see Florence M. Grimm, Astronomical Lore in Chaucer, U. of Nebraska Studies in Language, Literature, and Criticism, No. 2 (Lincoln, 1919). Reference should also of course be made to the admirable edition by Dr. Derek Price of the recently discovered Equatorie of the Planetis, doubtfully attributed to Chaucer (Cambridge, 1955).

Prologue

1 *sone.* On the ambiguity of this word see the introductory note just preceding. For examples of its use by a tutor or adviser Professor Kittredge (MP, XIV, 515) cites The Babees Book, ed. Furnivall, EETS, 1868, pp. 27, 34; Henry Scogan's Moral Balade, Oxf. Chau., VII, 237. For the reasonable observation that Chaucer had in mind other readers than "little Lewis" see K. E. Elmquist, MLN, LVI, 530.

6 *a philosofre.* Skeat quotes Cicero's Laelius, c. xiii: "Haec igitur prima lex amicitiae sanciatur, ut . . . amicorum causa honesta faciamus." But the sense is not very close to Chaucer's.

Professor Kittredge (p. 516) argues that the use of *frend* here favors the supposition that Chaucer was not addressing his own son.

7 *Condescendith,* accedes.

24 *ten yeer.* The younger Lewis Clifford may have been anywhere from four to seventeen years of age in 1391. Skeat, on the assumption that Lewis was Chaucer's own son, conjectures that his mother was the Cecelia de Chaumpaigne who, on May 1, 1380, released Chaucer from all liability "de raptu meo." But this involves an interpretation of "raptus" which is not now generally adopted. See the Biographical Introduction.

39 f. Proverbial: "All roads lead to Rome."

42 *redith or herith.* The occurrence of this formula here, as well as in Chaucer's tales, is noteworthy. It implies, unless its use is purely formal, that even an educational treatise may have been read aloud. Cf. also the *Retractation*, X, 1081.

45 Cf. *HF*, 861 ff.

56 f. This reference to "the King's English" is interesting as coming so soon after English supplanted French as the language of the sovereign and the court.

64 f. *And with this swerd shal I sleen envie.* In thus deprecating envy in his Prologue, Chaucer follows a long-established literary convention. See *Tr*, v, 1786, n.

65 ff. *The firste partie,* etc. Of the five parts here described Chaucer wrote only the first and a portion of the second. The third was intended to contain tables of latitude, longitude, and declination; the fourth was to treat the motions of the heavenly bodies, especially the moon; and the fifth was to teach general astronomical theory, apparently including matter which would now be called astrology.

73 *portatif aboute,* which can be carried about.

74 *smallist,* very small; perhaps a Latinism. Cf. *thikkest,* i, 3, 1.

85 f. On John Somer and Nicholas Lynne (or of Lynne) see, besides the articles in the DNB, A. G. Little, The Greyfriars in Oxford, Oxford, 1892, pp. 245 f.; M.R. James, A Descriptive Catalogue of the MSS. in the Library of St. John's College, Cambridge, 1913, p. 269; R. T. Gunther, Early Science in Oxford, II, 60 ff.

Somer, who was a Minorite of the Franciscan house at Bridgewater, made for Joan, mother of Richard II, a calendar dated 1380 in certain MSS. At that time he was probably at Oxford. Other astronomical and astrological writings ascribed to him are cited by Little, pp. 245 f. He is also credited with the authorship of a short chronicle of the Bridgewater house (Chronica quaedam brevis . . . de conventu Ville Briggewater). A versification of parts of the Bible (Compendium Bibliae metrice) in the same MS. as the chronicle and sometimes attributed to him, is said by Montfaucon to be anonymous. See Bibliotheca Bibliothecarum Manuscriptorum Nova, Paris, 1739, I, 46, no. 1423.

Nicholas of Lynne was a Carmelite friar and lecturer in theology at Oxford. His calendar, which was composed for John of Gaunt in 1386, is preserved in the Arundel MSS. 207 and 347. He was an astronomer of considerable reputation in the reign of Edward III. According to Houzeau and Lancaster (I, 641, no. 3218), a treatise on the astrolabe, ascribed to him, exists in MS. There is also a tradition, without sufficient support, that Lynne made voyages to the far north and presented charts to Edward III. See Hakluyt's Voyages, Edinburgh, 1885–90, I, 93 ff., and Little's comments, p. 245.

Part I

§ 5, 11 *principales*. On the French form of the plural see the Grammatical Introduction. Cf. *sterres fixes*, i, 21, 5; *lettres capitals*, ii, 3, 52.

§ 7, 6 *noumbres of augrym*, Arabic numerals. Cf. *MillT*, I, 3210, n.

§ 8, 13 *Alkabucius*, Alchabitius (Al-Qabīsi), 10th century. The reference is to his Introductorium ad scientiam judicialem astronomiae, Differentia Prima.

§ 10 The statements here are confused and partly erroneous. In the first place the names of the months are Roman, not Arabic. Secondly, Julius Caesar did not make the changes which Chaucer attributes to him. He did give July 31 days, but took none from February's 29, to which, on the contrary, he added a 30th in the bissextile year. It was Augustus Caesar who took 1 day (not 2) from February, to give August as many days as July. It was only after this and other changes made in his reign that the calendar assumed the form in which Chaucer gives it.

§ 11, 3 *the A B C*, the so-called Sunday letters, used in reckoning the ecclesiastical calendar.

§ 12 Cf. Messahala, ll. 444 ff.

§ 14, 6 *the hors*, Lat. "equus," Arabic "Al-Faras." Messahala (i, 6, in Gunther, II, 147, 201 f.) says that the wedge was so called because it was sometimes made in the shape of a horse. But the name may refer rather to its function. For other applications of the term see NED, s.v. Horse, 8.

§ 17 With this account of the Tropic of Cancer, which is not in Messahala, cf. Sacrobosco, De Sphaera, ii, 5 (fol. b 4 verso).

9 *Ptholome* (St. John's MS. *Ptolomeys almagest*). On the Almagest, see *MillT*, I, 3208, n. The reference here is to lib. i, table following cap. 12, where the exact declination is given as 23° 51′ 20″. Skeat notes that the true value in Chaucer's time was about 23° 31′.

12 *tropos*, Gr. τρόπος, a turning ("conversio," Sacrobosco, fol. b 3 verso).

14 ff. With this description of the equinoctial circle cf. Sacrobosco, ii, 1 (fol. a 7 recto).

19 *the speer solide*. Chaucer had apparently used a globe to illustrate to Lewis the motions of the heavenly bodies. See also, ii, 26, 1, n.

36 Sacrobosco, ii, 1 (fol. a 7 verso): "Et dicitur cingulus primi motus. Unde sciendum quod primus motus dicitur motus primi mobilis: hoc est nonae spherae, sive coeli ultimi," etc. The Primum Mobile was sometimes reckoned as part of the eighth sphere, outside of the "firmamentum" of the fixed stars, and sometimes as the ninth sphere. Chaucer, unless 8 is an error for 9 here, follows the former system; Sacrobosco, the latter. In *FranklT*, V, 1283, Chaucer makes the Primum Mobile the ninth.

45 ff. With the description of the Tropic of Capricorn again cf. Sacrobosco, ii, 5 (fol. b 4 recto).

§ 18, 2 *certeyn cercles that highten almycanteras*; Messahala (l. 8); "circulus almucantherath"; Arabic "Almuqantarat" (pl., with article, of "muqantarah"). They are circles to indicate altitude. On the best astrolabes they were marked for every degree of latitude; on Chaucer's, only for every other degree.

11 *compowned by 2 and 2*. The instrument was engraved with 45 circles for alternate degrees of latitude, instead of with the whole 90. The Arabians termed this smaller type of astrolabe "nisfi," as distinguished from one that was "tamm," complete.

§ 19, 6 *azimutz*, vertical circles passing from the zenith through the horizon and indicating the position of any heavenly body "in azimuth" (Arabic "as-sumut," pl., with article, of "samt," way, direction).

10 *cenyth of the sonne*, the point of the horizon denoting the sun's position in azimuth.

§ 20, 4 On *houres of planetes*, or "unequal hours," see ii, 12, n.

§ 21 In Skeat's note are the names of the stars marked in the diagram in MS. Dd. 3, 53, which is reproduced as fig. 2, Oxf. Ch., III. For further information see Gunther, Early Science in Oxford, II, 192, 201, 205, 222 ff.

13 The stars of the North are so called with reference to the zodiac, not to the equator. Aldebaran and Algomeisa are south of the ecliptic, but being north of the equator they rise north of the *est lyne*.

19 *arisen rather than the degre of her longitude*, rise earlier than the point where their meridian crosses the ecliptic.

27 Chaucer does not reach this explanation of eclipses. There is a brief statement of it in Sacrobosco, ii, 2 (fol. b 1 recto); iv, 2 is entitled "De eclipsi Lunae" (fol. d 5 recto).

35 ff. The heavenly zodiac is 12° in breadth, with the ecliptic in the center. But Chaucer's astrolabe shows only the northern half.

52 The "zodiac" (Gr. ζῴδιον, diminutive of ζῷον, living creature) is so named because of the fancied resemblance of many of the constellations to various animals.

55 ff. The doctrines here referred to belong to what would now be called astrology, and illustrations will be found in any standard treatise on the subject. Skeat gives a general reference to Porphyrius Philosophus, Introductio in Claudii Ptolemaei opus de affectibus astrorum, and cites extracts from a tract in MS., R. 15. 18, Trin. Coll., Camb. For a figure showing the supposed relation of the signs of the zodiac to the parts of the human body see the drawing in the Brussels MS. reproduced in photograph by Pintelon (after p. 127).

90 *almury* (Arabic "al-mur'ī," indicator), called also "denticulus" and "ostensor." The edge of the rete, near the head of Capricorn, is cut down to a small projecting tongue or pointer.

Part II

§ 1 Cf. Messahala, ll. 33 ff.

Rubric: *his cours*, Skeat *hir cours*. In Germanic grammar the sun is feminine; in Lat. and Fr., masculine. Usage varied in Mid. Eng.

7 In Chaucer's time the Sun entered Aries on March 12th. Reckoned by the new style, the date is March 20–21st.

7 f. *I wolde knowe*, I wished to know. The past tense is appropriate from the point of view of readers who are afterwards to use the treatise. Chaucer was probably writing in the year 1391, to which he refers.

§ 2 Cf. Messahala, ll. 41 ff.

2 *thi lift syde*, the left side of the body, which would correspond to the right or eastern edge of the astrolabe.

§ 3 Cf. Messahala, ll. 47 ff.

37 For a long note inserted after *ascendent* in MS. Bl¹ see the textual note.

43 *Alhabor* (Arabic "al-'abūr"), Sirius, the Dog-star.

§ 4 This section, which deals with astrology, is not from Messahala.

16 ff. A "house" in astrology covers a space of 30° and corresponds to a sign of the zodiac. Each planet has its "house" in a certain sign where its influence is held to be especially powerful. Every house is divided into three "faces," of 10°, and the faces are also assigned to the various planets.

30 ff. An ascendant is fortunate when the so-called "lord of the ascendant," the planet to which the house belongs, is in the rising sign, or else in the succeeding one, with other planets in friendly aspect, where he may see the ascendant. It is unfortunate if he is retrograde (that is, moving in a direction contrary to that of the sun in the ecliptic), or combust (that is, too near the sun), or joined with an evil planet in the same sign, or himself descending, or if other planets are in unfriendly aspect. For an example of unfortunate conditions see *MLT*, II, 295, and n. Cf. further *Gen Prol*, I, 417, n.

36 "the point where a planet (especially the moon) passed from the northern to the southern side of the ecliptic" (Skeat).

57 ff. On Chaucer's own attitude toward astrology, cf. *FranklT*, V, 1133, n.

68 *eleccion*, choice of a favorable time for an undertaking. See *MLT*, II, 312, and n.

§ 5 Cf. Messahala, ll. 55 ff.

§ 6 Cf. Messahala, ll. 72 ff. This conclusion depends upon the fact that light of the sun reaches us when the sun is 18° below the horizon. *Nadir* (Arabic, "nazīr," opposite), a point in the heavens, or degree of the zodiac, that is directly opposite to some other given point.

§ 7 Cf. Messahala, ll. 81 ff.

§ 8 Cf. Messahala, ll. 96 ff.

§ 9 Not in Messahala.

2 *the 2 chapitre before*; really in § 6.

4 *day vulgar*, the whole period of daylight, from the beginning of the morning twilight till the end of the evening twilight.

§ 10 Cf. Messahala, ll. 91 ff.

2 The term *houres of planetes* (not used here by Messahala) refers to an astrological supposition which is explained in ii, 12, n.

7 *contenen 30 degrees of the bordure*, i.e., taken together, they equal two hours, or one-twelfth of the equinoctial circle.

§ 11 Cf. Messahala, ll. 104 ff.

16 ff. Chaucer never reached the fourth part of the treatise in which this explanation was to be made.

§ 12 This section again deals with astrology and is not taken from Messahala. According to the theory of "hours of planets" the first unequal hour of each day belongs to the planet for which the day is named. Thus the first hour of Saturday belongs to Saturn. The successive hours are then assigned to the various planets according to the order Sun, Venus, Mercury, Moon, Saturn, Jupiter, Mars.

The 22nd hour of Saturday will fall to Saturn, the 23rd to Jupiter, the 24th to Mars, and the first hour of Sunday to the Sun. Chaucer makes rather elaborate use of the scheme for narrative purposes in the *KnT*. See I, 2217 ff., and n.

2 The nadir of the sun is said to show the hour of the planet in the morning because that hour is conceived as "entering upon the west horizon" (ll. 14 ff.). In the evening the sun itself marks the hour and continues to do so all the night.

§ 13 Cf. Messahala, ll. 122 ff.

§ 14 Cf. Messahala, ll. 149 ff. The procedure here is the reverse of that described in § 13.

§ 15 Cf. Messahala, ll. 156 ff.

§ 16 Cf. Messahala, ll. 142 ff. Logically this might be expected to precede § 14, as it does in Messahala.

§ 17 Cf. Messahala, ll. 341 ff. (which deal, however, merely with finding the degree of a planet). The method is as follows: Determine the altitude of the star before it souths, and find the ascending degree of the zodiac. Then find the ascending degree at an equal interval after it souths, when the star has the same altitude as before. The mean between them will be the degree that ascends when the star is on the meridian. Set this degree upon the eastern part of the "horizon obliquus," and the degree which souths with the star will then be on the meridian line. Skeat notes that this method is liable to considerable error because it does not distinguish between right ascension (reckoned from the equator) and longitude (reckoned from the ecliptic). The error is slight when the observations are taken very close to the meridian.

3 *tak an assendent*; as in ii, 3.

8 *eny thyng the south westward*, a little west of the south line.

§ 18 Cf. Messahala, ll. 160 ff.

1 *the centre*, the end of the metal tongue representing the star on the rete of the astrolabe.

§ 19 Not in Messahala.

8 *north or south fro the equinoxiall*, rather, from the ecliptic, as the rest of the discussion implies.

§ 20 Cf. Messahala, ll. 203 ff. The declination of a given degree of the zodiac is the difference between its meridian altitude and that of the 1st point of Aries.

§ 21 Cf. Messahala, ll. 236 ff. The latitude of a given place equals the number of degrees between the zenith and the south point of the equinoctial circle. The number of degrees from the pole to the northern point of the "horizon obliquus" is the same.

§ § 22–23 Not in Messahala.

§ 23, 28 ff. Some MSS. have here a set of observations calculated nearly for the latitude of Rome.

§ 24 Cf. Messahala, ll. 232 ff.

4 *make a nombre*, add together.

§ 25 Cf. Messahala, ll. 215 ff.

23 Several MSS. give the more accurate reckoning 38° 25', with its (inexact) complement 51° 50'. But Chaucer's own statement just below makes it probable that he used only the rough reckoning. The true latitude of Oxford, Skeat notes, is between 51° 45' and 51° 46'.

§ 26 Not in Messahala. It corresponds in substance to Sacrobosco's De Sphaera, iii, 1, 2.

1 *the spere solide* is taken by Professor Liddell

to refer to Sacrobosco's work. But both here and in i, 17, 19 it is more likely to mean a globe such as Chaucer had used in some of his demonstrations to Lewis.

5 *These auctours*, i.e., authorities (in general). On the generalizing use of *thise* see *KnT*, I, 1531, and n.

6 *right ascensioun*, to be carefully distinguished from "right ascension" as used in modern astronomy for longitude reckoned from the equator. The reference here is to those signs which ascend more directly, that is, at a greater angle to the horizon than the rest. See the further explanation in § 28, below.

11–16 *Ferther-over . . . right orisonte*; these lines, which are essential to the thought, are omitted in nearly all the MSS.

24 f. *ascensions . . . in the right cercle*, in modern terminology "right ascensions."

§ 27 Cf. Messahala, ll. 284 ff. The problem is to determine how many degrees of the equinoctial pass the meridian with a given sign.

§ 28 Cf. Messahala, ll. 292 ff. The problem is to determine how many degrees of the equinoctial ascend while a given sign is crossing the horizon. Cf. § 26, above.

27 The oblique, or tortuous, signs are said to obey the direct signs.

§ 29 Cf. Messahala, ll. 182 ff.

§ 30 Cf. Messahala, ll. 352 ff.

Rubric: by *the wey of the sonne* is meant here the sun's apparent motion on any given day.

§ 31 Cf. Messahala, ll. 176 ff.

Rubric: *cenyth*, zenith, not in the usual sense, but with reference to a point on the horizon.

8 Seamen divided the horizon into thirty-two parts, as in the modern mariners' compass. This information is not in Messahala.

§ 32 Not in Messahala. The problem is simply to find the sun's azimuth at a given time.

§ 33 Cf. Messahala, ll. 165 ff.

Rubric: *cenyth*, azimuth (as in § 31).

§ 34 Cf. Messahala, ll. 323 ff.

4 *upon the mones syde*, i.e., in nearly the same azimuth as the moon.

13 ff. The moon's latitude is never more than $5\frac{1}{4}°$ from the ecliptic, and this distance is commonly neglected in treatises of the astrolabe.

§ 35 Cf. Messahala, ll. 361 ff. A planet is said to have "direct" motion when it follows the succession of the signs of the zodiac; "retrograde" when it moves in the opposite direction.

25 *as in hir epicicle*. The moon was held to revolve in an epicycle about a center which itself revolved about the earth. The motion of the center was supposed to be direct; that of the moon in the epicycle, retrograde. See the Almagest, iv, 5, and ix, 5. See the study of Miss Florence M. Grimm on astronomy in Chaucer, U. of Nebraska Stud. in Lang., Lit. and Crit., No. 2, p. 44.

§ 36 Cf. Messahala, ll. 372 ff. For the definition of a "house" see ii, 4, 16, n. The present section and the following deal with the method of dividing the sphere correctly into the twelve houses.

§ 37 Cf. Messahala, ll. 388 ff.

§ § 38–40 Not in Messahala. Mr. R. T. Gunther (Early Science in Oxford, II, 203) has pointed out the similarity of § 38 to a section Ad meridien in-

veniendum in the De Mensura Horologii ascribed to the Venerable Bede. But Pintelon (edition of the *Astrolabe*, p. 10) finds the analogy "not quite convincing."

§ 38, 1 *for werpyng*, to provide against warping. Cf. *For percynge, Thop*, VII, 862, n.

§ 39 With the definition of the meridian line cf. Sacrobosco, ii, 4 (fol. b 2 verso).

22 *thei chaungen her almykanteras*, they differ in latitude.

25 ff. By *longitude* and *latitude* of a *climat* Chaucer means "length" and "breadth" respectively. His treatment of "climates," or zones, is very brief. Seven were regularly reckoned in his time, and they are discussed fully by Sacrobosco, iii, 9 (fol. d 1 verso et seq.). See further Gunther, II, 211 f.

§ 40 The problem is to find with what degree of the zodiac a planet ascends, its latitude and longitude being known.

19 *upward*, i.e., inward, or northward, on the astrolabe.

82 *thou shalt do wel ynow* may have been added by a scribe to finish the sentence. See the textual note.

Colophon. — In MS. Dd. 3. 53, according to Skeat, after *houre after houre*, the rest of the page is blank except for the following colophon: "Explicit tractatus de Conclusionibus Astrolabii, compilatus per Galfridum Chauciers ad Filium suum Lodewicum, scolarem tunc temporis Oxonie, ac sub tutela illius nobilissimi philosophi Magistri N. Strode, &c." The authority of this statement has been questioned by Gollancz, who suggested that the initial N should perhaps be read R, and that the whole note was a late and unauthorized explanation of Chaucer's dedication of the *Troilus* to Ralph Strode. See *DNB*, s.v., Strode, Ralph.

§ § 41–46 The conclusions or propositions which follow are of doubtful authenticity. They are preserved only in late MSS.; the style is rather different from that of the body of the work; and they follow what appears to be the unfinished sentence in § 40. But they have been included here because their genuineness is not absolutely disproved, and some of them illustrate certain points in Chaucer's writings. They do not correspond exactly to the text of Messahala, though the substance of § 41 is similar to Messahala, ll. 483 ff., and that of § § 42–43 to ll. 497 ff.

It may be further noted that § § 44–45 refer to tables which showed the position of the planets on Dec. 31, 1397. If these were real tables, and the date was not merely set down for purpose of illustration, it is unlikely that Chaucer would have been using them in 1391. The sections in question, then, if by Chaucer at all, were probably added several years after the main part of the *Astrolabe* was composed.

§ § 41–43 By *umbra recta*, or "extensa," is meant the shadow cast on a horizontal plane by an upright object; *umbra versa* is the shadow cast on a perpendicular plane by a style which projects from it at right angles. It is generally understood that for calculations by *umbra recta* the sun's altitude shall be greater than 45°, and by *umbra versa*, less than 45°.

§ 41, 5 The *rewle* here used is represented (in Skeat's drawing, Fig. 1) on the back of the astrolabe.

It is divided into twelve parts. Hence the calculations in the text are based upon twelve.

§ 44 This conclusion and the following explain the use of tables calculated to show the position of a planet at any given date. In those to which the author refers the basis of calculation was Dec. 31, 1397. The positions of the planets were shown for that date, and their changes of position indicated by the so-called tables of *anni collecti et expansi*. The *anni collecti* showed the motion for collective periods of years (from 20 to 3000, according to the text); the *anni expansi*, for the shorter periods from 1 to 20.

For an interesting reference to the use of such tables see *FranklT*, V, 1275 ff.

2 *rote*, root; the data used as a basis of calculation.

§ 45, 2 *Arsechieles tables*, doubtless the Astronomical Tables of Arzachel (Ibn al-Zarqālī). There is a copy in Merton College MS. 259, formerly the property of William Rede, Bishop of Chichester (d. 1385) (Gunther, II, 384).

§ 46 This follows § 40 in MS. Bl[1].

Skeat prints five additional sections (numbered 41[a], 41[b], 42[a], 43[a], 42[b]) which are generally conceded to be spurious.

The Romaunt of the Rose

The belief that Chaucer translated the Roman de la Rose rests upon his own testimony in the *Prologue* to the *Legend of Good Women*, confirmed — if confirmation were necessary — by Lydgate's Prologue to Bk. i of The Fall of Princes and a ballade of Deschamps (no. 285, Œuvres, SATF, II, 138). The only Middle English translation known to exist is the fragmentary poem here printed. It is preserved in a single Glasgow MS., which lacks the beginning and has no ascription to any author. Thynne included the work in his Chaucer of 1532, and it was long afterwards regarded as Chaucerian. But modern criticism has questioned its authenticity. It was rejected in whole or in part by Bradshaw, Furnivall, Ten Brink, and Skeat, whose changes of opinion are registered by Miss Hammond, pp. 451–52. In 1890 Kaluza (Acad., XXXVIII, 11) argued that the translation is really in three fragments (1–1705, 1706–5810, 5811–7696), and this conclusion has been generally agreed upon as a basis of later discussion. But judgments have continued to differ on the question of authorship. Kaluza assigned fragments A and C to Chaucer, and held B to be by another poet. Skeat's final opinion was that fragment A alone was Chaucer's. The authenticity of the entire poem was defended by Lounsbury, whose arguments were answered in detail by Professor Kittredge. At the opposite extreme from Lounsbury stands Professor Koch, who would deny Chaucer any part of the work.

Most recently a new examination of the evidence was made by A. Brusendorff in The Chaucer Tradition (London and Copenhagen, 1925, pp. 308 ff.). Rejecting Kaluza's division of the poem at line 1705, Professor Brusendorff recognized only two fragments (lines 1–5810 and 5811–end). Both of them, in their original form, he held to have been written by Chaucer. But he thought the text was handed down by a "transmitter" who depended on his memory and was able to produce only a fragmentary and mutilated copy. Dialectal forms not proper to Chaucer he explained on the theory that the transmitter was from a northerly locality. He believed Chaucer's translation of the Roman to have been complete, and pointed out passages in both Chaucer and Lydgate which he thought to be based upon portions of the work not represented in the existing fragments. Holding that the transmit-

ter, when his memory failed, resorted freely to composition, Professor Brusendorff undertook by the boldest sort of emendation to restore this supposed Chaucerian original.

Such is the variety of opinion about Chaucer's authorship of the *Romaunt*, and the question can perhaps never be positively decided on the internal evidence which appears to be alone available. Fragment A — to revert to the subdivision of Kaluza, which is still valid in spite of Brusendorff's criticism — accords well enough with Chaucer's usage in language and meter. If there is no definite evidence in favor of Chaucer's authorship, there is also no conclusive reason for rejecting it. But fragment B, on the testimony of the dialect alone, can hardly be Chaucer's; and the non-Chaucerian forms in fragment C, though fewer than in B, would probably be held evidence enough for the rejection of an independent poem. It seems more reasonable to assign B and C to a second translator, perhaps a Northern Chaucerian, than to explain them as works of Chaucer corrupted in transmission. In fact Professor Brusendorff's hypothesis of a transmitter by memory is a rather desperate measure to save the Chaucerian authorship of the whole poem.

Full references on the question of authorship are given by Brusendorff; see also Miss Hammond, pp. 451 ff., and Wells, pp. 649 ff. Of preceding discussions of the subject the following are representative: T. R. Lounsbury, Studies in Chaucer, New York, 1892, II, Chap. iv; G. L. Kittredge [Harv.] Stud. and Notes, I, 1 ff.; Kaluza, Chaucer und der Rosenroman, Berlin, 1893, and later articles in ESt, XXIII, 336, XXIV, 343; Skeat, The Chaucer Canon, Oxford, 1900, pp. 65 ff.; J. Koch, ESt, XXVII, 61–73, 227–34, XXX, 451–56; A. D. Schoch, MP, III, 339 ff. (a survey of the evidence).

Authors other than Chaucer to whom the translation has been ascribed are the writer of the Testament of Love, King James I of Scotland (for fragment B), and Lydgate (for fragments B and A). See Lindner, ESt, XI, 172; Skeat, Canon, pp. 84 ff.; Lange, ESt, XXIX, 397 ff.; Koch, ESt, XXVII, 61 ff., 227 ff.

The English poem covers about one-third of the French Roman de la Rose, specifically lines 1–5154, 10679–12360. It is to be noted that the English fragment A does not contain the heresy against

Love with which Chaucer is charged in the *Legend of Good Women*. The passages in condemnation of women to which the God of Love might have objected are all in Jean de Meun's part of the French poem (i.e., after line 4058). Some of them are included in fragment B of the English, and some do not appear at all in the translation.

The date of Chaucer's translation is not definitely known. It must have preceded the *Prologue to the Legend* (circa 1386), and is usually assigned to the earliest years of his literary production. Professor Brusendorff, because of the association of the work with the *Troilus* in the *Prologue to the Legend*, would date it near 1380. But he himself recognizes that the metrical form of the existing fragments is more like that of the *Book of the Duchess* than that of the *House of Fame*. E. P. Kuhl (PQ, XXIV, 33 ff.) argued for a date shortly before the death of Blanche. The influence of the French Roman is apparent in every period of Chaucer's work. See Fansler, Chaucer and the Roman de la Rose, New York, 1914; Miss L. Cipriani, Studies in the influence of the Romance of the Rose on Chaucer, PMLA, XXII, 552 ff.

Editions of the French poem have been numerous since it was first printed about 1480. The earliest to be based upon a comparison of MSS. is that of Méon, 4 v., Paris, 1814. The editions of F. Michel, 2 v., Paris, 1864, and P. Marteau, 5 v., Orléans, 1878–80, rest upon Méon's. A new critical text by E. Langlois has recently been published by the SATF, 5 v., Paris, 1914–24. The parts of the poem which correspond to the English *Romaunt* were printed by Kaluza, mainly from Michel's text, parallel with his edition of the Glasgow MS. (Ch. Soc., 1891). Skeat (Oxf. Ch. I, 93 ff.) printed from Méon's text the portion which corresponds to fragment A. References to the Roman made by recent editors and other investigators of Chaucer are usually to the edition by Méon (as in Skeat's notes) or to that of Michel (as in Fansler's study). Fansler (pp. 240 ff.) gives a table of correspondences in the line-numbers of Méon, Michel, and Marteau. In the present edition references are to the text of Langlois.

In the following notes, as in the case of the *Boece* and other translations, no attempt is made at a detailed collation of Chaucer's text with his original. The French version is cited only for the elucidation of the English. References to the sources of the Roman are added for the convenience of readers who wish to trace further the history of the ideas. Fuller information on the subject will be found in Langlois's notes and in his treatise, Origines et Sources du Roman de la Rose, Paris, 1891. On illustrations in the MSS., which are of exceptional interest, see A. Kuhn, Jahrbuch der Kunsthistorischen Sammlungen des allerhöchsten Kaiserhauses, XXXI, 1–66, and E. Winkler, Guillaume de Lorris: der Roman von der Rose, Vienna, 1921.

On the principles followed in the present edition of the English text, see the introduction to the Textual Notes on the *Romaunt*.

1 With this whole discussion of dreams cf. *NPT*, VII, 2922 ff., and n.; *HF*, 1–52, and n.

7 *Macrobes*, Macrobius, the commentator on Cicero's Somnium Scipionis.

9 *undoth* can mean either "expounds" or "re-

lates" (Fr. "escrist"). In *BD*, 284 and *NPT*, VII, 3123, Chaucer speaks of Macrobius as if he were the author of the Somnium, an impression he might have derived from this line of Lorris. But in *PF*, 31, he names *Tullyus* as the author.

22 *cariage*, Liddell's emendation (Globe edn.) of *corage*; Fr. "paage," toll.

42 In this and later allusions to the lady for whom the poem was written the English simply follows the French. The person intended by Guillaume de Lorris is unknown.

61–62 Cf. *LGW ProlF*, 125–26, *G*, 113–14.

63 Cf. Alain de Lille, De Planctu Naturae (Migne, Pat. Lat., CCX, 447 ff.).

71 The description which follows has many parallels in mediæval poetry. For illustrations and possible sources see Langlois's note, which refers to O. M. Johnston, ZRPh, XXXII, 705 ff.

98 *aguler*, needle-case (Fr. "aguillier"), seems not to be recorded elsewhere in English.

104 The sleeves were tightly laced or sewn with a thread. Cf. l. 570, below. Langlois notes several other examples from French poems. See also his article in Rom., XXXIII, 405.

118 *Seyne*, the river Seine.

119 *strayghter wel away*, much broader; Fr. "plus espandue."

129 *Beet*, struck, bordered; Fr. "Batoit."

140 The images described were painted on the wall. Langlois compares the garden wall in Floire et Blanceflor, ed. Du Méril, Paris, 1856, I, 71.

149 For *moveresse* Globe reads *meveresse*, Fr. "moverresse." The Glasgow MS. and Thynne have *mynoresse*, which may be due to the reading "meneresse" in certain Fr. MSS. (See Brusendorff, p. 308.)

191 *smale harlotes*, petty criminals. For the generalizing use of *these* cf. l. 411, below (Fr. "ces"); see also *KnT*, I, 1531, n.

225 *perche*, a horizontal pole, such as was put up in bedrooms for hanging clothes.

233–34 Fr. "Car sachiez que mout li pesast Se cele robe point usast." The English does not quite correspond.

247 ff. The portrait of Envy is based upon Ovid, Met., ii, 775 ff.

276 *for pure wood*, from sheer madness. Cf. *for hor*, line 356; *For moiste*, line 1564; *for wod*, *HF*, 1747; *for pure ashamed*, *Tr*, ii, 656; and see *KnT*, I, 2142, n.

292 *baggyngly*, askance; Fr. "borgneiant."

325 *tere hir swire*, tear her throat. This is not in the Fr.

356 *for hor*, "because (of being) hoary"; possibly to be read *for-hor*, "very hoary." See *KnT*, I, 2142, n.

358 *synne*, pity; Fr. "pechiez."

363 Here again the English departs from the original. Fr. "Les oreilles avoit mossues," var. "velues" (wrinkled? hairy?).

366 *her hondes lorne*. Fr. "E toutes les denz si perdues." But some MSS. read "mains," hands, for "denz," teeth.

369 ff. Cf. *ML Prol*, II, 20 ff.

387 Cf. "Tempus edax rerum," Met., xv, 234 ff.

413 *don there write*, cause to be written; Fr. "escrite"; here used of portrayal in painting.

415 *Poope-holy*, hypocritical; Fr. "Papelardie." The original meaning of "papelard" appears to have been "glutton" (from Fr. "paper," eat, and "lard," bacon). The English form "pope-holy" is due to popular etymology.

442 *ay*, ever (rather than the verb *agh*, ought, from AS. "áh," as Skeat suggested).

446 Matt. vi, 16.

468 Job iii, 3.

490 *daungerous*, stingy; Fr. "dangereus ne chiches." Langlois has "desdeigneus."

544 *The openyng of hir yen clere*, Fr., "Li entriauz," i.e., the space between her eyes. Langlois in his note cites other instances where a "large entrueil" is mentioned as a beautiful trait.

564 *werede ... upon*, wore (upon her). For the construction cf. *WB Prol*, III, 559, n.

579 *journe*, day's work; Fr. "jornee."

593 With the allegory of Idleness as the porter of Love's garden Langlois compares Ovid, Rem. Am., 139: "Otia si tollas, periere Cupidinis arcus."

611 The pictures were "full of sorrow and woe" to repel visitors.

624 For this proverbial use of India cf. *PardT*, VI, 722, and n.

648 The comparison with the Earthly Paradise was familiar. For other examples see Langlois's note.

668 *That other*, used with a pl. noun. Cf. line 991, below.

676 *of man that myghte dye*, i.e., of mortal man.

684 *sereyns*, Sirens. In *Bo*, i, pr. 1, 68, Chaucer has *mermaydenes* for the Lat. "Sirenes."

692 *erst*. For the idiom cf. *KnT*, I, 1566, n.

720 *reverdye*, rejoicing; Fr. "reverdie." The NED records no other case of *reverdye*, and perhaps the MS. reading, *reverye*, should be retained (as in Globe).

766 Langlois cites another reference to songs of Lorraine in the Galerent, ll. 1171–72.

768 *this contre*, Orléans.

791 *Ne bede I*, I would never ask.

868 *likyng*, agreeable; Fr. "plaisant" (Kaluza). Langlois reads: "Que vos iroie je disant?"

892 *amorettes*, Fr. "par fines amoretes," which may mean "by beautiful girls." The English fragment B (line 4755) has *amourettes* in this sense. In the present passage Skeat interprets it "with love-knots," and argues that *with* cannot mean "by" in this phrase and "with" in the rest of the sentence. Langlois cites in this connection ll. 155–57 from the Jugement d'Amour: "Cotes orent de roses pures, Et de violetes çaintures Que par soulaz firent amors" (Barbazan and Méon, Fabliaux et Contes, IV, 359).

907–8 E. P. Kuhl (PQ, XXIV, 33 ff.) would see in the insertion of lines on the Red Rose here and in line 1680 compliments to the Duke and Duchess of Lancaster.

915 *archaungell*, titmouse? (Fr. "mesenges.") The word is not known elsewhere in this sense and two emendations for it have been suggested: *acaunthyll*, a corruption of *acanthyllus*, "goldfinch," proposed by D'Arcy W. Thompson in N & Q, CLXXV, 332; and *wariangel*, the red-backed shrike, by J. G. Kunstmann in MLN, LV, 269. The latter word occurs in *FrT*, III, 1409.

923 ff. With the idea of the two bows and two sets of arrows cf. Ovid, Met., i, 468 ff. Langlois cites parallels from mediæval literature.

997 The explanation here promised was never written.

1007 Cf. line 952, above.

1014 *byrde*, bride (though the words may be of different origin); Fr. "esposee."

1018 *wyndred*, trimmed? painted?; Fr. "guigniee." Liddell cites "winrede bruwes" from the O. E. Homilies, 2nd Ser. (ed. Morris, EETS, 1873, p. 213), where the meaning is apparently "ogling glances." That interpretation seems less likely here, though the Fr. "guignier" is ambiguous. Cotgrave gives "guigner," to wink, and Godefroy has "guign(i)er," meaning "parer," "farder."

1031 *Sore plesaunt*, etc.; a difficult line. The Fr. has: "Sade, plaisant, aperte e cointe." Skeat emends *Wys* for *Sore*, and Kaluza suggests *Sade*. Probably *Sore* is the correct reading and is used merely for emphasis. Cf. line 4305, below.

1089 *durst*, needed. The verbs *dar* and *tharf* were often confused. Cf. line 1324, below.

1093 *Frise*, Friesland; added in the English. Explained by A. S. Cook (MLN, XXXI, 442) as Phrygia rather than Friesland, which did not abound in gold. He compares Rom. de Thèbes, 6630, but an English parallel would make his case stronger.

1106 *besaunt*, a gold coin, named for Byzantium, where it was struck. The weight was less than that of an English sovereign.

1117 *jagounces*, jacinths or hyacinths. Lydgate (Chorl and Bird, st. 34, Minor Poems, Percy Soc., 1840, p. 188) describes the *jagounce* as "Cytryne of colour, lyke garnettes of entayle."

1152 Alexander is here a type of liberality, as King Arthur, in line 1199, below, is of chivalry.

1158 *sende*, sent; Chaucer's usual preterite is *sente*.

1182 *adamaunt*, loadstone. On its meanings see *KnT*, I, 1990, n.

1232 *sukkenye*, Fr. "sorquenie," a frock. It was not made of hempen hards, but probably of fine linen.

1235 *ridled*, gathered, or pleated, like a curtain (OF. "ridel"). The Fr. here has "cuillie e jointe," and Langlois renders "cuillie" by "ajustée."

1240 *roket*, here synonymous with *sukkenye*; now used of the short surplice of a bishop.

1250 The lord of Windsor, when Guillaume de Lorris wrote, was Henry III. His son Edward (afterwards Edward I) was born in 1239. Perhaps, however, the reference was not to contemporary history but to Arthurian romance. Langlois cites Cligés, 1237 ff., and Rigomer, 13188, for the association of Windsor with King Arthur. For the order of words in *The lordis sone of Wyndesore* cf. *ClT*, IV, 1170, n.

1314 *olmeris*, elms; Fr. "moriers" (perhaps misread as "ormiers").

1324 See l. 1089, above.

1341 Skeat's emendation, *wol ... shete* (inf.): *mete* (pres. ind.), provides correct rimes, but breaks the sequence of tenses. Possibly *shette* is for a past participle *shĕte(n)*, instead of the more regular *shŏte(n)*.

1353 Fr. "Il n'est nus arbres qui fruit charge, Se n'est aucuns arbres hisdeus, Don il n'i ait ou un ou deus Ou vergier, ou plus, se devient." That is to say, all kinds of fruit trees, except a few which would have been too hideous, were represented in the orchard. The English misses the point.

1369 *greyn de parys*, Fr. "Graine de parevis." Skeat emends *parys* to *paradys*, but "greyn(s) de Parys" is recorded several times in Middle English. It is a corruption of "graine(s) de parais (pareys, pareis)," the popular form which existed in Old French alongside of the learned formation "graine de paradis." See Angl. Beibl., XXIX, 46.

1374 *coynes*, quins (whence, by misunderstanding of the plural, "quince").

1377 *aleys*, the fruit of the wild service tree; Fr. "alies." No other case has been noted of the occurrence of the word in English.

1383 With the tree list here cf. those in *PF*, 176 ff., and *KnT*, I, 2921 ff.

1414 *condys*, conduits; Fr. "conduiz." For the loss of the *t* in the English plural, comparison may be made with *avocas*, the reading of several MSS., in *PardT*, VI, 291.

1426 *myster*, need.

1436 *poudred*, Fr. "pipolee" (var. "piolee").

1453 *at good mes*, from a favorable point; Fr. "en bon leu." Cf. line 3462. The figure is that of a good range, or shot, in hunting.

1458 *Pepyn*, Pepin, king of the Franks, father of Charlemagne. One French MS. reads: "Mais puis Karles le fils Pepin." (Langlois reads: "Mais puis Charle ne puis Pepin.")

1469 The source of the story of Narcissus is Ovid, Met., iii, 356 ff.

1537 *warisoun*, reward? By confusion of Fr. "guerredon" with "guerison"?

1591 *accusith*, discloses; Fr. "accusent" (Kaluza); Langlois has "encusent."

1604 *to ligge upright*, to lie flat, i.e., to die.

1610 *Yblent*, blinded? deceived? Fr. "mis en rage" (Kaluza); Langlois has "mis a glaive."

1652 *enclos*, enclosed; a French form.

1674 *ron*, bush? Fr. "soz ciaus."

1705 According to the usual view, there is a break here in both rime and sense, which marks the end of the first fragment. Kaluza put the division after line 1704, but it comes better, as Skeat showed, after line 1705. Various proposals have been made to complete the sentence. Skeat suggested that a line had been lost, such as, *Fulfild of baume, withouten doute*; Liddell (Globe edn.) that an original couplet with the rimes *swete*, adj.: *swete*, vb. ("sweat"), or *swete: replete* (for Fr. "replenist"), had been corrupted in copying. Professor W. P. Reeves (MLN, XXXVIII, 124) would avoid the necessity of any emendation by taking *dide* (Th *dyed*) as "dyed" and giving it an unusual application to fragrance. In the opinion of Professor Liddell the work of the second poet, if there is a change of authors, does not begin until line 1715. Professor Brusendorff (pp. 320–21) argued that it is not necessary to assume any new fragment at all. In a case of such complete uncertainty it is best to let the MS. reading stand unaltered.

Lists of imperfect rimes and other forms in fragment B which do not accord with Chaucerian usage will be found in Skeat's introduction, Oxf. Ch., I, 4 ff. Examples of the various irregularities are pointed out in the following notes.

1721 *botoun* (misspelt *bothom* or *bothum*) is used in fragment B to translate Fr. "bouton," which was rendered *knoppe* in fragment A.

1728 On this conception of love entering the heart by way of the eye see *KnT*, I, 1096, n.

1733 *in [a] stounde*; Fr. "tantost."

1776 *withouten were*, without warning; Fr. "senz menacier." Skeat notes that similar tags, like *withouten doute*, *withouten wene*, are common in fragment B. But in this instance the phrase has appropriateness and force.

1785–86 *desir: ner*, an imperfect rime. Other examples are ll. 2037–38, *joynt: queynt*; 2441–42, *desyr: ner*; 2779–80, *desir: maner*; 4181–82, *ademant: foundement*; 4685–86, *ler: desir*.

1794–95 Not in the Fr. Apparently a proverb or quotation. Cf. lines 2084 ff., below.

1802 The third arrow is here named *Curtesie*. In ll. 955 ff., it was called *Fraunchise, . . . fethred . . . With valour and with curtesye*.

1811–12 The rime *hit* (pp.): *flit* (inf.) is un-Chaucerian. For other cases of the disregard of the final -*e* of the infinitive see lines 1873–74, 1939–40, 1981–82, 2615–16, 2627–28, 2629–30, 2645–46, 2755–56, 3099–3100.

1813–14 Another irregular rime, in which the final -*e* of the weak preterite, *wroughte*, is clipped.

1818 *ner*, positive, as in line 1848. It is usually comparative in Chaucer. But cf. *KnT*, I, 1439, n.

1820 Fr. "Qu'eschaudez doit eve doter." The translation gives the proverb in the form more familiar in English. Cf. *CYT*, VIII, 1407; also Proverbs of Hendyng, l. 184 (in Morris and Skeat, Specimens of Early English, II, Oxford, 1872, p. 40). See further Herrig's Arch., LXXXVIII, 376; Haeckel, p. 21, no. 68.

1847 Loose translation. Fr. "E durement 'm'abelissoit Ce que jou veoie a bandon."

1849–50 *I: malady* (for *maladye*), an example of the un-Chaucerian *y: ye* rime. Other instances are in lines 1861, 2179, 2209, 2493, 2737, 3241, 4145.

1853–54 *thore: more*, for *thar: mar*, a Northern rime. Chaucer's forms would be *there* and *more*.

1906 *Rokyng*, apparently the same word as *rouken*, "crouch," "cower," in *KnT*, I, 1308. The line is not in the French.

1928 *lepande*, a Northern participle.

1965 "The healing of love must be found where they [the lovers] got their wound." Professor Liddell suggests that *love* is personal (= "lover") and should perhaps be plural. The general idea that only the weapon that gives a wound can cure it — as in the Greek story of Achilles and Telephus — is familiar, and its application to love is not unusual.

2002 *sauff . . . vouche*, vouchsafe.

2028 The figure of the prison may be due, as Professor Liddell suggests, to the misunderstanding of Fr. "aprison," instruction. "Dedenz lui ne puet demorer Vilanie ne mesprison Ne nule mauvaise aprison."

2037 This was the regular posture of the vassal in doing homage.

2038 *made it . . . queynt* bore myself with due ceremony; Fr. "mout me fis cointes." For the idiom cf. line 3863; *Gen Prol*, I, 785, n.

2044 *taken*, perhaps to be emended to *tan* (Northern), as Skeat suggests.

2051 *And*, if.

2076 *disseise*, dispossess.

2077–78 *justice*, government? control? (punishment? Liddell). The translation is obscure and not quite parallel to Kaluza's Fr. text: "Tel garnison i avés mise, Qui le guerroie a vostre guise." Langlois reads: "Tel garnison i avez mise Qui le garde bien e jostise."

2088 For this conception of the key Langlois refers to Chrétien de Troyes, Ivain, 4632 ff.; Perceval, 3810 ff.

2092 *loke and knette*, locked and fast bound.

2149–52 These lines, in the French, follow line 2144 and form part of a speech of the god of Love.

2157–62 Not in the French.

2161 *poyntith*, punctuates, i.e., in reading. The MSS. were not punctuated.

2170 *Romance*, the French language.

2181 f. Cf. *WBT*, III, 1158.

2185–2202 Not in the Fr. For the ideas cf. *WBT*, III, 1109 ff., which, Skeat remarked, may have suggested the passage to the translator of fragment B. Brusendorff (pp. 392 ff.) insisted that the parallels here and elsewhere strongly support Chaucer's authorship of the whole translation.

2203 Cf. Ovid, Ars. Amat., ii, 604.

2206 References might be multiplied to passages in which Kay appears as the type of *vilanye*, or Gawain, of courtesy. Langlois, in his note, gives instances from Old French. On Gawain, cf. *SqT*, V, 95. An example of Kay's rudeness may be found in Malory's Morte d'Arthur, vii, ch. 1.

2230 *to thy power*, to the extent of thy power.

2255–84 With this counsel cf. Ovid, Ars. Amat., i, 513–24.

2263 *sittand*, the Northern form of the participle, is here established by the rime.

2269 *sitte so pleyn*, fit so closely, smoothly.

2271 The MS. spelling *awmere* (*aumere*, Th) here is probably only a scribal error.

2293 ff. Fr. "C'est maladie mout courtoise, Ou l'en jeue e rit e envoise."

2301–04 Not in the Fr.

2311–12 "If you are accomplished in any art, do not be distant and offish about performance." For the following counsel cf. Ovid, Ars. Amat., i, 595 ff.

2323 Kaluza, in a foot-note, proposed to emend *foote* to *floyte* (Fr. "fleüter"). Brusendorff (p. 418) suggested also changing the third person to the second, for consistency.

2325–28 Not in the Fr. *Among*, adverbial, "from time to time."

2326 *that thou make*, apparently an independent hortatory subjunctive. See the textual note.

2329 *scarce*, miserly; Fr. "aver."

2349 ff. Cf. Horace, Ars. Poet., 335 ff.

2355 *joyne*, enjoin; Fr. "enjoing."

2362 ff. Fr. "Vueil je e comant que tu aies En un seul leu tot ton cuer mis, Si qu'il n'i soit mie demis, Mais toz entiers, senz tricherie." The reading and sense are both doubtful in the translation. Skeat, keeping *For trecherie*, explains it "Against treachery, in all security." Liddell emends, *Of trecherie*, and interprets "half treacherous, half faithful."

The phrase *halfen dool* preserves an archaic form of the adjective in -*n* (from AS. "healfne dæl").

2367 For the ellipsis of the subject here cf. line 2416, below.

2383 ff. On the proverbial character of these lines, see Whiting, Chaucer's Use of Proverbs, p. 23.

2386 *maugre his*, in spite of himself.

2421 For this conceit of the separation of the lover's heart from his body Langlois cites Cligés, lines 5180 ff.

2427 Cf. the proverb "Ubi amor, ibi oculus," of which Langlois notes several versions.

2463 *lete*, cease.

2478 Proverbial; cf. *Tr*, i, 449, n.

2497 ff. Obscure and only partly paralleled in the Fr. See the textual note.

2522 The observance of secrecy was one of the fundamental principles of courtly love. See *NPT*, VII, 2914 ff., n.

2564 "Like a man defeated in war." The Fr. differs: "Come ome qui a mal as denz."

2573 "Castles in Spain" are still proverbial. On the history of the expression see Morel-Fatio in the Mélanges Picot, Paris, 1913, I, 335; cf. also Haeckel, p. 19, no. 60.

2592 *Fro joye*, MS. *The joye*. Skeat keeps *The* and makes *joye* the object of *langoure* — a difficult construction.

2604 *warned*, refused.

2621 *of hir*, Liddell's suggestion; the MS. reads *on hir*; Skeat and Globe *on me*.

2628 *liggen*, a Northern form, which should perhaps be corrected, since *ly(e)* occurs in rime below in lines 2629, 2645.

2631 Fr. "Gesirs est enuieuse chose."

2641 *contene*, contain thyself? (Skeat); continue? (Liddell). Perhaps a mistake for *contende*; Fr. "te contendras."

2643 This departs from the Fr.: "Se j'onques mal d'amer conui" (in the first person).

2660 *score*, crack; Fr. "fendeüre."

2673 ff. This departs from the Fr. and is perhaps corrupt. See the textual note to l. 2676.

With the use of *relyk* here and in l. 2907 as a term of endearment cf. *LGW ProlF*, 321, and n.

2684 Cf. Ovid, Ars. Amat., i, 729, 733.

2695 Cf. Ars. Amat., ii, 251 ff.

2709 *mare* (: *fare*), a Northern form.

2710 Cf. Ars. Amat., ii, 357 ff.; also the proverb "Out of sight, out of mind," to which Langlois cites numerous parallels.

2738 ff. The ideas are proverbial. Langlois cites the Latin line quoted by Rabelais (Pantagruel, iii, 41): "Dulcior est fructus post multa pericula ductus."

2755 Cf. Ovid, Pont., i, 6, 37.

2775 Fr. "Esperance par sofrir vaint." The French is nearer than the English to the proverb, "Qui patitur vincit."

2833–36 Not in the Fr. The negative in line 2836 seems necessary to the sense.

2840 Gaston Paris (Hist. Litt. de la France, XXVIII, 373, n.) took this to be an allusion to the lady of Fayel. But the identification is uncertain. Guillaume de Lorris appears, as Langlois notes, to be quoting the words of a song. The English version is free and considerably expanded. The lady's words, in the original, refer only to hearing speech about her lover. In the English, they include speaking about him herself, and this of course is involved, in both versions, in the advice which follows about selecting a confidant.

2881 "Then shall he [go] further."

2884 With this allusion to the institution of "sworn brotherhood" cf. the story of Palamon and Arcite. See *KnT*, I, 1132, n.

2951 "When the god of Love had taught," etc. The inversion is unusual.

3043 ff. Fr. "Chasteé, qui dame doit estre E des roses e des boutons, Iert assaillie des gloutons Si qu'ele avoit mestier d'aïe." The English translation departs from the original, perhaps through some confusion.

3088 *but it rise*, unless it happen (?). Cf. line 3115, where *arise* translates Fr. "avenir."

3130 The description of *Daunger* is characteristic of the "vilain," or peasant, as he appears in mediæval literature. Many features are also matched in the accounts of giants in the romances and chansons de geste. For illustrations see Langlois's note; also G. M. Vogt, The Peasant in Mid. Eng. Lit., unpublished Harv. diss., 1923.

3137 *kirked*, crooked? Form unexplained. Fr. "le nés froncié."

3146 Proverbial; cf. Haeckel, pp. 40 f., no. 139.

3185 "I could not hold out against the pain." Not in the Fr.

3205 ff. Langlois compares, for the idea, Ivain, 1492 ff., and P. Meyer, Recueil d'Anciens Textes, Paris, 1874–77, p. 372. See also the remarks about Nature in *PhysT*, VI, 9 ff., and n.

3233 *Ne hadde*, etc., if Idleness had not led thee.

3253–54 Fr. "E de Dangier neient ne monte Envers que de ma fille Honte."

3256 "Like one who is no sluggard." Fr. "Con cele qui n'est pas musarde." For the idiom cf. line 4235, below; also *MLT*, II, 1090, n.

3269 ff. Such references to the folly of love were commonplace in mediæval literature. Cf., for example, the speech of Theseus, *KnT*, I, 1785 ff., and n.

3294 "And to leave off is a masterly course." Fr. "Mes au lessier a grant mestrise" (Kaluza); "Mais a l'issir a grant maistrise" (Langlois).

3303 *leve*, believe; Fr. "croit."

3326 *in the peyne*, by torture. Cf. *KnT*, I, 1133.

3336 *Forwery*, very weary? Cf. *KnT*, I, 2142, n.

3346 *a Freend*, a proper name in the Fr.: "Amis ot non." It is apparently not to be so taken in the English.

3373 The rime *manace* (with silent *-e*): *caas* is un-Chaucerian.

3377 This departs from the French, which has the comparison (still proverbial): "Je le conois come un denier."

3401 *burdoun*, Fr. "baston d'espine."

3422 *That*; perhaps to be emended to *And*; Fr. "e."

3432 ff. A commonplace sentiment. Cf. *KnT*, I, 1606, and n.

3437 Obscure. Fr. "Mout trovai Dangier dur e lent De pardoner son mautalent." Skeat interprets *fil*, "condescended"; Liddell, "failed."

3454 *tall*, unusual spelling for *tale*, which here rimes with *all*.

3462 *at good mes*, at a favorable opportunity; Fr. "en bon point." See the note to line 1453, above.

3463 Cf. Prov. xv, 1; also passages cited by Langlois in his note to l. 2627 (= *Rom*, 2775).

3489 ff. Fr. "E tant qu'il a certainement Veü a mon contenement Qu' Amors malement me jostise," etc.

3502 *bothen*, Liddell's emendation of *bothom*, which Skeat refers to the *botoun*. But cf. the Fr.,

"Car l'une e l'autre me voudroit Aidier, s'eus pueent, volentiers."

3539 Cf. Ovid, Ex Ponto, ii, 9, 11.

3548 *This*, this is.

3604 *dar*, for *thar*, need. See the note to line 1089, above.

3674 Langlois compares Robert de Blois, Chast. des Dames, ll. 124 ff. (Barbazan and Méon, Fabliaux et Contes, II, 188).

3677 A commonplace. See Whiting, p. 28.

3687 f. Proverbial. Langlois cites parallels from Latin and French. Cf. Haeckel, pp. 13 f., no. 44.

3715 *of religioun*, of a religious order.

3733 Here and in line 3796 Liddell would give *beaute* three syllables. But this seems unlikely. The same question arises in the *KnT*, I, 2385.

3773 See Whiting, p. 24.

3774 The emendation *nille*, for MS. *ville*, may be unnecessary. Cf. *Intro to MLT*, II, 49, n.

3779 ff. The vicissitudes of love made a common topic. Cf. *KnT*, I, 1785 ff., and n.

3784 *The*; emended to *That* by Brusendorff, p. 376.

3795 Cf. l. 42, and n.

3811 *an Irish womman*; Fr. "Irese" (or "iraise"), interpreted by some as "Irish," by others as the common adjective "iroise," "angry, a virago." Langlois (I, 192, n.) suggests that the French poet intended a pun on the two words. The scornful mention of an Irishwoman is in keeping with the character often ascribed to the Irish in mediæval literature. For an extended account of the "Wild Irish" tradition see Professor E. D. Snyder, MP, XVII, 687 ff.

3826 *Reynes*, Rennes, in Brittany. *Amyas* is apparently only a mistake for Meaux; Fr. "Estre a Estampes ou a Miauz."

3832 *reward*, regard.

3851 *hadde*, (that he) had, as to have (?). A difficult ellipsis, but not impossible. Cf. *MLT*, II, 1091, n. Other editors supply [*Ne*], [*Nor*], perhaps correctly.

3863 *made it symple*, behaved with simplicity. Cf. the note to line 2038, above.

3878 Langlois compares Pamphilus de Amore, l. 417: "Sepius immeritas incusat fama puellas" (ed. Baudouin, Paris, 1874).

3912 For the idiom *to blere the eye*, "beguile, deceive," cf. *RvT*, I, 4049, *CYT*, VIII, 730.

3928 "I must (have) new counsel."

3931 f. Proverbial. Cf. *Tr*, v, 1266 f.

3978 A proverbial expression in French, of which Langlois cites examples.

3995 f. Possibly the *-e* of the inf. *withstonde* should be kept, and *londe* allowed an (irregular) dat. *-e*; so also in the case of *stonde*: *hond*, ll. 4091 f.

4012–13 For very free emendation see Brusendorff, p. 331.

4021 Fr. "Estiez vos ore couchiez? Levez tost sus," etc.

4030 "A churl changes his nature, ceases to play his part, when he is courteous." Fr. "Vilains qui est cortois enrage."

4032 A proverb in Fr. Cf. Li Proverbe au Vilain, 41 (ed. Tobler, Leipzig, 1895, p. 19). Other parallels are cited in Langlois's note. See also Haeckel, p. 35, no. 117.

4096 *me*, one. Skeat emends to *men*, which is perhaps more natural under the accent.

4123 *allas*: *face* (with silent *e*); an un-Chaucerian rime.

4137–40 Not in the Fr. The familiar sentiment might have been suggested by *Tr*, iii, 1625 ff., or *Boece*, ii, pr. 4, 7–9, or Dante, Inf., v, 121 ff.

4145–300 The English translation here shows a number of omissions and insertions, as compared with the Fr. (ll. 3797–936).

4176 *skaffaut*, scaffold, a shed on wheels which covered the approach of besiegers.

4180 Langlois cites, for mediæval recipes for mortar, G. Anelier, Hist. de la Guerre de Navarre, ed. F. Michel in Collection de Documents Inédits sur l'Hist. de France, Paris, 1856, p. 602, n. In none of them, he adds, is vinegar mentioned.

4181–82 *ademant*: *foundement*, an imperfect rime.

4191 *Spryngoldes*, catapults (from OF. "espringale"). The Fr. here has "perrieres."

4194 *who*, i.e., the men "who might be close at hand."(?) Skeat emends, [*whiche*].

4199 *maad*: *brad*, a Northern rime.

4218 *conestablerye*, ward of the castle; Fr. "conestablie," troop.

4229 *for stelyng*, to prevent stealing.

4235 "As being the one that causes all the strife." Cf. l. 3256.

4247 *Discordaunt*, apparently due to a misunderstanding of the Fr. "descorz," a type of *chanson*.

4249 *fayle*, make mistakes. The reading *fall* (: *Cornewall*) suggested by Liddell, is unlikely.

4250 *hornepipes*, pipes made of horn; Fr. "estives," pipes of straw. *Cornewaile*, probably Cornouaille, a town in Brittany.

4254 Since the abuse of women is here ascribed to *Wikked Tunge*, it is not probable that the blame of Chaucer in *LGW ProlF*, 322 ff., *G*, 248 ff. rests especially on this passage.

4279 *garisoun*, a mistaken rendering of Fr. "garnison."

4286 ff. With the description of La Vieille Langlois compares Pamphilus, ll. 281–82, 425.

4300 The phrase, which became proverbial, is used by Chaucer, *Gen Prol*, I, 476. See the note.

4305 Cf. l. 1031, n.

4322 *I wende a bought*, I supposed (myself) to have bought; Fr. "Jes cuidoie avoir achetez."

4328 Fr. "Que s'onques ne l'eüsse eüe." There is an ellipsis of *if* after *Thanne*.

4335 Langlois compares Ovid, Met., i, 269 ff.; Virgil, Georg., i, 226.

4353 A typical account of Fortune, and doubtless the source of various references to her in Chaucer. See *KnT*, I, 925 f., n.

4358 The reading *turne* (MS. G and Globe) would have to be taken as a protasis in the subjunctive.

4389 Cf. the proverb: "Qui plus castigat, plus amore ligat."

4429 This ends Guillaume de Lorris's part of the poem. Fr. "Que je n'ai mais aillors fiance." Jean de Meun begins: "E si l'ai je perdue, espeir."

4441 *what and*, what if.

4443 ff. Cf. Ovid, Her., xvi (xvii), 234; Langlois notes also the beginning, "Spes fallax," of the Elegia de Spe, Anthologia veterum Latinorum ... Poematum, ed. Meyer, Leipzig, 1835, no. 932.

4475 This sounds proverbial. Langlois compares Huon de Mery's Tornoiemenz Antecrist,

1662 ff. (ed. Wimmer, Ausgaben und Abhandlungen, LXXVI).

4493 *And yit moreover*, Fr. "Enseurquetout"; cf. *KnT*, I, 2801, n.

4495 *ronne in age*, advanced in age. Cf. *NPT*, VII, 2821, and n.

4499 *enforced*, enhanced; Fr. "enforcera."

4527 *my*, MS. *faire*, probably copied from next line; Fr. "ma priere."

4532 *lowe*, appraise; Fr. "De la value d'une pome." Liddell reads *love*, with rime of *v* and *w*.

4559 *cunne hym mawgre*, Fr. "mal gré saveir." Cf. *Kan hem ... thank*, *KnT*, I, 1808, and n.

4568 *wynke*, close the eyes (in sleep). Cf. *NPT*, VII, 3431.

4634 *greved*, or some similar word, must be supplied. Skeat has *pyned*; Liddell suggests *harmed*.

4681 Cf. line 2037, above.

4685 ff. This description of Love is based upon Alanus de Insulis, De Planctu Naturae (Migne, Pat. Lat., CCX, 455 f.; quoted by Langlois).

4693–94 Not in the Fr.

4705 *fret full*, fully furnished. Cf. *LGW*, 1117. Skeat mentions and rejects the emendation *bret ful* (= brim full).

4718 So MS. and Th; doubtless to be emended by interchanging *wisdom* and *kunnyng* (Brusendorff, p. 318). Fr. "C'est sapience sans science, C'est science sans sapience" (Langlois var.).

4732 *withoute*, on the outside; Globe, *oute*.

4751 f. *slowe*, moth (?). So Skeat. But no other occurrence of the word in this sense seems to be known. He takes *were* to mean "wear away." But this does not suit the context. The Fr. reads: "C'est teigne qui riens ne refuse, Les pourpres e les bureaus use." Liddell conjectures that the Engl. version followed a reading "caigne," which it rendered by *slowe*, vagabond.

4755–56 Proverbial. See Cotgrave, s.v., Amourette; also Rom., XIII, 533. Langlois cites several literary parallels.

4764 Previous editors have either supplied *ne* or changed *That* to *But*. But for a similarly inconsequent construction see l. 3774, above, and cf. *Intro to MLT*, II, 49, n.

4768 A reference to another passage in the De Planctu Naturae. Genius excommunicates every man who "legitimum Veneris obliquat incessum," or who "a regula Veneris exceptionem facit anormalam" (Migne, 482 A; cf. 432 A). On the history of Genius as an allegorical figure see E. C. Knowlton, MLN, XXXIX, 89. In his character as priest of Nature he appears later in the Fr. RR, (ll. 16285 ff.). In Gower's Conf. Am., he is the priest of Venus.

4783 f. Proverbial; see Haeckel, pp. 3 f., no. 12.

4790 *avaunt*, ahead, advanced.

4796 *par cuer*, by heart.

4809 Langlois notes the similarity of this definition to that in Andreas Capellanus, De Amore, bk. i, caps. 1, 2 (ed. E. Trojel, Copenhagen, 1892, pp. 3–7).

4821–24 Not in the Fr. Cf. *NPT*, VII, 3344 ff.

4831 *paramours*, adverbial, "with passionate love." Fr. "Mais par amour amer ne deignent." Cf. *KnT*, I, 1155, and n.

4838 *ernes*, passion, desire. Cf. *LGW*, 1287.

4840 ff. Proverbial; cf. Haeckel, p. 54.

4856 Proverbial; cf. Haeckel, p. 43, no. 146.

4859 *Oure sectis*, of our species, race.

4875 *fortened crece*, destroyed increase, i.e., abortion? So Skeat. Liddell reads *for tene crece.* The couplet is not in the Fr.

4884 The reference is to Cicero's De Senectute. See particularly chap. xii.

4917 *doth*, here apparently not causative, but used as in modern English.

4943 *Demande*; on readings and interpretation see the textual note.

5022 The translator seems to have forgotten the conclusion — "E qu'ele a sa vie perdue Se dou futur n'est secourue." Liddell suggests supplying *Al her lyf she hath forlorn.*

5123–24 Not in the Fr. Perhaps from *HF*, 1257 f. (see n.); cf. also *Intro to MLT*, II, 20 ff. and n.

5136 "Love that was so grafted in my thought, destroyed Reason's teaching."

5151 f. Still proverbial; cf. *Tr*, iv, 432 ff., n.

5169–71 Obscure. Fr. "Mais espeir que je comparrai Plus la haïne au darrenier, Tout ne vaille amour un denier." (Michel reads "me" for "ne.")

5201 *Love of freendshipp*, friendly love. Cf. *Tr*, ii, 371, 962; and, for the same construction, cf. *KnT*, I, 1912 and n. With the definition of friendship Langlois compares Cicero, De Amicitia, chaps. v, vi, xiii, xvii.

5223–24 Fr. "Teus meurs aveir deivent e seulent Qui parfaitement amer veulent."

5234–35 Proverbial. "Satis emit qui petit." Langlois cites parallels from Latin and French.

5259–60 A commonplace sentiment, if not exactly proverbial. Not in the Fr.

5266 Another proverb, and not in the Fr.; cf. Haeckel, p. 19, no. 61.

5274 *moleste*, used reflexively, unless *He* should be emended to *It* or *That.*

5278 *fered*, fired; properly a Kentish form, though used by Chaucer and other writers for convenience in rime.

5281 Cf. De Amicitia, ch. vi.

5286 Here the reference to Cicero is explicit. The passages immediately involved are chaps. xii, xiii, xvii.

5290 Obscure. Perhaps: "Unless it were too unreasonable." See the textual note.

5311 ff. Cf. De Amicitia, chap. xiv.

5330 *bit*, abides.

5351 *take*, Fr. "afuble."

5379 *vice*, with silent *-e*, making an un-Chaucerian rime with *wys.*

5384 *goot*, goat; Fr. "cers."

5399–400 *wat* (MS. *wote*): *estat*, a Northern rime.

5409 ff. The argument here is based upon Boethius, ii, pr. 8.

5417 *cherish* (inf.): *norys*, an irregular rime.

5419 *deles*, Northern form of the third person singular.

5443 *maken it hool*, perform it wholly (?). So Skeat.

5445–46 Fr. "Jusqu'au despendre les chemises."

5455 ff. A commonplace. See Whiting, p. 31; cf. also 5551, below.

5467 ff. The sentence is not completed.

5473–74 Perhaps *And* should be shifted from line 5474. Cf. the Fr. "E leur assiet, come marrastre, Au cueur un douloureus emplastre."

5484 *arn*, the Northern form, for which Chaucer almost invariably has *ben.*

5486 Not in the Fr. Cf. *Fort*, 34, for the distinction between *freend of effect* and *freend of chere* (*countenaunce*). This supports the emendation to *effect* (MS. Th *affecte*). See also ll. 5549–50, below. For full discussion of the *Fortune* passages see Brusendorff, pp. 404 ff.

5493 "Misfortune leaves not one (remaining)." Or perhaps emend *lat* to *leveth*, Fr. "remaint."

5507 "In the voice in which they had flattered" (?). Skeat suggests that *japerye*, "mockery," would be more appropriate than *flaterie*. Fr. "a voiz jolie."

5510 For this proverb, which is not in the Fr., cf. *Tr*, iii, 861, and n.

5513 Cf. Prov. xvii, 17.

5520 Proverbial; cf. Haeckel, p. 4, no. 13.

5523 ff. Cf. Ecclus. xxii, 22.

5534 Cf. Eccl. vii, 28.

5535–36 "For there is no wealth which may be compared to friendship, in respect to worthiness."

5538 *valoure*, value; Fr. "valeur."

5540 Proverbial. "Verus amicus omni praestantior auro." Langlois cites a number of variants. See also Haeckel, pp. 4 f., no. 15.

5552 Cf. *Fort*, 10.

5573 *And*, if.

5583 f. Proverbial; cf. Haeckel, p. 11, no. 36.

5590 *mowis* (MS. *mavis*), bushels; Fr. "muis."

5649 Cf. *BD*, 1167. The works of Pythagoras are lost. Hierocles of Alexandria (5th cent.) wrote a commentary on the Golden Verses. Langlois suggests that the source of Jean de Meun's information was the commentary of Chalcidius on the Timaeus, ch. cxxxvi, which says: "Pythagoras etiam in suis aureis versibus: Corpore deposito cum liber ad aethera perges, Euades hominem factus deus aetheris almi" (ed. Wrobel, Leipzig, 1876, p. 198).

5659 ff. From Boethius, *Bo*, i, pr. 5, 8 ff.; v, pr. 1, 12 ff. Cf. also *Truth*, 17, 19.

5666 Both Jean de Meun and Chaucer translated Boethius.

5572 Cf. *Fort*, 25.

5681 *eispendith*, a Southern plural form used here for the rime.

5706 Cf. Boethius, ii, m. 2.

5710 "To drink up the river Seine." Proverbial; cf. Haeckel, p. 18, no. 58.

5739 ff. Not in the Fr. Lounsbury (Studies, II, 222) traced the pun on *fy* ("fier"?) to La Bible of Guiot de Provins (in Fabliaux et Contes, ed. Barbazan and Méon, II, 390). The rest of the word-play may turn on English *syen* or *syken*. The point seems to be that *fysic* goes from *fying*, "trusting," to *sying*, "sighing." Skeat's interpretation of *fy* as "fie" and *sy* as "si" ("if") is less probable.

5759 Proverbial. Cf. *RvT*, I, 4320 f., and n.

5763–64 Cf. the *Pard Prol*, passim (especially, VI, 407 ff.).

5781 ff. Langlois compares the Latin couplet: "Dives divitias non congregat absque labore, Non tenet absque metu nec deserit absque dolore" (J. Werner, Lateinische Sprichwörte und Sinnsprüche des Mittelalters, Heidelberg, 1912, p. 22, no. 117).

5810 Here ends fragment B. There is no break in the MS., but the translation passes from line 5154 to line 10679 of the French original. In the omitted passage Reason continues her discourse, but fails to persuade the Lover to abandon the service of the god of Love. The Lover then consults

L'Ami, who advises him to approach Belacueil's prison by a road called Trop-Donner, constructed by Largesse. L'Ami also instructs the Lover at length about the Golden Age, the corruption of society, and his proper course of conduct toward his mistress and wife. The Lover then approaches the castle, but Richesse bars his entrance. The god of Love comes to his assistance, first convoking a council of his barons. Fragment C begins with the account of the assembly.

On the authorship of the fragment see the introduction to these notes. Skeat gives in his introduction (Oxf. Ch. I, pp. 3–11) lists of the departures from Chaucerian usage. In the following notes examples are cited, but no complete collection is attempted.

5837 *To-Moche-Yevyng*, Fr. "Trop Doner."

5856 *Fair-Welcomyng*, called *Bialacoil* in fragment B.

5857 *Wel-Heelynge*, Fr. "Bien Celer."

5869 The rime *entent: present* departs from Chaucer's usage. He regularly has *entente*. Other cases of the dropping of final *-e* in rime are ll. 6105–06 (*atte last (e): agast*), ll. 6565–66 (*wrought*, pl.: *nought*), and six instances of *I* or words ending in *-y*, riming with words in which Chaucer regularly has a final *-e*, at ll. 6111 f., 6301 f., 6339 f., 6373 f., 6875 f., 7317 f.

5883 *nedes*; the translator has confused "besoignes," affairs, with "besoinges," needs. See also the textual note.

5894 *tan*, a Northern form.

5919 the rime *hors: wors* departs from Chaucer's usage. He rimes *wors* with *curs* (*Ck Prol*, I, 4349) and *pervers* (*BD*, 813). Other irregular cases in fragment C are *force: croce*, ll. 6469–70; *pacience: vengeaunce*, ll. 6429–30; *Abstynaunce: penaunce*, ll. 7481–82 (Chaucer's form being *Abstinence*); *science: ignorence*, ll. 6717–18. The last three instances, however, are exactly paralleled in the Fr.

5954 Aphrodite, according to one account, was the daughter of Cronos and Euonyme. The wife of Cronos was Rhea. In the Roman religion Aphrodite was identified with Venus, and Cronos with Saturn.

5966 *pol*, pool; Fr. "La palu d'enfer."

5988 "Unless they spring up, increase (Fr. 'sourdent') in his garner."

6028–30 Cf. *KnT*, I, 1951 f.

6041 f. For *thankynges* Kaluza proposes *thwakkynges* (Fr. "colees"), and Liddell would emend *talkynges* to *wakynges* (Fr. "acolees").

6044 *leve*, remain? Fr. "demourra."

6068 *kyng of harlotes*, king of rascals; Fr. "reis des ribauz." This was the actual title of an officer of the court, a kind of provost marshal. See Méon's edition for references. Skeat notes that the name was also jocularly conferred on any conspicuous vagabond.

6083 *kepe*, desire; so in line 6093.

6111 *let*, leads.

6135 ff. Langlois suggests that the description of Fals-Semblant may owe something to John of Salisbury, Policraticus, vii, ch. 21. It served in turn as a model for Chaucer's portraiture of the Pardoner.

6141 *worldly folk*, Fr. "au siecle," which apparently means the secular clergy as opposed to the regular orders.

6174 *nedes*, Fr. "besoignes"; cf. line 5883, above.

6191 *a croked brere*, one of the numerous figures of worthlessness. See *Gen Prol*, I, 177, n. The Fr. has "un coutel troine."

6192 A familiar proverb: "Cucullus non facit monachum." Cf. Haeckel, p. 39, no. 133.

6198 *kut*, contraction of *cutteth*; Fr. "trenche." Skeat suggests that Guile is said to cut them into thirteen branches because thirteen was the regular number of a convent.

6204 *Gibbe*, a common English name for a tom-cat; Fr. "dans Tiberz," also the name of the cat in the Roman de Renard.

6226 The reference here, as ll. 6234 ff. show, is to the laity, not to the secular clergy.

6259 f. For *a wether* the Fr. has "dam Belin" and for *a wolf*, "Sire Isengrin," both names from the Roman de Renard.

6264 *wery*, worry.

6281–83 A mistranslation of the Fr.; "E se d'aus ne la veauz rescourre, Anceis les laisses par tout courre; Laisses! mais se tu leur comandes," etc. The translator misread "d'aus" (var. "d'eus") as "deus," and failed to see that the Church (in the second person) is subject of the whole passage.

6282 *in this colour*, in this manner.

6290 *stuffen*, garrison; Fr. "garnir."

6319 Proteus, the sea god, whose power of transformation has given its meaning to the adjective "Protean."

6337 *Robert*, a gentleman; *Robyn*, a common man. Langlois notes that in Le Jeu de Robin et Marion the knight is called Robert, and the shepherd, Robin.

6338 *Frere Menour*, Franciscan; *Jacobyn*, Dominican.

6339 *loteby*, wench; Fr. "compaigne."

6341 *Abstinence-Streyned*. Fr. "Astenance Contrainte."

6352 *alle religiouns*, all religious orders.

6354 "I take the worthless and leave the good." Fr. "J'en lais le grain e preing la paille" (but some MSS. transpose "lais" and "preing"). Langlois notes that the expression occurs frequently in mediæval French.

6355 [*blynde*], infinitive; Fr. "avugler" (Kaluza); "embacler" (Langlois).

6371 f. Liddell reads: *But where my sleight is aperceyved, Of hem I am nomore resceyved*. Fr. "Mais mes traiz ont aperceüz, Si n'en sui mais si receüz." (Langlois does not include these lines in his text. Kaluza includes 110 lines, corresponding to *Rom*, 6361–6472, which Langlois prints in his notes at line 11222 of the RR.)

6385 *Onys a yeer*, namely, at Easter. See *ParsT*, X, 1027.

6424 "Whose name is not Friar Wolf." Fr. "frere Louvel." This is said, of course, in irony.

6434 *yeve me my Savyour*, admit me to Holy Communion.

6440 *kepe not dele*, care not to deal.

6452 *this*, this is. See Prov. xxvii, 23; John x, 14.

6502 Proverbial. Langlois (citing Recueil Rawlinson, II, 191) compares "Mal done a sun vassal qui son coutel leche."

6528 A reference to the Aristotelian doctrine of the mean. Cf. *LGW ProlF*, 165.

6532 Prov. xxx, 8, 9.

6541 *mycher*, thief; Fr. "lierres."

6552 Langlois cites Guillaume de Saint-Amour, De Periculis, xii, pp. 50 f. He is mentioned by name in l. 6763, below. The references to Saint-Amour in the following notes are taken from Langlois.

6571 An allusion, doubtless, to the fine houses built by the mendicant orders.

6573 ff. Cf. De Periculis, xii, p. 48.

6583 The reference is to St. Augustine's work, De Opere Monachorum. The six lines of Kaluza's Fr. corresponding to ll. 6583–88 occur in only a few MSS. and are held by Langlois to be an interpolation.

6595 ff. Cf. Matt. xix, 20 f.; see also l. 6653, below.

6604 "Use his praying as a pretext for idleness."

6613 Fr. "Car l'escriture s'i acorde Qui la verité nous recorde."

6615 Justinian the famous emperor of the Eastern Empire and compiler of the Code. See bk. xi, tit. 25 (26), De Mendicantibus Validis (cited in De Periculis, ii, p. 52).

6631 Langlois notes that Guillaume de Saint-Amour uses similar caution about discussing the power of popes and bishops (De Periculis, ii, p. 25).

6636 Probably a reference to Matt. xxiii, 14. But see also De Periculis, xii, p. 52, and Collectiones Catholice Canonice Scripture, p. 218 (ascribed to Saint-Amour).

6653 Matt. xix, 20–21. Cf. also De Periculis, xii, p. 49.

6654 *the good-man,* Fr. "li preudon."

6661 ff. See I Thess. iv, 11–12 (quoted in De Periculis, xii, p. 48).

6665 *honden* is a strange archaism for the period and dialect; perhaps to be emended to *honde.*

6671 ff. Cf. De Periculis, xiv, p. 67.

6679 See Acts xx, 33 ff.

6685 ff. Cf. De Periculis, xii, pp. 49–51.

6691 St. Augustine is mentioned here in only a few Fr. MSS. The correct text has "selonc le comant De l'escriture." Jean de Meun, as Langlois notes, got both the quotation and the name of the author from Saint-Amour's De Periculis, xii, p. 48, and Responsiones, pp. 90–91. The instances that follow are of course not to be attributed to the ancient authority, but are Jean de Meun's own illustrations.

6693 ff. The Knights Templars were founded in 1119, the Hospitallers, circa 1087. *Chanouns Regulers,* as distinguished from secular canons, are members of certain orders who follow a rule. The White Monks were Cistercians, a reformed order of the Benedictines; the Black, the unreformed.

6712 Proverbial; cf. Haeckel, p. 36, no. 119.

6749 "In the rescue of our faith."

6763 *William Seynt Amour,* a doctor of the Sorbonne in the middle of the 13th century, and a strong partisan of the secular clergy in their controversy with the friars. Jean de Meun's debt to his Tractatus Brevis De Periculis Novissimorum Temporum has been indicated in preceding notes. The book was condemned by Pope Alexander IV in 1256 and Guillaume was banished from France. But the statement in ll. 6769 ff. as to the sympathies of the university and community of Paris seems to be substantially true. For a fuller account of the episode see Langlois's notes (to ll. 11506–13).

6782 *The noble,* Fr. "Le vaillant ome."

6795 *foxerie,* Fr. "renardie."

6797 *What devel,* what the devil, etc.

6804 *on her owne,* Fr. "douleur."

6820 They do not scald them before skinning, as a butcher does a hog.

6823 f. Langlois compares Rustebeuf, Estat du Monde, lines 43–46 (Œuvres, ed. Jubinal, Paris, 1874–75, II, 18).

6835 *It cometh right,* i.e., it is replenished. Cf. *Gen Prol,* I, 705.

6837 Cf. *Pard Prol,* VI, 403.

6838 See *Gen Prol,* I, 256, and n.

6845 f. Cf. *Pard Prol,* VI, 443 ff.

6861 *bygyns,* Beguines; members of a lay sisterhood in the Netherlands. Cf. l. 7254, n.

6862 Fr. "dames palatines," ladies of the court.

6867 *clad or naked,* i.e., under all circumstances. See *Gen Prol,* I, 534, n.

6871 ff. On the prying inquisitiveness of the friars Langlois cites De Periculis, v, p. 32.

6875 *Ayens,* in comparison with. For the idea of the passage see De Periculis, iv, p. 12.

6888 Matt. xxiii, 1–8, 13–15.

6907 *sadde,* heavy (in the physical sense).

6911 *bordurs,* phylacteries; Fr. "philateres."

6923 ff. Langlois compares De Periculis, xiv, p. 69.

6926 *as oon,* Fr. "par acort."

6948 *oure alder,* of us all. Cf. *Gen Prol,* I, 586, and n.

6971 *brokages,* match-making.

6973 *executour,* executor of wills. Langlois cites Rustebeuf, Vie dou Monde, ll. 144–45 (Œuvres, II, 42).

6993–94 Cf. De Periculis, i, p. 21.

6998 John the Baptist because of his austere life in the wilderness was regarded as the founder of asceticism.

7010 Matt. vii, 15.

7013 *lambren,* an interesting archaic form from AS. "lombru." (Cf. "children" from "cildru.") Chaucer's plural was apparently *lambes.*

7017 Cf. Matt. xxiii, 15.

7022 *bouger,* Fr. "bougre," sodomite (Th *bourgerons,* MS. *begger*). For the association of heretics with Milan, Langlois cites Li Tornoiement Antecrist, ll. 2772 ff., and the Chronique Métrique of G. Guiart, ll. 255–56 (in Buchon, Collection des Chroniques Nationales Françaises, VII, Paris, 1828, p. 35).

7037 *me* (Th *we) pray,* Fr. "Par trestouz les sainz que l'en preie."

7043 *caleweis,* pears named (probably) from Cailloux in Burgundy. See Langlois's note to l. 11746; also Barbazan et Méon, Fabliaux et Contes, Paris, 1808, II, 279, n. 2.

7057 *smerten,* smart for; Fr. "Ou sera puniz dou mesfait."

7059 ff. "But if a man owns a castle, even of inferior construction, and gives the friars acceptable gifts, they will quickly release him."

7063 *vounde ston;* Fr. "Ne li chausist ja de quel pierre." For *vounde* Skeat suggests *founde* or *founded.* If *vounde* is right, it is probably a form of *founde(n),* preterite participle of *find;* perhaps used here for building-material "found" or "provided" in the neighborhood.

7064 "Wrought by the mason's square and according to pattern." Fr. "Fust senz compas ou senz esquierre."

7076 *equipolences;* Fr. "equipolances" (Kaluza) -a form which seems also required by the rime in

English. (Langlois: "equipolences.") Skeat interprets it "equivocations"; Langlois, "des arguments équivalents."

7096 Cf. De Periculis, viii, p. 38, and see Langlois's note to RR, 11796. The true date is 1254 (not 1255, as given in both the Fr. and the Eng. texts). In that year the Minorite Gérard de Borgo San Donnino published, under the title Evangelium Eternum sive Spiritus Sancti, the Concordia Novi et Veteris Testamenti of the Abbot Joachim. He prefixed to Joachim's work a Liber Introductorius in Evangelium Eternum. This gospel of the Holy Spirit, it was claimed, was to supersede the gospel of the Son, as preserved in the New Testament. The Liber Introductorius was condemned by Alexander IV upon representations made by the theologians of the Sorbonne.

7108 "In the parvis, or porch, before the Cathedral of Notre Dame."

7118 Fr. "Ne cuidiez pas que je vous moque."

7134 Fals Semblant means that the book has been suppressed for a time by the friars to be brought forward again when Antichrist, their leader, shall appear. Langlois notes that the Introductorius was actually lost.

7172 The English lacks a couplet, necessary to the sense, which would translate the Fr.: "Par Pierre veaut le pape entendre."

7215 *my moder*, i.e., Hypocrisy.

7254 *beggers*, Fr. "beguins." The Beguins (or Beguards) were members of lay brotherhoods which arose in the Low Countries. They got their name from Lambert Bègue. Skeat suggests that the description here really applies to the Franciscans, or Gray Friars.

7259 *quaile pipe*, inaccurately translated; Fr. "Houseaus fronciez e larges botes, Qui resemblent bourse a caillier" (a net for quails?).

7286 Prov. xxvi, 11; cf. also II Pet. ii, 22.

7287 Cf. the Pardoner's remark, *PardT*, VI, 918.

7300 See l. 6068, above, and n.

7312 ff. Proverbial. Cf. "Le loup mourra en sa peau, qui ne l'escorchera vif" (cited with other parallels by Langlois).

7323 *Streyned-Abstinaunce*, Fr. "Contrainte Astenance."

7346 *batels*, battalions.

7386 Cf. Rustebeuf, Diz des Règles, ll. 168 f. (Œuvres, I, 231); Li Romans de Bauduin de Sebourc, vii, 351 (ed. Boca, Valenciennes, 1841); Triumphe des Carmes, ll. 94–100 (Langlois).

7391 Rev. vi, 8.

7401 *burdown*, staff; Fr. "bourdon."

7406 *saynt*, for *ceynt*, girt (like a Franciscan)? Or to be emended to *faynt*, pale? Fr. "qui bien se ratourne."

7413 *squierly*, like a squire? Fr. "Apres s'en va son escuier" (Kaluza). (Langlois: "Emprès s'en va senz escuier.")

7420 *Coupe-Gorge*, Cut-Throat.

7453 On Jolly Robin, the dancer, see *Tr*, v, 1174, and n.

7454 *Jacobyn*, a Dominican. Cf. *Freres preachours*, l. 7456.

7457 *beren*, would sustain. Fr. "Mauvaisement l'ordre tendraient, Se tel menesterel estaient."

7459 ff. The Augustinians, Franciscans (*Cordyleres*), and Carmelites (*Carmes*), together with the Dominicans, were usually reckoned as the four orders. The *Sacked Freers* were the Friars De Penitentia, also called di Sacco from the form of their robe.

7465 ff. Cf. *HF*, 265–66.

7490 ff. Matt. iv, 19; Luke v, 10. For its use by friars cf. *SumT*, III, 1820.

7505 Cf. *MancT*, IX, 332 ff.

7511 f. Proverbial; cf. Haeckel, p. 16, no. 51.

7517 Cf. ll. 3815 ff., above.

7544 Proverbial; cf. Haeckel, p. 39, no. 132.

7576 Fr. "cul (var. "puis") d'enfer," meaning, doubtless, with either reading, "the pit of hell." The Fr. "cul" may have led the English translator to introduce the idea which appears in the *Sum Prol*, III, 1665 ff. For further information on the matter see the introduction to the Explanatory Notes to *Sum Prol*.

7579 *with myschaunce*; here, as frequently, a curse.

7607 f. This sounds proverbial. Langlois compares Gautier de Coincy, Les Miracles de la Sainte Vierge, ed. Poquet, Paris, 1857, col. 662, ll. 594 f. Cf. Haeckel, p. 39, no. 134.

7634 "Though one pierced him with a spear" (reading *me* for Thynne's *he*). Fr. "S'en le deüst tout vif larder."

7643 *The maugre*, the blame.

7662 *jolyly*, apparently an adverb of emphasis; Fr. "bien."

7677 ff. With the friar's claim here cf. *Gen Prol*, I, 218 ff., and n.

T E X T U A L   N O T E S

The Canterbury Tales

As explained in the Preface to this revised edition, the textual notes to the *Canterbury Tales* have been reprinted here, except for a few factual corrections and additions, as they stood in the original edition. They will show the evidence on the basis of which the editor established his text. No attempt has been made to incorporate in them the vast body of new information about manuscripts in the Manly-Rickert edition. But, as was to be expected, a considerable number of readings have been changed in the text, chiefly in the light of the new evidence now available, and a list of the alterations is printed here.

A Table of Altered Readings in The Canterbury Tales

Tale, Fragment, and Line	Old Reading	Altered Reading
Gen Prol, I, 1	Aprille	Aprill
Gen Prol, I, 338	verraily	verray
Gen Prol, I, 466	Seint Jame	Seint-Jame
Gen Prol, I, 599	governyng,	governynge,
Gen Prol, I, 600	rekenyng,	rekenynge,
Gen Prol, I, 715	shortly,	soothly,
Gen Prol, I, 858	in this manere.	as ye may heere.
KnT, I, 914	heere,	heere. [period for comma]
KnT, I, 915	And seyde,	She seyde,
KnT, I, 1156	seyn?	seyen?
KnT, I, 1156	wistest	woost
KnT, I, 1462	in May,	of May [omit comma]
KnT, I, 1584	seyd	told
KnT, I, 1608	muche as thou art	muche thou art
KnT, I, 1862	Tho	The
KnT, I, 2212	larke,	larke)
KnT, I, 2212	also)	right tho [omit parenthesis]
KnT, I, 2420	me the victorie,	me victorie,
KnT, I, 2513	peples	peple
KnT, I, 2671	trompes,	trompours,
KnT, I, 2789	seyn,	seyen,
KnT, I, 2831	So greet a wepyng	So greet wepyng
KnT, I, 2854	Casteth	Caste
KnT, I, 2904	is al the strete	is the strete
KnT, I, 3028	nedeth,	nedes,
KnT, I, 3036	The which	That
Mill Prol, I, 3183	So was the Reve, and othere manye mo,	So was the Reve [omit comma] eek and othere mo,
MillT, I, 3256	tour	Tour
MillT, I, 3350	wyf ne took	wyf took
MillT, I, 3571	broke	breke
MillT, I, 3672	tyme wake	tyme to wake
MillT, I, 3697	semysoun:	semy soun:
Rv Prol, I, 3864	yow	thee
RvT, I, 4037	how that	howgates
RvT, I, 4056	I counte	ne counte I
RvT, I, 4064	loos,	laus,
RvT, I, 4074	out,	of,
RvT, I, 4088	nadstow	ne had thow
RvT, I, 4098	they goon!	he gooth!
RvT, I, 4104	do	dide
RvT, I, 4163	snorteth	fnorteth
RvT, I, 4308	This	Thise

Tale, Fragment, and Line	Old Reading	Altered Reading
MLT, II, 790	snorteth	fnorteth
MLT, II, 802	chargen	charge
MLT, II, 802	hire she	hire that she
WB Prol, III, 117	And for what profit was	And of so parfit wys
WB Prol, III, 193	sires,	sire,
WB Prol, III, 210	love, ther	love, ye, ther
WB Prol, III, 313	thogh thou	thogh that thou
WB Prol, III, 393	hym	hem
WB Prol, III, 394	he	they
WB Prol, III, 395	it	I [¶ at 395 instead of 393]
WB Prol, III, 540	face ful often	face often
WBT, III, 908	shal	wol
WBT, III, 990	his	this
WBT, III, 1038	desiren have	desiren to have
WBT, III, 1080	a	the
FrT, III, 1318	book;	book.
FrT, III, 1319	And thanne	Thanne
FrT, III, 1324	wher hym	wher that hym
FrT, III, 1428	laborious,	laborous,
FrT, III, 1584	clappeth there?"	clappeth?"
FrT, III, 1596	procutour	procuratour
SumT, III, 1838	"*je vous dy*	"now *je vous dy*
SumT, III, 1864	triklyng	trillyng
SumT, III, 1949	as in a fewe yeres,	as I in fewe yeres,
SumT, III, 1950	I have	Have
SumT, III, 2015	eke	certes
SumT, III, 2186	swich	that
ClT, IV, 522	on	in
ClT, IV, 552	to kisse,	to blisse,
ClT, IV, 553	it blisse.	it kisse.
ClT, IV, 772	markys	Markys
MerchT, IV, 1523	among his othere	amonges othere
MerchT, IV, 1686	ye	we
MerchT, IV, 1978	day,	day [omit comma]
MerchT, IV, 1979	For pitee	Of pitee
MerchT, IV, 2011	proyneth	preyneth
MerchT, IV, 2133	Juyl,	Juyn,
MerchT, IV, 2137	this	his
MerchT, IV, 2290	that sit in Trinitee.	but neither he ne she.
MerchT, IV, 2340	"That I	"For I
MerchT, IV, 2380	medicyne al fals;	medicyne fals;
MerchT, IV, 2395	thy brest."	his brest."
SqT, V, 99	seith	seide
SqT, V, 173	unto	to
SqT, V, 267	that	as
SqT, V, 284	so fresshe	swiche fresshe
SqT, V, 299	that a	that at a
SqT, V, 359	dreem,	dreem [omit comma]
SqT, V, 419	ne so	ne noon so
SqT, V, 455	love	ire
SqT, V, 491	chastised	chasted
SqT, V, 499	harde	ilke
SqT, V, 514	love, this ypocryte,	loves ypocryte,
SqT, V, 574	lasteth	laste
FranklT, V, 1050	lightned	lighted
FranklT, V, 1257	his	this
FranklT, V, 1265	of	or
FranklT, V, 1409	Melesie	Milesie
FranklT, V, 1534	surement	serement
FranklT, V, 1540	lyf.	lyf." [add quote]
FranklT, V, 1544	drede."	drede. [omit quote]
FranklT, V, 1621	wolde	wol
PardT, VI, 760	ye	yow
PardT, VI, 871	borwed hym	borwed of hym
ShipT, VII, 1	Seint Denys	Seint-Denys

Tale, Fragment, and Line	Old Reading	Altered Reading
ShipT, VII, 59	Seint Denys	Seint-Denys
ShipT, VII, 67	Seint Denys	Seint-Denys
ShipT, VII, 308	Seint Denys	Seint-Denys
ShipT, VII, 326	Seint Denys	Seint-Denys
Pr Prol, VII, 479	thurgh	of
PrT, VII, 663	synge I moot	synge moot
PrT, VII, 678	heryen	herying
Thop, VII, 871	by his syde;	bisyde;
Mel, VII, 1034	thise olde wise men,	this olde wise man,
Mel, VII, 1314	acounte	accompte
Mel, VII, 1328	yow	the
MkT, VII, 2210	sente	lente
MkT, VII, 2289	dayes	wikes
MkT, VII, 2340	feeldes	feeld
MkT, VII, 2477	as	al
MkT, VII, 2748	science	sentence
NPT, VII, 3248	that it was	that I was
SecN Prol, VIII, 19	seen	syn
SecN Prol, VIII, 21	swynke.	swynke, [comma for period]
SecNT, VIII, 139	or	and
SecNT, VIII, 158	sholden	shullen
SecNT, VIII, 197	right	but
SecNT, VIII, 330	myracle Goddes	myracle heigh Goddes
CYT, VIII, 764	glas,	glas; [semi-colon for comma]
CYT, VIII, 765	muchel	of muche
CYT, VIII, 814	othre	oure
CYT, VIII, 1157	cole	coles
CYT, VIII, 1189	harde	sory
CYT, VIII, 1226	that was	that ne was
CYT, VIII, 1433	How that	How be that
CYT, VIII, 1481	Amen.	[deleted]
Manc Prol, IX, 3	weye?	Weye?
Manc Prol, IX, 96	drynke we with	drynke with
MancT, IX, 310	I	ye
MancT, IX, 356	leef or	nevere so
Pars Prol, X, 59	make a protestacioun	make protestacioun
ParsT, X, 93	laste ende, hooly	laste, hooly
ParsT, X, 95	that a man	that if a man
ParsT, X, 95	synned./	synned,/ [comma for period]
ParsT, X, 104	men in	men communly in
ParsT, X, 133	confessioun."/	confusioun."/
ParsT, X, 274	discordaunces	disordinaunces
ParsT, X, 364	that thilke	that the love of thilke
ParsT, X, 370	synnes./	synnes;/ [semi-colon for period]
ParsT, X, 371	Soothly	soothly
ParsT, X, 405	whan men speken to muche biforn folk, and clappen as a mille, and taken no keep what they seye./	whan a man speketh to muche biforn folk, and clappeth as a mille, and taketh no keep what he seith./
ParsT, X, 417	chisel	chisels
ParsT, X, 451	gentrie	gentrice
ParsT, X, 604	geomancie,	nigromancie,
ParsT, X, 629	"A servant	"The servant
ParsT, X, 669	scourge	scoure
ParsT, X, 722	is blent,	is so blent,
ParsT, X, 747	is the thraldom	is in the thraldom
ParsT, X, 819	devouren	savouren
ParsT, X, 900	fedden	feden
ParsT, X, 996	giltes of a man,	giltes of o man,
ParsT, X, 1007	shryven to thy curaat,	shryven of thy curaat,
ParsT, X, 1029	almesses:	almesse:
ParsT, X, 1052	sikernesse	swetenesse
Retract, X, 1085	.xix.	.xxv.

The Canterbury Tales

Authorities: — At least eighty-three (or, if the Morgan fragment of the *Pardoner's Tale* be counted, eighty-four) MSS. of the *Canterbury Tales*, either complete or fragmentary, are known. With them may be reckoned also six early prints — two by Caxton (Cx¹ Cx²), two by Pynson (Pyn¹ Pyn²), one by Wynkyn de Worde (Ww), and Thynne's (Th) — though they are of little value for the establishment of the text. The relations of the prints to each other and to the MSS. have been examined by Professor W. W. Greg, PMLA, XXXIX, 737 ff. From the collation of a short passage of the *Knight's Tale* he concludes that Cx¹ alone ranks with the MSS. as an authority. Its text is poor, having been derived from an inferior copy resembling Trinity College, Cambridge, MS. R. 3. 15. In Cx² alterations were made by comparison with a MS. of uncertain affinities, and the four succeeding prints were all derived, directly or indirectly, from Cx², with supplementary use of unidentified MSS. Miss M. Kilgour, PMLA, XLIV, 186 ff., tries to show that the authority used was British Museum MS. Additional 35286, or one closely related to it. Wynkyn de Worde's edition, according to information furnished by Professor Manly, was derived partly from Cx², and partly from a different source, probably a MS.

The list of MSS. follows. The editor is indebted to Professor Manly for information about several, which have either been recently discovered or are imperfectly described in previous lists. Photographic reproductions of all the MSS. were brought together by Mr. Manly at the University of Chicago for use in the preparation of his critical edition, which contains an account of the authorities, as well as a full registration of variant readings. Descriptions of most of the MSS. may be found in Miss Hammond's Manual, pp. 163 ff. Another list, not quite complete, is given by Koch in his edition of the *Pardoner's Prologue* and *Tale*, Chaucer Society, 1902, and another, not including fragmentary copies, will be found in Manly's edition of the *Canterbury Tales*. The names by which certain copies are known have varied from time to time with changes of ownership. Those here adopted are the same as those employed in the Manly-Rickert critical edition. Professor Manly very kindly supplied the editor with the list before the publication of the first edition of the present work, and it is hoped that this uniformity of names and abbreviations may be a convenience to the users of both texts. The eight of the more extensive and important MSS. from which the *Canterbury Tales* have been printed in full by the Chaucer Society, the text of each, wherever defective, being pieced out from other sources, are designated by stars.

Ad¹ Additional 5140, British Museum.
Ad² Additional 25718, British Museum.
Ad³ Additional 35286, British Museum (formerly Ashburnham 125).
Ad⁴ Additional 10340, British Museum (a fragment quoted from memory).
Ar Arundel 140, British Museum (*Melibee* only).
Bo¹ Bodley 414, Bodleian.
Bo² Bodley 686, Bodleian.

Bw Barlow 20, Bodleian.
Ch Christ Church 152, Oxford.
Cn Cardigan MS., now the property of the Brudenell estate.
*Cp Corpus 198, Corpus Christi College, Oxford.
Ct Chetham 6709, Chetham's Library, Manchester.
*Dd Dd. 4, 24, University Library, Cambridge (perhaps formerly Hodley or Hoadley).
Dl Delamere MS., property of Boies Penrose II, Esq.
Do Douce d. 4, Bodleian (a single leaf, containing *General Prologue*, I, 298–368).
Ds¹ Devonshire MS., property of the Duke of Devonshire.
Ds² Devonshire fragment, property of the Duke of Devonshire.
Ee Ee, 2. 15, University Library, Cambridge (*Man of Law's Tale* only).
*El Ellesmere 26 c. 12, formerly Lord Ellesmere's, now in the Huntington Library, California.
En¹ Egerton 2726, British Museum (formerly Haistwell, and probably a Chandos MS.).
En² Egerton 2863, British Museum (formerly the Norton, later a Hodson MS.).
En³ Egerton 2864, British Museum (formerly the Ingilby, later a Hodson MS.).
Fi Fitzwilliam (McClean, 181), Fitzwilliam Museum, Cambridge (formerly Ashburnham 127).
*Gg Gg. 4. 27, University Library, Cambridge.
Gl Glasgow MS., Hunterian Museum U. 1. 1.
Ha¹ Harley 1239, British Museum.
Ha² Harley 1758, British Museum.
Ha³ Harley 7333, British Museum.
*Ha⁴ Harley 7334, British Museum.
Ha⁵ Harley 7335, British Museum.
Hl¹ Harley 1704, British Museum (*Prioress's Tale* only).
Hl² Harley 2251, British Museum (*Prioress's Tale* only).
Hl³ Harley 2382, British Museum (*Prioress's Tale* and *Second Nun's Tale*).
Hl⁴ Harley 5908, British Museum (a fragment).
He Helmingham MS., property of the Tollemache estate.
*Hg Hengwrt 154 (or Peniarth 392 D), National Library of Wales, Aberystwyth.
Hk Holkham MS., property of the Earl of Leicester.
Hn Huntington (H M 144), Huntington Library, California (formerly Huth; *Melibee* and *Monk's Tale* only).
Ht Hatton Donat 1, Bodleian.
Ii Ii. 3. 26, University Library, Cambridge.
Kk. Kk 1. 3, University Library, Cambridge (a fragment).
*La Lansdowne 851, British Museum.
Lc Lichfield 2, property of Lichfield Cathedral.
Ld¹ Laud 600, Bodleian.
Ld² Laud 739, Bodleian.
Ll¹ Longleat 257, property of the Marquess of Bath.
Ll² Longleat 29, property of the Marquess of Bath (fragments of the *Parson's Tale*).
Ln Lincoln 110, property of Lincoln Cathedral.
Ma Manchester English 113, John Rylands Library (formerly Hodson 39).

Mc Professor McCormick's MS., now property of the University of Chicago (formerly Ashburnham 126).

Me Merthyr, property of the Rev. L. C. Simons, Merthyr Mawr, Wales (part of the *Nun's Priest's Tale*).

Mg Morgan 249, Morgan Library, New York (formerly Ashburnham 124). The last leaf contains an additional fragment of the *Pardoner's Tale*.

Mm Mm. 2. 5, University Library, Cambridge (formerly Ely).

Ne New College, Oxford, D. 314, deposited in Bodleian.

Nl Northumberland MS., property of the Duke of Northumberland.

Np XIII. B. 29, Royal Library, Naples (*Clerk's Tale* only).

Ox¹ Manchester English 63, John Rylands Library (part of Oxford).

Ox² Oxford, property of A. S. W. Rosenbach Co., New York (part of Manchester English 63).

Ph¹ Phillips 6570, formerly owned by Mrs. Fenwick, Cheltenham; now property of A. S. W. Rosenbach Co., New York.

Ph² Phillips 8136, also a Cheltenham MS., formerly Canby, property of A. S. W. Rosenbach Co., New York.

Ph³ Phillips 8137, also a Cheltenham MS., property of A. S. W. Rosenbach Co., New York.

Ph⁴ Phillips 8299, also a Cheltenham MS., now H M 140, Huntington Library, California (*Clerk's Tale* only).

Pl Plimpton MS., property of G. A. Plimpton, Esq., New York (formerly Phillips 9970; a single sheet containing fragments of the *Merchant's Epilogue*, the *Squire's Prologue*, and the *Franklin's Tale*).

Pp Pepys 2006, Magdalene College, Cambridge (*Melibee* and *Parson's Tale*).

Ps Paris MS., fonds anglais 39, Bibliothèque Nationale.

*Pw Petworth MS., property of Lord Leconfield.

Py Royal College of Physicians 13, London.

Ra¹ Rawlinson Poetry 141, Bodleian.

Ra² Rawlinson Poetry 149, Bodleian.

Ra³ Rawlinson Poetry 223, Bodleian.

Ra⁴ Rawlinson C. 86, Bodleian (parts of the *Prioress's Tale* and the *Clerk's Tale*).

Ry¹ Royal 17. D. xv, British Museum.

Ry² Royal 18. C. ii, British Museum.

Se Arch. Selden B. 14, Bodleian.

Si Sion College, London, Arch. L. 40. 2. E.

Sl¹ Sloane 1685, British Museum.

Sl² Sloane 1686, British Museum.

Sl³ Sloane 1009, British Museum.

St Stonyhurst B. XXIII, Stonyhurst College, Lancashire.

Tc¹ R. 3. 3, Trinity College, Cambridge.

Tc² R. 3. 15, Trinity College, Cambridge.

Tc³ R. 3. 19, Trinity College, Cambridge (*Monk's Tale* only).

To Trinity Arch. 49, Trinity College, Oxford.

In the foregoing list are included all the MSS. that have been discovered by the diligent search of Professor Manly, Miss Edith Rickert, and their associates. Still other names appear in early lists,

but it is often impossible to determine whether they represent lost copies or are identical with some of those mentioned above. Thus Miss Hammond (p. 165) cites from Bernard's Catalogi references to Clarendon, Hodley (or Hoadley), Worseley, and Gresham College MSS.; and Urry mentioned Chandos and Ely copies which he used for his edition. Several of these have been identified more or less positively with known MSS., and some account of them will be found in Miss Rickert's communication to TLS, 1931, p. 1028. In the same article Miss Rickert makes inquiry about a number of MSS., possibly still in existence, the identity of which is entirely unknown.

Among unidentified MSS. is a "Scotch copy of Chaucer" mentioned by Gerard Langbaine in a letter to Selden, Oct. 11, 1652. See Miss Ethel Seaton, JEGP, XLVII, 352. She concludes that it may have been an unidentified Chaucer MS. among the Scottish Records, or conceivably a copy of the *Canterbury Tales* owned at some time by Lauderdale. On the latter, see M-R CT, I, pp. 625–6.

Of the MSS. enumerated above several have not been described with any fulness, a few contain short fragments not exceeding one or two tales, and others are decidedly incomplete. Eight of the more important, as already indicated, have been printed in full by the Chaucer Society. The Ellesmere copy and the edition of Thynne (1532) have been published in facsimile. Thus nine of the authorities are accessible as a whole. From forty-four of the remaining MSS., together with the two editions of Caxton and that of Thynne, specimen passages covering the Doctor-Pardoner link and the *Pardoner's Prologue* and *Tale* have been printed by the Chaucer Society. From eight other MSS., which lack the *Pardoner's Tale* — namely, Si Ra¹ Mc Ha¹ (completed by Ha⁵) Np Hk Ph⁴ (completed by Ha³) and Ll¹ (completed by Ma¹) — specimen passages have been printed covering the *Clerk's Prologue* and *Tale*.

Full information as to the readings and classification of all copies are supplied for the first time by Professor Manly's edition, which was not yet published when the basic text of this edition was prepared. But valuable tentative studies, based upon the published materials, have long been available, and served for the guidance of the present editor. The publication of M-R CT has influenced a number of the textual changes in this 2nd edition, which changes are listed separately on p. 883. On the basis of the specimens and the complete reprints named above, fifty-five authorities have been classified by Zupitza and Koch in the following groups. The abbreviations and designations of groups are those employed in the present edition.

α — El Hg Py.

β — Dd En¹ Ma¹ Ds¹ En³ Ni Ch Ad¹.

γ — Gg Ph¹ Bo¹.

δ — Ha⁴ Ha⁵ Ad³ Ps.

ε — Se Ht, and the original of the Pw-group, which includes Pw En² Bw Ln Ha² Lc Mg Fi Ry¹ Ry² Ld¹ Ld² Bo¹ Ph² Ph³ Mm Sl¹ Dl Ra² To.

ζ — Tc¹ Ra³ Gl Ad², and the original of the Cp-group, which includes Cp La Sl² Tc² Ne Ha³ He Ii Cx¹ Cx² Th.

The relations of the MSS. within the several groups are fully discussed in Zupitza's and Koch's prefaces to the specimens, and their conclusions are further exhibited in a chart drawn up by Professor Liddell, Specimens, Pt. iv, p. xlvii. The results of their investigations have been criticized by various scholars. See, for some of these comments, Miss Hammond's Manual, p. 169, and for an extensive re-examination of the whole question, The Chaucer Tradition, by Aage Brusendorff, Oxford, 1925. Professor Brusendorff's treatise is especially valuable for the information it supplies about unpublished MSS. A very acute criticism of the Zupitza-Koch classification, laying stress upon evidences of contamination in various MSS., was privately printed by the late Sir William McCormick, and the editor is indebted for copies to Lady McCormick and Miss Janet Heseltine. McCormick's results were published as The MSS. of Chaucer's Canterbury Tales: A Critical Description of their Contents. By Sir William McCormick with the assistance of Miss Janet E. Heseltine (Oxford, 1933).

It is by no means certain that the Zupitza-Koch classification is valid in all particulars, even for the *Pardoner's Tale,* and how far the same classification holds for other tales will be made clear by Professor Manly's collations. Zupitza and Koch gave too much weight, in the data they used for evidence, to trivial variations in spelling, and, as McCormick argued, they made too little allowance for contamination, of which Koch takes more account in his later work on the eight published MSS. (Chaucer Society, 1913). But there is general agreement, for the *Pardoner's Tale,* about the primary division of authorities into the six groups mentioned above, and so far as the published MSS. are concerned, the same grouping seems to hold in the main throughout the work. A few instances where MSS. depart from their usual class will be noted in the list of variant readings. It is further clear that classes ϵ and ζ, which include the great majority of authorities, belong to an inferior type (B), and they have so many common errors that they can be safely traced to a single source. Classes α, β, and γ, on the other hand, which usually agree in superior readings (type A), are not definitely united by errors in the *Pardoner's Tale.* In the other tales the printed representatives of these groups — MSS. El Hg Dd Gg — agree in a fair number of inferior readings, but the evidence hardly proves that there was a single archetype. Professor Brusendorff, who examined a dozen unpublished copies of the *Nun's Priest's Tale,* left the point undecided. The relation of α, β, and γ to one another is also a matter of dispute. Koch, from the evidence of the *Pardoner's Tale,* argued for a combination of α and β, as against γ; Brusendorff, on the basis of his collation combined α and γ. But in both Hg and Gg there is evidence of contamination with type B. Class δ (Brusendorff's "London group") occupies a curiously intermediate position between types A and B. Koch includes it with B, but allows for extensive contamination with A (perhaps especially with γ). Brusendorff, on the contrary, classed it with the superior type (his "all-England tradition"). Since in the tales as a whole the errors common to Ha[4] Cp Pw La are too numerous to be satisfactorily accounted for by contamination, Koch's classification of δ with type B is here adopted.

On all these disputed questions new light may be expected from Professor Manly's edition.

In addition to the readings of the nine published authorities, there are recorded in the following notes many variants from two unpublished copies to which the editor has had access: the Cardigan MS., which he was generously allowed to collate while it was temporarily in the possession of President Mac-Cracken of Vassar College, and the Morgan MS., which was very kindly placed at his disposal by Miss Belle da Costa Greene of the Morgan Library. The Morgan copy, as shown by the *Pardoner's Tale* specimen, belongs to the Petworth group (class ϵ). The Cardigan MS., which was long inaccessible to scholars, has recently been described by Miss Clara Marburg in PMLA, XLI, 229 ff. She prints the text of the *Pardoner's Prologue* and *Tale,* and shows that the MS. belongs to class β, being most closely related to Ma[1]. The common ancestor of the two MSS. was apparently contaminated with type B.

In accordance with the opinion and practice of all recent editors, the Ellesmere MS. has been made the basis of the text, and preference has ordinarily been given to the readings of type A. B has been followed only where it corrected errors in A or offered readings so superior intrinsically that they demanded adoption. The editor's practice with regard to unique readings of Ellesmere or of Harleian 7334, which often present difficult problems, is discussed in the section on textual method in the General Introduction. It may merely be added here that independent authority, that is to say, access to a good copy in addition to its own archetype, might be assumed not unreasonably in the case of several individual MSS. or groups. Thus Brusendorff argued that groups β and δ both derive some readings from a source superior to the common ancestor of all the MSS. He does not make this claim for the peculiar unique readings of Harleian 7334, which are discussed in the General Introduction. But in the case of Ellesmere he admits the possibility of independent authority for readings peculiar to that MS. alone. They may have been derived from Chaucer's own MS., or from an excellent copy now lost. Ellesmere as a whole, however, cannot be held to be a direct copy of the ultimate original. For the existence of a few errors common to all or nearly all MSS. suggests that one or more copies intervened between the author's original and the source of A and B.

There is great variation in the MSS. with respect to the order of the tales and the presence or absence of connecting links, and a tentative classification based upon these data was made by Miss Hammond, Manual, pp. 169 ff. It does not correspond altogether with the genealogy constructed by Zupitza and Koch from the study of the text. For MSS. which are classified together for their textual readings do not always agree in arrangement. Thus Hengwrt, which is closely related to Ellesmere in Koch's group α, has the tales in a disordered and inconsistent sequence partly resembling that of the Petworth group. And the arrangement of most of the best MSS. (classes α, β, and γ) is shared by members of groups δ and ϵ. The conditions are very complicated and do not admit of a simple explanation. They point to contamination, to the exercise of scribal independence, and possibly to a limited circulation of separate tales. An ingenious attempt to reconstruct the successive stages in the arrangement was made by Skeat in The Evolution of the Canterbury Tales, Chaucer Society, 1907. His conclusions are restated, with modifications, in his monograph on the Eight-Text Edition of the Canterbury Tales, Chaucer Society, 1909. For additional information see R. L. Campbell, Extra-Textual Data for a Classification of the MSS. of the Canterbury Tales, Univ. of Chicago Abstracts of Theses, Humanistic Series, V, 453 ff.; also Professor Manly's introduction to his edition, pp. 77 ff.

The appearance of the Manly-Rickert edition of the *Canterbury Tales*, which was eagerly awaited at the time of the first edition of the present work, has stimulated afresh the discussion of the history of Chaucer's text. Numerous articles have been published dealing with the arrangement of the tales and the genuineness of various links and other passages. But scholars have not yet reached agreement on these matters, and no attempt is made in this edition to reconstruct the successive stages in the composition of the work. The matters in question have been taken up only when they relate to practical decisions about the inclusion or exclusion of doubtful passages or to the order of the tales. But references are given at appropriate places in the Explanatory and Textual Notes to more extensive discussions of the questions involved.

One general problem of arrangement — and perhaps the only one of serious interest to the reader — may be mentioned here in conclusion. The order of tales which has the overwhelming support of the best MSS. is the following: Fragments I (Group A), II (B¹ = Man of Law), III (D), IV (E), V (F), VI (C), VII (B² = Shipman-Nun's Priest), VIII (G), IX (H), X (I). But by this arrangement a reference to Sittingbourne (forty miles from London) in the *Wife of Bath's Prologue* is made to precede a reference to Rochester (thirty miles from London) in the *Monk's Prologue*. To correct this obvious inconsistency the editor of the Six-Text reprint, on the authority of a single inferior MS. (Arch. Selden B. 14) combined II (B¹) and VII (B²) and assigned the *Man of Law's Epilogue* to the Shipman, printing it as the *Shipman's Prologue*. He also moved up Fragment VI (the tales of the Physician and the Pardoner), which comes after V in all MSS. (even following VIII in some copies), and placed it after II–VII (his B) to fill out the tales of the second day. Now there is no real support for this order in the MSS., and no reason for supposing that Chaucer adopted it. The Selden MS., which is the sole authority for combining II and VII, puts II–VII (B) between V and VIII, and VI between VIII and IX. If Chaucer had ever reached the final revision of the tales, he might himself have made one or both of the shifts of the Six-Text editor, and Professor Pratt, in the article already noted on p. 696, has argued very persuasively that he was practically committed at least to the former, the so-called Bradshaw shift. But there is no evidence that he ever took the step. And there are so many small discrepancies in the work that the misplacing of Rochester and Sittingbourne may be regarded as an oversight of Chaucer's own which he left uncorrected. He not only failed to complete the tales, but he never made a final arrangement of what he had written, or worked out a consistent scheme for the pilgrimage. Under the circumstances an editor must now choose between keeping the arrangement of the best MSS., with all its imperfections, or making the unauthorized adjustment adopted in the Six-Text and several succeeding editions. The former is undoubtedly the sounder procedure. It was in fact recommended by Skeat in his Evolution of the Canterbury Tales, pp. 27 ff. (although he afterwards defended the superior authority of the Harleian arrangement), and it has been recently adopted in Koch's edition and in Manly's selections. It reverts, moreover, to the venerable tradition of Tyrwhitt. In spite, therefore, of certain inconveniences in departing from the system of groups used in references in the prolific Chaucer "literature" of the past fifty years, the Ellesmere order has been followed in the present edition.

The position of Fragment VI (C) is of course largely independent of the question just discussed. In the MSS. it always occurs late — in the superior Ellesmere class after V — and it was shifted by the Six-Text edition to follow II–VII (B¹–B²) in order to fill out a programme of tales for the second day. But it is now recognized that in view of the incompleteness of the work it is not worth-while to try to make a consistent time-table for the pilgrimage. On other grounds it has been proposed to put VI before II (against the consistent testimony of the MSS.) or to put VI–VII immediately after II (thus preserving the combination VI–VII which appears in every MS. except Selden). See Shipley, MLN, X, 130; XI, 145; and S. Moore, PMLA, XXX, 116. There are reasons for both these suggestions which would deserve the consideration of an editor who thought it justifiable to make a new editorial arrangement. But they are not decisive enough to warrant a departure from the Ellesmere order.

In the citations below references are simply to the nine authorities followed, unless special mention is made of others. Thus Type A will refer to MSS. El Hg Dd (or En¹) Gg, Type B to MSS. Ha (i.e., Ha⁴) Cp Pw La and Thynne's edition (Th); α will be used for El Hg, and ζ for Cp La Th. Specific references will be made in each case to Cn and Mg, for which the editor's collations are incomplete. The former belongs to Type A, the latter to Type B. The references to Tatlock are (unless otherwise specified) to the Harleian MS. 7334, Chaucer Society, 1909; references to Manly are to his selections from the *Canterbury Tales*. No attempt will be made to record minor variations in spelling among MSS. which show verbal agreement.

FRAGMENT I

General Prologue

8 *halve*] *halfe* Ha Pw Th; rest (incl. Mg) *half*. Final *-e* is metrically necessary, and the pronunciation with *v* is probable.

40 *weren* Ha (also Ha³); rest (incl. Mg) *were*.

60 *armee* (*armeye*, etc.) El Pw ζ (also Se Cx²); *aryve* Hg (Skeat, Eight-Text Edition, p. 55) En¹ Gg Ha (also Cx¹); Mg ambiguous (*arme* or *arive*).

120 *seinte* Pw Ha (flourish?) Cp (?); rest (incl. Mg) *seint*.

179 *recchelees*] *Cloysterles* Ha.

252a,b This couplet occurs only in Hg among

the printed MSS. It is also in Th, and (Tatlock, p. 23) in Ld² Tc¹ Ch Ha² Py. Probably genuine, though perhaps canceled by Chaucer.

338 *verraily* Ha; rest (incl. Cn Mg) *verray, verrey,* etc.

363 Ha *Weren with uss eeke clothed in oo lyvere.*

396 *I-drawe* Gg; rest (incl. Cn Mg) *drawe.*

430 *Rufus* Cn Pw Mg (?); *Rufijs* Gg; *Rusus* Hg Dd Ha Cp La; *Russus* Th (?); *Risus* El.

485 *ypreved*] *I-proved* Ha; *preysed* Cn; rest (incl. Mg) *preved* (*proved*).

509 *seinte* Cn Ha Cp; rest (incl. Mg) *seint.*

510 *chaunterie* B (exc. Mg Th); *chauntrie* α Gg Cn (*chauntry*) En¹ Mg Th.

514 *noght a*] *no* Ha (perhaps correctly).

516 *to senful man nought* Ha; rest (incl. Mg) *nat* (*nought*) *to* (*with*) *sinful man* (*men*). (Cn *nat with symple men;* Ld¹ (Tatlock, p. 9) *nat to dispetous.*)

559 *greet*] *wyde* Ha.

607 *I-shadewed* Gg Ha; rest (incl. Cn Mg) *shad*(*o*)*wed.*

697 *seinte* Cn; rest (incl. Mg) *seint* (sometimes with final flourish).

714 *the murierly* α Gg; *so mery and so loude* En¹ Cn; *ful meriely* Ha; *so meriely* Pw Mg ζ.

715 *shortly* El Ha; rest (incl. Cn Mg) *soothly* (perhaps correctly, but cf. *MLT*, II, 428).

741 *that* Ha; rest (incl. Cn Mg) om.

752 *han been* Ha; rest (incl. Cn Mg) *been.*

764 *saugh nat*] *ne saugh* Ha.

782 *I wol yeve yow*] *smyteth of* Ha.

791 *oure* α Pw Mg La Sl¹; *youre* Dd Cn Ha Cp; others Ha.

803 *myselven* Ha Cp Pw La Sl¹; *myself* α Dd Cn Mg. *Goodly*] *gladly* Ha.

829 *I* Ha Cp Pw La Sl¹ Mg; α om.; *if ye it* Dd Cn.

The Knight's Tale

943 *yslawe* Cn Ha; rest (incl. Mg) *slawe.*

992 *housbondes* El En¹ Ha Th; *freendes* Hg Gg Cp Pw La; *lordes* Mg.

1031 *This Palamon and his felawe Arcite* El Cn Gg Ha; *Dwellen this P. and eek Arcite* Hg Cp Pw Mg La (perhaps correctly); *Dwellen thise P. and his felawe Arcite* En¹; *Dwelleth P. & his felowe Arcyte* Th.

1039 *fyner* El Cn Gg Ha; *fairer* Hg En¹ Pw Mg Cp Th; *feireste* La.

1212 *o* Dd; rest (incl. Cn Mg) *or.*

1248 *helpe* Hg Gg Ha Cp Pw Mg La; *heele* El Dd Cn Th.

1323 *lete I*] *I lete* Ha.

1376 *Biforen*] *Biforn*(*e*) all MSS. Th; *in* Ha; rest om.; *his*] *his owen*(*e*) El Dd Cn Gg.

1424 *long* El Dd Cn Gg Ha; *strong* Pw Mg ζ.

1573 *after he* El; *afterward he* Hg En¹ Gg Cp Pw Th; *he afterward* La; *afterward* Ha Mg.

1595 *for* Cn Ha; rest (incl. Mg) *or.*

1614 *le*(*e*)*f* Hg Gg Ha Cp; rest (incl. Cn Mg) *leve* (pl. or sbj.).

1637 *Tho* Cn Ha; rest (incl. Mg) *To* (*They gan to chaunge colour* En¹).

1906 *And on the gate west*(*e*)*ward in memorye* Cn and (Tatlock, p. 30) Ad³ To; *On the Weste gate in memorie* Ii (Tatlock); *And westward in memorie* En¹; *And westward also in memorie* Mg; *And west-*

ward in the mynde and in memory Ha; rest *And on* (*of, in*) *the west*(*ward*) (*side*) *in memorye.*

1986 *gate* A (incl. Cn); *gates* B (incl. Mg).

2030 *twynes* α; *twyned*(*e*) Dd Cn Gg Cp Pw Mg Th; *twyne* Ha La.

2037 *sterres* Cn Ha and (Tatlock, p. 30) Ch Bo¹ Ad³ Ha⁵; rest *sertres, certres* (Mg), *cercles, septres, storyes,* etc.

2049 *depeynted was* Ha; rest (incl. Cn Mg) *was depeynted* (Th *paynted*); Skeat em. *was depeynt.*

2060 *peynted* all authorities (Gg corrupt); Skeat em. *peynt.* Ha⁴ Ha⁵ (Tatlock, p. 10, n. 1) om. *yow* (perhaps correctly).

2142, 2144 *for old*(*e*), *for blak,* written separately in all eight MSS., also in Cn Mg Th.

2202 *and* α; rest (incl. Mg) *or.* The Cn reading, *pley best and syng,* suggests that *dauncen* in the other MSS. may have been incorrectly repeated from the line before.

2385 *the beautee*] *the gret bewte* Ha Ii (Tatlock, p. 30); *the fayre beaute* Th.

2488 *But* El B (incl. Mg.); *And* Hg Dd Gg Cn.

2681–82 Om. El Hg Gg; here printed from Cp.

2683 *was* El Cp Pw La Mg; *she was* Hg Dd and (Brusendorff, p. 112) En¹ Py (*As she was*); Cn *Therfore she was all his in chere and herte;* Ha³ *And was al his as by chere of herte* (Brusendorff); Tyrwhitt em. *And was all his in chere, as his in herte;* Koch em. *And was al his in chiere as in hir herte.*

2684 *furie* α Gg Mg; *fyr*(*e*) Dd Cn Ha Cp Pw La.

2725 *O* El Dd; *On* Gg; *One* Th; rest (incl. Cn Mg) *A.*

2770 Metrically suspicious. Possibly a headless line; perhaps to be em. to [*ne*] *may, may* [*now*], or [*no lenger*] *may endure.*

2801 Ha om. *for.*

2834 *renting*(*e*) Cn Gg Pw Mg Th; *rending*(*e*) Dd Ha Cp La.

2840 *chaunge*(*n*) *bothe* Hg Dd Cn; *torne* Ha; rest (incl. Mg) om.

2892 *that weren* Ha; rest (incl. Mg) om.; Cn *stedes grete and lilye white* (perhaps correctly).

3015 *And nat eterne be withoute lye* Ha.

3036 *The which* Ha; rest (incl. Cn Mg) *That.*

3059 *the* Dd Cn B (incl. Mg); rest om.

3090 *the Knight* Hg Dd ζ and (Brusendorff, p. 98, n. 1) Ha⁵ Ad³; *ful right* El Gg Ha.

3104 *also* Ha Ch (Tatlock); rest (incl. Mg) *so*; Cn *And he hire ageyne so gentilly.*

The Miller's Prologue and Tale

3170 *me* (*m'*) *athynketh* α Dd Cn Cp La Ha; *me thynkyth* Gg; *me for-thenketh* Pw Mg Th.

3176 *yheere* α; rest (incl. Cn Mg) (*to*) *here.*

3236 *eek* Ha; rest (incl. Cn Mg) om.

3238 *broyden* α; rest (incl. Cn Mg) (*y*)*bruded, embrouded, enbrauded.*

3322 *Schapen with goores in the newe get* Ha (conceivably Chaucer's revision, as Tatlock remarks, p. 20).

3451, 3457 *astromye* α Cn; *arstromye* La; rest (incl. Mg) have full form (also La Cn, l. 3457).

3483 *seynte* Cn Ha; rest (incl Mg) *seint* (some with final flourish).

3485 *verye* α Gg Cp Pw Mg La; *verray* Ha; *mare* Dd Cn Th.

3486 *wentestow(e), wentest thou* α Cp Pw Mg La; *wonestow, wonest thou,* etc. Gg Dd Ha Th; Cn uncertain. *Seinte* Hg Gg Ha Cp La; *seynt* El Dd Pw Mg Th.

3571 *broke* El Pw Mg Cp; rest (incl. Cn) *breke.*

3624 *His owne hand he made* Hg Dd Pw Mg ζ; El om. *he; With his owene hand he made* Cn Gg; *His owne hand than made* Ha.

3643 *very* αζ Pw Mg; *verray* Cn Gg Dd Ha (perhaps correctly).

3709 *pa* α Dd Gg Cp Pw Mg (*compaine* Ha La); *ba* Cn and (Skeat) Ha⁵ Ii Tc¹ Ra¹ Ra³ Bo¹ Ld²; *As helpe me God and swete seynte James* Th.

3721–22 In El Th; rest om.

3770 *viritoot(e)* α Cp Pw Mg; *veritot(e)* Dd Cn La Th; *verytrot* Ha; *merytot* Gg.

The Reeve's Prologue and Tale

3906 *half-wey(e)* A ζ; *passed* Ha Ii (Tatlock, p. 5, n.); *almost* Pw and (Tatlock) Ra¹ Lc.

3941, 3959 *Symkyn*] *Symekyn* (Ha only) would give relief from awkwardly short lines. Cf. *Janekyn* (El only) in *WB Prol,* III, 303. Skeat's *deÿnous* seems impossible.

3953 *(y)bounde(n)* El Gg Ha Pw; *wounde(n)* Hg Dd Cn Mg ζ.

4027 *boes* El; *bihoves* Hg Dd Cp Mg; *bihoveth* Cn ζ *falles* Ha; *muste* Gg.

4028 *fool*] *fon* Ha. In the following dialogue some MSS. have more dialect forms than El. It is hard to determine how many were intended by Chaucer.

4064 *laus* α Cp La; *lo(o)s* Dd Gg Ha Mg; *loce* Th; *louse* Cn Pw.

4085 *Lay*] *Leg* Ha.

4089 f. *fon: speeden hem anoon* Ha (possibly Chaucerian?).

4111 *fooles*] *fonnes* Dd En¹ (Brusendorff, p. 90) Cn.

4118 Koch em. [*han*] *hym bisoght* (omitting *they*) to avoid rare weak pret. ind. without *-e.* He makes a similar correction in *FranklT,* V, 1273.

4134 *na(ne)* Dd Ha Cp Mg; *no(ne)* α Gg Cn Th; *no(uh)t(e)* Pw La.

4166 *two* El Gg; α Hg Dd B (copied from line above?).

4171 *compline* La; rest (incl. Cn Mg) *complyng, complyng(e), cowplyng, copil.*

4254 *makes* Dd Ha; rest (incl. Cn Mg) *maketh.* Ga Ha.

4255 *wat . . . mysgaa* Dd and (Brusendorff, p. 91, n. 1) Ad¹ (dialectically more consistent).

4256 *lyes . . . alswa* Dd and (Brusendorff, p. 91, n. 1) Ad¹.

FRAGMENT II

The Introduction to the Man of Law's Tale

4 *ystert* α Dd Cn; *expert* Ha² ζ Pw Mg; om. Ha.

5 *eightetethe*] *xviij*ᵗʰᵉ Hg; *eytenthe* Mg; *eyghtene (xviije)* ζ Ha² Pw; *eighte and twentithe* El; *xviij* Cn; *eight and twenty* Dd; *threttenthe* Ha.

37 *now of*] *and holdeth* Ha only.

47 *But* Dd Cn En² Ad¹; *That* α Gg Pw ζ Mg.

The Man of Law's Tale

185 *ceriously* α Dd Cp Pw Mg Th; *certeynly* Gg; *so ryally* Ha; *curiousely* La; *so curiously* Cn.

497 *wook*] *awok* Ha. Skeat inserts [*that*] for the meter.

621 Skeat inserts [*ful*] for the meter.

791 *til*] *unto* Ha; *to* Dd Pw; Skeat em. *until.*

882 *eek*], inserted by Skeat for the meter, is supported by Cn.

1060 *alle* Ha; rest om.

The Man of Law's Epilogue

Lines 1163–90, which constitute the so-called *Shipman's Prologue,* are not found in the published MSS. of Type A. They have been printed by the Chaucer Society (Six-Text Edition, pp. 11* ff., 167) from 23 MSS., and additional copies have been reported as occurring in MSS. Ln Py En² Fi Gl Ne Dl Ph³ Mc and in Cx¹ Cx². See Tatlock, Harl. MS. 7334, p. 22 n. 2; Brusendorff, p. 70, n. 2; Manly, *CT,* pp 570 ff.; and C. R Kase, pp. 32 ff., in Three Chaucer Studies, N.Y., 1932 (not fully utilized by the editor). On the authenticity of the passage and its assignment to the Shipman see the introduction to the Explanatory Notes on the *ML Epil.* The present text is based upon Cp, compared with the other printed MSS.

1174 *Now* Ha Ha³ Th Ra¹ Ra² Ra³ Ht Tc¹ Tc² He Ry¹; rest *How.*

1179 *Shipman* Se; *Som(p)nour* Ha and (Tatlock, Manly) Ra³ Ry¹ Ln Py Mc; rest *Squier, Swyere,* etc.

1189 *phislyas*] so most MSS. (var. *phillyas, fisleas,* etc.); (*of*) *phisik* (var. sp.) Ra¹ Ra² Tc² Ht Th; *phisicians* Mm.

FRAGMENT III

The Wife of Bath's Prologue

For spurious links connecting the Wife's *Tale* with the Merchant's and the Squire's see the Textual Notes on the *Merch Epil* and the *SqT.*

44ª⁻ᶠ These lines occur in Dd Cn and (Manly, p. 576) Ch Cx² Ds¹ En¹ He Ma Ne Ry¹ Se Si Tc², and (Tatlock, p. 23, n.) Ii. They are probably genuine, but whether Chaucer added them late and meant to keep them, or wrote them early and meant to reject them, is uncertain. They are here printed from Dd.

44ᶠ *scoleiyng* Dd; *scolyng* Cn; *scoleying* Ch (Tatlock, p. 23, n.); Skeat, following Tyrwhitt, has *scolering* (incorrectly).

59 *Wher(e) can ye seye (seen)* Hg Dd Cn Pw Mg ζ; *Whanne saugh ye evere* El; *Whan sawe ye* Ha.

75 *up for* Hg Dd Gg La Pw; *up of* El (perhaps correctly; cf. "bravium virginitatis"); *uppe fro* Cp; *upon* Ha.

260 For this line Cp Pw La Mg have: *Thus saistow, Wernard, God yive thee meschaunce.*

303, 383 *Janekyn* El; rest (incl. Cn Mg) *Jankyn, Jenkyn.*

361 *so moot I thee*] *though queynte he be* Ha.

368 *maner* Cp Pw La; *of thy* Ha; *of these* Gg; om. α Dd Cn Mg Th.

575–84 Om. in many MSS.

595 For *Jankyn*, in all authorities, perhaps we should read *Janekyn*, since *ourë* is very improbable.
604 *seinte*] *seint* all MSS.; *dame* Th.
609-12 Om. in many MSS. Brusendorff (p. 86) suggests transposing the passage to a position after l. 618.
619-26 Om. in many MSS.
660 *sawe* α Cn Gg Ha Mg Th; *lawe* Dd Cp Pw La.
717-20 Om. in many MSS.

The Wife of Bath's Tale

881 *but* α Dd Ha Cp Pw La Mg and (Manly, p. 584) 26 others; *no(n)* Gg Cn Th and (Manly) 13 others.
941 *kike* El Dd Gg Th; *like* Hg Cn Ha; *loke* Cp Pw La Mg.
1112 *is*] *nis* Cp Pw (perhaps correctly, to avoid hiatus).

The Friar's Prologue and Tale

1295-96 In Ha this couplet stands between ll. 1308 and 1309.
1324 *wele* Dd; Skeat adopts *wher that*, from Cp Pw (also Mg). Perhaps we should insert *best*, with Ad¹ En² (Brusendorff, p. 110, n. 3), or *ought*, with Ha⁵ Ad³ (Brusendorff).
1329 *his* α Cn Gg Th; *her(e)* Dd Ha Cp Pw La Mg.
1377 *Ro(o)d(e)* for Dd Cp Pw La Mg Ha Th, etc. (27 in all, acc. to Manly); *Wente for* Gg Ps (Manly); *Redy for* Gl Nl Ra³ Ry¹ (Manly); *For* El Hg Cn En¹ (Brusendorff, p. 79, n. 3; 21 in all, acc. to Manly).
1406 *and pleye(n)* Hg Dd Cn En¹ Gg Ha Ha¹ Ad³; *hire wey(e)* El Pw ζ Mg.
1426 *eke* Dd Ha (avoids hiatus).
1428 *laborious* Dd Cp; rest (incl. Cn Mg) *laborous* (with hiatus).
1445 *and* Gg; rest (incl. Cn Mg) om. (*right* Dd).
1647 *and* is supplied after *Crist* by some editors for the meter. Ha reads *Powel*. But Chaucer may have permitted a pause or rest in such a list. Cf. *Prol Mel*, VII, 951.
1663 *these somonours hem* α Dd; *this* (*oure* Ha) *Somonour him* B (incl. Mg) Gg.

The Summoner's Prologue and Tale

1692 *that*] *than* Ha Pw (perhaps correctly; but cf. l. 1856).
1887 *mountayne* Hg; rest (incl. Cn Mg) *mount(e)*.
2004 Ha inserts spurious couplets after ll. 2004, 2012, 2037, 2048.
2015 *e(e)k(e)* El Cn Gg Pw Mg Th; *certes* Hg Dd Cp La; *also* Ha.
2201 *what*] *all what* Pw (perhaps correctly, since it improves the meter). Or read *hered*? or *what* [that]?
2224 *Certes it was a shrewed conclusioun* El.
2289 *dyd* or Th; *or elles* Ha. Skeat em. *or* [*as*]. *Pt(h)olome* La Ha² Mg Th; rest (incl. Cn) *Protholome(e)*, the corrupt form, which would make the extra word metrically unnecessary.

FRAGMENT IV
The Clerk's Prologue and Tale

For the *Clerk's Prologue* and *Tale* use has been made of the eight additional MSS. printed in the Chaucer Society Specimens, namely Si Ra¹ Mc Ha¹ (and for the *Prologue*, Ha⁵) Np (supplemented by Ad³) Hk Ph⁴ (and for the *Prologue*, Ha³) and Ll¹ (completed, where defective, from Ma).

31 *Petrak(e)* El (*Perak*) Hg Sl¹ Dd Cn Cp Pw La Ha³ (*Patrak*) Ma Mg; *Petrark(e)* Ha Si Mc Ra¹ (*Petark*) Ha⁵ Ad³ Hk Th. The division of authorities is almost identical in l. 1147, below.
137 *lynage* Dd Cn Ha Cp Pw La Si Mg Ra¹ Mc Ha¹ Ph⁴ Ll¹ Th; *lyne* El Hg (*ligne*); *lyf* Gg Np; Hk corrupt.
199 *site* El Hg Np, *cite* Cp La; *syth* Mc; *sight(e)* Cn Pw Gg Dd Ha Si Ra¹ Ph⁴ Ll¹ Ha¹ Th; *sigh* Mg.
266 *last* El Hg Cn Gg Cp Np La; *laste* Mg; *lasteth* Dd Ha Pw Th Si Ra¹ Hk Ph⁴; *lasted* Mc.
429 *homlynesse* Cp La Ha¹ Hk (Lat. "domestica"); *humlinesse* Ph⁴; rest (incl. Cn Mg) *humblenesse*, *humblesse*, etc.
508 *ye(e)* El Hg (in margin) Dd Cn Ha Pw Mg Th Si Ra¹ Mc Np Ph⁴ Ma; *the(e)* El Hg (in text) Gg Cp La Ha¹; *you quod shee* Hk.
537 Second *al* om. El Cn Cp La Th Np Ma Ra¹ Mg.
552-53 *kisse: blisse* El Cn Ma; rest (incl. Mg) *blisse: kisse* (Lat. "exosculans benedixit").
590 *Panik* Ha Cp Ha¹; *Paynyk* Mc; *Paynyd* Ra¹; rest (incl. Cn Mg) *Pavyk(e)*, *Pavye* (Lat. "Panico").
667 *youre*] *oure* Cp La Mg only; Lat. "nostro"; perhaps a deliberate change by Chaucer.
764, 939 *Panyk(e)* Ha Cn Cp Ra¹ Mc Ha¹; rest (incl. Mg) *Pavyk(e)*, *Pavy(e)*.
867 *your*] *my* Si Np El Hg Dd Ha Gg (*myn*).
868 *your* Ra¹ Mc Ph⁴ Cp La; rest (incl. Mg) *my(n)*.
915 *he*] *she* Ra¹ Mc; om. Gg.
996 *fane* Dd Cn Gg Pw Cp La Th Ha Si Ha¹ Np Ma Hk Mg; *vane* El Hg Ra¹ Mc; *wane* Ph⁴.
1067 *disposed* Dd Cn Pw Th Ra¹ Mc Ma Hk Mg; *purposed* Ha Si Cp La Np Ph⁴; *supposed* El Hg Gg Ha¹.
1088 *God thanke it yow* Hg Cn (*thanked*) Dd Ha Th Np Ma; *God thanke yow* Gg Ph⁴ Mg; *God I thanke it yow* Si Cp Ra¹ Mc; *God I thanked* (*thank*) *yow* La Pw; *good Lord I thanke you* Hk; *I thank yt you* Ha¹; *that thank I yow* El.
1181 *trust* Hg Dd Cn Gg Np Pw Ll¹ Mg Ha³ Ph⁴ Th; *hope* El Ha Si Ra¹ Mc Ha¹ Cp La.

The Host's Stanza

Lines 1212^{a-g} are preserved in El Hg Py Dd Cn Gg Se Bo² Bw Ne Ch Tc² Ln Ha² Ha³ Ry² Ad¹ En¹ Ma Np En³ Th. (See Miss Hammond, p. 303, and Tatlock, p. 23, n.) They are probably part of a canceled link, originally intended to follow l. 1169. But since they are without doubt genuine, it seems best to leave them standing in the text. Brusendorff (p. 76) argued that it was Chaucer's final plan to retain the stanza, for humorous relief, between the *Envoy* and the *Merchant's Prologue*.

In a number of MSS. *ClT* is followed by *FranklT*, and eight of them (Bw Ha² Ld² Lc Mg Ry² Sl¹ Nl) contain the following spurious link (printed by Manly, p. 84):

> *I haue a wyf quod oure Ost though she pore be*
> *Yit hath she an heep of vices lo*
> *For of hir tonge a moche shrewe is she*
> *For to my wille the contrary wol she do*
> *Therof no force lat alle suche thinges go*
> *But wite ye what in counsail be it said*
> *Me reweth sore that I am to hir tayd*
>
> *Sire Frankeleyn cometh nere zif it youre wil be*
> *And say vs a tale as ye are a gentilman*
> *It shal be don trewely host quod he*
> *I wol you telle as hertely as I can*
> *Holdeth me excused though I vnworthy am*
> *To telle you a tale for I wol Not rebell*
> *Azeinst youre wille a tale now wol I telle.*

For a full list of variants see M-R CT, III, 374.

The Merchant's Prologue and Tale

1228   *liven* Se; rest (incl. Cn) *lyve* (metrically less satisfactory).

1305-06   Om. Cp La and (Brusendorff, p. 66) Ra³ Ne Tc¹ Tc² Sl² Ha³ Ad¹ En³; also, as Professor Tatlock has informed the editor by letter, Ln; in other MSS. the couplet appears in various forms, nearly all manifestly spurious. Tatlock suggests that Chaucer wrote only *And if thou take a wyf*, the remainder having been pieced out by scribes. The version in the text is that of El Gg. Other forms are given below, as noted by Skeat, Oxf. Chau., V, 354; Brusendorff, pp. 65 f.; and Tatlock's letter. Professor Brusendorff made the variants in this passage a basis for classifying the MSS.

And if thow take a wiff in thin age oolde
Ful lightly maist thow be a cokewoolde (Se).

And if thou take a wyf [she wole destroye
Thy good substaunce, and thy body annoye] (Hg; bracketed words written on a blank in lighter ink. Tatlock thinks the hand is different, but contemporary).

And if that thou take a wif be (wel) (y-)war
Of oon peril which declare I ne dar (Ha Ps Ha⁵ Bo²).

And if thou take a wif (that) to the (is) untrewe
Ful ofte tyme it shal the (sore) r[e]we (Pw En² Mg Ha⁶ Ha² Ld² Lc Ld¹ To Ii Mm Ry² Sl¹ Th; also editions of 1550 and 1561).

And if thow take a wyf of heye lynage
She shal be hauteyn and of gret costage (Dd Cn En¹ Ry¹ Ch).

And if thou take a wif
And life in disese and langour al thi lif (Ht Ra²).

And if thow take a wif and she be faire
By-war the thanne of the repaire (Bw; obviously mended from *WBT*, III, 1224).

And if thow take a wif in dede
In sorow and care thi lif shaltow leede (Py).

1307   *thinges* A (exc. Cn; om. Gg); *sithe(s)* B (incl. Mg) Cn.
1358-61   Om. El.
1417   *twenty (xx)* α Gg; *sixtene (xvj)* Dd Cn Hɜ Cp Pw La Mg; *fyftene* Th.
1421   *thritty (xxxᵗⁱ)* α Dd Cn Gg Pw Mg Th; *twenty (xx)* Ha Cp La.
1514   *stapen* α; *schapyn* Gg; *stopen* Dd Ha Th Cp Mg; *stoupin* La Cn; *stoupeth* Pw.
1686   *ye]* *we* Hg Dd Cn; adopted by Skeat, who puts ll. 1684-87 in parentheses, taking them out of Justinus's speech. Tatlock (Dev. and Chron., p. 204) defends the reading of the majority of the MSS.
1780   *as* Ha; rest om.
1824   *thikke* Dd Cn Ha Cp Th; *thilke* α Gg Pw La Mg.
1888   *abyden* Hg Dd Gg Ha Cp Mg; *byden* Cn Pw La Th.
2127   *love* Dd Cn En¹ (adopted by Tyrwhitt); rest (incl. Mg) *he.*
2194   *my lord]* *that ben my lord* Dd Cn (perhaps correctly).
2230   So (with var., acc. to Brusendorff, p. 99) Ha⁵ Ad³ *(ethena)* Ps *(Sithea)* Sl² *(Ethea)* Mg *(Cecilia)*; Cn *(Cithia)* Cp Pw La and (Brusendorff) Ld¹ Ld² Bw Ra³ Se Mm Tc¹ En² Ry¹ Ry² Sl¹ read *Proserpyna.* El Dd Gg Ha Th and (Brusendorff) Bo² En¹ En³ Ad¹ Ch read *Ech after other right as any (a) lyne,* apparently a scribal substitute for the lost line. Hg has *Whos answere hath doon many a man pyne;* Py *Walkyng to and fro in the gardyne* (Brusendorff) — both manifestly corrupt. For an argument in support of the reading in the text see Brusendorff, pp. 99 f., citing Claudian, De Raptu Proserpinae, ii, 72 (variant). Koch reads *Sicilia.*
2240   *[tales]* in no MS.; inserted by Globe; Skeat inserts *[stories].*
2405   *(y)satled* α Dd; *(y)stabled* Sl¹ Se Pw La Mg Th.

The Merchant's Epilogue

2420   *Now swich a wyf]* *Alle evel wyves* Pw and others, referring to the *Clerk's Envoy,* which preceded in the Petworth arrangement.
2424   *the soothe]* *theᵗ soth* Pw Cn La; *a soth* α Dd Ha Se; *a sothe* Ha⁵.
2425   Pw and other MSS. read *By mony ensamples it proveth well,* removing the reference to the Merchant.
2440   In a considerable number of MSS. *MerchT* is followed by *WBT.* Three of them (Bw Ld² Ry²) contain the following spurious link (as printed by Manly, p. 84):

> *Oure Ost gan tho to loke vp anoon*
> *Gode men quod he herkenyth euerychon*
> *As euer I mote drynke wyn or ale*
> *This marchant hath Itole a mery tale*
> *How Ianuarie hade a lether Iape*
> *His wif put in his hoode an ape*
> *But here of I wil leue of as nowe*
> *Dame wif of bath quod he I pray yow*
> *Telle vs a tale now next aftir this*

Sir ost quod she so god my soule blis
As I fully therto wil consente
And fully it is myn holly entente
To don yow alle disport that I can
But holdith me excused I am a woman
I con not rehersen as thise clerkes can
And right a non she hath hir tale bygune.

FRAGMENT V

The Squire's Tale

12 ff. Here and elsewhere throughout the *Tale* the name is spelled *Cambyuscan* in α (apparently) Dd; *Cambuscan* in Cn Th; *Cambynskan* B (exc. Th) Gg.

20 *pitous*] *pietous* Hg (*Pietous and just and evere moore yliche*); *piteous* Cn.

201 *of* B (incl. Mg); *a* A (incl. Cn; Gg *as fayr as*).

265 *Aldiran* Hg Dd Cn (apparently); rest (incl. Mg) *A(l)drian*.

266 Second *this* Ha; rest om.

330 *by* Ha; rest om.

346 Between Part i and Part ii MSS. Cp Pw and (Manly, p. 83) Gl Ha² Lc Mg Mm Ry² have the unexplained inscription *The Stag of an Hert*, possibly an enigmatic reference to the name of the scribe of the MS. in which it originally appeared.

455 *love* El Gg; rest (incl. Cn Mg) *ire*.

517 *sownen* Hg Gg; rest (incl. Cn Mg) *sowneth*.

602 *hire* A (incl. Cn); *him* B (incl. Mg).

617–1223 Lacking in Ha.

650 *Pyes*] *And pyes* α Dd. Tyrwhitt, with this reading, transposed ll. 649–50, perhaps correctly. But Manly notes that most MSS. do not have *And*. In Cp La Sl² (Manly, p. 83) *WBT* immediately follows *SqT*, and La contains the following spurious conclusion:

Bot I wil here nowe maake a knotte
To the time it come next to my lotte
For here be felawes behinde an hepe treulye
That wolden talke ful bisilye
And have her sporte as wele as I
And the daie passeth fast certanly
Therefore oste taketh nowe goode heede
Who schall next tell and late him speede
Than schortly answarde the wife of Bathe
And swore a wonder grete hathe
Be goddes bones I wil tel next
I will nouht glose bot saye the text.

The Franklin's Prologue and Tale

For a spurious Clerk-Franklin link see the Textual Notes on the *Host's Stanza*, IV, 1212ᵃ⁻ᵍ.

726 *to me* En¹ Cn Pw Th; *me to* Cp La Sl¹ Mg; α om. *me*.

801 *Pennmark(e)* Cn La; *Denmarke* Th; rest (incl. Mg) *Pedmark(e)*.

999 f. This couplet is moved down to follow l. 1006 in Ha⁵ Ps Bw Ha³. That order is preferred by Brusendorff (pp. 103 f.) and Manly, and may represent a genuine tradition.

1161 *wowke* El; *day* Hg Dd Gg; *yeer* ζ Pw Mg.

1273 Koch inserts *hath*, to avoid the un-Chaucerian rime of a weak pret. with a form in -*t*.

1430 *a* Cp La Mg Th; rest om. Skeat reads

hemselven, but all MSS. have (*t*)*hemself*. The Cn reading, *slowen*, would also mend the meter.

1455–56, 1493–98 Only in El Ad³ (Tatlock, p. 23, n.) and (1455–56) Th, but apparently genuine.

The following short spurious link, connecting the *Franklin's Tale* with the *Physician's Tale*, was printed by Tyrwhitt:

Ye let that passen, quod our Hoste, as now.
Sire Doctour of Physike, I prey you,
Tell us a tale of som honest matere.
It shal be don, if that ye wol it here,
Said this doctour, and his tale began anon.
Now, good men, quod he, herkeneth everich on.

FRAGMENT VI

The Physician's Tale

On MSS. in which the *Physician's Tale* is preceded by the *Canon's Yeoman's Tale*, and for two spurious links connecting the two, see the Textual Notes on the *CYT*.

16 *A(p)pelles* α Dd Th; *Ap(p)ollus* Cn Ha Sl¹ Cp Pw La; *Appollo* Mg. *Zanzis* (or perhaps *Zauzis*) α Dd Cn; *Zeusis* Th; rest (incl. Mg) *Zephirus*.

49 *as* Sl¹ Pw Mg ζ; rest om. (Possibly to be read: *wise Pallas*, as in α Cn.)

59 *dooth* α Dd Cn; *do(o)n(e)* B (incl. Mg) Gg.

92 *bitrayseth* α Dd; *bitray(e)th* B (incl. Mg) Gg Cn. Cf. *MkT*, VII, 2380.

94 *mo*] *two* El Ad¹ Pw Sl¹.

103–04 Om. El.

238 *leyser* α Dd Cn; *leve* Gg B (incl. Mg).

The Words of the Host

For the *Pardoner's Tale* and the introductory passages the forty-six additional authorities published in the Chaucer Society's Specimens have been available; also Koch's critical edition, Ch. Soc., 1902, which was based upon them.

291 *advocatz*] *advocas(s)(e)* Sl¹ Pw and 15 other B authorities (perhaps correctly); *So falle upon his body and his bones* Ha Cp La and 12 other B authorities.

292 *The devel I bekenne him al at ones* Ha Cp La and 10 other B authorities.

297–98 In Cn Ha Cp La and 16 other B authorities. They are regarded as spurious by Koch and Manly. If genuine, they may belong between ll. 293–94. Several MSS. insert them after l. 300. Brusendorff (pp. 101 ff.) suggested that Chaucer meant to cancel them and composed later ll. 299–300 (not found in Ha Ps Lc Mg) to take their place.

299 Cp La and 4 other ζ MSS., also Cx¹ Cx² Th, have this spurious line: *But herof wol I nat procede as now*.

300 *for* nearly all A MSS.; om. B MSS. (also Ma Ds¹ Cn).

305–306 *jurdones: Galiones* most A MSS.; *jo(u)rdanes: Galianes* Py and most B MSS.

313 *cardynacle* El Hg Dd and 4 others; rest (incl. Cn) *cardiacle* (some corrupt).

319–20 Ha Ha⁵ Ps Ad³ read:

Tel(le) us a tale (for) thou canst many oon
Hit s(c)hal be don quod he and that ano(o)n.

326–27 Ha Ha⁵ Ps Ad³ read:

> *Gladly quod he and sayde as ye s(c)hal heer(e)*
> *But in the cuppe wil I me bethynke.*

Both these couplets were held by Brusendorff
(pp. 102 f.) to be genuine but rejected readings.

The Pardoner's Tale

492 *Senec*] *Seneca* Ha; *Seneke* Tc² Mm Pg³ Th.
The nine-syllable line may be emended by adopting
either of these readings or by following a number of
B MSS. which read *eek good(e) wordes.*
532 *That they* Cx¹ Cx²; *They* Ha and 9 others;
That Py Tc¹ Ra³ Gl; rest (incl. Cn) (*That) ther.* Cf.
ParsT, X, 820: *that (thei) ben.*
598 *yholden* Cp La and 3 other B MSS. This
avoids the hiatus, unusual with Chaucer, but here
occurring in two successive lines.
636 *swere*] *seye* El Ha.
659 *Lete (Late)* most A MSS. (incl. Cn); *Leveth*
Gg Ha Cp Pw La and most B MSS.
736 *in* Py Dd Ha Cn Th and 17 others; rest om.
747 *if*] *yif* Gg Cn and 11 others (perhaps correctly, to avoid hiatus).
777 *kep*] *hede* En¹ Ds¹ En³ Ad¹ Nl Tc¹ and ε
(exc. Se). *what that* Hg Dd Ch Ad³ Mm; rest (incl.
Cn) *what* (perhaps correctly).
826 *that right* El Hg Dd Cn Gg and 4 others;
thou right Cx²; *right* 5 MSS. Most authorities read
and that or *and thanne.* The best MSS. show a
broken construction, with the imv. *aris(e)* after
that. Possibly *Lookewhan* means "whenever" (MLN,
XXXI, 442), in which case *and that anoon* ("and no
delay") might follow, and the imv. would be regular.
871 *botelles*] *botels* El Hg Py Ha La and at least
15 others. Skeat keeps the shorter form and inserts
of without MS. support.
928 *miles*] *townes* B (exc. Se Cx²) Ma Cn.
944 *the*] *my* El Gg and 4 others.
In sixteen MSS. (Pw Bw En² Fi Ha² Ii Ld² Lc
Mg Ra² Ry² Sl¹ Bo¹ Mm Gl Ht) there is a spurious
link connecting *PardT* with *ShipT.* See Manly,
p. 85. The passage is printed from nine MSS. in the
Six-Text Edition, x*f. (Specimen ii of Moveable
Prologues). In Pw the text is as follows:

> *Nowe frendes seide our hoost so dere*
> *How liketh you by John the pardonere*
> *For he hath vnbokeled wel the male*
> *He hath vs tolde right a thrifty tale*
> *As touching of mysgouernaunce*
> *I prey to god yeve hym good chaunche*
> *As ye han herd of thise retourues thre*
> *Now gentil Marynere hertely I preye the*
> *Telle vs a good tale and that right anon*
> *It shal be done by god & by seint John*
> *Seide this marinere as wel as euer I can*
> *And right anoon his tale he bygan.*

MS. La alone has the following, also spurious:

> *Bot than spak oure Oste vnto Maister schipman*
> *Maister quod he to vs summe tale tel ye can*
> *Where-withe ye myht glad al this company*
> *If it were youre pleseing I wote wele sekurlye*
> *Sertes quod this Schipman a tale I can tell*
> *And the[r]-fore herkeneth hyderward how that I wil spell.*

FRAGMENT VII

The Shipman's Tale

131 *here* Gg; rest om.
202 *flankes* A (incl. Cn) Th; *shankes* Ha Cp
Pw Mg La.
214 *Quy (est) la* B (incl. Mg); *Who (is) there* A
(incl. Cn) (apparently from a gloss).
228 *tweye (tweyne, two)* B (incl. Mg; exc. Th);
ten A; Th *Scarsly amonge twenty twelve shal thrive.*
331 *sheeld* α Gg; *she(e)ldes* Dd B (incl. Mg);
scutes Cn.
350 *ar* A (incl. Cn) Ha; *be(n)* Pw Mg ζ.
359 *yow* A (incl. Cn); *hir(e)* B (incl. Mg).
432 *my* B (incl. Mg); *thy* Hg En¹ Cn; *oure* El.
434 *Taillynge* α En¹ Pw Mg; *Tailyng* Cn;
Toylyng Cp La; *Talynge* Ha Sl¹ Th.

The Prioress's Tale

564 *your(e)* Ha Pw La Mg Th; *oure* A (incl. Cn)
Cp (perhaps correctly).
636 *masse* Cp Pw La Mg; *the masse* A (incl. Cn)
Ha Th.
676 *ben* B (incl. Mg); *leyn* A (incl. Cn).

The Prologue and Tale of Sir Thopas

691 *al* α Gg; rest om.
805 In Dd only among the published MSS.;
also in Cn and (Skeat) Ry¹.
835 *For now* Pw ζ Mg; rest (incl. Cn) om.
(perhaps correctly). Manly cites Sir Bevis, l. 3, for
such a short verse.
881 *was*] *it was* El (perhaps correctly).

The Prologue and Tale of Melibee

951 *Marke* Th Cn (and possibly El Ha Ry² Cp
Pw, which have a flourish after -*k*). The ending is of
doubtful support in grammar. Either insert *and* or
leave the line with one syllable lacking. Chaucer
may have found such a rest or pause unobjectionable
in a list. Cf. *FrT,* III, 1647; *PF,* 380. The lack of
an unaccented syllable within a line is not uncommon
in Lydgate.
1062–63 Not in MSS. The passage, which is
necessary to the sense, was supplied by Tyrwhitt
and the Six-Text edition from the French *Mélibee.*
Cf. *Le Ménagier de Paris,* ed. Pichon, Soc. de Bib.
Fr., Paris, 1846, I, 193.
1070 *and he . . . book* om. El; the text follows
Hg.
1223 *conseillours*] *conseil* Ha Th (perhaps correctly); Fr. "conseil" (Ménagier, I, 203).
1276 *encreesceden* A (incl. Cn) Pw Cp La and
(Tatlock, p. 5, n. 1) 22 other MSS.; *entreteden* Th
Mg and (Tatlock) Lc. *Han shewed you* Ha and
(Tatlock) Ld¹; *proposid* Bo¹ (Tatlock); *hadden* Ii
(Tatlock) Fr. "adjoustèrent" (Ménagier, I, 206).
1324 *From* Hg; El om.
1335–36 *appertyneth . . . toures* Cp La; rest om.
And grete edifices supplied from the Fr. (Ménagier,
I, 209).
1433–34 Missing in all MSS. and Th; supplied
by Tyrwhitt and the Six-Text edn. from the Fr.
Ménagier, I, 214).

1445 *strong* A (incl. Cn) Pw Th; *straunge* Cp La; *strayt* Ha; Fr. "fors" (Ménagier, I, 215).
1497 *Gregorie*] *Poul* Ha; Fr. "Grégoire" (Ménagier, I, 218).
1556 *which . . . housbonde* om. El Gg Cp Pw La.
1560 *al(l)o(o)ne* Gg Cn B; *al alloone* α Dd.
1576 *sokyngly* Gg Cn B; *sekyngly* α Dd.
1643 *arn* α Dd Cn; *are* Pw; rest *ben*.
1664 *if he be* El; rest (incl. Cn) *if it be*. The French words are from Le Ménagier, I, 226; they are not represented in any of the published MSS. of the English or in Th.
1678 *thyng*] *thinges* Dd Ha.
1777 *And he seith . . . remissioun* om. El Dd Cn Gg Th wholly, Hg Ha Cp in part; from Pw. Fr. "et dit autre part: cellui est presque innocent qui a honte de son péchié et le recongnoist" (Ménagier, I, 231).

The Monk's Prologue and Tale

1889 *my*] *the* Cp La Th and (Brusendorff, p. 69, n. 4) Sl² Ha³ Tc¹ Mm Fi Ch Py; *this* Sl¹ and (Brusendorff) Ad¹ En² Ha². Miss Hammond (p. 258) takes *the* to be the original reading and *my* to be Chaucer's own revision.
1895 *For* B; om. α Dd Cn.
1957–58 El om.
2055 *Ciser* α; *siser* Ha; *Sythir* Gg Pw La; *cyder* Cp; *sydir* Cn; *sider* Mg.
2272 ff. *Odenak(e)* B (Th *Odenat*; Mg *Odonake*); *Onedake* A (incl. Cn).
2325 *Petrak* El Hg Dd Gg Cn La Mg and (Brusendorff, p. 119, n. 2) En¹ En² Ad¹ Ad³; *Petrarke* Cp Pw Th; *Perark* Ha. See textual note on *Cl Prol*, IV, 31.
2333 *maden* Mg; rest (incl. Cn) *made, maad*.
2340 *fe(e)ldes* A (incl. Cn); *fe(e)ld(e)* B (incl. Mg).
2363 *Biforen*] all MSS. have *Bifore, Biforn(e)*.
2380 *bitraysed* α Gg; *bitrayed* B (incl. Mg) Cn. Cf. *PhysT*, VI, 92.
2426 *spak(e)* α Dd Cn Th; *saugh, sawe, segh*, etc. Ha Cp Pw La Sl¹ Mg. Line deficient; Globe inserts *ne*.
2438 *but* α Dd Cn Th; *save (sauf)* Ha² Ha Cp Pw La Mg.
2467 [*south*] *north* A (incl. Cn); om. B (incl. Mg). The emendation seems necessary to the sense. Koch suggests, however, that Chaucer wrote *Noth* (for *Nothus*, which is mentioned along with "septem triones" in the passage in Boethius which lies behind the English text).
2544 *ful* B (incl. Mg; exc. Th); om. A (incl. Cn) Th (perhaps correctly, with the reading *fyre*, as in Cn Pw La Th).
2563 Globe inserts *ne* to avoid hiatus.
2720 *Valerie* Th (*Valery*); *Valirien* Ha, rest (incl. Cn Mg) *Valerius* (metrically difficult). Koch objects to *Valerie* here on the ground that it seems to mean in Chaucer the author of the Epistola ad Rufinum. See the introduction to the Explanatory Notes on the *WBT*.
2721 *word and ende* all MSS. and Th; doubtless a corruption of *ord and ende*. See the explanatory note on this line.

The Nun's Priest's Prologue

A shorter form of this link, omitting ll. 2771–90, is found in Hg Cp Pw Mg and several other MSS. (See Miss Hammond, p. 241 f. Cn has the full form.) In l. 2767 Ad¹ En³ Tc² Cx¹ read *Hoste* for *Knyght*, possibly representing Chaucer's first intention.
2783 *als* Ry¹ Dd Ha; *also* El Cn Ry² Sl¹ Ad¹ La Mg Th.
2786 *als* El Dd Sl¹ Ry¹ La Mg Th; *also* Ha Ry² Ad¹; *eke* Cn.
2792 *or* Pw; *o* Hg Dd Cn; rest (incl. Mg) om.

The Nun's Priest's Tale

2821 *stape* α *stope(n)* En¹ Sl¹ Cn Ha Cp Pw; *stoupe* La Mg; *ystept* Th.
2870 En¹ Th insert a couplet:

> *He fethered hir an hundred tyme a day*
> *And she hym pleseth all that ever she may.*

2896 *recche* A (exc. Cn) Th; *rede* Ha Cp Pw Mg La; *dressyn* Cn.
2929 *drede(n)* A (exc. Cn) Th; *dreme(n)* Cn B (incl. Mg; exc. Th).
2984 *auctour* α Dd Cp Pw La Mg; *au(c)tour(y)s* Gg Cn Th; *auctorite* Ha.
3036 *went(e) as it were* Hg Gg Ha; *as it were* El Th; *went for* Dd; *went to* Cn; *as he went(e)* Cp Pw La Mg.
3042 *he lith* Dd Pw Cn ζ (incl. Mg); *heere he lith* α Gg; *he lith heer* Ha.
3076 *But* Dd Cn; rest (incl. Mg) *But herken(e)(th)* (Alexandrine?).
3155 *venymous* B (incl. Mg) Dd Cn; *venymes* α Gg.
3189 *passed*] *i-passed* Dd Cn.
3386 *So feered for the* Dd; *So fered for* α; *So aferede for* Cn; *So were they fered for* Ha; *For they so sore a ferde were of the dogges* Th; *For fered for* Gg; *Sore afer(e)d(e) for* Cp Pw La Mg.
3395 *shrille*] *shill(e)* El Dd La Cn (perhaps correctly).
3418 *the cok* Dd Cn; rest (incl. Mg) *he* (Ha reading *ygon* to fill out the meter).

The Nun's Priest's Epilogue

This occurs in Dd Cn Ad¹ Ry¹ Ch Th and (Tatlock, p. 23, n.) Ds¹ En¹ En³ Ma. It is printed by the Chaucer Society from Dd Ad¹ Ry¹ Ch; the present text is based on Dd, collated with the Six-Text print and with Th. The passage is doubtless genuine, but seems likely to have been canceled to avoid repetition of material in the *Monk's Prologue*. Six more lines (surely spurious) are added in several MSS. to join the *NPT* to the *SecNT*. They are found in Cn and (Miss Hammond, p. 170) En³ Ad¹ Ma and are here printed from Cn.

> *Madame and y durst y wold you pray*
> *To telle us a tale y furtheryng of our way*
> *Then myght ye do unto us gret ease*
> *Gladly qᵈ she so that y myght you please*
> *You and this wurthy company*
> *And began hir tale ryght thus full sobyrly.*

3462 *another*] *the Nunne* Cn Ad¹; *another man* Th.

FRAGMENT VIII

The Second Nun's Prologue and Tale

18 *encrees* B (exc. Mg) Cn; *n'encrees* α; *ne encrees* Dd; *noon encrees* Mg; Gg corrupt.
139 *or* B (incl. Mg Sl¹); *and* α Dd Cn.
277 *Valerians*] *Cecilies* MSS. (incl. Cn Mg) Th; Lat. "Valeriani."
363 *ap(p)osed* Ha Cn Mg Th; *rest opposed* (also good mediæval usage).

The Canon's Yeoman's Prologue and Tale

The *Canon's Yeoman's Prologue* and *Tale* are not in Hg; they are supplied in the Six-Text edition by Lc (of the Pw group, according to Zupitza's classification).
562 *hors* B (incl. Lc Sl¹ Mg); *hakeney(e)* El Dd Cn.
564–65 Om. El.
Prima Pars inserted to correspond to the later headings found in El.
803 *purpos if* El Dd Cn; *craft if that* Gg B (incl. Lc Mg).
855 End of Dd; supplemented in Ch. Soc. edition by En¹.
881 *brat(e)* El En¹ Cn Th; *bak(ke)* Gg B (exc. Th; incl. Mg).
1100 Metrically harsh; perhaps to be emended, *Consumed han and wasted* or *Consumed and wastid have(n)*.
1171 *terued* En¹ Cn; *rest* (incl. Mg) *terned(e)*, *torned, turned*, etc. Cf. l. 1274.
1238–39 Om. El En¹ Cn Ry¹.
1274 *terve* El; *ter(e)* Cn; *rest* (incl. Mg) *terne, torne*, etc. (as in l. 1171).
1283–84 *The prest supposede nothing but wel, But busied him faste and was wonder fayn* B (exc. Ha; incl. Mg Lc). Ha has the A (incl. Cn) reading in a later hand.
1303 *werk*] *hert(e)* El En¹ Cn.
1427 *What*] *What that the* all MSS. and Th (which would make an Alexandrine verse).
In many MSS. *CYT* precedes *PhysT*, and 17 of them (Bw Bc¹ En² Fi Ht Ii Ld² Lc Mm Mg Ra² Ry¹ Ry² Sl² Bo² Py Se, acc. to Manly) contain the following spurious link (printed by him, p. 86):

Whan that this yoman his tale ended hadde
Of this fals Chanon whiche that was so badde
Oure host gan seye trewely and certain
This preest was bigiled sothly forto sayn
He wenynge forto be a philosophre
Til he right no gold lefte in his cofre
And sothly this preest hadde a luder iape
This cursed Chanon putte in his hood an ape
But al this passe I ouer as now
Sir doctour of physik I pray you
Tell vs a tale of som honest matere
It shal be don yif that ye wole it here
Saide this doctoure and his tale began anon
Now goode men quod he herkeneth everychon.

MS. La alone has the following link, also spurious:

Nowe trewly quod oure Oste this is a prati tale
For litel merveile it is that thou lokest so pale
Sethen thou hast medeled with so mony thinges
With bloweinge att the cole to melte bothe brochez and ringes
And othere many Jewels dar I vndertake
And that thi lorde couthe vs tel if we myht him oueretake
Bot lat him go a devel waye the compaigny is neuer the wers
And al suche fals harlotes I sette not be hem a kers
Bot latt pas ouere nowe al thes subtilitees
And sume worthi man tel vs summe veritees
As ye worschipful Maister of Phisike
Telleth vs somme tale that is a cronyke
That we may of yowe leren sum witte
Quod the Maister of Phisik a tale that I finde writte
In cronyke passed of olde tyme
Herkeneth for I wil tel it yow in rime.

FRAGMENT IX

The Manciple's Tale

147 *in ydel* El Gg; *rest* (incl. Cn Mg) *for noght*.
173 *yif* Gg; *if* α Cn Pw; *if that* En¹; *whan* Ha Cp La Mg Th.

FRAGMENT X

The Parson's Prologue and Tale

5 *Foure*] so (Tatlock, p. 20, n. 3) Ch Ad¹; *ten* (.x.) all published MSS. (La corrupt) Th Cn Mg and (Tatlock) 19 others; *thre* Ii (Tatlock).
11 *I me(e)ne* A (incl. Cn) Pw Mg ζ; equivalent in 20 other MSS. (Tatlock, p. 20, n. 3); *in mena* Ha Ld¹ (Tatlock); *in mene* Ry² (Tatlock).
73–74 In the MSS. this couplet — apparently through scribal error — follows l. 68.
190 *ther . . . dignitee* om. El; printed from Hg.
232 *lost* Ha² Cp Pw Mg La; *left* α En¹ Th.
254 *in so much* Th; *rest* (incl. Cn Mg) *noght (nat) so much* (which is harder).
273 *And therfore . . . manere* Gg Th; *rest* om.
281 *for oure felonies* El Th; *by oure felonies* Hg En¹ Cn Gg Ha Pw Mg (*vilenyes*) Cp La; Vulg. "propter scelera nostra."
290 End of Cp; supplemented in the Six-Text edition by Se.
365 Koch would supply *the love of* before *thilke worldly thinges*, thus improving both grammar and sense.
387 *spryng(e) of* Hg Th; *spryngen of* El En¹ Ha² Pw La; *springers of* Ha; *of hem springen* Se.
390 *De Superbia* here Hg; before l. 387 El La; part of longer title in Ha² Pw; *rest* om.
443 *Laban* and *Pharao* interchanged in all MSS. Th. The error may possibly be Chaucer's.
475 *Remedium* etc. after *spryngeth* El En¹ Se; in margin Gg; *rest* om.
551 End of Hg; supplemented in Six-Text edition by Ch.
616 *be-traysyn* Gg; *betray* Th; *betrayeth* En¹; *rest* (incl. Cn) *bitray(s)ed*. Tyrwhitt (followed by Skeat), apparently without MS. support, reads: *betrayed [God; and thise flaterers betrayen] man*, etc. The Latin supports the shorter reading: "Sub spe enim osculi ad modum Jude hominem tradit hosti-

bus suis" (K. O. Petersen, Sources of the Parson's Tale, Boston, 1901, p. 55).

630 *A* Mg; rest (incl. Cn) *I*.

649 *sygne] synne* El Gg.

670 *broghte] and broght(e)* all MSS. Th. *Scourge* Ch; *scoure with* El; rest (incl. Mg) *scoure* (perhaps correctly); *beate* Th.

698 *that seeth . . . recreaunt* om. El.

748 *is the thraldom* El Ch En¹ Cn Hg Th; *is thral to* Se La; *hath more (his) hope in (his) thraldom* Pw Ha² Mg. Perhaps to be read (with Skeat): *is in the thraldom*; but Eph. v, 5 reads: "aut avarus, quod est idolorum servitus" (so Peraldus, Petersen, p. 67).

858 *busshes* eds. em. for *beautees* all MSS.; *benches* Th.

869 *centesimus fructus secundum Ieronimum contra Iovinianum* Ha.

955 *David] Daniel* El Gg Th; Lat. "David" (Petersen, p. 78).

965 *til . . . bysshop* om. El Gg En¹.

983 *Ezechiel* all authorities, but Ezechias is meant (Is. xxxviii, 15). Of course the error may have been Chaucer's, and may even have stood in his source.

1000 *and no* El Gg Th; *and in no* Ch *and at no* En¹; *and is in no* Se Pw Mg La *and not* Ha.

1051 *ete by mesure*; Ha alone repeats *ete*, making two items instead of one; Lat. "largitas, laetitia, hora, et mensura" (Petersen, p. 29).

Chaucer's Retractation

Printed by the Chaucer Society from El Ad¹ Ha² Se (supplemented by Ht) Pw La Ha En¹ (completed in a modern hand); also found in Cn and (Tatlock, PMLA, XXVIII, 525, n.) Ry² Bo¹ Ra² Ra³ Ne Ii Mm Tc² Lc; that is, in all MSS. thus far described which have the immediately preceding part of the *Parson's Tale* unmutilated. But it is not in Th.

Rubric: So (with slight variations) El Ha² Se Pw En¹; *Hic capit Autor licenciam* Ad¹; *Composito huius libri hic capit licenciam suam* La; *Preces de Chauceres* Ha.

1086 *xix* Cn; *xxv (25)* El En¹ (late hand) Ad¹ Ha² Se Pw; *xv* La Ha.

1092 *Qui cum patre &c* El; written out fully in Ad¹.

The Book of the Duchess

Authorities: three MSS. and Thynne's edition:

F   Fairfax 16, Bodleian.
B   Bodley 638, Bodleian.
T   Tanner 346, Bodleian.
Th Thynne's edition, 1532.

All these copies have been printed by the Chaucer Society. On their relations see J. Koch, Angl., IV, Anz., 95; M. Lange, Untersuchungen über Chaucer's Boke of the Duchesse, Halle, 1883; and Mr. Heath's introduction in the Globe edition, p. xxxiii. F and B are, as usual, closely related, and in the case of this poem offer the best text. T belongs to the same group with the source of F and B. Th apparently stands by itself.

The present edition is based upon F, corrected by comparison with the other authorities. Numerous ungrammatical forms (chiefly bad final -*e*'s) have had to be corrected, and the spelling has been normalized to bring it into general conformity with that of the Ellesmere MS. of the *Canterbury Tales*. With regard to certain special problems see the Introduction on the Text. The authorities agree in supporting many readings which are either unsatisfactory in sense or metrically inferior to most of Chaucer's verse, and such readings have been sparingly corrected. Perhaps the editor has erred on the side of conservatism, but it appeared unsafe to indulge in wholesale emendation to improve the text of an early poem in a meter of rather rough and free traditions. Skeat's text is much more freely corrected. The important emendations of the various editors are recorded below.

23 *thus* em. Skeat, Koch; MSS., Globe *this*.

73 *founden* em. Skeat, Koch to avoid hiatus; MSS., Globe *founde*.

76 *of] of Alcyone* F Th; probably a gloss taken into the text.

80 *erme] yerne* F Th; emendation for rime.

82 *[he dwelte]* Skeat, Globe; *he taried* Koch; *her thoughte* F Th (apparently repeated from l. 81).

91–94 Globe transposes these couplets.

120 *knowen] know(e)* MSS.; em. Skeat, Globe, Koch to avoid hiatus.

128 *tooke*; read *took*? But the form may be subjunctive.

158 *no thing* em. Skeat, Globe, Koch; *noght* MSS. (which looks like corrupt repetition).

185 *axed] MSS. and axed (asked)*.

204 *nam]* MSS. *am*, followed by Globe; Skeat, Koch em. *nam*, restoring the usual idiom.

206 Skeat supplied *[look]* to mend an unusual construction. But the independent subjunctive (retained by Koch) is a possible idiom. Cf. *MerchT*, IV, 1942. Globe transfers *for* from l. 207 (metri gratia).

334 *Of* Skeat, Koch; MSS., Globe *And*.

338 *gilde* F, Koch; *gyldy(e)* B Th; *gilti* T; Skeat, Globe em. *gilden*.

383 *over shot* Th; *ovyrshotte* B; *overshet(te)* F T (perhaps correctly).

391 *crepte]* so Globe, Koch; Skeat em. *creep* (Chaucer's more usual form).

437 *rekened]* Skeat em. for *rekene*, MSS., Globe, Koch.

480 After l. 479 Th inserts *And thus in sorowe lefte me alone*. To preserve the customary numbering the next line is called l. 481. Thynne's line, with its un-Chaucerian rime (*aloon* for *alone*), is held by Skeat, Globe to be spurious. If it is genuine, possibly (as Professor Koch suggests) l. 478 should follow it. This would give the rime sequence aab, but the order seems unnatural.

498 *was* Skeat, Globe; *is* MSS., Koch.

584 *That]* so Globe, Koch; Skeat *Thogh*.

586 *hym*] so Globe, Koch; Skeat *hit*, to avoid unnatural change of gender.

599 *song* Skeat, Globe, Koch; *sorowe* MSS.

660 *the mid(de)* MSS., which makes the line suspiciously long.

681 *she my fers* MSS.; Skeat, Globe, Koch *my fers she*, for the meter.

721 *syr*] *good sire* MSS., Koch; *yis* om. Skeat; *good* om. Globe.

734 Skeat inserts *a!* after *fals.* Read *falsë* Th T (with inorganic *-e*)?

802 So Koch; Skeat *And al my thoghtes varyinge;* Globe *That tyme, and thoghtes varyinge.*

829 *so*] *and so* MSS.

832 *as* T; *al* B F Th.

855 *on*] so Globe; *upon* Skeat, Koch.

905 Skeat, Globe om. *whit*; Koch transposes *fresh* and *rody* — both changes being made to improve the meter. Here and at ll. 942, 948 there is a marginal note "blanche" in Stowe's hand.

932 *ther* supplied by Skeat, Globe, Koch.

942 So Koch; *whit* (Globe om.) again overloads the verse and may be wrong; Skeat om. *pure.*

943 *or* MSS., Koch; *and* Skeat; *nor* Globe.

948 *White*; the *-e* is clipped in the verse, but may be correctly written as the weak ending of the adjective.

959 *pure sewynge*] *pure* om. Skeat; *nere pursewyng(e)* Globe, Koch.

1020 *wolde not*] so Globe; Skeat, Koch *nolde.*

1028 *to* Skeat, Koch; *into* MSS., Globe.

1029–30 *Carrenar: war*] *Carrenare: ware* MSS.; but the singular form of the adjective seems to be required.

1039–40 *blesse* Th; rest *blisse.* The rare form *blesse* (accepted by Koch) rimes properly with *goddesse.* Skeat em. *goddesse* to *lisse*, Globe *goode lisse*, to rime with *blisse.*

1041 *and everydel(e)* MSS., Globe; Skeat *And I hirs hoolly, everydel* (so Koch, retaining *and*).

1075 *trewly* om. Skeat.

1126 Skeat supplies [*right*] before *tho.*

1133 *knewe* F T Th, supported by the meter, though *knew* (as in B) is the regular strong preterite indicative. Possibly this is subjunctive in indirect question.

1147 *not never* MSS.

1173 *the* om. MSS.; editors supply.

1188 *nam*] *am* MSS.; emendation to conform to the usual idiom.

1234 *to* om. Skeat.

1266 *And* MSS.; Lange, p. 20, *That* (to follow *so*).

1285 *al* (2nd)] Skeat, Globe, Koch em. *alle.*

1315 *homwardes* Globe em.; *hom(e)warde* MSS.; Skeat supplies [*quikly*] after *gan*, Koch *faste.*

The House of Fame

Authorities: three MSS. and the editions of Caxton and Thynne, grouped as follows:

α { B Bodley 638, Bodleian.
    { F Fairfax 16, Bodleian.

β { P Pepys 2006, hand B, Magdalene College, Cambridge (ends at l. 1483).
   { Cx Caxton's edition, 1483.
   { Th Thynne's edition, 1532.

All the texts are accessible in the Chaucer Society reprints. Th derived from Cx but made use of other authorities.

Mr. Heath held β to be superior and based the Globe text on P as far as it reaches. (See his introduction, p. xliv.) Brusendorff (p. 153, n.) also expressed a preference for β. The present editor finds the readings of α preferable in the majority of cases, and has consequently made F the basis of his text. The same choice was made by Willert (ed. *HF*, Berlin, 1883), Skeat and Koch, and is supported by Miss Hammond in MLN, XXIII, 20. But as a matter of fact, whichever group is adopted, a good many readings of the other have to be substituted. In this text, too, as in the *Book of the Duchess*, the readings of all MSS. are unsatisfactory and considerable emendation is necessary. Though the spelling of F does not conform altogether to that of the best MSS. of the *Canterbury Tales* and the *Troilus*, most of its peculiarities (such as the double vowels in *too, froo, loo, mee*, etc.) have been allowed to stand. Forms that appear inconsistent with Chaucer's usage have been corrected, and inflectional endings

have been made regular. In several instances *-n* has been silently added to infinitives to break a hiatus or mend the rhythm.

Professor Koch's readings are cited from his *Kleinere Dichtungen.*

Book I

Title. *The House of Fame* F B P Th; *The book of Fame made by Gefferey Chaucer*, Cx.

40 (*to*) *have visions* β; *avisions* α.

63 *now* F B P Th, Koch; Cx om.; Skeat, Globe *dide.*

73 *me(n) clepeth* α; *that men clepe(n)* β.

115 *forgo*; possibly to be read as two words: *for go*, "because of having gone."

119 *slepte*] so Koch; Skeat, Globe *sleep.*

127 *olde* α; *gold(e)* β.

143 *singe* β; *say* α.

153 Skeat, Globe, Koch supply *That* before *with.* The ellipsis of the subject relative here is certainly difficult though perhaps not impossible.

160 *Polytes* Th; *Polite* F B; *Plite* P; *Plyto* Cx.

184 *not*] Skeat [*but*] *noot*; Globe, Koch *ne wot.*

237 Globe, Koch transpose: *his folk he shulde.*

244 *Al(le) that* β; *That that* α.

285 *or* (before *double*) om. α P (perhaps correctly: *privy double*, "secretly double"?); *fals provyd or* Cx.

329 [*I*] supplied by Skeat, Globe.

347 *myn* β; *your(e)* α.

362 *Al*, Skeat, Globe; MSS. *But al; But* perhaps repeated from l. 361.

370 *him* Th; rest om.

397 *lo* α; *loke* β.
399 *Enone* α; *Oenone* β.
428 *grete* β; α om.
478 *any stiryng*] so Globe, Koch; *sterynge any* Th, Skeat.

Book II

536 *smote* α; *smyte* β (Machaut "mist"; see expl. n. to l. 534). *To* β; *of* α.
543 *in* α; *at* β.
603 *To do*] so Koch; Skeat, Globe *to done.*
618 *Venus [goddesse]* Skeat; *[dame] Venus* Globe. The line may be headless, but it is suspiciously short. Koch retains it.
675 *And of* β; *Of* α. The β reading makes the unusual dative *folkë* unnecessary.
718 *way* β; *aire* α.
756 *Ther as* β; *As ther* α.
786 *nede* α; *nedes* β.
797 *Wydder* α; *Brod(d)er* β.
817 *another* em. Willert, Koch; *in other* β; *other* α.
827 *same place* Globe; *sum place stide* F; *som styde* B; *some stede* Th; Skeat *the mansioun;* Koch *every stede.* P Cx om. ll. 827–64.
872 *[Quod he]* supplied by Skeat, Globe; Koch supplies *right* after *A.*
896 *gan* Skeat, Globe; *gan to* Cx Th; *to* F B P, Koch (conceivably an historical infinitive, but unlikely).
911–12 *And seide seyst thou eny token Or ought thow knowest yonder down* P; *And seyde seest thou ony token Or aught that in the (this) world is of spoken* Cx Th; α om.
919 *wrechche* F B Th; *wryght* Cx P.
946 *gonne] goome* P; rest *gan. Launce* α; *daunce* P Cx; *praunce* Th.
950 *ferde* α; *fer(e)* β.
957 *grete* β; *mochil* α.
961 *alwey upper* β; *upper alwey for* α.
1044 *byten* B Th; *beten* F P; *greve* Cx.
1066 *Seynte] seynt* MSS.
1079 *verrey* P; *very* Cx Th; *were* α.

Book III

1114 *site] cite* P; *cyte* Cx Th B; *citee* F.
1124 *alum de] alymde* P; *a lymed* Cx Th; *a thynge of* α, Skeat; Globe em. *alyned,* "aligned"; but Bradley (Athen., 1902, I, 563 f.) argued that the original reading was probably *alum de* (Fr. "alun de glace," crystallized alum). This is accepted by Brusendorff (p. 153, n.) and Koch.
1161–62 Lines transposed in α Th.
1170 *no* α Th; *the* P Cx. Reading doubtful; *compas* (noun) ought not to have final *-e.* Either emend the rime-word to *plas,* or take *no* as "nor" and *compace* as infinitive.
1177 All MSS. om. *craft* in l. 1177; β inserts in l. 1178, from which the editors have transferred it.
1189 *Babewynnes* Skeat, Globe, Koch em.; *Rabewynnes* B; *Rabewyures* F; *Babeweuries* P; *As babeuwryes* Cx; *As babeuries* Th.
1227–28 Lines transposed in α. *Atiteris* α; *Cytherus* β; Koch *Cytharis* ("Name eines Spielmanns?").
1228 *Pseustis* α; *Presentus* P; *Proserus* Cx Th.
1303 *they hatte* α; *the hackyng(e)* β.

1304 *full of* B; om. F; *and* β.
1351 *Ful* P Cx; rest *Fyne.*
1356 *lusty and riche* α Th; *riche lusty* P Cx.
1372 So β; *This was gret marvaylle to me* α. Perhaps originally *This was gret marvaylle to me, she* (Globe footnote).
1390 *on bestes* α; *on a(n) best(e) ben* β.
1415 *Thus] And thus* MSS.; *And* om. Skeat, Globe, Koch.
1425 *hy and* all om.; supplied by Globe from Th, l. 1426; Koch inserts *ful; greet [and hy]* Skeat.
1483 Skeat supplies *[dan]* before *Virgile,* comparing l. 1499.
1515 *olde* β; *al of the olde* F; *of the olde* B.
1551 *yet* β; *ryght* α.
1568 *messager(e)* B Cx; *messangere* F; *messenger* Th; *masynger* P; spellings vary throughout *HF;* the older form (without *n*) has been adopted.
1595 *forth* α; *fast(e)* β.
1623 *And thou dan Eolus quod she* β; *Have do(o)n Eolus let se(e)* α; cf. l. 1765, below.
1686 *pot] pot(te)ful* α Th; *pyt ful* Cx; *pitteful* P. To avoid over-long line, editors om. *of* or *ful* (perhaps repeated from l. 1687).
1702 *clew* α; *turned* β.
1717 *lyven* em. Skeat, Globe; *lyen* α Th, Koch; *be* P; om. Cx.
1725 *Al so* α Th, Koch; *And so* P Cx, Globe; Skeat *So kenely* α; *kynd(e)ly* β.
1726 *so* α; *That their fame was blowe a lofte* Cx Th; P om.
1735 *a* β; α om.
1738 *acheved* α Th; *eschewyd* P Cx. *Lestes* α; *bestes* P Cx; *questes* Th.
1761 *glive* α Th; *blowe* P Cx.
1765 *let se* α; *quod she* β; cf. l. 1623, above.
1779 *wher(e)* β; or α.
1781 *rought(e)* α; *thought* β.
1783 *sweynt(e)* α; *slepy* β.
1803 *beloweth* α; *belleth* β.
1812 *traytery(e)* α; *trechery(e)* β.
1813 *gretest* Willert, Skeat, Globe; *gret(e)* MSS., Koch. (Perhaps to be emended: *The grettest harm and wikkednesse.*)
1823 *lepynge* α Th; *crepyng(e)* P Cx.
1824 *choppen* α; *clappe(n)* β.
1843 End of P.
1895 *mene of* α; *ment of* Th; *mente* Cx.
1897 *wiste* Skeat, Globe, Koch; *wote* MSS.
1908 *[thus]* supplied by Skeat, Globe; Koch om. line.
1926 *it styl* Th; rest *still(e) (h)it.*
1940 *hottes* Skeat, Globe, Koch; *hattes* α Cx; *hutches* Th.
1944 So β; B om.; F starts the line *As ful this lo* (perhaps preserving a correct but uncompleted text).
1948 *roof* Cx; *rofe* Th; *rove* F; *rone* B, perhaps a real dative.
1962 *reste* Skeat, Globe, Koch; *restes* MSS.
1967 *wyndes* α; *wether* β. *and] and eke* MSS.
2004 *gynne* α; *the gyn(ne)* β. (Possibly *the gin,* "the device," riming with *therin.*)
2009 *these* MSS., Globe, Koch; but *thesë* is not regular; Skeat em. *swiche.*
2017 *fruit* Skeat, Koch (very doubtful); *frot* F; *foot* B; *swote* Cx Th, Globe. *Rote,* "root," is another possible emendation.

2018 *languysshe* Cx Th; *laugh* α.
2026 *here anoon* α; *anoon* om. β; *anoon here* Skeat, Globe, Koch transpose (for the meter).
2036 From β; α om. Koch regards the line as spurious and suggests: *Many a thousand in a route.*
2049 Metrically suspicious; Skeat em. *the other* for *he*; Koch supplies *sire* before *quod.*
2076 *tydyng* Cx Th; *mouth* α; Skeat *word*; Globe, Koch *thyng.* Read *ech tydyng?*
2079 *sparke* α; *sparcle* β.
2081 *ysprong(e)* α; *up spronge* β.
2083 *[hit]* and MSS.
2090 *drawe* β, Skeat, Globe; *thrawe* α (so Koch, who interprets it "eilen," hasten).
2094 Rest missing in Cx, which adds, however, 12 lines apparently spurious. See below.
2104 *oon [of us] two* Koch; *that oon [of] two* Skeat, Globe; *on(e) two* F Th; *that oon* B.
2152 *nose and yen* B, Globe; *noyse an highen* F; *noyse on hyghen* Th; Skeat, Koch *nose on hye* (perhaps correctly).

2156 *[nevene]* Skeat, Koch; *Whiche that y nat (naught) ne kan* MSS.; *ne wot, ne kan,* Globe.
2157 Cx adds at end:

> And wyth the noyse of them wo
> I sodeynly awoke anon tho
> And remembryd what I had seen
> And how hye and ferre I had been
> In my ghoost and had grete wonder
> Of that the god of thonder
> Had lete me knowen and began to wryte
> Lyke as ye have herd me endyte
> Wherfor to studye and rede alway
> I purpose to doo day by day
> Thus in dremyng and in game
> Endeth thys lytyl book_of Fame.

Th alters the first three lines:

> And therwithal I abrayde
> Out of my slepe halfe a frayde
> Remembrig wel what I had sene.

Anelida and Arcite

Authorities: eight MSS. of the whole poem and four of the *Complaint* alone; all of which, together with Caxton's edition, are printed by the Chaucer Society.

α {
  1 {
    F   Fairfax 16, Bodleian.
    B   Bodley 638, Bodleian.
    Hl¹ Harley 372, British Museum.
  }
  2 {
    T   Tanner 346, Bodleian.
    Ff   Cambridge University Library, Ff. 1. 6.
  }
  3 {
    L   Longleat 258, in the possession of the Marquess of Bath.
    D   Digby 181, Bodleian.
  }
}

β {
  1 {
    Hl² Harley 7333, British Museum (copied from Shirley).
    R   Trinity College, Cambridge, R. 3. 20,   both written
    Add Additional 16165, British Museum.   by Shirley.
  }
  2 {
    P   Pepys 2006, Magdalene College, Cambridge.
    Ph   Phillipps 8299, Cheltenham (contaminated with a MS. of the α³ type, perhaps with L).
    Cx   Caxton's edition, 1477–8? (perhaps contaminated with Hl²).
  }
}

Ll. 290–98 are omitted in β. Ll. 351–57 are in MSS. T D L Ff only; this portion of the text is based upon T. MSS. Ff R P Ph contain only the *Complaint.*

A thorough investigation of the MSS. of the *Anelida* will be found in Mr. Joseph Butterworth's uncompleted dissertation on the Textual Tradition of Chaucer's Minor Poems. The editor has had the advantage of consulting this study. It confirms the accepted view as to the classification of the authorities, but shows that in group β¹ MSS. R and Add have a common source as opposed to MS. Hl². It also adduces evidence, not previously noted, that Caxton's text is a contamination of β¹ and β².

Neither of the archetypes, α or β, affords a clearly superior text. Perhaps there is a slightly larger number of good readings in β. But, for orthographical reasons, MS. F has been taken as the basis of the present text, and β readings have been substituted where they appear more probable. The spellings in F have occasionally been corrected when they depart from the prevailing usage of the best Chaucer MSS., and a number of final -*e*'s have been supplied for grammatical regularity. A few variants peculiar to F, B, and Hl¹ (α¹) present a special problem. They are sometimes accepted as representing a version due to Chaucer himself. Several of them are tempting and one or two are manifestly superior to the critical text. But taken all together they are hardly sure enough or important enough to prove the author's revision of the poem, though some of them may represent corrections that stood in his original manuscript. See ll. 223, 229, 236, 257, 269, 278–79, 318, 331, 334, 349.

31 *token* α; *tokenyng* β.
53 *everich other to*] *eche other to* Cx; *yche othir for to* Hl² (perhaps correctly).
59 *slayn* MSS. Read *slawen?* or *slayn [was]?* But *proudë* (weak) is regular with the proper name. *Campaneus*] *Carpaneus* L T; for *Capaneus*; conceivably Chaucer's error.
63 *care* α; *fare* β.
68 *dwell(en)* α; *wonnen (women* Cx) β.
76 *is ther;* read *ther is* (L, Globe) or *nis ther* (Koch em.), to avoid hiatus?
77 *worlde;* final -*e* doubtful, though possible as dat. Perhaps to be read *worold* (dissyllabic).
82 *hath*] *bothe* α¹.
85 *Arcite* all MSS. om.
91 *trusted*] *trusteth* Hl² T. Read *trust* (Skeat, Globe), or *truste* (Koch)?

98 *As α; Al β.*

112 *hit did her ese β; hit did her herte an ese* (var.) *α.*

119 *heste β; herte α.*

132 *So β; For so α.*

143 *of β; for α.*

149 *kinde β; the kinde α.*

171 *Craumpyssheth] Al craumpisshed* Hl²; *Craumpysed alle* Add.

174 *Noon β; Ne noon α.*

182 *never α; not (nought) β.*

183 *him* Hl² Cx; rest *him up* (T om. *him*).

185 *dredeth* B D L Add; *dred hit* F T Hl¹; *drad* Hl² Cx.

193 *fee α; mete β.*

198 *Arcite] fals Arcite* T D L (and Hl¹ later in margin).

199 *dere herte β; her dere herte α.*

209 *with α; of β.*

223 *called] cleped α¹* only.

229 *Now is he fals, alas! and causeles] Alas now hath he left me causeles α¹.*

236 *For to] That I ne α¹.*

241 *ferther wol I never be founde α; (for) ther shal (I) never be founde β.* Both apparently mistake *founde* (infinitive) for *founde* (past partic. of *finde*).

250 *And α¹* Ph.

257 *cause] causer α¹.*

264–65 *But for I was so pleyn, Arcite, In al my werkes, much and lyte β.*

268 *this] the α¹.*

269 *Alas! ye] And als ye* Hl² P Cx (*also*); *of me α¹; Of my wo ye* Add; *And of my sorowe* Ph.

278 *come α¹ β* (exc. Ph); *turne* T D Ph L Ff. *And yit be pleyn* T D L P Ph Hl²; *and be al pleyn α¹; and be pleyn* R Ff; *and be thou playn* Cx; *and me pleyn* Add.

279 *And than shal this, that now is mis, be game] And turne al this that hath be mys to game α¹.*

286 *be(n) α* Ph; *lye, lyn, lyth β* (exc. Ph).

300 *deth α; dye β. foul α* Ph; *cruel (a) β* (exc. Ph).

301 *gilt(e)les α; causeles β.*

303 *Yow rekketh not α; Than wol ye laughe β.*

309 *holde] kepe* Hl² Add R Ph. *Aperil? Averyll* Hl² Add R P; rest *Appryll(e)* (var. sp.).

316 *renne α; fle(e)(n) β.*

318 *seyd oght amis, I prey α¹*; rest *oght seyd out of the way* (var. sp.). *α¹* possibly contains author's correction to avoid identical rime.

319 *al aweye α; half aweye β.*

331 *profren] swere yet α¹.*

332 *and merci me to preye α; and love me til I (he, ye) deye β.*

334 *thilke β; this α¹; such α² α³.*

346 *seyd α¹ α²; telle* R; rest *say.*

349 *so] to α¹.*

The Parliament of Fowls

Authorities: fourteen MSS. and Caxton's early print, all accessible in the Chaucer Society reprints.

B   Bodley 638, Bodleian.
D   Digby 181, Bodleian.
F   Fairfax 16, Bodleian.
Ff   Cambridge University Library Ff. 1. 6.
Gg   Cambridge University Library Gg. 4. 27.
H   Harley 7333, British Museum.
Hh   Cambridge University Library Hh. 4. 12.
J   St. Johns College, Oxford, LVII.
L   Laud 416, Bodleian.
Lt   Longleat 258, in the possession of the Marquess of Bath.
P   Pepys 2006, Magdalene College, Cambridge.
R   Trinity College, Cambridge, R. 3. 19.
S   Arch. Selden B. 24, Bodleian.
T   Tanner 346, Bodleian.
Cx   Caxton's edition, 1477–78.

These were partially classified by Professor Koch, Angl., IV, Anz., 97, and afterwards completely by Miss Hammond, University of Chicago Decennial Publications, First Series, VII, 3–25. According to Miss Hammond the authorities fall into the following groups (with changes of lettering):

Type A
- α   Gg Ff
- β   H R S Hh Cx
- γ   P J L

Type B
- δ   F B
- ε   T Lt D

Groups α, β, and γ belong to a type A, of which Gg is the best representative verbally, though its spellings, here as in the *Canterbury Tales*, the *Legend of Good Women*, and the *Troilus*, depart considerably from prevailing Chaucerian usage. Groups δ and ε belong to a second general type B.

Miss Hammond's results were criticized in turn by Koch in Herrig's Arch., CXI–CXII, 64 ff., 299 ff., 46 ff. See also his Versuch einer kritischen Textausgabe von Chaucers Parlement of Foules, Berlin, 1904. Koch's classification, which puts P with Hh, Cx, and S, and separates them all from H and R, assumes a double source for Ff, and in general makes extensive allowance for contamination.

Skeat used F (of Type B) as the basis of his edition. But Koch, and the Globe editor, Mr. Heath, have agreed in regarding the A type as slightly superior. Miss Hammond finds the authority of the two groups to be about equal. Professor Root's suggestion (JEGP, V, 189–93) that Type B contains the results of Chaucer's revision lacks adequate support. (See Tatlock, Dev. and Chron., p. 44, n. 2.) The present text is based upon MS. Gg with occasional normalization of its peculiar spellings. The special problem which is raised by the unique readings of Gg is discussed in the General Introduction on the Text. In the notes which follow are recorded the most important departures from Gg and retentions of Gg readings as against a "critical" text. Extended lists of variant readings are given by Professor Koch in his critical edition and in his [Chaucer's] Kleinere Dichtungen.

Title. So Gg; *The Parlament of Foules* H P B Lt D; *The Parlement of Briddes* F T; *Here foloweth the parlement of Byrdes reducyd to love, etc.* R; *Of the assemble of the byrdis on Seint Volantins day* L.

2 *so hard, so sharp*] *so sharp so hard* Gg Ff L J.

5 *his wonderful* Type A; *his* (or *a*) *dredeful* Type B (which inserts *so* before *with*).

26 *(as) of this* Type A; *of my first* Type B.

35 *sey(n)* Type A; *telle* Type B.

39 *it*] *he* all MSS. *al* Cx H Hh P S T D F B Lt; om. R; rest *of*.

54 *Nis* Gg Cx; *Meneth* Ff H R and Type B (*mornyth* D); *Ment* Hh L P; *In* J; *Was* S.

65 So Cx Hh P S H R J L, Skeat, Globe; *And was sumdel disseyvable and ful of harde grace* Gg; *And was sumdel ful of harde grace* Type B Ff (but om. *ful*). Koch em. *And sumdel fals and ful of harde grace.* Possibly Chaucer intended *And disseyvable and ful of harde grace.*

82 *And that foryevyn is his weked dede* Gg (possibly a case of the use of *that* to repeat *til*).

117 *north-north-west*] *north nor west* Gg; *north(e)west* R Ff. See explanatory note.

133 *sped*] *hy* Ff and Type B.

170 *wente in*] *that as* Gg.

214 *Wille*] *wel* Gg S; *whill* H; *whiele* Ff. (Boccaccio says "Voluttade," which may have been corruptly written "Voluntade," or mistaken for that word by Chaucer.)

215 *file*] *wile* Gg Cx J Ff Hh P S; *vyle* R; *wyel* H.

216 *touchede* R Cx B; *ordanyt* S; rest *couched(e).*

221 *don* (1st)] *go(n)* Type B. *By force*] *before* Gg Ff and Type B. Compare Teseide, vii, 55: "Di fare altrui a forza far follia."

305 *cast(e)* Gg Ff; *tast* Cx; rest *craft.*

313 *eyr* Gg Ff; rest *see.*

353 *foules*] *flyes* R; *bryddis* Ff.

356 *clothes* Gg; rest *fetheres.*

364 *old* all MSS. Koch em. *cold.*

379 *the vicaire*] *vicarye* Gg.

380 Skeat, Globe, Koch insert *and* before *moyst*, metri gratia. But the "Lydgatian" movement, with the missing unstressed syllable, should perhaps be allowed. See the textual note to *Prol Mel,* VII, 951.

381 *noumberis* Gg; *membris* Ff; *mesure* S; rest *noumbre* (sing.). (*Bo,* iii, m. 9, 18 has *nombres proporcionables*).

389 All MSS. exc. Gg Ff prefix *With*. The Gg reading is better metrically, and the broken construction is not without parallel.

391 *lete*] *breke* Gg.

455 *fullonge* Gg; *al hole* S; rest *alone.*

490 *drow* Gg; rest *wente.*

507 *spede*] *profit* Gg J. *Take* R; rest *take on (me).*

511 *fayr*] *good* P and Type B (T om.).

551 *sittyngest* Gg; *best sitting* S; rest *sitting.*

567 *love another*] *take a nothir* Gg.

573 *wit*] *mygh* (=*myght*) Gg.

594 *doke*] *goos* H R J P S (perhaps correctly, since the remark agrees perfectly with the former speech of the goose).

613 *rewthelees* em. Skeat, Globe; *reufulles* Gg; *rowthfull* P; rest *rewfull(e),* some with a weak -*e*, which is metrically possible but makes unsatisfactory sense.

632 *I* (1st)] *it* R H Cx Ff J. *Certis* Gg; rest om.

637 *hit* om. Gg (which improves the meter); *That it ought to be to you a suffisaunce* B (perhaps correctly).

641 *everich other* H R Ff P and Type B; *a nothir lyvis* Gg; *eny othir* J (with *like* before *as*).

647 *gon* Gg; rest *don.*

659 *tercelets*] *tersellis* Cx. Koch reads *tersels* because eagles, not falcons, are meant. But the distinction is doubtful.

672 *goddesse*] *queen* Gg.

680-92 The roundel is complete only in Gg, in a later fifteenth-century hand. It is partly preserved in J and D. The title *Qui bien aime (a) tard oublie,* which takes its place in Cx R F B, seems to refer to a tune (the *note* that was made in France). On the French song see further the explanatory note to l. 677.

697 *I*] *In* Gg (perhaps correctly; compare *KnT,* I, 1512, *In hope that I som grene gete may*).

Colophon. The title *Parliamentum Avium* is found in Gg Ff. T F B read: *Explicit tractatus de congregacione volucrum die Sancti Valentini, etc.*; D Lt *Here endith the Parlement of Foules*; Cx *Explicit the temple of bras.* See Schick, ed. Lydgate's Temple of Glas, EETS, 1891, p. xvii.

Boece

Authorities: ten MSS. and the early prints of Caxton and Thynne, classified (with one exception) by the Globe editor as follows:

α C¹ Cambridge University Library Ii. 1. 38.
   A² Additional 16165, British Museum.
   H   Harley 2421, British Museum.
   B   Bodley 797, Bodleian.
   Cx Caxton's edition, 1477–78.
   Th Thynne's edition, 1532.

β C²   Cambridge University Library Ii. 3. 21.
   Hn   Hengwrt 393, Peniarth.
   A¹   Additional 10340, British Museum.
   Sal Salisbury 13, Salisbury Cathedral.
   Auct Auct. F. 3. 5, Bodleian (Bk. i only, somewhat altered).

On the "revamped" text of Auct see Liddell, Acad., XLIX, 199, and Miss Hammond, English Verse between Chaucer and Surrey, Durham, N.C., 1927, p. 393. The tenth MS., Phillipps 9472, is cited by Skeat (Oxf. Chau., II, xliv), but no account is given of it. C² and A¹ have been published by the Chaucer Society. A collation of Cx, which belongs to Group α but shows contamination with Group β, was printed by Kellner in ESt, XIV, 1 ff. Bk. i, m. 1 of Sal was printed in Angl., II, 373; it resembles A¹. Th seems to follow Cx closely.

Groups α and β differ very little in their text. C¹, which was followed by Liddell (Globe), seems also to the present editor slightly the best, and this edition is based upon a photograph of that MS. Comparison has been made with A¹ C² Cx (Kellner's col-

lation) and Th, and account taken of such other
variants from other MSS. as are recorded by Liddell.
Readings of Cx are cited only when explicitly noted
by Kellner or Liddell, though it is fair to assume that
in many passages not listed by Kellner Cx agrees
with A¹ and C². Readings from the French translation (ascribed to Jean de Meun) are from Liddell.
Citations of the Latin original are from the edition
of Peiper, Leipzig, 1871.

Although the orthographic system of C¹ differs
considerably from that of the MSS. followed in the
Canterbury Tales and the *Troilus*, its spellings have
been kept except when they might be regarded as
downright errors. Final -*e*'s and inflectional endings
have been corrected when necessary.

Book I

m. **1, 16** *arn* C¹ C² Cx Th; *ben* A¹.
17 *of myn emptid* C¹ C² Cx Th; *upon myn emty*
A¹.
pr. **1, 55** *corn(e)* C² Th; *cornes* C¹ A¹ A²; Lat.
"segetem."
57 *hertes* C¹ C² Cx Th; *the hertes* A¹ (perhaps correctly).
m. **2, 1** *man* C² A¹; *this man* C¹ Cx Th (perhaps
correctly, though the reference is general in the Lat.).
14 *nombres* C¹; *nombre* C² A¹ Th; Lat. "numeris."
32 *fool* C² Th; *foul(e)* C¹ A¹ A² H B Cx; Lat.
"stolidam"; Fr. "fole."
m. **3, 2** *forlete(n)* C¹ Th; *forlefte(n)* C² A¹ Cx.
12 *kave* Cx Th; *kaves* C¹ C² A¹; Lat. "antro."
pr. **3, 5** *byholde* C² A¹; *byhelde* C¹ Th; Lat.
"respicio."
6 *house* Cx Th; *houses* C¹ C² A¹; Lat. "laribus."
56 *Soronas* C¹; *Soranos* Cx Th; *Sorans* C²;
Sorancis A¹.
65 *tempestes* C²; *tempeste* A¹; om. C¹ Cx Th.
78 *palis* C²; *paleys* C¹ Th; *palays* A¹; Lat.
"vallo." Cf. Bk. ii, m. 4, 17.
m. **4, 9** *writhith* C¹ Cx Th; *writith* C²; *wircheth* A¹;
Lat. "torquet."
11 *thonder leit* C¹ Cx Th; *thonder ly(g)ht* C² A¹.
pr. **4, 15** *sege* C¹ A¹ Th; *sete* C²; Lat. "sedem."
19 Gloss: *q(uasi) d(iceret) non* C¹ A¹.
24 *gerdouns* C¹ C²; *guerdon* A¹ Th; Lat.
"praemia."
26 *confermedest* C¹; *conformedest* C²; *enfo(u)rme-
dist* A¹ Th; Lat. "sanxisti."
66 *tourmentid* A¹; *turmentyden* C¹ C² B Cx Th
(perhaps a grammatical slip of Chaucer's, though
the Lat. has "vexabat").
183 *by* C² A¹; *of* Cx Th; *byfore* C¹; Lat. "a G.
Caesare."
244 *studie* C² A¹; *studies* C¹ Th; Lat. "studium."
262 *was* A¹ Th; *is* C¹ A² H B; om C².
279 *but (y)if (that)* C² A¹ Cx Th; *but that* C¹;
Lat. "nisi."
pr. **5, 20** f. *is lord*] *he is lord* B; *that is lord* C¹ C²
A¹ Th (and apparently the rest of the MSS.; possibly the superfluous *that* is Chaucer's).
pr. **6, 13** [*folie*] Liddell's conjecture; MSS.
fortune; Lat. "fortuita temeritate"; Fr. "fortunele
folie."
36 f. [*thorw*] supplied by Liddell; *chynynge*]
s(c)hynyng A¹ Th; [*and*] Liddell's conjecture for *is*
of the MSS.; Lat. "velut hiante valli robore."

75 *felonus*] *felouns* (possibly *felonus*?) C¹; and so
in several other instances.
84 *norissing* Cx Th; *noryssynges* C¹ C² A¹; *trust*
B; Lat. "fomitem" (Peiper; Obbarius, edn., Jena,
1843); Liddell cites "fomentum," apparently from
a MS.
88–90 *but to the resoun. . . . shine* om. C¹.
97 f. *that derknesse*] *and that derknesse* MSS.
m. **7, 18** *four(e)* C² A¹ Th Hn; om. C¹.

Book II

pr. **1, 27** *and despisen* C² Hn Cx Th; om. A¹ C¹.
m. **1, 12** *laugheth* A¹ Th; *leygheth* C¹; *lyssheth*
C²; Lat. "ridet."
pr. **2, 34** [*hem*] supplied by Liddell from Fr.;
perhaps unnecessary. B om. *of* and reads *to have* for
that thou hast.
57 After *axeth it* [*Wystestow nat thanne my
maneris?*] is supplied by Liddell from Lat. and Fr.
pr. **3, 23** *and ajust(e)* B (*aiuse*) Cx Th; om. C¹
C² Hn A¹; Fr. "aiusterai."
59 *fulfildest*] *and fulfildest* C¹ C² A¹ Th. (Both
Skeat and Liddell om. *and*, doubtless correctly.)
64 *feffedest* C² A¹ Th; *feddestow* C¹.
85 *seld(e)* Cx Th; *yelde* MSS; Lat. "rara."
Similar confusion of *s* and *y* (*z*) in ii, m. 3, 17;
pr. 6, 24.
86 *fortunous* A¹ Th; *fortunes* C¹; *fortune* C²; Lat.
"fortuitis."
90 *thar* A¹; *ther* B; *dar* C¹ C²; *dare* Cx Th. Possibly [*thee*] should be inserted, as Liddell suggests.
pr. **4, 45** *eldefader*] *eldyrfadyr* C² (two words? So
printed by Th and Skeat).
70 *delices*] *delites* C²; Lat. "delicias."
99 *is* A² Cx Th; om. A¹ C¹ C².
109 [*is*] supplied by Skeat and Liddell from Lat.
"nihil est miserum."
m. **4, 14** *site* C¹ C² A¹; *sete* Hn Cx; *seate* Th;
cite(e) A² H B; Lat. "sortem sedis amoenae."
pr. **5, 148** *desert*] *desertes* C².
173–74 So C¹ (and Liddell); C² A¹ A² Hn om.
is (also Skeat); *is for his wikkednesse the more* Cx Th;
of his wikkednesse is the more B.
pr. **6, 100** *as of wil* C² A¹; *of wil* C¹; *offt times* A²;
and . . . contrarie om. Cx Th.
m. **6, 15** *hide* C² Th; *hidde* C¹ A¹.
pr. **7, 3** *hadde*] *hadden* C¹ C² A¹ Th. (The grammatical slip may have been Chaucer's or the scribe's.)
7 *list that* C² A¹; *list it* C¹; *leste* Cx Th; A² om.
that. (Skeat supplies [*him*], taking *leste* as a verb;
Liddell follows MSS., and interprets *list* as the conjunction "lest.")
47 *conteneth*] *coveyteth* C² (and Skeat); Lat.
"habeat."
158 *of noon othir thyng, ne*] *of no glorye* C² Hn
Cx Th; A¹ om. whole sentence.
m. **7, 5** *se(e)te* C¹ A¹ Th; *cyte* C²; Lat. "situm."
Perhaps read *site* (with Skeat)? So also in iii, pr. 2, 3.
m. **8, 16** *heven(e)* C¹ Cx Th; *hevenes* A¹ C²; Lat.
"caelo."

Book III

pr. **1, 15** *that* (after *herbyforn*) om. A¹ C² (perhaps correctly). But *that weren* may be for *that* (*they*)
weren.
pr. **2, 3** *seete*] *cyte* C²; Lat. "sedem." Cf. ii, m.
7, 5.

110 [*ne*] Liddell; [*nat*] Skeat; Lat. "nam non esse anxiam," etc.
pr. **4, 45** ff. C¹ A² B H Cx om. *wykked* and *the fowlere and* and A² B H om. *so much more*; Hn C² om. *in* before *so mochel*; C² Hn A² B place *the which . . . folk* after *reverence*; A¹ alters the passage.
m. **5, 2** *corages* C¹ Cx Th; *corage* A¹ C²; Lat. "animos."
m. **6, 10** *thow* C¹ C² A¹; *ye* Hn H B Cx Th; Lat. "spectes."
pr. **7, 25** *Euripidis* Th; *Euripides* H; *Euridippis* C¹; *Euridippus* A¹; *Eurydyppys* C²; Lat. "Euripidis" (gen.).
pr. **8, 48** *of* (*the*), before *feblesse* A² Cx Th; *or* C¹ C² (corrupt).
pr. **9, 60** After *thynges* C¹ inserts *so that there ne be amonges hem no difference* (probably miscopied from the sentence below).
115 *honours* C² A¹; *honour* C¹ Cx Th; Lat. "honoribus."
174 *lyknesses* C²; *lyknesse* A¹ C¹ Th; Lat. "imagines."
199 *founded* C¹ Th; *founden* C² A¹; Lat. "fundatur."
m. **9, 1** *soowere and*] *sovereigne and* H Cx Th; om. C² A¹ Hn; Lat. "sator."
28 [*and*] supplied by Liddell; Lat. "Quae cum secta duos motum glomeravit in orbes, In semet reditura meat mentemque profundam Circuit," etc.
pr. **10, 71** *the fader* Cx Th; *the prince* C¹; *this prince* C² A¹; Lat. "hunc patrem."
73 Liddell, following the Lat. and Fr., suggests the insertion, after *ful*, of *or wenestow that he hath it naturely in himself*.
98 *hir* C¹ A² H Cx Th; *his* A¹ C². Perhaps Chaucer used the singular, following the Lat. construction.
143 [*men ben maked just*] supplied from Lat. and Fr.
178 [*of*] supplied by Liddell from Fr.
pr. **11, 214** *hyen to* C¹ Cx Th; *hyen* A¹.
m. **11, 33** *wyndes* C¹ Cx Th; *wynde* C².
37 *depe* C¹ Th; *depthe* C².
pr. **12, 135** *disposid*(*e*) C¹ C² A¹ Th; Skeat *deposede* (perhaps correctly); Lat. "disposuit."

Book IV

pr. **1, 38** *abaysschinge* C¹ Th; *an enbaissynge* A¹ C².
67 *arysen* A¹ Th; *areisen* C¹ C².
m. **1, 1** *I have for thi* C¹; *I have forsothe* C² A¹; *Than for thy* Cx Th; Lat. "Sunt etenim."
9 *areiseth* C² A¹; *aryseth* C¹ Th.
pr. **2, 142** *alwey* om. C¹ A² H B; *awey* C².
219 *undirstonde* C¹ C² A¹; *understondes*(*t*) A² B H Cx Th.
m. **2, 11** *floodes* C² A¹; *flood* C¹ A² H B Cx Th; Lat. "fluctus."
17 *tyranyes*] A¹ *tyrauntis*, perhaps correctly; Lat. "tyrannos."
pr. **3, 27** *rejoised*(*e*) C¹ Cx Th; *rejoyse* C²; *rejoiseth* A¹; Lat. "laetaretur."
pr. **4, 30** *power* C¹; *mowyng*(*e*) C² Th; *moevynge* A¹.
32 *thre* C¹ A¹; *the* C² H Cx; *theyr* A²; *her* Th; Lat. "triplici infortunio."
45 *shrewednesse* A¹ Th; *shrewednesses* C¹ C².
pr. **5, 27** *confusioun* C¹ A¹; *conclusion* C² Th; Lat. "confusionis."
pr. **6, 157** *fro* C² A¹ Th; *of* C¹.
333 *to men* C¹ H A² B; *for men* Th; *for man* Cx; *to man* C²; *to no man* A¹; Lat. "homini."
346 *or thinges* C¹ Cx Th; om. C² A¹; *of thinges* A² H.

Book V

pr. **3, 41** *ytravayled* C² A¹ Th (C¹ *y travailed*, unjoined); *travailed* H Cx. Liddell takes *y* as "I." Lat. "quasi vero . . . laboretur"; Fr. "nous travaillons."
167 [*ther*] supplied by Liddell from Fr.
m. **4, 52** *hurt*(*e*)*lith* C² A¹; *hurteth* C¹ A²; *hurleth* H Cx Th.
pr. **6, 74** *discresith* C¹; *disencresith* C² A¹ H Cx Th A² B; Fr. "descraist."
116 *previdence* C¹ (Th? indistinct); *purvidence* C²; *providence* A¹.
267 *quod she* C¹ Cx Th; *quod I* C²; om. A¹; Lat. "(B). Minime. (P.) Omne namque," etc. Liddell is perhaps right in reading *No, quod I. No, forsothe, quod sche*; but there is nothing in the Lat. which strictly corresponds to the second part.

Troilus and Criseyde

Authorities: Twenty manuscripts (four containing only brief fragments) and three early prints:

A   British Museum, Additional 12044 (incomplete).
Cm   Campsall, Doncaster.
Cp   Corpus Christi College, Cambridge, 61.
Cx   Caxton's edition, c. 1483.
D   Durham V. ii. 13 (Bishop Cosin's Library).
Dg   Digby 181, Bodleian.
Gg   Cambridge University Library, Gg. 4. 27.
Hl¹ Harley 2280, British Museum.
Hl² Harley 3943, British Museum.
Hl³ Harley 1239, British Museum.
Hl⁴ Harley 2392, British Museum.
Hl⁵ Harley 4912, British Museum (incomplete).

J   St. John's College, Cambridge, L. 1.
Ph   Phillipps 8250, Cheltenham.
R   Rawlinson Poet. 163, Bodleian.
S¹   Arch. Selden B. 24, Bodleian.
S²   Arch. Selden Supra 56, Bodleian.
Th   Thynne's edition, 1532.
W   Wynkyn de Worde's edition, 1517.

Short fragments are preserved in Trinity College MS. R. 3. 20 (Bk. i, 631–37) and Cambridge University Library Ff. 1. 6 (Bk. iii, 302–22), (both printed in the Ch. Soc. Odd Texts, Appendix, pp. ix-xii) and in R. 4. 20 and the Ellesmere Lydgate MS. (printed by MacCracken in MLN, XXV, 126 f.). Two other fragments (v, 1443–98), preserved on strips of vellum in a book-binding, are described in the Report of the

Cambridge Antiquarian Society, VI, 331–35. William Thomas's copy of the first stanza of the *Canticus Troili* (Bk. i, 400–6) from MS. Cotton Otho A XVIII, is printed by G. B. Pace in Speculum, XXVI, 307–8. Two unidentified MSS., apparently of the *Troilus*, which belonged to the library of the Duke of Burgundy in 1467 and 1487, are cited by Miss Hammond, in MLN, XXVI, 32, from Barrois, Bibliothèque Protypographique, Paris, 1830. There is an early print by Pynson (1526), but it is derived from Caxton and has no independent value.

Of the complete, or nearly complete, texts the following seven have been printed in full by the Chaucer Society: Cm Hl¹ Gg J Cp Hl³ Hl² (the last named in parallel columns with Rossetti's translation of the Italian original). From the remaining nine MSS. and the editions of Caxton and Thynne Specimen Extracts have been edited by McCormick and Root, and Thynne's text is also accessible in Skeat's photographic facsimile of his edition. In addition to this printed material, the present editor has made use of a complete copy of A, which was presented to the Harvard Library by Dr. Furnivall. And he has also taken account of the variant readings from unpublished MSS. printed by Sir William McCormick in the Globe Chaucer and by Professor Root both in his edition and in his volume on the Textual Tradition of Chaucer's Troilus (Chau. Soc., 1916). Root's appendix contains a valuable list of corrections of the Chaucer Society reprints.

The relations of the *Troilus* MSS. are very puzzling, and the problem of editing has been discussed above in the General Introduction on the Text. According to the investigations of McCormick and Root there are three discernible states of the text, α, β and γ, which represent either two or three distinct versions. The three types are distributed as follows among the different MSS. and editions:

$$\alpha \begin{cases} \text{Ph} \\ \text{Hl}^2 \ \ (\text{partly } \beta) \\ \text{Hl}^4 \ \ (\text{partly } \beta) \\ \text{W} \ \ \ \ (\text{to i, 546; then from Cx}) \end{cases}$$

$$\beta \begin{cases} \text{Gg} \ \ (\text{partly } \alpha) \\ \text{Hl}^5 \ \ (\text{partly } \alpha) \\ \text{J} \ \ \ \ (\text{partly } \alpha) \\ \text{R} \\ \text{Hl}^3 \ \ (\text{partly } \gamma \text{ and } \alpha) \\ \text{S}^1 \ \ (\text{partly } \gamma) \\ \text{Cx} \end{cases}$$

$$\gamma \begin{cases} \text{A} \\ \text{D} \end{cases} (\text{occasionally contaminated with } \alpha \text{ or } \beta) \\ \begin{cases} \text{S}^2 \\ \text{Dg} \\ \text{Cp} \end{cases} (\text{corrupt and marked by Northern dialect}) \\ \text{Cm} \\ \text{Hl}^1 \\ \text{Th} \ \ (\text{partly } \alpha \text{ and } \beta)$$

For reasons stated in the Introduction on the Text, Type γ has been adopted as authoritative by the present editor. Of the three best MSS., Cp, Cm, and Hl¹, the first has been made the basis of the text. Variations between it and Cm or Hl¹ are on the whole unimportant. Such readings of Types α and β as seem of literary interest or editorial significance are recorded in the notes that follow. It was the editor's original intention to give a much

longer list of variant readings. But for such detailed information scholars can now consult the complete apparatus in Professor Root's admirable edition. It should be observed that the letters α, β, and γ, as here employed, do not stand regularly for the same MSS., but designate the readings of the supposed three versions as restored by McCormick and Root. The classification of the MSS., as indicated above, varies in different parts of the poem. After iv, 430, for example, MS. J changes from β to α. It is even questioned whether the β readings represent a single version or revision of the text. On the general character of the revision see, besides Root's discussion, Tatlock, Dev. and Chron., Ch. Soc., 1907, pp. 1 ff.; Kittredge, The Date of Chaucer's Troilus, Ch. Soc., 1909, pp. 30 ff.; Brusendorff, pp. 167 ff.

In the matter of orthography the editor's method has been similar to that pursued in the *Canterbury Tales*. Since the Corpus MS., like the Ellesmere, represents a good scribal tradition, its spellings have been generally preserved. Grammatical errors have been corrected, especially incorrect final -*e*'s, as have also a few forms which appear not to be consistent with Chaucer's usage. Inflectional endings have occasionally been supplied when necessary for the meter or for clearness of meaning. But no attempt has been made at the regular restoration of unpronounced final -*e*'s, which are omitted rather more freely in the Corpus MS. than in the Ellesmere. The present text of the *Troilus*, then, like that of the *Canterbury Tales*, gives on the whole a faithful reproduction of the practice of a good Chaucerian scribe.

Book I

9 *Furie*] *wight* α.
13 *A woful wight to han*] *Unto a woful wighte* α.
19 *if this may don*] *myght I do yit* α; *yit myhte I do* Hl⁴.
24–28 α:

Remembre you of olde passid hevynesse
For goddis love and on adversitee
That other suffren thynke how somtyme that ye
Fownde how love durst you displese
Or ellis ye wonne hym with to grete ease.

33 *That I have*] *He yeve me* α.
44 *That God hem graunte ay good*] *On* (*In* Hl²) *love that God hem* (*them* Hl²) *graunte* α.
46 *Love*] *hem* α; *them* Hl² Hl⁴.
57 *Yt is wel wist*] *knowe*(*n*) *thyng is* α (exc. Hl²).
63 *By Paris don*] *Ful besily* α (exc. Ph). *Wroughten*] *diden* α Hl⁵.
78 *For which for to departen*] *Wherefor to departe al* α.
83 *In trust that he hath*] *Hopyng in hym* α; (Ital. "Da lui sperando").
85 *The noise*] *Gret rumour* α (Ital. "Fu romor grande").
88–91 α:

With her foos and wilned to be wrokyn
On hym that falsly had his trouthe brokyn
And sworen that he and al his kin at onys
Were worthy (*to be*) *brent bothe fell and bonys.*

93 *Al unwist*] *Unknowyng* α.
96 *Ne in al this world she nyst* (*not*) *what to rede* α.
101 *So fair was none for over every wight* α.

104 *doth* γ α; *is* β. *Hevenyssh perfit*] *perfit hevenly* α.

108 *for sorwe and fere*] *for pure fere* α.

111 *With chere and voys ful pytous and wepynge* α (Ital. "E con voce e con vista assai pietosa").

118 *Forth with meschaunce*] *To sory hap* α (Ital. "con la ria ventura").

137 *no thing softe*] *al* (as Hl⁴) *unsoft* α.

150–51 α:

> The old usage (For al Hl⁴) nold they of Troy lettyn
> As for to honour her goddis and (to) loute.

157 *lusty*] *joly* α.

159 *sondry*] *meny* α.

163–67 α:

> In general went every manere wight
> That thryfty was to heryn her servise
> And that so meny a thousand lusty knyght
> So meny a fressh mayde and lady bryght
> Ful wel byseyn the meste meyne and leeste.

167 *both(e) moeste meyne* Cp; *both most meyne* Hl¹; *bothe meene meste* Cm; *men bothe mest* A; *bothe moste menne* D; *bothe most mene* S¹; *the meste meyne* Ph; *the meste mene* Hl⁴; *the most and eke* Hl²; *bothe (the or tho) meste (moste)* J Gg Hl³ Th. Root (Text. Trad. p. 44) holds that *meyne*, which stood in the α text, meant *meynee*, "retinue," and was deleted in revision. But it may be the adjective *meene*, "mean," intermediate between *meste* and *leste*; and the revision is by no means certain.

169 *Among thise othere folk*] *Among the which(e)* α (Ital. "tra' quali").

176 *As was Criseyde, as folk seyde*] *As she was as thei seydyn* α.

183, 215 *This*] *Daun* α.

195 *God woot*] *O (a) lord* α.

202–03 α:

> O verrey folys may ye no thing se
> Kan none of yow yware by other be.

206–09 α:

> But trowe ye not that love tho lokyd row
> For that despit and shop to bene ywrokyn
> Yes certein loves bow was not ybrokyn
> For be myn heed he hit hym atte fulle.

255 *Refuseth*] *Ne grucchith* α.

257 *Betir is the wand (bond)* α.

259 *hym*] *love* β.

274 *And sodenly for wondyr he wex astoyned* (with variants) α Th.

276 *mercy*] *verrey* α.

324 *his* γ S¹ Th Cx; *the* J Gg Hl³ Ph Hl² Hl⁴ Hl⁵ (Ital. "al palazzo").

342 *But told y which were the worst y leve* α.

345 *Or elles*] *For good or* α.

363 *a* (before *temple*) Cm; *and* Cp Hl¹ A J Gg Hl³ Th; *at* R; *in the* Hl² Ph Hl⁵ S² Dg; om. Cx.

395 α (corrupt) perhaps read: *But eke save (that) in our spech is difference.*

403 *If he be* α.

442 *day by day* γ; *day fro day* α β (Ital. "di giorno in giorno").

458 *and* Cm A Gg Hl⁵ Th W; *in* S² Dg; rest om. Perhaps to be read: *whom to serven I laboure* (to whom to serven D).

466 *This* Cm Hl¹ D Hl² S¹ Ph W; *his* Cp A J Hl³ Gg Th (perhaps correctly).

483 *the Grekes*] *al the Grekes* α.

540 *to*] *mo* α Hl⁵ R Th.

563 *wo (to)* γ R; rest *sorwe*.

640 *may ben inly glad*] *wot(e) what gladnes is* α J Gg Hl⁵ Th.

682 *final* α R Cx Th Hl⁵; *finally* Cp Cm Hl¹ A J Gg Hl³ (probably wrong).

747 Hl² Ph Hl³ Hl⁴ Cx Th om. *a* (perhaps correctly).

755 *But lete me myn infortune waylyn* (*my fortune bewaylen* Hl⁴) α.

773 *No, certes, brother*] *Why no parde sir* α Th.

786 α has *Sisyphus* (in various spellings) for *Tityus* (*Ticius*).

796 *a resoun*] *o word, (ye)* α Th.

904 Cm D J R Hl⁵ Th om. second *that* (perhaps correctly).

914 *mucche*] *monche(n)* α.

949 *The lilie wexith white smothe and soft* α.

976 *wyse* γ Th S¹ J; *old(e)* α R; rest om.

1001 *moost*] *moste* Hl³ Cx; *to greve* (or *to-greve?*) γ (exc. D S¹); *ay greve* J R S¹; *greve* Hl² Gg Hl³ D Cx Th. Root's reading, *moste* (vb.) *his foos greve*, is very difficult.

1002 *wise* γ (om. A); *grete* α β.

1074 *the* J Dg D Hl⁴ Hl⁵ Hl² A Th; *tho* Cp Cm Hl¹ S¹ Hl³.

1075 *a-day* Cp Hl¹ S¹ J; rest *that day*.

Book II

40 *doyng*] *delyng* α.

46 *seid*] *don* α.

69 *Tereus* Hl⁴ R Cx; *Tireux* Cp Cm D Dg S¹ S²; *Tereux* J; *Tryeux* Hl¹; *Terous* Hl³; *Thereus* Ph Hl² Th; *Cireux* A; *Terius* Hl⁵. The rime *Tereus : thus* in *LGW*, 2315 shows that Chaucer knew the correct form.

86 γ S¹ read *With al yowre faire bok and (al) the companye*; Cp adds *faire* before *companye*; rest om. *faire*. Possibly Chaucer meant to revise, as in text: *With al youre fayre book and compaignie.*

110 *barbe* γ S¹ α; rest *wympel*.

115 *By God*] *by Joves* Ph Hl² Hl⁴ Gg Hl⁵. The latter reading may be right; Tatlock, p. 5, n. 3, defends it on the ground that Chaucer's revision elsewhere does not destroy local color.

128 *I* (interjection) so spelled in Cp Cm Hl¹ A J Gg; *eighe* Cx Th; om. Hl³; *y leve it not ywis* Hl².

248 *fremde* A D; *fremed* Th; rest *frende, friende*, etc.

253 *eighen down* γ α; *look down* for β.

339 *ye* Cp Cm Hl¹ A Gg; rest *we*.

403 *grow(en)* γ J R Th; rest *waxe(n), wox.*

406 *Nece* γ S¹ Th; rest om.

434 *is* α γ; *were* β.

478–79 α:

> Ne love a (no) man that can no wight ne may
> Aye(i)ns his wil(le).

482 *drede*] *dredde* (pret.?) Cp Th A (possibly right).

516 *af(f)er* J R; *after* A D Gg Hl³ Hl⁴ Hl⁵ Cx Th; *therafter* Cp Cm Hl¹ S¹ S² Dg; *yn a fere* Ph Hl² (Ital. "Io non gli era vicin").

603 *wax (wex, woxe)* α Gg Hl⁵ Th; rest *was*.

615 yates] latis Hl² only.
636 weldy γ α; worthy β.
675 first] tho α Th.
677 hir(e) hert(e) Ph Hl² Hl³ S² Dg Cx; rest om. herte (R Th var.).
734–35 Hl² Ph Gg Hl⁵ Th A (late hand over erasure):

> Men lovyn wymmen al this toun(e) about(e)
> Be they the wors (whi) nay without(yn) dout(e)

736–38 J R Hl⁴:

> Ek (Yit) wot I wel he worthy is to have
> Of wommen in this world the thriftyeste
> As ferforth as she may hir honour save

738 That woman is so (if) she Hl² Ph Gg Hl⁵ Th.
745 noon γ; rest no man.
777 why A Gg; wex J; rest wey(e), way (Hl² corrupt).
800 dremen] demen A S¹ Gg Hl² Ph Hl⁴ Th. Either reading makes good sense, but dremen is supported by iii, 585, below.
860 hym (hem) J R Hl² Ph Hl⁵ Th; it Cp Cm A Hl¹ Hl³ Gg. The next line favors the personification.
884 sike all MSS. Th. Skeat would emend to site, to avoid the assonant rime.
922 Of love which that made his (her Hl² Ph) herte gay J R Gg Hl⁵ Hl⁴.
956 trow(en) γ Th; rest trust(en) in (on, to) (trostyn Gg).
1083–85 J R Hl² Hl⁴ Ph Gg Hl⁵ Gg (enfeyned):

> But that was infenit (endles) for ay and o
> And how he wolde in trowth alwey hym holde
> And his adieux made and gan it folde

1093 This Pandare up therwith and that bytyme α J R Gg Hl⁵.
1095–97 α J R Gg Hl⁵:

> And seide slepe ye (yit) and it is pryme
> And gan to jape and seide thus myn herte
> So fresh it is though love do it smerte

1108 it thoughte] as thogh Hl² Ph Hl⁵ R S¹.
1196 that ye woot] that he wrote Hl² Ph (possibly the first form of the line).
1202 sat γ Th Hl³ S¹; rest fel (Hl⁵ knelid lowe).
1225 γ Hl³ om. ay.
1240 the om. γ (exc. A) S¹. (For the omission of the, possibly correct, compare the variant playde tho leoun, i, 1074, n.)
1291 shame γ S¹ Hl³ Th; rest speche (perhaps correctly).
1333 encrees of] encresseth J Gg Hl⁵ D. McCormick suggests the very likely emendation encresse (subj. 3 sing.).
1347 thise γ (exc. A D) Hl³; rest his(e) (perhaps correctly).
1429–30 So γ (exc. D) S¹ Hl³; rest But tel me how (for) thow woost of this matere, It myghte best availlen now lat se (A corrupt).
1624 helpe γ Hl³; rest frend(es).
1663 yow] me Cp Cm Hl¹ S² Dg; it Gg R Hl⁴ Th.
1665 his] this γ S¹ Cx (perhaps correctly).
1669 alweies γ Hl³; rest algate.
1749 Lest(e) Hl² Hl⁵ R Th; Last Hl³ D; Allas Hl⁴; Thus Cx; rest Las(se).
Between ll. 1750 and 1751 a single MS., R, inserts the following:

> Compleined ek heleyne of his siknes
> And feithfully that pitee was to heere

> For ye must outher chaungen your face
> That is so ful of mercy and bountee
> Or elles must ye do this man sum grace
> For this thyng folweth of necessytee
> As sothe as god ys in his magestee
> That crueltee with so benigne a chier
> Ne may not last in o persone yfere.

The first two lines are 1576–77 repeated. The word vacat, written against them in the margin, may indicate that the lines are to be canceled, or that the rest of the stanza is missing. The unique stanza which follows has every appearance of being genuine. But it is uncertain where Chaucer wished it to stand, or whether he meant to preserve it. McCormick, who first printed it (in the Furnivall Miscellany, Oxford, 1901, p. 297), suggested that it represents Chaucer's first intention, for which he afterward substituted ll. 1737–50. It does not seem to be in place after l. 1750, and still less so near l. 1576.

Book III

17 him] hem all MSS. (incorrectly).
28 hym Hl² Cx; hyt Ph; om. Hl⁴; rest it. Perhaps we should keep it and read joye.
56 kan] gan Cm Hl¹ Hl² Ph Hl⁴ Cx.
58 shorte] sor(e) J R Cx.
90 resons γ Hl³ Th; werkis Gg Hl⁵ R; rest wordes.
101 ferforthly] feythfully γ Th Hl³.
110 wreththe] herte γ Hl³ S¹ Hl² Cx (probably carried over from l. 109; but cf. iii, 887).
158 softely γ Hl³ Th; rest sobrely (Gg sekyrly).
189 merveille Cm Cp Hl¹ S² Dg; rest miracle.
230 mery γ Th Hl³; rest blisful.
256 So γ Hl³ Th S¹; rest (var. sp.) Thow woost thi selven what I wolde meene. (R combines the two.)
269 For that man is unbore γ Hl³ Th Hl² Ph R; rest For nevere was ther wight.
282 So γ Hl³ Hl⁵ S¹ Gg Th; The preye ich eft (al)thogh thou sholdest deye α J R Cx. (Root, Text. Trad., p. 178, suggests that the "return to the original reading" was deliberate.)
303 Hath mad] Hastow mad(e) γ Hl³ S¹ Th Gg Hl⁵.
354 liketh γ S¹; rest listeth (var. sp.).
371 wight] man J R Cx.
427 good(e) γ Hl³ S¹ Th; rest wyse.
442 I nyl nat seyn that though he lay(e) (ful) softe β.
455 So as they durste] In every thing J Hl⁴ R S¹.
461 grace] space α Gg Hl⁵ J.
489 man α γ Hl³ Th; wight β.
490 than he, withouten drede] to don his frend to spede β.
503 Neigh half this book] An hondred vers β.
518 out of doute] as hym thought β S¹.
525 wiste] thoughte β S¹.
528 Now] Thus β S¹.
529 fremed] wild(e) β Hl³ S¹.
535 gret γ Hl³ S¹ Th; rest his.
546 helpen in this nede γ α; that he wolde hym spede β.
554 come γ α Hl³; there β.

568   *And she agayne gan to hym for to rowne* β.
572   Most MSS. and Th have *thurste, thorste, durste,* etc.; S¹ Hl⁵ *thurft;* Skeat *thurfte* (with acc. pron.).
573   *myghte] sholde* β Hl⁴ S¹; *men* om. Hl³.
588   *and do now] for I do* β.
589   *yis* γ S¹ Hl⁸; Cx *tho;* Hl² Ph Hl⁴ om.; rest *this.*
591   *soule] fel* β.
598   *And of her wymmen wel a nyne or ten* α.
601   *Thurgh out an hole with yn a litil stewe* α.
604   *But to the point: now] But now to purpos* β; *But to the poynt whan that* Gg.
626   *That made(n) such a reyn fro heve(n) avale* α.
635   *For-whi] For Nece* β.
636   *For* γ Th; rest *Now (And* Hl³ S¹).
668   *And there I seyde] And al withinne* β.
672   *Than is it tyme for to gon to reste* (with var.) β.
677   *And alweye in this meene while it ron* β.
702   *werk] thing* β.
705   *blisful] seint(e)* β.
712   *blisful* γβ; *seynt* α.
759   *secre] lite(l)* β.
773   *holde in love] holde(n) longe* β.
800–01   β S¹:

> *Gan therewith al aboute hir herte colde*
> *And with a sik she sodeynly answerde*

882   *bounte] wisdom* J Hl⁴ R; *wysely* Cx.
937   *and that we han] and this matere* β; *and that ye han* Gg Th Hl³.
945   *al] as* β.
958   *kouthe] myghte* β.
971   *fynde] wot* J Hl⁴ R; *rede* Cx.
1096   *certeyn] alwey* β.
1101–02   *Allas . . . Iwis] Iwis . . Allas* β.
1115   *wete] ek(e)* β.
1136   *This light, nor I, ne] I nor this candel* Hl⁴; *Me thynk this candel* R.
1163, 1177   *And she] Criseide* β.
1165   *bought* γ Hl³ Th; rest *wroght(e).*
1203   *blisful* γ S¹ Th; rest *bryghte.*
1214   *ofte] al day* β.
1218   *al] now* β.
1225   *if] when* β; *of* Hl¹.
1239   *hym] al* β.
1245   *Was] Is* β.
1258   *that] yow* β; *the* Cm.
1260   *which] that* β; *As I that* J; *Than I that* Hl³; *As I which* Cp Hl² Cm Th.
1264   *For] And* β.
1280   *which] whom* β.
1283   *that] this* β.
1284   *to so swete a wight] to you (my) lady bright* β.
1295   *yow be] do yow* β; *thow be* Gg (over erasure); *be to you* Hl⁵.
1307   *it suffiseth, this] this suffiseth which* β.
1316   *Felten] They felte* J Hl⁴ Hl³ Cx.
1323   *al ne kan I] no man kan it* β.
1324–37   These stanzas come after l. 1414 in J Hl³ R S¹ Cx, and stand in both places in Hl⁴. Root (Text. Trad., pp. 157, 167) argues that the β position is the revised one because of the echo of *telle* in ll. 1323 and 1324, and because of the change in the β reading of l. 1415.
1324   *soth is] how al* β.
1327   *al holy his] the gret of* β.
1329   *any word] any thing* β; *ony world* Gg.

1334   *it al] hem hool* β.
1348   *it] this* β.
1354   *swich] this* β; *al the* A.
1360   *an hondred] a thousand* ρ (Ital. "Mille").
1362   *wo] sorwe* β.
1375   *Crecche* Hl⁵ Gg (*crache*); adopted by Root as variant of "cratch," to scrape together. Other readings are *kecche,* J Cm Cx Th; *tecche* Cp A D Hl⁸ Hl⁴; *theche,* Hl¹ S¹ R Ph.
1392–93   β:

> *To techen hem that coveitise is vice*
> *And love is vertu thogh men holde it nyce*

1395   *wel] ful* β (Cx *fully*).
1399   *swich] that* β.
1402   *thing* γ (exc. A) Th; rest *wo.*
1415   *But whan] whan that* β; Ital. "Ma poich' e' galli . . . udiro Cantar." Root (Text. Trad., p. 169) notes that the change may have been made to avoid the repetition of *But* after the shifting of ll. 1324–37.
1418   *bemes] stremes* β.
1420   *that anoon;* Skeat would emend to *than anoon,* to avoid the difficult ellipsis.
1441   *For thurgh thy rakel hying out of Troye* β.
1451   *nyght and love] love and nyght* β.
1455   *why sekestow] what sekestow (in)* β.
1464   *sonne, Titan] same tyme than* Hl³. *gan he] wolde he* β.
1473   *The welle and roote] The verray rote* β.
1482   *biteth* Cp A D S² Th; *bitleth* Hl¹; *brenneth* Cm; rest *streyneth* (Ital. "strigne"). *Syn]* so Hl² and om. so before *streineth.*
1492   *right] thus* β.
1496   *dowves] hawkes* β (defended by Root, Text Trad., p. 171).
1524   *wordes as* γ Th; rest *voys as thogh (thoght).*
1561   *I trowe, hire hedes ake] for god our (his) (hir) hed may ake* β.
1563   *mury] bright(e)* β.
1576   *chargeth] nedeth* β D.
1582   *fully] hoolly* β.
1595   *An hondred] A thousand* β.
1600   *Flegetoun] Contoun* Hl⁴; *Coichyton* R; *Cochita* Cx; *Conciton* Hl³ (all corruptions of "Cocytus," an inappropriate substitution in β, not likely to be due to Chaucer).
1622   *That I shal seyn] For love of god* β.
1643   *this matere ofte] al day this thing* Hl² Ph Gg Hl⁵ A. *stere* Hl³ R S¹ Cx; rest *tere.*
1645   *God woot] By god* β.
1703   *Pirous (Pyrous)* Hl² Ph A Th; others *Piros, Pirus, Pirora, Pirors, Pireys;* Ovid "Pyrois."
1720   *alwey, out of drede] ay without(en) drede* β.
1744–71   Troilus' Song om. Hl² Ph (inserted later in Ph).
1745   *heven(e)* α γ (exc. A) Hl³ Th; *hevenes* β.
1748   *knetteth* γ S¹ Th (Hl³ *kennyth*); rest *endytyth (endueth, endith);* Boethius "dictat." But *knetteth* translates "nectit," which is in the immediately preceding clause in Boethius. Both verbs occur in Chaucer's translation of the passage (*Bo,* ii, m. 8, 23 ff.). *Enditeth,* which represents the more literal rendering, may have been Chaucer's first version, afterwards revised in γ.
1754   *Holden] Hold(en)* in J R Cx Gg Hl⁵ Ph; Hl² corrupt; Boethius, "Foedus perpetuum tenent."
1820   The γ MSS. show confusion as to the point

at which Book iii ends. In Cp Cm Hl¹ the colophon is wrongly placed after iv, 28. D S², on the other hand, end Bk. iii at l. 1806.

Book IV

7   *the mowe*] *a mowe* β; Hl³ om. *a*.
25   *Mars*] *god* Hl² Hl³ Ph Hl⁵ (the first reading?).
37   *fighten*] *issen* J; *issu* Ph; perhaps Chaucer's first version from Ital. "uscii"?
39-40   This is the order of γ S¹ Th Hl⁵; rest transpose.
57-59   So (with variants) Cp Cm Hl¹ A D S² Hl² Ph Th; *To Pryamus . . . at his requeste* Hl³ Hl⁵ (*a gret request*); J Hl⁴ R S¹ Cx (= β) read (with var.):

> *But natheles a trewe was ther take*
> *At grekys* (or *gret*) *requeste and tho they gonnen trete*
> *Of prisoners a chaunge for to make.*

Ital.:

> "Chiese Priamo triegua, e fugli data;
> E cominciossi a trattare infra loro
> Di permutar prigioni quella fiata."

The reading of Hl³ or Hl⁵ is closest to the Italian and may well represent Chaucer's first version, which seems (as Root argues) to have been twice revised. The β version looks like the latest, but it is not clearly due to the author. The change of the request from Priam to the Greeks may have been made under the influence of Benoît and Guido.
87   *lefte* A D Hl³ S¹ S² J Cx Th; *le(e)ste* Cp Hl¹; rest *lost(e)*.
102   *right soone, douteles*] *for that is doutelees* α.
105   *have al this hevynesse*] *am broght in wrecchidnes* α.
114   *feithfully*] *sikerly* α.
123   *That they wol brynge*] *They wol eft bring* β.
126   *of Troie shal ben set on-fire*] *shal yit be set (up)on a fire* β.
131   *socour*] *mercy* α.
132   *sorwes*] *sikes* β.
139   *save-guarde*] *sauf conduyt* α; *sone gan sende* Hl³.
143   *Let*] *Gan* α (is *to holde* after *let* due to the fact that *gan* was the original auxiliary?).
156   *lordes wolde unto it*] *other lordes wolde* β.
160   *th'eschaunge of hire*] *(the) grauntinge* α.
197   *trewe* γ S¹ Th; rest *soth*.
212   *To yilde anon for Antenor Crisseyde* α.
222   *bad*] *dede* α.
238   *woodnesse*] *distresse* α.
247   *So wepyn that they semyn welles tweye* α. (Ital. "Forte piangeano, e parean due fontane"; ed. Paris, 1789, "Piangono sì che paion due fontane").
258   *wonder is*] *wel onethe* α (Ital. "appena").
261   *the* (pron.) A D S² S¹; *ye* Th; rest *thus* (Ital. "t'ho io fatto").
280   *ever(e)* γ Th; rest *alwey*.
282   *whider . . . me*] *whiderward* β.
286   *gerful*] *gery* α.
290   *What*] *How* α (Ital. "come").
295   *What shal I don*] *What I may don* γ Th (Ital. "Che farò io").
296   *On lyve*] *In wo* α.
300-01   α:

> *Ne hevenys lyght and thus (I) in derknesse*
> *My(n) woful lyf wel enden for (in) distresse*

Hl³:

> *Ne see no lyght and thus in derkenesse*
> *My sorowful lyfe wyl enden in distresse.*

306   *out of myn herte, and lat it*] *anon and do myn herte* α.
326   *youre lif*] *ye* α.
341   *peynes*] *sorwes* α.
347   *yelden*] *chaungen* α.
359   *For sorwe of this*] *Ny dede for wo* α.
365   *woful*] *sorweful* α.
373   *Neigh ded for smert*] *For crewel smert* α.
386   *For*] *O* α.
388   *Straunger*] *Strenger(e)* Hl³ Gg Hl⁵ Ph Cx α (exc. Hl²).
397   *felte*] *fond* α.
398   *lokyng*] *castyng* α.
404   *on or two*] *two or thre* α; *one or twey* Th.
409   *If*] *What* α.
418   *shal*] *moot* β.
430   *don*] *make* α.
445   *What Pandarus syn I have hir behight* α.
464   *wight*] *man* α.
491-532   Om. Cp; here printed from Cm.
498   *Nay god wot* γ Th; *Nay nay god wot* β; *Nay Pandarus* α. Perhaps the headless line in γ is due to corruption.
499   *But douteless for aught that may befalle* α.
506-07   *Or deth me slowe I wolde han yiven hire But now his comyng* α J Hl³ (om. *his*) Gg Ph Hl⁵ (Ital. "Morte, tu mi sarai tanto soave").
532   *fare* γ Cx Th Ph S¹; rest *care*.
537   *wepyng*] *sorwe* α.
560   *lettre*] *honour* α.
581   *For why in love is litel hertes reste* α.
590   *corteisly*] *preciously* α; *preciently* R; *curyously* Cx (with some support from Ital. "sottilmente").
594   *in blame a lite(l) yfounde* γ Th; *(a) lite(l) in blame ifownde* α; *in blame a litel stounde* β.
596   *shame unto yow*] *rape in my dom* α.
602   *weyveth*] *fleeth fro(m)* α Cx (Ital. "e' timidi rifiuta").
630   *spede*] *have* α.
644   *if that Jove*] *any aungel* α.
647   *why thow art thus gon* α.
674   *iset*] *biset* α.
680   *in towne, and*] *in townes* α.
696-98   *For al this while hir herte (tyme hire thouzt Gg) on oother thyng is . . . God wot hir advertence is elliswhere* α.
706   *So that she wende anon right for to dye* α.
708-14   Om. γ doubtless by mere oversight; here printed from J.
724   *tales*] *wordes* α (Ital. "parole").
747   *Wo worth that day and namely that nyght* α.
750-56   In α this stanza follows l. 735 (a position which corresponds to the order of the Filostrato), and begins:

> *The salte teeres from her eyen tweyne*
> *Out ronne as shoure in april ful swithe*
> *Hir white brest she bet and for the peyne*

757   *What shal he don what shal I do also* α.
762-63   α:

> *And corsed be that day which that Argyve*
> *Me of hir body bar to ben on lyve*

767 *lyves] oother α.*
770 *rooteles] ertheles α.*
781 *setten] holden α.*
790 *That highte Elisos] Ther Pluto regneth α.*
793 *chaunged] yolden α.*
794 *sorwful] woful α.*
819 *hire herte gan] for wo she gan α.*
820 *sorwe] shame α* (Ital. "vergogna").
823 *hous] chambre α.*
828–29 *α:*

> *Myn em Pandare of joyes mo than two*
> *Was cause causyng first to me Criseyde*

835 *alle worldly blisse] every worldly joye α.*
843 *woful] sorwful α.*
854 *This] This message* Cp Hl¹ S² D Hl⁴ Th. Root (Text. Trad., p. 187) suggests that Chaucer may have written: *This message which thi Troilus the sente.*
867 *ek hire] other α.*
868 *lith now Criseyde] for hem she lith α.*
876 *wel α* R S¹; *rest om.*
881 *erthely] worldly α.*
882 So γ S¹ Th; rest (with variants) *As he that shortly shapeth him to deye* (Ital. "Il qual del tutto in duol ne vuol morire"; ed. Paris, 1789, "Che cerca disperato di morire"). The γ reading repeats l. 357, above, — whether erroneously or by Chaucer's intention is uncertain.
891 *And ek the beste as my wit kan comprehende α.*
903 *this] his α* Cx.
906 *To sen hym in that wo that he is inne α* (Ital. "di veder Troilo afflitto").
910 *beteth* Gg Hl³ Ph Hl⁴ Cx Th; *rest he beteth* (so Root, interpreting, "that [vital] spirit which he is assailing in my heart").
915 *hastily] softly α; shortly* Ph.
924 *So lef] Lat be α.*
950–52 So all but Ph Hl³; which read:

> *He fast made hys compleynt and his moon*
> *Besyking hem to sende hym other grace*
> *Or fro thys worlde to doon hym sone pace*

Root suggests (Text. Trad., p. 218) that the change was made when stanza 155 (ll. 1079–85) was added.
953–1085 The whole soliloquy is omitted in Hl³ Ph Hl⁴, and all but the last stanza is omitted in Gg J. The passage is added later in Ph and J (in J by the original scribe). For a detailed account of the MSS. at this point see Root, Text. Trad., pp. 216 ff. They indicate pretty clearly that the soliloquy was inserted after the main body of the narrative was composed.
1038 *his om.* Ph S² (making a better line metrically).
1093 *many α yer] al (of, often in) thy lyf α.*
1097 *Lat be, and thynk right thus] Kanstow nat thinken thus α.*
1099 *Right so in love] In love also α* (exc. Gg).
1113 *Destourbe al this] Stynt al this thing α.*
1129 *peyne] sorwe α.*
1131 *toke, and after] hente and softe α.*
1133 *Wher that he was] What for to don α* Cx.
1138–39 *α:*

> *So bittre teris wep(te) nat thurgh the rynde*
> *The woful Mirra writen as I fynde*

1165 *in nothyng] in no cas α.*

1183 *hem] folk α* J Hl³.
1199 *low or hye] forth in hye* J α.
1214 *Lady] herte* J α.
1218 *to glade] conforte* J α (Ital. "la confortò"); *to gladder* Hl².
1222–23 *Ayein into her herte al softe wente So at the laste α.*
1250 *al hire blisse ylorn] hir joyes alle lorn α.*
1251 *Seying allas that evere they were born α.*
1294 *in effect] fynal(l)y α.*
1301 *As in thys cas lat dryve it oute of mynde* Hl³ only. (In this and several other unique Hl³ readings which follow, Root (Text. Trad., p. 216) suggests that we have a record of the text in its most primitive form.)
1304 *Ful cruelly oure hertis wolde anoye* Hl³ only.
1312–13 Hl³ only:

> *Considereth now that tyme it is of trewe*
> *Ye may not faille of myn estat to here*

1321 *erste* Cp Hl¹; *rest erst.* Perhaps the form in -e is used here and in HF, 512.
1322 *That we shul (wil Ph) everemo togeddre dwelle α; That I may have a liberte to dwelle* Hl³.
1325 *That for the beste] Of pourviaunce* Hl³ only.
1336 *as wyd] as muche α; as brode* Hl³.
1363–65 Hl³ only (Ital. "Ed a che far tra' Greci mi terebbe Che come vedi son sempre nell' armi"):

> *In hoste amonge the Grekys ever in fere*
> *Hit nyl not bee and gode soo wysly rede*
> *My soule as ye have cause noon to drede*

1388 (second half) — **1409** (first half) Om. Cp; here printed from Cm.
1392–93 Hl³ only:

> *To doo the wrathe of pyramus to passe*
> *Towardys hym and don hym stonde in grace*

1402 *If that I lye] Yif thys be les* Hl³ only.
1404 *In myddys hys werk* Hl³ only.
1411 *Whan he from Delphos to the Grekys sterte* Hl³ only.
1442 *Shal I never as in thys worlde have joye* Hl³ only.
1654 *no cause] no thought α; No thing* Hl³.

Book V

8 *gold-ytressed,* an emendation; most MSS. *gold(e) tressed; golde dressed* A; *gold tresses* S¹; *Auricomus tressed* Hl²; Gg lacks leaf.
9 *shene* Hl² Hl⁴ R S¹; *cleene* J Ph; *clere* γ Hl³ Cx Th.
60–61 α β transpose.
67 *valeye] wallys* R only; Hl³ *wey*; Ital. "vallo" (mistranslation by Chaucer?).
107 *Whan this was don* γ Th; *rest Whan tyme was.*
181 *fader fer] fadres tent* Hl³.
202 *nothyng] no wight α; non man* Gg (over erasure).
211 *walwith* Gg Hl⁴ Cx; *waltryth* R; *whieleth* J; *swellith* Ph; *rest wayleth or waileth.*
245 *langour] γ* S¹ Th; *rest longyng(e).*
412 *wene γ* S¹ Th; *rest sey(n)* (Ital. "diria").
436 *largesse] prowesse γ* S¹ Th (apparently wrong in this context).

565   γ S¹ Th *Lo yonder saugh ich myn owene lady daunce* (probably an error in γ).

594   *o*(= one) A J Hl⁴; *on* Gg; *a* Cp Cm Hl¹ Hl³ Hl² Th.

655   *Lat(h)ona* so all MSS.; Cx Th read *Lucyna*.

726   *nedede* Cm; rest *neded, nedith*. *No*] *none* Cp Gg A. Read either *nededë no* or *neded none*.

924   *lord* γ S¹ Th; rest *king* (Ital. "re").

992   *nevere yit I* Ph Hl⁴ Cx; *nevere yit ne* Gg; *I never yit* J; *I never* Hl² Hl³ R; *I never(e) er(e)* γ Th (possible, but metrically harder).

1095   *punysshed*] *publisshed* Hl² R Ph Cx Th.

1213   *the* Cp Cm Hl³ Ph D; rest om.

1233–74   Om. Cp; printed here from Cm.

1413   *As ye* γ S¹ Cx Th; rest *As she*.

1498   The following Latin argument of the twelve books of the Thebaid is inserted in the MSS. (exc. Hl⁴ R) after l. 1499, where it breaks the continuity of the text. Skeat shifted it to a position after l. 1484. Hl² contains an additional line: "Fervidus ypomedon timidique in gurgite mersus." The text is that of Cp, with a few corrections.

"Associat profugum Tideo primus Polymytem;
Tidea legatum docet insidiasque secundus;
Tercius Hemoniden canit et vates latitantes;
Quartus habet reges ineuntes prelia septem;
Mox furie Lenne quinto narratur et anguis;
Archymori bustum sexto ludique leguntur;

Dat Grayos Thebes et vatem septimus umbris;
Octavo cecidit Tideus spes vita Pelasgis;
Ypomedon nono moritur cum Part(h)onopea;
Fulmine percussus, decimo Capaneus superatur;
Undecimo sese perimunt per vulnera fratres;
Argivam flentem narrat duodenus et ignem."

1502–04   J Gg only:

And how Ypomedon with blody wownde ;
And ek (om. Gg) *Parthonope in litel stownde*
Ben slayn and how Cappaneus the proude

This (as Root, Text. Trad., p. 239, observes) is either corrupt, or it is the original version corrected later on reference to Statius.

1618   *Come*] *comen* R; so also Skeat and Globe, with avoidance of headless line.

1631   *La vostre C.* added by Hl¹ D S¹ S² and editors.

1807–27   These three stanzas are omitted in Hl² Hl⁴ and inserted later, on an inset leaf, in Ph. For a discussion of the reasons, with the conclusion that the passage was not present in Chaucer's earliest draft of the poem, see Root, Text. Trad., pp. 245 ff.

1809   *eighth(e)* J (*viij*) R (*viijᵗʰᵉ*) Cx (*eyght*); rest *seventhe* (Ital. "ottava").

1866   *Trine unite us from oure cruel foone* Hl² R only.

The Legend of Good Women

Authorities: twelve MSS. and one early edition, as follows:

A¹   Additional 9832, British Museum.
A²   Additional 12524, British Museum.
A³   Additional, 28617, British Museum.
B   Bodley 638, Bodleian.
F   Fairfax 16, Bodleian.
Ff   Cambridge University Library Ff. 1. 6.
Gg   Cambridge University Library Gg. 4. 27.
P   Pepys 2006, Magdalene College, Cambridge (hands B and C).
R   Rawlinson C. 86, Bodleian.
S   Arch. Selden B. 24, Bodleian.
T   Tanner 246, Bodleian.
Th   Thynne's edition, 1532.
Tr   Trinity College, Cambridge, R. 3. 19.

Several of these MSS. are fragmentary. R contains only the Dido, and Ff only the Thisbe. P has ll. 1–1377; A¹ has ll. 1–1985; A², ll. 1640–end; A³, nine fragmentary passages. All the texts have been printed by the Chaucer Society.

Incomplete and tentative classification of the MSS. was made by Skeat and by Pollard in the preparation of their editions. More detailed studies have been published by Kunz, Das Verhältnis der Handschriften von Chaucers Legend of Good Women, Berlin, 1889; by Bilderbeck, Chaucer's Legend of Good Women, London, 1902; by Amy, The Text of Chaucer's Legend of Good Women, Princeton, 1918, and by Koch, in Angl., XLIII, 197–244, XLIV, 23–71. See also his edition of the text, in [Chaucer's] Kleinere Dichtungen, Heidelberg, 1928. Differences in the conclusions of Amy and Koch are set forth in detail by Amy in JEGP, XXI, 107 ff. Their most important disagreement is in the estimate of MS. Gg, which Koch regards as the earlier version. In the opinion of the present editor, Dr. Amy's conclusions are substantially correct. They were also approved by Professor Brusendorff, Chaucer Tradition, p. 137, n. 5. For a few corrections of the Chaucer Society reprints, see Amy, p. 103.

MS. Gg stands by itself, since it contains the sole copy of the revised version of the Prologue. The other MSS. fall into two groups:

$$\alpha \begin{cases} 1 & \text{Tr A}^1 \\ 2 & \text{S A}^2 \\ 3 & \text{Ff P R A}^3 \end{cases}$$
$$\beta \begin{cases} 1 & \text{F B} \\ 2 & \text{T} \end{cases}$$

Thynne's edition runs mainly with Group β (standing closest to T), but shows contamination with Group α. Group α³ seems to be composite, deriving in part from β and in part from Gg or a lost MS. The relation of Gg to the two main Groups is not certain, but on the whole it stands nearer to Group α. Throughout the Legends, and particularly in the first six, it offers unique readings which have been held to indicate that Chaucer's revision went beyond the Prologue. See Bilderbeck, pp. 36 ff. The matter is by no means clear. But in the opinion of the present editor the readings in question are probably scribal variants. Compare also Amy, p. 101, n.

In the present edition the text of the earlier (F) version of the Prologue is based upon the Fairfax MS. because of its superior orthography, but the readings of Group α are given the preference. The text of the Legends is based upon MS. Gg, corrected by critical comparison of Groups α and β. Readings of Gg, even when unsupported, have been given serious consideration and sometimes accepted. For although Chaucer's revision seems not to have gone further than the Prologue, the MS. has special authority because of its independent derivation from his working copy. For the revised (G) Prologue, Gg is naturally the sole authority, and is made the basis of the text. But it is often difficult to determine whether variations between its readings and those of the other MSS. represent deliberate changes or merely scribal variants. Some unique readings of Gg are manifestly errors, and some readings which it shares with one or more MSS. of Version F seem so clearly inferior that they have been corrected by the editor. But many other variants, whether peculiar to Gg or shared with other MSS., are of a doubtful character. They may be scribal errors in Gg; or inferior readings of the first version inadvertently kept in revision; or variants in the first version which Chaucer deliberately approved and retained. In view of the peculiar authority of Gg, it has seemed safest to preserve such readings, and to call attention to the more important of them in the notes. The spelling of Gg, which departs widely from the usage of most Chaucer MSS., has been normalized throughout; that of MS. F has required very slight correction.

Prologue, Version F

(Variants which are clearly due to the revision will not be listed here.)

1 *tymes* α F T; *sythes* β Gg (apparently not a case of revision). *Have I* Tr Gg S A[1]; *I have* T F B Th.

50 *sighte*] all *sight*.

67 *Suffisa(u)nt* β Th; *Sufficient* Tr S; *Sufficia(u)nt* A[1] P.

196 *stryf* Tr S A[1] (also Gg); rest *thing*.

221 *fyne* β Tr S P; *fyn(e) and* A[1] (also Gg). Perhaps *fyne* is a mere spelling, though the form with final -e occurs in Chaucer. This seems unlikely to be a case of revision.

261 *for love* Tr A[1] S (also Gg); *of love* β P Th.

338 *seynt* all MSS., possibly to be emended to *seynte*, though the headless line is equally probable.

387 *half-goddes*] Langhans, Untersuchungen, p. 209, emends unnecessarily to *a goddes half*.

404 *sorweful*] *dredeful* β P.

427 *sithen* S only; rest *is* (which is metrically suspicious).

493 *shal charge his servantz*] *his servaunts charge* Tr A[1] only. A tempting reading for both versions, but perhaps due to scribe's mending of meter.

529 *florouns* F Th only (probably the first reading); rest *floures* (which was retained in Gg).

Prologue, Version G

6 *helle or hevene* Gg (also Tr); *hevin or helle* S; rest *hevene or in helle*. (Perhaps a mere scribal variant retained in Gg.)

16 *say* Gg (also Tr); perhaps we should read *saugh* with S P β? Both forms are common in Chaucer MSS., but *say* (*sey*) seems best established in rime.

34 *make* Gg; rest *maketh*. The Gg reading may be an error, but is retained as being possibly an intentional subjunctive. *from myne* Gg only; mere spelling.

51 *gynneth*] *begynnys* Gg (dialectic and probably scribal).

111 *surmountede* Gg; Version F has *surmounteth* (not a certain case of revision).

116 *th' atempre*] *the tempre* Gg only (*a tempre* Tr A[1]).

127 Meter suspicious; read *somĕ*, or insert *layes* (Skeat)? The next twelve lines in Gg are very defective. It looks as if Chaucer's revision had been either left incomplete, or had been badly corrupted by a scribe.

128 Meter defective in Gg; insert *May* (Skeat) or adopt reading of Version F (Globe). It is not certain that there is any revision here.

131 [*They*] *That* Gg, Skeat, with awkward construction; Globe [*And*].

132 *For on*] *At* Gg only; probably an error, rather than a deliberate variant.

135 *The honour and the humble obeysaunce* Gg only. This makes no sense, and the reading of Version F has been adopted (so Globe). Very likely a real alteration is concealed in Gg; Skeat em. *They dide honour and humble obeysaunces.*

137 *Ryght on to love and to natures* Gg only. Metrically defective; *longing* (so Globe) is supplied by comparison with Version F (*that longeth*); Skeat supplies *plesing*; Langhans, Untersuchungen, p. 104, would read: *Right as it longeth to love and to nature, Did eche of hem as other creature.*

138 Defective in Gg and not paralleled in Version F. Skeat supplies *doth wel. cryaturys* and *natures* (l. 137) are hardly possible; Version F has *nature: cure.* The whole passage is corrupt.

144 *loken*] Gg *loke*.

149, 152 *flourys* Gg (also Tr A[1] S P); *florouns* β. Hence not a deliberate revision. Chaucer simply used a MS. of the type which had substituted *floures.*

153 *fyn and* Gg (also A[1]); rest *fyne.*

157 *the* Gg; *her* Version F; perhaps revision.

159 *Of* Gg; *In* Version F; probably error in Gg.

192 *world* Gg; *wyde world* Version F. Perhaps a scribal omission in Gg.

213, 218 *Eek* Gg only; *And* Version F. Perhaps not revision.

317 *worthyeste*] Skeat em. for *worthyere* Gg.

412 *besynesse*] *holynes(se)* Version F. Apparently revision.

440 *And* Gg; *I* Version F. Perhaps deliberate revision.

451 *put*] *put me* Gg F T only.

472 *tyme*] *lyf* Gg P only; probably a mistake allowed to stand in revision.

Legend of Cleopatra

Heading. *Martiris* appears in F B T only, but is probably due to the author, though neglected in revision.

641 *rennyth* Gg; *ran* Th; *and* F B T; *raf* Tr; *rase* A[1]; *than* S; *thenn* P. There is MS. support for *renneth* or *ran*. The former is favored by the authority of Gg and the sequence of tenses, and the grammatical difficulty is removed by the emendation *renne*.

Explicit, etc., from F throughout the poem.

Legend of Thisbe

Headings from F throughout the poem.
718 *That tho was in that lond Estward dwellynge* Gg only; most other MSS. *That est(e)ward in the world was tho dwellynge*. (Possibly revision?)
724 *called* Gg α; *cleped* β.
794 *hast(e)* Gg Ff P; rest *lykinge*.
882 *she*] *he* Gg A¹ P.
890 *my* Gg (*myn*, corrected) Ff only; rest *thy* (which is wrong unless something has fallen out, as Globe suggests).

Legend of Dido

928 *In Naso and Eneydos* Gg only; rest *In thyn Eneyde* (*Ovide* S R) *and Naso*. (Possibly revision.)
944 *olde*] *owene* Gg.
964 *called*] *clepid* Gg.
1107 *ornementes* Gg Tr A¹; rest *pavement(e)s*.
1126 *Thus can this honurable quene hire gestis calle* Th Gg F B T (*his gistes*) Tr S (*gan*) A¹ (*ganne . . . to calle*) P (*gyfles*) R (*gafe . . . gyftes alle*). No MS. reading can be right. Skeat em. *Thus can this noble quene her gestes calle;* but *noble* is unsupported and *calle* is strangely employed. Globe *Thus gan this queene honoure hir gestes talle*, also suggesting *Thus yaf this noble queene hir giftes talle*. *Talle* for *calle* is a likely restoration on palaeological grounds, but it introduces a word which occurs only once elsewhere in Chaucer, and which is there used in a doubtful sense. Dr. Amy (p. 63) suggests the reading in the text, meaning "Thus, her guests have every reason to call this queen honorable." But the order is unusual.
1145 *take* Gg α; *make* β Th.
1160 2nd *to*] *comyth* Gg only. (Possibly revision.)
1166 *waketh, walweth*] *waylith and sche* Gg only. (Possibly revision.)
1170 *dere*] *leve* Gg. (Possibly revision.)
1171 *drem*] *slep* Gg only.
1175 *therwithal*] *ek thereto* Gg; *withal* F B T; *therwith* Th R.
1187 *thing* Gg P R; rest *wyght*.
1217 *These bestys wilde* Gg only; *The wild(e) hertes* β Th; *The wild(e) bestes* P R; *These wild(e) bestes* Tr S A¹.
1238 Metrically suspicious. Skeat em. *to been his wyf*; Koch om. the first *And*.
1269 *And waytyn* Gg only; *And plesen* Tr A¹; *And* T S; rest *To* (defective).
1283 *land than of*] *landes than* Gg (om. α before *quene*). Possibly revision.
1338 Globe em. *Jove* for *Jupiter*, which is the reading of all MSS. In Tr S A¹ the line is mended by the omission of *swete*; but this translates the Latin "dulces" (Aen., iv, 651), and is not likely to have been inserted by a scribe. It looks as if Chaucer wrote the alexandrine.
1339 *unbynd me*] *and brynge it* Gg.
1360 *contraire*] *contrair* S; rest *contrary(e), contrarious(e)*.

Legend of Hypsipyle and Medea

1382 *sekte* Gg A¹; *sleight(e)* F B only; *seeyte* A³; *seite* T; *set(t)* Tr S; *disceyte* Th.
1396 *as (and) Guido* Gg α; *and (as) Ovyde* β.
1404 *gentilesse* F B T S Th A³; rest *gentilnes(se)*.
1538 *almychti* S only; perhaps a scribe's emendation, but the short line seems impossible.
1545 *was*] *was mad* Tr only.
1605 *a leoun*] *lyo(u)n* F T S.
1607 *the art and craft* Tr S A¹; *craft and art* β; *the craft and art* Gg Th (extra syllable?); *the Craffte* A³.
1647 *stynten* β; *stynted, stynt* α Gg.
1659 *chefe traitour* F B T S Th; rest *theef (and) traitour* with variations.

Legend of Lucrece

1682 *And* A² only (*And especially*); rest om. The short line is metrically possible, but does not follow l. 1681 naturally unless *here* is there emended to *the*.
1716 *pryvely* Tr A¹; rest *ful prively* (perhaps correctly).
1728 *to*] *sore* Gg (possibly revision).
1764 *new(e)* F T Th B A²; *now* Gg S A³; om. A¹ Tr.
1836-1907 Om. Gg; printed from F, but with corrected readings.
1879 *himselve*] all MSS. *himself(e)*; metrically difficult.
1881 *that* α; *the lond* β.

Legend of Ariadne

From F as far as l. 1907

1936 *Unto Minos* Tr A¹; *To Minos* β S A² A³; *To Theseus* Gg only. Possibly Chaucer wrote the wrong name here and in l. 1964; compare the slip in l. 1966.
1964 *Mynos*] *King Mynos* S only; *Thesius* Gg only (cf. l. 1936).
1966 *Of Athenes*] *In moche(ll) myrth(e)* Tr A¹; *Of the towne* Th. Lowes suggests that the slip was Chaucer's, and was due to the Teseida. See the explanatory note.
1967 *happede*] *happid (happed)* Gg and all MSS. (exc. S *happinit*). Either the full form *happedē* or *happed ther* (Tr A¹) would mend the meter.
1971 *compleynyng(e)* Gg Tr A¹ A² S; *compleynt* F T B A³ Th.
1995 *he dar his lyf (to) kepe* Gg α; *his lyf (he) dar kepe* β.
2020 *drede*] *stede* β.
2053 *men*] *man* Gg (which is grammatically possible; see *ClT*, IV, 212, n.).
2069 *go* S; *goth* Gg Tr A² A³; *mot go* β. (Reading very doubtful.)
2075 *a* Gg; rest om.
2083 *lene* Gg β A³; *leve* A² S; *let* Tr.
2086 *leve* Gg A² F B; *lyve* S; *lene* T A³ Th; *graunt* Tr.
2094 *no profre* Gg α; *no(t) profyt* β.
2138 *was performed*] so all MSS.; Skeat, Koch em. *performed was*, for the meter.
2160 *newe*] *noble* β.
2186 *gropeth*] *graspeth* Gg Tr; *gaspeth* A².

2215 *shyp or boot* Tr only; *any bote* S A²; *bot(e) noon* β; *boote* A³; *boot . . . ne* Gg (clearly wrong).

Legend of Philomela

Heading from F (which reads *formatorum,* corruptly)

2261 *say* Gg Tr; rest *saugh (saw).*
2286 *she loveth (loved)* Gg α; *hir longeth* β.
2291 *beaute] bounte* B; *bounde* F.
2324 *he* Gg; rest om. *that* Gg only; rest α.
2359 *2nd that]* Tr S; rest om. (a possible reading, taking *by* as conjunction in the sense of "by the time that").

Legend of Phyllis

2422 *Chorus* Th; *Thorus, Thora* MSS. See the explanatory note.
2470 *As] And* F T B.
2506-07 Om. Gg; here printed from F.

Legend of Hypermnestra

2606 *utterly] witterly* F B T.
2612 *fyre] fuyr out* Gg (perhaps correctly).
2666 *costret(e)* Gg α; *costrel(e)* β.

Short Poems

The textual authorities for the Short Poems have nearly all been published by the Chaucer Society. References to them and other reprints, and to previous discussions of the relations of the MSS., are given below for each poem. Readings from the Leyden MS. (Vossius 9) are taken from a copy made by the present editor in 1896 and never published. The editor has made free use of the editions of Skeat, Heath, and Koch, and of the textual observations of Professor Brusendorff in his Chaucer Tradition. He would also express grateful acknowledgments to Mr. Joseph Butterworth for having communicated to him some of the results of an exhaustive study of the MSS. of the Minor Poems. Since the publication of the first edition of the present work a number of valuable articles, containing unpublished texts of the Short Poems and textual notes, have been published by Professor G. B. Pace. They will be noted under the poems with which they deal.

Since the authorities used for the text of the Short Poems often depart from the orthographical practice of the best Chaucer MSS., it has seemed best to the editor to normalize the spelling of these pieces.

An A B C

Authorities: thirteen copies in MS. and Speght's edition, all printed by the Chaucer Society:

α
1
F Fairfax 16, Bodleian.
B Bodley 638, Bodleian.
H¹ Harley 7578, British Museum (fragmentary).
2 P Pepys 2006, Magdalene College, Cambridge (two copies, both fragmentary).
3 Gg Cambridge University Library Gg. 4. 27.
Sp Speght's second edition, 1602.

β
1
Ff Cambridge University Library Ff. 5. 30.
G Hunterian Museum, Glasgow, U. 3. 12.
J St. John's College, Cambridge, G. 21.
L Laud Misc. 740, Bodleian.
S Sion College, London, Arc. $\frac{\text{L. 40. 2}}{\text{E. 44}}$
2
A Additional 36983, British Museum (formerly Bedford).

MS. Harley 2251 (H²), British Museum, appears to belong to Group α, but shows signs of contamina-

tion. The copies in Ff J G L S occur in a prose translation of Deguilleville's Pèlerinage de la Vie Humaine.

Group β offers the better text; Ff, with corrected spellings, is made the basis of the present edition.

35 *Unto mercy hastow receyved me* H² α.
39 *me wel chastyse]* S only; *me chastyse* Ff A; rest (perhaps correctly) *That but thou er that day correcte me (my folise* J). See J. B. Severs, MLN, LXIV, 306 ff., who defends the change of rime scheme, comparing *Former Age,* st. 6.
45 *wille* β; *wit* H² α.
83 *bothes* Ff G Gg; *bather* J; *both(e)* F L. *youre bothes,* though supported by good MSS., is a strange construction. Perhaps the reading should be *youre bother* (supported by J), as in *Tr,* iv, 168.
86 *Convict] Convicted* H²; *Committee* J.
132 *is his* H² α; *it is (hys* Ff margin) β. Koch em. (perhaps correctly) *hit his* ("hits, strikes his"), and compares Fr. "Son chastoy si fiert a hie."
146 *deprived* all but J L (*pryved*).
163 All MSS. insert *suff(e)red,* apparently repeated from l. 162. *pighte]* eds. em. *prighte* (perhaps correctly).
181 *bryght* Gg Sp only.

The Complaint unto Pity

Authorities: nine MSS., all published by the Chaucer Society, and Thynne's edition, 1532 (Th), available in Skeat's facsimile. The MSS. are classified as follows:

α
H¹ Harley 78, British Museum (by Shirley).
A Additional 34360, British Museum (formerly Phillipps 9053; copied from a Shirley MS).
H² Harley 7578, British Museum.

β
F Fairfax 16, Bodleian.
B Bodley 638, Bodleian.
T Tanner 346, Bodleian.
Ff Cambridge University Library Ff. 1. 6.
L Longleat 258, in the possession of the Marquess of Bath.
R Trinity College, Cambridge, R. 3. 19.

Th apparently belongs to Group β. According to the Globe editor, Ff is derived from T, and R shows contamination of the sources of L and of T and Ff. But both these opinions are questioned by Mr. Butterworth in his unpublished study of the MSS. Group β has a somewhat better text, though frequent corrections have to be made with the aid of Group α. F is taken as the basis of the present edition. References to Ten Brink are to his critical edition of the poem in the Chaucer Society's Essays, Part ii (n.d.), pp. 165 ff.

9 *a tyme sought* α; *sought a tyme* β Th.
21 *nas*] *was* MSS. Th; but Chaucer's usual idiom seems to have demanded a negative. Cf. l. 105.
24 *hold* β Th; *heve* α.
41 Ten Brink, Skeat, Koch, and Globe insert *and* before *drede*.
50 *Then leve (we) alle vertues save only Pite* β Th.
52 So A H¹; *alle* om. H²; *Confedered by bonde and (by) cruelte* β (*Unto Cruelte* Th).
61 *yfalle*] Th only (*yfal*); rest *fall(e)*.
67 *lo*] A H¹ only. Koch, following Ten Brink, reads [*ne*] *shulde*.
70 *hight(e)* α; *is high (hy)* β Th (*is hys* Ff); *Grace*] *your grace* β Th.
76 *wanten*] *want(e)* all MSS.
79 *With you benigne and faire creature* α.
80 *your(e)* β Th; *now oure* α.
83 *that perilous* β Th; *these (of thoo) persones* α.
89 *than* α (exc. H²); *also* β Th H².
92 *herenus (heremus, herenius?)* β Th; *vertuous(e)* α; *serenous* Globe em.
93 *tenderly* β Th; *trew(e)ly* α.
96 *the* H²; *the hevy* H¹ A; *so* β Th.
105 [*ne*] supplied by Ten Brink. Cf. l. 21.
117 *ye*] β (*ye*) *yet*; *Now pite that I have sought so yore agoo* α.

A Complaint to his Lady

Authorities: two MSS., Harley 78 (H) and Additional 34360 (A), formerly Phillipps 9053, both of the British Museum, and both printed by the Chaucer Society under Shirley's title, *The Balade of Pite*; and Stowe's edition (St), 1561. The copy in H was written by Shirley; that in A seems to be derived from it, but contains an additional stanza at the end. St closely resembles H. The spelling of all is very bad, and is normalized in the present text. A number of verbal corrections have also been accepted, though fewer than in Skeat's edition. On the MSS. see Koch, ESt, XXVII, 41 ff. (with textual notes), and Kleinere Dichtungen, p. 22; Miss Hammond, Angl., XXVIII, 25 f.; and Brusendorff, pp. 272 ff.

1 *nightes*] so all copies; Skeat *night*.
14 This line is repeated by Skeat at the beginning of the terza rima, to get a rime for *fulfille* (l. 16). The sense is also incomplete in the sentence beginning with l. 15.
16 [*he*] *never wol* Skeat; *wol never he* Globe; MSS. *wol (wil) never* all copies.
18 *yit*] so all copies; Skeat [*fro*].
22 After this line Skeat supplies *For this day in hir servise shal I dye*, from *Mars*, 189.
23 Before this series in terza rima Skeat supplies, from *Pity*, 22, 17, and *Anel*, 307:

Thus am I slain, with sorwes ful dyverse;
Ful longe agoon I oghte have taken hede.

25 *youthe*] so all copies; Koch em. *thought*.
32 Skeat suggests *Than al this worldes richest (or riche) creature.*
41 [*eek*] supplied by eds.
43 *I mis*] so all copies; Koch would em. *is mis*, for the grammar.
50-57 In all copies this stanza has but eight lines. Skeat supplies after l. 51 *Yow rekketh never wher I flete or sinke*; and after l. 53 *For on my wo yow deyneth not to thinke.* Cf. *Anel*, 181–82.
71 *fayner noon*] all copies *no(o)n fayner.*
72 *yow*] all copies *your(e).*
73 *to* [*yow distresse*] Skeat; *to your(e) hyenesse* all copies; Koch em. *hevynesse.*
92 *nil*] all copies *ne wil.*
114 *verrayly*] so *verrayly* MSS.; *verely* St; Skeat, Koch [*man than me*], to avoid the false rime.
117 *to be*] so H St; *triewly* A (which removes the false rime).
118-27 The last stanza is found in A only.
120 [*is*] supplied by Skeat.
123 *yow mighte*] so A; Skeat, Koch *mighte yow.*

The Complaint of Mars

Authorities: eight MSS., all printed by the Chaucer Society, and two early editions, that of Julian Notary (1499–1501), printed by the Chaucer Society, and that of Thynne (1532), available in Skeat's facsimile edition. The classification is as follows:

α {
F	Fairfax 16, Bodleian.
L	Longleat 258, in the possession of the Marquess of Bath.
T	Tanner 346, Bodleian.
Th	Thynne's edition.

β {
Pb	Pepys 2006 (Hand B, complete), Magdalene College, Cambridge.
S	Arch. Selden B. 24, Bodleian.
N	Julian Notary's edition.
Pe	Pepys 2006 (Hand E, fragmentary).
R	Trinity College, Cambridge, R. 3. 20.
H	Harley 7333, British Museum.

S appears to be contaminated with an α MS. resembling L. The readings of the archetype β are in most cases superior to those of α. But no single MS. of this group is very satisfactory. F therefore, because of its general conformity to the spelling of the best MSS. of other pieces, has been used as the basis of the present edition, but the readings of Group β have ordinarily been given the preference.

1 *foules* β (exc. *fooles* R, *floures* H); *lovers* α; *of* Pb N R S; *on* F H; *in* T Th; *at* Pe.
17 *yow your*] so S; *you a* R; *ye your* N; rest om. *yow.*
19 This line stands before l. 17 in F; before l. 18 in Th.
54 *and ther abyde* Pb N R S; *and abide* Pe; *ther abide* H; (*for*) *to abyde* α.
67 *ther* β; α om.
68 *wo* β; *sorowe* α.
141 *al alone* Pb N (metrically easier).
146 *doth (did)* β; *maketh* α.
191 *than pleyne* R; rest om. *than*; *compleyne* S; *pleynen* Pb.

207 *depraven* β (exc. *depeynen* S) Th; *departen* α (exc. Th).
227 *made* α N S; *make* R; *maketh* Pb.

To Rosemounde

Authority: a single copy in MS. Rawlinson Poet. 163, Bodleian, reproduced in facsimile in Skeat's Twelve Facsimiles of Old English Manuscripts, Oxford, 1892. For notes, textual and explanatory, based on fresh examination of the MS., see H. Kökeritz, MLN, LXIII, 310 ff. The spelling is here normalized.

11 *semy*, so the MS. Skeat em. *semly*.
21 *refreyde*] MS. *be refreyde* (with *be* above the line); Skeat transposed.

Womanly Noblesse

Authority: a single copy in MS. Additional 34360, British Museum, first printed by Skeat in Athen., 1894, I, 742. The title is Skeat's. The spelling is here somewhat normalized. The readings from Mac-Cracken are taken from his College Chaucer, pp. 565–66.

Subheading. *Chaucier*] *Chauncier* MS. (See Miss Hammond, Angl., XXVIII, 4.)
5 *womanly*] Skeat suggests em. *wyfly*.
10 [*you*] suppl. by Skeat, probably correctly.
12 After this line the editors insert a line as follows: [*I pray yow, do to me som daliaunce*] Skeat (Athen.); [*Taketh me, lady, in your obeisaunce*] Furnivall (adopted by Skeat, Oxf. Chau., IV, xxvi); [*Take my service in gre, and nat grevaunce*] Mac-Cracken.
15 [*loke*] Skeat; [*lo*] MacCracken. *humb[le]ly* Skeat em.; MS. *humbly*; *And* [*hoveth humblely*] Globe.
17 *peynes for* MS.; *for* om. Skeat.
21 *don*] Skeat em. (Oxf. Chau., IV, xxvi); MS. *do*.
24 *And thynkith be raison that* MS., Globe (which suggests em. *Me thynkith*); *And think resoun* Skeat (Stud. Chau.).
25 *for til do the* MS.; *the* om. Skeat.
29 *myn*] Skeat em.; MS. *my*.

Adam Scriveyn

Authorities: only one MS., Shirley's R. 3. 20, in the library of Trinity College, Cambridge. Stowe's edition (1561) also has the piece, in a text essentially identical with Shirley's, though different in spelling. Both copies are printed by the Chaucer Society. Shirley's MSS. are often untrustworthy in verbal detail, and in the present poem some previous editors have omitted *long* in l. 3 and *more* in l. 4, which on metrical grounds are open to suspicion. Skeat, for the same reason, omits *for* in l. 2. The spelling here is normalized.

The Former Age

Authorities: two MSS., Ii. 3. 21 and Hh. 4. 12, both in the Cambridge University Library, and both printed by the Chaucer Society. The former is superior, and is made, with normalization of the spelling, the basis of the present text.

3 *the fruites* MSS.; Skeat, Globe om. *the*.
42 MSS. om. second *in*.
44 *parfyt joye reste and quiete* Ii; *parfite joy and quiete* Hh.
55 After this line there is a line missing. Skeat proposes [*Fulfilled erthe of olde curtesye*]; Koch [*Yit hadden in this worlde the maistrie*]; MacCracken [*And Charite, thise koude hem beter gye*].
Finit &c. from Hh.

Fortune

Authorities: ten MSS. and the editions of Caxton and Thynne (Th), classified as follows:

α Ii Cambridge University Library Ii. 3. 21.

β { A Ashmole 59, Bodleian.
   { H Harley 2251, British Museum.
   { R Trinity College, Cambridge, R. 3. 20.

γ { F Fairfax 16, Bodleian.
  { B Bodley 638, Bodleian.
  { P Pepys 2006, Magdalene College, Cambridge.
  { Ld Lansdowne 699, British Museum.
  { Leyd Leyden University Library Vossius 9.
  { S Arch. Selden B. 10, Bodleian.
  { Cx Caxton's edition, c. 1477–78.

Th, which apparently belongs to Group γ, is available in Skeat's facsimile edition. All the rest except the Leyden copy, which most nearly resembles Ld and S, are printed by the Chaucer Society. The Leyden readings, from a copy made by the editor, are included in the following citations. MS. Ii is decidedly the best and contains a number of superior unique readings. It is therefore made the basis of the present text.

8, 16, 24 *thee* Ii only; rest om.
9 *light* Ii only; rest *si(g)ht*.
11 *mochel* Ii only; rest *moche, mych, muche. whirlynge* Ii; rest *t(o)urnyng(e)*.
30 *why wolt thou* Ii; rest *thou shalt nat*.
36 *derkyd* Ii; rest *derk(e), dirk*, etc.
64 After l. 64 all copies have a wrong rubric (*Le pleintif* in Ii).
72 Ld S Leyd om. *Lenvoy*.
76 Ii only; rest om. line.
77 *And*] *That* Ii R.

Truth

Authorities: twenty-one MS. copies (or twenty-two if MS. Phillipps 11409 is included), and the editions of Caxton and Thynne (Th). The sixteen MSS. published by the Chaucer Society have been classified as follows. See Koch, ESt, XXVII, 13 ff., and Kleinere Dichtungen, p. 33; and Brusendorff, p. 245.

α { A¹ Additional 10340, British Museum.
  { Ph Phillipps 8299, property of T. F. Fenwick, Esq., Cheltenham.

β { Gg Cambridge University Library Gg. 4. 27.
  { C Cotton Cleopatra D. vii, British Museum.
  { E Ellesmere MS., Huntington Library, San Marino, Calif.
  { A² Additional 22139, British Museum.

γ {
F   Fairfax 16, Bodleian (two copies, designated F₁, F₂).
R   Trinity College, Cambridge, R. 3. 20 (two copies, designated R₁, R₂).
Ld   Lansdowne 699, British Museum.
S¹   Arch. Selden B. 10 Bodleian.
H   Harley 7333, British Museum.
S²   Arch. Selden B. 24, Bodleian.
Kk   Cambridge University Library Kk. 1. 5.
Hat Hatton 73, Bodleian.
Cp   Corpus Christi College, Oxford, 203.
Cx   Caxton's edition, ca. 1477–78.
}

Other copies:

Lam Lambeth Palace Library 344 (a copy of Hat), published by H. N. MacCracken in MLN, XXIII, 212 ff.
A³   Additional 36983, British Museum (formerly Bedford).
Pep Pepys 2006, Magdalene College, Cambridge. Both A³ and Pep were published by G. B. Pace, MLN, LXIII, 458–9.
Co   Cotton Otho A XVIII, a manuscript made by William Thomas before the Cotton fire, published by G. B. Pace in Spec., XXVI, 306–7.
Leyd Leyden University Library Vossius 9, unpublished; the readings here cited are from a copy made by the editor in 1896, but since lost.

C. Brown (Register of Mid. Eng. Relig. Verse, II, Oxford, 1920, no. 515) adds, with a query, MS. Phillipps 11409 (unpublished), and Mr. Pace (MLN, LXIII, 462 n.) also leaves undecided the question of such a copy. This MS. and Pep are unclassified. Th, which apparently belongs to Group γ, is available in Skeat's facsimile edition. Groups α and β have a similar text, superior in general to that of γ. The present edition is based upon A¹, the only MS. which contains the *Envoy*. For an argument against the authority of A¹ see Brusendorff, pp. 246 ff.

2 *the thy good* F₁; *the thyne owne* Ph; *thin owen thing* A¹; *unto thy(n) thing* Gg C; *(un)to thy good(e)* E γ (exc. F₁ Cx); *(un)to the good* Leyd Cx Th; *unto thi lyvynge* A².
6 *Reule* α Ld Leyd Kk (line shifted) S¹; *Rede* Cp Cx Th; *Werke* β; *Do* R₁ R₂ Hat S² H F₁ F₂ Lam.
7 *thee* Ph A² γ Leyd Th; om. A¹ Gg E C.
8 *Tempest* α Gg E C; *Restreyne* A²; *Ne study* Cp; rest *Peyne*.
10 *Gret(e) reste* Gg A² γ (exc. Cp Kk) Leyd Th; *Meche rest* Cp; *For gret reste* E C Kk; *Muche wele* α.
11 *Bewar also* γ (exc. Cp, which has a different line) Leyd Th; *Bewar therfore* α; *And eek bewar* β (exc. A², which has a different line).
19 *Knowe thy contre* α β; *Lyft up thyne ene* Kk; *Lyfte up thy hert* Cp; rest *Looke up on hye and*.
20 *Holde the heye wey* α β; *Weyve (Weye) thy lust* γ Leyd Th.

Gentilesse

Authorities: nine MSS. and the editions of Caxton and Thynne (Th). The nine copies published by the Chaucer Society are classified as follows:

α {
C   Cotton Cleopatra D. vii, British Museum.
Add Additional 22139, British Museum.
H¹   Harley 7578, British Museum.
H²   Harley 2251, British Museum.
R¹   Trinity College, Cambridge, R. 14. 51 (first stanza only).
Cx   Caxton's edition, ca. 1477–78.
}

β {
R²   Trinity College, Cambridge, R. 3. 20.
H³   Harley 7333, British Museum.
A   Ashmole 59, Bodleian.
}

Th (which belongs to α) is available in Skeat's facsimile edition. Cambridge University Library MS. Gg. 4. 27. 1 (b), listed by C. Brown, Register of Mid. Eng. Relig. Verse, II, no. 2143, is unpublished and unclassified. Group α is superior; MS. C, which is one of the earliest and best, is taken as the basis of the present text. The β MSS. are by Shirley or derived from his copy.

1 *gentylesse* A R²; rest *gentilnes(se)*.
2 *(that) claymeth* A R¹ H² Cx Th; *that coveyteth* Add; *desireth* C R² H¹ H³.
6 *saufly* H² Cx (apparently Chaucer's regular form); rest *savely*.
20 *hem his heyres*; *heyre him* A; *Eyre suche*, H; other MSS. have plural. See R. E. Brittain, MLN, LI, 433 ff.

Lak of Stedfastnesse

Authorities: fourteen MS. copies and Thynne's edition (1532).

A   Additional 22139, British Museum.
B   Advocates Library i. 1. 6, Edinburgh.
C   Cotton Cleopatra D. vii, British Museum.
Co   Cotton Otho A. xviii, British Museum.
D   Trinity College, Dublin, No. 432.
F   Fairfax 16, Bodleian.
H¹   Harley 7333, British Museum.
H²   Harley 7578, British Museum.
Ht   Hatton 73, Bodleian.
L   Lambeth Palace Library, No. 344.
M   Pepys 2553 (the "Maitland Folio MS.") Magdalene College, Cambridge.
R¹   Trinity College, Cambridge, R. 3. 20.
R²   Trinity College, Cambridge, R. 3. 21 (two identical copies of the *Envoy* only).
R³   Trinity College, Cambridge, R. 14. 51.
Th   Thynne's edition (1532).

Nine of the MS. copies (A B C F H¹ H² Ht R¹ R³) and Thynne's edition have been published by the Chaucer Society. For the text of L see H. W. MacCracken, MLN, XXIII, 214. M was printed in Ancient Scottish Poems, ed. J. Pinkerton, London, 1786. Like B it contains Scottish dialect features. The copies of the *Envoy* in R² were printed by MacCracken in the article just cited. The last three stanzas occur in D and have been printed by R. Brotanek, Mittelenglische Dichtungen aus der Handschrift 432, etc. (Halle, 1940) and G. B. Pace in MLN, LXIII, 460–1. Co is preserved in a transcript made by William Thomas in 1721. It is printed by Pace in Spec., XXVI, 306–7. For a full account of the authorities and a thorough study of their classification see again Pace, Studies in Bibliography, IV, 105 ff. His text, which is based upon C, differs very slightly from that of the present editor, who also accepted the superior authority of the group to which C belongs.

5 *lyk(e)* A C F H² B M Th; *oon* H¹ H L R¹; *els* R³. Rubric. *Lenvoye to Kyng Richard* R³; rest (L) *envoy(e)*.
28 *wed* A C F H² R³; *drive* H¹ R² Ht L R¹; *bring* B; *leid* M.

The Complaint of Venus

Authorities: eight MS. copies (one fragmentary) and the editions of Julian Notary and Thynne (Th). The nine copies available in the Chaucer Society prints are classified as follows:

α { A   Ashmole 59, Bodleian.
{ R   Trinity College, Cambridge, R. 3. 20.

β { F   Fairfax 16, Bodleian.
{ T   Tanner 346, Bodleian.

{ Ff   Cambridge University Library Ff. 1. 6.
{ N   Julian Notary's edition, 1499–1501.
{ Pb   Pepys 2006 (Hand B), Magdalene College, Cambridge.
γ {
{ Pe   Pepys 2006 (Hand E), Magdalene College, Cambridge (ll. 45–82 only).
{ S   Arch. Selden B. 24, Bodleian.

Th (which often agrees with β) is available in Skeat's facsimile. Group β offers the best text, and F is adopted as the basis of the present edition. Group α, which is preferred by Heath, appears to the present editor to be inferior both verbally and orthographically to the Fairfax MS.

5 *on* F Ff S only; but it prevents hiatus.
8 *For (Sith) he is croppe and roote of gentylesse* α.
15 *assure* F Ff S N; *ensure* α T Pb.
22 *oght(e) I blesse wel* β; *oght I wel (to) blesse* Ff S N; *ought I blesse* Pb; *aught me wel to blesse* α.
27 *fasten* β; rest *fastyng* (perhaps correctly).
30 *often* β Ff N Pb; *ofttymes* R; *oft tyme* S; *offt sythes* A. *hew(e)* α S Pb; rest *visage*.
31 *Pley(e)* all copies; but Fr. "Plaindre" (see explanatory notes).
63 *wil I not* β; *wold(e) (I) not* γ; *ne shal I never* α.
71 *lay] this lay* all exc. N.
73 *Pryncess* α; *Prynces* βγ.
81 Skeat proposes for the meter: *To folowe in word the curiositee.*

Lenvoy de Chaucer a Scogan

Authorities: three MSS.: Gg 4. 27 (Gg) of the Cambridge University Library, Fairfax 16 (F) of the Bodleian, and Pepys 2006 (P) of Magdalene College, Cambridge; and the editions of Caxton, 1477–78 (Cx), first three stanzas only, and of Thynne, 1532 (Th). The first four copies have been printed by the Chaucer Society; Th is available in Skeat's facsimile edition. There is no clear evidence for a classification of the MSS. Cx and Th correspond most nearly to P. The three MSS. are of about equal value; F is taken as the basis of the present text.

15 *the goddes] this goddis* F only.
16 *rekelnesse* F Th; *rek(e)lesnes(se)* Gg P Cx; probably for *rakelnesse.*
28 *him* F Gg Th; *hem* P (possibly correctly, referring to the arrows).

Lenvoy de Chaucer a Bukton

Authorities: MS. Fairfax 16 (F), Bodleian, Julian Notary's edition, 1499–1501 (N), and Thynne's edition, 1532 (Th), all printed by the Chaucer Society. The text is practically the same in all three. MS. F is the basis of the present edition.

In N the poem has the following superscription: *Here foloweth the counceyll of Chaucer touchyng Maryag &c. whiche was sente to Bucketon &c.*

20 *wives] wifes* F. *these* F Th; *the* N.
27 *Unwys] Unwyse* all copies. The final *-e* is perhaps correct; cf. the Mod. Eng. pronunciation.

The Complaint of Chaucer to his Purse

Authorities: eleven MSS. and the editions of Caxton and Thynne (Th). The variations are slight and the classification of the texts is therefore uncertain. Their relations have been examined most fully by Professor G. B. Pace, The Text of Chaucer's Purse, Papers of the Bibliographical Society of the Univ. of Virginia, I, 105 ff., and Otho A. XVIII, Spec., XXVI, 306 f. He classifies the copies in three groups as follows:

{ F   Fairfax 16, Bodleian.
{ Ff   Camb. Univ. Library Ff. 1. 6.

{ A   Additional 22139, Brit. Museum.
{ CC₁   MS. 176, Gonville and Caius College, Cambridge.
{ P   Pepys 2006, Magdalene College, Cambridge.
{ Cx   Caxton's *Anel. and Arcite.*

{ H²   Harley 7333, Brit. Museum.
{ CC₂   MS. 176, Gonville and Caius College, Cambridge.
{ H   Harley 2251, Brit. Museum.
{ M   MS. 4, Morgan Library.
{ A²   Additional 34360, Brit. Museum.
{ Co   Cotton Otho A. XVIII.

Mr. Pace's tree (on p. 107) exhibits in more detail the relations he has worked out. He gives a table of variant readings (pp. 120–121), also full references to earlier discussions of the text.

In the present edition, as in the Globe, the text is based upon MS. F. Brusendorff (pp. 253 f.) gave the preference to A¹. He also preferred the French title, *La Complainte de Chaucer à sa Bourse Voide,* which occurs in P. Professor Pace bases his text on Ff, which is closely related to F.

7, 14, 21 *Be(e)th* F Ff H H²; *Be* A P Cx Th.
25 *oure harmes* H¹ Ff; *harmes* P Cx Th; *myn harme* F.

Short Poems of Doubtful Authorship

Against Women Unconstant

Authorities: three MSS. and Stowe's edition, 1561. They are apparently related as follows:

α   F Fairfax 16, Bodleian.

β {   H Harley 7578, British Museum.
     γ {   C Cotton Cleopatra D. vii, British Museum.
           St Stowe's edition, 1561.

The copy in C is printed by the Chaucer Society; variants from the other copies are registered by Skeat (Oxf. Chau., I, pp. 409 f.) and the Globe editor. Type α is superior; the C text has here been corrected by comparison with it.

Title. From St: *A Balade which Chaucer made agaynst woman unconstaunt.*
4 *have lyves* F; *to lyve have* C St; *have lyne and* H.
6 *ay so* F; *ay* St; *ever so* H C.
8 *nothing* F; *rest that nothing.*
16 *Bet* eds. em. for MSS. *Better.*
17 *stant*] MSS. *stondeth.*

Complaynt d'Amours

Authorities: three MSS., Harley 7333, British Museum (H), Fairfax 16, Bodleian (F), and Bodley 638, Bodleian (B). None of these copies has been printed exactly, but Skeat (Oxf. Chau., I, 411 ff.) gives a text based upon H and records numerous variants of F and B. The Globe edition also used H as a basis. F and B are, as usual, in close agreement. Their readings appear to be on the whole inferior to those of H, but occasionally deserve the preference. The spelling of H (probably written by Shirley or copied from him) is bad and has been normalized here, as also by Skeat and the Globe editor.

4 *right thus*] so F B; *right* om. H, Skeat, Globe.
9 *Nay* em. Koch; *Ne* MSS.; [*For*] Skeat.
14 *best*] so H; om. F B.
24 *sing(e)* F B; *say* H.
25–28 F is incomplete and B corrupt.
45 *oon* H; *a* F B.
47 *But* MSS.; *But* [*why*] Skeat.
55 *so* H; *all(e)* F B.
66 *sorwes* F B; *shoures* H.
69 *unkonnynge* F B; *unknowynge* H.
70 *word*] Skeat, Globe *worde,* an unlikely form.

Read [*un*]*to?* Without some emendation the line is defective.
76 So H; *on yow have pleyned* F B.
82 *Alwey in oon* F B; *And I ay oon* H.
86 *foughel* H; *foule* B; *soule* F; Skeat *foul* (monosyllabic, as regularly in Chaucer), supplying [*ther*].
90 *evermore* MSS.; [*for*] *evermore* Skeat, Koch.

Merciles Beaute

Authority: a single copy in MS. Pepys 2006, Magdalene College, Cambridge, printed by the Chaucer Society. The repeated lines are not written out in full in the MS.

1 *Youre yen two*] *Yowre two yen* MS. But in ll. 6 and 11 it reads *Youre yen &c.,* and the line is quoted in the form *Your eyen two* in the poem To my Soverain Lady, attributed to Lydgate. (See Skeat, Oxf. Chau., VII, 281.)
28 Skeat suggested (MLQ, II, no. 5, p. 38) the omission of *in* for the sake of the meter. Then he interpreted *prison* as "prisoner," an established Mid. Eng. meaning of the word, but one for which authority is lacking in Chaucer.
30 *this and that* MS.; Skeat, Globe read *this or that* (without comment).
36 [*ther*] Skeat em.; *this* MS.

A Ballade of Complaint

Authority: a single MS., British Museum Additional 16165, written by Shirley. It was first printed by Skeat in Academy, XXXIII, 292. Except for the spelling, which is regularized here, as by previous editors, the copy appears to be correct.

Proverbs

Authorities: three MSS., printed by the Chaucer Society, which fall into two groups, as follows:

α {   F Fairfax 16, Bodleian.
     H Harley 7578, British Museum.

β   A Additional 16165, British Museum (written by Shirley).

F is taken as the basis of the present text.

A Treatise on the Astrolabe

Authorities: twenty-five MSS., complete or fragmentary, of which twenty-two are listed by Skeat, and on the basis of the order of the sections the majority are classified by him in two main groups, as follows. The sigla are those employed in the first edition of the present work and used in the variant readings recorded below. But for convenience of comparison those employed in later studies have been added in parentheses.

α
Dd¹	Cambridge University Library Dd. 3. 53. (A)
Dd²	Cambridge University Library Dd. 12. 51. (P)
Cp	Corpus Christi College, Cambridge, 424. (F)
R	Trinity College, Cambridge, R. 15. 18. (G)
M¹	E Museo 54, Bodleian. (B)
A¹	Ashmole 391, Bodleian. (D)
Bl¹	Bodley 619, Bodleian. (E)
Rl¹	Rawlinson Misc. 1370 (now Rawlinson D-913), Bodleian. (C)

β
J	St. John's College, Cambridge, E. 2. (M)
A²	Ashmole 360, Bodleian. (O)
Dg	Digby 72, Bodleian. (N)
Rl²	Rawlinson Misc. 3 (now Rawlinson D-3), Bodleian. (K)
Add¹	Additional 23002, British Museum. (L)
Eg	Egerton 2622, British Museum. (R)
Sl¹	Sloane 261, British Museum. (I)
Sl²	Sloane 314, British Museum. (H)

Skeat left unclassified:

M²	E Museo 116, Bodleian. (W)
A³	Ashmole 393, Bodleian. (Q)
Bl²	Bodley 68, Bodleian. (U)
Add²	Additional 29250, British Museum. (S)
Ph	Phillipps 11955, Cheltenham; now in Library of Institute of Electrical Engineers, London. (T)
Brus	Brussels 1591. (X)

To these should be added:

Pl	Plimpton, now in Columbia University Library. (Pl)
Pen	Penrose, now owned by Mr. Boies Penrose, Philadelphia. (Y)
Harv	Harvard University Library. (Z)

Miss Hammond (p. 359) notes that Bernard's *Catalogus* mentions a Hatton MS. which does not appear in Skeat's list. If such a copy ever existed, it has not been identified. MS. Pl was in the library of the Earl of Ashburnham (Appendix No. CXXIII) and was once the property of Sir Kenelm Digby. It was acquired by Mr. G. A. Plimpton of New York, who gave it to the Columbia University Library. It contains diagrams of eclipses for 1417–33, and is probably to be dated in that period. The editio princeps of Thynne (Th) falls with group β; Brae's edition (Br, London, 1870) followed three MSS. of the same group (Add¹ Sl¹ Sl²). Since the publication of the first edition of the present work there has appeared an important comprehensive study of the manuscripts of the *Astrolabe* by P. Pintelon, *Chaucer's Treatise of the Astrolabe*

(posthumously printed, Antwerp, 1940). It contains a photographic reproduction of the Brussels MS., a tabulation of the order of conclusions in twenty-two MSS., and a list of the variant readings of the *Prologue* in seventeen MSS. Pintelon's study confirms Skeat's main division of the MSS. into two classes, and on the basis of his additional evidence he makes a further classification of the MSS. within each group. He also gives useful orthographical and grammatical notes on the text of MS. Brus. The Penrose and Harvard MSS. were unknown to Pintelon, but they have been carefully examined by Mr. Derek J. Price, and his reports on them have been made available to the present editor. The former is in a letter to Mr. Penrose and the latter in a statement which came to the Harvard Library with the MS., which was recently acquired as a gift of Mr. David Wheatland of Cambridge. In Mr. Price's opinion both MSS. Penrose and Harvard occupy a peculiar position in the *stammbaum*, perhaps representing a missing link between the two main groups.

Skeat's edition (Chau. Soc., 1872; Oxf. Chau., III) is based upon Dd¹, with which M¹ is in close agreement. Professor Liddell, in the Globe edition, made a further classification of five MSS. of Group α, and adopted Bl¹ as the basis of his text. The present editor has based his text upon a photograph of Bl¹, which he has compared throughout with readings of Dd¹ as recorded by Skeat, and with the β readings as represented in the editions of Thynne and Brae. For the introduction comparison has also been made with Mone's print of the *Proheme* from the Brussels MS. (QF, I, 550 f.); and for § 39 of Part ii use has been made of the version of Rl¹ printed by Skeat (Ch. Soc., pp. 68 f.; Oxf. Chau., III, 237 f.). Through the kindness of Mr. Plimpton his MS., while still in his hands, was collated by the editor, and many of its readings are noted below. Mr. Penrose has also kindly placed his MS. at the disposal of the editor, and variant readings from it and from the Harvard MS. are added in the second edition. Account has also been taken of the numerous variant readings recorded by Brae, Skeat, and Liddell.

It should be added that in some MSS. of both Chaucer and Messahala the text is accompanied by valuable illustrative drawings. MS. Dd¹ has a particularly fine series of over sixty, which may well correspond to illustrations in Chaucer's original copy. For reproductions see R. C. Gunther, *Chaucer and Messahalla on the Astrolabe*, Oxford, 1929 (Vol. V of Early Science at Oxford), and *The Astrolabes of the World* (Oxford, 1932). Mr. Gunther also gives collotype facsimiles of the Latin text of Messahala's treatise, with the accompanying drawings.

Pintelon's edition of the Brussels text contains a full list of variants from seventeen MSS. for the Prologue (ll. 1–65 of the present edition). For the main body of the treatise Pintelon cites numerous variants from MSS. Dd. 3. 53 and Rawl. D-913.

Title: *Tractatus de Conclusionibus Astrolabii* Dd¹ (colophon); *Tractatus Astrolabii* Cp; *The conclusions of the Astrolabie* Th; *The Conclusiouns of the Astrolabie compyled by Geoffry Chaucer newlye amendyd* Sl¹. Pl has none, but at the end *Explicit tractatus Astrolabij. Heere begynneth the tretyyce* [?] *of the declaracioun up on the conclusions of the Astrolabie,* Harv.; no title in Pen. A distinct title *Brede and milke for children* is found in Bl¹ Bl² M¹.

Prologue

1   Harv has the reading (not recorded by Pintelon): *Certayn evydences my lytel sone lewes have do me to understande thyne abylte.*

6   *a*] *the* Pen Harv; *wrappith* Harv. Brussels MS. alone has *lappeth* (Pintelon); *frend*] *frend hond* Pen.

18   *eny* Harv; *eche* Pen.

25 f.   *divided*] *is divided* Harv Pen; *under full*] *wondirful* Harv.

40   *folk*] *folkys* Harv.

41   *mekely … persone*] *every meke persone devouteliche* Pen.

48   *unto a child*] *to a lernere* Harv.

56   *preie* so Harv and Pen (omitting *we*, which follows in Brus.); *the king* om. Pen.

57   *these langagis,* Harv.

58   *obeieth, everich*] *to hym obeyeth, ech* Pen; *obedience, everich* Harv.

61   *engyn*] so Pen; *wyt* Harv.

64   *And … envie*] om. Pen; *swerd*] *swerd only* Harv.

70   *worken*] *to know* Pen.

73   *wel ye vote and every astrologien* Pen.

75 f.   *as in subtile tables calculed for a cause*] *as bethe calclyd in tables of Astronomy as Mynutis secundis tercies* [?] *quartes and othir* Pen.

84   *kalenders*] *kalendere* Harv.

85 f.   *Somyr and Lynne* Pen; *frere Jon Som. and frere H lynne* Harv.

107   *notefull*] *nedfull* Pen.

108   *the Maide*] *Mary* Harv, *the blessid mayd* Pen.

Part I

§ 1, 5   *the rewle* Bl¹ Pl Th Br Harv; *thy rewle* Dd¹; *this reule* Pen.

§ 3, 1   *thikkest* Bl¹ Dd¹ M¹; *the thikkest(e)* J Pl Harv (and Rl¹ margin) Th. Here, and frequently afterwards, Dd¹ adds *And for the more declaracioun, lo here thy* (or *the*) *figure.*

The following spurious sentence precedes § 3 in A² Add¹ Sl¹ Sl² Th, and is substituted for § 3 in Br Pen: *The moder of thyn Astrolabye is thickest by the brinkes, that is the utmoste rynge with degrees; and al the myddle within the rynge shal be thinner, to receyve the plates for dyvers clymates, and also for the rethe, that is shape in maner of a nette, or els after the webbe of a loppe.*

§ 5, 7   *centre* Rl¹ Rl² Pl Harv; *hool* Bl¹; *oriental* A¹; Bl² Brae's MSS. Th; + M¹ Dd¹; (*centre* was conjectured by Br).

§ 10, 6   *were clepid thus* Bl¹ Pen; *were cleped in Arabiens* Dd¹; *were yeven* Rl¹ Pl Harv; *ben consideryd* A¹ Rl²; *taken* (*t*)*her names* Th Br.

7   *lordes Arabiens* Bl¹; *clerkys Arabiens* Rl² A¹ (var.); *Arabiens* Bl² A² Pen; *Emperours* Pl Th Br Harv; *lordes* Dd¹.

21   Bl¹ contains a Latin note correcting Chaucer's statement.

§ 12, 7 ff.   *Umbra Recta* and *Umbra Versa* are er-

roneously interchanged here in the MSS. (exc. Sl¹), either by Chaucer or by an early scribe. Sl² has the error corrected in the margin.

§ 17, 2   *3 principal* Rl¹ Pl Harv Pen; *3 tropical* M¹ Dd¹; *tropik* Bl¹; *three* J Th Br.

36   *gurdel of the first moeving, or ellis of the first moevable* Bl¹; *girdel of the firste moeving, or elles of the angulus primi motus vel primi mobilis* Dd¹; *girdil of the first* Pl; *midway of the firste mevynge or els of the sonne* Th Br; *the gerdil of the fyrste moving or ellis of the sonne* Harv; om. Pen.

39   The figure *8* here seems to be an error for *9.* Perhaps [*ninthe*] should be inserted before *spere* in l. 47. Sacrobosco supports both corrections.

§ 21, 16   Bl¹ inserts after *Aldeberan* the words *Menkar Algevze* (*Algenze*?) *cor Leonis* and notes that they are found on the Merton College astrolabe.

78   *8 speer* here, as in § 17, 43 above, apparently a mistake for *9 speer.*

85   *streight* Bl¹ Th Br; *strait* Pl; *streit* Dd¹.

Part II

Skeat prints from J Latin headings to the propositions.

§ 1, 10   *knowe* Bl¹ Dd¹ Pl; *knew* A² Bl² Th Br.

15   *knowe* Bl¹ Dd¹ Pl; *knew* Bl² Rl² Th Br.

Between § 2 and § 3 a spurious short section, which merely repeats § 1, is inserted in late MSS. and in Th Br.

§ 3, 37   Bl¹ inserts after *ascendent* the following long note, which corresponds to Messahala's paragraph "De noticia stellarum incognitarum positarum in astrolabio" (Skeat, Chau. Soc. edn., p. 98): *Nota. That by this conclusioun thou may knowe also where ben at that same tyme alle othir sterres fixed that ben sette in thin Astrelabie, and in what place of the firmament; and also her arising in thy orizonte, and how longe that thei wol ben above the erthe with the Arke of the nyght. And loke evermore how many degrees thou fynde eny sterre at that tyme sitting upon thin Almycanteras, and upon as many degrees sette thou the reule upon the altitude in the bordere; and by the mediacioun of thy eye thorugh the 2 smale holes shalt thou se the same sterre by the same altitude aforseid. And so by this conclusioun may thou redely knowe which is oo sterre from a nother in the firmament, for as many as ben in the Astrelabie. For by that same altitude shal thou se that same sterre, & non othir, for there ne woll non othir altitude accorde therto* (Skeat, Chau. Soc. edn., p. 81; Oxf. Chau., III, 360 f.).

45, 47   *12 degrees* Bl¹ M¹ Dd¹ (corrected to *18*); *18 degrees* Pl A² Th Br Rl¹ (added in a later hand, in l. 52, Liddell) Harv.

55   *9 of the clokke* Bl¹ M¹; *8* (altered from *9*) Dd¹ Pl Sl¹; *5* Rl¹; *7* A² Bl² Rl² Th Br Harv.

10 degrees Bl¹ M¹; *2 degrees* Dd¹ (altered from *10* Rl¹ Pl Harv; *11 degrees* A² Bl² Rl² Th Br.

57   *10 degrees of Scorpius* Bl¹; *23 degrees of Libra* (corrected from *10 degrees of Taurus*) Dd¹; *20 degrees of Libra* Rl¹ Th Br Harv; *10 degrees of Taurus* M¹.

§ 4, 11–14   *degre than hath … which that is the* Bl¹ only.

25   *25 degres*] all MSS. *15 degrees* (Pl. om. figures entirely); but Brae cites Ptolemy's Tetrabiblos iii, 12: "viginti quinque."

§ 5, 4   *by 3 and 3*] so Dd² Pl; *by 2 and 2* Bl¹ Rl¹ Rl² Dd¹ R; *by 2* A² Th Br; left blank in M¹.

§ 10, 7   *30* Bl[1] Dd[1] Pl Br; *360 degrees* A[2] Bl[2] Rl[1] Rl[2] Sl[1] Th.

§ 11, 15   *ariste*] *arysing* Th Br Harv Pen; *rysinge* Pl; *arise* Bl[1] Dd[1] (difficult to construe; perhaps subj. For the emendation *arist* cf. § 12, 16).

§ 13–18 follow § 21 in many authorities (namely in those of Liddell's Group γ: A[2] Eg M[2] Add[1] Bl[2] Rl[2] Th Br).

§ 17 Rubric: Add[1] Sl[1] Sl[2] A[2] Th read *latitude*; J has *latitudinem*; Br. em. *altitude*. But *longitude*, as in Bl[1] Dd[1] Pl Harv Pen is clearly right.

9 *cacche* Bl[1] Th Br Harv Pen; *hath* Dd[1] M[1]; *take* A[2] Pl; *sett* Bl[2].

36 *(the) site* Bl[1] Dd[1]; *the syght* Rl[2] Pl Th Br; *that it sytteth* A[2] Bl[2]; *that it sit* Harv; *that he sit* Pen.

39 *site* Bl[1] Dd[1] Pen; *syght* Rl[2] Pl Th Br; *syttyng* A[2] Harv.

§ 19 Rubric: *his dwelling* Bl[1] Dd[1] Pl Harv Pen; *his orizonte* Rl[2]; *the orizonte* Th Br; *ejus orizon* J.

§ 22 Rubric: *oure countre* Bl[1] Dd[1] Harv; *the countre* M[1]; *oure centre* Rl[2] Pl Th Br Pen; *nostri centri* J.

18 *place* Bl[1] Dd[1] Sl[1] Br Pen; *planete* M[1] A[2] Bl[2] Sl[2] Add[1] Rl[1] Rl[2] Th; *planete place* Pl; om. Harv.

§ 23, 28 ff.   This example is adapted to the latitude of Oxford in Bl[1] Dd[1]. The rest (Liddell's Group β: Rl[1] Dd[2] γ) have a set of observations yielding a latitude about that of Rome. *56 . . . 48*] *62 . . . 21* Pl Th Harv Pen; *32 . . . 21* Br.

§ 25, 23 ff.   Bl[1] A[2] Bl[2] Pen (but not Harv) insert *and 25 minutes* after *38 degrees* and read (with minor variants) *so leveth there 51 degrees and 50 minutes that is the latitude*. This is an evident attempt, says Liddell, to make the problem fit the latitude of Oxford exactly; but the following sentence implies that the calculation was only rough.

27 *as thou might preve* om. A[1] A[2] Rl[1] Rl[2] Dd[2] Th Br Harv; *as y might prove* Dd[1]; *thow might preve the same* Bl[1] Pen; *thow might preve the* M[1].

39 ff.   The text follows Bl[1] (which, however, reads *17* for *10*) M[1] Dd[1]. Acc. to Liddell the remaining MSS. (his Group β, including also Pl), except for some contamination, read *10 degrees of Leo almost 56 of height at noon . . . declinacioun . . . 18 . . .; abate . . . 18 than leveth 38.*

§ 26, 11–16 *Ferther-over . . . right orizonte* om. Dd[1] Pl Th Br Harv Pen and "nearly all the MSS." (Skeat)

§ 28, 32 *end* Bl[2] Harv and (apparently) Brae's MSS.; others *heved, heed*, etc.; So Pen.

§ 30 Rubric: *altitude*] *latitude* Bl[1] Harv Pen.

17 Liddell's Group β (including Pl) adds *for on the morowe wyl the sonne be on another degre*, etc.; also in Harv Pen.

§ 33, 3 *Azimut(z)* Bl[1] Dd[1] M[1] Rl[1] Harv Pen; *minute(s)* Dd[2] Pl Th Br.

After § 36 the MSS. vary. The text follows Bl[1] Dd[1], with which M[1] Rl[1] agree. Rl[2] ends with § 35, Bl[2] with § 36. Other (late) MSS. insert a number of spurious conclusions either between § 35 and § 36 or after § 40.

§ 37, 14 *by thy label lith in the zodiak* Bl[1]; *by thy label in which degree of the zodiak* Dd[1] (Sk. adds *is*); *by thi (the) label in the zodiake* Pl Th Br; *and be thy zodiak* Harv Pen.

§ 38, 12 *fro the centre amiddes* Bl[1]; *fro the centre* Dd[1]; *fro thi pin* Pl; *fro the pyn* Rl[1] Add[1] Sl[2] Th Pen (propositions 38–41 not in Harv); om. Sl[1] Br.

30 ff   *than the nadir of the south lyne is the north lyne* Dd[1]; *than is the south lyne the north* Bl[1]; *the oppositife that is southe and northe* Th Br; om. Pen.

After § 38 Bl[1], which closely resembles Dd[1] M[1], becomes very inaccurate. § 39 is corrected in the text by the aid of Rl[1], which Skeat prints in full.

§ 39, 26 f.   *I-like distaunte fro the equinoxial* Rl[1]; *ilike distant fro the lyne meridional* Bl[1]; *y-lyke distant by-twene them alle* Dd[1]; whole sentence om. Pl Th Br Pen. Sacrobosco reads: "Longitudo autem climatis potest appellari linea ducta ab oriente in occidentem aeque distans ab aequinoctiali" (Venice, 1478, fol. d 4 recto).

30 *evene direct ageyns the pool artyke* Rl[1] Dd[2] Pl Th Br Pen; *evene directe ageyns from north to south* Bl[1] Dd[1] M[1]; Sacrobosco "versus polum arcticum" (fol. d 3 verso).

§ 40, 9 ff.   The figures in the text follow Dd[1]. Bl[1] makes the longitude of Venus 1° of Capricorn and its latitude 4° north, and then concludes that it ascends with 8° of Capricorn — an impossible result. In Pl Rl[1] Th Br Pen the figures are not filled in, but Brae gives them (from Sl[1]) in footnotes.

41 *2 degrees*] the number, om. in MSS., is supplied by Skeat.

42 *6 degree in* Dd[1]; *8 degre fro* Bl[1]; figure om. Pl Th Br Pen.

51 ff.   Bl[1] makes the latitude of Jupiter 2° south and its ascendant the 8° of Pisces; Dd[1], 3° south and 14° of Pisces. Either of these computations works out roughly with the globe. Sl[1] inserts *3* for the latitude and *6* for the ascendant. Pen om. figures.

75 Pen stops after *as I first seyd*.

79 *hir longitude* Pl Th Br; *his* Bl[1] Dd[1] M[1] Rl[1].

82 *thou shalt do wel ynow(e)* Pl Dd[2] J Th Br; om. most of the best MSS., which stop short with *houre —*. In Bl[1] § 46 follows in the next line.

Supplementary Propositions

The sections which follow are lacking in the best MSS. (exc. § 46, found in Bl[1]), and are of doubtful authenticity. The text of §§ 41–43 follows J (as printed by Skeat), compared with Th Br. Pl has §§ 41–43, but with figures corrupt. A few variants from other MSS. are recorded by Skeat, §§ 44, 45 follow Dg (as printed by Skeat); § 46 follows Bl[1], corrected by the aid of such variants as Skeat notes. The spelling in all six propositions has been somewhat normalized. Five other sections, generally recognized as spurious, are printed by Brae (pp. 60 ff.) and by Skeat (Chau. Soc. edn., pp. 57 ff.; Oxf. Chau., III, 230 ff.) and numbered 41a, 41b, 42a, 43a, 42b.

§ 42, 18 f.   *10 is . . . 10 feet* so Th (corrupt) Br; om. J; supplied by Skeat from Add[1] Dg Dd[2] Eg.

21 ff.   The figures are badly confused in the MSS. Thus, in ll. 23 f. J has *6* for *2* and *4* for *3*, and in ll. 25 f. interchanges *2* and *6* and omits *and 2 is 4 parties of 12*. Several modes of emendation might be adopted, but the reading of the text, proposed by Skeat, is simplest and best.

§ 44, 15 f.   *or what . . . or* om. Dg J; supplied by Skeat from A[2] Add[1].

18 *wryt*] Skeat's em. (*wryte*) for *wreten* Dg.

32 *lasse*] Skeat's em. for *passid* Add[1] Dg A[2]; om. J.

The Romaunt of the Rose

Authorities: MS. V. 3. 7 in the Hunterian Museum, Glasgow (G), edited by Kaluza, Chaucer Society, 1891, and Thynne's edition of 1532 (Th), accessible in Skeat's facsimile edition and in the Chaucer Society reprint (1911). The two authorities are independent, but closely similar. The present text is based upon G, completed and corrected by Th. Some eleven leaves appear to have been lost from G. The spelling in the text is corrected to conform to grammatical standards. In particular, the numerous ungrammatical final -*e*'s have been removed. But in view of the doubtful authorship of the poem strict Chaucerian usage has not been restored. Although final -*e*'s may not have been pronounced in rime in Fragments B and C, they have not been removed if they are etymologically justified in both rime-words of a couplet. Apart from inflectional adjustments the orthography of G has been allowed to stand, even where Thynne's edition has spellings more nearly in accord with those of most Chaucer MSS. For the same reason the editor has very sparingly adopted emendations to improve the meter. Many lines are easy to mend, as Skeat and other editors have done, by supplying words or changing their order. But in verse that is either non-Chaucerian or the work of Chaucer's youth it is hardly justifiable to introduce the smoothness of his later technique.

No record will ordinarily be made here of cases where missing words are supplied from Th, or of obvious corrections of the text. Instances of the latter (such as *falle*: *calle* for *fal*: *cal*, ll. 13, 14) are numerous, and most of them have been made in earlier editions. Attention will be called, however, to doubtful readings and noteworthy emendations, whether adopted or rejected. Many readings common to several modern editions are simply credited to "eds.," without any attempt to trace the history of the emendations.

Citations of the French original are made from Langlois's edition (SATF, 1914–24), except where other readings seem better to explain the English. The English text, as Langlois remarks, for the most part follows the French so closely that it ought to be possible to identify the translator's French MS., if it is still in existence. But Langlois himself does not furnish, either in his treatise on Les Manuscrits du Roman de la Rose (Lille, 1910) or in his edition, enough data to fix with certainty even the place of the MS. in his classification. Kaluza printed Michel's French text in parallel columns with the English, substituting for many of Michel's readings variants which corresponded more closely to the translation. Of the readings in which the English is there shown to depart from Michel a large number are not registered at all by Langlois; others have been adopted in his critical text; and many others occur in more than a single group of MSS. The group most often concerned, especially in the earlier part of the translation, is that designated by Langlois as L. In Fragment C, Group F is frequently a possible source. Of the variants recorded by Kaluza, it may be further noted, the proportionate number differs considerably in the different fragments. These facts suggest that the fragments were based upon different MSS., and to that extent support the prevalent opinion that they were the work of different translators. But it is of course possible that a single MS., like many of those examined by Langlois, was the product of contamination.

For textual notes and emendations by Professor Lange, see Angl., XXXV, 338 ff.; XXXVI, 479 ff., XXXVII, 146 ff.

1–44 From Th; om. G.

4 *that false ne bene* Th; *ne false been* Skeat; Globe suggests *to falseen ben*; Fr. "mençongier."

6 *warraunt*] Skeat *waraunte* (: *apparaunte*), perhaps correctly.

22 *cariage* Globe; *corage* Th; Fr. "paage" (= "toll").

37 [*the*] inserted for meter; Globe [*wil I*]; Fr. "je vueil."

66 *hath*] *had* G Th.

103 *lefe* Th; *swete* G; Globe suggests *newe*; Fr. "novele." The reading *leve is* would make the best rime (: *slevis*). But the weak adjective is not natural.

138 *enclosed was* G Th; Skeat *enclos it was* (cf. l. 1652).

149 *moveresse* eds.; *Mynoresse* G Th; Fr. "moverresse."

196 *myscounting* eds.; *myscoveiting* G Th; Fr. "mesconter."

211 *fade* Globe; Fr. "maigre"; *sad(d)e* G Th.

240 [*doun*] supplied by eds.; Globe suggests *hengde*.

248 *peynted* G Th; Skeat *peynt*.

256 Skeat inserts [*ful*] and Urry *right* for meter. *Than*] Globe *That*; Fr. "Ice."

275 [*wo*] om. G Th; supplied from Fr. "duel."

277 *so brekith*] Skeat *to-breketh*.

298 *se*] eds. *yse*, perhaps correctly. Cf. l. 1401.

299 *fair or worthi*] *fairer or worthier* G.

307 Skeat [*as*] *of lenesse*.

333–380 From Th; om. G.

379 [*er*] eds.; Fr. "ainz"; Th om.

401 *in*] *in* [*with*] Skeat; *within* Urry.

442 *ay(e)* G Th; Skeat [*shal*] (to correspond with Fr.).

444 *face*] *grace* G Th; Fr. "vis."

451 *wolde* G; *holde* Th, perhaps correctly.

483 [*y*]*wrought*] *wrought* G Th.

485 *laddre*] *laddris* G; *ladders* Th; Fr. "eschiele."

501 *nolde*] *wolde* G Th; but the correction seems necessary.

505 *god kepe it fro care* G Th; Skeat *god* [*it kepe and were*], Lange *God* [*it kepe fro were*], to obtain a Chaucerian rime.

516 [*o*]-*where* Skeat; *where* G Th; Globe suggests *there*; Kaluza suggests *any where*.

520 *Ful*] *For* G Th; Fr. "mout"; Globe *For-wo*, "very weary." On *for-* as a prefix see *KnT*, I, 2142, n.

532 [*so*] *fetys* eds., perhaps correctly.

535 *and oft*] *al* Th; *and of* G; Fr. "par maintes foiz escoutai."

567 [*in honde*] supplied by eds.; Fr. "en sa main."

586 *mayde(n)* eds.; *may* G Th.

602 *Alexandryn*] *of Alexandryne* G Th, perhaps the English translator's mistake; Fr. "terre Alexandrins," var. "terre as Sarradins."

603 *be*] possibly to be omitted; Fr. "Fist . . . aporter."

645 *inne*] [*ther*]*inne* eds., perhaps rightly.

657 *places* G Th; Lange *place* (Angl., XXXVII, 161).

662 *and*] *and* [*of*] eds.

673 *wel* G; *me* Th; Fr. "bien." *whan* Th; *that* G; Globe *than*; Fr. "quant."

684 *clepe* G Th; Skeat *clepen*, perhaps correctly.

716 *iargonyng* Th; *yarkonyng* G.

720 *reverdye*] *reverye* G; *revelrye* Th; Fr. "reverdie."

749 *make*] *couthe make* G Th (*couthe* repeated from l. 747?); Globe om. *And.*

761 *made* G Th; eds. *make* (Fr. "faire"), perhaps correctly.

773 Skeat *henten* [*hem*]; Globe suggests *casten* and [*hem*] *hente.*

791 *bede* Skeat; *bode* G Th (apparently corrupt).

798 *to God* G Th; Skeat, Kaluza om. *to* for meter.

801 Globe *Come* [*here*]; Fr. "ça venez"; Skeat *Come* [*neer*].

861 Kaluza [*Broun and*] *bent*; Globe *hir* [*browne*] *browis*; Fr. "bruns et enarchiez."

865 *wot not . . . I shal descryve* G Th.

879 *and* G Th; Skeat om. and supplies [*to*] before *be.*

923 After *two* G Th have *full wel devysed*, which is not in Fr. and overloads the meter.

932 Eds. om. *ful*; Fr. "de bone (var. 'gente') facon."

959 *sheten*] *shoten* G Th; but cf. l. 989.

960 *right* G Th; Kaluza conjectures *nigh*; Fr. "de près."

978 *al* Globe; *as* G Th; Fr. "toute."

984 *on* G Th; Skeat *of.*

1007 *As*] *And* G Th; Fr. "Ausi come"; Skeat *As* [*was*].

1010 Skeat *as* [*is*].

1018 *wyndred*] so Skeat, to correspond with l. 1020; *wyntred* G Th.

1026 Kaluza *toucheth*; *thought* G Th; Skeat *thinketh*; Fr. "touche."

1031 *Sore* G Th; Fr. "Sade," var. "Sage"; reading doubtful. Skeat reads [*Wys*] and conjectures also *Queint* or *Fine.* Kaluza says "perhaps read *Sade.*"

1037 *word*] *werk* G Th; Fr. "par faiz ne par diz."

1043 *leste* Globe; *best*(*e*) G Th; Fr. "li graignor e li menor."

1058 *prik*(*k*)*e* Skeat, Kaluza; *prile* G; *prill* Th; Globe suggests *thrill*, perhaps correctly.

1063 *Han hyndred and ydon* Th; *An hundrid have do* G. The reading of the couplet is doubtful. Fr. "Mainz prodomes ont encusez Li losengier par lor losenges."

1065 *And make*] *And maketh* Th; *Have maad* G.

1080 *ameled*] *amyled* Th; *enameled* G.

1089 *durst*] Skeat [*thurfe*]. But for confusion of *dar* and *tharf* cf. ll. 1324, 3604.

1166 *craftely* Th; *tristely* G.

1188 *Sarsynesh*] *Sarlynys*(*s*)*h*(*e*) G Th; Fr. "sarrazinesche," var. "sarradinesche."

1231 *elles*] *ell* G; *al* Th.

1236 *a* G Th; Skeat *oo*, perhaps correctly.

1282 [*Youthe*] Ten Brink (Chaucer Studien, p. 30); *And she* G Th; Fr. "Jonece."

1303 *thus*] *that* G Th; Fr. "ensi."

1313 *loreres*] *loreyes* G; *laurelles* Th; Fr. "loriers."

1314 *olmeris* Th; *oliveris* G; Fr. "moriers"; Globe suggests that *olmeris* was due to "moriers" being read as "ormiers."

1315 *ended* Th; *eended* G, which Skeat prints *y-ended*, perhaps correctly.

1324 *durst* G Th; Skeat [*thurte*].

1334 *bad him bende it* eds.; *had*(*de*) *hym bent* G Th.

1341–42 *hadde me shette*: *mette* G; *had me shete*: *mete* Th; Skeat [*wol*] . . . *shete*, and in l. 1343 [*wol me greven*]. It is barely possible that *shete* is a strong past part. from *sheten*, though the normal form is *shote*(*n*).

1348 *in al*(*l*) *the gardyn* G Th; Kaluza proposes *al the yerde in*, which Skeat adopts. Cf. l. 1447.

1363 *alemandres* Skeat; *almandres* G Th; *almanderes* Globe; Fr. "alemandiers."

1365 *wexen* G; *weren* Th.

1369 *parys* G Th; Fr. "Graine de paradis," var. "parevis."

1387–1482 From Th; om. G.

1447 [*in*] supplied for the sense; Skeat, Kaluza read [*yerde in*], as in l. 1348.

1453 *shoten* Th; Skeat *shete*, perhaps correctly.

1534 *comfort*] *comforte* G Th (possibly infinitive, though more probably the noun).

1538 *For* G Th; Globe *Fro*; Fr. "de la meschine." Globe suggests further that the translator confused Fr. "guerredon" with "guerison" (*warisoun*).

1581 *flour*] *foule* G Th; Fr. "flors."

1593–94 *he* Skeat, Kaluza; *ye* G Th; Fr. "il."

1608 *lovyng* eds.; *laughyng* G Th; Fr. "d'amer."

1623 *briddes*] *bridde* G; *byrde* Th.

1644 *The vertu and* [*the*] *strengthe*] *The vertue*(*s*) *and strengthes* G Th.

1663 *be*] *me* G Th; Fr. "fusse."

1683 [*al*] supplied by Kaluza; Fr. "tuit."

1705 Sentence incomplete and rime (with l. 1706) imperfect. Various emendations are possible (*filde* for *dide*, *replete* (: *swete*) for *aboute*), but the usual view is that a second translator begins at this point. See the introduction to Explanatory Notes.

1713 *mych* G; perhaps (here and elsewhere) to be read *moch*(*e*), as in Th.

1733 [*a*] Globe; Kaluza [*that*].

1750 [*that*] Globe; *it* G; om. Th.

1766 *certeynly* Skeat, Kaluza; *certis evenly* G Th, perhaps correctly (= "certainly in equal measure"?).

1771 *a* Skeat; *this* Globe; *his* G Th.

1797–98 *feyne*: *peyne* G; *fyne*: *pyne* Th. Perhaps an imperfect rime (*fyne*: *peyne*).

1814 *felt*(*e*) Skeat, Globe; *lefte* G Th.

1848 *it mighte* Skeat, perhaps correctly; Globe suggests *nere* or *nerwe.*

1892 So Th; *That he hadde the body hole made* G (in later hand).

1913–14 Transposed in G Th.

1924 *softenyng*] *softyng* G Th.

1965 *love*] Skeat *lovers*, perhaps correctly.

1984 Written by a later hand on a line originally left blank.

2002 *of*] Skeat suggests *to.*

2006 *kysse* probably to be read *kesse* (Kentish) for the rime.

2024 *And also*] Globe em. *Nede is*, to complete the sense.

2038 Skeat suggests *quoint* for rime.

2067 *susprised* G Th, Globe; Skeat em. *surprised*, but the other form occurs, though rarely.
2074 Skeat supplies [*it*] before *turne*, perhaps correctly.
2076 *disseise*] *desese* G; *disese* Th; Fr. "dessaisir."
2092 *jowelles*] *jowel*(*l*) G Th.
2116 *degre*(*e*) G Th; eds. *gree*.
2141 [*erre*] supplied by Urry; om. G Th; Skeat [*sinne*]; Fr. "issir hors de voie."
2261 Eds. supply [*hem*], perhaps correctly.
2285 *Fard*] *Farce* G Th; Fr. "farde."
2294 *laughith*] *knowith* G Th; Fr. "rit."
2302 *pleyeth* Skeat, Globe; *pleyneth* G Th.
2326 *that*] Globe [*se*] *that*. But the hortatory *that*, like Fr. "que," is used in Middle English. Cf. *BD*, 206 and the textual note.
2333 *kan* Globe; *ben* G Th; Fr. "sot."
2336 *loves* eds.; *londes* G Th.
2341 *swich gift* eds.; *this swif*(*f*)*te* G Th; Globe suggests *After so riche gift*; Fr. "après si riche don."
2365 *Of* Globe; *For* G Th; Skeat *For trecherie,* [*in*] *sikernesse.*
2395–2442 From Th; om. G.
2413 *As*] *A* Th; Fr. "Ausi come."
2427 *sende*] *sene* Th; Fr. "enveier."
2473 *Thou* Kaluza; *Thought* G Th.
2497–99 Text apparently corrupt. Globe suggests [*though*] *thou . . . But* [*that*] (for *But yitt*) which corresponds pretty well with Fr.: "Car se tu n'en peüsses traire Fors solement un bel salu, Si t'eüst il cent mars valu." Skeat *But yif.*
2532 [*thy*] om. G Th; Fr. "ta."
2563 *a-bred*] *a brede* Th; *abrode* G.
2564 *forwerreyd*] *forweriede* G; *forwerede* Th.
2569 *seme* eds.; *se* G Th.
2592 *Fro* Globe; *The* G Th. Globe punctuates: *why nyl ye me socoure Fro joye?*
2617 *not* eds.; *wote not* G Th.
2621 *of*] *on* G Th; Fr. "de li uns regarz"; Skeat *A loke on* [*me*], perhaps correctly.
2628 *liggen* G Th; eds. *lye*, which is supported by rimes in ll. 2629, 2645.
2650 *weder* eds.; *whider* G Th.
2675 *whom* Skeat, Kaluza; *whan*(*ne*) G Th; Fr. "De qui," var. "De quoi."
2676 This departs from Fr.; Kaluza suggests *Thou kisse the dore er thou go away*; Fr. "Au departir (var. 'Au revenir') la porte baise."
2682 *wakyng* Globe; *walkyng* G Th; Fr. "veilliers."
2752 *yet* eds.; *that* G Th; Fr. "toutes-voies."
2775 *caccheth*] em. for *cacche* G Th; Skeat [*to*] *cacche*; Globe *hathe.*
2783 *bonde* Globe; *londe* G Th; Fr. "Iceste te garantira, Ne ja de toi ne partira."
2796 *Thenkyng* G Th; Skeat, Kaluza *Thought.*
2824 *ben*] *not ben* G Th; Fr. "seroies."
2833 [*hem*] *me* G Th; apparently an error anticipating l. 2845.
2917 *they* eds.; *thou* G Th.
2921 [*he*] supplied by Skeat.
2934 *the eyen* Globe; *they* G Th; Fr. "li ueil"; Skeat *they . . . that* [*that*].
2968 *hegge* G Th; Globe em. *haye* because this form occurs later. See ll. 2971, 2987, 3007.
2992 [*I be*] supplied by eds.; Globe *You warrante*

may [*I*], which is closer to Fr. "Je vos i puis bien garantir."
3029 [*no*] *good* Skeat; *good* [*ne*] Globe.
3035 Line apparently defective. Skeat supplies [*On lyve*]; perhaps read *Y-brought forth* (Urry).
3125 Before *growe* G Th have *late it*; eds. om. (probably repeated from l. 3124).
3127–28 The rime is doubtless to be read *wer: ber,* though a subjunctive *bere* is possible.
3136 From Th, but doubtless corrupt; om. G.
3137 *kirked* G Th; meaning doubtful, perhaps "crooked" (*kroked*?) as Morris and Skeat suggest; Fr. "Le nés froncié, le vis hisdeus."
3150 *I*] *it* G; *he* Th; Fr. "je."
3175 *haye* Globe; *hayes* G Th; Fr. "la haie."
3179 [*wot*] Skeat; Globe [*not*]; Morris [*wiste*].
3264 *seyne* Skeat *feyne*, perhaps correctly.
3274 *a clerk*] eds. om. *a*; Fr. "s'il est clers."
3294 Kaluza em. G Th *And to love of his great maistri*(*e*); Fr. "Mes au lessier (var. 'a l'issir') a grant mestrise."
3319 *taughte* eds.; *thought* G Th.
3331 *chastith* Globe; Skeat om. *that.*
3429 *al your wil,* suggested by Bell; *elles well* G; *al wel* Th; Fr. "Toutes voz autres volontez."
3433 *sith*(*en*) eds.; *sichen* G; *suche* Th; Fr. "puis qu'il me siet."
3450 *So* Globe; *I ony tyme to passe* G; Fr. "Se tu passes jamais"; Th, Skeat *In any tyme to passe,* perhaps correctly.
3454 *tall = tale,* with final *-e* apocopated for rime.
3482 Something omitted? Morris, Skeat [*hard*]; Globe [*nat*].
3489 *demying* G Th; Globe *demenyng,* perhaps correctly; Fr. "E tant qu'il a certainement Veü a mon contenement Qu'Amors malement me jostise."
3490 *Than*] *That* G Th. In G the line is added in a later hand.
3491 *That*] *Than*(*ne*) G Th.
3502 *bothen*] so Globe; *bothom* G Th; Skeat *botoun.* But there is no mention of the Rosebud here in the Fr.
3522 *he*] *ye* G Th; Fr. "il."
3525 *is it*] *it is* G Th.
3566 *hym*] Globe *hem*; Fr. "ses enuiz."
3595–3690 From Th; om. G.
3604 *dare* Th; Skeat [*thar*].
3643 *God it blesse*] *the god of blesse* Th; Fr. "Deus la beneïe."
3694 *Thought* Skeat; *Though* G Th.
3697 *rewyng,* eds. em. for *rennyng* G Th.
3698 *to me* Skeat; *come* G Th.
3710 *hertes* eds.; *hert*(*e*) *is* G Th.
3751 *to* eds.; *ye* G Th.
3774 *nille*] *wille* (*wyl*) G Th (perhaps correctly).
3851 *In* G Th; eds. [*Ne*] *in,* perhaps correctly.
3895 *trecherous*] *trechours* G Th; but the rime word is *envyous.* Globe *trechours: envyou*[*r*]*s.*
3907 *lowde* eds.; *lowe* G Th.
3928 *Counsel I* [*mot take*] *newe, y-wis* Skeat.
3942 *To* eds.; *Do* G Th.
3943 *T'enclose* eds.; *Than*(*ne*) *close* G Th.
3979 *ashamed* eds.; *shamed* G Th.
3998 Fr. "S'ele le cuilloit en haine," which Globe suggests may have been misread as "Se belacueil l'ait en haine."
4137 *wel the more* Globe; *welthe, the more* G Th.
4177 Skeat, Kaluza supply [*For*]; Fr. "car."

4188 *Rosers*] *Roses* G Th; Fr. "rosier[s]."
4194 *who* G Th; Skeat [*whiche*].
4214 *part*[*i*]*e*, Globe em. for *parte* G Th.
4272 *waketh* eds.; *walketh* G Th. Cf. l. 2682.
4285 *Ther* eds.; *Which*(*e*) G Th.
4291 *expert* eds.; *except* G Th.
4293 Skeat [*loveres*] *wyle.*
4322 *wende a bought* eds.; *went aboute* G Th; Fr. "Jes cuidoie avoir achetez."
4339 *tylyer*] *tylyers* G; *tyllers* Th; Fr. "au vilain."
4366 *change* eds.; *charge* G Th.
4372 *wal*(*le*) eds.; *wol*(*e*) G Th.
4416 *corajous* (*coragious*) G Th and Skeat; Kaluza, Globe em. *curious.*
4472 *stounde* G Th; Globe suggests *wounde.*
4478 [*me have*] supplied by Skeat, Kaluza from Fr. "Aveir me lait."
4510 *symply* G Th; Globe *symplely.*
4527 *my* Globe; *faire* G Th; Fr. "par ma priere."
4532 *lowe* G Th (= "value"); Globe reads *love* (in same sense), taking *w* as Northern way of writing *v.*
4550 *lord* eds.; *love* G Th; Fr. "mon seigneur."
4561 (*y*)*if God wille* eds.; *yeve good will*(*e*) G Th; Fr. "se Deu plaist."
4617 *not* G Th; perhaps to be emended to *niste* (pret.).
4634 *grevid* supplied by Urry; Skeat *pyned*; Globe *harmed* (note). Some such word appears necessary.
4689 [*wite*] Globe; Skeat [*here lerne*]; Fr. "savras."
4705 *A trouthe* eds.; *And thurgh the* G Th.
4712 *awey to we*(*a*)*re* G Th; Globe *alwey to ware*, "always to be avoided."
4721 *sike* eds.; *like* G Th.
4722 *thurst* or *thrust* (= "thirst") eds. *trust*(*e*) G Th; Fr. "seif."
4723 Eds. em. *An* for *And* here and in l. 4725, perhaps correctly.
4725 *hunger* eds.; *angre* G Th; Fr. "fain."
4736 [*stat*] Skeat, Globe; *stedefastnesse* Kaluza; Fr. "estaz."
4755 *be*(*n*) eds. (= Fr. "sont"?); *by* G Th.
4764 *That*] *But* Skeat; Globe inserts [*ne*]; but neither change may be necessary. See the explanatory note.
4793 [*I*] supplied by eds.; *er ever* G Th; but Fr. has "devant," and rime word is *fer.*
4796 *par cuer*, from Fr.; *by partuere* G Th.
4807 *diffyne it er*(*e*) eds.; *diffyned he*(*e*)*re* G Th; Fr. "defenir onques."
4812 *which* eds.; *with* G Th.
4846 *What man* Kaluza; *That what* G Th; *That* [*who*] Skeat; *What wight* Globe.
4871 *Thus hath sotilled* Globe; *This hadde sotille* G; *This had subtyl* Th; Fr. "Ainsinc . . . soutiva."
4892 *tyme* Skeat; *perell* G; *parel* Th.
4935 *youthe, his chamberere* eds.; *youthes chamb*(*e*)*re* G Th; Fr. "Jennece sa chamberiere."
4943 *Demand*(*e*) eds.; *And mo*(*o*) G Th; Fr. "demant." Globe suggests that *moo* may mean "ask," or be a corruption of a word with that meaning. Cf. l. 5290.
4955 *can* eds.; *gan* G Th.
4960 *neither* G Th; eds. *ne*, perhaps correctly.
5004 *stont* eds.; *stondith* G Th.

5051 *she* eds.; *so* G Th; perhaps we should read *sho* (a Northern form).
5068 *But* Skeat, Kaluza; *That* G Th.
5085 *they* eds.; *to* G Th. But the anacoluthon is possible.
5107 *herberedest than* eds.; *herberest hem* G; *herborest* Th; Fr. "receüs."
5117 *thy youth*(*e*) eds.; *by thought* G Th; Fr. "ta jouvente."
5144 *alway* Skeat; *ay*(*e*) G Th; *al day* Globe.
5165–66 Bracketed words, supplied by Skeat, seem necessary.
Rubric (following **5200**) *Amistie* eds.; *Aunsete* G Th.
5223 Bracketed words supplied by Skeat.
5283 *his* eds.; *this* G Th.
5284 *wel* Globe; *wol*(*e*) G Th; Fr. "a dreit."
5287 *Man* Globe; *And* G Th; Skeat, Kaluza [*A man*].
5290 So G Th and Skeat; Globe em. *But if the more,* "Unless the request," etc. (comparing *moo,* l. 4943).
5292 *causes* Th; *cause* G; Skeat [*cases*].
5353 *Hidith* G Th; Skeat *It hit* (or *hidith*).
5360 *groweth* eds.; *greueth* G Th both times (which may represent *greveth* or *greweth*).
5389 Doubtful line; Skeat *To kepe* [*it ay is*] *his purpose*; Globe *To kepen alway his purpos.*
5401 *For* G Th; Globe (note) *Full*; Fr. "Mout."
5408 *all* Th; *it all* G; Skeat [*in*] *al*; Globe *at all.*
5451 Skeat supplies [*greet*] before *spekyng.*
5452 *ther-of* eds.; *che*(*e*)*r*(*e*) of G Th.
5542 Eds. insert [*is*] or [*his*], perhaps correctly.
5544 *fallyng* eds.; *fablyng* G Th; Fr. "cheanz."
5556 *doth* eds.; *depe* G Th.
5569 *yove* Globe; *yow* G Th; Skeat [*yeve*].
5577 *receyveth* eds.; *perceyveth* G Th; Fr. "receit."
5585–86 So Globe; G Th read *For* (*Lor* G) *he that hath mycches tweyne Ne value in his demeigne*; Fr. "Car teus n'a pas vaillant deus miches"; Skeat *hath* [*but*] . . . *Ne* [*more*] *value.*
5598 [*it*] Skeat; *that* G Th.
5611 *nought* Skeat; *not* G; *nat* Th.
5620 Globe supplies *Or*; Fr. "Ou espeir qu'il ne pense point," etc.
5627 [*it*] Skeat, [*that*] Globe.
5638 *nought* eds.; *not* G; *nat* Th; Globe suggests *But suffrith frost as hot ne ware*; Fr. "Ainz viegnent li freit e li chaut."
5641 *taketh* eds.; *take* G Th.
5643 Skeat, Globe [*the*] *deth*, perhaps correctly.
5649 *Pythagoras* Th; *Pictigoras* G.
5700 *more* eds.; om. G Th; Fr. "plus."
5701 *ynogh have* eds.; *though he hath* G Th; Fr. "assez aquis."
5755 *shewen* Skeat, Kaluza; *shewing* G Th. Globe *An* for *And.*
5855 *kepte* G Th; Skeat, Kaluza *kepeth*, perhaps correctly.
5879 [*at*] *al* eds.; *al*(*l*) G Th; Fr. "dou tout."
5883 *Al my nedis* eds.; *As my nede is* G Th; Fr. "A mes besoignes achever."
5942 *fully* eds.; *folyly* G Th.
5958 *sikerere* Kaluza, Globe: *s*(*e*)*urere* G Th.
5959, 6006 *leaute* eds.; *beaute* G Th.
5976 Eds. om. *ful*, perhaps correctly.
6002 *gnede* eds.; *grede* G Th.

6041 *thankynges* G Th; Kaluza *thwakkynges*; Fr. "colees."

6042 *talkynges* G Th; Globe suggests *wakynges*; Fr. "acolees."

6165 *swich* Skeat, Kaluza; *which*(*e*) G Th; Fr. "teus."

6174 *nedes* eds.; *nede* G Th; Fr. "besoignes."

6264 *the* G Th; *ther* Globe; Fr. "leur sanc."

6281 Fr. "E se d'aus (var. "d'eus," translated as "deus") ne la veauz rescourre."

6317–18 Bracketed words supplied by eds. following Fr.: "Mais tant est fort la decevance Que trop est grief l'aparcevance." *But so sligh*(*e*) *is the aperceyvyng* G Th; l. 6318 om. G; *That al to late cometh knowynge* Th (which appears spurious).

6341 *Streyned* eds.; *and reyned* G Th; Fr. "Contrainte."

6342 Skeat [*y-*]*feyned*, perhaps correctly.

6354 *lete* eds.; *be*(*a*)*te* G Th; Fr. "J'en lais."

6355 [*blynde*] *folk* [*ther*] Skeat; *To joly*(*e*) *folk I enhabite* G Th; Fr. "Por gens avugler (var. 'embacler') i abit, Je n'en quier, senz plus, que l'abit."

6359 *wre* Globe; *were* G; *beare* Th; *bere* Skeat, Urry; Fr. "Mout est en mei muez li vers."

6372 Om. G Th; supplied by Morris, Skeat, etc. from Fr.; Globe *But where my sleight is aperceyved, Of hem I am nomore resceyved.*

6425 *cheveys* G; *chuse* Th; Fr. "chevir" (Kaluza).

6469 *with force* G Th; Skeat *with* [*the*] *force*; Kaluza suggests "by seint Joce" and compares *WB Prol*, III, 483.

6515 *mot* eds.; *not* G Th.

6532 *thrittethe*, eds. em. for *thrittene* G Th; the reference is to chap. xxx.

6541 Globe supplies [*is*] after *Unnethe*.

6565 *hir* eds.; *the*(*i*)*r* G Th (a Northern form).

6606 *Blynne* Globe; *Ben somtyme in* G Th; Fr. "Entrelaissier"; Skeat, Kaluza *Somtyme* [*leven*].

6653 *ther* Globe (note); om. G Th; Skeat *wher*; Kaluza *though*; Fr. "la ou."

6688 From Th; Globe reads *nede is*; G has, in later hand over a blank space, *And wole but only done that. . . .*

6711 *his* G Th; read *this* (= "these," Fr. "les") as in Globe?

6786 From Th; G has in late hand *Of thyngis that he beste myghte.* Perhaps *endite* should be substituted for *write.*

6810 [*hir*] eds.; om. G Th; Fr. "leur."

6823–24 *robbed, giled* eds.; *robbyng, gilying* G Th; Fr. "lobez," "robez."

6911 *bordurs* Globe; *burdons* G Th; Fr. "philateres."

7013 ff. In G Th ll. 7110–58 are misplaced before ll. 7013–109, and ll. 7159–208 after ll. 7209–304.

7022 *bouger* Kaluza; *begger* G; Th, Skeat *bougerons*; Globe *bourgerons*; Fr. "bougre."

7029 [*thefe, or*] Skeat; *these that* G Th; Fr. "Ou lierres ou symoniaus."

7056 *our* Skeat; *his* G Th, Globe; Fr. "S'il ne nous a bien procurez." Possibly *his* is right, *his frendship* meaning "friendship or favor for him."

7063 *vounde* G Th is of uncertain meaning. Skeat suggests *founde* or *founded.* See explanatory note.

7076 Read *equipolaunces*? Fr. "equipolences" (: "pitances").

7092 From Th; om. G, which has in later hand *Of al that here axe juste their dome.*

7109 Om. G; *That they ne myght the booke by The sentence pleased hem wel trewly To the copye if him talent toke Of the Evangelystes booke* Th, the second and fourth lines of which seem to be spurious. L. 7109 is printed as emended by Skeat, Globe; Fr. "Qui lors aveir ne le peüst, A transcrivre s'il l'i pleüst."

7116 *troubler*(*e*) G Th; Globe *trouble*; Fr. "plus trouble."

7137 *never* Kaluza; *no more* Th; *more* G.

7145 *ne* eds.; *no* G Th, possibly correct (= "nor").

7172–73 Apparently lines are lost here corresponding to Fr. "Par Pierre veaut le pape entendre." Skeat inserts two lines, thus changing his numbering for the remainder of the poem.

7197 *ynowe*] *ynough* G Th (metrically suspicious).

7219 *maistres* eds.; *mynystres* G Th; Fr. "nous reinons."

7235 *comunably* G Th; Kaluza suggests *comunly*.

7252 Skeat, Globe supply *it*; Kaluza suggests *despit.*

7315 *al defyle* Th; *alto defyle* G; possibly to be emended *al tofyle* (Kaluza).

7316 *nil* Kaluza; *wol*(*e*) G Th; Fr. "ne triche e lobe."

7334 *Thankyng* Th; *Thankyth* G; Kaluza *and on his knees gan loute.*

7366 *graithe* eds.; *gracche* G Th; Fr. "s'atourne."

7383–7574 From Th; om. G.

7387 *devyse* eds.; *devysed* Th; Fr. "devis."

7442 *thanne* Th; eds. [*as*] *than*(*ne*), perhaps correctly.

7486 *dusty* eds.; *doughty* Th; Fr. "poudreus."

7546 Eds. [*for*] *to reprove*, perhaps correctly.

7634 *me* (the impersonal *me*(*n*)?)] *he* G Th, Globe; *ye* eds.

7660 *doth* eds.; *wote* G Th; Fr. "fait."

GLOSSARY

THE following glossary is not a complete Chaucer dictionary. Limitations of space have made it impossible to record Chaucer's entire vocabulary, or to register any considerable number of the occurrences of words and phrases. But it has been the editor's intention to include all words which, by reason of changes of form or meaning, need to be explained, and references are given in many places to notes in the body of the book which supply additional information. The glossary in Skeat's Oxford Chaucer gives a fuller list of words and many citations, and the Concordance of Professors Tatlock and Kennedy records every occurrence of all but a few of the commonest words.

Grammatical forms, except the regular endings that are easily recognized, are fully registered here. Thus the principal parts of strong verbs and of irregular weak verbs, and exceptional forms like the contracted third singular of the present indicative, are all noted; also the more common of the stereotyped phrases in which the dative ending of nouns is preserved. Nouns and adjectives of which Chaucer used two forms in the nominative — one with -e, and one without — are entered with an -e in parentheses: *bliss(e)*, *cler(e)*.

It has not been possible to register the very numerous varieties of spelling that occur in the text. In the case of common words the orthography has been normalized in accordance with the system long familiar to readers of Skeat's text. Long *e* and *o* are doubled in monosyllables (*meed*, *good*) and written single in longer words (*meten*, *gode*). The sound of long *i* is usually represented by *y*, and that of short *i* by *i*. The diphthong *ou* is written with *u* rather than *w*, and *sh* (or *ssh*) is used instead of the frequent *sch* of the MSS. But no attempt has been made to regularize the spelling of the diphthong *ai*, *ei* (*saint*, *seint*, *saynt*, *seynt*), and if the reader fails to find a word entered under one form he should look under the others. The same procedure may sometimes be necessary, for example, in the case of the variation between *an* and *aun* (*dance* and *daunce*), *i* and *y* (*icleped* and *ycleped*, *roially* and *royally*, *lien* and *lyen*), *ou* and *ow* (*toun* and *town*), or *sh* and *sch* (*shal* and *schal*). Cross references have been given for spellings that present real difficulty, and words of rare occurrence are entered in the glossary in the forms in which they appear in the text. This method makes the orthography of the glossary inconsistent, but has been adopted as a practical compromise for the convenience of the reader.

To aid the reader in pronunciation, long open *e* and *o* have been printed with a hook (*ẹ*, *ọ*). The difference between the open and close sounds of these letters is explained in the grammatical introduction.

Parentheses are used here, as in the grammatical introduction, to indicate letters or syllables that may or may not be written.

A

A, prep., on, in, by.

A, int., ah!

A, vb., have (shortened form).

A, An, the indefinite article; sometimes meaning "one" (of which it is in origin an unemphatic form); *al a*, the whole of a. On idiomatic use with numerals, etc., *an eighte*, *a certein*, see *ShipT*, VII, 334, n.

Abaissen, abash, disconcert. See Abasshen.

Abak, aback, backwards.

Abandoun, sbst., lack of control, freedom; *in abandoun*, fully, without check or restraint.

Abasshen, abash, make afraid. See Abaissen.

Abaten, abate, lower, put down, reduce.

Abaundonen, abandon, devote.

Abaved, Abawed, confounded, disconcerted, amazed.

Abaysschinge, amazement, bewilderment.

Abaysshed, pp., cast down.

Abayst; see Abaissen.

Abbey(e), abbey.

Abc, alphabet.

A-begged, a-begging. See *Pard Prol*, VI, 406, n.

Abeggen, Kentish form of Abyen.

Abet, abetting, aid.

Abeyen; see Abyen.

Abhominable, abominable, hateful.

Abit; see Habit.

Able, capable, fit, adapted, deserving.

Ablyng, enabling, lifting; fitting.

Aboght(e); see Abyen.

Abọọd, delay, abiding, continuance.

Abọọd; see Abyden.

Aboute, adv., about, around; in turn; *been aboute*, go about, set out, undertake.

Aboven, adv., above; hence, in good plight or fortune.

A-brẹd, adv., abroad.

Abreggen, abridge, shorten.

Abreyden, pt. *abreyd* (str.) and *abreyde* (wk.); awake, start up; break out.

Abrọchen, broach.

Abrọọd, abroad, wide open.

Absenten, abstain, refrain.

Abusioun, abuse; deceit; witchcraft; shame, scandal.

Abyden, pt. sg. *abọọd*, pl. *abiden*, pp. *abiden*; abide, dwell; await, expect, watch for; endure; stop, be still.

Abydinge, expectation, delay.

Abyen, pt. *aboghte*, pp. *aboght*; pay for, atone for, buy dearly; suffer, undergo. See Abeggen, Abeyen.

Accesse, attack of fever.

Accident, occurrence, incident; especially, an unusual occurrence or appearance; in philosophy, a property, attribute, or outward appearance as opposed to essential nature or substance. (See *PardT*, VI, 537, n.).

Accidie, sloth (one of the Deadly Sins).

Accioun, action, accusation.

Accomplicen, Accomplishen, accomplish; comprehend.

929

Accord, concord, agreement; peace.

Accordaunce, concord, harmony.

Ac(c)orden, reconcile, compose; agree; suit, befit; concern (?); grant, allow, consent.

Accusement, accusation.

Accusen, accuse, blame; reveal, disclose.

Achat, purchase.

Achatours, purchasers, caterers.

A-chekked, checked, hindered.

Acheven, achieve.

Achoken, choke.

Acloyen, overburden.

A-compas, round about, in a circle.

A-coold, adj. (probably from pp.), cold, chilly.

Acord, Acorden; see **Accord**, etc.

Acordable, harmonious.

Acorn(e), acorns; fruits.

Acorsen; see **Acursen**.

Acounten, reckon, consider; take account of; value.

Acoyen, quiet, allay; coax, caress.

Acquitaunce, release; deed of release.

Act, act, deed; pl., records.

Actif, active.

Acursen, Acorsen, curse.

Acustumaunce, custom, habitual mode of life.

Adama(u)nt, Atthamaunt, adamant; loadstone.

Adawen, awake, recover.

A-day, in the day, by day.

Adjeccioun, addition.

A(d)minystren, administer.

Ado, to do (lit. *at do*).

A-doun, downwards, down, below, at the bottom.

Adowryng, adoration.

Adrad (pp. of *adreden*), afraid.

Adressynge, directing.

Adversaire, adversary.

Adversarie, sbst. and adj., adversary; hostile.

Advertence, attention, heed.

Advocacies, pleas.

Afer, afar.

A-fere, Kentish form of **A-fyre**, afire.

Aferen, pp. *afer(e)d*; frighten.

Affeccioun, affection, devotion.

Affect, desire; feeling.

Affermen, affirm; agree upon; establish.

Affiance, trust.

Affilen, file, make smooth.

Afforced, forced.

Affounden, be numb, turn cold.

Affray, terror, fright; quarrel, fray.

Affrayen, terrify; arouse; pp. *affrayed*, terrified, afraid; roused, excited.

Affyen, trust.

Afore, Aforn, adv., before, formerly.

Aforyeyn, opposite, over against.

Afright, (pp. of *afrighten*), frightened.

After, adv., afterwards.

After, prep., after (of time or place); according to; for, in expectation of; towards, for (i.e., to obtain).

Afyn, adv., utterly, completely.

A-fyre; see **Fyr**.

A-game, in sport, in mockery.

Agasten, pt. *agaste*, pp. *agast*; terrify, deter; take fright.

Agayn, Ageyn, adv., again; in reply, in return.

Agayn(es), Ageyn, prep., against; opposite to or contrary to; towards; so as to meet; before, in the presence of; towards (of time), just before; in comparison with.

Agayn-ward, backward, back again.

Ageyn; see **Agayn**.

Ageyn-coming, return.

Agilten, pt. *agilte*, pp. *agilt*; offend, be guilty, sin.

Agon, pp. *agon, ago*; go away, depart; die.

Agreablely, complacently; pleasantly.

Agreabletee, agreeableness; equability.

A-gree (lit. *in gree*), in favor, in good part.

A-greef, in grief; sadly; amiss, in vexation.

Agreggen, aggravate.

Agreven, aggrieve, vex.

A-grief; see **A-greef**.

Agroos, pt. of **Agrysen**.

Agroted, surfeited, cloyed.

Agrysen, pt. *agroos*, pp. *agrisen*; shudder, tremble; dread, feel terror.

Agu, ague.

Aguler, needle-case.

A-heigh, on high, aloft.

Aiel, grandfather.

Ajournen, adjourn.

Ajugen, pp. *ajuged*; judge.

Aken, ache.

Aketoun, acton, a short sleeveless tunic, worn under the hauberk.

Aknowen (pp. of *aknowen*, acknowledge), conscious; *I am acknowe*, I acknowledge.

Akornes; see **Acorn(e)s**.

Akyngge, aching, pain

Al, awl. See also **Oules**.

Al, (occasionally **Alle**), adj., all, every; gen. sg. *alles-*, in *alles-kinnes*, of every sort; gen. pl. *aller, alder, alther; oure aller*, of us all; used also in composition with superlatives, as in *alder-best*, best of all; *al a*, the whole of a; *at al* wholly, at all; *in al*, entirely; *al and som*, the whole and every part; *al and somme*, one and all; *with alle*, therewith, moreover, also.

Al, adv., wholly, quite, altogether; *al only*, merely, simply; *al thus*, just so.

Al, concessive conj., as in *al be (it), al were (it)*, etc.

Alambik, Lambic, alembic.

Alaunt, large dog; wolf-hound.

Alayes, alloys.

Albificacioun, whitening (alchemical term).

Al-day, always, continually, at any time.

Alder, Alder-best, Alder-firste, etc.; see **Al**.

Alderman, alderman (either the municipal officer or the officer of a guild).

Aleggement, alleviation.

Aleggen; see **Alleggen**.

Alemandres, almond trees.

Alembyk; see **Alambik**.

Alenge; see **Elenge**.

Aley, alley.

Aleys, service-berries.

Ale-stake, signpost of an inn.

Algate(s), in every way, wholly; by all means; at all hazards; anyhow, nevertheless.

Alienen, alienate.

Alighten, pt. *alighte*, pp. *alight*; alight.

Alkaly, alkali.

Alkamystre, alchemist.

Alleggeaunce, alleviation. See **Alleggen (2)**.

Alleggen (1), allege, adduce.

Alleggen (2), allay, alleviate.

Aller; see Al.

Alliaunce, Alyaunce, alliance; marriage; kindred.

Allowen (1), allow, admit.

Allowen (2), applaud, praise.

Allye, ally.

Allyen, vb., ally one's self, supply with aid.

Almesse, alms.

Almest, almost.

Almury, the denticle or point on the rete of an astrolabe.

Almykanteras, small circles of declination in the celestial sphere; parallels of altitude.

Aloes, aloe, the resin or wood of the agalloch; *lignealoes*, lignum aloes.

Alofte, aloft, on high.

A-londe, on land, ashore.

Along on, along of, because of, owing to.

Al-only; see Aloonly.

Aloon(e), alone; alone of, without.

Aloonly, solely, only, alone.

Alosen, praise, commend.

Al-out, outright, altogether.

Al-outerly, all utterly, wholly, absolutely.

Alpes, pl. bull-finches.

Also, Als, adv., all so, also, besides.

Also, Als, As, conj., as.

Alswa, Northern form of Also.

Alther; see Al.

Altitude, in astronomy, the elevation of a celestial body above the horizon.

Alum glas, crystallized alum.

Al-utterly; see Al-outerly.

Alwey, always, continually; all the while; anyhow (= *algate(s)*).

Alyaunce; see Alliaunce.

Alyne, in a line.

Alyve, alive (from *on lyve*).

Amadrides, hamadriads.

Amalgamyng, forming an amalgam.

Amanusen; see Amenusen.

Amasen, amaze.

Amayen, pp. *amayed*; dismay.

Ambages, circumlocutions, equivocations, ambiguities.

Ambel, amble, a walking pace; *an ambel*, in an ambling pace.

Ambes as, double aces.

Amblere, an ambling horse.

Amelen, pp. *ameled*; enamel.

Amendement, amends.

Amenden, make amends; improve; succeed; surpass.

Amenusen, diminish, lessen; grow less.

Amercimentz, exactions, fines.

Ameven, Amo(e)ven, move; change.

Amiddes, adv., in the midst.

Amidde(s), prep., amid, in the midst of.

Ammonicioun, designation, pointing out.

Amoeven; see Ameven.

Amonesten, admonish; advise, recommend.

Among, adv., therewith, meanwhile; all the while; *ever among*, every now and then.

Amonges, adv., sometimes, variously.

Amonten; see Amounten.

Amorettes, sweethearts; love-knots.

Amorwe, on the morrow, in the morning.

Amo(u)nten, amount, amount to; mean.

Amoven; see Ameven.

Amphibologies, ambiguities.

Amy, friend.

An, prep., on; *an heigh, an hye*, on high.

Ancille, handmaiden.

Ancre, anchor.

And, conj., and; if.

Anes, once (Northern dial.).

Anexen; see Annexen.

Angerly, cruelly.

Angle, geometrical angle; corner, coign; in astronomy, angular distance from the meridian; in astrology, the four "houses" at the cardinal points of the compass.

Angle-hok, fish-hook.

Angre, anguish; anger.

Angren, enanger; vex.

Angry, wrathful; irritable, cruel.

Anguissh, anguish; anxiety.

Anguiss(h)ous, anxious; sorry; causing of feeling distress.

Angwisschen, wound, cause pain.

Anhangen, pp. *anhanged, anhonged*; hang.

Anientissen, annihilate.

A-night, in the night.

A-nightes, by night.

Anker, anchoress.

Anlaas, anlace, a short, two-edged knife or dagger.

An(n)exen, annex, attach.

Annueleer, a priest who celebrates anniversary masses, known as "annuals."

Annunciat, pre-announced, foretold.

Anoon, adv., at once, forthwith.

Anoon-right(es), immediately.

Anoy, annoyance, vexation; trouble; torture; sadness.

Anoyful, annoying, tiresome.

Anoyinge, injurious.

Anoynt, Enoynt, pp., anointed.

Anoyous, annoying, tiresome; disagreeable; harmful.

Anslet, short jacket. See Hainselin.

Answere, answer.

Answeren, answer; correspond to, be suitable for; be responsible for.

Antartik, antarctic, southern.

Antiphoner, antiphonary, anthem-book.

Antony, fyr of seint, erysipelas.

Anvelt, anvil.

Any, Eny, Ony, any.

Any-thing, used adverbially, at all, in any degree; *for anything*, on all accounts, at all hazards.

Aornement, adornment.

Apallen, make pale, pallid; weaken; pp. *ap(p)alled*, pale, weakened, languid.

Aparailen, vb., apparel, prepare, adorn; clothe (one's self).

Aparaille, apparel, ornament.

Aparceyven; see Aperceiven.

Apas; see Pas.

Apassen, pass, pass away.

Apayen, satisfy, please; *yvel apayd*, ill pleased.

Apayren, impair, injure; grow worse, perish.

Apaysen; see Ape(i)sen.

Ape, ape; *putte in the mannes hood an ape*, made a fool of him. See *Intro to PrT*, VII, 440, n.

Apeiren; see Apayren.

Ape(i)sen, appease, pacify; mitigate; settle.

Aperceiven, perceive, conceive.

Aperceyving, perception, observation.

Apert, open, manifest; also adv.

Apertena(u)nt, appertaining, belonging to; suitable.

Apertenen, appertain, belong.

Apetiten, vb., seek; desire.

Apiken, trim, adorn.

Apocalips, apocalypse.

Apointen, appoint, determine, resolve; settle (one's self).

Aposen; see **A(p)posen.**

Apotecarie, apothecary.

Apparaunt, clear, distinct.

Apparence, appearance; seeming; apparition; false show.

Apperen, appear.

Appert; see **Apert.**

Appetyt, appetite; desire.

Appieren; see **Apperen.**

Applyen, apply; be attached to.

Ap(p)osen, appose, question.

Apprentys, adj., unskilled, like an apprentice.

Appreven, Approven, approve; confirm as true.

Appropren, vb., appropriate.

Approver (var. reading), approver, informer.

Approwour, steward, bailiff; hence, agent.

Apreynten, imprint.

Aprochen, approach.

Aqueyntable, approachable, affable.

Aqueynten, pt. *aqueinte,* pp. *aqueint(ed)*; acquaint.

Aquyten, requite.

Aracen, eradicate, uproot; tear away.

Araisen; see **Areisen.**

Aray, array, dress; arrangement, order; state, condition.

Arayen, array, dress, adorn; order, appoint.

Arbitr(i)e, will, choice.

Arblasters, men with crossbows.

Arch; see **Ark.**

Archaungell, bird of uncertain identification. Possibly a corruption of *wariangel.* See *Rom,* 915, n.

Archewyves, arch-wives; strong, assertive, dominating wives (or women).

Ardaunt, ardent.

Areden, counsel, advise; explain, interpret, divine.

Areisen, raise, exalt; praise.

Aresonen, engage in reasoning or argument.

Arest, arrest; detention, delay; restraint; rest (for a spear).

Aresten, arrest; stop.

Aretten, impute, ascribe.

Arewe, in a row, one after another.

Argoille, crude tartar.

Argument, argument; astronomical term for a mathematical quantity from which another may be deduced.

Aright, aright; well, properly; exactly; certainly.

Arist, rising.

Ark, Arch, arc; with various uses in astronomy, as for the arc of the horizon from sunrise to sunset, or the apparent distance traversed by the sun in a given period.

Arm, arm; dat. phr. *by arme.*

Armee, army; armed expedition, "armada."

Armonyak, ammoniac.

Armonye, harmony.

Armure, armour.

Armurers, armourers.

Armypotente, powerful in arms.

Arn, are; see **Ben.**

Aroos; see **Arysen.**

A-roume, at large, in an open space.

A-rowe, in (on) a row; in succession.

Arowe; see **Arwe.**

Arracen; see **Aracen.**

Arrerage, arrears.

Arretten; see **Aretten.**

Arryvage, coming to shore.

Ars-metrike, arithmetic (from Lat. "ars metrica," due to misunderstanding of "arismetica," from ἀριθμητική).

Arst; see **Erst.**

Art, art, skill.

Arte; See **Artow.**

Artelries, engines for discharging missiles.

Arten, urge, constrain.

Artificial, artificial; *day artificial,* in astronomy, the length of the day from sunrise to sunset.

Artik, arctic, northern.

Artow, Arte, art thou.

Arwe, Arowe, arrow.

Arysen, pt. sg. *aroos,* pl. *arisen,* pp. *arisen*; arise, stand up.

As, as; also in combination *as that; as (as though, as that)* used in place of modern construction with "as if"; frequently employed as an expletive with imperatives or subjunctives: *as lat, as keep, as go we;* also with advs. and adv. phrases: *as nowthe, as in her tyme.* On these last uses (now felt to be pleonastic) see *KnT,* I, 2302, n., and *Gen Prol,* I, 462, n.

As, ace. See also **Ambes as.**

Asay; see **Assay.**

Ascapen, Escapen, escape.

Ascaunce(s), as if, as if to say; perhaps. See *SumT,* III, 1745, n.

Ascencioun, ascension, ascending degree (in astronomy); ascent, rising (in alchemy).

Ascenden, ascend; rise from the horizon (astronomical term).

Ascendent, ascendant; the degree of the ecliptic that is rising at a given time.

Ascry, outcry, alarm.

Aseüraunce, assurance.

Ashamed (pp. of *ashamen*), ashamed; put to shame, humiliated.

Aslaken, diminish; assuage.

Aslepe; asleep. See **Sleep.**

A-slope, aside, awry.

Asonder, A-sundir, asunder; hence, diversely.

Aspe, aspen tree.

Aspect, aspect; in astronomy, the angular distance between two planets.

Aspen, adj., of an aspen tree; also sbst.

Aspre, harsh, sharp, bitter; vexatious; angry, fierce; irritated.

Aspye, sbst., spy.

Aspyen, vb., spy, see.

Assaut, assault.

As(s)ay, trial, attempt; test; quality, temper.

Assayen, try, endeavor; test, prove.

Asse, ass.

Assege, sbst., siege.

Assegen, besiege.

Assemblee, assembly.

Assembling, union.

Assent, assent, consent; agreement; opinion.

Asseth, enough, sufficiency; satisfaction.

Asshe (1), ash-tree.

Asshe (2), pl. *asshen, asshes*; ash (of a burnt substance).

Asshy, sprinkled with ashes.

Assoilen, absolve, pardon; pay, discharge (a debt); loosen; resolve, explain.

Assoiling, absolution.

Assuren, feel sure, trust, rely; assure (another or one's self); make sure or secure; pp. *assured*, assured, self-possessed, etc.

Assyse, assize, session; judgment; order, position.

Astat, state.

Asterten, escape (trans. or intrans.); withdraw (?), desist (?).

Astonien, pp. *astonied, astoned*; astonish, confound.

Astoren, pp. *astored*; store, provide.

Astrelabie, Astrolabie, astrolabe.

Astrologien, astrologer, astronomer.

Astronomye, also perhaps **Astromye**, astronomy; astrology.

A-sundir; see **Asonder**.

Asure, sbst., assurance, protestation.

Asure, azure.

Aswagen, assuage, mitigate; reduce, diminish.

Asweved (pp. of *asweven*), dazed, put to sleep.

A-swone; see **Aswown**.

Aswown, fainted, in a swoon (from AS. pp. "aswogen"). Also a form *a-swowne* (and *a-swone*), as if from dat. phr. *on swowne*. But the sbst. is not recorded early.

At, at, by, with; with respect to; from (*ask at*). In numerous phrases: *at erste*, at first; *at on*, at one; *at shorte wordes*, briefly; *at regard*, with regard; *at yë*, at the eye, hence, visibly.

Ataken, pp. *atake(n)*; overtake.

Atasten, taste.

Ataynt; see **Atteinen**.

Atazir, influence. See *MLT*, II, 305, n.

Atempraunce, temperament; temperance, moderation; adjustment.

Atempren, temper, regulate; control (refl.)

Athinken, displease; impersonal, cause to regret or repent.

At-ones, at once, at the same time; once for all.

Atoon, at one.

Atreden, outwit, surpass in counsel.

Atrennen, outrun.

Attamen, pp. *attamed*; broach.

Atte, at the; used in adv. phrases, *atte fulle, beste, leste*, etc.

At(t)einen, attain, reach, achieve; pp. *at(t)eint*, apprehended, experienced.

At(t)empre(e), temperate, moderate, mild; modest; discreet.

Attendaunce, attendance; attention.

Attenden, attend; belong, pertain, attach itself. See also **Entenden**.

Atthamaunt; see **Adama(u)nt**.

Attour, array.

Attricioun, attrition; in theology, a state of imperfect sorrow for sin (less complete than contrition).

Attry, poisonous, venomous.

A-tweyn, in twain, in two.

A-twinne, apart.

Atwixen, betwixt.

A-two, in two, in twain.

Atyr, attire, dress.

Aucto(u)r, author, maker, creator.

Auctoritee, authority; text (of scripture, etc.); authoritative statement.

Audience, audience, assembly; hearing.

Aughte; see **Owen**.

Augrym, algorism; Arabic numerals. See *MillT*, I, 3210, n.

Augurye, augury.

Aurcessour, ancestor.

Auncestre, ancestor.

Auncetrye, ancestry.

Aungel, angel.

Auntren, adventure, risk (sometimes refl.).

Auntrous, adventurous.

Autentyk, authentic.

Auter, altar.

Autoritee; see **Auctoritee**.

Autour; see **Aucto(u)r**.

Autumpne, autumn.

Availen, avail, be of avail, aid; prevail.

Avalen, fall down, sink; doff, take off.

Avantage, advantage.

Avarous, avaricious.

Avauncen, advance, promote; aid; benefit; be profitable.

Avaunt, vaunt, boast.

Avaunt, adv., forward, in advance.

Avaunten, vb. refl., vaunt, boast one's self; extol.

Avauntour, boaster.

Avenaunt, graceful, comely; pleasant, friendly; convenient.

Aventaille, ventail; front or mouthpiece of a helmet.

Aventure, adventure; chance, luck, fortune; circumstance, accident; misfortune, danger; *of aventure*, *per aventure*, by chance; *on aventure*, in case of accident or misfortune; *in aventure*, in the hands of fortune.

Avisee; see **Avyse**.

Avisioun, vision, dream.

Avout(e)rye, adultery.

Avow, vow.

Avowen, vow, acknowledge, declare.

Avowtier, adulterer.

Avoy, fie.

Avys, advice, counsel, opinion; consideration.

Avyse, adj., deliberate.

Avysement, consideration, deliberation; counsel; determination; observation, attention.

Avysen, consider, deliberate; observe; often refl.; *avysed*, considered, deliberate, forewarned.

Await, watch, observation; watchfulness, waiting; ambush; plot.

Awaiten, await, watch, observe; lie in wait (for).

Awaken, pt. *awook*, pp. *awaked*; awake, wake; rouse one's self, resume speech or action.

Awaytour, lier in wait.

Awen, own (Northern dial.).

A-wepe, a-weeping, in or into tears.

A-werke, at work. See **Werk**.

Aweye, away, out of the way; from home. See **Wey(e)**.

Aweyward, backwards.

Awhapen, amaze, confound.

Awmener(e), purse for alms.

Awook; see **Awaken**.

Awreken, pp. *awreken, awroken*; avenge.

Awrie, awry, on one side.

Awroken; see **Awreken**.

Axen, ask; seek; require.

Axes; see **Accesse.**
Axing, asking, question.
Ay, aye, ever; *ay whyl that,* all the time that.
Ay-dwellinge, everlasting, perpetual.
Ayein, against, over against, opposite to.
Ayein, again, back; in reply.
Ayein-lẹdinge, returning, leading back.
Ayeinward, again, back again; on the other hand.
Aylen, ail.
Ayr, heir; see **Eyr.**
Azimut, azimuth.

B

Ba, kiss; see **Pa.**
Baas, base.
Babeuries; see **Babewynnes.**
Babewynnes, baboons; grotesque figures, gargoyles.
Bacheler, bachelor; young knight or aspirant to knighthood; bachelor of law, arts, etc.
Bachelrye, bachelor-hood; collective young men, candidates for knighthood.
Bacoun, bacon.
Bacyn, basin.
Bad; see **Bidden.**
Badde, bad.
Badder, worse.
Baden; see **Beden, Bidden.**
Bagge, purse.
Baggen, look askew, squint.
Baggepype, bagpipe.
Baggyngly, squintingly.
Baillye (1), castle wall; enclosure.
Baillye (2), jurisdiction; custody.
Bak, back; clothing for the back, coarse cloak or mantle.
Bake-mẹtes, baked meats, pasties.
Baken, pp. *ybaken;* bake.
Bakhalf, back side (of the astrolabe).
Bak-side, back side (of the astrolabe).
Balade, ballade. See *LGW Prol F,* 417, n.
Balaunce, balance; suspense, uncertainty.
Bale, bale, sorrow, misfortune.
Balke, balk, beam.
Balled, bald.
Band; see **Binden.**
Bane, slayer (orig. personal); destruction.
Banes, bones (Northern dial.).
Bar; see **Bẹren.**
Barbe, barb, a piece of pleated linen reaching from the chin to the waist.
Barbre, barbarian.
Bare, bare; desolate; insufficient; barren of results, useless.
Baren; see **Bẹren.**
Bareyne, barren.
Barge, barge, ship.
Barm, bosom.
Barm-clọoth, apron.
Barre, bar; transverse metal strips on a girdle, buckle, or saddle.
Barred, furnished with bars.
Barringe, adorning with bars (in heraldry).
Basilicok, basilisk.
Bataile, battle, fight; battalion, troop.
Batailed, battlemented, notched with indentations.
Batailen, vb., battle, fight.
Bate, strife.
Bateren, batter.

Bathe, both (Northern dial.).
Bathen, bathe, bask (refl.).
Baud, adj., lively, joyous, gay.
Baude, bawd.
Bauderye (1), jollity, mirth.
Bauderye (2), bawdry.
Baudy, dirty.
Baume, balm.
Baundon, power, control.
Bawdryk, baldric, belt.
Bay, bay-colored.
Bayard, a horse's name (from the color).
Be-; for words with this prefix see also **Bi-** and **By-.**
Beau, fair (Fr.).
Beautee, beauty.
Bebled, covered with blood.
Beblotten, blot.
Bed, bed; dat. phr. *on* (*to*) *bedde.*
Bẹdel, beadle; officer.
Beden, pt. sg. *bẹd,* pl. *bẹden, baden,* pp. *bọden;* offer; direct, tell, command. See also **Bidden.**
Bẹdes, beads.
Bedọten, make a fool of.
Bedrede, bedridden.
Bee, pl. *bees, been;* bee.
Beechen, made of beech.
Bẹẹk, beak.
Bẹẹm, balk, beam.
Bẹẹr; see **Bẹren.**
Bẹẹst, beast, animal; *beest roial,* Leo (the zodiacal sign).
Beet; see **Bẹten.**
Beggere, beggar; **Beguin,** hence mendicant.
Beggestere, beggar (properly feminine). See *Gen Prol,* I, 241, n.
Behewen, pp. *behewen;* hew, carve.
Bekken, nod, beckon.
Bel, fem. *bele;* fair (Fr.); *bel amy,* fair friend (formula of address).
Belle, bell.
Belwen, bellow.
Bely (1), belly.
Bely (2), bellows.
Beme, trumpet.
Ben, to be; for inflection see the Grammatical Introduction.
Benched, provided with benches.
Bend, band; in heraldry, a horizontal band across a shield.
Bendinge, providing with heraldic bends.
Bendiste, contr. of **Benedicite.**
Bẹne, bean.
Benedicite, bless ye (the lord); apparently contracted into both *ben'cite* and *bendiste.*
Bẹne-straw, bean-straw.
Benigne, benign, gracious.
Benisoun, benison, blessing.
Bent, slope, hillside.
Beraft; see **Birẹven.**
Berd, beard; *make a* (*his*) *berd,* deceive, delude; *in the berd,* face to face.
Bẹre (1), sbst., bear.
Bẹre, (2), sbst., bier.
Bẹr(e) (3), sbst., pillow-case; also *pilwe-beer.*
Bẹren, pt. sg. *bar, bẹer,* pl. *baren, bẹren,* pp. (*y*) *bọren;* bear, carry, possess, etc.; pierce; conduct (one's self); *bore doun,* overcome by testimony; *beren on*

honde, assure (him), assert (to him); accuse, bear witness against. See *MLT*, II, 620, n.

Berie, berry.

Berien, bury.

Berken, bark; pp. *borken*, shrieked, screamed.

Berme, barm, yeast.

Bern(e), barn.

Beryle, beryl.

Besaunt, bezant (gold coin of Byzantium); cf. also *besaunt-wight*.

Bespreynt; see **Bisprengen.**

Bestial, like a beast; stupid.

Bestialitee, nature or condition as a beast.

Besy; see **Bisy.**

Bet, adj. and adv., better.

Beten, pt. sg. *beet*, pl. *bet(t)en*, pp. *beten, bet*; beat, smite, hammer, flap; scourge; ornament, decorate, embroider.

Beten, remedy, heal; mend, improve; kindle.

Beth, are; see **Ben.**

Betraysynge, betrayal. See **Bitraisen.**

Bever, made of beaver.

Bewar, beware.

Beyen, buy; dial. var. of **Byen.**

Bibben, imbibe.

Bicched, cursed (lit. "bitched"); *bicched bones*, dice. See *PardT*, VI, 656, n.

Biclappen, clasp, enclose, catch.

Bicomen, pt. sg. *bicom*, pl. *bicomen*, pp. *bicomen*; become; go, depart.

Bidaffed, fooled.

Bidden, pt. sg. *bad*, pl. *baden, beden*, pp. *bidden, beden* (from AS. "biddan," sometimes confused with **Beden** (q.v.), offer, from AS. "beodan"); ask, request, pray; command, direct.

Bidding, request.

Bidelven, pp. *bidolven*; bury.

Biden; see **Byden.**

Bidewen, bedew.

Bifallen, pt. sg. *bifel, bifil*, pp. *bifallen*; befall, happen.

Bifallinge, befalling, coming to pass.

Bifor(e)n, adv., before, in front; in a favorable position; first; of old.

Bifor(e)n, prep., before.

Bifornseyd, aforesaid.

Bigamye, bigamy; marrying twice. See *WB Prol*, III, 33, n.

Bigeten, pt. sg. *bigat*, pp. *bigeten*, beget.

Biginnen, pt. sg. *bigan*, pl. *bigonnen*, pp. *bigonnen*; begin.

Bigoon (pp. of *bigoon*, lit. "gone about," "surrounded"), provided, ornamented, established, etc.; *wel bigon*, well provided, contented, happy, fortunate; *wo bigon*, wretched, distressed; cf. also, *sorwfully bigon, wers bigon.*

Bigylen, beguile, deceive.

Bihalve, behalf.

Bihaten, hate, detest.

Bihelden; see **Biholden.**

Biheste, behest, promise, command.

Biheten, Bihoten, pt. sg. *bihette, bihighte*, pp. *bihight*; promise.

Bihighte; see **Biheten.**

Bihinde(n), behind.

Biholden, Bihelden, pt. sg. *biheeld*, pp. *biholden*; behold, look upon.

Bihoof, behoof, profit, advantage; dat. phr. *til . . . behove.*

Bihoten; see **Biheten.**

Bihove; see **Bihoof.**

Bihovely, helpful, necessary.

Bihoven, befit, suit; be necessary. (Used both personally and impersonally.)

Bijapen, jest at, play trick upon.

Biker, quarrel.

Biknowen, pt. sg. *biknew*, pl. *biknewen*, pp. *biknowen*; acknowledge, confess; *I am biknowen*, I acknowledge.

Bilafte; see **Bileven.**

Bilden, build.

Bilder, builder; hence, as adj., used for building.

Bile, bill (of a bird).

Bilefte; see **Bileven.**

Bileve, belief, faith; creed.

Bileven, believe.

Bileven, Bleven, pt. *bilefte, bilafte*; remain, stay.

Bilinnen, Blinnen, cease, stop.

Bille, bill, petition; writ; letter.

Bimenen, bemoan; used reflexively.

Binden, contr. pr. 3 sg. *bint*, pt. sg. *bond, band*, pl. *bounden*, pp. *bounden, bonden*; bind, fasten.

Binding, constraint.

Binimen, pp. *binomen*; take away.

Bint, see **Binden.**

Biquethen, pp. *bequethen*; bequeath.

Biraft; see **Bireven.**

Bireven, pt. *birafte, birefte*, pp. *biraft, bireft*; bereave; take away; rob, deprive; prevent, restrain.

Biscorned, scorned.

Bisechen, Biseken, pt. *biso(u)ghte*, pp. *biso(u)ght*; beseech, implore.

Bisemare, shame; mockery, scorn.

Bisetten, employ; bestow, apply; establish, fix.

Biseye, Biseyn (pp. of *biseen*), beseen, provided; *wel (goodly, richely) biseye*, in good plight, of good (splendid) appearance, etc.; *yvel biseye*, ill-looking.

Bishenden, injure, ruin.

Bishetten, shut up.

Bishrewen, beshrew, curse (usually in a mild imprecation).

Bisien, busy (one's self); employ; trouble, disturb.

Bisily, busily, attentively, eagerly; completely; well.

Bisinesse, business, diligence; industry, labor, work; occupation; careful attention, care, anxiety.

Bismokede, soiled with smoke.

Bismotered, besmutted, marked with spots of dirt etc.

Biso(u)ght(e); see **Bisechen.**

Bispet, pp., spit upon.

Bispotten, bespot, smirch.

Bisprengen, pp. *bispreynt*; sprinkle, bedew.

Bisted, pp., placed, bestead, beset; hard pressed, endangered.

Bistowen, bestow, place, dispose; spend.

Bistryden, pt. sg. *bistrood*; bestride.

Bisy, Besy, busy, industrious, active; attentive, careful, anxious.

Bisyde, beside, near; *bisyde his leve*, without his leave.

Bisydes, besides; on one side.

Bit, contr. of *biddeth*.

Bitaken, pt. sg. *bitook*, pp. *bitaken*; betake, commit, entrust, deliver.

Bitechen, commit (to), give over (to).

Biternesse; see **Bitternesse.**

Bithinken, pt. *bitho(u)ghte*, pp. *bitho(u)ght*; bethink (often refl.); think of, imagine, consider.

Bitit, contr. of *bitydeth*.

Bitook; see **Bitaken**.

Bitor, bittern.

Bitraisen, Bitraisshen, betray.

Bitrenden, contr. pr. 3 sg. *bytrent*; encircle; twine around.

Bitternesse, bitterness; pl. *-es*, bitter things.

Bitwix(e)(n), between.

Bityden, betide, happen.

Bitymes, betimes, early.

Biwaren, spend, expend, lay out.

Biwepen, pt. *biwepte*, pp. *biwopen*; beweep, bemoan.

Biwreyen, Bewrayen, Biwryen, reveal, make known; betray.

Blake, black writing, ink (probably the wk. adj. used as a sbst.).

Blakeberyed, blackberrying. See *Pard Prol*, VI, 406, n.

Blaked, pp., blackened.

Blamen, blame; *to blame*, to be blamed. See *Gen Prol*, I, 375, n.

Blandisen, fawn; flatter.

Blanket, cut or dressing of meat (?). See *KnT*, I, 2951, n.

Blankmanger (lit. "white food"), creamed fowl or other meat stewed with eggs, rice, almonds, and sugar.

Blase, blaze.

Blasen, blow.

Blasten, blow (a trumpet blast).

Blaunche, white (Fr.). See **Fevere**.

Blechen, bleach.

Blenchen, pt. *bleynte*, pp. *bleynt*; blench, start back, turn aside.

Blenden, contr. pr. 3 sg. *blent*, pt. *blente*, pp. *blent*; blind; deceive.

Blent, contr. of *blendeth*.

Bleren, blear, dim; *blere hir yë*, deceive, cajole, hoodwink. See *RvT*, I, 3865, n.

Blering, dimming; hoodwinking.

Blessen, Blissen, bless; used refl., cross one's self.

Bleven; see **Bileven**.

Blew, blue; as sbst., blue clothing.

Bleyne, blain, blemish.

Bleynt(e); see **Blenchen**.

Blinnen; see **Bilinnen**.

Bliss(e), bliss, happiness.

Blissed, happy.

Blissen; see **Blessen**.

Blondren; see **Blundren**.

Bloo, blue, livid, smoke-colored.

Blosmen, blossom, bud.

Blosmy, blossoming, budding.

Blotte, blot, blemish.

Blowen, pt. *blew*, pp. *blowen*; blow; fill with wind.

Blundren, flounder, rush heedlessly, fall into confusion.

Blynden, blind. See also **Blenden**.

Blythe, blithe, glad, happy.

Blyve, Bylyve (lit. "by life"), quickly, soon, forthwith.

Boba(u)nce, boast, presumption.

Boce, Bos, boss, protuberance.

Bocler, Bokeler, buckler.

Bode (1), omen.

Bode (2), abiding, delay.

Boden, proclaim.

Boden; see **Beden**.

Body, body; person; corpse; *my body*, myself.

Boef, beef.

Boes, (it) behooves (Northern dial.).

Bokel, buckle.

Bokeler; see **Bocler**.

Boket, bucket.

Bolas, pl., bullaces.

Bolden, grow bold.

Bole, bull.

Bolle, bowl.

Bolt, bolt (of a crossbow).

Bolt-upright, flat on the back. See **Upright**.

Bomblen, bumble, boom.

Bon, good (Fr.).

Bond, bond, obligation; band, fetter.

Bond, Bonden; see **Binden**.

Bonde, bondman.

Bonde-folk, -men, bondmen.

Bone, boon, prayer, request.

Bontee; see **Bountee**.

Bood; see **Byden**.

Boole armonyak, "an astringent earth brought from Armenia, and formerly used as an antidote and styptic" (NED).

Boon, bone; ivory.

Boor, boar.

Boost, noise, outcry; boast, loud talk.

Boot, boat.

Boot; see **Bote**.

Boot; see **Byten**.

Booteles, without remedy.

Boras, borax.

Bord, board, plank; table, meals; dat. phr. *to borde, over borde*(?); *into shippes bord*, on board.

Bordel, brothel.

Bordillers, brothel-keepers.

Bordure, border; rim (of astrolabe).

Bore, sbst., bore, hole.

Borel, Burel, coarse, lay, unlearned; as sbst., coarse woolen clothes.

Bore(n); see **Beren**.

Borken; see **Berken**.

Bornen, Burnen, burnish, smoothe.

Borw, Borugh, pledge, surety; dat. phr. *to borwe*.

Borwen, borrow.

Bos; see **Boce**.

Bosard, buzzard.

Bosses, bushes.

Bosten, boast.

Bote, good, profit, advantage (cf. Mod. Eng. "to boot"); help, healing, salvation; *doth bote*, gives the remedy.

Botel, bottle (of hay).

Boterflye, butterfly.

Bothe, both; *your bothes, your bother*, of you both.

Bothon, Bothun; see **Botoun**.

Botiler, butler.

Botme, bottom.

Botoun, Bothon, Bothun bud.

Bouger, sodomite.

Bough, pl. *bowes*; bough.

Bouk, belly, trunk (of the body).

Boun, prepared, ready.

Bounde, bound, limit.

Bounden; see **Binden**.

Bountee, Bontee, goodness, kindness; virtue, excellence.

Bountevous, bounteous.

Bour, bower, bed-chamber; inner room; ladies' apartments.

Bourde, sbst., jest.

Bourden, jest.

Bowe, bow.

Bowen, pt. *bowed*; bow, bend; yield.

Bowes; see Bough and Bowe.

Box (1), box-tree.

Box (2), blow.

Box (3), box.

Boy, knave, rascal.

Boydekin, dagger (cf. Shak. "bodkin").

Boyste, box.

Boystous, rude, rough.

Bracer, arm-guard (in archery).

Bragot, bragget, a drink made of honey and ale.

Braid, start, quick movement.

Brak; see Breken.

Brasil, the red dye-stuff obtained from brazil-wood.

Brast(en); see Bresten.

Brat, cloak of cloth.

Braun, brawn, muscle; flesh (of the boar).

Braunche, branch.

Braunched, adj., having many branches.

Brayd; see Breyden.

Brede, breath, space; *on brede*, abroad.

Brede, roast meat.

Breden, breed; grow; increase; arise, originate.

Breech, breeches (orig. pl. of AS. "bróc," but usually sg. in Mid. Eng.).

Breed, bread.

Breem, bream, a fish with high arched back.

Breeth, breath.

Breken, pt. sg. *brak*, pl. *breken, broken*, pp. *broken*; break; break off; wreck; *breken his day*, to fail to pay on the appointed day.

Brekers, transgressors.

Brekke, break, breach, flaw.

Bremble-flour, bramble-flower, dog-rose.

Breme, furious; also adv.

Bren, bran.

Brennen, burn; be burnt, take fire; pp. *brend, 'brent*, burnt, forged, bright (as in *brend gold*), perhaps confused with *burned*, burnished.

Brere, briar; *breres*, underwood.

Bresten, contr. pr. 3 sg. *brest*, pt. sg. *brast*, pl. *brasten, brosten, brusten, bresten* (?), pp. *brosten*; burst, break; burst out; afflict.

Bretful, brimful.

Bretherhede, brotherhood, fraternity; guild.

Breve, adj., brief, short.

Brewen, pt. sg. *brew*; brew; contrive.

Breyden, pt. sg. *breyde*, pp. *brayd, browded*, but also in str. form *broyden*; start, awake, bestir one's self; snatch; embroider.

Briberyes, methods of stealing or cheating.

Brid, bird; young of birds.

Brigge, bridge.

Brighte, adv., brightly.

Brike, trap, snare.

Brim, brim, water's edge; dat. phr. *to the brimme*(?).

Brimme, fierce, cruel. See Breme.

Bringen, pt. *broghte*, pp. *broght*; bring, lead, conduct, introduce.

Brinnen, burn. See Brennen.

Bristilede, bristly.

Brocage, mediation; contract.

Broche, brooch; bracelet.

Brode, adv., broadly, plainly; far and wide; wide awake.

Broiden, pp. *broyded*; braid. See Breyden.

Brokkinge, of uncertain meaning; perhaps, using a quavering or broken voice.

Brond(e), torch; firebrand.

Brood, brood.

Brood, broad; thick, large; enlarged.

Broom, broom (the plant); pl. *bromes*, bushes.

Brosten; see Bresten.

Brotel, Brutel, brittle, fragile; frail, fickle; insecure, transitory.

Brouded, embroidered; braided, plaited; from Fr. "brouder," confused with the native str. pp. *browden* (AS."brogden.")

Brouken, enjoy, use; profit by.

Browded; see Breyden.

Browdynge, embroidery.

Browe, brow, eye-brow.

Broyden; see Breyden.

Brusten; see Bresten.

Brutel; see Brotel.

Bryben (Mod. Eng. "bribe"), steal, rob.

Bryge, strife, contention.

Buffet, blow.

Bugle-horn, drinking-horn made from the horn of the "bugle" or wild ox.

Buk, buck.

Bulden, build.

Bulle, papal bull.

Bulten, bolt, sift.

Burdoun, ground melody.

Burel; see Borel.

Burgeys, burgess; citizen.

Burgh, borough.

Burieles, burial places; the Catacombs.

Burnen; see Bornen.

Burnet, made of coarse brown cloth; also sbst., dress of such material.

Burthe, birth.

Busk, bush.

But, used as sbst., a but, an exception.

But and, but if.

Butiller; see Botiler.

Buxom, submissive, obedient.

By-; for words with this prefix see also Bi-.

By, prep., by; with respect to, concerning; *by me*, near, beside me; *by proces*, in process; *by this*, by now, already; *by the morwe*, by morning; *by that*, by the time that.

By and by, one after another, in order; side by side; precisely.

Byden, pt. sg. *bood*, pp. *biden*; wait, stay.

Byen, pt. *boghte*, pp. *boght*; buy, pay for; redeem.

Bygyn, Beguin.

Byle; see Bile.

Bylyve; see Blyve.

Bynne, bin, chest.

Bynt, Bint, contr. of *bindeth*.

Byrde, maiden, lady.

Byreynen, rain upon.

Byten, pt. sg. *boot*, pp. *biten*; bite; cut; sting; burn.

Bytinge, sbst., wound.

C (see also K and S)

Caas; see **Cas**.

Cacchen, Kecchen, pt. *caughte*, pp. *caught*; catch, take, obtain; pull, draw; perceive, conceive.

Cadence, cadence; rhythmic prose (?). See *HF*, 623, n.

Caitif, captive; wretch.

Cake, loaf (of bread).

Calcenynge, calcination.

Calcinacioun, calcination.

Calculen, calculate.

Calculer, calculator or pointer (of an astrolabe).

Caleweis, pears (from Cailloux in Burgundy).

Calle, caul; hair-net; head-dress; *maken him an howve above a calle*, make a fool of him.

Calme, calm.

Cam; see **Comen**.

Camaille, camel.

Camelyne, camel's hair stuff.

Camus, Kamus, low, flat, concave.

Can, Con, pl *connen*, pt. *coude*, inf. *connen*; understand; learn; know; know how, be able, have skill or experience; *can on governaunce*, knows of government, conduct; *can hir good*, knows her advantage (see *M L Epil*, II, 1169, n.); *can thank*, owes or feels thanks; *conne him maugree*, show him ill-will.

Cancre, cancer.

Candele, candle, torch; star.

Canel-boon (lit. "channel-bone"), collarbone.

Canelle, cinnamon.

Canevas, canvas.

Cankerdort; see **Kankedort**.

Canoun, canon, rule; table (of a calendar). On "The Canon" of Avicenna see *PardT*, VI, 889, n.

Cantel, portion.

Capel, horse; cart-horse, nag.

Capen; see **Gapen**.

Cappe, cap; *sette hir aller cappe*, made fools of them all.

Cardinacle, probably intentional blunder for *cardiacle*, disease or pain of the heart.

Careful, full of care, trouble, or sorrow.

Caren, vb., care, be anxious or troubled.

Careyne, carrion, dead body.

Carf; see **Kerven**.

Cariage, carrying off; *upon cariage*, in the way of carrying off; feudal *cariages*, feudal tolls imposed in place of service as carrier; hence, taxes.

Carl, man; fellow, boor, rustic.

Carmes, Carmelites, White Friars.

Carole, carol, a dance, accompanied by song.

Carolen, dance or sing a carol.

Carpen, talk.

Carrik, barge, ship.

Cart(e), cart; chariot.

Cartere, carter; charioteer.

Cas (1), **Caas**, case, affair; condition; accident, chance, mischance, adventure; *upon cas*, by chance; *in no mannes cas*, in no respect; *set a cas*, assume, suppose; *to deyen in the cas*, though death were to result.

Cas (2), case, quiver (for arrows).

Cast, casting, throwing; turn, occasion; contrivance, device.

Castelled, castellated.

Casten, pt. *caste*, pp. *cast*, and once *casten* (as if str. vb.); throw; vomit; cast (accounts); conjecture,

contrive, consider; plan, plot; refl., apply one's self; *cast biforn*, forecasted, premeditated, foreordained; *cast out*, overcome.

Casting, vomit.

Casuelly, accidentally.

Catapuce, caper-spurge (Lat. "Euphorbia Lathyris").

Catel, property, goods.

Caterwawed, caterwauling. See *Pard Prol*, VI, 406, n.

Cause, cause, reason; sake, benefit; plea (at law); *in cause*, to blame; *Cause causinge*, philosophical term for First Cause (Lat. "Causa Causans").

Causer, causer, creator.

Cave, cave; technical for the astrological "puteus." See *Mars*, 117, n.

Cavillacioun, cavilling.

Cedir, cedar.

Celebrable, worthy to be celebrated, honorable.

Celerer, cellarer, keeper of a cellar.

Celle (1), cell.

Celle (2), boarding, sill (Kentish form of *syll*).

Centre, center; point on the rete of an astrolabe.

Cenyth, Senith, zenith; point of intersection of an azimuth line with the horizon; the point of sunrise; the point of the sky directly overhead.

Ceptre, scepter.

Cered, waxed.

Cerial (var. **Serial**), of evergreen oak (Lat. "Quercus cerris").

Ceriously, minutely, in detail.

Certein, adj., certain, sure; a certain number or amount of (*certein gold, a certein yeres, a certein holes*); also used as sbst., a certain number; certainty.

Certein, adv., certainly, indeed.

Ceruce, white lead (compounded of carbonate and hydrate of lead).

Ces(s)en, cease; cause to cease, stop.

Cetewale, zedoary, a plant of the ginger tribe.

Ceynt, cincture, girdle.

Ceynt, Saynt, adj. from pp., girded, girdled.

Chaar; see **Char**.

Chafen, irritate.

Chaffare, sbst., trafficking; trading; merchandise, wares; matter, subject.

Chaffaren, vb., trade, traffic, barter.

Chair; see **Chayer**.

Chalangen, challenge, claim, arrogate.

Chalaundre, calander, lark.

Chalk-stoon, piece of chalk.

Chalons, blankets.

Chamberere, chambermaid, lady's maid.

Champartie, partnership in power; used by Lydgate and some later writers to denote rivalry; see NED.

Champioun, champion, fighting man; defender in judicial lists.

Chano(u)n, canon.

Chaped, mounted (with silver).

Chapelet, chaplet, fillet, circlet for the head.

Chapeleyn, chaplain; *nonne chapeleyne*, secretary and assistant to the Prioress. See *Gen Prol*, I, 164, n.

Chapman, merchant, trader.

Chapmanhede, bargaining, trading.

Char, chariot.

Charbo(n)cle, carbuncle (the precious stone).

Charge, load, burden; weight; care, responsibility;

tax; importance; *no charge*, no matter; *in his charge*, if he be responsible.

Chargeant, heavy, burdensome.

Chargen, load; weigh down, oppress; command, implore.

Char-hors, pl. chariot-horses.

Charme, charm.

Charmeresses, female charmers, workers with charms, witches.

Chartre, charter, document, agreement, deed.

Chasteleyn, castellan, governor of a castle.

Chasteleyne, wife of a *chasteleyn*.

Chasten, Chastien, chasten, teach, reprove, chastise.

Chasteyn, chestnut.

Chastysen, chastise, rebuke, restrain.

Chaunce, chance, luck; destiny; incident; technical term in the game of hazard. See *ML Prol*, II, 124, n.

Chaunten, chant; sing.

Chauntepleure, sing and weep; a song upon grief following joy; then, a proverbial term. See *Anel*, 320, n.

Chaunterie, chantry; endowment to provide masses for the souls of the founders or others.

Chayer, chair; professor's chair; throne.

Cheeke, cheek; cheekbone.

Cheep, market bargain; cheapness; time of cheapness; *greet cheep, good cheep*, good bargain, low price.

Chees; see **Chesen**.

Cheeste, quarreling, wrangling.

Cheeven, thrive, succeed; finish, bring to an end.

Chek, check (at chess).

Chekkere, chess-board.

Chekmat, checkmate.

Chelaundre; see **Chalaundre**.

Chepen, vb., trade; bargain.

Chere, face, appearance; look, glance; behavior; good cheer; friendly greeting.

Cherete; see **Chiertee**.

Cherissen, Chericen, cherish.

Cherl, churl, fellow; rough fellow; slave.

Cherubin, one of the cherubim.

Cherys, coll., cherries.

Ches, chess.

Chesen, pt. sg. *chees*, pl. *chosen*, pp. *chosen*; choose.

Cheste, Chiste, chest, box, trunk; coffin.

Chesteyn; see **Chasteyn**.

Chevache; see **Chyvachie**.

Cheveren; see **Shyveren**.

Chevesaile, ornamental collar.

Chevisaunce, accomplishing, bringing to an end; resource, remedy, device; borrowing or lending money; dealing for profit.

Chevisen, Cheveysen, achieve, accomplish one's desire; succeed; manage (on one's behalf), settle one's cause.

Cheveys; see **Chevisen**.

Chiche; see **Chinche**.

Chidde; see **Chyden**.

Chideresse, female scold. See **Chyden**.

Chidestere, female scold.

Chieftayn (var. **Cheventeyn**), chieftain.

Chiertee, Cherete, fondness, affection.

Chike, chicken.

Child, child; young man, fighting man; dat. phr. *with childe*.

Childly, childlike.

Chilyndre, cylinder, sun-dial.

Chinche, Chiche, adj., miserly, mean, avaricious; also sbst.

Chincherye, miserliness.

Chinchy, niggardly, miserly. See also **Chinche**.

Chirche, church.

Chirchehawe, churchyard.

Chirche-reve, church robbery.

Chirken, make a harsh or strident noise; chirp (like a bird).

Chisel, chisel; perhaps also scissors.

Chiste; see **Cheste**.

Chit; see **Chyden**.

Chiteren, chatter, twitter.

Chivalrye, chivalry; knighthood, valor; knightly deed or accomplishment; coll., a body of knights.

Chogh, Cow, chough.

Choppen, chop, knock, strike.

Chuk, chuck, noise made by a cock.

Chukken, cluck, make a clucking noise.

Chyden, contr. pr. 3 sg. *chit*, pt. *chidde*; chide, scold, reproach, reprove; complain.

Chymbe, rim (of a cask).

Chymben, chime.

Chymenee, chimney; fireplace.

Chynyng, yawning, gaping.

Chyvachie, Chevache, cavalry raid or expedition; feat of horsemanship; ride, course.

Cierge, wax-taper.

Cipre(e)ss, cypress; also collective.

Circumscriven, enclose, comprehend.

Circumstaunces, circumstances; accessory matters, accompaniments.

Ciser, strong drink.

Citole, stringed instrument, somewhat like a zither.

Citrinacioun, citronising (in alchemy).

Citryn, citron-colored.

Clad, Cladde; see **Clothen**.

Clamb(en); see **Climben**.

Clapers, burrows (for rabbits).

Clappe, noise, stroke; thunderclap; noisy talk, chatter.

Clappen, clap, chatter, talk; knock; shut.

Clapping, chatter.

Clarion, clarion, trumpet.

Clarioning, music of the clarion.

Clarre(e), drink of wine, honey, and spices.

Claspen, clasp; tie.

Clause, clause, sentence; agreement; *in a clause*, briefly.

Claw, pl. *clawes, clowes*; claw.

Clawen, pt. sg. *clew, clawed*; rub, scratch.

Cled(de); see **Clothen**.

Cleer, Clere, clear, bright; well-sounding; free; noble, splendid (Lat. "clarus").

Cleerly, entirely.

Cleernesse, brightness; glory.

Clefte; see **Cleven** (1).

Clene, clean; pure, unmixed; also adv., clean, entirely.

Clennesse, purity.

Clepen, call, name, mention; *clepen ayein*, recall.

Clere; see **Cleer**.

Clere, adv., clearly.

Cleren, grow clear; shine brightly.

Clergeoun, pupil; choir-boy. See *PrT*, VII, 495, n.

Clergial, clerkly, learned.

Clerk, cleric, one admitted to a religious order; ecclesiastic; scholar.

Cleven (1), pt. *clefte,* pp. *cloven;* cleave, split, cut; *clove,* dimpled.

Cleven (2), **Clyven,** cleave, adhere.

Clew; see **Clawen.**

Clewe, clew.

Cley, clay.

Cleymen, claim.

Clifte, cleft, chink.

Cliket, latch-key.

Climben, pt. sg. *clamb, clomb,* pl. *clamben, clomben,* pp. *clo(u)mben;* climb.

Clippen (1), embrace.

Clippen (2), clip, cut.

Clipsi, eclipsed, dim.

Clobbed, club-shaped.

Cloisterer, member or resident of a cloister.

Cloke, cloak.

Clom, interj., mum, be still.

Clomb(en); see **Climben.**

Cloos, close; secret; closed.

Clooth, cloth; garment; covering.

Cloothlees, naked.

Clos, sbst., close, yard.

Closen, enclose.

Closet, private room, chamber.

Closing, enclosure, boundary.

Closure, enclosure.

Clote-leef, burdock-leaf.

Cloth; see **Clooth.**

Clothen, pt. *cladde, cledde,* pp. *clad, cled;* clothe.

Clothered, clotted, coagulated.

Cloude, cloud; sky.

Cloumben; see **Climben.**

Clout, piece of cloth; clout, rag.

Clouted, clothed in patched garments, patched up.

Clove(n); see **Cleven** (1).

Clowes; see **Claw.**

Clow-gelofre, clove-gillyflower; clove (the spice).

Clustred, pp., covered with clouds.

Clyf, pl. *clyves, clyffes;* cliff.

Clymat, belt or zone of the earth; *clymates,* sets of almicanteras calculated for different latitudes.

Clyven; see **Cleven** (2).

Clyves; see **Clyf.**

Coagulat, pp., coagulated, clotted.

Cod, bag; stomach.

Coempcioun, coemption, joint purchase; the buying up of the whole supply of a commodity.

Coeterne, coeternal.

Cofre, coffer, chest, money-box; coffin.

Cogge, cock-boat.

Coghen, Coughen, cough.

Coillons, testicles.

Cok (1), cock; used to designate time, *the firste, the thridde cok.*

Cok (2), corruption of *God.* See *Manc Prol,* IX, 9, n.

Cokenay, cockney; effeminate fellow, milksop.

Cokewold, cuckold.

Cokkel, cockle; used to translate "zizania," *Lat.* "lollia," in Matt. xiii ("tares" in the King James Bible).

Cokkow, cuckoo.

Cold, cold, chilling; disastrous, fatal. See *NPT,* VII, 3256, n.

Colde, sbst., cold, chill.

Colden, grow cold.

Cole, coal.

Coler, collar.

Colera, choler, the humor (Lat.).

Colere, choler.

Colerik, choleric; hence, hot-tempered.

Col-fox, coal fox, fox with black tips.

Collacioun, comparison; conference.

Collateral, subordinate, lying aside from the main purpose.

Collect, pp., collected (in groups).

Collegge, college building.

Colour, color; appearance, complexion; excuse, pretence; way, manner; figures of speech, fine phrases (technical term in rhetoric).

Colpon, cutting, strip, slice; hence, gathering, shred; billet.

Columbyn, like a dove.

Com; see **Comen.**

Combren, pp. *combred;* encumber; *combreworld,* one who encumbers the world.

Combust, pp. burnt; quenched (used technically of a planet which is too near the sun).

Come, coming.

Comen, pt. sg. *cam, com,* pl. *comen,* pp. *comen;* come; *come therby,* come by it, obtain it; *com of,* come off, come along.

Comeven, Comm(o)even, move, instigate, induce.

Comlily, in a comely way.

Comm(o)even; see **Comeven.**

Com(m)une, common, general; ordinary; *in commune,* commonly, generally; used as sbst. for "the Commons," commoners; commonwealth; common property; technical term in law for common right.

Com(m)unely, publicly.

Compaignable, companionable.

Compaignye, Companye, company; companionship.

Comparysoned, compared.

Compas, compass, circuit; circle, circumference; zone; circlet, wreath; contriving; *compasses,* circles, or compasses; *tryne compas,* the threefold world (earth, sea, and heaven).

Compassement, plotting, contriving.

Compassen, plan, contrive; draw with compasses; surround, enclose; study, observe closely, comprehend.

Compassing, dimension; contrivance.

Compeer, fellow godfather; familiar friend, comrade.

Compellen, compel; bribe.

Compilatour, compiler.

Complexioun, also -plex-, complexion, temperament (mixture of humors in the system).

Compleynen, complain; lament.

Compleynt(e), complaint; technical term for ballad of complaint or lament.

Complisshen, accomplish.

Complyn, compline, evening service.

Comporten, bear, endure.

Composicioun, agreement; arrangement.

Compotent, master of itself (translates Lat. "sui compos").

Compounen, compound, compose; mix, temper; construct, draw, mark.

Comprehenden, comprehend; consider; comprise; include in an explanation or description.

Comprenden, contr. of **Comprehenden.**

Compte, account.

Comunabletes, communities.

Comunably, commonly, usually.

Comunalite, Comynalite, empire, dominion; community, commonwealth.

Comune; see **Commune.**

Comunte, community, common possession.

Comyn, cummin.

Comynalite; see **Comunalite.**

Con; see **Can.**

Conceite, conception, idea, thought; fancy, notion.

Concluden, conclude; include, summarize; succeed.

Conclusioun, conclusion, decision, judgment; summary, result (of an experiment); plan, purpose; end, fate; theorem, proposition (in mathematics).

Concorden, concord, agree.

Concours, course, result.

Condescenden, condescend, stoop to; agree upon; settle or fix upon; settle down to; come to particulars; yield, accede.

Condicioun, proviso, stipulation; state of being (inner character as well as external circumstances); conduct; state, circumstances; nature, sort, kind.

Condit, pl. *condys*; conduit.

Conestablerye, ward of a castle (under a constable).

Confederacye, conspiracy.

Confed(e)red, confederate, joined together.

Confermen, confirm, strengthen; decree.

Confiteor, I confess (Lat.).

Confiture, confection, mixture, preserve.

Confort, comfort, pleasure.

Conforten, comfort; strengthen, fortify, encourage.

Confounden, confound, destroy, ruin; confuse, perturb; subdue.

Confus, adj. (from pp.), confused, abashed; confusedly mixed, disorderly.

Congeled, congealed.

Congeyen, grant leave (Fr. "congé"), dismiss.

Congregacioun, congregation, assemblage; gathering together.

Conisaunce, cognizance, understanding; acquaintance.

Conjecten, conjecture, suppose; plot, conspire.

Conjoynen, pp. *conjoint;* compose, make up.

Conjunccioun, conjunction; technical in astrology for the apparent proximity of two heavenly bodies.

Conjuracioun, conjuring (in necromancy); conspiracy.

Conjuren, conjure, adjure; pray, beseech.

Connen; see **Can.**

Conning, adj., cunning, skilful.

Conscience, feeling, sensibility, pity, sympathy.

Consecrat, contr. pp., consecrated.

Conseil, council; counsel, advice; purpose, intention; secret; confidential adviser.

Conseilere, councillor; Roman consul.

Conseilour, counsellor; senator.

Consentant, consenting, agreeing.

Consentement, consenting.

Consentrik, concentric; having the same center or altitude.

Consequent, consequence, sequel.

Conservatyf, preserving. See *HF,* 847, n.

Conseyte; see **Conceite.**

Consistorye, consistory, council; court.

Constable, governor.

Constablesse, governor's wife.

Constaunce, constancy.

Constellacioun, constellation; cluster of stars; combination of heavenly bodies or influences.

Constreynaunce, constraint.

Constreynen, constrain, compel; refl., contract one's self).

Constreynte, constraint; distress.

Construen, understand, interpret; divine, explain.

Consulers, consuls.

Consumpt, pp., consumed.

Contagious, contiguous.

Contek, strife, conflict.

Contemplaunce, contemplation.

Contenance, countenance; appearance, demeanor; gesture; expression of feeling; self-possession; pretence; *fond his contenance*, composed himself.

Contenen, contain; hold together; remain; refl., bear, contain, maintain one's self.

Continued, pp., followed, completed.

Contract, pp., contracted.

Contraire, adj., contrary, opposed; also sbst., opponent, opposition.

Contrarie, contrary.

Contrarien, oppose.

Contrarious, contrary, adverse.

Contre, country; fatherland; *contre-folk*, people of his country; *contre-houses*, homes. See *Anel,* 25, n.

Controven, invent; compose.

Contubernyal, familiar, intimate.

Contunen, continue.

Convenient, suitable, fitting.

Convers, converse, reverse.

Conversacioun, conversation, way of living.

Converten, change (both trans. and intrans.); alter habit or opinion; swerve.

Conveyen, accompany, conduct; introduce.

Convict, contr. pp., overcome.

Conyng, cony, rabbit.

Cop, top; summit.

Cope, cope; cape, cloak; canopy (of heaven).

Coper, copper.

Copie, copy.

Coppe, Cuppe, cup.

Corage, heart, mind; nature, disposition; desire, will, ardor; courage, encouragement.

Corbetz, corbels.

Cord, cord, string; perhaps musical chord.

Corden, accord, agree.

Cordewane, Cordovan leather.

Cordyler, Franciscan (so named from his girdle of rope).

Corfew, curfew.

Cormeraunt, cormorant.

Corn, grain, crop; a grain (of corn); a cornstalk; fig., the best portion.

Cornemuse, bagpipe.

Corniculer, clerk, registrar.

Corny, strong of corn or malt.

Corone, Coroun(e), Croun, crown, garland; crown of the head; tonsure; in astronomy, the Northern Crown.

Correccioun, penalty, fine.

Cor(r)igen, correct.

Corrumpable, corruptible.

Corrumpen, corrupt.

Corrupcioun, corruption, destruction.

Cors, body; corpse.

Corsednesse, abomination.

Corseint (lit. "holy body"), saint; shrine.

Corsen, curse.

Corven; see **Kerven.**

Cos, kiss.

Cosin, cousin; also adj., akin, related, suitable.

Cosinage, kinship.

Cost (1), cost, expense.

Cost (2), way, manner, course; quality; *nedes cost,* of necessity.

Costage, cost.

Cǫste, coast; region (of earth or sky).

Cǫsteying, coasting.

Costlewe, costly. See *PardT,* VI, 495, n.

Costret (var. **Costrel**), flask, bottle.

Cǫte (1), cot, cote; room in a prison or dungeon.

Cǫte (2), coat, jacket; coat-of-arms; skirt; outer garment.

Cǫte-armure, coat-armor, coat-of-arms.

Cotidien, quotidian, daily.

Couchen, place, lay down, lay flat; impose; lie low, cower; pp. *couched,* set, laid; set with jewels.

Coude; see **Can.**

Counseil; see **Conseil.**

Counten, count, reckon, account.

Countenaunce; see **Contenance.**

Counting-bord, table in counting-house.

Countour (1), arithmetician; auditor (or perhaps pleader?). See *Gen Prol,* I, 359, n.

Contour (2), abacus, counting-board; counting-house.

Countour-hous, counting-house.

Countrepeisen, counterbalance, countervail; render equivalent.

Countrepleten, counterplead, argue against.

Countretaille, countertally, correspondence (of sound); hence, reply, retort.

Countrewaiten, watch over or against.

Coupable, culpable.

Coupe, cup.

Couren, cower.

Cours, course; course of life; in astronomy, orbit; in hunting, a run at the game.

Courser, courser, steed.

Courtepy, upper short coat.

Court-man, courtier.

Couth, Kouth, known, familiar, manifest.

Couthe; see **Can.**

Couthe, adv., manifestly, familiarly.

Coveityse, covetousness; bodily lust, desire.

Covenable, suitable, fitting; convenient.

Covent, convent.

Coverchief, head-covering, kerchief.

Covercle, pot-lid.

Coveren, cover; recover.

Covert, secret, hidden.

Coverture, covering; concealment; disguise.

Covetour, one who covets.

Covyne, deceitful agreement; deceitfulness.

Cow (1), pl. *keen, kyn;* cow.

Cow (2), see **Chogh.**

Coward, cowardly.

Cowardye, Cowardyse, cowardice.

Coy, quiet; modest, shy.

Coyen, make quiet, calm; cajole.

Coynes, quinces.

Crabbed, crabbed, cross, bitter.

Cracching, scratching.

Craft, skill, cunning; trade, art; secret; might, power; contrivance.

Crafty, skilful; clever; intelligent.

Craken, utter loudly or boldly; sing harshly (like a corn-crake).

Crampisshen, cramp, contract convulsively.

Crased, cracked, broken.

Creant (contr. of *recreant?*), *seith creant,* acknowledges defeat.

Creat, created.

Creaunce, credence, belief; object of belief.

Creauncen, borrow on credit.

Crece, increase, progeny.

Creep, see **Crepen.**

Crekes, tricks, wiles.

Crepel, cripple.

Crepen, pt. *creep, crepte,* pp. *cropen, crept;* creep.

Crevace, crevice, crack.

Crew; see **Crowen.**

Crinkled, full of turns and twists.

Crips, crisp, curly.

Cristen, Christian.

Cristendom, Christianity; the Christian faith.

Cristianitee, Christian people.

Croce, cross; crozier; staff, stick.

Crois, cross.

Croked, crooked; tortuous.

Crokes, crooks, hooks.

Crokke, crock, pot.

Crommes, crumbs.

Crop, top, sprout, new shoot; *crop and rote,* top and root; hence, altogether.

Cropen; see **Crepen.**

Croper, crupper.

Cros, cross.

Croslet, crucible.

Crouchen, mark with the sign of the cross.

Crouden, push, press.

Crouke, jug, pitcher.

Croun; see **Corone.**

Crouned, crowned; hence, surpassing, supreme.

Croupe(r); see **Croper.**

Crowen, pt. *crew,* pp. *crowen;* crow.

Crownet, coronet.

Croys; see **Crois.**

Crul, curly.

Crydestow, contr. of *criedest thou.*

Cryke, creek.

Cucurbites, chemical vessels for distillation.

Cuer, heart (Fr.); *par cuer,* by heart.

Culpe, guilt, culpability.

Culter, coulter (of a plough).

Culver, dove.

Cunnen; see **Can.**

Cunning, Konning, cunning, skill, knowledge, learning, experience.

Cuppe; see **Coppe.**

Curacioun, cure; method of cure.

Curat, one entrusted with the cure of souls; parish-priest.

Cure, care, heed; charge, attention, supervision; diligence; cure, remedy; *I do no cure,* I do not care; *besy cure,* occupation, busy employment or occupation; *his lyves cure,* his constant thought or care; *honest cure,* care for honor, self-respect; *in cuer,* in one's power.

Curiositee, elaborate workmanship; intricacy.

Curious, careful, diligent; skilful; eager; carefully or skilfully made; of strange or erudite interest (applied to magic).

Currour, courier, runner.

Cursednesse, wickedness; malice, shrewishness.

Cursen, curse; excommunicate.

Curteisye, courtesy.
Curteys, courteous; gentle, compassionate.
Customere, adj., accustomed.
Custume, custom; pl., payments; customs duties.
Cut, lot.
Cutten, contr. pr. 3 sg. *cut,* pt. *kitte,* pp. *cutted, cut;* cut.
Cynk, cinque, five.

D

Daf, fool.
Dag, tag, shred of cloth; hanging point of a garment slashed at the lower margin; tag of a lace or shoe-latchet.
Dagged, cut into tags or hanging peaks; slashed.
Dagginge, cutting into tags.
Dagoun, piece.
Dale, dale.
Dalf; see **Delven.**
Daliaunce, social conversation, chat, gossip; playfulness, mirth; caressing; wanton toying.
Damageous, damaging, injurious.
Dame, dame, madame; mother; dam; good wife.
Damiselle, damsel.
Dampnacioun, damnation, condemnation.
Dampnen, damn, condemn.
Dan, Daun, sir, lord (from Lat. "dominus").
Dar, pt. pr. vb., pt. *dorste,* inf. *dorren, durren;* dare.
Daren, lie in torpor or terror; crouch.
Darreynen, settle a right or a claim to; decide.
Dart, dart, given as a prize.
Daswen, daze, be dazzled.
Daun; see **Dan.**
Daunger, lordship, power, control; ungraciousness, disdain; hesitation, offishness, the quality of being "difficile." See *Gen Prol,* I, 517, n.
Daungerous, imperious, disdainful; offish, "difficile," fastidious; niggardly, sparing; grudging, hard to please.
Daunten, daunt, terrify; tame, overcome.
Dawen, dawn.
Daweninge, dawn.
Dawing, dawn.
Dayerye, dairy.
Dayesye (lit. "day's eye"), daisy.
Debaat, strife, conflict; war; debate.
Debaten, fight, make war; contend, quarrel.
Debonaire (lit. "of good disposition"), gentle, gracious, courteous; meek, calm.
Deceivable, deceitful.
Declamen, declaim, discuss.
Declinacioun, declination; in astronomy, the angular distance from the equator.
Declynen, decline, turn aside; in astronomy, possess declination.
Declyning, sloping.
Decoped, slashed, cut in openwork patterns.
Dede, pl. *dedes, dede;* deed, act; dat. phr. *in dede.*
Dede; see **Doon.**
Deden, grow dead, torpid, stupefied.
Dedicat, contr. pp., dedicated.
Deduyt, delight, pleasure.
Deed, dead; torpid, sluggish.
Deedly, deadly, mortal; dying; deathly.
Deef, pl. *deve;* deaf.
Deel, part, portion, share; bit, whit.
Deep, comp. **Depper;** deep.
Deer, pl. *deer;* animal.

Deerelyng, darling.
Dees (1); see **Deys.**
Dees (2), **Dys,** dice.
Deeth, death; plague, pestilence; dat. phr. *to dethe.*
Defamen, dishonor.
Defaute, fault, defect, lack; in hunting, the check or *stynt* of the pursuit when the scent is lost.
Defence, defense, resistance; covering; hindrance; prohibition; denial.
Defenced, defended.
Defendaunt, defense; *in his defendaunt,* in his defense (Fr. "en son defendant").
Defenden, defend; forbid.
Defensable, helping to defend.
Defet (lit. "undone"), injured, marred, disfigured.
Defoulen, trample down, defile; disgrace.
Defylen, bruise, maul.
Defynen, define, pronounce, declare.
Degisé, elaborate.
Degisynesse, elaborateness.
Degree, step or tier (of a theater); rank, status, condition; horizontal stripe; degree of an angle or arc.
Deignous; see **Deynous.**
Dekne, deacon.
Delen, deal; apportion; distribute; deal with; argue.
Deliberen, deliberate.
Delicasie, luxuriousness; voluptuousness; pleasure, delight.
Delicat, delicate, dainty; delicious.
Deliciously, delightfully; luxuriously.
Delitable, delightful.
Delitous, delightful, delicious.
Deliver(e), adj., active, agile; quick.
Deliveren, deliver; set free; do away with.
Delivernesse, activity.
Delven, pt. sg. *dalf,* pl. *dolven, dulven,* pp. *dolven;* delve, dig.
Delyces, delights; delicate feelings; loose pleasures; favorites.
Delye, delicate, dainty, fine.
Delyten, give or take pleasure; sometimes refl.
Demaunde, question.
Demeigne; see **Demeynen.**
Demen, deem, decide, suppose; judge, give a verdict, condemn.
Demeyne, domain, dominion; possession, ownership.
Deme(y)nen, manage, conduct; handle, manipulate; express, exhibit.
Demonstratif, demonstrable.
Denticle, pointer (on an astrolabe).
Depardieux, in God's name or authority; by God (an oath, Fr. "de par Dieu").
Departen, part, separate, divide; distinguish.
Departinge, separation, dividing; departure.
Depeynted, painted, depicted; stained.
Depper; see **Deep.**
Depraven, calumniate.
Depressioun, angular distance below the horizon.
Dere, comp. *derre;* dear; also adv.
Deren, hurt, injure.
Dereworth, amiable, friendly.
Derk, dark; inauspicious.
Derke, darkness.
Derken, Dirken, become dark; make dark; lie hidden, lurk.
Derne, secret.

Derre; see **Dere.**
Derthe, dearth.
Des-; see also **Dis-.**
Descensioun, descension; in astronomy, the degree of the celestial equator which sets with a given heavenly body; in astrology, the part of the zodiac in which a planet has least influence.
Descensories, in alchemy, vessels used for distillation by descent.
Descernen, discern.
Desceyvaunce, deception.
Deschargen, discharge, disburden.
Descryven, Discreven, describe.
Desert, adj., deserted, lonely.
Desert, Dissert, merit, deserving.
Desespeir, despair.
Desesperaunce, despair.
Deseveraunce; see **Disseveraunce.**
Desheriten, disinherit.
Deshonestee, dishonor, unseemliness.
Desirous, desirous; eager, ardent, ambitious.
Deslavee, immoderate, inordinate; dissolute.
Desordeynee, inordinate, disorderly.
Desordinat, inordinate.
Despeiren, despair; pp. *dispeired,* filled with despair.
Despenden, spend; waste.
Despense, expense; money for expenditure.
Desperaunce, desperation.
Despitous, spiteful; scornful; angry; cruel.
Desponen; see **Disponen.**
Desport, amusement, diversion, sport; merriment, mirth.
Desporten, rejoice; cheer, entertain.
Despoylen, despoil, rob.
Despyt, scorn, contempt; spite, malice; ill-humor.
Desray, disorder, confusion.
Destempred, distempered.
Destinal, pertaining to destiny; destined, fatal.
Destourben, disturb; hinder, interrupt.
Destract, distracted.
Destroubled, Distourbled, disturbed.
Destroyen, demolish, ruin; dissolve, consume; kill; lay waste, ravage; disturb, harass.
Determinat, determinate, fixed; properly placed (on the astrolabe).
Determynen terminate, come to an end; determine, settle.
Dette, debt.
Deus hic, a blessing: "God (be) here" (Lat.).
Deve; see **Deef.**
Dever; see **Devoir.**
Devil, devil; used as a curse or expletive in various expressions: *how devil, what devil, a devil weye.*
Devocioun, devotion; devoted application.
Devoid, free (from), destitute (of).
Devoiden, remove.
Devoir, Dever, duty; endeavor.
Devyaunt, divergent, turned aside.
Devyn, Divyn, diviner; astrologer.
Devynen; see **Divynen.**
Devyneresse, female diviner.
Devys, device, contrivance; supposition; disposal, will; direction; heraldic device; *at point devys,* with exactitude.
Devysen, devise, contrive, ordain; plan; arrange; imagine; relate, describe, discourse.
Dewe, Duwe, due.
Dexter, war-horse.

Deye, dairy-woman.
Deyen; see **Dyen.**
Deynen, deign.
Deynous, Deignous, disdainful, scornful.
Deyntee, sbst. (Fr. *dainté,* L. "dignitatem"), estimation, value, worth; delight, pleasure; a dainty, a delicacy.
Deyntee, adj., dainty, rare; fine, superior.
Deyntivous, dainty.
Deys, daïs, platform; high table.
Diapred, decorated with a small uniform pattern, or fret-work.
Dich, ditch.
Dichen; see **Dyken.**
Diete, diet.
Diffame, evil report.
Diffamen, defame.
Diffinicioun, definition, exposition.
Diffinitif, definitive, final.
Diffusion, diffuseness.
Diffyen, renounce; repudiate; challenge; defy.
Diffynen, define; conclude.
Diffyniss(h)en, define.
Dighten, pt. *dighte,* pp. *dight;* prepare, make ready; equip, array; place, ordain; lie with; also refl., prepare, betake one's self, hasten.
Digne, worthy, honorable; suitable; disdainful; scornful.
Dignitee, dignity, worth, rank; in astrology, the situation of a planet in which its influence is heightened, or the advantages it enjoys when in such a favorable situation.
Dilatacioun, dilating, diffuseness.
Diluge, deluge.
Dint, stroke.
Direct (really a contr. pp.), directed, addressed; direct; in astrology, motion in the same direction as that of the sun in the zodiac.
Dirken; see **Derken.**
Dis-; for words with this prefix see also **Des-.**
Disavauncen, set back, defeat.
Disaventure, misadventure, misfortune.
Disblamen, exonerate, free from blame.
Disceyven, deceive.
Dischevele, disheveled, with loose or disordered hair.
Disciplyne, discipline; mortification of the flesh.
Disclaunderen, slander; reproach.
Discomfit, discomfited, disconcerted.
Disconfiture, discomfiture.
Disconfort, discomfort; grief; discouragement.
Disconforten, discourage.
Discorden, disagree.
Discoveren, pp. *discovered, discovert;* uncover, reveal; *at discovert,* unprotected.
Discreet, wise, discerning; courteous (?).
Discreven; see **Descryven.**
Discuren, discover, reveal.
Discussen, discuss; dispel.
Disdeinous, disdainful.
Disencresen, decrease.
Disese, discomfort, inconvenience, uneasiness; displeasure; disease; misery; sorrow, grief.
Disesen, trouble, vex, distress.
Disesperat, desperate, without hope.
Disfigurat, disguised.
Disgysen, dress in new fashion; decorate, adorn; disguise, conceal.

Dishonest, dishonorable, shameful; unfair, unreasonable; unfaithful; immodest.

Disjoynt, difficult or perilous position; evil plight.

Dismal, unlucky day.

Disobeysaunt, disobedient.

Disordenaunce, violation of rules.

Disparage, disparagement; disgrace.

Disparagen, dishonor; misally.

Dispeired; see Despeiren.

Displayen, display, spread.

Displesaunce, displeasure; offense.

Displesaunt, displeasing.

Disponen, dispose; regulate.

Disposen, arrange; plan, purpose; pp. *disposed*, prepared, ready; *wel disposed*, in good health.

Disposicioun, disposition; state of mind; disposal.

Dispreisen, dispraise, blame, disparage.

Disputisoun, argument, debate; dispute.

Disrewlely, irregularly, without rule.

Dissert; see Desert.

Disserven, deserve.

Disseveraunce, dissevering, separation.

Disshevele; see Dischevele.

Dissh-metes, food cooked in dishes; pies, pastry.

Dissimulen, dissimulate, dissemble.

Disslaundren; see Disclaunderen.

Dissolucioun, dissoluteness.

Dissolven, cause the death of; cause to disappear, undo, destroy.

Distant, distant; *evene distantz*; (Fr. pl. in *-s*), equidistant.

Distemperaunce, inclemency.

Distempre, distempered, enraged.

Distempren, vex; be vexed.

Disteynen, stain, bedim.

Distincten, distinguish.

Distoned, out of tune.

Distourbled; see Destroubled.

Distreynen, seize, grasp; constrain; afflict; assess, tax.

Disturnen, turn aside.

Distyngwed, distinguished.

Ditee, ditty; discourse.

Diurne, diurnal.

Divinistre, divine, theologian.

Divisioun, act of dividing; distinction; difference; dividing line; detachment, company.

Divyn, divine, theologian.

Divynailes, divinations.

Divyne, sbst., divinity, theology.

Divynen, guess; declare.

Divynour, diviner, soothsayer.

Doand, Northern form of pr. p.; see Doon.

Dogerel, doggerel; bad or trivial verse.

Dogge, dog.

Doghter, pl. *doghtren*; daughter.

Doke, duck.

Dokke, dock (herb).

Dokken, dock, cut short.

Dolven; see Delven.

Dom, Do(u)mb, dumb.

Domesday, doomsday.

Domesman, judge.

Dominacioun, domination, control; ascendancy; used technically in astronomy and physiology.

Don, contr. of *do on*, put on.

Dong, dung.

Dongeoun, dungeon, keep-tower.

Don(n); see Dun.

Dool, grief, lamentation.

Dool, portion, share; *halfen dool*, half portion.

Doom, judgment; opinion; sentence, decision.

Doon, pt. *dide*, pp. *(y)doon*, inflected inf. *to done*; force; commit; fulfil; do, act, cause; frequently used as a causal auxiliary with infinitives, *do fecche, do come, dide don sleen*; also with participles, *hath don yow kept*; *don*, put on; *dide off*, doffed.

Dore, door; *out at dore*, out of doors.

Dormant, permanent. See *Gen Prol*, I, 353, n.

Dorren; see Dar.

Dorste; see Dar.

Dortour, dormitory.

Doseyn, dozen.

Dosser, basket to carry on the back.

Dotard, imbecile, fool; also adj.

Doten, dote, become foolish; behave foolishly.

Double, two-fold; deceitful.

Doublenesse, duplicity.

Doucet, dulcet, sweet-sounding; sbst., dulcet (pipe).

Doumb; see Dom.

Doun, down, feathers.

Doun, hill; dat. phr. *by doune*.

Doun-right, adv., straightway.

Doutable, doubtful; unstable, uncertain.

Doutance, doubt; perplexity.

Doute, doubt; fear; peril; lack; *out of doute*, doubtless.

Douten, doubt; fear.

Doutous, doubtful.

Doutremer, from beyond the sea.

Dowaire, dower.

Dowen, bequeath, give (as an endowment).

Downer, more downward, farther down.

Dowve, dove.

Drad(de); see Dreden.

Draf, draff; chaff.

Draf-sak, sack full of draff.

Dragoun, dragon; *tayl of the Dragoun*, the Dragon's tail. See *Astr*, ii, 4, 36, n.

Drasty, filthy, worthless.

Drat; see Dreden.

Draught, drink; move at chess.

Drawen, pt. sg. *dro(u)gh*, *drow*, *drew*, pl. *drowen*, pp. *drawen*; carry, haul; draw; incline, attract; bring forward or back; recall; move; draw near; withdraw.

Drecchen, delay, tarry; be slow or tedious; vex, annoy.

Drecchinge, delaying, prolonging.

Drede, dread, fear; doubt; *withouten*, or *out of, drede*, without doubt.

Dredeless, adj., fearless; adv., without doubt.

Dreden, contr. pr. 3 sg. *drat*, pt. *dredde*, *dradde*, pp. *drad*; dread, fear; sometimes refl.

Dredful, dreadful, terrible; timid.

Drenchen, pt. *dreynte*, *dreinte*, pp. *dreynt*, *drenched*; drown; be drowned; be overwhelmed.

Drenching, drowning.

Drerihed, dreariness, sorrow.

Dressen, address, direct; prepare, make ready, dress, array; set in order; often refl.

Drew; see Drawen.

Dreye, Drye, dry.

Dreyen, vb., dry.

Dreynt(e); see Drenchen.

Drogges, drugs.

Dronkelewe, drunken, addicted to drink. See *PardT*, VI, 495, n.

Dro(u)gh; see **Drawen**.

Dro(u)ghte, drought; thirst.

Droupen, droop, hang low, be draggled.

Drovy, dirty, muddy.

Drow(en); see **Drawen**.

Druerye, love; love-making; sometimes, wanton love.

Druggen, drudge.

Dryen, dree, endure; suffer.

Dryven, pt. sg. *droof*, pl. *driven*, pp. *driven*; drive, hasten; incite; continue, complete, include; pass (time).

Duetee, duty; debt.

Dulcarnoun, puzzle, dilemma. See *Tr*, iii, 931, n.

Dullen, feel or make dull; stupefy; make of no effect.

Dulven; see **Delven**.

Dun, dun-colored, dusty, swarthy.

Duren, endure, last; remain, continue, survive.

Duresse, hardship.

Durren; see **Dar**.

Dusken, grow dark or dim; darken (trans.).

Duwe; see **Dewe**.

Dwale, sleeping potion, narcotic drink.

Dwellen, pt. *dwelled*, *dwelte*, pp. *dwelled*, *dwelt*; dwell, remain, tarry; survive.

Dwelling, habitation; delay.

Dwyned, pp., dwindled, wasted away.

Dy, say (Fr.).

Dyamaunt, diamond; adamant.

Dyen, Deyen, die.

Dyere, dyer.

Dyete; see **Diete**.

Dyken, Dichen, make dikes or ditches.

Dys; see **Dees (2)**.

Dyte; see **Ditee**.

Dyversen, diversify, vary.

Dyversitee, diversity, variety.

E

Ebbe, ebb-tide, low water.

Ecclesiaste, divine, minister, preacher.

Ech, Ich, Ych, each.

Echen, eke out, increase, enlarge; add; help, aid.

Echoon, each one.

Echynnys, sea-urchins.

Edifien, edify; build up.

Eek, Eke, eke, also; moreover.

Eem, uncle.

Eet; see **Eten**.

Effect, result; effect; deed; cause; reality; *in effect*, in fact, in result.

Eft, again; later.

Eft-sone(s), immediately afterwards; very soon; hereafter; again.

Egal, equal; also adv.

Egalitee, equality; equanimity.

Egaly, equably; impartially.

Egge, edge; sword.

Eggement, instigation.

Eggen, egg on, incite, instigate.

Egging, instigation.

Egle, eagle; used by Chaucer as a generic term, covering the goshawk, falcon, sparrowhawk, and merlin.

Egre, sharp, bitter, fierce; acid, sour; keen; also adv.

Egremoyne, agrimony, a plant.

Egren, make eager, incite.

Eighe; see **Eye**.

Eighte, eight; also ordinal.

Eighteteene, eighteen.

Eightetethe, eighteenth.

Eir, Eyr, Air, air.

Eisel, vinegar.

Eke; see **Eek**.

Ekko, echo.

Elaat, adj., elate.

Elacion, elation.

Elbowe, elbow.

Elde, age, old age; lapse of time.

Eldefader (var. **Eldefather**), grandfather.

Elden, grow old; make old.

Eldres, Eldren, ancestors.

Eleccioun, election, choice; in astrology, choice of a favorable time. See *MLT*, II, 312, n.

Element, one of the four elements (fire, air, earth, and water); in astronomy, one of the celestial spheres.

Elenge, wretched, miserable.

Elengenesse, sadness.

Elevacioun, elevation; in astronomy, the altitude of the pole, or of any heavenly body, above the horizon.

Elevat, elevated.

Elf-queen, fairy queen.

Ellebor, hellebore.

Elles, else, otherwise, in other respects.

Elongacioun, angular distance.

Elvish, elvish; mysterious; elf-like, absent in demeanor, not of this world.

Em-; for words beginning with this prefix see also **En-**.

Embassadour, ambassador.

Embassadrye, embassy, negotiation.

Embelif, oblique, acute; also adv.

Embelis(sh)en, embellish.

Embosed, Enbosed, embossed, raised; in hunting, covered with flecks or bosses of foam; hence, exhausted.

Embracen, Enbracen, embrace; surround; hold fast.

Embrouden, Enbrouden, embroider.

Embusshementz, ambushes, ambuscades.

Emeraude, emerald.

Emforth, to the extent or measure of, according to, in proportion to.

Emisperie; see **Hemisper(i)e**.

Empeiren, Enpeiren, impair, injure.

Emperesse, Emperyce, empress.

Emplastren, plaster over, bedaub.

Emplien, enwrap.

Empoysonen, poison.

Emprenten, Enprienten, imprint; impress.

Empressen, press, impress. See also **Impressen**.

Empryse, Enprise, enterprise, undertaking; purpose, design; difficulty; value; estimation, renown; conduct, privilege, rule.

Empten, empty; exhaust, wear out.

En-; for words beginning with this prefix see also **Em-**.

Enbatailled, embattled.

Enbaumen, embalm; cover with balm.

Enbibyng, absorbing, soaking (alchemical term).

Enbosed; see **Embosed**.

Enbracen; see **Embracen.**

Enbrouden; see **Embrouden.**

Encens, incense.

Encensen, offer incense; cense.

Enchantours, enchanters, wizards.

Encharged, imposed, laid upon.

Enchaunten, enchant.

Enchęsoun, occasion, reason; cause.

Enclǫs, pp., enclosed.

Enclynen, incline (before), bow down (to), respect.

Enclyning, inclination.

Encomb(e)rous, cumbrous, burdensome.

Encombren, encumber, make weary; endanger; hinder, hamper; importune, vex, annoy.

Encorporing, incorporation.

Encręęs, increase; assistance.

Encręsen, increase, enlarge; enrich.

Endamagen, damage, harm; imperil; discredit, compromise.

Ende, end; limit; point; purpose.

Ended, finite.

End(e)long, adv., all along; lengthwise.

Endelong, prep., along, all along, down along.

Endentinge, indentation; in heraldry, notching with regular indentations.

Endere, ender; he who, or that which, ends.

Endetted, indebted.

Ending-day, death-day.

Enditement, indictment.

Endlong; see **End(e)long.**

Endouted, feared.

Endyten, indict; write, compose; dictate; relate.

Enfamyned, starved.

Enfaunce, infancy, youth.

Enfecten, infect.

Enforcen, enforce; strengthen, fortify; compel; gain strength; endeavor.

Enformen, inform, instruct.

Enfortuned, endowed with a power or a quality.

Engendrure, engendring, procreation; progeny; fraternity.

Engreggen, weigh down, burden.

Engreven, displease.

Engyn, Engin, skill; contrivance, device; machine.

Engyned, tortured, racked.

Enhabit, pp., inhabited; hence, possessed, devoted.

Enhansed, exalted, elevated (above the horizon).

Enhauncen, Enhaunsen, exalt, raise; promote.

Enhorten, exhort.

Enlacen, entangle; involve.

Enlangoured, made weak or pale with langour.

Enluminen, illumine.

Enluting, daubing with "lute," clay, etc.

Enoynten, pp. *enoynt(ed)*; anoint.

Enpeiren; see **Empeiren.**

Enprenten; see **Emprenten.**

Enpryse; see **Empryse.**

Enqueren, enquire.

Enqueste, inquest, legal inquiry.

Ensaigne, ensign, standard.

Ensa(u)mple, example, pattern; warning; instance, illustrative story.

Ensaumpler, exemplar; prototype.

Ensęled, sealed; confirmed by seal.

Enspyren; see **Inspiren.**

Ensuren, assure.

Entaile, carving, intaglio-work; figure, description.

Entaillen, carve.

Entalenten, stimulate, excite.

Entamen, cut; hence, open (a conversation, etc.).

Entecchen, stain, infect; endue with qualities, good or bad.

Entencioun, intention, purpose; design; meaning; understanding; endeavor; diligence; occupation; *of entencioun*, intentionally.

Entendement, perception; intention.

Entenden, Ententen, attend, give attention (to); aim, apply one's self; look intently, perceive; belong, pertain.

Entente, intent; intention; attention; design, purpose, plan; endeavor; meaning.

Ententyf, attentive; careful; devoted.

Enter-; for words beginning with this prefix see **Entre-.**

Entraille, entrails, inward parts.

Entrechaungen, interchange, exchange; confuse; mingle.

Entrecomunen, intercommunicate.

Entredited, interdicted.

Entree, entry; entrance; access.

Entrelaced, interlaced, intricate.

Entremedlen, intermingle; mix.

Entremes, entremets, intermediate course (at table).

Entremet(t)en, often refl., interfere, meddle.

Entren, enter.

Entreparten, share.

Entryken, ensnare, entrap; hold fast.

Entunen, intone.

Entunes, pl., tunes.

Entysinge, enticing, allurement.

Envenymen, envenom, poison; infect.

Enviroun, roundabout.

Envirounen, surround, encompass, include; go round about.

Envirouninge, circumference; surface.

Envoluped, enveloped, wrapped up.

Envoy, epilogue or postscript of a poem (Fr. "envoi").

Envye, envy; desire, longing.

Envyen (1), envy.

Envyen (2), vie; strive.

Envyned, stocked with wine.

Eny; see **Any.**

Episicle, epicycle; in astronomy, a small sphere or circle the center of which moves along the circumference of a larger one.

Equacioun, equation; calculation; equal division.

Equinoxial, equinoxial circle.

Equipolence, in logic, an equivalence between two or more propositions.

Ęr, adv., formerly.

Ęr, conj., ere, before.

Ęr, prep., before; as in *er now, er that, er tho.*

Ęrand(e), errand.

Erbe, herb; *erbe yve*, ground ivy.

Erber; see **Herber.**

Erche-, arch-; as in *erchebisshop, erchedeken.*

Ęre (1), ear; *at ere*, in (one's) ear.

Ęre (2), ear (of corn), spike.

Ęren, plough.

Erk, weary, wearied.

Erl, earl.

Ermen, grieve, be sad.

Ernest (1), Ernes, ardor (of love).

Ernest (2), earnest, pledge.

Ernestful, serious.

Erratik, wandering.

Erraunt, errant; stray; wandering.

Erren, err, transgress; wander.

Errour, error; wandering; doubt, perplexity.

Ers, buttocks.

Ęrst, first, at first; before; *erst than,* before; *dat.* phr. *at erste.*

Erthe, earth; land, country.

Eschaufen, burn, heat; grow warm.

Eschaunge, exchange; interchange.

Eschew, Eschu, averse.

Eschewen, Eschu(w)en, escape; avoid, shun.

Ęse, Eyse, ease; pleasure, delight.

Ęsement, easement, benefit.

Ęsen, ease, relieve; entertain, set at ease.

Ęspace, space (of time).

Especes, species, kinds, varieties.

Espiaille, coll., spies, espionage system.

Espirituel, spiritual.

Espleiten, perform, carry out.

Espye, spy.

Espyen, espy, observe, see; inquire.

Essoyne, excuse.

Ęst, sbst. and adj., east; also adv.

Estable, stable.

Establen, establish; settle.

Establissen, establish.

Establisshing, decree.

Estat, estate, state; rank, condition.

Estatlich, Estatly, stately, dignified; in accordance with rank.

Estatuts, statutes, ordinances.

Estoryal; see **Historial.**

Estraunge, strange.

Estres, inward parts; interior.

Esy, easy; moderate; slow; gentle.

Ęten, pt. sg. ęęt, ęt, pl. ęten, pp. *eten;* eat.

Ęterne, eternal; also sbst.

Ethe, Eythe, easy.

Evangyle, Evaungelie, gospel.

Evel; see **Yvel.**

Eve(n), evening.

Ęven, even, equal; exact; moderate; tranquil; also adv., *evene joynant,* just adjoining.

Ęvene-Cristen, fellow Christian.

Ęven(e)-lyk, similar.

Even-tyde, evening.

Ever(e), ever, always; *evere in oon,* always alike, continually, consistently.

Everich, each, every one; every; *everich a,* each.

Everichoon, every one.

Every-dayes, daily.

Every-dęęl, every bit, altogether.

Evidently, by observation.

Ew, yew-tree; also coll.

Exaltacioun, exaltation; in astrology, the position in which a planet exerts its strongest influence.

Exaltat, exalted.

Exametron, hexameter.

Exces, excess, extravagance of feeling.

Excusa(s)cioun, excuse; plea.

Executour, executor.

Executrice, executrix; causer.

Exercen, exercise.

Exercitacioun, exercise.

Existence, actuality, reality.

Exorsisacions, exorcisms.

Expans, calculated separately. See *FranklT,* V, 1275, n.

Experience, experience; experiment.

Expert, expert, skilled; experienced.

Expoun(d)en, expound, explain.

Expres, expressed, made clear; also adv.

Expressen, express; declare, relate.

Extre, axle-tree.

Ey, egg.

Eye, Eighe, Yë, pl. *eyen, yën;* eye; *at yë,* to sight, manifestly.

Eyed, furnished with eyes.

Eylen, ail.

Eyr (1); see **Eir.**

Eyr (2), heir.

Eyrish, aerial.

Eyse; see **Ęse.**

Eythe; see **Ethe.**

F

Fable, fable, tale; falsehood, deceit.

Face, face; in astrology, the third part (ten degrees) of a sign of the zodiac.

Facound, eloquent.

Facounde, eloquence, fluency.

Faculte(e), capacity; power; branch of study; profession; official position.

Fade, faded.

Fader, Feder, gen. sg. *fader, fadres;* father; parent, ancestor; origination; pl. *fadres,* Roman senators (Lat. "patres conscripti").

Fad(o)me, fathom.

Faille, failure.

Fail(l)en, fail, grow dim; cease; pp. *failed,* as adj., lacking, defective.

Fainen, pt. *fainte;* see **Feynen.**

Fair, fair, good; lovely; excellent; specious.

Faire, fairly, well; clearly; courteously; suitably; successfully.

Faire, fair, market.

Fair-Semblaunt, Fair-Semblance.

Fairye; see **Fayerye.**

Falding, coarse woolen cloth, frieze; a garment of that material.

Fallaces, deceits.

Fallen, pt. sg. *fel, fil,* pl. *fellen, fillen,* pp. *fallen;* fall, befall, happen; suit, befit; belong; pass into (some condition); prosper; *fil of his acord,* agreed with him.

Falsen, falsify; deceive, betray.

Falshęde, falsehood.

Falwe, fallow, yellow; sbst. pl. *falwes,* fallow-ground.

Fame, fame, renown; rumor, report; good report.

Famil(i)er, Famul(i)er, adj., familiar, intimate; affable; also sbst.

Fane (var. Vane), Fan, vane, weather-cock; apparently used of the revolving vane or bar in the game of quintain.

Fanne, fan.

Fantastyk, pertaining to the fancy.

Fantasye, fancy, imagination; delight; desire.

Fantome, phantom; illusion, dream.

Farcen, Farsen, stuff.

Fardel, load, bundle.

Farden, paint.

Fare, fare; procedure, business; stir, ado; behavior, conduct, fortune, condition, welfare.

Fare-cart, traveling-cart.

Faren, pt. *ferde,* pp. *faren, ferd;* fare; go, walk, travel; proceed; depart, vanish; behave; succeed;

take place, happen; be; *wel-farynge*, well-conditioned, well-appearing, handsome. See *FranklT*, V, 932, n.

Farsen; see **Farcen.**

Fasoun, fashion; shape; construction.

Faste, adv., closely, tight; near, close by; quickly; hard, eagerly.

Fastnen, Festnen, fasten, fix, plant.

Fatten, fatten.

Fattish, plump.

Faucon, falcon.

Faught; see **Fighten.**

Faunen, fawn (on).

Faute, fault, defect.

Fawe(n); see **Fayn.**

Fawnes, fauns; Roman deities of fields and herds.

Fay; see **Fey.**

Fayerye, Fairye, company of fairies; land of fairies; a fairy; magic, enchantment; a magical contrivance.

Fayn, Feyn, Fawe(n), glad, willing, eager; fond; also adv.

Faynt; see **Feynt.**

Feble, Fieble, feeble, weak.

Feblesse, weakness.

Fecche, vetch.

Fecchen, pt. *fette* pp. *fet*; fetch, bring; reach, get.

Feden, pt. *fedde*; feed.

Feder; see **Fader.**

Fee, reward, pay; possession; property, fief; *fee simple*, unrestricted possession.

Feeld, field, plain.

Feend, fiend, devil; foe.

Feendly, fiendish.

Feer, fear; see **Fere.**

Feere, company. See **Fere** (1).

Feeste; see **Feste.**

Feet, feat; performance.

Feffen, enfeoff, endow, put in possession.

Feirs; see **Fers,** adj.

Feithful, faithful; believing (Christian).

Fel, skin.

Fel, adj., comp. *feller*; terrible; cruel; deadly; fierce.

Fel; see **Fallen.**

Felawe, fellow, companion, comrade; *good felawe*, boon companion; hence (sometimes), rascal.

Felaw(e)shipe, fellowship, company; partnership.

Felawschipen, accompany.

Feldefare, fieldfare.

Fele, much, many.

Felefolde, manifold.

Felen, feel, perceive (by other senses, as well as by touch); experience; became aware; understand by experiment; investigate.

Felenous; see **Felonous.**

Fellen, fell, cause to fall; cut down.

Fellen; see **Fallen.**

Felliche, Felly, severely, bitingly.

Felnesse, fierceness, cruelty.

Felonous, Felenous, wicked, fierce; violent; criminal; impious.

Felonye, crime; wickedness, injustice; impiety; treachery.

Feloun, adj., fierce, cruel; evil, wicked.

Felthe; see **Filthe.**

Femele, female.

Fen, chapter, subdivision. See *PardT*, VI, 889, n.

Fenel, fennel.

Fenix, phoenix.

Fer, adj., comp. *ferre, ferrer, ferther*, sup. *ferrest(e), ferthest*; far; also adv.

Ferd(e); see **Faren.**

Ferd(e) perhaps pp. of *feren* used as sbst.), fear; dat. phr. *for ferde*.

Fere, Feer, fear, terror; panic.

Fere (1), companion; mate; wife.

Fere (2), dat. of *feer*, Kentish form of *fyr*, fire.

Fered, Kentish for *fyred*, fired, enflamed.

Feren, frighten, terrify.

Forforth, far; *as forforth as*, as far as, as long as, exactly as if, to such a degree.

Ferforthly, completely, thoroughly; to such an extent.

Ferly, strange.

Fermacies, medicines.

Ferme, sbst., rent.

Ferme, firm; durable.

Fermen, confirm, make firm.

Fermerer, friar in charge of an infirmary.

Fermour, farmer of taxes.

Fern, adj., remote, distant; past; *of ferne yere*, of last year.

Fern, adv., long ago.

Ferre, Ferrer, Ferrest(e); see **Fer.**

Fers, queen (at chess); pl. *ferses*, the chessmen.

Fers, Feirs, Fiers, adj., fierce.

Ferste; see **Firste.**

Ferthe, fourth.

Ferther, Ferthest; see **Fer.**

Ferther-over, moreover.

Ferthing, farthing; bit; small gift.

Fery, fiery.

Fesaunt, pheasant.

Fest, Kentish for *fist*.

Feste, feast; merriment; *feeste maketh*, pays court, honors, shows favor; *have feeste of*, delight in.

Festen, feast.

Festeyinge, feasting, entertaining.

Festlich, festive, convivial.

Festnen; see **Fastnen.**

Fet; see **Fecchen.**

Fether, feather; wing.

Fethered, provided with feathers or wings.

Fetheren, grow wings; stroke with the wings (in caress).

Fette; see **Fecchen.**

Fetys, well-made, neat, graceful, handsome.

Fevere, fever; *fevere terciane*, intermittent fever; *blaunche fevere*, white fever.

Fewe, sbst. and adj., few; not many; used, as in Mod. Eng., with the article, *a fewe welles, a wordes fewe*.

Fey, Fay, faith; *par ma fay*, by my faith.

Feyn; see **Fayn.**

Feynen, Feignen, Faynen, pt. *feyned, feynte*; feign, pretend; dissimulate; sometimes refl.

Feynt, Faynt, adj., feigned.

Feynten, faint; weaken, enfeeble.

Feyntyse, deceit, guile.

Fiaunce, trust, confidence.

Ficchen, fix.

Fieble; see **Feble.**

Fiers; see **Fers,** adj.

Fifte, fifth.

Fige, fig; fig-tree.

Fighten, contr. pr. 3 sg. *fight*, pt. sg. *faught*, pp. *fo(u)ghten*, fight.

Figure, figure, shape, form; marking; appearance; figure of speech.

Figuren, signify, symbolize.

Figuringe, form; similitude, figure.

Fikelnesse, fickleness.

Fil; see **Fallen.**

Filet, fillet, headband.

Fille, fill, sufficiency.

Fillen; see **Fallen.**

Filthe, Felthe, filth; shame, disgrace.

Finden, contr. pr. 3 sg. *fint,* pt. sg. *fond,* pl., pp. *founden;* find, discover; devise, invent; provide, provide for; in hunting, discover the game after it has begun to run.

Finding, provision.

Fined, refined, delicately made.

Fint; see **Finden.**

Firre, fir-tree.

Firste, Ferste, adj., first; *with the firste,* very soon.

Fit (1), canto, "passus."

Fit (2), dangerous or exciting situation or experience; mood, feeling; bout, turn, spell.

Fithele, fiddle.

Fix, adj. from pp., fixed; solidified; pl. *fixe, fixes (sterres).*

Flatour, flatterer.

Flaugh; see **Fleen** (1).

Fla(u)mbe, Flawme, flame.

Flawnes, flawns; "a dish composed of new cheese, eggs, powdered sugar, colored with saffron and baked in small tins called 'coffins' " (Skeat).

Flayn; see **Fleen** (3).

Fled(de); see **Fleen** (2).

Flee, pl. *fleen;* flea.

Fleen (1), pt. sg. *flaugh, fleigh, fley, fly,* pl. *flowen, flyen,* pp. *flow(e)n;* fly.

Fleen (2), pt. sg. *fleigh, fledde,* pp. *fled;* flee, escape.

Fleen (3), pp. *flayn;* flay.

Flees, fleece.

Fleet; see **Fleten.**

Fleigh; see **Fleen** (1) and (2).

Flekked, flecked, spotted.

Flemen, banish.

Flemere, banisher, one who puts to flight.

Fleshly, adv., carnally.

Fleten, contr. pr. 3 sg. *fleet;* float, bathe; flow, spread abroad; abound.

Flex, flax.

Fley; see **Fleen** (1).

Flight, flight; dat. phr. *to flighte.*

Flikeren, flutter.

Flitten, flit, shift, pass away; *flitting,* fleeting.

Flo, arrow.

Flokmele, in a flock or troop, in crowds.

Flood, flood-tide.

Floor, floor; domain.

Floroun, floret; petal.

Floteren, flutter, waver, fluctuate.

Flotery, waving, fluttering.

Flour, flower; choice part; supreme beauty or excellence; flourishing time; flour.

Flouren, flourish; bloom.

Flourette, floweret, bud.

Floury, flowery.

Flo(e)n; see **Fleen** (1).

Flowte, Floyte, flute.

Flowtour, flute-player.

Floytynge, playing on the flute (?); whistling (?).

Fly; see **Fleen** (1).

Flye, fly.

Flyen; see **Fleen** (1).

Fnesen, puff, snort.

Fnorten; snort; snore.

Fo, pl. *foon, foos;* foe.

Fode, food.

Foghten; see **Fighten.**

Foisoun, plenty, abundance.

Folde, fold, sheepfold.

Foled, foaled.

Folily, foolishly; idly.

Fol(o)wen, follow; imitate.

Foly, foolish; also adv.

Folye, folly, foolishness; silly thing; wantonness, dissipation.

Folyen, act foolishly.

Fomen, foe-men.

Fomy, foamy.

Fond, foolish.

Fond; see **Finden.**

Fonden, try, endeavor; attempt to persuade.

Fongen, receive.

Fonne, fool (Northern dial.).

Fool, fool, jester; also adj.

Fool-large, foolishly generous.

Foom, foam.

Foon; see **Fo.**

Foore, path, track; trace of steps.

Foot, Fote, pl. *feet;* foot; dat. phrases *to fote, to fete* (pl.), etc.; extended use, *half a fote thikke.*

Footen, dance.

Foot-hoot, "hot-foot," instantly.

Foot-mantel, foot-cloth, to wear over the skirt in riding.

For, for; in regard to; because of; for the sake of; against, to prevent; in spite of; *knew for subtil,* knew to be subtle; *for old, mad,* etc., because of age, madness, etc. See *KnT,* I, 2142, n.

Forage, fodder; food; winter-food.

Forbeden, contr. pr. 3 sg. *forbet,* pt. *forbad, forbed,* pp. *forboden;* forbid.

Forberen, pt. sg. *forbar;* bear, endure; forbear; forgive; disregard; spare; abstain; let alone.

Forbisen, instruct by examples.

Forblak (?), extremely black (?). See *KnT,* I, 2142, n.

Forbode, prohibition.

Forboden; see **Forbeden.**

Forbreken, pt. sg. *forbrak;* break off, interrupt.

Forbrused, badly bruised.

Forby, by, past.

Forcracchen, scratch severely.

Forcutten, cut to pieces.

Fordoon, pt. *fordide,* pp. *fordoon;* destroy; kill; overcome.

Fordriven, driven about, scattered.

Fordronken (?), very drunken (?); in some places doubtless to be read *for dronken.* See *Mill Prol,* I, 3120, n.

Fordrye (?), very dry (?). See *SqT,* V, 409, n.

Fordwyned, shrunken.

Forehed, Forheed, Foreheved, forehead.

For(e)ward, promise, agreement.

For(e)wardis, adv., forwards.

Foreyn, outer, exterior, extraneous.

Foreyne, sbst., "chambre foreyne," privy.

Forfaren, perish.

Forfered, pp. of *forferen*; afraid, terrified. Sometimes hard to distinguish from *for fered*, because afraid, or *for ferde*, from fear. See *SqT*, V, 527, n.; also Ferd(e), sbst.

Forfeten, forfeit; do wrong.

For-fyn (?), very ingenious (?). See *Tr*, iv, 477, n.

Forgaf; see Foryeven.

Forgat; see Foryeten.

Forgo, pp., exhausted with walking (?). See *HF*, 115, n.

Forgon, pt. *foryede*, pp. *forgon*; forego, give up; lose.

Forgyft, forgiveness.

Forheed; see Forhed.

For-hoor, very hoar (?). But see *Rom*, 356, n.

Forkerven, cut in pieces. See Kerven.

Forlaft; see Forleven.

Forlesen, pp., *forlorn*; lose.

Forleten, pp. *forleten*; leave, abandon, forsake; yield up; cease.

Forleven, pp. *forlaft*; abandon, forsake.

Forliven, vb., degenerate; pp., *forlived*, ignoble, degenerate.

Forlong; see Furlong.

Forlorn; see Forlesen.

Forlost, utterly lost.

Forloyn, signal that the dogs are far off from the game; hence, a recall from the hunt.

Forme, Fourme, form; formality; technical use, Lat. *forma*; lair (of a hare).

Forme-fader, first father, forefather.

Formel, companion, mate (of a bird).

Former, Maker, Creator.

Formest, first, foremost.

Forn-cast, premeditated, foreordained.

Forneys, Fourneys, furnace.

For-ofte, very often.

For-old (?), very old (?). See *KnT*, I, 2142, n.

Forpampred, exceedingly pampered.

Forpeyned, distressed.

Forpyned, tormented; wasted by torture or suffering.

Fors, Force, force; importance, consequence; *no fors*, no matter; *do no fors*, care not; *what fors*, what matter.

Forsaken, pt. sg. *forsook*, pp. *forsaken*; forsake, leave; deny, refuse, withstand.

Forseid, aforesaid.

Forshapen, transformed.

Forshright, exhausted with shrieking (but possibly to be read *for shright*).

Forslewen, waste idly.

Forslewthen, waste by sloth.

Forsluggen, spoil, allow to spoil.

Forsongen, exhausted by singing.

Forsothe, dat. phr., forsooth, verily.

Forster, forester, game-keeper.

Forstraught, distracted.

Forsweren, pt. sg. *forswor*, pp. *forsworen*; forswear, swear falsely; sometimes refl.

Fortened, destroyed (?), obstructed (?).

Forth, Furth, forth, further, forward; out; still, continually; *tho forth*, henceforth.

Forthenken; see Forthinken.

Forther, Further, further; more forward.

Forth(e)ren, Furth(e)ren, further, advance; help, assist.

Forther-moor, furthermore; moreover.

Forther-over, furthermore; moreover.

Forthinken, pt. *forthoghte*; displease, seem wrong or unfortunate; regret.

Forthright, straightforwardly.

Forthward, forwards.

Forthwith, also, therewith.

Forthy, therefore, for that reason; *no(gh)t forthy*, nevertheless.

For to, prep. with inf., to, in order to; *for to dye*, though one were to die. See *KnT*, I, 1133, n.

Fortreden, pp. *fortroden*; tread down, trample upon.

Fortuit, fortuitous.

Fortunel, accidental.

Fortunen, happen, befall; render fortunate; interpret favorably; in astrology, to choose a fortunate combination of influences. See *Gen Prol*, I, 417, n.

Fortunous, fortuitous.

Forwaked, exhausted with watching.

Forwandred, spent with wandering.

Forward, foremost.

Forward, sbst.; see For(e)ward.

Forwelked, withered, wrinkled.

Forweped, exhausted with weeping.

Forwered, worn out.

Forwerreyd, put down in battle, defeated.

Forwery (?), very weary (?). See *PF*, 93, n.

Forwe; see Furwe.

Forwhy, wherefore, why; because.

Forwiten, pt. pr. *forwo(o)t*; foreknow.

Forwiting, foreknowledge.

Forwo(o)t; see Forwiten.

Forwounded, severely wounded.

Forwrapped, wrapped up; covered.

Foryaf; see Foryeven.

Foryat; see Foryeten.

Foryede; see Forgon.

Foryelden, yield in return; repay, reward.

Foryetelnesse, forgetfulness.

Foryeten, Forgeten, contr. pr. 3 sg. *foryet, forget*, pt. *foryat, forgat*, pp. *foryeten, forgeten*; forget.

Foryeven, pt. sg. *foryaf, forgaf*, pl. *foryeven*, pp. *foryiven*; forgive.

Fostren, foster, bring up; nourish, feed; cherish.

Fote; see Foot.

Fote-brede, foot-breadth.

Fother, load; large quantity.

Foudre, thunderbolt.

Foul, Fow(e)l, sbst., bird.

Foul, adj., foul, vile, filthy; wretched; ugly; disgraceful.

Foule, adv., foully; wickedly; disgracefully; meanly; hideously.

Foun, young deer of first year; for metaphorical use, see *Tr*, i, 465, n.

Foundement, foundation.

Founden (1); see Fonden.

Founden (2), found, establish.

Foure, four.

Fourmed, formed, shaped.

Fourneys; see Forneys.

Fow(e)l; see Foul.

Foynen, thrust, parry.

Fraknes, freckles.

Franchise, liberty; privilege; nobleness; bounty; generosity; frankness.

Frank, franc (French coin).

Frankeleyn, franklin.

Frape, troop, company; pack.

Fraten; see Freten.

Fraught, pp., freighted.
Fraynen; see **Freynen**.
Free, free; noble; generous, liberal, lavish; gracious.
Freedom, freedom; liberality.
Freele, frail, fragile; transitory.
Freend, pl. *frendes* and (perhaps) *freend*; friend.
Freletee, frailty.
Frem(e)de, strange; foreign; wild.
Frendes; see **Freend**.
Frenesye, frenzy, madness.
Frenetik, frantic.
Frenge, fringe, border.
Frere, friar.
Fresen, freeze.
Fressh (and perhaps *fresshe*), fresh, bright, lively; bold.
Fresshe, adv., freshly, newly.
Fresshen, refresh.
Fret, ornament.
Freten, contr. pr. 3 sg. *fret*, pt. pl. *freten*, *fraten*, pp. *freten*; eat, devour, consume; swallow up.
Fretted, **Fret(t)**, decorated; set.
Freynen, **Fraynen**, ask, inquire.
Fro, from.
From, conj., from the time when.
Froten, rub.
Frothen, froth, become covered with foam.
Frounce, wrinkle.
Frouncen, pp. *frounced*; wrinkle, show wrinkles.
Frownt, front, countenance.
Fructifyen, be fruitful.
Fructuous, fruitful.
Fruit, **Frut**, fruit; essence; result.
Frutestere, fruit-seller (properly fem.).
Fulfillen, fulfill; fill full, satiate, satisfy; complete, perform.
Fulliche, fully.
Fulsomnesse, fulness, abundance, excess.
Fume, vapor.
Fumetere, fumitory.
Fumositee, vaporous humor (arising from the stomach).
Fundement, foundation; fundament.
Furial, furious, tormenting.
Furlong, furlong; short distance; race-course; brief period of time.
Furre, fur.
Furred, trimmed with fur.
Furringe, trimming of fur.
Furth; see **Forth**.
Furth(e)ren; see **Forth(e)ren**.
Further-over; see **Forther-over**.
Furwe, **Forwe**, furrow.
Furye, fury (the monster); rage.
Fusible, susceptible of being fused.
Fustian, fustian, thick cotton cloth.
Futures, sbst. pl., future events or times.
Fyf, **Fyve**, five.
Fyle, file.
Fyn, end; aim; result; death.
Fyn, fine, refined; delicate; superior, excellent; pure, absolute; *of fyne force*, from sheer need, necessity.
Fynch, finch; *pulle a fynch*, see *Gen Prol*, I, 652, n.
Fyne, adv., finely, closely, excellently.
Fynen, finish, end; cease.
Fynt; see **Finden**.
Fyr, fire; dat. phr. *on fyre, a-fyre; fyr of Seint Antony*, erysipelas; *fyr-makynge*, building of the pyre.

Fysicien, physician.
Fyve; see **Fyf**.

G

Gabben, mock; lie, speak idly; boast.
Gabbyng, lying.
Gadeling, vagabond, idle fellow.
Gad(e)ren, gather.
Gad(e)ring, gathering, accumulation.
Gaillard, **Gaylard**, gay, joyous, merry.
Galaxye, the Galaxy, Milky Way.
Galen, sing, cry out; exclaim.
Galentyne, galantine; a sauce.
Galingale, a flavor prepared from sweet cyperus.
Galiones, medicines. See *Words of Host*, VI, 306, n.
Galle (1), gall; metaphorically, envy.
Galle (2), sore spot.
Galoche, shoe.
Galon, gallon.
Galpen, gape.
Galwes, gallows.
Game(n), pl. *games*; game, sport; fun, amusement; joke, jest; contest.
Gamen, impers. vb., please.
Gan; see **Ginnen**.
Ganen, yawn.
Gapen, **Capen**, gape, open the mouth; gasp; stare.
Gapinges, greedy desires.
Gappe, gap.
Gargat, throat.
Garisoun, defense, deliverance; healing; garrison.
Garleek, garlic.
Garnement, garment.
Garner, **Gerner**, garner, granary.
Garnisoun, defense; garrison. See also **Garisoun**.
Gas, Northern dial. for *gooth*.
Gastly, terrible.
Gastnesse, terror.
Gat; see **Geten**.
Gate (1), gate, door. See also **Yate**.
Gate (2), way, wise. See also **Algate(s)**, **Othergate**.
Gat-tothed, with teeth set wide apart. See *Gen Prol*, I, 468, n.
Gaude, trick, prank; pretense; toy, gaud.
Gaudé, dyed with weld.
Gauded, furnished with *gauds*, i.e., beads. See *Gen Prol*, I, 159, n.
Gauren, gaze, stare.
Gay, joyous, merry; wanton; bright, lively; showily dressed.
Gaye, gayly, finely.
Gaynen, **Geynen**, gain, profit; avail.
Gaylard; see **Gaillard**.
Gayler(e), jailer.
Gaytres beryis, berries of the gay-tree or gait-tree, or dogwood.
Geaunt, giant.
Gebet, gibbet.
Geen, pp. of *goon* (Northern dial.).
Geery, changeable. See **Gere** (2).
Gees; see **Goos**.
Geesten, tell a tale, a *geste*; used perhaps with reference to metrical form in *Pars Prol*, X, 43; see n.
Geeth; see **Goon**.
Gemme, gem.
Gendres, kinds.

General, general; liberal, broad; *in general,* generally, universally; in a company.

Generally, everywhere; as a general principle.

Gent, refined, exquisite; genteel; slender, graceful.

Gent(e)rye, gentility, nobility, rank; mark of good birth.

Gentil, adj., gentle of birth or character; noble; excellent, worthy; well-bred; charming; mild, tender; also sbst.

Gentilesse, gentleness of birth or character; nobility; courtesy, high breeding; delicacy; slenderness.

Gentrice, gentility.

Geomancie, divination by figures made, commonly, on the ground. See *KnT,* I, 2045, n.

Geometriens, geometricians.

Gerdonen; see **Guerdonen.**

Gerdoun, guerdon.

Gẹre (1), equipment; apparel; gear, armor; utensils; contrivance; property.

Gẹre (2), change; changeful manner, vacillation. (Perhaps the *e* is close in *Gere, Gerful,* etc.)

Gẹrful, changeable.

Gerl, girl; young person of either sex.

Gerland, Gerlond, garland.

Gerner; see **Garner.**

Gesse, guess; doubt.

Gessen, guess, suppose, imagine; judge of.

Gessing, opinion; estimation.

Gest, guest.

Geste, occurrence, exploit; history; tale, romance; romance-form, perhaps with special reference to alliteration. See *Prol Mel,* VII, 933, n.

Gestours, Gestiours, story-tellers.

Get; see **Jet.**

Geten, contr. pr. 3 sg. *get,* pt. sg. *gat,* pp. *geten;* get, obtain; beget.

Geven; see **Yeven.**

Geyn, gain, profit.

Geyne; see **Gaynen.**

Gif, if (Northern dial.).

Gigges, squeaking noises (?). See *MLN,* LXV, 529.

Gigginge, fitting the arm-strap (Fr. "guige") to a shield.

Gilde(n), of gold, golden.

Giler; see **Gylour.**

Gilt, guilt, sin.

Gilt, adj., gilt, golden.

Gilt(e)lẹes, guiltless.

Giltif, guilty.

Gin, device, contrivance; engine of war; trap, snare.

Ginglen, jingle.

Ginnen, pt. sg. *gan,* pl., pp. *gonnen, gunnen;* begin, undertake; also as mere auxiliary for past time (= did). See *Gen Prol,* I, 301, n.

Gipser, purse, pouch; game-bag.

Girdel, girdle; in astronomy, central line or great circle.

Girden, contr. pr. 3 sg. *girt,* pp. *girt;* strike, pierce.

Girdilstẹde, waist.

Girl; see **Gerl.**

Gisarme, a weapon; battle-ax or halberd.

Giste, stage of a journey. See *Tr,* ii, 1349, n.

Giterne, cittern, guitar.

Giternen, play on the guitar.

Gladen, gladden, cheer; comfort, console; rejoice.

Gladere, gladdener.

Gladly, gladly, willingly; fain; by preference; commonly, as a general rule. See *NPT,* VII, 3224, n.

Glaren, glisten, shine; stare.

Glasen, glaze, furnish with glass; *glase his howve,* give him a glass cap, a useless defense. See *MkT,* VII, 2372, n.

Glede, live coal.

Gledy, glowing, burning (as a coal).

Glee, music; entertainment; instrument.

Glẹem, gleam.

Glenten, glance.

Gleyre, white (of an egg).

Gliden; see **Glyden.**

Gliwen, glue, fasten.

Glọọd; see **Glyden.**

Glọse, gloss, marginal explanation; comment, exposition.

Glọsen, interpret, explain; comment upon; flatter, cajole.

Glotonye, gluttony.

Glotoun, glutton.

Glowmben, look glum, scowl, frown.

Glyden, pt. sg. *glọọd,* pp. *gliden;* glide, slip; pass; rise.

Glymsyng, glimpse, imperfect view.

Gnawen, pt. sg. *gnow;* gnaw; eat.

Gnede, stingy person.

Gnodden, rub.

Gnof, churl, lout; thief.

Gnow; see **Gnawen.**

Gobet, piece, fragment; lump.

Godhẹde, godhead, divinity.

Godlihẹde; see **Goodlihẹed(e).**

Godsib; see **Gossib.**

Gold-bẹte, gilt, adorned with beaten gold; embroidered with gold. See *KnT,* I, 979, n.

Gold-hewen, cut or hewn out of gold.

Goldlẹes, without money.

Golee, gabble (lit. "throatful").

Golet, gullet, throat.

Goliardeys, jester, buffon. See *Gen Prol,* I, 560, n.

Gomme, gum.

Gonfanoun, gonfanon, gonfalon, banner.

Gong, privy.

Gonne, gun, cannon.

Gonnen; see **Ginnen.**

Good, sbst., property, wealth, goods; benefit, advantage; dat. phr. *to gode,* etc.; *can his good,* knows his advantage, how to act or succeed, etc. See *ML Epil,* II, 1169, n.

Good, adj., good; dat. phr. *for gode.*

Goodlich, kindly, bountiful.

Goodlihẹed(e), goodliness, seemliness; beauty.

Good-man, master; householder.

Gooldes, marigolds.

Gọọn, pr. 3 sg. *gọọth, geeth, gas* (Northern), pp. *gọn;* go, move, proceed; walk, roam; *out gooth,* goes off, is discharged (of a gun). See also **Wenden** and **Yede.**

Gọọre, gore or piece of a garment; also the whole garment.

Goos, pl. *gees;* goose.

Goosish, goose-like, silly.

Gọọst, spirit, ghost; soul; mind.

Gọọt, goat.

Gorge, throat.

Goshauk, goshawk.

Gossib, Godsib, fellow sponsor in baptism; spiritual relative; intimate friend.

Gossomer, gossamer.

Gostly, spiritually, mystically; devoutly, truly. See *Tr,* v, 1030, n.

Goter, gutter; watercourse; eaves-trough.

Goune, Gowne, gown.

Gourde, gourd.

Goute, gout.

Governaille, mastery, control.

Governaunce, government, rule, control; subjection; management, care; self-control, demeanor.

Governeresse, female governor, ruler, mistress.

Grace, rarely **Gras,** favor; grace; mercy, pardon; honor, distinction; *graces,* thanks; *harde grace, sory grace,* ill favor, disfavor, severity, misfortune, etc. (often in imprecations).

Gracious, gracious, agreeable; acceptable.

Graithen; see **Greythen.**

Grame, anger, grief; harm.

Grange, granary, barn.

Granten, grant, consent; fix, settle upon.

Grant mercy, Gramercy, much thanks.

Grapenel, grapnel.

Gras (1), Gres, grass.

Gras (2); see **Grace.**

Graspen, grope.

Graunge, Graunt, etc.; see **Grange, Grant,** etc.

Grave, grave; pit.

Gravel, gravel; pl. *gravelis,* sands.

Graven, pp. *graven;* dig, bury; engrave.

Grayn, Greyn, grain, corn; grain (of paradise), cardamom; pearl; dye (made of the cochineal grain); *in grayn,* of a fast color.

Graythen; see **Greythen.**

Grece, Greesse, grease.

Gree (1), favor, good will.

Gree (2), degree, rank, supremacy.

Greef, grievance.

Greet, comp. *gretter,* sup. *grettest;* great; chief, principal; *the grete,* the chief or essential part.

Grehound, greyhound.

Greithen; see **Greythen.**

Grene, green, fresh; vigorous, flourishing; pallid.

Grenehede, greenness, wantonness.

Grennying, grinning.

Gres; see **Gras (1).**

Greten (1), greet.

Greten (2), lament (Northern dial.).

Gretter, Grettest; see **Greet.**

Greve, brushwood; pl. branches; thicket.

Greven, grieve, vex; harm, aggrieve.

Greyn; see **Grayn.**

Greythen, Greithen, Graythen, prepare, make ready; dress, clothe, adorn.

Grifphon, griffin.

Grinden, contr. pr. 3 sg. *grint,* pt. sg. *grond,* pp. *grounden;* grind.

Grinding, toll for grinding.

Grinten, pt. *grynt(e)* gnash (with the teeth).

Grisel, gray-haired old man.

Gris(e)ly, terrible, awful, horrible.

Grobben, grub, dig.

Groff; see **Gruf.**

Groinen, grumble, complain.

Grome, man.

Grond; see **Grinden.**

Gronten, pt. *gronte,* grunt; groan.

Gropen, grope; try, test, search out.

Grot, particle, bit.

Grote, groat (Dutch coin).

Ground, ground; foundation; texture (of cloth); dat. phr. *to grounde.*

Growen, pt. sg. *grew, growed,* str. pp. *growen;* grow.

Groyn (1), snout (of swine).

Groyn (2), murmur, complaint.

Grucchen, grumble, murmur at.

Gruf, face downward, groveling.

Gruwel, gruel.

Gryl, horrible.

Grynt(e); see **Grinten.**

Gryntynge, gnashing (of teeth).

Grypen, sieze, grasp.

Grys, sbst., a costly gray fur.

Grys, adj., gray.

Guerdonen, Gwerdonen, Gerdonen, reward.

Gunnen; see **Ginnen.**

Gyde, guide.

Gyden, guide, direct; conduct; instruct; govern.

Gyderesse, conductress.

Gyen, guide, direct; control, govern.

Gyle, guile, deceit; trick.

Gylour, Giler, beguiler, deceiver; trickster.

Gyngebreed, gingerbread.

Gype, frock; smock.

Gypoun, tunic (worn under the hauberk).

Gyse, guise, manner, way; plan.

Gyser, gizzard, liver.

Gyte, apparently dress, gown, or mantle, whereas OF. "guite" meant hat (Godefroi, s.v.).

H

Ha, contr. form of **Have.**

Haberdasshere, seller of hats and miscellaneous small wares.

Habergeoun, Haubergeoun, hauberk, coat of mail.

Habit, habit; disposition, mood; bodily condition; practice; dress, religious garb.

Habitacle, habitable space; niche.

Hab(o)undaunt, abundant, abounding.

Habounden, abound.

Habyten, inhabit.

Hacches, hatches.

Had(d)e; see **Haven.**

Haf; see **Heven.**

Hainselin, short jacket.

Haire; see **Heyre.**

Hakeney, hackney, horse used for ordinary riding or hauling; an old horse.

Halden, Northern form of **Holden.**

Halen, draw, pull; attract.

Half, sbst., pl. *halves;* side, part; behalf; *a Goddes half,* in God's name (adjuration).

Half, adj., wk. and pl. *halfe, halve;* half; *halve cours,* half-course; *halvendel,* half (part).

Half-goddes, Halve goddes, demi-gods.

Halke, corner, nook; hiding-place.

Halle, hall; dining-hall; parlor.

Halowen, halloo; set on the dogs with the halloo.

Halp; see **Helpen.**

Hals, neck, throat.

Halsen, conjure, implore.

Halt; see **Halten** and **Holden.**

Halten, contr. pr. 3 sg. *halt;* halt, limp, go lame.

Halve goddes; see **Half-goddes.**

Halve(s); see **Half,** sbst, and adj.

Halvendel; see **Half,** adj.

Halwe, saint; *halwes,* shrines or relics.

Halwen, hallow; consecrate.

Halyday, holy day, religious feast day; holiday. (The combined and uncombined forms were freely confused in early English.)

Ham, Northern dial. for **Hoom.**

Hameled, mutilated, lamed. See *Tr,* ii, 964, n.

Hamer, hammer.

Hampred, hampered, burdened.

Han; see **Haven.**

Handebręde, hand's breadth.

Handwerk, handiwork, created things.

Hangen, Hongen, pt. sg. *heng,* pl. *hengen,* pp. *hanged;* hang, hang down; linger.

Hap, chance, luck; good fortune; occurrence.

Happen, happen, befall.

Happenen, happen.

Happy, fortunate.

Hard, Herd, hard, difficult; callous, cruel; *of hard,* with difficulty; *herd-herted,* hard-hearted.

Harde, tightly; firmly.

Hardely, Hardily, boldly; certainly, surely; without hesitation.

Hardiment, Hardement, boldness.

Hardinesse, boldness; fool-hardiness; insolence.

Hardnesse, hardship; cruelty; affliction.

Hardy, bold, brave; rash; sturdy.

Hardyng, hardening, tempering.

Harlot (common gender), low fellow; rascal; thief.

Harlotrye, low or evil conduct; wickedness; ribaldry.

Harm, hurt, injury; grief, suffering, misfortune; *broken harm,* petty injury or annoyance (?). See *MerchT,* IV, 1425, n.

Harneised, equipped, armed, mounted.

Harneys, Herneys, armor; outfit, equipment; provision; privy members; *plough harneys,* plough fittings.

Harpe, harp.

Harpour, harper.

Harre, hinge.

Harrow!, help!, a cry of distress.

Harwen, harry, despoil.

Haryen, drag; pull violently.

Hasard, hazard, a game of dice.

Hasardour, player at hazard, gamester.

Hasardrye, playing at hazard, gaming.

Hasel, hazel; *haselwodes shaken,* a proverbial phrase for what is obvious, no news. See *Tr,* iii, 890, n.

Haspe, hasp.

Hastif, hasty.

Hastow, hast thou.

Hat, hot (Northern form).

Haten; see **Hǫten.**

Hatręde, hatred.

Hatte; see **Hǫten.**

Hatter; see **Hǫot.**

Haubergeoun; see **Habergeoun.**

Hauberk, armor for breast and back, mail plates.

Haunche-boon, thigh-bone, haunch-bone.

Haunt, abode; "limit"; practice; skill.

Haunten, practice, be accustomed to; employ; resort to, frequent.

Hauteyn, haughty, proud, arrogant; loud.

Haven, Han, pt. *had(d)e,* pp. *had;* have; hold, keep, possess; take, obtain; *hath,* impers., there is (Fr. "y a"); *hadde lever,* had rather, would rather.

Havinge, possession.

Havoir, having, possession.

Hawe (1), haw, hedge; yard.

Hawe (2), perhaps the same word as **Hawe** (1),

haw, fruit of the hawthorn; *hawe-bake,* baked haws.

Hay, hedge.

Hayt, Heyt, get up! (in urging on a horse).

He, gen. sg. *his,* dat. *him,* pl. *they,* gen. *hire,* dat. *hem;* he; *he . . . he,* this one . . . that one; *him Arcite,* that Arcite. See *KnT,* I, 1210, n. On *his* as substitute for the genitive ending of a noun (*Mars his venim*) see *LGW,* 2593, n.

Hed; see **Hyden.**

Hede, heed.

-hęde, less often **-heed,** abstract suffix, equivalent to -hood as in *wommanhede, youthhede,* etc.

Hęden, head, provide with a head.

Hęed, Hęved, head; source, beginning; *maugree hir heed,* in spite of all she could do; dat. phr. *for hir hede* (?).

Hę(ę)f; see **Hęven.**

Heeld; see **Hǫlden.**

Hęęlp; see **Helpen.**

Hęęp, heap, large quantity; crowd, host; dat. phr. *to-hepe,* all together.

Hęęr, hair.

Heer, Here, here.

Heer-agayns, against this.

Heer-biforn, before this.

Heerdis, "hards," coarse flax.

Heer-forth, in this direction.

Hęęr-męle, a hair's breadth.

Hęęt; see **Hęte.**

Heet; see **Hǫten.**

Hęęth, heath, heather.

Hegge, hedge.

Heigh, Hey, Hy, high; *in heigh and lowe,* in high things and low, in all respects (see *Gen Prol,* I, 817, n.); *an heigh,* on high.

Heighe, Hye, adv., high, on high; loudly; proudly.

Heighly, highly; deeply.

Heighte, Highte, height.

Helden, bend, incline.

Helden; see **Hǫlden.**

Helden; see **Hielden.**

Hele, heel.

Hęle, health; recovery; prosperity.

Hęleles, out of health.

Hęlen (1), pp. *heled;* conceal.

Hęlen (2), pp. *heled;* heal.

Helle, hell.

Helm, helmet.

Helmed, equipped with a helmet.

Helpe, helper, assistant.

Helpen, pt. sg. *halp, hęęlp,* pp. *holpen;* help, aid; heal, cure.

Helply, helpful.

Hem, border; phylactery.

Hemisper(i)e, hemisphere.

Hend(e), ready to hand, convenient, handy; pleasant, courteous, gentle.

Heng(en); see **Hangen.**

Henne(s), hence.

Henten, contr. pr. 3 sg. *hent,* pl. *hente,* pp. *hent;* seize, obtain, catch, get.

Hentere, filcher.

Hepe, hip of the dog-rose.

Hępen, heap; accumulate, augment.

Heraud, herald.

Herauden, proclaim like a herald.

Herbe, Erbe, herb.

Herber, garden; arbor.
Herbergage, abode; lodging.
Herbergeour, Herberger, provider of lodgings, host; harbinger.
Herberw(e) lodging, dwelling; inn; harbor.
Herber(w)en, take shelter or harbor; lodge.
Herby, hereby, with respect to this; hence.
Herd (1); see **Hard**.
Herd (2), haired.
Herde (1), herd.
Herde (2), Hierde, herdsman; shepherd.
Herd(e); see **Heren**.
Herde-gromes, herdsmen.
Herdesse Hierdesse, shepherdess; protectress.
Her(e) (1), Hir(e), her (pers. pron.).
Her(e) (2), Hir(e), her (poss. pron.).
Her(e) (3), Hir(e), their (poss. pron.).
Here-agayns, -ayeins, against this, in reply to this.
Here and howne, explanation doubtful. See *Tr*, iv, 210, n.
Her(e)myte, hermit.
Heren (also close ē), pt. *herde*, pp. *herd*; hear.
Herien, praise, honor, worship.
Herken, hearken.
Herknen, hearken.
Herne, corner.
Herneys; see **Harneys**.
Heroner, falcon for herons; also adj.
Heronsew, heron-shaw, young heron.
Herse, hearse.
Hert, hart.
Herte, gen. sg. *hertes, herte*; heart; courage; beloved; *herte roote*, root (bottom) of the heart.
Hert(e)ly, heartfelt, hearty; of true heart.
Herten; see **Hurten**.
Herte-spoon, the spoon-shaped depression at the end of the breast-bone.
Heryinge, praising, praise.
Heste, behest, command; promise.
Het, pp.. heated.
Hete, heat; boiling surge; passion.
Heten; see **Hoten**.
Heterly, violently, fiercely.
Hethen, heathen.
Hethen, hence (Northern dial.).
Hethenesse, heathendom.
Hethyng, contempt.
Hette; see **Hoten**.
Heved; see **Heed**.
Heven, pt. sg. *haf, he(e)f, heved*; heave, lift.
Heven(e), gen. sg. *hevenes, hevene*; heaven; one of the spheres; metaphorically for joy or glory.
Hevenys(s)h, heavenly.
Hevy, heavy; sad; difficult.
Hevyen, weigh down, make heavy.
Hevynesse, heaviness, sorrow; slowness, torpor, indolence.
Hewe (1), Huwe, hue, complexion; appearance; pretense.
Hewe (2), domestic servant.
Hewed, hued, colored.
Hewen, hew, cut.
Hey, hay; grass.
Hey, comp. Heyer, etc.; see **Heigh**.
Heyen, rise.
Heyne, wretch.
Heyre, Haire, hair-shirt; also adj.
Heysoge, hedge-sparrow.

Heyt; see **Hayt**.
Hid(de); see **Hyden**.
Hider, hither.
Hidous, hideous, terrible, ugly.
Hielden, Helden, pour out, shed.
Hierde; see **Herde** (2).
Hierdesse; see **Herdesse**.
Hight(e); see **Hoten**.
Highte; see **Heighte**.
Highten, adorn; delight.
Hil (perhaps Hille), hill.
Hindrest, hindmost.
Hir(e); see **Her(e)**, in various meanings.
Hirës, hers.
Hirnia, hernia.
Hirs, theirs.
His, his, its; sometimes used with gen. of proper name, *Mars his*; often pluralized (*hise*) in the MSS.
Historial Estoryal, historical.
Hit, it.
Hit; see **Hyden**.
Ho, interj., stop! hold!; also subst.
Hochepot, hotchpotch, mixture.
Hoked, hooked, barbed.
Hoker, scorn, disdain.
Hokerly, scornfully.
Hold, hold, grasp, possession; stronghold, castle.
Holden, contr. pr. 3 sg. *halt, holt*, pt. sg. *heeld*, pl. *helden*, pp. *holden*; hold, keep; continue; remain firm; restrain; esteem, deem, account; *holden in honde*, cajole, put off with promises. See *HF*, 692, n.
Hole, hole.
Holinesse, holiness, sanctity; religious form or sect.
Holly, Hoolly, wholly.
Holm, holm-oak, evergreen oak.
Holnesse, integrity.
Holour, lecher, adulterer, ribald.
Holpen; see **Helpen**.
Holsom, wholesome; healing.
Holsomnesse, health.
Holt; see **Holden**.
Holt, plantation.
Holughnesse, concavity.
Holwe, adj., hollow; also adv.
Homager, vassal.
Hommen, hum.
Homycide, murderer; murder, manslaughter.
Hond, hand; dat. phr. *on (in) honde*; *beren on honde*, accuse, testify against; assure, persuade; *holden in honde*, cajole, put off with false promises or hopes. See **Beren, Holden**.
Honest, honorable, worthy; decent; respectable, appropriate to persons of standing.
Honestee, honor; virtue (of a woman); good or honorable character; rank, dignity.
Honestetee, honor; modesty; neatness.
Hongen; see **Hangen**.
Hony, honey; a term of endearment.
Hony-comb, honeycomb; used also as a term of endearment.
Hook, hook; sickle; crozier.
Hool, adj., whole; sound, in health; unwounded; perfect, entire; also adv.
Hoom, home; also adv., home, homewards.
Hoomlinesse, domesticity; familiarity.
Hoomly, belonging to house or home; familiar, informal; native.

Hoor, hoary, white-haired.

Hoost, host, army.

Hoot, comp. *hotter*, *hatter*; hot, fervent; violent; voracious.

Hopen, hope, expect; suppose, think; sometimes transitive.

Hoper, hopper.

Hoppen, hop; dance.

Hoppesteres, dancing-girls; used as adj., *shippes hoppesteres*. See *KnT*, I, 2017, n.

Hord, hoard, store; store-house; avarice.

Horn-pipes, pipes made of horn.

Horowe, adj. pl., foul, filthy, scandalous.

Hors, pl. *hors*, dat. phr. *on horse*; horse; a name for a wedge on an astrolabe.

Hors, adj., hoarse.

Horsly, horse-like, with the qualities of an excellent horse.

Hose, pl. *hosen*, *hoses*; hose, covering for feet and legs.

Hospitaliers, Knights Hospitallers.

Host(e), Ost(e), host, innkeeper.

Hostel, hostelry.

Hostesse, O(o)stesse, hostess.

Hostiler, innkeeper; servant at an inn.

Hote, adv., hotly.

Hoten, Haten, Heten, pt. *heet*, *hatte*, *hette*, *highte*, pp. *hoten*, *hight*; command; promise; most commonly used in the passive sense of AS. "hatte," be called, named.

Hotte, basket carried on the back.

Hound, dog.

Houndfish, dogfish.

Houpen, whoop.

Houre (var. Oure), hour.

Hous, house; in astronomy, the "mansion" of a planet (a sign of the zodiac), or a division of the celestial sphere. See *MLT*, II, 295, n.

Housbonde, husband.

Housbondrye, household goods; economy, economical use (of).

Hous(e)len, housel, administer the eucharist (to).

Hoven, hover, abide; linger about, wait in readiness.

How, adv., how; *how that*, however it be that.

Howgates, in what way. See Gate (2).

How, interj., ho!

Howne, unexplained word. See *Tr*, iv, 210, n.

Howve, hood; *sette his howve*, make a fool of him. See *Gen Prol*, I, 586, n.

Hulstred, covered, hidden, concealed.

Humb(e)ly, Humblely, humbly.

Humblesse, humility, meekness.

Humblynge, humming, low murmur or growl.

Hunte, hunter, huntsman.

Hunteresse, huntress.

Hurt(e)len, push; dash together.

Hurten, contr. pr. 3 sg. *hurt*; hurt, harm.

Hust, pp., hushed, silent; used also as imp.

Huwe; see Hewe (1).

Hy; see Heigh.

Hyden, contr. pr. 3 sg. *hit*, pt. *hidde*, pp. *hid*, *hed*; hide, conceal; lie hidden.

Hye, haste; in phr. *in hye*, in haste.

Hye, adv.; see Heighe.

Hyen, hie, hasten; bring quickly; often refl.

Hyene, hyena.

Hynde, hind.

Hyne, hind, servant, farm laborer.

Hyre, hire, payment; reward; ransom.

I (see also Y)

I-, common verbal prefix (AS. "ge-"). For words beginning with this prefix see Y-.

I, Ich, Ik, pron., I.

I, interj., Ey!

Icchen, itch.

Ich; see I, Ech.

Idus, ides.

If, Yif, if; commonly *if that*.

Ik; see I.

Il, evil (Northern dial.).

Il-hayl, bad luck (Northern dial.).

Ilke, same. See Thilke.

Ill(e), adv., evilly, ill.

Ilyk; see Yliche.

Immoevablete, immobility.

Impen, graft.

Imperie (var. Emperie), government, rank.

Impertinent, irrelevant.

Impetren, ask for, impetrate.

Importable, intolerable.

Impossible, Inpossible, impossible; also sbst.

Impressen, impress, make an impression; imprint.

In-; for words beginning with this prefix see also Im-, Em-, En-.

In, inn, lodging, dwelling.

Inche, inch.

Inclyned, bent.

Inconstance, inconstancy.

Inconvenient, sbst., inconvenience.

Incubus, an evil spirit supposed to lie upon persons in their sleep, and to have intercourse with women.

Indeterminat, indeterminate; not marked on the astrolabe.

Indifferently, impartially.

Indignacion, contemptuous behavior or treatment; anger (against evil or injustice), hence, rebellious wrath.

Induracioun, induration, hardening.

Inequal, unequal; on *houres inequales* see *KnT*, I, 2271, n., and *Astr*, ii, 8 and 10.

Inestimable, invaluable, beyond estimate.

Infect, not valid, defective (title); dimmed.

In-fere, together (lit. "in company").

Infermetee, Infirmite, infirmity.

Infirme, weak, insufficient.

Informaciouns, instructions, directions.

Infortunat, unfortunate, inauspicious.

Infortune, ill fortune.

Infortuned, ill-starred.

Infortuning, unfortunate condition or situation.

Ingot, ingot, mould for metal.

Inhelden, Inhielden, pour in.

Injure, injury.

Inke, ink.

Inly, inwardly, intimately; greatly, completely, perfectly.

In-mid, into, amid.

Inne, adv., in, within.

Innen, vb., house, lodge.

Innerest, innermost.

Inobedience, disobedience.

Inordinat, immoderate, excessive.

Inset, pp., implanted.

Insighte, insight; understanding.

Inspiren, quicken; breathe upon.

Instance, presence; instance, request; suggestion.
Intercept, pp., intercepted.
Intervalle, interval.
In-til, unto, as far as.
Into, into; unto.
Intresse, interest.
Introductorie, sbst., introduction.
In-with, within, in.
Ipocrisye, hypocrisy.
Ipocrite, Ypocryte, hypocrite.
Ire, ire, anger; irritability.
Iren, iron.
Irous, angry, wrathful.
Irreguler, a monk or "regular" who violates the rules of his order.
Issen, issue.
Issue, outlet; result.
Iwis; see Ywis.

J

Jade, jade, cart-horse, draught-horse.
Jagounce, jacinth or hyacinth (precious stone).
Jalous; see Jelous.
Jambeux, leggings, leg-armor.
Jane, small coin (named from Genoa).
Jang(e)ling, idle talk; dispute.
Janglen, jangle, chatter, babble.
Jangleresse, female prattler, chatterbox.
Janglerye, chatter, gossip.
Jape, jest, joke; truck; butt; laughing-stock.
Japen, jest, play a trick.
Japerie, joking, buffoonery.
Jape-worthi, laughable, ridiculous.
Jargon, talk.
Jaunyce, jaundice.
Jeet, jet.
Jelous, Jalous, jealous.
Jet, Get, contrivance; fashion, mode.
Jeupardye; see Jupartye.
Jewel, Jowel, Juwel, jewel.
Jewerye, Jewry.
Jo, come to pass (?); fit (?), suit (?). See *Tr*, iii, 33, n.
Jogelour, juggler.
Jogelrye, jugglery.
Joignen; see Joynen.
Jolif, Joly, jolly, merry, lively; pretty.
Jolily, in jolly fashion, merrily; neatly; emphatically, very well (colloquial).
Jolitee, jollity, merriment, sport; happiness; passion, lust.
Joly; see Jolif.
Jompren, jumble.
Jossa, down here.
Jouken, lie at rest; remain.
Journee, day's work or march; journey.
Jowel; see Jewel.
Jowes, jaws.
Joye, joy.
Joynant, adjoining.
Joynen, Joignen, join; enjoin.
Joynture, union.
Jubbe, vessel for ale or wine.
Jugen, Juggen, judge; deem.
Jug(g)e, judge; referee.
Juparten, jeopardize, endanger.
Jupartye, Jeupardye, jeopardy, peril; problem at chess.
Jurdon, chamber-pot.

Jurisdiccioun, jurisdiction.
Justen, joust, tourney.
Justyse, justice; judgment; administration of justice
Juwel; see Jewel.
Juwise, Juyse, justice, judgment; sentence.

K (see also C)

Kalender, calendar; hence, directory, example, model.
Kalendes, Kalends, first day of the month; hence, beginning, introduction.
Kamus; see Camus.
Kankedort (var. Cankerdort), an unexplained term apparently meaning a state of suspense, or difficult position. See *Tr*, ii, 1752, n.
Karf; see Kerven.
Kaynard, dotard.
Kecchen; see Cacchen.
Kechil, small cake.
Keen; see Cow.
Keep, sbst., care, heed, notice; in phr. *taken keep*.
Kek; see Quek.
Kemben, pt. *kembde, kempte*, pp. *kembd, kempt*; comb.
Kemp, coarse, stout.
Ken, Kentish for Kin.
Kene, keen, sharp; bold; eager; cruel.
Kene, adv., keenly.
Kennen, perceive, discern; teach, show.
Kepen, keep, preserve, take care of; intend, care to; regard, reck.
Kernel (1), seed; kernel (of a nut).
Kernel (2), battlement.
Kers, cress (symbol of worthlessness).
Kerven, pt. sg. *carf, karf*, pl. *corven, korfen*, pp. *corven, korven*; carve, cut, pierce.
Kervere, carver.
Kessen, Kentish for Kissen.
Keveren, cover; recover.
Keye, key; rudder (Lat. "clavus").
Kid(de); see Kythen.
Kiken, peep, gaze.
Kiken, kick.
Kin, kin, kindred; race; kind; *som kinnes, alles kinnes, noskinnes*, of some, every, no kind.
Kinde, sbst., nature; race, stock; species; sort; natural disposition; *of kinde*, by nature.
Kinde, adj., kind; natural; also adv.
Kindely, natural; also adv.
Kinrede, kindred; family, relatives; birth.
Kirked (?), crooked (?).
Kirtel, kirtle.
Kissen, Kessen, kiss.
Kitte; see Cutten.
Knakkes, tricks; evil ways.
Knarre, knot in wood; hence, stout, sturdy fellow.
Knarry, knotted, gnarled.
Knave, boy, page, servant; peasant; *knavechild*, male child.
Kneden, knead.
Knee, Know, knee; dat. phr. *on knowe*.
Knelen, kneel.
Knetten; Kentish for Knitten.
Knewe(n); see Knowen.
Knitten, knit, join; wed; gather together.
Knobbes, knobs, pimples.
Knok, knock.
Knoppe, bud.

Knopped, fastened with a button (*knoppe*).

Knotte, knot; difficulty; gist or point of a story.

Know; see **Knee.**

Knoweleche, Knowliche, knowledge.

Knowen, pt. sg. *knew,* pl. *knewen,* pp. *knowen;* know; make known, disclose.

Knowinge, conscious, aware; *knowinge with me,* my witnesses.

Knowlechen, acknowledge.

Knowleching, knowing.

Knyf, knife, dagger.

Konning; see **Cunning.**

Korfen, Korven; see **Kerven.**

Krecche, scrape together.

Kukkow!, cuckoo!

Kyde, kid.

Kymelin, shallow tub.

Kyn; see **Cow.**

Kynde; see **Kinde.**

Kyte, kite (bird).

Kythen, pt. *kythed, kidde,* pp. *kythed, kid;* make known, show, display, declare.

L

Laas; see **Las.**

Labbe, blab, tell-tale.

Labben, blab, tattle, gossip.

Label, rod or rule on the front of an astrolabe.

Laborious (var. **Laborous**), laborious.

Labouren, labor, toil; take pains.

Lacche, snare, spring.

Laced, caught, entangled.

Lacerte, muscle.

Lache, lazy, slack, dull.

Lachesse, indolence.

Lad(de); see **Leden.**

Laddre, ladder.

Laden, load; cover.

Lady, gen. sg. *lady;* lady.

Laft(e); see **Leven** (1).

Lak, lack, defect; want; fault; blame.

Lake (1), lake, pond.

Lake (2), fine linen cloth.

Lakken, find fault, disparage; fall short; lack (impers.).

Lambic; see **Alambik.**

Lambren; see **Lomb.**

Lame, lame, feeble; halting; afflicted (in mind).

Lampe, thin plate.

Lampes, pl., lamps.

Land, Lond, land, country; dat. phr. *to* (*on*) *lande; upon lond,* in the country.

Lang, long (Northern dial.).

Langour, languishing; weakness, sickness, slow starvation.

Langouren, languish.

Lanterne, lantern.

Lapidaire, "Lapidarium," treatise on precious stones.

Lappe, flap, corner, fold, edge (of cloth); wrapper; lap.

Lappen, enfold.

Large, large, broad; liberal, generous, lavish; free; *at his large,* free, "at large."

Large, adv., freely.

Largely, fully; broadly speaking.

Largenesse, liberality.

Largesse, liberality; bounty.

Larke, lark.

Las, Laas, lace; leash, string; snare, entanglement.

Lasse, Lesse, adj., less; also adv.

Lasshe, lash; stroke.

Last, load, burden; hence, a great number.

Laste, last; lowest (?), basest (?). See *Bo,* ii, pr. 5, 49, n.

Lasten, contr. pr. 3 sg. *last,* pt. *laste*(*d*); last, endure; delay; extend.

Lat(en); see **Leten.**

Late, late, tardy; slow; also adv.

Laterede, slow, tardy.

Lathe, barn (Northern dial.).

Latis, lattice.

Latitude, breadth, especially the breadth of a climate; the angular distance of a body from the ecliptic; the distance of a place north or south of the equator.

Latoun, latten, a mixed metal compounded chiefly of copper and zinc.

Latter, adv., later, more slowly.

Laude, laud, honor, praise; *laudes,* pl., lauds (the canonical hour).

Laughen, Lauhwen, Leighen, pt. sg. *lough, laughed,* pp. *laughen, laughed;* laugh.

Launcegay (*lance* + Arab. "zaghāyah"), a slender lance of hard wood.

Launcen, Launchen, push, throw one's self, rear.

Launde, glade, clearing in the forest (used for hunting-ground).

Laure, Laurel, Laurer, Lorer, laurel-tree.

Lauriol, spurge-laurel.

Laus; see **Loos.**

Laven, draw up (water); exhaust, i.e., answer (a question) perfectly.

Lavender(e), laundress.

Laverokkes, larks.

Lavours, lavers, basins.

Lawe, law, custom; a religious system, body of religious faith.

Laxatyf, laxative.

Lay (1), lay, song.

Lay (2), law; belief, creed.

Lay, Lay(e)n; see **Lyen** (1).

Laynere, strap, thong.

Layser; see **Leyser.**

Lazar, leper.

Leche, physician.

Lechecraft, leechcraft, medicine; medical skill.

Lecher, healer.

Lechour, lecher.

Leden, contr. pr. 3 sg. *let,* pt. *ledde, ladde,* pp., *led, lad;* lead, conduct; draw; carry; guide; govern; continue, pass, spend; bring about.

Leden, (lit. "Latin"), language, speech; talk.

Leden, leaden.

Leed, sbst., lead; a caldron.

Leef; see **Leven** (1).

Leef, pl. *leves;* leaf.

Leef, Lief, comp. *lever, leefer,* sup. *levest;* lief; dear, beloved; pleasant, agreeable; *ful leef were me,* I should like; also sbst.

Leefful; see **Leveful.**

Leefsel, Levesel, the bush used as a sign of a tavern; leafy arbor.

Leek, leek.

Leep; see **Lepen.**

Leere, flank, loin; properly flesh, muscle (AS. "líra," ON. "lær").

Lẹẹs (1), leash.
Lẹẹs (2), false, untrue; also sbst., deceit, fraud.
Lẹẹs; see Lesen.
Lẹẹse, pasture.
Lẹẹste, least; *atte leeste, atte leeste weye*, at the very least.
Leet; see Leten.
Leful; see Leveful.
Legende, life of a saint or martyr; sad tale; story.
Leggen (1); see Leyen.
Leggen (2); see Alleggen (2).
Leid(e), Leyd(e); see Leyen.
Leigh; see Lyen (2).
Leigheth; see Laughen.
Lemaille; see Limaille.
Lẹmes, flames; rays.
Lemes; see Lim.
Lemman (*leef-man*), lover, sweetheart (of either gender); concubine.
Lendes, loins.
Lẹne, lean, slender; weak.
Lẹnen (1), lend, give; grant, allow; *in lening*, as a loan.
Lẹnen (2), lean, incline.
Lẹnesse, leanness.
Leng, adv., longer.
Lenger, Lengest; see Long.
Lengthe, length.
Lengthing, lengthening; inf. *lengthen*.
Lente, Lent.
Leonesse, lioness.
Leonyn, leonine.
Leopart, Leopard, Lybard, leopard.
Leos (Gk. λεώς), people.
Leoun, Lyoun, lion.
Lẹpand, Northern pr. p. of Lẹpen.
Lẹpen, pt. sg. *leep*; leap, spring; run; run about, exercise.
Lẹred, learned.
Lẹren, teach; learn.
Lerne, learn; teach.
Lesen, pt. sg. lẹẹs, pp. lọr(e)n; lose; destroy; *loren*, forlorn, wretched, wasted.
Lẹsinge, lie, falsehood; deceit.
Lesinge, loss.
Lẹsse; see Lasse.
Lẹsse(n), lessen, diminish.
Lest, Kentish for *list*; see Listeth.
Lest, Kentish for Lust.
Lẹste, least.
Lesteth, Kentish for Listeth.
Let; see Lẹden, Leten, Letten.
Leten, Laten, contr. pr. 3 sg. *let*, imp. *let, lat*, pt. sg. *leet*, pl. *leten*, pp. *leten, laten*; let, allow; yield; leave; abandon, forsake; omit, desist; deem, consider; frequently used in a causative sense with an infin., *let calle*; also combined with the causative *don, let don cryen*.
Lette, hindrance, delay.
Lette-game, "let-game," one who spoils or hinders sport.
Letten, contr. pr. 3 sg. *let*, pt. sg. *lette, letted*, pp. *let*; hinder, thwart; cut off, conceal; delay, be hindered; wait, hesitate; cease, desist.
Lett(e)rure, literature; learning.
Letuarie, electuary, remedy.
Lẹve, leave, permission.
Lẹveful, Lẹ(ẹ)f(f)ul, permissible, allowable.

Lẹven, imp. 2 sg. *le(e)f*, pt. sg. *lefte, lafte*, pp. *left, laft*; leave, let alone; abandon, forsake; permit, grant; cease, omit, desist; refrain; remain.
Leven, believe.
Leven, grant, allow.
Leven; see Liven.
Levene, flash of lightning.
Lever(e), comp. of Leef; *me were lever, hadde I lever*, etc., I had rather; *had hire levere*, she had rather.
Levesel; see Leefsel.
Levest; see Leef.
Lẹwed, ignorant, unlearned; coarse, rude; wicked; wanton.
Lẹwednesse, ignorance; coarseness.
Ley; see Lyen (1).
Leyen, Leggen, pt. *leyde*, pp. *leyd*; lay; lay up; lay out, expend; bet, pledge.
Leyser, Layser, leisure, opportunity; deliberation.
Leyt, flame (of a candle); also in *thonder-leyt*, lightning.
Libel, written statement or accusation.
Licenciat, a man licensed by the pope to hear confessions and administer penance.
Liche, adj., like; also adv.
Licoryce, Lycorys, licorice.
Licour, liquor, moisture; juice.
Lief; see Leef.
Lift, Left, adj., left.
Lige, Liege, Leege, liege, subject, vassal.
Ligeaunce, allegiance.
Liggen; see Lyen (1).
Light, light (of weight); light-hearted, joyous; fickle, trifling; active, nimble; lightly clothed; transitory; easy (to do).
Lighte, adv., brightly, brilliantly.
Lighten (1), pt. *lighte*; make light, alleviate; render glad or cheerful; feel light or glad.
Lighten (2), pt. *lighte*; alight, descend.
Lighten (3), pp. *light(ed)*; shine; illumine.
Lighter, adv., more lightly, more easily.
Lightly, lightly, carelessly; joyfully; easily, quickly; equally.
Lightnen, lighten, clear, illumine.
Lightnesse (1), brightness.
Lightnesse (2), levity, agility.
Lightsom, lightsome, gay, cheerful.
Ligne, line.
Ligne-aloes, wood of the aloe.
Likerous, lecherous, licentious; greedy, gluttonous; eager, desirous; base, vile.
Lilie, lily.
Lilting-horn, horn for playing a lilt.
Lim, pl. *lim(m)es, lemes*; limb.
Limaille, Lemaille, Lymaille, metal filings.
Limitacioun, a friar's limit.
Limitour, a friar licensed to beg within a definite limit.
Linage, lineage, race, descent; birth, family; kinsfolk; consanguinity.
Lippe, lip.
Lipsen, lisp.
Lisse, relief, alleviation; comfort, solace.
Lissen, assuage, relieve, alleviate.
List; see Lust.
List(e); see Listeth.
Listen, listen, hear.
Listes (1), lists (for a tournament).
Listes (2), wiles, devices.

Listeth, Lesteth, Lusteth, impers. vb., usually with dat., contr. pr. 3 sg. *list, lest, lust,* pt. *liste,* etc.; it pleases; also pers., is pleased, wishes; *him liste,* it pleased him, he wished; *me list right evel,* I had no desire to.

Litarge, litharge; protoxide of lead.

Litargye, lethargy.

Litel, comp. *lasse, lesse,* sup. *leeste;* little; *into litel,* within a little, almost.

Litestere, dyer.

Lith, limb.

Litherly, adv., ill.

Liven, Leven; live.

Liveree, livery.

Lixt; see **Lyen** (2).

Lode, load.

Lodemenage, pilotage.

Lode-sterre, lodestar, polar star.

Lodman (var. **Lodesman**), pilot.

Loft, air; height; loft, upper room; dat. phr. *on lofte,* aloft, on high; in the air; *kepte on lofte,* sustained.

Logge, lodge, inn; resting-place.

Logged, lodged.

Loigne, rope, tether.

Loken, look, regard; see, behold; consider; contemplate; take heed; *looke who, whan, what,* whoever, whenever, etc. See *WBT,* III, 1113, n., and cf. *wayte what.*

Loken, vb. wk., lock up.

Loken, str. pp. of *louken,* lock.

Loking, look, gaze; glance; appearance, aspect, countenance; power of sight.

Lollere, loller; Lollard.

Lomb, Lamb, pl. *lombren, lambren;* lamb.

Lond; see **Land.**

Long, sbst., lung.

Long, adj., comp. *lenger,* sup. *lengest;* long; tall; high.

Long, prep., "along of," because of; *long of the fyrmaking,* because of the fire.

Longe, adv., long; at great length.

Longen (1), long for, desire.

Longen (2), be appropriate to, befit; belong; concern.

Longitude, the distance between two given meridians; the distance on the ecliptic from the vernal equinoctial point to a circle perpendicular to the ecliptic and passing through the heavenly body whose longitude is required; a line parallel to the equator which measures the length of a climate.

Loof, pl. *loves;* loaf.

Loone, loan.

Loos, praise, fame, report.

Loos, Laus, Lous, loose; free.

Looth, loath; loathsome, hateful; *me were looth,* it would be displeasing to me, I should be loath (to do it), etc.; also sbst.

Looth, adv., unwillingly, with dislike.

Loothly, hideous, ugly.

Loppe, spider.

Lopwebbe, cobweb.

Lorden, rule over as lord.

Lordings, sirs, gentlemen.

Lordshipe, lordship, rank; rule, control, authority; post of authority; patronage.

Lore, lore, learning, knowledge; instruction, doctrine; experience.

Lorel, wretch, worthless fellow.

Lor(e)n; see **Lesen.**

Lorer; see **Laure.**

Los; loss; ruin, cause of perdition.

Los; see **Loos.**

Losenger, Losengeour, flatterer.

Losengerie, flattery.

Losenges, lozenges; small diamond-shaped figures (commonly used as bearings in heraldry).

Los(i)en, pt. *loste,* pp. *lost;* lose.

Lost, sbst., loss.

Loteby, paramour.

Lothen, loathe.

Lotinge, lurking.

Loude, adv., loudly.

Lough, adj., low.

Lough; see **Laughen.**

Louren, lour, frown.

Lous; see **Loos.**

Louten, bend, bow down; do obeisance.

Love-dayes, days for settling disputes by arbitration.

Love-drury(e), passionate love, affection.

Loveknotte, love-knot (an intertwined device).

Loves; see **Loof.**

Lovyere, lover. See *Gen Prol,* I, 80, n.

Low(e), Lough, Lawe, low, humble; small, contemptible, wretched.

Lowe, adv., low, humbly; in a low tone, softly.

Lowen, appraise, value.

Lowke, confederate, accomplice.

Luce, luce, pike.

Lufsom, lovely; amiable.

Lunarie, lunary, moon-wort.

Lure, lure or bait for a hawk; enticement.

Lurken, lurk, lie concealed (not necessarily with the idea of ambush; see NED, s.v.).

Lussheburghes, pl., spurious coins.

Lust, Lest, List, pleasure, delight; desire, wish; interest; thing which gives delight.

Lust(eth); see **Listeth.**

Lustihed(e), Lustinesse, joy, delight, cheerfulness; vigor.

Lusty, lusty; joyous, happy; pleasant; vigorous.

Luxures, pl., lusts.

Luxurie, lust, licentiousness.

Luxurious, lecherous; outrageous, excessive.

Lyard, gray.

Lybard; see **Leopart.**

Lyche-wake, wake over a corpse.

Lycorys; see **Licoryce.**

Lye, lie.

Lyen (1), **Liggen,** pt. sg. *lay, ley,* pl. *layen,* pp. *leyn, layn;* lie; recline; remain, lodge, reside; belong or pertain (to).

Lyen (2), 2 sg. pres. *lixt,* pt. *leigh;* tell a lie.

Lyen (3), blaze, flame.

Lyes, pl., lees, dregs, sediment.

Lyf, gen. sg. *lyves,* dat. phr. *on (to, of) lyve,* acc. *lyf* (also *lyve,* by extension from dat.?), pl. *lyves;* life; lifetime; *lyves,* gen. sg. used as adj., living, alive.

Lyflode, livelihood, means of support.

Lyfly, adj., lively; bright, vivid.

Lyfly, Lyvely, adv., in a lively or lifelike way.

Lyken, please; often impers.; *us lyketh yow,* it pleases us with respect to you; rarely personal, like, enjoy, find agreeable.

Lykinge, adj., pleasing; thriving.

Lyklihed(e), likelihood.

Lykly, similar; probable, likely to occur; apparently able or fitted.

Lyknen, liken, compare.

Lyknesse, likeness; parable.

Lym, lime; quicklime.

Lymaille; see **Limaille.**

Lymen, cover with birdlime; hence, ensnare, catch.

Lymere, limmer, tracking-hound, which was kept on a lime or leash.

Lymrod, lime-rod.

Lynde, linden-tree.

Lyne, line; lineage.

Lyne-right, exactly in a line with.

Lyonesse; see **Leonesse.**

Lyoun; see **Leoun.**

Lystes; see **Listes** (1) and (2).

Lyte, Lite, little; also adj., little, small, slight; and adv.

Lythe, easy; soft, delicate.

Lyve, Lyves; see **Lyf.**

M

M', me (before a vowel).

Ma(a)d, Ma(a)de; see **Maken.**

Ma(a)t, dead (the lit. sense, from Arab. "māt"); checkmated; defeated, subdued, dejected, exhausted.

Madden, go mad, be mad or angry.

Mader, sbst., madder.

Magestee, Majestee, majesty.

Magistrat, magistracy.

Magnificence, great and generous welldoing, magnanimity (see *ParsT*, X, 736); splendor, glory.

Maheym, maim, maiming.

Maille, mail-armor.

Maister, master, lord; doctor (of divinity, law, etc.); *maister-hunte*, master of the game or of the hunt; *maister strete, tour, town, temple*, etc., chief street, tower, etc.

Maistresse, mistress; governess, instructress.

Maistrise, strength, power, domination.

Maistrye, mastery, control; superiority; skill; a masterly performance; art, elegance; *for the maistrye*, surpassing all others; hence, extremely.

Majestee; see **Magestee.**

Make, sbst., mate; match, opponent; husband or wife.

Makelees, unmatched, peerless.

Maken, pt. *maked(e)*, *ma(a)de*, pp. *maked*, *ma(a)d*; make; produce; compose, write; pretend, counterfeit; cause.

Maken, match (?).

Makere, maker, composer.

Making, poetry, composition.

Malapert, forward, impudent.

Male (1), bag, wallet.

Male (2), male.

Malefice, maleficent act or device.

Malencolie, black bile, one of the humors.

Malencolyk, melancholy.

Malgre; see **Maugre(e).**

Malice, wickedness; inclination to evil; ill-will, spite.

Malisoun, curse.

Malliable, malleable.

Malt; see **Melten.**

Maltalent, ill-humor, ill-will, resentment.

Malvesye, malmsey; a sweet wine, named from Monemvasia in the Morea and originally obtained from that place or the neighborhood.

Man, pl. *men*; man; mankind; hero; servant, retainer; used indefinitely (sometimes in the unemphatic form *men*): *men seith*, they say (Germ. "man sagt"); *as man that*, like one who.

Manace, menace, threat.

Manacen, Manasen, menace, threaten.

Mandement, summons.

Mane, techel, phares, for Heb. "Mene, mene, tekel, upharsin" (Dan. v, 25).

Maner, manor.

Manére, Máner, manner; method, way, conduct, deportment; courtesy; kind, sort, as in *maner wight, maner thinges* (used without *of*); *maners*, pl., manners (Lat. "mores").

Mangonel, engine for casting stones and other missiles.

Manhede, manhood, manliness.

Manly, adv., boldly, in manly fashion.

Mannish, like a man; unwomanly; human; also adv.

Mansioun, abiding-place, dwelling; in astrology, the daily positions of the moon, or the sign (or signs) of the zodiac in which a planet exerts especially great influence.

Mansuete, meek, mild, courteous.

Mansuetude, meekness, gentleness.

Mantel, mantle, cloak; *foot-mantel*, riding skirt.

Mantelet, short mantle.

Many, many; often used directly with a sg. noun, *many knight*, many a knight.

Manye, mania.

Mappemounde, map of the world.

Marchal, Marshal, marshal.

Marchandyse, merchandise; trading.

Marcha(u)nt, merchant.

Marcial, martial, warlike.

Marcien, Martian, having the temperament of one subject to the planet Mars.

Mar(e), adj. and adv., more, greater (Northern dial.).

Mareys, marsh.

Marie, interj., marry!, by St. Mary!

Mark (1), **Merk,** mark, point, spot; race, sex; sign; image.

Mark (2), **Marc,** a monetary unit of the value of 13 *s.* 4 *d.* (two-thirds of a pound).

Market-betere, loafer or swaggerer in a market.

Markis, marquis.

Markissesse, marchioness.

Marle-pit, marl-pit.

Marren, mar, disfigure.

Martyre, martyrdom.

Martyren, make a martyr of, torment.

Mary, marrow, pith.

Mary-bones, marrow-bones.

Mase, maze, labyrinth; state or position of bewilderment.

Masednesse, amazement, bewilderment.

Maselyn, mazer or bowl of maple-wood.

Masen, be in a state of bewilderment; pp. *mased*, stunned.

Masse, Messe, mass.

Masse-peny, offering for a mass.

Mast (1), mast of a ship.

Mast (2), mast, fruit of various trees; acorns and beechnuts.

Masty, sluggish ("fattened on mast").

Mat; see Ma(a)t.

Matere, Matiere, matter, subject; affair, business; material; theme, subject-matter; cause.

Matins, morning-prayers.

Maugre (e), Malgre, ill-will; reproach; also as prep., in spite of.

Maumet, idol (corruption of "Mahomet").

Maumetrye, Mohammedanism; idolatry.

Maunciple, manciple; steward of an inn or college.

Mavis, song-thrush.

Mawe, maw, stomach.

May; see Mowen.

May, maiden.

Mayde(n), maiden, girl.

Maydenhęd(e), maidenhood, virginity.

Maymen, Meymen, maim, injure.

Mayntenen, maintain, uphold.

Maysondew, hospital (Fr. "Maison Dieu").

Meche(l); see Muche(l).

Męde, meed, reward; bribe; pl. to medes, for reward.

Mede, Meeth, mead, a drink made from honey.

Med(e)len, mix, mingle; dye; stir up; meddle.

Medewe, meadow.

Medlee, cloth of mixed weave; used as adj.

Medler, medlar (the fruit).

Męęl, meal.

Męęltide, meal-time.

Meeth; see Mede.

Męgre, meager, slender.

Mei(g)nee; see Meynee.

Meke, meek; also adv.

Meken, become meek; have mercy; make meek, mollify; refl., humble one's self.

Męle, meal (of flour).

Melk, milk.

Melle, Mille, mill.

Melten, pt. malt, pp. molten; melt.

Memorial, adj., preserving in memory.

Memorye, memory; state of consciousness.

Men; see Man.

Menden, mend; gain, profit.

Mendience, mendicancy.

Mendynant(y)z, mendicants.

Męne, means, course; instrument; mediator, go-between; intermediary; middle state or course of action.

Męne, middle; mean; intermediate.

Męnelich, moderate.

Męnen, pt. mente, menede, pp. ment; mean, intend; say, declare; signify; menen wel, be favorably disposed.

Menour, Minorite.

Menstralcie; see Minstralcye.

Ment(e); see Męnen.

Mentes, plants of mint.

Menyver, miniver.

Merciable, merciful.

Mercurie, mercury (quicksilver).

Mercy, mercy; thanks; graunt mercy, many thanks.

Męre, mare.

Meridian, adj., southern; exactly on the meridian.

Meridie, midday.

Meridional, southern.

Meritorie, meritorious.

Merk; see Mark (1).

Merken, brand.

Merlioun (var. Emerlion), merlin, small falcon.

Mermayde(n), mermaid, siren.

Mersshy, marshy.

Merveille, Mervaille, marvel.

Mery(e), Murye, Myrie, merry, glad, gay; pleasant.

Meryte, merit, deserving; reward.

Mes, range, distance; at good mes, at good, favorable range for a shot.

Meschaunce, mischance, misfortune; bad conduct; evil condition; with meschaunce, ill luck to him (a frequent curse).

Meschief, Mescheef, Mischeef, misfortune, mishap; harm, trouble.

Męsel, leper.

Męselrie, leprosy.

Message, message, errand; messenger.

Messager, Messanger, messenger.

Messagerie, sending of messages.

Messe; see Masse.

Meste, most; highest; superl. of Muche(l), Moche(l), etc.

Mester, Myster, occupation, office; service; what myster men, what sort of men.

Mesuage, messuage, dwelling-house.

Mesure, measure; moderation, temperance.

Mesuren, measure.

Met, measure of capacity.

Met; see Meten and Męten.

Męte, meat, food.

Mete, meet, fitting, suitable; equal.

Metely, well-proportioned.

Meten, pt. mette, pp. met; meet (trans. and intrans.). arrive at the point (of); succeed (in).

Męten (1), contr. pr. 3 sg. met, pt. mette, pp. met; dream.

Męten (2), measure.

Meting, meeting.

Męting, dream.

Mette; see Meten, Męten.

Meven; see Moeven.

Mewe, Muwe, mew; coop, pen; hiding-place.

Meymen; see Maymen.

Meynee, Mei(g)nee, household; retinue, suit; army; crew; company, assembly.

Meynt, Meynd, pp., mixed, mingled.

Meyntenaunce, demeanor.

Mich(el); see Muche(l).

Midel, adj., of moderate height.

Mighte; see Mowen.

Mikel; see Muche(l).

Milde, mild.

Milksop, bread sopped in milk; hence, weakling.

Mille; see Melle.

Milne-stọnes, mill-stones.

Minde; see Mynde.

Ministre, minister; officer.

Ministren, administer.

Minstralcye, minstrelsy; music; musical instruments.

Miracle, miracle; wonder; legend; pleyes of miracles, miracle-plays.

Mirre, myrrh.

Mirthe, Murthe, mirth, joy; amusement.

Mis, adj., wrong, bad; amiss; also sbst. and adv.

Misacounten, miscount.

Misaunter, misadventure.

Misavysen, vb. refl., act ill-advisedly.

Misbeden, pp. misbọden; offer evil, injure, insult.

Misbileve, suspicion of deception.

Misbileved, adj., infidel; also sbst.

Misboden; see Misbeden.

Misborn, pp., misbehaved.

Miscarien, miscarry, go amiss, come to harm.

Mischeef; see Meschief.

Misdemen, misjudge.

Misdeparten, divide amiss.

Misdrawynge, way of drawing apart.

Misericorde, mercy; pity.

Misese, discomfort; trouble; harm.

Misesed, troubled, disturbed.

Misfallen, pt. sbj. *mysfille*; misbefall, happen amiss (for).

Misforyiven, pt. *misforyaf*; misgive.

Misgon, pp., *misgon, miswent*; go amiss or astray.

Misgovernaunce, misconduct.

Misgyed, misguided. See Gyen.

Mishappen, happen ill (for); also personal.

Misknowynge, sbst., ignorance.

Misknowynge, adj., ignorant.

Misleden, mislead; misconduct.

Misledynge, misdirection.

Mislyen, pt. *mislay*; lie in an uncomfortable position.

Mislyken, displease.

Mislyved, of evil life, wicked, treacherous.

Mismetren, scan wrongly.

Missen, miss, fail; approach an end; lack, want.

Misset, pp., misplaced; badly timed.

Misseyen, speak amiss; speak evil (of), slander.

Missitten, pt. *missat*; be out of place; misbecome.

Misspeken, pt. *misspak*; speak amiss.

Mistaken, pp. *mistaken*; make a mistake; transgress.

Mister; see Mester.

Misterye, ministry; calling, vocation.

Mistihede, mystery.

Mistornen, turn aside; mislead.

Mistyden, be unlucky.

Miswanderynge, erring, going astray.

Miswent; see Misgon.

Miswey, adv., astray.

Misweyes, by-paths.

Miswryten, miswrite.

Mitayn, Miteyn, mitten, glove.

Mixen, dunghill.

Mo, adj. comp., more; greater; another, others; *na mo*, no others, none else; also adv.

Mochel, sbst., size.

Moche(l); see Muche(l).

Mocioun, motion; proposal; feeling, desire.

Moder, mother; the thickest plate of an astrolabe.

Moeble, adj., movable; also sbst., movable possessions.

Moedes, moods, strains (of music).

Moerdre; see Mordre.

Moevable, movable; impressionable, changeable; *the firste moevable*, the "primum mobile."

Moeven, Meven, move, stir up; begin; disturb.

Moevere, mover, cause.

Moiste, moist; new (not worn); fresh (not stale).

Mok(e)ren, hoard up.

Mokerere, miser.

Moleste, molestation; trouble.

Mollificacioun, mollifying, softening.

Molten; see Melten.

Mone, moon; position of the moon.

Mone, moan, complaint.

Monen, bemoan, lament.

Monesten, admonish.

Mon(e)th, month.

Monyour, coiner.

Mood, state of anger; thought.

Moornen, mourn; yearn for.

Moot (1), note of a horn or bugle.

Moot (2), motion (of a heavenly body).

Moot, pt. pr. vb., 2 sg. *most*, pt. *moste*; may, am permitted; must, shall, am obliged (to); frequent in adjurations, *so moot I thee*, so may I prosper; sometimes impers., *us moste*.

Mo(o)te, mote, atom.

Moralitee, morality; moral writing; the moral (of a fable or tale).

Mordre, Moerdre, murder.

More, sbst., root.

More, adj. comp., greater, larger; higher (in station); also sbst. and adv.

Moreover, besides, in addition, still further; *and yet moreover*, translates Lat. "ad haec."

Mormal, sore, gangrene.

Morne, morning.

Morter, mortar; bowl of wax with a wick; later, a thick candle (NED).

Mortifyen, mortify; deaden; in alchemy, change quick-silver (*argentum vivum*) into silver.

Mortreux, thick soup, stew (properly pl. of *mortrel*, but used also as sg.).

Morwe(n), morning; morrow.

Morwenynge, morning.

Morwe-tyde, morning-time.

Mosel, muzzle.

Most, Moste; see Moot.

Moste, greatest; chief.

Motren, mutter.

Mottelee, motley; parti-colored cloth.

Motyf, motive; suggestion, idea.

Mountance, amount, quantity; value.

Mourdant, chape or tag (of girdle).

Mous, pl. *mys*; mouse.

Moustre, pattern.

Moveresse, stirrer up (of quarrels).

Mowe, grimace.

Mowen, pt. pr. vb., sg. *may*, pl. *mowen*, wk. pt. *mighte*; be able, have power; be permitted; sometimes used absolutely, without dependent inf.

Mowis, bushels.

Mowlen, become mouldy; decay.

Mowynge, ability.

Moysoun, harvest; crop, growth.

Moysty, new (ale).

Muable, mutable; changeable.

Mucchen, munch.

Muche(l), Moche(l), Meche(l), Mich(el), Mikel, adj., much, great; also adv.

Mullok, heap of refuse; confused pile.

Multiplicacio(u)n, multiplication; technical for alchemy, the art of transmuting baser substances into silver and gold.

Multiplye, practise alchemy; increase the population (*world to multiplye*).

Murierly, more merrily. See Mery(e).

Murmuracion, murmuring.

Murthe; see Mirthe.

Murye; see Mery(e).

Musard, muser; hence, sluggard; dolt.

Muscle, mussel.

Musen, consider, be in a study; gaze intently.

Muwe; see Mewe.

Glossary

Muwet, mute.
Mycche, loaf of bread.
Mycher, thief.
Myle, mile; *myle wey*, space of a mile; also used as a measure of time (twenty minutes).
My(n), my; mine.
Mynde, Minde, mind; memory, recollection; sound mind, sanity; reason.
Mynen, mine; undermine.
Mynnen, remember; mention.
Mynour, miner.
Mynten, intend.
Myrie; see **Mery(e)**.
Mys-; for words beginning with this prefix see **Mis-**.
Mys; see **Mous**.
Myster; see **Mester**.
Myte (1), mite (small Flemish coin); something without value.
Myte (2), mite (the insect).

N

N', contr. for **Ne** before a vowel.
Na, no (Northern dial.); *na mo, na more*, no more, no other.
Nacioun, nation; perhaps also birth (Fr. "naissance").
Nadde, contr. for **Ne hadde**.
Naddre, Neddre, adder; serpent.
Nadir, the point of the ecliptic opposite to the position of the sun.
Naillen, Naylen, nail, fasten.
Naken, pp. *naked*; make naked, strip; *naked*, bare; plain; destitute, wretched.
Naker, kettle-drum.
Nale, in *atte nale*, at the ale (-house).
Nam; see **Nimen**.
Name, name; title; reputation.
Namely, Namelich(e), especially.
Namo, Namore; see **Na**.
Nappen, take a nap; nod.
Nar(o)we, adj., narrow, tight, close; small; also adv.
Nat, not.
Natal, presiding over nativities.
Nat forthy, nevertheless, notwithstanding.
Naught, nought, nothing.
Naught, not.
Nave, nave (of a wheel).
Navele, navel.
Navye, Naveye, navy, fleet.
Nay, adv., nay, no; also sbst., denial.
Naylen; see **Naillen**.
Nayten, refuse; deny.
Ne, not; *ne ... ne*, neither ... nor; occasionally used, where it would not be in Mod. Eng., after vbs. of neg. meaning. See *Tr*, ii, 716, n.
Nece, niece; cousin.
Necessen, compel.
Neddre; see **Naddre**.
Nede; need, necessity; extremity, emergency, peril; matter of business; specific need or necessity (esp. in pl.).
Nede(s), adv., needs, necessarily.
Nedeful, needy.
Nedelees, needless, unnecessary; also adv.
Nedely, necessarily, of necessity.
Neden, be needful or necessary; commonly impersonal, *us neded*, we should need.
Nedes-cost, of necessity.

Neen, no (Northern dial.).
Ne(e)r, adv., nearer; comp. of **Neigh**, but sometimes used as pos.
Neet, pl., neat, cattle.
Negardye; see **Nigardye**.
Neghen; see **Neighen**.
Ne(i)gh, Ney, Nygh, Ny, adj., comp. *ne(e)r, ner(r)e*, sup. *nexte*; near, nigh; also adv., almost, well nigh.
Neighebour(e), neighbor.
Ne(i)ghen, Nyghen, draw near; *neigh it nere*, approach it more closely.
Neither nother, neither the one nor the other.
Nekke, neck.
Nel; see **Nil**.
Nempnen, name.
Ner; see **Ne(e)r**.
Nercotikes, narcotics.
Nere, contr. of **Ne were**.
Nerf, nerve (sinew).
Ner(r)e; see **Neigh**.
Nether, lower.
Net-herd, cow-herd.
Netherest, nethermost.
Nevenen, name, mention.
Neveradel, never a bit, not at all.
Never(e), never.
Nevew, nephew.
Newe, new; fresh; *of newe*, anew; also adv.
Newefangel, fond of novelty.
Neweliche, recently.
Newe-thought, Inconstancy (personified).
Nexte, adj. sup., nearest; next; last; easiest; see **Neigh**.
Ney; see **Neigh**.
Nigard, miserly, niggardly; also sbst.
Nigardye, niggardliness.
Night, night; dat. phr. *by nighte*; *a nighte*, by night; the phr. *to-night* may mean the present night (now passing), the night following the present day, or the night just past. See *NPT*, VII, 2926, n.
Nighten, become night, grow dark.
Nighter-tale, night-time.
Nigromancier, necromancer.
Nil (Ne wil), Nel, will not.
Nillynge, refusing, not wishing (to be).
Nimen, pt. sg. *nam*, pp., *nomen*; take, put.
Niste (Ne wiste), knew not; see **Witen**.
No, neg. adv., no; perhaps also nor. See *HF*, 1170, n.
Noble, a coin (worth 6 *s*. 8 *d*.).
Noblen, ennoble.
Noblesse, nobility, nobleness; rank; magnificence; conduct worthy of a nobleman.
Nobleye, nobility; noble rank; splendor; collectively, an assembly of nobles.
Noel, Nowel, birthday; hence, Christmas.
Noght, not; not at all, by no means; *noght but for*, only because.
Nokked, notched.
Nolde, contr. of **Ne wolde**; see **Wil(e)**.
Nombre, Noumbre, number; quantity; sum.
Nomen; see **Nimen**.
Noncerteyn; see **Nouncerteyn**.
Nones, nonce, in the phrases *for the nones, with the nones*, properly *for (with) then ones*, where *then* is the dat. of the demonstrative pron. or article; *for the nones*, for the time or occasion, on the spur of the moment; for the special purpose; then a

colorless tag, sometimes apparently serving merely for emphasis (see *Gen Prol*, I, 379, n., 545, n.); *with the nones*, provided only, on condition that. See also Ǫnes.

Nonne, gen. sg. *nonnes*, *nonne*; nun.

Nonnerye, nunnery.

Nǫǫn, none, no.

Nǫǫt, contr. of Ne wǫǫt; see Witen.

Norice, Norys, nurse.

Noricen, Norissen, Norishen, nourish; raise, bring up; foment.

Noriss(h)inge, nourishing; nutriment, sustenance; up-bringing; growth.

Noriture; see **Norture**.

Nor(r)y, pupil.

Nortelrye, nurture, education.

Norture, nourishment; nurture, breeding; good manners.

Norys; see **Norice**.

Nǫse-thirles, nostrils.

Nǫskinnes, from *nones kinnes*, of no kind; see **Kin**.

Nǫst, contr. of Ne wost; see **Witen**.

Not, closely cropped or shaven; *not heed*, head with hair cut short.

Nǫt, contr. of Ne wǫt; see **Witen**.

Nǫtabilitee, notable fact or observation.

Notaries, scribes.

Nǫte (1), note, mark; musical note or tune (on *the kinges note* see *MillT*, I, 3217, n.); musical notation; *by note*, according to notes, or in concord, all together.

Nǫte (2), business, task.

Nǫte (pronounced *nŭte*), nut.

Nǫteful, useful.

Nǫtemuge, Nǫtemigge, nutmeg.

Nǫther, neither.

Nǫthing, adv., not at all, in no degree; *for nothing*, on no account.

Nǫtificacioun, hint.

Nǫtifyen, indicate, make known, declare; take note of.

Nought; see **Noght**.

Nouncerteyn, uncertainty; also adj.

Noun-power, impotence, powerlessness.

Nouthe, now (lit. "now then"); *as nouthe*, at present.

Novelrye, novelty.

Novys, novice.

Now, now; *now and now*, now and then, from time to time.

Nowche, setting for jewels, clasp; jewelled ornament; also *an ouche*.

Nowel; see **Noel**.

Noy, hurt, injury.

Noyen, annoy, vex, injure.

Noyous, annoying, troublesome.

Noyse, outcry; report; evil report.

Noysen, make a noise, cry out.

Ny; see **Neigh**.

Nyce, ignorant; foolish, weak; wanton; careful, scrupulous.

Nycetee, ignorance, simplicity; folly; lust; foolish or trivial conduct; shyness; scrupulousness.

Nyfles, trifles, silly stories.

Nygh, Nyghen; see **Ne(i)gh, Ne(i)ghen**.

Nymphe, nymph.

O

Ǫ; see **Ǫǫn**.

Obedient, obedient; in astronomy, the eastern signs of the zodiac, regarded as subject to the western signs. See *Astr*, ii, 28.

Obeisant, obedient.

Obeisaunce, obedience; act of obedience, submission, or attention.

Obeysshyng, obedience, submission.

Obeysynge, obedient.

Object, adj., presented.

Obligacioun, bond, surety.

Obligen, oblige, compel; *obligen to*, impose an obligation on.

Observaunce, observance; duty; ceremony; attention, heed; respect, homage.

Observen, observe, pay regard or heed; favor.

Occian, ocean.

Occupyen, take possession of, seize upon; occupy, inhabit; take up, fill; hold to; follow closely.

Octogamye, marrying eight times.

Of, prep., of; from; by; concerning, with regard to; because of, as a result of; during (*of al a tyde, of al my lyf*); sometimes in a partitive sense (*of smale houndes had she*).

Of, adv., off, away.

Offence, injury, harm, discomfort; hindrance; guilt.

Offencioun, Offensioun, crime, offense; injury, damage.

Offenden, offend; injure; attack.

Offertorie, offertory (said or sung during the collection of the offering in church).

Office, office; secular employment; duty, function; natural property; place of office; *houses of office*, storerooms devoted to household service.

Offrynge, offering of alms at the altar; contribution in church.

Of-newe, newly, lately, of late; anew, again.

Of-showven, shove off, repel.

Of-taken, taken off, removed.

Ofte, adv., often; sometimes also adj. in early English, as perhaps in the phrases *ofte sythe(s), ofte tyme*, oftentimes.

Ofthowed, pp., thawed away.

Oght, Ought, Aught, aught, anything; sometimes used as adv., at all.

Oghte; see **Ǫwen**.

Oille, oil.

Ǫkes; see **Ǫǫk**.

Olifaunt, elephant.

Olyve, olive-tree.

Olyver, olive-tree; olive-yard.

Omelie, homily.

On, on, upon; at; in; with regard to; toward, against.

Onde, envy.

Ǫnen, unite, complete.

Ǫnes, once; of one mind, in agreement; *atones* (North. *atanes*), at one time. See also **At-ǫnes, Nǫnes**.

Onethe; see **Unethe(s)**.

Ǫnliche, only.

On-lofte; see **Loft**.

On-lyve; see **Lyf**.

Ony, Onything; see **Any**, etc.

Ǫǫ; see **Ǫǫn**.

Ǫǫk, oak.

Ǫǫn, Ǫn, Ǫǫ, Ǫ, one; one single; one and the same; one continuous and uniform; *that oon*, the one; *ever in oon*, always alike, continually; *after oon*, according to one standard, uniformly good; *oon and oon*, one by one; *at oon*, at one, in agreement; *oon the faireste*, one of the fairest (see *ClT*, IV, 212, n.).

Oostesse; see Hostesse.

Ooth, oath.

Op(e)nen, open.

Open-ers, fruit of the medlar.

Open-heeded (var. -heveded), bare-headed.

Opie, opium, opiate.

Opposen, oppose; accuse (of); appose, examine.

Opposicion, opposition; in astronomy, the relation of two planets when they are 180° apart.

Oppressen, oppress, suppress; violate.

Or, oar.

Or, conj., ere, before.

Or, prep., before.

Or, conj., or. See Other, conj.

Oratorie, oratory, chapel or closet for private devotions.

Ord, point; beginning. See Word.

Ordal, ordeal.

Ordenaunce, Ordinaunce, arrangement, order; regulation, command; preparation, provision, plan; determination.

Ordenee, Ordeyne, well ordered or regulated; symmetrical.

Ordeynen, ordain, order, determine; provide; prepare; appoint.

Ordeynly, in due order, conformably.

Ordeynour, ruler.

Ordinat, ordered, regulated; in due order.

Ordre, order, law; class, set; orderly tabulation; religious (monastic) order; *by ordre*, in order.

Ordred, ordained, in (clerical) orders.

Ordure, filth; mire; rubbish.

Ore, favor, mercy, grace.

Ore, ore (of metal).

Orfrays, orphrey, gold embroidery, braid, or fringe.

Organs, organ (formerly pl.).

Orgon, organ (construed as pl. in *NPT*, VII, 2851).

Orisonte, horizon.

Orisoun, orison, prayer.

Orlog(g)e, horologe, clock.

Orphelin, orphaned.

Orpiment, orpiment (trisulphide of arsenic).

Osanne, Hosannah.

Ost, host, army.

Ostage, hostage.

Ost(e); see Host(e).

Ostelementes, furniture, household goods.

Ostesse; see Hostesse.

Otes, oats.

Other, adj., second; other; different; recent (*this other night*); *that oon ... that other*, the one ... the other.

Other, Outher, conj., either; or.

Othergate, otherwise. See Gate (2).

Other-wey(e)s, otherwise; diversely.

Otherwhyle, Outherwhyle, sometimes.

Otherwyse, on other terms or conditions.

Ouche; see Nowche.

Ought; see Oght.

Oughte; see Owen.

Oule, owl.

Oules, pl., awls, spiked irons.

Ounce, ounce; small bunch or portion.

Ounded, wavy.

Ounding, sbst., adornment with waved lines.

Oundy, wavy.

Our(e), pron., our; *oure(s), ours.* On the special use in phrases of intimacy (the "domestic *our*") see *ShipT*, VII, 69, n.

Out, adv., out; completely, fully; *out and out*, entirely; *out of*, without; out of.

Out, interj., alas!

Out-breken, break out.

Out-bresten, burst out.

Out-bringen, express, utter.

Out-drawe, pp., drawn out.

Oute, away; out, disclosed, made known, uttered.

Outen, put forth, show; utter; offer.

Out(e)reste; see Utt(e)reste.

Outerly; see Utterly.

Outermost(e), uttermost.

Outfleyinge, flying out.

Outhees, outcry, clamor, alarm.

Outher; see Other, conj.

Outlandish, foreign.

Outlawe, outlaw.

Outrage, excess; inordinateness; violence, cruelty, injustice; wrong.

Outrageous, excessive, immoderate; superfluous; violent; over-bold.

Outrance, excess; *to (into) outrance*, beyond all limits, to the utmost.

Outrayen, Outreyen, be outrageous, excessive; fall into a passion.

Outrely, utterly, absolutely, entirely.

Outridere, rider abroad; an officer of a monastery who rode about to inspect granges.

Outslyngen, cast out.

Out-springen, pt. *-sprong*; spring forth, come to light; spread abroad.

Out-strecchen, pp. *-straught*; stretch out.

Out-take(n), excepted.

Out-twynen, twist out; utter.

Out-wenden, come forth, proceed.

Out-yede, went out. See Yede.

Over-, prefix to denote excess; cf. *overgreet, overhaste, overlight, overlonge*, etc.

Over, adj., superl. *overest(e)*; upper.

Over, adv., very, exceedingly.

Over, prep., above; besides; beyond, exceeding.

Overal, everywhere; in every respect; *overal ther*, wherever; *over al and al*, beyond every other.

Overblowe, pp., blown over, past.

Overbyden, outlive.

Overcomen, pt. sg. *overcom*, pp., *overcomen*; overcome, defeat; come to pass.

Over-gilt, gilded over.

Overgoon, pass away; overspread; trample upon.

Overkerven, cut across, cross.

Overlad, pp., overborne, brow-beaten (lit. "over-led").

Overloken, look over.

Overlyen, overlie, lie upon.

Overmacchen, overmatch.

Over-nyght, the night before.

Over-old, too old, out of date.

Overpassen, surpass; exceed, overstep.

Overraughte, reached over (horses), urged on.

Overshaken, shake off.

Oversheten, pp. *overshoten* (var. *oversheten*); overrun the scent (in hunting).

Oversloppe, upper- or over-garment, gown, cassock.

Overspreden, contr. pr. 3 sg. *-sprat*, pt. *-spradde*; spread over, cover.

Qverspringen, overpass.
Qverstrecchen, stretch or extend over.
Qverswimmen, swim or float over or across.
Qvert, overt, open.
Qverthrowen, pp. *qverthrqwen*; be overthrown, ruined.
Qverthrowinge, sbst., overturning, destruction.
Qverthrowinge, pr. p. used as adj., headlong; over-whelming; headstrong; revolving.
Qverthwart, across, crosswise; askance; opposite.
Qvertymeliche, adv., untimely.
Qverwhelmen, turn or roll over.
Qverwhelven, overturn, agitate.
Qwen, pt. pr. vb., pt. *o(u)ghte, aughte*; owe, own, possess; be under obligation; ought; often used impersonally, *him (hir, us) oghte*, it behoved him, etc.
Qwen, Qw(e)ne, own.
Owh, interj., alas!
Qwher, Qwghwhere, anywhere.
Oxe, pl. *oxen*; ox.
Oynement, ointment.
Oynon, onion.

P

Pa, kiss; see also **Ba.**
Paas; see **Pas.**
Pacen; see **Passen.**
Pacience, patience.
Page, page, servant; attendant in service or in training for knighthood; boy.
Paillet, pallet.
Paire, Peire, Peyre, pair; set, series (not necessarily two in number, as *a peire of bedes*).
Paisible; see **Pęsible.**
Palais, Paleys, palace; mansion (in astrology).
Palasie, palsy.
Palasyn, belonging to the palace or court.
Pale, perpendicular stripe.
Paleis, Paleys; see **Palais, Palis.**
Palen, render pale.
Palestral, pertaining to wrestling or athletic games.
Palfrey, palfrey, riding-horse.
Palis, Palays, paling; palisade, stockade.
Palled, aphetic form of *ap(p)alled*, pale, weak, languid.
Pallet, straw bed or mattress; couch.
Palmere, palmer; originally a pilgrim to the Holy Land; then used for pilgrims more generally.
Palynge, adorning with heraldic pales or stripes.
Pan, brain-pan, skull.
Panade, large knife, cutlass.
Panne, pan.
Panter, fowling net.
Panyer, pannier, bread-basket.
Papeer, Pepir, pepper.
Papejay, Papingay, Popinjay, popinjay; parrot or woodpecker.
Papelard, hypocrite.
Papelardye, hypocrisy.
Paper, Papir, paper; account-book; certificate.
Par, Per, by (Fr. "par").
Parage, birth, lineage; rank.
Paramentz, Parementz, rich hangings or clothing.
Paramour, sbst., paramour; concubine; love-making.
Paramour(s), adv., for love (Fr. "par amour"); with passionate or romantic devotion; passionately. See *KnT*, I, 1155, n.

Paraunter, Paraventure, peradventure, perhaps.
Par cas; see **Percas.**
Parcel, part; small portion.
Parchemyn, Perchemyn, parchment.
Parcuer; see **Cuer.**
Pardee, Pardieux (lit. "by God"), a common oath or asseveration: certainly, verily.
Pardoner, pardoner, seller of indulgences.
Paregal, fully equal.
Paremed; see **Paramentz.**
Parentele, relationship, kinship.
Parfey, Parfay, by (upon) my faith.
Parfit, Perfit, perfect.
Parfournen, Perfournen, perform, execute; complete, fulfil; be equivalent to.
Parisshe, parish.
Parisshen, parishioner.
Paritorie, pellitory of the wall.
Parlement, parley, deliberation; decree; parliament.
Parodie, period, duration.
Parsener, Parsoner, partner.
Part, party, side; share.
Parten, divide into parts; separate; depart from; take leave, depart; disperse; share; participate (in); *partynge felawes*, sharing partners.
Partener, partner, partaker.
Partlęs, without part or share.
Partrich, partridge.
Party, adj., mixed, variegated (cf. "parti-colored").
Partye, part, portion; share; side; partisan; party.
Parvys, porch; room above a church-porch. On other possible meanings see *Gen Prol*, I, 310, n.
Pas, Paas, pl. *pas*; pace, step, gate; yard; distance; grade, degree; *goon a paas*, walk at a footpace; *thousand pas*, a mile.
Passage, passage, way; period (of time).
Passant, excelling, surpassing.
Passen, Pacen, surpass, excel, outdo; conquer; pass by, pass away; depart.
Passing, surpassing, excellent.
Passioun, passion, suffering; passive impression or feeling.
Pastee, pasty.
Pasture, act of feeding.
Patente, letter patent; papal license.
Paternoster, the Lord's prayer.
Patren, recite the paternoster.
Patrimoine, patrimony.
Patroun, patron; pattern.
Paunche, paunch.
Pawmes, palms (of the hand).
Pax, the "osculatorium," used at mass for the "kiss of peace."
Pay, pleasure; satisfaction.
Payen, pay; satisfy, please; appease.
Payen, adj., pagan.
Payndemayn, fine white bread.
Payne, see **Peyne.**
Pęche, peach.
Pęcok, peacock; *pecok-arwes*, arrows with peacock's feathers.
Pecunial, pecuniary.
Peer; see **Pere.**
Pę(ę)rle, pearl.
Peert (aphetic form of *apert*), forward, saucy, bold.
Pęęs, peace.
Peire; see **Paire.**

Peiren, impair, damage.

Pekke, peck (measure).

Pel, peel, small castle.

Peler; see Pile(e)r.

Pelet, pellet, cannon-ball.

Penaunt, penitent.

Pencel (1), pencil, brush.

Pencel (2), Pensel (for *penoncel*), small pennon or streamer; lady's token borne by a knight.

Penitauncer, confessor who imposes penance.

Penitence, penance.

Penne, pen.

Penner, pen-case.

Penoun, pennon; ensign of knight-bachelor.

Pensel; see Pencel (2).

Peny, pl. *penyes, pens;* penny; money.

Penyble, painstaking; inured (to pain).

Pepir; see Papeer.

Peple; see Poeple.

Percas, Par cas, perchance.

Percely, Persly, parsley.

Percen, pierce; stab.

Perchaunce, perchance; probably, doubtless.

Perche, perch; bar; horizontal rod.

Perchemyn; see Parchemyn.

Pere, peer, equal.

Peregryn, pilgrim, foreign.

Pere-jonette, early pear.

Peres, pears.

Perfit; see Parfit.

Perfournen; see Parfournen.

Perissen, perish; destroy.

Perled, studded with drops like pearls.

Perree, Perrye, jewelry; precious stones.

Pers, adj., Persian blue, blue-gray; also sbst., cloth of that color.

Persaunt, piercing; keen, sharp.

Perséveren, endure; continue.

Persone, Persoun, person; parson.

Pertinacie, pertinacity.

Pervinke, Pervenke, periwinkle.

Pesen, sbst. pl., peas.

Pesen, vb., appease.

Pesible, Paisible, peaceable, gentle, tranquil.

Pestilence, pestilence, plague; harm, disaster (common in curses).

Peter, a common oath, by St. Peter!

Peyne, Payne, pain, grief, distress; trouble, care; effort, toil; penalty; pain of torture; *in the peyne,* under torture.

Peynen, usually refl., take pains or trouble; strive, endeavor.

Peynten, pt. *peynte, peynted(e),* pp. *peynt(ed);* paint, color; smear over.

Peyntour, painter.

Peynture, painting.

Peyre; see Paire.

Peytrel, poitril, collar for horse (originally breast-plate of horse in armor).

Phares; see Mane.

Phislias, word of uncertain form and meaning. See *ML Epil,* II, 1189, n.

Phitonissa, Phitonesse, pythoness, witch. See *FrT,* III, 1510, n.

Pich, pitch.

Pichen, pt. *pighte;* pitch; prick, pierce.

Piëtee, Piëtous; see Pitee, Pitous.

Piggesnye (lit. "pig's eye"), a flower (perhaps the trillium); then, a term of endearment. See *MillT,* I, 3268, n.

Pighte; see Pichen.

Piken (1), pick; pick at; adorn; despoil.

Piken (2), peek, peep.

Pikerel, young pike.

Pilche, outer garment with fur.

Pile(e)r, Peler, pillar, column; used as adj., supporting, propping up.

Piled, pp. used as adj., deprived of hair, bald. See Pillen. Possibly, in some passages, the adj. means covered with pile or hair. See *RvT,* I, 3935, n.

Pilen, pillage, plunder, rob.

Pillen, rob, plunder; peel.

Pilour, pillager, robber, spoiler.

Pil(o)we, pillow.

Pilwe-beer, pillow-case.

Piment, spiced and sweetened wine.

Pin, pin; brooch; thin wire; *hangeth on a joly pin,* is in high spirits (original meaning uncertain).

Pinchen, pinch, pleat; *pinchen at,* fig., find fault (with), blame.

Piper, piper; used as adj., suitable for making pipes.

Pissemyre, pismire, ant.

Pistel, epistle, letter; message, communication.

Pit, Put (North. dial.), pit.

Pit; see Putten.

Pitaunce, pittance, allowance of food to inmates of a religious house; gifts.

Pitee, Piëtee, pity; a pity.

Pith, strength, vigor; marrow.

Pitous, Piëtous, pitiful, merciful; sorrowful, mournful; piteous, sad; pitiable; excusable.

Place, Plas, place; manor-house.

Plage, region; quarter, direction.

Plane, plane-tree.

Planete, planet.

Plantayn, plantain.

Plante, Plaunte, plant; slip; piece of cut wood; staff, cudgel.

Plas; see Place.

Plat, flat; blunt, downright, certain, plain; also adv.

Plate, plate (used in armor); the sight on the rule of an astrolabe.

Playn, Pleyn, even, smooth, flat; clear, plain; also adv.

Plé, plea.

Pleadour, pleader, lawyer.

Pleden, Pleten, plead, argue, sue at law.

Plegge, pledge.

Plein, Pleinen, Pleinte; see Pleyn, etc.

Plentee, plenty, plenitude; fulness, abundance.

Plentevous, plenteous, plentiful.

Plesaunce, pleasure, delight; happiness; amusement; kindly or pleasant behavior; pleasing object or experience.

Plesen, please.

Pleten, see Pleden.

Pley, Play, play, sport; game; entertainment; delusion; joke, jest; amorous or wanton dalliance.

Pleyen, play, be amused or playful; rejoice; amuse one's self, take a holiday; play (on an instrument).

Pleyn (1) (Lat. "plenus"), full, complete; also adv.

Pleyn (2) (Lat. "planus"); see Playn.

Pleynen (sometimes refl.), complain, lament; make complaint (against); whinny (as a horse).

Pleyner, plenary, full.

Pleynte, plaint, complaint, lament.

Plicchen (? var. of *plukken*), pt. *plighte*, pp. *plight*; pluck, pull; draw or tear out.

Plight(e); see **Plicchen** and **Plighten**.

Plighten, pt. *plighte*, pp. *plight*; plight, pledge.

Pliten, fold; turn backward and forward.

Plogh, Plough, plough.

Plomet, plummet, weight.

Plom-rewle, plumb-rule.

Plo(u)ngen, plunge.

Plowman, ploughman.

Plowmes, plumes.

Plowngy, stormy, rainy (lit. "plunging," or "causing plunges").

Plyt(e), plight, unhappy state or condition.

Pocok; see **Pęcok**.

Poeple, Peple, People, Puple, people, populace.

Poeplish, popular, pertaining to the populace.

Poeste; see **Pouste**.

Poesye, poetry.

Point, point, position; part; end, tag; object; state, condition; *in good point*, in good condition; *at point devys*, exactly, to perfection; *point for point*, in every particular.

Pointel, stylus, writing implement.

Pointen, stab, pierce; point; describe.

Pǫke, bag.

Pǫken, poke, nudge; incite.

Poket, small bag.

Pokkes, pocks, pustules.

Pǫlax, pole-axe, battle-axe.

Pollut, pp., polluted.

Polyve, pulley.

Pome-garnettys, pomegranates.

Pomel, top.

Pomely, dappled, marked with round spots like an apple.

Pompe, pomp.

Pǫol (1), pole, staff.

Pǫol (2), pole, northern or southern point of the heavens or of the earth's surface.

Pool, pool.

Popelote, doll, pet, darling.

Popet, puppet; dainty little person.

Popler, poplar-tree; also collective.

Poplexye, apoplexy.

Poppen, adorn, trick out.

Poppere, small dagger.

Poraille, poor people.

Porche, porch.

Pore; see **Povre**.

Porfurie, porphyry (used as a mortar).

Porisme, corollary.

Portatif, portable.

Porte-colys, portcullis.

Porter, Portour, porter.

Porthors, portesse, breviary.

Portreytour, portrayer.

Pǫse, cold in the head.

Pǫsen, suppose, assume for the sake of argument.

Posicioun, thesis, supposition, hypothesis.

Positif, positive; *positif lawe*, law of decree or enactment, as opposed to natural law.

Possen, push, toss.

Possessioner, member of an endowed religious order.

Post, post, support, pillar.

Postum, imposthume, abscess.

Potage, soup.

Potente, staff; crutch.

Potestat, potentate.

Pothecarie; see **Apotecarie**.

Pouche, pouch, bag; pocket.

Poudre, powder, dust; gunpowder; *poudre-marchant*, a flavoring powder.

Poun, pawn (at chess).

Poupen, puff, blow.

Pouren (1), pore, gaze steadily; pore over, examine closely; peep.

Pouren (2), pour.

Pous, pulse.

Pouste, Poeste, power.

Povre, Pore, Poure, poor; also adv.

Povreliche, Poureliche, Povrely, Pourely, Porely, poorly, in poverty.

Pownage, pannage, food for swine.

Pownsonen, pierce or punch with holes; stamp.

Poynaunt, Poinant, Pugnaunt, poignant, pungent, hot with spices.

Poynt, Poyntel, Poynten; see **Point**, etc.

Praktisour, practitioner.

Prauncen, prance, run about.

Praye, sbst.; see **Preye**.

Preambulacioun, preambling.

Pręcen; see **Presen**.

Pręchen, preach.

Pręchour, preacher.

Precious, precious, valuable; fastidious, over-nice.

Predestinat, pp., predestinated.

Predestinee, predestination.

Predicacioun, preaching; sermon.

Preef, Proef, Preve, proof; test; experience; experiment; *with yvel preef*, bad luck to you (a curse).

Pręes, press, crowd, throng; stress of battle; *putte in prees*, push one's self, compete, take a risk. See also **Presse**, the relation of which to **Pręes** is not quite clear.

Pręesen; see **Presen**.

Preest, priest.

Preferren, have preference or precedence over; precede.

Preignant, urgent, pressing.

Preisen, praise; appraise, estimate; prize, esteem.

Prenostik, prognostic.

Prente, print.

Prenten, print, imprint.

Prentis, apprentice.

Pręsen, press forward, throng; constrain, hasten.

Present, adv., presently, at once; also adj.

Presentarie, ever-present.

Presently, at present, at the moment.

Presoun, Prison, prison.

Presse, instrument for pressing; cupboard; clothes-press, linen-press; mold; *on presse*, under a press, suppressed, low-spirited. See also **Pręes**.

Pręssen; see **Presen**.

Pressure, wine-press.

Prest, adj., ready, prepared; prompt.

Pretenden, aim, tend, seek after.

Preterit, past time.

Pretorie, the Pretorian cohort, the imperial guard.

Preve; see **Preef**.

Preven, prove, approve; exemplify; test; undergo a test; succeed.

Prevetee; see **Privetee**.

Prev(e)y; see **Privee**.

Previdence, foresight.

Preye, Praye, prey.
Preyen, Prayen, pray, beg, beseech.
Preyere, Prayere, prayer.
Preynen; see Proynen.
Preys, praise.
Preysen, praise.
Prikasour, hunter on horseback.
Prikinge, pricking, spurring (a horse), hard riding; tracking the hare by footprints.
Prikke, prick, point, dot; small mark; pin's point; degree, pitch; critical moment; sting; puncture, stab.
Prik(k)en, pt. *prighte*, *priked*; prick, spur; incite, rouse; ache.
Prime, prime, the canonical hour (beginning at 6 A.M.); then the period from six till nine (ending at *high prime*, *prime large*).
Principal, principal, chief; cardinal.
Pris; see Prys.
Privee, sbst., privy.
Privee, Privy, Prev(e)y, adj., privy, secret, private, intimate; closely attendant; also adv.
Privetee, privacy; private affairs or counsel; secrecy; private apartments; private parts.
Probleme, problem.
Proces, process, proceeding; matter, argument, story; course of time or events.
Procuratour, Procutour, proctor, agent, attorney; collector of alms.
Proef; see Preef.
Proeven; see Preven.
Prohemye (var. Proheme), proem, prologue.
Prolacioun, utterance.
Prollen, prowl, search widely.
Prologe, prologue; prelude.
Pronouncen, pronounce; declare, announce.
Prophecye, prophecy.
Prophete, prophet.
Propre, own; especial, peculiar; complete, perfect; handsome, comely, well formed or grown.
Proprely, properly, fitly, appropriately; naturally; exactly, literally.
Propretee, peculiar property, individual character or characteristic; quality; possession, property.
Prosen, write in prose.
Prospectyves, perspective-glasses, lenses; magic glasses to reveal the future.
Prospere, prosperous.
Provende, provision, stipend, allowance.
Proverb, proverb, saying.
Proverben, pp. *proverbed*; said in proverbs.
Provost, prefect, praetor, magistrate.
Provostrye, office of provost, praetorship.
Prow, profit, benefit, advantage.
Prowesse, prowess, valor; excellence; profit.
Proynen, Preynen, prune, trim, make neat.
Pryde, Pruyde, pride.
Pryen, pry, peer, gaze, spy.
Prymerole, primrose.
Pryme temps, beginning; the spring.
Prys, price, value; worth; excellence; praise, esteem, reputation; prize, reward.
Publisshen, publish, proclaim.
Publysschen, var. Puplisshen, refl. vb., repopulate themselves, be propagated.
Pugnaunt; see Poynaunt.
Pullaylle, poultry.
Pullen, pull, draw; pluck; *pulle a finch*, see *Gen Prol*, I, 652, n.

Pulpet, Pulpit, pulpit.
Pultrye, poultry.
Puniss(h)en, Punycen, punish.
Puple; see Poeple.
Purchacen, Purchasen, purchase, buy; procure, acquire; obtain, win; contrive, provide, bring about; transfer by conveyancing.
Purchas, gain, acquisition; proceeds of begging or stealing.
Purchasour, conveyancer, or purchaser of land for one's self.
Pure, adj., pure; very; utter; also adv.
Puren, cleanse; pp. *pured*, refined, very pure.
Purfiled, trimmed at the edges.
Purpre, purple.
Purprise, enclosure, precinct.
Pursevaunt, pursuivant.
Pursu(y)t(e), pursuit; perseverance, continuance; prosecution.
Purtreyen, Portreyen, draw.
Purveyable, provident, careful.
Purveyaunce, providence, foresight; provision, equipment.
Purveyen, provide; foresee.
Put; see Pit.
Put(e)rie, whoredom.
Putours, procurers.
Putten, contr. pr. 3 sg. *put*, pt. *putte*, pp. *put* (North. dial. *pit*); put, lay; suppose, take for granted; impose; set; add; settle, establish.
Pye, magpie.
Pyk, pike (fish).
Pykepurs, pick-purse.
Pyled; see Piled.
Pyn, pine-tree.
Pyne, pain, torment, suffering; place of torment; toil, effort.
Pynen, torture, examine by torture; suffer, grieve; pine away.
Pypen, pipe, whistle; play on a pipe; make a faint or squeaking noise; hiss; *piping-hoot*, piping-hot.
Pyrie, pear-tree.

Q

Qua(a)d, evil, bad.
Quaille, Quayle, quail.
Quaken, pt. *quook*, pp. *quaked*; quake, tremble, shiver, shake.
Quakke, hoarseness.
Qualm, plague, pestilence; death; loss, damage; croak (of raven).
Quappen, shake, toss, heave; beat, palpitate.
Quarel, arrow or square bolt used with the crossbow.
Quarele, Querele, quarrel; complaint.
Quarter-night, nine o'clock, when a quarter of the night is gone.
Quarteyne, quartan fever.
Queint; see Queynt.
Quek, Kek, quack (of a duck or goose).
Quellen, kill; smite.
Quemen, please, subserve.
Quenchen, pt. *queynte*, pp. *queynt*; quench, extinguish; put an end to.
Quene, queen.
Quene, quean, concubine.
Querele; see Quarele.
Querne, hand-mill.

Querrour, quarry-worker.
Questemongeres, questmen, jurymen.
Quęthen, pt. *quod*; say, declare; *quethe him quyte*, cry him quit; commonly restricted in use to pt. *quod*, quoth.
Queynt(e); see **Quenchen**.
Queynte, sbst., pudendum.
Queynt(e), adj., strange; curious, curiously contrived; elaborate, ornamented; neat; artful, sly; graceful; *make it queynt(e)*, be offish or disdainful, make it strange or difficult; also, show pleasure or satisfaction.
Queynte, adv., skilfully, artfully.
Queyntelyche, adv., strangely, curiously; cunningly, skilfully.
Queyntyse, finery, ornament; elegance.
Quiet, quiet, rest.
Quik, alive; lively, quick, ready; intelligent.
Quisshin, cushion.
Quitly, adv., freely, entirely.
Quit(te); see **Quyten**.
Quod; see **Quęthen**.
Quoniam, pudendum.
Quook; see **Quaken**.
Quynyble, "a part in music, one octave above the treble" (NED).
Quyrboilly, boiled skin (leather).
Quystroun, scullion.
Quyten, pt. *quitte*, pp. *quit*; requite, repay; reward, recompense; ransom, set free, discharge; *quyte hir whyle*, repay her time (or trouble).

R

Raa, roe (North. dial.).
Raby, rabbi.
Racyne, root.
Rad(de); see **Ręden**.
Radevore, tapestry. See *LGW*, 2352, n.
Rafles, raffles.
Raft(e); see **Ręven**.
Rage, rage, madness, folly; passion, violent grief or desire; blast, violent rush.
Ragen, indulge in amorous or wanton dalliance.
Ragerye, wantonness, passion.
Rakel, rash; hasty.
Rakelnesse, Rekelnesse, rashness.
Raken, pp. *raked, y-reken*; rake.
Rake-stęle, rake-handle.
Raket, the game of rackets.
Raklen, behave rashly.
Ram, ram; Aries (in the zodiac).
Ramage, wild.
Rammish, ramlike (in odor).
Rampen, romp, rear, behave violently.
Rape, haste.
Rape, adv., quickly.
Rapen, vb., in phr. *rape and renne*, seize and carry away.
Rascaille, mob.
Rasour, razor.
Rated, pp., berated, scolded (of uncertain etymology).
Rathe, adv., quickly, soon; early.
Rather, adj., former, earlier; also adv., sooner, more willingly.
Raughte; see **Ręchen**.
Raunsoun, ransom.
Raven, rave, be mad; act or speak madly.

Ravisshen, Ravysen, seize, snatch; appropriate; carry off; take greedily; ravish, violate.
Ravyne, ravening, greediness; rapine, plunder, theft; prey.
Ravynour, Ravyner, plunderer.
Ravysable, ravishing, eager for prey.
Ravysen; see **Ravisshen**.
Rayed, striped.
Rëal, Rial, regal, royal.
Rëalme, Rëaume, Rë(a)wme, Ręme, realm.
Rëaltee, royalty.
Rebating, abatement.
Rebekke, old woman. See *FrT*, III, 1377, n.
Rebel, adj., rebellious.
Rebounden, rebound, return.
Recchelęes, reckless, careless; regardless of duty or discipline. See *Gen Prol*, I, 179, n.
Recchen, Rekken (1), pt. *ro(u)ghte*; reck, care, heed.
Recchen (2), interpret, expound.
Receite, receipt, recipe.
Receyven, Resceiven, Resseyven, pp. *received*; receive; in astrology, applied to a planet which is favorably situated with respect to other planets.
Rechasen, chase, pursue.
Ręchen, pt. *reighte, raughte*; reach, touch; stretch out; deliver, hand over.
Reclaymen, bring a hawk to the lure; entice.
Recomaunden, Recomenden, recommend; command; commit.
Recomforten, Reconforten, comfort or encourage again.
Recompensacioun, recompense.
Reconciled, Reconsiled, reconciled; reconsecrated.
Reconforten; see **Recomforten**.
Reconsilen, reconcile.
Reconyssaunce, recognizance.
Record, record, report, testimony.
Recorden, record; witness; bear in mind, remember; call to mind.
Recours, recourse, return; resort; orbit.
Recoveren, Rekeveren, recover, regain, get; heal; retrieve.
Recoverer, recovery, remedy.
Recreaundise, cowardliness.
Recreaunt, recreant, confessing himself defeated; cowardly.
Recured, recovered.
Red(de); see **Ręden**.
Reddour, severity, rigor; harshness.
Rede, adj., made of reed (musical instrument).
Rędelęes, without counsel.
Rędely, Rędily, readily, soon; easily; truly.
Ręden, contr. pr. 3 sg. *ręt*, pt. *redde, radde*, pp. *red, rad*; read; advise, counsel; interpret; study, describe, give an account of.
Redouten, fear, respect, revere.
Redressen, amend, reform; assert, vindicate; refl., rise again.
Reducen, sum up.
Rędy, ready; prepared, dressed; at hand.
Ręęd, advice, counsel; plan; help, remedy; profit; adviser, helper; dat. phr. *to rede*; *I can no reed*, I am at a loss, without counsel.
Ręęd, adj., red; also sbst.
Reeft, rift.
Ręęs, haste, rush.
Refect, pp., refreshed, restored.
Referren, refer, bring back; reduce.

Refreininge, refrain, burden.

Refreyden, cool down, grow cold.

Refreynen, bridle, curb.

Reft(e); see **Reven.**

Refus, pp., as adj., refused, rejected.

Refut, Refuyt, refuge; safety.

Regal, regal, royal; pl. as sbst., royal attributes.

Regalye, royal rule, authority.

Registre, register, list, table of contents.

Rehercen, Rehersen, rehearse, repeat, enumerate.

Rehersaille, rehearsal, enumeration.

Reheten, cheer, console, encourage.

Reighte; see **Rechen.**

Re(i)gne, Reine, Reyne, kingdom, realm; rule, government.

Re(i)gnen, Reynen, reign, rule; rule over, prevail in.

Reine; see **Re(i)gne.**

Rejoyen, rejoice.

Rekelnesse; see **Rakelnesse.**

Reken, reek, smoke.

Rek(e)nen, reckon.

Rekeveren; see **Recoveren.**

Rekken; see **Recchen** (1).

Relay, set of fresh hounds (or horses) posted to take up the chase.

Relees, release; relief; ceasing; *out of relees,* without ceasing.

Releevynge, remedy.

Relenten, melt.

Reles(s)en, release, give up, relieve; remit, forgive.

Releven, relieve; revive; recompense; restore (to life, wealth, etc.).

Religioun, religion; religious life; a religious order, or the life of the member of one.

Religious, pious; belonging or devoted to a religious order; also sbst., a monk or nun.

Reme; see **Realme.**

Remede, Remedye, remedy.

Remembren, remember; remind; come to mind; call to mind; sometimes refl.

Remena(u)nt, remnant, remainder, rest.

Remeven, Remoeven, Remu(w)en, remove.

Remorden, cause remorse; vex, trouble.

Remounten, strengthen, comfort.

Remuable, changeable, variable; capable of motion.

Remu(w)en; see **Remeven.**

Ren, run (imp.).

Renably, fluently, readily.

Renden, Renten, pt. *rente,* pp. *rent;* rend, tear.

Rendren, render, recite.

Renegat, renegade.

Reneyen, deny, renounce.

Renge, rank, file.

Renged, pp. ranged in rows.

Rennen (1), pt. sg. *ran,* pl. and pp. *ronnen;* run, go; be current; spread; flow, continue.

Rennen (2); see **Rapen.**

Renomed, renowned.

Renomee, renown.

Renoun, renown.

Renovelance, renewal.

Renovellen, renew, be renewed.

Rente, rent; tribute; revenue, regular income.

Rent(e)(n); see **Renden.**

Repair, resort.

Repairen, Repeyren, repair, go, betake one's self; resort to; return; go home; dwell.

Repeled, pp., repealed.

Repentaunt, penitent.

Repeyren; see **Repairen.**

Repleccioun, repletion.

Repleet, replete, full.

Replenyss(h)en, replenish, fill.

Reportour, reporter, narrator; judge, referee (?).

Rep(p)licacioun, folding; reply, retort; *withouten repplicaccioun,* without reply being allowed.

Rep(p)lyen, reply; object.

Repreef; see **Repreve.**

Reprehencioun, reprehension, reproof.

Reprehenden, reprehend, reproach, blame.

Reprevable, reprehensible; discreditable.

Repreve, Repreef, reproof; shame, reproach.

Repreven, Reproeven, Reproven, reprove, reproach; blame; discredit, stultify.

Repugnen, be repugnant (to).

Requerable, desirable.

Requeren, require, demand; ask, seek; beg, entreat.

Requeste, request.

Resalgar, realgar, disulphide of arsenic.

Resceiven; see **Receyven.**

Resc(o)us, rescue, aid, support.

Rescowen, rescue, save.

Resemblable, similar.

Resen, shake, tremble.

Resolven, flow out; melt, dissolve; be held in solution.

Resonable, reasonable; ready of speech.

Resort, resource.

Resoun, reason; right; correct way; argument, speech, opinion; cause; consideration, regard; estimation; order (technical term in rhetoric).

Resounen, resound.

Resport, regard, respect.

Respyt, respite, delay.

Respyten, hesitate, delay, refuse.

Resseyven; see **Receyven.**

Reste, rest, repose; time of repose.

Resteles, adj., restless; also adv.

Resten, rest, remain; repose.

Restreynen, restrain; cut short.

Ret; see **Reden.**

Retenue, retinue; suite, troop.

Rethor, orator, rhetorician.

Rethorien, adj., rhetorical; also sbst.

Rethoryke, rhetoric.

Reto(u)rnen, return; revolve; bring back.

Retraccioun, retraction; something withdrawn.

Retreten, treat again, reconsider.

Retrograd, retrograde: "moving in a direction contrary to that of the sun's motion in the ecliptic" (Skeat).

Reule, Rewle, rule; revolving plate or rod, on the back of an astrolabe, used for measuring and taking altitudes.

Reulen, Rewlen, rule, guide, control.

Reuthe, Rewthe, Routhe, ruth, pity, compassion; lamentation; a pitiful sight or occurrence.

Reve, reeve, bailiff.

Revel, revelry; minstrelsy.

Revelour, reveller.

Revelous, given to revelry.

Reven, pt. *refte, rafte,* pp. *reft, raft;* rob, plunder; take away; bereave.

Reverdye (var. **Reverye**), joy, delight.

Reverten, bring back.

Revesten, clothe again.

Revǫken, recall.

Reward, regard, consideration.

Rewde; see **Rude**.

Rewe, row, order, line; *a-rewe, by rewe*, in order, one after another.

Rew(e)ful, rueful, lamentable, sad; also sbst.

Rewel-bǫon, ivory (perhaps that of the narwhale).

Rewen, rue, be sorry; have pity; do penance (for); sometimes impers.

Rewle; see **Reule**.

Rewlich, pitiable.

Rewme; see **Rëalme**.

Rewthe; see **Reuthe**.

Reye, rye.

Reyes, pl., round dances.

Reyn, Rein, rain; rain-storm.

Reyne; see **Re(i)gne**.

Reyne, rein, bridle.

Reynen (1), pt. *rǫn, reyned*; rain, rain down.

Reynen (2); see **Re(i)gnen**.

Reynes, pl., reins, kidneys, loins.

Reysen (1), raise; build up; obtain, exact.

Reysen (2), make a raid or military expedition (with special reference to Prussian campaigns).

Reysyns, grapes.

Rial; see **Rëal**.

Riban, ribbon.

Ribaned, adorned with ribbons or gold-lace.

Ribanynge, ribbon-work; trimming or border of silk.

Ribaud, laborer; coarse or ribald person.

Ribaudye, ribaldry, coarse jesting.

Ribibe, term of contempt for an old woman; probably an application of *ribibe, ribible*, fiddle. See *FrT*, III, 1377, n.

Ribible, Rubible, rebeck; lute or fiddle.

Riche, rich.

Richesse, riches, wealth.

Riden; see **Ryden**.

Ridled, plaited, gathered in folds.

Riet, rete, or net, of an astrolabe.

Right, right; justice; pl., rights; true reasons; *at alle rightes*, in all respects; *have right*, be in the right (Fr. "avoir raison"); *right circle*, circle perpendicular to the equator.

Right, adv., just, exactly; completely; very, extremely.

Rightful, rightful, lawful, correct; just; perfect; *rightful age*, best age, prime.

Rightwis, righteous; just.

Rigour, rigor, severity.

Rinde, rind, bark, skin.

Ringen, pt. sg. *rong*, pl. and pp. *rongen, rungen*; ring; resound.

Riot; see **Ryot**.

Rioten, indulge in wanton or riotous living.

Riotour, riotous liver.

Risshe, rush.

Rist; see **Rysen**.

Rit; see **Ryden**.

Rivelyng, puckering.

Rivér(e), river; river-bank, hawking-ground.

Robbour, robber.

Roche, rock.

Rochet, Roket, outer garment, smock-frock, cloak.

Rode, complexion.

Rode, rood, cross.

Rody, ruddy.

Roggen, shake.

Rogh, pl. *rowe*; rough.

Roghte; see **Recchen** (1).

Roignous, Roynous, scurvy, rotten.

Roket; see **Rochet**.

Rok(ke), rock.

Rok(k)en, vb., rock.

Rolle, roll.

Rollen, roll, revolve; turn over; talk over, discuss.

Romblen; see **Rumblen**.

Rǫmen, roam, wander; travel, go.

Rǫn, rose-bush.

Rǫn; see **Reynen** (1).

Rond, round.

Rong(en); see **Ringen**.

Rong, sbst., rung.

Ronnen; see **Rennen** (1).

Rǫǫ, roe.

Rǫǫd; see **Ryden**.

Rǫǫde-bęem, beam which supports a cross.

Rǫǫf; see **Ryven**.

Roof, dat. *rove*; roof.

Rǫǫre, uproar.

Rǫǫs, see **Rysen**.

Rǫǫst, roast meat.

Rǫpen (pp.), of *ripen, rǫpen*), reaped.

Rǫren, roar; resound; lament loudly.

Rǫsen, rosy; made of roses.

Rǫser, rose-bush.

Rǫse-ręed, red as a rose.

Rǫsten, roast.

Rǫte, a stringed instrument.

Rote, root; source; basic principle; in astronomy, a number written opposite a date as a basis for calculation of corresponding quantities for other dates; in astrology, the "epoch" of a nativity.

Roten, rotten; currupt.

Rotien, rot; cause to rot.

Roughte; see **Recchen** (1).

Rouken, cower, crouch.

Roulen, roll, gad about.

Roum, room, space; dat. phr. *a-roume*.

Roum, Rowm, spacious, roomy.

Rouncy, carthorse, nag; strong, powerful horse.

Rounde, roundly, easily; freely, with full tone.

Roundel, roundel, roundelay; small circle.

Roundnesse, roundness; orbit.

Rounen, whisper.

Route, rout, company, band; number; flock.

Routen (1), assemble.

Routen (2), roar, make a noise or murmur; snore.

Routhe; see **Reuthe**.

Rove; see **Roof**.

Rowe, row; line; ray.

Rowe, roughly, angrily; also adj. pl. (see **Rogh**).

Rown; see **Roum**.

Royalliche, royally.

Roylen, roll, wander, meander.

Royne, roughness.

Roynous; see **Roignous**.

Rubee, ruby.

Rubible; see **Ribible**.

Rubifying, rubefaction, making red. See *CYT*, VIII, 797, n.

Rubriche, rubric.

Ruddock, robin.

Rude, Rewde, rude, rough; poor, humble, boorish; also sbst.

Rudeliche, rudely, roughly.

Ruggy, rough.

Rum, ram, ruf, meaningless words used to illustrate alliteration.

Rumble, rumbling sound; rumor.

Rumblen, rumble, make a murmuring noise.

Rungen; see **Ringen.**

Rusen, make a detour to escape the hounds.

Ryal; see **Rëal.**

Ryden, contr. pr. 3 sg. *rit,* pt. sg. *rǫǫd,* pl. and pp. *riden, ride;* lie at anchor; *ryden out,* go on an expedition; go out on a tour of inspection.

Ryding, procession; jousting.

Rym, rime.

Rymen, rime.

Rymeyed, rimed.

Rympled, wrinkled.

Ryot, Riot, riotous or wanton living, debauchery; extravagance.

Rype, ripe, mature; seasonable.

Rys, twig, spray.

Rysen, contr. pr. 3 sg. *rist,* pt. sg. *rǫǫs,* pl. and pp. *risen;* rise, arise.

Ryte, rite, observance.

Ryven, pt. sg. *rǫǫf;* pierce, cut, tear; thrust.

S (see also C)

Saaf; see **Sauf.**

Sachel, satchel, bag.

Sacrifyen, sacrifice.

Sacrilege, outrage or violence upon sacred persons or things; applied to sorcery in *Bo,* i, pr. 4, 257 ff.

Sad, heavy; firm, stable; steady, fixed, settled; sober, earnest, serious, staid; sorrowful; discreet.

Sadel, saddle.

Saffronen, color or flavor with saffron; used figuratively in *Pard Prol,* VI, 345.

Saffroun, saffron.

Sailen, assail, attack.

Saillour, dancer.

Sak, sack, bag.

Sakked Frẹres, Friars of the Sack.

Sakken, pp. *sakked;* put in a sack.

Sal, shall (North. dial.).

Sal armǫnyak, sal ammoniac. See *CYT,* VIII, 798, n.

Salewen, Salu(w)en, Salowen, salute.

Sal peter, saltpeter; rock-salt.

Sal preparat, prepared salt.

Sal tartre, salt of tartar; carbonate of potash.

Sa(l)vacioun, salvation; safety; *withoute any sa(l)-vacioun,* without saving any.

Salwes, willow-twigs, osiers.

Samit, samite, silk.

Samon, salmon.

Sang, song (North. dial.).

Sangwyn, blood-red; also sbst., red cloth.

Sanz, Sa(u)ns, without.

Sapience, wisdom.

Sarge, serge.

Sarpler, canvas sack.

Sarsynesh, Saracen.

Sauf, adj., safe, secure.

Sauf, Save, prep., save, except.

Saufly, Savely, safely; with safety.

Saugh; see **Seen.**

Sa(u)le, North. form of **Soule.**

Sa(u)ns; see **Sanz.**

Sauter, psalter.

Sautrye, psaltery.

Savacioun; see **Sa(l)vacioun.**

Save, a decoction of herbs (Lat. "sapa" = "mustum coctum," Ducange).

Save, prep., save, except; *save your grace,* saving (keeping safe or intact) your grace.

Save-garde, safeguard, safe-conduct.

Savely; see **Saufly.**

Saverous, pleasant, agreeable.

Savoren; see **Savo(u)ren.**

Savory, pleasant.

Savour, savor, flavor; smell, odor, pleasure, interest.

Savoured, perfumed.

Savo(u)ren (var. **Saveren**), impers., taste; smell; pers., enjoy, relish, care for.

Sawceflẹẹm, having pimples or eruptions (Lat. "salsum phlegma").

Sawe, saw, saying; word, speech.

Sawen, Say; see **Seen.**

Sayen, essay, endeavor.

Sayn; see **Seyen, Seen.**

Saynt; see **Ceynt.**

Scabbe, scab; a disease (of animals).

Scaffold, Skaffaut, scaffold, shed on wheels; used sometimes for a stage; also to cover the approach of a battering-ram.

Scalle, a scabby disease.

Scalled, having the scall, scabby.

Scantilon, pattern.

Scantitee, scantiness, scarcity.

Scapen, escape.

Scarmishyng, skirmishing.

Scarmuch(e), skirmish.

Scars, scarce; niggardly.

Scathe, harm, misfortune; *that was scathe,* that was a pity.

Scathelẹẹs, harmlessly.

Sch-; see **Sh-.**

Science, science, knowledge; wisdom; a branch of learning; learned composition.

Sclat, slate.

S(c)laundre, slander, scandal, disgrace.

Sclave, slave.

Sclendre, slender, thin; poor.

Scochoun, escutcheon.

Scoleiyng, schooling.

Scole-matere, matter for the schools, scholastic question.

Scole-ward, school-ward, toward school.

Scoleyen, study, attend school.

Scomes, scums, foamings.

Scọre, hole, crack.

Scorklen, scorch, shrivel.

Scornen, scorn; deride, jest at.

Scouren, cleanse; scourge, beat.

Scripture, writing, inscription; passage, text; used especially of Holy Scripture.

Scrit, writ, deed.

Scriveyn, scribe.

Scryvenyssh, like a scrivener.

Sechen, Seken, seek.

Secree, sbst., secret.

Secree, secret; trusty, confidential; able to keep secrets; also adv.

Secte, sect, company; religion.

Seculer, layman.

Seden, bear seed.

See (1), sea; *fulle see*, high tide.
See (2), seat; seat of power.
Seed-foul, birds living on seeds.
Seek; see **Sik**.
Seel (1), bliss, joy.
Seel (2), seal.
Seen, pt. sg. *s(e)y, say, seigh, sigh, saugh*, pl. *seyen, sawen, syen*, pp. *seyen, seyn, sayn, seen*; infl. infin. *to sene*; see, behold; look.
Seer, sere, dry.
Se(e)stow, seest thou; see **Seen**.
Seet; see **Sitten**.
Seeth; see **Sethen**.
Sege, seat, throne; siege.
Seggen; see **Seyen**.
Seigh; see **Seen**.
Seignorye, domain; dominion.
Sein; see **Seyen**.
Seintuarie, sanctuary; holy object, relic.
Seisen; see **Sesen**.
Seistow, sayest thou; see **Seyen**.
Seken, Sechen, pt. *so(u)ghte*, pp. *so(u)ght*; seek, search; *seken to*, resort to, press towards; *return to seke upon*, attack, harass; *to seke*, to be sought, hard to find, at a loss, at fault.
Seker, Sekir; see **Siker**.
Sekernesse, Sikernesse, security.
Selde(n), seldom.
Seled, sealed.
Selinesse, happiness, bliss.
Sellen, pt. *solde*, pp. *sold*; sell, barter.
Sely, happy, blessed; innocent, good, kind, poor, wretched, hapless.
Semblable, similar.
Semblaunce, semblance, appearance; resemblance.
Semblaunt, semblance, appearance.
Semlihede, seemliness, gracefulness.
Sem(e)ly, seemly, comely; becoming, pleasing; also adv.
Semen, seem, appear; often impers.
Semes, seams.
Semicope, short cope, half-cope.
Seminge, seeming, appearance; *to my seminge*, in my judgment.
Semisoun, half-sound.
Semy, thin, small.
Sen, since. See **Sin**.
Senatorie, senatorial rank.
Sencer, censer.
Sendal, thin silk.
Senden, contr. pr. 3 sg. *sent*, pt. *sente*, pp. *sent*; send.
Sene, inflected inf. of **Seen**, see.
Sene, adj., visible, apparent, to be seen.
Sengen, pp. *seynd*; singe, broil.
Sengle, single.
Senith; see **Cenyth**.
Sensibilities, perceptions.
Sensible, perceptible.
Sensynge, censing (with incense).
Sent, Sente; see **Senden**.
Sentement, sentiment, feeling; passion; sensibility, susceptibleness.
Sentence, meaning, significance; contents, subject, theme; opinion, decision, judgment, verdict, sentence.
Septemtrional, northern.
Septemtrioun, north.
Serchen, search; visit, haunt.

Seremant, oath.
Sereyns, sirens.
Sergeaunt, sergeant. See the description of the Man of Law in the Explanatory Notes to *Gen Prol*.
Serial; see **Cerial**.
Sermonen, preach, harangue.
Sermoning, discourse, argument.
Servage, servitude.
Serva(u)nt, servant; lover.
Serviable, serviceable.
Servisable, serviceable, willing to serve; useful.
Servitute, servitude.
Servyse, service; religious service; musical performance.
Serye, process, sequence of thought, argument.
Sesen, Seisen, seize; possess (tech. legal term); pp. *sesed*, seized, possessed.
Sesoun, season; flourishing time.
Set; see **Setten**.
Sete, seat, throne.
Seten; see **Sitten**.
Setewale; see **Cetewale**.
Sethen, pt. *seeth*, pp. *soden*; seethe, boil.
Setten, contr. pr. 3 sg. *set*, pt. *sette*, pp. *set*; set, put; appoint; suppose, imagine; reckon, count, care, esteem; stake (in a game); *sette hir cappe*, made fools of them; *wel set*, seemly, suitable.
Seur, sure; also adv.
Seurly, surely.
Seur(e)tee; see **Sur(e)tee**.
Sewen (1), **Su(w)en**, pursue, follow; ensue.
Sewen (2); see **Sowen** (2).
Sewes, juices, gravies; broths.
Sewynge, conformable, similar.
Sexte, sixth.
Sexteyn, sacristan.
Sexti, sixty.
Sey, Seyen; see **Seen**.
Seyen, Seggen, say.
Seyl, sail.
Seyn; see **Seen**.
Seynd; see **Sengen**.
Seynt, saint; holy.
Shaar, plough-share.
Shad, Shadde; see **Sheden**.
Shadowing, shadow; shaded spot.
Shadwe, shadow.
Shadwed, shadowed, shaded.
Shaken, pt. sg. *shook*, pl. *shoken*, pp. *shaken*; shake.
Shal, pt. pr. vb., pl. *shul(len)*, pt. *sholde, shulde*; shall, must, is to, ought to; owes.
Shale, shell, husk.
Shalemyes, shawms, reed-pipes.
Sham(e)fast, modest, shy; ashamed.
Shamen, put to shame, make ashamed.
Shap, shape, form; privy member.
Shapen, pt. sg. *shoop*, pl. *shopen*, pp. *shapen*; shape, make; devise, contrive, plot; prepare, provide, intend; dispose (used especially of fate).
Shaply, shapely, suitable; likely.
Shar; see **Sheren**.
Sharp, sharp; keen.
Sharpe, adv., sharply; shrilly.
Shaven, pp. *shaven*; shave.
Shawe, wood.
Sheden, pt. *shedde, shadde*, pp. *shad*; shed, pour; diffuse, distribute; divide.
Sheef, sheaf.

Sheeld, shield; French coin ("écu").

Shelden, Kentish form of **Shilden**.

Shenden, pt. *shente*, pp. *shent*; harm, injure, defile; destroy, ruin, spoil; disgrace, reproach, scold; come to harm, be injured.

Shendshipe, shame, disgrace.

Shene, bright, shining; fair, beautiful; also adv.

Shent, Shente; see **Shenden**.

Shepe; see **Shipe**.

Shepne, Shipne, stable, shed.

Shẹre, pair of shears.

Shẹren, pt. *shar*, pp., *shọr(e)n*; shear, cut.

Sherte, shirt.

Shẹrynge-hokes, shearing-hooks (to cut ropes in a sea-fight.

Shet; see **Shetten**.

Shete, sheet.

Sheten, pp. *shoten*; shoot.

Sheter (lit. "shooter"), fit for shooting.

Shẹthe, sheath.

Shetten, Shitten, pt. *shette*, pp. *shet* (Kentish); shut, close, fasten; clasp.

Shewen, show; appear, portend; see, behold (*fair to shewe*).

Shewinge, sbst., showing, exhibiting; evidence; demeanor.

Shewinge, evident.

Shiften, provide, ordain; distribute, assign.

Shilden, Shelden, shield, defend; forbid.

Shimering, shimmer, glimmer.

Shine, shin.

Ship, ship; dat. phr. *to shippe*.

Shipe, Shepe, hire, reward.

Shipne; see **Shepne**.

Shirreve, sheriff.

Shiten, pp., defiled, foul.

Shitten; see **Shetten**.

Shitting, shutting.

Shọde, parting of the hair; temple.

Shoken; see **Shaken**.

Sholde; see **Shal**.

Sholder-bọọn, bone of the shoulder-blade.

Shonde, shame; harm.

Shoo, pl. *shoos, shoon*; shoe.

Shọọf; see **Shouven**.

Shook; see **Shaken**.

Shoon; see **Shoo**.

Shọọn; see **Shynen**.

Shoop, Shopen; see **Shapen**.

Shoppe, shop.

Shor(e)n; see **Shẹren**.

Short(e)ly, briefly, in short.

Shot, arrow, dart, missile.

Shoten; see **Sheten**.

Shot-wyndowe, window with a hinge or bolt.

Shour, shower; attack, onslaught.

Shouven, pt. sg. *shọọf*, pl. and pp. *shoven*; shove, push, advance; bring into notice.

Shrẹdden, shred, cut.

Shrewe, wicked person, scoundrel, wretch; ill-tempered person, shrew; also adj.

Shrewed, wicked, cursed.

Shrewen, beshrew, curse.

Shrifte, shrift, confession.

Shrighte; see **Shryken**.

Shrill (var. **Shill**), shrill.

Shrimp, small, puny creature.

Shrọọf; see **Shryven**.

Shryken, Skryken, pt. *shrighte*; shriek.

Shryne, shrine.

Shryned, enshrined; canonized.

Shryven, pt. sg. *shrọọf*, pl. and pp. *shriven*; shrive, confess.

Shulde, Shul(len); see **Shal**.

Shyned; see **Shynen**.

Shynen, pt. sg. *shọọn, shyned(e)*, pp. *shyned*; shine.

Shynken (var. **Skynken**), pour out.

Shyvere, thin slice.

Shyveren, Cheveren, shiver; break.

Sib, related, akin.

Sigh; see **Seen**.

Sight(e), sight, look; foresight.

Sighte; see **Syken**.

Signal, sign, token.

Signe, sign, symptom; proof.

Signet, signet-ring.

Signifiaunce, significance, signification.

Sik, Seek, Syk, sick, ill.

Siker, sure, certain; safe, secure; also adv.

Sikeren, assure.

Sikerer, comp. of **Siker**.

Siklich(e), Sikly, sickly, ill, with ill will; *sikly berth*, bears with difficulty (Lat. "aegre fert").

Similacioun, simulation; dissimulation.

Similitude, similitude, comparison; likeness; counterpart; statement, proposition.

Simplely, simply.

Simplesse, simplicity; unity.

Simplicitee, simplicity.

Sin, since.

Singen, pt. sg. *sang, song*, pl. and pp. *songen*; sing; recite.

Singularitees, singular parts, particulars.

Singuler, single, particular; separate, private, peculiar; especial.

Singulerly, singly.

Sinken, pt. *sank*, pl. and pp. *sonken*; sink; cause to sink.

Sinne, sin.

Sire, sire, father; master; *sir* (usually without final -*e*), sir, a title in address.

Sisoures, scissors.

Sit; see **Sitten**.

Site, site, situation.

Sith, adv., afterwards; thereupon.

Sith, since.

Sithe, scythe.

Sithen, conj. and adv., since.

Sitten, contr. pr. 3 sg. *sit*, pt. sg. *sat, sẹẹt*, pl. *sẹten*, pp. *seten*; sit; dwell; remain; be situated; suit, befit; affect.

Sitting(e), North. dial. *sittand*; fitting.

Sixe, six.

Sixte, sixth.

Sk-; see also **Sc-**.

Skaffaut; see **Scaffold**.

Skale (1), scale (for measuring), graduated line or arc.

Skale (2), scale (of a fish or reptile).

Skant, sparing, niggardly.

Skile, reason, cause, argument; claim.

Skilful, reasonable (both pers. and impers.).

Skillynge, reason.

Skryken; see **Shryken**.

Skryppe, scrip, bag, wallet.

Skulle, skull.

Skye, cloud.

Slaken, slacken; loosen; assuage; appease, abate; cease, desist, omit.

Slak(k)e, slack, loose; slow, late; soft.

Slaughtre, slaughter, murder.

Slaundre; see **S(c)laundre.**

Slawen, Slayn; see **Sleen.**

Sled, sledge; carriage.

Sleen, Sloon, pt. sg. *slow(h), slough,* pl. *slowen,* pp. *slayn, slawen;* slay; destroy, extinguish.

Sleep; see **Slepen.**

Sleep, sleep; dat. phr. *on-slepe, aslepe,* asleep.

Sleëre, slayer.

Sleigh, Sley, Sly, Sligh, skilful, artful; subtle, crafty, sly; deceitful; skilfully contrived.

Sleighte, Slighte, sleight, craft, cunning; skill, dexterity, nimbleness; trick, device; plan.

Slepen, pt. sg. *sleep, slepte,* pl. *slepen, slepten;* sleep.

Slepy, sleepy; sleep-inducing, soporific.

Slewthe, Slouthe, sloth.

Sley; see **Sleigh.**

Slider, slippery.

Sligh; see **Sleigh.**

Slighte; see **Sleighte.**

Slingen, pt. *slong;* sling; fling (one's self).

Slit; see **Slyden.**

Slogardye, Slogardrye, sluggishness, sloth.

Sloggy; see **Sluggy.**

Slombren, slumber.

Slombry, sleepy.

Slong; see **Slingen.**

Sloo, sloe.

Sloon; see **Sleen.**

Sloppe, loose over-garment.

Slough, Slow, slough.

Slough, adj.; see **Slow(e).**

Slough; see **Sleen.**

Slouthe; see **Slewthe.**

Slow; see **Slough,** sbst., and **Sleen,** vb.

Slowe, sbst., moth.

Slow(e), Slough, slow; slack, slothful, idle.

Slowen, Slowh; see **Sleen.**

Sluggy, sluggish.

Sly; see **Sleigh.**

Slyden, contr. pr. 3 sg. *slit;* slide, move; pass away.

Slyding, sliding, slippery; unstable.

Slyk, sleek, smooth.

Slyk, such (North. dial.).

Slyvere, strip, slice, piece.

Smal, small, little; high, thin (of the voice); also sbst. *a smal,* a little; *but smal,* but little.

Smal, adv., little.

Smalish, smallish.

Smatren, smatter, defile.

Smert, adj., smart, quick; sharp, painful.

Smert(e), sbst., smart, pain.

Smerte, sharply, smartly; sorely.

Smerten, smart, feel or cause pain or grief; suffer.

Smeten; see **Smyten.**

Smit; see **Smyten.**

Smithed, forged.

Smitted, smutted, sullied.

Smok, smock.

Smoklees, without a smock.

Smoot; see **Smyten.**

Smoterliche, besmirched, sullied (in reputation).

Smothe, smooth; also adv.

Smyten, contr. pr. 3 sg. *smit,* pt. *smoot,* pp. *smiten, smeten;* smite, strike; strike off.

Snare, snare, noose; trap.

Snewen, Snowen, snow; abound.

Snibben, chide, rebuke (lit. "snub").

Snorten, snort; sniff.

Snoute, snout, nose.

Snow, snow; argent (in heraldry).

So, adv., so; to such a degree.

So (that), conj., provided that; whereas.

Sobre, sober, grave; demure.

Sobrenesse, sobriety.

Socour, Socours, succor, help.

Socouren, vb., succor, help.

Soden; see **Sethen.**

Sodeyn, sudden; quick, prompt, forward.

Softe, soft; also adv.

Softely, softly, gently; quietly.

Soght(e); see **Seken.**

Sojour, sojourn; dwelling.

Sojournen, sojourn, dwell; tarry, remain.

Soken, toll.

Sokyngly, gradually, slowly.

Sol, Sol (Lat.), the sun.

Solacen, cheer, comfort; amuse, refresh.

Solas, comfort, consolation; amusement, entertainment; pleasure; rest.

Sold, Solde; see **Sellen.**

Solempne, formal, ceremonious, pompous, splendid; important, of public character; impressive, distinguished; festive, merry.

Solempnitee, pomp; ceremony.

Soleyn, solitary; unmated; sullen.

Solsticium, solstice, "the point of the ecliptic most remote from the equator" (Skeat).

Som, pl. *som(m)e;* indef. pron. and pronom. adj.; some; one, a certain one; *som ... som* (correlative), one ... another; *al and som, alle and some,* all and each, one and all; *his tenthe som,* one of ten, he and nine others.

Somdel, somewhat.

Somer, summer; the warm season (sometimes including spring).

Som(m)e; see **Som.**

Somnour, summoner, apparitor.

Somonce, summons.

Som(p)nen, summon.

Sompnolence, somnolence.

Somtyme, once; sometime; sometimes.

Sond, sand.

Sonde, sending; message or messenger; visitation.

Sonded, sanded.

Sondry, sundry, various.

Sone, son.

Sone, soon; straightway, at once.

Song, Songen; see **Singen.**

Sonken; see **Sinken.**

Sonne, Sunne, sun.

Sonner, sooner.

Sonnish, sun-like, golden.

Sool, sole, single.

Soor, sore; wounded; sad.

Sooth, true; wk. form as sbst., *the sothe;* dat. phr. *for sothe.*

Soothfastnesse, truth.

Sooty, sooty, soiled with soot.

Soper, Souper, supper.

Sophistrye, wicked cunning.

Sophyme, sophism; subtlety, deceit.

Sop(p)e, sop (of bread).

Sore, sore, wound; pain; misery.

Sore, adv., sorely; ill, badly; strictly, closely; eagerly, ardently.

Sormounten, Sour-, Sur-, surmount; surpass.

Sort (1), lot, chance; destiny; divination.

Sort (2), sort, kind, class.

Sorted, allotted.

Sorwe, sorrow; mourning; sympathy; in imprecation, *with sorwe*.

Sorwen, sorrow.

Sory, sorry, sorrowful, sad; sore; wretched, ill; unlucky; also adv.

Soster; see Suster.

Sote; see Swete.

Sotel; see Sotil.

Soteltee, subtlety, cunning; device.

Soth-sawe, true saying; proverb.

Sotil, subtle, skilful; subtly woven; thin. See also Subtil.

Sotted, besotted, foolish.

Soudiour, soldier.

Soughe, Sowe, sow.

Sought, Soughte; see Seken.

Soul, sole.

Soule, Sowle, soul.

Soulfre, sulphur.

Soun, sound; boast, vaunt.

Sound, unhurt; in good health.

Sounden, make sound, heal.

Sounen, sound, play upon (an instrument); utter; mean, signify; declare, proclaim, rehearse; sound or speak like; *sounen in (to, into)*, tend toward, make for, be consonant with. See *Gen Prol*, I, 307, n.

Soupen, sup.

Souper; see Soper.

Souple, supple, pliant; yielding.

Souplen, bend, make supple.

Sour, sour, bitter, cruel.

Sourden, arise; originate, be derived.

Soure, sourly, bitterly.

Sourmounten; see Sormounten.

Sours, source; upward leap or flight.

Souter, cobbler.

Souvenaunce, remembrance.

Soveraynetee, Sovereyntee, sovereignty; supremacy.

Sovereyn, adj., supreme, chief; very high; superior; in astrology, the western signs of the zodiac, regarded as superior to the eastern; also sbst., sovereign; lord, master, lady; superior.

Sovereyntee; see Soveraynetee.

Sowdan, sultan.

Sowdanesse, sultaness.

Sowded, fastened, united; hence, confirmed.

Sowe; see Soughe.

Sowen (1), pp. *sowen*; sow.

Sowen (2), Sewen, pt. *sowed*; sew.

Sowken, suck; cheat, embezzle.

Sowle; see Soule.

Sowled, endowed with a soul.

Sownen; see Sounen.

Sowres, sorrels, bucks.

Space, space, room; space of time; opportunity; *the space*, meanwhile (?).

Spak, Spaken; see Speken.

Span; see Spinnen.

Spanne, span.

Span-newe, span-new, new as a chip just cut (ON. "span-nýr").

Sparen, spare, leave unhurt; cease, refrain; also reflex., be haughty, reserved, offish.

Sparhauk; see Sperhauk.

Sparke, spark.

Sparkle, small spark.

Sparre, spar, wooden beam.

Sparred, Sper(r)ed, barred, sparred, fastened.

Sparth, battle-axe.

Spaunysshing, expanding, extending.

Spaynel, spaniel.

Spece, species, kind, sort.

Speche, speech, discourse.

Spectacle, glass, eye-glass.

Speculacioun, contemplation.

Speden, speed, succeed, prosper; cause to prosper; hasten, expedite, accomplish.

Speed, success; help, benefit; advantage; dat. phr. *for comune spede*, for the good of all.

Speken, pt. sg. *spak*, pl. *speken, spaken*, pp. *spoken*; speak.

Spell, story, narrative; incantation (in *night-spell*).

Spence, buttery.

Spere, spear.

Spere, sphere, orbit; globe.

Spered; see Sparred.

Sperhauk, sparrowhawk.

Sperme, seed.

Sper(r)ed; see Sparred.

Speten; see Spitten.

Spewen, spew, vomit.

Spiced, spiced; over-fastidious, scrupulous. See *Gen Prol*, I, 526, n.

Spicerye, mixture of spices; oriental goods (including fruits, cloths, and other products).

Spie, sbst., spy.

Spillen, spill; waste; destroy; kill; perish.

Spinnen, pt. sg. *span*, pl. *sponnen*; spin.

Spir, spire, stalk, stem; shoot, sprout.

Spirit, spirit; on the tech. use in physiology see *KnT*, I, 2749, n.; in alchemy, see *CYT*, VIII, 820 n.

Spitel, hospital.

Spitous, spiteful, malicious; inhospitable.

Spitten, Speten, spit.

Sponnen; see Spinnen.

Spore, spur.

Spornen, Spurnen, spurn, trample on; kick; trip one's self, stumble.

Spousaille, espousal, wedding.

Spouse, spouse, husband, wife.

Spousen, espouse, marry.

Sprang; see Springen (1).

Spraynd, Spreynd; see Springen (1).

Spreden, pt. *spradde*, pp. *sprad*; spread, open; cover; disperse.

Sprengen; see Springen (2).

Spring (1), beginning, first growth; dawn.

Spring (2), lively dance.

Springen (1), pt. *sprang, sprong*, pp. *sprongen*; spring, leap; spring up; rise; spread, increase; *sprongen*, advanced.

Springen (2), Sprengen, pp. *spreynd, spraynd*; sprinkle, scatter; sow.

Sprong, Sprongen; see Springen (1).

Spryngoldes, catapults.

Spurnen; see **Spornen.**

Squames, scales.

Square, square.

Squaymous, squeamish.

Squieren, play the squire to, attend.

Squierly, like a squire.

Squyer, squire.

Squyre, carpenter's square; rule for measuring.

Stablen, establish.

Stablenesse, stability.

Stablissen, establish.

Stadie, stadium, race-course.

Staf, g. sg. *staves*; staff, stick; shaft of a car or wagon (?). See *Anel*, 184, n.

Staf-slyng, sling, attached to a staff or handle.

Stage, place, position.

Staire; see **Steyre.**

Stak; see **Stiken.**

Stakeren, stagger.

Stal; see **Stelen.**

Stalke, stalk, stem; piece of straw; upright of a ladder.

Stalken, stalk, move or walk stealthily or slowly, creep up.

Stall(e), stall.

Stamin, tamine, coarse cloth of woolen or worsted.

Stampen, bray (in a mortar).

Stanchen; see **Staunchen.**

Standen; see **Stonden.**

Stank, pond, pool.

Stant; see **Stonden.**

Stapen, Stopen, pp., as adj., advanced (lit. "stepped").

Stare, starling.

Starf; see **Sterven.**

Stark, strong; severe; downright.

Startlynge, Stertlynge, starting, leaping, skittish; making a sudden movement.

Staunchen, stanch, satisfy.

Stede, stead, place.

Stede, steed.

Stedfast, Stid(e)fast, steadfast.

Steel, steel; dat. phr. *of stele.*

Steep, large, protruding (eyes).

Steer, bullock.

Steeren, steer; control.

Steked; see **Stiken.**

Stele, handle; end. See **Rake-stele.**

Stelen, pt. *stal*, pp. *stolen*; steal; steal away.

Stellifyen, transform into a constellation.

Stemen, shine, gleam.

Stenten; see **Stinten.**

Steppes, foot-tracks.

Stere (1), helm, rudder; *in stere*, a-stern.

Stere (2), pilot, helmsman.

Sterelees, without a rudder.

Steren, Stiren, stir, move, instigate, excite, provoke.

Steren, steer; control.

Steresman, steersman.

Sterling, sterling (the monetary unit).

Sterne, Stierne, stern; violent.

Sternely, sternly.

Sterre, star, planet; constellation.

Stert, start; *at a stert*, in an instant.

Sterten, Stirten, contr. pr. 3 sg. *stert*, pt. *sterte, stirte*, pp. *stert, stirt*; start, leap, move quickly; depart; leave suddenly; *depe ystert in lore*, far advanced in learning.

Stertlynge; see **Startlynge.**

Sterven, pt. sg. *starf*, pl. and pp. *storven*; die; die of hunger.

Stevene (1), voice, sound; talk, fame, report.

Stevene (2), time, occasion, appointment.

Stewe (1), **Stuwe,** fish-pond or tank.

Stewe (2), **Stuwe, Styve,** stew, heated room; closet, small room; brothel.

Stewe-door, closet-door.

Steyen; see **Styen.**

Steyre, Staire, stair, staircase; degree.

Stiborn, stubborn.

Stid(e)fast; see **Stedfast.**

Stierne; see **Sterne.**

Stif, stiff, strong; hard; bold.

Stiken, pt. *stak, stiked, steked*; stick, stick fast; stab, pierce; fix, insert.

Stikke, stick, twig; paling.

Stile (1), stile (for climbing a barrier).

Stile (2), style (in writing).

Stillatorie, still.

Stille, adj., still, silent; also adv.

Stingen, pp. *stongen*; sting, pierce.

Stinken, pt. *stank*; stink.

Stinten, Stenten (originally causative), stint, cease, leave off, stop; stay; cause to cease, restrain.

Stiren; see **Steren.**

Stiropes, stirrups.

Stirt(e)(n); see **Sterten.**

Stith, anvil.

Stod(en); see **Stonden.**

Stok, stock; stump, block, post; race, origin.

Stoken, stab, pierce.

Stokked, pp., put in the stocks.

Stol, stool, chair; frame for making tapestry or embroidery.

Stole, long robe; stole (of a priest).

Stomak, stomach; appetite; compassion (cf. "bowels of mercy").

Stonden, Standen, contr. pr. 3 sg. *stont, stant*, pt. sg. *sto(o)d*, pl. *stoden*, pp. *stonden*; stand, take a position; stick fast; abide (by); be set up or fixed in place.

Stongen; see **Stingen.**

Stoon, stone, rock; gem.

Stoor, perhaps also **Store,** store, stock; possession; live-stock; value, estimation.

Stoor, great, strong.

Stopen; see **Stapen.**

Storial, historical.

Storie, story, tale; history; a narrative portion of the liturgy (Lat. "historia").

Storven; see **Sterven.**

Stot, stallion, horse; heifer (as term of abuse for old woman).

Stounde, space of time; season; short time, moment; hard time; pain, fierce attack.

Stoundemele, from hour to hour, from time to time; also adj., momentary.

Stoupen, stoop; droop.

Stour, battle, combat.

Stout, proud, obstinate; strong.

Straight; see **Streight.**

Straken, move, proceed; *straken forth*, return homeward from the hunt, or sound the horn to announce the return.

Strange; see **Straunge.**

Strangenesse, strangeness, estrangement.

Strangien, strangle, choke; kill by strangulation; destroy.

Straught(e); see **Strecchen.**

Straunge, strange; foreign, external; estranged, distant, unfriendly; unusual, difficult; in astronomy, a star not represented in the rete of the astrolabe, or the degrees in the equator and ecliptic not belonging to a given star.

Strawen, pp. *strawed;* strew.

Strayte, strait.

Strecchen, pt. *streighte, straughte,* pp. *streight, straught, strecched;* stretch, extend; reach.

Strẹẹ, straw.

Strẹẹm, stream, river, current; beam (of light).

Streen, strain, stock, race.

Streight, Straight, adj. from pp., stretched, extended; straight; also adv.; see **Strecchen.**

Streit, strait, narrow; small, scanty; mean; strict; *with streite swerd,* with drawn sword (Lat. "strictus").

Streite, strictly; tightly; closely.

Streng, string.

Strenger, Strengest; see **Strong.**

Strengthe, strength, force; *slee with strengthe,* kill in the chase with horses and hounds (Fr. "à force").

Strepen, strip.

Strete, street; road.

Streynen, strain; press; constrain, force; compress; hold, confine.

Streyt; see **Streit.**

Strike, hank, bunch (of flax).

Strọk; see **Stryken.**

Strompet, strumpet.

Stronde, strand, shore.

Strong, comp. *strenger,* sup. *strengest;* strong; difficult, hard.

Stronge, strongly; securely.

Strọọf; see **Stryven.**

Strọọk, stroke.

Strouten, spread out.

Stroyer, destroyer.

Stryf, strife, quarrel.

Stryke, stroke, mark.

Stryken, pt. *strọọk, stryked,* pp. *striken;* strike; stroke; strike out, run.

Stryven, pt. *strọọf,* pp. *striven;* strive; fight; oppose; vie.

Stubbes, stubs, stumps.

Stubble-goos, an old goose fed on stubble.

Studie, study, meditation; eager desire, endeavor; library.

Studien, study; give heed; deliberate; be in perplexity, wonder, muse.

Stuffen, garrison, supply with defenders and munitions.

Sturdy, cruel, harsh; stern; firm.

Stuwe; see **Stewe** (1) and (2).

Sty, pig-sty.

Styen, Steyen, rise, mount.

Styve; see **Stewe** (2).

Styward, steward.

Suasioun, suasion, persuasiveness.

Subdẹkne, subdeacon.

Subgit, subject.

Subjeccion, subjection; suggestion.

Sublymatories, vessels used in sublimation.

Sublymed, sublimated.

Substance, substance, the essence of a thing (tech.,

as opposed to *accident;* see *PardT,* VI, 537, n.); the majority.

Subtil, subtle, skilful; finely wrought. See also **Sotil.**

Subtil(i)tee, subtlety; skill, craft; device, trick; specious argument.

Succident, in astrology, a succedent house. See *Astr,* ii, 4, 30, n.

Sucre, Sugre, sugar.

Suen; see **Sewen.**

Suertee; see **Sur(e)tee.**

Suffisaunce, sufficiency; contentment.

Suffysen, suffice; be able, *suffyse unto,* be satisfied with (?).

Suffrable, patient.

Suffraunce, patience, endurance, longsuffering; permission; receptivity.

Suffraunt, patient, tolerant; also sbst.

Suffren, suffer, endure; permit, submit.

Suggestioun, accusation; suggestion.

Sukkenye, short frock, smock.

Summitten, submit, subject.

Sunne; see **Sonne.**

Superficie, Superficie, surface.

Supplyen, supplicate, pray.

Supportacioun, support.

Supprysen, Susprysen, surprise; take possession of, overcome.

Surcọte, surcoat, outer coat.

Sur(e)tee, Seur(e)tee, Su(e)rtee, surety, security; careless confidence.

Surfeet, surfeit.

Surmounten; see **Sormounten.**

Surplys, surplice; loose robe.

Surquidrie, Surquidrye, arrogance, presumption.

Sursanure, a wound healed over on the surface.

Surtee; see **Suretee.**

Surveiaunce, surveillance.

Suspecioun, suspicion.

Suspect, sbst., suspicion.

Suspect, adj., suspicious; suspected.

Susprysen; see **Supprysen.**

Sustenen, sustain; maintain, preserve; uphold, hold up; endure.

Sustening(e), sustenance.

Suster, Soster, g. sg. *suster,* pl. *sustren, sustres;* sister.

Suwen; see **Sewen.**

Suyte, Sute, suit; kind; dress, array.

Swa, so (North. dial.).

Swal; see **Swellen.**

Swalowen; see **Swelwen.**

Swappe, swoop (of a bird of prey).

Swappen, strike; dash, fall.

Swar; see **Swẹren.**

Swartish, dark, swarthy.

Swatte; see **Swẹten.**

Swayn, young man, servant.

Sweigh, motion, sway.

Swellen, pt. sg. *swal,* pp. *swollen;* swell.

Sweller, inflater.

Swelten, die; faint.

Swelwen, Swalowen, Swolwen, swallow.

Swerd, sword.

Swẹren, pt. sg. *swor, swar,* pl. *sworen,* pp. *swọren, sworn;* swear.

Swete, Sote, Swote, sweet; also sbst. On possible distinctions in meaning, see J. H. Fisher, *JEGP,* X, 326 ff.

Swęten, pt. *swatte*; sweat.

Swetter, comp. of **Swete**.

Swęty, sweaty.

Sweven, dream.

Sweynt, pp. of *swenchen*, tired out, exhausted; slothful.

Swich, such; idiomatic, *swiche seven*, seven times as many. See *BD*, 408, n.

Swimmen, pt. pl. *swommen*; swim; be filled with swimming things.

Swink, labor, toil.

Swinken, pp. *swonken*; labor, toil.

Swire, neck, throat.

Swolow, gulf.

Swolwen; see **Swelwen**.

Swommen; see **Swimmen**.

Swoning(e), **Swowninge**, swooning.

Swonken; see **Swinken**.

Swǫǫt, sweat.

Swor, Swor(e)n; see **Swęren**.

Swote; see **Swete**.

Swo(u)gh, **Swow**, sough, low sound; sigh, groan; noise (of wind, etc.); swoon.

Swounen, swoon, faint.

Swow; see **Swo(u)gh**.

Swowne, swoon.

Swythe, quickly; *as swythe*, immediately.

Swyven, copulate, lie with; play the harlot.

Sy; see **Seen**.

Sy, if (Fr. "si").

Sycamour, sycamore.

Syen, sink, descend.

Syen; see **Seen**.

Syk, sbst., sigh.

Syk; see **Sik**.

Syken, pt. *syked, sighte*; sigh.

Syklatoun; a costly cloth. See *Thop*, VII, 734, n.

Sylvre, silver.

Symonyals, simoniacs.

Symonye, simony.

Symphonye, term used for various musical instruments; commonly for a tabor.

Synwes, sinews.

Syn; see **Sin**.

Syre; see **Sire**.

Sys, Sis, six; *sys cink*, six-five (one of the best throws in hazard).

Systen (var. of **Syken**), grieve. See *Tr*, ii, 884, n.

Syth, time; pl. *sythes, sythe* (orig. gen. or dat. pl., preserved in phrases); *ofte sythe*, oftentimes.

Syve, sieve.

T

T', abbreviation of **To**, before vowels.

Taa(n), North. dial. for **Taken**.

Taas, heap, pile.

Tabard, loose coat of laborer; herald's coat-of-arms. See *Gen Prol*, I, 20, n.

Tabernacle, tent; shrine.

Table, table; tablet; plate (of an astrolabe); pl. *tables*, the game of backgammon; *table dormant*, see *Gen Prol*, I, 353, n.

Tabour, tabor, small drum.

Tabouren, drum.

Tache, Tecche, blemish, defect; quality, characteristic.

Taffata, taffeta.

Taillage, Taylage, tax.

Taille, tally, an account scored upon notched sticks.

Taillyng, reckoning, credit, business dealings. See *ShipT*, VII, 434, n.

Takel, apparatus, gear; weapons, especially arrows.

Taken, pt. sg. *took*, pl. *token*, pp. *taken*; take, seize; give, offer; hit; refl., betake (one's self); take place, happen; *taken keep*, take heed.

Tal, meek (?), humble (?); or quick (?), prompt (?).

Tald, North. dial. for *told*; see **Tellen**.

Talen, tell a story; talk; converse; discuss.

Talent, wish, desire; appetite, longing.

Talke, talk.

Tame, tame.

Tapinage, hiding; sneaking.

Tapiten, cover with tapestry.

Tappe, tap.

Tappestere, female tapster, barmaid.

Tapycer, weaver of tapestry.

Tar; see **Tęren**.

Tare, tare, weed.

Targe, shield; protection.

Tarien, tarry, delay; waste; cause to delay.

Tart, adj., tart, pungent.

Tarte, sbst., tart.

Tartre, tartar; *oille of tartre*, cream of tartar.

Tasseled, provided with tassels, fringed.

Tast, taste; relish.

Tasten, test, try; feel; experience.

Taught, Taughte, see **Tęchen**.

Tatarwagges, tatters.

Taverne, tavern.

Taverner, innkeeper.

Taylage; see **Taillage**.

Taylagier, tax-gatherer.

Tecche; see **Tache**.

Techel; see **Mane**.

Tęchen, pt. *taughte, tęched*, pp. *taught*; teach, inform; show; tell.

Tellen, pt. *tǫlde*, pp. *tǫld*; tell, relate; reckon, compute; account, esteem.

Teme; see **Theme**.

Temen, bring.

Tempesten, perturb; refl., distress one's self violently.

Tempestous, tempestuous.

Temple, temple; inn of court.

Tempre; see **At(t)empre(e)**.

Tempren, temper, moderate; control; in alchemy, adjust the heat for melting.

Temprure, tempering, mixing.

Temps, tense; time; *at prime temps*, at first, the first time.

Temptour, tempter.

Tene, grief, sorrow; trouble, vexation; ruin, destruction.

Tenour, tenor, general purport, drift.

Tente, tent.

Tentifly, attentively.

Tercel, male eagle.

Tercelet, Terslet, male falcon or hawk.

Terciane, tertian, recurring every third (i.e., alternate) day.

Tęre, sbst., tear.

Tęren, pt. *tar*, pp. *tǫrn*; tear, scratch; treat (a matter), stir up an issue (?). See *Tr*, iii, 1643.

Terins, tarins, siskins (a kind of finch).

Terme, term, set time, period; end, goal; boundary, limit; phrase, tech. term, jargon; *in terme*, with formal accuracy; a portion of the zodiac (see *FranklT*, V, 1288, n.).

Terme-day, appointed day.

Termynen, determine; set down in definite terms.

Terrestre, terrestrial.

Terslet; see **Tercelet.**

Terven, flay, strip, skin.

Tery, teary, tearful.

Tester, head-armor (of man or horse). See *KnT*, I, 2499.

Testes, vessels for assaying metals.

Testif, testy, headstrong, irritable.

Tẹte, teat.

Textuel, learned in texts, well-read.

Teyd, tied, bound.

Teyne, thin metal rod or plate.

Th', frequent abbreviation of **The** before vowels; less frequently used for **Thee.**

Thakken, stroke; pat.

Thank, sbst., thanks, gratitude; adv. gen., *his (my) thankes,* of his (my) will, willingly, voluntarily; *can thank,* owes (lit."knows") thanks, feels gratitude.

Thanken, Thonken, thank.

Than(ne), then.

Thar, impers. vb., pt. *thurte, thurfte;* it is necessary. On confusion with forms of *dar, durste,* see *Rom,* 1089, n.

Thar, adv., there.

That, rel. pron., that, whom; that which.

That, conj., that; so that; as; because; also used to repeat *if, when,* etc. (see *Pars Prol,* X, 39, n.).

The, old instr. of the demonstrative, as in *the bet, the better,* etc.

Thedam (var. **Thedom**), success.

Theech, Theek; see **Theen.**

Theef, thief, robber; criminal.

Theen, thrive, prosper; *so theech, so theek,* as I hope to prosper.

Thefly, like a thief.

Thefte, theft.

Theme, Teme, theme, text, thesis.

Then, than.

Thenken, Thenchen, sometimes **Thinken,** pt. *tho(u)ghte,* pp. *tho(u)ght;* think; consider; intend; sometimes apparently confused with **Thinken,** seem.

Thenne, Kentish for **Thinne.**

Thenne, then.

Thenne(s), thence.

Theorik, theory; theoretical explanation.

Theraboute, thereabout, thereupon; concerned with that matter.

Ther-agayns, Ther-ayeyns, Ther-geyn, against that, in reply to that.

Theras, there, where; whereas; wherever.

Therbifore, Therbiforn, before that, beforehand, previously.

Therby, thereby; by it, to it, near it.

Ther(e), there; where, wherever; whereas; wherewith; on the idiomatic use with optative clauses of blessing and cursing see *KnT*, I, 2815, n.

Ther-geyn; see **Ther-agayns.**

Theroute, out from it, thence; outside.

Therwhyle(s), while; meanwhile.

Thẹw, habit, custom; quality; virtue; *thewes,* morals, manners (used by Chaucer only in pl.).

The-ward, to, toward thee.

Thẹwed, possessed of qualities, virtues, etc.; *wel thewed,* of good character or habits.

Thider, thither.

Thider-ward, thither.

Thikke, thick; stout; substantial; frequent, repeated; also adv.

Thikke-hẹrd, thick-haired.

Thikke-sterred, thickly covered with stars.

Thilke, that, that same, that very, such.

Thing, pl. *thing, thinges;* thing; wealth, property; affair; deed, legal document; religious service or rite; poem or other production; *for any thing,* in spite of everything, at any cost.

Thinken, pt. *tho(u)ghte;* impers. vb., seem; *me (hir, him) thinketh,* it seems to me (her, him).

Thinken, occasionally used for **Thenken.**

Thinne, Thenne, thin, slender; poor, feeble; meager, scanty.

Thirlen, pp., *thirled, thrilled;* pierce.

This, contr. of *this is.*

Thọ (1), pron., those.

Thọ (2), adv., then.

Thogh, though; yet, still, however.

Thoght, Thoghte; see **Thenken, Thinken.**

Thoght, thought; anxiety, care.

Thoghtful, anxious, moody.

Thọlen, suffer, endure.

Thombe, thumb.

Thonder, thunder; *thonder-dint,* thunder-clap, stroke of lightning; *thonder-leyt,* thunder-bolt, flash of lightning.

Thondren, vb., thunder.

Thonken; see **Thanken.**

Thorgh; see **Thurgh.**

Thorn, thorn; thorn-tree; hawthorn.

Thor(o)ugh; see **Thurgh.**

Thorp, Throp, village.

Thought, Thoughte; see **Thenken, Thinken.**

Th(o)urgh-girt, struck through.

Thral, thrall, slave, subject; also adj.

Thrallen, enthrall, subject.

Thraste; see **Thresten.**

Thrẹden, vb., thread.

Thrẹed, sbst., thread.

Threpen, assert, affirm positively.

Threshfold, threshold.

Thresshen, thrash.

Thresten, pt. *threste, thraste;* thrust, push.

Thrẹten, threaten.

Thretty, Thritty, thirty.

Threw, Threwen; see **Throwen.**

Thridde, third.

Thrift, success, prosperity, welfare; used in adjuration, *by my thrift.*

Thrifty, profitable, serviceable; provident.

Thrilled; see **Thirlen.**

Thringen, pt. *throng,* pp. *thrungen;* press, thrust; throng.

Thristen, pt. *thriste,* pp. *thrist;* thrust against, support.

Thrittene, thirteen.

Thritty; see **Thretty.**

Thrọf; see **Thryven.**

Throgh; see **Thurgh.**

Throng; see **Thringen.**

Throp; see **Thorp.**

Throstel, Thrustel, throstle. song-thrush.

Thrọte, throat.

Throte-bolle, Adam's apple.

Throwe, time, while, short time.

Throwen, pt. sg. *threw*, pl. *threwen*, pp. *throwen*; throw, cast; twist, turn.

Throwes, throes, torments.

Thrungen; see Thringen.

Thrustel; see Throstel.

Thrustel-cok, throstlecock, male thrush.

Thrye(s), thrice.

Thryven, pt. *throf*, pp. *thriven*; thrive, prosper; grow, flourish.

Thurfte; see Thar.

Thurgh, Thorgh, Thro(u)gh, Thor(o)ugh, Thurw, through; commonly used as prefix.

Thurghfare, thoroughfare.

Thurghout, throughout; out through, all through.

Thurgh-shoten, shot through.

Thurgh-soght, searched through, thoroughly examined.

Thurrok, sink (in ship's hull).

Thurst, thirst.

Thursten, thirst; both pers. and impers.

Thurte; see Thar.

Thurw; see Thurgh.

Thwitel, large knife.

Thwyten, pp. *thwiten*; whittle; carve.

Tid; see Tyden.

Tidif, pl. *tidyves*; tidy, a small bird.

Tikel, unsteady, unstable.

Tikelnesse, instability, unsteadiness.

Tiklen, tickle.

Til, prep., to (North. form); *til and fra*, to and fro.

Til, conj., till, until.

Tilien, till, cultivate.

Tiliere, tiller.

Timbre, timbrel, tambourine.

Tipet, Typet, tippet, cape.

Tiptoon, tiptoes.

Tissu, Tissew, tissue; a band.

Titering, hesitation, vacillation.

Title, name, description.

Tixted, learned in texts.

To- (1), prepositional prefix, as in *to-forn*, before.

To- (2), prefix indicating separation, destruction, or emphasis, as in *to-bresten*, *to-hewen*.

To, pl. *toon*, *toos*; toe.

To, contr. of *toon* in *the toon*, that one.

Tobeten, beat severely.

Tobreken, break in pieces. See Breken.

Tobresten, burst or break in pieces. See Bresten.

Tocleven, cleave in twain. See Cleven (1).

Todasshen, dash in pieces.

Tode, toad.

Todrawen (1), draw toward one, allure.

Todrawen (2), pt. pl. *todrowen*, pp. *todrawen*; tear apart, distract.

Todryven, drive apart, scatter. See Dryven.

Toforn, prep. and adv., before.

Togeder, Togider, Togedre(s), Togidre(s), together.

Toght, taut (probably pp. of *togen*, tow, draw).

Togon, disperse. But see *LGW*, 653, n.

To-hepe, together, into a heap.

Tohewen, pp., *tohewen*; hew in pieces.

Token; see Taken.

Toknen, mark, designate.

Told, Tolde; see Tellen.

Tollen (1), take toll.

Tollen (2), Tullen, attract, allure.

Tombe, Toumbe, tomb.

Tombestere, dancing girl.

Tomelten, melt away.

To-morwe, tomorrow.

Tonge, Tunge, tongue; speech, language.

Tonged, tongued.

Tonges, tongs.

Tonne, tun, cask.

Tonne-gret, as big as a cask.

Too; see To.

Took; see Taken.

To(o)l, weapon; instrument.

Toon; see To.

To(o)n, one; in *the toon*, that one, the one.

Toquaken, quake, tremble very much.

Toracen, tear into pieces.

Torche, torch.

Tord, turd, piece of dung.

Torenden, rend in pieces; distract.

Toret; see Tourette.

Tormenten, Turmenten, torment, torture.

Tormentise, torment.

Tormentour, tormentor; executioner; also adj.

Tormentrye, Turmentrye, pain, torture.

Torn; see Teren.

Torn, turn.

Tornen, Turnen, turn; return; shape in a lathe.

Torney, tourney.

Torombelen (?), rumble heavily, crash (*LGW*, 1218, probably to be read *to rombelen*).

Tortuo(u)s, tortuous; in astronomy, the signs of the zodiac which ascend most obliquely. See *MLT*, II, 302, n.

Toscatered, scattered, dispersed.

Toshaken, pp., shaken to pieces; tossed about.

Toshenden, pp. *toshent*; destroy utterly.

Tosheren, pt. *toshar*; cut in two.

Toshivered, broken to pieces.

Toshreden, cut into shreds.

Toslitered, slashed with cuts.

Tospreden, spread apart, open (perhaps to be read *to spreden*; see *LGW Prol F*, 202).

Tosterten, start asunder, burst.

Tostoupen, stoop down (? probably to be read *to stoupen*; see *FrT*, III, 1560).

Toswinken, labor hard (probably to be read *to swinken*?; see *PardT*, VI, 519).

Totar; see Toteren.

Totelere, tatler; also adj.

Toteren, pt. *totar*, pp. *totor(e)n*; tear in pieces.

Tother, in *the tother* (that other), the other.

Totreden, tread down, trample under foot.

Toty, dizzy.

Touchen, touch; reach; touch on; concern.

Touching, sbst., touch.

Touchinge, pr. p., touching; *as touchinge*, with reference to, concerning.

Tough, tough, hard, troublesome; on *make it tough* see *Tr*, ii, 1025, n.

Toumbe; see Tombe.

T(o)umblynge, transitory, perishing, unstable.

Toun, town; farm; dat. phr. *in* (at, out of, etc.) *toune*.

Tour, tower, citadel; in astronomy, mansion.

Touret, turret.

Tourette, Toret, ring; swivel-ring to attach a dog's leash to the collar.

T(o)urneiynge, fighting in a tournament.

Tourneyment, tournament.
Toute, buttocks.
Towayle, towel, cloth.
Towinden, pt. *towond*; break in pieces.
To-yẹre, this year.
Trace, Tra(a)s, trace, trail; procession.
Tracen, trace, follow; go.
Trad; see **Trẹden.**
Tragedie, tragedy, tragic story. See *Mk Prol*, VII, 1973, n.
Traisoun, Tresoun, treason.
Traitorye, Traiterye, treachery.
Transmewen, Transmuwen, transmute, transform.
Transporten, transport; extend.
Trappe, trap, snare; trap-door.
Trapped, furnished with trappings.
Trappures, trappings (for horses).
Trasshen, pp. *trasshed*; betray.
Traunce, trance, state of partial insensibility; study, fit of musing.
Trauncen, tramp about.
Travaile, Travel, labor, work; pains.
Travailen, labor, toil; endeavor; suffer; travel, journey.
Trave, wooden frame for holding horses.
Travel; see **Travaile.**
Travers, curtain, screen.
Trayen, Traysen, betray.
Trays, traces.
Traysen; see **Trayen.**
Trayteresse, Traytouresse, traitress.
Treble, triple.
Trechour, traitor.
Trẹde-foul, treader of fowls.
Trẹden, contr. pr. 3 sg. *trẹt*, pt. sg. *trad*, pl. and pp. *troden*; tread, step; copulate (of male bird).
Trẹdyng, treading; procreation.
Tree, tree; wood; the cross.
Treget, jugglery, trickery, guile; trap, snare.
Tregetour, juggler, magician.
Tregetrye, trickery.
Tremour, tremor.
Trench, trench; alley cut through shrubbery.
Trenden, revolve.
Trentals, series of thirty masses for the dead.
Trepeget, trebuchet, machine for hurling large stones.
Tresor, treasure, wealth.
Tresorere, treasurer.
Trẹsoun; see **Traisoun.**
Trespacen, Trespassen, trespass, transgress, sin.
Trespas, trespass, wrong; fault, sin.
Tresse, tress, braid of hair.
Tressen, dress or plait the hair.
Tressour, head-dress.
Trẹt; see **Trẹden.**
Trẹtable, tractable, yielding; docile; affable.
Trẹtee, treaty, agreement; discussion.
Trẹten, treat; tell of, relate; write, speak, discourse.
Trẹtys, Trẹtice, sbst., treatise, story; treaty; contract.
Tretys, adj., well-formed, graceful.
Trewe, Truwe, sbst., truce.
Trewe, adj., true, faithful; honest; also adv.
Trew(e)liche, Trew(e)ly, truly, certainly.
Trewe-love, true-love (herb paris?).
Treye, "tray," three.
Triacle, remedy.

Trichour, treacherous.
Trillen, turn, twirl.
Trinitee, the Trinity.
Trippen, dance.
Trist, trust.
Triste (var. **Tristre**), sbst., tryst; hunting station where the bowman stands to shoot the deer.
Tristen, Trusten, Trosten, trust, trust to.
Troden; see **Trẹden.**
Trogh, trough.
Trompe (1), trumpet.
Trompe (2), trumpeter.
Trompen, sound the trumpet.
Trompour, trumpeter.
Tronchoun, truncheon (of a spear).
Trọne, throne.
Tropik, turning-point; solstitial point.
Trosten; see **Tristen.**
Troublable, disturbing.
Trouble, adj., troubled, turbid, dim; troublous, tempestuous; anxious; vexed.
Tr(o)ubly, cloudy.
Trouthe, truth; troth, promise; fidelity.
Trowandyse; see **Truaundyse.**
Trowen, trow, believe; think.
Truaunding, idling, shirking.
Truaundyse, Trowandyse, fraudulent begging; knavery; idleness.
Truaunt, vagabond, idler, rogue.
Trubly; see **Tr(o)ubly.**
Trufles, trifles.
Trussed, packed.
Truwe; see **Trewe,** sbst.
Trycen, draw, drag, pull.
Trye, excellent, choice.
Tryne compas, the threefold world (earth, sea, and sky).
Trype, small piece.
Tubbe, tub.
Tuel, Tuwel, pipe; chimney; hole.
Tullen; see **Tollen** (2).
Tumblen, tumble, perform athletic feats.
Tumblynge; see **T(o)umblynge.**
Tunge; see **Tonge.**
Turmenten; see **Tormenten.**
Turmentrye; see **Tormentrye.**
Turnen; see **Tornen.**
Turtel, turtle-dove.
Turves, pl. of *turf*, turf.
Tuwel; see **Tuel.**
Tweye, two; twain.
Tweyne, twain.
Twicchen, pt. *twighte*, pp. *twight*; twitch; draw, pull; *twight*, distraught.
Twinnen, separate, part in two; set out, depart.
Twiste, twig; tendril.
Twisten, twist, wring, torture.
Twyë(s), twice.
Twyn, twine.
Twynen, twine, twist.
Tyde, time, hour; season; tide of the sea.
Tyden, pp. *tid*; betide; happen.
Tydif; see **Tidif.**
Tyle, tile; row of bricks.
Tylynge, tilling, tillage.
Tymbestere, female timbrel-player.
Tyne, brewing vat; cask.
Typet; see **Tipet.**

Tyren, tear, rend.
Tythere, payer of tithes.
Tytled, dedicated.

ʋ

Unagreable, disagreeable; miserable.
Unapt, indisposed.
Unaraced, unbroken, untorn.
Unavysed, unadvised, unaware; unpremeditated; reckless, foolish.
Unbityden, fail to take place.
Unbodien, leave the body.
Unbokelen, unbuckle.
Unbore(n), unborn.
Unbounden, pp., unbound, separated, divorced.
Unbrent, Unbrend, unburnt.
Unbroyden, unbraided.
Unbuxumnesse, unsubmissiveness.
Uncircumscript, unbounded.
Unclosed, unfastened; unenclosed.
Unclosen, become open.
Uncommitted, not entrusted (to one).
Unconninge, Uncunninge, ignorant; unskillful; foolish.
Uncouplen, let loose (the hounds).
Uncouth (lit. "unknown"), strange, alien, foreign; marvelous, curious.
Uncouthly, strangely, strikingly.
Uncovenable, unfit; unseemly.
Uncunninge; see **Unconninge.**
Under, under; among.
Underfongen, undertake.
Undermeles, undern-times. See **Undren.**
Undernimen, pt. *undernoom,* pp. *undernomen;* understand, perceive; reprove.
Underpicchen, pt. *underpighte;* stuff, pack full beneath.
Underput, pp., subjected.
Undersporen, thrust under, pry up.
Understonden, pt. sg. *understood,* pl. *understoden,* pp. *understonden;* understand; know.
Undertaken, pt. *undertook,* pp. *undertaken;* undertake; conduct an enterprise; declare, warrant, dare say.
Undigne, unworthy.
Undon, pt. *undide,* pp. *undon;* undo, unfasten; come undone; unfold, disclose.
Undren, a designation of time, of shifting application; originally, the third hour, nine o'clock in the morning; also used for noon; sometimes, apparently, for mid-forenoon, the time of the morning meal; and later, for mid-afternoon.
Uneschuable, inevitable.
Unese, lack of ease; discomfort; trouble.
Unethe(s), Unnethe(s), hardly (lit. "uneasily"); scarcely at all; with difficulty.
Unfestlich, unfestive, not in festival times.
Ungiltif, guiltless, innocent.
Ungrobbed, not digged around.
Unhap, mishap, misfortune.
Unhardy, cowardly.
Unheele, sickness, misfortune.
Unholsom, sick, weak.
Unhyden, disclose, reveal.
Universe; *in universe,* universally.
Universitee, universality; the universal.
Unjoignen, Unjoynen, disjoin.
Unkinde, unnatural; cruel; ungrateful.

Unknitten, unknit.
Unkonninge; see **Unconninge.**
Unkorven, uncut.
Unkouth; see **Uncouth.**
Unkunninge; see **Unconninge.**
Unlaced, disentangled.
Unleful, Unleveful, not permissible, illicit.
Unloven, cease to love.
Unlust, disinclination.
Unlykly, displeasing.
Unmanhod, unmanly deed.
Unmeke, not meek, proud.
Unmete, unmeet, unfit; displeasing.
Unmighty, unable; impotent.
Unmoevable, immovable.
Unnesten, leave the nest.
Unnethe(s); see **Unethe(s).**
Unordred, not belonging to a religious order.
Unparygal, unequal.
Unplitable, unreasonable (? Lat. "inexplicabilis").
Unplyten, unplait, unfold, explain; evolve (Lat. "explicat").
Unpurveyed, unprovided.
Unrelesed, unrelieved.
Unremeved, unmoved.
Unright, wrong, injury.
Unsad, unsettled.
Unsavory, displeasing.
Unscience, false knowledge, error.
Unsely, unhappy; unfortunate.
Unset, unappointed.
Unshethen, unsheathe, remove.
Unshetten, pt. *unshette,* pp. *unshett;* unlock.
Unshewed, unconfessed.
Unslekked, unslacked (of lime).
Unsolempne, uncelebrated.
Unso(u)ght, not sought; ready at hand.
Unsowe, not sown.
Unsowen, unsew.
Unspeedful, unprofitable.
Unsperd, unsparred, unbolted.
Unstaunchable, inexhaustible.
Unstaunched, insatiate.
Unstraunge, not strange; used of the familiar stars represented on the rete of an astrolabe.
Unswellen, decrease in fulness.
Unteyen, untie; set free.
Unthank, the opposite of thanks; a curse.
Unthrift, lack of profit, wastefulness; nonsense.
Unto, prep., unto; conj., until.
Untold, uncounted.
Untressed, unplaited; unarranged; with hair loose.
Untretable, inexorable.
Untrewe, untrue; also adv.
Untristen, distrust.
Untrust, sbst., distrust.
Untyme; *in untyme,* out of season.
Unusage, lack of use.
Unwar, unaware; unexpected; accidental; also adv.
Unweelde, Unweeldy, unwieldy, hard to move or control; weak.
Unwemmed, unspotted.
Unwened, unexpected.
Unwist, unknown; uninformed.
Unwit, lack of wit; folly.
Unwiting, Unwot, etc.; see **Witen.**
Unwryen, uncover, disclose.
Unyolden, without having yielded.

Up, adv., up; open; *up and doun*, in all respects, in every way.

Up, prep., on, upon.

Upborn, borne up, valued.

Upbounde, bound up.

Upbreyden, upbraid, rebuke.

Updressen, set up, make ready.

Updrow; see **Drawen.**

Uphaf, lifted up; see **Heven.**

Uphepynge, heaping up.

Upon, prep., on, upon; besides; against; also adv.

Uppe, up; open.

Upper, adv., higher.

Uppereste, adj., uppermost.

Up-plight, pp., plucked up, pulled up.

Upright, Upryght, adv., upright; supine.

Uprist, contr. of *upryseth.*

Upriste, up-rising.

Up-so-doun, upside down.

Upspringen, rise; spring up.

Upsterten, Upstirten, start up, arise.

Up-yaf; see **Yeven.**

Up-yolden; see **Yelden.**

Urchoun, hedgehog.

Urne, urn.

Usaunce, custom, usage.

Usaunt, accustomed; addicted.

Usen, use; accustom; be accustomed, wont.

Using, use.

Us-self, Us-selve, ourselves.

Usure, usury.

Utter, outer.

Utt(e)reste, Out(e)reste, outermost; farthest; supreme.

Utterly, Outerly, utterly, entirely.

V

Vache, cow, beast.

Vailen, avail.

Valaunse, perhaps used for a sign of the zodiac opposite the mansion of a given planet. See *Mars,* 145, n.

Valerian, valerian, a medicinal herb.

Valewe, Value, value.

Valey(e), valley.

Valour, worth; valor.

Vanishen, vanish, disappear; shrink up, waste away.

Vapour, vapor, mist; influence.

Variaunce, variation; difference.

Vassalage, Vasselage, prowess.

Vavasour, sub-vassal; substantial landholder. See *Gen Prol,* I, 360, n.

Veel, veal.

Vekke, hag, old woman.

Veluët, velvet.

Vendable, vendible, venal.

Venerien, influenced by Venus.

Venerye, hunting.

Vengen, revenge.

Vengeresses, avenging goddesses.

Venim, venom, poison; corruption; malice; dye.

Venjaunce, Vengeaunce, vengeance.

Venquissen, Venquisshen, vanquish.

Ventusinge, cupping (in surgery).

Ver, the spring.

Veray; see **Ver(r)ay.**

Verdegrees (var. **Vertgrees**), verdigris.

Verdit, Voirdit, verdict.

Verger, orchard.

Vermayle, vermillion.

Vernage, a strong, sweet white wine of Italy.

Vernisshed, varnished, smeared with a glossy substance.

Vernycle, a reproduction of the sacred handkerchief which bore the miraculous impression of Christ's face.

Ver(r)ay, Verrey, true, real; exact, just; apparently not used as adv. by Chaucer.

Ver(r)ayly, -liche, Verreyly, -liche, verily, truly.

Verrayment, verily, truly.

Verre, glass.

Verrey; see **Ver(r)ay.**

Vers, pl. *vers;* verse, line.

Versifiour, versifier, poet.

Vertu, virtue; power, efficacy, efficiency; mental faculty; magical influence; valor.

Vertuous, possessing virtue or power; efficacious, capable; holy.

Verye, a word of uncertain meaning. See *MillT,* I, 3485, n.

Vessel, vessel; coll., plate (Fr. "vaisselle").

Vestiment, clothing.

Veyne, vein; sap-vessel; *seken every veyne,* try every means; *touchid on som good veyne,* approached in an advantageous way.

Veyne-blood, letting blood at a vein.

Veze, rush, blast.

Viage, voyage, journey; expedition, undertaking.

Vicair(e), Viker, vicar, deputy; deputed ruler.

Vigile, wake.

Vigilyes, vigils, meetings on the eve of a festival.

Viker; see **Vicair(e).**

Vileins, villainous; rude; sinful.

Vileinye, character or conduct of a *vilain* or churl; vile, shameful deed; harm, wrong; coarse or unfitting speech; reproach; disgrace; rudeness; discourtesy.

Vinolent, full of wine, addicted to drinking wine.

Violes, pl., vials, phials.

Virelay, ballad with a return of rime. See *LGW Prol F,* 417, n.

Viritoot, swift movement (?).

Viritrate, hag.

Visagen, put a face (on it), disguise.

Vitaille, coll., victuals, provisions; also pl., *vitailes.*

Vitaillen, provide with victuals.

Vitaillier, victualler.

Vitremyte, woman's cap or headdress. See *MkT,* VII, 2372, n.

Vitriole, vitriol.

Voide, "voidee," light dessert, with wine and spices, and sometimes comfits, taken before retiring.

Voide, solitary; void.

Voiden, Voyden, make void; frustrate; remove, expel; empty; quit, depart.

Voirdit; see **Verdit.**

Vois, Voys, voice.

Volage, volatile, flighty, wanton.

Volatyl, coll., fowls.

Voltor, pl. *volturies;* vulture.

Volunte, will, desire.

Volupe(e)r, night-cap; woman's cap.

Vouchen, call, declare; used by Chaucer only in the phrase *vouchen sauf,* pt. *vouched sauf;* vouchsafe, grant, permit.

Vounde (?), dial. form of *founden*, pp., found (?); hence, excellent (?). See *Rom*, 7063, n.

Vulgar, *day vulgar*, the "artificial" day with the morning and evening twilight added; cf. also *vulgar nyght*.

Vyce, vice; fault, error; defect.

W

Waast, waist.

Waat, wot, knows (North. dial.).

Wacche, watch, sentinel; also abstr., watching, lying awake.

Waden, wade, advance with difficulty; go, pass, descend; enter.

Waf; see **Weven**.

Wafereres, makers of wafer-cakes, confectioners.

Waget, watchet, light blue.

Waiten, wait, watch; seek occasion; expect; observe; attend.

Waken, pt. *wook*, pp. *waked*; wake; be, or remain, awake; keep awake, carouse; rouse one's self, resume speech or action.

Wake-pleyes, funeral games.

Waker, watchful, vigilant.

Waking, being awake, watching; vigils; period of wakefulness.

Walet, wallet.

Walked, sbst., walking; *go walked*, gone a-walking. See *Pard Prol*, VI, 406, n.

Walken, pt. *welk*, *walked*, pp. *walked*; walk, roam; go.

Walowen; see **Walwen**.

Walsh-note, walnut.

Walwen, wallow, roll; tumble, toss; cause to roll.

Wan; see **Winnen**.

Wanges, molar teeth.

Wang-tooth molar tooth (lit. "cheek-tooth").

Wanhope, despair.

Wan(i)en, wane.

Wanten, want; lack; fail, be lacking.

Wantown, wanton (lit. "ill-governed"); undisciplined, unruly; lascivious, lewd; sportive, merry. See *Gen Prol*, I, 208, n.

Wantownesse, wantonness; affectation.

Wantrust, distrust.

War, ware, aware; wary, cautious, discreet, prudent; *ben war*, beware; observe.

Waranten; see **Warenten**.

Warde, ward (abstr.), guard, keeping, care.

Wardecors, body-guard.

Warderere, i.e., *warde rere*, look out behind.

Wardrobe, privy. See *PrT*, VII, 572, n.

Ware, coll., wares, goods, merchandise.

Waren, vb., reflex., beware; avoid, make way for.

Warenten, **Waranten**, warrant, protect.

Wariangle, shrike, butcher-bird.

Waricen; see **Warisshen**.

Warien, curse.

Warisoun, payment, requital.

Warisshen, cure; be cured, recover.

Warly, warily.

Warnen (1), **Wernen**, warn, caution, notify; summon, invite.

Warnen (2), **Wernen**, refuse, deny; forbid.

Warnestoren, fortify, garrison; provision.

Wasshen, pt. *wes(s)h*, *wis(s)h*, pp. *wasshen*; wash.

Waste, wasted, partially destroyed.

Wastel-breed, fine white bread. See *Gen Prol*, I, 147, n.

Wastour, waster.

Watering, place for watering horses.

Wawe, wave.

Wax, Waxen; see **Wexen**.

Waxen, pt. *waxed*; coat with wax.

Wayk, weak.

Wayken, weaken, diminish; grow weak.

Waymenten, lament.

Wayn, wain, wagon, car.

Wayten (1), lie in wait (for), beset; attend, escort; *wayten upon*, observe, watch; *wayte what*, whatever.

Wayten, (2), show, put upon, inflict.

Webbe, weaver.

Wed, sbst., pledge; dat. phr. *to wedde*.

Wedden, wed, marry.

Wede, weed, garment; religious habits.

Weder, weather; storm.

Weel, well (cf. Scottish "weel").

We(e)lden, pt. *welte*, *weelde(d)*; wield, control; control one's self, move with ease.

Weeldinge, power, control (lit. "wielding").

Weep, pt.; see **Wepen**.

Weep, sbst., weeping; dat. phr. *a-weep(e)*.

Weeply, tearful.

Weerdes; see **Wyerdes**.

Weet, wet.

We(e)x; see **Wexen**.

Wegge, wedge.

Wehee, whinnying (of a horse).

We(i)lawey, Weylawey, alas!

Wel, well; many, much; used emphatically, as in *wel royal*; fully, completely (with numerals), *wel nyne and twenty*.

Welawey; see **We(i)lawey**.

Welde (1), power, control.

Welde (2), weld.

Weldy, wieldy, active.

Wele, weal, well-being, happiness, success.

Weleful, happy, prosperous.

Wel-faring, well-favored. See *FranklT*, V, 932, n.

Wel-Heelynge, Good-concealment.

Welk; see **Walken**.

Welked, withered.

Welken, sbst., welkin, heaven, sky.

Welken, vb., wither, waste away (Lat. "emarcescere").

Welmen, gush, well forth.

Welte; see **We(e)lden**.

Wel-willy, well-wishing, beneficent, benevolent.

Wem, blemish; hurt.

Wemmelees, without blemish, spotless.

Wenden, pt. *wente*, pp. *(y)went*; wend, go; pass; pass away, depart. See also **Goon**.

Wene, supposition, doubt.

Wenen, ween, suppose, imagine.

Wenged, winged.

Went, Wente; see **Wenden**.

Wente, sbst., path, passage; turn.

Wepen, pt. *weep*, *wepte*, pp. *wepen*, *wopen*, *wept*; weep.

Wepen, weapon.

Werbul, warble, tune.

Werchen, Werken, Wirchen, Wirken, Worchen, Wurchen, pt. *wro(u)ghte*, pp. *wro(u)ght*; work; act; ache; make, create, contrive; form; compose; perform its function (give relief).

Were, doubt, state of anxiety or uncertainty; *withouten were*, without doubt.

Were, weir.

Weren (1), pt. *wer(e)de, wered*; wear, bear on one's person; *weren upon*, have on.

Weren (2), ward off; defend, protect.

Werk, work; dat. phr. *a werke*.

Werken; see Werchen.

Wernen; see Warnen (1) and (2).

Werning, hindrance, forbidding.

Werre, war, hostility; trouble.

Werre, adv., worse.

Werreyen, make war; oppose.

Werreyour, warrior.

Wers, worse.

Werste, worst.

Werte, wart.

Wery, weary, exhausted; tired (of doing something).

Weryen, worry, strangle.

Wesele, weasel.

Wes(s)h; see Wasshen.

West, west; dat. phr. *by weste*.

Westen, turn toward the west.

Westren, go toward the west.

Wete, sweat, perspiration.

Weven, pt. *waf*, pp. *woven*; weave.

Wex, wax.

Wexen, Waxen, pt. *we(e)x, wax, wox*, pp. *waxen, woxen*; wax, grow, increase; become.

Wey(e), way, path; used adverbially (like "away") in *go wey, do wey*.

Weyen, weigh.

Weyer, the "weigher," the equator.

Weyk, weak.

Weyked, pp., weakened; feeble.

Weymentinge, Waymentinge, lamenting.

Weyven, waive; put aside; neglect, abandon; turn aside.

What, what; whatever; why; what!; somewhat, something; *what ... what*, partly ... partly; *a litel what*, slightly, somewhat.

Wheelen, wheel, cause to turn.

Whelkes, pimples, blotches.

Whelp, pup; cub.

Whenne(s), whence.

Wher, where; wherever.

Wher, contr. of Whether.

Whete, wheat.

Whether, which (of two).

Whetten, pt. *whette*; whet, sharpen.

Which, which; what kind of (Lat. "qualis").

Whider, whither.

Whilk, which (North. dial.).

Whilom; see Whylom.

Whippe, whip.

Whippeltree, cornel-tree.

Who, who; whoever; one who.

Whyl-er, erewhile, formerly.

Whyles (gen. sg. of *whyle*), whilst.

Whylom, whilom, formerly; once.

Whynen, whine, whinny.

Whyt, white; innocent; specious, flattering; *whyte monkes*, Cistercians.

Widwe, widow.

Wight, person, man, creature; thing, bit, whit.

Wight, adj., active; swift.

Wighte, weight.

Wiket, wicket-gate.

Wikke, Wikked, wicked, bad, evil.

Wilde, wild; *wilde fyr*, Greek fire; erysipelas; also a burning pudding-sauce.

Wil(e), Wol(e), irreg. vb., 2 sg. pr. *wilt, wolt*, pl. *wollen*, pt. *wolde*; will, wish, desire.

Wilful, willing, voluntary.

Wilnen, desire.

Wiltow, contr. of *wilt thou*.

Wimpel, wimple, a garment of women, folded to cover the head, chin, sides of the face, and neck.

Wimplen, cover (as with a wimple).

Windas, windlass.

Winden; see Wynden.

Windy, unstable (like wind).

Winken, wink, shut the eyes; nod; sleep, try to sleep.

Winnen, pt. sg. *wan*, pl. and pp. *wonnen*; win, gain; conquer; get profit.

Winsinge, pr. p., wincing, starting aside, skittish.

Wirchen; see Werchen.

Wirdes; see Wyerdes.

Wirken; see Werchen.

Wis; see Ywis.

Wisly, certainly, surely, verily.

Wissen, instruct, teach; tell, show; guide, direct.

Wis(s)h; see Wasshen.

Wisshe, wish.

Wist(e); see Witen.

Wit, wit; mind, reason; understanding, knowledge; judgment, wisdom; opinion; *wittes*, senses.

Witen, pt. pr. vb., sg. *wo(o)st, wo(o)t*, pl. *witen*, pt. *wiste*, pp. *wist*; know, discover. See also Noot, Niste, etc.

With, with; by; *with alle*; see under Al.

Withdrawen, pt. *withdrow(gh)*; withdraw; subtract.

Witholden, pp. *witholden*; withhold, retain, detain; retain in service. See *Gen Prol*, I, 511, n.

Withinne-forth, everywhere within; inwardly.

Withoute-forth, outwardly.

Withouten, without; besides; excepting.

Withseyen, gainsay, deny; refuse; renounce.

Withstonden, pt. *withstood*, pp. *withstonden*; withstand, oppose.

Witing, knowledge.

Witnesfully, publicly.

Witterly, plainly, surely, truly.

Wivere, wyvern, snake.

Wlatsom, abominable, disgusting; heinous.

Wo, woe; also adj., *me is as wo For hym as evere I was for any man*, *LGW*, 1985 f.

Wodebinde, woodbine, honeysuckle.

Wodedowve, wood-pigeon.

Wodewale, green woodpecker.

Wodnesse, madness.

Wold, possession; dat. phr. *in wolde*.

Wol(d)(e); see Wil(e).

Wolle, wool.

Wol(le)n, Wolt(ow); see Wil(e).

Wombe, womb; belly; the depression on an astrolabe.

Wond(en); see Wynden.

Wonden, cease, desist.

Wonder, adj., wonderful, strange; also adv.

Wonderly, -liche, wondrously.

Wondermost, most wonderful.

Wonders, adv., wondrously.

Wone, wont, custom; abode.

Wonen, Wonien, dwell, inhabit; pp. *woned*, dwelt; accustomed, wont.

Wonger, pillow.

Woning, dwelling, habitation.

Wonnen; see **Winnen.**

Woọd, woad.

Wood, mad, angry; *for wood,* because angry; hence, madly, furiously.

Wooden, be mad, rage.

Wook; see **Waken.**

Woọn, resource; number; abundance, plenty; dwelling-place, retreat.

Woọst(ow), Woọt; see **Witen.**

Wopen; see **Wepen.**

Worchen; see **Werchen.**

Worcher, worker, maker.

Word, word; *at shorte wordes,* briefly; *hadde the wordes,* was spokesman.

Word and ende, corruption of *ord and ende,* beginning and end. See *MkT,* VII, 2721, n.

Wort, wort, unfermented beer.

Wortes, herbs.

Worthen, pp. *yworthen;* become; be, dwell; get into or upon; *wel (wo) worth,* may it be well (ill) with respect to.

Worthy, having worth, rank, or standing; deserving; excellent (in a general sense).

Woọst(ow), Woọt; see **Witen.**

Wouke, Wowke, Wyke, week.

Wounde, wound; plague.

Woọven; see **Weọven.**

Wowen, woo.

Wox(en); see **Wexen.**

Wrak; see **Wreken.**

Wrak, sbst., wreck.

Wrang, wrongly (North. dial.).

Wrastlen, wrestle.

Wrathen, enanger.

Wraw, angry; fretful.

Wrecche, wretch, sorrowful person; also adj.

Wrecchednesse, wretchedness, misery, poverty; poor or miserable act or performance.

Wreche, vengeance; punishment; wretchedness.

Wreen; see **Wryen** (1).

Wreigh; see **Wryen** (1).

Wreken, pt. *wrak,* pp. *wreken, wroken;* wreak, avenge.

Wrench, trick, fraud.

Wresten, wrest, force, constrain.

Wreyen, Wrien, betray, disclose.

Wrighte, workman.

Wringen, pt. *wrong;* wring, pinch, squeeze; drive, compel; force a way.

Wroken; see **Wreken.**

Wrong, wrong; *had wrong,* was wrong.

Wrong, adv., amiss, astray.

Wroọt; see **Wryten.**

Wrooth, wroth, angry.

Wroten, tear with the snout, root.

Wro(u)ght, Wro(u)ghte; see **Werchen.**

Wryen (1), **Wreen,** pt. *weigh;* hide, cover; clothe, disguise; conceal.

Wryen (2); see **Wreyen.**

Wryen (3), turn, bend; turn aside.

Wryten, contr. pr. 3 sg. *writ,* pt. sg. *wroọt,* pl. and pp. *writen;* write.

Wrythen, contr. pr. 3 sg. *wryth;* writhe, wriggle; wreathe; cast forth wreaths or rings.

Wurchen; see **Werchen.**

Wurching, Worching, machination.

Wyde-where, far and wide.

Wyerdes, Weerdes, Wirdes, weirds, fates, destinies.

Wyf, gen. sg. and pl. *wyves;* woman; wife; housewife; dat. phr. *to wyve.*

Wyfhoọd, womanhood.

Wyke; see **Wouke.**

Wyld(e)nesse, wildness.

Wyle, wile, stratagem; subtlety.

Wyn, wine; *wyn ape,* see *Manc Prol,* IX, 44, n.

Wynden, contr. pr. 3 sg. *wynt,* pt. *wond,* pp., *wo(u)nden;* wind, turn; revolve; bend, direct; entwine, intertwine; wander about.

Wynd-melle, windmill (Kentish dial.).

Wyndren, trim.

Wyr, wire; bit.

Wys, wise, prudent; *make it wys,* deliberate, hold off, etc. See *Gen Prol,* I, 785, n.

Wyse, wise, way, manner.

Wyte, blame, reproach; charge, accusation.

Wyten, blame, reproach; accuse.

Y (see also I)

Y, pers. pron., I.

Y- I-, a prefix (AS. "ge-," Germ. "ge-") commonly used with past participles; rare, in Mid. Eng., as a general verbal prefix (*yseen,* from AS. "geseon"). Participles in *y-* are not entered here separately from their verbs unless the forms might not be recognized or the meaning calls for special record.

Ya; see **Ye.**

Yaf; see **Yeven.**

Yald, Yalt; see **Yelden.**

Yare, ready.

Yate, gate.

Yaven; see **Yeven.**

Ybedded, pp., put to bed.

Ybenched, supplied with benches.

Yblent; see **Blenden.**

Ybleynt; see **Blenchen.**

Yblọwe(n), blown; rumored.

Ybowed, diverted.

Ybrend, Ybrent, burnt.

Ycchyng (var. **Yecching**), itching.

Ych; see **Ech.**

Ychaped, furnished with chapes or metal caps.

Yclenched, clinched, riveted.

Ycontinued, continuous.

Ycorven; see **Kerven.**

Ycrased, cracked, crushed, broken.

Ycrowe; see **Crowen.**

Ydarted, pierced with a dart.

Ydel, idle, vain, empty; *in (on) ydel,* in vain.

Ydolastre, idolater.

Ydole, idol.

Ydrad; see **Dreden.**

Yë; see **Eye.**

Ye, Ya, yea.

Yedding, song, ballad.

Yede, pt. sg., pl. *yeden;* went, walked.

Yẹẹr, rarely **Yẹre,** pl. *yeer, yeres;* year; dat. phr. *to yere, yeer by yere.*

Yefte; see **Yifte.**

Yeldehalle, gildhall.

Yelden, Yilden, contr. pr. 3 sg. *yelt, yalt,* pt. sg. *yald,* pl. *yolden;* yield, submit; pay, restore, requite; refl., betake one's self.

Yelding, produce.

Yelpen, boast.

Yelt; see **Yelden.**
Yelwe, yellow.
Yeman, pl. *yemen;* yeoman.
Yemanly, in yeomanlike fashion.
Yën; see **Eye.**
Yerd, yard, garden.
Yerde, rod, stick; correction; yard (measure).
Yerne, eager, lively; quick; also adv.
Yernen, yearn; long for, desire.
Yerning, yearning, longing; affection.
Yeten, pp. *yeten;* pour, shed.
Yeven, **Geven, Yiven,** pt. sg. *yaf,* pl. *yaven,* imp.
  2 sg. *yif,* pp. *yeven;* give.
Yevere, giver.
Yexen, hiccough.
Yfare; see **Faren.**
Yfere; see **Infere.**
Yfet; see **Fecchen.**
Yfinden, pp. *yfounden;* find.
Yflit, carried, whirled along.
Yfounded, founded, based, set on a foundation.
Yfreten; see **Freten.**
Yfrounced, wrinkled.
Ygerdoned, rewarded.
Ygeten; see **Geten.**
Yglased, glazed.
Yglewed, glued, fixed fast.
Yglosed, flattered.
Ygrave, cut, graven; engraved; dug up or out;
  buried.
Ygreved, grieved; injured.
Ygrounde, ground; sharpened.
Yharded, hardened.
Yheeren, hear.
Yherd, haired, covered with hair.
Yhevied, weighed down.
Yhight, hight, called.
Yif, if; see **If.**
Yif, imp., give; see **Yeven.**
Yifte, **Yefte,** gift.
Yilden; see **Yelden.**
Ying, young (North. dial.).
Yis, yes; more emphatic than *ye, ya.*
Yiven; see **Yeven.**
Ykempt, combed.
Yknet, **Yknit,** knotted; joined together.
Yknowen, know; discern, recognize. See **Knowen.**
Ykorven; see **Kerven.**
Ykoud, known.
Ylad, **Yled;** see **Leden.**
Ylaft; see **Leven.**
Ylaid; see **Leyen.**
Yle, isle, island.
Ylet, hindered, obstructed. See **Letten.**
Yleten, allowed, left. See **Leten.**
Yleyd; see **Leyen.**
Yliche, **Ylyk,** like, alike, similar; also adv.
Ylissed, eased, relieved.
Yloren, lost. See **Lesen.**
Ylost, lost.
Ylyk; see **Yliche.**
Ylyke, adv., alike, equally.
Ylymed, caught (as with bird-lime).
Ymaad, **Ymaked,** made; caused.
Ymagerie, carved work.
Ymaginatyf, given to imagining; suspicious.
Ymagined, considered, deliberate.
Ymaked; see **Ymaad.**

Ymasked, enmeshed.
Ymedled, mixed, mingled; confounded.
Ymel, among (North. dial.).
Ymeynd, mingled, mixed.
Ymp, graft, scion.
Ympne, hymn; lyric poem.
Ymused, mused, reflected.
Ynde, indigo, blue.
Ynogh, adj., pl. *ynowe;* enough; also adv.
Ynome, caught, seized; taken; overcome. See
  Nimen.
Yok, yoke.
Yolden; see **Yelden.**
Yollen, **Yellen,** yell.
Yomanrye (var. **Yemanrye**), yeomanry.
Yon, adj., yon.
Yond, yonder.
Yong, young.
Yonghede, youth.
Yore, yore, of old, long ago; for a long time; *yore
  ago*(n), long ago.
Youling, howling; lamentation.
Your, your; *youre*(s), yours.
Youthe, youth.
Youthhede, youth. See **-hede,** suffix.
Ypiked, picked over.
Ypleynted, full of complaint.
Ypocras, a cordial drink.
Ypocryte; see **Ipocrite.**
Yprayed, bidden, invited.
Ypreved, proved.
Ypulled, plucked (of hairs or feathers).
Ypurveied, foreseen.
Yqueynt, quenched. See **Quenchen.**
Yquiked, quickened; kindled.
Yraft, bereft; snatched away. See **Reven.**
Yre, **Ire,** ire, anger.
Yreke (pp. of *reken*), raked together, covered up.
Yren, iron.
Yrent, torn; taken
Yronge; see **Ringen.**
Yronne; see **Rennen.**
Yse, ice.
Yseen, pp. *yseye, yseyn;* see, behold; look.
Ysene, adj., visible, manifest.
Yseye, seen. See **Seen**
Yshad, shed, scattered, spread abroad.
Yshaken, shaken; quivering, sparkling.
Yshent, injured, ruined; blamed; humiliated. See
  Shenden.
Yshett, shut.
Yshore, shorn.
Yshove, shoved, borne about.
Ysmite, smitten; wounded.
Ysounded, sunk.
Ysped, sped; advanced; worked out. See **Speden.**
Yspreynd, sprinkled. See **Springen** (2).
Ystalled, set in a seat, installed.
Ystonde, stood, been. See **Stonden.**
Ystorve, dead. See **Sterven.**
Ystrawed, strewn, bestrewn.
Ystrike, struck.
Ysweped, swept.
Ythen, prosper; thrive.
Ythewed, mannered, disposed; *wel ythewed,* well-
  conducted.
Ythrongen, confined.
Ythrungen; see **Thringen.**

Ytressed, plaited in tresses.
Yve, ivy; *erbe yve*, ground ivy.
Yvel, adj., evil, ill; also adv.
Yvory, Yvoire, ivory.
Ywar, aware.
Ywent (1), gone. See **Wenden**.
Ywent (2), weened, supposed. See **Wenen**.
Ywet, wetted.
Ywhet, whetted.
Ywimpled, covered with a wimple.
Ywis, Iwis, Wis, certainly, truly, surely, assuredly.
Ywist, known.

Yworthe, pp., become.
Ywoxen, grown. See **Wexen**.
Ywrapped, involved.
Ywrithen, wreathed, wrapped about.
Ywroken, avenged. See **Wreken**.
Ywronge, wrung, forced. See **Wringen**.
Ywryen, concealed, hidden. See **Wryen** (1).
Yyeve, Yyve, given.

Z

Zeles, pl., zeals.
Zodiak, zodiac.

PROPER NAMES

A

Abigayl, Abigail, wife of Nabal (I Sam. xxv).

Absolon, Absalom; (1) son of David; (2) character in *MillT*.

Achademycis, translating Lat. "Academicis," the Academic school of philosophy.

Achaleous, Acheleous, Acheloys (gen.), Achelous, a river in Greece; the river-god who took the form of a bull against Hercules.

Achate(s), companion of Aeneas.

Achemenye, Persia.

Achetofel, Achitofel, Achitophel (Ahithophel). See II Sam. xv, 12.

Achille(s), Achilles.

Adam, (1) first man; (2) Chaucer's scrivener.

Adoon, Adoun, Adonis.

Adrastus, king of Argos, one of the Seven against Thebes.

Adriane, Ariadne, daughter of Minos.

Affrican, Scipio Africanus Major.

Affrike, Auffrike, Africa.

Agamenon, Agamemnon, Greek leader against the Trojans.

Agaton, Agathon (or Agatho). See *LGW Prol F*, 526, n.

Agenor, father of Europa.

Aglawros, sister of Herse; turned by Mercury to stone.

Alayn; see **Aleyn.**

Albon, Alban.

Albyn, probably Decius Albinus, a contemporary of Boethius.

Albyon, Albion, Britain.

Alcathoe, the citadel of Megara.

Alcebiades, Alcipyades, Alcibiades.

Alceste, Alcestis, wife of Admetus.

Alcion(e), Alcyone or Halcyone, wife of Ceÿx.

Aldeberan, Aldebaran, the star.

Aldiran, the name of a star. See *SqT*, V, 263, n.

Alete, Alecto, one of the Furies.

Aleyn, Alayn, (1) Alanus de Insulis, Alain de Lille (c. 1128–1202); (2) a character in *RvT*.

Alfonce; see **Piers.**

Algarsyf, a character in *SqT*.

Algezir, Algeciras in Spain.

Algomeyse, the star α Canis Minoris.

Alhabor, Sirius, the dog-star.

Alisa(u)ndre, (1) Alexander the Great; (2) Alexandria.

Aliso(u)n, Alison; (1) characters in *WBT* and *MillT*; (2) see **Alys.**

Alkabucius, Alchabitius, an Arabian astronomer of the 10th century. See *Astr*, i, 8, 13, n.

Alkaron, the Koran.

Alla, Aella, king of Northumberland.

Almachius, Almache, a character in *SecNT*.

Almageste, the Almagest of Ptolemy. See *MillT*, I, 3208, n.

Almena, Alcmena, mother of Hercules.

Alnath, the star α in Aries.

Alocen, Alhazen, Arabian mathematician of the 11th century, famous for discoveries in optics.

Alys, Alisoun, Alice, the wife of Bath.

Ambrose, St. Ambrose (c. 340–97), bishop of Milan.

Amete, Admetus, king of Pherae in Thessaly and husband of Alcestis.

Amphiorax, Amphiaraus, husband of Eriphyle, and one of the Seven against Thebes.

Amphioun, Amphion, king of Thebes and husband of Niobe.

Anaxogore, Anaxagoras, the Greek philosopher.

Anchises, father of Aeneas.

Androgeus, Androgeos, son of Minos.

Andromacha, Andromache, wife of Hector.

Anelida; see the introduction to the Explanatory Notes to *Anel*.

Anne, (1) St. Anna, mother of the Virgin; (2) Anna, sister of Dido.

Anselm, St. Anselm (c. 1033–1109), archbishop of Canterbury.

Anteclaudian, the Anticlaudianus of Alanus de Insulis, a philosophical poem.

Antecrist, Antichrist.

Antenor(e), Anthenor, Antenor, Trojan warrior.

Antheus, Antaeus, the giant wrestler, killed by Hercules.

Ant(h)iochus, Antiochus Epiphanes, king of Syria 175–64 B.C.

Antigone, a Trojan maiden.

Antonius, (1) Mark Antony; (2) Antoninus, or Caracalla, emperor of Rome, A.D. 211–17.

Antony, Seint, St. Anthony, born in Egypt c. 250.

Antylegyus, Antilochus. See *BD*, 1069, n.

Apennyn, the Apennine range.

Apia, Via, the Appian Way.

Apius, Appius, a character in *PhysT*.

Ap(p)elles, Appelles, celebrated Grecian painter, contemporary of Alexander the Great.

Ap(p)ollo, Apollo, the Greek divinity.

Appollonius, hero of the romance Apollonius of Tyre.

Aquarius, Aquarie, a sign of the zodiac.

Aquilon, Aquilo, the north wind.

Arabik, Arabic.

Arab(y)e, Arabia.

Aragon, a kingdom of Spain.

Arcadye, Arcadia in Peloponnesus.

Archymoris, used as gen. of Archemorus, a name applied by the Seven against Thebes to the child Opheltes, killed by a dragon and buried by the Seven.

Arcita, Arcite, a character in *KnT*.

Arcturus, Arctour, the constellation Boötes; also star α in Boötes.

Ardea, a town in Latium.

Arge, Argon, Argos.

Argeyes, Argives.

Argonautycon (g. pl.), the Argonautica, heroic poem of Valerius Flaccus.

Argus, (1) the hundred-eyed; (2) the builder of the Argo; (3) Algus; see *BD*, 435, n.

Argyve, Argiva, mother of Cressida.

Aries, Ariete, the Ram, a sign of the zodiac.

Arionis harpe, Arion's harp, the constellation Lyra.

Aristoclides, the tyrant of Orchomenos.

Aristotle, Aristotile, Aristotles, the Greek philosopher.

Armorik(e), Armorica, Brittany; Armorican.
Arnold of the Newe Toun, Arnaldus de Villanova, or Arnaud de Villeneuve, 13th century.
Arpies, Arpiis, the Harpies.
Arras, a town in France.
Arrius, a character in the Epistola Valerii of Walter Map.
Arsechiel, Arzachel. See *Astr*, ii, 45, 2, n.
Arthemisie, Artemisia of Caria, who built the Mausoleum to the memory of her husband Mausolus.
Arthour, Artour, Arthur, king of Britain.
Artoys, Artois.
Arveragus, a character in *FranklT*.
Ascanius, Askanius, son of Aeneas.
Assuer(e), Assuerus, Ahasuerus.
Asye, Asia.
Athalantes doughtres, daughters of Atlas, the constellation of the Pleiades.
Athalus, Attalus III Philometor, king of Pergamus 138–33 B.C., fabled inventor of chess.
Athamantes, Athamas, king of Orchomenos in Boeotia.
Atiteris; see *HF*, 1227, n.
At(t)halante, Atalanta.
At(t)henes, (1) Athens; (2) the Athenians.
Attheon, Actaeon.
Attilla, Attila the Hun.
Attrides, Atrides, son of Atreus, Agamemnon.
At(t)ropos, Atropos, the Fate.
Augustyn, Austyn, St. Augustine (354–430).
Aurelian, Roman emperor, A.D. 270–75.
Aurelius, Aurelie, a character in *FranklT*.
Aurora, (1) goddess of the dawn; (2) see *BD*, 1169, n.
Auster, the south wind.
Austyn; see Augustyn.
Averrois, Averroes, Arabian physician and philosopher (12th cent.).
Avycen, Avicenna (980–1037), Arabian philosopher, author of the Canon of Medicine.

B

Babilan, Babylonian.
Babiloigne, Babiloyne, Babylon.
Bacus, Bachus, Bacchus, the Greek divinity.
Baldeswelle, Baldeswell (Bawdeswell) in Norfolk.
Ballenus. See *HF*, 1273, n.
Balthasar, Belshazzar.
Barbarie, barbarian territory.
Barnabo, Bærnabò, Viscount of Milan. See *MkT*, VII, 2399, n.
Basilie, St. Basil (329–79), bishop of Caesarea.
Basilius, one of the accusers of Boethius.
Bayard, a name for a horse.
Belial, the devil.
Belle, the Bell, a Southwark inn.
Bellona, goddess of war.
Belmarye, Benmarin, a Moorish kingdom in Africa. See *CT*, I, 59, n.
Benedight, Beneit, St. Benedict (c. 480–544).
Bernard, (1) St. Bernard; (2) see *LGW ProlF*, 16, n.; (3) 14th cent. physician. See *Gen Prol*, I, 429, n.
Berwyk, (probably) Berwick-on-Tweed.
Bethulia, Bethulie, city of the Israelites besieged by Holofernes; perhaps Shechem or Sichem.
Beves, hero of the romance Sir Beves of Hamtoun.
Biblis, Byblis, twin sister of Caunus. See Ovid, Met., ix, 453 ff.
Bilyea, Bilia. See *FrT*, V, 1455, n.

Blaunche, the Duchess of Lancaster.
Blee, Blean forest. See *CYT*, VIII, 556, n.
Bobbe-up-and-doun. See *Manc Prol*, IX, 2, n.
Boece, Boethius.
Boetes, Boötes, the constellation.
Boghtoun under Blee. See Blee.
Bole, Bull, the sign Taurus in the zodiac.
Boloigne, (1) Boulogne in France; (2) Bologna in Italy.
Boreas, the north wind.
Bradwardyn, Thomas Bradwardine (c. 1290–1349), theologian and archbishop of Canterbury.
Breseyda, Brixseyde, Briseis.
Bret, Briton, Welshman. See *HF*, 1208, n. on Glascurion.
Britaigne, Britayne, Briteyne, Brittany, Britain.
Brito(u)n, Briton, Breton.
Brixseyde; see Breseyda.
Brok, Brock, a horse's name.
Bromeholm, Bromholm (Norfolk).
Brugges, Bruges.
Brut, Brutus, legendary founder of the Celtic kingdom of Britain.
Brutus, (1) L. Junius Brutus, consul in 509 B.C.; (2) M. Brutus, the so-called tyrannicide. Brutus Cassius; see *MkT*, VII, 2697, n.
Bukton. See the introduction to the Explanatory Notes to *Buk*.
Burdeux, Bordeaux.
Burgoyne, Burgundy.
Burnel the Asse, Brunellus the Ass. See *NPT*, VII, 3312, n.
Busirus, Busyrides, Busiris, king of Egypt, slain by Hercules.

C (see also K, S)

Cacus, Kacus, a giant slain by Hercules.
Cadme, Cadmus of Thebes, husband of Harmonia.
Calipsa, Calypso, nymph who loved Ulysses.
Calistopee, Calyxte, Callisto, an Arcadian nymph changed by Zeus into a bear and subsequently slain by Artemis.
Calkas, Calchas, the Trojan priest, father of Cressida in *Tr*.
Cal(l)iope, the Muse.
Calydoigne, Calydoyne, Calydon, ruled over by Oeneus, grandfather of Diomedes.
Calyxte; see Calistopee.
Cambalo, Cambalus, son of Cambiuskan. See *SqT*, V, 29 ff., n.
Cambises, Cambyses, king of Persia.
Cambyuskan, Cambiuskan, a character in *SqT*. See *Sq T*, V, 12, n.
Campaneus, Cap(p)aneus, Capaneus, one of the Seven against Thebes.
Campayne, Campania in Italy.
Canace(e), (1) a character in *SqT*; (2) character referred to in *ML Prol*, II, 78 and *LGW Prol G*, 219.
Cananee, Canaanite.
Cancer, Cancre, a sign of the zodiac.
Candace, an Indian queen.
Cane, Cana.
Cantebregge, Cantebrigge, Cambridge.
Canyos, the Canii, the followers of Canius.
Canyus, Julius Canius (or Canus). See *Bo*, i, pr. 3, 56, n.
Capricorn(e), Capricorn, a sign of the zodiac.
Caribdis, Charybdis, the whirlpool.

Carrenar, the Kara-Nor. See *BD*, 1028, n.

Cartage, Carthage, Cartagena, Spanish Mediterranean port.

Cassandra, Cassandre, the daughter of Priam who had power of prophecy.

Cassidor(i)e, Cassidorus, Magnus Aurelius Cassiodorus.

Castor, twin brother of Pollux, with whom he is associated in the constellation of Gemini.

Cataloigne, Catalonia, a province of Spain.

Cato(u)n, (1) Cato of Utica; (2) Dionysius Cato, reputed author of the *Disticha de Moribus ad Filium.*

Catullus, the Latin poet.

Caucasus, Kaukasous, a mountain range in southwestern Asia.

Caunterbury, Canterbury.

Caym, Cain.

Cecil(i)e, St. Cecilia, who probably perished in Sicily under Marcus Aurelius between 176 and 180.

Cedasus, Scedasus, of Leuctra in Boeotia.

Cenobia, Cenobie, Zenobia, queen of Palmyra, defeated by Aurelian, A.D. 273.

Cerberus, the dog who guarded the entrance to the Lower World.

Cerce, Circes, Circe, mythical sorceress who charmed Ulysses.

Ceres, the Roman divinity.

Cesar, Caesar.

Cesiphus, Sisyphus; possibly used for Tityus.

Ceys, Seys, Ceÿx, husband of Alcyone.

Chaldeye, Chaldea.

Charles, Charlemagne.

Chauntecleer, name of a cock in *NPT.*

Chepe, Cheapside, in London; perhaps also Eastcheap.

Chichevache, a fabulous cow. See *ClT*, IV, 1188, n.

Chiron, the Centaur, tutor of Achilles.

Chorus, (1) Caurus, the northwest wind, a stormy wind in Italy; (2) used as name of a sea-god; but see *LGW*, 2422, n.

Cibella, Cybele, the Greek divinity, mother of the gods.

Cilenius, Cyllenius, Mercury, born on Mt. Cyllene.

Cinthia, Cynthia, another name for Diana.

Cipioun; see **Scipioun.**

Cipre, Cyprus.

Cipris, Cipride, Cypris, Venus.

Cirrea, Cirra, a town near Delphi and Mt. Parnassus.

Cirus, Cyrus the Elder, founder of the Persian Empire.

Cithe, Cithia, Scithia, Scythia.

Citherea, Cytherea, Venus.

Cithero(u)n, Mt. Cithaeron, sacred to Bacchus and the Muses apparently confused with the island of Cythera, sacred to Venus.

Clare, St. Clara or Clare (1194–1253), founder of the Fransciscan nuns.

Claudian, Claudius Claudianus (4th cent.), author of De Raptu Proserpinae.

Claudius, (1) M. Aurelius Claudius, Roman emperor, A.D. 268–70; (2) a character in *PhysT.*

Clemence, Clemency, Pity.

Cleo, Clio, the Muse.

Cleopat(a)ras, Cleopatre, Cleopatra.

Clitermystra, Clytemnestra, wife of Agamemnon.

Colatyn, L. Tarquinius Collatinus, husband of Lucretia.

Colcos, Colchis, country of the Golden Fleece.

Colle, (1) name of juggler; see *HF*, 1277, n.; (2) name of a dog.

Coloigne, Cologne.

Conigaste, Conigastus, adversary of Boethius.

Constantyn, Constantinus Afer. See *Gen Prol*, I, 429, n.

Coribantes, Corybantes, priests of Cybele.

Corynne, probably Corinna, a Theban poetess. See the introduction to the Explanatory Notes to *Anel.*

Crassus, Marcus, the triumvir.

Creon, tyrant of Thebes.

Creseyde; see **Cris(s)eyde.**

Cresus, Croesus.

Creusa, wife of Aeneas.

Cris(s)eyde, Creseyde, Cressida, heroine of *Tr.*

Crisippus, Chrysippus. See *WB Prol*, III, 670 ff., n.

Crist, Christ.

Cristopher, St. Christopher.

Cupide, Cupido, Cupid.

Custance, Constance, a character in *MLT.*

Cutberd, St. Cuthbert (d. 687).

Cymerie, Cimmerii, a mythical people mentioned by Homer.

Cyprian, an accuser of Boethius.

D

Dalida, Delilah.

Damascien, Damascenus. See *Gen Prol*, I, 429, n.

Damasie, seint, Pope Damasus I (336–84).

Damyan, a character in *MerchT.*

Damyssene, Damascene; used for Damascus.

Dane, Daphne.

Danao, Danaus, father of Hypermnestra.

Dant(e), Daunte, the Italian poet.

Dardanus, mythical ancestor of the Trojans.

Dares, D. Frygius, Dares the Phrygian, or Trojan, to whom was ascribed a work on the Trojan war.

Darius, king of Persia.

Daunte; see **Dant(e).**

David, Davit, king of the Jews.

Decorat, Decoratus, quaestor c. 508.

Decrees, Book of, the Decretals of Gratian.

Dedalus, Daedalus, builder of the labyrinth in Crete.

Deiphebus, Deiphebe, Deiphobus, son of Priam, a character in *Tr.*

Delphos, Delphi.

Delphyn, the Dolphin.

Demetrius, king of Parthia.

Democion, Demotion. See *FranklT*, V, 1426, n.

Demopho(u)n, Demophon (or Demophoön), the betrothed of Phyllis.

Denys, seint, St. Denis (Dionysius), first bishop of Paris and patron saint of France.

Depeford, Deptford.

Dertemouthe, Dartmouth.

Deyscorides, Dioscorides, a Greek physician of the 2nd century.

Dianira, Dianire, Dejanira, wife of Hercules.

Dido, queen of Carthage.

Diogenes, Greek philosopher.

Diomede(s), (1) son of Tydeus; (2) Thracian king killed by Hercules.

Dite, Dictys of Crete, the reputed author of a work on the Trojan war.
Dives, the rich man in the parable.
Donegild, a character in *MLT*.
Dorigen(e), a character in *FranklT*.
Drye See, The Gobi Desert. See *BD*, 1038, n. and F. P. Magoun, Jr. Med. Stud., XVII, 125.
Duche, Dutch (German).
Dunmowe, (Little?) Dunmow in Essex.
Dunstan, Seint, St. Dunstan, archibishop of Canterbury in 959.
Dyone, Dione, mother of Venus.

E

Eacides, Aeacides, grandson of Aeacus, Achilles.
Ebrayk, Hebrayk, Hebraic, Hebrew.
Ebrew, Hebrew.
Ecclesiaste, Ecclesiasticus.
Echo, Ecquo, Ekko, the nymph, whose love for Narcissus was not returned.
Eclympasteyr; see *BD*, 167, n.
Ector, Hector, son of Priam.
Ecuba, Hecuba, wife of Priam.
Edippus, Edippe, Oedipus, king of Thebes.
Edward, Seint, the Confessor.
Egeus, Aegeus, father of Theseus.
Egipt(e), Egypt.
Egiste(s), Aegyptus, brother of Danaus and father of Lynceus.
Eglentyne, the Prioress.
Ekko; see **Echo**.
Elcanor; see *HF*, 514 ff., n.
Eleaticis, translating Latin "Eleaticis," of the Eleatic school of philosophy.
Eleyne, (1) Helen of Troy; (2) St. Helen.
Eliachim, Eliakim, a priest. See Judith iv, 7 (Vulg.).
Elicon(e), Mt. Helicon in Boeotia.
Elise, Elisha.
Elisos, Elysium.
Elpheta, wife of Cambiuskan. See *SqT*, V, 29 ff., n.
Eltham, in Kent.
Elye, Elijah.
Emele-ward, to, towards the Emilia, N. Italy.
Emelya, Emelye, Emilia, Emily, a character in *KnT*.
Emetreus; see *KnT*, I, 2155–86, n.
Eneas, Enyas, Enee, Aeneas.
Eneydos (i.e., "Aeneidos liber"), Aeneid.
Engelond, England.
Ennok, Enoch.
Ennopye, Oenopia, later Aegina.
Enyas; see **Eneas**.
Eolus, Aeolus, god of winds.
Epicurus, the Greek philosopher.
Epist(e)les, Epistles; used of Ovid's Heroides.
Epycuriens, Epicureans.
Ercules, Hercules.
Eriphilem, Eriphyle, wife of Amphiaraus.
Ermony, Armenia.
Ermyn, Armenian.
Erro; see **Herro**.
Erudice, Eurydice, wife of Orpheus.
Escaphilo, Ascalaphus, changed into an owl by Proserpina.
Esculapius, Aesculapius, god of the medical art.
Eson, Æson, father of Jason.
Esperus; see **Hesperus**.
Ester, Hester, Esther.

Ethiocles, Eteocles, brother of Polynices.
Ethiopeen, Ethiopian.
Ethna, Aetna.
Eva, Eve, the first woman.
Eufrates, Euphrates.
Euripidis, Euripides, the Greek tragic poet.
Eurippe, Euripus, a strait between Euboea and Boeotia.
Europe, Europa.
Eurus, the southeast wind.
Evander, early Trojan settler in Italy.
Ezechias, Ezechie, Hezekiah.
Ezechiel, Ezekiel.

F

Fabricius, C. Fabricius Luscinus, Roman hero.
Fawny (Lat. "Fauni"), fauns, deities of fields and herds.
Femenye, the country of the Amazons.
Ferrare, Ferrara.
Feverer, February.
Flaundres, Flanders.
Flaundryssh, Flemish.
Flegetoun, Phlegethon, the river of fire in the Lower World.
Flexippe, a character in *Tr*.
Flora, goddess of flowers.
Fraunceys, Francis.
Frise, Friesland.
Frydeswyde, seinte, St. Frideswide.
Fynystere, Cape Finisterre in the province of Galicia, Spain. See *Gen Prol*, I, 408, n.
Fysshstrete, Fish Street, now Fish Hill Street.

G

Gabriel, the archangel.
Gaius Cesar, Caligula (in *Bo*, i, pr. 4).
Galathee, Galatea, heroine of the Latin dialogue Pamphilus de Amore. See *Mel*, VII, 1556, n.
Galgopheye, probably the valley of Gargaphia in Boeotia.
Galice, Galicia in Spain.
Galien, (1) Galen, the famous physician; (2) Gallienus, Roman emperor, A.D. 260–68.
Galiones, drinks named after Galen.
Gallus, Symplicius, Sulpicius Gallus, consul at Rome in 166 B.C.
Ganymede, Ganymede, cup-bearer to Jove.
Gatesden, John of Gaddesden (or Gatesden) of Oxford, physician of the 14th century.
Gaudencius, mentioned in *Bo*, i, pr. 4, 116.
Gaufred, Gaufride, (1) Geoffrey of Monmouth; (2) Geoffroi de Vinsauf. See *NPT*, VII, 3347, n.
Gaunt, Ghent, in E. Flanders.
Gawayn, Gaweyn, Gawain, knight of Arthur's court.
Gazan, Gaza.
Gemini(s), the sign of the zodiac.
Genelloun, Genylo(u)n, Ganelon, the betrayer of Roland.
Gerland, Garland, a dog.
Germayn, Germanicus.
Gernade, Granada.
Gerounde, the river Gironde.
Gerveys, a character in *MillT*.
Gilbertyn, Gilbertus Anglicus, 13th century writer on medicine.

Gile(s), Seint, St. Aegidius, St. Giles, 6th or 7th century.
Gille, Jill.
Glascurion, Glasgerion. See *HF*, 1208, n.
Golias, Goliath.
Go(o)delief, the Host's wife (?). See *Mk Prol*, VII, 1894, n.
Gootlond, Gottland, an island in the Baltic Sea.
Gower, the poet.
Graunson, Sir Otes (or Oton) de Granson, the French poet. See *Ven*, 82, n.
Grece, Greece; See of Grece, the Mediterranean.
Gregorie, Seint, Gregory the Great (c. 540–604), first Pope of that name.
Grekissch, Grekyssh, Grykyssche, Greek.
Grenewych, Greenwich.
Grete See, the Mediterranean.
Grisilde, Grisildis, Griselda, heroine of *ClT*.
Guydo de Columpnis, Guido delle Colonne, author of the Historia Trojana.
Gy, hero of the romance Guy of Warwick.
Gysen, the river Gyndes in Assyria.

H

Habradate, Abradates. See *FranklT*, V, 1414, n.
Haly, Hali. See *Gen Prol*, I, 429, n.
Hanybal, Hannibal.
Hasdrubal, king of Carthage in 146 B.C.
Hayles, the Abbey of Hailes in Gloucestershire.
Hebrayk; see Ebrayk.
Helie, Eli (I Sam. i–iv).
Helowys, Heloïse, wife of Abelard.
Hemonydes, the son of Haemon.
Herenus, Herynes, Erinyes, the Furies, avenging deities.
Hereos, Eros. See *KnT*, I, 1372, n.
Hermanno, son of Zenobia.
Hermengyld, a character in *MLT*.
Hermes, Hermes Trismegistus. See *CYT*, VIII, 1434, n.
Hermus, a large river of Asia Minor.
Hermyon, Hermione, daughter of Menelaus.
Herodes, Herod.
Herro, Erro, Hero, priestess of Venus in Sestus, beloved by Leander.
Herry Bailly, Harry Bailly, or Baillif, the Host.
Hesperus, Esperus, the evening star.
Hester; see Ester.
Hierse, Herse, sister of Aglauros and beloved of Mercury.
Hogge, Hodge, nickname for Roger.
Holdernesse, Holderness (Yorkshire).
Homer, Omer, Homer.
Horaste, a character in *Tr*.
Horn Childe, hero of the romances King Horn, Horn Childe, etc.
Huberd, Hubert, the Friar.
Hugelyn, Ugolino of Pisa.
Hugh, of Lincoln, the child martyr.
Huwe, Hugh, name of a priest.
Hulle, Hull (Yorkshire).

I (see also Y)

Idra, Idre, Hydra, the monster slain by Hercules.
Ilyoun, Ilion, Troy.
Imeneus, Hymenaeus, god of marriage.
Inde, India.
Indus, the great river of India.

Innocent, Pope Innocent III.
Ipomedo(u)n, Hippomedon, one of the Seven against Thebes.
Isaude, Isawde, Isoude, Isolde (or Iseult).
Isaye, Isaiah.
Isiphile(e), Hypsipyle, daughter of Thoas, and deserted by Jason.
Isope, Aesop.
Isoude, see Isaude.
Itayl(l)e, Italy.
Iulo, Iulus (or Ascanius), son of Aeneas.
Ixion, king of the Lapithæ, chained to a wheel in the Lower World.

J

Jaconitos, Jaconites, in Colchos.
Jakke, Jack.
Jame, Seint, (1) St. James; (2) the shrine of Santiago at Compostela.
Jankin, Janekyn, Jenkin (dimin. of John).
Janicula, Janicle, a character in *ClT*.
Januarie, January; (1) the name of the month; (2) an old man in *MerchT*.
Janus, used for January.
Jason, leader of the Argonauts.
Jepte, Jephthah, son of Gilead (Judges xi–xii).
Jeremye, Jeremiah, the Hebrew prophet.
Jerome, St. Jerome (c. 340–420).
Jewerye, Juerie, (1) kingdom of the Jews; (2) Jews' quarter, Jewry.
Jhesus Syrak, Jesus, son of Sirach.
Joab, leader in David's army.
Joce, St. Joce (Judocus), a Breton saint.
Johan, John.
John, a character in *RvT*.
John, Seint, (1) St. John; (2) St. John the Baptist; (3) St. John Chrysostom.
Jonas, Jonah.
Jonathas, Jonathan.
Joseph, son of Jacob.
Josephus, author of history of the Jews.
Jove(s), Jove, Jupiter.
Jovinian, St. Jerome's adversary.
Jubaltare, Gibraltar.
Judas, (1) J. Maccabeus; (2) J. Iscariot.
Judith, slayer of Holofernes.
Juerie; see Jewerye.
Julian, St. Julian, patron of hospitality, said to have lived in early 4th century.
Julius, (1) Julius Caesar; (2) July.
Juno, Roman divinity.
Jup(p)iter, Jupiter; (1) Roman divinity; (2) planet.
Justinus, a character in *MerchT*.
Juvenal, the Roman poet.
Juyl, July. See also Julius.

K (see also C)

Kacus; see Cacus.
Kaukasous; see Caucasus.
Kayrrud; see *SqT*, V, 808, n.
Kenelm, Seint, son of Kenulphus.
Kenulphus, king of Mercia. See *NPT*, VII, 3110, n.

L

Laban, father of Rachel (Gen. xxix–xxxi).
Laboryntus, the labyrinth of Daedalus in Crete.
Lachesis, the Fate.
Lacidomye, Lacedaemon.

Ladomya, Laodomea, Laudomia, Laodamia, wife of Protesilaus.

Lameadoun, Lamedon, Laomedon, king of Troy.

Lamek, Lameth, Lamech (Gen. iv, 19 ff.).

Lamuel, Lemuel (Prov. xxxi).

Laodomea; see **Ladomya.**

Latumyus; see *WB Prol*, III, 757, n.

Latyne, Latinus, king of Latium.

Laudomia; see **Ladomya.**

Launcelot (de Lake), Lancelot of the Lake, knight of Arthur's court.

Lavina; see **Lavyne** (1).

Lavyne, (1) Lavinia, Italian wife of Aeneas; (2) Lavinium, ancient town of Latium.

Layus, Laius, father of Oedipus.

Lazar, Lazarus.

Leandre, Leander of Abydos.

Lemnoun, Lemnos, a large island in the Aegean.

Lenne; see *Astr Prol*, 86 f., n.

Leonard, St. Leonard, patron saint of captives.

Leo, Leoun, the sign of the zodiac.

Leoun, (1) see **Leo;** (2) the Book of the Lion; see *Retractation*, X, 1087, n.

Lepe, a town in Spain.

Lete, Lethe, river of oblivion in the Lower World.

Lettow, Lithuania.

Lia, Leah; see *SecNT*, VIII, 85 ff., n.

Libra, a sign of the zodiac.

Libie, Libya.

Limote, probably Elymas. See *HF*, 1274, n.

Lollius; see *HF*, 1467 ff., n.

Longius, more commonly called Longinus. See *A B C*, 163, n.

Looth, Lot.

Loreyn(e), Lorraine.

Lowys, Lewis, probably Chaucer's son. See the introduction to the explanatory notes on *Astr*.

Loy, Seinte, St. Eligius. See *Gen Prol*, I, 120, n.

Luc, St. Luke.

Lucan, the Latin poet.

Lucifer, (1) Satan; (2) the morning star.

Lucina, a name of Diana.

Lucrece, Lucresse, Lucretia.

Lucye, Lucia, Lucilia, wife of the poet Lucretius.

Lumbardes, Lombards.

Lumbardye, Lombardy.

Lybeux, hero of the romance Libeaus Desconus.

Lyde, Lydia.

Lydyens, the Lydians.

Lyeys, Lyas, Ayas, in Armenia.

Lygurge, Lycurgus, king of Thrace.

Lyma, error for Livia, who murdered her husband, Drusus Caesar (i.e., Drusus Junior).

Lyno, Lynceus, son of Aegyptus, and husband of Hypermnestra.

Lynyan, Giovanni da Lignaco (or Legnano), Italian jurist of the 14th century.

M

Mabely, Mabel, a character in *FrT*.

Macedo, the Macedonian.

Macedoyne, Macidonye, Macidoyne, Macedonia.

Machabee, (1) Judas Maccabeus; (2) the books of the Maccabees.

Macrobes, Macrobeus, Macrobye, Macrobius, the Latin author.

Madrian, possibly St. Materne or St. Mathurin. See *MkT*, VII, 1892, n.

Magdale(y)ne, Magdalene.

Mahoun, Makomete, Mahomet.

Maius, May.

Makomete; see **Mahoun.**

Malkyn, a girl's name.

Malle, Moll (name of a sheep).

Malyne, Molly.

Manes, departed spirits inhabiting the Lower World. See *Tr*, v, 892, n.

Mantoan, of Mantua in Italy.

Marcia, Marsyas (wrongly considered feminine by Chaucer).

Marcia Catoun, Marcia, daughter of M. Cato Uticensis.

Marcian, Marcien, Martianus Mineus Felix Capella, a native of Carthage (5th century), author of "De Nuptiis Philologiae et Mercurii."

Marcius, March.

Marcus Tullius, Tulyus, Cicero.

Mardochee, Mordecai, in the Book of Esther.

Marie, Seinte, (1) the Blessed Virgin; (2) St. Mary the Egyptian.

Mark, St. Mark.

Marmoryke, Marmarica or Barca, in northern Africa.

Marrok, Morocco.

Mars, Marte, the god of war.

Martyn, St. Martin (c. 316–400), bishop of Tours.

Massynisse, Masinissa, king of the Numidians.

Mathew, St. Matthew.

Maudelayne, Maudeleyne, (1) Magdalen, the name of a ship; (2) the treatise De Maria Magdalena, commonly attributed to Origen.

Maure, St. Maur (Maurus), d. 565.

Maurice, Mauricius, a character in *MLT*.

Maxime, Maximus, a character in *SecNT*.

Mecene, Messene (or Messenia).

Medea, daughter of Aeëtes, king of Colchis.

Medes, inhabitants of Media in western Asia.

Megera, Megaera, one of the Furies.

Melan, Milayn, Milan.

Meleagre, Meleager, who slew the Calydonian boar.

Melibeus, Melibee, hero of *Mel*.

Menelaus, brother of Agamemnon and husband of Helen of Troy.

Mercenrike, the kingdom of Mercia.

Mercurye, Mercury, the Roman divinity.

Messenus, Misenus, Trojan trumpeter.

Metellius; see *WB Prol*, III, 460, n.

Methamorphosios, Ovid's Metamorphoses. See *ML Intro*, II, 93, n.

Michelmesse, Michaelmas.

Michias, Micah, Hebrew prophet.

Mida, Midas, wealthy king of Phrygia.

Middelburgh, Middelburg, in Holland.

Milayn; see **Melan.**

Milesie, Miletus.

Minerva, the Roman divinity.

Minos, king of Crete.

Minotaur, monstrous offspring of Pasiphaë and a bull.

Mirra, Myrrha, mother of Adonis.

Moises, Moses.

Monesteo, Mnestheus, a Trojan hero.

Morpheus, god of sleep.

N

Nabal, an enemy of David (I Sam. xxv.).

Nabugodonosor, Nebuchadnezzar.

Narcisus, Narcissus.

Narice, used by Chaucer for Ithaca (Boethius, iv, m. 3, 1, adj. "Neritii," var. "Naricii.").

Naso, P. Ovidius Naso, Ovid.

Nazarenus, the Nazarene.

Nembrot, Nimrod (Gen. x, 8 ff.).

Neptunus, Neptune, the Roman divinity.

Nero, **Neroun**, the Roman emperor.

Nessus, a Centaur, slain by Hercules.

Newegate, Newgate prison.

Newe Toun, Villeneuve. See *CT*, VII, 1428, n.

Nicerates, Niceratus, put to death by the Thirty Tyrants.

Nichanore, Nicanor; (1) an officer of Alexander the Great at the time of his capture of Thebes; (2) a general defeated and slain by Judas Maccabeus.

Nicholas, a clerk in *MillT*.

Nynus, Ninus, traditional founder of Nineveh.

Noe, Noah.

Nonyus, Nonius, satirized by Catullus.

Northfolk, Norfolk.

Note, St. Neot (9th cent.).

Nothus, Notus, the south wind.

Nowel, Noël.

Nowelis, humorous for **Noes**, Noah's.

Nynyvee, Nineveh.

Nyobe, Niobe.

Nysus, Nisus, king of Megara, father of Scylla.

O

Octovyan, **Octovyen**, Octavian; (1) the Roman emperor Augustus; (2) see *BD*, 368, n.

Odenake, Odenathus, ruler of Palmyra, husband of Zenobia.

Oenone, wife of Paris before he carried off Helen.

Oëtes, Aeëtes, father of Medea.

Oloferne, **Olofernus**, Holofernes, Assyrian king slain by Judith.

Olyver, Oliver, friend of Roland.

Omer; see **Homer**.

Opilion, Opilio, adversary of Boethius.

Oreb, Mt. Horeb.

Orewelle, Orwell Haven.

Origenes, Origen, early Christian writer.

Orion, Arion, an ancient Greek bard.

Orkades, the Orkney and Shetland Islands.

Orliens, Orleans.

Orpheus, mythical bard, husband of Eurydice.

Osenay, **Oseneye**, Osney, near Oxford.

Osewold, Oswald, the Reeve.

Ovide, Ovid, the Latin poet.

Oxenford, Oxford.

Oyse, the river Oise.

P

Padowe, Padua.

Palamon, a character in *KnT*.

Palatye, Palathia, probably Turkish Balat.

Palinurus, helmsman of Aeneas's ship.

Palladion, the Palladium, a statue of Pallas Athena.

Pallas, the Greek divinity.

Palymerie, Palmyra, a celebrated city of Syria.

Pamphilus, **Pamphilles**, hero of the Latin dialogue Pamphilus de Amore. See *Mel*, VII, 1556, n.

Pan, the sylvan deity.

Pandarus, **Pandare**, a character in *Tr*.

Pandion, king of Athens, father of Procne (or Progne) and Philomela.

Panik, name of an old countship near Bologna.

Papynian, Aemilius Papinianus, a celebrated Roman jurist, put to death by Caracalla.

Parcas (acc. of Lat. pl. "Parcae"), Fates.

Paris, (1) the son of Priam; (2) the French city.

Parmanydes, Parmenides, Greek philosopher.

Parnaso, **Pernaso**, Mt. Parnassus, the home of the Muses.

Parthes, Parthians.

Parthonope, Parthenopaeus, one of the Seven against Thebes.

Pathmos, the island of Patmos.

Paul, **Poul**, (1) St. Paul; (2) St. Paul's Cathedral.

Paulus, (1) Ludius Aemilius Paulus, the Roman consul; (2) St. Paul.

Paulyn, Decius Paulinus, consul in 498.

Pavie, Pavia.

Pedmark; see **Penmark**.

Pegasee, the Pegasean (horse), Pegasus.

Pelleus, Peleus, king of Thessaly and father of Achilles.

Pemond, Piedmont.

Pene, the Punic Land.

Penmark, **Pedmark**, Penmarch, in Brittany.

Penelope(e), **Penalopee**, Penelope, wife of Ulysses.

Penneus, Peneus, river-god, father of Daphne.

Pepyn, Pepin, king of the Franks.

Perce, Persia.

Percien, **Persien**, Persian; pl., the Persians.

Percyvell, hero of the romance Sir Percyvelle of Galles.

Perkyn, Perkin, a character in *CkT*.

Pernaso; see **Parnaso**.

Perotheus, Pirithous, friend of Theseus.

Perses, Persians.

Persien; see **Percien**.

Pertelote, Partlet, a hen in *NPT*.

Peter, (1) St. Peter; (2) **P.** Alfonce, Petrus Alphonsus. See **Piers**.

Petrak, Petrarch.

Petro, Pedro, Peter; (1) king of Spain; (2) king of Cyprus.

Phanye, daughter of Croesus.

Pharao, **Pharoo**, Pharaoh.

Phasipha, Pasiphaë, wife of King Minos of Crete and mother of the Minotaur.

Phebus, (1) Apollo; (2) the sun.

Phebuseo, a Trojan hero mentioned in *Tr*.

Phedra, Phaedra, wife of Theseus.

Pheton, Phaëthon, son of Helios, the god of the sun.

Phidoun, Phidon, slain by the Thirty Tyrants.

Philistiens, Philistines.

Philomene, Philomela, sister of Procne.

Philostrate, Philostratus, a character in *KnT*.

Philotetes, Philoctetes.

Phisiologus, Physiologus. See *NPT*, VII, 3271, n.

Phitonissa, Pythoness; the witch of Endor.

Phitoun, the Python.

Phyllis, beloved of Demophon.

Pictagoras, **Pithagores**, **Pittagoras**, Pythagoras, the Greek philosopher.

Pierides, the Muses; from Pieria, near Mt. Olympus; or, daughters of Pierus.

Piers, Pierce, Peter; **P.** Alphonce (or **Alfonce**), Petrus Alphonsus, a Spaniard, author of the Disciplina Clericalis.

Pigmalion, Pygmalion.

Piramus, Pyramus, lover of Thisbe.

Pirous, Pyrois, a horse in the sun's chariot.
Pirrus, Pyrrhus, son of Achilles.
Pisces, a sign of the zodiac.
Pithagores, Pittagoras; see **Pictagoras.**
Pize, Pisa.
Placebo, a character in *MerchT*.
Plato, Platon, the Greek philosopher.
Pleyndamour; see *Thop*, VII, 897, n.
Pleynte of Kynde, the De Planctu Naturae of Alanus de Insulis.
Pluto, god of the Lower World.
Poilleys, Apulian.
Poliphemus, Polyphemus, chief of the Cyclopes.
Poliphete, Polyphoetes (?). See *Tr*, ii, 1467, n.
Polite(s), Polites, son of Priam.
Polixena, Polixene, Polyxena, daughter of Priam, betrothed to Achilles.
Pollux, twin brother of Castor.
Polydamas, a Trojan hero.
Polymestore, Polymestor (or Polymnestor), king of Thracian Chersonesus, who fought at Troy.
Polymya, the Muse Polyhymnia.
Polymyte(s), Polynices, son of Oedipus and Jocasta, one of the Seven against Thebes.
Pompe, Pompei, Pompeye, Pompeus, Pompey, the Roman general and triumvir.
Poo, the Po river.
Poperyng, Poperinghe. See *Thop*, VII, 720, n.
Porcia, Portia, wife of M. Brutus.
Portyngale, Portugal.
Poul; see **Paul.**
Priam, Priamus, king of Troy.
Priapus, god of fertility.
Proigne, Procne (or Progne), wife of Tereus and sister of Philomela.
Proserpyna, Proserpyne, Proserpina, wife of Pluto.
Protheselaus, Protesilaus, husband of Laodamia.
Pruce, Pruyse, Pusssia, Prussian.
Prudence, wife of Melibeus.
Pseustis, Presentus (?). See *HF*, 1227, n.
Ptholome(e), Tholome, Ptolemy.
Puella, figure in geomancy.
Pycardie, Picardy.

Q

Quyryne, Quirinus, Romulus.

R

Rachel, wife of Jacob, and mother of Joseph.
Raphael, the archangel.
Rauf, Ralph, name of a priest.
Ravenne, Ravenna.
Razis, Rhazes, 9th–10th century physician of Baghdad.
Rebekka, Rebekke, Rebekah, wife of Isaac.
Rede See, Red Sea.
Regulus, Marcus, consul in 256 B.C.
Remedie of Love, Ovid's Remedium Amoris.
Renard, Reynard, common name for a fox.
Reynes, Rennes in Brittany.
Richard, kyng, Richard I.
Ripheo, Ripheus (or Rhipeus), a Trojan hero.
Robert, sir, name of a priest.
Robyn, Robin, a man's name.
Rochele (The), La Rochelle.
Rodogone, Rhodogone, daughter of Darius.
Rodopeya, Rodopeye, Rhodope, a range of mountains in Thrace.

Roger, (1) the Cook; (2) Ruggieri, bishop of Pisa.
Romance of the Rose, French poem by Guillaume de Lorris and Jean de Meun.
Romulus, legendary founder of Rome.
Ronyan. See *Words of Host*, VI, 310, n.
Rosarie, Rosarium Philosophorum, a treatise on alchemy by Arnaldus de Villanova.
Rosemounde, Rosamond.
Rouchestre, Rochester.
Rouncivale; see *Gen Prol*, I, 670, n.
Rowland, Roland, hero of the Chanson de Roland.
Rubeus, figure in geomancy.
Ruce, Russye, Russia.
Rufus, a Greek physician of Ephesus in the time of Trajan (A.D. 98–117).
Russell, reddish; name of the fox in *NPT*.
Russye; see **Ruce.**

S (see also C)

Sagittarius, Sagittarie, the Archer, a sign of the zodiac.
Salamon, Salomon, Solomon.
Saluce(s), Saluzzo, town and marquisate.
Samaritan, the woman of Samaria.
Sampsoun, Samson.
Samuel, the Hebrew prophet.
Santippe, Santippo (Antipus?), a character in *Tr.*
Sapor, Shapur I, king of Persia (3d cent. A.D.).
Sarpedo(u)n, Sarpedon, a Trojan.
Sarra, Sarah, wife of Abraham.
Sarray, Saraï Berké, or New Saraï, trading center on the Akhtuba branch of the Lower Volga. See Magoun, Med. Stud., XVII, 138.
Satalye, ancient Attalia, on the southeast coast of Asia Minor.
Sathan(as), Satan.
Satiry (Lat. "Satyri"), satyrs, wood-deities.
Saturne, Saturnus, Saturn; (1) the Roman divinity; (2) the planet.
Sayne; see **Seyne.**
Scariot, Iscariot.
Scipioun, Cipioun, Scipio Africanus Minor.
Scithero, Cicero.
Scithia; see **Cithe.**
Scogan; see the introduction to the Explanatory Notes to *Scog.*
Scorpio, Scorpioun, a sign of the zodiac.
Scot, a horse's name.
Seint-Denys, St. Denis-sur-Seine, a suburb of Paris.
Semyrame, Semyramis, Semyramus, Semiramis, queen of Assyria.
Seneca, Senec, Senek, the Roman author.
Seneciens, the followers of Seneca.
Senior, the name of a book. See *CYT*, VIII, 1450, n.
Septe, Ceuta in Morocco, or the ridge, Septem Fratres. See *MLT*, II, 947, n.
Septem Tryones, Lat. "septentriones," the seven plough-oxen, used of Ursa Major and Ursa Minor; hence, the north.
Serapion, a physician. See *Gen Prol*, I, 429, n.
Seryen, Syrien, Serian, Chinese; a name derived from σήρ, silk-worm.
Seyne, Sayne, the river Seine.
Seynt Amour, William; French writer. See *Rom*, 6763, n.
Seynt-Jame, Santiago (in Compostela).
Seys; see **Ceys.**
Sheene, Sheen, now Richmond (Surrey).

Sheffeld, Sheffield.
Sibil(l)e, Sibyl; (1) the Cumaean Sibyl; (2) Cassandra.
Sidyngborne, Sittingbourne.
Signifer, the zodiac.
Silla, Scylla, daughter of Nisus of Megara.
Simon, Symoun, Symond, (1) St. S. the Canaanite (apostle); (2) S. the Pharisee; (3) S. Magus (see Acts viii, 9); (4) a character in *RvT*.
Socrates, the Greek philosopher.
Sol, Lat. for Sun, a name for gold.
Soler Halle, probably King's Hall at Cambridge.
Somer; see *Astr Prol*, 85 f., n.
Sophie, daughter of Melibeus.
Soranas; see *Bo*, i, pr. 3, 56, n.
Southwerk, Southwark.
Spaigne, Spayne, Spain.
Stace, Statius.
Stilboun; see *PardT*, VI, 603, n.
Stix, Styx, river of the Lower World.
Stoyciens, Stoics.
Stratford atte Bowe, Stratford at Bow.
Strode, Ralph Strode. See *Tr*, v, 1856, n. (at end).
Strother; see *RvT*, I, 4014, n.
Stymphalides, Stymphalis.
Surrien, Syrian.
Surrye, Syria.
Susanna, Susanne, Susannah.
Swetonius, Swetoun, Suetonius, the Roman historian.
Symacus, Symmachus, father-in-law of Boethius.
Symkyn, Simkin (dim. of Simon), a character in *RvT*.
Symois, Simoïs, a river near Troy.
Symond, Symoun; see **Simon.**
Symplicius Gallus; see **Gallus.**
Synay, Mt. Sinai.
Synoun, Sinon, who betrayed Troy into the hands of the Greeks.
Syrien; see **Seryen.**
Syrius, Sirius, the dog-star.
Sysile, Sicily.
Sytheo, Sichaeus, Dido's husband.

T

Tabard, an inn in Southwark.
Tagus, the river Tajo in Spain.
Talbot, a dog.
Tantalus, Tantale, father of Pelops.
Tarbe, Tharbe, a female character in *Tr*.
Tarquinius, Tarquyn, Tarquyny, Sextus, son of L. Tarquinius Superbus.
Tars, Tartary.
Tartarye, Tartary.
Tartere, Tartar.
Taurus, Taur, Tawr, (1) a sign of the zodiac; (2) the constellation.
Tereus, husband of Procne.
Termagaunt, Termagant, a supposed heathen idol.
Tertulan, probably Tertullian (c. 160-240).
Tesbee; see **Thisbe.**
Tessalie; see **Thessalye.**
Teuta, queen of Illyria, 231 B.C.
Tewnes, Tunis.
Tharbe; see **Tarbe.**
Thebes, (1) in Greece; (2) in Egypt.
Thelophus, Telephus, wounded and healed by Achilles's spear.
Theodomas, Thiodamas, a Theban augur.
Theodora, wife of Algarsif. See *SqT*, V, 663, n.

Theodoric, the Great, king of the Ostrogoths (A.D. 474-526), who condemned and executed Boethius.
Theofraste, Theophrastus, author of the Liber Aureolus de Nuptiis.
Theseus, duke of Athens.
Thesiphone, Tisiphone, one of the Furies.
Thessalye, Tessalie, Thessaly.
Thetis, a Nereid, mother of Achilles.
Thisbe, Tesbee, Tisbe, a Babylonian maiden, beloved by Pyramus.
Thoas, Toas, father of Hypsipyle.
Thobie, (1) Tobit; (2) Tobias, son of Tobit.
Tholome; see **Ptholome(e).**
Tholosan, of Toulouse (wrongly applied to Statius).
Thomas, (1) St. T. the apostle; (2) St. T. à Becket; (3) a character in *SumT*.
Thopas, hero of *Sir Thopas*.
Thymalao, son of Zenobia.
Thymeo, the Timaeus of Plato.
Thymothee, Timotheus.
Tiburce, Tiburtius, a character in *SecNT*.
Ticius, Tityus, tortured by vultures in the Lower World.
Tisbe; see **Thisbe.**
Titan, the sun.
Titus Livius, Livy, the historian.
Toas; see **Thoas.**
Tolletanes (pl.), of Toledo. See *FranklT*, V, 1274, n.
Trace, Thrace.
Tramyssene, Tremessen (Tlemçen).
Trist(r)am, the lover of Isolde.
Triton, a sea god.
Troian, Trojan.
Troianysshe, Trojan.
Troilus, hero of *Tr*.
Trophee; see *MkT*, VII, 2117, n.
Trotula, person of uncertain identification. See *WBT*, III, 670, n.
Trumpyngtoun, near Cambridge.
Trygwille, Triguilla, adversary of Boethius.
Tubal, Tubal-cain, son of Lamech (Gen. iv, 19, 22).
Tullius, (1) M. Tullius Cicero; (2) Tullus Hostilius, king of Rome.
Turkeys, Turkish.
Turkye, Turkey.
Turnus, king of the Rutuli who fell by the hand of Aeneas.
Tybre, Tiber river.
Tydeus, father of Diomedes.
Tyle, Thule.
Tyrene, Tyrrhenian, Tuscan.
Tyresie, Tiresias, the Theban soothsayer.
Tyrie, Tyre.
Tyro, of Tyre.
Tytus; (1) see **Titus;** (2) for **Dite** (?), Dictys of Crete.

U

Ulixes, Ulysses.
Urban, Pope Urban I, A.D. 222.
Ursa, Ursa Major.

V

Valence, probably Valence near Lyons, France.
Valentyn(e), St. Valentine.
Valeria, wife of Servius.
Valerian, a character in *SecNT*.

Valerius, Valerie, (1) Valerius Maximus, Latin author; (2) see *LGW Prol G*, 268 ff., n.
Venus, (1) the goddess; (2) the planet.
Venyse, Venice.
Verone, Verona.
Vesulus, Monte Viso, in the Maritime Alps.
Vincent, of Beauvais, 13th century author of Speculum Historiale, etc.
Virgile, Virgilius, Virgil, the Latin poet.
Virginia, a character in *PhysT*.
Virginius, a character in *PhysT*.
Virgo, a sign of the zodiac.
Visevus, Vesuvius.
Vitulon, Witelo, Polish physicist of the 13th century.
Vulcano, Vulcanus, Roman divinity.

W

Wade; see *MerchT*, IV, 1424, n.
Walakye, Wallachia, now part of Rumania.
Walter, a character in *ClT*.
Walys, Wales.
Ware, in Hertfordshire.
Waterynge of Seint Thomas, St. Thomas Watering (Surrey).
Watlynge Street, Watling Street, i.e., the Milky Way.
Watte, Wat (for Walter).
Wilkyn, a character in *WB Prol*.
William, (1) the Conqueror; (2) see **Seynt Amour.**
Wyndesore, Windsor.

X

Xantippa, Xantippe, wife of Socrates.

Y (see also I)

Yarbas, Iarbas, rejected suitor of Dido.
Ykarus, Icarus, son of Daedalus.
Yole, Iole, beloved by Hercules.
Ypermystra, Ypermystre, Hypermnestra, daughter of Danaus.
Ypocras, (1) Hippocrates (5th cent. B.C.); (2) a cordial named after him.
Ypolita, Hippolyte, according to one tradition a leader of the Amazons and married to Theseus.
Ypotys; see *Thop*, VII, 297, n.
Ypres, a city in Flanders.
Ysaac, Isaac.
Ysidis, Isis, an Egyptian divinity. See *HF*, 1844, n.
Ysidre, Seint, St. Isidore.
Ysoude; see **Isaude.**
Ytacus, Ithacus, the Ithacan (Ulysses).
Yve, St. Ives. See *ShipT*, VII, 227, n.

Z

Zacharie, Zakarie, Zechariah.
Zanzis (or perhaps **Zauzis**), apparently for Zeuxis, the Greek painter.
Zeno, of Elea in Italy, b. about 488 B.C.; may have perished in an attempt to deliver his native country from a tyrant.
Zepherus, Zephirus, Zephyrus (or Zephyr), the west wind.